CAT

Common Admission Test

33 *Years'*

Topic-Wise & Year-Wise

SOLVED PAPERS

1990-2022

by

Gautam Puri

(Alumnus IIM Bangalore)

Title : CAT : 33 Years' Topic-Wise & Year-Wise Solved Papers 1990-2022

Language : English

Author's Name : Gautam Puri

Typeset & Published by :

Career Launcher Infrastructure (P) Ltd.

A-45, Mohan Cooperative Industrial Area, Near Mohan Estate Metro Station, New Delhi - 110044

Marketed by :

G.K. Publications (P) Ltd.

Plot No. 9A, Sector-27A, Mathura Road, Faridabad, Haryana-121003

ISBN : **978-93-5681-304-5**

Printer's Details: Printed in India, New Delhi.

For product information :

Visit ***www.gkpublications.com*** or email to ***gkp@gkpublications.com***

Contents

English Usage

Quantitative Aptitude

CHAPTER

Verbal Logic

PARA-COMPLETION

1991

DIRECTIONS for Questions 1 to 6: Each of these questions contains a sentence followed by four choices. Select from among these choices the one which most logically completes the idea contained in the given sentence.

1. Particularly today, when so many difficult and complex problems face the human species, the development of broad
(a) and powerful shoulders is necessary.
(b) plans of action is not possible.
(c) moral values is required.
(d) and powerful thinking is desperately needed.

2. In the European Community countries there has been talk of an energy tax to raise funds
(a) by burdening the rich who can afford higher taxes.
(b) to penalise heavy users of energy.
(c) by raising the price of energy-intensive implements.
(d) to search for alternative sources of energy.

3. "Look before you leap" reflects an attitude expressed in such a saying as
(a) 'Forewarned is forearmed.'
(b) 'A stitch in time saves nine.'
(c) 'No risk no gain.'
(d) 'Fools rush where the angels fear to tread.'

4. This is the ancient kingdom of Sumeria and you are its venerated ruler. The fate of Sumeria' economy and of your royal subjects
(a) is written in their horoscopes.
(b) is as unknown as the name of your kingdom.
(c) is entirely in your hands.
(d) is allocated according to their needs.

5. Furthermore, to be radical means to be ready and willing to break with the predominant cultural, political and social beliefs and values in order to
(a) investigate the essential realities that they conceal.
(b) investigate the root cause of malaise in a society.
(c) shape a new economic order.
(d) re-construct the system in terms of new realities.

6. Entrepreneurs are never satisfied with the status quo, they are intent on shaping the future, rather than being shaped by it. As one Chief Executive once said,
(a) "The future is the sum total of actions in the present and past."
(b) "If you are not alert, before you realize it the future is on you."
(c) "I do not want our competitors making decisions for us."
(d) "It is a sound business policy to anticipate change than being swamped by it."

1993

DIRECTIONS for Questions 7 to 10: Each question is a logical sequence of statements with a missing link, the location of which is shown parenthetically. From the four choices available you are required to choose the one which best fits the sequence logically.

7. Many of us live one-eyed lives. We rely largely on the eye of the mind to form our images of reality. It is a mechanical world based on fact and reason. (_______). So today more and more of us are opening the other eye, the eye of the heart, looking for realities to which the mind's eye is blind. This is a world warmed and transformed by the power of love, a vision of community beyond the mind's capacity to see. Either eye alone is not enough. We need "wholesight", a vision of the world in which mind and heart unite.
(a) It had led to unprecedented scientific growth and material well – being.
(b) In the nuclear age, our mind-made world has been found flawed and dangerous, even lethal,
(c) The question is irrelevant, whether or not they can be seen and reasoned.
(d) We have built our lives based on it because it seemed predictable and safe.

8. People arguing for a position have been known to cast the opposite in an unnecessarily feeble light. (______). People who indulge in this fallacy may be fearful or ignorant of a strong counter argument. Detecting this fallacy often depends on having already heard a better refutation, or having information with which to construct one.

(a) Casting the opposite as weaker than it really is, is a very effective strategy.
(b) This portrayal of a refutation as weaker than it really is, is a sure way of proving your point.
(c) Casting the opposite as weaker than it really is, is not a very effective strategy.
(d) This portrayal of refutation as weaker than it really is, is unwarranted.

9. The question of what rights animals should enjoy is a vexatious one, Hundreds of millions of animals are put to death for human use each year. Contrariwise, it can be argued that slowing down scientific research would retard discovery of antidotes to diseases such as cancer which kill humans and animals alike. (________). What if super intelligent beings from Alpha Centauri landed on earth and decided to use us for their experiments, arguing that they could save far more of their and our lives by so doing?

(a) It will benefit both in the long run.
(b) Is the argument truly fair to animals?
(c) But the progress of human civilization cannot be made contingent on some hypothetical rights of animals.
(d) There is no question of equating human rights with those of animals.

10. A deliberation is a form of discussion in which two people begin on different sides of an issue. (_______) Then each decides, in the light of the other argument whether to adopt the other position, to change his or her position somewhat, or to maintain the same position. Both sides realize that to modify one's position is not to lose; the point is to get closer to the truth of the matter.

(a) Each person argues his or her position most sincerely.
(b) The prerequisite for deliberation to be productive is that persons involved must keep an open mind.
(c) The purpose is to resolve the issue to the satisfaction of both parties.
(d) The trick is to state your viewpoint from a position of strength.

1996

11. When we call others dogmatic, what we really object to is ___.

(a) their giving the dog a bad name
(b) their holding dogmas that are different from our own
(c) the extremism that goes along with it
(d) the subversion of whatever they actually believe in concomitantly

12. I am an entertainer ___, I have to keep smiling because in my heart laughter and sorrow have an affinity.

(a) Even if I have tears in my eyes
(b) Even though I am depressed inside
(c) While entertaining people
(d) In the entertainment business

13. The stock markets ___. The state they are in right now speaks volumes about this fact.

(a) is the barometer of public confidence
(b) are the best indicators of public sentiment
(c) are used to trade in expensive shares
(d) are not used to taking stock of all markets

14. Political power is just as permanent as today's newspaper. Ten years down the line, ___ the most powerful man in any state today.

(a) who cares
(b) nobody will remember what was written in today's newspaper or
(c) few will know, or care about
(d) when a lot of water will have passed under the bridge, who will care

15. ___, the more they remain the same.

(a) People all over the world change
(b) The more people change
(c) The more they are different
(d) The less people change

16. Although, it has been more than 50 years since Satyajit Ray made *Pather Panchali*, ___ refuse to go away from the mind.

(a) the haunting images
(b) its haunting images
(c) its haunted images
(d) the haunt of its images.

2005

DIRECTIONS for Questions 17 to 20: Each of the following questions has a paragraph from which the last sentence has been deleted. From the given options, choose that one that completes the paragraph in the most appropriate way.

17. The audiences for crosswords and sudoku, understandably, overlap greatly, but there are differences, too. A crossword attracts a more literary person, while sudoku appeals to a keenly logical mind. Some crossword enthusiasts turn up their noses at sudoku because they feel it lacks depth. A good crossword requires vocabulary, knowledge, mental flexibility and sometimes even a sense of humor to complete.

It touches numerous areas of life and provides an "Aha!" or two along the way. ________

(a) Sudoku, on the other hand, is just a logical exercise, each one similar to the last.

(b) Sudoku, incidentally, is growing faster in popularity than crosswords, even among the literati.

(c) Sudoku, on the other hand, can be attempted and enjoyed even by children.

(d) Sudoku, however, is not exciting in any sense of the term.

18. Most firms consider expert individuals to be too elitist, temperamental, egocentric, and difficult to work with. Force such people to collaborate on a high-stakes project and they just might come to fisticuffs. Even the very notion of managing such a group seems unimaginable. So most organizations fall into default mode, setting up project teams of people who get along nicely. ________

(a) The result, however, is disastrous

(b) The result is mediocrity.

(c) The result is creation of experts who then become elitist.

(d) Naturally, they drive innovations.

19. Federer's fifth grand slam win prompted a reporter to ask whether he was the best ever. Federer is certainly not lacking in confidence, but he wasn't about to proclaim himself the best ever. "The best player of this generation, yes", he said. "But nowhere close to ever. Just look at the records that some guys have. I'm a minnow." ________

(a) His win against Agassi, a genius from the previous generation, contradicts that.

(b) Sampras, the king of an earlier generation, was as humble.

(c) He is more than a minnow to his contemporaries.

(d) The difference between 'the best of this generation' and 'the best ever' is a matter of perception.

20. Thus the end of knowledge and the closing of the frontier that it symbolizes is not a looming crisis at all, but merely one of many embarrassing fits of hubris in civilization's long industry. In the end, it will pass away and be forgotten. Ours is not the first generation to struggle to understand the organizational laws of the frontier, deceive itself that it has succeeded, and go to its grave having failed. ________

(a) One would be wise to be humble.

(b) But we might be the first generation to actually reach the frontier.

(c) But we might be the first generation to deal with the crisis.

(d) However, this time the success is not illusory.

2006

DIRECTIONS for Questions 21 to 32: Each of the following questions has a paragraph from which the last sentence has been deleted. From the given options, choose the one that completes the paragraph in the most appropriate way.

21. Relations between the factory and the dealer are distant and usually strained as the factory tries to force cars on the dealers to smooth out production. Relations between the dealer and the customer are equally strained because dealers continuously adjust prices — make deals — to adjust demand with supply while maximizing profits. This becomes a system marked by a lack of long-term commitment on either side, which maximizes feelings of mistrust. In order to maximize their bargaining positions, everyone holds back information — the dealer about the product and the consumer about his true desires.

(a) As a result, 'deal making' becomes rampant, without concern for customer satisfaction.

(b) As a result, inefficiencies creep into the supply chain.

(c) As a result, everyone treats the other as an adversary, rather than as an ally.

(d) As a result, fundamental innovations are becoming scarce in the automobile industry.

(e) As a result, everyone loses in the long run.

22. We can usefully think of theoretical models as maps, which help us navigate unfamiliar territory. The most accurate map that it is possible to construct would be of no practical use whatsoever, for it would be an exact replica, on exactly the same scale, of the place where we were. Good maps pull out the most important features and throw away a hugo amount of much less valuable information. Of course, maps can be bad as well as good — witness the attempts by medieval Europe to produce a map of the world. In the same way, a bad theory, no matter how impressive it may seem in principle, does little or nothing to help us understand a problem.

(a) But good theories, just like good maps, are invaluable, even if they are simplified.

(b) But good theories, just like good maps, will never represent unfamiliar concepts in detail.

(c) But good theories, just like good maps, need to balance detail and feasibility of representation.

(d) But good theories, just like good maps, are accurate only at a certain level of abstraction.

(e) But good theories, just like good maps, are useful in the hands of a user who knows their limitations.

23. In the evolving world order, the comparative advantage of the United States lies in its military force.

Diplomacy and international law have always been regarded as annoying encumbrances, unless they can be used to advantage against an enemy. Every active player in world affairs professes to seek only peace and to prefer negotiation to violence and coercion.

(a) However, diplomacy has often been used as a mask by nations which intended to use force.

(b) However, when the veil is lifted, we commonly see that diplomacy is understood as a disguise for the rule of force.

(c) However, history has shown that many of these nations do not practice what they profess.

(d) However, history tells us that peace is professed by those who intend to use violence.

(e) However, when unmasked, such nations reveal a penchant for the use of force.

24. I am sometimes attacked for imposing 'rules'. Nothing could be further from the truth. I hate rules. All I do is report on how consumers react to different stimuli. I may say to a copywriter, "Research shows that commercials with celebrities are below average in persuading people to buy products. Are you sure you want to use a celebrity?" Call that a rule? Or I may say to an art director, "Research suggests that if you set the copy in black type on a white background, more people will read it than if you set it in white type on a black background."

(a) Guidance based on applied research can hardly qualify as 'rules'.

(b) Thus, all my so called 'rules' are rooted in applied research.

(c) A suggestion perhaps, but scarcely a rule.

(d) Such principles are unavoidable if one wants to be systematic about consumer behaviour.

(e) Fundamentally it is about consumer behaviour — not about celebrities or type settings.

25. Age has a curvilinear relationship with the exploitation of opportunity. Initially, age will increase the likelihood that a person will exploit an entrepreneurial opportunity because people gather much of the knowledge necessary to exploit opportunities over the course of their lives, and because age provides credibility in transmitting that information to others. However, as people become older, their willingness to bear risks declines, their opportunity costs rise, and they become less receptive to new information.

(a) As a result, people transmit more information rather than experiment with new ideas as they reach an advanced age.

(b) As a result, people are reluctant to experiment with new ideas as they reach an advanced age.

(c) As a result, only people with lower opportunity costs exploit opportunity when they reach an advanced age.

(d) As a result, people become reluctant to exploit entrepreneurial opportunities when they reach an advanced age.

(e) As a result, people depend on credibility rather than on novelty as they reach an advanced age.

2007

26. Characters are also part of deep structure. Characters tie events in a story together and provide a thread of continuity and meaning. Stories can be about individuals, groups, projects, or whole organizations, so from an organizational studies perspective, the focal actor(s)determine the level and unit of analysis used in a study. Stories of mergers and acquisitions, for example, are commonplace. In these stories whole organizations are personified as actors. But these macro-level stories usually are not told from the perspective of the macro-level participants, because whole organizations cannot narrate their experiences in the first person.

(a) More generally, data concerning the identities and relationships of the characters in the story are required, if one is to understand role structure and social networks in which that process is embedded.

(b) Personification of a whole organization abstracts away from the particular actors and from traditional notions of level of analysis.

(c) The personification of a whole organization is important because stories differ depending on who is enacting various events.

(d) Every story is told from a particular point of view, with a particular narrative voice, which is not regarded as part of the deep structure.

(e) The personification of a whole organization is a textual device we use to make macro-level theories more comprehensible.

27. Nevertheless, photographs still retain some of the magical allure that the earliest daguerreotypes inspired. As objects, our photographs have changed; they have become physically flimsier as they have become more technologically sophisticated. Daguerre produced pictures on copper plates: today many of our photographs never become tangible things, but instead remain filed away on computers and cameras, part of the digital ether that envelops the modern world. At the same time, our patience for the creation of images has also eroded. Children today are used to being tracked from birth by digital cameras and video recorders and they expect to see the results of their poses and performances instantly.

The space between life as it is being lived and life as it is being displayed shrinks to a mere second.

(a) Yet, despite these technical developments, photographs still remain powerful because they are reminders of the people and things we care about.

(b) Images, after all, are surrogates carried into battle by a soldier or by a traveller on holiday.

(c) Photographs, be they digital or traditional, exist to remind us of the absent, the beloved, and the dead.

(d) In the new era of the digital image, the images also have a greater potential for fostering falsehood and trickery, perpetuating fictions that seem so real we cannot tell the difference.

(e) Anyway, human nature being what it is, little time has passed after photography's invention became means of living life through images.

28. Mma Ramotswe had a detective agency in Africa, at the foot of Kgale Hill. These were its assets: a tiny white van, two desks, two chairs, a telephone, and an old typewriter. Then there was a teapot, in which Mma Ramotswe - the only private lady detective in Botswana - brewed redbush tea. And three mugs - one for herself, one for her secretary, and one for the client. What else does a detective agency really need? Detective agencies rely on human intuition and intelligence, both of which Mma Ramotswe had in abundance.

(a) But there was also the view, which again would appear on no inventory.

(b) No inventory would ever include those, of course.

(c) She had an intelligent secretary too.

(d) She was a good detective and a good woman.

(e) What she lacked in possessions was more than made up by a natural shrewdness.

2008

29. Most people at their first consultation take a furtive look at the surgeon's hands in the hope of reassurance. Prospective patients look for delicacy, sensitivity, steadiness, perhaps unblemished pallor. On this basis, Henry Perowne loses a number of cases each year. Generally, he knows it's about to happen before the patient does: the downward glance repeated, the prepared questions beginning to falter, the overemphatic thanks during the retreat to the door.

(a) Other people do not communicate due to their poor observation.

(b) Other patients don't like what they see but are ignorant of their right to go elsewhere.

(c) But Perowne himself is not concerned.'

(d) But others will take their place, he thought.

(e) These hands are steady enough, but they are large.

30. Trade protectionism, disguised as concern for the climate, is raising its head. Citing competitiveness concerns, powerful industrialized countries are holding out threats of a levy **on** imports of energy-intensive products from developing countries that refuse to accept their demands. The actual source of protectionist sentiment in the OECD countries is, of course, their current lacklustre economic performance, combined with the challenges posed by the rapid economic rise of China and India - in that order.

(a) Climate change is evoked to bring trade protectionism through the back door.

(b) OECD countries are taking refuge in climate change issues to erect trade barriers against these two countries.

(c) Climate change concerns have come as a convenient stick to beat the rising trade power of China and India.

(d) Defenders of the global economic status quo are posing as climate change champions.

(e) Today's climate change champions are the perpetrators of global economic inequity.

31. Mattancherry is Indian Jewry's most famous settlement. Its pretty streets of pastel coloured houses, connected by first-floor passages and home to the last twelve saree-and-sarong-wearing, white-skinned Indian Jews are visited by thousands of tourists each year. Its synagogue, built in *1568,* with a floor of blue-and-white Chinese tiles, a carpet given by Haile Selassie and the frosty Yaheh selling tickets at the door, stands as an image of religious tolerance.

(a) Mattancherry represents, therefore, the perfect picture of peaceful co-existence.

(b) India's Jews have almost never suffered discrimination, except for European colonizers and each other.

(c) Jews in India were always tolerant.

(d) Religious tolerance has always been only a façade and nothing more.

(e) The pretty pastel streets are, thus, very popular with the tourists.

32. Given the cultural and intellectual interconnections, the question of what is 'Western' and what is 'Eastern' (or 'Indian')is often hard to decide, and the issue can be discussed only in more dialectical terms. The diagnosis of a thought as 'purely Western' or 'purely Indian' can be very illusory.

(a) Thoughts are not the kind of things that can be easily categorized.
(b) Though 'occidentalism' and 'orientalism' as dichotomous concepts have found many adherents.
(c) 'East is East and West is West' has been a discredited notion for a long time now.
(d) Compartmentalizing thoughts is often desirable.
(e) The origin of a thought is not the kind of thing to which 'purity' happens easily.

(a) CD (b) BD
(c) AB (d) None of these

MEMORY BASED QUESTIONS

2009

33. There are two gaps in the sentence/paragraph given below. From the pairs of words given, choose the one that fills the gaps most appropriately.

It goes without saying that the vast majority of sporty kids weren't bullies at all – but like a ________ blaming anyone vaguely brown for the actions of 19 people on 9/11, I developed my ________ long ago and still enjoy feeling it fester.

(a) bigot, prejudice (b) chauvinist, belief
(c) fanatic, conviction (d) philistine, aversion

34. There are two gaps in the sentence/paragraph given below. From the pairs of words given, choose the one that fills the gaps most appropriately.

According to this thesis, Amundsen approached the hardships ________, applying practical lessons from his experience with Eskimos in the north and relying on well-trained dogs to pull sledges. Scott, by contrast, took a more _______ view of exploration, in which hardships simply were to be endured as a test of heroism.

(a) rationally, impractical
(b) shrewdly, fanciful
(c) pragmatically, naïve
(d) realistically, romantic

35. A paragraph is given below from which the last sentence has been deleted. From the given options, choose the one that completes the paragraph in the most appropriate way.

Since the gods are super parents and super leaders, they must necessarily have large houses in which to 'meet' with their followers. Anyone flying low over human settlements in a spacecraft and ignorant of our ways would notice immediately that in many of the villages and towns and cities there were one or two homes much bigger than the rest.

(a) These – the houses of the gods-the temples, the mosques, the churches and the cathedral – are buildings apparently made for giants.
(b) Mere mortals do not require buildings that large.
(c) Their followers repeatedly visit them and bow down before them, but they themselves are invisible.
(d) The visitors would then imagine what purpose they would serve.

36. A paragraph is given below from which the last sentence has been deleted. From the given options, choose the one that completes the paragraph in the most appropriate way.

Camera phones, a gimmick and a luxury a few years ago, have become ubiquitous. The International Telecommunications Union estimates that 4.6 billion mobile phones are in use at the moment. Of those, more than a billion are equipped with cameras, according to Tom Hausken, an analyst at Strategies Unlimited, a market research firm based in Mountain View, California. Dr Hausken estimates that some 800m camera-phones will be sold this year. Yet most of the photos taken with these phones will be grainy and of low resolution—fine for capturing the essence of a moment to send to friends and family, but not good enough to frame for the wall. The reason is that both camera and lens have to be small, to fit with all the other gubbins on a phone.

(a) Phone cameras with up to five megapixels are becoming available, but InVisage, hopes to leap from that to 12 megapixels, without any increase in size.
(b) In a typical camera-phone, the image is focused by the lens onto a photosensitive silicon chip.
(c) A typical camera-phone is equipped with a one- or two-megapixel silicon-based camera chip that is about 8mm across.
(d) After all one buys a phone not for the camera alone; the camera is merely another feature.

37. A paragraph is given below from which a sentence has been deleted. From the given options, choose the one that completes the paragraph in the most appropriate way.

Dr James Ost, senior lecturer in psychology at the University of Portsmouth, specialises in the study of memory. He says not remembering much of your childhood is normal, mostly because it is mundane.________________________. He had a simpler idea: "If you want to remember something that happened at a particular place, go back to that place." It's called context reinstatement and is what the police use in crime re-enactment.

(a) Recently, after the birth of my second son, Rufus, I was inspired to go looking for tangible memories of my mother.

(b) He debunked the idea that a major trauma may have wiped out my memory, or that hypnosis would help me to remember.

(c) Clearly, memory does play tricks on us.

(d) I asked James how I can best help my children remember their childhood: "The more I learn about memory, the less I rely on my own," he said.

2010

38. A paragraph is given below from which the last sentence has been deleted. From the given options, choose the one that completes the paragraph in the most appropriate way.

The realist at last loses patience with ideals altogether, and sees in them only something to blind us, something to numb us, something to murder self in us, something whereby, instead of resisting death, we can disarm it by committing suicide. The idealist, who has taken refuge with the ideals because he hates himself and is ashamed of himself, thinks that all this is so much the better.

(a) And it is not the ignorant and stupid who maintain this error, but the literate and the cultured.

(b) The idealist says, 'Realism means egotism; and egotism means depravity.'

(c) The realist, who has come to have a deep respect for himself and faith in the validity of his own will, thinks it so much the worse.

(d) Unfortunately, this is the sort of speech that nobody but a realist understands.

39. A paragraph is given below from which the last sentence has been deleted. From the given options, choose the one that completes the paragraph in the most appropriate way.

Christopher Dell's "Monsters: A Bestiary of the Bizarre" is a visual typology of the monstrous. Dell draws on images from across centuries and continents to celebrate the hideous fecundity of the human imagination. 'Resistance to monsters is clearly futile,' he writes. 'While we may no longer worry about being eaten by trolls on the way home, there remains a fascination with, and fear of, these creatures that have shadowed us throughout history.

(a) It shows us what man's imagination can do to man.'

(b) After all, we should remember God is our creator.'

(c) After all, we should remember who created them: not the gods, not Echidna, but man.'

(d) Believe in God, not in fantasy.'

40. A paragraph is given below from which the last sentence has been deleted. From the given options, choose the one that completes the paragraph in the most appropriate way.

Months after its debut, "Hillary: The Movie" faces the supreme court. The justices' review of the documentary financed by long term critics of Secretary of State Hillary Clinton could bring more than just a thumbs up or thumbs down.

(a) It may win all time high approval ratings for the Secretary of State.

(b) It will vindicate the faith of movie goers the world over.

(c) It may settle the question of whether Hillary deserves to be so popular.

(d) It may settle the question of whether the government can regulate a politically charged film as a campaign ad.

2011

41. A paragraph is given below from which the last sentence has been deleted. From the given options, choose the one that completes the paragraph in the most appropriate way.

The answers to these questions about reality were many, but in Germany they tended to posit the idea of an evolving harmony, a movement towards equilibrium between the two poles of an objective reality and subjective human consciousness. The work of Mommsen, Eucken and Heyse was characterized by this spirit of willingness to see reality in an explicable, idealized light, whereas Hauptmann, the consummate naturalist, rejected all attempts to embellish reality. Like other naturalists he adopted a critical position, under the banner of "truth", towards hypocrisy and convention and under the banner of "modernity", towards the fashion for historical themes and subjects within literature.

(a) It is this dichotomy that should be considered in evaluating these German prize winners' works.

(b) And thus there existed a dichotomy between the idealized and the naturalistic view of beauty.

(c) Equally important is that the industrial revolution introduced Germany to pragmatic thinking.

(d) This gave rise to a crisis within the educated bourgeoisie, nurtured by Goethean ideals of good.

42. A paragraph is given below from which the last sentence has been deleted. From the given options, choose the one that completes the paragraph in the most appropriate way.

Policy failures come in many shapes and sizes. But they are almost invariably accentuated by the choices that have to be made in periods of financial shortage. Yesterday the coalition government found itself confronted by two of them, one in policing policy and the other in higher education. The failures are radically different in many details. But they have this in common: they are both serious failures, and they were both foreseeable. They could both have been mitigated by clearer policymaking at an earlier stage.

(a) On the policing cuts, it is the opinion that Britain has more police officers than it needs.
(b) Instead each has been allowed to fester and become more difficult to solve politically.
(c) Downing Street must be thanking Prince Andrew for providing some distraction.
(d) Police numbers have increased without proper regard to social need.

2012

43. Given below is a paragraph from which the last sentence has been deleted. From the given options, choose the one that completes the paragraph in the most appropriate way.

It might not sound like a recipe for success – but this is the most important piece of theatre happening anywhere in the country. Some 40 years ago, director Augusto Boal began experimenting with invisible theatre – rehearsing and performing semi-improvised pieces in public spaces to the unsuspecting public. Meanwhile in the bohemian lofts of New York City, a new generation of visionaries were embedding their art ever further into the everyday. Lurking in the corner of a diner, Vito Acconci sat quietly rubbing his arm to produce a sore, while Allan Kaprow created instructions for almost unseen activities to be carried out on the streets of the city. ________________

(a) Such theatre is not as successful as that which happens in an auditorium.
(b) Even audiences were transformed, no longer limited to those who knew they were an audience.
(c) In this way, theatre broke free of the auditorium, art tore itself from the gallery and the museum.
(d) Theatre veterans are least bothered about praise or criticism.

44. Given below is a paragraph from which the last sentence has been deleted. From the given options, choose the one that completes the paragraph in the most appropriate way.

There is much to commend in this novel, a witty parable of India's changing society, yet there is much to ponder. The scales have fallen from the eyes of some Indian writers, many either living abroad, or educated there like Adiga. The home country is invariably presented as a place of brutal injustice and sordid corruption, one in which the poor are always dispossessed and victimised by their age-old enemies, the rich. Characters at the colourful extremities of society are Dickensian grotesques, Phiz sketches, adrift in a country that is lurching rapidly towards bland middle-class normality. ________________

(a) My hunch is this is fundamentally an outsider's view and a superficial one.
(b) There are so many alternative Indias, uncontacted and unheard which Adiga can never hope to explore.
(c) Adiga is a genius of this age who has written a pathbreaking book.
(d) Presenting the home country as a poverty-stricken place has become a means of getting cheap popularity.

45. Given below is a paragraph from which the last sentence has been deleted. From the given options, choose the one that completes the paragraph in the most appropriate way.

Warschawski describes the atrocities of the occupation—from the sack of Ramallah to the massacre in Jenin, the razing of houses and refugee camps, shooting at ambulances and hospitals, the use of Palestinian civilians as human shields—showing how each of these pushes back the boundaries of what was previously thinkable. Warschawski has the keen eye of an Israeli insider. ________________.

(a) He keenly observes the destructive movements of Palestinians and develops a powerful critique of their terrorist activities with a persuasive power drawn from his Jewish origins.
(b) He develops a powerful critique of Israeli policies with a persuasive power drawn from his own Jewish origins.
(c) Palestinian occupation of Israel is the subject that worries him the most, and he writes a powerful critique with a comprehensive account of massacre and plunder.
(d) He blindly supports the Palestinian cause and even expects the U.S. to stand by an independent state for them.

2013

46. A paragraph is given below from which the last sentence has been deleted. From the given options, choose the one that completes the paragraph in the most appropriate way.

Twenty some years ago I took my family (wife, toddler, and infant) to the National Gallery of Art, in Washington, D.C. At one point I found myself alone, and I suddenly questioned my assumption that the toddler, my son, was with my wife, who also had the infant. As I stood in a gallery looking around for them, I saw a security guard framed in the door of an adjacent room. He was at first (as guards often are) as staid and unmoving as the statuary he was protecting. ____________

(a) Suspecting the worst, I ran into the room and saw my son, who wasn't with my wife, swinging on the frame of a huge painting.
(b) My eyes then moved on to the painting that I had almost become the proud owner of, Peter Paul Rubens' Daniel in the Lions' Den.
(c) As I glanced at him again, there came a crowd streaming inside the hall which made me curious for the reason of the commotion.
(d) Suddenly he flinched, gasped, and pointed agitatedly, horror smearing across his face.

47. A paragraph is given below from which the last sentence has been deleted. From the given options, choose the one that completes the paragraph in the most appropriate way.

Historians have established that parts of Bangalore were inhabited since the time of the Western Ganga dynasty (AD 350 to AD 550) and played a role in the fortunes of the Chola, Hoysala and Vijaynagar empires, as the place was situated in a strategic location at the center of the South Indian peninsula. In spite of this hoary history, the founding date of the city is usually given as AD 1537 when Kempe Gowda I built a mud fort which was later fortified by Haider Ali in the 18th century. This fort was the nucleus of what is now commonly known as the "pete" area, a Bangalore that preceded the arrival of the British. With the defeat of Tipu Sultan in Srirangapatnam, the British army garrisoned itself in the vicinity of the old city area of Bangalore, thus laying the foundation of Bangalore Cantonment in the early 19th century. ____________

(a) For a significant part of its history, Bangalore was a divided city.
(b) Through the 19th century the Cantonment gradually expanded and acquired a distinct cultural and political salience as it was governed directly by the British.
(c) This was the beginning of a very different Bangalore from the one that existed around the old fort.
(d) The overwhelming influence of the British also bequeathed a particularly libertarian cultural character to the Cantonment that the conservative residents of the city both loathed and longed for at the same time.

48. A paragraph is given below from which the last sentence has been deleted. From the given options, choose the one that completes the paragraph in the most appropriate way.

When India revised its policy with respect to foreign investment, the country's balance of payments difficulties had not been resolved. However, the presumption was that foreign firms would use India as a base for world market production, earning the country vast amounts of foreign exchange. However, that expectation has been belied. ____________

(a) This makes the foreign exchange cost of liberalization high and its implications for India's balance of payments adverse.
(b) Unable to limit foreign presence as a result, the government in those years opted for regulation to reduce the cost of foreign presence.
(c) That experience suggested that policy favouring foreign capital partly explained India's retarded development.
(d) Foreign firms do not engage in export, but their principal target remains the domestic market.

PARA-JUMBLES

1991

DIRECTIONS for Questions 1 to 69: Sentences given in each question, when properly sequenced, form a coherent paragraph. Each sentence is labelled with a letter. Choose the most logical order of the sentences from among the four given choices to construct a coherent paragraph.

1. A. And that the pursuit of money by whatever design within the law is always benign.
B. And it holds broadly that the greater the amount of money, the greater the intelligence.
C. This is the institutional truth of Wall Street, this you will be required to believe.
D. The institutional truth of the financial world holds that association with money implies intelligence.

(a) ACBD
(b) CDBA
(c) DBAC
(d) DCAB

2. A. Then think of by how much our advertising could increase the sales level.

B. Advertising effectiveness can be best grasped intuitively on a per capita basis.

C. Overall effectiveness is easily calculated by considering the number of buyers and the cost of advertising.

D. Think of how much of our brand the average individual is buying now.

(a) DCAB (b) DACB
(c) BCDA (d) ABCD

3. A. The age of pragmatism is here, whether we like it or not.

B. The staple rhetoric that was for so long dished out also belongs to the bipolar world of yesterday.

C. The old equations, based on the cold war and on non-alignment no longer holds good.

D. But contrary to much of what is being said and written, it is a multipolar rather than unipolar world that appears to be emerging out of recent events.

(a) ABCD (b) ACBD
(c) ADBC (d) ADCB

4. A. Past research has uncovered the fact that cognitive age is inversely related to life satisfaction among the elderly.

B. A person may feel young or old irrespective of chronological age.

C. That is, the 'younger' an elderly person feels, the more likely she or he is to be satisfied with life in general.

D. Cognitive age is a psychological construct that refers to one's subjective assessment of one's age.

(a) BDAC (b) DBAC
(c) DCAB (d) ABCD

5. A. It was a fascinating tempting green, like the hue of the great green grasshopper.

B. Her teeth were very white and her voice had a cruel and at the same time a coaxing sound.

C. While she was uncorking the bottle I noticed how green her eyeballs were.

D. I saw, too, how small her hands were, which showed that she did not use them much.

(a) ACBD (b) BACD
(c) CADB (d) BADC

6. A. By intelligence we mean a style of life, a way of behaving in various situations, and particularly in new, strange and perplexing situations.

B. When we talk about intelligence, we do not mean the ability to get a good score on a certain kind of test, or even the ability to do well at school.

C. The true test of intelligence is not how to do, but how we behave when we don't know what to do.

D. These are at best only indicators of something large, deeper and far more important.

(a) BDAC (b) CDBA
(c) ABCD (d) CABD

7. A. In formal speech, syllables are likely to be more deliberately sounded than in informal speech.

B. Yet dictionary editors have no choice but to deal with each word as an individual entity.

C. The pronunciation of words is influenced by the situation.

D. Further, the pronunciation of a word is affected by its position in the sentence and by the meaning it carries.

(a) ACBD (b) ACDB
(c) ABCD (d) CADB

1992

8. A. It is turning off the tap.

B. And with no consensus of the exit policy, the government is damned if it supports loss making units and damned if it doesn't.

C. The private sector did the same in the past because securing legal sanction for closure was virtually impossible.

D. After years of funding the losses of public sector companies, the government is doing the unthinkable.

(a) DACB (b) CADB
(c) DCAB (d) BDAC

9. A. Trade protocols were signed, the dollar as the medium of exchange was ignored, trade was denominated in rupees and the exchange rate between the two countries was to be fixed outside the ambit of free markets.

B. A young India, some years after independence fashioning her foreign policy of nonalignment, found it prudent to stay close to the former Soviet Union.

C. Once upon a time there was a super power named Soviet Union that attracted nations apprehensive of the global aspirations of the other superpower, the U.S.A.

D. One way of doing this was to evolve a bilateral relations in trade that could be called upon provide a buffer against the arm-twisting by the U.S.A.

(a) CBAD (b) BADC
(c) BCAD (d) CBDA

10. A. I had heard that sort of thing before.

B. He said that his generation was the first to believe that it had no future.

C. A young American made earthling stopped by my house the other day to talk about some book of mine he had read.

D. He was the son of a Boston man who had died an alcoholic vagrant.

(a) CDBA (b) ABCD
(c) CBAD (d) ABDC

11. A. This is probably one of the reasons why the number of women and men remain roughly equal in most societies.

B. Fortunately or unfortunately, individual couples cannot really be concerned about this overall 'error'.

C. Population growth then can be considered the error of this central process.

D. Purely at the human level, it appears that most couples like to have at least one living daughter and one living son when they are in the middle ages.

(a) CBDA (b) DACB
(c) DCBA (d) CDAB

12. A. Against this background, the current target of 12.8 percent does not seem that high a figure.

B. A better vantage point to evaluate the 12.8 percent target for export growth is our performance in the 'golden years' between 1986 – 87 and 1990 – 91, during which time exports in dollar terms increased by 17.1 percent.

C. In fact, the rate of growth would have to increase still further if we are to achieve the eighth plan target of export growth in value terms of 13.6 percent per annum.

D. Even in 1990 – 91, the year of the Gulf War, exports went up by 9 percent.

(a) BDAC (b) BCAD
(c) DABC (d) ACBD

13. A. Their growing costs and a growing economy-must be reckoned with realistically.

B. Central programmes persist and in some cases grow.

C. As demand expands, programmes expand.

D. It is extremely difficult to curtail them.

(a) CDAB (b) BCDA
(c) DABC (d) ACBD

14. A. It was never denied and seemed to be integrated into the city life.

B. The poverty was there right in the open in all the streets.

C. But, somehow it did not depress me as much as I had feared.

D. Indian society is associated with great poverty, and indeed I saw a lot of poverty in Bombay.

(a) ADBC (b) BCAD
(c) BCDA (d) DCBA

15. A. This has been going on now for nearly 200 years.

B. They haven't even been noticed much by central, state, or local governments, no matter how insolent or blasphemous or treasonous those writers may be.

C. But writers of novels, plays, short stories or poems have never been hurt or hampered much.

D. Journalists and teachers are often bullied or fired in my country for saying this or that.

(a) DCBA (b) ABCD
(c) BCDA (d) DCAB

1993

16. A. In emission trading, the government fixes the total amount of pollution that is acceptable to maintain a desired level of air quality.

B. Economists argue this approach makes air pollution control more cost – effective than the current practice of fixing air pollution standards and expecting all companies to pollute below these standards.

C. USA uses emission trading to control air pollution.

D. It then distributes emission permits to all companies in the region, which add up to the overall acceptable level of emission.

(a) BADC (b) ACDB
(c) CADB (d) DBAC

17. A. Realists believe that there is an objective reality "out there" independent of ourselves.

B. This reality exists solely by virtue of how the world is, and it is in principle discoverable by application of the methods of science.

C. They believe in the possibility of determining whether or not a theory is indeed really true or false.

D. I think it is fair to say that this is the position to which most working scientists subscribe.

(a) ABCD (b) CDBA
(c) DCBA (d) BCAD

18. A. All levels of demand, whether individual, aggregate, local, national, or international are subject to change.

B. At the same time, science and technology add new dimensions to products, their uses, and the methods used to market them.

C. Aggregate demand fluctuates with changes in the level of business activity, GNP, and national income.

D. The demands of individuals tend to vary with changing needs and rising income.

(a) CBDA (b) DCAB
(c) BCAD (d) ADCB

19. A. There is a strong manufacturing base for a variety of products.

B. India has come a long way on the technology front.

C. But the technology adopted has been largely of foreign origin.

D. There are however areas such as atomic energy, space, agriculture, and defense where significant strides have been made in evolving relevant technologies within the country.

(a) ADCB (b) DBAC
(c) BACD (d) CBAD

20. A. Secret persons shall strike with weapons, fire or poison.

B. Clans mutually supporting each other shall be made to strike at the weak points.

C. He shall destroy their caravans, herds, forests and troop reinforcements.

D. The conqueror shall cause enemy kingdom to be destroyed by neighboring kings, jungle tribes, pretenders or unjustly treated princes.

(a) DCBA (b) ABCD
(c) BDCA (d) ADCB

21. A. The individual companies vary in size, from the corner grocery to the industrial giant.

B. Policies and management methods within firms range from formal well-planned organization and controls to slipshod day-to-day operations.

C. Various industries offer a wide array of products or services through millions of firms largely independent of each other.

D. Variation in the form of ownership contributes to diversity in capital investment, volume of business, and financial structure.

(a) DBCA (b) CADB
(c) BADC (d) ADCB

1994

22. A. To have settled one's affairs is a very good preparation to leading the rest of one's life without concern for the future.

B. When I have finished this book I shall know where I stand.

C. One does not die immediately after one has made one's will; one make's one's will as a precaution.

D. I can afford then to do what I choose with the years that remain to me.

(a) DBAC (b) CABD
(c) BDAC (d) CBDA

23. A. It is sad that India has always been in a hurry to conform to the western thought, especially the American.

B. Even the smaller countries have the guts to take a firm contrarian stand if they feel the policies happen to compromise their country's interest.

C. It's one thing to sprout theories on liberalization, and entirely another to barter the interests of the nation in it's name.

D. In this case too, while a large number of countries are yet to ratify the GATT, India has not only ratified the treaty, but is also preparing to amend the Patents Act.

(a) CABD (b) DCAB
(c) CBDA (d) BDCA

24. A. But instead you are faced with another huge crag and the weary trail continues.

B. No, the path wind on and another mountain bars your way.

C. When for days you have been going through a mountain pass, a moment comes when you are sure that after winding around the great mass of rock in front of you, you will come upon the plain.

D. Surely after this you will see the plain.

(a) CDBA (b) BADC
(c) CADB (d) BCAD

25. A. During one exhibition, however, some air became mixed with the hydrogen, and in the words of the shaken performer: "The explosion was so dreadful that I imagined all my teeth had been blown out!"

B. An entertainer would finish his acts by blowing the hydrogen he had inhaled towards a lighted candle; as the hydrogen caught fire, flames would shoot menacingly from his lips.

C. A paper bag filled with hydrogen amazed guests by zooming off into space.

D. When people learned about its unique lighter-than-air property, they began to use it in all sorts of parlor stunts.

(a) DCBA (b) DBAC
(c) CABD (d) ACBD

26. A. It is exciting and various.

B. I am a writer as I might have been a doctor or a lawyer.

C. The writer is free to work in what he believes.

D. It is so pleasant a profession that it not surprising if a vast number of persons adopt it who have no qualifications for it.

(a) CADB (b) ABDC
(c) DBCA (d) BDAC

27. A. there was the hope that in another existence a greater happiness would reward one

B. previous existence, and the effort to do better would be less difficult too when

C. it would be less difficult to bear the evils of one's own life if

D. one could think that they were but the necessary outcome of one's errors in a

(a) CABD (b) BDCA
(c) BADC (d) CDBA

28. A. he can only renew himself if his soul

B. he renews himself and

C. the writer can only be fertile if

D. is constantly enriched by fresh experience

(a) CBAD (b) CADB
(c) BDCA (d) BACD

29. A. but a masterpiece is

B. untaught genius

C. a laborious career than as the lucky fluke of

D. more likely to come as the culminating point of

(a) CDAB (b) ADCB
(c) CDBA (d) ACDB

30. A. what interests you is the way in which you have a created the illusion

B. they are angry with you, for it was

C. the public is easily disillusioned and then

D. the illusion they loved; they do not understand that

(a) ACBD (b) BDCA
(c) CBDA (d) BCAD

31. A. an adequate physical and social infrastructure level

B. the pattern of spatial growth in these towns as also to

C. the failure of the government to ensure

D. the roots of the riots are related to

(a) ACBD (b) DBCA
(c) ABDC (d) CBDA

1995

32. A. Where there is division there must be conflict, not only division between man and woman, but also division on the basis of race, religion and language.

B. We said the present condition of racial divisions, linguistic divisions has brought out so many wars.

C. Also we went into the question as to why does this conflict between man and man exist.

D. May we continue with what we were discussing last evening?

(a) ABCD (b) DBCA
(c) BCAD (d) BDAC

33. A. No other documents give us so intimate a sense of the tone and temper of the first generation poets.

B. Part of the interest of the journal is course historical.

C. And the clues to Wordsworth's creative processes which the journal affords are of decisive significance.

D. Not even in their own letters do Wordsworth and Coleridge stand so present before us than they do through the references in the journal.

(a) BACD (b) BDAC
(c) CBAD (d) DABC

34. A. These high plans died, slowly but definitively, and were replaced by the dream of a huge work on philosophy.

B. In doing whatever little he could of the new plan, the poet managed to write speculations on theology,and political theory.

C. The poet's huge ambitions included writing a philosophic epic on the origin of evil.

D. However, not much was done in this regard either, with only fragments being written.

(a) ABCD (b) CBAD
(c) CDAB (d) CADB

35. A. We can never leave off wondering how that which has ever been should cease to be.
B. As we advance in life, we acquire a keener sense of the value of time.
C. Nothing else, indeed, seems to be of any consequence; and we become misers in this sense.
D. We try to arrest its few last tottering steps, and to make it linger on the brink of the grave.
(a) ACDB (b) BCDA
(c) BDCA (d) ABCD

36. A. There is no complete knowledge about anything.
B. Our thinking is the outcome of knowledge, and knowledge is always limited.
C. Knowledge always goes hand in hand with ignorance.
D. Therefore, our thinking which is born out of knowledge, is always limited under all circumstances.
(a) BCAD (b) BCDA
(c) DABC (d) CBDA

1996

37. A. Still, Sophie might need an open heart surgery later in life and now be more prone to respiratory infections.
B. But with the news that his infant daughter Sophie has a hole in her heart, he appears quite vulnerable.
C. While the condition sounds bad, it is not life threatening, and frequently corrects itself.
D. Sylvester Stallone has made millions and built a thriving career out of looking invincible.
(a) DCAB (b) DBAC
(c) DBCA (d) DCBA

38. A. However, the severed head could not grow back if fire could be applied instantly to the amputated part.
B. To get rid of this monstrosity was truly a Herculean task, for as soon as one head was cut off, two new ones replaced it.
C. Hercules accomplished this labour with the aid of an assistant who cauterized the necks as fast as Hercules cut off the heads!
D. One of the twelve labours of Hercules was the killing of hydra, a water monster with nine heads.
(a) DCBA (b) ABCD
(c) DBAC (d) BDCA

39. A. That Hollywood is a man's world is certainly true, but it is not the whole truth.
B. Even Renaissance film actress, Jodie Foster, who hosts this compendium of movie history, confesses surprise at this.
C. She says that she had no idea that women were so active in the industry even in those days.
D. During the silent era, for example, female scriptwriters outnumbered males 10 to 1.
(a) ADBC (b) ABDC
(c) DCAB (d) ABCD

40. A. Its business decisions are made on the timely and accurate flow of information.
B. It has 1,700 employees in 13 branch and representative offices across the Asia-Pacific region.
C. For employees to maintain a competitive edge in a fast-moving field, they must have quick access to JP Morgan's proprietary trade related data.
D. JP Morgan's is one of the largest banking institutions in the US and a premier international trading firm.
(a) DBAC (b) DCBA
(c) CDAB (d) DCAB

41. A. The Saheli Programme, run by the US Cross-Cultural Solutions, is offering a three week tour of India that involves a lot more than frenzied sightseeing.
B. Participants interested in women's issues will learn about arranged marriages, dowry and infanticide.
C. Holiday packages include all sorts of topics, but female infanticide must be the first for tourism.
D. Interspersed with these talks and meetings are visits to cities like New Delhi and Agra, home to the Taj Mahal.
(a) ACBD (b) CDBA
(c) ADBC (d) CABD

42. A. Something magical is happening to our planet.
B. Some are calling it a paradigm shift.
C. Its getting smaller.
D. Others call it business transformation.
(a) ABDC (b) ACDB
(c) ABCD (d) ACBD

1997

43. A. It begins with an ordinary fever and a moderate cough.

B. India could be under attack from a class of germs that cause what are called atypical pneumonias.

C. Slowly, a sore throat progresses to bronchitis and then pneumonia and respiratory complications.

D. It appears like the ordinary flu, but baffled doctors find that the usual drugs don't work.

(a) ABCD (b) BDAC
(c) ADCB (d) BCDA

44. A. Chemists mostly don't stock it: only a few government hospitals do but in limited quantities.

B. Delhi's building boom is creating a bizarre problem: snakes are increasingly biting people as they emerge from their disturbed underground homes.

C. There isn't enough anti-snake serum, largely because there is no centralised agency that distributes the product.

D. If things don't improve, more people could face paralysis, and even death.

(a) BCAD (b) DBCA
(c) ABCD (d) CABD

45. A. But the last decade has witnessed greater voting and political participation by various privileged sections.

B. If one goes by the earlier record of mid-term elections, it is likely that the turnout in 1998 will drop by anything between four and six percentage points over the already low polling of 58 per cent in 1996.

C. If this trend offsets the mid-term poll fatigue, the fall may not be so steep.

D. Notwithstanding a good deal of speculation on this issue, it is still not clear as to who benefits from a lower turnout.

(a) BACD (b) ABCD
(c) DBAC (d) CBDA

46. A. After several routine elections there comes a 'critical' election which redefines the basic pattern of political loyalties, redraws political geography and opens up political space.

B. In psephological jargon, they call it realignment.

C. Rather, since 1989, there have been a series of semi-critical elections.

D. On a strict definition, none of the recent Indian elections qualifies as a critical election.

(a) ABCD (b) ABDC
(c) DBAC (d) DCBA

47. A. Trivial pursuits marketed by the Congress, is a game imported from Italy.

B. The idea is to create an imaginary saviour in times of crisis so that the party doesn't fall flat on its collective face.

C. Closest contenders are Mani Shankar Aiyar, who still hears His Master's Voice and V. George, who is frustrated by the fact that his political future remains Sonia and yet so far.

D. The current champion is Arjun for whom all roads lead to Rome, or in this case, 10 Janpath.

(a) ABDC (b) ABCD
(c) DCBA (d) CDBA

48. A. Good advertising can make people buy your products even if it sucks.

B. A dollar spent on brainwashing is more cost-effective than a dollar spent on product improvement.

C. That's important because it takes pressure off you to make good products.

D. Obviously, there's a minimum quality that every product has to achieve: it should be able to withstand the shipping process without becoming unrecognizable.

(a) BACD (b) ACBD
(c) ADCB (d) BCDA

49. A. Almost a century ago, when the father of the modern automobile industry, Henry Ford, sold the first Model T car, he decided that only the best would do for his customers.

B. Today, it is committed to delivering the finest quality with over six million vehicles a year in over 200 countries across the world.

C. And for over 90 years, this philosophy has endured in the Ford Motor Company.

D. Thus, a vehicle is ready for the customer only if it passes the Ford 'Zero Defect Programme'.

(a) ABCD (b) ACDB
(c) ACBD (d) CDAB

50. A. But, clearly, the government still has the final say.

B. In the past few years, the Reserve Bank of India might have wrested considerable powers from the government when it comes to monetary policy.

C. The RBI's announcements on certain issues become effective only after the government notifies them.

D. Isn't it time the government vested the RBI with powers to sanction such changes, leaving their ratification for later?

(a) ACDB (b) ACBD
(c) BACD (d) DACB

51. A. I sat there frowning at the checkered tablecloth, chewing the bitter cud of insight.
B. That wintry afternoon in Manhattan, waiting in the little French restaurant, I was feeling frustrated and depressed.
C. Even the prospect of seeing a dear friend failed to cheer me as it usually did.
D. Because of certain miscalculations on my part, a project of considerable importance in my life had fallen through.
(a) ADBC (b) BCDA
(c) BDCA (d) ABCD

52. A. Perhaps the best known is the Bay Area Writing Project, founded by James Gray in 1974.
B. The decline in writing skills can be stopped.
C. Today's back-to-basics movement has already forced some schools to place renewed emphasis on writing skills.
D. Although the inability of some teachers to teach writing successfully remains a big stumbling block, a number of programmes have been developed to attack this problem.
(a) BCDA (b) ADCB
(c) ACBD (d) CABD

1998

53. A. He was carrying his jacket and walked with his head thrown back.
B. As Annette neared the lamp she saw a figure walking slowly.
C. For a while Michael walked on and she followed 20 paces behind.
D. With a mixture of terror and triumph of recognition she slackened her pace.
(a) ABCD (b) BADC
(c) BCDA (d) ACBD

54. A. However, the real challenge today is in unlearning, which is much harder.
B. But the new world of business behaves differently from the world in which we grew up.
C. Learning is important for both people and organisations.
D. Each of us has a 'mental model' that we've used over the years to make sense.
(a) CADB (b) BDAC
(c) CDAB (d) ACBD

55. A. There was nothing quite like a heavy downpour of rain to make life worthwhile.
B. We reached the field, soaked to the skin, and surrounded it.
C. The wet, as far as he was concerned, was ideal.
D. There, sure enough, stood Claudius, looking like a debauched Roman emperor under a shower.
(a) DCBA (b) BDCA
(c) BADC (d) BACD

56. A. Alex had never been happy with his Indian origins.
B. He set about rectifying this grave injustice by making his house in his own image of a country manor.
C. Fate had been unfair to him; if he had had his wish, he would have been a count or an Earl on some English estate, or a medieval monarch in a chateau in France.
D. This illusion of misplaced grandeur, his wife felt, would be Alex's undoing.
(a) ACDB (b) ABDC
(c) ACBD (d) CABD

57. A. The influence is reflected the most in beaded evening wear.
B. Increasingly, the influence of India's colours and cuts can be seen on western styles.
C. And even as Nehru jackets and Jodhpurs remain staples of the fashion world, designers such as Armani and McFadden have turned to the sleek silhouette of the churidar this year.
D. Indian hot pink, paprika and saffron continue to be popular colours, year in and year out.
(a) BADC (b) ABCD
(c) BCAD (d) DABC

58. A. Such a national policy will surely divide and never unite the people.
B. In fact, it suits the purpose of the politicians; they can drag the people into submission by appealing to them in the name of religion.
C. In order to inculcate the unquestioning belief they condemn the other states, which do not follow their religion.
D. The emergence of the theocratic states, where all types of crimes are committed in the name of religion, has revived the religion of the Middle Ages.
(a) ABCD (b) DBCA
(c) DBAC (d) CDAB

59. A. His left-hand concealed a blackjack, his right-hand groped for the torch in his pocket.
B. The meeting was scheduled for 9 o'clock, and his watch showed the time to be a quarter to nine.
C. The man lurked in the corner, away from the glare of light.
D. His heart thumped in his chest, sweat beads formed themselves on his forehead, his mouth was dry.
(a) CABD (b) BDAC
(c) BADC (d) ABCD

60. A. The director walked into the room and took a look around the class.
B. Mitch wanted to scream — the illogicality of the entire scene struck him dumb.
C. The managers stared at him with the look of fear that no democratic country should tolerate in its people.
D. He walked out of the room — it was his irrevocable protest against an insensible and insensitive situation.
(a) ACBD (b) BDAC
(c) BCAD (d) ABCD

61. A. The establishment of the Third Reich influenced events in American history by starting a chain of events which culminated in war between Germany and the United States.
B. The Neutrality Acts of 1935 and 1936 prohibited trade with any belligerents or loans to them.
C. While speaking out against Hitler's atrocities, the American people generally favoured isolationist policies and neutrality.
D. The complete destruction of democracy, the persecution of Jews, the war on religion, the cruelty and barbarism of the allies, caused great indignation in this country and brought on fear of another World War.
(a) ABCD (b) CBDA
(c) CDBA (d) ADCB

62. A. An essay which appeals chiefly to the intellect is Francis Bacon's *Of Studies*.
B. His careful tripartite division of studies expressed succinctly in aphoristic prose demands the complete attention of the mind of the reader.
C. He considers studies as they should be; for pleasure, for self-improvement, for business.
D. He considers the evils of excess study: laziness, affectation, and preciosity.
(a) DCBA (b) ABCD
(c) CDBA (d) ACBD

63. A. By reasoning we mean the mental process of drawing an inference from two or more statements or going from the inference to the statements, which yield that inference.
B. So logical reasoning covers those types of questions, which imply drawing an inference from the problems.
C. Logic means, if we take its original meaning, the science of valid reasoning.
D. Clearly, for understanding arguments and for drawing the inference correctly, it is necessary that we should understand thc statements first.
(a) ACBD (b) CABD
(c) ABCD (d) DBCA

1999

64. A. In rejecting the functionalism in positivist organization theory, either wholly or partially, there is often a move towards a political model of organization theory.
B. Thus, the analysis would shift to the power resources possessed by different groups in the organization and the way they use these resources in actual power plays to shape the organizational structure.
C. At the extreme, in one set of writings, the growth of administrators in the organization is held to be completely unrelated to the work to be done and to be caused totally by the political pursuit of self-interest.
D. The political model holds that individual interests are pursued in organizational life through the exercise of power and influence.
(a) ADBC (b) CBAD
(c) DBCA (d) ABDC

65. A. Group decision-making, however, does not necessarily fully guard against arbitrariness and anarchy, for individual capriciousness can get substituted by collusion of group members.
B. Nature itself is an intricate system of checks and balances, meant to preserve the delicate balance between various environmental factors that affect our ecology.
C. In institutions also, there is a need to have in place a system of checks and balances which inhibits the concentration of power in the hands of only some individuals.
D. When human interventions alter this delicate balance, the outcomes have been seen to be disastrous.
(a) CDAB (b) BCAD
(c) CABD (d) BDCA

66. A. He was bone-weary and soul-weary, and found himself muttering, "Either I can't manage this place, or it's unmanageable."
B. To his horror, he realized that he had become the victim of an amorphous, unwitting, unconscious conspiracy to immerse him in routine work that had no significance.
C. It was one of those nights in the office when the office clock was moving towards four in the morning and Bennis was still not through with the incredible mass of paper stacked before him.
D. He reached for his calendar and ran his eyes down each hour, half-hour, and quarter-hour, to see where his time had gone that day, the day before, the month before.
(a) ABCD (b) CADB
(c) BDCA (d) DCBA

67. A. With that, I swallowed the shampoo, and obtained the most realistic results almost on the spot.

B. The man shuffled away into the back regions to make up a prescription, and after a moment I got through on the shop-telephone to the Consulate, intimating my location.

C. Then, while the pharmacist was wrapping up a six-ounce bottle of the mixture, I groaned and inquired whether he could give me something for acute gastric cramp.

D. I intended to stage a sharp gastric attack, and entering an old-fashioned pharmacy, I asked for a popular shampoo mixture, consisting of olive oil and flaked soap.

(a) DCBA (b) DACB

(c) BDAC (d) BCDA

2000

68. A. The likelihood of an accident is determined by how carefully the motorist drives and how carefully the pedestrian crosses the street.

B. An accident involving a motorist and a pedestrian is such a case.

C. Each must decide how much care to exercise without knowing how careful the other is.

D. The simplest strategic problem arises when two individuals interact with each other, and each must decide what to do without knowing what the other is doing.

(a) ABCD (b) ADCB

(c) DBCA (d) DBAC

2001

69. A. The situations in which violence occurs and the nature of that violence tends to be clearly defined at least in theory, as in the proverbial Irishman's question: "Is this a private fight or can anyone join in?"

B. So the actual risk to outsiders, though no doubt higher than our societies, is calculable.

C. Probably the only uncontrolled applications of force are those of social superiors to social inferiors and even here there are probably some rules.

D. However, binding the obligation to kill, members of feuding families engaged in mutual massacre will be genuinely appalled if by some mischance a bystander or outsider is killed.

(a) DABC (b) ACDB

(c) CBAD (d) DBAC

DIRECTIONS for Questions 70 to 100: The sentences given in each question, when properly sequenced, form a coherent paragraph. Each sentence is labelled with a letter. Choose the most logical order of sentences from among the four given choices to construct a coherent paragraph.

1999

70. A. Since then, intelligence tests have been mostly used to separate dull children in school from average or bright children, so that special education can be provided to the dull.

B. In other words, intelligence tests give us a norm for each age.

C. Intelligence is expressed as intelligence quotient, and tests are developed to indicate what an average child of a certain age can do .... What a five-year-old can answer, but a four-year-old cannot, for instance.

D. Binet developed the first set of such tests in the early 1900s to find out which children in school needed special attention.

E. Intelligence can be measured by tests.

(a) CDABE (b) DECAB

(c) EDACB (d) CBADE

2000

71. A. If caught in the act, they were punished, not for the crime, but for allowing themselves to be caught another lash of the whip.

B. The bellicose Spartans sacrificed all the finer things in life for military expertise.

C. Those fortunate enough to survive babyhood were taken away from their mothers at the age of seven to undergo rigorous military training.

D. This consisted mainly of beatings and deprivations of all kinds like going around barefoot in winter, and worse, starvation so that they would be forced to steal food to survive.

E. Male children were examined at birth by the city council and those deemed too weak to become soldiers were left to die of exposure.

(a) BECDA (b) ECADB

(c) BCDAE (d) ECDAB

2000

72. A. This very insatiability of the photographing eye changes the terms of confinement in the cave, our world.

B. Humankind lingers unregenerately in Plato's cave, still revelling, its age-old habit, in mere images of truth.

C. But being educated by photographs is not like being educated by older images drawn by hand; for one thing, there are a great many more images around, claiming our attention.

D. The inventory started in 1839 and since then just about everything has been photographed, or so it seems.

E. In teaching us a new visual code, photographs alter and enlarge our notions of what is worth looking at and what we have a right to observe.

(a) EABCD (b) BDEAC
(c) BCDAE (d) ECDAB

73. A. To be culturally literate is to possess the basic information needed to thrive in the modern world.

B. Nor is it confined to one social class; quite the contrary.

C. It is by no means confined to 'culture' narrowly understood as an acquaintance with the arts.

D. Cultural literacy constitutes the only sure avenue of opportunity for disadvantaged children, the only reliable way of combating the social determinism that now condemns them.

E. The breadth of that information is great, extending over the major domains of human activity from sports to science.

(a) AECBD (b) DECBA
(c) ACBED (d) DBCAE

74. A. Both parties use capital and labour in the struggle to secure property rights.

B. The thief spends time and money in his attempt to steal (he buys wire cutters)and the legitimate property owner expends resources to prevent the theft (he buys locks).

C. A social cost of theft is that both the thief and the potential victim use resources to gain or maintain control over property.

D. These costs may escalate as a type of technological arms race unfolds.

E. A bank may purchase more and more complicated and sophisticated safes, forcing safecrackers to invest further in safecracking equipment.

(a) ABCDE (b) CABDE
(c) ACBED (d) CBEDA

2001

75. A. Michael Hofman, a poet and translator, accepts this sorry fact without approval or complaint.

B. But thanklessness and impossibility do not daunt him.

C. He acknowledges too — in fact, he returns to the point often — that best translators of poetry always fail at some level.

D. Hofman feels passionately about his work and this is clear from his writings.

E. In terms of the gap between worth and rewards, translators come somewhere near nurses and street-cleaners.

(a) EACDB (b) ADEBC
(c) EACBD (d) DCEAB

76. A. Passivity is not, of course, universal.

B. In areas where there are no lords or laws, or in frontier zones where all men go armed, the attitude of the peasantry may well be different.

C. So indeed it may be on the fringe of the unsubmissive.

D. However, for most of the soil-bound peasants the problem is not whether to be normally passive or active, but when to pass from one state to another.

E. This depends on an assessment of the political situation.

(a) BEDAC (b) CDABE
(c) EDBAC (d) ABCDE

2002

77. A. As officials, their vision of a country shouldn't run too far beyond that of the local people with whom they have to deal.

B. Ambassadors have to choose their words.

C. To say what they feel they have to say, they appear to be denying or ignoring part of what they know.

D. So, with ambassadors as with other expatriates in black Africa, there appears at a first meeting a kind of ambivalence.

E. They do a specialized job and it is necessary for them to live ceremonial lives.

(a) BCEDA (b) BEDAC
(c) BEADC (d) BCDEA

78. A. "This face-off will continue for several months given the strong convictions on either side," says a senior functionary of the high-powered task force on drought.

B. During the past week-and-half, the Central Government has sought to deny some of the earlier apprehensions over the impact of drought.

C. The recent revival of the rains had led to the emergence of a line of divide between the two.

D. The state governments, on the other hand, allege that the Centre is downplaying the crisis only to evade its full responsibility of financial assistance that is required to alleviate the damage.

E. Shrill alarm about the economic impact of an inadequate monsoon had been sounded by the Centre as well as most of the states, in late July and early August.

(a) EBCDA (b) DBACE
(c) BDCAE (d) ECBDA

79. A. This fact was established in the 1730s by French survey expeditions to Equador near the Equator and Lapland in the Arctic, which found that around the middle of the earth the arc was about a kilometer shorter.

B. One of the unsettled scientific questions in the late 18th century was that of exact nature of the shape of the earth.

C. The length of one-degree arc would be less near the equatorial latitudes than at the poles.

D. One way of doing that is to determine the length of the arc along a chosen longitude or meridian at one degree latitude separation.

E. While it was generally known that the earth was not a sphere but an 'oblate spheroid', more curved at the equator and flatter at the poles, the question of 'how much more' was yet to be established.

(a) BECAD (b) BEDCA
(c) EDACB (d) EBDCA

2003

80. A. A few months ago I went to Princeton University to see what the young people who are going to be running our country in a few decades are like.

B. I would go to sleep in my hotel room around midnight each night, and when I awoke, my mailbox would be full of replies—sent at 1:15 a.m., 2:59 a.m., 3:23 a.m.

C. One senior told me that she went to bed around two and woke up each morning at seven; she could afford that much rest because she had learned to supplement her full day of work by studying in her sleep.

D. Faculty members gave me the names of a few dozen articulate students, and I sent them e-mails, inviting them out to lunch or dinner in small groups.

E. As she was falling asleep she would recite a math problem or a paper topic to herself; she would then sometimes dream about it, and when she woke up, the problem might be solved.

(a) DABCE (b) DACEB
(c) ADBCE (d) AECBD

81. A. Four days later, Oracle announced its own bid for PeopleSoft, and invited the firm's board to a discussion.

B. Furious that his own plans had been endangered, PeopleSoft's boss, Craig Conway, called Oracle's offer "diabolical", and its boss, Larry Ellison, a "sociopath".

C. In early June, PeopleSoft said that it would buy J.D. Edwards, a smaller rival.

D. Moreover, said Mr. Conway, he "could imagine no price nor combination of price and other conditions to recommend accepting the offer."

E. On June 12th, PeopleSoft turned Oracle down.

(a) CABDE (b) CADBE
(c) CEDAB (d) CAEBD

82. A. Surrendered, or captured, combatants cannot be incarcerated in razor wire cages; this 'war' has a dubious legality.

B. How can then one characterize a conflict to be waged against a phenomenon as war?

C. The phrase 'war against terror', which has passed into the common lexicon, is a huge misnomer.

D. Besides, war has a juridical meaning in international law, which has codified the laws of war, imbuing them with a humanitarian content.

E. Terror is a phenomenon, not an entity—either State or non-State.

(a) ECDBA (b) BECDA
(c) EBCAD (d) CEBDA

83. A. I am much more intolerant of a human being's shortcomings than I am of an animal's, but in this respect I have been lucky, for most of the people I have come across have been charming.

B. Then you come across the unpleasant human animal—the District Officer who drawled, 'We chaps are here to help you chaps,' and then proceeded to be as obstructive as possible.

C. In these cases of course, the fact that you are an animal collector helps; people always seem delighted to meet someone with such an unusual occupation and go out of their way to assist you.

D. Fortunately, these types are rare, and the pleasant ones I have met more than compensated for them—but even so, I think I will stick to animals.

E. When you travel round the world collecting animals you also, of necessity, collect human beings.

(a) EACBD (b) ABDCE
(c) ECBDA (d) ACBDE

84. A. To avoid this, the QWERTY layout put the keys most likely to be hit in rapid succession on opposite sides. This made the keyboard slow, the story goes, but that was the idea.

B. A different layout, which had been patented by August Dvorak in 1936, was shown to be much faster.

C. The QWERTY design (patented by Christopher Sholes in 1868 and sold to Remington in 1873) aimed to solve a mechanical problem of early typewriters.

D. Yet the Dvorak layout has never been widely adopted, even though (with electric typewriters and then PCs)the anti-jamming rational for QWERTY has been defunct for years.

E. When certain combinations of keys were struck quickly, the type bars often jammed.

(a) BDACE (b) CEABD
(c) BCDEA (d) CAEBD

85. A. The wall does not simply divide Israel from a putative Palestinian state on the basis of the 1967 borders.

B. A chilling omission from the road map is the gigantic 'separation wall' now being built in the West Bank by Israel.

C. It is surrounded by trenches, electric wire and moats; there are watchtowers at regular intervals.

D. It actually takes new tracts of Palestinian and, sometimes five or six kilometres at a stretch.

E. Almost a decade after the end of South African apartheid this ghastly racist wall is going up with scarcely a peep from Israel's American allies who are going to pay for most of it.

(a) EBCAD (b) BADCE
(c) AEDCB (d) ECADB

86. A. Luckily the tide of battle moved elsewhere after the American victory at Midway and an Australian victory over Japan at Milne Bay.

B. It could have been no more than a delaying tactic.

C. The Australian military, knowing the position was hopeless, planned to fall back to the south-east in the hope of defending the main cities.

D. They had captured most of the Solomon Islands and much of New Guinea, and seemed poised for an invasion.

E. Not many people outside Australia realize how close the Japanese got.

(a) EDCBA (b) ECDAB
(c) ADCBE (d) CDBAE

87. A. Call it the third wave sweeping the Indian media.

B. Now they are starring in a new role, as suave dealmakers who are in a hurry to strike alliances and agreements.

C. Look around and you will find a host of deals that have been inked or are ready to be finalized.

D. Then the media barons wrested back control from their editors, and turned marketing warriors with the brand as their missile.

E. The first came with those magnificent men in their mahogany chambers who took on the world with their mighty fountain pens.

(a) ACBED (b) CEBDA
(c) CAEBD (d) AEDBC

88. A. The celebrations of economic recovery in Washington may be as premature as that 'Mission Accomplished' banner hung on the USS Abraham Lincoln to hail the end of the Iraq war.

B. Meanwhile, in the real world, the struggles of families and communities continue unabated.

C. Washington responded to the favourable turn in economic news with enthusiasm.

D. The celebrations and high-fives up and down Pennsylvania Avenue are not to be found beyond the Beltway.

E. When the third quarter GDP showed growth of 7.2% and the monthly unemployment rate dipped to six per cent euphoria gripped the US capital.

(a) ACEDB (b) CEDAB
(c) ECABD (d) ECBDA

89. A. To much of the Labour movement, it symbolises the brutality of the upper classes.

B. And to everybody watching, the current mess over foxhunting symbolises the government's weakness.

C. To foxhunting's supporters, Labour's 1991 manifesto commitment to ban it symbolises the party's metropolitan roots and hostility to the countryside.

D. Small issues sometimes have large symbolic power.

E. To those who enjoy thundering across the countryside in red coats after foxes, foxhunting symbolises the ancient roots of rural lives.

(a) DEACB (b) ECDBA
(c) CEADB (d) DBAEC

90. A. In the case of King Merolchazzar's courtship of the Princess of the Outer Isles, there occurs a regrettable hitch.

B. She acknowledges the gifts, but no word of a meeting date follows.

C. The monarch, hearing good reports of a neighbouring princess, dispatches messengers with gifts to her court, beseeching an interview.

D. The princess names a date, and a formal meeting takes place; after that everything buzzes along pretty smoothly.

E. Royal love affairs in olden days were conducted on the correspondence method.

(a) ACBDE (b) ABCDE
(c) ECDAB (d) ECBAD

91. A. Who can trace to its first beginnings the love of Damon for Pythias, of David for Jonathan, of Swan for Edgar?

B. Similarly with men.

C. There is about great friendships between man and man a certain inevitability that can only be compared with the age-old association of ham and eggs.

D. One simply feels that it is one of the things that must be so.

E. No one can say what was the mutual magnetism that brought the deathless partnership of these wholesome and palatable foodstuffs about.

(a) ACBED (b) CEDBA
(c) ACEBD (d) CEABD

92. A. Events intervened, and in the late 1930s and 1940s, Germany suffered from 'over-branding'.

B. The British used to be fascinated by the home of Romanticism.

C. But reunification and the federal government's move to Berlin have prompted Germany to think again about its image.

D. The first foreign package holiday was a tour of Germany organized by Thomas Cook in 1855.

E. Since then Germany has been understandably nervous about promoting itself abroad.

(a) ACEBD (b) DECAB
(c) BDAEC (d) DBAEC

2004

93. A. The two neighbours never fought each other.

B. Fights involving three male fiddler crabs have been recorded, but the status of the participants was unknown

C. They pushed or grappled only with the intruder.

D. We recorded 17 cases in which a resident that was fighting an intruder was joined by an immediate neighbour, an ally.

E. We therefore tracked 268 intruder males until we saw them fighting a resident male.

(a) BEDAC (b) DEBAC
(c) BDCAE (d) BCEDA

94. A. In the west, Allied Forces had fought their way through southern Italy as far as Rome.

B. In June 1944 Germany's military position in World War too appeared hopeless

C. In Britain, the task of amassing the men and materials for the liberation of northern Europe had been completed.

D. Red Army was poised to drive the Nazis back through Poland.

E. The situation on the eastern front was catastrophic.

(a) EDACB (b) BEDAC
(c) BDECA (d) CEDAB

95. A. He felt justified in bypassing Congress altogether on a variety of moves.

B. At times he was fighting the entire Congress.

C. Bush felt he had a mission to restore power to the presidency.

D. Bush was not fighting just the democrats.

E. Representatives democracy is a messy business, and a CEO of the white House does not like a legislature of second guessers and time wasters.

(a) CAEDB (b) DBAEC
(c) CEADB (d) ECDBA

96. A. But this does not mean that death was the Egyptians' only preoccupation.

B. Even papyri come mainly from pyramid temples.

C. Most of our traditional sources of information about the Old Kingdom are monuments of the rich like pyramids and tombs.

D. Houses in which ordinary Egyptian lived have not been preserved, and when most people died they were buried in simple graves.

E. We know infinitely more about the wealthy people of Egypt than we do about the ordinary people, as most monuments were made for the rich.

(a) CDBEA (b) ECDAB
(c) EDCBA (d) DECAB

97. A. Experts such as Larry Burns, head of research at GM, reckon that only such a full hearted leap will allow the world to cope with the mass motorization that will one day come to China or India.

B. But once hydrogen is being produced from biomass or extracted from underground coal or made from water, using nuclear or renewable electricity, the way will be open for a huge reduction in carbon emissions from the whole system.

C. In theory, once all the bugs have been sorted out, fuel cells should deliver better total fuel economy than any existing engines.

D. That is twice as good as the internal combustion engine, but only five percentage points better than a diesel hybrid.

E. Allowing for the resources needed to extract hydrogen from hydrocarbon, oil coal or gas, the fuel cell has an efficiency of 30%.

(a) CEDBA (b) CEBDA
(c) AEDBC (d) ACEBD

2005

98. A. Similarly, turning to caste, even though being lower caste is undoubtedly a separate cause of disparity, its impact is all the greater when the lower-caste families also happen to be poor.

B. Belonging to a privileged class can help a woman to overcome many barriers that obstruct women from less thriving classes.

C. It is the interactive presence of these two kinds of deprivation – being low class and being female – that massively impoverishes women from the less privileged classes.

D. A congruence of class deprivation and gender discrimination can blight the lives of poorer women very severely.

E. Gender is certainly a contributor to societal inequality, but it does not act independently of class.

(a) EABDC (b) EBDCA
(c) DAEBC (d) BECDA

99. A. What identity is thus 'defined by contrast', divergence with the West becomes central.

B. Indian religious literature such as the *Bhagavad Gita* or the Tantric texts, which are identified as differing from secular writings seen as 'western', elicits much greater interest in the West than do other Indian writings, including India's long history of heterodoxy.

C. There is a similar neglect of Indian writing on non-religious subjects, from mathematics, epistemology and natural science to economics and linguistics.

D. Through selective emphasis that point up differences with the West, other civilizations can, in this way, be redefined in alien terms, which can be exotic and charming, or else bizarre and terrifying, or simply strange and engaging.

E. The exception is the *Kamasutra* in which western readers have managed to cultivate an interest.

(a) BDACE (b) DEABC
(c) BDECA (d) BCEDA

100. A. This is now orthodoxy to which I subscribe – up to a point.

B. It emerged from the mathematics of chance and statistics.

C. Therefore the risk is measurable and manageable.

D. The fundamental concept: Prices are not predictable, but the mathematical laws of chance can describe their fluctuations.

E. This is how what business schools now call modern finance was born.

(a) ADCBE (b) EBDCA
(c) ABDCE (d) DCBEA

DIRECTIONS for Questions 101 to 104: In each question, there are five sentences/paragraphs. The sentence/paragraph labelled A is in its correct place. The four that follow are labelled B, C, D and E, and need to be arranged in the logical order to form a coherent paragraph/passage. From the given options, choose the **most appropriate** one.

2007

101. A. In America, highly educated women, who are in stronger position in the labour market than less qualified ones, have higher rates of marriage than other groups.

B. Some work supports the Becker thesis, and some appears to contradict it.

C. And, as with crime, it is equally inconclusive.

D. But regardless of the conclusion of any particular piece of work, it is hard to establish convincing connections between family changes and economic factors using conventional approaches.

E. Indeed, just as with crime, an enormous academic literature exists on the validity of the pure economic approach to the evolution of family structures.

(a) BCDE (b) DBEC
(c) BDCE (d) ECBD
(e) EBCD

102. A. Personal experience of mothering and motherhood are largely framed in relation to two discernible or "official" discourses: the "medical discourse and natural childbirth discourse". Both of these tend to focus on the "optimistic stories" of birth and mothering and underpin stereotypes of the "good mother".

B. At the same time, the need for medical expert guidance is also a feature for contemporary reproduction and motherhood. But constructions of good mothering have not always been so conceived - and in different contexts may exist in parallel to other equally dominant discourses.

C. Similarly, historical work has shown how what are now taken-for-granted aspects of reproduction and mothering practices result from contemporary "pseudoscientific directives" and "managed constructs". These changes have led to a reframing of modern discourses that pattern pregnancy and motherhood leading to an acceptance of the need for greater expert management.

D. The contrasting, overlapping, and ambiguous strands within these frameworks focus to varying degrees on a woman's biological tie to her child and predisposition to instinctively know and be able to care for her child.

E. In addition, a third, "unofficial popular discourse" comprising "old wives" tales and based on maternal experiences of childbirth has also been noted. These discourses have also been acknowledged in work exploring the experiences of those who apparently do not "conform" to conventional stereotypes of the "good mother".

(a) EDBC (b) BCED
(c) DBCE (d) EDCB
(e) BCDE

103. A. Indonesia has experienced dramatic shifts in its formal governance arrangements since the fall of President Soeharto and the close of his centralized, authoritarian "New Order" regime in 1997.

B. The political system has taken its place in the nearly 10 years since *Reformasi* began. It has featured the active contest for political office among a proliferation of parties at central, provincial and district levels; direct elections for the presidency (since 2004); and radical changes in centre-local government relations towards administrative, fiscal, and political decentralization.

C. The mass media, once tidily under Soeharto's thumb, has experienced significant liberalization, as has the legal basis for non-governmental organizations, including many dedicated to such controversial issues as corruption control and human rights.

D. Such developments are seen optimistically by a number of donors and some external analysts, who interpret them as signs of Indonesia's political normalization.

E. A different group of analysts paint a picture in which the institutional forms have changed, bitt power relations have not. Vedi Hadiz argues that Indonesia's "democratic transition" has been anything but linear.

(a) BDEC (b) CBDE
(c) CEBD (d) DEBC
(e) BCDE

104. A. I had six thousand acres of land, and had thus got much spare land besides the coffee plantation. Part of the farm was native forest, and about one thousand acres were squatters' land, what [the Kikuyu] called their *shambas*.

B. The squatters' land was more intensely alive than the rest of the farm, and was changing with the seasons the year round. The maize grew up higher than your head as you walked on the narrow hard-trampled footpaths in between the tall green rustling regiments.

C. The squatters are Natives, who with their families hold a few acres on a white man's farm, and in return have to work for him a certain number of days in the year. My squatters, I think, saw the relationship in a different light, for many of them were born on the farm, and their fathers before them, and they very likely regarded me as a sort of superior squatter on their estates.

D. The Kikuyu also grew the sweet potatoes that have a vine like leaf and spread over the ground like a dense entangled mat, and many varieties of big yellow and green speckled pumpkins.

E. The beans ripened in the fields, were gathered and thrashed by the women, and the maize stalks and coffee pods were collected and burned, so that in certain seasons thin blue columns of smoke rose here and there all over the farm.

(a) CBDE (b) BCDE
(c) CBED (d) DBCE
(e) EDBC

DIRECTIONS for Questions 105 to 108: The sentences given in each question, when properly sequenced, form a coherent paragraph. Each sentence is labelled with a letter. Choose the most logical order of sentences from among the given choices to construct a coherent paragraph.

2001

105. A. Although there are large regional variations, it is not infrequent to find a large number of people sitting here and there and doing nothing.

B. Once in office, they receive friends and relatives who feel free to call any time without prior appointment.

C. While working, one is struck by the slow and clumsy actions and reactions, indifferent attitudes,procedure rather than outcome orientation, and the lack of consideration for others.

D. Even those who are employed often come late to the office and leave early unless they are forced to be punctual.

E. Work is not intrinsically valued in India.

F. Quite often people visit ailing friends and relatives or go out of their way to help them in their personal matters even during office hours.

(a) ECADBF (b) EADCFB
(c) EADBFC (d) ABFCBE

106. A. But in the industrial era destroying the enemy's productive capacity means bombing the factories which are located in the cities.

B. So in the agrarian era, if you need to destroy the enemy's productive capacity, what you want to do is burn his fields, or if you're really vicious, salt them.

C. Now in the information era, destroying the enemy's productive capacity means destroying the information infrastructure.

D. How do you do battle with your enemy?

E. The idea is to destroy the enemy's productive capacity, and depending upon the economic foundation, that productive capacity is different in each case.

F. With regard to defence, the purpose of the military is to defend the nation and be prepared to do battle with its enemy.

(a) FDEBAC (b) FCABED
(c) DEBACF (d) DFEBAC

2002

107. A. Branded disposable diapers are available at many supermarkets and drug stores.

B. If one supermarket sets a higher price for a diaper, customers may buy that brand elsewhere.

C. By contrast, the demand for private-label products may be less price sensitive since it is available only at a corresponding supermarket chain.

D. So the demand for branded diapers at any particular store may be quite price sensitive.

E. For instance, only SavOn Drugs stores sell SavOn Drugs diapers.

F. Then stores should set a higher incremental margin percentage for private label diapers.

(a) ABCDEF (b) ABCEDF
(c) ADBCEF (d) AEDBCF

108. A. Having a strategy is a matter of discipline.

B. It involves the configuration of a tailored value chain that enables a company to offer unique value.

C. It requires a strong focus on profitability and a willingness to make tough tradeoffs in choosing what not to do.

D. Strategy goes far beyond the pursuit of best practices.

E. A company must stay the course even during times of upheaval, while constantly improving and extending its distinctive positioning.

F. When a company's activities fit together as a self-reinforcing system, any competitor wishing to imitate a strategy must replicate the whole system.

(a) ACEDBF (b) ACBDEF
(c) DCBEFA (d) ABCEDF

DIRECTIONS for Questions 109 to 173: Sentences given in each question, when properly sequenced, form a coherent paragraph. The first and last sentences are 1 and 6, and the four in between are labelled A, B, C and D. Choose the most logical order of these four sentences from among the four given choices to construct a coherent paragraph from sentences 1 to 6.

1992

109. 1. Amount of published information available varies widely by industry.

A. Unfortunately for the researcher, many industries do not meet these criteria, and there may be little published information available.

B. Generally, the problem the researcher will face in using published data for analysing an economically meaningful industry is that they are too broad or too arranged to fit the industry.

C. However, it is always possible to gain some important information about an industry from published sources and these sources should be aggressively pursued.

D. Larger the industry, the older it is, and the slower the rate of technological change, better is the available published information.

6. If a researcher starts a searching for data with this reality in mind, the uselessness of broad data will be better recognized and the tendency to give up will be avoided.

(a) ACBD (b) CBAD
(c) DACB (d) BDAC

110. 1. The main source of power in industrial undertaking is electricity.

A. Electricity from water also requires enormous rivor valley projects involving huge expenditure.

B. In contrast, electricity from atomic power stations will result in a tremendous saving in expenditure.

C. Besides, the mineral resources of the world required for generation of electricity are being rapidly depleted.

D. But the production of electricity needs huge quantities of coal.

6. The installation of atomic plants will help in meeting the shortage of these resources.

(a) ABDC (b) CBAD
(c) DABC (d) BCAD

111. 1. Intensity of competition in an industry is neither a matter of coincidence nor bad luck.

A. The collective strength of these forces determines the ultimate profit potential in the industry where profit potential is measured in terms of long run returns on invested capital.

B. Rather, competition in an industry is rooted in its underlying economic structure and goes well beyond the behavior of current competitors.

C. Not all industries have the same potential.

D. The state of competition in an industry depends on five basic competitive forces.

6. They differ fundamentally in their ultimate profit potential as the collective strength of the forces differ.

(a) CDBA (b) DCAB
(c) BDAC (d) ABDC

112. 1. The general enemy of mankind, as people have discovered, is not science, but war.

A. It is found that there is peace, science is constructive; when there is war science is perverted to destructive ends.

B. Science merely reflects the social forces by which it is surrounded.

C. Until now, they have brought us to the doorstep of doom.

D. The weapon which science gives us do not necessarily create war, these make war increasingly more terrible.

6. Our main problem, therefore, is not to curb science, but to stop war, to substitute law for force and international governments for anarchy in the relations between nations.

(a) ADBC (b) BADC
(c) CDAB (d) DABC

113. 1. It will be foolish to deny that the countryside has many attractions to offer.

A. One soon gets tired of the same old scenes and creatures day in and day out.

B. But there is another side of the picture.

C. The honesty and frankness of the country-folk, too, is a refreshing change from the dishonesty and selfishness we find in so many urban people.

D. There is the lovely scenery, the interesting and varied wildlife, the long rambles through the woods and fields and the clean, healthy air.

6. The loneliness and monotony in the countryside soon begin to make themselves felt and we long for the familiar sidewalks and street corners of the town.

(a) ABCD
(b) DCAB
(c) DABC
(d) DCBA

114. 1. A welfare state in the attainment of its objective must avoid coercion and violence.

A. But communism implies the loss of freedom of expression and action and introduces a regimentation of life.

B. Communism implies the loss of freedom of expression and action and introduces a regimentation of life.

C. There are all serious disadvantages which perhaps outweigh the economic gains.

D. Communism aims at the welfare state and perhaps the completest form of the welfare state in most respects.

6. A true welfare state can develop only by following the path of peace and democracy.

(a) CADB (b) ACDB
(c) DCAB (d) DABC

115. 1. Human experience tends to show that the more we mix with a man, the more we come to dislike him.

A. When the acquaintance with him ripens into intimacy, we are likely to become very keenly aware of his defects and imperfections.

B. In the beginning, we may feel greatly attracted by someone because of certain qualities that we find in him.

C. But on closer acquaintance we will begin to perceive his faults and shortcomings.

D. The truth is that nobody is free from faults and weaknesses.

6. But while a man makes a show of his strong points and his good qualities, he generally tries to conceal or cover his faults and defects.

(a) ACBD (b) BCAD
(c) CDBA (d) DCAB

1993

116. 1. India's experience of industrialization is characteristic of the difficulties faced by a newly independent developing country.

A. In 1947, India was undoubtedly an under – developed country with one of the lowest per capita incomes in the world.

B. Indian industrialization was the result of a conscious deliberate policy of growth by an indigenous political elite.

C. Today India ranks fifth in the international comity of nations if measured in terms of purchasing power.

D. Even today however, the benefits of Indian industrialization since independence have not reached the masses.

6. Industrialization in India has been a limited success; one more example of growth without development.

(a) CDAB (b) DCBA
(c) CABD (d) BACD

117. 1. What does the state do in a country where tax is very low?

A. It tries to spy upon the taxpayers.

B. It investigates income sources and spending patterns.

C. Exactly what the tax authority tries to do now even if inconsistently.

D. It could also encourage people to denounce to the tax authorities any conspicuously prosperous neighbours who may be suspected of not paying their taxes properly.

6. The ultimate solution would be an Orwellian System.

(a) BADC (b) DBAC
(c) ABCD (d) DCBA

118. 1. It is significant that one of the most common objections to competition is that it is blind.

A. This is important because in a system of free enterprise based on private property chances are not equal and there is indeed a strong case for reducing the inequality of opportunity.

B. Rather it is a choice between a system where it is the will of few persons that decides who is to get what and one where it depends at least partly, on the ability and the enterprise of the people concerned.

C. Although competition and justice may have little else in common, it is as much a commendation of competition as of justice that it is no respecter of persons.

D. The choice today is not between a system in which everybody will get what he deserves according to some universal standard and one where individuals' shares are determined by chance of goodwill.

6. The fact that opportunities open to the poor in a competitive society are much more restricted than those open to the rich, does not make it less true that in such a society the poor are more free than a person commanding much greater material comfort in a different type of society.

(a) CDBA (b) DCBA
(c) ABCD (d) BADC

119. 1. The fragile Yugoslav state has an uncertain future.

A. Thus, there will surely be chaos and uncertainty if the people fail to settle their differences.

B. Sharp ideological differences already exist in the country.

C. Ethnic, regional, linguistic and material disparities are profound.

D. The country will also lose the excellent reputation it enjoyed in the international arena.

6. At worst, it will once more become vulnerable to international conspiracy and intrigue.

(a) BCAD (b) ADCB
(c) ACBD (d) DBCA

120. 1. The New Economic Policy comprises the various policy measures and changes introduced since July 1991.

A. There is a common thread running through all these measures.

B. The objective is simple to improve the efficiency of the system.

C. The regulator mechanism involving multitude of controls has fragmented the capacity and reduced competition even in the private sector.

D. The thrust of the new policy is towards creating a more competitive environment as a means to improving the productivity and efficiency of the economy.

6. This is to be achieved by removing the banners and restrictions on the entry and growth of firms.

(a) DCAB (b) ABCD
(c) BDAC (d) CDBA

121. 1. Commercial energy consumption shows an increasing trend and poses the major challenge for the future.

A. The demand, for petroleum, during 1996 – 97 and 2006 – 07 is anticipated to be 81 million tonnes and 125 million tonnes respectively.

B. According to the projections of the 14th Power Survey Committee Report, the electricity generation requirements from utilities will be about 416 billion units by 1996 – 97 and 825 billion units by 2006 – 07.

C. The production of coal should reach 303 million tonnes by 1996 – 97 to achieve Plan targets and 460 million tonnes by 2006 – 07.

D. The demand for petroleum products has already outstripped indigenous production.

6. Electricity is going to play a major role in the development of infrastructural facilities.

(a) DACB (b) CADB
(c) BADC (d) ABCD

122. 1. The necessity for regional integration in South Asia is underlined by the very history of the last 45 years since the liquidation of the British Empire in this part of the world.

A. After the partition of the Indian Subcontinent, Pakistan was formed in that very area which the imperial powers had always marked out as the potential base for operations against the Russian power in Central Asia.

B. Because of the disunity and ill-will among the South Asian neighbours, particular India and Pakistan, great powers from outside the area could meddle into their affairs and thereby keep neighbours apart.

C. It needs to be added that it was the bountiful supply of sophisticated arms that emboldened Pakistan to go for warlike bellicosity towards India.

D. As a part of the cold war strategy of the US, Pakistan was sucked into Washington's military alliance spreading over the years.

6. Internally too, it was the massive induction of American arms into Pakistan which empowered the military junta of that country to stuff out the civilian government and destroy democracy in Pakistan.

(a) ACBD (b) ABDC
(c) CBAD (d) DCAB

123. 1. The success of any unit in a competitive environment depends on prudent management sources.

A. In this context it would have been more appropriate if the concept of accelerated depreciation, together with additional incentives towards capital allowances for recouping a portion of the cost of replacements out of the current generations, had been accepted.

B. Added to this are negligible retention of profits because of inadequate capital allowances and artificial disallowance's of genuine outflows.

C. One significant cause for poor generation of surpluses is the high cost of capital and its servicing cost.

D. The lack of a mechanism in India tax laws for quick recovery of capital costs has not received its due attention.

6. While this may apparently look costly from the point of view of the exchequer, the ultimate cost of the Government and the community in the form of losses suffered through poor viability will be prohibitive.

(a) ADBC (b) BCDA
(c) CBDA (d) DBAC

124. 1. Count Rumford is perhaps best known for his observations on the nature of heat.

A. He undertook several experiments in order to test the theories of the origin of frictional heat.

B. According to the calorists, the heat was produced by the "caloric" squeezed out of he chips in the process of separating them from the larger pieces of metal.

C. Lavoisier had introduced the term "caloric" for the weightless substance heat, and had included it among the chemical elements, along with carbon, nitrogen and oxygen.

D. In the munitions factory in Munich, Rumford noticed that a considerable degree of heat developed in a brass gun while it was being bored.

6. Rumford could not believe that the big amount of heat generated could have come from the small amount of dust created.

(a) ABCD (b) CBDA
(c) ADCB (d) CDAB

125. 1. Visual recognition involves storing and retrieving of memories.

A. Psychologists of the Gestalt School maintain that objects are recognised as a whole in a procedure.

B. Neural activity, triggered by the eye, forms an image in the brain's memory system that constitutes an internal representation of the viewed object.

C. Controversy surrounds the question of whether recognition is a single one-step procedure or a serial step-by-step one.

D. When an object is encountered again, it is matched with its internal recognition and thereby recognised.

6. The internal representation is matched with the retinal image in a single operation.

(a) DBAC (b) DCAB
(c) BDCA (d) CABD

126. 1. The idea of sea-floor spreading actually preceded the theory of plate tectonics.

A. The hypothesis was soon substantiated by the discovery that periodic reversals of the earth's magnetic field are recorded in the oceanic crust.

B. In its original version, it described the creation and destruction of ocean floor, but it did not specify rigid lithospheric plates.

C. An explanation of this process devised by F.J. Vine and D.H. Mathews of Princeton is now generally accepted.

D. The sea-floor spreading hypothesis was formulated chiefly by Harry H. Hess of Princeton University in the early 1960's.

6. As magma rises under the mid-ocean, ferromagnetic minerals in the magma become magnetised in the direction of the geomagnetic field.

(a) DCBA (b) ABDC
(c) CBDA (d) DBAC

127. 1. The history of mammals dates back at least to Triassic time.

A. Miocene and Pliocene time was marked by culmination of several groups and continued approach towards modern characters.

B. Development was retarded, however, until the sudden acceleration of evolutional change that occurred in the oldest Paleocene.

C. In the Oligocene Epoch, there was further improvement, with appearance of some new lines and extinction of others.

D. This led in Eocene time to increase in average size, larger mental capacity, and special adaptations for different modes of life.

6. The peak of the career of mammals in variety and average large size was attained in this epoch.

(a) BDCA (b) ACDB
(c) BCDA (d) ACBD

128. 1. The death of cinema has been predicted annually.

A. It hasn't happened.

B. It was said that the television would kill it off and indeed audiences plummeted reaching a low in 1984.

C. Film has enjoyed a renaissance, and audiences are now roughly double of what they were a decade ago.

D. Then the home computer became the projected nemesis, followed by satellite television.

6. Why? Probably because, even in the most atomized of societies, we human beings feel the need to share our fantasies and our excitement.

(a) CADB (b) BDAC
(c) ABDC (d) DABC

1994

129. 1. It is often said that good actors can get out of play more than the author has put into it.

A. A good actor, bringing to a part his own talent, often gives it a value that the layman on reading the play had not seen in it, but at the utmost he can do no more than reach the ideal that the author has seen in his mind's eye.

B. In all my plays I have been fortunate enough to have some of the parts acted as I wanted; but in none have I had all the parts so acted.

C. That is not true.

D. He has to be an actor of address to do this; for the most part the author has to be satisfied with an approximation of the performance he visualized.

6. This is obviously inevitable, for the actor who is suited to a certain role may well be engaged and you have to put up with the second or third best, because there is no help for it.

(a) BACD (b) DACB
(c) CADB (d) DCBA

130. 1. I can think of no serious prose play that has survived the generation that gave it birth.

A. They are museum pieces.

B. They are revived now and then because a famous part tempts a leading actor, or a manager in want of a stop-gap thinks he will put on a play on which he has no loyalties to pay.

C. A few comedies have haphazardly traveled down a couple of centuries or so.

D. The audience laugh at their wit with politeness and at their farce with embarrassment.

6. They are not held nor taken out of themselves.

(a) CDBA (b) CBAD
(c) ABDC (d) BACD

131. 1. The wind had savage allies.

A. If it had not been for my closely fitted helmet, the explosions might have shattered my eardrums.

B. The first clap of thunder came as a deafening explosion that literally shook my teeth.

C. I didn't hear the thunder, I actually felt it – an almost unbearable physical experience.

D. I saw lighting all around me in every shape imaginable.

6. It was raining so torrentially that I thought I would drown in mid air.

(a) BCAD (b) CADB
(c) CBDA (d) ACDB

132. 1. All human beings are aware of the existence of a power greater than that of the mortals – the name given to such a power by individuals is an outcome of birth, education and choice.

A. Logically, therefore such a power should be remembered in good times also.

B. Their other philanthropic contributions include the construction and maintenance of religious places such as temples or gurudwaras.

C. Industrial organizations also contribute to the veneration of this power by participating in activities such as religious ceremonies and festivities organized by the employees.

D. This power provides an anchor in times of adversity, difficulty and trouble.

6. The top management/managers should participate in all such events, irrespective of their personal choice.

(a) CADB (b) BCAD
(c) DACB (d) DBCA

133. 1. A thorough knowledge of the path or course to be followed is essential for achieving success.

A. Seniors must show the path clearly by laying down the precise expectations of the management in terms of job description, key result areas and personal targets.

B. They should also 'light the path' by personal example.

C. Advice tendered or help offered must be objectively evaluated for its effectiveness in achieving the desired goal.

D. A display of arrogance and a false sense of 'self-worth', in order to belittle those who come to help prove dysfunctional.

6. The individuality of each employee must be respected.

(a) CDAB (b) CADB
(c) BADC (d) ABCD

1995

134. 1. Currency movements can have a dramatic impact on equity returns for foreign investors.

A. This is not surprising as many developing economies try to peg their exchange rates to the US dollar or to a basket of currencies.

B. Many developing economies manage to keep exchange rate volatility lower than that in the industrial economies.

C. India has also gone in for the full float on the current account and abolished the managed exchange rate.

D. Dramatic exceptions are Argentina, Brazil and Nigeria.

6. Another emerging market specific risk is liquidity risk.

(a) ADBC
(b) CDAB
(c) BDAC
(d) CABD

135. 1. All human beings are aware of the existence of a power greater than that of the mortals — the name given to such a power by individuals is an outcome of birth, education and choice.

A. This power provides an anchor in times of adversity, difficulty and trouble.

B. Industrial organisations also contribute to the veneration of this power by participating in activities such as religious ceremonies and festivities organised by the employees.

C. Their other philanthropic contributions include the construction and maintenance of religious places such as temples or gurdwaras.

D. Logically, therefore, such a power should be remembered in good times also.

6. The top management/managers should participate in all such events, irrespective of their personal choice.

(a) ADBC (b) BCAD
(c) CADB (d) DACB

136. 1. Total forgiveness for a mistake generates a sense of complacency towards target achievement among the employees.

A. In such a situation the work ethos gets distorted and individuals get a feeling that they can get away with any lapse.

B. The feeling that they develop is: whether I produce results or not, the management will not punish me or does not have the guts to punish me.

C. Also, excess laxity damages management credibility, because for a long time, the management has maintained that dysfunctional behaviour will result in punishment, and when something goes wrong, it fails to take specific punitive action.

D. The severity of the punishment may be reduced, by modifying it, but some action must be taken against the guilty so as to serve as a reminder for all others in the organization.

6. Moreover, it helps establish the management's image of being firm, fair and yet human.

(a) DCBA (b) BACD
(c) DBCA (d) CABD

137. 1. But the vessel kept going away.

A. He looked anxiously around.

B. There was nothing to see but the water and empty sky.

C. He could now barely see her funnel and masts when heaved up on a high wave.

D. He did not know for what.

6. A breaking wave slapped him in the face, choking him.

(a) ADBC (b) ACDB
(c) CADB (d) ABCD

138. 1. Managers must lead by example; they should not be averse to giving a hand in manual work; if required.

A. They should also update their competence to guide their subordinates; this would be possible only if they keep in regular touch with new processes, machines, instruments, gauges, systems and gadgets.

B. Work must be allocated to different groups and team members in clear, specific terms.

C. Too much of wall-building is detrimental to the exercise of the 'personal charisma' of the leader whose presence should not be felt only through notices, circulars or memos, but by being seen physically.

D. Simple, clean living among one's people should be insisted upon.

6. This would mean the maintaining of an updated organization chart; laying down job descriptions; identifying key result areas; setting personal targets; and above all, monitoring of performance, to meet organizational goals.

(a) BDAC (b) BCDA
(c) ADCB (d) ACDB

139. 1. The top management should perceive the true worth of people and only then make friends.

A. Such 'true friends' are very few and very rare.

B. Factors such as affluence, riches, outward sophistication and conceptual abilities are not prerequisites for genuine friendship.

C. Such people must be respected and kept close to the heart.

D. Business realities call for developing a large circle of acquaintances and contacts; however, all of them will be motivated by their own self-interest and it would be wrong to treat them as genuine friends.

6. There is always a need for real friends to whom one can turn for balanced, unselfish advice, more so when one is caught in a dilemma.

(a) ABCD
(b) ADBC
(c) ACDB
(d) ACBD

140. 1. Managers, especially the successful ones, should guard against ascribing to themselves qualities and attributes which they may not have, or may have in a measure much less than what they think they have!

A. External appearances can be deceptive.

B. To initiate action, without being in possession of full facts, can lead to disastrous results.

C. Also, one should develop confidants who can be used as sounding boards, in order to check one's own thinking against that of the others.

D. It is also useful to be receptive to feedback about oneself so that a real understanding of the 'self' exists.

6. A false perception can be like wearing coloured glasses — all facts get tainted by colour of the glass and the mind interprets them wrongly to fit into the perception.

(a) DCAB (b) BADC
(c) DABC (d) BCAD

141. 1. Conflicting demands for resources are always voiced by different functions/departments in an organization.

A. Every manager examines the task entrusted to him and evaluates the resources required.

B. Availability of resources in full measure makes task achievement easy, because it reduces the effort needed to somewhat make-do.

C. A safety cushion is built into demand for resources, to offset the adverse impact of any cut imposed by the seniors.

D. This aspect needs to be understood as a reality.

6. Dynamic, energetic, growth-oriented and wise managements are always confronted with the inadequacy of resources with respect to one of the four Ms (men, machines, money and materials)and the two Ts (time and technology).

(a) DABC (b) ACBD
(c) ABCD (d) BCDA

142. 1. Despite the passage of time, a large number of conflicts continue to remain alive, because the wronged parties, in reality or in imagination, wish to take revenge upon each other, thus creating a vicious circle.

A. At times, managers are called upon to take ruthless decisions in the long-term interests of the organization.

B. People hurt others, at times knowingly, to teach them a lesson and, at other times, because they lack correct understanding of the other person's stand.

C. The delegation of any power, to any person, is never absolute.

D. Every ruthless decision will be accepted easily if the situation at the moment of committing the act is objectively analysed, shared openly and discussed rationally.
6. Power is misused; its effects can last only for a while, since employees are bound to confront it some day, more so, the talented ones.

(a) BCAD (b) ADBC
(c) DABC (d) BADC

143. 1. Managers need to differentiate among those who commit an error once, those who are repetitively errant but can be corrected, and those who are basically wicked.
A. The persons in this category will resort to sweet-talk and make all sorts of promises on being caught, but, at the first opportunity will revert to their bad ways.
B. Managers must take ruthless action against the basically wicked and ensure their separation from the organization at the earliest.
C. The first category needs to be corrected softly and duly counselled; the second category should be dealt with firmly and duly counselled till they realize the danger of persisting with their errant behaviour.
D. It is the last category of whom the managers must be most wary.
6. The punishment must be fair and based on the philosophy of giving all the possible opportunities and help prior to taking ruthless action.

(a) ADCB (b) CDAB
(c) CADB (d) BDAC

1996

144. 1. It doesn't take a highly esteemed medical expert to conclude that women handle pain better than men.
A. First the men would give birth, and then take six months to recover.
B. As for labour pains, the human species would become extinct if men had to give birth.
C. They do, however, make life hell for everyone else with their non-stop complaining about how bad they feel.
D. The men in my life, including my husband and my father, would not take a Tylenol for pain even if their lives depends on it.
6. And by the time they finish sharing their excruciating experience with their buddies, all reproduction would come to a halt.

(a) ABDC (b) DCBA
(c) CDBA (d) BACD

145. 1. A few years ago, hostility towards Japanese-Americans was so strong that I thought they were going to reopen the detention camps here in Kolkata.
A. Today Asians are a success story.
B. I cannot help making a comparison to the anti-Jewish sentiment in Nazi Germany when Jewish people were successful in business.
C. But do people applaud President Clinton for improving foreign trade with Asia?
D. Now, talk about the 'Arkansas-Asia Connection' is broadening that hatred to include all Asian-Americans.
6. No, blinded by jealousy, they complain that it is the Asian-Americans who are reaping the wealth.

(a) DBAC (b) ABDC
(c) DABC (d) ACBD

146. 1. Michael Jackson, clearly no admirer of long engagements, got married abruptly for the second time in three years.
A. The latest wedding took place in a secret midnight ceremony in Sydney, Australia.
B. It is also the second marriage for the new missus, about whom little is known.
C. The wedding was attended by the groom's entourage and staff, according to Jackson's publicist.
D. The bride, 37-year-old Debbie Rowe, who is carrying Jackson's baby, wore white.
6. All that is known is that she is a nurse for Jackson's dermatologist.

(a) ACDB (b) BDCA
(c) DABC (d) CDBA

147. 1. Liz Taylor isn't just unlucky in love.
A. She, and husband Larry Fortensky, will have to pay the tab — $4,32,600 in court costs.
B. The duo claimed that a 1993 story about a property dispute damaged their reputations.
C. Taylor has just filed a defamation suit against the *National Enquirer*.
D. She is unlucky in law too.
6. Alas, all levels of the California court system disagreed.

(a) CDAB (b) DCAB
(c) DABC (d) CDBA

148. 1. Hiss was serving as Head of the Endowment on August 3, 1948, when Whittaker Chambers reluctantly appeared before the House Un-American Activities Committee.

A. Chambers, a portly rumpled man with a melodramatic style, had been a Communist courier but had broken with the party in 1938.

B. When Nixon arranged a meeting of the two men in New York, Chambers repeated his charges and Hiss his denials.

C. Summoned as a witness, Hiss denied that he had ever been a Communist or had known Chambers.

D. He told the Committee that among the members of a secret Communist cell in Washington during the 1930s was Hiss.

6. Then, bizarrely, Hiss asked Chambers to open his mouth.

(a) CBAD (b) ADBC

(c) ADCB (d) ACDB

149. 1. Since its birth, rock has produced a long string of guitar heroes.

A. It is a list that would begin with Chuck Berry and continue with Hendrix, Page and Clapton.

B. These are musicians celebrated for their sheer instrumental talent, and their flair for expansive, showy and sometimes self-indulgent solos.

C. It would also include players of more recent vintage, like Van-Halen and Living Colour's Vemon Reid.

D. But with the advent of alternative rock and grunge, guitar heroism became uncool.

6. Guitarists like Peter Buck and Kurt Cobain shy away from exhibitionism.

(a) ACBD (b) ABCD

(c) BCAD (d) BADC

150. 1. For many scientists, oceans are the cradle of life.

A. But all over the world, chemical products and nuclear waste continue to be dumped into them.

B. Coral reefs, which are known to be the most beautiful places of the submarine world, are fast disappearing.

C. The result is that many species of fish die because of this pollution.

D. Of course man is the root cause behind these problems.

6. Man has long since ruined the places he visits — continents and oceans alike.

(a) ACBD (b) BACD

(c) ABDC (d) BCAD

151. 1. Am I one of the people who are worried that Bill Clinton's second term might be destroyed by the constitutional crisis?

A. On the other hands, ordinary citizens have put the campaign behind them.

B. In other words, what worries me is that Bill Clinton could exhibit a version of what George Bush used to refer to as Big Mo.

C. That is, he might have so much campaign momentum that he may not be able to stopcampaigning.

D. Well, it's true that I've been wondering whether a President could be impeached for refusing to stop talking about the bridge we need to build to the 21st century.

6. They now prefer to watch their favourite soaps and ads on TV rather than senators.

(a) DBCA (b) ABDC

(c) BACD (d) CBDA

152. 1. So how big is the potential market?

A. But they end up spending thousands more each year on hardware overhaul and software upgradation.

B. Analysts say the new machines will appeal primarily to corporate users.

C. An individual buyer can pick up a desktop computer for less than $2,000 in America.

D. For them, the NCs best-drawing card is its promise of much lower maintenance costs.

6. NCs, which automatically load the latest version of whatever software they need could put an end to all that.

(a) BCAD (b) DABC

(c) BDCA (d) DCAB

153. 1. Historically, stained glass was almost entirely reserved for ecclesiastical spaces.

A. By all counts, he has accomplished that mission with unmistakable style.

B. "It is my mission to bring it kicking and screaming out of that milieu," says Clarke.

C. The first was the jewel-like windows he designed for a Cistercian Church in Switzerland.

D. Two recent projects show his genius in the separate worlds of the sacred and the mundane.

6. The second was a spectacular, huge skylight in a shopping complex in Brazil.

(a) CBAD (b) BADC

(c) ABDC (d) DBAC

1997

154. 1. Whenever technology has flowered, it has put man's language — developing skills into overdrive.

A. Technical terms are spilling into mainstream language almost as fast as junk — mail is slapped into e-mail boxes.

B. The era of computers is no less.

C. From the wheel with its axle to the spinning wheel with its bobbins, to the compact disc and its jewel box, inventions have trailed new words in their wake.

D. "Cyberslang is huge, but it's parochial, and we don't know what will filter into the large culture," said Tom Dalzell, who wrote the slang dictionary *Flappers 2 Rappers*.

6. Some slangs already have a pedigree.

(a) BCAD (b) CBAD
(c) ABCD (d) DBCA

155. 1. Until the MBA arrived on the scene the IIT graduate was king.

A. A degree from one of the five IITs was a passport to a well-paying job, great prospects abroad and, for some, a decent dowry to boot.

B. From the day he or she cracked the Joint Entrance Examination, the IIT student commanded the awe of neighbours and close relatives.

C. IIT students had, meanwhile, also developed their own special culture, complete with lingo and attitude, which they passed down.

D. True, the success stories of IIT graduates are legion and they now constitute the cream of the Indian diaspora.

6. But not many alumni would agree that the IIT undergraduate mindset merits a serious psychological study, let alone an interactive one.

(a) BACD (b) ADCB
(c) BADC (d) ABCD

156. 1. Some of the maharajas, like the one at Kapurthala, had exquisite taste.

A. In 1902, the Maharaja of Kapurthala gave his civil engineer photographs of the Versailles Palace and asked him to replicate it, right down to the gargoyles.

B. Yeshwantrao Holkar of Indore brought in Bauhaus aesthetics and even works of modern artists like Brancusi and Duchamp.

C. Kitsch is the most polite way to describe them.

D. But many of them, as the available light photographs show, had execrable taste.

6. Like Ali Baba's caves, some of the palaces were like warehouses with the downright ugly next to the sublimely aesthetic.

(a) BACD (b) BDCA
(c) ABCD (d) ABDC

157. 1. There, in Europe, his true gifts unveiled.

A. Playing with Don Cherie, blending Indian music and jazz for the first time, he began setting the pace in the late 70s for much of what present—day fusion is.

B. John McLaughlin, the legendary guitarist whose soul has always had an Indian stamp on it, was seduced immediately.

C. Fusion by Gurtu had begun.

D. He partnered Gurtu for four years, and 'natured' him as a composer.

6. But for every experimental musician there's a critic nestling nearby.

(a) ABCD (b) BCAD
(c) ADBC (d) ABDC

158. 1. India, which has two out of every five TB patients in the world, is on the brink of a major public health disaster.

A. If untreated, a TB patient can die within five years.

B. Unlike AIDS, the great curse of modern sexuality, the TB germ is airborne, which means there are no barriers to its spread.

C. The dreaded infection ranks fourth among major killers worldwide.

D. Every minute, a patient falls prey to the infection in India, which means that over five lakh people die of the disease annually.

6. Anyone, anywhere can be affected by this disease.

(a) CADB (b) BACD
(c) ABCD (d) DBAC

1998

159. 1. Buddhism is a way to salvation.

A. But Buddhism is more severely analytical.

B. In the Christian tradition there is also a concern for the fate of human society conceived as a whole, rather than merely as a sum or network of individuals.

C. Salvation is a property, or achievement of individuals.

D. Not only does it dissolve society into individuals, the individual in turn is dissolved into component parts and instants, a stream of events.

6. In modern terminology, Buddhist doctrine is reductionist.

(a) ABDC (b) CBAD
(c) BDAC (d) ABCD

160. 1. The problem of improving Indian agriculture is both a sociological and an administrative one.

A. It also appears that there is a direct relationship between the size of a state and development.

B. The issues of Indian development, and the problem of India's agricultural sector, will remain with us long into the next century.

C. Without improving Indian agriculture, no liberalisation and delicensing will be able to help India.

D. At the end of the day, there has to be a ferment and movement of life and action in the vast segment of rural India.

6. When it starts marching, India will fly.

(a) DABC (b) CDBA
(c) ACDB (d) ABCD

161. 1. Good literary magazines have always been good because of their editors.

A. Furthermore, to edit by committee, as it were, would prevent any magazine from finding its own identity.

B. The more quirky and idiosyncratic they have been, the better the magazine is, at least as a general rule.

C. But the number of editors one can have for a magazine should also be determined by the number of contributions to it.

D. To have four editors for an issue that contains only seven contributions, it is a bit silly to start with.

6. However, in spite of this anomaly, the magazine does acquire merit in its attempt to give a comprehensive view of the Indian literary scene as it is today.

(a) ABCD (b) BCDA
(c) ABDC (d) CBAD

162. 1. It is the success story of the Indian expatriate in tho US which today hogs much of the media coverage in India.

A. East and West, the twain have met quite comfortably in their person, thank you.

B. Especially in its more recent romancing — the-NRI phase.

C. Seldom does the price of getting there — more like not getting there — or what's going on behind those sunny smiles get so much media hype.

D. Well groomed, with their perfect Colgate smiles, and hair in place, they appear the picture of confidence which comes from having arrived.

6. The festival of feature films and documentaries made by Americans of Indian descent being screened this fortnight, goes a long way in filling those gaps.

(a) ACBD (b) DABC
(c) BDAC (d) ABCD

163. 1. A market for Indian art has existed ever since the international art scene sprang to life.

A. But interest in architectural conceits is an unanticipated fallout of the Festivals of India of the '80s, which were designed to increase exports of Indian crafts.

B. Simultaneously, the Indian elite discarded their synthetic sarees and kitsch plastic furniture and a market came into being.

C. Western dealers, unhappy in a market afflicted by violent price fluctuations and unpredictable profit margins, began to look East, and found cheap antiques with irresistible appeal.

D. The fortunes of the Delhi supremos, the Jew Town dealers in Cochin and myriad others around the country were made.

6. A chain of command was established, from the local contacts to the provincial dealers and up to the big boys, who entertain the Italians and the French, cutting deals worth lakhs in warehouses worth crores.

(a) ABCD (b) DCAB
(c) CBAD (d) CABD

1999

164. 1. Making people laugh is tricky.

A. At times, the intended humour may simply not come off.

B. Making people laugh while trying to sell them something is a tougher challenge, since the commercial can fall flat on two grounds.

C. There are many advertisements which do amuse but do not even begin to set the cash registers ringing.

D. Again, it is rarely sufficient for an advertiser simply to amuse the target audience in order to reap the sales benefit.

6. There are indications that in substituting the hardsell for a more entertaining approach, some agencies have rather thrown out the baby with the bath-water.

(a) CDBA (b) ABCD
(c) BADC (d) DCBA

165. 1. Picture a termite colony, occupying a tall mud hump on an African plain.

A. Hungry predators often invade the colony and unsettle the balance.

B. The colony flourishes only if the proportion of soldiers to workers remains roughly the same, so that the queen and workers can be protected by the soldiers, and the queen and soldiers can be serviced by the workers.

C. But its fortunes are presently restored, because the immobile queen, walled in well below the ground level, lays eggs not only in large enough numbers, but also in the varying proportions required.

D. The hump is alive with worker termites and soldier termites going about their distinct kinds of business.

6. How can we account for a mysterious ability to respond like this to events on the distant surface?

(a) BADC (b) DBAC
(c) ADCB (d) BDCA

166. 1. According to recent research, the critical period for developing language skills is between the age of three and five years.

A. The read-to child already has a large vocabulary and a sense of grammar and sentence structure.

B. Children who are read to in these years have a far better chance of reading well in school, indeed, of doing well in all their subjects.

C. And the reason is actually quite simple.

D. This correlation is far and away the highest yet found between home influences and school success.

6. Their comprehension of language is therefore very high.

(a) DACD (b) ADCB
(c) ABCD (d) BDCA

167. 1. High-powered outboard motors were considered to be one of the major threats to the survival of the Beluga whales.

A. With these, hunters could approach Belugas within hunting range and profit from its inner skin and blubber.

B. To escape an approaching motor, Belugas have learnt to dive to the ocean bottom and stay there for up to 20 min, by which time the confused predator has left.

C. Today, however, even with much more powerful engines, it is difficult to come close, because the whales seem to disappear suddenly just when you thought you had them in your sights.

D. When the first outboard engines arrived in the early 1930s, one came across 4 HP and 8 HP motors.

6. Belugas seem to have used their well-known sensitivity to noise to evolve an 'avoidance' strategy to outsmart hunters and their powerful technologies.

(a) DACB (b) ACDB
(c) ADCB (d) DBAC

168. 1. The reconstruction of history by post-revolutionary science texts involves more than a multiplication of historical misconstructions.

A. Because they aim quickly to acquaint the student with what the contemporary scientific community thinks it knows, textbooks treat the various experiments, concepts, laws and theories of the current normal science as separately and as nearly seriatim as possible.

B. Those misconstructions render revolutions invisible; the arrangement of the still visible material in science texts implies a process that, if it existed, would deny revolutions a function.

C. But when combined with the generally unhistorical air of science writing and with the occasional systematic misconstruction, one impression is likely to follow.

D. As pedagogy, this technique of presentation is unexceptionable.

6. Science has reached its present state by a series of individual discoveries and inventions that, when gathered together, constitute the modern body of technical knowledge.

(a) BADC (b) ADCB
(c) DACB (d) CBDA

2000

169. 1. Security inks exploit the same principle that causes the vivid and constantly changing colours of a film of oil on water.

A. When two rays of light meet each other after being reflected from these different surfaces, they have each travelled slightly different distances.

B. The key is that the light is bouncing off two surfaces, that of the oil and that of the water layer below it.

C. The distance the two rays travel determines which wavelengths, and hence colours, interfere constructively and look bright.

D. Because light is, an electromagnetic wave, the peaks and troughs of each ray then interfere either constructively, to appear bright, or destructively, to appear dim.

6. Since the distance the rays travel changes with the angle as you look at the surface, different colours look bright from different viewing angles.

(a) ABCD (b) BADC
(c) BDAC (d) DCAB

170. 1. Commercially reared chicken can be unusually aggressive, and are often kept in darkened sheds to prevent them pecking at each other.

A. The birds spent far more of their time — up to a third — pecking at the inanimate objects in the pens, in contrast to birds in other pens which spent a lot of time attacking others.

B. In low light conditions, they behave less belligerently, but are more prone to ophthalmic disorders and respiratory problems.
C. In an experiment, aggressive head-pecking was all but eliminated among birds in the enriched environment.
D. Altering the birds' environment, by adding bales of wood-shavings to their pens, can work wonders.
6. Bales could diminish aggressiveness and reduce injuries; they might even improve productivity, since a happy chicken is a productive chicken.

(a) DCAB (b) CDBA
(c) DBAC (d) BDCA

171. 1. The concept of a 'nation-state' assumes a complete correspondence between the boundaries ofthe nation and the boundaries of those who live in a specific state.
A. Then there are members of national collectivities who live in other countries, making a mockery of the concept.
B. There are always people living in particular states who are not considered to be (and often do not consider themselves to be) members of the hegemonic nation.
C. Even worse, there are nations which never had a state or which are divided across several states.
D. This, of course, has been subject to severe criticism and is virtually everywhere a fiction.
6. However, the fiction has been, and continues to be, at the basis of nationalist ideologies.

(a) DBAC (b) ABCD
(c) BACD (d) DACB

172. 1. In the sciences, even questionable examples of research fraud are harshly punished.
A. But no such mechanism exists in the humanities — much of what humanities researchers call research does not lead to results that are replicable by other scholars.
B. Given the importance of interpretation in historical and literary scholarship, humanities researchers are in a position where they can explain away deliberate and even systematic distortion.
C. Mere suspicion is enough for funding to be cut off; publicity guarantees that careers can be effectively ended.
D. Forgeries which take the form of pastiches in which the forger intersperses fake and real partscan be defended as mere mistakes or aberrant misreading.
6. Scientists fudging data have no such defences.

(a) BDCA (b) ABDC
(c) CABD (d) CDBA

173. 1. Horses and communism were, on the whole, a poor match.
A. Fine horses bespoke the nobility the party was supposed to despise.
B. Communist leaders, when they visited villages, preferred to see cows and pigs.
C. Although a working horse was just about tolerable, the communists were right to be wary.
D. Peasants from Poland to the Hungarian Pustza preferred their horses to party dogma.
6. "A farmer's pride is his horse; his cow may be thin but his horse must be fat," went a Slovak saying.

(a) ACDB (b) DBCA
(c) ABCD (d) DCBA

MEMORY BASED QUESTIONS

2009

174. Five sentences are given below, labeled A, B, C, D and E. They need to be arranged in a logical order to form a coherent paragraph/passage. From the given options, choose the most appropriate option.
A. When he does track down soothsayers he is disappointed or bored and worries about how much they are going to charge him.
B. His aim is to uncover pre-colonial spiritual and magical beliefs.
C. So it goes for the other countries he visits—Nigeria, Ghana, Côte d'Ivoire, Gabon and South Africa.
D. The shrines are "lavatorial and disagreeable".
E. But the Africa he sees is a pretty filthy place.

(a) CBEDA (b) BDECA
(c) CEDBA (d) ECDAB

175. Five sentences are given below, labeled A, B, C, D and E. They need to be arranged in a logical order to form a coherent paragraph/passage. From the given options, choose the most appropriate option.
A. The status of the husband ultimately determines the status of the woman.
B. For a "good woman" to be qualified as thus, her life cycle should necessarily progress from being a virgin daughter to a chaste and dutiful wife, daughter-in-law and a mother under the sanction of her father, husband and son, respectively.
C. Womanhood as seen within this normative framework is suddenly challenged in the absence of a man either through desertion or widowhood.

D. If this trajectory is followed then she brings honour to the family.

E. These realities then pose a challenge to men and the society at large, as the question of their identity becomes a matter of concern.

(a) BCAED (b) BDCEA
(c) ABCDE (d) ABDEC

2010

176. Five sentences are given below, labeled A, B, C, D and E. They need to be arranged in a logical order to form a coherent paragraph. From the given options, choose the most appropriate one.

A. In 1986 it was renamed Recent Acquisitions because, as the museum's director Philippe de Montebello wrote, the rise in art prices "has limited the quantity and quality of acquisitions to the point where we can no longer expect to match the standards of just a few years ago."

B. And as the museum's buying power fades, public experience of art is impoverished, and the brain drain of gifted young people from curatorship into art dealing accelerates.

C. From the point of view of American museums, the art-market boom is an unmitigated disaster.

D. The symbol of the Metropolitan Museum of Art's plight is an annual booklet that used to be titled Notable Acquisitions.

E. These institutions voice a litany of complaints, a wrenching sense of disfranchisement and weakness, as their once adequate annual buying budgets of $2 million to $5 million are turned to chicken feed by art inflation.

(a) ABECD (b) DABEC
(c) CEDAB (d) DABCE

2012

177. The sentences given below, when properly sequenced, form a coherent paragraph. Each sentence is labelled with a letter. Choose the most logical order of sentences from among the given choices.

A. On the whole, we have not arrived at any general consensus over the nature and causes of fascism in our time.

B. Historians, sociologists, social psychologists, and political theorists have been debating this question since Mussolini's seizure of power in 1922.

C. However, with limited success.

D. What is the 'true' nature of fascism?

E. Is it something radically new to political experience, a unique creation of the 20th century; or is it merely old tyranny possessed of new, more efficient techniques for gaining and holding power?

(a) ABCDE (b) DEABC
(c) DEBCA (d) ADEBC

178. The sentences given below, when properly sequenced, form a coherent paragraph. Each sentence is labelled with a letter. Choose the most logical order of sentences from among the given choices.

A. Those who don't recognize wisdom latent in the foolishness?

B. There is always a knowing wink in these tales, but who is being laughed at?

C. In an imaginary East European scene, these paragons of scholarship and righteousness are shown to be fools.

D. The wise men of Chelm may be among the most familiar folk characters in the Jewish tradition.

E. The fools who don't realize they are fools?

(a) DCEAB (b) AEDCB
(c) BDCEA (d) DCBEA

179. The sentences given below, when properly sequenced, form a coherent paragraph. Each sentence is labelled with a letter. Choose the most logical order of sentences from among the given choices.

A. In addition to being one of Mr. De Palma's signature set pieces — a deft and dazzling aria of surveillance, suspense and partial nudity — this sequence seems especially designed to beguile critics who have covered the annual carnival of cinematic indulgence and bureaucratic intransigence that is Cannes.

B. The loot in question is a serpentine diamond-studded gold brassiere that adorns the otherwise naked torso of a willowy model named Veronica (Rie Rasmussen), who strolls up the famed red carpet at the Palais des Festivals on the arm of the French filmmaker Regis Wargnier.

C. *Femme Fatale*, the breathtakingly convoluted new thriller from Brian De Palma, opens with a daring jewel heist carried out in the middle of the Cannes International Film Festival.

D. If this conjures up an image of diamonds tastefully stashed in a velvet drawstring bag, think again.

E. Veronica is abruptly summoned to the ladies room — whose sparkling cleanliness is a notably unrealistic touch — for some heavy-breathing sex with Laure Ash (Rebecca Romijn-Stamos), a thief posing as a member of the paparazzi.

(a) CBDAE (b) CBDEA
(c) CDBEA (d) CDAEB

2013

180. Five sentences are given below labeled A, B, C, D and E. They need to be arranged in a logical order to form a coherent paragraph/passage. From the given options, choose the most appropriate one.

A. At the critical moment, a canopy conceals the act of anointment, by a priest not a civil official.

B. The conferring of state headship is an exclusive Anglican ritual, steeped in the Henrician Reformation.

C. The Queen is serene and vulnerable, flanked by fussing bishops and ranks of hereditary peers, symbolising the legitimacy of inherited office.

D. Succession is sanctioned and blessed by God, with a staged cry of assent from the congregation.

E. The Queen's 1953 coronation, to be reprised many times on television this weekend, now seems medieval in its costumes and ritual.

(a) BDACE (b) EBCAD
(c) BECAD (d) ECBAD

181. Five sentences are given below, labeled A, B, C, D and E. They need to be arranged in a logical order to form a coherent paragraph/passage. From the given options, choose the most appropriate one.

A. Logic suggests that Japanese food should not do well in North Indian fish-hating markets.

B. But sushi is all the rage because teenagers love it.

C. Over the last decade, new restaurants have opened and turned the conventional wisdom on its head.

D. Similarly, the fast food chains which survive on wheat (pizzas, pasta, hamburger buns, etc.) should all flop in the rice-loving South.

E. My guess is that the differences will be ironed out as the new generation comes of age.

(a) ECABD (b) ABDEC
(c) CABED (d) EABDC

182. Four sentences are given below labeled (a), (b), (c) and (d). Of these, three sentences need to be arranged in a logical order to form a coherent paragraph/passage. From the given options, choose the one that does not fit the sequence.

(a) In case of a loss of coolant accident, where there is no supply of light water coolant to circulate around the core, and fuel meltdown, the highly radioactive molten fuel core will drop down into the core catcher.

(b) It is a huge vessel, weighing 101 tonnes and made of stainless steel.

(c) Extensive research was done at the Kurchatov institute in Moscow before the catcher's design and the bricks' composition were finalized.

(d) Another safety feature special to the reactors is the core catcher situated on the floor of the reactor building.

183. Four sentences are given below labeled (a), (b), (c) and (d). Of these, three sentences need to be arranged in a logical order to form a coherent paragraph/passage. From the given options, choose the one that does not fit the sequence.

(a) Nostalgia and wonder are the two emotions that dominate visitors' minds when they view the quaint collection of artwork harking back to an idyllic Bangalore, in Fernandes' small gallery, aPaulogy.

(b) Thus nostalgia works at several levels, and as humans think that the condition of their lives is improving as they head into the future, a part of their mind also harks back to a supposedly simpler time when life was more peaceful.

(c) Nostalgia can exist only when there is a linear conception of time and modernity, with its notion of progress, is deeply intertwined with the concept of nostalgia.

(d) And Fernandes' work satiates that hunger for nostalgia an old Bangalorean would have.

2014

184. Five sentences are given below, labeled A, B, C, D and E. They need to be arranged in a logical order to form a coherent paragraph/passage. From the given options, choose the most appropriate sequence.

A. Two and a half years ago, her father received the grim news that he was suffering from the early symptoms of Alzheimer's.

B. She is focusing on her other career as a successful children's book author.

C. Her latest, *What's Happening to Grandpa?* is a touching, compassionate story about a young girl who learns that her grandfather is suffering from Alzheimer's disease.

D. As an author, she has taken up the challenge of tackling subjects that kids often don't understand and parents don't know how to talk about.

E. Sadly, this book - like her past two children's best-sellers *What's Heaven?* and *What's wrong with Timmy?* — stems from a firsthand family drama.

(a) BDCEA (b) BEDCA
(c) ABEDC (d) None of the above

185. Five sentences are given below, labeled A, B, C, D and E. They need to be arranged in a logical order to form a coherent paragraph/passage. From the given options, choose the most appropriate sequence.

A. The knowledge worker is gaining importance since the opening up of global competition.

B. So the bait is no longer fatter bonus, but much beyond that.

C. Indian companies see the need to attract and retain good workers.

D. From training sessions to spruce up their skills to fun parties — anything to keep them happy.

E. Moreover, the employers recognize the importance of peaceful personal relationships in keeping employees happy.

(a) ACEBD (b) CEABC
(c) ABCDE (d) ADEBC

186. Five sentences are given below, labeled A, B, C, D and E. They need to be arranged in a logical order to form a coherent paragraph/passage. From the given options, choose the most appropriate sequence.

A. He also mentions the existential burdens on his brother with as much delicacy as the subject will permit.

B. Many will be disappointed that there is little introspective dwelling on his relationship with Hillary.

C. Even from the early part of his life, he seems to have inspired extraordinary loyalty from his friends, most of whom he managed to involve in his presidency.

D. They will be disappointed because his early life in Arkansas is particularly well told.

E. The early life contains description of his troubled family life with an abusive stepfather, the dilemmas of his mother.

(a) ABEDC
(b) BEDAC
(c) ABCDE
(d) BDEAC

187. Four sentences are given below, labeled (a), (b), (c) and (d). Of these, three sentences need to be arranged in a logical order to form a coherent paragraph/passage. From the given options, choose the one that does not fit the sequence.

(a) With footage including wallowing hippos, galloping herds of antelope and lunching hyenas, it really shows the potential of drones in wildlife filmmaking.

(b) So whether it's an aerial shot of surfers riding giant waves off the coast of Oahu, Hawaii or an eerie journey through ice caves in Alaska, we've rounded up six of the best videos filmed by drones around the world.

(c) By using a drone, he gives you a rare look at the shape of the waves coming in, the flow of the surfers around the bay and the motion of the barrels as they break.

(d) A state-of-the-art video being the one created by photographer Will Burrard-Lucas using his "BeetleCopter" - this stunning film takes a drone on a safari in the Serengeti.

188. Four sentences are given below, labeled (a), (b), (c) and (d). Of these, three sentences need to be arranged in a logical order to form a coherent paragraph/passage. From the given options, choose the one that does not fit the sequence.

(a) If that's what it is, there's little wonder Britain is no longer capable of marching into somebody else's country and forcing the indigenous population to wear ill-fitting suits and make us all a fried breakfast.

(b) I should think that when the English Spirit of Cricket waddles self-deprecatingly into view looking down at the ground, the Australian Spirit of Cricket spits, readjusts its box and growls, "Strewth, what happened to you mate? Did you blow all the housekeeping money at the pie stall?"

(c) Andrew Strauss went to Radley and all I can say is that is the sort of sharp practice they are teaching in English public schools these days.

(d) And that to me is what was truly galling about England's final-session shenanigans on Sunday – the complete schoolboy amateurishness of it.

189. Four sentences are given below, labeled (a), (b), (c) and (d). Of these, three sentences need to be arranged in a logical order to form a coherent paragraph/passage. From the given options, choose the one that does not fit the sequence.

(a) According to Amnesty International: "In August [2012], despite the failure of Mexican authorities to meet human rights conditions set by the US Congress as part of the Merida initiative, the US State Department recommended that Congress release the 15% of funds subject to the conditions."

(b) The Americas must follow the progressive lead of countries such as Uruguay and Bolivia in exploring alternatives to a military response to the war on drugs, which has been an unmitigated failure of violence, corruption and oppression.

(c) It is undeniable that the US dishes out extravagant amounts of military aid to Mexico with a scandalous lack of oversight as to how it is used.

(d) This aid may have since been spent on equipment and training of the same security services that prosecutors are now accusing of the extrajudicial execution of students, many of whom are teenagers.

2015

190. Five sentences related to a topic are given below. Four of them can be put together to form a meaningful and coherent short paragraph. Identify the odd one out. Choose its number as your answer and key it in.

(a) The poets in question have, like other poets, various faults.

(b) But they were, at best, engaged in the task of trying to find the verbal equivalent for states of mind and feeling.

(c) And this means both that they are more mature, and that they wear better, than later poets of certainly not less literary ability.

(d) Poetry comes from the heart and not from random philosophical concepts.

(e) It is not a permanent necessity that poets should be interested in philosophy, or in any other subject.

191. Five sentences related to a topic are given below. Four of them can be put together to form a meaningful and coherent short paragraph. Identify the odd one out. Choose its number as your answer and key it in.

(a) The opening words of James Joyce's Ulysses seem initially to come from the realist world.

(b) However, the appearances are going to be deceptive, and they become more so as we go through the novel.

(c) Joyce, after all, was a grand master.

(d) Its stylistic deviations become more obvious, even though they are at base founded in remarkably accurate history.

(e) The primary modernist technique here lies in Joyce's making of allusions, which lead us to feel the presence of underlying conceptual or formal structures.

192. Five sentences related to a topic are given below. Four of them can be put together to form a meaningful and coherent short paragraph. Identify the odd one out. Choose its number as your answer and key it in.

(a) The planet is tidally locked to its star, much as the moon is to Earth, and has one face in permanent daylight, the other in darkness.

(b) Given the world's size and mass, researchers suspect it is rocky, like the inner planets of our solar system.

(c) It orbits 1.4m miles from its star, far closer than Mercury, which is never less than 36m miles from the sun.

(d) Red dwarfs are by far the most common type of star in the Milky Way but because of their low luminosity, individual red dwarfs cannot easily be observed.

(e) Because the red dwarf is so small, and the planet is on such a close orbit, astronomers should find it fairly easy to detect and study any atmosphere the world has.

193. Five sentences are given below, labeled a, b, c, d and e. They need to be arranged in a logical order to form a coherent paragraph. Write the correct answer in the space given below.

(a) It is less than a year since Bellerín was "abandoned" by Per Mertesacker to endure a gruelling ordeal in a bruising Arsenal defeat by Stoke at the Britannia Stadium.

(b) And he contributes plenty in attack, too, thanks to blinding speed and smart choices.

(c) At 20 he offers ample scope to get even better, and it is an encouraging sign that in matches where it had initially looked as if his rapid opponent might get the better of him, he has quickly risen to the challenge and come out emphatically on top.

(d) Bellerín has gone on not only to prove he can cut it in the Premier League but that he is a cut above most other defenders.

(e) Héctor Bellerín (Arsenal) is another young Spaniard about whom there were once questions over Premier League suitability.

194. Five sentences are given below, labeled a, b, c, d and e. They need to be arranged in a logical order to form a coherent paragraph. Write the correct answer in the space given below.

(a) Another features a hostage-taking in a hospital.

(b) Elsewhere, an old lover surprises a lounge pianist, sending her reeling back into painful memories.

(c) An overbearing mother remembers visititing her wary son and his boisterous, pregnant wife.

(d) Most stories turn on some kind of betrayal.

(e) One story takes place at the funeral reception of a man whose wife has just learned of his infidelity.

195. Five sentences are given below, labeled a, b, c, d and e. They need to be arranged in a logical order to form a coherent paragraph. Write the correct answer in the space given below.

(a) There is, however, a gap of at least a billion years between the formation of the earth and these first signs of living organisms.

(b) Cyanobacteria are still abundant on earth today.

(c) The principal kinds of bacteria were cyanobacteria: the name refers to the blue-green colour, not the production of cyanide.

(d) A small amount of evidence, mostly still controversial, records the presence of bacteria and perhaps other microbial life in Archaean rocks from Australia and South Africa dated at 3.5 b yr ago.

(e) At some point in that interval, life arose on earth in the form of relatively simple self replicating molecules.

196. Five sentences are given below, labeled 1, 2, 3, 4 and 5. They need to be arranged in a logical order to form a coherent paragraph. Write the correct answer in the space given below.

(a) Olive bursts into tears when she meets an anorexic young woman.

(b) "I don't know who you are," she confesses, "but young lady, you're breaking my heart."

(c) "You're not starving," the girl replies, looking at this large woman, with her thick wrists and hands, her "big lap."

(d) "Sure I am," Olive says. "We all are."

(e) "I'm starving, too," Olive tells her, "Why do you think I eat every doughnut in sight?"

2016

197. The following question consists of a set of five sentences. These sentences need to be arranged in a coherent manner to create a meaningful paragraph. Type in the correct order of the sentences in the space provided below the question.

(a) The 1800's were transitional years in the struggle for individual democratic human rights.

(b) The controversy surrounding the Women question is but one example of the shifting sands underlying the so-called firm foundation of the period's attitudes toward faith, morality, and "every assertion [was] met with a counter-assertion."

(c) Most people today still believe the myth that the Victorian era was a period of a universally accepted value system; that most women lived leisurely, inactive lives, and that husbands and wives remained serenely together, both serving their separate functions in making life pleasant and meaningful.

(d) As Walter Houghton has argued so forcefully in The Victorian Frame of Mind, the Victorian period could best be characterized by the word "doubts."?

(e) Such, however, was not the case, as recent scholarship has shown.

198. The following question consists of a set of five sentences. These sentences need to be arranged in a coherent manner to create a meaningful paragraph. Type in the correct order of the sentences in the space provided below the question.

(a) The emergence of life might not be the luck of atoms arranging themselves in the right way, it says, but an inevitable event if the conditions are correct.

(b) But a new theory, proposed by a researcher at MIT and first reported in Quanta Magazine, proposes that when a group of atoms is exposed for a long time to a source of energy, it will restructure itself to dissipate more energy.

(c) "You start with a random clump of atoms, and if you shine light on it for long enough, it should not be so surprising that you get a plant," England said.

(d) Paul Rosenberg, writing this week on Richard Dawkins' site, said that the theory could make things "a whole lot worse for creationists".

(e) The problem for scientists attempting to understand how life began is understanding how living beings – which tend to be far better at taking energy from the environment and dissipating it as heat – could come about from non-living ones.

199. The following question consists of a set of five sentences. These sentences need to be arranged in a coherent manner to create a meaningful paragraph. Type in the correct order of the sentences in the space provided below the question.

(a) The fundamental idea behind any such theory—which we may call *the immediacy thesis*—is that judgments of beauty are not (or at least not primarily) mediated by inferences from principles or applications of concepts, but rather have all the immediacy of straightforwardly sensory judgments.

(b) It was against this, and against more moderate forms of rationalism about beauty, that mainly British philosophers working mainly within an empiricist framework began to develop theories of taste.

(c) Rationalism about beauty is the view that judgments of beauty are judgments of reason, i.e., that we judge things to be beautiful by reasoning it out, where reasoning it out typically involves inferring from principles or applying concepts.

(d) It is the idea, in other words, that we do not reason to the conclusion that things are beautiful, but rather "taste" that they are.

(e) At the beginning of the 18th century, rationalism about beauty had achieved dominance on the continent, and was being pushed to new extremes by "les géomètres," a group of literary theorists who aimed to bring to literary criticism the mathematical rigor that Descartes had brought to physics.

200. The following question consists of a set of five sentences. These sentences need to be arranged in a coherent manner to create a meaningful paragraph. Type in the correct order of the sentences in the space provided below the question.

(a) Game theory can also help us to understand how the ongoing Greek bank run could be quelled by European policymakers signalling that a "Grexit" is out of the cards, dispelling asymmetric information in what's known to game theorists as a "Bayesian game."

(b) Using this type of analysis can help us understand better why a "Grexit" is a non-credible threat and what is known to game theorists as a "strictly dominated strategy".

(c) One key question to ask is what makes this default stand-off difference from previous Greek defaults in the past few years?

(d) The Nash equilibrium, named after Nash who proved its ubiquitous existence in his 28-page Nobel-prize winning 1951 Ph.D. thesis, was a revolutionary concept that essentially a way to predict the outcome of events in matters of conflict and non-cooperation much like between Greece and Europe in their present stand-off.

(e) To understand how the "game" works and identify the Nash equilibrium (the predicted outcome), one must first understand the incentives of all players, namely those of Greece and the rest of Europe.

2017

201. The five sentences (labelled a, b, c, d, e) given in this question, when properly sequenced, form a coherent paragraph. Each sentence is labelled with a number. Decide on the proper order for the sentences and key in this sequence of five numbers as your answer.

(a) The implications of retelling of Indian stories, hence, takes on new meaning in a modern India.

(b) The stories we tell reflect the world around us.

(c) We cannot help but retell the stories that we value - after all, they are never quite right for us - in our time.

(d) And even if we manage to get them quite right, they are only right for us - other people living around us will have different reasons for telling similar stories.

(e) As soon as we capture a story, the world we were trying to capture has changed.

202. The five sentences (labelled a, b, c, d, e) given in this question, when properly sequenced, form a coherent paragraph. Each sentence is labelled with a number. Decide on the proper order for the sentences and key in this sequence of five numbers as your answer.

(a) Before plants can take life from atmosphere, nitrogen must undergo transformations similar to ones that food undergoes in our digestive machinery.

(b) In its aerial form nitrogen is insoluble, unusable and is in need of transformation.

(c) Lightning starts the series of chemical reactions that need to happen to nitrogen, ultimately helping it nourish our earth.

(d) Nitrogen - an essential food for plants - is an abundant resource, with about 22 million tons of it floating over each square mile of earth.

(e) One of the most dramatic examples in nature of ill wind that blows goodness is lightning.

203. The five sentences (labelled a, b, c, d, e) given in this question, when properly sequenced, form a coherent paragraph. Each sentence is labelled with a number. Decide on the proper order for the sentences and key in this sequence of five numbers as your answer.

(a) This has huge implications for the health care system as it operates today, where depleted resources and time lead to patients rotating in and out of doctor's offices, oftentimes receiving minimal care or concern (what is commonly referred to as "bed side manner") from doctors.

(b) The placebo effect is when an individual's medical condition or pain shows signs of improvement based on a fake intervention that has been presented to them as a real one and used to be regularly dismissed by researchers as a psychological effect.

(c) The placebo effect is not solely based on believing in treatment, however, as the clinical setting in which treatments are administered is also paramount.

(d) That the mind has the power to trigger biochemical changes because the individual believes that a given drug or intervention will be effective could empower chronic patients through the notion of our bodies' capacity for self-healing.

(e) Placebo effects are now studied not just as foils for "real" interventions but as a potential portal into the self-healing powers of the body.

204. The five sentences (labelled a, b, c, d, e) given in this question, when properly sequenced, form a coherent paragraph. Each sentence is labelled with a number. Decide on the proper order for the sentences and key in this sequence of five numbers as your answer.

(a) Johnson treated English very practically, as a living language, with many different shades of meaning and adopted his definitions on the principle of English common law - according to precedent.

(b) Masking a profound inner torment, Johnson found solace in compiling the words of a language that was, in its coarse complexity and comprehensive genius, the precise analogue of his character.

(c) Samuel Johnson was a pioneer who raised common sense to heights of genius, and a man of robust popular instincts whose watchwords were clarity, precision and simplicity.

(d) The 18th century English reader, in the new world of global trade and global warfare, needed a dictionary with authoritative acts of definition of words of a language that was becoming seeded throughout the first British empire by a vigorous and practical champion.

(e) The Johnson who challenged Bishop Berkeley's solipsist theory of the nonexistence of matter by kicking a large stone ("I refute it thus") is the same Johnson for whom language must have a daily practical use.

2018 Slot 1

205. The four sentences (labelled a,b,c,d) given in this question, when properly sequenced, form a coherent paragraph. Each sentence is labelled with a number. Decide on the proper sequence of order of the sentences and key in this sequence of four numbers as your answer:

(a) Impartiality and objectivity are fiendishly difficult concepts that can cause all sorts of injustices even if transparently implemented.

(b) It encourages us into bubbles of people we know and like, while blinding us to different perspectives, but the deeper problem of 'transparency' lies in the words "...and much more".

(c) Twitter's website says that "tweets you are likely to care about most will show up first in your timeline...based on accounts you interact with most, tweets you engage with, and much more."

(d) We are only told some of the basic principles, and we can't see the algorithm itself, making it hard for citizens to analyse the system sensibly or fairly or be convinced of its impartiality and objectivity.

206. The four sentences (labelled a, b, c, and d) given in this question, when properly sequenced, form a coherent paragraph. Decide on the proper order for the sentences and key in this sequence of four numbers as your answer.

(a) The eventual diagnosis was skin cancer and after treatment all seemed well.

(b) The viola player didn't know what it was; nor did her GP.

(c) Then a routine scan showed it had come back and spread to her lungs.

(d) It started with a lump on Cathy Perkins' index finger.

207. The four sentences (labelled a,b,c,d) given in this question, when properly sequenced, form a coherent paragraph. Each sentence is labelled with a number. Decide on the proper sequence of order of the sentences and key in this sequence of four numbers as your answer:

(a) But now we have another group: the unwitting enablers.

(b) Democracy and high levels of inequality of the kind that have come to characterize the United States are simply incompatible.

(c) Believing these people are working for a better world, they are, actually, at most, chipping away at the margins, making slight course corrections, ensuring the system goes on as it is, uninterrupted.

(d) Very rich people will always use money to maintain their political and economic power.

208. The four sentences (labelled a, b, c, and d) given in this question, when properly sequenced, form a coherent paragraph. Decide on the proper order for the sentences and key in this sequence of four numbers as your answer.

(a) The woodland's canopy receives most of the sunlight that falls on the trees.

(b) Swifts do not confine themselves to woodlands, but hunt wherever there are insects in the air.

(c) With their streamlined bodies, swifts are agile flyers, ideally adapted to twisting and turning through the air as they chase flying insects – the creatures that form their staple diet.

(d) Hundreds of thousands of insects fly in the sunshine up above the canopy, some falling prey to swifts and swallows

2018 Slot 2

209. The four sentences (labelled a, b, c, and d) given in this question, when properly sequenced, form a coherent paragraph. Decide on the proper order for the sentences and key in this sequence of four numbers as your answer.

(a) It was his taxpayers who had to shell out as much as $1.6bn over 10 years to employees of failed companies.

(b) Companies in many countries routinely engage in such activities which means that the employees are left with unpaid entitlements

(c) Deliberate and systematic liquidation of a company to avoid liabilities and then restarting the business is called phoenixing.

(d) The Australian Minister for Revenue and Services discovered in an audit that phoenixing had cost the Australian economy between $2.9bn and $5.1bn last year.

210. The four sentences (labelled a,b,c,d) given in this question, when properly sequenced, form a coherent paragraph. Each sentence is labelled with a number. Decide on the proper sequence of order of the sentences and key in this sequence of four numbers as your answer:

(a) In the era of smart world, however, 'Universal Basic Income' is an ineffective instrument which cannot address the potential breakdown of the social contract when large swathes of the population would effectively be unemployed.

(b) In the era of industrial revolution, the abolition of child labour, poor laws and the growth of trade unions helped families cope with the pressures of mechanised work.

(c) Growing inequality could be matched by a creeping authoritarianism that is bolstered by technology that is increasingly able to peer into the deepest vestiges of our lives.

(d) New institutions emerge which recognise ways in which workers could contribute to and benefit by economic growth when, rather than if, their jobs are automated.

211. The four sentences (labelled a,b,c,d) given in this question, when properly sequenced, form a coherent paragraph. Each sentence is labelled with a number. Decide on the proper sequence of order of the sentences and key in this sequence of four numbers as your answer:

(a) They would rather do virtuous side projects assiduously as long as these would not compel them into doing their day jobs more honourably or reduce the profit margins.

(b) They would fund a million of the buzzwordy programs rather than fundamentally question the rules of their game or alter their own behavior to reduce the harm of the existing distorted, inefficient and unfair rules.

(c) Like the dieter who would rather do anything to lose weight than actually eat less, the business elite would save the world through social-impact-investing and philanthrocapitalism.

(d) Doing the right thing — and moving away from their win-win mentality — would involve real sacrifice; instead, it's easier to focus on their pet projects and initiatives.

212. The four sentences (labelled a, b, c, and d) given in this question, when properly sequenced, form a coherent paragraph. Decide on the proper order for the sentences and key in this sequence of four numbers as your answer.

(a) Self-management is thus defined as the 'individual's ability to manage the symptoms, treatment, physical and psychosocial consequences and lifestyle changes inherent in living with a chronic condition'.

(b) Most people with progressive diseases like dementia prefer to have control over their own lives and health-care for as long as possible.

(c) Having control means, among other things, that patients themselves perform self-management activities.

(d) Supporting people in decisions and actions that promote self-management is called self-management support requiring a cooperative relationship between the patient, the family, and the professionals.

FACTS, INFERENCES, JUDGEMENTS

DIRECTIONS for Questions 1 to 15: Each question has a set of four sequentially ordered statements. Each statement can be classified as one of the following:

- Facts, which deal with pieces of information that one has heard, seen or read, and which are open to discovery or verification (the answer option indicates such a statement with an 'F').
- Inferences, which are conclusions drawn about the unknown, on the basis of the known (the answer option indicates such a statement with an 'I').
- Judgements, which are opinions that imply approval or disapproval of persons, objects, situations and occurrences in the past, the present or the future (the answer option indicates such a statement with a 'J')

Select the answer option that best describes the set of four statements.

1994

1. A. If India has embarked on the liberalization route, she cannot afford to go back.
   B. Under these circumstances, being an active supporter of WTO policies will be a good idea.
   C. The WTO is a truly global organization aiming at freer trade.
   D. Many member countries have already drafted plans to simplify tariff structures.
   (a) FJFI (b) IFJF
   (c) IJFF (d) IFIF
2. A. The Minister definitely took the wrong step.
   B. Under the circumstances, he had many other alternatives.
   C. The Prime Minister is embarrassed due to the Minister's decision.
   D. If he has put the government in jeopardy, the Minister must resign.
   (a) JFFI (b) IFJI
   (c) FFJI (d) IFIJ
3. A. The ideal solution will be to advertise aggressively.
   B. One brand is already popular amongst the youth.
   C. Reducing prices will mean trouble as our revenues are already dwindling.
   D. The correct solution will be to consolidate by aggressive marketing.
   (a) JFIJ (b) FJJI
   (c) IJFF (d) JJIF
4. A. If democracy is to survive the people must develop a sense of consumerism.
   B. Consumerism has helped improve the quality of goods in certain countries.
   C. The protected environment in our country is helping the local manufacturers.
   D. The quality of goods suffers if the manufacturers take undue advantage of this.
   (a) IJFJ (b) JFJI
   (c) IJJF (d) IFJJ
5. A. Unless the banks agree to a deferment of the interest, we cannot show profits this year.
   B. This would not have happened had we adopted a stricter credit scheme.
   C. The revenues so far cover only the cost and salaries.
   D. Let us learn a lesson: we cannot make profits without complete control over credit.
   (a) IIJF (b) IJFI
   (c) FJIF (d) FJFI
6. A. Qualities cannot be injected into one's personality.
   B. They are completely dependent on the genetic configuration that one inherits.
   C. Hence changing our inherent traits is impossible as the genes are unalterable.
   D. The least one can do is to try and subdue the "bad qualities".
   (a) FIJI (b) JFFI
   (c) JFIJ (d) JIFI
7. A. Everything is purposeless.
   B. Nothing before and after the existence of the universe is known with certainty.
   C. Man is a part of the purposeless universe; hence man is also purposeless.
   D. There is only one way of adding purpose to this universe: Union with Him.
   (a) JFIJ (b) FJJI
   (c) JFFI (d) IJFJ
8. A. Everyday social life is impossible without interpersonal relationships.
   B. The root of many misunderstandings has been cited in poor relations among individuals.
   C. Assuming the above to be true, social life will be much better if people understand the importance of good interpersonal relations.
   D. A study reveals that interpersonal relations and hence life in general can be improved with a little effort on the part of individuals.
   (a) FJIJ (b) JFIF
   (c) FIFJ (d) IFFJ
9. A. The prices of electronic goods are falling.
   B. Sine we have substantial reductions in import duties, this is obvious.
   C. The trend is bound to continue in the near future.
   D. But the turnover of the electronic industry is still rising, because the consumers are increasing at a rapid rate.
   (a) IFJF (b) FJII
   (c) FIJF (d) JIFF
10. A. In the past, it appears, wealth distribution, and not wealth creation has dominated the economic policy.
    B. Clearly, the government has not bothered to eradicate poverty.
    C. Today's liberalization is far from the hitherto Nehruvian socialism.
    D. Results are evident I n the form of a boom in the manufacturing sector output and turnover of all industries.
    (a) FJIF (b) FIFJ
    (c) IJIF (d) JIFF

2006

11. A. According to all statistical indications, the Sarva Shiksha Abhiyan has managed to keep pace with its ambitious goals.

B. The Mid-day Meal Scheme has been a significant incentive for the poor to send their little ones to school, thus establishing the vital link between healthy bodies and healthy minds.

C. Only about 13 million children in the age group of 6 to 14 years are out of school.

D. The goal of universalisation of elementary education has to be a pre-requisite for the evolution and development of our country.

(a) IIFJ (b) JIIJ
(c) IJFJ (d) IJFI
(e) JIFI

12. A. We should not be hopelessly addicted to an erroneous belief that corruption in India is caused by the crookedness of Indians.

B. The truth is that we have more red tape — we take eighty-nine days to start a small business, Australians take two.

C. Red tape leads to corruption and distorts a people's character.

D. Every red tape procedure is a point of contact with an official, and such contacts have the potential to become opportunities for money to change hands.

(a) JFIF (b) JFJJ
(c) JIJF (d) IFJF
(e) JFJI

13. A. So much of our day-to-day focus seems to be on getting things done, trudging our way through the tasks of living — it can feel like a treadmill that gets you nowhere; where is the childlike joy?

B. We are not doing the things that make us happy; that which brings us joy; the things that we cannot wait to do because we enjoy them so much.

C. This is the stuff that joyful living is made of — identifying your calling and committing yourself wholeheartedly to it.

D. When this happens, each moment becomes a celebration of you; there is a rush of energy that comes with feeling completely immersed in doing what you love most.

(a) IIIJ (b) IFIJ
(c) JFJJ (d) JJJJ
(e) JFII

14. A. Inequitable distribution of all kinds of resources is certainly one of the strongest and most sinister sources of conflict.

B. Even without war, we know that conflicts continue to trouble us — they only change in character.

C. Extensive disarmament is the only insurance for our future; imagine the amount of resources that can be released and redeployed.

D. The economies of the industrialized western world derive 20% of their income from the sale of all kinds of arms.

(a) IJJI (b) JIJF
(c) IIJF (d) JIIF
(5) IJIF

15. A. Given the poor quality of service in the public sector, the HIV/AIDS affected should be switching to private initiatives that supply anti-retroviral drugs (ARVs)at a low cost.

B. The government has been supplying free drugs since 2004, and 35000 have benefited up to now — though the size of the affected population is 150 times this number.

C. The recent initiatives of networks and companies like AIDSCare Network, Emcure, Reliance-Cipla-Cil, would lead to availability of much-needed drugs to a larger number of affected people.

D. But how ironic it is that we should face a perennial shortage of drugs when India is one of the world's largest suppliers of generic drugs to the developing world.

(a) JFIJ (b) JIIJ
(c) IFIJ (d) IFFJ
(e) JFII

MEMORY BASED QUESTIONS

2009

Directions for questions 16 to 19: *The passage given below is followed by a set of questions. Choose the most appropriate answer to each question.*

In March this year, the home ministry proposed a change in the rules governing the Arms Act as well as an amendment in the Act itself. The proposed changes would make police verification of the applicant for a gun licence compulsory and take away the discretionary powers of the local authorities to grant such licences. These changes would also have provided the ministry with a veto on giving gun licences. Under present rules, police verification is necessary, but in case the police do not give the verification report the district authorities were empowered to grant the applicant the licence to carry firearms. Henceforth, it has been made mandatory for the police to give their verification report, giving clear reasons for their decision. The final issuance of the gun licence would depend on what the police says. The home ministry has argued that this will reduce the number of people who wrangle gun licences with false claims, while also providing the government with a centralised database on gun ownership.

The gun lobby, which includes parliamentarians from the Bharatiya Janata Party, the Samajwadi Party and the Congress, met the prime minister and has launched a media campaign arguing that this amendment to the Arms Act was illegal and unethical. They argue that any amendment needs to be made through Parliament and cannot be done via changes in the Rules, while on a larger political note, the gun lobby argues for the "right" of every citizen to carry arms.

The right to carry arms was a part, even if minor, of the agenda of anti-colonialism in India. This was in response to the Arms Act of 1878 which put severe restrictions on the ownership of guns by Indians while exempting the British from such controls. That the Arms Act was perceived, rightfully so, as an attempt to disarm the colonised and reduce their capacity to revolt against colonial oppression, more so since that Act explicitly drew from the "experiences" of 1857. The post-colonial law laid down strict rules for gun ownership, reducing the number of firearms which could be owned by one person but made them uniform for all citizens.

But the purported right to own a gun is argued on another, more utilitarian, level. As the press release of the National Association for Gun Rights in India states, gun possession by civilians protects their life and property when attacked by criminals with illegal weapons. Also, it is argued, that reducing the number of legal weapons owned by law-abiding citizens does nothing to bring down the number of illegal arms with criminals but merely lessens the ability of the law-abiding citizen to protect himself. Using this logic the gun lobby in India has urged the government to not only drop its proposed amendment but rather make guns easily available to all citizens who are not disqualified.

This is a dangerous proposal. The cunning mix of residual anti-colonial sentiments, purported rights of citizens, appeal to people's need for safety and top-level lobbying can actually weaken gun control laws and make the situation worse. The solution to the spread of small arms and guns in society is not to legalise and encourage gun possession by citizens, but rather to work towards elimination of all arms in society. The government should move towards banning the possession of guns by all civilians, no matter what the excuse. Once gun possession is totally outlawed, it will be far easier to identify those who possess and flaunt arms. When arms possession is totally banned, any display of weapon by civilians will be, prima facie, illegal. This would, in fact, directly help in reducing illegal weapons. Reduction in firearms and making their public possession and display illegal will not only increase public safety, it will also strengthen democracy and the voice of the oppressed. It is no surprise that most gun lobbyists are representatives of feudal and other parasitical social classes, despite their attempt to speak in the name of the "citizen".

16. Which one of these is not given as an argument against the proposed amendment to the Arms act?

(a) The amendment is a part of the colonial agenda that seeks to disarm the colonized.

(b) The legal process through which the amendment is proposed is incorrect.

(c) The amendment would have no effect on illegal possession of guns.

(d) The amendment restricts the rights of the citizen to protect himself or his property.

17. Which one of the following is a criticism levelled against the gun lobby by the author?

(a) The author accuses them of having an inadequate understanding of the situation.

(b) The author claims that they do not truly represent the group they claim to speak for.

(c) The author accuses them of being cunning.

(d) The author claims that they do not want to reduce illegal possession of arms.

18. How was the perceived bias in the Arms Act of 1878 addressed by the post-colonial law?

(a) All citizens now had the right to possess guns.

(b) The laws for gun possession were made stricter.

(c) The number of guns that a person could own was brought down.

(d) Laws for gun possession were made uniform for all citizens.

19. Which of the following best expresses the main idea of the passage?

(a) An argument against the lobby that seeks to weaken gun control laws in India.

(b) An analysis of gun possession laws in India.

(c) An appeal to reduce illegal possession of weapons.

(d) An endorsement of the amendment to the Arms act proposed by the home ministry.

20. A paragraph is given below from which the last sentence has been deleted. From the given options, choose the one that completes the paragraph in the most appropriate way.

The good news is that policy experiments carried out by governments, NGOs, academics and international institutions are slowly building up a body of evidence about methods that work. A large-scale evaluation in Andhra Pradesh in southern India has shown, for example, that performance pay for teachers is three times as effective at raising pupils' test scores as the equivalent amount spent on school supplies. In Rajasthan, teachers were paid only on showing a date-stamped photograph to prove they had been in class on a given day.

(a) The World Bank hopes to bring such innovations to the notice of other governments during the summit, if it can.

(b) And in Uganda the government, appalled that money meant for schools was not reaching them, took to publicising how much was being allotted, using radio and newspapers.

(c) This led not just to a massive decline in absenteeism, but also to better pupil performance.

(d) Money needs to be spent, therefore, not merely on building more schools or hiring more teachers, but on getting them to do what they are paid for.

Directions for questions 21 to 23: *The passage given below is followed by a set of questions. Choose the most appropriate answer to each question.*

Since its Platonic beginnings, philosophical aesthetics has been impelled by an alternative that is as enlightening as it is misleading. Aesthetic perception has been attributed the capacity either to gain a genuine access to being or to disclose a genuine sphere of illusion [Schein]. In the first figure of thought, aesthetic perception is seen as an encounter with how things truly are, as a penetration of illusionary conditions of everyday life. In the second figure of thought, however, aesthetic perception appears inversely as a turning away from the stability of the reliable world and thus as a penetration of the power of the real.

To my mind, this is one of the incorrect contrasts from which aesthetics ought to escape. The way of doing so becomes evident once it is clear that the alternative paths are just variations of a third path that is already well trodden, where intuition and reflection are on a pilgrimage to being or appearance.

The classical aesthetics of being understands the aesthetic process as the revelation of an otherwise concealed higher sense or being. In current discussions, though, a non-classical variation, one frequently formulated in media theory, plays a big part; in the objects of art, this variation sees at work a discovery of the constructiveness of all relations of the real. Both variations of an aesthetics of being do, however, assume that general structures of reality can be recognized in or by means of aesthetic perception; the basic constitution of the reality becomes visible in the constitution of aesthetic perception.

An aesthetics of illusion [aesthetik des Scheins], by contrast, rejects this close liaison between reality and aesthetic reality, and, correspondingly, between the aesthetic, epistemological and ethical theory of the one reality. For the aesthetics of illusion the field - or, more radically, the time span - of the aesthetic is a separate zone from which nothing can be inferred about the constitution of reality. It describes the process of aesthetic experience as entering the sphere of illusion, an illusion that is otherwise ignored, one that is located outside the continuity of being.

Each of these positions has been defended in very different variations and with enormously varying willingness to form alliances. One need only recall Hegel's hugely influential discussion of the absolute's sensuous illusion [sinnlicher Schein], Nietzsche's ideas about artistically exposing the illusionary character [Scheincharakter] of the cultural world, or Bloch's aesthetics of anticipating [Vorschein] a better society in the future. Nonetheless, the preoccupation with being or appearance, which goes back to Plato, presents an especially unfortunate alternative. According to this fixation, aesthetic consciousness paves the way either to a higher reality or out of the lower reaches of reality (or it goes both ways simultaneously). Either way, aesthetic perception is conceived of as flight from the phenomenal presence of human life. In effect, aesthetic consciousness is understood in both perspectives as an inattentiveness to the concrete here and now of its acts of perception.

21. A suitable title to the above passage would be:

(a) Aesthetic perception – a flight from the phenomenal presence of human life.

(b) The aesthetics of illusion and its power.

(c) Understanding aesthetic perception and its various manifestations.

(d) Aesthetics of being and its non- classical variation.

22. Which of the following can't be inferred from the passage?

(a) The sphere of illusion is disjoint from the continuity of being.

(b) Reality reveals the general characteristics of aesthetic illusion.

(c) General structures of reality are recognized by aesthetic perception.

(d) None of the above.

23. Which of the following is not a part of 'aesthetic perception', as explained in the passage?

(a) A flight from the lower reaches of reality to the higher.

(b) Discovering the constructiveness of all relations of the real.

(c) Anticipating a better society in future.

(d) Exposing the being which is illusionary in character.

Directions for questions 24 to 26: *The passage given below is followed by a set of questions. Choose the most appropriate answer to each question.*

Lucian Freud has some intriguing opinions about other artists. He has no time for Leonardo da Vinci. He wonders if Raphael's Madonna of the Pinks, bought by the National Gallery after a popular campaign, is really by Raphael at all because "normally I can't bear Raphael, but I like that one a little bit". His own hero is Titian, whose paintings mean infinitely more to him than the works of Poussin – let alone Vermeer, whose people he thinks bizarrely absent.

How do we know all this? No, Freud hasn't started his own blog. Instead, the famously reticent painter imparted these views to a friend, the critic Martin Gayford (who does blog, over at Bloomberg). In his new book, Man with a Blue Scarf, Gayford tells how – having known Freud for years – he finally popped the question: would the greatest living painter of portraits paint his portrait? He was surprised when the answer was yes, and that Freud wanted to get cracking right away.

When he paints, Freud talks, and he likes to go to a restaurant with the sitter after each session to carry on talking. So finally, after all these years and with his subject's full cooperation, Martin Gayford is able to give readers the eloquent and pugnacious voice of Lucian Freud – on art, artists and life. In reviews of the book, which are very positive, it is the quotes from Freud that tend to steal the show. But this book is not just for Freud fans, or a sombre intellectual document for art students. The fascination of Freud's persona and ideas comes across so well because of the writer's skill. Freud's style is unmistakable. Gayford downplays his own, but actually it is his craft as a storyteller that turns what were actually a fractured series of encounters – in the sense that all life is a series of fractured encounters – into a gripping, dramatic read. It is, I think, a new style of art writing in which the critic does not assume the lofty position of a pontiff or professor, between artist and public. He is unpretentious and natural, and above all wants to capture Freud as a person, not just a painter (or maybe, since the book is very directly about the making of a work of art, as a person painting).

If it is Freud who dominates the book, it is Gayford's achievement to bring him out and to do so with wit and humour as well as acute intelligence. Man with a Blue Scarf is literally inimitable – no one else is going to get this opportunity – but it contains a lot that critics and even novelists can learn from. It's the real deal.

24. Which of the following cannot be inferred about Lucien Freud?

(a) He is usually a reticent person.

(b) He was enthusiastic about painting Gayford's portrait.

(c) He's a gifted story teller.

(d) He likes to interact with his subjects even after the process of painting.

25. According to the author, which of the following is true about Gayford's book on Lucien Freud?

(a) Freud comes across as unpretentious and natural in the book.

(b) Quotes from Freud steal the show away from Gayford's writing.

(c) The book is primarily for Freud's fans and supporters.

(d) Although Freud dominates the book, it works because of Gayford's writing.

26. Where could the passage have been taken from?

(a) An article on Lucien Freud.

(b) A review of 'Man with a Blue Scarf'.

(c) An article on Freud and Gayford.

(d) An article on 'Man with a Blue Scarf'.

2010

Directions for questions 27 to 29: *The passage given below is followed by a set of three questions. Choose the most appropriate answer to each question.*

Don't shoot the messenger is usually a good rule to live by. But it is hard when it comes to Bernie Madoff, the former billionaire serving a 150-year jail term for running history's biggest Ponzi scheme.

Yet, in recent jailhouse interviews, Madoff has given a valuable insight into causes of the Great Recession, whose awful impact has blighted millions of lives across America and around the world. No one can deny Madoff's activities were an appalling fraud, but, he insists, what about the involvement of everyone else in the global financial system.

"They had to know," Madoff told the New York Times, referring to the banks and hedge funds that greedily reaped millions in fees from his operations. He pointed out to New York magazine that he refused to give the banks any information as to how he got such high returns and would not let them do due diligence. Yet they never complained. "These banks and these funds had to know there were problems," he said.

No wonder that Irving Picard, the trustee representing Madoff's victims, has filed a civil suit seeking damages from banks who did business with Madoff. They include big Wall Street names like HSBC, Citigroup, JP Morgan and Merrill Lynch. Just because Madoff is a crook sitting in jail does not mean he isn't right when he tells us to look elsewhere, too.

Yet, unfortunately, Madoff is the only one behind bars. That is the worst thing about the whole sorry saga. Madoff and his scheme have become a useful foil for the entire finance industry – and a distraction from its venality. It's always Madoff that the tabloids put on the front pages. It's Madoff who is the ultimate banking bogey man. It's Madoff who spurs public outrage and whose jailing has satiated a quest for justice. It is the classic "one bad apple" defence of the kind banks and Wall Street specialise in. It is not the system's or the bosses' fault, they say, it is just a few rogue operators and they have been dealt with.

But we should not be fooled. We should listen to Madoff when he fingers the whole financial sector and the giant firms within it as part of the problem, too. He told New York magazine:

"It's unbelievable ... no one has has any criminal convictions. The whole new regulatory reform is a joke."

He's not alone in being amazed that, despite the astonishing frauds and manipulations by Wall Street during the boom years, not one top banking or hedge fund executive sits in jail. It is indeed jaw-dropping.

27. Which of these can be inferred as the 'insight' given by Madoff?

(a) The Recession was caused by a few rogue operators.
(b) The Recession was caused by the failure of the banks and financial organizations.
(c) The Recession was caused by the venality of the finance industry.
(d) The Recession was caused, in part, by the actions of the banking and financial industry.

28. Why does the author call Madoff the ultimate banking bogeyman?

(a) Madoff has come to represent the wrongs committed by the banking industry.
(b) Madoff has come to represent the type of agent that caused the recession.
(c) Madoff's actions were like those of a bogeyman.
(d) Madoff was to blame for the banking industry losing millions.

29. Which one of these would be the best title for the passage?

(a) Bernie Madoff – The new banking poster boy
(b) Beyond Madoff - Who else is to blame for the Recession?
(c) How did Bernie Madoff cause the Recession?
(d) How did the financial sector contribute to the Recession?

Directions for questions 30 and 31: *The passage given below Is followed by a set of two qustions. Choose the most appropriate answer to each question.*

The British monarch, Elizabeth II, in a green dress and leprechaun hat daintily sipping a glass of Guinness through a straw would have been a most fantastic depiction anytime in her past 59-year reign. But on Wednesday a cartoon in London's Independent came close to reality, excepting perhaps the frothy beer mug dancing in the air. For the first time in a century, ever since her grandfather, George V, crossed the Irish Sea, a reigning British monarch has set foot on Ireland. That absence of a hundred years puts into relief the bloodshed, bitter enmity and mistrust that have marked Anglo-Irish relations and cleaved the two nations all along. As a foil, her presence has been invested, not very surprising for Dublin, by a high degree of symbolism — some real, some exaggerated. The real: the queen's laying of the wreath at the Garden of Remembrance to honour the Irish patriots who fought against the British. The exaggerated: her green cloak to go with the Emerald Isle.

The queen's visit is meant to symbolise more than anything else an acknowledgment that history should not be allowed to stand in the way of the future; that the two nations have come a long way since the Easter Rising and the Irish War of Independence and the many fraught years since. While Sinn Fein's black balloons, the largely deserted streets and the heavy security presence reminded that history could not be too easily wished away, the queen took the first step towards a new rapprochement between the old adversaries. A year ago, British Prime Minister David Cameron had already apologised for the Bloody Sunday of 1972.

As Stephen said in Ulysses, "History is a nightmare from which I am trying to awake." That is quite like what the British and the Irish are trying to do.

30. Which of the following can be inferred from the passage?

I. Relations between England and Ireland are cordial now.
II. Both Irish and British have been making efforts to ease the tension between the two nations.
III. The queen had chosen her attire to match Irish colours.

(a) Only I (b) II and III
(c) I and II (d) None of the above

31. How is the quote from Ulysses relevant to Britain and Ireland?

(a) After years of conflict between Britain and Ireland, efforts are being made to resolve issues.
(b) After years of shared misfortune, Britain and Ireland are trying to make amends.
(c) Both Britain and Ireland have a tragic past that they are trying to recover from.
(d) Britain and Ireland have had bitter enmity and mistrust toward each other but that is now a thing of the past.

Directions for questions 32 to 35 : The passage given below is followed by a set of four questions. Choose the most appropriate answer to each question.

But I wonder how much real attention Dickens's books will get. In America at least, he seems to be an author more known than read. (Find me someone who claims to have read "Martin Chuzzlewit" and I will show you a goddamned liar.) Yet even if you've read only one of his books, his stamp is such that it feels like you've read them all. The virtues that kept him famous, prosperous and never out of print—that he is easily grasped and eternally inventive in his visuals and jokes—have served to make him iconic. His characters, of course, deserve most of the credit. They possess those funny allegorical names, behave just as fixedly, and get thrown into one melodramatic scene after another. But taken as a whole, those 989 characters make up an unforgettable universe of humanity matched only by Shakespeare, whom Dickens worshipped.

George Orwell, in his famous essay on Dickens, pegged the novelist as a cynic who was neither a radical nor an idle bourgeois, but a self-made mystery who unswervingly championed the underdog, typically the working poor. He went on to assert that Dickens's reticence to take a definitive position on class and rights carried over to his characters, who tend to feel unreal. While Orwell claimed he could conduct a conversation with a chap like Leopold Bloom, he held that he couldn't imagine one with any of the folks imagined by Dickens.

The Orwell essay is a long one and is interesting because there is a palpable tension between his obvious love for Dickens and his need to bring a clear, socialist critique to the table, if for no other reason than to prevent Dickens from being 'stolen' by others with their own specious agendas. For example, Orwell couldn't say enough about how amazing Dickens was in writing the way children think, but on the other hand it rankles him that Dickens never talks about actual work and what people do when they're not standing around in some literary scene.

But despite persistent and, to my mind, niggling quarrels that Orwell picks with Dickens, he couldn't bring himself to condemn him. He went on to concede that he couldn't imagine a day when he wouldn't be reminded of a particular Dickensian scene or moment. It is this aspect of Dickens, the sheer scope of the world he created and the widescreen variety of his novels, that is his true legacy. Yes, his novels are of a piece, but when you fit the jigsaw together it's a remarkable picture, whirling and alive. Its intricacies and moving parts far outweighing the surprise coincidences, occasional mawkishness and deus ex machina endings.

32. Which of these best expresses the central theme of the passage?

(a) The passage explores why Dickens is an important author and will always be read.

(b) The author wants to argue that despite some weaknesses Dickens as a writer is second only to Shakespeare.

(c) The passage captures the universal legacy of Dickens' writings.

(d) The passage captures the author's analysis of a George Orwell essay on Dickens.

33. All of the following are criticisms of Dickens' novels except:

I. Dickens' novels feature characters that have funny allegorical names.

II. Dickens is too sentimental at times.

III. Dickens' characters' opinion on class and rights is not clear which makes them feel unreal.

IV. Dickens' novels feature surprising coincidences.

(a) Only I (b) I and III

(c) II and IV (d) II, III and IV

34. According to author, what is the most important feature of Dickens' writings?

(a) The fact that his writing is easily understood by everybody.

(b) The whimsical characters that he created.

(c) The inventive visuals and jokes.

(d) The complete range and variety of his writings.

35. Which of the following best describes the tone of the passage?

(a) Analytical (b) Pedantic

(c) Descriptive (d) Nostalgic

36. The passage given below is followed by a question. Choose the most appropriate answer to the question.

Why should this absolutely God-given faculty of memory retain so much better the events of yesterday than those of last year, and, best of all, those of an hour ago? Why, again, in old age should its grasp of childhood's events seem firmest? Why should repeating an experience strengthen our recollection of it? Why should drugs,fevers, asphyxia, and excitement resuscitate things long since forgotten? . . . such peculiarities seem quite fantastic; and might, for aught we can see *a priori*, be the precise opposites of what they are. Evidently, then, the faculty does not exist absolutely, but works under conditions; and the quest of the conditions becomes the psychologist's most interesting task.

Which one of the following can be inferred from the passage?

(a) We tend to misunderstand our brains' status quo.

(b) The functions of faculty of memory are beyond human comprehension.

(c) Psychologists are trying to understand how memory functions.

(d) Psychologists believe that understanding the conditions under which faculty of memory operates is the key to understand this faculty.

2011

Directions for questions 37 to 40: *The passage given below is followed by a set of four questions. Choose the most appropriate answer to each question.*

Three judgments by the Supreme Court in the month of July mark a sharp departure from pedantic legalism and point to the possibilities of a transformative constitutionalism that sustains and elaborates the idea of constitutional morality developed in the *Naz Foundation* judgment of the Delhi High Court in 2009. The three cases are also very different pieces that speak to different realities in similar fashion: *Ram Jethmalani v Union of India* (SIT); *Nandini Sundar and Others v State of Chhattisgarh* (SJ); and *Delhi Jal Board v National Campaign for Dignity and Rights of Sewerage and Allied Workers* (DJB). It might be argued, and rightly too, that radical jurisprudence by the Supreme Court is not a recent phenomenon — it has an older history rooted in struggles for civil and political rights. While that is the genealogy of this jurisprudence, we need yet to celebrate each signpost in the development of deliberative jurisprudence that responds not merely to the manifestations of a case, narrowly construed, but sees the larger socio-political context as an inextricable part of the bare facts, so to speak.

The guarantee of public goods — security, infrastructure for governance, law making and enforcement, provision of material and cultural goods especially for classes that lack the power, privilege and status to secure these for themselves — is state obligation. Neither markets (which cater to self-centered activities of individuals and groups) nor purely private social action can be expected to stand in for the state and provide public goods. Central to the delineation of the problem in these cases is the opening out of the idea of constitutionalism to include a broader idea of justice that enables the mapping of injustice in all its complexity. Tracing the link between the existence of perennial channels for unaccounted monies abroad and the erosion of developmental goals of the state, the Supreme Court contextualizes the need to reign in cash flows and ensure total accountability with reference to the structure of a neo-liberal economy. Gunnar Myrdal's caution about the dangers of a "soft state" that spawns the "unholy nexus between the law maker, the law keeper, and the law breaker" is immediately relevant.

"Carried away by the ideology of neo-liberalism, it is entirely possible that the agents of the State entrusted with the task of supervising the economic and social activities may err more on the side of extreme caution, whereby signals of wrongdoing may be ignored even when they are strong. Instances of the powers that be ignoring publicly visible stock market scams, or turning a blind eye to large-scale illegal mining have become all too familiar, and may be readily cited."

The framework of justice by this token stretches illimitably beyond the narrow confines of constitutional law and decided cases to the letter and spirit of the constitution. "Modern constitutionalism posits that no wielder of power should be allowed to claim the right to perpetrate state's violence against anyone, much less its own citizens, unchecked by law, and notions of innate human dignity of every individual."

37. Which of the following options correctly sums up the areas that the author seeks to cover through the passage?

(a) Jurisprudence, Justice and the Constitution

(b) Jurisprudence, Neo-liberalism and Politics

(c) Society, Politics and Jurisprudence

(d) The Constitution, Jurisprudence and Enforcement of justice

38. "Central to the delineation of the problem in these cases is the opening out of the idea of constitutionalism to include a broader idea of justice that enables the mapping of injustice in all its complexity." Which of the following statements would correctly paraphrase the above line?

(a) The main way to define the problem is to merge the understanding of constitutionalism and justice so that all aspects of injustice are covered.

(b) The essential way to define the problem is to include the understanding of constitutionalism and justice with all aspects of injustice.

(c) The crucial aspect of defining the problem is to broaden the understanding of constitutionalism and hence justice to include aspects of injustice.

(d) The crucial aspect of defining the problem is to widen the understanding of constitutionalism and hence justice so that all complexities of injustice are covered.

39. How does the author develop the central idea?

(a) By making a reference to three cases which form the core of the discussion.

(b) By making a reference to the Naz foundation judgment which forms the base for the core of the discussion.

(c) By making a reference to recent judicial developments and referring to the lineage of jurisprudence that includes the socio-political context.

(d) By making a reference to recent judicial developments and referring to the lineage of jurisprudence in the context of neo-liberalism.

40. It can be inferred that the tone of the author in the third paragraph is

(a) critical (b) forgiving

(c) objective (d) disparaging

Directions for questions 41 and 42: *Answer the questions on the basis of the information given below.*

Four teams – Alveston, Blackpool, Chelsea and Dunstable – reached the semifinal stage in a football tournament. Two of the four teams played against each other in the first semifinal and the rest two played against each other in the second semifinal. The winners of these two matches played the final and the winner of the final match was declared the Champion of the tournament. The following observations were made during the semifinals and the final match:

(i) Ten goals were scored in the three matches. At least one goal was scored by each of the four teams. Each team scored a distinct number of goals.

(ii) The team that scored the maximum number of goals in the three matches was not the Champion of the tournament.

(iii) Alveston did not play against Blackpool but Chelsea played against Dunstable.

(iv) Neither Blackpool nor Dunstable was the Champion of the tournament. The absolute difference between the total goals scored by these two teams in the three matches was 2.

41. How many goals were scored in the final match of the tournament?

(a) 1 (b) 2

(c) 3 (d) 4

42. How many goals did the Champion of the tournament score in its semifinal match?

(a) 1 (b) 2

(c) 3 (d) 4

Directions for questions 43 and 44: *The passage given below is followed by a set of two questions. Choose the most appropriate answer to each question.*

Meditation is the natural process of withdrawing attention from environmental, physical, and mental processes and consciously directing it inward to a chosen focus of attention. But not many people know how to practice meditation for personal benefit and spiritual growth.

The beneficial side-effects of regular meditation practice include stress reduction, strengthening of the body's immune system, more orderly thinking, improvement in power of concentration, and a slowing of the biological ageing process. For these reasons, meditation practice is recommended by an increasing number of doctors as a harmless way for patient-clients to be more responsible for their own total well-being. The primary purpose of meditation practice, however, is to bring forth clear states of awareness that will make authentic spiritual growth easier to experience.

Cultivation of inner contentment prevents us from getting swept away by circumstances. Engaging in self-examination and self-discipline is important in order to clear away any of the psychological conflicts that might pose a problem. Study of 'lower' or secular knowledge helps us function effectively in the world. Many get educated so that they can live more effectively. But also important is the acquisition of higher knowledge or metaphysics to inquire about God, cosmic mind, manifestation of universes, our relationship with God — why are we here, and for what purpose?

When engaged in daily activities and relationships, endeavour to maintain a state of mental calmness and Self-awareness. Cultivate cheerfulness and optimism. Maintain your emotional balance. Adhere to wholesome routines of activity and rest. Maintain a healthy lifestyle: choose a nutritious diet and exercise regularly. Let all of your thoughts, feelings, and actions be wholesome and constructive. You will then be empowered to live enjoyably, effectively, and successfully.

43. Which of the following sums up the central idea of the passage most effectively?

(a) Meditation and its side-effects

(b) Meditation is essential for enjoying life

(c) Meditation- personal benefits and spiritual growth

(d) A spiritual journey for growth and self awareness

44. According to the passage, what is the most important purpose of meditation?

(a) To improve the workings of the mind and hence lead to an improvement in the biological processes.

(b) To help a follower reach states of calm and peace and allow her to live in optimism and happiness.

(c) To help a follower reach heightened states of awareness through which she can grow spiritually.

(d) To guide followers through states of lower knowledge and subsequently higher knowledge so that they can achieve their ultimate goal.

45. The paragraph given below is followed by a question. Choose the most appropriate answer to the question.

People repeatedly complain that they see advertisements everywhere, but advertisers should not be blamed for this. No one is forced to advertize his property - for many companies it is an important part of their income. Football teams would have much less money if they were not sponsored. And no one is forced to look at advertising - you can turn the TV off between shows, or just flick past adverts in newspapers. If you don't want to see the adverts, then just ignore them.

Which of the following statements would weaken the above argument?

(a) Advertisers use many devious methods to get their message across.

(b) Some adverts today are even being hidden in what seem like pieces of art or public information so people don't realize they are being marketed to.

(c) By targeting people's unconscious thoughts adverts are a form of brainwashing that take away people's freedoms to make choices.

(d) Ignoring something that surrounds you all the time is not easy.

46. The paragraph given below is followed by a question. Choose the most appropriate answer to the question.

Anorexia Nervosa is an eating disorder defined as severe, self- inflicted starvation and loss in body weight to at least 15% below that expected for the individual's sex and height. Anorexia is typically associated with women and body image and is classified as a mental illness. Mortality varies between 5% and 18%. Patients who are dangerously thin are sometimes force-fed through a naso-gastric (through the nose) tube. This force-feeding is undignified. The patient's right to refuse treatment should be respected even if they are mentally ill.

Which of the following statements would weaken the above argument?

(a) In the case of mentally ill patients, their distorted perceptions of reality may render them unable to make a choice.

(b) Many medical treatments are unpleasant or painful but they are necessary to preserve life.

(c) Medical ethics say that a doctor has a responsibility to keep the patient alive to administer treatment.

(d) Anorexics are characterized by self-denial and often do not come forward voluntarily.

Directions for questions 47 to 49: *The passage given below is followed by a set of three questions. Choose the most appropriate answer to each question.*

"The lions had escaped, but the tiger was there. He was starving; one soldier tried to feed it and the other soldier shot and killed it after it bit the soldier's hand off." In brief, that is the play's first scene.

From there, the action bursts into a plethora of issues, each more disturbing than the next. On one level, it's a political drama about the war in Iraq, on another, an existential tract with the tiger as a contemporary Godot, and on still another, it's a ghost story. When I ask Joseph about the ghosts, he is finally at home and easily forthcoming as he delves into the story line. "The Tiger explains in his first monologue as a ghost that suddenly the knowledge and the stuff of the universe is floating into him.

This is a basic reality of dying in this world that I've created, that once you're dead and you're a ghost, you learn at an accelerated pace. Suddenly, the ghost knows about Dante and suddenly Kev (the Marine-turned-ghost) knows about the bones in his hand, about the Arabic roots of the word algebra, and all of a sudden he's praying in Arabic."

In Bengal Tiger emotional reality is clouded by the problems of translation. By using Arabic dialogue (without subtitles), Joseph underlines the failure of communication. As he points out, "US soldiers, by and large, don't speak Arabic. When you're in a very stressful and violent situation, the act of translation takes on huge importance. And yet, because those situations are so stressful, what is lost in translation in those moments can be grave."

Indeed, the language barrier leads to a harrowing scene when Kev (Brad Fleischer), the Marine, who shot the tiger, enters an Iraqi home in pursuit, he imagines, of the enemy. Upon entering, Kev draws his gun and starts shouting at the women in English while they respond by screaming at him wildly in Arabic. The miscommunication and the mass confusion it fuels make for a situation much more frightening than any ghost story.

Much as I try to probe for the psychological roots to Joseph's often disturbing work, the playwright diverts me from his personal experience to his aesthetic. "Story-telling", he imparts, "can get boring if you're not dealing with the issues of life or death, or on the edge of something. Now that doesn't mean that every story has to have violence in it, but I'm attracted to it for a number of reasons, and part of it is the movies that I was raised on, most of which employed violence in some way."

47. It can be inferred that the purpose of the first paragraph is

(a) to describe the real-life incident on which the play is based.

(b) to inform the reader about the first scene of the play.

(c) to arouse interest about the article.

(d) to set the tone for the rest of the article.

48. Which of the following describes a technique that the author frequently uses in the passage?

(a) She frequently moves from the general to the specific.

(b) She frequently moves from the specific to the general and back again.

(c) She frequently starts with an analysis and then uses a quote to elaborate on a point.

(d) None of the above

49. According to the passage, why does Joseph refer to disturbing issues in his work?

(a) These issues resonate with contemporary political realities.

(b) It allows him to reflect on and critique harsh social realities.

(c) His audience have come to expect explorations of such issues in his work.

(d) He feels that they are important to the story-telling in his plays.

2012

Directions for Questions 50 to 52: The passage given below is followed by a set of questions. Choose the most appropriate answer to each question.

Ask anyone on the street: "what is Romanticism?" and you will certainly receive some kind of reply. Everyone claims to know the meaning of the word romantic. The word conveys notions of sentiment and sentimentality, a visionary or idealistic lack of reality. It connotes fantasy and fiction. It has been associated with different times and with distant places: the island of Bali, the world of the Arabian Nights, the age of the troubadours and even Manhattan. Advertising links it with the effects of lipstick, perfume and soap. If we could ask the advertising genius who, fifty years ago came up with the brilliant cigarette campaign, "blow some my way," he may have responded with "it's romantic."

These meanings cause few problems in every day life — indeed, few of us wonder about the meaning of Romanticism at all. Yet we use the expression freely and casually ("a romantic, candle-lit dinner"). But literary historians and critics as well as European historians have been quarreling over the meaning of the word Romanticism for decades. One of the problems is that the Romantics were liberals and conservatives, revolutionaries and reactionaries. Some were preoccupied with God; others were atheistic to the core. Some began their lives as devout Catholics, lived as ardent revolutionaries and died as staunch conservatives. The expression Romantic gained currency during its own time, roughly 1780-1850. However, even within its own period of existence, few Romantics would have agreed on a general meaning. Perhaps this tells us something. To speak of a Romantic era is to identify a period in which certain ideas and attitudes arose, gained currency and in most areas of intellectual endeavor, became dominant. That is, they became the dominant mode of expression. Which tells us something else about the Romantics: expression was perhaps everything to them — expression in art, music, poetry, drama, literature and philosophy. Just the same, older ideas did not simply wither away. Romantic ideas arose both as implicit and explicit criticisms of 18th century Enlightenment thought. For the most part, these ideas were generated by a sense of inadequacy with the dominant ideals of the Enlightenment and of the society that produced them.

Romanticism appeared in conflict with the Enlightenment. You could go as far as to say that Romanticism reflected a crisis in Enlightenment thought itself, a crisis which shook the comfortable 18th century *philosophe* out of his intellectual single-mindedness. The Romantics were conscious of their unique destiny. In fact, it was self-consciousness which appears as one of the keys elements of Romanticism itself.

The *philosophes* were too objective — they chose to see human nature as something uniform. The *philosophes* had also attacked the Church because it blocked human reason. The Romantics attacked the Enlightenment because it blocked the free play of the emotions and creativity. The *philosophe* had turned man into a soulless, thinking machine — a robot. In a comment typical of the Romantic thrust, William Hazlitt (1778-1830) asked, "*For the better part of my life all I did was think.*" And William Godwin (1756-1836), a contemporary of Hazlitt's asked, "*what shall I do when I have read all the books?*" Christianity had formed a matrix into which medieval man situated himself. The Enlightenment replaced the Christian matrix with the mechanical matrix of Newtonian natural philosophy. For the Romantic, the result was nothing less than the demotion of the individual. Imagination, sensitivity, feelings, spontaneity and freedom were stifled — choked to death. Man must liberate himself from these intellectual chains.

50. How does the author use the arguments of the *philosophes* and the Romantics attacking the church for different reasons to make a point regarding the Romantics' problem with the *philosophes*?

(a) By mentioning how both opposed the same thing – the Church's treatment of human beings as being uniform.

(b) By talking about how both opposed the Church on different grounds, which in the end were quite similar.

(c) By quoting the views of the leaders of the Romantics and the *philosophes* and showing how they actually meant the same thing.

(d) By showing how one fought for logic and the other for sentiments thereby proving the Romantics' support of the spirit opposing dependence on rationality.

51. What specific instance of the Romantics' self-consciousness is mentioned by the author in the passage?

(a) The author talks of their acceptance of emotions and sentimentality, all of which is possible only in a faith that is about self-consciousness.

(b) The author mentions the Romantics' insistence on ideas and concepts, which is the best expression of self-consciousness.

(c) The author talks about the Romantics' consciousness of their ordinance nonpareil.

(d) The author points out the anomalies between the Romantics and their *philosophes* where self-consciousness is mentioned.

52. What makes the author deduce "for the Romantics, expression was everything"?

(a) Passion was important to the Romantics.

(b) The Romantics opposed Enlightenment and objectivity.

(c) The existence of atheism in the Romantics.

(d) The romantics could not be submissive.

Directions for Questions 53 to 56: The passage given below is followed by a set of questions. Choose the most appropriate answer to each question.

In the 1950 movie *All About Eve*, the theatre critic is a dapper, cynical charmer with the Old World moniker Addison DeWitt. He's no hero, but his wry assessments can make or break a production. Characters repeat his phrases throughout the film, in both scornful and reverent tones.

Almost a half-century later, the television show *The Critic* presented an animated schlemiel, paunchy and balding, voiced by the nerdy comic endomorph Jon Lovitz. This character's influence on the world in which he lives is nonexistent. His impact comes down to serving as the butt of jokes.

Does this series tell us something about the way the world view those who make cultural judgments for a living? In the decade since that show's run, many critics report, they've gotten even less respect. Or ceased to matter entirely.

"You get arts journalists together these days," says Doug McLennan, editor of Arts Journal.com and a longtime Seattle music writer, "and it's what they talk about: their declining influence. They say Frank Rich was the last critic who could close a show." Most remember when *Time* and *Newsweek* had full rosters of arts critics.

What happened? Besides the Internet and its rash of blogs, suspected culprits include the culture of celebrity, anti-intellectual populism, stingy newspaper owners and what some critics say is a loss of vitality or visibility in their art forms. While many lament the situation, some think the decentralization of authority means the arts — and the conversation around them — will flourish without these stern, doctrinaire figures.

The nonprofit arts, with their limited marketing budgets, have typically depended more on criticism than the promotion-driven world of entertainment, which is sometimes called "critic-proof." But as late as the 1970s, the feisty Pauline Kael was spurring American outlaw filmmakers toward their most daring work.

But it's less common, critics say, for one of their kind to draw an audience's attention to an overlooked work. Some arts critics, such as Peter Schjeldahl of the New Yorker, Charles Rosen of the New York Review of Books and former Time critic Robert Hughes, continue to do this.

Part of the problem seems to be the general tarnishing of the press in recent years. "Two decades ago," concludes "Trends 2005," a Pew Research Center study, "just 16 per cent of readers said they could believe little or nothing of what they read in their daily paper; in the most recent survey, that number nearly tripled, to 45 per cent.".

Dave Hickey, an art critic best known for the book *Air Guitar: Essays on Art & Democracy*, doesn't think the Internet is the problem. "But I *do* think that we're over," he says. "Being an art critic was one of those jobs like night-time disk jockey or sewing machine repairman: It was a one- or two-generation job."

For Hickey, art criticism lost its lustre and excitement the same time art did. "There was a sense that things had a forward tilt," he says of American art after World War II, when it seemed to be moving toward a consummation. "Jackson Pollock changed the way the world looked, Andy Warhol changed the way the world looked."

But the high couldn't last forever, and the power went to the curators.

"I'm like Wolfman Jack," Hickey groans. "The times have passed me by."

53. It can be inferred from the passage that the world of entertainment is less dependent now on the critics because

(a) the audience does not pay heed to critics.

(b) their big marketing budgets get people interested irrespective of the reviews.

(c) they draw people courtesy the star power which is unaffected by criticism.

(d) one failure does not end an entertainment empire.

54. By citing the example of Charles Rosen, what aspect of a critic's personality is being highlighted by the author?

(a) Controversial and opinionated

(b) Capricious

(c) One who draws attention towards a work which is not so well-known

(d) Wine connoisseurs who want to seek the advice of a critic

55. What is the author trying to prove by mentioning: "*Characters repeat his phrases throughout the film, in both scornful and reverent tones*" while talking about the critic?

(a) Even films acknowledged the important role of a critic.

(b) People loved him or hated him, but they could not ignore him.

(c) Films in earlier times tried to get favourable reviews by creating characters who were critics.

(d) The critic was seen as a multidimensional individual in the earlier times.

56. What is Hickey trying to say by calling art criticism "a one – or two – generation job"?

(a) It can be done by only one generation in a family unlike law

(b) The industry he was involved in was vibrant for only a few decades

(c) Such jobs only capture the fancy of one or two generations

(d) Every generation has a different approach towards it

Directions for Questions 57 to 59: Read the passage given below and choose the best answers for the questions that follow.

On the first page of the novel I am writing, I describe a horse — a gray mare named Mathilde. The mare is not a principal character in my novel; on page 23, when she briefly reappears in the hold of a ship crossing the Atlantic Ocean on her way to South America, I may, in the confusion of a stormy passage, easily forget about her and call her a pony; worse still, on page 84 where Mathilde is galloping on the plains of the Gran Chaco in Paraguay, I could have her become a filly. My point is that there is a huge difference between a mare, a pony and a filly. My Mathilde is long-legged, elegant, reliable, whereas a pony is tricky, often mean and tends to nip, and a filly is skittish, untrained, ready to bolt and do who knows what.

Misspellings and inaccurate quotations and/or inaccurately rendered foreign phrases (and the writer herself is often the one to notice these most) stop the reader cold on the page. The same is true of typos.

Writing consistently goes beyond getting the facts right. "If it is one, say one," says a Chinese proverb (and not eighteen minus seventeen nor five-sixths plus one-sixth). This is not, I think, a question of keeping it simple but of making it as true as possible. Not an easy task: At every turn, the sentence invites me to show how much I know, to show how smart I think I am; every metaphor, every analogy has the potential for fraudulence. Adverbs are hills I must climb to get to my destination; adjectives are furniture blocking my way. English is a naming language; its power derives from nouns.

"Art," Ken Kesey said, "is a lie in the service of truth," a statement which may appear to be contradictory but is not. Interesting, too, how often a true story sounds both false and boring while a lie sounds quite plausible.; the truth is right there in front of your nose. A lie is more trouble. As the liar/writer, I have to convince. I have to appear sincere and be twice as clever so as not to get caught. One way of doing this is to use a lot of details, to distract the reader: "Making things up — as in fiction — sounds easy and like fun and it may be at first. By page three, to say nothing of by chapter five or six, I guarantee, it becomes harder and harder to sustain that lie or whatever the story is that you have made up. Harder still to continue to sustain the belief of your reader as well as to convince him of the worth of your endeavor; hardest of all for him to trust you with it.

In my case, some of my writing is based on my experience .And if I'm successful, in the end, I won't be able to remember — like a good liar, I suppose — what is true and what is made up. Or I like to write about stuff the average reader may not know a whole lot about: Sufis, Thai culinary customs, Guarani lace-making. Or I do a lot of research and then try my damndest to hide it all — another form of deceit — because every fact, every date, every statistic (however accurate and consistent)in fiction is like a stone hurled into the hull of a boat and with each stone the boat sinks further in the water.

57. It can be inferred that the author talks about the mistakes with the horse, filly and mare in order to

(a) Present herself as an easygoing person who is not afraid to admit to her mistakes

(b) Showcase instances where she had also committed mistakes

(c) Highlight the details that need to be taken care of while writing a book

(d) Provide a framework for young writers

58. What does the author mean by saying "English is a naming language"?

(a) English is most conducive to indulge in name-calling.

(b) The main focus of English literature is names.

(c) The power of name-calling is immense in English.

(d) English is most suited to talking about different people.

59. What is the author trying to convey by using the imagery of throwing stones into a boat, which sinks further to talk about fiction?

(a) It becomes more and more difficult to hide the truth.

(b) Each section makes the story more accurate.

(c) The stones indicate the burden of being a writer.

(d) The feeling of claustrophobia and entrapment as a writer.

2013

Directions for questions 60 to 62: The passage given below is followed by a set of questions. Choose the most appropriate answer to each question.

It's argued that retribution is used in a unique way in the case of the death penalty. Crimes other than murder do not receive a punishment that mimics the crime - for example rapists are not punished by sexual assault and people guilty of assault are not ceremonially beaten up.

Camus and Dostoevsky argued that the retribution in the case of the death penalty was not fair, because the anticipatory suffering of the criminal before execution would probably outweigh the anticipatory suffering of the victim of their crime. Others argue that the retribution argument is flawed because the death penalty delivers a 'double punishment'; that of the execution and the preceding wait, and this is a mismatch to the crime.

Many offenders are kept 'waiting' on death row for a very long time; in the USA the average wait is 10 years. In Japan, the accused are only informed of their execution moments before it is scheduled. The result of this is that each day of their life is lived as if it was their last.

Some lawyers argue that capital punishment is not really used as retribution for murder, or even consistently for a particular kind of murder. They argue that, in the USA at least, only a small minority of murderers is actually executed, and that imposition of capital punishment on a "capriciously selected random handful" of offenders does not amount to a consistent programme of retribution. Since capital punishment is not operated retributively, it is inappropriate to use retribution to justify capital punishment. This argument would have no value in a society that applied the death penalty consistently for particular types of murder.

Some people who believe in the notion of retribution are against capital punishment because they feel the death penalty provides insufficient retribution. They argue that life imprisonment without possibility of parole causes much more suffering to the offender than a painless death after a short period of imprisonment.

The death penalty doesn't seem to deter people from committing serious violent crimes. The thing that deters is the likelihood of being caught and punished. The general consensus among social scientists is that the deterrent effect of the death penalty is at best unproven.

60. Which of the following options presents the main idea of the given passage?

(a) The death penalty itself does not serve its purpose of retribution for heinous crimes and neither does it act as a means of deterrence.

(b) The use of the death penalty as a means of retribution needs to be reconsidered as it fails to serve its purpose.

(c) The argument of retribution in the favour of death penalty is flawed as it amounts to a punishment not matching the crime, owing to the anticipatory suffering of the guilty.

(d) Capital punishment as a just means of retribution and as a deterrent is debatable.

61. Which of the following has not been mentioned as an argument against capital punishment?

A. It may not be retribution enough.

B. It can be misused to punish the innocent.

C. As a punishment, it may not match the crime committed.

D. No other crime, apart from murder, receives a punishment that mimics the crime.

(a) A and B (b) Only B
(c) Only C (d) C and D

62. Why does the author state that retribution in the case of the death penalty is unique?

(a) Barring cases of murder, the death penalty does not deliver punishment that is similar to the crime.

(b) The punishment mirrors the crime, unlike in crimes other than murder.

(c) It brings with it an anticipatory suffering that was in all probability absent in the case of the victim of the crime.

(d) The death penalty leaves no opportunity for remorse in the case of the criminal.

Directions for questions 63 to 65: The passage given below is followed by a set of questions. Choose the most appropriate answer to each question.

Scheibitz's paintings are often difficult to read, though most contain human presences, and many are titled as if they are portraits: Portrait Tracy Berglund; Henry Stand; Ret Marut. The names sound as invented as the shapes that make and unmake the figures in the paintings. Look long enough and Tracy Berglund appears to resolve into a female figure in a long skirt and grey jacket, holding a slice of watermelon. Or it could be cheese. Or a megaphone.

Everything looks deliberate and calculated, but at some point things stop making sense – or rather, start making a kind of sense that is all Scheibitz's own. Flat planes drift into emptiness; distracted brushstrokes wander away like someone getting lost on a walk. Perspectives warp, geometries fall apart. The spaces between things become more insistent than the things themselves. These are very unreasonable paintings.

That's part of the pleasure. Scheibitz's work has been called "conceptual painting". I have always thought painting is a conceptual as well as a physical activity. Using fragments of graphic symbols, compound forms and motifs whose origins are often impossible to trace, the artist arrives at a kind of figuration that is at odds with itself. "I can't invent anything and I can't use what I find as it is," he recently told one interviewer. He also told me, as we looked around his show, that everything connects to everything else.

Part of Scheibitz's collection of source materials is laid out on tables at Baltic – not that they're much help. Here is a gift pack of multicoloured Harrods golf tees, then two patterned cigarette lighters, some dice, a walnut and several stones with naturally occurring right angles. How odd. And now, he has painted various objects yellow: a plaster tortoise, a paintbrush stiff with pigment, a toy car. Among all these things, traces of the shapes and contours in his paintings might be found, like lines of a song or a bit of a tune that goes round your head. There are dozens of these objects. How they are translated into elements in his paintings is anybody's guess.

The overall impression is that nothing is random. There are affinities here. Scheibitz has a good eye for an ambiguous but characterful shape. One "portrait", called John Held, is painted on a small, asymmetrically carved gravestone that sits on a plinth. It looks a bit like a face but has no features.

63. Which of the following options best explains why the author terms Scheibitz's paintings as unreasonable?

(a) The paintings serve to confuse more than to illuminate.

(b) The paintings are not what they seem at first and need further pondering.

(c) The paintings do not depend on the interpretation of the onlooker but on that of their artist.

(d) The paintings require an understanding of art and its related philosophy.

64. Which of the following options can be inferred from the given passage?

(a) As an artist, Scheibitz deliberately thrives on creating an art that is difficult to fathom and place.

(b) The paintings of Scheibitz are hard to categorise; however, this makes them all the more invigorating.

(c) In Scheibitz's paintings nothing is arbitrary; everything has a reason and a place for its existence.

(d) The understanding of art cannot be devoid of a philosophical conception; that is what gives art its conceptual framework.

65. Which of the following options best presents the significance of the penultimate paragraph?

(a) It indicates that everything that the painter is inspired by is interlinked.

(b) It allows for the understanding that Scheibitz's paintings though inspired by real life may portray things in an abstract light.

(c) It attests that there is a method to the painter's madness.

(d) It supports the author's assertion that his paintings have to draw from real life and cannot be entirely invented.

Directions for questions 66 to 68: The poem given below is followed by a set of questions. Choose the most appropriate answer to each question.

I would not exchange the sorrows of my heart
For the joys of the multitude.
And I would not have the tears that sadness makes
To flow from my every part turn into laughter.
I would that my life remain a tear and a smile.
A tear to purify my heart and give me understanding
Of life's secrets and hidden things.
A smile to draw me nigh to the sons of my kind and
To be a symbol of my glorification of the gods.
A tear to unite me with those of broken heart;
A smile to be a sign of my joy in existence.
I would rather that I died in yearning and longing than that I live Weary and despairing.
I want the hunger for love and beauty to be in the
Depths of my spirit, for I have seen those who are
Satisfied the most wretched of people.
I have heard the sigh of those in yearning and Longing, and it is sweeter than the sweetest melody.
With evening's coming the flower folds her petals
And sleeps, embracing her longing.
At morning's approach she opens her lips to meet
The sun's kiss.
The life of a flower is longing and fulfilment.
A tear and a smile.
The waters of the sea become vapour and rise and come
Together and area cloud.
And the cloud floats above the hills and valleys
Until it meets the gentle breeze, then falls weeping
To the fields and joins with brooks and rivers to Return to the sea, its home.
The life of clouds is a parting and a meeting.
A tear and a smile.
And so does the spirit become separated from
The greater spirit to move in the world of matter
And pass as a cloud over the mountain of sorrow
And the plains of joy to meet the breeze of death
And return whence it came.
To the ocean of Love and Beauty——to God.

66. Which of the following options best reflects the theme of the poem?

(a) Misery is necessary as it inspires the poor to find new meaning in their lives.

(b) The yearning of the heart helps unite those in need and opens a greater space for growth and development.

(c) Despair and contentment are both necessary for the growth of the individual self.

(d) The challenges and joys that one experiences are a necessary part of the journey of life and of one's destiny.

67. Which of the following options best explains why the poet feels that those who are Satisfied are the most wretched?

(a) Such people have achieved satisfaction through deplorable means.

(b) They lack the longing that brings with it a sense of fulfillment and the ability to understand the secrets of life.

(c) They cease to hunger for love and beauty.

(d) Their lives no longer have a destiny to fulfill and all the happiness no longer forms a part of it.

68. Which of the following does the author attempt to signify while stating the example of the clouds?

(a) The cycle of give and take

(b) The fact that all forms complete their life-cycle going through a series of partings and meetings

(c) The reality that every occurrence has significance apart from the obvious

(d) The co-existence of the spiritual and the worldly

2014

69. Read the following arguments and answer the questions that follow.

A letter from a Japanese ex-student to his American Professor:

Do you believe if I say that language can make a person different? What I mean is this. Now I can speak Japanese and English. When I was mainly speaking Japanese, I did not express myself much to other people. It can be because of the circumstances I had or the culture I have. Then I started speaking English and learnt how to express myself, and came to know who I was, what I was aiming for in the future ... Now I'm back in Japan and my mind has started thinking in Japanese. Again, I seem to stop expressing myself. If I tell you which part of mine I like better, I prefer me speaking in English even though my Japanese is far better than my English.

A possible explanation for the predicament could be:

(a) the strong distinction of levels in Japanese society, which makes free communication very difficult.

(b) we all lack appropriate words to express ourselves.

(c) the Japanese ex-student did not grasp anything that he was taught within the precincts of the American classroom.

(d) All of the above

Directions for questions 70 to 73: The passage given below is followed by a set of four questions. Choose the most appropriate answer to each question.

For as long as it has existed, fashion, being a language, has always been used as a means of communication. This very peculiar kind of communication takes place on two levels: an open one, and a hidden one. There is in fact an underlying fact, a creative value left to each individual that allows the transmission of ambiguous and equivocal messages; think of the eroticism of neglected lace, the hardness of riding boots or the provocativeness of some metal details.

If we agree that fashion is a language we should emphasize that it is a very sophisticated one and, in a way, a complementary one — a tool for articulating and supporting words rather than substituting them. And if we agree that fashion is distinct from style, we must admit that its acknowledged codes are variable. This variation can occur at different levels mainly, but not only, visually, often revamping outdated meanings. The system of constantly shifting meanings, codes and values is in fact fundamental to fashion, as we understand it in our culture. Designers know this well and they are the first to perceive signs of instability. The instabilities, ambiguities and ambivalences, described by Fred Davis in his excellent book on the subject, drive creativity to and fro between opposites such as young/old, male/female, work/play, simplicity/complexity, revelation/concealment, freedom/constraint, conformism/rebellion, eroticism/chastity, discretion/overstatement and so on. The field where the game of change is played is framed within couples of constantly recurring antithetic meanings. Fashion delights us by playing on the tensions between these couples — we derive a frisson from the contradictions they suggest. We may tire of a look but whenever one of these themes returns, its freshness is restored; our fascination with them seems endless. James Carse, a professor of philosophy at New York University, and a friend of mine, in one of his books, divides the world of human relations into 'finite and infinite games'. What is the difference? In the former case, the goal of the game is to select a winner; in the latter, it is to play the game forever. Incidentally, the latter is typical of the game of children, which were in fact the author's chief source of inspiration. Without doubt, fashion is an infinite game, since nobody is interested in starting the ultimate trend, the final one.

Though changes in fashion correspond to macro-changes in cultures or societies, they nevertheless require human action, the work of creative people, of industry and the complicity of consumers. Fashion, after all, does not happen by accident.

The fashion industry purposefully identifies garments and accessories as indicators of social status. Historians have suggested that this has been so since the fourteenth century. Nowadays, this identification has become a carefully planned and greatly accelerated activity. In the eternal ping-pong game between antithetical meanings, the motivating force for creativity within fashion is nearly always, or often, cultural. When Chanel urged her wealthy clients to dress like their maids, she was playing on the dialectics between the rich and the poor, the high and the low status; but the reason for her attraction to these particular themes, and the reason for the fashion's success, was her ability to intuit the predominant social tensions of the moment (in this case ideas about the uncertainties of wealth and power initiated by the economic unrest of the 1930s).

70. According to the passage, which of the following statements correctly describes one of the levels of communication through fashion?

(a) The open level leads to creative value which is easily understood by everyone but is shrouded by the transmission of ambiguous and equivocal messages.

(b) The close level leads to creative value left for the individual which needs to be properly aligned with the open level communication.

(c) The hidden level communicates creative value which can lead to transmission of ambiguous and equivocal messages.

(d) All of the above

71. According to the passage, what is the relevance of the distinction between fashion and style?

(a) There can be significant variation in the fashion codes used by designers.

(b) There is significant variation in the style codes used by designers.

(c) Understanding the variability of fashion codes may make fashion more universal (which was achieved by Chanel).

(d) All of the above

72. According to the passage, what is the role of contradictions, as mentioned by Fred Davis?

(a) Designers often avoid these contradictions in order to avoid being controversial.

(b) Designers may use these well-known contradictions in order to be more creative.

(c) Designers may utilize these contradictions in order to specialize in a particular genre and achieve fame and recognition.

(d) Designers often collude with fashion magazines in order to resolve these contradictions.

73. What does the author wish to convey when he states that fashion is an infinite game?

(a) Fashion trends are numerous and cyclical.

(b) No one in fashion talks about the ultimate trend.

(c) Though designers believe in the ultimate trend, fashion magazines are skeptical.

(d) The author calls fashion an infinite game based on its mass appeal.

Directions for questions 74 to 77: The passage given below is followed by a set of four questions. Choose the most appropriate answer to each question.

You see, society feels that it must control or discipline the citizen, shape his mind according to certain religious, social, moral and economic patterns. One of our most difficult problems is what we call discipline, and it is really very complex. Now, is discipline necessary at all? Most of us feel, especially while we are young, that there should be no discipline, that we should be allowed to do whatever we like, and we think that is freedom. But merely to say that we should or should not have discipline, that we should be free, and so on, has very little meaning without understanding the whole problem of discipline. The keen athlete is disciplining himself all the time, is he not? His joy in playing games and the very necessity to keep fit makes him go to bed early, refrain from smoking, eat the right food and generally observe the rules of good health. His discipline is not an imposition or a conflict, but a natural outcome of his enjoyment of athletics.

Now, does discipline increase or decrease human energy? Human beings throughout the world, in every religion, in every school of thought, impose discipline on the mind, which implies control, resistance, adjustment, suppression; and is all this necessary? If discipline brings about a greater output of human energy, then it is worthwhile, then it has meaning; but if it merely suppresses human energy, it is very harmful and destructive. All of us have energy, and the question is whether through discipline that energy can be made vital, rich and abundant, or whether discipline destroys whatever energy we have. I think this is the central issue. Many human beings do not have a great deal of energy, and what little energy they have is soon smothered and destroyed by the controls, threats and taboos of their particular society with its so-called education; so they become imitative, lifeless citizens of that society. And does discipline give increased energy to the individual who has a little more to begin with? Does it make his life rich and full of vitality?

When you are very young, as you all are, you are full of energy, are you not? You want to play, to rush about, to talk — you can't sit still, you are full of life. Then what happens? As you grow up, your teachers begin to curtail that energy by shaping it, directing it into various moulds; and when at last you become men and women, the little energy you have left is soon smothered by society, which says that you must be proper citizens, you must behave in a certain way. Through so-called education and the compulsion of society, this abounding energy you have when you are young is gradually destroyed.

Now, can the energy you have at present be made more vital through discipline? If you have only a little energy, can discipline increase it? If it can, then discipline has meaning; but if discipline really destroys one's energy, then discipline must obviously be put aside.

What is this energy which we all have? This energy is thinking, feeling; it is interest, enthusiasm, greed, passion, lust, ambition, and hate. Painting pictures, inventing machines, building bridges, making roads, cultivating the fields, playing games, writing poems, singing, dancing, going to the temple, worshipping — these are all expressions of energy; and energy also creates illusion, mischief and misery. The very finest and the most destructive qualities are equally the expressions of human energy. But, you see, the process of controlling or disciplining this energy and letting it out in one direction and restricting it in another becomes merely a social convenience; the mind is shaped according to the pattern of a particular culture, and thereby its energy is gradually dissipated.

So, our problem is, can this energy, which in one degree or another we all possess, be increased, given greater vitality — and if so, to do what? What is energy for? Is it the purpose of energy to make war? Is it to invent jet planes and innumerable other machines, to pursue some guru, to pass examinations, to have children, to worry endlessly over this problem and that? Or can energy be used in a different way so that all our activities have significance in relation to something which transcends them all? Surely, if the human mind, which is capable of such astonishing energy, is not seeking reality or God, then every expression of its energy becomes a means of destruction and misery. To seek reality requires immense energy; and if man is not doing that, he dissipates his energy in ways which create mischief, and therefore society has to control him. Now, is it possible to liberate energy in seeking God or truth and, in the process of discovering what is true, to be a citizen who understands the fundamental issues of life and whom society cannot destroy? Are you following this, or is it a little bit too complex? You see, man is energy, and if man does not seek truth, this energy becomes destructive; therefore society controls and shapes the individual, which smothers this energy. That is what has happened to the majority of grown-up people all over the world. And perhaps you have noticed another interesting and very simple fact: that the moment you really want to do something, you have the energy to do it. What happens when you are keen to play a game? You immediately have energy, do you not? And that very energy becomes the means of controlling itself, so you don't need outside discipline. In the search for reality, energy creates its own discipline. The man who is seeking reality spontaneously becomes the right kind of citizen, which is not according to the pattern of any particular society or government.

74. The athlete's example proves that

(a) When discipline is in-born, we enjoy it.

(b) Games generate discipline naturally.

(c) When one really enjoys doing something, discipline will follow as a natural outcome.

(d) Athletes do not need the imposition of discipline, they are naturally disciplined.

75. As per the passage, the general effect of education is

(a) An organized society

(b) Destruction of energy

(c) Resistance and suppression

(d) None of the above

76. The author believes that controlling discipline is

(a) Merely a social gimmick

(b) Merely a social convenience at the cost of human potential

(c) A necessary evil

(d) Completely undesirable

77. According to the author, energy is

(a) Greed (b) Lust

(c) Enthusiasm (d) All of the above

Directions for questions 78 to 81: The passage given below is followed by a set of four questions. Choose the most appropriate answer to each question.

Conscious of her approaching death, she has broken at last a lifetime's practice of concealment, of stashing the truth away in the manner of the papers and mementoes mouldering in her battered travel trunk. The woman in her eighties (her bones aching in the humid heat of summer, her step cautious in winter's frozen treachery) unwinds the past, sends it twisting and spiralling in an unstoppable black flow across the pages. The urgency of the project is insistent: impending foreclosure flays her on, reopening old wounds, forcing her to confront life in all its bewilderment and pain.

This, in the sparest of terms, is the framework of *The Blind Assassin*, the novel which has won for the Canadian writer, Margaret Atwood, this year's Booker Prize. Her previous near-winners were *The Handmaid's Tale*, *Cat's Eye*, and *Alias Grace*. In her latest book, Atwood explores again a theme central to her fictional universe: what happens to relationships, to human potential, to the possibility of happiness when women are kept subordinate, stultified by their inferior status and locked in silence.

Iris Chase, the woman who unravels her past across the pages of *The Blind Assassin*, is at first sight an improbable victim of history. The granddaughter of an entrepreneur who built an empire out of the manufacture of buttons and cheap clothing for the masses, she has lived, for the most part of her life, cocooned from economic hardship. In her narrative, she conjures up the whimsical splendours of Avilion, the evocatively titled domain her grandparents built in celebration of their new wealth and status and the place where she spent her childhood. Reliving her marriage to a young tycoon with political ambitions, she takes us into the sumptuous between-the-Wars world of the highly moneyed: the fur-draped fashions, the dinner parties, the Atlantic crossings on luxury liners. Such landscapes, replete with nostalgia, have in our own times yielded rich pickings to advertisers and commercial film-makers aware of the power of the past. In Atwood's case, however, evoking a class experience characterized by profligacy and privilege is not done to beguile us or set the book on course for film rights. Rather, it establishes a polarity between material advantage and emotional poverty, between the possibilities opened up by access to plenty and the reality of futile, empty lives. In a real sense, this is not only a political novel but also a morality tale.

In the book's opening pages, information is thrown at the reader from a variety of sources: from a narrative we do not yet understand to be Iris', from newspaper clippings, and from a book written by Laura Chase (Iris' sister). The last carries immediate poignancy, for we already know Laura to be dead, her car having plunged from a bridge; there is speculation that it was suicide.

This choice of structure allows Atwood to introduce, from the start, a sense of the contentious nature of experience: there is a world of difference between the clipped prose of the pro-establishment local paper and the dead Laura's unfolding of emotion (her novel is a high-intensity story of unmarried love which generated shock waves following its publication in the late 1940s). The structure also builds in elasticity, enabling the writer not only to throw the past against the present but also to change pace, to intensify and then release, in a way that tightens her hold on our sensibilities, propelling us deeper into the mystery.

There is a further dimension to this structure: through it we, the readers, find ourselves repeatedly revising the assumptions we formed at the novel's beginning. In the manner of a landscape viewed from a moving vantage point, the story shifts, rearranges itself, discloses elements once hidden from view. To specify the changes would be to give away too much of the plot, reducing the novel's capacity to surprise and challenge. What Atwood is attempting, one senses, is not a bid for authorial cleverness designed to leave the reader stunned and bemused, but rather a journey towards the truth which invites her reader to question, reformulate and reinterpret. Despite its old technology form, this is an interactive novel.

For the reader who accepts the invitation, this is a journey into pain. Atwood wields her pen like the most deadly and delicate of knives, cutting through to the raw edge of emotion, exposing our areas of greatest vulnerability: our relationships with others. Part of the stiletto sharpness of her writing derives from a use of language that is precise and alive to the sheer potency of words.

Atwood's use of analogy, too, can bring the reader up short. When Iris' father, lamed and broken, returns home in his uniform from the First World War, his medals "are like holes shot in the cloth, through which the dull gleam of his real, metal body can be seen". On board a ship at the start of her honeymoon, Iris watches professional dancers perform a passionless tango accompanied by music that is "... jagged, hobbled — like a four-legged animal lurching on three legs; a crippled bull with its head down, lunging".

This is also a book rich in tongue-in-cheek humour that at several points had me laughing out loud. In a narrative that has a strong aural quality to it, a pervasive sense of voice play, Atwood makes artful use of the character of Renee, the housekeeper at the ancestral home to whom Iris and Laura, having lost their own mother, turn for maternal attention. A working class woman with a no-nonsense outlook on life, Renee offers, through her repertoire of proverbs, sayings and catch-phrases, a running commentary on events that both entertains and unsettles. But the primary source of humour is Iris herself: curmudgeonly and difficult in old age, she is possessed of a capacity for wry observation, an ability to lay bare the incongruities of life, with humour jostling the sadness.

78. If medals "are like holes shot in the cloth", then Atwood is a critic of

(a) Perpetrators of war

(b) Third grade tailoring

(c) Glorification of war

(d) All medals and awards

79. Pick the odd one out:

(a) A sense of the contentious nature of experience

(b) An interactive novel

(c) A moving vantage point

(d) A capacity for wry observation

80. What does the author mean by 'the contentious nature of experience'?

(a) That quality of experience which makes us satisfied with our lot

(b) Contextual nature of experience

(c) Converging nature of experience

(d) Collaborative nature of experience

81. Identify the central theme of Atwood's novel.

(a) Potential effects of female-subjugation

(b) Presence of the past in the working of the present

(c) Communality of human experience

(d) None of the above

Directions for questions 82 to 85: The passage given below is followed by a set of four questions. Choose the most appropriate answer to each question.

Attempts to explain prophecy must make suppositions about the future. The most fundamental supposition is that events in the future do not yet exist and cannot, therefore, produce effects in the present. The path of explanation that stems from this view leads necessarily to various ideas of the future as a potential that somehow exists in the present.

In their simplest form, these ideas follow the analogy of the seed and flower. A gardener can examine a seed and predict what flower it will produce. Some premonitions may indeed stem from clues scarcely noticed in a conscious way. An unfamiliar noise in a car, for example, may give rise to an accurate premonition of danger. The weakness of the theory, in this form, is that it requires of the precogniser an uncanny ability to analyze signs and indications that are not only imperceptible to the ordinary eye but also impossible to deduce theoretically. What clues in a dreamer's environment could prompt an accurate precognition of a disaster six months and 3,000 miles away? Some extraordinary suggestions have been made to explain how the future may be unrealized but cognizable in the present. One such suggestion, by Gerhard Dietrich Wasserman, a mathematical physicist at the University of Durliam in England, is that all events exist as timeless mental patterns, with which every living and non-living particle in the universe is associated.

This idea owes something to the ancient belief that the universe — the macrocosm — contains innumerable microcosms, each recapitulating the features and order of the large whole. Thus man was seen as a microcosm of the earth, his veins and arteries corresponding to streams and rivers, and so on.

By the end of the 17th century, the idea had undergone many transformations but was still potent. The great philosopher and mathematician Baron Gottfried Wilhelm von Leibniz, for example wrote, "All the different classes of being which taken together make up the universe are, in the ideas of God who knows distinctly their essential graduations, only so many ordinates of a single curve so closely united that it would be impossible to place others between any two of them, since that would imply disorder and imperfection."

Accordingly, the various orders of beings, animate and inanimate, so gradually approximate each other in their attributes and properties that they form a single chain, "so closely linked one to another that it is impossible to determine precisely the point at which one ends and the next begins." In this concept of a "chain of being" then, the animate, and therefore the spiritual or psychic, are connected with the inanimate by a gradation of shared attributes. For Leibniz the implication was that someone with enough insight "would see the future in the present as in a mirror." Another version of the idea that the future lies hidden in the present was advanced by Adrian Dobbs, a mathematician and physicist at the University of Cambridge, in 1965. As events unfold, he proposed, they actualize a relatively small number of the possibilities for change that exist at a subatomic level. In the process, disturbances are caused that create another dimension of time or what Dobbs calls a psitronic wave-front. This wave-front can be registered by the brain's neurons, at least in certain especially sensitive people, and be interpreted. A metaphor may help to clarify the process.

Imagine a pond, at one side of which a toy ship is launched; at the other side of the pond is a very small person. He is unable to see the ship, but as the ship travels forward, the waves it makes reach the shore on which he stands. As they travel across the pond, these waves pass around certain objects — weeds, leaves, a log — that are fixed or slowly drifting on its surface. The objects thus create disturbances in the wave-front, which the small person, who has a lifetime's experience in these things, is able to note in fine detail. From what he learns of the wave-fronts he not only obtains an image of the objects that produced them but also calculates how long it will be before they drift to the shore.

In this metaphor, the toy ship represents an event unfolding in time. Its course across the pond represents one of many paths it might take and the dimension of time it occurs in. The pond itself represents Dobbs's "psitronic wave-front," and the small person is, of course, the neuronal apparatus that receives the wave-front and converts it to a prediction. Granting that Dobbs's theory is purely hypothetical and that no psitronic wave has been discovered, the difficulty is in suggesting a neuronal mechanism by which the observer distinguishes the wave-front of a particular event from the presumable maelstrom of wave-fronts produced by simultaneously unfolding events. Again, the farther away the event is in the future, the more numerous the wave-fronts and the more complex the problem.

Such in general, are some of the theories that regard the future as being, in some way, a potential implicitly accessible in the present, and such are the difficulties and limitations attending them.

82. The given passage mentions each of the following EXCEPT
- (a) Extraordinary skills of perception may be required in order to have premonitions.
- (b) The future does not yet exist.
- (c) Tremendous insight may be required in order to have premonitions.
- (d) Psitronic fronts are extremely elusive and stay hidden.

83. In the toy ship example, the author is least likely to agree with the statement that
- (a) It is not possible for several events to unfold simultaneously.
- (b) Seemingly intangible wave-fronts can be converted to tangible predictions.
- (c) The toy ship could have followed different paths in the pond.
- (d) An analogy to Dobbs' wave-front can be drawn.

84. Which of the following is not correct as per the passage?
- (a) Leibniz's theory did not permit the addition of new beings on the "chain of being".
- (b) Leibniz was convinced that animate beings share common attributes only with animate ones.
- (c) Animate beings, as per Leibniz, share attributes with inanimate ones also.
- (d) None of above

85. The word "uncanny" in the passage specifically refers to:
- (a) The innumerable microcosms, each recapitulating the features and order of the large whole
- (b) The ability to analyse symptoms and indications that are not visible to the ordinary eye
- (c) Dobbs' version of the idea that the future lies hidden in the present
- (d) Premonitions that originate from hints and clues that are hardly noticed at the conscious level

2015

Directions for questions 86 to 91: The passage given below is followed by a set of six questions. Choose the most appropriate answer to each question.

"Myth has two main functions," the poet and scholar Robert Graves wrote in 1955. "The first is to answer the sort of awkward questions that children ask, such as 'Who made the world? How will it end? Who was the first man? Where do souls go after death?'...The second function of myth is to justify an existing social system and account for traditional rites and customs." In ancient Greece, stories about gods and goddesses and heroes and monsters were an important part of everyday life. They explained everything from religious rituals to the weather, and they gave meaning to the world people saw around them.

In Greek mythology, there is no single original text like the Christian Bible or the Hindu Vedas that introduces all of the myths' characters and stories. Instead, the earliest Greek myths were part of an oral tradition that began in the Bronze Age, and their plots and themes unfolded gradually in the written literature of the archaic and classical periods. The poet Homer's 8th-century BC epics the Iliad and the Odyssey, for example, tell the story of the (mythical) Trojan War as a divine conflict as well as a human one. They do not, however, bother to introduce the gods and goddesses who are their main characters, since readers and listeners would already have been familiar with them.

Around 700 BC, the poet Hesiod's Theogony offered the first written cosmogony, or origin story, of Greek mythology. The Theogony tells the story of the universe's journey from nothingness (Chaos, a primeval void) to being, and details an elaborate family tree of elements, gods and goddesses who evolved from Chaos and descended from Gaia (Earth), Ouranos (Sky), Pontos (Sea) and Tartaros (the Underworld).

Later Greek writers and artists used and elaborated upon these sources in their own work. For instance, mythological figures and events appear in the 5th-century plays of Aeschylus, Sophocles and Euripides and the lyric poems of Pindar. Writers such as the 2nd-century BC Greek mythographer Apollodorus of Athens and the 1st-century BC Roman historian Gaius Julius Hyginus compiled the ancient myths and legends for contemporary audiences.

At the center of Greek mythology is the pantheon of deities who were said to live on Mount Olympus, the highest mountain in Greece. From their perch, they ruled every aspect of human life. Olympian gods and goddesses looked like men and women (though they could change themselves into animals and other things) and were–as many myths recounted–vulnerable to human foibles and passions.

86. Which of the following is one of the main functions of Myth?

(a) To answer questions that are yet unexplained by science

(b) To satisfy the curiosity of children about our world

(c) To explain the rationale behind everyday rituals

(d) To answer the unanswerable questions

87. What is the difference between Hindu and Greek Mythology?

(a) There are texts explaining Hindu Mythology but no such texts exist about Greek mythology.

(b) In Hindu mythology all stories and characters can be explained by a single text (or collection) but this is not true of Greek mythology.

(c) Hindu mythology was passed on through written text but Greek mythology was passed on through oral recitation.

(d) In Greek mythology the main characters of a story are not as well explained as in Hindu mythology.

88. Who created the first story of Greek Mythology?

(a) Homer

(b) Hesiod

(c) Apollodorus

(d) Cannot be determined from the passage

89. What is the role played by Theogony in Greek mythology?

(a) It tells the story of how the world began.

(b) It introduces the four main characters of Greek Mythology.

(c) It helps explain the myth of Chaos.

(d) It tells the story of the Earth and the Sky.

90. What does the author mean by '*pantheon of deities*'?

(a) Temple of all gods

(b) The realm of the heroes

(c) Place of worship

(d) Group of gods

91. What were the similarities between Olympian Gods and Human Beings?

A. These Gods looked like humans.

B. They had weaknesses like humans.

C. They were as passionate as humans.

(a) A and B (b) B and C

(c) C and A (d) A, B and C

Directions for questions 92 to 97: The passage given below is followed by a set of six questions. Choose the most appropriate answer to each question.

From Billie Holiday to Kurt Cobain, Jeff Buckley to Lana Del Rey, we enjoy the music of suffering and sadness, songs that help us through our worst moments – broken relationships, melancholy, mania. Summed up by John Cusack's indie-sad lad in the film of High Fidelity – "What came first? The music or the misery?" – we espouse the miserable and the hopeless.

However, the musicians behind the songs are often an afterthought. Or if not that, they're subject to the notion that their depression is a creative spark and their mental illness the driving force behind compelling art. As someone who has suffered from severe depression, the romantic notion of the doomed artist is not all that. You put on weight and then lose it, you sleep too much or too little, and the myriad other symptoms dictate that it's not the gladiola-swinging, woe-is-me fest it's talked up to be. But does this connection between art and angst have any foundation?

Research earlier this year linked high childhood IQ to an increased risk of experiencing bipolar traits in later life. "There is something about the genetics underlying the disorder that are advantageous," said Daniel Smith of the University of Glasgow, who led the study. "One possibility is that serious disorders of mood such as bipolar disorder – are the price that human beings have had to pay for more adaptive traits such as intelligence, creativity and verbal proficiency."

Marjorie Wallace, chief executive of Sane, a mental health charity, considers this concept potentially harmful, given that not all cases of bipolar disorder are the same. Although tormented geniuses exist – figures such as Robert Schumann and Van Gogh – she says their talents are not necessarily a byproduct of being bipolar. "The majority of people may have the illness but not the gift."

"There is," she adds, "the possibility that somebody who has fragile mental health can be sensitive to other dimensions. I also think that there is a 'tormented genius' link, particularly with people who have bipolar disorder. However, not everybody with mental illness can possibly be gifted artistically or musically. So it can make people who aren't feel even less adequate, and even more of a failure."

So is the troubled artist fallacy damaging the music industry? Alanna McArdle, formerly of Joanna Gruesome, believes so."It's a harmful trope that leads to ignorance and a lack of awareness of what mental illness actually is and what it can do to a person," she says. "I went out with a guy who told me that I shouldn't be so resentful of my mental illness because it's allowed me to create some amazing art. But I think that's wrong, and I also think it's a very offensive stance to take. I would much rather never write another song if the trade-off was to not have my illness."

The idea of mental illness as a creative force is, to most people who suffer from it, a myth. The chronic lack of self-esteem caused by mental illness, the numbing effect of antidepressants and the grip of anxiety on a performer who looks as if they have it easy are barriers that can prevent a musician from doing their job. Pete Doherty, for example, cancelled a number of Libertines shows in September after suffering from a severe anxiety attack. "Depression and anxiety, in different ways, have the effect of limiting someone's capacity for expression and reaching out towards the world," says Simon Procter, a programme director at music therapy charity Nordoff Robbins, who has co-headed a paper on music therapy and depression.

92. Which of the following options depict the main idea of the passage?

(a) The idea of mental illness as a positive creative force is unhelpful to the people who suffer from it – and some of them claim it's damaging the music industry.

(b) Attitudes towards mental health, while improving, are still poor, and when it involves people making music we love, we tend to ignore it.

(c) Glorifying the angsty artist leaves those suffering from mental illness more in the dark than ever.

(d) Music can work wonders as therapy for mental illness, but is unhelpful to the people who suffer from it.

93. Which of the following statements by a famous musician can substantiate the perspective that mental illness helps creativity?

(a) The coming out of the depression is often the period of time where I can create the most.

(b) I always have a desire to write out my depression, so I'll make a song as catharsis.

(c) High-profile musicians' panic attacks and breakdowns help lift the stigma from mental illness.

(d) Both (a) and (b)

94. How is the idea of mental illness as a creative force harmful to people in general?

(a) People with mental illness give it as an excuse for their bad behavior.

(b) People feel it is ok to have a mental illness if the by-product is creative genius.

(c) People with mental illness might not be able to convert their creativity into success.

(d) It makes those with the illness, but not the artistic genius, feel like a failure.

95. Which of the following can be inferred from the given passage?

(a) It is not clear if there exists a connection between art and angst.

(b) Mental disorders, as a by product of creative genius, is a myth.

(c) In most successful artists the presence of a mental disorder is a likely result of their lifestyles.

(d) Ignoring mental disorders because it adds to creativity is a common occurrence.

96. What can be inferred about Alanna McArdle from the passage?

(a) She is an art prodigy.

(b) She has suffered from mental illness.

(c) She appreciates that her illness has allowed her to be creative.

(d) She does not like people commenting on her illness.

97. Which of the following can most likely be the view of Simon Procter?

(a) Music therapy is a plausible remedy for depression

(b) Depression can limit the ability to express oneself

(c) Mental illness is most definitely not a cause of creative genius

(d) All of the given

Directions for questions 98 to 100: The passage given below is followed by a set of three questions. Choose the most appropriate answer to each question.

Hundreds of protesters gathered outside Downing Street Thursday to protest David Cameron's invitation to Egyptian President Abdel Fattah el-Sisi. Seven people were arrested during Thursday's demonstration, including two people for assault. Five others were arrested after holding a "die-in" to block the Egyptian president from entering No. 10, Metropolitan police told BuzzFeed News. All seven are still being held by police officers, BuzzFeed News has been told.

Sisi arrived in London on Wednesday night and met Thursday with Cameron and senior members of the cabinet. He is also expected to meet defence secretary Michael Fallon later today to discuss issues surrounding regional security and counterterrorism.

At a press conference held in Downing Street on Thursday afternoon, both Sisi and Cameron stated that security services were doing all they could to ensure the security of tourists in the Egyptian resort of Sharm el Sheikh. Cameron also said that the UK and Egypt would work together in ensuring the safety of British tourists.

"We are working intensively together in the spirit of close cooperation and I'm immensely grateful for all the efforts the Egyptian authorities have made so far," Cameron said. Sisi claimed that the British government had been satisfied with Egyptian airport security when it requested information 10 months ago, but asserted that Egypt was "completely ready to co-operate with all of our friends" to strengthen security.

Sisi's Downing Street invitation has been highly criticised by activists who accuse the British government of ignoring human rights concerns regarding the Egyptian regime, in particular the death of over 800 people at the hands of Egyptian military forces in Ra'baa in 2013.

On Wednesday night, a number of Egyptian activists addressed a crowd of protesters. Among those who spoke were the sisters of Ibrahim Halawa, a 19-year-old Irish man who has been held in an Egyptian prison since 2013 for participating in the Ra'baa protests against the regime.Human rights groups such as Amnesty International and Human Rights Watch have urged the British government to confront Sisi on human rights issues.

"David Cameron needs to show that he's got what it takes to stand up to repressive leaders not just give them a handshake and a grand tour of No. 10," Amnesty International's Egypt researcher, Nicholas Piachaud, told the *IB Times*. "That means raising serious human rights concerns including the repressive laws which are putting peaceful protesters behind bars."

David Mepham, UK director at Human Rights Watch, said the British government should show its "support for an international inquiry into grave crimes committed by the Egyptian security forces" and call for the release of prisoners arrested "solely for peaceful protest or their political or religious sympathies".

98. Which of the following statements states the main idea of this passage appropriately?

(a) Press, media and people did not very well take to the idea of David Cameron inviting the Egyptian President as an act of socio-political friendliness.

(b) The visit of the Egyptian President Sisi was as controversial as it was necessary and opened multiple discussions on whether it was the best course of action by Cameron.

(c) Whenever there is some terroristic activity involved, the nations concerned are always under pressure to rectify the political tension by extending friendly invitations as is the case for the UK and Egypt.

(d) The proposed and realized visit of the Egyptian President Sisi to the UK was an event marked with concern and hope on behalf of both the host country and the home country of the invitee because of recent unrest.

99. In the given context, what is the role that para 4 plays in shedding some light on the relationship between the UK and Egypt?

(a) Para 4 acts as a stamp of good intent and positive outlook on parts of both Cameron and Sisi as they state their motivations in trying to reconcile the differences created between the two nations.

(b) Para 4 is a connecting link between the invitation extended by Cameron and the positive response from Sisi, which in turn reflects well on both parties as they shake hands.

(c) Para 4 is an attempt to prove that both Cameron and Sisi have only the best intentions for their respective countries' benefit as they come together to forget past disasters.

(d) Just like Germany has done for Greece and the US has for Iraq, the UK is now doing the same for Egypt by extending a friendly hand when the latter needs one the most.

100. Based on the information furnished in the passage above, all of the following statements are correct EXCEPT

(a) David Cameron and President Sisi have met at least once to discuss the political-military unrest caused by events in 2013.

(b) There were protestations and exhibition of disagreement and dislike amongst people at the venue of Sisi's proposed visit and there were security measures required.

(c) The demonstrations by Halawa's family were supported by Human Rights Watch and Amnesty International as a sign of their allegiance to the Ra'baa victims.

(d) There has been insistence following the Ra'baa events to question the Egyptian forces on their past acts of unjustified violence against peaceful protestors.

Directions for questions 101 to 103: The passage given below is followed by a set of three questions. Choose the most appropriate answer to each question.

People in monogamous relationships catch sexually transmitted diseases just as often as those in open relationships, a new survey suggests, largely due to infidelity spreading infections.

Reported in the current *Journal of Sexual Medicine*, the survey of 554 people found that monogamous couples are less likely to use condoms and get tested for STDs — even when they're not being faithful to their partner.

"It turns out that when monogamous people cheat, they don't seem to be very good about using condoms," Justin Lehmiller, a psychologist at Ball State University and author of the study, told Fox News by email. "People in open relationships seem to take a lot of precautions to reduce their sexual health risks."

The finding matters because people who think they are in monogamous relationships may face higher odds of an infection than they suspect, Lehmiller and other researchers told Fox News. And a stigma around open relationships that views such couples as irresponsible — even among researchers who conduct studies — may be skewing the evidence.

One in four of the 351 monogamous-relationship participants in Lehmiller's survey said they had cheated on their partners, similar to rates of sexual infidelity reported in other surveys. About 1 in 5, whether monogamous or not, reported they had been diagnosed with an STD. Participants averaged between 26 to 27 years old, and most (70%) were women.

For people in supposedly exclusive relationships, Lehmiller said, "this risk is compounded by the fact that cheaters are less likely to get tested for (STDs), so when they pick something up, they are probably less likely to find out about it before passing it along."

Psychologist Terri Conley of the University of Michigan told Fox News that the survey results echoed her team's findings in a 2012 *Journal of Sexual Medicine* study that found people in open relationships were more likely to use condoms correctly in sexual encounters than people in exclusive relationships.

To bolster confidence in the results, Conley said, more funding is needed to test research subjects for STDs directly, rather than relying on their own notoriously unreliable self-reporting of infections.

She compared just assuming that monogamous relationships are safer to assuming abstinence education will really stop teenagers from having sex: "Sure, abstinence would be great, but we know that isn't reality."

To put it another way, Lehmiller said, "There's a potential danger in monogamy in that if your partner puts you at risk by cheating, you're unlikely to find out until it's too late."

In a commentary on Lehmiller's study in *Journal of Sexual Medicine*, Conley argued that sex researchers are "committed to the belief that monogamy is best" and are "reluctant to consider contradictory evidence."

"I'm not saying monogamy is bad," Conley said. "What I found is that the level of hostility among reviewers to suggesting people in consensual non-monogamous relationships are more responsible is really over the top."

Conley said she initially struggled to publish her 2012 study. When she changed the framing of its conclusion to find that "cheaters" in monogamous relationships were more irresponsible, the study was suddenly published.

"Even in a scientific review process, challenging researchers' preconceived notions is perilous," she wrote in her commentary.

Other relationship researchers disagree, however, saying that sociologists have cast shade on monogamy — finding declines in happiness, sexual satisfaction, and frequency of intercourse — for decades. "This is about as widespread a finding as one gets," Harry Reis, a psychologist at the University of Rochester, told Fox News. He called the idea that social scientists are biased against studies showing the value of non-monogamous relationships was "poppycock."

101. Which of the following options can most appropriately continue the passage?

(a) Sex researcher Debbie Herbernick of Indiana University echoed this view, saying funding is not an issue: "I've never seen much negative reaction or pushback."

(b) More critically, Reis said, reviewers might be dubious about the data collected on open relationships, given their relative rarity making reliable data collection difficult.

(c) Although Lehmiller published his study, he agreed with Conley that a stigma still marks open relationships, even in science.

(d) "People, including many sex researchers," he said, "have a tendency to put monogamy on a pedestal and to be very judgmental when it comes to consensual non-monogamy."

102. From the statements given below, choose the one that can be easily inferred from the lines 'Conley said...suddenly published'. (lines 39-41)

(a) People in monogamous relationships tend to be defensive about their cheating habits and hence will do everything they can to avoid being exposed.

(b) Scientific studies often have difficulty obtaining validation when they feature issues concerning people's private lives and sexual behaviour.

(c) Conley's research put at risk the non-monogamous relationship status of those researchers who otherwise touted their status as monogamous and faithful partners.

(d) Conley faced difficulty in publishing her research because she was challenging the preconceived and well-defended notion that monogamous relationships are preferable.

103. How does the author use the word 'stigma' in the fourth paragraph?

(a) A pessimistic opinion

(b) A mark of disgrace or infamy

(c) A negative reputation

(d) A sense of notoriety

Directions for questions 104 to 109: The passage given below is followed by a set of six questions. Choose the most appropriate answer to each question.

Did you know that the Impressionists favored the elimination of the color black from their painter's palette? According to Wilkins et al, Impressionism encouraged this:

"The new color theory emphasized the presence of color within shadows and, in asserting that there was no black in nature, inspired the Impressionists to ban black from their palette."

The founder of Impressionism is Claude Monet (1840-1926), a French painter born in Paris. He was a close associate of the French painter, Edouard Manet, who helped art move away from Realism in the nineteenth century. Monet served along with fellow artist Edgar Degas and author Emile Zola as a pall bearer at Manet's funeral in 1883. Degas later created ballet scenes including 1874's Ballet Rehearsal which showed some qualities of Impressionism.

Early in his career, Monet created a style of painting that focused on the light in the shadows. This study of natural light is the focus of his landmark painting, Impression – Sunrise, completed in 1872. This work is the source of the term "Impressionism." Impression – Sunrise is full of powerful shades of blue, gray, and orange, and a few fishermen in small boats float in the foreground as the sun rises at the top of the painting.

Art historians note that Impressionist paintings such as Impression – Sunrise were rejected by the Paris Salon, leading the painters to hold their own autonomous shows. Monet first exhibited this work in Paris in 1874 in a non-Salon-approved exhibition. Honour and Fleming note that the independent exhibitions by the Impressionists showed how the artists were trying to escape the "tyranny of the official art-world." In other words, if an artist could not get accepted by the Salon, he or she would have no method of becoming a professional artist in France.

Monet contributed many other paintings to the art world over the remainder of his career. He consistently explored how the human eye sees landscapes or scenes in the outdoors. He wanted to capture real events and watch how they related to the light. In Gare St.-Lazare (1877), Monet showed that a Paris train station could be the center point of the natural light shining through the glass roof on a sunny day.

The Impressionists also painted "a typically middle-class vision of happiness" in keeping with their bourgeois backgrounds, according to Honour and Fleming. The authors use the example of Monet's sketch for The Picnic which predates Impression – Sunrise by six years. It was never finished, but it shows middle-class ladies and gentleman at a picnic beneath a beautiful canopy of trees.

As the founder of this a new style of painting, Monet left a huge mark on the art worlds of the 19th and 20th centuries. He died of lung cancer in 1926 and was buried at the church in Giverny, France.

104. Why did the Impressionists favor the elimination of the color black from their painter's palette?

(a) There is no black in nature.

(b) Black is the colour of shadows and not of real things.

(c) There exists colour in everything, even shadows.

(d) They wanted to imitate nature in minute detail.

105. What was the most significant contribution of Manet to art?

(a) He helped art to move away from Realism and towards Impressionism.

(b) He influenced art towards newer movements in techniques.

(c) He helped artists in breaking away from influence of Realism.

(d) Cannot be determined from the passage

106. Which of the following is true of Impressionism?

A. It received its name from a painting of Monet.

B. It is a study of light in shadows.

C. In its early stage, it was rejected by the Paris Salon.

(a) A and B (b) B and C

(c) C and A (d) A, B and C

107. The passage is most likely

(a) an article on Monet

(b) an article on impressionist art

(c) an article on impressionist artists

(d) an article on movement of art from Realism to Impressionism

108. What does the author mean by 'a typically middle-class vision of happiness'?

(a) depiction of a middle class family

(b) depiction of middle class people having a good time

(c) depiction of normal ladies and gentleman in everyday scenarios

(d) depiction of the normality of a middle class life

109. Which of the following was/were artists' attempt(s) to escape the tyranny of the official art-world?

(a) Holding independent art shows

(b) Creating painting that were not commissioned

(c) Holding non-Salon-approved exhibition

(d) All of the given

SUMMARY TYPE QUESTIONS

2003

DIRECTIONS for Questions 1 to 9: Four alternative summaries are given below each text. Choose the option that best captures the essence of the text.

1. It is important for shipping companies to be clear about the objectives for maintenance and materials management — as to whether the primary focus is on service level improvement or cost minimization. Often when certain systems are set in place, the cost minimization objective and associated procedure become more important than the flexibility required for service level improvement. The problem really arises since cost minimization tends to focus on out of pocket costs which are visible, while the opportunity costs, often greater in value, are lost sight of.

(a) Shipping companies have to either minimize costs or maximize service quality. If they focus on cost minimization, they will reduce quality. They should focus on service level improvement, or else opportunity costs will be lost sight of.

(b) Shipping companies should determine the primary focus of their maintenance and materials management. Focus on cost minimization may reduce visible costs, but ignore greater invisible costs and impair service quality.

(c) Any cost minimization programme in shipping is bound to lower the quality of service. Therefore, shipping companies must be clear about the primary focus of their maintenance and materials management before embarking on cost minimization.

(d) Shipping companies should focus on quality level improvement rather than cost cutting. Cost cutting will lead to untold opportunity costs. Companies should have systems in place to make the service level flexible.

2. Try before you buy. We use this memorable saying to urge you to experience the consequences of an alternative before you choose it, whenever this is feasible. If you are considering buying a van after having always owned sedans, rent one for a week or borrow a friend's. By experiencing the consequences first hand, they become more meaningful. In addition, you are likely to identify consequences you had not even thought of before. May be you will discover that it is difficult to park the van in your small parking space at work, but that, on the other hand, your elderly father has a much easier time getting in and out of it.

(a) If you are planning to buy a van after being used to sedans, borrow a van or rent it and try it before deciding to buy it. Then you may realize that parking a van is difficult while it is easier for your elderly father to get in and out of it.

(b) Before choosing an alternative, experience its consequences if feasible. If, for example, you want to change from sedans to a van, try one before buying it. You will discover aspects you may never have thought of.

(c) Always try before you buy anything. You are bound to discover many consequences. One of the consequences of going in for a van is that it is more difficult to park than sedans at the office car park.

(d) We urge you to try products such as vans before buying them. Then you can experience consequences you have not thought of such as parking problems. But your father may find vans more comfortable than cars.

3. Physically, inertia is a feeling that you just can't move; mentally, it is a sluggish mind. Even if you try to be sensitive, if your mind is sluggish, you just don't feel anything intensely. You may even see a tragedy enacted in front of your eyes and not be able to respond meaningfully. You may see one person exploiting another, one group persecuting another, and not be able to get angry. Your energy is frozen. You are not deliberately refusing to act; you just don't have the capacity.

(a) Inertia makes your body and mind sluggish. They become insensitive to tragedies, exploitation, and persecution because it freezes your energy and decapacitates it.

(b) When you have inertia you don't act although you see one person exploiting another or one group persecuting another. You don't get angry because you are incapable.

(c) Inertia is of two types — physical and mental. Physical inertia restricts bodily movements. Mental inertia prevents mental response to events anacted in front of your eyes.

(d) Physical inertia stops your body from moving; mental inertia freezes your energy, and stops your mind from responding meaningfully to events, even tragedies, in front of you.

4. Some decisions will be fairly obvious — 'no-brainers'. Your bank account is low, but you have a two-week vacation coming up and you want to get away to some place warm to relax with your family. Will you accept your in-laws' offer of free use of their Florida beachfront condo? Sure. You like your employer and feel ready to move forward in your career. Will you step in for your boss for three weeks while she attends a professional development course? Of course.

(a) Some decisions are obvious under certain circumstances. You may, for example, readily accept a relative's offer of free holiday accommodation. Or step in for your boss when she is away.

(b) Some decisions are no-brainers. You need not think when making them. Examples are condo offers from in-law and job offers from bosses when your bank account is low or boss is away.

(c) Easy decisions are called 'no-brainers' because they do not require any cerebral activity. Examples such as accepting free holiday accommodation abound in our lives.

(d) Accepting an offer from in-laws when you are short on funds and want a holiday is a no-brainer. Another no-brainer is taking the boss's job when she is away.

2004

5. The human race is spread all over world, from the polar regions to the tropics. The people of whom it is made up eat different kinds of food, partly according to the climate in which they live, and partly according to the kind of food which their country produces. In hot climates; meat and fat are not much needed; but in the Arctic regions they seem to be very necessary for keeping up the heat of the body. Thus, in India, people live chiefly on different kinds of grains, eggs, milk, or sometimes fish and meat. In Europe people eat more meat and less grain. In the Arctic regions, where no grains and fruits are produced, the Eskimo and others races live almost entirely on meat and fish.

(a) Food eaten by people in different regions of the world depends on the climate and produce of the region, and varies from meat and fish in the Arctic to predominantly grains in the tropics.

(b) Hot climates require people to eat grains while cold regions require people to eat meat and fish.

(c) In hot countries people eat mainly grains while in the Arctic, they eat meat and fish because they cannot grow grains.

(d) While people in Arctic regions like meat and fish and those in hot regions like India prefer mainly grains, they have to change what they eat depending on the local climate and the local produce.

6. You seemed at first to take no notice of your school-fellows, or rather to set yourself against them because they were strangers to you. They knew as little of you as you did of them; this would have been the reason for their keeping aloof from you as well, which you would have felt as a hardship. Learn never to conceive a prejudice against others because you know nothing of them. It is bad reasoning, and makes enemies of half the world. Do not think ill of them till they behave ill to you; and then strive to avoid the faults, which you see in them. This will disarm their hostility sooner than pique or resentment or complaint.

(a) The discomfort you felt with your school fellows was because both sides knew little of each other. You should not complain unless you find others prejudiced against you and have attempted to carefully analyze the faults you have observed in them.

(b) The discomfort you felt with your school fellows was because both sides knew little of each other. Avoid prejudice and negative thoughts till you encounter bad behaviour from others, and then win them over by shunning the faults you have observed.

(c) You encountered hardship amongst your school fellows because you did not know then well. You should learn not to make enemies because of your prejudices irrespective of their behaviour towards you.

(d) You encountered hardship amongst your school fellows because you did not know them well. You should learn to not make enemies because of your prejudices unless they behave badly with you.

7. Local communities have often come in conflict with agents trying to exploit resources, at a faster pace, for an expanding commercial-industrial economy. More often than not, such agents of resource-intensification are given preferential treatment by the state, through the grant of generous long leases over mineral or fish stocks, for example, or the provision of raw material at an enormously subsidized price. With the injustice so compounded, local communities at the receiving end of this process have no recourse expect direct action, resisting both the state and outside exploiters through a variety of protest techniques. These struggles might perhaps be seen as a manifestation of a new kind of class conflict.

(a) A new kind of class conflict arises from preferential treatments given to agents of resource-intensification by the state, which the local community sees as unfair.

(b) The grant of long leases to agents of resource-intensification for an expanding commercial-industrial economy leads to direct protests from the local community, which sees it as unfair.

(c) Preferential treatment given by the state to agents of resource-intensification for an expanding commercial-industrial economy exacerbates injustice to local communities and leads to direct protests from them, resulting in a new type of class conflict.

(d) Local communities have no option but to protest against agents of resource-intensification and create a new type of class conflict when they are given raw material at subsidized prices for an expanding commercial-industrial economy.

8. Although almost all climate scientists agree that the Earth is gradually warming, they have long been of two minds about the process of rapid climate shifts within larger periods of change. Some have speculated that the process works like a giant oven or freezer, warming or cooling the whole planet at the same time. Others think that shifts occur on opposing schedules in the Northern and Southern Hemisphere, like exaggerated seasons. Recent research in Germany examining climate patterns in the Southern Hemisphere at the end of the last Ice Age strengthens the idea that warming and cooling occurs at alternate times in the two hemispheres. A more definitive answer to this debate will allow scientists to better predict when and how quickly the next climate shift will happen.

(a) Scientists have been unsure whether rapid shifts in the Earth's climate happen all at once or on opposing schedules in different hemispheres; research will help find a definitive answer and better predict climate shifts in future.

(b) Scientists have been unsure whether rapid shifts in the Earth's climate happen all at once or on opposing schedules in different hemispheres; finding a definitive answer will help them better predict climate shifts in future.

(c) Research in Germany will help scientists find a definitive answer about warming and cooling of the Earth and predict climate shifts in the future in a better manner.

(d) More research rather than debates on warming or cooling of the Earth and exaggerated seasons in its hemisphere will help scientists in Germany predict changes better in future.

9. Modern bourgeois society, said Nietzsche, was decadent and enfeebled – a victim of the excessive development of the rational faculties at the expense of will and instinct. Against the liberal-rationalist stress on the intellect, Nietzsche urged recognition of the dark mysterious world of instinctual desires – the true forces of life. Smother the will excessive intellectualizing and you destroy the spontaneity that sparks cultural creativity and ignites a zest for living. The critical and theoretical outlook destroyed the creative instincts. For man's manifold potential to be realized, he must forego relying on the intellect and nurture again the instinctual roots of human existence.

(a) Nietzsche urges the decadent and enfeebled modern society to forego intellect and give importance to creative instincts.

(b) Nietzsche urges the decadent and enfeebled modern society to smother the will with excessive intellectualizing and ignite a zest for living.

(c) Nietzsche criticizes the intellectuals for enfeebling the modern bourgeois society by not nurturing man's creative instincts.

(d) Nietzsche blames excessive intellectualization for the decline of modern society and suggests nurturing creative instincts instead.

2016

10. The following question consists of a paragraph which is followed by four options. Among the given options, choose the one which captures the essence of the paragraph accurately and clearly. Type in that option as the answer in the space provided below the question.

There is a difference between knowingness and knowledge, but what is it? Knowingness comes after knowledge; it is only the echo of its source, and it is proud to be the echo. One of the liberties of our connected age is that we can be almost infinitely knowing, consoling our lack of true knowledge with an easy cynicism of acquisition. It is cheaply glorious to be able to discover almost any fact about the world. On the machine I am using to write this review: I experience that liberty as the reward it is, and also as a punishment; as both a gift of the digital world and a judgment on my scant acquaintance with the actual world. Speak for yourself, you may say. Who is this "we," so easily invoked? If knowingness is capitalism's gift to those metropolitan élites who haven't earned it, there are also multitudes of people, constrained by poverty and political oppression and the bad luck of obscurity, who don't deserve the brutal "knowledge" that is being meted out daily on their lives; they would be very grateful for the privileges of knowingness.

(a) Those overlooked by capitalism would willingly choose knowledge and this diminishes the value of the argument of cynicism made by the sheltered elites about knowledge.

(b) Capitalism shields the elites from a full acquaintance with the world while exposing the poor to the world and this explains their different attitudes towards privileges.

(c) The ease of acquisition is a reward for the underprivileged that would be grateful for even the 'cheap glory' associated with it.

(d) The cynical argument of the ease of knowingness wanes when one grasps that those less fortunate would gladly embrace this 'ease' rather than an immersed acquaintance with the world.

11. The following question consists of a paragraph which is followed by four options. Among the given options, choose the one which captures the essence of the paragraph accurately and clearly. Type in that option as the answer in the space provided below the question.

As in the 18th century, so in the 21st. Cognitive psychologists with their innatist views tell us that women work with a finer mesh of emotional understanding than men. The novel - by that view the most feminine of forms - answers to their biologically ordained skills. From other rooms in the teeming mansion of the social sciences, there are others who insist that it is all down to conditioning. But perhaps the causes are less interesting than the facts themselves. Reading groups, readings, breakdowns of book sales all tell the same story: when women stop reading, the novel will be dead.

(a) In the 21st century too, the survival of the novel depends on female readership, which is to say it depends on their innate inclination towards fine emotional understanding.

(b) As psychology has shown, both women and the novel share a deep reservoir of emotional understanding, which underscores the reason for the dependence of the novel on female readership.

(c) Some social sciences argue that women are conditioned by society to have finer emotional understanding, which explains why the novel depends on women readers for its survival.

(d) It may be down to nature or nurture, but even in the 21st century one thing is clear: if women read on, the novel lives on.

12. The following question consists of a paragraph which is followed by four options. Among the given options, choose the one which captures the essence of the paragraph accurately and clearly. Type in that option as the answer in the space provided below the question.

The century since Franz Kafka was born has been marked by the idea of "modernism"—self-consciousness new among centuries, a consciousness of being new. Sixty years after his death, Kafka epitomizes one aspect of this modern mind-set: a sensation of anxiety and shame whose center cannot be located and therefore cannot be placated; a sense of an infinite difficulty within things, impeding every step; a sensitivity acute beyond usefulness, as if the nervous system, flayed of its old hide of social usage and religious belief, must record every touch as pain. In Kafka's peculiar and highly original case this dreadful quality is mixed with immense tenderness, oddly good humor, and a certain severe and reassuring formality. The combination makes him an artist; but rarely can an artist have struggled against greater inner resistance and more sincere diffidence as to the worth of his art.

(a) Despite Kafka's shyness and struggles he is a quintessential modernist artist, as he, quite unlike any other, manages to juxtapose tenderness and humor with pain and an implacable sense of anxiety and shame.

(b) Kafka's ability to lace his literature with themes of modernism such as anxiety, shame and pain intermingled with humor and tenderness makes him an original modernist.

(c) Kafka was ahead of his time as he exemplifies the modernist mindset of anxiety and pain, but he is raised to the level of an artist only when he manages to mix this with humor and tenderness.

(d) Kafka's shyness and inner struggles are an outcome of the modernism he displays wherein the thoughts are permeated with anxiety and pain, but as he is an artist he uses humor and formality as a reassurance.

2017

13. The passage given below is followed by four summaries. Choose the option that best captures the author's position.

North American walnut sphinx moth caterpillars (Amorpha juglandis) look like easy meals for birds, but they have a trick up their sleeves – they produce whistles that sound like bird alarm calls, scaring potential predators away. At first, scientists suspected birds were simply startled by the loud noise. But a new study suggests a more sophisticated mechanism: the caterpillar's whistle appears to mimic a bird alarm call, sending avian predators scrambling for cover. When pecked by a bird, the caterpillars whistle by compressing their bodies like an accordion and forcing air out through specialised holes in their sides. The whistles are impressively loud - they have been measured at over

SO dB from 5 cm away from the caterpillar - considering they are made by a two-inch long insect.

(a) North American walnut sphinx moth caterpillars will whistle periodically to ward off predator birds - they have a specialized vocal tract that helps them whistle.

(b) North American walnut sphinx moth caterpillars can whistle very loudly; the loudness of their whistles is shocking as they are very small insects.

(c) North American walnut sphinx moth caterpillars, in a case of acoustic deception, produce whistles that mimic bird alarm calls to defend themselves.

(d) North American walnut sphinx moth caterpillars, in a case of deception and camouflage, produce whistles that mimic bird alarm calls to defend themselves.

14. The passage given below is followed by four summaries. Choose the option that best captures the author's position.

Both Socrates and Bacon were very good at asking useful questions. In fact, Socrates is largely credited with coming up with a way of asking questions, 'the Socratic method', which itself is at the core of the 'scientific method', popularised by Bacon. The Socratic method disproves arguments by finding exceptions to them, and can therefore lead your opponent to a point where they admit something that contradicts their original position. In common with Socrates, Bacon stressed it was as important to disprove a theory as it was to prove one - and real-world observation and experimentation were key to achieving both aims. Bacon also saw science as a collaborative affair, with scientists working together, challenging each other.

(a) Both Socrates and Bacon advocated clever questioning of the opponents to disprove their arguments and theories.

(b) Both Socrates and Bacon advocated challenging arguments and theories by observation and experimentation.

(c) Both Socrates and Bacon advocated confirming arguments and theories by finding exceptions.

(d) Both Socrates and Bacon advocated examining arguments and theories from both sides to prove them.

15. The passage given below is followed by four summaries. Choose the option that best captures the author's position.

A fundamental property of language is that it is slippery and messy and more liquid than solid, a gelatinous mass that changes shape to fit. As Wittgenstein would remind us, "usage has no sharp boundary."

Oftentimes, the only way to determine the meaning of a word is to examine how it is used. This insight is often described as the "meaning is use" doctrine. There are differences between the "meaning is use" doctrine and a dictionary-first theory of meaning. "The dictionary's careful fixing of words to definitions, like butterflies pinned under glass, can suggest that this is how language works. The definitions can seem to ensure and fix the meaning of words, just as the gold standard can back a country's currency." What Wittgenstein found in the circulation of ordinary language, however, was a free-floating currency of meaning. The value of each word arises out of the exchange. The lexicographer abstracts a meaning from that exchange, which is then set within the conventions of the dictionary definition.

(a) Dictionary definitions are like 'gold standards' - artificial, theoretical and dogmatic. Actual meaning of words is their free-exchange value.

(b) Language is already slippery; given this, accounting for 'meaning in use' will only exasperate the problem. That is why lexicographers 'fix' meanings.

(c) Meaning is dynamic; definitions are static. The 'meaning in use' theory helps us understand that definitions of words are culled from their meaning in exchange and use and not vice versa.

(d) The meaning of words in dictionaries is clear, fixed and less dangerous and ambiguous than the meaning that arises when words are exchanged between people.

2018 Slot 1

16. The passage given below is followed by four summaries. Choose the option that best captures the author's position.

Artificial embryo twinning is a relatively low-tech way to make clones. As the name suggests, this technique mimics the natural process that creates identical twins. In nature, twins form very early in development when the embryo splits in two. Twinning happens in the first days after egg and sperm join, while the embryo is made of just a small number of unspecialized cells. Each half of the embryo continues dividing on its own, ultimately developing into separate, complete individuals. Since they developed from the same fertilized egg, the resulting individuals are genetically identical.

(a) Artificial embryo twinning is just like the natural development of twins, where during fertilization twins are formed.

(b) Artificial embryo twinning is low-tech unlike the natural development of identical twins from the embryo after fertilization.

(c) Artificial embryo twinning is low-tech and mimetic of the natural development of genetically identical twins from the embryo after fertilization.

(d) Artificial embryo twinning is low-tech and is close to the natural development of twins where the embryo splits into two identical twins.

17. The passage given below is followed by four summaries. Choose the option that best captures the author's position.

Production and legitimation of scientific knowledge can be approached from a number of perspectives. To study knowledge production from the sociology of professions perspective would mean a focus on the institutionalization of a body of knowledge. The professions-approach informed earlier research on managerial occupation, business schools and management knowledge. It however tends to reify institutional power structures in its understanding of the links between knowledge and authority. Knowledge production is restricted in the perspective to the selected members of the professional community, most notably to the university faculties and professional colleges. Power is understood as a negative mechanism, which prevents the non-professional actors from offering their ideas and information as legitimate knowledge.

(a) The study of knowledge production can be done through many perspectives.

(b) Professions-approach aims at the institutionalization of knowledge but restricts knowledge production as a function of a select few.

(c) Professions-approach focuses on the creation of institutions of higher education and disciplines to promote knowledge production

(d) The professions-approach has been one of the most relied upon perspective in the study of management knowledge production.

18. The passage given below is followed by four summaries. Choose the option that best captures the author's position.

The conceptualization of landscape as a geometric object first occurred in Europe and is historically related to the European conceptualization of the organism, particularly the human body, as a geometric object with parts having a rational, three-dimensional organization and integration. The European idea of landscape appeared before the science of landscape emerged, and it is no coincidence that Renaissance artists such as Leonardo da Vinci, who studied the structure of the human body, also facilitated an understanding of the structure of landscape. Landscape which had been a subordinate background to religious or historical narratives, became an independent genre or subject of art by the end of sixteenth century or the beginning of the seventeenth century.

(a) The Renaissance artists were responsible for the study of landscape as a subject of art.

(b) The three-dimensional understanding of the organism in Europe led to a similar approach towards the understanding of landscape.

(c) Landscape became a major subject of art at the turn of the sixteenth century.

(d) The study of landscape as an independent genre was aided by the Renaissance artists.

2018 Slot 2

19. The passage given below is followed by four summaries. Choose the option that best captures the author's position.

Should the moral obligation to rescue and aid persons in grave peril, felt by a few, be enforced by the criminal law? Should we follow the lead of a number of European countries and enact bad Samaritan laws? Proponents of bad Samaritan laws must overcome at least three different sorts of obstacles. First, they must show the laws are morally legitimate in principle, that is, that the duty to aid others is a proper candidate for legal enforcement. Second, they must show that this duty to aid can be defined in a way that can be fairly enforced by the courts. Third, they must show that the benefits of the laws are worth their problems, risks and costs.

(a) A number of European countries that have successfully enacted bad Samaritan laws may serve as model statutes.

(b) Bad Samaritan laws may be desirable but they need to be tested for legal soundness.

(c) Everyone agrees that people ought to aid others, the only debate is whether to have a law on it.

(d) If bad Samaritan laws are found to be legally sound and enforceable they must be enacted.

20. The passage given below is followed by four summaries. Choose the option that best captures the author's position.

The early optimism about sport's deterrent effects on delinquency was premature as researchers failed to find any consistent relationships between sports participation and deviance. As the initial studies were based upon cross-sectional data and the effects captured were short-term, it was problematic to test and verify the temporal sequencing of events suggested by the deterrence theory. The correlation between sport and delinquency could not be disentangled from class and cultural variables known. Choosing individuals to play sports in the first place was problematic, which became more acute in the subsequent decades as researchers began to document just how closely sports participation was linked to social class indicators.

(a) Contradicting the previous optimism, latter researchers have proved that there is no consistent relationship between sports participation and deviance.

(b) Sports participation is linked to class and cultural variables such as education, income, and social capital.

(c) There is a direct relationship between sport participation and delinquency but it needs more empirical evidence.

(d) Statistical and empirical weaknesses stand in the way of inferring any relationship between sports participation and deviance.

21. The passage given below is followed by four summaries. Choose the option that best captures the author's position:

A Japanese government panel announced that it recommends regulating only genetically modified organisms that have had foreign genes permanently introduced into their genomes and not those whose endogenous genes have been edited. The only stipulation is that researchers and businesses will have to register their modifications to plants or animals with the government, with the exception of microbes cultured in contained environments. Reactions to the decision are mixed. While lauding the potential benefits of genome editing, an editorial opposes across-the-board permission. Unforeseen risks in gene editing cannot be ruled out. All genetically modified products must go through the same safety and labeling processes regardless of method.

(a) Excepting microbes cultured in contained environments from the regulations of genome editing is premature.

(b) Exempting from regulations the editing of endogenous genes is not desirable as this procedure might be risk-prone.

(c) A government panel in Japan says transgenic modification and genome editing are not the same.

(d) Creating categories within genetically modified products in terms of transgenic modification and genome editing advances science but defies laws.

SYLLOGISMS

1990

DIRECTIONS for Questions 1 to 63: Each of these questions contains six statements followed by four sets of combinations of three. Choose the set in which the statements are most logically related.

1. A. Some of my closest friends disapprove of me.
B. Some of my closest friends are aardvarks.
C. All of my closest friends disapprove of me.
D. All who disapprove of me are aardvarks.
E. Some who disapprove of me are aardvarks.
F. Some of my closest friends are no aardvarks.

(a) BCD (b) ABD
(c) BCE (d) ABE

2. A. All those who achieve great ends are happy.
B. All young people are happy.
C. All young people achieve great ends.
D. No young people achieve great ends.
E. No young people are happy,
F. Some young people are happy.

(a) ADE (b) ABF
(c) ACB (d) ADF

3. A. All candid men are persons who acknowledge merit in a rival.
B. Some learned men are very candid.
C. Some learned men are not persons who acknowledge merit in a rival.
D. Some learned men are persons who are very candid.
E. Some learned men are not candid.
F. Some persons who recognize merit in a rival are learned.

(a) ABE (b) ACF
(c) ADE (d) BAF

4. A. All roses are fragrant.
B. All roses are majestic.
C. All roses are plants.
D. All roses need air.
E. All plants need air.
F. All plants need water.

(a) CED (b) ACB
(c) BDC (d) CFE

5. A. All men are men of scientific ability.
B. Some women are women of scientific ability.
C. Some men are men of artistic genius.
D. Some men and women are of scientific ability.
E. All men of artistic genius are men of scientific ability.
F. Some women of artistic genius are women of scientific ability.
(a) ACD (b) ACE
(c) DEF (d) ABC

6. A. No fishes breathe through lungs.
B. All fishes have scales.
C. Some fishes breed up stream.
D. All whales breathe through lungs.
E. No whales are fishes.
F. All whales are mammals.
(a) ABC (b) BCD
(c) ADE (d) DEF

7. A. Some mammals are carnivores.
B. All whales are mammals.
C. All whales are aquatic animals.
D. All whales are carnivores.
E. Some aquatic animals are mammals.
F. Some mammals are whales.
(a) ADF (b) ABC
(c) AEF (d) BCE

8. A. First-year students of this college like to enter for the prize.
B. All students of this college rank as University students.
C. First-year students of this college are entitled to enter for the prize.
D. Some who rank as University students are First-year students.
E. All University students are eligible to enter for the prize.
F. All those who like to are entitled to enter for the prize.
(a) AEF (b) ABC
(c) BEC (d) CDF

9. A. Some beliefs are uncertain.
B. Nothing uncertain is worth dying for.
C. Some belief is worth dying for.
D. All beliefs are uncertain.
E. Some beliefs are certain.
F. No belief is worth dying for.
(a) ABF (b) BCD
(c) BEF (d) BDF

10. A. No lunatics are fit to serve on a jury.
B. Everyone who is sane can do logic.
C. None of your sons can do logic.
D. Some who can do logic are fit to serve on a jury.
E. All who can do logic are fit to serve on a jury.
F. Everyone who is sane is fit to serve on a jury.
(a) BDE (b) BEF
(c) BDF (d) ADE

1991

11. A. No attendants are qualified.
B. Some nurses are qualified.
C. Some nurses are not qualified.
D. All nurses are attendants.
E. All attendants are qualified.
F. Some attendants are qualified.
(a) ABF (b) CDF
(c) BDF (d) BDE

12. A. Mary is John's wife.
B. Mary and John danced together.
C. Mary wears John's ring.
D. Husband and wives danced the last waltz.
E. John loves Mary.
F. John danced last with Mary.
(a) ADF (b) ABD
(c) ACE (d) AEF

13. A. All roses are fragrant.
B. All roses are majestic.
C. All roses are plants.
D. All plants need air.
E. All roses need air.
F. All plants need water.
(a) ABC (b) BCD
(c) CDE (d) CEF

14. A. Laxman is a man.
B. Meera is Laxman's wife.
C. Some women are islands.
D. No man is an island.
E. Meera is not an island.
F. Laxman is not a island.
(a) ADE (b) ABE
(c) ADF (d) CDE

15. A. College students are intelligent.
B. Intelligence is a collegian's attribute.
C. Ram's sister is a college student.
D. Ram is a college student.
E. All intelligent persons go to college.
F. Ram is an intelligent person.
(a) ADF (b) BCD
(c) ABF (d) ABD

16. A. Smoking causes cancer.
B. All cigarettes are hazardous to health.
C. Smoking doesn't cause cancer sometimes.
D. One brand of cigarettes is cham – cham.
E. Brand X causes cancer.
F. Cham – cham is bad for health.
(a) ABE (b) BDF
(c) ABD (d) ABC

17. A. All good bridge players play good chess.
B. Many good chess players are not bridge players.
C. Goren is a good bridge player.
D. Goren plays chess well.
E. Spassky plays chess well.
F. Spassky plays bridge badly.
(a) ABD (b) BEF
(c) ACE (d) ACD

18. A. All snakes are reptiles.
B. All reptiles are not snakes.
C. All reptiles are cold blooded.
D. All snakes lay eggs.
E. All reptiles lay eggs.
F. Snakes are cold blooded.
(a) ADE (b) BDE
(c) ABE (d) ACF

19. A. All leaves are green.
B. All leaves have chlorophyll.
C. Chlorophyll is green.
D. All plants have leaves.
E. All plants have chlorophyll.
F. Only leaves have chlorophyll.
(a) BDE (b) BEF
(c) BDF (d) AEF

20. A. Some men are bald.
B. Bald people are intelligent.
C. Raman is a man.
D. Raman is bald.
E. Raman is intelligent.
F. All men are intelligent.
(a) ABF (b) BDE
(c) BCD (d) BEF

21. A. No barbarian is gentleman.
B. Some gentlemen are barbarians.
C. Some gentlemen are rude.
D. No gentlemen are rude.
E. Some barbarians are not rude.
F. All barbarians are rude.
(a) ABE (b) BCE
(c) ADF (d) BDE

22. A. Metal is good material for desks.
B. Desks are made of metal.
C. This object is not a desk.
D. This object is a desk.
E. This object is not made of metal.
F. This is made of metal.
(a) ADF (b) BCE
(c) ABD (d) BDF

23. A. Mathew and Paul are brothers.
B. Siblings are known to quarrel often.
C. Mathew and Paul don't quarrel.
D. All those who quarrel are siblings.
E. Paul and Mathew quarrel often.
F. Mathew and Paul cannot be siblings.
(a) BDE (b) ADF
(c) CDE (d) ABE

24. A. Painting and music is art.
B. Art is symptom of culture.
C. Culture and art are complementary.
D. Music is a form of art.
E. Painting is a form of art.
F. Music shows culture.
(a) BDF (b) AEF
(c) ACE (d) CEF

25. A. Different hues are obtained from primary colours.
B. A rainbow consists of several hues.
C. Blue and red can give different hues.
D. Red is a primary color.
E. Blue can give different hues.
F. Red can give different hues.
(a) ACE (b) AEF
(c) ADF (d) CDF

1992

26. A. All boys are good.
B. Some girls are bad.
C. Good people are educated.
D. Boys are educated.
E. Ram is an educated boy.
F. Lata is an educated girl.
(a) BCF (b) ACD
(c) DEF (d) ADC

27. A. All who are sincere are graduates.
B. Some graduates are not sincere.
C. All who are sincere are dull.
D. All graduates are dull.
E. Some who are dull are graduates.
F. No one who is dull is sincere.

(a) BEF (b) ADF
(c) ABF (d) ADC

28. A. Sham won a lottery.
B. Sham lost in a chess game.
C. Sham is not intelligent.
D. One need not be intelligent to win a lottery.
E. One need not be intelligent to win a chess game.
F. Sham plays chess.
(a) BEF (b) ACD
(c) BDE (d) BDF

29. A. Good managers are intuitive.
B. Some managers are women.
C. Supriya is a good manager.
D. Supriya is a woman.
E. Some women are intuitive.
F. Supriya is intuitive.
(a) BCE (b) ABD
(c) ACF (d) ADF

30. A. Some college athletes are professionals.
B. No college athlete is a professional.
C. Some professionals are well paid.
D. All professionals are well paid.
E. All well – paid persons are professionals.
F. No well – paid person is a college athlete.
(a) BEF (b) ABF
(c) BDF (d) ACF

31. A. Some intolerant are poor – thinkers.
B. Some poor – thinker is intolerant.
C. All people with high ideals are intolerant.
D. No poor thinker is intolerant.
E. No poor thinker has high ideals.
F. Some people with high ideals are not poor thinkers.
(a) CDE (b) CDF
(c) ABD (d) BCF

32. A. All engineers can sing.
B. No music lover can sing.
C. All who can sing are music lovers.
D. All music lovers can sing.
E. Some who can sing are engineers.
F. All engineers are music lovers.
(a) ACE (b) ACF
(c) ABF (d) ACD

33. A. Some well-dressed people are sociable.
B. All sociable people are well-dressed.
C. Some well dressed people are dull.
D. No dull person is well-dressed.
E. Some sociable people are dull.
F. Some dull ones are well-dressed.
(a) ACE (b) BCE
(c) ADE (d) BEF

34. A. Iran and Iraq are members of the UN.
B. Iran and Iraq are not friends.
C. Iran and Iraq are neighbours.
D. Some UN members are friends.
E. Not all members of the UN are friends.
F. All neighbours are not friends.
(a) ABE (b) ABD
(c) CDF (d) AEF

1994

35. A. All vegetarians eat meat.
B. All those who eat meat are not vegetarians.
C. All those who eat meat are herbivorous.
D. All vegetarians are carnivorous.
E. All those who eat meat are carnivorous.
F. Vegetarians are herbivorous.
(a) BCE (b) ABE
(c) ACD (d) ACF

36. A. All roses have thorns.
B. All roses have nectar.
C. All plants with nectar have thorns.
D. All shrubs have roses.
E. All shrubs have nectar.
F. Some roses have thorns.
(a) BEF (b) BCF
(c) BDE (d) ACF

37. A. No spring is a season.
B. Some seasons are springs.
C. Some seasons are autumns.
D. No seasons are autumns.
E. Some springs are not autumns.
F. All springs are autumns.
(a) DFA (b) BEF
(c) CEB (d) DEB

38. A. All falcons fly high.
B. All falcons are blind.
C. All falcons are birds.
D. All birds are yellow.
E. All birds are thirsty.
F. All falcons are yellow.
(a) ABC (b) CDF
(c) DEF (d) BCA

39. A. No wires are hooks.
B. Some springs are hooks.
C. All springs are wires.
D. Some hooks are not wires.
E. No hook is a spring.
F. All wires are springs.
(a) AED (b) BCF
(c) BEF (d) ACE

40. A. Some abra are dabra.
B. All abra are cabra.
C. All dabra are abra.
D. All dabra are not abra.
E. Some cabra are abra.
F. Some cabra are dabra
(a) AEF (b) BCF
(c) ABD (d) BCE

41. A. No plane is a chain.
B. All manes are chains.
C. No mane is a plane.
D. Some manes are not planes.
E. Some planes are manes.
F. Some chains are not planes.
(a) ACD (b) ADF
(c) ABC (d) CDF

42. A. All dolls are nice.
B. All toys are nice.
C. All toys are dolls.
D. Some toys are nice.
E. Some nice things are dolls.
F. No doll is nice.
(a) CDE (b) CEF
(c) ACD (d) BEF

43. A. Some buildings are not sky-scrappers.
B. Some sky-scrappers are not buildings.
C. No structure is a sky-scrapper.
D. All sky-scrappers are structures.
E. Some sky-scrappers are buildings.
F. Some structures are not buildings.
(a) ACE (b) BDF
(c) CDE (d) ACF

44. A. All bins are buckets.
B. No bucket is a basket.
C. No bin is a basket.
D. Some baskets are buckets.
E. Some bins are baskets.
F. No basket is a bin.
(a) BDE (b) ACB
(c) CDF (d) ABF

1995

45. A. Some bubbies are not dubbles
B. Some dubbles are not bubbles
C. Noone who is rubbles is dubbles
D. All dubbles are rubbles
E. Some dubbles are bubbles
F. Some who are rubbles are not bubbles
(a) ACF (b) DEF
(c) ABC (d) BDF

46. A. Some men are bad
B. All men are sad
C. All bad things are men
D. All bad things are sad
E. Some sad things are men
F. Some sad things are bad
(a) AFE (b) BCF
(c) BDA (d) BCE

47. A. All Toms are bright
B. No bright Toms are Dicks
C. Some Toms are Dicks
D. Some Dicks are bright
E. No Tom is a Dick
F. No Dick is a Tom
(a) ABC (b) BEF
(c) ABF (d) CDA

48. A. All witches are nasty
B. Some devils are nasty
C. All witches are devils
D. All devils are nasty
E. Some nasty are devils
F. No witch is nasty
(a) BCD (b) CDA
(c) DEC (d) FEC

49. A. No tingo is a bingo
B. All jingoes are bingoes
C. No jingo is a tingo
D. Some jingoes are not tingoes
E. Some tingoes are jingoes
F. Some bingoes are not tingoes
(a) ABC (b) ACB
(c) DFA (d) BDA

1996

50. A. Some pins are made of tin
B. All tin is made of copper
C. All copper is used for pins
D. Some tin is copper
E. Some pins are used for tin
F. Some copper is used for tin
(a) ABC (b) CEF
(c) CDA (d) ABE

51. A. An ostrich lays eggs
B. All birds lay eggs
C. Some birds can fly
D. An ostrich cannot fly
E. An ostrich is a bird
F. An ostrich cannot swim
(a) BEA (b) ABE
(c) DEC (d) ECB

52. A. Some paper is wood
B. All wood is good
C. All that is good is wood
C. All wood is paper
D. All paper is good
E. Some paper is good
(a) BED (b) BDF
(c) FAB (d) FBA

53. A. All bricks are tricks
B. Some tricks are shrieks
C. Some that are shrieks are bricks
D. Some tricks are not bricks
E. All tricks are shrieks
F. No tricks are shrieks
(a) EAC (b) BCD
(c) ABC (d) EDC

54. A. Some sand is band
B. All sandal is band
C. All band is sandal
D. No sand is sandal
E. No band is sand
F. Some band is sandal
(a) BCA (b) AFE
(c) DEC (d) CED

55. A. No wife is a life
B. All life is strife
C. Some wife is strife
D. All that is wife is life
E. All wife is strife
F. No wife is strife
(a) BEF (b) FCB
(c) ABF (d) BDE

56. A. Some crows are flies
B. Some flies are mosquitoes
C. All mosquitoes are flies
D. Some owls are flies
E. All owls are mosquitoes
F. Some mosquitoes are not owls
(a) ABC (b) CEF
(c) ADE (d) EDB

57. A. Six is five
B. Five is not four
C. Some five is ten
D. Some six is twelve
E. Some twelve is five
F. Some ten is four
(a) ADE (b) ABC
(c) AEF (d) EDC

58. A. Poor girls want to marry rich boys
B. Rich girls want to marry rich boys
C. Poor girls want to marry rich girls
D. Rich boys want to marry rich girls
E. Poor girls want to marry rich girls
F. Rich boys want to marry poor girls
(a) ADE (b) ABC
(c) BCD (d) DEF

1997

59. A. No bird is viviparous.
B. All mammals are viviparous.
C. Bats are viviparous.
D. No bat is a bird.
E. No bird is a mammal.
F. All bats are mammals.
(a) ADC (b) ABE
(c) FBA (d) AFC

60. A. No mother is a nurse.
B. Some nurses like to work.
C. No woman is a prude.
D. Some prude are nurses.
E. Some nurses are women.
F. All women like to work.

(a) ABE (b) CED
(c) FEB (d) BEF

61. A. Oranges are sweet.
B. All oranges are apples.
C. Some sweet are apples.
D. Some oranges are apples.
E. All sweet are sour.
F. Some apples are sour.
(a) DAC (b) CDA
(c) BCA (d) FEC

62. A. Zens are Marutis.
B. Zens are fragile.
C. Marutis are fragile.
D. Opels are fragile.
E. Marutis are Opels.
F. Opels are stable.
(a) ACB (b) EFD
(c) CEA (d) ABC

63. A. Dogs sleep in the open.
B. Sheep sleep indoors.
C. Dogs are like sheep.
D. All indoors are sheep.
E. Some dogs are not sheep.
F. Some open are not sheep.
(a) AFE (b) DCA
(c) ABE (d) FBD

1998

DIRECTIONS for Questions 64 to 77: Each question has a set of four statements. Each statement has three segments. Choose the alternative where the third segment in the statement can be logically deduced using both the preceding two, but not just from one of them.

64. A. Some Xs are Ps. Some Ps are Ys. Some Xs are Ys.
B. All Sonas are bright. Some bright are crazy. Some Sonas are crazy.
C. No faith is strong. Only strong have biceps. No faith has biceps.
D. All men are weak. Some weak are strong. Some strong are weak.
(a) A and D (b) C only
(c) D only (d) None of these

65. A. Some icicles are cycles. All cycles are men. Some icicles are men.
B. All girls are teeth. No teeth is yellow. No girls are yellow.
C. No hand is foot. Some foot are heads. Some hands are heads.
D. Every man has a wife. All wives are devoted. No devoted has a husband.
(a) A, B and C (b) A and B
(c) C and B (d) all of these

66. A. No sun is not white. All moon is sun. All moon is white.
B. All windows are open. No open space is allocated. All window is closed space.
C. No German can fire. All Americans bombard. Both, Germans and Americans can fight.
D. No X is Z. No Z is Y. No X is Y.
(a) A only (b) B only
(c) C only (d) D only

67. A. All Ts are square. All squares are rectangular. All Ts are rectangular.
B. Some fat are elongated. Some elongated things are huge. Some fat are huge.
C. Idiots are bumblers. Bumblers fumble. Idiots fumble.
D. Water is good for health. Health foods are rare. Water is rare.
(a) D only (b) C only
(c) Both A and C (d) All of these

1999

68. A. No cowboys laugh. Some who laugh are sphinxes. Some sphinxes are not cowboys.
B. All ghosts are florescent. Some ghost do not sing. Some singers are not florescent.
C. Cricketers indulge in swearing. Those who swear are hanged. Some who are hanged are not cricketers.
D. Some crazy people are pianists. All crazy people are whistlers. Some whistlers are pianists.
(a) A and B (b) C only
(c) A and D (d) D only

69. A. All good people are knights. All warriors are good people. All knights are warriors.
B. No footballers are ministers. All footballers are tough. Some ministers are players.
C. All pizzas are snacks. Some meals are pizzas. Some meals are snacks.
D. Some barkers are musk deer. All barkers are sloth bears. Some sloth bears are musk deer.
(a) C and D (b) B and C
(c) A only (d) C only

70. A. Dinosaurs are prehistoric creatures. Water-buffaloes are not dinosaurs. Water-buffaloes are not prehistoric creatures.

B. All politicians are frank. No frank people are crocodiles. No crocodiles are politicians.

C. No diamond is quartz. No opal is quartz. Diamonds are opals.

D. All monkeys like bananas. Some GI Joes like bananas. Some GI Joes are monkeys.

(a) C only (b) B only
(c) A and D (d) B and C

71. A. All earthquakes cause havoc. Some landslides cause havoc. Some earthquakes cause landslides.

B. All glass things are transparent. Some curios are glass things. Some curios are transparent.

C. All clay objects are brittle. All XY are clay objects. Some XY are brittle.

D. No criminal is a patriot. Ram is not a patriot. Ram is a criminal.

(a) D only (b) B only
(c) C and B (d) A only

72. A. MD is an actor. Some actors are pretty. MD is pretty.

B. Some men are cops. All cops are brave. Some brave people are cops.

C. All cops are brave. Some men are cops. Some men are brave.

D. All actors are pretty ; MD is not an actor ; MD is not pretty.

(a) D only (b) C only
(c) A only (d) B and C

73. A. All IIMs are in India. No BIMs are in India. No IIMs are BIMs.

B. All IIMs are in India. No BIMs are in India. No BIMs are IIMs.

C. Some IIMs are not in India. Some BIMs are not in India. Some IIMs are BIMs.

D. Some IIMs are not in India. Some BIMs are not in India. Some BIMs are IIMs.

(a) A and B (b) C and D
(c) A only (d) B only

74. A. Citizens of Yes Islands speak only the truth. Citizens of Yes Islands are young people. Young people speak only the truth.

B. Citizens of Yes Islands speak only the truth. Some Yes Islands are in Atlantic. Some citizens of Yes Islands are in the Atlantic.

C. Citizens of Yes Islands speak only the truth. Some young people are citizens of Yes Islands. Some young people speak only the truth.

D. Some people speak only the truth. Some citizens of Yes Islands speak only the truth. Some people who speak only the truth are citizens of Yes Islands.

(a) A only (b) B only
(c) C only (d) D only

75. A. All mammals are viviparous. Some fish are viviparous. Some fish are mammals.

B. All birds are oviparous. Some fish are not oviparous. Some fish are birds.

C. No mammal is oviparous. Some creatures are oviparous and some are not. Some creatures are not mammals.

D. Some creatures are mammals. Some creatures are viviparous. Some mammals are viviparous.

(a) A only (b) B only
(c) C only (d) D only

76. A. Many singers are not writers. All poets are singers. Some poets are not writers.

B. Giants climb beanstalks. Some chicken do not climb beanstalks. Some chicken are not giants.

C. All explorers live in snowdrifts. Some penguins live in snowdrifts. Some penguins are explorers.

D. Amar is taller than Akbar. Anthony is shorter than Amar. Akbar is shorter than Anthony.

(a) A only (b) B only
(c) B and C (d) D only

77. A. A few farmers are rocket scientists. Some rocket scientists catch snakes. A few farmers catch snakes.

B. Poonam is a kangaroo. Some kangaroos are made of teak. Poonam is made of teak.

C. No bulls eat grass. All matadors eat grass. No matadors are bulls.

D. Some skunks drive Cadillacs. All skunks are polar bears. Some polar bears drive Cadillacs.

(a) B only (b) A and C
(c) C only (d) C and D

DIRECTIONS for Questions 78 to 87: Each question consists of five statements followed by options consisting of three statements put together in a specific order. Choose the option which indicates a valid argument, that is, where the third statement is a conclusion drawn from the preceding two statements.

Example:

A. All cigarettes are hazardous to health.

B. Brand X is a cigarette.

C. Brand X is hazardous to health.

ABC is a valid option, where statement C can be concluded from statements A and B.

78. A. All software companies employ knowledge workers.
B. Tara Tech employs knowledge workers.
C. Tara Tech is a software company.
D. Some software companies employ knowledge workers.
E. Tara Tech employs only knowledge workers.
(a) ABC (b) ACB
(c) CDB (d) ACE

79. A. Traffic congestion increases carbon monoxide in the environment.
B. Increase in carbon monoxide is hazardous to health.
C. Traffic congestion is hazardous to health.
D. Some traffic congestion does not cause increased carbon monoxide.
E. Some traffic congestion is not hazardous to health.
(a) CBA (b) BDE
(c) CDE (d) BAC

80. A. Apples are not sweets.
B. Some apples are sweet.
C. All sweets are tasty.
D. Some apples are not tasty.
E. No apple is tasty.
(a) CEA (b) BDC
(c) CBD (d) EAC

81. A. Some towns in India are polluted.
B. All polluted towns should be destroyed.
C. Town Meghana should be destroyed.
D. Town Meghana is polluted.
E. Some towns in India should be destroyed.
(a) BDE (b) BAE
(c) ADE (d) CDB

82. A. No patriot is a criminal.
B. Bundledas is not a criminal.
C. Bundledas is a patriot.
D. Bogusdas is not a patriot.
E. Bogusdas is a criminal.
(a) ACB (b) ABC
(c) ADE (d) ABE

83. A. Anteaters like ants.
B. Boys are anteaters.
C. Balaram is an anteater.
D. Balaram likes ants.
E. Balaram may eat ants.
(a) DCA (b) ADC
(c) ABE (d) ACD

84. A. All actors are handsome.
B. Some actors are popular.
C. Ram is handsome.
D. Ram is a popular actor.
E. Some popular people are handsome.
(a) ACD (b) ABE
(c) DCA (d) EDC

85. A. Modern industry is technology-driven.
B. BTI is a modern industry.
C. BTI is technology-driven.
D. BTI may be technology-driven
E. Technology driven industry is modern.
(a) ABC (b) ABD
(c) BCA (d) EBC

86. A. All Golmal islanders are blue-coloured people.
B. Some smart people are not blue-coloured people.
C. Some babies are blue-coloured.
D. Some babies are smart.
E. Some smart people are not Golmal islanders.
(a) BCD (b) ABE
(c) CBD (d) None of these

87. A. MBAs are in great demand.
B. Ram and Sita are in great demand.
C. Ram is in great demand.
D. Sita is in great demand.
E. Ram and Sita are MBAs.
(a) ABE (b) ECD
(c) AEB (d) EBA

CRITICAL REASONING

DIRECTIONS for Questions 1 to 19: This section contains statements followed by questions based on the statements. Read the statements and select the best option as the answer.

***Q.1 to 3*:** We have planned development with a view to raising standard of living of our teeming millions. Hence our economic development is inspired by social justice.

1990

1. Which of the following will weaken the argument?
(a) Without economic development standard of living cannot be raised.
(b) Social justice implies economic prosperity.
(c) Development cannot be planned.
(d) None of these.

2. The argument is based on which of the following assumptions?
I. Social justice is our aim and economic development is the means.

II. There is overpopulation in India.

III. Economic development will lead to social justice.

(a) Only I (b) Both I and II

(c) Both I and III (d) Both II and III

3. Which of the following will strengthen the argument?

(a) Social justice can be done by raising the standard of living

(b) Economic planning is necessary for every state.

(c) For economic development production should be increased.

(d) None of these.

Q.4 to 5: We will have to take more interest in hydro-electric projects. As the prices of oil have increased, it has become vital that such renewable sources of energy are tapped.

4. The assumption/assumptions of the argument is / are which of the following?

I. Hydro electric power is a renewable source of energy.

II. Hydro electric power is comparatively cheaper.

(a) Only I (b) Only II

(c) Both I and II (d) Neither I nor II

5. Which of the following will weaken the argument?

(a) Generation of hydroelectric power is more costly than oil.

(b) OPEC increased oil prices.

(c) Without energy we cannot manage.

(d) None of these.

Q6 to 8: There can be no civilization without music, dance or art, for one is not fully, vibrantly alive without them.

6. The assumption/assumptions of the argument is / are which of the following?

I. Civilization and art are closely linked up.

II. If people are not full of life there can be no civilization.

(a) Only I (b) Only II

(c) Both I and II (d) Neither I nor II.

7. Which of the following would weaken the argument?

(a) Music is the life of man.

(b) Living persons like music.

(c) Art has no relation with civilization.

(d) None of these.

8. Which of the following would strengthen the argument?

(a) Music, dance and art are human activities.

(b) Only the vibrantly alive can contribute to civilization.

(c) Music injects new life in man.

(d) None of these.

Q9 to 11: It is sometimes mooted that there can be democracy in a two party system. That would be correct if politics were a game like cricket or football; but politics is not sports.

9. Which of the following would strengthen the argument?

(a) Two party system functions well

(b) Politics is a dirty game.

(c) Two political parties limit the choice of the voters.

(d) None of these.

10. Which of the following would weaken the argument?

(a) The game of politics is played like any other game, for example, football.

(b) Politics is not a sport.

(c) Political parties struggle for power.

(d) None of these.

11. The assumption/assumptions of the argument is/are which of the following?

I. Politics is not a game.

II. Two party system is ideal for democracy.

III. Cricket is played by two teams.

(a) Only I (b) Only II

(c) Only III (d) I, II, III

Q12 to 14: Kya –Kya is an obscure island which is inhabited by two types of people: the 'Yes' type and the 'No' type. Native of type 'Yes' ask only questions the right answer to which is 'Yes' while those of type 'No' ask only questions the right answer to which is 'No'. For example. The 'Yes' type will ask questions like "Is 2 plus 2 equal to 4?" while the 'No' type will ask questions like "Is 2 plus 2 equal to five?" The following questions are based on your visit to the island of Kya – Kya.

1992

12. If an islander asks, "Do I belong to the 'No' type", which of the following is correct?

(a) He is a 'No'.

(b) He is a 'Yes'.

(c) It is impossible for him to have asked such a question.

(d) His type cannot be identified.

13. Ram and Laxman are brothers from the Island. Laxman asks you, "Is at least one of us brothers of type 'No"? You can conclude that

(a) Ram is 'NO', Laxman is 'Yes '.

(b) both are 'Yes'.

(c) Ram is 'Yes', Laxman is 'No'.

(d) both are 'No'.

14. You are approached by one of the islanders and asked, "Am I of type 'Yes"? You can infer that

(a) he was a 'No'.

(b) he was a 'Yes'.

(c) such a situation is not possible.

(d) no conclusion is possible.

15. Unless you decide your whole life to it, you will never learn to speak the language of another country to perfection; you will never know its people and its literature with complete intimacy.

Which of the following is likely to undermine the above argument?

(a) I can speak 10 foreign languages already.

(b) I do not travel to foreign countries.

(c) I am happy with the languages I know and do not need to learn any other language.

(d) I should spend time to understand my own people and literature first, only then can I appreciate other languages and cultures.

16. The writer can only be fertile if he renews himself and he can only renew himself, if his soul is constantly enriched by fresh experience.

Which of the following is most likely to support the above thought?

(a) Only out of fresh experience can the writer get germs for new writing.

(b) The writer can meet new people.

(c) The writer must see new places.

(d) None of these

1995

17. But because the idea of private property has been permitted to override with its selfishness, the common good of humanity it does not follow that there are not limits within which that idea can function for the general convenience and advantage.

Which of the following is most likely to weaken the argument?

(a) All the people of the society should progress at an equitable rate and there should be no disparities and private property does bring about a tremendous disparity.

(b) One should not strive for the common good of humanity at all, instead one should be concerned with maximising one's own wealth.

(c) One should learn from the experiences of former communist nations and should not repeat his mistakes at all.

(d) Even prosperous capitalist countries like the USA have their share of social problems.

18. Now the audience is a very curious animal. It is shrewd rather than intelligent. Its mental capacity is less than that of its most intellectual members. If these were graded from A to Z, decreasing with succeeding letters to the zero of the hysterical shop-girl, I should say its mental capacity would come around about the letter O.

According to the above statement,

(a) some members in the audience are more intelligent than any of its other members.

(b) the net intelligence of the audience is a little less than average.

(c) Only (a)

(d) Both (a) and (b)

19. I have been studying it, consciously and subconsciously, for 40 years and I still find men unaccountable; people I know intimately can surprise me by some action of theirs which I never thought them capable of or by the discovery of some trait which exhibit a side of themselves that I never even suspected.

The idea in this sentence can be best summarised as

(a) men are inconsistent and therefore one should not be confident even about one's closest friends.

(b) men are unpredictable, one can never tell what they will do next; hence, one should be very careful in one's dealings.

(c) no matter how closely you know somebody there still exists an unknown facet of his personality.

(d) None of these

DIRECTIONS for Questions 20 to 47: Read the passages given below and answer the questions that follow.

1998

20. Efficiency is all right in its place, in the shop, the factory, the store. The trouble with efficiency is that it wants to rule our play as well as our work; it won't be content to reign in the shop, it follows us home.

It can be inferred from the above passage that

(a) efficiency can become all-pervading.

(b) efficiency does not always pay.

(c) efficiency can be more of a torture than a blessing.

(d) None of these

21. In order to ease the traffic congestion, the transport planners decided to have a sophisticated system of elevated monorail travel in the city. However, it was pointed out by somebody that a metro rail system would be a more effective solution to the traffic problem. The plan was thus stalled. Moreover, since a budget had not been drawn up for the project, it was deemed fit to stall the work of the monorail for some time. In the meanwhile, the traffic planners of the city decided to build an efficient system of subways and flyovers in the city with the aim of easing the same problem. At the instant when the planners were preparing to award the contracts to the concerned parties, the transport planners came up with the contention that the subways interfered with the site of a pillar of the monorail system. The traffic planners had to give up the idea and think of other possible solutions.

Which of the following can we infer from the above passage?

(a) The city authorities felt that the monorail system was essentially impractical.

(b) There is a strong contention between the two groups of planners in the city.

(c) The projects would be stalled for an indefinite period.

(d) None of these

22. The company encourages its managers to interact regularly, without a pre-set agenda, to discuss issues concerning the company and society. This idea has been borrowed from the ancient Indian concept of religious congregation, called satsang. Designations are forgotten during these meetings; hence, it is not uncommon in these meetings to find a sales engineer questioning the CEO on some corporate policy or his knowledge of customers.

Based on the information provided in the above passage, it can be inferred that

(a) the company is concerned about its reputation with its employees.

(b) the company believes in fostering the spirit of dialogue without degenerating it into a positioning based debate.

(c) the company had some inter-personnel problems in the past due to which it felt the need for these corporate satsangs.

(d) All of these

23. From Cochin to Shimla, the new culture vultures are tearing down acres of India's architectural treasures. Ancestral owners are often fobbed off with a few hundred rupees for an exquisitely carved door or window, which fetches fifty times that much from foreign dealers, and yet more from the drawing room sophisticates of Europe and the US. The reason for such shameless rape of the Indian architectural wealth can perhaps, not wrongly, be attributed to the unfortunate blend of activist disunity and the local indifference.

It can be inferred from the above passage that

(a) the environment created by the meeting between activist disunity and local indifference is ideal for antique dealers to strive in India.

(b) only Indians are not proud of their cultural heritage and are hungry for the foreign currency that is easily available in return of artifacts.

(c) most Indian families have heirlooms which can be sold at high prices to Europeans and Americans.

(d) India provides a rich market for unscrupulous antique dealers.

24. Deepa Metha's *Fire* is under fire from the country's self-appointed moral police. Their contention is that the film is a violation of the Indian cultural mores and cannot be allowed to influence the Indian psyche. According to them, such films ruin the moral fabric of the nation, which must be protected and defended against such intrusions at all cost, even at the cost of cultural dictatorship.

Based on the information in the above passage, it can be inferred that

(a) the assumption underlying the moral police's critique of *Fire* is that the Indian audience is vulnerable to all types of influence.

(b) the assumption underlying the moral police's critique of *Fire* is that the Indian audience is impressionable and must be protected against 'immoral' influences.

(c) the moral police thinks it has the sole authority to pass judgement on films screened in India.

(d) None of these

25. The dominant modern belief is that the soundest foundation of peace would be universal prosperity. One may look in vain for historical evidence that the rich have regularly been more peaceful than the poor, but then it can be argued that they have never felt secure against the poor; that their aggressiveness stemmed from fear; and that the situation would be quite different if everybody were rich.

It can be inferred from the above passage that

(a) a lot of aggression in the world stems from the desire of the haves to defend themselves against the have-nots.

(b) universal prosperity as a foolproof measure of peace can no longer be accepted.

(c) Both (a) and (b)

(d) Neither (a) nor (b)

26. The effect produced on the mind by travelling depends entirely on the mind of the traveller and on the way in which he conducts himself. The chief idea of one very common type of traveller is to see as many objects of interest as he possibly can. If he can only after his return home say that he has seen such and such temple, castle, picture gallery, or museum, he is perfectly satisfied. Far different is the effect of travels upon those who leave their country with a mind prepared by culture to feel intelligent admiration for all the beauties of nature and art to be found in foreign lands. When they visit a new place, instead of hurrying from temple to museum to picture gallery, they allow the spirit of the place to sink into their minds, and only visit such monuments as the time they have at their disposal allows them to contemplate without irreverent haste.

It can be inferred from the above passage that

(a) the writer prefers the second type of traveller.

(b) the first type of traveller is the lay traveller who does not understand the worth of any place he travels to.

(c) the objective of the second type of traveller is not to see much, but to see well.

(d) All of these

27. Whether we look at the intrinsic value of our literature, or at the particular situation of this country, we shall see the strongest reason to think that of all foreign tongues, the English tongue is that which would be the most useful to our native subjects.

It can be inferred that

(a) the speaker is a die-hard colonist.

(b) the speaker has the good of the nation at heart.

(c) the speaker is addressing an issue related to a colonial empire.

(d) None of these

28. Where the film *Bombay* loses out is where every commercial film congenitally goes awry—becoming too simplistic to address serious issues and failing to translate real life to reel.

Which of the following can be inferred from the above line?

(a) The film's director aimed at recreating real life on the silver screen.

(b) The film was too simplistic for the audience's taste.

(c) The film was successful in spite of its shortcomings.

(d) None of these

29. Aspiration is nothing new. Neither is the debate over what the Indian middle class is, what it wants and what it buys. Since the mid-80s, that has been the focus of the economic policy papers so called pro- and anti-poor budgets and marketing strategies that have successfully broken the barrier of urban selling and reached deeper into rural India with increasing income levels and aspirations.

Based on the above passage, it can be inferred that

(a) the Indian middle class has been the focus of economic policies for a long time.

(b) the Indian middle class has graduated from being the 'deprived' middle class to the 'pampered' middle class.

(c) Both (a) and (b)

(d) Neither (a) nor (b)

1999

30. Three airlines — IA, JA and SA — operate on the Delhi- Mumbai route. To increase the number of seats sold, SA reduced its fares and this was emulated by IA and JA immediately. The general belief was that the volume of air travel between Delhi and Mumbai would increase as a result.

Which of the following, if true, would add credence to the general belief?

(a) Increase in profitability of the three airlines.

(b) Extension of the discount scheme to other routes.

(c) A study that shows that air travellers in India are price-conscious.

(d) A study that shows that as much as 80 per cent of air travel in India is company-sponsored.

31. According to McNeill, a Brahmin priest was expected to be able to recite at least one of the Vedas. The practice was essential for several centuries when the Vedas had not yet been written down. It must have had a selective effect, since priests would have been recruited from those able or willing to memorize long passages. It must have helped in the dissemination of the work, since a memorized passage can be duplicated many times.

Which of the following can be inferred from the above passage?

(a) Reciting the Vedas was a Brahmin's obligation.

(b) The Vedic priest was like a recorded audio cassette.

(c) McNeill studied the behaviour of Brahmin priests.

(d) Vedic hymns had not been scripted.

32. Developed countries have made adequate provisions for social security for senior citizens. State insurers (as well as private ones)offer medicare and pension benefits to people who can no longer earn. In India, with the collapse of the joint family system, the traditional shelter of the elderly has disappeared. And the state faced with a financial crunch is not in a position to provide social security. So, it is advisable that the working population give serious thought to building a financial base for itself.

Which one of the following, if it were to happen, weakens the conclusions drawn in the above passage the most?

(a) The investible income of the working population, as a proportion of its total income, will grow in the future.

(b) The insurance sector is underdeveloped and trends indicate that it will be extensively privatized in the future.

(c) India is on a path of development that will take it to a developed country status, with all its positive and negative implications.

(d) If the working population builds a stronger financial base, there will be a revival of the joint family system.

33. Various studies have shown that our forested and hilly regions and, in general, areas where biodiversity — as reflected in the variety of flora — is high, are the places where poverty appears to be high. And these same areas are also the ones where educational performance seems to be poor. Therefore, it may be surmised that, even disregarding poverty status, richness in biodiversity goes hand in hand with educational backwardness.

Which one of the following statements, if true, can be said to best provide supporting evidence for the surmise mentioned in the passage?

(a) In regions where there is little variety in flora, educational performance is seen to be as good as in regions with high variety in flora, where poverty levels are high.

(b) Regions which show high biodiversity also exhibit poor education performance, at low levels of poverty.

(c) Regions which show high biodiversity reveal high levels of poverty and poor educational performance.

(d) In regions where there is low biodiversity, at all levels of poverty, educational performance is seen to be good.

34. Cigarettes constitute a mere 20 per cent of tobacco consumption in India, and fewer than 15 per cent of the 200 million tobacco users consume cigarettes. Yet these 15 per cent contribute nearly 90 per cent of the tax revenues to the exchequer from the tobacco sector. The punitive cigarette taxation regime has kept the tax base narrow, and reducing taxes will expand this base.

Which of the following best bolsters the conclusion that reducing duties will expand the tax base?

(a) The cigarette manufacturers' association has decided to indulge in aggressive promotion.

(b) There is a likelihood that tobacco consumers will shift to cigarette smoking if cigarette prices were to reduce.

(c) The cigarette manufacturers are lobbying for a reduction on duties.

(d) An increase in duties on non-cigarette tobacco may lead to a shift in favour of cigarette smoking.

35. Thomas Malthus, the British clergyman-turned economist, predicted that the planet would not be able to support the human population for long. His explanation was that human population grows at a geometric rate, while the food supply grows only at an arithmetic rate.

Which one of the following, if true, would not undermine the thesis offered by Malthus?

(a) Population growth can be slowed down by the voluntary choices of individuals and not just by natural disasters.

(b) The capacity of the planet to feed a growing human population can be enhanced through biotechnological means.

(c) Human systems, and natural systems like food supply, follow natural laws of growth which have remained constant, and will remain unchanged.

(d) Human beings can colonize other planetary systems on a regular and ongoing basis to accommodate a growing population.

36. The company's coffee crop for 1998-99 totalled 8,079 tonnes, an all-time record. The increase over the previous year's production of 5,830 tonnes was 38.58 per cent. The previous highest crop was 6,089 tonnes in 1970-71. The company had fixed a target of 8,000 tonnes to be realized by the year 2000-01, and this has been achieved two years earlier, thanks to the emphasis laid on the key areas of irrigation, replacement of unproductive coffee bushes, intensive refilling and improved agricultural practices. It is now our endeavour to reach the target of 10,000 tonnes in 2001-02.

Which one of the following would contribute most to making the target of 10,000 tonnes in 2001-02 unrealistic?

(a) The potential of the productivity enhancing measures implemented up to now has been exhausted.

(b) The total company land under coffee has remained constant since 1969 when an estate in the Nilgiri Hills was acquired.

(c) The sensitivity of the crop to climatic factors makes predictions about production uncertain.

(d) The target-setting procedures in the company had been proved to be sound by the achievement of the 8,000 tonnes target.

37. Animals, in general, are shrewd in proportion as they cultivate society. Elephants and beavers show the greatest signs of this sagacity when they are together in large numbers, but when man invades their communities they lose all their spirit of industry. Among insects, the labours of the bee and the ant have attracted the attention and admiration of naturalists, but all their sagacity seems to be lost upon separation, and a single bee or ant seems destitute of every degree of industry. It becomes the most stupid insect imaginable, and it languishes and soon dies.

Which of the following can be inferred from the above passage?

(a) Humankind is responsible for the destruction of the natural habitat of animals and insects.

(b) Animals, in general, are unable to function effectively outside their normal social environment.

(c) Naturalists have great admiration for bees and ants, despite their lack of industry upon separation.

(d) Elephants and beavers are smarter than bees and ants in the presence of human beings.

2000

38. In a recent report, the gross enrolment ratios at the primary level, that is, the number of children enrolled in classes one to five as a proportion of all children aged six to ten, were shown to be very high for most states; in many cases they were way above 100 per cent! These figures are not worth anything, since they are based on the official enrolment data compiled from school records. They might as well stand for 'gross exaggeration ratios'.

Which one of the following options best supports the claim that the ratios are exaggerated?

(a) The definition of gross enrolment ratio does not exclude, in its numerator, children below six years or above ten years enroled in classes one to five.

(b) A school attendance study found that many children enrolled in the school records were not meeting a minimum attendance requirement of 80 per cent.

(c) A study estimated that close to 22 per cent of children enrolled in the class one records were below six years of age and still to start going to school.

(d) Demographic surveys show shifts in the population profile which indicate that the number of children in the age group six to ten years is declining.

39. Szymanski suggests that the problem of racism in football may be present even today. He begins by verifying an earlier hypothesis that clubs' wage bills explain 90 per cent of their performance. Thus, if players' salaries were to be only based on their abilities, clubs that spend more should finish higher. If there is pay discrimination against some group of players — fewer teams bidding for black players thus lowering the salaries for blacks with the same ability as whites — that neat relation may no longer hold. He concludes that certain clubs seem to have achieved much less than what they could have, by not recruiting black players.

Which one of the following findings would best support Szymanski's conclusion?

(a) Certain clubs took advantage of the situation by hiring above-average shares of black players.

(b) Clubs hired white players at relatively high wages and did not show proportionately good performance.

(c) During the study period, clubs in towns with a history of discrimination against blacks, under-performed relative to their wage bills.

(d) Clubs in one region, which had higher proportions of black players, had significantly lower wage bills than their counterparts in another region which had predominantly white players.

40. The pressure on Italy's 257 jails has been increasing rapidly. These jails are old and overcrowded. They are supposed to hold up to 43,000 people — 9,000 fewer than now. San Vittore in Milan, which has 1,800 inmates, is designed for 800. The number of foreigners inside jails has also been increasing. The minister-in-charge of prisons fears that tensions may snap, and so has recommended to the government an amnesty policy.

Which one of the following, if true, would have most influenced the recommendation of the minister?

(a) Opinion polls have indicated that many Italians favour a general pardon.

(b) The opposition may be persuaded to help since amnesties must be approved by a two-thirds majority in parliament.

(c) During a recent visit to a large prison, the Pope, whose pronouncements are taken seriously, appealed for 'a gesture of clemency'.

(d) Shortly before the recommendation was made, 58 prisons reported disturbances in a period of two weeks.

41. The offer of the government to make iodised salt available at a low price of one rupee per kilogram is welcome, especially since the government seems to be so concerned about the ill effects of non-iodised salt. But it is doubtful whether the offer will actually be implemented. Way back in 1994, the government, in an earlier effort, had prepared reports outlining three new and simple but experimental methods for reducing the costs of iodisation to about five paise per kilogram. But these reports have remained just those — reports on paper.

Which one of the following, if true, most weakens the author's contention that it is doubtful whether the offer will be actually implemented?

(a) The government proposes to save on costs by using the three methods it has already devised for iodisation.

(b) The chain of fair-price distribution outlets now covers all the districts of the state.

(c) Many small-scale and joint-sector units have completed trials to use the three iodisation methods for regular production.

(d) The government which initiated the earlier effort is in place even today and has more information on the effects of non-iodised salt.

42. About 96 per cent of Scandinavian moths have ears tuned to the ultrasonic pulses that bats, their predators, emit. But the remaining 4 per cent do not have ears and are deaf. However, they have a larger wingspan than the hearing moths, and also have higher wing-loadings — the ratio between a wing's area and its weight — meaning higher manoeuvrability.

Which one of the following can be best inferred from the above passage?

(a) A higher proportion of deaf moths than hearing moths fall prey to bats.

(b) Deaf moths may try to avoid bats by frequent changes in their flight direction.

(c) Deaf moths are faster than hearing moths, and so are less prone to becoming a bat's dinner than hearing moths.

(d) The large wingspan enables deaf moths to better receive and sense the pulses of their bat predators.

43. Argentina's beef cattle herd has dropped to under 50 million from 57 million ten years ago in 1990. The animals are worth less, too: prices fell by over a third last year, before recovering slightly. Most local meat packers and processors are in financial trouble, and recent years have seen a string of plant closures. The Beef Producers Association has now come up with a massive advertisement campaign calling upon Argentines to eat more beef — their 'juicy, healthy, rotund, plate-filling' steaks.

Which one of the following, if true, would contribute most to a failure of the campaign?

(a) There has been a change in consumer preference towards eating leaner meats like chicken and fish.

(b) Prices of imported beef have been increasing, thus making locally grown beef more competitive in terms of pricing.

(c) The inability to cross-breed native cattle with improved varieties has not increased production to adequate levels.

(d) Animal rights pressure groups have come up rapidly, demanding better and humane treatment of farmyard animals like beef cattle.

44. The problem of traffic congestion in Athens has been testing the ingenuity of politicians and town planners for years. But the measures adopted to date have not succeeded in decreasing the number of cars on the road in the city centre. In 1980, an odds and evens number-plate legislation was introduced, under which odd and even plates were banned in the city centre on alternate days, thereby expecting to halve the number of cars in the city centre. Then in 1993 it was decreed that all cars in use in the city centre must be fitted with catalytic converters; a regulation had just then been introduced, substantially reducing import taxes on cars with catalytic converters, the only condition being that the buyer of such a 'clean' car offered for destruction a car at least 15-year-old.

Which one of the following options, if true, would best support the claim that the measures adopted to date have not succeeded?

(a) In the 1980s, many families purchased second cars with the requisite odd or even number plate.

(b) In the mid-1990s, many families found it feasible to become first-time car owners by buying a car more than 15-year-old and turning it in for a new car with catalytic converters.

(c) Post-1993, many families seized the opportunity to sell their more than 15-year-old cars and buy 'clean' cars from the open market, even if it meant forgoing the import tax subsidy.

(d) All of the above

45. Although in the limited sense of freedom regarding appointments and internal working, the independence of the Central Bank is unequivocally ensured, the same cannot be said of its right to pursue monetary policy without coordination with the Central Government. The role of the Central Bank has turned out to be subordinate and advisory in nature.

Which one of the following best supports the conclusion drawn in the passage?

(a) A decision of the chairman of the Central Bank to increase the bank rate by two percentage points sent shock-waves in industry, academic and government circles alike.

(b) Government has repeatedly resorted to monetisation of the debt despite the reservations of the Central Bank.

(c) The Central Bank does not need the Central Government's nod for replacing soiled currency notes.

(d) The inability to remove coin shortage was a major shortcoming of this government.

46. The Shveta-chattra or the 'White Umbrella' was a symbol of sovereign political authority placed over the monarch's head at the time of the coronation. The ruler so inaugurated was regarded not as a temporal autocrat but as the instrument of protective and sheltering firmament of supreme law. The white umbrella symbol is of great antiquity and its varied use illustrates the ultimate common basis of non-theocratic nature of states in the Indian tradition. As such, the umbrella is found, although not necessarily a white one, over the head of Lord Ram, the Mohammedan sultans and Chatrapati Shivaji.

Which one of the following best summarises the above passage?

(a) The placing of an umbrella over the ruler's head was a common practice in the Indian subcontinent.

(b) The white umbrella represented the instrument of firmament of the supreme law and the non-theocratic nature of Indian states.

(c) The umbrella, not necessarily a white one, was a symbol of sovereign political authority.

(d) The varied use of the umbrella symbolised the common basis of the non-theocratic nature of states in the Indian tradition.

47. The theory of games is suggested to some extent by parlour games such as chess and bridge. Friedman illustrates two distinct features of these games. First, in a parlour game played for money, if one wins the other (others)loses (lose). Second, these games are games involving a strategy. In a game of chess, while choosing what action is to be taken, a player tries to guess how his/her opponent will react to the various actions he or she might take. In contrast, the card-pastime, 'patience' or 'solitaire' is played only against chance.

Which one of the following can best be described as a 'game'?

(a) The team of Tenzing Norgay and Edmund Hillary climbing Mt. Everest for the first time in human history.

(b) A national level essay writing competition.

(c) A decisive war between the armed forces of India and Pakistan over Kashmir.

(d) Oil Exporters' Union deciding on world oil prices, completely disregarding the countries which have at most minimal oil production.

MEMORY BASED QUESTIONS

2015

48. The passage given below is followed by four alternative summaries. Choose the option that best captures the essence of the passage. Key in the number of the option you choose as your answer

The study of Buddhism over the past century or so has resembled the encounter of the blind men and the elephant in many ways. Students of Buddhism have tended to fasten onto a small part of the tradition and assume their conclusions held true about the whole. Often the parts they have seized on have been a little like the elephant's tusks — a striking, but unrepresentative, part of the whole animal. As a result, many erroneous and sweeping generalizations about Buddhism have been made, such as that it is 'negative', 'world-denying', 'pessimistic', and so forth. Although this tendency to over generalize is now less common, it is still found in some of the older literature where authors tended to exaggerate certain features of the tradition or assume that what was true of Buddhism in one culture or historical period held good everywhere.

1. The story of three blind men and the elephant can tell us much about Buddhism.
2. Buddhism has been generalized and many of its facets over-exaggerated by its perpetuators over the years.
3. The way the three blind men make conclusions about the elephant is analogous to how the world views Buddhism.
4. Authors in general are unable to grasp the nuances of Buddhism.

49. The passage given below is followed by four alternative summaries. Choose the option that best captures the essence of the passage. Key in the number of the option you choose as your answer

Volkswagen, trying to get to the bottom of its emissions-cheating scandal, pressured employees to tell what they know, announcing an amnesty program for informants that will expire soon. The company has yet to explain publicly who was responsible for installing software in 11 million diesel vehicles that was designed to disguise the output of nitrogen oxide, a pollutant harmful to the lungs. Volkswagen also admitted that it underreported the levels of carbon dioxide produced by about 800,000 of its diesel and gasoline vehicles in Europe and that had it exaggerated their fuel economy.

1. Volkswagen exaggerated their fuel economy and is now trying to pressurize the employees to take the blame.
2. Volkswagen, is pressurizing its employees to spill the beans by stating that the amnesty program will soon end.
3. Volkswagen has been underreporting the levels of carbon dioxide produced by its diesel and gasoline vehicles in Europe.
4. Volkswagen, trying to get to the bottom of its emissions cheating scandal, pressured employees to tell what they know.

50. The passage given below is followed by four alternative summaries. Choose the option that best captures the essence of the passage. Key in the number of the option you choose as your answer

A major glacier in Greenland that holds enough water to raise global sea levels by half a metre has begun to crumble into the North Atlantic Ocean, scientists say. The huge Zachariae Isstrom glacier in northeast Greenland started to melt rapidly in 2012 and is now breaking up into large icebergs where the glacier meets the sea, monitoring has revealed. The calving of the glacier into chunks of floating ice will set in train a rise in sea levels that will continue for decades to come, the US team warns. "Even if we have some really cool years ahead, we think the glacier is now unstable," said Jeremie Mouginot at the University of California, Irvine. "Now this has started, it will continue until it retreats to a ridge about 30km back which could stabilise it and perhaps slow that retreat down."

1. Huge Zachariae Isstrom glacier has begun to break up, starting a rapid retreat that could continue to raise sea levels for decades to come.
2. Global Warming and other related factors are breaking up glaciers that are raising the level of North Atlantic ocean.
3. The huge Zachariae Isstrom glacier is now breaking up into large icebergs where the glacier meets the sea.
4. Huge Zachariae Isstrom glacier will continue to melt until it retreats to a ridge about 30km back which could stabilise it.

LOGICAL CONSISTENCY

1997

DIRECTIONS for Questions 1 to 14: Each question has a main statement followed by four statements labelled A, B, C and D. Choose the ordered pair of statements where the first statement implies the second, and the two statements are logically consistent with the main statement.

1. Either Sam is ill, or he is drunk.

A. Sam is ill.

B. Sam is not ill.

C. Sam is drunk.

D. Sam is not drunk.

(a) AB (b) DA

(c) AC (d) CD

2. Whenever Ram hears of a tragedy, he loses sleep.

A. Ram heard of a tragedy.

B. Ram did not hear of a tragedy.

C. Ram lost sleep.

D. Ram did not lose sleep.

(a) CA (b) BD

(c) DB (d) AD

3. Either the train is late, or it has derailed.

A. The train is late.

B. The train is not late.

C. The train is derailed.

D. The train is not derailed.

(a) AB (b) DB

(c) CA (d) BC

4. When I read a horror story I have a nightmare.

A. I read a story.

B. I did not read a horror story.

C. I did not have a nightmare.

D. I had a nightmare.

(a) CB (b) AD

(c) BC (d) AC

5. When I eat berries I get rashes.

A. I ate berries.

B. I did not get rashes.

C. I did not eat berries.

D. I got rashes.

(a) DA (b) BC

(c) CB (d) None of these

1998

6. Either Sita is sick or she is careless.

A. Sita is not sick.

B. Sita is not careless.

C. Sita is sick.

D. Sita is careless.

(a) AB (b) AD

(c) BA (d) DA

7. Ram gets a swollen nose whenever he eats hamburgers.

A. Ram gets a swollen nose.

B. Ram does not eat hamburgers.

C. Ram does not get a swollen nose.

D. Ram eats hamburgers.

(a) AB (b) DC

(c) AC (d) BC

8. Either the employees have no confidence in the management or they are hostile by nature.

A. They are not hostile by nature.

B. They are hostile by nature.

C. They have confidence in the management.

D. They have no confidence in the management.

(a) BA (b) CB

(c) DA (d) BD

9. Whenever Ram reads late into the night, his father beats him.

A. His father does not beat Ram.

B. Ram reads late into the night.

C. Ram reads early in the morning.

D. Ram's father beats him in the morning.

(a) CD (b) BD

(c) AB (d) None of these

10. All irresponsible parents shout if their children do not cavort.

A. All irresponsible parents do not shout.

B. Children cavort.

C. Children do not cavort.

D. All irresponsible parents shout.

(a) AB

(b) BA

(c) CA

(d) All of these

1999

11. Either the orangutan is not angry, or he frowns upon the world.

A. The orangutan frowns upon the world.

B. The orangutan is not angry.

C. The orangutan does not frown upon the world.

D. The orangutan is angry.

(a) CB only (b) DA only

(c) AB only (d) CB and DA

12. Either Ravana is a demon, or he is a hero.

A. Ravana is a hero.

B. Ravana is a demon.

C. Ravana is not a demon.

D. Ravana is not a hero.

(a) CD only (b) BA only

(c) CD and BA (d) DB and CA

13. Whenever Rajeev uses the Internet, he dreams about spiders.

A. Rajeev did not dream about spiders.

B. Rajeev used the Internet.

C. Rajeev dreamt about spiders.

D. Rajeev did not use the Internet.

(a) AD (b) DC

(c) CB (d) DA

14. If I talk to my professors, then I do not need to take a pill for headache.

A. I talked to my professors.

B. I did not need to take a pill for headache.

C. I needed to take a pill for headache.

D. I did not talk to my professors.

(a) AB only (b) DC only

(c) CD only (d) AB and CD

Odd Sentence Out

2016

1. The following question consists of a set of five sentences. Out of these, four sentences can be arranged to make a coherent paragraph. One sentence doesn't belong to the paragraph. Type in that option as the odd one out in the space provided below the question.
   (a) Management of tropical forests could stabilize current CO_2 concentrations while nations transition from fossil fuels to clean, renewable energy.
   (b) Forests' carbon-storing abilities cannot compare to the potential emissions in the planet's current fossil fuel reserves
   (c) But a fresh look at forests might reveal a solution.
   (b) Negotiators in Paris face a tough job hammering out a global agreement to slash greenhouse gas emissions far enough and fast enough to prevent the worst effects of climate change.
   (d) If governments could reverse tropical deforestation; the planet could buy some time.

2. The following question consists of a set of five sentences. Out of these, four sentences can be arranged to make a coherent paragraph. One sentence doesn't belong to the paragraph. Type in that option as the odd one out in the space provided below the question.
   (a) More and more land is being cleared for people to plant crops like cotton and tobacco, creating runoff downriver that silts up rivers and shrinks waterholes for Africa's remaining hippo population.
   (b) Low-slung with big bellies, hippos appear awkward on land, but they are fast runners for their size (more than 9,000 pounds for some adult males) and can cover great distances when defending their territory or searching for food.
   (c) Male hippos regularly take over a length of riverbank to establish mating territory.

(d) With a name derived from the Greek words for "river horse," hippopotamuses are semiaquatic herbivores that live their lives in water, except for evening rituals when they follow well-worn paths up riverbanks to feeding grounds.

(e) Sometimes, these squatting rights result in fierce battles, during which the males bellow loudly and bare their huge canine teeth.

3. The following question consists of a set of five sentences. Out of these, four sentences can be arranged to make a coherent paragraph. One sentence doesn't belong to the paragraph. Type in that option as the odd one out in the space provided below the question.

(a) Neanderthals, the closest extinct relatives of humans, lived in Eurasia from about 200,000 to 30,000 years ago.

(b) To investigate this question, the researchers examined the facial bones of Neanderthals.

(c) Some scientists think that Neanderthals and humans are on the same branch of the family tree.

(d) "However, our findings, based upon facial growth patterns, indicate they are indeed sufficiently distinct from one another," Lacruz said.

(e) Bone is created with bone-forming cells called osteoblasts, and it's broken down with bone-absorbing cells called osteoclasts.

2017

4. Five sentences related to a topic are given below. Four of them can be put together to form a meaningful and coherent short paragraph. Identify the odd one out.

(a) Although we are born with the gift of language, research shows that we are surprisingly unskilled when it comes to communicating with others.

(b) We must carefully orchestrate our speech if we want to achieve our goals and bring our dreams to fruition.

(c) We often choose our words without thought, oblivious of the emotional effects they can have on others.

(d) We talk more than we need to, ignoring the effect we are having on those listening to us.

(e) We listen poorly, without realising it, and we often fail to pay attention to the subtle meanings conveyed by facial expressions, body gestures, and the tone and cadence of our voice.

5. Five sentences related to a topic are given below. Four of them can be put together to form a meaningful and coherent short paragraph. Identify the odd one out.

(a) Over the past fortnight, one of its finest champions managed to pull off a similar impression.

(b) Wimbledon's greatest illusion is the sense of timelessness it evokes.

(c) At 35 years and 342 days, Roger Federer became the oldest man to win the singles title in the Open Era – a full 14 years after he first claimed the title as a scruffy, pony-tailed upstart.

(d) Once he had survived the opening week, the second week witnessed the range of a rested Federer's genius.

(e) Given that his method isn't reliant on explosive athleticism or muscular ball-striking, both vulnerable to decay, there is cause to believe that Federer will continue to enchant for a while longer.

6. Five sentences related to a topic are given below. Four of them can be put together to form a meaningful and coherent short paragraph. Identify the odd one out.

(a) Those geometric symbols and aerodynamic swooshes are more than just skin deep.

(b) The Commonwealth Bank logo - a yellow diamond, with a black chunk sliced out in one corner - is so recognisable that the bank doesn't even use its full name in its advertising.

(c) It's not just logos with hidden shapes; sometimes brands will have meanings or stories within them that are deliberately vague or lost in time, urging you to delve deeper to solve the riddle.

(d) Graphic designers embed cryptic references because it adds a story to the brand; they want people to spend more time with a brand and have that idea that they are an insider if they can understand the hidden message

(e) But the CommBank logo has more to it than meets the eye, as squirrelled away in that diamond is the Southern Cross constellation.

2018 Slot 1

7. Five sentences related to a topic are given below. Four of them can be put together to form a meaningful and coherent short paragraph. Identify the odd one out.

(a) Displacement in Bengal is thus not very significant in view of its magnitude.

(b) A factor of displacement in Bengal is the shifting course of the Ganges leading to erosion of river banks.

(c) The nature of displacement in Bengal makes it an interesting case study.

(d) Since displacement due to erosion is well spread over a long period of time, it remains invisible.

(e) Rapid displacement would have helped sensitize the public to its human costs.

8. Five sentences related to a topic are given below. Four of them can be put together to form a meaningful and coherent short paragraph. Identify the odd one out. Choose its number as your answer and key it in.

(a) Translators are like bumblebees.

(b) Though long since scientifically disproved, this factoid is still routinely trotted out.

(c) Similar pronouncements about the impossibility of translation have dogged practitioners since Leonardo Bruni's De interpretatione recta, published in 1424.

(d) Bees, unaware of these deliberations, have continued to flit from flower to flower, and translators continue to translate.

(e) In 1934, the French entomologist August Magnan pronounced the flight of the bumblebee to be aerodynamically impossible

2018 Slot 2

9. Five sentences related to a topic are given below. Four of them can be put together to form a meaningful and coherent short paragraph. Identify the odd one out.

(a) In many cases time inconsistency is what prevents our going from intention to action.

(b) For people to continuously postpone getting their children immunized, they would need to be constantly fooled by themselves.

(c) In the specific case of immunization, however, it is hard to believe that time inconsistency by itself would be sufficient to make people permanently postpone the decision if they were fully cognizant of its benefits.

(d) In most cases, even a small cost of immunization was large enough to discourage most people.

(e) Not only do they have to think that they prefer to spend time going to the camp next month rather than today, they also have to believe that they will indeed go next month.

10. Five sentences related to a topic are given below. Four of them can be put together to form a meaningful and coherent short paragraph. Identify the odd one out.

(a) Much has been recently discovered about the development of songs in birds.

(b) Some species are restricted to a single song learned by all individuals, others have a range of songs.

(c) The most important auditory stimuli for the birds are the sounds of other birds.

(d) For all bird species there is a prescribed path to development of the final song,

(e) A bird begins with the subsong, passes through plastic song, until it achieves the species song.

11. Five sentences related to a topic are given below. Four of them can be put together to form a meaningful and coherent short paragraph. Identify the odd one out.

(a) As India looks to increase the number of cities, our urban planning must factor in potential natural disasters and work out contingencies in advance.

(b) Authorities must revise data and upgrade infrastructure and mitigation plans even if their local area hasn't been visited by a natural calamity yet.

(c) Extreme temperatures, droughts, and forest fires have more than doubled since 1980.

(d) There is no denying the fact that our baseline normal weather is changing.

(e) It is no longer a question of whether we will be hit by nature's fury but rather when.

12. Five sentences related to a topic are given below. Four of them can be put together to form a meaningful and coherent short paragraph. Identify the odd one out. Choose its number as your answer and key the number in:

(a) Our smartphones can now track our diets, our biological cycles, even our digestive systems and sleep-patterns.

(b) Researchers have even coined a new term, "orthosomnia", to describe the insomnia brought on by paying too much attention to smartphones and sleep-tracking apps.

(c) Sleep, nature's soft nurse, is a blissful, untroubled state all too easily disturbed by earthly worries or a guilty conscience.

(d) The existence of a market for such apps is unsurprising: shift work, a long-hours culture and blue light from screens have conspired to rob many of us of sufficient rest.

(e) A new threat to a good night's rest has emerged – smart-phones, with sleep-tracking apps.

■■

ANSWERS

PARA-COMPLETION

1. d **2.** d **3.** a **4.** c **5.** d **6.** b **7.** b **8.** c
9. b **10.** a **11.** b **12.** a **13.** b **14.** c **15.** b **16.** b
17. a **18.** b **19.** c **20.** a **21.** e **22.** a **23.** b **24.** c
25. d **26.** e **27.** a **28.** b **29.** b **30.** d **31.** b **32.** e
33. a **34.** d **35.** a **36.** c **37.** b **38.** c **39.** c **40.** d
41. a **42.** b **43.** c **44.** a **45.** b **46.** d **47.** c **48.** d

PARA-JUMBLES

1. c **2.** c **3.** b **4.** b **5.** c **6.** a **7.** d **8.** a
9. d **10.** a **11.** b **12.** a **13.** b **14.** d **15.** a **16.** c
17. a **18.** d **19.** c **20.** a **21.** b **22.** b **23.** a **24.** c
25. a **26.** d **27.** d **28.** a **29.** b **30.** c **31.** b **32.** b
33. a **34.** d **35.** b **36.** d **37.** c **38.** c **39.** a **40.** a
41. a **42.** d **43.** b **44.** a **45.** a **46.** b **47.** a **48.** b
49. c **50.** c **51.** c **52.** a **53.** b **54.** a **55.** b **56.** c
57. a **58.** b **59.** a **60.** a **61.** d **62.** b **63.** b **64.** a
65. d **66.** b **67.** a **68.** d **69.** a **70.** c **71.** a **72.** c
73. a **74.** b **75.** c **76.** d **77.** c **78.** d **79.** b **80.** c
81. a **82.** d **83.** a **84.** b **85.** b **86.** a **87.** d **88.** d
89. a **90.** c **91.** c **92.** c **93.** a **94.** b **95.** d **96.** c
97. a **98.** b **99.** d **100.** b **101.** d **102.** a **103.** e **104.** c
105. c **106.** a **107.** c **108.** a **109.** d **110.** c **111.** c **112.** b
113. d **114.** d **115.** b **116.** d **117.** c **118.** a **119.** a **120.** b
121. a **122.** b **123.** c **124.** c **125.** d **126.** a **127.** a **128.** c
129. c **130.** b **131.** a **132.** c **133.** d **134.** d **135.** d **136.** b
137. c **138.** d **139.** d **140.** a **141.** b **142.** d **143.** b **144.** a
145. a **146.** a **147.** b **148.** c **149.** a **150.** a **151.** a **152.** c
153. b **154.** b **155.** c **156.** d **157.** d **158.** a **159.** b **160.** d
161. b **162.** c **163.** c **164.** c **165.** b **166.** d **167.** a **168.** a
169. b **170.** d **171.** a **172.** c **173.** c **174.** a **175.** b **176.** c
177. c **178.** d **179.** c **180.** d **181.** a **182.** c **183.** a **184.** a
185. a **186.** d **187.** c **188.** b **189.** b **190.** 4 **191.** 3 **192.** 4
193. eadbc **194.** eabcd **195.** dcbae **196.** abecd **197.** ceadb **198.** ebacd **199.** cebad **200.** dbaec
201. (becda) **202.** (ecdba) **203.** (bedca) **204.** (dceab) **205.** (acbd) **206.** (dbac) **207.** (bdac) **208.** (adcb)
209. (cdab) **210.** (bdac) **211.** (cbda) **212.** (bcad)

FACTS, INFERENCES, JUDGEMENTS

1. c	**2.** a	**3.** a	**4.** b	**5.** d	**6.** c	**7.** a	**8.** b
9. c	**10.** d	**11.** c	**12.** e	**13.** d	**14.** b	**15.** a	**16.** a
17. b	**18.** d	**19.** a	**20.** c	**21.** c	**22.** b	**23.** d	**24.** c
25. d	**26.** d	**27.** d	**28.** b	**29.** b	**30.** d	**31.** a	**32.** c
33. a	**34.** d	**35.** a	**36.** c	**37.** a	**38.** d	**39.** c	**40.** c
41. a	**42.** b	**43.** c	**44.** c	**45.** b	**46.** a	**47.** b	**48.** c
49. d	**50.** d	**51.** c	**52.** d	**53.** b	**54.** c	**55.** b	**56.** b
57. c	**58.** b	**59.** a	**60.** d	**61.** b	**62.** b	**63.** c	**64.** c
65. c	**66.** d	**67.** c	**68.** b	**69.** a	**70.** c	**71.** a	**72.** b
73. b	**74.** c	**75.** b	**76.** b	**77.** d	**78.** c	**79.** d	**80.** b
81. a	**82.** d	**83.** a	**84.** b	**85.** b	**86.** b	**87.** b	**88.** d
89. a	**90.** d	**91.** a	**92.** a	**93.** d	**94.** d	**95.** a	**96.** b
97. b	**98.** d	**99.** a	**100.**c	**101.**b	**102.**d	**103.**b	**104.**a
105.b	**106.**c	**107.**a	**108.**b	**109.**c			

SUMMARY TYPE QUESTIONS

1. b	**2.** b	**3.** b	**4.** a	**5.** a	**6.** b	**7.** c	**8.** b
9. d	**10.** d	**11.** d	**12.** a	**13.** c	**14.** d	**15.** c	**16.** c
17. b	**18.** d	**19.** b	**20.** d	**21.** b			

SYLLOGISMS

1. c	**2.** c	**3.** d	**4.** a	**5.** b	**6.** c	**7.** d	**8.** c
9. d	**10.** b	**11.** c	**12.** a	**13.** c	**14.** c	**15.** a	**16.** b
17. d	**18.** d	**19.** a	**20.** b	**21.** d	**22.** d	**23.** d	**24.** a
25. c	**26.** b	**27.** d	**28.** b	**29.** c	**30.** a	**31.** a	**32.** b
33. d	**34.** a	**35.** d	**36.** c	**37.** a	**38.** b	**39.** d	**40.** b
41. c	**42.** a	**43.** b	**44.** d	**45.** d	**46.** b	**47.** c	**48.** b
49. a	**50.** c	**51.** a	**52.** b	**53.** a	**54.** a	**55.** d	**56.** d
57. a	**58.** a	**59.** b	**60.** c	**61.** a	**62.** a	**63.** a	**64.** b
65. b	**66.** a	**67.** c	**68.** c	**69.** a	**70.** b	**71.** c	**72.** b
73. a	**74.** c	**75.** c	**76.** b	**77.** d	**78.** b	**79.** d	**80.** a
81. b	**82.** a	**83.** d	**84.** b	**85.** a	**86.** b	**87.** c	

CRITICAL REASONING

1. c	**2.** c	**3.** a	**4.** c	**5.** a	**6.** b	**7.** c	**8.** b
9. c	**10.** a	**11.** c	**12.** c	**13.** a	**14.** d	**15.** d	**16.** a
17. a	**18.** d	**19.** c	**20.** a	**21.** c	**22.** b	**23.** a	**24.** b
25. a	**26.** c	**27.** d	**28.** d	**29.** a	**30.** c	**31.** b	**32.** c
33. c	**34.** b	**35.** c	**36.** a	**37.** b	**38.** c	**39.** b	**40.** d
41. c	**42.** b	**43.** a	**44.** d	**45.** b	**46.** d	**47.** c	**48.** c
49. d	**50.** a						

LOGICAL CONSISTENCY

1. b	**2.** c	**3.** d	**4.** a	**5.** b	**6.** b	**7.** d	**8.** b
9. d	**10.** a	**11.** d	**12.** d	**13.** a	**14.** d		

ODD SENTENCE OUT

1. b	**2.** a	**3.** a	**4.** b	**5.** d	**6.** a	**7.** e	**8.** b
9. (acbd*)	**10.** c	**11.** c	**12.** d				

EXPLANATIONS

PARA-COMPLETION

1. d Broad and powerful thinking is needed to solve the problems.

2. d The funds are being 'raised' for the purpose of having money to spend on the search of alternative sources of energy.

3. a If you look before you leap you will be forewarned and thus can be forearmed.

4. c As the king, the fate of the economy and the subjects would be in the ruler's hands.

5. d We should be prepared to 'break' something to 'reconstruct' it.

6. b If the future is upon us before we realize it, it will shape us rather than the other way round.

7. b What follows the blank shows that what has been happening till now has led to some undesirable things and hence a change is now coming in. (b). is the only choice that shows what wrong has happened.

8. c (c) suggests that the strategy adopted by some people is not very effective, and the idea is continued with in the passage when the author refers to it as 'this fallacy'.

9. b What follows the blank shows that the author is against the argument projected in the beginning of the passage. (b) is the only choice which would support this.

10. a The passage begins with the situation of two people on two different sides of the issue. Each gets a chance to argue his or her position and after listening to each other they decide whether they wish to change their position or not. The use of 'then' after the blank shows that some action has taken place before it, and a. is the only choice showing an action.

11. b This is the only phrase that fits here.

12. a 'Even if I have tears in me' goes perfectly with 'I have to keep smiling'.

13. b Stock markets indicate public sentiment, not just confidence.

14. c 'Few will know about' is the most concise way to express the meaning.

15. b It is a well-known saying in English.

16. b 'Its haunting images' refers to the haunting images of the movie.

17. a The passage contrasts crosswords with Sudoku. A crossword touches numerous areas of life and provides a few surprises along the way. So the next sentence needs to talk about Sudoku along these lines. Option (a) which describes Sudoku as "just a logical exercise" (unlike the crossword which touches numerous areas of life) with each one similar to the last (unlike the surprises that a good crossword can provide).

18. b Since expert individuals are left out of such groups, the result is most likely to be mediocrity.

19. c Option (b) talks about humility which is not talked about in the passage, option (c) is an extension of the concept of being a minnow.

20. a The passage has a decidedly negative tone. The author states that just like other generations before it, this generation has also struggled to understand the organizational laws of the frontier, has suffered from unwarranted pride, and has also failed like those before. So only (a) can complete the paragraph by stating the need for humility in front of this failure.

21. e The paragraph stresses on the relationships between the factories, dealers and the consumers. Every entity has certain short-term expectations from each other. This makes these relationships strenuous. This strain leads to feelings of mistrust and lack of commitment. So the longer this continues, the more the chances of everyone succumbing to this vicious trap and they would soon realize that they have sacrificed long-term stability and gain for short-term benefits. Hence Option (e). Option (d) is too specific to industry (at the cost of the other players – dealers and customers), option (b) suffers from the same short-comings together with throwing the technical (unexplained) jargon 'supply chain' to us. Option (a) takes into account only 2 players and repeats what is stated in the passage about "dealers adjusting prices and making deals" in the term 'Deal making'; option (c) seems close but can be eliminated as the word 'adversary' is too strong. The passage implies that everyone tries to maximize his benefits, not that they 'oppose' one another.

22. a The passage heads towards describing the functions that bad / good maps (and therefore theories) serve. Just as a 'Bad theory' does not help us understand a problem, a 'good theory' is invaluable to us, though it may be simplified. 'Simplified' here implies that less valuable information is left out. According to this logic, option (b), (c), (d), get eliminated. Option (e) is close but more negative in tone than required. The word 'limitation' here indicates a short coming whereas the passage implies that it is a simplification as it would not be of practical use otherwise.

23. b Going with the direction of the passage, the last line is stating 'now all players "profess" to seek only peace'. Profess means to mask or to pretend. Thus option (b) which talks about the veil being lifted is the most logical statement that completes the passage. More so this also follows from the source of the text.

24. c The answer is very direct. With every statement of his, the author seeks to show how foolish those people are who call his advice 'rules'. After his first statement he has posed the rhetorical question "Call that a rule?" The same should follow after his second "scarcely a rule!"

25. d In the first part of the passage, the author seeks to explain why one who is young would exploit an entrepreneurial opportunity. Thus, in the second part of the passage once the "however" is established, evidence will seek to show how older people will be reluctant to exploit entrepreneurial opportunity. Option (b) seems correct but it only gives a general statement that with age, people become reluctant to new ideas. Between option (b) and (d), option (d) goes in continuation with the text as it states that at a mature age, people are unwilling to utilize entrepreneurial opportunities. So option (d) is correct.

26. e "The personification of a whole organization is a textual device ..." is the choice which continues the theme in the last two lines of the paragraph in the best possible way. The latter half of the paragraph is talking about personification of whole organizations and this is the choice which completes the paragraph satisfactorily. The choice justifies why whole organizations are personified even though they cannot speak as characters.

27. a 'Yet despite these technical developments...... ...care about'.

In the first line of the paragraph the author speaks about the magical allure still retained by photographs. Then he goes on to describe the negative effects of technological advancements on the same. Thus, in line with the first idea (a) describes how photographs are still holding out against these negative effects.

28. b 'No inventory would ever include those, ofcourse'.The para starts with listing out 'the inventory'.The option which says 'what she lacked..........natural shrewdness' is beyond the scope of the argument. All the options can be easily eliminated. 'Those' in the option 'No inventory would ever include those, ofcourse', refers to human intuition and intelligence of Mma Ramotswe.

29. b In the paragraph the author suggests why the doctor loses some of his patients. Option 5 can be easily eliminated as the pronoun "these" has no antecedent in the para. Option (c) & (d) are farfetched as they are to do with the doctor's attitude towards the problem, which the para does not indicate in any way. Option (a) can also be done away with as it suggests those patients who fail to speak up and not about those who leave his treatment, as indicated in the para. Option (b) fits in perfectly as it speaks of those who have no other alternative but to seek his treatment.

30. d Options (a) and (c) are very generalized statements. Option (b) is a repetition of the idea presented in the beginning of the paragraph. The para talks about how developed countries indulge in trade protectionism as a move against China and India's economic rise , under the guise of climate concern. Option (d) and (e) talk about the same thing but (d) goes along with the subtle suggestive tone of the para while (e) is more curt in its accusation of 'perpetrators of inequity'.

31. b The para is a description of the Jewry settlement,. (d) can be eliminated as it brings in a hint of skepticism. (c) is a mere repetition of an idea already discussed in the para (that of jews being tolerant). (e) can also be eliminated as it is brings an alien concept – that of Mattancherry's popularity with the tourists . Between (a) and (b), we will eliminate (a) as it has a more conclusive tone, which is not in sync with the descriptive nature of the paragraph.

32. e Option (a) can be easily eliminated as it is a mere repetition of the ideas presented in the para. Option (b) is a little farfetched as it should come one or two more sentences later in the para . Option (c) does not match with the idea presented in the passage. Option (d) does not match with the tone of the paragraph. Option (e) completes the idea as the emphasis in the last line of the para is that the idea of 'pure Western and pure Indian thoughts' is deceptive.

33. a The author admits to disliking an entire group of people based on the actions of a few. Hence, the word 'bigot', which means 'one who regards or treats the members of a group (as a racial or ethnic group) with hatred and intolerance', fits best. 'Chauvinist' means 'a person who has undue partiality or attachment to a group or place to which he/she belongs or has belonged'. A 'fanatic' is also similar in meaning, it means 'marked by excessive enthusiasm and often intense uncritical devotion'. Both these words are inappropriate as the author is shown to be critical of a particular group and not excessively devoted or attached to any group. 'Philistine' means 'a person who is guided by materialism and is usually disdainful of intellectual or artistic values' and is completely irrelevant in the given context. Also, for the second blank we need a word with negative connotations since the author mentions that it 'festers'. Prejudice would therefore be appropriate.

34. d To answer this question we essentially need two contrasting words. Also, these words must describe accurately both Amundsen's and Scott's approaches. Options (a), (c) and (d) all have words which can fit in the first blank. However, the best word for how Scott viewed exploration is 'romantic' which means 'marked by the imaginative or emotional appeal of what is heroic, adventurous, remote, mysterious, or idealized.'

35. a Option (a) continues the idea of how these buildings would appear to someone flying over human settlements.

36. c The paragraph highlights the popularity of a camera phone and the limitations it suffers from because of its size. Option (c) continues in the same vein and tells us about a small camera chip (about 8 mm across) that is used in these phones. Option (a) is completely different in tone – it tells us about an endeavour by a particular firm. Option (b) is out of the question as it goes into the technicalities of how an image is formed. Option (d) focuses on the camera being a fringe-benefit.

37. b The sentence immediately after the blank states "He had a simpler idea". Therefore the sentence in the blank needs to have another idea/suggestion by the psychologist. Option (b) is the only one that fits.

38. c The paragraph discusses differences between idealists and realists. The next sentence should be option (c) as it brings out this difference. The paragraph ends with 'The idealist… thinks that all this is so much the better.' Option (c) features a similar construction- 'The realist… thinks it so much the worse.'

39. c The deleted sentence is a part of Dell's statement. Dell says we are no longer afraid of monsters and trolls but continue to be fascinated by them. (c) is the logical continuation as it tells us why we are not afraid of them but still fascinated by them.

40. d Only (d) gives a sensible reason for the review bringing more than just a thumbs up or thumbs down— the review would likely settle an important question on the scope of government regulation. Since the "Justices review" is being discussed , only (d) can be the logical continuation.

41. a The paragraph discusses the idea of reality – on one hand an idealized reality and on the other a naturalistic reality. This paragraph indicates a dichotomy in viewpoints. Option (c) can be ruled out because there is no reference to a third view in the paragraph. Option (d) is ruled out as the educated bourgeoisie are not the subject of the paragraph – it is the works and the views of artistes (writers). Option (b) does not match with the central idea of the passage as this option talks about beauty and not reality. Option (a) is the best answer as it considers the dichotomy as well as the works of the German artistes with respect to *reality*.

42. b The paragraph is about policy failures – specifically the policing policy and the higher education policy. The paragraph has a negative tone. Option (c) can be ruled out as it has a tone of relief – a positive tone. Options (a) and (d) can be ruled out as they are only specific to the policing policy. Option (b) is the answer as it refers to both the policing and higher education policies. It also follows from the penultimate line in the paragraph that states that both failures could have been mitigated – option (b) logically completes the paragraph by stating that instead they were allowed to fester.

43. c The tone of the paragraph is predominantly narrative and in the past tense. Option (a) is repetitive and is abruptly in the present. Even option (d) abruptly jump to the present and do not continue the tone. Option (b) seems to follow option (c)- note that option (b) starts with 'even audiences were transformed' which is logical after option (c) which talks of transformation of theatre. Option (c) is closely linked to the para end which talks of unseen activities. Option (c) not only continues the paragraph but defines what this invisible theatre is all about.

44. a The first line of the paragraph-'much to commend and much to ponder'- gives away the tone of the author- which is moderate and not extreme. Option (b) is too definitive in 'Adiga can never hope to explore'. Option (c) is too laudatory. Option (d) is extreme in its negative tone. Option (a) continues the author's view. Also note the words 'my hunch is .....' which is moderate in its import.

45. b The correct answer is (b). (a) is incorrect: the author talks about atrocities caused by Israelis and not Palestinians. (c)' is incorrect: the author talks about Israeli occupation and not of Palestinian occupation. (d) is incorrect: it is far fetched. Option (b) goes with the theme and development of the passage.

46. d Here, the sentence "He was at first..." indicates that while at first the guard seemed stoic, something about him will change in the next moment.

Option (a) does not mention the guard at all, as an ideal follow up sentence should.

Same is the case with option (b), where the author mentions a painting, previously unmentioned in the passage.

Option (c) does mention the guard, but does not depict any change in him. A logical extension of a sentence such as "He was at first..." will depict a change in the subject's actions or reactions whereas option (c) shifts the focus from the guard to the author as it states "*As I glanced...*"

Option (d) describes a sudden change in the guard's expressions and bodily movements. Hence, it aptly follows the previous sentence in the passage. Thus, option (d) is the correct answer.

47. c As the given paragraph is about an overall broad historical view of Bangalore, option (c) best fits in as the last line of the passage.

Option (b) seems to be appropriate too but, as pointed out earlier, the given paragraph is about a broad overview of Bangalore's history, rather than the history of the cantonment per se.

Option (a) is incorrect as it is more like an introduction to the topic, rather than the concluding line of the paragraph.

Option (d) talks about an issue not touched upon in the given paragraph.

48. d Option (d) is the correct answer as it explains how and why the expectations of foreign firms earning vast amounts of foreign exchange for India, were belied.

Option (c) is incorrect as nowhere does the paragraph mention that a policy 'favoring' foreign capital was adopted by India. It merely mentions that India's policy with respect to foreign investment had been 'revised'. Moreover, the paragraph mentions that the revised policies did not live up to their expectations. This does not imply that the policies caused India's retarded development.

Option (a) is incorrect as, again, the paragraph only talks about the failure of foreign firms in earning forex for India. There is no mention of how this affected the cost of liberalization.

Option (b) is negated as it refers to events beyond those covered in the given paragraph.

PARA-JUMBLES

1. c D. introduces the 'institutional truth of the financial world', B. elaborates the idea, A continues with B. and C. presents the conclusion.

2. c B. introduces the subject of the passage, C. elaborates on the idea, and use of 'then' in A. shows that it should follow D.

3. b A. introduces the age of pragmatism as the topic of the passage, C. explains what has changed in the new age, B. explains the characteristic of the old world and D. comments on the position today.

4. b D. shows that the passage is about cognitive age, B. explains what it implies, A. talks about a research related to the subject and C. explains the implications of the research.

5. c The sentence C. introduces 'her eyes', and should be the first sentence. A. elaborates on the eyes, so A should follow C. No other option has CA as the mandatory pair. So, answer is (c).

6. a B. shows that the topic is 'intelligence', D. uses 'these' to refer to the different abilities associated with intelligence, as presented in B. A. explains what intelligence actually is and C. talks about the true test of intelligence.

7. d The passage is about difference in pronunciation of words in different situations. A. explains what the difference is. Use of 'further' and 'yet' in D. and B. respectively show the order in which they should occur.

8. a D introduces an action of the government, A. explains what it is, C. relates it to another action and B. concludes the passage by stating the consequences of the action.

9. d C starts with 'once upon a time' indicating that this should be the beginning of the passage. B. talks about how C. prompted Indians to stay closer to Soviet Union, D. states how this could be done and A. elaborates on the same.

10. a C introduces an American to the passage, D. states who he was, B. talks about something he said, and A. shows the author's reaction to it.

11. b D introduces the topic of the passage, A. talks about consequences of D. C. elaborates on the idea and refers to an error which is again referred to in B. as 'this error". Therefore B. should follow C.

12. a B states how to evaluate our target for export growth, D. continues with it by using 'even', A. uses D. as a background to compare the current target and C. concludes the passage.

13. b B introduces central programmes as the subject of the passage, C. shows how they grow, D. states that it is difficult to curtail them and A. concludes the passage.

14. d D shows that the passage is about poverty in Indian society, and about the author seeing it in Bombay. C. states the effect it had on the author, B. talks about poverty being in the open and A., by using 'it' for the poverty shows that it should follow B.

15. a D introduces the fact that journalists and teachers are often criticized for speaking out their mind. C. starts by using 'but' and states that unlike journalists and teachers writers are not hampered much. B. continues with the idea, and uses the pronoun 'they' for the writers, showing that it should follow C. and A. concludes the passage.

16. c C. introduces the topic of the passage, A. and D. explain it, B. presents the Economists' view of the whole idea.

17. a A. introduces the view of realists regarding reality, B. refers to 'this reality' and should follow A. C. refers to the realists again by using 'they' and should follow A. and B. D. presents the author's view about the given position.

18. d A. introduces 'changes in demands' as the topic sentence, D. gives some factors leading to the changes, C. elaborates on them and B. shows the effect of some more factors on the same issue.

19. c B. talks about the positive aspect of India's technological front, A. continues with the same, C. introduces the other side of the issue by using 'but' and D. contradicts C. by giving certain examples.

20. a D. introduces the topic of destruction of enemy kingdom by conquerors, C. uses the pronoun 'he' thus should follow D., B. and A. present more methods adopted by the conqueror in destroying the enemy.

21. b C. introduces the idea of various industries offering services through millions of firms, A. states that the individual firms vary in size, D. talks about other variations and B. about the variations in policies etc. within the firms.

22. b C. introduces the idea of making a will, A. gives a reason for doing so, B. and D. exemplify it through an example from author's life.

23. a C. introduces the topic of the passage, A. states how India is doing what C. has warned against. B. compares India's attitude with that of the smaller countries and D. refers to a specific case to prove the point.

24. c C. states a situation, A. contradicts by using 'but', D. states that as the trail continues one feels that one would son see the plain, but B. shows that this hope is not fulfilled.

25. a D. introduces an idea of using something in tricks. C. gives an example of one such trick B. talks of something entertainers would do and D. tells us about something that happened during one such show.

26. d B. introduces the author, D. says that he enjoys his profession, A. and C. continue with it.

27. d C. should precede D. as D. uses 'they' to refer to 'the evils of one's own life' mentioned in C.B. and A. logically follow.

28. a Only C. uses the noun 'the writer', which is referred to as 'he' in all other choices, hence C. should be the first one in the series. Also B should logically follow C. So this makes option (a) correct.

29. b The subject of the sentence has been introduced in A. as 'the masterpiece', so should be the first part of the sentence. A masterpiece cannot be a career, or untaught genius. Only D. can follow A.

30. c C. introduces the central point of the sentence as 'the public being easily disillusioned'. It should be the first part in the series. B., D. and then A. logically follow.

31. b D. introduces the subject as 'the roots of the riots', B. states what the roots are related to, C. gives another point of relation, which has to logically precede A.

32. b D tells us that the passage is about continuation of previous night's discussion. B states what the discussion was about. C adds a point to it by using 'also'. A answers the question raised in C about the reason of conflicts.

33. a B states that the document tells us about history, A states which part of history does it relate to, D elaborates further on the first generation poets by referring to Wordsworth and Coleridge.

34. d C introduces the poet's large plans, A shows how they were replaced by new plans, D states how even these plans remained unfulfilled and B tells us what was the ultimate outcome of the plans.

35. b B states our attitude towards value of time as we advance in life; C refers to the same by using the phrase 'we become miser in this sense'; and D shows how we become misers. A presents the concluding statement.

36. d C relates knowledge to ignorance; B relates our thinking to our knowledge and states that our knowledge is always limited, a fact which leads to D that states that as knowledge is limited, our thinking is also limited. A concludes the passage.

37. c D introduces Sylvestor Stallone as being a successful man, B states the condition of his daughter as a contrast to his career, C states that the condition might correct itself and A states that in spite of the possible cure, how the girl might suffer.

38. c D introduces one of the twelve labours of Hercules, B states the problem involved in the task, A states how the problem could be tackled and C states how Hercules finally accomplished the task.

39. a A makes a statement that is proved by an example in D. B shows the reaction of Jodie Foster to the given fact and C continues with it.

40. a D introduces JP Morgan as one of the largest banking institutes, B states some facts to corroborate it, A tells us about how it makes its business decisions and C states the importance of JP Morgan's proprietary related data.

41. a A states an offer being made by the Saheli programme, C states that it will include all sorts of topics, B further states what the participants will learn, and D states that the tour would also include some sightseeing.

42. d A states that something magical is happening to our planet, C states what it is, B states what it is being called by some people and D states what others are calling it.

43. b B introduces atypical pneumonia as the subject of the passage, D states that it appears like an ordinary flu, A states its symptoms and C states how these symptoms progress to give rise to complications.

44. a B introduces the problem of snakes, C states why there is not enough anti-snake serum, A elaborates on non-availability of the same, and D concludes the passage by stating what the final outcome could be.

45. a B talks about the previous records of mid-term elections, and its implications on the present situation, A presents a contradictory fact, and C states the implications of this fact. D concludes the passage.

46. b A introduces critical elections as the subject of the passage, B explains it, D states that none of the Indian elections so far has been a critical election, instead as C states, there have been many semi-critical ones.

47. a A introduces the subject, B elaborates on it, D states who is the current champion of the game and C states who other contenders are.

48. b A introduces the benefit of good advertising, C states why this benefit is important, B gives an example and D concludes by saying that in spite of this a minimum quality has to be maintained.

49. c B uses the word 'it' that refers to the 'philosophy' in C and so CB is a mandatory pair. Moreover, A 'century ago', C 'for 90 years', and B 'today', makes a chain and D concludes the passage.

50. c B states that RBI has wrested many powers from the government, A states that in spite of this the government has the final say, C elaborates on this fact and D questions this state of affairs.

51. c B introduces the fact that the author was depressed, D gives a reason for the same, C shows the extent of his depression and A concludes the passage.

52. a B introduces the idea of the possibility of stopping the decline in writing skills, C states how this is being done, D talks about a number of programmes being developed for the same and A gives the example of one such programme.

53. b (B) introduces a figure walking slowly, (A) describes it. (D) states that Annete followed the figure with a triumph of recognition, and (C) tells us the name of the figure and states that 'she' followed him.

54. a (C) states that learning is important. (A) states that in contrast today unlearning is the real challenge. (D) followed by (B) states why unlearning is a real challenge.

55. b (B) states that 'we' reached the field soaked. (D) states that Claudius was standing there. (C) states the effect of being wet on Claudius, and (A) elaborates on it.

56. c (A) states that Alex had never been happy with his origins. (C) states what he would rather have been. (B) states what he tries to do to rectify the facts, and (D) shows his wife's reaction to his actions.

57. a (B) states the influence of Indian colours and cuts on Western styles. (A) states that it is seen most on the beaded evening wear. (D) tells us the most popular colours and (C) states how the international fashion scene has been affected by the Indian outfits.

58. b (D) introduces the point of emergence of theocratic states. (B) states how it benefits the politicians. (C) shows how the politicians act and (A) concludes the paragraph.

59. a (C) introduces the subject of the passage. (A) describes him. (B) shows why he was in that place, and (D) describes his mental state.

60. a (A) shows the director walking into the room. (C) tells us that the managers stared at him. (B) states Mitch's reaction, and (D) states what he finally did.

61. d (A) states the influence of Third Reich. (D) elaborates on the events that accompanied the Third Reich. (C) states that while speaking out against Hitler, Americans favoured isolationist policies, and (B) elaborates on such policies.

62. b (A) introduces *Of Studies* as the main idea of the passage. (B) states that the essay requires complete attention of the reader. (C) states Bacon's stand on studies, and (D) continues with the same.

63. b (C) relates logic to reasoning. (A) states what reasoning means. (B) states what logical reasoning covers, and (D) states how we can understand arguments and draw inferences correctly.

64. a (a) ADBC is the correct answer choice. AD is a closely-connected pair. A introduces the shift from functional model in organization theory to a political model and D defines the political model.

'Thus' in B and 'At the extreme' in C carry the discussion on the political model further, and C ends by highlighting that the organization structure develops unrelated to functional requirements, in the extreme case.

(b) CBAD also has the linked pair AD, but the overall flow of thoughts is not logical. Starting with A and ending with C takes us logically from rejection of one model to discussion on another, as in ADBC.

(c) DBCA: Though DBC flows smoothly, A at the end is out of place.

(d) ABDC: B intrudes between A and D as we cannot talk of 'analysis of power resources' in B, unless we have defined the political model in D first.

65. d (d) BDCA is the correct answer choice.

BD is a mandatory pair, as the pronoun 'this' delicate balance in D refers to nature's delicate balance in B. The 'also' in C guides us towards the analogy between institutions and nature, both requiring a system of checks and balances. And A ends by stating that group decision-making is not necessarily the answer because groups can also function like individuals.

(a) CDAB and (c) CABD: The 'also' in C disqualifies it as a contender for the introductory sentence.

(b) BCAD: Though C can also follow B smoothly, D at the end is then totally out of place.

66. b (b) CADB is the correct answer choice.

C makes a good introductory sentence as it introduces Bennis and his predicament . A, B and D all use pronouns: 'he', 'him', 'his' and 'himself', all referring to Bennis.

67. a (a) DCBA is the correct answer choice.

D introduces the intention of the person 'to stage a gastric attack' and the rest explain the sequence of events: D: I ... asked for shampoo mixture ...

C: 'Then' feigns gastric attack and asks for some medicine.

B: uses shop-telephone to inform the Consulate of his location (probably he also informs the Consulate of his gastric attack).

A: 'With that', swallows the shampoo to induce actual gastric attack.

The reason for the author's intention, however, remains unclear.

(b) DACB also correctly starts with D, but A cannot follow D as he cannot swallow the shampoo mixture in A, untill he gets it from the pharmacist in C.

(c) BDAC and (d) BCDA. B can possibly start the paragraph, but A cannot come directly after D.

68. d DB is a mandatory pair as B is an example of what is being stated in D. A — 'likelihood of an accident' follows B — 'accident'. C describes the outcome.

69. a BC is a mandatory pair with 'calculable' and 'only uncontrolled applications (exceptions to B).

70. c (c) EDACB is the correct answer choice.

DA is a mandatory pair, as 'in the early 1990s' in D links chronologically with 'since then' in A links chronologically with 'in the early 1900s' in D. Furthermore, D refers to 'such tests' and, therefore cannot start the paragraph.

CB also emerges as a closely-linked pair. 'In other words' in B summarizes succinctly the idea introduced in C.

Other options do not meet all the above requirements and hence do not flow logically from start to finish.

71. a EC is the mandatory pair, as 'those' in C refers to male children in E. B opens the paragraph as it introduces 'Bellicose spartans'. 'military training' in C is described in D and A.

72. c B opens the paragraph by introducing the motion of 'human being drawing images in cave'. C introduces the new means of image making, i.e. photography. The inventory in D refers to the images in C. 'everything has been photographed' in D should be followed by 'insatiability' in A. 'confinement' in A is then followed by 'enlarge our notions' in E.

73. a AE is a mandatory pair because 'breadth of information' mentioned in E is in reference to 'basic information' in A. 'extending over' in E should be followed by 'confined' in C as a contrast. B follows with 'nor' — the same concept. D gives the 'contrary' view in B.

74. b C introduces the paragraph with the concept of social cost of theft. 'Both parties' in A refer to 'thief and victim' in C. B describes simple property rights. DE describes escalating costs and methods.

75. c Only E can start this paragraph, work it out. AC follows in (a) and (c). B with 'but' is the point of inflexion and D ends the paragraph on an optimistic note.

76. d Between the options, the best options for the opening sentence seem to be A and B. Again the option with B as the first sentence does not flow logically. A-B is a better sequence as it moves from general (universal) to specific (in areas..). This makes choice (d) correct.

77. c B starts the paragraph. C is too abrupt to follow. E links job to ambassador in A. Ambivalence in D is illustrated in C.

78. d Only E can start the paragraph. C continues with the temporal reference and mentions division between 2 parties.

79. b Given B, E cannot start the paragraph. Rather, E follows with the question. D offers an answer to E. C supports with facts. A ends with the discoverers of the fact.

80. c ADB is a clear sequence. So is CE. A has a suitable opening with *A few months ago*. The invitation and the response follow in DB. *she* in E has a clear reference to *One senior* in C.

81. a CA gives the sequence of action. BD follows with reaction. The outcome is in E. CA outlines the consecutive bids. BD gives Mr. Conway's statements. *Moreover* in D adds to B.

82. d C is the best beginning to the paragraph. C spells out the *misnomer*. E makes a statement on *terror* that is justified though B and in D as *Besides*. The humanitarian context of D is given in A.

83. a The "these types are rare" of D should follow B. AC also is mandatory as "these cases" of C is an explanation of A. Also D looks like the logical ending and E the logical beginning. Hence the correct ans. is (a)

84. b CE gives the *problem*. A gives the solution. BD gives the *Dvorak* angle. Pay attention to the openers, *To avoid this* answers the problem. Similarly, D presents a contrast with *Yet*.

85. b AD is clearly a mandatory pair as D talks about the extra enclosures. Also 'this . . ., wall' of E should follow from A, D and C.

86. a ED is a mandatory pair as the 'they' of D are 'the Japanese' off E. Only (a) has ED in that order.

87. d A is the general sentence. ED and B have to come one after another because they represent a sequence.

88. d Option (c) also looks correct but actually option (d) is right because (A) is just an analogy to explain the phenomenal mentioned in sentence (D). Also EC forms a mandatory pair.

89. a D is the general sentence. E and A form a mandatory pair because the 'it' mentioned in sentence A talks about the 'fox hunting' mentioned in sentence E.

90. c It seems as if CB is mandatory. However, looking at it closely reveals that the 'she' of B and the princess of D are two different entities. The monarch and the princess of C are general. The 'she' of B is the princess of A. Therefore, EC and CD and DA are mandatory.

91. c CE is mandatory as can be seen by the 'these . . ., food stuffs' of E. However, this still leaves us with three answer choices. B should follow E as can be seen by the word 'similarly', hence (c) becomes the answer.

92. c Link between BD 'British'-'foreign policy' and then AE from 'overbranding' and 'since then . . . nervous on promoting' and the EC 'but reunification .... think again'.

93. a AC is a mandatory pair and DAC is a mandatory sequence.

94. b B is the opening statement as it introduces the subject and the date. EDA is a sequence that describes the situation from the east to the west. Statement C is a stand-alone statement.

95. d CDBA is a mandatory sequence. "Bush was not fighting just the democrats" in statement D, relates directly with "At times he was fighting..." in statement B.

96. c Both statements C and B (papyri is the plural for Egyptian papers and documents) are talking about sources of information, making CB a mandatory pair.

97. a ED is a mandatory pair as 'the fuel cell efficiency has an efficiency of 30%' in E connects with 'That is twice as good' in D. BA is a pair because 'the way will be open for a huge reduction…' in B connects with 'only such a full-hearted leap will allow the world to cope with mass motorization' in A.

98. b DC is the mandatory pair, which makes (c) and (d) incorrect. E is the opening statement. A concludes the argument by substantiating the argument in EBCD. Therefore, the analogy from the previous argument is being extended in 'A' (keyword – "similarly")

99. d From the options, it can be ascertained that 'B' is the opening statement. Also, B explains "greater interest… than", hence 'C' is the natural antecedent to 'B', wherein "a similar neglect" has been talked, about. Hence (d) is the correct option.

100. b After reading statement B the first question that comes to mind is what does 'it' stand for. The question is answered by statement (E) which should be the logical antecedent. This makes EB a mandatory pair and that is present only in option (b).

101. d ECBD

EC is a mandatory pair which is linked by 'crime'. This pair is contained in options (b) and (d). D cannot follow A as 'particular piece of work' is mentioned in B. Thus D should follow B.

102. a EDBC

E must follow A as it talks about the third discourse. BC is a mandatory pair as C continues the thought that there is a need for greater expert management.

103. e BCDE

B and C explain the positive developments after 'the fall of President Soeharto and the close of his centralized, ……… In 1997'. DE is a mandatory pair as D speaks about the opinion of analysts and E speaks about another group of analysts.

104. c CBED

A talk about squatters' land. C describes who the squatters were. B follows C as it gives the description of squatters' land.

E carries on the idea of what happens in the squatters' land (ripening, gathering, thrashing, collecting etc.) and finally D gives additional information about what is grown in these fields which is indicated by the word 'also'.

105. c Out of the options for first sentence E/A, E seems better. Then, E–A forms a mandatory pair as it moves from the general "India" to specific "regional variations".

D–B' is the second mandatory pair with "office" being mentioned in D and then B starting with "office".

This makes choice (c) correct.

106. a Between D and F, you are more likely to choose D as the opening sentence as it is a question, but if D comes first, sentence F would be general and will take the sequence of information back. Therefore, choose F as the opening sentence. F–D seems better than F–C. Also B–A–C is a mandatory sequence as they are all comparing the scenario between different contexts. This makes choice (a) correct.

107. c The reason why the demand for branded diapers may be price-sensitive is given in A. This is supported by DB. C contrasts, supported by the example in E. F can be linked with private-labels.

108. a (c) is a haphazard choice with no definite beginning, middle or end. Discipline goes better with strong focus as in AC. E further elaborates. DBF talks about making strategy foolproof through the value chain.

109. d B shows the problem faced by a researcher, D. elaborates why this happens, A continues with it and C., by using 'however' introduces the way out of the problem.

110. c D starts with 'but' and states why use of electricity in industries poses problems. A. continues with the idea and the word 'also' shows that it should follow D. B. presents an alternate to the costly options by using ' in contrast', C. states another reason to avoid using mineral resources for generating electricity and leads to 6.

111. c The user of word 'rather' in B. indicates that it should follow 1. D. states that the competition depends on five basic competitive forces, A. continues with the same idea. C. states that not all industries have the same potential an this is elaborated in 6.

112. b B supports the fact presented in 1., A. gives reasons for the argument. D. talks about how science affects war and C. states its overall result, leading to the conclusion in 6.

113. d. D talks about a lovely scenery in a countryside, which was introduced in 1. C. talks about other positive points of a countryside, B. uses 'but' to state that there are negative points too, A. elaborates on the idea and leads to 6.

114. d D introduces communism as a kind of a welfare state introduced in 1. A. presents the other side of communism, B. elaborates on the idea, and C. leads to the conclusion stated in 6.

115. b B states how we start knowing a man, C. talks about growing acquaintance, A. about it leading to intimacy and D leads to the conclusion as presented in 6.

116. d B. starts at the beginning of Indian industrialization, A. elaborates on it, C. talks about the scenario today, D. states a common element between the beginning and today. The word 'However' in D makes it the conclusive statement AC is mandatory pair. Thus option D (BACD) is the best option.

117. c The correct sequence is ABCD. The question in (1) is answered by A. B follows A by talking about how the state spies upon the taxpayers. C follows B and likens the state's possible behavior to what the tax authority tries to do inconsistently. D talks about an Orwellian System (a despotic form of government described in Orwell's novel 1984) thereby linking it to sentence 6.

118. a C. makes a comparison between competition and justice. D. states what the choice is 'not between', and B. by using 'rather' shows that it should follow D. A continues with the idea and leads to 6. Also DB is a mandatory pair and hence, we are left with only one option i.e. A.

119. a A. uses 'thus' to show the effect of the disparities in Yugoslavia mentioned in B. and C. It should thus follow the two. D. uses the phrase 'will also'..., thus showing that it should follow A.

120. b The use of 'these measures' in A. refers to the measures stated in 1., so it should be the first sentence in the series. B talks about the objectives of these measures and C. and D. elaborate on the idea.

121. a D. introduces the problem related to petroleum products, A. presents statistics to support it. B. talks about electricity, an idea which is continued in 6., so B. should be the last sentence in the series.

122. b A. starts at the beginning of the last 45 years, B. states how external powers tried to control the region, D. continues with the idea. C. talks about supply of arms to Pakistan, an idea that is continued in 6.

123. c C. states a cause for the problem introduced in 1. B. starts with 'added to this', showing that it should follow C. A. introduces a way out of the situation and 6. analyses the solution. Therefore A. should precede 6.

124. c A. introduces us to Rumford's experiments, D. tells us about his observations. C. introduces the term 'caloric', B. explains the term.

125. d C. introduces a controversy regarding 'recognition', A. states an aspect of that controversy, B. talks about what happens when an object is encountered and D. talks about what happens when the same object is countered again. BD is a mandatory pair and D has to be the sentence that makes a pair with sentence 6.

126. a D. continues with the idea introduced in 1. C. states an explanation about the phenomenon, B. refers to this explanation and A. states how it was substantiated. Also A will be the last sentence as it forms a mandatory pair with sentence 6.

127. a There are two mandatory pairs in the questions. BD and A6. B. talks about the beginning of evolution changes, D. about adaptations, C. about further improvements as well as about extinctions, and A. about the approach towards modern lines.

128. c A. states that what has been predicted annually, according to 1. has not happened. B., and then D., talk about events that led to such a prediction. The use of 'then' in D. shows that it should follow B. C. makes a statement that is analysed in 6.

129. c C. should be the first sentence as it states that the logic presented in 1. is not true. A. and D. talk about the qualities of a good actor. B. talks about the author's own plays and 6. continues with his observation in B.

130. b C. introduces the idea that some comedies have survived over many years. B. gives a reason for it and A. continues with the reason.

131. a B. introduces 'an ally of the wind', hinted at in 1. C. states that the author did not hear it and A. gives the reason for it.

132. c D. talks about the 'power' introduced in 1. A. states that if 'it is an anchor in difficulties it should be remembered in good times too'. C. states the work done by some organizations and B. adds to it.

133. d A. suggests that seniors should help in showing the path. B. continues by referring to 'the seniors' mentioned in A. C. and D. state how one should accept the help provided by seniors.

134. d C states India's position on exchange rate; A states why India's position is not surprising; B continues with the idea; D gives examples of exceptions to B.

135. d D talks about the 'power' introduced in 1. A states that if 'it is an anchor in difficulties, it should be remembered in good times too'. C states the work done by some organizations and B adds to it.

136. b B states what happens in the absence of punishment; A talks about the effect of such a situation; C adds to it by using 'also' and D states what can be done instead.

137. c C continues with the fact that the vessel was moving away; A states that he looked around; D states that it was of no use; B explains why there was no use of looking around.

138. d A continues with the idea introduced in 1. C states that the leader should be personally seen; D states what else should be insisted upon. B talks of allocating work to members in clear terms, and this should precede 6, which states how this has to be done.

139. d A states that true friends are very rare; C states that as they are rare, they should be respected; B states some factors which should not be considered while making friends; and D states that in business realities, all the acquaintances are motivated by self interest and thus cannot be treated as genuine friends.

140. a 1 states what managers should guard against; D states how one can do so; C continues by using 'also'. A states that external appearances can be deceptive; B elaborates on the fact and leads to 6.

141. b A states how demands for resources are made; C states what is done to offset adverse effects of cuts imposed by seniors; B states the importance of availability of adequate resources; and D re-emphasizes the point made in B.

142. d B continues with the idea introduced in 1. A relates the idea to managers in an organization, who have to take ruthless decisions; D states how these decisions can be made easier to accept. C talks about delegation of power, an idea that is continued in 6.

143. b C states how the first two categories mentioned in 1 should be dealt with, D talks about the last category; A continues by referring to 'the persons in this category'. B states how the wicked must be dealt with and leads to 6.

144. a Starts with telling how women handle pain better than men. Given example of child birth in A followed by consequences in B, D states that men in authors' life do not take painkillers, C tells about their complaining.

145. a D States the position now, as opposed to a 'few years ago' mentioned in 1. B makes a comparison with a similar situation which A continues with. C asks a question that is answered by 6.

146. a A talks about where the wedding took place, C states who all attended marriage, D tells us about the bride and B states that little is known about her, a fact that is continued in 6.

147. b D states that in addition to being unlucky in love, Liz Taylor is unlucky in law too. C states the reason for that observation, A states the consequences of C and B states what the lawsuit was about.

148. c A tells us who Chambers was, D states why he had appeared before the Committee, C states Hiss' reaction to charges against him. B states that Nixon arranged a meeting between the two, and 6 continues with what happened at the meeting.

149. a A gives some names of the guitar heroes, C adds to the list, B states why these musicians were popular and D states why their popularity came down.

150. a A states that though oceans are the cradles of life, waste is dumped into them, C talks about the results of the same, B continues with it and D concludes that man has caused these problems.

151. a D tries to answer the question raised in 1, B simplifies the statement made in D, C further simplifies it and A talks about the position of ordinary citizens regarding the issue, which is continued in 6.

152. c B answers the question raised in 1, D gives a reason for the stand taken by the analysts regarding the new machine, C highlights that a desktop computer can come just for $2,000 in America, and A states a disadvantage of these computers.

153. b B states Clarke's determination to make stained glass more popular, A states his success in the mission, D talks about his two projects and C elaborates on the first project while 6 talks about the second.

154. b C gives some examples to support 1. B introduces the era of computers as another example, A talks about the increasing technical terms, D introduces the idea of slangs, which is continued in 6.

155. c 6 speaks of a study of IIT undergraduates' mindset. C speaks of culture developed by IIT students. Therefore, C6 is mandatory. D speaks of success stories of IIT graduates and therefore follows A.

156. d A talks about the taste of the Maharaja of Kapurthala, B introduces another Maharaja with an exquisite taste, D introduces something in contrast to this, C continues with the idea which is exemplified in 6.

157. d A shows how 'his' gifts were unveiled, B states the effect it had on McLaughlin, D states his reaction to the same and C states the ultimate outcome.

158. a C states why India is on the brink of a major public health disaster, A states what happens if TB is untreated for 5 years, D presents some statistics to highlight the point, B states how the disease spreads and 6 continues with the fact.

159. b After 1, (C) states a fact about salvation. (B) states the Christian belief in that regard. (A) opposes it to Buddhism, by using 'but'. (D) elaborates the fact.

160. d After the factors stated in 1, (A) states the relationship between size of a state and development. (B) states that the problems of agricultural sector will remain with us in the next century. (C) emphasizes the need to improve agriculture. (D) states that rural India has to start moving, an idea that is continued in (6).

161. b (B) shows the relationship between a magazine and its editor, 'editors' are referred to as 'they'. (C) states that the number of editors should be determined by the contributions it gets. (D) continues with this fact. (A) follows by using 'furthermore'.

162. c (B) follows (1) by using 'especially'. (D) explains the 'NRI phase'. (A) states that the East and the West meet in the NRIs. (C) states a fact that has been overlooked, and (6) tells us that the festival of feature films and documentaries is trying to fill this gap.

163. c (C) gives a reason for a market for Indian art coming into being. (B) states what simultaneously happened in India. (A) states what happened as a fallout of the festivals of India. (D) elaborates on it and leads to (6).

164. c (c) BADC is the correct answer choice.

B connects up well with 1 to introduce the topic: 'Use of Humour in Advertising'. There are 'two grounds' why an ad can be ineffective. 'At times' in A and 'Again' in D guide the reader to the "two grounds." B–A–D are, hence, logically connected. 1-B is a good pair because 'making people laugh' is qualified further in B.

165. b (b) DBAC is the correct answer choice.

1. places focus on a "mud hump" and D describes "the hump is alive ...". Hence, 1D is a mandatory pair.

BA is another mandatory pair. B talks about 'the proportion of soldiers to workers' and A talks about 'unsettling the balance'.

A–C–6 are also connected. C talks about 'restoring of fortunes' by the 'queen termite laying eggs on a as-required basis' to make up the losses. And 6 wonders at this 'mysterious ability' of the queen termite.

166. d (d) BDCA is the correct answer choice.

'these years' in B connects to 'three to five years' in 1. Then 'this correlation' in D connects to what is elaborated in B.

C then talks about 'the reason' for this correlation, which is elaborated in A: 'a large vocabulary and a sense of grammar and sentence structure,' and is summed up in 6 as: "comprehension of language is high.

Hence, we get 1–BDCA–6.

167. a (a) DACB is the correct answer choice.

1 introduces the topic: 'High-powered outboard motors (OBM) ... threats to ... Beluga whales'. D takes us back to the low-powered 'first OBMs' ... in the early 1930s'. 'With these' in A refers to the first OBMs' in D and not to 'high powered OBMs' in 1, as the context makes clear later. Hence, A follows D rather than 1. This rules out option (b) and (c). C brings us back to the present, contrasting ('however') the ineffectiveness of 'much more powerful engines' of today with the effectiveness of 'the first OBMs' of the early 1930s. B and 6 then explain the reason for the ineffectiveness of today's high-powered OBMs: the 'avoidance strategy' of the Beluga whales.

Hence, 1 – DACB – 6 flows logically as explained above.

168. a (a) BADC is the correct answer choice.

The paragraph is trying to say that science textbooks and other scientific writings do not present the advance of science in the correct historical perspective and thereby present science as 'a series of individual discoveries and inventions ... (6)'.

'Those misconstructions' in B connects it with 1, leading to BADC as the correct answer choice. B is followed by A, which tells us why science textbooks are arranged as they are and D praises 'this technique of presentation' as 'unexceptionable as pedagogy.' 'But' in C contrasts with D and guides the reader to the incorrect 'impression that is likely to follow.' This impression is elaborated in 6.

169. b B has to follow 1 as it exemplifies the principle mentioned in 1. A continues the explanation of what happens when light bounces off 2 surfaces. D explains further and C6 gives the result.

170. d B follows 1 as low light conditions are same as darkened conditions. DCA discuss the experiment and 6 the happy result.

171. a D follows 1 as 'this' in D is in reference to nation state concept in 1. B follows D by explaining why that concept is being criticized. A continues with other reasons and C makes a further addition with "Even worse....". (C-6) also forms a mandatory pair, thereby making choice (a) correct.

172. c C follows 1 as a logical continuation, the questionable — suspicion link A logically follows C by comparing position in humanities. B and D give reasons for distortions in humanities. (D-6) is a mandatory pair since 'D — mentions "Can be defended" and 6 mentions ...."... no such defences". This makes choice (c) correct.

173. c A gives the reason why communists despised horses in 1. What they preferred instead is given in B. C makes allowances and D6 presents the alternate view.

174. a (D-A) would be a mandatory pair here as they connect the ideas of soothsayers and shrines. Similarly (E-D) fit together as they both convey the idea of a filthy place. The only option where we find this combination is option (a).

175. b (B-D) is a mandatory pair as "the life cycle" in B is referred to as "this trajectory" in D. Similarly, (C-E) should come together as they discuss the idea of when this framework ceases to function in the absence of men. Statement A then follows as a conclusion.

176. c The sequence should start with sentence C as it introduces a topic – the repercussions of the art-market boom. C is followed by E (as there is a reference in the plural) and both sentences are linked with the reference to museums. E also is an elaboration of the point being made in sentence C. D and A are clearly linked through the reference to the annual booklet. B comes in as the ending sentence as it mentions the consequence of the weakening in the buying power of museums. The correct sequence is CEDAB, option (c).

177. c DE and BC must surely go together for the movie references. If DE goes together then B ('this question') must follow E. And A would follow C as it sums up the discussion. So, (c) is the answer.

178. d DC must go together and it must begin the paragraph. The paragraph cannot begin with A or B. At the same time, B must follow C as 'these tales' in B refer to 'shown as' in C.
So, the answer is (d).

179. c Though B can follow C, D has to follow C or it cannot be fitted in anywhere else. B 'the loot in question' must follow D. So, the answer has to be (c).

180. d The paragraph follows a general to specific format. Starting with general statements on the Queen's coronation to bringing in more specific details - as those given in statement C. BAD is a mandatory sequence wherein sentence B states that conferring of state headship is an exclusive Anglican ritual; sentence A states what happens in the ritual – act of anointment by a priest – and sentence D states how the ritual ends – succession is sanctioned and is followed by a sort of applause by the people who have gathered there.

181. a CAB forms a logical sequence. Statement C mentions the fact that conventional wisdom (accepted norms) have been turned over. Statement A introduces an example of this – how Japanese food should logically not be accepted in the fish-hating North Indian markets. Statement B presents a contrast by stating that though Sushi is a Japanese item, it is all the rage among North Indians. It also gives the reason why conventional logic has not played out with reference to the acceptance of Japanese restaurants in North India. Options (b) and (d) can be ruled out as they do not contain this mandatory sequence. Statement D should follow CAB as it provides an example that is similar to the one in CAB. Also, statement E should either start or end the sequence as it is a general statement, while all the other statements refer to specific examples. Hence, option (c) can be ruled out and option (a) is the answer.

182. c Options (d), (b) and (a) form a sequence as they talk about the core catcher, its structure and its functionality, respectively. Option (d) introduces the core catcher. Option (b) provides further details on its structure while option (a) explains how the core catcher functions in the eventuality of an accident. These options thus form a mandatory sequence. Option (c), though related, does not fit this sequence as it talks about the background of the core catcher's design and mentions bricks' composition which is a wider concern.

183. a Options (c) and (b) are a mandatory pair as the deep intertwining between modernity and nostalgia is summed up and explained in option (b). Similarly, options (b) and (d) are also a mandatory pair and 'that hunger' mentioned in option (d) refers to the harking back of the human mind to 'a supposedly simpler time' in the past 'when life was more peaceful'. This sequence therefore deals with nostalgia and how such a sense of nostalgia finds expression in the artist's work. Option (a), though on seemingly related lines, actually talks about the reaction of observers of the artist's work rather than how the work evokes such a reaction and therefore it does not fit into the sequence.

184. a Sentence B talks about the other career of a person; sentence D talks about what direction that has taken and sentence C mentions her latest book. Sentence E talks about how it has been inspired by an instance in her life and sentence A goes on to describe that instance. This makes option (a) the correct answer.

185. a AC is a mandatory pair as both these sentences discuss the importance of knowledge workers in the face of global competition. E, B and D are connected to each other as they discuss means of keeping workers happy. Thus, option (a) is the correct answer.

186. d BD is a mandatory pair. Sentence B mentions that many would be disappointed. Sentence D mentions the reason for this disappointment; sentence E then goes on to mention aspects of his early life and sentence A further adds to this. Sentence C ends the sequence with a comment about his relationship with his friends. This makes option (d) the correct answer.

187. c The coherent sequence is bda. Statement b begins the discussion about filming of videos by drones around the world and d talks about one such video recorded on a safari in the Serengeti. Statement a should follow d because it carries forward the idea of the video recorded on the safari by giving details of what the video contains. Option (c) is the odd sentence because it talks about waves and surfers, which have nothing to do with the safari. Thus, option (c) is the correct answer.

188. b The coherent sequence is dca. Statement d criticizes England's trickeries and amateurishness in the final session. Statement c carries forward this idea by giving an example and questioning the practice in English public schools. Statement a should follow c as it states the consequence of the situation mentioned in c. Only option (b) contrasts England's and Australia's spirit of cricket and hence, is the odd sentence. Thus, option (b) is the correct answer.

189. b The coherent sequence is cad. Sentence c states that the US dishes out military aid to Mexico without bothering about how it is used and a further elaborates on this. Statement d discusses the possibility of the aid (mentioned in a) being spent on extrajudicial executions. Only option (b) discusses that America should look at alternatives to a military response. Thus, option (b) is the correct answer.

190. d The correct sequence is (abce). The paragraph talks about poets. Sentence (d) talks about the origin of poetry. Hence, it is the odd one out. It is too general in context too.

191. (c) The correct sequence is (abde). (b) and (b) make a mandatory pair (The pronoun "Its" in (d) refers to "the novel" in (b)). (a) best introduces the paragraph as it mentions the name of the novel under discussion (*Ulysses*). (e) follows (d) as it mentions the word "here" which makes it contextually appropriate. The entire paragraph refers to a novel by James Joyce. Sentence (c) is the odd one out. It is a conclusion about Joyce which is too broad. There is no precedent to justify the usage of "after all" in the sentence.

192. (d)The correct sequence is (abce) as they form a mandatory sequence. Sentence (d) talks about Red dwarfs. The entire paragraph talks about one specific planet. Hence, (d) doesn't fit the paragraph.

193. (eadbc)

(e) mentions the full name of the sportsperson. Hence, it will be the opening sentence. (db) make a mandatory pair. The word "too" in (b) adds to the idea mentioned in (d). (a) will come before (d) because it mentions the situation (being abandoned by Per Mertesacker) which leads to (d). (c) is the concluding statement.

194. (eabcd)

(ea) make a mandatory pair (One-another). (b) mentions the word "elsewhere". Thus, it continues the idea of plot setting. (c) and (d) can come after (b). (d) is the concluding statement ("most stories").

195. (dcbae)

(d) begins the paragraph by introducing the subject: bacteria. (c) follows (d) since it talks about the principle kinds of bacteria. (cb) is a mandatory pair. (c) introduces cyanobacteria and (b) gives general information about it. (a) follows by giving general information. The presence of the word 'however' in (a) suggests that (a) cannot begin the paragraph, it will only come at a later point. (e) follows (a). 'that interval' in (e) refers to the 'gap' mentioned in (a).

196. (abecd)

ab make a mandatory pair (anorexic young woman – young lady). (e) continues the explanation for why the young girl is breaking Olive's heart. (c) is the young girl's response to Olive. (d) will, thus, be the last sentence logically.

197. Sentence (c) introduces the topic. (ce) make a mandatory pair as the word "however" in (e) contradicts the theme of sentence (c). (a) follows next as it explains the latest findings of the scholars which is mentioned in (e). (d) gives an example of (a). (b) is the final sentence as it gives the author's opinion.

198. (e) introduces the paragraph and hence, can be the topic sentence. (b) will come next as the word "but" suggests a slight change in the theme. (b) changes the theme mentioned in (e). (ea) make a mandatory pair as the pronoun "it says" in (a) refers to the theory or study mentioned in (e). (c) will come next as England is the researcher who has been mentioned in (b) and (a). (d) will come next as Paul Rosenberg reviews the theory mentioned in the previous sentences.

199. Sentence (c) introduces the topic under discussion i.e. Rationalism and beauty. (e) takes the idea forward by providing the historical backdrop. (eb) make a mandatory pair as the pronoun "this" in (b) has been defined in (e). (ba) also make a mandatory pair as the phrase "any such theory" in (a) has been defined in (b). (d) explains the ideas mentioned in (a). Hence (ad) also make a mandatory pair.

200. (d) introduces the concept of Nash equilibrium and also its relation with the Greece and Europe stand-off. (db) make a mandatory pair as (b) has a pronoun "this" which has been explained in (d). (a) takes the idea forward as is evident by the phrase "can also help us". (e) will come after (a) as it talks about the "game" which has been mentioned in the previous sentences. (c) is the last sentence as it raises a question. This question will be answered in the subsequent paragraphs.

201. (b) is the opening sentence of the paragraph which introduces the topic 'The stories we tell reflect the world around us'. follows (b), which further justifies the above mentioned statement. It is followed by (c) which tells us that we often retell the stories which we value. and (a) form a mandatory pair justifying sentence (c).

202. The paragraph begins with sentence (e) talking about the goodness of lightning. It is followed by (c) which discusses the useful nature of lightning, helping Nitrogen to react. It is further followed by (d) which in continuation with (c) introduces the need of Nitrogen for plants. and (a) form a mandatory pair as they go on discussing the process by which Nitrogen reacts and help the plants.

203. Sentence (b) introduces the topic defining the placebo effect. It is sequentially followed by (e) which showcases the study of this effect. and (c) form a mandatory pair discussing in details how this placebo effect works. The paragraph ends with (a) which showcases the implications this placebo effect has in the health care system.

204. This is an impossible to attempt question. Due to lack of any key words in the sentences, one can come to multiple possible arrangements. Hence, one should have left this question. Only (c) and (e) make a mandatory pair. As (e) is the explanation of (c).

205. The arrangement given as the answer by CAT makes no sense. Sentence 1 is clearly the opening sentence. However, 3 after sentence 1 is too abrupt. There is no 'linking word or phrase'. 1324 is the official answer. 1432 also looks like a possible sequence. This question seems incorrect.

206. Sentence 4 opens the paragraph with the full name, Cathy Perkins. 'The viola player' in sentence 2 refers to 'Cathy Perkins'. So, 42 is a mandatory pair. 1 and 3 come in sequence because of 'then' in 3 which creates a chronological sequence with 1. So, 4213 is the correct order.

207. The clue is 'but' in sentence 1. It contradicts sentences 2 and 4. 2 is broader in scope. So, 24 is a better pair. 3 ('these people') refers to sentence 1. So, 2413 is the correct order.

208. Sentence 1 clearly opens the paragraph as it introduces the canopy of the woodlands. 14 is a pair (sunlight-sunshine). 2 is a better conclusion as it introduces a new insight into the dietary habits of the swifts. 3 comes after 4. 'Their' in 3 refers to the swifts in 4. So, 1432 is the correct order. However, 1423 is also close.

209. Option (c) will be the starting statement as it introduces the concept of " phoenixing", followed by option (d), which talks more about it. Option (a), it was his taxpayers....refers to the Australian economy, mentioned in (d) option.

210. Option (b) is the introductory sentence followed by option (d) which has the related information based upon option (b), making a mandatory pair. Option (a) talks about the problem related to (b) and (d) options, consequently option (c) being the closing sentence.

211. Option (c) is the introductory sentence as other options have used pronouns in relation with option (c). Next likely to be followed sentence would option (b) because of the pronoun used "they" in option (b) which refers to the business elite and the similarity of logic used in option (c) is stated in option (b), like the dieter who would.....they would fund a million of the buzzwordy....Similarly option (d) should be 3rd sentence as it has the resemblance of option (b), keeping option (a) as the last sentence where "they" is again used for business elite.

212. Option (a) cannot be the introductory sentence as "thus" is used which indicates the fact that there is something more talked about, similarly options (c) and (d). Thus, introductory sentence should be option (a). Option (c) talks about the control means which has a reference in introductory sentence, therefore being the (b) sentence, consequently followed by option (a) and then option (d) being the last.

FACTS, INFERENCES, JUDGEMENTS

1. c C and D both present facts and no other choice gives that as an option.
2. a A presents a judgement on part of the author, B and C present facts and D presents a logical conclusion based on the facts.
3. a B presents a fact and no other choice gives that as an option C Presents an inference based on a logical conclusion of the fact that the revenues are already dwindling.
4. b We can see that B presents a fact and D presents an inference.
5. d A and C clearly present facts. B is an opinion of the author based on common sense. D presents an inference.
6. c A is based on common sense. B is a well known fact. C is a logical conclusion based on B.
7. a B is a well known fact which logically leads to the inference drawn in C. Other two are opinions of the author and hence judgements.
8. b B and D clearly present facts. C presents an inference based on these facts.
9. c A and D present facts, B presents a logical conclusion based on these facts and C presents a judgement on part of the author.
10. d A is not a fact as it uses the phrase 'it appears'. C and D clearly present facts.
11. c Statement C is a fact because it is open to discovery or verification. This eliminates option (b). The words "has to be...." make statement D a judgement as it expresses a personal viewpoint. This eliminates options (d) & (e). As "... statistical indications..." have been referred to in statement A, it is definitely an inference. This is because it is a conclusion about the unknown which is based on the known. The second statement is a judgement because this statement is open to debate. Therefore option (c) is the correct answer.
12. e Statement C is a judgement because it expresses a personal viewpoint regarding the consequences of red tape. This eliminates option (a). Statement B is a fact because the latter half of the sentence is given by way of an example and not by way of a conclusion. This eliminates option (c). Statement A describes what "we should...." do. This statement explains the speaker's disapproval regarding the consequences of red tape. Therefore, it is a judgement. This eliminates option (d). Statement D is an inference. It is known to us that a red tape procedure is a point of contact with an official. That this point of contact offers a potential opportunity is a conclusion based on this information. This makes option (e) correct.
13. d Statement A is a judgement as it is based on the author's opinion. This eliminates option (a) & (b). Statement B uses the general term "we ". This makes it a judgement. If it had been about "I" or "us" then it would have been a fact. Statements C and D are personal opinions. Hence, the correct answer is option (d).
14. b Looking at the A statement, if you mark the keywords 'is certainly' then it gives us a clear idea that it is a point of view expressed by the author. Therefore, it is a judgement. The B statement is an inference as it arrives at a conclusion from a stated premise. The C statement, where the author mentions 'is the only insurance' (although there may be other insurances, that the author negates) qualifies it as a judgement. The D statement is a pure fact. So, option (b) is correct.
15. a Statement A is a judgement because it expresses an approval/disapproval. It is a subjective opinion-an advice given to HIV affected patients. So, options (c) & (d) can be eliminated. Statement B is clearly factual. This eliminates option (b). Statement C is a conclusion about the future scenario which is based on the "recent initiatives". Hence, this statement is an inference. In statement D, "But how ironic ..." shows the author's disapproval. So statement D is a judgement. Thus, option (a) is the correct answer.
16. a All the other options are mentioned in the passage but option (a) is true of the Arms Act of 1878 and not the amendment.
17. b Refer to the lines *"It is no surprise that most gun lobbyists are representatives of feudal and other parasitical social classes, despite their attempt to speak in the name of the "citizen".*
18. d Refer to the lines *"The post-colonial law laid down strict rules for gun ownership, reducing the number of firearms which could be owned by one person but made it uniform for all citizens."* Options (b) and (c) are mentioned but they do nothing for the perceived bias. Option (d) effectively eliminates the bias by making the laws uniform for all citizens.

Option (a) cannot be inferred from the passage. We do not know if all citizens have the **right** to possess guns.

19. a Option (b) is incorrect as the passage does not describe all the aspects of gun possession laws. Option (c) is also incorrect. Although the author does argue in favour of measures that would curtail illegal possession of guns, it is not the main idea. Option (d) is not appropriate as the author does not actively endorse the amendments rather he/she opposes people or arguments against the amendments.

20. c The passage ends with a specific instance of teachers in Rajasthan. Option (c) is the only one that continues with this idea. All the other options bring in new ideas or conclusions.

21. c Option (a) is only one of the ways in which aesthetic perception has been understood by the author. Option (b) can be eliminated, as the passage does not mention the power of aesthetic perception. Option (d) again talks about only one of the two main alternatives. Option (c) is the correct choice as the passage is about the alternative paths/modes/theories of aesthetic perception.

22. b Option (a) is encompassed by the aesthetics of illusion in paragraph 4. Option (c) is talked about in paragraph 3 as part of the aesthetics of being. Refer to the lines *"Both variations of an aesthetics of being do, however, assume that general structures of reality can be recognized in or by means of aesthetic perception."* But option (b) is not talked about in the passage. No alternative leads to the being disclosing the characteristics of illusion. Hence option (b) is correct.

23. d Option (a) can be inferred from the lines in the last paragraph. *"According to this fixation, aesthetic consciousness paves the way either to a higher reality or out of the lower reaches of reality or it goes both ways simultaneously."* Option (b) is explicit in the last lines of paragraph 3. Option (c) is referred to in paragraph 5 among the examples of aesthetic perception "Bloch's aesthetics of anticipating [Vorschein] a better society in the future." All the examples are variations of aesthetic perception. Option (d) is correct as we cannot infer the being to be illusionary in character, but we can infer that there is an illusion which can reveal characteristics of a higher being.

24. c All the other options are supported by the passage. Option (a) is mentioned in the second paragraph. Refer to the lines *"Instead, the famously reticent painter....".* Option (b) can be inferred from these lines in the second paragraph *"He was surprised when the answer was yes, and that Freud wanted to get cracking right away."* Option (d) can be inferred from the third paragraph *"When he paints, Freud talks, and he likes to go to a restaurant with the sitter after each session to carry on talking".* Option (c) is actually a statement about Gayford. *"Gayford downplays his own, but actually it is his craft as a storyteller that turns…"*

25. d All the other options are incorrect according to the passage. Option (a) is incorrect as it is a statement about Gayford. Refer to these lines in the second last paragraph *"He is unpretentious and natural, and above all wants to capture Freud as a person".* Option (b) also cannot be inferred as the passage only mentions that quotes from Freud steal the show, we cannot infer that this happens to the detriment of Gayford's writing. Option (c) is also incorrect as the passage clearly mentions – *"But this book is not just for Freud fans, or a sombre intellectual document for art students."*

26. d The focus of the article is not on Lucien Freud or Martin Gayford, rather it is on how they collaborated for the book 'Man with a blue scarf'. At the same time the passage is not a book review as it does not really evaluate the book. It works more as a piece of writing that describes the book and how it was written.

27. d Throughout the passage the author has argued that the banks and the financial sector had an important role in causing the Great Recession. Bernie Madoff is guilty but he is hardly the only person who deserves to go to prison. Refer to the lines *"Just because Madoff is a crook sitting in jail does not mean he isn't right when he tells us to look elsewhere, too."* Option (a) cannot be the answer as it cannot be the insight given by Madoff. Also, option (a) is contradictory to the author's opinion- *"It is the classic "one bad apple" defence of the kind banks and Wall Street specialise in. It is not the system's or the bosses' fault, they say, it is just a few rogue operators and they have been dealt with...".* Option (b) states that the recession was caused by the failure of banking organizations , which is incorrect. The option does not state what exactly this failure was. Option (c) is not the answer as the author merely mentions the venality of the finance industry. He/She does not attribute the Recession to it.

28. b The answer can be inferred from the lines *"Madoff and his scheme have become a useful foil for the entire finance industry... … It's Madoff who spurs public outrage and whose jailing has satiated a quest for justice".* The author says that it is Madoff who is ultimately cast as the villain and the cause of the recession by the entire finance industry.

Option (b) comes closest to expressing this. Option (a) is incorrect as it does not specifically discuss discusses the role of banking industry in causing recession .

29. b The central idea of the passage is how Bernie Madoff is not the only person responsible for the recession. The author argues that we need to consider the role of the entire financial sector also. Hence, option (b) works best. Options (a) is contradictory to the ideas presented in the passage. Option (d) is incorrect as the author does not discuss 'how' the financial sector contributed to the Recession. He/she only states that it played a part.Option (c) is incorrect as it stresses how Madoff was responsible for the recession .

30. d None of the statements can be inferred from the passage. (I) cannot be inferred; refer to the lines *"While Sinn Fein's black balloons, the largely deserted streets and the heavy security presence reminded that history could not be too easily wished away".* They seem to suggest that there is still some tension between the two countries. (II) can be inferred from the passage. (III) also cannot be inferred as the author writes, *"The exaggerated: her green cloak to go with the Emerald Isle"* The author says that looking for symbolism in the queen's choice of a cloak is an exaggeration.

31. a Option (a) best expresses how Britain and Ireland are trying to make things right. We cannot assume that everything has been resolved because there is evidence in the passage against this. Therefore, option (d) can be eliminated. Options (b) and (c) (*shared misfortune* and *tragic past*) are too broad in scope and can be construed to mean anything.

32. c The major part of the passage discusses Orwell's essay on Dickens. Option (d) is inappropriate because Orwell's opinion of Dickens is discussed only in the context of the essay that he (Orwell) wrote. This essay has been used as an example to illustrate author's view. Throughout the passage author has tried to show why, despite criticism, Dickens' writings have had a universal appeal.

33. a All except (I) are mentioned as criticisms of Dickens' writings. (II) and (IV) can be found in the lines *"...far outweighing the surprise coincidences, occasional mawkishness and deus ex machina endings."* (III) is one of the criticisms that Orwell levels at Dickens. *" ... Dickens's reticence to take a definitive position on class and rights carried over to his characters, who tend to feel unreal."*

34. d The answer can be found in the last paragraph *"... the sheer scope of the world he created and the wide screen variety of his novels, that is his true legacy."*

35. a The tone of the passage can be best described as analytical. The author does not merely describe the features of Diocken's writings . He goes on to analyse the various aspects of his writing. The author uses Orwell's essays to dissect the writings of Charles Dickens.

36. c Option (d) is incorrect because 'the quest of conditions being the psychologist's most interesting task' is the opinion of the author and not of psychologists. The passage does not state/ imply the opinion of the psychologists, it talks about the opinion of the author only. Option (c) is correct as it can be inferred from the last line of the passage.

37. a The author makes reference to three judgments by the Supreme Court and asserts the significance of social action. She draws an important connection among courts, social sciences and social movements. The second paragraph also makes a reference to the importance of the State in social development - that in certain areas it cannot be substituted by the private sector or the private social sector. The last two paragraphs also bring out the importance of the constitution and for the legal framework to include "the letter and the spirit of the constitution". Option (a) is the answer. Options (b) and (c) can be ruled out because there is not reference to politics - to the socio-political context only. Option (d) can also be ruled out because though the author hints at correct governance or strict governance (when he refers to a "soft state") it does not talk about enforcement of justice.

38. d The second paragraph provides the answer to this question. Option (d) is the best paraphrasing of the highlighted text which indicates that the understanding of constitutionalism needs to be widened so that a broader understanding of justice can be included. And this will help cover all complexities of injustice. Option (a) is incorrect as it is incorrect to infer that the understanding of constitutionalism and justice need to be merged. Option (b) is incorrect as it states that the understanding of constitutionalism and justice should include aspects of injustice – not all complexities of injustice. Option (c) is ambiguous as from it one can infer that aspects of injustice are to be included/a part of an understanding of constitutionalism and justice.

39. c The first paragraph starts with a reference to three recent judgments with a reference to a previous judgment (Naz foundation). In the next few sentences the author asserts that these pronouncements have a lineage in jurisprudence. She also indicates that every such case that is viewed and judged from the socio-political context is to be celebrated. Option (c) is the answer. Option (a) is incorrect – the three cases do not form the core of the discussion. Similarly option (b) is also incorrect. Option (d) can be ruled out as the author does not state that jurisprudence has a lineage that includes neo-liberalism. In fact, she states that agents of the state are carried away by the ideology of neo-liberalism – this is with reference to the problem of a "soft state".

40. c The third paragraph is in inverted commas indicating that it is quoted from some other source. The paragraph envisages a situation where the State, "carried away by the ideology of neo-liberalism" and overly cautious, ignores the signals of wrongdoing even when they are strong. The tone of paragraph is cautionary and objective. It is not particularly critical of anything in particular nor does it have a disparaging tone. Option (c) is the correct answer.

41. a 1

42. b Chelsea, the Champion of the tournament, scored 2 goals in the semifinal.

43. c The last line of the first paragraph states that meditation can be used for personal benefit and spiritual growth. The rest of the paragraphs all present information to the reader on how this is so. Option (c) is the answer. Option (a) is incorrect as it mentions the side effects of meditation indicating a negative connotation. But the passage only refers to positive side effects. Option (b) is incorrect as the passage does not imply that meditation is necessary for enjoying life. It only argues why and how meditation is beneficial. Option (d) does not fit in with the scope of the passage. The option itself could have been considered had there been reference only to a specific spiritual journey in the passage.

44. c The last line of the second paragraph states the primary purpose of meditation - "The primary purpose of meditation practice, however, is to bring forth clear states of awareness that will make authentic spiritual growth easier to experience." Link this with the last paragraph and option (c) emerges as the answer. Option (a) can be ruled out as there is no mention that meditation improves biological processes – it only strengthens of the immune system and leads to slowing of the biological ageing processes. These are also mentioned as beneficial side effects and not the main purpose of meditation. Option (b) has been mentioned in the passage but not as the main purpose of meditation – they are benefits of meditation and elements of living a wholesome life. Option (d) can be ruled out because the ultimate goal of a follower has not been mentioned and only acquisition of knowledge is not the main purpose of meditation.

45. b The author argues that the consumers have a choice weather or not to view advertisements and therefore, they should not complain about increasing adverts. Option (b) weakens this argument. If people are not aware that the piece of art or public information they are viewing is a form of adverts, then it is impossible to consciously avoid it.

46. a The argument revolves around a patient's right to choose weather or not a treatment should be administered to him/her. Option (a) states that in case of mental illness, a patient loses the ability to exercise this right as he/she is unable to take rational decisions. Hence, option (a) weakens the argument.

47. b The first paragraph starts with a narration of an incident between the tiger and the soldiers. It ends by saying that this is the first scene of the play. Option (b) is correct. Option (c) is incorrect as the second paragraph takes forward the thread of thought (discussing the structure of the play). Option (d) is incorrect as there is no assertion or tone in the first paragraph itself. Option (a) is incorrect since the passage does not mention whether the scene described is based on a real-life incident or not.

48. c A careful reading of the passage will help identify that the author uses the analysis and quotation approach. She makes her point and then uses a quote from Joseph to substantiate that point. This can be seen from the second, third, fourth and sixth paragraphs. Option (c) is the answer. Options (a) and (b) are incorrect as the author never moves from specific to general or vice versa.

49. d The last paragraph has the answer. Refer to the lines ""Story-telling", he imparts, "can get boring if you're not dealing with the issues of life or death, or on the edge of something."" Option (a) is incorrect as violence has not been explicitly linked to contemporary political realities. Option (c) is incorrect as Joseph never states this. Option (b) can't be inferred as there is no reference to critiques of social realities.

50. d The author talks about this in the fourth paragraph at the beginning – "The *philosophes* had also attacked the Church because it blocked human reason. The Romantics attacked the Enlightenment because it blocked the free play of the emotions and creativity. The *philosophe* had turned man into a soulless, thinking machine — a robot." This proves that the Romantics who came after the philosophes were fighting against the over dependence on reason and harking back to emotions. This makes choice (d) correct.

51. c The author mentions this at the end of the third paragraph. "The Romantics were conscious of their unique destiny. In fact, it was self-consciousness which appears as one of the key elements of Romanticism itself" making choice (c) correct.

52. d The author mentions in the second paragraph – "To speak of a Romantic era is to identify a period in which certain ideas and attitudes arose, gained currency and in most areas of intellectual endeavor, became dominant. That is, they became the dominant mode of expression. Which tells us something else about the Romantics: expression was perhaps everything to them". None of (a), (b) or (c) talks about this.

53. b The author mentions in the fifth paragraph – "promotion-driven world of entertainment" which is "critic proof". This makes option (b) correct. Option 1 is too general. Options (c) and (d) are too specific and can be part of option (b).

54. c The author mentions Rosen's names among others in the sixth paragraph which he begins by saying "But it's less common, critics say, for one of their kind to draw an audience's attention to an overlooked work". This makes option (c) correct.

55. b The author starts the passage with the example and in the rest of the passage looks at this phenomenon. This example showed the way films reflected the reality of the time when a critic was an important figure. The sentence mentioned in the quote in the question also highlights how characters gave a lot of importance to the critic in the film and irrespective of whether they respected what he said or looked down upon it, they acknowledged it. This makes option (b) correct. Option (a) is true but not specific to the question asked. Option (c) is incorrect. Option (d) is not mentioned in the passage.

56. b The author mentions this in the eighth paragraph. Hickey compares the job of the art critic with "a night-time disk jockey or a sewing machine repairman". Both of these are professions that were at their peak for only a few decades (one-two generations).

57. c The author mentions the mistakes in the first paragraph of the passage and later moves on to mention other mistakes that are easy to make while writing. Her intention is as stated in option (c).

58. b The author mentions this at the end of the third paragraph and talks about how the power of English is in its names. This makes option (b) correct. Name-calling is different and is not what the author means in this context.

59. a The author mentions the details in the story as being stones thrown into a boat. With each stone being thrown the boat sinks even more. This is what details do to a story – they make it more and more difficult to sustain its accuracy. This makes option (a) correct.

60. d The passage presents arguments against the death penalty – right from the fact that it is seen as a mismatch to the crime committed, that it is not retribution enough and to the fact that it does not deter people from committing crime. The fact that the death penalty is unfair is given in the first three paragraphs. That it does not serve its purpose can be inferred from the fourth and the fifth paragraphs. The sixth paragraph asserts that the death penalty does not deter people from committing crime. Option (d) aptly sums up these main arguments in the passage and is thus the correct answer.

Option (a) is incorrect because rather than presenting different sides of the argument, it sticks to only one of the views.

Option (b) is incorrect because the passage does not focus on reconsidering (or lobbying for) the use of the death penalty.

Option (c) states only one of the points mentioned in the passage as a reason for the argument of death penalty being flawed and hence becomes incorrect.

61. b Sentence A can be inferred from the first line of the second last paragraph.

Sentence C can be inferred from the second paragraph, which indicates that death penalty may cause double suffering to the accused due to the dreadful wait before death.

Sentence D can be inferred from the first line of the first paragraph itself.

Sentence B cannot be evidenced from the passage. Thus, option (c) is the answer.

62. b According to the passage, all crimes, except murder, do not receive a punishment that is similar to the crime. The author has made a hidden assumption here that the death penalty is handed over only in the case of murder and thus, it mirrors the crime. This fact, that it mirrors the crime, is what makes death penalty unique. Thus, option (b) is correct.

Option (a) is incorrect because, as pointed out before, the death penalty is assumed to be given only for murder. The option states that the death penalty is given for crimes besides murder too, which cannot be inferred from the passage.

Option (c) is incorrect because anticipatory suffering is not mentioned as a feature that makes the death penalty unique but one that makes it unfair.

Option (d) is not discussed and is beyond the scope of the passage.

63. c The last line of the second paragraph refers to Scheibitz's paintings as unreasonable. Refer to the first two paragraphs in order to understand why the author draws such a conclusion. The first paragraph refers to the fact that the paintings are not what they seem at first or even second glance (refer to the last three sentences of this paragraph). The second paragraph indicates a sense of contradiction in the paintings. The first sentence of this paragraph also indicates that the paintings make sense but if one enters Scheibitz's realm. The next few lines explain the fact that the paintings force the individual to see the subtle – 'The spaces between things become more insistent than the things themselves.' It is indicated that the onlooker is thus forced to see things beyond the obvious and to understand the paintings not from their individual perspectives but from the artist's (Scheibitz's) perspective. Option (c) is, thus, the answer.

Option (a) is ruled out because it fails to present a complete perspective.

Option (b) is also ruled out as it is incomplete and doesn't answer the question.

Option (d) can be ruled out because it is not derived from the information in the passage. There is no indication that one must understand art and its related philosophy in order to understand Scheibitz's paintings.

64. c Option (a) cannot be inferred on the basis of the passage because there is no indication that the artist deliberately creates art that is difficult to fathom and place. In fact, in the third paragraph the artist is quoted as saying that, "I can't invent anything and I can't use what I find as it is." This indicates that the artist does not deliberately confuse. The last sentence of this paragraph also indicates, that in the artist's mind, everything in his paintings is interconnected with the inspirations he draws from real life.

Option (b) is incorrect because it is not evidenced from the passage that Scheibitz's paintings are hard to categorize.

Option (c) is correct and can be inferred from the last line of the third paragraph and the entire fourth paragraph.

Option (d) is incorrect because it seeks to explain the passage in a philosophical light. While the philosophical link can be briefly inferred ("The spaces between things become more insistent than the things themselves" and "The overall impression is that nothing is random" etc.), it does not form the mainstay of the discussion and the option cannot be concretely inferred.

65. c Though it is true according to the passage that everything the artist is inspired by has a reason, but option (a) makes too general a statement. According to the passage, the source materials are interconnected which necessarily may not be the source of his inspiration.

Option (b), which says Scheibitz's paintings may portray things in an abstract light, contradicts the last line of the third paragraph and hence, is incorrect.

Option (d) talks about the author's assertion, which is incorrect because the assertion mentioned in the option is that of the painter.

Refer to the lines, "The overall impression is that nothing is random. There are affinities here." These lines, paraphrased into option (c), provide the correct significance of the penultimate paragraph and therefore option (c) is the correct answer.

66. d The poem 'A Tear and A Smile' by Kahlil Gibran reflects the poet's philosophical musings. The poet feels that both tears and smiles are necessary in his life – refer to the fifth line of the poem and the stanza after this line. The poet feels that tears purify his heart while smiles bring him closer to the gods (a symbol of my glorification of the gods). The poet also uses the last four stanzas to illustrate that challenges and joys form part of every being's life and that these two elements play their part in the fulfilment of one's destiny. Refer to the last stanza – 'the spirit become separated' and 'return whence it came' – which indicates that one lives this life to fulfil a destiny and to ultimately return to the original source. Option (d) is hence the answer.

Option (a) can be ruled out because the poet does not mention the poor. He only mentions those in yearning and longing – this does not indicate poverty.

Option (b) can be ruled out because the main theme is the importance of 'a tear and a smile' and not the unification of those in need.

Option (c) is incorrect because it is incomplete and does not bring in the fact that 'a tear and a smile' are instrumental in moving one towards one's destiny – towards one's final goal.

67. c Refer to lines 12-17. In line 12, the poet feels that it is better to live a life in which one constantly aspires (yearns) for fulfilment, instead of leading a life that is dull and tired (dull because there is nothing to aspire for – refer to line 15). The poet goes on to state further that the sighs of an individual who longs for fulfilment are sweet to hear. One can infer that the author is in favour of the individual strife towards fulfilment. The poet also clearly indicates that a person who is Satisfied cannot experience the joys that yearning and longing bring with them. Option (c) can thus be inferred to be the answer.

Option (a) can be ruled out because it judges the manner in which people find satisfaction; information on the means used to find satisfaction is not stated or implied in the poem.

Option (b) is incorrect because the poet links the ability to understand the secrets of life with the presence of challenges (tears). The poem, however, does not provide any information on why an individual would lack the ability to understand the secrets of life.

Option (d) presumes more than the poem indicates – there is no implication that Satisfied individuals are already in a state of happiness that ceases to exist as soon as they become Satisfied.

68. b Refer to lines 24-32 in which the author brings in the example of the clouds to convey that one eventually returns to one's origins. Line 24 states that the clouds start from the sea (water vapour that rise from the sea form clouds). Line 28 indicates that after a time, the clouds return to their origin, the sea. Thus, option (b) is correct.

Option (a) is incorrect because give and take indicates that an exchange is taking place – whereas the author mentions a parting and a meeting and the return to one's origins.

Option (c) is incorrect because the author does not imply that there are obvious and subtle explanations for the formation of clouds.

Option (d) is incorrect because there is no demarcation of spiritual and worldly phenomenon in the poem.

69. a Option (b) is a very general statement and suggests that everyone should always have trouble while trying to express himself. But the paragraph indicates that the student "... started speaking English and learnt how to express ..." Option (c) also contradicts this information. Option (a) gives a plausible explanation for the student's predicament. Refer to the line "It can be because of the circumstances I had or the culture I have." Thus, option (a) is the correct answer.

70. c Refer to the first paragraph "This very peculiar kind ... some metal details'. This makes option (c) the correct answer.

71. a The second paragraph delves into this issue and the author mentions that: "And if we agree ... perceive signs of instability". Thus, option (a) is the correct answer.

72. b Refer to the lines "Designers know this well and they are the first to perceive signs of instability ... Fashion delights us by playing on the tensions between these couples". Thus, option (b) is the correct answer.

73. b Refer to the last line of the second paragraph "...nobody is interested in starting the ultimate trend, the final one". Thus, option (b) is the correct answer.

74. c Refer to the last 3 lines of the first paragraph. Option (c) follows from this and hence, is the correct answer.

75. b Refer to the second and third paragraphs. The author explains that education results in the destruction of energy. Thus, option (b) is the correct answer.

76. b Refer to the fifth paragraph "... controlling or disciplining this energy and letting it out in one direction and restricting it in another becomes merely a social convenience; the mind is shaped according to the pattern of a particular culture, and thereby its energy is gradually dissipated". Thus, option (b) is the correct answer.

77. d Refer to the fifth paragraph "What is this energy which we all have? This energy is thinking, feeling; it is interest, enthusiasm, greed, passion, lust, ambition, and hate". Thus, option (d) is the correct answer.

78. c Medals are symbols of the glorification of war. By stating that medals are nothing more than holes in a cloth, Atwood is criticizing the glorification of war. Thus, option (c) is the correct answer.

79. d Options (a), (b) and (c) are various attributes of Atwood's novel, as described by the author of this passage. Option (d) is the odd one out – the author has used this term to describe an attribute of Iris, a character in the novel. The author has not used this term to describe the novel itself. Option (d) is thus, the odd one out and hence, is the correct answer.

80. b Refer to the fifth paragraph "...a sense of the contentious nature of experience: there is a world of difference between the clipped prose of the pro-establishment local paper and the dead Laura's unfolding of emotion ..." Thus, option (b) is the correct answer.

81. a Refer to the second paragraph, the author states explicitly "In her latest book Atwood explores again a theme central to her fictional universe: what happens to relationships, to human potential, to the possibility of happiness when women are kept subordinate, stultified by their inferior status and locked in silence". Thus, option (a) is the correct answer.

82. d All of the above have been mentioned in the passage, except option (d). Thus, option (d) is the correct answer.

83. a Refer to the line "Its course across the pond represents one of many paths it might take..." Option (a) contradicts this and hence, is the correct answer.

84. b Refer to the fifth paragraph. Option (b) contradicts this and hence, is the correct answer.

85. b Refer to the second paragraph. Option (b) is the correct answer.

86. b Refer to the first paragraph. It clearly states the two main functions of myth. a is wrong because it refers to Science as a discipline which is not mentioned in the first paragraph. c talks about rituals which is factually wrong. d mentions the word unanswerable which is undefined in the paragraph.

87. b Refer to the first line of the second paragraph ("In Greek mythology, there is no single original text like the Christian Bible or the Hindu Vedas that introduces all of the myths' characters and stories"). a is wrong because the passage doesn't state that there is no such text in Greek mythology. c and d are irrelevant options.

88. d The passage doesn't state this fact. It simply mentions the authors. But the phrase "first story of Greek mythology" is not mentioned in the passage. Hesiod's story simply mentions the origin of Greek mythology.

89. a Refer to the third paragraph ("Around 700 BC, the poet Hesiod's Theogony...Tartaros (the Underworld)". a is the clear answer. b, c, and d can't be inferred from the passage.

90. d It is mentioned in the last paragraph. It talks about deities who lived on Mount Olympus. a is incorrect. It doesn't talk about a temple of all Gods. b and c are incorrect too. d can be contextually inferred.

91. a A and B can be derived from the last line of the paragraph. C is factually incorrect as the paragraph simply mentions that the Olympian Gods were vulnerable to weaknesses and passion. But it doesn't mention the degree of passion. The phrase "as passionate as humans" will be factually wrong.

92. a It is a central idea question. c and d can be eliminated because they are too narrow in scope. b is wrong because the central idea of the passage is "the troubled artist fallacy". The passage doesn't focus on how attitude of the world towards mental issues has improved. a is the best answer.

93. d The passage talks about the "troubled artist fallacy". It talks about the perception that people who suffer from mental illness create great work as a result of their struggle. Both a and b highlight such a situation. c is irrelevant as it doesn't mention the creation of artistic work. a mentions the period of recuperation as the period of artistic fertility. It too is a part of the mental illness.

94. d Refer to the lines "However, not everybody with mental illness... more of a failure" in the last but two paragraph. d is the correct option. a mentions bad behaviour which is not mentioned in the paragraph. b and c are incorrect options.

95. a b is too extreme an opinion to be derived from the passage. c is incorrect because the passage doesn't mention lifestyle as a reason for their artistic genius. d is wrong because of the phrase "common occurrence". a can be inferred from the entire passage as the author's tone is cautious on the matter .

96. b Refer to the penultimate paragraph. (Lines: "...I shouldn't be so resentful of my mental illness.") a mentions the word prodigy which can't be inferred due to lack of data. c is wrong because she doesn't appreciate the view point. d is an extreme conclusion. She resents the view point that her illness was the reason for her success as an artist. She might not disapprove a general comment on her mental struggle.

97. b Refer to the last paragraph. Simon Procter clearly mentions b. Hence, it is the best option.

98. d The passage is about the visit initiated by Cameron and the graceful acceptence by Sisi and how the two political figures tried to mend bonds between the two countries. a makes the event sound unsuccessful. b puts the onus onto Cameron, which is not the case either. c is just another general statement made with the main subjects in the passage but with no real relation to the passage. d correctly sums up the fact that the visit was a political action and had relevance for both nations. Hence, d is correct.

99. a The role of a paragraph should always be determined in context of the ongoing argument. a does it best by stating how the invitation and the visit of Sisi affected the situation between Egypt and the UK. The other options state the same as well, but change a few details here and there which makes them slightly incorrect and thus bad choices. b calls it a connecting link, where it is an independent paragraph and not linked to any other paragraph. c states that there were disasters in the past, and that is factually incorrect and d brings in analogies which, as we know, is a bad strategy when answering questions in reading comprehension. Hence, a is correct.

100.c The information given in a can be found in para 2, and b can be found in paras 1 and 3. d is clearly indicated in para 6. c is not mentioned anywhere. Hence, c is correct.

101.b Since this is a question about continuity, we have to find something that takes forth the last sentence with sufficient logic. a introduces the question of funding which has not yet been mentioned. c goes on to talk about the discussion that the two main researchers in the passage have, but we have not yet come to that point in our given extract. d includes a point that would flow very well after statement b but not on its own. b talks about the paucity of evidence which links itself nicely to the last sentence which aims at ridiculing the believability of such research as 'poppycock'. This statement furthers the argument that it is still nascent as a research field. Hence, (b) is correct.

102.d Questions on inference tend to always include statements of generic intent. a and b do just that, but make sweeping generalizations on people's behaviour and scientific study and its viability in publishing. c assumes that there was foul play involved at the research stage and that there were researchers involved in affecting publication of Conley's work. This is incorrect. d correctly infers that since the study was revelatory in nature, it did not sit well with the group that it aimed at exposing. Hence, d is correct.

103.b The term 'stigma' means a sense of infamy or disgrace associated with a concept or an idea. Stigma is not an opinion but a universally accepted notion. Options (c) and (d) indicate that it is to do with the status of a person (by using the words 'notoreity' and 'reputation') which is also incorrect by definition. Hence, b is correct.

104.a Refer to the lines "The new color theory...in asserting that there was no black in nature...their palette."ais the clear answer. b is a twisted option. The passage doesn't state that black is the colour of shadows. Similarly, we can eliminate c and d.

105.b It is a factual question. The answer can be located in the third paragraph. Refer to the line "Edouard Manet, who helped art move away from Realism in the nineteenth century". b is the only correct option.

106.c Only A and C can be located in the passage. B is not mentioned in the passage.

107.a The entire passage focuses on Monet as a proponent of impressionism. Hence a is the best answer. b, c, and d don't focus on Monet. Due to insufficient data, they can be eliminated.

108.b From the penultimate paragraph, b is the clear answer. a is wrong because the author doesn't talk about only one family. c is a twisted option. The normal ladies and gentlemen might refer to any class. d twists the line. Normality is not defined in the paragraph.

109.c It is mentioned in the fifth paragraph. After being rejected by the Paris Salon, the artists held their own exhibitions. a doesn't mention this aspect. Hence it can be eliminated. b talks about commissioned paintings, which is beyond the scope of the passage. d can be eliminated as a and b are wrong. c is the best option.

SUMMARY TYPE QUESTIONS

1. b (a) is wrong because 'if they focus on cost . . . they will reduce' [too definite]. (c) is wrong 'Any cost minimization' — is too broad. (d) is wrong because 'quality improvement rather than cost cutting' is not implied. Both should be done. Hence, choice (b) is correct.

2. b (a) is wrong because there is no mention of choices. (c) is wrong because 'always try' [too extreme]. (d) is wrong because 'we urge . . . to buy vans' is too narrow. Hence, choice (b) is correct.

3. b There is only one type of inertia which has both mental and physical effects. That is why (c) and (d) are wrong. (a) which says 'freezes . . . decapitates' is too extreme. Hence, choice (b) is correct.

4. a (a) is unambiguous, (b) is not right because the boss did not offer any job. (c) is wrong because free holiday accommodation does not come that frequently in our lives. (d) is wrong because you never take the boss's job when she is away.

5. a Statement (b) is only partially true. It only talks of requirements and not of what grows in those regions. Similarly, statement (c) talks only of produce and not requirement. The passage is not concerned with what people like or prefer but with what is locally available or required.

6. b The last sentence of the passage is only conveyed fully in option (b).

7. c Statement (b) and (d) are partially true, as they do not cover all the examples of preferential treatment. Statement a is incomplete, as it does not mention direct protest.

8. b Statement (c) is factually wrong as we don't know if further research can happen only in Germany. Option (d) wrongly brings out a contest between research and debate. Between options (a) and (b), choice (a) is inappropriate because we don't know if 'research' will help find a 'definitive answer'.

9. d Option (b) is factually wrong. Option (b) is wrong because Nietzsche does not criticize 'intellectuals'. Option (a) is wrong because he does not talk of 'the decline of modern society' only Option (d) captures the essence of the paragraph.

10. The author explains cynically the ease of acquiring knowledge and makes a distinction between knowledge and knowingness. He proceeds to state how it has no value as compared to actual experience. He counters the view of the first paragraph in the second one by mentioning less fortunate people's point of view. Option (d) is the correct summation of the points of cynicism and those points which are later disputed by the less fortunate. The other options are either too narrow or too broad to be the summary of this passage.

11. The passage is an analysis of the novel and its survivability and its relationship with female readers. Option (d) uses 'nature' to relate to innatism and mentions nurture to equate with 'conditioning'. Then later it proceeds to state the clear conclusion of the passage. This is an accurate summation of the passage.

12. In this passage the author has explained Kafka's work and the way he impacted modernism. Option (a) is correct as it includes all the themes i.e. Kafka's inner problems, modernism, humour, pain etc. Option (b) is incorrect because it mentions 'literature' which is not mentioned in the passage.

13. According to the given paragraph the North American walnut sphinx moth caterpillar often whistles which is very loud in nature. The birds often mimic these whistles by which they understand the location of these prey birds and they get time to take cover. Option (a) is incorrect since it talks about vocal tracks, which is out of scope. Option (b) is partially correct since it does not talk about the correct use of the whistling. Option (d) uses the word 'camouflage' which is also beyond the scope of the given context. Option (c) describes the passage correctly and accurately.

14. According to the given paragraph, both Socrates and Bacon stressed on arguments from both ends, that is, to prove as well as disprove. To both, it was important to disprove a theory as is to prove it when it came to asking questions. Option (a) is incorrect since it only talks about disapproving arguments. Option (b) is beyond the scope of the context since it fails to capture the main theme of the passage. Option (c) is partially correct, since it only talks about confirming an argument and not the other way. Option (d) is the only correct answer.

15. The passage talks about the importance of meaning which is dynamic in nature whereas definitions are dynamic. Definitions are extracted from the meanings and not the other way round. Hence (c) is the correct option here. Option (a) is incorrect since it talks about the dogmatic nature of meaning. Option (b) is also incorrect factually. Option (d) is beyond the scope of the given context.

16. All the options look close. But in the paragraph, the author talks about 'mimicking or imitating.' So, the word 'mimetic' makes option 3 the best summary of the paragraph. Option 1 says 'just like the natural development' which is not mentioned in the paragraph. Options 2 and 4 are distorted options.

17. The author mentions two important points in the paragraph: the pros and cons of professions-approach. Only option 2 mentions this point. Option 3 is partially correct. Option 1 is too narrow and vague. Option 4 is factually not supported by the paragraph.

18. This seems to be a wrong answer. The focus here is not on Renaissance. Option 2 seems to be a better option. The option given by CAT is 4. However, all the four options look incomplete. Option 1 is wrong as the author doesn't say that the Renaissance artists were responsible for the subject. They just introduced a new type of approach to the subject of landscape art. Option 3 is clearly too narrow and doesn't mention the main point.

19. 4-6 lines talk about the obstacles of Samaritan law, which is being talked in further lines, the link is to testify the laws. Thus, option (b) is the right answer.

20. Option (a) is contradicting to the passage. Option (b) is used as an example to strengthen the point. Option (c) talks about the direct relation which is not quite evident. Thus, option (d) is the right answer that covers the whole point of the passage.

21. Options (a),(c) and (d) are mentioned as the stances while the whole passage talks about exemption from regulation for the editing of endogenous genes....So the right answer is option (b).

SYLLOGISMS

1. c

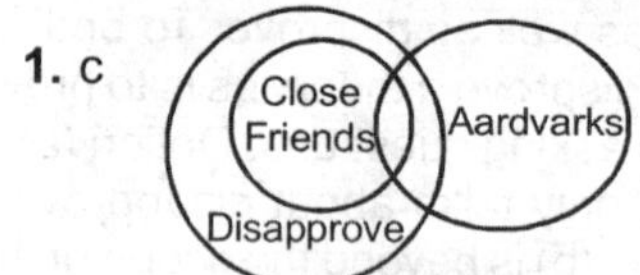

2. c

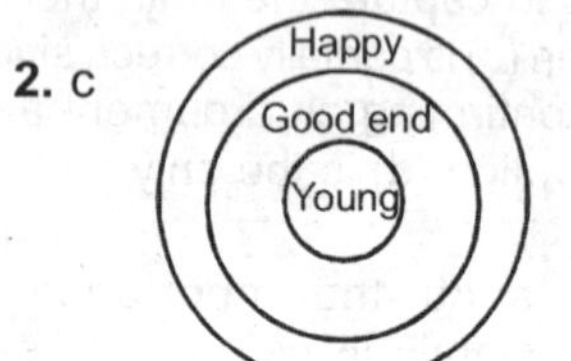

3. d

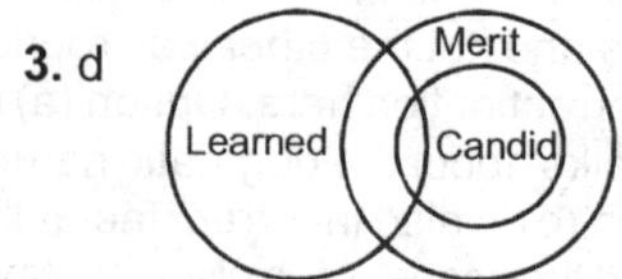

4. a

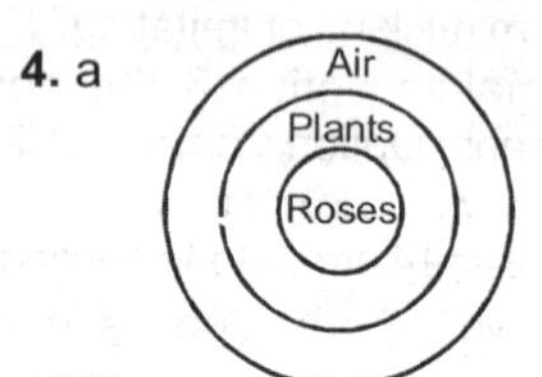

5. b

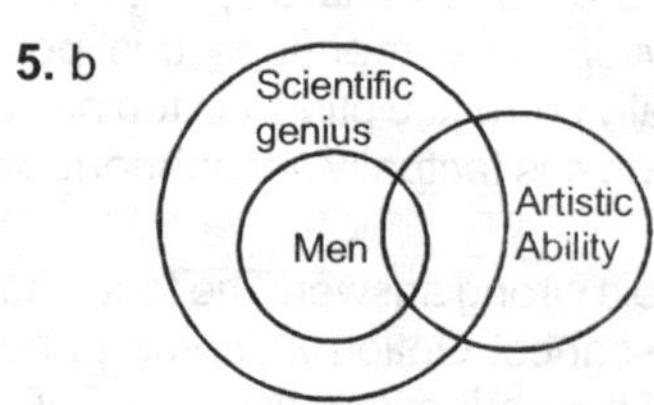

6. c

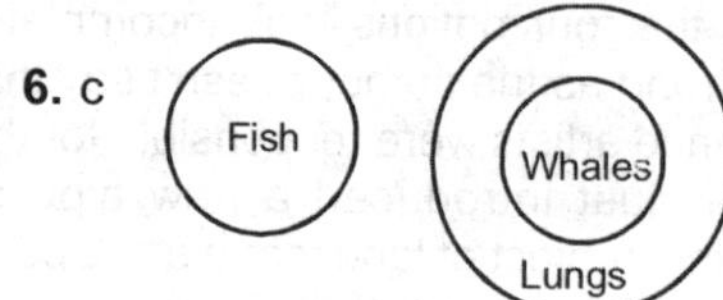

7. d

8. c

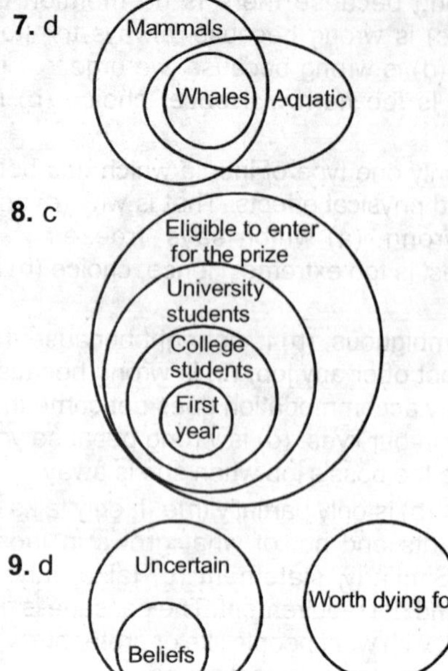

9. d

10. b

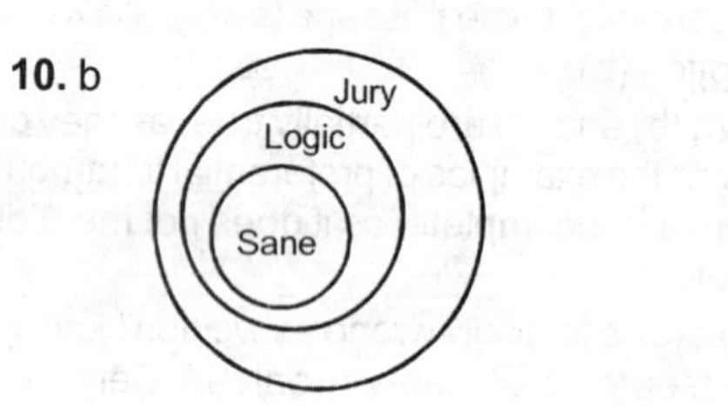

11. c

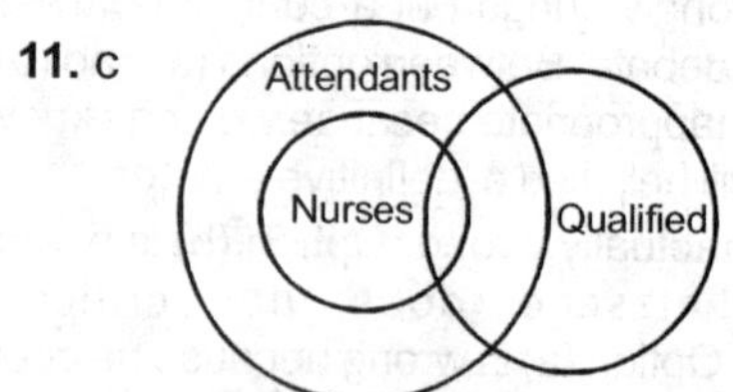

12. a If Mary and John are wife and husband and the last waltz was danced by husbands and wives, it follows that John danced last with Mary.

13. c

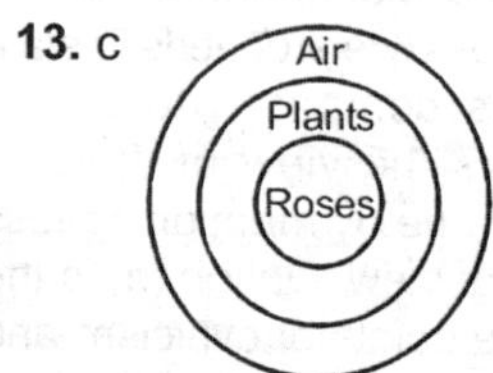

14. c Laxman is a man and no man is an island, so Laxman cannot be an island.

15. a If college students are intelligent and Ram is a college student, it follows that Ram is intelligent.

16. b If all cigarettes are hazardous to health and cham-cham is a brand of cigarette, then cham-cham would also be hazardous to health.

17. d If all good bridge players play good chess, then Goran being a good bridge player should also play good chess.

18. d

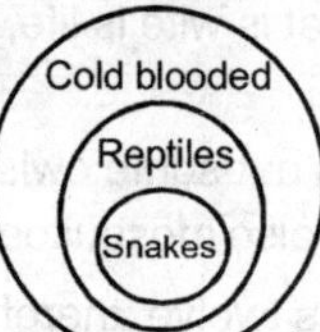

19. a

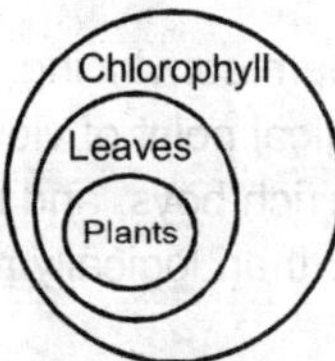

20. b If bald people are intelligent and Raman is bald, it follows that Raman is intelligent.

21. d

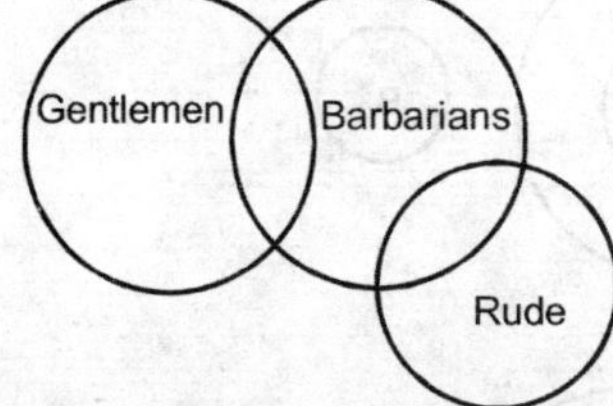

22. d Desks are made of metals. So if an object is a desk it should be made of metal.

23. d Mathew and Paul are siblings and siblings are known to quarrel often. Therefore it follows that Mathew and Paul quarrel often.

24. a Art is a symptom of culture and music is a form of art, therefore music also shows culture.

25. c If primary colours give different hues, and red is a primary colour, it implies that red also gives different hues.

26. b

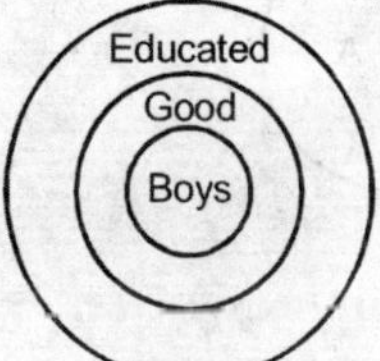

27. d

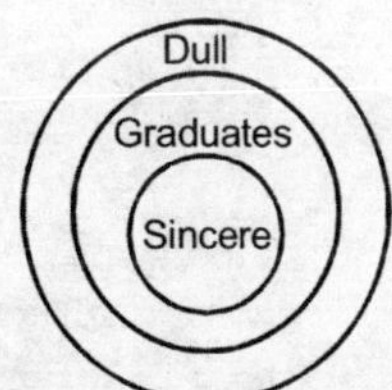

28. b Sham won a lottery though he is not intelligent. This shows that intelligence is not needed to win a lottery.

29. c If good managers are intuitive and Supriya is a good manager it follows that she is intuitive.

30. a

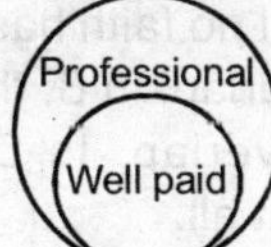

31. a

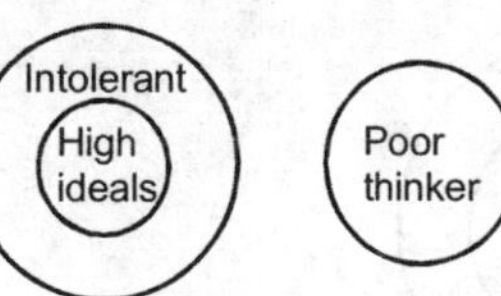

32. b

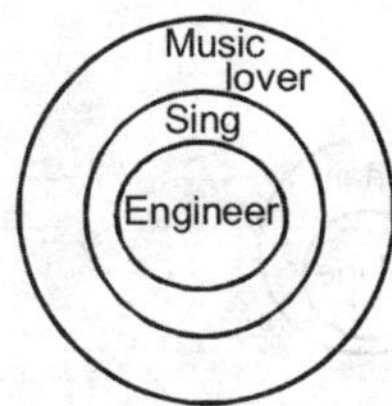

33. d

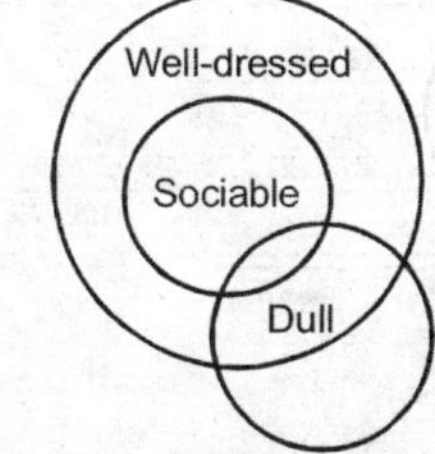

34. a Though Iran and Iraq are members of the UN, they are not friends, implying that all members of the UN are not friends.

35. d

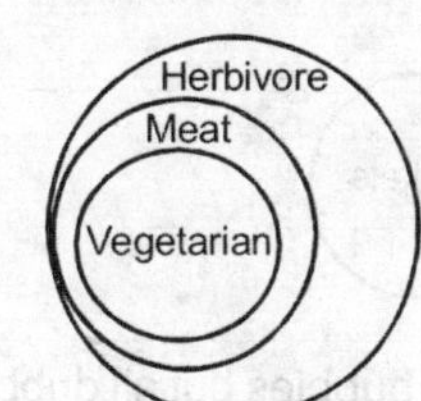

36. c

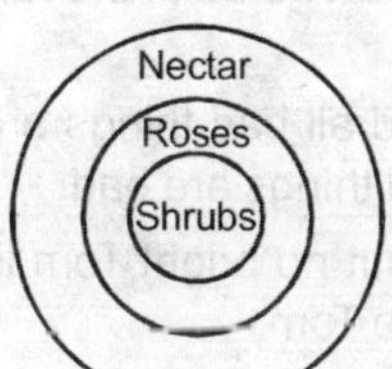

37. a

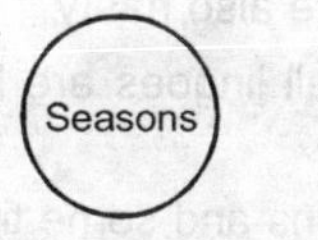

38. b

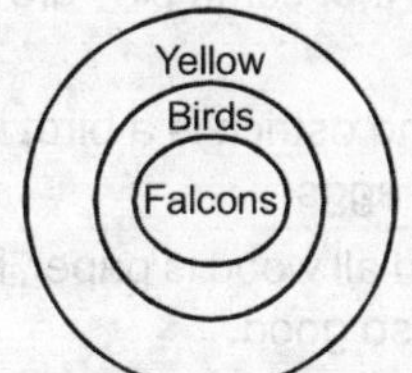

39. d

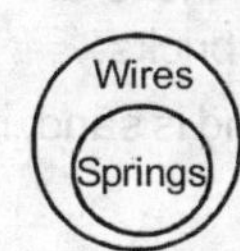

40. b

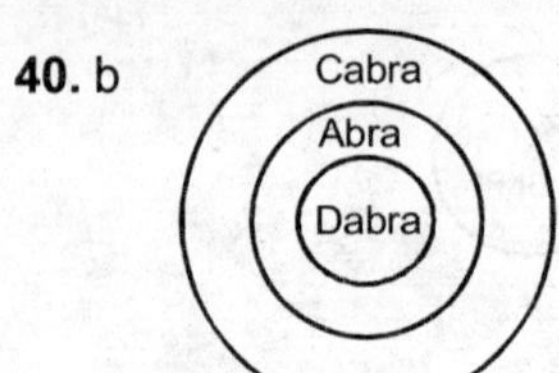

41. c

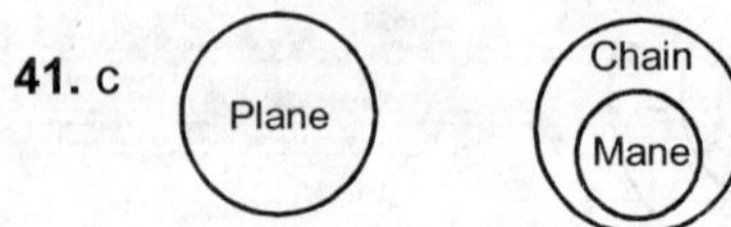

42. a

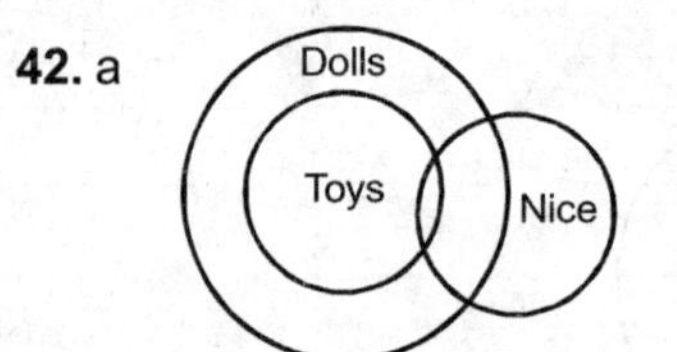

43. b

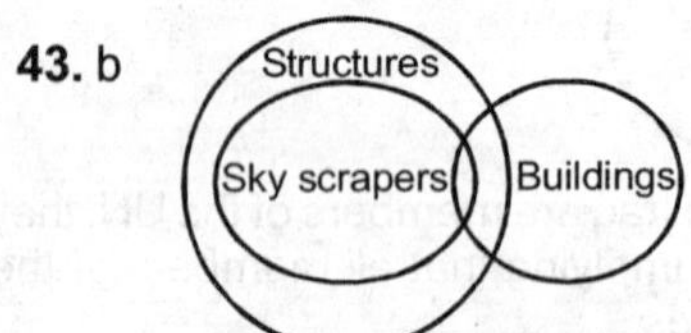

44. d

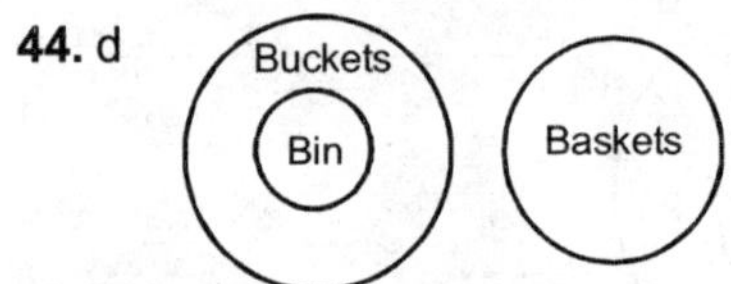

45. d Some dubbles are not bubbles but all dubbles are rubbles, so it follows that some of the rubbles are not bubbles.

46. b If all men are sad and all bad things are men, it follows that some sad things are bad.

47. c All Toms are bright, but no bright Tom is a Dick. Therefore, no Dick is a Tom.

48. b If all witches are devils and all devils are nasty, it implies that all witches are also nasty.

49. a No tingo is a bingo but all jingoes are bingoes. Hence, no jingo is a tingo.

50. c If all copper is used for pins and some tin is also copper, then it follows that some pins are made of tin.

51. a If all birds lay eggs and ostrich is a bird, it follows that ostrich also lays eggs.

52. b If all wood is good and all wood is paper, it follows that some paper is also good.

53. a If all bricks are tricks and all tricks are shrieks, then some shrieks should be bricks.

54. a If all sandal is band and all band is sand, it follows that some sand is band.

55. d All life is strife and all that is wife is life, therefore all wife is also strife.

56. d All owls are mosquitoes but some owls are flies, therefore some flies are also mosquitoes.

57. a Six is five but some six is twelve, therefore some twelve is also five.

58. a Although this doesn't seem convincing, but if we look at it from purely logical point of view, then if poor girls want to marry rich boys, and rich boys want to marry rich girls, then logically poor girls want to marry rich girls.

59. b

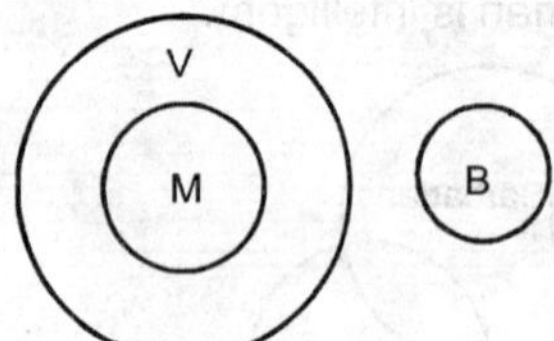

60. c

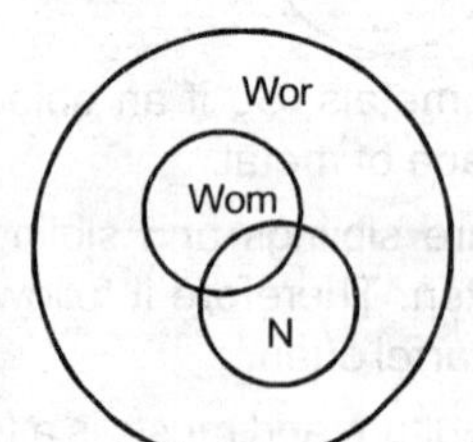

61. a

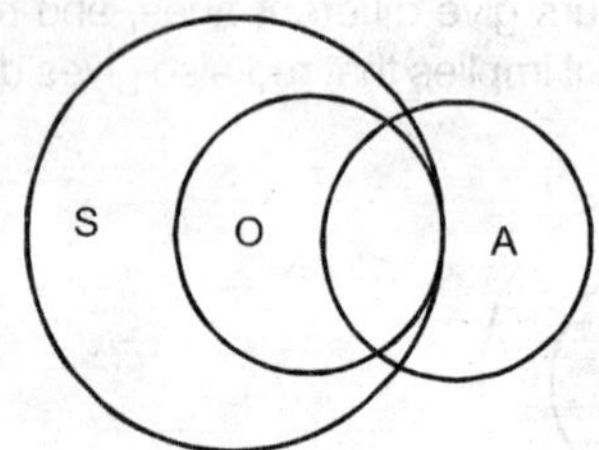

62. a

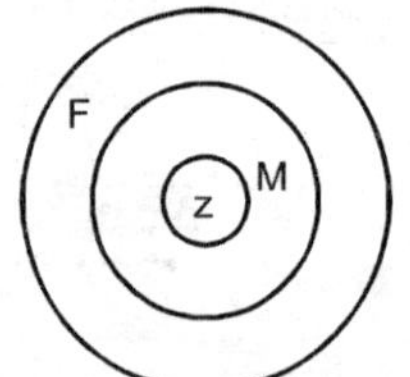

63. a

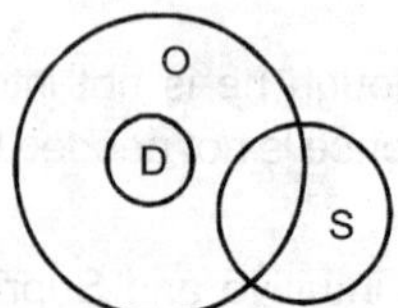

64. b If only strong have biceps and no faith is strong, it follows that no faith has biceps. In A, X and Y need not overlap. In B, the Sona and crazy set need not overlap. In D there is no logical conclusion at all.

65. b In (C) and (D) the first two statements do not logically lead to the third. In C, we do not know if the hand and the head set overlap. D leads to an unpredictable conclusion. The icicles which are cycles are at least men. In B, if no teeth is yellow, no girl can be yellow, since all girls are teeth.

66. a If no sun is not white, it implies that all sun is white. All moon is sun, so it follows that all moon is white. B and C lead to undefined conclusions. In D, there is a possibility that X and Y sets can intersect.

67. c If all Ts are square and all squares are rectangular, it follows that all Ts are rectangular. Also, if idiots are bumblers and bumblers fumble, it follows that idiots fumble. In B, there is a possibility that fat and huge sets need not intersect. D plays with words and leads to uncertain conclusion again.

68. c (c) 'A and D' is the correct answer choice

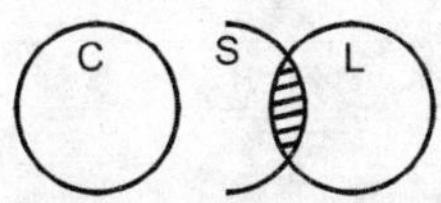

Statement A is valid:

The shaded portion represents those some sphinxes that laugh and, therefore, are not cowboys as no cowboys laugh.

Statement B is invalid.

All G are F.

Some G are not S.

∴ Some S are not F.

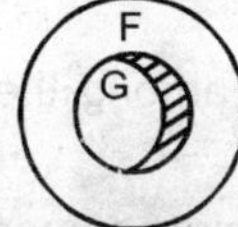

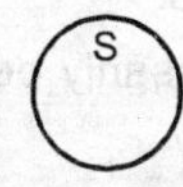

F = Florescent things

G = Ghosts

S = Singers

The valid conclusion is: Some F(shared position) are not S. (V) and not the converse: Some S are not F. (X)

(The some ghosts who are not singers (in shaded portion) are also the 'some florescent things that are not singers')

Statement C is invalid:

All C are S.

All S are H.

∴ Some H are not C.

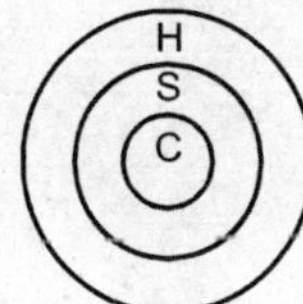

C = Cricketers

S = Those who swear

H = Those who are hanged

The valid conclusion is:

All C are H (✓) and not its negation: Some H are not (C) (x)

Statement D is valid.

Some CP are P.

All CP are W.

∴ Some W are P.

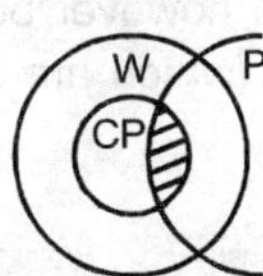

CP = Crazy people

W = Wrestlers

P = Pianists

The shaded portion represents those some pianists who are crazy people and are, therefore, wrestlers. And conversely, they are those some wrestlers who are pianists.

69. a (a) 'C and D' is the correct answer choice.

Statement A is invalid: The valid conclusion would be 'All W are K', rather than its converse, 'All K are W'.

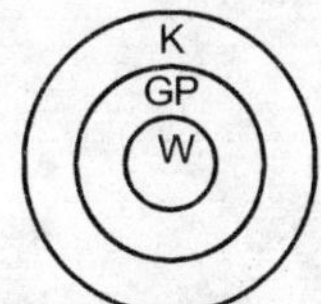

K = Knights

GP = Good People

W = Warriors

Statement B is invalid, because it has four terms: footballers, ministers, tough people and players.

Statement C is valid: The 'some M' that are P are also S. (shaded position).

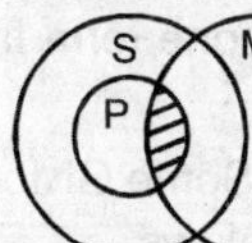

S = Snacks

P = Pizzas

M = Meals

Statement D is valid: The 'some MD' that are B are also SB. (shaded portion).

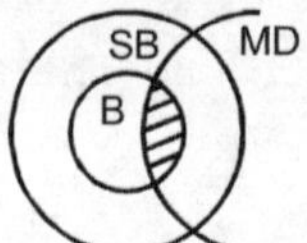

SB = Sloth bears

B = Barkers

MD = Musk deer

70. b (b) B only is the correct answer choice.

Statement A is invalid, as 'No WB are PC' cannot be validly concluded. What can, however, be validly concluded is that 'Some PC (which are all D in shaded position) are not WB'.

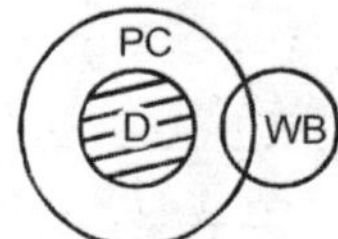

D = Dinosaurs

PC = Prehistoric creatures

WB = Water buffaloes

Statement B is valid as evident from the Venn diagram

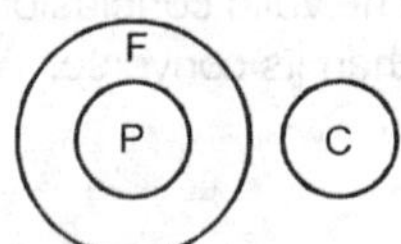

F = Frank creatures

P = Politicians

C = Crocodiles

P is a subset of F.

F and C are disjoint sets.

As the main set F can never intersect with C, the subset D will also never intersect or coincide with C.

Statement C is invalid: No valid conclusion can follow from two negative premises, as negatives have the effect of separating one term from the others.

Statement D is invalid, as the 'Some GI Joes' who like bananas need not be monkeys.

71. c (c) 'C and B' is the correct answer choice.

Statement A is invalid because it has four terms:

a. Earthquakes

b. Things that cause havoc

c. Landslides

d. Things that cause landslides

Statement B is valid as the 'Some C' which are GT are also T (shaded portion).

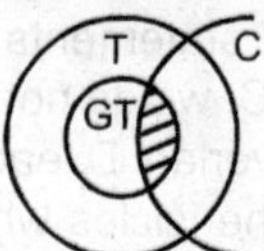

T = Transparent

GT = Glass things

C = Curios

As all glass things (GT) are transparent (T), those curios (C) that are GT are definitely T.

Statement C is valid:

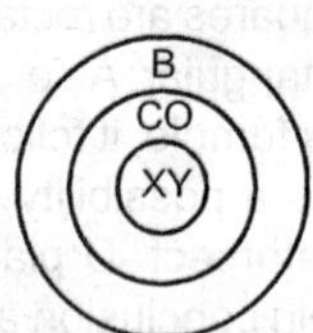

B = Brittle things

CO = Clay objects

CO is a subset of B.

XY is a subset of CO.

Therefore, XY is also a subset of B.

Thus, all XY are also brittle.

Statement D is invalid.

No valid conclusion can follow from two negative premises, as negatives have the effect of separating one term from the other.

72. b (b) C is the only correct answer choice.

Statement A is invalid.

MD need not necessarily be among the some actors who are pretty.

Statement B is invalid, as the third segment is not a conclusion logically deduced using both the first and second segments. In fact, the conclusion can directly be deduced from the second segment alone. Another way to check for this error is to see whether the middle term 'Cops', that appears in the premises also appears in the conclusion. Here, 'Cops' appears in all three segments and option (b) is therefore, not a valid syllogism.

Statement C is valid. Those 'Some men', who are cops are also brave people (shaded portion).

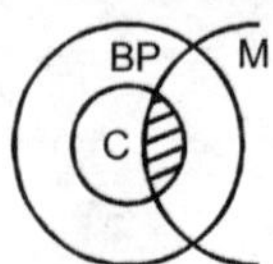

BP = Brave people

C = Cops

M = Men

C is a subset of BP

Some M is C.

Therefore, those M that are C, are also BP.

Statement D is invalid, MS may still be pretty without being an actor.

73. a (a) 'A and B' is the correct answer choice.

A and B are both valid: 'No IIMs are BIMs' or its converse,

'No BIMs are IIMs' are both equally valid.

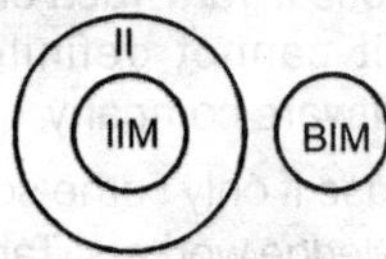

II = Institutes in India.

IIMs is a subset of II.

No II is a BIM

As the mainset II can never intersect with the disjoint set BIM, the subset IIM will also never intersect or coincide with BIM.

C and D are both invalid: The 'Some IIMs' and the 'Some BIMs' need not have any relationship between them, just because they are not in India.

74. c (c) Only C is the correct answer choice.

Statement A is invalid. We cannot conclude about 'all YP', but only about 'Some YP' (shaded portion) who are, incidentally, 'all CY'.

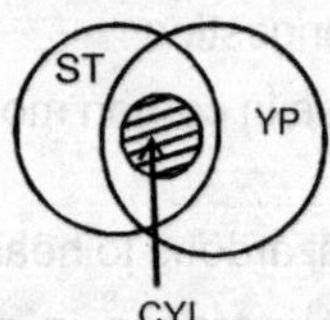

CYI = Citizens of Yes Islands

ST = People who speak only the truth

YP = Young people

Statement B is invalid, because it has four terms:

a. Citizens of Yes Islands

b. People who speak only the truth

c. Things that are in the Atlantic

d. Yes Islands

Statement C is valid. The 'Some YP' who are CYI also are people who speak only the truth. (shaded portion)

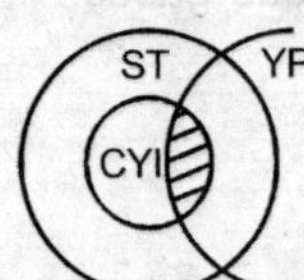

Statement D is invalid, because the 'some people' and the 'some CYI' need not have any relationship between them, just because both speak only the truth.

75. c (c) C only is the correct answer choice.

Statement A is invalid, as the some fish that are viviparous need not be mammals.

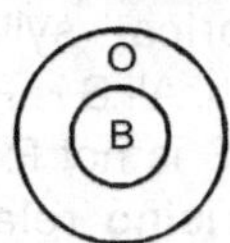

Statement B is invalid. We can validly conclude that the 'Some fish (shaded portion)' that are not oviparous are definitely not birds as well. But, based on this, we cannot conclude that 'Some fish are birds', as we have no knowledge about the 'remaining fish'.

Statement C is valid, as we can validly conclude that the 'Some C' which are inside the circle O cannot be mammals. But nothing definite can be said about the 'Some C' which are outside the circle O.

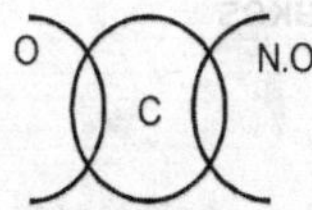

Statement D is invalid, because the 'Some C', which are V and the 'Some C', which are M, need not have any relationship between them, as evident from the Venn diagram.

76. b (b) B only is the correct answer choice.

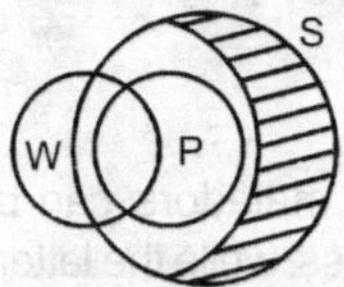

Statement A is invalid, as no definite relationship between P and W can be established.

Note: 'Many' is translated as 'Some' to convert the statement in standard form.

The 'Some S (shared portion)' are not W, but some other S could be W, as shown in the Venn diagram above.

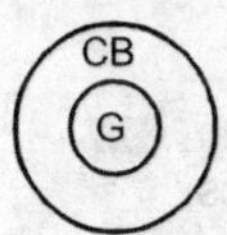

Statement B is valid, as the 'Some C (shaded portion)' that do not climb beans stalks cannot be giants.

G = Grants

C = Children

CB = Creatures which climb beanstalks

C is invalid, the 'Some penguins' that live in snowdrifts need not be explorers.

D is invalid, as Amar is the tallest among the three, but it is not clear how the heights of Akbar and Anthony are compared.

Note: This is not a 'Categorical' syllogism comprising statements, as such. All S is P, No S is P, Some S is P and some S is not P. It is a 'relational' syllogism comprising relational statements that normally feature in analytical reasoning. Be alert: CAT examiner is in the habit of jumbling up questions to throw you off gear.

77. d (d) 'C and D' is the correct answer choice.

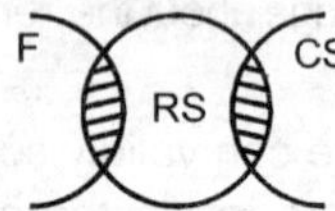

Statement A is invalid: The 'Some F' who are RS and the 'Some RS' who can catch snakes need not have any relationship between them.

CS = People who catch snakes

RS = Rocket scientists

F = Farmers

Note: 'Many' or 'a few' are both translated as 'some' to convert the statements in the standard form.

Statement B is invalid. Poonam need not be among the some kangaroos that are made of teak.

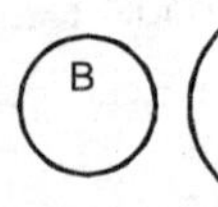

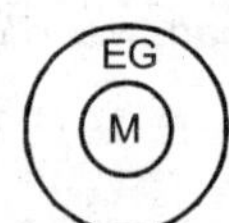

Statement C is valid. No matadors can be bulls because the former eat grass, while the latter do not.

EG: Creatures that eat grass

M: Matadors

B: Bulls

Statement D is valid. The some PB (shaded portion) are in effect the 'Some skunks' that drive Cadillacs.

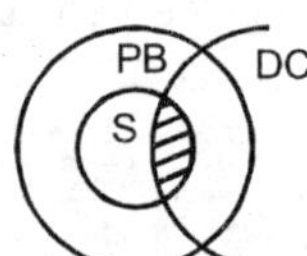

DC: Creature that drive Cadillacs

PB: Polar bears

S: Skunks

78. b (b) ACB is the correct answer choice. as it forms a valid syllogism.

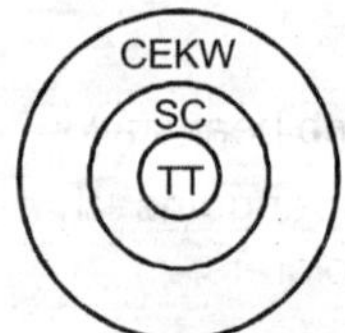

CEKW = Companies that employ knowledge workers

SC = Software companies

TT = Tara Tech

The premises state that all software companies employ knowledge workers and Tara Tech is a software company. Therefore, Tara Tech employs knowledge workers.

(a) ABC is invalid, because if Tara Tech employs knowledge workers, it cannot definitely be concluded that it is a software company.

(c) CDB is invalid, because if only some software companies employ knowledge workers, Tara Tech may not be among them.

(d) ACE introduces a fourth term. 'Companies that employ only knowledge workers' and, therefore, violates the very definition of a syllogism, which must have 3 and only 3 terms.

79. d (d) BAC is the correct answer choice, as it forms a valid syllogism.

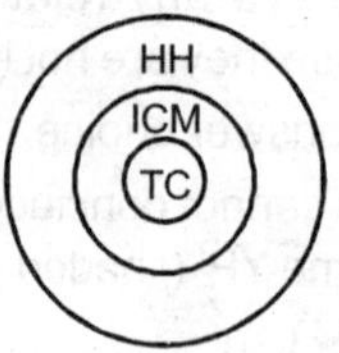

TC = Instances of traffic congestion

ICM = Instances of increase in carbon monoxide in the environment.

HH = Instances that are hazardous to health.

The premises state that increase in carbon monoxide is hazardous to health and traffic congestion increases carbon monoxide in the environment. Therefore, traffic congestion is hazardous to health.

(a) CBA is invalid, because if TC and ICM are both separately hazardous to health (HH), no definite relationship between TC and ICM necessarily follows.

(b) BDE is invalid, because the some TC that are not ICM need not necessarily be free of any hazard to health (HH): they could possibly pollute the environment with other noxious gases.

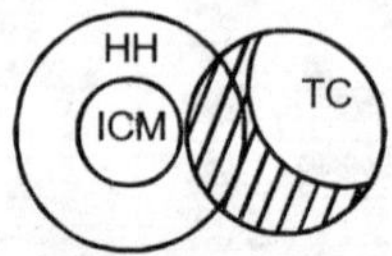

The shaded portion shows those some TC that are not ICM, but could possibly be hazardous to health (HH).

(c) CDE is invalid, because the conclusion E is a negation of one of the premises C. Another check reveals the TC is the middle term, which appears in both the premises C and D, and E, therefore, should not appear in the conclusion E, as per the basic definition of a syllogism.

80. a (a) CEA is the correct answer choice, as it forms a valid syllogism.

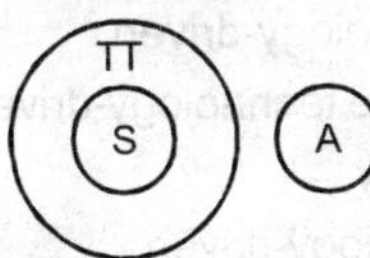

Figures S = Sweets

TT = Tasty things

A = Apples

Sweets are a subset of tasty things. Apples are not tasty things. As apples are not a part of the main set of tasty things, they can also not be a part of the subset of sweets.

(b) BDC is invalid, because the set of some A that are S and the set of some A that are not TT may have no relationship with each other (disjoint sets).

(c) CBD is invalid, because some A that are S are definitely TT, but we have no knowledge of the remaining A, and hence can reach no conclusion about them.

(d) EAC is invalid, because if all A are neither S nor TT, we cannot establish a definite relationship between S and TT.

81. b (b) BAE is the correct answer choice, as it forms a valid syllogism.

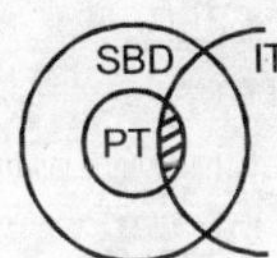

PT = Polluted towns

SBD = Things that should be destroyed

IT = Indian towns or towns in India.

The shaded portion are those IT which are polluted (PT) and hence should be destroyed (SBD).

The premises state that polluted towns should be destroyed and that some towns in India are polluted. The 'some' in statement E refers to the polluted Indian towns that should be destroyed.

(a) BDE is invalid, because with B and D as premises, the only valid conclusion that follows is C. Town Meghana should be destroyed. 'Town Meghana' cannot be simply replaced by 'Some town in India,' as in E.

(c) ADE is invalid, because the syllogism has more than 3 terms. The term SBD does not appear in the premises A and D, but appears in the conclusion E as a new and fourth term.

(d) CDB is invalid, because we can't talk of all PT in the conclusion B, when we only have information about Town Meghana in both the premises C and D. In deductive reasoning, we cannot proceed from specific cases to general cases. It would, however, be valid to conclude that 'some polluted towns should be destroyed.'

82. a (a) ACB is the correct answer choice, as it forms a valid syllogism.

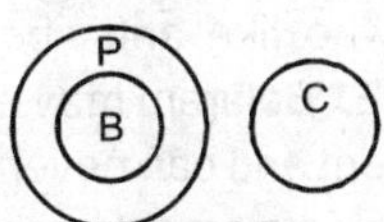

P = Patriots

C = Criminals

B = Bundledas

Since patriot and criminal are two distinct sets, what is patriot, cannot be criminal. Therefore, if Bundeldas is a patriot, Bundeldas cannot be a criminal.

(b) ABC is invalid, because if no P is C and B is not C, we cannot be definite that B is not P.

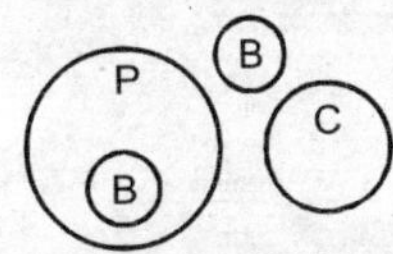

Bundledas (B) may be a patriot (P) or not. Nothing definite can be concluded.

(c) ADE is invalid, on similar lines as explained in the case of (b).

(d) ABE is invalid, because the syllogism has four terms: patriots, criminals, Bundledas and Bogusdas.

83. d (d) ACD is the correct answer choice, as it forms a valid syllogism.

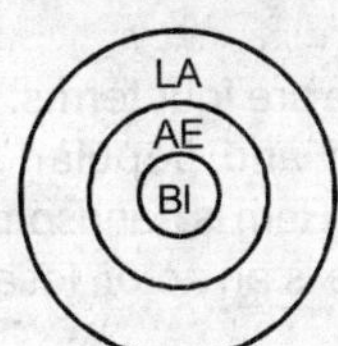

BI = Balaram

AE = Anteaters

LA = Creatures who like ants

Anteaters like ants and Balram is an anteater. Therefore, Balram likes ants.

(a) DCA is invalid. Just because Balaram likes ants and he is also an anteater, it does not logically follow that all anteaters like ants. It would, however, be valid to conclude that 'some anteaters like ants.'

(b) ADC is invalid, because if Balaram like ants, we cannot definitely conclude that Balaram is an anteater, as evident from the Venn diagram.

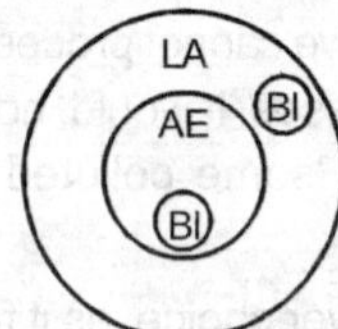

(c) ABC is invalid, because it has four terms: Anteaters, creatures who like ants, boys and Balaram. Furthermore, E: 'Balaram may eat ants' is a tantologous statement and can never feature in a valid syllogism. A 'may' statement implies 'may not' and is always true (tantalogous), and can always stand on its own, without any supporting premises. Hence, such a statement is of no use to a student of logic, who is concerned with the process of reasoning, arriving at a definite conclusion from definite information given in the premises.

84. b (b) ABE is the correct answer choice, as it forms a valid syllogism.

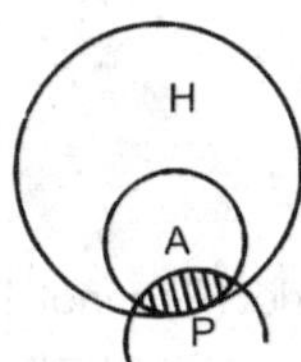

H = Handsome people

A = Actors

P = Popular people

The shaded portion are some popular people who are actors and hence are handsome people.

All actors are handsome and some of those actors are also popular. Therefore, some who are popular are also handsome.

(a) ACD is invalid, as there are four terms: actors, handsome people, Ram and popular actors. Furthermore, just because Ram is handsome does not definitely mean that he is an actor, let alone 'a popular actor'.

(c) and (d) are similarly invalid as option (a), because they each have four terms.

85. a (a) ABC is the correct answer choice, as it forms a valid syllogism.

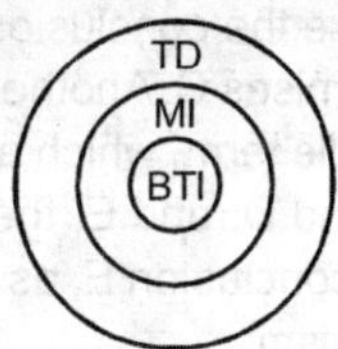

BTI = BTI

MI = Modern Industry

TD = Thing that is technology-driven

All modern industries are technology-driven.

BTI is a modern industry

Therefore, BTI is technology-driven.

(b) ABD is invalid, although it is similar to the correct option ABC.

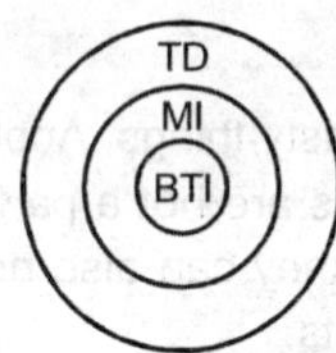

It is invalid simply because the statement D: 'BTI may be technology-driven, is a tantalogous statement (that is, it is always true, regardless of what the premises say).

(c) BCA is invalid. Just because BTI is a modern industry and it is technology-driven, it does not mean that all MI are TD. It would, however, be valid to conclude that 'Some MI are TD'.

(d) EBC is invalid, because if BTI is a modern industry, we cannot definitely conclude that it is technology- driven, as evident from the Venn diagram.

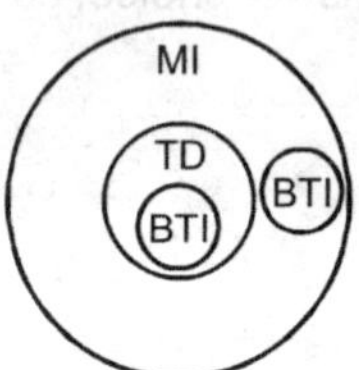

86. b (b) ABE is the correct answer choice, as it forms a valid syllogism.

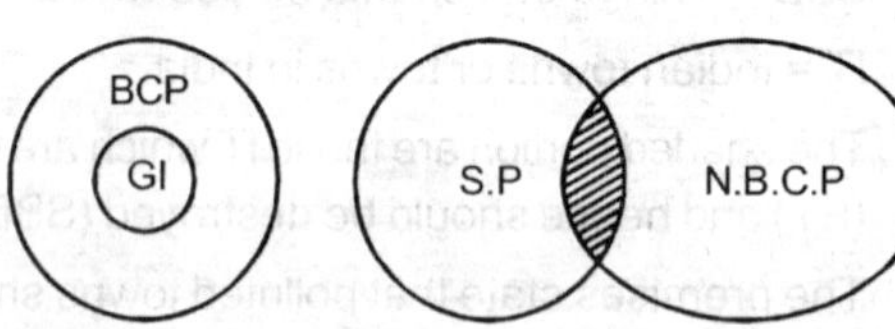

GI = Golmal islanders

BCP = Blue-coloured people

SP = Smart people

NBCP = Not blue-coloured people

Those smart people who are not blue-coloured people (shaded portion) are definitely not Golmal islanders.

(a) BCD is invalid, because there is no connection between some babies that are BCP and the some SP who are not BCP.

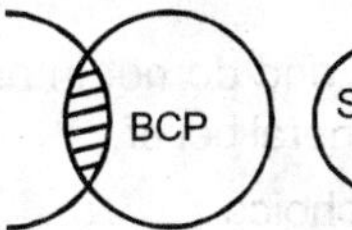

(c) CBD is invalid, because there need not necessarily be any relationship between the some B that are BCP and the some B that are SP.

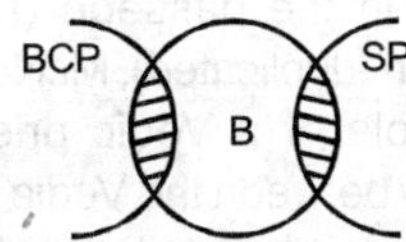

87. c (c) AEB is the correct answer choice, as it forms a valid syllogism.

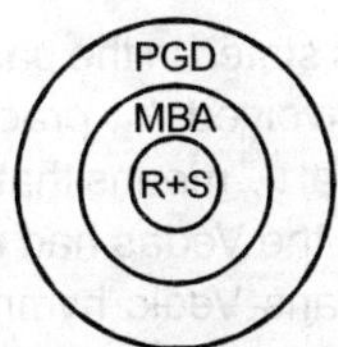

R + S = Ram and Sita

PGD = People in great demand

MBA = MBA

As all MBAs are in great demand and Ram and Sita belong to the set of MBAs, Ram and Sita are also in great demand.

(a) ABE is invalid because R + S need not be MBAs, just because both are in great demand.

(b) ECD makes no sense.

(d) EBA is invalid. Just because R + S are MBAs and in great demand does not mean that 'all MBAs are in great demand'. It would, however, be valid to conclude the 'some MBAs are in great demand'.

CRITICAL REASONING

1. c The whole argument is based on the fact that we are planning our development with a purpose in mind. If development cannot be planned, the argument is weakened.

2. c The statement that our economic development is inspired by social justice implies both the assumptions.

3. a The argument suggests that our economic development will lead to better standard of living and it will in turn bring social justice.

4. c The reasons given for taking interest in hydro electric projects are that oil prices are increasing and that renewable sources should be tapped.

5. a If hydroelectric power is costlier, then such projects will not help in the face of rising oil prices.

6. b The statement suggests that without music, dance or art one cannot be fully alive; hence there can be no civilization.

7. c If art has no relation with civilization, the whole argument is nullified.

8. b The statement considers being vibrantly alive as being a necessary condition for being civilized.

9. c If two parties limit the choice of the voters, we cannot have a true democracy.

10. a If politics were also played like any other game then two parties would be enough to play that game.

11. c The author states that democracy would be possible with just two parties if it were a game like cricket, thus assuming that cricket is played by two parties, or teams.

12. c The answer to this question can be neither 'No' nor 'Yes' as both would contradict the given conditions.

13. a The answer to the question has to be 'yes' implying that Laxman is 'Yes' hence Ram has to be 'No'

14. d The answer to this question can be 'No' as well as 'Yes'.

15. d One cannot devote one's whole life to understanding another culture, if to appreciate other cultures first one has to spend time understanding one's own culture and people.

16. a Fresh experience enriches the writers soul, thus renewing him, in turn leading to the writer being fertile.

17. a An idea that brings in a tremendous disparity would not be able to work for general convenience and advantage, as stated in the argument.

18. d

19. c The passage states that even those whom we intimately know, can surprise us at times with some unknown facet of their personality.

20. a As the passage says that efficiency won't be content to reign in the shop, but will follow us home, it implies that efficiency can become all-pervading. (b) is not the focus of the questions. (c) goes beyond the scope of the argument.

21. c As each project is being stalled for some reason or the other and no consensus has been reached on any of the projects, we can infer that the projects will be stalled for an indefinite period. (a) is stated in the argument, and (b) is likely to be a conclusion.

22. b The passage states that designations are forgotten during the meetings and even a sales engineer can question the CEO on company policies. The company's ulterior motive is not the focus of the argument, so (a) and (c) are ruled out.

23. a The passage states that the rape of Indian architectural wealth can be attributed to the blend of activist disunity and local indifference. (b) may not be true as Indians may be gullible. (c) and (d) are stated in the passage.

24. b The moral police feel that *Fire* would influence the Indian psyche and ruin the moral fabric of the nation, which it should not be allowed to do. (a) is not true, as Indian audiences may be discriminating. (c) is not an inference, it is true to a certain extent.

25. a The passage states that the rich have never felt secure against the poor and their aggressiveness stemmed from fear of the poor. (b) refutes the conclusion in the argument.

26. c The passage states that the second kind of traveller visits only such monuments as the time at his disposal allows him to contemplate without irreverent haste. The preference of the writer is not the focus of the argument, hence (a) is wrong. (b) is too caustic.

27. d None of the given options is supported by the passage. (c) may not be true in the immediate temporal context of the argument. (b) is clear from the argument, it is not an inference. (a) is, of course, wrong.

28. d The passage supports none of the given options. (c) does not seem to be true in light of facts presented in the passage. (b) is stated anyway in the passage. What the director aimed at does not seem to be the focus of the argument, which discusses a general consequence.

29. a The Indian middle-class, what it wants and what it buys has been the focus of economic policies since the mid-80s. (b) infers far beyond what can be reasonably inferred from the argument.

30. c (c) is the correct answer choice.

All three airlines have reduced their fares to make up for this loss in increased volumes. This decision is obviously based on the general belief or assumption that air travellers in India are price-conscious. If there is a market research study that shows exactly that, then it would add credence to the general belief.

(a) The general belief relates reduced fares to increased volumes, not to increased profitability. It is possible to increase profitability by cutting costs, even if volumes do not increase. Hence, the cause – and – effect relationship between reduced fares and increased volumes is not directly supported by this statement.

(b) and (d) are irrelevant and do not in any way support or weaken the general belief.

31. b (b) is the correct answer choice

Apparently McNeill is a Westerner who is doing some sort of research on the role of the Brahmin priest in ancient Indian society. From the way his thoughts are evolving in the passage (recite–memorize–dissemination–duplicated), McNeill can only understand the role of a Vedic priest by drawing a direct analogy between the Vedic priest, whom he does not understand except superficially, and a recorded audio casette, which is an essential and ubiquitous item in McNeill's world.

(a) and (d) are more or less stated in the passage, so there is no inference involved. '... practice of reciting Vedas was essential ...' means that it was an obligation and '... when the Vedas had not yet been written down ...' means Vedic hymns had not been scripted. (c) also is less of an inference and more of a surmise.

32. c (c) is the correct answer choice.

The arrangement emerges somewhat like this:-

Premise – I: If developed country, then social security for the elderly.

Premise – II: No social security for the elderly in India, as it is not a developed country and also the traditional support system for them is vanishing.

Conclusion: Therefore, working people in India must save for their old age.

(c) announces the good news for Indian working people:

'India will become a developed country in the future,' implying social security for the elderly, thereby weakening the conclusion.

(a) and (b) indicate some encouraging future trends, but do not obviate the necessity for Indian working people to save for their old age.

(d) Strengthens the conclusion, rather than weakening it.

33. c (c) is the correct answer choice.

The surmise or hypothesis in the passage implies that:

biodiversity is inversely proportional to educational performance, with poverty playing no role in this relationship.

(d) merely confirms the inverse relationship, at all levels of poverty.

(a) relates good education performance with high levels of poverty, regardless of biodiversity (variety of flora). It is, therefore, irrelevant.

(b) and (c) also support the inverse relationship between biodiversity and educational performance, but each reserves a role for poverty in this relationship. (c) summarizes better, hence (c).

34. b (b) is the only option that explains how reducing taxes will broaden the tax base. If taxes on cigarettes (which constitute 90% of the revenues) are reduced, the prices of cigarettes will come down, thereby increasing the demand for cigarettes. More the cigarette smokers, the broader the tax base. Options (a) and (c) mention peripheral matters. (d) is talking about increasing duties (taxes) whereas the last sentence of the paragraph has only looked at "reducing taxes".

35. c (c) is the correct answer choice.

(a) undermines Mathews' theory by showing how population need not follow geometric rate of growth and (b) undermines it by showing how food need not follow arithmetic rate of growth.

(d) undermines his theory by pointing out that the inability of our planet to support the growing human population need not lead to disastrous consequences for humans. There are ways that these can be averted.

(c) is the only option that does not undermine his theory. It also does not support his theory by referring to the different rates of growth in human and natural systems, but merely asserts that these rates of growth remain constant and cannot be changed.

36. a (a) is the correct answer choice.

The picture that emerges from the passage is:

Year	Production (in tonnes)	% increase over previous year
1970–71	6,089	—
—		
1997–98	5,830	—
1998–99	8,079	38.58%

This shows that the average production has remained well below 6,000 tonnes in the previous years. The significant increase of over 2,000 tonnes in 1998–99 was achieved by using all possible productivity enhancing measures.

If all areas have been properly irrigated, if all unproductive coffee bushes have been replaced, if intensive refilling and improved agricultural practices have been used — how much more can be done?

Obviously, the target of 10,000 tonnes (about 70% increase over average of less than 6000 tonnes) is unrealistic, as explained by option (a). Options (b) and (c) also indirectly contribute to making the target of 10,000 tonnes unrealistic. But (a) contributes MOST.

(d), on the other hand, supports the target as realistic, by placing faith in the soundness of the target-selling produces.

37. b (b) is the correct answer choice.

The first sentence of the passage asserts that:

Intelligence of animals is proportionate to the extent of their socializing.

Then the passage gives examples of how animals are effective when they are in their own social group and ineffective when they are alone.

This is exactly what is given in option (b).

(a) and (c) are partly stated in the passage, but do not convey the central message.

(d) cannot be inferred as the passage does not compare the behaviour of elephants and beavers with the behaviour of bees and ants.

38. c If the number of students enrolled for a certain class do not fit into that age interval, they are in excess and hence, unrepresentative, thus resulting in bloated ratios. (a) is wrong because the definition of gross enrollment ratio itself is flawed. Attendance is not the focus of our argument. We are also not concerned with demographic trends, but only with given data.

39. b The argument states that 'clubs that spend more should finish at a higher ranking'. This is reflected in 'highly paid white players returned a low ranking'. (a) focuses on clubs that recruited black players, a consequence Szymanski is not immediately concerned with. (c) also throws no light on the relation 'clubs that spend more should finish higher'. Nor does (d).

40. d Only (d) connects the recommendation directly to the cause 'rising tensions' in prisons and not to any marginal political factors. (a), (b) and (c) may have contributed, but peripherally, to the minister's decision.

41. c (a) and (d) cover the government's honourable intentions, which look best on paper. (b) discusses one feasiblilty factor. (c) is the best choice as it shows how the project has reached the implementation stage from the pilot stage.

42. b 'Manoeuvrability' is linked to 'flight direction changes' in (d). (c) just vaguely mentions 'faster'. (a) makes no inference, as such. It may or may not be true. There is insufficient evidence to infer (d), it sounds rather far-fetched.

43. a (b) does not attack the argument, it helps the Association's cause. (c) is pointless, if there isn't adequate consumption. (d) has little to do with the core issue in the argument. But (a) if true, would render the cumulative efforts of the Association fruitless.

44. d (a) would only result in more cars per family. (b) and (c) defeat Athens' purpose as citizens devise ingenious methods to maintain status quo both in terms of number of cars and congestion.

45. b The Central Bank can only express 'reservations' on 'monetisation' to the government. It cannot be the 'boss', it only advises. (c) does not support the conclusion in any way. (a) and (d) are specific observations, but they do not contribute to our answer.

46. d (d) is a summary for the general words 'varied use', 'common basis' pertaining to the 'symbol' in the geographical and historical context. (c) does not present the complete picture. (a) refuses to divulge the significance of the umbrella. (b) is wrong as the ruler is regarded as the instrument of firmament of the supreme law.

47. c This answer goes without guessing. There are two parties in the game, and each has its own strategy and a guess on the opponent's move. (a) involves more of cooperation strategies than game plans. (b) is competition involving more than two candidates. (d) is about cartels.

48. c1 is too narrow and it doesn't mention the central idea of the paragraph. 4 is wrong as the paragraph doesn't mention authors as the central idea. 2 could have been the right answer but it doesn't match the tone of the author, which is slightly negative. Proponents of Buddhism haven't exaggerated rather it was done by few authors. 3 is the best answer as it contains the central idea of the paragraph.

49. d1 is wrong because Volkswagen is not trying to shift the blame onto the employees. Rather it has encouraged employees to share information and has announced an amnesty plan. 3 is wrong as it is too narrow. 2 is too narrow and is a twisted option. The amnesty programme will end soon but that is not the reason why Volkswagen is pressurizing the employees. 4 is the best option.

50. a2 is not mentioned in the paragraph. Only one glacier is the focal point of the paragraph. 3 mentions the sub idea and misses the central idea of the paragraph i.e. the ecological impact of the disintegration of the glacier. 4, too, is a narrow option. Option (a) mentions the central idea and it is the best answer.

LOGICAL CONSISTENCY

1. b Sam is not drunk, so he must be ill. One of the either ... or condition is true.

2. c As Ram did not lose sleep, it shows that he did not hear of the tragedy. When A, then B. Not B, hence not A.

3. d The train is not late, so it must have derailed. One of the either ... or condition is true.

4. a I did not have a nightmare, so I must not have read a horror story. When A, then B. Not B, hence not A.

5. b I did not get rashes which shows that I did not eat berries. When A, then B. Not B, hence not A.

6. b If Sita is not sick, it follows that she is careless. One of the either/or conditions hold good.

7. d Ram does not eat hamburgers, so it follows that he does not get a swollen nose. When X, then Y. Not Y, hence not X.

8. b If the employees have confidence in the management, it follows that they are hostile. The first of the either/ or condition is false, so the second one has to be true.

9. d None of the given options relates logically to the given statements.

10. a As all irresponsible parents do not shout, it follows that the children cavort. When X, then Y. X, hence Y.

11. d The main statement clearly states that if the orangutan (O)belongs to the set of not angry (NA), he cannot belong to the set of frowns (F). Also, O must belong to either of the two sets.

CB states that O is not F and is NA. And DA states that O is not NA and is F. Therefore, both CB and DA are logically valid.

12. d The main statement clearly states that Ravana (R) is either a demon (D)or a hero (H). He has to be at least one of the two, and if he is one, he cannot be the other.

DB states that R is not H but is D.

And CA states that R is not D but is H.

Therefore, both DB and CA are logically valid.

13. a The question statement clearly states that whenever Rajeev uses the Internet, he dreams about spiders. However, this does not mean that he dreams about spiders only when he uses the Internet. Therefore, using the Internet is only one possible condition for Rajeev to dream about spiders.

Thus, the Venn diagram for the question will be:

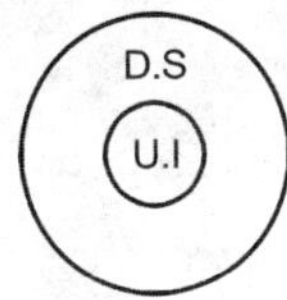

Where,

UI → Uses Internet

DS → Dreams of spiders

Answer choice (a)AD states that Rajeev did not dream about spiders, and hence he did not use the Internet. This logically follows the above Venn diagram. If the main set does not occur, the subset will also not occur.

Thus, AD is the right option.

14. d P = I talk to my professors

Q = I do not need to take a pill for headache.

Therefore, both AB($P \Rightarrow Q$) and CD(neg $Q \Rightarrow$ neg P)are logically consistent, not BA and DC.

(d)'AB and CD' is the correct answer choice.

ODD SENTENCE OUT

1. Misfit sentence is (b) with correct sequence being (dcea). The theme of the passage is introduced by (d) where challenge to slash greenhouse gas emission is faced. (b) follows the idea giving a ray of hope. (ea) go on further to suggest that what can be done to care of such a problem. (b) only tells about the existing limitation.
2. (a) is the misfit sentence with correct sequence being (dbce). (d) introduces the subject - hippo of the passage. (b) further gives details of the description. (ce) is a mandatory pair that describes the behaviour of the creature. (a) is out of context that introduces a new element of habitat issues of the hippos.
3. (a) is the misfit sentence with the correct sequence being (cdbe). The theme of the passage is that we are trying to draw similarity between humans and Neanderthals. (c) initiates the discussion and (d) states the opposite idea. This is followed by (b) which says to answer 'this question', researchers are studying facial bones followed by description of facts about bone formation.
4. The sentences if arranged sequentially form a coherent paragraph on the importance of communication of which speech is an integral part. Leaving aside the 2nd sentence all of them talk on this topic. although may seem correct but actually it is farfetched ("achieve our goals and bring our dreams to fruition") as far as the context of the given paragraph is concerned.
5. The jumbled paragraph if arranged sequentially, IT talks about Federer achieving greatness in spite of his age. He is the oldest tennis player to win a singles title. But, option (d) is an anomaly. It talks about some ongoing tournament, which Federer may be a part of. However, even the third sentence can be the odd one out as it talks about a very specific technique of Federer.
6. This is a wrong answer. The correct answer should have been. The entire paragraph talks about subtlety. The second sentence talks about something else.
7. It is a difficult question. All the sentences talk about erosion. The main idea of the paragraph is difficult to grasp. However, 5 talks about 'human cost'. So, this introduces a new idea. So, 5 is the best answer.
8. The second sentence has the phrase 'this factoid'. There is no clear precedence for this pronoun in the paragraph. So, sentence 2 is the odd one out.
9. The arrangement given as the answer by CAT makes no sense. Sentence (a) is clearly the opening sentence. However, (c) after sentence (a) is too abrupt. There is no 'linking word or phrase'. adcb also looks like a possible sequence. This question seems incorrect.
10. The best way to eliminate the odd one out, 4 sentences only refers to song while option (c) only refers to the sound. Thus right answer is option (c).
11. Options (a,b,d) and (e) talk about the urbanisation and mitigation strategies while option (c) is talking about the consequences which is not related to urban areas, like forest fires.
12. Options (a) and (b), options (b) and (c) form a mandatory pair resulting in option (e) being the irrelevant point. So, right answer is option (e).

2
CHAPTER

Vocabulary

MATCH THE MEANING

2001

DIRECTIONS for Questions 1 to 10: Answer the questions based on the following information.

For the word given at the top of each table, match the dictionary definitions on the left (A, B, C, D) with their corresponding usage on the right (E, F, G, H). Out of the four possibilities given in the boxes below the table, select the one that has all the definitions and their usages correctly matched.

1. Exceed

Dictionary definition

A. To extend outside of or enlarge beyond used chiefly in strictly physical relations
B. To be greater than or superior to
C. Be beyond the comprehension of
D. To go beyond a limit set by (as an authority or privilege)

Usage

E. The mercy of God exceeds our finite minds
F. Their accomplishments exceeded our expectation.
G. He exceeded his authority when he paid his brother's gambling debts with money from the trust.
H. If this rain keeps up, the river will exceed its banks by morning.

(a)

A	H
B	F
C	E
D	G

(b)

A	H
B	E
C	F
D	G

(c)

A	G
B	F
C	E
D	H

(d)

A	F
B	G
C	H
D	E

2. Infer

Dictionary definition

A. To derive by reasoning or implication
B. To surmise
C. To point out
D. To hint

Usage

E. We see smoke and infer fire.
F. Given some utterance, a listener may infer from it all sorts of things which neither the utterance nor the utterer implied.
G. I waited all day to meet him. From this you can infer my zeal to see him.
H. She did not take part in the debate except to ask a question inferring that she was not interested in the debate.

(a)

A	G
B	E
C	H
D	F

(b)

A	F
B	H
C	E
D	G

(c)

A	H
B	G
C	F
D	E

(d)

A	E
B	F
C	G
D	H

3. Mellow

Dictionary definition

A. Adequately and properly aged so as to be free of harshness
B. Freed from the rashness of youth
C. Of soft and loamy consistency
D. Rich and full but free from stridency

Usage

E. He has mellowed with age.
F. The tones of the old violin were mellow.
G. Some wines are mellow.
H. Mellow soil found in the Gangetic plains.

(a)

A	E
B	G
C	F
D	H

(b)

A	E
B	F
C	G
D	H

(c)

A	G
B	E
C	H
D	F

(d)

A	H
B	G
C	F
D	E

4. Relief

Dictionary definition

A. Removal or lightening of something distressing
B. Aid in the form of necessities for the indigent
C. Diversion
D. Release from the performance of duty

Usage

E. A ceremony follows the relief of a sentry after the morning shift.
F. It was a relief to take off the tight shoes.
G. The only relief I get is by playing cards.
H. Disaster relief was offered to the victims

(a)

A	F
B	H
C	E
D	G

(b)

A	F
B	H
C	G
D	E

(c)

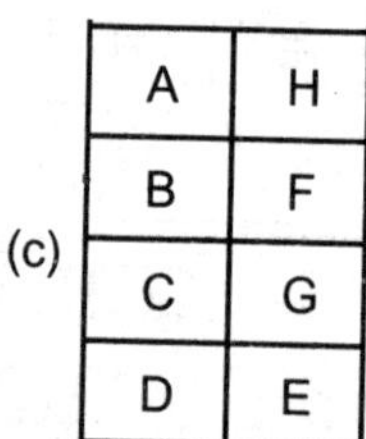

A	H
B	F
C	G
D	E

(d)

A	G
B	E
C	H
D	F

5. Purge

Dictionary definition

A. Remove a stigma from the name of
B. Make clean by removing whatever is superfluous, foreign
C. Get rid of
D. To cause evacuation of

Usage

E. The opposition was purged after the coup.
F. The committee heard his attempt to purge himself of a charge of heresy.
G.. Drugs that purge the bowels are often bad for the brain.
H. It is recommended to purge water by distillation.

(a)

A	E
B	G
C	F
D	H

(b)

A	F
B	E
C	H
D	G

(c)

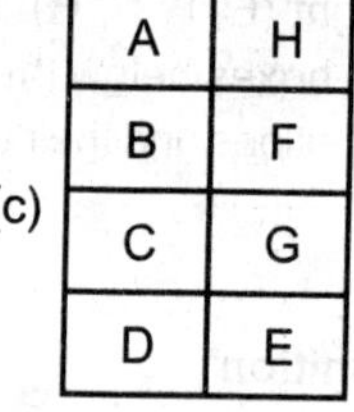

A	H
B	F
C	G
D	E

(d)

A	F
B	H
C	E
D	G

2002

6. Measure

Dictionary definition

A. Size or quantity found by measuring
B. Vessel of standard capacity
C. Suitable action
D. Ascertain extent or quantity

Usage

E. A measure was instituted to prevent outsiders from entering the campus.
F. Sheila was asked to measure each item that was delivered.
G. The measure of the cricket pitch was 22 yards.
H. Ramesh used a measure to take out one litre of oil.

(a)

A	H
B	F
C	E
D	G

(b)

A	G
B	E
C	F
D	H

(c)

A	G
B	H
C	E
D	F

(d)

A	F
B	H
C	E
D	G

7. Bound

Dictionary definition

A. Obliged, constrained
B. Limiting value
C. Move in a specified direction
D. Destined or certain to be

Usage

E. Dinesh felt bound to walk out when the discussion turned to kickbacks.

F. Buffeted by contradiuctory forces he was bound to lose his mind.

G. Vidya's story strains the bounds of credulity

H. Bound for a career in law, Jyoti was reluctant to study Milton.

(a)

A	F
B	H
C	G
D	E

(b)

A	E
B	G
C	H
D	F

(c)

A	E
B	H
C	F
D	G

(d)

A	F
B	G
C	E
D	H

8. Catch

Dictionary definition

A. Capture

B. Grasp with senses or mind

C. Deception

D. Thing or person worth trapping

Usage

E. All her friends agreed that Prasad was a good catch.

F. The proposal sounds very good but where is the catch?

G. Hussain tries to catch the spirit of India in this painting.

H. Sorry, I couldn't catch you.

(a)

A	H
B	F
C	E
D	G

(b)

A	F
B	G
C	E
D	H

(c)

A	G
B	F
C	E
D	H

(d)

A	G
B	H
C	F
D	E

9. Deal

Dictionary definition

A. Manage, attend to

B. Stock, sell

C. Give out to a number of people

D. Be concerned with

Usage

E. Dinesh insisted on dealing the cards.

F. This contract deals with handmade cards.

G. My brother deals in cards.

H. I decided not to deal with handmade cards.

(a)

A	F
B	E
C	G
D	H

(b)

A	H
B	G
C	E
D	F

(c)

A	F
B	H
C	G
D	E

(d)

A	H
B	E
C	G
D	F

10. Turn

Dictionary definition

A. Give new direction to

B. Send

C. Change in form

D. Opportunity coming successively for each person

Usage

E. It was now his turn to be angry.

F. Leena never turned away a beggar.

G. Ashish asked Laxman to turn his face to the left.

H. The old school building has been turned into a museum.

(a)

A	H
B	E
C	F
D	G

(b)

A	G
B	F
C	E
D	H

(c)

A	G
B	E
C	F
D	H

(d)

A	G
B	F
C	H
D	E

CLOZE TEST

2002

DIRECTIONS for Questions 1 to 6: Fill the gaps in the passages below with the most appropriate word from the options given for each gap. The right words are the ones used by the author. Be guided by the author's overall style and meaning when you choose the answers.

Von Nuemann and Morgenstern assume a decision

framework in which all options are thoroughly considered, each option being independent of the others, with a numerical value derived for the utility of each possible outcome (these outcomes reflecting, in turn, all possible combinations of choices). The decision is then made to maximize the expected utility. ... 1 ... such a model reflects major simplifications of the way divisions are made in the real world. Humans are not able to process information as quickly and effectively as the model assumes; they tend not to think ... 2 ... as easily as the model calls for; they often deal with a particular option without really assessing its ... 3 ... and when they do assess alternatives, they may be extremely nebulous about their criteria of evaluation.

1. (a) Regrettably (b) Firstly
   (c) Obviously (d) Apparently
2. (a) quantitatively (b) systematically
   (c) scientifically (d) analytically
3. (a) implications (b) disadvantages
   (c) utility (d) alternatives

In a large company, ... 4 ... people is about as common as using a gun or a switch-blade to ... 5 ... an argument. As a result, most managers have little or no experience of firing people, and they find it emotionally traumatic; as result, they often delay the act interminably, much as an unhappy spouse will prolong a bad marriage. And when the firing is done, it's often done clumsily, with far worse side effects than are necessary.

Do the world-class software organizations have a different way of firing people? No, but they do the deed swiftly, humanely, and professionally.

The key point here is to view the fired employee as a 'failed product' and to ask how the *process* ... 6 ... such a phenomenon in the first place.

4. (a) dismissing (b) punishing
   (c) firing (d) admonishing
5. (a) resolve (b) thwart
   (c) defeat (d) close
6. (a) derived (b) engineered
   (c) produced (d) allowed

2004

DIRECTIONS for Questions 7 to 16: Fill up the blanks, numbered [7], [8] ...... up to [16], in the two passages below with most appropriate word from the options given for each blank.

"Between the year 1946 and the year 1955, I did not file any income tax returns." With that [7] statement, Ramesh embarked on an account of his encounter with the income tax department. "I originally owed Rs. 20,000 in unpaid taxes. With [8] and [9], the 20,000 became 60,000. The Income tax Department then went into action, and I learned first hand just how much power the Tax Department wields. Royalties and trust funds can be [10]; automobiles may be [11], and auctioned off. Nothing belongs to the [12] until the case is settled."

7. (a) devious (b) blunt
   (c) tactful (d) pretentious
8. (a) interest (b) taxes
   (c) principal (d) returns
9. (a) sanctions (b) refunds
   (c) fees (d) fines
10. (a) closed (b) detached
    (c) attached (d) impounded
11. (a) smashed (b) seized
    (c) dismantled (d) frozen
12. (a) purchaser (b) victim
    (c) investor (d) offender

At that time the white house was as serene as a resort hotel out of season. The corridors were [13]. In the various offices, [14] gray men in waistcoats talked to one another in low-pitched voices. The only color, or choler, curiously enough, was provided by President Eisenhower himself. Apparently, his [15] was easily set off; he scowled when he [16] the corridors.

13. (a) striking (b) hollow
    (c) empty (d) white
14. (a) quiet (b) faded
    (c) loud (d) stentorian
15. (a) laughter (b) curiously
    (c) humour (d) temper
16. (a) paced (b) strolled
    (c) stormed (d) prowled

WORD / PHRASE REPLACEMENT

1990

DIRECTIONS for Questions 1 to 5: Choose from among the given alternatives the one which will be a suitable substitute for the underlined expression in each of the following.

1. The <u>marriage of the princess with the commoner</u> caused a furore among the royalty.
   (a) mesalliance (b) misalliance
   (c) elopement (d) romance
2. The victim's <u>involuntary responses to stimulus</u> proved that he was still living.
   (a) reactions (b) reflexes
   (c) feedback (d) communication

3. The art and science of good eating and drinking is now a lost art.
(a) Gastronomy (b) Osteopathy
(c) Gluttony (d) Cooking

4. The thrilling narrative caused the hair on the skin to stand erect.
(a) tension (b) horrification
(c) terror (d) horror

5. The body of Macedonian infantry drawn up in close order was like a formidable castle of steel.
(a) phalanx (b) phagocyte
(c) phenomenon (d) phaeton

2001

DIRECTIONS for Questions 6 to 10: For each of the words below, a contextual usage is provided. Pick the word from the alternatives given that is most inappropriate in the given context.

6. Specious: A specious argument is not simply a false one but one that has the ring of truth.
(a) Deceitful (b) Fallacious
(c) Credible (d) Deceptive

7. Obviate: The new mass transit system may obviate the need for the use of personal cars.
(a) Prevent (b) Forestall
(c) Preclude (d) Bolster

8. Disuse: Some words fall into disuse as technology makes objects obsolete.
(a) Prevalent (b) Discarded
(c) Obliterated (d) Unfashionable

9. Parsimonious: The evidence was constructed from very parsimonious scraps of information.
(a) Frugal (b) Penurious
(c) Thrifty (d) Altruistic

10. Facetious: When I suggested that war is a method of controlling population, my father remarked that I was being facetious.
(a) Jovian (b) Jovial
(c) Jocular (d) Joking

2002

DIRECTIONS for Questions 11 to 15: For each of the words below a context is provided. From the alternatives given pick the word or phrase that is closest in meaning in the given context.

11. **Opprobrium:** The police officer appears oblivious to the opprobrium generated by his blatantly partisan conduct.
(a) Harsh criticism
(b) Acute distrust
(c) Bitter enmity
(d) Stark oppressiveness

12. **Portend:** It appears to many that the US 'war on terrorism' portends trouble in the Gulf.
(a) Introduces (b) Evokes
(c) Spells (d) Bodes

13. **Prevaricate:** When a videotape of her meeting was played back to her and she was asked to explain her presence there, she started prevaricating.
(a) Speaking evasively
(b) Speaking violently
(c) Lying furiously
(d) Throwing a tantrum

14. **Restive:** The crowd became restive when the minister failed to appear even by 10 pm.
(a) Violent (b) Angry
(c) Restless (d) Distressed

15. **Ostensible:** Manohar's ostensible job was to guard the building at night.
(a) Apparent
(b) Blatant
(c) Ostentatious
(d) Insidious

2005

DIRECTIONS for Questions 16 to 19: Each of the following questions has a paragraph with one italicized word that does not make sense. Choose the most appropriate replacement for that word from the options given below the paragraph.

16. Intelligent design derives from an early 19th-century explanation of the natural world given by an English clergyman, William Paley. Paley was the populariser of the famous watchmaker analogy. Proponents of intelligent design are *crupping* Paley's argument with a new gloss from molecular biology.
(a) destroying (b) testing
(c) resurrecting (d) questioning

17. Women squat, heads covered, beside huge piles of limp fodder and *blunk* oil lamps, and just about all the cows in the three towns converge upon this spot. Sinners, supplicants and yes, even scallywags hand over a few coins for a crack at redemption and a handful of grass.
(a) shining (b) bright
(c) sputtering (d) effulgent

18. It is *klang* to a sensitive traveler who walks through this great town, when he sees the streets, the roads and cabin doors crowded with beggars, mostly women, followed by three, four, or six children, all in rags and importuning every passenger for alms.
(a) amusing (b) irritating
(c) disgusting (d) distressing

19. Or there is the most *fingummy* diplomatic note on record: when Philip of Macedon wrote to the Spartans that, if he came within their borders, he would leave not one stone of their city, they wrote back the one word – "If".
(a) witty (b) rude
(c) simple (d) terse

ONE-BLANK FIB

1990

DIRECTIONS for Questions 1 to 22: In each of the following questions, a part of a sentence has been left blank. Select from among the four options given below each question, the one which would best fill in the blank.

1. The insurance claim was __________ by the relevant documents
(a) sustained (b) backed out
(c) backed up (d) proved

2. The recent disturbances in the country will ______ and peace will be restored.
(a) blow past (b) blow over
(c) pass through (d) come to pass

1994

3. One dark night a Darvesh ________ passing by a dry well.
(a) wasn't (b) happened to be
(c) discovered in (d) found to

4. Nordisk have recently __________ a product called Glucometer.
(a) started (b) commissioned
(c) launched (d) begun

5. I had already published a novel and it was an unexpected success. I thought my _______.
(a) days were up (b) chances were good
(c) ladyluck was happy (d) fortune was made

6. The neighbour grabbed the boy, and rolled him on the road to _______ the flames.
(a) smother (b) kill
(c) burn out (d) fizz out

7. Sam asked me to keep his secret ___________.
(a) secret (b) in myself
(c) amongst us (d) between us

8. Sometimes the greatest inventions _______ an idea of starting simplicity
(a) stumbles upon (b) hinge upon
(c) starves without (d) lacks

9. Real friends, genuinely wanting the best for the organization, _______different garbs.
(a) come in (b) clad in
(c) dressed in (d) clothed in

1997

10. An act of justice closes the book on a misdeed; an act of vengeance ___.
(a) is reprehensible
(b) is sordid
(c) reopens the first chapter
(d) writes an epilogue

11. This is about ___ a sociological analysis can penetrate.
(a) as far as
(b) the outer limits that
(c) just how far into the subject
(d) just the relative distance that

12. I am always the first to admit that I have not accomplished everything that I ___ achieve five years ago.
(a) set out to (b) went to
(c) thought to (d) thought of

13. This is not the first time that the management has done some ___.
(a) tough talk (b) tough talking
(c) firm talk (d) firm talking

14. In India the talent is prodigious, and it increases ___.
(a) each year (b) year by year
(c) annually (d) progressively

15. The present constitution will see ___ amendments but its basic structure will survive.
(a) much more (b) many more
(c) too many more (d) quite a few more

16. Taking risks, breaking the rules, and being a maverick have always been important for companies, but, today, they are ___.
(a) more crucial than ever
(b) more crucial
(c) much more crucial
(d) very crucial

17. Education is central because electronic networks and software-driven technologies are beginning to ___ the economic barriers between nations.
(a) break down (b) break
(c) crumble (d) dismantle

1998

18. When children become more experienced with words as visual symbols, they find that they can gain meaning without making ___ sounds.

(a) aural (b) audible
(c) vocal (d) intelligible

19. As a step towards protesting against the spiralling prices, the farmers have decided to stage a picket in an effort to ___.

(a) show their virility
(b) make themselves heard
(c) curb the prices
(d) topple the government

20. Science is a sort of news agency comparable ___ to other news agencies.

(a) principally (b) in principle
(c) in principal (d) in spirit and form

21. Most political leaders acquire their position by causing a large number of people to believe that these leaders are ___ by altruistic desires.

(a) actuated (b) convinced
(c) categorised (d) led

22. Everyone will admit that swindling one's fellow beings is a necessary practice; upon it is based the really sound commercial success formula — ___.

(a) sell what you cannot buy back
(b) buy what you will sell to another at a higher price
(c) buy cheap and sell dear
(d) sell what you can, do not buy from a competitor

TWO-BLANK FIB

1990

DIRECTIONS for Questions 1 to 31: Each of the following questions has one or more blank spaces indicating where a word / words has been left out. Following each sentence, four words or sets of words lettered a to d have been given. You have to select the appropriate word or set of words to make the sentence most meaningful.

1. The ________, those cellular bodies which contain the ________ particles, the genes, provide us with basic facts of genetic transmission.

(a) protoplasm, microscopic
(b) globules, fat
(c) cytoplasm, minute
(d) chromosomes, hereditary

2. I should not have ________ to talk in such a ________ strain especially when I had not studied the man to whom I was talking.

(a) daring, commanding
(b) try, bold
(c) ventured, peremptory
(d) emboldened, reckless

3. High prices are often the ______ of ______ of goods

(a) accompaniment, dearth
(b) concomitant, scarcity
(c) cause, destitution
(d) result, glut

1998

4. Football evokes a ___ response in India compared to cricket, that almost ___ the nation.

(a) tepid ... boiling
(b) lukewarm ... electrifies
(c) turbid ... fascinating
(d) apocryphal ... genuinely fascinates

5. Social studies, science matters of health and safety, the very atmosphere of the classroom — these areas are few of the ___ for the ___ of proper emotional reactions.

(a) things ... growth
(b) fertile areas ... basis
(c) fertile fields ... inculcation
(d) important areas ... formation

6. Learning is more efficient when it is ___. It is less efficient when it is ___.

(a) fast ... slow
(b) rapid ... turtle-slow
(c) tedious ... like a joy ride
(d) fun ... drudgery

7. To a greater or lesser degree all the civilized countries of the world are made up of a small class of rulers ___ and of a large class of subjects ___.

(a) formed by a small minority ... who are uncivilized
(b) powerfully corrupt ... pointless crusaders
(c) corrupted by too much power ... corrupted by too much passive obedience
(d) who are ruled ... who ruled

8. Simple arithmetic tells us that there is more ___ than ___.

(a) imitation ... innovation
(b) improvisation ... improvement
(c) impracticality ... knowledge
(d) improbability ... probability

2000

9. Though one eye is kept firmly on the ___, the company now also promotes ___ contemporary art.
(a) present ... experimental
(b) future ... popular
(c) present ... popular
(d) market ... popular

10. The law prohibits a person from felling a sandalwood tree, even if it grows on one's own land, without prior permission from the government. As poor people cannot deal with the government, this legal provision leads to a rip-roaring business for ___, who care neither for the ___, nor for the trees.
(a) middlemen ... rich (b) the government ... poor
(c) touts ... rich (d) touts ... poor

11. It will take some time for many South Koreans to ___ the conflicting images of North Korea, let alone to ___ what to make of their northern cousins.
(a) reconcile ... decide
(b) understand ... clarify
(c) make out ... decide
(d) reconcile ... understand

12. In these bleak and depressing times of ___ prices, non-performing governments and ___ crime rates, Sourav Ganguly has given us, Indians, a lot to cheer about.
(a) escalating ... increasing
(b) spiralling ... booming
(c) spiralling ... soaring
(d) ascending ... debilitating

13. The manners and ___ of the nouveau riche is a recurrent ___ in the literature.
(a) style ... motif (b) morals ... story
(c) wealth ... theme (d) morals ... theme

14. But ___ are now regularly written not just for tools, but well-established practices, organisations and institutions, not all of which seem to be ___ away.
(a) reports ... withering (b) stories ... trading
(c) books ... dying (d) obituaries ... fading

15. The Darwin who ___ is most remarkable for the way in which he ___ the attributes of the world class thinker and head of the household.
(a) comes ... figures
(b) arises ... adds
(c) emerges ... combines
(d) appeared ... combines

2001

16. Since her face was free of ___ there was no way to ___ if she appreciated what had happened.
(a) make-up ... realise (b) expression ... ascertain
(c) emotion ... diagnose (d) scars ... understand

17. In this context, the ___ of the British labour movement is particularly ___.
(a) affair ... weird
(b) activity ... moving
(c) experience ... significant
(d) atmosphere ... gloomy

18. Indian intellectuals may boast, if they are so inclined, of being ___ to the most elitist among the intellectual ___ of the world.
(a) subordinate ... traditions
(b) heirs ... cliques
(c) ancestors ... societies
(d) heir ... traditions

2003(L)

19. The British retailer, M&S, today formally ______ defeat in its attempt to _____ King's, its US subsidiary, since no potential purchasers were ready to cough up the necessary cash.
(a) admitted, acquire (b) conceded, offload
(c) announced, dispose (d) ratified, auction

20. Early ______ of maladjustment to college culture is _______ by the tendency to develop friendship networks outside college which mask signals of maladjustment.
(a) treatment, compounded
(b) detection, facilitated
(c) identification, complicated
(d) prevention, helped

21. The ______ regions of Spain all have unique cultures, but the _______ views within each region make the issue of an acceptable common language of instruction an even more contentious one.
(a) different, discrete (b) distinct, disparate
(c) divergent, distinct (d) different, competing

22. A growing number of these expert professionals _____ having to train foreigners as the students end up ______ the teachers who have to then unhappily contend with no jobs at all or new jobs with drastically reduced pay packets.
(a) resent, replacing
(b) resist, challenging
(c) welcome, assisting
(d) are, supplanting

23. Companies that try to improve employees' performance by _____ rewards encourage negative kinds of behavior instead of _____ a genuine interest in doing the work well.

(a) giving, seeking
(b) bestowing, discouraging
(c) conferring, discrediting
(d) withholding, fostering

2003(R)

24. The best punctuation is that of which the reader is least conscious; for when punctuation, or lack of it, ___ itself, it is usually because it ___.

(a) obtrudes ... offends
(b) enjoins ... fails
(c) conceals ... recedes
(d) effaces ... counts

25. The argument that the need for a looser fiscal policy to ____ demand outweighs the need to ___ budget deficits is persuasive.

(a) assess ... minimize (b) outstrip ... eliminate
(c) stimulate ... control (d) restrain ... conceal

26. The Athenians on the whole were peaceful and prosperous; they had ___ to sit at home and think about the universe and dispute with Socrates, or to travel abroad and ___ the world.

(a) leisure ... explore (b) time ... ignore
(c) ability ... suffer (d) temerity ... understand

27. Their achievement in the field of literature is described as ___; sometimes it is even called ___.

(a) magnificent ... irresponsible
(b) insignificant ... influential
(c) significant ... paltry
(d) unimportant ... trivial

28. From the time she had put her hair up, every man she had met had grovelled before her and she had acquired a mental attitude toward the other sex which was a blend of ___ and ___.

(a) admiration ... tolerance
(b) indifference ... contempt
(c) impertinence ... temperance
(d) arrogance ... fidelity

29. This simplified ___ to the decision-making process is a must read for anyone ___ important real estate, personal, or professional decisions.

(a) primer ... maximizing
(b) tract ... enacting
(c) introduction ... under
(d) guide ... facing

30. Physicians may soon have ___ to help paralysed people move their limbs by bypassing the ___ nerves that once controlled their muscles.

(a) instruments ... detrimental
(b) ways ... damaged
(c) reason ... involuntary
(d) impediments ... complex

31. The Internet is a medium where users have nearly ___ choices and ___ constraints about where to go and what to do.

(a) unbalanced ... non-existent
(b) embarrassing ... no
(c) unlimited ... minimal
(d) choking ... shockinge

2008

Directions for Questions 32 to 35: Each of the following questions has a sentence with two blanks. Given below each question are five pairs of words. Choose the pair that best completes the sentence.

32. The genocides in Bosnia and Rwanda, apart from being mis-described in the most sinister and ________ manner as 'ethnic cleansing', were also blamed, in further hand-washing rhetoric, on something dark and interior to ________ and perpetrators alike.

(a) innovative; communicator
(b) enchanting; leaders
(c) disingenuous; victims
(d) exigent; exploiters
(e) tragic; sufferers

33. As navigators, calendar makers, and other ________ of the night sky accumulated evidence to the contrary, ancient astronomers were forced to ________ that certain bodies might move in circles about points, which in turn moved in circles about the earth.

(a) scrutinizers; believe (b) observers; agree
(c) scrutinizers; suggest (d) observers; concede
(e) students; conclude

34. Every human being, after the first few days of his life, is a product of two factors: on the one hand, there is his ________ endowment; and on the other hand, there is the effect of environment, including ______

(a) constitutional; weather
(b) congenital; education
(c) personal; climate
(d) economic; learning
(e) genetic; pedagogy

35. Exhaustion of natural resources, destruction of individual initiative by governments, control over men's minds by central _______ of education and propaganda are some of the major evils which appear to be on the increase as a result of the impact of science upon minds suited by _________ to an earlier kind of world.
(a) tenets; fixation
(b) aspects; inhibitions
(c) institutions; inhibitions
(d) organs; tradition
(e) departments; repulsion

MEMORY BASED QUESTIONS

2011

36. There are two gaps in the sentence given below. From the pairs of words given, choose the one that fills the gaps most appropriately.
To call their fervor a .... of the media was a/ an .... of an out-of-touch intellectual elite, and an insult to basic human integrity and intelligence.
(a) gimmick; cachet
(b) torridity; delusion
(c) contrivance; illusion
(d) pun; opinion

37. There are two gaps in the sentence given below. From the pairs of words given, choose the one that fills the gaps most appropriately.
What distinguishes the book from many other collective volumes with similar .... coverage is its unifying theme of regional disparities, and a common methodological ....
(a) distinct; behaviour
(b) diverse; turnpike
(c) sundry; formula
(d) disparate; heuristic

2012

38. There are two blanks in the following sentence. From the pair of words given, choose the one that fills the blanks most appropriately. The first word in the pair should fill the first blank.
Even those who do not _________ Mahatma Gandhi's ideas __________ him as a champion who has daringly refused give up his convictions.
(a) shrink from....... condemn
(b) concur with....... recognize
(c) disagree with....... envision
(d) dissent from....... remember

2013

39. There are two gaps in the sentence/paragraph given below. From the pairs of words given, choose the one that fills the gaps most appropriately.
It's the vulnerability of the political father-figure, played strategically to bring out something deeper from the __________ than civil obedience, something more like __________ love.
(a) populace, unquestioning
(b) society, irrevocable
(c) generality, unrequited
(d) opposition, inevitable

40. There are two gaps in the sentence/paragraph given below. From the pairs of words given, choose the one that fills the gaps most appropriately.
For Septimius Severus stood as a __________ reminder of what Libya had once been: a Mediterranean region of immense cultural and economic wealth, anything but __________ from the world beyond the sea.
(a) constant, analogous
(b) wistful, isolated
(c) steady, different
(d) nostalgic, indistinguishable

2014

41. There are two gaps in the sentence/paragraph given below. From the pairs of words given, choose the one that fills the gaps most appropriately.
However, the adults in the audience may find even these _____ effects a relief, given the overwhelming _____ of most of the film.
(a) Gaffe, Tempo
(b) Gauche, Blandness
(c) Gauche, Traction
(d) Gaffe, Speed

42. There are two gaps in the sentence/paragraph given below. From the pairs of words given, choose the one that fills the gaps most appropriately.
Despite the _______ that has characterized much of Vietnamese history, a nationalist ______ has remained in the form of anti-colonization and anti-imperialism.
(a) Divisiveness, Continuity
(b) Divisions, Colony
(c) Schisms, Bridge
(d) Tumult, Consistency

COMMON CONFUSABLES

2007

DIRECTIONS for Questions 1 to 3: In each question, there are four sentences. Each sentence has pairs of words/phrases that are italicized and highlighted. From the italicized and highlighted word(s)/phrase(s), select the **most appropriate** word(s)/phrase(s) to form correct sentences. Then, from the options given, choose the best one.

1. The cricket council that ***was*** [A] / ***were*** [B] elected last March ***is*** [A] ***are*** [B] at sixes and sevens over new rules.

   The critics ***censored*** [A] / ***censured*** [B] the new movie because of its social unacceptability.

   Amit's explanation for missing the meeting was ***credulous*** [A] / ***credible*** [B].

   She coughed ***discreetly*** [A] / ***discretely*** [B] to announce her presence.

   (a) BBAAA (b) AAABA
   (c) BBBBA (d) AABBA
   (e) BBBAA

2. The ***further*** [A] / ***farther*** [B] he pushed himself, the more disillusioned he grew.

   For the crowds it was more of a ***historical*** [A] / ***historic*** [B] event; for their leader, it was just another day.

   The old man has a healthy ***distrust*** [A] / ***mistrust*** [B] for all new technology.

   This film is based on a ***real*** [A] / ***true*** [B] story.

   One suspects that the ***compliment*** [A] / ***complement*** [B] was backhanded.

   (a) BABAB (b) ABBBA
   (c) BAABA (d) BBAAB
   (e) ABABA

3. ***Regrettably*** [A] / ***Regretfully*** [B] I have to decline your invitation.

   I am drawn to the poetic, ***sensual*** [A] / ***sensuous*** [B] quality of her paintings.

   He was ***besides*** [A] / ***beside*** [B] himself with rage when I told him what I had done.

   After brushing against a ***stationary*** [A] / ***stationery*** [B] truck my car turned turtle.

   As the water began to rise ***over*** [A] / ***above*** [B] the danger mark, the signs of an imminent flood were clear.

   (a) BAABA (b) BBBAB
   (c) AAABA (d) BBAAB
   (e) BABAB

2008

DIRECTIONS for Questions 4 to 7: In each question, there are five sentences. Each sentence has a pair of words that are italicized and highlighted. From the italicized and highlighted words, select the most appropriate words (A or B) to form correct sentences. The sentences are followed by options that indicate the words, which may be selected to correctly complete the set of sentences. From the options given, choose the **most appropriate** one.

4. Anita wore a beautiful ***broach (A)/brooch (B)*** on the lapel of her jacket.

   If you want to complain about the amenities in your neighbourhood, please meet your ***councillor(A)/counsellor(B).***

   I would like your ***advice(A)/advise(B)*** on which job I should choose.

   The last scene provided a ***climactic(A)/climatic(B)*** ending to the film.

   Jeans that ***flair(A)/flare(B)*** at the bottom are in fashion these days.

   (a) BABAA (b) BABAB
   (c) BAAAB (d) ABABA
   (e) BAABA

5. The cake had lots of ***currents(A)/currants(B)*** and nuts in it.

   If you engage in such ***exceptional(A)/exceptionable(B)*** behaviour, I will be forced to punish you.

   He has the same capacity as an adult to ***consent(A)/assent(B)*** to surgical treatment.

   The minister is ***obliged (A)/compelled(B)*** to report regularly to a parliamentary board.

   His analysis of the situation is far too ***sanguine(A)/genuine(B).***

   (a) BBABA (b) BBAAA
   (c) BBBBA (d) ABBAB
   (e) BABAB

6. She managed to bite back the ***ironic(A)/caustic(B)*** retort on the tip of her tongue.

   He gave an impassioned and ***valid(A)/cogent(B)*** plea for judicial reform.

   I am not ***adverse(A)/averse(B)*** to helping out.

   The ***coupé(A)/coup(B)*** broke away as the train climbed the hill.

   They heard the bells ***peeling(A)/pealing(B)*** far and wide.

   (a) BBABA (b) BBBAB
   (c) BAABB (d) ABBAA
   (e) BBBBA

7. We were not successful in ***defusing(A)/diffusing(B)*** the Guru's ideas.
The students ***baited(A)/bated(B)*** the instructor with irrelevant questions.
The ***hoard(A)/horde(B)*** rushed into the campus.
The prisoner's ***interment(A)/interment(B)*** came to an end with his early release.
The hockey team could not deal with his ***unsociable(A)/unsocial(B)*** tendencies.
(a) BABBA (b) BBABB
(c) BABAA (d) ABBAB
(e) AABBA

ODD WORD OUT

1992

DIRECTIONS for Questions 1 to 33: Each of these questions has four items. You are required to select that item which does not belong to the group.

1. (a) authority (b) cruel
(c) kind (d) loyal
2. (a) revenue (b) income
(c) expenditure (d) receivables
3. (a) courage (b) strength
(c) valour (d) warrior
4. (a) democracy
(b) voting
(c) monarchy
(d) dictatorship
5. (a) Gold medalist
(b) Athlete
(c) Olympic Champion
(d) Record holder
6. (a) Managers use their authority.
(b) Scientists use their logical abilities.
(c) Artists use their creative abilities
(d) Engineers use their technical skills.
7. (a) Air travel is expensive.
(b) Most people travel to Australia by air.
(c) Businessmen travel a lot by air.
(d) Aeroplanes are expensive.

1993

8. (a) Invoice (b) Sales Tax
(c) Octroi (d) Quotation
9. (a) Equestrian (b) Neigh
(c) Derby (d) Bark
10. (a) Apt (b) Relevant
(c) Appropriate (d) Adept
11. (a) Ring (b) Shoulder
(c) Finger (d) Write
12. (a) Abstract (b) Conceptual
(c) Material (d) Idealist

1995

13. (a) Couple (b) Sever
(c) Rend (d) Lacerate
14. (a) Quell (b) Ruffle
(c) Allay (d) Control
15. (a) Cease (b) Launch
(c) Initiate (d) Commence
16. (a) Brink (b) Hub
(c) Verge (d) Brim
17. (a) Eulogy (b) Panegyric
(c) Ignominy (d) Glorification
18. (a) Detest (b) Abhor
(c) Ardour (d) Loathe
19. (a) Adroit (b) Adept
(c) Dexterous (d) Awkward
20. (a) Taciturn (b) Reserved
(c) Clamorous (d) Silent
21. (a) Sporadic (b) Frequent
(c) Intermittent (d) Scarce
22. (a) Fanatic (b) Zealot
(c) Maniac (d) Rational

1996

23. (a) Impetuosity (b) Equanimity
(c) Zealousness (d) Effervescence
24. (a) Drip (b) Intrusion
(c) Percolation (d) Effluence
25. (a) Duplicity (b) Guilelessness
(c) Artfulness (d) Shrewdness
26. (a) Taxi (b) Cruiser
(c) Amble (d) Cab
27. (a) Hiatus (b) Break
(c) Pause (d) End

1997

28. (a) Keen (b) Kin
(c) Enthusiastic (d) Willing
29. (a) Adept (b) Adapt
(c) Skilful (d) Proficient
30. (a) Ring (b) Round
(c) Bell (d) Circle
31. (a) Computer (b) Internet
(c) Grid (d) Network

32. (a) Suffer (b) Endure
(c) Bear (d) Withstand

33. (a) Break (b) Hiatus
(c) Chasm (d) Bridge

ANALOGY

1990

DIRECTIONS for Questions 1 to 47: Each of the following questions has a pair of CAPITALIZED words followed by four pairs of words. Choose the pair of words which best expresses the relationship similar to that expressed in the capitalized pair.

1. CAR : ROAD
(a) electricity : cable (b) ink : pencil
(c) bomb : missile (d) fly : bird

2. FORESIGHT : FARSIGHTEDNESS
(a) long : lengthy (b) further : farther
(c) short : dwarf (d) thinker : visionary

3. FLEET : NAVY
(a) chapter : book (b) seats : auditorium
(c) letter : word (d) drop : ocean

4. FEATHER : WING
(a) down : goose
(b) cotton : mattress
(c) subheading : heading
(d) brick : wall

5. SUGAR : TEA
(a) paper : editor (b) weapon : murderer
(c) button : buttonhole (d) umbrella : rain

1992

6. SYMPHONY : COMPOSER
(a) rain : flood (b) light : switch
(c) novel : author (d) song : music

7. TREE : TRUNK
(a) pen : ink (b) car : chassis
(c) cabin : log (d) arm : body

8. CIRCLE : ARC
(a) line : segment (b) part : whole
(c) percent : fraction (d) small : big

9. COW : HERD
(a) grass : green (b) child : family
(c) bald : hair (d) horse : jockey

10. WOOL : ACRYLIC
(a) rayon : silk (b) plastic : rubber
(c) winter : spring (d) cotton : terylene

11. DOCTOR : DISEASE
(a) policeman : criminal (b) dentist : drill
(c) politician : electorate (d) teacher : ignorance

12. BIRD : ORNITHOLOGY
(a) zoology : animal (b) stars : galaxy
(c) archeology : antiquity (d) plants : botany

13. FOOD : HUNGER
(a) sleep : weariness (b) night : slumber
(c) dream : sleep (d) thirst : drink

14. SPEAR : DART
(a) knife : sword (b) door : window
(c) mountain : molehill (d) cannon : gun

15. BUILDING : BRICK
(a) lime : cement (b) highway : asphalt
(c) river : bridge (d) vehicle : road

1993

16. BRAND : PRODUCT
(a) Dalda : Rath
(b) Aircraft : Flying Machine
(c) Shoes : Reebok
(d) Sports car : Automobiles

17. FOOD : GOURMET
(a) Book : Critic (b) Art : Connoisseur
(c) Sports : Fans (d) Craft : Skill

18. NORTH : SOUTH
(a) Black : White (b) Yellow : orange
(c) Red : Maroon (d) Red : Indigo

19. DROUGHT : FAMINE
(a) Poverty : Plenty (b) Drip : Fluid
(c) Camera : Film (d) Training : Skill

20. NUTS : BOLTS
(a) Nitty : Gritty (b) Bare : Feet
(c) Naked : Clothes (d) Hard : Soft

21. SALT : SALTY
(a) Sweet : Sugar (b) Cow : Bovine
(c) Bitter : Sour (d) Taste : Flavor

22. JUST : ARBITRARY
(a) Order : Chaos (b) Bare : Clothed
(c) Hope : Surprise (d) Proper : Impropr

23. CRIME : PUNISHMENT
(a) Lawyer : Judge (b) Court : Room
(b) Accused : Defendant (d) Homicide : Penalty

24. ATMOSPHERE : STRATOSPHERE
(a) Nimbus : Cloud
(b) Instrument : Calibration
(c) Aircraft : Jet
(d) Climate : Rain

25. DIVIDE : UNITE
(a) Split : Apart (b) Marriage : Divorce
(b) Fission : Fusion (d) Chasm : Gap

1994

26. LYING : PERJURY
(a) statement : testimony
(b) seeing : observing
(c) taking : stealing
(d) eating : dining

27. PREHISTORIC : MEDIEVAL
(a) Akbar : British
(b) present : future
(c) Shakesphere : Tennyson
(d) colossus : elephant

28. LOUD : STENTORIAN
(a) mild : noisy (b) painful : prickly
(c) adjective : descriptive (d) bright : resplendent

1995

29. LIMPID : MURKY
(a) Dazed : Clouded (b) Obscure : Vague
(c) Bright : Gloomy (d) Nebulous : Dim

30. EASE : ALLEVIATE
(a) Hint : Allocative (b) Revolt : Repudiate
(c) Collapse : Rise (d) Question : Interrogate

31. SECRET : CLANDESTINE
(a) Overt : Furtive (b) Covert : Stealthy
(c) Open : Closed (d) News : Rumour

32. DRAMA : AUDIENCE
(a) Brawl : Vagabonds (b) Game : Spectators
(c) Art : Critics (d) Movie : Actors

33. BUILDING : STOREY
(a) Book : Chapter (b) Sentence : Adjective
(c) Tree : Stem (d) Elephant : Tusk

1996

34. LIQUID : GASEOUSNESS
(a) Serum : Fume (b) Humid : Arid
(c) Thaw : Distil (d) Smoke : Cloud

35. FISSION : FUSION
(a) Implosion : Explosion
(b) Separation : Combination
(c) Intrusion : Extrusion
(d) Enemy : Friend

36. DOUBT : FAITH
(a) Atheist : Religion (b) Sceptic : Pious
(c) Iconoclast : Idol (d) Apostate : State

37. BRICK : BUILDING
(a) Word : Dictionary (b) Alphabet : Letter
(c) Platoon : Soldier (d) Idiom : Language

38. DULCET : RAUCOUS
(a) Sweet : Song
(b) Crazy : insane
(c) Palliative : Exacerbating
(d) Theory : Practical

39. ACTION : REACTION
(a) Introvert : Extrovert (b) Assail : Defend
(c) Diseased : Treatment(d) Death : Rebirth

40. MALAPROPISM : WORDS
(a) Anachronism : Time
(b) Ellipsis : Sentence
(c) Jinjanthropism : Apes
(d) Catechism : Religion

41. ANTERIOR : POSTERIOR
(a) In : Out (b) Top : Bottom
(c) Head : Tail (d) Front : Rear

1997

42. PEEL : PEAL
(a) Coat : Rind (b) Laugh : Bell
(c) Rain : Reign (d) Brain : Cranium

43. DOGGEREL : POET
(a) Symphony : Composer
(b) Prediction : Astrologer
(c) Wine : Vintner
(d) Pulp fiction : Novelist

44. PREMISE : CONCLUSION
(a) Assumption : Inference
(b) Hypothesis : Theory
(c) Knowledge : Ideas
(d) Brand : Marketing

45. BARGE : VESSEL
(a) Shovel : Implement (b) Book : Anthology
(c) Rim : Edge (d) Training : Preparation

46. LOVE : OBSESSION
(a) Happiness : Joy (b) Amity : Harmony
(c) Enemy : Hatred (d) Sorrow : Misery

47. REPTILE : ADDER
(a) Skeleton : Flesh
(b) Method : System
(c) Plant : Genus
(d) Dinosaur : Tyrannosaurus

1990

DIRECTIONS for Questions 48 to 57: Answer the questions based on the following information.
In each of these questions, a related pair of words or phrases is followed by a pair of words or phrases. Select the lettered pair that best expresses a relationship that is least similar to the one expressed in the original pair.

48. RENT : LEASE
(a) interest : borrow (b) salary : employ
(c) price : buy (d) tax : govern

49. TEMPERATURE : HEAT
(a) votes : popularity (b) IQ : intelligence
(c) ohms : resistance (d) speed : distance

50. PROGRESS : PROGRESSIVE
(a) terror : terrorist
(b) sympathy : sympathizer
(c) revolution : revolutionary
(d) reform : reformist

51. STUBBORN : ADAPTABLE
(a) stupid : bright (b) moral : amoral
(c) inherent : extraneous (d) friend : enemy

52. CLIPS : PAPER
(a) thread : beads (b) cement : bricks
(c) ribbon : hair (d) bag : vegetables

1995

53. GERMANE : PERTINENT
(a) Apt : Appropriate (b) Quick : Urgent
(c) Dull : Sluggish (d) Excited : Serene

54. SAIL : SHIP
(a) Propeller : Aeroplane
(b) Radar : Satellite
(c) Hydrogen : Balloon
(d) Accelerator : Car

55. COSMIC : UNIVERSE
(a) Terrestrial : Earth (b) Lunar : Moon
(c) Connubial : Youth (d) Annular : Ring

56. CANINE : DOG
(a) Feline : Cat (b) Aquiline : Parrot
(c) Serpentine : Cobra (d) Vulpine : Fox

57. XENOPHOBIA : FOREIGNERS
(a) Claustrophobia : Height
(b) Anglophobia : Englishmen
(c) Bibliophobia : Book
(d) Hemophobia : Blood

MISCELLANEOUS

1994

DIRECTIONS for Questions 1 to 5: Four statements with blanks have been given. These statements are followed by four alternatives. Choose the one which fits into the set of statements the maximum number of times.

1. A. Professional studies has become the _______ of the rich.
B. Every citizen has the _______ to speak, travel and live as he pleases.
C. He has a definite _______ over all his rivals.
D. Sheron no longer has the ________ of the company's bungalow and car.
(a) advantage
(b) privilege
(c) right
(d) concession

2. A. People sensed _________.
B. A bad ________ case had come in – a person with a smashed arm.
C. And then, without warning, ________ struck.
D. The dogs were the first to recognize the signs of oncoming ________.
(a) tragedy (b) accident
(c) disaster (d) calamity

3. A. The men there have fought _________ and emotional withdrawal, and were more capable of helping Jim.
B. But _______ does occasionally inflict all the adults.
C. A person who is deeply hurt feels very _________.
D. It is hard to survive this feeling of _______.
(a) dejection (b) lonely
(c) trouble (d) depression

4. A. I have had a small power of ________.
B. Down with a very high fever, he suffers from frequents fits of ________.
C. They are now bitter enemies – all because of a small ________.
D. Her _________ is the most creative thing she has ever possessed.
(a) illusion (b) imagination
(c) hallucination (d) misunderstanding

5. A. Communism states that every individual must live for the _________.
B. The _________ of the affairs of the nation is deplorable.
C. _________ have been laid down by the United States : states The Statesman.
D. No _________ has succeeded in gaining complete autonomy from the Federal government.
(a) state (b) nation
(c) government (d) condition

■■

ANSWERS

MATCH THE MEANING

1. (a) 2. (d) 3. (c) 4. (b) 5. (d) 6. (c) 7. (b) 8. (d) 9. (b) 10. (d)

CLOZE TEST

1. (c) 2. (a) 3. (d) 4. (c) 5. (a) 6. (d) 7. (b) 8. (a) 9. (d) 10. (c)
11. (b) 12. (d) 13. (c) 14. (a) 15. (d) 16. (a)

WORD / PHRASE REPLACEMENT

1. (b) 2. (b) 3. (a) 4. (d) 5. (a) 6. (c) 7. (d) 8. (a) 9. (d) 10. (a)
11. (a) 12. (d) 13. (a) 14. (c) 15. (a) 16. (c) 17. (c) 18. (d) 19. (d)

ONE-BLANK FIB

1. (c) 2. (b) 3. (b) 4. (c) 5. (d) 6. (a) 7. (d) 8. (b) 9. (a) 10. (c)
11. (a) 12. (a) 13. (b) 14. (b) 15. (b) 16. (a) 17. (a) 18. (b) 19. (b) 20. (b)
21. (a) 22. (c)

TWO-BLANK FIB

1. (d) 2. (c) 3. (b) 4. (b) 5. (d) 6. (d) 7. (c) 8. (a) 9. (b) 10. (d)
11. (a) 12. (c) 13. (d) 14. (d) 15. (c) 16. (b) 17. (c) 18. (d) 19. (b) 20. (c)
21. (a) 22. (a) 23. (d) 24. (a) 25. (c) 26. (a) 27. (d) 28. (b) 29. (d) 30. (b)
31. (c) 32. (c) 33. (d) 34. (b) 35. (d) 36. (c) 37. (d) 38. (b) 39. (a) 40. (b)
41. (b) 42. (a)

COMMON CONFUSABLES

1. (d) 2. e 3. (b) 4. (c) 5. (b) 6. (b) 7. (a)

ODD WORD OUT

1. (a) 2. (c) 3. (d) 4. (b) 5. (a) 6. (a) 7. (d) 8. (d) 9. (d) 10. (d)
11. (d) 12. (c) 13. (a) 14. (b) 15. (a) 16. (b) 17. (c) 18. (c) 19. (d) 20. (c)
21. (b) 22. (d) 23. (b) 24. (b) 25. (b) 26. (c) 27. (d) 28. (b) 29. (b) 30. (c)
31. (a) 32. (d) 33. (d)

ANALOGY

1. (a) 2. (d) 3. (a) 4. (d) 5. (c) 6. (c) 7. (b) 8. (a) 9. (b) 10. (d)
11. (d) 12. (d) 13. (a) 14. (d) 15. (b) 16. (d) 17. (b) 18. (a) 19. (d) 20. (a)
21. (b) 22. (a) 23. (d) 24. (c) 25. (c) 26. (a) 27. (b) 28. (d) 29. (c) 30. (d)
31. (b) 32. (b) 33. (a) 34. (a) 35. (b) 36. (a) 37. (a) 38. (c) 39. (b) 40. (a)
41. (d) 42. (c) 43. (d) 44. (b) 45. (a) 46. (d) 47. (d) 48. (d) 49. (d) 50. (b)
51. (b) 52. (d) 53. (d) 54. (b) 55. (c) 56. (b) 57. (a)

MISCELLANEOUS

1. (b) 2. (c) 3. (d) 4. (b) 5. (a)

EXPLANATIONS

MATCH THE MEANING

1. a A–H: Here 'exceed' would mean 'flowing beyond' the 'banks' (physical boundaries).

B–F: Here their accomplishments 'were superior to' the expectation.

C–E: It is difficult for us to 'comprehend' the infinite mercy of God.

D–G: He 'crossed limits' when he embezzled from the fund.

2. d A–E: We see smoke and 'deduce' that there must be a fire.

B–F: The listener makes all sorts of guesses about the 'utterance'.

C–G: 'You' can be sure from 'the long wait' that the person is definitely inclined to meet 'him'.

D–H: She had distanced herself from the debate but for a perfunctory question, thereby 'hinting' that she was not exactly excited by the debate.

3. c A–G: The wines have been preserved for a long time so as to 'age' it.

B–E: He has been "freed from the rashness of youth" in his old age.

C–H: The soil in the Gangetic plains are 'rich' with the flow of time.

D–F: The violin tunes were 'rich and pleasant'.

4. b A–F: The author felt "light after removing something distressing 'shoes'

B–H: The victims were given relief 'aid'.

C–G: The only 'diversion' I get is by playing cards.

D–E: The sentry was 'released from the performance of duty'.

5. d A–F: The committee heard his attempt to "remove the stigma" from his name.

B–H: Water had to be purified of "foreign/ superfluous" ingredients by distillation.

C–E: The opposition was "gotten rid of" after the coup.

D-G: Drugs that empty the bowels have a bad effect on the brain.

6. c The size of the pitch is the usage of measure.

The vessel is used to take out a litre of oil.

Action against tresspassers was instituted in the campus.

Sheila ascertained the measurement of each item.

7. b Dinesh could not stand the discussion and he was forced to walk out.

Vidya's story is the limit, very hard to believe.

Jyoti wanted to go to the Bar.

The forces were such that he was certain to go over the edge.

8. d Hussain tried to capture the spirit of India in this painting (on the canvas).

Sorry, I could not understand what you just said.

Is there some deception (vanishing act) in this proposal?

All her friends agreed that Prakash was a person worth entrapping in the snares of romance.

9. b I decided not to do business in handmade cards.

My brother is a trader of cards.

Dinesh insisted on giving out the cards to the players.

This contract is concerned with handmade cards.

10. d Ashish asked Laxman to turn his face in a new direction.

Leena never sent a beggar away without offering anything.

The old school building has taken the form of a museum.

Now he had the opportunity to voice his protest.

CLOZE TEST

1. c Obviously is the right answer as it matches the tone of great simplifications.

2. a Numerical value in the earlier paragraph points to quantitatively as the answer.

3. d Assess alternatives that follows the blank gives the answer alternatives.

4. c The passage deals with firing employees.

5. a Resolve means to find a solution to something.

6. d The failed product would not be present had it not passed through the process.

7. b Ramesh makes a direct, blatant statement that he did not file his income tax returns. Devious means scheming, deceitful.

8. a The principal tax is already mentioned as Rs. 20000. He hasn't filed his income tax returns. Due to the delay he will also have to pay interest on the principal amount.

9. d There are no sanctions involved with the income tax. It's not possible for him to get a refund unless he files his returns. Due to the delay he will be charged a fine and not a fee.

10. c To impound means to seize property (usually by force of power)and is used normally and here talking about trust fund. So attached here refers to attaching property by legal writ is the best option.

11. b Automobiles can only be seized before being auctioned off (and not smashed, dismantled or frozen!).

12. d An income tax defaulter is an offender and not a purchaser, victim or investor.

13. c The words in the previous sentence and the tone of the passage indicate that the corridors were empty.

14. a This choice is appropriate because the men were talking in low-pitched voices. Stentorian means marked by loud voice.

15. d The word 'choler' (which means anger or irritability) in the previous sentence indicates a direct relationship with temper.

16. a He couldn't have strolled the corridors because he was angry. The President would not prowl in the corridors. Also one does not storm a corridor but may storm in and out of a corridor or a room. But one can pace up and down.

WORD / PHRASE REPLACEMENT

1. b Misalliance refers to an alliance between people not normally looked upon as suitable for each other.

2. b 'Reflexes' implies a movement made in response to something.

3. a The art and science of good eating and drinking is called gastronomy.

4. d 'Horror' as a noun can mean an enjoyable feeling of fear from listening to a story or from watching a movie, and is thus different from 'terror', which cannot be enjoyable.

5. a 'Phalanx' means a number of people standing close together for a specific purpose.

6. c A specious argument sounds true but is actually false. 'Credible' has a positive note against the other three choices.

7. d To obviate is to make something unnecessary, this meaning is elucidated in (a), (b) and (c). 'Bolster' on the other hand strengthens the cause of driving personal cars.

8. a Easy. (b) (c) and (d) actually mean something that is no longer in use. (a) talks about prevailing practices.

9. d Parsimonious means being stingy. Choices (a), (b) and (c) are similar making choice (d) the answer.

10. a To say that war is a remedy for the burgeoning population problem is to speak flippantly. (b), (c) and (d) convey this light tone. Jovian relates to the planet Jupiter.

11. a Opprobrium is the state of being abused or scornfully criticized.

12. d Portend means to predict or foreshadow.

13. a Prevaricate means to speak evasively with intent to deceive.

14. c Restive means to be restless or nervous.

15. a Ostensible means what is apparent or seeming to be the situation.

16. c Resurrecting i.e. bring back to practice is the best choice. (a), (b) and (d) are negative options.

17. c Sputtering is a light popping sound of a flame which is dying out. The ideas conveyed are dim and grim so 'shining', bright and effulgent are out.

18. d Such a scene should be distressing to a sensitive traveler. Irritating and disgusting are negative options. 1 can be clearly ruled out.

19. d The one word reply conveys that it is terse. As it has no element of humour we can easily rule out – "witty".

ONE-BLANK FIB

1. c 'Backed up' a claim is the correct idiomatic usage.

2. b The correct usage is - disturbances 'blow over' (which means to fade away without serious consequences).

3. b Only 'happened to be ' or 'wasn't' can grammatically fit here. 'Wasn't' does not give the sentence the appropriate meaning.

4. c One 'launches' a product.

5. d 'Unexpected success' goes best with 'fortune was made'.

6. a The correct idiomatic usage is 'smothering the flames', which means to extinguish the flames.

7. d Because there is a reference of two peoples Sam and I, there is a need to use 'Between'.

8. b 'Hinge upon' means 'depends upon'.

9. a Only 'come in' fits here, in the sense of "appear in".

10. c An act of vengeance relates to the 'beginning' of the misdeeds, and thus reopens the first chapter. Look for a suitable complement in sentences split with a semicolon. When there is a semicolon in the sentence, one has to look for a logical complement — 'closes : reopens'.

11. a The correct idiomatic usage is 'as far as' something can go. (b) and (d) sound extremely confusing as they add parameters. (c) sounds needlessly verbose.

12. a One sets out to achieve something. 'thought of' is not right as it should be followed by 'achieving'. 'thought to' does not sound as active as the author might wish it to be. 'went to' sounds similarly vague.

13. b One does 'tough talking'. 'talk tough' is a general idiomatic expression. 'has done some' should be followed by an -ing form of the verb, such as 'investigating' or 'probing'.

14. b 'Year by year' is the correct idiomatic usage here. 'annually' and 'progressively' are not the right words to use as we are just making a general observation, not dealing with statistics. The singular stress on 'each' is unwarranted in this sentence.

15. b 'Amendments' is a countable noun and so 'many' should be used as a quantifier for it. (c) and (d) tamper with the pronouncement in the sentence by using weak quantifiers.

16. a 'More crucial than ever' shows that though they were important earlier too, now they are even more important. (a) matches the verbal tense in the sentence 'more crucial than (they have) ever (been)'.

17. a 'Break down' is the correct idiomatic use here. 'barriers' are not 'crumbled' or 'dismantled'. We can 'break' a record. For an erect barrier, the appropriate verb would be 'break down'.

18. b 'Audilble' sounds as opposed to 'visual' symbols, fits here.'without making intelligible sounds' does not make sense in the sentence. 'aural' and 'vocal' are technical words that draw attention away from the crux of the sentence i.e. one need not be heard all the time to gain meaning.

19. b The farmers are protesting and want their voice to be heard. (a) and (d) do not fit into the semantic context of the sentence. The farmers, by themselves, cannot curb the prices, so (c) is not right.

20. b In terms of general rules, science as a news agency is comparable to other news agencies. 'principal' means 'chief' and this is not the meaning that the sentence is trying to convey, so (a) and (c) are wrong. 'in spirit and form' also sounds directionless, when the sentence is saying that the underlying values are the same.

21. a 'Actuated' means motivated. Leaders cannot be 'led'. One cannot categorise people 'by' desires. 'convinced' similarly sounds vague.

22. c 'Buy cheap and sell dear' is the only option that will, without any doubt, lead to a commercial success. (d) gives an unwarranted warning. (a) is not sound commerce. (b) is needlessly verbose, as compared to (c). (c) sounds like a formula, it is also the best choice after the hyphen.

TWO-BLANK FIB

1. d The first blank should have a plural. Hence either b or d is the right choice. And genes are hereditary particles, making (d) the right option.

2. c Only 'ventured' fits in the first blank properly.

3. b A scarcity of goods is usually accompanied by or causes a rise in prices. So (d) does not follow logically. (*glut* means an excessive supply of something) *Destitution* (poverty) cannot be applied to inanimate objects. So (c) is also eliminated. *Accompaniment* means something incidental or added for ornament, symmetry, etc. This does not fit the context of the sentence. So (a) is also eliminated. *Concomitant* as a noun is used to mean "a phenomenon that naturally accompanies or follows something." This makes (b) the correct option.

4. b 'Lukewarm' fits in the first blank, and in the second, we need a verb. So 'electrifies' is the best suited of all the given choices. 'boiling' and 'fascinating' cannot grammatically fit the second blank. 'almost' and 'genuinely' are unlikely to go together.

5. d Social studies, science matters of health and safety and the atmosphere of the classroom, help in formation of proper emotional responses. Hence these can be referred to as the 'important areas'. 'things' is too vague a word to fill the first blank. Emotional reactions cannot be 'inculcated'. Given 'basis' and 'formation', the second word is more appropriate to fill in the second blank.

6. d Learning is always more efficient when it is fun and less efficient when it is a drudgery (boring). Learning need not be efficient when it is fast or rapid, this may lead to loss of retention. Never can learning be more efficient when it is tedious.

7. c The rulers get too much power while those who are ruled show passive obedience. (d) makes an incomplete sentence with the second phrase. It is unlikely that a crusade is pointless. (a) does not make sense. (c) shows a proper parallel and logical structure.

8. a (a) has is the only pair of words that fits in without creating any contradictions. When it comes to arithmetic, you can count the number of copy cats (imitation). This inference does not come across in choices (b), (c) and (d).

9. b Future is what the company also needs to keep in mind when selling popular contemporary art. (a) and (c) are wrong because we need not keep an eye on the present, it's already here. Remember that we have the word 'though' in the sentence and hence, the words must contrast 'future-popular (now)'.

10. d Choice (b) is ruled out since the government cannot make money in this case. Choices (a) and (c) are ruled out since they introduce 'rich' into the context. In the scenario presented in the sentence, it's obvious that (d) is the best choice since touts (middlemen who are illegal/without proper authority). This makes (d) correct.

11. a Choice (c) is ruled out as 'make out' is a rather informal usage. 'Let alone' means what will follow will be a stronger/more concrete expression than 'reconciliation'. In this case, decide is a better opinion than understand and choice (a) is correct.

12. c 'Depressing times of spiraling prices' and 'soaring crime rates' fits in best. (b) is out, because 'booming' and 'crime rates' don't go well together. 'spiralling' prices are prices that rise out of order. Crime rates cannot 'debilitate', and 'soaring' matches the depressing tone of 'spiralling'.

13. d Choice (a) is ruled out as 'style' and 'manners' are similar. Choice (c) is ruled out as nouveau riche means 'new rich'. 'Manners and Morals' is a phrase and goes well. Choice (b) is incorrect as a 'recurrent story in literature' is incorrect. A recurrent theme which means many works which are similar in that they have this theme makes sense. This makes choice (d) correct.

14. d It's choice (d). You don't write reports or stories or books for tools, but 'obituaries' — yes, as tools do get obsolete. Also 'practices' do not wither or trade or die away, but they do fade away with time.

15. c You do not add or figure two attributes, but you do combine them into one. 'Appear' again is too abrupt when you are discerning a personality, 'emerges' would be more appropriate.

16. b The sentence is drawing a correlation between her face and her understanding. Scars and make-up are irrelevant in this context and can be removed as possible options. "To diagnose if she appreciated" is incorrect, you diagnose on the basis of symptoms. This leaves us option (b) which fits in well to make a coherent sentence.

17. c Choice (a) with "weird" as an option can be removed and similarly choice (d) with "gloomy". They are both using words that are not first-priority as they are somewhat informal. Out of the other choices, "activity" is not qualified as "moving' (emotional). Choice (c) fits in the best and is the answer.

18. d Choice (a) can be easily eliminated since "being subordinate" and "boasting" of it do not go together. Choice (c) is incorrect because 'intellectuals' (individuals) being ancestors to societies (collectivity) is incorrect. Also present Indian intellectuals cannot possibly be ancestors either. Choice (b) is incorrect because "intellectual cliques" is odd especially since "cliques" is used in a somewhat negative sense. Choice (d) is correct.

19. b *conceded* and *offload* are the most appropriate pair of words to fit here. *announced* do not go with *formally*, so (c) is out. Nor does *ratified*, so (d) is out. *Acquire* does not go logically with *purchasers*, so (a) is out.

20. c If you have friends outside college, they tend to mask adjustment problems with college colleagues. *treatment* cannot be *compounded*, so (a) is out. If *signals* are *masked*, nothing is *facilitated*, so (b) is out. For similar reasons, *helped* in (d) cannot fill the second blank. *Identification* and *complicated* is thus the right pair.

21. a In the first blank the confusion could be between "different" and "distinct". However once you know that certain regions of Spain are unique, only then can you call them distinct, not before. Which is why the first blank can't be distinct. So the first blank should be different. Now between (a) and (d) the correct answer is (a) because discrete means distinct and so we are carrying forward the thought of difference between regions and then in the regions themselves.

22. a *resent* and *replacing* is the most appropriate pair of words to fit here. *welcome* cannot go with the implication in *unhappy* so (c) is out. *Resist* is too extreme to fit in a teacher's situation, so (b) is out. *are* in (d) also indicate a compulsive situation which is not evident in the sentence, so (d) is out.

23. d Negative reinforcements foster negative behavior. (a), (b) and (c) are easily ruled out as *giving, bestowing* or *conferring* rewards cannot possibly encourage negative behaviour. *Withholding* and *fostering* thus presents the right situation here.

24. a The first part talks about how punctuation should be. The second part gives reasons for it. If punctuation makes the reader 'least conscious' then it should be least 'obtruding'.

25. c 'stimulate' and 'control' should be on almost opposite tangents as the passage talks of why a looser fiscal policy is better than the 'control' of budget.

26. a 'leisure' and 'explore' go with 'peaceful and prosperous'. (b) is wrong because when you 'travel abroad' you don't 'ignore' the world. (c) is obviously wrong — you don't 'suffer' the world. (d) is wrong as 'temerity' means audacity.

27. d Reading this sentence tells us that the second blank has to be of a slightly higher degree but on the same theme. Only (d) fits this criterion.

28. b If men had groveled before her then her attitude would definitely be negative.

29. d The second blank cannot be filled by any other choice other than 'facing'.

30. b Again the second blank can only be filled by 'damaged'.

31. c The two blanks should have contrasting words as 'choices' and 'constraints' are also contrasting. (c) fits in.

32. c The word 'disingenuous' means insincere and is suitable in the given context (suggested by the word- 'sinister') . The word 'victims' brings out the contrast with 'perpetrators' most aptly.

33. d In the first blank the word 'scrutinizers' is inappropriate as the context suggests observation and not analysis, therefore 'observers' is the right word. In the second blank 'concede' would be more appropriate than 'agree' as the sense is that of yielding ground as suggested by the expression 'forced to...'

34. b The best option is (b) (congenital, education) as the word 'environment' in the sentence is used figuratively to suggest the overall surroundings/conditions which shape a person. Option (c) seems close but is incorrect as the word 'climate' is insufficient to convey this figurative sense of environment.

35. d Going by the first blank, option (c) and (d) are close. In the second blank the context requires a word which goes along with the sense of 'minds' which are accustomed to the former or the old school of thought and hence the word 'tradition' aptly fits in here.

36. c The lines talk about the response of the media to a particular issue (the issue has not been mentioned). The author has a good opinion about the response of the media as understood by the word 'fervor'. The elites have presented their views about the response but their opinion is disliked by the author as revealed by the words 'insult to the basic integrity and intelligence'. So, we need a negative word for the first as well as the second blank.

The word 'gimmick' and 'contrivance' are apt for the first blank. 'Gimmick' means an unusual trick or unnecessary device that is intended to attract attention or to persuade people to buy something. 'Contrivance' is (usually disapproving) something that causes things to happen in a story in a way that does not seem natural or believable; a clever trick or plan. 'Cachet' which means 'prestige' makes option (a) unfit for the blanks. 'Illusion' which means a false idea or belief, especially about somebody or about a situation is apt for the second blank. Thus, option (c) is the correct option.

'Torrid' means emotional and passionate, so 'torridity' is incorrect for the first blank. 'Pun' means the clever or humorous use of a word that has more than one meaning, or of words that have different meanings but sound the same; double-meaning. Thus, option (b) and (d) are negated.

37. d The author is speaking on a positive note about the book and mentions its goodness. The author talks about the regional disparities related to the subject that are covered with a unifying theme in the book. 'Sundry' which means various is inappropriate is the given context. 'Turnpike' which refers to a wide road, where traffic can travel fast for long distances and that drivers must pay a toll to use is inappropriate. Thus, options (b) and (c) are negated.

'Disparate' which means made up of parts or people that are very different from each other (example: a disparate group of individuals) matches with the theme of the sentence. 'Distinct' means easily or clearly heard, seen, felt, etc; clearly different or of a different kind is less apt than disparate for the first blank.

'Heuristic' means involving or serving as an aid to learning, discovery, or problem-solving by experimental and especially trial-and-error methods; *also*: of or relating to exploratory problem-solving techniques that utilize self-educating techniques to improve performance. Thus, 'heuristic' is the apt word for the second blank. Option (d) is the correct answer.

38. b The question can be easily answered by following the tone of the sentence. The sentence can be completed by using words which can give the opposing meaning to the two parts of the sentence. Following this logic, options (c) and (d) can be rejected. Option (a) is incorrect as the second blank does not communicate the meaning of the sentence properly. 'Condemn' is not the apt word here as the idea that follows the second blank is not in concurrence with the sentence that follows it. The second part of the sentence requires a word with a positive connotation. Option (b) is the correct answer as it highlights that even amongst his critics, Gandhiji was respected for his conviction for his ideas.

39. a This question can be done by elimination. It is clear that the first blank will be filled up by some word similar to society or the population. In the second blank, an adjective for the word 'love' is required.

Option (b) can be eliminated because 'irrevocable', which means irreversible, doesn't fit in as something that a political father-figure may demand from the people.

Option (c) is also incorrect because 'unrequited' means unreturned, and going by the statement, does not logically fit in.

Option (d) is incorrect because 'civil obedience' cannot be demanded from the opposition, but from the civilians.

The word populace, meaning the ordinary people of a country or an area, aptly fits in the first blank. 'Unquestioning' goes perfectly with obedience, that is demanded of the people, and hence option (a) is correct.

40. b All the four options are grammatically appropriate for the first blank, but logically, only option (b) fits in. Since the sentence talks about a yearning for the glorious past, the word 'wistful', which means 'full of yearning or desire tinged with melancholy' aptly fits in the blank and makes it meaningful. The other options do not fit in the given context and hence are incorrect.

41. b Gauche means unsophisticated/socially awkward and Blandness describes the quality of being boring, plain, insipid. Thus, option (b) is the correct answer.

42. a Divisiveness means creating dissension or discord. Nationalist would refer to a common thread, a binding force. Thus, option (a) is the correct answer.

COMMON CONFUSABLES

1. d AABBA

Cricket Council is a collective noun so it takes a singular verb. The reference is made to a group as a whole and not to an individual.

Censure implies harsh criticism.

Censor means to put a ban on something objectionable.

Credible means capable of being believed.

Credulous means tending to believe without evidence.

Discretely means distinct whereas discreetly means to carefully avoid social embarrassment or distress; tactful.

2. e ABABA

Farther is used specifically for physical distance. Further is not used in the physical context and is used to indicate something of a greater degree or extent.

Historical is something pertaining to history while historic is something significant.

Distrust means having a sense of fear anticipation of discomfort of danger whereas mistrust is believing that a particular party has a hidden agenda.

True means not false or not fictional while real means existing or occurring in the physical world.

Compliment means a remark or an act expressing respect or admiration

Complement means a person or thing that completes something

3. b BBBAB

Regretfully would refer to the subject 'I'

Sensual is more related to sense organs (bodily)

Sensuous is aesthetically appealing to the senses.

Beside oneself means overwhelmed

For example: Beside oneself with grief

Stationary means something that is at rest

Stationery means any writing material

'Over' refers to a more symbolic sense whereas 'above' confirms with the idea of crossing the physical mark.

4. c In option (a) Anita wore a *brooch* is the correct option. As broach means to mention and suggest for the first time. While *brooch* means a clasp or an ornament. In the second sentence one has to meet a *councillor* to complain about neighbourhood amenities as a *councillor* draws from the word council - which is responsible for keeping the county in order. A *counsellor* is one who helps you take an informed decision about one or more of your concerns, therefore *councillor* is the right option here. In the third sentence *advice* has to take the noun form and not the verb form, therefore *advice* is the right option. *When Mr. Raymond advises people, he gives them advice. Climactic* refers to climax, while *climatic* to weather conditions, therefore climactic is the right option. *Flair* refers to a natural talent; it is commonplace to say that one has a *flair for writing. Flare* means to spread gradually outward, as the end of a trumpet, the bottom of a wide skirt, or the sides of a ship. Therefore, BAAAB (c) is the right option.

5. b *Currents* refer to prevailing or flowing, while *currants* are deciduous shrubs; therefore B is the right option. In the second sentence, *exceptional* means unusual or extraordinary. While, *exceptionable* means objectionable. *Assent* means to concur to or subscribe to. While *consent* means to agree, comply or yield. In the third sentence *obliged* refers to bind morally or legally, as by a promise or contract. While, *compelled* refers to being forced. Therefore, A is the correct option. *Sanguine* refers to being cheerfully optimistic, 'far too' in the sentence provides the cue to choose option A. While *genuine* refers to authenticity and is usually not used with *far too.* Therefore BBAAA (b) is the right option.

6. b *Caustic* refers to severely critical or sarcastic, while *ironic* draws from irony which refers to the use of words to convey a meaning that is the opposite of its literal meaning. Therefore B is the correct option. *Cogent* refers to clear, or an incisive presentation. While *valid* refers to being sound. And, being impassionate usually does not necessitate being valid. *Averse* means having a strong feeling of opposition, or antipathy. While *adverse* refers to something being unfavourable. Therefore B is the correct option. *Coup* is a clever action or accomplishment. A *coupé* is the end compartment in a European railroad car. Therefore, A is the correct option. *Peal* refers to a ringing of a set of bells, especially a change or set of changes rung on bells. While, *peel* refers to that which is peeled from something, as a piece of the skin or rind of a fruit. Therefore, B is the right option. Therefore, BBBAB (b) is the right option.

7. a *Defusing* means to remove the fuse from a bomb, mine etc. *Diffuse* means to spread or scatter widely or disseminate. Therefore B is the right option. *Baited* means to entice, especially by trickery or strategy. While, *bated* means to lessen or diminish; abate. Therefore, A is the right option. In sentence three *hoard* refers to a supply or accumulation that is hidden or carefully guarded for preservation. While, *horde* refers to a large group, mass or crowd. Therefore B is the correct option. In sentence four *interment* refers to burial, while *internment* refers to restrict to or confine within prescribed limits. Therefore B is the correct option. In sentence five *unsociable* refers to showing, or marked by a disinclination to friendly social relations; withdrawn and *unsocial* comes close in meaning to *unsociable* and is used more specifically when talking about predispositions or tendencies. Therefore, your answer choice should have corresponded with the options in the previous sentences treating these two words as synonyms. Therefore BABBA (a) is the correct answer.

ODD WORD OUT

1. a All others are adjectives.

2. c All others refer to something one receives.

3. d All others are synonyms.

4. b All others are kinds of governments.

5. a All others refer to individuals who have been honoured in some way.

6. a All others refer to individuals who use their skills or abilities. Authority cannot be called a skill.

7. d All others refer to 'travel'.

8. d All others relate to payments made for something.

9. d Equestrian means of or pertaining to horseback riding. Neigh is the cry of a horse. A derby is an annual horse race. Bark is the odd word out.

10. d All others are synonyms.

11. d All others are nouns, while write is a verb.

12. c All others are synonyms.

13. a All others are synonyms meaning 'to tear or cut'.

14. b All others are synonyms of control.

15. a All others mean 'to start'; cease means to stop.

16. b All others mean 'on the edge'.

17. c All others refer to something said in praise.

18. c All others refer to a feeling of hatred.

19. d All others are adjectives meaning 'skillful'.

20. c All others are adjectives for persons who do not speak much.

21. b All others are synonyms.

22. d All others refer to persons who are madly enthusiastic about something.

23. b All others have a quality of excitement in them.

24. b All others refer to a flow of a liquid.

25. b All others refer to deception in some form.

26. c All others are modes of transport.

27. d All others refer to a break in a continuous action.

28. b All others except 'kin' are synonyms.

29. b All others except 'adapt' are synonyms.

30. c All others except 'bell' refer to circular shapes. Bell is an object.

31. a All others except 'computer' refer to some kind of a network.

32. d Withstand is almost the opposite of the other three words.

33. d All others except 'bridge' refer to some kind of a gap or opening.

ANALOGY

1. a Just as a road is a medium for a car, a cable is a medium for electricity.

2. d Both the pairs are synonyms with two nouns.

3. a A fleet is a part of navy, just as a chapter is a part of a book. Moreover, both a fleet and a chapter are complete entities in themselves unlike a drop, a letter or a chair.

4. d Many feathers together make a wing and many bricks together make a wall.

5. c Just as sugar goes into tea, a button goes into the buttonhole.

6. c A composer composes a symphony and an author writes a novel.

7. b Like a trunk holds a tree upright, a chassis holds a car together.

8. a An arc is a part of a circle, just as a segment is a part of a line.

9. b A cow is a part of herd and a child is a part of a family.

10. d Wool is natural and acrylic is man made. Similarly cotton is natural and terelyene is man made.

11. d A doctor treats diseases and a teacher treats ignorance.

12. d Ornithology is a study of birds and botany is a study of plants.

13. a One eats food when one experiences hunger and one sleeps when one experiences weariness.

14. d A spear can be said to be a bigger kind of a dart, similarly a cannon is a bigger gun.

15. b Bricks are used to make a building, asphalt is used to make a highway.

16. d A brand is a type of product and a sports car is a type of an automobile.

17. b A gourmet is an expert on food and a connoisseur is an expert on art.

18. a North is the opposite of south and black of white.

19. d Drought and famine are synonyms as are training and skill.

20. a Nuts and bolts are used together as a phrase just as nitty-gritty are also used together.

21. b Salty is the adjective for the noun 'salt'. Bovine is the adjective for the noun 'cow'.

22. a Lack of being just is the defining characteristic of arbitrary just as lack of having order is a characteristic of chaos.

23. d A crime leads to punishment, just as a homicide leads to a penalty.

24. c Stratosphere is a layer of atmosphere, jet is a kind of an aircraft.

25. c The first word of both the pairs implies 'to cut or break up something into parts' while the second word in both means 'bringing things together'.

26. a Perjury is delibrate, willful giving of false evidence under oath i.e. lying under oath.

Similarly testimony is a statement given under oath.

27. b Medieval follows prehistoric, just as future follows present.

28. d Both the pairs are pairs of synonyms.

29. c Both are pairs of antonyms.

30. d 'Alleviate' is an extended form of 'ease' and 'interrogate' is an extended form of 'question'.

31. b Both are pairs of synonyms. All four words mean 'secret'.

32. b Audience watch a drama and spectators watch a game.

33. a Just as a building can have many stories, a book can have many chapters.

34. a The first pair shows two states of matter and the second pair gives examples of those states.

35. b The first word of each pair refers to breaking up of something and the second pair refers to joining of something.

36. a Both are pairs of antonyms.

37. a Bricks put together make a building, just as words put together make a dictionary.

38. c Both are pairs of antonyms.

39. b In both the pairs, the first is interrupted or followed by the second.

40. a Using words in a wrong place is malapropism and placing something in a wrong period of time is anachronism.

41. d Anterior means front and posterior means rear.

42. c (c) is a pair of homophones. (a), (b) and (d) do not have pairs of homophones.

43. d Doggerel is a badly written verse, which is written by a poet. Pulp fiction is a badly written piece of fiction, written by a novelist. (a), (b) and (c) do not show this derogatory relationship.

44. b A premise is evidence which leads to a conclusion. An assumption does not lead to an inference. An assumption, if wrong, will weaken an inference. But a hypothesis does lead to a theory. A hypothesis is a suggested explanation for a group of facts or phenomena that is accepted as likely to be true.

45. a A barge is a kind of a vessel, and a shovel is a kind of an implement. (b), (d) and (e) do not show this item to categorise relationship.

46. d The second word in the pair is a higher degree of the first. (a), (b) and (c) do not display such a relationship.

47. d The second word belongs to the family in the first word. (a), (b) and (c) do not display such a relationship.

48. d Just as one pays rent when one takes something on a lease, one pays interest on borrowing something, pays salary on employing someone and pays a price to buy something. But one does not pay tax on governing someone.

49. d In all other pairs the first word is used to measure the second.

50. b Just as a progressive person leads to progress, the second word of the pair in all other choices except b. leads to the first word of the pair. A sympathizer 'gives', and not 'leads to' sympathy.

51. b All others pairs have words that are opposites of each other. "Amoral" means not caring about right or wrong; neither moral nor immoral.

52. d In all other pairs, the first word holds the second together. For example clips hold papers together and a ribbon holds hair together. But vegetables are put inside a bag.

53. d All others are pairs of synonyms.

54. b In all other pairs, the first word is a part of the second word.

55. c In all other pairs, the first word is an adjective referring to the second word.

56. b In all other pairs, the first word is an adjective derived from the second pair.

57. a In all other pairs, the first word refers to a fear of the second word.

MISCELLANEOUS

1. b Privilege can be used in A., B. and D.

2. c Disaster can fit in A., C. and D.

3. d Depression fits in A., B. and D.

4. b Imagination fits in A. and D.

5. a State fits in A., B. and D.

■■

Grammar

SENTENCE SELECTION

1990

DIRECTIONS for Questions 1 to 40: In each of the questions below, four different ways of writing a sentence are indicated. Choose the best way of writing the sentence.

1. (a) The Excel Company has greatly enhanced it's advertising expense.
(b) The Excel Company has greatly increased its advertising expense.
(c) The Excel Company has greatly enhanced its advertising expense.
(d) The Excel Company has greatly increased it's advertising expense.

2. (a) Today we love, what tomorrow we hate; today we seek, what tomorrow we shun, today we desire, what tomorrow we fear.
(b) Today, we love what tomorrow we hate, today, we seek what tomorrow we shun, today, we desire what tomorrow we fear.
(c) Today we love what tomorrow we hate, today we seek what tomorrow we shun, today we desire what tomorrow we fear.
(d) Today we love what tomorrow we hate; today we seek what tomorrow we shun; today we desire what tomorrow we fear.

3. (a) There's Mr. Som, whom they say is the best singer in the country.
(b) There's Mr. Som, who they say is the best singer in the country.
(c) There is Mr. Som, whom they say is the best singer in the country.
(d) There is Mr. Som who, they say is the best singer in the country.

4. (a) I am not one of those who believe everything they hear.
(b) I am not one of those who believes everything I hear.
(c) I am not one of those who believes everything he hears.
(d) I am not one of those who believes in everything one hears.

5. (a) The Board of Directors will hold its next meeting in July.
(b) The Board of Directors will hold it's next meeting in July.
(c) The Board of Directors shall hold the next meeting in July.
(d) The Board of Directors shall hold it's next meeting in July.

6. (a) The state of his affairs were such as to cause anxiety to his creditors.
(b) The state of his affairs was such as to cause anxiety to his creditors.
(c) The state of his affairs are such as to cause anxiety to his creditors.
(d) The state of his affairs are such as to cause anxiety to his creditors.

7. (a) Cannot one do what one likes with one's own?
(b) Cannot one do that one likes to do with his own?
(c) Cannot one do that one likes with his own?
(d) Cannot one do what he likes with his own?

8. (a) Each of the students has done well.
(b) Each of the student has done well.
(c) Each of the students have done well.
(d) Each of the student have done well.

9. (a) None of us were comfortable with what was happening.
(b) None of us was comfortable with what was happening.
(c) None among us were comfortable with what was happening.
(d) None amongst us were comfortable with what was happening.

10. (a) Neither the king nor his ministers desires war.
(b) Neither king nor his ministers desires war.
(c) Neither the king nor his ministers desire war.
(d) Neither king nor his ministers desire war.

11. (a) The history of Modern Industry's performance, which is marginal at best, may be an indication of solvency problems that will occur in the future.
(b) Modern industry's history of marginal performance may indicate solvency problems in the future.
(c) The history of marginal performance of Modern Industry may indicate future solvency problems.
(d) Modern Industry's history of performance, which is marginal at best, may indicate future solvency problems.

12. (a) On the whole food front one may say that we can enjoy festivals in the consciousness that though some things are dear, the basic foods are better in quality and still low in price.
(b) We can enjoy festivals knowing that though some things are clear, the basic foods are of better quality and still low in price.
(c) Although we know that some things are dear, we can still enjoy festivals because the basic foods are better in quality and low in price.
(d) On the whole food front, although some things are dear, we can still enjoy festivals as the basic foods are of better quality and quite cheap.

13. (a) The dull are likely to have a limited conceptual grasp.
(b) It is unlikely that the dull would have adequate conceptual grasp.
(c) The dull are not likely to grasp concepts easily.
(d) It is unlikely that the dull can grasp concepts easily.

14. (a) I request you to kindly deliver to me a tin of milk powder.
(b) Could you please send me a tin of milk powder?
(c) May I request you to please send me a tin of milk powder?
(d) Can I have milk powder sent to me please?

15. (a) There is no question of it not being possible to freeze you to death and wake you up as and when you want.
(b) There is no question of it not being possible to freeze you to death and wake you up whenever you want.
(c) Undoubtedly, it should be possible to freeze you to death and wake you up whenever you want.
(d) Undoubtedly, it should be possible to freeze you to death and wake you up when you want.

16. (a) Finally, there will be unexpected, unanticipated implicational consequences of this development concerning human life.
(b) This development concerning human life will finally have unanticipated consequences.
(c) This development concerning human life will finally have unexpected and unanticipated implications.
(d) This development concerning human life will finally have unexpected implications.

17. (a) His definition of reality has first to be made coincident with the point of view adopted by the author whom he is discussing.
(b) His definition of reality has first to be made coincident with the point of view adopted by the author who he is discussing.
(c) His definition has to first agree with the point of view adopted by the author he is discussing.
(d) His definition of reality has first to coincide with the point of view adopted by the author he is discussing.

18. (a) I should be very much obliged if you could be kind enough to send me the required material.
(b) I should be much obliged if you could send me the required material.
(c) I should be very much obliged if you could kindly send me the required material.
(d) I should be grateful and very much obliged if you could kindly send me the required material.

19. (a) I am sorry, a prior engagement prevents me from joining you at dinner on Monday.
(b) I regret to say that I am very sorry that a previous engagement will prevent me from joining you at dinner on Monday.
(c) I regret to inform you that because of a previous engagement I will be prevented from joining you at dinner on Monday.
(d) I am sorry to say that I am unable to join you at dinner on Monday because of a prior engagement.

20. (a) Looking back, our inability to confirm speakers gave us the maximum headaches.
(b) Looking at it with hindsight our inability to confirm speakers gave us the maximum headaches.
(c) On hindsight we find that our inability to confirm speakers gave us the maximum headaches.
(d) On hindsight, our inability to confirm speakers gave us the maximum headaches.

1991

21. (a) The best part of the programme is the dances.
(b) The best part of the programme are the dances.
(c) The best part of the programme are the dance.
(d) The best parts of the programme is the dances.

22. (a) The professor, as well as the students, was pleased with their results.
(b) The professor, as well as the students, were pleased with their results.
(c) The professor as well as the students were pleased with their results.
(d) The professor as well as the students were pleased with their results.

23. (a) He was unwilling to testify, he was afraid of the defendant.
(b) Because he was afraid of the defendant, he was unwilling to testify.
(c) He was unwilling to testify: he was afraid of the defendant.
(d) Because he was afraid of the defendant he was unwilling to testify.

24. (a) When you have good health, one should feel fortunate.
(b) When you have good health, you should feel fortunate.
(c) When one have good health, you should feel fortunate.
(d) When one has good health, he should feel fortunate.

25. (a) Either you or he have to be here.
(b) Either you or he has to be here.
(c) Neither you nor he have to be here.
(d) Neither you nor they has to be here.

26. (a) Children begin by loving their parents; as they grow older they judge them; sometimes they forgive them.
(b) Children begin by loving their parents, as they grow older they judge them; sometimes they forgive them.
(c) Children begin by loving their parents; as they grow older they judge them, sometimes they forgive them.
(d) Children begin by loving their parents, as they grow older they judge them; sometimes they forgive them.

27. (a) Gopal and Ramesh have not finished his work.
(b) Gopal and Ramesh has not finished his work.
(c) Neither Gopal nor Ramesh have finished their work.
(d) Neither Gopal nor Ramesh has finished his work.

28. (a) The fact that Raghu was a good student he had many offers for good jobs.
(b) The fact that Raghu was a good student resulted in his having many offers for good jobs.
(c) The fact Raghu was a good student resulted in him having offers for good jobs.
(d) The fact that Raghu was a good student resulted in him having many offers for good jobs.

29. (a) The people of this company, have always been aware, of the needs for products of better quality and lower price.
(b) The people of this company, havc always been aware of the need for products of better quality and lower price.
(c) The people of this company have always been aware of the need for products of better quality and lower price.
(d) The people of this company, have always been aware of the need for products of better quality, and lower price.

30. (a) The Dean finally agreed to see me. To talk about my financial problems.
(b) The Dean finally agreed to see me, to talk about my financial problems.
(c) The Dean, finally agreed to see me to talk about my financial problems.
(d) The Dean finally agreed to see me to talk about my financial problems.

31. (a) We invited only the people who he said were his friends.
(b) We invited only the people whom he said were his friends.
(c) We invited only the people whom he said was his friends.
(d) We invited only the person whom he said were his friends.

2002

32. (a) The main problem with the notion of price discrimination is that it is not always a bad thing, but that it is the monopolist who has the power to decide who is charged what price.
(b) The main problem with the notion of price discrimination is not that it is always a bad thing, it is the monopolist who has the power to decide who is charged what price.
(c) The main problem with the notion of price discrimination is not that it is always a bad thing, but that it is the monopolist who has the power to decide who is charged what price.
(d) The main problem with the notion of price discrimination is not it is always a bad thing, but that it is the monopolist who has the power to decide who is charged what price.

33. (a) A symbiotic relationship develops among the contractors, bureaucracy and the politicians, and by a large number of devices costs are artificially escalated and black money is generated by underhand deals.
(b) A symbiotic relationship develops among contractors, bureaucracy and politicians, and costs are artificially escalated with a large number of devices and black money is generated through underhand deals.

(c) A symbiotic relationship develops among contractors, bureaucracy and the politicians, and by a large number of devices costs are artificially escalated and black money is generated on underhand deals.

(d) A symbiotic relationship develops among the contractors, bureaucracy and politicians, and by large number of devices costs are artificially escalated and black money is generated by underhand deals.

34. (a) The distinctive feature of tariffs and export subsidies is that they create difference of prices at which goods are traded on the world market and their price within a local market.

(b) The distinctive feature of tarriffs and export subsidies is that they create a difference of prices at which goods are traded with the world market and their prices in the local market.

(c) The distinctive feature of tariffs and export subsidies is that they create a difference between prices at which goods are traded on the world market and their prices within a local market.

(d) The distinctive feature of tariffs and export subsidies is that they create a difference across prices at which goods are traded with the world market and their prices within a local market.

35. (a) Any action of government to reduce the systemic risk inherent in financial markets will also reduce the risks that private operators perceive and thereby encourage excessive hedging.

(b) Any action by government to reduce the systemic risk inherent in financial markets will also reduce the risks that private operators perceive and thereby encourage excessive gambling.

(c) Any action by government to reduce the systemic risk inherent in financial markets will also reduce the risks that private operators perceive and thereby encourages excessive gambling.

(d) Any action of government to reduce the systemic risk inherent in financial markets will also reduce the risks that private operators perceive and thereby encourages excessive gambling.

2003(L)

36. (a) The running of large businesses consist of getting somebody to make something that somebody else sold to somebody else for more than its cost.

(b) The running of a large business consists of getting somebody to make something that somebody else will sell to somebody else for more than it costs.

(c) The running of a large business consists of getting somebody to sell something that somebody else made for more than it cost.

(d) The running of large businesses consist of getting somebody to make something else that somebody else will sell to somebody else for more than it costs.

37. (a) From the sixteenth century onwards, people started feeling disdainful and self-conscious about their body and its products that led to a heightened focus on emotional and bodily regulations.

(b) The heightened focus on controlling the body and emotions comes from disdain and self-consciousness about the body and its products, found in the sixteenth century.

(c) From the sixteenth century onwards, a growing disdain for and self-consciousness about the body and its products took hold, leading to a heightened focus on emotional and bodily regulation.

(d) The heightened focus on emotional and bodily regulations started from the sixteenth century onwards, when people felt disdain and self-consciousness about the body and its products.

38. (a) We are forced to fall back on fatalism as an explanation of irrational events.

(b) We are forced to falling back on the fatalism as an explanation of irrational events.

(c) We are forced to fall back on fatalism as explanations of irrational events.

(d) We are forced to fall back to fatalism as an explanation of irrational events

39. (a) Creativity in any field is regarded not only as valuable for itself but also as a service to the nation.

(b) Creativity in any field is not regarded only as valuable on its own, but also as a service to the nation.

(c) Creativity, in any field, is not only regarded as valuable, but also as a service to the nation.

(d) Creativity in any field is regarded not only as valuable in itself but also as a service to the nation.

40. (a) If precision of thought had facilitated precision of behaviour, and if reflection had preceded action, it would be ideal for humans.

(b) It would be ideal for humans if reflection preceded action and precision of thought facilitated precision of behaviour.

(c) It would be ideal for humans if precedence of reflection was followed by action and precision of thought, by precise behaviour.

(d) It would have been ideal for humans, if precise action and behaviour preceded precise reflection.

1992

DIRECTIONS for Questions 41 to 45: In each of the three questions, a sentence has been divided into four parts and marked (a), (b), *(c) and (d). One of these parts contains a mistake in grammar, idiom or syntax. Identify that part and mark it as the answer.*

41. (a) Pakistan was the team
(b) whom most people thought
(c) would win the World Cup
(d) held in 1987.

42. (a) When you turn to your right,
(b) you will find a big house
(c) with a beautiful garden on the front side of it
(d) and that is my residence.

43. (a) I have been postponing calling
(b) on my friend in the hospital,
(c) but I am planning
(d) I would go there tomorrow.

44. (a) I wondered who could be calling me at midnight
(b) and when I took the phone
(c) I found it was not other
(d) Than my fiancé from Paris.

45. (a) I want you to take the first bus
(b) and to go to the Bank
(c) and remit this cheque and then
(d) come back straight here.

MEMORY BASED QUESTIONS

2011

46. Given below are five sentences. Each sentence has a pair of words that are italicized. From the italicized words, select the most appropriate words (A or B) to form correct sentences. The sentences are followed by options that indicate the words, which may be selected to correctly complete the set of sentences. From the options given, choose the most appropriate one.

A man came *floundering (A) / foundering (B)* through the snow towards us.

For some *persevere (A) / perverse (B)* reason he is refusing to see a doctor.

His *mordent (A) / mordant (B)* wit appealed to students.

She set off at a *cantor (A) / canter (B)*.

The fire *chard (A) / charred (B)* the paper.

(a) ABAAB
(b) BABAA
(c) ABBBB
(d) BAABB

47. Given below are five sentences. Each sentence has a pair of words that are italicized. From the italicized words, select the most appropriate words (A or B) to form correct sentences. The sentences are followed by options that indicate the words, which may be selected to correctly complete the set of sentences. From the options given, choose the most appropriate one.

The white marble sculpture of the saint in the throes of divine ecstasy is strikingly offset by a gilt *aureole (A) / oriole (B)*.

Conflicts among the various groups do not *auger (A) / augur (B)* well for the future of the peace talks.

Sometimes shipbuilders *sheath (A) / sheathe (B)* a ship's bottom with copper for extra protection from barnacles and other threats.

She was so tired, her eyelids were beginning to *drupe (A) / droop (B)*.

She developed *complications (A) / complexities (B)* after the surgery.

(a) AAAAA (b) BBBAA
(c) BAABB (d) ABBBA

2012

48. Given below are five sentences or parts of sentences that form a paragraph. Identify the sentence(s) or part(s) of sentence(s)that is/are correct in terms of grammar and usage. Then, choose the most appropriate option.

1. In every democratic and more-or-less secular countries,
2. similar questions arise about precise extent to which religious sub-cultures
3. should be allowed to live on their own rules and laws.
4. One set of questions emerge when believers demand, and often get,
5. an opt-out from the law of the land.

(a) 3 & 5
(b) 3 only
(c) 5 only
(d) 2, 3 & 5

2013

49. Given below are five sentences or parts of sentences that form a paragraph. Identify the sentence(s) or part(s) of sentence(s) that is/are incorrect in terms of grammar and usage. Then, choose the most appropriate option.

A. Since the breakdown of political formality, pictures have stood for a different message, for which the umbrella term is "down to earth".

B. This down-to-earthness has myriad elements, most of it contradictory or impossible.

C. For instance, to be down-to-earth you have to like sport; to like sport you have to choose a team; but if you go and see your team, you are no longer down-to-earth because you can afford a ticket.

D. If you pretend that you can't afford a ticket, you're disingenuous; if you shrug and say, "I can get a free ticket to anything, I'm prime minister", you're reasonable but you have squandered the advantage you gained in liking sport in the first place.

E. Realistically, all one can do is pretend you're too busy to watch sport, which works OK for the harassed, sleep-deprived, Thatcher-model premier, but couldn't possibly wash for David "Fruit Ninja" Cameron.

(a) A, C and E
(b) B, D and E
(c) B, C and D
(d) A, B and E

50. Given below are five sentences or parts of sentences that form a paragraph. Identify the sentence(s) or part(s) of sentence(s) that is/are incorrect in terms of grammar and usage. Then, choose the most appropriate option.

A. The central question to answering in judging the proportionality of this sentence is whether the desire to punish a whistleblower driven by moral outrage stems from the alleged harm he did US military and diplomatic interests, or whether it derives more from sheer embarrassment.

B. The judge presiding, Col Denise Lind, had already thrown out the gravest of charge, that of "aiding the enemy".

C. Col Lind had also limited the admissibility of evidence regarding the "chilling effects" that Mr Manning's actions had on US diplomacy by releasing 250,000 state department cables.

D. A military witness conceded there was no evidence that anyone had been killed after being named in the releases.

E. Mr Manning's recent apology for his actions does not, and should not, detract from the initial defence he gave for it, when he spoke of his shock at the "delightful bloodlust" displayed by that helicopter crew, or his belief that stimulating a debate about the wars was the right thing to do.

(a) A, B and E
(b) B, C and D
(c) A, C and D
(d) A, C and E

2014

51. Given below are four sentences or parts of sentences that form a paragraph. Identify the sentence(s) or part(s) of sentence(s) that is/are incorrect in terms of grammar and usage. Then, choose the most appropriate option.

1. Herbivores birds do not have teeth to grind up the vegetation they eat.
2. Teeth would make their skulls too heavy and make flight difficult.
3. Instead, a part of their digestive system, called the crop, contains stones, which grind up the plant material they eat.
4. Some herbivores are called ruminants.

(a) 1 & 2 (b) 1
(c) 2 (d) 3 & 2

52. Given below are five sentences. Each sentence has a pair of words that are italicized. From the italicized words, select the most appropriate words (A or B) to form correct sentences. The sentences are followed by options that indicate the words, which may be selected to correctly complete the set of sentences. From the options given, choose the most appropriate option.

I. It would not be wrong to say that the politicians today are leeches (A) / leaches (B) feeding off the hard-working majority.

II. He had been gulled (A) / culled (B) into believing that the documents were authentic

III. The sole of the shoe should be designed in a manner such that it can take constant abrasion (A) / aberration (B).

IV. He attenuated (A) / accentuated (B) the eccentricity of the already freakish costume by adopting theatrical attitudes and an air of satisfied negligence.

V. She is the object of his unabashed amorphous (A) / amorous (B) intentions.

(a) BAAAB (b) BBBAB
(c) AAABB (d) ABAAA

53. Given below are five sentences. Each sentence has a pair of words that are italicized. From the italicized words, select the most appropriate words (A or B) to form correct sentences. The sentences are followed by options that indicate the words, which may be selected to correctly complete the set of sentences. From the options given, choose the most appropriate option.

I. The animal approached us bellowing (A) / billowing (B) and pawing the ground with the strength of many earthly bulls.

II. I have seen this whole body of soldiers, upon a word of command, draw their swords at once, and brandish (A) / blandish (B) them in the air.

III. I am surprised that plaintiffs' hyperbolic allegations and inflated damage claims are given any credence (A) / cadence (B).

IV. A number of the species are edible, while others have been recorded as deleterious (A) / delirious (B).

V. From the top of the hill I decried (A) / descried (B) a solitary rider.

(a) BABAB
(b) BBBAB
(c) ABAAB
(d) AAAAB

54. Given below are five sentences. Each sentence has a pair of words that are italicized. From the italicized words, select the most appropriate words (A or B) to form correct sentences. The sentences are followed by options that indicate the words, which may be selected to correctly complete the set of sentences. From the options given, choose the most appropriate option.

I. A survey of the history of Christianity tells a disturbing tale, one wherein diffident (A) / dissident (B) cries for reform resulted in dangerous accusation of heresy and witchcraft.

II. Certainly the Arabs have no interest in seeing another war conflagrate (A) / conflate (B) in the Gulf region.

III. The government operates according to its own rules, bringing enormous benefits to the chosen few, and suffering and immiseration (A) / commiseration (B) to millions.

IV. If the minority in such case cedes (A) / secedes (B) rather than acquiesces, it will make a precedent which in turn will divide and ruin them.

V. The full moon beams like a beckon (A) / beacon (B) in the clear sky.

(a) BBAAB
(b) BAABB
(c) ABBBA
(d) AAABB

55. Given below is a sentence, part of which is missing. Beneath the sentence you will find four ways of phrasing the missing part. Select the correct answer in terms of grammar and usage.

The bamboo sharks are just as easy to breed, ________not much market for them.

(a) but they grow much larger, and are so common that there are
(b) but they grow much larger, and thus are so common that there are
(c) but they grow much larger, and thus are so common that their is
(d) but they grow much larger, and are so common that there is

56. Given below are four sentences or parts of sentences that form a paragraph. Identify the sentence(s) or part(s) of sentence(s) that is/are incorrect in terms of grammar and usage. Then, choose the most appropriate option.

1. William Butler Yeats wrote two poems, which are together known as the Byzantium series.
2. The first is "Sailing to Byzantium," and their sequel is simply named "Byzantium."
3. The former is considered easier of the two to understand.
4. It contains multiple meanings and emotions, and the poet uses various literary devices to communicate them.

(a) 1 & 4 (b) 2 & 3
(c) 2 & 4 (d) 1 & 3

SENTENCE CORRECTION

1991

DIRECTIONS for Questions 1 to 15: Each sentence below has been broken up into four parts sequentially. Choose that part which contains a mistake.

1. (a) A feasibility survey has now
(b) been completed in India to establish
(c) a network of felicitate contacts
(d) between small and medium enterprises.

2. (a) Privatization generally represents
(b) an ideological response
(c) to the perceived problem
(d) in the public sector.

3. (a) The Indian government's choice
(b) of the EEC as a partner
(c) stem from the fact
(d) that the community is the most important market for India.

4. (a) A person who earns a
(b) few thousand rupees
(c) and decides to save
(d) many of it must be a miser.

5. (a) Had you been in my
(b) position, you were definitely
(c) shown your displeasure
(d) at the turn of events.

6. (a) I definitely disagree (b) with the position that
(c) requires that money (d) is a key motivator.

7. (a) This has slowed the progress
(b) of reforms in many countries
(c) because the choice of either of the extreme
(d) positions inevitably invite criticism.

8. (a) Gavaskar was a great batsman who
(b) having played more than 100
(c) test matches, he then decided
(d) to call it a day.

9. (a) When we sold of all our
(b) furniture, crockery and
(c) other household goods,
(d) the room looked bare.

10. (a) In the history of mankind
(b) it has always been
(c) minority which have been
(d) able to change the world.

11. (a) Management education is
(b) becoming highly sought after
(c) by aspiring ambitious students
(d) because of high demand in the job market.

1993

12. (a) You did not wait (b) for us before you
(c) went to meet him. (d) Isn't it?

13. (a) The police have prevented
(b) Rajan in leaving the
(c) city without informing them
(d) two days in advance.

14. (a) I would have
(b) given you the
(c) documents yesterday if
(d) you had asked for it.

15. (a) Who have you
(b) invited for the lecture
(c) on astrophysics
(d) this evening?

2004

DIRECTIONS for Questions 16 to 18: Identify the incorrect sentence or sentences.

16. A. It was a tough situation and Manasi was taking pains to make it better.
B. Slowly her efforts gave fruit and things started improving.
C. Everyone complemented her for her good work.
D. She was very happy and thanked everyone
(a) A (b) D
(c) B and C (d) A and C

17. A. Harish told Raj to plead guilty.
B. Raj pleaded guilty of stealing money from the shop.
C. The court found Raj guilty of all the crimes he was charged with.
D. He was sentenced for three years in jail
(a) A and C (b) B and D
(c) A, C, and D (d) B, C, and D

18. A. Last Sunday, Archana had nothing to do.
B. After waking up, she lay on the bed thinking of what to do.
C. At 11 o' clock she took shower and got ready.
D. She spent most of the day shopping
(a) B and C (b) C
(c) A and B (d) B, C, and D

2005

DIRECTIONS for Questions 19 to 22: Each question consists of four sentences on a topic. Some sentences are grammatically incorrect or inappropriate. Select the option that indicates the grammatically correct and appropriate sentence(s).

19. A. When virtuoso teams begin their work, individuals are in and group consensus is out.
B. As project progresses, however, the individual stars harness themselves to the product of the group.
C. Sooner or later, the members break through their own egocentrism and become a plurality with single-minded focus on the goal.
D. In short, they morph into a powerful team with a shared identity.
(a) A&C (b) A&D
(c) B&D (d) A, C&D

20. A. Large reductions in the ozone layer, which sits about 15-30 km above the Earth, take place each winter over the polar regions, especially the Antarctic, as low temperatures allow the formation of stratospheric clouds that assist chemical reactions breaking down ozone.

B. Industrial chemicals containing chlorine and bromine have been blamed for thinning the layer because they attack the ozone molecules, making them to break apart.

C. Many an offending chemicals have now been banned.

D. It will still take several decades before these substances have disappeared from the atmosphere.

(a) D (b) B&D
(c) A&D (d) A&C

21. A. The balance of power will shift to the East as China and India evolve.

B. Rarely the economic ascent of two still relatively poor nations has been watched with such a mixture of awe, opportunism, and trepidation.

C. Postwar era witnessed economic miracles in Japan and South Korea, but neither was populous enough to power worldwide growth or change the game in a complete spectrum of industries.

D. China and India, by contrast, posses the weight and dynamism to transform the 21st-century global economy.

(a) A, B&C (b) A&D
(c) C (d) C&D

22. A. People have good reason to care about the welfare of animals.

B. Ever since Enlightenment, their treatment has been seen as a measure of mankind's humanity.

C. It is no coincidence that William Wilberforce and Sir Thomas Foxwell Buxton, two leaders of the movement to abolish the slave trade, helped found the Royal Society for the Prevention of Cruelty to Animals in 1820s.

D. An increasing number of people go further: mankind has a duty not to cause pain to animals that have the capacity to suffer.

(a) A&D (b) B
(c) A&C (d) C&D

2007

DIRECTIONS for Questions 23 to 29: In each question, there are five sentences or parts of sentences that form a paragraph. Identify the sentence(s) or part(s) of sentence(s) that is/are correct in terms of grammar and usage. Then, choose the **most appropriate option.**

23. A. When I returned to home, I began to read

B. everything I could get my hand on about Israel.

C. That same year Israel's Jewish Agency sent

D. a *Shaliach* a sort of recruiter to Minneapolis.

E. I became one of his most active devotees.

(a) C & E (b) C only
(c) E only (d) B, C & E
(e) C, D & E

24. A. So once an economy is actually in a recession,

B. the authorities can, in principle, move the economy

C. out of slump - assuming hypothetically

D. that they know how to - by a temporary stimuli.

E. In the longer term, however, such polices have no affect on the overall behaviour of the economy.

(a) A, B & E (b) B, C & E
(c) C & D (d) E only
(e) B only

25. A. It is sometimes told that democratic

B. government originated in the city-states

C. of ancient Greece. Democratic ideals have been handed to us from that time.

D. In truth, however, this is an unhelpful assertion.

E. The Greeks gave us the word, hence did not provide us with a model.

(a) A, B & D (b) B, C & D
(c) B & D (d) B only
(e) D only

2008

26. A. In 1849, a poor Bavarian imigrant named Levi Strauss

B. landed in San Francisco, California,

C. at the invitation of his brother-in-law David Stern

D. owner of dry goods business.

E. This dry goods business would later became known as Levi Strauss & Company.

(a) B only (b) B and C
(c) A and B (d) A only
(e) A, B and D

27. A. In response to the allegations and condemnation pouring in,

B. Nike implemented comprehensive changes in their labour policy.

C. Perhaps. sensing the rising tide of global labour concerns,

D. from the public would become a prominent media issue,

E. Nike sought to be a industry leader in employee relations.

(a) D and E (b) D only
(c) A and E (d) A and D
(e) B, C and E

28. A. Charges and countercharges mean nothing
B. to the few million who have lost their home.
C. The nightmare is far from over, for the government
D. is still unable to reach hundreds who are marooned.
E. The death count have just begun.
(a) A only (b) C only
(c) A and C (d) A, C and D
(e) D only

29. A. I did not know what to make of you.
B. Because you'd lived in India, I associate you more with my parents than with me.
C. And yet you were unlike my cousins in Calcutta, who seem so innocent and obedient when I visited them.
D. You were not curious about me in the least.
E. Although you did make effort to meet me.
(a) A only (b) A and B
(c) A and E (d) D only
(e) A and D

MEMORY BASED QUESTIONS

2010

30. Given below are a few sentences. Identify the sentence(s)/ part(s) of the sentence(s) that is/are correct in terms of grammar and usage (including spelling, punctuation and logical consistency). Then choose the most appropriate option.
(A) Many a men dated their ruin from some murder or other that perhaps they thought little of at the time.
(B) Afterwards, when fascinated by the man, as you will be, turn immediately to this excellent, detailed and often harrowing biography.
(C) After they had finished the meal they asked the waiter the bill.
(D) By the time she arrives, we will have finished our homework.
(a) A and B (b) A and D
(c) B and D (d) Only C

31. Given below are a few sentences. Identify the sentence(s)/ part(s) of the sentence(s) that is/are correct in terms of grammar and usage (including spelling, punctuation and logical consistency). Then choose the most appropriate option.
(A) Imagine a speck of dust close to a planet a billion times the size of earth. The speck of dust represents the odds in favour of your being born.
(B) The huge planet would be the odds against itself. So stop sweating the small stuff.
(C) Don't be like the ingrate who got a castle as a present and worried about the mildew in the bathroom.
(D) Stop looking at the gift horse in the mouth- remember that you are a Black Swan.
(a) A & B (b) A & D
(c) C & D (d) C

2012

32. Given below are five sentences that form a paragraph. Identify the sentence(s)or part(s) of sentence(s) that is/are correct in terms of grammar and usage (including spelling, punctuation and logical consistency). Then, choose the most appropriate option.
A. A tarot is one of the most wonderful of human inventions.
B. Despite all the outcry of philosophers, this pack of pictures,
C. in whom destiny is reflected as in a mirror with multiple facets,
D. remains so vital and exercises so irresistible an attraction on
E. imaginative minds that it is hardly possible that it could ever be abolished.
(a) A only (b) A and B
(c) D and E (d) D only

PHRASE REPLACEMENT

1996

DIRECTIONS for Questions 1 to 24: In each of the following questions, a part of the paragraph or sentences has been underlined. From the choices given to you, you are required to choose the one which would best replace the underlined part.

1. The Romanians may be restive under Soviet direction — but they are tied to Moscow by ideological and military links.
(a) they are tied to Moscow by ideological and military links
(b) they are preparing for a great revolution
(c) secretly they rather enjoy the prestige of being protected by the mighty Soviets
(d) there is nothing they can do about it

2. In a penetrating study, CBS-TV focuses on these people without hope, whose bodies are cared for by welfare aid, but whose spirit is often neglected by a disinterested society.
(a) whose bodies are cared for by welfare aid
(b) who do not have enough to eat
(c) whose hopelessness may be alleviated
(d) who may be physically satiated

3. Contemplating whether to exist with an insatiable romantic temperament, he was the author and largely the subject of a number of memorable novels.
   (a) Contemplating whether to exist
   (b) Combining realistic details
   (c) Miscegenating a brilliant mind
   (d) Aware that he had been born
4. How many times have I asked myself: when is the world going to start to make sense? There is a monster out there, and it is rushing towards me over the uneven ground of consciousness.
   (a) There is a monster out there
   (b) It is as if the world is on my shoulders
   (c) The answer is out there somewhere
   (d) There is a sea of sensibility in me
5. In Martin Amis' new novel, the narrator is trapped — and hurtling towards a terrible secret, its resolution and the dreadful revelations it brings, ally to give an excruciating vision of guilt.
   (a) ally to give an excruciating vision of guilt
   (b) to us give a vivid picture of guilt
   (c) is a painful picture of a guilt ridden world
   (d) does not really solve all the questions in the narrator's mind
6. Victory is everything in the Indian universe and Tendulkar will be expected to translate his genius to that effect. To contemplate any other option is to contemplate the risk of failure.
   (a) To contemplate any other option is to contemplate the risk of failure.
   (b) Failure is not an action that can be contemplated.
   (c) Any other action has the potential of failure.
   (d) Failure is not an option.

1997

7. This government has given subsidies to the Navratnas but there is no telling whether the subsequent one will do.
   (a) whether the subsequent government will do so
   (b) if the government to follow will accept the policy
   (c) if the government to follow will adhere to the policy
   (d) whether the subsequent one will do so
8. Rahul Bajaj has done a great job of taking the company to its present status, but it is time that he let go off the reins.
   (a) let go of the reins (b) stepped down
   (c) let go off the reins (d) delegated responsibility
9. With the pick up in the standard of education, expensive private schools have started blooming up in every corner of the country.
   (a) started blooming in every corner of the country
   (b) started mushrooming all over the country
   (c) started mushrooming in every corner of the country
   (d) blossomed all over the country
10. It is important that whatever else happens, these two factors should not be messed around with.
    (a) It is important that
    (b) It is a fact that
    (c) It should be urgently understood that
    (d) It should be understood that
11. It must be noticed that under no circumstance should the company go in for diversification.
    (a) It must be noticed
    (b) It must be noted
    (c) It must be pointed out
    (d) It should be noticed

1998

12. British Airspace has been focusing on building European links.
    (a) concentrating on creating European links
    (b) pursuing ways of building European connectivity
    (c) stressing on building European links
    (d) focusing on forging European links
13. The appetite of banks for funds was lost under the onslaught of the slowdown, corporates refused to borrow even as bank deposits flourished.
    (a) bank deposits flourished
    (b) bank deposits swelled
    (c) bank deposits were enhanced
    (d) bank deposits flummoxed
14. The 8th-century revival of Byzantine learning is an inexplicable phenomenon, and its economic and military precursors have yet to be discovered.
    (a) a phenomenon yet to be discovered
    (b) a phenomenon incompletely explained
    (c) an inexplicable phenomenon
    (d) an unidentifiable phenomenon
15. The management can still hire freely but cannot scold freely.
    (a) cannot scold at will
    (b) cannot give umbrage
    (c) cannot take decisions to scold
    (d) cannot scold willfully
16. Many people mistake familiarity for a vulgar style, and suppose that to write without affectation is to write at random speed.
    (a) is to write at random (b) is to write randomly
    (c) is to write fast (d) is to do speed writing

1999

17. It was us who had left before he arrived.

(a) we who had left before time he had arrived.

(b) us who had went before he arrived.

(c) us who had went before had arrived.

(d) we who had left before he arrived.

18. The MP rose up to say that in her opinion, she thought the Women's Reservation Bill should be passed on unanimously.

(a) rose to say that she thought the Women's Reservation Bill should be passed

(b) rose up to say that, the Women's Reservation Bill should be passed on

(c) rose to say that, in her opinion, she thought that the Women's Reservation Bill should be passed

(d) rose to say that, in her opinion, the Women's Reservation Bill should be passed on

19. Mr Pillai, the president of the union and who is also a member of the community group, will be in charge of the negotiations.

(a) since he is a member of the community group

(b) also being a member of the community group

(c) a member of the community group

(d) in addition, who is a member of the community group

20. Since the advent of cable television, at the beginning of this decade, the entertainment industry took a giant stride forward in our country.

(a) this decade saw the entertainment industry taking

(b) this decade, the entertainment industry has taken

(c) this decade, the entertainment industry had taken

(d) this decade, the entertainment industry took

21. His mother made great sacrifices to educate him, moving house on three occasions, and severing the thread on her loom's shuttle whenever Mencius neglected his lessons to make him understand the need to persevere.

(a) severing the thread on her loom's shuttle whenever Mencius neglected his lessons to make him understand the need to persevere.

(b) severed the thread on her loom's shuttle whenever Mencius neglected his lessons to make him understand the need to persevere.

(c) severed the thread on her loom's shuttle whenever Mencius neglected his lessons to make him understand the need for persevering.

(d) severing the thread on her loom's shuttle whenever Mencius neglected his lessons to make them understand the need to persevere.

22. If you are in a three-month software design project and, in two weeks, you've put together a program that solves part of the problem, show it to your boss without delay.

(a) and, you've put together a program that solves part of the problem in two weeks

(b) and, in two weeks, you've put together a program that solves part of the problem

(c) and, you've put together a program that has solved part of the problem in two weeks

(d) and, in two weeks, you put together a program that solved only part of the problem

23. Many of these environmentalists proclaim to save nothing less than the planet itself.

(a) to save nothing lesser than

(b) that they are saving nothing lesser than

(c) to save nothing less than

(d) that they save nothing less than

24. Bacon believes that the medical profession should be permitted to ease and quicken death where the end would otherwise only delay for a few days and at the cost of great pain.

(a) be delayed for a few days

(b) be delayed for a few days and

(c) be otherwise only delayed for a few days and

(d) otherwise only delay for a few days and

2004

DIRECTIONS for Questions 25 to 27: Each statement has a part missing. Choose the best option from the four options given below the statement to make up the missing part.

25. Many people suggest ___ and still other would like to convince people not to buy pirated cassettes.

(a) to bring down audiocassette prices to reduce the incidence of music piracy, others advocate strong legal action against the offenders,

(b) bringing down audiocassette prices to reduce the incidents of music piracy, others are advocating strong legal action against offenders,

(c) bringing down audiocassette prices to reduce the incidents of music piracy, others advocate strong legal action against offenders,

(d) audiocassette prices to be brought down to reduce incidents of music piracy, others advocate that strong legal action must be taken against offenders,

26. The ancient Egyptians believed ___ so that when these objects were magically reanimated through the correct rituals, they would be able to function effectively.
   (a) that it was essential that things they portrayed must have every relevant feature shown as clearly as possible
   (b) it was essential for things they portray to have had every relevant feature shown as clearly as possible,
   (c) it was essential that the things they portrayed had every relevant feature shown as clearly as possible.
   (d) that when they portrayed things, it should have every relevant feature shown as clearly as possible
27. Archaeologists believe that the pieces of red – ware pottery excavated recently near Bhavnagar and ___ shed light on a hitherto dark 600-year period in the Harappan history of Gujarat.
   (a) estimated with a reasonable certainty as being about 3400 years old,
   (b) are estimated reasonably certain to be about 3400 years old,
   (c) estimated at about 3400 years old with reasonable certainty,
   (d) estimated with reasonable certainty to be about 3400 years old,

WORD USAGE

2003(L)

DIRECTIONS for Questions 1 to 13: In each question, the word at the top of the table is used in four different ways, numbered (a) to (d). Choose the option in which the usage of the word is INCORRECT or INAPPROPRIATE.

1. Bundle
   (a) The newborn baby was a bundle of joy for the family.
   (b) Mobile operators are offering a bundle of additional benefits.
   (c) He made a bundle in the share market.
   (d) It was sheer luck that brought a bundle of boy-scouts to where I was lying wounded.

2. Distinct
   (a) He is distinct about what is right and what is wrong.
   (b) Mars became distinct on the horizon in the month of August.
   (c) The distinct strains of Ravi's violin could be heard above the general din.
   (d) Ghoshbabu's is a distinct case of water rising above its own level.

3. Implication
   (a) Everyone appreciated the headmaster's implication in raising flood relief in the village.
   (b) This letter will lead to the implication of several industrialists in the market scam.
   (c) Several members of the audience missed the implication of the minister's promise.
   (d) Death, by implication, is the only solution the poem offers the reader.

4. Host
   (a) If you host the party, who will foot the bill?
   (b) Kerala's forests are host to a range of snakes
   (c) Ranchi will play the host to the next national film festival.
   (d) A virus has infected the host computer.

5. Sort
   (a) What sort of cheese do you use in pizza?
   (b) Farmers of all sort attended the rally.
   (c) They serve tea of a sort on these trains.
   (d) Let's sort these boys into four groups.

2003(R)

6. Help
   (a) This syrup will help you cold.
   (b) I can't help the colour of my skin.
   (c) Ranjit may help himself with the beer in the fridge.
   (d) Do you really expect me to help you out with cash.

7. Paper
   (a) Your suggestions look great on the paper, but are absolutely impractical.
   (b) Do you know how many trees are killed to make a truckload of paper?
   (c) So far I have been able to paper over the disagreements among my brothers.
   (d) Dr. Malek will read a paper on criminalization of politics.

8. Service
   (a) Customers have to service themselves at this canteen.
   (b) It's a service lift; don't get into it.
   (c) I'm not making enough even to service the loan.
   (d) Jyoti's husband has been on active service for three months.

9. Reason
   (a) Your stand is beyond all reason.
   (b) Has she given you any reason for her resignation?
   (c) There is little reason in your pompous advice.
   (d) How do you deal with a friend who doesn't listen to a reason?

10. Business
   (a) I want to do an MBA before going into business.
   (b) My wife runs profitable business in this suburb.
   (c) If we advertise we will get twice as much business as we have now.
   (d) How you spend your money is as much my business as yours.

2004

11. Bolt

(a) The shopkeeper showed us a bolt of fine silk.

(b) As he could not move, he made a bolt for the gate.

(c) Could you please bolt the door?

(d) The thief was arrested before he could bolt from the scene of the crime.

12. Fallout

(a) Nagasaki suffered from the fallout of nuclear radiation.

(b) People believed that the political fallout of the scandal would be insigficant.

(c) Who can predict the environmental fallout of the WTO agreements?

(d) The headmaster could not understand the fallout of several of his good students at the public examination.

13. Passing

(a) She did not have passing marks in mathematics.

(b) The mad woman was cursing everybody passing her on the road.

(c) At the birthday party all the children enjoyed a game of passing the parcel.

(d) A passing taxi was stopped to rush the accident victims to the hospital.

2005

DIRECTIONS for Questions 14 to 16: In each question, the word at the top of the table is used in four different ways, numbered (a) to (d). Choose the option in which the usage of the word is incorrect or inappropriate.

14. Near

(a) I got there just after you left – a near miss!

(b) She and her near friend left early.

(c) The war led to a near doubling of oil prices.

(d) They came near to tears seeing the plight of the victims.

15. Hand

(a) I have my hand full, I cannot do it today.

(b) The minister visited the jail to see the breach at first hand.

(c) The situation is getting out of hand here!

(d) When the roof of my house was blown away, he was willing to lend me a hand.

16. For

(a) He has a great eye for detail.

(b) We are waiting for the day.

(c) I can't bear for her to be angry.

(d) It couldn't be done for ever.

Directions for Questions 17 to 20: In each of the questions, a word has been used in sentences in five different ways. Choose the option corresponding to the sentence in which the usage of the word is **incorrect or inappropriate.**

2008

17. Run

(a) I must run fast to catch up with him.

(b) Our team scored a goal against the run of play.

(c) You can't run over him like that.

(d) The newly released book is enjoying a popular run.

(e) This film is a run-of-the-mill production.

18. Round

(a) The police fired a round of tear gas shells.

(b) The shop is located round the corner.

(c) We took a ride on the merry-go-round.

(d) The doctor is on a hospital round.

(e) I shall proceed further only after you come round to admitting it.

19. Buckle

(a) After the long hike our knees were beginning to buckle.

(b) The horse suddenly broke into a buckle.

(c) The accused did not buckle under police interrogation.

(d) Sometimes, an earthquake can make a bridge buckle.

(e) People should learn to buckle up as soon as they get into a car.

20. File

(a) You will find the paper in the file under C.

(b) I need to file an insurance claim.

(c) The cadets were marching in a single file.

(d) File your nails before you apply nail polish.

(e) When the parade was on, a soldier broke the file.

MEMORY BASED QUESTIONS

2009

21. The word given below has been used in sentences in four different ways. Choose the option corresponding to the sentence in which the usage of the word is **incorrect or inappropriate.**

Cover

(a) The band became successful after doing cover versions of hits from the '80s.

(b) The cover story in this edition of the magazine is on Barack Obama.

(c) Rahul wanted to take the day off so he asked his colleague to cover up for him at work.

(d) The lecture is supposed to cover the feminist movement from its inception to its present state.

22. The word given below has been used in sentences in four different ways. Choose the option corresponding to the sentence in which the usage of the word is **incorrect or inappropriate.**

Figure

(a) He cut a fine figure in his new designer suit.

(b) The child drew a stick figure of himself.

(c) The accounts showed a discrepancy because he forgot to figure some additional expenditure.

(d) The archer did not figure in the final selection much to the surprise of his supporters.

2010

23. The word given below has been used in sentences in four different ways. Choose the option corresponding to the sentence in which the usage of the word is incorrect or inappropriate.

THROW

(a) When I bought my motorbike, they threw in free insurance.

(b) He loves the new project and has thrown himself into it with great gusto.

(c) Shah Rukh Khan has not been able to throw off the romantic hero image.

(d) We're not going to throw the towel just because we lost one game.

24. The word given below has been used in sentences in four different ways. Choose the option corresponding to the sentence in which the usage of the word is incorrect or inappropriate.

SIT

(a) My partner just sits and expects things to get done.

(b) I was new to the job, so I sat in on the meetings to learn the procedures.

(c) He had to sit out most of the matches due to injury.

(d) He sat on many committees dealing with environmental issues.

25. Given below are five sentences. Each sentence has a pair of words that are italicised. From the italicised words, select the most appropriate words (A or B) to form correct sentences. The sentences are followed by options that indicate the words, which may be selected to correctly complete the set of sentences. From the options given, choose the most appropriate one.

He showed us *grisly* (A)/*grizzly* (B) photos of the crime scene.

Salman's *last* (A)/*latest* (B) movie which was released yesterday is a big hit.

The trees cast a big *shade* (A)/*shadow* (B), so he sat under it.

The vice-president must now take on the *mantle* (A)/ *mettle* (B) of supreme power.

The garden *blazed* (A)/*braised*(B) with colour.

(a) AABAB

(b) BBBBA

(c) ABBAA

(d) BBAAB

26. Given below are five sentences. Each sentence has a pair of words that are italicised. From the italicised words, select the most appropriate words (A or B) to form correct sentences. The sentences are followed by options that indicate the words, which may be selected to correctly complete the set of sentences. From the options given, choose the most appropriate one.

I haven't seen him *for* (A)/ *since* (B) over five years.

The teacher asked us to use our *fantasy* (A)/ *imagination* (B)while writing essays.

He should be arriving *briefly* (A)/*shortly* (B).

Unfortunately inflation is on the *rise* (A)/ *raise* (B) again.

The opposition parties are making political *capital* (A) / *capitol* (B)out of the government's problems.

(a) ABABA (b) ABBAA

(c) BBBAB (d) AABAB

2011

27. The word given below has been used in sentences in four different ways. Choose the option corresponding to the sentence in which the usage of the word is *incorrect or inappropriate.*

Wash

(a) He decided to wash down the meal with a glass of red wine.

(b) The first day of the play was washed out after only 90 minutes.

(c) The body was found washed over on a beach.

(d) She always helps to wash up after dinner even if she is the guest.

28. The word given below has been used in sentences in four different ways. Choose the option corresponding to the sentence in which the usage of the word is *incorrect or inappropriate.*

Whip

(a) She had the whip hand and it was useless to resist.

(b) However difficult the task she will always whip through it.

(c) Shivi whipped up a delicious dinner for us in 10 minutes.

(d) The police officer whipped at her radio and called for back-up.

29. The word given below has been used in sentences in four different ways. Choose the option corresponding to the sentence in which the usage of the word is *incorrect or inappropriate.*

Zip

(a) The sleeping bags can zip together.

(b) This jacket zips up right to the neck.

(c) I put out my hand to ask the auto rickshaw driver to stop but he just zipped past me.

(d) She zipped into class as if nothing had happened and she was not 45-minutes late!

2012

30. The word given below is used in sentences in four different ways. Choose the option in which the usage of the word is *incorrect or inappropriate.*

HIT

(a) In his new book he hits off the American temperament with amazing insight.

(b) What will happen when the story hits the front page?

(c) This course will hit the high spots of ancient history.

(d) Critics hit off at the administration's new energy policy.

31. The word given below has been used in sentences in four different ways. Choose the option corresponding to the sentence in which the usage of the word is **incorrect or inappropriate.**

Note

(a) The author included a note on the usage of the term.

(b) The chess player of note was invited to inaugurate the Sports Complex.

(c) Her photograph rings a note but I still can't remember who she is.

(d) There was a note of sorrow in her manner.

2013

32. The word given below has been used in the given sentences in four different ways. Choose the option corresponding to the sentence in which the usage of the word is *incorrect or inappropriate.*

Buy

(a) The negotiators kept the gunman talking to buy time for the hostages.

(b) She had never bought into the idea that to be attractive you have to be thin.

(c) Joe finally bought it in a plane crash in Tunisia.

(d) Supermarkets have been buying out champagne for Christmas.

2014

33. For the word given at the top of the table, match the dictionary definitions on the left with their corresponding usages on the right. Out of the four choices given in the columns below the table, select the one that has all the definitions and their usages correctly matched.

Cast

Dictionary Definition	Usage
A. Throw forcefully	E. The fisherman decided to cast his net into the sea only thrice a day.
B. Direct or cause to fall	F. The director cast new actors in his latest venture.
C. Register a vote	G. She cast a glance at him which made him crazy.
D. Actors in a play	H. Every responsible citizen must cast his or her vote.

(a) A–E, B–H, C–G, D–F (b) A–F, B–H, C–G, D–E

(c) A–H, B–G, C–F, D–E (d) A–E, B–G, C–H, D–F

34. The word given below has been used in the given sentences in four different ways. Choose the option corresponding to the sentence in which the usage of the word is *incorrect or inappropriate.*

Neck

(a) The company that he founded in 1983 is now an albatross around his neck, making losses of several hundreds of thousands a year.

(b) Your little brother who cannot sit for still for five seconds is a pain in the neck.

(c) He stuck his neck out for the deal because he thought he could make some big money.

(d) The two companies are neck to neck in the competition to win over customers.

35. The word given below has been used in the given sentences in four different ways. Choose the option corresponding to the sentence in which the usage of the word is *incorrect or inappropriate.*

Eyes

(a) She cried her eyes after her husband died in a gruesome car accident.

(b) We had a bird's eye view of the old town from the top of the city walls.

(c) Martha married an abusive younger man with a roving eye and a habit of spending his days at the country inn.

(d) She was a girl with stars in her eyes and dreams of becoming famous.

IDENTIFY THE ERRONEOUS PART

1995

DIRECTIONS for Questions 1 to 5: Answer the questions based on the following information.

In these questions, each sentence has been divided into four parts, marked (a), (b), (c) and (d). Identify that part of the sentence which needs to be changed for the sentence to be grammatically correct.

1. (a) Almost all school teachers insist that
   (b) a student's mother
   (c) is responsible for the student's conduct
   (d) as well as his dress.
2. (a) In the forthcoming elections
   (b) every man and woman
   (c) must vote for the candidate
   (d) of their choice.
3. (a) If one has to decide
   (b) about the choice of a career
   (c) you should choose that option
   (d) which is really beneficial.
4. (a) It is essential that diseases like tuberculosis
   (b) are detected and treated
   (c) as early as possible in order to
   (d) assure a successful cure.
5. (a) The Mumbai police have found
   (b) the body of a man
   (c) who they believe to be
   (d) the prime suspect in a murder case.

■■

ANSWERS

SENTENCE SELECTION

1. (b) **2.** (d) **3.** (b) **4.** (a) **5.** (a) **6.** (b) **7.** (a) **8.** (a) **9.** (b) **10.** (c)
11. (c) **12.** (c) **13.** (c) **14.** (b) **15.** (c) **16.** (b) **17.** (c) **18.** (b) **19.** (d) **20.** (a)
21. (a) **22.** (a) **23.** (b) **24.** (b) **25.** (b) **26.** (a) **27.** (d) **28.** (b) **29.** (c) **30.** (d)
31. (a) **32.** (c) **33.** (b) **34.** (c) **35.** (b) **36.** (b) **37.** (c) **38.** (a) **39.** (d) **40.** (b)
41. (b) **42.** (d) **43.** (d) **44.** (c) **45.** (b) **46.** (c) **47.** (d) **48.** (c) **49.** (b) **50.** (a)
51. (b) **52.** (c) **53.** (d) **54.** (b) **55.** (d) **56.** (b)

SENTENCE CORRECTION

1. (c) **2.** (c) **3.** (c) **4.** (d) **5.** (b) **6.** (c) **7.** (d) **8.** (c) **9.** (a) **10.** (c)
11. (c) **12.** (d) **13.** (b) **14.** (d) **15.** (a) **16.** (c) **17.** (b) **18.** (a) **19.** (b) **20.** (c)
21. (b) **22.** (a) **23.** (a) **24.** e **25.** (c) **26.** (a) **27.** (d) **28.** (c) **29.** (a) **30.** (c)
31. (d) **32.**c

PHRASE REPLACEMENT

1. (a) **2.** (a) **3.** (b) **4.** (c) **5.** (a) **6.** (c) **7.** (d) **8.** (a) **9.** (c) **10.** (a)
11. (b) **12.** (d) **13.** (b) **14.** (c) **15.** (a) **16.** (a) **17.** (d) **18.** (a) **19.** (c) **20.** (b)
21. (a) **22.** (b) **23.** (d) **24.** (c) **25.** (c) **26.** (c) **27.** (d)

WORD USAGE

1. (d) **2.** (a) **3.** (a) **4.** (c) **5.** (b) **6.** (c) **7.** (a) **8.** (a) **9.** (d) **10.** (b)
11. (b) **12.** (d) **13.** (b) **14.** (b) **15.** (a) **16.** (c) **17.** (c) **18.** (d) **19.** (b) **20.** e
21. (c) **22.** (c) **23.** (d) **24.** (a) **25.** (c) **26.** (b) **27.** (c) **28.** (d) **29.** (d) **30.** (d)
31. (c) **32.** (d) **33.** (d) **35.** (a)

IDENTIFY THE ERRONEOUS PART

1. (c) **2.** (d) **3.** (c) **4.** (d) **5.** (c)

EXPLANATIONS

SENTENCE SELECTION

1. b "Enhanced' means to increase or improve the quality or value of something. The correct usage here would be 'increased'. The contracted form 'its' and not 'it's' shows the possessive form of the pronoun.
2. d The sentence is divided into three different clauses hence each should be separated by a semicolon.
3. b We need to use 'who' for the subject Mr. Som. Choice d. is not correct due to the wrong placement of the comma after 'who'.
4. a The plural pronoun 'those' should take a plural verb 'believe'.
5. a 'Its' and not 'it's' is the correct contracted possessive form for 'it'.'It's' means 'it is'.
6. b The nouns or pronouns used after a preposition are treated as an object so they are not subjects. So the verb is going to agree with the noun or pronoun used before the preposition. The subject is "state" which is singular in number, so the verb must be "was".
7. a If we use 'one' as our subject all following pronouns must be according to 'one' i.e One (Subjective); One (Objective); One's (Possessive); Oneself (Emphatic or Reflexive) etc.
8. a We are talking about each individual student among a group of students, so the verb should be singular.
9. b None can be used as a singular or a plural number pronoun. In this sentence it is used to represent 'no one' so requires a singular number verb. Therefore, the right answer is (b).
10. c Because we are talking about a particular king we should use 'the king'. Moreover the verb should be consistent with the noun after 'nor'. The noun is a plural one hence should take a plural verb desire.
11. c Here "marginal performance" has to be emphasized. The sentence in option (c) does that most convincingly. In option (b), using "of" after the possessive makes the sentence awkward. Option (a) and (d) talk about the marginal nature of performance as additional information rather than foregrounding it.
12. c The constructions in (a) and (d) are wordy and awkward. The use of the concessive clause in (c) (Although we know that some things are dear) clearly communicates why we can still enjoy festivals.
13. c Choice c. uses the simplest and most concise words. 'Conceptual grasp' is incomplete and needs to be followed by a prepostion and an object.
14. b Choice b. uses the appropriate degree of politeness. Choice d. is wrong as it does not tell how much milk powder is required. Others are overtly polite.
15. c 'Whenever' implies at any time, hence c. is a better choice than d. Other choices are unnecessarily wordy.
16. b 'Unexpected' and 'unanticipated' are synonyms, so using both in a sentence is redundant. Moreover 'consequence' is a better word to suggest the result of something on something else.
17. c The appropriate idiomatic use is 'definition should agree with'.
18. b "Much obliged' serves the same purpose as 'very much obliged' and is thus preferable.
19. d The sentence in (a) features a comma splice error. A comma has been used to connect two independent clauses. (b) and (c) feature awkward sentence constructions. In sentence (d) the simple present tense is used to talk about a future event/ schedule.
20. a "Looking back' is the correct idiomatic usage. It means "remembering" or "reflecting" something.
21. a The subject here is 'the best part', which is singular and should therefore be followed by a singular verb.
22. a When using 'as well as' to introduce a complex subject, the phrase should be set off by commas, and the verb agrees with the main subject, which in this case is 'the professor'.
23. b As the first part of the sentence provides the reason for his being unwilling to testify, 'because' should be used to introduce it. Moreover a comma should always be used to separate two distinct phrases in a sentence.
24. b The pronoun should remain consistent throughout the sentence.
25. b When 'either' and 'neither' are followed by 'or' and 'nor' respectively, the verb depends on the noun following 'or' and 'nor'.
26. a The sentence has three different clauses, which should be separated by semi colons.
27. d When 'neither' is followed by 'nor', the verb depends on the noun following 'nor'. In this case it is singular, hence the verb should also be singular.
28. b Before a gerund a noun should appear in the possessive form.
29. c The sentence does not need any commas.
30. d The sentence needs no commas.
31. a We should use 'who' for subjects who do the action. In the given sentence 'who' is the subject of the verb 'were'.
32. c This is a simple question of parallelism, not that it is ... but that it is.

33. b You generate money through deals, and not by deals or on deals. The two factors — escalated costs and black money — are lucidly given in (b).

34. c We always have to use the conjunction between to compare prices at two levels.

35. b Reduce and encourage will make a parallel construction. Action is taken by someone, not of someone.

36. b *Running … consists* has singular subject-verb agreement. Again, *more than it costs* is the right diction.

37. c (b) and (d) have inappropriate temporal references. A is also wrong as *products* did not lead to the *heightened focus*. (c) is the answer as the second and third part of the sentence when put together is complete by itself.

38. a Improper use as in "falling back" and "explanations" rule out (b) and (c). Fall back on is the right prepositional phrase and thus A is right.

39. d *is regarded* should go together. *Valuable in itself* is the right expression. *Not only as …but also as* has parallel construction.

40. b *it would be ideal* expresses a satisfactory proposition. R*eflection* should precede *action*, and *thought* should facilitate *behavior*.

41. b 'Which' should be used for an inanimate noun 'team'.

42. d The correct and more concise usage is 'garden in its front'.

43. d The correct usage is 'planning to go there'

44. c The correct pronoun to be used is 'none' instead of 'not'.

45. b The use of 'to' before 'go' is redundant in answer (b). Therefore, the correct answer is option (b).

46. c ABBBB

In the given context, 'flounder' means to struggle to move or get somewhere in water, mud, etc. 'Founder' as a verb means to fail because of a particular problem or difficulty. For example: The peace talks foundered on a basic lack of trust. It also means to fill with water and sink. For example: Our boat foundered on a reef. So 'floundering' is the apt word for the first sentence. 'Persevere' means to continue trying to do or achieve something despite difficulties. 'Perverse' means showing deliberate determination to behave in a way that most people think is wrong, unacceptable or unreasonable. Thus, 'perverse' is apt for the second sentence. 'Mordent' means a musical decoration in which either the note above or below is played as well as the written note; a musical ornament made by a quick alternation of a principal tone with the tone immediately below it. 'Mordant' means critical and unkind, but funny. Thus, 'mordant' is the apt word for the third sentence. 'Cantor' refers to the person who leads the singing in a synagogue or in a church choir. 'Canter' as a noun means a movement of a horse at a speed that is fairly fast but not very fast; a ride on a horse moving at this speed. So, 'canter' is apt for the fourth sentence. 'Chard' refers to a vegetable with large leaves and thick white, yellow or red stems. 'Charred' means burnt and black. So 'charred' is the apt word for the fifth sentence.

47. d ABBBA

'Gilt' refers to a thin layer of gold, or something like gold that is used on a surface for decoration. 'Aureole' means a circle of light. 'Oriole' refers to a bird. In the context of gilt, the word 'aureole' is appropriate. 'Auger' refers to a tool that looks like a large corkscrew and is used for making holes in wood. 'Augur' means to be a sign that something will be successful or not successful in the future; bode. Thus, 'augur' is apt for the second sentence. 'Sheath' refers to any covering that fits closely over something for protection. It is a noun. 'Sheathe' on the other hand is its verb form and means to cover something in a material, especially in order to protect it. As the sentence requires a verb, 'sheathe' is the apt word. 'Drupe' is a noun and refers to one-seeded indehiscent fruit having a hard bony endocarp, a fleshy mesocarp, and a thin exocarp that is flexible (as in the cherry) or dry and almost leathery (as in the almond). 'Droop' means to bend, hang or move downwards, especially because of being weak or tired. In the given context, 'droop' is the apt word. 'Complication' in the given context means a new problem or illness that makes treatment of a previous one more complicated or difficult. 'Complexity' means the state of being difficult to understand example: the complexities of the system. One develops complications after surgeries; complexities is inappropriate in the given context.

48. c In '1' it should be 'country' not countries; in '2' it should be 'about the..' because an article is required here; in '3' it should be 'live by..' not 'live on..' and; in '4' it should be 'emerges' not 'emerge' because it is referring to 'one set..' and not to 'questions..'.

49. b Sentences A and C are correct in terms of grammar and usage.

In sentence B, the pronoun 'it' (singular pronoun) has been incorrectly used to refer to the noun 'elements' (plural). Since 'elements' is plural, a plural pronoun should be used here. The correct sentence will be – "…elements, most of them…"

In sentence D, the phrase 'gained in' is incorrect and should be replaced by the phrase 'gained by'. The phrase 'gained in' is used to indicate an increase or growth in something. For example, 'The shares gained in value'.

Sentence E is incorrect because the same pronouns should be used in the whole sentence. Since the entire paragraph is in second person, the pronoun 'one' should be replaced by 'you' to make the sentence correct. Therefore, the correct answer is option (b).

50. a Sentences C and D are correct in terms of grammar and usage.

Sentence A should contain the word 'answer' instead of 'answering' because an 'infinitive' is never followed by the '-ing' form of the verb.

Sentence B is wrong because instead of 'gravest of charge', it should be 'gravest of charges'.

Sentence E has a subject-verb agreement error. The word 'actions' (plural) should have been referred to by the pronoun 'them' (plural pronoun) and not 'it' (singular pronoun). Hence, the correct answer is option (a).

51. b Herbivorous birds would be correct; herbivorous is an adjective, herbivores is a noun. The other sentences are correct. Thus, option (b) is the correct answer.

52. c The correct answer is AAABB. Leech is a noun which refers to bloodsucking parasites that feed on others while leach is a verb which means to drain away from soil, ash, or similar material by the action of a percolating liquid, especially rainwater. Gulled means fooled while culled means slaughtered (generally used for killing animals). Abrasion refers to the process of wearing down or rubbing away by means of friction and aberration means deviation or abnormality. To attenuate means to lessen the intensity of something and to accentuate means to intensify or emphasize. Amorphous means shapeless while amorous means passionate and lustful. Thus, option (c) is the correct answer.

53. d The correct answer is AAAAB. Bellow means to roar or to shout while billow means to puff, swell or fill with something. Blandish means to coax someone with kind words or flattery and brandish means to exhibit something aggressively. Credence means belief in something or accepting something as true and cadence means rhythm or beat. Delirious means to be in a disturbed state of mind while deleterious means harmful. To decry means to denounce or criticize someone while descry means to catch sight of something. Thus, option (d) is the correct answer.

54. b The correct answer is BAABB. Diffident means lacking self-confidence while dissident means a rebel or a non-conformist. Conflagrate means to inflame or incite and conflate means to mix different types of elements together. Immiseration means economic impoverishment and commiseration means pity or sympathy. Secede means to withdraw or disaffiliate from an organization/group while cede means to yield or surrender. Beacon means a shining example or a guiding light while beckon refers to a gesture to summon someone. Thus, option (b) is the correct answer.

55. d Option (c) uses 'their' instead of 'there'. The other incorrect options have subject verb agreement errors. Option (d) is the correct answer.

56. b Sentence 2 should be corrected to 'its sequel' and sentence 3 should contain 'the easier'. Thus, option (b) is the correct answer.

SENTENCE CORRECTION

1. c The correct usage would be, 'a network to facilitate contacts'.

2. c The correct phrase would be, 'to the perceived problems'.

3. c 'The Indian Government's choice' is a singular noun and should have a singular verb 'stems'.

4. d The correct quantifier to be used here is 'most'.

5. b Here we should use the verb in past participle, i.e. 'you would have' as we are talking about an unreal past condition.

6. c 'Requires' should be replaced with 'assumes'.

7. d The noun 'choice' is singular and should be followed by a singular verb 'invites'.

8. c We already have a subject 'who' for the verb 'decided', so 'he then' is wrongly used here.

9. a 'Of' should be replaced with 'off'.

10. c Here minorities are being treated as a specific group and should therefore be preceded by 'the'.

11. c 'Aspiring' cannot be used as an adjective for students here, as those who are studying management are already students.

12. d The correct tag question should use the same auxiliary verb as in the main clause, hence the correct tag question here would be, 'did you?'.

13. b The correct idiomatic usage is 'prevented someone from leaving'.

14. d The 'documents' are a plural noun, so should be referred to by them and not it.

15. a Here who is acting as an object for the verb invited, hence should be replaced by 'whom'.

16. c Sentence B is wrong because efforts 'bear fruit' and not 'give fruit'. Sentence C is incorrect because 'complimented' should have been used, comple mented means 'something that completes, makes up a whole'.

17. b Sentence B is wrong because you don't plead 'guilty of' but plead 'guilty to' a crime. Sentence D is wrong because one gets 'sentenced to' prison.

18. a Sentence B is incorrect because the correct usage of its last part would be – 'thinking what to do'. Sentence C is wrong because the article 'a' should precede 'shower'.

19. b The second sentence does not use the article. It should be 'As a/the project progresses" in sentence C there should be the indefinite article 'a' before single-minded which leaves us with option (b) as the correct answer.

20. c Sentence B should have "making them break apart". Sentence C should have "many offending chemicals".

21. b B should be "rarely has ..."
C should begin with 'The'.

22. a Option B should be "since the Enlightenment.
Option C should be "in the 1820's"

23. a C and E
In (A) 'to' is redundant.
In (B) 'hands on about Israel'.
In (D) a Shaliach, a sort of recruiter to Minneapolis.

24. e B only
In (A) 'into' should be used in place of 'in'
In (C) the article is missing before the word 'slump'
In (D) the singular form 'stimulus' should be used in place of 'stimuli'
In (E) 'effect' should be used in place of 'affect'

25. c B and D
In (A) 'said' should be used instead of 'told'
In (C) 'handed down to' should be used in place of 'handed to'
In (E) a subject is required after 'hence'. Another way of correcting (E) is to replace 'hence' by 'but'.

26. a Sentence A is incorrect as the spelling of 'imigrant' is not correct , should be 'immigrant'. Sentence D is incorrect because of a missing article and should be ' the owner of a dry goods ....'. Sentence E is incorrect and should be '..... would later be known as.....'. Sentence C is incorrect. We require a comma between 'brother-in-law' and 'David Stern'.

27. d Sentence B should be'.....its labour policy' because the subject is Nike and we can't substitute it with the plural pronoun 'their'. Sentence C should be 'Perhaps sensing that the rising tide...' as without 'that' the sentence structure is incomplete. Sentence E should be ' ....an industry..' as the word industry begins with a vowel so the appropriate article is 'an'.

28. c Sentence B should be '...few millions.... 'Sentence D should be ... reach the hundreds who are marooned.. Sentence E is incorrect as per subject verb agreement and should be '...death count has begun'.

29. a Sentence B has tense inconsistency, it should be '...I associated you...'. Sentence C has a similar error and should be '....who seemed...'. Sentence D has an error of modifier placement and should be '...not in the least curious..' Sentence E has a missing article, should be'...you did make an effort...'.

30. c B and D
'A' is incorrect . The correct statement should be "Many a men dated their ruin from some murder or other that perhaps they thought little of at *that* time."
'C' is incorrect. The correct statement should be "After they had finished the meal they asked the waiter for the bill."

31. d B and D are correct.
(A) is incorrect. The correct expression is 'Imagine a speck of dust close to a planet a billion times the size of *the* earth' or alternatively, 'Imagine a speck of dust close to a planet a billion times the size of *Earth.'*
(B) is incorrect. The correct expression is 'the huge planet would be the odds against *it* (i.e. the odds against your being born). (D) is incorrect. The correct expression is 'stop looking a gift horse in the mouth' which means questioning the value of something you have received for free (You look a gift horse in the mouth when you receive a gift and then you question the value of that gift).

32. c A is incorrect it should use 'the' before 'tarot'. B uses the singular 'outcry' incorrectly; it should be 'outcries', C is incorrect as it uses the pronoun 'whom' instead of 'which' for a non living object.

PHRASE REPLACEMENT

1. a No other choice states why they are tied to Moscow.

2. a The sentence refers to the people who are 'physically looked after' by the welfare aid. No other choice states the involvement of welfare aid.

3. b The best possible and logical answer is (b) combining realsitic details.

4. c The given phrase obviously refers to the answer to the question that is bothering the author.

5. a The original phrase is best suited here.

6. c The sentence means that any other action will most probably lead to failure.

7. d The sentence is incomplete as 'will do' does not have an object. It should therefore be followed by 'so'. (a) is not correct as 'government' is repeated. 'policy' is undefined in (b) and (c).

8. a We let go 'of' something, but we turn 'off' the lights. The proposals in (b) and (d) might go beyond the scope of the sentence.

9. c The correct idiomatic usage to refer to a proliferation of something is 'have mushroomed'. 'blooming' and 'blossoming' are not words that we use to indicate that a lot of schools have come up overnight. 'Mushrooming' is most apt, literally and figuratively, in this regard. 'all over' is a more generic term than 'in every corner'; the latter term is more specific.

10. a The phrase used is grammatically correct. There is a huge difference between 'important' and 'fact'. (d) similarly overlooks the serious tone of the sentence. (c) sounds verbose.

11. b We take 'note' of an important clause. There is nothing to 'notice' in the sentence, so (a) and (d) are ruled out. (c) sounds awkward when read along with the rest of the sentence.

12. d 'To forge' implies to create a lasting relationship based on hard work. 'forge ... links' (smithy) makes better enginering sense than 'build links' or 'create links'. 'Links' also goes with the purpose - Aeroplanes.

13. b Bank deposits 'swelled' implies that they increased to a great extent. The banking industry can flourish, not the deposits. Bank deposits cannot be 'enhanced' or 'flummoxed'.

14. c The original phrase is the best suited for the given sentence. The 'revival' has taken place, hence (a) is not true. (d) also cannot be true in light of the 'revival'. (c) is a more precise choice than (b).

15. a 'At will' fits here perfectly in contrast to 'freely'. 'umbrage' can be given without intention, so (b) is not right. (d) does not make sense. 'scolding' happens spontaneously most of the times, hence it is unlikely that it involves a decision-making process.

16. a 'To write at random' is more concise than 'to write at a random speed' and conveys the meaning perfectly. 'writing without affectation' in no sense means writing 'fast' or 'with speed'. We choose (a) over (b) because of the parallel construction with 'write without affectation'.

17. d (d) is the correct answer choice.

The question relates to choosing the correct pronoun case: Subjective (we) or objective (us). The answer to the question 'who had left before he arrived?' is 'we', not 'us': 'We' is the subject of the verb 'had left' and the referent of the relative pronoun 'who,' which is also in the subjective case.

(b) and (c) are incorrect because they use 'Us' the objective case. They also have other obvious errors.

(a) Uses the correct pronoun case (We), but incorrectly places both verbs 'had left' and 'had arrived' in the past perfect tenses. For indicating that one event has occurred in the past before another, the former should be placed in past perfect tense, while the latter in simple past tense.

18. a (a) is the correct answer, as it corrects all the errors in the original sentence. Other options do not.

Redundancy:

(i) 'rose up': 'rise' includes the idea of upward motion.

(ii) 'in her opinion, she thought': use either 'in her opinion' or 'she thought'.

Idiom (iii) 'passed on': Bills are always 'passed' in Parliament. 'Pass on' is a phrasal verb and has its own uses.

19. c (c) is the correct answer choice.

This question tests you for parallelism. There are two possible parallel structures:

(i) Mr Pillai, X and Y, will be ... (phrase X and Y placed in apposition).

(ii) Mr Pillai, who is X and also Y, will be ... (use of who-clause)

There are also other ways to express the same idea but with different shades of meaning/emphasis:

(iii) Since Mr Pillai is X and Y, he will be ... (two main clauses joined by 'some' as a conjunction).

(iv) Being X and Y, Mr Pillai will be ...(use of participial clause).

Answer choice (c) matches with (i) above. Other choices do not match with any of the other possible grammatical structures.

20. b (b) is the correct answer choice.

This question tests you for use of the correct verb tense. Possible constructions could be:

(i) At the beginning of this decade, X took a giant stride ...

(ii) Use present perfect, when we talk of a period of time extending from a point in the past and completion of an action 'since' then, as seen from today's perspective.

(b) matches with (ii) above and correctly uses the present perfect tense. The phrase 'at the beginning of this decade' is merely placed in opposition to inform us about the 'advent of cable television,' and does not in any way affect the structure of the sentence.

21. a (a) is the correct answer choice.

The main verb 'made great scarifices' in the main clause is modified by both participial clauses to explain the sacrifices she made:

(i) 'moving house on three occasions'.

(ii) 'severing the thread ... to make him understand the need to persevere.'

In (b) and (c), 'severed' (simple past tense) is used parallel with 'made', thereby producing two parallel main clauses. This is not grammatically incorrect, but changes the intended meaning, which was to highlight 'severing of the thread ...' as a 'sacrifice' the mother made.

(d) uses 'severing' correctly, but incorrectly replaces 'him' referring to Mencius by 'them.'

22. b (b) is the correct answer choice.

The question tests you for the correct positioning of the adverbial phrase 'in two weeks.' Since this phrase relates to 'putting together a programme,' it should be positioned closest to the verb phrase it modifies. The possible positions are examined below:

(i) 'You've put together (in two weeks) a programme ...'

[Incorrect. Adverb cannot come between the verb and its object.]

(ii) 'You've put together a programme (in two weeks) that solves ...'

[Incorrect. Here the adverb cannot separate the noun 'program' and the relative pronoun. 'that', which modifies it.]

(iii) '(in two weeks) you've put together a programme ...'

[Correct. The adverbial phrase is close to the verb it modifies and is not intrusive in this position.]

In (a) and (c), the intended meaning changes. It appears that 'the problem is solved in two weeks,' rather than 'the programme being put together in two weeks'.

(d) in incorrect as the adverbial phrase 'in two weeks' should be cordoned off by two commas, and introduction of "only" changes the meaning.

23. d (d) is the correct answer choice.

The question tests you for the correct idiomatic structure to be used with the verb 'proclaim.' 'Proclaim,' unlike 'claim,' cannot be followed by a to-infinitive. It should be followed by a that-clause in this case. Therefore, (d) is correct, while (a) and (c) are incorrect.

Though (b) correctly uses the that-clause, the present continuous tense 'are saving' changes the meaning.

The simple present tense 'save' is appropriate here to indicate a general sense. Furthermore, 'less' itself is a comparative (little → less → least) and need not be replaced by the double comparative 'lesser,' which is used only in certain standard idiomatic phrases, such as, 'the lesser of the two evils.'

24. c (c) is the correct answer choice.

The question tests you for the correct use of passive voice and the positioning of adverbs. First, 'end' cannot be the doer of the action: 'would delay,' but it should correctly be at the receiving end: 'would be delayed (passive voice).' Second, both the adverbs 'otherwise'and 'only' are required for the intended meaning to emerge clearly. Third, these adverbs should be positioned closest to the verb they modify. What better place than to be sandwiched between the auxiliary verb and the main verb: 'Would be otherwise only delayed.'

25. c Between options (b) and (c), the difference is inthe word advocate and advocating. Both options have the word "incidents". We need a verb (advocate) and not a gerund (advocating). Hence, the option (c). In option (a), the usage 'suggest to bring down is incorrect'. In option (d) audiocassette prices 'should' be (and not 'to' be) brought down. Between options (b) and (c), 'incidence' of music piracy can be reduced and not 'incidents'.

26. c Option (b) is incorrect due to the usage of the simple present tense in 'they portray'. Option (d) is incorrect due to the usage if the singular 'it' for the plural 'things'. Option (a) is wrong because of the unnecessary usage of 'must have' after using 'essential'.

27. d Option (b) is incorrect because we cannot say that 'archeologists ... are estimated'. Options (a) and (c) have the problems of misplaced modifiers.

WORD USAGE

1. d *bundle of boy-scouts* is incorrect usage. The correct usage is *a group of boy-scouts*.

2. a *He is clear about what is* would have been a better expression. The correct usage is "clear" about certain things.

3. a *appreciated the headmaster's gesture of raising* is the correct expression, implication implies negativity.

4. c *Ranchi will play the host to* is incorrect. The correct sentence should be '*Ranchi will host*' the next national film festival.

5. b *Farmers of "all sorts"* is the correct expression.

6. c The phrase 'help with the beer' is incorrect as it should be 'help to the beer'.

7. a It's always 'suggestions look great on paper'.

8. a It should be 'serve themselves' in stead of 'service themselves'.

9. d The correct phrase is 'listen to reason' and not 'listen to a reason'.

10. b The phrase 'profitable business' should be 'a profitable business'.

11. b The correct usage would have been – 'he bolted for the gate'.

12. d Fallout does not mean failure. It refers to consequence or argument.

13. b The usage of 'passing her ' is inappropriate, one can simply say 'passing on the road ' or ' passing by '.

14. b Option (b)talks about a 'near' friend. There is nothing like a near friend. It should have been 'close' friend

15. a It should have been "I have my hands full".

16. c It should have been "I can't bear her being angry".

17. c In Sentence (c)'run over' as a phrasal verb means being physically mowed down and it is not appropriate to convey the symbolic sense of brow beating somebody.

18. d Sentence (d)is incorrect and should be ' The doctor is on a round/the doctor is on a round of the hospital.'

19. b The expression 'the horse suddenly broke into a buckle' is idiomatically incorrect. The correct idiomatic expression is "broke into a gallop".

20. e In sentence (e), the expression '...a soldier broke the file...' is grammatically incorrect. The correct idiomatic expression is "broke ranks".

21. c The correct usage would have been "cover for him" which would mean "substitute or take the place of someone".

22. c The correct usage would have been "figure in some additional expenditure". "Figure in" means "take into consideration".

23. d (a) is correct. To 'throw in' means to add to something. (b) is correct. To 'throw oneself into something' means to do something with great enthusiasm. (c) is correct. To 'throw off' means to free yourself from something. (d) is incorrect. The correct expression is " throw in the towel " which means to stop trying.

24. a (a) is incorrect. The correct expression is 'sit back'- to sit back means to wait for something to happen while deliberately not being involved. (b) is correct. To 'sit in on something' means to be present during a meeting but not participate. (c) is correct. To 'sit out' means to wait for something to finish. (d) is correct. To 'sit on' means to be on a committee or panel (to be a member). Radhika has sat on the finance committee from the beginning.

25. c ABBAA

Grisly means gruesome while *grizzly* is a type of bear. *Latest* which means most recent suits the context of the sentence. When used as a noun, *shade* is relative darkness; *shadow* is what causes the darkness. A tree casts a *shadow* which causes *shade*. *Mantle* means the role and responsibilities of an important person or job, especially when they are passed on from one person to another. *Mettle* means the ability and determination to do something successfully despite difficult conditions. *Blaze* means to shine brightly whereas *braise* means to cook meat or vegetables very slowly with a little liquid in a closed container.

26. b ABBAA

For is used to describe period of time of an action while *since* denotes the starting time of an action. The word we want here is 'for'. *Fantasy* means extravagant and unrestrained imagination. The word we want here is 'imagination'. *Briefly* means for a short time, whereas *shortly* means soon. Hence, 'shortly' is the word to be used here. *Rise / raise*- both the words can mean 'to move upwards', but they are not interchangeable. *Rise* is an intransitive verb and *raise* is a transitive verb. *Raise* requires an object to cause the motion. 'Rise' is the word to be used here. *Capital* means an advantage or a gain whereas *capitol* means a building in which the state legislature body meets. So, 'capital' is correct in the given context.

27. c To *wash over* means to suddenly affect somebody strongly, so that they are not aware of anything else or to happen to or around somebody without affecting them. This is incorrect in the given context. The correct sentence should be "The body was found washed up on a beach". *Washed up* here means to carry something onto land. So (c) is incorrect.

Wash down means to drink in order to swallow something solid. So, (a) is correct. *Wash out* means to make a game, an event, etc. end early or prevent it from starting. Thus (b) is correct. *Wash up* means to clean the plates and dishes after a meal. Thus, (d) is correct.

28. d Sentence (d) is incorrect. The correct phrasal verb is *whip out* which means to remove quickly. The correct sentence is "The police officer whipped out her radio and called for back-up."

Have/hold the whip hand (over somebody/something) means to be in a position where you have power or control over somebody/something. So (a) is correct. To *whip through* means to do something quickly. Thus, (b) is correct. To *whip up* is to make food quickly. So (c) is correct.

29. d *Zip somebody/yourself into something* means to fasten clothes, bags, etc. with a zip/zipper. For example: The children were safely zipped into their sleeping bags. However, in the context given in (d) *zip into* is incorrect. The correct usage should have been *strode into* which means to walk in with long strides sometimes indicating confidence. Thus option (d) is incorrect.

Zip together means to be fastened with a zip/zipper. So (a) is correct. *Zip up* or *zip somebody/something up* means to be fastened with a zip/zipper; to fasten something with a zip/zipper. So (b) is correct. *Zip past* means to move very quickly or to make something move very quickly in the direction mentioned. Thus, (c) is correct.

30. d Option (a) is correct. 'Hit off' means to represent or describe precisely or aptly. Option (b) is correct. 'Hit' also means to be published in or appear in a newspaper or a magazine. Option (c) is correct. 'Hit the high spots' means paying attention to only the most important or obvious facets or items. Option (d) is incorrect. The correct sentence should be "Critics hit out at the administration's new energy policy". 'Hit out' means to make a violent verbal attack.

31. c Option (a) uses the word appropriately. 'Note' here refers to an explanatory comment that the author decided to include in his work. Option (b) uses the word appropriately. When reference is made to a man of 'note' it is suggested that the person is distinguished or famous. In the given option, the chess player who is famous because of the sport that he pursues is invited for the inauguration. Option (c) is the correct choice because it does not use the word 'note' appropriately. The word has been incorrectly used in place of 'rings a bell'. When something 'rings a bell', it evokes some memory or recollection. Therefore, the sentence conveys that even though her photograph evoked some memory of this person, he still could not recall her identity. Hence, in this sentence 'rings a note' shows incorrect usage of the idiom 'rings a bell'. Option (d) uses the word appropriately. 'Note' here means a characteristic emotional quality.

32. d Option (a) has the correct usage of the word 'buy'. 'Buy time' means to delay something.

Option (b) is also correct for 'bought into an idea' means to believe in an idea.

'Bought it', as mentioned in option (c), means to die.

'Buying out' means to pay somebody for their share in a business, usually in order to get total control of it for yourself or to pay money so that somebody can leave an organization before the end of an agreed period. It is incorrect in the given sentence and the correct usage is 'buying in', which means to buy something in large quantities. Therefore, option (d) is the correct answer.

33. d This question can be solved simply by working out the options for C. You can easily arrive at CH, which will give you option (d) as the answer

34. d The correct idiom in option (d) is 'neck and neck'. If two people who are competing are neck and neck, they are very close and either of them could win. To stick one's neck out for someone or something means to take a risk. If someone is described as a pain in the neck, he/she is an annoyance. If something is an albatross around your neck, it's something that you have done or are connected with that keeps causing you problems. Thus, option (d) is the correct answer.

35. a Option (a) is erroneous as the correct phrase is 'to cry one's eyes out' and therefore the correct sentence should have been "She cried her eyes out after her husband died in a gruesome car accident." A bird's eye view refers to a view from a very high place which allows you to see a large area. If someone has a roving eye, they are sexually attracted to people other than their partner. The idiom "stars in one's eyes" means to be dazzled or enraptured. Thus, option (a) is the correct answer.

IDENTIFY THE ERRONEOUS PART

1. c 'The student's' should be replaced with 'his'.

2. d We are talking about 'every man or woman', therefore the pronoun used should be singular 'his/her', instead of 'their'.

3. c The pronoun should remain consistent throughout the sentence, hence 'you' should be replaced with 'one'.

4. d 'Assure' is an intransitive verb and should be followed by an object. The correct usage here would be 'be sure of'.

5. c The man being referred here is the object to the verb, hence 'who' should be replaced with 'whom'.

4 CHAPTER Reading Comprehension

READING COMPREHENSION

1990

Directions: Read the following passages and answer the questions that follow each passage. Your answer to the questions should be based on the passages only.

Passage – 1

The motive force that has carried the psychoanalytic movement to a voluminous wave of popular attention and created for it considerable following among those discontent with traditional methods and attitudes, is the frank direction of the psychological instruments of exploration to the insistent and intimate problems of human relations. However false or however true its conclusions, however weak or strong its arguments, however effective or defective or even pernicious its practice, its mission is broadly humanistic. Psychological enlightenment is presented as a program of salvation. By no other appeal could the service of psychology have become so glorified. The therapeutic promise of psychoanalysis came as the most novel, most ambitious, most releasing of the long procession of curative systems that mark the history of mental healing.

To the contemporary trends in psychology, psychoanalysis actually offered a rebuke, a challenge, a supplement, though it appeared to ignore them. With the practical purpose of applied psychology directed to human efficiency it had no direct relation and thus no quarrel. The solution of behaviorism, likewise bidding for popular approval by reducing adjustment to a program of conditioning, it inevitably found alien and irrelevant, as the behaviorist in reciprocity found psychoanalytic doctrine mystical, fantastic, assumptive, remote. Even to the cognate formulations of mental hygiene, as likewise in its contacts with related fields of psychology, psychoanalysis made no conciliatory advances. Towards psychiatry, its nearest of kin, it took an unfriendly position, quite too plainly implying a disdain for an unprogressive relative. These estrangements affected its relations throughout the domain of mind and its ills; but they came to head in the practice.

From the outset in the days of struggle, when it had but a sparse and scattered discipleship, to the present position of prominence, Freudianism went its own way, for the most part neglected by academic psychology. Of dreams, lapses and neuroses, orthodox psychology had little say. The second reason for the impression made by psychoanalysis when once launched against the tide of academic resistance was its recognition of depth psychology, so much closer to human motivation, so much more intimate and direct than the analysis of mental factors.

Most persons in trouble would be grateful for relief without critical examination of the theory behind the practice that helped them. Anyone at all acquainted with the ebb and flow of cures – cures that cure cures that fail – need not be told that the scientific basis of the system is often the least important factor. Many of these systems arise empirically within a practice, which by trial, seems to give results. This is not the case in psychoanalysis. Psychoanalysis belongs to the typical groups of therapies in which practice is entirely a derivative of theory. Here the pertinent psychological principle reads: "Create a belief in the theory, and the fact will create themselves".

1. The distinctive feature of psychoanalysis is that
   (a) it provided the laymen with a scientific basis to the theories of psychology.
   (b) it blasted the popular theory that the conscious mind could be aptly linked the tip of an iceberg.
   (c) it provided effective means for the cure of mental disorders.
   (d) it rendered existing trends in psychology defunct.
2. The distinction between behaviorism and psychoanalysis that is heightened here is which of the following?
   (a) Behaviorism is wide in scope; psychoanalysis more restricted.
   (b) Behaviorism are more tolerant in their outlook; psychoanalysis more dogmatic.
   (c) Behaviorism traces all action to conditioning by habit; psychoanalysis to the depths of the human mind.
   (d) Behaviorism are more circumspect and deliberate in their propagation of theory; psychoanalysis jump to conclusion impetuously.
3. The statement which is refuted by the passage is this:
   (a) The popularity enjoyed by psychoanalysis is partly due to the disenchantment with traditional methods of psychology.
   (b) Psychoanalysis wooed people dissatisfied with other branches of psychology to swell their ranks.
   (c) Psychoanalysis were pioneers in the realm of analysis of the subconscious mind.
   (d) Psychoanalysis alienated allied branches of psychology.

4. Create a belief in theory and
   (a) belief will be created itself.
   (b) theory will be created itself.
   (c) facts will be created themselves .
   (d) All of the above.
5. Psychoanalysis are of the opinion that
   (a) methods of psychoanalysis must be in keeping with individual needs.
   (b) inferences can be drawn empirically from repeated experiments with any given theory.
   (c) theory leads to practice.
   (d) practice culminates into theory.
6. Freudian psychoanalysis was ignored by academic psychology because of which of the following?
   (a) Its theories were not substantiated by practical evidence.
   (b) It probed too deep into the human mind thereby divesting it of its legitimate privacy.
   (c) It did not have a large following.
   (d) It was pre-occupied with unfamiliar concepts such as dreams and the subconscious mind.
7. The only statement to receive support from the passage is which of the following?
   (a) Psychoanalysis concentrated more on the theoretical remedies than their practical implementation.
   (b) Psychoanalysis broke the shackles of convention in its involvement with humanistic issues.
   (c) The attitude of psychoanalysis towards allied branches of psychology could at best be described as indifferent.
   (d) Psychoanalysis dispelled the prevalent notion that dreams were repressed desires.
8. The popularity enjoyed by the psychoanalytical movement may be directly attributed to
   (a) dissatisfaction with existing methods of psychology.
   (b) its logical, coherent process of ratiocination.
   (c) its novel unconventionality in both postulate and practice.
   (d) its concentration upon the humanistic aspect of psychological analysis.

Passage – 2

It is undeniable that some very useful analogies can be drawn between the relational systems of computer mechanism and the relational systems of brain mechanism. The comparison does not depend upon any close resemblance between the actual mechanical links which occur in brains and computers; it depends on what the machines do. Further more, brains and computers can both be organized so as to solve problems. The mode of communication is very similar in both the cases, so much so that computers can now be designed to generate artificial human speech and even, by accident, to produce sequences of words which human beings recognize as poetry. The implication is not that machines are gradually assuming human forms, but that there is no sharp break of continuity between what is human, what is mechanical.

9. From the passage, it is evident that the author thinks
   (a) computers are now naturally programmed to produce poetry.
   (b) computers are likely to usurp the place of intellectual superiority accorded to the human brain.
   (c) the resemblance that the computer bears to the human brain is purely mechanical.
   (d) the unintentional mixing up of word sequences in the computer can result in poetry.
10. Computers have acquired a proven ability of performing many of the functions of the human brain because
   (a) the brain of modern man is unable to discharge its functions properly on account of over-reliance on machines.
   (b) the sophisticated computer mechanism is on the verge of outstripping human mental faculties.
   (c) the process of organizing and communicating are similar in both cases.
   (d) the mechanics of the human brain have been introduced in the computer.
11. The resemblance between the human brain and the computer is
   (a) imaginary. (b) intellectual.
   (c) mechanical. (d) functional.
12. The passage implies that
   (a) computers are assuming human forms.
   (b) human are assuming mechanical forms.
   (c) computers and humans are substitutable.
   (d) there is continuity between what is human and what is mechanical.
13. The author uses the word 'recognize' in relation to computer poetry to convey a
   (a) sense of sorrow at the reluctant admission of the superiority of machines by mankind.
   (b) feeling that computers have yet to conquer the emotional heights that man is capable of attaining.
   (c) feeling of derision for the popular faith in the omnipotence of the computer.
   (d) feeling of a fatalistic acceptance of the computer's encroachment upon human bastions.

14. Points of dissimilarity between the human brain and the computer don't extend to

(a) the faculty of composing poetry.

(b) methods of communication.

(c) the faculty of composing poetry.

(d) the faculty of speaking naturally

Passage – 3

A distinction should be made between work and occupation. Work implies necessity; it is something that must be done as contributing to the means of life in general and to one's own subsistence in particular. Occupation absorbs time and energy so long as we choose to give them; it demands constant initiative, and it is its own rewar (d) For the average person the element of necessity in work is valuable, for he is saved the mental stress involved in devising outlets for his energy. Work has for him obvious utility, and it bring the satisfaction of tangible rewards. Where as occupation is an end in itself, and we therefore demand that it shall be agreeable, work is usually the means to other ends – ends which present themselves to the mind as sufficiently important to compensate for any disagreeableness in the means. There are forms of work, of course, which since external compulsion is reduced to a minimum, are hardly to be differentiated from occupation. The artist, the imaginative writer, the scientist, the social worker, for instance, find their pleasure in the constant spontaneous exercise o creative energy and the essential reward of their work is in the doing of it. In all work performed by a suitable agent there must be a pleasurable element, and the greater the amount of pleasure that can be associated with work, the better. But for most people the pleasure of occupation needs the addition of the necessity provided in work. It is better for them to follow a path of employment marked out for them than to have to find their own.

When, therefore, we look ahead to the situation likely to be produced by the continued rapid extension of machine production, we should think not so much about providing occupation for leisure as about limiting the amount of leisure to that which can be profitably use (d) We shall have to put the emphasis on the work – providing rather than the goods – providing aspect of the economic process. In the earlier and more ruthless days of capitalism the duty of the economic system to provide work was overlooke(d) The purpose of competitive enterprise was to realize a profit. When profit ceased or was curtailed, production also ceased or was curtaile (d) Thus the workers, who were regarded as units of labour forming part of the costs of production, were taken on when required and dismissed when not require (d) They hardly thought of demanding work as a right. And so long as British manufacturers had their eyes mainly on the markets awaiting them abroad, they could conveniently neglect the fact that since workers are also consumers, unemployment at home means loss of trade. Moral considerations did not yet find a substitute in ordinary business prudence. The labour movements arose largely as a revolt against the conception of workers as commodities to be bought and sold without regard to their needs as human beings. In a socialist system it is assumed that they will be treated with genuine consideration, for, the making of profit not being essential, central planning will not only adjust the factors of production to the best advantage but will secure regularity of employment. But has the socialist thought about what he would do if owing to technological advance, the amount of human labour were catastrophically reduced? So far as I know, he has no plan beyond drastically lining the hours of work, and sharing out as much work as there may be. And, of course, he would grant monetary relief to those who were actually unemploye (d) But has he considered what would be the moral effect of life imagined as possible in the highly mechanized state of future? Has he thought of the possibility of bands of unemployed and under-employed workers marching on the capital to demand not income (which they will have) but work?

15. Future, according to the passage, may find the workers

(a) without money. (b) without work.

(c) replacing machines. (d) without leisure.

16. The main defect of socialism at present is that

(a) it has not evolved a satisfactory system of making workers co-sharers in prosperity.

(b) it has not made work less burdensome for the mass of workers.

(c) it has not taken into consideration the possibility of an immense reduction of human labour in the wake of mechanization

(d) it is not concerned with improving and streamlining the method of production.

17. The labour movement was the outcome of

(a) an effort to increase productivity.

(b) a move to make workers share in the prosperity of the capitalists.

(c) a revolt against the conception of workers as commodities.

(d) a move to avert mass unemployment because of the mechanization.

18. The chief purpose of competitive enterprise is to

(a) create more job opportunities.

(b) produce as much as possible.

(c) create more wealth in the country.

(d) realize the maximum profit.

19. In the situation created by the rapid extension of machine production, our object should be to

(a) make work as light as possible.

(b) provide increased opportunities for interesting occupation.

(c) limit the amount of leisure to that which can be profitably used.

(d) produce more and more goods.

20. The activities of the artist, the writer, the scientist etc. may be considered to be occupations because

(a) they often does not have any utilitarian value.

(b) external compulsion is reduced to a minimum and they are agreeable and require quite a lot of initiative.

(c) they occupies time and energy only so long as the workers choose to give them.

(d) they care only for the pleasure which brings them without any consideration of reward.

21. Which of the following statements is not true according to the information contained in the passage?

(a) Work is something done as contributing to the means of life in general and to one's own subsistence in particular.

(b) Occupation is something that requires initiative and can be done at one's will and pleasure and not as a task.

(c) Work brings in tangible rewards while occupation is not utilitarian.

(d) There is no form of work which shows approximation to occupation.

22. The chief reason for a person taking up an occupation may be stated to be :-

(a) a desire to make profit.

(b) an irresistible urge to do something uncommon.

(c) a wish to do something useful to society.

(d) a desire to do something which requires initiative and doing it at his will and pleasure.

23. The distinction between work and occupation is as follows :-

(a) Work at all times is unpleasant and occupation is always agreeable.

(b) In work there is an element of necessity which is totally wanting in occupation.

(c) Work has obvious utility and brings tangible rewards, while occupation is an end in itself.

(d) Work and occupation often seem to be so very much alike that no distinction can be made between them.

Passage – 4

If the more articulate members of a community formed a coherent and united class with a common interest, democracy would probably replace in to the rule of that intelligent, educated minority; even as it is, the democracies of the modern world are much closer to this fate than they are to the much-canvassed dangers of mob rule. Far from oppressing the cultured minority, or any other minorities, democracy gives more of them more scope to have their way than any other system does. This is the lesson of experience. It might also have been derived from an analysis of the concept of democracy, if the concept had been accurately analyzed.

24. The word articulate here refers to

(a) the elite.

(b) people who are endowed with a native intelligence.

(c) that class which is well educated.

(d) people who are endowed with clarity of speech.

25. What emerges as the truth from a reading of the paragraph is that

(a) forms of government other than democracy give the mobs great scope for self expression.

(b) democracy provides greater scope for mob rule.

(c) democracy provides greater scope for the rule of the minority.

(d) forms of government other than democracy give the educated minority greater scope for self expression.

26. Our appreciation of the virtues of the democratic system

(a) is the result of an illusory concept.

(b) is the result of our negative response to other forms of government.

(c) is the result of a proven record of the success of democracy.

(d) is the result of centuries of accurate research on the theoretical aspects of democracy.

27. The wide scope that democracy offers to the minorities can be made known

(a) by our common sense.

(b) by our political theories.

(c) by our native intelligence.

(d) by proper analysis.

28. The author seems to be

(a) a supporter of mob rule.

(b) a supporter of democracy

(c) against intelligence in minorities.

(d) analysing the flaws of democracy.

29. The institution of democracy, in modern times
   (a) is on the brink of extinction.
   (b) has become vulnerable to the dangers of proletariat rule.
   (c) should be prepared for the inevitability of mob rule.
   (d) has become prone to the rule of particular class of people.

Passage – 5

A difficult readjustment in the scientist's conception of duty is imperatively necessary. As Lord Adrain said in his address to the British Association, "unless we are ready to give up some of our old loyalties, we may be forced into a fight which might end the human race". This matter of loyalty is the crux. Hitherto, in the East and in the West alike, most scientists, like most other people, have felt that loyalty to their own state is paramount. They have no longer a right to feel this. Loyalty to the human race must take its place. Everyone in the West will at once admit this as regards Soviet scientists. We are shocked that Kapitza who was Rutherford's favourite pupil, was willing when the Soviet government refused him permission to return to Cambridge, to place his scientific skill at the disposal of those who wished to spread communism by means of H-bombs. We do not so readily apprehend a similar failure of duty on our own side. I do not wish to be thought to suggest treachery, since that is only a transference of loyalty to another national state. I am suggesting a very different thing; that scientists the world over should join in enlightening mankind as to the perils of a great war and in devising methods for its prevention. I urge with all the emphasis at my disposal that this is the duty of scientists in East and West alike. It is difficult duty, and one likely to entail penalties for those who perform it. Bu after all it is the labours of scientists which have caused the danger and on this account, if on no other, scientists must do everything in their power to save mankind from the madness which they have made possible. Science from the dawn of history, and probably longer, has been intimately associated with war. I imagine that when our ancestors descended from the trees they were victorious over the arboreal conservatives because flints were sharper than coconuts. To come to more recent times, Archimedes was respected for his scientific defense of Syracuse against the Romans; Leonardo obtained employment under the Duke of Milan because of his skill in fortification, though he did mention in a postscript that he could also paint a bit. Galileo similarly derived an income from the Grant Duke of Tuscany because of his skill in calculating the trajectories of projectiles. In the French Revolution those scientists who were not guillotined devoted themselves to making new explosives. There is therefore no departure from tradition in the present day scientist's manufacture of A-bombs and H-bomb. All that is new is the extent of their destructive skill.

I do not think that men of science can cease to regard the disinterested pursuit of knowledge as their primary duty. It is true that new knowledge and new skills are sometimes harmful in their effects, but scientists cannot profitably take account of this fact since the effects are impossible to foresee. We cannot blame Columbus because the discovery of the Western Hemisphere spread throughout the Eastern Hemisphere an appallingly devastating plague. Nor can we blame James Watt for the Dust Bowl although if there had been no steam engines and no railways the West would not have been so carelessly or so quickly cultivate (d) To see that knowledge is wisely used in primarily the duty of statesmen, not of science; but it is part of the duty of men of science to see that important knowledge is widely disseminated and is not falsified in the interests of this or that propaganda.

Scientific knowledge has its dangers; but so has every great thing. And over and beyond the dangers with which it threatens the present, it opens up, as nothing else can, the vision of a possible happy world, a world without poverty, without war, with little illness. And what is perhaps more than all, when science has mastered the forces which mould human character, it will be able to produce populations in which few suffer from destructive fierceness and in which the great majority regard other people, not as competitors, to be feared, but as helpers in a common task. Science has only recently begun to apply itself to human beings except in their purely physical aspect. Such science as exists in psychology and anthropology has hardly begun to affect political behaviour or private ethics. The minds of men remain attuned to a world that is fast disappearing. The changes in our physical environment require, if they are to bring well being, correlative changes in our beliefs and habits. If we cannot effect these changes, we shall suffer the fate of the dinosaurs, who could not live on dry land.

I think it is the duty of science – I do not say of every individual man of science – to study the means by which we can adapt ourselves to the new worl(d) There are certain things that the world quite obviously needs; tentativeness, as opposed to dogmatism in our beliefs: an expectation of co-operation, rather than competition, in social relations, a lessening of envy and collective hatre(d) These are things which education could produce without much difficulty. They are not things adequately south in the education of the present day.

It is progress in the human sciences that we must look to undo the evils which have resulted from a knowledge of the physical world hastily and superficially acquired by populations unconscious of the changes in themselves that the new knowledge has made imperative. The road to a happier world than any known in the past lies open before us if atavistic destructive passion can be kept in leash while the necessary adaptations are made. Fears are inevitable in our time, but hopes are equally rational and far more likely to bear good fruit. We must learn to think rather less of the dangers to be avoided than of the good that will be within our grasp if we believe in it and let it dominate our thoughts. Science, whatever unpleasant consequences it may have by the way, is in its very nature a liberator, a liberator of bondage to physical nature and, in time to come a liberator from the weight of destructive passion. We are on the threshold of utter disaster or unprecedented glorious achievement. No previous age has been fraught with problems so momentous and it is to science that we must look for happy issue.

30. The duty of science, according to the author is :-

(a) to realize the vision of a happy new world

(b) to pursue knowledge for its own sake

(c) to see that only such discoveries as conducive to the progress of humanity should be made

(d) to study the means by which we can adapt ourselves to the new world

31. Archimedes, Leonardo and Galileo have been mentioned to substantiate the statement that

(a) science has always been intimately associated with war

(b) from ancient times science has played a leading part in the life of man

(c) all learning has flourished only under the patronage of royalty and eminent personages

(d) in the past pursuit of knowledge was done for its own sake

32. The ground on which the author suggests that all scientists should join in educating mankind regarding the perils of a great war is that

(a) scientists being among the most learned among people, should take the lead in this process of education.

(b) it is the work of scientists which has led to this perilous situation and so they should do something to undo the mischief.

(c) science has always been associated with war and in the fitness of things, scientists should take the lead in trying to end it.

(d) all others like politicians and soldiers have vested interest in perpetuating war and by elimination, scientists alone may be trusted to work for its abolition.

33. In modern times, the crux of the matter as far as scientists are concerned is that

(a) their loyalty to the state should be declared in no uncertain terms.

(b) a readjustment in the scientist's conception of duty is imperatively necessary.

(c) they should not object to stringent control by the state over their activities.

(d) they should assert their independence and refuse to subject themselves to any kind of control.

34. The instance of Kaptiza cited by the author goes to prove that

(a) every scientist has his price.

(b) in Soviet Russia, communists do not tolerate independent scientists.

(c) scientists, whether in the East or West, have hitherto felt that loyalty to their own state is paramount.

(d) scientists in the West have a higher sense of responsibility than their counterparts in the East.

35. Which among the following statements is not true according to the information provided in the passage?

(a) If there is no readjustment in the scientist's conception of duty, the extinction of the human race by war is a distinct possibility.

(b) Up till now, scientists all over the world have felt that loyalty to their own state is paramount

(c) It is the labours of scientists which have caused the danger of annihilation of mankind.

(d) The tradition up to now has been that scientists have been respected for their pursuit of knowledge and not for their part in devising potent weapons of destruction

36. The duty of the scientist, according to the passage, is

(a) to further the interests of his state with as much devotion as possible

(b) to pursue knowledge regardless of the consequences of their discoveries and inventions

(c) to see that important knowledge is widely disseminated and is not falsified in the interests of propaganda

(d) to refuse to serve national interests

37. The evils which have resulted from knowledge of the physical world can only be overcome by

(a) a more intensive pursuit of scientific knowledge

(b) making scientists more responsible to society

(c) adequate progress in the human sciences

(d) enlightening the general public about the evils

38. Science may be considered a liberator in the sense that :-

(a) ultimately it may bring the nations of the world together

(b) it may make man's life a great deal happier than what it is now

(c) it may free man from bondage to physical nature and the weight of destructive passions

(d) it may end the tyranny of age old beliefs and superstitions.

Passage – 6

Humans have probably always been surrounded by their kin – those to whom they have been related by blood or marriage. But the size, the composition, and the functions of their families and kinship groups have varied tremendously. People have lived not only in the "nuclear family", made up of just the parents and their offspring, which is standard in the West and has been found almost everywhere, they have lived in extended families and in formal clans; they have been "avunculocal"; they have been "ultrolateral", they have been conscious of themselves as heirs of lineages hundred of generations deep. However constructed, the traditional kinship group has usually provided those who live in it with security, identity, and indeed with their entire scheme of activities and beliefs. The nameless billions of hunter-gatherers who have lived and died over the past several million years have been embedded in kinship groups, and when people started to farm about ten thousand years ago, their universe remained centered on kinship. Now that there was a durable form of wealth which could be hoarded-grain–some families became more powerful than other; society became stratified, and genealogy became an important means of justifying and perpetuating status.

During the past few centuries, however, in part of the world-in Europe and the countries that have been developing along European lines-a process of fragmentation has been going on. The ties and the demands of kinship have been weakening, the family has been getting smaller and, some say, less influential, as the individual, with a new sense of autonomy and with new obligations to himself (or, especially in the last decade and a half, to herself),has come to the foreground. A radically different mental order-self-centered and traceable not to any single historical development as much as to the entire flow of Western history since at least the Renaissance has taken over. The political and economic effects of this rise in individual self-consciousness have been largely positive: civil rights are better protected and opportunities are greater in the richer, more dynamic countries of the West; but the psychological effects have been mixed , at best. Something has been lost: a warmth, a sanity, and a supportiveness that are apparent among people whose family networks are still intact. Such qualities can be found in most of the Third World and in rural pockets of the U.S., but in the main stream of post-industrial society the individual is increasingly left to himself, to find meaning, stability, and contentment however he can.

An indication of how far the disintegration of traditional kinship has advanced is that a surprising number of Americans are unable to name all four of their grandparents. Such people have usually grown up in step-families, which are dramatically on the rise. So is the single – parent family-the mother-child unit, which some anthropologists contend is the real nucleus of kinship, having already contracted to the relatively impoverished nuclear family, partly as an adaptation to industrialization kinship seems to be breaking down even further. With the divorce rate in America at about fifty percent and the remarriage rate at about seventy five, the traditional Judeo-Christian scheme of marriage to one person for life seems to be shading into a pattern of serial monogamy, into a sort of staggered polygamy, which some anthropologists, who believe that we aren't naturally monogamous to begin with, see as "a return of normality". Still other anthropologists explain what is happening somewhat differently; we are adopting delayed system of marriage, they say, with the length of the marriage chopped off at both ends. But many adults aren't getting married at all; they are putting "self-fulfillment" before marriage and children and are having nothing further to do with kinship after leaving their parents' home; their family has become their work associate or their circle of best friends. This is the most distressing trend of all; the decline in the capacity of long-term intimate bonding.

1991

39. The traditional kinship group provides:

(a) Security

(b) Identity

(c) Entire scheme of activity

(d) All of the above

40. Which of the following is indicative of the extent of disintegration of kinship groups?

(a) A large number of Americans are unable to name all four of their grandparents.

(b) Growing number of single-parent families.

(c) Increase in the average age at which males get married.

(d) Both (a) and (b).

41. Which of the following statements is not true?

(a) When people started to farm ten thousand years ago, kinship became less important.

(b) Some families became more powerful than others after farming was initiated.

(c) Genealogy became an important means of perpetuating status after the advent of farming.

(d) Stratification of society was a result of hunter – gatherers taking up farming.

42. According to the author, what has been sacrificed with the rise in individual self-consciousness?

(a) Sanity (b) Supportiveness

(c) Warmth (d) All of the above

43. The theme of the passage is which of the following?

(a) The impact of the deterioration of kinship of groups on third world countries.

(b) The correlation between the decline of traditional kinship groups and stratification of society.

(c) The changes that have occurred to kinship group pattern and the effect of those changes on the individuals.

(d) The political and economic repercussions of the decline of the nuclear family.

44. What does the author mean by serial monogamy?

(a) Judeo-Christian scheme of marriage.

(b) Marriage to one person for life.

(c) A sequence of marriages and divorces.

(d) Delayed marriage.

45. Which of the following statements cannot be inferred from the above passage?

(a) Smaller families are more autonomous and influential.

(b) The rise of the individuals can largely be viewed as a western phenomenon.

(c) A different mental order is in evidence and can be traced to the renaissance period.

(d) Mainstream post-industrial society would benefit from a resurgence of kinship groups.

46. The word "genealogy" refers to:

(a) family history (b) kinship groups

(c) family authority (d) nuclear family

47. According to the passage, the most distressing trend is:

(a) Many adults are putting "self fulfillment" before marriage and children and aren't getting married at all.

(b) The American divorce rate of 50 percent and remarriage rate of 75 percent.

(c) The contraction of the nuclear family to the mother – child unit.

(d) The inability to develop lasting personal relationship.

48. According to the passage, which statement is not true of kinship group fragmentation?

(a) It is apparent that in Europe and countries developing along European lines a process of fragmentation has been taking place during the past few centuries.

(b) A self-centered mental order has replaced the earlier kin-centered mental order and it can be traced to a specific historical development.

(c) The political and economic benefits of the rise of the individuals have not been largely positive.

(d) Psychological effects of the rise of the individuals have been both positive and negative.

Passage – 7

In 1787, the twenty-eighth year of the reign of King George III, the British Government sent a fleet to colonize Australia. Never had a colony been founded so far from its parent state, or in such ignorance of the land it occupied. There had been no reconnaissance. In 1770 Captain James Cook had made landfall on the unexplored east coast of this utterly enigmatic continent, stopped for a short while at a place named Botany Bay and gone north again. Since then, no ship had called – not a word, not an observation, for 17 years, each one of which was exactly like the thousands that had preceded it, locked in its historical immensity of blue heat, blush, sandstone and the measured booming of glassy pacific rollers.

Now, this coast was to witness a new colonial experiment, never tried before, not repeated since. An unexplored continent would become a jail. The space around it, the very air and sea, the whole transparent labyrinth of the South pacific, would become a wall 14,000 miles thick.

The late 18th century abounded in schemes of social goodness thrown off by its burgeoning sense of revolution. But here, the process was to be reversed: not utopia, but Dystopia; not Rousseau's natural man moving in moral grace amid free social contract, but man coerced, deracinated, in chains. Other parts of the Pacific, especially Tahiti, might seem to conform Rousseau. But the intellectual patrons of Australia, in its first colonial years, were Hobbes and Sade.

In their most sanguine moments, the authorities hoped that it would eventually swallow a whole class-the "criminal class", whose existence was one of the prime sociological beliefs of late Georgian and early Victorian England. Australia was settled to defend English property not from the frog-eating invader across the Channel but from the marauder within. English lawmakers wished not only to get rid of the "Criminal class" but if possible to forget about it. Australia was a Cloaca, invisible, its contents filthy and unnamable.

To most Englishmen this place seemed not just a mutant society but another planet-an exiled world, summed up in its popular name, "Botany Bay". It was remote and anomalous to its white creators. It was strange but close, as the unconscious to the conscious mind. There was as yet no such thing as "Australian" history or culture. For its first forty years, everything that happened in the thief-colony was English. In the whole period of convict transportation, the Crown shipped more than 160,000 men, women and children(due to defects in the records, the true number will never be precisely known) in bondage to Australia. This was the largest forced exile of citizens at the behest of a European government in pre-modern history. Nothing in earlier penology compares with it. In Australia, England drew the sketch for our own century's vaster and more terrible fresco of repression, the Gulag. No other country had such a birth, and its pangs may be said to have begun on the afternoon of January 26, 1788, when a fleet of eleven vessels carrying 1,030 people, including 548 male and 188 female convicts, under the command of captain Arthur Phillip in his flagship Sirius, entered Port Jackson or, as it would presently be called, Sydney Harbor.

49. When the author refers to "the marauder within", he is referring to:

(a) the working class. (b) the lower class.

(c) the criminal class. (d) the Loch Ness monster.

50. According to the passage, the intellectual mentors of Australia could be :

(a) Hobbes and Cook (b) Hobbes and Sade

(c) Phillip and Jackson (d) Sade and Phillip

51. Which of the following does not describe what the English regarded Australia to be :

(a) a mutant society.

(b) an exiled world.

(c) an enigmatic continent.

(d) a new frontier.

52. Elsewhere, according to the author, the late eighteenth century saw a plethora of:

(a) moral grace

(b) social welfare programs

(c) free social contracts

(d) social repression

53. The word "sanguine" means:

(a) wise (b) pessimistic

(b) shrewd (d) confident

54. The primary theme of the passage is

(a) the colonization of Australia

(b) the first forty years of Australian history.

(c) the rise of the "criminal class" and its impact on the life of Georgian England.

(d) the establishment of Australia as a penal colony.

55. One of the hallmarks of the late Georgian and early Victorian England was the belief in:

(a) repression of the "criminal class".

(b) convict transportation.

(c) colonization as a solution to social problems.

(d) the existence of a "criminal" class of people.

56. What is penology?

(a) The study of transportation of criminals.

(b) The study of punishment in its relation to crime.

(c) The study of pens.

(d) The study of ink flow of pens.

57. According to the passage, which of the following statements is not true?

(a) During the seventeen years after Captain James Cook made landfall at Botany Bay, the British made several observation trips to Australia.

(b) Australia was settled by the British to protect their property from some of their own kin.

(c) The author implies that while Rousseau was vindicated in the functioning of the society of Tahiti, the process in Australia presented a contrary picture.

(d) Both (a) and (b).

58. Sydney Harbor was earlier known as:

(a) Port Jackson (b) Botany Bay

(c) Storm Bay (d) Norfolk Bay

Passage – 8

The fact is often obscured by the widespread confusion about the nature and role of emotions in man's life. One frequently hears the statement, "Man is not merely a rational being, he is also an emotional being", which implies some sort of dichotomy, as if, in effect, man possessed a dual nature, with one part in opposition to the other. In fact, however, the content of man's emotions is the product of his rational faculty; his emotions are a derivative and a consequence, which, like all of man's other psychological characteristics, cannot be understood without reference to the conceptual power of his consciousness.

As man's tool of survival, reasons has two basic functions: cognition and evaluation. The process of cognition consists of discovering what things are, of identifying their nature, their attributes and properties. The process of evaluation consists of man discovering the relationship of things to himself, of identifying what is beneficial to him and what is harmful, what should be sought and what should be avoided.

"A 'value' is that which one acts to gain and/or keep." It is that which one regards as conducive to one's welfare. A value is the object of an action. Since man must act in order to live, and since reality confronts him with many possible goals, many alternative courses of action, he cannot escape the necessity of selecting values and making value judgements.

"Value" is a concept pertaining to a relation – the relation of some aspect of reality to man(or to some other living entity). If a man regards a things(a person, an object, an event, mental state, etc.) as good for him, as beneficial in some way, he values it and, when possible and appropriate, seeks to acquire, retain and use or enjoy it; if a man regards a thing as bad for him, as inimical or harmful in some way, he disvalues it – and seeks to avoid or destroy it. If he regards a thing as of no significance to him, as neither beneficial nor harmful, he is indifferent to it – and takes no action in regard to it.

Although his life and well-being depend on a man selecting values that are in fact good for him, i.e., consonant with his nature and needs, conducive to his continued efficacious functioning, there are no internal or external forces compelling him to do so. Nature leaves him free in this matter. As a being of volitional consciousness, he is not biologically "programmed" to make the right value-choices automatically. He may select values that are incompatible with his needs and inimical to his well-being, values that lead him to suffering and destruction. But whether his values are life-serving or life-negating, it is a man's values that direct his actions. Values constitute man's basic motivational tie to reality.

In existential terms, man's basic alternative of "for me" or "against me", which gives rise to the issue of values, is the alternative of life or death. But this is an adult, conceptual identification. As a child, a human being first encounters the issue of values through the experience of physical sensations of pleasure and pain.

To a conscious organism, pleasure is experienced, axiomatically, as a value; pain, as disvalue. The biological reason for this is the fact that pleasure is a life-enhancing state and that pain is a signal of danger, of some disruption of the normal life process.

There is another basic alternative, in the realm of consciousness, through which a child encounters the issue of values, of the desirable and the undesirable. It pertains to his cognitive relations to reality. There are times when a child experiences a sense of cognitive efficacy in grasping reality, a sense of cognitive control, of mental clarity(within the range of awareness possible to his stage of development). There are times when he suffers from a sense of cognitive inefficacy, of cognitive helplessness, of mental chaos, the sense of being out of control and unable to assimilate the date entering his consciousness. To experience a state of efficacy is to experience it as a value; to experience a state of inefficacy is to experience it as a disvalue. The biological basis of this fact is the relationship of efficacy to survival.

The value of sense of efficacy as such, like the value of pleasure as such, is introspectively experienced by man as primary. One does not ask a man: "Why do you prefer pleasure to pain?" Nor does one ask him: "Why do you prefer a state of control to a state of helplessness?" It is through these two sets of experiences that man first acquires preferences, i.e. values.

A man may choose, as a consequence of his errors and/or evasions, to pursue pleasure by means of values that in fact can result only in pain; and he can pursue a sense of efficacy by means of values that can only render him impotent. But the value of pleasure and the disvalue of pain, as well as the value of efficacy and the disvalue of helplessness, remain the psychological base of the phenomenon of valuation.

59. The author subtly suggests that
- (a) there is a dual nature in man.
- (b) there is dichotomy between man as an emotional being and man as a rational being.
- (c) there should be no dichotomy between man as a rational being and man as an emotional being.
- (d) man's emotions cannot be understood.

60. The biological basis of choosing efficacy as value
- (a) cannot be understood easily.
- (b) is the relationship of efficacy to survival.
- (c) is the association of efficacy to pleasure.
- (d) is the biological relationship to cognition.

61. The author defines value as
- (a) something that results as good.
- (b) something that is chosen by man.
- (c) that which gives pleasure over pain.
- (d) that which increases efficacy.

62. The basic theme of the passage is that
- (a) man can choose his own values, irrespective of whether they are life sustaining or not.
- (b) man chooses values that are life sustaining.
- (c) values are given to man on account of his emotive process.
- (d) emotions and rationality are derived from each other.

63. According to this passage, through which of the following set of experiences, does man first acquire preferences?

A. Good and bad

B. Pleasure and pain

C. Child and adult

D. Efficacy and inefficacy

(a) A (b) A and B

(c) B and D (d) C

64. Reason has the following basic functions:
- (a) Wisdom and judgement.
- (b) Identifying what is beneficial to man.
- (c) Identifying the nature of pleasure and its value.
- (d) Cognition and evaluation.

65. The difference between a child's and adult's conceptual identification of issues relating to value is that
(a) the former experiences them through physical sensations.
(b) the latter experiences them through physical sensations.
(c) the latter's is more volitional in nature.
(d) the adults' choice is existential in nature.

66. According to the author, while man chooses his own values, it does not mean that
(a) he is always successful.
(b) it guarantees the basic reason for choosing them.
(c) they are incompatible with his needs.
(d) his environment has a say in it.

67. What man experiences as primary, according to the author,
(a) is questionable merit.
(b) changes overtime.
(c) is the value of pain and pleasure.
(d) is not debatable.

68. While a man can choose his values
(a) he is biologically programmed to choose those of survival.
(b) he is biologically programmed to choose those of destruction.
(c) his volitional consciousness can lead him to the wrong choice.
(d) his volitional consciousness leads him to the correct choice.

Passage – 9

When you first arrive in a new culture, there is a period of confusion that comes from the new situation and from a lack of information. It leaves you quite dependent and in need of help in the form of information and above. The second stage begins as you start to interact with the new culture. It is called the stage of small victories. Each new encounter with the culture is fraught with peril. It is preceded by anxiety and information collection and rehearsal. Then the even occurs and you return home either triumphant or defeated. When successful, the feelings really are very much as though a major victory has been won. A heightened roller coaster effect is particularly characteristic of this stage. The support needed is emotional support, people who appreciate what you are going through and who can cheer you onward. It often happens that once some of the fundamentals of life are mastered, there is time to explore and discover the new culture. This is the honeymoon stage of wonder and infatuation, in it there is a heightened appreciation of the new, the different, the aesthetic. Depending on the degree of cultural immersion and exploration it may continue for a considerable period of time. During this time there is no interest in attending to the less attractive downsides of the culture.

After a while, a self-correction takes place. No honeymoon can last forever. Irritation and anger begin to be experienced. Why in the world would anyone do it that way? Can't these people get their act together? Now the deficits seem glaringly apparent. For some people, they overwhelm the positive characteristics and become predominant.

Finally, if you are lucky enough to chart a course through these stages and not get stuck(and people do get stuck in these stages), there is a rebalance of reality. There is the capacity to understand and enjoy the new culture without ignoring those features that are less desirable.

This cultural entry and engagement process is both cognitive and affective. New information is acquired and remembered; old schema and perceptions are revised and qualified. An active learning process occurs. At the same time, anxiety arises in reaction to uncertainties and the challenges of the learning processes. It must be managed, as must the extremes of feeling that occur in this labile period. Thus, I am describing a learning process that results in valuing and affirming the best in the culture while at the same time seeing it in its completeness, seeing it whole. The capacity to affirm the whole- including those aspects that are less desirable yet are part of the whole – is critically important.

An appreciative process, "appreciative inquiry" is proposed as a way of helping members of different cultures recognize and value their differences and create a new culture where different values are understood and honoured. Executives - those who must lead this culture–change projects – need to understand that equal employment opportunity, affirmative action and sexual harassment policies, as viewed and implemented in organizations, are problem oriented change strategies. They focus on correcting what is wrong rather than creating a valued future. Executives themselves will need to inquire appreciatively into cultures that are not known to them before they are equipped to lead cultural change in their own organizations.

69. Which of the following statements is not true?
(a) A particular effect of interaction with a new culture is an opportunity to enjoy a roller coaster ride.
(b) Entering a new culture brings about a shift in processes of thinking and feeling.
(c) An initial sense of wonder and awe makes a new entrant oblivious to the less pleasant side of the new culture.
(d) Some people can forever remain angry and dissatisfied with the new culture.

70. Entering new cultures can predominantly help the entrant in

(a) understanding the appreciative process.

(b) appreciating stages in cultural development.

(c) appreciating diversity.

(d) understanding the problem solving process.

71. Opening a bank account in a new culture is an example of which stage?

(a) Confusion. (b) Small victories.

(c) Honeymoon. (d) (b) and (c).

72. According to the passage, entering a culture that is very different from your own is overall

(a) an infatuating process.

(b) a learning process.

(c) an exhausting process.

(d) a depressing process.

73. Which of the following statements cannot be inferred from the above passage?

(a) Acts that are meaningful in the familiar culture cannot be taken for granted in a new one.

(b) Social interaction becomes less predictable in a new culture.

(c) Seeing someone in completeness means accepting him with his strengths and weaknesses.

(d) Modifications in organization culture must result in appreciative inquiry.

74. Which of the following is true?

(a) Infatuation and heightened appreciation with a new culture can be maintained forever.

(b) Entry to a new culture evokes an extremely negative feeling.

(c) Affirmation of a new culture involves viewing it in its entirety with its strengths as well as weak points.

(d) Organizational policies to deal with sexual harassment can bring about a change in the organizational culture.

Passage – 10

In 1787, Jeremy Bentham published a lengthy pamphlet entitled, "Defense of Usury: showing the Impolicy of the Present Legal Restraints on the Terms of pecuniary bargains he was concerned with loans between individuals or business enterprises. The legal restraints were limits on interest rates paid or received. Usury was and is the popular term for charging interest rates in excess of legal limits.

Bentham makes an overwhelmingly persuasive case for the proposition he sets forth at the beginning of the pamphlet, "viz. that no man of ripe years and sound mind, acting freely, and with his eyes open, ought to be hindered, with a view of his advantage from making such bargain, in the way of obtaining money, as he thinks fit; and nor (what is necessary consequence) nobody is hindered from supplying him upon any terms he thinks proper to accede to".

During the nearly two centuries since Bentham's pamphlet was published his arguments have been widely accepted by economists and as widely neglected by politicians. I know of no economist of any standing from that time to this who has favored a legal limit on the rate of interest that borrowers could pay or lenders receive though there must have been some. I know of no country that does not limit by law the rates of interest and I doubt that there are any. As Bentham wrote, "in great political questions wide indeed is the distance between conviction and practice."

Bentham's explanation of the "grounds of the prejudices against usury" is as valid today as when he wrote: "The business of a money lender has no where, nor any time, been a popular one. Those who have the resolution to sacrifice the present to the future, are natural objects of envy to those who have sacrificed the future to the present. The children who don't have their cake to eat are the natural enemies of the children who have theirs. While the money is hoped for, and for a short time after it has been received, he who lends it is a friend and benefactor: by the time the money is spent, and the evil hour of reckoning has come, the benefactor is found to have changed his nature, and to have put on the image of the tyrant and the oppressor. It is an oppression for a man to reclaim his money: it is none to keep it from him."

Bentham's explanation of the "mischief of the anti-usurious laws" is also as valid today as when he wrote that these laws preclude "many people altogether, from getting the money they stand in need of, to answer their respective exigencies." For still others, they render "he terms so much the worse – While, out of loving kindness, or whatsoever other motive, the law precludes the man from borrowing, upon terms which it deems too disadvantageous, it does not preclude him from selling, upon any terms, howsoever disadvantageous." His conclusion : "The sole tendency of the law is to heap distress upon distress."

Developments since Bentham's days have increased the mischief done by usury legislation. Economic progress has provided the ordinary man with the means to save. The spread of banks, savings-and-loan associations, and the like has given the ordinary man the facilities for saving. For the first time in history, the working class may well be net lenders rather than net borrowers. They are also the ones who have fewest alternatives, who find it hardest to avoid legal regulations, and who are therefore hardest hit by them.

Under the spur of(Congressman)Wright Patman and his ilk, the Federal Reserve (1970) now limits the interest rate that commercial banks may pay to a maximum of 4 percent for small savers but to 7 percent for deposits of $100,000 or more. And the deposits of small savers have been relatively stable or growing, while those of large depositors have been declining sharply because they have still better alternatives.

That is the way the self-labeled defenders of the "people" look after their interests – by keeping them from receiving the interests they are entitled to. Along with Bentham, "I would wish to learn why the legislator should be more anxious to limit the rate of interest one way, than the other? Why he should make it his business to prevent their getting more than a certain price for the use of it than to prevent their getting less? — Let any one that can, find an answer to these questions: it is more than I can do."

75. The author is making a case for

(a) varying interest rates on loans.

(b) withdrawing the legislation on usury.

(c) reducing the interest rate difference on large deposits as against small.

(d) ensuring that owners get interest rates, which are determined by free market operations.

76. The lament of the author is that the mischief that the law makes is that

(a) it puts a ceiling on interest rates.

(b) it overlooks economic theory.

(c) it accepts the selling of a product at an exorbitant price while lending at high interest rates as illegal.

(d) many needy people do not get money.

77. The author suggests that

(a) usury is desirable.

(b) there should be no legal restrictions on interest rates.

(c) one should have one's cake and eat it too.

(d) he has no answer to the question of usury legislation.

78. How is usury defined?

(a) Charging interest rates in excess of legal limits.

(b) Charging exorbitant interest rates.

(c) Allowing any amount to be borrowed.

(d) None of the above.

79. Bentham was primarily concerned with

(a) all loans in the economy.

(b) loans by money lenders.

(c) loans by individuals and businesses.

(d) loans by banks and financial institutions.

80. To reclaim his own money, man becomes an oppressor because

(a) he will reclaim it with high interest.

(b) the borrower cannot repay.

(c) borrowers do not like to part with money.

(d) the critical need being over, the money lent is of less value to the borrower.

81. Who should be allowed to borrow and lend at any interest rate?

(a) Individuals and businesses.

(b) Money lenders.

(c) Sane men acting freely and with full knowledge.

(d) Small lenders and borrowers.

82. The author is

(a) a politician.

(b) a plutocrat.

(c) a reformed post glasnost Marxist.

(d) a staunch supporter of free market operations.

83. Mischief of usury legislation has increased as

(a) loans have increased.

(b) more people have become lenders.

(c) small lenders are hardest hit by the legislation.

(d) more people, among the working class, are net lenders.

Passage – 11

Long before I disbanded formally, the Eclipse Group, in order to assist the company in applying for patents on the new machine, had gathered and had tried to figure out which engineers had contributed to Eagle's patentable features. Some who attended found those meetings painful. There was bickering. Harsh words were occasionally exchanged. Alsing, who during the project had set aside the shield of technical command, came in for some abuse – why should his name go on any patents, what had he done? Someone even asked that question regarding West. Ironically, perhaps, those meetings illustrated that the building of Eagle really did constitute a collective effort, for now that they had finished, they themselves were having a hard time agreeing on what each individual had contributed. But, clearly, the team was losing its glue. 'It has no function anymore. It's like an afterbirth,' said one old hat after the last of the patent meetings. Shortly after those meetings, Wallach, Alsing,

Rasala and West received telegrams of congratulations from North-Carolina's leader. That was a classy gesture, all agreed. The next day Eagle finally went out the Company's door.

In New York City, in faded elegance of the Roosevelt Hotel, under gilded chandeliers, on April 29, 1980, Data General announced Eagle to the world. On days immediately following, in other parts of the country and in Canada and Europe, the machine was presented to salesmen and customers, and some members of the Eclipse Group went off on so-called road shows. About dozen of the team attended the big event in New York. There was a slick slide show. There were speeches. Then there was an impressive display in a dining hall-128 terminals hooked up to a single Eagle. The machine crashed during this part of the program, but no one except the company engineers noticed, the problem was corrected so quickly and deftly. Eagle – this one consisted of the boards from Gollum –looked rather fine in skins of off – white and blue, but also unfamiliar.

A surprising large number of reporters attended, and the next day Eagle's debut was written up at some length in both the Wall Street Journal and the financial pages of the New York Times. But it wasn't called Eagle anymore. Marketing had rechristened it the Eclipse MV/8000. This also took some getting used to.

The people who described the machine to the press had never, of course, had anything to do with making it. Alsing -who was at the premiere and who had seen Marketing present machines before, ones he's worked on directly-said : After Marketing gets through, you go home and say to yourself, "Wow! Did I do that?" And in front of the press, people who had not even been around when Eagle was conceived were described as having had responsibility for it. All of that was to be expected – just normal flak and protocol.

As for the machine's actual inventors-the engineers, most of whom came, seemed to have a good time, although some did seem to me a little out of place, untutored in this sort of performance. Many of them had brought new suits for the occasion. After the show, there were cocktails and then lunch, they occupied a table all their own. It was a rather formal luncheon, and there was some confusion at the table as to whether it was proper to take first the plate of salad on the right or the one on the left.

West came, too, He did not sit with his old team, but he did talk easily and pleasantly with many of them during the day. "I had a great talk with West!". Remarked one of the Microkids. He wore a brown suit, conservatively tailored. He looked as though he'd been wearing a suit all his life. He had come to this ceremony with some reluctance, and he was decidedly in the background. At the door to the show, where name tags were handed out, West had been asked what his title was. "Business Development" he'd said. At the cocktail party after the formal presentation, a reporter came up to him: "You seem to know something about this machine. What did you have to do with it?" West mumbled something, waving a hand, and changed the subject. Alsing overheard this exchange. It offended his sense of reality. He couldn't let the matter stand there. So he took the reporter aside and told him, 'That guy was the leader of the whole thing'. I had the feeling that West was just going through emotions and was not really present at all.

When it was over and we were strolling down a busy street towards Penn Station, his mood altered. Suddenly there was no longer a feeling of forbidden subjects, as there had been around him for many months. I found myself all of a sudden saying to him: "It's just a computer. It's really a small thing in the world, you know."

West smiled softly. 'I know it'. None of it, he said later, had come out the way he had imagined it would, but it was over and he was glad. The day after the formal announcement, Data General's famous sales force had been introduced to the computer in New York and elsewhere. At the end of the presentation for the sales personnel in New York, the regional sales manager got up and gave his troops a pep talk. 'What motivates people?' he asked. He answered his own question, saying, 'Ego and the money to buy things that they and their families want?' It was a different game now. Clearly, the machine no longer belonged to its makers.

84. Bickering during the meetings were indicative of the fact that

(a) there was heavy competition among the engineers.

(b) everyone wanted to take credit for Eagle.

(c) Eagle constituted a collective effort.

(d) it was hard to decide on the leader.

85. In this passage, the author seems to suggest that

(a) hard work does lead to grand results.

(b) some individuals stand out in scientific programmes.

(c) those who get credit earn it.

(d) once a new product is launched, the pains and pleasure that preceded it are lost.

86. The 'afterbirth', a simile expressed by an old hand was with reference to

(a) the Eclipse MV/8000 (b) the Eagle

(c) Mr. Alsing (d) the Eclipse Group

87. It appears from Mr. West's conversation with the author that

(a) he was quite upset over the way things turned out.

(b) he was glad to forget all about it.

(c) he preferred to keep his thoughts to himself.

(d) nothing motivated him.

88. A telegram by the North Carolina leader
(a) implicitly identified those who deserved credit for Eagle.
(b) was a worthy gesture before the launch.
(c) was an implicit invitation to Wallach, Alsing, Rasala and West to be at the dinner.
(d) indicated that Eagle would be launched the next day.

89. Apparently, one of the things that the younger computer professionals considered an honour was
(a) to be invited to the party.
(b) to talk to Mr. West.
(c) to be part of the Eclipse group.
(d) to sell Eagle.

90. The launching of Eagle in New York was a gala affair
(a) but for the fact that the machine crashed during the programme.
(b) in spite of the fact that the machine crashed during the progamme.
(c) because 128 terminals were hooked up to a single Eagle.
(d) because a new machine was being launched.

91. According to the passage, even as the premiere of the Eagle launch seemed a grand success among those who appeared incongruous were
(a) people from the Wall Street Journal and New York times.
(b) the marketing people.
(c) people who were never around when Eagle was conceived.
(d) the engineers responsible for Eagle.

92. "Just normal flak and protocol" refers to
(a) the grandeur of the launching ceremony.
(b) giving credit for Eagle to even those who weren't responsible for it.
(c) the marketing people who rechristened the machine.
(d) Mr. Alsing who was present at the premiere.

93. The author states that the machine no longer belonged to its makers
(a) because the marketing people had changed its name.
(b) because the engineers seemed to have lost interest in the machine.
(c) because of the expressed attitude towards what motivated people.
(d) because Mr. West refused to get involved.

Passage – 12

The core of modern doctoring is diagnosis, treatment and prognosis. Most medical schools emphasize little else. Western doctors have been analyzing the wheezes and pains of their patients since the 17th century to identify the underlying disease of the cause of complaints. They did it well and good diagnosis became the hall mark of a good physician. They were less strong on treatment. But when sulphonamides were discovered in 1935 to treat certain bacterial infections, doctors found themselves with powerful new tools. The area of modern medicine was born. Today there is a ever-burgeoning array of complex diagnostic tests, and of pharmaceutical and surgical methods of treatment. Yet what impact has all this had on health?

Most observers ascribe recent improvements in health in rich countries to better living standards and changes in lifestyle. The World Health Organization cities the wide differences in health between Western and Eastern Europe. The two areas have similar pattern of diseases: heart disease, senile dementia, arthritis and cancer are the most common cause of sickness and death. Between 1947 and 1964, both parts of Europe saw general health improve , with the arrival of cleaner water, better sanitation and domestic refrigerators. Since the mid 1960s, however, E. European countries, notable Poland and Hungary, have seen mortality rates rise and life expectancy fall. Why? The WHO ascribes the divergence to differences in lifestyle-diet, smoking habits, alcohol, a sedentary way of life (factors associated with chronic and degenerative diseases) rather than differences in access in modern medical care.

In contrast, the huge sum now spent in the same of medical progress produce only marginal improvements in health. America devotes nearly 12% of its GNP to it high technology medicine, more than any other developed country. Yet, overall, Americans die younger, lose more babies and are at least as likely to suffer from chronic diseases. Some medical producers demonstrably do work: mending broken bones, the removable of cataracts, drugs for ulcers, vaccination, aspirin for headaches, antibiotics for bacterial infections, techniques that save new born babies, some organ transplant, yet the evidence is scant for many other common treatments. The coronary bypass, a common surgical technique, is usually to overcome the obstruction caused by a blood clot in arteries leading to the heart. Deprived of oxygen, tissues in the heart might otherwise die. Yet, according to a 1988 study conducted in Europe, coronary bypass surgery is beneficial only in the short term. A bypass patient who dies within five years has probably lasted longer than if he had simply taken drugs. But among those who get to or past five years, the drug-takers live longer than those who have surgery.

An American study completed in 1988 concluded that removing tissue from the prostate gland after the appearance of (non-cancerous) growth, but before the growths can do much damage, does not prolong life expectancy. Yet the operation was performed regularly and cost Medicare, the federally – subsidized system for the elderly, over $1 billion a year.

Though they have to go through extensive clinical trials, it is not always clear that drugs provide health benefits. According to Dr. Louise Russell, a professor of economics at Rutgers University, in New Jersey, although anti – cholesterol drugs have been shown in clinical trails to reduce the incidence of deaths due to coronary heart disease, in ordinary life there is no evidence that extend the individual drug taker's life expectancy. Medical practice varies widely from one country to another. Each year in America about 60 of every 100,000 people have a coronary by-pass; In Britain about six Anti-diabetic drugs are far more commonly used in some European countries than others. One woman in five, in Britain, has a hysterectomy (removal of the womb) at some time during her life; In America and Denmark, seven out of ten do so.

Why? If coronary heart problems were far commoner in America than Britain, or diabetes in one part of Europe than another, such differences would be justified. But that is not so. Nor do American and Danish women become evidently healthier than British ones. It is the medical practice, not the pattern of illness or the outcome, that differs. Perhaps American patients expect their doctors to "do something" more urgently than British ones? Perhaps American doctors are readier to comply? Certainly the American medical fraternity grows richer as a result. No one else seems to have gained through such practices.

To add injury to insult, modern medical procedures may not be just of questionable worth but sometimes dangerous. Virtually all drugs have some adverse side-effects on some people. No surgical procedure is without risk. Treatments that prolong life can also promote sickness: the heart attack victim may be saved but survive disabled.

Attempts have been made to sort out this tangle. The "outcomes movement" born in America during the past decade, aims to lessen the use of inappropriate drugs and pointless surgery by reaching some medical consensus– which drug to give? whether to operate or medicate?–through better assessment of the outcome of treatments.

Ordinary clinical trials measure the safety and immediate efficacy of products or procedures. The outcomes enthusiasts try to measure and evaluate far wider consequences. Do patients actually feel better? What is the impact on life expectancy and other health statistics? And instead of relying on results from just a few thousand patients, the effect of treating tens of thousands are studied retrospectively. As an example of what this can turn up, the adverse side-effects associated with Opren, an anti-arthritis drug, were not spotted until it was widely used.

Yet Dr. Arnold Epstein, of the Harvard Medical School, argues that, worthy as it may be, the outcomes movement is likely to have only a modest impact on medical practice. Effectiveness can be difficult to measure: patients can vary widely in their responses. In some, a given drug may relieve pain, in others not: is highly subjective. Many medical controversies will be hard to resolve because of data conflict.

And what of the promised heart-disease or cancer cures? Scientists accept that they are unlikely to find an answer to cancer, heart disease or degenerative brain illness for a long while yet. These diseases appear to be highly complex, triggered when a number of bodily functions go awry. No one pill or surgical procedure is likely to be the panacea. The doctors probably would do better looking at the patient's diet and lifestyle before he becomes ill than giving him six pills for the six different bodily failure that are causing the illness once he has got it.

Nonetheless modern medicine remains entrenched. It is easier to pop pills than change a lifetime" habits. And there is always the hope of some new miracle cure —or some individual miracle.

Computer technology has helped produce cameras so sensitive that they can detect the egg in the womb, to be extracted for test tube fertilization. Bio-materials have created an artificial heart that is expected to increase life expectancy among those fitted with one by an average of 54 months. Bio-technology has produced expensive new drugs for the treatment of cancer. Some have proved life-savers against some rare cancers; none has yet had a substantial impact on overall death rates due to cancer.

These innovations have vastly increased the demand and expectations of health care and pushed medical bills even higher – not lower, as was once hoped. Inevitably, governments, employers and insurers who finance health care have rebelled over the past decade against its astronomic costs, and have introduced budgets and rationing to curb them.

Just as inevitably, this limits access to health care: rich people get it more easily than poor ones.

Some proposed solutions would mean no essential change, just better management of the current system. But others, mostly from American academics, go further, aiming to reduce the emphasis on modern medicine and its advance. Their trust is two headed:

(i) prevention is better – and might be cheaper – than cure; and

(ii) if you want high-tech, high-cost medicine, you (or your insurers, but not the public) must pay for it, especially when its value is uncertain.

Thus the finance of health-care systems, private or public, could be skewed to favour prevention rather than cure. Doctors would be reimbursed for preventive practices, whilst curative measures would be severely rationed. Today the skew is all the other way: Governments or insurers pay doctors to diagnose disease and prescribe treatment, but not to give advise on smoking or diet.

Most of the main chronic diseases are man-made. By reducing environmental pollution, screening for and treating biological risk indicators such as high blood pressure, providing vaccination and other such measures – above all, by changing people's own behavior – within decades the incidence of these diseases could be much reduced. Governments could help by imposing ferocious "Sin taxes" on unhealthy products such as cigarettes, alcohol, maybe even fatty foods, to discourage consumption.

The trouble is that nobody knows precisely which changes – apart from stopping smoking – are really worth putting into effect, let alone how. It is clear that people whose blood pressure is brought down have a brighter future than if it stayed high; It is not clear that cholesterol screening and treatment are similarly valuable. Today's view of what constitutes a good diet may be judged wrong tomorrow.

Much must change before any of these "caring" rather than "cure" schemes will get beyond the academic drawing-board. Nobody has yet been able to assemble a coherent preventive programme. Those countries that treat medicine as a social cost have been wary of moves to restrict public use of advanced and / or costly medical procedures, while leaving the rich to buy what they like. They fear that this would simply leave ordinary people with third-class medicine.

In any case, before fundamental change can come, society will have to recognize that modern medicine is an imprecise science that does not always work: and that questions of how much to spend on it, and how, should not be determined almost incidentally, by doctor's medical preferences.

1992

94. The discovery of sulphonamides

(a) helped the doctors to diagnose better.

(b) led to better treatment of some bacterial infections.

(c) eventually led to pharmaceutical and surgical methods of treatment.

(d) None of the above.

95. The current medical practice as carried out in America benefits mostly the

(a) doctors

(b) rich

(c) biotechnology companies

(d) None of the above

96. In some European countries anti-diabetic drugs are far more commonly used than others because

(a) the drugs are fairly easy to take.

(b) more people in those countries suffer from diabetes than in others.

(c) medical practice in different countries varies.

(d) the sedentary way of life which marks their lifestyle results in more people becoming diabetic.

97. Which of the following statements is false?

(a) Coronary by-pass operation is entirely ineffective.

(b) Drug taking is sometimes better than undergoing coronary by-pass surgery.

(c) Removing tissue from prostrate gland after non-cancerous growths appear is a risky operation.

(d) The American medicare is billed about a billion dollars annually for prostrate operations.

98. Which of the following measures if undertaken under 'Care rather than Cure' movement could prove to be controversial?

(a) 'Sin' taxes on harmful substances such as tobacco and alcohol.

(b) Screening for high blood pressure.

(c) Providing vaccinations.

(d) Cholesterol screening.

99. The outcomes movement could make a significant impact on medical practice if only

(a) the efficacy of all drugs could be tested fast.

(b) the results from just a few thousands patients could be relied on.

(c) the patient had responded uniformly to drugs and medical procedure.

(d) pain could be easily relieved.

100. Modern cure are known to be expensive because

(a) bio-material are expensive.

(b) employing biotechnological process in making medicines is an expensive process.

(c) there is a huge demand for them but the supply is limited.

(d) None of these.

101. The main objection to 'care rather cure' approach is that it

(a) might leave the poor to fend for themselves.

(b) will lead to confusion as far as the choice of medical technique to be followed.

(c) is not possible to put togethor coherent preventive programme.

(d) will lead to the neglect to curative techniques.

Passage – 13

Smith did not invent economics. Joseph Schumpter observed that "The Wealth of the Nations" did not contain "a single analytic idea, principle or method that was entirely new". Smith's achievement was to combine an encyclopaedic variety of insight, information and anecdote, and to distill from it a revolutionary doctrine. The resulting masterpiece is the most influential book about economics ever published. Remarkably, much of it speaks directly to questions that are still of pressing concern.

The pity is that Smith's great book, like most classics (of 900 pages), is more quoted than read. All sides in today's debates about economic policy have conspired to peddle a conveniently distorted version of its idea. If his spirit is still monitoring events, it will undoubtedly have celebrated the collapse of communism. But it must also long to meet the politicians who have taken charge of a fine reputation and not so fine profile. And put them right on one or two points.

Today Smith is widely seen as intellectual champion of self-interest. This is a misconception. Smith saw no moral virtue in selfishness ; on the contrary he saw its dangers. Still less was he a defender of capital over labour (he talked of the capitalist's "mean rapacity"), of the rising bourgeoisie over the common folk. His suspicion of self – interest and his regard for the people as a whole come through clearly in one of his best-known remarks: "People of the same trade often meet together, even have merriment and diversion, but the conversation ends in a conspiracy against the public, or in some contrivance to raise prices."

Far from praising self-interest as a virtue, Smith merely observed it to be a driving economic force. In "The Wealth of Nations" he explained how this potentially destructive impulse is harnessed to the social good. What is to prevent greedy producers raising their prices until their customers can afford to pay no more? The answer is competition. If producers raise their prices too high, they create an opportunity for one or more among them to profit by charging less and thus selling more. In this way competition tames selfishness and regulates prices and quality. At the same time it regulates quantities. If buyers want more bread and less cheese, their demand enables bakers to charge more and obliges cheese-mongers to charge less. Profits in bread-making would rise and profits in cheese-making would fall; effort and capital would move from one task to the other.

Through Smith's eyes, it is possible to marvel afresh at this fabulously powerful mechanism and to relish, as he did, the paradox of private gain yielding social good. Only more so, for the transactions that deliver a modern manufactured good to its customer are infinitely more complicated than those described by Smith. In his day, remember, the factory was still a novel idea: manufacturing meant pins and coats.

A modern car is made of raw materials that have been gathered from all over the world, combined into thousands of intermediate products, sub-assembled by scores of separate enterprises. The consumer need know nothing of all this, any more than the worker who tapped the rubber for the tyres knows or cares what its final use will be. Every transaction is voluntary. Self-interest and competition silently process staggering quantities of information and direct the flow of good. Services, capital and labour – just as in Smith's much simpler world. Far-sighted as he was, he would surely have been impressed. Mind you, modern man has also discovered something else. With great effort and ingenuity, and the systematic denial of personal liberty, governments can supplant self-interest and competition, and replace the invisible hand of market forces with collective endeavour and a visible input- output table. The result is a five-year waiting list for Trabants.

Because Smith was convinced that the market would, literally, deliver the goods, he wanted it, by and large, left alone. He said that governments should confine themselves to three main tasks: defending the people from the "violence and invasion of other independent societies", protecting every member of society from the "injustice or oppression of every other member of it"; and providing "certain public works and certain public institutions, which it can never be for the interest of any individual, or small number of individuals, to erect and maintain."

Each of these jobs arises because the market in some ways fails. In the first two cases-collective defence and the administration of justice - the failure is the so-called free-rider problem. People disguise what they are willing to pay for a service that must be provided to everybody or not at all; they want to consume it and let others meet the cost. However the third job the provision of "certain public works and certain public institutions" goes much wider. Indeed, to modern minds, it threatens to be all encompassing. It recognizes not only the free-rider problem but also other species of market failure notably, the effects of private transactions on third parties, or "externalities". Smith has in mind roads, public education, and help for the destitute. As it turned out, millions of teachers, nurses, firemen, postmen, rubbish collectors, bus drivers and 57,000 varieties of civil servant have since marched through this opening.

Smith's thinking already seems to permit a great deal of government intervention. Add some modern economics and the floodgates open. For instance, theorists have shown that if just one price in an economy is different from price under competition, efficiency may require other every price to be somewhat distorted as well. Less government intervention, it seems to follow, cannot be assumed to be better. Competition itself has changed out of recognition. Modern economies, it is said, are driven not by countless small producers, but by handful of giant enterprises and monopolistic trade unions. And the rapid pace of industrial change has made the externality of pollution for more obvious than before. Smith, admittedly, is a bit thin on global warming.

Above all, many have forgotten something than Smith saw clearly: that every advantage granted by government to one part of the economy puts the rest at a disadvantage. Accordingly, he talked not of "intervention" -a too-neutral word-but of "preference" and "restraint". Modern governments offer preference as though it costs nothing: the beneficiaries demand it as of right.

But Smith went further than revealing the penalty in every preference. He also understood that ministers,like markets, fail. A great virtue of unfettered competition, he said, was that "the sovereign is completely discharged from a duty, in the attempting to perform which he must always be exposed to innumerable delusions, and for the proper performance of which no human wisdom or knowledge could ever be sufficient. " Many of the reasons why markets fail are also reasons why governments fail at the same task. If the consumer refuses to reveal his preferences in a market setting, how are governments to discover them? All too often, moreover, government intervention is itself a cause of the market breaking down which becomes the reason for further rounds of intervention, and so on. In Britain think of tax preferences for housing, rent controls, planning, regulations; America think of tax preferences for borrowing, deposit insurance, leverage buy-outs, financial-market regulation.

In one crucial respect, Smith's arguments are even more powerful now than in this day. Naturally, he favoured free trade to prevent market failure: "By means of glasses, hotbeds, and hotwalls, very good grapes can be raised in Scotland, and very good wine too can be made of them at about thirty times the expense for which at least equally good can be brought from foreign countries. Would it be a reasonable law to prohibit the importation of all foreign wines, merely to encourage the making of claret and burgundy in Scotland?" Two centuries later, free trade is not just a matter of the cheapest supply; it is also the best way to force producers that might otherwise be near-monopolies to compete. It is perfect folly to complain that today's big companies render the invisible hand powerless, and to conclude that barriers to trade must go up: trade and competition need each other more than ever before.

Smith was a pragmatist. The principles he expounded on the proper role of government are flexible if anything, too flexible. They are a remainder that imperfect markets are usually cleverer than imperfect governments, but they cannot draw a line to separate good intervention from bad. If governments and voters could be guided by two Smithian precepts, however, the market system that has worked so well would work even better.

First, the competitive clash of self interest against self-interest, however imperfect, has built-in safeguards. Before governments exert their monopoly power to displace it, they must justify themselves. Let the burden of proof always be on them, Second, when preference or restraint are judged to be necessary, use market forces to apply them. Tariffs are better than quotas; taxes are better than bans or direct controls; allocating resources by price (e.g. in health or education) is better than allocating them by fiat, even if the services are then provided "free"(but never forget those inverted commas) to their consumers.

102. Smith's attitude to the virtues of self interest can be best described as

(a) pragmatic (b) cynical

(c) skeptical (d) supportive

103. According to Adam Smith

(a) selfishness is dangerous.

(b) competition is the result of 'mean rapacity'

(c) self interest always leads to competition.

(d) competition regulates quantities.

104. All of the following are reasons for market failure except:

(a) The effects of private transactions on third parties.

(b) People would like to consume goods without paying for them.

(c) Unfettered and unbridled trade.

(d) Government intervention.

105. Adam Smith is most likely to agree with the statement:

(a) It is necessary for capital to exploit labour if competition and low prices are to be engendered.

(b) Businessmen would form cartels given the chance.

(c) Lesser government intervention is better.

(d) Collective endeavour could be the basis of economic growth.

106. Which of the following situations is not an instance of market failure?

(a) A government practising apartheid.

(b) A specialist doctor charging high fees.

(c) Poor development of roads and railways.

(d) A murderer going scot-free.

107. The 'free rider' problem results in the need for all of the following except

(a) government laws to prevent crime.

(b) a national defence budget.

(c) a national R & D centre for an industry.

(d) a United Nations peace keeping force.

108. Based on the passage, competitions will directly affect all of the following except:

(a) quantity of a good produced.

(b) quality of a good produced

(c) direction of flow of goods.

(d) price of goods sold.

109. We can conclude from the passage that:

(a) government control is often self propagating.

(b) rulers are prone to delusions.

(c) governments often fail because markets also fail.

(d) government actions rarely have justifications.

110. Based on the passage, we could say that Adam Smith would not support

(a) government intervention.

(b) corporation

(c) taxes.

(d) import licences.

111. All the following characteristics of the modern world are used as arguments for government intervention except.

(a) advanced and costly research in basic science.

(b) the far greater complexity of the modern manufacturing process.

(c) increased pollution and environmental hazards.

(d) the pre-eminence of large corporations.

112. Based on the passage, the following can be inferred, except which of the following?

(a) Governments must act only when necessary.

(b) High customs duties are an acceptable way to restrict a change.

(c) High taxation is better than bans.

(d) The role of governments must be more flexible.

113. The most serious problem of modern government is that they

(a) hire too many people.

(b) offer advantages to groups as if it costs nothing.

(c) are often unwise in their decisions.

(d) tax the citizens to much.

Passage – 14

Atmospheric jet streams were discovered towards the end of World War II by U.S. bomber pilots over Japan and by German reconnaissance aircraft over the Mediterranean. The World Meteorological Organization defines a jet stream as a strong, narrow air current that is concentrated along nearly horizontal axis in the upper troposphere or stratosphere (10 to 50 km altitude), characterized by wind motions that produce strong vertical lateral shearing action and featuring one of more velocity maximum. Normally a jet stream is thousands of kilometers long, hundreds of kilometers wide and several kilometers deep. The vertical wind shear is of the order of 5 to 10 m/sec per kilometer, and the lateral shear is of the order of 5 m/sec per 100 km. An arbitrary lower limit of 30m/sec is assigned to the speed of the wind along the axis of a jet stream.

With abundant radio-sonic data now available over the Northern Hemisphere it is possible to map the jet streams in the upper troposphere (near 10 to 12 km) in their daily occurrence and variation and to forecast them reasonably well with numerical prediction techniques. Upper-air information from the Southern Hemisphere is still sparse. Constant-level balloons (the so-called GHOST balloons) and satellite information on temperature structure and characteristic cloud formations in the atmosphere are serving to close the data on the global jet stream distribution. The strongest winds known in jet streams have been encountered over Japan, where speeds up to 500 km/hr (close to 300 knots) occur. A persistent band of strong winds occurs during the winter season over this region, flowing from the southwest and leading tropical air northern India into juxtaposition with polar and arctic air from Siberia. A similar region of confluence of air masses with vastly different temperatures exists over the central and eastern United States, leading to a maximum frequency of occurrence of jet streams during winter and spring.

The main impact on weather and climate comes from two distinct jet stream system: the Polar - Front Jet Stream, which is associated with the air mass contracts (the fronts) of middle latitudes and which gives rise to the formation of squalls, storms, and cyclones in this latitude belt; and the Subtropical Jet Stream, which lies over the subtropical high-pressure belt, and which is characterized by predominant subsidence motions and, hence, with fair weather. During summer, a belt of strong easterly winds is found over Southeast Asia, India, the Arabian Sea, and tropical Africa, this tropical, easterly jet streams is tied in with the weather disturbances of the Indian and African summer monsoons and their heavy rainfalls.

Because of their strong winds, jet streams play an important role in the economy of air traffic. Head winds must be outlasted by extra fuel, which takes up useful cargo space. Clear air turbulence (CAT) is often associated with the strong vertical wind shears found in the jet stream region. It is a hazard to passenger and crew safety, and, because of the increased stresses on the air frame, it decreases the useful life of the aircraft.

114. An atmospheric jet stream is

(a) a rare phenomenon.

(b) three dimensional.

(c) concentrated in the northern hemisphere.

(d) more common in summer.

115. Detailed studies of atmospheric streams have been made over
(a) South Africa (b) Europe
(c) Australia (d) Antarctica

116. The atmospheric jet stream consists of
(a) cumulous clouds bearing saturated moisture.
(b) debris caused by meteorites.
(c) air currents.
(d) effluents from speeding aircraft.

117. According to present knowledge, jet streams are caused when
(a) polar and Arctic air meet.
(b) air masses with considerably different temperatures meet.
(c) winds with different speeds meet.
(d) squalls, storms and cyclones get dispersed.

118. Jet streams affect air-traffic by
I. delaying flights.
II. Increased fuel consumption.
III. Their propensity to cause accidents.
IV. Damaging the air frame.
(a) I, II, III & IV (b) II & IV only
(c) II, III & IV only (d) II & III only

119. The summer monsoon over India is caused by
(a) the rotation of the earth.
(b) jet streams from the subtropical regions.
(c) juxtaposition of tropical air with Arctic air in the upper atmosphere.
(d) a tropical and easterly jet stream.

120. The result of the Subtropical Jet Stream is
(a) the occurrence of cyclones.
(b) the prevalence of fair weather.
(c) head winds which affect air traffic.
(d) high wind speed over Japan.

Passage – 15

A conservation problem equally as important as that of soil erosion is the loss of soil fertility. Most agriculture was originally supported by the natural fertility of the soil; and, in areas in which soils were deep and rich in minerals, farming could be carried on for many years without the return of any nutrients to the soil other than those supplied through the natural breakdown of plant and animal wastes. In river basins, such as that of the Nile, annual flooding deposited a rich layer of silt over the soil, thus restoring its fertility. In areas of active volcanism, such as Hawaii, soil fertility has been renewed by the periodic deposition of volcanic ash. In other areas, however, natural fertility has been quickly exhausted. This is true of most forest soils, particularly those in the humid tropics. Because continued cropping in such areas caused a rapid decline in fertility and therefore in crop yields, fertility could be restored only by abandoning the areas and allowing the natural forest vegetation to return. Over a period if time, the soil surface would be rejuvenated by parent materials, new circulation channels would form deep in the soil, and the deposition of forest debris would restore minerals to the topsoil. Primitive agriculture in such forests was of shifting nature: areas were cleared of trees and the woody material burned to add ash to the soil; after a few years of farming, the plots would be abandoned and new sites cleared. As long as populations were sparse in relation to the area of forestland, such agricultural methods did little harm. They could not, however, support dense populations or produce large quantities of surplus foods.

Starting with the most easily depleted soils, which were also the easiest to farm, the practice of using various fertilizers was developed. The earliest fertilizers were organic manures, but later, larger yields were obtained by adding balanced combinations of those nutrients (e.g. potassium, nitrogen, phosphorus and calcium) that crop plants require in greatest quantity. Because high yields are essential, most modern agriculture depends upon the continued addition of chemical fertilizers to the soil. Usually these substances are added in mineral form, but nitrogen is often added as urea, an organic compound.

Early in agricultural history, it was found that the practice of growing the same crop year after year in a particular plot of ground not only caused undesirable changes in the physical structure of the soil, but also drained the soil of its nutrients. The practice of crop rotation was discovered to be a useful way to maintain the condition of the soil, and also to prevent the buildup of those insects and other plant pests that are attracted to a particular kind of crop. In rotation systems, a grain crop is often grown the first year, followed by a leafy-vegetable crop in the second year, and pasture crop in the third. The last usually contains legumes (e.g. clover, alfalfa), because such plants can restore nitrogen to the soil through the action of bacteria that live in nodules on their roots.

In irrigation agriculture, in which water is brought in to supply the needs of crops in an area with insufficient rainfall, a particular soil-management problem that develops is the salinization(concentration of salts)of the surface soil. This most commonly results from inadequate drainage of the irrigated land; because the water cannot flow freely, it evaporates, and the salts dissolved in the water are left on the surface of the soil. Even though the water does not contain a large concentration of dissolved salts, the accumulation over the years can be significant enough to make the soil unsuitable for crop production. Effective drainage solves the problem; in many cases, drainage canals must be constructed, and drainage tiles must be laid beneath the surface of the soil. Drainage also requires the availability of an excess of water to flush the salts from the surface soil. In certain heavy soils with poor drainage, this problem can be quite severe; for example, large areas of formerly irrigated land in the Indus basin, in the Tigris-Euphrates region, in the Nile Basin, and in the Western United States, have been seriously damaged by salinization.

121. The areas most prone to salinization are
(a) those irrigated with well-water.
(b) those in which crop rotation is not practiced.
(c) sub-tropical forests.
(d) flat land irrigated from reservoirs.

122. The most appropriate title to this passage is
(a) Problems of soil erosion.
(b) Agriculture in Volcanic islands.
(c) The importance of chemical fertilizers.
(d) Causes of and remedies of soil-infertility.

123. Natural fertility exhausts most quickly in
(a) river valley lands (b) humid tropical forests
(c) volcanic areas (d) lands near urban areas

124. The factor that can restore fertility to the soil not mentioned in the passage is
(a) alluvium brought by rivers
(b) bacterial action
(c) fertilizer fixation through lightning
(d) organic manure

125. Crop rotation helps to
I. increase the farmer's seasonal income.
II. preserve soil condition.
III. desalinize the soil.
IV. destroy pests.
(a) I, II, III & IV (b) I, II & IV only.
(c) II & IV only (d) II, III & IV only

126. One of the characteristics of agricultural land in Nile basin is
(a) it contains a lot of bacteria.
(b) it consists of heavy soil with poor drainage properties.
(c) the Nile water contains an excess of salts.
(d) it contains nutritive minerals.

127. Plants with nodules on their roots are known as
(a) debris (b) leafy-vegetables
(c) legumes (d) grain crop

Passage – 16

Scientism has left humanity in our technical mastery of inanimate nature, but improvised us in our quest for an answer to the riddle of the universe and of our existence in it. Scientism has done worse than that with respect to our status as social beings, that is, to our life with our fellow human beings. The quest for the technical mastery of social life, comparable to our mastery over nature, did not find scientism at a loss for an answer: reason suggested that physical nature and social life were fundamentally alike and therefore proposed identical methods for their domination. Since reason in the form of causality reveals itself most plainly in nature, nature became the model for the social world and the natural sciences the image of what the social sciences one day would be. According to scientism, there was only one truth, the truth of science, and by knowing it, humanity would know all. This was, however, a fallacious argument, its universal acceptance initiated an intellectual movement and a political technique which retarded, rather than furthered, human mastery of the social world.

The analogy between the natural and social worlds is mistaken for two reasons. On the one hand human action is unable to model the social world with the same degree of technical perfection that is possible in the natural world. On the other hand, the very notion that physical nature is the embodiment of reason from which the analogy between natural and social worlds derives, is invalidated by modern scientific thought itself.

Physical nature, as seen by the practitioner of science consists of a multitude of isolated facts over which human action has complete control. We know that water boils at a temperature of 212 degrees Fahrenheit and, by exposing water to this temperature, we can make it boil at will. All practical knowledge of physical nature and all control over it are essentially of the same kind.

Scientism proposed that the same kind of knowledge and of control held true for the social world. The search for a single cause, in the social sciences, was but a faithful copy of the method of the physical sciences. Yet in the social sphere, the logical coherence of the natural sciences finds no adequate object and there is no single cause by the creation of which one can create a certain effect at will. Any single cause in the social sphere can entail an indefinite number of different effects, and the same effect can spring from an indefinite number of different effects, and the same effect can spring from an indefinite number of different causes.

128. The author's attitude towards the application of scientism to the social sciences is best described as one of
(a) committed scrutiny (b) dismissal
(c) criticism (d) approval

129. According to the author, causes and effects in the social world are

(a) unrelated to each other

(b) difficult to identify or predict.

(c) subject to manipulation at will.

(d) reducible to a single cause for each effect.

130. Which of the following statements about scientism is best supported by the passage?

(a) Scientism provides the basis for mastery of the social world.

(b) Scientism is only superficially concerned with cause-and –effect relationships.

(c) Scientism is poorly suited to explain social behaviour.

(d) Scientism is no longer applicable to the study of the natural sciences.

131. As is used in the passage, the term 'scientism' can best be defined as

(a) belief that the methods of the physical sciences can be applied to all fields of enquiry.

(b) faith that human beings can master their own physical limitations.

(c) desire to keep the social sciences separate from the physical sciences

(d) opinion that scientists must take moral responsibility for their actions

132. In the passage, the author is most concerned with doing which of the following?

(a) Upholding the primacy of reason over superstition.

(b) Attacking a particular approach to the social sciences.

(c) Describing a method for achieving control over human social behaviour.

(d) Demonstration the superiority of the social sciences over the natural sciences.

Passage – 17

From a vantage point in space, an observer could see that the Earth is engaged in a variety of motions. First, there is its rotation on its own axis, causing the alternation of day and night. This rotation, however, is not altogether steady. Primarily because of the moon's gravitational action, the Earth's axis wobbles like that of an ill-spun top. In this motion, called 'precession', the North and South Poles each traces out the base of a cone in space, completing a circle every 25,800 years, In addition, as the Sun and the Moon change their positions with respect to the Earth, their changing gravitational effects result in a slight 'nodding' of the earth's axis, called 'mutation', which is superimposed on precession. The Earth completes one of these 'nods' every 18.6 years.

The earth also, of course, revolves round the Sun, in a 6-million mile journey that takes 365.25 days. The shape of this orbit is an ellipse, but it is not the center of the Earth that follows the elliptical path. Earth and Moon behave like an asymmetrical dumb-bell, and it is the center of mass of this dumb-bell that traces the ellipse around the sun. The center of the Earth-Moon mass lies about 3000 miles away from the center of the Earth, and the Earth thus moves in an S-curve that crosses and re-crosses its orbital path. Then too, the Earth accompanies the sun in the sun's movements: first, through its local star cloud, and second, in a great sweep around the hub of its galaxy, the Milky Way that takes 200 million years to complete.

133. The passage is most likely directed towards an audience of

(a) geologists.

(b) astronauts.

(c) meteorologists interested in weather prediction.

(d) person with little technical knowledge of astronomy.

134. Which of the following best describes the main subject of the passage?

(a) The various types of the Earth's motions

(b) Past changes in the Earth's position

(c) The moon gravitational effect on the earth

(d) Oddities of the Earth's rotation of its axis.

135. The passage indicates that a single cycle of which of the following motions is completed in the shortest period of time?

(a) Mutation.

(b) Precession.

(c) The Earth's rotation on its axis.

(d) The movement of the dumb-bell formed by the center of mass of Earth-Moon.

136. Which of the following techniques does the author use in order to make the descriptions of motion clear?

I. Comparison with familiar objects.

II. Reference of geometric forms.

III. Allusions to the works of other authors.

(a) I only (b) II only

(c) I and II only (d) II and III only

Passage – 18

The connective tissues are heterogeneous group of tissues derived from the mesenchyme, a meshwork of stellate cells that develop in the middle layer of the early embryo. They have the general function of maintaining the structural integrity of organs, and providing cohesion and internal support for the body as a whole. The connective tissues include several types of fibrous tissue that vary only in their density and cellularity, as well as more specialized variants ranging from adipose tissue through cartilage to bone. The cells that are responsible for the specific function of an organ are referred to as its parenchyma, while the delicate fibrous meshwork that blinds the cells together into functional units, the fibrous partitions or septa that enclose aggregations of functional units, and the dense fibrous capsule that encloses the whole organ, collectively make up its connective-tissue framework, or stroma. Blood vessels, both large and small, course through connective tissues, which is therefore closely associated with the nourishment of tissues and organs throughout the body. All nutrient materials and waste products exchanged between the organs and the blood must traverse peri-vascular spaces occupied by connective tissue. One of the important functions of the connective – tissue cells is to maintain conditions in the extra-cellular spaces that favour this exchange.

Some organs are suspended from the wall of a body cavity by thin sheets of connective tissues called mesenteries; others are embedded in adipose tissue a form of a connective tissue in which the cells are specialized for the synthesis and storage of energy-rich reserves of fat, or lipid. The entire body is supported from within by a skeleton composed of bone, a type of connective tissue endowed with great resistance to stress owing to its highly ordered, laminated structure and to its hardness, which results from deposition of mineral salts in its fibres and amorphous matrix. The individual bones of the skeleton are held firmly together by ligaments, and muscles are attached to bone by tendons, both of which are examples of dense connective tissue in which many fibre bundles are associated in parallel array to provide great tensile strength. At joints, the articular surfaces of the bones are covered with cartilage, a connective tissue with an abundant intercellular substance that gives it a firm consistency well adopted to permit smooth gliding movements between the opposed surfaces. The synovial membrane, which lines the margins of the joint cavity and lubricates and nourishes the joint surfaces, is also a form of connective tissue.

137. The passage has most probably been taken from a book on

(a) neurology (b) nutrition
(c) physiology (d) calisthenics

138. Mesenteries are

(a) adipose tissue in which some organs are embedded.
(b) referred to as parenchyma, and are responsible for specific functions of an organ.
(c) thin sheets from which some organs are suspended.
(d) cells through which blood flows.

139. Through peri-vascular spaces exchange takes place between

(a) blood and organs.
(b) cells and embryo.
(c) nutrients and waste products.
(d) septa and stroma.

140. The connective tissue in which fat is stored is called

(a) adipose tissue (b) mesenteries
(c) ligaments (d) adipose tissue

141. The connective tissues originate in the

(a) cartilage (b) bone
(c) embryo (d) nutrients.

142. Some instances of connective tissues are

I. Cartilage
II. Stroma
III. Lipid
IV. Synovia

(a) I, II, III & IV (b) I, III & IV only
(c) I, II, & IV only (d) I and II only

143. The tissue which enables smooth gliding movements of neighbouring surface is

(a) adipose tissue (b) cartilage
(c) synovial membrane (d) stellate cells

Passage – 19

Emile Durkheim, the first person to be formally recognized as a sociologist and the most scientific of the pioneers, conducted a study that stands as a research model for sociologists today. His investigation of suicide was, in fact, the first sociological study to use statistics. In *suicide* (1964, originally published in 1897) Durkheim documented his contention that some aspects of human behaviour – even something as allegedly individualistic as suicide – can be explained without reference to individuals.

Like all of Durkheim's work, suicide must be viewed within the context of his concern for social integration. Durkheim wanted to see if suicide rates within a social entity (for example, a group, organization, or society) are related to the degree to which individuals are socially involved (integrated and regulated). Durkheim describes three types of suicide: egoistic, anomic, and altruistic. Egoistic suicide is promoted when individuals do not have sufficient social ties. Since single (never married) adults, for example, are not heavily involved with the family life, they are more likely to commit suicide than are married adults. Altruistic suicide on the other hand, is more likely to occur when social integration is too strong. The ritual suicide of Hindu widows on their husbands funeral pyres is one example. Military personnel, trained to lay down their lives for their country, provide another illustration.

Durkheim's third type of suicide – anomic suicide increases when the social regulation of individuals is disrupted. For example, suicide rates increase during economic depressions. People who suddenly find themselves without a job or without hope of finding one are more prone to kill themselves. Suicides may also increase during period of prosperity. People may loosen their social ties by taking new jobs, moving to new communities, or finding new mates.

Using data from the government population reports of several countries (much of it from the French Government Statistical Office), Durkheim found strong support for his line reasoning. Suicide rates were higher among single than married people, among military personnel than civilians, among divorced than married people, and among people involved in nationwide economic crises.

It is important to realize that Durkheim's primary interest was not in the empirical(observations)indicators he used such as suicide rates among military personnel, married people, and so forth. Rather, Durkheim used the following indicators to support several of his contentions: (1) Social behavior can be explained by social rather than psychological factors; (2) suicide is affected by the degree of integration and regulation within social entities; and (3) Since society can be studied scientifically, sociology is worthy of recognition in the academic world. Durkheim was successful on all three counts.

1993

144. Higher suicide rate during rapid progress in a society is a manifestation of

(a) altruistic suicide. (b) anomic suicide.

(c) egoistic suicide. (d) None of the above.

145. In his study of suicide Durkheim's main purpose was

(a) to document that suicide can be explained without reference to the individual.

(b) to provide an explanation of the variation in the rate of suicide across societies.

(c) to categorize various types of suicides.

(d) to document that social behavior can be explained by social rather than psychological factors.

146. Increase in the suicide rate during economic depression is an example of

(a) altruistic suicide. (b) anomic suicide.

(c) egoistic suicide. (d) Both a and c.

147. Single adults not heavily involved with family life are more likely to commit suicide. Durkheim categorized this as

(a) anomic suicide.

(b) altruistic suicide.

(c) egoistic suicide.

(d) Both (b) and (c)

148. According to Durkheim, suicide rates within a social entity can be explained in terms of

(a) absence of social ties.

(b) disruption of social regulation.

(c) nature of social integration.

(d) All of the above.

149. According to Durkheim, altruistic suicide is more likely among

(a) military personnel than among civilians.

(b) single people than among married people.

(c) divorcees than among married people.

(d) people involved in nationwide economic crises.

150. Basing himself on his own indicators. Durkheim was

(a) right on some counts, not others.

(b) vindicated on all counts.

(c) wrong but did not realize that he was right.

(d) substantially correct but formally wrong.

151. To support his contentions, Durkheim relied on the following indicators

(a) social behaviour is explicable predominantly through social factors.

(b) suicide is contingent upon the degree of regulation and interaction.

(c) recognizing sociology is to acknowledge that society is susceptible to scientific investigation.

(d) All of the above.

152. Ritual suicide of Hindu widows on their husband's funeral pyres is

(a) a manifestation of strong social integration.

(b) an example of brutality against women.

(c) an example of anomic suicide.

(d) an example of egoistic suicide.

Passage – 20

How quickly things change in the technology business! A decade ago, IBM was the awesome and undisputed king of the computer trade, universally feared and respected. A decade ago, two little companies called Intel and Microsoft were mere blips on the radar screen of the industry, upstart start-ups that had signed on to make the chips and software for IBM's new line of personal computers. Though their products soon became industry standards, the two companies remained protected children of the market leader.

What happened since is a startling reversal of fortune. IBM is being ravaged by the worst crisis in the company's 79 year history. It is undergoing its fifth restructuring in the past seven years as well as seemingly endless rounds of job cuts and firings that have eliminated 100,000 jobs since 1985. Last week IBM announced to its shell-shocked investors that it lost $4.97 billion last year – the biggest loss in American corporate history.

And just when IBM is losing ground in one market after another, Intel and Microsoft have emerged as the computer industry's most fearsome pair of competitors. The numbers on Wall Street tell a stunning story. Ten years ago, the market value of the stock of Intel and Microsoft combined amounted to about a tenth of IBM's. Last week, with IBM's stock at an 11-year low Microsoft's value surpassed its old mentor's for the first time ever ($26.76 billion to $26.48 billion) and Intel ($24.3 billion) is not far behind. While IBM is posting losses, Intel's profits jumped 30% and Microsoft's rose 44%.

Both Intel, the world's largest supplier of computer chips, and Microsoft, the world's largest supplier of computer software, have assumed the role long played by Big Blue as the industry's pacesetter. What is taking place is a generational shift unprecedented in the information age – one recalls a transition in the US auto industry 70 years ago, when Alfred Sloan's upstart General Motors surpassed Ford Motor as America's No. 1 car maker. The transition also reflects the decline of computer manufacturers such as IBM. Wang and Unisys and the rise of companies like Microsoft, Intel and AT&T that create the chips and software to make the computers work. "Just like Dr. Frankenstein, IBM created these two monster competitors, "says Richard Shaffer publisher of the Computer Letter "Now even IBM is in danger of being trampled by the creations it unleashed."

Although Intel and Microsoft still have close relationships with Big Blue, there is little love lost between IBM and its potent progeny. IBM had an ugly falling-out with former partner Microsoft over the future of personal-computer software. Microsoft developed the now famous disk operating system for IBM-PC – called DOS – and later created the operating software for the next generation of IBM personal computers, the Personal System/2. When PS/2 and is operating system, OS/2, failed to catch on, a feud erupted over how the two companies would upgrade the system. Although they publicly patched things up, the partnership was tattered. IBM developed its own version of OS/2, which has so far failed to capture the industry's imagination. Microsoft's competing version, dubbed New Technology, or NT, will debut in a few months and will incorporate Microsoft's highly successful Windows program, which lets users juggle several programs at once. Windows NT, however, will offer more new features, such as the ability to link many computers together in a network and to safeguard them against unauthorized use.

IBM and Intel have also been parting company. After relying almost exclusively on the Santa Clara, California company for the silicon chips that serve as computer brains, IBM has moved to reduce its dependence on Intel by turning to competing vendors. In Europe, IBM last year began selling a low-cost line of PC's called Ambra, which runs on chips made by Intel rival Advanced Micro Devices. IBM also demonstrated a sample PC using a chip made by another Intel enemy, Cyrix. And that October IBM said it would begin selling the company's own chips to outsiders in direct competition with Intel.

IBM clearly fells threatened. And the wounded giant still poses the biggest threat to any further dominance by Intel and Microsoft. Last year, it teamed up with both companies most bitter rivals – Apple Computers and Motorola – to develop advanced software and microprocessors for a new generation of desktop computers. In selecting Apple and Motorola, IBM bypassed its longtime partners. Just as Microsoft's standard operating system runs only on computers built around Intel's computer chips, Apple's software runs only on Motorola's chips. Although IBM has pledged that the new system will eventually run on a variety of machines, it will initially run only computer programs written for Apple's Macintosh or IBM's OS/2. Its competitive juice now flowing, IBM last week announced that it and Apple Computer will deliver the operating system in 1994 – a year ahead of schedule.

153. As a result of greater competition in the US Computer industry

(a) some computer companies are expanding while others are contracting.

(b) employment in the industry is going down.

(c) the industry is becoming more monopolized.

(d) the share value of IBM is going up relative to that of Intel and Microsoft.

154. Which of the following statements is <u>not</u> implied by the passage?

(a) The market of microchips and software's are becoming leaders in the computer industry.

(b) Wang and Unisys are primarily manufacturers of computers.

(c) IBM laying off workers in the biggest job cut in American corporate history.

(d) Intel is based in California.

155. The personal computer called Ambra is marketed by:

(a) Cyrix.

(b) IBM.

(c) Intel.

(d) Microsoft.

156. Why is something that happened 70 years ago in the US auto industry being mentioned here?

(a) General Motors broke away from Ford Motors.

(b) A new company went ahead of an established market leader.

(c) Like Dr. Frankenstein, Ford Motor created a monster in General Motors.

(d) Microsoft, Intel and AT & T were originally created by IBM.

157. Who is mentioned as the principal supplier of silicon chips to IBM?

(a) AT&T. (b) Microsoft.

(c) Cyrix. (d) Intel.

158. One possible conclusion from the passage is that

(a) share prices are not a good indicator of a company's performance.

(b) firing workers restores a company's health.

(c) all companies ultimately regret being a Dr. Frankenstein to some other company.

(d) consumers gain as a result of competition among producers.

159. Which of the following statements is true?

(a) IBM plans to introduce a new system that will run on a variety of machines.

(b) IBM's new generation desk top computers will run only on Motorola's chips.

(c) IBM is working out a joint strategy with Apple to force Motorola to supply chips at a lower price.

(d) IBM is going to sell its own chips to Apple and Motorola.

160. Many computers will be linked together through a network in a system developed by

(a) IBM. (b) Apple.

(c) Microsoft. (d) None of the above.

161. What was the original reason for the feud between IBM and Microsoft?

(a) The two companies developed competing software's.

(b) Microsoft and Intel teamed up against IBM.

(c) IBM began to purchase microchips from Intel instead of Microsoft.

(d) IBM made loses while Microsoft made profits.

Passage – 21

Environmental protection and management is deservedly attracting a lot of attention these days. This is a desirable development in the face of the alarming rate of natural resource degradation which greatly hampers their optimal utilization. When waste waters emanating from municipal sewage, industrial effluent, agriculture and land runoffs, find their way either to ground water reservoirs or other surface water sources, the quality of water deteriorates, rendering it unfit for use. The natural balance is distributed when concentrated discharges of waste water is not controlled. This is because the cleansing forces of nature cannot do their job in proportion to the production of filthy matter.

According to the National Environment Engineering and Research Institute (NEERI), a staggering 70 percent of water available in the country is polluted. According to the Planning Commission "From the Dal lake in the North to the Chaliyar river in the South From Damodar and Hoogly in the East to the Thane Creek in the West, the picture of water pollution is uniformly gloomy. Even our large perennial rivers, like the Ganga, are today are heavily polluted".

According to one study, all the 14 major rivers of India are highly polluted. Beside the Ganga, these rivers include the Yamuna, Narmada, Godaveri, Krishna and Cauvery. These rivers carry 85 percent of the surface runoff and their drainage basins cover 73 percent of the country. The pollution of the much revered Ganga is due in particular to municipal sewage that accounts for ¾th of its pollution load. Despite India having legislation on water pollution [The Water (Prevention and Control of Pollution) Act, 1974] and various water pollution control boards, rivers have today become synonymous with drains and sewers.

Untreated community wastes discharged into water courses from human settlements account for four times as much waste water as industrial effluent. Out of India's 3,119 towns and cities, only 217 have partial (209) or full (8) sewerage treatment facilities and cover less than a third of the urban population. Statistics from a report of the Central Board for Prevention and Control of Water Pollution. Statistics from a report of the Central Board for Prevention and Control of Water Pollution reveal that 1,700 of 2,700 water using industries in India are polluting the water around their factories. Only 160 industries have waste water treatment plants. One estimate suggests that the volume of waste water of industrial origin will be comparable to that of domestic sewerage in India by 2000 AD. Discharges from agricultural fields, which carry fertilizing ingredients of nitrogen, phosphorous and pesticides are expected to be three times as much as domestic sewage. By that date, thermal pollution generated by discharges from thermal power plants will be the largest in volume.

Toxic effluents deplete the levels of oxygen in the rivers, endanger all aquatic life and render water absolutely unfit for human consumption, apart from affecting industrial production. Sometimes these effects have been disastrous. A recent study reveals that the water of the Ganga, Yamuna, Kali and Hindon rivers have considerable concentrations of heavy metals due to inflow of industrial wastes, which pose a serious health hazard to the millions living on their banks. Similarly, the Cauvery and Kapila rivers in Karnataka have been found to contain metal pollutants, which threaten the health of people in riverine towns. The Periyar, the largest river of Kerala, receives extremely toxic effluent that result in high incidence of skin problems and fish kills. The Godavari of Andhera Pradesh and the Damodar and Hoogly in West Bengal receive untreated industrial toxic wastes. A high level of pollution has been found in the Yamuna, while the Chambal of Rajasthan is considered the most polluted river in Rajasthan. Even in industrially backward Orissa, the Rushikula river is extremely polluted. The fate of the Krishna in Andhra Pradesh, the Tungabhadra in Karnataka, the Chaliyar in Kerala, the Gomti in U.P., the Narmada in M.P. and the Sone and the Subarnarekha rivers in Bihar is no different.

According to the W.H.O.- eighty percent of diseases prevalent in India are water-borne; many of them assume epidemic proportions. The prevalence of these diseases heighten under conditions of drought. It is also estimated that India loses as many as 73 million man-days every year due to water prone diseases, costing Rs.600 crore by way of treatment expenditure and production losses. Management of water resources with respect to their quality also assumes greater importance especially when the country can no more afford to waste water.

The recent Clean-the Ganga Project with an action plan estimated to cost the exchequer Rs.250 crore (which has been accorded top priority) is a trend setter in achieving this goal. The action plan evoked such great interest that offers of assistance have been received from France, UK, US and the Netherlands as also the World Bank. This is indeed laudable. Poland too has now joined this list. The very fact that these countries have volunteered themselves to contribute their mite is a healthy reflection of global concern over growing environmental degradation and the readiness of the international community to participate in what is a truly formidable task. It may be recalled that the task of cleansing the Ganga along the Rishikesh – Hardwar stretch under the first phase of the Ganga Action Plan has been completed and the results are reported to be encouraging.

The reasons for the crisis of drinking water resources are drying up and the lowering of ground water through overpumping; this is compounded by the pollution of water sources. All these factors increase the magnitude of the problem. An assessment of the progress achieved by the end of March 1985, on completion of the first phase of the International Drinking Water Supply and Sanitation Decade (1981 – '91) reveals that drinking water has been available to 73 percent of the urban population and 56 percent of the rural population only. This means that nearly half the country's rural population has to get drinking water facilities. This needs to be urgently geared up especially when considered against the Government's professed objective of providing safe drinking water and sanitation to all by the end of the International Drinking Water Supply and Sanitation Decade i.e. March 1991. The foremost action in this would be to clean up our water resources.

As per surveys conducted by the NEERI, per capita drinking water losses in different cities in the country range between 11,000 to 31,000 litres annually. This indicates a waste level of 20 to 35 percent of the total flow of water in the distribution system primarily due to leaks in main and household service pipes. Preventive maintenance programme would substantially reduce losses, wastages and would certainly go a long way in solving the problem.

According to the Union Ministry of Works and Housing, of the 2.31 lakhs problem villages most have been provided with at least one source of drinking water as of March, 1986. The balance (38,748) villages are expected to be covered during the seventh plan. A time bound national policy on drinking water is being formulated by Government, wherein the task is proposed to be completed by the end of the seventh plan. An outlay of Rs.6,522.47 crores has been allotted for the water supply and sanitation sector in the seventh plan period against an outlay of Rs.3,922.02 crores in the sixth plan. Of this, outlay for rural water supply sector is Rs.3,454.47 crores. It is expected that this outlay would help to cover about 86.4 percent of the urban and 82.2 percent of the rural population with safe drinking water facilities by March 1991. Hygienic sanitation facilities would be provided to 44.7 percent and 1.8 percent of the urban and rural population respectively within the same period.

162. According to NEERI

(a) the extent of water pollution in the Dal Lake is grim.

(b) 70 percent of the total water available in the country is polluted.

(c) only 217 out of 3119 towns and cities have sewage treatment facilities.

(d) all the 14 major rivers of India are highly polluted.

163. The degradation of natural resources will necessarily lead to

(a) poor economic utilization of resources.

(b) contamination of water from municipal sewage.

(c) water unfit for human consumption.

(d) none of the above.

164. Which of the following statements has/ have been made by the W.H.O?

(a) Water-borne diseases account for 80 percent of all diseases prevalent in India.

(b) Water-borne diseases in India create a loss of Rs.600 crores every year.

(c) Both (a) and (b).

(d) None of the above.

165. Which of the following statements is correct?

(a) The river Periyar is in the South India.

(b) The river Periyar is the largest river of Kerala.

(c) The river Gomti is also extremely polluted.

(d) All of the above are correct.

166. Municipal sewage pollutants account for

(a) the lowest percentage of water pollution

(b) 75 percent of the Ganga's water pollution load.

(c) twice the volume of the waste water of industrial origin.

(d) three times as much as the discharge from agricultural fields.

167. The crisis of drinking water is caused chiefly by

(a) the green house effect.

(b) water pollution caused by industrial development.

(c) drying up of water sources and over pumping.

(d) increasing urbanization.

168. The cost of the 'Clean-the –Ganga Pollution' Project Action Plan is likely to be sourced from

(a) the Indian exchequer.

(b) France, UK, US and the Netherlands.

(c) the World Bank, Poland, UK.

(d) the US, UK, Netherlands, Poland, France, the World Bank and India.

169. Considerable amounts of metal pollutants are found in the river(s)

(a) Chambal of Rajasthan.

(b) Rushikula in Orissa.

(c) Damodar, Hoogly, Krishna and Gomti.

(d) Ganga, Yamuna, Kali, Hindon, Cauvery and Kapila.

170. Out of the total outlay for water supply and sanitation in the seventh plan, rural water supply sector would receive

(a) about 53 percent.

(b) over 80 percent.

(c) between 65 to 80 percent.

(d) equal to 44.7 percent.

171. The best remedy for shortage lies in

(a) putting up more pumps in rural areas.

(b) cleaning up polluted water.

(c) reducing the waste level of 25-30 percent of the total flow of water.

(d) constructing large sized dams.

Passage – 22

To teach is to create a space in which obedience to truth is practiced. Space may sound a vague, poetic metaphor until we realize that it describes experiences of everyday life. We know what it means to be in a green and open field; we know what it means to be on a crowded rush hour bus. These experiences of physical space have parallels in our relations with others. On our jobs we know what it is to be pressed and crowded, our working space diminished by the urgency of deadlines and competitiveness of colleagues. But then there are times when deadlines disappear and colleagues cooperate, when everyone has a space to move, invent and produce with energy and enthusiasm. With family and friends, we know how it feels to have unreasonable demands placed upon us, to be boxed in by the expectations of those nearest to us. But then there are times when we feel accepted for who we are (or forgiven for who we are not), times when a spouse or a child or a friend gives us the space, both to be and to become.

Similar experiences of crowding and space are found in education. To sit in a class where the teacher stuffs our minds with information, organizes it with finality, insists on having the answers while being utterly uninterested in our views, and focus us into a grim competition for grades – to sit in such a class is to experience a lack of space for learning. But to study with a teacher, who not only speaks but also listens, who not only answers but asks questions and welcomes our insights, who provides information and theories that do not close doors but open new ones, who encourages students to help each other learn – to study with such a teacher is to know the power of a learning space.

A learning space has three essential dimensions: openness, boundaries and an air of hospitality. To create open learning space is to remove the impediments to learning that we find around and within us; we often create them ourselves to evade the challenge of truth and transformation. One source of such impediments is our fear of appearing ignorant to others or to ourselves. The oneness of a space is created by the firmness of its boundaries. A learning space cannot extend indefinitely; if it did, it would not be a structure for learning but an invitation for confusion and chaos. When space boundaries are violated, the quality of space suffers. The teacher who wants to create an open learning space must define and defend its boundaries with care. Because the pursuit of truth can be painful and discomforting, the learning space must be hospitable. Hospitable means receiving each other, our struggles, our new-born ideas with openness and care. It means creating an ethos in which the community of truth can form and the pain of its transformation be borne. A learning space needs to be hospitable not to make learning painless, but to make painful things possible, things without which no learning can occur, things like exposing ignorance, testing tentative hypotheses, challenging false or partial information, and mutual criticism of thought.

The task of creating learning space with qualities of openness, boundaries and hospitality can be approached at several levels. The most basic level is the physical arrangement of the classroom, Consider the traditional classroom setting with row of chairs facing the lectern where learning space is confined to the narrow alley of attention between each student and teacher. In this space, there is no community of truth, hospitality of room for students to relate to the thoughts of each other. Contrast it with the chairs placed in a circular arrangement creating an open space within which learners can interconnect. At another level, the teacher can create conceptual space-space with words in two ways. One is through assigned reading; the other is through lecturing, assigned reading, not in the form of speed reading several hundred pages but contemplative reading which opens, not fills, our learning space. A teacher can also create a learning space by means of lectures. By providing critical information and a framework of interpretation, a lecturer can lay down boundaries within which learning occurs.

We also create learning space through the kind of speech we utter and the silence from which true speech emanates. Speech is a precious gift and a vital tool, but too often our speaking is an evasion of truth, a way of buttressing our self-serving reconstructions of reality. Silence must therefore be an integral part of learning space. In silence, more than in arguments, our mind made world falls away and we are open to the truth that seeks us. Words often divide us, but silence can unite. Finally teachers must also create emotional space in the class-room, space that allows feelings to arise and be dealt with because submerged feelings can undermine learning. In an emotionally honest learning space, one created by a teacher who does not fear dealing with feelings, the community of truth can flourish between us and we can flourish in it.

172. The task of creating learning space with qualities of openness, boundaries and hospitality is multidimensional. It involves operating at

(a) psychological and conceptual levels.

(b) physical, perceptual and behavioral levels.

(c) physical, conceptual and emotional levels.

(d) conceptual, verbal and sensitive levels.

173. The statement 'the openness of a space is created by the firmness of its boundaries' appears contradictory. Which of the following statements provides the best justification for the proposition?

(a) We cannot have a space without boundaries.

(b) Bounded space is highly structured.

(c) When space boundaries are violated, the quality of space suffers.

(d) A teacher can effectively defend a learning space without boundaries.

174. According to the author, learning is a painful process because

(a) it exposes our ignorance.

(b) our views and hypotheses are challenged.

(c) it involves criticizing the views of other.

(d) All of the above reasons.

175. Understanding the notion of space in our relations with other is

(a) to acknowledge the beauty of a poetic metaphor.

(b) exclusively rooted in our experiences of physical space.

(c) to accept a spiritual dimension in our dealings with our peers.

(d) to extend the parallel of physical space to our experiences in daily life.

176. Which of the following statements best describes the author's conception of learning space?

(a) Where the teacher is friendly.

(b) Where there is no grim competition for grades.

(c) Where the students are encouraged to learn about space.

(d) Where the teacher provides information and theories which open new doors and encourages students to help each other learn.

177. According to the author, silence must be an integral part of learning space because

(a) silence helps to unite us with others to create a community of truth.

(b) silent contemplation prepares us to construct our mind –made world.

(c) speaking is too often an exercise in the evasion of truth.

(d) speaking is too often a way of buttressing our self – serving reconstruction of reality.

178. Another way of describing the author's notion of learning space can be summarized in the following manner

(a) It is vital that learning be accompanied by unlearning.

(b) Learning encompasses such elements as courage, dignity and endeavour.

(c) An effective teacher recognizes the value of empathy.

(d) Encourage good learners, discourage indifferent ones.

179. According to the author, an effective teacher does not allow

(a) feelings to arise within the learning space.

(b) silence to become an integral part of the learning space.

(c) learning space to be filled by speed reading of several hundred pages of assigned reading.

(d) violation of learning space boundaries.

180. An emotionally honest learning space can only be created by

(a) a teacher committed to joining the community of truth.

(b) a teacher who is not afraid of confronting feelings.

(c) a teacher who takes care not to undermine the learning process.

(d) a teacher who worships critical silence.

181. Conceptual space with words can be created by

(a) assigned reading and lecturing.

(b) speed reading and written comprehension.

(c) gentle persuasion and deliberate action.

(d) creative extrapolation and illustrations.

Passage – 23

Management education gained new academic stature within US Universities and greater respect from outside during the 1960's and 1970's. Some observers attribute the competitive superiority of US corporations to the quality of business education. In 1978, a management professor, Herbert A. Simon of Carnegie Mellon University, won the Nobel Prize in economics for his work in decision theory. And the popularity of business education continued to grow, since 1960, the number of master's degrees awarded annually has grown from under 5000 to over 50,000 in the mid 1980's as the MBA has become known as 'the passport to the good life'.

By the 1980's, however, US business schools faced critics who charged that learning had little relevance to real business problems. Some went so far as to blame business schools for the decline in US competitiveness.

Amidst the criticisms, four distinct arguments may be discerned. The first is that business schools must be either unnecessary or deleterious because Japan does so well without them. Underlying this argument is the idea that management ability cannot be taught, one is either born with it or must acquire it over years of practical experience. A second argument is that business schools are overly academic and theoretical. They teach quantitative models that have little application to real world problems. Third, they give inadequate attention to shop floor issues, to production processes and to management resources. Finally, it is argued that the encourage undesirable attitudes in students, such as placing value on the short term and 'bottom line' targets, while neglecting longer term development criteria. In summary, some business executives complain that MBAs are incapable of handing day to day operational decisions, unable to communicate and to motivate people, and unwillingly to accept responsibility for following through on implementation plans. We shall analyze these criticisms after having reviewed experiences in other countries.

In contrast to the expansion and development of business education in the United States and more recently in Europe, Japanese business schools graduate no more than two hundred MBAs each year. The Keio Business School (KBS) was the only graduate school of management in the entire country until the mid 1970's and it still boasts the only two year masters programme. The absence of business schools in Japan would appear in contradiction with the high priority placed upon learning by its Confucian culture. Confucian colleges taught administrative skills as early as 1630 and Japan wholeheartedly accepted Western learning following the Meiji restoration of 1868 when hundreds of students were dispatched to universities in US, Germany, England and France to learn the secrets of western technology and modernization. Moreover, the Japanese educational system is highly developed and intensely competitive and can be credited for raising the literary and mathematical abilities of the Japanese to the highest level in the world.

Until recently, Japan corporations have not been interested in using either local or foreign business schools for the development of their future executives. Their in-company training programs have sought the socialization of newcomers, the younger the better. The training is highly specific and those who receive it have neither the capacity nor the incentive to quit. The prevailing belief, says Imai, 'is a management should be born out of experience and many years of effort and not learnt from educational institutions.' A 1960 survey of Japanese senior executives confirmed that a majority (54%) believed that managerial capabilities can be attained only on the job and not in universities.

However, this view seems to be changing: the same survey revealed that even as early as 1960. 37% of senior executives felt that the universities should teach integrated professional management. In the 1980's a combination of increased competitive pressures and greater multi-nationalisation of Japanese business are making it difficult for many companies to rely solely upon internally trained managers. This has led to a rapid growth of local business programmes and a greater use of American MBA programmes. In 1982-83, the Japanese comprised the largest single group of foreign students at Wharton, where they not only learnt the latest techniques of financial analysis, but also developed worldwide contacts through their classmates and became Americanized, something highly useful in future negotiations. The Japanese, then do not 'do without' business schools, as is sometimes contended. But the process of selecting and orienting new graduates, even MBAs, into corporations is radically different than in the

US. Rather than being placed in highly paying staff positions, new Japanese recruits are assigned responsibility for operational and even menial tasks. Success is based upon Japan's system of highly competitive recruitment and intensive in-company management development, which in turn are grounded in its tradition of universal and rigorous academic education, life-long employment and strong group identification.

The harmony among these traditional elements has made Japanese industry highly productive and given corporate leadership a long term view. It is true that this has been achieved without much attention to university business education, but extraordinary attention has been devoted to the development of managerial skills, both within the company and through participation in programmes sponsored by the Productivity Center and other similar organizations.

182. The author argues that the Japanese system

(a) is better than the American system.

(b) Is highly productive and gives corporate leadership a long term view as a result of its strong traditions.

(c) is slowly becoming Americanized.

(d) succeeds without business schools, where as the US system fails because of it.

183. The growth of popularity of business schools among students was most probably due to

(a) Herbert A. Simon a management professor winning the Nobel Prize in economics.

(b) the gain in academic stature.

(c) the large number of MBA degree awarded.

(d) a perception that it was a 'passport to good life.'

184. According to the passage

(a) learning, which was useful in the 1960's and 1970's became irrelevant in the 1980's.

(b) management education faced criticisms in the 1980's

(c) business schools are insensitive to the needs of industry.

(d) by the 1980's business schools contributed to the decline in US competitiveness.

185. A criticism that management education did not face was that

(a) it imparted poor quantitative skills to MBAs.

(b) it was unnecessarily and deleterious.

(c) it was irrevocably irrelevant.

(d) it inculcated undesirable attitudes in students.

186. The absence of business schools in Japan

(a) is due to the prevalent belief that management ability can only be acquired over years of practical experience.

(b) was due to the high priority placed on learning as opposed to doing in Confucian culture.

(c) is hard to explain for the proponents of business education.

(d) contributed a great deal to their success in international trade and business.

187. The 1960's and 1970's can best be described as a period

(a) when quality business education contribute to the superiority of US corporations.

(b) when the number of MBAs rose from under 5,000 to over 50,000.

(c) when management education gained new academic stature and greater respect.

(d) when the MBA became more disreputable.

188. US business schools faced criticism in the 1980's because

(a) of the decline in Japanese competitiveness.

(b) many critics felt the learning had little relevance to business problems.

(c) people realized that management ability cannot be taught.

(d) MBAs were unwilling to accept responsibility for implementation on the shop floor.

189. Training programmes in Japanese corporations have

(a) been based upon Confucian culture.

(b) sought the socialization of newcomers.

(c) been targeted at people who have neither the capacity nor the incentive to quit.

(d) been teaching people to do menial tasks.

190. The Japanese modified their views on management education because of

(a) greater exposure to US MBA programmes.

(b) the need to develop worldwide contacts and become Americanized.

(c) the outstanding success of business schools in the US during the 1960's and 1970's.

(d) a combination of increased competitive pressures and greater multi-nationalisation of Japanese business.

191. The Japanese were initially able to do without business schools as a result of

(a) their highly developed and intensively competitive education system.

(b) dispatching hundreds of Western technology and modernization.

(c) their highly specific in-company training programmes.

(d) prevailing beliefs regarding educational institutions.

192. The main difference between US and Japanese corporations is

(a) that one employs MBAs, the other does not.

(b) that US corporations do not employ Japanese people.

(c) that US corporations pay more to fresh recruits.

(d) in the process of selecting and orienting new recruits.

193. The author argues that

(a) Japanese do not do without business schools as is generally perceived.

(b) Japanese corporations do not hire MBAs because of traditions of universal and rigorous academic education, life long employment and strong group identification.

(c) placing MBAs in operational and menial tasks is a major factor in Japanese business success.

(d) US corporations should emulate the Japanese and change the way new recruits are induced.

Passage – 24

The communities of ants are sometimes very large, numbering even up to 500, individuals: and it is a lesson to us that no one has ever yet seen quarrel between any two ants belonging to the same community. On the other hand, it must be admitted that they are in hostility not only with most other insects, including ants of different species, but even with those of the same species if belonging to different communities. I have over and over again introduced ants from one of my nests into another nest of the same species; and they were invariably attacked, seized by a leg or an antenna, and dragged out. It is evident, therefore, that the ants of each community all recognize one another, which is very remarkable. But more than this, I several times divided a nest into two halves and found that even after separation of a year and nine months they recognize one another and were perfectly friendly, while they at once attacked ants from a different nest, although of the same species.

It has been suggested that the ant of each nest have some sign or password by which they recognize one another. To test this I made some of them insensible, first I tried chloroform; but this was fatal to them, and I did not consider the test satisfactory. I decided therefore to intoxicate them. This was less easy than I had expected. None of my ants would voluntarily degrade themselves by getting drunk. However, I got over the difficulty by putting them into whisky for a few moments. I took fifty specimens - - twenty five percent from one nest and twenty five percent from another made them dead drunk, market each with a spot of paint, and put them on a table close to where other ants from one the nests were feeding. The table was surrounded as usual with a moat of water to prevent them from straying. The ants, which were feeding, soon noticed those, which I had made drunk. They seemed quite astonished to find their comrades in such a disgraceful condition, and as much at a loss to know what to do with their drunkards as we were. After a while, however, they carried them all away; the strangers they took to the edge of the moat and dropped into the water, while they bore their friends home into the nest, where by degrees they slept off the effects of the spirits. Thus it is evident that they know their friends even when incapable of giving any sign or password.

1994

194. An appropriate title for this passage might be

(a) Nature's Mysteries

(b) Human Qualities in the Insect world

(c) Drunken Ants

(d) Communication in Ant Communities

195. Attitudes of ants towards strangers of the same species may be categorized as

(a) indifferent (b) curious

(c) hostile (d) passive

196. The author's anecdotes of the inebriated ants would support all the following inductions except the statement that

(a) ants take unwillingly to intoxicants

(b) ants aid comrades in distress

(c) ants have invariable recognition of their community members

(d) ants recognize their comrades by a mysterious password.

197. According to the passage, chloroform was less successful than alcohol for inhibiting communication because of

(a) its expense

(b) its unpredictable side effects

(c) its unavailability

(d) its fatality

198. Although the author is a scientist, his style of writing also exhibits a quality of

(a) sophistry (b) whimsy

(c) hypocrisy (d) tragedy

Passage – 25

Compared with other experimental sciences, astronomy has certain limitations. First, apart from meteorites, the Moon, and the nearer planets, the objects of study are inaccessible and cannot be manipulated, although nature sometimes provides special conditions, such as eclipses and other temporary effects. The astronomer must content himself with studying radiation emitted or reflected from celestial bodies.

Second, from the Earth's surface these are viewed through a thick atmosphere that completely absorbs most radiation except within certain "windows", wavelength regions in which the radiation can pass through the atmosphere relatively freely in the optical, near-infrared, and radio bands of the electromagnetic spectrum; and even in these windows the atmosphere has considerable effects. For light, these atmospheric effects are as follows: (1) some absorption that dims the radiation somewhat, even in a clear sky; (2) refraction, which causes slight shift in the direction so that the object appears in a slightly different place; (3) scintillation (twinkling); i.e., fluctuations in brightness of effectively point – like sources such as stars, fluctuations that are, however, averaged out for objects with larger images, such as planets (the ionosphere, an ionized layer high in the atmosphere, and interplanetary medium have similar effects on radio sources); (4) image movement because of atmospheric turbulence ("bad seeing") spreads the image of a tiny point over an angle of nearly one arc second or more on the celestial sphere (one arc second equals 1/3, 600 degrees); and (5) background light from the night sky. The obscuring effects of the atmosphere and its clouds are reduced by placing observing stations on mountains, preferably in desert regions (e.g., southern California and Chile), and away from city lights. The effects are eliminated by observing from high-altitude aircraft, balloons, rockets, space probes, and artificial satellites. From stations all or most of the atmosphere, gamma rays and X-rays-that is, high-energy radiation at extremely short wave-lengths and far-ultraviolet rays and far-infrared radiation, all completely absorbed by the atmosphere at ground level observatories can be measured, At radio wave-lengths between about one centimeter and 20 meters, the atmosphere (even when cloudy) has little effect, and man-made radio signals are the chief interference.

Third, the Earth is a spinning, shifting, and wobbling platform. Spin on its axis causes alternation of day and night and an apparent rotation of the celestial sphere with stars moving from east to west. Ground – based telescopes use a mounting that makes it possible to neutralize the rotation of Earth relative to the stars; with an equatorial mounting driven at a proper speed, the direction of the telescope tube can be kept constant for hours while the Earth turns under the mounting. Large radio telescopes usually have vertical and horizontal axes (altazimuth mounting), with their pointing continuously controlled by a computer.

In addition to the daily spin, there are much more gradual effects, called precession and nutation. Gravitational action of the Sun and Moon on the Earth's equatorial bulge causes the Earth's axis to process like a top or gyroscope, gradually tracing out a circle on the celestial sphere in about 26,000 years, and also to nutate or wobble slightly in a period of 18.6 years. The Earth's rotation and orbital motion provide the basic standard of directions of stars, so that uncertainties in the rate of these motions can lead to quite small but important uncertainties in measurements of stellar movements.

199. One of the type of radiations that cannot pass through the atmospheric 'windows' without distortion is

(a) near infra-red spectrum.

(b) far-ultraviolet spectrum.

(c) optical band in the spectrum.

(d) radio band in the spectrum.

200. One of the atmospheric effects earth – based experiments that is not mentioned in the passage is

(a) twinkling.

(b) refraction.

(c) image movement.

(b) clouds from volcano eruptions.

201. The purpose of telescope mounting is to neutralize

(a) atmospheric interference.

(b) the effect of precession.

(c) the effect of nutation.

(d) the effect of diurnal spinning.

202. The precession period of Earth is

(a) 24 hours (b) 365.25 days

(c) 18.6 years (d) 26,000 years

203. Gravitational action of the Sun and the Moon on Earth causes

I. diurnal spinning

II. Precession

III. Nutation

(a) I only (b) I and II only

(c) II and III only (d) I, II and III

204. The orbital motion of the Earth

(a) is partly caused by the moon.

(b) can have uncertain rates.

(c) has a periodicity of 18.6 years.

(d) is neutralized by telescope mounting.

205. The man-made radio signals have wave-lengths of

(a) more than 20 meters.

(b) less than one centimeter.

(c) between one centimeter and 20 meters.

(d) gamma rays.

Passage – 26

If American policy towards Europe in the postwar years had been a conspicuous success, and towards Asia a disappointing balance between success and failure, it could be said that the most conspicuous thing about relations with Latin America was the absence of any policy. Franklin Roosevelt, to be sure, had launched a "Good Neighbour" policy, but being a good neighbour was, it seemed, a negative rather than a positive affair, a matter of keeping hands off, of making the Monroe Doctrine, in form at least, multilateral. All through the postwar years, the states of Latin America - - Mexico and Chile were partial exceptions - - were in the throes of major economic and social crises. Population was growing faster than in any other part of the globe, without a comparable increase in wealth or productivity; the gap between the poor and the rich was widening; and as the rich and powerful turned to the military for the preservation of order and privilege, the poor turned to revolution.

Deeply involved in other quarters of the globe, the United States paid little attention to the fortunes or misfortunes of her neighbours to the south, and when she did intervene, it appeared to be on the side of order and the status quo rather than on the side of reform. So frightened was the United States of "Communism" in Latin America that it preferred military dictatorship to reformers who might drift too far to the "left", and sustained a Batista in Cuba, a Trujillo in the Dominican Republic, a Peron in Argentina, and a Jimenez in Venezuela.

In his last two years, President Eisenhower had tried to mend his Latin American fences. Though rejecting a Brazilian proposal of a Marshall Plan for Latin America, he did take the initiative in setting up an Inter-American development Bank with a capital of one billion dollars, almost half of it supplied by the United States. Other government investments in Latin America ran to some four million dollars, while private investments exceeded nine billion. Yet though to most Americans, all this seemed a form of economic aid, many Latin Americans regarded it as economic imperialism. In September 1960, came a co-operative plan that could not be regarded as other than enlightened: the Act of Bogota, which authorized a grant of half a billion dollars to subsidize not only economic but social and educational progress in Latin America. "We are not saints", said President Eisenhower when he visited Santiago de Chile, "We know we make mistakes, but our heart is in the right place".

But was it? President Kennedy was confronted by the same dilemma that had perplexed his predecessors. Clearly it was essential to provide a large-scale aid to the countries south of Rio Grande, but should this aid go to bolster up established regimes and thus help maintain status quo, or should it be used to speed up social reforms, even at the risk of revolt? As early as 1958, the then Senator Kennedy had asserted that "the objective of our aid program in Latin America should not be to purchase allies, but to consolidate a free and democratic Western Hemisphere, alleviating those conditions which might foster opportunities for communistic infiltration and uniting our peoples on the basis of constantly increasing living standards".

This conviction that raising the standards of living was the best method of checking Communism now inspired President Kennedy's bold proposal for the creation of the alliance for progress - - a ten year plan designed to do for Latin America what Marshall Plan had done for Western Europe. It was to be "a peaceful revolution on a hemispheric scale, a vast co-operative effort, unparalleled in magnitude and nobility of purpose, to satisfy the basic needs of the American people for homes, work, land, health and schools. "To achieve this, the United States pleaded an initial grant of one billion dollars, with the promise of additional billions for the future.

206. Following World War II, which problem was the United States most concerned with regarding Latin America?

(a) Economic stability. (b) Political ideology.

(c) Religious persecution. (d) Military dictatorship.

207. A key reason why Latin Americans rejected the Inter-American development Bank was that

(a) it primarily provided money for social reform subsidies.

(b) the moneys provided were only for specific performance projects.

(c) it constituted an extension of the Marshall Plan into Latin America

(d) it was being used as a means to control the economic destiny of Latin America.

208. Which of the following is most closely associated with the concept of a Marshall Plan for Latin America?

(a) The Good Neighbour Policy.

(b) The Alliance for Progress.

(c) The Act of Bogota.

(d) The Monroe Doctrine.

209. According to the passage, the fundamental change in U.S. foreign policy directed towards Latin America

(a) resulted in a deterioration of U.S. Latin American relations.

(b) was responsible for Peron remaining as a dictator in Peru.

(c) recognized that economic aid alone would prevent social revolutions.

(d) provided for increased military and economic aid to prevent the spread of communism in Latin America.

210. Which of the following statements is not true?

(a) Mexico and Chile did not experience the general social crises that are common to the majority of Latin American countries.

(b) President Eisenhower continued in practice the theory that economic aid was the best defense against communist incursion into Latin America

(c) The Good Neighbour Policy favoured a multilateral interpretation of the Monroe Doctrine.

(d) The traditional U.S. approach in Latin America was to protect the status quo.

211. Which of the inferences can be drawn if everything said in the passage were assumed to be true?

(a) Rebellions are fuelled by social reforms and avoided by supporting established authorities or continuing the present state of affairs.

(b) The American policy towards Asia can be called an overall success, though small in magnitude.

(c) Kennedy, in 1958, wanted America to aid South American countries to acquire more support in their fight against communism.

(d) Eisenhower rejected the Marshall Plan, whereas Kennedy implemented a similar one.

Passage – 27

In order to better understand conservation in China, it is essential that one has a grasp of what the term "Chinese conservatism" means. Chinese conservatism is markedly different from the conservatism of the modern West. The political term "conservative" came about during the French Revolution and inspired men who were determined to preserve Christian and aristocratic elements in European society. Chinese conservatism began around the time of the Taiping Rebellion and had as its primary objectives the preservation of both Confucian society and non-feudal strains of pre-Opium War Chinese society. While western conservatism believes in sacredness of private property and distrust of cosmopolitanism, the Chinese conservatism is the defense of a rational cosmopolitan order. Thus, the only common area of agreement between European and Chinese conservatism is the intent to conserve.

During the Tung-chin Restoration, the great aim was the revival of Confucian values and institutions. But these aims had to be modified so that they might endure. Restoration statesmen had no desire to create a new society – they wanted to restore a society that they believed had been based on truth. The statesmen of the Restoration stretched the traditional ideology to its limits in an effort to make the Confucian system under new conditions. They were true conservatives in a great tradition, living in an age when revolutionary change was unavoidable. The aim of the Restoration was to restore to their original vitality the best of the ancient institutions. During the Restoration, the two immediate problems were the suppression of rebellion and the stabilization of foreign relations. In addition, the people were striving for a restoration of the system of government by superior civil officials.

The men in the hierarchy of the Restoration rose to prominence through proven ability in both civil and military affairs. They emphasized human and social training – that is, indoctrination, morality, and the art of leadership through the cultivation of character. The great majority of the officials rose through the examination system.

During the chaos of this period, the examination system had lost much of its effectiveness. This is important and must be noted because the examination system was the traditional avenue for selecting officials. The senior official of Restoration realized that their policies would be ineffective unless the quality of the junior official was improved, so it was their duty to weed out the officials who had attained office in irregular ways and to promote the examination system as the only way to high position. But these men of the Restoration had enough foresight to determine that it was impossible to select officials automatically on the basis of objective tests alone. As a result, the system of recommendation was ushered in, whereby; a high official sponsored the career of a promising young man. This acted as an important supplement to the examination system.

212. The traditional method for selecting officials was

(a) approximately by the civil government.

(b) the examination system.

(c) through a subjective testing system.

(d) sponsorship by a high government official.

213. A primary objective in the development of Restoration thought was

(a) to modify traditional Chinese society to reflect new conditions.

(b) to create a new society based on truth.

(c) the knowledge that Chinese conservatism is superior to western conservatism.

(d) the desire to familiarized China with military technology.

214. The major similarity between Chinese and western conservatism is

(a) that Chinese conservatism attempted to preserve traditions.

(b) that Chinese conservatism developed during the Taiping Revolution.

(c) the cosmopolitan nature of western conservatism.

(d) that Chinese conservatism is primarily land oriented.

215. The most significant Chinese philosopher mentioned in the passage is

(a) Tung-chin. (b) I. Ching.

(c) Buddha (d) None of the above.

216. During the Restoration, ancient institutions

(a) were no longer accepted as a viable alternative to western technology.

(b) were studied only as classical examples of a former glorious past.

(c) were to be the cornerstones of a changing but traditional society.

(d) were considered as a primary reason for the decline of traditional China.

217. The western conservatives intended to preserve all the following except

(a) Christianity. (b) private property.

(c) cosmopolitanism. (d) aristocratic elements.

218. The most appropriate title for the passage will be

(a) The Chinese examination system.

(b) Chinese Conservatism

(c) How the officials rose

(d) Impact of the Taiping Rebellion

Passage – 28

Every state has a constitution, since every state functions on the basis of certain rules and principles. It has often been asserted that the United States has a written constitution, but that the constitution of Great Britain is unwritten. This is true only in the sense that, in the United States, there is a formal document called the Constitution, whereas there is no such document in Great Britain. In fact, however, many parts of the British constitution exist in written form, whereas important aspects of the American constitution are wholly unwritten. The British constitution includes the bill of Rights (1689), the Act of Settlement (1700 – 01), the Parliament Act of 1911, the successive Representation of the People Acts (which extended the suffrage), the statutes dealing with the structure of the courts, the various local government acts, and many others. These are not ordinary statutes, even though they are adopted in the ordinary legislative way, and they are not codified within the structure of single orderly document. On the other hand, such institutions in the United States as the presidential cabinet and the system of political parties, though not even mentioned in the written constitution, are most certainly of constitutional significance. The presence or absence of a formal written document makes a difference, of course, but only one of degree. A single-document constitution has such advantages as greater precision, simplicity, and consistency. In a newly developing state as Israel, on the other hand, the balance of advantage has been found to lie with an uncodified constitution evolving through the growth of custom and the medium of statutes. Experience suggests that some codified constitutions are much too detailed. An overlong constitution invites disputes and litigation is rarely read or understood by the ordinary citizen and injects too much rigidity in cases in which flexibility is often preferable. Since a very long constitution says to many things on too many subjects, it must be amended often, and this makes it still longer. The United States Constitution of 7,000 words is a model of brevity, whereas many of that country's state constitutions are much too long - the longest being hat of the sate of Louisiana, whose constitution now has about 255,000 words. The very new, modern constitutions of the recently admitted states of Alaska and Hawaii and the Commonwealth of Puerto Rico have, significantly, very concise constitutions ranging from 9,000 to 15,000 words. The 1949 constitution of India, with 395 articles, is the wordiest of all national constitutions. In contract, some of the world's new constitutions, such as those of Japan and Indonesia, are very short indeed.

Some constitutions are buttressed by powerful institutions such as an independent judiciary, whereas other, though committed to lofty principles, are not supported by governmental institutions endowed with the authority to defend these principles in concrete situation. Accordingly, many juristic writers distinguish between "normative" and "normal" constitutions. A normative constitution is the one that not only has the status of supreme law but it also fully activated and effective; it is habitually obeyed in the actual life of the state. A nominal constitution may express high aspirations, but it does not, in fact, reflect the political realities of the state. Article 125 of the 1936 constitution of the Soviet Union and the article 87 of the 1954 constitution of the People's Republic of China both purport to guarantee freedom of speech, but in those countries even mild expressions of dissent are likely to be swiftly and sternly repressed. Where the written constitution is only nominal, behind the verbal façade will be found the real constitution containing the basic principles according to which power is exercised in actual fact. Thus in the Soviet Union, the rules of the

Communist Party describing its organs and functioning are more truly the constitution of that country than are the grand phases of the 1936 Stalin constitution. Every state, in short has a constitution, but in some, real constitution operates behind the façade of a nominal constitution.

219. The lengthiest constitution in the world is that of
(a) Great Britain.
(b) India
(c) Puerto Rico.
(d) Soviet Union.

220. The instance of a country without a written constitution mentioned in the passage is
(a) People's Republic of China
(b) Japan.
(c) Israel.
(d) Indonesia.

221. The unwritten parts of the US constitution deal with
(a) Courts.
(b) presidential cabinet.
(c) relationship between the Centre and the States.
(d) fundamental rights.

222. In the United States
(a) the newly admitted states have lengthy constitutions.
(b) the newly admitted states have concise constitutions.
(c) the political parties have no constitutional significance.
(d) the constitution can be termed 'normal'.

223. In countries with 'normative' constitutions
(a) there will be very little freedom of speech.
(b) there are effective instruments to enforce their provisions.
(c) political realities are different from what are enshrined in them.
(d) there are frequent amendments to them.

224. By 'normal' constitution, the author means
(a) a written constitution.
(b) one that contains lofty ideals.
(c) a lengthy constitution.
(d) a constitution that is not being enforced.

225. One of the drawbacks of a long constitution is
(a) its publication is expensive.
(b) it is difficult to understand.
(c) it may require to be amended frequently.
(d) it is difficult to enforce.

226. According to the author, the difference between a written and an unwritten constitution
(a) has no significance.
(b) is just one of degree.
(c) has been exaggerated by politicians.
(d) cannot be defined.

Passage – 29

An urgent problem is now threatening libraries throughout the world. Their collections, which are crucial for diverse purposes as economic development, educational research and recreational pursuits, are in danger of disintegrating.

The problem is mainly due to one cause – the type of paper on which books have been printed for the past one and a half centuries. Until the 1850s, paper was produced from linen or cotton rags and proved to be relatively long-lasting. In the mid-19th century, however, the popular demand for paper and the commercial need for an economic method of production led to the use of mechanically ground wood pulp. Paper manufactured for wood pulp is highly acidic and therefore inherently unstable. It contains lignin – a major factor in causing paper to discolour and disintegrate. The useful lifespan of most 20th-century book papers has been estimated to be no more than a few decades.

Libraries comprise an important part of the market for printed books and they are increasingly aware of the fragility of this material. The extent of the deterioration of library collections is alarming. Surveys conducted at various major institutions reveal that 26% to 40% of the books they hold are seriously embrittled and thus unavailable for normal use.

Programmes are now being developed with two main aims in mind – on the one hand, to improve the physical condition of library collections, especially by the process called 'mass de-acidification'(which is designed to eliminate acid from the paper of published books and insert a buffer compound that will provide protection against future acid attack from the environment); and on the other, to transfer the contents of existing books to another medium (such as microfilm or optical disk).

Libraries will only be able to carry out these special tasks with the assistance of other experts such as book conservators and high-technology specialists. But here is another group with whom librarians have traditionally enjoyed strong affinities and whose co-operation will be crucial if the problem of decaying collections is to be arrested – namely, the printing and publishing industries. The existing problem – that of book collections already assembled in libraries – is of vast proportions, but it is intensified by the continuing use of acid-based paper in book publishing. The key issue is how to preserve the books of the future, not simply those of the past.

If the future dimensions of the conservation problem are to be curbed, there will need to be widespread adoption of paper which is of archival quality.

This change does not relate to a narrowly perceived need because the long term preservation of library collections is important – both for the overall social benefits they bring as well as for the special advantages they bestow on the printing and publishing industries.

In the first place, libraries are of critical importance to the future well-being of citizens since they provide the knowledge base of society. They contain the record of humanity – the accumulation of ideas and insights and discoveries on which social effort and progress are possible. The destruction of libraries would represent an immense cultural loss, a form of amnesia which would affect every member of society.

In the second place, printers and publishers have an economic interest in turning to paper of archival quality. So long as the libraries are acquiring books with a short lifespan they will be forced to devote an increasing share of their budgets to conservation. These budgets are severely strained by the combined impact of inflation and currency devaluation, and there is scarcely any prospect of enlarged government funding. As a result, libraries will be compelled to balance the preservation of their collections against the expansion of those collations. In short, the choice will be between conservation and acquisition – and the funds for conservation are likely to come from acquisition budgets. This unpalatable choice will damage both libraries and the printing and publishing industries and can only be minimized in its effects by a bold decision to convert to use of permanent paper.

227. The tone of the passage is one of

(a) informed concern. (b) destructive criticism.

(c) derisive ridicule. (d) helpless alarm.

228. The phrase 'archival quality' implies

(a) a smooth paper. (b) thick paper.

(c) long-lasting paper. (d) alkaline paper.

229. Wood-pulp as raw material for paper was developed because of

(a) the need to produce large quantities of paper.

(b) the shortage of linen.

(c) the need to develop non-acidic paper.

(d) scientific research.

230. If paper has to last long ...

(a) it should be made of cotton rags.

(b) it should be non-acidic.

(c) it should be alkaline.

(d) preservatives must be used.

231. On of the reasons not mentioned in the passage in favour of producing long-lasting paper is

(a) it will help preserve the knowledge-base of society.

(b) it will enable more books to be brought by libraries.

(c) it will lead to more governmental allocation to libraries.

(d) it will help the publishing industry.

232. Purchase of new books by libraries are bound to be curtailed because of all the following reasons except

(a) drastic reduction in governmental funding.

(b) the need for spending more money for conservation of old books.

(c) the need to microfilm books.

(d) inflationary trends.

233. Continued use of wood-pulp paper in book will affect

I. libraries.

II. General public.

III. the publishing industry.

IV. The governments.

(a) I and III only (b) II and III only

(c) I, II, III and IV (d) I, II, and III only

234. The substance which causes paper to discolour is

(a) acid. (b) linen.

(c) lignin. (d) preservatives.

Passage – 30

The Japanese want their Emperor to reign for long, very long, but their Prime Ministers to have very short tenures. During the 61 years Hirohito has been on the Chrysanthemum throne, 38 Prime Ministers have come and gone(or at least 32, if returns to power are left out of account). Eisaku Sato's eight uninterrupted years as Prime Minister in the Sixties and early Seventies provoked fears about the possible ill-effects of one-man leadership on Japanese democracy, and led the dominant Liberal Democratic Party (LDP) to lay down the norm of a two-year for a party chief and head of Government. Mr.Yasuhiro Nakasone, now bowing out, has served for an unusual five years. His success as Prime Minister was evidenced by the ruling party re-electing him leader more than once. But his plan to push through the Diet a Bill to levy a 5% indirect tax as part of financial reforms failed, in spite of the LDP majority in both the chambers. It was time then for him to go.

The quick turnover of Primate Minister has contributed to the functioning of the LDP through factions. In the party that has ruled Japan for 32 years continuously, factionalism is not something unseemly. The leader is chosen by hard bargaining – some foreigners call it horse-trading– among the faction leaders, followed, if necessary, by a party election. For the decision in favour of Noboru Takeshita as the next President of the LDP and Primate Minister of Japan, voting was not necessary. His hopes were stronger than those of he other two candidates – Finance Minister Kiichi Miyazawa and former Foreign Minister, Shintaro Abe – if only because he had proved himself more skillful in the game of factional politics. A one-time protégé of Mr. Kakuei Tanaka, he thrust himself forward when the leader was disgraced on a charge of accepting bribes for sale of Lockheed aircraft to Japan and debilitated by physical ailments. Mr. Takeshita took away most of Mr. Tanaka's following and now leads the biggest faction in the LDP. Mr. Nakasone persuaded Mr. Miyazawa and Mr. Abe to accept Mr. Takeshita's leadership. An election would most probably have led to the same result. Mr. Takeshita seemed to have forged a firm alliance with at least two other factions and put in his bag the votes necessary for a win.

How Mr. Takeshita will fare after taking over the reins of Government in 1987 is not so certain. He will be Japan's first Prime Minister with a humble rural origin. A dichotomy in his nature shows through his record of teaching English in a junior high school and not trying to speak that language in public later. When he was the Minister of Finance, he gave the impression of an extremely cautious man with a reverence for consensus but challengingly titled a book on his ideas 'Going My Way'. Mr. Takeshita says that continuing Mr. Nakasone's programmes would be the basis of his policy. This is not saying enough. Japan faces two main issues, tax reforms and relations with United States. Mr. Nakasone's plan to impose an indirect tax ran into effective opposition, and the friction with the U.S. over trade continues. Mr. Takeshita cannot be facing an easy future as Japan's next leader and there is nothing to show yet that he will be drawing on secret reserves of dynamism.

235. The politician who had been Prime Minister for the longest period since the Second World War was

(a) Hirohito (b) Kakuei Tanaka

(c) Nakasone (d) Eisaku Sato

236. When did Hirohito ascend the throne?

(a) 1946

(b) 1926

(c) In the early fifties

(d) 1936

237. Mr. Tanaka ceased to be Prime Minister because

(a) he could not get a favourable legislative bill passed by Parliament.

(b) he had completed the prescribed two years term.

(c) he was involved in a bribe scandal.

(d) of horse-trading among his party members.

238. The politician who had just recently ceased to be Prime Minister is

(a) Eisaku Sato.

(b) Yasuhiro Nakasone.

(c) Shintaro Abe.

(d) Kiichi Miyazawa.

239. Mr. Takeshita's success in the Prime Ministerial quest is due to

(a) his financial wizardry.

(b) his loyalty to his predecessor's policies.

(c) his skill in manipulating fractional politics.

(d) his good knowledge of English.

240. The author's assessment of the potential of Mr. Takeshita to be a successful Prime Minister can be summarized as one of

(a) cautious optimism.

(b) enthusiastic adulation.

(c) objective skepticism.

(d) undisguised derision.

241. Factionalism in the Liberal Democratic Party is mainly due to

(a) the clash between urban and rural interests.

(b) the long reign of the Emperor.

(c) fears about one-man leadership.

(d) frequent changes in Prime Ministers.

242. Most of the erstwhile Prime Ministers of Japan

(a) were English educated.

(b) were from rural areas.

(c) had urban backgrounds.

(d) have been former Finance Ministers.

243. The number of erstwhile Prime Ministers mentioned by name in the passage is

(a) 2. (b) 3.

(c) 4. (d) 5.

Passage – 31

The Republican Party has lost its mind. To win elections, a party obviously needs votes and constituencies. However first, it needs an idea. In 1994-95, the Republican Party had after a long struggle advanced a coherent, compelling set of political ideas expressed in a specific legislative agenda. The political story of 1996 is that this same party, within the space of six weeks, became totally, shockingly intellectually deranged.

Think back. The singular achievement of the House Speaker Newt Gingrich's 1994 revolution was that it swept into power united behind one comprehensive ideological goal: dismantling the welfare state. Just about anything in the contract with America and the legislative agenda of the 104th Congress is a mere subheading: welfare reform, tax cuts, entitlement reform, returning power to the states, the balanced budget (a supremely powerful means for keeping the growth of government in check).

The central Republican idea was that the individual, the family, the church, the schools — civil society — were being systematically usurped and strangled by the federal behemoth Republicans who were riding into Washington to slay it.

With this idea they met Clinton head-on in late 1995. And although they were tactically defeated — the government shutdown proved a disaster for Republicans — they won philosophically. Clinton conceded all their principles. He finally embraced their seven year balanced budget. Then, in a State of the Union speech that might have been delivered by a moderate Republican, he declared, "The era of Big Government is over," the dominant theme of the Gingrich Revolution.

It seems so long ago. Because then, astonishingly, on the very morrow of their philosophical victory, just as the Republicans prepared to carry these ideas into battle in November, came cannon fire from the rear. The first Republican renegade to cry 'Wrong!' and charge was Steve Forbes. With his free-lunch, tax-cutting flat tax, he declared the balanced budget, the centrepiece of the Republican revolution, unnecessary. Then, no sooner had the Forbes mutiny been put down then Pat Buchanan declared a general insurrection. He too declared war on the party's central ideology in the name not supply side theory but of class welfare, the Democratic weapon of choice against Republicanism.

The enemy, according to Buchanan, is not the welfare state. It is that conservative icon, capitalism, with its ruthless captains of industry, greedy financiers and political elite (Republicans included, of course). All three groups collaborate to let foreigners — immigrants, traders, parasitic foreign-aid loafers — destroy the good life of the ordinary American worker.

Buchananism holds that what is killing the little guy in America is the Big Guy, not Big Government. It blames not an overreaching government that tries to insulate citizens from life's buffeting to the point where it creates deeply destructive dependency, but an uncaring government that does not protect its victim-people enough from that buffeting. Buchanan would protect and wield a mighty government apparatus to do so, government that builds trade walls and immigrant — repelling fences, that imposes punitive taxes on imports, that policies the hiring and firing practices of business with the arrogance of the most zealous affirmative action enforcer.

This is Reaganism standing on its head. Republicans have focused too much on the mere technical dangers posed by this assault. Yes, it gives ammunition to the Democrats. Yes, it puts the eventual nominee through a bruising campaign and delivers him tarnished and drained into the ring against Bill Clinton.

But the real danger is philosophical, not tactical. It is axioms, not just policies, that are under fire. The Republican idea of smaller government is being proud to dust — by Republicans. In the middle of an election year, when they should be honing their themes against Democratic liberalism, Buchanan's rise is forcing a pointless rearguard battle against a philosophical corpse, the obsolete Palaeo conservatism — a mix of nativism, protectionism and isolationism of the 1930s.

As the candidates' debate in Arizona last week showed, the entire primary campaign will be fought on Buchanan's grounds, fending off his Smoot-Hawley-Franco populism. And then what? After the convention, what does the nominee do? Try to resurrect the anti-welfare state themes of the historically successful 1994 congressional campaign? Well, yes, but with a terrible loss of energy and focus — and support. Buchanan's constituency, by then convinced by their leader that the working man's issues have been pushed aside, may simply walk on election day or, even worse, defect to the Democrats. After all, Democrats fight class war very well.

Political parties can survive bruising primary battles. They cannot survive ideological meltdown. Dole and Buchanan say they are fighting for the heart and soul of the Republican Party, heart and soul, however, will get you nowhere when you've lost your way — and your mind.

1995

244. Which broad ideology helped Newt Gingrich lead the Republican revolution of 1994?
(a) Tax cuts
(b) Entitlement reform
(c) Welfare reform
(d) Welfare state dismantling

245. Assuming the passage to be truthful, what does a party not need to win elections?
(a) Votes (b) Money
(c) Constituencies (d) Ideas

246. Which of the following is not a Republican?
(a) Newt Gingrich (b) Pat Buchanan
(c) Bob Dole (d) None of these

247. The Republicans were tactically defeated by the Democrats because
(a) of the shutdown of the government.
(b) the balanced budget plan failed.
(c) Steve Forbes led a revolution.
(d) Bill Clinton pre-empted them.

248. Which of the following would be a suitable title for the passage?

(a) *The Democrats: Victory in Sight*

(b) *Follies and Foibles of the Republican Party*

(c) *Republicans — Are You Crazy?*

(d) *Mutinies on the Republican Party.*

249. The word 'obsolete' in the context of the passage means

(a) antiquated. (b) absolute.

(c) boring. (d) miasmic.

250. What, according to the author, is the real danger for Republicans?

(a) The fact that small government is being ground to dust.

(b) The fact that Bill Clinton is gaining popularity.

(c) The fact that it is axioms, and not just policies that are under fire.

(d) The fact that the eventual nominee would be too tired to fight an election against Clinton.

251. Which of the following, according to Buchanan, is not an enemy?

(a) Big government (b) Immigrants

(c) Captains of industry (d) Foreign-aid requesters

Passage – 32

Icicles — two metres long and, at their tips, as bright and sharp as needles — hang from the caves: wild ice stalactites, dragon's teeth. I peer through them to see the world transformed to abstract. Little snow tornadoes twirl across the blank. The car is out there somewhere, represented by a subtle bump in the snow-field. The old geep truck, a larger beast, is up to its door handles, like a sinking remnant: dinosaur yielding to ice age. The town's behemoth snow-plow passes on the road, dome light twirling, and casts aside a frozen doe that now lies, neck broken, upon the roadside snow-bank, soon to vanish under the snowfall still to come.

There is double-jointed consciousness at work in the dramatics of big weather. Down in the snowstorm, we are as mortal as the deer. I sink to my waist in a drift; I panic, my arms claw for an instant, like a drowning swimmer's, in the powder. Men up and down the storm collapse with coronaries, snow shovels in their hands, cheeks turned into a deathly colour, like frost-bitten plums.

Yet when we go upstairs to consult the Weather Channel, we settle down, as cosy gods do, to hover high above the earth and watch the play with a divine perspective. Moist air labelled L for low rides up the continent from the Gulf of Mexico and collides with the high that has slid down from the North Pole. And thus is whipped up the egg-white fluff on the studio map that, down in the frozen, messy world, buries mortals.

An odd new metaphysics of weather: It is not that weather has necessarily grown more apocalyptic. The famous 'Winter of the Blue Snow' of 1886-87 turned rivers of the American West into glaciers that when they thawed, carried along inundation of dead cattle. President Theodore Roosevelt was virtually ruined as a rancher by the weather that destroyed 65 per cent of his herd. In 1811 Mississippi river flowed briefly because of the New Madrid earthquake. What's new in America is the theatre of it. Television does not create weather; any more than it creates contemporary politics. However, the ritual ceremonies of televised weather have endowed a subject often previously banal with an amazing life as mass entertainment, nationwide interactive preoccupation and a kind of immense performance art.

What we have is weather as electronic American Shintoism, a casual but almost mystic daily religion, wherein nature is not inert but restless, stirring alive with kinetic fronts and meanings and turbulent expectations (forecasts, variables, prophecies). We have installed an elaborate priesthood and technology of interpretation: acolytes and satellites preside over snow and circuses. At least major snowstorms have about them an innocence and moral neutrality that is more refreshing than the last national television spectacle, the O. J. Simpson trial.

One attraction is the fact that these large gestures of nature are political. The weather in the mirabilis mode can, of course, be dragged onto the opened page to start a macro-argument about global warning or a micro-spat over a mayor's fecklessness in deploying snowplows. Otherwise, traumas of weather do not admit of political interpretation. The snow Shinto reintroduces an element of what is almost charmingly uncontrollable in life. And, as shown last week, surprising, even as the priests predict it. This is welcome — a kind of ideological relief- in a rather stupidly politicised society living under the delusion that everything in life (and death) is arguable, political and therefore manipulable — from diet to DNA. None of the old earthbound Marxist Who-Whom here in meteorology, but rather sky gods that bang around at higher altitudes and leave the earth in its misery, to submit to the sloppy collateral damage.

The moral difference of weather, even when destructive, is somehow stimulating. Why? The sheer levelling force is pleasing. It overrides routine and organises people into a shared moment that will become a punctuating memory in their lives ('Lord, remember the blizzard in 1996?').

Or perhaps one's reaction is no more complicated than a child's delight in dramatic disruption. Anyone loves to stand on the beach with a hurricane coming — a darkly lashing Byronism in surf and wind gets the blood up. The God's, or child's, part of the mind welcomes big weather — floods and blizzards. The coping, grown-up human part curses it, and sinks.

The paradox of big weather, it makes people feel important even while it, dramatises their insignificance. In some ways, extreme weather is a brief moral equivalent of war — as stimulating as war can sometimes be, through without most of the carnage.

The sun rises upon diamond-scattered snow-fields and glistens upon the lucent dragon's teeth. In the distance, three deer, roused from their shelter under pines, venture forth. They struggle and plunge undulously through the opulent white.

Upstairs, I switch on the Shinto Weather Channel and the priests at the map show me the next wave — white swirls and eddies over Indiana, heading ominously east.

252. How many vehicles does the author mention in the passage?

(a) One (b) Two
(c) Three (d) Four

253. The author compares the weather bulletin channel reportage to

(a) a war (b) the O. J. Simpson trial
(c) a ritual ceremony (d) a theatre

254. Which of the following was not the result of the 'Winter of Blue Snow'?

(a) It almost ruined Theodore Roosevelt
(b) It made the Mississippi flow northward
(c) It turned rivers into glaciers
(d) It killed a lot of cattle

255. The moral indifference of the weather is stimulating in spite of being destructive because

(a) it shows no mercy.
(b) it organises people into a shared moment.
(c) Both (a) and (b)
(d) Neither (a) nor (b)

256. The author's reaction to the snowstorm may be said to be

(a) fascinated (b) scared
(c) cynical (d) deadpan

257. According to the author, one of the greatest attractions of the weather is that

(a) it is politicized (b) it is apolitical
(c) it is reckless (d) it is beautiful

258. What is most probably the physical position of the author of the passage?

(a) In his house (b) In a snowstorm
(c) In his office (d) In a bunk

259. Which of the following is not true of the weather?

(a) It is a moral equivalent of war
(b) It is pleasantly manipulable
(c) It is a levelling force
(d) It dramatises man's insignificance

260. The word 'undulously' in the context of the passage means

(a) unduly (b) indomitably
(c) powerful (d) curved

Passage – 33

Among those who call themselves socialists, two kinds of persons may be distinguished. There are, in the first place, those whose plans for a new order of society, in which private property and individual competition are to be superseded and other motives to action substituted, are on the scale of a village community or township, and would be applied to an entire country by the multiplication of such self-acting units; of this character are the systems of Owen, of Fourier, and the more thoughtful and philosophic socialists generally. The other class, which is more a product of the continent than of Great Britain and may be called the revolutionary socialists, has people who propose to themselves a much bolder stroke. Their scheme is the management of the whole productive resources of the country by one central authority, the general government. And with this view some of them avow as their purpose that the working classes, or somebody on their behalf, should take possession of all the property of the country, and administer it for the general benefit.

Whatever may be the difficulties of the first of these two forms of socialism, the second must evidently involve the same difficulties and many more. The former, too, has the great advantage that it can be brought into operation progressively, and can prove its capabilities by trial. It can be tried first on a select population and extended to others as their education and cultivation permit. It need not, and in the natural order of things would not, become an engine of subversion until it had shown itself capable of being also a means of reconstruction. It is not so with the other; the aim of that is to substitute the new rule for the old at a single stroke, and to exchange the amount of good realised under the present system, and its large possibilities of improvement, for a plunge without any preparation into the most extreme form of the problem of carrying on the whole round of the operations of social life without the motive power which has always hitherto worked the social machinery. It must be acknowledged that those who would play this game on the strength of their own private opinion, unconfirmed as yet by any experimental verification — who would forcibly deprive all who have now a comfortable physical existence of their only present means of preserving it, and would brave the frightful bloodshed and misery that would ensue if the attempt was resisted — must have a serene confidence in their own wisdom on the one hand and the recklessness of other people's sufferings on the other, which Robespierre and St. Just, hitherto the typical instances of those united attributes, scarcely came up to. Nevertheless this scheme has great elements of popularity which the more cautious and reasonable form of socialism has not; because what it professes to do, it promises to do quickly, and holds out hope to the enthusiastic of seeing the whole of their aspirations realised in their own time and at a blow.

261. Who among of the following is not a socialist?
 (a) Robespierre
 (b) Fourier
 (c) Owen
 (d) All are socialists

262. Which of the following, according to the author, is true?
 (a) The second form of socialism has more difficulties than the first.
 (b) The second form of socialism has the same difficulties as the first.
 (c) The second form of socialism has less difficulties than the first.
 (d) The author has not compared the difficulties of the two.

263. According to the author, the difference between the two kinds of socialists is that
 (a) one consists of thinkers and the others are active people.
 (b) the first have a definite philosophy and the second don't have any definite philosophy.
 (c) the first believe in gradual change while the others believe in revolutionary change.
 (d) the first are the products of Britain, while the others are products of Russia.

264. Which of the following were characteristics of St. Just and Robespierre?
 (a) Unconcern for other's suffering
 (b) Full confidence in their own wisdom
 (c) Both (a) and (b)
 (d) Neither (a) nor (b)

265. Which of the following according to the author, may not be the result of not verifying the desirability of socialism experimentally first?
 (a) Bloodshed
 (b) Deprivation of current comfortable existence
 (c) Corruption in high places
 (d) Misery caused by resisting the change

266. According to the philosophy of revolutionary socialism,
 (a) the government takes over the villages first, and then gradually the whole country.
 (b) the government takes over all productive resources of the country at one stroke.
 (c) the government declares a police state and rules by decree.
 (d) there is no government as such: the people rule themselves by the socialist doctrine.

267. The word 'avow' in the context of the passage means
 (a) proclaim (b) vow
 (c) affirm (d) deny

268. It may be inferred from the passage that the author's sympathies are for
 (a) neither side.
 (b) the side of the socialist doctrine.
 (c) the second type of socialism.
 (d) the first type of socialism.

Passage – 34

Whatever philosophy may be, it is in the world and must relate to it. It breaks through the shell of the world in order to move into the infinite. But it turns back in order to find in the finite its always unique historical foundation. It pushes into the furthest horizons beyond being-in-the-world in order to experience the present in the eternal. But even the profoundest meditation acquires its meaning by relating back to man's existence here and now. Philosophy glimpses the highest criteria, the starry heaven of the possible, and seeks in the light of the seemingly impossible the way to man's dignity in the phenomenon of his empirical existence. Philosophy addresses itself to individuals. It creates a free community of those who rely on each other in their will for truth. Into this community the philosophic man would like to enter. It is there in the world all the time, but cannot become a worldly institution without losing freedom of its truth. He cannot know whether he belongs to it. No authority decides on his acceptance. He wants to live in his thinking in such a way as to make his acceptance possible. But how does the world relate to philosophy? There are chairs of philosophy at the universities. Nowadays they are an embarrassment. Philosophy is politely respected because of tradition, but despised in secret. The general opinion is: it has nothing of importance to say. Neither has it any practical value. It is named in public but does it really exist? Its existence is proved at least by the defence measures it provokes. We can see this in the form of comments like: Philosophy is too complicated. I don't understand it. It's beyond me. It's something for professionals. I have no gift for it. Therefore it doesn't concern me. But that is like saying : I don't need to bother work or scholarship without thinking or questioning its meaning, and, for the rest, have 'opinions' and be content with that. The defence becomes fanatical. A benighted vital instinct hates philosophy. It is dangerous. If I understood it I would have to change my life. I would find myself in another frame of mind, see everything in a different light, have to judge anew. Better now think philosophically! Then come the accusers, who want to replace the obsolete philosophy by something new and totally different. It is mistrusted as the utterly mendacious end product of a bankrupt theology. The meaninglessness of philosophical propositions is made fun of. Philosophy is denounced as the willing handmaiden of political and other powers. For many politicians, their wretched trade would be easier if philosophy did not exist at all. Masses and functionaries are easier to manipulate when they do not think but only have a regimented intelligence. People must be prevented from becoming serious. Therefore, it is better for philosophy to be boring. Let the chairs of philosophy rot. The more piffle is taught, the sooner people will be blinkered against the light of philosophy. Thus philosophy is surrounded by enemies, most of whom are not conscious of being such. Bourgeois complacency, conventionality, the satisfactions of economic prosperity, the appreciation of science only for its technical achievements, the absolute will to power, the bonhomie of politicians, the fanaticism of ideologies, the literary self-assertiveness of talented writers — in all these things people parade their anti-philosophy. They do not notice it because they do not realise what they are doing. They are unaware that their anti-philosophy is in itself a philosophy, but a perverted one, and that this anti-philosophy, if elucidated, would annihilate itself.

269. A suitable title for the passage would be
(a) *Man and Philosophy*
(b) *Philosophical Angst*
(c) *A Defence of Philosophy*
(d) *The Enemies of Philosophy*

270. Which of the following is true, keeping the passage in mind?
(a) Philosophy is evidently respected
(b) Philosophy is secretly despised
(c) Both (a) and (b)
(d) Neither (a) nor (b)

271. Which of the following is not a charge against philosophy?
(a) That it is obsolete
(b) That it is mendacious
(c) That it is the handmaiden of political powers
(d) That it is immoral

272. Which of the following is not mentioned as a function of philosophy in the passage?
(a) It shows the way to man's dignity in the face of his empirical existence.
(b) It breaks through the shell of the world in order to move into the infinite.
(c) It pushes into the furthest horizons beyond being in the world.
(d) It makes the world a better place to live in.

273. Why according to the passage, would the politicians be happy if philosophy did not exist?
(a) Masses would be easier to manipulate as they would not think for themselves.
(b) They would not have to make false allegiances to ideologies.
(c) They would not have to face allegations of ignoring philosophy.
(d) They would not have to be philosophical about losing an election.

274. The word 'chairs', in the context of the passage, means
(a) wooden-faced people.
(b) departments.
(c) separate chairs for philosophers.
(d) reserved seats for students of philosophy.

275. According to the author, the existence of philosophy is proved by
(a) the fact that there are still chairs of philosophy in universities.
(b) the defence measures it provokes.
(c) the polite respect it gets.
(d) the fact that it answers the fundamental questions of life.

Passage – 35

Even if we're a bit snooty about them, we should go down on our knees and thank heaven for movies like *Jurassic Park* and directors like Steven Spielberg who make them. They fill the cinemas, if only because the hype is virtually irresistible. And because they do so, hundreds of maniacs all over the world continue to finance films. But is this is an example of a worldwide jackpot movie? Yes and no. Yes, because it delivers dinosaurs by the dozen, in as weird a fashion as have been seen on the screen before. And no, because the accompanying story, courtesy Michael Crichton, has little of the real imagination that made Spielberg's *ET* and *Close Encounters* into the jackpot movies of their time. Technically, it works like a dream but, as a cinematic dream, it's unmemorable. This may be because of its cardboard human characters, dwarfed by the assemblage of their prehistoric ancestors and serviced by a screenplay that makes the abortive mating calls of this weirdly asexual zoo seem eloquent in comparison. What kind of park is this?, enquiries Sam Neil. "Oh, it's right up your alley", says Richard Attenborough. More likely, though it has something to do with the development of the story which at no point engages us properly on the human level, except perhaps to hope that the kids and Neil's grumpy scientist who learns to love them will finally escape from the grasp of the velociraptors chasing them. We're looking at nothing but stunts, and they get tiresome laid end to end. Crichton's book was scarcely much better but at least it had a convincing villain in John Hammond, *Jurassic Park's* billionaire developer, whereas Attenborough's approximation seems merely enthusiastically misguided. And Crichton's warning of what might happen if we muck about with nature becomes weaker in the film. What we actually have in *Jurassic Park* is a non-animated Disney epic with affiliations to *Jaws* which seems to amuse and frighten but succeeds in doing neither well enough to count. Its real interest lies in how Spielberg's obsession with childhood now manifests itself in his middle age. It looks like being on automatic pilot — gestural rather than totally convinced but determined to remain the subject of analytical study. The whole thing, of course, is perfectly adequate fun once the ludicrously simplistic explanation of DNA has been traversed in Hammond's costly futuristic, computerised den. Even I could understand it. Thereafter, the theme park's creaky inability to deal with an ordinary old typhoon as its VIPs travel around hoping the investment will work, leads to predictable disasters, proficiently worked out but never truly frightening. But then this is a film for children of all ages, except perhaps those under 12, and one shouldn't expect sophistication on other than the technological level. *Jurassic Park* is more of a roller-coaster ride than a piece of real cinema. It delivers, but only on a certain plane. Even the breaking of the barriers between our civilization and a monstrous past doesn't have the kick it could have had.

Possibly one is asking for a different film which in the end would not have appealed across the box-office spectrum as well as this obviously does. But still one leaves it vaguely disappointed. All that work and just a mouse that roars. It's wonderful story, but told with more efficiency than inspiration — possibly a sign of the times, along with the merchandising spree which follows it so readily.

276. Which of the following has not been mentioned as a Steven Spielberg movie in the passage?

(a) *Jaws* (b) *ET*
(c) *Close Encounters* (d) *Jurassic Park*

277. In which way does the author find the film inferior to the original book?

(a) The book is more interesting.
(b) The book had a more convincing villain.
(c) The book is easier to understand.
(d) The story had a good author but a bad director.

278. The passage is most probably

(a) a book review. (b) a film critic's comments.
(c) a film review. (d) a magazine article.

279. The book *Jurassic Park* is written by

(a) Crichton (b) Attenborough
(c) Hammond (d) Neil

280. Which of the following does the author say of the film?

(a) The film is technically inferior and does not have a good storyline.
(b) The film is technically inferior but has a good storyline.
(c) The film is technically slick but does not have a good storyline.
(d) The film is technically slick and has a good storyline.

281. The writer's opinion of the film *Jurassic Park* may be said to be

(a) very favourable. (b) very depressing.
(c) excellent. (d) not very favourable.

282. Why according to the author, should we thank heaven for movies like *Jurassic Park*, even though they may not be very good aesthetically?

(a) Because they fill the halls, and thus people will finance more films.
(b) Because it is one of the major hits of the year.
(c) Because the film has brilliant technical wizardry.
(d) Because of the hundreds of films being produced, this is one of the few excellent ones.

283. According to the author, *Jurassic Park*

(a) is very amusing. (b) is very frightening.
(c) Both (a) and (b) (d) Neither (a) nor (b)

284. The phrase 'muck about', in the context of the passage, means

(a) make dirty (b) interfere with
(c) be frivolous about (d) to mask

Passage – 36

The opinion polls had been wrong. Although they were signalling a weakening in Labour's lead in the days before the general election — which pointed to a hung parliament — many working-class voters had been embarrassed to tell middle-class pollsters that they were intending to vote Labour. The final result on April 9, 1992, which gave Neil Kinnock a working majority of 30, was a turnaround of the century.

As John Major cleared his desk in Downing Street, pundit after pundit lined up to criticise his lacklustre campaign. The trouble was, they all agreed, that the Conservative Party no longer had a message or political purpose. Its representation in the north of England was decimated; its future as a national party doubtful.

For Kinnock the victory was a sweet reward for nine years of Herculean labour in making his party electable. Not only had he a working majority, but the divisions in Conservative ranks — between anti-Europeans, free marketers and moderates — threatened to split the party. Having set himself the objective of heading a two or three term government, Kinnock made his cabinet appointments with the long haul in mind. There were few surprises. John Smith, with whom he coexisted uneasily, was made chancellor; Roy Hattersley became home secretary; Gerald Kaufmann went to the foreign office; inveterate Euro-sceptic Bryan Gould took over environment; and Gordon Brown went to trade. It was, as many commentators conceded, a much more heavyweight cabinet than any of the Conservatives could have mustered.

But the new cabinet was to have its first trial of strength very soon. The problem was the foreign exchange markets. Although both Kinnock and Smith had, throughout, the election campaign, reaffirmed their commitment to hold the pound's parity at 2.95 DM inside the ERM, the foreign exchange markets simply did not believe them. Every previous Labour government had devalued; what reason was there to suppose this one would be different?

The pressure built up immediately. On Friday, April 10, the Bank of England managed to hold the line only by spending £4 billion — around a sixth of its total reserves — to support the exchange rate. But late that night, as the New York markets closed, the Governor of the Bank of England led the deputation to a meeting at 11, Downing Street with Smith and the permanent secretary to the Treasury, Sir Terence Burns. If, said the governor, the pound was to survive the coming week inside the ERM, then Smith would have to demonstrate his resolve by raising interest rates — by at least 2 per cent. It would also help, added the officials, if the government were to commit Britain to full monetary union and to meet the Maastricht criteria for a single currency. This would mean that both the taxation from Smith's first budget would have to be used to reduce government borrowing and the manifesto promises to raise child benefit and pensions be postponed.

Smith listened to Eddie George — number two at the Bank of England and the arbiter of British exchange rate policy — explain that, at the current rate of reserve loss, Britain's reserves would have run out by the following weekend. The markets needed decisive action. And they needed to know, by the night of Sunday, April 12, at the very latest, what the government would do when the far-eastern markets opened after the weekend. Sir Terence advised that once the markets recognised the government was resolved to hold the exchange rate, pressure would quickly subside and the interest rate increases could be reversed. The name of the game was earning credibility.

Although Smith had been warned to expect a Treasury/Bank of England move to assert the cannons of economic orthodoxy, he had hoped to have been more than a few hours into his chancellorship before the pressures started to mount. As it stood, he felt like the victim of a coup and wondered to what extent the foreign exchange market selling had been prompted by the Bank of England's ham fisted intervention — almost designed to manufacture a run on the pound. In any case, he could do nothing without conferring with the prime minister.

In fact Kinnock had asked Smith to have the preliminary Bank of England meeting without him. Although he was not at one with his chancellor over economic policy and distrusted his judgement, he wanted to complete his cabinet appointments — and confer with his own advisers about how to react to what he knew the bank and treasury recommendations would be. He was determined to avoid being bounced into decisions before he had decided his line.

The alternative was to apply to the EC for a realignment conference, in which many more currencies would be devalued. But that could hardly be done then; it would have to wait until the following weekend. And it was not clear if the pound would be devalued sufficiently, or if other countries would follow the British lead. Not only might Britain have to devalue alone, it might not secure a devaluation large enough to make a difference; and be accompanied by higher interest rates.

285. The word 'pundit', in the context of the passage, means
(a) a religious leader
(b) a psychologist
(c) an expert
(d) a paleontologist

286. What was the main problem facing the new cabinet?
(a) The dissension in the ranks of the party.
(b) The devaluation of the currency.
(c) The foreign exchange market problem.
(d) The monetary union problem.

287. Who, according to the passage, is the leader of the Labour Party?
(a) Neil Kinnock
(b) John Smith
(c) Gerald Kaufmann
(d) Roy Hattersley

288. What, according to the treasury secretary, was the only way out of the exchange problem?
(a) Devaluation of the currency
(b) Rise in interest rates
(c) Government spending
(d) Raising taxes

289. It may be inferred from the passage that

(a) the Bank of England would go along with whatever the government decided.

(b) the prime minister was a puppet in the hands of the Bank of England.

(c) the Bank of England was completely independent of the government.

(d) the Bank of England could put enormous pressure on the government to formulate policy.

290. Why did Kinnock ask Smith to attend the Bank of England meeting without him?

(a) Because he did not get along with Smith.

(b) Because he wanted to use that time to confer with others.

(c) Because he already met them and did not want to meet them again.

(d) Because he was afraid of being censured by them.

291. Why, according to the author, was the realignment conference not a viable option for the government?

(a) Because other countries may not follow the British lead in devaluation.

(b) Because the higher interest rates to be given by Britain may deplete resources further.

(c) Both (a) and (b)

(d) Neither (a) nor (b)

292. Which of the following do not belong to the Labour cabinet?

(a) Mr John Smith (b) Mr Bryan Goul

(c) Mr Maastricht (d) Mr G. Brown

293. What, according to the passage, was not a reason for the defeat of the Conservative Party?

(a) A lacklustre campaign

(b) Wrong policies

(c) No special message

(d) No political purpose

Passage – 37

I want to stress this personal helplessness we are all stricken with in the face of a system that has passed beyond our knowledge and control. To bring it nearer home, I propose that we switch off from the big things like empires and their wars to more familiar little things. Take pins for example! I do not know why it is that I so seldom use a pin when my wife cannot get on without boxes of them at hand; but it is so; and I will therefore take pins as being for some reason specially important to women.

There was a time when pinmakers would buy the material; shape it; make the head and the point; ornament it; and take it to the market, and sell it and the making required skill in several operations. They not only knew how the thing was done from beginning to end, but could do it all by themselves. But they could not afford to sell you a paper of pins for the farthing. Pins cost so much that a woman's dress allowance was calling pin money.

By the end of the 18th century Adam Smith boasted that it took 18 men to make a pin, each man doing a little bit of the job and passing the pin on to the next, and none of them being able to make a whole pin or to buy the materials or to sell it when it was made. The most you could say for them was that at least they had some idea of how it was made, though they could not make it. Now as this meant that they were clearly less capable and knowledgeable men than the old pin-makers, you may ask why Adam Smith boasted of it as a triumph of civilisation when its effect had so clearly a degrading effect. The reason was that by setting each man to do just one little bit of the work and nothing but that, over and over again, he became very quick at it. The men, it is said, could turn out nearly 5000 pins a day each; and thus pins became plentiful and cheap. The country was supposed to be richer because it had more pins, though it had turned capable men into mere machines doing their work without intelligence and being fed by the spare food of the capitalist just as an engine is fed with coals and oil. That was why the poet Goldsmith, who was a farsighted economist as well as a poet, complained that 'wealth accumulates, and men decay'.

Nowadays Adam Smith's 18 men are as extinct as the diplodocus. The 18 flesh-and-blood men have been replaced by machines of steel which spout out pins by the hundred million. Even sticking them into pink papers is done by machinery. The result is that with the exception of a few people who design the machines, nobody knows how to make a pin or how a pin is made: that is to say, the modern worker in pin manufacture need not be one-tenth so intelligent, skilful and accomplished as the old pinmaker; and the only compensation we have for this deterioration is that pins are so cheap that a single pin has no expressible value at all. Even with a big profit stuck on to the cost-price you can buy dozens for a farthing; and pins are so recklessly thrown away and wasted that verses have to be written to persuade children(without success) that it is a sin to steal, if even it's a pin.

Many serious thinkers, like John Ruskin and William Morris, have been greatly troubled by this, just as Goldsmith was, and have asked whether we really believe that it is an advance in wealth to lose our skill and degrade our workers for the sake of being able to waste pins by the ton. We shall see later on, when we come to consider the Distribution of Leisure, that the cure for this is not to go back to the old free for higher work than pin-making or the like. But in the meantime the fact remains that the workers are now not able to make anything themselves even in little bits. They are ignorant and helpless, and cannot lift their finger to begin their day's work until it has all been arranged for them by their employer's who themselves do not understand the machines they buy, and simply pay other people to set them going by carrying out the machine maker's directions.

The same is true for clothes. Earlier the whole work of making clothes, from the shearing of the sheep to the turning out of the finished and washed garment ready to put on, had to be done in the country by the men and women of the household, especially the women; so that to this day an unmarried woman is called a spinster. Nowadays nothing is left of all this but the sheep shearing; and even that, like the milking of cows, is being done by machinery, as the sewing is. Give a woman a sheep today and ask her to produce a woollen dress for you; and not only will she be quite unable to do it, but you are likely to find that she is not even aware of any connection between sheep and clothes. When she gets her clothes, which she does by buying them at the shop, she knows that there is a difference between wool and cotton and silk, between flannel and merino, perhaps even between stockinet and other wefts; but as to how they are made, or what they are made of, or how they came to be in the shop ready for her to buy, she knows hardly anything. And the shop assistant from whom she buys is no wiser. The people engaged in the making of them know even less; for many of them are too poor to have much choice of materials when they buy their own clothes.

Thus the capitalist system has produced an almost universal ignorance of how things are made and done, whilst at the same time it has caused them to be made and done on a gigantic scale. We have to buy books and encyclopaedias to find out what it is we are doing all day; and as the books are written by people who are not doing it, and who get their information from other books, what they tell us is twenty to fifty years out of date knowledge and almost impractical today. And of course most of us are too tired of our work when we come home to want to read about it; what we need is cinema to take our minds off it and feel our imagination.

It is a funny place, this word of capitalism, with its astonishing spread of education and enlightenment. There stand the thousands of property owners and the millions of wage workers, none of them able to make anything, none of them knowing what to do until somebody tells them, none of them having the least notion of how it is made that they find people paying them money, and things in the shops to buy with it. And when they travel they are surprised to find that savages and Esquimaux and villagers who have to make everything for themselves are more intelligent and resourceful! The wonder would be if they were anything else. We should die of idiocy through disuse of our mental faculties if we did not fill our heads with romantic nonsense out of illustrated newspapers and novels and plays and films. Such stuff keeps us alive, but it falsifies everything for us so absurdly that it leaves us more or less dangerous lunatics in the real world.

Excuse my going on like this; but as I am a writer of books and plays myself, I know the folly and peril of it better than you do. And when I see that this moment of our utmost ignorance and helplessness, delusion and folly, has been stumbled on by the blind forces of capitalism as the moment for giving votes to everybody, so that the few wise women are hopelessly overruled by the thousands whose political minds, as far as they can be said to have any political minds at all, have been formed in the cinema, I realise that I had better stop writing plays for a while to discuss political and social realities in this book with those who are intelligent enough to listen to me.

1996

294. A suitable title to the passage would be

(a) *You Can't Hear a Pin-drop Nowadays.*

(b) *Capitalism and Labour Disintegration: Pinning the Blame.*

(c) *The Saga of the Non Safety Pins.*

(d) *Reaching the Pinnacle of Capitalistic Success.*

295. Why do you think that the author gives the example of Adam Smith?

(a) Because he thinks that Adam Smith was a boaster without any facts to back his utterance.

(b) Because he wants to give us an example of something undesirable that Adam Smith was proud of.

(c) Because he is proud to be a believer in a tenet of production that even a great man like Adam Smith boasted about.

(d) Because he feels that Adam Smith was right when he said that it took 18 men to make a pin.

296. Which of the following is true as far as pins are concerned?

(a) The cost of pins is more nowadays to produce.

(b) Earlier, workmen made pins with a lot of love and care.

(c) Pinball machines are the standard pin producing gadgets nowadays.

(d) It took much longer to make a pin earlier.

297. The reason that children have to be taught that stealing a pin is wrong is that

(a) they have an amazing proclivity to steal them right from childhood.

(b) pins are so common and cheap that taking one would not even be considered stealing by them.

(c) stealing a pin would lead to stealing bigger and bigger things in the future.

(d) stealing an insignificant thing like a pin smacks of kleptomania.

298. It may be inferred from the passage that the author

(a) is a supporter of the craftsmanship over bulk mechanised production.

(b) is a supporter of assembly line production over socialistic systems of the same.

(c) is a defender of the faith in capitalistic production.

(d) None of the above

299. Which of the following is not against the modern capitalistic system of mass production?

(a) John Ruskin (b) Goldsmith

(c) Adam Smith (d) William Morris

300. Goldsmith's dictum, "wealth accumulates, and men decay," in the context of the passage, probably means

(a) the more wealthy people get, they become more and more corrupt.

(b) the more rich people get, they forget the nuances of individual ability.

(c) people may have a lot of money, but they have to die and decay someday.

(d) the more a company gets wealthy the less they take care of people.

301. When the author says that a woman now is likely to know about any connection between sheep and clothes, he is probably being

(a) vindictive (b) chauvinistic

(c) satirical (d) demeaning

302. Which of the following can be a suitable first line to introduce the hypothetical next paragraph at the end of the passage?

(a) The distribution of leisure is not a term that can be explained in a few words.

(b) If people wear clothes they hardly seem to think about the method of production.

(c) Machines are the gods of our age and there seems to be no atheists.

(d) None of the above.

Passage – 38

Now let us turn back to inquire whether sending our capital abroad, and consenting to be taxed to pay emigration fares to get rid of the women and men who are left without employment in consequence, is all that capitalism can do when our employers, who act for our capitalists in industrial affairs, and are more or less capitalists themselves in the earlier stages of capitalistic development, find that they can sell no more of their goods at a profit, or indeed at all, in their own country.

Clearly they cannot send abroad the capital they have already invested, because it has all been eaten up by the workers, leaving in its place factories and railways and mines and the like; and these cannot be packed into a ship's hold and sent to Africa. It is only the freshly saved capital that can be sent out of the country. This, as we have seen, does go abroad in heaps of finished products. But the British land held by him on long lease, must, when once he has sold all the goods at home that his British customers can afford to buy, either shut up his works until the customers have worn out their stock of what they have bought, which would bankrupt him(for the landlord will not wait), or else sell his superfluous goods somewhere else; that is, he must send them abroad. Now it is not easy to send them to civilized countries, because they practise Protection, which means that they impose heavy taxes (customs duties) on foreign goods. Uncivilized countries, without Protection, and inhabited by natives to whom gaudy calicoes and cheap showy brassware are dazzling and delightful novelties, are the best places to make for at first.

But trade requires a settled government to put down the habit of plundering strangers. This is not a habit of simple tribes, who are often friendly and honest. It is what civilized men do where there is no law to restrain them. Until quite recent times it was extremely dangerous to be wrecked on our own coasts, as wrecking, which meant plundering wrecked ships and refraining from any officious efforts to save the lives of their crews, was a well-established business in many places on our shores. The Chinese still remember some astonishing outbursts of looting perpetrated by English ladies of high position, at moments when law was suspended and priceless works of art were to be had for the grabbing. When trading with aborigines begins with the visit of a single ship, the cannons and cutlasses carried may be quite sufficient to overawe the natives if they are troublesome. The real difficulty begins when so many ships come that a little trading station of white men grows up and attracts the white ne'er-do-wells and violent roughs who are always being squeezed out of civilization by the pressure of law and order. It is these riff-raff who turn the place into a sort of hell in which sooner or later missionaries are murdered and traders plundered.

Their home governments are appealed to put a stop to this. A gunboat is sent out and inquiry made. The report after the inquiry is that there is nothing to be done but set up a civilized government, with a post office, police, troops and the navy in the offing. In short, the place is added to some civilized Empire. And the civilized taxpayer pays the bill without getting a farthing of the profits.

Of course the business does not stop there. The riff-raff who have created the emergency move out just beyond the boundary of the annexed territory, and are as great a nuisance as ever to the traders when they have exhausted the purchasing power of the included natives and push on after fresh customers. Again they call on their home government to civilize a further area; and so bit by bit the civilized Empire grows at the expense of the home taxpayers, without any intention or approval on their part, until at last although all their real patriotism is centred on their own people and confined to their own country, their own rulers, and their own religious faith; they find that the centre of their beloved realm has shifted to the other hemisphere. That is how we in the British Islands have found our centre moved from London to the Suez Canal, and are now in the position that out of every hundred of our fellow-subjects, in whose defence we are expected to shed the last drop of our blood, only 11 are whites or even Christians. In our bewilderment some of us declare that the Empire is a burden and a blunder, whilst others glory in it as a triumph. You and I need not argue with them just now, our point for the moment being that, whether blunder or glory, the British Empire was quite unintentional. What should have been undertaken only as a most carefully considered political development has been a series of commercial adventures thrust on us by capitalists forced by their own system to cater to foreign customers before their own country's needs were one-tenth satisfied.

303. It may be inferred that the passage was written
(a) when Britain was still a colonial power.
(b) when the author was in a bad mood.
(c) when the author was working in the foreign service of Britain.
(d) when the author's country was overrun by the British.

304. According to the author, the habit of plundering the strangers
(a) is usually not found in simple tribes but civilized people.
(b) is usually found in the barbaric tribes of the uncivilized nations.
(c) is a habit limited only to English ladies of high position.
(d) is a usual habit with all white-skinned people.

305. Which of the following does not come under the aegis of capital already invested?
(a) Construction of factories
(b) Development of a mine
(c) Trade of finished products
(d) All of the above

306. Which of the following may be called the main complaint of the author?
(a) The race of people he belongs to are looters and plunderers.
(b) The capitalists are taking over the entire world.
(c) It is a way of life for English ladies to loot and plunder.
(d) The English taxpayer has to pay for the upkeep of territories he did not want.

307. Why do the capitalistic traders prefer the uncivilized countries to the civilized ones?
(a) Because they find it easier to rule them.
(b) Because civilized countries would make them pay protection duties.
(c) Because civilized countries would make their own goods.
(d) Because uncivilized countries like the cheap and gaudy goods of bad quality all capitalists produce.

308. The word 'officious', in the context of the passage, means
(a) self-important. (b) official.
(c) rude. (d) oafish.

309. According to the author, the main reason why capitalist go abroad to sell their goods is
(a) that they want to civilize the under developed countries of the world by giving them their goods.
(b) that they have to have new places to sell their surplus goods some where in new markets.
(c) that they actually want to rule new lands and selling goods is an excuse.
(d) None of the above

Passage – 39

That the doctrines connected with the name of Mr Darwin are altering our principles has become a sort of commonplace thing to say. And moral principles are said to share in this general transformation. Now, to pass by other subjects, I do not see why Darwinism need change our ultimate moral ideas. It was not to modify our conception of the end, either for the community, or the individual, unless we have been holding views, which long before Darwin were out of date. As to the principles of ethics I perceive, in short, no sign of revolution. Darwinism has indeed helped many to truer conception of the end, but I cannot admit that it has either originated or modified that conception.

And yet in ethics Darwinism after all perhaps be revolutionary, it may lead not to another view about the end, but to a different way of regarding the relatively importance of the means. For in the ordinary moral creed those means seem estimated on no rational principle. Our creed appears rather to be an irrational mixture of jarring elements. We have the moral code of Christianity, accepted in part; rejected practically by all save a few fanatics. But we do not realise how in its very principle the Christian ideals is false. And when we reject this code for another and in part a sounder morality, we are in the same condition of blindness and of practical confusion. It is here that Darwinism, with all the tendencies we may group under that name, seems destined to intervene. It will make itself felt, I believe, more and more effectually. It may force on us in some points a correction of our moral views, and a return to a non-Christian and perhaps a Hellenic ideal. I propose to illustrate here these general statements by some remarks on Punishment.

Darwinism, I have said, has not even modified our ideas of the Chief Good. We may take that as — the welfare of the community realised in its members. There is, of course, a question as to meaning to be given to welfare. We may identify that with mere pleasure, or gain with mere system, or may rather view both as inseparable aspects of perfection and individuality. And the extent and nature of the community would once more be a subject for some discussion. But we are forced to enter on these controversies here. We may leave welfare undefined, and for present purpose need not distinguish the community from the state. The welfare of this whole exists, of course, nowhere outside the individuals, and the individuals again have rights and duties only as members in the whole. This is the revived Hellenism — or we may call it in the organic view of things — urged by German Idealism early in the present century.

310. What is most probably the author's opinion of the existing moral principles of the people?

(a) He thinks they have to be revamped in the light of Darwinism.

(b) He thinks that they are okay as they are and do not need any major change.

(c) He thinks that it may be a good idea to have a modicum of the immortal Darwinism in us.

(d) Cannot be determined from the passage.

311. According to the author, the doctrines of Mr Darwin

(a) have changed our physical and moral principles.

(b) have to be re-evaluated to correct the faults endemic in them.

(c) do not have to change our moral ideas.

(d) are actually new versions of old moral rules.

312. What, according to the passage, is the Chief Good?

(a) Being good and kind to all fellow human beings.

(b) The greatest good of the greatest number.

(c) The welfare of the community realised in its members.

(d) Cannot be determined from the passage.

313. It is implied in the passage that

(a) a Hellenic ideal is not a proper substitute of the Christian ideal.

(b) what mankind needs is a Hellenic ideal rather than a Christian one.

(c) Darwinism is more Christian than Hellenic.

(d) fanatics do not understand what Darwinism really is.

314. According to the author, the moral code of Christianity

(a) is not followed by most people.

(b) is in danger due to opposition of Darwinism.

(c) is followed by a vast majority of people.

(d) is totally ignored by all true Christians.

Passage – 40

Governments looking for easy popularity have frequently been tempted into announcing give-aways of all sorts; free electricity, virtually free water, subsidised food, cloth at half price, and so on. The subsidy culture has gone to extremes. The richest farmers in the country get subsidised fertiliser. University education, typically accessed by the wealtier sections, is charged at a fraction of cost. Postal services are subsidised, and so are railway services. Bus fares cannot be raised to economical levels because there will be violent protests, so bus travel is subsidised too. In the past, price control on a variety of items, from steel to cement, meant that industrial consumers of these items got them at less than actual cost, while the losses of the public sector companies that produced them were borne by the taxpayer! A study, done a few years ago, came to the conclusion that subsidies in the Indian economy total as much as 14.5 per cent of gross domestic product. At today's level, that would work out to about Rs. 1,50,000 crore.

And who pays the bill? The theory — and the political fiction on the basis of which it is sold to unsuspecting voters — is that subsidies go to the poor, and are paid for by the rich. The fact is that most subsidies go to the 'rich' (defined in the Indian context as those who are above the poverty line), and much of the tab goes indirectly to the poor. Because the hefty subsidy bill results in fiscal deficits, which in turn push up rates of inflation — which, as everyone knows, hits the poor the hardest of all. Indeed, that is why taxmen call inflation the most regressive form of taxation.

The entire subsidy system is built on the thesis that people cannot help themselves, therefore governments must do so. That people cannot afford to pay for a variety of goods and services, and therefore the government must step in. This thesis has been applied not just in the poor countries but in the rich ones as well; hence the birth of the welfare state in the West, and an almost Utopian social security system; free medical care, food aid, old age security, et al. But with the passage of time, most of the wealthy nations have discovered that their economies cannot sustain this social safety net, which infact reduces the desire among people to pay their own way, and takes away some of the incentive to work. In short, the bill was unaffordable, and their societies were simply not willing to pay. To the regret of many, but because of the laws of economics are harsh, most Western societies have been busy pruning the welfare bill.

In India, the lessons of this experience — over several decades, and in many countries — do not seem to have been learnt. Or, they are simply ignored in the pursuit of immediate votes. People who are promised cheap food or clothing do not in most cases look beyond the gift horses — to the question of who picks up the tab. The uproar over higher petrol, diesel and cooking gas prices ignored this basic question: if the user of cooking gas does not want to pay for its cost, who should pay? Diesel in the country is subsidised, and if the trucker or owner of a diesel generator does not want to pay for its full cost, who does he or she think should pay the balance of the cost? It is a simple question, nevertheless it remains unasked.

The Deve Gowda government has shown some courage in biting the bullet when it comes to the price of petroleum products. But it has been bitten by a much bigger subsidy bug. It wants to offer food at half its cost to everyone below the poverty line, supposedly estimated at some 380 million people. What will be the cost? And, of course, who will pick up the tab? The Andhra Pradesh Government has been bankrupted by selling rice at Rs. 2 per kg. Should the Central Government be bankrupted too, before facing up to the question of what is affordable and what is not? Already, India is perenially short of power because the subsidy on electricity has bankrupted most electricity boards, and made private investment wary unless it gets all manner of state guarantees. Delhi's subsidised bus fares have bankrupted the Delhi Transport Corporation., whose buses have slowly disappeared from the capital's streets. It is easy to be soft and sentimental, by looking at programmes that will be popular. After all, who doesn't like a free lunch? But the evidence is surely mounting that the lunch isn't free at all. Somebody is paying the bill. And if you want to know who, take a look at the country's poor economic performance over the years.

315. Which of the following should not be subsidised now, according to the passage?

(a) University education (b) Postal services

(c) Steel (d) All of the above

316. The statement that subsidies are paid for by the rich and go to the poor is

(a) fiction.

(b) fact.

(c) fact, according to the author.

(d) fiction, according to the author.

317. Why do you think that the author calls the Western social security system Utopian?

(a) The countries' belief in the efficacy of the system was bound to turn out to be false.

(b) The system followed by these countries is the best available in the present context.

(c) Every thing under this system was supposed to be free but people were charging money for them.

(d) The theory of system followed by these countries was devised by Dr Utopia.

318. It can be inferred from the passage that the author

(a) believes that people can help themselves and do not need the government.

(b) believes that the theory of helping with subsidy is destructive.

(c) believes in democracy and free speech.

(d) is not a successful politician.

319. Which of the following is not a victim of extreme subsidies?

(a) The poor

(b) The Delhi Tranport Corporation

(c) The Andhra Pradesh Government

(d) None of these

320. What, according to the author, is a saving grace of the Deve Gowda government?

(a) It has realised that it has to raise the price of petroleum products.

(b) It has avoided been bitten by a bigger subsidy bug.

(c) Both (a) and (b).

(d) Neither (a) and (b).

321. A suitable title to the passage would be-

(a) *There's No Such Thing as a Free Lunch.*

(b) *The Economic Overview.*

(c) *Deve Gowda's Government and its Follies.*

(d) *It Takes Two to Tango.*

322. Which of the following is not true, in the context of the passage?

(a) Where subsidies are concerned, the poor ultimately pay the tab.

(b) Inflation is caused by too much subsidies.

(c) Experts call subsidies the most regressive form of taxation.

(d) Fiscal deficits are caused due to heavy subsidy bills.

Passage – 41

The membrane-bound nucleus is the most prominent feature of the eukaryotic cell. Schleiden and Schwann, when setting forth the cell doctrine in the 1830s, considered that it had a central role in growth and development. Their belief has been fully supported even though they had only vague notions as to what that role might be, and how the role was to be expressed in some cellular action. The membraneless nuclear area of the prokaryotic cell, with its tangle of fine threads, is now known to play a similar role.

Some cells, like the sieve tubes of vascular plants and the red blood cells of mammals, do not possess nuclei during the greater part of their existence, although they had nuclei when in a less differentiated state. Such cells can no longer divide and their life span is limited. Other cells are regularly multinucleate. Some, like the cells of striated muscles or the latex vessels of higher plants, become so through cell fusion. Some, like the unicellular protozoan paramecium, are normally binucleate, one of the nuclei serving as a source of hereditary information for the next generation, the other governing the day-to-day metabolic activities of the cell. Still other organisms, such as some fungi, are multinucleate because cross walls, dividing the mycelium into specific cells, are absent or irregularly present. The uninucleate situation, however, is typical for the vast minority of cells, and it would appear that this is the most efficient and most economical manner of partitioning living substance into manageable units. This point of view is given credence not only by the prevalence of uninucleate cells, but because for each kind of cell there is a ratio maintained between the volume of the nucleus and that of the cytoplasm. If we think of the nucleus as the control centre of the cell, this would suggest that for a given kind of cell performing a given kind of work, one nucleus can 'take care of' a specific volume of cytoplasm and keep it in functioning order. In terms of material and energy, this must mean providing the kind of information needed to keep flow of materials and energy moving at the correct rate and in the proper channels. With the multitude of enzymes in the cell, materials and energy can of course be channelled in a multitude of ways; it is the function of some information molecules to make channels of use more preferred than others at any given time. How this regulatory control is exercised is not entirely clear.

The nucleus is generally a rounded body. In plant cells, however, where the centre of the cell is often occupied by a large vacuole, the nucleus may be pushed against the cell wall, causing it to assume a lens shape. In some white blood cells, such as polymorphonucleated leukocytes, and in cells of the spinning gland of some insects and spiders, the nucleus is very much lobed. The reason for this is not clear, but it may relate to the fact that for a given volume of nucleus, a lobate form provides a much greater surface area for nuclear-cytoplasmic exchanges, possibly affecting both the rate and the amount of metabolic reactions. The nucleus, whatever its shape, is segregated from the cytoplasm by a double membrane, the nuclear envelope, with the two membranes separated from each other by a perinuclear space of varying width. The envelope is absent only during the time of cell division, and then just for a brief period. The outer membrane is often continuous with the membranes of the endoplasmic reticulum, a possible retention of an earlier relationship, since the envelope, at least in part, is formed at the end cell division by coalescing fragments of the endoplasmic reticulum. The cytoplasmic side of the nucleus is frequently coated with ribosomes, another fact that stresses the similarity and relation of the nuclear envelope to the endoplasmic reticulum. The inner membrane seems to posses a crystalline layer where it abuts the nucleoplasm, but its function remains to be determined.

Everything that passes between the cytoplasm and the nucleus in the eukaryotic cell must transverse the nuclear envelope. This includes some fairly large molecules as well as bodies such as ribosomes, which measure about 25 mm in diameter. Some passageway is, therefore, obviously necessary since there is no indication of dissolution of the nuclear envelope in order to make such movement possible. The nuclear pores appear to be reasonable candidates for such passageways. In plant cells these are irregularly, rather sparsely distributed over the surface of the nucleus, but in the amphibian oocyte, for example, the pores are numerous, regularly arranged, and octagonal and are formed by the fusion of the outer and inner membrane.

323. Which of the following kinds of cells never have a nuclei?

(a) Sieve Tubes

(b) Red blood cells of mammals

(c) Prokaryotic cells

(d) None of these

324. According to the first paragraph, the contention of Schleiden and Schwann that the nucleus is the most important part of the cell has

(a) been proved to be true.

(b) has been true so far but false in the case of the prokaryotic cell.

(c) is only partially true.

(d) has been proved to be completely false.

325. It may be inferred from the passage that the vast majority of cells are

(a) multinucleate. (b) binucleate.

(c) uninucleate. (d) anunucleate.

326. What is definitely a function of the nuclei of the normally binucleate cell?

(a) To arrange for the growth and nourishment of the cell.

(b) To hold hereditary information for the next generation.

(c) To make up the basic physical structure of the organism.

(d) To fight the various foreign diseases attacking the body.

327. The function of the crystalline layer of the inner membrane of the nucleus is

(a) generation of nourishment of the cell.

(b) holding together the disparate structures of the endoplasmic reticulum.

(c) helping in transversal of the nuclear envelope.

(d) Cannot be determined from the passage

328. Why, according to the passage, is the polymorpho-nucleated leukocyte probably lobed?

(a) Because it is quite convoluted in its functions.

(b) Because it is the red blood cell which is the most important cell in the body.

(c) Because it provides a greater area for metabolism reactions.

(d) Because it provides greater strength to the spider web due to greater area.

329. Why, according to the passage, are fungi multinucleate?

(a) Because they need more food to survive.

(b) Because they frequently lack walls dividing the mycelium.

(c) Because the mycelium is areawise much bigger than other cells.

(d) Cannot be determined from the passage

Passage – 42

The second plan to have to examine is that of giving to each person what she deserves. Many people, especially those who are comfortably off, think this is what happens at present: that the industrious and sober and thrifty are never in want, and that poverty is due to idleness, improvidence, drinking, betting, dishonesty, and bad character generally. They can point to the fact that a labour whose character is bad finds it more difficult to get employment than one whose character is good; that a farmer or country gentleman who gambles and bets heavily, and mortgages his land to live wastefully and extravagantly, is soon reduced to poverty; and that a man of business who is lazy and does not attend to it becomes bankrupt. But this proves nothing that you cannot eat your cake and have it too; it does not prove that your share of the cake was a fair one. It shows that certain vices make us rich. People who are hard, grasping, selfish, cruel, and always ready to take advantage of their neighbours, become very rich if they are clever enough not to overreach themselves. On the other hand, people who are generous, public spirited, friendly, and not always thinking of the main chance, stay poor when they are born poor unless they have extraordinary talents. Also as things are today, some are born poor and others are born with silver spoons in their mouths: that is to say, they are divided into rich and poor before they are old enough to have any character at all. The notion that our present system distributes wealth according to merit, even roughly, may be dismissed at once as ridiculous. Everyone can see that it generally has the contrary effect; it makes a few idle people very rich, and a great many hardworking people very poor.

On this, intelligent Lady, your first thought may be that if wealth is not distributed according to merit, it ought to be; and that we should at once set to work to alter our laws so that in future the good people shall be rich in proportion to their goodness and the bad people poor in proportion to their badness. There are several objections to this; but the very first one settles the question for good and all. It is, that the proposal is impossible and impractical. How are you going to measure anyone's merit in money? Choose any pair of human beings you like, male or female, and see whether you can decide how much each of them should have on her or his merits. If you live in the country, take the village blacksmith and the village clergyman, or the village washerwoman and the village schoolmistress, to begin with. At present, the clergyman often gets less pay than the blacksmith; it is only in some villages he gets more. But never mind what they get at present: you are trying whether you can set up a new order of things in which each will get what he deserves. You need not fix a sum of money for them: all you have to do is to settle the proportion between them. Is the blacksmith to have as much as the clergyman? Or twice as much as the clergyman? Or half as much as the clergyman? Or how much more or less? It is no use saying that one ought to have more the other less; you must be prepared to say exactly how much more or less in calculable proportion. Well, think it out. The clergyman has had a college education; but that is not any merit on his part: he owns it to his father; so you cannot allow him anything for that. But through it he is able to read the New Testament in Greek; so that he can do something the blacksmith cannot do. On the other hand, the blacksmith can make a horse-shoe, which the parson cannot. How many verses of the Greek Testament are worth one horse-shoe? You have only to ask the silly question to see that nobody can answer it.

Since measuring their merits is no use, why not try to measure their faults? Suppose the blacksmith swears a good deal, and gets drunk occasionally! Everybody in the village knows this; but the parson has to keep his faults to himself. His wife knows them; but she will not tell you what they are if she knows that you intend to cut off some of his pay for them. You know that as he is only a mortal human being, he must have some faults; but you cannot find them out. However, suppose he has some faults he is a snob; that he cares more for sport and fashionable society than for religion! Does that make him as bad as the blacksmith, or twice as bad, or twice and quarter as bad, or only half as bad? In other words, if the blacksmith is to have a shilling, is the parson to have six pence, or five pence and one-third, or two shillings? Clearly these are fools' questions: the moment they bring us down from moral generalities to business particulars it becomes plain to every sensible person that no relation can be established between human qualities, good or bad, and sums of money, large or small. It may seem scandalous that a prize-fighter, for hitting another prize-fighter so hard at Wembley that he fell down and could not rise within ten seconds, received the same sum that was paid to the Archbishop of Canterbury for acting as Primate of the Church of England for nine months; but none of those who cry out against the scandal can express any better in money the difference between the two. Not one of the persons who think that the prize-fighter should get less than the Archbishop can say how much less. What the prize-fighter got for his six or seven months' boxing would pay a judge's salary for two years; and we all agree that nothing could be more ridiculous, and that any system of distributing wealth which leads to such absurdities must be wrong. But to suppose that it could be changed by any possible calculation that an ounce of archbishop of three ounces of judge is worth a pound of prize-fighter would be sillier still. You can find out how many candles are worth a pound of butter in the market on any particular day; but when you try to estimate the worth of human souls the utmost you can say is that they are all of equal value before the throne of God. And that will not help you in the least to settle how much money they should have. You must simply give it up, and admit that distributing money according to merit is beyond mortal measurement and judgement.

330. Which of the following is not a vice attributed to the poor by the rich?

(a) Idleness

(b) Drug addition

(c) Gambling

(d) Alcoholism

331. What, according to the author, do the generous and public spirited people need to become rich?

(a) A criminal mind

(b) To be born with silver spoons

(c) Extraordinary talents

(d) Strength of character

332. In the passage, which kind of people are not mentioned as likely to get rich quickly?

(a) Selfish people (b) Grasping people

(c) Hard people (d) Ambitious people

333. What, according to the author, is the main problem in distributing wealth according to the goodness or badness of human beings?

(a) Because the bad people will as always, cheat the good people of their fair share of the money.

(b) Because there are too many people in the world and it will take a long time to categorise them into good or bad.

(c) Because there are no standards by which to judge good or bad in relation to money.

(d) None of the above

334. Which of the following about the author's thinking may be inferred from the passage?

(a) The poor should work hard to become rich.

(b) The present system of distribution of wealth is biased in favour of the rich.

(c) The honest men should resort to trickery if they want to become rich.

(d) The present system of government should give way to a more progressive one.

335. This passage most probably is a part of

(a) a newspaper article.

(b) an anthropological document.

(c) a letter to someone.

(d) an ecclesiastical liturgy.

336. The word 'improvidence' in the context of the passage, means

(a) extravagance. (b) lasciviousness.

(c) corruption. (d) indelicacy.

337. The author gives the example of the Archbishop of Canterbury and the prize-fighter to

(a) prove that there cannot be any division of wealth based on moral standards.

(b) prove that in this day and age might always scores over religion and love.

(c) prove the existence of a non-discriminating god.

(d) prove that a pound of butter is worth more than any amount of candles any day.

Passage – 43

The conventional wisdom says that this is an issue-less election. There is no central personality of whom voters have to express approval or dislike; no central matter of concern that makes this a one-issue referendum like so many elections in the past; no central party around which everything else revolves — the Congress has been displaced from its customary pole position, and no one else has been able to take its place. Indeed, given that all-seeing video cameras of the Election Commission, and the detailed pictures they are putting together on campaign expenditure, there isn't even much electioning: no slogans on the walls, no loudspeakers blaring forth at all hours of the day and night, no cavalcades of cars heralding the arrival of a candidate at the local bazaar. Forget it being an issue-less election, is this an election at all?

Perhaps the 'fun' of an election lies in its featuring someone whom you can love or hate. But Narasimha Rao has managed to reduce even a general election, involving nearly 600 million voters, to the boring non-event that is the trademark of his election rallies, and indeed of everything else that he does. After all, the Nehru-Gandhi clan has disappeared from the political map, and the majority of voters will not even be able to name P.V.Narasimha Rao as India's Prime Minister. There could be as many as a dozen prime ministerial candidates ranging from Jyoti Basu to Ramakrishna Hegde, and from Chandra Shekar to (believe it or not) K.R.Narayanan. The sole personality who stands out, therefore, is none of the players, but the umpire: T.N.Seshan.

As for the parties, they are like the blind men of Hindustan, trying in vain to gauge the contours of the animal they have to confront. But it doesn't look as if it will be the mandir-masjid, nor will it be Hindutva or economic nationalism. The Congress will like it to be stability, but what does that mean for the majority? Economic reform is a non-issue for most people with inflation down to barely 4 per cent, prices are not top of the mind either. In a strange twist, after the hawala scandal, corruption has been pushed off the map too.

But ponder for a moment, isn't this state of affairs astonishing, given the context? Consider that so many ministers have had to resign over the hawala issue; that a governor who was a cabinet minister has also had to quit, in the wake of judicial displeasure; that the prime minister himself is under investigation for his involvement in not one scandal but two; that the main prime ministerial candidate from the opposition has had to bow out because he too has been changed in the hawala case; and that the head of the 'third force' has his own little (or not so little) fodder scandal to face. Why then is corruption not an issue — not as a matter of competitive politics, but as an issue on which the contenders for power feel that they have to offer the prospect of genuine change? If all this does not make the parties (almost all of whom have broken the law, in not submitting their audited accounts every year to the income tax authorities) realise that the country both needs — and is ready for-change in the Supreme Court; the assertiveness of the Election Commission, giving new life to a model code of conduct that has been ignored for a quarter country; the independence that has been thrust upon the Central Bureau of Investigation; and the fresh zeal on the part of tax collectors out to nab corporate no-gooders. Think also that at no other point since the Emergency of 1975-77 have so many people in power been hounded by the system for their misdeeds.

Is this just a case of a few individuals outside the political system doing the job, or is the country heading for a new era? The seventies saw the collapse of the national consensus that marked the Nehruvian era, and ideology took over in the Indira Gandhi years. That too was buried by Rajiv Gandhi and his technocratic friends. And now, we have these issue-less elections. One possibility is that the country is heading for a period of constitutionalism as the other arms of the state reclaim some of the powers they lost, or yielded, to the political establishment. Economic reform free one part of Indian society from the clutches of the political class. Now, this could spread to other parts of the system. Against such a dramatic backdrop, it should be obvious that people (voters) are looking for accountability, for ways in which to make a corrupted system work again. And the astonishing thing is that no party has sought to ride this particular wave; instead all are on the defensive, desperately evading the real issues. No wonder this is an 'issue-less' election.

338. Why does the author probably say that the sole personality who stands out in the elections is T.N.Seshan?

(a) Because all the other candidates are very boring.

(b) Because all the other candidates do not have his charisma.

(c) Because the shadow of his strictures are looming large over the elections.

(d) None of the above

339. A suitable title to the passage would be

(a) *Elections: A Oreview.*

(b) *The Country's Issue-less Elections.*

(c) *T.N.Seshan — the Real Hero.*

(d) *Love or Hate Them, But Vote For Them.*

340. Which of the following are not under scrutiny for alleged corruption, according to the passage?

(a) The opposition prime ministerial candidate

(b) P.V. Narasimha Rao

(c) The leader of the 'third force'

(d) Ramakrishna Hegde

341. Why does the author say that almost all parties have broken the law?

(a) Because they all indulge in corrupt electoral process.

(b) Because they all have more income than recorded sources.

(c) Because they are all indicted on various charges.

(d) Because they have failed to submit audited accounts to tax authorities.

342. According to the passage, which of the following has not been responsible for the winds of change blowing throughout the country?

(a) Greater awareness on the part of the general public.

(b) Enforcement of a model code of conduct by the Election Commission.

(c) Greater independence to the Central Bureau of Investigation.

(d) Fresh zeal on the part of tax collectors.

343. According to the passage, which of the following is not mentioned as even having the potential to be an issue in the current elections?

(a) The mandir-masjid issue

(b) The empowerment of women

(c) Economic nationalism

(d) Hindutva

Passage – 44

I think that it would be wrong to ask whether 50 years of India's Independence are an achievement or a failure. It would be better to see things as evolving. It's not an either-or question. My idea of the history of India is slightly contrary to the Indian idea. India is a country that, in the north, outside Rajasthan, was ravaged and intellectually destroyed to a large extent by the invasions that began in about AD 1000 by forces and religions that India had no means of understanding.

The invasions are in all the schoolbooks. But I don't think that people understand that every invasion, every war, every campaign, was accompanied by slaughter, a slaughter always of the most talented people in the country. So these wars, apart from everything else led to a tremendous intellectual depletion of the country. I think that in the British period, and in the 50 years after the British period, there has been a kind of regrouping or recovery, a very slow revival of energy and intellect. This isn't an idea that goes with the vision of the grandeur of old India and all that sort of rubbish. That idea is a great simplification and it occurs because it is intellectually, philosophically easier for Indians to manage.

What they cannot manage, and what they have not yet come to terms with, is that ravaging of all the north of India by various conquerors. That was ruined not by the act of nature, but by the hand of man. It is so painful that few Indians have begun to deal with it. It is much easier to deal with British imperialism. That is a familiar topic, in India and Britain. What is much less familiar is the ravaging of India before the British.

What happened from AD 1000 onwards, really, is such a wound that it is almost impossible to face. Certain wounds are so bad that they can't be written about. You deal with that kind of pain by hiding from it. You retreat from reality. I do not think, for example, that the Incas of Peru or the native people of Mexico have ever got over their defeat by the Spaniards. In both places the head was cut off. I think the pre-British ravaging of India was as bad as that.

In the place of knowledge of history, you have various fantasies about the village republic and the Old Glory. There is one big fantasy that Indians have always found solace in: about India having the capacity for absorbing its conquerors. This is not so. India was laid low by its conquerors. I feel the past 150 years have been years of every kind of growth. I see the British period and what has continued after that as one period. In that time, there has been a very slow intellectual recruitment. I think every Indian should make the pilgrimage to the site of the capital of the Vijayanagar empire, just to see what the invasion of India led to. They will see a totally destroyed town. Religious wars are like that. People who see that might understand what the centuries of slaughter and plunder meant. War isn't a game. When you lost that kind of war, your town was destroyed, the people who built the towns were destroyed. You are left with a headless population. That's where modern India starts from. The Vijayanagar capital was destroyed in 1565. It is only now that the surrounding region has begun to revive.

A great chance has been given to India to start up again, and I feel it has started up again. The questions about whether 50 years of India since Independence have been a failure or an achievement are not the questions to ask.

In fact, I think India is developing quite marvelously, people thought — even Mr Nehru thought — that development and new institutions in a place like Bihar, for instance, would immediately lead to beauty. But it doesn't happen like that. When a country as ravaged as India, with all its layers of cruelty, begins to extend justice to people lower down, it's a very messy business. It's not beautiful, it's extremely messy. And that's what you have now, all these small politicians with small reputations and small parties. But this is part of growth, this is part of development. You must remember that these people, and the people they represent, have never had rights before. When the oppressed have the power to assert themselves, they will behave badly. It will need a couple of generations of security, and knowledge of institutions, and the knowledge that you can trust institutions — it will take at least a couple of generations before people in that situation begin to behave well.

People in India have known only tyranny. The very idea of liberty is a new idea. The rulers were tyrants. The tyrants were foreigners. And they were proud of being foreign. There's a story that anybody could run and pull a bell and the emperor would appear at his window and give justice. This is a child's idea of history — the slave's idea of the ruler's mercy. When the people at the bottom discover that they hold justice in their own hands, the earth moves a little. You have to expect these earth movements in India. It will be like this for a hundred years. But it is the only way. It's painful and messy and primitive and petty, but it's better that it should begin. It has to begin. If we were to rule people according to what we think fit, that takes us back to the past when people had no voices.

With self-awareness all else follows. People begin to make new demands on their leaders, their fellows, on themselves. They ask for more in everything. They have a higher idea of human possibilities. They are not content with what they did before or what their fathers did before. They want to move. That is marvellous. That is as it should be.

I think that within every kind of disorder now in India there is a larger positive movement. But the future will be fairly chaotic. Politics will have to be at the level of the people now. People like Nehru were colonial — style politicians. They were to a large extent created and protected by the colonial order. They did not begin with the people. Politicians now have to begin with the people. They cannot be too far above the level of the people. They are very much part of the people.

It is important that self-criticism does not stop. The mind has to work, the mind has to be active, there has to be an exercise of the mind. I think it's almost a definition of a living country that it looks at itself, analyses itself at all times. Only countries that have ceased to live can say it's all wonderful.

1997

344. The central thrust of the passage is that
(a) India is gearing up for a new awakening.
(b) India is going back to its past status.
(c) India is yet to understand itself.
(d) India's glorious past is a figment of the imagination.

345. The writer's attitude is
(a) excessively critical of India.
(b) insightful.
(c) cynical.
(d) col (d)

346. The writer has given the example of the Vijayanagar kingdom in order to drive home the point that
(a) Indians should know their historical sites.
(b) Indians should be aware of the existence of such a historic past.
(c) it is time that India came to terms with the past.
(d) All of these

347. The writer is against
(a) the child's view of history.
(b) taking a critical stand on history.
(c) indulging in the details of the past.
(d) None of these

348. According to the writer, India's regeneration and revival took place
(a) in the British period.
(b) after the British period.
(c) during and after the British period.
(d) a long time after the British left.

349. According to the passage, self-awareness is followed by
(a) self-righteousness.
(b) a higher idea of human possibilities.
(c) a desire for more in everything.
(d) Both (b) and (c)

350. According to the passage, India's current situation is
(a) bleak. (b) horrific.
(c) primitive and messy. (d) None of these

351. For a country to be alive and progressive, it is important that
(a) self-criticism does not stop.
(b) self-criticism does not exceed a certain limit.
(c) it feels that all is right with itself.
(d) None of these

352. The writer's prognosis for India's future is that
(a) it will be stable.
(b) it will be chaotic.
(c) it will reflect the manipulations of the present.
(d) it will give way to self-criticism.

353. One of the main features of the tyranny of foreign rulers was
(a) the decimation of the country's artists.
(b) the decimation of the country's wealth.
(c) the decimation of the country's talented people.
(d) All of these

Passage – 45

When talks come to how India has done for itself in 50 years of independence, the world has nothing but praise for our success in remaining a democracy. On other fronts, the applause is less loud. In absolute terms, India hasn't done too badly, of course, life expectancy has increased. So has literacy. Industry, which was barely a fledging, has grown tremendously. And as far as agriculture is concerned, India has been transformed from a country perpetually on the edge of starvation into a success story held up for others to emulate.

But these are competitive times when change is rapid, and to walk slowly when the rest of the world is running is almost as bad as standing still or walking backwards. Compared with large chunks of what was then the developing world — South Korea, Singapore, Malaysia, Thailand, Indonesia, China and what was till lately a separate Hong Kong — India has fared abysmally.

It began with a far better infrastructure than most of these countries had. It suffered hardly or not at all during the World War II. It had advantages like an English speaking elite, quality scientific manpower (including a Nobel laureate and others who could be ranked among the world's best) and excellent business acumen. Yet, today, when countries are ranked according to their global competitiveness, it is tiny Singapore that figures at the top. Hong Kong is an export powerhouse. So is Taiwan. If a symbol were needed of how far we have fallen back, note that while Korean Cielos are sold in India, no one in South Korea is rushing to buy an Indian car.

The reasons list themselves. Topmost is economic isolationism. The government discouraged imports and encouraged self-sufficiency. Whatever the aim was, the result was the creation of a totally inefficient industry that failed to keep pace with global trends and, therefore, became absolutely uncompetitive. Only when the trade gates were opened a little did this become apparent. The years since then have been spent in merely trying to catch up.

That the government actually sheltered its industrialists from foreign competition is a little strange. For, in all other respects, it operated under the conviction that businessmen were little more than crooks who were to be prevented from entering the most important areas of the economy, who were to be hamstrung in as many ways as possible, who were to be tolerated in the same way as an inexcisable wart. The high, expropriatory rates of taxation, the licensing laws, the reservation of whole swathes of industry for the public sector, and the granting of monopolies to the public sector firms were the principal manifestations of this attitude. The government forgot that before wealth could be distributed, it had to be created. The government forgot that it itself could not create, but only squander wealth.

Some of the manifestations of the old attitude have changed. Tax rates have fallen. Licensing has been all but abolished. And the gates of global trade have been opened wide. But most of these changes were forced by circumstances partly by the foreign exchange bankruptcy of 1991 and the recognition that the government could no longer muster the funds to support the public sector, leave alone expand it. Whether the attitude of the government itself, or that of more than a handful of ministers, has changed, is open to question.

In many other ways, however, the government has not changed one whit. Business still has to negotiate a welter of negotiations. Transparency is still a longer way off. And there is no exit policy. In defending the existing policy, politicians betray an inability to see beyond their noses. A no-exit policy for labour is equivalent to a no-entry policy for new business. If one industry is not allowed to retrench labour, other industries will think a hundred times before employing new labour.

In other ways too, the government hurts industries. Public sector monopolies like the department of telecommunications and Videsh Sanchar Nigam Ltd. make it possible for Indian businesses to operate only at a cost several times that of their counterparts abroad. The infrastructure is in shambles partly because it is unable to formulate a sufficiently remunerative policy for private business, and partly because it does not have the stomach to change market rates for services.

After a burst of activity in the early nineties, the government is dragging its feet. At the rate it is going, it will be another 50 years before the government realises that a pro-business policy is the best pro-people policy. By then of course, the world would have moved even farther ahead.

354. The writer's attitude towards the government is

(a) critical. (b) ironical.

(c) sarcastic. (d) derisive.

355. The writer is surprised at the government's attitude towards its industrialists because

(a) the government did not need to protect its industrialists.

(b) the issue of competition was non-existent.

(c) the government looked upon its industrialists as crooks.

(d) the attitude was a conundrum.

356. The government was compelled to open the economy due to

(a) pressure from international markets.

(b) pressure from domestic market.

(c) foreign exchange bankruptcy and paucity of funds with the government.

(d) All of these

357. The writer ends the passage on a note of
(a) cautious optimism.
(b) pessimism.
(c) optimism.
(d) pragmatism.

358. According to the writer, India should have performed better than the other Asian nations because
(a) it had adequate infrastructure.
(b) it had better infrastructure.
(c) it had better politicians who could take the required decisions.
(d) All of these

359. India was in a better condition than the other Asian nations because
(a) it did not face the ravages of the World War II.
(b) it had an English speaking populace and good business sense.
(c) it had enough wealth through its exports.
(d) Both (a) and (b)

360. The major reason for India's poor performance is
(a) economic isolationism.
(b) economic mismanagement.
(c) inefficient industry.
(d) All of these

361. One of the features of the government's protectionist policy was
(a) encouragement of imports.
(b) discouragement of exports.
(c) encouragement of exports.
(d) discouragement of imports.

362. The example of the Korean Cielo has been presented to highlight
(a) India's lack of stature in the international market.
(b) India's poor performance in the international market.
(c) India's lack of creditability in the international market.
(d) India's disrepute in the international market.

363. According to the writer,
(a) India's politicians are myopic in their vision of the country's requirements.
(b) India's politicians are busy lining their pockets.
(c) India's politicians are not conversant with the needs of the present scenario.
(d) All of these

Passage – 46

When Deng Xiaoping died a few months ago, the Chinese leadership barely paused for a moment before getting on with the business of governing the country. Contrast that with the chaotic contortions on India's political stage during the past month, and it is easy to conclude that democracy and democratic freedoms are serious obstacles to economic progress.

When the Chinese leadership wants a power plant to be set up, it just goes ahead. No fears of protracted litigation, of environmental protests, or of lobbying by interested parties. It — or the economy — is not held to ransom by striking truckers or air traffic controllers. Certainly, there is much that is alluring about an enlightened dictatorship.

But there the trouble begins. First, there is no guarantee that a dictatorship will be an enlightened one. Myanmar has been ruled by a dictator for decades, and no one would claim that it is better off than even Bangladesh which has itself suffered long stretches of dictatorship. Nor can Mobuto Sese Seko, much in the news these days, be described as enlightened by any reckoning. The people of Israel, almost the only democracy in a region where dictatorships (unenlightened ones) are the norm, are much better off than their neighbours.

Second, dictatorships can easily reverse policies. China was socialist as long as Mao Zedong was around. When Deng Xiaoping took over in what was essentially a palace coup, he took the country in the opposite direction. There is little to ensure that the process will not be repeated. In India such drastic reversals are unlikely.

Six years ago Indian politicians agreed that industries should be de-licensed, that imports should be freed or that investment decisions should be based on economic considerations. Now few think otherwise. Almost all politicians are convinced of the merits of liberalisation though they may occasionally lose sight of the big picture in pandering to their constituencies. India has moved slower than China on liberalisation, but whatever moves it has made are more permanent.

Democracies are also less likely to get embroiled in destructive wars. Had Saddam Hussain been under the obligation of facing free elections every five years, he would have thought ten times before entangling his people in a long confrontation with the West. Germany, Italy and Japan were all dictatorships when they launched the World War II. The price was paid by the economies.

Democracies make many small mistakes. But dictatorships are more susceptible to making huge ones and risking everything on one decision — like going to war. Democracies are the political equivalent of free markets, Companies know they can't fool the consumer too often; he will simply switch to the competition. The same goes for political parties. When they fail to live up to their promises in government, the political consumer opts for the competition.

Democratic freedoms too are important for the economy, especially now that information is supreme. Few doubt that the Internet will play an important part in the global economy in the decades to come. But China, by preventing free access to it, is already probably destroying its capabilities in this area. As service industries grow in importance, China may well be at a disadvantage though that may not be apparent today when its manufacturing juggernaut is rolling ahead.

India has stifled its entrepreneurs through its licensing policies. That was an example of how the absence of economic freedom can harm a country. But right-wing dictatorships like South Korea erred in the opposite direction. They forced their businesses to invest in industries, which they (the dictators) felt had a golden future. Now many of those firms are trying to retreat from those investments. Statism is bad, no matter what the direction in which it applies pressure. At this moment, China and other dictatorships may be making foolish investment decisions. But as industries are subsidized and contrary voices not heard, the errors will not be realised until the investments assume gargantuan proportions.

India's hesitant ways may seem inferior to China's confident moves. But at least we know what the costs are. That is not the case with China. It was only years after the Great Leap Forward and only such experiments that the cost in human lives (millions of them) became evident to the world. What the cost of China's present experiments is we may not know for several years more. A nine per cent rate of growth repeated year after year may seem compelling. But a seven per cent rate of growth that will not falter is more desirable. India seems to be on such a growth curve, whatever the shenanigans of our politicians.

364. According to the passage,

(a) India needs a benevolent dictatorship.

(b) India has failed as a democracy.

(c) India should go the way of China.

(d) None of these

365. The passage says that

(a) benevolent dictators are not easy to find.

(b) not all dictators will be enlightened.

(c) dictators can make or break a country.

(d) an enlightened dictatorship is better than a corrupt democracy.

366. It can be implied from the passage that

(a) a lower rate of growth is preferred to a higher rate of growth.

(b) a higher rate of growth is preferred to a lower rate of growth.

(c) a low but stable rate of growth is preferred to a high rate of growth.

(d) a low but faltering rate of growth is a sign of stability amidst growth.

367. Vis-a-vis democracies, dictatorships run the risk of

(a) losing all for a single mistake.

(b) making bigger mistakes.

(c) making huge mistakes and risking everything.

(d) None of these

368. The writer's conclusion in the passage is that

(a) under no circumstances should a country encourage a corrupt democrat.

(b) under no circumstances should statism be a welcome move.

(c) a statist will not give due importance to the voice of the people.

(d) a statist will always look to his own welfare.

369. Democracy has been compared to the free market, as

(a) both have a high degree of competition.

(b) both offer a multitude of options to choose from.

(c) consumer satisfaction plays an important role in both.

(d) All of these

370. It can be inferred from the passage that

(a) China stands to lose out in the global market because it has blocked the Internet.

(b) India stands to gain in the global market because of its policy vis-à-vis the Internet.

(c) Internet will play a crucial role in the global market in the years to come.

(d) All of these

371. According to the passage, a democratic set up works as a check on the

(a) actions and decisions of its leaders.

(b) functioning of its economy.

(c) Both (a) and (b)

(d) None of these

372. India's moves on liberalisation are more permanent than China's because

(a) India's politicians are in agreement over the need for reforms.

(b) India is not at the mercy of dictators.

(c) unlike China, India is unlikely to have drastic policy reversals.

(d) India is not in a hurry to reform

373. According to the passage,

(a) Israel is the only democracy in West Asia.

(b) Israel is better off than Bangladesh or Myanmar.

(c) Israel does not face policy reversals.

(d) None of these

Passage – 47

Of each of the great leaders, it is said by his followers, long after he is gone, he made us do it. If leadership is the art of persuading your people to follow your bidding, without their realising your involvement, the archetype of its practice is N. R. Narayana Murthy, the chairman and managing director of the Rs. 143.81 crore Infosys Technologies (Infosys). For, the 52-year-old CEO of the globalised software corporation — which he founded with six friends, and a combined capital of Rs. 10,000 in 1981 and which now occupies the front ranks of the country's most admired corporations, leads with the subtlest of weapons: personal example.

Infosys ranks only 578th among the country's listed companies, and sixth in the software sector, in terms of its turnover. But it is setting new standards for India Inc. through its practices of inter alia awarding stock options to its employees, putting the value of its intellectual assets and its brands on its balancesheet, and conforming to the disclosure standards of the Securities and Exchange Commission (SEC) of the US. Behind all this is the stubborn personal subscription of its CEO to the underlying causes of wealth-creation-people-power and transparency. "What were choices earlier are compulsions now," asserts Murthy.

In fact, the mirror images of Murthy, the Man, can be found all over Infosys, his company. His egalitarianism — which finds expression in such habits as using the same table and chair as anyone else in the organisation — is practised firmly when it comes to charting a course for the company's future: everyone has a voice. "We have no hierarchy just for the sake of control."

Brimming with the conviction that customer satisfaction is the key to success, Murthy has built a fleet-footed human resource management system that treats employees as customers, using the resources of the organisation to meet their professional and personal needs. His instruments are not just top-of-the-market salaries, but also operational empowerment as well as every facility that an employee needs to focus on the job.

Just what methods does Murthy use to ensure that his DNA is replicated in his company? Not for him are the classical leadership genre — transactional or transformational, situational or visionary. His chosen style, instead, is to lead by example, ensuring that the CEO's actions set the template for all Infoscions.

Murthy believes that the betterment of man can be brought about through the 'creation of wealth, legally and ethically'. The personal example that he has set enabled his company to mirror those beliefs, tying his own rewards, and measuring his value to the company, to his ability to create wealth, and erecting systems for the company's wealth to be shared by its people. Sums up Nandan Nilekani, 41, deputy managing director, Infosys: "This is the future model of the corporation. Run an excellent company, and let the market increase its value to create wealth."

Although Murthy is one of the prime beneficiaries of the philosophy — his 10 per cent stake in Infosys is worth Rs. 130 crore today — in his book, the leader leads not by grabbing the booty but by teaching others to take what they deserve. That's why, on the Infosys' balancesheet, the value of Murthy's intellectual capital is nowhere near the top, on the rationale, that the CEO, at 52, is worth far less to his company than, say, a bright young programmer of 26. To spread the company's wealth, Murthy has instituted stock options — the first to do so in the country — for employees, creating 300 millionaires already. By 2000, he wants the number to climb to 1000.

To act as a beacon for his version of the learning organisation, Murthy not only spends an hour a day surfing the Internet to learn about new technological developments in his field, he also makes as many luncheon appointments as he can with technical people and academicians — dons from the Indian Institutes of Technology for instance — systematically plumbing their depths for an understanding of new developments in infotech. Murthy's objective is not just to stay abreast of the state-of-the-art, but also to find a way to use that knowledge for the company.

Following Murthy's example, Infosys has set up a technology advancement unit, whose mandate is to track, evaluate, and assimilate new techniques and methodologies. In fact, Murthy views learning not just as amassing data, but as a process that enables him to use the lessons from failure to achieve success. This self-corrective loop is what he demonstrates through his leadership during a crisis.

In 1995, for example, Infosys lost a Rs. 15 crore account — then 20 per cent of its revenues — when the $69 billion GE yanked its business from it. Instead of recriminations, Murthy activated Infosys' machinery to understand why the business was taken away and to leverage the learning for getting new clients instead. Feeling determined instead of guilty, his employees went on to sign up high profile customers like the $20 billion Xerox, the $7 billion Levi Strauss, and the $14 billion Nynex.

"You must have a multi-dimensional view of paradigms," says the multi-tasking leader. The objective is obvious: ensure that Infosys' perspective on its business and the world comes from as many vantage points as possible so that corporate strategy can be synthesised not from a narrow vision, but from a wide angle lens. In fact, Murthy still regrets that, in its initial years, Infosys didn't distil a multi-pronged understanding of the environment into its strategies, which forced it onto an incremental path that led revenues to snake up from Rs. 0.02 crore to just Rs. 5 crore in the first 10 years.

It was after looking around itself instead of focusing on its initial business of banking software, that Infosys managed to accelerate. Today the company operates with stretch targets setting distant goals and working backwards to get to them. The crucial pillar on which Murthy bases his ethical leadership is openness. Transparency, he reckons, is the clearest signal that one has nothing to hide. The personal manifestations of that are inter alia the practice of always giving complete information whenever any employee, customer, or investor asks for it: the loudly proclaimed insistence that every Infoscion pay taxes and file returns: and a perpetually open office into which anyone can walk.

But even as he tries to lead Infosys into cloning his own approach to enterprise, is Murthy choosing the best future for it? If Infosys grows with the same lack of ambition, the same softness of style, and the same absence of aggression, is it not cutting off avenues of growth that others may seize? As Infosys approaches the 21st century it is obvious that Murthy's leadership will have to set ever-improving role models for his ever-learning company. After all, men grow old; companies shouldn't.

374. One of the ways in which Infosys spreads the company's wealth among its employees is

(a) by awarding stock options.

(b) by giving an extravagant bonus at the end of each year.

(c) Both (a) and (b)

(d) None of these

375. According to the passage, at Infosys

(a) control is exerted through a system of hierarchy.

(b) control is not exerted through a system of hierarchy.

(c) hierarchy does not have pride of place.

(d) popular opinion is the most respected voice.

376. Murthy believes in

(a) betterment of man through learning.

(b) betterment of man through ethical creation of wealth.

(c) betterment of man through experimentation.

(d) All of these

377. The example of the Rs. 15 crore account highlights

(a) Murthy's ability to see his company through a crisis.

(b) Murthy's ability to turn failure into success.

(c) Murthy's potential to handle a crisis.

(d) All of these

378. According to Murthy, learning is

(a) the essence of a employee.

(b) the art of amassing data.

(c) a process that helps him to learn from failure.

(d) All of these

379. According to the passage,

(a) Infosys could not have succeeded without working backward.

(b) Infosys succeeded because it worked backwards.

(c) working backwards contributed to Infosys' success.

(d) working backwards is a hallmark of Infosys' functioning today.

380. Openness at Infosys includes

(a) the payment of taxes.

(b) giving complete information.

(c) sharing secrets.

(d) Both (a) and (b)

381. It is evident from the passage that

(a) Infosys will have to devise new strategies to meet the challenges of the 21st century.

(b) Infosys will stagnate if it does not become aggressive.

(c) Infosys may have to become more aggressive in order to retain its market.

(d) None of these

382. The cornerstone of Murthy's human resource management system is

(a) the employee as God.

(b) optimum utilization of human potential.

(c) customer satisfaction.

(d) satisfaction of personal needs.

383. According to the passage,

(a) Infosys is a reflection of its CEO.

(b) Infosys brings the best out in Murthy.

(c) Infosys and Murthy are synonymous.

(d) Murthy, the man, and Murthy the CEO are incompatible.

Passage – 48

Last fortnight, news of a significant development was tucked away in the inside pages of newspapers. The government finally tabled a bill in Parliament seeking to make primary education a fundamental right. A fortnight earlier, a Delhi-based newspaper had carried a report about a three-month interruption in the Delhi Government's 'Education for All' programme. The report made for distressing reading. It said that literacy centres across the city were closed down, volunteers beaten up and enrolment registers burnt. All because the state government had, earlier this year, made participation in the programme mandatory for teachers in government schools. The routine denials were issued and there probably was a wee bit of exaggeration in the report. But it still is a pointer to the enormity of the task at hand.

That economic development will be inherently unstable unless it is built on a solid base of education, specially primary education, has been said so often that it is in danger of becoming a platitude. Nor does India's abysmal record in the field need much reiteration. Nearly 30 million children in the six to ten age group do not go to school — reason enough to make primary education not only compulsory but a fundamental right. But is that the solution? More importantly, will it work? Or will it remain a mere token, like the laws providing for compulsory primary education? It is now widely known that 14 states and four Union Territories have this law on their statute books. Believe it or not, the list actually includes Bihar, Madhya Pradesh (MP) and Rajasthan, where literacy and education levels are miles below the national average. A number of states have not even notified the compulsory education law.

This is not to belittle the decision to make education a fundamental right. As a statement of political will, a commitment by the decision-makers, its importance cannot be undervalued. Once this commitment is clear, a lot of other things like resource allocation will naturally fall into place. But the task of universalizing elementary education (UEE) is complicated by various socio-economic and cultural factors which vary from region to region and within regions.

If India's record continues to appall, it is because these intricacies have not been adequately understood by the planners and administrators. The trouble has been that education policy has been designed by grizzled mandarins ensconced in Delhi and is totally out of touch with the ground reality. The key then is to decentralise education planning and implementation. What's also needed is greater community involvement in the whole process. Only then can school timings be adjusted for convenience, school children given a curriculum they can relate to and teachers made accountable.

For proof, one has only to look at the success of the district primary education programme, which was launched in 1994. It has met with a fair degree of success in the 122 districts it covers. Here the village community is involved in all aspects of education — allocating finances to supervising teachers to fixing school timings and developing curriculum and textbooks — through district planning teams. Teachers are also involved in the planning and implementation process and are given small grants to develop teaching and learning material, vastly improving motivational levels. The consequent improvement in the quality of education generates increased demand for education.

But for this demand to be generated, quality will first have to be improved. In MP, the village panchayats are responsible for not only constructing and maintaining primary schools but also managing scholarships, besides organising non-formal education. How well this works in practice remains to be seen (though the department claims the schemes are working very well) but the decision to empower panchayats with such powers is itself a significant development. Unfortunately, the Panchayat Raj Act has not been notified in many states. After all, delegating powers to the panchayats is not looked upon too kindly by vested interests. More specifically, by politicians, since decentralisation of education administration takes away from them the power of transfer, which they use to grant favours and build up a support base. But if the political leadership can push through the bill to make education a fundamental right, it should also be able to persuade the states to implement the laws on Panchayat Raj. For, UEE cannot be achieved without decentralisation. Of course, this will have to be accompanied by proper supervision and adequate training of those involved in the administration of education. But the devolution of powers to the local bodies has to come first.

384. One of the problems plaguing the education system in India is

(a) poverty.

(b) diverse cultural and socio-economic factors.

(c) male chauvinism.

(d) All of these

385. In the context of the passage, the term 'grizzled mandarins' means

(a) old hags.

(b) decrepit men.

(c) ineffective old men.

(d) None of these

386. One of the reasons contributing to India's poor performance on the education front is that

(a) its leaders do not have the conviction required to improve the education system.

(b) male members of society do not want their female counterparts to be educated.

(c) administrators in charge of education are out of touch with ground realities.

(d) the country does not have the law for implementation of education policies in its statute books.

387. The only way in which the education system can be improved is by

(a) decentralising education planning and implementation.

(b) introducing fresh blood in the planning body.

(c) injecting funds into the exchequer solely for the purpose.

(d) educating the people on the need for primary education.

388. Very low education levels are visible in

(a) Bihar, Rajasthan and Uttar Pradesh.

(b) Rajasthan, West Bengal and Madhya Pradesh.

(c) Rajasthan, Bihar and Madhya Pradesh.

(d) West Bengal, Uttar Pradesh and Bihar.

389. The district primary education programme

(a) was launched in 1994 in 22 states.

(b) was launched in 1994 in 12 states.

(c) launched in 1994 has been successful in 122 districts.

(d) launched in 1994 has met with dubious success.

390. The village panchayats in Madhya Pradesh are responsible for

(a) implementing adult education policies for the villages.

(b) organising non-formal education.

(c) scholarships and construction and maintenance of primary schools.

(d) Both (b) and (c)

391. The successful implementation of education policies is obstructed by

(a) vested interests.

(b) panchayat officials.

(c) politicians.

(d) bureaucrats.

392. Primary education

(a) is a fundamental right.

(b) will be made a fundamental right.

(c) is only for the privileged sections of society.

(d) None of these

393. One of the ways in which education policy can be successfully implemented as mentioned in the passage, is

(a) greater community involvement.

(b) greater community development.

(c) greater community awareness.

(d) Both (a) and (b)

Passage – 49

The narrator of *Midnight's Children* describes it as a kind of collective fantasy. I suppose what he, or I, through him was trying to say, was that there never had been a political entity called India until 1947. The thing that became independent had never previously existed, except that there had been an area, a zone called India. So it struck me that what was coming into being, this idea of a nation-state, was an invention. It was an invention of the nationalist movement. And a very successful invention.

One could argue that nation-states are a kind of collective fantasies. Very similar things happened with the unification of Italy, and also with the unification of Germany. The history of India is a history of independent nation-states. It is a history of Oudh or Bengal or Maratha kingdoms. All those independent histories agreed to collectivise themselves into the idea of the nation of India. In the case of Pakistan, it was less successful. Pakistan was under-imagined. It did not survive as a nation-state.

If you ask people in general, they would have absolutely no problem with the idea of India at all. I think, in a way the strength of the nationalist idea is shown by its ability to survive the extraordinary stresses that it was placed under. I think the stresses of things — communalism, the high degree of public corruption, of regional rivalries, of the tension between the centre and the state, the external pressures of bad relations with Pakistan — these are colossal pressures which any state could be forgiven for being damaged by. I think the thing to say about the success of the idea is that it remains an idea though people might not find it very easy to give a simple definition of it. But that it does exist and that it is something to which people feel they belong, I think is now the case. That it survives these stresses is an indication of its strength.

I'm not interested in an idealised, romantic vision of India, I know it is the great pitfall of the exile. So you know for me, always, the issue of writing about India has been not to write as an outsider. On the other hand, evidently something has changed in the last 10 years, which is that as a result of various circumstances, I've not been able to return. All I can say is that I have felt it as the most profound loss and I still do. There have been many losses in the last decade but the loss of the easy return to India has been for me an absolute anguish, an inescapable anguish. I feel as if I've lost a limb. I am very anxious to bring that period to an end.

I do not think that one of the most interesting phenomena for India as a country is the phenomenon of the Indian Diaspora. I often think Indian — Indian Indians — find that very hard to understand. In England, when people call themselves British Indian, they mean both halves of that. And yet, what it means to be a British Indian is very alien to an Indian Indian. The same is true in the Caribbean, in Africa, in Canada, in the United States, and so on. The thing that has interested me is that there are now many, many ways of being something which you can legitimately call Indian. Being an Indian in India is just one of those ways.

The forces of disintegration are always there. I think in every society there is the tension between the forces that bring it together and the forces that pull it apart. I'm worried, above all, of the communal issue because half a century is no time at all in the eye of history, and half a century ago something of colossally horrible proportion took place. The fact that it hasn't happened for 50 years on quite the same scale means nothing. It could still happen tomorrow. One of the things that I remember very vividly, being there 10 years ago at about the time of the killings that took place in Assam, is discussing this with good friends and fellow writers. And I remember somebody said to me, until we understand that we are capable of these things, we can't begin to move beyond them. Because it's a very easy response to atrocities, to say: oh those terrible people did that, and we are not like that. I think the difficult response is to accept we are also capable of that, the thing that happened there could also, in certain circumstances, be something that we were able to perpetrate. The civilising influence is what prevents most of us from giving vent to those terrible urges. Those urges are part of humanity as well as the more civilized urges.

Of course, I fear in India the recurrence of communal or regionalist inter-community violence. I fear the long-term damage to a democracy that can be done by mass corruption. I think corruption is in a way a subversion of democracy and the commonplace view in India is that corruption is everywhere. In a sense, you could say that is not a democratic society. If money, favour and privilege is what makes the place work, then that's not a democracy. At least it runs the danger of being no longer able to call itself a democracy.

What was happening, I thought, was that people were trying to seize control of that rhetoric. That is to say, special interest groups. You could say Hindus are a very large special interest group. If any group inside such a complex and many faceted country tries to define the nation exclusively in its own terms, then it begins to create terrible stresses. I do think that the kind of attempt to define India in Hindu terms is worrying for that reason. It creates backlashes, it creates polarisation, and it creates the risk of more upheaval. Partly, I am saying this as a kind of objective observer, but nobody is an objective observer.

I come from an Indian minority, I no doubt have a minority perspective. I can't ignore that and nor would I wish to. Partly, also I am speaking temperamentally. That is to say, the kind of religious language in politics is something I find temperamentally unpleasant. I don't like people who do that, whether they be sectarians in Northern Ireland or India. I believe in, if possible, separating one's personal spiritual needs and aspirations from the way in which a country is run. I think in those countries where that separation has not taken place, one can see all kinds of distortions of social and ordinary life which are unpleasant. Iran is an obvious example. The country in which that kind of separation has completely fragmented it.

Where Naipaul is right, although I don't share his conclusions about it, but I think where he is right, is in saying that this is a great historical moment. One reason why the 50th anniversary is interesting is that it does seem to represent the end of the first age and the beginning of second age. And to that extent that is true now, if someone was born today, they would be born into a very different set of cultural assumptions and hopes than somebody born 50 years ago. We were entirely sold on the Nehru-Gandhi kind of plan. We grew up and that was the portrait of the nation we had hung on our wall, and to the extent that you never entirely lose those formative ideas, that's still the picture of the country I've got on my wall. But it's clear that for somebody being born now, they are being born into a very different country.

I also think of taking the Naipaul point on what would happen if the BJP were to form a government. Well, what I would like to think is that in order for the BJP or anybody of that persuasion to form a government, they would have to change. There is even some kind of suggestion that it may even be happening a little bit because they are intelligent people. They understand their weaknesses as well as their strengths. Clearly, for a Hinduist party to form the government of the country is not at all unlikely. So I think one does have to engage with that in the same way as many people in the country who, like myself, were not remotely in tune with the Thatcherite revolution but have to engage with it because it was in fact happening, and kept winning elections, and the world was not going to go back. So, of course, both people inside the Hindu political enterprise and people outside it will have to shift. I am optimistic about India's ability to force those changes that are necessary because I do believe it is not fundamentally an intolerant country and will not fundamentally accept intolerant politics.

On the other hand, there has to be reckoning with the fact that these are ideas, which are gaining in popularity. I'll tell you where I would draw the line myself. I think there was a great historical mistake made in Europe about the Nazi Party. People attempted to see whether they could live with it and discovered very rapidly that was a mistake, that appeasement was a great historical mistake. So, it seems to me, the question is: What do we make of this political enterprise? Is it fundamentally democratic or fundamentally anti-democratic? If democratic, then we must all learn to make the best of it. If anti-democratic, then we must fight it very hard.

What happened in India happened before the book (*Satanic Verses*) had actually entered. It happened because of an article in *India Today*, which, I must say, I thought was an irresponsibly written article, because it was written by somebody, who, as a friend, asked me for an early copy of the book, and then presented that book in the most inflammatory sort of way.

This was one of the things that disappointed me, that after a lifetime of having written from a certain sensibility, and a certain point of view, I would have expected people in India to know about it since it was all entirely about India. It was written from a deep sense of connection and affection for India. I would have expected that I had some money in the bank. That is to say, if Salman Rushdie wrote any book, then we know who he is. He is not some idiot who just arrived from nowhere shouting abuse. This is somebody whose work, whose opinions, whose lectures and whose stories we know. I would have hoped that my work would have been judged in the context of what people already knew about me. Instead, it seemed as if everything I had been in my life up to that point suddenly vanished out of the window and this other Rushdie was invented who was this complete bastard who had done this terrible thing. There did not seem to be any attempt to correct that or to combat that. I was surprised and disappointed it did not. It didn't happen here either. It didn't happen anywhere in the world. It was as if the force of history, the force of a historical event was so huge that it erases all that goes before it.

The negative response to the *Satanic Verses*, let us remember that there was also a positive response, was such that it erased my personality and put in its place some other guy who they didn't recognize at all. Anybody who knows anything about these countries, and I do know something about these countries, knows that every cheap politician can put a demonstration in the street in five minutes. That doesn't represent in any sense the people's will. It represents a certain kind of political structure, political organization. It doesn't represent truth.

But I always believed and I still believe that India would come back. I never believe that the loss of India is forever. Because India is not Iran, it's not even Pakistan, and I thought good sense will prevail in India because that's my life experience of Indian people and of the place.

1998

394. The idea of India that inspired the writer's generation was the one dominated or formed by

(a) the Nehru-Gandhi politics.

(b) the Nehru-Gandhi ideology.

(c) the Nehru-Gandhi idea regarding India's formative years.

(d) the Nehruvian idea of socialism.

395. The writer does not share

(a) Naipaul's stand that the 50th anniversary is a historical moment.

(b) Naipaul's stand that the 50th anniversary is not a historical moment.

(c) Naipaul's conclusion on the 50th anniversary being a historical moment.

(d) Naipaul's conclusion on the 50th anniversary not being a historical moment.

396. The writer shows faith in India's basic

(a) stability. (b) resilience.

(c) fortitude. (d) democracy.

397. According to the writer,

(a) politicians incite the general public to demonstrate against writers.

(b) a politician's demonstration does not reflect the people's will.

(c) Both (a) and (b)

(d) Neither (a) nor (b)

398. The writer's view of India is determined mainly by

(a) his experience.

(b) his fondness for the country.

(c) his love for the resilience of the Indian people.

(d) his love of writing about India.

399. According to the writer's friend,

(a) we should fight against communal pressure.

(b) the fact that communal conflagrations haven't occurred in India for half a century, is something to be proud of.

(c) we can move beyond things, only after we know we are capable of those things.

(d) we have to identify with the people who were involved in inciting communal passions.

400. What according to the passage prevents us from giving in to violent, terrible urges?

(a) Our education

(b) Our upbringing

(c) Our cultural influences

(d) The civilising influence

401. According to the writer, what disqualifies India from being called a democracy?

(a) Its communalism

(b) Its corruption

(c) Its anti-minority stance

(d) All of these

402. The writer contradicts his assertion of being an 'objective observer' on the basis that

(a) no one can be an 'objective observer'.

(b) no one is an 'objective observer'.

(c) he is a subjective observer.

(d) everybody is a subjective observer.

403. In the first paragraph of the passage, the writer questions

(a) the existence of a political entity called India prior to independence.

(b) the contention that a political entity called India did not exist.

(c) the stand that India was an invention.

(d) the stand that India needs to think in terms of its being a nation-state.

404. According to the writer, the difference between India and Pakistan was that

(a) India survived as a nation-state, Pakistan did not.

(b) Indians were full of fantastic ideas in 1947.

(c) Pakistan was born out of another nation.

(d) the creation of Pakistan suffered from under-imaginativeness.

405. According to the passage, the secret of India's survival lies in

(a) its ability to fight back in the face of tremendous stress and strains.

(b) the highly fertile imagination of the Indian people.

(c) a sense of belonging that people feel for it.

(d) Both (a) and (c)

Passage – 50

If Western civilization is in a state of permanent crisis, it is not far-fetched to suggest that there may be something wrong with its education. No civilization, I am sure, has ever devoted more energy and resources to organised education, and if we believe in nothing else, we certainly believe that education is, or should be, the key to everything. In fact, the belief in education is so strong that we treat it as the residual legatee of all our problems. If the nuclear age brings new danger; if the advance of genetics engineering opens the doors of new abuses; if commercialism brings new temptations, the answer must be more and better education. The modern way of life is becoming more complex: this means that everybody must become more highly educated. "By 1984," it was said recently, "it will be desirable that the most ordinary of men is not embarrassed by the use of a logarithm table, the elementary concepts of the calculus, and by the definitions and uses of such words as electron, coulomb, and volt. He should further have become able not only to handle a pen, and ruler but also a magnetic tape, valve, and transistor. The improvement of communications between individuals and groups depends on it." Most of all, it appears, the international situation calls for prodigious educational efforts. The classical statement on this point was delivered by Sir Charles(now Lord)Snow in his *Rede Lecture* some years ago: To say that we must educate ourselves or perish, is a little more melodramatic than the facts warrant. To say we have to educate ourselves or watch a steep decline in our lifetime, is about right. According to Lord Snow, the Russians are apparently doing much better than anyone else and will 'have a clear edge', unless and until the Americans and we educate ourselves both sensibly and imaginatively'.

Lord Snow, it will be recalled, talked about 'The Two Cultures and the Scientific Revolution' and expressed his concern that 'the intellectuals life of the whole of western society is increasingly being split into two polar groups . . . At one pole we have the literary intellectuals . . . at the other the scientists'. He deplores the 'gulf of mutual incomprehension' between these two groups and wants it bridged. It is quite clear how he thinks this 'bridging' operation is to be done; the aims of his educational policy would be, first, to get as many 'alpha-plus scientists as the country can throw up'; second, to train 'a much larger stratum of alpha professionals' to do the supporting research, high class design and development; third, to train 'thousands upon thousands' of other scientists and engineers; and finally, to train 'politicians, administrators, and entire community, who know enough science to have a sense of what the scientists are talking about'. If this fourth and last group can at least be educated enough to 'have sense' of what the real people, the scientists and engineers, are talking about, so Lord Snow seems to suggest, the gulf of mutual incomprehension between the 'Two Cultures' may be bridged.

These ideas on education, which are by no means unrepresentative of our times, leave one with the uncomfortable feeling that ordinary people, including politicians, administrators, and so forth, are really not much use, they have failed to make the grade: but, at least, they should be educated enough to have a sense of what is going on, and to know what the scientists mean when they talk to quote Lord Snow's example about the Second Law of Thermodynamics. It is an uncomfortable feeling, because the scientists never tire of telling us that the fruits of their labours are 'neutral': whether they enrich humanity or destroy it depends on how they are used. And who is to decide how they are used? There is nothing in the training of scientists and engineers to enable them to take such decision, or else, what becomes of the neutrality of science?

If so much reliance is today being placed in the power of education to enable ordinary people to cope with the problems thrown up by scientific and technological progress, then there must be something more to education than Lord Snow suggests. Can education help us to turn the potentiality into a reality to the benefit of man?

To do so, the task of education would be, first and foremost the transmission of ideas of value, of what to do with our lives. There is no doubt also the need to transmit know-how but this must take second place, for it is obviously somewhat foolhardy to put great powers into the hands of people without making sure that they have a reasonable idea of what to do with them. At present, there can be little doubt that the whole of mankind is in mortal danger, not because we are short of scientific and technological know-how, but because we tend to use it destructively, without wisdom. More education can help us only if it produces more wisdom.

The essence of education, I suggested, is the transmission of values, but values do not help us to pick our way through life unless they have become our own, a part, so to say, of our mental make-up. This means that they are more than mere formulae or dogmatic assertions: that we think and feel with them, that they are the very instruments through which we like and interpret, and experience the world. When we think, we do not just think: we think with ideas. Our mind is not a blank, a tabula rasa. When we begin to think we can do so only because our mind is already filled with all sorts of ideas with which to think. All through our youth and adolescence, before the conscious and critical mind begins to act as a sort of censor and guardian at the threshold, ideas seep into our mind, multitudes of them. These years are, one might say, our Dark Ages during which we are nothing but inheritors; it is only in later years that we can gradually learn to sort out our inheritance.

First of all, there is language. Each word is an idea. If the language which seeps into us during our Dark Ages is English, our mind is thereby furnished by a set of ideas which is significantly different from the set represented by Chinese, Russian, German, or even American. Apart from words there are the rules of putting them together: grammar, another bundle of ideas, the study of which has fascinated some modern philosophers to such an extent that they thought they could reduce the whole of philosophy to a study of grammar.

All philosophers and others have always paid a great deal of attention to ideas seen as the result of thought and observation; but in modern times all too little attention has been paid to the study of the ideas which form the very instruments by which thought and observation proceed. On the basis of experience and conscious thought small ideas may easily be dislodged, but when it comes to bigger, more universal, or more subtle ideas, it may not be so easy to change them. Indeed, it is often difficult to become aware of them, as they are the instruments and not the result of our thinking just as you can see what is outside you, but cannot easily see that with which you see, the eye itself. And even when one has become aware of them it is often impossible to judge them on the basis of ordinary experience.

We often notice the existence of more or less fixed ideas in other people's minds — ideas with which they think without being aware of doing so. We then call them prejudices, which is logically quite correct because they have merely seeped into the mind and are in no way the result of judgement. But the word prejudice is generally applied to ideas that are patently erroneous and recognisable as such by anyone except the prejudiced man. Most of the ideas with which we think are not of that kind at all. To some of them, like those incorporated in words and grammar, the notions of truth or error cannot even be applied, others are quite definitely not prejudices but the result of a judgement; others again are tacit assumptions or presuppositions which may be very difficult to recognise.

I say, therefore, that we think with or through ideas and that what we call thinking is generally the application of pre-existing ideas to a given situation or set of facts. When we think about, say the political situation we apply to that situation our political ideas, more or less systematically, and attempt to make that situation' 'intelligible' to ourselves by means of these ideas. Similarly, everywhere else we evaluate the situation in the light of our value-ideas.

The way in which we experience and interpret the world obviously depends very much indeed on the kind of ideas that fill our minds. If they are mainly small, weak, superficial, and incoherent, life will appear insipid, uninteresting, petty and chaotic. It is difficult to bear the resultant feeling of emptiness, and the vacuum of our minds may only too easily be filled by some big, fantastic notion-political or otherwise — which suddenly seem to illumine everything and to give meaning and purpose to our existence. We feel that education will help solve each new problem or complexity that arises. It needs no emphasis that herein lies one of the great dangers of our times.

When people ask for education they normally mean something more than mere training, something more than mere knowledge of facts, and something more than a mere diversion. Maybe they cannot themselves formulate precisely what they are looking for; but I think what they are really looking for is ideas that could make the world, and their own lives, intelligible to them. When a thing is intelligible you have a sense of participation; when a thing is unintelligible you have a sense of estrangement. 'Well, I don't know', you hear people say, as an impotent protest against the unintelligibility of the world as they meet it. If the mind cannot bring to the world a set — or, shall we say, a tool box — of powerful ideas, the world must appear to it as a chaos, a mass of unrelated phenomena, of meaningless events. Such a man is like a person in a strange world and without any signs of civilization, without maps or signposts or indicators of any kind. Nothing has any meaning to him; nothing can hold his vital interest; he has no means of making anything intelligible to himself.

406. The writer's contention in the passage is that the crisis in Western civilization can be explained by
(a) the presence of some flaws in its education.
(b) some inherent lack of coordination among its various elements.
(c) some basic misunderstanding in its society.
(d) the energy it has devoted to education.

407. According to the writer, Lord Snow sees the intellectual life of Western society as split between
(a) the educated and the uneducated.
(b) the government servants and the plebeians.
(c) scientists and literary intellectuals.
(d) administrators and intellectuals.

408. The writer seems to criticise the belief that
(a) education gives rise to further complexities as civilization progresses.
(b) all new problems and complexities can be tackled and solved by more and better education.
(c) people need to learn more in order to earn more.
(d) None of these

409. What, according to the author, would be the definition of 'prejudice'?
(a) Ideas that help people to identify with new situations.
(b) Fixed ideas with which people think without being aware of doing so.
(c) Ideas that people cull from experience in order to judge a situation.
(d) Fixed ideas that see a person through the trials and tribulations of life.

410. According to Lord Snow, which of the following groups needs to be educated enough to at least understand the works of scientists and engineers?
(a) Politicians, administrators, and the entire community
(b) Politicians and literary intellectuals
(c) Politicians and the layman
(d) All of these

411. In the passage, the writer questions
(a) the neutrality of science.
(b) scientists' stand on the neutrality of science.
(c) scientists' stand on the neutrality of their labours.
(d) Lord Snow's assertion regarding the potential of intellectuals in society.

412. The author's assertion in the passage is that education's main responsibility is to
(a) transmit ideas of value.
(b) transmit technical knowledge.
(c) Both (a) and (b)
(d) transmit the values regarding human and societal norms.

413. The author believes that
(a) the gulf between science and literature needs to be bridged.
(b) ideas should be maintained for a holistic view of society and its problems.
(c) words are not ideas.
(d) None of these

414. Which of the following sentences is not true according to the author?
(a) Values must be part of one's psyche.
(b) Values are merely dogmatic assertions.
(c) One identifies with values.
(d) Values are the means to interpret and experience the world.

415. Thinking is
(a) being.
(b) knowing.
(c) application of pre-existing ideas to a situation.
(d) application of fixed ideas to a situation.

Passage – 51

The highest priced words are ghost-written by gagmen who furnish the raw material for comedy over the air and on the screen. They have a word-lore all their own, which they practise for five to fifteen hundred dollars a week, or fifteen dollars a gag at piece rates. That's sizable rate for confounding acrimony with matrimony, or extracting attar of roses from the otter.

Quite apart from the dollar sign on it, gagmen's word-lore is worth a close look, if you are given to the popular American pastime of playing with words — or if you're part of the 40 per cent who make their living in the word trade.

Gag writers' tricks with words point up the fact that we have two distinct levels of language: familiar, ordinary words that everybody knows; and more elaborate words that don't turn up so often, but many of which we need to know if we are to feel at home in listening and reading today.

To be sure gagmen play hob with the big words, making not sense but fun of them. They keep on confusing bigotry with bigamy, illiterate with illegitimate, monotony with monogamy, osculation with oscillation. They trade on the fact that for many of their listeners, these fancy terms linger in a twilight zone of meaning. It's their deliberate intent to make everybody feel cozy at hearing big words, jumbled up or smacked down. After all, such words loom up over-size in ordinary talk, so no wonder they get the bulldozer treatment from the gagmen.

Their wrecking technique incidentally reveals our language as full of tricky words, some with 19 different meanings, others which sound alike but differ in sense. To ring good punning changes, gag writers have to know their way around in the language. They don't get paid for ignorance, only for simulating it.

Their trade is a hard one, and they regard it as serious business. They never laugh at each other's jokes; rarely at their own. Like comediennes, they are usually melancholy men in private life.

Fertile invention and ingenious fancy are required to clean up 'blue' burlesque gags for radio use. These shady gags are theoretically taboo on the air. However, a gag writer who can leave a faint trace of bluing when he launders the joke is all the more admired — and more highly paid.

A gag that keeps the blue tinge is called a 'double intender', gag-land jargon for double entendre. The double meaning makes the joke funny at two levels. Children and other innocents hearing the crack for the first time take it literally, laughing at the surface humour; listeners who remember the original as they heard it in vaudeville or burlesque, laugh at the artfulness with which the blue tinge is disguised.

Another name for a double meaning of this sort is 'insinuendo'. This is a portmanteau word or 'combo', as the gagmen would label it, thus abbreviating combination. By telescoping insinuation and innuendo, they get insinuendo, on the principle of blend words brought into vogue by Lewis Caroll.

'Shock logic' is another favourite with gag writers. Supposedly a speciality of women comediennes, it is illogical logic more easily illustrated than defined. A high school girl has to turn down a boy's proposal, she writes:

Dear Jerry,

I'm sorry, but I can't get engaged to you. My mother thinks I am too young to be engaged and besides, I'm already engaged to another boy.

Yours regretfully.

Guess who.

Gag writers' lingo is consistently funnier than their gags. It should interest the slang-fancier. And like much vivid jargon developed in specialised trades and sports, a few of the terms are making their way into general use. Gimmick, for instance, in the sense either of a trick devised or the point of a joke, is creeping into the vocabulary of columnists and feature writers.

Even apart from the trade lingo, gagmen's manoeuvres are of real concern to anyone who follows words with a fully awakened interest. For the very fact that gag writers often use a long and unusual word as the hinge of a joke, or as a peg for situation comedy, tells us something quite significant: they are well aware of the limitations of the average vocabulary and are quite willing to cash in on its shortcomings.

When Fred Allens' joke-smiths work out a fishing routine, they have Allen referring to the bait in his most arch and solemn tones: "I presume you mean the legless invertebrate." This is the old minstrel trick, using a long fancy term, instead of calling a worm a worm.

Chico Marx can stretch a pun over 500 feet of film, making it funnier all the time, as he did when he rendered, "Why a duck?"

And even the high-brow radio writers have taken advantage of gagmen's technique. You might never expect to hear on the air such words as lepidopterist and entymologist. Both occur in a very famous radio play by Norman Corvine, 'My client Curly', about an unusual caterpillar which would dance to the tune 'yes, sir, she's my baby' but remained inert to all other music. The dancing caterpillar was given a real New York buildup, which involved calling in the experts on butterflies and insects which travel under the learned names above. Corvine made mild fun of the fancy professional titles, at the same time explaining them unobtrusively.

There are many similar occasions where any one working with words can turn gagmen's trade secrets to account. Just what words do they think outside the familiar range? How do they pick the words that they 'kick around'? It is not hard to find out.

416. According to the writer, a larger part of the American population

(a) indulges in playing out the role of gag writers.

(b) indulges in the word trade.

(c) seeks employment in the gag trade for want of something better.

(d) looks down on gag writers.

417. The hallmark of gag writers is that they

(a) ruin good, simple language.

(b) have fun with words.

(c) make better sense of words.

(d) play with words to suit the audience's requirements.

418. According to the passage, the second level of language is important if

(a) one wants to feel at home reading and listening today.

(b) one wants to be a gag writer.

(c) one wants to understand clean entertainment.

(d) All of these

419. According to the writer, gag writers thrive on

(a) the double-layered aspect of language.

(b) audience craze for double entendres.

(c) vulgar innuendoes.

(d) commonplace jugglery with language.

420. In gag writers' trade

(a) long words are abbreviated for effect.

(b) parts of words are combined to produce a hilarious portmanteau effect.

(c) long words play a major role.

(d) Both (b) and (c)

421. When the writer says, "They don't get paid for ignorance, only for simulating it," he means to say

(a) the audience likes to think the gag writers are an ignorant lot.

(b) gag writers are terrific with insinuations.

(c) simulating ignorance is the trick that makes gag writers tick.

(d) None of these

422. Gag writers have influenced

(a) television artistes. (b) radio writers.

(c) circus clowns. (d) All of these

Passage – 52

From ancient times, men have believed that, under certain peculiar circumstances, life could arise spontaneously: from the ooze of rivers could come eels and from the entrails of dead bulls, bees; worms from mud, and maggots from dead meat. This belief was held by Aristotle, Newton and Descartes, among many others, and apparently the great William Harvey too. The weight of centuries gradually disintegrated men's beliefs in the spontaneous origin of maggots and mice, but the doctrine of spontaneous generation clung tenaciously to the question of bacterial origin.

In association with Buffon, the Irish Jesuit priest John Needham declared that he could bring about at will the creation of living microbes in heat-sterilised broths, and presumably, in propitiation, theorised that God did not create living things directly but bade the earth and water to bring them forth. In his *Dictionaire Philosophique*, Voltaire reflected that it was odd to read of Father Needham's claim while atheists conversely should deny a Creator yet attribute to themselves the power of creating eels. But, wrote Thomas Huxley, 'The great tragedy of science — the slaying of a beautiful hypothesis by an ugly fact — which is so constantly being enacted under the eyes of philosophers, was played, almost immediately, for the benefit of Buffon and Needham.

The Italian Abbé Spallanzani did an experiment. He showed that a broth sealed from the air while boiling never develops bacterial growths and hence never decomposes. To Needham's objection that Spallanzani had ruined his broths and the air above them by excessive boiling, the Abbé replied by breaking the seals of his flasks. Air rushed in and bacterial growth began! But the essential conflict remained. Whatever Spallanzani and his followers did to remove seeds and contaminants was regarded by the spontaneous generationists as damaging to the 'vital force' from whence comes new life.

Thus, doubt remained, and into the controversy came the Titanic figure of Louis Pasteur. Believing that a solution to this problem was essential to the development of his theories concerning the role of bacteria in nature, Pasteur freely acknowledged the possibility that living bacteria very well might be arising anew from inanimate matter. To him, the research problem was largely a technical one: to repeat the work of those who claimed to have observed bacterial entry. For the one that contended that life did not enter from the outside, the proof had to go to the question of possible contamination. Pasteur worked logically. He found during the experiments that after prolonged boiling, a broth would ferment only when air was admitted to it. Therefore, he contended, either air contained a factor necessary for the spontaneous generation of life or viable germs were borne in by the air and seeded in the sterile nutrient broth. Pasteur designed ingenious flasks whose long S-shaped necks could be left open. Air was trapped in the sinuous glass tube. Broths boiled in these flask tubes remained sterile. When their necks were snapped to admit ordinary air, bacterial growth would then commence — but not in every case. An occasional flask would remain sterile presumably because the bacterial population of the air is unevenly distributed. The forces of spontaneous generation would not be so erratic. Continuous scepticism drove Pasteur almost to fanatical efforts to control the ingredients of his experiments to destroy the doubts of the most sceptical. He ranged from the mountain air of Montanvert, which he showed to be almost sterile, to those deep, clear wells whose waters had been rendered germfree by slow filtration through sandy soil. The latter discovery led to the familiar porcelain filters of the bacteriology laboratory. With pores small enough to exclude bacteria, solutions allowed to percolate through them could be reliably sterilised.

The argument raged on and soon spilled beyond the boundaries of science to become a burning religious and philosophical question of the day. For many, Pasteur's conclusions caused conflict because they seemed simultaneously to support the Biblical account of creation while denying a variety of other philosophical systems. The public was soon caught up in the crossfire of a vigorous series of public lectures and demonstrations by leading exponents of both views, novelists, clergymen, their adjuncts and friends. Perhaps the most famous of these evenings in the theatre — competing perhaps with a great debate between Huxley and Bishop Wiberforce for elegance of rhetoric — was Pasteur's public lecture at the Sorbonne on April 7, 1864. Having shown his audience the swan necked flasks containing sterile broths, he concluded, "And, therefore, gentlemen, I could point to that liquid and say to you, I have taken my drop of water from the immensity of creation, and I have taken it full of the elements appropriated to the development of inferior beings. And I wait, I watch, I question it! — begging it to recommence for me the beautiful spectacle of the first creation. But it is dumb, dumb since these experiments were begun several years ago; It is dumb because I have kept it from the only thing man does not know how to produce: from the germs that float in the air, from life, for life is a germ and a germ is life. Never will the doctrine of spontaneous generation recover from the mortal blow of this simple experiment." And it is not. Today these same flasks stand immutable: they are still free of microbial life.

It is an interesting fact that despite the ringing declaration of Pasteur, the issue did not die completely. And although far from healthy, it is not yet dead. In his fascinating biography of Pasteur, Rene Dubos has traced the later developments which saw new eruptions of the controversy, new technical progress and criticism, and new energetic figures in the breach of the battle such as Bastion, for, and the immortal Tyndall, against, the doctrine of spontaneous generation. There was also new 'sorrow' for Pasteur as he read years later, in 1877, the last jottings of the great physiologist Claude Bernard and saw in them the 'mystical' suggestion that yeast may arise from grape juice. Even at this late date, Pasteur was stirred to new experiments again to prove to the dead Bernard and his followers the correctness of his position.

It seems to me that spontaneous generation is not only a possibility, but a completely reasonable possibility which should never be relinquished from scientific thought. Before men knew of bacteria, they accepted the doctrine of spontaneous generation as the 'only reasonable alternative' to a belief in supernatural creation. But today, as we look for satisfaction at the downfall of the spontaneous generation hypothesis, we must not forget that science has rationally concluded that life once did originate on earth by spontaneous generation. It was really Pasteur's evidence against spontaneous generation that for the first time brought the whole difficult question of the origin of life before the scientific world. In the above controversy, what was unreasonable was the parade of men who claimed to have 'proved' or who resolutely 'believed in' spontaneous generation on the face of proof — not that spontaneous generation cannot occur — but that their work was shot through with experimental error. The acceptable evidence also makes it clear that spontaneous generation, if it does not occur, must obviously be a highly improbable event under present conditions. Logic tells us that science can only prove an event improbable: it can never prove it impossible — and Gamow has appropriately remarked that nobody is really certain what would happen if a hermetically sealed can were opened after a couple of million years. Modern science agrees that it was highly improbable for life to have arisen in the pre-Cambrian seas, but it concluded, nevertheless, that there it did occur. With this, I think, Pasteur would agree.

Aside from their theoretical implications, these researchers had the great practical result of putting bacteriology on a solid footing. It was now clear how precisely careful one had to be to avoid bacterial contamination in the laboratory. We now knew what 'sterile' meant and we knew that there could be no such thing as 'partial sterilization'. The discovery of bacteria high in the upper atmosphere, in the mud of the deep sea bottom, in the waters of hot springs, and in the Arctic glaciers established bacterial ubiquity as almost absolute. In recognition of this Lord Lister introduced aseptic technique into the practice of surgery. It was the revolution in technique alone that made possible modern bacteriology and the subsequent research connecting bacteria to phenomena of human concern, research, which today is more prodigious than ever. We are just beginning to understand the relationship of bacteria to certain human diseases, to soil chemistry, nutrition, and the phenomenon of antibiosis, wherein a product of one organism (e.g. penicillin) is detrimental to another.

It is not an exaggeration then to say that the emergence of the cell theory represents biology's most significant and fruitful advance. The realisation that all plants and animals are composed of cells which are essentially alike, that cells are all formed by the same fundamental division process, that the total organism is made up of activities and inter-relations of its individual cells, opened up horizons we have not even begun to approach. The cell is a microcosm of life, for in its origin, nature and continuity resides the entire problem of biology.

423. Needham's theory that 'God did not create living things directly' was posited as

(a) an attempt to support his assertion by religious doctrine.

(b) an attempt to placate his religious peers.

(c) an attempt at propitiating a possibly offended God or the religious psyche of the time.

(d) All of these

424. It can be inferred from the passage that

(a) Huxley, Buffon and Needham were contemporaries.

(b) Buffon, Needham, Voltaire and Huxley were contemporaries.

(c) Voltaire wrote a treatise on Needham's claim.

(d) None of these

425. According to the passage,
(a) Pasteur's precursors in the field worked on the basis of spontaneous generation.
(b) unlike his predecessors, Pasteur worked on logical premises rather than arbitrary and spontaneous discoveries.
(c) Pasteur stood to benefit largely from the work of his predecessors.
(d) Pasteur developed the ideas set forth by Voltaire and Needham.

426. Pasteur began his work on the basis of the contention that
(a) either air contained a factor necessary for the spontaneous generation of life or viable germs were borne in by the air and seeded in the sterile nutrient broth.
(b) after prolonged boiling, a broth would ferment only when air was admitted to it.
(c) Both (a) and (b)
(d) Neither (a) nor (b)

427. The porcelain filters of the bacteriology laboratories owed their descent to
(a) Pasteur's homeland.
(b) the well water of Montanvert that had been rendered germ-free by slow filtration through sandy oil.
(c) Both (a) and (b)
(d) None of these

428. What according to the passage was Pasteur's declaration to the world?
(a) Nobody could deny the work done by him.
(b) Science would forever be indebted to his experiments in bacteriology.
(c) The doctrine of spontaneous generation would never recover from the mortal blow dealt to it by his experiments.
(d) Those who refused to acknowledge his experiments would regret their scepticism.

429. What according to the writer, was the problem with the proponents of spontaneous generation?
(a) Their work had no scientific basis.
(b) Their work was ruined by experimental errors.
(c) Both (a) and (b)
(d) Neither (a) nor (b)

430. One of the results of the theoretical cross fire regarding bacteriology was that
(a) partial sterilization as a possibility was ruled out.
(b) aseptic technique was introduced in surgery.
(c) the meaning of sterile was clear to all.
(d) All of these

431. One of the reasons for the conflict caused by Pasteur's experiments was that
(a) they denied the existence of God as the creator.
(b) they seemed simultaneously to support the Biblical account of creation while denying a variety of other philosophical systems.
(c) academicians and scientists refused to accept his theories.
(d) there were too many debates on the topic and this left the people confused.

432. According to the author,
(a) it is an exaggeration to say that cell theory represents biology's most significant and fruitful advance.
(b) Pasteur could not hold his own against the contenders.
(c) cell theory rendered null and void all the other bacteriological theories of the time.
(d) the emergence of the cell theory represents biology's most significant and fruitful advance.

Passage – 53

The end of mutual funds, when it came, was sudden but not unexpected. For over 10 years, mutual fund has been scripting its own growth demise, embarking on a reckless course of high risks, unhealthy pastimes, and unchecked maladies. Ironically but fittingly too, the very hand that had supported and sustained it through the turbulent early period of its existence was the one that, finally wielded the euthanasian syringe. The individual investor it was who had made the mutual fund post-liberalisation, India's most vibrant vehicle for individual investment. The individual investor it was who brought the curtain down on an act that had started with a virtuoso performance, only to putrefy into a show of ineptitude, imprudence, and irresponsibility.

The mutual fund, as we know it, may be dead. It died of many things. But, primarily, of a cancer that ate away at its innards. A cancer that destroyed the value of the investments, the mutual funds was made to service the Rs. 85,000 crore that India's investors had entrusted them with ever since they began life way back in 1964 as The Unit Trust Of India's (UTI), now disgraced Unit Scheme 64 (US 64). A cancer that grew from the refusal of the men and women to manage the mutual fund to exercise a mixture of caution and aggression, but to adopt, instead, an indisciplined, unplanned, fire-from-the hip approach to investment. A cancer that ultimately, robbed the mutual funds of the resources they would have to use to pay back their investors, leaving them on Death Row.

Indeed, the scandal that US 64 had been brewing for years, was only one, but not the first, of the warning-bells that pointed to the near emptiness of many a mutual fund's coffers. In quick succession have emerged reports of more and more fund-schemes that have been laid bare, their corpuses empty, their ability to meet their promises of assured returns to investors demolished. At least 37 per cent of the 235 fund schemes in operation in the country have promised investors assured returns of over 15 per cent for 5 years, and repurchase-prices well above their Net Asset Values (NAVs).

According to a study conducted by the Delhi-based Value Research, at least 18 big schemes due for redemption over the next three years will be unable to service their investors, or even return their money at the time of redemption. The shortfall? Rs. 4,685.10 crore. Or 75.87 per cent of the amount handed over by trusting investors to fund managers. Worries Ajai Kaul, 38, president, Alliance Capital Asset Management: "When an assured-returns scheme runs into problems, investors view it as one more let-down by the mutual funds."

Had they but known of the actual practices seen in the offices and hallways of the mutual funds, which have translated into these results, investors would have shown their disgust long ago. Take the case of a mutual fund company that manages more than a dozen schemes. According to an unwritten, but formalised, principle, each scheme takes it in turn to sell some of its holdings to its sister-schemes, booking fat notional gains and posting NAVs. While investors responded by pouring in even more of their savings, the profits were clearly only on paper. In the offices of another asset management company half way across Mumbai, the demand for cellular-phones peaked six months ago.

Its employees had, suddenly, realised that making their personal deals using information gathered in the course of their professional work, was best done over cell phones so that the company's records wouldn't show the call being made. Obviously, the hot tips went to fatten their — and not investors' — pockets. Earlier, quite a few merchant bankers entered the mutual funds industry to use the corpus to subscribe to the issues they were managing. It took a crash in the primary market — not ethics or investigations — for this practice to stop.

Filled with fear and loathing — and righteous anger — the investor has, therefore, decided to adjure the mutual fund. According to Marketing And Development Research Associates (MDRA) opinion poll of 342 investors conducted last fortnight in the five metros — Bangalore, Kolkata, Chennai, Delhi and Mumbai — mutual funds as an investment instrument now ranks a lowly fourth on safety — after bank deposits, gold, and real estate — and fifth on returns — ahead only of bank deposits and gold. And only 14.20 per cent of the sample will even consider investing in a mutual fund in the future.

Still, it is the species that has died, not its every member. The ones that have survived are the bright performers who beat the market benchmark — the 100 — scrip. The Bombay Stock Exchange (BSE) National Index — by the widest margins within their three genres: growth, income and balance. However, even their star turns have not been able to stave off the stench of death over the business. In fact, an autopsy of the late — and, at the moment not particularly lamented — mutual funds reveal a sordid saga of callousness and calumny.

Sheer disaster stares the mutual funds in the face and a cataclysm could destroy the savings of lakhs of investors too. A Value Research estimate of probable shortfall that 18 assured-returns schemes will face at the time of their scheduled redemptions over the three years adds up to a sense-numbing Rs. 4,685 crore. An independent audit of the 60 assured-returns schemes managed by the public sector mutual funds conducted by Price Waterhouse Coopers at the behest of the Securities and Exchange Board of India (SEBI) estimated a shortfall of between Rs. 2,500 crore and Rs. 3,000 crore. In 1999 alone judging from their present NAVs, the four schemes due for redemption — Canbank Asset Management Company's Cantriple, IndBank Asset Management Company's IndPrakash, SBI Funds Management's Magnum Triple Plus, and BOI Mutual Fund's (BOIMF) Double Square Plus — are heading for a collective shortfall of Rs. 1,639.55 crore.

As of June 30, 1998, the country's 252 fund-schemes managed assets with a market value of Rs. 69,599 crore, with the UTI alone controlling the fate of Rs. 50,000 crore. That is Rs. 11,000 crore less than the money invested in these schemes as of June 30, 1997, which means that the mutual funds have wiped out Rs. 11,000 crore from the investors' hard earned money in the intervening 12 months. Of course, every fund is paying for the sins of the black sheep. For, the villain of the piece was UTI and the 95 funds managed by the public sector banks and institutions, the value of whose corpuses fell from Rs. 66,748 crore to Rs. 57,350 crore in the past year. In fact, these funds contributed 85.40 per cent of the overall value-loss, with the private sector funds boosting their corpuses from Rs. 4,000 crore to Rs. 4,120 crore to lower the extent of the erosion.

For investors, that has translated into an option of either exiting at a loss — or holding on in vain hope. On November 20, 1998, a depressing 77 per cent of the 58 listed fund schemes were quoting at discounts of between 5 per cent and 40 per cent to their NAVs. And what of the NAVs themselves? The units of a shoulder-slumping 15 per cent of the schemes were worth less than their par values. And US 64, of course continued to languish, with an estimated NAV of Rs. 9.68. Even if there are schemes that have performed individually well, that the mutual funds have collectively failed to deliver couldn't be more obvious. So investors' murderous mood can hardly be debated.

Their genesis and growth reveals just what blinded the mutual funds to the possibility of failure. Forty per cent of the banks-and-insurance companies-promoted funds in operation were launched between 1987 and 1993, when the stock markets were bull-dominated. In a period that saw only one bear phase, the BSE Sensitivity Index (the Sensex) climbed by 346 per cent. Being successful with equity investments required no skills; only investible funds. Nor was fund-raising a problem, as investors desperately sought ways to grab a piece of equity boom. Between 1984 and 1989, the mutual funds collected Rs. 13,455 crore as subscriptions, but, in the next five years, they picked up Rs. 45,573 crore.

In January, 1994, the UTI's Mastergain mopped up a stunning Rs. 4,700 crore while the most awaited Morgan Stanley Growth — a showcase for the fabled fund-management metier of the foreign mutual funds — took in Rs. 1,000 crore in just three days. Low entry-barriers — a so called sound track-record, a general reputation of fairness and integrity, an application-fee of Rs. 25,000, a registration fee of Rs. 25 lakh and an annual fee of Rs. 2.50 lakh — made entering the business a snap. Explains Ajay Srinivasan, 34, CEO, Prudential ICICI Mutual Fund: "Mutual funds were misunderstood by investors. Everyone thought they were a one way ticket to a jackpot."

Intoxicated, fund-managers poured in more and more of their corpuses into equity, ignoring the downsides, confident that the boom would last forever. In the process, they ignored the very concept of risk-management, blithely ignoring the safety net of fixed-income instruments, and accusing those who advised caution of being cowards. In 1995, for instance, ABN estimated 70 per cent of the money being managed by the mutual funds had been funnelled into equity. Whether they knew it or not, they were breaking away from the trend set by the mutual funds in the US, where the industry began by investing primarily in the money market, with only 25 per cent of their corpus set aside for stocks. Only in the past 15 years, after operating for more than seven decades, have those funds ventured into equity. Unfortunately, their success blinded the fund-managers to the fact that they were riding a wave-not navigating the treacherous seas. As Vivek Reddy, 36, CEO, Kothari-Pioneer Mutual Fund, puts it: "It was the stock market conditions that helped the mutual funds deliver returns, not superior investment skills." Then, the stock markets collapsed and never quite recovered. Between July 1997 and October 1998, the Sensex free-fell from 4306 to 2812 finally nullifying the theory that if you wait long enough, share-prices are always bound to rise. And the mutual fund, unused to a diet of falling equity indices, collapsed too.

The quantum of money mopped up by the mutual fund may suggest that the reports of its extinction have been greatly exaggerated. In 1997-98, Indians entrusted Rs. 18,701 crore to the mutual funds, with new schemes alone mopping up Rs. 12,279 crore. Questions R. G Sharma, 58, CEO, LIC Mutual Fund: "How do you explain that Dhanvarsha 12 and Dhanvarsha 13, floated in April and September 1998, managed to mop up Rs. 335 crore?" Not quite a loss of faith, would you say? Think again. In those 12 months, those very investors also took away Rs. 16,227 crore in the form of repurchases and redemptions, leaving only Rs. 2,474 crore more in the hands of fund-managers. What's more, since none of the withdrawals could have been made from the new schemes, the old schemes, obviously, gave it all up, effectively yielding Rs. 9,805 crore to angry investors who took away their money. It is the same story this year: in the first quarter of 1998-99, old schemes collected Rs. 2,340 crore, compared to the new schemes' Rs. 1,735 crore but they gave up Rs. 2,749 crore ending up Rs. 409 crore poorer.

Sure, some people are still putting money into the mutual funds. The real reason: money is flowing in from two genres of investors — neither of whom is the quintessential urban. The first comprises people in the semi-urban and rural areas, for whom names like the LIC and GIC still represent safety and assured schemes of income. Importantly, this category investor isn't clued into the financial markets, and is not, accordingly, aware of the problems that confront the mutual funds. Confirms Nikhil Khatau, 38, Managing Director, Sun F & C Asset Management: "That market is fairly stable. "However, as soon as the fundamental problems hit their dividend-paying ability, even the die hard mutual fund investor from India's villages and small towns — who, don't forget, has already been singed by the disappearance of thousands of non- banking finance companies — will swear off their favourite investment vehicle.

The second genre of investor explains why the private sector funds have been successful in soaking up large sums: 31.10 per cent of the total takings in 1997-98, and 10.70 per cent in the first quarter of 1998-99. They are the so called high net worth players — corporates and individuals — who in Khatau's terms, 'are aggressive about managing their wealth, and look closely at comparative performance'. While their fastidiousness has forced them to pick the private sector mutual funds, whose disclosures and performance has both been ahead of their public sector cousins, their interest does not represent every investor's disillusionment.

433. The amount of money entrusted to the care of the mutual funds was

(a) Rs. 75,000 crore. (b) Rs. 80,000 crore.

(c) Rs. 85,000 crore. (d) Rs. 82,000 crore.

434. The end of mutual funds was carried out at the hands of

(a) the government.

(b) non-banking finance companies.

(c) the individual investors.

(d) banks.

435. According to the passage, the flaws of the mutual funds lay in their
(a) post-liberalisation syndrome.
(b) imprudent and irresponsible handling.
(c) stagnation.
(d) All of these

436. According to the passage, one of the reasons for the failure of the mutual funds was
(a) their indisciplined approach to investment.
(b) their devil-may-care approach to the world of finance.
(c) their ability to deceive investors.
(d) their inability to read the pulse of their investors.

437. According to the writer, one of the fallouts of the end of mutual funds is that
(a) at least some of the big schemes due for redemption over the next three years will be unable to service their investors.
(b) only very few of the big schemes due for redemption over the next three years will be unable to service their investors.
(c) none of the big schemes due for redemption over the next three years will be able to service their investors.
(d) None of these

438. It can be inferred from the passage that
(a) money was siphoned away outside the country by the mutual funds.
(b) many of the mutual fund offices indulged in malpractice.
(c) money invested in the mutual fund schemes were never returned to the investors.
(d) a sustained attack by the media exposed the anomalies in the mutual fund industry.

439. The current rank of the mutual fund industry in terms of safety and returns on deposits respectively is
(a) third and fourth.
(b) tenth and twelfth.
(c) fourth and fifth.
(d) It is not ranked at all.

440. The increase in the number of cell phone subscriptions in the office of an asset management company was due to the fact that
(a) calls made by employees for personal deals couldn't be lodged in the company's records.
(b) employees found it easier to deal with investors without involving the company.
(c) the company was scrupulous about maintaining correct records.
(d) the company was unscrupulous in granting personal deals to the employees.

441. According to the passage, mutual funds caused a loss of
(a) Rs. 10,000 crore of the investors' money.
(b) Rs. 11,000 crore of the investors' money.
(c) Rs. 5,000 crore of the investors' money.
(d) Rs. 8,000 crore of the investors' money.

442. On the basis of the passage, it may be said that, in terms of retrieving their money, the investors
(a) are caught between the devil and the deep blue sea.
(b) have a no-exit route.
(c) have to make do with little or no gain.
(d) will trust the few bright stars in the mutual fund industry.

443. According to the passage, one of the reasons for the euphoria in the mutual fund industry can be attributed to
(a) the stock market boom in the late eighties and early nineties.
(b) failure of the primary market.
(c) Both (a) and (b)
(d) Neither (a) nor (b)

Passage – 54

Unseasonableness is a tendency to do socially permissible things at the wrong time. The unseasonable man is the sort of person who comes to confide in you when you are busy. He serenades his beloved when she is ill. He asks a man who has just lost money by paying a bill for a friend to pay a bill for him. He invites a friend to go for a ride just after the friend has finished a long car trip. He is eager to offer services which are not wanted, but which cannot be politely refused. If he is present at an arbitration, he stirs up dissension between the two parties, who were really anxious to agree. Such is the unseasonable man.

1999

444. He tends to
(a) entertain women.
(b) be a successful arbitrator when dissenting parties are anxious to agree.
(c) be helpful when solicited.
(d) tell a long story to people who have heard it many times before.

445. The unseasonable man tends to

(a) bring a higher bidder to a salesman who has just closed a deal.

(b) disclose confidential information to others.

(c) sing the praises of the bride when he goes to a wedding.

(d) sleep late and rise early.

Passage – 55

The World Trade Organization (WTO) was formed in the early 1990s as a component of the Uruguay Round negotiation. However, it could have been negotiated as part of the Tokyo Round of the 1970s, since that negotiation was an attempt at a 'constitutional reform' of the General Agreement on Tariffs and Trade (GATT). Or it could have been put off to the future, as the US Government wanted. What factors led to the creation of the WTO in the early 1990s?

One factor was the pattern of multilateral bargaining that developed late in the Uruguay Round. Like all complex international agreements, the WTO was a product of a series of trade-offs between principal actors and groups. For the United States, which did not want a new organization, the dispute settlement part of the WTO package achieved its longstanding goal of a more effective and more legal dispute settlement system. For the Europeans, who by the 1990s had come to view GATT dispute settlement less in political terms and more as a regime of legal obligations, the WTO package was acceptable as a means to discipline the resort to unilateral measures by the United States. Countries like Canada and other middle and smaller trading partners were attracted by the expansion of a rules-based system and by the symbolic value of a trade organization, both of which inherently support the weak against the strong. The developing countries were attracted due to the provisions banning unilateral measures. Finally, and perhaps most important, many countries at the Uruguay Round came to put a higher priority on the export gains than on the import losses that the negotiation would produce, and they came to associate the WTO and a rules-based system with those gains. This reasoning — replicated in many countries — was contained in US Ambassador Kantor's defence of the WTO, and it amounted to a recognition that international trade and its benefits cannot be enjoyed unless trading nations accept the discipline of a negotiated rules-based environment.

A second factor in the creation of the WTO was pressure from lawyers and the legal process. The dispute settlement system of the WTO was seen as a victory of legalists over pragmatists but the matter went deeper than that. The GATT, and the WTO, are contract organizations based on rules, and it is inevitable that an organization created to further rules will in turn be influenced by the legal process. Robert Hudec has written of the 'momentum of legal development', but what is this precisely? Legal development can be defined as promotion of the technical legal values of consistency, clarity (or, certainty) and effectiveness: these are values that those responsible for administering any legal system will seek to maximize. As it played out in the WTO, consistency meant integrating under one roof the whole lot of separate agreements signed under GATT auspices; clarity meant removing ambiguities about the powers of contracting parties to make certain decisions or to undertake waivers: and effectiveness meant eliminating exceptions arising out of grandfather-rights and resolving defects in dispute settlement procedures and institutional provisions. Concern for these values is inherent in any rules-based system of cooperation, since without these values, rules would be meaningless in the first place. Rules, therefore, create their own incentive for fulfilment.

The momentum of legal development has occurred in other institutions besides the GATT, most notably in the European Union (EU). Over the past two decades the European Court of Justice (ECJ) has consistently rendered decisions that have expanded incrementally the EU's internal market, in which the doctrine of 'mutual recognition' handed down in the case Cassis de Dijon in 1979 was a key turning point. The court is now widely recognized as a major player in European integration, even though arguably such a strong role was not originally envisaged in the Treaty of Rome, which initiated the current European Union. One means the court used to expand integration was the 'teleological method of interpretation', whereby the actions of member states were evaluated against 'the accomplishment of the most elementary community goals set forth in the Preamble to the [Rome] Treaty'. The teleological method represents an effort to keep current policies consistent with stated goals, and it is analogous to the effort in GATT to keep contracting party trade practices consistent with stated rules. In both cases legal concerns and procedures are an independent force for further cooperation.

In large part, the WTO was an exercise in consolidation. In the context of a trade negotiation that created a near-revolutionary expansion of international trade rules, the formation of the WTO was a deeply conservative act needed to ensure that the benefits of the new rules would not be lost. The WTO was all about institutional structure and dispute settlement: these are the concerns of conservatives and not revolutionaries, which is why lawyers and legalists took the lead on these issues. The WTO codified the GATT institutional practice that had developed by custom over three decades, and it incorporated a new dispute settlement system that was necessary to keep both old and new rules from becoming a sham. Both the international structure and the dispute settlement system were necessary to preserve and enhance the integrity of the multilateral trade regime that had been built incrementally from the 1940s to the 1990s.

446. What could be the closest reason why the WTO was not formed in the 1970s?

(a) The US government did not like it.

(b) Important players did not find it in their best interest to do so.

(c) Lawyers did not work for the dispute settlement system.

(d) The Tokyo Round negotiation was an attempt at constitutional reform.

447. The most likely reason for the acceptance of the WTO package by nations was that

(a) it had the means to prevent the US from taking unilateral measures.

(b) they recognized the need for a rule-based environment to protect the benefits of increased trade.

(c) it settles disputes more legally and more effectively.

(d) its rule-based system leads to export gains.

448. According to the passage, WTO promoted the technical legal values partly through

(a) integrating under one roof the agreements signed under GATT.

(b) rules that create their own incentive for fulfilment.

(c) grandfather-rights exceptions and defects in dispute settlement procedures.

(d) ambiguities about the powers of contracting parties to make certain decisions.

449. In the method of interpretation of the European Court of Justice,

(a) current policies needed to be consistent with stated goals.

(b) contracting party trade practices needed to be consistent with stated rules.

(c) enunciation of the most elementary community goals needed to be emphasised.

(d) actions of member states needed to be evaluated against the stated community goals.

450. In the statement " .... it amounted to a recognition that international trade and its benefits cannot be enjoyed unless trading nations accept the discipline of a negotiated rules-based environment", 'it' refers to

(a) Ambassador Kantor's defence of the WTO.

(b) the higher priority on export gains placed by many countries at the Uruguay Round.

(c) the export gains many countries came to associate with a rule-based system.

(d) the provision of a rule-based system by the WTO.

451. The importance of Cassis de Dijon is that it

(a) gave a new impetus to the momentum of legal development at the European Court of Justice.

(b) resulted in a decision that expanded incrementally the EU's internal market.

(c) strengthened the role of the court more than envisaged in the Treaty of Rome.

(d) led to a doctrine that was a key turning point in European integration.

Passage – 56

Have you ever come across a painting, by Picasso, Mondrian, Miro, or any other modern abstract painter of this century, and found yourself engulfed in a brightly-coloured canvas which your senses cannot interpret? Many people would tend to denounce abstractionism as senseless trash. These people are disoriented by Miro's bright, fanciful creatures and two-dimensional canvases. They click their tongues and shake their heads at Mondrian's grid works, declaring that the poor guy played too many scrabble games. They silently shake their heads in sympathy for Picasso, whose gruesome, distorted figures must be a reflection of his mental health. Then, standing in front of a work by Charlie Russell, the famous western artist, they'll declare it a work of God. People feel more comfortable with something they can relate to and understand immediately without too much thought. This is the case with the work of Charlie Russell. Being able to recognize the elements in his paintings — trees, horses and cowboys — gives people a safety line to their world of 'reality'. There are some who would disagree when I say abstract art requires more creativity and artistic talent to produce a good piece than does representational art, but there are many weaknesses in their arguments.

People who look down on abstract art have several major arguments to support their beliefs. They feel that artists turn abstract because they are not capable of the technical drafting skills that appear in a Russell: therefore, such artists create an art form that anyone is capable of and that is less time consuming, and then parade it as artistic progress. Secondly, they feel that the purpose of art is to create something of beauty in an orderly, logical composition. Russell's compositions are balanced and rational: everything sits calmly on the canvas, leaving the viewer satisfied that he has seen all there is to see. The modern abstractionists, on the other hand, seem to compose their pieces irrationally. For example, upon seeing Picasso's Guernica, a friend of mine asked me, "What's the point?" Finally, many people feel that art should portray the ideal and real. The exactness of detail in Charlie Russell's work is an example of this. He has been called a great historian because his pieces depict the lifestyle, dress, and events of the times. His subject matter is derived from his own experiences on the trial, and reproduced to the smallest detail.

I agree in part with many of these arguments, and at one time even endorsed them. But now, I believe differently. Firstly, I object to the argument that abstract artists are not capable of drafting. Many abstract artists, such as Picasso, are excellent draftsmen. As his work matured, Picasso became more abstract in order to increase the expressive quality of his work. Guernica was meant as a protest against the bombing of that city by the Germans. To express the terror and suffering of the victims more vividly, he distorted the figures and presented them in a black and white journalistic manner. If he had used representational images and colour, much of the emotional content would have been lost and the piece would not have caused the demand for justice that it did. Secondly, I do not think that a piece must be logical and aesthetically pleasing to be art. The message it conveys to its viewers is more important. It should reflect the ideals and issues of its time and be true to itself, not just a flowery, glossy surface. For example, through his work, Mondrian was trying to present a system of simplicity, logic, and rational order. As a result, his pieces did end up looking like a scrabble board.

Miro created powerful, surrealistic images from his dreams and subconscious. These artists were trying to evoke a response from society through an expressionistic manner. Finally, abstract artists and representational artists maintain different ideas about 'reality'. To the representational artist, reality is what he sees with his eyes. This is the reality he reproduces on canvas. To the abstract artist, reality is what he feels about what his eyes see. This is the reality he interprets on canvas. This can be illustrated by Mondrian's Trees series. You can actually see the progression from the early recognizable, though abstracted Trees, to his final solution, the grid system.

A cycle of abstract and representational art began with the first scratchings of prehistoric man. From the abstractions of ancient Egypt to representational, classical Rome, returning to abstractionism in early Christian art and, so on up to the present day, the cycle has been going on. But this day and age may witness its death through the camera. With film, there is no need to produce finely detailed, historical records manually; the camera does this for us more efficiently. Maybe, representational art would cease to exist. With abstractionism as the victor of the first battle, maybe, a different kind of cycle will be touched off. Possibly, some time in the distant future, thousands of years from now, art itself will be physically non-existent. Some artists today believe that once they have planned and constructed a piece in their mind, there is no sense in finishing it with their hands; it has already been done and can never be duplicated.

452. The author argues that many people look down upon abstract art because they feel that

(a) modern abstract art does not portray what is ideal and real.

(b) abstract artists are unskilled in matters of technical drafting.

(c) abstractionists compose irrationally.

(d) All of the above

453. The author believes that people feel comfortable with representational art because

(a) they are not engulfed in brightly-coloured canvases.

(b) they do not have to click their tongues and shake their heads in sympathy.

(c) they understand the art without putting too much strain on their minds.

(d) paintings like Guernica do not have a point.

454. In the author's opinion, Picasso's Guernica created a strong demand for justice since

(a) it was a protest against the German bombing of Guernica.

(b) Picasso managed to express the emotional content well with his abstract depiction.

(c) it depicts the terror and suffering of the victims in a distorted manner.

(d) it was a mature work of Picasso, painted when the artist's drafting skills were excellent.

455. The author acknowledges that Mondrian's pieces may have ended up looking like a scrabble board because

(a) many people declared the poor guy played too many scrabble games.

(b) Mondrian believed in the 'grid-works' approach to abstractionist painting.

(c) Mondrian was trying to convey the message of simplicity and rational order.

(d) Mondrian learned from his Tree series to evolve a grid system.

456. The main difference between the abstract artist and the representational artist in matter of the 'ideal' and the 'real', according to the author, is

(a) how each chooses to deal with 'reality' on his or her canvas.

(b) the superiority of interpretation of reality over production of reality.

(c) the different values attached by each to being a historian.

(d) the varying levels of drafting skills and logical thinking abilities.

Passage – 57

Each one has his reasons: for one, art is a flight; for another, a means of conquering. But one can flee into a hermitage, into madness, into death. One can conquer by arms. Why does it have to be writing? Because, behind the various aims of authors, there is a deeper and more immediate choice which is common to all of us. We shall try to elucidate this choice, and we shall see whether it is not in the name of this very choice of writing that the engagement of writers must be required.

Each of our perceptions is accompanied by the consciousness that human reality is a 'revealer'. That is, it is through human reality that 'there is' being , or, to put it differently, that man is the means by which things are manifested. It is our presence in the world which multiplies relations. It is we who set up a relationship between this tree and that bit of sky. Thanks to us, that star which has been dead for millennia, that quarter moon, and that dark river are disclosed in the unity of a landscape. It is the speed of our auto and our airplane which organizes the great masses of the earth. With each of our acts, the world reveals to us a new face. But, if we know that we are directors of being, we also know that we are not its producers. If we turn away from this landscape, it will sink back into its dark permanence. At least, it will sink back: there is no one mad enough to think that it is going to be annihilated. It is we who shall be annihilated, and the earth will remain in its lethargy until another consciousness comes along to awaken it. Thus, to our inner certainty of being 'revealers' is added that of being inessential in relation to the thing revealed.

One of the chief motives of artistic creation is certainly the need of feeling that we are essential in relationship to the world. If I fix on canvas or in writing a certain aspect of the fields or the sea or a look on someone's face which I have disclosed, I am conscious of having produced them by condensing relationships, by introducing order where there was none, by imposing the unity of mind on the diversity of things. That is, I think myself essential in relation to my creation. But this time it is the created object which escapes me; I cannot reveal and produce at the same time. The creation becomes inessential in relation to the creative activity. First of all, even if it appears to others as definitive, the created object always seems to us in a state of suspension; we can always change this line, that shade, that word. Thus, it never forces itself . A novice painter asked his teacher, 'When should I consider my painting finished'? And the teacher answered, "When you can look at it in amazement and say to yourself 'I'm the one who did that!"

Which amounts to saying 'never'. For, it is virtually considering one's work with someone else's eyes and revealing what has been created. But it is self-evident that we are proportionally less conscious of the thing produced and more conscious of our productive activity. When it is a matter of poetry or carpentry, we work according to traditional norms, with tools whose usage is codified; it is Heidegger's famous 'they' who are working with our hands. In this case, the result can seem to us sufficiently strange to preserve its objectivity in our eyes. But if we ourselves produce the rules of production, the measures, the criteria, and if our creative drive comes from the very depths of our heart, then we never find anything but ourselves in our work. It is we who have invented the laws by which we judge it, it is our history, our love, our gaiety that we recognize in it. Even if we should regard it without touching it any further, we never receive from it that gaiety or love. We put them into it. The results which we have obtained on canvas or paper never seem to us objective. We are too familiar with the processes of which they are the effects. These processes remain a subjective discovery: they are ourselves, our inspiration, our ruse, and when we seek to perceive our work, we create it again, we repeat mentally the operations which produced it; each of its aspects appears as a result. Thus, in the perception, the object is given as the essential thing and the subject as the inessential. The latter seeks essential in the creation and obtains it, but then it is the object which becomes the inessential.

The dialectic is nowhere more apparent than in the art of writing, for the literary object is a peculiar top which exists only in movement. To make it come into view a concrete act called reading is necessary, and it lasts only as long as this act can last. Beyond that, there are only black marks on paper. Now, the writer cannot read what he writes, whereas the shoemaker can put on the shoes he has just made if they are of his size, and the architect can live in the house he has built. In reading, one foresees: one waits. He foresees the end of the sentence, the following sentence, the next page. He waits for them to confirm or disappoint his foresights. The reading is composed of a host of hypotheses, followed by awakenings, of hopes and deceptions. Readers are always ahead of the sentence they are reading in a merely probable future which partly collapses and partly comes together in proportion as they progress, which withdraws from one page to the next and forms the moving horizon of the literary object. Without waiting, without a future, without ignorance, there is no objectivity.

457. The author holds that

(a) there is an objective reality and a subjective reality.

(b) nature is the sum total of disparate elements.

(c) it is human action that reveals the various facets of nature.

(d) apparently disconnected elements in nature are unified in a fundamental sense.

458. It is the author's contention that

(a) artistic creations are results of human consciousness.

(b) the very act of artistic creation leads to the escape of the created object.

(c) man can produce and reveal at the same time.

(d) an act of creation forces itself on our consciousness leaving us full of amazement.

459. The passage makes a distinction between perception and creation in terms of

(a) objectivity and subjectivity.

(b) revelation and action.

(c) objective reality and perceived reality.

(d) essentiality and non-essentiality of objects and subjects.

460. The art of writing manifests the dialectic of perception and creation because

(a) reading reveals the writing till the act of reading lasts.

(b) writing to be meaningful needs the concrete act of reading.

(c) this art is anticipated and progresses on a series of hypotheses.

(d) this literary object has a moving horizon brought about by the very act of creation.

461. A writer, as an artist,

(a) reveals the essentiality of revelation.

(b) makes us feel essential vis-à-vis nature.

(c) creates reality.

(d) reveals nature in its permanence.

Passage – 58

Since Second World War, the nation state has been regarded with approval by every political system and every ideology. In the name of modernization in the West, of socialism in the Eastern Bloc, and of the development in the Third World, it was expected to guarantee the happiness of individuals as citizens and of people as societies. However, the state today appears to have broken down in many parts of the world. It has failed to guarantee either security or social justice, and has been unable to prevent either international wars or civil wars. Distributed by the claims of communities within it, the nation state tries to repress their demands and to proclaim itself as the only guarantor of security of all. In the name of national unity, territorial integrity, equality of all its citizens and non-partisan secularism, the state can use its powerful resources to reject the demands of the communities; it may even go so far as genocide to ensure that order prevails.

As one observes the awakening of communities in different parts of the world, one cannot ignore the context in which identity issues arise. It is no longer a context of sealed frontiers and isolated regions but is one of the integrated global systems. In a reaction to this trend towards globalization, individuals and communities everywhere are voicing their desire to exist, to use their power of creation and to play an active part in national and international life.

There are two ways in which the current upsurge in demands for the recognition of identities can be looked at. On the positive side, the efforts by certain population groups to assert their identity can be regarded as 'liberation movements', challenging oppression and injustice. What these groups are doing — proclaiming that they are different, rediscovering the roots of their culture or strengthening group solidarity — may accordingly be seen as legitimate attempts to escape from their state of subjugation and enjoy a certain measure of dignity. On the downside, however, militant action for recognition tends to make such groups more deeply entrenched in their attitude and to make their cultural compartments even more watertight. The assertion of identity then starts turning into self-absorption and isolation, and is liable to slide into intolerance of others and towards ideas of 'ethnic cleansing', xenophobia and violence.

Whereas continuous variations among people prevent drawing of clear dividing lines between the groups, those militating for recognition of their group's identity arbitrarily choose a limited number of criteria such as religion, language, skin colour, and place of origin so that their members recognize themselves primarily in terms of the labels attached to the group whose existence is being asserted . This distinction between the group in question and other groups is established by simplifying the feature selected. Simplification also works by transforming groups into essences, abstractions endowed with the capacity to remain unchanged through time. In some cases, people actually act as though the group has remained unchanged and talk, for example, about the history of nations and communities as if these entities survived for centuries without changing, with the same ways of acting and thinking, the same desires, anxieties, and aspirations.

Paradoxically, precisely because identity represents a simplifying fiction, creating uniform groups out of disparate people, that identity performs a cognitive function. It enables us to put names to ourselves and others, form some idea of who we are and who others are, and ascertain the place we occupy along with the others in the world and society. The current upsurge to assert the identity of groups can thus be partly explained by the cognitive function performed by identity. However, that said, people would not go along as they do, often in large numbers, with the propositions put to them, in spite of the sacrifices they entail, if there was not a very strong feeling of need for identity, a need to take stock of things and know 'who we are', 'where we come from' and 'where we are going'.

Identity is thus a necessity in a constantly changing world, but it can also be a potent source of violence and disruption. How can these two contradictory aspects of identity be reconciled? First, we must bear the arbitrary nature of identity categories in mind, not with a view to eliminating all forms of identification — which would be unrealistic since identity is a cognitive necessity — but simply to remind ourselves that each of us has several identities at the same time. Second, since tears of nostalgia are being shed over the past, we recognize that culture is constantly being recreated by cobbling together fresh and original elements and counter-cultures. There are in our own country a large number of syncretic cults wherein modern elements are blended with traditional values or people of different communities venerate saints or divinities of particular faiths. Such cults and movements are characterized by a continual inflow and outflow of members which prevent them from taking on a self-perpetuating existence of their own and hold our hope for the future, indeed, perhaps for the only possible future. Finally, the nation state must respond to the identity urges of its constituent communities and to their legitimate quest for security and social justice. It must do so by inventing what the French philosopher and sociologist, Raymond Aron, called 'peace through law'. That would guarantee justice both to the state as a whole and its parts, and respect the claims of both reason and emotions. The problem is one of reconciling nationalist demands with exercise of democracy.

462. According to the author, happiness of individuals was expected to be guaranteed in the name of
(a) development in the Third World.
(b) socialism in the Third World.
(c) development in the West.
(d) modernization in the Eastern Bloc.

463. Demands for recognition of identities can be viewed
(a) positively and negatively.
(b) as liberation movements and militant action.
(c) as efforts to rediscover cultural roots which can slide towards intolerance of others.
(d) All of the above

464. Going by the author's exposition of the nature of identity, which of the following statements is untrue?
(a) Identity represents creating uniform groups out of disparate people.
(b) Identity is a necessity in the changing world.
(c) Identity is a cognitive necessity.
(d) None of the above

465. According to the author, the nation state
(a) has fulfilled its potential.
(b) is willing to do anything to preserve order.
(c) generates security for all its citizens.
(d) has been a major force in preventing civil and international wars.

466. Which of the following views of the nation state cannot be attributed to the author?
(a) It has not guaranteed peace and security.
(b) It may go as far as genocide for self-preservation.
(c) It represents the demands of communities within it.
(d) It is unable to prevent international wars.

Passage – 59

The persistent patterns in the way nations fight reflect their cultural and historical traditions and deeply-rooted attitudes that collectively make up their strategic culture. These patterns provide insights that go beyond what can be learnt just by comparing armaments and divisions. In the Vietnam War, the strategic tradition of the United States called for forcing the enemy to fight a massed battle in an open area, where superior American weapons would prevail. The United States was trying to re-fight Second World War in the jungles of South-east Asia, against an enemy with no intention of doing so.

Some British historians describe the Asian way of war as one of indirect attacks, avoiding frontal attacks meant to overpower an opponent. This traces back to Asian history and geography: the great distances and harsh terrain have often made it difficult to execute the sort of open field clashes allowed by the flat terrain and relatively compact size of Europe. A very different strategic tradition arose in Asia.

The bow and arrow were metaphors for an Eastern way of war. By its nature, the arrow is an indirect weapon. Fired from a distance of hundreds of yards, it does not necessitate immediate physical contact with the enemy. Thus, it can be fired from hidden positions. When fired from behind a ridge, the barrage seems to come out of nowhere, taking the enemy by surprise. The tradition of this kind of fighting is captured in the classical strategic writing of the East. The 2,000 years worth of Chinese writings on war constitutes the most subtle writing on the subject in any language. Not until Clausewitz, did the West produce a strategic theorist to match the sophistication of Sun-tzu, whose *Art of War* was written 2,300 years earlier.

In Sun-tzu and other Chinese writings, the highest achievement of arms is to defeat an adversary without fighting. He wrote: "To win one hundred victories in one hundred battles is not the acme of skill. To subdue the enemy without fighting is the supreme excellence." Actual combat is just one among many means towards the goal of subduing an adversary. War contains too many surprises to be a first resort. It can lead to ruinous losses, as has been seen time and again. It can have the unwanted effect of inspiring heroic efforts in an enemy, as the United States learned in Vietnam, and as the Japanese found out after Pearl Harbour.

Aware of the uncertainties of a military campaign, Sun-tzu advocated war only after the most thorough preparations. Even then, it should be quick and clean. Ideally, the army is just an instrument to deal the final blow to an enemy already weakened by isolation, poor morale, and disunity. Ever since Sun-tzu, the Chinese have been seen as masters of subtlety who take measured actions to manipulate an adversary without his knowledge. The dividing line between war and peace can be obscure. Low level violence often is the backdrop to a larger strategic campaign. The unwitting victim, focused on the day-to-day events, never realizes what's happening to him until it's too late. History holds many examples. The Viet Cong lured French and US infantry deep into the jungle, weakening their morale over several years. The mobile army of the United States was designed to fight on the plains of Europe, where it could quickly move unhindered from one spot to the next. The jungle did more than make quick movement impossible; broken down into smaller units and scattered in isolated bases, US forces were deprived of the feeling of support and protection that ordinarily comes from being part of a big army.

The isolation of US troops in Vietnam was not just a logistical detail, something that could be overcome by, for instance, bringing in reinforcements by helicopter. In a big army reinforcements are readily available. It was Napoleon who realized the extraordinary effects on morale that come from being part of a larger formation. Just the knowledge of it lowers the soldier's fear and increases his aggressiveness. In the jungle and on isolated bases, this feeling was removed. The thick vegetation slowed down the reinforcements and made it difficult to find stranded units. Soldiers felt they were on their own.

More important, by altering the way the war was fought, the Viet Cong stripped the United States of its belief in the inevitability of victory, as it had done to the French before them. Morale was high when these armies first went to Vietnam. Only after many years of debilitating and demoralizing fighting did Hanoi launch its decisive attacks, at Dien Bien Phu in 1954 and against Saigon in 1975. It should be recalled that in the final push to victory the North Vietnamese abandoned their jungle guerrilla tactics completely, committing their entire army of twenty divisions to pushing the South Vietnamese into collapse. This final battle, with the enemy's army all in one place, was the one that the United States had desperately wanted to fight in 1965. When it did come out into the open in 1975, Washington had already withdrawn its forces and there was no possibility of re-intervention.

The Japanese early in Second World War used a modern form of the indirect attack, one that relied on stealth and surprise for its effects. At Pearl Harbour, in the Philippines, and in South-east Asia, stealth and surprise were attained by sailing under radio silence so that the navy's movements could not be tracked, Moving troops aboard ships into South-east Asia made it appear that the Japanese army was also 'invisible'. Attacks against Hawaii and Singapore seemed, to the American and British defenders, to come from nowhere. In Indonesia and the Philippines the Japanese attack was even faster than the German blitz against France in the West.

The greatest military surprises in American history have all been in Asia. Surely, there is something going on here beyond the purely technical difficulties of detecting enemy movements. Pearl Harbour, the Chinese intervention in Korea, and the Tet offensive in Vietnam all came out of a tradition of surprise and stealth. US technical intelligence — the location of enemy units and their movements — was greatly improved after each surprise, but with no noticeable improvement in the American ability to foresee or prepare what would happen next. There is a cultural divide here, not just a technical one. Even when it was possible to track an army with intelligence satellites, as when Iraq invaded Kuwait or when Syria and Egypt attacked Israel, surprise was achieved. The United States was stunned by Iraq's attack on Kuwait even though it had satellite pictures of Iraqi troops massing at the border.

The exception that proves the point that cultural differences obscure the West's understanding of Asian behaviour was the Soviet Union's 1979 invasion of Afghanistan. This was fully anticipated and understood in advance. There was no surprise because the United States understood Moscow's world view and thinking. It could anticipate Soviet action almost as well as the Soviets themselves, because the Soviet Union was really a western country.

The difference between the eastern and the western way of war is striking. The West's great strategic writer, Clausewitz, linked war to politics, as did Sun-tzu. Both were opponents of militarism, of turning war over to the generals. But there, all similarity ends. Clausewitz wrote that the way to achieve a larger political purpose is through destruction of the enemy's army. After observing Napoleon conquer Europe by smashing enemy armies to bits, Clausewitz made his famous remark in *On War* (1932) that combat is the continuation of politics by violent means. Morale and unity are important, but they should be harnessed for the ultimate battle. If the eastern way of war is embodied by the stealthy archer, the metaphorical western counterpart is the swordsman charging forward, seeking a decisive showdown, eager to administer the blow that will obliterate the enemy once and for all. In this view, war proceeds along a fixed course and occupies a finite extent of time, like a play in three acts with a beginning, a middle, and an end. The end, the final scene, decides the issue for good.

When things don't work out quite this way, the western military mind feels tremendous frustration. Sun-tzu's great disciples, Mao Zedong and Ho Chi Minh, are respected in Asia for their clever use of indirection and deception to achieve an advantage over stronger adversaries. But in the West their approach is seen as underhanded and devious. To the American strategic mind, the Viet Cong guerilla did not fight fairly. They should have come out into the open and fought like men, instead of hiding in the jungle and sneaking around like a cat in the night.

467. According to the author, the main reason for theUS losing the Vietnam War was
- (a) the Vietnamese understood the local terrain better.
- (b) the lack of support for the war from the American people.
- (c) the failure of the US to mobilize its military strength.
- (d) their inability to fight a war on terms other than those they understood well.

468. Which of the following statements does not describe the 'Asian' way of war?
- (a) Indirect attacks without frontal attacks.
- (b) The swordsman charging forward to obliterate the enemy once and for all.
- (c) Manipulation of an adversary without his knowledge.
- (d) Subduing an enemy without fighting.

469. Which of the following is not one of Sun-tzu's ideas?
- (a) Actual combat is the principal means of subduing an adversary.
- (b) War should be undertaken only after thorough preparation.
- (c) War is linked to politics.
- (d) War should not be left to the generals alone.

470. The difference in the concepts of war of Clausewitz and Sun-tzu is best characterized by
- (a) Clausewitz's support for militarism as against Sun-tzu's opposition to it.
- (b) their relative degrees of sophistication.
- (c) their attitude to guerilla warfare.
- (d) their differing conceptions of the structure, time and sequence of a war.

471. To the Americans, the approach of the Viet Cong seemed devious because
- (a) the Viet Cong did not fight like men out in the open.
- (b) the Viet Cong allied with America's enemies.
- (c) the Viet Cong took strategic advice from Mao Zedong.
- (d) the Viet Cong used bows and arrows rather than conventional weapons.

472. According to the author, the greatest military surprises in American history have been in Asia because
- (a) the Americans failed to implement their military strategies many miles away from their own country.
- (b) the Americans were unable to use their technologies like intelligence satellites effectively to detectenemy movements.
- (c) the Americans failed to understand the Asian culture of war that was based on stealth and surprise.
- (d) Clausewitz is inferior to Sun-tzu.

Passage – 60

The current debate on intellectual property rights (IPRs) raises a number of important issues concerning the strategy and policies for building a more dynamic national agricultural research system, the relative roles of public and private sectors, and the role of agribusiness multinational corporations (MNCs). This debate has been stimulated by the international agreement on Trade Related Intellectual Property Rights (TRIPs), negotiated as part of the Uruguay Round. TRIPs, for the first time, seeks to bring innovations in agricultural technology under a new worldwide IPR regime. The agribusiness MNCs (along with pharmaceutical companies) played a leading part in lobbying for such a regime during the Uruguay Round negotiations. The argument was that incentives are necessary to stimulate innovations, and that this calls for a system of patents which gives innovators the sole right to use (or sell/lease the right to use) their innovations for a specified period and protects them against unauthorised copying or use. With strong support of their national governments, they were influential in shaping the agreement on TRIPs, which eventually emerged from the Uruguay Round.

The current debate on TRIPs in India—as indeed elsewhere —echoes wider concerns about 'privatization' of research and allowing a free field for MNCs in the sphere of biotechnology and agriculture. The agribusiness corporations, and those with unbounded faith in the power of science to overcome all likely problems, point to the vast potential that new technology holds for solving the problems of hunger, malnutrition and poverty in the world.

The exploitation of this potential should be encouraged and this is best done by the private sector for which patents are essential. Some, who do not necessarily accept this optimism, argue that fears of MNC domination are exaggerated and that farmers will accept their products only if they decisively outperform the available alternatives. Those who argue against agreeing to introduce an IPR regime in agriculture and encouraging private sector research are apprehensive that this will work to the disadvantage of farmers by making them more and more dependent on monopolistic MNCs. A different, though related apprehension is that extensive use of hybrids and genetically engineered new varieties might increase the vulnerability of agriculture to outbreaks of pests and diseases. The larger, longer-term consequences of reduced biodiversity that may follow from the use of specially-bred varieties are also another cause for concern. Moreover, corporations, driven by the profit motive, will necessarily tend to underplay, if not ignore, potential adverse consequences, especially those which are unknown and which may manifest themselves only over a relatively long period. On the other hand, high-pressure advertising and aggressive sales campaigns by private companies can seduce farmers into accepting varieties without being aware of potential adverse effects and the possibility of disastrous consequences for their livelihood if these varieties happen to fail. There is no provision under the laws, as they now exist, for compensating users against such eventualities.

Excessive preoccupation with seeds and seed material has obscured other important issues involved in reviewing the research policy. We need to remind ourselves that improved varieties by themselves are not sufficient for sustained growth of yields. In our own experience, some of the early high yielding varieties (HYVs) of rice and wheat were found susceptible to widespread pest attacks; and some had problems of grain quality. Further research was necessary to solve these problems. This largely successful research was almost entirely done in public research institutions. Of course, it could in principle have been done by private companies, but whether they choose to do so depends crucially on the extent of the loss in market for their original introductions on account of the above factors and whether the companies are financially strong enough to absorb the 'losses', invest in research to correct the deficiencies and recover the lost market. Public research, which is not driven by profit, is better placed to take corrective action. Research for improving common pool resource management, maintaining ecological health and ensuring sustainability is both critical and also demanding in terms of technological challenge and resource requirements. As such research is crucial to the impact of new varieties, chemicals and equipment in the farmer's field, private companies should be interested in such research. But their primary interest is in the sale of seed material, chemicals, equipment and other inputs produced by them. Knowledge and techniques for resource management are not 'marketable' in the same way as those inputs. Their application to land, water and forests has a long gestation and their efficacy depends on resolving difficult problems such as designing institutions for proper and equitable management of common pool resources. Public or quasi-public research institutions informed by broader, long-term concerns can only do such work.

The public sector must therefore continue to play a major role in the national research system. It is both wrong and misleading to pose the problem in terms of public sector versus private sector or of privatization of research. We need to address problems likely to arise on account of the public-private sector complementarity, and ensure that the public research system performs efficiently. Complementarity between various elements of research raises several issues in implementing an IPR regime. Private companies do not produce new varieties and inputs entirely as a result of their own research. Almost all technological improvement is based on knowledge and experience accumulated from the past, and the results of basic and applied research in public and quasi-public institutions (universities, research organizations). Moreover, as is increasingly recognised, accumulated stock of knowledge does not reside only in the scientific community and its academic publications, but is also widely diffused in traditions and folk knowledge of local communities all over.

The deciphering of the structure and functioning of DNA forms the basis of much of modern biotechnology. But this fundamental breakthrough is a 'public good' freely accessible in the public domain and usable free of any charge. Varieties/techniques developed using that knowledge can however be, and are, patented for private profit. Similarly, private corporations draw extensively, and without any charge, on germ plasm available in varieties of plants species (neem and turmeric are by now famous examples). Publicly funded gene banks as well as new varieties bred by public sector research stations can also be used freely by private enterprises for developing their own varieties and seek patent protection for them. Should private breeders be allowed free use of basic scientific discoveries? Should the repositories of traditional knowledge and germ plasm be collected which are maintained and improved by publicly funded institutions? Or should users be made to pay for such use? If they are to pay, what should be the basis of compensation? Should the compensation be for individuals or for communities/ institutions to which they belong? Should individuals/ institutions be given the right of patenting their innovations? These are some of the important issues that deserve more attention than they now get and need serious detailed study to evolve reasonably satisfactory, fair and workable solutions. Finally, the tendency to equate the public sector with the government is wrong. The public space is much wider than government departments and includes cooperatives, universities, public trusts and a variety of non-governmental organizations (NGOs). Giving greater autonomy to research organizations from government control and giving non-government public institutions the space and resources to play a larger, more effective role in research, is therefore an issue of direct relevance in restructuring the public research system.

2000

473. Which one of the following statements describes an important issue, or important issues, not being raised in the context of the current debate on IPRs?

(a) The role of MNCs in the sphere of biotechnology and agriculture.

(b) The strategy and policies for establishing an IPR regime for Indian agriculture.

(c) The relative roles of public and private sectors.

(d) Wider concerns about 'privatization' of research.

474. The fundamental breakthrough in deciphering the structure and functioning of DNA has become a public good. This means that

(a) breakthroughs in fundamental research on DNA are accessible by all without any monetary considerations.

(b) the fundamental research on DNA has the characteristic of having beneficial effects for the public at large.

(c) due to the large scale of fundamental research on DNA, it falls in the domain of public sector research institutions.

(d) the public and other companies must have free access to such fundamental breakthroughs in research.

475. In debating the respective roles of the public and private sectors in the national research system, it is important to recognise

(a) that private companies do not produce new varieties and inputs entirely on their own research.

(b) that almost all technology improvements are based on knowledge and experience accumulated from the past.

(c) the complementary role of public and private-sector research.

(d) that knowledge repositories are primarily the scientific community and its academic publications.

476. Which one of the following may provide incentives to address the problem of potential adverse consequences of biotechnology?

(a) Include IPR issues in the TRIPs agreement.

(b) Nationalize MNCs engaged in private research in biotechnology.

(c) Encourage domestic firms to patent their innovations.

(d) Make provisions in the law for user compensation against failure of newly-developed varieties.

477. Which of the following statements is not a likely consequence of emerging technologies in agriculture?

(a) Development of newer and newer varieties will lead to increase in biodiversity.

(b)MNCs may underplay the negative consequences of the newer technology on environment.

(c) Newer varieties of seeds may increase vulnerability of crops to pests and diseases.

(d) Reforms in patent laws and user compensation against crop failures would be needed to address new technology problems.

478. The TRIPs agreement emerged from the Uruguay Round to

(a) address the problem of adverse consequences of genetically engineered new varieties of grain.

(b) fulfil the WTO requirement to have an agreement on trade related property rights.

(c) provide incentives to innovators by way of protecting their intellectual property.

(d) give credibility to the innovations made by MNCs in the field of pharmaceuticals and agriculture.

479. Public or quasi-public research institutions are more likely than private companies to address the negative consequences of new technologies, because of which of the following reasons?

(a) Public research is not driven by profit motive.

(b) Private companies may not be able to absorb losses arising out of the negative effects of the new technologies.

(c) Unlike new technology products, knowledge and techniques for resource management are not amenable to simple market transactions.

(d) All of the above

480. While developing a strategy and policies for building a more dynamic national agricultural research system, which one of the following statements needs to be considered?

(a) Public and quasi-public institutions are not interested in making profits.

(b) Public and quasi-public institutions have a broader and long-term outlook than private companies.

(c) Private companies are incapable of building products based on traditional and folk knowledge.

(d) Traditional and folk knowledge cannot be protected by patents.

Passage – 61

One of the criteria by which we judge the vitality of a style of painting is its ability to renew itself — its responsiveness to the changing nature and quality of experience, the degree of conceptual and formal innovation that it exhibits. By this criterion, it would appear that the practice of abstractionism has failed to engage creatively with the radical change in human experience in recent decades. It has, seemingly, been unwilling to re-invent itself in relation to the systems of artistic expression and viewers' expectations that have developed under the impact of the mass media.

The judgement that abstractionism has slipped into 'inter gear' is gaining endorsement, not only among discerning viewers and practitioners of other art forms, but also among abstract painters themselves. Like their companions elsewhere in the world, abstractionists in India are asking themselves an overwhelming question today: Does abstractionism have a future? The major crisis that abstractionists face is that of revitalising their picture surface; few have improvised any solutions beyond the ones that were exhausted by the 1970s. Like all revolutions, whether in policies or in art, abstractionism must now confront its moment of truth: having begun life as a new and radical pictorial approach to experience, it has become an entrenched orthodoxy itself. Indeed, when viewed against a historical situation in which a variety of subversive, interactive and richly hybrid forms are available to the art practitioner, abstractionism assumes the remote and defiant air of an aristocracy that has outlived its age; trammelled by formulaic conventions yet buttressed by a rhetoric of sacred mystery, it seems condemned to being the last citadel of the self-regarding 'fine art' tradition, the last hurrah of painting for painting's sake.

The situation is further complicated in India by the circumstances in which an indigenous abstractionism came into prominence here during the 1960s. From the beginning it was propelled by the dialectic between two motives, one revolutionary and the other conservative — it was inaugurated as an act of emancipation from the dogmas of the nascent Indian nation state, when art was officially viewed as an indulgence at worst, and at best, as an instrument for the celebration of the republic's hopes and aspirations. Having rejected these dogmas, the pioneering abstractionists also went on to reject the various figurative styles associated with the Santiniketan circle and others. In such a situation, abstractionism was a revolutionary move. It led art towards the exploration of the subconscious mind, the spiritual quest and the possible expansion of consciousness. Indian painting entered into a phase of self-inquiry, a meditative inner space where cosmic symbols and non-representational images ruled. Often, the transition from figurative idioms to abstractionist ones took place within the same artist.

At the same time, Indian abstractionists have rarely committed themselves wholeheartedly to a non-representational idiom. They have been preoccupied with the fundamentally metaphysical project of aspiring to the mystical-holy without altogether renouncing the symbolic. This has been sustained by a hereditary reluctance to give up the murti, the inviolable iconic form, which explains why abstractionism is marked by the conservative tendency to operate with images from the sacred repertoire of the past. Abstractionism thus entered India as a double-edged device in a complex cultural transaction. Ideologically, it served as an internationalist legitimisation of the emerging revolutionary local trends. However, on entry, it was conscripted to serve local artistic preoccupations — a survey of indigenous abstractionism will show that its most obvious points of affinity with European and American abstract art were with the more mystically oriented of the major sources of abstractionist philosophy and practice, for instance, the Kandinsky-Klee School. There have been no takers for Malevich's Suprematism, which militantly rejected both the artistic forms of the past and the world of appearances, privileging the new-minted geometric symbol as an autonomous sign of the desire for infinity.

Against this backdrop, we can identify three major abstractionist idioms in Indian art. The first develops from a love of the earth, and assumes the form of a celebration of the self's dissolution in the cosmic panorama; the landscape is no longer a realistic transcription of the scene, but is transformed into a visionary occasion for contemplating the cycles of decay and regeneration. The second idiom phrases its departures from symbolic and archetypal devices as invitations to heightened planes of awareness. Abstractionism begins with the establishment or dissolution of the motif, which can be drawn from diverse sources, including the hieroglyphic tablet, the Sufi meditation dance or the Tantric diagram. The third idiom is based on the lyric play of forms guided by gesture or allied with formal improvisations like the assemblage. Here, sometimes, the line dividing abstract image from patterned design or quasi-random expressive marking may blur. The flux of forms can also be regimented through the policies of pure colour arrangements, vector-diagrammatic spaces and gestural design.

In this genealogy, some pure lines of descent follow their logic to the inevitable point of extinction, others engage in cross-fertilization, and yet others undergo mutation to maintain their energy. However, this genealogical survey demonstrates the wave at its crests, those points where the metaphysical and the painterly have been fused in images of abiding potency, ideas sensuously ordained rather than fabricated programmatically to a concept. It is equally possible to enumerate the troughs where the two principles do not come together, thus arriving at a very different account. Uncharitable as it may sound, the history of Indian abstractionism records a series of attempts to avoid the risks of abstraction by resorting to an overt and near-generic symbolism, which many Indian abstractionists embrace when they find themselves bereft of the imaginative energy to negotiate the union of metaphysics and painterliness.

Such symbolism falls into a dual trap: it succumbs to the pompous vacuity of pure metaphysics when the burden of intention is passed off as justification; or then it is desiccated by the arid formalism of pure painterliness, with delight in the measure of chance or pattern guiding the execution of a painting. The ensuing conflict of purpose stalls the progress of abstractionism in an impasse. The remarkable Indian abstractionists are precisely those who have overcome this and addressed themselves to the basic elements of their art with a decisive sense of independence from prior models. In their recent work, we see the logic of Indian abstractionism pushed almost to the furthest it can be taken. Beyond such artists stands a lost generation of abstractionists whose work invokes a wistful, delicate beauty but stops there.

Abstractionism is not a universal language; it is an art that points up the loss of a shared language of signs in society. And yet, it affirms the possibility of its recovery through the effort of awareness. While its rheotoric has always emphasised a call for new forms of attention, abstractionist practice has tended to fall into a complacent pride in its own incomprehensibility; a complacency fatal in an ethos where vibrant new idioms compete for the viewers' attention. Indian abstractionists ought to really return to basics, to reformulate and replenish their understanding of the nature of the relationship between the painted image and the world around it. But will they abandon their favourite conceptual habits and formal conventions, if this becomes necessary?

481. Which one of the following is not stated by the author as a reason for abstractionism losing its vitality?

(a) Abstractionism has failed to reorient itself in the context of changing human experience.

(b) Abstractionism has not considered the developments in artistic expression that have taken place in recent times.

(c) Abstractionism has not followed the path taken by all revolutions, whether in politics or art.

(d) The impact of mass media on viewers' expectations has not been assessed, and responded to, by abstractionism.

482. Which of the following, according to the author, is the role that abstractionism plays in a society?

(a) It provides an idiom that can be understood by most members in a society.

(b) It highlights the absence of a shared language of meaningful symbols which can be recreated through greater awareness.

(c) It highlights the contradictory artistic trends of revolution and conservatism that any society needs to move forward.

(d) It helps abstractionists invoke the wistful, delicate beauty that may exist in society.

483. According to the author, which one of the following characterises the crisis faced by abstractionism?

(a) Abstractionists appear to be unable to transcend the solutions tried out earlier.

(b) Abstractionism has allowed itself to be confined by set forms and practices.

(c) Abstractionists have been unable to use the multiplicity of forms now becoming available to an artist.

(d) All of the above

484. According to the author, the introduction of abstractionism was revolutionary because it

(a) celebrated the hopes and aspirants of a newly independent nation.

(b) provided a new direction to Indian art, towards self-inquiry and non-representational images.

(c) managed to obtain internationalist support for the abstractionist agenda.

(d) was an emancipation from the dogmas of the nascent nation state.

485. Which one of the following is not part of the author's characterization of the conservative trend in Indian abstractionism?

(a) An exploration of the subconscious mind.

(b) A lack of full commitment to non-representational symbols.

(c) An adherence to the symbolic while aspiring to the mystical.

(d) Usage of the images of gods or similar symbols.

486. Given the author's delineation of the three abstractionist idioms in Indian art, the third idiom can be best distinguished from the other two idioms through its

(a) depiction of nature's cyclical renewal.

(b) use of non-representational images.

(c) emphasis on arrangement of forms.

(d) limited reliance on original models.

487. According to the author, the attraction of the Kandinsky-Klee School for Indian abstractionists can be explained by which one of the following?

(a) The conservative tendency to aspire to the mystical without a complete renunciation of the symbolic.

(b) The discomfort of Indian abstractionists with Malevich's Suprematism.

(c) The easy identification of obvious points of affinity with European and American abstract art, of which the Kandinsky-Klee School is an example.

(d) The double-edged nature of abstractionism which enabled identification with mystically-oriented schools.

488. Which one of the following, according to the author, is the most important reason for the stalling of abstractionism's progress in an impasse?

(a) Some artists have followed their abstractionist logic to the point of extinction.

(b) Some artists have allowed chance or pattern to dominate the execution of their paintings.

(c) Many artists have avoided the trap of a near-generic and an open symbolism.

(d) Many artists have found it difficult to fuse the twin principles of the metaphysical and the painterly.

Passage – 62

In a modern computer, electronic and magnetic storage technologies play complementary roles. Electronic memory chips are fast but volatile (their contents are lost when the computer is unplugged). Magnetic tapes and hard disks are slower, but have the advantage that they are non-volatile, so that they can be used to store software and documents even when the power is off.

In laboratories around the world, however, researchers are hoping to achieve the best of both worlds. They are trying to build magnetic memory chips that could be used in place of today's electronic ones. These magnetic memories would be non-volatile; but they would also be faster, would consume less power, and would be able to stand up to hazardous environments more easily. Such chips would have obvious applications in storage cards for digital cameras and music players; they would enable handheld and laptop computers to boot up more quickly and to operate for longer; they would allow desktop computers to run faster; they would doubtless have military and space-faring advantages too. But although the theory behind them looks solid, there are tricky practical problems that need to be overcome.

Two different approaches, based on different magnetic phenomena, are being pursued. The first, being investigated by Gary Prinz and his colleagues at the Naval Research Laboratory (NRL) in Washington DC, exploits the fact that the electrical resistance of some materials changes in the presence of a magnetic field — a phenomenon known as magneto-resistance. For some multi-layered materials, this effect is particularly powerful and is, accordingly, called 'giant' magneto-resistance (GMR). Since 1997, the exploitation of GMR has made cheap multi-gigabyte hard disks commonplace. The magnetic orientations of the magnetised spots on the surface of a spinning disk are detected by measuring the changes they induce in the resistance of a tiny sensor. This technique is so sensitive that it means the spots can be made smaller and packed closer together than was previously possible, thus increasing the capacity and reducing the size and cost of a disk drive.

Dr. Prinz and his colleagues are now exploiting the same phenomenon on the surface of memory chips, rather than spinning disks. In a conventional memory chip, each binary digit (bit) of data is represented using a capacitor reservoir of electrical charge that is either empty of full — to represent a zero or a one. In the NRL's magnetic design, by contrast, each bit is stored in a magnetic element in the form of a vertical pillar of magnetisable material. A matrix of wires passing above and below the elements allows each to be magnetised, either clockwise or anticlockwise, to represent zero or one. Another set of wires allows current to pass through any particular element. By measuring an element's resistance you can determine its magnetic orientation, and hence whether it is storing a zero or a one. Since the elements retain their magnetic orientation even when the power is off, the result is non-volatile memory. Unlike the elements of an electronic memory, a magnetic memory's elements are not easily disrupted by radiation. And compared with electronic memories, whose capacitors need constant topping up, magnetic memories are simpler and consume less power. The NRL researchers plan to commercialize their device through a company called Non-volatile Electronics, which recently began work on the necessary processing and fabrication techniques. But it will be some years before the first chips roll off the production line.

Most attention in the field is focused on an alternative approach based on magnetic tunnel-junctions (MTJs), which are being investigated by researchers at chip makers, such as IBM, Motorola, Siemens and Hewlett-Packard. IBM's research team, led by Stuart Parkin, has already created a 500 element working prototype that operates at 20 times the speed of conventional memory chips and consumes one per cent of the power. Each element consists of a sandwich of two layers of magnetisable material separated by a barrier of aluminium oxide just four or five atoms thick. The polarisation of lower magnetisable layer is fixed in one direction, but that of the upper layer can be set (again, by passing a current through a matrix of control wires) either to the left or to the right, to store a zero or a one. The polarisations of the two layers are then in either the same or opposite directions.

Although the aluminium-oxide barrier is an electrical insulator, it is so thin that electrons are able to jump across it via a quantum-mechanical effect called tunnelling. It turns out that such tunnelling is easier when the two magnetic layers are polarised in the same direction than when they are polarised in opposite directions. So by measuring the current that flows through the sandwich, it is possible to determine the alignment of the topmost layer, and hence whether it is storing a zero or a one.

To build a full-scale memory chip based on MTJs is, however, no easy matter. According to Paulo Freitas, an expert on chip manufacturing at the Technical University of Lisbon, magnetic memory elements will have to become far smaller and more reliable than current prototypes if they are to compete with electronic memory. At the same time, they will have to be sensitive enough to respond when the appropriate wires in the control matrix are switched on, but not so sensitive that they respond when a neighbouring element is changed. Despite these difficulties, the general consensus is that MTJs are the more promising ideas.

Dr Parkin says his group evaluated the GMR approach and decided not to pursue it, despite the fact that IBM pioneered GMR in hard disks. Dr. Prinz, however, contends that his plan will eventually offer higher storage densities and lower production costs.

Not content with shaking up the multi-billion-dollar market for computer memory, some researchers have even more ambitious plans for magnetic computing. In a paper published last month in *Science*, Russell Cowburn and Mark Welland of Cambridge University outlined research that could form the basis of a magnetic microprocessor a chip capable of manipulating (rather than merely storing) information magnetically. In place of conducting wires, a magnetic processor would have rows of magnetic dots, each of which could be polarised in one of two directions. Individual bits of information would travel down the rows as magnetic pulses, changing the orientation of the dots as they went. Dr. Cowburn and Dr. Welland have demonstrated how a logic gate(the basic element of a microprocessor)could work in such a scheme. In their experiment, they fed a signal in at one end of the chain of dots and used a second signal to control whether it propagated along the chain.

It is admittedly, a long way from a single logic gate to a full microprocessor, but this was true also when the transistor was first invented. Dr. Cowburn, who is now searching for backers to help commercialize the technology, says he believes it will be at least 10 years before the first magnetic microprocessor is constructed. But other researchers in the field agree that such a chip is the next logical step. Dr. Prinz says that once magnetic memory is sorted out 'the target is to go after the logic circuits'. Whether all-magnetic computers will ever be able to compete with other contenders that are jostling to knock electronics off its perch — such as optical, biological and quantum computing — remains to be seen. Dr Cowburn suggests that the future lies with hybrid machines that use different technologies. But computing with magnetism evidently has an attraction all its own.

489. In developing magnetic memory chips to replace the electronic ones, two alternative research paths are being pursued. These are approaches based on

(a) volatile and non-volatile memories.

(b) magneto-resistance and magnetic tunnel-junctions.

(c) radiation disruption and radiation neutral effects.

(d) orientation of magnetized spots on the surface of a spinning disk and alignment of magnetic dots on the surface of a conventional memory chip.

490. A binary digit or bit is represented in the magneto-resistance based magnetic chip using

(a) a layer of aluminium oxide.

(b) a capacitor.

(c) a vertical pillar of magnetized material.

(d) a matrix of wires.

491. In the magnetic tunnel-junctions (MTJs) tunnelling is easier when

(a) two magnetic layers are polarised in the same direction.

(b) two magnetic layers are polarised in the opposite directions.

(c) two aluminium-oxide barriers are polarised in the same direction.

(d) two aluminium-oxide barriers are polarised in the opposite directions.

492. A major barrier on the way to build a full-scale memory chip based on MTJs is

(a) the low sensitivity of the magnetic memory elements.

(b) the thickness of aluminium oxide barriers.

(c) the need to develop more reliable and far smaller magnetic memory chips.

(d) All of the above

493. In the MTJs approach, it is possible to identify whether the top most layer of the magnetized memory element is storing a zero or one by

(a) measuring an element's resistance and thus determining its magnetic orientation.

(b) measuring the degree of disruption caused by radiation in the elements of the magnetic memory.

(c) magnetizing the elements either clockwise or anticlockwise.

(d) measuring the current that flows through the sandwich.

494. A line of research which is trying to build a magnetic chip that can both store and manipulate information, is being pursued by

(a) Paul Freitas. (b) Stuart Parkin.

(c) Gray Prinz. (d) None of them

495. Experimental research currently underway, using rows of magnetic dots, each of which could be polarised in one of the two directions, has led to the demonstration of

(a) working of a microprocessor.

(b) working of a logic gate.

(c) working of a magneto-resistance based chip.

(d) working of a magneto tunnelling-junction (MTJ) based chip.

496. From the passage, which of the following cannot be inferred?

(a) Electronic memory chips are faster and non-volatile.

(b) Electronic and magnetic storage technologies play a complementary role.

(c) MTJs are the more promising idea, compared to the magneto-resistance approach.

(d) Non-volatile Electronics is the company set up to commercialize the GMR chips.

Passage – 63

The story begins as the European pioneers crossed the Alleghenies and started to settle in the Midwest. The land they found was covered with forests. With incredible effort they felled the trees, pulled the stumps and planted their crops in the rich, loamy soil. When they finally reached the western edge of the place, we now call Indiana, the forest stopped and ahead lay a thousand miles of the great grass prairie. The Europeans were puzzled by this new environment. Some even called it the 'Great Desert'. It seemed untillable. The earth was often very wet and it was covered with centuries of tangled and matted grasses. With their cast iron plows, the settlers found that the prairie sod could not be cut and the wet earth stuck to their plowshares. Even a team of the best oxen bogged down after a few years of tugging. The iron plow was a useless tool to farm the prairie soil. The pioneers were stymied for nearly two decades. Their western march was halted and they filled in the eastern regions of the Midwest.

In 1837, a blacksmith in the town of Grand Detour, Illinois, invented a new tool. His name was John Deere and the tool was a plow made of steel. It was sharp enough to cut through matted grasses and smooth enough to cast off the mud. It was a simple tool, the 'sod buster' that opened the great prairies to agricultural development.

Sauk County, Wisconsin is the part of the prairie where I have a home. It is named after the Sauk Indians. In 1673, Father Marquette was the first European to lay his eyes upon their land. He found a village laid out in regular patterns on a plain beside the Wisconsin river. He called the place Prairie du Sac. The village was surrounded by fields that had provided maize, beans and squash for the Sauk people for generations reaching back into the unrecorded time.

When the European settlers arrived at the Sauk prairie in 1837, the government forced the native Sauk people, west of the Mississippi river. The settlers came with John Deere's new invention and used the tool to open the area to a new kind of agriculture. They ignored the traditional ways of the Sauk Indians and used their sod-busting tool for planting wheat. Initially, the soil was generous and the farmers thrived. However, each year the soil lost more of its nurturing power. It was only 30 years after the Europeans arrived with their new technology that the land was depleted. Wheat farming became uneconomic and tens of thousands of farmers left Wisconsin seeking new land with sod to bust.

It took the Europeans and their new technology just one generation to make their homeland into a desert. The Sauk Indians who knew how to sustain themselves on the Sauk prairie land were banished to another kind of desert called a reservation. And they even forgot about the techniques and tools that had sustained them on the prairie for generations unrecorded. And that is how it was that three deserts were created — Wisconsin, the reservation and the memories of people. A century later, the land of the Sauks is now populated by the children of a second wave of European farmers who learned to replenish the soil through the regenerative powers of dairying, ground cover crops and animal manures. These third and fourth generation farmers and townspeople do not realise, however, that a new settler is coming soon with an invention as powerful as John Deere's plow.

The new technology is called 'bereavement counselling'. It is a tool forged at the great state university, an innovative technique to meet the needs of those experiencing the death of a loved one, a tool that can 'process' the grief of the people who now live on the Prairie of the Sauk. As one can imagine the final days of the village of the Sauk Indians before the arrival of the settlers with John Deere's plow, one can also imagine these final days before the arrival of the first bereavement counsellor at Prairie du Sac. In these final days, the farmers and the towns people mourn at the death of a mother, brother, son, or friend. The bereaved is joined by neighbours and kin. They meet grief together in lamentation, prayer and song. They call upon the words of the clergy and surround themselves in community.

It is in these ways that they grieve and then go on with life. Through their mourning they are assured of the bonds between them and renewed in the knowledge that this death is a part of the Prairie of the Sauk. Their grief is common property, an anguish from which the community draws strength and gives the bereaved the courage to move ahead.

It is into this prairie community that the bereavement counsellor arrives with the new grief technology. The counsellor calls the invention a service and assures the prairie folk of its effectiveness and superiority by invoking the name of the great university while displaying a diploma and certificate. At first, we can imagine that the local people will be puzzled by the bereavement counsellor's claim. However, the counsellor will tell a few of them that the new technique is merely to assist the bereaved's community at the time of death. To some other prairie folk who are isolated or forgotten, the counsellor will approach the Country Board and advocate the right to treatment for these unfortunate souls. This right will be guaranteed by the Board's decision to reimburse those too poor to pay for counselling services. There will be others, schooled to believe in the innovative new tools certified by universities and medical centres, who will seek out the bereavement counsellor by force of habit. And one of these people will tell a bereaved neighbour who is unschooled that unless his grief is processed by a counsellor, he will probably have major psychological problems in later life. Several people will begin to use the bereavement counsellor because, since the Country Board now taxes them to insure access to the technology, they will feel that to fail to be counselled is to waste their money, and to be denied a benefit, or even a right.

Finally, one day, the aged father of a Sauk woman will die. And the next door neighbour will not drop by because he doesn't want to interrupt the bereavement counseller. The woman's kin will stay home because they will have learned that only the bereavement counsellor knows how to process grief the proper way. The local clergy will seek technical assistance from the bereavement counsellor to learn the correct form of service to deal with guilt and grief. And the grieving daughter will know that it is the bereavement counsellor who really cares for her because only the bereavement counsellor comes when death visits this family on the Prairie of the Sauk.

It will be only one generation between the bereavement counsellor arrival and the community of mourners disappearance. The counsellor's new tool will cut through the social fabric, throwing aside kinship, care, neighbourly obligations and community ways of coming together and going on. Like John Deere's plow, the tools of bereavement counselling will create a desert where a community once flourished. And finally, even the bereavement counsellor will see the impossibility of restoring hope in clients once they are genuinely alone with nothing but a service for consolation. In the inevitable failure of the service, the bereavement counsellor will find the deserts even in herself.

497. Which one of the following best describes the approach of the author?

(a) Comparing experiences with two innovations tried, in order to illustrate the failure of both.

(b) Presenting community perspectives on two technologies which have had negative effects on people.

(c) Using the negative outcomes of one innovation to illustrate the likely outcomes of another innovation.

(d) Contrasting two contexts separated in time, to illustrate how 'deserts' have arisen.

498. According to the passage, bereavement handling traditionally involves

(a) the community bereavement counsellors working with the bereaved to help him/her overcome grief.

(b) the neighbours and kin joining the bereaved and meeting grief together in mourning and prayer.

(c) using techniques developed systematically in formal institutions of learning, a trained counsellor helping the bereaved cope with grief.

(d) the Sauk Indian Chief leading the community with rituals and rites to help lessen the grief of the bereaved.

499. According to the author, due to which of the following reasons, will the bereavement counsellor find the deserts even in herself?

(a) Over a period of time, working with Sauk Indians who have lost their kinship and relationships, she becomes one of them.

(b) She is working in an environment where the disappearance of community mourners makes her work place a social desert.

(c) Her efforts at grief processing with the bereaved will fail as no amount of professional service can make up for the loss due to the disappearance of community mourners.

(d) She has been working with people who have settled for a long time in the Great Desert.

500. According to the author, the bereavement counsellor is

(a) a friend of the bereaved helping him or her handle grief.

(b) an advocate of the right to treatment for the community.

(c) a kin of the bereaved helping him/her handle grief.

(d) a formally trained person helping the bereaved handle grief.

501. The prairie was a great puzzlement for the European pioneers because

(a) it was covered with thick, untillable layers of grass over a vast stretch.

(b) it was a large desert immediately next to lush forests.

(c) it was rich cultivable land left fallow for centuries.

(d) it could be easily tilled with iron plows.

502. Which of the following does the 'desert' in the passage refer to?

(a) Prairie soil depleted by cultivation of wheat.

(b) Reservations in which native Indians were resettled.

(c) Absence of, and emptiness in, community kinship and relationships.

(d) All of the above

503. According to the author, people will begin to utilize the service of the bereavement counsellor because

(a) new Country regulations will make them feel it is a right, and if they don't use it, it would be a loss.

(b) the bereaved in the community would find her a helpful friend.

(c) she will fight for subsistence allowance from the Country Board for the poor among the bereaved.

(d) grief processing needs tools certified by universities and medical centres.

504. Which of the following parallels between the plow and bereavement counselling is not claimed by the author?

(a) Both are innovative technologies.

(b) Both result in migration of the communities into which the innovations are introduced.

(c) Both lead to 'deserts' in the space of only one generation.

(d) Both are tools introduced by outsiders entering existing communities.

Passage – 64

The teaching and transmission of North Indian classical music is, and long has been, achieved by largely oral means. The *raga* and its structure, the often breathtaking intricacies of *tala* or rhythm, and the incarnation of *raga* and *tala* as *bandish* or composition, are passed thus, between *guru* and *shishya* by word of mouth and direct demonstration, with no printed sheet of notated music, as it were, acting as a go-between. Saussure's conception of language as a communication between addresser and addressee is given, in this model, a further instance, and a new, exotic complexity and glamour.

These days, especially with the middle-class having entered the domain of classical music and playing not a small part in ensuring the continuation of this ancient tradition, the tape recorder serves as a handy technological slave and preserves, from oblivion, the vanishing, elusive moment of oral transmission. Hoary gurus, too, have seen the advantage of this device, and increasingly use it as an aid to instruct their pupils; in place of the shawls and other traditional objects that used to pass from *shishya* to *guru* in the past, as a token of the regard of the former for the latter, it is not unusual, today, to see cassettes changing hands.

Part of my education in North Indian classical music was conducted via this rather ugly but beneficial rectangle of plastic, which I carried with me to England when I was an undergraduate. One cassette had stored in it various *talas* played upon the tabla, at various tempos, by my music teacher's brother-in-law, Hazarilalji, who was a teacher of Kathak dance, as well as a singer and a tabla player. This was a work of great patience and prescience, a one and half hours performance without any immediate point or purpose, but intended for some delayed future moment when I'd practise the *talas* solitarily.

This repeated playing out of the rhythmic cycles on the tabla was inflected by the noises — an irate auto driver blowing a horn; the sound of overbearing pigeons that were such a nuisance on the banister; even the cry of a kulfi seller in summer — entering from the balcony of the third floor flat we occupied in those days, in a lane in a Mumbai suburb, before we left the city for good. These sounds, in turn, would invade, hesitantly, the ebb and flow of silence inside the artificially heated room, in a borough of West London, in which I used to live as an undergraduate. There, in the trapped dust, silence and heat, the theka of the tabla, qualified by the imminent but intermittent presence of the Mumbai suburb, would come to life again. A few years later, the tabla and, in the background, the pigeons and the itinerant kulfi seller, would inhabit a small graduate room in Oxford.

The tape recorder, though, remains an extension of the oral transmission of music, rather than a replacement of it. And the oral transmission of North Indian classical music remains, almost uniquely, a testament to the fact that the human brain can absorb, remember and reproduce structures of great complexity and sophistication without the help of the hieroglyph or written mark or a system of notation. I remember my surprise on discovering that Hazarilalji — who had mastered Kathak dance, *tala* and North Indian classical music, and who used to narrate to me, occasionally, compositions meant for dance that were grand and intricate in their verbal prosody, architecture and rhythmic complexity — was near illiterate and had barely learnt to write his name in large and clumsy letters.

Of course, attempts have been made, throughout the 20th century, to formally codify and even notate this music, and institutions set up and degrees created, specifically to educate students in this 'scientific' and codified manner. Paradoxically, however, this style of teaching has produced no noteworthy student or performer; the most creative musicians still emerge from the *guru-shishya* relationship, their understanding of music developed by oral communication.

The fact that North Indian classical music emanates from, and has evolved through, oral culture, means that this music has a significantly different aesthetic, and that this aesthetic has a different politics, from that of Western classical music. A piece of music in the Western tradition, at least in its most characteristic and popular conception, originates in its composer, and the connection between the two, between composer and the piece of music, is relatively unambiguous precisely because the composer writes down, in notation, his composition, as a poet might write down and publish his poem. However far the printed sheet of notated music might travel thus from the composer, it still remains his property; and the notion of property remains at the heart of the Western conception of 'genius', which derives from the Latin *gignere* or 'to beget'.

The genius in Western classical music is, then, the originator, begetter and owner of his work — the printed, notated sheet testifying to his authority over his product and his power, not only for expression or imagination, but of origination. The conductor is a custodian and guardian of this property. Is it an accident that Mandelstam, in his notebooks, compares — the conductor's baton to a policeman's, saying all the music of the orchestra lies mute within it, waiting for its first movement to release it into the auditorium?

The *raga* — transmitted through oral means — is, in a sense, no one's property; it is not easy to pin down its source, or to know exactly where its provenance or origin lies. Unlike the Western classical tradition, where the composer begets his piece, notates it and stamps it with his ownership and remains, in effect, larger than, or the father of, his work, in the North Indian classical tradition, the *raga* — unconfined to a single incarnation, composer or performer — remains necessarily greater than the artiste who invokes it.

This leads to a very different politics of interpretation and valuation, to an aesthetic that privileges the evanescent moment of performance and invocation over the controlling authority of genius and the permanent record. It is a tradition, thus, that would appear to value the performer, as medium, more highly than the composer who presumes to originate what, effectively, cannot be originated in a single person — because the *raga* is the inheritance of a culture.

505. The author's contention that the notion of property lies at the heart of the Western conception of genius is best indicated by which one of the following?

(a) The creative output of a genius is invariably written down and recorded.

(b) The link between the creator and his output is unambiguous.

(c) The word 'genius' is derived from a Latin word which means 'to beget'.

(d) The music composer notates his music and thus becomes the 'father' of a particular piece of music.

506. Saussure's conception of language as a communication between addresser and addressee, according to the author, is exemplified by the

(a) teaching of North Indian classical music by word of mouth and direct demonstration.

(b) use of the recorded cassette as a transmission medium between the music teacher and the trainee.

(c) written down notation sheets of musical compositions.

(d) conductor's baton and the orchestra.

507. The author holds that the 'rather ugly but beneficial rectangle of plastic' has proved to be a 'handy technological slave' in

(a) storing the *talas* played upon the tabla, at various tempos.

(b) ensuring the continuance of an ancient tradition.

(c) transporting North Indian classical music across geographical borders.

(d) capturing the transient moment of oral transmission.

508. The oral transmission of North Indian classified music is an almost unique testament of the

(a) efficacy of the *guru-shishya* tradition.

(b) learning impact of direct demonstration.

(c) brain's ability to reproduce complex structures without the help of written marks.

(d) the ability of an illiterate person to narrate grand and intricate musical compositions.

509. According to the passage, in the North Indian classical tradition, the *raga* remains greater than the artiste who invokes it. This implies an aesthetic which

(a) emphasises performance and invocation over the authority of genius and permanent record.

(b) makes the music no one's property.

(c) values the composer more highly than the performer.

(d) supports oral transmission of traditional music.

510. From the author's explanation of the notion that in the Western tradition, music originates in its composer, which one of the following cannot be inferred?

(a) It is easy to transfer a piece of Western classical music to a distant place.

(b) The conductor in the Western tradition, as a custodian, can modify the music, since it 'lies mute' in his baton.

(c) The authority of the Western classical music composer over his music product is unambiguous.

(d) The power of the Western classical music composer extends to the expression of his music.

511. According to the author, the inadequacy of teaching North Indian classical music through a codified, notation-based system is best illustrated by

(a) a loss of the structural beauty of the *ragas*.

(b) a fusion of two opposing approaches creating mundane music.

(c) the conversion of free-flowing *ragas* into stilted set pieces.

(d) its failure to produce any noteworthy student or performer.

512. Which of the following statements best conveys the overall idea of the passage?

(a) North Indian and Western classical music are structurally different.

(b) Western music is the intellectual property of the genius while the North Indian *raga* is the inheritance of the culture.

(c) Creation as well as performance are important in the North Indian classical tradition.

(d) North Indian classical music is orally transmitted while Western classical music depends on written down notations.

Passage – 65

The Union Government's present position vis-a-vis the upcoming United Nations conference on racial and related discrimination world-wide seems to be the following: discuss race please, not caste; caste is our very own and not at all as bad as you think. The gross hypocrisy of that position has been lucidly underscored by *Kancha Ilaiah*. Explicitly, the world community is to be cheated out of considering the matter on the technicality that caste is not, as a concept, tantamount to a racial category. Internally, however, allowing the issue to be put on agenda at the said conference would, we are patriotically admonished, damage the country's image. Somehow, India's virtual beliefs elbow out concrete actualities. Inverted representations, as we know, have often been deployed in human histories as balm for the forsaken — religion being the most persistent of such inversions. Yet, we would humbly submit that if globalising our markets is thought as good for the 'national' pocket, globalising our social inequities might not be so bad for the mass of our people. After all, racism was as uniquely institutionalised in South Africa as caste discrimination has been within our society; why then can't we permit the world community to express itself on the latter with a fraction of the zeal with which, through the years, we pronounced on the former?

As to the technicality about whether or not caste is admissible into an agenda about race (that the conference is also about 'related discriminations' tends to be forgotten), a reputed sociologist has recently argued that where race is a 'biological' category caste is a 'social' one. Having earlier fiercely opposed implementation of the Mandal Commission Report, the said sociologist is at least to be complemented now for admitting, however tangentially, that caste discrimination is a reality, although, in his view, incompatible with racial discrimination. One would like quickly to offer the hypothesis that biology, in important ways that affect the lives of many millions, is in itself perhaps a social construction. But let us look at the matter in another way.

If it is agreed — as per the position today at which anthropological and allied scientific determinations rest — that the entire race of *homo sapiens* derived from an originary black African female (called 'Eve'), then one is hard put to understand how, one some subsequent ground, ontological distinctions are to be drawn either between races or castes. Let us also underline the distinction between the supposition that we are all god's children and the rather more substantiated argument about our descent from 'Eve', lest both positions are thought to be equally diversionary. It then stands to reason that all subsequent distinctions are, in modern parlance, 'constructed' ones, and like all ideological constructions, attributable to changing equations between knowledge and power among human communities through contested histories here, there, and elsewhere.

This line of thought receives, thankfully, extremely consequential buttress from the findings of the Human Genome project. Contrary to earlier (chiefly 19th-century colonial) persuasions on the subject of race, as well as, one might add, the somewhat infamous Jensen offerings in the 20th century from America, those finding deny genetic difference between 'races'. If anything, they suggest that environmental factors impinge on gene-function, as a dialectic seems to unfold between nature and culture. It would thus seem that 'biology' as the constitution of pigmentation enters the picture first only as a part of that dialectic. Taken together, the originary mother stipulation and the Genome findings ought indeed to furnish ground for human equality across the board, as well as yield policy initiatives towards equitable material dispensations aimed at building a global order where, in Hegel's stirring formulation, only the rational constitutes the right. Such, sadly, is not the case as everyday fresh arbitrary grounds for discrimination are constructed in the interests of sectional dominance.

2001

513. When the author writes 'globalising our social inequities', the reference is to

(a) going beyond an internal deliberation on social inequity.

(b) dealing with internal poverty through the economic benefits of globalisation.

(c) going beyond an internal delimitation of social inequity.

(d) achieving disadvantaged people's empowerment, globally.

514. According to the author, 'inverted representations as balm for the forsaken'

(a) is good for the forsaken and often deployed in human histories.

(b) is good for the forsaken, but not often deployed historically for the oppressed.

(c) occurs often as a means of keeping people oppressed.

(d) occurs often to invert the *status quo*.

515. Based on the passage, which broad areas unambiguously fall under the purview of the UN conference being discussed?

A. Racial prejudice

B. Racial pride

C. Discrimination, racial or otherwise

D. Caste-related discrimination

E. Race-related discrimination

(a) A and E (b) C and E

(c) A, C and E (d) B, C and D

516. According to the author, the sociologist who argued that race is a 'biological' category and caste is a 'social' one,

(a) generally shares the same orientation as the author's on many of the central issues discussed.

(b) tangentially admits to the existence of 'caste' as a category.

(c) admits the incompatibility between the people of different race and caste.

(d) admits indirectly that both caste-based prejudice and racial discrimination exist.

517. An important message in the passage, if one accepts a dialectic between nature and culture, is that

(a) the results of the Human Genome Project reinforces racial differences.

(b) race is at least partially a social construct.

(c) discrimination is at least partially a social construct.

(d) caste is at least partially a social construct.

Passage – 66

Studies of the factors governing reading development in young children have achieved a remarkable degree of consensus over the past two decades. The consensus concerns the causal role of 'phonological skills in young children's reading progress. Children who have good phonological skills, or good 'phonological awareness' become good readers and good spellers. Children with poor phonological skills progress more poorly. In particular, those who have a specific phonological deficit are likely to be classified as dyslexic by the time that they are 9 or 10 years old.

Phonological skills in young children can be measured at a number of different levels. The term phonological awareness is a global one, and refers to a deficit in recognising smaller units of sound within spoken words. Development work has shown that this deficit can be at the level of syllables, of onsets and rimes, or phonemes. For example, a 4-year old child might have difficulty in recognising that a word like *valentine* has three syllables, suggesting a lack of syllabic awareness. A five-year-old might have difficulty in recognising that the odd work out in the set of words *fan, cat, hat, mat* is *fan*. This task requires an awareness of the sub-syllabic units of the *onset* and the *rime*. The onset corresponds to any initial consonants in a syllable words, and the rime corresponds to the vowel and to any following consonants. Rimes correspond to rhyme in single-syllable words, and so the rime in *fan* differs from the rime in *cat*, *hat* and *mat*. In longer words, rime and rhyme may differ. The onsets in *val:en:tine* are */v/* and */t/*, and the rimes correspond to the selling patterns '*al*', '*en*' and' *ine*'.

A six-year-old might have difficulty in recognising that *plea* and *pray* begin with the same initial sound. This is a *phonemic* judgement. Although the initial phoneme */p/* is shared between the two words, in *plea* it is part of the onset '*pl*' and in *pray* it is part if the onset '*pr*'. Until children can segment the onset(or the rime), such phonemic judgements are difficult for them to make. In fact, a recent survey of different developmental studies has shown that the different levels of phonological awareness appear to emerge sequentially. The awareness of syllables, onsets, and rimes appears to merge at around the ages of 3 and 4, long before most children go to school. The awareness of phonemes, on the other hand, usually emerges at around the age of 5 or 6, when children have been taught to read for about a year. An awareness of onsets and rimes thus appears to be a precursor of reading, whereas an awareness of phonemes at every serial position in a word only appears to develop as reading is taught. The onset-rime and phonemic levels of phonological structure, however, are not distinct. Many onsets in English are single phonemes, and so are some rimes (e.g. *sea, go, zoo*).

The early availability of onsets and rimes is supported by studies that have compared the development of phonological awareness of onsets, rimes, and phonemes in the same subjects using the same phonological awareness tasks. For example, a study by Treiman and Zudowski used a same/different judgement task based on the beginning or the end sounds of words. In the beginning sound task, the words either began with the same onset, as in *plea* and *plank*, or shared only the initial phoneme, as in plea and pray. In the end-sound task, the words either shared the entire rime, as in *spit* and *wit*, or shared only the final phoneme, as in *rat* and *wit*. Treiman and Zudowski showed that four- and five-year-old children found the onset-rime version of the same/different task significantly easier than the version based on phonemes. Only the six-year-olds, who had been learning to read for about a year, were able to perform both versions of the tasks with an equal level of success.

518. From the following statements, pick out the true statement according to the passage.
(a) A mono-syllabic word can have only one onset.
(b) A mono-syllabic word can have only one rhyme but more than one rime.
(c) A mono-syllabic word can have only one phoneme.
(d) All of these

519. Which one of the following is likely to emerge last in the cognitive development of a child?
(a) Rhyme (b) Rime
(c) Onset (d) Phoneme

520. A phonological deficit in which of the following is likely to be classified as dyslexia?
(a) Phonemic judgement
(b) Onset judgement
(c) Rime judgement
(d) Any one or more of the above

521. The Treiman and Zudowski experiment found evidence to support which of the following conclusions?
(a) At age six, reading instruction helps children perform both, the same-different judgement task.
(b) The development of onset-rime awareness precedes the development of an awareness of phonemes.
(c) At age four to five children find the onset-rime version of the same/different task significantly easier.
(d) The development of onset-rime awareness is a necessary and sufficient condition for the development of an awareness of phonemes.

522. The single-syllable words *Rhyme* and *Rime* are constituted by the exact same set of
A. rime(s)
B. onset(s)
C. rhyme(s)
D. phonemes(s)
(a) A and B (b) A and C
(c) A, B and C (d) B, C and D

Passage – 67

Billie Holiday died a few weeks ago. I have been unable until now to write about her, but since she will survive many who receive longer obituaries, a short delay in one small appreciation will not harm her or us. When she died we — the musicians, critics, all who were ever transfixed by the most heart-rending voice of the past generation — grieved bitterly. There was no reason to. Few people pursed self-destruction more whole-heartedly than she, and when the pursuit was at an end, at the age of 44, she had turned herself into a physical and artistic wreck. Some of us tried gallantly to pretend otherwise, taking comfort in the occasional moments when she still sounded like a ravaged echo of her greatness. Others had not even the heart to see and listen any more. We preferred to stay home and, if old and lucky enough to own the incomparable records of her heyday from 1937 to 1946, many of which are not even available on British LP, to recreate those coarse-textured, sinuous, sensual and unbearable sad noises which gave her a sure corner of immortality. Her physical death called, if anything, for relief rather than sorrow. What sort of middle age would she have faced without the voice to earn money for her drinks and fixes, without the looks — and in her day she was hauntingly beautiful — to attract the men she needed, without business sense, without anything but the disinterested worship of ageing men who had heard and seen her in her glory?

And yet, irrational though it is, our grief expressed Billie Holiday's art, that of a woman for whom one must be sorry. The great blues singers, to whom she may be justly compared, played their game from strength. Lionesses, though often wounded or at bay (did not Bessie Smith call herself 'a tiger, ready to jump'?), their tragic equivalents were Cleopatra and Phaedra; Holiday's was an embittered Ophelia. She was the Puccini heroine among blues singers, or rather among jazz singers, for though she sang a cabaret version of the blues incomparably, her natural idiom was the pop song. Her unique achievement was to have twisted this into a genuine expression of the major passions by means of a total disregard of its sugary tunes, or indeed of any tune other than her own few delicately crying elongated notes, phrased like Bessie Smith or Louis Armstrong in sackcloth, sung in a thin, gritty, haunting voice whose natural mood was an unresigned and voluptuous welcome for the pains of love. Nobody has sung, or will sing, Bess's songs from *Porgy* as she did. It was this combination of bitterness and physical submission, as of someone lying still while watching his legs being amputated, which gives such a blood-curdling quality to her Strange Fruit, the anti-lynching poem which she turned into an unforgettable art song. Suffering was her profession; but she did not accept it.

Little need be said about her horrifying life, which she described with emotional, though hardly with factual, truth in her autobiography *Lady Sings the Blues*. After an adolescence in which self-respect was measured by a girl's insistence on picking up the coins thrown to her by clients with her hands, she was plainly beyond help. She did not lack it, for she had the flair and scrupulous honesty of John Hammond to launch her, the best musicians of the 1930s to accompany her — notably Teddy Wilson, Frankie Newton and Lester Young — the boundless devotion of all serious connoisseurs, and much public success. It was too late to arrest a career of systematic embittered self-immolation. To be born with both beauty and self-respect in the Negro ghetto of Baltimore in 1915 was too much of a handicap, even without rape at the age of 10 and drug-addiction in her teens. But, while she destroyed herself, she sang, unmelodious, profound and heartbreaking. It is impossible not to weep for her, or not to hate the world which made her what she was.

523. Why will Billie Holiday survive many who receive longer obituaries?

(a) Because of her blues creations.

(b) Because she was not as self-destructive as some other blues exponents.

(c) Because of her smooth and mellow voice.

(d) Because of the expression of anger in her songs.

524. According to the author, if Billie Holiday had not died in her middle age

(a) she would have gone on to make a further mark.

(b) she would have become even richer than what she was when she died.

(c) she would have led a rather ravaged existence.

(d) she would have led a rather comfortable existence.

525. Which of the following statements is not representative of the author's opinion?

(a) Billie Holiday had her unique brand of melody.

(b) Billie Holiday's voice can be compared to other singers in certain ways.

(c) Billie Holiday's voice had a ring of profound sorrow.

(d) Billie Holiday welcomed suffering in her profession and in her life.

526. According to the passage, Billie Holiday was fortunate in all but one of which of the following ways?

(a) She was fortunate to have been picked up young by an honest producer.

(b) She was fortunate to have the likes of Louis Armstrong and Bessie Smith accompany her.

(c) She was fortunate to possess the looks.

(d) She enjoyed success among the public and connoisseurs.

Passage – 68

The narrative of Dersu Uzala is divided into two major sections, set in 1902, and 1907, that deal with separate expeditions which Arseniev conducts into the Ussuri region. In addition, a third time frame forms a prologue to the film. Each of the temporal frames has a different focus, and by shifting them Kurosawa is able to describe the encroachment of settlements upon the wilderness and the consequent erosion of Dersu's way of life. As the film opens, that erosion has already begun. The first image is a long shot of a huge forest, the trees piled upon one another by the effects of the telephoto lens so that the landscape becomes an abstraction and appears like a huge curtain of green. A title informs us that the year is 1910. This is as late into the century as Kurosawa will go. After this prologue, the events of the film will transpire even farther back in time and will be presented as Arseniev's recollections. The character of Dersu Uzala is the heart of the film, his life the example that Kurosawa wishes to affirm. Yet the formal organization of the film works to contain, to close, to circumscribe that life by erecting a series of obstacles around it. The film itself is circular, opening and closing by Dersu's grave, thus sealing off the character from the modern world to which Kurosawa once so desperately wanted to speak. The multiple time frames also work to maintain a separation between Dersu and the contemporary world. We must go back father even than 1910 to discover who he was. But this narrative structure has yet another implication. It safeguards Dersu's example, inoculates it from contamination with history, and protects it from contact with the industrialised, urban world. Time is organised by the narrative into a series of barriers, which enclose Dersu in a kind of vacuum chamber, protecting him from the social and historical dialectics that destroyed the other Kurosawa heroes. Within the film, Dersu does die, but the narrative structure attempts to immortalise him and his example, as Dersu passes from history into myth.

We see all this at work in the enormously evocative prologue. The camera tilts down to reveal felled trees littering the landscape and an abundance of construction. Roads and houses outline the settlement that is being built. Kurosawa cuts to a medium shot of Arseniev standing in the midst of the clearing, looking uncomfortable and disoriented. A man passing in a wagon asks him what he is doing, and the explorer says he is looking for a grave. The driver replies that no one has died here, the settlement is too recent. These words enunciate the temporal rupture that the film studies. It is the beginning of things (industrial society) and the end of things (the forest), the commencement of one world so young that no one has had time yet to die and the eclipse of another, in which Dersu had died. It is his grave for which the explorer searches. His passing symbolises the new order, the development that now surrounds Arseniev. The explorer says he buried his friend three years ago next to huge cedar and fir trees, but now they are all gone. The man on the wagon replies they were probably chopped down when the settlement was built, and he drives off. Arseniev walks to a barren, treeless spot next to a pile of bricks. As he moves, the camera tracks and pans to follow, revealing a line of freshly built houses and a woman hanging her laundry to dry. A distant train whistle is heard, and the sounds of construction in the clearing vie with the cries of birds and the rustle of wind in the trees. Arseniev pauses, looks around for the grave that once was, and murmurs desolately, 'Dersu'. The image now cuts farther into the past, to 1902, and the first section of the film commences, which describes Arseniev's meeting with Dersu and their friendship.

Kurosawa defines the world of the film initially upon a void, a missing presence. The grave is gone, brushed aside by a world rushing into modernism, and now the hunter exists only in Arseniev's memories. The hallucinatory dreams and visions of Dodeskaden are succeeded by nostalgic, melancholy ruminations. Yet by exploring these ruminations, the film celebrates the timelessness of Dersu's wisdom. The first section of the film has two purposes: to describe the magnificence and in human vastness of nature and to delineate the code of ethics by which Dersu lives and which permits him to survive in these conditions. When Dersu first appears, the other soldiers treat him with condescension and laughter, but Arseniev watches him closely and does not share their derisive response. Unlike them, he is capable of immediately grasping Dersu's extraordinary qualities. In camp, Kurosawa frames Arseniev by himself, sitting on the other side of the fire from his soldiers. While they sleep or joke among themselves, he writes in his diary and Kurosawa cuts in several point-of-view shots from his perspective of trees that appear animated and sinister as the fire light dances across their gnarled, leafless outlines. This reflective dimension, this sensitivity to the spirituality of nature, distinguishes him from the others and forms the basis of his receptivity to Dersu and their friendship. It makes him a fit pupil for the hunter.

527. How is Kurosawa able to show the erosion of Dersu's way of life?

(a) By documenting the ebb and flow of modernisation.

(b) By going back farther and farther in time.

(c) By using three different time frames and shifting them.

(d) Through his death in a distant time.

528. Arseniev's search for Dersu's grave

(a) is part of the beginning of the film.

(b) symbolises the end of the industrial society.

(c) is misguided since the settlement is too new.

(d) symbolises the rediscovery of modernity.

529. The film celebrates Dersu's wisdom

(a) by exhibiting the moral vacuum of the pre-modern world.

(b) by turning him into a mythical figure.

(c) through hallucinatory dreams and visions.

(d) through Arseniev's nostalgic, melancholy ruminations.

530. According to the author, the section of the film following the prologue

(a) serves to highlight the difficulties that Dersu faces that eventually kills him.

(b) shows the difference in thinking between Arseniev and Dersu.

(c) shows the code by which Dersu lives that allows him to survive his surroundings.

(d) serves to criticize the lack of understanding of nature in the pre-modern era.

531. In the film, Kurosawa hints at Arseniev's reflective and sensitive nature

(a) by showing him as not being derisive towards Dersu, unlike other soldiers.

(b) by showing him as being aloof from other soldiers.

(c) through shots of Arseniev writing his diary, framed by trees.

(d) All of these

532. According to the author, which of these statements about the film is correct?

(a) The film makes its arguments circuitously.

(b) The film highlights the insularity of Arseniev.

(c) The film begins with the absence of its main protagonist.

(d) None of these

Passage – 69

Democracy rests on a tension between two different principles. There is, on the one hand, the principle of equality before the law, or, more generally, of equality, and, on the other, what may be described as the leadership principle. The first gives priority to rules and the second to persons. No matter how skilfully we contrive out schemes, there is a point beyond which the one principle cannot be promoted without some sacrifice of the other.

Alexis do Tocqueville, the great 19th-century writer on democracy, maintained that the age of democracy, whose birth he was witnessing, would also be the age of mediocrity, in saying this he was thinking primarily of a regime of equality governed by impersonal rules. Despite his strong attachment to democracy, he took great pains to point out what he believed to be its negative side: a dead level plane of achievement in practically every sphere of life. The age of democracy would, in his view, be an unheroic age; there would not be room in it for either heroes or hero-worshippers.

But modern democracies have not been able to do without heroes: this too was foreseen, with much misgiving, by Tocqueville. Tocqueville viewed this with misgiving because he believed, rightly or wrongly, that unlike in aristocratic societies there was no proper place in a democracy for heroes and, hence, when they arose they would sooner or later turn into despots. Whether they require heroes or not, democracies certainly require leaders, and, in the contemporary age, breed them in great profusion; the problem is to know what to do with them.

In a world preoccupied with scientific rationality the advantages of a system based on an impersonal rule of law should be a recommendation with everybody. There is something orderly and predictable about such a system. When life is lived mainly in small, self-contained communities, men are able to take finer personal distinctions into account in dealing with their fellow men. They are unable to do this in a large and amorphous society, and organised living would be impossible here without a system of impersonal rules. Above all, such a system guarantees a kind of equality to the extent that everybody, no matter in what station of life, is bound by the same explicit, often written, rules and nobody is above them.

But a system governed solely by impersonal rules can at best ensure order and stability; it cannot create any shining vision of a future in which mere formal equality will be replaced by real equality and fellowship. A world governed by impersonal rules cannot easily change itself, or when it does, the change is so gradual as to make the basic and fundamental feature of society appear unchanges. For any kind of basic or fundamental change, a push is needed from within, a kind of individual initiative which will create new rules, new terms and conditions of life.

The issue of leadership thus acquires crucial significance in the context of change. If the modern age is preoccupied with scientific rationality, it is no less preoccupied with change. To accept what exists on its own terms is traditional, not modern, and it may be all very well to appreciate tradition in music, dance and drama, but for society as a whole the choice has already been made in favour of modernisation and development. Moreover, in some countries the gap between ideal and reality has become so great that the argument for development and change is now irresistible.

In these countries no argument for development has greater appeal or urgency than the one which shows development to be the condition for the mitigation, if not the elimination, of inequality. There is something contradictory about the very presence of large inequalities in a society which profess to be democratic. It does not take people too long to realise that democracy by itself can guarantee only formal equality; beyond this, it can only whet people's appetite for real or substantive equality. From this arises their continued preoccupation with plans and schemes that will help to bridge the gap between the ideal of equality and the reality which is so contrary to it.

When pre-existing rules give no clear directions of change, leadership comes into its own. Every democracy invests its leadership with a measure of charisma, and expects from it a corresponding measure of energy and vitality. Now, the greater the urge for change in a society the stronger the appeal of a dynamic leadership in it. A dynamic leadership seeks to free itself from the constraints of existing rules: in a sense that is the test of its dynamism. In this process it may take a turn at which it ceases to regard itself as being bound by these rules, placing itself above them. There is always a tension between 'charisma' and 'discipline' in the case of a democratic leadership, and when this leadership puts forward revolutionary claims, the tension tends to be resolved at the expense of discipline.

Characteristically, the legitimacy of such a leadership rests on its claim to be able to abolish or at least substantially reduce the existing inequalities in society. From the argument that formal equality or equality before the law is but a limited good, it is often one short step to the argument that it is a hindrance or an obstacle to the establishment of real or substantive equality. The conflict between a 'progressive' executive and a 'conservative' judiciary is but one aspect of this larger problem. This conflict naturally acquires added piquancy when the executive is elected and the judiciary appointed.

533. Dynamic leaders are needed in democracies because

(a) they have adopted the principles of 'formal' equality rather than 'substantive' equality.

(b) 'formal' equality whets people's appetite for 'substantive' equality.

(c) systems that rely on the impersonal rules of 'formal' equality lose their ability to make large changes.

(d) of the conflict between a 'progressive' executive and a 'conservative' judiciary.

534. What possible factor would a dynamic leader consider a 'hindrance' in achieving the development goals of a nation?

(a) Principle of equality before the law

(b) Judicial activism

(c) A conservative judiciary

(d) Need for discipline

535. Which of the following four statements can be inferred from the above passage?

A. Scientific rationality is an essential feature of modernity.

B. Scientific rationality results in the development of impersonal rules.

C. Modernisation and development have been chosen over traditional music, dance and drama.

D. Democracies aspire to achieve substantive equality.

(a) A, B, D but not C (b) A, B but not C, D

(c) A, D but not B, C (d) A, B, C but not D

536. Tocqueville believed that the age of democracy would be an un-heroic age because

(a) democractic principles do not encourage heroes.

(b) there is no urgency for development in democratic countries.

(c) heroes that emerged in democracies would become despots.

(d) aristocratic society had a greater ability to produce heroes.

537. A key argument the author is making is that

(a) in the context of extreme inequality, the issue of leadership has limited significance.

(b) democracy is incapable of eradicating inequality.

(c) formal equality facilitates development and change.

(d) impersonal rules are good for avoiding instability but fall short of achieving real equality.

538. Which of the following four statements can be inferred from the above passage?

A. There is conflict between the pursuit of equality and individuality.

B. The disadvantages of impersonal rules can be overcome in small communities.

C. Despite limitations, impersonal rules are essential in large systems.

D. Inspired leadership, rather than plans and schemes, is more effective in bridging inequality.

(a) B, D but not A, C (b) A, B but not C, D

(c) A, D but not B, C (d) A, C but not B, D

Passage – 70

In the modern scientific story, light was created not once but twice. The first time was in the Big Bang, when the universe began its existence as a glowing, expanding, fireball, which cooled off into darkness after a few million years. The second time was hundreds of millions of years later, when the cold material condensed into dense suggests under the influence of gravity, and ignited to become the first stars.

Sir Martin Rees, Britain's astronomer royal, named the long interval between these two enlightements the cosmic 'Dark Age'. The name describes not only the poorly lit conditions, but also the ignorance of astronomers about that period. Nobody knows exactly when the first stars formed, or how they organised themselves into galaxies — or even whether stars were the first luminous objects. They may have been preceded by quasars, which are mysterious, bright spots found at the centres of some galaxies.

Now two independent groups of astronomers, one led by Robert Becker of the University of California, Davis, and the other by George Djorgovski of the Caltech, claim to have peered far enough into space with their telescopes (and therefore backwards enough in time) to observe the closing days of the Dark age.

The main problem that plagued previous efforts to study the Dark Age was not the lack of suitable telescopes, but rather the lack of suitable things at which to point them. Because these events took place over 13 billion years ago, if astronomers are to have any hope of unravelling them they must study objects that are at least 13 billion light years away. The best prospects are quasars, because they are so bright and compact that they can be seen across vast stretches of space. The energy source that powers a quasar is unknown, although it is suspected to be the intense gravity of a giant black hole. However, at the distances required for the study of Dark Age, even quasars are extremely rare and faint.

Recently some members of Dr Becker's team announced their discovery of the four most distant quasars known. All the new quasars are terribly faint, a challenge that both teams overcame by peering at them through one of the twin Keck telescopes in Hawaii. These are the world's largest, and can therefore collect the most light. The new work by Dr Becker's team analysed the light from all four quasars. Three of them appeared to be similar to ordinary, less distant quasars. However, the fourth and most distant, unlike any other quasar ever seen, showed unmistakable signs of being shrouded in a fog because new-born stars and quasars emit mainly ultraviolet light, and hydrogen gas is opaque to ultraviolet. Seeing this fog had been the goal of would-be Dark Age astronomers since 1965, when James Gunn and Bruce Peterson spelled out the technique for using quasars as backlighting beacons to observe the fog's ultraviolet shadow.

The fog prolonged the period of darkness until the heat from the first stars and quasars had the chance to ionise the hydrogen (breaking it into its constituent parts, protons and electrons). Ionised hydrogen is transparent to ultraviolet radiation, so at that moment the fog lifted and the universe became the well-lit place it is today. For this reason, the end of the Dark Age is called the 'Epoch of Re-ionisation'. Because the ultraviolet shadow is visible only in the most distant of the four quasars, Dr Becker's team concluded that the fog had dissipated completely by the time the universe was about 900 million years old, and one-seventh of its current size.

539. In the passage, the Dark Age refers to

(a) the period when the universe became cold after the Big Bang.

(b) a period about which astronomers know very little.

(c) the medieval period when cultural activity seemed to have come to an end.

(d) the time that the universe took to heat up after the Big Bang.

540. Astronomers find it difficult to study the Dark Age because

(a) suitable telescopes are few.

(b) the associated events took place aeons ago.

(c) the energy source that powers a quasars is unknown.

(d) their best chance is to study quasars, which are faint objects to begin with.

541. The four most distant quasars discovered recently

(a) could only be seen with the help of large telescopes.

(b) appear to be similar to other ordinary, quasars.

(c) appear to be shrouded in a fog of hydrogen gas.

(d) have been sought to be discovered by Dark Age astronomers since 1965.

542. The fog of hydrogen gas seen through the telescopes

(a) is transparent to hydrogen radiation from stars and quasars in all states.

(b) was lifted after heat from starts and quasars ionised it.

(c) is material which eventually became stars and quasars.

(d) is broken into constituent elements when stars and quasars are formed.

Passage – 71

The production of histories of India has become very frequent in recent years and may well call for some explanation. Why so many and why this one in particular? The reason is a two-fold one: changes in the Indian scene requiring a re-interpretation of the facts and changes in attitudes of historians about the essential elements of Indian history. These two considerations are in addition to the normal fact of fresh information, whether in the form of archeological discoveries throwing fresh light on an obscure period or culture, or the revelations caused by the opening of archives or the release of private papers. The changes in the Indian scene are too obvious to need emphasis. Only two generations ago British rule seemed to most Indian as well as British observers likely to extend into an indefinite future; now there is a teenage generation which knows nothing of it. Changes in the attitudes of historians have occurred everywhere, changes in attitudes to the content of the subject as well as to particular countries, but in India there have been some special features. Prior to the British, Indian historiographers were mostly Muslims, who relied, as in the case of Sayyid Ghulam Hussain, on their own recollection of events and on information from friends and men of affairs. Only a few like Abu'l Fazl had access to official papers. These were personal narratives of events, varying in value with the nature of the writer. The early British writers were officials. In the 18th century they were concerned with some aspect of Company policy, or like Robert Orme in his *Military Transactions* gave a straight narrative in what was essentially a continuation of the Muslim tradition. In the early 19th century the writers were still, with two notable exceptions, officials, but they were now engaged in chronicling, in varying moods of zest, pride, and awe, the rise of the British power in India to supremacy. The two exceptions were James Mill, with his critical attitude to the Company and John Marchman, the Baptist missionary. But they, like the officials, were anglo-centric in their attitude, so that the history of modern India in their hands came to be the history of the rise of the British in India.

The official school dominated the writing of Indian history until we get the first professional historian's approach. Ramsay Muir and P. E. Roberts in England and H. H. Dodwell in India. Then Indian historians trained in the English school joined in, of whom the most distinguished was Sir Jadunath Sarkar and the other notable writers: Surendranath Sen, Dr Radhakumud Mukherji, and Professor Nilakanta Sastri. They, it may be said, restored India to Indian history, but their bias was mainly political. Finally have come the nationalists who range from those who can find nothing good or true in the British to sophisticated historical philosophers like K. M. Panikker.

Along the types of historians with their varying bias have gone changes in the attitude to the content of Indian history. Here Indian historians have been influenced both by their local situation and by changes of thought elsewhere. It is this field that this work can claim some attention since it seeks to break new ground, or perhaps to deepen a freshly turned furrow in the field of Indian history. The early official historians were content with the glamour and drama of political history from Plassey to the Mutiny, from Dupleix to the Sikhs. But when the *raj* was settled down, glamour departed from politics, and they turned to the less glorious but more solid ground of administration. Not how India was conquered but how it was governed was the theme of this school of historians. It found its archpriest in H. H. Dodwell, its priestess in Dame Lilian Penson, and its chief shrine in the Volume VI of the *Cambridge History of India*. Meanwhile, in Britain other currents were moving, which led historical study into the economic and social fields. R. C. Dutt entered the first of these currents with his *Economic History of India* to be followed more recently by the whole group of Indian economic historians. W. E. Moreland extended these studies to the Mughal Period. Social history is now being increasingly studied and there is also of course a school of nationalist historians who see modern Indian history in terms of the rise and the fulfillment of the national movement.

All these approaches have value, but all share in the quality of being compartmental. It is not enough to remove political history from its pedestal of being the only kind of history worth having if it is merely to put other types of history in its place. Too exclusive an attention to economic, social, or administrative history can be as sterile and misleading as too much concentration on politics. A whole subject needs a whole treatment for understanding. A historian must dissect his subject into its elements and then fuse them together again into an integrated whole. The true history of a country must contain all the features just cited but must present them as parts of a single consistent theme.

2002

543. Which of the following may be the closest in meaning to the statement 'restored India to Indian history'?
(a) Indian historians began writing Indian history.
(b) Trained historians began writing Indian history.
(c) Writing India-centric Indian history began.
(d) Indian history began to be written in India.

544. Which of the following is the closest implication of the statement 'to break new ground, or perhaps to deepen a freshly turned furrow'?
(a) Dig afresh or dig deeper.
(b) Start a new stream of thought or help establish a recently emerged perspective.
(c) Begin or conduct further work on existing archeological sites to unearth new evidence.
(d) Begin writing a history free of any biases.

545. Historians moved from writing political history to writing administrative history because
(a) attitudes of the historians changed.
(b) the *raj* was settled down.
(c) politics did not retain its past glamour.
(d) administrative history was based on solid ground.

546. According to the author, which of the following is not among the attitudes of Indian historians of Indian origin?
(a) Writing history as personal narratives.
(b) Writing history with political bias.
(c) Writing non-political history due to lack of glamour.
(d) Writing history by dissecting elements and integrating them again.

547. In the table given below, match the historians to the approaches taken by them.

A. Administrative	B. Political
C. Narrative	D. Economic
E. Robert Orme	F. H.H. Dodwell
G. Radha Kumud Mukherji	H. R.C. Dutt

(a)

A	F
B	G
C	E
D	H

(b)

A	G
B	F
C	E
D	H

(c)

A	E
B	F
C	G
D	H

(d)

A	G
B	F
C	H
D	E

Passage – 72

There are a seemingly endless variety of laws, restrictions, customs and traditions that affect the practice of abortion around the world. Globally, abortion is probably the single most controversial issue in the whole area of women's rights and family matters. It is an issue that inflames women's right groups, religious institutions, and the self-proclaimed 'guardians' of public morality. The growing worldwide belief is that the right to control one's fertility is a basic human right. This has resulted in a worldwide trend towards liberalization of abortion laws. Forty per cent of the world's population live in countries where induced abortion is permitted on request. An additional 25 per cent live in countries where it is allowed if the women's life would be endangered if she went to full term with her pregnancy. The estimate is that between 26 and 31 million legal abortions were performed in that year. However, there were also between 10 and 22 million illegal abortions performed in that year.

Feminists have viewed the patriarchal control of women's bodies as one of the prime issues facing the contemporary women's movement. They observe that the defintion and control of women's reproductive freedom have always been the province of men. Patriarchal religion, as manifest in Islamic fundamentalism, traditionalist Hindu practice, orthodox Judaism, and Roman Catholicism, has been an important historical contributory factor for this and continues to be an important presence in contemporary societies. In recent times, governments, usually controlled by men, have 'given' women the right to contraceptive use and abortion access when their countries were perceived to have an overpopulation problem. When these countries are perceived to be underpopulated, that right had been absent. Until the 19th century, a woman's rights to an abortion followed English common law; it could only be legally challenged if there was a 'quickening', when the first movements of the fetus could be felt. In 1800, drugs to induce abortions were widely advertised in local newpapers. By 1900, abortion was banned in every state except to save the life of the mother. The change was strongly influenced by medical profession, which focussed its campaign ostensibly on health and safety issues for pregnant women and the sancity of life. Its position was also a means of control of non-licensed medical practitioners such as midwives and women healers who practiced abortion.

The anti-abortion campaign was also influenced by political considerations. The large influx of eastern and southern European immigrants with their large families was seen as a threat to the population balance of the future United States. Middle and upper-classes Protestants were advocates of abortion as a form of birth control. By supporting abortion prohibitions the hope was that these Americans would have more children and thus prevent the tide of immigrant babies from overwhelming the demographic characteristics of Protestant America.

The anti-abortion legislative position remained in effect in the United States through the first 65 years of the 20th century. In the early 1960s, even when it was widely known that the drug thalidomide taken during pregnancy to alleviate anxiety was shown to contribute to the formation of deformed 'flipper-like' hands or legs of children, abortion was illegal in the United States. A second health tragedy was the severe outbreak of rubella during the same time period, which also resulted in major birth defects. These tragedies combined with a change of attitude towards a woman's right to privacy led a number of states to pass abortion-permitting legislation.

On one side of the controversy are those who call themselves 'pro-life'. They view the foetus as a human life rather than as an unformed complex of cells; therefore, they hold to the belief that abortion is essentially murder of an unborn child. These groups cite both legal and religious reasons for their opposition to abortion. Pro-lifers point to the rise in legalised abortion figures and see this as morally intolerable. On the other side of the issue are those who call themselves 'pro-choice'. They believe that women, not legislators or judges, should have the right to decide whether and under what circumstances they will bear children. Pro-choicers are of the opinion that laws will not prevent women from having abortions and cite the horror stories of the past when many women died at the hands of 'backroom' abortionists and in desperate attempts to self-abort. They also observe that legalized abortion is especially important for rape victims and incest victims who became pregnant. They stress physical and mental health reasons why women should not have unwanted children.

To get a better understanding of the current abortion controversy, let us examine a very important work by Kristin Luker titled *Abortion and the Politics of Motherhood*. Luker argues that female pro-choice and pro-life activists hold different world views regarding gender, sex, and the meaning of parenthood. Moral positions on abortions are seen to be tied intimately to views on sexual bahavior, the care of children, family life, technology, and the importance of the individual. Luker identified 'pro-choice' women as educated, affluent, and liberal. Their contrasting counterparts, 'pro-life' women, support traditional concepts of women as wives and mothers. It would be instructive to sketch out the differences in the world views of these two sets of women. Luker examines California, with its liberalized abortion law, as a case history. Public documents and newspaper accounts over a 26-year period were analysed and over 200 interviews were held with both pro-life and pro-choice activists.

Luker found that pro-life and pro-choice activists have intrinsically different views with respect to gender. Pro-life women have a notion of public and private life. The proper place for men is in the public sphere of work; for women, it is the private sphere of the home. Men benefit through the nurturance of women; women benefit through the protection of men. Children are seen to be the ultimate beneficiaries of this arrangement of having the mother as a full-time loving parent and by having clear role models. Pro-choice advocates reject the view of separate spheres. They object to the notion of the home being the 'women's sphere'. Women's reproductive and family roles are seen as potential barriers to full equality. Motherhood is seen as a voluntary, not a mandatory or 'natural' role.

In summarizing her findings, Luker believes that women become activists in either of the two movements as the end result of lives that centre around different conceptualizations of motherhood. Their beliefs and values are rooted to the concrete circumstances of their lives, their educations, incomes, occupations, and the different marital and family choices that they have made. They represent two different world views of women's roles in contemporary society and as such the abortion issues represent the battleground for the justification of their respective views.

548. According to your understanding of the author's arguments, which countries are more likely to allow abortion?

(a) India and China

(b) Australia and Mongolia

(c) Cannot be inferred from the passage

(d) Both (a) and (b)

549. Which amongst these was not a reason for banning of abortions by 1900?

(a) Medical professionals stressing the health and safety of women

(b) Influx of eastern and southern European immigrants

(c) Control of unlicensed medical practitioners

(d) A tradition of matriarchal control

550. A pro-life woman would advocate abortion if

(a) the mother of an unborn child is suicidal.

(b) bearing a child conflicts with a woman's career prospects.

(c) the mother becomes pregnant accidentally.

(d) None of these

551. Pro-choice women object to the notion of the home being the 'women's sphere' because they believe

(a) that home is a 'joint sphere' shared between men and women.

(b) that reproduction is a matter of choice for women

(c) that men and women are equal

(d) Both (b) and (c)

552. Two health tragedies affecting the US society in the 1960s led to

(a) a change in attitude to women's right to privacy.

(b) retaining the anti-abortion laws with some exceptions.

(c) scrapping of anti-abortion laws.

(d) strengthening of the pro-life lobby.

553. Historically, the pro-choice movements has got support from, among others,

(a) major patriarchal religions.

(b) countries with low population density.

(c) medical profession.

(d) None of these

Passage – 73

The conceptions of life and the world which we call 'philosophical' are a product of two factors: one inherited religious and ethical conceptions; the other, the sort of investigation which may be called 'scientific', using this word in its broadest sense. Individual philosophers have differed widely in regard to the proportions in which these two factors entered into their systems, but it is the presence of both, in some degree, that characterizes philosophy.

'Philosophy' is a word which has been used in many ways, some wider, some narrower. I propose to use it in a very wide sense, which I will now try to explain.

Philosophy, as I shall understand the word, is something intermediate between theology and science. Like theology, it consists of speculations on matters as to which definite knowledge has, so far, been unascertainable; but like science, it appeals to human reason rather than to authority, whether that of tradition or that of revelation. All definite knowledge so I should contend belongs to science; all dogma as to what surpasses definite knowledge belongs to thelogy. But between theology and science there is a 'No Man's Land', exposed to attack from both sides; this 'No Man's Land' is philosophy. Almost all the questions of most interest to speculative minds are such as science cannot answer, and the confident answers of theologians no longer seem so convincing as they did in former centuries. Is the world divided into mind and matter, and if so, what is mind and what is matter? Is mind subject to matter, or is it possessed of independent powers? Has the universe any unity or purpose? Is it evolving towards some goal? Are there really laws of nature, or do we believe in them only because of our innate love of order? Is man what he seems to the astronomer, a tiny lump of carbon and water impotently crawling on a small and unimportant planet? Or is he what he appears to Hamlet? Is he perhaps both at once? Is there a way of living that is noble and another that is base, or are all ways of living merely futile? If there is a way of living that is noble, in what does it consist, and how shall we achieve it? Must the good be eternal in order to deserve to be valued, or is it worth seeking even if the universe is inexorably moving towards death? Is there such a thing as wisdom, or is what seems such merely the ultimate refinement of folly? To such questions no answer can be found in the laboratory. Theologies have professed to give answers, all too definite; but their definiteness causes modern minds to view them with suspicion. The studying of these questions, if not the answering of them, is the business of philosophy.

Why, then, you may ask, waste time on such insoluble problems? To this one may answer as a historian, or as an individual facing the terror of cosmic loneliness.

The answer of the historian, in so far as I am capable of giving it, will appear in the course of this work. Ever since men became capable of free speculation, their actions in innumerable important respects, have depended upon their theories as to the world and human life, as to what is good and what is evil. This is as true in the present day as at any former time. To understand an age or a nation, we must understand its philosophy, and to understand its philosophy we must ourselves be in some degree philosophers. There is here a reciprocal causation: the circumstances of men's lives do much to determine their philosophy, but, conversely, their philosophy does much to determine their circumstances.

There is also, however, a more personal answer. Science tells us what we can know, but what we can know is little, and if we forget how much we cannot know we may become insensitive to many things of very great importance. Theology, on the other hand, induces a dogmatic belief that we have knowledge, where in fact we have ignorance, and by doing so generates a kind of impertinent insolence towards the universe. Uncertainty, in the presence of vivid hopes and fears, is painful, but must be endured if we wish to live without the support of comforting fairy tales. It is good either to forget the questions that philosophy asks, or to persuade ourselves that we have found indubitable answers to them. To teach how to live without certainty, and yet without being paralyzed by hesitation, is perhaps the chief thing that philosophy, in our age, can still do for those who study it.

554. The purpose of philosophy is to

(a) reduce uncertainty and chaos.

(b) help us to cope with uncertainty and ambiguity.

(c) help us to find explanations for uncertainty.

(d) reduce the terror of cosmic loneliness.

555. Based on the passage, what can be concluded about the relation between philosophy and science?

(a) The two are antagonistic.

(b) The two are complementary.

(c) There is no relation between the two.

(d) Philosophy derives from science.

556. From reading the passage, what can be concluded about the profession of the author? He is most likely not to be a

(a) historian.

(b) philosopher.

(c) scientist.

(d) theologian.

557. According to the author, which of the following statements about the nature of universe must be definitely true?

(a) The universe has unity.

(b) The universe has a purpose.

(c) The universe is evolving towards a goal.

(d) None of these

Passage – 74

Cells are the ultimate multi-taskers: they can switch on genes and carry out their orders, talk to each other, divide in two, and much more, all at the same time. But they couldn't do any of these tricks without a power source to generate movement. The inside of a cell bustles with more traffic than Delhi roads, and, like all vehicles, the cell's moving parts need engines. Physicists and biologists have looked 'under the hood' of the cell and laid out the nuts and bolts of molecular engines.

The ability of such engines to convert chemical energy into motion is amazing nanotechnology researchers are looking for ways to power molecule-sized devices. Medical researchers also want to understand how these engines work. Because these molecules are essential for cell division, scientists hope to shut down the rampant growth of cancer cells by deactivating certain motors. Improving motor-driven transport in nerve cells may also be helpful for treating diseases such as Alzheimer's, Parkinson's or ALS, also known as Lou Gehrig's disease.

We wouldn't make it far in life without motor proteins. Our muscles wouldn't contract. We couldn't grow, because the growth process requires cells to duplicate their machinery and pull the copies apart. And our genes would be silent without the services of messenger RNA, which carries genetic instructions over to the cell's protein-making factories. The movements that make these cellular activities possible occur along a complex network of threadlike fibers, or polymers, along which bundles of molecules travel like trams. The engines that power the cell's freight are three families of proteins, called myosin, kinesin and dynein. For fuel, these proteins burn molecules of ATP, which cells make when they break down the carbohydrates and fats from the foods we eat. The energy from burning ATP causes changes in the proteins' shape that allow them to heave themselves along the polymer track. The results are impressive: In one second, these molecules can travel between 50 and 100 times their own diameter. If a car with a five-foot-wide engine were as efficient, it would travel 170 to 340 kilometres per hour.

Ronald Vale, a researcher at the Howard Hughes Medical Institute and the University of California at San Francisco, and Ronald Milligan of the Scripps Research Institute have realized a long-awaited goal by reconstructing the process by which myosin and kinesin move, almost down to the atom. The dynein motor, on the other hand, is still poorly understood. Myosin molecules, best known for their role in muscle contraction, form chains that lie between filaments of another protein called actin. Each myosin molecule has a tiny head that pokes out from the chain like oars from a canoe. Just as rowers propel their boat by stroking their oars through the water, the myosin molecules stick their heads into the actin and hoist themselves forward along the filament. While myosin moves along in short strokes, its cousin kinesin walks steadily along a different type of filament called a microtubule. Instead of using a projecting head as a lever, kinesin walks on two 'legs'. Based on these differences, researchers used to think that myosin and kinesin were virtually unrelated. But newly discovered similarities in the motors' ATP-processing machinery now suggest that they share a common ancestor — molecule. At this point, scientists can only speculate as to what type of primitive cell-like structure this ancestor occupied as it learned to burn ATP and use the energy to change shape. "We'll never really know, because we can't dig up the remains of ancient proteins, but that was probably a big evolutionary leap," says Vale.

On a slightly larger scale, loner cells like sperm or infectious bacteria are prime movers that resolutely push their way through to other cells. As L. Mahadevan and Paul Matsudaira of the Massachusetts Institute of Technology explain, the engines in this case are springs or ratchets that are clusters of molecules, rather than single proteins like myosin and kinesin. Researchers don't yet fully understand these engines' fueling process or the details of how they move, but the result is a force to be reckoned with. For example, one such engine is a spring-like stalk connecting a single-celled organism called a vorticellid to the leaf fragment it calls home. When exposed to calcium, the spring contracts, yanking the vorticellid down at speeds approaching three inches (eight centimetres) per second.

Springs like this are coiled bundles of filaments that expand or contract in response to chemical cues. A wave of positively charged calcium ions, for example, neutralizes the negative charges that keep the filaments extended. Some sperm use spring-like engines made of actin filaments to shoot out a barb that penetrates the layers that surround an egg. And certain viruses use a similar apparatus to shoot their DNA into the host's cell. Ratchets are also useful for moving whole cells, including some other sperm and pathogens. These engines are filaments that simply grow at one end, attracting chemical building blocks from nearby. Because the other end is anchored in place, the growing end pushes against any barrier that gets in its way.

Both springs and ratchets are made up of small units that each move just slightly, but collectively produce a powerful movement. Ultimately, Mahadevan and Matsudaira hope to better understand just how these particles create an effect that seems to be so much more than the sum of its parts. Might such an understanding provide inspiration for ways to power artificial nano-sized devices in the future? "The short answer is absolutely," says Mahadevan. "Biology has had a lot more time to evolve enormous richness in design for different organisms. Hopefully, studying these structures will not only improve our understanding of the biological world, it will also enable us to copy them, take apart their components and recreate them for other purpose."

558. According to the author, research on the power source of movement in cells can contribute to

(a) control over the movement of genes within human systems.
(b) the understanding of nanotechnology.
(c) arresting the growth of cancer in a human being.
(d) the development of cures for a variety of diseases.

559. The author has used several analogies to illustrate his arguments in the article. Which of the following pairs of words are examples of the analogies used?

A. Cell activity and vehicular traffic
B. Polymers and tram tracks
C. Genes and canoes
D. Vorticellids and ratchets

(a) A and B (b) B and C
(c) A and D (d) A and C

560. Read the five statements below: A, B, C, D, and E. From the options given, select the one which includes a statement that is not representative of an argument presented in the passage.

A. Sperms use spring like engines made of actin filament.
B. Myosin and kinesin are unrelated.
C. Nanotechnology researchers look for ways to power molecule-sized devices.
D. Motor proteins help muscle contraction.
E. The dynein motor is still poorly understood.

(a) A, B and C (b) C, D and E
(c) A, D and E (d) A, C and D

561. Read the four statements below: A, B, C and D. From the options given, select the one which includes only statements that are representative of arguments presented in the passage.

A. Protein motors help growth processes.
B. Improved transport in nerve cells will help arrest tuberculosis and cancer.
C. Cells, together, generate more power than the sum of power generated by them separately.
D. Vorticellid and the leaf fragment are connected by a calcium engine.

(a) A and B but not C
(b) A and C but not D
(c) A and D but not B
(d) C and D but not B

562. Read the four statements below: A, B, C and D. From the options given, select the one which includes statements that are representative of arguments presented in the passage.

A. Myosin, kinesin and actin are three types of protein.
B. Growth processes involve a routine in a cell that duplicates their machinery and pulls the copies apart.
C. Myosin molecules can generate vibrations in muscles.
D. Ronald and Mahadevan are researchers at Massachusetts Institute of Technology.

(a) A and B but not C and D
(b) B and C but not A
(c) B and D but not A and C
(d) A, B and C but not D

Passage – 75

If translated into English, most of the ways economists talk among themselves would sound plausible enough to poets, journalists, businesspeople, and other thoughtful though *non-economical* folk. Like serious talk anywhere — among boat desingers and baseball fans, say — the talk is hard to follow when one has not made a habit of listening to it for a while. The culture of the conversation makes the words arcane. But the people in the unfamiliar conversation are not Martians. Underneath it all (the economist's favourite phrase) conversational habits are similar. Economics uses mathematical models and statistical tests and market arguments, all of which look alien to the literary eye. But looked at closely they are not so alien. They may be seen as figures of speech-metaphors, analogies, and appeals to authority.

Figures of speech are not mere frills. They think for us. Someone who thinks of a market as an 'invisible hand'

and the organization of work as a 'production function' and his coefficients as being 'significant', as an economist does, is giving the language a lot of responsibility. It seems a good idea to look hard at his language.

If the economic conversation were found to depend a lot on its verbal forms, this would not mean that economics would be not a science, or just a matter of opinion, or some sort of confidence game. Good poets, though not scientists, are serious thinkers about symbols; good historians, though not scientists, are serious thinkers about data. Good scientists also use language. What is more(though it remains to be shown) they use the cunning of language, without particularly meaning to. The language used is a social object, and using language is a social act. It requires cunning (or, if you prefer, consideration), attention to the other minds present when one speaks.

The paying of attention to one's audience is called 'rhetoric', a word that I later exercise hard. One uses rhetoric, of course, to warn of a fire in a theatre or to arouse the xenophobia of the electorate. This sort of yelling is the vulgar meaning of the word, like the president's 'heated rhetoric' in a press conference or the 'mere rhetoric' to which our enemies stoop. Since the Greek flame was lit, though, the word has been used also in a broader and more amiable sense, to mean the study of all the ways of accomplishing things with language: inciting a mob to lynch the accused, to be sure, but also persuading readers of a novel that its characters breathe, or bringing scholars to accept the better argument and reject the worse.

The question is whether the scholar- who usually fancies himself an announcer of 'results' or a stater of 'conclusions' free of rhetoric — speaks rhetorically. Does he try to persuade? It would seem so. Language, I just said, is not a solitary accomplishment. The scholar doesn't speak into the void, or to himself. He speaks to a community of voices. He desires to be heeded, praised, published, imitated,honoured, en-Nobeled. These are the desires. The devices of language are the means.

Rhetoric is the proportioning of means to desires in speech. Rhetoric is an economics of language, the study of how scarce means are allocated to the insatiable desires of people to be heard. It seems on the face of it a reasonable hypothesis that economists are like other people in being talkers, who desire listeners whey they go to the library or the laboratory as much as when they go to the office or the polls. The purpose here is to see if this is true, and to see if it is useful: to study the rhetoric of economic scholarship.

The subject is scholarship. It is not the economy, or the adequacy of economic theory as a description of the economy, or even mainly the economist's role in the economy. The subject is the conversation economists have among themselves, for purposes of persuading each other that the interest elasticity of demand for investment is zero or that the money supply is controlled by the Federal Reserve.

Unfortunately, though, the conclusions are of more than academic interest. The conversations of classicists or of astronomers rarely affect the lives of other people. Those of economists do so on a large scale. A well known joke describes a May Day parade through Red Square with the usual mass of soldiers, guided missiles, rocket launchers. At last come rank upon rank of people in gray business suits. A bystander asks, "Who are those?" "Aha!" comes the reply, "Those are economists: you have no idea what damage they can do!" Their conversations do it.

563. According to the passage, which of the following is the best set of reasons for which one needs to 'look hard' at an economist's language?

A. Economists accomplish a great deal through their language.

B. Economics is an opinion-based subject.

C. Economics has a great impact on other's lives.

D. Economics is damaging.

(a) A and B (b) C and D
(c) A and C (d) B and D

564. In the light of the definition of rhetoric given in the passage, which of the following will have the least element of rhetoric?

(a) An election speech
(b) An advertisement jingle
(c) Dialogues in a play
(d) Commands given by army officers

565. As used in the passage, which of the following is the closest meaning to the statement 'The culture of the conversation makes the words arcane'?

(a) Economists belong to a different culture.
(b) Only mathematicians can understand economists.
(c) Economists tend to use terms unfamiliar to the lay person, but depend on familiar linguistic forms.
(d) Economists use similes and adjectives in their analysis.

566. As used in the passage, which of the following is the closest alternative to the word 'arcane'?

(a) Mysterious
(b) Secret
(c) Covert
(d) Perfidious

567. Based on your understanding of the passage, which of the following conclusions would you agree with?

(a) The geocentric and the heliocentric views of the solar system are equally tenable.

(b) The heliocentric view is superior because of better rhetoric.

(c) Both views use rhetoric to persuade.

(d) Scientists should not use rhetoric.

Passage – 76

At the heart of the enormous boom in wine consumption that has taken place in the English speaking world over the last two decades or so is a fascinating, happy paradox. In the days when wine was exclusively the preserve of a narrow cultural elite, bought either at auctions or from gentleman wine merchants in wing collars and bow-ties, to be stored in rambling cellars and decanted to order by one's butler, the ordinary drinker didn't get a look-in. Wine was considered a highly technical subject, in which anybody without the necessary ability could only fall flat on his or her face in embarrassment. It wasn't just that you needed a refined aesthetic sensibility for the stuff if it wasn't to be hopelessly wasted on you. It required an intimate knowledge of what came from where, and what it was supposed to taste like.

Those were times, however, when wine appreciation essentially meant a familiarity with the great French classics, with perhaps a smattering of other wines — like sherry and port. That was what the wine trade dealt in. These days, wine is bought daily in supermarkets and high-street chains to be consumed that evening, hardly anybody has a cellar to store it in and most don't even possess a decanter. Above all, the wines of literally dozens of countries are available in our market. When a supermarket offers its customers a couple of fruity little numbers from Brazil, we scarcely raise an eyebrow.

It seems, in other words, that the commercial jungle that wine has now become has not in the slightest deterred people from plunging adventurously into the thickets in order to taste and see. Consumers are no longer intimidated by the thought of needing to know their Pouilly-Fume from their Pouilly-Fuisse, just at the very moment when there is more to know than ever before.

The reason for this new mood of confidence is not hard to find. It is on every wine label from Australia, New Zealand, South Africa and the United States: the name of the grape from which the wine is made. At one time that might have sounded like a fairly technical approach in itself. Why should native English-speakers know what Cabernet Sauvignon or Chardonnay were? The answer lies in the popularity that wines made from those grape varieties now enjoy. Consumer effectively recognize them as brand names, and have acquired a basic lexicon of wine that can serve them even when confronted with those Brazilian upstarts.

In the wine heartlands of France, they are scared to death of that trend—not because they think their wine isn't as good as the best from California or South Australia (what French winemaker will ever admit that?) but because they don't traditionally call their wines Cabernet Sauvignon or Chardonnay. They call them Chateau Ducru Beaucaillou or Corton-Charlemagne, and they aren't about the change. Some areas, in the middle of southern France, have now produced a generation of growers using the varietal names on their labels and are tempting consumers back to French wine. It will be an uphill struggle, but there is probably no other way if France is to avoid simply becoming a specialty source of old-fashioned wines for old-fashioned connoisseurs.

Wine consumption was also given a significant boost in the early 1990s by the work of Dr. Serge Renaud, who has spent many years investigating the reasons for the uncannily low incidence of coronary heart disease in the south of France. One of his major findings is that the fat-derived cholesterol that builds up in the arteries and can eventually lead to heart trouble, can be dispersed by the tannins in wine. Tannin is derived from the skins of grapes, and is therefore present in higher levels in red wines, because they have to be infused with their skins to attain the red colour. That news caused a huge upsurge in red wine consumption in the United States. It has not been accorded the prominence it deserves in the UK, largely because the medical profession still sees all alcohol as a menace to health, and is constantly calling for it to be made prohibitively expensive. Certainly, the manufacturers of anticoagulant drugs might have something to lose if we all got the message that we would do just as well by our hearts by taking half a bottle of red wine every day!

2003(L)

568. The tone that the author uses while asking "what French winemaker will ever admit that?" is best described as

(a) caustic (b) satirical

(c) critical (d) hypocritical

569. What according to the author should the French do to avoid becoming a producer of merely old-fashioned wines?

(a) Follow the labeling strategy of the English-speaking countries

(b) Give their wines English names

(c) Introduce fruity wines as Brazil has done

(d) Produce the wines that have become popular in the English-speaking world

570. The development which has created fear among winemakers in the wine heartland of France is the

(a) tendency not to name wines after the grape varieties that are used in the wines.

(b) 'education' that consumers have derived from wine labels from English speaking countries.

(c) new generation of local winegrowers who use labels that show names of grape varieties.

(d) ability of consumers to understand a wine's qualities when confronted with "Brazilian upstarts".

571. Which one of the following, if true, would provide most support for Dr. Renaud's findings about the effect of tannins?

(a) A survey showed that film celebrities based in France have a low incidence of coronary heart disease.

(b) Measurements carried out in southern France showed red wine drinkers had significantly higher levels of coronary heart incidence than white wine drinkers did.

(c) Data showed a positive association between sales of red wine and incidence of coronary heart disease.

(d) Long-term surveys in southern France showed that the incidence of coronary heart disease was significantly lower in red wine drinkers than in those who did not drink red wine.

572. Which one of the following CANNOT be reasonably attributed to the labeling strategy followed by wine producers in English speaking countries?

(a) Consumers buy wines on the basis of their familiarity with a grape variety's name.

(b) Even ordinary customers now have more access to technical knowledge about wine.

(c) Consumers are able to appreciate better quality wines.

(d) Some non-English speaking countries like Brazil indicate grape variety names on their labels.

Passage – 77

Right through history, imperial powers have clung to their possessions to death. Why, then, did Britain in 1947 give up the jewel in its crown, India? For many reasons. The independence struggle exposed the hollowness of the white man's burden. Provincial self-rule since 1935 paved the way for full self-rule. Churchill resisted independence, but the Labour government of Atlee was anti-imperialist by ideology. Finally, the Royal Indian Navy mutiny in 1946 raised fears of a second Sepoy mutiny, and convinced British waverers that it was safer to withdraw gracefully. But politico-military explanations are not enough. The basis of empire was always money. The end of empire had much to do with the fact that British imperialism had ceased to be profitable. World War II left Britain victorious but deeply indebted, needing Marshall Aid and loans from the World Bank. This constituted a strong financial case for ending the no-longer profitable empire.

Empire building is expensive. The US is spending one billion dollars a day in operations in Iraq that fall well short of full scale imperialism. Through the centuries, empire building was costly, yet constantly undertaken because it promised high returns. The investment was in armies and conquest. The returns came through plunder and taxes from the conquered.

No immorality was attached to imperial loot and plunder. The biggest conquerors were typically revered (hence titles like Alexander the Great, Akbar the Great, and Peter the Great). The bigger and richer the empire, the more the plunderer was admired. This mindset gradually changed with the rise of new ideas about equality and governing for the public good, ideas that culminated in the French and American revolutions. Robert Clive was impeached for making a little money on the side, and so was Warren Hastings. The white man's burden came up as a new moral rationale for conquest. It was supposedly for the good of the conquered. This led to much muddled hypocrisy. On the one hand, the empire needed to be profitable. On the other hand, the white man's burden made brazen loot impossible.

An additional factor deterring loot was the 1857 Sepoy Mutiny. Though crushed, it reminded the British vividly that they were a tiny ethnic group who could not rule a gigantic subcontinent without the support of important locals. After 1857, the British stopped annexing one princely state after another, and instead treated the princes as allies. Land revenue was fixed in absolute terms, partly to prevent local unrest and partly to promote the notion of the white man's burden. The empire proclaimed itself to be a protector of the Indian peasant against exploitation by Indian elites. This was denounced as hypocrisy by nationalists like Dadabhoy Naoroji in the 19th century, who complained that land taxes led to an enormous drain from India to Britain. Objective calculations by historians like Angus Maddison suggest a drain of perhaps 1.6 percent of Indian Gross National Product in the 19th century. But land revenue was more or less fixed by the Raj in absolute terms, and so its real value diminished rapidly with inflation in the 20th century. By World War II, India had ceased to be a profit center for the British Empire.

Historically, conquered nations paid taxes to finance fresh wars of the conqueror. India itself was asked to pay a large sum at the end of World War I to help repair Britain's finances. But, as shown by historian Indivar Kamtekar, the independence movement led by Gandhiji changed the political landscape, and made mass taxation of India increasingly difficult. By World War II, this had become politically impossible. Far from taxing India to pay for World War II, Britain actually began paying India for its contribution of men and goods. Troops from white dominions like Australia, Canada and New Zealand were paid for entirely by these countries, but Indian costs were shared by the British government. Britain paid in the form of non-convertible sterling balances, which mounted swiftly. The conqueror was paying the conquered, undercutting the profitability on which all empire is founded. Churchill opposed this, and wanted to tax India rather than owe it money. But he was overruled by Indian hands who said India would resist payment, and paralyze the war effort. Leo Amery, Secretary of State for India, said that when you are driving in a taxi to the station to catch a life-or-death train, you do not loudly announce that you have doubts whether to pay the fare. Thus, World War II converted India from a debtor to a creditor with over one billion pounds in sterling balances. Britain, meanwhile, became the biggest debtor in the world. It's not worth ruling over people you are afraid to tax.

573. Why didn't Britain tax India to finance its World War II efforts?

(a) Australia, Canada and New Zealand had offered to pay for Indian troops.

(b) India has already paid a sufficiently large sum during World War I.

(c) It was afraid that if India refused to pay, Britain's war efforts would be jeopardized.

(d) The British empire was built on the premise that the conqueror pays the conquered.

574. What was the main lesson the British learned from the Sepoy Mutiny of 1857?

(a) That the local princes were allies, not foes.

(b) That the land revenue from India would decline dramatically.

(c) That the British were a small ethnic group.

(d) That India would be increasingly difficult to rule.

575. Which of the following was NOT a reason for the emergence of the 'white man's burden' as a new rationale for empire-building in India?

(a) The emergence of the idea of the public good as an element of governance.

(b) The decreasing returns from imperial loot and increasing costs of conquest.

(c) The weakening of the immorality attached to an emperor's looting behaviour.

(d) A growing awareness of the idea of equality among peoples.

576. Which of the following best captures the meaning of the 'white man's burden', as it is used by the author?

(a) The British claim to a civilizing mission directed at ensuring the good of the natives.

(b) The inspiration for the French and American revolutions.

(c) The resource drain that had to be borne by the home country's white population.

(d) An imperative that made open looting of resources impossible.

577. Which one of the following best expresses the main purpose of the author?

(a) To present the various reasons that can lead to the collapse of an empire and the granting of independence of the subjects of an empire.

(b) To point out the critical role played by the 'white man's burden' in making a colonizing power give up its claims to native possessions.

(c) To highlight the contradictory impulse underpinning empire building which is a costly business but very attractive at the same time.

(d) To illustrate how erosion of the financial basis of an empire supports the granting of independence to an empire's constituents.

Passage – 78

The controversy over genetically modified food continues unabated in the West. Genetic modification (GM) is the science by which the genetic material of a plant is altered, perhaps to make it more resistant to pests or killer weeds, or to enhance its nutritional value. Many food biotechnologists claim that GM will be a major contribution of science to mankind in the 21st century. On the other hand, large numbers of opponents, mainly in Europe, claim that the benefits of GM are a myth propagated by multinational corporations to increase their profits, that they pose a health hazard, and have therefore called for government to ban the sale of genetically-modified food.

The anti-GM campaign has been quite effective in Europe, with several European Union member countries imposing a virtual ban for five years over genetically-modified food imports. Since the genetically-modified food industry is particularly strong in the United States of America, the controversy also constitutes another chapter in the US-Europe skirmishes which have become particularly acerbic after the US invasion of Iraq.

To a large extent, the GM controversy has been ignored in the Indian media, although Indian biotechnologists have been quite active in GM research. Several groups of Indian biotechnologists have been working on various issues connected with crops grown in India. One concrete achievement which has recently figured in the news is that of a team led by the former vice-chancellor of Jawaharlal Nehru university, Asis Datta — it has successfully added an extra gene to potatoes to enhance the protein content of the tuber by at least 30 percent. It is quite likely that the GM controversy will soon hit the headlines in India since a spokesperson of the Indian Central government has recently announced that the government may use the protato in its midday meal programme for schools as early as next year.

Why should "scientific progress", with huge potential benefits to the poor and malnourished, be so controversial? The anti-GM lobby contends that pernicious propaganda has vastly exaggerated the benefits of GM and completely evaded the costs which will have to be incurred if the genetically-modified food industry is allowed to grow unchecked. In particular, they allude to different types of costs.

This group contends that the most important potential cost is that the widespread distribution and growth of genetically-modified food will enable the corporate world (alias the multinational corporations – MNCs) to completely capture the food chain. A "small" group of biotech companies will patent the transferred genes as well as the technology associated with them. They will then buy up the competing seed merchants and seed-breeding centers, thereby controlling the production of food at every possible level. Independent farmers, big and small, will be completely wiped out of the food industry. At best, they will be reduced to the status of being subcontractors.

This line of argument goes on to claim that the control of the food chain will be disastrous for the poor since the MNCs, guided by the profit motive, will only focus on the high-value food items demanded by the affluent. Thus, in the long run, the production of basic staples which constitute the food basket of the poor will taper off. However, this vastly overestimates the power of the MNCs. Even if the research promoted by them does focus on the high-value food items, much of biotechnology research is also funded by governments in both developing and developed countries. Indeed, the protato is a by-product of this type of research. If the protato passes the field trials, there is no reason to believe that it cannot be marketed in the global potato market. And this type of success story can be repeated with other basic food items.

The second type of cost associated with the genetically modified food industry is environmental damage. The most common type of "genetic engineering" involved gene modification in plants designed to make them resistant to applications of weed-killers. This then enables farmers to use massive dosages of weed-killers so as to destroy or wipe out all competing varieties of plants in their field. However, some weeds through genetically-modified pollen contamination may acquire resistance to a variety of weed-killers. The only way to destroy these weeds is through the use of ever-stronger herbicides which are poisonous and linger on in the environment.

578. The author doubts the anti-GM lobby's contention that MNC control of the food chain will be disastrous for the poor because

(a) MNCs will focus on high-value food items.

(b) MNCs are driven by the motive of profit maximization.

(c) MNCs are not the only group of actors in genetically-modified food research.

(d) Economic development will help the poor buy MNC-produced food.

579. Using the clues in the passage, which of the following countries would you expect to be in the forefront of the anti-GM campaign?

(a) USA and Spain.

(b) India and Iraq.

(c) Germany and France.

(d) Australia and New Zealand.

580. Genetic modification makes plants more resistant to killer weeds. However, this can lead to environmental damage by

(a) wiping out competing varieties of plants which now fall prey to killer weeds.

(b) forcing application of stronger herbicides to kill weeds which have become resistant to weak herbicides.

(c) forcing application of stronger herbicides to keep the competing plants weed-free.

(d) not allowing growth of any weeds, thus reducing soil fertility.

581. According to the passage, biotechnology research

(a) is of utility only for high value food items.

(b) is funded only by multinational corporations.

(c) allows multinational corporations to control the food basket of the poor.

(d) addresses the concerns of rich and poor countries.

582. Which of the following about the Indian media's coverage of scientific research does the passage seem to suggest?

(a) Indian media generally covers a subject of scientific importance when its mass application is likely.

(b) Indian media's coverage of scientific research is generally dependent on MNCs interests.

(c) Indian media, in partnership with the government, is actively involved in publicizing the results of scientific research.

(d) Indian media only highlights scientific research which is funded by the government.

Passage – 79

Social life is an outflow and meeting of personality, which means that its end is the meeting of character, temperament, and sensibility, in which our thoughts and feelings, and sense perceptions are brought into play at their lightest and yet keenest.

This aspect, to my thinking, is realized as much in large parties composed of casual acquaintances or even strangers, as in intimate meetings of old friends. I am not one of those superior persons who hold cocktail parties in contempt, looking upon them as barren or at best as very tryingly kaleidoscopic places for gathering, because of the strangers one has to meet in them; which is no argument, for even our most intimate friends must at one time have been strangers to us. These large gatherings will be only what we make of them if not anything better, they can be as good places to collect new friends from as the slave-markets of Istanbul were for beautiful slaves or New Market for race horses.

But they do offer more immediate enjoyment. For one thing, in them one can see the external expression of social life in appearance and behaviour at its widest and most varied, where one can admire beauty of body or air, hear voices remarkable either for sweetness of refinement, look on elegance of clothes or deportment. What is more, these parties are schools for training in sociability, for in them we have to treat strangers as friends. So, in them we see social sympathy in widest commonality spread, or at least should. We show an atrophy of the natural human instinct of getting pleasure and happiness out of other human beings if we cannot treat strangers as friends for the moment. And I would go further and paraphrase Pater to say that not to be able to discriminate every moment some passionate attitude in those about us, even when we meet them casually, is on this short day of frost and sun which out life is, to sleep before evening.

So, it will be seen that my conception of social life is modest, for it makes no demands on what we have, though it does make some on what we are. Interest, wonder, sympathy, and love, the first two leading to the last two, are the psychological prerequisites for social life; and the need for the first two must not be underrated. We cannot make the most even of our intimate social life unless we are able to make strangers of our oldest friends everyday by discovering unknown areas in their personality, and transform them into new friends. In sum, social life is a function of vitality.

It is tragic, however, to observe that it is these very natural springs of social life which are drying up among us. It is becoming more and more difficult to come across fellow-feeling for human beings as such in our society and in all its strata. In the poor middle class, in the course of all my life. I have hardly seen any social life properly so-called. Not only has the grinding routine of making a living killed all desire for it in them, it has also generated a standing mood of peevish hostility to other human beings. Increasing economic distress in recent years has infinitely worsened this state of affairs, and has also brought a sinister addition class hatred. This has become the greatest collective emotional enjoyment of the poor middle class, and indeed they feel most social when they form a pack, and snarl or howl at people who are better off than they.

Their most innocent exhibition of sociability is seen when they spill out from their intolerable homes into the streets and bazaars. I was astonished to see the milling crowds in the poor suburbs of Calcutta. But even there a group of flippant young loafers would put on a conspiratorial look if they saw a man in good clothes passing by them either on foot or in a car. I had borrowed a car from a relative to visit a friend in one of these suburbs, and he became very anxious when I had not returned before dusk. Acid and bombs, he said, were thrown at cars almost every evening in that area. I was amazed. But I also know as a fact that my brother was blackmailed to pay five rupees on a trumped up charge when passing in a car through one such locality.

The situation is differently inhuman, but not a whit more human, among the well-to-do. Kindliness for fellow human beings has been smothered in them, taken as a class, by the arrogance of worldly position, which among the Bengalis who show this snobbery is often only a third-class position.

583. The word 'they' in the first sentence of the third paragraph refers to
(a) Large parties consisting of casual acquaintances and strangers.
(b) Intimate meetings of old friends.
(c) New friends.
(d) Both (a) and (b).

584. In this passage the author is essentially
(a) showing how shallow our social life is.
(b) poking fun at the lower middle class people who howl at better off people.
(c) lamenting the drying up of our real social life.
(d) criticizing the upper class for lavish showy parties.

585. The author's conception of 'social life' requires that
(a) people attend large gatherings.
(b) people possess qualities like wonder and interest.
(c) people do not spend too much time in the company of intimate friends.
(d) large parties consist of casual acquaintances and intimate friends.

586. The word 'discriminate' in the last sentence of the third paragraph means
(a) recognize (b) count
(c) distinguish (d) analyse

587. What is the author trying to show through the two incidents in the paragraph beginning, "Their most innocent exhibition of sociability..."?

(a) The crowds in poor Calcutta suburbs can turn violent without any provocation.

(b) Although poor, the people of poor Calcutta suburbs have a rich social life.

(c) It is risky for rich people to move around in poor suburbs.

(d) Achieving a high degree of sociability does not stop the poor from hating the rich.

Passage – 80

Modern science, exclusive of geometry, is a comparatively recent creation and can be said to have originated with Galileo and Newton. Galileo was the first scientist to recognize clearly that the only way to further our understanding of the physical world was to resort to experiment. However obvious Galileo's contention may appear in the light of our present knowledge, it remains a fact that the Greeks, in spite of their proficiency in geometry, never seem to have realized the importance of experiment. To a certain extent, this may be attributed to the crudeness of their instruments of measurement. Still an excuse of this sort can scarcely be put forward when the elementary nature of Galileo's experiments and observations is recalled. Watching a lamp oscillate in the cathedral of Pisa, dropping bodies from the leaning tower of Pisa, rolling balls down inclined planes, noticing the magnifying effect of water in a spherical glass vase, such was the nature of Galileo's experiments and observations. As can be seen, they might just as well have been performed by the Greeks. At any rate, it was thanks to such experiments that Galileo discovered the fundamental law of dynamics, according to which the acceleration imparted to a body is proportional to the force acting upon it.

The next advance was due to Newton, the greatest scientist of all time if account be taken of his joint contributions to mathematics and physics. As a physicist, he was of course an ardent adherent of the empirical method, but his greatest title to fame lies in another direction. Prior to Newton, mathematics, chiefly in the form of geometry, had been studied as a fine art without any view to its physical applications other than in very trivial cases. But with Newton all the resources of mathematics were turned to advantage in the solution of physical problems. Thenceforth, mathematics appeared as an instrument of discovery, the most powerful one known to man, multiplying the power of thought just as in the mechanical domain the lever multiplied our physical action. It is this application of mathematics to the solution of physical problems, this combination of two separate fields of investigation, which constitutes the essential characteristic of the Newtonian method. Thus, problems of physics were metamorphosed into problems of mathematics.

But in Newton's day the mathematical instrument was still in a very backward state of development. In this field again Newton showed the mark of genius by inventing the integral calculus. As a result of this remarkable discovery, problems, which would have baffled Archimedes, were solved with ease. We know that in Newton's hands this new departure in scientific method led to the discovery of the law of gravitation. But here again the real significance of Newton's achievement lay not so much in the exact quantitative formulation of the law of attraction, as in his having established the presence of law and order at least in one important realm of nature, namely, in the motions of heavenly bodies. Nature thus exhibited rationality and was not mere blind chaos and uncertainty. To be sure, Newton's investigations had been concerned with but a small group of natural phenomena, but it appeared unlikely that this mathematical law and order should turn out to be restricted to certain special phenomena; and the feeling was general that all the physical processes of nature would prove to be unfolding themselves according to rigorous mathematical laws.

When Einstein, in 1905, published his celebrated paper on the electrodynamics of moving bodies, he remarked that the difficulties, which surrounded the equations of electrodynamics, together with the negative experiments of Michelson and others, would be obviated if we extended the validity of the Newtonian principle of the relativity of Galilean motion, which applies solely to mechanical phenomena, so as to include all manner of phenomena: electrodynamics, optical etc. When extended in this way the Newtonian principle of relativity became Einstein's special principle of relativity. Its significance lay in its assertion that absolute Galilean motion or absolute velocity must ever escape all experimental detection. Henceforth absolute velocity should be conceived of as physically meaningless, not only in the particular realm of mechanics, as in Newton's day, but in the entire realm of physical phenomena. Einstein's special principle, by adding increased emphasis to this relativity of velocity, making absolute velocity metaphysically meaningless, created a still more profound distinction between velocity and accelerated or rotational motion. This latter type of motion remained absolute and real as before. It is most important to understand this point and to realize that Einstein's special principle is merely an extension of the validity of the classical Newtonian principle to all classes of phenomena.

588. According to the author, why did the Greeks NOT conduct experiments to understand the physical world?

(a) Apparently they did not think it necessary to experiment.

(b) They focused exclusively on geometry.

(c) Their instruments of measurement were very crude.

(d) The Greeks considered the application of geometry to the physical world more important.

589. The statement "Nature thus exhibited rationality and was not mere blind chaos and uncertainty" suggests that

(a) problems that had baffled scientists like Archimedes were not really problems.

(b) only a small group of natural phenomena was chaotic.

(c) physical phenomena conformed to mathematical laws.

(d) natural phenomena were evolving towards a less chaotic future.

590. Newton may be considered one of the greatest scientists of all time because he

(a) discovered the law of gravitation.

(b) married physics with mathematics.

(c) invented integral calculus.

(d) started the use of the empirical method in science.

591. Which of the following statements about modern science best captures the theme of the passage?

(a) Modern science rests firmly on the platform built by the Greeks.

(b) We need to go back to the method of enquiry used by the Greeks to better understand the laws of dynamics.

(c) Disciplines like Mathematics and Physics function best when integrated into one.

(d) New knowledge about natural phenomena builds on existing knowledge.

592. The significant implication of Einstein's special principle of relativity is that

(a) absolute velocity was meaningless in the realm of mechanics.

(b) Newton's principle of relativity needs to be modified.

(c) there are limits to which experimentation can be used to understand some physical phenomena.

(d) it is meaningless to try to understand the distinction between velocity and accelerated or rotational motion.

Passage – 81

The invention of the gas turbine by Frank Whittle in England and Hans von Ohain in Germany in 1939 signalled the beginning of jet transport. Although the French engineer Lorin had visualized the concept of jet propulsion more than 25 years earlier, it took improved materials and the genius of Whittle and von Ohain to recognize the advantage that a gas turbine offered over a piston engine, including speeds in excess of 350 miles per hour. The progress from the first flights of liquid propellant rocket and jet-propelled aircraft in 1939 to the first faster-than-sound (supersonic) manned airplane (the Bell X-1) in 1947 happened in less than a decade. This then led very rapidly to a series of supersonic fighters and bombers, the first of which became operational in the 1950s. World War II technology foundations and emerging Cold War imperatives then led us into space with the launch of Sputnik in 1957 and the placing of the first man on the moon only 12 years later — a mere 24 years after the end of World War II.

Now a hypersonic flight can take you anywhere in the planet in less than four hours. British Royal Air Force and Royal Navy and the air forces of several other countries are going to use a single-engine cousin to the F/A-22, called the F-35 Joint Strike Fighter. These planes exhibit stealthy angles and coatings that make it difficult for radar to detect them, among aviation's most cutting-edge advances in design. The V-22, known as tilt-rotor, part helicopter, part airplane, takes off vertically, then tilts its engine forward for winged flight. It provides speed, three times the payload, five times the range of the helicopters it's meant to replace. The new fighter, F/A-22 Raptor, with more than a million parts, shows a perfect amalgamation of stealth, speed, avionics and agility.

It seems conventional forms, like the Predator and Global Hawk are passé, the stealthier unmanned aerial vehicles (UAVs) are in. They are shaped like kites, bats and boomerang, all but invisible to the enemy radar and able to remain over hostile territory without any fear of getting grilled if shot down. Will the UAVs take away pilots' jobs permanently? Can a computer-operated machine take a smarter and faster decision in a war-like situation? The new free-flight concept will probably supplement the existing air traffic control system by computers on each plane to map the altitude, route, weather and other planes; and a decade from now, there will be no use of radar any more.

How much bigger can the airplanes get? In the '50s they got speed, in the '80s they became stealthy. Now they are getting smarter thanks to computer automation. The change is quite huge: from the four-seater to the A380 airplane. It seems we are now trading speed for size as we build a new superjumbo jet, the 555 seater A380, which will fly at almost the same speed of the Boeing 707, introduced half a century ago, but with an improved capacity, range, greater fuel economy. A few years down the line will come the truly larger model, to be known as 747X. In the beginning of 2005, the A380, the world's first fully double-decked superjumbo passenger jet, weighing 1.2 million punds, may carry a load of about 840 passengers.

Barring the early phase, civil aviation has always lagged behind the military technologies (of jet engines, lighweight composite materials, etc.). There are two fundamental factors behind the decline in commercial aeronautics in comparison to military aeronautics. There is no collective vision of our future such as the one that drove us in the past. There is also a need for a more aggressive pool of airplane design talents to maintain an industry that continues to find a multibillion dollar-a-year market for its product.

Can the history of aviation technology tell us something about the future of aeronautics? Have we reached a final state in our evolution to a mature technology in aeronautics? Are the challenges of coming out with the 'better, cheaper, faster' designs somehow inferior to those that are suited for 'faster, higher, further'? Safety should improve greatly as a result of the forthcoming improvements in airframes, engines, and avionics. Sixty years from now, aircraft will recover on their own if the pilot loses control. Satelites are the key not only to GPS (global positioning system) navigation but also to in-flight communications, uplinked weather, and even in-flight e-mail. Although there is some debate about what type of engines will power future airplanes — lightweight turbines, turbocharged diesels, or both — there is little debate about how these power plants will be controlled. Pilots of the future can look forward to more and better on-board safety equipment.

2003(R)

593. Why might radars not be used a decade from now?

(a) Stealth technology will advance so much that it is pointless to use radar to detect aircraft.

(b) UAVs can remain over hostile territory without any danger of being detected.

(c) Computers on board may enable aircraft to manage safe navigation on their own.

(d) It is not feasible to increase the range of radars.

594. According to the author, commercial aeronautics, in contrast to military aeronautics, has declined because, among other things.

(a) Speed and technology barriers are more easily overcome in military aeronautics.

(b) The collective vision of the past continues to drive civil and commercial aeronautics.

(c) Though the industry has a huge market, it has not attracted the right kind of aircraft designers.

(d) There is a shortage of materials, like light weight composites, used in commercial aeronautics.

595. According to the first paragraph of the passage, which of the following statements is NOT false?

(a) Frank Whittle and Hans von Ohain were the first to conceive of jet propulsion.

(b) Supersonic fighter planes were first used in World War II.

(c) No man had travelled faster than sound until the 1950s.

(d) The exploitation of jet propulsion for supersonic aviation has been remarkably fast.

596. What is the fourth paragraph of the passage, starting, "How much bigger . . . ", about?

(a) Stealth, speed, avionics, and agility of new aircraft.

(b) The way aircraft size has been growing.

(c) Use of computer automation in aircraft.

(d) Super-jumbo jets that can take more than 500 passengers.

597. What is the most noteworthy difference between V-22 and a standard airplane?

(a) It can take off vertically.

(b) It has winged flight.

(c) It has excellent payload.

(d) Its range is very high.

Passage – 82

Pure love of learning, of course, was a less compelling motive for those who became educated for careers other than teaching. Students of law in particular had a reputation for being materialistic careerists in an age when law was becoming known as 'the lucrative science' and its successful practice the best means for rapid advancement in the government of both church and state. Medicine too had its profit-making attractions. Those who did not go on to law or medicine could, if they had been well trained in the arts, gain positions at royal courts or rise in the clergy. Eloquent testimony to the profit motive behind much of 12th-century education was the lament of a student of Abelard around 1150: "Christians educate their sons . . . for gain, in order that the one brother, if he be a clerk, may help his father and mother and his other brothers, saying that a clerk will have no heir and whatever he has will be ours and the other brothers." With the opening of positions in law, government and the church, education became a means for advancement not only in income but also in status. Most who were educated were wealthy, but in the 12th century, more often than before, many were not and were able to rise through the ranks by means of their education. The most familiar examples are Thomas Becket, who rose from a humble background to become chancellor of England and then archbishop of Canterbury, and John of Salisbury, who was born a 'plebeian' but because of his reputation for learning died as bishop of Chartres.

The instances of Becket and John of Salisbury bring us to the most difficult question concerning 12th-century education: To what degree was it still a clerical preserve? Despite the fact that throughout the 12th century the clergy had a monopoly of instruction, one of the outstanding medievalists of our day, R. W. Southern, refers with good reason to the institutions staffed by the clergy as 'secular schools'. How can we make sense out of the paradox that 12th-century schools were clerical and yet 'secular'?

Let us look at the clerical side first. Not only were all 12th-century teachers except professionals and craftsmen in church order, but in northern Europe students in schools had clerical status and looked like priests. Not that all really were priests, but by virtue of being students all were awarded the legal privileges accorded to the clergy. Furthermore, the large majority of 12th-century students, outside of the possible exception of Italy, if not already priests became so after their studies were finished. For these reasons, the term 'cleric' was often used to denote a man who was literate and the term 'layman' one who was illiterate. The English word for cleric, clerk, continued for a long time to be a synonym for student or for a man who could write, while the French word clerc even today has the connotation of intellectual.

Despite all this, 12th-century education was taking on many secular qualities in its environment, goals, and curriculum. Student life obviously became more secular when it moved out from the monasteries into the bustling towns. Most students wandered from town to town in search not only of good masters but also of worldly excitement, and as the 12th century progressed they found the best of each in Paris. More important than environment was the fact that most students, even though they entered the clergy, had secular goals. Theology was recognized as the 'queen of the sciences', but very few went on to it. Instead they used their study of the liberal arts as a preparation for law, medicine, government service, or advancement in the ecclesiastical hierarchy.

This being so, the curriculum of the liberal arts became more sophisticated and more divorced from religion. Teaching was still almost exclusively in Latin, and the first book most often read was the Psalter, but further education was no longer similar to that of a choir school. In particular, the discipline of rhetoric was transformed from a linguistic study into instruction in how to compose letters and documents; there was a new stress on logic; and in all the liberal arts and philosophy texts more advanced than those known in the early Middle Ages were introduced.

Along with the rise of logic came the translation of Greek and Arabic philosophical and scientific works. Most important was the translation of almost all the writings of Aristotle, as well as his sophisticated Arabic commentators, which helped to bring about an intellectual revolution based on Greek rationalism. On a more prosaic level, contact with Arabs resulted in the introduction in the 12th century of the Arabic numeral system and the concept of zero. Though most westerners first resisted this and made crude jokes about the zero as an ambitious number 'that counts for nothing and yet wants to be counted', the system steadily made its inroads first in Italy and then throughout Europe, thereby vastly simplifying the arts of computation and record-keeping.

598. According to the passage, what led to the secularisation of the curriculum of the liberal arts in the 12th century?

(a) It was divorced from religion and its influences.

(b) Students used it mainly as a base for studying law and medicine.

(c) Teaching could no longer be conducted exclusively in Latin.

(d) Arabic was introduced into the curriculum.

599. According to the author, in the 12th century, individuals were motivated to get higher education because it

(a) was a means for material advancement and higher status.

(b) gave people with wealth an opportunity to learn.

(c) offered a coveted place for those with a love of learning.

(d) directly added to the income levels of people.

600. According to the passage, 12th-century schools were clerical and yet secular because

(a) many teacher were craftsmen and professionals who did not form part of the church.

(b) while the students had the legal privileges accorded to the clergy and looked like priests, not all were really priests.

(c) the term 'cleric' denoted a literate individual rather than a strict association with the church.

(d) though the clergy had a monopoly in education, the environment, objectives and curriculum in the schools were becoming secular.

601. What does the sentence 'Christians educate their sons . . . will be ours and the other brothers' imply?

(a) The Christian family was a close-knit unit in the 12th century.

(b) Christians educated their sons not so much for the love of learning as for material gain.

(c) Christians believed very strongly in educating their sons in the Church.

(d) The relationship between Christian parents and their sons was exploitative in the 12th century.

602. According to the passage, which of the following is the most noteworthy trend in education in 12th-century Europe?

(a) Secularization of education.

(b) Flowering of theology as the queen of the sciences.

(c) Wealthy people increasingly turning to education.

(d) Rise of the clergy's influence on the curriculum.

Passage – 83

At first sight, it looks as though panchayati raj, the lower layer of federalism in our polity, is as firmly entrenched in our system as is the older and higher layer comprising the Union Government and the State. Like the democratic institutions at the higher level, those at the panchayat level, the panchayati raj institutions (PRIs), are written into and protected by the Constitution. All the essential features, which distinguish a unitary system from a federal one, are as much enshrined at the lower as at the upper level of our federal system. But look closely and you will discover a fatal flaw. The letter of the Constitution as well as the spirit of the present polity have exposed the intra-State level of our federal system to a dilemma of which the inter-State and Union-State layers are free. The flaw has many causes. But all of them are rooted in an historical anomaly, that while the dynamics of federalism and democracy have given added strength to the rights given to the States in the Constitution, they have worked against the rights of panchayats.

At both levels of our federal system there is the same tussle between those who have certain rights and those who try to encroach upon them if they believe they can. Thus, the Union Government was able to encroach upon certain rights given to the States by the Constitution. It got away with that because the single dominant party system, which characterised Centre-State relations for close upon two decades, gave the party in power at the Union level many extra-constitutional political levers. Second, the Supreme Court had not yet begun to extend the limits of its power. But all that has changed in recent times. The spurt given to a multi-party democracy by the overthrow of the Emergency in 1977 became a long-term trend later on because of the ways in which a vigorously democratic multi-party system works in a political society which is as assertively pluralistic as Indian society is. It gives political clout to all the various segments which constitute that society. Secondly, because of the linguistic reorganisation of States in the 1950s, many of the most assertive segments have found their most assertive expression as States. Thirdly, with single-party dominance becoming a thing of the past at the Union level, governments can be formed at that level only by multi-party coalitions in which State-level parties are major players. This has made it impossible for the Union Government to do much about anything unless it also carries a sufficient number of State-level parties with it. Indian federalism is now more real than it used to be, but an unfortunate side-effect is that India's panchayati raj system, inaugurated with such fanfare in the early 1980s, has become less real.

By the time the PRIs came on the scene, most of the political space in our federal system had been occupied by the Centre in the first 30 years of Independence, and most of what was still left after that was occupied by the States in the next 20. PRIs might have hoped to wrest some space from their immediate neighbour, the States, just as the States had wrested some from the Centre. But having at last managed to checkmate the Centre's encroachments on their rights, the States were not about to allow the PRIs to do some encroaching of their own.

By the 1980's and early 1990s, the only nationally left, the Congress, had gone deeper into a siege mentality. Finding itself surrounded by State-level parties, it had built walls against them in stead of winning them over. Next, the States retaliated by blocking Congress proposals for panchayati raj in Parliament, suspecting that the Centre would try to use panchayats to by-pass State Governments. The suspicion fed on the fact that the powers proposed by the Congress for panchayats were very similar to many of the more lucrative powers of State Governments. State-level leaders also feared, perhaps, that if panchayat-level leaders captured some of the larger PRIs, such as district-level panchayats, they would exert pressure on State-level leaders through intra-State multi-party federalism.

It soon became obvious to Congress leaders that there was no way the panchayati raj amendments they wanted to write into the Constitution would pass muster unless State-level parties were given their pound of flesh. The amendments were allowed only after it was agreed that the powers of panchayats could be listed in the Constitution. Illustratively, they would be defined and endowed on PRIs by the State Legislature acting at its discretion.

This left the door wide open for the States to exert the power of the new political fact that while the Union and State Governments could afford to ignore panchayats as long as the MLAs were happy, the Union Government had to be sensitive to the demands of State-level parties. This has given State-level actors strong beachheads on the shores of both inter-State and intra-State federalism. By using various administrative devices and non-elected parallel structures, State Governments have subordinated their PRIs to the State administration and given the upper hand to State Government officials against the elected heads of PRIs. Panchayats have become local agencies for implementing schemes drawn up in distant State capitals. And their own volition has been further circumscribed by a plethora of 'Centrally-sponsored schemes'. These are drawn up by even more distant Central authorities but at the same time tie up local staff and resources on pain of the schemes being switched off in the absence of matching local contribution. The 'foreign aid' syndrome can be clearly seen at work behind this kind of 'grass roots development'.

603. The central theme of the passage can be best summarized as

(a) our grassroots development at the panchayat level is now driven by the 'foreign aid' syndrome.

(b) panchayati raj is firmly entrenched at the lower level of our federal system of governance.

(c) a truly federal polity has not developed since PRIs have not been allowed the necessary political space.

(d) the Union Government and State-level parties are engaged in a struggle for the protection of their respective.

604. The sentence in the last paragraph, "And their own volition has been further circumscribed. . ." refers to

(a) the weakening of the local institutions' ability to plan according to their needs.

(b) the increasing demands made on elected local leaders to match central grants with local contributions.

(c) the empowering of the panchayat system as implementers of schemes from State capitals.

(d) the process by which the prescribed Central schemes are reformulated by local elected leaders.

605. What is the 'dilemma' at the intra-State level mentioned in the first paragraph of the passage?

(a) Should the state governments wrest more space from the Union, before considering the panchayati system?

(b) Should the rights similar to those that the States managed to get be extended to panchayats as well?

(c) Should the single party system which has withered away be brought back at the level of the States?

(d) Should the States get 'their pound of flesh' before allowing the Union Government to pass any more laws?

606. Which of the following most closely describes the 'fatal flaw' that the passage refers to?

(a) The ways in which the democratic multi-party system works in an assertively pluralistic society like India's are flawed.

(b) The mechanisms that our federal system uses at the Union Government level to deal with States are imperfect.

(c) The instruments that have ensured federalism at one level, have been used to achieve the opposite at another.

(d) The Indian Constitution and the spirit of the Indian polity are fatally flawed.

607. Which of the following best captures the current state of Indian federalism as described in the passage?

(a) The Supreme Court has not begun to extend the limits of its power.

(b) The multi-party system has replaced the single party system.

(c) The Union, State and panchayati raj levels have become real.

(d) There is real distribution of power between the Union and State-level parties.

Passage – 84

While I was in class at Columbia, struggling with the esoterica du jour, my father was on a bricklayer's scaffold not far up the street, working on a campus building. Once we met up on the subway going home — he was with his tools, I with my books. My father wasn't interested in Thucydides, and I wasn't up on arches. My dad has built lots of places in New York City he can't get into: colleges, condos, office towers. He made his living on the outside. Once the walls were up, a place took on a different feel for him, as though he wasn't welcome anymore. Related by blood, we're separated by class, my father and I. Being the white-collar child of a blue-collar parent means being the hinge on the door between two ways of life. With one foot in the working-class, the other in the middle class, people like me are Straddlers, at home in neither world, living a limbo life.

What drove me to leave what I knew? Born blue-collar, I still never felt completely at home among the tough guys and anti-intellectual crowd of my neighbourhood in deepest Brooklyn. I never did completely fit in among the preppies and suburban royalty of Columbia, either. It's like that for Straddlers. It was not so smooth jumping from Italian old-world style to US professional in a single generation. Others who were the first in their families to go to college, will tell you the same thing: the academy can render you unrecognisable to the very people who launched you into the world. The ideas and values absorbed in college challenge the mom-and pop orthodoxy that passed for truth for 18 years. Limbo folk may eschew polyester blends for sea-isle cotton, prefer Brie to Kraft slices. They marry outside the neighbourhood and raise their kids differently. They might not be in church on Sunday.

When they pick careers (not jobs), it's often a kind of work their parents never heard of or can't understand. But for the white-collar kids of blue-collar parents, the office is not necessarily a sanctuary. In Corporate America, where the rules are based on notions foreign to working-class people, a Straddler can get lost. Social class counts at the office, even though nobody likes to admit it. Ultimately, corporate norms are based on middle-class values, business types say. From an early age, middle-class people learn how to get along, using diplomacy, nuance, and politics to grab what they need. It is as though they are following a set of rules laid out in a manual that blue-collar families never have the chance to read.

People born into the middle class to parents with college degrees have lived lives filled with what French sociologist Pierre Bourdieu calls 'cultural capital'. Growing up in an educated environment, they learn about Picasso and Mozart, stock portfolios and crème brulee. In a home with cultural capital, there are networks: someone always has an aunt or golfing buddy with the inside track for an internship or some entry-level job. Dinner-table talk could involve what happened that day to mom and dad at the law firm, the doctor's office, or the executive suite. Middle-class kids can grow up with a sense of entitlement that will carry them through their lives. This 'belongingness' is not just related to having material means, it also has to do with learning and possessing confidence in your place in the world. Such early access and direct exposure to culture in the home is the more organic, 'legitimate' means of appropriating cultural capital, Bourdieu tells us. Those of us possessing 'ill-gotten Culture' can learn it, but never as well. Something is always a little off about us, like an engine with imprecise timing. There's a greater match between middle-class lives and the institutions in which the middle class works and operates — universities or corporations. Children of the middle and upper classes have been speaking the language of the bosses and supervisors forever.

Blue-collar kids are taught by their parents and communities to work hard to achieve, and that merit is rewarded. But no blue-collar parent knows whether such things are true in the middle-class world. Many professionals born to the working-class report feeling out of place and out of place and outmanoeuvred in the office. Soon enough, Straddlers learn that straight talk won't always cut. Resolving conflicts head-on and speaking your mind doesn't always work, no matter how educated the Straddler is.

In the working-class, people perform jobs in which they are closely supervised and are required to follow orders and instructions. That, in turn, affects how they socialise their children. Children of the working-class are brought up in a home in which conformity, obedience and intolerance for back talk are the norm — the same characteristics that make a good factory worker.

608. According to the passage, which of the following statements about 'cultural capital' is NOT true?

(a) It socializes children early into the norms of middle class institutions.

(b) It helps them learn the language of universities and corporations.

(c) It creates a sense of enlightenment in middle-class children.

(d) It develops bright kids into Straddlers.

609. According to the passage, the patterns of socialization of working-class children make them most suited for jobs that require

(a) diplomacy.

(b) compliance with orders.

(c) enterprise and initiative.

(d) high risk-taking.

610. When Straddlers enter white collar jobs, they get lost because

(a) they are thrown into an alien value system.

(b) their families have not read the rules in corporate manuals.

(c) they have no one to guide them through the corporate maze.

(d) they miss the 'mom and pop orthodoxy'.

611. What does the author's statement, "My father wasn't interested in Thucydides, and I wasn't up on arches," illustrate?

(a) Organic cultural capital

(b) Professional arrogance and social distance

(c) Evolving social transformation

(d) Breakdown of family relationships

612. Which of the following statements about Straddlers does the passage NOT support explicitly?

(a) Their food preferences may not match those of their parents.

(b) They may not keep up some central religious practices of their parents.

(c) They are at home neither in the middle class nor in the working-class.

(d) Their political ideologies may differ from those of their parents.

Passage – 85

The endless struggle between the flesh and the spirit found an end in Greek art. The Greek artists were unaware of it. They were spiritual materialists, never denying the importance of the body and ever seeing in the body a spiritual significance. Mysticism on the whole was alien to the Greeks, thinkers as they were. Thought and mysticism never go well together and there is little symbolism in Greek art. Athena was not a symbol of wisdom but an embodiment of it and her statues were beautiful grave women, whose seriousness might mark them as wise, but who were marked in no other way. The Apollo Belvedere is not a symbol of the sun, nor the Versailles Artemis of the moon. There could be nothing less akin to the ways of symbolism than their beautiful, normal humanity. Nor did decoration really interest the Greeks. In all their art they were preoccupied with what they wanted to express, not with ways of expressing it, and lovely expression, merely as lovely expression, did not appeal to them at all.

Greek art is intellectual art, the art of men who were clear and lucid thinkers, and it is therefore plain art. Artists than whom the world has never seen greater, men endowed with the spirit's best gift, found their natural method of expression in the simplicity and clarity which are the endowment of the unclouded reason. "Nothing in excess," the Greek axiom of art, is the dictum of men who would brush aside all obscuring, entangling superfluity, and see clearly, plainly, unadorned, what they wished to express. Structure belongs in an especial degree to the province of the mind in art, and architectonics were pre-eminently a mark of the Greek. The power that made a unified whole of the trilogy of a Greek tragedy, that envisioned the sure, precise, decisive scheme of the Greek statue, found its most conspicuous expression in Greek architecture. The Greek temple is the creation, par excellence, of mind and spirit in equilibrium.

A Hindoo temple is a conglomeration of adornment. The lines of the building are completely hidden by the decorations. Sculptured figures and ornaments crowd its surface, stand out from it in thick masses, break it up into a bewildering series of irregular tiers. It is not a unity but a collection, rich, confused. It looks like something not planned but built this way and that as the ornament required. The conviction underlying it can be perceived: each bit of the exquisitely wrought detail had a mystical meaning and the temple's exterior was important only as a means for the artist to inscribe thereon the symbols of the truth. It is decoration, not architecture.

Again, the gigantic temples of Egypt, those massive immensities of granite which look as if only the power that moves in the earthquake were mighty enough to bring them into existence, are something other than the creation of geometry balanced by beauty. The science and the spirit are there, but what is there most of all is force, unhuman force, calm but tremendous, overwhelming. It reduces to nothingness all that belongs to man. He is annihilated. The Egyptian architects were possessed by the consciousness of the awful, irresistible domination of the ways of nature; they had no thought to give to the insignificant atom that was man.

Greek architecture of the great age is the expression of men who were, first of all, intellectual artists, kept firmly within the visible world by their mind, but, only second to that, lovers of the human world. The Greek temple is the perfect expression of the pure intellect illumined by the spirit. No other great buildings anywhere approach its simplicity. In the Parthenon straight columns rise to plain capitals; a pediment is sculptured in bold relief; there is nothing more. And yet — here is the Greek miracle — this absolute simplicity of structure is alone in majesty of beauty among all the temples and cathedrals and palaces of the world. Majestic but human, truly Greek. No superhuman force as in Egypt; no strange supernatural shapes as in India; the Parthenon is the home of humanity at ease, calm, ordered, sure of itself and the world. The Greeks flung a challenge to nature in the fullness of their joyous strength. They set their temples on the summit of a hill overlooking the wide sea, outlined against the circle of the sky. They would build what was more beautiful than hill and sea and sky and greater than all these. It matters not at all if the temple is large or small; one never thinks of the size. It matters not how much it is in ruins. A few white columns dominate the lofty height at Sunion as securely as the great mass of the Parthenon dominates all the sweep of sea and land around Athens. To the Greek architect man was the master of the world. His mind could understand its laws; his spirit could discover its beauty.

613. "The Greeks flung a challenge to nature in the fullness of their joyous strength." Which of the following best captures the 'challenge' that is being referred to?

(a) To build a monument matching the background colours of the sky and the sea.

(b) To build a monument bigger than nature's creations.

(c) To build monuments that were more appealing to the mind and spirit than nature's creations.

(d) To build a small but architecturally perfect monument.

614. Which of the following is NOT a characteristic of Greek architecture, according to the passage?

(a) A lack of excess

(b) Simplicity of form

(c) Expression of intellect

(d) Mystic spirituality

615. From the passage, which of the following combinations can be inferred to be correct?

(a) Hindoo temple — power of nature

(b) Parthenon — simplicity

(c) Egyptian temple — mysticism

(d) Greek temple — symbolism

616. According to the passage, what conception of man can be inferred from Egyptian architecture?

(a) Man is the centre of creation.

(b) Egyptain temples save man from unhuman forces.

(c) Temples celebrate man's victory over nature.

(d) Man is inconsequential before the tremendous force of nature.

617. According to the passage, which of the following best explains why there is little symbolism in Greek art?

(a) The Greeks focused on thought rather than mysticsm.

(b) The struggle between the flesh and the spirit found an end in Greek art.

(c) Greek artists were spiritual materialists.

(d) Greek statues were embodiments rather than symbols of qualities.

Passage – 86

The painter is now free to paint anything he chooses. They are scarcely any forbidden subjects, and today everybody is prepared to admit that a painting of some fruit can be as important as a painting of a hero dying. The Impressionists did as much as anybody to win this previously unheard-of freedom for the artist. Yet, by the next generation, painters began to abandon the subject altogether, and began to paint abstract pictures. Today the majority of pictures painted are abstract.

Is there a connection between these two developments? Has art gone abstract because the artist is embarrassed by his freedom? Is it that, because he is free to paint anything, he doesn't know what to paint? Apologists for abstract art often talk of it as the art of maximum freedom. But could this be the freedom of the desert island? It would take to long to answer these questions properly. I believe there is a connection. Many things have encouraged the development of abstract art. Among them has been the artists' wish to avoid the difficulties of finding subjects when all subjects are equally possible.

I raise the matter now because I want to draw attention to the fact that the painter's choice of a subject is a far more complicated question than it would at first seem. A subject does not start with what is put in front of the easel or with something which the painter happens to remember. A subject starts with the painter deciding he would like to paint such-and-such because for some reason or other he finds it meaningful. A subject begins when the artist selects something for *special mention.* (What makes it special or meaningful may seem to the artist to be purely visual – its colours or its form.) When the subject has been selected, the function of the painting itself is to communicate and justify the significance of that selection.

It is often said today that subject matter is unimportant. But this is only a reaction against the excessively literary and moralistic interpretation of subject matter in the nineteenth century. In truth the subject is literary the beginning and end of a painting. The painting begins with a selection(I will paint this and not everything else in the world); it is finished when that selection is justified (now you can see all that I saw and felt in this and how it is more than merely itself).

Thus, for a painting to succeed it is essential that the painter and his public agree about what is significant. The subject may have a personal meaning for the painter or individual spectator; but there must also be the possibility of their agreement on its general meaning. It is at this point that the culture of the society and period in question precedes the artist and his art. Renaissance art would have meant nothing to the Aztecs –and vice versa. If, to some extent, a few intellectuals can appreciate them both today it is because their culture is an historical one; its inspiration is history and therefore it can include within itself, in principle if not in every particular, all known developments to date.

When a culture is secure and certain of its values, it presents it presents its artists with subjects. The general agreement about what is significant is so well established that the significance of a particular subject accrues and becomes traditional. This is true, for instance, of reeds and water in China, of the nude body in Renaissance, of the animal in Africa. Furthermore, in such cultures the artist is unlikely to be a free agent: he will be employed *for the sake of particulars subjects,* and the problem, as we have just described it, will not occur to him.

When a culture is in a state of disintegration or transition the freedom of the artist increases – but the question of subject matter becomes problematic for him: he, himself, has to choose for society. This was at the basis of all the increasing, crises in European art during the nineteenth century. It is too often forgotten how many of the art scandals of that time were provoked by the choice of subject (Gericault, Courbet, Daumier, Degas, Lautrec, Van Gogh, etc.).

By the end of the nineteenth century there were, roughly speaking, two ways in which the painter could meet this challenge of deciding what to paint and so choosing for society. Either he identified himself with the people and so allowed their lives to dictate his subjects to him; or he had to find his subjects within himself as painter. By *people* I mean everybody except the bourgeoisie. Many painters did of course work of the bourgeoisie according to their copy-book of approved subjects, but all of them, filling the Salon and the Royal Academy year after year, are now forgotten, buried under the hypocrisy of those they served so sincerely.

2004

618. When a culture is insecure, the painter chooses his subject on the basis of:

(a) The prevalent style in the society of his time.

(b) Its meaningfulness to the painter.

(c) What is put in front of the easel.

(d) Past experience and memory of the painter

619. In the sentence, "I believe there is a connection" (second paragraph), what two developments is the author referring to?

(a) Painters using a dying hero and using a fruit as a subject of painting.

(b) Growing success of painters and an increase in abstract forms.

(c) Artists gaining freedom to choose subjects and abandoning subjects altogether.

(d) Rise of Impressionists and an increase in abstract forms.

620. Which of the following is NOT necessarily among the attributes needed for a painter to succeed:

(a) The painter and his public agree on what is significant.

(b) The painting is able to communicate and justify the significance of its subject selection.

(c) The subject has a personal meaning for the painter.

(d) The painting of subjects is inspired by historical developments.

621. In the context of the passage, which of the following statements would NOT be true?

(a) Painters decided subjects based on what they remembered from their own lives.

(b) Painters of reeds and water in China faced no serious problem of choosing a subject.

(c) The choice of subject was a source of scandals in nineteenth century European art.

(d) Agreement on the general meaning of a painting is influenced by culture and historical context.

622. Which of the following views is taken by the author?

(a) The more insecure a culture, the greater the freedom of the artist.

(b) The more secure a culture, the greater the freedom of the artist.

(c) The more secure a culture, more difficult the choice of subject.

(d) The more insecure a culture, the less significant the choice of the subject.

Passage – 87

Recently I spent several hours sitting under a tree in my garden with the social anthropologist William Ury, a Harvard University professor who specializes in the art of negotiation and wrote the bestselling book, *Getting to Yes.* He captivated me with his theory that tribalism protects people from their fear of rapid change. He explained that the pillars of tribalism that humans rely on for security would always counter any significant cultural or social change. In this way, he said, change is never allowed to happen too fast. Technology, for example, is a pillar of society. Ury believes that every time technology moves in a new or radical direction, another pillar such as religion or nationalism will grow stronger - in effect, the traditional and familiar will assume greater importance to compensate for the new and untested. In this manner, human tribes avoid rapid change that leaves people insecure and frightened.

But we have all heard that nothing is as permanent as change. Nothing is guaranteed. Pithy expressions, to be sure, but no more than cliches. As Ury says, people don't live that way from day-to-day. On the contrary, they actively seek certainty and stability. They want to know they will be safe.

Even so, we scare ourselves constantly with the idea of change. An IBM CEO once said: 'We only re-structure for a good reason, and if we haven't re-structured in a while, that's a good reason.' We are scared that competitors, technology and the consumer will put us out of business so we have to change all the time just to stay alive. But if we asked our fathers and grandfathers, would they have said that they lived in a period of little change? Structure may not have changed much. It may just be the speed with which we do things.

Change is over-rated, anyway. Consider the automobile. It's an especially valuable example, because the auto industry has spent tens of billions or dollars on research and product development in the last 100 years. Henry Ford's first car had a metal chassis with an internal combustion, gasoline-powered engine, four wheels with rubber tyres, a foot operated clutch assembly and brake system, a steering wheel, and four seats, and it could safely do 18 miles per hour. A hundred years and tens of thousands of research hours later, we drive cars with a metal chassis with an internal combustion, gasoline-powered engine, four wheels with rubber tyres, a foot operated clutch assembly and brake system, a steering wheel, four seats - and the average speed in London in 2001 was 17.5 miles per hour!

That's not a hell of a lot of return for the money. Ford evidently doesn't have much to teach us about change. The fact that they're still manufacturing cars is not proof that Ford Motor Co. is a sound organization, just proof that it takes very large companies to make cars in great quantities - making for an almost impregnable entry barrier.

Fifty years after the development of the jet engine, planes are also little changed. They've grown bigger, wider and can carry more people. But those are incremental, largely cosmetic changes.

Taken together, this lack of real change has come to mean that in travel - whether driving or flying — time and technology have not combined to make things much better.

The safety and design have of course accompanied the times and the new volume of cars and flights, but nothing of any significance has changed in the basic assumptions of the final product.

At the same time, moving around in cars or aeroplanes becomes less and less efficient all the time. Not only has there been no great change, but also both forms or transport have deteriorated as more people clamour to use them. The same is true for telephones, which took over hundred years to become mobile, or photographic film, which also required an entire century to change.

The only explanation for this is anthropological. Once established in calcified organizations, humans do two things: sabotage changes that might render people dispensable, and ensure industry-wide emulation. In the 1960s, German auto companies developed plans to scrap the entire combustion engine for an electrical design. (The same existed in the 1970s in Japan, and in the l980s in France.). So for 40 years we might have been free of the wasteful and ludicrous dependence on fossil fuels. Why didn't it go anywhere? Because auto executives understood pistons and carburettors, and would loath to cannibalize their expertise, along with most of their factories.

623. According to the passage, which of the following statements is true?

(a) Executives of automobile companies are inefficient and ludicrous.

(b) The speed at which an automobile is driven in a city has not changed much in a century.

(c) Anthropological factors have fostered innovation in automobiles by promoting use of new technologies.

(d) Further innovation in jet engines has been more than incremental.

624. Which of the following views does the author fully support in the passage?

(a) Nothing is as permanent as change.

(b) Change is always rapid.

(c) More money spent on innovation leads to more rapid change.

(d) Over decades, structural change has been incremental.

625. Which of the following best describes one of the main ideas discussed in the passage?

(a) Rapid change is usually welcomed in society.

(b) Industry is not as innovative as it is made out to be.

(c) We should have less change than what we have now.

(d) Competition spurs companies into radical innovation.

626. According to the passage, the reason why we continues to be dependent on fossil fuels is that:

(a) Auto executives did not wish to change.

(b) No alternative fuels were discovered.

(c) Change in technology was not easily possible

(d) German, Japanese and French companies could not come up with new technologies.

Passage – 88

The viability of the multinational corporate system depends upon the degree to which people will tolerate the unevenness it creates. It is well to remember that the 'New Imperialism' which began after 1870 in a spirit of Capitalism Triumphant, soon became seriously troubled and after 1914 was characterized by war, depression, breakdown of the international economic system and war again, rather than free Trade, Pax Britannica and Material Improvement. A major reason was Britain's inability to cope with the by-products of its own rapid accumulation of capital; i.e., a class-conscious labour force at home; a middle class in the hinterland; and rival centres of capital on the Continent and in America. Britain's policy tended to be atavistic and defensive rather than progressive-more concerned with warding off new threats than creating new areas of expansion. Ironically, Edwardian England revived the paraphernalia of the landed aristocracy it had just destroyed. Instead of embarking on a 'big push' to develop the vast hinterland of the Empire, colonial administrators often adopted policies to arrest the development of either a native capitalist class or a native proletariat which could overthrow them.

As time went on, the centre had to devote an increasing share of government activity to military and other unproductive expenditures; they had to rely on alliances with an inefficient class of landlords, officials and soldiers in the hinterland to maintain stability at the cost of development. A great part of the surplus extracted from the population was thus wasted locally.

The New Mercantilism (as the Multinational Corporate System of special alliances and privileges, aid and tariff concessions is sometimes called) faces similar problems of internal and external division. The centre is troubled: excluded groups revolt and even some of the affluent are dissatisfied with the roles. Nationalistic rivalry between major capitalist countries remains an important divisive factor, Finally, there is the threat presented by the middle classes and the excluded groups of the underdeveloped countries. The national middle classes in the underdeveloped countries came to power when the centre weakened but could not, through their policy of import substitution manufacturing, establish a viable basis for sustained growth. They now face a foreign exchange crisis and an unemployment (or population) crisis-the first indicating their inability to function in the international economy and the second indicating their alienation from the people they are supposed to lead. In the immediate future, these national middle classes will gain a new lease of life as they take advantage of the spaces created by the rivalry between American and non-American oligopolists striving to establish global market positions.

The native capitalists will again become the champions of national independence as they bargain with multinational corporations. But the conflict at this level is more apparent than real, for in the end the fervent nationalism of the middle class asks only for promotion within the corporate structure and not for a break with that structure. In the last analysis their power derives from the metropolis and they cannot easily afford to challenge the international system. They do not command the loyalty of their own population and cannot really compete with the large, powerful, aggregate capitals from the centre. They are prisoners of the taste patterns and consumption standards set at the centre.

The main threat comes from the excluded groups. It is not unusual in underdeveloped countries for the top 5 per cent to obtain between 30 and 40 per cent of the total national income, and for the top one-third to obtain anywhere from 60 to 70 per cent. At most, one-third of the population can be said to benefit in some sense from the dualistic growth that characterizes development in the hinterland. The remaining two-thirds, who together get only one-third of the income, are outsiders, not because they do not contribute to the economy, but because they do not share in the benefits. They provide a source of cheap labour which helps keep exports to the developed world at a low price and which has financed the urban-biased growth of recent years. In fact, it is difficult to see how the system in most underdeveloped countries could survive without cheap labour since removing it(e.g. diverting it to public works projects as is done in socialist countries)would raise consumption costs to capitalists and professional elites.

627. According to the author, the British policy during the 'New Imperialism' period tended to be defensive because
(a) it was unable to deal with the fallouts of a sharp increase in capital.
(b) its cumulative capital had undesirable side-effects.
(c) its policies favoured developing the vast hinterland.
(d) it prevented the growth of a set-up which could have been capitalistic in nature.

628. Under New Mercantilism, the fervent nationalism of the native middle classes does not create conflict with the multinational corporations because they (the middle classes)
(a) negotiate with the multinational corporations.
(b) are dependent on the international system for their continued prosperity.
(c) are not in a position to challenge the status quo.
(d) do not enjoy popular support.

629. In the sentence, "They are prisoners of the taste patterns and consumption standards set at the center." (fourth paragraph), what is the meaning of 'center'?
(a) National government (b) Native capitalists.
(c) New capitalists. (d) None of the above.

630. The author is in a position to draw parallels between New Imperialism and New Mercantilism because
(a) both originated in the developed Western capitalist countries.
(b) New Mercantilism was a logical sequel to New Imperialism
(c) they create the same set of outputs – a labour force, middle classes and rival centers of capital.
(d) both have comparable uneven and divisive effects.

Passage – 89

Fifty feet away three male lions lay by the road. They didn't appear to have a hair on their heads. Noting the color of their noses(leonine noses darken as they age, from pink to black), Craig estimated that they were six years old-young adults. "This is wonderful!" he said, after staring at them for several moments. "This is what we came to see. They really are maneless." Craig, a professor at the University of Minnesota, is arguably the leading expert on the majestic Serengeti lion, whose head is mantled in long, thick hair. He and Peyton West, a doctoral student who has been working with him in Tanzania, had never seen the Tsavo lions that live some 200 miles east of the Serengeti. The scientists had partly suspected that the maneless males were adolescents mistaken for adults by amateur observers. Now they knew better.

The Tsavo research expedition was mostly Peyton's show. She had spent several years in Tanzania, compiling the data she needed to answer a question that ought to have been answered long ago: Why do lions have manes? It's the only cat, wild or domestic, that displays such ornamontation. In Tsavo she was attacking the riddle from the opposite angle. Why do its lions not have manes? (Some "maneless" lions in Tsavo East do have partial manes, but they rarely attain the regal glory of the Serengeti lions'.) Does environmental adaptation account for the trait? *Are* the lions of Tsavo, as some people believe, a distinct subspecies of their Serengeti cousins?

The Serengeti lions have been under continuous observation for more than 35 years, beginning with George Schaller's pioneering work in the l960s. But the lions in Tsavo, Kenya's oldest and largest protected ecosystem, have hardly been studied. Consequently, legends have grown up around them. Not only do they look different, according to the myths, they *behave* differently, displaying greater cunning and aggressiveness. "Remember too," *Kenya: The Rough Guide* warns, "Tsavo's lions have a reputation of ferocity." Their fearsome image became well-known in 1898, when two males stalled construction of what is now Kenya

Railways by allegedly killing and eating 135 Indian and African laborers. A British Army officer in charge of building a railroad bridge over the Tsavo River, Lt. Col. J. H. Patterson, spent nine months pursuing the pair before he brought them to bay and killed them. Stuffed and mounted, they now glare at visitors to the Field Museum in Chicago. Patterson's account of the leonine reign of terror, *The Man-Eaters of Tsavo,* was an international best-seller when published in 1907. Still in print, the book has made Tsavo's lions notorious. That annoys some scientists. "People don't want to give up on mythology," Dennis King told me one day. The zoologist has been working in Tsavo off and on for four years. "I am so sick of this man-eater business. Patterson made a helluva lot of money off that story, but Tsavo's lions are no more likely to turn man-eater than lions from elsewhere."

But tales of their savagery and wiliness don't all come from sensationalist authors looking to make a buck. Tsavo lions are generally larger than lions elsewhere, enabling them to take down the predominant prey animal in Tsavo, the Cape buffalo, one of the strongest, most aggressive animals of Earth. The buffalo don't give up easily: They often kill or severely injure an attacking lion, and a wounded lion might be more likely to turn to cattle and humans for food.

And other prey is less abundant in Tsavo than in other traditional lion haunts. A hungry lion is more likely to attack humans. Safari guides and Kenya Wildlife Service rangers tell of lions attacking Land Rovers, raiding camps, stalking tourists. Tsavo is a tough neighborhood, they say, and it breeds tougher lions.

But are they really tougher? And if so, is there any connection between their manelessness and their ferocity? An intriguing hypothesis was advanced two years ago by Gnoske and Peterhans: Tsavo lions may be similar to the unmaned cave lions of the Pleistocene. The Serengeti variety is among the most evolved of the species-the latest model, so to speak-while certain morphological differences in Tsavo lions (bigger bodies, smaller skulls, and maybe even lack of a mane) suggest that they are closer to the primitive ancestor of all lions. Craig and Peyton had serious doubts about this idea, but admitted that Tsavo lions pose a mystery to science.

631. The book *Man-Eaters of Tsavo* annoys some scientists because

(a) it revealed that Tsavo lions are ferocious.

(b) Patterson made a helluva lot of money from the book by sensationalism.

(c) it perpetuated the bad name Tsavo lions had.

(d) it narrated how two male Tsavo lions were killed.

632. The sentence which concludes the first paragraph, "Now they knew better", implies that:

(a) The two scientists were struck by wonder on seeing maneless lions for the first time.

(b) Though Craig was an expert on the Serengeti lion, now he also knew about the Tsavo lions.

(c) Earlier, Craig and West thought that amateur observers had been mistaken.

(d) Craig was now able to confirm that darkening of the noses as lions aged applied to Tsavo lions as well.

633. According to the passage, which of the following has NOT contributed to the popular image of Tsavo lions as savage creatures?

(a) Tsavo lions have been observed to bring down one of the strongest and most aggressive animals — the Cape buffalo.

(b) In contrast to the situation in traditional lion haunts, scarcity of non-buffalo prey in the Tsavo makes the Tsavo lions more aggressive.

(c) The Tsavo lion is considered to be less evolved than the Serengeti variety.

(d) Tsavo lions have been observed to attack vehicles as well as humans.

634. Which of the following, if true, would weaken the hypothesis advanced by Gnoske and Peterhans most?

(a) Craig and Peyton develop even more serious doubts about the idea that Tsavo lions are primitive.

(b) The maneless Tsavo East lions are shown to be closer to the cave lions.

(c) Pleistocene cave lions are shown to be far less violent than believed.

(d) The morphological variations in body and skull size between the cave and Tsavo lions are found to be insignificant.

Passage – 90

Throughout human history the leading causes of death have been infection and trauma. Modem medicine has scored significant victories against both, and the major causes of ill health and death are now the chronic degenerative diseases, such as coronary artery disease, arthritis, osteoporosis, Alzheimer's, macular degeneration, cataract and cancer. These have a long latency period before symptoms appear and a diagnosis is made. It follows that the majority of apparently healthy people are pre-ill.

But are these conditions inevitably degenerative? A truly preventive medicine that focused on the pre-ill, analysing the metabolic errors which lead to clinical illness, might be able to correct them before the first symptom. Genetic risk factors are known for all the chronic degenerative diseases, and are important to the individuals who possess them. At the population level, however, migration studies confirm that these illnesses are linked for the most part to lifestyle factors—exercise, smoking and nutrition. Nutrition is the easiest of these to change, and the most versatile tool for affecting the metabolic changes needed to tilt the balance away from disease.

Many national surveys reveal that malnutrition is common in developed countries. This is not the calorie and/or micronutrient deficiency associated with developing nations (Type A malnutrition); but multiple micronutrient depletion, usually combined with calorific balance or excess (Type B malnutrition). The incidence and severity of Type B malnutrition will be shown to be worse if newer micronutrient groups such as the essential fatty acids, xanthophylls and flavonoids are included in the surveys. Commonly ingested levels of these micronutrients seem to be far too low in many developed countries.

There is now considerable evidence that Type B malnutrition is a major cause of chronic degenerative diseases. If this is the case, then it is logical to treat such diseases not with drugs but with multiple micronutrient repletion, or 'pharmaco-nutrition'. This can take the form of pills and capsules-'nutraceuticals', or food formats known as 'functional foods'. This approach has been neglected hitherto because it is relatively unprofitable for drug companies-the products are hard to patent-and it is a strategy which does not sit easily with modem medical interventionism. Over the last 100 years, the drug industry has invested huge sums in developing a range of subtle and powerful drugs to treat the many diseases we are subject to. Medical training is couched in pharmaceutical terms and this approach has provided us with an exceptional range of therapeutic tools in the treatment of disease and in acute medical emergencies. However, the pharmaceutical model has also created an unhealthy dependency culture, in which relatively few of us accept responsibility for maintaining our own health. Instead, we have handed over this responsibility to health professionals who know very little about health maintenance, or disease prevention.

One problem for supporters of this argument is lack of the right kind of hard evidence. We have a wealth of epidemiological data linking dietary factors to health profiles / disease risks, and a great deal of information on mechanism: how food factors interact with our biochemistry. But almost all intervention studies with micronutrients, with the notable exception of the omega 3 fatty acids, have so far produced conflicting or negative results. In other words, our science appears to have no predictive value. Does this invalidate the science? Or are we simply asking the wrong questions?

Based on pharmaceutical thinking, most intervention studies have attempted to measure the impact of a single micronutrient on the incidence of disease. The classical approach says that if you give a compound formula to test subjects and obtain positive results, you cannot know which ingredient is exerting the benefit, so you must test each ingredient individually. But in the field of nutrition, this does not work. Each intervention on its own will hardly make enough difference to be measured. The best therapeutic response must therefore combine micronutrients to normalise our internal physiology. So do we need to analyse each individual's nutritional status and then tailor a formula specifically for him or her? While we do not have the resources to analyse millions of individual cases, there is no need to do so. The vast majority of people are consuming suboptimal amounts of most micronutrients, and most of the micronutrients concerned are very safe. Accordingly, a comprehensive and universal program of micronutrient support is probably the most cost-effective and safest way of improving

635. The author recommends micronutrient-repletion for large-scale treatment of chronic degenerative diseases because

(a) it is relatively easy to manage.

(b) micronutrient deficiency is the cause of these diseases.

(c) it can overcome genetic risk factors.

(d) it can compensate for other lifestyle factors.

636. Tailoring micronutrient-based treatment plans to suit individual deficiency profiles is not necessary because

(a) it very likely to give inconsistent or negative results.

(b) it is a classic pharmaceutical approach not suited to micronutrients.

(c) most people are consuming suboptimal amounts of safe-to-consume micronutrients.

(d) it is not cost effective to do so.

637. Type-B malnutrition is a serious concern in developed countries because

(a) developing countries mainly suffer from Type-A malnutrition.

(b) it is a major contributor to illness and death.

(c) pharmaceutical companies are not producing drugs to treat this condition.

(d) national surveys on malnutrition do not include newer micronutrient groups.

638. Why are a large number of apparently healthy people deemed pre-ill?

(a) They may have chronic degenerative diseases.

(b) They do not know their own genetic risk factors which predispose them to diseases.

(c) They suffer from Type-B malnutrition.

(d) There is a lengthy latency period associated with chronically degenerative diseases.

Passage – 91

A game of strategy, as currently conceived in game theory, is a situation in which two or more "players" make choices among available alternatives (moves). The totality of choices determines the outcomes of the game, and it is assumed that the rank order of preferences for the outcomes is different for different players. Thus the "interests" of the players are generally in conflict. Whether these interests are diametrically opposed or only partially opposed depends on the type of game.

Psychologically, most interesting situations arise when the interests of the players are partly coincident and partly opposed, because then one can postulate not only a conflict among the players but also inner conflicts within the players. Each is torn between a tendency to cooperate, so as to promote the common interests, and a tendency to compete, so as to enhance his own individual interests.

Internal conflicts are always psychologically interesting. What we vaguely call "interesting" psychology is in very great measure the psychology of inner conflict. Inner conflict is also held to be an important component of serious literature as distinguished from less serious genres. The classical tragedy, as well as the serious novel reveals the inner conflict of central figures. The superficial adventure story on the other hand, depicts only external conflict; that is, the threats to the person with whom the reader (or viewer)identifies stem in these stories exclusively from external obstacles and from the adversaries who create them. On the most primitive level this sort of external conflict is psychologically empty. In the fisticuffs between the protagonists of good and evil, no psychological problems are involved or, at any rate, none are depicted in juvenile representations of conflict.

The detective story, the "adult" analogue of a juvenile adventure tale, has at times been described as a glorification of intellectualized conflict. However, a great deal of the interest in the plots of these stories is sustained by withholding the unraveling of a solution to a problem. The effort of solving the problem is in itself not a conflict if the adversary (the unknown criminal) remains passive, like Nature, whose secrets the scientist supposedly unravels by deduction. If the adversary actively puts obstacles in the detective's path toward the solution, there is genuine conflict. But the conflict is psychologically interesting only to the extent that it contains irrational components such as a tactical error on the criminal's part or the detective's insight into some psychological quirk of the criminal or something of this sort. Conflict conducted in a perfectly rational manner is psychologically no more interesting than a standard Western. For example, Tic-tac-toe, played perfectly by both players, is completely devoid of psychological interest. Chess may be psychologically interesting but only to the extent that it is played not quite rationally. Played completely rationally, chess would not be different from Tic-tac-toe.

In short, a pure conflict of interest (what is called a zero-sum game) although it offers a wealth of interesting conceptual problems, is not interesting psychologically, except to the extent that its conduct departs from rational norms.

2005

639. According to the passage, internal conflicts are psychologically more interesting than external conflicts because

(a) internal conflicts, rather than external conflicts, form an important component of serious literature as distinguished from less serious genres.

(b) only juveniles or very few "adults" actually experience external conflict, while internal conflict is more widely prevalent in society.

(c) in situations of internal conflict, individuals experience a dilemma in resolving their own preferences for different outcomes.

(d) there are no threats to the reader (or viewer) in case of external conflicts.

640. Which, according to the author, would qualify as interesting psychology?

(a) A statistician's dilemma over choosing the best method to solve an optimization problem.

(b) A chess player's predicament over adopting a defensive strategy against an aggressive opponent.

(c) A mountaineer's choice of the best path to Mt. Everest from the base camp.

(d) A finance manager's quandary over the best way of raising money from the market.

641. According to the passage, which of the following options about the application of game theory to a conflict-of-interest situation is true?

(a) Assuming that the rank order of preferences for options is different for different players.

(b) Accepting that the interests of different players are often in conflict.

(c) Not assuming that the interests are in complete disagreement.

(d) All of the above.

642. The problem solving process of a scientist is different from that of a detective because

(a) scientists study inanimate objects, while detectives deal with living criminals or law offenders.

(b) scientists study known objects, while detectives have to deal with unknown criminals or law offenders.

(c) scientists study phenomena that are not actively altered, while detectives deal with phenomena that have been deliberately influenced to mislead.

(d) scientists study psychologically interesting phenomena, while detectives deal with "adult" analogues of juvenile adventure tales.

Passage – 92

Crinoline and croquet are out. As yet, no political activists have thrown themselves in front of the royal horse on Derby Day. Even so, some historians can spot the parallels. It is a time of rapid technological change. It is a period when the dominance of the world's superpower is coming under threat. It is an epoch when prosperity masks underlying economic strain. And, crucially, it is a time when policy-makers are confident that all is for the best in the best of all possible worlds. Welcome to the Edwardian Summer of the second age of globalisation.

Spare a moment to take stock of what's been happening in the past few months. Let's start with the oil price, which has rocketed to more than \$65 a barrel, more than double its level 18 months ago. The accepted wisdom is that we shouldn't worry our little heads about that, because the incentives are there for business to build new production and refining capacity, which will effortlessly bring demand and supply back into balance and bring crude prices back to \$25 a barrel. As Tommy Copper used to say, 'just like that'.

Then there is the result of the French referendum on the European Constitution, seen as thick-headed luddites railing vainly against the modern world. What the French needed to realize, the argument went, was that there was no alternative to the reforms that would make the country more flexible, more competitive, more dynamic. Just the sort of reforms that allowed Gate Gourmet to sack hundreds of its staff at Heathrow after the sort of ultimatum that used to be handed out by Victorian mill owners. An alternative way of looking at the French "non" is that our neighbours translate "flexibility" as "you're fired".

Finally, take a squint at the United States. Just like Britian a century ago, a period of unquestioned superiority is drawing to a close. China is still a long way from matching America's wealth, but it is growing at a stupendous rate and economic strength brings geo-political clout. Already, there is evidence of a new scramble for Africa as Washington and Beijing compete for oil stocks. Moreover, beneath the surface of the US economy, all is not well. Growth looks healthy enough, but the competition from China and elsewhere has meant the world's biggest economy now imports far more than it exports. The US is living beyond its means, but in this time of studied complacency a current account deficit worth 6 perfect of gross domestic product is seen as a sign of strength, not weakness.

In this new Edwardian summer, comfort is taken from the fact that dearer oil has not had the savage inflationary consequences of 1973-1974, when a fourfold increase in the cost of crude brought an abrupt end to a postwar boom that had gone on uninterrupted for a quarter of a century. True, the cost of living has been affected by higher transport costs, but we are talking of inflation at 2.3 per cent and not 27 per cent. Yet the idea that higher oil prices are of little consequence is fanciful. If people are paying more to fill up their cars it leaves them with less to spend on everything else, but there is a reluctance to consume less. In the 1970s unions were strong and able to negotiate large, compensatory pay deals that served to intensify inflationary pressure. In 2005, that avenue is pretty much closed off, but the abolition of all the controls on credit that existed in the 1970s means that households are invited to borrow more rather than consume less. The knock-on effects of higher oil prices are thus felt in different ways – through high levels of indebtedness, in inflated asset prices, and in balance of payments deficits.

There are those who point out, rightly, that modern industrial capitalism has proved mightily resilient these past 250 years, and that a sign of the enduring strength of the system has been the way it apparently shrugged off everything – a stock market crash, 9/11, rising oil prices – that have been thrown at it in the half decade since the millennium. Even so, there are at least three reasons for concern. First, we have been here before. In terms of political economy, the first era of globalisation mirrored our own. There was a belief in unfettered capital flows, in free migration. Eventually, though, there was a backlash, manifested in a struggle between free traders and protectionists, and in rising labour militancy.

Second, the world is traditionally as its most fragile at times when the global balance of power is in flux. By the end of the nineteenth century, Britain's role as the hegemonic power was being challenged by the rise of the United States, Germany, and Japan while the Ottoman and Hapsburg empires were clearly in rapid decline. Looking ahead from

2005, it is clear that over the next two or three decades, both China and India – which together account for half the world's population – will flex their muscles.

Finally, there is the question of what rising oil prices tell us. The emergence of China and India means global demand for crude is likely to remain high a t a time when experts say production is about to top out. If supply constraints start to bite, any decline in the prices are likely to be short-term cyclical affairs punctuating a long upward trend.

643. By the expression 'Edwardian Summer', the author refers to a period in which there is

(a) unparalleled luxury and opulence.

(b) a sense of complacency among people because of all-round prosperity.

(c) a culmination of all-round economic prosperity.

(d) an imminent danger lurking behind economic prosperity.

644. What, according to the author, has resulted in a widespread belief in the resilence of modern capitalism?

(a) Growth in the economies of Western countries despite shocks in the form of increase in levels of indebtedness and inflated asset prices.

(b) Increase in the prosperity of Western countries and China despite rising oil prices.

(c) Continued growth of Western economies despite a rise in terrorism, an increase in oil prices and other similar shocks.

(d) The success of continued reforms aimed at making Western economies more dynamic, competitive and efficient.

645. Which of the following best represents the key argument made by the author?

(a) The rise in oil prices, the flux in the global balance of power and historical precedents should make us question our belief that the global economic prosperity would continue.

(b) The belief that modern industrial capitalism is highly resilient and capable of overcoming shocks will be belied soon.

(c) Widespread prosperity leads to neglect of early signs of underlying economic weakness, manifested in higher oil prices and a flux in the global balance of power.

(d) A crisis is imminent in the West given the growth of countries like China and India and the increase in oil prices.

646. What can be inferred about the author's view when he states 'As Tommy Cooper used to say "just like that"?

(a) Industry has incentives to build new production and refining capacity and therefore oil prices would reduce.

(b) There would be a correction in the price levels of oil once new production capacity is added.

(c) The decline in oil prices is likely to be short-term in nature.

(d) It is not necessary that oil prices would go down to earlier levels.

Passage – 93

While complex in the extreme, Derrida's work has proven to be a particularly influential approach to the analysis of the ways in which language structures our understanding of ourselves and the world we inhabit, an approach he termed *deconstruction*. In its simplest formulation, deconstruction can be taken to refer to a methodological strategy which seeks to uncover layers of hidden meaning in a text that have been denied or suppressed. The term 'text', in this respect, does not refer simply to a written form of communication, however. Rather, texts are something we all produce and reproduce constantly in our every day social relations, be they spoken, written or embedded in the construction of material artifacts. At the heart of Derrida's deconstructive approach is his critique of what he perceives to be the totalitarian impulse of the Enlightenment pursuit to bring all that exists in the world under the domain of representative language, a pursuit he refers to as *logocentrism*. Logocentrism is the search for a rational language that is able to know and represent the world and all its aspects perfectly and accurately. Its totalitarian dimension, for Derrida at least, lies primarily in its tendency to marginalize or dismiss all that does not neatly comply with its particular linguistic representations, a tendency that, throughout history, has all too frequently been manifested in the form of authoritarian institutions. Thus logocentrism has, in its search for the truth of absolute representation, subsumed difference and oppressed that which it designates as its alien 'other'. For Derrida, western civilization has been built upon such a systematic assault on alien cultures and ways of life, typically in the name of reason and progress.

In response to logocentrism, deconstruction posits the idea that the mechanism by which this process of marginalization and the ordering of truth occurs is through establishing systems of binary opposition. Oppositional linguistic dualisms, such as rational/irrational, culture/nature and good/bad are not, however, construed as equal partners as they are in, say, the semiological structuralism of Saussure. Rather, they exist, for Derrida, in a series of hierarchical relationships with the first term normally occupying a superior position. Derrida defines the relationship between such oppositional terms using the neologism *différance*. This refers to the realization that in any statement, oppositional terms differ from each other (for instance, the difference between rationality and irrationality is constructed through oppositional usage), and at the same time, a hierarchical relationship is maintained by the deference of one term to the other (in the positing of rationality over irrationality, for instance). It is this latter point which is perhaps the key to understanding Derrida's approach to deconstruction.

For the fact at any given time one term must defer to its oppositional 'other', means that the two terms are constantly in a state of interdependence. The presence of one is dependent upon the absence or 'absent-presence' of the 'other', such as in the case of good and evil, whereby to understand the nature of one, we must constantly relate it to the absent term in order to grasp its meaning. That is, to do good, we must understand that our act is not evil, for without that comparison the term becomes meaningless. Put simply, deconstruction represents an attempt to demonstrate the absent-presence of this oppositional 'other', to show that what we say or write is in itself not expressive simply of what is present, but also of what is absent. Thus, deconstruction seeks to reveal the interdependence of apparently dichotomous terms and their meanings relative to their textual context; that is, within the linguistic power relations which structure dichotomous terms hierarchically. In Derrida's own words, a deconstructive reading "must always aim at a certain relationship, unperceived by the writer, between what he commands and what he does not command of the patterns of a language that he uses. ...[It] attempts to make the not-seen accessible to sight."

Meaning, then, is never fixed or stable, whatever the intention of the author of a text. For Derrida, language is a system of relations that are dynamic, in that all meanings we ascribe to the world are dependent not only on what we believe to be present but also on what is absent. Thus, any act of interpretation must refer not only to what the author of a text intends, but also to what is absent from his or her intention. This insight leads, once again, to Derrida's further rejection of the idea of the definitive authority of the intentional agent or subject. The subject is decentred; it is conceived as the outcome of relations of *différance*. As author of its own biography, the subject thus becomes the ideological fiction of modernity and its logocentric philosophy, one that depends upon the formation of hierarchical dualisms, which repress and deny the presence of the absent 'other'. No meaning can, therefore, even be definitive, but is merely an outcome of a particular interpretation.

647. According to the passage, Derrida believes that:

(a) Reality can be construed only through the use of rational analysis.

(b) Language limits our construction of reality.

(c) A universal language will facilitate a common understanding of reality.

(d) We need to uncover the hidden meaning in a system of relations expressed by language.

648. To Derrida, 'logocentrism' does not imply:

(a) A totalitarian impulse.

(b) A domain of representative language.

(c) Interdependence of the meanings of dichotomous terms.

(d) A strategy that seeks to suppress hidden meanings in a text.

649. According to the passage, Derrida believes that the system of binary opposition

(a) represents a prioritization or hierarchy.

(b) reconciles contradictions and dualities.

(c) weakens the process of marginalization and ordering of truth.

(d) deconstructs reality.

650. Derrida rejects the idea of 'definitive authority of the subject' because

(a) interpretation of the text may not make the unseen visible.

(b) the meaning of the text is based on binary opposites.

(c) the implicit power relationship is often ignored.

(d) any act of interpretation must refer to what the author intends.

Passage – 94

Our propensity to look out for regularities, and to impose laws upon nature, leads to the psychological phenomenon of dogmatic thinking or, more generally, dogmatic behaviour: we expect regularities everywhere and attempt to find them even where there are none; events which do not yield to these attempts we are inclined to treat as a kind of 'background noise'; and we stick to our expectations even when they are inadequate and we ought to accept defeat. This dogmatism is to some extent necessary. It is demanded by a situation which can only be dealt with by forcing our conjectures upon the world.

Moreover, this dogmatism allows us to approach a good theory in stages, by way of approximations: if we accept defeat too easily, we may prevent ourselves from finding that we were very nearly right.

It is clear that this dogmatic attitude, which makes us stick to our first impressions, is indicative of a strong belief; while a critical attitude, which is ready to modify its tenets, which admits doubt and demands tests, is indicative of a weaker belief. Now according to Hume's theory, and to the popular theory, the strength of a belief should be a product of repetition; thus it should always grow with experience, and always be greater in less primitive persons. But dogmatic thinking, an uncontrolled wish to impose regularities, a manifest pleasure in rites and in repetition as such, is characteristic of primitives and children; and increasing experience and maturity sometimes create an attitude of caution and criticism rather than of dogmatism.

My logical criticism of Hume's psychological theory, and the considerations connected with it, may seem a little removed from the field of the philosophy of science. But the distinction between dogmatic and critical thinking, or the dogmatic and the critical attitude, brings us right back to our central problem. For the dogmatic attitude is clearly related to the tendency to verify our laws and schemata by seeking to apply them and to confirm them, even to the point of neglecting refutations, whereas the critical attitude is one of readiness to change them — to test them; to refute them; to falsify them, if possible. This suggests that we may identify the critical attitude with the scientific attitude, and the dogmatic attitude with the one which we have described as pseudo-scientific. It further suggests that genetically speaking the pseudo-scientific attitude is more primitive than, and prior to, the scientific attitude: that it is a pre-scientific attitude. And this primitivity or priority also has its logical aspect. For the critical attitude is not so much opposed to the dogmatic attitude as super-imposed upon it: criticism must be directed against existing and influential beliefs in need of critical revision — in other words, dogmatic beliefs. A critical attitude needs for its raw material, as it were, theories or beliefs which are held more or less dogmatically.

Thus, science must begin with myths, and with the criticism of myths; neither with the collection of observations, nor with the invention of experiments, but with the critical discussion of myths, and of magical techniques and practices. The scientific tradition is distinguished from the pre-scientific tradition in having two layers. Like the latter, it passes on its theories; but it also passes on a critical attitude towards them. The theories are passed on, not as dogmas, but rather with the challenge to discuss them and improve upon them.

The critical attitude, the tradition of free discussion of theories with the aim of discovering their weak spots so that they may be improved upon, is the attitude of reasonableness, of rationality. From the point of view here developed, all laws, all theories, remain essentially tentative, or conjectural, or hypothetical, even when we feel unable to doubt them any longer. Before a theory has been refuted we can never know in what way it may have to be modified.

2006

651. In the context of science, according to the passage, the interaction of dogmatic beliefs and critical attitude can be best described as:

(a) A duel between two warriors in which one has to die.

(b) The effect of a chisel on a marble stone while making a sculpture.

(c) The feedshare (natural gas) in fertilizer industry being transformed into fertilizers.

(d) A predator killing its prey.

(e) The effect of fertilizers on a sapling.

652. According to the passage, the role of a dogmatic attitude or dogmatic behaviour in the development of science is

(a) critical and important, as, without it, initial hypotheses or conjectures can never be made.

(b) positive, as conjectures arising out of our dogmatic attitude become science.

(c) negative, as it leads to pseudo-science.

(d) neutral, as the development of science is essentially because of our critical attitude.

(e) inferior to critical attitude, as a critical attitude leads to the attitude of reasonableness and rationality.

653. Dogmatic behaviour, in this passage, has been associated with primitives and children. Which of the following best describes the reason why the author compares primitives with children?

(a) Primitives are people who are not educated, and hence can be compared with children, who have not yet been through school.

(b) Primitives are people who, though not modern, are as innocent as children.

(c) Primitives are people without a critical attitude, just as children are.

(d) Primitives are people in the early stages of human evolution; similarly, children are in the early stages of their lives.

(e) Primitives are people who are not civilized enough, just as children are not.

654. Which of the following statements best supports the argument in the passage that a critical attitude leads to a weaker belief than a dogmatic attitude does?

(a) A critical attitude implies endless questioning, and, therefore, it cannot lead to strong beliefs.

(b) A critical attitude, by definition, is centred on an analysis of anomalies and "noise".

(c) A critical attitude leads to questioning everything, and in the process generates "noise" without any conviction.

(d) A critical attitude is antithetical to conviction, which is required for strong beliefs.

(e) A critical attitude leads to questioning and to tentative hypotheses.

655. According to the passage, which of the following statements best describes the difference between science and pseudo-science?

(a) Scientific theories or hypotheses are tentatively true whereas pseudo-sciences are always true.

(b) Scientific laws and theories are permanent and immutable whereas pseudo-sciences are contingent on the prevalent mode of thinking in a society.

(c) Science always allows the possibility of rejecting a theory or hypothesis, whereas pseudo-sciences seek to validate their ideas or theories.

(d) Science focuses on anomalies and exceptions so that fundamental truths can be uncovered, whereas pseudo-sciences focus mainly on general truths.

(e) Science progresses by collection of observations or by experimentation, whereas pseudo-sciences do not worry about observations and experiments.

Passage – 95

Fifteen years after communism was officially pronounced dead, its spectre seems once again to be haunting Europe. Last month, the Council of Europe's parliamentary assembly voted to condemn the "crimes of totalitarian communist regimes," linking them with Nazism and complaining that communist parties are still "legal and active in some countries." Now Goran Lindblad, the conservative Swedish MP behind the resolution, wants to go further. Demands that European Ministers launch a continent-wide anti-communist campaign — including school textbook revisions, official memorial days, and museums — only narrowly missed the necessary two-thirds majority. Mr. Lindblad pledged to bring the wider plans back to the Council of Europe in the coming months.

He has chosen a good year for his ideological offensive: this is the 50th anniversary of Nikita Khrushchev's denunciation of Josef Stalin and the subsequent Hungarian uprising, which will doubtless be the cue for further excoriation of the communist record. Paradoxically, given that there is no communist government left in Europe outside Moldova, the attacks have if anything, become more extreme as time has gone on. A clue as to why that might be can be found in the rambling report by Mr. Lindblad that led to the Council of Europe declaration. Blaming class struggle and public ownership, he explained "different elements of communist ideology such as equality or social justice still seduce many" and "a sort of nostalgia for communism is still alive." Perhaps the real problem for Mr. Lindblad and his right-wing allies in Eastern Europe is that communism is not dead enough — and they will only be content when they have driven a stake through its heart.

The fashionable attempt to equate communism and Nazism is in reality a moral and historical nonsense. Despite the cruelties of the Stalin terror, there was no Soviet Treblinka or Sorbibor, no extermination camps built to murder millions. Nor did the Soviet Union launch the most devastating war in history at a cost of more than 50 million lives — in fact it played the decisive role in the defeat of the German war machine. Mr. Lindblad and the Council of Europe adopt as fact the wildest estimates of those "killed by communist regimes" (mostly in famines) from the fiercely contested Black Book of Communism, which also underplays the number of deaths attributable to Hitler. But, in any case, none of this explains why anyone might be nostalgic in former communist states, now enjoying the delights of capitalist restoration. The dominant account gives no sense of how communist regimes renewed themselves after 1956 or why Western leaders feared they might overtake the capitalist world well into the 1960s. For all its brutalities and failures, communism in the Soviet Union, Eastern Europe, and elsewhere delivered rapid industrialization, mass education, job security, and huge advances in social and gender equality. Its existence helped to drive up welfare standards in the West, and provided a powerful counterweight to Western global domination.

It would be easier to take the Council of Europe's condemnation of communist state crimes seriously if it had also seen fit to denounce the far bloodier record of European colonialism — which only finally came to an end in the 1970s. This was a system of racist despotism, which dominated the globe in Stalin's time. And while there is precious little connection between the ideas of fascism and communism, there is an intimate link between colonialism and Nazism. The terms lebensraum and konzentrationslager were both first used by the German colonial regime in south-west Africa (now Namibia), which committed genocide against the Herero and Nama peoples and bequeathed its ideas and personnel directly to the Nazi party.

Around 10 million Congolese died as a result of Belgian forced labour and mass murder in the early twentieth century; tens of millions perished in avoidable or enforced famines in British-ruled India; up to a million Algerians died in their war for independence, while controversy now rages in France about a new law requiring teachers to put a positive spin on colonial history. Comparable atrocities were carried out by all European colonialists, but not a word of condemnation from the Council of Europe. Presumably, European lives count for more.

No major twentieth century political tradition is without blood on its hands, but battles over history are more about the future than the past. Part of the current enthusiasm in official Western circles for dancing on the grave of communism is no doubt about relations with today's Russia and China. But it also reflects a determination to prove there is no alternative to the new global capitalist order — and that any attempt to find one is bound to lead to suffering. With the new imperialism now being resisted in the Muslim world and Latin America, growing international demands for social justice and ever greater doubts about whether the environmental crisis can be solved within the existing economic system, the pressure for alternatives will increase.

656. Among all the apprehensions that Mr. Goran Lindblad expresses against communism, which one gets admitted, although indirectly, by the author?

(a) There is nostalgia for communist ideology even if communism has been abandoned by most European nations.

(b) Notions of social justice inherent in communist ideology appeal to critics of existing systems.

(c) Communist regimes were totalitarian and marked by brutalities and large scale violence.

(d) The existing economic order is wrongly viewed as imperialistic by proponents of communism.

(e) Communist ideology is faulted because communist regimes resulted in economic failures.

657. What, according to the author, is the real reason for a renewed attack against communism?

(a) Disguising the unintended consequences of the current economic order such as social injustice and environmental crisis.

(b) Idealising the existing ideology of global capitalism.

(c) Making communism a generic representative of all historical atrocities, especially those perpetrated by the European imperialists.

(d) Communism still survives, in bits and pieces, in the minds and hearts of people.

(e) Renewal of some communist regimes has led to the apprehension that communist nations might overtake the capitalists.

658. The author cites examples of atrocities perpetrated by European colonial regimes in order to

(a) compare the atrocities committed by colonial regimes with those of communist regimes.

(b) prove that the atrocities committed by colonial regimes were more than those of communist regimes.

(c) prove that, ideologically, communism was much better than colonialism and Nazism.

(d) neutralise the arguments of Mr. Lindblad and to point out that the atrocities committed by colonial regimes were more than those of communist regimes.

(e) neutralise the arguments of Mr. Lindblad and to argue that one needs to go beyond and look at the motives of these regimes.

659. Why, according to the author, is Nazism closer to colonialism than it is to communism?

(a) Both colonialism and Nazism were examples of tyranny of one race over another.

(b) The genocides committed by the colonial and the Nazi regimes were of similar magnitude.

(c) Several ideas of the Nazi regime were directly imported from colonial regimes.

(d) Both colonialism and Nazism are based on the principles of imperialism.

(e) While communism was never limited to Europe, both the Nazis and the colonialists originated in Europe.

660. Which of the following cannot be inferred as a compelling reason for the silence of the Council of Europe on colonial atrocities?

(a) The Council of Europe being dominated by erstwhile colonialists.

(b) Generating support for condemning communist ideology.

(c) Unwillingness to antagonize allies by raking up an embarrassing past.

(d) Greater value seemingly placed on European lives.

(e) Portraying both communism and Nazism as ideologies to be condemned.

Passage – 96

My aim is to present a conception of justice which generalizes and carries to a higher level of abstraction the familiar theory of the social contract. In order to do this we are not to think of the original contract as one to enter a particular society or to set up a particular form of government. Rather, the idea is that the principles of justice for the basic structure of society are the object of the original agreement. They are the principles that free and rational persons concerned to further their own interests would accept in an initial position of equality. These principles are to regulate all further agreements; they specify the kinds of social cooperation that can be entered into and the forms of government that can be established. This way of regarding the principles of justice, I shall call justice as fairness. Thus, we are to imagine that those who engage in social cooperation choose together, in one joint act, the principles which are to assign basic rights and duties and to determine the division of social benefits. Just as each person must decide by rational reflection what constitutes his good, that is, the system of ends which it is rational for him to pursue, so a group of persons must decide once and for all what is to count among them as just and unjust. The choice which rational men would make in this hypothetical situation of equal liberty determines the principles of justice.

In 'justice as fairness', the original position is not an actual historical state of affairs. It is understood as a purely hypothetical situation characterized so as to lead to a certain conception of justice. Among the essential features of this situation is that no one knows his place in society, his class position or social status, nor does anyone know his fortune in the distribution of natural assets and abilities, his intelligence, strength, and the like. I shall even assume that the parties do not know their conceptions of the good or their special psychological propensities. The principles of justice are chosen behind a veil of ignorance. This ensures that no one is advantaged or disadvantaged in the choice of principles by the outcome of natural chance or the contingency of social circumstances. Since all are similarly situated and no one is able to design principles to favor his particular condition, the principles of justice are the result of a fair agreement or bargain.

Justice as fairness begins with one of the most general of all choices which persons might make together, namely, with the choice of the first principles of a conception of justice which is to regulate all subsequent criticism and reform of institutions. Then, having chosen a conception of justice, we can suppose that they are to choose a constitution and a legislature to enact laws, and so on, all in accordance with the principles of justice initially agreed upon. Our social situation is just if it is such that by this sequence of hypothetical agreements we would have contracted into the general system of rules which defines it. Moreover, assuming that the original position does determine a set of principles, it will then be true that whenever social institutions satisfy these principles, those engaged in them can say to one another that they are cooperating on terms to which they would agree if they were free and equal persons whose relations with respect to one another were fair. They could all view their arrangements as meeting the stipulations which they would acknowledge in an initial situation that embodies widely accepted and reasonable constraints on the choice of principles. The general recognition of this fact would provide the basis for a public acceptance of the corresponding principles of justice. No society can, of course, be a scheme of cooperation which men enter voluntarily in a literal sense; each person finds himself placed at birth in some particular position in some particular society, and the nature of this position materially affects his life prospects. Yet a society satisfying the principles of justice as fairness comes as close as a society can to being a voluntary scheme, for it meets the principles which free and equal persons would assent to under circumstances that are fair.

661. A just society, as conceptualized in the passage, can be best described as:

(a) A Utopia in which everyone is equal and no one enjoys any privilege based on their existing positions and powers.

(b) A hypothetical society in which people agree upon principles of justice which are fair.

(c) A society in which principles of justice are not based on the existing positions and powers of the individuals.

(d) A society in which principles of justice are fair to all.

(e) A hypothetical society in which principles of justice are not based on the existing positions and powers of the individuals.

662. The original agreement or original position in the passage has been used by the author as:

(a) A hypothetical situation conceived to derive principles of justice which are not influenced by position, status and condition of individuals in the society.

(b) A hypothetical situation in which every individual is equal and no individual enjoys any privilege based on the existing positions and powers.

(c) A hypothetical situation to ensure fairness of agreements among individuals in society.

(d) An imagined situation in which principles of justice would have to be fair.

(e) An imagined situation in which fairness is the objective of the principles of justice to ensure that no individual enjoys any privilege based on the existing positions and powers.

663. Which of the following best illustrates the situation that is equivalent to choosing 'the principles of justice' behind a 'veil of ignorance'?

(a) The principles of justice are chosen by businessmen, who are marooned on an uninhabited island after a shipwreck, but have some possibility of returning.

(b) The principles of justice are chosen by a group of school children whose capabilities are yet to develop.

(c) The principles of justice are chosen by businessmen, who are marooned on an uninhabited island after a shipwreck and have no possibility of returning.

(d) The principles of justice are chosen assuming that such principles will govern the lives of the rule makers only in their next birth if the rule makers agree that they will be born again.

(e) The principles of justice are chosen by potential immigrants who are unaware of the resources necessary to succeed in a foreign country.

664. Why, according to the passage, do principles of justice need to be based on an original agreement?

(a) Social institutions and laws can be considered fair only if they conform to principles of justice.

(b) Social institutions and laws can be fair only if they are consistent with the principles of justice as initially agreed upon.

(c) Social institutions and laws need to be fair in order to be just.

(d) Social institutions and laws evolve fairly only if they are consistent with the principles of justice as initially agreed upon.

(e) Social institutions and laws conform to the principles of justice as initially agreed upon.

665. Which of the following situations best represents the idea of justice as fairness, as argued in the passage?

(a) All individuals are paid equally for the work they do.

(b) Everyone is assigned some work for his or her livelihood.

(c) All acts of theft are penalized equally.

(d) All children are provided free education in similar schools.

(e) All individuals are provided a fixed sum of money to take care of their health.

Passage – 97

Human Biology does nothing to structure human society: age may enfeeble us all, but cultures vary considerably in the prestige and power they accord to the elderly. Giving birth is a necessary condition for being a mother, but it is not sufficient. We expect mothers to behave in maternal ways and to display appropriately maternal sentiments. We prescribe a clutch of norms or rules that govern the *role* of a mother. That the social role is independent of the biological base can be demonstrated by going back three sentences. (giving birth is certainly not sufficient to be a mother but, as adoption and fostering show, it is not even necessary!

The fine detail of what is expected of a mother or a father or a dutiful son differs from culture to culture, but everywhere behaviour is coordinated by the *reciprocal* nature of roles. Husbands and wives, parents and children, employers and employees, waiters and customers, teachers and pupils, warlords and followers: each makes sense only in its relation to the other. The term 'role' is an appropriate one. because the metaphor of an actor in a play neatly expresses the rule-governed nature or scripted nature of much of social life and the sense that society is a joint production. Social life occurs only because people play their parts (and that is as true for war and conflicts as for peace and love) and those parts make sense only in the context of the overall show. The drama metaphor also reminds us of the artistic licence available to the players. We can play a part straight or, as the following from J.P. Sartre conveys, we can ham it up.

Let us consider this waiter in the café. His movement is quick and forward, a little too precise, a little too rapid. He comes towards the patrons with a step a little too quick. He bends forward a little too eagerly: his voice, his eyes express an interest a little too solicitous for the order of the customer. Finally there he returns, trying to imitate in his walk the inflexible stiffness of some kind of automation while carrying his tray with the recklessness of a tightropewalker .....All his behaviour seems to us a game....But what is he playing? We need not watch long before we can explain it: he is playing at being a waiter in a café.

The American sociologist Frying Goffman built an influential body of social analysis on elaborations of the metaphor of social life as drama. Perhaps his most telling point was that it is only through acting out a part that we express character. It is not enough to be evil or virtuous: we have to be seen to be evil or virtuous.

There is distinction between the roles we play and some underlying self. Here we might note that some roles are more absorbing than others. We would not be surprised by the waitress who plays the part in such a way as to signal to us that she is much more than her occupation. We would be surprised and offended by the father who played his part 'tongue in cheek'. Some roles are broader and more far-reaching than others. Describing someone as a clergyman or faith healer would say far more about that person than describing someone as a bus driver.

2007

666. What is the thematic highlight of the passage?

(a) In the absence of strong biological linkages, reciprocal roles provide the mechanism for coordinating human behaviour.

(b) In the absence of reciprocal roles, biological linkages provide the mechanism for coordinating human behaviour.

(c) Human behaviour is independent of biological linkages and reciprocal roles.

(d) Human behaviour depends on biological linkages and reciprocal roles.

(e) Reciprocal roles determine normative human behaviour in society.

667. Which of the following would have been true if biological linkages structured human society?

(a) The role of mother would have been defined through her reciprocal relationship with her children.

(b) We would not have been offended by the father playing his role 'tongue in cheek'.

(c) Women would have adopted and fostered children rather than giving birth to them.

(d) Even if warlords were physically weaker than their followers, they would still dominate them.

(e) Waiters would have stronger motivation to serve their customers.

668. It has been claimed in the passage that "some roles are more absorbing than others". According to the passage, which of the following seem(s) appropriate reason (s) for such a claim?

A. Some roles carry great expectations from the society preventing manifestation of the true self.

B. Society ascribes so much importance to some roles that the conception of self may get aligned with the roles being performed.

C. Some roles require development of skill and expertise leaving little time for manifestation of self.

(a) A only (b) B only

(c) C only (d) A & B

(e) B & C

Passage – 98

Every civilized society lives and thrives on a silent but profound agreement as to what is to be accepted as the valid mould of experience. Civilization is a complex system of dams, dykes. and canals warding off, directing, and articulating the influx of the surrounding fluid element: a fertile fenland, elaborately drained and protected from the high tides of chaotic, unexercised, and inarticulate experience. In such a culture, stable and sure of itself within the frontiers of 'naturalized' experience, the arts wield their creative power not so much in width as in depth. They do not create new experience, but deepen and purify the old. Their works do not differ from one another like a new horizon from a new horizon, but like a madonna from a madonna.

The periods of art which are most vigorous in creative passion seem to occur when the established pattern of experience loosens its rigidity without as yet losing its force. Such a period was the Renaissance, and Shakespeare its poetic consummation. Then it was as though the discipline of the old order gave depth to the excitement of the breaking away, the depth of job and tragedy, of incomparable conquests and irredeemable losses. Adventurers of experience set out as though in lifeboats to rescue and bring back to the shore treasures of knowing and feeling which the old order had left floating on the high seas. The works of the early Renaissance and the poetry of Shakespeare vibrate with the compassion for live experience in danger of dying from exposure and neglect. In this compassion was the creative genius of the age. Yet, it was a genius of courage, not of desperate audacity. For, however elusively, it still knew of harbours and anchors, of homes to which to return, and of barns in which to store the harvest. The exploring spirit of art was in the depths of its consciousness still aware of a scheme of things into which to fit its exploits and creations.

But the more this scheme of things loses its stability, the more boundless and uncharted appears the ocean of potential exploration. In the blank confusion of infinite potentialities flotsam of significance gets attached to jetsam of experience: for everything is sea, everything is at sea-

...The sea is all about us;

The sea is the land's edge also, the granite

Into which it reaches, the beaches where it tosses

Its hints of earlier and other creation...

– and Rilke tells a story in which, as in T.S. Eliot's poem, it is again the sea and the distance of 'other creation' that becomes the image of the poet's reality. A rowing boat sets out on a difficult passage. The oarsmen labour in exact rhythm. There is no sign yet of the destination. Suddenly a man. seemingly idle, breaks out into song. And if the labour of the oarsmen meaninglessly defeats the real resistance of the real waves, it is the idle single who magically conquers the despair of apparent aimlessness. While the people next to him try to come to grips with the element that is next to them, his voice seems to bind the boat to the farthest distance so that the farthest distance draws it towards itself. 'I don't know why and how,' is Rilke's conclusion, 'but suddenly I understood the situation of the poet, his place and function in this age. It does not matter if one denies him every place — except this one. There one must tolerate him.'

669. In the passage, the expression "like a madonna from a madonna" alludes to

(a) The difference arising as a consequence of artistic license.

(b) The difference between two artistic interpretations.

(c) The difference between 'life' and 'interpretation of life'.

(d) The difference between 'width' and 'depth' of creative power.

(e) The difference between the legendary character and the modern day singer.

670. The sea and 'other creation' leads Rilke to

(a) Define the place of the poet in his culture.

(b) Reflect on the role of the oarsman and the singer.

(c) Muse on artistic labour and its aimlessness.

(d) Understand the elements that one has to deal with.

(e) Delve into natural experience and real waves.

671. According to the passage, the term "adventurers of experience" refers to

(a) Poets and artists who are driven by courage.

(b) Poets and artists who create their own genre.

(c) Poets and artists of the Renaissance.

(d) Poets and artists who revitalize and enrich the past for us.

(e) Poets and artists who delve in flotsam and jetsam in sea.

Passage – 99

To discover the relation between rules, paradigms, and normal science, consider first how the historian isolates the particular loci of commitment that have been described as accepted rules. Close historical investigation of a given specialty at a given time discloses a set of recurrent and quasi-standard illustrations of various theories in their conceptual, observational, and instrumental applications. These are the community's paradigms, revealed in its textbooks, lectures, and laboratory exercises. By studying them and by practicing with them, the members of the corresponding community learn their trade. The historian, of course, will discover in addition a penumbral area occupied by achievements whose status is still in doubt, but the core of solved problems and techniques will usually be clear. Despite occasional ambiguities, the paradigms of a mature scientific community can be determined with relative ease.

That demands a second step and one of a somewhat different kind. When undertaking it, the historian must compare the community's paradigms with each other and with its current research reports. In doing so, his object is to discover what isolable elements, explicit or implicit, the members of that community may have abstracted from their more global paradigms and deploy it as rules in their research. Anyone who has attempted to describe or analyze the evolution of a particular scientific tradition will necessarily have sought accepted principles and rules of this sort. Almost certainly, he will have met with at least partial success. But, if his experience has been at all like my own, he will have found the search for rules both more difficult and less satisfying than the search for paradigms. Some of the generalizations he employs to describe the community's shared beliefs will present more problems. Others, however, will seem a shade too strong. Phrased in just that way, or in any other way he can imagine, they would almost certainly have been rejected by some members of the group he studies. Nevertheless, if the coherence of the research tradition is to be understood in terms of rules, some specification of common ground in the corresponding area is needed. As a result, the search for a body of rules competent to constitute a given normal research tradition becomes a source of continual and deep frustration.

Recognizing that frustration, however, makes it possible to diagnose its source. Scientists can agree that a Newton, Lavoisier, Maxwell, or Einstein has produced an apparently permanent solution to a group of outstanding problems and still disagree, sometimes without being aware of it, about the particular abstract characteristics that make those solutions permanent. They can, that is, agree in their identification of a paradigm without agreeing on, or even attempting to produce, a full interpretation or rationalization of it. Lack of a standard interpretation or of an agreed reduction to rules will not prevent a paradigm from guiding research. Normal science can be determined in part by the direct inspection of paradigms, a process that is often aided by but does not depend upon the formulation of rules and assumption. Indeed, the existence of a paradigm need not even imply that any full set of rules exists.

672. What is the author attempting to illustrate through this passage?

(a) Relationships between rules, paradigms, and normal science

(b) How a historian would isolate a particular 'loci of commitment'

(c) How a set of shared beliefs evolves into a paradigm

(d) Ways of understanding a scientific tradition

(e) The frustrations of attempting to define a paradigm of a tradition

673. The term 'loci of commitment' as used in the passage would most likely correspond with which of the following?

(a) Loyalty between a group of scientists in a research laboratory

(b) Loyalty between groups of scientists across research laboratories

(c) Loyalty to a certain paradigm of scientific inquiry

(d) Loyalty to global patterns of scientific inquiry

(e) Loyalty to evolving trends of scientific inquiry

674. The author of this passage is likely to agree with which of the following?

(a) Paradigms almost entirely define a scientific tradition.

(b) A group of scientists investigating a phenomenon would benefit by defining a set of rules.

(c) Acceptance by the giants of a tradition is a sine qua non for a paradigm to emerge.

(d) Choice of isolation mechanism determines the type of paradigm that may emerge from a tradition.

(e) Paradigms are a general representation of rules and beliefs of a scientific tradition.

Passage – 100

The difficulties historians face in establishing cause-and-effect relations in the history of human societies are broadly similar to the difficulties facing astronomers, climatologists, ecologists, evolutionary biologists; geologists, and palaeontologists. To varying degrees each of these fields is plagued by the impossibility of performing replicated, controlled experimental interventions, the complexity arising from enormous numbers of variables, the resulting uniqueness of each system, the consequent impossibility of formulating universal laws, and the difficulties of predicting emergent properties and future behaviour. Prediction in history, as in other historical sciences, is most feasible on large spatial scales and over long times, when the unique features of millions of small-scale brief events become averaged out. Just as I could predict the sex ratio of the next 1,000 newborns but not the sexes of my own two children. the historian can recognize factors that made inevitable the broad outcome of the collision between American and Eurasian societies after 13,000 years of separate developments, but not the outcome of the 1960 U.S. presidential election. The details of which candidate said what during a single televised debate in October 1960 could have given the electoral victory to Nixon instead of to Kennedy, but no details of who said what could have blocked the European conquest of Native Americans.

How can students of human history profit from the experience of scientists in other historical sciences? A methodology that has proved useful involves the comparative method and so-called natural experiments. While neither astronomers studying galaxy formation nor human historians can manipulate their systems in controlled laboratory experiments, they both can take advantage of natural experiments, by comparing systems differing in the presence or absence (or in the strong or weak effect)of some putative causative factor. For example, epidemiologists, forbidden to feed large amounts of salt to people experimentally, have still been able to identify effects of high salt intake by comparing groups of humans who already differ greatly in their salt intake: and cultural anthropologists, unable to provide human groups experimentally with varying resource abundances for many centuries, still study long-term effects of resource abundance on human societies by comparing recent Polynesian populations living on islands differing naturally in resource abundance.

The student of human history can draw on many more natural experiments than just comparisons among the five inhabited continents. Comparisons can also utilize large islands that have developed complex societies in a considerable degree of isolation (such as Japan, Madagascar. Native American Hispaniola, New Guinea, Hawaii, and many others), as well as societies on hundreds of smaller islands and regional societies within each of the continents. Natural experiments in any field, whether in ecology or human history, are inherently open to potential methodological criticisms. Those include confounding effects of natural variation in additional variables besides the one of interest, as well as problems in inferring chains of causation from observed correlations between variables. Such methodological problems have been discussed in great detail for some of the historical sciences. In particular, epidemiology, the science of drawing inferences about human diseases by comparing groups of people (often by retrospective historical studies), has for a long time successfully employed formalized procedures for dealing with problems similar to those facing historians of human societies.

In short, I acknowledge that it is much more difficult to understand human history than to understand problems in fields of science where history is unimportant and where fewer individual variables operate. Nevertheless, successful methodologies for analyzing historical problems have been worked out in several fields. As a result, the histories of dinosaurs, nebulae, and glaciers are generally acknowledged to belong to fields of science rather than to the humanities.

675. Why do islands with considerable degree of isolation provide valuable insights into human history?

(a) Isolated islands may evolve differently and this difference is of interest to us.

(b) Isolated islands increase the number of observations available to historians.

(c) Isolated islands, differing in their endowments and size may evolve differently and this difference can be attributed to their endowments and size.

(d) Isolated islands. differing in their endowments and size, provide a good comparison to large islands such as Eurasia, Africa, Americas and Australia.

(e) Isolated islands, in so far as they are inhabited, arouse curiosity about how human beings evolved there.

676. According to the author, why is prediction difficult in history?

(a) Historical explanations are usually broad so that no prediction is possible.

(b) Historical outcomes depend upon a large number of factors and hence prediction is difficult for each case.

(c) Historical sciences, by their very nature, are not interested in a multitude of minor factors, which might be important in a specific historical outcome.

(d) Historians are interested in evolution of human history and hence are only interested in long-term predictions.

(e) Historical sciences suffer from the inability to conduct controlled experiments and therefore have explanations based on a few long-term factors.

677. According to the author, which of the following statements would be true?

(a) Students of history are missing significant opportunities by not conducting any natural experiments.

(b) Complex societies inhabiting large islands provide great opportunities for natural experiments.

(c) Students of history are missing significant opportunities by not studying an adequate variety of natural experiments.

(d) A unique problem faced by historians is their inability to establish cause and effect relationships.

(e) Cultural anthropologists have overcome the problem of confounding variables through natural experiments.

Passage – 101

When I was little, children were bought two kinds of ice cream, sold from those white wagons with canopies made of silvery metal: either the two-cent cone or the four-cent ice-cream pie. The two-cent cone was very small, in fact it could fit comfortably into a child's hand, and it was made by taking the ice cream from its container with a special scoop and piling it on the cone. Granny always suggested I eat only a part of the cone, then throw away the pointed end, because it had been touched by the vendor's hand (though that was the best part, nice and crunchy, and it was regularly eaten in secret, after a pretence of discarding it).

The four-cent pie was made by a special little machine, also silvery, which pressed two disks of sweet biscuit against a cylindrical section of ice cream. First you had to thrust your tongue into the gap between the biscuits until it touched the central nucleus of ice cream; then, gradually, you ate the whole thing, the biscuit surfaces softening as they became soaked in creamy nectar. Granny had no advice to give here: in theory the pies had been touched only by the machine; in practice, the vendor had held them in his hand while giving them to us, but it was impossible to isolate the contaminated area.

I was fascinated, however, by some of my peers, whose parents bought them not a four-cent pie but two two-cent cones. These privileged children advanced proudly with one cone in their right hand and one in their left; and expertly moving their head from side to side, they licked first one, then the other. This liturgy seemed to me so sumptuously enviable, that many times I asked to be allowed to celebrate it. In vain. My elders were inflexible: a four-cent ice, yes; but two two-cent ones, absolutely no.

As anyone can see, neither mathematics nor economy nor dietetics justified this refusal. Nor did hygiene, assuming that in due course the tips of both cones were discarded. The pathetic, and obviously mendacious, justification was that a boy concerned with turning his eyes from one cone to the other was more inclined to stumble over stones, steps, or cracks in the pavement. I dimly sensed that there was another secret justification, cruelly pedagogical, but I was unable to grasp it.

Today, citizen and victim of a consumer society, a civilization of excess and waste (which the society of the thirties was not), I realize that those dear and now departed elders were right. Two two-cent cones instead of one at four cents did not signify squandering, economically speaking, but symbolically they surely did. It was for this precise reason, that I yearned for them: because two ice creams suggested excess. And this was precisely why they were denied to me: because they looked indecent, an insult to poverty, a display of fictitious privilege, a boast of wealth. Only spoiled children ate two cones at once, those children who in fairy tales were rightly punished, as Pinocchio was when he rejected the skin and the stalk. And parents who encouraged this weakness, appropriate to little parvenus, were bringing up their children in the foolish theatre of "I'd like to but I can't." They were preparing them to turn up at tourist-class check-in with a fake Gucci bag bought from a street peddler on the beach at Rimini.

Nowadays the moralist risks seeming at odds with morality, in a world where the consumer civilization now wants even adults to be spoiled, and promises them always something more, from the wristwatch in the box of detergent to the bonus bangle sheathed, with the magazine it accompanies, in a plastic envelope. Like the parents of those ambidextrous gluttons I so envied, the consumer civilization pretends to give more, but actually gives, for four cents, what is worth four cents. You will throwaway the old transistor radio to purchase the new one, that boasts an alarm clock as well, but some inexplicable defect in the mechanism will guarantee that the radio lasts only a year. The new cheap car will have leather seats, double side mirrors adjustable from inside, and a panelled dashboard, but it will not last nearly so long as the glorious old Fiat 500, which, even when it broke down, could be started again with a kick.

The morality of the old days made Spartans of us all, while today's morality wants all of us to be Sybarites.

2008

678. Which of the following cannot be inferred from the passage?

(a) Today's society is more extravagant than the society of the 1930s.

(b) The act of eating two ice cream cones is akin to a ceremonial process.

(c) Elders rightly suggested that a boy turning eyes from one cone to the other was more likely to fall.

(d) Despite seeming to promise more, the consumer civilization gives away exactly what the thing is worth.

(e) The consumer civilization attempts to spoil children and adults alike.

679. In the passage, the phrase "little parvenus" refers to

(a) naughty midgets. (b) old hags.

(c) arrogant people. (d) young upstarts.

(e) foolish kids.

680. The author pined for two two-cent cones instead of one four-cent pie because

(a) it made dietetic sense.

(b) it suggested intemperance.

(c) it was more fun.

(d) it had a visual appeal.

(e) he was a glutton.

681. What does the author mean by "nowadays the moralist risks seeming at odds with morality"?

(a) The moralists of yesterday have become immoral today.

(b) The concept of morality has changed over the years.

(c) Consumerism is amoral.

(d) The risks associated with immorality have gone up.

(e) The purist's view of morality is fast becoming popular.

682. According to the author, the justification for refusal to let him eat two cones was plausibly

(a) didactic. (b) dietetic.

(c) dialectic. (d) diatonic.

(e) diastolic.

Passage – 102

Language is not a cultural artifact that we learn the *way* we learn to tell time or how the federal government works. Instead, it is a distinct piece of the biological makeup of our brains. Language is a complex, specialized skill, which develops in the child spontaneously, without conscious effort or formal instruction, is deployed without awareness of its underlying logic, is qualitatively the same in every individual, and is distinct from more general abilities to process information or behave intelligently. For these reasons some cognitive scientists have described language as a psychological faculty, a mental organ, a neural system, and a computational module. But I prefer the admittedly quaint term "instinct". It conveys the idea that people know how to talk in more or less the sense that spiders know how to spin webs. Web-spinning was not invented by some unsung spider genius and does not depend on having had the right education or on having an aptitude for architecture or the construction trades. Rather, spiders spin spider webs because they have spider brains, which give them the urge to spin and the competence to succeed. Although there are differences between webs and words, I will encourage you to see language in this way, for it helps to make sense of the phenomena we will explore.

Thinking of language as an instinct inverts the popular wisdom, especially as it has been passed down in the canon of the humanities and social sciences. Language is no more a cultural invention than is upright posture. It is not a manifestation of a general capacity to use symbols: a three-year-old, we shall see, is a grammatical genius, but is quite incompetent at the visual arts, religious iconography, traffic signs, and the other staples of the semiotics curriculum. Though language is a magnificent ability unique to *Homo sapiens* among living species, it does not call for sequestering the study of humans from the domain of biology, for a magnificent ability unique to a particular living species is far from unique in the animal kingdom. Some kinds of bats home in on flying insects using Doppler sonar. Some kinds of migratory birds navigate thousands of miles by calibrating the positions of the constellations against the time of day and year. In nature's talent show, we are simply a species of primate with our own act, a knack for communicating information about who did what to whom by modulating the sounds we make when we exhale.

Once you begin to look at language not as the ineffable essence of human uniqueness hut as a biological adaptation to communicate information, it is no longer as tempting to see language as an insidious shaper of thought, and, we shall see, it is not. Moreover, seeing language as one of nature's engineering marvels — an organ with "that perfection of structure and co-adaptation which justly excites our admiration," in Darwin's words - gives us a new respect for your ordinary Joe and the much-maligned English language (or any language). The complexity of language, from the scientist's point of view, is part of our biological birthright; it is not something that parents teach their children or something that must be elaborated in school — as Oscar Wilde said, "Education is an admirable thing, but it is well to remember from time to time that nothing that is worth knowing can be taught." A preschooler's tacit knowledge of grammar is more sophisticated than the thickest style manual or the most state-of-the-art computer language system, and the same applies to all healthy human beings, even the notorious syntaxfracturing professional athlete and the, you know, like, inarticulate teenage skateboarder. Finally, since language is the product of a well-engineered biological instinct, we shall see that it is not the nutty barrel of monkeys that entertainer-columnists make it out to be.

683. According to the passage, which of the following does not stem from popular wisdom on language?

(a) Language is a cultural artifact.

(b) Language is a cultural invention.

(c) Language is learnt as we grow.

(d) Language is unique to *Homo sapiens.*

(e) Language is a psychological faculty.

684. Which of the following can be used to replace the "spiders know how to spin webs" analogy as used by the author?

(a) A kitten learning to jump over a wall

(b) Bees collecting nectar

(c) A donkey carrying a load

(d) A horse running a Derby

(e) A pet clog protecting its owner's property

685. According to the passage, which of the following is unique to human beings?

(a) Ability to use symbols while communicating with one another.

(b) Ability to communicate with each other through voice modulation.

(c) Ability to communicate information to other members of the species.

(d) Ability to use sound as means of communication.

(e) All of the above.

686. According to the passage, complexity of language cannot be taught by parents or at school to children because

(a) children instinctively know language.

(b) children learn the language on their own.

(c) language is not amenable to teaching.

(d) children know language better than their teachers or parents.

(e) children are born with the knowledge of semiotics.

687. Which of the following best summarizes the passage?

(a) Language is unique to *Homo sapiens.*

(b) Language is neither learnt nor taught.

(c) Language is not a cultural invention or artifact as it is made out.

(d) Language is instinctive ability of human beings.

(e) Language is use of symbols unique to human beings.

Passage – 103

To summarize the Classic Maya collapse, we can tentatively identify five strands. I acknowledge, however, that Maya archaeologists still disagree vigorously among themselves in part, because the different strands evidently varied in importance among different parts of the Maya realm; because detailed archaeological studies are available for only some Maya sites; and because it remains puzzling why most of the Maya heartland remained nearly empty of population and failed to recover after the collapse and after re-growth of forests.

With those caveats, it appears to me that one strand consisted of population growth outstripping available resources: a dilemma similar to the one foreseen by Thomas Malthus in 1798 and being played out today in Rwanda, Haiti and elsewhere. As the archaeologist David Webster succinctly puts it, "Too many farmers grew too many crops on too much of landscape." Compounding that mismatch between population and resources was the second strand: the effects of deforestation and hillside erosion, which caused a decrease in the amount of useable farmland at a time when more rather than less farmland was needed, and possibly exacerbated by an anthropogenic drought resulting from deforestation, by soil nutrient depletion and other soil problems, and by the struggle to prevent bracken ferns from overrunning the fields.

The third strand consisted of increased fighting, as more and more people fought over fewer resources. Maya warfare, already endemic, peaked just before the collapse. That is not surprising when one reflects that at least five million people, perhaps many more, were crammed into an area smaller than the US state of Colorado (104,000 square miles). That warfare would have decreased further the amount of land available for agriculture, by creating no-man's lands between principalities where it was now unsafe to farm. Bringing matters to a head was the strand of climate change. The drought at the time of the Classic collapse was not the first drought that the Maya had lived through, but it was the most severe. At the time of previous droughts, there were still uninhabited parts of the Maya landscape, and people at a site affected by drought could save themselves by moving to another site. However, by the time of the Classic collapse the landscape was now full, there was no useful unoccupied land in the vicinity on which to begin anew, and the whole population could not be accommodated in the few areas that continued to have reliable water supplies.

As our fifth strand, we have to wonder why the kings and nobles failed to recognize and solve these seemingly obvious problems undermining their society. Their attention was evidently focused on their short-term concerns of enriching themselves, waging wars, erecting monuments, competing with each other, and extracting enough food from the peasants to support all those activities. Like most leaders throughout human history, the Maya kings and nobles did not heed long-term problems, insofar as they perceived them.

Finally, while we still have some other past societies to consider before we switch our attention to the modern world, we must already he struck by some parallels between the Maya and the past societies. As on Mangareva, the Maya environmental and population problems led to increasing warfare and civil strife. Similarly, on Easter Island and at Chaco Canyon, the Maya peak population numbers were followed swiftly by political and social collapse. Paralleling the eventual extension of agriculture from Easter Island's coastal lowlands to its uplands, and from the Mimbres floodplain to the hills, Copan's inhabitants also expanded from the floodplain to the more fragile hill slopes, leaving them with a larger population to feed when the agricultural boom in the hills went bust. Like Easter Island chiefs erecting ever larger statues, eventually crowned by pukao, and like Anasazi elite treating themselves to necklaces of 2,000 turquoise beads, Maya kings sought to outdo each other with more and more impressive temples, covered with thicker and thicker plaster — reminiscent in turn of the extravagant conspicuous consumption by modern American CEOs. The passivity of Easter chiefs and Maya kings in the face of the real big threats to their societies completes our list of disquieting parallels.

688. According to the passage, which of the following best represents the factor that has been cited by the author in the context of Rwanda and Haiti?
- (a) Various ethnic groups competing for land and other resources
- (b) Various ethnic groups competing for limited land resources
- (c) Various ethnic groups fighting with each other
- (d) Various ethnic groups competing for political power
- (e) Various ethnic groups fighting for their identity

689. By an anthropogenic drought, the author means
- (a) a drought caused by lack of rains.
- (b) a drought caused due to deforestation.
- (c) a drought caused by failure to prevent bracken ferns from overrunning the fields.
- (d) a drought caused by actions of human beings.
- (e) a drought caused by climate changes.

690. According to the passage, the drought at the time of Maya collapse had a different impact compared to the droughts earlier because
- (a) the Maya kings continued to be extravagant when common people were suffering.
- (b) it happened at the time of collapse of leadership among Mayas.
- (c) it happened when the Maya population had occupied all available land suited for agriculture.
- (d) it was followed by internecine warfare among Mayans.
- (e) irreversible environmental degradation led to this drought.

691. According to the author, why is it difficult to explain the reasons for Maya collapse?
- (a) Copan inhabitants destroyed all records of that period.
- (b) The constant deforestation and hillside erosion have wiped out all traces of the Maya kingdom.
- (c) Archaeological sites of Mayas do not provide any consistent evidence.
- (d) It has not been possible to ascertain which of the factors best explains as to why the Maya civilization collapsed.
- (e) At least five million people were crammed into a small area.

692. Which factor has not been cited as one of the factors causing the collapse of Maya society?
- (a) Environmental degradation due to excess population
- (b) Social collapse due to excess population
- (c) Increased warfare among Maya people
- (d) Climate change
- (e) Obsession of Maya population with their own short-term concerns

Passage – 104

A remarkable aspect of art of the present century is the range of concepts and ideologies which it embodies. It is almost tempting to see a pattern emerging within the art field - or alternatively imposed upon it a *posteriori* - similar to that which exists under the umbrella of science where the general term covers a whole range of separate, though interconnecting, activities. Any parallelism is however - in this instance at least - misleading. A scientific discipline develops systematically once its bare tenets have been established, named and categorized as conventions. Many of the concepts of modern art, by contrast, have resulted from the almost accidental meetings of groups of talented individuals at certain times and certain places. The ideas generated by these chance meetings had twofold consequences. Firstly, a corpus of work would be produced which, in great part, remains as a concrete record of the events. Secondly, the ideas would themselves be disseminated through many different channels of communication - seeds that often bore fruit in contexts far removed from their generation. Not all movements were exclusively concerned with innovation. Surrealism, for instance, claimed to embody a kind of insight which can be present in the art of any period. This claim has been generally accepted so that a sixteenth century painting by Spranger or a mysterious photograph by Atget can legitimately be discussed in surrealist terms. Briefly, then, the concepts of modern art are of many different (often fundamentally different) kinds and resulted from the exposures of painters, sculptors and thinkers to the more complex phenomena of the twentieth century, including our ever increasing knowledge of the thought and products of earlier centuries. Different groups of artists would collaborate in trying to make sense of a rapidly changing world of visual and spiritual experience. We should hardly be surprised if no one group succeeded completely, but achievements, though relative, have been considerable. Landmarks have been established - concrete statements of position which give a pattern to a situation which could easily have degenerated into total chaos. Beyond this, new language tools have been created for those who follow - semantic systems which can provide a springboard for further explorations.

The codifying of art is often criticized. Certainly one can understand that artists are wary of being pigeon-holed since they are apt to think of themselves as individuals - sometimes with good reason. The notion of self-expression, however, no longer carries quite the weight it once did; objectivity has its defenders. There is good reason to accept the ideas codified by artists and critics, over the past sixty years or so, as having attained the status of independent existence - an independence which is not without its own value. The time factor is important here. As an art movement slips into temporal perspective, it ceases to be a living organism - becoming, rather, a fossil. This is not to say that it becomes useless or uninteresting. Just as a scientist can reconstruct the life of a prehistoric environment from the messages codified into the structure of a fossil, so can an artist decipher whole webs of intellectual and creative possibility from the recorded structure of a 'dead' art movement. The artist can match the creative patterns crystallized into this structure against the potentials and possibilities of his own time. As T.S. Eliot observed, no one starts anything from scratch; however consciously you may try to live in the present, you are still involved with a nexus of behaviour patterns bequeathed from the past. The original and creative person is not someone who ignores these patterns, but someone who is able to translate and develop them so that they conform more exactly to his - and our - present needs.

693. Many of the concepts of modern art have been the product of

(a) ideas generated from planned deliberations between artists, painters and thinkers.

(b) the dissemination of ideas through the state and its organizations.

(c) accidental interactions among people blessed with creative muse.

(d) patronage by the rich and powerful that supported art.

(e) systematic investigation, codification and conventions.

694. In the passage, the word 'fossil' can be interpreted as

(a) an art movement that has ceased to remain interesting or useful.

(b) an analogy from the physical world to indicate a historic art movement.

(c) an analogy from the physical world to indicate the barrenness of artistic creations in the past.

(d) an embedded codification of pre-historic life.

(e) an analogy from the physical world to indicate the passing of an era associated with an art movement.

695. In the passage, which of the following similarities between science and art may lead to erroneous conclusions?

(a) Both, in general, include a gamut of distinct but interconnecting activities.

(b) Both have movements not necessarily concerned with innovation.

(c) Both depend on collaborations between talented individuals.

(d) Both involve abstract thought and dissemination of ideas.

(e) Both reflect complex priorities of the modern world.

696. The range of concepts and ideologies embodied in the art of the twentieth century is explained by
(a) the existence of movements such as surrealism.
(b) landmarks which give a pattern to the art history of the twentieth century.
(c) new language tools which can be used for further explorations into new areas.
(d) the fast changing world of perceptual and transcendental understanding.
(e) the quick exchange of ideas and concepts enabled by efficient technology.

697. The passage uses an observation by T.S. Eliot to imply that
(a) creative processes are not 'original' because they always borrow from the past.
(b) we always carry forward the legacy of the past.
(c) past behaviours and thought processes recreate themselves in the present and get labeled as 'original' or 'creative'.
(d) 'originality' can only thrive in a 'greenhouse' insulated from the past biases.
(e) 'innovations' and 'original thinking' interpret and develop on past thoughts to suit contemporary needs.

DIRECTIONS for Questions 698 to 702: The poem given below is followed by five questions. Choose the best answer to each question.

As you set out for Ithaka
hope the journey is a long one,
full of adventure, full of discovery.
Laistrygonians and Cyclops,
angry Poseidon – don't be afraid of them:
you'll never find things like that on your way
as long as you keep your thoughts raised high,
as long as a rare excitement
stirs your spirit and your body.
Laistrygonians and Cyclops,
wild Poseidon – you won't encounter them
unless you bring them along inside your soul,
unless your soul sets them up in front of you.
Hope the voyage is a long one,
may there be many a summer morning when,
with what pleasure, what joy,
you come into harbours seen for the first time;
may you stop at Phoenician trading stations
to buy fine things,
mother of pearl and coral, amber and ebony,
sensual perfume of every kind –
as many sensual perfumes as you can;
and may you visit many Egyptian cities
to gather stores of knowledge from their scholars.
Keep Ithaka always in your mind.
Arriving there is what you are destined for.
But do not hurry the journey at all.
Better if it lasts for years,
so you are old by the time you reach the island,
wealthy with all you have gained on the way,
not expecting Ithaka to make you rich.
Ithaka gave you the marvelous journey,
without her you would not have set out.
She has nothing left to give you now.
And if you find her poor, Ithaka won't have fooled you.
Wise as you will have become, so full of experience,
you will have understood by then what these Ithakas mean.

2003(L)

698. Which of the following best reflects the central theme of this poem?
(a) If you don't have high expectations, you will not be disappointed.
(b) Don't rush to your goal; the journey is what enriches you.
(c) The longer the journey the greater the experiences you gather.
(d) You cannot reach Ithaka without visiting Egyptian ports.

699. The poet recommends a long journey. Which of the following is the most comprehensive reason for it?
(a) You can gain knowledge as well as sensual experience.
(b) You can visit new cities and harbours.
(c) You can experience the full range of sensuality.
(d) You can buy a variety of fine things.

700. In the poem, Ithaka is a symbol of
(a) the divine mother. (b) your inner self.
(c) the path to wisdom. (d) life's distant goal.

701. What does the poet mean by 'Laistrygonians' and 'Cyclops'?
(a) Creatures which, along with Poseidon, one finds during a journey.
(b) Mythological characters that one should not be afraid of.
(c) Intra-personal obstacles that hinder one's journey.
(d) Problems that one has to face to derive the most from one's journey.

702. Which of the following best reflects the tone of the poem?
(a) Prescribing (b) Exhorting
(c) Pleading (d) Consoling

2016

Directions for questions 703 to 708: The passage given below is followed by a set of six questions. Choose the most appropriate answer to each question.

My mother, deeply rooted in the peasant culture of her native Punjab, was always immersed in the supernatural. She was born into Sikhism, but – like many Indians of her generation – her knowledge of her religion was never strong. She could never name its 10 founding gurus; nor had she any interest in its monist theology which encourages an internal experience of God through meditation.

Her Sikhism was an emotionally driven, personal mish-mash of various customs from across the subcontinent – most of it Hindu. She visited temples daily, prayed each morning and chanted Sanskrit hymns – without understanding a word – while wafting incense through the house. And she fasted – a lot.

Her religion was disordered, ad-hoc and impossible to pin down, but it was a constant in my life and it inspired me. I have an abiding love of myth – the first book I took out of a library was about the Greek heroes – and I find India and its spiritual traditions enchanting. I've made dozens of pilgrimages there to sites of Sikh martyrdom, birthplaces of Hindu avatars and the shrines of Sufi babas. I have a lasting fascination with yoga and mystical experiences.

Mum's supernatural thinking – her certainty that creation was shaped by divine beings and magical forces, and influenced by spells and curses – was, I felt, a link between myself and my ancestors, stretching back millennia. I loved talking to her about the stories in the *Puranas*, about Krishna battling snake-devils and Shiva churning the oceans for the nectar of immortality, on her terms – as things that actually happened – and seeing her light up with excitement at the tales.

But last year she found Jesus – and all her fantastical pagan ways went out of the window. She had begun to seek Him in earnest the year before. My mother works for a catering company in Southall, west London, cleaning the dishes that come off the planes at nearby Heathrow Airport, and it was an evangelist colleague, a former Sikh, who invited her to a Christian prayer service in a local church. "I felt peace straight away," Mum said. "From the first time I went and listened to people's testimonies, about how Jesus had healed and changed their lives, I felt peace."

She continued visiting the church, which has a north-Indian congregation and conducts its services in Punjabi, and lost interest in her old ways. Then Jesus came to her in a dream: "He held my hand," she told me. "He said he was with me and wouldn't leave me. I woke up and I could still feel it."

Her conversion itself wasn't too surprising. The story of Jesus is, by Indian standards, a plausibly humdrum one. Most Indian villagers could point you towards someone who cures the sick, raises the dead and knows the secret of eternal life. And the morphing of religions has always been a common occurrence there. What unnerved me was my sense of betrayal, the painful sense of rejection as Mum turned her back on what had been our abiding bond. It felt like she'd turned her back on me.

703. According to the passage, which of the following cannot be inferred to be true about the author's mother?

(a) She did not experience a lasting connection with her original religion.

(b) She looked towards religion as an answer to her problems.

(c) She had always felt a disconnect with the Sikhism.

(d) She came from a humble background.

704. According to the passage, which of the following options would best explain the original religious philosophy of the author's mother?

(a) She felt a oneness in the diversity of religion.

(b) She was staunch in following every custom of her religion.

(c) She turned to religion for emotional fulfilment over the spiritual.

(d) She would follow the religious creed according to her whims and fancies.

705. According to the passage, it can be inferred that the author's mother stepped over to another religion because

(a) she felt assured that she was not alone in her suffering.

(b) people from her community were doing so.

(c) she did not feel a major difference in following the new religion.

(d) she finally felt the peace that she had been searching for long.

706. From the passage, it can be best inferred that the author

(a) is nonchalant about his mother's religious affiliations.

(b) has mixed feelings on his mother's conversion.

(c) feels betrayed that she left his religion and moved to another.

(d) viewed his own reaction in an objective manner.

707. According to the passage, the story of Jesus is, by Indian standards

(a) unbelievable (b) polemic

(c) unexciting (d) misunderstood

708. According to the author, what happened after the author's mother discovered Jesus?

(a) She stopped practicing fasts and other rituals.

(b) She started regularly dreaming about Jesus.

(c) She abandoned her faith and her family.

(d) She betrayed her son's trust.

Directions for questions 709 to 714: The passage given below is followed by a set of six questions. Choose the most appropriate answer to each question.

I enjoyed *Imaginary Friends*. Lurie's keen eye for detail, plot twists, and subtle, laugh-out-loud humour brings the Festinger study to another level. Lurie includes and goes beyond the participant-observer point of view of the sociologist. She deftly choreographs how cults can affect and change those who study them, just as sociologists can change the cults they study. In many ways, Lurie explores critiques of Festinger's theory and methodology while she sustains the reasoning behind them.

Imaginary Friends is the story of two male professors, one seasoned and the other just out of graduate school. Doctor Tom McMann as the lead sociologist is a large, fit, middle-aged, never-married fellow. He has established a powerful reputation among his colleagues after just one important publication. McMann convinces his new, young colleague Roger Zimmern, a non-practicing Jew, to help him find a charismatic group so that the two can test a sociological theory. It has been decades since McMann has published anything of significance. He is anxious that no other colleague knows about the project until he gathers his data. Zimmern finds a small, newly formed cult in the nearby town of Sophis—Lurie mimics Festinger's Seekers with her cult the Truth Seekers. The two men successfully infiltrate the group that exhibits little suspicion of their motives, save for one member, Ken. McMann wants to observe how unexpected change and unfulfilled prophecies affect group dynamics. He predicts that, after cognitive dissonance from a "disconfirmation," the group will adjust through rationalizations and by increased recruiting. The sociologists expect to participate for months, if necessary.

Roger narrates the story from the perspective of reflection months after things have fallen apart. The comic events originally occurred when Roger got in over his head in more ways than one during the project. The story is his effort to make sense of all the apparent nonsense that happened then.

The core of the cult depends on Verena, a college dropout at age 19, who moves in with her Aunt Elsie, an avid Spiritualist. Elsie encourages Verena's mediumistic sensibilities. Through automatic writing, Verena makes contact with an alien race of Guardians from the planet Varna. The Varnian leader Ro channels information to the group through Verena's cryptic scrawls written after she enters a trance state. The group also hears from Mo and Ko of Varna in this way.

Roger describes Verena as both a nut and a sensitive, alluring waif with sculpted features, and hypnotic and liquid eyes. McMann poses as the professor that he is, but in personality more like an affable, accommodating car salesman. Throughout the text, Roger refers to himself as both Roger Zimmern, the objective scholar, and as "Stupid Roger," the klutzy, shy professor truly interested in contact with Varna. His split persona adds to the tension he feels and the confusion he exhibits, all of which cause uncomfortable, if comic, moments. He eventually wonders who is crazy: Is it he, McMann, or the group?

During weeks of meetings with six or seven others in Elsie's house, Roger endures progressive changes in diet and belief structures. He tries ineffectively to memorize layers of lessons derived from Ro, Spiritualist doctrine, and idiosyncratic truths that members add to group metaphysics. McMann and Zimmern try their best to be nondirective and participatory, but some circumstances push their acting abilities.

709. Which of the following, according to the passage, can best be inferred from the passage?

(a) The study of cult and group behaviour is an exhausting process.

(b) Sociologists are affected by the behaviour and lives of those they study.

(c) In the study of cults, the observer and the observed can both be affected by each other.

(d) Roger, in his enthusiasm to impress the group, becomes progressively stupid.

710. According to the passage, which of the following can be said to be untrue about *Imaginary Friends*?

(a) Lurie bases her protagonists on the actual sociologists who undertook the Festinger study.

(b) Lurie takes her book beyond a level that the Festinger study achieved.

(c) The book is a ficti on based on a study conducted on a cult.

(d) The plot is a first person account of one of the sociologists and his effort to understand his experiences with the cult.

711. Which of the following has been mentioned in the passage as a result of an unfulfilled prophecy within a cult?
   (a) There is an effect on group dynamics.
   (b) There is a cognitive dissonance within the group.
   (c) The group has to go through the unexpected change that follows.
   (d) The group adjusts through a process of rationalisations.

712. From the passage, which of the following cannot be inferred about the indoctrination process of the cult that Roger joins?
   (a) A comic pairing of a new recruit and an older member of the cult.
   (b) A requirement to inculcate the new beliefs of the cult.
   (c) Change in food consumption.
   (d) The memorisation of truths which are specific to the cult.

713. Which of the following is an apt title for the passage?
   (a) The Festinger Study – A Critical Analysis
   (b) McMann and Roger – An Unlikely Pair
   (c) *Imaginary Friends* – A Review
   (d) Sociological Integration in Cults

714. According to the passage, which of the following can be true about Verena?
   (a) She was an insane yet alluring waif with attractive features.
   (b) She had a certain charisma that appealed to Roger.
   (c) She was way too young to be a part of a cult.
   (d) She had been exploited and brainwashed by her aunt into joining the cult.

Directions for questions 715 to 717: The passage given below is followed by a set of three questions. Choose the most appropriate answer to each question.

Why do sensible and rational people seem to lose the ability to act sensibly and rationally when they are in conflict? What makes some families tear themselves apart in a variety of squabbles which to outsiders may seem petty but which result in family members not speaking to each other for years? What drives neighbours to blight their daily lives with unpleasant, bitter, and confrontational disputes? And how can otherwise placid and restrained people become almost unrecognizable when involved in road rage incidents – or even trolley rage in supermarkets?

The answer may be distilled down to one psychological phenomenon: self-esteem. It is one of the strongest motivating factors in conflict and generates powerful emotions. We all have self-esteem, whether corporate or individual; we all have a need to think well of ourselves, and for others to think well of us. Self-esteem governs many of the decisions we make daily, as we expend huge amounts of time and effort constantly maintaining and protecting our self-image.

The flipside of our desire for approval is our aversion to disapproval – or worse still, our dread of humiliation. An example of this is the fear of public speaking – a dread that can be greater than that of flying or even of death. It is explained by the fact that the disapproval of each person in the audience constitutes a potentially significant attack on our self-image. The larger the audience, the more overwhelming is the prospect of humiliation.

There is now neurological evidence demonstrating the effect that attacks on our self-esteem have on the brain. One study showed that "social pain" activated the same circuits of the brain as physical pain. Consequently any attack on our self-image is interpreted by the brain as physical pain. When we speak of "hurt" feelings, we acknowledge that any form of censure, from slight criticism to outright condemnation or rejection, affects our self-esteem and is felt as physical pain – hence our aversion to admitting fault or to accepting liability. The word "sorry" is one of the most difficult to express, despite it being the quickest, cheapest, and most effective form of resolving a dispute. But our brain seems to indicate to us that saying sorry will be as painful as putting our hand into a fire.

715. What is the theme of the first two paragraphs of this passage?
   (a) Inability to act rationally in a conflict
   (b) Lack of conversation between family members
   (c) Behaviour of people in road rage incidents
   (d) Response of people to injured self-esteem

716. According to the passage, what kind of evidence does the author cite in support of his claim that we react with various degrees of violence to attacks on our self-esteem?
   (a) Empirical (b) Sociological
   (c) Neurological (d) None of the -above

717. According to the passage, the author would agree with all of the following except:
   (a) The desire for approval is ubiquitous.
   (b) Since the brain interprets any attack on our self esteem as physical pain such pain can be treated and cured like a physical pain.
   (c) Some people have a far greater fear of public speaking than that of death because the former incurs the displeasure of so many people.
   (d) Self esteem plays a major role in our lives.

Directions for questions 718 to 720: The passage given below is followed by a set of three questions. Choose the most appropriate answer to each question.

At a nondescript tin shed in Mumbai's Lower Parel, a young man lights a lamp in front of a photo of *Hanuman* before stepping into the red mud pit where he is being trained in *kushti* by Prakash Ranwade, national wrestler and secretary of the Bombay Wrestling Association. This is the 85-year-old Laxmi Narayan VayamShala, possibly among the oldest *kushti akharas* in India.

In the 18th century, the Maratha rulers of Kolhapur promoted *kushti* enthusiastically, including encouraging women to take up training. Later, the British encouraged *pehelwans* by employing them in security services and the police force, etc. Then, in the early 20th century, it was the turn of the mills to play patron by employing the *pehelwans.*

But *kushti* is finally vanishing from Mumbai. The *taleems* or training houses have been slowly shutting down. "Earlier we used to have at least 25 *taleems* around Parel and Lower Parel. But today there are only four or five, and they are struggling to survive," says Tanwade. At Laxmi Narayan VayamShala, there are only eight wrestlers, who practice on the ground floor and live on the first floor. They used to come from all over Maharashtra, but not so much anymore.

"I used to learn *kushti* but now I play cricket. There is no partner to wrestle with and no future either," says Class 10 student Akanksha, the daughter of Ramachandra Patil. Her father represented Maharashtra twice in the national wrestling championships, and she would have liked to make him proud.

But some signs of hope are sprouting. A State-level championship was held in Nagpur after 28 years, and the Maharashtra Chief Minister has also promised to lend support. The few remaining *taleems* might yet get back their glory days.

718. According to the passage, why is *kushti* vanishing from Mumbai?

(a) because cricket is more popular

(b) because there are no state level competition

(c) because there are no patrons

(d) because of lack of space

719. According to the passage, what does the author mean when he says that the Maratha rulers promoted *kushti*?

(a) They honoured the winners of contests.

(b) They attended kushti championships.

(c) They invited the wrestlers to the court.

(d) They gave financial encouragement to those who took up *kushti.*

720. Which of the following can be inferred from the passage?

(a) Political recognition is necessary for any sport to flourish.

(b) Wrestling is dying in Mumbai for lack of state government's encouragement.

(c) The former wrestlers do not encourage their children to take up *kushti* anymore.

(d) Material reward and the prospect of livelihood are needed to attract people to *kushti.*

Directions for questions 721 to 726: The passage given below is followed by a set of six questions. Choose the most appropriate answer to each question.

Why is it that during the Renaissance, China fell behind Europe in technology? Often people assume that it has something to do with the Confucian tradition in China supposedly making the Chinese ultra-conservative, whereas the Judeo-Christian tradition in Europe supposedly stimulated science and innovation. Well, first of all, just ask Galileo about the simulating effects of the Judeo-Christian tradition on science. Then, secondly, just consider the state of technology in medieval Confucian China. China led the world in innovation and technology in the early Renaissance. Chinese inventions include canal lock gates, cast iron, compasses, deep drilling, gun powder, kites, paper, porcelain, printing, stern-post rudders, and wheelbarrows — all of those innovations are Chinese innovations. So the real question is, why did China lose its enormous technological lead to late-starter Europe? Why did the Renaissance affected Europe and not China?

We can get insight by seeing why China lost its lead in ocean-going ships. As of the year 1400, China had by far the best, the biggest, and the largest number of, ocean-going ships in the world. Between 1405 and 1432 the Chinese sent 7 ocean-going fleets, the so-called treasure fleets, out from China. Those fleets comprised hundreds of ships; they had total crews of 20,000 men; each of those ships dwarfed the tiny ships of Columbus; and those gigantic fleets sailed from China to Indonesia, to India, to Arabia, to the east coast of Africa, and down the east coast of Africa. It looked as if the Chinese were on the verge of rounding the Cape of Good Hope, coming up the west side of Africa, and colonizing Europe.

Well, China's tremendous fleets came to an end through a typical episode of isolationism, such as one finds in the histories of many countries. There was a new emperor in China in 1432. In China there had been a Navy faction and an anti-Navy faction. In 1432, with the new emperor, the anti-Navy faction gained ascendancy. The new emperor decided that spending all this money on ships is a waste of money. Okay, there's nothing unusual about that in

China; there was also isolationism in the United States in the 1930's, and Britain did not want anything to do with electric lighting until the 1920s. The difference, though, is that this abandoning of fleets in China was final, because China was unified under one emperor. When that one emperor gave the order to dismantle the shipyards and stop sending out the ships, that order applied to all of China and China's tradition of building ocean-going ships was lost because of the decision by one person. China was a virtual gigantic island, like Tasmania.

Now contrast that with what happened with ocean-going fleets in Europe. Columbus was an Italian, and he wanted an ocean-going fleet to sail across the Atlantic. Everybody in Italy considered this a stupid idea and wouldn't support it. So Columbus went to the next country, France, where everybody considered it a stupid idea and wouldn't support it. So Columbus went to Portugal, where the king of Portugal considered it a stupid idea and wouldn't support it. So Columbus went across the border to a duke of Spain who considered this stupid. And Columbus then went to another duke of Spain who also considered it a waste of money. Finally, on the seventh try, Columbus went back to the king and queen of Spain, who said, all right, you can have three ships, but they were small ships. Columbus sailed across the Atlantic and, as we all know, discovered the New World, came back, and brought the news to Europe. Cortez and Pizarro followed him and brought back huge quantities of wealth. Within a short time, as a result of Columbus having shown the way, 11 European countries jumped into the colonial game and got into fierce competition with each other. The essence of these events is that Europe was fragmented, so Columbus had many different chances.

721. What was the impact of the Renaissance on China?
   (a) It led to an intellectual rebirth.
   (b) It had the effect of resuscitating knowledge.
   (c) It gave birth to intellectual fermentation.
   (d) It did not affect China.

722. What was the relation between China's maritime strength and inventions?
   (a) China became military strong and so could devote time to inventions.
   (b) Chinese maritime trade made China wealthy and allowed her to pursue new ideas.
   (c) Chinese sea farers visited many lands which led to a cross pollination of thought and this in turn gave birth to new concepts.
   (d) The sea farers of China sailed far and wide, thus, putting a premium or the proper maintenance of the craft which forced the crew of these ships to come up with new ideas.

723. What does the author mean when he refers to Galileo and the influences of the Judeo Christian tradition?
   (a) It is generally believed that then Judas Christian tradition encouraged science.
   (b) England and Europe use their phenomenal achievements in sciences and innovation to the Judas Christian tradition.
   (c) The Judas Christian tradition stifled science.
   (d) The Judas Christian tradition played no role but get the credit for the flowering of sciences and innovation.

724. What is the message of this passage?
   (a) Maritime buyer is essential for sciences and innovation.
   (b) The Renaissance played a major role in shifting the balances of power.
   (c) Italian curiosity in conjunction with European wealth led to the development of Europe.
   (d) Concentration of power in one hand can as easily destroy a country as it can strengthen it.

725. What is the author's opinion about isolationism?
   (a) It is nothing unusual.
   (b) Several countries including the United States have practised isolationism at one time or another and they have not come to any harm.
   (c) The isolation resulting from the dismantling of navies did not harm China in any way or affect its science and innovation.
   (d) The absolute power of the Chinese emperor brought about the isolation of China, which has the potential to kill science & innovation.

726. Why does the author refer to the colonial game?
   (a) The colonies enriched the European countries.
   (b) The colonies facilitated transfer of large chunks of population thereby enriching the lives of remaining populations.
   (c) The colonies necessitated the build-up of military strength.
   (d) The colonies gave rise to fierce competition.

2017

Question Numbers (727 to 732) : *The passage below is accompanied by a set of six questions. Choose the best answer to each question.*

Creativity is at once our most precious resource and our most inexhaustible one. As anyone who has ever spent any time with children knows, every single human being is born creative; every human being is innately endowed with the ability to combine and recombine data, perceptions, materials and ideas, and devise new ways of thinking and doing. What fosters creativity? More than anything else: the presence of other creative people. The big myth is that creativity is the province of great individual geniuses. In fact creativity is a social process. Our biggest creative breakthroughs come when people learn from, compete with, and collaborate with other people.

Cities are the true fonts of creativity... With their diverse populations, dense social networks, and public spaces where people can meet spontaneously and serendipitously, they spark and catalyze new ideas. With their infrastructure for finance, organization and trade, they allow those ideas to be swiftly actualized.

As for what staunches creativity, that's easy, if ironic. It's the very institutions that we build to manage, exploit and perpetuate the fruits of creativity – our big bureaucracies, and sad to say, too many of our schools. Creativity is disruptive; schools and organizations are regimented, standardized and stultifying.

The education expert Sir Ken Robinson points to a 1968 study reporting on a group of 1,600 children who were tested over time for their ability to think in out-of-the-box ways. When the children were between 3 and 5 years old, 98 percent achieved positive scores. When they were 8 to 10, only 32 percent passed the same test, and only 10 percent at 13 to 15. When 280,000 25-year-olds took the test, just 2 percent passed. By the time we are adults, our creativity has been wrung out of us.

I once asked the great urbanist Jane Jacobs what makes some places more creative than others. She said, essentially, that the question was an easy one. All cities, she said, were filled with creative people; that's our default state as people. But some cities had more than their shares of leaders, people and institutions that blocked out that creativity. She called them "squelchers."

Creativity (or the lack of it) follows the same general contours of the great socio-economic divide - our rising inequality - that plagues us. According to my own estimates, roughly a third of us across the United States, and perhaps as much as half of us in our most creative cities - are able to do work which engages our creative faculties to some extent, whether as artists, musicians, writers, techies, innovators, entrepreneurs, doctors, lawyers, journalists or educators - those of us who work with our minds. That leaves a group that I term "the other 66 percent," who toil in low-wage rote and rotten jobs - if they have jobs at all - in which their creativity is subjugated, ignored or wasted.

Creativity itself is not in danger. It's flourishing is all around us - in science and technology, arts and culture, in our rapidly revitalizing cities. But we still have a long way to go if we want to build a truly creative society that supports and rewards the creativity of each and every one of us.

727. In the author's view, cities promote human creativity for all the following reasons EXCEPT that they

(a) contain spaces that enable people to meet and share new ideas.

(b) expose people to different and novel ideas, because they are home to varied groups of people.

(c) provide the financial and institutional networks that enable ideas to become reality.

(d) provide access to cultural activities that promote new and creative ways of thinking.

728. The author uses 'ironic' in the third paragraph to point out that

(a) people need social contact rather than isolation to nurture their creativity.

(b) institutions created to promote creativity eventually stifle it.

(c) the larger the creative population in a city, the more likely it is to be stifled.

(d) large bureaucracies and institutions are the inevitable outcome of successful cities.

729. The central idea of this passage is that

(a) social interaction is necessary to nurture creativity.

(b) creativity and ideas are gradually declining in all societies.

(c) the creativity divide is widening in societies in line with socio-economic trends.

(d) more people should work in jobs that engage their creative faculties.

730. Jane Jacobs believed that cities that are more creative

(a) have to struggle to retain their creativity.

(b) have to 'squelch' unproductive people and promote creative ones.

(c) have leaders and institutions that do not block creativity.

(d) typically do not start off as creative hubs.

731. The 1968 study is used here to show that

(a) as they get older, children usually learn to be more creative.

(b) schooling today does not encourage creative thinking in children.

(c) the more children learn, the less creative they become.

(d) technology today prevents children from being creative.

732. The author's conclusions about the most 'creative cities' in the US (paragraph 6) are based on his assumption that

(a) people who work with their hands are not doing creative work.

(b) more than half the population works in non-creative jobs.

(c) only artists, musicians, writers, and so on should be valued in a society.

(d) most cities ignore or waste the creativity of low-wage workers.

Questions Numbers (733 to 738) : *The passage below is accompanied by a set of six questions. Choose the best answer to each question.*

During the frigid season...it's often necessary to nestle under a blanket to try to stay warm. The temperature difference between the blanket and the air outside is so palpable that we often have trouble leaving our warm refuge. Many plants and animals similarly hunker down, relying on snow cover for safety from winter's harsh conditions. The small area between the snowpack and the ground, called the subnivium...might be the most important ecosystem that you have never heard of.

The subnivium is so well-insulated and stable that its temperature holds steady at around 32 degree Fahrenheit (0 degree Celsius). Although that might still sound cold, a constant temperature of 32 degree Fahrenheit can often be 30 to 40 degrees warmer than the air temperature during the peak of winter. Because of this large temperature difference, a wide variety of species...depend on the subnivium for winter protection.

For many organisms living in temperate and Arctic regions, the difference between being under the snow or outside it is a matter of life and death. Consequently, disruptions to the subnivium brought about by climate change will affect everything from population dynamics to nutrient cycling through the ecosystem.

The formation and stability of the subnivium requires more than a few flurries. Winter ecologists have suggested that eight inches of snow is necessary to develop a stable layer of insulation. Depth is not the only factor, however. More accurately, the stability of the subnivium depends on the interaction between snow depth and snow density. Imagine being under a stack of blankets that are all flattened and pressed together. When compressed, the blankets essentially form one compacted layer. In contrast, when they are lightly placed on top of one another, their insulative capacity increases because the air pockets between them trap heat. Greater depths of low-density snow are therefore better at insulating the ground.

Both depth and density of snow are sensitive to temperature. Scientists are now beginning to explore how climate change will affect the subnivium, as well as the species that depend on it. At first glance, warmer winters seem beneficial for species that have difficulty surviving subzero temperatures; however, as with most ecological phenomena, the consequences are not so straightforward. Research has shown that the snow season (the period when snow is more likely than rain) has become shorter since 1970. When rain falls on snow, it increases the density of the snow and reduces its insulative capacity. Therefore, even though winters are expected to become warmer overall from future climate change, the subnivium will tend to become colder and more variable with less protection from the above-ground temperatures.

The effects of a colder subnivium are complex...For example, shrubs such as crowberry and alpine azalea that grow along the forest floor tend to block the wind and so retain higher depths of snow around them. This captured snow helps to keep soils insulated and in turn increases plant decomposition and nutrient release. In field experiments, researchers removed a portion of the snow cover to investigate the importance of the subnivium's insulation. They found that soil frost in the snow-free area resulted in damage to plant roots and sometimes even the death of the plant.

733. The purpose of this passage is to

(a) introduce readers to a relatively unknown ecosystem: the subnivium.

(b) explain how the subnivium works to provide shelter and food to several species.

(c) outline the effects of climate change on the subnivium.

(d) draw an analogy between the effect of blankets on humans and of snow cover on species living in the subnivium.

734. All of the following statements are true EXCEPT

(a) Snow depth and snow density both influence the stability of the subnivium.

(b) Climate change has some positive effects on the subnivium.

(c) The subnivium maintains a steady temperature that can be 30 to 40 degrees warmer than the winter air temperature.

(d) Researchers have established the adverse effects of dwindling snow cover on the subnivium.

735. Based on this extract, the author would support which one of the following actions?

(a) The use of snow machines in winter to ensure snow cover of at least eight inches.

(b) Government action to curb climate change.

(c) Adding nutrients to the soil in winter.

(d) Planting more shrubs in areas of short snow season.

736. In paragraph 6, the author provides the examples of crowberry and alpine azalea to demonstrate that

(a) Despite frigid temperatures, several species survive in temperate and Arctic regions.

(b) Due to frigid temperatures in the temperate and Arctic regions, plant species that survive tend to be shrubs rather than trees.

(c) The crowberry and alpine azalea are abundant in temperate and Arctic regions.

(d) The stability of the subnivium depends on several interrelated factors, including shrubs on the forest floor.

737. Which one of the following statements can be inferred from the passage?

(a) In an ecosystem, altering any one element has a ripple effect on all others.

(b) Climate change affects temperate and Artie regions more than equatorial or arid ones.

(c) A compact layer of wool is warmer than a similarly compact layer of goose down.

(d) The loss of the subnivium, while tragic, will affect only temperate and regions.

738. In paragraph 1, the author uses blankets as a device to

(a) evoke the bitter cold of winter in the minds of readers.

(b) explain how blankets work to keep us warm.

(c) draw an analogy between blankets and the snowpack.

(d) alert readers to the fatal effects of excessive exposure to the cold.

Questions (739 to 744) : The end of the age of the internal combustion engine is in sight. There are small signs everywhere: the shift to hybrid vehicles is already under way among manufacturers. Volvo has announced it will make no purely petrol-engined cars after 2019 ... and Tesla has just started selling its first electric car aimed squarely at the middle classes: the Tesla 3 sells for $35,000 in the US, and 400,000 people have put down a small, refundable deposit towards one. Several thousand have already taken delivery, and the company hopes to sell half a million more next year. This is a remarkable figure for a machine with a fairly short range and a very limited number of specialised charging stations.

Some of it reflects the remarkable abilities of Elon Musk, the company's founder, as a salesman, engineer, and a man able to get the most out his factory workers and the governments he deals with ... Mr Musk is selling a dream that the world wants to believe in.

This last may be the most important factor in the story. The private car is ... a device of immense practical help and economic significance, but at the same time a theatre for myths of unattainable self-fulfilment. The one thing you will never see in a car advertisement is traffic, even though that is the element in which drivers spend their lives. Every single driver in a traffic jam is trying to escape from it, yet it is the inevitable consequence of mass car ownership.

The sleek and swift electric car is at one level merely the most contemporary fantasy of autonomy and power. But it might also disrupt our exterior landscapes nearly as much as the fossil fuel-engined car did in the last century. Electrical cars would of course pollute far less than fossil fuel-driven ones; instead of oil reserves, the rarest materials for batteries would make undeserving despots and their dynasties fantastically rich. Petrol stations would disappear. The air in cities would once more be breathable and their streets as quiet as those of Venice. This isn't an unmixed good. Cars that were as silent as bicycles would still be as dangerous as they are now to anyone they hit without audible warning.

The dream goes further than that. The electric cars of the future will be so thoroughly equipped with sensors and reaction mechanisms that they will never hit anyone. Just as brakes don't let you skid today, the steering wheel of tomorrow will serve you away from danger before you have even noticed it...

This is where the fantasy of autonomy comes full circle. The logical outcome of cars which need no driver is that they will become cars which need no owner either. Instead, they will work as taxis do, summoned at will but only for the journeys we actually need. This the future towards which Ubem.is working. The ultimate development of the private car will be to reinvent public transport. Traffic jams will be abolished only when the private car becomes a public utility. What then will happen to our fantasies of independence? We'll all have to take to electrically powered bicycles.

739. Which of the following statements best reflects the author's argument?

(a) Hybrid and electric vehicles signal the end of the age of internal combustion engines.

(b) Elon Musk is a remarkably gifted salesman.

(c) The private car represents an unattainable myth of independence.

(d) The future Uber car will be environmentally friendlier than even the Tesla.

740. The author points out all of the following about electric cars EXCEPT

(a) Their reliance on rare materials for batteries will support despotic rule.

(b) They will reduce air and noise pollution.

(c) They will not decrease the number of traffic jams.

(d) They will ultimately undermine rather than further driver autonomy.

741. According to the author, the main reason for Tesla's remarkable sales is that
(a) in the long run, the Tesla is more cost effective than fossil fuel-driven cars.
(b) the US government has announced a tax subsidy for Tesla buyers.
(c) the company is rapidly upscaling the number of specialised charging stations for customer convenience
(d) people believe in the autonomy represented by private cars.

742. The author comes to the conclusion that
(a) car drivers will no longer own cars but will have to use public transport.
(b) cars will be controlled by technology that is more efficient than car drivers.
(c) car drivers dream of autonomy but the future may be public transport.
(d) electrically powered bicycles are the only way to achieve autonomy in transportation.

743. In paragraphs 5 and 6, the author provides the example of Uber to argue that
(a) in the future, electric cars will be equipped with mechanisms that prevent collisions.
(b) in the future, traffic jams will not exist.
(c) in the future, the private car will be transformed into a form of public transport.
(d) in the future, Uber rides will outstrip Tesla sales.

744. In paragraph 6, the author mentions electrically powered bicycles to argue that
(a) if Elon Musk were a true visionary, he would invest funds in developing electric bicycles.
(b) our fantasies of autonomy might unexpectedly require us to consider electric bicycles.
(c) in terms of environmental friendliness and safety, electric bicycles rather than electric cars are the future
(d) electric buses are the best form of public transport.

Question Numbers (745 to 747) : Typewriters are the epitome of a technology that has been comprehensively rendered obsolete by the digital age. The ink comes off the ribbon, they weigh a ton, and second thoughts are a disaster. But they are also personal, portable and, above all, private. Type a document and lock it away and more or less the only way anyone else can get it is if you give it to them. That is why the Russians have decided to go back to typewriters in some government offices, and why in the US, some departments have never abandoned them. Yet it is not just their resistance to algorithms and secret surveillance that keeps typewriter production lines – well one, at least – in business (the last British one closed a year ago). Nor is it only the nostalgic appeal of the metal body and the stout well-defined keys that make them popular on eBay. A typewriter demands something particular: attentiveness. By the time the paper is loaded, the ribbon tightened, the carriage returned, the spacing and the margins set, there's a big premium on hitting the right key. That means sorting out ideas, pulling together a kind of order and organising details before actually striking off. There can be no thinking on screen with a typewriter. Nor are there any easy distractions. No online shopping. No urgent emails. No Twitter. No need even for electricity - perfect for writing in a remote hideaway. The thinking process is accompanied by the encouraging clack of keys, and the ratchet of the carriage return. Ping!

745. Which one of the following best describes what the passage is trying to do?
(a) It describes why people continue to use typewriters even in the digital age.
(b) It argues that typewriters will continue to be used even though they are an obsolete technology.
(c) It highlights the personal benefits of using typewriters.
(d) It shows that computers offer fewer options than typewriters.

746. According to the passage, some governments still use typewriters because:
(a) they do not want to abandon old technologies that may be useful in the future.
(b) they want to ensure that typewriter production lines remain in business.
(c) they like the nostalgic appeal of typewriter.
(d) they can control who reads the document.

747. The writer praises typewriters for all the following reasons EXCEPT
(a) Unlike computers, they can only be used for typing.
(b) You cannot revise what you have typed on a typewriter.
(c) Typewriters are noisier than computers.
(d) Typewriters are messier to use than computers.

Question Numbers (748 to 750) : Despite their fierce reputation, Vikings may not have always been the plunderers and pillagers popular culture imagines them to be. In fact, they got their start trading in northern European markets, researchers suggest.

Combs carved from animal antlers, as well as comb manufacturing waste and raw antler material has turned up at three archaeological sites in Denmark, including a medieval marketplace in the city of Ribe. A team of researchers from Denmark and the U.K. hoped to identify the species of animal to which the antlers once belonged by analyzing collagen proteins in the samples and comparing them across the animal kingdom, Laura Geggel reports for Live Science. Somewhat surprisingly, molecular analysis of the artifacts revealed that some combs and other material had been carved from reindeer antlers.... Given that reindeer (Rangifer tarandus) don't live in Denmark, the researchers posit that it arrived on Viking ships from Norway. Antler craftsmanship, in the form of decorative combs, was part of Viking culture. Such combs served as symbols of good health, Geggel writes. The fact that the animals shed their antlers also made them easy to collect from the large herds that inhabited Norway.

Since the artifacts were found in marketplace areas at each site it's more likely that the Norsemen came to trade rather than pillage. Most of the artifacts also date to the 780s, but some are as old as 725. That predates the beginning of Viking raids on Great Britain by about 70 years. [Traditionally, the so-called "Viking Age" began with these raids in 793 and ended with the Norman conquest of Great Britain in 1066.) Archaeologists had suspected that the Vikings had experience with long maritime voyages [that] might have preceded their raiding days. Beyond Norway, these combs would have been a popular industry in Scandinavia as well. It's possible that the antler combs represent a larger trade network, where the Norsemen supplied raw material to craftsmen in Denmark and elsewhere.

748. The primary purpose of the passage is:

(a) to explain the presence of reindeer antler combs in Denmark.

(b) to contradict the widely-accepted beginning date for the Viking Age in Britain, and propose an alternate one.

(c) to challenge the popular perception of Vikings as raiders by using evidence that suggests their early trade relations with Europe.

(d) to argue that besides being violent pillagers, Vikings were also skilled craftsmen and efficient traders.

749. The evidence – "Most of the artifacts also date to the 780s, but some are as old as 725" – has been used in the passage to argue that:

(a) the beginning date of the Viking Age should be changed from 793 to 725.

(b) the Viking raids started as early as 725.

(c) some of the antler artifacts found in Denmark and Great Britain could have come from Scandinavia.

(d) the Vikings' trade relations with Europe pre-dates the Viking raids.

750. All of the following hold true for Vikings EXCEPT

(a) Vikings brought reindeer from Norway to Denmark for trade purposes.

(b) Before becoming the raiders of northern Europe, Vikings had trade relations with European nations.

(c) Antler combs, regarded by the Vikings as a symbol of good health, were part of the Viking culture

(d) Vikings, once upon a time, had trade relations with Denmark and Scandinavia.

2018 Slot 1

Question Numbers (751 to 755): *The passage below is accompanied by a set of four questions. Choose the best answer to each question.*

Economists have spent most of the 20th century ignoring psychology, positive or otherwise. But today there is a great deal of emphasis on how happiness can shape global economies, or — on a smaller scale — successful business practice. This is driven, in part, by a trend in "measuring" positive emotions, mostly so they can be optimized. Neuroscientists, for example, claim to be able to locate specific emotions, such as happiness or disappointment, in particular areas of the brain. Wearable technologies, such as Spire, offer data-driven advice on how to reduce stress.

We are no longer just dealing with "happiness" in a philosophical or romantic sense — it has become something that can be monitored and measured, including by our behavior, use of social media and bodily indicators such as pulse rate and facial expressions.

There is nothing automatically sinister about this trend. But it is disquieting that the businesses and experts driving the quantification of happiness claim to have our best interests at heart, often concealing their own agendas in the process. In the workplace, happy workers are viewed as a "win-win." Work becomes more pleasant, and employees, more productive. But this is now being pursued through the use of performance-evaluating wearable technology, such as Humanyze or Virgin Pulse, both of which monitor physical signs of stress and activity toward the goal of increasing productivity.

Cities such as Dubai, which has pledged to become the "happiest city in the world," dream up ever-more elaborate and intrusive ways of collecting data on well-being — to the point where there is now talk of using CCTV cameras to monitor facial expressions in public spaces. New ways of detecting emotions are hitting the market all the time: One company, Beyond Verbal, aims to calculate moods conveyed in a phone conversation, potentially without the knowledge of at least one of the participants. And Facebook [has] demonstrated . . . that it could influence our emotions through tweaking our news feeds — opening the door to ever-more targeted manipulation in advertising and influence.

As the science grows more sophisticated and technologies become more intimate with our thoughts and bodies, a clear trend is emerging. Where happiness indicators were once used as a basis to reform society, challenging the obsession with money that G.D.P. measurement entrenches, they are increasingly used as a basis to transform or discipline individuals.

Happiness becomes a personal project, that each of us must now work on, like going to the gym. Since the 1970s, depression has come to be viewed as a cognitive or neurological defect in the individual, and never a consequence of circumstances. All of this simply escalates the sense of responsibility each of us feels for our own feelings, and with it, the sense of failure when things go badly. A society that deliberately removed certain sources of misery, such as precarious and exploitative employment, may well be a happier one. But we won't get there by making this single, often fleeting emotion, the over-arching goal.

751. According to the author, wearable technologies and social media are contributing most to:
   (a) depression as a thing of the past.
   (b) disciplining individuals to be happy.
   (c) happiness as a "personal project".
   (d) making individuals aware of stress in their lives.

752. From the passage we can infer that the author would like economists to:
   (a) correlate measurements of happiness with economic indicators.
   (b) work closely with neuroscientists to understand human behaviour.
   (c) incorporate psychological findings into their research cautiously.
   (d) measure the effectiveness of Facebook and social media advertising.

753. In the author's opinion, the shift in thinking in the 1970s:
   (a) put people in touch with their own feelings rather than depending on psychologists.
   (b) reflected the emergence of neuroscience as the authority on human emotions.
   (c) introduced greater stress into people's lives as they were expected to be responsible for their own happiness.
   (d) was a welcome change from the earlier view that depression could be cured by changing circumstances.

754. The author's view would be undermined by which of the following research findings?
   (a) A proliferation of gyms that are collecting data on customer well-being.
   (b) There is a definitive move towards the adoption of wearable technology that taps into emotions.
   (c) Stakeholders globally are moving away from collecting data on the well-being of individuals.
   (d) Individuals worldwide are utilising technologies to monitor and increase their well-being.

755. According to the author, Dubai:
   (a) collaborates with Facebook to selectively influence its inhabitants' moods.
   (b) incentivises companies that prioritise worker welfare.
   (c) develops sophisticated technologies to monitor its inhabitants' states of mind.
   (d) is on its way to becoming one of the world's happiest cities.

Question Numbers (756 to 759) : The passage below is accompanied by a set of five questions. Choose the best answer to each question.

When researchers at Emory University in Atlanta trained mice to fear the smell of almonds (by pairing it with electric shocks), they found, to their consternation, that both the children and grandchildren of these mice were spontaneously afraid of the same smell. That is not supposed to happen. Generations of school children have been taught that the inheritance of acquired characteristics is impossible. A mouse should not be born with something its parents have learned during their lifetimes, any more than a mouse that loses its tail in an accident should give birth to tailless mice. . . .

Modern evolutionary biology dates back to a synthesis that emerged around the 1940s-60s, which married Charles Darwin's mechanism of natural selection with Gregor Mendel's discoveries of how genes are inherited. The traditional, and still dominant, view is that adaptations – from the human brain to the peacock's tail – are fully and satisfactorily explained by natural selection (and subsequent inheritance). Yet [new evidence] from genomics, epigenetics and developmental biology [indicates] that evolution is more complex than we once assumed. . . .

In his book On Human Nature (1978), the evolutionary biologist Edward O Wilson claimed that human culture is held on a genetic leash. The metaphor [needs revision]. . . . Imagine a dog-walker (the genes) struggling to retain control of a brawny mastiff (human culture). The pair's trajectory (the pathway of evolution) reflects the outcome of the struggle. Now imagine the same dog-walker struggling with multiple dogs, on leashes of varied lengths, with each dog tugging in different directions. All these tugs represent the influence of developmental factors, including epigenetics, antibodies and hormones passed on by parents, as well as the ecological legacies and culture they bequeath. . . .

The received wisdom is that parental experiences can't affect the characters of their offspring. Except they do. The way that genes are expressed to produce an organism's phenotype – the actual characteristics it ends up with – is affected by chemicals that attach to them. Everything from diet to air pollution to parental behaviour can influence the addition or removal of these chemical marks, which switches genes on or off. Usually these so-called 'epigenetic' attachments are removed during the production of sperm and eggs cells, but it turns out that some escape the resetting process and are passed on to the next generation, along with the genes. This is known as 'epigenetic inheritance', and more and more studies are confirming that it really happens. Let's return to the almond-fearing mice. The inheritance of an epigenetic mark transmitted in the sperm is what led the mice's offspring to acquire an inherited fear. . . .

Epigenetics is only part of the story. Through culture and society, [humans and other animals] inherit knowledge and skills acquired by [their] parents. . . . All this complexity . . . points to an evolutionary process in which genomes (over hundreds to thousands of generations), epigenetic modifications and inherited cultural factors (over several, perhaps tens or hundreds of generations), and parental effects (over single-generation timespans) collectively inform how organisms adapt. These extra-genetic kinds of inheritance give organisms the flexibility to make rapid adjustments to environmental challenges, dragging genetic change in their wake – much like a rowdy pack of dogs.

756. The Emory University experiment with mice points to the inheritance of:

(a) psychological markers
(b) acquired characteristics
(c) acquired parental fears
(d) personality traits

757. Which of the following options best describes the author's argument?

(a) Darwin's and Mendel's theories together best explain evolution.
(b) Darwin's theory of natural selection cannot fully explain evolution.
(c) Mendel's theory of inheritance is unfairly underestimated in explaining evolution.
(d) Wilson's theory of evolution is scientifically superior to either Darwin's or Mendel's.

758. The passage uses the metaphor of a dog walker to argue that evolutionary adaptation is most comprehensively understood as being determined by:

(a) genetic, epigenetic, developmental factors, and ecological legacies.
(b) ecological, hormonal, extra genetic and genetic legacies.
(c) extra genetic, genetic, epigenetic and genomic legacies.
(d) socio-cultural, genetic, epigenetic, and genomic legacies

759. Which of the following, if found to be true, would negate the main message of the passage?

(a) A study indicating the primacy of ecological impact on human adaptation.
(b) A study affirming the influence of socio-cultural markers on evolutionary processes.
(c) A study highlighting the criticality of epigenetic inheritance to evolution.
(d) A study affirming the sole influence of natural selection and inheritance on evolution.

Question Numbers (760 to 764) : The passage below is accompanied by a set of five questions. Choose the best answer to each question.

The only thing worse than being lied to is not knowing you're being lied to. It's true that plastic pollution is a huge problem, of planetary proportions. And it's true we could all do more to reduce our plastic footprint. The lie is that blame for the plastic problem is wasteful consumers and that changing our individual habits will fix it.

Recycling plastic is to saving the Earth what hammering a nail is to halting a falling skyscraper. You struggle to find a place to do it and feel pleased when you succeed. But your effort is wholly inadequate and distracts from the real problem of why the building is collapsing in the first place. The real problem is that single-use plastic- the very idea of producing plastic items like grocery bags, which we use for an average of 12 minutes but can persist in the environment for half a millennium-is an incredibly reckless abuse of technology. Encouraging individuals to recycle more will never solve the problem of a massive production of single-use plastic that should have been avoided in the first place.

As an ecologist and evolutionary biologist, I have had a disturbing window into the accumulating literature on the hazards of plastic pollution. Scientists have long recognized that plastics biodegrade slowly, if at all, and pose multiple threats to wildlife through entanglement and consumption. More recent reports highlight dangers posed by absorption of toxic chemicals in the water and by plastic odors that mimic some species' natural food.

Plastics also accumulate up the food chain, and studies now show that we are likely ingesting it ourselves in seafood. . . .

Beginning in the 1950s, big beverage companies like Coca-Cola and Anheuser-Busch, along with Phillip Morris and others, formed a non-profit called Keep America Beautiful. Its mission is/was to educate and encourage environmental stewardship in the public. . . . At face value, these efforts seem benevolent, but they obscure the real problem, which is the role that corporate polluters play in the plastic problem. This clever misdirection has led journalist and author Heather Rogers to describe Keep America Beautiful as the first corporate greenwashing front, as it has helped shift the public focus to consumer recycling behavior and actively thwarted legislation that would increase extended producer responsibility for waste management. . . . [T]he greatest success of Keep America Beautiful has been to shift the onus of environmental responsibility onto the public while simultaneously becoming a trusted name in the environmental movement. . . .

So what can we do to make responsible use of plastic a reality? First: reject the lie. Litterbugs are not responsible for the global ecological disaster of plastic. Humans can only function to the best of their abilities, given time, mental bandwidth and systemic constraints. Our huge problem with plastic is the result of a permissive legal framework that has allowed the uncontrolled rise of plastic pollution, despite clear evidence of the harm it causes to local communities and the world's oceans. Recycling is also too hard in most parts of the U.S. and lacks the proper incentives to make it work well.

760. It can be inferred that the author considers the Keep America Beautiful organisation:

(a) a "greenwash" because it was a benevolent attempt to improve public recycling habits.

(b) an innovative example of a collaborative corporate social responsibility initiative.

(c) an important step in sensitising producers to the need to tackle plastics pollution.

(d) a sham as it diverted attention away from the role of corporates in plastics pollution.

761. Which of the following interventions would the author most strongly support:

(a) having all consumers change their plastic consumption habits.

(b) recycling all plastic debris in the seabed.

(c) completely banning all single-use plastic bags.

(d) passing regulations targeted at producers that generate plastic products.

762. In the second paragraph, the phrase "what hammering a nail is to halting a falling skyscraper" means:

(a) focusing on single-use plastic bags to reduce the plastics footprint.

(b) relying on emerging technologies to mitigate the ill-effects of plastic pollution.

(c) focusing on consumer behaviour to tackle the problem of plastics pollution.

(d) encouraging the responsible production of plastics by firms.

763. The author lists all of the following as negative effects of the use of plastics EXCEPT the:

(a) slow pace of degradation or non-degradation of plastics in the environment.

(b) poisonous chemicals released into the water and food we consume.

(c) air pollution caused during the process of recycling plastics.

(d) adverse impacts on the digestive systems of animals exposed to plastic.

764. In the first paragraph, the author uses "lie" to refer to the:

(a) blame assigned to consumers for indiscriminate use of plastics.

(b) understatement of the enormity of the plastics pollution problem.

(c) understatement of the effects of recycling plastics.

(d) fact that people do not know they have been lied to.

Question Numbers (765 to 769) : The passage below is accompanied by a set of five questions. Choose the best answer to each question.

[The] Indian government [has] announced an international competition to design a National War Memorial in New Delhi, to honour all of the Indian soldiers who served in the various wars and counter-insurgency campaigns from 1947 onwards. The terms of the competition also specified that the new structure would be built adjacent to the India Gate - a memorial to the Indian soldiers who died in the First World War. Between the old imperialist memorial and the proposed nationalist one, India's contribution to the Second World War is airbrushed out of existence.

The Indian government's conception of the war memorial was not merely absent-minded. Rather, it accurately reflected the fact that both academic history and popular memory have yet to come to terms with India's Second

World War, which continues to be seen as little more than mood music in the drama of India's advance towards independence and partition in 1947. Further, the political trajectory of the postwar subcontinent has militated against popular remembrance of the war. With partition and the onset of the India-Pakistan rivalry, both of the new nations needed fresh stories for self-legitimisation rather than focusing on shared wartime experiences.

However, the Second World War played a crucial role in both the independence and partition of India. . . . The Indian army recruited, trained and deployed some 2.5 million men, almost 90,000 of which were killed and many more injured. Even at the time, it was recognised as the largest volunteer force in the war. . . .

India's material and financial contribution to the war was equally significant. India emerged as a major military-industrial and logistical base for Allied operations in south-east Asia and the Middle East. This led the United States to take considerable interest in the country's future, and ensured that this was no longer the preserve of the British government.

Other wartime developments pointed in the direction of India's independence. In a stunning reversal of its long-standing financial relationship with Britain, India finished the war as one of the largest creditors to the imperial power.

Such extraordinary mobilization for war was achieved at great human cost, with the Bengal famine the most extreme manifestation of widespread wartime deprivation. The costs on India's home front must be counted in millions of lives.

Indians signed up to serve on the war and home fronts for a variety of reasons. . . . [M]any were convinced that their contribution would open the doors to India's freedom. . . . The political and social churn triggered by the war was evident in the massive waves of popular protest and unrest that washed over rural and urban India in the aftermath of the conflict. This turmoil was crucial in persuading the Attlee government to rid itself of the incubus of ruling India. . . .

Seventy years on, it is time that India engaged with the complex legacies of the Second World War. Bringing the war into the ambit of the new national memorial would be a fitting - if not overdue - recognition that this was India's War.

765. The author claims that omitting mention of Indians who served in the Second World War from the new National War Memorial is:

(a) a reflection of misplaced priorities of the post-independence Indian governments.

(b) appropriate as their names can always be included in the India Gate memorial.

(c) a reflection of the academic and popular view of India's role in the War.

(d) is something which can be rectified in future by constructing a separate memorial.

766. In the first paragraph, the author laments the fact that:

(a) the new war memorial will be built right next to India Gate.

(b) there is no recognition of the Indian soldiers who served in the Second World War.

(c) funds will be wasted on another war memorial when we already have the India Gate memorial.

(d) India lost thousands of human lives during the Second World War.

767. The author lists all of the following as outcomes of the Second World War EXCEPT:

(a) large-scale deaths in Bengal as a result of deprivation and famine.

(b) the large financial debt India owed to Britain after the War.

(c) independence of the subcontinent and its partition into two countries.

(d) US recognition of India's strategic location and role in the War.

768. The author suggests that a major reason why India has not so far acknowledged its role in the Second World War is that it:

(a) blames the War for leading to the momentous partition of the country.

(b) wants to forget the human and financial toll of the War on the country.

(c) views the War as a predominantly Allied effort, with India playing only a supporting role.

(d) has been focused on building an independent, non-colonial political identity.

769. The phrase "mood music" is used in the second paragraph to indicate that the Second World War is viewed as:

(a) a tragic period in terms of loss of lives and national wealth.

(b) a part of the narrative on the ill-effects of colonial rule on India.

(c) a backdrop to the subsequent independence and partition of the region.

(d) setting the stage for the emergence of the India–Pakistan rivalry in the subcontinent.

Question Numbers (770 to 774) : The passage below is accompanied by a set of five questions. Choose the best answer to each question.

. . . "Everybody pretty much agrees that the relationship between elephants and people has dramatically changed," [says psychologist Gay] Bradshaw. . . . "Where for centuries humans and elephants lived in relatively peaceful coexistence, there is now hostility and violence. Now, I use the term 'violence' because of the intentionality associated with it, both in the aggression of humans and, at times, the recently observed behavior of elephants." ...

Typically, elephant researchers have cited, as a cause of aggression, the high levels of testosterone in newly matured male elephants or the competition for land and resources between elephants and humans. But. . . Bradshaw and several colleagues argue. . . that today's elephant populations are suffering from a form of chronic stress, a kind of species-wide trauma. Decades of poaching and culling and habitat loss, they claim, have so disrupted the intricate web of familial and societal relations by which young elephants have traditionally been raised in the wild, and by which established elephant herds are governed, that what we are now witnessing is nothing less than a precipitous collapse of elephant culture. . . .

Elephants, when left to their own devices, are profoundly social creatures. . . . Young elephants are raised within an extended, multitiered network of doting female caregivers that includes the birth mother, grandmothers, aunts and friends. These relations are maintained over a life span as long as 70 years. Studies of established herds have shown that young elephants stay within 15 feet of their mothers for nearly all of their first eight years of life, after which young females are socialized into the matriarchal network, while young males go off for a time into an all-male social group before coming back into the fold as mature adults. . . .

This fabric of elephant society, Bradshaw and her colleagues [demonstrate], ha[s] effectively been frayed by years of habitat loss and poaching, along with systematic culling by government agencies to control elephant numbers and translocations of herds to different habitats. . . . As a result of such social upheaval, calves are now being born to and raised by ever younger and inexperienced mothers. Young orphaned elephants, meanwhile, that have witnessed the death of a parent at the hands of poachers are coming of age in the absence of the support system that defines traditional elephant life. "The loss of elephant elders," [says] Bradshaw . . . "and the traumatic experience of witnessing the massacres of their family, impairs normal brain and behavior development in young elephants."

What Bradshaw and her colleagues describe would seem to be an extreme form of anthropocentric conjecture if the evidence that they've compiled from various elephant researchers. . . weren't so compelling. The elephants of decimated herds, especially orphans who've watched the death of their parents and elders from poaching and culling, exhibit behavior typically associated with post-traumatic stress disorder and other trauma-related disorders in humans: abnormal startle response, unpredictable asocial behavior, inattentive mothering and hyperaggression. . . .

[According to Bradshaw], "Elephants are suffering and behaving in the same ways that we recognize in ourselves as a result of violence. . . . Except perhaps for a few specific features, brain organization and early development of elephants and humans are extremely similar."

770. Which of the following measures is Bradshaw most likely to support to address the problem of elephant aggression?
   (a) Increased funding for research into the similarity of humans and other animals drawing on insights gained from human-elephant similarities.
   (b) Funding of more studies to better understand the impact of testosterone on male elephant aggression.
   (c) The development of treatment programmes for elephants drawing on insights gained from treating post-traumatic stress disorder in humans.
   (d) Studying the impact of isolating elephant calves on their early brain development, behaviour and aggression.

771. In paragraph 4, the phrase, "The fabric of elephant society . . . has[s] effectively been frayed by . . ." is:
   (a) a metaphor for the effect of human activity on elephant communities.
   (b) an accurate description of the condition of elephant herds today.
   (c) an exaggeration aimed at bolstering Bradshaw's claims.
   (d) an ode to the fragility of elephant society today.

772. The passage makes all of the following claims EXCEPT:
   (a) human actions such as poaching and culling have created stressful conditions for elephant communities.
   (b) elephants establish extended and enduring familial relationships as do humans.
   (c) elephant mothers are evolving newer ways of rearing their calves to adapt to emerging threats.
   (d) the elephant response to deeply disturbing experiences is similar to that of humans.

773. Which of the following statements best expresses the overall argument of this passage?
   (a) The brain organisation and early development of elephants and humans are extremely similar.
   (b) The relationship between elephants and humans has changed from one of coexistence to one of hostility.

(c) Recent elephant behaviour could be understood as a form of species-wide trauma-related response.

(d) Elephants, like the humans they are in conflict with, are profoundly social creatures.

774. In the first paragraph, Bradshaw uses the term "violence" to describe the recent change in the human-elephant relationship because, according to him:

(a) both humans and elephants have killed members of each other's species.

(b) elephant herds and their habitat have been systematically destroyed by humans.

(c) human-elephant interactions have changed their character over time.

(d) there is a purposefulness in human and elephant aggression towards each other.

2018 Slot 2

Question Numbers (775 to 779) : The passage below is accompanied by a set of five questions. Choose the best answer to each question.

Will a day come when India's poor can access government services as easily as drawing cash from an ATM? . . . [N]o country in the world has made accessing education or health or policing or dispute resolution as easy as an ATM, because the nature of these activities requires individuals to use their discretion in a positive way. Technology can certainly facilitate this in a variety of ways if it is seen as one part of an overall approach, but the evidence so far in education, for instance, is that just adding computers alone doesn't make education any better. . . .

The dangerous illusion of technology is that it can create stronger, top down accountability of service providers in implementation-intensive services within existing public sector organisations. One notion is that electronic management information systems (EMIS) keep better track of inputs and those aspects of personnel that are 'EMIS visible' can lead to better services. A recent study examined attempts to increase attendance of Auxiliary Nurse Midwife (ANMs) at clinics in Rajasthan, which involved high-tech time clocks to monitor attendance. The study's title says it all: Band-Aids on a Corpse . . . e-governance can be just as bad as any other governance when the real issue is people and their motivation.

For services to improve, the people providing the services have to want to do a better job with the skills they have. A study of medical care in Delhi found that even though providers, in the public sector had much better skills than private sector providers their provision of care in actual practice was much worse.

In implementation-intensive services the key to success is face-to-face interactions between a teacher, a nurse, a policeman, an extension agent and a citizen. This relationship is about power. Amartya Sen's . . . report on education in West Bengal had a supremely telling anecdote in which the villagers forced the teacher to attend school, but then, when the parents went off to work, the teacher did not teach, but forced the children to massage his feet. . . . As long as the system empowers providers over citizens, technology is irrelevant.

The answer to successfully providing basic services is to create systems that provide both autonomy and accountability. In basic education for instance, the answer to poor teaching is not controlling teachers more . . . The key . . . is to hire teachers who want to teach and let them teach, expressing their professionalism and vocation as a teacher through autonomy in the classroom. This autonomy has to be matched with accountability for results—not just narrowly measured through test scores, but broadly for the quality of the education they provide.

A recent study in Uttar Pradesh showed that if, somehow, all civil service teachers could be replaced with contract teachers, the state could save a billion dollars a year in revenue and double student learning. Just the additional autonomy and accountability of contracts through local groups—even without complementary system changes in information and empowerment—led to that much improvement. The first step to being part of the solution is to create performance information accessible to those outside of the government. . . .

775. The author questions the use of monitoring systems in services that involve face-to-face interaction between service providers and clients because such systems:

(a) improve the skills but do not increase the motivation of service providers.

(b) do not improve services that need committed service providers.

(c) are not as effective in the public sector as they are in the private sector.

(d) are ineffective because they are managed by the government.

776. According to the author, service delivery in Indian education can be improved in all of the following ways EXCEPT through:

(a) elimination of government involvement.

(b) use of technology.

(c) access to information on the quality of teaching.

(d) recruitment of motivated teachers.

777. In the context of the passage, we can infer that the title "Band Aids on a Corpse" (in paragraph 2) suggests that:

(a) the electronic monitoring system was a superficial solution to a serious problem.

(b) the nurses who attended the clinics were too poorly trained to provide appropriate medical care.

(c) the nurses attended the clinics, but the clinics were ill-equipped.

(d) the clinics were better funded, but performance monitoring did not result in any improvement.

778. Which of the following, IF TRUE, would undermine the passage's main argument?

(a) Empowerment of service providers leads to increased complacency and rigged performance results.

(b) If absolute instead of moderate technological surveillance is exercised over the performance of service providers.

(c) If it were proven that service providers in the private sector have better skills than those in the public sector.

(d) If it were proven that increase in autonomy of service providers leads to an exponential increase in their work ethic and sense of responsibility.

779. The main purpose of the passage is to:

(a) find a solution to the problem of poor service delivery in education by examining different strategies.

(b) argue that some types of services can be improved by providing independence and requiring accountability.

(c) critique the government's involvement in educational activities and other implementation-intensive services.

(d) analyse the shortcomings of government-appointed nurses and their management through technology.

Question Numbers (780 to 784) : The passage below is accompanied by a set of five questions. Choose the best answer to each question.

More and more companies, government agencies, educational institutions and philanthropic organisations are today in the grip of a new phenomenon: 'metric fixation'. The key components of metric fixation are the belief that it is possible – and desirable – to replace professional judgment (acquired through personal experience and talent) with numerical indicators of comparative performance based upon standardised data (metrics); and that the best way to motivate people within these organisations is by attaching rewards and penalties to their measured performance.

The rewards can be monetary, in the form of pay for performance, say, or reputational, in the form of college rankings, hospital ratings, surgical report cards and so on. But the most dramatic negative effect of metric fixation is its propensity to incentivise gaming: that is, encouraging professionals to maximise the metrics in ways that are at odds with the larger purpose of the organisation. If the rate of major crimes in a district becomes the metric according to which police officers are promoted, then some officers will respond by simply not recording crimes or downgrading them from major offences to misdemeanours. Or take the case of surgeons. When the metrics of success and failure are made public – affecting their reputation and income – some surgeons will improve their metric scores by refusing to operate on patients with more complex problems, whose surgical outcomes are more likely to be negative. Who suffers? The patients who don't get operated upon.

When reward is tied to measured performance, metric fixation invites just this sort of gaming. But metric fixation also leads to a variety of more subtle unintended negative consequences. These include goal displacement, which comes in many varieties: when performance is judged by a few measures, and the stakes are high (keeping one's job, getting a pay rise or raising the stock price at the time that stock options are vested), people focus on satisfying those measures – often at the expense of other, more important organisational goals that are not measured. The best-known example is 'teaching to the test', a widespread phenomenon that has distorted primary and secondary education in the United States since the adoption of the No Child Left Behind Act of 2001.

Short-termism is another negative. Measured performance encourages what the US sociologist Robert K Merton in 1936 called 'the imperious immediacy of interests ... where the actor's paramount concern with the foreseen immediate consequences excludes consideration of further or other consequences'. In short, advancing short-term goals at the expense of long-range considerations. This problem is endemic to publicly traded corporations that sacrifice long-term research and development, and the development of their staff, to the perceived imperatives of the quarterly report.

To the debit side of the ledger must also be added the transactional costs of metrics: the expenditure of employee time by those tasked with compiling and processing the metrics in the first place – not to mention the time required to actually read them. . . .

780. All of the following can be a possible feature of the No Child Left Behind Act of 2001, EXCEPT:

(a) standardised test scores can be critical in determining a student's educational future.

(b) the focus is more on test-taking skills than on higher order thinking and problem-solving.

(c) assessment is dependent on the teacher's subjective evaluation of students' class participation.

(d) school funding and sanctions are tied to yearly improvement shown on tests.

781. Of the following, which would have added the least depth to the author's argument?

(a) Assessment of the pros and cons of a professional judgment-based evaluation system.

(b) An analysis of the reasons why metrics fixation is becoming popular despite its drawbacks.

(c) A comparative case study of metrics- and non-metrics-based evaluation, and its impact on the main goals of an organisation.

(d) More real-life illustrations of the consequences of employees and professionals gaming metrics-based performance measurement systems.

782. What is the main idea that the author is trying to highlight in the passage?

(a) All kinds of organisations are now relying on metrics to measure performance and to give rewards and punishments.

(b) Long-term organisational goals should not be ignored for short-term measures of organisational success.

(c) Performance measurement needs to be precise and cost-effective to be useful for evaluating organisational performance.

(d) Evaluating performance by using measurable performance metrics may misguide organisational goal achievement.

783. What main point does the author want to convey through the examples of the police officer and the surgeon?

(a) Critical public roles should not be evaluated on metrics-based performance measures.

(b) Some professionals are likely to be significantly influenced by the design of performance measurement systems.

(c) Metrics-linked rewards may encourage unethical behaviour among some professionals.

(d) The actions of police officers and surgeons have a significantly impact on society.

784. Which of the following is NOT a consequence of the 'metric fixation' phenomenon mentioned in the passage?

(a) Deviating from organisationally important objectives to measurable yet less important objectives.

(b) Finding a way to show better results without actually improving performance.

(c) Short-term orientation induced by frequent measurement of performance.

(d) Improving cooperation among employees leading to increased organisational effectiveness in the long run.

Question Numbers (785 to 788) : The passage below is accompanied by a set of four questions. Choose the best answer to each question.

. . . Grove snails as a whole are distributed all over Europe, but a specific variety of the snail, with a distinctive white-lipped shell, is found exclusively in Ireland and in the Pyrenees mountains that lie on the border between France and Spain. The researchers sampled a total of 423 snail specimens from 36 sites distributed across Europe, with an emphasis on gathering large numbers of the white-lipped variety. When they sequenced genes from the mitochondrial DNA of each of these snails and used algorithms to analyze the genetic diversity between them, they found that. . . a distinct lineage (the snails with the white-lipped shells) was indeed endemic to the two very specific and distant places in question.

Explaining this is tricky. Previously, some had speculated that the strange distributions of creatures such as the white-lipped grove snails could be explained by convergent evolution—in which two populations evolve the same trait by coincidence—but the underlying genetic similarities between the two groups rules that out. Alternately, some scientists had suggested that the white-lipped variety had simply spread over the whole continent, then been wiped out everywhere besides Ireland and the Pyrenees, but the researchers say their sampling and subsequent DNA analysis eliminate that possibility too. "If the snails naturally colonized Ireland, you would expect to find some of the same genetic type in other areas of Europe, especially Britain. We just don't find them," Davidson, the lead author, said in a press statement.

Moreover, if they'd gradually spread across the continent, there would be some genetic variation within the white-lipped type, because evolution would introduce variety over the thousands of years it would have taken them to spread from the Pyrenees to Ireland. That variation doesn't exist, at least in the genes sampled. This means that rather than the organism gradually expanding its range, large populations instead were somehow moved en mass to the other location within the space of a few dozen generations, ensuring a lack of genetic variety.

"There is a very clear pattern, which is difficult to explain except by involving humans," Davidson said. Humans, after all, colonized Ireland roughly 9,000 years ago, and the oldest fossil evidence of grove snails in Ireland dates to roughly the same era. Additionally, there is archaeological evidence of early sea trade between the ancient peoples of Spain and Ireland via the Atlantic and even evidence that humans routinely ate these types of snails before the advent of agriculture, as their burnt shells have been found in Stone Age trash heaps.

The simplest explanation, then? Boats. These snails may have inadvertently traveled on the floor of the small, coast-hugging skiffs these early humans used for travel, or they may have been intentionally carried to Ireland by the seafarers as a food source. "The highways of the past were rivers and the ocean–as the river that flanks the Pyrenees was an ancient trade route to the Atlantic, what we're actually seeing might be the long lasting legacy of snails that hitched a ride...as humans travelled from the South of France to Ireland 8,000 years ago," Davidson said.

785. All of the following evidence supports the passage's explanation of sea travel/trade EXCEPT:

(a) archaeological evidence of early sea trade between the ancient peoples of Spain and Ireland via the Atlantic Ocean.

(b) the coincidental existence of similar traits in the white-lipped grove snails of Ireland and the Pyrenees because of convergent evolution.

(c) absence of genetic variation within the white-lipped grove snails of Ireland and the Pyrenees, whose genes were sampled.

(d) the oldest fossil evidence of white-lipped grove snails in Ireland dates back to roughly 9,000 years ago, the time when humans colonised Ireland.

786. In paragraph 4, the evidence that "humans routinely ate these types of snails before the advent of agriculture" can be used to conclude that:

(a) white-lipped grove snails may have inadvertently traveled from the Pyrenees to Ireland on the floor of the small, coast-hugging skiffs that early seafarers used for travel.

(b) the seafarers who traveled from the Pyrenees to Ireland might have carried white-lipped grove snails with them as edibles.

(c) 9,000 years ago, during the Stone Age, humans traveled from the South of France to Ireland via the Atlantic Ocean.

(d) rivers and oceans in the Stone Age facilitated trade in white-lipped grove snails.

787. Which one of the following makes the author eliminate convergent evolution as a probable explanation for why white-lipped grove snails are found in Ireland and the Pyrenees?

(a) The distinct lineage of white-lipped grove snails found specifically in Ireland and the Pyrenees.

(b) The coincidental evolution of similar traits (white-lipped shell) in the grove snails of Ireland and the Pyrenees.

(c) The absence of genetic similarities between white-lipped grove snails of Ireland and snails from other parts of Europe, especially Britain.

(d) The absence of genetic variation between white-lipped grove snails of Ireland and the Pyrenees.

788. The passage outlines several hypotheses and evidence related to white-lipped grove snails to arrive at the most convincing explanation for:

(a) how the white-lipped variety of grove snails might have migrated from the Pyrenees to Ireland.

(b) how the white-lipped variety of grove snails independently evolved in Ireland and the Pyrenees.

(c) why the white-lipped variety of grove snails were wiped out everywhere except in Ireland and the Pyrenees.

(d) why the white-lipped variety of grove snails are found only in Ireland and the Pyrenees.

Question Numbers (789 to 793) : The passage below is accompanied by a set of five questions. Choose the best answer to each question.

NOT everything looks lovelier the longer and closer its inspection. But Saturn does. It is gorgeous through Earthly telescopes. However, the 13 years of close observation provided by Cassini, an American spacecraft, showed the planet, its moons and its remarkable rings off better and better, revealing finer structures, striking novelties and greater drama. . . .

By and large the big things in the solar system—planets and moons—are thought of as having been around since the beginning. The suggestion that rings and moons are new is, though, made even more interesting by the fact that one of those moons, Enceladus, is widely considered the most promising site in the solar system on which to look for alien life. If Enceladus is both young and bears life, that life must have come into being quickly. This is also believed to have been the case on Earth. Were it true on Enceladus, that would encourage the idea that life evolves easily when conditions are right.

One reason for thinking Saturn's rings are young is that they are bright. The solar system is suffused with comet dust, and comet dust is dark. Leaving Saturn's ring system (which Cassini has shown to be more than 90% water ice) out in such a mist is like leaving laundry hanging on a line downwind from a smokestack: it will get dirty. The lighter the rings are, the faster this will happen, for the less mass they contain, the less celestial pollution they can absorb before they start to discolour. . . . Jeff Cuzzi, a scientist at America's space agency, NASA, who helped run Cassini, told the Lunar and Planetary Science Conference in Houston that combining the mass estimates with Cassini's measurements of the density of comet-dust near Saturn suggests the rings are no older than the first dinosaurs, nor younger than the last of them—that is, they are somewhere between 200m and 70m years old.

That timing fits well with a theory put forward in 2016, by Matija Cuk of the SETI Institute, in California and his colleagues. They suggest that at around the same time as the rings came into being an old set of moons orbiting Saturn destroyed themselves, and from their remains emerged not only the rings but also the planet's current suite of inner moons—Rhea, Dione, Tethys, Enceladus and Mimas. . . .

Dr Cuk and his colleagues used computer simulations of Saturn's moons' orbits as a sort of time machine. Looking at the rate at which tidal friction is causing these orbits to lengthen they extrapolated backwards to find out what those orbits would have looked like in the past. They discovered that about 100m years ago the orbits of two of them, Tethys and Dione, would have interacted in a way that left the planes in which they orbit markedly tilted. But their orbits are untilted. The obvious, if unsettling, conclusion was that this interaction never happened—and thus that at the time when it should have happened, Dione and Tethys were simply not there. They must have come into being later. . . .

789. The phrase "leaving laundry hanging on a line downwind from a smokestack" is used to explain how the ringed planet's:
(a) atmosphere absorbs comet dust.
(b) moons create a gap between the rings.
(c) rings discolour and darken over time.
(d) rings lose mass over time.

790. Based on information provided in the passage, we can infer that, in addition to water ice, Saturn's rings might also have small amounts of:
(a) rock particles and comet dust.
(b) methane and rock particles.
(c) helium and methane.
(d) helium and comet dust.

791. Based on information provided in the passage, we can conclude all of the following EXCEPT:
(a) Saturn's rings were created from the remains of older moons.
(b) Thethys and Dione are less than 100 million years old.
(c) Saturn's lighter rings discolour faster than rings with greater mass.
(d) none of Saturn's moons ever had suitable conditions for life to evolve.

792. The main objective of the passage is to:
(a) demonstrate how the orbital patterns of Saturn's rings and moons change over time.
(b) highlight the beauty, finer structures and celestial drama of Saturn's rings and moons.
(c) provide evidence that Saturn's rings and moons are recent creations.
(d) establish that Saturn's rings and inner moons have been around since the beginning of time.

793. Data provided by Cassini challenged the assumption that:
(a) there was life on earth when Saturn's rings were being formed.
(b) new celestial bodies can form from the destruction of old celestial bodies.
(c) Saturn's ring system is composed mostly of water ice.
(d) all big things in the solar system have been around since the beginning.

Question Numbers (794 to 798) : The passage below is accompanied by a set of five questions. Choose the best answer to each question.

. . . The complexity of modern problems often precludes any one person from fully understanding them. Factors contributing to rising obesity levels, for example, include transportation systems and infrastructure, media, convenience foods, changing social norms, human biology and psychological factors. . . . The multidimensional or layered character of complex problems also undermines the principle of meritocracy: the idea that the 'best person' should be hired. There is no best person. When putting together an oncological research team, a biotech company such as Gilead or Genentech would not construct a multiple-choice test and hire the top scorers, or hire people whose resumes score highest according to some performance criteria. Instead, they would seek diversity. They would build a team of people who bring diverse knowledge bases, tools and analytic skills. . . .

Believers in a meritocracy might grant that teams ought to be diverse but then argue that meritocratic principles should apply within each category. Thus the team should consist of the 'best' mathematicians, the 'best' oncologists, and the 'best' biostatisticians from within the pool. That position suffers from a similar flaw. Even with a knowledge domain, no test or criteria applied to individuals will produce the best team. Each of these domains possesses such depth and breadth, that no test can exist. Consider the field of neuroscience. Upwards of 50,000 papers were published last year covering various techniques, domains of enquiry and levels of analysis, ranging from molecules and synapses up through networks of neurons. Given that complexity, any attempt to rank a collection of neuroscientists from best to worst, as if they were competitors in the 50-metre butterfly, must fail. What could be true is that given a specific task and the composition of a particular team, one scientist would be more likely to contribute than another. Optimal hiring depends on context. Optimal teams will be diverse.

Evidence for this claim can be seen in the way that papers and patents that combine diverse ideas tend to rank as high-impact. It can also be found in the structure of the so-called random decision forest, a state-of-the-art machine-learning algorithm. Random forests consist of ensembles of decision trees. If classifying pictures, each tree makes a vote: is that a picture of a fox or a dog? A weighted majority rules. Random forests can serve many ends. They can identify bank fraud and diseases, recommend ceiling fans and predict online dating behaviour. When building a forest, you do not select the best trees as they tend to make similar classifications. You want diversity. Programmers achieve that diversity by training each tree on different data, a technique known as bagging. They also boost the forest 'cognitively' by training trees on the hardest cases – those that the current forest gets wrong. This ensures even more diversity and accurate forests.

Yet the fallacy of meritocracy persists. Corporations, non-profits, governments, universities and even preschools test, score and hire the 'best'. This all but guarantees not creating the best team. Ranking people by common criteria produces homogeneity. . . . That's not likely to lead to breakthroughs.

794. Which of the following conditions, if true, would invalidate the passage's main argument?

(a) If a new machine-learning algorithm were developed that proved to be more effective than the random decision forest.

(b) If assessment tests were made more extensive and rigorous.

(c) If it were proven that teams characterised by diversity end up being conflicted about problems and take a long time to arrive at a solution.

(d) If top-scorers possessed multidisciplinary knowledge that enabled them to look at a problem from several perspectives.

795. On the basis of the passage, which of the following teams is likely to be most effective in solving the problem of rising obesity levels?

(a) A team comprised of nutritionists, psychologists, urban planners and media personnel, who have each performed well in their respective subject tests.

(b) A specialised team of nutritionists from various countries, who are also trained in the machine-learning algorithm of random decision forest.

(c) A team comprised of nutritionists, psychologists, urban planners and media personnel, who have each scored a distinction in their respective subject tests.

(d) A specialised team of top nutritionists from various countries, who also possess some knowledge of psychology.

796. Which of the following conditions would weaken the efficacy of a random decision forest?

(a) If a large number of decision trees in the ensemble were trained on data derived from easy cases.

(b) If a large number of decision trees in the ensemble were trained on data derived from easy and hard cases.

(c) If the types of ensembles of decision trees in the forest were doubled.

(d) If the types of decision trees in each ensemble of the forest were doubled.

797. The author critiques meritocracy for all the following reasons EXCEPT that:

(a) diversity and context-specificity are important for making major advances in any field.

(b) criteria designed to assess merit are insufficient to test expertise in any field of knowledge.

(c) modern problems are multifaceted and require varied skill-sets to be solved.

(d) an ideal team comprises of best individuals from diverse fields of knowledge.

798. Which of the following best describes the purpose of the example of neuroscience?

(a) Neuroscience is an advanced field of science because of its connections with other branches of science like oncology and biostatistics.

(b) Unlike other fields of knowledge, neuroscience is an exceptionally complex field, making a meaningful assessment of neuroscientists impossible.

(c) In narrow fields of knowledge, a meaningful assessment of expertise has always been possible.

(d) In the modern age, every field of knowledge is so vast that a meaningful assessment of merit is impossible.

ANSWERS

1. (c) **2.** (c) **3.** (b) **4.** (c) **5.** (c) **6.** (d) **7.** (b) **8.** (d) **9.** (d) **10.** (c)
11. (d) **12.** (d) **13.** (b) **14.** (b) **15.** (b) **16.** (c) **17.** (c) **18.** (d) **19.** (c) **20.** (b)
21. (d) **22.** (d) **23.** (c) **24.** (c) **25.** (c) **26.** (c) **27.** (d) **28.** (b) **29.** (d) **30.** (d)
31. (a) **32.** (b) **33.** (b) **34.** (c) **35.** (d) **36.** (c) **37.** (c) **38.** (c) **39.** (d) **40.** (d)
41. (a) **42.** (d) **43.** (c) **44.** (c) **45.** (a) **46.** (a) **47.** (d) **48.** (c) **49.** (c) **50.** (b)
51. (d) **52.** (b) **53.** (d) **54.** (d) **55.** (d) **56.** (b) **57.** (a) **58.** (a) **59.** (c) **60.** (b)
61. (b) **62.** (a) **63.** (c) **64.** (d) **65.** (a) **66.** (b) **67.** (d) **68.** (c) **69.** (a) **70.** (c)
71. (b) **72.** (b) **73.** (d) **74.** (c) **75.** (b) **76.** (c) **77.** (b) **78.** (a) **79.** (c) **80.** (c)
81. (c) **82.** (d) **83.** (c) **84.** (c) **85.** (d) **86.** (d) **87.** (b) **88.** (b) **89.** (b) **90.** (b)
91. (d) **92.** (b) **93.** (c) **94.** (b) **95.** (d) **96.** (c) **97.** (a) **98.** (d) **99.** (c) **100.** (b)
101. (a) **102.** (a) **103.** (d) **104.** (c) **105.** (b) **106.** (d) **107.** (c) **108.** (b) **109.** (a) **110.** (d)
111. (b) **112.** (d) **113.** (b) **114.** (b) **115.** (b) **116.** (c) **117.** (b) **118.** (c) **119.** (d) **120.** (b)
121. (d) **122.** (d) **123.** (b) **124.** (c) **125.** (c) **126.** (b) **127.** (c) **128.** (c) **129.** (b) **130.** (c)
131. (a) **132.** (b) **133.** (d) **134.** (a) **135.** (c) **136.** (c) **137.** (c) **138.** (c) **139.** (c) **140.** (d)
141. (c) **142.** (c) **143.** (b) **144.** (b) **145.** (a) **146.** (b) **147.** (c) **148.** (d) **149.** (a) **150.** (b)
151. (d) **152.** (a) **153.** (a) **154.** (c) **155.** (b) **156.** (b) **157.** (d) **158.** (c) **159.** (a) **160.** (c)
161. (a) **162.** (b) **163.** (a) **164.** (c) **165.** (d) **166.** (b) **167.** (c) **168.** (d) **169.** (d) **170.** (a)
171. (b) **172.** (c) **173.** (c) **174.** (d) **175.** (d) **176.** (d) **177.** (a) **178.** (c) **179.** (c) **180.** (b)
181. (a) **182.** (b) **183.** (d) **184.** (b) **185.** (c) **186.** (a) **187.** (c) **188.** (b) **189.** (b) **190.** (d)
191. (a) **192.** (d) **193.** (a) **194.** (d) **195.** (c) **196.** (d) **197.** (d) **198.** (b) **199.** (b) **200.** (d)
201. (d) **202.** (d) **203.** (c) **204.** (b) **205.** (c) **206.** (b) **207.** (d) **208.** (a) **209.** (c) **210.** (b)
211. (a) **212.** (b) **213.** (a) **214.** (a) **215.** (d) **216.** (c) **217.** (c) **218.** (b) **219.** (b) **220.** (c)
221. (b) **222.** (b) **223.** (b) **224.** (d) **225.** (c) **226.** (b) **227.** (a) **228.** (c) **229.** (a) **230.** (b)
231. (c) **232.** (a) **233.** (d) **234.** (c) **235.** (d) **236.** (b) **237.** (c) **238.** (b) **239.** (c) **240.** (c)
241. (d) **242.** (c) **243.** (b) **244.** (d) **245.** (b) **246.** (d) **247.** (a) **248.** (b) **249.** (a) **250.** (c)
251. (a) **252.** (c) **253.** (c) **254.** (b) **255.** (b) **256.** (a) **257.** (b) **258.** (a) **259.** (b) **260.** (d)
261. (d) **262.** (a) **263.** (c) **264.** (c) **265.** (c) **266.** (b) **267.** (a) **268.** (a) **269.** (c) **270.** (c)
271. (d) **272.** (d) **273.** (a) **274.** (b) **275.** (b) **276.** (a) **277.** (b) **278.** (c) **279.** (a) **280.** (c)
281. (d) **282.** (a) **283.** (d) **284.** (b) **285.** (c) **286.** (c) **287.** (a) **288.** (b) **289.** (d) **290.** (b)
291. (a) **292.** (c) **293.** (b) **294.** (b) **295.** (b) **296.** (d) **297.** (b) **298.** (a) **299.** (c) **300.** (b)
301. (c) **302.** (d) **303.** (a) **304.** (a) **305.** (c) **306.** (d) **307.** (b) **308.** (a) **309.** (c) **310.** (b)
311. (c) **312.** (c) **313.** (b) **314.** (a) **315.** (d) **316.** (d) **317.** (a) **318.** (b) **319.** (d) **320.** (a)
321. (a) **322.** (c) **323.** (d) **324.** (a) **325.** (c) **326.** (b) **327.** (d) **328.** (c) **329.** (b) **330.** (b)
331. (c) **332.** (d) **333.** (c) **334.** (b) **335.** (c) **336.** (a) **337.** (b) **338.** (c) **339.** (b) **340.** (d)
341. (d) **342.** (a) **343.** (b) **344.** (c) **345.** (b) **346.** (c) **347.** (a) **348.** (c) **349.** (d) **350.** (c)
351. (a) **352.** (b) **353.** (c) **354.** (a) **355.** (c) **356.** (c) **357.** (b) **358.** (b) **359.** (d) **360.** (a)
361. (d) **362.** (b) **363.** (a) **364.** (d) **365.** (b) **366.** (c) **367.** (c) **368.** (b) **369.** (d) **370.** (c)
371. (d) **372.** (b) **373.** (d) **374.** (a) **375.** (b) **376.** (b) **377.** (d) **378.** (c) **379.** (d) **380.** (d)
381. (a) **382.** (d) **383.** (a) **384.** (b) **385.** (d) **386.** (c) **387.** (a) **388.** (c) **389.** (c) **390.** (d)
391. (c) **392.** (d) **393.** (a) **394.** (b) **395.** (c) **396.** (b) **397.** (c) **398.** (a) **399.** (c) **400.** (d)
401. (b) **402.** (b) **403.** (a) **404.** (d) **405.** (d) **406.** (a) **407.** (c) **408.** (b) **409.** (b) **410.** (a)
411. (c) **412.** (a) **413.** (d) **414.** (b) **415.** (c) **416.** (b) **417.** (b) **418.** (a) **419.** (a) **420.** (d)
421. (c) **422.** (b) **423.** (c) **424.** (b) **425.** (b) **426.** (a) **427.** (b) **428.** (c) **429.** (b) **430.** (a)
431. (b) **432.** (d) **433.** (c) **434.** (c) **435.** (b) **436.** (a) **437.** (a) **438.** (b) **439.** (c) **440.** (a)
441. (b) **442.** (a) **443.** (a) **444.** (d) **445.** (a) **446.** (b) **447.** (b) **448.** (a) **449.** (d) **450.** (c)
451. (d) **452.** (d) **453.** (c) **454.** (b) **455.** (c) **456.** (a) **457.** (c) **458.** (b) **459.** (d) **460.** (a)
461. (b) **462.** (a) **463.** (d) **464.** (d) **465.** (b) **466.** (c) **467.** (d) **468.** (b) **469.** (a) **470.** (d)

471. (a) **472.** (c) **473.** (b) **474.** (a) **475.** (c) **476.** (d) **477.** (a) **478.** (c) **479.** (d) **480.** (b)
481. (d) **482.** (b) **483.** (d) **484.** (b) **485.** (a) **486.** (c) **487.** (a) **488.** (d) **489.** (b) **490.** (c)
491. (a) **492.** (c) **493.** (d) **494.** (d) **495.** (b) **496.** (a) **497.** (d) **498.** (b) **499.** (c) **500.** (d)
501. (a) **502.** (d) **503.** (a) **504.** (b) **505.** (c) **506.** (a) **507.** (d) **508.** (c) **509.** (a) **510.** (b)
511. (d) **512.** (b) **513.** (a) **514.** (c) **515.** (a) **516.** (b) **517.** (b) **518.** (a) **519.** (d) **520.** (d)
521. (b) **522.** (b) **523.** (a) **524.** (c) **525.** (d) **526.** (b) **527.** (c) **528.** (a) **529.** (d) **530.** (c)
531. (d) **532.** (c) **533.** (c) **534.** (a) **535.** (a) **536.** (a) **537.** (d) **538.** (c) **539.** (b) **540.** (b)
541. (a) **542.** (b) **543.** (c) **544.** (b) **545.** (c) **546.** (d) **547.** (a) **548.** (a) **549.** (d) **550.** (d)
551. (d) **552.** (b) **553.** (d) **554.** (b) **555.** (b) **556.** (d) **557.** (d) **558.** (d) **559.** (a) **560.** (a)
561. (b) **562.** (a) **563.** (c) **564.** (d) **565.** (c) **566.** (a) **567.** (c) **568.** (b) **569.** (a) **570.** (b)
571. (d) **572.** (c) **573.** (c) **574.** (c) **575.** (b) **576.** (a) **577.** (d) **578.** (c) **579.** (c) **580.** (b)
581. (d) **582.** (a) **583.** (a) **584.** (c) **585.** (b) **586.** (a) **587.** (d) **588.** (a) **589.** (c) **590.** (b)
591. (d) **592.** (c) **593.** (c) **594.** (c) **595.** (d) **596.** (b) **597.** (a) **598.** (c) **599.** (a) **600.** (d)
601. (b) **602.** (a) **603.** (c) **604.** (a) **605.** (b) **606.** (c) **607.** (b) **608.** (d) **609.** (b) **610.** (a)
611. (c) **612.** (d) **613.** (c) **614.** (d) **615.** (b) **616.** (d) **617.** (a) **618.** (b) **619.** (c) **620.** (c)
621. (a) **622.** (a) **623.** (b) **624.** (d) **625.** (b) **626.** (a) **627.** (a) **628.** (c) **629.** (d) **630.** (d)
631. (c) **632.** (c) **633.** (c) **634.** (c) **635.** (b) **636.** (c) **637.** (b) **638.** (b) **639.** (c) **640.** (b)
641. (b) **642.** (c) **643.** (b) **644.** (c) **645.** (a) **646.** (d) **647.** (d) **648.** (c) **649.** (a) **650.** (a)
651. (b) **652.** (a) **653.** (d) **654.** (e) **655.** (c) **656.** (c) **657.** (b) **658.** (e) **659.** (a) **660.** (d)
661. (c) **662.** (a) **663.** (d) **664.** (b) **665.** (d) **666.** (e) **667.** (b) **668.** (d) **669.** (b) **670.** (a)
671. (d) **672.** (d) **673.** (c) **674.** (e) **675.** (c) **676.** (b) **677.** (c) **678.** (c) **679.** (d) **680.** (b)
681. (b) **682.** (a) **683.** (e) **684.** (b) **685.** (b) **686.** (a) **687.** (d) **688.** (a) **689.** (d) **690.** (c)
691. (d) **692.** (e) **693.** (c) **694.** (e) **695.** (a) **696.** (d) **697.** (e) **698.** (b) **699.** (a) **700.** (d)
701. (c) **702.** (b) **703.** (c) **704.** (c) **705.** (d) **706.** (b) **707.** (c) **708.** (a) **709.** (c) **710.** (a)
711. (d) **712.** (a) **713.** (c) **714.** (b) **715.** (d) **716.** (d) **717.** (b) **718.** (c) **719.** (d) **720.** (d)
721. (d) **722.** (c) **723.** (c) **724.** (d) **725.** (d) **726.** (d) **727.** (d) **728.** (b) **729.** (a) **730.** (c)
731. (b) **732.** (a) **733.** (c) **734.** (b) **735.** (b) **736.** (d) **737.** (a) **738.** (c) **739.** (c) **740.** (d)
741. (d) **742.** (c) **743.** (c) **744.** (b) **745.** (a) **746.** (d) **747.** (d) **748.** (c) **749.** (d) **750.** (a)
751. (b) **752.** (c) **753.** (c) **754.** (c) **755.** (c) **756.** (b) **757.** (b) **758.** (a) **759.** (d) **760.** (d)
761. (d) **762.** (c) **763.** (c) **764.** (a) **765.** (c) **766.** (b) **767.** (b) **768.** (d) **769.** (c) **770.** (c)
771. (a) **772.** (c) **773.** (c) **774.** (d) **775.** (b) **776.** (a) **777.** (a) **778.** (a) **779.** (b) **780.** (c)
781. (b) **782.** (d) **783.** (c) **784.** (d) **785.** (b) **786.** (b) **787.** (d) **788.** (d) **789.** (c) **790.** (a)
791. (d) **792.** (c) **793.** (d) **794.** (d) **795.** (a) **796.** (a) **797.** (d) **798.** (d)

EXPLANATIONS

1. c Psychoanalysis has been referred to a curative system for mental healing.
2. c Behaviorism bid for approval by reducing adjustment to a program of conditioning while psychoanalysis analysed mental factors.
3. b The passage states that psychoanalysis created for itself a considerable following among those content with traditional methods and attitudes.
4. c Create a belief in the theory and the facts will create themselves.
5. c Psychoanalysts believe that practice is entirely a derivative of theory.
6. d Freudian psychoanalysis was neglected by academic psychology because orthodox psychology largely ignored dreams, lapses and neuroses.
7. b The mission of psychoanalysis has been described as humanistic and one that was the most novel and releasing of the curative systems that mark the history of mental healing.
8. d The psychoanalytical movement became popular due to its exploration of intimate problems of human relations.
9. d Computers produce by accident sequences of words that humans recognize as poetry.
10. c Both can be organized to solve problems and both have a similar mode of communication.
11. d The comparison between the two depends upon what the two can do.
12. d The author says that there is no sharp break of continuity between what is human and what is mechanical.
13. b The author implies that computers are not yet capable of producing poetry.
14. b The mode of communication is very similar in both.
15. b The author states that in future due to mechanization there would be many unemployed people.
16. c Socialism at present does not think of the possibility of unemployment in the wake of mechanization.
17. c A revolt against the conception of a worker as a commodity led to the labour movement.
18. d The main purpose of competitive enterprise is to realize a profit.
19. c In the given context we should think of limiting the amount of leisure to that which can be profitably used.
20. b In the given activities the external compulsion is minimum and they have an element of pleasure and require initiative.
21. d There are forms of work like that of an artist or a scientist where external compulsion is reduced to the minimum and which can thus be hardly differentiated from occupation.
22. d Occupation absorbs time and energy so long as we choose to give them.
23. c Work implies necessity and contributes to one's subsistence in particular while an occupation is an end in itself.
24. c The articulate minority refers to the educated and intelligent class.
25. c The passage states that democracy gives more minorities more scope to have their own way than any other system.
26. c We have come to appreciate the virtues of democracy through experience.
27. d The author states that the lesson about the scope offered by democracy to minorities could have been derived by an analysis of the concept of democracy.
28. b The author talks about the virtues of democracy.
29. d Democracies of the world are closer to being ruled by intelligent, educated minorities.
30. d The author thinks it is the duty of science to study the means by which we can adapt ourselves to the new world.
31. a The examples of these scientists have been given to show that scientists have always been associated with war.
32. b The author says that it is the labour of scientists that has led to all these dangers so scientists have to work to save mankind from this madness.
33. b Till now the scientists felt loyalty to their own state was paramount. But now the loyalty to human race should replace it.
34. c The example has been used to prove how scientists felt that loyalty to their states, to whatever ends it led to, was paramount.
35. d The passage states that scientists have always been associated with war and always have been respected.
36. c The passage states that it is part of the duty of men of science to see that important knowledge is widely disseminated and is not falsified in the interests of this or that propaganda.
37. c Only an adequate progress in human sciences can overcome evils that have resulted from the knowledge of the physical world.
38. c Science is in its very nature a liberator, a liberator of bondage to physical nature and, in time to come a liberator from the weight of destructive passion.

39. d A traditional kinship group provides security, identity as well as an entire scheme of things.

40. d Both the examples have been cited in the passage to show the extent of disintegration of kinship.

41. a The passage states that farming led to kinship becoming more important.

42. d The rise in individual self consciousness has led to the loss of sanity, supportiveness as well as warmth.

43. c The passage deals with the changes in kinship patterns over time and their effect on the individuals.

44. c The author says that serial monogamy is a series of marriages and divorces.

45. a According to the passage, smaller families are less influential.

46. a 'Genealogy refers to family history.

47. d The most distressing trend is the decline in the ability to form long term intimate bonding.

48. c The passage states that the political and economic benefits of the rise of the individuals have been positive.

49. c 'The marauder within' refers to the criminal class.

50. b The intellectual patrons of Australia in its first colonial years were Hobbes and Sade.

51. d The English did not regard Australia as a new frontier. It was settled to defend the English property from the criminal class.

52. b The late 18th century abounded in schemes of social goodness.

53. d 'Sanguine' means confident or hopeful.

54. d The passage primarily deals with the settlement of Australia as a penal colony to defend the English property from the criminal class.

55. d The existence of the criminal class was one of the prime sociological beliefs of late Georgian and early Victorian England.

56. b "Penology' is the study of punishment in relation to crime.

57. a For seventeen years no observation was made on the island.

58. a Sydney Harbor is the new name for Port Jackson.

59. c The author says that man's emotions are the product of his rational faculty; his emotions cannot be understood without reference to the conceptual power of his consciousness.

60. b The biological basis of choosing efficacy has been said to be the relationship of efficacy to survival.

61. b Nature has left man free in choosing values.

62. a The passage clearly states that man chooses his own values, irrespective of their actual effect on his life.

63. c The passage states that man first acquires preferences through pleasure and pain as well as through efficacy and inefficacy.

64. d Reason serves the dual function of cognition as well as of evaluation.

65. a As a child a human being experiences issues relating to values through physical sensations of pleasure and pain.

66. b Since man must act to live, he is actually forced to select values.

67. d The passage clearly states that man experiences efficacy as well as pleasure as primary, hence the question is not debatable.

68. c As a being of volitional consciousness, man is not biologically programmed to make right value choices automatically.

69. a A heightened roller coaster effect, and not an opportunity for a roller coaster ride, is a characteristic of the stage of small victories.

70. c Entering a new culture involves an appreciative process, to help members of different cultures value the differences.

71. b Opening a bank account is an example of a small victory as it is preceded by anxiety and information collection.

72. b Entering a new culture is a learning process that results in valuing and affirming the best in a culture, while at the same time seeing it as a whole.

73. d The passage states that appreciative inquiry must precede cultural changes in an organization.

74. c The passage emphasizes that affirmation of a new culture involves viewing the whole, including the points that are less desirable.

75. b The author does not approve of legal limits on interest charged on money lent to people. The last paragraph shows his support for the free market operations.

76. c The author states that though the law precludes the man from borrowing, upon terms, which it deems too disadvantageous, it does not preclude him from selling, upon any terms, howsoever disadvantageous.

77. b The author states that he knows of no economist of any standing who has favoured a legal limit on the rate of interest on borrowed money.

78. a 'Usury' is defined as charging rates on money that are in excess of the legal limits.

79. c Bentham was primarily concerned with loans to individuals or business enterprises.

80. c The author laments that 'it is an oppression for a man to claim his money, but not to keep it from him.' Thus he implies that a man becomes an oppressor only because the borrower does not return the money.

81. c The passage states that no man of sound mind and with his eyes open should be hindered from obtaining money.

82. d The author emphasizes the importance of free market operations throughout the passage, and draws attention to the validity of the "mischief of the anti-usurious laws." He also condemns politicians and so (d) is the most fitting description for the author.

83. c The author states that the working class that may be the lender for the first time in history, will be the hardest hit by the legal regulations.

84. c The bickering illustrated that Eagle constituted a collective effort, and now they were having a hard time deciding on the contribution of each individual.

85. d The author seems to suggest that with the launch of the machine everything that preceded it becomes past. Even the team started losing its glue and instead bickering started.

86. d The word 'after birth' was used for 'the team that was losing its glue', that is the Eclipse Group.

87. b During the conversation West said that none of it had come out the way he had expected and that he was glad it was all over.

88. b The telegram was described as a 'classy gesture' by all.

89. b One of the 'Microkids' exclaimed that he had a 'great talk with West', showing that it as an honour for him.

90. b The machine had crashed during the programme but no one except the company engineers noticed and the problem was fast corrected. The event was written up at length in both the Wall Street Journal and the New York Times, the next day.

91. d Some of the engineers seemed to the author to be out of place, being untutored in that sort of a performance.

92. b It refers to the fact that in front of the Press even those who had not been around when Eagle was conceived were described as having had the responsibility for it.

93. c The author states that ego and money motivates people and clearly the machine no longer belonged to the makers.

94. b The discovery led to treatment of some bacterial infections.

95. d The medical fraternity has grown richer due to the current medical practices in America.

96. c The reason is simply that medical practices differ in different countries.

97. a It is beneficial in the short term.

98. d Cholesterol screening applied under 'Care rather than cure' movement could be controversial as today's view of what constitutes a good diet may prove to be wrong tomorrow.

99. c The outcomes movement is likely to have only a modest affect because effectiveness of drugs is not same in all patients.

100. b Bio technologies have produced new drugs but they are very expensive.

101. a It will restrict the public use of costly medicines, leaving the poor to fend for themselves.

102. a Smith deals with virtues of self interest in a very practical, factual way. He has been referred to as a pragmatist.

103. d Smith says competition leads to regulation of quantity.

104. c Smith favoured free trade to prevent market failure.

105. b Smith says that if free trade is not there, producers might try to form near monopolies.

106. d The passage states that government has to try to defend people from violence, injustice, and oppression and has to provide certain public works because the market has in some way failed.

107. c A free rider problem arises due to failure of collective defence and administration of justice, and an R & D department of an industry cannot be used to solve it.

108. b According to Smith competition directly affects prices, quality of goods and quantity of goods produced.

109. a Government intervention is often a cause of market breaking down, requiring more intervention on Government's part.

110. d Smith is against laws prohibiting import.

111. b The greater complexity in the modern manufacturing process has not been presented as an argument for government intervention.

112. d The passage does not talk about flexibility in the role of the government. Infact it states that government should confine itself only to certain tasks.

113. b Modern government offers preferences as if it costs nothing.

114. b A jet stream has length, width as well as depth.

115. b Most data is available over the Northern hemisphere.

116. c A jet stream is defined as 'a strong, narrow air current'.

117. b Jet streams are caused by confluence of air masses with very different temperatures.

118. c Jet streams have not been shown to cause flight delays.

119. d The strong easterly jet streams causes summer monsoon over India.

120. b The subtropical jet stream is associated with fair weather.

121. d In the lands with insufficient rainfall, where water is brought in from outside for irrigation, salinization can take place.

122. d The passage talks about problems as well as remedies for soil infertility.

123. b Natural fertility exhausts the fastest in humid tropical forests.

124. c The passage does not talk of fertilizer fixation through lightning.

125. c Crop rotation preserves soil and prevents build up of pests.

126. b The Nile basin contains heavy soil with poor drainage properties.

127. c Legumes have nodules in their roots.

128. c The author criticizes the application of scientism to social sciences.

129. b The last paragraph highlights that in social sphere there is no single cause by the creation of which one can create a certain effect at will.

130. c The author has tried to show that scientism cannot be properly applied to explain social behaviour.

131. a According to scientism there is only one truth the truth of science and the methods of physical science can thus be applied to other fields of enquiry, like the social sciences.

132. b The author has attacked the approach of scientism towards social sciences.

133. d The passage uses comparisons with familiar objects and very simple language, indicating that it is aimed at people with little technical knowledge of astronomy.

134. a The first sentence of the passage shows that the passage is about the variety of motions of the earth.

135. c The Earth's rotation on its axis causes the alternation between day and night, which we all know takes only 24 hours.

136. c The author has used comparisons with objects like a top and references to geometric shapes like cones.

137. c Physiology is a study of the way living things function, hence the passage must have been taken from a book on physiology.

138. c Mesentries are thin sheets of connective tissues from which certain organs are suspended.

139. c The nutrients and waste materials are exchanged between blood and organs through the peri-vascular spaces.

140. d The cells of adipose tissue are specialized for storage of fat.

141. c The connective tissues develop in the middle layer of the early embryo.

142. c Cartilage, stroma and synovia are examples of connective tissues.

143. b Cartilage permits smooth gliding movements between opposed surfaces.

144. b It is a manifestation of anomic suicide.

145. a Furkheim was trying to document the fact that something as individualistic as suicide can be explained without reference to individuals.

146. b It is also a manifestation of anomic suicide.

147. c This was categorised as egoistic suicide.

148. d Durkheim uses all three as explanations for suicide within a social entity.

149. a Military personnel, trained to lay their lives for the country are more likely to commit suicide.

150. b Durkheim was successful on all three indicators that he based his contentions on.

151. d He has used all the given indicators to support his contentions.

152. a This would happen due to a manifestation of strong individual ties.

153. a The passage shows that though IBM is losing ground in one market after another, Intel and Microsoft have emerged as the computer industry's most fearsome pair of competitors.

154. c IBM's 'loss' and not the 'lay off' was the biggest in the corporate history.

155. b IBM marketed Ambra.

156. b General Motors, a relatively new company, had surpassed Ford as America's No. 1 car maker.

157. d Intel was the major supplier of silicon chips to IBM.

158. c The passage states that each company feels threatened by its own creations.

159. a The passage states that IBM plans to introduce a new system that would run on a variety of machines.

160. c Windows NT, developed by Microsoft will link together many computers through a network.

161. a Both marketed their own versions of Os2.

162. b NEERI has reported that 70% of the total water available in the country is polluted.

163. a The degradation of natural resources will lead to poor economic utilization of resources.

164. c W.H.O. has made both the observations.

165. d All the given statements are supported by the passage.

166. b 75% of Ganga's pollution comes from municipal sewage.

167. c Drying up of water resources and over pumping causes drinking water crisis.

168. d US, UK, Netherlands, Poland, France, World Bank and India are together going to fund the project.

169. d Ganga, Yamuna, kali, Hindon, cauvery and Kapila, have all shown great amounts of metal pollutants in their waters.

170. a Out of a total outlay of 6,522.47 crores, rural water supply would receive 3,454.47 crores.

171. b The shortage can be best tackled by cleaning up polluted water.

172. c This task should operate at the physical, conceptual as well as at the emotional levels.

173. c Violation of space boundaries makes the quality of space suffer, hence openness of space can be created only by the firmness of its boundaries.

174. d The author has given all three as reasons that make learning a painful process.

175. d Our experiences in the physical world have parallels in our relationships with others, where the concept of space also works.

176. d The author feels that a learning space would be one where the teacher provides information and theories which encourage the process of learning.

177. a Silence unites us and we also become more open to truth.

178. c An effective teacher would be one who is not afraid of dealing with feelings.

179. c An effective teacher would never allow the learning space to be filled by reading of a big number of pages of assigned reading.

180. b An emotionally honest learning space is created by a teacher who is not afraid of dealing with feelings.

181. a Assigned reading and lecturing can create a conceptual space.

182. b The author states that the harmony among these traditional elements has made Japanese industry highly productive and given corporate leadership a long term view.

183. d It was widely perceived that management education was a passport to good life.

184. b In 1980's management education had started getting criticism from various quarters.

185. c Management education faced all other criticisms in the 1980's

186. a Japan has traditionally believed that management ability can only be acquired through years of practical experience.

187. c In 1960's and 1970's management education gained academic stature. A management professor was even awarded the Nobel prize. It also gained more respect.

188. b In 1980's critics charged that learning had little relevance to real business problems.

189. b Training programmes in Japanese corporations have sought the socialization of new comers.

190. d Increased competitive pressures and greater multi nationalism of Japanese business made Japan change its attitude towards management education.

191. a The author states that the Japanese educational system is highly developed and intensely competitive, raising the mathematical and literary capabilities of the Japanese to the highest in the world.

192. d The two differ in their process of selecting and orienting new recruits.

193. a The author has given the example of Wharton to argue that Japanese do not 'do without' business schools.

194. d The passage is basically about how ants communicate.

195. c Ants attack strangers who might belong to the same species.

196. d If they did so they would have been unable to communicate with the drunken ants.

197. d Chloroform killed the ants.

198. b The author has a playful, whimsical way of writing.

199. b All others can pass through the atmospheric windows without distortion.

200. d Clouds from volcanic eruptions do not find a mention in the passage.

201. d Telescope mounting is used to neutralize the Earth's rotation relative to the stars.

202. d The precession period of the Earth is 26,000 years.

203. c The diurnal spinning is the spinning of the Earth on its own axis, having no relation to the gravitational force of the Sun or the Moon.

204. b The last passage states that there can be uncertainty in the rate of orbital motion of the Earth.

205. c Man made signals can interfere with the radio wavelengths between 1cm. And 20m. implying that they also fall in the same range.

206. b US was more concerned with 'order' than with reforms of any kind.

207. d Latin Americans regarded it as economic imperialism.

208. a The Act of Bogota was most closely related to the Marshall Plan or Latin America.

209. c US preferred dictatorship to the spread of communism in Latin America.

210. b The President's initiative to present financial economic aid to Latin America has been presented as an example of his efforts to mend his 'Latin Ameriacn fences'. Thus he was not acting to continue to keep communism from intruding the country.

211. a The passage states that speeding up social reforms implied a risk of revolt, which could be avoided by maintaining status quo.

212. b The examination system was the traditional avenue of selecting the officials.

213. a The Restoration statesmen tried to restore the society, and not create a new one. They tried to stretch the traditional ideology in order to make the Confucian system under the new conditions.

214. a The only similarity was their intent to conserve.

215. d None of these philosphers has been mentioned in the passage.

216. c The aim of the Restoration was to restore to their original vitality the best of the ancient institutes.

217. c Western conservatism distrusted cosmopolitanism.

218. b The passage is basically about Chinese Conservatism.

219. b India has the lengthiest constitution in the world.

220. c Israel does not have a written constitution.

221. b Presidential cabinet is not even mentioned in the American constitution.

222. b The constitutions of new states in the US are very concise.

223. b A normative constitution has the status of supreme law and is fully activate and effective.

224. d Where the written constitution is only nominal, behind the verbal façade will be found the real constitution containing the basic principles according to which power is exercised in actual fact.

225. c Since a long constitution says too many things, on too many subjects, it has to be amended often.

226. b The presence or absence of a written constitution makes a difference, but only of a degree.

227. a The author is concerned about the books and is also well informed about the topic.

228. c The paper of 'archival quality' refers to a long lasting paper.

229. a Wood pulp helped in producing large quantities of paper.

230. b Paper that is acidic is highly unstable.

231. c This is not a reason mentioned in the passage, for producing long lasting paper.

232. a Reduction in government funding has not been mentioned as a reason for curtailing purchase of new books.

233. d The continued use of wood pulp will not have any effect on the governments.

234. c Lignin is a major factor that causes paper to discolour.

235. d Eisaku Sato was the Prime Minister for eight years.

236. b Hirohito has been said to be on throne for 61 years at the time of writing of the passage, which was in 1987.

237. c Mr. Tanaka was involved in a bribe scandal.

238. b The passage says that Mr. Yasuhiro Nakasone is 'now bowing out'.

239. c He has proved himself more skillful in the game of factional politics and thus his hopes are stronger.

240. c The author states that how Mr. Takeshita will fare after taking over the reins of the government is not certain, and reasons about this in an objective manner.

241. d The quick turnover of Prime Ministers has led to factionalism in LDP.

242. c Mr. Takeshita will be the first Prime Minister with humble rural origins.

243. b The three Prime Ministers mentioned by name here are Mr. Nakasone, Mr. Eisaku Sato and Mr. Kakue Tanaka.

244. d The dismantling of the welfare state helped Gingrich lead to the Republican revolution of 1994. Refer second paragraph line 2.

245. b Money has not been mentioned as what a party needs to win elections. Refer first paragraph, line 1.

246. d All of the mentioned names belong to the Republicans.

247. a They were tactically defeated by the Democrats because of the government shutdown. Refer fourth paragraph line 2.

248. b The passage is basically about the mistakes committed by the Republicans and their odd ways of thinking.

249. a 'Obsolete' has been used to imply old/antiquated.

250. c The real danger to the Republicans is the fact that its axioms, and not its policies, are under fire. Refer ninth paragraph line 1.

251. a The idea of small governments is being ground to dust by Buchman. Refer seventh paragraph line 1.

252. c A car, a jeep and a snowplough have been mentioned here.

253. c The weather bulletin has been compared to a ritual ceremony. Refer fifth paragraph line 2.

254. b An earthquake had caused the Mississippi to flow northward.

255. b The author says that weather organizes people into a shared moment, hence inspite of being destructive, it can be said to be stimulating.

256. a The use of the language to describe the snow storm reflects the author's fascination with it.

257. b The greatest attractions of weather, for the author, is that it is apolitical.

258. a The author is watching the weather channel, thus he is in his house.

259. b The weather is not manipulable.

260. d 'Undulously' means curved.

261. d All are socialists, though Robespierre has been mentioned as an example of a person who till now was thought to be a typical instance of attributes needed for being a revolutionary socialist, does come up to them.

262. a The second form of socialism involves all the difficulties of the first one and much more.

263. c The difference is in their attitude towards change.

264. c Both have been mentioned as the characteristics of the two persons.

265. c Corruption in high places has not been mentioned in the passage.

266. b The aim of the revolutionary socialism is to substitute the new rule for the old one at one stroke.

267. a 'Avow' means to proclaim.

268. a The author does not symapthize with either of the two sides.

269. c The author has tried to defend philosophy in the passage.

270. c The passage states that philosophy is politely respected but secretly despised.

271. d Philosophy has not been said to be immoral.

272. d Philosophy has not been mentioned as being responsible for making the world a better place to live in.

273. a If philosophy did not exist, masses would not think for themselves, and would thus be easier to manipulate for the politicians.

274. b 'Chairs at the universities' refers to the departments at the universities.

275. b The existence of philosophy is proved by the defence measures it provokes.

276. a *Jaws* has not been mentioned as Spielberg's movie.

277. b The author says that at least the book had a convincing villain

278. c The passage is obviously talking about a film review.

279. a The book was written by Crichton.

280. c The author praises the film for its technical effects and sophistication at the technological level, but is disappointed with its story line.

281. d The writer says, "one leaves it vaguely disappointed."

282. a He is thankful for such films because they fill the cinemas, and this leads people to continue financing films.

283. d The author finds it neither frightening nor amusing.

284. b 'Muck about with nature' implies 'interfere with nature'.

285. c 'Pundit' in the passage means an expert.

286. c The problem the new cabinet faced was of the foreign exchange market. Refer first line paragraph fourth.

287. a Neil Kinnock has been mentioned as being the leader of the Labour Party. Refer first line paragraph third.

288. b The only way out was to raise the interest rates by at least 2 per cent. Refer fifth paragraph line 6.

289. d We can infer that the Bank of England could exert enormous pressure on the government in its policy formulation.

290. b He wanted to complete his cabinet appointments and to consult his own advisors.

291. a It was not clear if the other countries would follow the lead, hence realignment was not a viable option.

292. c Maastricht has not been mentioned as part of the Labour cabinet.

293. b The wrong policies have not been mentioned as a reason for the defeat of the Conservative Party.

294. b The passage is about how capitalism has led to disintegration of labour.

295. b The author feels that Adam Smith boasted about something that was actually undesirable.

296. d It takes much less time to make pins by machines today.

297. b Pins are so cheap that a child stealing it would not even feel that he is actually stealing something.

298. a The author is clearly against machines taking the place of men.

299. c Adam Smith was a supporter of mass production.

300. b The statement means that as people get richer they lose out on individual abilities.

301. c He is attacking this fact by making fun of it.

302. d None of the given statements continue with what the author has said in the last paragraph.

303. a The passage refers to the British Government as the 'Empire', and talks about the way it takes over foreign territories.

304. a The aulhor says that simple tribes are often friendly and honest.

305. c Trade of finished products falls under the capital freshly saved.

306. d He says that the civilized empire grows at the expense of the home tax payers, without any intention or approval on their parts.

307. b Civilized countries practise protection, which means there is an imposition of heavy taxes on imported goods.

308. a 'Officious' means 'self-important'.

309. c Though they seem to come with the intention of trade, soon gun boats follow and a government is set up by the capitalists in the new land.

310. b He perceives no sign of a revolution in ethical matters.

311. c The author finds no reason why the doctrines of Darwin should change our moral ideas.

312. c The Chief Good refers to the welfare of the community realized in its members.

313. b He advocates a return to a non-Christian and perhaps a Hellenic ideal.

314. a The moral code of Christianity has been rejected by all except fanatics.

315. d The passage is obviously against all the subsidies.

316. d The author believes that actually the poor pays for the subsidies and most subsidies go to the rich.

317. a Utopia is an imaginary perfect world.

318. b The author believes that subsidies do more harm than good.

319. d All are victims of subsidies.

320. a Deve Gowda's government has shown some courage when it came to petroleum prices.

321. a The passage is about the fact that ultimately subsidies are not really beneficial.

322. c Experts call inflation and not subsides the most regressive form of taxation. Refer paragraph second line 6.

323. d They had nuclei in a less differentiated state.

324. a The contention has been proved to be true.

325. c There is prevalence of uninucleate cells.

326. b Nuclei of a binucleate cell serve as a source of hereditary information.

327. d The function of the crystalline layer has not been mentioned in the passage.

328. c A lobate form provides a much greater surface area for nuclear cytoplasmic exchanges.

329. b Fungi are multinucleate because the cross walls are either absent or irregularly present.

330. b Drug addiction has not been mentioned as a reason for poverty.

331. c Such people need extraordinary talent to become rich.

332. d Ambitious people have not been mentioned as the ones likely to get rich quickly.

333. c The author says that there is no way by which to judge the goodness or badness of a person.

334. b He rejects the notion that the wealth is distributed according to merit and feels that it is biased in favour of the rich.

335. c The author refers to someone as ' intelligent lady' implying that he is probably writing to someone.

336. a 'Improvidence' means spending too much of money.

337. b The example proves that might scores over love and religion.

338. c He has been referred to as the umpire, and the passage also mentions the assertiveness being shown by the Election Commission regarding code of conduct during the elections.

339. b The passage is about an issue-less election, as highlighted even by the last sentence of the passage.

340. d Ramakrishna Hegde's involvement in any alleged corruption case has not been mentioned in the passage.

341. d All the parties have failed to submit audited returns every year.

342. a The greater awareness among the public has not been credited with the changes coming in the system.

343. b The empowerment of women has not been mentioned as a possible issue of the elections.

344. c In the first five paragraphs, the author makes it clear that Indians do not understand themselves yet. (a) is far from the truth. (b) is unlikely and (d) is not true.

345. b The author tries to show what exactly was India's history like and what are the prospects for the future. The writer is making observations and analysing these, hence there is no reason why the attitude should be critical, cynical or cold.

346. c Through the example he has tried to show us what centuries of slaughter and plunder actually meant for the country. (a) and (b) are not true, the writer is not glorifying the Vijayanagar empire.

347. a The author is critical of people having a child's view of history and equates it with the slave's idea of the ruler's mercy. (b) is not true as the writer does take a critical stand on history. (c) is besides the fact.

348. c The writer says that during British rule, and for 50 years after that, there was a revival of energy and intellect. (d) is not true in light of facts presented in the passage. (a) and (b) are not true in an isolated context.

349. d With self-awareness, people ask for more of everything. (b) and (c) are both found in the ninth paragraph. (a) is simply not true.

350. c He says that India's present situation is 'primitive and messy'. The writer has not expressed any pessimistic opinion 'bleak' or an extreme opinion 'horrific'.

351. a Self-criticism is important for a country to be alive and progressive. Refer to the last paragraph. (b) and (c) are thus not true.

352. b The writer says that the future will be fairly chaotic. (a), (c) and (d) find no mention in the passage.

353. c Every invasion was accompanied by slaughter of the country's most talented people. (a) and (b) did take place, but it is (c) which is the main feature of the tyranny of foreign rulers.

354. a The author is critical of the government policies. Refer to the beginning of each paragraph. The writer is not rude enough to be derisive. There is no reason for the writer to be sarcastic or ironical.

355. c He is surprised as in all other cases government looked at the industrialists as crooks. (a) is a different point of view. (b) is a fact presented in the passage that does not contribute to the writer's surprise. (d) is not true as the reason is cited below the writer's feelings.

356. c Foreign exchange bankruptcy and paucity of funds compelled government to open up its economy. (a) and (b) in no way influenced the government's move.

357. b The author says that in another 50 years the world would have moved even further ahead. Hence, there is no room for any kind of optimism or pragmatism.

358. b Its infrastructure should have helped India to perform better than other Asian countries. (c) is not cited in the passage. Given (b), (a) cannot be a better answer as India's infrastucture is compared with the infrastructure of the other countries.

359. d (a) and (b) are reasons for India being in a better condition than other nations. Refer to the third paragraph. (c) is not stated in the passage.

360. a Economic isolationism has led to India's poor performance. Refer to the beginning of the fourth paragraph. Hence, (b) and (c) are rendered void.

361. d Government tried to protect its own industries through discouraging imports. Refer to the beginning of the fourth paragraph. Hence, (a), (c) and (b) are not the best answers.

362. b While Korean Cielos are sold in India, no Indian cars are sold abroad. (a), (c) and (d) are opinionated answers, hence, not necessarily true.

363. a Indian politicians are unable to see beyond their noses. Whether (b) and (c) are true or not is unclear from the passage.

364. d The passage actually talks about the advantages of democracy. Hence, the opinions expressed in (a), (b) and (c) find no place in the passage.

365. b The passage says that there is no guarantee that all dictatorships will be enlightened. Refer to the beginning of the third paragraph. Hence, there is no reason to mark (a), (c) or (d), though they may have a shade of truth.

366. c The author sees a low but unfaltering rate of growth as a sign of stability amidst growth. (b) and (d) are not true. (a) is also doubtful, after all, how low can the growth be?

367. c Dictatorships are more prone to making huge mistakes and risking everything on a single decision. (c) is a more complete answer as compared to (a) and (b).

368. b The writer does not support statism under any circumstances. Refer to the penulitmate paragraph. (a) is a confusing response. (c) and (d) do not address the question.

369. d All the choices (a), (b) and (c) have been implied in the sixth paragraph.

370. c The passage states that Internet will play an important role in the decades to come. Refer to the eighth paragraph. We cannot infer (b) for sure. (a) is almost stated in the passage.

371. d Though (a) and (b) are desirable outcomes, they are not specifically stated in the passage.

372. b The main reason is (b), the dictatorship factor that figures so often in the passage. (a), (c) and (d) may be desirable factors, but not conclusive.

373. d (a), (b) or (c) have not been distinctly mentioned in the passage.

374. a Infosys has awarded stock options among its employees. (b) has not been mentioned in the passage. Refer to the second paragraph.

375. b Infosys does have a hierarchy, it does not have a hierarchy 'just' for control. Refer to the third paragraph. (d) may be true, but it is a rather vague response. (a) and (c) are not true.

376. b He believes that betterment of man can happen through creation of wealth, ethically and legally. Refer to the sixth paragraph. Given (b), (a) and (c) are weaker choices.

377. d The example highlights all the given facts. The qualities stated in (a), (b) and (c) are evident in the case.

378. c Murthy believes that learning is a process that helps him learn through failure. (a) is not the focus of the question. Learning transcends (b) as per information given in paragraph 9.

379. d Today the company works backwards to achieve its goals. Refer to the penultimate paragraph. Given (d), the other choices (a), (b) and (c) are weak.

380. d Openness at Infosys includes payment of taxes as well as giving complete information. (c) sounds rather ambiguous.

381. a (a) is stated in the last paragraph. (b) and (c) sound rather extreme.

382. d Infosys' HR treats its employees as customers. (d) is directly stated in the passage in paragraph 4, line 3. (a), (b) and (c) are generic and not very strong contenders for the answer.

383. a The CEO's actions set the template for all Infoscians. (b), (c) and (d) do not reflect the truth as per the passage.

384. b The diverse cultural and socio-economic factors are a major problem affecting the Indian education system. (a) and (c) are not stated in the passage.

385. d 'Grizzled mandarins' refers to bureaucrats. It would be unfair to label the mandarins as (a), (b) or (c).

386. c Those in charge of education are totally out of touch with the ground reality. This point is given in the fourth paragraph. Hence, it will not be necessary to mark (a), (b) or (d) as the answer.

387. a The author advocates decentralizing education planning and implementation to improve the education system. This point is given in the fourth paragraph. Hence, it will not be necessary to mark (b), (c) or (d) as the answer.

388. c Rajasthan, Bihar and Madhya Pradesh show very low education levels. The answer is given in the second paragraph. We are not sure about (a), (b) or (d).

389. c The programme, launched in 1994, has been successful in 122 districts. The answer is given in the fifth paragraph. Choices (a), (b) and (d) are thus rendered void.

390. d The village panchayats are responsible for scholarships, construction and maintenance of primary schools and for organizing non-formal education. We do not know if (a) forms part of the portfolio.

391. c Politicians are specially responsible for obstructing the implementation of education policies as decentralization of educational administration will take away certain powers from them. We are not sure about the intentions of (a), (b) or (d).

392. d None of the given statements can be related to primary education, on the basis of the passage.

393. a The author advocates greater community involvement for successful implementation of education policy. This point is given in the fourth paragraph. We are not sure about either (b) or (c).

394. b The Nehru-Gandhi ideologies led to the formation of the idea of India that inspired the writer's generation. This answer is given in the tenth paragraph. Don't be misled by (c); the writer mentions 'formative ideas', not 'formative years'. (a) and (d) are again imprecise answers.

395. c The writer agrees that the 50th anniversary is a great moment, but does not share Naipaul's conclusions about it. Refer to the tenth paragraph. Hence, (a), (b) and (d) are not correct.

396. b The writer believes that India will come back and does not feel that India's loss is forever. Refer to the last paragraph. (a), (c) and (d) are inaccurate observations.

397. c The writer feels that the politicians incite the general public to demonstrate against writers and also that it does not reflect the people's will. Refer to the penultimate paragraph.

398. a Whatever he says about India is based on his experience, as is shown by the last line of the passage. There is insufficient evidence in the passage to support (b), (c) and (d) as the answer.

399. c The writer's friend says that we can move beyond things only after we know we are capable of those things. The answer is given vividly in the sixth paragraph. (a) and (b) are not mentioned in the passage. (d) is not an exact representation of the writer's views.

400. d The passage states that the civilizing influence prevents us from giving in to violent, terrible urges. (d) is again stated explicitly in the sixth paragraph. (a), (b) and (c) may be partially true.

401. b The writer fears the long-term damage to democracy that the corruption can bring about, as it is a subversion of democracy, and says that it will harm India too as corruption is everywhere in India. The answer is given in the seventh paragraph. Hence, (a) and (c) are imperfect answers.

402. b The writer says that no one is an objective observer. The answer is given in the eighth paragraph. Hence, (a), (c) and (d) are imperfect answers.

403. a The writer says that there never had been a political entity called India prior to 1947. (a) is the best representation of the writer's views. (b), (c) and (d) do not give the exact picture.

404. d The writer feels that the difference lies in the fact that Pakistan was under-imagined. The answer is given in the second paragraph. (a), (b) and (c) are not substantiated by the passage.

405. d The writer feels that the strength of the nationalist idea is shown by its ability to survive great stress that it is placed under and in the sense of belonging that the people feel for it. Refer to the third paragraph. (b) has not been stated in the passage.

406. a The writer says that if Western civilisation is in a state of a permanent crisis, something is wrong with its education. The opening statement confirms (a). There is insufficient evidence to support (b), (c) and (d) as the answer.

407. c Lord Snow seems to see the intellectual life of the Western society as split between scientists and literary intellectuals. The answer is given in the second paragraph. (a), (b) and (d) are not stated in the passage.

408. b The writer does not agree that education can help in tackling all new problems and complexities. The answer is given in the penultimate paragraph. The views expressed in (a) and (c) find no mention in the passage.

409. b He defines prejudice as fixed ideas with which people think, without being aware of doing so. Refer to the ninth paragraph. (a), (c) and (d) are imprecise definitions of prejudice.

410. a Lord Snow says that the politicians, administrators and the entire community needs to be educated to understand the works of scientists and engineers. Refer to the second paragraph. (b) and (c) are partially correct answers.

411. c The writer does not agree with the scientists' stand on the neutrality of their labours. (c) can be amply inferred from the third paragraph. (a), (b) and (d) are imprecise answers.

412. a The author feels that the main purpose of education is to transmit ideas of value. (a) is clearly given in the fifth paragraph. (b) and (d) are not supported by the passage.

413. d (a) is not stated anywhere in the passage. (b) and (c) also find no explicit mention in the passage.

414. b The author says that values are more than mere dogmatic assertions. Refer to paragraph 6, line 3. (a), (c) and (d) are stated in the same paragraph.

415. c According to the passage, thinking is application of pre-existing ideas to a situation. Refer to paragraph 10, line 2. In light of (c), it will be a folly to mark (a), (b) or (d).

416. b The writer says that a large part of the American population indulges in word trade. Refer to the second paragraph. (a), (c) and (d) cannot be even remotely inferred from the passage.

417. b The hallmark of gag writers is that they have fun with words. Refer to paragraph 4, line 1. (a), (c) and (d) are not stated in the passage.

418. a The second level of language is important if one wants to be comfortable listening and reading. (a) is stated in the third paragraph. (b) and (c) are not stated in the passage.

419. a The writer says that the gag writers thrive on the double layered aspect of the language. The middle portion of the passage amply demonstrates (a). (b), (c) and (d) may be isolated aspects of the trade.

420. d In gag writing, both, long words as well as combining of parts of words to produce a hilarious effect are important. (a) cannot be inferred from the passage. (b) and (c) can be inferred from the fourth paragraph as well as various examples in the passage.

421. c Gag writers simulate ignorance. The answer is given in the fifth paragraph. (b) is an isolated observation and (a) is not true.

422. b According to the passage, radio artistes have taken advantage of the techniques of gag writers. (a) and (c) are not mentioned in the passage.

423. c The theory has been suggested to be an attempt at appeasing the religious psyche of that time by stating that God indirectly created life. (c) is stated in the second paragraph. (a) and (b) are misleading answers.

424. b All four have been referred to as working or writing at the same time. This is evident in the second paragraph. (a) is only partially right. (c) is not true.

425. b Pasteur did not work on arbitrary or spontaneous discoveries. He worked on logical premises. This is evident in the fourth paragraph. (a) is certainly not true, considerable differences of opinion existed even then. (c) and (d) are nor true either.

426. a Pasteur based his work on the belief that either air contained a factor necessary for the spontaneous generation of life or viable germs were borne in by the air and seeded in the sterile nutrient broth. (b) is only an observaation, not the hypothesis. (a) is stated in the fourth paragraph.

427. b The well water of Montanvert led to the discovery of the porcelain filters. (a) is nowhere stated in the paragraph. (b) is clear from the fourth paragraph.

428. c Pasteur declared that his experiments had dealt a mortal blow to the spontaneous generation doctrine. The conclusion of the fifth paragraph makes (c) a clear choice. (a), (b) and (d) are rather extreme.

429. b The writer feels that the works of the proponents of spontaneous generation was ruined by experimental errors. (b) is mentioned in the seventh paragraph. (a) is clearly not true.

430. a This cross fire ruled out the possibility of partial sterilisation. (b) is clear from the penultimate paragraph. (b) is not directly stated in the passage and (c) sounds vague.

431. b Pasteur's experiments supported the Biblical version of creation of life, but denied many other philosophical systems. (b) is explicitly given in the fifth paragraph. Given (b), the other choices (a), (c) and (d) seem extreme.

432. d The author says that the cell theory represents biology's most significant and fruitful advance. Refer last paragraph, line 1. (a) is thus wrong and (b) and (c) are not supported by the passage.

433. c Rs. 85,000 crore has been entrusted to the care of mutual funds. (c) is stated in the second paragraph.

434. c The individual investors led the move for the end of mutual funds. Refer to the first paragraph. (a), (b) and (d) are wrong choices.

435. b The mutual funds were flawed in their imprudent and irresponsible handling. Refer to the end of the first paragraph. (a) and (c) are not valid reasons.

436. a The indisciplined attitude of the mutual funds in their approach to investment led to their fall. Refer to the second paragraph. The claims in (b), (c) and (d) are not completely substantiated by the passage.

437. a The passage states that at least 18 of the big schemes due for redemption over the next 3 years will be unable to service their investors. Refer to the fourth paragraph. (b) plays with words 'only very few' and (c) is not correct.

438. b The passage shows the facts that lead to the inference that many of the mutual funds offices indulged in malpractices. Refer to the fifth and sixth paragraphs. (a), (c) and (d) are not stated in the passage.

439. c Mutual fund industry ranks fourth on safety and fifth in terms of returns on deposits. Refer to the seventh paragraph. (a), (b) and (d) are thus wrong.

440. a More cellphones were subscribed as calls made on them could not be lodged in the company records. Refer to the fifth and sixth paragraphs. (b), (c) and (d) are not stated in the passage.

441. b Mutual funds have caused a loss of Rs. 11,000 crore of the investors' money. Refer to the tenth paragraph. (a), (c) and (d) are wrong.

442. a Investors have the option of either exiting at a loss or holding on in vain hope. Refer to the eleventh paragraph. (b), (c) and (d) are not very perfect choices.

443. a The stock market boom in the late eighties and early nineties led to the initial euphoria in the mutual funds industry. Refer to the passage from the twelfth paragraph onwards. (b) is clearly not true.

444. d (d) is the correct answer choice. It is an example of doing the right thing, 'at the wrong time.'

In (d), telling a long story could be entertaining or interesting, but not when others have heard it many times before. The intention in (b) and (c) contradicts the definition of an unseasonable man. (a) is irrelevant.

445. a (a) is the correct answer choice. It is also an example of doing the right thing, 'at the wrong time.'

In (a), getting a higher bidder is helpful to the salesman, but not when he has just closed a deal. He will only curse himself and you. (d) is a matter of choice, not unseasonableness. (b) may be undesirable, but not unseasonable. There is nothing unseasonable about (c) either.

446. b (b) is the correct answer choice: This answer emerges from para 2, second sentence: "... WTO was a product of a series of trade-offs between principal actors and groups." The important players were essentially the United States; Europeans; countries like Canada and other middle and smaller trading partners; and the developing countries, which continued negotiations as part of the Uruguay Round till the 1990s. The Tokyo Round of the 1970s was an attempt at a 'constitutional reform' of the GATT, while what the important players eventually settled for in the WTO was the evolution of a rules–based system through multiple negotiations which obviously required time.

(a): Though it is mentioned in para 1 that 'the US government wanted to put off the Tokyo Round of the 1970s to the future', but it is clear from para 2 that other important players also first wanted to evolve a rules-based system through negotiations before agreeing to anything binding on them.

(c) is factually incorrect in light of para 3, and as such has no relevance to the non-formation of WTO in the 1970s. (d) is incomplete as 'the Tokyo Round negotiation was an attempt at constitutional reform of GATT,' and not related to formation of a new organization, WTO, as such.

447. b (b) is the summary of what is discussed in the second paragraph and emerges from the last sentence of the paragraph. (a), (c) and (d) are also stated in the second paragraph but as individual considerations that went into the formulation of the WTO package. (b) sums it up succinctly.

448. a (a) is the correct answer choice.

In paragraph 3, the passage defines 'legal development' as 'the promotion of the technical legal values of consistency, clarity and effectiveness. And these values were achieved in the WTO through (a) consistency: integrating under one roof the agreements signed under GATT.

(b) Clarity: removing ambiguities about the powers of constructing parties to make certain decisions.

(c) Effectiveness: eliminating grandfather rights exceptions and defects in dispute settlement procedure.

Option (a) only covers how the value of consistency was achieved, option (c) relates to the value of effectiveness, but omits the word 'eliminating' and option (d) relates to the value of clarity, but omits the word 'removing'. This omissions render these options incomplete, and hence disqualifies them as possible correct answers. Thus, option (a) 'partly' (as in the question stem) answers the question how technical legal values were promoted in the WTO. Option (b) is an observation, not a step.

449. d (d) is the correct answer choice The question stem alludes to the 'teleological method of interpretation,' whereby action of member states were evaluated against the accomplishment of community goals. (paragraph 4, lines 7 and 8). The other choices (a), (b) and (c) do not touch this main point.

450. c (c) is the correct answer choice. The 'benefits of international trade' (para 2, lines 11 and 12) refer to 'the export gains' (para 2, line 14) as brought out in option (c). Whereas option (b) only talks about the export gains and option (d) only about a rule-based system. (a) is a misleading choice.

451. d (d) is the correct answer choice.

Since 'the doctrine of mutual recognition handed down (by the European Court and Justice) in the case Cassis de Dijon was a key turning point,' and 'the court is recognized as a major player in European integration', join these together and you get option (d) as the correct option (para 4, lines 3 to 5). Options (a), (b) and (c) are also mentioned in para 4, but are not directly related to the Cassis de Dijon case as such.

452. d (d) is the correct answer choice.

All the three issues raised in options (a), (b) and (c) are arguments against abstract art, as discussed in para 2.

453. c (c) is the correct answer choice.

It echoes the words in para 1, lines 7 and 8.

'Something they can relate to and understand immediately without too much thought'. (a), (b) and (d) are peripheral observations.

454. b (b) is the correct answer choice.

This can be inferred from para 3, lines 6 and 7. 'If he had used representational images and colour, much of the emotional content would have been lost and the piece (Guernica) would not have caused the demand for justice that it did.' (c) is a shocking choice. (d) is not true at all. (a) is just the background for the painting.

455. c (c) is the correct answer choice and directly emerges from para 3, last two lines. (a) may be an isolated opinion. (b) and (d) are irrelevant to the question.

456. a (a) is the correct answer choice.

Para 4 discusses how each deals with 'reality' on canvas:-

(i) Representational artist: What he sees with his eyes – he reproduces on canvas.

(ii) Abstract artist: What he feels about what his eyes see – he interprets on canvas.

Option (b) is incorrect as nowhere in the passage does the author talk about one being superior to the other. The author's point of view is that the critics of abstract art fail to see its merit, both forms are different and have their own merits.

Options (c) and (d) are irrelevant to the question asked. (c) is refuted in the passage and (d) is rather a tall claim. (a) is a lopsided observation.

457. c (c) is the correct answer choice.

The concept that because humans can perceive the world around them, they are the 'revealers' of reality, has been highlighted in the second para: '... that man is the means by which things are manifested'. — 'With each of our acts, the world reveals to us a new face'.

Option (a), though implicit in the passage, is not the central point of the author.

Option (b) and (d) talk of the unity of nature, but it is not relevant to the central idea of the passage.

458. b (b) is the correct answer choice. Refer para 3, lines 4 - 6 especially the fifth line.

459. d (d) is the correct answer choice.

The author distinguishes between perception and creation in the following manner:-

(i) Perception: Man, the subject, is essential as 'revealer' of objects around him but not essential to the existence of the objects.

In other words, if there is no object, there is nothing for men to perceive or 'reveal', but object can exist whether man is there to perceive it or not.

(ii) creation: Man creates in order to feel essential in the world around him. So, it is the creative activity that is essential, not man's creations (paintings, writing, etc.)

All other options are either irrelevant or do not capture the essence of the meaning.

460. a (a) is the correct answer.

The writer is the creator (subject) of the 'literary work' (object). To the writer, the very act of writing is essential, not his literary work. On the other hand, the reader (subject) is essential as the revealer of this literary work/the object of someone else's creation. But the reader is not essential to the existence of this literary work, which can exist even if these is no one to read it. This is how the dialectic of perception and creation manifests itself in the art of writing. Only option (a) captures the essence.

461. b (b) is the correct answer choice, because the writer makes us (readers) essential as revealers of what is written in the writer's literary work (the created object which is now part of the world around us). Can be inferred from para 2. (a), (c) and (d) are not accurate inferences from the passage.

462. a (a) is the correct answer choice.

The nation-state was expected to guarantee the happiness of individuals in the name of (para 1, lines 2 and 3):-

– Modernization in the West [not development in the West, as in option (c).]

– Socialism in the Eastern Bloc [not modernization in the Eastern Bloc, as in option (d).]

– Development in the Third World [as in option (a), not socialism in the Third World, as in option (b).]

463. d (d) is the correct answer choice.

Para 3 highlights that demands of communities and groups for recognition of their identities can be viewed:

(i) positively: as liberation movements, against oppression and injustice.

(ii) negatively: as militant action, when the search and assertion for their identity can result in intolerance of others.

Options (a), (b) and (c) together cover the full group. Hence, (d) all of these is the correct answer.

464. d (d) None of the above is the correct answer. Choice as option (a), (b) and (c) are all true about the nature of identity as per the author.

Option (a) – para 5, line 1

Option (b) – para 6, line 1

Option (c) – para 5, line 2

465. b (b) is the correct answer choice, as emerges from the last two lines of para 1: 'the state can use its powerful resources to reject the demand of its communities; it may even go so far as genocide to ensure that order prevails'. Other options are not correct as per para 1, which on the contrary, discusses the failures of the nation state.

466. c (c) is the correct answer choice, as nowhere has the author said that the nation state represents the demands of communities within it. On the contrary, para 1, lines 6 and 7 state: 'Distributed by the claims of communities within it, the nation state tries to repress their demands ...'

Options (a), (b) and (d), on the other hand, are true about the nation state as per para 1.

467. d (d) The primary purpose of this passage is to compare the Western 'strategic culture' with that of Asians and highlight the 'cultural divide', rather than a technical one. Options (a) and (c) deal with technical issues of war, whereas option (b) deals with the issue of morale. Only option (d) supports the 'cultural divide'. Paras 7-8 reveal some of the reasons for America's defeat at Vietnam.

468. b (b) is the correct answer choice, and is the metaphor for the western way of war, as opposed to 'a stealthy archer', which embodies the eastern way of war (last but one para, lines 7 and 8).

Options (a) (para 2, line 1), (c) (para 5, line 4 and 5) and (d) (para 4, line 1 to 3) all describe the 'Asian' way of war.

469. a (a) is the correct answer choice.

Sun-tzu believed in 'subduing an adversary without fighting (para 4, lines 1 to 3), and not through actual combat, as stated in option (a).

Other options: (b) is stated at para 5, lines 1 and 2; (c) and (d) are stated in last but one para, lines 1 and 2, where it is stated that both Sun-tzu and Clausewitz had similar views on (c) and (d).

470. d (d) is the correct answer choice.

The important differences in the concept of war of Clausewitz and Sun-tzu are summarized below:

		Clausewitz	Sun-tzu
(i)	Structure	Massed Battle in an open area	Persistent indirect attacks to weaken enemy through isolation, poor morale and disunity
(ii)	Time	Finite extent of time, say, few months	Long drawn-out, over several years
(iii)	Sequence of War	Fixed course with a beginning, a middle and an end.	No fixed sequence. But use full might of the army in a final quick and clean operation, when enemy has been considerably weakened

Option (a) is incorrect, as both were opponents of militarism, of turning the war over to the generals.

Option (b) is incorrect, as both were sophisticated as strategic theorists.

Option (c) does highlight a difference, but (d) is far more comprehensive.

471. a (a) is the correct answer choice, and directly emerges from the last para, last two lines.

Option (b) and (c) are nonsensical.

As regards option (d), 'bows and arrows' metaphorically represent the Asian way of war, not literally.

472. c (c) is the correct answer choice, as it captures the essence of the passage: difference in strategic culture between the West and Asia leading to America's failure to understand the Asian culture of war. (a) and (b) are minor reasons. (d) is doubtful. The ninth para and specifically lines 1-3 deal with this aspect.

473. b The second paragraph clearly makes choice (b) correct.

474. a (a) is given in the opening lines of the fifth paragraph. (b), (c) and (d) are imprecise interpretations.

475. c Choices (b) and (d) are general observations. Choice (c) is also explicitly stated in the 3rd line of the fourth paragraph.

476. d Refer to the end of paragraph 2, where both the problem and the concern have been addressed. (a), (b) and (c) sound far-fetched in this regard.

477. a (b), (c) and (d) are clearly given in paragraph 2. 'reduced biodiversity' suggests that (a) is the answer.

478. c The essence of paragraph 1 is captured in (c). Thus, (a), (b) and (d) are irrelevant.

479. d (a), (b) and (c) are outlined in paragraph 3. Hence, (d) is the answer.

480. b Refer to the concluding sentence of paragraph 3 and the opening sentence of paragraph 4 to mark (b) with confidence. (a) and (c) are not the main concerns. (d) is an obtuse observation with regard to our question.

481. d All the reasons are cited in the first paragraph itself. Choice (a) is mentioned in the 2nd line, (b) in the second last line, (c) in the last line and (d) is not mentioned. Instead mass media's impact is also stated in the para. This makes choice (d) correct.

482. b The opening lines of the final paragraph are represented suitably in (b). (a), (c) and (d) are doubtful choices.

483. d (a), (b) and (c) are stated vividly in the second paragraph, hence (d) is the answer.

484. b The author mentions this aspect in the third and fourth last lines of the third para. This makes choice (b) correct.

485. a (a) has been described as revolutionary in the third paragraph. (b), (c) and (d) are given in the fourth paragraph as the conservative tendency.

486. c The latter part of the fifth paragraph makes it clear that (c) is the answer. (a), (b) and (d) are not mentioned.

487. a (a) is stated in the opening lines of the fourth paragraph. (b), (c) and (d) are thus peripheral observations.

488. d The first line of the seventh paragraph begins with considering a "dual trap" and this till the fifth line tells us about the details of the same. This makes choice (d) correct.

489. b Refer to the beginning of paragraph 2, paragraph 3 and paragraph 5 to get (b) as the answer.

490. c Refer to the second sentence of paragraph 4 to mark (c) as the answer.

491. a The third line of the sixth paragraph makes choice (a) the answer.

492. c The third sentence of the seventh paragraph makes choice (c) the answer.

493. d Refer to the last sentence of paragraph 6 to mark (d) as the answer.

494. d Russell Cowburn and Mark Welland are trying to build the magnetic chip that can store and manipulate information. Hence (d) is the answer.

495. b The last lines of the eighth paragraph make choice (b) correct.

496. a Refer to the second sentence of paragraph 1 to mark (a) as the answer. (b) is stated in the opening lines of the passage. The opening lines of the sixth paragraph confirm (c). The concluding lines of the fourth paragraph confirm (d).

497. d Choice (a) is incorrect because the author is not talking about the failure otherwise he'd have looked at reasons for the failure. Choice (b) is incorrect because community perspectives are not presented, instead technology's impact on the community is mentioned. Choice (c) is incorrect because the negative effects of both are present. Choice (d) is the best choice as the author is providing an analogy.

498. b (b) can be easily inferred from the latter half of the passage. (a) and (c) are clearly not true. (d) does not find support in the passage.

499. c (c) is the obvious answer as can be amply inferred from the last paragraph. (a), (b) and (d) are uncertain choices.

500. d The introduction of the bereavement counsellor in the ninth paragraph points towards (d) as the answer.

501. a (b), (c) and (d) can be immediately ruled out. The first paragraph shows that (a) is the answer.

502. d Refer to the fourth sentence in the sixth paragraph and the concluding sentence of the passage to get (a), (b) and (c) as valid choices.

503. a (b) may be right. (c) and (d) are unlikely answers. (a) is stated in the concluding sentence of the ninth paragraph.

504. b (a), (c) and (d) are stated overtly in the passage. (b) is not true as the second innovation did not lead to the migration of the community.

505. c (c) is the best answer as can be derived from the concluding lines of paragraph 7 and explained further in detail in paragraph 8.

506. a The answer is (a) as is explicitly given in paragraph 1.

507. d Refer to the second paragraph third line 'preserves from'. The best answer is thus (d).

508. c The second sentence of the fifth paragraph makes it clear that (c) is the best answer.

509. a The opening lines of the last paragraph make it clear that (a) is the answer.

510. b (a), (c) and (d) can be inferred from paragraphs 7 and 8. But it is not mentioned that the conductor can modify the music, hence (b) is the answer.

511. d Information presented in the last line of paragraph 6 makes choice (d) correct.

512. b (d) is an observation, not the overall idea. (a) and (c) are also observations. (b) best captures the central idea of the passage as is evident from the latter half of the passage.

513. a The reference is to an open discussion of the caste issue on a global platform.

514. c Referring to paragraph 1, lines (7-8) its obvious that choice (c) is correct. "Inverted representations .... such inversions".

515. a Clearly, the UN conference is looking at discriminations based on caste, especially looking at paragraph 1. Choices (A) and (E) mention that choice (B) is a positive area and is not being addressed and choices (C) and (D) are too broad. This makes choice (a) correct.

516. b Paragraph 2, line 5 clearly indicates that choice (b) is correct.

517. b The author mentions in paragraph 2, line 3 – "race is a biological category" and in the last paragraph line 5 – "It would thus seem ... that dialectic". This means all biological constructs are social constructs of which race is one. This makes choice (b) correct.

518. a A mono-syllabic word has only one syllable. So it can have only one onset. A phoneme, according to the passage, can be 'initial' and 'final'.

519. d According to second last paragraph, line seven, it's obvious that choice (d) is correct.

520. d The last part of the first paragraph makes it clear that (d) is correct.

521. b According to the last para, lines 7-10. The Treiman and Zudowski experiment showed that '4 and 5-year-old children found the onset-rime version ... significantly easier ... only the 6-year-old ... were able to perform both versions ... with an equal level of success'.

522. b Refer to the sentence in paragraph 2 — 'rimes correspond to rhymes in single-syllabus words'.

523. a Choice (b) is false because the author says in paragraph one, line 4 "Few people ...". Choice (c) is false because the author says " ... Coarse-textured ...." in the fifth last line of the first para. Choice (d) is also incorrect as revealed in the last part of the passage. Choice (a) is correct as the author's appreciation is for her singing though he does pay attention to other aspects of her life.

524. c The answer is presented in the fourth last line of the first para, "what middle age ..". This makes choice (c) correct.

525. d The answer to this is also presented directly in the last line of the second paragraph — "suffering was her ....". This makeschoice (d) correct.

526. b Billie Holiday was fortunate to have 'the best musicians of the 1930s to accompany her — notably Teddy Wilson, Frankie Newton and Lester Young ...'

527. c The author mentions in the first paragraph, lines 3-5, "Each of the ....". This makes choice (c) correct.

528. a Refer to the part 'The film itself ... opening by Dersu's grave'. Besides (a) can be easily inferred from the second paragraph.

529. d The answer is presented directly in lines 2-4 of the third paragraph. "... nostalgic, melancholy...".

530. c The answer is in lines 4-6 of the third paragraph. "First section of ....". This makes choice (c) is correct.

531. d This aspect is highlighted in the last paragraph and choice (d) is the answer.

532. c Refer to the part 'Kurosawa defines the world of the film initially upon a void, a missing presence'.

533. c Refer to the seventh paragraph lines 4-5 '... the greater the urge for change in a society, the stronger the appeal of a dynamic leadership ...' This makes choice (c) correct.

534. a The answer to this question is present in the last paragraph in the second line "From the argument...." This makes choice (a) correct.

535. a Choice (A) is present in paragraph four, line one, choice (B) is mentioned in the last line of the fourth paragraph and choice (D) is mentioned in the 3rd last line of the seventh para. This makes choice (a) correct.

536. a The answer is presented in lines 1 to 4 of paragraph 2. This makes choice (a) correct.

537. d Refer to the first line of the fifth paragraph — 'But a system governed solely by impersonal rules can at best ensure order and stability; it cannot ... formal equality will be repiaced by real equality ...' This makes choice (d) correct.

538. c A can be inferred, refer to the part — 'Democracy rests on two different principles ... the principle of equality before the law ... the leadership principle ... one principle cannot be promoted without some sacrifice of the other... ' D can be inferred, refer to the part — 'their continued preoccupation with plans and schemes ... to bridge the gap between the ideal of equality and the reality which is so contrary to it ... leadership with a measure of charisma ...' B and C venture too far by using the words 'disadvantages' and 'limitations' respectively which have no contextual relevance.

539. b The second and third lines of the second paragraph mention "Dark Age..." this makes choice (b) correct.

540. b Lines one to three of the fourth paragraph mention "The main problem..." making choice (b) the answer.

541. a Lines three-five of the fifth paragraph "Recently, some members ..." makes choice (a) correct.

542. b As revealed in the first line of the last paragraph, choice (b) is correct.

543. c Refer 2nd para, especially to the part: 'Then Indian historians trained in ... mainly political.'

544. b (a), (c) and (d) seem to be superficial answers. (b) matches the syntax of the statement given in the question.

545. c Refer to the part glamour departed from politics.

546. d (d) is mentioned as a desirable characteristic towards the end of the passage.

547. a In (a), the writers and their respective approaches are correctly matched as per the information given in the passage.

548. a Refer to the part abortion access when their countries were perceived to have an overpopulation problem.

549. d (a), (b) and (c) are stated towards the end of the second paragraph and the beginning of the third paragraph.

550. d (a), (b) and (c) are too far-fetched and find no place in the passage.

551. d (a) need not be necessarily true as an inference. (b) and (c) are explicitly stated towards the end of the penultimate paragraph.

552. b Refer towards the end of the fourth paragraph. (b) comes closest to what the writer wants to say.

553. d (a), (b) and (c) find no place in the passage to support the pro-choice lobby.

554. b Simple. Just read the last line of the passage.

555. b (a), (c) and (d) are factually incorrect as per information given in the 3rd paragraph. (b) comes closest to the central idea in the third paragraph.

556. d The writer does not harbour a very favorable view of theologians, refer to all too definite.

557. d (a), (b) and (c) take the form of questions raised by the writer in the course of the passage.

558. d Refer towards the end of the second paragraph.

559. a Refer to inside of a cell bustles with more traffic and polymers, along which bundles of molecules travel like trams.

560. a Refer to 'The dynein motor ... is still poorly understood and without motor proteins. Our muscles wouldn't contract'.

561. b Refer to the part without motor proteins ... We couldn't grow and these particles create an effect that seems to be so much more than the sum of its parts.

562. a Refer to the part three families of proteins, called myosin, kinesin and dynein and the growth process requires cells to duplicate their machinery and pulls the copies apart.

563. c Refer to the part They think for us and is giving the language a lot of responsibility.

564. d (d) does not qualify as rhetoric on the basis of information given in the fourth paragraph. Commands are, at best, staid.

565. c (a), (b) and (d) cannot qualify as an answer as they sound extreme or implausible. (c) comes closest to what the writer would like to suggest.

566. a Arcane in the context of usage in the passage means esoteric.

567. c Refer to the part bringing scholars to accept the better argument and reject the worse.

568. b The writer is using satire to mildly tease the French winemaker. (a), (c) and (d) are rather extreme choices.

569. a Refer to the part *some areas have now produced a generation of growers using the varietal names on their labels.* The writer says that (a) is probably the only option left for French winemakers.

570. b Refer to the part *it is on every wine label ... the name of the grape from which the wine is made ... acquired a basic lexicon.* (b) well describes that the French winemakers are scared of this trend.

571. d Option (d) is the most substantiated reason to support Dr. Renaud's findings. The development in (d) would support Dr. Renaud's findings that fat-derived cholesterols can be dispersed by the tannins in wine.

572. c (a), (b) and (d) are stated in the 4th paragraph. (c) is unlikely. A consumer may still not be enough of a connoisseur to discriminate wine tastes.

573. c Refer to the part *India would resist payment, and paralyze the war effort.* (c) is clearly the answer.

574. c Refer to the part *it reminded the British vividly.* (c) is clearly the answer. (a) was an outcome, not a cause. (b) is a minor factor. (d) is far-sighted.

575. b (a), (c) and (d) are stated in the third paragraph. (b) is not a reason for the emergence of the 'white man's burden'. It is a consequence, not a cause.

576. a Refer to the part *it was supposedly for the good of the conquered.* (a) entirely captures the meaning of the 'white man's burden'.

577. d Refer to the last line of the first paragraph, the second paragraph and the last line of the passage. They amply support (d) as the answer. (a) does not touch on the financial implications. White man's burden *is a single aspect of the passage, not the main idea, so (b) is not right. (c) can be ruled out straightaway.*

578. c Refer to the part *much of biotechnology research is also funded by governments.* (c) is clearly the answer.

579. c Refer to the part *anti-GM campaign has been quite effective in Europe.* (c) is clearly the answer.

580. b Refer to the part *use of ever-stronger herbicides which are poisonous.* The last line specifically supports (b) as the answer and not (a) which is discussed in a different context. The passage has no intention of keeping competing plants standing at all, let alone keeping them weed-free, so (c) is wrong.

581. d Refer to the part *much of biotechnology research is also funded by governments in both developing and developed countries.* (d) is the answer. (a), (b) and (c) are disputed in the passage.

582. a Refer to the part *GM controversy will soon hit the headlines in India ... use the protato in its midday meal program for schools.* (a) can be inferred. (b) is, of course, wrong. (c) is doubtful. (d) is also not true.

583. a The last sentence of the 2nd paragraph states *these large gatherings* which continues as *they* in the 3rd paragraph. (a) is clearly the answer.

584. c The passage begins with description of social life and towards the last few paragraphs, moves on to show drying up of our social life. ...(c) is clearly the answer. (b) and (d) are rather extreme observations. (a) is also a blunt statement, whereas the passage does have a subtle tone.

585. b Refer to the part *Interest, wonder ... the need of the first two must not be underrated.* (b) is clearly the answer.

586. a *Discriminate* means to recognize *passionate attitude, distinguish* is too technical a word to fit the requirement. (b) and (d) are irrelevant.

587. d The correct ans. is (d) as can be seen by the first line of the second last para. If you read the previous para also you'll find that what the author is actually saying is that the so called social life is not as per the real definitions. (a). is not right as the author is nowhere showing that the crowds in poor Calcutta can turn violent anytime. He is just giving a couple of instances to prove his point. We can't generalize like this. (b) is the opposite of what the author is trying to show. (c) again is a generalization.

588. a Refer to the part *it remains a fact that the Greeks...never seem to have realized the importance of experiment.* (a) is clearly the answer. The Greek preference for geometry is not mentioned in the passage, so (b) and (d) are out. (c) is a superficial answer.

589. c Refer to the part *physical processes of nature would prove to be unfolding themselves according to rigorous mathematical laws.* (c) is clearly the answer. (a) is not true. (b) is also refuted and (d) is irrelevant.

590. b Refer to the part *account be taken of his joint contributions to mathematics and physics.* (b) is clearly the answer. (a), (c) and (d) are specific aspects.

591. d Refer to the part *extension of the validity.* The writer states that Einstein's special principle is an extension of the validity of the classical Newtonian principle. This being the concluding sentence makes (d) the best answer. (a) and (b) are not correct observations. (c) sounds plausible but it is actually a vague observation.

592. c the correct ans is (c) If you read the 6th line of last para it's given that the principle's assertion was that "absolute velocity must ever escape all experimental detection." Which means that sometimes we can't experiment. This is very similar to (c). Ans. choice (a) is a fact and not an "implication". (b). Is again a fact and in (d). The word "meaningless" is too strong and this choice is a generalization from a specific point. Generalizations need not be correct.

593. c See third paragraph last two lines. It is clearly mentioned that 'new free-flight concept . . . and other planes'.

594. c Paragraph 5, fourth line says that there is 'also a need for . . ., design talents . . .'

595. d First paragraph fifth line says '. . ., happened in less than a decade'.

596. b Paragraph 4 clearly talks about the increase in size of the aircraft.

597. a Paragraph 2, fourth line talks about the differences and explicitly mentions 'takes off vertically.'

598. c Refer to paragraph 5, line 1 'became . . . more divorced from religion.'

599. a Refer to paragraph 1, line 10 '. . . a means for advancement not only in income but also in status.'

600. d Refer to paragraph 3: 'Let us look at the clerical side first' and paragraph 4, line 5 'even though they entered the clergy, had secular goals.'

601. b Refer to para 1, line 7 'Christians educate their sons . . . for gain . . .'

602. a Refer to paragraph 4, line 1 'edu' was taking on many secular qualities . . .

603. c Refer to the part *while the dynamics of federalism and democracy have given added strength to the rights given to the States in the Constitution, they have worked against the rights of Panchayats*

604. a Refer to the words *volition* which means *preference* and *circumscribe* which means *confine*

605. b Refer to the part *while the dynamics of federalism and democracy have given added strength to the rights given to the States in the Constitution, they have worked against the rights of Panchayats*

606. c Refer to the part *exposed the intra-State level of our federal system to a dilemma of which the inter-State and Union-State layers are free*

607. b Refer to the part *The spurt given to a multi-party democracy by the overthrow of the Emergency in 1977 became a long-term trend later*

608. d (a), (b) and (c) are specifically stated in the paragraph starting *People born into the middle class to parents*

609. b Refer to the part *jobs in which they are closely supervised and are required to follow orders.*

610. a Refer to the part *Ultimately, corporate norms are based on middle-class values*

611. c Refer to the part *We're separated by class*

612. d (a), (b) and (c) are specifically stated in the passage at the end of the first[t] paragraph and the second paragraph.

613. c Refer to last paragraph, line 10 'they would build what was more beautiful than . . .'

614. d Refer to paragraph 1, line 3 'Mysticism on the whole was alien' and last paragraph lines 6 and 7.

615. b Refer to last paragraph, lines 3 and 4 'Simplicity in the Parthenon St. Columns . . .'

616. d Paragraph 4, last line '. . . insignificant atom that was man.'

617. a Paragraph 1, line 3 'Mysticism on the whole was alien' and paragraph 2 line 1 'Greek art is intellectual are . . .'

618. b According to the passage, when "a culture is in a state of disintegration or transition ... he, himself has to choose for society." So (b) is the correct option.

619. c The first paragraph details the "two developments" -a greater freedom in choosing subjects and the concurrent abandoning of the subject by artists. The second paragraph explores the connection between these two developments.

620. c The second sentence of the fifth paragraph says 'the subject may have a personal meaning ... ; but there ... general meaning.' This is quite the opposite of what answer choice (c) states, and so it becomes the answer.

621. a The third paragraph, second line says 'a subject does not start ... or with something which the painter has to remember'.

622. a According to the passage-"When a culture is in a state of disintegration or transition the freedom of the artist increases..."

623. b The answer directly follows from the fourth paragraph where the author asserts that change is overrated and uses the example of the automobile to support his assertion.

624. d The author reinforces the point again and again in the passage that even though "we scare ourselves constantly with the idea of change ...Structure may not have changed much."

625. b This is a main idea question; if you look at the complete passage, the author through examples of aeroplanes and cars and even telephones etc. is trying to show that innovation has not happened as much as it has been made out to be. The changes have been basically incremental and cosmetic.

626. a In the last paragraph, the passage states that the dependence on fossil fuels has continued because the auto executives did not want to let go of their field of expertise and adopt new technology.

627. a According to the passage one of the major reasons for the British policy during 'New Imperialism' period tended to be defensive was that Britain was unable "to cope with the by-products of its own rapid accumulation of capital."

628. c The second-last paragraph talks of the various factors that are responsible for this. Answer choice (c) combines all of them.

629. d The centre as can be seen from the first paragraph is the - 'rival centers of capital on the Continont and in America,' therefore none of these is the answer.

630. d It follows from the third paragraph that "The New Mercantilism ... faces similar problems of internal and external division", which the passage goes on to discuss.

631. c In the third paragraph, the passage states-" ... the book has made Tsavo's lions notorious. That annoys some scientists."

632. c It follows from the first paragraph that Craig and Peyton West "had partly suspected ... mistaken for adults by amateur observers."

633. c All the other three answer choices are in the fourth and fifth paragraphs.

634. c If (c) is true and if Tsavo lions are similar to the cave lions, then the Tsavo lions should also be less violent, whereas the hypothesis tries to give reasons for the Tsavo lions being more ferocious.

635. b According to the author, "Type B malnutrition is a major cause of chronic degenerative diseases."

636. c In the fifth paragraph, the author discusses a possible way of ensuring micronutrient repletion on a global scale. He explains that since the "vast majority of people are consuming suboptimal amounts of most nutrients ...

637. b The fourth paragraph, first line says Type B malnutrition is the major cause of chronic degenerative diseases. The first paragraph says chronic degenerative diseases are the major causes of ill-health and death, hence answer choice (b) follows.

638. b Check the first paragraph for the answer.
Answer choices (a) and (d) seem to be very close. However if you look at the first paragraph 4th line it says- " These have a long latency period <u>before symptoms appear and a diagnosis is made.</u>" So the latency period is quite specific. It is not just any latency period as suggested by answer choice (d). What one needs to ask in answer choice (d) is "which latency period?" Also answer choice a includes the latency period i.e. it includes answer choice (d). What this means is that a large number of apparently healthy people are deemed pre-ill because <u>they may have chronic degenerative diseases</u> as "These (*chronic degenerative diseases*) have a long latency period <u>before symptoms appear and a diagnosis is made</u>".

639. c In para number 2 "Each is torn ..." and then further in para 3 "Internal ..." These lines in paras 2 and 3 talk about external conflict being psychologically empty, and no psychological problems involved therein. This makes internal conflicts psychologically interesting.

640. b In paragraph 4, refer to line 11, "Chess may be psychologically..... rationally." According to the author, only when someone acts irrationally will that act be considered psychologically interesting and out of the given choices only option (b) qualifies, wherein adopting a defensive strategy against an aggressive opponent will be irrational. Option (c) is incorrect as the choice that the mountaineer would make would depend on external conditions and there would not be any internal conflicts as such, and the decisions that he would need to make would have to be rational.

641. b In the first paragraph refer to line 4- "Thus the "interests" of the players are generally in conflict." Choice (c) may also be correct but choice (b) is more appropriate as it is stated directly in the passage whereas choice (c) is an inference. Choice (a) is a consequence of applying game theory to a situation, not one of its pre-requisites, Therefore option 4 is also ruled out.

642. c In paragraph 4 lines 3 onwards- "The effort... genuine" According to this, in case of the detective , if the criminal remains passive, there is no conflict, whereas the scientist has to unravel the secrets of nature (which is "passive") by deduction .

643. b Answer choice (d), says that the danger being talked about is 'imminent', which is not necessarily the case as per the author in the passage, whereas the fact that everyone is complacent about it, is being talked about throughout the passage, which makes option (b) correct.

644. c In the sixth paragraph, the author explains why a belief in the "enduring strength of the system" might not be warranted. He also explains the reason behind such a belief-"... a sign of the enduring strength of the system ...since the millennium."

645. a This is the correct option as choice (b) is too narrow. Choice (c) is a universal truth which may not be the case. There could be a problem between 1 and 4 but 4 is ruled out because this option is one of the reasons supporting the author's argument but is not his key argument as such. Moreover, the author does not say that the crisis is imminent.

646. d In the 2nd paragraph, the author is being sarcastic about the fact that the new production and refining capacity will effortlessly bring demand and supply back to balance. (line 2 onwards "the accepted ...just like that") and he quotes Tommy Cooper to emphasize his sarcasm. It must be remembered that we have to consider the author's point of view, not Tommy Cooper's. Therefore option (d) is correct

647. d Option (a) and (c) are contrary to what Derrida says in the passage which makes them incorrect. There can be a confusion between 2 and 4. Option (b) could have been an inference if the statement had been "Language limits our interpretations of reality". But the word 'construction' is incorrect. Therefore only option (d) according to the passage, is correct.

648. c According to the passage, Derrida is against logocentrism and choices (a), (b) and (d) are pro logocentrism which leaves option (c) which is different from logocentrism.

649. a This is a fact based question. In paragraph 2, refers to line 5 "Rather, they exist ... position". Option (a) directly follows from this line.

650. a Answer choice (d) is contrary to what is being said. Answer choice (c) is irrelevant. There can be a confusion between 1 and 2 but it must be noted that it is not the meaning of the text which is based on binary opposites but the interpretation. This leaves us only with answer choice (a).

651. b According to the passage, "A critical attitude needs for its raw material, as it were, theories or beliefs which are held more or less dogmatically". Therefore, our critical attitude is the tool by which we shape our dogmatic beliefs. Thus, the relationship of dogmatic beliefs and critical attitude is equivalent to that of a chisel and that of a marble stone.

652. a Option (c), (d) and (e) are ruled out because they are not supported by the passage. (negative, neutral, inferior) - Option (a) and (b) are close but (a) is better because the question is about the role of dogmatic behaviour with respect to the development of science.

In the third paragraph, 8th line, it is mentioned that dogmatic attitude is pseudo/pre-scientific attitude. Science needs dogmatic beliefs for their critical revision. Beginning of fourth paragraph states that science begins with myths and criticism of myths. Thus, dogmatic behavior is required to develop science because the former serves as the base on which science is made.

653. d Refer to the last sentence of the second paragraph. It is clear from the context (especially from the words - 'experience', 'maturity') that time has a direct effect on the evolution of thinking. Option (d) is the only option which takes into account the element of time (the word - 'stages').

654. e Option (e) is correct because this statement suggests that critical attitude is a process of questioning which leads to tentative hypothesis. A critical attitude by itself is not opposed to conviction, but it tries to modify the conviction according to reason.

655. c Refer to the third last paragraph of the passage; dogmatic attitude is pseudo-scientific because its aim is only to verify its laws and schemata even if it has to neglect the refutations. Whereas critical attitude is flexible enough to change, refute or falsify its tenets and therefore has a questioning attitude.

656. c We refer to the tenth line of the third paragraph. Here Mr. Goran Lindblad admits that communism did commit brutalities but it also had positive consequences like rapid industrialization. Hence option (c) is the best answer.

657. b Option (d) is very blatant, but is not the 'real' reason for the attack. The reason that the West repeatedly attacks communism (as stated by the author in the last para) is that they want to establish the current capitalist order as supreme i.e. they idealise 'global capitalism'. Option (e) is close, but wrongly states that communist nations might overtake the capitalists. This is not given in the passage.

658. e The answer can be found in the first line of the last paragraph, which in essence implies that it is important to go beyond and look at the motives of atrocities perpetrated by different regimes. The motive is global capitalism as described in the last paragraph. Therefore, Option (e) is correct.

659. a (a) is the correct answer. In the fourth paragraph the author explains the 'intimate link' between colonialism and Nazism. A peripheral view of this relationship suggests that the answer should be (c) which explains the terms and ideas that were imported and used by the Nazi party. But the next few lines explain the deeper relationship that exists between the two. These lines refer to the atrocities that one race has committed upon the other. The British imposed their rule on the Indian people. Similarly, the Belgian forced labour and mass murder led to the death of 10 million Congolese. These references are clearly race centric. Therefore, (a) is correct.

660. d On the basis of the given choices the best answer is option (d). In the second last paragraph, the author attempts to portray the magnitude of the atrocities committed by the European Colonialists. In doing so he mentions in a sarcastic tone "Presumably European lives count for more." Thus, this is not an inference that can be drawn from the passage. The rest of the statements can be easily inferred from the passage.

661. c A careful scrutiny of the second paragraph reveals that the concept of "justice as fairness" is a hypothetical situation in a real society. Thus options (a), (b) and (e) can be eliminated. The possible answers are (c) or (d). (c) is more specific in comparison to option (d). Thus (c) is the correct answer.

662. a Refer to para 1. "Rather, the idea is that the principles...initial position of equality." Associate these lines with paragraph 2. So, option (a) can be inferred from the passage.

663. d Refer to the latter half in the second paragraph. In essence it states that the principles of justice should be so chosen that they neither favour or disfavour a particular class of society. A law maker who chooses the principle of justice without being aware of his status in society in the next birth exemplifies the situation that has been described as choosing the principles of justice behind a veil of ignorance. Thus option (d) is the most appropriate choice. Option (a) is incorrect because if there is a possibility of return then the businessmen would obviously choose those principles which will favour their situation. Option (b) is incorrect because the reference to school children is quite vague. Option (c) is incorrect because if businessmen were to choose these principles then they might choose those which favour their family. Also, these businessmen are aware that there is no possibility of their return. Option (e) is incorrect because they may or may not migrate ('potential immigrants'). It also suggests that the current principles of justice in their society do not contribute to their success. If they are unsuccessful in their own society then why would they choose certain principles which do not favour their situation.

664. b Option (b) is correct because 'fair' in this option means 'just'. We cannot choose option (d) though it's a close choice because 'fairly' means 'gradually'. Here, the choice clearly depends upon the usage and the context of this word.

665. d When all children are provided free education, it indicates that the decision to do so has not been taken with any other consideration in mind, save the children's benefit. Thus, the children's family background and social status do not matter, in accordance with the passage's theme.

666. e 'Reciprocal roles determine normative human behaviour in society'.

This is the main idea of the passage that is carried throughout. Note that 'role of biology' is negated and 'reciprocal roles' are affirmed in paragraph 1 and 2.

667. b 'We would not have been offended by the father playing his role 'tongue in cheek''.

All the other options would have been false if biological linkages would have structured human society.

668. d The last para where the author mentions the examples of a waitress and a clergyman and a driver refers to the alignment of self with the rules being performed and society preventing manifestation of the true self.

669. b 'The difference between two artistic interpretations'

Refer the last three lines of the 1st para where the author talks about the gap between the two artistic interpretations within the depth of the creative power and doesn't mention width.

670. a 'Define the place of the poet in his culture'.

The lines starting with "But suddenly I understood ….."define the position of the poet in his culture.

671. d Refer to the 5th line of the 2nd para. Here the term "adventures of experience" refers to the poet & artists who over vitalize and enrich the past for us.

672. d 'ways of understanding a scientific tradition '.

The idea is implicitly throughout the passage.

673. c 'Loyalty to a certain paradigm of scientific inquiry'. This is an analogy question where we can draw comparison from the line that says "loci of commitment that have been described as accepted rules." Options 1 and 2 talk about a bohemical structure rather than conformity. It is 'loyalty to something' and not 'loyalty among people' talked about in the passage. Option 4 talks about adherence to an accepted norm which goes out of the scope of the argument. Option 5 talks about evolving trends which is not mentioned in the paragraph. Therefore option (c) is the best choice.

674. e From the theme and tone of the passage it can be inferred that paradigms are predominant as compared to rules. It is difficult to define rules.

Paradigms in part determine normal science and also need not depend on the formulation of rules and assumptions. Hence the author would agree with the choice "Paradigms are a general representation of rules and beliefs of a scientific tradition."

675. c Option (c) is the most logical explanation. Refer to lines "those include ... correlations between variables"

676. b 'Historical outcomes depend......... each case'. Refer to the 1st para where it says "Prediction in history... became averaged out". This is further supported by the example.

677. c Note the tone with which the third paragraph starts it emphasizes that students can do much more!

678. c Refer to the 4th paragraph of the passage. The elders were of the opinion that turning of the eyes by the child while having the ice-creams in both hands could make the child fall down or trip over stones, steps in the pavement. The phrase 'rightly suggested' changes the meaning of the given sentence and hence it cannot be inferred from the passage.

679. d 'Parvenus' refer to persons who have suddenly risen to a higher social and economic class but have not yet received social acceptance by others in that class. Hence, the phrase 'little parvenus' would appropriately refer to 'young upstarts'.

680. b Refer to the 5th paragraph of the passage. The sentence 'two two-cent ....suggested excess' clearly tell us that it was intemperance on part of the author which made him pine for two two-cent ice-cream cones instead of one four-cent pie.

681. b In the lines 'Nowadays the moralist ....spoiled'. The author is talking about morality in the context of the present day world. The rest of the options are out of the scope of the passage.

682. a Refer to the last line of the 4th paragraph of the passage. Here the author says that the intentions of his elders in not letting him eat two-cent cones was 'cruelly pedagogical'. This implies that the justification was 'didactic' in nature. This makes option (a) correct. The rest of the options are incorrect in context of the passage. 'Dietetic' refers to anything related with diet or the use of food. 'Dialectic' refers to the nature of logical argumentation. 'Diatonic' refers to using only the seven tones of a standard scale without chromatic alterations. 'Diastolic' refers to the rhythmically occurring relaxation and the dilation of the heart chambers.

683. e According to popular wisdom, language is a cultural artifact or cultural invention or it is part of the leaning process or it is unique to *Homo sapiens*. But option(e) has been stated as the viewpoint of the cognitive scientists as can be seen in the lines 'Language is a complex specialized......module'. The author also agrees with the cognitive scientists' view as he confirms to the view that language comes by instinct. He further corroborates this by saying that people know how to talk in the same manner as spiders know how to spin the web.

684. b "Spiders know how to spin webs" highlights the inherent qualities of living species. This analogy can be replaced in a similar way by "Bees collecting nectar" which is also a part of their inane trait. Options(a), (c), (d), (e) mention traits which are acquired over a period of time by putting in some kind of effort in order to be adept at them.

685. b Refer to the last sentence of the 2nd paragraph of the passage. It states that 'In nature's talent show, we are simply a species of primate with our own act, a knack for communicating information about who did what to whom by modulating the sounds we make when we exhale'. Hence, communicating with each other through voice modulation is the unique quality of human beings as per the passage.

686. a Refer to the 3rd paragraph of the passage where the author says that the scientists believe that the complexity of language is part of our biological birthright. He further illustrates the scientists' point of view that it cannot be taught. The author strengthens this view by quoting Oscar Wilde, making option(a) as the correct answer option. The rest of the options are not mentioned in the passage.

687. d Throughout the passage, the author is talking about language as a type of instinct that is existent is human beings and not any specific attribute or skill that is learnt by them over a period of time. In the first paragraph, the author claims 'But I prefer the admittedly quaint term instinct'. Similarly in the last paragraph of the passage, the author concludes by saying that 'Finally, since language is the product of a well engineered biological instinct, we shall see that it is not the nutty barrel of monkeys that entertainer-columnists make it out to be'.

688. a The 2nd paragraph of the passage begins with 'With those caveats, it appears to me that one strand consisted ....to prevent bracken ferns from over running the fields'. Hence in the context of Rwanda and Haiti, the author is referring to the existence of too many people fighting for limited land and other resources. Hence, option (a) is the most appropriate answer.

689. d 'Anthropogenic' refers to being caused or produced by human beings. So 'anthropogenic drought' refers to the drought caused by actions of human beings. Further hint is given in the 8th line of the 2nd paragraph of the passage.

690. c In the 3rd paragraph, refer to the lines 'At the time of previous droughts.......to have reliable water supplies'. Hence, it is evident that the final drought which caused the collapse of the Maya civilization was different from the previous droughts because man had left no unoccupied land away from agriculture to start life in a new way.

691. d The first paragraph of the passage states that 'To summarize the Classic Maya collapse, we can tentatively identify five strands. I acknowledge, however, that Maya archaeologists still disagree vigorously among themselves-in part, because the different strands evidently varied in importance among different parts of the Maya realm; because detailed archaeological studies are available for only some Maya sites, and because it remains puzzling why most of the Maya heartland remained nearly empty of population and failed to recover after the collapse and after re-growth of forests'. Hence, there is not one specific factor that can individually explain the collapse of the Maya civilization. Therefore, the correct answer would be option 4.

692. e The answer is clearly indicated in the 4th paragraph of the passage where it is mentioned that the Maya kings and leaders were more focussed on their short-term concerns of enriching themselves. The entire Maya population was not obsessed with its short-term interests. Hence, it cannot be cited as one of the factors causing the collapse of the Maya society.

693. c In the first paragraph of the passage, refer to the lines 'Many of the concepts of modern art, by contrast, have resulted from the almost accidental meetings of groups of talented individuals at certain times and certain places'. Hence, option 3 is the reason for the emergence of the concepts of modern art.

694. e According to the author, with the passage of time an art movement ceases to be a living organism and it becomes a fossil. The author then takes the example of a scientist who reconstructs the life of the past era which are codified in the form of messages in the structure of a fossil. He goes on to say similarly an artist also analyses the intellectual and creative possibilities from the art movements of the past. 'Fossil' here signifies the temporal phasing of an era associated with the art movement. This makes option 5 the correct option. Option 1 is contradictory to the facts mentioned in the passage. In option 2, the word 'historic' means significant which is not being indicated by the author. Option 3 is contradictory to the author's point of view. Option 4 is out of the scope of the argument.

695. a Refer to the first sentence of the first paragraph of the passage where science and art have been stated as similar in including a whole range of separate, though interconnecting activities. Hence, option(a) is the correct answer.

696. d In the first paragraph of the passage, refer to the lines 'Briefly, then, the concepts of modern art are of legitimately......visual and spiritual experience'. Hence, the ideologies of the art of the twentieth century can be better realised by the fast changing world of visual and metaphysical understanding. The rest of the options have no link with the concepts and ideologies of the art of the twentieth century.

697. e In the last paragraph of the passage, refer to the lines 'As T.S Eliot observed, no one starts anything from the scratch however consciously you may try to live in the present, you are still involved with a nexus of behaviour patterns bequeathed from the past. The original and creative person is not someone who ignores these patterns but someone who is able to translate and develop them so that they conform more exactly to his and our present needs'. Hence, new and original thinking is always developed on the basis of the past thoughts in order to cater to the modern needs. Therefore, option(e) is the most appropriate answer.

698. b Refer to the part *better if it lasts for years …wealthy with all you have gained on the way.* (b) is clearly the answer. (c) is far-fetched. (a) is an isolated observation. (d) is totally incorrect.

699. a Refer to the part *as many sensual perfumes as you can … to gather stores of knowledge.* (a) is clearly the answer. (b), (c) and (d) are short-sighted observations.

700. d Refer to the part *Keep Ithaka always in your mind. Arriving there is what you are destined for.* (d) is undoubtedly the answer.

701. c Refer to the part *you bring them along inside your soul.* (c) is undoubtedly the answer.

702. b Refer to the part *Ithaka gave you the marvelous journey, without her you would not have set out.* The poem has a tone of encouragement and promise. (b) is clearly the answer. (a), (c) and (d) are ridiculous choices.

703. Option (a) can be inferred from the passage. The author's mother feels the need to convert later in her life. It shows that she did not experience a lasting connection with her original religion. Option (b) can also be inferred from the passage as the author's mother followed her religion seriously as a mean to cope with her life. Option (c) cannot be inferred even though the first paragraph indicates that her knowledge of Sikhism was not strong and that she had no interest in its monist theology. The second paragraph indicates that she had her own interpretation of the religion - a more emotional one. This paragraph helps argue against the claim that she felt a disconnect with her religion. The word "always" also makes it inappropriate. Option (c) is thus the answer. Option (d) can be inferred from the first sentence of the passage ...'*deeply rooted in the peasant culture of her native Punjab'*.

704. The first four paragraphs in the passage help place the religious philosophy of the author's mother when she followed Sikhism. She followed Sikhism but brought in a variety of customs from the subcontinent; most of these customs were Hindu. It is clear that she did not follow the monist theology of the religion - the understanding that a variety of existing things can be explained in terms of a single reality or substance eluded her. Hence, option (a) can be ruled out. Option (b) is incorrect because there is no mention that she followed every custom. Option (c) can be inferred from the first sentence of the second paragraph. This sentence indicates that the author's mother was looking for emotional security in religion. The third paragraph points to the fact that she followed certain customs for her personal goals. The last sentence of the first paragraph also indicates that she was not looking for spiritual fulfilment in religion. Option (d) is a negative portrayal of the reason why the author's mother followed religious customs. However, the passage only indicates her lack of understanding and her personal motivation. It does not indicate a whimsical nature.

705. The last sentence of the fifth paragraph indicates that the reason she continued visiting church was that she felt peace. The penultimate paragraph also indicates that she felt assured that Jesus was with her and she was not alone. It is also clear from these two paragraphs that she had not felt this way previously and hence, it is safe to infer that she felt the peace she had been searching for. Option (b) is the answer. Option (a) is incorrect because the author's mother was looking for an answer to her suffering and not reassurance that there were others who were suffering too. Option (b) is incorrect because even though the congregation at the church was north-Indian, this would not have been a factor in her move away from Sikhism as latter also had followers from her community (native Punjab). Option (c) cannot be inferred because the sixth and seventh paragraphs indicate that she felt a difference from her previous religion and hence moved over to Christianity.

706. The last paragraph states that the author was not too surprised by his mother's conversion. However, what surprised him was his own feeling of hurt and betrayal that he felt by what he understood to be his mother's rejection of their bond over religion. Option (a) can be ruled out. The author has mixed feeling about this mother's conversion - an understanding of why she converted and yet a feeling of hurt on her betrayal of their religious bond. Option (b) is the answer. Option (c) is not the full portrayal of the author's feelings. Option (d) is incorrect because the author says he was surprised (*unnerved)* at his own reaction to his mother's conversion. In such an instance, he could not have viewed his reaction in an objective manner.

707. Refer to the line "The story of Jesus is, by Indian standards, a plausibly humdrum one" in the last paragraph. The word "humdrum" means unexciting. Hence, option (c) is the best answer. Option (a) can be ruled out because the exact opposite has been stated in the passage. Every Indian village has a story like that of Jesus. Hence, people will readily believe it. Option (b) is wrong because "polemic" means confrontational. The passage doesn't talk about Jesus's story being confrontational for the Indians. Option (d) is not factually supported by the passage. Hence, (c) is the best answer.

708. Option (b) is wrong because the passage mentions that she dreamt of the Jesus once. Option (c) is wrong because the passage has not given us any information regarding the author's mother abandoning her family. Option (d) is wrong because the author feels betrayed but it can't be inferred that his mother deliberately betrayed him. Option (a) is mentioned in the passage. Refer to the lines –" and lost interest in her old ways.". Hence, Option (a) is the best answer.

709. The passage is a review of a book (*Imaginary Friends*) that has links with the Festinger study. The third sentence of the first paragraph also states that this book looks at *"how cults can affect and change those who study them, just as sociologists can change the cults they study"*. The rest of the passage focuses on this subject matter and does not move into the broader topic of group behaviour. Hence (a) can be ruled out (Mark the word "exhaustive"). Option (b) is a partial assessment of the statement in the first paragraph and hence it is not the answer. It is also too generic in nature. Option (c) correctly infers the third sentence of the first paragraph and is thus the answer. The word "can be" makes it the correct deduction. Option (d) is incorrect because the narrator calls himself stupid on occasions. However, whether he undergoes any cerebral deterioration in the process of the study can't be determined.

710. Option (a) cannot be determined based on the information in the passage. The Festinger study was undertaken by sociologists but there is no confirmation, in the passage, that the protagonists of *Imaginary Friends* are based on the sociologists who undertook the Festinger study. Option (b) can be inferred from the second sentence of the first paragraph. It is clear that the book is a fiction and takes the Festinger study to another level. There is also the mention of the detailed and multi-layered description of the characters. Option (c) can be inferred from the first paragraph. The fourth sentence of this paragraph also indicates that the Festinger study was conducted on (a) cult/cults. Option (d) can be inferred from the third paragraph. Hence, Option (a) is the answer.

711. The result of an unfulfilled prophecy or a disconfirmation, on a cult, is mentioned in the last half of the second paragraph. While an unfulfilled prophecy or an unexpected change may take place, the group usually adjusts through a process or rationalisation and increase in recruitment. This is mentioned in the penultimate sentence of the second paragraph. Option (d) is the answer. Refer to the last two lines of the second paragraph. Option (a) can be ruled out because it is an effect and not the end result. Option (b) can be ruled out because it is a preliminary effect of an unfulfilled prophecy but not the result. Option (c) can be ruled out because the unexpected change and unfulfilled prophecy have been used as synonyms in the passage (Refer to the third last sentence of the second paragraph). Option (c) is, thus, incorrect.

712. Option (a) cannot be inferred from the passage as there is no reference, at all, to 'a pairing' of a new recruit and an older member. Option (a) and Option (c) can be inferred from the first sentence of the last paragraph. Option (d) can be inferred from the second sentence of the last paragraph - *"He tries ineffectively to memorize... idiosyncratic truths that members add to group metaphysics."* The reference to idiosyncratic truths indicates that these truths are specific to the cult. E can be inferred from the last two lines of the passage. Roger desperately tries to remember all that he has been taught so as to become a part of the group. So, Option (a) is the answer.

713. The passage focuses entirely upon the book and its analysis. Option (a) can be ruled out because the main idea of the passage is not to critically analyse The Festinger Study. The focus is its application in the book. Option (b) is too narrow to be the central idea. Hence, it can't be the title. Option (d) is too broad as this passage only talks about one fictional cult. It can't be applied to cults everywhere. Option (c) is the best fit. Though the passage doesn't read like a conventional book review, this option best captures the essence of the passage. Hence, Option (c) is the answer.

714. The personality of Verena is mentioned in the fourth paragraph. The fifth paragraph mentions Roger's impression of Verena. Option (a) is the way Roger describes Verena. It may or may not be true regarding her personality. Hence, option (a) can't be inferred from the passage. Option (c) is untrue as the passage mentions her as a 19 year old. The passage doesn't talk about the normal age group of cult members. There may have been other members who were quite young. So, Option (c) can't be the answer. Option (d) is partially correct as the fourth paragraph says that Verena's aunt encouraged her. The words 'exploitation' and 'brainwashed' make the option too extreme to be inferred from the limited data given in the passage. Hence, Option (b) is the best option. The fifth paragraph makes it clear that Roger is obsessed with Verena's personality and appeal.

715. Option (d) best captures the central idea of the first two paragraphs. Option (a), (b), and (c) are too narrow to be the theme. They are the separate things mentioned in the first paragraph. The author asks why people act in certain manners. The first line of the second paragraph supplies part of the answer – self esteem.

716. No empirical or sociological evidence has been cited in the passage while discussing the main idea of the passage. In the last paragraph the author talks about some neurological evidence. He refers to a study. But he does not cite any neurological evidence himself.

717. Option (a) is stated in the second paragraph. Refer to the line "we all have a need to think well of ourselves, and for others to think well of us". Hence, the author will agree with option (a). Option (c) is mentioned in the third paragraph. Refer to the line "An example of this is the fear of public speaking – a dread that can be greater than that of flying or even of death". The author will agree with Option (c). Option (d) Is the central theme of the passage. The author talks about road rage incidents to highlight this point. But nowhere does the author suggest that the pain of injured self esteem is identical to physical pain. The brain interprets any attack on our self esteem as a physical pain but it does not follow that the brain of the body reacts to it in the same ways they would to physical pain. The passage also doesn't talk about cure. Option (b) is the answer.

718. The passage does not say that the popularity of cricket is the reason for the decline of *kushti*. The passage states that after 28 years a state level championship was held. But it does not say that the absence of state level championships led to the decline of *kushti*. The passage does not talk about lack of space anywhere. Similarly, the passage mentions that Akanksha, the daughter of an erstwhile wrestler would have loved to make her father proud. So, it can't be inferred that youngsters are not interested in *kushti*. But the passage does say that earlier *pehelwans* were employed by the British & the mills. Now there is no employer or growth opportunity. Option (c) is the answer.

719. Promoting a sport means giving it sustained encouragement. The Maratha rulers encouraged even women to take up the sport. So they acted like patrons. Option (d) is the best option. Option (a) is incorrect because the passage doesn't give factual information regarding honours bestowed by the Maratha rulers on winners. Option (b) is also factually unsupported by the passage. Option (c) has not been mentioned in the passage. The British employed *pehelwans*, according to the passage. The correct answer is, thus, Option (d).

720. Option (a) can't be inferred. The Marathas' encouragement of wrestling does not mean that political encouragement is essential. We can't also apply the information given in the passage to any sport as the passage focuses solely on *kushti*. Option (b) cannot be inferred from the passage. The last paragraph praises the effort of the state government. So, we can't say that the state government is to be solely blamed for the decline in *kushti*.. Option (c) is wrong because the passage talks about the daughter of a former wrestler. The author doesn't talk about the opinion of the parents. Option (d) is not directly stated; rather it is implied. The passage highlights lack of prospects as one of the reasons why youngsters are not taking up *kushti*. It makes E the best answer.

721. The Renaissance was an European development. The Church and Christian theology had killed science and the pursuit of knowledge. The Renaissance marked the rebirth and revival of science and the quest for knowledge. China was never a Christian country and hence the Renaissance did not affect it. Hence the solutions is (d).

722. Chinese seafarers travelled far and wide interacted with many races and nations and encountered many new ideas & concepts. Their tales gave rise to curiosity among the native Chinese who came up with conflations as well as original ideas. The fermentation of ideas was the source of Chinese science. Hence the answer is option (c). Military strength wealth and long voyages are all irrelevant.

723. The Judes Christian tradition refers to the beliefs & practices of Judaism, which is older than Christianity and Christianity itself. Both these religions hold that what is given in their scriptures is the word of god and hence, cannot be wrong. When science challenged these ideas it became necessary to put science and scientists down with a heavy hand. Hence the influence of Judeo Christian tradition instead of stimulating science actually killed it. Hence the word 'supposedly'. Correct answer is option (c).

724. The message of the passage is that when a single person wields absolute power a single wrong decision can play havoc. China which led the world bill about the 14th century because backward when the emperor ordered the dismantling of the navy thus in a way making China insular. The correct answer is option (d). Option (a) is irrelevant because maritime trade & not maritime power is the source of cross-fertilization of ideas. Option (b) is irrelevant because the Renaissance played no role in China. Option (c) is irrelevant because Europe was not exactly wallowing in wealth and further the curiosity of Columbus does not mean that all Italians were equally curious.

725. Option (a) is irrelevant because the question is not whether isolationism is usual or unusual but rather, whether it is good or bad. Option (c) is irrelevant because in the ultimate analysis the dismantling of the navies isolated China and this led in the long run to the intellectual decay of China. Hence the correct answer is option (d).

726. Option (a) is irrelevant because any amount of wealth is spent overtime. It cannot last forever. Similarly, option (b) is incorrect as the one time transfer of population is not a permanent solution. Likewise option (c) is irrelevant because the increase in military might was a temporary phenomenon. The correct answer is option (d). When there is fierce competition it gives rise to a quest for new solutions, new ideas, and new science.

727. Option (d) is the correct answer as in paragraph 2 of the given passage, where the author talks about the promotion of creativity in cities, he does not mention that cities provide access to cultural activities. This is nowhere stated in the passage.

728. Option (b) is the correct answer as in paragraphs 3 and 4 of passage it is presented that organizations that were supposed to foster creativity, actually stifle it.

729. Option (a) is the correct answer as the entire passage revolves around the idea how cities help in flourishing of creativity. The author describes the importance of social interaction and how the lack of it, spoils creativity. Option (b) is ruled out because the author explicitly states that "creativity itself is not in danger". Option (c) is incorrect since it is discussed only in the last 2 paragraphs. Option (d) is too generic. It can't be the main idea.

730. Option (c) is the correct answer as from paragraph 5 it can be easily inferred that Jane Jacobs holds leaders responsible for promoting creativity in people and cities.

731. Option 2 is the correct answer as after talking about what stifles creativity (in paragraph 3), the author presents the 1968 report(in order to validate the previous point). Option 1 states exactly the opposite of what is stated in the passage. Option 3 is incorrect because the reduction of creativity cannot be attributed to learning more. Option 4 is unrelated. The passage does not talk about technology. However, the second option is only the best option. "Schools today" makes it a dicey option.

732. In the 2nd last paragraph of the passage, it is stated that the creativity of only those people can be utilized who use their minds to work. This implies that people who work with their hands are not creative. Hence, option (a) is the correct answer.

733. Option (c) is the correct answer as the entire passage presents the effects of climate change on Subnivium. This rules out options (a) and (b) that keep Subnivium (and not the effects of climate change on it) as the point of focus. Option (d) is used as an example only in the first paragraph of the passage and therefore it can't be the purpose of the passage.

734. Option (b) is the correct answer as the entire passage does not mention even a single positive effect of climate change on the Subnivium. Though one may infer that there may be some hints of positive impact, the overall effect is not positive. All other options are stated in the passage.

735. All options (a), (c) and (d) address the symptoms of climate change. They fail to attack the main cause, let alone providing a solution to that cause. Option (b) addresses the cause and even provides a solution to the issue of climate change. Hence it is the correct answer.

736. Options (a) and (c) are too generic. Option (b) is incorrect because such information has not been provided. In the last paragraph of the passage it is stated that the effects of colder Subnivium are interrelated and multilayered. This has been substantiated through the example of shrubs. Therefore, option (d) is the correct answer.

737. Option (a) is correct as the entire passage is about how the effects of climate change are interrelated. Options (b), (c) and (d) are incorrect because the passage does not give us enough information to claim them.

738. Clearly, option (c) is the correct answer as the passage uses the example of blankets to draw an analogy. First it is shown that having spaces between the layers of a blanket increases the insulating property. Next, using the same logic, the effects of increase in snow density is explained.

739. Option (c) is the correct answer as it is explicitly stated in paragraph 2 of the passage. Other options are beyond the scope of the passage.

740. Options (a) and (c) are ruled out since they are stated in paragraph 3. Option (b) is stated towards the end of paragraph Option (d) cannot be inferred from anywhere in the passage. Hence, it is correct answer.

741. Option (d) is the correct answer and can be inferred from paragraph Options (a) and (b) cannot be inferred from anywhere in the passage. Option (c) is incorrect because this distorted information about charging stations is not there in the passage.

742. Towards the end of the passage, the author states that though car drivers want autonomy, public transport will be the future as this is the only solution to traffic problem. This makes option (c) correct. Options (a) and (d) are beyond the scope of the passage. Option (b) is ambiguous.

743. Option (d) is ruled out since the passage does not compare the sales of Uber and Tesla. Option (b) is incorrect since this cannot be determined. Option (a) is beyond the passage's scope. Option (c) is correct as it is clearly demonstrated in paragraphs 5 and 6- private cars will operate as taxis so that one can use them in the hour of need. And this is the future towards which Uber is working.

744. Option (b) is stated in the last paragraph of the passage, where we are told that traffic jams will not exist if personal cars become public utility products. And the only way one can get autonomy is through the use of bicycle. Option (a) is not stated in the passage. The comparison drawn between electric powered bicycle and electrics is not in the passage. Hence, option (c) is ruled out. Option (d) is a personal judgment, which is nowhere in the passage.

745. Option (a) is the correct answer as the author provides examples of the US and Russia to tell that these countries have taken up the use of typewriter. The author also supports their using of typewriters by providing us with positive aspects of the typewriters. Option (b) is beyond the scope of the passage. Option (c) is incorrect since clearly it is not the main aim of the passage. There is no hint to make that claim. Option (d) is incorrect since this difference has nowhere been made.

746. "Type a document and lock it away and more or less the only way anyone else can get.......... some departments have never abandoned them". This information, which says that using of typewriters helps one control who views the document, makes option (d) correct.

747. Towards the end of the passage, it is written- "Nor are there any easy distractions." – i.e that typewriters can be used only for one single thing-writing. Hence 1 is stated in the passage and is therefore not the answer. It is also stated- "there's a big premium on hitting the right key." This means that once something has been typed, it cannot be revised. Hence option (b) is also stated. It is also stated- "....encouraging clack of keys". This is associated with typewriters making more noise than computers. Hence option (c) is also stated. Nothing in the passage points towards option (d). Therefore, it is the correct answer.

748. The main aim of the author appears to dismiss the popular believe that Vikings were pillagers. The passage revolves around the idea that Vikings started out as traders. This makes option (c) correct. Option (a) is ruled out because the example of combs has been used only as an illustration. Option (d) is incorrect because the passage discusses a period before Vikings turned into pillagers. Option (b) is beyond the scope of the passage.

749. Option (d) is the correct answer. The author states that the age of Viking started in 793 and extended till the Norman conquest of Great Britain in 1066. This means that Vikings had trade relations with Britain before the Viking age.

750. In the passage it is stated that Vikings only brought the combs from Norway to Denmark. Hence option (a) cannot be concluded from the passage, making it the correct answer.

751. Refer to the last line of the penultimate paragraph. Option 2 is the clear answer.

752. Refer to the main idea of the passage. This question is very close to question number 4. The author would definitely support any step that relieves the common man of the pressure of 'being happy'. So, option 3 will be supported by the author.

753. This can be located in the last two paragraphs. The author doesn't mention the example of 1970 in a positive tone. The main idea of the passage has a negative tone. So, option 3 is the correct answer. The other options have positive undertones.

754. This requires us to use the fundamentals of critical reasoning. The author warns us against the use of technology to bully or manipulate individuals to become obsessed with 'becoming happy'. This 'happiness' is not actually happiness. The author clearly blames the many companies that analyse and monitor consumer behaviour. So, option 3, if true, will weaken the author's argument. If these companies are not using such data, then the author's warning is misplaced. So, option 3 is the correct answer.

755. Refer to the first two lines of the fourth paragraph. Option 3 is the clear answer.

756. Refer to the last three lines of the first paragraph. Option 2 is the clear answer.

757. In the passage, the author doesn't compare Darwin and Mendel. He doesn't blame one or praise the other. The author also doesn't state that either Darwin or Mendel is better. So, option 2 is the best choice.

758. Refer to the third paragraph. The question refers to this paragraph. Options 2 and 3 come in the last paragraph. So, they are out of context. Option 4 too goes outside the scope of the third paragraph. So, option 1 is the clear answer.

759. The main message of the passage is that the current theory of natural selection doesn't look adequate to explain the process of evolution. So, option 3 would challenge this notion. Hence, option 4 is the answer.

760. The clue is the word 'sham'. It is the only option where the Keep America Beautiful organization is mentioned in a negative light. The other options are all too positive. The author has clearly taken a negative view of the organisation. So, option 4 is the correct answer.

761. Refer to the first paragraph. The author says that consumers are wrongly blamed and held responsible for the rise in plastic pollution. According to the author, companies that manufacture plastic unnecessarily are to be held responsible. So, he will support option 4 the most.

762. Refer to the line where the phrase is mentioned. The author is talking about the responsibility ascribed to consumers to control the increase in plastic pollution across the globe. Option 3 is the clear answer.

763. This is not mentioned anywhere in the passage. The other options can be located in the passage.

764. Refer to the first paragraph, especially the first two lines. So, option 1 is the clear answer.

765. The author uses a very neutral tone to talk about this issue. So, option 1 can be eliminated as it is too negative. Option 4 goes beyond the scope of the discussion. Refer to the first line of the second paragraph. So, option 3 is the clear answer.

766. The first paragraph focuses on option 2. So, it is the correct answer.

767. Refer to the lines that come before and after the line where 'mood music' is mentioned. Option 2 is the clear answer. The other options are irrelevant.

768. This is a main idea based question. The entire passage focuses on India's lack of acknowledgement of the second world war. So, only options 3 and 4 are relevant. However, the passage doesn't mention 'non-colonial political identity' anywhere. So, option 3 should be the right answer as it is mentioned towards the end of the passage. But the word 'only' might have been perceived as being too extreme. So, CAT has given option 4 as the answer.

769. Refer to the lines that come before and after the line where 'mood music' is mentioned. Option 3 is the clear answer. The other options are irrelevant.

770. It is an easy answer. Option 3 talks about the main idea of the passage. As PTSD like symptoms in elephants is the main focus of the passage, option 3 is the best answer. Option 2 is irrelevant. Optlon 4 goes beyond the scope of the passage. Option 1 is close but it talks about 'all animals'. So, it is too broad.

771. This answer given by CAT is dicey. A metaphor is an indirect reference. The given line is neither a metaphor nor an ode. It is also not an exaggeration. Refer to the first line of the penultimate paragraph. Refer to the line: "What Bradshaw and her colleagues describe would seem to be an extreme form of anthropocentric conjecture if the evidence that they've compiled from various elephant researchers. . . weren't so compelling." Option 2 is a close answer and may appear to be a better choice too. However, CAT has given option 1 as the answer.

772. The passage nowhere mentions option 3. The author does talk about orphaned elephants. But there is no mention of mothers of these elephants evolving newer ways. The other options can be located in the passage. So, option 3 is the correct answer.

773. In the passage, the author focuses on PTSD in elephants. Option 1 is too generic. Option 4 is too narrow and misleading. The focus of the passage is not on conflict. Option 2 is too narrow. It only talks about one part of the first paragraph. Option 3 best captures the essence of the passage.

774. This is a fact based question. Refer to the last line of the first paragraph. The words 'intentionality' and 'purposefulness' are synonyms. So, option 4 is the correct answer.

775. The paragraph 3 and 4 talks about the face-to-face interaction between service providers and clients, where the results been not fruitful. Therefore, the right answer should be option (b).

776. Need to check for the option not present in the passage. Option (a) isn't mentioned, option (b) is present in the 1st paragraph, Option (c) and Option (d) have resemblance in 2nd last and last paragraph. The right answer is option (a).

777. In 2nd paragraph, e-governance can be just as bad as any other....from this line it can be inferred that the electronic monitoring system was a superficial solution to a serious problem. The right answer is option (a).

778. The overall passage talks about the complacency with the service providers, with the instances given makes the option (a) the right answer.

779. Option (a),(c) and (d) talk about the specific issues or are the examples of a common issue which is clearly mentioned in Option (b), the right answer.

Question Numbers (780 to 784):

780. If the evaluation could be subjective then what is the use of the test as proper measures or guidelines might not be included on being subjective. Therefore, the right answer is option (c).

781. The author isn't protesting about the cause but in general talking about the pros and cons on the matter. The right answer is option (b).

782. The author introduced the matter, mentioned a few benefits about the cause and then has only projected the negative outcome of evaluating performance measurement. The right answer is option (d).

783. The correct answer can be inferred from the 2nd paragraph where author talks in general about the professionals. Thus, the right answer is option (c).

784. Option (d) isn't mentioned in the passage, the right option.

Question Numbers (785 to 788):

785. Option (b) isn't mentioned in the passage therefore being the right answer.

786. Since the time period mentioned in the passage belong to an ancient time, one can infer from the paragraph that snails were edible. The right answer is option (b).

787. The answer can be inferred from the paragraph 4 and 5 of the passage, the right answer is option (d).

788. The answer can be referred from 1st paragraph, lines 1 to 5..The right answer is option (d).

Question Numbers (789 to 793)

789. 3rd paragraph, lines 6-9, it refers to the Saturn's rings discolour and darken over time. Thus the right answer is option (c).

790. There is no mention of the methane and helium in the passage, therefore it can be inferred that the close option and answer is option (a).

791. Option a, b and c are mentioned in the passage while option d isn't. The right answer is option (d).

792. 2nd paragraph, d-e lines, it can be inferred from the passage that the author has provided evidence that Saturn's rings and moons are recent creations. In addition to this, author has talked in depth about the rings and moons creation. The right answer is option (c).

793. It can be inferred from the 1st and 3rd paragraph that all big things in the solar system have been around since the beginning, therefore the right answer is option (d).

794. The main idea of the passage is to find the best person for a job, thus option (d) is the right answer.

795. 2nd passage, 1-8 lines, it can be referred from the lines that the option (a) is the right answer.

796. 2nd last paragraph, last d-e lines, it can be inferred from the lines that the right answer is option (a).

797. It can be inferred from 2nd and 3rd paragraph, the right answer is option (d).

798. 3rd and 4th paragraph, proves option (d) to be the right answer.

Quantitative Aptitude

CHAPTER

Number System

DIVISIBILITY

1990

1. If n is any positive integer, then $n^3 - n$ is divisible
   (a) Always by 12 (b) Never by 12
   (c) Always by 6 (d) Never by 6

Directions for Questions 2 and 3: Each of the following questions is followed by two statements. MARK,

(a) if the question can be answered with the help of statement I alone,
(b) if the question can be answered with the help of statement II alone,
(c) if both, statement I and statement II are needed to answer the question, and
(d) if the statement cannot be answered even with the help of both the statements.

2. If R is an integer between 1 & 9, P – R = 2370, what is the value of R?
   I. P is divisible by 4.
   II. P is divisible by 9.
3. x, y and z are three positive odd integers, is x + z divisible by 4?
   I. y – x = 2.
   II. z – y = 2.

1991

4. Let k be a positive integer such that k + 4 is divisible by 7. Then the smallest positive integer n, greater than 2, such that k + 2n is divisible by 7 equals
   (a) 9 (b) 7
   (c) 5 (d) 3
5. If x is a positive integer such that 2x + 12 is perfectly divisible by x, then the number of possible values of x is
   (a) 2 (b) 5
   (c) 6 (d) 12
6. A positive integer is said to be a prime number if it is not divisible by any positive integer other than itself and 1. Let p be a prime number greater than 5. Then $(p^2 - 1)$ is
   (a) never divisible by 6
   (b) always divisible by 6, and may or may not be divisible by 12.
   (c) always divisible by 12, and may or may not be divisible by 24.
   (d) always divisible by 24.

1993

7. The number of positive integers not greater than 100, which are not divisible by 2, 3 or 5 is
   (a) 26 (b) 18
   (c) 31 (d) None

1995

8. For the product n(n + 1)(2n + 1), $n \in N$, which one of the following is not necessarily true?
   (a) It is even
   (b) Divisible by 3
   (c) Divisible by the sum of the square of first n natural numbers
   (d) Never divisible by 237

1996

9. If a number 774958A96B is to be divisible by 8 and 9, the respective values of A and B will be
   (a) 7 and 8
   (b) 8 and 0
   (c) 5 and 8
   (d) None of these
10. If n is any odd number greater than 1, then $n(n^2 - 1)$ is
    (a) divisible by 96 always
    (b) divisible by 48 always
    (c) divisible by 24 always
    (d) None of these

1997

11. If m and n are integers divisible by 5, which of the following is not necessarily true?
    (a) m – n is divisible by 5
    (b) $m^2 - n^2$ is divisible by 25
    (c) m + n is divisible by 10
    (d) None of these

Direction for Question 12: The question is followed by two statements. As the answer,

Mark (a) if the question can be answered with the help of one statement alone.

Mark (b) if the question can be answered with the help of any one statement independently.

Mark (c) if the question can be answered with the help of both statements together.

Mark (d) if the question cannot be answered even with the help of both statements together.

12. Is the number completely divisible by 99?

I. The number is divisible by 9 and 11 simultaneously.

II. If the digits of the number are reversed, the number is divisible by 9 and 11.

1998

13. How many five-digit numbers can be formed using the digits 2, 3, 8, 7, 5 exactly once such that the number is divisible by 125?

(a) 0 (b) 1

(c) 4 (d) 3

2000

14. Let N = $55^3 + 17^3 - 72^3$. N is divisible by

(a) both 7 and 13 (b) both 3 and 13

(c) both 17 and 7 (d) both 3 and 17

15. Let D be a recurring decimal of the form D = 0. a_1 a_2 a_1 a_2 a_1 a_2 ..., where digits a_1 and a_2 lie between 0 and 9. Further, at most one of them is zero. Which of the following numbers necessarily produces an integer, when multiplied by D?

(a) 18 (b) 108

(c) 198 (d) 288

16. Let S be the set of integers x such that

I. $100 \le x \le 200$,

II. x is odd and

III. x is divisible by 3 but not by 7.

How many elements does S contain?

(a) 16 (b) 12

(c) 11 (d) 13

2001

17. Let b be a positive integer and a = $b^2 - b$. If $b \ge 4$, then $a^2 - 2a$ is divisible by

(a) 15 (b) 20

(c) 24 (d) All of these

2002

18. $7^{6n} - 6^{6n}$, where n is an integer > 0, is divisible by

(a) 13 (b) 127

(c) 559 (d) All of these

2003(R)

19. Let n (>1) be a composite integer such that $\sqrt{n}$ is not an integer. Consider the following statements:

A : n has a perfect integer-valued divisor which is greater than 1 and less than $\sqrt{n}$.

B : n has a perfect integer-valued divisor which is greater than $\sqrt{n}$ but less than n.

(a) Both A and B are false

(b) A is true but B is false

(c) A is false but B is true

(d) Both A and B are true

20. If a, a + 2 and a + 4 are prime numbers, then the number of possible solutions for a is

(a) one (b) two

(c) three (d) more than three

2003(L)

21. How many even integers n, where $100 \le n \le 200$, are divisible neither by seven nor by nine?

(a) 40 (b) 37

(c) 39 (d) 38

22. The number of positive integers n in the range $12 \le n \le 40$ such that the product (n–1)(n–2)...3.2.1 is not divisible by n is

(a) 5 (b) 7

(c) 13 (d) 14

2005

23. The digits of a three-digit number A are written in the reverse order to form another three-digit number B. If B > A and B – A is perfectly divisible by 7, then which of the following is necessarily true?

(a) 100 < A < 299

(b) 106 < A < 305

(c) 112 < A < 311

(d) 118< A < 317

24. Let S be a set of positive integers such that every element n of S satisfies the conditions

I. $1000 \le n \le 1200$

II. Every digit in n is odd

Then how many elements of S are divisible by 3?

(a) 9 (b) 10

(c) 11 (d) 12

MEMORY BASED QUESTIONS

2009

25. The digits of all the two digit multiples of 8 are reversed. How many of the resulting numbers would be divisible by 4 but not by 8?

(a) 3 (b) 4
(c) 2 (d) 1

2015

26. Which of the following will completely divide $(106^{90} - 49^{90})$?

(a) 589 (b) 186
(c) 124 (d) None of these

2016

27. Find the smallest number which when divided by 3, 5 and 7 leaves remainders 2, 4 and 6 respectively.

(a) 104 (b) 105
(c) 209 (d) None of these

PROPERTY

Direction for Question 1: The question is followed by two statements. As the answer,

Mark (a) if the question can be answered with the help of statement I alone,

Mark (b) if the question can be answered with the help of statement II alone,

Mark (c) if both the statement I and statement II are needed to answer the question, and

Mark (d) if the question cannot be answered even with the help of both the statements.

1991

1. What is the value of prime number x?

I. $x^2 + x$ Is a two digit number greater than 50.

II. x^3 is a three digit number.

2. Three times the first of three consecutive odd integers is 3 more than twice the third. What is the third integer?

(a) 15 (b) 9
(c) 11 (d) 5

3. $2^{73} - 2^{72} - 2^{71}$ is the same as

(a) 2^{69} (b) 2^{70}
(c) 2^{71} (d) 2^{72}

4. The sum of two integers is 10 and the sum of their reciprocals is 5/12. Then the larger of these integers is

(a) 2 (b) 4
(c) 6 (d) 8

5. x, y and z are three positive integers such that $x > y > z$. Which of the following is closest to the product xyz?

(a) $(x - 1)yz$ (b) $x(y - 1)z$
(c) $xy(z - 1)$ (d) $x(y + 1)z$

6. A third standard teacher gave a simple multiplication exercise to the kids. But one kid reversed the digits of both the numbers and carried out the multiplication and found that the product was exactly the same as the one expected by the teacher. Only one of the following pairs of numbers will fit in the description of the exercise. Which one is that?

(a) 14, 22 (b) 13, 62
(c) 19, 33 (d) 42, 28

7. To decide whether a n digits number is divisible by 7, we can define a process by which its magnitude is reduced as follows: ($i_1, i_2, i_3, \ldots$, are the digits of the number, starting from the most significant digit). $i_1 i_2 \ldots i_n \Rightarrow i_1 . 3^{n-1} + 1_2 . 3^{n-2} + \ldots + i_n . 3^0$.

E.g. 259 $\Rightarrow 2.3^2 + 5.3^1 + 9.3^0 = 18 + 15 + 9 = 42$

Ultimately the resulting number will be seven after repeating the above process a certain number of times. After how many such stages, does the number 203 reduce to 7?

(a) 2 (b) 3
(c) 4 (d) 1

8. If 8 + 12 = 2, 7 + 14 = 3, then 10 + 18 = ?

(a) 10 (b) 4
(c) 6 (d) 18

Directions for Questions 9 and 10 : Each of these items has a question followed by two statements. As the answer,

Mark (a) if the question can be answered with the help of statement I alone,

Mark (b) if the question can be answered with the help of statement II, alone,

Mark (c) if both, statement I and statement II are needed to answer the question, and

Mark (d) if the question cannot be answered even with the help of both the statements.

1993

9. What are the values of 3 integers a, b and c?

I. ab = 8

II. bc = 9

10. What are the ages of the three brothers?

I. The product of their ages is 21.

II. The sum of their ages is not divisible by 3.

11. Suppose one wishes to find distinct positive integers x, y such that $\frac{x+y}{xy}$ is also a positive integer. Identify the correct alternative.
(a) This is never possible.
(b) This is possible and the pair (x, y) satisfying the stated condition is unique.
(c) This is possible and there exist more than one but a finite number of ways of choosing the pair (x, y).
(d) This is possible and the pair (x, y) can be chosen in infinite ways.

12. Given odd positive integers x, y and z, which of the following is not necessarily true?
(a) $x^2 y^2 z^2$ is odd
(b) $3(x^2 + y^3)z^2$ is even.
(c) $5x + y + z^4$ is odd
(d) $z^2 (x^4 + y^4)/2$ is even

13. Let x < 0.50, 0 < y < 1, z > 1. Given a set of numbers, the middle number, when they are arranged in ascending order, is called the median. So the median of the numbers x, y and z would be
(a) less than one
(b) between 0 and 1
(c) greater than 1
(d) cannot say

14. Let x < 0, 0 < y < 1, z > 1. Which of the following may be false?
(a) $(x^2 - z^2)$ has to be positive.
(b) yz can be less than one.
(c) xy can never be zero.
(d) $(y^2 - z^2)$ is always negative.

15. A young girl counted in the following way on the fingers of her left hand. She started calling the thumb 1, the index finger 2, middle finger 3, ring finger 4, little finger 5, then reversed direction, calling the ring finger 6, middle finger 7, index finger 8, thumb 9, then back to the index finger for 10, middle finger for 11, and so on. She counted up to 1994. She ended on her
(a) thumb (b) index finger
(c) middle finger (d) ring finger

16. Let x, y and z be distinct positive integers satisfying x < y < z and x + y + z = k. What is the smallest value of k that does not determine x, y, z uniquely?
(a) 9 (b) 6
(c) 7 (d) 8

1995

17. 72 hens cost Rs.__ 96.7__. Then what does each hen cost, where two digits in place of '__' are not visible or are written in illegible hand?
(a) Rs.3.23 (b) Rs.5.11
(c) Rs.5.51 (d) Rs.7.22

18. The value of $\frac{55^3 + 45^3}{55^2 - 55 \times 45 + 45^2}$ is
(a) 100 (b) 105
(c) 125 (d) 75

19. Three consecutive positive even numbers are such that thrice the first number exceeds double the third by 2, then the third number is
(a) 10 (b) 14
(c) 16 (d) 12

Directions for Questions 20 and 21: Each of these questions is followed by two statements, I and II. Mark the answer as:
(a) if the question can be answered with the help of statement I alone.
(b) if the question can be answered with the help of statement II alone.
(c) if both statement I and statement II are needed to answer the question.
(d) if the question cannot be answered even with the help of both the statements.

20. If x, y and z are real numbers, is z – x even or odd?
I. xyz is odd.
II. xy + yz + zx is even.

21. Is x + y – z + t even?
I. x + y + t is even.
II. t and z are odd.

DirectionS for Questions 22 and 23: Each of these questions is followed by two statements, I and II. Mark the answer as:
(a) if the question cannot be answered even with the help of both the statements taken together.
(b) if the question can be answered by any one of the two statements.
(c) if each statement alone is sufficient to answer the question, but not the other one (e.g. statement I alone is required to answer the question, but not statement II and vice versa).
(d) if both statements I and II together are needed to answer the question.

1995

22. If a, b and c are integers, is
$(a - b + c) > (a + b - c)$?
I. b is negative.
II. c is positive.

23. How old is Sachin in 1997?
I. Sachin is 11 years younger than Anil whose age will be a prime number in 1998.
II. Anil's age was a prime number in 1996.

1997

24. If n is an integer, how many values of n will give an integral value of $\frac{(16n^2 + 7n + 6)}{n}$?
(a) 2 (b) 3
(c) 4 (d) None of these

25. P and Q are two positive integers such that PQ = 64. Which of the following cannot be the value of P + Q?
(a) 20 (b) 65
(c) 16 (d) 35

26. Which of the following is true?
(a) $7^{3^2} = (7^3)^2$ (b) $7^{3^2} > (7^3)^2$
(c) $7^{3^2} < (7^3)^2$ (d) None of these

27. P, Q and R are three consecutive odd numbers in ascending order. If the value of three times P is 3 less than two times R, find the value of R.
(a) 5 (b) 7
(c) 9 (d) 11

Direction for Question 28: The question is followed by two statements. As the answer,
Mark (a) if the question can be answered with the help of one statement alone.
Mark (b) if the question can be answered with the help of any one statement independently.
Mark (c) if the question can be answered with the help of both statements together.
Mark (d) if the question cannot be answered even with the help of both statements together.

28. What is the value of $a^3 + b^3$?
I. $a^2 + b^2 = 22$ II. ab = 3

1998

29. n^3 is odd. Which of the following statement(s) is(are) true?
I. n is odd. II. n^2 is odd.
III. n^2 is even.
(a) I only (b) II only
(c) I and II (d) I and III

30. $(BE)^2$ = MPB, where B, E, M and P are distinct integers. Then M =
(a) 2 (b) 3
(c) 9 (d) None of these

31. Five-digit numbers are formed using only 0, 1, 2, 3, 4 exactly once. What is the difference between the maximum and minimum number that can be formed?
(a) 19800 (b) 41976
(c) 32976 (d) None of these

32. I started climbing up the hill at 6 a.m. and reached the top of the temple at 6 p.m. Next day I started coming down at 6 a.m. and reached the foothill at 6 p.m. I walked on the same road. The road is so short that only one person can walk on it. Although I varied my pace on my way, I never stopped on my way. Then which of the following must be true?
(a) My average speed downhill was greater than that of uphill
(b) At noon, I was at the same spot on both the days.
(c) There must be a point where I reached at the same time on both the days.
(d) There cannot be a spot where I reached at the same time on both the days.

Direction for Question 33: The question is followed by two statements. As the answer,
Mark (a) if the question can be answered with the help of any one statement alone but not by the other statement.
Mark (b) if the question can be answered with the help of either of the statements taken individually.
Mark (c) if the question can be answered with the help of both statements together.
Mark (d) if the question cannot be answered even with the help of both statements together.

33. Is n odd?
I. n is divisible by 3, 5, 7 and 9.
II. $0 < n < 400$

1999

34. Let a, b, c be distinct digits. Consider a two-digit number 'ab' and a three-digit number 'ccb', both defined under the usual decimal number system, if $(ab)^2 = ccb > 300$, then the value of b is
(a) 1 (b) 0
(c) 5 (d) 6

35. If $n = 1 + x$ where x is the product of four consecutive positive integers, then which of the following is/are true?

A. n is odd

B. n is prime

C. n is a perfect square

(a) A and C only

(b) A and B only

(c) A only

(d) None of these

36. If $n^2 = 12345678987654321$, what is n?

(a) 12344321 (b) 1235789

(c) 111111111 (d) 11111111

2000

37. Let x, y and z be distinct integers, that are odd and positive. Which one of the following statements cannot be true?

(a) xyz^2 is odd

(b) $(x - y)^2 z$ is even

(c) $(x + y - z)^2 (x + y)$ is even

(d) $(x - y)(y + z)(x + y - z)$ is odd

38. Let S be the set of prime numbers greater than or equal to 2 and less than 100. Multiply all elements of S. With how many consecutive zeros will the product end?

(a) 1 (b) 4

(c) 5 (d) 10

39. Convert the number 1982 from base 10 to base 12. The result is

(a) 1182 (b) 1912

(c) 1192 (d) 1292

2001

40. Let x, y and z be distinct integers. x and y are odd and positive, and z is even and positive. Which one of the following statements cannot be true?

(a) $y(x - z)^2$ is even

(b) $y^2(x - z)$ is odd

(c) $y(x - z)$ is odd

(d) $z(x - y)^2$ is even

41. In a number system, the product of 44 and 11 is 3414. The number 3111 of this system, when converted to the decimal number system, becomes

(a) 406 (b) 1086

(c) 213 (d) 691

Directions for Questions 42 and 43: Each question is followed by two statements, I and II.

Mark

(a) if the question can be answered by one of the statements alone and not by the other.

(b) if the question can be answered by using either statement alone.

(c) if the question can be answered by using both the statements together, but cannot be answered by using either statement alone.

(d) if the question cannot be answered even by using both statements together.

42. What are the values of m and n?

I. n is an even integer, m is an odd integer, and m is greater than n.

II. Product of m and n is 30.

43. What is the value of X?

I. X and Y are unequal even integers, less than 10, and $\frac{X}{Y}$ is an odd integer.

II. X and Y are even integers, each less than 10, and product of X and Y is 12.

2003(R)

44. Let x and y be positive integers such that x is prime and y is composite. Then,

(a) $y - x$ cannot be an even integer

(b) xy cannot be an even integer

(c) $\frac{(x+y)}{x}$ cannot be an even integer

(d) None of these

2005

45. For a positive integer n, let p_n denote the product of the digits of n and s_n denote the sum of the digits of n. The number of integers between 10 and 1000 for which $p_n + s_n = n$ is

(a) 81 (b) 16

(c) 18 (d) 9

2007

46. Consider four-digit numbers for which the first two digits are equal and the last two digits are also equal. How many such numbers are perfect squares?

(a) 3 (b) 2

(c) 4 (d) 0

(e) 1

MEMORY BASED QUESTIONS

2009

47. $N = 4^7 \times 5^9 + 2^4 \times 7 + 3 \times 5^3 + 2^6 \times 5^8$

How many distinct digits are there in the number N?

(a) 8 (b) 7
(c) 5 (d) 6

48. $a^6 + b^6$ is a prime number. If a and b are distinct integers, then what is their sum?

(a) 0 (b) 2
(c) 1 (d) Data Inconsistent

49. If $a = \frac{\sqrt{8}-\sqrt{7}}{\sqrt{8}+\sqrt{7}}$ and $b = \frac{\sqrt{8}+\sqrt{7}}{\sqrt{8}-\sqrt{7}}$, then what is the value of $\frac{\frac{1}{a}+\frac{1}{b}}{1+\frac{1}{ab}}$?

(a) 15 (b) 113
(c) 23 (d) None of these

50. If $x = \sqrt{15} - \sqrt{11}$, $y = \sqrt{27} - \sqrt{23}$, $z = 2\left(\sqrt{6} - \sqrt{5}\right)$, then which of the following is correct?

(a) $x > y > z$
(b) $x < y < z$
(c) $x < z < y$
(d) $x > z > y$

2010

51. A 3-digit natural number 'abc', where a, b and c are distinct digits, when increased by 33.33% becomes 'cab'. When 'cab' is increased by 33.33% it becomes 'bca'. How many such numbers are there?

(a) 0 (b) 1
(c) 2 (d) 5

52. If a and b are real numbers such that $a^{a^b} = b$ and $a \neq b$, then what is the value of $a^b - b$?

(a) –1 (b) 0
(c) 1 (d) 2

53. $M = \sqrt{3-\sqrt{5}+\sqrt{9-4\sqrt{5}}}$ and $N = \sqrt{\sqrt{7}-1-\sqrt{11-4\sqrt{7}}}$. What is the value of $\frac{M-N}{M+N}$?

(a) 0 (b) 1
(c) –1 (d) None of these

54. N is a five-digit perfect square whose unit digit is same as the tens digit. How many such N are there?

(a) 31 (b) 30
(c) 33 (d) 32

2011

55. Which of the following number(s) is/are not prime?

(i) $2^{5001} + 1$
(ii) $2^{5002} + 1$
(iii) $2^{5003} + 1$

(a) (i) and (ii) (b) (i) and (iii)
(c) (ii) and (iii) (d) (i), (ii) and (iii)

56. How many positive integer pairs (x, y) satisfy $\sqrt{x} + \sqrt{y} = \sqrt{2003}$?

(a) 0 (b) 1
(c) 2 (d) 3

57. The sum of thirty-two consecutive natural numbers is a perfect square. What is the least possible sum of the smallest and the largest of the thirty-two numbers?

(a) 81 (b) 36
(c) 49 (d) 64

2012

58. The number 44 is written as a product of 5 distinct integers. If 'n' is the sum of these five integers then what is the sum of all the possible values of n?

(a) 11 (b) 23
(c) 26 (d) 32

2013

59. Arrange the numbers $2^{\frac{7}{6}}, 3^{\frac{3}{4}}$ and $5^{\frac{2}{3}}$ in ascending order.

(a) $2^{\frac{7}{6}} > 3^{\frac{3}{4}} > 5^{\frac{2}{3}}$ (b) $3^{\frac{3}{4}} > 2^{\frac{7}{6}} > 5^{\frac{2}{3}}$
(c) $5^{\frac{2}{3}} > 3^{\frac{3}{4}} > 2^{\frac{7}{6}}$ (d) None of these

2014

60. If $7^a = 26$ and $343^b = 676$ then what is the relation between a and b?

(a) a = b
(b) a = 2b
(c) 2a = 3b
(d) 3a = 2b

2015

61. A four-digit number is divisible by the sum of its digits. Also, the sum of these four digits equals the product of the digits. What could be the product of the digits of such a number?

(a) 6 (b) 8
(c) 10 (d) 12

62. Let P be the set of all odd positive integers such that every element in P satisfies the following conditions.

I. $100 \le n < 1000$

II. The digit at the hundred's place is never greater than the digit at tens place and also never less than the digit at units place.

How many elements are there in P?

(a) 93 (b) 94
(c) 95 (d) 96

63. If $3x + y + 4 = 2xy$, where x and y are natural numbers, then find the ratio of the sum of all possible values of x to the sum of all possible values of y.

(a) $\frac{2}{3}$ (b) $\frac{15}{19}$
(c) $\frac{17}{21}$ (d) $\frac{7}{9}$

2016

64. How many natural numbers less than or equal to 15 have 4 factors each?

2017

65. Let a_1, a_2, a_3, a_4, a_5 be a sequence of five consecutive odd numbers. Consider a new sequence of five consecutive even numbers ending with $2a_3$.

If the sum of the numbers in the new sequence is 450, then a_5 is

2018 Slot 1

66. While multiplying three real numbers, Ashok took one of the numbers as 73 instead of 37. As a result, the product went up by 720. Then the minimum possible value of the sum of squares of the other two numbers is

2018 Slot 2

67. If the sum of squares of two numbers is 97, then which one of the following cannot be their product?

(1) 48 (2) –32
(3) 16 (4) 64

68. The smallest integer n for which $4^n > 17^{19}$ holds, is closest to

(1) 35 (2) 37
(3) 33 (4) 39

FACTORIAL AND ITS APPLICATION

1991

1. What is the greatest power of 5 which can divide 80! exactly?

(a) 16 (b) 20
(c) 19 (d) None of these

1993

2. The product of all integers from 1 to 100 will have the following numbers of zeros at the end.

(a) 20 (b) 24
(c) 19 (d) 22

1997

3. ABC is a three-digit number in which A > 0. The value of ABC is equal to the sum of the factorials of its three digits. What is the value of B?

(a) 9 (b) 7
(c) 4 (d) 2

2005

4. Let $n! = 1 \times 2 \times 3 \times \ldots \times n$ for integer $n \ge 1$.

If $p = 1! + (2 \times 2!) + (3 \times 3!) + \ldots + (10 \times 10!)$, then $p + 2$ when divided by 11! leaves a remainder of

(a) 10 (b) 0
(c) 7 (d) 1

MEMORY BASED QUESTIONS

2009

5. N is a natural number which has 4 factors. If $10 \le N \le 70$, then how many values are possible for N?

(a) 19 (b) 20
(c) 21 (d) 22

2010

6. $N = 70! \times 69! \times 68! \times \ldots\ldots 3! \times 2! \times 1!$

Which of the following represents the 147th digit from the right end of N?

(a) 2 (b) 0
(c) 5 (d) 7

2012

7. 500! + 505! + 510! + 515! is completely divisible by 5^n, where n is a natural number. How many distinct values of n are possible?

(a) 120
(b) 121
(c) 124
(d) 125

2013

8. 'ab' is a two-digit prime number such that one of its digits is 3. If the absolute difference between the digits of the number is not a factor of 2, then how many values can 'ab' assume?

(a) 5 (b) 3
(c) 6 (d) 8

9. The number of factors of the square of a natural number is 105. The number of factors of the cube of the same number is 'F'. Find the maximum possible value of 'F'.

(a) 208 (b) 217
(c) 157 (d) 280

10. Let $R(x) = mx^3 - 100x^2 + 3n$, where m and n are positive integers. For how many ordered pairs (m, n) will $(x - 2)$ be a factor of $R(x)$?

(a) 16 (b) 17
(c) 18 (d) 15

11. How many natural numbers divide exactly one out of 1080 and1800, but not both?

(a) 20 (b) 42
(c) 24 (d) 36

2014

12. 'P' is the product of ten consecutive two-digit natural numbers. If 2^a is one of the factors of P, then the maximum value that 'a' can assume is

(a) 11 (b) 12
(c) 13 (d) 14

2015

13. P is the product of the first 100 multiples of 15 and Q is the product of the first 50 multiples of 25^{20}. Find the number of consecutive zeroes at the end of $\frac{P^2}{Q} \times 10^{1767}$.

(a) 1968 (b) 1914
(c) 3 (d) 2024

2016

14. $N = 5^{1!+2!+3!+4!}$

The digits of the number N are added to get another number. Then the digits of the number obtained are added to get yet another number. The process is repeated till a single digit number is obtained. What is that single digit number?

HCF AND LCM

1993

1. The smallest number which when divided by 4, 6 or 7 leaves a remainder of 2, is

(a) 44 (b) 62
(c) 80 (d) 86

1994

2. What is the smallest number which when increased by 5 is completely divisible by 8, 11 and 24?

(a) 264 (b) 259
(c) 269 (d) None of these

3. Which is the least number that must be subtracted from 1856, so that the remainder when divided by 7, 12 and 16 is 4.

(a) 137 (b) 1361
(c) 140 (d) 172

1995

4. Three bells chime at an interval of 18 min, 24 min and 32 min. At a certain time they begin to chime together. What length of time will elapse before they chime together again?

(a) 2 hr and 24 min (b) 4 hr and 48 min
(c) 1 hr and 36 min (d) 5 hr

Direction for Question 5: The question is followed by two statements, I and II. Mark the answer as:

(a) if the question can be answered with the help of statement I alone.

(b) if the question can be answered with the help of statement II alone.

(c) if both statement I and statement II are needed to answer the question.

(d) if the question cannot be answered even with the help of both the statements.

5. What is the number x?

I. The LCM of x and 18 is 36.

II. The HCF of x and 18 is 2.

1998

6. Three wheels can complete 60, 36 and 24 revolutions per minute. There is a red spot on each wheel that touches the ground at time zero. After how much time, all these spots will simultaneously touch the ground again?

(a) $\frac{5}{2}$ s (b) $\frac{5}{3}$ s
(c) 6 s (d) 7.5 s

7. A is the set of positive integers such that when divided by 2, 3, 4, 5, 6 leaves the remainders 1, 2, 3, 4, 5 respectively. How many integers between 0 and 100 belong to set A?
(a) 0 (b) 1
(c) 2 (d) None of these

8. Number of students who have opted for subjects A, B and C are 60, 84 and 108 respectively. The examination is to be conducted for these students such that only the students of the same subject are allowed in one room. Also the number of students in each room must be same. What is the minimum number of rooms that should be arranged to meet all these conditions?
(a) 28 (b) 60
(c) 12 (d) 21

1999

9. For two positive integers a and b define the function **h**(a, b) as the greatest common factor (G.C.F) of a, b. Let A be a set of n positive integers. G(A), the G.C.F of the elements of set A is computed by repeatedly using the function **h**. The minimum number of times **h** is required to be used to compute G is
(a) $\frac{1}{2}n$ (b) $(n-1)$
(c) n (d) None of these

2001

10. A red light flashes three times per minute and a green light flashes five times in 2 min at regular intervals. If both lights start flashing at the same time, how many times do they flash together in each hour?
(a) 30 (b) 24
(c) 20 (d) 60

11. Of 128 boxes of oranges, each box contains at least 120 and at most 144 oranges. The number of boxes containing the same number of oranges is at least
(a) 5 (b) 103
(c) 6 (d) Cannot be determined

2002

12. At a bookstore, 'MODERN BOOK STORE' is flashed using neon lights. The words are individually flashed at the intervals of $2\frac{1}{2}$ s, $4\frac{1}{4}$ s and $5\frac{1}{8}$ s respectively, and each word is put off after a second. The least time after which the full name of the bookstore can be read again is
(a) 49.5 s (b) 73.5 s
(c) 1744.5 s (d) 855 s

13. Three pieces of cakes of weights $4\frac{1}{2}$ lb, $6\frac{3}{4}$ lb and $7\frac{1}{5}$ lb respectively are to be divided into parts of equal weight. Further, each part must be as heavy as possible. If one such part is served to each guest, then what is the maximum number of guests that could be entertained?
(a) 54 (b) 72
(c) 20 (d) None of these

2006

14. Which among $2^{\frac{1}{2}}$, $3^{\frac{1}{3}}$, $4^{\frac{1}{4}}$, $6^{\frac{1}{6}}$ and $12^{\frac{1}{12}}$ is the largest?
(a) $2^{1/2}$ (b) $3^{1/3}$
(c) $4^{1/4}$ (d) $6^{1/6}$
(e) $12^{1/12}$

MEMORY BASED QUESTIONS

2014

15. The ratio of two numbers whose is 600 is 7 : 8. What is the LCM of the given two numbers?
(a) 1120 (b) 560
(c) 2240 (d) 1152

2015

16. Out of 4 numbers a, b, c, and d, each pair of numbers has the same highest common factor. Find the highest common factor of all the four numbers if the least common multiple of a and b is 310 and that of c and d is 651.

17. How many ordered triplets (a, b, c) exist such that LCM (a, b) = 1000, LCM(b, c) = 2000, LCM (c, a) = 2000 and HCF (a, b) = k × 125?
(a) 32 (b) 28
(c) 24 (d) 20

REMAINDER

1990

1. The remainder when 2^{60} is divided by 5 equals
(a) 0 (b) 1
(c) 2 (d) None of these

1991

2. Find the minimum integral value of n such that the division 55n/124 leaves no remainder.
(a) 124 (b) 123
(c) 31 (d) 62

1995

3. $5^6 - 1$ is divisible by

(a) 13 (b) 31

(c) 5 (d) None of these

4. The remainder obtained when a prime number greater than 6 is divided by 6 is

(a) 1 or 3 (b) 1 or 5

(c) 3 or 5 (d) 4 or 5

1998

5. A certain number, when divided by 899, leaves a remainder 63. Find the remainder when the same number is divided by 29.

(a) 5

(b) 4

(c) 1

(d) Cannot be determined

6. What is the digit in the unit's place of 2^{51}?

(a) 2 (b) 8

(c) 1 (d) 4

7. A number is formed by writing first 54 natural numbers in front of each other as 12345678910111213 ... Find the remainder when this number is divided by 8.

(a) 1 (b) 7

(c) 2 (d) 0

1999

8. The remainder when 7^{84} is divided by 342 is

(a) 0 (b) 1

(c) 49 (d) 341

2000

9. Let N = 1421 × 1423 × 1425. What is the remainder when N is divided by 12?

(a) 0 (b) 9

(c) 3 (d) 6

10. The integers 34041 and 32506, when divided by a three-digit integer n, leave the same remainder. What is the value of n?

(a) 289 (b) 367

(c) 453 (d) 307

11. When 2^{256} is divided by 17, the remainder would be

(a) 1 (b) 16

(c) 14 (d) None of these

2002

12. After the division of a number successively by 3, 4 and 7, the remainders obtained are 2, 1 and 4 respectively. What will be the remainder if 84 divides the same number?

(a) 80 (b) 75

(c) 41 (d) 53

Directions for Question 13: The question is followed by two statements, A and B. Answer the question using the following instructions.

Choose 1 if the question can be answered by one of the statements alone but not by the other.

Choose 2 if the question can be answered by using either statement alone.

Choose 3 if the question can be answered by using both the statements together, but cannot be answered by using either statement alone.

Choose 4 if the question cannot be answered even by using both statements together.

13. Four students were added to a dance class. Would the teacher be able to divide her students evenly into a dance team (or teams) of 8?

A. If 12 students were added, the teacher could put everyone in teams of 8 without any leftovers.

B. The number of students in the class is currently not divisible by 8.

(a) 1 (b) 2

(c) 3 (d) 4

2003(R)

14. What is the sum of all two-digit numbers that give a remainder of 3 when they are divided by 7?

(a) 666 (b) 676

(c) 683 (d) 777

15. What is the remainder when 4^{96} is divided by 6?

(a) 0 (b) 2

(c) 3 (d) 4

Directions for Question 16: The question is followed by two statements, A and B. Answer each question using the following instructions.

Choose (a) if the question can be answered by one of the statements alone but not by the other.

Choose (b) if the question can be answered by using either statement alone.

Choose (c) if the question can be answered by using both the statements together, but cannot be answered by using either statement alone.

Choose (d) if the question cannot be answered even by using both the statements together.

2003(L)

16. Is $a^{44} < b^{11}$, given that a = 2 and b is an integer?

A. b is even

B. b is greater than 16

2004

17. The remainder, when $(15^{23} + 23^{23})$ is divided by 19, is

(a) 4 (b) 15
(c) 0 (d) 18

2005

18. If $x = (16^3 + 17^3 + 18^3 + 19^3)$, then x divided by 70 leaves a remainder of

(a) 0 (b) 1
(c) 69 (d) 35

19. The rightmost non-zero digit of the number 30^{2720} is

(a) 1 (b) 3
(c) 7 (d) 9

2008

20. What are the last two digits of 7^{2008}?

(a) 21 (b) 61
(c) 01 (d) 41
(e) 81

MEMORY BASED QUESTIONS

2015

21. There are 40 students in a class. A student is allowed to shake hand only once with a student who is taller than him or equal in height to him. He can't shake hand with anyone who is shorter than him. Average height of the class is 5 feet. What is the difference between the maximum and minimum number of handshakes that can take place in the class?

(a) $\left(\frac{^{40}C_2}{2} - 20\right)$ (b) 361

(c) $^{40}C_2 - 40$ (d) $^{40}C_2$

MISCELLANEOUS

2000

Direction for Question 1: The question is followed by two statements, I and II. Answer the question using the following instructions.

Mark the answer as:

(a) if the question can be answered by one of the statements alone, but cannot be answered by using the other statement alone.

(b) if the question can be answered by using either statement alone.

(c) if the question can be answered by using both the statements together, but cannot be answered by using either statement alone.

(d) if the question cannot be answered even by using both statements together.

1. What are the ages of two individuals, X and Y?

I. The age difference between them is 6 years.

II. The product of their ages is divisible by 6.

2002

2. Number S is obtained by squaring the sum of digits of a two-digit number D. If difference between S and D is 27, then the two-digit number D is

(a) 24 (b) 54
(c) 34 (d) 45

3. If u, v, w and m are natural numbers such that $u^m + v^m = w^m$, then which one of the following is true?

(a) $m \geq \min(u, v, w)$ (b) $m \geq \max(u, v, w)$
(c) $m < \min(u, v, w)$ (d) None of these

Directions for Questions 4 to 6: Answer the questions on the basis of the information given below.

The seven basic symbols in a certain numeral system and their respective values are as follows:

I = 1, V = 5, X = 10, L = 50, C = 100, D = 500 and M = 1000

In general, the symbols in the numeral system are read from left to right, starting with the symbol representing the largest value; the same symbol cannot occur continuously more than three times; the value of the numeral is the sum of the values of the symbols. For example, XXVII = 10 + 10 + 5 + 1 + 1 = 27. An exception to the left-to-right reading occurs when a symbol is followed immediately by a symbol of greater value; then the smaller value is subtracted from the larger.

For example, XLVI = (50 – 10) + 5 + 1 = 46.

2003(R)

4. The value of the numeral MDCCLXXXVII is

(a) 1687 (b) 1787
(c) 1887 (d) 1987

5. The value of the numeral MCMXCIX is

(a) 1999 (b) 1899
(c) 1989 (d) 1889

6. Which of the following represent the numeral for 1995?

I. MCMLXXV II. MCMXCV
III. MVD IV. MVM

(a) Only I and II (b) Only III and IV
(c) Only II and IV (d) Only IV

2003(L)

7. A positive whole number M less than 100 is represented in base 2 notation, base 3 notation, and base 5 notation. It is found that in all three cases the last digit is 1, while in exactly two out of the three cases the leading digit is 1. Then M equals

(a) 31 (b) 63
(c) 75 (d) 91

2004

8. Suppose n is an integer such that the sum of digits of n is 2, and $10^{10} < n < 10^{11}$. The number of different values of n is

(a) 11 (b) 10
(c) 9 (d) 8

2006

9. The sum of four consecutive two-digit odd numbers, when divided by 10, becomes a perfect square.

Which of the following can possibly be one of these four numbers?

(a) 21 (b) 25
(c) 41 (d) 67
(e) 73

2008

10. Suppose, the seed of any positive integer n is defined as follows:

seed(n) = n, if n < 10
= seed(s(n)), otherwise,

where s(n) indicates the sum of digits of n. For example, seed(7) = 7, seed(248) = seed(2 + 4 + 8) = seed(14) = seed(1 + 4) = seed(5) = 5 etc. How many positive integers n, such that n < 500, will have seed (n) = 9?

(a) 39 (b) 72
(c) 81 (d) 108
(e) 55

MEMORY BASED QUESTIONS

2011

11. In a three-digit number, the unit digit is twice the tens digit and the tens digit is twice the hundreds digit. The same number is written as 1XY and 1YX in base 8 and base 9 respectively. Find the sum of X and Y in the decimal system.

(a) 15
(b) 7
(c) 11
(d) Cannot be determined

2015

12. If $x^2 + (x + 1)(x + 2)(x + 3)(x + 6) = 0$, where x is a real number, then one value of x that satisfies this equation is

(a) $3-\sqrt{3}$
(b) $3+\sqrt{3}$
(c) $(-3+\sqrt{3})$
(d) 0

13. If $x^4 - y^4 = 15$, where x and y are natural numbers, then find the value of the expression $x^4 + y^4$.

2016

14. The absolute difference between the average of first N1 natural numbers and that of the first N2 natural numbers is 10. What is the absolute difference between N1 and N2?

15. A rational number $\frac{A}{B}$, where A and B are co-prime, is converted into a decimal number. If both A and B are less than 100, then for how many values of B will $\frac{A}{B}$ always be a terminating decimal?

(a) 40 (b) 60
(c) 14 (d) 15

16. How many terms of the sequence given below are integers?

$$21, 7, \frac{21}{5}, \ldots, \frac{21}{2n-1}, n \in N$$

(a) 2
(b) 3
(c) 4
(d) 5

17. A florist sells only two kinds of flowers – Rose and Tulip. On a particular day, he sold 70 Roses and 90 Tulips. If none of his customers bought more than one flower of each type, what is the minimum number of customers that must have visited his shop on that day?

2017

18. The numbers 1, 2, ... 9 are arranged in a 3 × 3 square grid in such a way that each number occurs once and the entries along each column, each row, and each of the two diagonals add up to the same value.

If the top left and the top right entries of the grid are 6 and 2, respectively, then the bottom middle entry is

19. If the product of three consecutive positive integers is 15600 then the sum of the squares of these integers is

(a) 1777 (b) 1785

(c) 1875 (d) 1877

20. How many different pairs (a, b) of positive integers are there such that a ≤ b and $\frac{1}{a}+\frac{1}{b}=\frac{1}{9}$?

2018 Slot 2

21. The value of the sum 7 x 11 + 11 x 15 + 15 x 19 + ...+ 95 x 99 is

(a) 80730 (b) 80773

(c) 80707 (d) 80751

ANSWERS

Divisibility

1. (c)	2. (b)	3. (c)	4. (a)	5. (c)	6. (d)	7. (a)	8. (d)	9. (b)	10. (c)
11. (c)	12. (b)	13. (c)	14. (d)	15. (c)	16. (d)	17. (d)	18. (d)	19. (d)	20. (a)
21. (c)	22. (b)	23. (b)	24. (a)	25. (c)	26. (a)	27. (a)			

Property

1. (a)	2. (a)	3. (c)	4. (c)	5. (a)	6. (b)	7. (a)	8. (a)	9. (c)	10. (d)
11. (a)	12. (d)	13. (b)	14. (a)	15. (b)	16. (d)	17. (c)	18. (a)	19. (b)	20. (a)
21. (c)	22. (d)	23. (a)	24. (d)	25. (d)	26. (b)	27. (c)	28. (d)	29. (c)	30. (b)
31. (c)	32. (c)	33. (c)	34. (a)	35. (a)	36. (c)	37. (d)	38. (a)	39. (c)	40. (a)
41. (a)	42. (c)	43. (a)	44. (d)	45. (d)	46. (e)	47. (b)	48. (a)	49. (a)	50. (d)
51. (c)	52. (b)	53. (a)	54. (a)	55. (d)	56. (a)	57. (c)	58. (a)	59. (c)	60. (c)
61. (b)	62. (c)	63. (d)	64. (e)	65. (51)	66. (40)	67. (d)	68. (d)		

Factorial and its Application

1. (c)	2. (b)	3. (*)	4. (d)	5. (b)	6. (b)	7. (c)	8. (b)	9. (d)	10. (a)
11. (a)	12. (c)	13. (b)	14. (8)						

HCF and LCM

1. (d)	2. (b)	3. (d)	4. (b)	5. (c)	6. (*)	7. (b)	8. (d)	9. (b)	10. (a)
11. (c)	12. (b)	13. (d)	14. (b)	15. (c)	16. 31	17. (b)			

Remainder

1. (b)	2. (a)	3. (b)	4. (b)	5. (a)	6. (b)	7. (c)	8. (b)	9. (c)	10. (d)
11. (a)	12. (d)	13. (a)	14. (b)	15. (d)	16. (a)	17. (c)	18. (a)	19. (a)	20. (c)
21. (d)									

Miscellaneous

1. (d)	2. (b)	3. (d)	4. (b)	5. (a)	6. (c)	7. (d)	8. (a)	9. (c)	10. (e)
11. (c)	12. (c)	13. 17	14. (20)	15. (c)	16. (c)	17. (90)	18. (c)	19. (d)	20. (c)
21. (c)									

EXPLANATIONS

Divisibility

1. c $n^3 - n = n(n^2 - 1) = (n - 1)n(n + 1)$

Above expression is the product of three consecutive numbers. So at least one number is even and one number is a multiple of 3. So the product is always divisible by 6.

2. b From the question we can figure out that P lies between 2371 and 2379.

Using statement I: P = 2372 or 2376

Using statement II: P = 2376

Hence, statement II alone is sufficient to get a unique value of R.

3. c As none of the statement gives information about all three – x, y and z, they alone are not sufficient to answer the question.

Using both statements together: x, y and z are three consecutive odd integers.

Therefore, x + z is not divisible by 4.

4. a a = k + 4 is divisible by 7

b = k + 2n is divisible by 7

$\Rightarrow$ b – a = 2n – 4 is divisible by 7

$\Rightarrow$ 2n – 4 = 0 or 7 or 14 ...

For minimum integral value of n,

2n – 4 = 14

$\Rightarrow$ n = 9.

5. c If (2x + 12) is perfectly divisible by x, then (2x + 12)/x has to be an integer as x is an integer. Now if we divide, the expression simplifies to (2 + 12/x). The only way in which this expression would be an integer is when 12/x is an integer or if 12 is perfectly divisible by x. This is possible if x takes either of these values : 1, 2, 3, 4, 6, 12. Hence, the answer is 6 values.

6. d As each prime number greater than or equal to 3 is of the form $6k \pm 1$, where k is a natural number,

$p = 6k \pm 1$.

$p^2 - 1 = (6k \pm 1)^2 - 1 = 12k(3k \pm 1)$

Above number is always divisible by 24 irrespective of value of k.

7. a The following Venn diagram shows the distribution of numbers between 1 and 100 that are divisible by 2, 3, 5 or a combination of two or more of them.

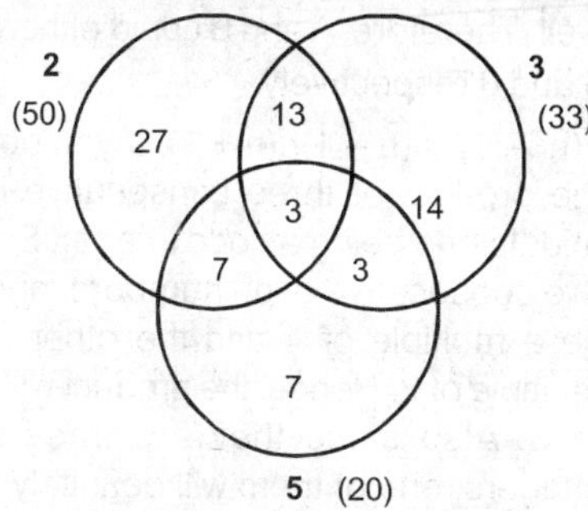

50 numbers are divisible by 2, 33 numbers are divisible by 3 and 20 numbers are divisible by 5.

3 numbers are divisible by all 2, 3 and 5.

16 numbers are divisible by both 2 and 3, therefore 13 numbers are divisible by 2 and 3 but not by 5.

10 numbers are divisible by both 2 and 5, therefore 7 numbers are divisible by 2 and 5 but not by 3.

6 numbers are divisible by both 3 and 5, therefore 3 numbers are divisible by 3 and 5 but not by 2.

Total number of numbers that are divisible by one or more among 2, 3 and 5 = 27 + 14 + 7 + 13 + 3 + 7 + 3 = 74

Hence, the required number = 100 – 74 = 26.

8. d Since n(n + 1) are two consecutive integers, one of them will be even and thus their product will always be even.

Also, sum of the squares of first 'n' natural numbers is given by $\frac{n(n+1)(2n+1)}{6}$.

Hence, our product will always be divisible by this. Also you will find that the product is always divisible by 3 (you can use any value of n to verify this).

However, we can find that option (d) is not necessarily true. **E.g.** If n = 118, (2n + 1) = 237 or if n = 236, then (n + 1) = 237 or if n itself is 237, etc.

9. b For the number to be divisible by 9, the sum of the digits should be a multiple of 9.

We find that the sum of all the digits (excluding A and B) = (7 + 7 + 4 + 9 + 5 + 8 + 9 + 6) = 55. The next higher multiple of 9 is 63 or 72.

Hence, the sum of A and B should either be 8 or 17. We find that (a) and (c) cannot be the answer.

For a number to be divisible by 8, the number formed by its last three digits should be divisible by 8. The last three digits are 96B. The multiples of 8 beginning with 96 are 960 and 968. Hence, B can either be 0 or 8. Both of which satisfy our requirement of the number being divisible by 9 as well. Therefore, A and B could either be 0 and 8 or 8 and 0 respectively.

10. c $n(n^2 - 1) = (n - 1)n(n + 1)$. If you observe, this is the product of three consecutive integers with middle one being an odd integer. Since there are two consecutive even numbers, one of them will be a multiple of 4 and the other one will be a multiple of 2. Hence, the product will be a multiple of 8. Also since they are three consecutive integers, one of them will definitely be a multiple of 3. Hence, this product will always be divisible by $(3 \times 8) = 24$.

Hint: Students, please note if a number is divisible by 96, it will also be divisible by 48 and 24. Similarly, if a number is divisible by 48, it will always divisible by 24. Since there cannot be more than one right answers, we can safely eliminate options (a) and (b).

11. c The best way to solve this is the method of simulation, E.g. let m = 10 and n = 5. Therefore, m – n = 5, which is divisible by 5.

$m^2 - n^2 = 100 - 25 = 75$, divisible by 25. m + n = 10 + 5 = 15 is not divisible by 10.

Hence, the answer is (c).

Note that for the sum of two multiples of 5 to be divisible by 10, either both of them should be odd (i.e. ending in 5) or both of them should be even (i.e. ending in 0).

12. b 11 and 9 are coprimes of 99, and hence the number divisible by 99 must be divisible by 9 and 11.

Certainly statement I alone is sufficient to answer the question. Statement II says when the digits of the number are reversed, the new number formed is divisible by 9 and 11. The best way to handle this particular case is by simulation. Let us select any number which is divisible by 9 and 11. Let us select 1386 which is divisible by 9 and 11. Hence, the original number will be 6831 which, in turn, is also divisible by 99. Hence, statement II also is independently sufficient to answer the question. Since both the statements are independently sufficient to answer the question, the answer is (b).

13. c Let us find some of the smaller multiples of 125. They are 125, 250, 375, 500, 625, 750, 875, 1000, ...

A five-digit number is divisible by 125, if the last three digits are divisible by 125. So the possibilities are 375 and 875, 5 should come in unit's place, and 7 should come in ten's place. Thousand's place should contain 3 or 8. We can do it in 2! ways. Remaining first two digits, we can arrange in 2! ways. So we can have 2! × 2! = 4 such numbers. There are: 23875, 32875, 28375, 82375.

14. d N can be written either as $(54 + 1)^3 + (18 - 1)^3 - 72^3$ or $(51 + 4)^3 + 17^3 - (68 + 4)^3$.

The first form is divisible by 3 and the second by 17.

15. c $99 \times D = a_1a_2$. Thus, $D = \frac{a_1 a_2}{99}$. Hence, D must be multiplied by 198 as 198 is a multiple of 99.

16. d There are 33 numbers between 100 and 200 which are divisible by 3.

Out of these, 17 are even and 16 are odd.

There are 5 numbers between 100 and 200 which are divisible by 21 (LCM of 3 and 7).

Out of these, 3 are odd.

Hence, the number of odd numbers divisible by 3, but not by 7 is (16 – 3) = 13.

17. d $a = b^2 - b$, $b \geq 4$

$a^2 - 2a = (b^2 - b)^2 - 2(b^2 - b) = (b - 2)(b - 1)\,b\,(b + 1)$

Using different values of $b \geq 4$, we will find that $a^2 - 2a$ is divisible by 15, 20 and 24.

Hence, all of these is the right answer.

18. d $7^{6n} - 6^{6n}$

Putting n = 1.

$7^6 - 6^6 = (7^3 - 6^3)(7^3 + 6^3)$

This is a multiple of $7^3 - 6^3 = 127$ and $7^3 + 6^3 = 559$ and $7 + 6 = 13$. Hence, all of these is the right answer.

19. d Let n = 6.

Therefore, $\sqrt{n} = \sqrt{6} \approx 2.4$.

Therefore, divisors of 6 are 1, 2 and 3.

If we take 2 as divisor, then, $\sqrt{n} > 2 > 1$.

Therefore, statement A is true.

If we take 3 as divisor, then $6 > 3 > 2.4$, i.e., $n > 3 > \sqrt{n}$.

Therefore, statement B is also true.

20. a Any prime number greater than 3 can be expressed in the form of $6n \pm 1$ and minimum difference between three consecutive prime numbers is 2 and 4. The values that satisfy the given conditions are only 3, 5 and 7, i.e., only one set is possible.

21. c There are 101 integers between 100 and 200, of which 51 are even.

Between 100 and 200, there are 14 multiples of 7, of which 7 are even.

There are 11 multiples of 9, of which 6 are even.

But there is one integer (i.e., 126) that is a multiple of both 7 and 9 and also even.

Hence, the answer is (51 – 7 – 6 + 1) = 39.

22. b From 12 to 40, there are 7 prime numbers, i.e., 13, 17, 19, 23, 29, 31 and 37 such that (n – 1)! is not divisible by any of them.

23. b Let A = abc. Then, B = cba.

Given, B > A ⇒ c > a

As B – A = (100c + 10b + a) – (100a + 10b + c)

⇒ B – A = 100 (c – a) + (a – c)

⇒ B – A = 99 (c – a). Also, (B – A) is divisible by 7.

But, 99 is not divisible by 7 (no factor like 7 or 7^2). Therefore, (c – a) must be divisible by 7 {i.e., (c – a) must be 7, 7^2, etc.}. Since c and a are single digits, value of (c – a) must be 7. The possible values of (c, a) {with c > a} are (9, 2) and (8, 1). Thus, we can write A as:

A : abc ≡ 1b8 or 2b9

As b can take values from 0 to 9, the smallest and largest possible value of A are:

A_{min} = 108 and A_{max} = 299

Only option (b) satisfies this.

Hence, (b) is the correct option.

24. a The 100th and 1000th position values will be only 1.

Different possibilities of unit and tens digits are (1, 3), (1, 9), (3, 1), (3, 7), (5, 5), (7, 3), (7, 9), (9, 1) and (9, 7).

Hence, there are 9 elements in S.

25. c Two digit multiples of 8 are 16, 24, 32, 40, 48, 56, 64, 72, 80, 88 and 96. Out of these only two numbers - 40 and 48 satisfy the given condition. So the answer is 2.

26. a $x = 106^{90} - 49^{90}$

$(x^n - a^n)$ is divisible by both (x – a) and (x + a) whenever n is even

⇒ $(106^{90} - 49^{90})$ is divisible by both 57 and 155

57 = 19 × 3

155 = 31 × 5

Therefore, $(106^{90} - 49^{90})$ will be divisible by (19 × 31) = 589 as well.

Also, note that $(106^{90} - 49^{90})$ will be odd and options (b) and (c) are even. Hence, they can be rejected.

27. a The form of a number which when divided by 3, 5 and 7 leaves remainders 2, 4 and 6 respectively

= k × (LCM of 3, 5 and 7) – 1,

where k is a natural number

= 105k – 1

For the number to be the smallest, k has to be 1.

Hence, the smallest such number = 105 × 1 – 1 = 104.

Property

1. a From statement I, $x^2 + x > 50$ and $x^2 + x < 100$

$\Rightarrow x(x+1) > 50$

Only prime number 7 satisfies the above equation. So the question can be answered from statement I alone.

2. a Let the 3 odd numbers be (x – 2), x and (x + 2). It is given that 3(x – 2) = 3 + 2(x + 2)

⇒ x = 13. Hence, the third integer is (x + 2) = 15.

3. c $2^{73} - 2^{72} - 2^{71} = 2^{71}(2^2 - 2 - 1) = 2^{71}(4 - 2 - 1) = 2^{71}$.

4. c Since the sum of reciprocals is $\frac{5}{12}$. The two numbers must have their LCM as 12 and their sum as given will be 10.

Possible numbers are 4 and 6 only.

5. a Going by the options:

(a) $(x-1)yz = xyz - yz$ (b) $x(y-1)z = xyz - xz$

(c) $xy(z-1) = xyz - xy$ (d) $x(y+1)z = xyz + xz$

Here, yz will be minimum out of yz, xz, xy, xz as x > y > z

Hence, the correct answer is option (a).

6. b The last digits obtained by multiplying the units place digits should be the same as that obtained by multiplying the tens place digits.

Hence, option (b) is the correct answer.

7. a $203 = 2.3^2 + 0.3^1 + 3.3^0 = 18 + 0 + 1 = 21$

$21 = 2.3^1 + 1.3^0 = 6 + 1 = 7$.

Therefore, we can reduce 203 to 7 in 2 steps.

8. a Here logic is:

A + B = (A + B) – 18

Hence, 10 + 18 = {(10 + 18) – 18} = 10.

9. c **From statement I:**

(a, b) can be (1, 8), (2, 4), (4, 2) and (8, 1).

Therefore, statement I alone cannot give the value of a, b and c.

From statement II:

(b, c) can be (1, 9), (3, 3) and (9, 1).

On combining statements I and II:

b = 1, a = 8 and c = 9

Hence, the answer is (c).

10. d From statement I, the ages could be either (1, 3, 7) or (1, 1, 21). Statement II doesn't simplify this further as none of the above combinations when added is divisible by 3.

Hence, the answer is (d).

11. a It can be very easy to figure out that (x + y) will always be greater than xy, only if one of them is 1.

E.g. If x = 1 and y = 2, then (x + y) = 3 and xy = 2.

Hence, (x + y) > xy.

Other than this, for all other values of x & y, (x + y) will always be less than xy, and hence, the ratio of $\frac{(x+y)}{xy} < 1$, and hence, cannot be an integer.

Also, even if one of the values is 1, $\frac{(x+y)}{xy}$ will never be an integer. Hence, the answer is (a).

12. d You can do this by the method of simulation. For eg. Let the three numbers be 1, 3 and 5. So option (a) is $1^2.3^2.5^2 = 225$, which is odd. (b) is $3(1^2 + 3^3)5^2 = 2100$, which is even.

$5 + 3 + 5^4 = 633$, which is odd. (d) is $\frac{5^2(1^4+3^4)}{2} = 1025$, which is not even and hence, the answer is (d).

13. b Since there are two numbers which are less than 1 (viz. x and y), it is obvious that the median will be less than 1. Hence, (c) cannot be the answer.

Since x < 0.5 and 0 < y < 1, the median will not be less than 0. Hence, the answer is (b).

14. a Let us evaluate each option.

Option (a):

As x < 0 and z > 1, let x = – 1 and z = 3, then $(x^2 - z^2) = -8$. Hence, this option is not true.

Option (b):

As 0 < y < 1 and z > 1, let $y = \frac{1}{4}$ and z = 2,

then $yz = \frac{1}{4} \times 2 = \frac{1}{2}$.

Therefore, yz can be less than 1.

Option (c):

Since none of the x and y is equal to zero, therefore xy can never be zero.

Option (d):

0 < y < 1 and z > 1, therefore $(y^2 - z^2)$ is always negative.

Hence, answer is (a).

15. b She counted thumb on 1, 9, 17, 25 and so on. So it forms an arithmetic progression.

She counted thumb closest of 1994 on

(1 + 1992 (multiple of 8)) = 1993

Hence, she would have counted 1994 on the index finger.

16. d In this case since x, y and z are distinct positive integers, our aim is figure out which of the answer choices cannot be expressed as the sum of 3 integers uniquely. **E.g.** 6 can only be expressed as (1 + 2 + 3). 7 can only be expressed as (1 + 2 + 4). But 8 can be expressed as either (1, 2, 5) or (1, 3, 4).

17. c **Hint:** The best way to solve this question is to multiply the alternatives by 72 and find which one gives you the middle three digits as 96.7.

To save time, you can multiply 72 by integer values only.

E.g. 72 × 3 = 216, 72 × 5 = 360 and 72 × 7 = 504.

It is to be noted that when the decimal part of the answer will be multiplied by 72, the actual answer will increase.

Let us now roughly multiply the decimal values of the options also by 72.

E.g. 72 x 0.2 = 14.4, 72 × 0.1 = 7.2 and 72 × 0.5 = 36.

So option (a) will yield (216 + 14) = 230 (approximately), (b) will yield (360 + 7) = 367 (approximately), (c) will yield (360 + 36) = 396 (approximately) and (d) will yield (504 + 14) = 528 (approximately).

Of these, only option (c) satisfies our requirement of 2nd and 3rd digits being 96.

18. a The given expression is of the form $\frac{[x^3+y^3]}{[x^2-xy+y^2]}$.

We know, $\mathbf{x^3} + \mathbf{y^3} = (x + y)(x^2 - xy + y^2)$.

Thus, required value = (x + y) = (55 + 45) = 100.

19. b If the numbers are (x – 2), x and (x + 2), then 3(x – 2) – 2 = 2(x + 2) ⇒ x = 12

∴ x + 2 = 14.

20. a Statement I suggests that xyz is odd. This is only possible if all three of them are odd.

Hence, z – x is even.

So only statement I is required to answer the question.

21. c This can be answered using both the statements. Statement II suggests that both t and z are odd.

Statement I suggests that (x + y + t) is even.

Since the difference between an even and an odd number is always odd, (x + y + t) – z will be odd.

22. d This question can be answered by using the two statements.

Given (a – b + c) > (a + b – c).

It is nothing but is (–b + c) > (b – c).

Since b is negative and c is positive,

⇒ c > b

Using both statements:

c > 0

b < 0

c > b

So always (a – b + c) > (a + b – c).

23. a We cannot answer the question using both the statements.

Given that Anil's ages are prime numbers in 1998 and 1996. It is of difference 2. There are so many prime numbers with difference 2. They are (17, 19), (41, 43), . . . so on.

So we cannot find out exact age of Sachin.

24. d The given expression can be written as

$$\left(\frac{16n^2}{n}\right)+\left(\frac{7n}{n}\right)+\left(\frac{6}{n}\right)=16n+7+\left(\frac{6}{n}\right)$$

Since n is an integer, the expression (16n + 7) will always be an integer. Hence, for the entire expression to be an integer, the part $\left(\frac{6}{n}\right)$ should also be an integer. This can be possible only if n is a factor of 6, viz.

n = 1, 2, 3, 6, –1, –2, –3 and –6.

Hence, n can have eight values.

25. d If we were to express 64 as product of two positive integers, we can get the following combinations: (64 × 1), (32 × 2), (16 × 4), (8 × 8).

Thus, we find that P + Q cannot be 35.

26. b $7^{3^2} = 7^9$ and $(7^3)^2 = 7^6$. Since $7^9 > 7^6 \Rightarrow 7^{3^2} > (7^3)^2$.

27. c As P, Q and R are consecutive odd numbers, Q = P + 2 and R = P + 4. Now 3P = 2(P + 4) – 3. On solving this equation, we get P = 5.

Therefore, R = 5 + 4 = 9

28. d $a^3 + b^3 = (a + b)(a^2 + b^2 – ab)$. Combining statements I and II, we get the value of (a + b) = $\sqrt{28}$ or $-\sqrt{28}$. Since we do not have the unique value of (a + b), we cannot get the unique answer $a^3 + b^3$.

29. c If n^3 is odd, then n should also be odd. Hence, n^2 should also be odd, not even. So only I and II are true.

30. b Since MPB is a three-digit number, and also the square of a two-digit number, it can have a maximum value of 961 viz. 31^2. This means that the number BE should be less than or equal to 31. ⇒ B can be 0, 1, 2 or 3.

Since the last digit of MPB is also B, it can only be 0 or 1 (as none of the squares end in 2 or 3). The only squares that end in 0 are 100, 400 and 900. But for this to occur the last digit of BE also has to be 0. Since E and B are distinct integers, both of them cannot be 0. Hence, B has to be 1. BE can be a number between 11 and 19 (as we have also ruled out 10), with its square also ending in 1.

Hence, the number BE can only be 11 or 19. 11^2 = 121. This is not possible as this will mean that M is also equal to 1. Hence, our actual number is 19^2 = 361. Hence, M = 3.

31. c The maximum and the minimum five-digit numbers that can be formed using only 0, 1, 2, 3, 4 exactly once are 43210 and 10234 respectively. The difference between them is 43210 – 10234 = 32976.

32. c Since the distance travelled was the same both ways and also it was covered in the same time, the average speed will be the same uphill and downhill. Hence, statement (a) is false. Statement (b) need not be true. It would be true and had the speeds (and not average speed) been the same both ways. But it is clearly indicated that he varied his pace throughout. Now it has to be noted that the journey uphill and the journey downhill started at the same time, i.e. 6 a.m. and also ended at the same time 6 p.m. (though on different days). So if we were to assume a hypothetical case in which one person starts downhill at 6 a.m. and other one starts uphill at 6 a.m., along the same path, then there would be a point on the path where they would meet (i.e. they would reach at the same time), irrespective of their speeds. Our case is similar to that, except for the fact that here, we have only one person moving both ways. So there has to be a point on the path, where he reached at the same time on both days.

33. c LCM of 3, 5, 7, 9 = 315. Hence, all the multiples of 315 will be divisible by 3, 5, 7 and 9. These may be even or odd. Hence, the statement I in itself is not sufficient to answer the question.

The statement II however suggests that the number is 315 itself (as it is the only multiple that lies between 0 and 400). Hence, n is indeed odd. We require both the statements together to answer this.

34. a $(ab)^2$ = ccb, the greatest possible value of 'ab' to be 31.

Since 31^2 = 961 and since ccb > 300, 300 < ccb < 961, so 18 < ab < 31. So the possible value of ab which satisfies $(ab)^2$ = ccb is 21. So 21^2 = 441,

∴ a = 2, b = 1, c = 4.

35. a Use the method of simulation, viz. take any sample values of x and verify that n is both odd as well as a perfect square.

Alternate solution:

Let $x = (a-1)\,a\,(a+1)(a+2)$

$= (a^2-1)\,a(a+2)$

$= a^4 + 2a^3 - a^2 - 2a$

$n = x + 1 = a^4 + 2a^3 - a^2 - 2a + 1$

$= (a^2 - a + 1)^2$

36. c The square root is 111111111.

37. d Take any three odd and positive integers and check all the options.

38. a There is only one 5 and one 2 in the set of prime numbers between 2 and 100. Hence, there would be only one zero at the end of the resultant product.

39. c

12	1982
12	165 – 2
12	13 – 9
	1 – 1

The answer is 1192.

40. a Check the answer choices basis the fact that:

Odd × Odd = Odd

Odd × Even = Even

Even × Even = Even

41. a The product of 44 and 11 is 484.

If base is x, then,

$3414 = 3x^3 + 4x^2 + 1x^1 + 4 \times x^0 = 484$

$\Rightarrow 3x^3 + 4x^2 + x = 480$

This equation is satisfied only when x = 5.

So base is 5.

In decimal system, the number 3111 can be written as 406.

42. c From statement II, m, n could be (2, 15) (5, 6), (3, 10) and (1, 30) but from statement I, we get m, n as (2, 15).

Hence, the question can be answered by using both the statements together.

43. a From statement I, unequal even integers less than 10 are 2, 4, 6 and 8.

$\frac{X}{Y}$ is an odd integer is possible only if X = 6 and Y = 2

From statement II, even integers less than 10 are 2, 4, 6 and 8.

XY = 12 ⇒ X = 6, Y = 2 or X = 2, Y = 6

Hence, question can be answered by using statement I alone but not by statement II.

44. d In option (a), take x = 7, y = 9. Then, 9 – 7 = 2, which is even.

In option (b), take x = 2, y = 9. Then, 2 × 9 = 18, which is even.

In option (c), take x = 3, y = 9. Then, $\frac{3+9}{3} = 4$, which is even.

Hence, option (d) is the correct choice.

45. d It is given that 10 < n < 1000.

Let n be a two digit number. Then,

$n = 10a + b \Rightarrow p_n = ab,\ s_n = a + b$

Then, ab + a + b = 10a + b

⇒ ab = 9a ⇒ b = 9

∴ There are 9 such numbers 19, 29, 39, …, 99.

Now, let n be a three digit number.

$\Rightarrow n = 100a + 10b + c \Rightarrow p_n = abc,\ s_n = a + b + c$

Then, abc + a + b + c = 100a + 10b + c

⇒ abc = 99a + 9b

$\Rightarrow bc = 99 + 9\frac{b}{a}$

But the maximum value of bc = 81 (when both b & c are 9)

and RHS is more than 99. Hence, no such number is possible.

Hence, there are 9 such integers.

46. e Let the four-digit number be denoted by aabb = 11 × (100a + b).

Now since aabb is a perfect square, 100a + b should be a multiple of 11.

The only pairs of values of a and b that satisfy the above mentioned condition is a = 7 and b = 4. Clearly 7744 is a perfect square.

47. b $4^7 \times 5^9 = 2^{14} \times 5^9 = 2^5 \times (10)^9$

$= 32000000000$

$2^4 \times 7 = 112$

$3 \times 5^3 = 375$

$2^6 \times 5^8 = 5^2 \times (10)^6 = 25000000$

Adding the four numbers we get:

N = 32025000487

The distinct digits in N are 3, 2, 0, 5, 4, 8 and 7.

48. a $a^6 + b^6 = (a^2 + b^2)(a^4 + b^4 - a^2b^2)$

Since $a^6 + b^6$ is divisible by $a^2 + b^2$, it can be prime only in two cases:

(i) $a^2 + b^2$ is 1: This is not possible since both a and b are integers.

(ii) $a^6 + b^6 = a^2 + b^2$: If a and b are distinct integers and $a^6 + b^6$ is prime, then this is possible only if

⇒ a = 1, b = –1

⇒ a = –1, b = 1

The sum of a and b is 0 in both the cases.

49. a Let $y = \frac{\frac{1}{a}+\frac{1}{b}}{1+\frac{1}{ab}} = \frac{a+b}{ab+1}$

$$ab = \left(\frac{\sqrt{8}-\sqrt{7}}{\sqrt{8}+\sqrt{7}}\right)\left(\frac{\sqrt{8}+\sqrt{7}}{\sqrt{8}-\sqrt{7}}\right) = 1$$

$\Rightarrow$ $y = \frac{a+b}{1+1} = \frac{a+b}{2}$

Also, $a = \frac{\sqrt{8}-\sqrt{7}}{\sqrt{8}+\sqrt{7}} = \left(\sqrt{8}-\sqrt{7}\right)^2 = 15-2\sqrt{8}\sqrt{7}$

and $b = \frac{\sqrt{8}+\sqrt{7}}{\sqrt{8}-\sqrt{7}} = \left(\sqrt{8}+\sqrt{7}\right)^2 = 15+2\sqrt{8}\sqrt{7}$

$$y = \frac{a+b}{2} = 15$$

50. d

$$x = \sqrt{15} - \sqrt{11}$$
$$y = \sqrt{27} - \sqrt{23}$$
$$z = \sqrt{24} - \sqrt{20}$$

Let $f(x) = \sqrt{(x+4)} - \sqrt{x}$ (where $x > 0$).

It can be observed that f(x) decreases as x increases.

So $x > z > y$.

51. c $abc \times 1.33 = \frac{4}{3}abc = cab$ ...(i)

$cab \times 1.33 = \frac{4}{3}cab = \frac{16}{9}abc = bca$ ...(ii)

From equation (ii), we can conclude that the resultant number is a multiple of 16 and the initial number is a multiple of 9. Hence, we can say that the resultant number should be a multiple of 16 as well as 9 i.e. a multiple of 144.

There are two multiples of 144 which satisfy the condition i.e. 432 and 864.

Thus the number 'abc' could be either 243 or 486.

52. b It is given that $a^{a^b} = b$

Putting the value of b in left-hand side, we get

$$a^{a^{a^{a^b}}} = b$$

On repeating the same step n times, we get

$$a^{a^{a^{\cdot^{\cdot^{b}}}}} = b$$

When n tends to infinity, we get

$$a^{a^{a^{\cdot^{\cdot^{b}}}}} = a^b = b$$

Hence $a^b - b = 0$.

Alternate Method:

$$a^2 = 2, \text{ then } a = \sqrt{2}$$

$$a^{a^2} = 2, \text{ then } a = \sqrt{2}$$

Similarly, if $a^{a^b} = b$, then $a = \sqrt[b]{b} = b^{\frac{1}{b}}$

Hence, $a^b - b = 0$.

53. a

$$M = \sqrt{3-\sqrt{5}+\sqrt{9-4\sqrt{5}}}$$
$$= \sqrt{3-\sqrt{5}+\sqrt{\left((\sqrt{5})^2 - 2\times 2\times\sqrt{5}+2^2\right)}}$$
$$= \sqrt{3-\sqrt{5}+\sqrt{(\sqrt{5}-2)^2}}$$
$$= \sqrt{3-\sqrt{5}+\sqrt{5}-2} = \sqrt{1} = 1$$
$$N = \sqrt{\sqrt{7}-1-\sqrt{11-4\sqrt{7}}}$$
$$= \sqrt{\sqrt{7}-1-\sqrt{\left(\sqrt{7}\right)^2 - \left(2\times 2\times\sqrt{7}\right)+(2)^2}}$$
$$= \sqrt{\sqrt{7}-1-\sqrt{\left(\sqrt{7}-2\right)^2}}$$
$$= \sqrt{\sqrt{7}-1-\sqrt{7}+2} = \sqrt{1} = 1$$

Hence, $\frac{M-N}{M+N} = \frac{1-1}{1+1} = 0$.

54. a The last two digits of such perfect squares could be either 00 or 44.

Also, the largest five digit perfect square is $(316)^2$ i.e. 99856. So the number must be less than 316.

Case I: The perfect square ends with 00.

Any multiple of 10 will always end up with two zeros. 100 would be the first such number and 310 the last. There are 22 such numbers.

Case II: The perfect square ends with 44.

For the square of a number to end with 4, its unit digit must be either 2 or 8.

(i) Let the number be 'ab2', where 'a' and 'b' are the digits at hundreds and unit place respectively.

$$(ab2)^2 = (ab\times 10 + 2)^2$$
$$= \left(a^2b^2 \times 100\right) + \left(4\times ab\times 10\right) + 4$$

The last digit will always be 4, but for the second last digit to be 4, '4 × b' must end with 4. Thus 'b' could be either 1 or 6.

Possible numbers are 112, 162, 212, 262 and 312.

(ii) Let the number be 'ab8', where 'a' and 'b' are the digits at hundred and unit place respectively.

$(ab8)^2 = (ab \times 10 + 8)^2$

$= \left(a^2b^2 \times 100\right) + \left(16 \times ab \times 10\right) + 64$

The last digit will always be 4, but for the second last digit to be 4, '6 × b + 6' must end with 4. Thus 'b' could be either 3 or 8.

Possible numbers are 138, 188, 238 and 288.

Total possible numbers = 22 + 5 + 4 = 31.

Alternate Method:

The last two digits of such perfect squares could be either 00 or 44.

Perfect squares ending with 00 are always of the form $N^2 \times 10^2$, where N is a natural number.

Total such numbers would be 22 i.e. 10000 to 96100.

Perfect squares ending with 44 are the squares of numbers of the form $50k \pm 12$, where k is whole number.

Total such numbers would be 9 i.e. 112^2, 138^2, 162^2, 188^2, 212^2, 238^2, 262^2, 288^2 and 312^2.

Total possible numbers = 22 + 9 = 31.

55. d $\frac{a^n + b^n}{a + b} \Rightarrow \text{Remainder} = 0, \text{if n is odd.}$

$\therefore$ $2^{5001} + 1$ and $2^{5003} + 1$ are divisible by 3.

Now, $2^{5002} + 1$ can be written as $4^{2501} + 1$.

$\therefore$ $4^{2501} + 1$ is divisible by 5.

Hence, none of the given numbers is a prime number.

56. a $\sqrt{x} = \sqrt{2003} - \sqrt{y}$

Squaring both the sides, we get

$$x = 2003 + y - 2\sqrt{2003 \times y}$$

For x to be an integer, y must be of the form $2003a^2$, where 'a' is a natural number.

Similarly, we can say that x must be of the form $2003a^2$, where 'b' is a natural number.

$\therefore$ $\sqrt{2003a^2} + \sqrt{2003b^2} = \sqrt{2003}$

$\Rightarrow a + b = 1$

Hence, no solution is possible.

57. c Let the numbers be a, a + 1, a + 2, ..., a + 31.

Sum of these numbers

$$= 32a + \frac{31 \times 32}{2} = 16(2a + 31)$$

As 16 is a perfect square, the least possible value of 2a + 31 = 49.

Therefore, a = 9 and a + 31 = 40.

The least possible sum = 49.

58. a Prime factorization of 44 leads to:

$$44 = 2 \times 2 \times 11$$

To express 44 as product of five distinct integers we'll have to introduce 1 and –1.

The only possible way comes out to be:

$$44 = 2 \times (-2) \times 11 \times 1 \times (-1)$$

In this case the value of n would be 11 which is also the only possible value.

59. c LCM of 6, 4 and 3 = 12

$\therefore$ $2^{\frac{7}{6}} = (2^{14})^{\frac{1}{12}}$

$3^{\frac{3}{4}} = (3^9)^{\frac{1}{12}}$

$5^{\frac{3}{4}} = (5^8)^{\frac{1}{12}}$

It is clear from the above numbers that $5^8 > 3^9 > 2^{14}$.

60. c $343^b = 676$

$\Rightarrow$ $7^{3b} = 26^2$

Now, $7^a = 26$

$\Rightarrow$ $7^{3b} = (7^a)^2$

$\Rightarrow$ $2a = 3b$.

61. b Check the options.

Option (a): If the product of the digits is 6, then the factors of 6 are 1, 2, 3 and 6. There is no combination of digits which satisfies the given conditions. So it is not the answer.

Option (b): If the product of the digits is 8, then the factors of 8 are 1, 2, 4 and 8. So only possible combination is 1, 1, 2, 4.

Hence, the number is 4112.

Similarly, we can check options (c) and (d).

62. c Let n be xyz and since n is odd z can take only odd values i.e. 1, 3, 5 and 9 Now, $x \le y$ and $x \ge z$

Possible values			
x	y	z	n
1	1, 2, 3, 4, ...9	1	9
2	2, 3, 4, ...9	1	8
3	3, 4, ...9	1, 3	14
4	4, 5, 6, ...9	1, 3	12
5	5, 6, ...9	1, 3, 5	15
6	6, 7,...9	1, 3, 5	12
7	7, 8, 9	1, 3, 5, 7	12
8	8, 9	1, 3, 5, 7	8
9	9	1, 3, 5, 7, 9	5

$\therefore$ Total number of elements in P = 95.

63. d $3x + y + 4 = 2x\,y \Rightarrow 3x + 4 = y\,(2x - 1)$

$$\Rightarrow y = \frac{(3x + 4)}{(2x - 1)}$$

When $x = 6 \Rightarrow y = 2$

When $x = 1 \Rightarrow y = 7$

These two are the only possible pairs of values of x and y. Where x and y are natural numbers.

$\therefore$ Required ratio $= \frac{(6+1)}{(2+7)} = \frac{7}{9}$.

64. e If a number which is of the form $a^p \times b^q \times \ldots$, where a, b, ... are prime numbers and p, q, ... are natural numbers, then the number of factors of the number is given by $(p + 1) \times (q + 1) \times \ldots$.

According to the question,

$(p + 1) \times (q + 1) \times \ldots = 4 = 1 \times 4 = 2 \times 2$

From the above equation, it can be concluded that the number in the given case can be of the form either a^3 or $a \times b$.

There is only one number of the form a^3 which is less than or equal to 15 i.e. 2^3. There are 4 numbers of the form $a \times b$ which are less than or equal to 15 and these numbers are 2×3, 2×5, 2×7 and 3×5.

Hence, the number of required numbers is 5.

65. 51 Let five consecutive odd numbers be

$x - 4, x - 2, x, x + 2, x + 4$.

Now new sequence in revenue order

$2x, 2x - 2, 2x - 4; 2x - 6, 2x - 8$

So, sum = 450

$10x - 20 = 450$

$10x = 470$

$x = 47$

$a_5 = x + 4$

$= 47 + 4 = 51$.

66. 40 Let the other two numbers are x and y

$\therefore 73\,xy - 37\,xy = 720$

$\Rightarrow xy = 20$

$x = \sqrt{20}$ and $y = \sqrt{20}$ will satisfy the above the equation and give the minimum value of $x^2 + y^2$.

So, $x^2 + y^2 = (\sqrt{20})^2 + (\sqrt{20})^2 = 40$

67. d Let the two numbers be x and y

Since, AP $\geq$ GP

$\Rightarrow \frac{x+y}{2} \geq \sqrt{xy}$

Squaring both sides we get,

$x^2 + y^2 \geq 2xy$

We know that $x^2 + y^2 = 97$

$\Rightarrow 97 \geq 2xy$

$\Rightarrow 48.5 \geq xy$

Hence, the value of xy cannot be 64.

68. d Given that: $4^n > 17^{19}$

At n = 38, LHS will become 16^{19} which is just less than 17^{19}

Hence, smallest possible required value of n will be 39.

Factorial and its Application

1. c Number of powers of 5 in 80!

$= \left(\frac{80}{5} = 16\right) + \left(\frac{80}{5^2} \Rightarrow 3\right) = 19.$

2. b Number of 2 in the product of all integers from

$1 \text{ to } 100 = \frac{100}{2} + \frac{100}{4} + \frac{100}{8} + \frac{100}{16} + \frac{100}{32} + \frac{100}{64}$

$= 50 + 25 + 12 + 6 + 3 + 1 = 97$ and number of 5 in the product of all integers from 1 to 100

$= \frac{100}{5} + \frac{100}{25} = 20 + 4 = 24$

Hence, number of zeros at the end

= Lowest of the (number of 2, number of 5) = 24.

3. The value of ABC, three-digit number should satisfy the condition 100A + 10B + C = A! + B! + C! ....(i)

The maximum value of three digit number is 999 and minimum is 100.

We observe that 7! = 5040 > 999

So the 3-digits of the number must be

6 as 6! = 720

and/or 5 as 5! = 120

and/or 4 as 4! = 24

and/or 3 as 3! = 6

and/or 2 as 2! = 4

and/or 1 as 1! = 1

If we consider 6 at the hundred's place digit we see that condition (i) is not satisfied as 600 < 720 (6!)

So we conclude that 6 cannot occupy any position in the number.

If we place '5' at the hundred's place then the number should lie between the range of 500 and 600. Considering the RHS of equation (i) by putting A + B = C = 5 we get the sum as 360 which is less than 500.

Similarly, putting 4, 3, 2 at the hundred's place does not satisfies the given condition (i).

Only 1 can be placed at hundred place and 5 should be one of the digit at other two position in order to make it a three digit number.

Thus, only combination we satisfies the given condition (i) is (1, 4, 5) i.e. 145 = 1! + 4! + 5! = 145.

4. d If p = 1! = 1, then

p + 2 = 3 when divided by 2! will give a remainder of 1.

If p = 1! + 2 × 2! = 5, then

p + 2 = 7 when divided by 3! will give a remainder of 1.

Hence, p = 1! + (2 × 2!) + (3 × 3!) + … + (10 × 10!) when divided by 11! leaves a remainder 1.

Alternative method:

P = 1 + 2.2! + 3.3! + … + 10.10!

= (2–1)1! + (3–1)2! + (4–1)3! + … + (11–1)10!

= 2! – 1! + 3! – 2! + …+ 11! –10! = 1 + 11!

Hence, the remainder is 1.

5. b Since N has 4 factors, N must be of the form P_1^3 or $P_2 \times P_3$ where P_1, P_2, P_3 are prime numbers.

If N takes the form P_1^3 then P_1 can only be 3.

If N takes the form $P_2 \times P_3$ then the possibilities are:

Nine possible values where 2 is the smaller factor: 2 × 5, 2 × 7, 2 × 11, 2 × 13, 2 × 17, 2 × 19, 2 × 23, 2 × 29, 2 × 31

Seven possible values where 3 is the smaller factor: 3 × 5, 3 × 7, 3 × 11, 3 × 13, 3 × 17, 3 × 19, 3 × 23

Three possible values where 5 is the smaller factor: 5 × 7, 5 × 11, 5 × 13

So N can take 1 + 9 + 7 + 3 = 20 values in all.

6. b We have to calculate the number of zeroes starting from the right end of the number N.

The number of zeroes from:

1! to 4! = 0

5! to 9! = 1× 5 = 5

10! to 14! = 2 × 5 = 10

15! to 19! = 3 × 5 = 15

20! to 24! = 4 × 5 = 20

25! to 29! = 6 × 5 = 30

30! to 34! = 7 × 5 = 35

35! to 39! = 8 × 5 = 40

So we get 155 zeroes till 39! only. From this we can easily conclude that the 147th digit from the right end of N will be zero.

7. c 500! + 505! + 510! + 515!

= 500!(1 + 5k) (where k is a natural number)

It can be seen that 5k + 1 won't be a multiple of 5.

Minimum value of n for which 500! Is divisible by 5^n = 1.

Maximum value of n for which 500! Is divisible by 5^n

$$\left[\frac{500}{5}\right]+\left[\frac{500}{5^2}\right]+\left[\frac{500}{5^3}\right]+\left[\frac{500}{5^4}\right] = 100+20+4=124$$

Hence, there are 124 possible values of n.

8. b Since 'ab' is a two-digit prime number and one of its digit is 3, it can assume any of the values among 13, 23, 31, 37 ,43, 53, 73 and 83.

As the absolute difference between the digits of the number is not a factor of 2, the number among the obtained numbers that satisfy the aforementioned condition are 37, 73 and 83. Hence, the number of values that 'ab' can assume is 3.

9. d Let the number be N.

In order to maximize the number of factors of N^3, N^2 must be expressed as a product of as many prime factors as possible.

No. of factors of N^2 = 105 = 3 × 5 × 7

$= (2+1)(4+1)(6+1)$

$\therefore$ $N^2 = (a)^2(b)^4(c)^6$, where a, b and c are prime numbers.

$\therefore$ $N^3 = (a)^3(b)^6(c)^9$

Hence, the number of factors of N^3

$= (3+1)\times(6+1)\times(9+1) = 4\times7\times10 = 280.$

10. a (x – 2) is a factor of R(x).

$\therefore$ R(2) = 0

$\Rightarrow$ $m(2)^3 - 100(2)^2 + 3n = 0$

$\Rightarrow$ 8m – 400 + 3n = 0

$$\Rightarrow m = \frac{400-3n}{8} = 50 - \frac{3n}{8}$$

As m and n are positive integers, so n must be a multiple of 8. For n = 8, 16, 24, …, 128, we get m = 47, 44, 41, …, 2 respectively.

Hence, the number of possible values of ordered pair (m, n) is 16.

11. a $1080 = 2^3 \times 3^3 \times 5^1$

$1800 = 2^3 \times 3^2 \times 5^2$

HCF of 1080 and 1800 = $2^3 \times 3^2 \times 5$

Number of factors of 1080 = 4 × 4 × 2 = 32

Number of factors of 1800 = 4 × 3 × 3 = 36

Number of factors of HCF of the two numbers

= 4 × 3 × 2

= 24

Hence, the required number of divisiors

= (32 + 36) – 2 × 24

= 20.

12. c In order to maximize the power of 2 in the product, one of the ten numbers has to be 64 as this is the highest two-digit number of the form 2^k, where k is a natural number.

There has to be maximum number of multiples of 8 among the ten numbers. In a set of ten consecutive natural numbers, there can be a maximum of two numbers that will be a multiple of 8.

The possible sets of ten consecutive natural numbers that satisfy the aforementioned conditions are 55 to 64, 56 to 65, 63 to 72 and 64 to 73. The highest power of 2 in the product of any of these sets of ten numbers will be 13.

13. b $P = 15^{100} (1 \times 2 \times 3 \times ... \times 100)$

$= 15^{100} \times 100!$

Highest power of 2 in P = 97 (2 will be deciding factor for number of zeroes because number of fives will be greater than number of zeroes in this number)

$Q = 25^{20\times50} (1 \times 2 \times 3x... \times 50) = 5^{2000} \times 50!$

Highest power of 2 in Q = 47

So Highest power of 2 in

$$\frac{P^2}{Q} \times 10^{1767} = 2 \times 97 + 1767 - 47$$

$$= 1914.$$

Hence, number of zeroes = 1914.

14. 8 The number finally obtained will be the "digit sum" of the original number. It can be directly obtained by dividing the original number by 9 and finding the remainder.

$$\text{Rem}\left[\frac{5^{1!+2!+3!+4!}}{9}\right] = \text{Rem}\left[\frac{5^{33}}{9}\right]$$

$$= \text{Rem}\left[\frac{(5^3)^{11}}{9}\right]$$

$$= \text{Rem}\left[\frac{(-1)^{11}}{9}\right]$$

$$= -1 = 8.$$

HCF and LCM

1. d Required number = LCM (4, 6, 7) + 2 = 86.

2. b Required number = LCM (8, 11, 24) – 5 = 259.

3. d The LCM of 7, 12 and 16 is 336. The closest multiple of 336 to 1856 is 1680. So 1684 when divided by 7, 12 and 16 leaves a remainder of 4. This is the closest such number, less than 1856. Hence, the number to be subtracted from 1856 to get 1684, must be the least such number.

So the answer is (1856 – 1684) = 172.

Alternate method:

Subtract options from 1856 and check.

4. b The bells will chime together after a time that is equal to the LCM of 18, 24 and 32 = 288 min = 4 hr and 48 min.

5. c We know that product of two numbers = LCM × HCF

$= 36 \times 2 = 72.$

So $\quad x = \frac{72}{18} = 4.$

Hence, both the statements are required to answer the question.

6. * The time taken by the red spots on all three wheels to simultaneously touch the ground again will be equal to the LCM of the times taken by the three wheels to complete one revolution. The first wheel completes 60 revolutions per minute i.e., to complete one revolution, it takes $\left(\frac{60}{60}\right) = 1$ sec

The second wheel completes 36 revolutions per minute i.e., to complete one revolution, it takes $\left(\frac{60}{36}\right) = \frac{5}{3}$ sec.

Similarly, the third wheel takes $\left(\frac{60}{24}\right) = \frac{5}{2}$ sec to complete one revolution.

$\therefore$ LCM of $1, \frac{5}{3}, \frac{5}{2} = \frac{\text{LCM}(1,5,5)}{\text{HCF}(1,3,2)} = \frac{5}{1} = 5$ sec

*** The correct answer is not available in the given options.**

7. b Note that the difference between the divisors and the remainders is constant.

2 – 1 = 3 – 2 = 4 – 3 = 5 – 4 = 6 – 5 = 1

In such a case, the required number will always be

[a multiple of LCM of (2, 3, 4, 5, 6) – (The constant difference)].

LCM of (2, 3, 4, 5, 6) = 60

Hence, the required number will be 60n – 1.

Thus, we can see that the smallest such number is (60 × 1) – 1 = 59

The second smallest is (60 × 2) – 1 = 119

So between 1 and 100, there is only one such number, viz. 59.

8. d HCF of 60, 84 and 108 is 12. Hence, 12 students should be seated in each room. So for subject A we would require $\left(\frac{60}{12}\right)$ = 5 rooms, for subject B we would require $\left(\frac{84}{12}\right)$ = 7 rooms and for subject C we would require $\left(\frac{108}{12}\right)$ = 9 rooms. Hence, minimum number of rooms required to satisfy our condition = 5 + 7 + 9 = 21 rooms.

9. b If there are n numbers, the function h has to be performed one time less.

10. a First light blinks after 20 s.

Second light blinks after 24 s.

They blink together after LCM (20 and 24) = 120 s = 2 min. Hence, the number of times they blink together in an hour = 30.

11. c We can put a minimum of 120 oranges and a maximum of 144 oranges, i.e., 25 oranges need to be filled in 128 boxes.

There are 25 different possibilities if there are 26 boxes.

In such a case, at least 2 boxes contain the same number of oranges. (i.e., even if each of the 25 boxes contain a different number of oranges, the 26th must contain one of these numbers).

Similarly, if there are 51 boxes, at least 3 boxes contain the same number of oranges.

Hence, at least 6 boxes have the same number of oranges in case of 128 boxes.

12. b Since each word is lit for a second, least time after which the full name of the bookstore can be read again

$$= \text{LCM}\left(\frac{5}{2}+1, \frac{17}{4}+1, \frac{41}{8}+1\right)$$

$$= \text{LCM}\left(\frac{7}{2}, \frac{21}{4}, \frac{49}{8}\right)$$

$$= \frac{\text{LCM}(7, 21, 49)}{\text{HCF}(2, 4, 8)} = \frac{49 \times 3}{2} = 73.5\text{ s}.$$

13. d $\text{HCF}\left(\frac{9}{2}, \frac{27}{4}, \frac{36}{5}\right) = \frac{\text{HCF}(9, 27, 36)}{\text{LCM}(2, 4, 5)} = \frac{9}{20}$ lb

= Weight of each piece

Also, total weight of three pieces of cakes = 18.45 lb

$\therefore$ Maximum number of guests that could be entertained = $\frac{18.45 \times 20}{9} = 41$.

14. b LCM of 2, 3, 4, 6, 12 = 12

We can rewrite the given surds as

$\sqrt[12]{2^6}, \sqrt[12]{3^4}, \sqrt[12]{4^3}, \sqrt[12]{6^2}, \sqrt[12]{12^1}$

$\therefore$ 3^4 is the greatest.

Note: $n^{1/n}$ is maximum when n = e (2.718). Among the given options, n = 3 is closest to the value of e.

15. c Let the numbers be a and b.

We know, $a + b = 600$ and $\frac{a}{b} = \frac{7}{8}$

Solving, the above two equations, we get

a = 280

b = 320

LCM (a, b) = LCM (280, 320)

= 2240.

16. 31 Let the four numbers be XK, XL, XM and XN, where X is the common factor of each pair possible pair of numbers and K, L, M, N are prime to each other.

310 = 2 × 5 × 31

651 = 31 × 21 = 3 × 7 × 31 $\therefore$ GCF (310, 651) = 31

which is the highest common factor of all.

17. b $1000 = 2^3 \times 5^3$ and $2000 = 2^4 \times 5^3$

Since LCM (c, a) and LCM (b, c) is $2^4 \times 5^3$ and LCM (a, b) = $2^3 \times 5^3$, so the factor 2^4 must be present in c.

Hence $c = 2^4 \times 5^x$, where x ranges from 0 to 3

Therefore, there are four possible values of C.

Since, HCF of (a, b) = K × 5^3, it means

$a = 2^y \times 5^3$

$b = 2^z \times 5^3$

x = 0 to 3, y = 0, then z = 3 → 4 cases.

x = 0 to 3, y = 1, then z = 3 → 4 cases.

x = 0 to 3, y = 2, then z = 3 → 4 cases.

x = 0 to 3, y = 3, then z = 3 → 4 cases.

x = 0 to 3, y = 3, then z = 2 → 4 cases.

x = 0 to 3, y = 3, then z = 1 → 4 cases.

x = 0 to 3, y = 3, then z = 0 → 4 cases.

Hence, total cases = 28.

Remainder

1. b $\text{Rem}\left[\frac{2^{60}}{5}\right] = \text{Rem}\left[\frac{(2^4)^{15}}{5}\right] = \text{Rem}\left[\frac{1^{15}}{5}\right] = 1.$

2. a As 55 does not have factor common with 124, for 55n to be exactly divisible by 124, n should be a multiple of 124.

Hence, the minimum value that n can have is 124 itself.

3. b $5^6 - 1 = (5^3)^2 - 1 = (125)^2 - (1)^2 = (125 + 1)(125 - 1)$ $= 124 \times 126 = 31 \times 4 \times 126.$

So among the given answer choices, it is divisible by 31.

4. b The best way to solve this question is by the method of simulation. Choose any prime number greater than 6 and verify the result.

When 7 is divided by 6, it gives a remainder 1. So our answer could be (a) or (b). When 11 is divided by 6, it gives a remainder 5. Hence, our answer is (b).

5. a Since 899 is divisible by 29, so you can directly divide the remainder of 63 by 29, so $\frac{63}{29}$ will give 5 as a remainder, option (a).

6. b Since 2 has a cyclicity of 4,

i.e. $2^1 = 2, 2^2 = 4, 2^3 = 8, 2^4 = 16, 2^5 = 32, 2^6 = 64, ...,$ the last digits (2, 4, 8, 6) are in four cycles.

$\therefore$ On dividing $\frac{51}{4}$, we get the remainder as 3.

$\therefore$ The last digit has to be $2^3 = 8$

Shortcut:

Since cyclicity of the power of 2 is 4, so 2^{51} can be written in $2^{4(12)+3}$ or unit digit will be $2^3 = 8$.

7. c The number formed by the last 3 digits of the main number is 354. The remainder is 2 if we divide 354 by 8. So the remainder of the main number is also 2 if we divide it by 8.

8. b **Note:** $342 = 7^3 - 1$. On further simplification we get,

$$= \frac{(7^3)^{28}}{342} = \frac{343^{28}}{342} = \frac{(342+1)^{28}}{342} = \frac{342\,N + 1}{342}$$

Hence, remainder = 1.

9. c $N = 1421 \times 1423 \times 1425$. When divided by 12, it shall look like $\frac{[(1416+5)\times(1416+7)\times(1416+9)]}{12}$.

Now the remainder will be governed by the term $5 \times 7 \times 9$, which when divided by 12 leaves the remainder 3.

10. d Let r be the remainder. Then, 34041 – r and 32506 – r are perfectly divisible by n. Hence, their difference should also be divisible by the same number.

$\therefore$ (34041 – r) – (32506 – r) = 1535, which is divisible by only 307.

11. a $(2^4)^{64} = (17-1)^{64} = 17n + (-1)^{64} = 17n + 1$

Hence, remainder = 1.

12. d $3(4(7x + 4) + 1) + 2 = 84x + 53$

Therefore, remainder is 53.

13. a From A, if by adding 12 students, the total number of students is divisible by 8. By adding 4 students, it will be divisible by 8.

14. b Such numbers are 10, 17, ..., 94.

These numbers are in AP. There are 13 numbers.

$\therefore$ Sum $= \frac{10+94}{2} \times 13 = 52 \times 13 = 676.$

15. d To find the remainder when $\frac{4^{96}}{6}$, let us use the basic property of dividing the power of 4 by 6, i.e.,

$$\frac{4^1}{6} = 4$$

$$\frac{4^2}{6} = 4$$

$$\frac{4^3}{6} = 4$$

$$\frac{4^4}{6} = 4$$

Hence, any power of 4 when divided by 6 leaves a remainder of 4.

16. a Since b can take any even number 2, 4, 6,…,we cannot say anything from statement A.

Consider statement B.

If b > 16, say b = 17, then $2^{44} < (16 + 1)^{11}$.

$\Rightarrow 2^{44} < (2^4 + 1)^{11}$

Hence, we can answer the question using statement B alone.

17. c $15^{23} = (19-4)^{23} = 19x + (-4)^{23}$, where x is a natural number.

$23^{23} = (19+4)^{23} = 19y + (4)^{23}$, where y is a natural number.

$15^{23} + 23^{23} = 19(x+y) + 4^{23} + (-4)^{23} = 19(x+y).$

Hence, remainder will be zero.

18. a $x = 16^3 + 17^3 + 18^3 + 19^3$ is an even number

Therefore, 2 divides x.

$a^3 + b^3 = (a+b)(a^2 - ab + b^2)$

$\Rightarrow$ a + b always divides $a^3 + b^3$.

Therefore, $16^3 + 19^3$ is divisible by 35.

$18^3 + 17^3$ is divisible by 35.

Thus, x is divisible by 70.

Hence, option (a) is the correct choice.

19. a $((30)^4)^{680} = (8100)^{680}$.

Hence, the right most non-zero digit is 1.

20. c The last two digits of any number in the form of 7^{4n} will always be equal to 01.

For example: $7^4 = 2401$ and $7^8 = 5764801$.

21. d If all are of equal height, number of handshakes $= {}^{40}C_2$.

If all are of different heights, number of handshakes = 0.

Difference $= {}^{40}C_2 - 0 = {}^{40}C_2$.

Miscellaneous

1. d Statement I implies $X - Y = 6$.

Statement II implies XY is divisible by 6.

You can see that many values of X and Y can satisfy statement I and II.

2. b Check choices.

Choice (b) 54 $\Rightarrow S = (5 + 4)^2 = 81$

$\Rightarrow D - S = 81 - 54 = 27$. Hence, the number = 54.

3. d $u^m + v^m = w^m$

$u^2 + v^2 = w^2$

Taking Pythagorean triplet 3, 4 and 5, we see that $m < \min(u, v, w)$.

Also, $1^1 + 2^1 = 3^1$ and hence, $m \le \min(u, v, w)$.

4. b MDCCLXXXVII = 1000 + 500 + 100 + 100 + 50 + 10 + 10 + 10 + 5 + 1 + 1 = 1787

5. a MCMXCIX = 1000 + (1000 – 100) + (100 – 10) + (10 – 1) = 1000 + 900 + 90 + 9 = 1999

6. c (I) MCMLXXV = 1000 + (1000 – 100) + 50 + 10 + 10 + 5 = 1975

(II) MCMXCV = 1000 + (1000 – 100) + (100 – 10) + 5 = 1995

(III) MVD = 1000 + (500 – 5) = 1495

(IV) MVM = 1000 + (1000 – 5) = 1995

Therefore, the answer is (II) and (IV), i.e. option (c).

7. d Since the last digit in base 2, 3 and 5 is 1, the number should be such that on dividing by either 2, 3 or 5 we should get a remainder 1. The smallest such number is 31. The next set of numbers are 61, 91.

Among these only 31 and 91 are a part of the answer choices.

Among these, $(31)_{10} = (11111)_2 = (1011)_3 = (111)_5$

Thus, all three forms have leading digit 1.

Hence, the answer is 91.

8. a We have

(a) $10^{10} < n < 10^{11}$

(b) Sum of the digits for 'n' = 2

Clearly,

(n) min = 10000000001 (1 followed by 9 zeros and finally 1)

Obviously, we can form 10 such numbers by shifting '1' by one place from right to left again and again.

Again, there is another possibility for 'n'

n = 20000000000

So number of different values of n = 10 + 1 = 11.

9. c By option (c), if four consecutive odd numbers are 37, 39, 41 and 43, then sum of these 4 numbers is 160.

When divided by 10, we get 16, which is a perfect square.

∴ 41 is one of the odd numbers.

10. e seed(n) function will eventually give the digit-sum of any given number, n.

All the numbers 'n' for which seed(n) = 9 will give the remainder 0 when divided by 9.

For all positive integers n, n < 500, there are 55 multiples of 9.

11. c Let the hundreds digit be n.

The tens digit will be 2n.

The unit digit will be 4n.

The possible values of 'n' are 1 and 2 and hence the possible numbers are 124 and 248 respectively.

On converting 248 in base 8 and base 9, the given condition gets violated.

On converting 124 in base 8 and base 9, we get

$(174)_8 = (147)_9$.

Required sum = 4 + 7 = 11.

12. c $(x+1)(x+2)(x+3)(x+6) = -x^2$

$(x^2+7x+6)(x^2+5x+6) = -x^2$

$x^2\left(x+7+\frac{6}{x}\right)\left(x+5+\frac{6}{x}\right) = -x^2$

Put $x + \frac{6}{x} = y$

$(y+7)(y+5) = -1$

$y^2 + 12y + 36 = 0 \Rightarrow (y+6)^2 = 0 \Rightarrow y = -6$

$\therefore\ x + \frac{6}{x} = -6$

$x^2 + 6x + 6 = 0$

$$x = \frac{-6 \pm \sqrt{36 - 4(6)}}{2} = \frac{-6 \pm 2\sqrt{3}}{2} = -3 \pm \sqrt{3}$$

13. 17 $(x^2 - y^2)(x^2 + y^2) = 15$

$\Rightarrow (x^2 - y^2)(x^2 + y^2) = 1 \times 15 = 3 \times 5$

$\Rightarrow x^2 - y^2 = 3$ and $x^2 + y^2 = 5$ (because x and y are natural numbers)

$\therefore 2x^2 = 8$

$\Rightarrow x^2 = 4$

$\therefore y^2 = 1$

$\Rightarrow x^4 + y^4 = 4^2 + 1^2 = 17.$

14. 20 According to the question,

$$\frac{N1+1}{2} - \frac{N2+1}{2} = 10$$

$$\Rightarrow \quad N1 - N2 = 20$$

15. 3 If $\frac{A}{B}$ is always a terminating decimal, then B can either be 1 or can have only two prime factors i.e. 2 and 5. The possible values of B are 1, 2, 4, 5, 8, 10, 16, 20, 25, 32, 40, 50, 64 and 80, i.e. 14 values in all.

16. 3 $\frac{21}{2n-1} = m(\text{say})$, where m is an integer.

For m to be an integer, (2n – 1) should be 1, 3, 7 or 21 i.e. one of the factors of 21.

Hence, the number of integers in the sequence is 4.

17. 90 His shop must have been visited by at least 90 customers.

The number of customers who bought both Rose and Tulip = 70.

The rest 20 customers must have bought just 1 Tulip each.

18. c Numbers in the square grid is shown below.

6	7	2
1	5	9
8	3	4

19. d $a(a + 1)(a + 2) = 15600.$

Now factors of 15600

$= 2 \times 2 \times 2 \times 2 \times 3 \times 5 \times 5 \times 13$

So, 15600 is the product of 24, 25, 26

So, sum of the squares of these integers is $24^2 + 25^2 + 26^2 = 1877.$

20. c $\frac{1}{a} + \frac{1}{b} = \frac{1}{9}$

$ab = 9(a + b)$

$ab = 9a + 9b$

$9a = b(a - 9)$

$$b = \frac{9a}{a-9} = \frac{9a - 81 + 81}{a-9}$$

$$= \frac{9(a-9)}{a-9} + \frac{81}{a-9}$$

$$b = \frac{81}{a-9} + 9$$

For b to be integer and $a \leq b$, the first term should be an integer. So factors of 81 are 1, 3, 9, 27, 81. Now put these values satisfying $a \leq b$. So only 3 values (1, 3, 9) will satisfy the given condition.

So, answer will be 3.

21. c The nth term of the given series

$= [4(n + 1) - 1][4(n + 2) - 1]$

$= (4n + 3)(4n + 7)$

$= 16n^2 + 40n + 21$

$\Rightarrow$ Required sum

$$= \frac{16[n(n+1)(2n+1)]}{6} + \frac{40n(n+1)}{2} + 21n \quad \text{....(1)}$$

As, n = 23 and all the individual terms are odd.

Hence, correct answer will be odd multiple of 23 which will be 80707.

2

CHAPTER

Arithmetic

PERCENTAGES AND FRACTION

1990

1. In a stockpile of products produced by three machines M1, M2 and M3, 40% and 30% were manufactured by M1 and M2 respectively. 3% of the products of M1 are defective, 1% of products of M2 defective, while 95% of the products of M3 are not defective. What is the percentage of defective in the stockpile?

(a) 3% (b) 5%

(c) 2.5% (d) 4%

2. Gopal went to a fruit market with certain amount of money. With this money he can buy either 50 oranges or 40 mangoes. He retains 10% of the money for taxi fare. If he buys 20 mangoes, then the number of oranges he can buy is

(a) 25 (b) 18

(c) 20 (d) None of these

Directions for Questions 3 to 5 : A dealer deals only in colour TVs and VCRs. He wants to spend up to Rs.12 lakhs to buy 100 pieces. He can purchase a colour TV at Rs.10,000 and a VCR at Rs.15,000. He can sell a colour TV at Rs.12,000 and a VCR at Rs.17,500. His objective is to maximize profits. Assume that he can sell all the items that he stocks.

3. For the maximum profit, the number of colour TVs and VCRs that he should respectively stock are

(a) 80, 20 (b) 20, 80

(c) 60, 40 (d) None of these

4. If the dealer would have managed to get an additional space to stock 20 more items, then for maximizing profit, the ratio of number of VCRs and number of TVs that he should stock is

(a) 7 : 3 (b) 0

(c) 1 : 2 (d) None of these

5. The maximum profit, in rupees lakh, the dealer can earn from his original stock if he can sell a colour TV at Rs. 12200 and VCR at Rs.18300 is

(a) 2.64 (b) 2.49

(c) 2.72 (d) 2.87

6. If equal numbers of people are born on each day, find the approximate percentage of the people whose birthday will fall on 29th February. (If we are to consider people born in 20th century and assuming no deaths).

(a) 0.374 (b) 0.5732

(c) 0.0664 (d) None of these

1991

7. Gopal went to a fruit market with certain amount of money. With this money he can buy either 50 oranges or 40 mangoes. He retains 10% of the money for taxi fare. If he buys 20 mangoes, then the number of oranges he can buy is

(a) 25 (b) 20

(c) 18 (d) 6

1993

8. The rate of increase of the price of sugar is observed to be two percent more than the inflation rate expressed in percentage. The price of sugar, on January 1, 1994, is Rs. 20 per kg. The inflation rate for the years 1994 and 1995 are expected to be 8% each. The expected price of sugar on January 1, 1996 would be

(a) Rs.23.60 (b) Rs.24.00

(c) Rs.24.20 (d) Rs.24.60

9. A report consists of 20 sheets each of 55 lines and each such line consist of 65 characters. This report is retyped into sheets each of 65 lines such that each line consists of 70 characters. The percentage reduction in number of sheets is closest to

(a) 20 (b) 5

(c) 30 (d) 35

1994

10. The number of votes not cast for the Praja Party increased by 25% in the National General Election over those not cast for it in the previous Assembly Polls, and the Praja Party lost by a majority twice as large as that by which it had won the Assembly Polls. If a total 2,60,000 people voted each time. How many voted for the Praja Party in the Assembly Elections.

(a) 1,10,000 (b) 1,50,000

(c) 1,40,000 (d) 1,20,000

1995

11. A person who has a certain amount with him goes to market. He can buy 50 oranges or 40 mangoes. He retains 10% of the amount for taxi fares and buys 20 mangoes and of the balance he purchases oranges. Number of oranges he can purchase is

(a) 36 (b) 40
(c) 15 (d) 20

12. $\frac{2}{5}$ of the voters promise to vote for P and the rest promised to vote for Q. Of these, on the last day 15% of the voters went back of their promise to vote for P and 25% of voters went back of their promise to vote for Q, and P lost by 2 votes. Then the total number of voters is

(a) 100 (b) 110
(c) 90 (d) 95

13. The rate of inflation was 1000%. Then what will be the cost of an article, which costs 6 units of currency now, 2 years from now?

(a) 666 (b) 660
(c) 720 (d) 726

Direction for Question 14: The question is followed by two statements, I and II. Mark the answer as:

(a) if the question can be answered with the help of statement I alone.
(b) if the question can be answered with the help of statement II alone.
(c) if both statement I and statement II are needed to answer the question.
(d) if the question cannot be answered even with the help of both the statements.

14. What is the price of bananas?

I. With Rs.84, I can buy 14 bananas and 35 oranges.
II. If price of bananas is reduced by 50%, then we can buy 48 bananas in Rs.12.

1996

15. I bought 5 pens, 7 pencils and 4 erasers. Rajan bought 6 pens, 8 erasers and 14 pencils for an amount which was half more what I had paid. What per cent of the total amount paid by me was paid for the pens?

(a) 37.5% (b) 62.5%
(c) 50% (d) None of these

16. The price of a Maruti car rises by 30% while the sales of the car come down by 20%. What is the percentage change in the total revenue?

(a) –4% (b) –2%
(c) +4% (d) +2%

1997

17. Fresh grapes contain 90% water while dry grapes contain 20% water. What is the weight of dry grapes obtained from 20 kg fresh grapes?

(a) 2 kg (b) 2.5 kg
(c) 2.4 kg (d) None of these

18. A man earns x% on the first Rs. 2,000 and y% on the rest of his income. If he earns Rs. 700 from income of Rs. 4,000 and Rs. 900 from if his income is Rs. 5,000, find x%.

(a) 20% (b) 15%
(c) 25% (d) None of these

Direction for Question 19: The question is followed by two statements, I and II. Answer the question based on the statements and mark the answer as:

(a) if the question can be answered with the help of any one statement alone but not by the other statement.
(b) if the question can be answered with the help of either of the statements taken individually.
(c) if the question can be answered with the help of both statements together.
(d) if the question cannot be answered even with the help of both statements together.

1998

19. Radha and Rani appeared in an examination. What was the total number of questions?

I. Radha and Rani together solved 20% of the paper.
II. Radha alone solved $\frac{3}{5}$ of the paper solved by Rani.

1999

20. Forty per cent of the employees of a certain company are men, and 75% of the men earn more than Rs. 25,000 per year. If 45% of the company's employees earn more than Rs. 25,000 per year, what fraction of the women employed by the company earn less than or equal to Rs. 25,000 per year?

(a) $\frac{2}{11}$ (b) $\frac{1}{4}$
(c) $\frac{1}{3}$ (d) $\frac{3}{4}$

2000

21. The table below shows the agewise distribution of the population of Reposia. The number of people aged below 35 years is 400 million.

Age group	Percentage
Below 15 years	30.00
15-24	17.75
25-34	17.00
35-44	14.50
45-54	12.50
55-64	7.10
65 and above	1.15

If the ratio of females to males in the 'below 15 years' age group is 0.96, then what is the number of females in that age group?

(a) 82.8 million (b) 90.8 million
(c) 80 million (d) 90 million

2001

22. The owner of an art shop conducts his business in the following manner: every once in a while he raises his prices by X%, then a while later he reduces all the new prices by X%. After one such up-down cycle, the price of a painting decreased by Rs. 441. After a second up-down cycle the painting was sold for Rs. 1,944.81. What was the original price of the painting?

(a) Rs. 2,756.25 (b) Rs. 2,256.25
(c) Rs. 2,500 (d) Rs. 2,000

Direction for Question 23: The question is followed by two statements, I and II.

Mark

(a) if the question can be answered by one of the statements alone and not by the other.
(b) if the question can be answered by using either statement alone.
(c) if the question can be answered by using both the statements together, but cannot be answered by using either statement alone.
(d) if the question cannot be answered even by using both statements together.

23. Two friends, Ram and Gopal, bought apples from a wholesale dealer. How many apples did they buy?

I. Ram bought one-half the number of apples that Gopal bought.
II. The wholesale dealer had a stock of 500 apples.

2002

24. Mayank, Mirza, Little and Jaspal bought a motorbike for \$60. Mayank paid one-half of the sum of the amounts paid by the other boys. Mirza pad one-third of the sum of the amounts paid by the other boys. Little paid one-fourth of the sum of the amounts paid by the other boys. How much did Jaspal have to pay?

(a) \$15 (b) \$13
(c) \$17 (d) None of these

2003(L)

25. At the end of year 1998, Shepard bought nine dozen goats. Henceforth, every year he added p% of the goats at the beginning of the year and sold q% of the goats at the end of the year where $p > 0$ and $q > 0$. If Shepard had nine dozen goats at the end of year 2002, after making the sales for that year, which of the following is true?

(a) $p = q$ (b) $p < q$
(c) $p > q$ (d) $p = q/2$

Direction for Question 26: The question is followed by two statements, A and B. Answer the question using the following instructions.

Choose (a) if the question can be answered by using one of the statements alone but not by using the other statement alone.

Choose (b) if the question can be answered by using either of the statements alone.

Choose (c) if the question can be answered by using both statements together but not by either statement alone.

Choose (d) if the question cannot be answered on the basis of the two statements.

2004

26. Zakib spends 30% of his income on his children's education, 20% on recreation and 10% on healthcare. The corresponding percentage for Supriyo are 40%, 25%, and 13%. Who spends more on children's education?

A. Zakib spends more on recreation than Supriyo.
B. Supriyo spends more on healthcare than Zakib.

2006

27. The length, breadth and height of a room are in the ratio 3 : 2 : 1. If the breadth and height are halved while the length is doubled, then the total area of the four walls of the room will

(a) remain the same
(b) decrease by 13.64%
(c) decrease by 15%
(d) decrease by 18.75%
(e) decrease by 30%

Directions for Questions 28 and 29: Each question is followed by two statements, A and B.

Answer each question using the following instructions:

Mark (a) if the question can be answered by using the statement A alone but not by using the statement B alone.

Mark (b) if the question can be answered by using the statement B alone but not by using the statement A alone.

Mark (c) if the question can be answered by using either of the statements alone.

Mark (d) if the question can be answered by using both the statements together but not by either of the statements alone.

Mark (e) if the question cannot be answered on the basis of the two statements.

2007

28. In a particular school, sixty students were athletes. Ten among them were also among the top academic performers. How many top academic performers were in the school?

A. Sixty per cent of the top academic performers were not athletes.

B. All the top academic performers were not necessarily athletes.

29. Thirty per cent of the employees of a call centre are males. Ten per cent of the female employees have an engineering background. What is the percentage of male employees with engineering background?

A. Twenty five per cent of the employees have engineering background.

B. Number of male employees having an engineering background is 20% more than the number of female employees having an engineering background.

MEMORY BASED QUESTIONS

2009

30. Mogambo has got some money which he can spend completely in buying either 50 mangoes or 40 oranges. If he wants to save 10% of the amount and buy at least 20 oranges, then what is the maximum possible number of mangoes that he can buy?

(a) 15 (b) 16

(c) 20 (d) 24

2010

31. One hundred ml of alcohol is mixed with y ml of water. Forty ml of this alcohol-water mixture is added to 2y ml of another alcohol-water mixture whose alcohol concentration is 26%. If the percentage of water in the resultant mixture is 2y%, then what is the value of y?

(a) 30 (b) 40

(c) 20 (d) 25

2011

32. If $12P + 3R + 4Q = 16$, where P, Q and R are positive real numbers, then what is the maximum possible value of $P^3R^3Q^2$?

(a) 1 (b) 2

(c) 4 (d) 8

2012

33. A contractor did not have space in his garage for 8 of his trucks. He, therefore, increased the size of his garage by 50% which gave him space for 8 more trucks than he owned altogether. How many trucks did he own?

(a) 32 (b) 48

(c) 40 (d) 45

34. The list price of an article was increased by 10%. It was then decreased by 10%. If the final price became Rs. 20, then find the initial list price (in Rs.)

(a) $\frac{10 \times 100^2}{100^2 - 20^2}$

(b) $\frac{20^2 \times 10^2}{100^2 - 10^2}$

(c) $\frac{20 \times 100^2}{100^2 - 10^2}$

(d) $20 \times \left(\frac{100^2 - 10^2}{100^2}\right)$

2014

35. There are two factories – A and B – in Kaarobaarnagar. In factory A, the number of male employees is 50% more than that of female employees. In factory B, the number of female employees is 40% less than that of male employees. The number of female employees in factory B is 60 more than that of male employees in factory A. Which of the following cannot be the total number of male employees in the two factories put together?

(a) 204 (b) 180

(c) 320 (d) 300

2017

36. Out of the shirts produced in a factory, 15% are defective, while 20% of the rest are sold in the domestic market. If the remaining 8840 shirts are left for export, then the number of shirts produced in the factory is

(a) 13600 (b) 13000
(c) 13400 (d) 14000

37. In a village, the production of food grains increased by 40% and the per capita production of food grains increased by 27% during a certain period. The percentage by which the population of the village increased during the same period is nearest to

(a) 16 (b) 13
(c) 10 (d) 7

2018 Slot 1

38. In an examination, the maximum possible score is N while the pass mark is 45% of N. A candidate obtains 36 marks, but falls short of the pass mark by 68%. Which one of the following is then correct?

(a) $201 \le N \le 242$. (b) $N \ge 253$.
(c) $N \le 200$. (d) $243 \le N \le 252$.

PROFIT, LOSS AND DISCOUNT

1991

Direction for Question 1: The question is followed by two statements. As the answer,

Mark (a) if the question can be answered with the help of statement I alone,

Mark (b) if the question can be answered with the help of statement II alone,

Mark (c) if both the statement I and statement II are needed to answer the question, and

Mark (d) if the question cannot be answered even with the help of both the statements.

1. Is it more profitable for Company M to produce Q?

I. Product R is sold at a price four times that of Q.

II. One unit of Q requires 2 units of labour, while one unit of R requires 5 units of labour. There is no other constraint on production.

1994

2. A dealer offers a cash discount of 20% and still makes a profit of 20%, when he further allows 16 articles to a dozen to a particularly sticky bargainer. How much percent above the cost price were his wares listed?

(a) 100% (b) 80%
(c) 75% (d) 66 2/3%

Directions for Questions 3 and 4: The question is followed by two statements. As the answer,

Mark (a) if the question can be answered with the help of statement I alone,

Mark (b) if the question can be answered with the help of statement II, alone,

Mark (c) if both, statement I and statement II are needed to answer the question, and

Mark (d) if the question cannot be answered even with the help of both the statements.

3. If the selling price were to be increased by 10%, the sales would reduce by 10%. In what ratio would profits change?

I. The cost price remains constant.

II. The cost price increased 10%.

1995

4. A stockist wants to make some profit by selling sugar. He contemplates about various methods. Which of the following would maximise his profit?

I. Sell sugar at 10% profit.

II. Use 900 g of weight instead of 1 kg.

III. Mix 10% impurities in sugar and selling sugar at cost price.

IV. Increase the price by 5% and reduce weights by 5%.

(a) I or III (b) II
(c) II, III and IV (d) Profits are same

Direction for Question 5: The question is followed by two statements, I and II. Mark the answer as:

(a) if the question can be answered with the help of statement I alone.

(b) if the question can be answered with the help of statement II alone.

(c) if both statement I and statement II are needed to answer the question.

(d) if the question cannot be answered even with the help of both the statements.

5. What is the profit percentage?

I. The cost price is 80% of the selling price.

II. The profit is Rs.50.

1996

6. Instead of a metre scale, a cloth merchant uses a 120 cm scale while buying, but uses an 80 cm scale while selling the same cloth. If he offers a discount of 20% on cash payment, what is his overall profit percentage?

(a) 20% (b) 25%
(c) 40% (d) 15%

Directions for Questions 7 and 8: Answer the questions based on the following information.

A watch dealer incurs an expense of Rs. 150 for producing every watch. He also incurs an additional expenditure of Rs. 30,000, which is independent of the number of watches produced. If he is able to sell a watch during the season, he sells it for Rs. 250. If he fails to do so, he has to sell each watch for Rs. 100.

7. If he is able to sell only 1,200 out of 1,500 watches he has made in the season, then he has made a profit of

(a) Rs. 90,000 (b) Rs. 75,000

(c) Rs. 45,000 (d) Rs. 60,000

8. If he produces 1,500 watches, what is the number of watches that he must sell during the season in order to break-even, given that he is able to sell all the watches produced?

(a) 500 (b) 700

(c) 800 (d) 1,000

9. I sold two watches for Rs. 300 each, one at the loss of 10% and the other at the profit of 10%. What is the percentage of loss(–)or profit(+) that resulted from the transaction?

(a) (+)10 (b) (–)1

(c) (+)1 (d) (–)10

Directions for Questions 10 and 11: Each question is followed by two statements, I and II. Mark the answer as:

(a) if the question cannot be answered even with the help of both the statements taken together.

(b) if the question can be answered by any one of the two statements.

(c) if each statement alone is sufficient to answer the question, but not the other one (E.g. statement I alone is required to answer the question, but not statement II and vice versa).

(d) if both statements I and II together are needed to answer the question.

10. What is the cost price of the article?

I. After selling the article, a loss of 25% on cost price is incurred.

II. The selling price is three-fourths of the cost price.

11. What is the selling price of the article?

I. The profit on sales is 20%.

II. The profit on each unit is 25% and the cost price is Rs. 250.

1997

12. A dealer buys dry fruits at Rs. 100, Rs. 80 and Rs. 60 per kilogram. He mixes them in the ratio 3 : 4 : 5 by weight, and sells at a profit of 50%. At what price per kilogram does he sell the dry fruit?

(a) Rs. 80 (b) Rs. 100

(c) Rs. 95 (d) None of these

13. After allowing a discount of 11.11%, a trader still makes a gain of 14.28%. At how many percentage above the cost price does he mark on his goods?

(a) 28.56%

(b) 35%

(c) 22.22%

(d) None of these

Directions for Questions 14 and 15: Answer the questions based on the following information.

A company purchases components A and B from Germany and USA respectively. A and B form 30% and 50% of the total production cost. Current gain is 20%. Due to change in the international scenario, cost of the German mark increased by 30% and that of USA dollar increased by 22%. Due to market conditions, the selling price cannot be increased beyond 10%.

1998

14. What is the maximum current gain possible?

(a) 10% (b) 12.5%

(c) 0% (d) 7.5%

15. If the USA dollar becomes cheap by 12% over its original cost and the cost of German mark increased by 20%, what will be the gain? (The selling price is not altered.)

(a) 10% (b) 20%

(c) 15% (d) 7.5%

Directions for Questions 16 and 17: The questions is followed by two statements, I and II. Answer the question using the following instructions.

Mark the answer as:

(a) if the question can be answered by one of the statements alone, but cannot be answered by using the other statement alone.

(b) if the question can be answered by using either statement alone.

(c) if the question can be answered by using both the statements together, but cannot be answered by using either statement alone.

(d) if the question cannot be answered even by using both statements together.

2000

16. Harshad bought shares of a company on a certain day, and sold them the next day. While buying and selling he had to pay to the broker 1% of the transaction value of the shares as brokerage. What was the profit earned by him per rupee spent on buying the shares?

I. The sales price per share was 1.05 times that of its purchase price.

II. The number of shares purchased was 100.

2002

17. A dress was initially listed at a price that would have given the store a profit of 20% of the wholesale cost. What was the wholesale cost of the dress?

A. After reducing the listed price by 10%, the dress sold for a net profit of $10.

B. The dress is sold for $50.

Directions for Questions 18 and 19: Answer the questions on the basis of the information given below.

A certain perfume is available at a duty-free shop at the Bangkok international airport. It is priced in the Thai currency Baht but other currencies are also acceptable. In particular, the shop accepts Euro and US Dollar at the following rates of exchange:

US Dollar 1 = 41 Bahts

Euro 1 = 46 Bahts

The perfume is priced at 520 Bahts per bottle. After one bottle is purchased, subsequent bottles are available at a discount of 30%. Three friends S, R and M together purchase three bottles of the perfume, agreeing to share the cost equally. R pays 2 Euros. M pays 4 Euros and 27 Thai Bahts and S pays the remaining amount in US Dollars.

2003(L)

18. How much does R owe to S in Thai Baht?

(a) 428 (b) 416

(c) 334 (d) 324

19. How much does M owe to S in US Dollars?

(a) 3 (b) 4

(c) 5 (d) 6

Directions for Questions 20 and 21: Answer the following questions based on the information given below:

Shabnam is considering three alternatives to invest her surplus cash for a week. She wishes to guarantee maximum returns on her investment. She has three options, each of which can be utilized fully or partially in conjunction with others.

Option A : Invest in a public sector bank. It promises a return of +0.10%.

Option B : Invest in mutual funds of ABC Ltd. A rise in the stock market will result in a return of + 5% while a fall will entail a return of –3%.

Option C: Invest in mutual funds of CBA Ltd. A rise in the stock market will result in a return of –2.5%, while a fall will entail a return of +2%.

20. The maximum guaranteed return to Shabnam is

(a) 0.25% (b) 0.10%

(c) 0.20% (d) 0.15%

(e) 0.30%

21. What strategy will maximize the guaranteed return to Shabnam?

(a) 100% in option A

(b) 36% in option B and 64% in option C

(c) 64% in option B and 36% in option C

(d) 1/3 in each of the three options

(e) 30% in option A, 32% in option B and 38% in option C

MEMORY BASED QUESTIONS

2014

22. A trader used to make 5% profit on an item by selling it at the usual marked price. One day, he tripled the marked price of the item and finally offered a discount of 30%. Find the percentage profit he made on the item that day.

(a) 120.5% (b) 100%

(c) 94.5% (d) None of these

2015

23. A shopkeeper sold 10 items, all of which are of the same cost price, such that profit percentage on no two item is the same. The profits made on the given items were in an arithmetic progression. If the profit percentage of the item the selling price of which is 4th highest and the item the selling price of which is 7th highest were 13 % and 10 % respectively, find the profit percentage on the whole.

(a) 11.5%

(b) 12%

(c) 12.5%

(d) Data insufficient

2016

24. The percentage profit earned by selling an article at Rs.1,920 is equal to the percentage loss incurred by selling the same article at Rs.1,280. At what price (in Rs.) should the article be sold to make a profit of 25%?

2017

25. The manufacturer of a table sells it to a wholesale dealer at a profit of 10%. The wholesale dealer sells the table to a retailer at a profit of 30%. Finally, the retailer sells it to a customer at a profit of 50%. If the customer pays Rs.4290 for the table, then its manufacturing cost (in Rs) is

(a) 1500 (b) 2000

(c) 2500 (d) 3000

26. Mayank buys some candies for Rs.15 a dozen and an equal number of different candies for Rs.12 a dozen. He sells all for Rs.16.50 a dozen and makes a profit of Rs.150. How many dozens of candies did he buy altogether?

(a) 50 (b) 30

(c) 25 (d) 45

2018 Slot 1

27. A wholesaler bought walnuts and peanuts, the price of walnut per kg being thrice that of peanut per kg. He then sold 8 kg of peanuts at a profit of 10% and 16 kg of walnuts at a profit of 20% to a shopkeeper. However, the shopkeeper lost 5 kg of walnuts and 3 kg of peanuts in transit. He then mixed the remaining nuts and sold the mixture at Rs. 166 per kg, thus making an overall profit of 25%. At what price, in Rs. per kg, did the wholesaler buy the walnuts?

(a) 98 (b) 86

(c) 84 (d) 96

RATIO AND PROPORTION

1991

1. An outgoing batch of students wants to gift PA system worth Rs.4200 to their school. If the teachers offer to pay 50% more than the students, and an external benefactor gives three times teachers' contribution, how much should the teachers donate?

(a) 600 (b) 840

(c) 900 (d) 1200

1993

2. From each of the two given numbers, half the smaller number is subtracted. Of the resulting numbers the larger one is three times as large as the smaller. What is the ratio of the two numbers?

(a) 2 : 1

(b) 3 : 1

(c) 3 : 2

(d) None

1996

3. The cost of diamond varies directly as the square of its weight. Once, this diamond broke into four pieces with weights in the ratio 1 : 2 : 3 : 4. When the pieces were sold, the merchant got Rs. 70,000 less. Find the original price of the diamond.

(a) Rs. 1.4 lakh (b) Rs. 2 lakh

(c) Rs. 1 lakh (d) Rs. 2.1 lakh

Direction for Question 4: The question is followed by two statements, I and II. Mark the answer as:

(a) if the question cannot be answered even with the help of both the statements taken together.

(b) if the question can be answered by any one of the two statements.

(c) if each statement alone is sufficient to answer the question, but not the other one (E.g. statement I alone is required to answer the question, but not statement II and vice versa).

(d) if both statements I and II together are needed to answer the question.

4. What is the number of type-2 widgets produced, if the total number of widgets produced is 20,000?

I. If the production of type-1 widgets increases by 10% and that of type-2 decreases by 6%, the total production remains the same.

II. The ratio in which type-1 and type-2 widgets are produced is 2 : 1.

1997

5. A student gets an aggregate of 60% marks in five subjects in the ratio 10 : 9 : 8 : 7 : 6. If the passing marks are 50% of the maximum marks and each subject has the same maximum marks, in how many subjects did he pass the examination?

(a) 2 (b) 3

(c) 4 (d) 5

6. The value of each of a set of coins varies as the square of its diameter, if its thickness remains constant, and it varies as the thickness, if the diameter remains constant. If the diameter of two coins are in the ratio 4 : 3, what should be the ratio of their thickness if the value of the first is four times that of the second?

(a) 16 : 9 (b) 9 : 4

(c) 9 : 16 (d) 4 : 9

1998

7. A yearly payment to the servant is Rs. 90 plus one turban. The servant leaves the job after 9 months and receives Rs. 65 and a turban. Then find the price of the turban.

(a) Rs. 10 (b) Rs. 15

(c) Rs. 7.50 (d) Cannot be determined

8. I have one-rupee coins, 50-paisa coins and 25-paisa coins. The number of coins are in the ratio 2.5 : 3 : 4. If the total amount with me is Rs. 210, find the number of one-rupee coins.

(a) 90 (b) 85

(c) 100 (d) 105

Direction for Question 9: The question is followed by two statements, I and II. Answer the question based on the statements and mark the answer as:

(a) if the question can be answered with the help of any one statement alone but not by the other statement.

(b) if the question can be answered with the help of either of the statements taken individually.

(c) if the question can be answered with the help of both statements together.

(d) if the question cannot be answered even with the help of both statements together.

9. What is the value of 'a'?

I. Ratio of a and b is 3 : 5, where b is positive.

II. Ratio of 2a and b is $\frac{12}{10}$, where a is positive.

1999

10. The speed of a railway engine is 42 kmph when no compartment is attached, and the reduction in speed is directly proportional to the square root of the number of compartments attached. If the speed of the train carried by this engine is 24 kmph when 9 compartments are attached, the maximum number of compartments that can be carried by the engine is

(a) 49 (b) 48

(c) 46 (d) 47

Directions for Questions 11 and 12: Answer the questions based on the following information.

Rajiv reaches city B from city A in 4 hours, driving at speed of 35 kmph for the first two hour and at 45 kmph for the next two hours. Aditi follows the same route, but drives at three different speeds: 30, 40 and 50 kmph, covering an equal distance in each speed segment. The two cars are similar with petrol consumption characteristics (km per litre)shown in the figure below.

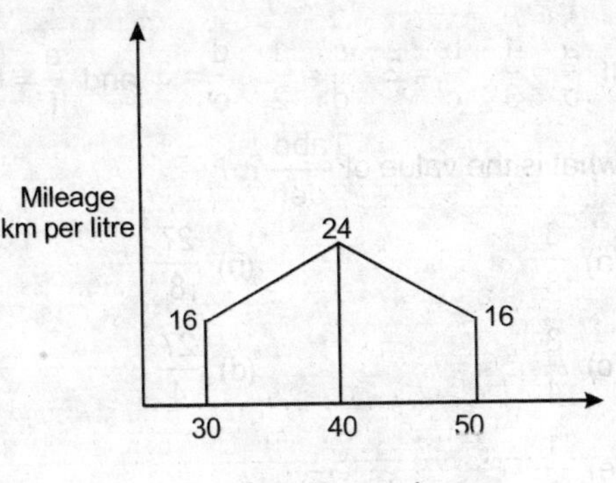

11. The quantity of petrol consumed by Aditi for the journey is

(a) 8.3 l (b) 8.6 l

(c) 8.9 l (d) 9.2 l

12. Zoheb would like to drive Aditi's car over the same route from A to B and minimize the petrol consumption for the trip. What is the quantity of petrol required by him?

(a) 6.67 l (b) 7 l

(c) 6.33 l (d) 6.0 l

2001

13. Fresh grapes contain 90% water by weight while dried grapes contain 20% water by weight. What is the weight of dry grapes available from 20 kg of fresh grapes?

(a) 2 kg (b) 2.4 kg

(c) 2.5 kg (d) None of these

2002

14. Three travellers are sitting around a fire, and are about to eat a meal. One of them has 5 small loaves of bread, the second has 3 small loaves of bread. The third has no food, but has 8 coins. He offers to pay for some bread. They agree to share the 8 loaves equally among the three travellers, and the third traveller will pay 8 coins for his share of the 8 loaves. All loaves were the same size. The second traveller (who had 3 loaves) suggests that he will be paid 3 coins, and that the first traveller be paid 5 coins. The first traveller says that he should get more than 5 coins. How much should the first traveller get?

(a) 5 (b) 7

(c) 1 (d) None of these

15. If pqr = 1, the value of the expression

$$\frac{1}{1+p+q^{-1}}+\frac{1}{1+q+r^{-1}}+\frac{1}{1+r+p^{-1}}$$ is equal to

(a) p + q + r (b) $\frac{1}{p+q+r}$

(c) 1 (d) $p^{-1}+q^{-1}+r^{-1}$

16. Flights A and B are scheduled from an airport within the next one hour. All the booked passengers of the two flights are waiting in the boarding hall after check-in. The hall has a seating capacity of 200, out of which 10% remained vacant. 40% of the waiting passengers are ladies. When boarding announcement came, passengers of flight A left the hall and boarded the flight. Seating capacity of each flight is two-third of the passengers who waited in the waiting hall for both the flights put together. Half the passengers who boarded flight A are women. After boarding for flight A, 60% of the waiting hall seats became empty. For every twenty of those who are still waiting in the hall for flight B, there is one air hostess in flight A. What is the ratio of empty seats in flight B to the number of air hostesses in flight A?

(a) 10 : 1 (b) 5 : 1
(c) 20 : 1 (d) 1 : 1

Direction for Question 17: The question is followed by two statements, A and B. Answer each question using the following instructions.

Choose (a) if the question can be answered by one of the statements alone but not by the other.

Choose (b) if the question can be answered by using either statement alone.

Choose (c) if the question can be answered by using both the statements together, but cannot be answered by using either statement alone.

Choose (d) if the question cannot be answered even by using both statements together.

17. A sum of Rs. 38,500 was divided among Jagdish, Punit and Girish. Who received the minimum amount?

A. Jagdish received $\frac{2}{9}$ of what Punit and Girish received together.

B. Punit received $\frac{3}{11}$ of what Jagdish and Girish received together.

2003(R)

18. Let a, b, c, d and e be integers such that a = 6b = 12c, and 2b = 9d = 12 e. Then which of the following pairs contains a number that is not an integer?

(a) $\left(\frac{a}{27}, \frac{b}{e}\right)$ (b) $\left(\frac{a}{36}, \frac{c}{e}\right)$

(c) $\left(\frac{a}{12}, \frac{bd}{18}\right)$ (d) $\left(\frac{a}{6}, \frac{c}{d}\right)$

19. In a coastal village, every year floods destroy exactly half of the huts. After the flood water recedes, twice the number of huts destroyed are rebuilt. The floods occurred consecutively in the last three years — 2001, 2002 and 2003. If floods are expected again in 2004, the number of huts expected to be destroyed is

(a) less than the number of huts existing at the beginning of 2001

(b) less than the total number of huts destroyed by floods in 2001 and 2003

(c) less than the total number of huts destroyed by floods in 2002 and 2003

(d) more than the total number of huts built in 2001 and 2002

Direction for Question 20: The question is followed by two statements, A and B. Answer the question using the following instructions:

Choose (a) if the question can be answered by using statement A alone but not by using B alone.

Choose (b) if the question can be answered by using statement B alone but not by using A alone.

Choose (c) if the question can be answered by using either statement alone and

Choose (d) if the question can be answered using both the statements together but not by either statement alone.

20. The members of a local club contributed equally to pay Rs. 600 towards a donation. How much did each one pay?

A. If there had been five fewer members, each one would have paid an additional Rs. 10.

B. There were at least 20 members in the club, and each one paid not more than Rs. 30.

2004

21. If $\frac{a}{b+c} = \frac{b}{c+a} = \frac{c}{a+b} = r$ then r cannot take any value except

(a) $\frac{1}{2}$ (b) –1

(c) $\frac{1}{2}$ or – 1 (d) $-\frac{1}{2}$ or – 1

2006

22. If $\frac{a}{b} = \frac{1}{3}$, $\frac{b}{c} = 2$, $\frac{c}{d} = \frac{1}{2}$, $\frac{d}{e} = 3$ and $\frac{e}{f} = \frac{1}{4}$, then what is the value of $\frac{abc}{def}$?

(a) $\frac{3}{8}$ (b) $\frac{27}{8}$

(c) $\frac{3}{4}$ (d) $\frac{27}{4}$

(e) $\frac{1}{4}$

23. The number of employees in Obelix Menhir Co. is a prime number and is less than 300. The ratio of the number of employees who are graduates and above, to that of employees who are not, can possibly be:
(a) 101 : 88 (b) 87 : 100
(c) 110 : 111 (d) 85 : 98
(e) 97 : 84

MEMORY BASED QUESTIONS

2012

24. Three men are gambling in Casino Royal. They start with sums of money in the ratio 7 : 6 : 5 and finish with sums of money in the ratio 6 : 5 : 4, in the same order as before. One of them won $ 12. How many dollars did he start with ? [The three men gambled amongst each other only]
(a) $1080 (b) $420
(c) $210 (d) None of these

2013

25. The ratio of alcohol to water in an alcohol-water solution is 9 : 1. The rate of evaporation per hour of alcohol and water on boiling is 20% and 5% respectively. The minimum number of hours for which the solution needs to be boiled so as it contains at least 18% of water?
(a) 3 (b) 4
(c) 3.5 (d) 4.5

2016

26. If $4x + 3y : y - 6x :: 14 : 1$, then find the value of $\frac{2x}{y}$.
(a) $\frac{1}{2}$ (b) $\frac{1}{4}$
(c) 2 (d) 4

2017

27. If a, b, c are three positive integers such that a and b are in the ratio 3 : 4 while b and c are in the ratio 2:1, then which one of the following is a possible value of (a + b + c)?
(a) 201 (b) 205
(c) 207 (d) 210

2018 Slot 1

28. Raju and Lalitha originally had marbles in the ratio 4:9. Then Lalitha gave some of her marbles to Raju. As a result, the ratio of the number of marbles with Raju to that with Lalitha became 5:6. What fraction of her original number of marbles was given by Lalitha to Raju?
(a) $\frac{1}{4}$ (b) $\frac{1}{5}$
(c) $\frac{6}{19}$ (d) $\frac{7}{33}$

2018 Slot 2

29. The scores of Amal and Bimal in an examination are in the ratio 11 : 14. After an appeal, their scores increase by the same amount and their new scores are in the ratio 47 : 56. The ratio of Bimal's new score to that of his original score is
(a) 4 : 3 (b) 3 : 2
(c) 5 : 4 (d) 8 : 5

AVERAGE

1991

Directions for Questions 1 to 3: Each of these items has a question followed by two statements. As the answer,
Mark (a) if the question can be answered with the help of statement I alone,
Mark (b) if the question can be answered with the help of statement II alone,
Mark (c) if both the statement I and statement II are needed to answer the question, and
Mark (d) if the question cannot be answered even with the help of both the statements.

1. The average of three unequal quotations for a particular share is Rs.110. If all are quoted in integral values of rupee, does the highest quotation exceed Rs.129?
I. The lowest quotation is Rs.100.
II. One of the quotations is Rs.115.

1993

2. Is the average of the largest and the smallest of four given numbers greater than the average of the four numbers?
I. The difference between the largest and the second largest numbers is greater than the difference between the second smallest and the smallest numbers.
II. The difference between the largest and the second largest numbers is less than the difference between the second largest and the second smallest numbers.

1994

3. What is the average weight of the 3 new team members who are recently included into the team?
I. The average weight of the team increases by 20 kg.
II. The 3 new men substitute earlier members whose weights are 64 kg, 75 kg and 66 kg.

Directions for Questions 4 to 6: Answer the questions based on the following information.

There are 60 students in a class. These students are divided into three groups A, B and C of 15, 20 and 25 students each. The groups A and C are combined to form group D.

1997

4. What is the average weight of the students in group D?
   (a) More than the average weight of A
   (b) More than the average weight of C
   (c) Less than the average weight of C
   (d) Cannot be determined
5. If one student from group A is shifted to group B, which of the following will be true?
   (a) The average weight of both groups increases
   (b) The average weight of both the groups decreases
   (c) The average weight of the class remains the same
   (d) Cannot be determined
6. If all the students of the class have the same weight, then which of the following is false?
   (a) The average weight of all the four groups is the same
   (b) The total weight of A and C is twice the total weight of B
   (c) The average weight of D is greater than the average weight of A
   (d) The average weight of all the groups remains the same even if a number of students are shifted from one group to another
7. The average marks of a student in 10 papers are 80. If the highest and the lowest scores are not considered, the average is 81. If his highest score is 92, find the lowest.
   (a) 55 (b) 60
   (c) 62 (d) Cannot be determined

1999

8. Total expenses of a boarding house are partly fixed and partly varying linearly with the number of boarders. The average expense per boarder is Rs. 700 when there are 25 boarders and Rs. 600 when there are 50 boarders. What is the average expense (in Rs.)per boarder when there are 100 boarders?
   (a) 550 (b) 580
   (c) 540 (d) 570

Direction for Question 9: The question is followed by two statements I and II.

Mark:

(a) if the question can be answered by any one of the statements alone, but cannot be answered by using the other statement alone.
(b) if the question can be answered by using either statement alone.
(c) if the question can be answered by using both the statements together, but cannot be answered by using either statement alone.
(d) if the question cannot be answered even by using both the statements together.

9. The average weight of students in a class is 50 kg. What is the number of students in the class?
   I. The heaviest and the lightest members of the class weigh 60 kg and 40 kg respectively.
   II. Exclusion of the heaviest and the lightest members from the class does not change the average weight of the students.

2000

10. Consider a sequence of seven consecutive integers. The average of the first five integers is n. The average of all the seven integers is
    (a) n
    (b) n + 1
    (c) k × n, where k is a function of n
    (d) $n + \left(\frac{2}{7}\right)$
11. A shipping clerk has five boxes of different but unknown weights each weighing less than 100 kg. The clerk weights the boxes in pairs. The weights obtained are 110, 112, 113, 114, 115, 116, 117, 118, 120 and 121 kg. What is the weight of the heaviest box?
    (a) 60 kg (b) 62 kg
    (c) 64 kg (d) Cannot be determined

2001

12. A student took five papers in an examination, where the full marks were the same for each paper. His marks in these papers were in the proportion of 6 : 7 : 8 : 9 : 10. In all papers together, the candidate obtained 60% of the total marks. Then the number of papers in which he got more than 50% marks is
    (a) 2 (b) 3
    (c) 4 (d) 5
13. A college has raised 75% of the amount it needs for a new building by receiving an average donation of Rs. 600 from the people already solicited. The people already solicited represent 60% of the people the college will ask for donations. If the college is to raise exactly the amount needed for the new building, what should be the average donation from the remaining people to be solicited?
    (a) Rs. 300 (b) Rs. 250
    (c) Rs. 400 (d) Rs. 500

14. Three classes X, Y and Z take an algebra test.

The average score in class X is 83.

The average score in class Y is 76.

The average score in class Z is 85.

The average score of all students in classes X and Y together is 79.

The average score of all students in classes Y and Z together is 81.

What is the average for all the three classes?

(a) 81 (b) 81.5
(c) 82 (d) 84.5

15. A set of consecutive positive integers beginning with 1 is written on the blackboard. A student came along and erased one number. The average of the remaining numbers is $35\frac{7}{17}$. What was the number erased?

(a) 7 (b) 8
(c) 9 (d) None of these

2002

16. Amol was asked to calculate the arithmetic mean of 10 positive integers, each of which had 2 digits. By mistake, he interchanged the 2 digits, say a and b, in one of these 10 integers. As a result, his answer for the arithmetic mean was 1.8 more than what it should have been. Then b – a equals

(a) 1 (b) 2
(c) 3 (d) None of these

Direction for Question 17: The question is followed by two statements, A and B. Answer the question using the following instructions.

Choose (a) if the question can be answered by one of the statements alone but not by the other.

Choose (b) if the question can be answered by uçing either statement alone.

Choose (c) if the question can be answered by using both the statements together, but cannot be answered by using either statement alone.

Choose (d) if the question cannot be answered even by using both statements together.

17. Is 500 the average (arithmetic mean) score in the GMAT?

A. Half of the people who take the GMAT score above 500 and half of the people score below 500.

B. The highest GMAT score is 800 and the lowest score is 200.

2007

18. Ten years ago, the ages of the members of a joint family of eight people added up to 231 years. Three years later, one member died at the age of 60 years and a child was born during the same year. After another three years, one more member died, again at 60, and a child was born during the same year. The current average age of this eight-member joint family is nearest to

(a) 23 years (b) 22 years
(c) 21 years (d) 25 years
(e) 24 years

Direction for Question 19: The question is followed by two statements A and B. Indicate your response based on the following directives.

Mark (a) if the questions can be answered using A alone but not using B alone.

Mark (b) if the question can be answered using B alone but not using A alone.

Mark (c) if the question can be answered using A and B together, but not using either A or B alone.

Mark (d) if the question cannot be answered even using A and B together.

19. The average weight of a class of 100 students is 45 kg. The class consists of two sections, I and II, each with 50 students. The average weight, W_I, of Section I is smaller than the average weight W_{II}, of the Section II. If the heaviest student say Deepak, of section II is moved to Section I, and the lightest student, say Poonam, of Section I is moved to Section II, then the average weights of the two sections are switched, i.e., the average weight of Section I becomes W_{II} and that of Section II becomes W_I. What is the woight of Poonam?

A: $W_{II} - W_I = 1.0$.

B: Moving Deepak from Section II to I (without any move I to II)makes the average weights of the two sections equal.

2016

20. During a fundraiser event for the elderly people, apart from all the members of the organising committee, a huge number of volunteers also donated some amount for the noble cause. The members of the organising committee made an average contribution of Rs.1,100 and this sum comprised 88% of the total amount raised through the event. The number of members in the organising committee was 40% more than the number of volunteers. Find the average contribution (in Rs.) made by the volunteers.

2017

21. The average height of 22 toddlers increases by 2 inches when two of them leave this group. If the average height of these two toddlers is one-third the average height of the original 22, then the average height, in inches, of the remaining 20 toddlers is

(1) 30 (2) 23
(3) 32 (4) 26

2018 Slot 1

22. A CAT aspirant appears for a certain number of tests. His average score increases by 1 if the first 10 tests are not considered, and decreases by 1 if the last 10 tests are not considered. If his average scores for the first 10 and the last 10 tests are 20 and 30, respectively, then the total number of tests taken by him is

23. In an apartment complex, the number of people aged 51 years and above is 30 and there are at most 39 people whose ages are below 51 years. The average age of all the people in the apartment complex is 38 years. What is the largest possible average age, in years, of the people whose ages are below 51 years?

(1) 26 (2) 25
(3) 28 (4) 27

2018 Slot 2

24. The arithmetic mean of x, y and z is 80, and that of x, y, z, u and v is 75, where $u = (x + y)/2$ and $v = (y + z)/2$. If $x \geq z$, then the minimum possible value of x is

SIMPLE INTEREST AND COMPOUND INTEREST

1991

1. A sum of money compounded annually becomes Rs.625 in two years and Rs.675 in three years. The rate of interest per annum is

(a) 7% (b) 8%
(c) 6% (d) 5%

Direction for Question 2 : The question is followed by two statements. As the answer,

Mark (a) if the question can be answered with the help of statement I alone,

Mark (b) if the question can be answered with the help of statement II, alone,

Mark (c) if both, statement I and statement II are needed to answer the question, and

Mark (d) if the question cannot be answered even with the help of both the statements.

1994

2. Little Beau Peep lost her sheep. She couldn't remember how many were there. She knew she would have 400 more next year, than the number of sheep she had last year. How many sheep were there?

I. The number of sheep last year was 20% more than the year before that and this simple rate of increase continues to be the same for the next 10 years.

II. The increase is compounded annually.

1995

3. Ram purchased a flat at Rs.1 lakh and Prem purchased a plot of land worth Rs.1.1 lakh. The respective annual rates at which the prices of the flat and the plot increased were 10% and 5%. After two years they exchanged their belongings and one paid the other the difference. Then

(a) Ram paid Rs.275 to Prem
(b) Ram paid Rs.475 to Prem
(c) Ram paid Rs.375 to Prem
(d) Prem paid Rs.475 to Ram

4. A man invests Rs.3,000 at the rate of 5% per annum. How much more should he invest at the rate of 8%, so that he can earn a total of 6% per annum?

(a) Rs.1,200 (b) Rs.1,300
(c) Rs.1,500 (d) Rs.2,000

Direction for Question 5 : The question is followed by two statements. As the answer, mark

(a) if the question cannot be answered even with the help of both the statements taken together.

(b) if the question can be answered by any one of the two statements.

(c) if each statement alone is sufficient to answer the question, but not the other one (E.g. statement I alone is required to answer the question, but not statement II and vice versa).

(d) if both statements I and II together are needed to answer the question.

1996

5. What is the total worth of Lakhiram's assets?

I. A compound interest at 10% on his assets, followed by a tax of 4% on the interest, fetches him Rs. 1,500 this year.

II. The interest is compounded once every four months.

Direction for Question 6: The question is followed by two statements, I and II.

Mark

(a) if the question can be answered by one of the statements alone and not by the other.

(b) if the question can be answered by using either statement alone.

(c) if the question can be answered by using both the statements together, but cannot be answered by using either statement alone.

(d) if the question cannot be answered even by using both statements together.

2001

6. Is Country X's GDP higher than country Y's GDP?
   I. GDPs of the countries X and Y have grown over the past 5 years at compounded annual rate of 5% and 6% respectively.
   II. Five years ago, GDP of country X was higher than that of country Y.

MEMORY BASED QUESTIONS

2015

7. An amount borrowed at simple interest gets tripled in 24 years. How many years does it take to get doubled, if the interest rate is same.

2018 Slot 1

8. John borrowed Rs. 2,10,000 from a bank at an interest rate of 10% per annum, compounded annually. The loan was repaid in two equal instalments, the first after one year and the second after another year. The first instalment was interest of one year plus part of the principal amount, while the second was the rest of the principal amount plus due interest thereon. Then each instalment, in Rs., is

2018 Slot 2

9. Gopal borrows Rs. X from Ankit at 8% annual interest. He then adds Rs. Y of his own money and lends Rs. X + Y to Ishan at 10% annual interest. At the end of the year, after returning Ankit's dues, the net interest retained by Gopal is the same as that accrued to Ankit. On the other hand, had Gopal lent Rs. X + 2Y to Ishan at 10%, then the net interest retained by him would have increased by Rs. 150. If all interests are compounded annually, then find the value of X + Y.

MIXTURE AND SOLUTIONS

1. A man buys spirit at Rs. 60 per litre, adds water to it and then sells it at Rs. 75 per litre. What is the ratio of spirit to water if his profit in the deal is 37.5%?

   (a) 9 : 1 (b) 10 : 1
   (c) 11 : 1 (d) None of these

2. Two liquids A and B are in the ratio 5 : 1 in container 1 and 1 : 3 in container 2. In what ratio should the contents of the two containers be mixed so as to obtain a mixture of A and B in the ratio 1 : 1?

   (a) 2 : 3 (b) 4 : 3
   (c) 3 : 2 (d) 3 : 4

Direction for Question 3: The question is followed by two statements, I and II. Mark the answer as:

(a) if the question cannot be answered even with the help of both the statements taken together.

(b) if the question can be answered by any one of the two statements.

(c) if each statement alone is sufficient to answer the question, but not the other one (E.g. statement I alone is required to answer the question, but not statement II and vice versa).

(d) if both statements I and II together are needed to answer the question.

1996

3. What is the ratio of the two liquids A and B in the mixture finally, if these two liquids kept in three vessels are mixed together? (The containers are of equal volume.)
   I. The ratio of liquid A to liquid B in the first and second vessel is 3 : 5, 2 : 3 respectively.
   II. The ratio of liquid A to liquid B in vessel 3 is 4 : 3.

1998

4. There are two containers: the first contains 500 ml of alcohol, while the second contains 500 ml of water. Three cups of alcohol from the first container is taken out and is mixed well in the second container. Then three cups of this mixture is taken out and is mixed in the first container. Let A denote the proportion of water in the first container and B denote the proportion of alcohol in the second container. Then

   (a) A > B (b) A < B
   (c) A = B (d) Cannot be determined

2004

5. A milkman mixes 20 litres of water with 80 litres of milk. After selling one-fourth of this mixture, he adds water to replenish the quantity that he had sold. What is the current proportion of water to milk?

   (a) 2 : 3 (b) 1 : 2
   (c) 1 : 3 (d) 3 : 4

MEMORY BASED QUESTIONS

2011

6. From a vessel containing 160 litres of milk, 'x' litres is drained out and replaced with water. Then 'x' litres of milk-water solution is drained out and replaced with water. If the quantity of milk left in the vessel is 90 litres, then what is the value of 'x'?

(a) 30 (b) 40
(c) 36 (d) 35

2014

7. An empty metal container (without its handle) weighs 15% of what it weighs when completely filled with a particular liquid. After adding the handle, the weight of the fully filled container increases by 5%. If the weight of a partly filled container is $\frac{1}{3}$ of the completely filled container with the handle attached, then what fraction of container is utilized?

(a) $\frac{4}{17}$ (b) $\frac{3}{17}$
(c) $\frac{6}{19}$ (d) $\frac{3}{19}$

8. The percentage volumes of milk in three solutions A, B and C form a geometric progression in that order. If we mix the first, second and third solutions in the ratio 2 : 3 : 4, by volume, we obtain a solution containing 32% milk. If we mix them in the ratio 3 : 2 : 1, by volume, we obtain a solution containing 22% milk. What is the percentage of milk in A?

(a) 6% (b) 12%
(c) 18% (d) 24%

2015

9. From a vessel completely filled up with pure wine, 140 litres of content is removed and replaced with equal quantity of water. The process is repeated one more time. In a 98 litres sample of the resulting solution 80 litres is water. Find the capacity (in litres) of the vessel.

2016

10. A 100 ml flask contains 30% acid solution. What quantity of the solution should be replaced with 12% acid solution so that the resultant solution contains 21% acid?

(a) 50 ml
(b) 44.44 ml
(c) 33.33 ml
(d) 64 ml

2017

11. Bottle 1 contains a mixture of milk and water in 7 : 2 ratio and Bottle 2 contains a mixture of milk and water in 9 : 4 ratio. In what ratio of volumes should the liquids in Bottle 1 and Bottle 2 be combined to obtain a mixture of milk and water in 3 : 1 ratio?

(a) 27 : 14 (b) 27 : 13
(c) 27 : 16 (d) 27 : 18

12. Consider three mixtures - the first having water and liquid A in the ratio 1 : 2, the second having water and liquid B in the ratio 1 : 3, and the third having water and liquid C in the ratio 1 : 4. These three mixtures of A, B, and C, respectively, are further mixed in the proportion 4 : 3 : 2. Then the resulting mixture has

(a) The same amount of water and liquid B
(b) The same amount of liquids B and C
(c) More water than liquid B
(d) More water than liquid A

2018 Slot 1

13. Two types of tea, A and B, are mixed and then sold at Rs. 40 per kg. The profit is 10% if A and B are mixed in the ratio 3 : 2, and 5% if this ratio is 2 : 3. The cost prices, per kg, of A and B are in the ratio

(a) 21 : 25 (b) 19 : 24
(c) 18 : 25 (d) 17 : 25

14. A trader sells 10 litres of a mixture of paints A and B, where the amount of B in the mixture does not exceed that of A. The cost of paint A per litre is Rs. 8 more than that of paint B. If the trader sells the entire mixture for Rs. 264 and makes a profit of 10%, then the highest possible cost of paint B, in Rs. per litre, is

(a) 16
(b) 20
(c) 22
(d) 26

2018 Slot 2

15. A 20% ethanol solution is mixed with another ethanol solution, say, S of unknown concentration in the proportion 1:3 by volume. This mixture is then mixed with an equal volume of 20% ethanol solution. If the resultant mixture is a 31.25% ethanol solution, then the unknown concentration of S is

(a) 50%
(b) 48%
(c) 55%
(d) 52%

16. The strength of a salt solution is p% if 100 ml of the solution contains p grams of salt. If three salt solutions A, B, C are mixed in the proportion 1 : 2 : 3, then the resulting solution has strength 20%. If instead the proportion is 3 : 2 : 1, then the resulting solution has strength 30%. A fourth solution, D, is produced by mixing B and C in the ratio 2 : 7. The ratio of the strength of D to that of A is

(a) 1 : 3 (b) 3 : 10

(c) 2 : 5 (d) 1 : 4

17. A jar contains a mixture of 175 ml water and 700 ml alcohol. Gopal takes out 10% of the mixture and substitutes it by water of the same amount. The process is repeated once again. The percentage of water in the mixture is now

(a) 20.5 (b) 25.4

(c) 35.2 (d) 30.3

18. There are two drums, each containing a mixture of paints A and B. In drum 1, A and B are in the ratio 18 : 7. The mixtures from drums 1 and 2 are mixed in the ratio 3 : 4 and in this final mixture, A and B are in the ratio 13 : 7. In drum 2, then A and B were in the ratio

(a) 220 : 149 (b) 251 : 163

(c) 229 : 141 (d) 239 : 161

TIME SPEED AND DISTANCE

1990

1. A car after traveling 18 km from a point A developed some problem in the engine and speed became 4/5 of its original speed. As a result, the car reached point B 45 minutes late. If the engine had developed the same problem after traveling 30 km from A, then it would have reached B only 36 minutes late. The original speed of the car (in km per hour) and the distance between the points A and B (in km.) is

(a) 25, 130 (b) 30,150

(c) 20, 90 (d) None of these

2. Two trains are traveling in opposite direction at uniform speed 60 and 50 km per hour respectively. They take 5 seconds to cross each other. If the two trains had traveled in the same direction, then a passenger sitting in the faster moving train would have overtaken the other train in 18 seconds. What are the lengths of trains (in metres)?

(a) 112, 78

(b) 97.78, 55

(c) 102.78, 50

(d) 102.78, 55

Directions for Questions 3 to 6 : Each of the following questions is followed by two statements. MARK,

(a) if the question can be answered with the help of statement I alone,

(b) if the question can be answered with the help of statement II alone,

(c) if both, statement I and statement II are needed to answer the question, and

(d) if the statement cannot be answered even with the help of both the statements.

3. Ramu went by car from Calcutta to Trivandrum via Madras, without any stoppages. The average speeds for the entire journey was 40 kmph. What was the average speed from Madras to Trivandrum?

I. The distance from Madras to Trivandrum is 0.30 times the distance from Calcutta to Madras.

II. The average speed from Madras to Trivandrum was twice that of the average speed from Calcutta to Madras.

4. How long did Mr. X take to cover 5000 km journey with 10 stopovers?

I. The ith stopover lasted i^2 minutes.

II. The average speed between any two stopovers was 66 kmph.

1991

5. A train started from Station A, developed engine trouble and reached Station B, 40 minutes late. What is the distance between Stations A and B?

I. The engine trouble developed after travelling 40 km from Station A and the speed reduced to $\frac{1}{4}$th of the original speed.

II. The engine trouble developed after travelling 40 km from station A in two hours and the speed reduced to $\frac{1}{4}$th of the original speed.

6. What is the time difference between New York and London?

I. The departure time at New York is exactly 9.00 a.m. local time and the arrival time at London is at 10.00 a.m. local time.

II. The flight time is 5 hours.

7. Every day Neera's husband meets her at the city railway station at 6.00 p.m. and drives her to their residence. One day she left early from the office and reached the railway station at 5.00 p.m. She started walking towards her home, met her husband coming from their residence on the way and they reached home 10 minutes earlier than the usual time. For how long did she walk?

(a) 1 hour (b) 50 minutes

(c) ½ hour (d) 55 minutes

Directions for Questions 8 to 10 : Use the following information:

Q started to move from point B towards point A exactly an hour after P started from A in the opposite direction. Q's speed was twice that of P. When P had covered one-sixth of the distance between the points A and B, Q had also covered the same distance.

1993

8. The point where P and Q would meet is
(a) Closer to A
(b) Exactly between A and B
(c) Closer to B
(d) P and Q will not meet at all

9. How many hours would P take to reach B?
(a) 2 (b) 5
(c) 6 (d) 12

10. How many more hours would P (compared to Q) take to complete his journey?
(a) 4 (b) 5
(c) 6 (d) 7

11. A ship leave on a long voyage. When it is 18 miles from the shore, a seaplane, whose speed is ten times that of the ship, is sent to deliver mail. How far from the shore does the seaplane catch up with the ship?
(a) 24 miles (b) 25 miles
(c) 22 miles (d) 20 miles

1994

12. Shyam went from Delhi to Shimla via Chandigarh by car. The distance from Delhi to Chandigarh is $\frac{3}{4}$ times the distance from Chandigarh to Shimla. The average speed from Delhi to Chandigarh was half as much again as that from Chandigarh to Shimla. If the average speed for the entire journey was 49 kmph. What was the average speed from Chandigarh to Shimla?
(a) 39.2 kmph (b) 63 kmph
(c) 42 kmph (d) None of these

13. A and B walk from X to Y, a distance of 27 km at 5 kmph and 7 kmph respectively. B reaches Y and immediately turns back meeting A at Z. What is the distance from X to Z?
(a) 25 km (b) 22.5 km
(c) 24 km (d) 20 km

14. The winning relay team in a high school sports competition clocked 48 minutes for a distance of 13.2 km. Its runners A, B, C and D maintained speeds of 15 kmph, 16 kmph, 17 kmph, and 18 kmph respectively. What is the ratio of the time taken by B to than taken by D?
(a) 5 : 16 (b) 5 : 17
(c) 9 : 8 (d) 8 : 9

Direction for Question 15: The question is followed by two statements. As the answer,

Mark (a) if the question can be answered with the help of statement I alone,
Mark (b) if the question can be answered with the help of statement II, alone,
Mark (c) if both, statement I and statement II are needed to answer the question, and
Mark (d) if the question cannot be answered even with the help of both the statements.

15. Is the distance from the office to home less than the distance from the cinema hall to home?
I. The time taken to travel from home to office is as much as the time taken from home to the cinema hall, both distance being covered without stopping.
II. The road from the cinema hall to home is bad and speed reduces, as compared to that on the road from home to the office.

1995

16. In a race of 200 m run, A beats S by 20 m and N by 40 m. If S and N are running a race of 100 m with exactly same speed as before, then by how many metres will S beat N?
(a) 11.11 m (b) 10 m
(c) 12 m (d) 25 m

17. I live X floors above the ground floor of a high-rise building. It takes me 30 s per floor to walk down the steps and 2 s per floor to ride the lift. What is X, if the time taken to walk down the steps to the ground floor is the same as to wait for the lift for 7 min and then ride down?
(a) 4 (b) 7
(c) 14 (d) 15

18. A man can walk up a moving 'up' escalator in 30 s. The same man can walk down this moving 'up' escalator in 90 s. Assume that his walking speed is same upwards and downwards. How much time will he take to walk up the escalator, when it is not moving?
(a) 30 s (b) 45 s
(c) 60 s (d) 90 s

1996

19. In a mile race, Akshay can be given a start of 128 m by Bhairav. If Bhairav can give Chinmay a start of 4 m in a 100 m dash, then who out of Akshay and Chinmay will win a race of one and half miles, and what will be the final lead given by the winner to the loser? (One mile is 1,600 m.)
(a) Akshay, $\frac{1}{12}$ mile (b) Chinmay, $\frac{1}{32}$ mile
(c) Akshay, $\frac{1}{24}$ mile (d) Chinmay, $\frac{1}{16}$ mile

20. A man travels three-fifths of a distance AB at a speed 3a, and the remaining at a speed 2b. If he goes from B to A and return at a speed 5c in the same time, then

(a) $\frac{1}{a}+\frac{1}{b}=\frac{1}{c}$ (b) $a + b = c$

(c) $\frac{1}{a}+\frac{1}{b}=\frac{2}{c}$ (d) None of these

21. A man travels from A to B at a speed x km/hr. He then rests at B for x hours. He then travels from B to C at a speed 2x km/hr and rests for 2x hours. He moves further to D at a speed twice as that between B and C. He thus reaches D in 16 hr. If distances A-B, B-C and C-D are all equal to 12 km, the time for which he rested at B could be

(a) 3 hr (b) 6 hr

(c) 2 hr (d) 4 hr

22. In a watch, the minute hand crosses the hour hand for the third time exactly after every 3 hr 18 min and 15 s of watch time. What is the time gained or lost by this watch in one day?

(a) 14 min 10 s lost

(b) 13 min 50 s lost

(c) 13 min 20 s gained

(d) 14 min 40 s gained

Directions for Questions 23 and 24: Answer the questions based on the following information.

A certain race is made up of three stretches: A, B and C, each 2 km long, and to be covered by a certain mode of transport. The following table gives these modes of transport for the stretches, and the minimum and maximum possible speeds (in km/hr) over these stretches. The speed over a particular stretch is assumed to be constant. The previous record for the race is 10 min.

		Min.	Max.
A	Car	40	60
B	Motorcycle	30	50
C	Bicycle	10	20

1997

23. Anshuman travels at minimum speed by car over A and completes stretch B at the fastest speed. At what speed should he cover stretch C in order to break the previous record?

(a) Maximum speed for C

(b) Minimum speed for C

(c) This is not possible

(d) None of these

24. Mr Hare completes the first stretch at the minimum speed and takes the same time for stretch B. He takes 50% more time than the previous record to complete the race. What is Mr Hare's speed for the stretch C?

(a) 10.9 km/hr (b) 13.3 km/hr

(c) 17.1 km/hr (d) None of these

25. Mr Tortoise completes the race at an average speed of 20 km/hr. His average speed for the first two stretches is four times that for the last stretch. Find the speed over stretch C.

(a) 15 km/hr (b) 12 km/hr

(c) 10 km/hr (d) This is not possible

26. An express train travelling at 80 km/hr overtakes a goods train, twice as long and going at 40 km/hr on a parallel track, in 54 s. How long will the express train take to cross a platform of 400 m long?

(a) 36 s (b) 45 s

(c) 27 s (d) None of these

Directions for Questions 27 to 29: Answer the questions based on the following information.

Boston is 4 hr ahead of Frankfurt and 2 hr behind India. X leaves Frankfurt at 6 p.m. on Friday and reaches Boston the next day. After waiting there for 2 hr, he leaves exactly at noon and reaches India at 1 a.m. On his return journey, he takes the same route as before, but halts at Boston for 1hr less than his previous halt there. He then proceeds to Frankfurt.

27. If his journey, including stoppage, is covered at an average speed of 180 mph, what is the distance between Frankfurt and India?

(a) 3,600 miles (b) 4,500 miles

(c) 5,580 miles (d) Data insufficient

28. If X had started the return journey from India at 2.55 a.m. on the same day that he reached there, after how much time would he reach Frankfurt?

(a) 24 hr (b) 25 hr

(c) 26 hr (d) Data insufficient

29. What is X's average speed for the entire journey (to and fro)?

(a) 176 mph (b) 180 mph

(c) 165 mph (d) Data insufficient

Directions for Questions 30 and 31: Answer the questions based on the following information.

A thief, after committing the burglary, started fleeing at 12 noon, at a speed of 60 km/hr. He was then chased by a policeman X. X started the chase, 15 min after the thief had started, at a speed of 65 km/hr.

30. At what time did X catch the thief?
(a) 3.30 p.m. (b) 3 p.m.
(c) 3.15 p.m. (d) None of these

31. If another policeman had started the same chase along with X, but at a speed of 60 km/hr, then how far behind was he when X caught the thief?
(a) 18.75 km (b) 15 km
(c) 21 km (d) 37.5 km

DirectionS for Questions 32 to 34: Each of these items has a question followed by two statements, I and II. Mark the answer

(a) if the question can be answered with the help of one statement alone.
(b) if the question can be answered with the help of any one statement independently.
(c) if the question can be answered with the help of both statements together.
(d) if the question cannot be answered even with the help of both statements together.

32. A person is walking from Mali to Pali, which lies to its north-east. What is the distance between Mali and Pali?
I. When the person has covered $\frac{1}{3}$ the distance, he is 3 km east and 1 km north of Mali.
II. When the person has covered $\frac{2}{3}$ the distance, he is 6 km east and 2 km north of Mali.

33. What is the speed of the car?
I. The speed of a car is 10 (km/hr) more than that of a motorcycle.
II. The motorcycle takes 2 hr more than the car to cover 100 km.

34. After what time will the two persons Tez and Gati meet while moving around the circular track? Both of them start at the same point and at the same time.
I. Tez moves at a constant speed of 5 m/s, while Gati starts at a speed of 2 m/s and increases his speed by 0.5 m/s at the end of every second thereafter.
II. Gati can complete one entire lap in exactly 10 s.

1998

35. Distance between A and B is 72 km. Two men started walking from A and B at the same time towards each other. The person who started from A travelled uniformly with average speed of 4 km/hr. While the other man travelled with varying speed as follows: in the first hour his speed was 2 km/hr, in the second hour it was 2.5 km/hr, in the third hour it was 3 km/hr, and so on. When will they meet each other?
(a) 7 hr
(b) 10 hr
(c) 35 km from A
(d) Mid-way between A and B

36. I started climbing up the hill at 6 a.m. and reached the top of the temple at 6 p.m. Next day I started coming down at 6 a.m. and reached the foothill at 6 p.m. I walked on the same road. The road is so short that only one person can walk on it. Although I varied my pace on my way, I never stopped on my way. Then which of the following must be true?
(a) My average speed downhill was greater than that of uphill
(b) At noon, I was at the same spot on both the days.
(c) There must be a point where I reached at the same time on both the days.
(d) There cannot be a spot where I reached at the same time on both the days.

1999

37. Navjivan Express from Ahmedabad to Chennai leaves Ahmedabad at 6.30 a.m. and travels at 50 kmph towards Baroda situated 100 km away. At 7.00 a.m. Howrah-Ahmedabad Express leaves Baroda towards Ahmedabad and travels at 40 kmph. At 7.30 a.m. Mr Shah, the traffic controller at Baroda realizes that both the trains are running on the same track. How much time does he have to avert a head-on collision between the two trains?
(a) 15 min (b) 20 min
(c) 25 min (d) 30 min

Directions for Questions 38 to 40: Answer the questions based on the following information.

A road network (shown in the figure below) connects cities A, B, C and D. All road segments are straight lines. D is the mid-point on the road connecting A and C. Roads AB and BC are at right angles to each other with BC shorter than AB. The segment AB is 100 km long.

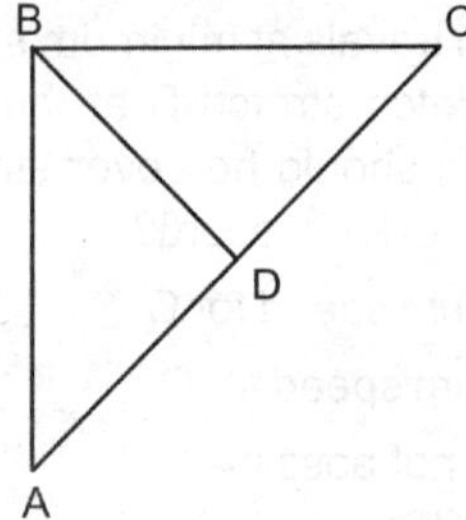

Ms X and Mr Y leave A at 8.00 a.m., take different routes to city C and reach at the same time. X takes the highway from A to B to C and travels at an average speed of 61.875 kmph. Y takes the direct route AC and travels at 45 kmph on segment AD. Y's speed on segment DC is 55 kmph.

38. What is the average speed of Y?

(a) 47.5 kmph (b) 49.5 kmph
(c) 50 kmph (d) 52 kmph

39. The total distance travelled by Y during the journey is approximately

(a) 105 km (b) 150 km
(c) 130 km (d) Cannot be determined

40. What is the length of the road segment BD?

(a) 50 km (b) 52.5 km
(c) 55 km (d) Cannot be determined

2000

41. A truck travelling at 70 km/hr uses 30% more diesel to travel a certain distance than it does when it travels at a speed of 50 km/hr. If the truck can travel 19.5 km/L of diesel at 50 km/hr, how far can the truck travel on 10 L of diesel at a speed of 70 km/hr?

(a) 130 km (b) 140 km
(c) 150 km (d) 175 km

Directions for Questions 42 and 43: Answer the questions based on the following information.

There are five machines — A, B, C, D, and E — situated on a straight line at distances of 10 m, 20 m, 30 m, 40 m and 50 m respectively from the origin of the line. A robot is stationed at the origin of the line. The robot serves the machines with raw material whenever a machine becomes idle. All the raw materials are located at the origin. The robot is in an idle state at the origin at the beginning of a day. As soon as one or more machines become idle, they send messages to the robot-station and the robot starts and serves all the machines from which it received messages. If a message is received at the station while the robot is away from it, the robot takes notice of the message only when it returns to the station. While moving, it serves the machines in the sequence in which they are encountered, and then returns to the origin. If any messages are pending at the station when it returns, it repeats the process again. Otherwise, it remains idle at the origin till the next message(s) is(are) received.

42. Suppose on a certain day, machines A and D have sent the first two messages to the origin at the beginning of the first second, and C has sent a message at the beginning of the 5th second and B at the beginning of the 6th second, and E at the beginning of the 10th second. How much distance has the robot travelled since the beginning of the day, when it notices the message of E? Assume that the speed of movement of the robot is 10 m/s.

(a) 140 m (b) 80 m
(c) 340 m (d) 360 m

43. Suppose there is a second station with raw material for the robot at the other extreme of the line which is 60 m from the origin, i.e. 10 m from E. After finishing the services in a trip, the robot returns to the nearest station. If both stations are equidistant, it chooses the origin as the station to return to. Assuming that both stations receive the messages sent by the machines and that all the other data remains the same, what would be the answer to the above question?

(a) 120 (b) 140
(c) 340 (d) 70

Direction for Question 44: The question is followed by two statements, I and II. Answer the question using the following instructions.

Mark the answer as:

(a) if the question can be answered by one of the statements alone, but cannot be answered by using the other statement alone.

(b) if the question can be answered by using either statement alone.

(c) if the question can be answered by using both the statements together, but cannot be answered by using either statement alone.

(d) if the question cannot be answered even by using both statements together.

44. Ghosh Babu has decided to take a non-stop flight from Mumbai to No-man's-land in South America, He is scheduled to leave Mumbai at 5 a.m., IST on December 10, 2000. What is the local time at No-man's-land when he reaches there?

I. The average speed of the plane is 700 km/hr.

II. The flight distance is 10,500 km.

2001

45. At his usual rowing rate, Rahul can travel 12 miles downstream in a certain river in 6 hr less than it takes him to travel the same distance upstream. But if he could double his usual rowing rate for this 24 miles round trip, the downstream 12 miles would then take only 1 hr less than the upstream 12 miles. What is the speed of the current in miles per hour?

(a) $\frac{7}{3}$ (b) $\frac{4}{3}$
(c) $\frac{5}{3}$ (d) $\frac{8}{3}$

46. Shyama and Vyom walk up an escalator (moving stairway). The escalator moves at a constant speed. Shyama takes three steps for every two of Vyom's steps. Shyama gets to the top of the escalator after having taken 25 steps, while Vyom (because his slower pace lets the escalator do a little more of the work)takes only 20 steps to reach the top. If the escalator were turned off, how many steps would they have to take to walk up?

(a) 40 (b) 50
(c) 60 (d) 80

47. Train X departs from station A at 11 a.m. for station B, which is 180 km so far. Train Y departs from station B at 11 a.m. for station A. Train X travels at an average speed of 70 km/hr and does not stop anywhere until it arrives at station B. Train Y travels at an average speed of 50 km/hr, but has to stop for 15 min at station C, which is 60 km away from station B enroute to station A. Ignoring the lengths of the trains, what is the distance, to the nearest kilometre, from station A to the point where the trains cross each other?

(a) 112 km (b) 118 km
(c) 120 km (d) None of these

48. Three runners A, B and C run a race, with runner A finishing 12 m ahead of runner B and 18 m ahead of runner C, while runner B finishes 8 m ahead of runner C. Each runner travels the entire distance at a constant speed. What was the length of the race?

(a) 36 m (b) 48 m
(c) 60 m (d) 72 m

Directions for Questions 49 and 50: Answer the questions based on the following information.

The petrol consumption rate of a new model car 'Palto' depends on its speed and may be described by the graph below.

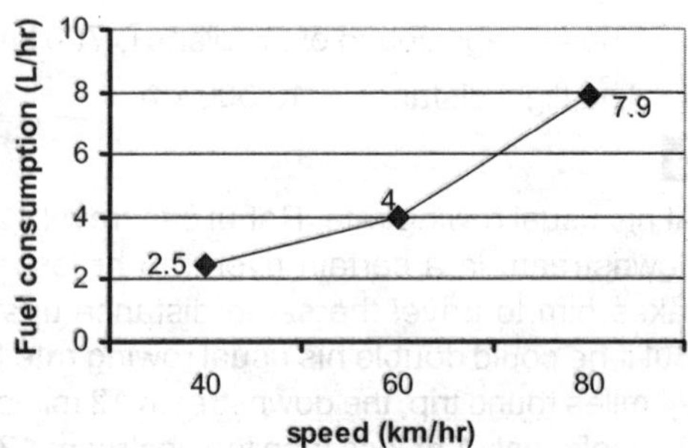

49. Manasa makes a 200 km trip from Mumbai to Pune at a steady speed of 60 km/hr. What is the volume of petrol consumed for the journey?

(a) 12.5 L (b) 13.33 L
(c) 16 L (d) 19.75 L

50. Manasa would like to minimize the fuel consumption for the trip by driving at the appropriate speed. How should she change the speed?

(a) Increase the speed
(b) Decrease the speed
(c) Maintain the speed at 60 km/hr
(d) Cannot be determined

Directions for Questions 51 and 52: Each question is followed by two statements, I and II.

Mark

(a) if the question can be answered by one of the statements alone and not by the other.
(b) if the question can be answered by using either statement alone.
(c) if the question can be answered by using both the statements together, but cannot be answered by using either statement alone.
(d) if the question cannot be answered even by using both statements together.

51. On a given day a boat ferried 1,500 passengers across the river in 12 hr. How many round trips did it make?

I. The boat can carry 200 passengers at any time.
II. It takes 40 min each way and 20 min of waiting time at each terminal.

52. What will be the time for downloading software?

I. Transfer rate is 6 kilobytes per second.
II. The size of the software is 4.5 megabytes.

2002

53. On a straight road XY, 100 m long, five heavy stones are placed 2 m apart beginning at the end X. A worker, starting at X, has to transport all the stones to Y, by carrying only one stone at a time. The minimum distance he has to travel is

(a) 472 m (b) 422 m
(c) 744 m (d) 860 m

54. Only a single rail track exists between stations A and B on a railway line. One hour after the north-bound super fast train N leaves station A for station B, a south-bound passenger train S reaches station A from station B. The speed of the super fast train is twice that of a normal express train E, while the speed of a passenger train S is half that of E. On a particular day, N leaves for B from A, 20 min behind the normal schedule. In order to maintain the schedule, both N and S increased their speeds. If the super fast train doubles its speed, what should be the ratio (approximately)of the speeds of passenger train to that of the super fast train so that the passenger train S reaches exactly at the scheduled time at A on that day?

(a) 1 : 3 (b) 1 : 4
(c) 1 : 5 (d) 1 : 6

55. On a 20 km tunnel, connecting two cities A and B, there are three gutters (1, 2 and 3). The distance between gutters 1 and 2 is half the distance between gutters 2 and 3. The distance from city A to its nearest gutter, gutter 1, is equal to the distance of city B from gutter 3. On a particular day, the hospital in city A receives information that an accident has happened at gutter 3. The victim can be saved only if an operation is started within 40 min. An ambulance started from city A at 30 km/hr and crossed gutter 1 after 5 min. If the driver had doubled the speed after that, what is the maximum amount of time would the doctor get to attend the patient at the hospital. Assume 1 min is elapsed for taking the patient into and out of the ambulance?

(a) 4 min

(b) 2.5 min

(c) 1.5 min

(d) The patient died before reaching the hospital

56. A car rental agency has the following terms. If a car is rented for 5 hr or less, then, the charge is Rs. 60 per hour or Rs. 12 per kilometre whichever is more. On the other hand, if the car is rented for more than 5 hr, the charge is Rs. 50 per hour or Rs. 7.50 per kilometre whichever is more. Akil rented a car from this agency, drove it for 30 km and ended up playing Rs. 300. For how many hours did he rent the car?

(a) 4 hr (b) 5 hr

(c) 6 hr (d) None of these

57. A train approaches a tunnel AB. Inside the tunnel is a cat located at a point that is $\frac{3}{8}$ of the distance AB measured from the entrance A. When the train whistles the cat runs. If the cat moves to the entrance of the tunnel A, the train catches the cat exactly at the entrance. If the cat moves to the exit B, the train catches the cat at exactly the exit. The speed of the train is greater than the speed of the cat by what order?

(a) 3 : 1 (b) 4 :1

(c) 5 : 1 (d) None of these

2003(R)

58. A car is being driven, in a straight line and at a uniform speed, towards the base of a vertical tower. The top of the tower is observed from the car and, in the process, it takes 10 min for the angle of elevation to change from 45° to 60°. After how much more time will this car reach the base of the tower?

(a) $5\left(\sqrt{3}+1\right)$ (b) $6\left(\sqrt{3}+\sqrt{2}\right)$

(c) $7\left(\sqrt{3}-1\right)$ (d) $8\left(\sqrt{3}-2\right)$

59. Two straight roads R1 and R2 diverge from a point A at an angle of 120°. Ram starts walking from point A along R1 at a uniform speed of 3 km/hr. Shyam starts walking at the same time from A along R2 at a uniform speed of 2 km/hr. They continue walking for 4 hr along their respective roads and reach points B and C on R1 and R2 respectively. There is a straight line path connecting B and C. Then Ram returns to point A after walking along the line segments BC and CA. Shyam also returns to A after walking along line segments BC and CA. Their speeds remains unchanged. The time interval (in hours) between Ram's and Shyam's return to the point A is

(a) $\frac{10\sqrt{19}+26}{3}$ (b) $\frac{2\sqrt{19}+10}{3}$

(c) $\frac{\sqrt{19}+26}{3}$ (d) $\frac{\sqrt{19}+10}{3}$

2003(L)

Directions for Questions 60 to 62: Answer the questions on the basis of the information given below.

A city has two perfectly circular and concentric ring roads, the outer ring road (OR)being twice as long as the inner ring road (IR). There are also four (straight line) chord roads from E1, the east end point of OR to N2, the north end point of IR; from N1, the north end point of OR to W2, the west end point of IR; from W1, the west end point of OR, to S2, the south end point of IR; and from S1 the south end point of OR to E2, the east end point of IR. Traffic moves at a constant speed of 30π km/hr on the OR road, 20π km/hr on the IR road, and $15\sqrt{5}$ km/hr on all the chord roads.

60. The ratio of the sum of the lengths of all chord roads to the length of the outer ring road is

(a) $(\sqrt{5}:2)$ (b) $(\sqrt{5}:2\pi)$

(c) $\sqrt{5}:\pi$ (d) None of the above.

61. Amit wants to reach N2 from S1. It would take him 90 minutes if he goes on minor arc S1 – E1 on OR, and then on the chord road E1 – N2. What is the radius of the outer ring road in kms?

(a) 60 (b) 40

(c) 30 (d) 20

62. Amit wants to reach E2 from N1 using first the chord N1 – W2 and then the inner ring road. What will be his travel time in minutes on the basis of information given in the above question?

(a) 60 (b) 45

(c) 90 (d) 105

63. In a 4000 meter race around a circular stadium having a circumference of 1000 meters, the fastest runner and the slowest runner reach the same point at the end of the 5th minute, for the first time after the start of the race. All the runners have the same starting point and each runner maintains a uniform speed throughout the race. If the fastest runner runs at twice the speed of the slowest runner, what is the time taken by the fastest runner to finish the race?

(a) 20 min (b) 15 min

(c) 10 min (d) 5 min

Directions for Question 64: In the question there are two statements: A and B.

Choose (a) if the question can be answered by one of the statements alone but not by the other.

Choose (b) if the question can be answered by using either statement alone.

Choose (c) if the question can be answered by using both the statements together but cannot be answered using either statement alone.

Choose (d) if the question cannot be answered even by using both the statements A and B.

64. If A and B run a race, then A wins by 60 seconds. If B and C run the same race, then B wins by 30 seconds. Assuming that C maintains a uniform speed what is the time taken by C to finish the race?

A. A and C run the same race and A wins by 375 metres.

B. The length of the race is 1 km.

2004

65. Two boats, traveling at 5 and 10 kms per hour, head directly towards each other. They begin at a distance of 20 kms from each other. How far apart are they (in kms)one minute before they collide.

(a) $\frac{1}{12}$ (b) $\frac{1}{6}$

(c) $\frac{1}{4}$ (d) $\frac{1}{3}$

66. If a man cycles at 10 km/hr, then he arrives at a certain place at 1 p.m. If he cycles at 15 km/hr, he will arrive at the same place at 11 a.m. At what speed must he cycle to get there at noon?

(a) 11 km/hr (b) 12 km/hr

(c) 13 km/hr (d) 14 km/hr

67. Karan and Arjun run a 100-meter race, where Karan beats Arjun 10 metres. To do a favour to Arjun, Karan starts 10 metres behind the starting line in a second 100 metre race. They both run at their earlier speeds. Which of the following is true in connection with the second race?

(a) Karan and Arjun reach the finishing line simultaneously.

(b) Arjun beats Karan by 1 metre

(c) Arjun beats Karan by 11 metres.

(d) Karan beats Arjun by 1 metre.

68. A sprinter starts running on a circular path of radius r metres. Her average speed (in metres/minute) is πr during the first 30 seconds, $\frac{\pi r}{2}$ during next one minute, $\frac{\pi r}{4}$ during next 2 minutes, $\frac{\pi r}{8}$ during next 4 minutes, and so on. What is the ratio of the time taken for the nth round to that for the previous round?

(a) 4 (b) 8

(c) 16 (d) 32

2005

69. A jogging park has two identical circular tracks touching each other, and a rectangular track enclosing the two circles. The edges of the rectangles are tangential to the circles. Two friends, A and B, start jogging simultaneously form the point where one of the circular tracks touches the smaller side of the rectangular track. A jogs along the rectangular track, while B jogs along the two circular tracks in a figure of eight. Approximately, how much faster than A does B have to run, so that they take the same time to return to their starting point?

(a) 3.88% (b) 4.22%

(c) 4.44% (d) 4.72%

Directions for Questions 70 and 71: Answer the questions on the basis of the information given below.

Ram and Shyam run a race between points A and B, 5 km apart, Ram starts at 9 a.m from A at a speed of 5 km/hr, reaches B, and returns to A at the same speed, Shyam starts at 9:45 a.m. from A at a speed of 10 km/hr, reaches B and comes back to A at the same speed.

70. At what time do Ram and Shyam first meet each other?

(a) 10 a.m.

(b) 10:10 a.m.

(c) 10:20 a.m.

(d) 10:30 a.m.

71. At what time does Shyam over take Ram?

(a) 10:20 a.m

(b) 10:30 a.m

(c) 10:40 a.m

(d) 10:50 a.m

2006

72. Arun, Barun and Kiranmala start from the same place and travel in the same direction at speeds of 30, 40 and 60 km per hour respectively. Barun starts two hours after Arun. If Barun and Kiranmala overtake Arun at the same instant, how many hours after Arun did Kiranmala start?

(a) 3 (b) 3.5
(c) 4 (d) 4.5
(e) 5

2007

Directions for Questions 73 and 74: Answer the following questions based on the information given below:

Cities A and B are in different time zones. A is located 3000 km east of B. The table below describes the schedule of an airline operating non-stop flights between A and B. All the times indicated are local and on the same day.

Departure		Arrival	
City	Time	City	Time
B	8:00 am	A	3:00 pm
A	4:00 pm	B	8:00 pm

Assume that planes cruise at the same speed in both directions. However, the effective speed is influenced by a steady wind blowing from east to west at 50 km per hour.

73. What is the time difference between A and B?

(a) 1 hour and 30 minutes
(b) 2 hours
(c) 2 hours and 30 minutes
(d) 1 hour
(e) Cannot be determined

74. What is the plane's cruising speed in km per hour?

(a) 700
(b) 550
(c) 600
(d) 500
(e) Cannot be determined.

2008

75. Rahim plans to drive from city A to station C, at the speed of 70 km per hour, to catch a train arriving there from B. He must reach C at least 15 minutes before the arrival of the train. The train leaves B, located 500 km south of A, at 8:00 am and travels at a speed of 50 km per hour. It is known that C is located between west and northwest of B, with BC at 60° to AB. Also, C is located between south and southwest of A with AC at 30° to AB. The latest time by which Rahim must leave A and still catch the train is closest to

(a) 6 : 15 am (b) 6 : 30 am
(c) 6 :45 am (d) 7 : 00 am
(e) 7 : 15 am

MEMORY BASED QUESTIONS

2009

76. Chaupat, Popat and Sarpat participate in a race of 'x' m. Chaupat finishes 18 m ahead of Popat and 24 m ahead of Sarpat. Popat finishes 8 m ahead of Sarpat. If none of the three changes his running speed during the race, then what is the value of x?

(a) 54 (b) 48
(c) 90 (d) 72

77. Himanshu, Saral and Vikas start running from the same point in the same direction along a straight line at 07 : 00 a.m., 08 : 00 a.m. and 10 : 00 a.m. with speeds of 2 kmph, 3 kmph and 4 kmph respectively. When Saral catches Himanshu he sends Himanshu back (along the straight line) immediately to deliver a message to Vikas. At what time would Himanshu meet Vikas?

(a) 10 : 30 a.m. (b) 11 : 00 a.m.
(c) 10 : 40 a.m. (d) 11 : 15 a.m.

2010

78. P and Q are two points 100 km apart. A starts running from P towards Q at 10 km/hr. B starts running from Q at exactly the same time and in the same direction as that of A at 20 km/hr. After an hour, B turns back and changes his speed to 10 km/hr. After another hour, B again turns back and changes his speed to 20 km/hr. He keeps on changing his speed and direction in this manner till the time he meets A. After how much time will A and B meet for the first time?

(a) 30 hours (b) 18 hours
(c) 10 hours (d) 20 hours

2011

79. Pawan and Qureshi working together can do a piece of work in 10 days whereas Qureshi and Rohit working together can do the same work in 12 days. All three work together to do a job for which they are paid Rs. 300. If Qureshi's share is Rs. 140, then what is Pawan's share?

(a) Rs. 100 (b) Rs. 60

(c) Rs. 80 (d) Cannot be determined

80. Yamini and Zora are standing 25 km apart. Zora starts moving towards Yamini. After 40 minutes Yamini also starts moving towards Zora. By the time Yamini covers 5 km, Zora has covered 15 km. They meet at a point 7 km from the starting point of Yamini. What is the speed of Yamini?

(a) 7.5 km/h (b) 10.5 km/h

(c) 17.5 km/h (d) 6 km/h

2013

81. Once upon a time, the king of a jungle planned a 2-kilometre race between a rabbit and a tortoise. Soon after the start of the race, the rabbit took a huge lead. On realizing that even after taking a nap of 't' min, he would beat the tortoise by 13 min, he stooped under a tree and went to sleep. Meanwhile the tortoise kept walking. When the rabbit woke up, he realized that he had slept for (14 + t) min, and immediately started running towards the target at a speed $\frac{3}{2}$ times his original speed. The race eventually ended in a dead heat. If the ratio of the original speed of the rabbit to that of the tortoise was 6 : 1 and the rabbit overstretched his nap by $1\frac{1}{6}$t min, then how long did the tortoise take to complete the race?

(a) 24 min (b) 30 min

(c) 28 min (d) 36 min

2014

82. P, Q and R start walking from the same point. P and Q start at 1 PM and R starts at 3 PM. R takes over P at 5 PM and then doubles his speed and takes over Q after another hour. What is the ratio of speed of A and speed of B?

(a) 8 : 5 (b) 3 : 4

(c) 4 : 3 (d) 5 : 8

2015

83. There is a string of length 100 m running from east to west. 1000 ants are dropped onto the string. Assume that each ant lands on the string facing either the east or the west direction. As soon as they land, each ant starts moving in the direction which is being faced by it at 50 m/ min till it falls off the string. But if an ant collides with another ant coming from the opposite direction, both of them reverse their directions and proceed to move now in the opposite directions. Ants fall only at either of the ends of the string. What is the minimum time by which the string is definitely free of ants?

(a) 1 min (b) 2 min

(c) 200 min (d) Infinite time

84. In a rowing competition, first boat rows over the course at an average speed of 4 yards/second. Second boat rows over the first half of the course at the rate of $3\frac{1}{2}$ yards /second and over the remaining half at $4\frac{1}{2}$ yards/second, thereby reaching the winning post 15 seconds after the first boat. Find the time taken (in minutes) by the second boat to cover the entire course.

2016

85. Two friends – Prakash and Arpit – started running simultaneously from a point P in the same direction along a straight running track. The ratio of the speeds of Prakash and Arpit was 2 : 5 respectively. Two hours later, Arpit turned back and started running backwards at one-fifth of his original speed. He met Prakash at a distance of 10 km from the point P. What was Prakash's speed?

(1) 1.25 km/hr (2) 2.5 km/hr

(3) 3.75 km/hr (4) 6.25 km/hr

86. Anu and Prem started running simultaneously from diametrically opposite points on a circular track. They ran in opposite directions and met after 12 minutes for the first time. After how long (in minutes) would they meet for the seventh time?

2017

87. In a 10 km race. A, B, and C, each running at uniform speed, get the gold, silver, and bronze medals, respectively. If A beats B by 1 km and B beats C by 1 km, then by how many metres does A beat C?

88. Arun drove from home to his hostel at 60 miles per hour. While returning home he drove half way along the same route at a speed of 25 miles per hour and then took a bypass road which increased his driving distance by 5 miles, but allowed him to drive at 50 miles per hour along this bypass road. If his return journey took 30 minutes more than his onward journey, then the total distance traveled by him is

(a) 55 miles (b) 60 miles

(c) 65 miles (d) 70 miles

89. A motorbike leaves point A at 1 pm and moves towards point B at a uniform speed. A car leaves point B at 2 pm and moves towards point A at a uniform speed which is double that of the motorbike. They meet at 3:40 pm at a point which is 168 km away from A. What is the distance, in km, between A and B?

(a) 364 (b) 378

(c) 380 (d) 388

2018 Slot 1

90. Point P lies between points A and B such that the length of BP is thrice that of AP. Car 1 starts from A and moves towards B. Simultaneously, car 2 starts from B and moves towards A. Car 2 reaches P one hour after car 1 reaches P. If the speed of car 2 is half that of car 1, then the time, in minutes, taken by car 1 in reaching P from A is

91. Train T leaves station X for station Y at 3 pm. Train S, traveling at three quarters of the speed of T, leaves Y for X at 4 pm. The two trains pass each other at a station Z, where the distance between X and Z is three-fifths of that between X and Y. How many hours does train T take for its journey from X to Y?

92. The distance from A to B is 60 km. Partha and Narayan start from A at the same time and move towards B. Partha takes four hours more than Narayan to reach B. Moreover, Partha reaches the mid-point of A and B two hours before Narayan reaches B. The speed of Partha, in km per hour, is

(a) 3 (b) 4

(c) 6 (d) 5

2018 Slot 2

93. On a long stretch of east-west road, A and B are two points such that B is 350 km west of A. One car starts from A and another from B at the same time. If they move towards each other, then they meet after 1 hour. If they both move towards east, then they meet in 7 hrs. The difference between their speeds, in km per hour, is

94. Points A, P, Q and B lie on the same line such that P, Q and B are, respectively, 100 km, 200 km and 300 km away from A. Cars 1 and 2 leave A at the same time and move towards B. Simultaneously, car 3 leaves B and moves towards A. Car 3 meets car 1 at Q, and car 2 at P. If each car is moving in uniform speed then the ratio of the speed of car 2 to that of car 1 is

(a) 1 : 4

(b) 2 : 9

(c) 2 : 7

(d) 1 : 2

95. Points A and B are 150 km apart. Cars 1 and 2 travel from A to B, but car 2 starts from A when car 1 is already 20 km away from A. Each car travels at a speed of 100 kmph for the first 50 km, at 50 kmph for the next 50 km, and at 25 kmph for the last 50 km. The distance, in km, between car 2 and B when car 1 reaches B is

TIME AND WORK

1990

1. A, B and C individually can finish a work in 6, 8 and 15 hours respectively. They started the work together and after completing the work got Rs.94.60 in all. When they divide the money among themselves, A, B and C will respectively get (in Rs.)

(a) 44, 33, 17.60 (b) 43, 27.20, 24.40

(c) 45, 30, 19.60 (d) 42, 28, 24.60

1991

2. Alord got an order from a garment manufacturer for 480 Denim Shirts. He brought 12 sewing machines and appointed some expert tailors to do the job. However, many didn't report to duty. As a result, each of those who did, had to stitch 32 more shirts than originally planned by Alord, with equal distribution of work. How many tailors had been appointed earlier and how many had not reported for work?

(a) 12, 4 (b) 10, 3

(c) 10, 4 (d) None of these

3. Three machines, A, B and C can be used to produce a product. Machine A will take 60 hours to produce a million units. Machine B is twice as fast as Machine A. Machine C will take the same amount of time to produce a million units as A and B running together. How much time will be required to produce a million units if all the three machines are used simultaneously?

(a) 12 hours (b) 10 hours

(c) 8 hours (d) 6 hour

Direction for Question 4 : The question is followed by two statements. As the answer,

Mark (a) if the question can be answered with the help of statement I alone,

Mark (b) if the question can be answered with the help of statement II, alone,

Mark (c) if both, statement I and statement II are needed to answer the question, and

Mark (d) if the question cannot be answered even with the help of both the statements.

1993

4. Two types of widgets, namely type A and type B, are produced on a machine. The number of machine hours available per week is 80. How many widgets of type A must be produced?

I. One unit of type A widget requires 2 machine hours and one unit of type B widget requires 4 machine hours.

II. The widget dealer wants supply of at least 10 units of type A widget per week and he would not accept less than 15 units of type B widget.

5. A group of workers was put on a job. From the second day onwards, one worker was withdrawn each day. The job was finished when the last worker was withdrawn. Had no worker been withdrawn at any stage, the group would have finished the job in two-third the time. How many workers were there in the group?
(a) 2 (b) 3
(c) 5 (d) 11

1994

6. One man can do as much work in one day as a woman can do in 2 days. A child does one third the work in a day as a woman. If an estate-owner hires 39 pairs of hands, men, women and children in the ratio 6 : 5 : 2 and pays them in all Rs. 1,113 at the end of the days work. What must the daily wages of a child be, if the wages are proportional to the amount of work done?
(a) Rs.14 (b) Rs.5
(c) Rs.20 (d) Rs.7

7. A water tank has three taps A, B and C. A fills four buckets in 24 minutes, B fills 8 buckets in 1 hour and C fills 2 buckets in 20 minutes. If all the taps are opened together a full tank is emptied in 2 hours. If a bucket can hold 5 litres of water, what is the capacity of the tank?
(a) 120 litres (b) 240 litres
(c) 180 litres (d) 60 litres

8. There is a leak in the bottom of the tank. This leak can empty a full tank in 8 hours. When the tank is full, a tap is opened into the tank which admits 6 litres per hour and the tank is now emptied in 12 hours. What is the capacity of the tank?
(a) 28.8 litres (b) 36 litres
(c) 144 litres (d) Cannot be determined

Direction for Question 9 : The question is followed by two statements. As the answer,
Mark (a) if the question can be answered with the help of statement I alone,
Mark (b) if the question can be answered with the help of statement II, alone,
Mark (c) if both, statement I and statement II are needed to answer the question, and
Mark (d) if the question cannot be answered even with the help of both the statements.

9. A and B work at digging a ditch alternately for a day each. If A can dig a ditch in *'a'* days and B can dig that ditch in *'b'* days, will work get done faster if A begins the work?
I. n is a positive integer such that $n\left(\frac{1}{a}+\frac{1}{b}\right)=1$
II. b > a

1995

10. A group of men decided to do a job in 8 days. But since 10 men dropped out every day, the job got completed at the end of the 12th day. How many men were there at the beginning?
(a) 165 (b) 175
(c) 80 (d) 90

11. Two typists undertake to do a job. The second typist begins working one hour after the first. Three hours after the first typist has begun working, there is still $\frac{9}{20}$ of the work to be done. When the assignment is completed, it turns out that each typist has done half the work. How many hours would it take each one to do the whole job individually ?
(a) 12 hr and 8 hr (b) 8 hr and 5.6 hr
(c) 10 hr and 8 hr (d) 5 hr and 4 hr

1997

Directions for Questions 12 and 13: Answer the questions based on the following information.
The Weirdo Holiday Resort follows a particular system of holidays for its employees. People are given holidays on the days where the first letter of the day of the week is the same as the first letter of their names. All employees work at the same rate.

12. Raja starts working on February 25, 1996, and finishes the job on March 2, 1996. How much time would T and J take to finish the same job if both start on the same day as Raja?
(a) 4 days (b) 5 days
(c) Either (a) or (b) (d) Cannot be determined

13. Starting on February 25, 1996, if Raja had finished his job on April 2, 1996, when would T and S together likely to have completed the job, had they started on the same day as Raja?
(a) March 15, 1996 (b) March 14, 1996
(c) March 22, 1996 (d) Data insufficient

1998

14. A company has a job to prepare certain number cans and there are three machines A, B and C for this job. A can complete the job in 3 days, B can complete the job in 4 days, and C can complete the job in 6 days. How many days will the company take to complete the job if all the machines are used simultaneously?
(a) 4 days (b) $\frac{4}{3}$ days
(c) 3 days (d) 12 days

2001

15. A can complete a piece of work in 4 days. B takes double the time taken by A, C takes double that of B, and D takes double that of C to complete the same task. They are paired in groups of two each. One pair takes two-thirds the time needed by the second pair to complete the work. Which is the first pair?

(a) A and B (b) A and C

(c) B and C (d) A and D

16. There's a lot of work in preparing a birthday dinner. Even after the turkey is in the oven, there's still the potatoes and gravy, yams, salad, and cranberries, not to mention setting the table. Three friends — Asit, Arnold and Afzal — work together to get all of these chores done. The time it takes them to do the work together is 6 hr less than Asit would have taken working alone, 1 hr less than Arnold would have taken alone, and half the time Afzal would have taken working alone. How long did it take them to do these chores working together?

(a) 20 min (b) 30 min

(c) 40 min (d) 50 min

2002

17. It takes six technicians a total of 10 hr to build a new server from Direct Computer, with each working at the same rate. If six technicians start to build the server at 11 am, and one technician per hour is added beginning at 5 pm, at what time will the server be completed?

(a) 6.40 pm (b) 7 pm

(c) 7.20 pm (d) 8 pm

18. Three small pumps and a large pump are filling a tank. Each of the three small pump works at $\frac{2}{3}$ the rate of the large pump. If all four pumps work at the same time, they should fill the tank in what fraction of the time that it would have taken the large pump alone?

(a) $\frac{4}{7}$ (b) $\frac{1}{3}$

(c) $\frac{2}{3}$ (d) $\frac{3}{4}$

2004

19. In Nuts And Bolts factory, one machine produces only nuts at the rate of 100 nuts per minute and needs to be cleaned for 5 minutes after production of every 1000 nuts. Another machine produces only bolts at the rate of 75 bolts per minute and needs to cleaned for10 minutes after production of every 1500 bolts. If both the machines start production at the same time, what is the minimum duration required for producing 9000 pairs of nuts and bolts?

(a) 130 minutes (b) 135 minutes

(c) 170 minutes (d) 180 minutes

2005

20. A chemical plant has four tanks (A, B, C and D), each containing 1000 litres of a chemical. The chemical is being pumped from one tank to anther as follows.

From A to B @ 20 litres/minute

From C to A @ 90 litres/minute

From A to D @ 10 litres/minute

From C to D @ 50 litres/minute

From B to C @ 100 litres/minute

From D to B @ 110 litres/minute

Which tank gets emptied first, and how long does it take (in minutes)to get empty after pumping starts?

(a) A, 16.66 (b) C, 20

(c) D, 20 (d) D, 25

MEMORY BASED QUESTIONS

2012

21. The radius of the cross-sections of pipes P_1 and P_2 are 7 m and 14 m respectively. Water flows through P_1 at a constant rate of 10 m/s and it can alone fill a tank in 2 hours. If P_1 is used as the inlet pipe and P_2 as the outlet pipe then together they fill the tank in 4 hours. What is the rate of water flow (in m/s) through P_2?

(a) 1.00 (b) 1.25

(c) 1.50 (d) 2.00

2013

22. Anushka and Anirudh working together can complete a piece of work in 20 days. They started the work togethor, but Anuslıka left after x days and Anirudh finished the remaining work in the next x/2 days. Had Anushka left after 3x/4 days, Anirudh would have taken x days to finish the remaining work. Find the ratio of the efficiency of Anushka to that of Anirudh.

(a) 2 : 3 (b) 3 : 2

(c) 2 : 1 (d) 1 : 1

2016

23. A contractor agreed to finish a piece of work in 150 days. He employed 75 men and made them work for 8 hours per day. However, after 90 days, he realized that only $\frac{2}{7}$th of the work was completed. How many more men would he need to employ to complete the work on time if he intended to make everybody work for 10 hours per day henceforth?

2017

24. A tank has an inlet pipe and an outlet pipe. If the outlet pipe is closed then the inlet pipe fills the empty tank in 8 hours. If the outlet pipe is open then the inlet pipe fills the empty tank in 10 hours. If only the outlet pipe is open then in how many hours the full tank becomes half-full?

(a) 20 (b) 30
(c) 40 (d) 45

2017

25. Amal can complete a job in 10 days and Bimal can complete it in 8 days. Amal, Bimal and Kamal together complete the job in 4 days and are paid a total amount of Rs 1000 as remuneration. If this amount is shared by them in proportion to their work, then Kamal's share, in rupees, is

(a) 100 (b) 200
(c) 300 (d) 400

2018 Slot 1

26. A tank is fitted with pipes, some filling it and the rest draining it. All filling pipes fill at the same rate, and all draining pipes drain at the same rate. The empty tank gets completely filled in 6 hours when 6 filling and 5 draining pipes are on, but this time becomes 60 hours when 5 filling and 6 draining pipes are on. In how many hours will the empty tank get completely filled when one draining and two filling pipes are on?

27. When they work alone, B needs 25% more time to finish a job than A does. They two finish the job in 13 days in the following manner: A works alone till half the job is done, then A and B work together for four days, and finally B works alone to complete the remaining 5% of the job. In how many days can B alone finish the entire job?

(a) 16 (b) 18
(c) 20 (d) 22

28. Humans and robots can both perform a job but at different efficiencies. Fifteen humans and five robots working together take thirty days to finish the job, whereas five humans and fifteen robots working together take sixty days to finish it. How many days will fifteen humans working together (without any robot) take to finish it?

(a) 45
(b) 32
(c) 40
(d) 36

2018 Slot 2

29. A water tank has inlets of two types A and B. All inlets of type A when open, bring in water at the same rate. All inlets of type B, when open, bring in water at the same rate. The empty tank is completely filled in 30 minutes if 10 inlets of type A and 45 inlets of type B are open, and in 1 hour if 8 inlets of type A and 18 inlets of type B are open. In how many minutes will the empty tank get completely filled if 7 inlets of type A and 27 inlets of type B are open?

30. Ramesh and Ganesh can together complete a work in 16 days. After seven days of working together, Ramesh got sick and his efficiency fell by 30%. As a result, they completed the work in 17 days instead of 16 days. If Ganesh had worked alone after Ramesh got sick, in how many days would he have completed the remaining work?

(a) 12 (b) 13.5
(c) 14.5 (d) 11

31. A tank is emptied everyday at a fixed time point. Immediately thereafter, either pump A or pump B or both start working until the tank is full. On Monday, A alone completed filling the tank at 8 pm. On Tuesday, B alone completed filling the tank at 6 pm. On Wednesday, A alone worked till 5 pm, and then B worked alone from 5 pm to 7 pm, to fill the tank. At what time was the tank filled on Thursday if both pumps were used simultaneously all along?

(a) 4:48 pm (b) 4:24 pm
(c) 4:36 pm (d) 4:12 pm

MISCELLANEOUS

1990

1. I brought 30 books on Mathematics, Physics, and Chemistry, priced at Rs.17, Rs.19, and Rs.23 per book respectively, for distribution among poor students of Standard X of a school. The physics books were more in number than the Mathematics books but less than the Chemistry books, the difference being more than one. The total cost amounted to Rs.620. How many books on Mathematics, Physics, and Chemistry could have been bought respectively?

(a) 5, 8, 17 (b) 5, 12, 13
(c) 5, 10, 15 (d) 5, 6, 19

2. The last time Rahul bought Diwali cards, he found that the four types of cards that he liked were priced Rs.2.00, Rs.3.50, Rs.4.50 and Rs.5.00 each. As Rahul wanted 30 cards, he took five each of two kinds and ten each of the other two, putting down the exact number of 10 rupees notes on the payment counter. How many notes did Rahul give?

(a) 8 (b) 9
(c) 10 (d) 11

Direction for Question 3: The question is followed by two statements, I and II. As the answer,

Mark (a) if the question can be answered with the help of statement I alone,

Mark (b) if the question can be answered with the help of statement II alone,

Mark (c) if both the statement I and statement II are needed to answer the question, and

Mark (d) if the question cannot be answered even with the help of both the statements.

1991

3. X says to Y, "I am 3 times as old as you were 3 years ago". How old is X?

I. Y's age 17 years from now will be same as X's present age.

II. X's age nine years from now is 3 times Y's present age.

1994

4. Two towns A and B are 100 km apart. A school is to be built for 100 students of town B and 30 students of Town A. Expenditure on transport is Rs. 1.20 per km per student. If the total expenditure on transport by all 130 students is to be as small as possible, then the school should be built at

(a) 33 km from Town A. (b) 33 km from Town B

(c) Town A (d) Town B

5. It takes the pendulum of a clock 7 seconds to strike 4 o'clock. How much time will it take to strike 11 o'clock?

(a) 18 seconds (b) 20 seconds

(c) 19.25 seconds (d) 23.33 seconds

Direction for Question 6 : Data is provided followed by two statements – I and II – both resulting in a value, say I and II. As your answer,

Mark (a) if I > II.

Mark (b) if I < II.

Mark (c) if I = II.

Mark (d) if nothing can be said.

6. Last week Martin received $ 10 in commission for selling 100 copies of a magazine. Last week Miguel sold 100 copies of this magazine. He received his salary of $ 5 per week plus a commission of 2 cents for each of the first 25 copies sold, 3 cents for each of next 25 copies sold and 4 cents for each copy thereafter. ($1 = 100 cents).

I. Martin's commission in the last week.

II. Miguel's total income for last week.

Direction for Question 7 : The question is followed by two statements. As the answer,

Mark (a) if the question can be answered with the help of statement I alone,

Mark (b) if the question can be answered with the help of statement II, alone,

Mark (c) if both, statement I and statement II are needed to answer the question, and

Mark (d) if the question cannot be answered even with the help of both the statements.

7. Ten boys go to a neighbouring orchard. Each boy steals a few mangoes. What is the total number of mangoes they steal?

I. The first boy steals 4 mangoes and the fourth boy steals 16 mangoes and the eight boy 32 mangoes and the tenth boy steals 40 mangoes.

II. The first boy stole the minimum number of mangoes and the tenth boy stole the maximum number of mangoes.

1996

8. Once I had been to the post office to buy five-rupee, two-rupee and one-rupee stamps. I paid the clerk Rs. 20, and since he had no change, he gave me three more one-rupee stamps. If the number of stamps of each type that I had ordered initially was more than one, what was the total number of stamps that I bought?

(a) 10 (b) 9

(c) 12 (d) 8

Directions for Questions 9 and 10: Answer the questions based on the following information.

A salesman enters the quantity sold and the price into the computer. Both the numbers are two-digit numbers. But, by mistake, both the numbers were entered with their digits interchanged. The total sales value remained the same, i.e. Rs. 1,148, but the inventory reduced by 54.

9. What is the actual price per piece?

(a) Rs. 82 (b) Rs. 41

(c) Rs. 6 (d) Rs. 28

10. What is the actual quantity sold?

(a) 28 (b) 14

(c) 82 (d) 41

11. Out of two-thirds of the total number of basketball matches, a team has won 17 matches and lost 3 of them. What is the maximum number of matches that the team can lose and still win more than three-fourths of the total number of matches, if it is true that no match can end in a tie?

(a) 4 (b) 6

(c) 5 (d) 3

Directions for Questions 12 and 13: Answer the questions based on the following information.

Production pattern for number of units (in cubic feet) per day.

Day	1	2	3	4	5	6	7
Number of units	150	180	120	250	160	120	150

For a truck that can carry 2,000 cubic ft, hiring cost per day is Rs. 1,000. Storing cost per cubic feet is Rs. 5 per day.

1998

12. If all the units should be sent to the market, then on which days should the trucks be hired to minimize the cost?
    (a) 2nd, 4th, 6th, 7th
    (b) 7th
    (c) 2nd, 4th, 5th, 7th
    (d) None of these
13. If the storage cost is reduced to Re. 0.80 per cubic feet per day, then on which day(s), should the truck be hired?
    (a) 4th (b) 7th
    (c) 4th and 7th (d) None of these
14. You can collect as many rubies and emeralds as you can. Each ruby is worth Rs. 4 crore and each emerald is worth Rs. 5 crore. Each ruby weighs 0.3 kg. And each emerald weighs 0.4 kg. Your bag can carry at the most 12 kg. What should you collect to get the maximum wealth?
    (a) 20 rubies and 15 emeralds
    (b) 40 rubies
    (c) 28 rubies and 9 emeralds
    (d) None of these
15. My son adores chocolates. He likes biscuits. But he hates apples. I told him that he can buy as many chocolates he wishes. But then he must have biscuits twice the number of chocolates and should have apples more than biscuits and chocolates together. Each chocolate cost Re. 1. The cost of apple is twice the chocolate and four biscuits are worth one apple. Then which of the following can be the amount that I spent on that evening on my son if number of chocolates, biscuits and apples brought were all integers?
    (a) Rs. 34
    (b) Rs. 33
    (c) Rs. 8
    (d) None of these

Direction for Question 16: The question is followed by two statements, I and II. Answer the questions based on the statements and mark the answer as:

(a) if the question can be answered with the help of any one statement alone but not by the other statement.
(b) if the question can be answered with the help of either of the statements taken individually.
(c) if the question can be answered with the help of both statements together.
(d) if the question cannot be answered even with the help of both statements together.

16. What is the price of tea?
    I. Price of coffee is Rs. 5 more than that of tea.
    II. Price of coffee is Rs. 5 less than the price of a cold drink which cost three times the price of tea.

1999

Directions for Questions 17 to 19: Answer the questions based on the following information.

Ten coins are distributed among four people P, Q, R and S such that one of them gets one coin, another gets two coins, the third gets three coins and the fourth gets four coins. It is known that Q gets more coins than P, and S gets fewer coins than R.

17. If the number of coins distributed to Q is twice the number distributed to P, then which one of the following is necessarily true?
    (a) R gets an even number of coins.
    (b) R gets an odd number of coins.
    (c) S gets an even number of coins.
    (d) S gets an odd number of coins.
18. If R gets at least two more coins than S, then which one of the following is necessarily true?
    (a) Q gets at least two more coins than S.
    (b) Q gets more coins than S.
    (c) P gets more coins than S.
    (d) P and Q together get at least five coins.
19. If Q gets fewer coins than R, then which one of the following is not necessarily true?
    (a) P and Q together get at least four coins.
    (b) Q and S together get at least four coins.
    (c) R and S together get at least five coins.
    (d) P and R together get at least five coins.

Directions for Questions 20 and 21: Answer the questions based on the following information.

There are blue vessels with known volumes $v_1, v_2, \ldots, v_m$, arranged in ascending order of volume, $v_1 > 0.5$ litre, and $v_m < 1$ litre. Each of these is full of water initially. The water from each of these is emptied into a minimum number of empty white vessels, each having volume 1 litre. The water from a blue vessel is not emptied into a white vessel unless the white vessel has enough empty volume to hold all the water of the blue vessel. The number of white vessels required to empty all the blue vessels according to the above rules was n.

20. Among the four values given below, which is the least upper bound on e, where e is the total empty volume in the white vessels at the end of the above process?
    (a) mv_m
    (b) $m(1-v_m)$
    (c) mv_1
    (d) $m(1-v_1)$

21. Let the number of white vessels needed be n_1 for the emptying process described above, if the volume of each white vessel is 2 litres. Among the following values, which is the least upper bound on n_1?

(a) $\frac{m}{4}$

(b) Smallest integer greater than or equal to $\left(\frac{n}{2}\right)$

(c) n

(d) Greatest integer less than or equal to $\left(\frac{n}{2}\right)$

MEMORY BASED QUESTIONS

2011

22. What are the last two digits of 9483^{67483}?

(a) 21 (b) 87

(c) 27 (d) None of these

2013

23. During his trip to England, Mr. Clockilal, a horologist, decided to visit 'The Cuckooland Museum' dedicated to the exhibition of cuckoo clocks. He entered the museum between 12 noon and 1 p.m. The moment he entered the museum, he observed that the angle between the minute hand and the hour hand of one of the clocks was 20°. While leaving the museum, he observed that the angle between the minute hand and the hour hand of the same clock was 220°. If he spent more than 3 hours and less than 4 hours in the museum, then how much time did he exactly spend in the museum?

(a) 3 hours $52\frac{8}{11}$ minutes

(b) 3 hours $53\frac{4}{11}$ minutes

(c) 3 hours $38\frac{2}{11}$ minutes

(d) Either (a) or (c)

24. Muniram made an investment of 10 lakh in Axim Dynamic Bond. The variation in fund value of the bond with respect to time follows a polynomial with degree 2. Due to precarious market condition, the fund value of the investment becomes 50% of the investment at the end of 2nd year. If the fund value becomes 150% of the investment at the end of 4th year, then what is the absolute difference (in lakh) between the investment and the fund value of the bond at the end of 8th year?

(a) 80 (b) 70

(c) 75 (d) 60

ANSWERS

Percentages and Fraction

1. (a)	2. (c)	3. (c)	4. (b)	5. (a)	6. (d)	7. (b)	8. (c)	9. (a)	10. (c)
11. (d)	12. (a)	13. (d)	14. (b)	15. (b)	16. (c)	17. (b)	18. (b)	19. (d)	20. (d)
21. (b)	22. (a)	23. (d)	24. (b)	25. (c)	26. (a)	27. (e)	28. (a)	29. (c)	30. (c)
31. (d)	32. (a)	33. (c)	34. (c)	35. (c)	36. (b)	37. (c)	38. (d)		

Profit, Loss and Discount

1. (c)	2. (a)	3. (b)	4. (b)	5. (a)	6. (a)	7. (b)	8. (b)	9. (b)	10. (a)
11. (c)	12. (d)	13. (a)	14. (a)	15. (b)	16. (a)	17. (a)	18. (d)	19. (c)	20. (c)
21. (b)	22. (a)	23. (a)	24. (2000)	25. (b)	26. (a)	27. (d)			

Ratio and Proportion

1. (c)	2. (a)	3. (c)	4. (b)	5. (c)	6. (b)	7. (a)	8. (d)	9. (d)	10. (b)
11. (c)	12. (a)	13. (c)	14. (b)	15. (c)	16. (a)	17. (c)	18. (d)	19. (c)	20. (a)
21. (c)	22. (a)	23. (e)	24. (b)	25. (b)	26. (b)	27. (c)	28. (d)	29. (a)	

Average

1. (a)	**2.** (a)	**3.** (d)	**4.** (d)	**5.** (c)	**6.** (c)	**7.** (b)	**8.** (a)	**9.** (d)	**10.** (b)
11. (b)	**12.** (c)	**13.** (a)	**14.** (b)	**15.** (a)	**16.** (b)	**17.** (d)	**18.** (e)	**19.** (c)	**20.** (210)
21. (c)	**22.** (60)	**23.** (c)	**24.** (105)						

Simple Interest and Compound Interest

1. (b)	**2.** (c)	**3.** (a)	**4.** (c)	**5.** (d)	**6.** (d)	**7.** 12	**8.** (121000)	**9.** (4000)

Mixture and Solutions

1. (b)	**2.** (d)	**3.** (a)	**4.** (c)	**5.** (a)	**6.** (d)	**7.** (b)	**8.** (c)	**9.** (245)	**10.** (a)
11. (b)	**12.** (c)	**13.** (b)	**14.** (b)	**15.** (a)	**16.** (a)	**17.** (c)	**18.** (d)		

Time speed and distance

1. (d)	**2.** (c)	**3.** (c)	**4.** (d)	**5.** (b)	**6.** (d)	**7.** (d)	**8.** (a)	**9.** (d)	**10.** (c)
11. (d)	**12.** (c)	**13.** (b)	**14.** (c)	**15.** (c)	**16.** (a)	**17.** (d)	**18.** (b)	**19.** (d)	**20.** (c)
21. (a)	**22.** (b)	**23.** (c)	**24.** (b)	**25.** (c)	**26.** (c)	**27.** (b)	**28.** (a)	**29.** (a)	**30.** (c)
31. (b)	**32.** (b)	**33.** (c)	**34.** (d)	**35.** (d)	**36.** (c)	**37.** (b)	**38.** (b)	**39.** (a)	**40.** (b)
41. (c)	**42.** (a)	**43.** (a)	**44.** (d)	**45.** (d)	**46.** (b)	**47.** (a)	**48.** (b)	**49.** (b)	**50.** (b)
51. (a)	**52.** (c)	**53.** (d)	**54.** (d)	**55.** (c)	**56.** (c)	**57.** *(b)	**58.** (a)	**59.** (b)	**60.** (c)
61. (c)	**62.** (d)	**63.** (c)	**64.** (c)	**65.** (c)	**66.** (b)	**67.** (d)	**68.** (c)	**69.** (d)	**70.** (b)
71. (b)	**72.** (c)	**73.** (d)	**74.** (b)	**75.** (b)	**76.** (d)	**77.** (b)	**78.** (d)	**79.** (a)	**80.** (a)
81. (b)	**82.** (d)	**83.** (b)	**84.** 16	**85.** (b)	**86.** 156	**87.** (1900)	**88.** (c)	**89.** (b)	**90.** (b)
91. (15)	**92.** (d)	**93.** (50)	**94.** (a)	**95.** (5)					

Time and Work

1. (a)	**2.** (c)	**3.** (b)	**4.** (c)	**5.** (b)	**6.** (d)	**7.** (b)	**8.** (c)	**9.** (a)	**10.** (a)
11. (c)	**12.** (c)	**13.** (c)	**14.** (b)	**15.** (d)	**16.** (c)	**17.** (d)	**18.** (b)	**19.** (c)	**20.** (c)
21. (b)	**22.** (d)	**23.** 150	**24.** (a)	**25.** (a)	**26.** (10)	**27.** (c)	**28.** (b)	**29.** (48)	**30.** (b)
31. (b)									

Miscellaneous

1. (c)	**2.** (d)	**3.** (a)	**4.** (d)	**5.** (d)	**6.** (a)	**7.** (d)	**8.** (a)	**9.** (b)	**10.** (a)
11. (a)	**12.** (c)	**13.** (b)	**14.** (b)	**15.** (a)	**16.** (c)	**17.** (d)	**18.** (b)	**19.** (a)	**20.** (d)
21. (b)	**22.** (b)	**23.** (d)	**24.** (b)						

EXPLANATIONS

Percentages and Fraction

1. a Let there be 100 products in the stockpile. Hence, products from M1 = 40, from M2 = 30 and from M3 = 30. Number of defective products from M1 = 0.03 x 40 = 1.2, from M2 = 0.01 x 30 = 0.3 and from M3 = 0.05 x 30 = 1.5.
Therefore, total number of defective products =3, Percentage of defective stockpile = 3.

2. c Let Gopal have Rs. 400. The price of an orange and that of a mango would be Rs.8 and Rs.10 respectively.
If he keeps 10% of the money for taxi fare, he is left with Rs.360.
Now if he buys 20 mangoes i.e. if he spends Rs. 200, he is left with Rs. 160, for which he can buy 20 oranges.

3. c Let the number of TVs and VCRs bought be t and v respectively. Therefore,

$t + v \le 100$ ... (i)

$10000t + 15000v \le 1200000 \Rightarrow 2t + 3v \le 240$ ... (ii)

Profit = 2000t + 2500v, to maximize profit we have to maximize v.
From (i) and (ii),

$2(100 - v) + 3v \le 240$

$v \le 40$ and $t \le 60$

For maximum profit: t = 60 and v = 40.

4. b Let the number of TVs and VCRs bought be t and v respectively. Therefore,

$t + v \le 120$ ... (i)

$10000t + 15000v \le 1200000 \Rightarrow 2t + 3v \le 240$ ... (ii)

Profit = 2000t + 2500v, to maximize profit we have to maximize v.
From (i) and (ii),

$2(120 - v) + 3v \le 240$

$v \le 0$ and $t \le 120$

For maximum profit: t = 120 and v = 0.
Required ratio = 0.

5. a Let the number of TVs and VCRs bought be t and v respectively. Therefore,

$t + v \le 100$ ... (i)

$10000t + 15000v \le 1200000 \Rightarrow 2t + 3v \le 240$ ...(ii)

Profit = 2200t + 3300v,
to maximize profit we have to maximize v.
From (i) and (ii),

$2(100 - v) + 3v \le 240$

$v \le 40$ and $t \le 60$

For maximum profit: t = 60 and v = 40.
Required profit = 2200 × 60 + 3300 × 40
= Rs.2.64 lakhs.

6. d Let 'p' people be born everyday. Since February 29 comes once in 4 years. In 20th century there were 25 leap years, hence number of people born on 29th February = 25p. Total number of people born in the century = (25 x 366 x p) + (75 x 365 x p) = 36525p. Therefore, percentage of people born on 29th February $= \frac{25}{36525} \times 100 = 0.0684$.

HINT: Students please note that this could well be solved by taking 1 set of leap year as well. In other words, in a 4 year period in 20th century number of people born = (3 x 365 x p) + 366p = 1461p and number of people born on 29th February in this 4 year period = p.
Hence, required percentage $= \frac{1}{1461} \times 100 = 0.0684$.
Thus the period has no significance in this problem.

7. b Let the amount with Gopal be Rs. 400. Therefore, price of an orange is then Rs. 8 and that of a mango is Rs.10. If he keeps 10% of the money for taxi fare, he is left with Rs.360. Now if he buys 20 mangoes, then he spends on mangoes Rs. 200. Now he is left with Rs.160, in which he can buy 20 oranges.

8. c Since the inflation rate is 8% in both the years 1994 and 1995, therefore, the rate of increase of the price of sugar is 10%.
∴ Price of sugar on January 1, 1996 = Price of sugar on January 1, 1994 $\times \left(1 + \frac{10}{100}\right)^2 = 20 \times 1.21$
= Rs.24.20 per kg.

9. a The total number of the characters = (20 x 55 x 65).
Let the number of pages in the new format be n.
Thus, the total number of the characters
= (65 x 70 x n).
Since the total number of the characters remains same, therefore, $n \approx 16$.
Hence, the required percentage

$= \frac{20 - 16}{20} \times 100 = 20\%$.

10. c Let x be the number of votes not cast for Praja Party in the previous polls.

So the number of votes not cast for the party in this assembly polls would be 1.25x.

Margin of victory in the previous polls

= (Votes cast) – (Votes not cast)

= (260000 – x) – x = (260000 – 2x).

Margin of loss in this years polls

= 1.25x – (260000 – 1.25x)

= (2.5x – 260000).

As per the given information,

margin of loss this year = 2 × Margin of victory last year.

Therefore, (2.5x – 260000) = 2(260000 – 2x).

$\Rightarrow$ x = 120000.

So the number of votes cast for the party in assembly election = 260000 – 120000 = 140000.

11. d Let us assume that the person has Rs.100.

With this, he can buy 50 oranges or 40 mangoes. In other words, the price of an orange is Rs.2 and that of a mango is Rs.2.50.

If he decides to keep 10% of his money for taxi fare, he would be left with Rs.90.

Now if he buys 20 mangoes, he would spend Rs.50 and will be left with Rs.40.

Thus, he can buy 20 oranges.

12. a Let there be 100 voters in all.

Initially, 40 of these promised to vote for P, while 60 of them promised to vote for Q.

On the last day, (15% of 40) = 6 voters went back of their promise and voted for Q.

Also, 25% of 60 = 15 voters shifted their interest from Q to P.

So finally, P end up getting (40 – 6 + 15) = 49 votes and Q end up getting (60 – 15 + 6) = 51 votes.

Hence, margin of victory for Q = (51 – 49) = 2, which is true. Hence, there were 100 voters in all.

13. d Required cost $= 6\left[1+\frac{1000}{100}\right]^2$

$= 6(11)^2 = 121 \times 6 = 726.$

14. b Statement II in itself suggests the price of a banana. Since we can buy 48 bananas in Rs.12, price of a banana = Re.0.25. And since this price is after 50% reduction, the actual price of a banana = Re.0.5.

15. b Let us look at the two equations. Let (5 pens + 7 pencils + 4 erasers)cost Rs. x. Hence, (6 pens + 14 pencils + 8 erasers)will cost Rs. 1.5x. Had, in the second case, Rajan decided to buy 10 pens instead of 6, the quantity of each one of them would have doubled over the first case and hence it would have cost me Rs. 2x. So (10 pens + 14 pencils + 8 erasers)= Rs. 2x. Now subtracting the second equation from the third, we get 4 pens cost Rs. 0.5x. Since 4 pens cost Re 0.5x, 5 of them will cost Re 0.625x. This is the amount that I spent on pens. Hence, fraction of the total amount paid = 0.625 = 62.5%.

16. c This can simply be solved by multiplying the two multiplication factors to get the effective multiplication factor. E.g. multiplication factor for 30% increase = 1.30. Multiplication factor for 20% decrease = 0.8.

Hence, 1.30 × 0.8 = 1.04. This multiplication factor (i.e. 1.04)indicates that there is a 4% increase in total revenue.

So the answer is +4%.

Alternative method:

By using the formula $x + y + \frac{xy}{100}$

$\therefore$ x = +30%; y = – 20%

$\Rightarrow 30 + 60 + \frac{50(-20)}{100} = 30 - 20 - 6 = +4\%.$

17. b 20 kg fresh grapes will contain (0.9 × 20) = 18 kg water and 2 kg mass. If the dry grape has to contain 2 kg mass, it should constitute 80% of that. Hence, if 80% of dry grapes corresponds to 2 kg, its total weight will be $\left(\frac{2}{0.8}\right) = 2.5$ kg.

18. b The two equations can be written as:

$$2000\left(\frac{x}{100}\right) + 2000\left(\frac{y}{100}\right) = 700$$

and $2000\left(\frac{x}{100}\right) + 3000\left(\frac{y}{100}\right) = 900$

The equations can be simplified to x + y = 35 and 2x + 3y = 90. Solving these two equations simultaneously, we get x = 15%.

19. d Even by using both the statements, we can only find out the proportion of the paper solved by Radha and Rani. In the light of the fact that the number of questions solved by either or both of them is not given, we cannot answer the question asked.

20. d

Men	Women
40%	60%

Out of 40% men, 75% earn more than Rs. 25,000.

Hence, 30% of the company (men) earn more than Rs. 25,000.

But, in all 45% of the employees earn more than Rs. 25,000.

Hence, among women 15% earn more than Rs. 25,000 and the remaining (60 – 15)% earn less than or equal to Rs. 25,000.

Therefore, the fraction of women = $\frac{45}{60} = \frac{3}{4}$.

21. b Total 400 million is for 64.75% of the population. Hence, total population is 617.76 million. Let females be F and males be M. Then $\frac{F}{M} = 0.96$ (in the class below 15).

Total population in the range is approximately 185.32 million. Hence, number of females is 90.8 million.

22. a In first updown cycle, the reduction price is Rs. 441. According to this, (b)and (d) are removed. Now we have to analyse (c), if the original price is Rs. 2,500, then after first operation, the price will be 2500 – 441= Rs. 2,059.

In second operation, it will come down to around Rs. 1688 $\left[\text{here decrease\%} = \frac{441}{2500} \times 100 \approx 18\%\right]$.

So the value is not equivalent to Rs. 1,944.81.

Hence, option (a) is the answer.

23. d Statement I gives a general figure of Ram and Gopal.

Statement II does not give any idea of how many apples Ram and Gopal purchased.

Both statements together also cannot give any result.

24. b Mayank paid $\frac{1}{2}$ of the sum paid by other three.

$\Rightarrow$ Mayank paid $\frac{1}{3}$rd of the total amount = \$20.

Similarly, Mirza paid \$15 and Little paid \$12.

Remaining amount of \$60 – \$20 – \$15 – \$12 = \$13 is paid by Jaspal.

25. c Given that Shephard had 9 dozens of goat at the end of 1998.

$\therefore$ Number of goats at the beginning of 1999 = (1 + p%) 9 dozens

He sells off q% of this at the end of the year 1999.

$\therefore$ Number of goats at the end of 1999 = (1 – q%) (1 + p%) 9 dozens

Since every year the same process is repeated and at the end of 2002, he has the same number as at the end of 1998,

we can get that (1 + p%)(1 – q%) = 1

$\Rightarrow 1 + p - q - pq = 1$

$\Rightarrow p - q = pq$

$\Rightarrow p > q$ (Since p > 0 and q > 0)

26. a Let incomes of Zakib and Supriyo be Z and S respectively.

Statement A: 20% of Z > 25% of S $\Rightarrow Z > \frac{5}{4}S$

Now, Zakia spent 30% of his income on education

$= 30\% \text{ of } Z > \frac{30}{100} \times \frac{5}{4}S = 0.375S$

From this we cannot say if 0.3 Z is greater than or less than 0.4 S.

Hence, statement A alone is not sufficient.

Statement B: 13% of S > 10% of Z

Multiplying both sides by 3, we get,

39% of S > 30% of Z

So 40% of S is definitely more than 30% of Z.

Hence, statement B alone is sufficient.

27. e Let the initial length, breadth and height of the room be 3x, 2x and x respectively.

Initial area of the four walls = $2(3x + 2x)x = 10x^2$

The new dimensions are: length = 6x, breadth = x and height $= \frac{x}{2}$.

New area of the four walls $= 2(6x + x)\frac{x}{2} = 7x^2$

Therefore, percentage decrease

$$= \frac{10x^2 - 7x^2}{10x^2} \times 100 = 30\%.$$

28. a From statement A, it is clear that 40% of top academic performers are athletes and that is equal to 10. So total number of academic performers can be calculated.

Statement B does not provide any relevant information.

So the answer is (a).

29. c Statement A alone is sufficient because 10% of the female employees have engineering background, 70% of the employees are females, so 7% of the employees are female and having engineering background. Hence, 18% of the employees are male and having engineering background. From statement B, we know the number of male employees having engineering background. So, the percentage of male employees having engineering background can be calculated. So, the answer is (c).

30. c As he wants to save 10% of the total money, he can buy either 45 mangoes or 36 oranges. If he buys exactly 20 oranges then he can buy 16 more oranges with the money left.

Let M be the price of a mango and O be the price of an orange.

So $45\text{ M} = 36\text{ O}$

$\Rightarrow \quad O = \frac{5}{4}M$

$\Rightarrow \quad 16\text{ O} = 16 \times \frac{5}{4}M$

$\Rightarrow \quad 16\text{ O} = 20\text{ M}$

So he can buy 20 mangoes with the money left.

31. d Volume of water in the 40 ml taken from the first alcohol-water mixture = $\left(\frac{y}{100+y}\right) \times 40$ ml

Volume of water in the 2y ml taken from the second alcohol-water mixture = $(1 - 0.26) \times 2y = 1.48y$ ml.

Total volume of the two mixtures taken
$= (40 + 2y)$ ml.

Hence, $\frac{\left(\frac{y}{100+y}\right) \times 40 + 1.48y}{40+2y} = \frac{2y}{100}$

Solving the above equation for y, we get

y = 25 or −108 (which is rejected)

Note: Instead of solving for y, the value can also be obtained by simply substituting the options in the last equation.

32. a **Note:** A.M. ≥ G.M.

$$\frac{4P+4P+4P+R+R+R+2Q+2Q}{8} \geq \sqrt[8]{256 \times P^3R^3Q^2}$$

$$\frac{12P+3R+4Q}{8} \geq 2\sqrt[8]{P^3R^3Q^2}$$

$$16 \geq 16\sqrt[8]{P^3R^3Q^2}$$

$1 \geq \sqrt[8]{P^3R^3Q^2}$ or $1 \geq P^3R^3Q^2$.

33. c Suppose the contractor had x trucks.

So, we have $\frac{x+8}{x-8} = \frac{3}{2}$

$\Rightarrow x = 40$

34. c List price first increases by 10% and then decreases by 10%.

$\Rightarrow \left(\frac{100+10}{100}\right) \times \left(\frac{100-10}{100}\right)$
$\times$ initial list price = final list price

$\Rightarrow$ Initial list price = $\frac{20 \times 100^2}{100^2 - 10^2}$

35. c Let the number of female employees in factory A and the number of male employees in factory B be 2a and 5b respectively. Therefore, the number of male employees in factory A and that of female employees in factory B will be 3a and 3b respectively.

$\therefore \quad 3b = 3a + 60$

$\Rightarrow \quad b - a = 20 \quad$ ...(i)

Total number of male employees in the two factories put together

$= 3a + 5b.$

$= 3a + 5 \times (20 + a)$

$= 8a + 100.$

Among the given options, only 8a + 100 = 320 will not give a positive integer value of 'a'.

36. b Let total shirts produced = 100x

Defective = 15x

Rest = 85x

Shirts sold in domestic market = 17x

Remaining shirts = 68x

So, $\quad 68x = 8840$

$\Rightarrow \quad 100x = 13000.$

37. c The required percentage $= \left(\frac{40}{127} - 1\right) \times 100 = 10\%$

38. d According to the question,

$$36 = \left(1 - \frac{68}{100}\right)\left(\frac{45}{100}N\right)$$

$$36 = \frac{32}{100} \times \frac{45}{100} \times N$$

$\Rightarrow \quad N = 250$

Hence, $243 \leq N \leq 252$

Profit, Loss and Discount

1. c The statement I only gives the comparison of the selling prices. You must realise that this information is not enough to answer the question as the profit also depends on cost. So we also need to analyze the statement II. And since there is no other constraint on production, we can solely compare the profitability of two products on the basis of labour. According to it, if 10 units of labour is available, it can produce 5 units of Q and 2 units of R. So, from 10 units of labour, I can earn (5 x 1)= 5 units of sales revenue from Q and (2 x 4)= 8 units of sales revenue from R. So by taking both statements together we can determine which would be more profitable.

2. a 16 articles sold at priced 12 articles, is equivalent to discount of $\left[\left(\frac{16-12}{16}\right) \times 100\right] = 25\%$

Hence, shop keepers offer two discounts of 20% and 25% respectively and still makes a profit of 20%.

If c is the cost price of an article and m is the marked price, then $1.2 \times c = m \times \frac{3}{4} \times \frac{4}{5}$

$\Rightarrow$ m = 2c.

This means that he had marked his goods 100% above his cost price.

3. b P = (SP – CP)x Sales. From the data given in the question we can figure out that P1 = (1.1SP – CP) x 0.9Sales.

Hence, $\frac{P}{P1} = \frac{1.11(SP - CP)}{(1.1SP - CP)}$.

To find this ratio we need to eliminate the variables CP & SP. This can only be done if in the denominator, CP is replaced by 1.1CP. In other words, if the CP increases by 10%, as in that case our ratio will be $\frac{1.11}{1.1} = 1.01$.

Hence, only statement II is required to answer the question.

4. b Profit percentage in each case is

(i) 10%

(ii) $\frac{100 \times 100}{900} = \frac{100}{9}\%$

(iii) $\frac{100 \times 1.1 - 100}{100} \times 100 = 10\%$

(iv) $\frac{10 \times 100}{95} = \frac{200}{19}\%$

5. a It is clear that only statement I is required to answer the question, if CP = 0.8 SP, then SP = $\left(\frac{1}{0.8}\right)$ CP.

$\therefore$ SP = 1.25 CP

Thus, profit percentage is 25.

6. a Let the price per metre of cloth be Re 1. The shopkeeper buys 120 cm, but pays for only 100 cm. In other words, he buys 120 cm for Rs. 100.

So his CP = $\left(\frac{100}{120}\right)$ = Re 0.833 per metre. Now he sells 80 cm, but charges for 100 cm. In other words, he sells 80 cm for Rs. 100. On this he offers a 20% discount on cash payment. So he charges Rs. 80 for 80 cm cloth. In other words, his SP = $\left(\frac{80}{80}\right)$ = Re 1 per metre. So his percentage profit in the overall transaction = $\frac{(1 - 0.833)}{0.833}$ = 20%.

7. b Total expense incurred in making 1,500 watches = (1500 x 150)+ 30000 = Rs. 2,55,000.

Total revenue obtained by selling 1,200 of them during the season = (1200 × 250) = Rs. 3,00,000. The remaining 300 of them has to be sold by him during off season.

The total revenue obtained by doing that = (300 × 100) = Rs. 30,000.

Hence, total revenue obtained = (300000 + 30000) = Rs. 3,30,000.

Hence, total profit = (330000 – 255000) = Rs. 75,000.

8. b From the previous solution, we can see that the total expense incurred by him in manufacturing 1,500 watches = Rs.2,55,000. In order to break-even, he has to make a minimum revenue in order to recover his expenditure. He gets Rs. 250 per watch sold and Rs. 100 on every watch not sold. Let him sell x watches to break-even. So our equation will be 250x + 100(1500 – x) = 255000. Solving this, we get x = 700 watches.

9. b In this case, we need not use the data that SP = Rs. 300 each. This has to be used only to figure out that the SP of both the articles is the same. Also since the profit percentage on one is equal to the loss percentage on the other, viz. 10% effectively, it will be a loss given by $\frac{(10)^2}{100}$ = 1%. Hence, the correct answer is (–)1.

10. a Both the statements are telling the same, that selling price is 75% of cost price.

So we cannot determine the actual cost of the article.

11. c By using statement II we can determine the selling price of the article.

Selling price = 1.25 × 250 = Rs. 312.50

But by using statement I we cannot determine the selling price.

12. d Let he mix 3 kg, 4 kg and 5 kg of dry fruits at Rs. 100, Rs. 80 and at Rs. 60 per kilogram respectively. Hence, his effective cost of the dry fruits per kilogram should be the weighted average

$= \frac{3 \times 100 + 4 \times 80 + 5 \times 60}{3 + 4 + 5} = \frac{920}{12}$

In order to make a 50% profit, he will have to sell it at

$\frac{920}{12} \times 1.5 = \frac{920}{12} \times \frac{3}{2} = \frac{920}{8}$ = Rs. 115 per kilogram.

Since none of the answer-choices confirms this, the answer is (d).

13. a **Hint:** Students please note that the percentages that are given are the basic percentages derived from basic fractions. E.g. 11.11% = $\frac{1}{9}$ and 14.28 = $\frac{1}{7}$. Hence, you should make use of the most of this kind of knowledge. So let the CP be Re 1.

Since he makes a profit of $\frac{1}{7}$, his SP = $(1 + \frac{1}{7})$ = Rs. $\frac{8}{7}$.

His marked price should be $\frac{1}{9}$ above this. So if we subtract $\frac{1}{9}$ of MP from the MP, we will get the SP.

So $(MP - \frac{1}{9} MP) = SP = \frac{8}{7}$

Hence, $MP = \frac{9}{7}$

Therefore, percentage of mark-up on CP = (MP – CP)/CP

$= (\frac{9}{7} - 1)/1 = \frac{2}{7} = 2(\frac{1}{7}) = 2 \times 14.28 = 28.56\%$

Alternative method:

We can use the formula $z = x - y - \frac{xy}{100}$, where

z = Gain percentage

x = Percentage above CP

y = Discount percentage

$\therefore$ $14.28\% = x - 11.11\% - \frac{11.11x}{100}$

or $14.28 = \frac{100x - 1111 - 11.11x}{100}$

or 1428 – 1111 = 88.89x

or x = 28.56% (Approximately)

For questions 14 and 15:

Let CP = 100

Current gain = 20

$\Rightarrow$ SP = 120

CP = Cost of A + Cost of B + Other

= 30% + 50% + 20%

14. a Since cost of German mark (A) increase by 30%

New cost of A = 30 + 30% of 30 = 39

Similarly,

New cost of B = 50 + 22% of 50 = 61

New CP = 39 + 61 + 20 = 120

New SP = 120 + 10% of 120 = 132

Maximum profit $= \frac{12}{120} = 10\%$

15. b New cost of A = 30 + 20% of 30 = 36

New cost of B = 50 – 12% of 50 = 44

New CP = 36 = 44 + 20 = 100

Gain = 20%

16. a Statement I implies that profit is 2.95%, but we want the profit per rupee spent on buying the shares. The cost of buying the shares for Harshad is CP + 0.01 CP = 1.01 CP.

The cost of selling is SP – 0.01 SP = 0.99 SP

The difference of the two is profit, i.e.

0.99 SP – 1.01 CP = 0.99 × 1.05 CP – 1.01 CP = 0.0295 CP. Hence, profit = 2.95%.

Statement II gives us no information regarding sales price and purchase price.

17. a Statement:

A. Let the wholesale price is x.

Thus, listed prices = 1.2x

After a discount of 10%, new price = 0.9 × 1.2x = 1.08x

$\therefore$ 1.08 – x = 10$.

Thus, we know x can be found.

B. We do not know at what percentage profit, or at what amount of profit the dress was actually sold.

For questions 18 and 19:

S, M and R in all spend 1248 Bahts.

Initially M pays 211 Bahts and R pays 92 Bahts.

Remaining is paid by S i.e; 945 Bahts.

If 1248 is divided equally among S, M and R, each has to spend 415 Bahts.

Hence, M has to pay 205 Bahts which is 5 Dollars to S.

and R has to pay 324 Bahts to S.

For questions 20 and 21:

To maximise Shabnam's return we need to evaluate all the given options in the question number 7. Assume Shabnam had one rupee to invest. Let the return be denoted by 'r'.

Consider the option (30% in option A, 32% in option B and 38% in option C): If the stock market rises, then

r = 0.1 × 0.3 + 5 × 0.32 – 2.5 × 0.38 = 0.653

If the stock market falls, then

r = 0.1 × 0.3 – 3 × 0.32 + 2 × 0.38 = – 0.197

Consider option (100% in option A): This will give a return of 0.1%.

Consider option (36% in option B and 64% in option C) : If the stock market rises, then

r = 5 × 0.36 – 2.5 × 0.64 = 0.2

If the stock market falls, then

r = – 3 × 0.36 + 2 × 0.64 = 0.2

Consider option (64% in option B and 36% in option C): If the stock market rises, then

$r = 5 \times 0.64 - 2.5 \times 0.36 = 2.1$

If the stock market falls, then

$r = -3 \times 0.64 + 2 \times 0.36 = -1.2$

Consider option (1/3 in each of the 3 options): If the stock market rises, then

$r = 0.1 \times 0.33 + 5 \times 0.33 - 2.5 \times 0.33 = 0.858$

If the stock market falls, then

$r = 0.1 \times 0.33 - 3 \times 0.33 + 2 \times 0.33 = -0.297$

We can see that only in option **(36% in option B and 64% in option C)**, Shabnam gets an assured return of 0.2% irrespective of the behaviour of the stock market. So right option for questions number 19 is **(0.20%)** and question number 20 is **(36% in option B and 64% in option C)**.

22. a Let the earlier cost price of the item = ₹ 100

$\Rightarrow$ Earlier marked price = ₹ 105.

On that day, 30% discount is offered on

₹ 3 × 105 = ₹ 315

Thus, new selling price = ₹ 220.50

$\Rightarrow$ New Profit percentage = 120.50%.

23. a If the profit amount are in A.P then the profit % ages are also in an A.P.

If P_4 = 13% and P_7 = 10% then P_5 = 12% and P_6 = 11%.

Average of the middle terms will give the profit % on the whole i.e. (11 + 12)/2 = 11.5 %

24. 2000 Let the C.P. of the article be Rs.x.

$$\therefore \quad \frac{1920 - x}{x} \times 100 = \frac{x - 1280}{x} \times 100$$

$$\Rightarrow \quad 1920 - x = x - 1280$$

$$\Rightarrow \quad 2x = 3200$$

$$\Rightarrow \quad x = 1600$$

Hence, to make a profit of 25%, the S.P.

= 125% of 1600 = Rs.2,000.

25. b Let the CP be x

$$\therefore x \times \frac{110}{100} \times \frac{130}{100} \times \frac{150}{100} = 4290$$

x = Rs. 000.

26. a Let he buys one dozen candies of each type IInd type

Total C.P. = Rs. 7

S.P. = Rs. 33

Profit = Rs. 6

For getting profit of Rs. 50

He must sold 50 dozens

27. 4 Let the price of the peanut bought by the wholesaler be Rs. x / kg and that of walnut be Rs.3x/kg.

For the shopkeeper, total price of 8 kg of peanuts and 16 kg of walnuts is

$$\frac{110}{100} \times 8x + \frac{120}{100} \times 16 \times 3x = \frac{332x}{5}$$

The shopkeeper sold the remaining mixture i.e. 16 kg at Rs. 166 /kg.

∴ Total S.P for him = 16 × 166 = Rs. 2656

He made overall profit of 25%

$$\therefore \text{Total C.P.} = \frac{100}{125} \times 2656 = \frac{4}{5} \times 2656$$

$$\therefore \frac{332x}{5} = \frac{4}{5} \times 2656$$

$$\Rightarrow X = 32$$

∴ The wholesaler bought the walnuts at 3 × 32 = Rs. 96 per kg.

Ratio and Proportion

1. c The ratios of the share of students, teachers and benefactor is 1 : 1.5 : 4.5. So, the proportion of teachers share is $\frac{1.5}{7}$. So teachers would donate:

$$\frac{(1.5 \times 4200)}{7} = \text{Rs.}900.$$

2. a Let the two given numbers be x and y such that x > y.

According to the question,

$$x - \frac{y}{2} = 3\left(y - \frac{y}{2}\right) \Rightarrow \frac{x}{y} = \frac{2}{1}.$$

3. c Let the original weight of the diamond be 10x. Hence, its original price will be $k(100x^2)$... where k is a constant. The weights of the pieces after breaking are x, 2x, 3x and 4x. Therefore, their prices will be kx^2, $4kx^2$, $9kx^2$ and $16kx^2$. So the total price of the pieces = $(1 + 4 + 9 + 16)kx^2$ = $30kx^2$. Hence, the difference in the price of the original diamond and its pieces = $100kx^2 - 30kx^2$ = $70kx^2$ = 70000.

Hence, kx^2 = 1000 and the original price = $100kx^2$ = 100 × 1000 = 100000 = Rs. 1 lakh.

4. b Consider the statement I:

Let number of type-1 widgets = x.

Number of type-2 widgets = y.

From the given question, x + y = 20000.

From statement I, 1.1 x + 0.94y = 20000.

So we can get x and y.

From statement II, number of type-2 widgets produced $= \frac{1}{3} \times 20000 = 6667$.

The question can be answered by using either of the statements alone.

5. c Let his marks be 100, 90, 80, 70 and 60 in the five subjects. Hence, totally he has scored 400 marks. This constitutes only 60% of the total marks. Hence, total marks $= \frac{400}{0.6} = 667$, Since the total marks in each subject is the same, hence maximum marks in each subject will be $\left(\frac{667}{5}\right) \simeq 133$. Out of this 50% is the passing marks. In other words, to pass in a subject he needs to score 66.5 marks. We can see that only in one subject he scored less than this, viz. 60. Hence, he passed in 4 subjects.

6. b Let D_1, T_1 and D_2, T_2 denote the diameters and the thickness of the two coins respectively. If V_1 and V_2 are the values of the two coins.

$$\frac{V_1}{V_2} = \left(\frac{D_1^2 T_1}{D_2^2 T_2}\right) = \left(\frac{D_1}{D_2}\right)^2 \left(\frac{T_1}{T_2}\right)$$

Therefore, $\frac{4}{1} = \left(\frac{4}{3}\right)^2 \left(\frac{T_1}{T_2}\right) \Rightarrow \left(\frac{T_1}{T_2}\right) = \frac{9}{4}$.

7. a Let the cost of the turban be T.

Total payment for one year = Rs. 90 + T. So the payment for 9 months should be Rs. $\frac{3}{4}(90 + T)$. But this is equal to (65 + T). Equating the two, we get T = Rs. 10.

8. d Since the number of coins are in the ratio 2.5 : 3 : 4, the values of the coins will be in the ratio (1 × 2.5) : (0.5 × 3): (0.25 × 4)

= 2.5 : 1.5 : 1 or 5 : 3 : 2

Since they totally amount to Rs. 210, if the value of each type of coins are assumed to be 5x, 3x and 2x, the average value per coin will be $\frac{210}{10x}$.

So the total value of one-rupee coins will be

$5 \times \left(\frac{210}{10x}\right)$ = Rs. 105

So the total number of one-rupee coins will be 105.

9. d Note that both the statements give the same piece of information that a : b = 3 : 5 and that a and b are both positive. But none of the statements either in itself or together can give the value of a.

10. b $18 \propto \sqrt{9}$

$42 \propto \sqrt{x}$; Here x = number of compartments

$$\frac{18}{42} = \frac{\sqrt{9}}{\sqrt{x}}$$

Simplifying, x = 49, but this is with reference to maximum speed. Hence, number of compartments would be one less in order to run i.e. 48.

11. c Distance between A and B = (35 × 2) + (45 × 2) = 160 km.

Distance covered by Aditi in each speed segment $= \frac{160}{3}$

Hence, total petrol consumed

$$= \left(\frac{160}{3} \times \frac{1}{16}\right) + \left(\frac{160}{3} \times \frac{1}{24}\right) + \left(\frac{160}{3} \times \frac{1}{16}\right) = 8.91$$

12. a For minimum petrol consumption, Zoheb should drive at 40 kmph, petrol consumption $= \frac{160}{24} = 6.67$ l.

13. c Fresh grapes contain 10% pulp.

∴ 20 kg fresh grapes contain 2 kg pulp.

Dry grapes contain 80% pulp.

∴ 2 kg pulp will contain $\frac{2}{0.8} = \frac{20}{8} = 2.5$ kg dry grapes.

14. b Each traveller had $\frac{8}{3}$ loaves.

⇒ First traveller has given $5 - \frac{8}{3}$ loaves to the third.

Second traveller sacrificed only $3 - \frac{8}{3} = \frac{1}{3}$rd of a loaf.

So, first should get 7 coins.

15. c Given pqr = 1 ⇒ $pq = \frac{1}{r}$ and $\frac{1}{p} = qr$

$$\frac{1}{1+p+q^{-1}} + \frac{1}{1+q+r^{-1}} + \frac{1}{1+r+p^{-1}}$$

$$= \frac{q}{1+q+pq} + \frac{r}{1+qr+r} + \frac{1}{1+r+qr}$$

$$= \frac{qr}{1+qr+r} + \frac{r}{1+qr+r} + \frac{1}{1+r+qr} = \frac{1+r+qr}{1+r+qr} = 1$$

Alternate solution: Putting x = y = z = 1, we get

$$\frac{1}{1+p+q^{-1}} + \frac{1}{1+q+r^{-1}} + \frac{1}{1+r+p^{-1}}$$

$$= \frac{1}{1+1+1} + \frac{1}{1+1+1} + \frac{1}{1+1+1} = \frac{1}{3} + \frac{1}{3} + \frac{1}{3} = 1.$$

16. a

Total seats in the hall	200
Seats vacant	20
Total waiting	180
Ladies	72

Seating capacity of flight $\frac{2}{3}\times 180 = 120$

Number of people in flight A = 100

For flight B = 180 – 100 = 80

Thus, airhostess for A = $\frac{80}{20} = 4$

Empty seats in flight B = 120 – 80 = 40

40 : 4 = 10 : 1

17. c Jagdish (J), Punit (P), Girish (G)

Statement A: J = $\frac{2}{9}$ [P + G]W

P + G + J = 38500

Thus, only J can be found.

Statement B: Similarly, from this only P can be found.

Combining we know J, P and G can be found.

18. d a = 6b = 12c and 2b = 9d = 12e.

Dividing the first equation by 12 and second by 36, we get $\frac{a}{12} = \frac{b}{2} = \frac{c}{1}$ and $\frac{b}{18} = \frac{d}{4} = \frac{e}{3}$

i.e. $\frac{a}{108} = \frac{b}{18} = \frac{c}{9}$ and $\frac{b}{18} = \frac{d}{4} = \frac{e}{3}$

$\therefore \frac{a}{108} = \frac{b}{18} = \frac{c}{9} = \frac{d}{4} = \frac{e}{3}$

$\therefore$ a : b : c : d : e = 108 : 18 : 9 : 4 : 3.

$\therefore \frac{c}{d} = \frac{9}{4}$ is not an integer.

19. c Let in 2001 the number of huts before floods = 32

$\therefore$ Huts destroyed = $\frac{32}{2} = 16$ and rebuilt = 32.

$\therefore$ Total huts after floods in 2001 = 16 + 32 = 48

Similarly, in 2002, destroyed = 24

Rebuilt = 48

Total = 24 + 48 = 72

Similarly, in 2003, destroyed = 36

Rebuilt = 72

Total = 36 + 72 = 108

$\therefore$ Checking with choices, the answer is (c).

20. a Let there be n members in the club.

From statement A, we have $\frac{600}{n-5} = \frac{600}{n} + 10$.

Solving this equation, we get n = 20. Therefore, we can find the payment of each member.

Hence, statement A alone is sufficient.

From statement B, we cannot determine anything.

21. c If $\frac{a}{b+c} = \frac{b}{c+a} = \frac{c}{a+b} = r$

then there are only two possibilities.

(i) If $a + b + c \neq 0$, then

$$\frac{a}{b+c} = \frac{b}{c+a} = \frac{c}{a+b} = \frac{a+b+c}{(b+c)+(c+a)+(a+b)}$$

$$= \frac{a+b+c}{2(a+b+c)} = \frac{1}{2}$$

(ii) If a+ b + c = 0, then

b + c = – a

c + a = – b

a + b = – c

Hence, $\frac{a}{b+c} = \frac{a}{(-a)} = -1$

Similarly, $\frac{b}{c+a} = \frac{c}{a+b} = -1$

Therefore, option (c)is the correct answer.

22. a $\frac{a}{b} = \frac{1}{3}, \frac{b}{c} = \frac{2}{1} \Rightarrow a : b : c = 2 : 6 : 3$

Similarly, a : b : c : d : e : f = 6 : 18 : 9 : 18 : 6 : 24

$\therefore \frac{abc}{def} = \frac{6\times 18\times 9}{18\times 6\times 24} = \frac{3}{8}$

Hence, option (a)is the correct answer.

Alternate method:

$$\frac{a}{b}\times\frac{b}{c}\times\frac{c}{d}\times\frac{d}{e}\times\frac{e}{f} = \frac{a}{f} = \frac{1}{3}\times 2\times\frac{1}{2}\times 3\times\frac{1}{4} = \frac{1}{4}$$

$$\frac{b}{c}\times\frac{c}{d} = \frac{b}{d} = 2\times\frac{1}{2} = 1$$

$$\frac{c}{d}\times\frac{d}{e} = \frac{c}{e} = \frac{1}{2}\times 3 = \frac{3}{2}$$

So, $\frac{abc}{def} = \frac{a}{f}\times\frac{b}{d}\times\frac{c}{e} = \frac{1}{4}\times 1\times\frac{3}{2} = \frac{3}{8}$.

23. e Using options, the sum of the numerator and denominator of the ratio should be a prime number. Only option (e)satisfies [97 + 84 = 181].

24. b Suppose that the total amount involved in this game in $K.

The first person has $\frac{7}{18}$K in the beginning and $\frac{6}{15}$K in the end. Thus he won something.

Second person has $\frac{6}{18}$K in the beginning and $\frac{5}{15}$K in the end. So he neither gains nor loses. At this point it is very clear that third person loses something.

$\Rightarrow \quad \frac{6}{15}K - \frac{7}{18}K = 12.$

So, K = 1080.

So,the winner must have started with $420.

25. b Let the required number of hour be h.

$$\therefore \frac{1\times\left(1-\frac{5}{100}\right)^h}{9\left(1-\frac{20}{100}\right)^h + 1\times\left(1-\frac{5}{100}\right)^h} \geq \frac{18}{100}$$

Going through the options, h = 4 comes out to be the correct answer.

26. b Let 4x + 3y = 14k, then xy = 2k and y – 6x = k.

On solving the first and the third equations,

we get $x = \frac{k}{2}$ and y = 4k.

$\Rightarrow \quad xy = 2k^2$

$$\therefore \frac{2x}{y} = \frac{2\times\frac{k}{2}}{4k} = \frac{1}{4}.$$

27. c a : b = 3 : 4

b : c = 2 : 1

a : b : c = 3 : 4 : 2

Let a = 3x, b = 4x, c = 2x.

So, a + b + c = 9x which is a multiple of 9.

So, among options, only 207 is a multiple of 9.

∴ The possible value of (a + b + c) is 207.

28. d Let Raju and Lalitha originally had 4 and 9 marbles respectively and Lalitha gave x marbles to Raju.

$$\therefore \frac{4+x}{9-x} = \frac{5}{6}$$

$$11x = 21$$

$$x = \frac{21}{11}$$

Hence, the fraction of her original number of marbles given by Lalitha to Raju was

$$\frac{\frac{21}{11}}{9} = \frac{21}{11\times 9} = \frac{7}{33}$$

29. a Let the new marks be 47 and 56 respectively.

Old marks are in the ratio of 11 : 14 and their difference is 3.

Therefore, the old marks has to be 33 and 42 so that the difference becomes 9 and equal to the new one.

Hence, required ratio for Bimal = 56 : 42 = 4 : 3.

Average

1. a Sum of all the three quotations = 110 × 3 = Rs. 330

From statement I, if the lowest quotation is Rs. 110 then the sum of other two quotations = 330 – 100 = Rs. 230.

Now, minimum value of second quotation = Rs. 101

Therefore, maximum value of third quotation = 230 –101 = Rs. 229.

2. a If the numbers are a, b, c and d such that a < b < c < d, then from statement I, we get (d – c) > (b – a).

So we can say, (d + a)> (b + c) or (d + a) + (d + a) > (b + c)+ (d + a). Dividing both the sides by 4, we get $\frac{(d+a)}{2} > \frac{(a+b+c+d)}{4}$.

This shows that the average of the largest and the smallest of four numbers is indeed greater than the average of all the 4 numbers. Hence, we can answer the question using statement I only.

3. d As neither average weight of the original members is not mentioned nor the number of members in original team, question cannot be answered.

4. d Although the number of students in group D is more than in any other group, we still cannot say anything about the average weight of this group as nothing is mentioned about the average weights of any of the groups or of the individual students.

5. c Although one student is shifted from group A to group B, the number of students in the class and the total weight of the students remain the same. Therefore, the average weight of the class remains the same.

6. c The total weight of any group will vary according to the number of students in that group. Hence, the total weight of group A and C which has (15 + 25)= 40 will be twice that of students in group B which has 20 students. However, it is clear that if all the students are of same weight, then the average weight of all groups remains same irrespective of how many students are present in each group. Hence, clearly the statement given in option (c) is false.

7. b Total marks scored by the student in 10 papers = (80 × 10)= 800. If we exclude the papers in which he scored the highest and the lowest marks, then the total marks scored by him in remaining 8 papers = (81 × 8)= 648. Hence, his total in these two papers in which he scored the highest and the lowest marks = (800 – 648) = 152. Since his highest score is 92, his lowest score is (152 – 92) = 60.

8. a Let x be the fixed cost and y the variable cost. Then,

$$17500 = x + 25y \quad \ldots (i)$$
$$30000 = x + 50y \quad \ldots (ii)$$

Solving the equation (i)and (ii), we get
x = 5000, y = 500

Now if the average expense of 100 boarders be 'A'. Then, 100 × A = 5000 + 500 × 100

$\Rightarrow$ A = Rs. 550.

9. d Statement I gives the weight of the heaviest and lightest members of the class but no indication as to the number of students in the class or the total weight of the students is there. The second statement is also inconclusive, making our answer choice as (d).

10. b Use any 7 consecutive numbers to check the answers.

$n = \frac{(1+2+3+4+5)}{5} = 3$, average of 7 integers is $k = \frac{(1+2+3+4+5+6+7)}{7} = 4$.

So k = n + 1.

Alternate Solution:

The average of the first 5 terms is the middle term which is third term, and the average of the first 7 terms is the middle term which is the fourth term. Hence, it is one more than the previous average.

11. b 60 kg is wrong because then to arrive at a total of 121, the other box will have to weigh 61 kg which will be obviously be the highest. 64 is wrong too, because then to add up to 121, the other weight will have to be 57 and to make up to a total of 120, the next box shall have a weight 63 which obviously makes the maximum possible total 64 + 63 = 127. 62 is the correct answer because the other boxes shall be 59, 54, 58, 56. These will give all the totals given in the question.

12. c Let the marks scored in five subjects be 6x, 7x, 8x, 9x and 10x (on a scale of 1).

Average score = 60%

$$\Rightarrow \frac{6x + 7x + 8x + 9x + 10x}{5} = \frac{60}{100} \Rightarrow 8x = 0.6$$

$\Rightarrow$ x = 0.075

So the marks are 0.45, 0.525, 0.6, 0.675 and 0.75.

Number of times the marks exceed 50% is 4.

13. a Let x be the total number of people the college will ask for donations.

$\therefore$ People already solicited = 0.6x

Amount raised from the people solicited = 600 × 0.6x = 360x

Now 360x constitutes 75% of the amount.

Hence, remaining 25% = 120x

Hence, average donation from remaining people $= \frac{120x}{0.4x}$ = Rs. 300.

14. b Let the number of students in classes X, Y and Z be a, b and c respectively. Then,

total of X = 83a; total of Y = 76b; total of Z = 85c

Also $\frac{83a + 76b}{a + b} = 79 \Rightarrow 4a = 3b;$

and $\frac{76b + 85c}{b + c} = 81 \Rightarrow 4c = 5b$

Hence, $b = \frac{4}{3}a$, $c = \frac{5}{4}b = \frac{5}{4} \times \frac{4}{3}a = \frac{5}{3}a$

Average of X, Y and Z $= \frac{83a + 76b + 85c}{a + b + c}$

$$= \frac{83a + 76 \times \frac{4}{3}a + 85 \times \frac{5}{3}a}{a + \frac{4}{3}a + \frac{5}{3}a}$$

$= \frac{978}{12} = 81.5.$

15. a Let the highest number be n and x be the number erased.

Then, $\frac{\frac{n(n+1)}{2} - x}{(n-1)} = 35\frac{7}{17} = \frac{602}{17}.$

Here, the denominator (n – 1) must be a multiple of 17.

For n – 1 = 68 $\Rightarrow$ n = 69, we have $\frac{\frac{69(70)}{2} - x}{68} = \frac{602}{17}$

$\Rightarrow$ x = 602 × 68 – 69 × 35 = 2415 – 2408 = 7.

Hence, n = 69 and x = 7 satisfy the above conditions.

16. b Let the number be 'ab'.

Arithmetic mean is more by 1.8 means sum is more by 18.

$\therefore$ (10b + a) – (10a + b)= 18 $\Rightarrow$ 9 (b – a) = 18

$\Rightarrow$ b – a = 2.

17. d A gives 500 as median and B gives 600 as range.

A and B together do not give average. Therefore, it cannot be answered from the given statements.

18. e The total age of all the eight people in the family = 231

As per the information given in the question, the total age of all the people in the family = 231 + 3 × 8 – 60 + 0 = 195

Similarly, the total age of the people in the family four years ago = 195 + 3 × 8 – 60 + 0 = 159.

Therefore, the current average age of all the people in the family = $\frac{159+32}{8}$ = 24 years.

19. c **Using A:** $W_{II} = 45.5$ and $W_I = 44.5$

Using B: Weight of Deepak = 70kg (Only after using statement A)

This is sufficient to find weight of Poonam using the data given in the question statement. Hence, option (c) is correct choice.

20. 210 Let the number of volunteers be x.

∴ the number of members = 1.4x

Total contribution made by the members

= 1100 × 1.4x = Rs.1540x

Now, Rs.1540x is 88% of the total amount raised, therefore, the remaining 12% = Rs.210x.

Hence, the average contribution made by the volunteers

$= \frac{210x}{x}$ = Rs.210.

21. c Let the average height of 22 toddlers be x.

Average height of two toddlers = $\frac{1x}{3}$.

Now, Average increases by 2 inches when two leave the group.

So, sum of the heights of 20 toddlers = 20(x + 2)

So,22x = (x + 2) × 20 + $\frac{2x}{3}$.

⇒ x = 30.

So, the average height of the remaining 20 toddlers is 30 + 2 = 32 inches.

22. 60 Let the number of tests taken by him be x and the average score be A.

The average score for the first 10 tests = 20

So, the sum of the scores for these first 10 tests = 200

Similarly, the sum of the scores for the last 10 tests = 30 × 10 = 300

$\therefore \frac{200+300+s}{x} = A$, where s is the sum of the scores for remaining tests.

$\frac{500+s}{x} = A$ ....(i)

Now, according to the question,

$\frac{s+300}{x-10} = A+1$ ....(ii)

$\frac{200+s}{x-10} = A-1$ ....(iii)

On solving eq. (i),(ii) and (iii), we get A = 25, x = 60.

∴ The total number of tests taken by him is 60.

23. c The maximum average of the people under 51 years is found when there are 30 people with 51 years of age.

∴ Sum of the age of those 30 people aged 51 years = 51 × 30 = 1530

Average of all people in the apartment complex = 38

∴ Sum of the age of all people = (30 + 39)38 = 2622

∴ Sum of the age of the people aged below 51 years = 2622 – 1530 = 1092

∴ Largest possible average of the people aged below 51 years

$= \frac{1092}{39} = 28$

24. 105 Given that: x + y + z = 240,

x + y + z + u + v = 375, 2u = x + y and 2v = y + z

⇒ u + v = 135

Using these equations, we get x + 2y + z = 270 and y = 30

Hence, x + z = 210 and minimum value of x = 105 $(\because x \geq z)$

Simple Interest and Compound Interest

1. b For a difference of 1 year, CI can be computed as SI. Hence, from the 2nd year to the 3rd year interest earned = (675 – 650)= Rs.50 on Rs.625.

Hence, the Rate of interest

$= \frac{50}{625} \times 100 = 8\%$ p.a.

2. c The statement I suggests that the number of sheep had increased by 20% last year over the previous year. But it does not suggest whether the rate of increase is annual or not.

E.g. 20% increase in a year can also be obtained by 9.5% increase over 6 months. i.e. 1.095 x 1.095 = 1.20.

The statement II however suggests that the increase is compounded annually.

Hence, now we can find the answer.

If the number of sheep last year was *x*, then $x + 400 = x(1.2)^2$

Hence, *x* = 909.

Thus, we require both statements to answer the question.

3. a After 2 years, the price of the flat will be $(1)(1.10)^2$ = Rs.1.21 lakh.

Correspondingly the price of the land will be $(1.1)(1.05)^2$ = Rs.1.21275 lakh.

Hence, the price of the plot = Rs.(1.21275 – 1.21) lakh = Rs.275 more than that of the flat.

Hence, if they exchange, Ram will have to pay this amount to Prem .

4. c Using alligation, the ratio of the amounts invested at both the rates = 2 : 1.

Since he has invested Rs.3,000 at 5%, he should further invest Rs.1,500 at 8% to earn a total interest of 6% per annum.

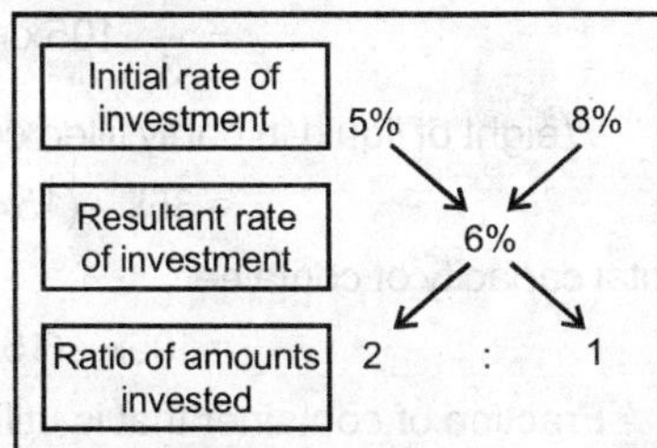

Alternative method:

Let the amount invested at 8% be Rs.x.

Then, $3000 \times \frac{105}{100} + x \times \frac{108}{100} = (3000 + x)\frac{106}{100}$

$\Rightarrow$ 0.02x = 30 $\Rightarrow$ x = 1,500

$\therefore$ He should further invest Rs.1,500 at 5% to earn a total interest of 6% per annum.

5. d Both the statements are needed to answer the questions. Since in statement I all the dates are given except the time to compound the interest. That date is given in the second statement.

6. d From statement I nothing can be said since exact figures are not given.

From statement II since X > Y (from B) we do not know how much X is greater than Y, because if it is slightly greater than it will be less than Y after 5 years whereas if the difference is very high, then X will be greater than Y even after 5 years.

7. 12 For the amount to get tripled, the increase is 200% of the principal. If it happens in 24 years then it will take 12 years for the increase to be 100% of the principal.

8. 121000 Let the two instalments be 'x'

After one year, 210000 × 1.1 = 231000

After paying the first instalment,

(231000 – x) × 1.1 = x

$\Rightarrow$ x = 121000

9. 4000 Let X = Rs. 100a and Y = Rs. 100b

Gopal owes Ankit an interest of Rs. 8a at the end of the year and similarly

Ishan owes Gopal an interest of Rs. (10a + 10b) at the end of the year.

Given that, 2 × 8a = 10a + 10b

$\Rightarrow$a : b = 5 : 3 or a = 5k and b = 3k

Also, additional amount equal to Y or 300k at 10% interest would fetch Gopal Rs. 150 more.

$\Rightarrow$ 30k = Rs. 150

Hence, X + Y = 800k = Rs. 4000.

Mixture and Solutions

1. b Since SP of spirit and solution water = Rs.75/l and there is a profit of 37.5%, CP of spirit and water solution = $\frac{75}{1.375}$ = Rs.54.54/l

This should indeed be the weighted average of the costs of spirit and water. So if we alligate, we can get the ratio of spirit : water (assuming that cost of water is 0).

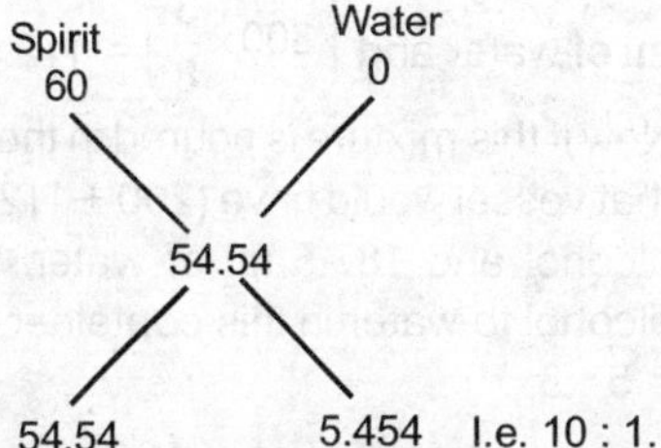

2. d We can solve this by alligation. But while we alligate, we have to be careful that it has to be done with respect to any one of the two liquids, viz. either A or B. We can verify that in both cases, we get the same result. E.g. the proportion of A in the first vessel is $\frac{5}{6}$ and that in the second vessel is $\frac{1}{4}$, and we finally require $\frac{1}{2}$ parts of A. Similarly, the proportion of B in the first vessel is $\frac{1}{6}$, that in the second vessel is $\frac{3}{4}$ and finally we want it to be $\frac{1}{2}$. With respect to liquid A

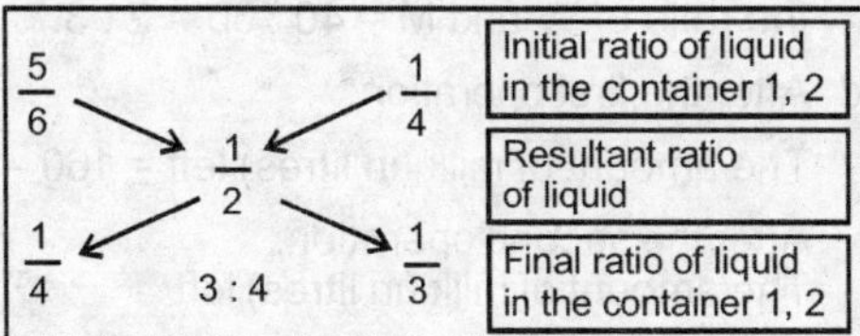

With respect to liquid B

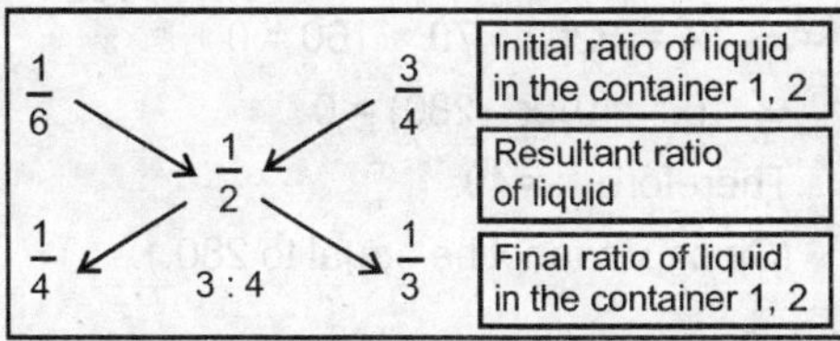

3. a Given that containers are in equal volume, that does not mean that quantities in each container are in equal volumes. Since we do not know the quantity of the liquid, we cannot find the ratio of the final mixture.

4. c Let the capacity of each cup be 100 ml. So 300 ml of alcohol is taken out from the first container and poured into the second one. So the first vessel will have 200 ml of alcohol and the second one will have 500 ml of water and 300 ml of alcohol. So the ratio of water to alcohol in the second vessel is 5 : 3.

Hence, proportion of alcohol in B = 3 : 8

Now if 300 ml of mixture is removed from the second container, it will have $\left(300\times\frac{5}{8}\right) = 187.5$ ml of water and $\left(300\times\frac{3}{8}\right) = 112.5$ ml of alcohol.

Now if this mixture is poured in the second vessel, that vessel would have (200 + 112.5)= 312.5 ml of alcohol and 187.5 ml of water. Hence, ratio of alcohol to water in this container = 312.5 : 187.5 = 5 : 3

Hence, proportion of water = A = 3 : 8

Hence, we find that A = B

Note: This result will be independent of the capacity of the cup.

5. a

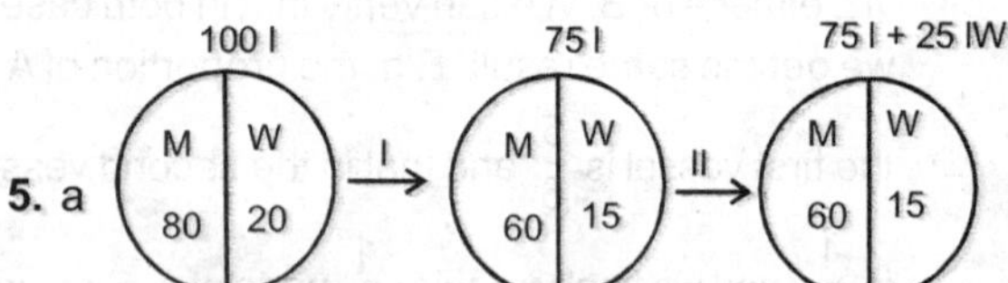

The diagram is self explanatory. Removal of 25 litres at stage I will result in volume of milk being reduced by 80% of 25 lit i.e. 20 lit and volume of water being reduced by the remaining 5 lit. So M = 60 lit and W = 15 lit. Addition of 25 lit water will finally given M = 60 lit and W = 40 M. Hence, the ratio of W and M = 40 : 60 = 2 : 3.

6. d After the first operation:

The amount of milk (in litres) left = 160 – x

After the second operation:
The amount of milk (in litres) left

$$=(160-x)-\frac{160-x}{160}\times x = 90$$

$\Rightarrow x^2 - 320x + 70 \times 160 = 0$

$\Rightarrow (x-40)(x-280) = 0$

Therefore, x = 40.

(Since x cannot be equal to 280.)

7. b Let the container (without the handle) weigh 100x when it is completely filled with a liquid.

∴ The empty metal container (without its handle) weighs 15x.

After handle is added weight of fully filled container = 105x.

∴ Weight of handle = 5x.

∴ Weight of partly filled container

$$= \frac{1}{3}\times 105x = 35x.$$

∴ Weight of liquid in partly filled container

$$= 35x - (15x + 5x) = 15x.$$

Total capacity of container

$$= 105x - (15x + 5x) = 85x.$$

∴ Fraction of container that is utilized

$$= \frac{15x}{85x} = \frac{3}{17}.$$

8. c Suppose percentage of milk in A, B and C vessels is a, ar and ar^2 respectively.

By the problem,

$$\frac{2a + 3ar + 4ar^2}{900} = \frac{32}{100} \quad \text{... (i)}$$

$$\frac{3a + 2ar + ar^2}{600} = \frac{22}{100} \quad \text{... (ii)}$$

From (i) & (ii), a = 12 and r = 2.

∴ The percentage of milk in A = 12%.

9. 245

Let x be the initial quantity of wine in the vessel. y litres of content is removed twice. The part of wine left is $x\left(1-\frac{y}{x}\right)^2$.

Now in 98 L of sample 18 L is wine which is same as $\frac{18}{98}$ part of the solution

$$\left(1-\frac{y}{x}\right)^2 = \frac{(x-y)^2}{x^2} = \frac{18}{98} = \frac{9}{49}$$

$$\Rightarrow \frac{(x-140)^2}{x^2} = \frac{9}{49} \Rightarrow x = 245.$$

10. a Let x ml of the solution be replaced with 12% acid solution. Therefore,

$$\frac{30}{100}\times(100-x)+\frac{12}{100}\times x = \frac{21}{100}\times 100$$

$\Rightarrow x = 50$

11. b

	Milk	Water
I.	7	2
II.	9	4

For milk, using allegation method,

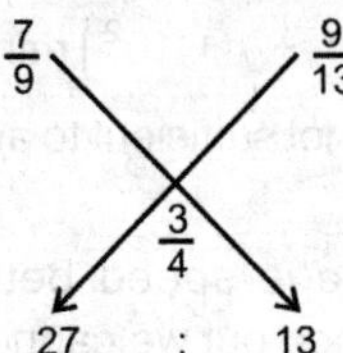

Hence, the required ratio = 27 : 13

12. c Ratio of liquid $A = \frac{\frac{2}{3} \times 4}{9} \Rightarrow \frac{8}{27}$

Ratio of liquid $B = \frac{\frac{3}{4} \times 3}{9} \Rightarrow \frac{1}{4}$

Ratio of liquid $C = \frac{\frac{4}{5} \times 2}{9} \Rightarrow \frac{8}{45}$

Ratio of water $= \frac{\frac{1}{3} \times 4 + \frac{1}{4} \times 3 + \frac{1}{5} \times 2}{9}$

$\Rightarrow \frac{\frac{4}{3} + \frac{3}{4} + \frac{2}{5}}{9}$

$\Rightarrow \frac{149}{60 \times 9} = \frac{149}{540}$

∴ Water in more than liquid B.

13. b Let the cost prices per kg of A and B be Rs. y and Rs. z respectively.

A B Profit

3x : 2x 10%

∴ Total C.P. when mixed in the ratio of 3 : 2

= (3xy + 2xz)

S.P.= 5x × 40 = 200 x

P = 10%

$200x = \frac{110}{100}(3xy + 2xz)$

33y + 22z = 2000 ....(i)

When A and B are mixed in the ratio of 2 : 3, then total C.P. = 2xy + 3xz

Profit = 5%

$200\,x = \frac{105}{100}(2xy + 3xz)$

42y + 63z = 4000 .... (ii)

On solving eq. (i) and (ii), we get,

$y = \frac{7600}{231}$ and $z = \frac{3200}{77}$

$\therefore \frac{y}{z} = \frac{19}{24}$

14. b Let the cost of paint B is Rs. x/litre and that of point A is Rs. (8 + x)/ litre.

Suppose, the quantity of paint A in the mixture be y litres and that of paint B be (10 – y) litres.

∴ Total cost of the mixture = (8 + x) y + x(10 – y)

SP. of the entire mixture = Rs. 264

Profit = 10%

$\therefore \quad C.P = \frac{100}{110} \times 264 = Rs.240$

$\therefore \quad (8 + x)y + x(10 - y) = 240$

⇒ 8y + 10x = 240

4y + 5x = 120

In order to get highest possible cost of paint B, put minimum value of y.

∴ y = 5 will give the highest possible value of x

∴ 5x = 120 – 20

x = 20

15. a Let the concentration of the ethanol solution 's' with which the 20% ethanol solution is mixed be x%.

Thus, concentration of the final mixture after the first step $= \left(\frac{20+3x}{1+3}\right)\%$

Now, this mixture is mixed with another 20% ethanol solution in equal proportion and we get resultant mixture of 31.25% ethanol solution.

$\Rightarrow \frac{\left(\frac{20+3x}{4} + 20\right)}{1+1} = 31.25$

Hence, x = 50%.

16. a Let the strength of A, B and C be a, b, c respectively.

$\Rightarrow \frac{a + 2b + 3c}{6} = 20$ or a + 2b + 3c = 120 ... (1)

Similarly,3a + 2b + c = 180 ... (2)

Subtracting, (1) from (2) we get: c = a – 30 and subtracting (1) from 3 × (2) we get: b = 105 – 2a

Given that, $\frac{2b + 7c}{9}$

$\Rightarrow \frac{210 - 4a + 7a - 210}{9} = \frac{a}{3}$

Hence, D : A = 1 : 3.

17. c Fraction of alcohol in the mixture $= \frac{700}{875} = \frac{4}{5}$

Fraction of alcohol after the secong substitution

$= \frac{4}{5} \times \frac{9}{10} \times \frac{9}{10} = 0.648 = 64.8\ \%$

Hence, percentage of water in the final mixture = 35.2%

18. d It is given that the parts of B in drum 1 and the final mixture are multiples of 7.

Therefore, parts of B in drum 2 has to be multiple of 7.

Hence, the correct answer will be 239 : 161.

Time speed and distance

1. d It can be seen that by travelling 12 km (30 –18) more at original speed, the car reaches 9 minutes earlier. So, in order to reach 45 minutes earlier, it has to travel a distance of 60 km more at original speed.

So the distance between points A & B = (18 + 60) = 78 kms.

Hence, the answer is (d).

2. c To completely cross each other the trains have to effectively travel a distance equal to the sum of their lengths.

They cover this distance at a effective speed of (60 + 50) = 110 kmph in 5 sec.

Hence, the sum of the lengths $= 110 \times \left(\frac{5}{3600}\right)$

= 0.152.78 km or 152.78 m.

For the passenger sitting in the faster train to cross the slower train completely, he should have moved through a distance equal to the length of the slower train.

Since the trains are moving in the same direction, effective speed = (60 – 50)= 10 kmph.

Since the distance equal to the length of the slower train is covered in 18 secs., the length of the slower train $= 10 \times \left(\frac{18}{3600}\right) = 0.05$ km or 50 m.

Thus the length of the faster train is (152.78 – 50) = 102.78 m.

3. c None of the statements alone is sufficient to answer the question.

Using both statements together: Let the distance and average speed between Calcutta and Madras be 'x' km and 'y' kmph respectively.

$$\text{Average speed} = \frac{\text{Total Dstance}}{\text{Total Time}}$$

$$= \frac{1.3x}{\left(\frac{x}{y} + \frac{0.3x}{2y}\right)} = \frac{1.3}{\left(\frac{1}{y} + \frac{0.3}{2y}\right)} = 40 \text{ kmph}$$

Since y is the only unknown, its value can be determined and hence the average speed between Madras and Trivandrum can be found. Thus we require both statements to answer the question.

4. d From statement I we can find that the stopping time was $\left(1^2 + 2^2 + 3^2 + 4^2 + \cdots + 10^2\right)$ minutes

But this statement alone is not sufficient to answer the question.

From statement II, average speed between stopovers can be determined but we cannot find total time from the source stop to the destination stop. Thus, this statement alone is also not sufficient.

We cannot answer the question even by using both the statements together.

5. b In order to solve the question, we need to know two things : (a)the original speed of the train or the new speed of the train and (b)at what distance from A or after how much time after leaving A the train brokedown. The statement II provides both of these data viz. original speed = 20 kmph and distance from A = 40 kms. and hence only this is required to answer the question.

E.g: If the distance between A & B is considered to be x, then time taken had it not broken down is x/20 hours. The new time taken is [2 + (x – 40)/5] hours and we know that this time is 40 min. more than the original time. The equation becomes : x/20 + 40/60 = [2 + (x – 40)/5], which can be easily solved to get value of x.

6. d **From both statements I and II:**

Arrival time of flight by New York local time will be 2 P.M.

Since we don't know whether the flight landed on same date or other we can not find the answer.

7. d Since her husband meets her mid way, the total time saved by him can be equally divided into time saved while going to station and that saved while returning home. In other words, he saved 5 min. while going and 5 min. while coming. So instead of usual time of 6.00 pm he must have met her at 5.55 pm. So she must have walked for 55 min.

8. a It is clear that after a particular amount of time P and Q are equidistant from A and B respectively and speed of Q is twice the speed of P, therefore, in the remaining time distance moved by Q will be twice than P. Hence, they would meet closer to A.

9. d Let the speed of P be x and the distance between A and B be d, so the speed of Q will be 2x.

According to the question,

$(1+t)v = 2vt = \frac{d}{6}$ (Let t be the travel time of Q)

$\Rightarrow t = 1$ and $d = 12v$

Hence, the time taken by P to reach to B $= \frac{d}{v} = 12$ hours.

10. c As P takes 12 hours to complete his journey, so Q moving with twice the speed of P will take $\frac{12}{2} = 6$ hours to complete his journey.

Hence, P will take 6 hours more than Q to complete the journey.

11. d The separation between the ship and the seaplane is 18 miles. Since the two are travelling in the same direction, the relative speed would be 9 times the speed of the ship (If speed of ship is x miles/hour, speed of the seaplane would be 10x and $10x - x = 9x$). Hence, to catch up with the ship, the seaplane would take $\frac{18}{9x} = \frac{2}{x}$ hours. Now, the ship covers x miles in an hour, so in $\frac{2}{x}$ hours it would cover 2 miles. So when the seaplane catches up with the ship, it would be 18 + 2 = 20 miles from the shore.

12. c It is clear that the ratio of the distances between (Delhi-Chandigarh): (Chandigarh-Shimla) = 3 : 4. The ratio of the speeds between (Delhi-Chandigarh) : (Chandigarh-Shimla)= 3 : 2.

Let the distances be 3x and 4x respectively and speeds be 3y and 2y.

So the time taken will be $\left(\frac{x}{y}\right)$ and $\left(\frac{2x}{y}\right)$ respectively. Average speed

$$= \frac{(\text{Total Distance})}{(\text{Total Time})} = \frac{(7x)}{\left(\frac{x}{y} + \frac{2x}{y}\right)} = \frac{7y}{3} = 49.$$

Hence, y = 21. So the average speed from Chandigarh to Shimla = 2y = 42 kmph.

13. b Let they meet at a distance x kms from X.

So the total distance travelled by A = x at the speed of 5 kmph.

Total distance travelled by B = 27 + (27 – x) = (54 – x)at the speed of 7 kmph.

Time taken by A = $\frac{x}{5}$.

Time taken by B = $\frac{(54 - x)}{7}$.

Since they have met at the same time, they would have travelled for the same time.

Hence, $\frac{x}{5} = \frac{(54 - x)}{7}$ or x = 22.5 kms.

14. c Since it is a relay race, all the runners ran the same distance.

Hence, for a same distance, ratio of times $= \frac{1}{\text{ratio of speeds}}$.

Hence, ratio of times taken by B & D = 18 : 16 = 9 : 8.

15. c Statement I tells us that the time taken to cover both distances is the same, but it does not tell us anything about the speeds at which these are covered. This information is given by the second statement, which says the speed from cinema hall to home is less than that between home to the office.

Hence, by using both the statements we can say that the distance between cinema hall to home is less than that between home to the office.

16. a In the same time as A runs 200 m in the race, S runs 180 m and N runs 160 m.

In other words, in the same time as S runs 180 m, N runs 160 m.

So in the same time as S runs 100 m, N will run $\left(100 \times \frac{160}{180}\right) = 88.89$ m.

Hence, in a 100 m race, S will beat N by (100 – 88.89) = 11.11 m.

17. d Since I live X floors above the ground floor and it takes me 30 s per floor to walk down and 2 s per floor to ride the lift, it takes 30X s to walk down and 2X s to ride the lift after waiting 420 s.

$\Rightarrow 30X = 2X + 420 \Rightarrow X = 15.$

Alternative method:

X > 14 as time taken to walk has to be greater than 7 min.

18. b Let the length of the escalator be 90 ft.

(There is no loss of generality in making this assumption.)

Let the speed of the escalator be y ft per second and the man's walking speed be x ft per second.

According to the question, we get

$$\frac{90}{30} = x + y$$

$$\frac{90}{90} = x - y$$

Adding the above equations, we get 2x = 4, i.e., x = 2.

$\therefore$ Time taken by the man to walk up the escalator when it is not moving = $\frac{90}{2}$ or 45 s.

19. d In a mile race, Akshay can be given a start of 128 m by Bhairav. This means that Bhairav can afford to start after Akshay has travelled 128 m and still complete one mile with him. In other words, Bhairav can travel one mile, i.e. 1,600 m in the same time as Akshay can travel (1600 – 128) = 1,472 m. Hence, the ratio of the speeds of Bhairav and Akshay = Ratio of the distances travelled by them in the same time = $\frac{1600}{1472}$ = 25 : 23. Bhairav can give Chinmay a start of 4 miles. This means that in the time Bhairav runs 100 m, Chinmay only runs 96 m. So the ratio of the speeds of Bhairav and Chinmay = $\frac{100}{96}$ = 25 : 24. Hence, we have B : A = 25 : 23 and B : C = 25 : 24. So A : B : C = 23 : 25 : 24. This means that in the time Chinmay covers 24 m, Akshay only covers 23 m. In other words, Chinmay is faster than Akshay. So if they race for $1\frac{1}{2}$ miles = 2,400 m, Chinmay will complete the race first and by this time Akshay would only complete 2,300 m. In other words, Chinmay would beat Akshay by 100 m = $\frac{1}{16}$ mile.

20. c Let the total distance be x. So the man travels a distance $\frac{3x}{5}$ at a speed 3a. Therefore, total time taken to travel this distance = $\frac{3x}{(15a)} = \frac{x}{(5a)}$

$\left[\text{Time} = \frac{\text{distance}}{\text{speed}}\right]$

He then travels a distance $\frac{2x}{5}$ at a speed 2b.

Hence, time taken to travel this distance = $\frac{2x}{(10b)}$ = $\frac{x}{(5b)}$. So total time taken in going from A to B = $\frac{x}{(5a)} + \frac{x}{(5b)}$. Now he travels from B to A and comes back. So total distance travelled = 2x at an average speed 5c.

Hence, time taken to return = $\frac{2x}{(5c)}$.

Since the time taken in both the cases remains the same, we can write $\frac{x}{5a} + \frac{x}{5b} = \frac{2x}{5c}$.

Therefore, $\frac{1}{a} + \frac{1}{b} = \frac{2}{c}$.

21. a Total time taken by the man to travel from A to D = 16 hr and total distance travelled = 36 km. The time that he would have taken had he not rested in between will be (16 – x – 2x) = (16 – 3x). But this time should be equal to the addition of the times that he takes to travel individual segments. This is given as : $\frac{12}{x} + \frac{12}{2x} + \frac{12}{4x} = \frac{84}{4x} = \frac{21}{x}$.

Therefore, $\frac{21}{x} = (16 - 3x)$.

So we get the equation $3x^2 - 16x + 21 = 0$. Solving this equation, we get x = 3 or x = $\frac{7}{3}$. This should be the time for which he rested at B.

22. b In a watch that is running correct, the minute hand should cross the hour hand once in every $65 + \frac{5}{11}$ min. So they should ideally cross three times once in $3 \times \left(\frac{720}{11}\right) = \frac{2060}{11}$ min = 196.36 min. But in the watch under consideration they meet after every 3 hr, 18 min and 15 s, i.e. $(3 \times 60 + 18 + \frac{15}{60})$ $= \frac{793}{4}$ min = 198.25 min. In other words, our watch is actually losing time (as it is slower than the normal watch). Hence, when our watch elapsed 198.25 min, it actually should have elapsed 196.36 min. So in a day, when our watch will elapse (60 × 24) = 1440, it should actually elapse $\left(1440 \times \frac{196.36}{198.25}\right)$ = 1426.27. Hence, the amount of time lost by our watch in one day = (1440 – 1426.27)= 13.73, i.e. 13 min and 50s (approximately).

23. c If he travels at minimum speed over stretch A (i.e. 40km/hr), the total time taken to cover this stretch = $\frac{2}{40} = \frac{1}{20}$ hr = 3 min.

If he then travels at the fastest speed over stretch B (i.e. 50 km/hr), the total time taken to cover this stretch = $\frac{2}{50} = \frac{1}{25}$ = 2.4 min.

Thus, total time taken over the first two stretches = 3 + 2.4 = 5.4 min.

In order to break the previous record he will have to cover the third stretch in (10 – 5.4) = 4.6 min.

To do this he will have to cover the third stretch at $\frac{2}{4.6}$ = 0.434 km per minute or 26.08 km/hr. But the maximum speed over the stretch C is 20 km/hr. Hence, it is not possible for C to break the previous record.

24. b The minimum speed in stretch A is 40 km/hr. If Mr Hare travels the first stretch at this speed, then the time taken by him to cover this stretch = $\frac{2}{40}$ = 3 min. Also he takes 3 min to cover stretch B. And he covers the entire race in (1.5 × 10)= 15 min. This means that he should have taken (15 – 3 – 3) = 9 min to cover stretch C. Hence, his speed over this stretch should be $\frac{2}{9}$ = 0.22 km per minute or 13.3 km/hr.

25. c Let his average speed over the last stretch be x. Hence, his average speed for first two stretches = 4x. So the total time taken to cover the three stretches = $\frac{4}{4x} + \frac{2}{x}$

His average speed over the race is 20 km/hr.

Hence, the time taken to complete the race = $\frac{6}{20}$

Hence, we have the equation $\frac{4}{4x} + \frac{2}{x} = \frac{6}{20}$

Solving this equation, we get x = 10 km/hr.

26. c Effective speed of two trains = 80 – 40 = 40 km/hr. (Since they are moving in the same direction as inferred from the word 'overtakes'). At this speed in 54 s, they would travel an effective distance of $\frac{40 \times 54}{3600}$ = 0.6 km or 600 m. This effective distance should be equal to the sum of the lengths of the two trains. So, if length of the express train is L, length of the goods train will be 2L. Hence, our equation will be L + 2L = 600 or L = 200 m.

So, the time taken by this train to cross a platform 400 m long will be = $\frac{(200 + 400)}{80 \times \frac{5}{18}}$ = 27 s.

(Note that we have converted the denominator in metres per second. Hence, the factor of $\frac{5}{18}$).

For questions 27 to 29 : Let us convert all the time to same time zone, viz. Boston. So X left Frankfurt at 6 p.m. on Friday (Frankfurt time) or 10 p.m. on Friday (Boston time). X reached Boston at 10 a.m. on Saturday (Boston time). In other words, X has taken 12 hr in all to go from Frankfurt to Boston. After 2 hr wait, X leaves at 12 noon (Boston time). Now X reaches India at 1 a.m. on Sunday (Indian time) or 11 a.m. on Saturday (Boston time). Thus, X takes 11 hr in all to go from Boston to India.

27. b Overall, X has travelled for 25 hr (including stoppages)at an average speed of 180 miles per hour. Hence, the distance between Frankfurt and India is (25 × 180)= 4500 miles.

28. a On the return journey, X halts at Boston for one hour less than his previous halt there. Therefore, X takes 24 hr for his return journey.

29. a Since distance between Frankfurt and India is 4,500 miles, overall distance travelled by him (to and fro) = 9000 miles. And he has taken $(25 + 24 + 1\frac{11}{12}{*}) = 50\frac{11}{12}$ hr in all to cover this distance.

***Note:** $1\frac{11}{12}$ hr has been accounted for the halt that he had in India (from 1 a.m. to 2.55 a.m.). Hence, his average speed for the entire journey

$= \frac{9000}{\left(50\frac{11}{12}\right)}$, i.e. 176.75 mph.

30. c Since the policeman started 15 min late, in this time the thief would have already covered $\frac{60}{4}$ = 15 km. To catch the thief, the policeman will have to make up for this distance of 15 km. Every hour the policeman is travelling (65 – 60) = 5 km more than the thief. Hence, to make up the distance of 15 km, he would take 3 hr. Since policeman started at 12.15 p.m., he would catch the thief at 3.15 p.m.

31. b Every hour the second policeman covers (65 – 60)= 5 km less than the first one. Since the first policeman catches the thief in 3 hr, in this time the second policeman will be (3 × 5) = 15 km behind.

32. b

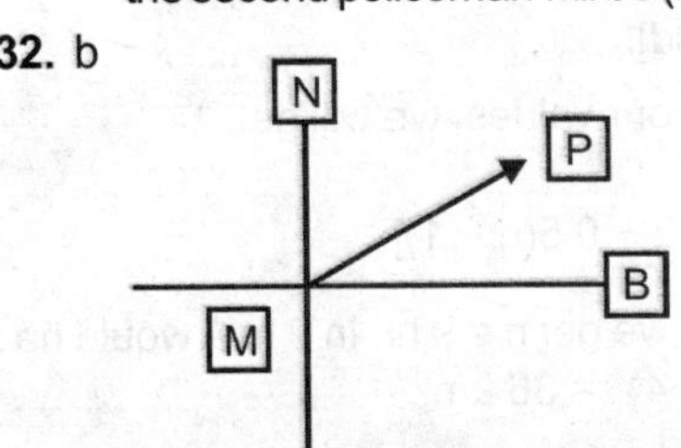

The diagram will be as shown. M is Mali and P is Pali.

Consider statement I. When the person covers $\frac{1}{3}$ distance, he is 3 km east and 1 km north of Mali. Based on this statement alone, we can easily find out where he will be on line MP by using Pythagoras' theorem. Once we find this distance, we can easily get distance MP by multiplying it by 3. Similarly, based on statement II alone also, we can find distance MP. Hence, both the statements are independently sufficient to answer the question. Hence, the answer is (b).

33. c Let the speed of the motorcycle be x km/hr. Therefore, speed of the car will be (x + 10) km/hr. From statement II, we can form the following equation.

$$\left(\frac{100}{(x+10)}\right) = \left(\left(\frac{100}{x}\right) + 2\right)$$

After solving this equation, we can get the speed of the car. Hence, this question can be answered by combining both the statements.

34. d None of the statements specifies the direction in which Tez and Gati are moving, which is very significant.

35. d Since A and B are moving in opposite directions, we will add their speeds to calculate the effective speeds. In other words, in the first hour they would effectively cover a distance of (4 + 2) = 6 km towards each other. In the second hours, they would effectively cover a distance of (4 + 2.5) = 6.5 km towards each other.

In the third hour, (4 + 3) = 7 km.

In the fourth hour, (4 + 3.5) = 7.5 km and so on.

We can see that the distances that they cover in each hour are in AP, viz. 6, 6.5, 7, 7.5, ... with a = 6 and d = 0.5. Since they have to effectively cover a distance of 72 km, the time taken to cover this much distance would be the time taken to meet each other. So the sum of the first n terms of our AP has to be 72.

If we are to express this in our equation of sum of first n terms of the AP, we will get $S_n = \frac{n}{2} \times [2a + (n-1)d]$.

Substituting our values, we will get

$72 = \frac{n}{2} \times [12 + 0.5(n-1)]$

Solving this, we get n = 9 hr. In 9 hr A would have covered (9 × 4) = 36 km.

So B would also have covered (72 – 36) = 36 km.

Hence, they would meet mid-way between A and B.

36. c Since the distance travelled was the same both ways and also it was covered in the same time, the average speed will be the same uphill and downhill. Hence, statement (a) is false. Statement (b)need not be true. It would be true and had the speeds (and not average speed) been the same both ways. But it is clearly indicated that he varied his pace throughout. Now it has to be noted that the journey uphill and the journey downhill started at the same time, i.e. 6 a.m. and also ended at the same time 6 p.m. (though on different days). So if we were to assume a hypothetical case in which one person starts downhill at 6 a.m. and other one starts uphill at 6 a.m., along the same path, then there would be a point on the path where they would meet (i.e. they would reach at the same time), irrespective of their speeds. Our case is similar to that, except for the fact that here, we have only one person moving both ways. So there has to be a point on the path, where he reached at the same time on both days.

37. b At 7.30 a.m., Navjivan Express is at 50 km from A at the same time, Howrah-Ahmedabad Express is at 20 km from B.

Hence, distance between the trains at 7.30 a.m. is 30 km.

Relative speed = 50 + 40 = 90 kmph

Hence, time left = $\frac{30}{90} = \frac{1}{3}$ hr = 20 min.

38. b

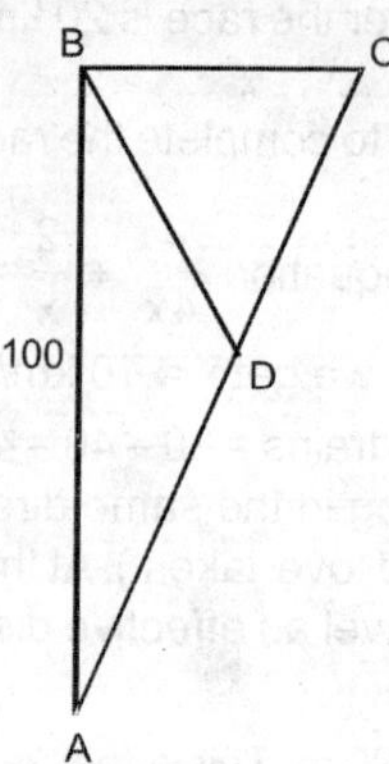

Since AD = DC, the distance travelled is same for the two stretches.

Hence, the average speed is given by

$\frac{2ab}{(a+b)} = \frac{(2 \times 45 \times 55)}{(45+55)} = 49.5$ kmph.

39. a Now, since X and Y reach C at the same time,

$\frac{100 + BC}{61.875} = \frac{AC}{49.5}$

Hence, you need to take help from options. i.e.

If AC = 105, $BC^2 = AC^2 - AB^2 = 105^2 - 100^2 = 1025$ or BC = 32

So, $\frac{100 + BC}{AC} = \frac{132}{105} = 1.25$

40. b In this triangle, AD = DC = BD = $\frac{105}{2}$ = 52.5 km

Note: The best way to solve this question is to treat questions 39 and 40 together. You would figure out that the answer to question 40 has to be half of the answer to question 39, and the only pairs of answer choices that fit into this condition are 105 and 52.5.

41. c The vehicle travels 19.5 km/L at the rate of 50 km/hr.

So it should travel $\frac{19.5}{1.3}$ km/L at the rate of 70 km/hr = 15 km/L.

The distance covered at 70 km/hr with 10 L = 10 × 15 = 150 km.

42. a The robot begins to give material to machine A and then to D, it thus covers 40 m in that time span and takes 4 s. Also then it returns to the origin, and takes 4 s, while covering 40 m again. When it arrives at the origin, the messages of B and C are already there, thus it moves to give the material to them, which takes it in total 6 s, and it covers 30 + 30 = 60 m in total. Hence, the distance travelled by the robot will be 40 m + 40 m + 60 m = 140 m.

43. a In this question, once the robot has delivered the material to machines A and D, it shall reach the origin 2 (nearest), taking 6 s, and covering 60 m.

Then it immediately moves to deliver material to machines C and B covering a distance of 40 m and finally back to the origin (nearest). Thus, it cover a distance of 60 m. Hence, it covers a total distance of 120 m.

44. d Here, by combining the two statements, we get the duration of the flight.
For the arrival time we should have information regarding the time zone difference of Mumbai and No-man's-land.

45. d Let x be the speed of Rahul, and y be the speed of current in mph.

$$\frac{12}{x-y}-\frac{12}{x+y}=6 \Rightarrow \frac{y}{x^2-y^2}=\frac{1}{4}$$

$$\Rightarrow y=\frac{x^2-y^2}{4} \quad \text{... (i)}$$

When Rahul doubles his rowing speed, then we have

$$\frac{12}{2x-y}-\frac{12}{2x+y}=1 \quad \Rightarrow \quad \frac{2y}{4x^2-y^2}=\frac{1}{12}$$

$$\Rightarrow y=\frac{4x^2-y^2}{24} \quad \text{... (ii)}$$

$\therefore$ From (i) and (ii), we have $2x^2 = 5y^2$

Putting $x^2 = \frac{5}{2}y^2$ in (i), we get $y=\frac{\frac{3}{2}y^2}{4} \Rightarrow y=\frac{8}{3}$.

46. b If Shyam takes 1 min for every 3 steps, then he takes $\frac{1}{3}$ min for every step.
For 25 steps, he takes $\frac{25}{3}$ min, i.e. 8.33 min.
So Vyom takes $\frac{1}{2}$ min for every step.
For 20 steps, he takes $\frac{20}{2}$ min, i.e. 10 min.
Difference between their time = 1.66 min.
Escalator takes 5 steps in 1.66 min and difference in number of steps covered = 5
Speed of escalator is 1 step for 0.33 min, i.e. 3 steps per minute.
If escalator is moving, then Shyam takes 25 steps and escalator also takes 25 steps.
Hence, total number of steps = 50.

47. a Total time taken by B to cover 60 km

$$=\frac{60}{50}\text{hr}=\frac{6}{5}\text{hr}$$

It stops at station C for $\frac{1}{4}$ hr.

Now, in $\left(\frac{6}{5}+\frac{1}{4}\right)$ hr train X travels

$$70 \times \frac{29}{20} = 101.5 \text{ km}$$

This implies that they do not cross each other by the time train Y finishes its stoppage at station C.
Let they meet after t hr.

Then $70t + 50(t - \frac{1}{4}) = 180 \Rightarrow t = \frac{192.5}{120}$ hr

Distance from A will be $(70 \times \frac{192.5}{120})$ km = 112 km approximately

48. b Let L be length in metres of the race which A finishes in t seconds.

Speed of A = $\frac{L}{t}$ m/s

Speed of B = $\frac{L-12}{t}$ m/s

Speed of C = $\frac{L-18}{t}$ m/s

Time taken by B to finish the race

$$=\frac{L}{(L-12)/t}\text{ s}=\left(\frac{L}{L-12}\right)t\text{ s}$$

In this time, C covers (L – 8) m

$$\left(\frac{L-18}{t}\right)\left(\frac{L}{L-12}\right)t=L-8$$

$$\Rightarrow L = 48 \text{ m}$$

49. b

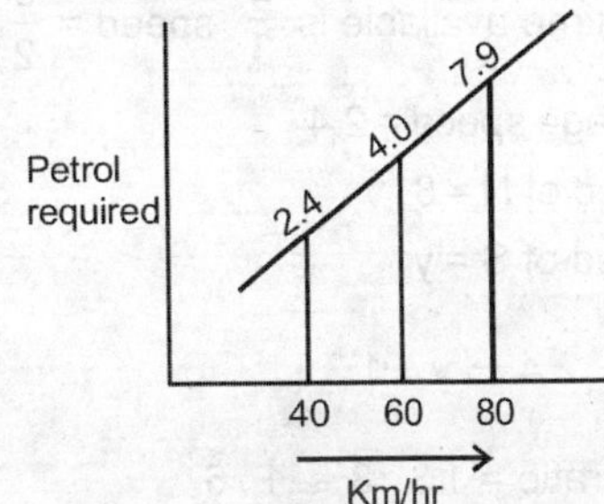

60 km/hr is travelled in 4 L petrol (from the graph).
$\therefore$ 1 L is required for 15 km, i.e. for 15 km, 1 L petrol is required.

For 200 km, $\frac{200}{15}$ = 13.33 L is required.

50. b The fuel consumption at various speeds would be

$$\frac{200}{40}\times 2.5 = 12.5 \text{ L};$$

$$\frac{200}{80}\times 7.9 = 19.75 \text{ L};$$

$$\frac{200}{60}\times 4 = 13.33 \text{ L}$$

If Manasa travels at 40 km/hr, the total consumption would be 12.5 L. Hence, Manasa has to decrease the speed.

51. a Statement I gives the capacity of boat and is of no help in finding out the number of round trips.

From statement II round trips can be calculated since we know the total time taken is 12 hr.

52. c Statement I gives the rate and statement II gives the size. It is like statement I gives the speed and statement II the distance and we are to find out time. So both statements are needed.

53. d Every trip will need more than 180 m and there are $4\frac{1}{2}$ trips. Hence, the distance covered will be greater than 750 m, for which there is only one option = 860.

Alternative method:

For the first stone, he will cover 100 m.

For second, 200 – 4 = 196 m

For third, 200 – 8 = 192 m

For fourth, 200 – 12 = 188 m

For fifth, 200 – 16 = 184 m

Hence, total distance = 860 m

54. d If speed of N = 4, speed of S = 1,

$\Rightarrow$ Average speed $= \frac{2 \times 4 \times 1}{4+1} = 1.6$

Because time available is $\frac{2}{3}$, speed = $\frac{3}{2}$

Now average speed = 2.4

Now speed of N = 8

Now speed of S = y

$\frac{2 \times 8 \times y}{8+y} = 2.4 \Rightarrow y = 1.3$

Required ratio = 1.3 : 8 $\approx$ 1 : 6

55. c

15 km

A 2.5 km G_1 G_2 G_3 2.5 km B

Let G_1, G_2 and G_3 be the three gutters such that $G_2G_3 = 2\,G_1G_2$.

AG_1 = 5 min × 30km/hr = 2.5 km

$\therefore$ G_1G_3 = 20 – 2 × 2.5 = 15 km

Time taken to cover AG_1 = 5 min

Time taken to cover $(G_1G_3 + G_3A)$

$= \frac{(15+17.5)\text{km}}{2 \times 30 \text{ km/hr}} = \frac{32.5}{60} \times 60 = 32.5$ minutes

The patient reaches the hospital in a total of (32.5 + 5) = 37.5 minutes

Maximum time that the doctor gets to attend the patient = 40 – 37.5 – 1 = 1.5 minutes.

56. c By trial and error:

30 × 12 = 360 > 300

30 × 7.5 = 225 < 300

50 × 6 = 300. Hence, he rented the car for 6 hr.

57. ***b** AB is the tunnel and 'd' km be its length.

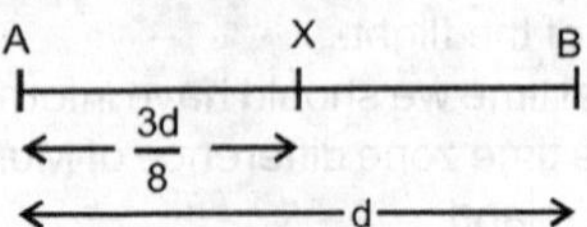

Let the current position of the cat be X. If it runs towards A, it would reach A at the same time as the train reaches A.

However, if it runs towards the other end B, it would reach point Y at the same time when the train reaches A.

Hence, point Y would be at a distance of $\frac{3d}{8}$ km from X

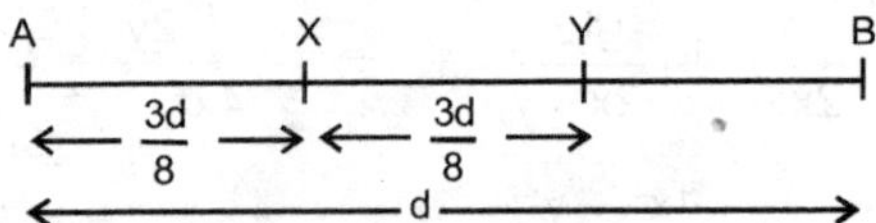

As the cat and the train would reach B simultaneously, the cat would cover the rest $\frac{2d}{8} = \frac{d}{4}$ km distance in the same time that the train takes to cover the whole tunnel i.e. d km.

Therefore, the speed of the train = 4 × the speed of the cat

Hence, ratio of the speeds of the train and cat is 4 : 1.

*** The language in the question is slightly ambiguous.** A possible interpretation is that the ratio of their speeds is to be determined which is correctly 4 : 1.

58. a Let AB be the tower and C and D be the initial and final positions of the car.

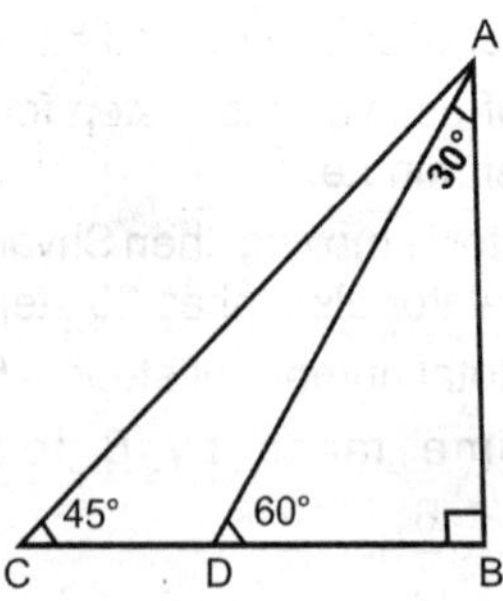

Let AB = 1

Therefore, BC = 1

$\therefore \tan 60 = \frac{AB}{BD} \Rightarrow \sqrt{3} = \frac{1}{BD} \Rightarrow BD = \frac{1}{\sqrt{3}}$

$\therefore CD = BC - BD = 1 - \frac{1}{\sqrt{3}}$

As time for traveling CD, i.e. $1-\frac{1}{\sqrt{3}}$ is 10 min

$\therefore$ Time required for traveling BD $= \frac{\frac{1}{\sqrt{3}}}{1-\frac{1}{\sqrt{3}}}\times 10$

$= \frac{1}{\sqrt{3}-1}\times 10 = \frac{10}{\sqrt{3}-1} = \frac{10}{\sqrt{3}-1}\times\frac{\sqrt{3}+1}{\sqrt{3}+1}$

$= \frac{10\left(\sqrt{3}+1\right)}{2} = 5\left(\sqrt{3}+1\right)$ min

59. b

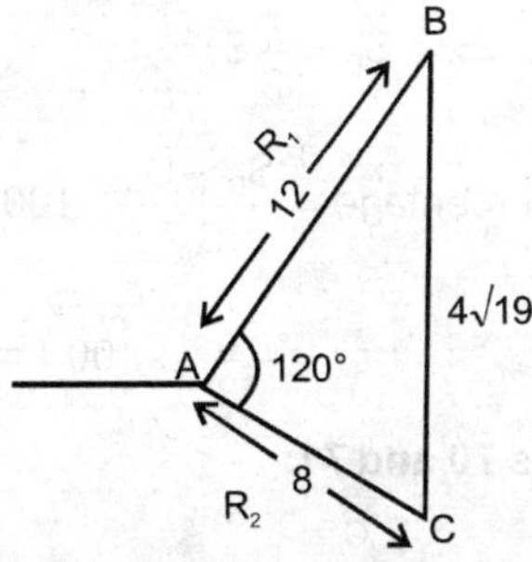

$BC^2 = (12)^2 + 8^2 - 2\times 12\times 8\times\cos 120°$

$\therefore BC = 4\sqrt{19}$

$\therefore t_1 = \frac{4\sqrt{19}+8}{3}$ and $t_2 = \frac{4\sqrt{19}+12}{2}$

[where t_1 and t_2 are time taken by Ram and Shyam to reach the starting point]

$t_2 - t_1 = \frac{4\sqrt{19}+12}{2} - \frac{4\sqrt{19}+8}{3}$

$= \frac{12\sqrt{19}+36-8\sqrt{19}-16}{6}$

$= \frac{4\sqrt{19}+20}{6} = \frac{2\sqrt{19}+10}{3}.$

For question 60 to 62 :

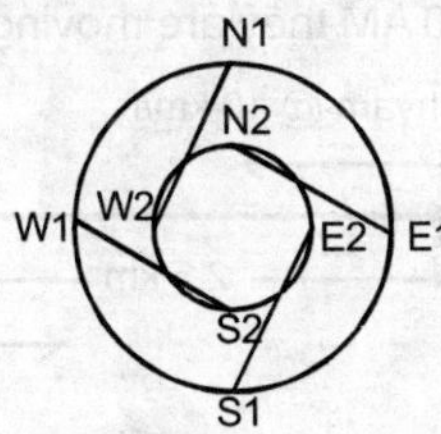

If the radius of the inner ring road is r, then the radius of the outer ring road will be 2r (since the circumference is double).

The length of IR = $2\pi r$, that of OR = $4\pi r$ and that of the chord roads are $r\sqrt{5}$ (Pythagoras theorem)

The corresponding speeds are 20π, 30π and $15\sqrt{5}$ kmph.

Thus time taken to travel one circumference of IR = $\frac{r}{10}$ hr, one circumference of OR = $\frac{r}{7.5}$ hr and one length of the chord road = $\frac{r}{15}$ hr

60. c Sum of the length of the chord roads = $4r\sqrt{5}$ and the length of OR = $4\pi r$.

Thus, the required ratio = $\sqrt{5} : \pi$

61. c The total time taken by the route given $= \frac{r}{30} + \frac{r}{15} = \frac{3}{2}$ (i.e. 90 min.)

Thus, r = 15 km. The radius of OR = 2r = 30 kms

62. d The total time taken = $\frac{r}{20} + \frac{r}{15} = \frac{7r}{60}$

Since r = 15, total time taken = $\frac{7}{4}$ hr = 105 min.

63. c The ratio of the speeds of the fastest and the slowest runners is 2 : 1. Hence, they should meet at only one point on the circumference i.e. the starting point (As the difference in the ratio in reduced form is 1). For the two of them to meet for the first time, the faster should have completed one complete round over the slower one. Since the two of them meet for the first time after 5 min, the faster one should have completed 2 rounds (i.e. 2000 m)and the slower one should have completed 1 round. (i.e. 1000 m) in this time. Thus, the faster one would complete the race (i.e. 4000 m)in 10 minutes.

64. c If A takes X seconds then B takes (x + 60) seconds to run 1000 m.

Ratio of speeds of A and C = 1000 : 625 = 8 : 5

Ratio of time taken by A and C = 5 : 8

If B takes y second then C takes (y + 30) seconds to run 1000 m, then

$5(y + 30) = 8x$ ...(i)

and $\frac{1000}{x+60} = \frac{1000}{y}$ ...(ii)

Solving, we get the values of x and y.

Hence, both statements are required.

65. c The boats will be colliding after a time which is given by

$t = \frac{20}{5+10} = \frac{4}{3}$ hours = 80 minutes.

After this time of 80 minutes, boat (1) has covered $80\times\frac{5}{60}$ kms $= \frac{20}{3}$ kms, whereas boat (2) has covered $80\times\frac{10}{60}$ kms $= \frac{40}{3}$ kms.

After 79 minutes, distance covered by the first boat $= d_1 = \left(\frac{20}{3} - \frac{5}{60}\right)$ kms

After 79 minutes, distance covered by the second boat $= d_2 = \left(\frac{40}{3} - \frac{10}{60}\right)$ kms

So the separation between the two boats $= 20 - (d_1 + d_2) = \frac{1}{4}$ kms

Alternative method:

Relative speed of two boats = 5 + 10 = 15 km/hr

i.e. in 60 min they cover (together) = 15 km

$\therefore$ in 1 min they will cover (together) $\frac{15}{60} = \frac{1}{4}$ km

66. b Let d be the distance to be travelled and t be the time taken to reach at 1 p.m.

If the man cycles at 10 km/hr, then $\frac{d}{t} = 10$ ... (i)

If the man cycles at 15 km/hr, then $\frac{d}{t-2} = 15$ ... (ii)

Solving (i)and (ii), we get t = 6 hours and d = 60 km

To reach the place by noon, he needs to cycle at

$= \frac{d}{t-1} = \frac{60}{6-1} = 12$ km/hr

67. d **Race 1:**

In whatever time Karan covers a distance of 100 m, Arjun covers 90 m in the same time.

$\therefore$ Ratio of their speeds = 10 : 9

Race 2:

Now Karan is 10 m behind the starting point. Once again to cover 100 m from this new point Karan will be taking the same time as before. In this time, Arjun will be covering 90 meters only. This means that now both of them will be at the same point, which will be 10 meters away from the finish point. Since both of them are required to cover the same distance of 10 m and Karan has a higher speed, he will beat Arjun. No need for calculations as option (d)is the only such option.

68. c As options are independent of n, let us assume n = 2.

Circumference of the track $= 2\pi r$

$\therefore$ Time taken for first round

$= \frac{1}{2} + 1 + 2 + 4 = 7.5$ minutes and time taken for second round = 8 + 16 + 32 + 64 = 120 minutes

Hence, ratio $= \frac{120}{7.5} = 16 : 1 = 16$

69. d Let r be the radius of the two circular tracks.

$\therefore$ The rectangle has dimensions 4r × 2r.

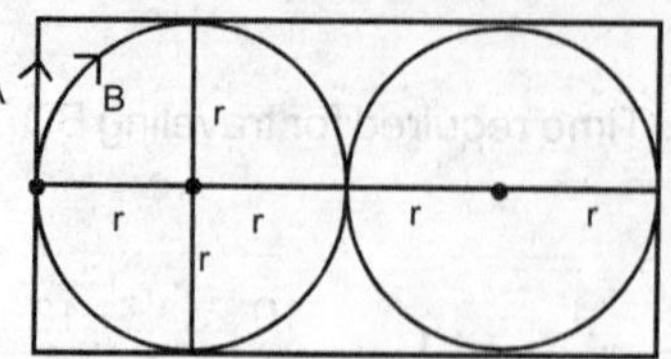

A covers a distance of 2r + 2r + 4r + 4r = 12 r

B covers a distance of $2\pi r + 2\pi r = 4\pi r$

Time taken by both of them is same.

$\therefore \frac{4\pi r}{S_B} = \frac{12r}{S_A} \Rightarrow S_B = \frac{\pi}{3} S_A$

$\therefore$ Required percentage $= \frac{S_B - S_A}{S_A} \times 100$

$= \frac{\pi - 3}{3} \times 100 = 4.72\%$.

For questions 70 and 71:

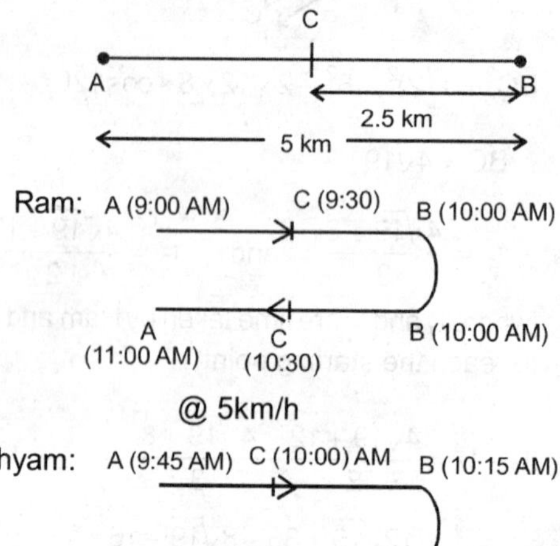

70. b It is clear that Ram and Shyam shall meet each other between C & B, sometime after 10:00 AM. At 10:00 AM they are moving as shown below:

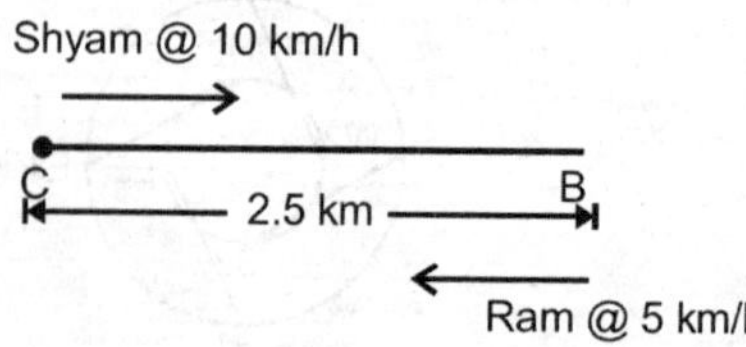

Fig. at 10:00 AM

From now, time taken to meet $= \frac{2.5}{(10+5)} \times 60$ min

= 10 minutes

So, they meet each other at 10:10 AM.

71. b It is clear from the diagram that at 10:30; Shyam overtakes Ram.

Alternate: At 10:15 the situation is as show:

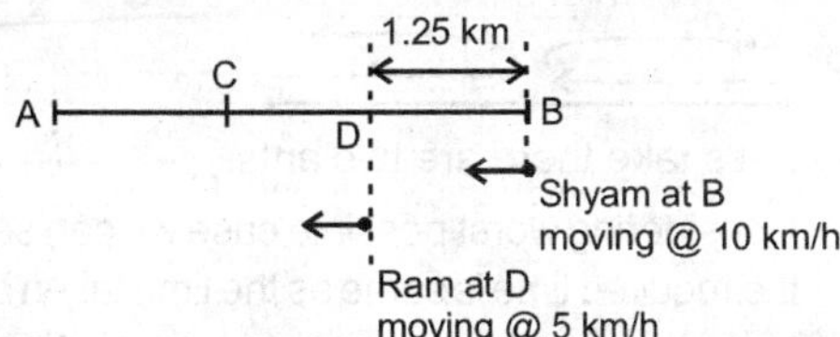

Time taken for Shyam to overtake Ram $= \frac{1.25}{(10-5)} \times 60 = 15$ min.

$\Rightarrow$ Shyam overtakes Ram at 10:30 AM.

72. c Let us assume that Arun started running at 10 a.m. and Barun started at 12 noon. So, in these two hours distance traveled by Arun is 60 km and the relative speed of Barun w.r.t Arun is 10 km/hr.

So Barun will overtake Arun after $= \frac{60}{10} = 6$ hours

So, Barun reaches there at 6 p.m.

So, Kiranmala also overtakes Arun at 6 p.m.

Let us assume Kiranmala takes 't' time to overtake Arun and the relative speed of Kiranmala w.r.t Arun is 30 km/hr and Arun ran for 8 hrs.

So, distance travelled by Arun is = 30 × 8 = 240 km

while distance travelled by Kiranmala = 60t

$\therefore$ 240 = 6t $\Rightarrow$ t = 4

Hence, Kiranmala start running 4 hours after Arun had st off.

For questions 73 and 74:

Let the cruising speed of the plane and the time difference between A and B be y km/hr and x hours respectively.

Distance between A and B = 3000 kilometers.

For the plane moving from city A to City B : 3000 = (7 – x)× (y – 50). This is satisfied for x = 1 and y = 550.

These are the only values given in the options that satisfy the above equation.

75. b As per the conditions given in the questions, we get the following figure.

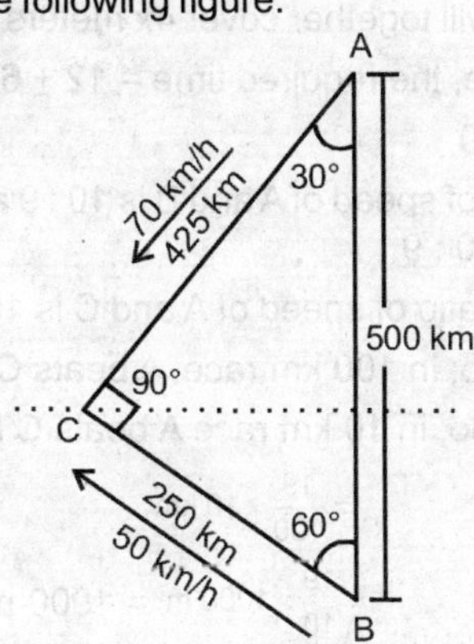

The train leaving at B reaches C at 1:00 p.m. taking a total time of 5 hours, which means that Rahim should reach C by 12:45 p.m.

Now total time taken by Rahim moving with a speed of 70 km/hr is 't'.

$$t = \frac{250\sqrt{3}}{70} \text{km/hr} = 6 \text{ hrs } 12 \text{ mins (approx)}$$

The time by which Rahim must start from A

= 13 : 00 – 0 : 15 – 6 : 12 = 6 : 33

Therefore, the latest time by which Rahim must leave A and still catch the train is closest to 6:30 a.m.

76. d In the time Chaupat covers x m, Popat covers (x – 18) m and Sarpat covers (x – 24) m.

And in the time Popat covers x m, Sarpat covers (x – 8) m.

So $\frac{x-18}{x-24} = \frac{x}{x-8}$

$\Rightarrow$ $x^2 - 26x + 144 = x^2 - 24x$

$\Rightarrow$ 2x = 144

$\Rightarrow$ x = 72

77. b Himanshu starts at 7 a.m. and Saral at 8 a.m. So Himanshu would have covered 2 km by the time Saral starts. Saral will catch Himanshu after $\frac{2}{3-2} = 2$ hours.

So Himanshu and Saral will be together at 10 a.m. after each has covered 6 km. Vikas also starts at 10 a.m. So the time taken by Himanshu to meet Vikas will be $\frac{6}{2+4} = \frac{6}{6} = 1$ hour.

So Himanshu and Vikas meet at 11 a.m.

78. d A covers 10 km in the first hour while B covers 20 km. As a result the distance between them increases by 10 km.

A covers 10 km in the next hour while B covers – 10 km. As a result the distance between them decreases by 20 km.

In the first two hours the distance between A and B decreases by 10 km.

The time taken by A and B to meet for the first time

$= \frac{100}{10} \times 2 = 20$ hours

79. a Let the work (in units) done in a day by Pawan, Qureshi and Rohit be P, Q and R respectively. Let the total work done be (L.C.M. of 10 and 12) 60 units.

$\therefore$ P + Q = 6 units and Q + R = 5 units.

Let Pawan's share be Rs. x. So Rohit's share will be

Rs. (160 – x).

Ratio of the amount received by Pawan and Qureshi together to the amount received by Qureshi and Rohit together

$$= \frac{x+140}{140+160-x} = \frac{6}{5} \text{ or } x = 100$$

80. a If Yamini covers 5 km in 't' hours, Zora will cover 15 km in $t + \frac{2}{3}$ hours.

The distance between the two at this moment is 5 km, and Yamini will cover 2 km more and Zora will cover 3 km more till they meet.

Therefore, the ratio of the speeds of Yamini to Zora is 2 : 3.

$$\frac{5}{t} \div \frac{15}{\left(t+\frac{2}{3}\right)} = \frac{2}{3}$$

Solving the above equation, we get $t = \frac{2}{3}$.

Speed of Yamini = 7.5 km/hr.

81. b The rabbit overstretched his sleeping time by $1\frac{1}{6}t$ min.

$$\therefore \quad t + 1\frac{1}{6}t = 14 + t \Rightarrow t = 12$$

Let the speed (in km/min) of the rabbit and tortoise be '6x' and 'x' respectively.

Had the rabbit not overstretched his nap, he would have beaten the tortoise by 13 min.

$$\therefore \quad \frac{2}{6x} + 12 + 13 = \frac{2}{x}$$

$$\Rightarrow x = \frac{1}{15}$$

Hence, the time taken by the tortoise to complete the race $= \frac{2}{x} = \frac{2}{1/15} = 30$ min.

82. d The distance covered by R in 2 hours (3 PM to 5 PM) is same as the distance covered by P in 4 hours (1 PM to 5 PM).

Ratio of speeds of P and R = 1 : 2.

Now, R tales over Q in another hour by doubling his speed, so R has covered a total distance in 3 hours (3 PM to 6 PM) which he would have covered in 4 hours without changing his speed.

To cover the same distance, a takes 5 hours (1 PM to 6 PM) Ratio of speed of Q and R = 4 : 5

⇒ Ratio of speed of P and Q = 5 : 8.

83. b

Let's take there are two ants.

Considering worst possible case we can see easily the required time is same as the time taken by an ant to reach one extreme point to another extreme point. Which will be same when there are 1000 ants.

ie, maximum time $= \frac{100}{50}$ min. = 2 min.

84. 16

Let the distance be x

$$\therefore 15 + \frac{x}{4} = \frac{x/2}{7/2} + \frac{x/2}{9/2}$$

Solving we have x = 15 × 252

Total time taken by the second boat

$$= \frac{15 \times 252}{7} + \frac{15 \times 252}{9}$$

= 960 sec = 16 min.

85. b Let the speeds of Prakash and Arpit be 2x and 5x respectively. Let's assume that Arpit turned back from point Q as shown in the figure given below, ran at a speed of x after turning back and met Prakash at point R, 't' hours after they started running.

P —— 10 km —— R —— a —— Q

From the given conditions,

$$2x \times t = 10 = 5x \times 2 - x \times (t-2)$$

$$\Rightarrow \quad t = 4$$

So the running speed of Prakash

$$= 2x = \frac{10}{4} = 2.5 \text{ km/hr.}$$

86. 156 Let the length of the track be 4x meters.

As they together cover 2x meters in 12 minutes, they will together cover 4x meters in 24 minutes.

Hence, the required time = 12 + 6 × 24 = 156.

87. 1900 900

Ratio of speed of A and B is 10 : 9 and that of B to C is 10 : 9

∴ Ratio of speed of A and C is 100 : 81

⇒ So, in 100 km race, A beats C by 19 km

⇒ So, in 10 km race A beats C by

$$= \frac{19}{100} \times 10 \text{ km}$$

$$= \frac{19}{10} \times 1000 \text{ m} = 1900 \text{ m}$$

88. c ← 2d →
A d C d B

Total time taken to cover distance AB = $\frac{2d}{60}$.

Time taken to cover BC = $\frac{d}{25}$.

Time taken to reach point A through bypass road

$= \frac{d+5}{50}$.

So, $\frac{d}{25} + \frac{(d+5)}{50} - \frac{2d}{60} = \frac{30}{60}$

$\Rightarrow \frac{12d + 6d + 30 - 10d}{5} = \frac{30}{60}$

$\Rightarrow$ 8d + 30 = 150

$\Rightarrow$ 8d = 120

$\Rightarrow$ d = 15

$\Rightarrow$ So, total distance travelled by him is 4d + 5

= 65 miles.

89. b 1pm → 3:40 pm ← 2pm
A ——— C ——— B
s ← 168 km → C d 2s

Time taken to cover distance AC = $2 + \frac{40}{60} = \frac{8}{3}$hrs.

So, speed of motorbike = $\frac{168}{8} \times 3$ = 63 km/hr

So, speed of car = 2 × 63 = 126 km/hr

BC (distance) $= 126 \times \left(1 + \frac{40}{60}\right) = 126 \times \frac{5}{3} = 210$km

So, total distance = 168 + 210 = 378 km.

90. b Let distance AP be x km.

∴ BP = 3x km.

Let the speed of car 1 be 2s then speed of car 2 will be s.

Now, according to the question,

$\frac{3x}{s} - \frac{x}{2s} = 1$

$\frac{6x - x}{2s} = 1$

$\Rightarrow \frac{x}{s} = \frac{2}{s}$

∴ Time taken by car 1 in reaching P from A is

$= \frac{x}{2s} = \frac{2}{5 \times 2} = \frac{1}{5} \times 60 = 12$ minutes.

91. 15

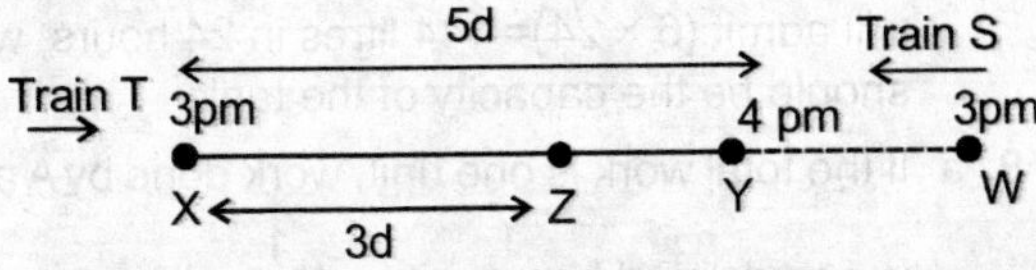

Let Train S is at point W at 3 pm and both the trains pass each other at point Z.

∴ Speed of train T be 4s and that of train S will be 3s.

Distance covered by train S from 3 pm to 4 pm i.e. (YW) = 3s × 1 = 3s.

∴ The time taken by the trains when both started simultaneously at 3 pm till they passed each other

$= \frac{5d + 3s}{(4s + 3s)} = \frac{5d + 3s}{7s}$

So, the speed of train T to cover distance XZ

$= \frac{3d}{5d + 3s} \times 7s$

$\Rightarrow 4s = \frac{3d \times 7s}{5d + 3s}$

∴ Time taken by train T to cover the distance

from X to Y $= \frac{5d}{4s} = \frac{5}{4} \times 12 = 15$ hours

92. d

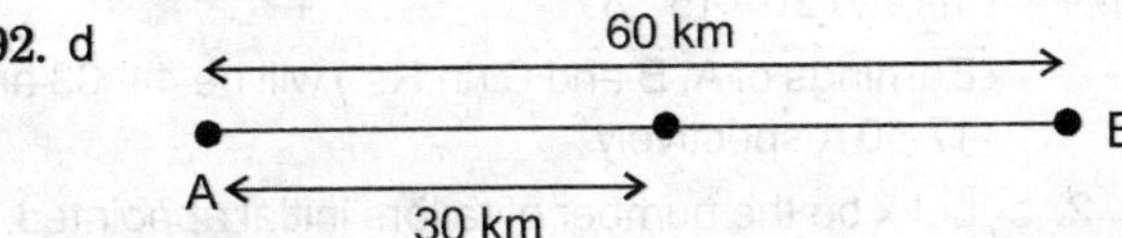

Partha →

Narayan →

Let Narayan takes t hours to cover the distance AB.

∴ Partha will take (t + 4) hours to cover the same distance.

Now, Partha reaches midpoint of AB two hours before Narayan reaches B.

∴ Partha takes (t – 2) hours to cover 30 km.

$\Rightarrow$ Remaining 30 km, is covered by Partha in (t + 4) – (t – 2) = 6 hours.

∴ Speed of Partha $= \frac{30}{6} = 5$km/hr.

93. 50 Let the speed of the cars starting from A and B be x km/hr and y km/hr respectively.

Applying the concept of relative speed we get:

$\frac{350}{x + y} = 1$ and $\frac{350}{y - x} = 7$

Solving the two equations, we get x = 150 km/hr and y = 200 km/hr.

Hence, required difference is 50.

94. a Ratio of speeds of car 1 and car 3 = 200 : 100 = 2 : 1

Similarly, ratio of speeds of car 3 and car 2

= 200 : 100 = 2 : 1

Hence, ratio of the speeds of car 2 and car 1 = 1 : 4.

95. 5 Time taken for Car 1 to reach B from the point when Car 2 starts:

First 30 km – 18 min

Second 50 km – 60 min

Third 50 km – 120 min

$\Rightarrow$ Total time = 198 minutes

In 198 minutes the distance covered by Car 2 will be:

First 50 km – 30 min

Second 50 km – 60 min

Therefore, in remaining time of 108 min the distance covered by Car 2 at 25 km/hr will be = 45 km.

Hence, required distance = 5 km.

Time and Work

1. a Ratio of working efficiently of A, B and C

$= \frac{1}{6} : \frac{1}{8} : \frac{1}{15}$ or 20 : 15 : 8

Total earnings would be divided among A, B and C in ratio 20 : 15 : 8.

Earnings of A, B and C (in Rs.) will be 44, 33 and 17.60 respectively.

2. c Let x be the number of tailors initial appointed.

Let n be the number of shirts that had to be stitched by each tailor initially

Let y be the number of tailors who did not come.

$x \times n = 480.$

$(x - y)(n + 32) = 480$

Only option (c)satisfies the equation.

3. b B being twice as fast as A, will take half of time of A to produce a million units i.e. = 30 hrs.

Since Machine C takes the same amount of time as A & B running together,

$\therefore \frac{1}{C} = \frac{1}{A} + \frac{1}{B}$ or $\frac{1}{A} + \frac{1}{B} + \frac{1}{C} = \frac{2}{A} + \frac{2}{B}.$

$\Rightarrow \frac{2}{60} + \frac{2}{30} = \frac{1}{10}.$

Hence, it will take 10 hours.

4. c **From statement I:** From this statement, exact number of widgets produced by machine A cannot be determined.

From statement II: From this statement also exact number of widgets produced by machine A cannot be determined.

On combining statements I and II: Dealer produced minimum 10 units of widget A and 15 units of widget B and for that he requires 10 × 2 + 15 × 4 = 80 machine hours and number of machine hours available per week is also 80 hours.

Hence, he produced 10 units of widget A.

5. b Let the work done by a worker be x units, w be the total work and n be the number of workers in the group. Then,

w = Work done on the nth day i.e. last day + Work done on the second last day + ... + Work done on the first day

$\Rightarrow w = x + 2x + \ldots + nx = \frac{n(n+1)x}{2}$ ... (i)

When none of the workers is removed, then

$w = nx \times \frac{2n}{3} = \frac{2n^2x}{3}$ ... (ii)

From equation (i)and (ii), we get

$\frac{n(n+1)x}{2} = \frac{2n^2x}{3} \Rightarrow n = 3.$

6. d There are 18 men, 15 women and 6 children.

Working efficiency of man : woman : child = 6 : 3 : 1.

So the ratio of the work done in a day by 18 men, 15 women and 6 children = (18 × 6) : (15 × 3) : (6 ×1) = 108 : 45 : 6.

Hence, the daily wage of Rs. 1,113 should be divided in this ratio. That makes it, Rs.756 for men, Rs.315 for women and Rs. 42 for children.

Hence, 6 children earn Rs. 42 in a day.

So the daily wage of a child should be Rs. 7.

7. b Since a bucket holds 5 litres of water, water discharged in one minute by tap A, B and C is $\frac{5}{6}$ litres, $\frac{2}{3}$ litres and $\frac{1}{2}$ litres respectively

If A, B and C are all opened simultaneously, total discharge in one minute $= \left(\frac{5}{6} + \frac{2}{3} + \frac{1}{2}\right)$ = 2 litres

So in 2 hours, the discharge would be 240 litres, that is the capacity of the tank.

8. c Since the leak can empty the tank in 8 hours, the rate of leak $= \frac{1}{8}$.

And since the leak along with the tap can empty it in 12 hours, the equation can be rewritten as:

$\frac{1}{x} - \frac{1}{8} = -\frac{1}{12}$ (where x is the time taken by the tap to fill the tank).

Simplifying we get, $\frac{1}{x} = \frac{1}{24}$ or x = 24.

This means that the tap can fill the tank in 24 hours. Since the tap admits 6 litres per hour, it will admit (6 × 24)= 144 litres in 24 hours, which should be the capacity of the tank.

9. a If the total work is one unit, work done by A and B in one day will be $\frac{1}{a}$ unit and $\frac{1}{b}$ unit respectively.

Using statement I: $\frac{n}{a} + \frac{n}{b} = 1,$

Since 'n' is an integer, if both A and B work for n days, work will be completed no matter who starts a work.

Using statement II, nothing can be concluded as total amount of work is not known.

10. a If x men were there on day one, there would be (x – 110)men on the 12th day.

Hence, on an average, there were (x – 55) men.

The job takes $\frac{3}{2}$ times the normal time.

Hence, the average number of people = $\frac{2}{3}$.

$\Rightarrow x - 55 = \frac{2}{3}x$

Hence, x = 165

11. c Let the first typist takes X hours and the second takes Y hours to do the whole job.

When the first was busy typing for 3 hr, the second was busy only for 2 hr.

Both of them did $\frac{11}{20}$ of the whole work.

$\therefore \frac{3}{X}+\frac{2}{Y}=\frac{11}{20}$.

When the assignment was completed, it was revealed that each typist had done half the work.

$\therefore$ The first one spent $\frac{X}{2}$ hr, and the second, $\frac{Y}{2}$ hr.

And since the first had begun one hour before the second, we have $\frac{X}{2}-\frac{Y}{2}=1 \Rightarrow X = 10$ hr, Y = 8 hr.

12. c As there is no day in the week whose first letter is R, it can be concluded that Raja does not have any holidays. Since 1996 is a leap year, we can figure out that Raja has totally worked for 7 days. Let his rate of doing the job be one unit per day. So he would complete 7 units of work in a week. J's situation is similar to Raja and does not have any holiday during the week. T will have two holidays in a week (Tuesday and Thursday). Since the rate of working for all the three of them is the same, the working pattern of J and T would be as follows.

We can see that depending on which day is February 25, 1996, to complete 7 units, they would either take 4 days or 5 days. Hence, the answer is (c).

Sun.	Mon.	Tue.	Wed.	Thurs.	Fri.	Sat.
2 units	2 units	1 unit	2 units	1 unit	2 units	2 units

13. c Now Raja has worked for (5 days in February + 31 days in March + 2 days in April) = 38 days. Let us assume his rate to be the same as in the previous question, viz. one unit a day. Hence, he completes 38 units totally. In a week, T takes holiday on Tuesday and Thursday, while S takes holiday on Saturday and Sunday. We can see that their working pattern would be as follows.

Sun.	Mon.	Tues.	Wed.	Thurs.	Fri.	Sat.
1 unit	2 units	1 unit	2 units	1 unit	2 units	1 unit

So in a week they work together 10 units work. Thus, in three weeks, they would complete 30 units work. It can be found out that February 25 is Sunday. So the remaining 8 units of work can be completed only on Friday, i.e. March 22.

14. b In one day, A would do $\frac{1}{3}$ of the job, B would do $\frac{1}{4}$ of the job and C would do $\frac{1}{6}$ of the job.

Hence, if all three of them work simultaneously, in one day they would do $\left(\frac{1}{3}+\frac{1}{4}+\frac{1}{6}\right)=\frac{3}{4}$ of the job.

Hence, to complete the entire job together they would take $\frac{4}{3}$ days.

Shortcut:

A can complete the job in 3 days. So A, B and C combined will take less days than A alone to finish the job. So straightway option (b).

15. d Work done in one day by A, B, C and D are $\frac{1}{4}, \frac{1}{8}, \frac{1}{16}$ and $\frac{1}{32}$ respectively.

Using answer choices, we note that the pair of B and C does $\frac{3}{16}$ of work in one day; the pair of A and D does $\frac{1}{4}+\frac{1}{32}=\frac{9}{32}$ of the work in one day.

Hence, A and D take $\frac{32}{9}$ days.

B and C take $\frac{16}{3}=\frac{32}{6}$ days.

Hence, the first pair must comprise of A and D.

16. c Let 't' be the time taken for all three together, then $\frac{1}{t+6}+\frac{1}{t+1}+\frac{1}{2t}=\frac{1}{t}$

Solving the above equation, we get

$3t^2 + 7t - 6 = 0$ or $t = \frac{2}{3}$ hr = 40 min

17. d Total amount of work = 60 man-hours

From 11 am to 5 pm, 6 technicians = 36 man-hours

From 5 pm to 6 pm, 7 technicians = 7 man-hours

From 6 pm to 7 pm, 8 technicians = 8 man-hours

From 7 am to 8 pm, 9 technicians = 9 man-hours

Total = 60 man-hours

18. b Three small pumps = Two large pumps

Three small + One large pumps = Three large pump

$\therefore \frac{1}{3}$rd of total time is taken by the large pump alone.

19. c **Machine I :**

Number of nuts produced in one minute = 100

To produce 1000 nuts time required = 10 min

Cleaning time for nuts = 5 min

Effective time to produce 1000 nuts = 15 min

Effective time to produce 9000 nuts = 15 × 9 – 5 = 130 min

Machine II :

To produce 75 bolts time required = 1 min

To produce 1500 bolts time required = 20 min

Cleaning time for bolts = 10 min

Effective time to produce 1500 bolts = 30 min

Effective time to, produce 9000 bolts = 30 × 6 – 10 = 170 min … (ii)

From (i) and (ii),

Minimum time to produce 900 pairs of nuts and bolts = 170 minutes

20. c

A	B	C	D
–20	20		
90		–90	
–10			10
		–50	50
	–100	100	
	110		–110
Total +60	30	–40	–50

D gets emptied first, it gets emptied in 20 minutes.

Hence, option (c) is the correct answer.

21. b Area of cross section for

$$P_1 = A_1 = \left(\frac{22}{7}\right)7^2 = 154 \text{ m}^2$$

Volume of water flowing through P_1 in one second

= 154 × 10 = 1540 m^3

Volume of tank = V = 1540 × 2 × 3600

= 11088 × 10^3 m^3

Area of cross section for

$$P_2 = A_2 = \left(\frac{22}{7}\right)14^2 = 616 \text{ m}^2$$

Let the rate of water flowing through P_2 = s m/s

Volume of water flowing through P_2 in one second = 616s m^3

Volume of water flow in the tank when P_1 is used as inlet and P_2 is used as outlet pipe: 1540 – 616s.

Time taken to fill = 4 hours = 4 x 3600 seconds

So,(1540 – 616s) × 4 × 3600 = V

= 11088 × 10^3

= 1540 × 2 × 3600

or 1540 – 616s = 770

or s = 1.25 m/s

22. d Let the efficiencies of Anirudh and Anushka be 'a' and 'b' units/day respectively.

$$\therefore (a+b)x + a \times \frac{x}{2} = (a+b)\frac{3x}{4} + a \times x \Rightarrow \frac{a}{b} = 1$$

Hence, the required ratio is 1 : 1.

23. 150 $\frac{m \times d \times h}{w}$ = constant, where

m = number of men

d = number of days

h = number of hours

w = amount of work

Let the number of additional men required be x.

$$\therefore \frac{75 \times 90 \times 8}{2} = \frac{(75+x) \times 60 \times 10}{5}$$

or x = 150

Hence, 150 additional men would be required.

24. a A → inlet pipe, B → outlet pipe

A takes 8 hours to fill the tank

(A and B) together takes 10 hours

So, total volume of the tank is LCM of 8, 10 i.e. 0 ltrs(say)

Half filled tank means $\frac{40}{2}$ = 20 ltrs.

In 1 hour, A fills $\frac{40}{8}$ = 5 ltrs and

(A + B) fills $\left(\frac{40}{10}\right)$ = 4 ltrs.

So, B empties in 1 hour = 5 – 4 = 1 ltr

So, total time taken by B to make the full tank half filled = $\frac{20}{1}$ = 20 hours.

25. a Amal can complete the work in 10 days

Bimla can complete the work in 8 days

(Amal + Bimla + Kamal) can complete the work in 4 days

Total work done = LCM of 10, 8 and 4 = 40 units.

So, Amal's 1 day work is 4 units.

Bimal's 1 day work is 5 units

Amal's + Bimal's + Kamal's together 1 day work is = 10 units

⇒ Kamal's 1 day work is 1 unit.

So, their amount of work done is in the ratio of 4 : 5 : 1

⇒ Share of Kamla = Rs.100

26. 10 Let the filling pipe be denoted by f and the draining pipe by d.

∴ 6(6f + 5d) = 60 (5f + 6d)

6f + 5d = 50f + 60d

$\Rightarrow \quad 4f + 5d = 0$

$5d = -4f$

$\frac{d}{f} = -\frac{4}{5}$

∴ Total quantity of the tank

$= 6\,(6 \times 5 + 5 \times (-4))$

$= 60$ units

One draining and two filling pipes will fill $= 1 \times -4 + 2 \times 5 = 6$ units in 1 hour

∴Number of hours when the empty tank will get completely filled $= \frac{60}{6} = 10$ hours

27. c Let A finishes the job in 4x days.

∴B finishes the job in $\frac{125}{100} \times 4x = 5x$ days.

Total work = LCM (4x, 5x) = 20x.

∴A does $\frac{20x}{4x} = 5$ units in 1 day.

∴ B does $\frac{20x}{5x} = 4$ units in 1 day.

$\frac{20x}{2} = 10x$	?	$\frac{5}{100} \times 20x = x$
A	(A + B) in 4 days	B

∴ In 4 days, A and B together does

$= 4\,(5 + 4) = 36$ units

∴ $36 = 20x - (10x + x)$

$9x = 36$

$x = 4$

∴ Total work done $= 20 \times 4 = 80$

Hence, B can alone finish the entire job in

$= \frac{80}{4} = 20$ days.

28. b According to the question,

$30(15H + 5R) = 60\,(5H + 15R)$

$15H + 5R = 10H + 30R$

$5H = 25R$

$\frac{H}{R} = \frac{5}{1}$

∴ Total work $= 30\,(15 \times 5 + 5 \times 1) = 2400$

∴ Number of days taken by fifteen humans working together without any robot to finish the job

$= \frac{2400}{15 \times 5} = 32$

29. 48Let the units of water bring in by A and B in 1 minute be 'a' and 'b' respectively.

$\Rightarrow 30 \times (10a + 45b) = 60(8a + 18b)$

$\Rightarrow 2a = 3b$ or $a : b = 3 : 2$

Therefore, total capacity of tank $= 30 \times (30 + 90)$

Hence, required time $= \frac{30(30 + 90)}{7 \times 3 + 27 \times 2} = 48$ minutes.

30. b Let the efficiencies of Ramesh and Ganesh be R and G respectively.

$\Rightarrow \quad 16(R + G) = 17G + 7R + 10 \times (0.7R)$

$\Rightarrow \quad G = 2R$

Thus, total Work $= 48R$

Work left after 7 days $= 48R - 7 \times 3R = 27R$

Hence, required time $= \frac{27R}{2R} = 13.5$ days.

31. b Work done by A in 3 hours i.e. from 5 pm to 8 pm is done by B in 2 hours i.e. from 5 pm to 7 pm

Thus, the ratio of rate of flow of water from A and B = 2 : 3

Therefore, we can assume the time taken by A and B to be 3x hours and 2x hours respectively. Now, it's given that 3x – 2x = 2 hours (A finishes at 8 pm and B at 6 pm)

Thus, time taken by A and B to fill the tank will be 6 hours and 4 hours respectively such that the starting time is 2 pm and capacity of the tank = 12 units.

Hence, required time $= \frac{12}{5} = 2.4$ hours which means they will fill the tank completely at 4.24 pm by starting at 2 pm.

Miscellaneous

1. c Options (b) and (d)can be eliminated as the difference in the number of books is 1. i.e.12,13 and 5,6 respectively.

Among option (a) and (c)we can quickly verify by multiplying only the last digits.

Eg. For option (a)the last digit of the total cost should be $(5 \times 7) + (8 \times 9) + (7 \times 3) = 5 + 2 + 1 = 8$. Which is not we are looking for as our total cost is Rs.620.

Hence, option (c)is correct choice.

2. d As total cost is an integral multiple of 10, number of cards bought by Rahul of Rs.3.50 and that of Rs.4.50 must be equal i.e. 5 or 10.

If Rahul bought 5 cards of Rs.3.50 and 5 cards of Rs.4.50, total cost of all cards $= 2 \times 10 + 3.50 \times 5 + 4.50 \times 5 + 5 + 10 =$ Rs. 110.

If Rahul bought 10 cards of Rs.3.50 and 10 cards of Rs.4.50, total cost of all cards $= 2 \times 5 + 3.50 \times 5 + 450 \times 10 + 5 \times 5 =$ Rs. 115. (not possible)

∴ Required number of notes $= \frac{110}{10} = 11$.

3. a Let present age of X and Y be x and y respectively.

We have, $x = 3(y-3)$ ... (i)

From statement I, $x = y + 17$ ... (ii)

From statement II, $x + 9 = 3y$ ... (iii)

From (i) and (ii)x = 37.5 years and y = 12.5 years

But, equations (i) and (iii)are same so we cannot find values of x and y.

4. d

Option	Location	Expenditure of Town A students	Expenditure of Town B students	Total Expenditure
(a)	33 km from A	33 x 1.2 x 30 = 1188	67 x 1.2 x 100 = 8040	1188 + 8040 = 9228
(b)	33 km from B	67 x 1.2 x 30 = 2412	33 x 1.2 x 100 = 3960	2412 + 3960 = 6372
(c)	Town A	0	100 x 100 x 1.2 = 12000	12000
(d)	Town B	30 x 100 x 1.2 = 3600	0	3600

Hence, we find that the least expenditure will be incurred if the school is located in town B.

HINT : Students please note that since there are more number of students from Town B, to minimise the total expenditure the school should be located as closer to town B as possible.

5. d If a clock has to strike 4 or 4 times, there are 3 time intervals between the 4 strikes (Since the first strike happens at the zeroth second).

So in 7 seconds the pendulum elapses 3 time intervals. To strike 11, there has to be 10 time intervals, which will take $\frac{10 \times 7}{3}$ = 23.33 seconds.

6. a Miguel's income

= 5 + (0.02 × 25)+ (0.03 × 25) + (0.04 × 50)
= $8.25.

Martin's commission = $10.

Hence, obviously I > II.

7. d From the statement I, we can only find the number of mangoes stolen by 4 of the 10 boys.

The statement II suggests that the number of mangoes stolen by each of the remaining six boys is more than 4 and less than 40. Although from the two statements that are given it is tempting to assume that the number of mangoes stolen by the boys must be in AP, since it is not mentioned explicitly we cannot answer the question.

8. a Since I paid Rs. 20 and because of lack of change, the clerk gave me Rs. 3 worth of stamps, it can be concluded that the total value of the stamp that I wanted to buy is Rs. 17. Since I ordered initially a minimum of 2 stamps of each denominations, if I buy exactly 2 stamps each, my total value is 2(5 + 2 + 1) = Rs. 16. The only way in which I make it Rs. 17 is buying one more stamp of Re 1. Hence, the total number of stamps that I ordered = (2 + 2 + 3) = 7.

In addition, the clerk gave me 3 more. Hence, the total number of stamps that I bought = (7 + 3) = 10 (viz. 2 five-rupee, 2 two-rupee and 6 one-rupee stamps).

For questions 9 and 10:

Hint: Students, please note that this sum could be intelligently solved by looking at both the questions together and also the answer choices. We know that the inventory has reduced by 54 units. This means two things: (i) actual quantity sold was less than the figure that was entered the computer (i.e. after interchanging digits), so the unit's place digit of the actual quantity sold should be less than its ten's place digit; and (ii) the difference between the actual quantity sold and the one that was entered in the computer is 54. From question 10, we can figure out that the only answer choice that supports both these conditions is (a), as (82 – 28 = 54).

So the actual quantity sold = 28. Now since the total sales is Rs.1,148, actual price per piece $= \frac{1148}{28}$ = Rs.41.

Hence, the answer to question is (b).

9. b

10. a

11. a The team has played a total of (17 + 3) = 20 matches. This constitutes $\frac{2}{3}$ of the matches. Hence, total number of matches played = 30.

To win $\frac{3}{4}$ of them, a team has to win 22.5, i.e. at least win 23 of them. In other words, the team has to win a minimum of 6 matches (since it has already won 17)out of remaining 10. So it can lose a maximum of 4 of them.

12. c We can see that there are two types of cost: (i) Transportation cost (viz. hiring truck) and (ii) storing cost. It can be seen that the daily production is far less than the capacity of the truck. So a truck can be hired to carry multiple days production at one go. So as long as the storing cost is less than the cost of hiring the truck (i.e. Rs. 1,000), it makes sense to store the production. When the storing cost exceeds Rs. 1,000, it is best that the entire lot be sent to the market.

The cost pattern is as given in the following table:

Units produced	Units to be stored	Cost of storing (Rs.)	Cost of sending to the market (Rs.)	Should you hire truck?	Cost Incurred (Rs.)
150	150	750	1,000	No	750
180	(150 + 180) = 330	1,650	1,000	Yes	1000
120	120	600	1,000	No	600
250	(120 + 250) = 370	1,850	1,000	Yes	1,000
160	160	800	1,000	No	800
120	(160 + 120) = 280	1,400	1,000	Yes	1,000
150	150	750	1,000	Yes*	1,000
			Total Cost		6,150

* In spite of the fact that storing is cheaper than hiring truck on the last day, we have to do with the latter option because everything that is manufactured has to be sent to the market.

So according to this table, if the truck is hired on 2nd, 4th, 6th and 7th days, total cost = Rs. 6,150. But is this the most cost-effective scheme? It can be seen that we are hiring truck on two consecutive days (6th and 7th). Hence, since everything that is manufactured has to be sent to the market, we have yet another option of hiring the truck on the 5th day and sending the 6th and 7th days production together on the last day. In that case, the cost on 5th day would be Rs. 1,000 (i.e. Rs. 200 more than the present cost), the cost on the 6th day would be (120 × 5) = Rs. 600 (i.e. Rs. 400 less than the present cost) and the cost on the 7th day would be Rs. 1,000 (the same as the present cost). Hence, we can say that the total cost would actually come down by (+200 – 400 = – 200) Rs. 200.

Hence, this becomes the most cost-effective scheme. So we should hire trucks on 2nd, 4th, 5th and 7th days.

13. b If the storage cost is reduced to Re. 0.8 per cubic feet, then the cost pattern is as given in the following table.

Units produced	Units to be stored	Cost of storing (Rs.)	Cost of sending to the market (Rs.)	Should you hire truck?	Cost incurred (Rs.)
150	150	120	1,000	No	120
180	(150 + 180) = 330	264	1,000	No	264
120	(330 + 120) = 450	360	1,000	No	360
250	(450 + 250)	560	1,000	No	560
160	(700 + 160)	688	1,000	No	688
120	(860 + 120)	784	1,000	No	784
150	(980 + 150)	904	1,000	Yes **	1,000
			Total cost		3,776

** In spite of the fact that storing is cheaper than hiring truck on the last day, we have to do with the latter option because everything that is manufactured has to be sent to the market.

Hence, the most cost-effective scheme would be sending the entire production on the 7th day.

14. b To maximise the value of the wealth, we must carry more of the one whose value per kilogram is more.

Value per kilogram of ruby = $\left(\frac{4}{0.3}\right)$ = Rs. 13.33 crore, and value per rupee of each emerald = $\left(\frac{5}{0.4}\right)$ = Rs. 12.5 crore.

It is obvious that we should carry entire 12 kg of ruby. This would amount to $\left(\frac{12}{0.3}\right)$ = 40 rubies.

15. a Let the number of chocolates be c.

Number of apples has to be more than 3c, lets say 3c + k, k is a positive integer.

	Chocolate	Biscuits	Apple
No.	c	2c	3c + k
Cost per piece	1	0.5	2
Total cost	c	c	6c + 2k

Total spend = 8c + 2k

for c = 4, k = 2

Total spend = 34

Hence, (a) is the answer.

The cost of each chocolate is Re. 1. So the cost of apple should be Rs. 2 and that of one biscuit should be Re. 0.5. Thus, if he eats x chocolates, he has to eat 2x biscuits. Hence, the total value of chocolates will be Rs. x and that of biscuits will be (0.5)(2x)= Rs. x. Hence, we see that the value of chocolates is to the value of biscuits will always be 1 : 1. As per our assumption he will have to eat more than (x + 2x)= 3x apples and hence the total value of the apples will be more than (2)(3x) = 6x. In other words, the ratio of value chocolates to apples or biscuits to apples will be more than 1 : 6. In other words, if the value of chocolates and biscuits is Re. 1 each, then the value of apples has to be more than Rs. 6, or the combined value will be more than Rs. 8. This means that the value of apples will always constitute more than $\frac{6}{8}$ or $\frac{3}{4}$ of the entire bill. It can further be observed that the total value of chocolates and biscuits together will always be an even integer and so will be the value of apples. This means that the combined value of all three of them has to be even and not odd. So Rs. 33 cannot be the answer. Also Rs. 8 cannot be the answer as, if we take the value of chocolates and biscuits to be minimum, i.e. Re. 1 each, then the value of apples can be a minimum of Rs. 8. Hence, the total value will always be Rs. 10 or higher. The only option possible is Rs. 34. To verify this let us find two even numbers (one of them higher than $\frac{3}{4}$ of 34) which adds 34.

We can find many such numbers E.g. 32 + 2, 30 + 4, 28 + 6 and 26 + 8. All of these could be a possible combination.

16. c From the statement II, we can frame the equation that: (Cold drink) = 3(Tea) and (Coffee) = (Cold drink) – 5 = 3(Tea) – 5. So we have one equation in terms of prices of tea and coffee. Although, this alone may not be sufficient to answer the question, in the light of the equation provided by the first statement, viz. (Coffee) = (Tea) + 5, we can solve the two equations simultaneously and get the price of tea.

For questions 17 to 19:

17. d It is given that Q > P and R > S.

Q	P	R	S
4	2	3	1
2	1	4	3

The distribution of coins can be of two types in both the cases, S gets an odd number.

18. b

P	Q	R	S
1	3	4	2
2	4	3	1

Clearly, Q gets more coins than S in both the cases.

19. a

R	S	Q	P
4	2	3	1
4	1	3	2
4	3	2	1

Looking at the possible distribution of coins, we find that option (a)is not always true.

20. d Let m = 1. So, option (a)will give the answer as V_m and option (c)will give the answer as V_1. Both of these cannot be the answers as V_m and V_1 are the amount of volume filled.

Let m = 2. So, option (b)will give the answer as $2(1 - V_2)$ and option (d)will give the answer as $2(1 - V_1)$. Now consider option (b).

Actual empty volume > $2(1 - V_2)$. Therefore, for this situation $m(1 - V_1)$is the only possible answer.

21. b Let m = 1 and n = 1. Option (a) gives the answer as $\frac{1}{4}$ and option (d) gives the answer as 'greatest integer less than or equal to $\frac{1}{2}$'. So, both of these cannot be the answer. Option (b) gives the answer as 'smallest integer greater than or equal to $\frac{1}{2}$' and option (c)gives the answer as 1. But the actual answer can be greater than 1 as the volume of the vessel is 2 l. Hence, (b) is the answer.

22. b If N is a natural number such that $N = a^p b^q c^r \ldots$ where a, b, c etc are prime numbers, then Euler's Totient function is given by

$$\phi(N) = N\left(1 - \frac{1}{a}\right)\left(1 - \frac{1}{b}\right)\left(1 - \frac{1}{c}\right).$$

If P is some other natural number which is prime to N, then the remainder when $P^{\phi(N)}$ is divided by N is 1.

To find the last two digits we need to find the remainder when 9483^{67483} is divided by 100.

$$\phi(100) = 100\left(1 - \frac{1}{2}\right)\left(1 - \frac{1}{5}\right) = 40$$

Required remainder = $83^{67483} = 83^{40k+3} = 83^3 = 87$.

23. d Let the time at which Mr. Clockilal entered the museum be 'm' minutes past 12 noon.

$$\therefore \left|\frac{11}{2}m - 30 \times 0\right| = 20 \Rightarrow m = 3\frac{7}{11}$$

As he spent more than 3 hours and less than 4 hours in the museum, and the angle between the minute and hour hands at the time of leaving was 220°, he must have left the museum between $3:3\frac{7}{11}$ p.m. and 4 p.m.

Let the time at which he left the museum be 'n' minutes past 3 p.m.

$$\therefore \left|\frac{11}{2}n - 30 \times 3\right| = 220 \Rightarrow n = 56\frac{4}{11} \text{ or } 41\frac{9}{11}$$

Hence, the time spent by Mr. Clockilal in the museum was either 3 hours $52\frac{8}{11}$ minutes or 3 hours $38\frac{2}{11}$ minutes.

24. b Let the fund value follow the quadratic polynomial

$$f(x) = ax^2 + bx + c.$$

When $x = 0, f(x) = 10 \Rightarrow c = 10$

When $x = 2, f(x) = 5$

$\Rightarrow 4a + 2b + 10 = 5$

$\Rightarrow 4a + 2b = -5$ ... (i)

When $x = 4, f(x) = 15$

$\Rightarrow 16a + 4b + 10 = 15$

$\Rightarrow 16a + 4b = 5$ ... (ii)

Solving (i) and (ii), we get

$$a = \frac{15}{8} \quad b = \frac{-25}{4}$$

∴ Required difference

$$= \left(\frac{15}{8} \times 8^2 - \frac{25}{4} \times 8 + 10\right) - 10 = 70.$$

■■

3 CHAPTER

Geometry and Mensuration

LINE

1994

Direction for Question 1 : Data is provided followed by two statements – I and II – both resulting in a value, say I and II. As your answer,

Mark (a) if I > II.

Mark (b) if I < II.

Mark (c) if I = II.

Mark (d) if nothing can be said.

1. k_1, k_2, k_3 are parallel lines. AD = 2 cm, BE = 8 cm and CF = 32 cm.

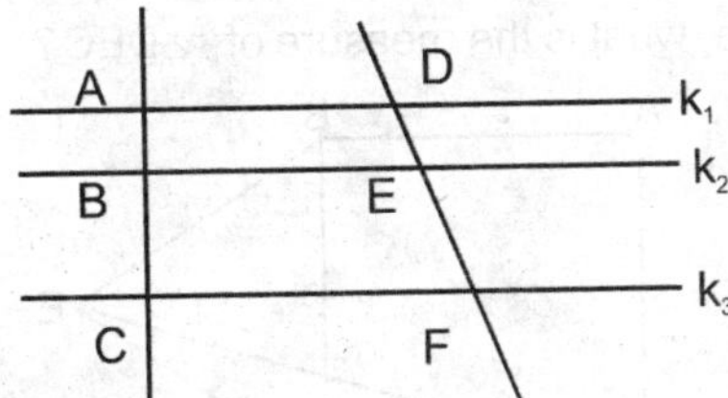

I. (AB) × (EF)

II. (BC) × (DE)

Direction for Question 2 : The question is followed by two statements. As the answer,

Mark (a) if the question can be answered with the help of statement I alone,

Mark (b) if the question can be answered with the help of statement II, alone,

Mark (c) if both, statement I and statement II are needed to answer the question, and

Mark (d) if the question cannot be answered even with the help of both the statements.

2. Is segment PQ greater than segment RS?

I. PB > RE, BQ = ES.

II. B is a point on PQ, E is a point on RS.

Direction for Question 3: The question is followed by two statements. As the answer,

Mark:

(a) if the question can be answered by any one of the statements alone, but cannot be answered by using the other statement alone.

(b) if the question can be answered by using either statement alone.

(c) if the question can be answered by using both the statements together, but cannot be answered by using either statement alone.

(d) if the question cannot be answered even by using both the statements together.

1999

3. A line graph on a graph sheet shows the revenue for each year from 1990 through 1998 by points and joins the successive points by straight-line segments. The point for revenue of 1990 is labelled A, that for 1991 as B, and that for 1992 as C. What is the ratio of growth in revenue between 1991-92 and 1990-91?

I. The angle between AB and X-axis when measured with a protractor is 40°, and the angle between CB and X-axis is 80°.

II. The scale of Y-axis is 1 cm = Rs. 100

TRIANGLE

1991

1. A man starting at a point walks one km east, then two km north, then one km east, then one km north, then one km east and then one km north to arrive at the destination. What is the shortest distance from the starting point to the destination?

(a) $2\sqrt{2}$ km (b) 7 km

(c) $3\sqrt{2}$ km (d) 5 km

1993

Directions for Questions 2 and 3: Use the following information:

ABC forms an equilateral triangle in which B is 2 km from A. A person starts walking from B in a direction parallel to AC and stops when he reaches a point D directly east of C. He, then, reverses direction and walks till he reaches a point E directly south of C.

2. Then D is

(a) 3 km east and 1 km north of A

(b) 3 km east and $\sqrt{3}$ km north of A

(c) $\sqrt{3}$ km east and 1 km south of A

(d) $\sqrt{3}$ km west and 3 km north of A

3. The total distance walked by the person is

(a) 3 km (b) 4 km

(c) $2\sqrt{3}$ km (d) 6 km

1994

Direction for Question 4 : Data is provided followed by two statements – I and II – both resulting in a value, say I and II. As your answer,

Mark (a) if I > II.

Mark (b) if I < II.

Mark (c) if I = II.

Mark (d) if nothing can be said.

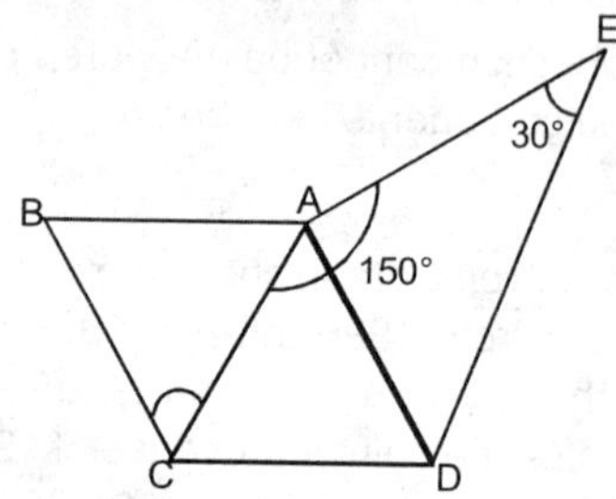

4. In ΔACD, AD = AC and $\angle C = 2\angle E$. The distance between parallel lines AB and CD is h. Then

   I. Area of parallelogram ABCD

   II. Area of ΔADE

1995

5. Which one of the following cannot be the ratio of angles in a right-angled triangle?

   (a) 1 : 2 : 3 (b) 1 : 1 : 2

   (c) 1 : 3 : 6 (d) None of these

6. AB ⊥ BC, BD ⊥ AC and CE bisects $\angle C$, $\angle A = 30°$. Then what is $\angle CED$?

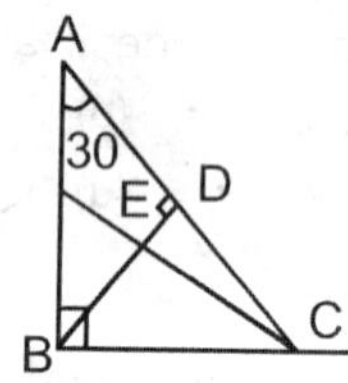

   (a) 30° (b) 60°

   (c) 45° (d) 65°

7. The sides of a triangle are 5, 12 and 13 units. A rectangle is constructed, which is equal in area to the triangle, and has a width of 10 units. Then the perimeter of the rectangle is

   (a) 30 units (b) 36 units

   (c) 13 units (d) None of these

8. The length of a ladder is exactly equal to the height of the wall it is leaning against. If lower end of the ladder is kept on a stool of height 3 m and the stool is kept 9 m away from the wall, the upper end of the ladder coincides with the top of the wall. Then the height of the wall is

   (a) 12 m (b) 15 m

   (c) 18 m (d) 11 m

Directions for Question 9: The question is followed by two statements, I and II. Mark the answer as:

(a) if the question can be answered with the help of statement I alone.

(b) if the question can be answered with the help of statement II alone.

(c) if both statement I and statement II are needed to answer the question.

(d) if the question cannot be answered even with the help of both the statements.

9. What is the area of the triangle?

   I. Two sides are 41 cm each.

   II. The altitude to the third side is 9 cm long.

1996

10. If ABCD is a square and BCE is an equilateral triangle, what is the measure of $\angle DEC$?

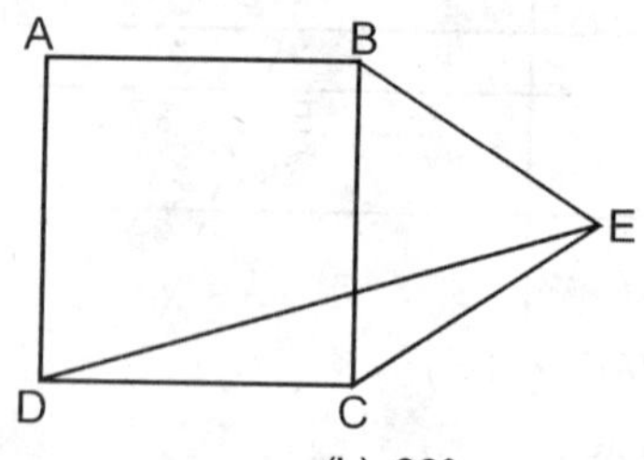

   (a) 15° (b) 30°

   (c) 20° (d) 45°

11. In ΔABC, $\angle B$ is a right angle, AC = 6 cm, and D is the mid-point of AC. The length of BD is

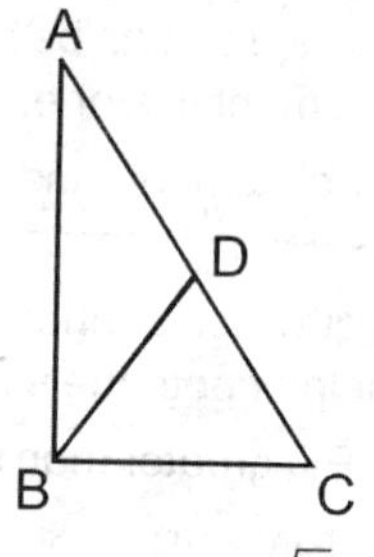

   (a) 4 cm (b) $\sqrt{6}$ cm

   (c) 3 cm (d) 3.5 cm

1997

12. In ΔABC, points P, Q and R are the mid-points of sides AB, BC and CA respectively. If area of ΔABC is 20 sq. units, find the area of ΔPQR.

   (a) 10 sq. units (b) $5\sqrt{3}$ sq. units

   (c) 5 sq. units (d) None of these

1998

Directions for Questions 13 and 14: Answer the questions based on the following information.

A cow is tethered at point A by a rope. Neither the rope nor the cow is allowed to enter ΔABC.

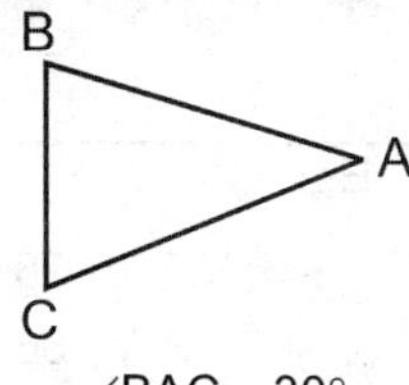

$\angle BAC = 30°$

$l(AB) = l(AC) = 10$ m

13. What is the area that can be grazed by the cow if the length of the rope is 8 m?

(a) $134\pi\frac{1}{3}$ sq. m (b) 121π sq. m

(c) 132π sq. m (d) $\frac{176\pi}{3}$ sq. m

14. What is the area that can be grazed by the cow if the length of the rope is 12 m?

(a) $133\pi\frac{1}{6}$ sq. m (b) 121π sq. m

(c) 132π sq. m (d) $\frac{176\pi}{3}$ sq. m

Direction for Question 15: The question is followed by two statements, I and II. Answer the question based on the statements and mark the answer as:

(a) if the question can be answered with the help of any one statement alone but not by the other statement.

(b) if the question can be answered with the help of either of the statements taken individually.

(c) if the question can be answered with the help of both statements together.

(d) if the question cannot be answered even with the help of both statements together.

15. Find the length of AB if

$\angle YBC = \angle CAX = \angle YOX = 90°$.

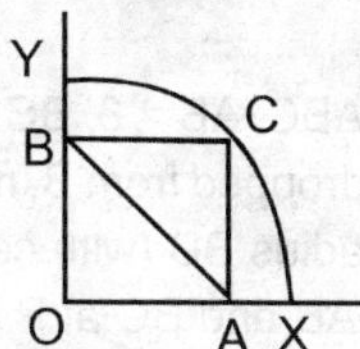

I. Radius of the arc is given.

II. OA = 5

2000

16. What is the number of distinct triangles with integral valued sides and perimeter 14?

(a) 6 (b) 5

(c) 4 (d) 3

17. If a, b and c are the sides of a triangle, and $a^2 + b^2 + c^2 = bc + ca + ab$, then the triangle is

(a) equilateral

(b) isosceles

(c) right-angled

(d) obtuse-angled

18.

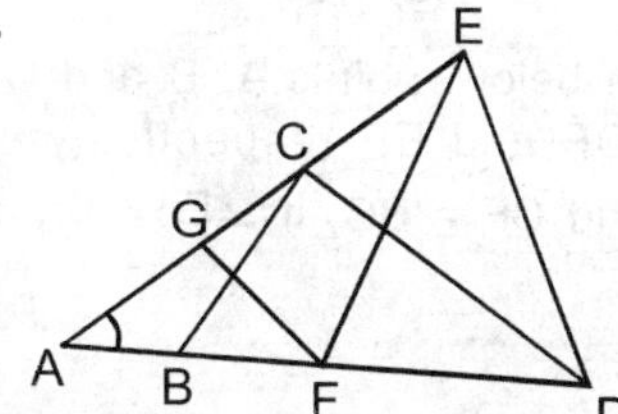

In the figure above, AB = BC = CD = DE = EF = FG = GA. Then $\angle DAE$ is approximately

(a) 15° (b) 20°

(c) 30° (d) 25°

2001

19. A certain city has a circular wall around it, and this wall has four gates pointing north, south, east and west. A house stands outside the city, 3 km north of the north gate, and it can just be seen from a point 9 km east of the south gate. What is the diameter of the wall that surrounds the city?

(a) 6 km (b) 9 km

(c) 12 km (d) None of these

20.

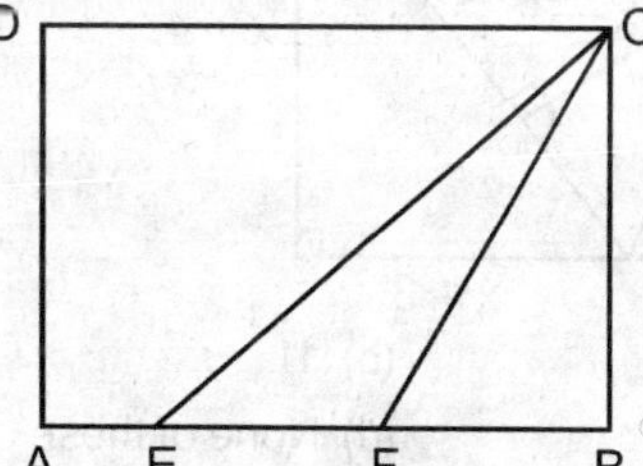

In the above diagram, ABCD is a rectangle with AE = EF = FB. What is the ratio of the areas of ΔCEF and that of the rectangle?

(a) $\frac{1}{6}$ (b) $\frac{1}{8}$

(c) $\frac{1}{9}$ (d) None of these

21. A ladder leans against a vertical wall. The top of the ladder is 8 m above the ground. When the bottom of the ladder is moved 2 m farther away from the wall, the top of the ladder rests against the foot of the wall. What is the length of the ladder?

(a) 10 m (b) 15 m

(c) 20 m (d) 17 m

22. Euclid has a triangle in mind. Its longest side has length 20 and another of its sides has length 10. Its area is 80. What is the exact length of its third side?

(a) $\sqrt{260}$ (b) $\sqrt{250}$

(c) $\sqrt{240}$ (d) $\sqrt{270}$

23. In ΔDEF shown below, points A, B and C are taken on DE, DF and EF respectively such that EC = AC and CF = BC. If $\angle D = 40^0$, then $\angle ACB$ =

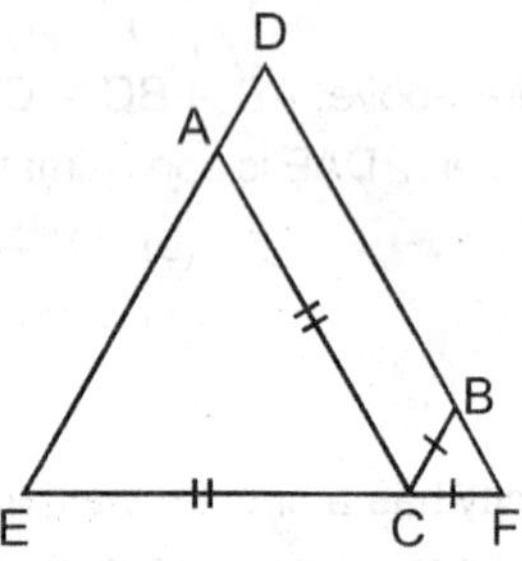

(a) 140° (b) 70°

(c) 100° (d) None of these

24. Based on the figure below, what is the value of x, if y = 10?

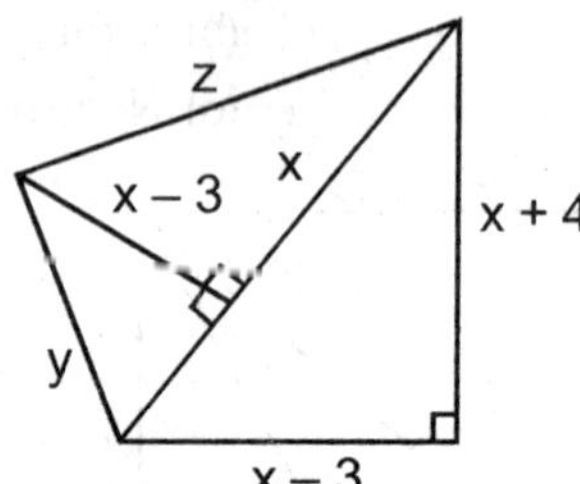

(a) 10 (b) 11

(c) 12 (d) None of these

2002

25. In ΔABC, the internal bisector of $\angle A$ meets BC at D. If AB = 4, AC = 3 and $\angle A = 60°$, then the length of AD is

(a) $2\sqrt{3}$ (b) $\frac{12\sqrt{3}}{7}$

(c) $\frac{15\sqrt{3}}{8}$ (d) $\frac{6\sqrt{3}}{7}$

26. In the figure given below, ABCD is a rectangle. The area of the isosceles right triangle ABE = 7 cm^2; EC = 3(BE). The area of ABCD (in cm^2) is

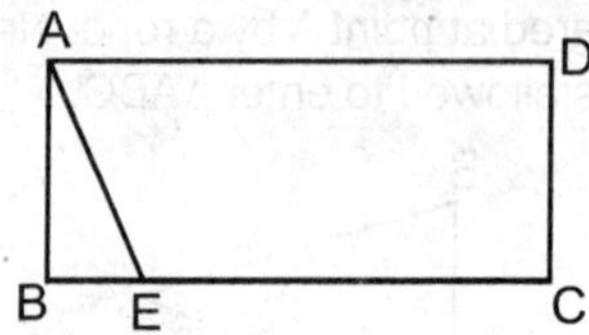

(a) 21 cm^2 (b) 28 cm^2

(c) 42 cm^2 (d) 56 cm^2

2003(R)

27. In the figure (not drawn to scale) given below, P is a point on AB such that AP : PB = 4 : 3. PQ is parallel to AC and QD is parallel to CP. In ΔARC, $\angle ARC$ = 90°, and in ΔPQS, $\angle PSQ$ = 90°. The length of QS is 6 cm. What is the ratio of AP : PD?

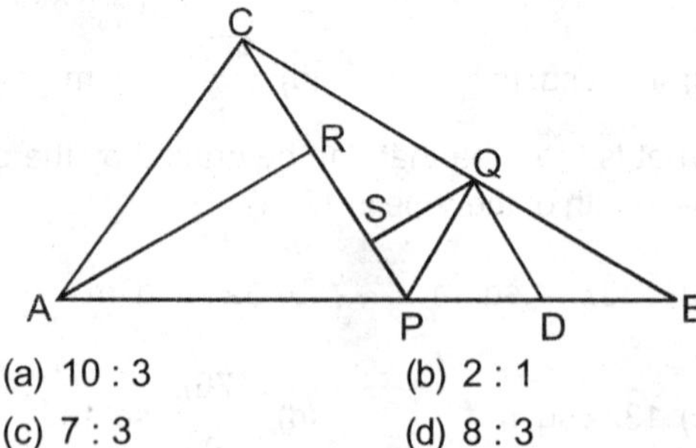

(a) 10 : 3 (b) 2 : 1

(c) 7 : 3 (d) 8 : 3

28. In the figure (not drawn to scale) given below, if AD = CD = BC and $\angle BCE = 96°$, how much is the value of $\angle DBC$?

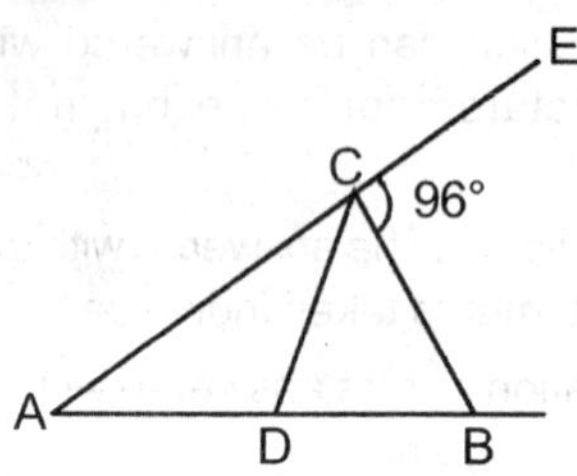

(a) 32°

(b) 84°

(c) 64°

(d) Cannot be determined

2003(L)

29. In the triangle ABC, AB = 6, BC = 8 and AC = 10. A perpendicular dropped from B, meets the side AC at D. A circle of radius BD (with center B) is drawn. If the circle cuts AB and BC at P and Q respectively, the AP:QC is equal to

(a) 1 : 1 (b) 3 : 2

(c) 4 : 1 (d) 3 : 8

30. In the diagram given below,

$\angle ABD = \angle CDB = \angle PQD = 90^\circ$.

If AB : CD = 3 : 1, the ratio of CD : PQ is

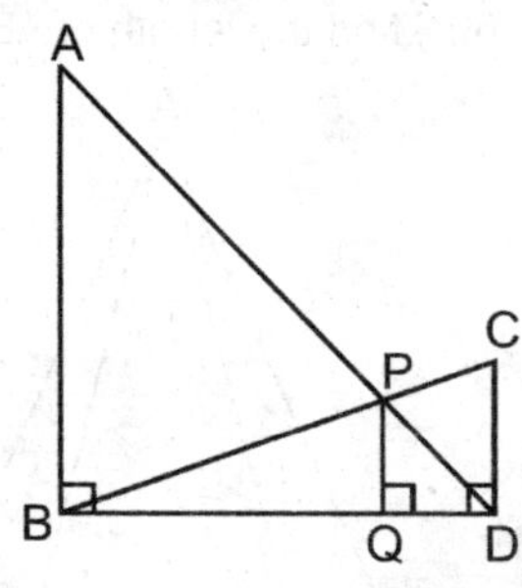

(a) 1 : 0.69 (b) 1 : 0.75

(c) 1 : 0.72 (d) None of the above

Direction for Question 31: The question is followed by two statements, A and B. Answer the question using the following instructions.

Choose (a) if the question can be answered by one of the statements alone but not by the other.

Choose (b) if the question can be answered by using either statement alone.

Choose (c) if the question can be answered by using both the statements together, but cannot be answered by using either statement alone.

Choose (d) if the question cannot be answered even by using both the statements together.

31. D, E, F are the mid points of the sides AB, BC and CA of triangle ABC respectively. What is the area of DEF in square centimeters?

A. AD = 1 cm, DF = 1 cm and perimeter of DEF = 3 cm

B. Perimeter of ABC = 6 cm, AB = 2 cm and AC = 2 cm.

2004

32. A father and his son are waiting at a bus stop in the evening. There is a lamp post behind them. The lamp post, the father and his son stand on the same straight line. The father observes that the shadows of his head and his son's head are incident at the same point on the ground. If the heights of the lamp post, the father and his son are 6 metres, 1.8 metres and 0.9 metres respectively, and the father is standing 2.1 metres away from the post then how far (in metres)is son standing form his father?

(a) 0.9 (b) 0.75

(c) 0.6 (d) 0.45

2005

33. Consider the triangle ABC shown in the following figure where BC = 12 cm, DB = 9 cm, CD = 6 cm and $\angle BCD = \angle BAC$

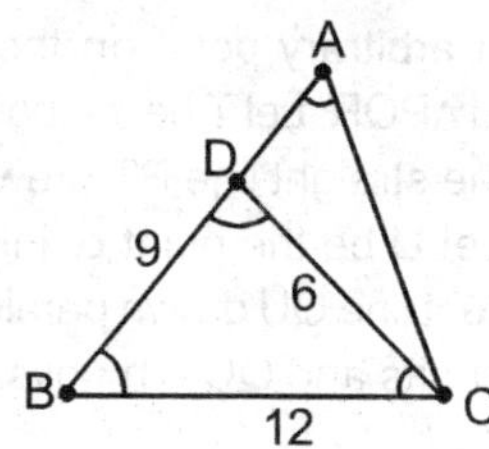

What is the ratio of the perimeter of ΔADC to that of the ΔBDC?

(a) $\frac{7}{9}$ (b) $\frac{8}{9}$

(c) $\frac{6}{9}$ (d) $\frac{5}{9}$

2008

34. Consider obtuse-angled triangles with sides 8 cm, 15 cm and x cm. If x is an integer, then how many such triangles exist?

(a) 5 (b) 21

(c) 10 (d) 15

(e) 14

MEMORY BASED QUESTIONS

2009

35. In the given figure, ABC is an isosceles triangle with AB = AC. If AE = AF and angle BAE = 30°, then what is the value of angle FEC?

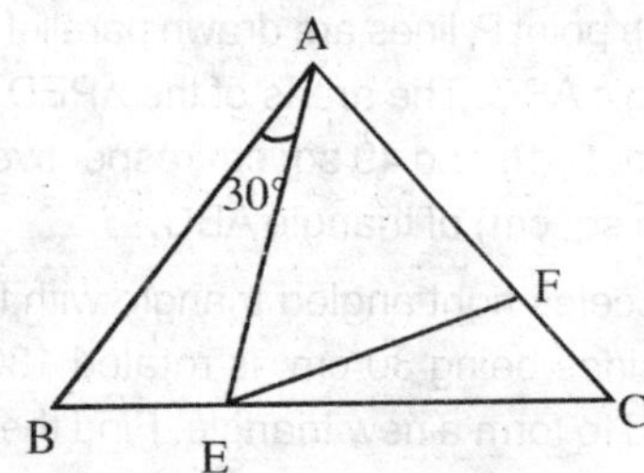

(a) 15° (b) 30°

(c) 60° (d) Cannot be determined

2013

36. E is a point on the side AB of a rectangle ABCD, the adjacent sides of which are in the ratio 2 : 1. If $\angle AED = \angle DEC$, then what is the measure of $\angle AED$?

(a) 15° (b) 45°

(c) 75° (d) Either (a) or (c)

2014

37. The length of the hypotenuse of a right-angled triangle is 240 units. The perimeter of the given triangle is a perfect square. If the perimeter of the given triangle is greater than 550 units, then which of the following can be the length of a side of the given right-angled triangle?

(a) 192 units (b) 168 units

(c) 144 units (d) Both (a) and (c)

38. Let S be an arbitrary point on the side PQ of an acute-angled ΔPQR. Let T be the point of intersection of QR and the straight line PT drawn parallel to SR through P. Let U be the point of intersection of PR and the straight line QU drawn parallel to SR through Q. If PT = a units and QU = b units, then the length of SR is

(a) $\frac{a+b}{ab}$ units (b) $\frac{a-b}{ab}$ units

(c) $\frac{ab}{a+b}$ units (d) $\frac{ab}{a-b}$ units

39. The bisector of ∠BAC of ΔABC cuts BC at D and the circumcircle of the triangle at E. If DE = 3 cm, AC = 4 cm and AD = 5 cm, then the length of AB is

(a) 7 cm (b) 8 cm

(c) 9 cm (d) 10 cm

2015

40.

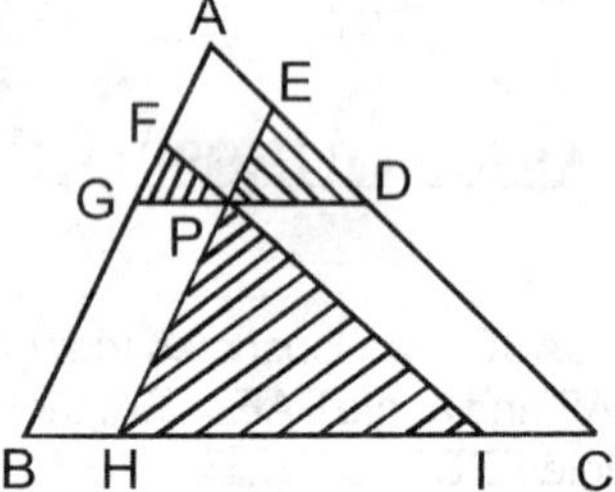

Through point P, lines are drawn parallel to the sides of triangle ABC. The areas of the ΔPED, ΔPFG and ΔPHI are 9, 16 and 49 sq. cm respectively. Find the area (in sq. cm) of triangle ABC.

41. An isosceles right angled triangle with length of its equal sides being 30 cm, is rotated 180° about its centroid to form a new triangle. Find the area of the region common to the original and the new triangles.

(a) 275 sq. cm

(b) 300 sq. cm

(c) 375 sq. cm

(d) 350 sq. cm

42. ΔABC is a right angled triangle, with ∠B = 90°, AB = 20 cm and BC = 21cm. A circle with centre O is inscribed in triangle ABC. OD, OE and OF are perpendiculars drawn on the sides AB, BC and CA respectively. Find the ratio of the area of the quadrilateral FOEC to the area of the quadrilateral ADOF.

(a) 15 : 14

(b) 14 : 15

(c) 12 : 11

(d) 7 : 5

2016

43. In the figure given below, AD = AE = 4 cm and BD = CE = 2 cm. If BC is a straight line and ∠ADE = 60°, find the length of AB.

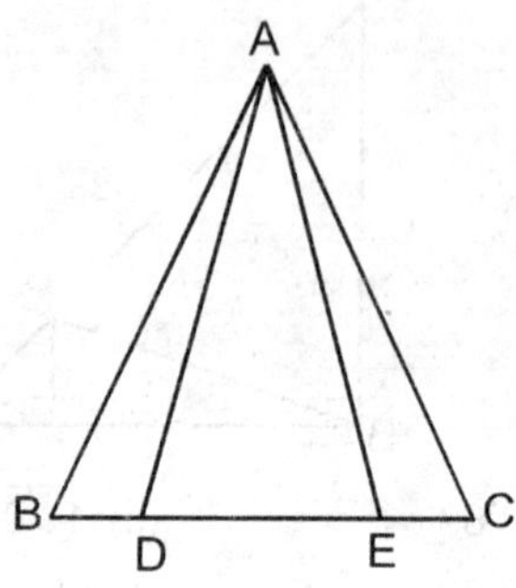

(a) $2\sqrt{7}$ cm (b) 5 cm

(c) $2\sqrt{5}$ cm (d) None of these

44. In an isosceles triangle ABC shown below, AB = AC, DE || BC, ∠ADF = 30° and ∠DFE = 70°. If DF = 4 cm, then find the length of DE.

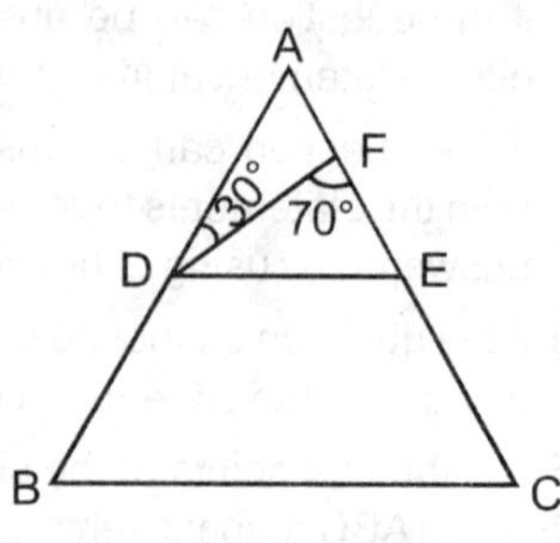

(a) 2 cm (b) 4 cm

(c) $2\sqrt{3}$ cm (d) $4\sqrt{3}$ cm

2018 Slot 1

45. Given an equilateral triangle T1 with side 24 cm, a second triangle T2 is formed by joining the midpoints of the sides of T1. Then a third triangle T3 is formed by joining the midpoints of the sides of T2. If this process of forming triangles is continued, the sum of the areas, in sq cm, of infinitely many such triangles T1, T2, T3,... will be

(a) $248\sqrt{3}$ (b) $192\sqrt{3}$

(c) $188\sqrt{3}$ (d) $164\sqrt{3}$

2018 Slot 2

46. A triangle ABC has area 32 sq units and its side BC, of length 8 units, lies on the line x = 4. Then the shortest possible distance between A and the point (0, 0) is

(a) 8 units (b) 4 units

(c) $2\sqrt{2}$ units (d) $4\sqrt{2}$ units

QUADRILATERALS

1990

1. A square is drawn by joining the midpoints of the sides of a given square. A third square is drawn inside the second square in the same way and this process is continued indefinitely. If side of the first square is 8 cm, the sum of the areas of all the squares such formed (in sq.cm.)is

(a) 128 (b) 120
(c) 96 (d) None of these

1991

Direction for Question 2 : The question is followed by two statements. As the answer,

Mark (a) if the question can be answered with the help of statement I alone,

Mark (b) if the question can be answered with the help of statement II alone,

Mark (c) if both the statement I and statement II are needed to answer the question, and

Mark (d) if the question cannot be answered even with the help of both the statements.

2. What is the area under the line GHI – JKL in the given quadrilateral OPQR, knowing that all the small spaces are squares of the same area?

I. Length ABCDEQ is greater than or equal to 60.

II. Area OPQR is less than or equal to 1512.

3. Let the consecutive vertices of a square S be A, B, C & D. Let E, F & G be the mid-points of the sides AB, BC & AD respectively of the square. Then the ratio of the area of the quadrilateral EFDG to that of the square S is nearest to

(a) 1/2 (b) 1/3
(c) 1/4 (d) 1/8

1994

4. Four friends start from four towns, which are at the four corners of an imaginary rectangle. They meet at a point which falls inside the rectangle, after travelling distances of 40, 50 and 60 metres. The maximum distance that the fourth could have traveled is (approximately) ....

(a) 67 metres (b) 52 metres
(c) 22.5 metres (d) Cannot be determined

1995

5. ABCD is a square of area 4, which is divided into four non-over lapping triangles as shown in figure. Then the sum of the perimeters of the triangles is

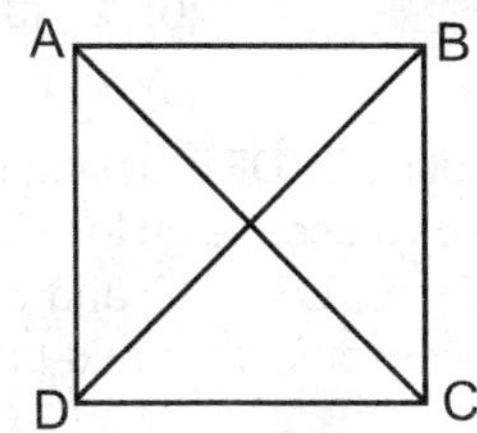

(a) $8(2 + \sqrt{2})$ (b) $8(1 + \sqrt{2})$
(c) $4(1 + \sqrt{2})$ (d) $4(2 + \sqrt{2})$

6. In the adjoining figure, AC + AB = 5AD and AC – AD = 8. Then the area of the rectangle ABCD is

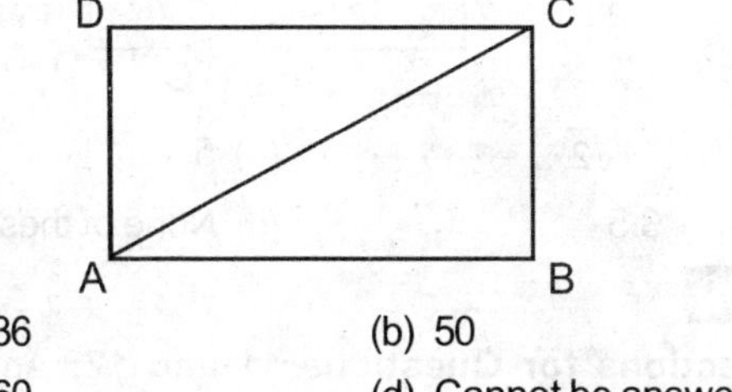

(a) 36 (b) 50
(c) 60 (d) Cannot be answered

Direction for Question 7: The question is followed by two statements, I and II. Mark the answer as:

(a) if the question can be answered with the help of statement I alone.

(b) if the question can be answered with the help of statement II alone.

(c) if both statement I and statement II are needed to answer the question.

(d) if the question cannot be answered even with the help of both the statements.

7. What is the length of rectangle ABCD?

I. Area of the rectangle is 48 square units.

II. Length of the diagonal is 10 units.

1997

8. The adjoining figure shows a set of concentric squares. If the diagonal of the innermost square is 2 units, and if the distance between the corresponding corners of any two successive squares is 1 unit, find the difference between the areas of the eighth and the seventh squares, counting from the innermost square.

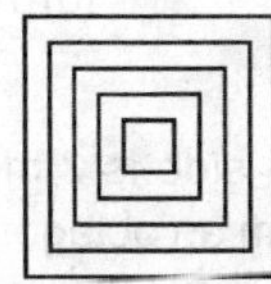

(a) $10\sqrt{2}$ sq. units (b) 30 sq. units
(c) $35\sqrt{2}$ sq. units (d) None of these

9. In a rectangle, the difference between the sum of the adjacent sides and the diagonal is half the length of the longer side. What is the ratio of the shorter to the longer side?

(a) $\sqrt{3} : 2$ (b) $1 : \sqrt{3}$

(c) 2 : 5 (d) 3 : 4

10. In the given figure, EADF is a rectangle and ABC is a triangle whose vertices lie on the sides of EADF and AE = 22, BE = 6, CF = 16 and BF = 2. Find the length of the line joining the mid-points of the sides AB and BC.

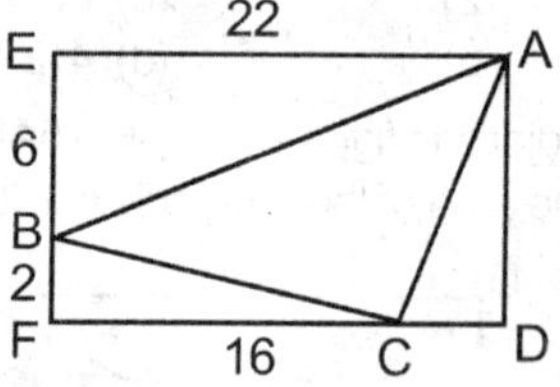

(a) $4\sqrt{2}$ (b) 5

(c) 3.5 (d) None of these

1999

Directions for Questions 11 and 12: Answer the questions based on the following information.

A rectangle PRSU, is divided into two smaller rectangles PQTU, and QRST by the line TQ. PQ = 10 cm.

QR = 5 cm and RS = 10 cm. Points A, B, F are within rectangle PQTU, and points C, D, E are within the rectangle QRST. The closest pair of points among the pairs (A, C), (A, D), (A, E), (F, C), (F, D), (F, E), (B, C), (B, D), (B, E)are $10\sqrt{3}$ cm apart.

11. Which of the following statements is necessarily true?

(a) The closest pair of points among the six given points cannot be (F, C)

(b) Distance between A and B is greater than that between F and C.

(c) The closest pair of points among the six given points is (C, D), (D, E), or (C, E).

(d) None of the above

12. AB > AF > BF ; CD > DE >CE ; and BF = $6\sqrt{5}$ cm.

Which is the closest pair of points among all the six given points?

(a) B, F (b) C, D

(c) A, B (d) None of these

2001

13. A square, whose side is 2 m, has its corners cut away so as to form an octagon with all sides equal. Then the length of each side of the octagon, in metres, is

(a) $\frac{\sqrt{2}}{\sqrt{2}+1}$ (b) $\frac{2}{\sqrt{2}+1}$

(c) $\frac{2}{\sqrt{2}-1}$ (d) $\frac{\sqrt{2}}{\sqrt{2}-1}$

2002

14. Instead of walking along two adjacent sides of a rectangular field, a boy took a short cut along the diagonal and saved a distance equal to half the longer side. Then the ratio of the shorter side to the longer side is

(a) $\frac{1}{2}$ (b) $\frac{2}{3}$

(c) $\frac{1}{4}$ (d) $\frac{3}{4}$

Directions for Questions 15 and 16: Answer the questions based on the following diagram.

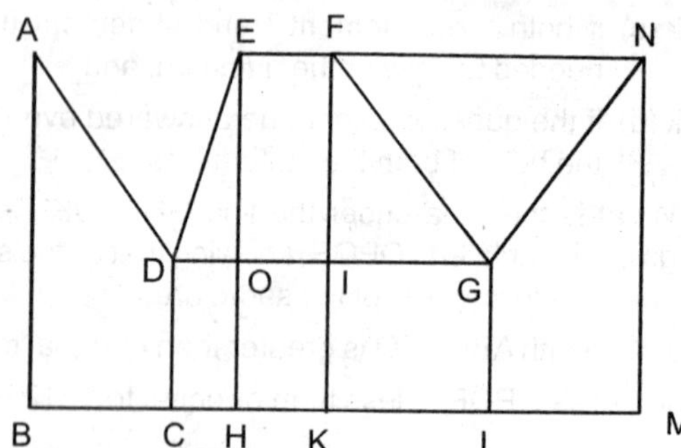

In the above diagram, $\angle ABC = 90° = \angle DCH = \angle DOE = \angle EHK = \angle FKL = \angle GLM = \angle LMN$ AB = BC = 2CH = 2CD = EH = FK = 2HK = 4KL = 2LM = MN

15. The magnitude of $\angle FGO$ =

(a) 30° (b) 45°

(c) 60° (d) None of these

16. What is the ratio of the areas of the two quadrilaterals ABCD to DEFG?

(a) 1 : 2 (b) 2 : 1

(c) 12 : 7 (d) None of these

2003(L)

17. A vertical tower OP stands at the center O of a square ABCD. Let h and b denote the length OP and AB respectively. Suppose $\angle APB = 60°$ then the relationship between h and b can be expressed as

(a) $2b^2 = h^2$

(b) $2h^2 = b^2$

(c) $3b^2 = 2h^2$

(d) $3h^2 = 2b^2$

2006

18. An equilateral triangle BPC is drawn inside a square ABCD. What is the value of the angle APD in degrees?

(a) 75 (b) 90

(c) 120 (d) 135

(e) 150

2007

Direction for Question 19: The question is followed by two statements A and B. Indicate your response based on the following directives.

Mark (a) if the questions can be answered using A alone but not using B alone.

Mark (b) if the question can be answered using B alone but not using A alone.

Mark (c) if the question can be answered using A and B together, but not using either A or B alone.

Mark (d) if the question cannot be answered even using A and B together.

19. Rahim plans to draw a square JKLM with point O on the side JK but is not successful. Why is Rahim unable to draw the square?

A : The length of OM is twice that of OL.

B : The length of OM is 4 cm.

MEMORY BASED QUESTIONS

2010

20. In the figure given below, a tangent is drawn at point P on a circle of radius 1 cm. A and B are two points on the tangent and ABCD is a rectangle, where C and D are two points on the circumference of the circle. What is the approximate area (in cm^2) of the rectangle ABCD if 2AB = BC?

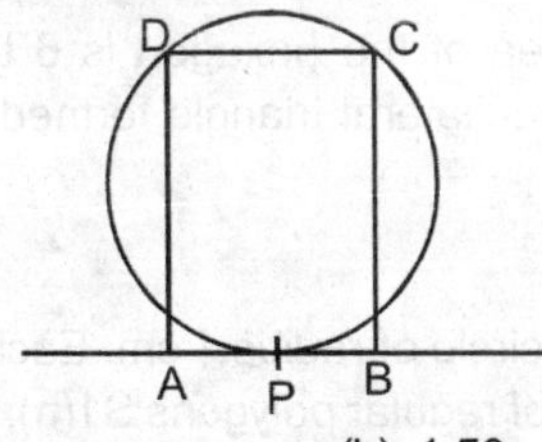

(a) 1.77 (b) 1.50

(c) 1.83 (d) 1.60

2011

21. In the figure given below ABCD is a square of side 4 cm. P is the midpoint of AD and is joined with vertex B. A perpendicular is drawn from vertex C on BP, which intersects BP at point E. What is the area of ΔBEC?

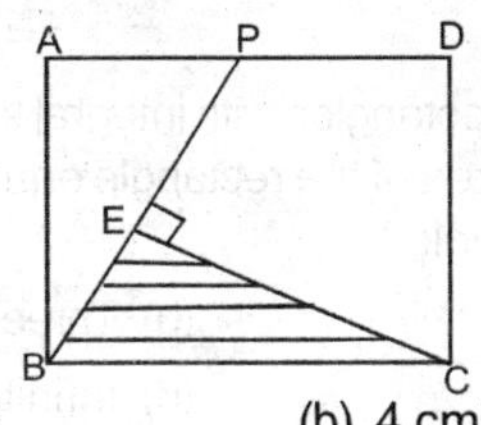

(a) 6.4 cm^2 (b) 4 cm^2

(c) 3.2 cm^2 (d) None of these

22. In the figure given below ABCD is a rectangle. The ratio of the length of EB to the length of BF is $2 : \sqrt{3}$. What is the ratio of the length of BF to the length of FC?

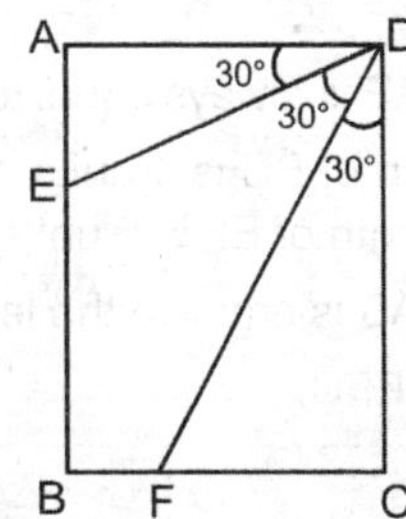

(a) $9 : 5\sqrt{3}$ (b) $2\sqrt{3} : 2$

(c) 2 : 3 (d) None of these

2012

23. A rectangle with perimeter 88 m is partitioned into 5 congruent rectangles, as shown in the diagram given below. The perimeter of each of the congruent rectangles is

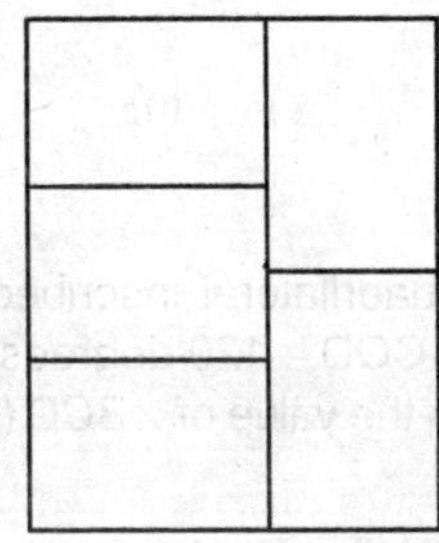

(a) 20 m (b) 32 m

(c) 48 m (d) 40 m

24. A trapezium DEFG is circumscribed about a circle that has centre at C. If DM = 1 cm, GN = 4 cm and the measure of $\angle DEF = \angle EFG = 90°$, then find the radius of the circle.

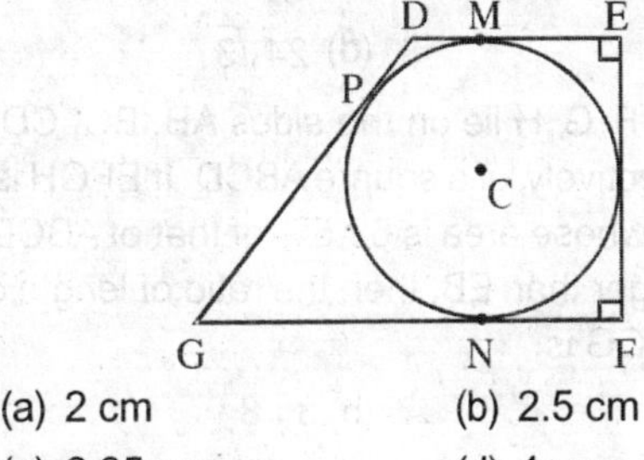

(a) 2 cm (b) 2.5 cm

(c) 2.25 cm (d) 4 cm

2014

25. How many rectangles with integral sides are possible where the area of the rectangle equals the perimeter of the rectangle?

(a) One (b) Three

(c) Two (d) Infinitely many

26. ABCD is a rectangle with points E and F lying on sides AB and CD respectively. If the area of quadrilateral AEFD equals the area of quadrilateral CBEF, then which of the following statements is necessarily false with respect to the rectangle ABCD?

(a) Length of AE is always equal to the length of CF.

(b) If the length of BC is 4 units, then the smallest integral length of EF is 5 units.

(c) Length of AE is equal to the length of DF.

(d) $\angle AEF = \angle EFC$.

2015

27. ABCD is an isosceles trapezium with BC = AD = 10 units, AB = 2 units and CD = 14 units. The mid-points of the sides of the trapezium are joined to form a quadrilateral PQRS. Find the ratio of the area of the circle inscribed in the quadrilateral PQRS to the area of trapezium ABCD.

(a) $\frac{3\pi}{8}$ (b) $\frac{3\pi}{16}$

(c) $\frac{\pi}{4}$ (d) $\frac{\pi}{8}$

2017

28. ABCD is a quadrilateral inscribed in a circle with centre O. If $\angle COD$ = 120 degrees and $\angle BAC$ = 30 degrees, then the value of $\angle BCD$ (in degrees) is

2018 Slot 1

29. In a parallelogram ABCD of area 72 sq cm, the sides CD and AD have lengths 9 cm and 16 cm, respectively. Let P be a point on CD such that AP is perpendicular to CD. Then the area, in sq cm, of triangle APD is

(a) $32\sqrt{3}$ (b) $18\sqrt{3}$

(c) $12\sqrt{3}$ (d) $24\sqrt{3}$

30. Points E, F, G, H lie on the sides AB, BC, CD, and DA, respectively, of a square ABCD. If EFGH is also a square whose area is 62.5% of that of ABCD and CG is longer than EB, then the ratio of length of EB to that of CG is

(a) 1 : 3 (b) 3 : 8

(c) 4 : 9 (d) 2 : 5

2018 Slot 2

31. From a rectangle ABCD of area 768 sq cm, a semicircular part with diameter AB and area 72π sq cm is removed. The perimeter of the leftover portion, in cm, is

(a) $80 + 16\pi$ (b) $82 + 24\pi$

(c) $86 + 8\pi$ (d) $88 + 12\pi$

32. A parallelogram ABCD has area 48 sqcm. If the length of CD is 8 cm and that of AD is s cm, then which one of the following is necessarily true?

(a) $5 \le s \le 7$ (b) $s \ne 6$

(c) $s \ge 6$ (d) $s \le 6$

33. The area of a rectangle and the square of its perimeter are in the ratio 1 : 25. Then the lengths of the shorter and longer sides of the rectangle are in the ratio

(a) 2:9 (b) 1:3

(c) 3:8 (d) 1:4

POLYGONS

1993

Direction for Question 1 : The question is followed by two statements. As the answer,

Mark (a) if the question can be answered with the help of statement I alone,

Mark (b) if the question can be answered with the help of statement II, alone,

Mark (c) if both, statement I and statement II are needed to answer the question, and

Mark (d) if the question cannot be answered even with the help of both the statements.

1. What is the area of a regular hexagon?

I. The length of the boundary line of the hexagon is 36 cm.

II. The area of the hexagon is 6 times the area of an equilateral triangle formed on one of the sides.

1999

2. There is a circle of radius 1 cm. Each member of a sequence of regular polygons S1(n), n = 4, 5, 6, ..., where n is the number of sides of the polygon, is circumscribing the circle: and each member of the sequence of regular polygons S2(n), n = 4, 5, 6, ... where n is the number of sides of the polygon, is inscribed in the circle. Let L1(n) and L2(n) denote the perimeters of the corresponding polygons of S1(n) and S2(n), then $\frac{\{L1(13) + 2\pi\}}{L2(17)}$ is

(a) greater than $\frac{\pi}{4}$ and less than 1

(b) greater than 1 and less than 2

(c) greater than 2

(d) less than $\frac{\pi}{4}$

Direction for Question 3: The question is followed by two statements I and II.

Mark:

(a) if the question can be answered by any one of the statements alone, but cannot be answered by using the other statement alone.

(b) if the question can be answered by using either statement alone.

(c) if the question can be answered by using both the statements together, but cannot be answered by using either statement alone.

(d) if the question cannot be answered even by using both the statements together.

3. Mr X starts walking northwards along the boundary of a field from point A on the boundary, and after walking for 150 m reaches B, and then walks westwards, again along the boundary, for another 100 m when he reaches C. What is the maximum distance between any pair of points on the boundary of the field?

I. The field is rectangular in shape.

II. The field is a polygon, with C as one of its vertices and A as the mid-point of a side.

2003(R)

4. Let ABCDEF be a regular hexagon. What is the ratio of the area of the Δ ACE to that of the hexagon ABCDEF?

(a) $\frac{1}{3}$ (b) $\frac{1}{2}$

(c) $\frac{2}{3}$ (d) $\frac{5}{6}$

2003(L)

5. Each side of a given polygon is parallel to either the X or the Y axis. A corner of such a polygon is said to be convex if the internal angle is 90° or concave if the internal angle is 270°. If the number of convex corners in such a polygon is 25, the number of concave corners must be

(a) 20 (b) 0

(c) 21 (d) 22

6. In the figure below, ABCDEF is a regular hexagon and $\angle AOF = 90°$. FO is parallel to ED. What is the ratio of the area of the triangle AOF to that of the hexagon ABCDEF?

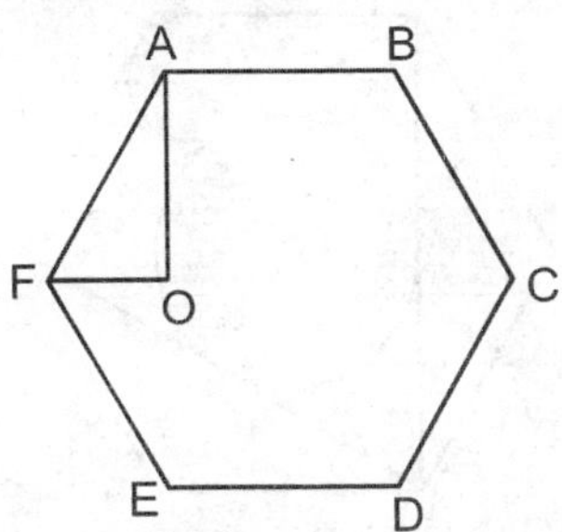

(a) $\frac{1}{12}$ (b) $\frac{1}{6}$

(c) $\frac{1}{24}$ (d) $\frac{1}{18}$

MEMORY BASED QUESTIONS

2009

7. ABCDEF is a regular hexagon with AB = 5 cm. Nine line segments are drawn in the hexagon in such a way that AB, DE and these line segments form eleven equidistant parallel lines. If the ends of each of the line segments lie on the perimeter of the hexagon, then what is the sum (in cm) of the lengths of the nine line segments?

(a) 80 (b) 60

(c) 70 (d) 75

2010

8. In the figure given below, ABCDEF is a regular hexagon whose diagonals intersect at point O. G is the centroid of triangle AOF and L is the midpoint of FO. The line segment HK joins the midpoints of AB and CD. Find the ratio of the shaded area marked 'x' to the shaded area marked 'y'.

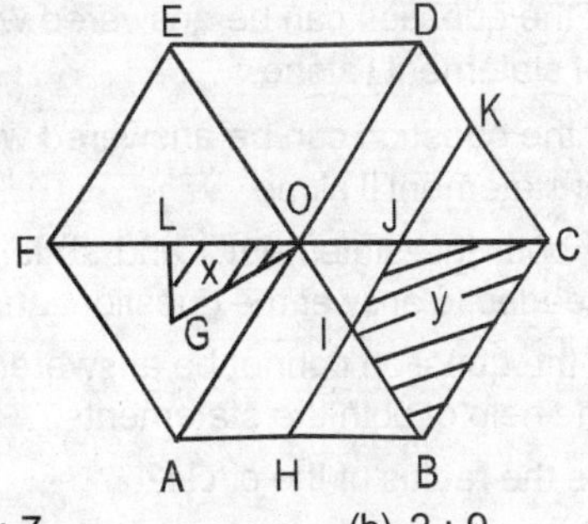

(a) 3 : 7 (b) 2 : 9

(c) 2 : 5 (d) 3 : 11

2012

9. In the regular hexagon shown below, what is the ratio of the area of the smaller circle to that of the bigger circle?

(a) $3:7+2\sqrt{3}$ (b) $3:7+\sqrt{3}$

(c) $3:16+4\sqrt{3}$ (d) $3:7+4\sqrt{3}$

2016

10. In a regular polygon, the number of diagonals is 'k' times the number of sides. If the interior angle of the polygon is θ, then the value of k is

(a) $\frac{3\theta-\pi}{2(\pi-\theta)}$ (b) $\frac{2(3\theta-\pi)}{\pi-\theta}$

(c) $\frac{2(\pi-\theta)}{3\theta-\pi}$ (d) $\frac{(\pi-\theta)}{2(3\theta-\pi)}$

2017

11. Let ABCDEF be a regular hexagon with each side of length 1 cm. The area (in sq cm) of a square with AC as one side is

(a) $3\sqrt{2}$ (c) 3

(c) 4 (d) $\sqrt{3}$

CIRCLE

1991

Direction for Question 1: The question is followed by two statements. As the answer,

Mark (a) if the question can be answered with the help of statement I alone,

Mark (b) if the question can be answered with the help of statement II alone,

Mark (c) if both the statement I and statement II are needed to answer the question, and

Mark (d) if the question cannot be answered even with the help of both the statements.

1. What is the radius of the circle?

   I. Ratio of its area to circumference is > 7.

   II. Diameter of the circle is ≤ 32.

2. A circle is inscribed in a given square and another circle is circumscribed about the square. What is the ratio of the area of the inscribed circle to that of the circumscribed circle?

(a) 2 : 3 (b) 3 : 4

(c) 1 : 4 (d) 1 : 2

3. A one rupee coin is placed on a table. The maximum number of similar one rupee coins which can be placed on the table, around it, with each one of them touching it and only two others is

(a) 8 (b) 6

(c) 10 (d) 4

1993

4. Three identical cones with base radius r are placed on their bases so that each is touching the other two. The radius of the circle drawn through their vertices is

(a) smaller than r

(b) equal to r

(c) larger than r

(d) depends on the height of the cones.

5. The line AB is 6 metres in length and is tangent to the inner one of the two concentric circles at point C. It is known that the radii of the two circles are integers. The radius of the outer circle is

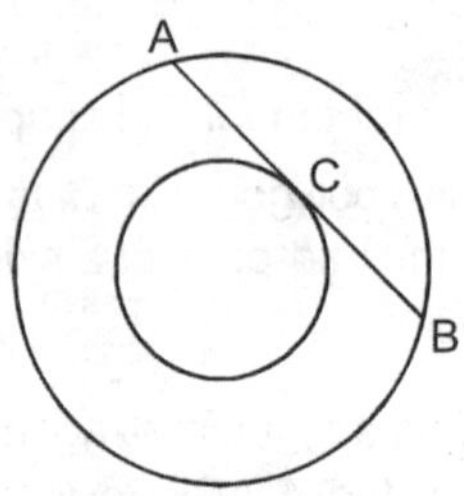

(a) 5 metres (b) 4 metres

(c) 6 metres (d) 3 metres

1995

6. PQRS is a square. SR is a tangent (at point S) to the circle with centre O and TR = OS. Then the ratio of area of the circle to the area of the square is

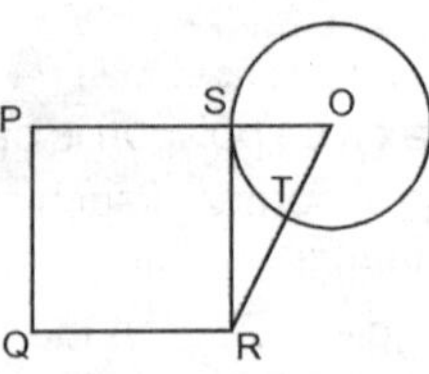

(a) $\frac{\pi}{3}$ (b) $\frac{11}{7}$

(c) $\frac{3}{\pi}$ (d) $\frac{7}{11}$

7. In the given figure, AB is diameter of the circle and points C and D are on the circumference such that $\angle CAD = 30°$ and $\angle CBA = 70°$. What is the measure of $\angle ACD$?

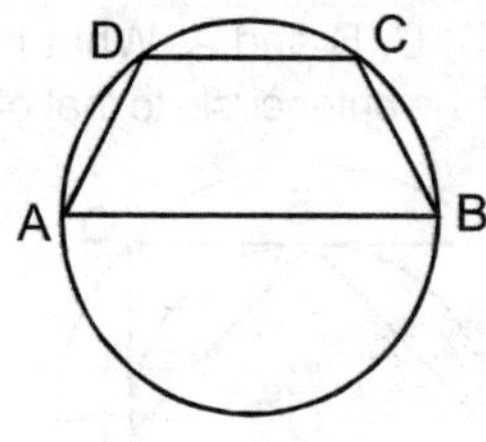

(a) 40° (b) 50°
(c) 30° (d) 90°

1996

8. From a circular sheet of paper with a radius 20 cm, four circles of radius 5 cm each are cut out. What is the ratio of the uncut to the cut portion?

(a) 1 : 3 (b) 4 : 1
(c) 3 : 1 (d) 4 : 3

9. The figure shows a circle of diameter AB and radius 6.5 cm. If chord CA is 5 cm long, find the area of ΔABC.

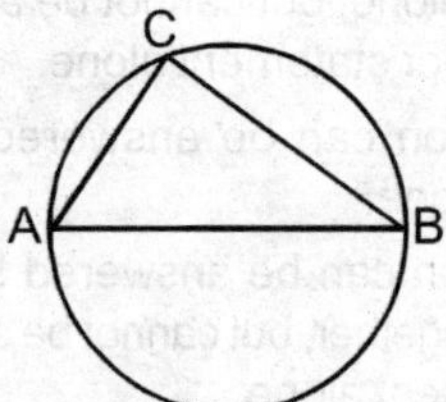

(a) 60 sq. cm (b) 30 sq. cm
(c) 40 sq. cm (d) 52 sq. cm

10. The figure shows the rectangle ABCD with a semicircle and a circle inscribed inside in it as shown. What is the ratio of the area of the circle to that of the semicircle?

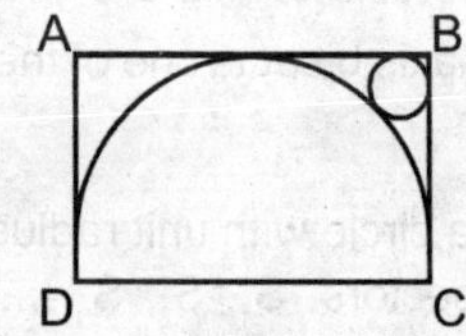

(a) $(\sqrt{2}-1)^2 : 1$ (b) $2(\sqrt{2}-1)^2 : 1$
(c) $(\sqrt{2}-1)^2 : 2$ (d) None of these

Direction for Question 11: The question is followed by two statements, I and II. Mark the answer as:

(a) if the question cannot be answered even with the help of both the statements taken together.
(b) if the question can be answered by any one of the two statements.
(c) if each statement alone is sufficient to answer the question, but not the other one (E.g. statement I alone is required to answer the question, but not statement II and vice versa).
(d) if both statements I and II together are needed to answer the question.

11. A tractor travelled a distance 5 m. What is the radius of the rear wheel?

I. The front wheel rotates 'N' times more than the rear wheel over this distance.
II. The circumference of the rear wheel is 't' times that of the front wheel.

1997

12.

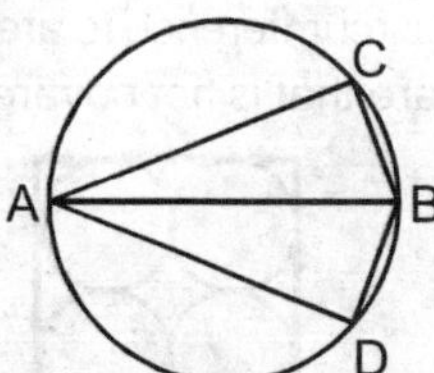

AB is the diameter of the given circle, while points C and D lie on the circumference as shown. If AB is 15 cm, AC is 12 cm and BD is 9 cm, find the area of the quadrilateral ACBD.

(a) 54π sq. cm (b) 216π sq. cm
(c) 162π sq. cm (d) None of these

13. In the adjoining figure, points A, B, C and D lie on the circle. AD = 24 and BC = 12. What is the ratio of the area of ΔCBE to that of ΔADE?

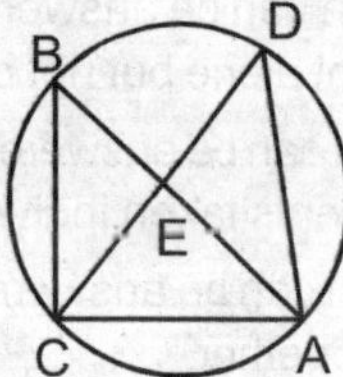

(a) 1 : 4
(b) 1 : 2
(c) 1 : 3
(d) Data insufficient

14. The sum of the areas of two circles, which touch each other externally, is 153π. If the sum of their radii is 15, find the ratio of the larger to the smaller radius.

(a) 4
(b) 2
(c) 3
(d) None of these

1998

15. Three circles, each of radius 20, have centres at P, Q and R. Further, AB = 5, CD = 10 and EF = 12. What is the perimeter of ΔPQR?

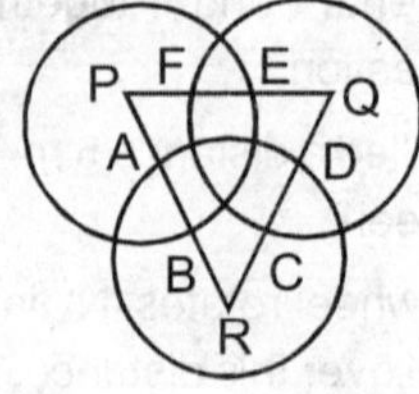

(a) 120 (b) 66
(c) 93 (d) 87

16. Four identical coins are placed in a square. For each coin the ratio of area to circumference is same as the ratio of circumference to area. Then find the area of the square that is not covered by the coins.

(a) $16(\pi - 1)$
(b) $16(8 - \pi)$
(c) $16(4 - \pi)$
(d) $16\left(4 - \frac{\pi}{2}\right)$

Directions for Questions 17 and 18: Each question is followed by two statements, I and II. Answer the questions based on the statements and mark the answer as:

(a) if the question can be answered with the help of any one statement alone but not by the other statement.
(b) if the question can be answered with the help of either of the statements taken individually.
(c) if the question can be answered with the help of both statements together.
(d) if the question cannot be answered even with the help of both statements together.

17. There are two concentric circles C_1 and C_2 with radii r_1 and r_2. The circles are such that C_1 fully encloses C_2. Then what is the radius of C_1?

I. The difference of their circumference is k cm.
II. The difference of their areas is m sq. cm.

18. A circle circumscribes a square. What is the area of the square?

I. Radius of the circle is given.
II. Length of the tangent from a point 5 cm away from the centre of the circle is given.

1999

19. The figure below shows two concentric circles with centre O. PQRS is a square inscribed in the outer circle. It also circumscribes the inner circle, touching it at points B, C, D and A. What is the ratio of the perimeter of the outer circle to that of polygon ABCD?

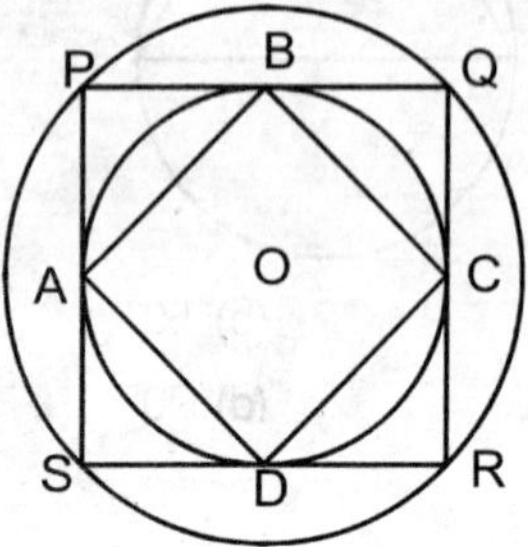

(a) $\frac{\pi}{4}$ (b) $\frac{3\pi}{2}$
(c) $\frac{\pi}{2}$ (d) π

Direction for Questions 20: The question is followed by two statements I and II.

Mark:

(a) if the question can be answered by any one of the statements alone, but cannot be answered by using the other statement alone.
(b) if the question can be answered by using either statement alone.
(c) if the question can be answered by using both the statements together, but cannot be answered by using either statement alone.
(d) if the question cannot be answered even by using both the statements together.

20. There is a circle with centre C at the origin and radius r cm. Two tangents are drawn from an external point D at a distance d cm from the centre. What are the angles between each tangent and the X-axis?

I. The coordinates of D are given.
II. The X-axis bisects one of the tangents.

2000

21. Consider a circle with unit radius. There are seven adjacent sectors, S_1, S_2, S_3, ... , S_7, in the circle such that their total area is $\frac{1}{8}$ of the area of the circle. Further, the area of the jth sector is twice that of the (j – 1)th sector, for j = 2, ..., 7. What is the angle, in radians, subtended by the arc of S_1 at the centre of the circle?

(a) $\frac{\pi}{508}$ (b) $\frac{\pi}{2040}$
(c) $\frac{\pi}{1016}$ (d) $\frac{\pi}{1524}$

Directions for Questions 22 and 23: Each question is followed by two statements, I and II. Answer each question using the following instructions.

Mark the answer as:

(a) if the question can be answered by one of the statements alone, but cannot be answered by using the other statement alone.

(b) if the question can be answered by using either statement alone.

(c) if the question can be answered by using both the statements together, but cannot be answered by using either statement alone.

(d) if the question cannot be answered even by using both statements together.

22. ΔPQR has $\angle PRQ = 90°$. What is the value of PR + RQ?

I. Diameter of the inscribed circle of the ΔPQR is equal to 10 cm.

II. Diameter of the circumscribed circle of the ΔPQR is equal to 18 cm.

23. 'O' is the centre of two concentric circles, AE is a chord of the outer circle and it intersects the inner circle at points 'B' and 'D'. 'C' is a point on the chord in between 'B' and 'D'.

What is the value of AC/CE?

I. BC/CD = 1

II. A third circle intersects the inner circle at 'B' and 'D' and the point 'C' is on the line joining the centres of the third circle and the inner circle.

2002

24. The length of the common chord of two circles of radii 15 cm and 20 cm, whose centres are 25 cm apart, is

(a) 24 cm (b) 25 cm

(c) 15 cm (d) 20 cm

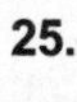

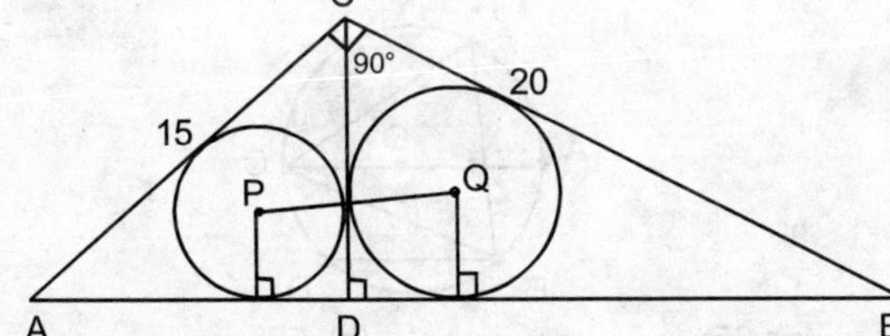

In the above figure, ACB is a right-angled triangle. CD is the altitude. Circles are inscribed within the ΔACD and ΔBCD. P and Q are the centres of the circles. The distance PQ is

(a) 5 (b) $\sqrt{50}$

(c) 7 (d) 8

2003(R)

26. In the figure below (not drawn to scale), rectangle ABCD is inscribed in the circle with centre at O. The length of side AB is greater than side BC. The ratio of the area of the circle to the area of the rectangle ABCD is $\pi : \sqrt{3}$. The line segment DE intersects AB at E such that $\angle ODC = \angle ADE$.

The ratio AE : AD is

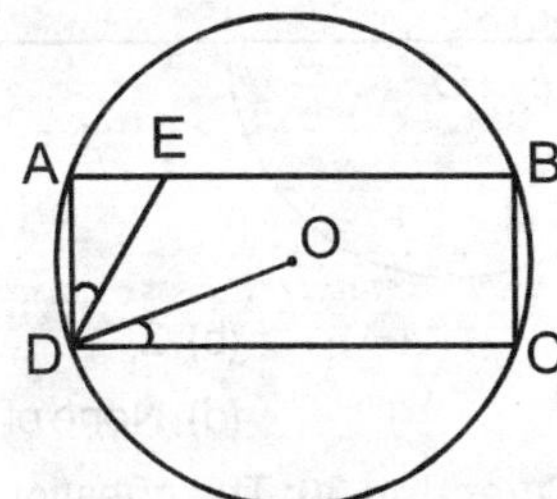

(a) $1 : \sqrt{3}$ (b) $1 : \sqrt{2}$

(c) $1 : 2\sqrt{3}$ (d) 1 : 2

27. In the figure given below (not drawn to scale), A, B and C are three points on a circle with centre O. The chord BA is extended to a point T such that CT becomes a tangent to the circle at point C. If $\angle ATC = 30°$ and $\angle ACT = 50°$, then the angle $\angle BOA$ is

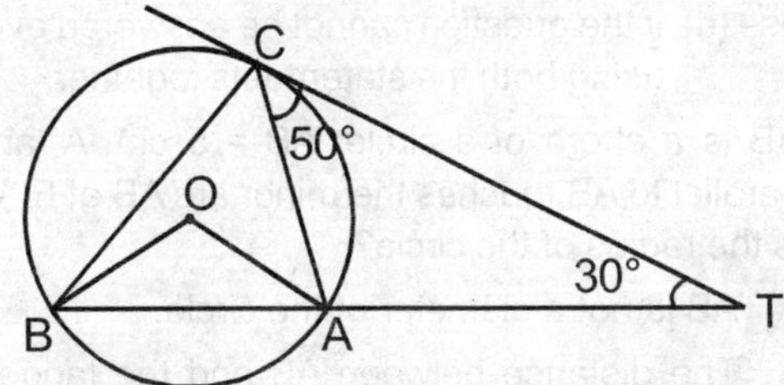

(a) 100°

(b) 150°

(c) 80°

(d) not possible to determine

2003(L)

28. There are two concentric circles such that the area of the outer circle is four times the area of the inner circle. Let A, B and C be three distinct points on the perimeter of the outer circle such that AB and AC are tangents to the inner circle. If the area of the outer circle is 12 square centimeters then the area (in square centimeters) of the triangle ABC would be

(a) $\pi\sqrt{12}$ (b) $\frac{9}{\pi}$

(c) $\frac{9\sqrt{3}}{\pi}$ (d) $\frac{6\sqrt{3}}{\pi}$

29. In the figure below, AB is the chord of a circle with center O. AB is extended to C such that BC = OB. The straight line CO is produced to meet the circle at D. If $\angle ACD$ = y degrees and $\angle AOD$ = x degrees such that x = ky, then the value of k is

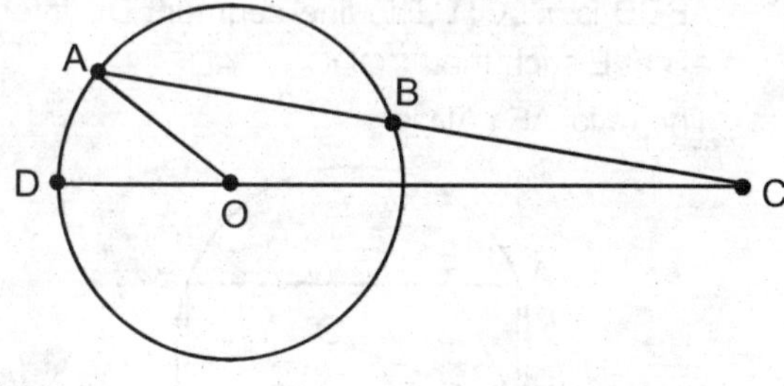

(a) 3 (b) 2
(c) 1 (d) None of the above

Direction for Question 30: The question is followed by two statements, A and B. Answer the question using the following instructions.

Choose (a) if the question can be answered by one of the statements alone but not by the other.
Choose (b) if the question can be answered by using either statement alone.
Choose (c) if the question can be answered by using both the statements together, but cannot be answered by using either statement alone.
Choose (d) if the question cannot be answered even by using both the statements together.

30. AB is a chord of a circle. AB = 5 cm. A tangent parallel to AB touches the minor arc AB at E. What is the radius of the circle?

A. AB is not a diameter of the circle.
B. The distance between AB and the tangent at E is 5 cm.

2004

Directions for Questions 31 to 33: Answer the questions on the basis of the information given below.

In the adjoining figure I and II, are circles with P and Q respectively, The two circles touch each other and have common tangent that touches them at points R and S respectively. This common tangent meets the line joining P and Q at O. The diameters of I and II are in the ratio 4 : 3. It is also known that the length of PO is 28 cm.

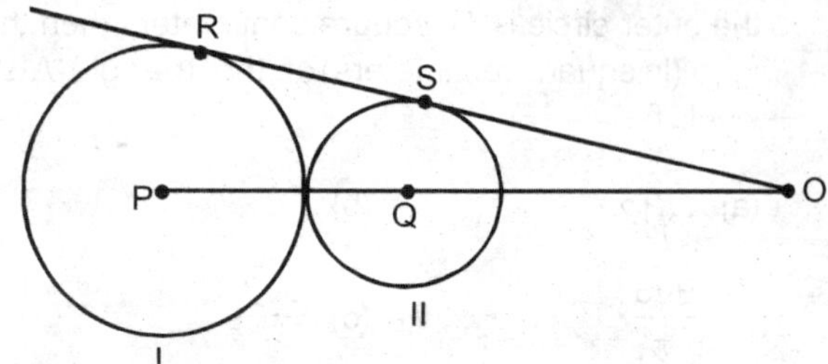

31. What is the ratio of the length of PQ to that of QO?
(a) 1 : 4 (b) 1 : 3
(c) 3 : 8 (d) 3 : 4

32. What is the radius of the circle II?
(a) 2 cm (b) 3 cm
(c) 4 cm (d) 5 cm

33. The length of SO is
(a) $8\sqrt{3}$ cm (b) $10\sqrt{3}$ cm
(c) $12\sqrt{3}$ cm (d) $14\sqrt{3}$ cm

34. On a semicircle with diameter AD, chord BC is parallel to the diameter. Further, each of the chords AB and CD has length 2, while AD has length 8. What is the length of BC?

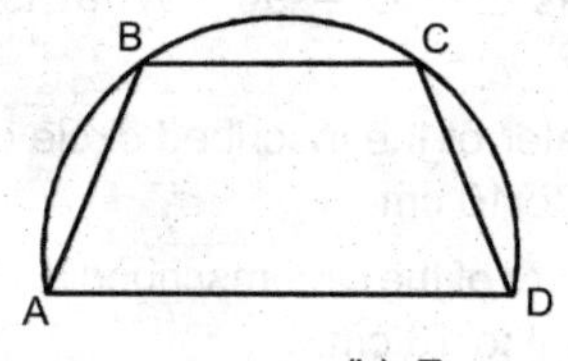

(a) 7.5 (b) 7
(c) 7.75 (d) None of the above

35. A circle with radius 2 is placed against a right angle. Another smaller circle is also placed as shown in the adjoining figure. What is the radius of the smaller circle?

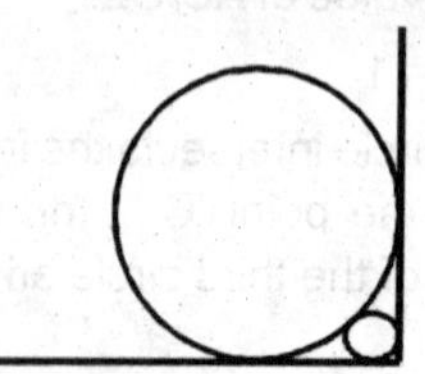

(a) $3-2\sqrt{2}$ (b) $4-2\sqrt{2}$
(c) $7-4\sqrt{2}$ (d) $6-4\sqrt{2}$

36. In the adjoining figure, chord ED is parallel to the diameter AC of the circle. If $\angle CBE = 65°$, then what is the value of $\angle DEC$?

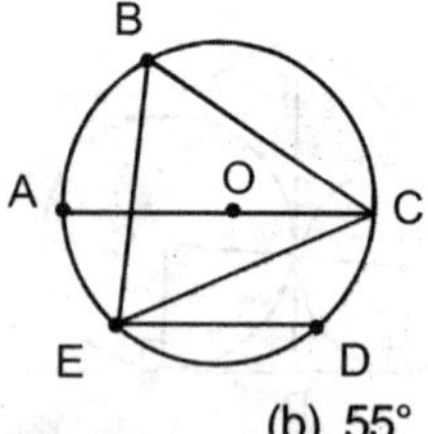

(a) 35° (b) 55°
(c) 45° (d) 25°

2005

37. What is the distance in cm between two parallel chords of lengths 32 cm and 24 cm in a circle of radius 20 cm?
(a) 1 or 7 (b) 2 or 14
(c) 3 or 21 (d) 4 or 28

38. In the following figure, the diameter of the circle is 3 cm. AB and MN are two diameters such that MN is perpendicular to AB. In addition, CG is perpendicular to AB such that AE : EB = 1 : 2, and DF is perpendicular to MN such that NL : LM = 1 : 2. The length of DH in cm is

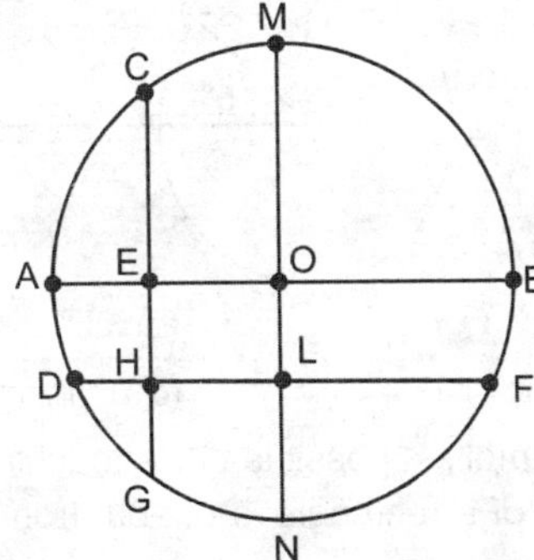

(a) $2\sqrt{2}-1$ (b) $\frac{(2\sqrt{2}-1)}{2}$

(c) $\frac{(3\sqrt{2}-1)}{2}$ (d) $\frac{(2\sqrt{2}-1)}{3}$

39. P, Q, S and R are points on the circumference of a circle of radius r, such that PQR is an equilateral triangle and PS is a diameter of the circle. What is the perimeter of the quadrilateral PQSR?

(a) $2r(1+\sqrt{3})$ (b) $2r(2+\sqrt{3})$

(c) $r(1+\sqrt{5})$ (d) $2r+\sqrt{3}$

2006

40. A semi-circle is drawn with AB as its diameter. From C, a point on AB, a line perpendicular to AB is drawn meeting the circumference of the semi-circle at D. Given that AC = 2 cm and CD = 6 cm, the area of the semi-circle (in sq. cm)will be:

(a) 32π (b) 50π

(c) 40.5π (d) 81π

(e) undeterminable

2007

41. Two circles with centres P and Q cut each other at two distinct points A and B. The circles have the same radii and neither P nor Q falls within the intersection of the circles. What is the smallest range that includes all possible values of the angle AQP in degrees?

(a) Between 0 and 90

(b) Between 0 and 30

(c) Between 0 and 60

(d) Between 0 and 75

(e) Between 0 and 45

2008

42. In a triangle ABC, the lengths of the sides AB and AC are equal to 17.5 cm and 9 cm respectively. Let D be a point on the line segment BC such that AD is perpendicular to BC. If AD = 3 cm, then what is the radius (in cm)of the circle circumscribing the triangle ABC?

(a) 17.05 (b) 27.85

(c) 22.45 (d) 32.25

(e) 26.25

MEMORY BASED QUESTIONS

2009

43. In the given figure, two equal circles (with radius 'R' units) intersect each other at two points M and N such that $\angle PMQ = 90°$. What is the area (in sq units) of the region that is common to both the circles?

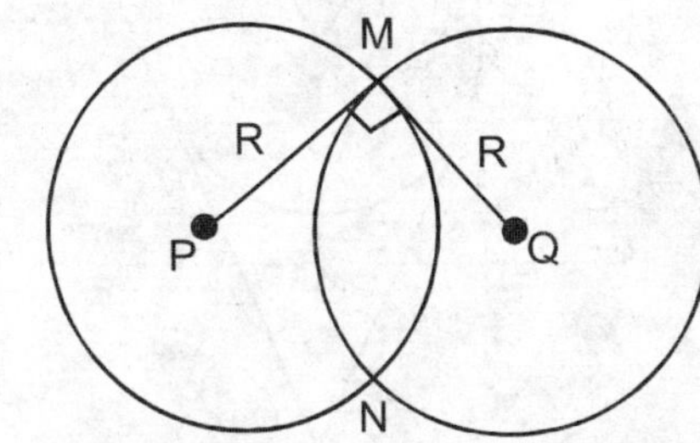

(a) $R^2 \times \left(\frac{\pi}{2}-1\right)$

(b) $\frac{1}{2}R^2 \times \left(\frac{\pi}{2}-1\right)$

(c) $\frac{1}{2}R^2 \times \left(1-\frac{\pi}{2}\right)$

(d) $R^2 \times \left(1-\frac{\pi}{2}\right)$

2012

44. A circle of radius 6.5 cm is circumscribed around a right-angled triangle with the sides a, b and c cm where a, b and c are natural numbers. What is the perimeter of the triangle?

(a) 30 cm (b) 26 cm

(c) 28 cm (d) 32 cm

45. Two circles with centers A and B touch each other at C. The radii of the two circles are 3 m and 6 m respectively. Ramu and Shamu start simultaneously from C with speeds 6π m/s and 3π m/s and travel along the circles with centers A and B respectively. If Ramu gives Shamu a start of 2 seconds, what time (in seconds)after Ramu's start would they be separated by a distance of 18 m?

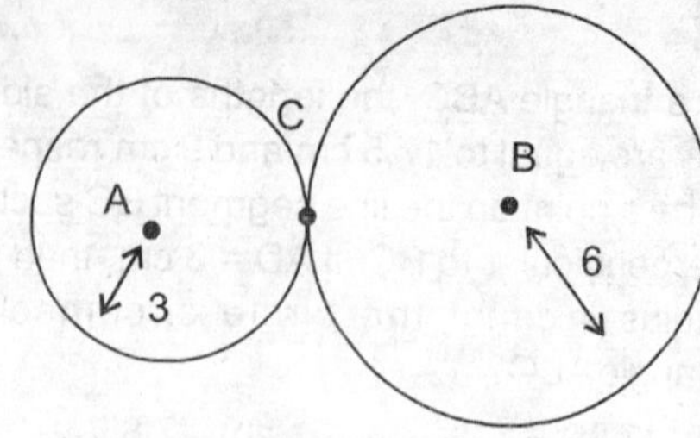

(a) 7 (b) 10
(c) 125 (d) Never

46. From a point P, the tangents PQ and PT are drawn to a circle with centre O and radius 2 units. From the centre O, OA and OB are drawn parallel to PQ and PT respectively. The length of the chord TQ is 2 units. Find the measure of the $\angle AOB$.

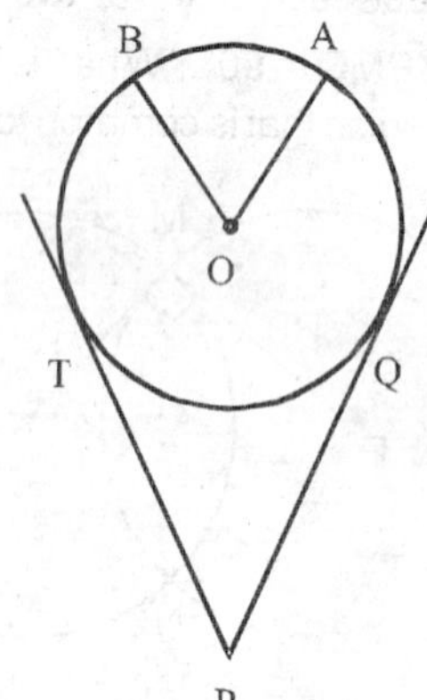

(a) 30° (b) 90°
(c) 120° (d) 45°

2013

47. In the figure given below, AB is a diameter of the circle. If AB II CD, AC II BE and $\angle BAE = 35°$, then the absolute difference between $\angle CDB$ and $\angle ABD$ is

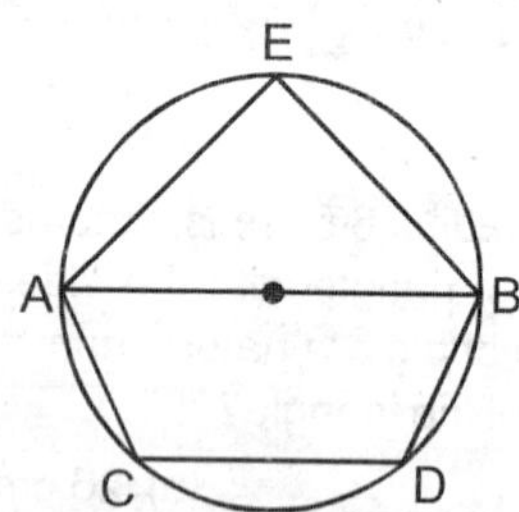

(a) 90° (b) 70°
(c) 55° (d) 125°

2014

48. AC is a chord of a circle whose centre is at O. If B is any point on the arc AC and $\angle OCA = 20°$, then the magnitude of $\angle ABC$ is

(a) 110° (b) 70°
(c) 140° (d) Either (a) or (b)

2015

49. In the given figure, AB is the diameter of the circle with centre O. If $\angle BOD = 15°$, $\angle EOA = 85°$, then find the measure of $\angle ECA$.

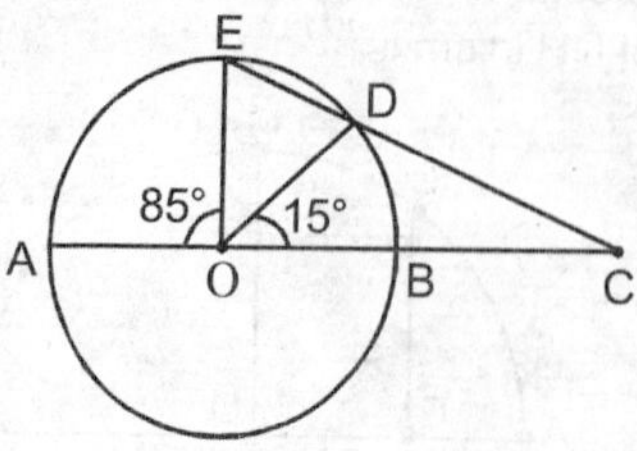

(a) 20° (b) 25°
(c) 35° (d) Cannot be determined

50. The smallest possible circle touching two opposite sides of a rectangle is cut-out from a rectangle of area 60 sq. units. If the area of this circle is $\frac{3}{2}$ times the area left out in the rectangle, find the length of the smaller side of the rectangle.

(a) $\frac{6}{\sqrt{\pi}}$ units (b) $\frac{9}{\sqrt{\pi}}$ units
(c) $\frac{12}{\sqrt{\pi}}$ units (d) $\frac{15}{\sqrt{\pi}}$ units

51.

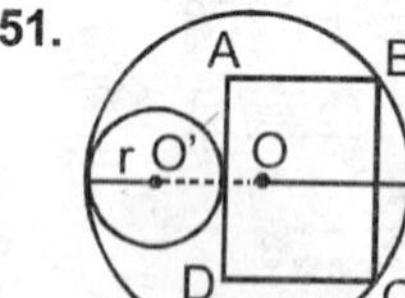

In the figure, O and O' are the centres of the bigger and smaller circles respectively and small circle touches the square ABCD at the mid point of side AD. The radius of the bigger circle is equal to 15 cm and the side of the square ABCD is 18 cm. Find the radius of the smaller circle.

(a) 4.25 cm (b) 4.5 cm
(c) 4.75 cm (d) 5 cm

2018 Slot 1

52. In a circle, two parallel chords on the same side of a diameter have lengths 4 cm and 6 cm. If the distance between these chords is 1 cm, then the radius of the circle, in cm, is

(a) $\sqrt{11}$ (b) $\sqrt{14}$
(c) $\sqrt{13}$ (d) $\sqrt{12}$

53. Let ABCD be a rectangle inscribed in a circle of radius 13 cm. Which one of the following pairs can represent, in cm, the possible length and breadth of ABCD?

(a) 24, 12 (b) 24, 10
(c) 25, 10 (d) 25, 9

54. In a circle with center O and radius 1 cm, an arc AB makes an angle 60 degrees at O. Let R be the region bounded by the radii OA, OB and the arc AB. If C and D are two points on OA and OB, respectively, such that OC = OD and the area of triangle OCD is half that of R, then the length of OC, in cm, is

(a) $\left(\frac{\pi}{6}\right)^{\frac{1}{2}}$ (b) $\left(\frac{\pi}{4}\right)^{\frac{1}{2}}$

(c) $\left(\frac{\pi}{3\sqrt{3}}\right)^{\frac{1}{2}}$ (d) $\left(\frac{\pi}{4\sqrt{3}}\right)^{\frac{1}{2}}$

2018 Slot 2

55. On a triangle ABC, a circle with diameter BC is drawn, intersecting AB and AC at points P and Q, respectively. If the lengths of AB, AC, and CP are 30 cm, 25 cm, and 20 cm respectively, then the length of BQ, in cm, is

56. A chord of length 5 cm subtends an angle of 60° at the centre of a circle. The length, in cm, of a chord that subtends an angle of 120° at the centre of the same circle is

(a) $6\sqrt{2}$ (b) 8

(c) $5\sqrt{3}$ (d) 2π

MENSURATION

1991

1. A square piece of cardboard of sides ten inches is taken and four equal squares pieces are removed at the corners, such that the side of this square piece is also an integer value. The sides are then turned up to form an open box. Then the maximum volume such a box can have is

(a) 72 cubic inches.

(b) 24.074 cubic inches.

(c) 2000/27 cubic inches

(d) 64 cubic inches.

1993

2. A slab of ice 8 inches in length, 11 inches in breadth, and 2 inches thick was melted and resolidified into the form of a rod of 8 inches diameter. The length of such a rod, in inches, is nearest to

(a) 3 (b) 3.5

(c) 4 (d) 4.5

3. The diameter of a hollow cone is equal to the diameter of a spherical ball. If the ball is placed at the base of the cone, what portion of the ball will be outside the cone?

(a) 50% (b) less than 50%

(c) more than 50% (d) 100%

1994

4. A right circular cone, a right circular cylinder and a hemisphere, all have the same radius, and the heights of the cone and cylinder equal to their diameters. Then their volumes are proportional, respectively to

(a) 1 : 3 : 1 (b) 2 : 1 : 3

(c) 3 : 2 : 1 (d) 1 : 2 : 3

5. A right circular cone of height h is cut by a plane parallel to the base and at a distance h/3 from the base, then the volumes of the resulting cone and the frustum are in the ratio

(a) 1 : 3 (b) 8 : 19

(c) 1 : 4 (d) 1 : 7

Direction for Question 6 : The question is followed by two statements. As the answer,

Mark (a) if the question can be answered with the help of statement I alone,

Mark (b) if the question can be answered with the help of statement II, alone,

Mark (c) if both, statement I and statement II are needed to answer the question, and

Mark (d) if the question cannot be answered even with the help of both the statements.

6. What will be the total cost of creating a 1- foot border of tiles along the inside edges of a room?

I. The room is 48 feet in length and 50 feet in breadth.

II. Every tile costs Rs. 10.

1996

7. A wooden box (open at the top) of thickness 0.5 cm, length 21 cm, width 11 cm and height 6 cm is painted on the inside. The expences of painting are Rs. 70. What is the rate of painting per square centimetres?

(a) Re. 0.7 (b) Re. 0.5

(c) Re. 0.1 (d) Re. 0.2

1997

Direction for Question 8 : The question is followed by two statements. As the answer,

(a) if the question can be answered with the help of one statement alone.

(b) if the question can be answered with the help of any one statement independently.

(c) if the question can be answered with the help of both statements together.

(d) if the question cannot be answered even with the help of both statements together.

8. What is the ratio of the volume of the given right circular cone to the one obtained from it?
   I. The smaller cone is obtained by passing a plane parallel to the base and dividing the original height in the ratio 1 : 2.
   II. The height and the base of the new cone are one-third those of the original cone.

1999

Direction for Question 9 : The question is followed by two statements. As the answer,

(a) if the question can be answered by any one of the statements alone, but cannot be answered by using the other statement alone.
(b) if the question can be answered by using either statement alone.
(c) if the question can be answered by using both the statements together, but cannot be answered by using either statement alone.
(d) if the question cannot be answered even by using both the statements together.

9. A small storage tank is spherical in shape. What is the storage volume of the tank?
   I. The wall thickness of the tank is 1 cm.
   II. When an empty spherical tank is immersed in a large tank filled with water, 20 l of water overflow from the large tank.

10. There is a square field of side 500 m long each. It has a compound wall along its perimeter. At one of its corners, a triangular area of the field is to be cordoned off by erecting a straight-line fence. The compound wall and the fence will form its borders. If the length of the fence is 100 m, what is the maximum area that can be cordoned off?

(a) 2,500 sq m (b) 10,000 sq m
(c) 5,000 sq m (d) 20,000 sq m

2000

11. A farmer has decided to build a wire fence along one straight side of his property. For this, he planned to place several fence-posts at 6 m intervals, with posts fixed at both ends of the side. After he bought the posts and wire, he found that the number of posts he had bought was 5 less than required. However, he discovered that the number of posts he had bought would be just sufficient if he spaced them 8 m apart. What is the length of the side of his property and how many posts did he buy?

(a) 100 m, 15 (b) 100 m, 16
(c) 120 m, 15 (d) 120 m, 16

2001

12. Two sides of a plot measure 32 m and 24 m and the angle between them is a perfect right angle. The other two sides measure 25 m each and the other three angles are not right angles.

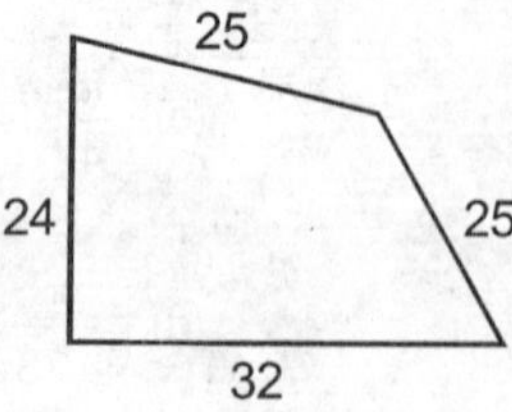

What is the area of the plot?

(a) 768 m^2 (b) 534 m^2
(c) 696.5 m^2 (d) 684 m^2

13. A rectangular pool 20 m wide and 60 m long is surrounded by a walkway of uniform width. If the total area of the walkway is 516 m^2, how wide, in metres, is the walkway?

(a) 43 m (b) 4.3 m
(c) 3 m (d) 3.5 m

Direction for Question 14: The question is followed by two statements, I and II.

Mark

(a) if the question can be answered by one of the statements alone and not by the other.
(b) if the question can be answered by using either statement alone.
(c) if the question can be answered by using both the statements together, but cannot be answered by using either statement alone.
(d) if the question cannot be answered even by using both statements together.

14. A square is inscribed in a circle. What is the difference between the area of the circle and that of the square?
   I. The diameter of the circle is $25\sqrt{2}$ cm.
   II. The side of the square is 25 cm.

2002

15. Four horses are tethered at four corners of a square plot of side 14 m so that the adjacent horses can just reach one another. There is a small circular pond of area 20 m^2 at the centre. Find the ungrazed area.

(a) 22 m^2 (b) 42 m^2
(c) 84 m^2 (d) 168 m^2

16. Neeraj has agreed to mow a lawn, which is a 20 m × 40 m rectangle. He mows it with 1 m wide strip. If Neeraj starts at one corner and mows around the lawn toward the centre, about how many times would he go round before he has mowed half the lawn?

(a) 2.5

(b) 3.5

(c) 3.8

(d) 4

2003(R)

Directions for Questions 17 to 19: Answer the questions on the basis of the information given below.

Consider three circular parks of equal size with centres at A_1, A_2 and A_3 respectively. The parks touch each other at the edge as shown in the figure (not drawn to scale). There are three paths formed by the triangles $A_1A_2A_3$, $B_1B_2B_3$ and $C_1C_2C_3$ as shown. Three sprinters A, B and C begin running from points A_1, B_1 and C_1 respectively. Each sprinter traverses her respective triangular path clockwise and returns to her starting point.

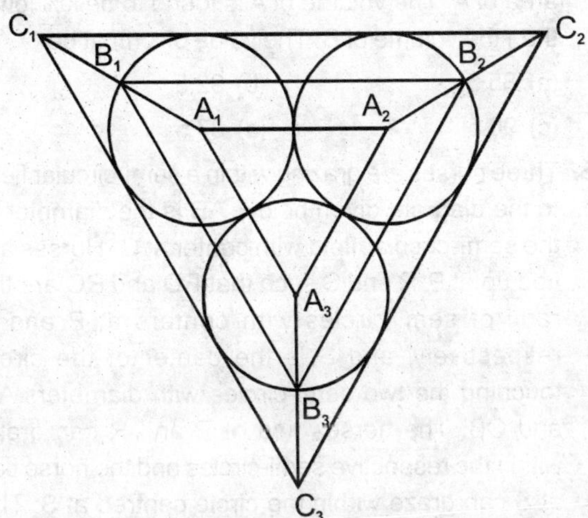

17. Let the radius of each circular park be r, and the distances to be traversed by the sprinters A, B and C be a, b and c respectively. Which of the following is true?

(a) $b - a = c - b = 3\sqrt{3}\,r$

(b) $b - a = c - b = \sqrt{3}\,r$

(c) $b = \frac{a+c}{2} = 2(1 + \sqrt{3})r$

(d) $c = 2b - a = (2 + \sqrt{3})r$

18. Sprinter A traverses distances A_1A_2, A_2A_3 and A_3A_1 at an average speeds of 20, 30 and 15 respectively. B traverses her entire path at a uniform speed of $(10\sqrt{3}+20)$. C traverses distances C_1C_2, C_2C_3 and C_3C_1 at an average speeds of $\frac{40}{3}(\sqrt{3}+1)$, $\frac{40}{3}(\sqrt{3}+1)$ and 120 respectively. All speeds are in the same unit. Where would B and C be respectively when A finishes her sprint?

(a) B_1, C_1

(b) B_3, C_3

(c) B_1, C_3

(d) B_1, Somewhere between C_3 and C_1

19. Sprinters A, B and C traverse their respective paths at uniform speeds of u, v and w respectively. It is known that $u^2 : v^2 : w^2$ is equal to Area A : Area B : Area C, where Area A, Area B and Area C are the areas of triangles $A_1A_2A_3$, $B_1B_2B_3$ and $C_1C_2C_3$ respectively. Where would A and C be when B reaches point B_3?

(a) A_2, C_3

(b) A_3, C_3

(c) A_3, C_2

(d) Somewhere between A_2 and A_3, Somewhere between C_3 and C_1

Directions for Questions 20 to 22: Answer the questions on the basis of the information given below.

Consider a cylinder of height h cm and radius $r = \frac{2}{\pi}$ cm as shown in the figure (not drawn to scale). A string of a certain length, when wound on its cylindrical surface, starting at point A and ending at point B, gives a maximum of n turns (in other words, the string's length is the minimum length required to wind n turns).

20. What is the vertical spacing between the two consecutive turns?

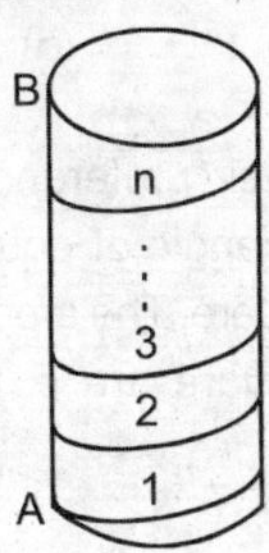

(a) $\frac{h}{n}$ cm

(b) $\frac{h}{\sqrt{n}}$ cm

(c) $\frac{h}{n^2}$ cm

(d) Cannot be determined

21. The same string, when wound on the exterior four walls of a cube of side n cm, starting at point C and ending at point D, can give exactly one turn (see figure, not drawn to scale). The length of the string is

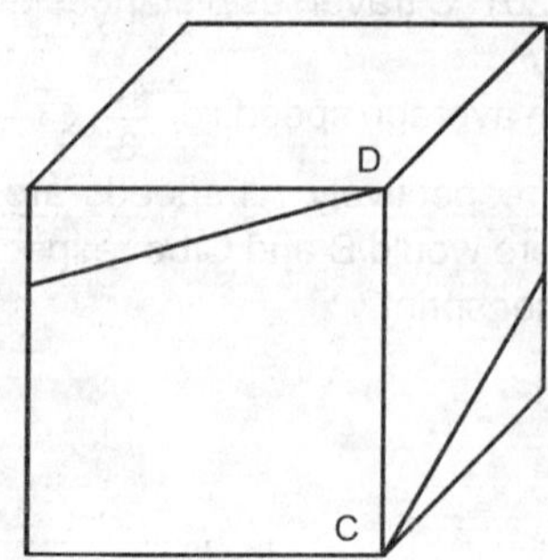

(a) $\sqrt{2}$ n cm (b) $\sqrt{17}$ n cm

(c) n cm (d) $\sqrt{13}$ n cm

22. In the set-up of the previous two questions, how is h related to n?

(a) h = $\sqrt{2}$ n (b) h = $\sqrt{17}$ n

(c) h = n (d) h = $\sqrt{13}$ n

23. Consider two different cloth-cutting processes. In the first one, n circular cloth pieces are cut from a square cloth piece of side *a* in the following steps: the original square of side *a* is divided into *n* smaller squares, not necessarily of the same size, then a circle of maximum possible area is cut from each of the smaller squares. In the second process, only one circle of maximum possible area is cut from the square of side *a* and the process ends there. The cloth pieces remaining after cutting the circles are scrapped in both the processes. The ratio of the total area of scrap cloth generated in the former to that in the latter is

(a) 1 : 1 (b) $\sqrt{2}$: 1

(c) $\frac{n(4-\pi)}{4n-\pi}$ (d) $\frac{4n-\pi}{n(4-\pi)}$

24. The length of the circumference of a circle equals the perimeter of a triangle of equal sides, and also the perimeter of a square. The areas covered by the circle, triangle, and square are c, t and s, respectively. Then,

(a) s > t > c

(b) c > t > s

(c) c > s > t

(d) s > c > t

25. A piece of paper is in the shape of a right-angled triangle and is cut along a line that is parallel to the hypotenuse, leaving a smaller triangle. There was 35% reduction in the length of the hypotenuse of the triangle. If the area of the original triangle was 34 square inches before the cut, what is the area (in square inches)of the smaller triangle?

(a) 16.665 (b) 16.565

(c) 15.465 (d) 14.365

26. A square tin sheet of side 12 inches is converted into a box with open top in the following steps. The sheet is placed horizontally. Then, equal-sized squares, each of side x inches, are cut from the four corners of the sheet. Finally, the four resulting sides are bent vertically upwards in the shape of a box. If x is an integer, then what value of x maximizes the volume of the box?

(a) 3 (b) 4

(c) 1 (d) 2

2003(L)

27. Let A and B be two solid spheres such that the surface area of B is 300% higher than the surface area of A. The volume of A is found to be k% lower than the volume of B. The value of k must be

(a) 85.5 (b) 92.5

(c) 90.5 (d) 87.5

28. Three horses are grazing within a semi-circular field. In the diagram given below, AB is the diameter of the semi-circular field with center at O. Horses are tied up at P, R and S such that PO and RO are the radii of semi-circles with centers at P and R respectively, and S is the center of the circle touching the two semi-circles with diameters AO and OB. The horses tied at P and R can graze within the respective semi-circles and the horse tied at S can graze within the circle centred at S. The percentage of the area of the semi-circle with diameter AB that cannot be grazed by the horses is nearest to

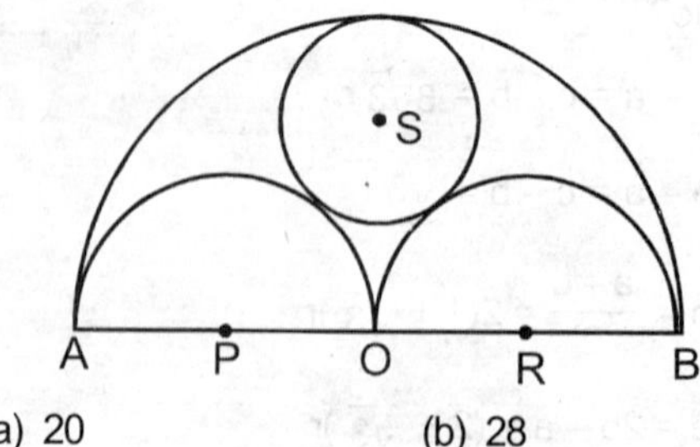

(a) 20 (b) 28

(c) 36 (d) 40

29. In the figure below, the rectangle at the corner measures 10 cm × 20 cm. The corner A of the rectangle is also a point on the circumference of the circle. What is the radius of the circle in cm?

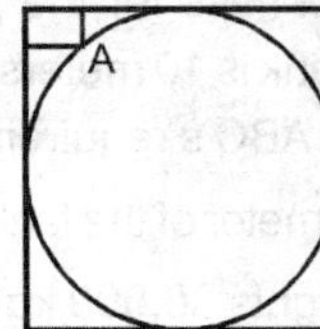

(a) 10 cm (b) 40 cm
(c) 50 cm (d) None of the above

2004

30. A rectangular sheet of paper, when halved by folding it at the mid point of its longer side, results in a rectangle, whose longer and shorter sides are in the same proportion as the longer and shorter sides of the original rectangle. If the shorter side of the original rectangle is 2, what is the area of the smaller rectangle?

(a) $4\sqrt{2}$ (b) $2\sqrt{2}$
(c) $\sqrt{2}$ (d) None of the above

31. Let C be a circle with centre P_0 and AB be a diameter of C. Suppose P_1 is the mid point of the line segment P_0B, P_2 is the mid point of the line segment P_1B and so on. Let C_1, C_2, C_3, ... be circles with diameters P_0P_1, P_1P_2, P_2P_3... respectively. Suppose the circles C_1, C_2, C_3, ... are all shaded. The ratio of the area of the unshaded portion of C to that of the original circle is

(a) 8 : 9 (b) 9 : 10
(c) 10 : 11 (d) 11 : 12

32. If the lengths of diagonals DF, AG and CE of the cube shown in the adjoining figure are equal to the three sides of a triangle, then the radius of the circle circumscribing that triangle will be

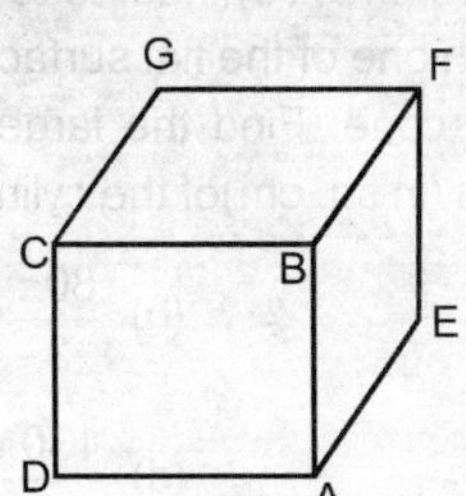

(a) equal to the side of cube

(b) $\sqrt{3}$ times the side of the cube

(c) $\frac{1}{\sqrt{3}}$ times the side of the cube

(d) impossible to find from the given information.

2005

33. Two identical circles intersect so that their centers, and the points at which they intersect, form a square of side 1 cm. The area in sq. cm of the portion that is common to the two circles is

(a) $\frac{\pi}{4}$ (b) $\frac{\pi}{2}-1$

(c) $\frac{\pi}{5}$ (d) $\sqrt{2}-1$

34. Four points A, B, C and D lie on a straight line in the X-Y plane, such that AB = BC = CD, and the length of AB is 1 metre. An ant at A wants to reach a sugar particle at D. But there are insect repellents kept at points B and C. The ant would not go within one metre of any insect repellent. The minimum distance in metres the ant must traverse to reach the sugar particle is

(a) $3\sqrt{2}$ (b) $1 + \pi$

(c) $\frac{4\pi}{3}$ (d) 5

35. Rectangular tiles each of size 70 cm by 30 cm must be laid horizontally on a rectangular floor of size 110 cm by 130 cm, such that the tiles do not overlap. A tile can be placed in any orientation so long as its edges are parallel to the edges of the floor. No tile should overshoot any edge of the floor. The maximum number of tiles that can be accommodated on the floor is

(a) 4
(b) 5
(c) 6
(d) 7

36. A rectangular floor is fully covered with square tiles of identical size. The tiles on the edges are white and the tiles in the interior are red. The number of white tiles is the same as the number of red tiles. A possible value of the number of tiles along one edge of the floor is

(a) 10
(b) 12
(c) 14
(d) 16

2006

Directions for Questions 37 and 38: Answer questions on the basis of the information given below:

A punching machine is used to punch a circular hole of diameter two units from a square sheet of aluminium of width 2 units, as shown below. The hole is punched such that the circular hole touches one corner P of the square sheet and the diameter of the hole originating at P is in line with a diagonal of the square.

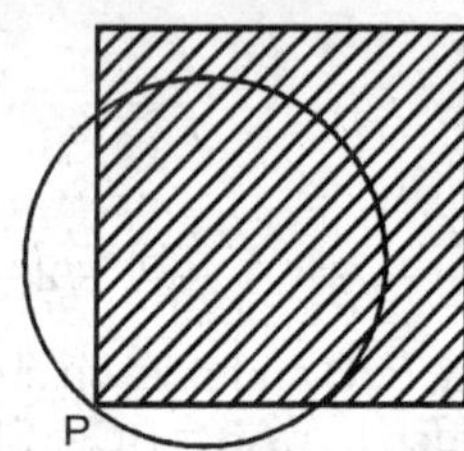

37. The proportion of the sheet area that remains after punching is:

(a) $\frac{(\pi+2)}{8}$ (b) $\frac{(6-\pi)}{8}$

(c) $\frac{(4-\pi)}{4}$ (d) $\frac{(\pi-2)}{4}$

(e) $\frac{(14-3\pi)}{6}$

38. Find the area of the part of the circle (round punch) falling outside the square sheet.

(a) $\frac{\pi}{4}$

(b) $\frac{(\pi-1)}{2}$

(c) $\frac{(\pi-1)}{4}$

(d) $\frac{(\pi-2)}{2}$

(e) $\frac{(\pi-2)}{4}$

2007

Direction for Question 39: The question is followed by two statements A and B. Indicate your response based on the following directives.

Mark (a) if the questions can be answered using A alone but not using B alone.

Mark (b) if the question can be answered using B alone but not using A alone.

Mark (c) if the question can be answered using A and B together, but not using either A or B alone.

Mark (d) if the question cannot be answered even using A and B together.

39. ABC Corporation is required to maintain at least 400 Kilolitres of water at all times in its factory, in order to meet safety and regulatory requirements. ABC is considering the suitability of a spherical tank with uniform wall thickness for the purpose. The outer diameter of the tank is 10 meters. Is the tank capacity adequate to meet ABC's requirements?

A : The inner diameter of the tank is at least 8 meters.

B : The tank weights 30,000 kg when empty, and is made of a material with density of 3 gm/cc.

2008

40. Consider a square ABCD with midpoints E, F, G and H of AB, BC, CD and DA respectively. Let L denote the line passing through F and H. Consider points P and Q, on L and inside ABCD, such that the angles APD and BQC both equal 120°. What is the ratio of the area of ABQCDP to the remaining area inside ABCD?

(a) $\frac{4\sqrt{2}}{3}$ (b) $2+\sqrt{3}$

(c) $\frac{10-3\sqrt{3}}{9}$ (d) $1+\frac{1}{\sqrt{3}}$

(e) $2\sqrt{3}-1$

41. Two circles, both of radii 1 cm, intersect such that the circumference of each one passes through the centre of the other. What is the area (in sq. cm.) of the intersecting region?

(a) $\frac{\pi}{3}-\frac{\sqrt{3}}{4}$ (b) $\frac{2\pi}{3}+\frac{\sqrt{3}}{2}$

(c) $\frac{4\pi}{3}-\frac{\sqrt{3}}{2}$ (d) $\frac{4\pi}{3}+\frac{\sqrt{3}}{2}$

(e) $\frac{2\pi}{3}-\frac{\sqrt{3}}{2}$

42. Consider a right circular cone of base radius 4 cm and height 10 cm. A cylinder is to be placed inside the cone with one of the flat surfaces resting on the base of the cone. Find the largest possible total surface area (in sq. cm)of the cylinder.

(a) $\frac{100\pi}{3}$ (b) $\frac{80\pi}{3}$

(c) $\frac{120\pi}{7}$ (d) $\frac{130\pi}{9}$

(e) $\frac{110\pi}{7}$

MEMORY BASED QUESTIONS

2009

43. A rectangular floor is fully covered with equal square tiles. All the tiles on the edges of the floor are white and the rest of them are red in colour. The total number of white tiles is half the total number of red tiles on the floor. What is the maximum possible difference between the number of red tiles and the number of white tiles on the floor?

(a) 70 (b) 48
(c) 78 (d) 40

2010

44. A cylindrical pipe of length 75 m, through which water flows at the rate of 54 km/hr, can fill 80% of a cuboidal tank of 118800 m^3 capacity in 14 hours. What is the radius (in cm) of the cross section of the pipe?

(a) 20 (b) 25
(c) 50 (d) Cannot be determined

45. A large cube is formed by bringing together 729 smaller identical cubes. Each face of the larger cube is painted with red colour. How many smaller cubes are there none of whose faces is painted?

(a) 216 (b) 256
(c) 343 (d) None of these

2011

46. A cube of edge 12 cm is cut into 64 equal cubes. All the cubes are now arranged on a table such that one face of each cube touches the table. The resulting figure is a solid cuboid whose length and breadth are in the ratio 4 : 1 respectively. What is the total surface area of the table occupied by the cuboid?

(a) 144 cm^2 (b) 288 cm^2
(c) 576 cm^2 (d) None of these

2013

47. A spherical ball of the maximum possible volume is placed inside a right-circular cone of height 'h' units. If the radius of the base of the cone is equal to $h/\sqrt{3}$ units, then the ratio of the volume of the sphere to that of the cone is

(a) 4 : 9 (b) 5 : 9
(c) $1:\sqrt{3}$ (d) $2:3\sqrt{3}$

2014

48. The top and bottom radii of a frustrum of a solid cone are 3 cm and 6 cm respectively. Its height is 8 cm. There is a conical cavity of height 3 cm and radius 6 cm at the bottom. The amount of material in the solid is

(a) 132 π cm^3 (b) 168 π cm^3
(c) 159 π cm^3 (d) Data Insufficient

2015

49. A field is in the form of a rectangle of dimension 24 m × 56 m. There is 2700 m of fencing that is available. The field has to be divided into many identical smaller square plots, having integral sides (in metres), each of which is to be fenced. Find the side of each of the square plots such that the fencing material that is left out is minimum.

(a) 1 m (b) 2 m
(c) 4 m (d) 8 m

2016

50. An unsharpened cylindrical pencil consists of a layer of wood surrounding a solid cylinder of graphite. The radius of a pencil is 7 mm, the radius of the graphite cylinder is 1 mm and the length of the pencil is 10 cm. Find the cost of the material used in a pencil, if the cost of wood is Rs.0.70/cm^3 and that of graphite is Rs.2.10/cm^3.

(1) Rs.8.76 (2) Rs.10.02
(3) Rs.11.22 (4) Rs.13.74

51. Two circles of radii 'r' units and '2r' units intersect each other in such a way that their common chord is of the maximum possible length. What is the area (in square units) of the region that is common to the two circles?

(1) $\frac{\pi r^2}{2}$ (2) $\frac{7\pi r^2}{6} - \sqrt{3}r^2$

(3) $\frac{11\pi r^2}{6} - \frac{\sqrt{3}r^2}{2}$ (4) $\frac{7\pi r^2}{6} - \frac{\sqrt{3}r^2}{2}$

52. A raindrop consists of 75% water and the rest is dust. However, by the time it reaches the surface of Earth, it is left with 70% water as 2 ml water evaporates on the way. Find the original volume of the raindrop.

(1) 12 ml (2) 15 ml
(3) 40 ml (4) 42 ml

53. A square is inscribed in a circle and the circle is inscribed in a regular octagon. Find the ratio of the area of the square to that of the octagon.

(1) $(1+\sqrt{2}):4$

(2) $(2\sqrt{2}-1):4$

(3) $(\sqrt{2}-1):4$

(4) Cannot be determined

54. From a rectangular sheet of dimensions 30 cm × 20 cm, four squares of equal size are cut from the four corners. Then the resulting four sides are bent upwards to give it the shape of an open box. If the volume of the box is 1056 cm^3, what is the length of the side of the squares cut from the corners?

(1) 2 cm (2) 4 cm
(3) 6 cm (4) 11 cm

2017

55. The base of a vertical pillar with uniform cross section is a trapezium whose parallel sides are of lengths 10 cm and 20 cm while the other two sides are of equal length. The perpendicular distance between the parallel sides of the trapezium is 12 cm. If the height of the pillar is 20 cm, then the total area, in sq cm, of all six surfaces of the pillar is

(1) 1300 (2) 1340
(3) 1480 (4) 1520

56. If three sides of a rectangular park have a total length 400 ft, then the area of the park is maximum when the length (in ft) of its longer side is

57. Let P be an Interior point of a right-angled isosceles triangle ABC with hypotenuse AB.If the perpendicular distance of P from each of AB, BC, and CA is $4(\sqrt{2}-1)$ cm, then the area, in sq cm, of the triangle ABC is

2018 Slot 1

58. A right circular cone, of height 12 ft, stands on its base which has diameter 8 ft. The tip of the cone is cut off with a plane which is parallel to the base and 9 ft from the base. With π = 22/7, the volume, in cubic ft, of the remaining part of the cone is

CO-ORDINATE GEOMETRY

1991

1. What is the distance between the points A(3, 8) and B(–2, –7)?

(a) $5\sqrt{2}$ (b) 5
(c) $5\sqrt{10}$ (d) $10\sqrt{2}$

1991

2. The points of intersection of three lines $2X + 3Y - 5 = 0$, $5X - 7Y + 2 = 0$ and $9X - 5Y - 4 = 0$

(a) form a triangle
(b) are on lines perpendicular to each other
(c) are on lines parallel to each other
(d) are coincident

1997

Direction for Question 3: The question is followed by two statements, I and II. Mark the answer

(a) if the question can be answered with the help of one statement alone.
(b) if the question can be answered with the help of any one statement independently.
(c) if the question can be answered with the help of both statements together.
(d) if the question cannot be answered even with the help of both statements together.

3. What is the area bounded by the two lines and the coordinate axes in the first quadrant?

I. The lines intersect at a point which also lies on the lines $3x - 4y = 1$ and $7x - 8y = 5$.

II. The lines are perpendicular, and one of them intersects the Y-axis at an intercept of 4.

1999

Directions for Questions 4 and 5: Answer the questions based on the following information.

A robot moves on a graph sheet with X and Y-axis. The robot is moved by feeding it with a sequence of instructions. The different instructions that can be used in moving it, and their meanings are:

Instruction	Meaning
GOTO (x, y)	Move to point with coordinates (x, y) no matter where you are currently
WALKX(p)	Move parallel to the X-axis through a distance of p, in the positive direction if p is positive, and in the negative direction if p is negative
WALKY(p)	Move parallel to the Y-axis through a distance of p, in the positive direction if p is positive, and in the negative direction if p is negative.

4. The robot reaches point (6, 6) when a sequence of three instructions is executed, the first of which is a GOTO(x, y)instruction, the second is WALKX(2) and the third is WALKY(4). What are the value of x and y?

(a) 2, 4 (b) 0, 0
(c) 4, 2 (d) 2, 2

5. The robot is initially at (x, y), $x > 0$ and $y < 0$. The minimum number of instructions needed to be executed to bring it to the origin (0, 0) if you are prohibited from using the GOTO instruction is

(a) 2 (b) 1
(c) x + y (d) 0

2000

6. ABCD is a rhombus with the diagonals AC and BD intersecting at the origin on the x-y plane. The equation of the straight line AD is x + y = 1. What is the equation of BC?

(a) x + y = –1

(b) x – y = –1

(c) x + y = 1

(d) None of these

Direction for Question 7: The question is followed by two statements, I and II. Answer the question using the following instructions.

Mark the answer as:

(a) if the question can be answered by one of the statements alone, but cannot be answered by using the other statement alone.

(b) if the question can be answered by using either statement alone.

(c) if the question can be answered by using both the statements together, but cannot be answered by using either statement alone.

(d) if the question cannot be answered even by using both statements together.

7. There are two straight lines in the x-y plane with equations:

ax + by = c; dx + ey = f

Do the two straight lines intersect?

I. a, b, c, d, e and f are distinct real numbers.

II. c and f are non-zero.

2002

8. The area of the triangle whose vertices are (a, a), (a + 1, a + 1) and (a + 2, a) is

(a) a^3 (b) 1

(c) 2a (d) $2^{1/2}$

2005

9. Consider a triangle drawn on the X-Y plane with its three vertices of (41, 0), (0, 41) and (0, 0), each vertex being represented by its (X, Y) coordinates. The number of points with integer coordinates inside the triangle (excluding all the points on the boundary) is

(a) 780 (b) 800

(c) 820 (d) 741

MEMORY BASED QUESTIONS

2011

10. Two lines P and Q intersect at point (3, 2) in the x-y plane. The slope of line P is 45° and line Q is parallel to the x-axis. What is the area (in sq. units) of the triangle formed by P, Q and a line perpendicular to P and passing through point (5, 4)?

(a) 12 (b) 8

(c) 6 (d) 4

2015

11. The line $\sqrt{3}y = x$ is the radius of the circle, it meets the circle centred at origin O at point M $(\sqrt{3}, 1)$. If PQ is the tangent to the circle at M as shown, find the length of the PQ.

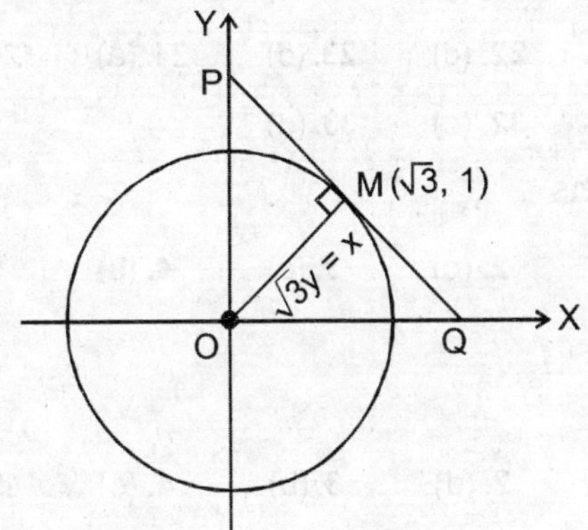

(a) $\frac{5}{2}\sqrt{3}$ units (b) $3\sqrt{3}$ units

(c) $2\sqrt{3}$ units (d) $\frac{8}{\sqrt{3}}$ units

12. The coordinates of two diagonally opposite vertices of a rectangle are (4, 3) and (-4,-3). Find the number of such rectangle(s), if the other two vertices also have integral coordinates.

(a) 1 (b) 4

(c) 5 (d) 10

2017

13. The points (2, 5) and (6, 3) are two end points of a diagonal of a rectangle. If the other diagonal has the equation y = 3x + c, then c is

(a) –5

(b) –6

(c) –7

(d) –8

ANSWERS

Line

1. (c) 2. (c) 3. (a)

Triangle

1. (d)	2. (b)	3. (d)	4. (c)	5. (c)	6. (b)	7. (d)	8. (b)	9. (c)	10. (*)
11. (c)	12. (c)	13. (d)	14. (a)	15. (d)	16. (c)	17. (a)	18. (d)	19. (b)	20. (a)
21. (d)	22. (a)	23. (c)	24. (b)	25. (b)	26. (d)	27. (c)	28. (c)	29. (d)	30. (b)
31. (b)	32. (d)	33. (a)	34. (c)	35. (a)	36. (c)	37. (d)	38. (c)	39. (d)	40. (196)
41. (b)	42. (a)	43. (a)	44. (b)	45. (b)	46. (b)				

Quadrilaterals

1. (a)	2. (c)	3. (a)	4. (a)	5. (b)	6. (c)	7. (c)	8. (b)	9. (d)	10. (b)
11. (a)	12. (d)	13. (b)	14. (d)	15. (d)	16. (c)	17. (b)	18. (e)	19. (a)	20. (a)
21. (c)	22. (c)	23. (d)	24. (a)	25. (c)	26. (b)	27. (d)	28. (90)	29. (a)	30. (a)
31. (d)	32. (c)	33. (d)							

Polygons

1. (a)	2. (c)	3. (c)	4. (b)	5. (c)	6. (a)	7. (c)	8. (b)	9. (d)	10. (a)
11. (b)									

Circle

1. (d)	2. (d)	3. (b)	4. (c)	5. (a)	6. (a)	7. (a)	8. (c)	9. (b)	10. (d)
11. (a)	12. (d)	13. (a)	14. (a)	15. (c)	16. (c)	17. (c)	18. (b)	19. (c)	20. (b)
21. (c)	22. (c)	23. (b)	24. (a)	25. (b)	26. (a)	27. (a)	28. (c)	29. (a)	30. (a)
31. (b)	32. (b)	33. (c)	34. (b)	35. (d)	36. (d)	37. (d)	38. (b)	39. (a)	40. (b)
41. (c)	42. (e)	43. (a)	44. (a)	45. (d)	46. (c)	47. (b)	48. (d)	49. (c)	50. (c)
51. (b)	52. (c)	53. (b)	54. (c)	55. (24)	56. (c)				

Mensuration

1. (a)	2. (b)	3. (c)	4. (a)	5. (b)	6. (d)	7. (c)	8. (b)	9. (c)	10. (a)
11. (d)	12. (d)	13. (c)	14. (b)	15. (a)	16. (c)	17. (a)	18. (c)	19. (b)	20. (a)
21. (b)	22. (c)	23. (a)	24. (c)	25. (d)	26. (d)	27. (d)	28. (b)	29. (c)	30. (b)
31. (d)	32. (a)	33. (b)	34. (b)	35. (c)	36. (b)	37. (b)	38. (d)	39. (b)	40. (e)
41. (e)	42. (a)	43. (a)	44. (a)	45. (c)	46. (c)	47. (a)	48. (a)	49. (b)	50. (c)
51. (b)	52. (a)	53. (a)	54. (b)	55. (c)	56. (200)	57. (16)	58. (198)		

Coordinate Geometry

1. (c)	2. (d)	3. (c)	4. (c)	5. (a)	6. (a)	7. (d)	8. (b)	9. (a)	10. (d)
11. (d)	12. (c)	13. (d)							

EXPLANATIONS

Line

1. c Since the lines are parallel, $\frac{AB}{BC} = \frac{DE}{EF}$, i.e.

AB × EF = BC × DE.

Hence, I = II.

2. c None of the statement alone is sufficient to answer the question.

Using both statements together:

PQ = PB + BQ and RS = RE + ES

If BQ = ES and PB > RE, PQ > PS.

3. a

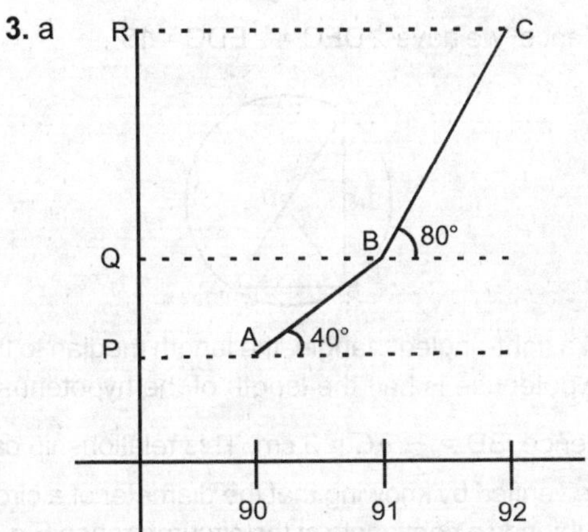

Ratio of revenues = $\frac{RQ}{QP}$

Since in a line graph, the years are uniformly spaced

$\Rightarrow \frac{RQ}{QP} = \frac{\tan 80°}{\tan 40°}$

So the ratio can be determined from statement I alone.

Statement II is immaterial because we intend to find the ratio and not absolute figures.

Triangle

1. d Following diagram shows the movement of the man.

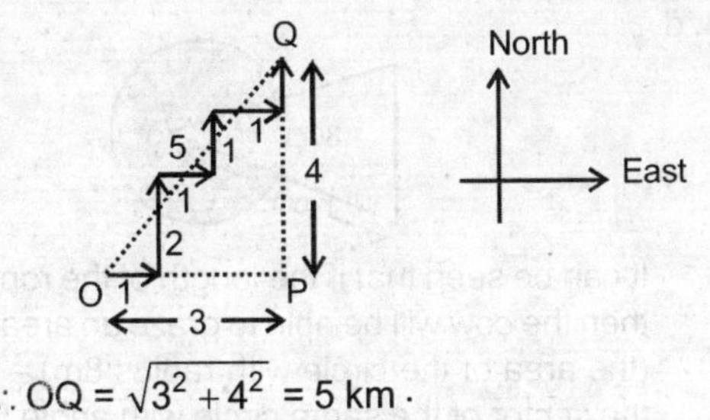

$\therefore OQ = \sqrt{3^2 + 4^2} = 5$ km.

For questions 2 and 3:

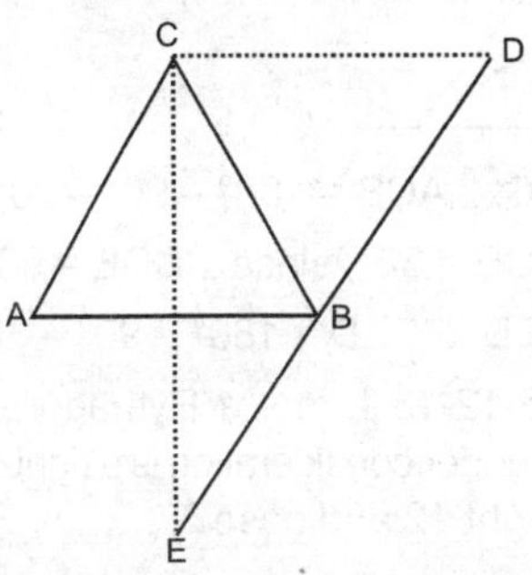

2. b Since ΔABC is an equilateral triangle with length of the side 2 km, so its altitude will be $\sqrt{3}$ km. As point D is directly east of C, so D is 3 km east and $\sqrt{3}$ km north of A.

3. d ABDC and AEBC, both are rhombus with each side 2 km.

Hence, the total distance walked by the person = BD + DB + BE = 2 + 2 + 2 = 6 km.

4. c Since $\angle C = 2\ \angle E$, therefore $\angle BCA = 60°$.

Also since ABCD is a parallelogram,

AB = CD and AD = BC = AC.

Hence, ΔABC and ΔACD are equilateral triangles.

Hence, area of this triangle = $\frac{s^2}{4}\sqrt{3}$, where s is the side of the triangle = AB = AD = DC = BC.

$\therefore$ Area of the parallelogram is twice this area = $\frac{s^2}{2}\sqrt{3}$.

Since $\angle CAD = 60°$, $\angle DAE = 90°$, so ΔEAD is a right triangle with side AD = s. Since it is a 30°-60°-90° triangle, hence side AE = $s\sqrt{3}$.

$\therefore$ Area of this triangle = $\frac{(s \times s\sqrt{3})}{2} = \frac{s^2}{2}\sqrt{3}$.

Hence, the required two areas are equal or I = II.

5. c The largest angle in a right-angled triangle is 90°, which corresponds to the highest part of the ratio.

Let us evaluate each option.

In (a), the remaining two angles would be 30° and 60°, which is possible.

In (b), the remaining two angles would be 45° each, which is again possible.

In (c), the remaining two angles would be 15° and 45°, which is not possible as the sum of the angles is not 180°.

6. b

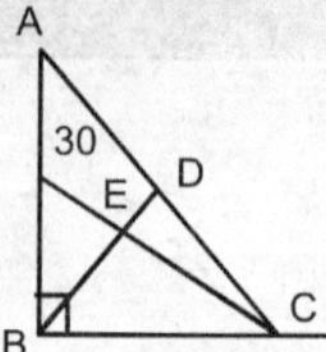

In ΔABC, $\angle ACB = 180° - 90° - 30° = 60°$.

$\therefore$ $\angle DCE = 30°$, since $\angle CDE = 90°$.

In ΔCED, $\angle CED = 180° - 90° - 30° = 60°$.

7. d Since 5-12-13 forms a Pythagorean triplet, the triangle under consideration is a right-angled triangle with height 12 and base 5.

So area of the triangle = $\left(\frac{1}{2}\right)(12)(5) = 30$ sq. units.

If area of the rectangle with width 10 units is 30 sq. units, its length = 3 units.

Hence, its perimeter = 2(10 + 3) = 26 units.

8. b

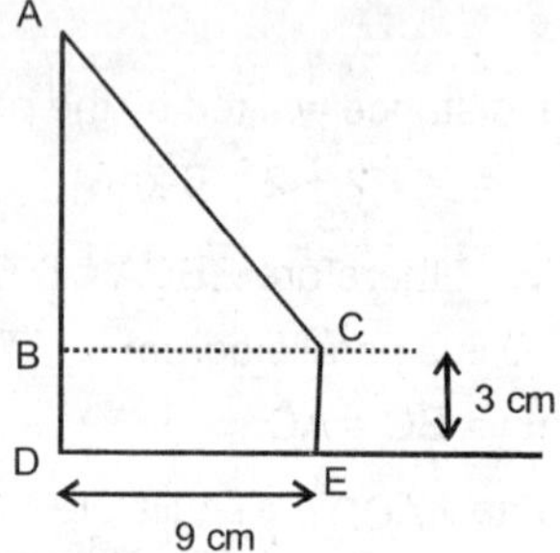

The figure can be drawn as shown above.

Height of the wall = AD = AC = (AB + 3) or AB = (AC – 3).

In right-angled triangle ABC, $AB^2 + BC^2 = AC^2$.

Thus, $(AC - 3)^2 + 81 = AC^2$.

$\therefore$ AC = 15 m.

Hence, height of the wall = 15 m.

Hint: Please note that the same multiple of all the triplets should also be triplets. E.g. if 3-4-5 is a triplet, then 3(3-4-5)should also be triplet or 9-12-15 is also a triplet.

Note that the base of the triangle is 9, so other two sides should be 12 and 15.

9. c Both statements are required to answer the question. Statement I tells us that the triangle is an isosceles triangle. In an isoceles triangle, the altitude is also the median and bisects the third side.

Hence, if we know the altitude length and the length of the congruent sides in an isoceles triangle, we can find its base. And if we know the base and the height of a triangle, we can find its area.

10. a

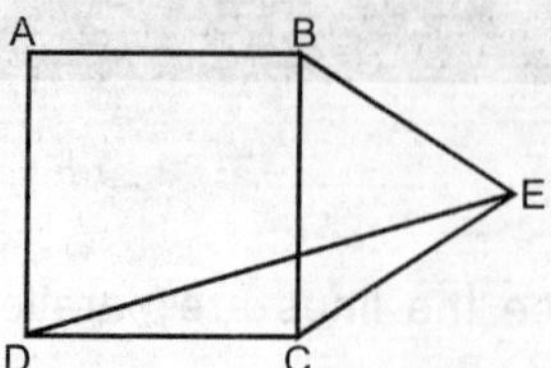

Since ΔBCE is an equilateral triangle, CE = BC = BE.

And since ABCD is a square, BC = CD. Hence, CD = CE. So in ΔCDE, we have CD = CE. Hence, $\angle EDC = \angle CED$. Now $\angle BCE = 60°$ (since equilateral triangle)and $\angle BCD = 90°$ (since square).

Hence, $\angle DCE = \angle DCB + \angle BCE = (60° + 90°) = 150°$.

So in ΔDCE, $\angle EDC + \angle CED = 30°$ (since three angles of a triangle add up to 180°).

Hence, we have $\angle DEC = \angle EDC = 15°$.

11. c

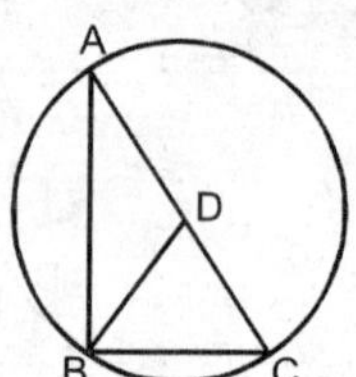

In a right-angled triangle, the length median to the hypotenuse is half the length of the hypotenuse.

Hence, BD = $\frac{1}{2}$ AC = 3 cm. This relationship can be verified by knowing that the diameter of a circle subtends a right angle at the circumference E.g. in the above figure D is the centre of the circle with AC as diameter. Hence, $\angle ABC$ should be 90°. So BD should be the median to the hypotenuse. Thus, we can see that BD = AD = CD = Radius of this circle.

Hence, BD = $\frac{1}{2}$ diameter = $\frac{1}{2}$ AC = $\frac{1}{2}$ × hypotenuse.

12. c In a triangle, the line joining the mid-points of any two sides is half the length of its third side. Hence, every side of ΔPQR would be half the sides of ΔABC. Hence, area of ΔPQR would be $\frac{1}{4}$ the area of ΔABC = $\frac{1}{4}$ × 20 = 5 sq. units.

13. d

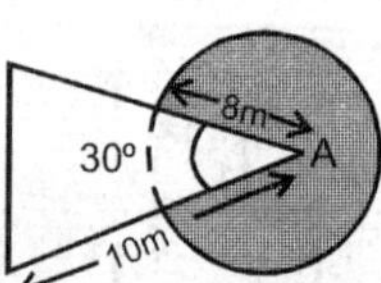

It can be seen that if the length of the rope is 8 m, then the cow will be able to graze an area equal to (the area of the circle with radius 8m) – (Area of the sector of the same circle with angle 30°)

$$= \pi(8)^2 - \frac{30}{360}\pi(8)^2$$

$$= 64\pi - \frac{1}{12}(64\pi)$$

$$= 64\pi\left(\frac{11}{12}\right) = \frac{176\pi}{3} \text{ sq. m}$$

Shortcut:

Area grazed without restriction is 64π m^2 it should be less than 64π sq. m. with restriction. So the correct choice is (d).

14. a

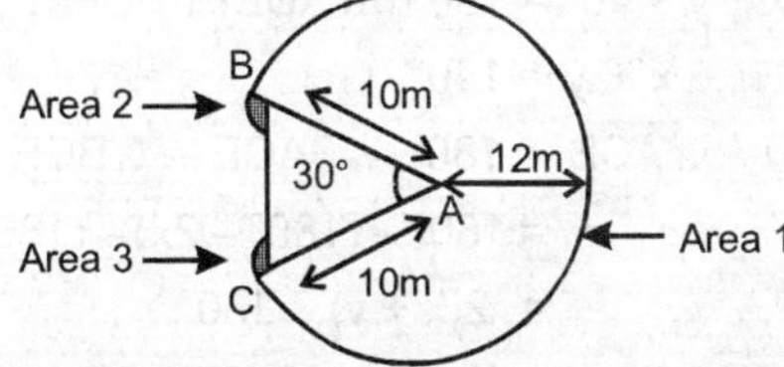

If the length of the rope is 12 m, then the total area that can be grazed by the cow is as depicted in the diagram. Area 1 is (the area of the circle with radius 12)– (Area of the sector of the same circle with angle 30°).

So area 1 = $\pi(12)^2 - \frac{30}{360}\pi(12)^2 = 132\pi$ sq.m.

Since the length of the rope is higher than the sides of the triangle (viz. AB and AC), if the cow reaches point B or C, there would still be a part of the rope (12 – 10) = 2 m in length. With this extra length available the cow can further graze an area equivalent to some part of the circle with radius = 2 m from both points, i.e. B and C. This is depicted as area 2 and area 3 in the diagram. Hence, the actual area grazed will be slightly more than 132π. The only answer choice that supports this is (a).

15. d

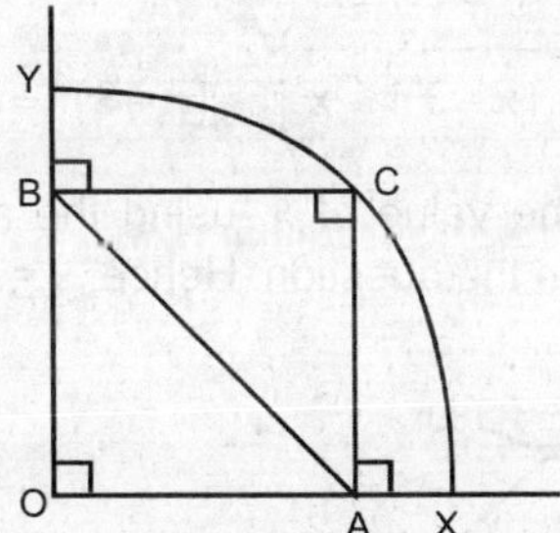

Do not make the mistake of assuming O to be the centre of the circle. Since the centre is not known, knowing radius is not of great help. It can be observed that $\angle BCA$ is also $90°$, as in the quadrilateral OBCA, the remaining three angles are $90°$. So the quadrilateral can either be a square or a rectangle. As we do not know even this, we cannot make use of the second statement as well. Hence, both the statements are not sufficient to answer the question.

16. c If the sides of the triangle are a, b and c, then a + b > c. Given a + b + c = 14.

Then the sides can be (4, 4, 6), (5, 5, 4), (6, 5, 3) and (6, 6, 2). Hence, four distinct triangles are possible.

17. a We know that $(a + b + c)^2 = a^2 + b^2 + c^2 + 2ab + 2bc + 2ac = 3ab + 3bc + 3ac$

Now assume values of a, b, c and substitute in this equation to check the options.

Short cut: $(a - b)^2 + (b - c)^2 + (c - a)^2 = 0$.

Hence, a = b = c.

18. d

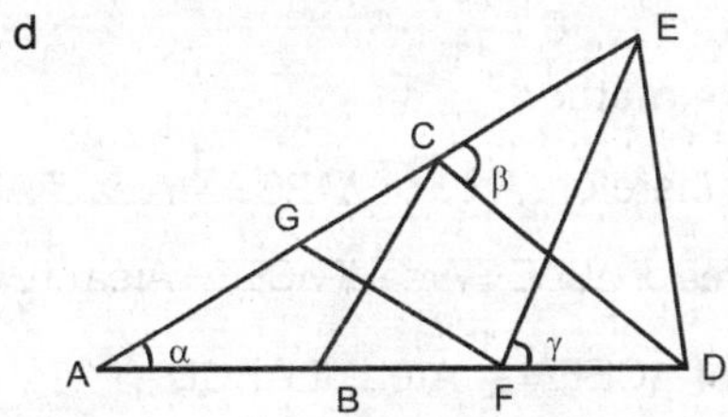

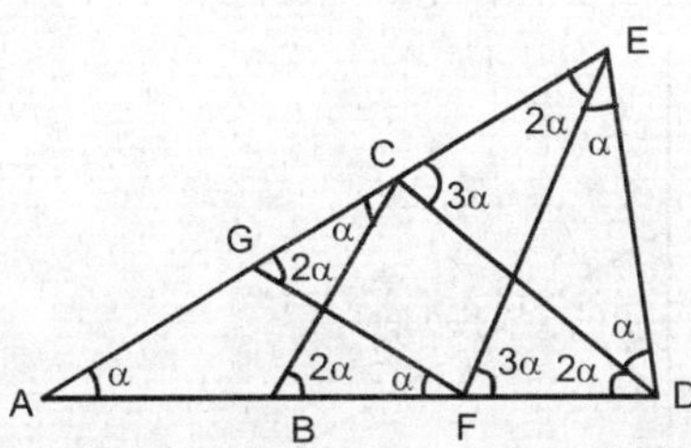

Let $\angle EAD = \alpha$. Then $\angle AFG = \alpha$ and also $\angle ACB = \alpha$.

Therefore, $\angle CBD = 2\alpha$ (exterior angle to ΔABC).

Also $\angle CDB = 2\alpha$ (since CB = CD).

Further, $\angle FGC = 2\alpha$ (exterior angle to ΔAFG).

Since GF = EF, $\angle FEG = 2\alpha$. Now $\angle DCE = \angle DEC = \beta$ (say). Then $\angle DEF = \beta - 2\alpha$.

Note that $\angle DCB = 180° - (\alpha + \beta)$.

Therefore, in ΔDCB, $180° - (\alpha + \beta) + 2\alpha + 2\alpha = 180°$ or $\beta = 3\alpha$. Further $\angle EFD = \angle EDF = \gamma$ (say).

Then $\angle EDC = \gamma - 2\alpha$. If CD and EF meet at P, then $\angle FPD = 180° - 5\alpha$ (because $\beta = 3\alpha$).

Now in ΔPFD, $180° - 5\alpha + \gamma + 2\alpha = 180°$ or $\gamma = 3\alpha$.

Therefore, in ΔEFD, $\alpha + 2\gamma = 180°$ or $\alpha + 6\alpha = 180°$ or $\alpha = 26°$ or approximately 25°.

19. b

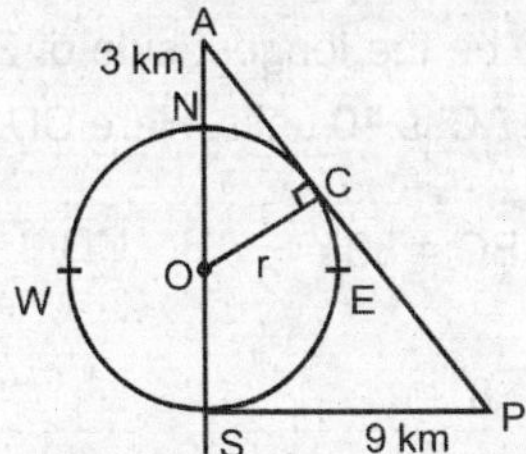

ΔAPS and ΔAOC are similar triangles.

Where OC = r

$$\therefore \frac{r}{r+3} = \frac{9}{\sqrt{81 + (2r + 3)^2}}$$

Now use the options. Hence, the diameter is 9 km.

20. a Let BC = y and AB = x.

Then area of ΔCEF = Area(ΔCEB) – Area(ΔCFB)

$$= \frac{1}{2}.\frac{2x}{3}.y - \frac{1}{2}.\frac{x}{3}.y = \frac{xy}{6}$$

Area of ABCD = xy

∴ Ratio of area of ΔCEF and area of ABCD is

$$\frac{xy}{6} : xy = \frac{1}{6}$$

Alternate method:

Join AC, therefore Area of $\Delta ABC = \frac{1}{2}$ Area of ABCD

Also, Area of ΔCAE = Area of ΔCEF = Area of ΔCFB

∴ Area of $\Delta CEF = \frac{1}{6}$ Area of ABCD

21. d

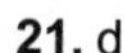

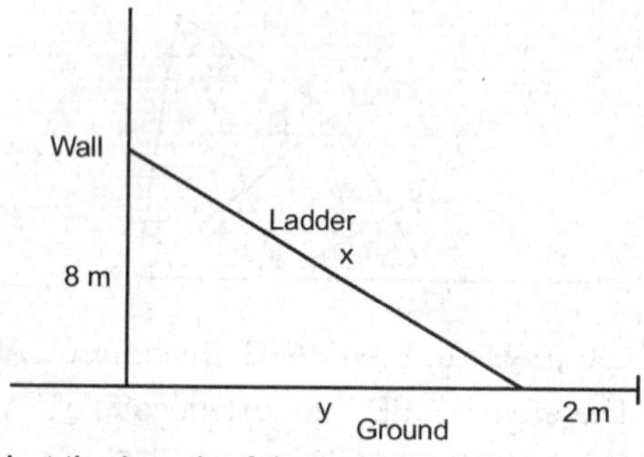

Let the length of the ladder be x meter. We have $8^2 + y^2 = x^2$ and $(y + 2) = x$

Hence, $64 + (x - 2)^2 = x^2$

$\Rightarrow 64 + x^2 - 4x + 4 = x^2$

$\Rightarrow 68 = 4x \quad \Rightarrow \quad x = 17$

22. a

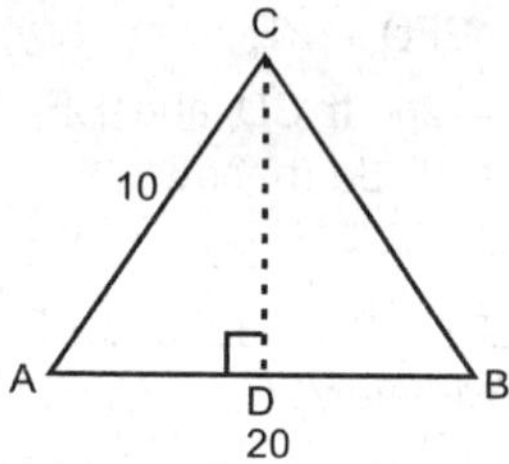

Let's assume AB be the longest side of 20 units and another side AC is 10 units. Here CD ⊥ AB.

Since area of $\Delta ABC = 80 = \frac{1}{2} AB \times CD$

So $CD = \frac{80 \times 2}{20} = 8$.

In ΔACD; $AD = \sqrt{10^2 - 8^2} = 6$

Hence, DB = 20 – 6 = 14.

So $CB = \sqrt{14^2 + 8^2} = \sqrt{196 + 64} = \sqrt{260}$ units.

23. c

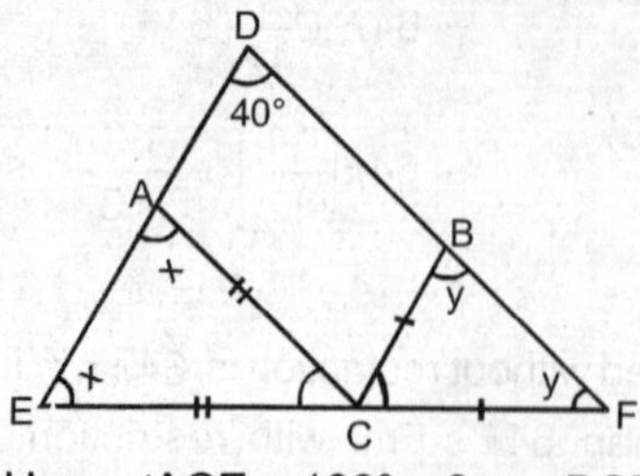

Here ∠ACE = 180° – 2x , ∠BCF = 180° – 2y

and x + y + 40° = 180° (In ΔDEF)

So x + y = 140°

So ∠ACB = 180° – ∠ACE – ∠BCF

= 180° – (180° – 2x) – (180° – 2y)

= 2(x + y) – 180°

= 2 × 140° – 180°

= 100°

24. b

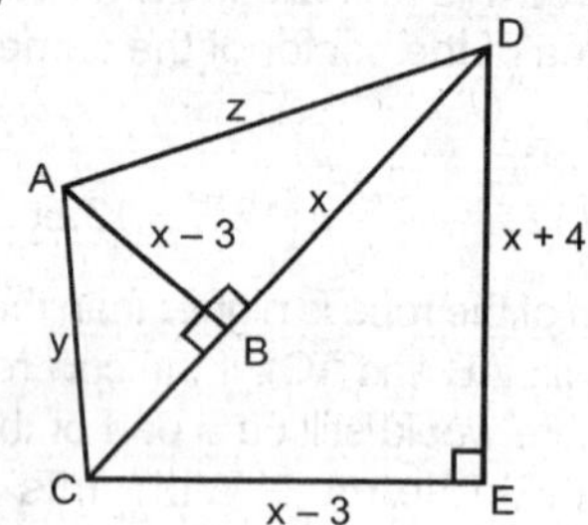

By Pythagoras Theorem,

$$DC = \sqrt{(x+4)^2 + (x-3)^2}$$

Again by Pythagoras Theorem,

$BC^2 + AB^2 = AC^2$

$$\Rightarrow \left(\sqrt{(x+4)^2 + (x-3)^2} - x\right)^2 + (x-3)^2 = 100$$

We can find the value of x, using the answer choices given in the question. Hence, x = 11.

25. b

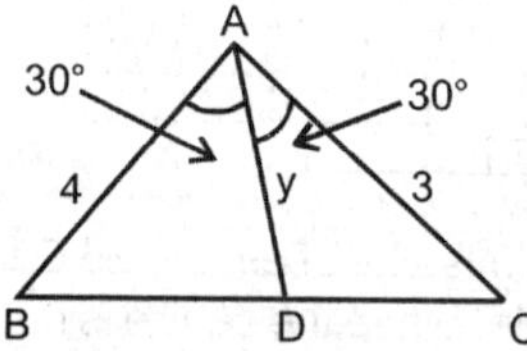

Let BC = x and AD = y.

As per Bisector Theorem, $\frac{BD}{DC} = \frac{AB}{AC} = \frac{4}{3}$

Hence, $BD = \frac{4x}{7}$; $DC = \frac{3x}{7}$

In ΔABD, $\cos 30° = \dfrac{(4)^2 + y^2 - \frac{16x^2}{49}}{2 \times 4 \times y}$

$\Rightarrow\ 2\times4\times y\times\frac{\sqrt{3}}{2}=16+y^2-\frac{16x^2}{49}$

$\Rightarrow\ 4\sqrt{3}y=16+y^2-\frac{16x^2}{49}$ ... (i)

Similarly, from ΔADC, $\cos30^\circ=\dfrac{9+y^2-\frac{9x^2}{49}}{2\times3\times y}$

$\Rightarrow\ 3\sqrt{3}y=9+y^2-\frac{9x^2}{49}$ ... (ii)

Now (i) × 9 – 16 × (ii), we get

$36\sqrt{3}y-48\sqrt{3}y=9y^2-16y^2\ \Rightarrow y=\frac{12\sqrt{3}}{7}$

Alternate solution:

Area of ΔABC = Area of ΔABD + Area of ΔADC

$\Rightarrow \frac{1}{2}\times4\times3\ \sin60^\circ=\frac{1}{2}\times4\times y$

$\sin30^\circ+\frac{1}{2}\times3\times y\times\sin30^\circ$

$\Rightarrow\quad 12\sqrt{3}=4y+3y$

$\Rightarrow\quad y=\frac{12\sqrt{3}}{7}$

26. d

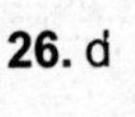

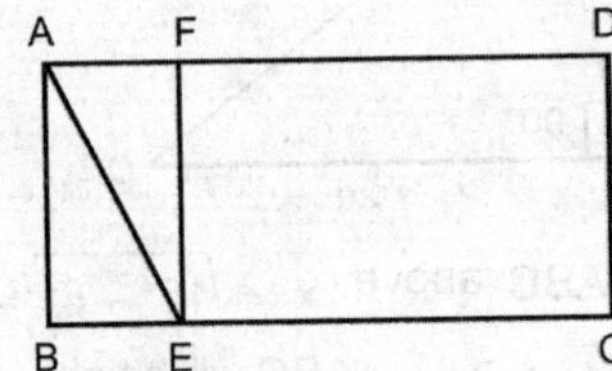

Area of ΔABE = 7 cm²

Area of rectangle ABEF = 14 cm²

$\therefore$ Area of ABCD = 14 × 4 = 56 cm²

27. c PQ || AC

$\therefore \frac{CQ}{QB}=\frac{AP}{PB}=\frac{4}{3}$

QD || PC

$\therefore \frac{PD}{DB}=\frac{CQ}{QB}=\frac{4}{3}$

As $\frac{PD}{DB}=\frac{4}{3}$

$\therefore PD=\frac{4}{7}PB$

$\therefore \frac{AP}{PD}=\frac{AP}{\frac{4}{7}PB}=\frac{7}{4}\times\frac{AP}{PB}=\frac{7}{4}\times\frac{4}{3}=7:3$

28. c

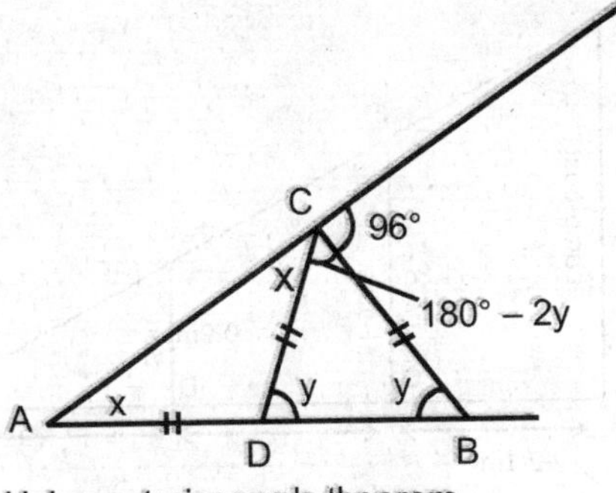

Using exterior angle theorem

$\angle A+\angle B=96^\circ$

i.e. x + y = 96° ... (i)

Also x + (180° – 2y)+ 96° = 180°

$\therefore$ x – 2y + 96° = 0

$\therefore$ x – 2y = –96° ... (ii)

Solving (i) and (ii),

y = 64° and x = 32°

$\therefore \angle DBC=y=64^\circ$

29. d

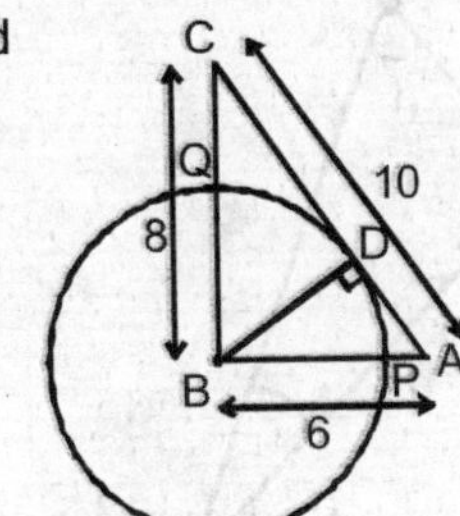

Triangle ABC is a right angled triangle.

Thus $\frac{1}{2}$ × BC × AB = $\frac{1}{2}$ × BD × AC

Or, 6 × 8 = BD × 10. Thus BD = 4.8.

Therefore, BP = BQ = 4.8.

So, AP = AB – BP = 6 – 4.8 = 1.2 and CQ = BC – BQ = 8 – 4.8 = 3.2.

Thus, AP : CQ = 1.2 : 3.2 = 3 : 8

30. b Using the Basic Proportionality Theorem, $\frac{AB}{PQ}=\frac{BD}{QD}$ and $\frac{PQ}{CD}=\frac{BQ}{BD}$.

Multiplying the two we get, $\frac{AB}{CD}=\frac{BQ}{QD}$ = 3 : 1.

Thus CD : PQ = BD : BQ = 4 : 3 = 1 : 0.75

31. b The question tells us that the area of triangle DEF will be $\frac{1}{4}$th the area of triangle ABC. Thus by knowing either of the statements, we get the area of the triangle DEF.

32. d

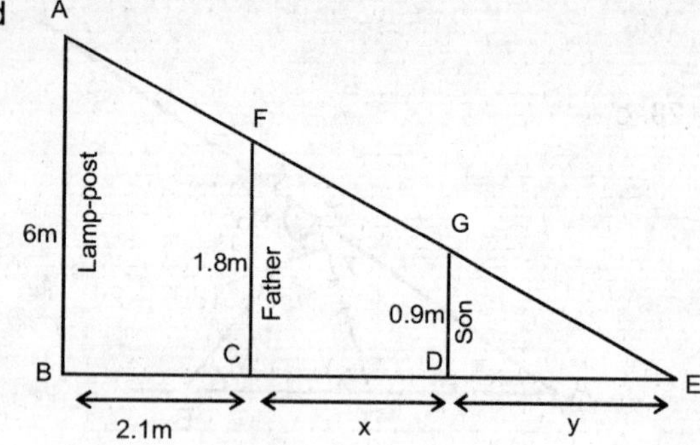

$\Delta ABE \sim \Delta FCE$

$$\therefore \frac{6}{1.8} = \frac{2.1 + x + y}{x + y} \quad ...(i)$$

Also $\Delta ABE \sim \Delta GDE$

$$\therefore \frac{6}{0.9} = \frac{2.1 + x + y}{y} \quad ...(ii)$$

From (i)and (ii), x = 0.45m.

33. a

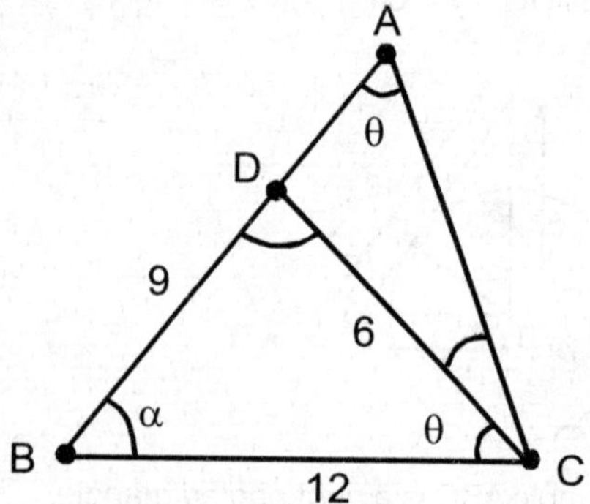

Here $\angle ACB = \theta + [180° - (2\theta + \alpha)] = 180° - (\theta + \alpha)$

So here we can say that triangle BCD and triangle ABC will be similar. $\Delta BCD \sim \Delta BAC$

Hence, from the property of similar triangles

$$\frac{AB}{12} = \frac{12}{9} \Rightarrow AB = 16$$

$$\frac{AC}{6} = \frac{12}{9} \Rightarrow AC = 8$$

$$\therefore \quad AD = 7$$

$$S_{ADC} = 8 + 7 + 6 = 21$$

$$S_{BDC} = 27$$

Hence, $r = \frac{21}{27} = \frac{7}{9}$

34. c The three sides of the obtuse triangle are 8 cm, 15 cm and x cm. As 15 is greater than 8, hence either x or 15 will be the largest side of this triangle. Consider two cases:

Case I:

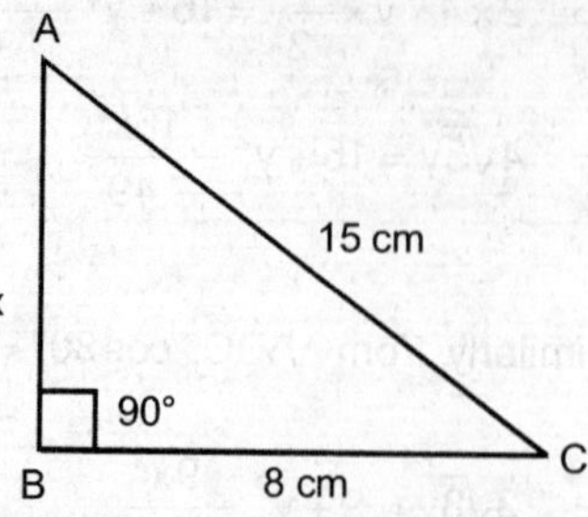

Consider the right ΔABC above,

$$x = \sqrt{15^2 - 8^2} = 12.68 \text{ cm}$$

For all values of x < 12.68, the ΔABC will be obtuse. But as the sum of two sides of triangle must be greater than the third side, hence (x + 8) > 15 or x > 7.

Thus, the permissible values of x are 8, 9, 10, 11 and 12.

Case II:

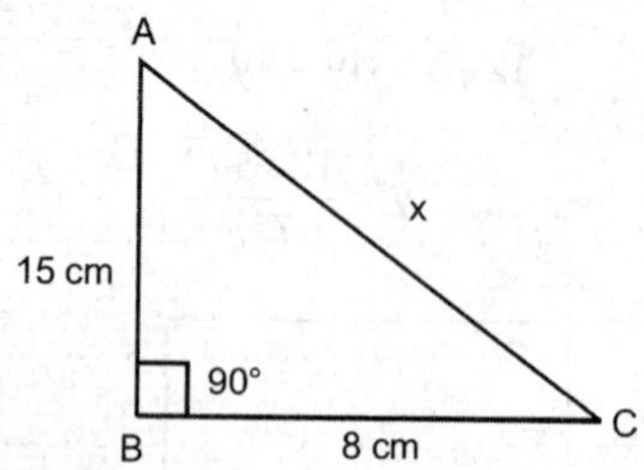

In the right ΔABC above, $x = \sqrt{15^2 + 8^2} = 17$.

For all values of x > 17, ΔABC will be obtuse. But, as the length of third side should be less than the sum of other two sides, hence x < (15 + 8) or x < 23. The permissible values of x are: 18, 19, 20, 21 and 22.

From Case I and II, x can take 10 values.

35. a

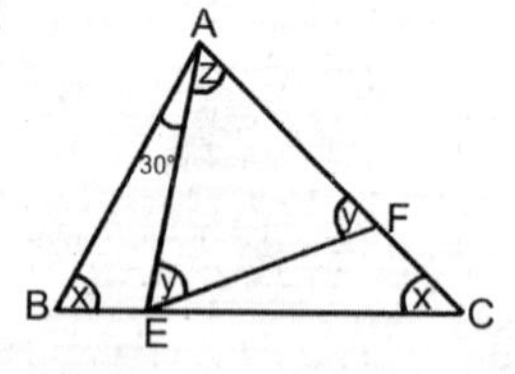

Let $\angle ACB = \angle ABC = x$,

$\angle AEF = \angle AFE = y$,

$\angle EAF = z$.

$$y = \angle FEC + x$$

$$\Rightarrow \quad \angle FEC = y - x$$

Now $\quad 2y = 180° - z \quad ...(i)$

Also $\quad 2x + 30° + z = 180°$

$\Rightarrow \quad 2x = 150° - z \quad ...(ii)$

From (i) and (ii): $2(y - x) = 30°$

$\Rightarrow \quad y - x = 15°$

So $\quad \angle FEC = 15°$

36. c Let the two sides of the rectangle be x and 2x and $\angle AED$ be θ.

$\therefore \angle DEC = \theta$

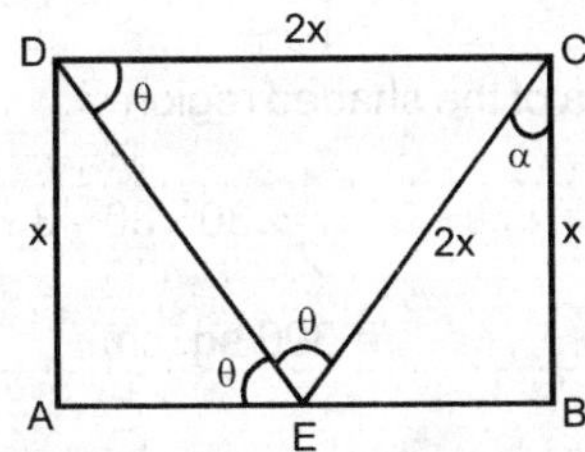

$\therefore \angle CEB = 180 - 2\theta$

Also, $\angle EDC = \angle AED = \theta$ (AB is parallel to CD.)

In ΔDEC,

$\angle DEC = \angle EDC \Rightarrow CD = EC = 2x$

In ΔBCE,

$$\cos\alpha = \frac{x}{2x} \Rightarrow \alpha = 60°$$

Now, in ΔBCE

$2\theta = 90° + 60°$ (Exterior angle is equal to the sum of opposite interior angles.)

$\Rightarrow \theta = 75°$.

37. d Let the length of the other two sides of the triangle be 'a' and 'b' respectively,

$\Rightarrow \quad a^2 + b^2 = 240^2 = 57600$

Also, a + b + 240 must be a perfect square.

Perimeter of a right angled triangle is maximized when the two sides other than its hypotenuse are equal in length.

Therefore, the maximum perimeter of the right angled triangle will be

$$120(\sqrt{2}) + 120(\sqrt{2}) + 240 = 579(\text{approx}).$$

Also, the perimeter of the triangle should be greater than twice of the length of the hypotenuse of the triangle.

Therefore, the perimeter of the triangle should be greater than 480 and less than 579.

Possible squares in the above range are 484, 529 and 576.

But, as per the information given in the question, the perimeter can only be equal to 576.

The values of 'a' and 'b' will be 192 and 144 units not necessarily in that particular order.

Hence, option (d) is the correct choice.

38. c

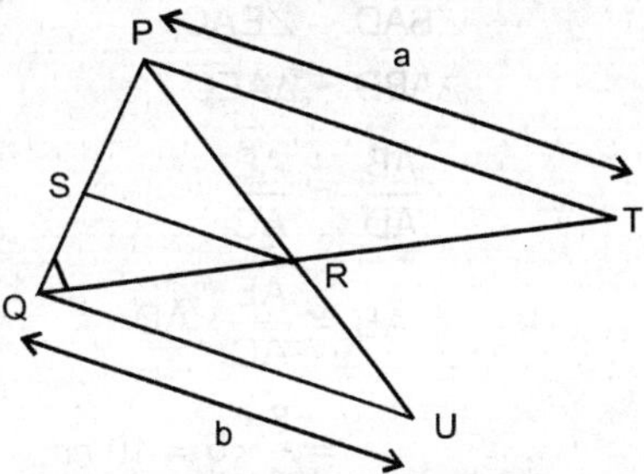

Given that PT || SR || QU

PT = a units, QU = b units.

ΔPTQ and ΔSRQ are similar.

$\therefore$ We have

$$\frac{PQ}{PT} = \frac{SQ}{SR}$$

or $\quad \frac{PQ}{a} = \frac{SQ}{SR} \quad$ ... (i)

ΔUQP and ΔRSP are similar.

$\therefore$ We have $\quad \frac{PQ}{QU} = \frac{PS}{SR}$

or $\quad \frac{PQ}{b} = \frac{PS}{SR} \quad$ ... (ii)

Combining (i) and (ii)

$$\frac{PQ}{a} + \frac{PQ}{b} = \frac{SQ + PS}{SR}$$

or $\quad PQ\left(\frac{1}{a} + \frac{1}{b}\right) = \frac{PQ}{SR}$ [As SQ + PS = PQ]

$$PQ\left[\frac{a+b}{ab}\right] = \frac{PQ}{SR}$$

or $\quad SR = \frac{ab}{a+b}$.

39. d

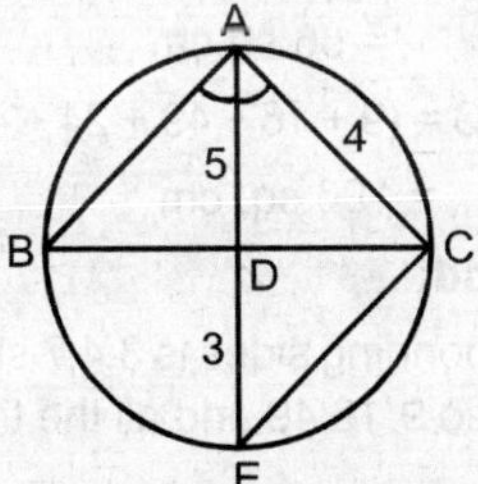

The figure would be as shown above.

Join EC.

Let $\quad \angle BAD = x°$

and $\quad \angle ABD = y°$.

$\Rightarrow \quad \angle DAC = x°$

and $\quad \angle AEC = y°$.

In ΔABD and ΔAEC,

$\angle ABD = \angle AEC$

$\angle BAD = \angle EAC$

$\therefore \quad \Delta ABD \sim \Delta AEC$

$\Rightarrow \quad \dfrac{AB}{AD} = \dfrac{AE}{AC}$

$\Rightarrow \quad AB = \dfrac{AE}{AC} \times AD$

$= \dfrac{8}{4} \times 5 = 10$ cm.

40. 196

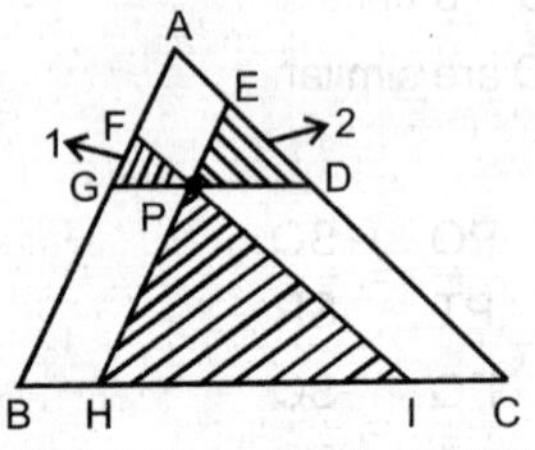

ΔPED is similar to ΔGFP

Ratio of area = 9 : 16

Therefore ratio of sides = $\sqrt{\dfrac{9}{16}} = 3 : 4$

Hence, P divides GD in the ratio 3 : 4.

$\Delta AGD = \left(\dfrac{7}{3}\right)^2 \times 9 = 49$ sq.cm

[ΔAGD similar to ΔFGP]

So area of AEPF = 49 – [16 + 9] = 24 sq. cm

Similarly area of BFI = $\left(\dfrac{10}{3}\right)^2 \times 9 = 100$ sq. cm

Therefore area of BHPG = $100 - (49 + 9) = 42$ sq. cm

Similarly area of PDCI = $\left(\dfrac{11}{7}\right)^2 \times 49 - 49 - 16$

= 56 sq.cm

Area of triangle ABC = (9 + 16 + 49 + 24 + 42 + 56)

= 196 sq. cm

Alternative method:

Ratio of the corresponding sides is 3:4:7 since the areas are in the ratio 9:16:49 and all the triangles are similar.

Hence GP + PD = BH+IC = HI. So HI is half of BC. Since triangle 3 is similar to Triangle ABC and HI is the corresponding Side to BC , and is half of it the area of triangle 3 must be $\dfrac{1}{4}$ the area of triangle ABC. So area of triangle ABC = 196 sq cm.

41. b

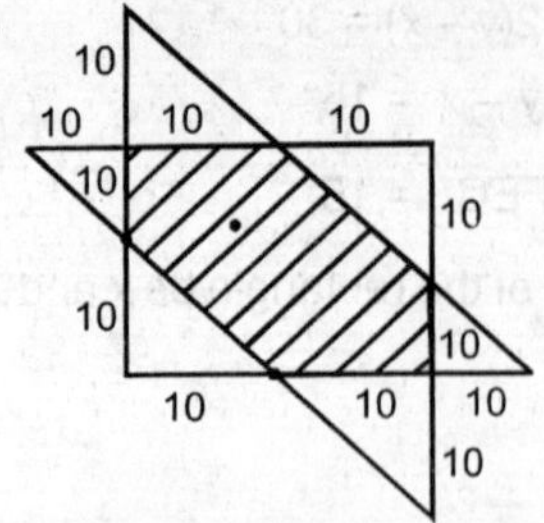

Area of the shaded region

$= \dfrac{1}{2} \times 30 \times 30 - 3 \times \left(\dfrac{1}{2} \times 10 \times 10\right)$

= 300 sq. cm.

42. a

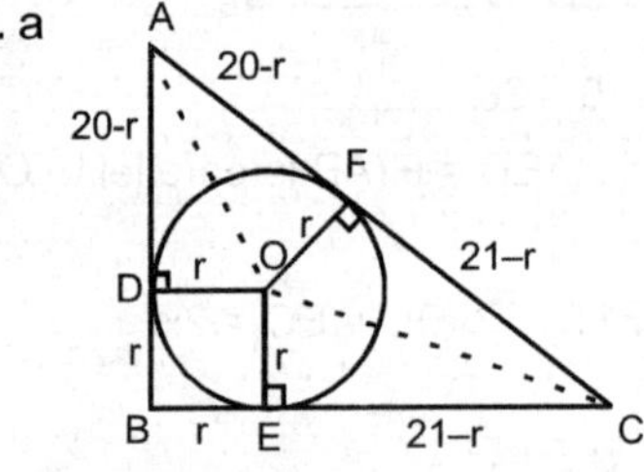

$AC = \sqrt{AB^2 + BC^2} = 29$ cm

and (20 – r) + (21 – r) = 29

or, 2r = 41– 29

⇒ r = 6 cm

$\Delta OEC \cong \Delta OFC$ (RHS)

Area(□FOEC) = 2 × Area (ΔOEC)

$= 2.\dfrac{1}{2}.15.6 = 90\,cm^2$

Similarly, $\Delta AOD \cong \Delta AOF$ (RHS)

Area(□ADOF) = 2 × Area (ΔAOD)

$= 2.\dfrac{1}{2}.14.6 = 84\,cm^2$

$\dfrac{\text{Area(□FOEC)}}{\text{Area(□ADOF)}} = \dfrac{90}{84} = \dfrac{15}{14}$.

43. a

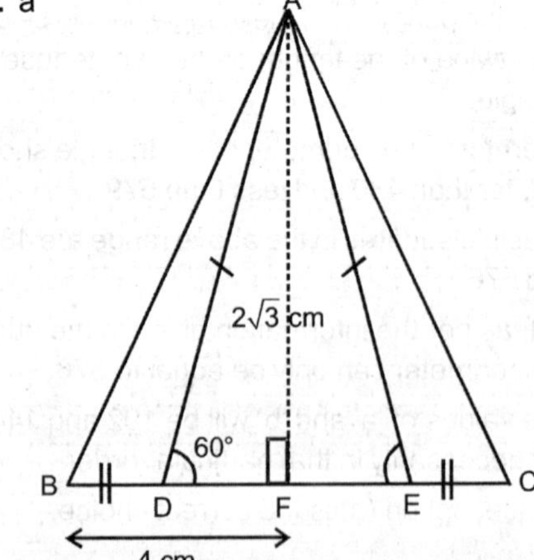

Let's draw AF perpendicular to BC.

In ΔADE, as AD = AE

$\angle AED = \angle ADE = 60°$

$\Rightarrow \angle DAE = 60°$

Hence, we can conclude that ΔADE is an equilateral triangle.

$\Rightarrow \quad AF = \frac{\sqrt{3}}{2} \times 4$

$= 2\sqrt{3}$ cm

and DF = FE = 2 cm

In ΔAFB, using Pythagoras' Theorem,

$AB = \sqrt{AF^2 + BF^2}$

=

$\sqrt{(2\sqrt{3})^2 + 4^2} = 2\sqrt{7}$ cm.

44. b In ΔABC, AB = AC

Let $\angle ABC = \angle ACB = x°$

and $\angle BAC = y°$

$\therefore \quad 2x + y = 180°$

In ΔFDE, $\angle FED = x°$

and $\angle FDE = x - 30°$ $(\because DE \parallel BC)$

$\Rightarrow \quad x + x - 30 + 70 = 180°$

$\therefore \quad x = 70°$

We see that $\angle FED = \angle DFE$

Hence, DFE is an isosceles triangle i.e.

DF = DE = 4 cm.

45. b The triangle formed by joining the mid-points of the sides of an equilateral triangle is itself an equilateral triangle having side length equal to half of that of bigger triangle.

$\therefore$ According to the question,

Sum of the areas of all triangles

$= \frac{\sqrt{3}}{4}\left[(24)^2 + (12)^2 + (6)^2 + (3)^2 + ...\right]$

$= \frac{\sqrt{3}}{4} \times \frac{(24)^2}{1 - \frac{1}{4}}$

$\left(\because \text{Sum of an Infinite G.P.} = \frac{a}{1-r}\right)$

$= 192\sqrt{3}$ sq.cm

46. b Point A will be at the shortest possible distance from the (0, 0) when it will lie at a perpendicular distance of 8 units from BC along the X-axis.

Hence, the coordinate of A will be (–8, 0) and the required distance will be 4 units.

Quadrilaterals

1. a The side of every inner square will be $\frac{1}{\sqrt{2}}$ times the side of the immediate outer square.

Hence, the area of every inner square will be half of the area of the immediate outer square.

The area of the outermost square = 64 sq. cm.

So the area of the 2nd square would be 32 sq.cm., the 3rd square would be 16 sq.cm. and so on.

Hence, the sum of all these areas

$= 64 + 32 + 16 + 8 + 4 + ...$

$= \frac{64}{(1 - \frac{1}{2})} = 128$ sq. cm.

2. c Let length of the smaller square be x.

From statement I, Length of ABCDEQ = $10x \geq 60$

$\Rightarrow \quad x \geq 6$

From statement II, Area of rectangle OPQR $= 42x^2 \leq 1512 \Rightarrow x^2 \leq 36$

$\therefore x \leq 6$

By combining results from statement I and II we have, x = 6

Now, area under the line GHI-JKL can be found out using x.

3. a Let side of square be a.

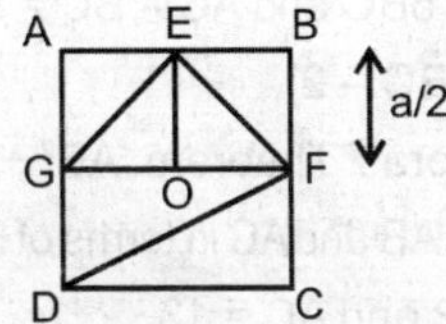

Area quadrilateral EFDG = Area ΔDGF + Area ΔGEF

$= \frac{1}{2} \times \frac{a}{2} \times a + \frac{1}{2} \times a \times \frac{a}{2}$

$= \frac{1}{2}a^2$

$\therefore Ar(EFDG) : Ar(S) = \frac{1}{2}$

4. a

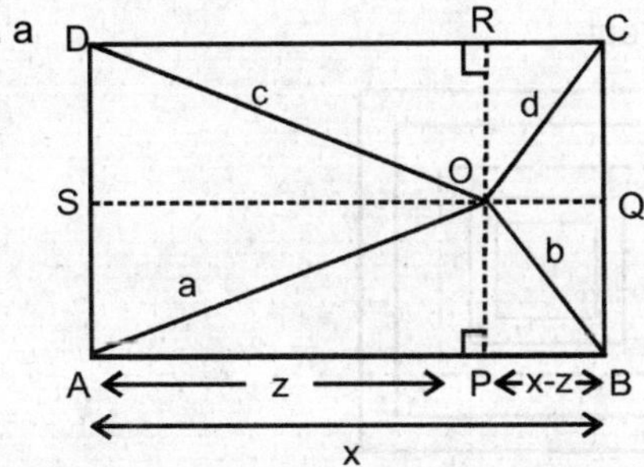

Let x and y be the sides of the rectangle ABCD and z be the length of AP.

Then CR = BP = x – z

By applying Pythagoras Theorem, we have

in ΔAPO, $a^2 = OP^2 + z^2$ ... (i)

in ΔBPO, $b^2 = OP^2 + (x - z)^2$ ... (ii)

in ΔCRO, $d^2 = OR^2 + (x - z)^2$ ... (iii)

in ΔDRO, $c^2 = OR^2 + z^2$ ... (iv)

Solving above equation, we have $a^2 + d^2 = b^2 + c^2$

$\therefore$ For any point inside a rectangle as shown,

$$a^2 + d^2 = b^2 + c^2$$

$\therefore$ Pairing up the distance so that d is to be the maximum, we get $40^2 + d^2 = 50^2 + 60^2$

$\Rightarrow$ d = 67 m.

5. b Since base of each triangle will be counted once,

Sum of perimeters of the triangles = Perimeter of the square + 2 × (Sum of its diagonals).

But each of the other two sides of the triangles is common to two triangles, so it will be counted twice.

Area of the square = 4, therefore length of its side = 2 and perimeter = 8.

Also its diagonal = $2\sqrt{2}$.

So the required perimeter = $(8 + 2 \times 4\sqrt{2}) = 8(1 + \sqrt{2})$.

6. c Since AD = BC (Opposite sides of a rectangle are equal.)

AB + AC = 5BC and AC – BC = 8 or AC = BC + 8

$\therefore$ AB = 4(BC – 2)

By Pythagoras' Theorem, $AB^2 + BC^2 = AC^2$

Expressing AB and AC in terms of BC we get, BC = 5.

$\therefore$ AB = 12 and AC = 13

So area of the rectangle = 5 × 12 = 60.

7. c This can be solved using both the statements together.

From statement I, we know that L × B = 48 or $B = \frac{L}{48}$.

From statement II, we know $L^2 + B^2 = 100$

Combining statements I and II, $L^2 + \left(\frac{L}{48}\right)^2 = 100$.

L is the only unknown in this equation and can be found out.

8. b

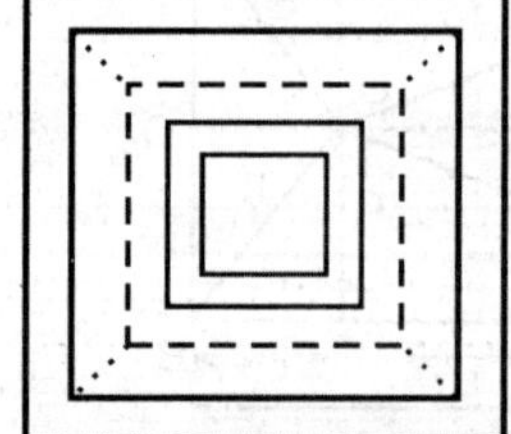

The diagonal of the innermost square is 2 units. The diagonal of every successive square would increase by 2 units (since corners are one unit apart). So the diagonal of the 7th square = 14 units and that of the 8th square = 16 units. Area of the 7th square $= \frac{1}{2}(14)^2$ and that of 8th square $= \frac{1}{2}(16)^2$, i.e. 98 and 128 respectively. Hence, the difference in their areas = 128 – 98 = 30 sq.units.

9. d Let L and B denote the length and the breadth of the rectangle. So the diagonal will be $\sqrt{(L^2 + B^2)}$.

Hence, from the condition given,

$$(L + B) - \sqrt{(L^2 + B^2)} = \frac{1}{2}L$$

$$\Rightarrow \sqrt{(L^2 + B^2)} = \frac{L}{2} + B$$

Squaring both sides, we get

$$(L^2 + B^2) = \left(\frac{L}{2} + B\right)^2$$

$$\Rightarrow L^2 = \frac{L^2}{4} + LB$$

$$\Rightarrow \frac{3L^2}{4} = LB$$

$$\Rightarrow \frac{B}{L} = \frac{3}{4}$$

Shortcut:

First write the relation $(L + B) - \sqrt{(L^2 + B^2)} = \frac{1}{2}L$.

or $\frac{L}{2} + B = \sqrt{L^2 + B^2}$

Putting the values of options. Option (d) satisfies. So the answer is (d).

10. b

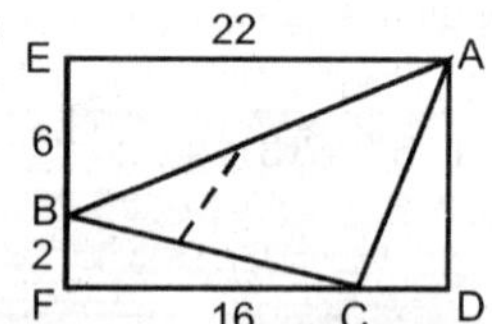

We know that length of the line joining the mid-points of two sides of a triangle is half the length of third side. Hence, the required length is half the length of side AC. Since EADF is rectangle, EF = AD = 8.

CD = (22 – 16) = 6.

So in the right-angled ΔADC, AD = 8 and CD = 6. Therefore, AC = 10. Hence, length of the line joining the mid-points of AB and BC = $\frac{1}{2}(10) = 5$.

For questions 11 and 12:

P 10 cm Q 5 cm R

A, B, F C,D, E

U T S

11. *a The sides of the rectangle PRSU are PR = 15 cm and RS = 10 cm.

$\therefore$ Its diagonal $= \sqrt{15^2 + 10^2} = \sqrt{325} \approx 18$ cm.

Given that the minimum distance between any pair of points formed by taking one from A, B and F and the other from C, D and E is $10\sqrt{3} = \sqrt{300} \approx 17$ cm, which is close to the length of the diagonal of PRSU. This implies that each of A, B and F are close to one of the vertices P or U and each of C, D and E are close to one of the vertices S or R.

Note that all the three points in one of the rectangles PQTU and QRST will be close to the same vertex (or else the minimum distance between one of these points and one of the three in the other rectangle will be less than $10\sqrt{3}$ cm). Also, the points (A, B, F) and (C, D, E) have to be diagonally opposite as maximum distance between two vertices on same side is 15 cm.

Option (a): The closest two points of the given six points have to be any two out of A, B, F or any two out of C, D, E (since they are closest to the same vertex). Therefore, (F, C)cannot be the closest pair of points as they are diagonally opposite.

Option (b): It is definitely false as A and B are close to the same vertex, while F and C are close to diagonally opposite vertices.

Option (c): It is possible but not necessary that the closest pair of points among the six given points is (C,D), (D, E)or (C, E). The other possibilities are (A, B), (B, F) or (A, F).

12. *d The maximum possible distance between the pairs (C, D), (D, E) or (C, E)is the length of the diagonal of the rectangle QRST, i.e. $\sqrt{10^2 + 5^2} = 5\sqrt{5}$ cm.

Since AB > AF > BF = $6\sqrt{5}$ cm, the closest pair of points of the given six points will be from the set (C, D, E).

As CD > DE > CE, so (C, E) will be the pair of closest points.

*__Note:__ There is slight inconsistency regarding the information given in the question. If BF = $6\sqrt{5} \approx 13.4$ cm, then A, B and F cannot be close to the same vertex as the length of the diagonal of rectangle PQTU is 14 cm approximately. This in turn will contradict the fact the minimum distance between any point of A, B, F and the other from C, D, E is $10\sqrt{3}$ cm.

A likely possibility is that the information regarding minimum distance between any point of (A, B, F) and the other from (C, D, E) is specific to question no. 11 only.

13. b

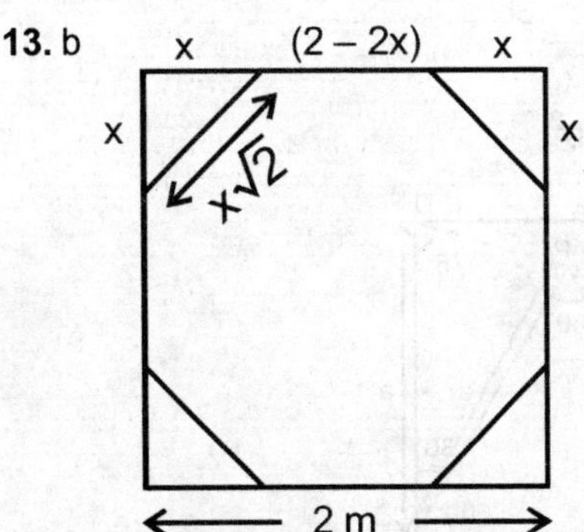

Let the length of the edge cut at each corner be x m. Since the resulting figure is a regular octagon,

$\therefore \sqrt{x^2 + x^2} = 2 - 2x \Rightarrow x\sqrt{2} = 2 - 2x$

$\Rightarrow \sqrt{2}\,x\,(1 + \sqrt{2}) = 2 \Rightarrow x = \dfrac{\sqrt{2}}{\sqrt{2}+1}$

$\therefore 2 - 2x = \dfrac{2}{\sqrt{2}+1}$.

14. d Check choices, E.g. $\frac{1}{2} \Rightarrow$ Diagonal = $\sqrt{5}$

Distance saved = $3 - \sqrt{5} \approx 0.75 \neq$ Half the larger side. Hence, incorrect.

$\frac{3}{4} \Rightarrow$ Diagonal = 5

Distance saved = (4 + 3)– 5 = 2 = Half the larger side.

15. d If KL = 1, then IG = 1 and FI = 2

Hence, $\tan\theta = \frac{2}{1} = 2$

Thus, θ none of 30°, 45° and 60°.

16. c Area of quadrilateral ABCD $= \frac{1}{2}(2x + 4x) \times 4x = 12x$

Area of quadrilateral DEFG $= \frac{1}{2}(5x + 2x) \times 2x = 7x$

Hence, ratio = 12 : 7

17. b

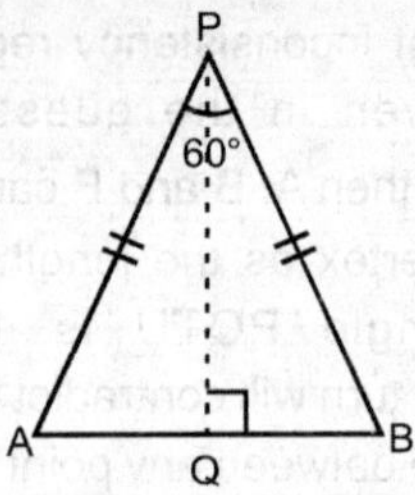

Given $\angle APB = 60°$ and AB = b.

$\therefore \ PQ = \frac{b}{2} \times \sqrt{3}$

Next, $\frac{b}{2}$, h and PQ form a right angle triangle.

$\therefore \ \frac{b^2}{4} + h^2 = \frac{3b^2}{4}$

$\Rightarrow \ 2h^2 = b^2$

18. e

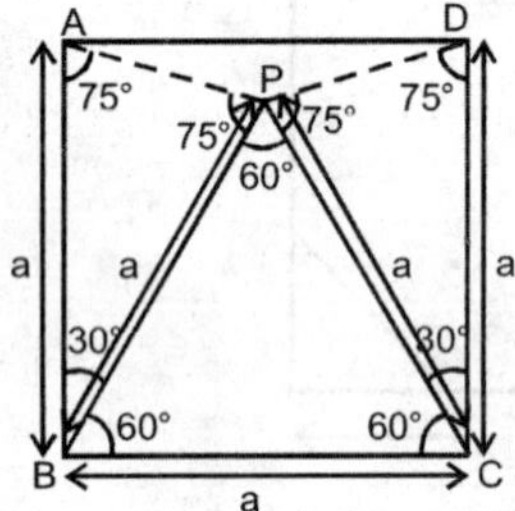

$\angle PBC = \angle CPB = \angle BPC = 60°$

(L's of equilateral triangle)

PC = CD = a

Also, $\angle CPD = \angle PDC = \frac{180° - 30°}{2} = 75°$

Similarly, $\angle BAP = \angle BPA = 75°$

$\angle APD = 360° - 75° - 75° - 60° = 150°$

19. a **Using A:** $\frac{OM}{OL} = \frac{2}{1}$

But if O lies on JK, maximum possible value of $\frac{OM}{OL}$ is $\frac{\sqrt{2}}{1}$ (when O lies on K)

So, Rahim is unable to draw such a square

Using B: Nothing specific can be said about the dimensions of the figure.

Hence, option (a)is the correct choice.

20. a

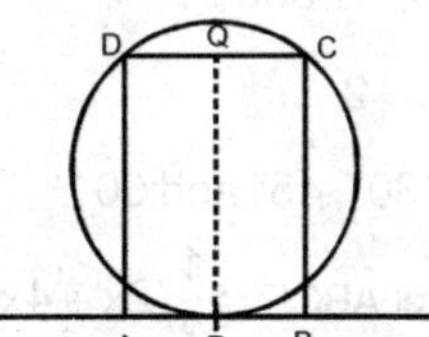

AP must be equal to PB.

Let's assume that the line segment PQ divides the rectangle ABCD into two equal parts (see the figure).

Let AB = 2a; hence, BC = 4a (all lengths in cm).

$$CP = \sqrt{(4a)^2 + a^2} = \sqrt{17}a = DP$$

Area of $\Delta CDP = \frac{1}{2} PQ.CD = 4a^2$

Radius of the circle = Circumradius of ΔCDP

$$= \frac{CD \times CP \times DP}{4(\text{Area of } \Delta CDP)} = \frac{17}{8}a = 1.$$

Hence, $a = \frac{8}{17}$ cm

Area of rectangle ABCD = 2a × 4a = $8a^2$

= 1.77 cm^2 approximately.

21. c

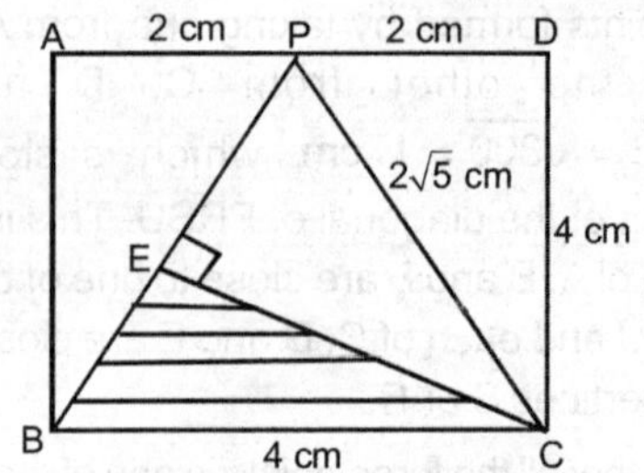

In right triangle PDC, using Pythagoras theorem,

$PD^2 + DC^2 = PC^2$

$\Rightarrow PC = 2\sqrt{5}$ cm ...(i)

Area $\Delta PBC = \frac{1}{2}$ area sq. ABCD ...(ii)

$= \frac{4 \times 4}{2} = 8\,cm^2$

Also, area $\Delta PBC = \frac{1}{2} \times CE \times PB$

From equations (i) and (ii), we get

$$\frac{1}{2} \times CE \times 2\sqrt{5} = 8 \ \text{ or } \ CE = \frac{8}{\sqrt{5}}$$

In right triangle CEB, by Pythagoras theorem,

$BE^2 + CE^2 = BC^2$

$\Rightarrow BE = \frac{4}{\sqrt{5}}$ cm

Required area $= \frac{1}{2} \times CE \times BE = 3.2\ cm^2$

22. c

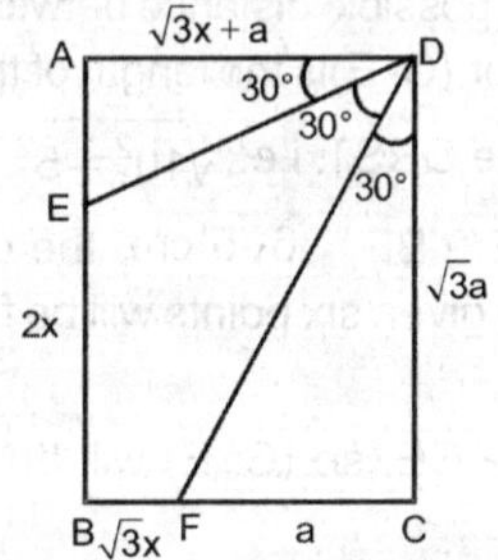

Let the length of EB be 2x units.

Therefore, the length of BF = $\sqrt{3}x$ units.
Let the length of FC be a units.

Therefore, the length of DC = $\sqrt{3}a$ units.
(Since triangle DFC is 30°- 60°- 90° triangle.)

In triangle AED,

$\therefore \quad \sqrt{3}(\sqrt{3}a - 2x) = \sqrt{3}x + a$

$\Rightarrow \quad \frac{\sqrt{3}x}{a} = \frac{2}{3}$

Required ratio = 2 : 3.

23. d Let the lengths and breadths of each of the small rectangles be 'b' m and 'a' m respectively.

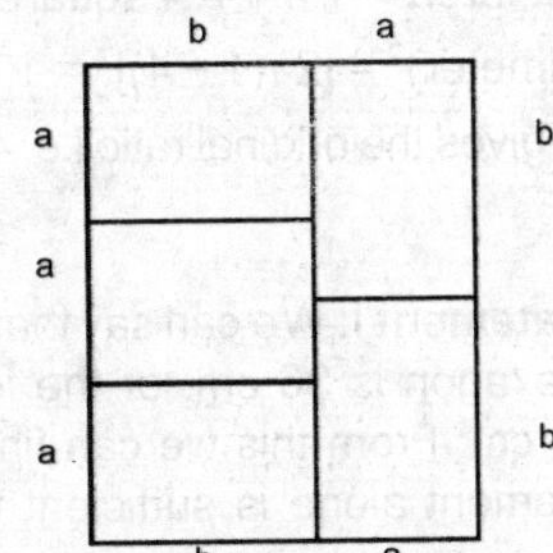

$\therefore$ 5a + 4b = 88 and 3a = 2b

$\Rightarrow$ a = 8 and b = 12

Perimeter of each small rectangle = 2(a + b) = 40

24. a

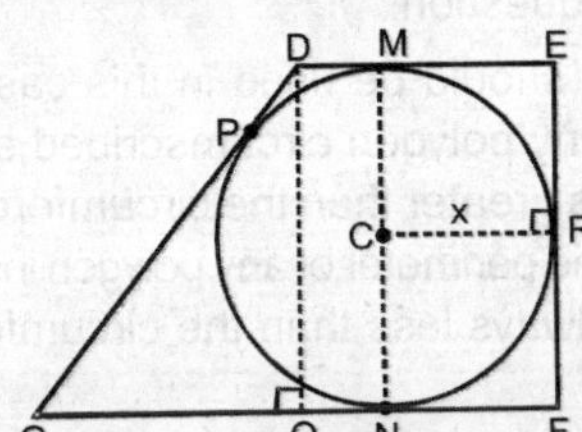

Let, the radius of circle be 'x' cm.

$\therefore$ CM = CN = CR = x

Given that GN = 4 cm

$\therefore$ GP = 4 cm

Also, DP = DM = QN = 1 cm

$\therefore$ GD = 5 cm

GQ = GM – QN = 4 – 1 = 3 cm

In $\Delta DGQ : DQ = \sqrt{GD^2 - GQ^2} = 4$ cm

$\Rightarrow$ 2x = 4 cm ($\because$ DQ = MN)

$\therefore$ x = 2 cm.

25. c Let the lengths of the sides of the rectangle be a units and b units.

By the problem,

ab = 2a + 2b

a = 2b / (b – 2)

Two cases are possible-

(i) a = 4, b = 4

(ii) a = 3 and b = 6

Thus, two different rectangles are possible.

26. b Option (a): This statement is always true.

Option (b): This statement is necessarily false as the smallest possible integral length of EF is 4 units.

Option (c): This statement is true when EF is parallel to BC.

Option (d): This statement is always true.

27. d

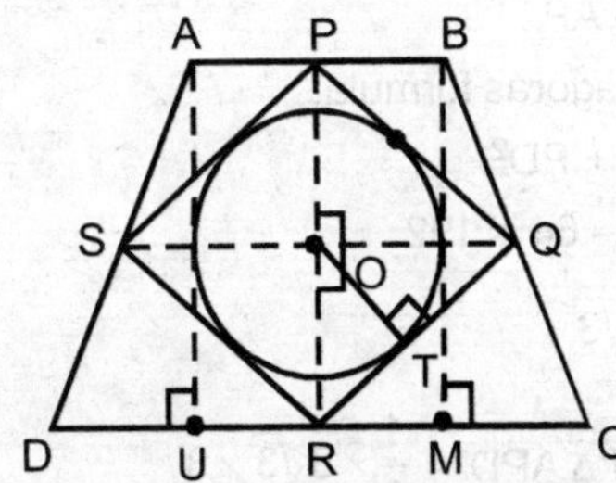

PQRS is a rhombus, so the centre of the inscribed circle will be the center of the rhombus PQRS

$SQ = \frac{1}{2}(AB + CD) = \frac{1}{2}(2 + 14) = 8$ units

$OR = \frac{1}{2}PR$

$DU = \frac{1}{2}(CD - MU) = \frac{1}{2}(14 - AB) = 6$ units

$PR = AU = \sqrt{AD^2 - DU^2} = \sqrt{10^2 - 6^2} = 8$ units

PR = SQ = 8

$\Rightarrow$ PQRS is a square.

$\Rightarrow OT = 2\sqrt{2}$ units

Area of trapezium $= \frac{1}{2}(AB + CD) \times PR$

= 64 sq. unit

Required ratio $= \frac{\pi OT^2}{64} = \frac{\pi \times 8}{64} = \frac{\pi}{8}$.

28. 90

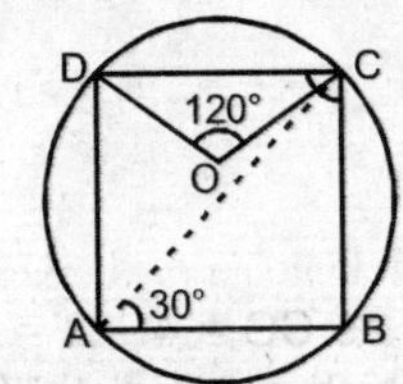

$\angle DOC = 120°$

So, $\angle DAC = 60°$

$\Rightarrow \angle DAB = 90°$

[Angle made at the circumference is half of the angle made at the centre]

As ABCD is a cyclic quadrilateral

So ∠DAB + ∠BCD = 180°

⇒ ∠BCD = 90°.

29. a

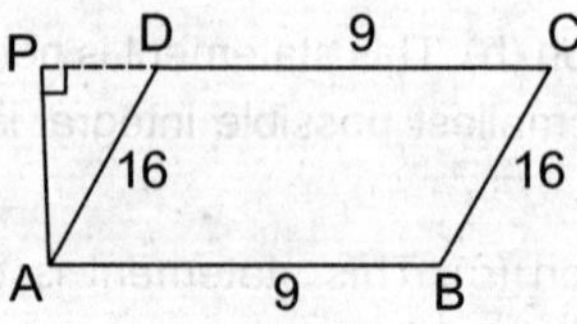

Area of parallelogram ABCD = Base × Height

72 = 9 × h

h = 8 cm = AP

Using Pythagoras formula,

$AD^2 = AP^2 + PD^2$.

$PD^2 = 256 - 64 = 192$

$\Rightarrow PD = 8\sqrt{3}$

$\therefore$ Area of Δ APD $= \frac{1}{2} \times 8\sqrt{3} \times 8$

$= 32\sqrt{3}$ sq. cm

30. a

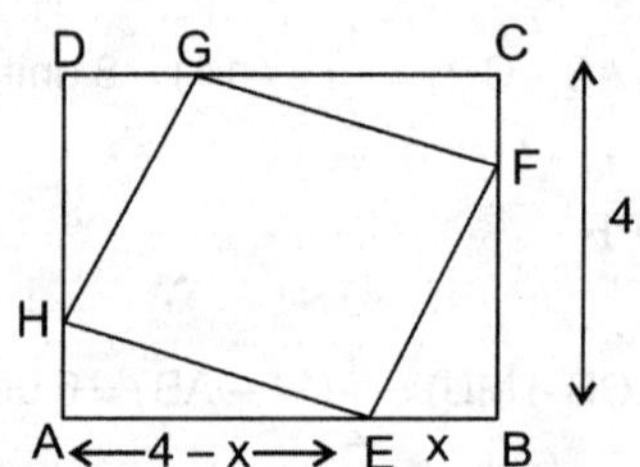

Let the side of the square ABCD be 4 units and EB = x

⇒ AE = 4 – x = CG

Area (EFGH) = 62.5% of Area (ABCD)

Area of EFGH = $(EF)^2$

$(EF)^2 = x^2 + (4 - x)^2$

$\therefore\ x^2 + (4 - x)^2 = \frac{5}{8} \times (4)^2$

$x^2 + 16 + x^2 - 8x = \frac{5}{8} \times 16$

$2x^2 - 8x + 6 = 0$

$x^2 - 4x + 3 = 0$

On solving it, we get,

x = 1, x = 3.

x = 3 is not possible as CG = 4 – 3 = 1, which implies CG < EB, which contradicts the given condition.

$\therefore \frac{EG}{CG} = \frac{x}{4-x} = \frac{1}{3} = 1:3$

31. d Given that : $\frac{\pi r^2}{2} = 72\pi$

⇒ r = 12 cm, AB = 24 cm and BC = 32 cm

Hence, perimeter of the leftover portion

= 32 × 2 + 24 × 1 + π × 12 = 88 + 12π.

32. c Given that AB = CD = 8 cm

⇒ Area of parallelogram = AB × AD sin ∠DAB

⇒ 8 × s × sin ∠DAB = 48

The maximum value of sin ∠DAB will be 1 at 90°

Thus, the minimum value of 's' will be 6 cm

Hence, correct answer will be S ≥ 6.

33. d Checking the options we get the required ratio as 1 : 4

Such that, area = 1 × 4 = 4 square units

and $(\text{perimeter})^2 = [2\times(1 + 4)]^2 = 100$

Hence, it gives the original ratio i.e. 4 : 100 = 1 : 25.

Polygons

1. a **From statement I:** We can say that the perimeter of the hexagon is 36 cm, or the length of each side is 6 cm. From this we can find its area. So this statement alone is sufficient to answer the question.

From statement II: It does not provide any other data, but merely states the property of a regular hexagon. So, this statement alone is not sufficient to answer the question.

2. c Following rule should be used in this case: The perimeter of any polygon circumscribed about a circle is always greater than the circumference of the circle and the perimeter of any polygon inscribed in a circle is always less than the circumference of the circle.

Since the circles is of radius 1, its circumference will be 2π. Hence, L1(13)> 2π and L2(17) < 2π. So {L1(13) + 2π } > 4π.

Hence, $\frac{\{L1(13) + 2\pi\}}{L2(17)}$ will be greater than 2.

3. c Statement I by itself does not solve the problem but it does tell us about the shape of the field. However, it fails to give information about the points A, B and C as to whether they be at the end of the field, etc. This data is given by the second statement, from which it is known that

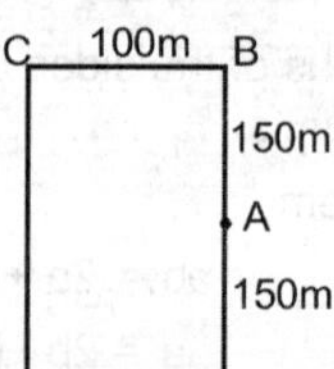

The polygon has the length = 150 × 2 = 300 m and the breadth = 100 m and also that it is a rectangle (from A). Thus, the maximum distance is the diagonal length of the rectangle.

4. b

$\because$ ΔACE is equilateral triangle with side $\sqrt{3}$ a.

Area of hexagon $= \frac{\sqrt{3}}{4} a^2 \times 6$

Area as $\Delta ACE = \frac{\sqrt{3}}{4}(\sqrt{3}a)^2$

Therefore, ratio $= \frac{1}{2}$

5. c In this kind of polygon, the number of convex angles will always be exactly 4 more than the number of concave angles.

NOTE : The number of vertices have to be even. Hence, the number of concave and convex corners should add up to an even number. This is true only for the answer choice (c).

6. a It is very clear, that a regular hexagon can be divided into six equilateral triangles. And triangle AOF is half of an equilateral triangle.

Hence, the required ratio = 1 : 12.

7. c

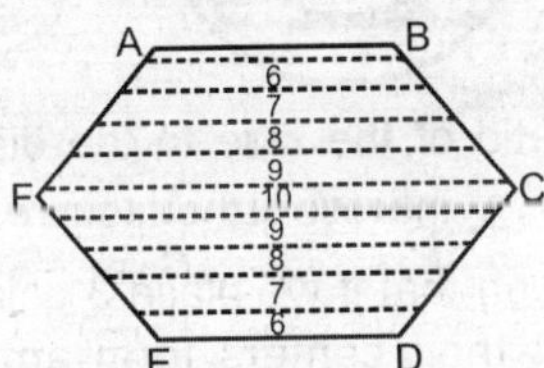

Since AB is 5 cm, CF would be 10 cm.

And the four equidistant lines drawn between them have to be of 6 cm, 7 cm, 8 cm and 9 cm long.

So the total length = 2(6 + 7 + 8 + 9) + 10 = 70 cm

8. b

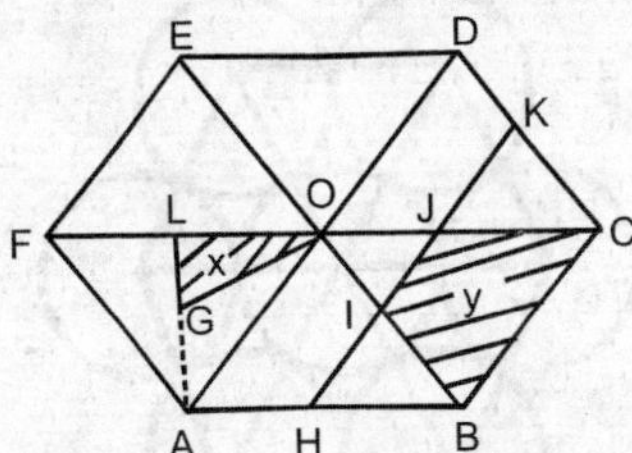

Let the length of the side of the hexagon be a units.

$\therefore$ ΔAFO and ΔBCO are equilateral triangles with the length of their side equal to a units and area (in sq. units) of each being $\frac{\sqrt{3}}{4}a^2$.

In ΔAFO, as G is the centroid and L is mid point of OF, AL is the median to the side OF.

Also, $AL = \frac{\sqrt{3}}{2}a$ units and $GL = \frac{\sqrt{3}}{6}a$ units

(Centroid divides medians in the ratio 2:1)

$$\text{Area of } \Delta GOL = \frac{1}{2} \times LG \times LO$$

$$= \frac{1}{2} \times \frac{\sqrt{3}}{6}a \times \frac{a}{2}$$

$$= \frac{\sqrt{3}}{24}a^2 \text{ sq. units} \qquad \text{...(i)}$$

As H and K are the mid points of AB and CD respectively, HK is parallel to AD. Thus, HI is parallel to AO and OD is parallel to JK. Hence, I is the mid point of OB and J is the mid point of OC.

$$\therefore \Delta OIJ \sim \Delta OBC \quad \frac{\text{Area } \Delta OIJ}{\text{Area } \Delta OBC} = \frac{IJ^2}{BC^2} = \frac{1}{4}$$

Area of quadrilateral BCJI

$$= \frac{3}{4}\text{area } \Delta OBC = \frac{\sqrt{3}}{4}a^2 \times \frac{3}{4} \text{ sq. units.} \qquad \text{...(ii)}$$

From (i) and (ii), required ratio = 2:9.

Alternate Method:

ΔAOF and ΔOBC are equilateral triangles with equal area (as length of the sides is the same for the two).

$$\text{Area } \Delta GOL = \frac{1}{2}\text{Area } \Delta FOG$$

$$= \frac{1}{2}\left(\frac{1}{3}\text{Area } \Delta AOF\right)$$

$$= \frac{1}{6}\text{Area } \Delta AOF \qquad \text{...(i)}$$

Area of quadrilateral

$$IJCB = \frac{3}{4}\text{Area } \Delta OBC. \qquad \text{...(ii)}$$

From (i) and (ii), required ratio = 2:9.

9. d

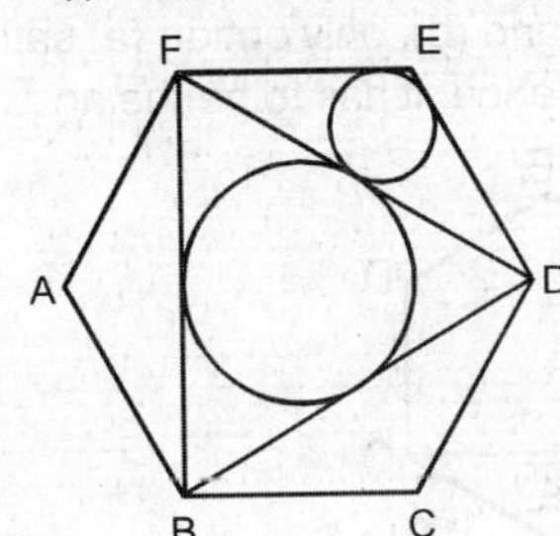

Let EF= s unit

In triangle DEF:

$$DF = 2EF\cos 30^0 = \sqrt{3}s$$

Semi perimeter of triangle DEF (in units) = S

$$= \left(1+\frac{\sqrt{3}}{2}\right)s.$$

Area of triangle DEF (in unit^2) = Δ

$$= \frac{1}{2}(EF\sin 30^0)DF = \frac{\sqrt{3}s^2}{4}.$$

Inradius of triangle DEF (in units) = r_1

$$= \frac{\Delta}{S} = \frac{\sqrt{3}s^2}{4\left(1+\frac{\sqrt{3}}{2}\right)s} = \frac{\sqrt{3}s}{4\left(1+\frac{\sqrt{3}}{2}\right)} = \frac{\sqrt{3}s}{2\left(2+\sqrt{3}\right)}$$

Inradius of triangle DEF (in units) = r_2

$$= \frac{1}{3}\left(\frac{\sqrt{3}}{2}DF\right) = \frac{DF}{2\sqrt{3}} = \frac{s}{2}.$$

Ratio of area = $r_1^2 : r_2^2 = 3 : 7 + 4\sqrt{3}$

10. a Interior angle of an n–sided regular polygon

$$= \frac{(n-2)\pi}{n} = \theta$$

$$\Rightarrow \quad n = \frac{2\pi}{\pi-\theta}$$

The number of diagonals in an n–sided polygon

$$= {}^nC_2 - n = kn$$

$$\Rightarrow \quad \frac{n(n-3)}{2} = kn$$

$$\Rightarrow \quad k = \frac{n-3}{2}$$

Hence, $\quad k = \dfrac{\left(\frac{2\pi}{\pi-\theta}\right)-3}{2} = \dfrac{3\theta-\pi}{2(\pi-\theta)}.$

Alternate solution:

If the polygon is an equilateral triangle, then, k = 0 and $\theta = 60°$. Only options (a) and (b) satisfy these conditions.

If the polygon is a square, then, $k = \frac{1}{2}$ and $\theta = 90°$.

Between (a) and (b), only option (a) satisfies these conditions. Hence, it has to be the answer.

11. b

$$\cos 120^o = \frac{1^2 + 1^2 - AC^2}{2 \times 1 \times 1}$$

$$-\frac{1}{2} = \frac{2 - AC^2}{2}$$

$$AC^2 = 2 + 1 = 3$$

$$AC = \sqrt{3}\text{ cm}$$

Area of square = AC^2 = 3 cm.

Circle

1. d Let the radius of the circle be r.

From statement I, $\dfrac{\pi r^2}{2\pi r} > 7$

$\Rightarrow r > 14$ ...(i)

From statement II, $2r \le 32$

$\Rightarrow r \le 16$ ...(ii)

Combining (i)and (ii), $14 < r \le 16$

So r can be 15 or 16.

2. d As it is apparent from the following diagram, the diameter of the inscribed circle is equal to the side of the square, while the diameter of the circumscribed square is equal to the diagonal of the square. Since the ratio of any two circles is equal to the ratio of the squares of their diameters, in this case the required ratio is equal to (side)^2 : (diagonal)^2.

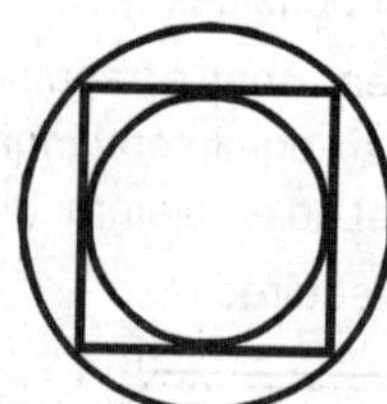

Now, the ratio of the side to the diagonal of a square = $1 : \sqrt{2}$, the ratio of their squares will be $1 : 2$.

3. b It can be seen that if we place 3 coins touching each other, their centers form an equilateral triangle. Hence, the angle made by the centers of the coins around the central coin is 60°. Since the total angle to be covered is 360°, there has to be 6 coins surrounding the central coin.

4. c

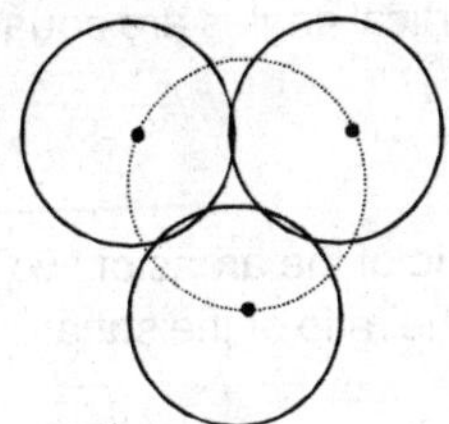

It can be seen that, if we place the 3 cones in such a way that they touch each other, it will be similar to placing 3 circles touching, with vertices of the cone corresponding to the centers of the circles. The centers of the circle form an equilateral triangle with each side being 2r. A circle that passes through the centers will be the circumcircle to such a triangle. The radius of the circumcircle of an equilateral triangle is $\left(\frac{1}{\sqrt{3}}\right)$ times its side.

Hence, in our case it would be $\left(\frac{2r}{\sqrt{3}}\right)$ and $\left(\frac{2r}{\sqrt{3}}\right) > r$, since $\sqrt{3} = 1.73$ (approx.).

5. a

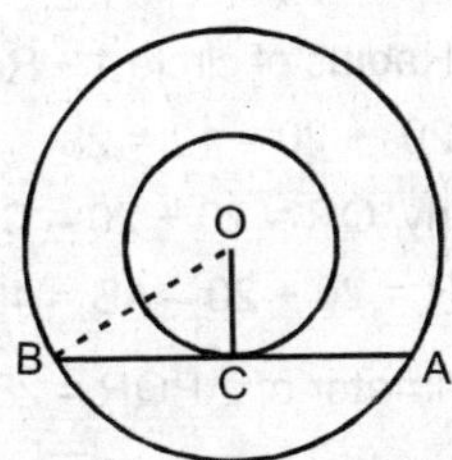

Let x meters and y meters be the radius of the outer and the inner circles respectively and O be their center.

In right angled Δ OCB,

$CB^2 = OB^2 - OC^2$

$\Rightarrow \quad 9 = x^2 - y^2$

$\Rightarrow \quad (x + y)(x - y) = 9 \times 1$

As x and y are integers, therefore, x + y = 9 and x – y = 1.

Thus, x = 5.

Hence, radius of the outer circle is 5 meters.

6. a In the given figure, the area of the circle = πr^2.

To find out the area of the circle, we need to find out the length of the side of the square.

We know, OR = OT + TR = OT + OS = 2r.

In right-angled triangle ORS, OR = 2r and OS = r.

So $SR^2 = OR^2 - OS^2$.

But SR^2 = Area of the square = $4r^2 - r^2 = 3r^2$.

Hence, the required ratio = $\frac{\pi}{3}$.

7. a

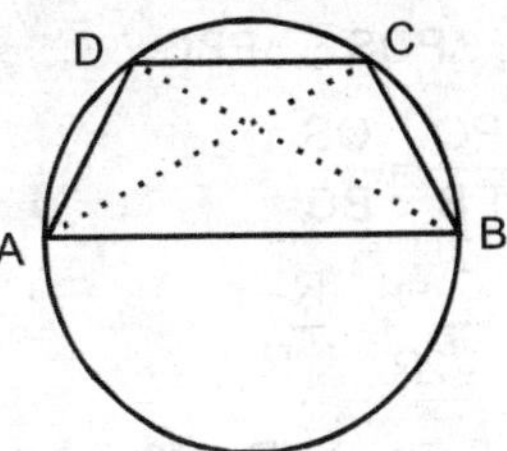

If we draw the imaginary lines AC and BD, we find that $\angle$CAD and $\angle$CBD are subtended by the same chord DC.

$\therefore \angle CAD = \angle CBD = 30°$.

Thus, $\angle DBA = (70° - 30°) = 40°$.

Also, $\angle$DBA and $\angle$ACD are subtended by the same chord DA.

Hence, $\angle ACD = \angle DBA = 40°$.

8. c

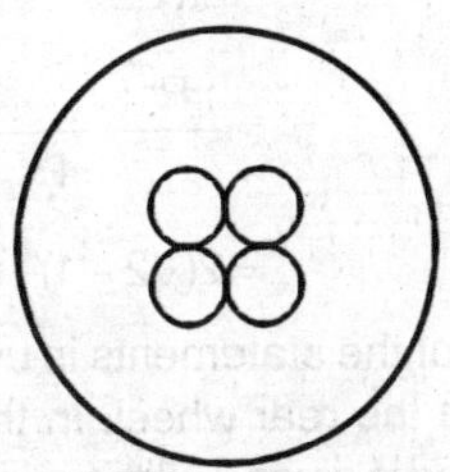

Area of the original paper = $\pi(20)^2 = 400\pi$ cm². The total cut portion area = $4(\pi)(5)^2 = 100\pi$ cm². Therefore, area of the uncut (shaded) portion = (400 – 100)= 300π cm².

Hence, the required ratio = $300\pi : 100\pi = 3 : 1$.

9. b The radius of the circle is 6.5 cm. Therefore, its diameter = 13 cm and AB = 13 cm. Since the diameter of a circle subtends 90° at the circumference, $\angle ACB = 90°$. So ΔACB is a right-angled triangle with AC = 5 cm, AB = 13 cm.

Therefore, CB should be equal to 12 cm (as 5-12-13 form a Pythagorean triplet).

Hence, the area of the triangle $= \frac{1}{2} \times AC \times CB$

$= \frac{1}{2} \times 5 \times 12 = 30$ sq.cm.

10. d

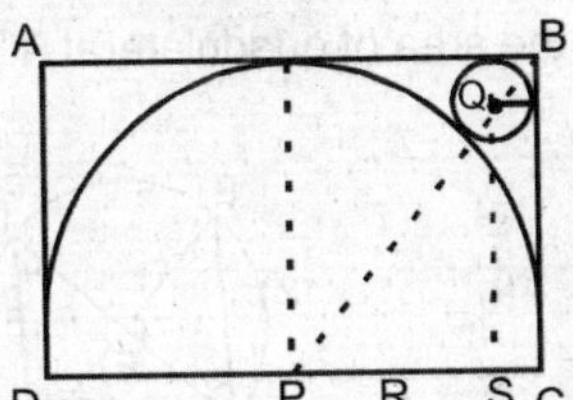

Let radius of the semicircle be R and radius of the circle be r.

Let P be the centre of semicircle and Q be the centre of the circle.

Draw QS parallel to BC.

Now, $\Delta PQS \sim \Delta PBC$

$\therefore \frac{PQ}{PB} = \frac{QS}{BC}$

$\Rightarrow \frac{R+r}{\sqrt{2}R} = \frac{R-r}{R}$

$\Rightarrow R+r = \sqrt{2}R - \sqrt{2}r$

$\Rightarrow r(1+\sqrt{2}) = R(\sqrt{2}-1)$

$\Rightarrow r = R\frac{(\sqrt{2}-1)}{(\sqrt{2}+1)} \times \frac{(\sqrt{2}-1)}{(\sqrt{2}-1)}$

$\Rightarrow r = R(\sqrt{2}-1)^2$

Required ratio $= \frac{\pi r^2}{\pi R^2} \times 2$

$= \frac{\pi R^2(\sqrt{2}-1)^4 \times 2}{\pi R^2}$

$= 2(\sqrt{2}-1)^4 : 1$

11. a None of the statements is useful in finding the radius of the rear wheel. In the question, distance travelled is given. But the number of rotations taken by it is not given.

12. d

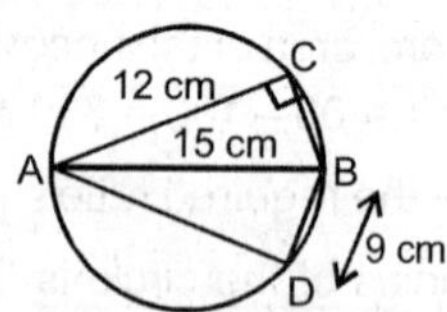

Since AB is the diameter of the circle, $\angle ACB$ would be right angle. In this triangle, we know AB = 15 and AC = 12. So we can find BC. Hence, BC = 9. Since BC = BD, AD = AC (similar triangles).

Hence, area of ΔACB = Area of ΔABD

$= \frac{1}{2} AC \times CB$

$= \frac{1}{2} \times 12 \times 9 = 54 \text{ cm}^2$

So the area of quadrilateral ACBD = 2 × 54 = 108 sq. cm.

13. a

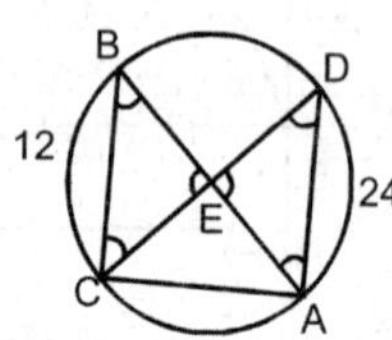

In ΔBEC and ΔAED

$\angle CBE = \angle CDE$ ($\because$ Angles in the same segment of a circle are equal)

Similarly, $\angle BCE = \angle EAD$ ($\because$ Angles in the same segment of a circle are equal)

$\angle BEC = \angle AED$ (Vertical angles are equal)

$\therefore$ By AAA similarity

$\Delta CEB \sim \Delta AED$

We know that the ratio of the areas of two similar triangles is equal to the ratio of the squares of the corresponding sides

$\therefore \frac{\text{Area}(\Delta BEC)}{\text{Area}(\Delta AED)} = \left(\frac{BC}{DA}\right)^2 = \left(\frac{12}{24}\right)^2 = \left(\frac{1}{2}\right)^2 = \frac{1}{4}$

14. a If the radii of two circles are r_1 and r_2, then the two equations can be written $\pi r_1^2 + \pi r_2^2 = 153\pi$ or $(r_1^2 + r_2^2) = 153$ and $r_1 + r_2 = 15$.

Now $r_1^2 + r_2^2 = (r_1 + r_2)^2 - 2r_1r_2$

Therefore, $153 = (15)^2 - 2r_1r_2$ or $r_1r_2 = 36$.

If 36 is to be expressed as the product of two integers, it could be (36 × 1), (18 × 2), (12 × 3), (9 × 4), (6 × 6).

The only two factors that add up to 15 are 12 and 3. Hence, $r_1 = 12$, $r_2 = 3$. Therefore, the ratio of larger radius to the smaller one is 12 : 3 = 4.

15. c PQ = PE + FQ – FE

= Radius of circle 1 + Radius of circle 2 – FE

= 20 + 20 – 12 = 28

Similarly, QR = 20 + 20 – CD = 40 – 10 = 30

and PR = 20 + 20 – AB = 40 – 5 = 35

So perimeter of ΔPQR = 28 + 30 + 35 = 93

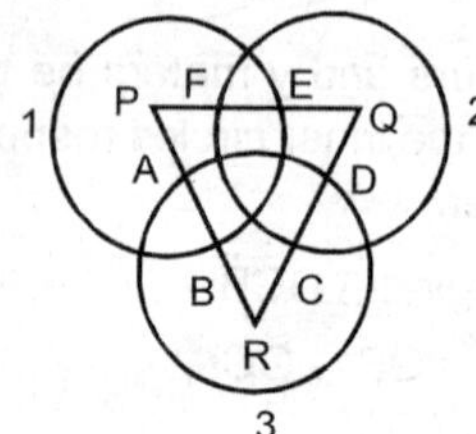

16. c Let R be the radius of each circle. Then $\frac{\pi R^2}{2\pi R} = \frac{2\pi R}{\pi R^2}$ which implies that $\frac{R}{2} = \frac{2}{R}$, i.e. $R^2 = 4$, i.e. R = 2.

Then the length of the square is 8. Thus, the area of the square is 64, while the area covered by each coin is $\pi \times 2^2 = 4\pi$. Since there are four coins, the area covered by coins is $4(4\pi) = 16\pi$.

Hence, the area not covered by the coins is $64 - 16\pi = 16(4 - \pi)$.

17. c The information given in the question implies that $r_1 > r_2$.

Statement I suggests that $(r_1 - r_2) = \frac{k}{2\pi}$.

Hence, this statement alone does not give the value of r_1.

Statement II implies that $(r_1^2 - r_2^2) = \frac{m}{\pi}$.

Hence, again this statement alone is not sufficient to answer the question. But in the second equation, we simplify $(r_1^2 - r_2^2)$as $(r_1 + r_2)(r_1 - r_2)$ and then substitute the value of $(r_1 - r_2)$ from the first equation, we will get the value of $(r_1 + r_2)$. Now we have two equations in r_1 and r_2, which can be solved simultaneously to get the value of r_1. Hence, both the statements when together taken can answer the question.

18. b

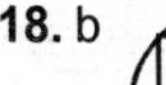

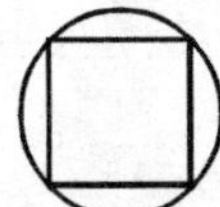

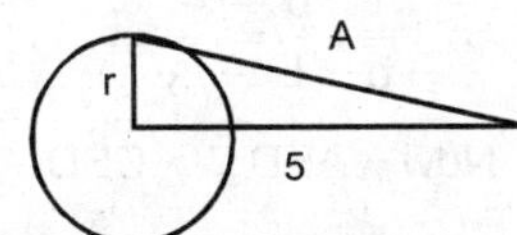

Statement I itself is sufficient to answer the question. As, if we know the radius of the circle we can find out the length of the diagonal of the square (which will be the diameter) and if we know the diagonal of a square we can find the length of its sides and hence the area.

Again, the second statement in itself can answer the question. As, from the data that is given we can find the radius of the circle and hence the area of the square (as given before). This can be explained from the diagram given. Since the tangent makes a right angle with the radius at the circumference, the triangle is a right-angled triangle. Hence, $A^2 = 5^2 + r^2$. Hence, knowing the value of A, we can find out r. Hence, both statements in itself can answer the question. Therefore, the answer is (b).

19. c Let the radius of the outer circle be OQ = x.

Hence, perimeter of the circle $= 2\pi x$

But OQ = BC = x (diagonals of the square BQCO)

Perimeter of ABCD = 4x

Hence, ratio = $\frac{2\pi x}{4x} = \frac{\pi}{2}$.

20. b

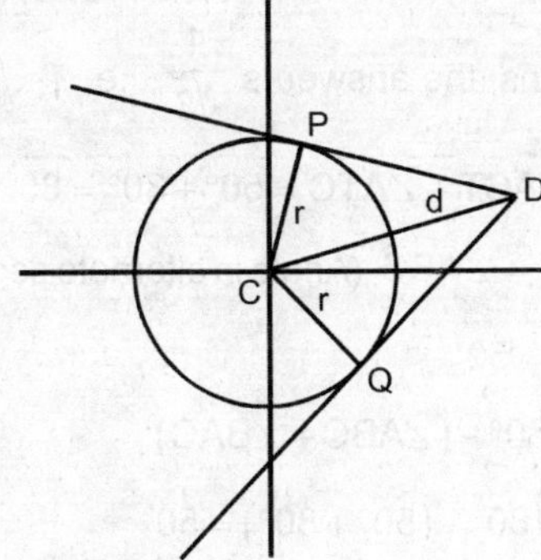

r and d are given

From **statement I,** when co-ordinates of D are given, only one pair of tangents can be drawn onto the given circle from D. So angle made by x-axis for each can be found out.

Hence, statement I alone is sufficient.

Consider **statement II.** Let the x-axis bisect the tangent QD, i.e. QA = AD.

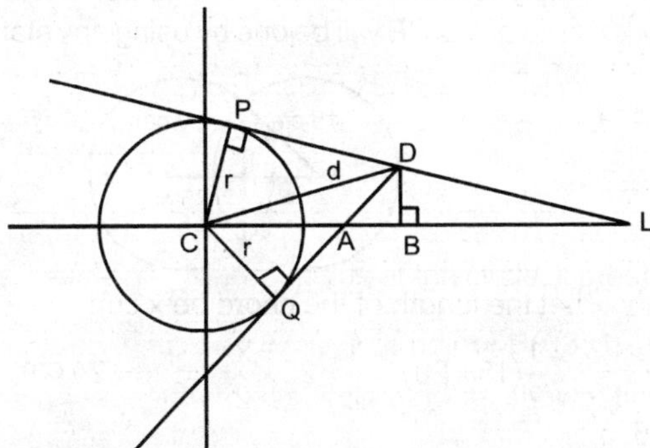

Here $QA = \frac{1}{2}QD = \frac{1}{2}\sqrt{d^2 - r^2}$. So using trigonometric ratios in right ΔCQA, we can determine $\angle CAQ$. Therefore, $\angle DAB$ is equal to $\angle CAQ$ (vertically opposite angles).

Consider the other tangent DP. Let it intersect x-axis at point L.

$\angle CDQ$ can be determined using trigonometric ratios (as two of the sides are given in right ΔCDQ). Also, $\angle CDQ$ is equal to $\angle CDP$ (since the two right ΔCQD and ΔCPD are congruent). Drop a perpendicular DB on x-axis. In right ΔDBL, we can find $\angle BDL = 180^\circ - (\angle ADB + \angle CDQ + \angle CDP)$ $= 180^\circ - 2\angle CDQ - \angle ADB$. Applying angle sum property of triangle, we can determine $\angle DLB$.

Hence, statement II alone is sufficient.

21. c Let the area of sector S_1 be x units. Then the area of the corresponding sectors shall be 2x, 4x, 8x, 16x, 32x and 64x. Since every successive sector has an angle that is twice the previous one, the total area then shall be 127x units. This is $\frac{1}{8}$ of the total area of the circle.

Hence, the total area of the circle will be 127x × 8

= 1016x units. Hence, angle of sector S_1 is $\frac{\pi}{1016}$.

22. c For a given inradius and circumradius, there is only one possible value of (PR + RQ).

Hence, both the statements are required to answer the question.

23. b You can see from the following diagram that both statements individually

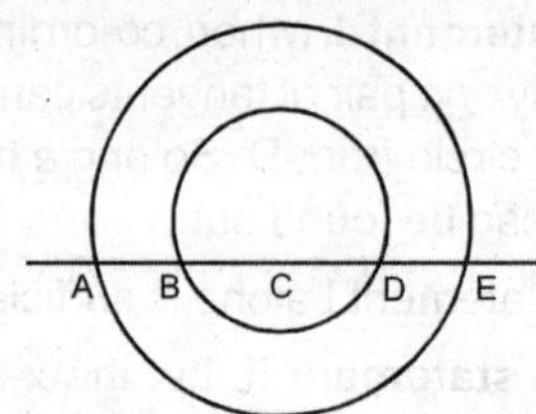

imply towards C being the mid-point of BD. The ratio of AC/CE will be one by using any statement.

24. a

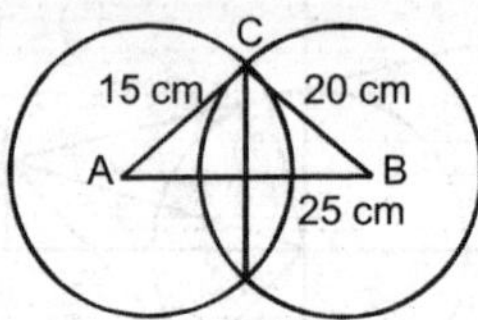

Let the length of the chord be x cm.

$\therefore \frac{1}{2}(15\times 20)=\frac{1}{2}\times 25\times\frac{x}{2} \Rightarrow x = 24$ cm

25. b

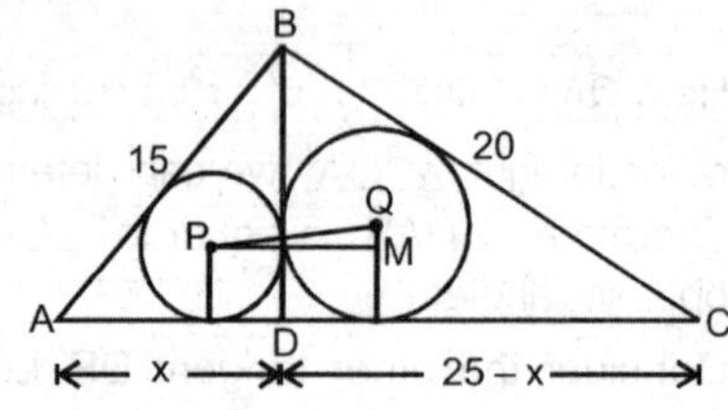

$(15)^2 - x^2 = (20)^2 - (25-x)^2$

$\Rightarrow x = 9$

$\Rightarrow BD = 12$

Area of $\Delta ABD = \frac{1}{2}\times 12\times 9 = 54$

$s = \frac{1}{2}(15+12+9) = 18$

$r_1 = \frac{\text{Area}}{s} \Rightarrow r_1 = 3$

Area of $\Delta BCD = \frac{1}{2}\times 16 \times 12 = 96$

$s = \frac{1}{2}(16+20+12) = 24$

$r_2 = \frac{\text{Area}}{s} \Rightarrow r_2 = 4$

In ΔPQM, $PM = r_1 + r_2 = 7$ cm

$QM = r_2 - r_1 = 1$ cm

Hence, $PQ = \sqrt{50}$ cm

26. a

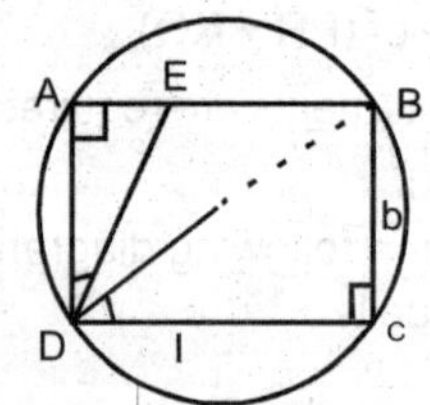

$BD = 2r$

$$\frac{\text{Area of circle}}{\text{Area of rectangle}} = \frac{\pi r^2}{lb} = \frac{\pi}{\sqrt{3}}$$

$$\frac{r^2}{lb} = \frac{1}{\sqrt{3}} \Rightarrow \frac{\frac{d^2}{4}}{lb} = \frac{1}{\sqrt{3}} \Rightarrow \frac{d^2}{4lb} = \frac{1}{\sqrt{3}}$$

$$\therefore \frac{l^2+b^2}{4lb} = \frac{1}{\sqrt{3}} \Rightarrow \frac{l^2+b^2}{lb} = \frac{4}{\sqrt{3}}$$

$$\Rightarrow \frac{l}{b}+\frac{b}{l} = \frac{4}{\sqrt{3}} \quad \text{... (i)}$$

Now $\Delta AED \sim \Delta CBD$

$$\therefore \frac{AE}{CB} = \frac{AD}{DC} \Rightarrow \frac{AE}{AD} = \frac{BC}{DC} \Rightarrow \frac{AE}{AD} = \frac{b}{l}$$

$\therefore$ We have to find $\frac{AE}{AD}$, i.e. $\frac{b}{l}$.

Let $\frac{b}{l} = x$

Therefore, from (i), we get

$$\frac{1}{x}+x = \frac{4}{\sqrt{3}}$$

$$\Rightarrow \frac{1+x^2}{x} = \frac{4}{\sqrt{3}}$$

$$\Rightarrow \sqrt{3}+\sqrt{3}x^2 = 4x$$

$$\Rightarrow \sqrt{3}x^2 - 4x + \sqrt{3} = 0$$

$$\therefore \quad x = \frac{-(-4)\pm\sqrt{16-4(\sqrt{3})\sqrt{3}}}{2\sqrt{3}}$$

$$= \frac{4\pm\sqrt{16-12}}{2\sqrt{3}} = \frac{4\pm 2}{2\sqrt{3}} = \frac{6}{2\sqrt{3}} \text{ OR } \frac{2}{2\sqrt{3}}$$

$$= \frac{\sqrt{3}}{1} \text{ OR } \frac{1}{\sqrt{3}}$$

From options, the answer is $\frac{1}{\sqrt{3}}$, i.e. $1:\sqrt{3}$.

27. a $\angle BAC = \angle ACT + \angle ATC = 50° + 30° = 80°$

And $\angle ACT = \angle ABC$ (Angle in alternate segment)

So $\angle ABC = 50°$

$\angle BCA = 180° - (\angle ABC + \angle BAC)$

$= 180° - (50° + 80°) = 50°$

Since $\angle BOA = 2\angle BCA = 2\times 50° = 100°$

Alternative Method:

Join OC

$\angle OCT = 90°$ (TC is tangent to OC)

$\angle OCA = 90° - 50° = 40°$

$\angle OAC = 40°$ (OA = OC being the radius)

$\angle BAC = 50° + 30° = 80°$

$\angle OAB = 80° - 40° = 40° = \angle OBA$

(OA = OB being the radius)

$\angle BOA = 180° - (\angle OBA + \angle OAB) = 100°$

28. c

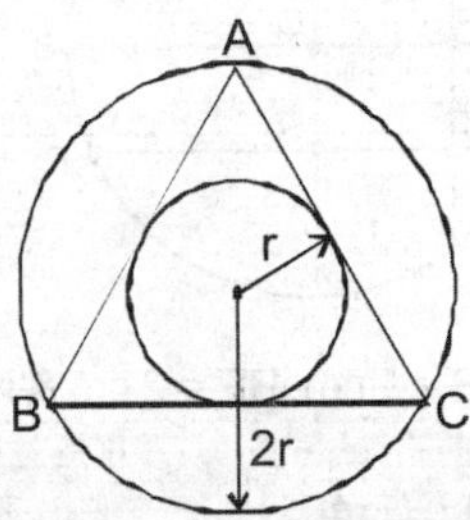

Since the area of the outer circle is 4 times the area of the inner circle, the radius of the outer circle should be 2 times that of the inner circle.

Since AB and AC are the tangents to the inner circle, they should be equal. Also, BC should be a tangent to inner circle. In other words, triangle ABC should be equilateral.

The area of the outer circle is 12.

Hence, the area of inner circle is 3 or the radius is $\sqrt{\dfrac{3}{\pi}}$.

The area of equilateral triangle = $3\sqrt{3}\ r^2$, where r is the inradius.

Hence, the answer is $\dfrac{9\sqrt{3}}{\pi}$.

29. a If y = 10°,

$\angle BOC = 10°$ (opposite equal sides)

$\angle OBA = 20°$ (external angle of ΔBOC)

$\angle OAB = 20$ (opposite equal sides)

$\angle AOD = 30°$ (external angle of ΔAOC)

Thus k = 3

30. a

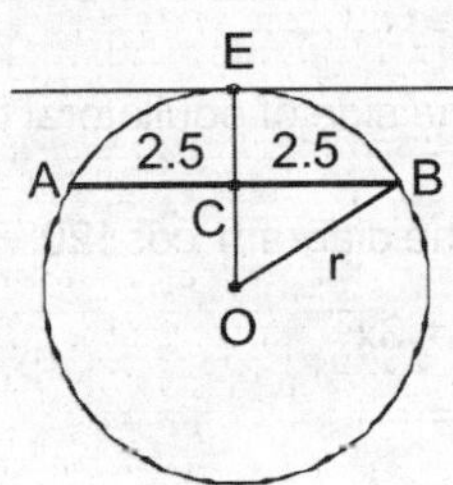

We can get the answer using the second statement only. Let the radius be r.

AC = CB = 2.5 and using statement B, CE = 5, thus OC = (r – 5).

Using Pythagoras theorem, $(r - 5)^2 + (2.5)^2 = r^2$

We get r = 3.125 cm.

NOTE: You will realize that such a circle is not possible (if r = 3.125 how can CE be 5). However we need to check data sufficiency and not data consistency. Since we are able to find the value of r uniquely using second statement the answer is (a).

31. b $\dfrac{OP}{OQ} = \dfrac{PR}{QS} = \dfrac{4}{3}$

OP = 28

OQ = 21

PQ = OP – OQ = 7

$\dfrac{PQ}{OQ} = \dfrac{7}{21} = \dfrac{1}{3}$

32. b PR + QS = PQ = 7 $= \dfrac{PR}{QS} = \dfrac{4}{3}$

$\Rightarrow QS = 3$ cm.

33. c $SO = \sqrt{OQ^2 - QS^2}$

$= \sqrt{21^2 - 3^2}$

$= \sqrt{24 \times 18} = 12\sqrt{3}$ cm.

34. b

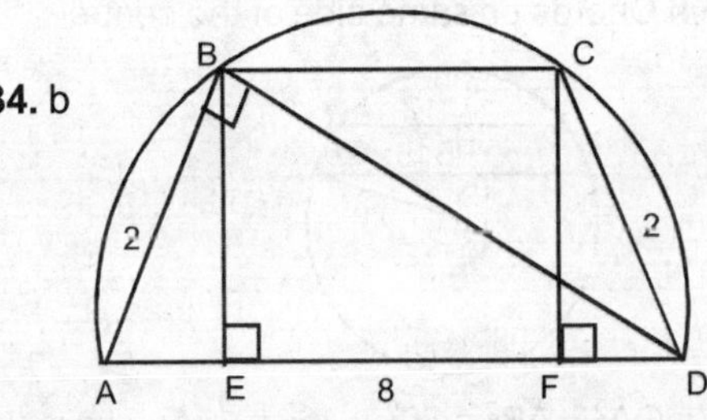

$\dfrac{1}{2} \times AB \times BD = \dfrac{1}{2} \times AD \times BE$

$\Rightarrow 2\sqrt{8^2 - 2^2} = 8 \times BE$

$\Rightarrow BE = \dfrac{\sqrt{60}}{4} = \dfrac{\sqrt{15}}{2}$

$AE = \sqrt{2^2 - \left(\dfrac{\sqrt{15}}{2}\right)^2} = \sqrt{4 - \dfrac{15}{4}} = \dfrac{1}{2}$

$BC = EF = 8 - \left(\dfrac{1}{2} + \dfrac{1}{2}\right) = 7$

35. d

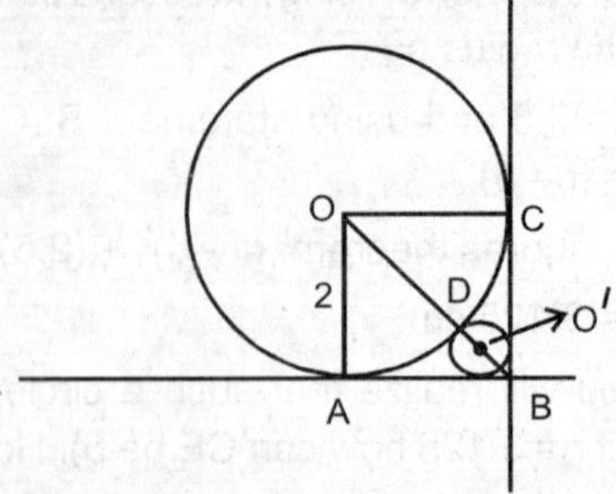

Let the radius of smaller circle be 'r'.

$\therefore \quad O'B = r\sqrt{2}$

$\therefore \quad OB = O'B + O'D + OD = r\sqrt{2} + r + 2$

Also OB = $2\sqrt{2}$

$\Rightarrow \quad r\sqrt{2} + r + 2 = 2\sqrt{2}$

$\Rightarrow \quad r = 6 - 4\sqrt{2}$

36. d

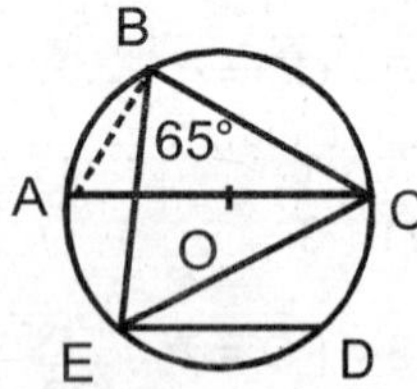

In ΔABC, $\angle B = 90°$ (Angles in semicircle)

Therefore, $\angle ABE = 90 - 65 = 25°$

Also, $\angle ABE = \angle ACE$ (Angle subtended by same arc AE)

Also, $\angle ACE = \angle CED$ [$AC \parallel ED$]

Therefore, $\angle CED = 25°$

37. d **Case I:** Chords on same side of the centre.

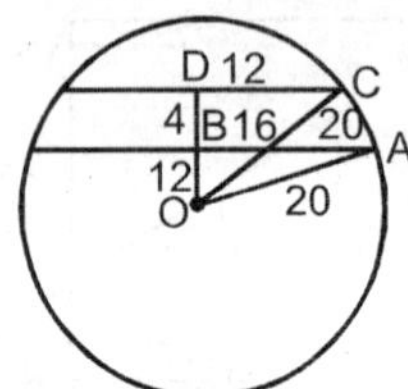

$OB^2 = OA^2 - AB^2 = 20^2 - 16^2 = 144$

$OB = 12$

$OD^2 = 20^2 - 12^2 = 400 - 144 = 256$

$OD = 16$

BD = 4 cm

Case II: Chords on opposite side of the centre.

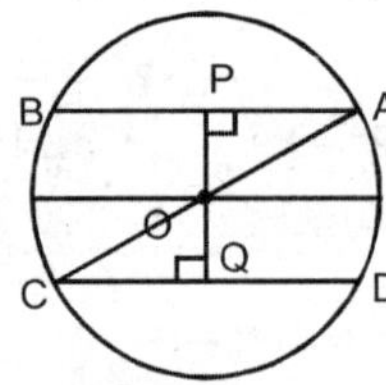

AB = 32 cm, CD = 24 cm

$OP = \sqrt{AO^2 - AP^2} = \sqrt{(20)^2 - (16)^2}$

OP = 12 cm

& $OQ = \sqrt{(OC)^2 - (CQ)^2} = \sqrt{(20)^2 - (12)^2}$

OQ = 16 cm

Distance = PQ = 12 + 16 = 28 cm.

38. b

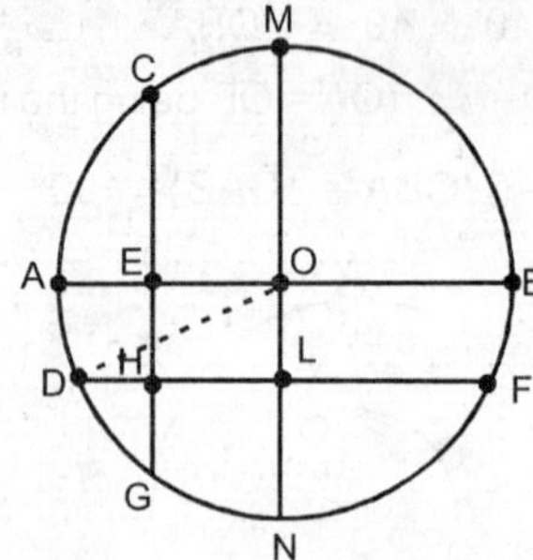

AE = 1 cm, BE = 2 cm & NL = 1 cm, ML = 2 cm

$HL = OE = \frac{1}{2}$

DL = DH + HL

$\Rightarrow \quad DL = DH + \frac{1}{2}$

OB = AO = radius = 1.5

$DO^2 = OL^2 + DL^2$

$\Rightarrow \quad \left(\frac{3}{2}\right)^2 = \left(\frac{1}{2}\right)^2 + \left(DH + \frac{1}{2}\right)^2$

$\Rightarrow \quad \left(DH + \frac{1}{2}\right)^2 = 2 \quad \Rightarrow \quad DH = \sqrt{2} - \frac{1}{2}.$

39. a

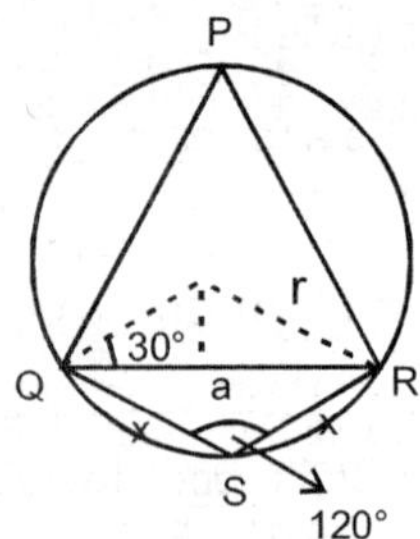

Here $\cos 30° = \frac{a}{2r}$

$\Rightarrow \quad a = r\sqrt{3}$

Here the side of equilateral triangle is $r\sqrt{3}$

From the diagram $\cos 120° = \frac{x^2 + x^2 - a^2}{2x^2}$

$\Rightarrow \quad a^2 = 3x^2$

$x = r$

Hence, the circumference will be $2r\left(1 + \sqrt{3}\right)$.

40. b

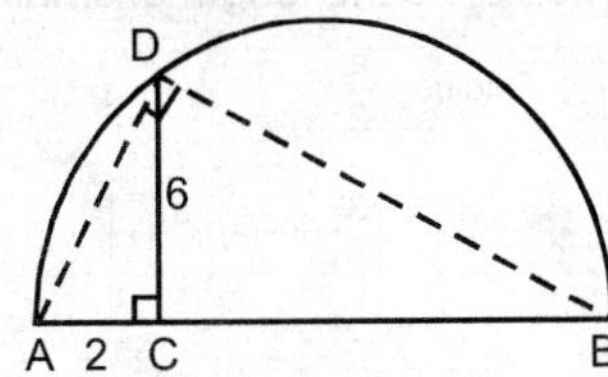

$\angle ADB = 90°$ (Angle in semicircle)

$CD^2 = AC \times CB$

$\Rightarrow (6)^2 = 2 \times CB$

$\Rightarrow 36 = 2 \times CB$

$\Rightarrow CB = 18$ cm

$\therefore AB = AC + CB = 20$ cm

Hence, area of semicircle $= \frac{1}{2}\pi(10)^2 = 50\pi$ sq. cm.

41. c

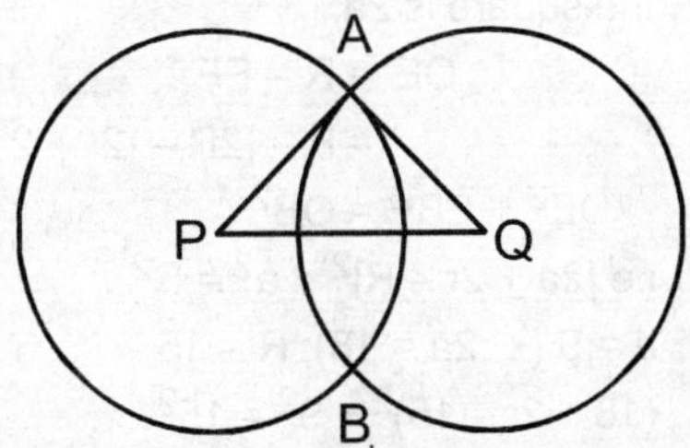

If P and Q lie on the intersections of the circles as shown in the figure given below.

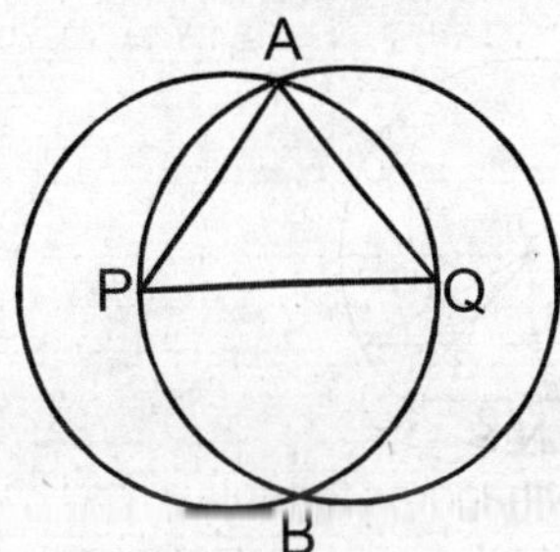

In this case triangle APQ is equilateral. So the maximum possible measure of the angle AQP is 60°. The answer is between 0 and 60.

42. e We can use the formula for the circum radius of a triangle:

$$R = \frac{a \times b \times c}{4 \times (\text{Area of the triangle})}$$

or $$R = \frac{a \times b \times c}{4 \times \left(\frac{1}{2} \times b \times AD\right)}$$

$$= \frac{a \times c}{2 \times AD}$$

$$= \frac{17.5 \times 9}{2 \times 3} = 26.25 \text{ cm}$$

43. a

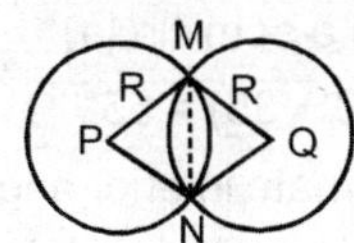

Area of $\Delta MNQ = \frac{1}{2} \times R \times R = \frac{1}{2}R^2$

Area of sector $MNQ = \frac{1}{4} \times \pi R^2$

So the required area $= 2\left[\frac{1}{4}\pi R^2 - \frac{1}{2}R^2\right]$

$= 2 \times \frac{1}{2}R^2\left[\frac{\pi}{2} - 1\right] = R^2\left[\frac{\pi}{2} - 1\right]$ sq units

44. a Centre of the circle will be mid-point of the hypotenuse of the triangle. So, hypotenuse = 2 × 6.5 = 13 cm.

Since all the sides are natural numbers, obviously other sides are 5 cm and 12 cms and the perimeter is 5 + 12 + 13 = 30 cm.

45. d If Ramu and Shamu are at the diametrically opposite ends (in which case distance = 18 m)

Then

1.5 + 3 x N = 4 M where M, N are natural numbers

This is never possible.

46. c

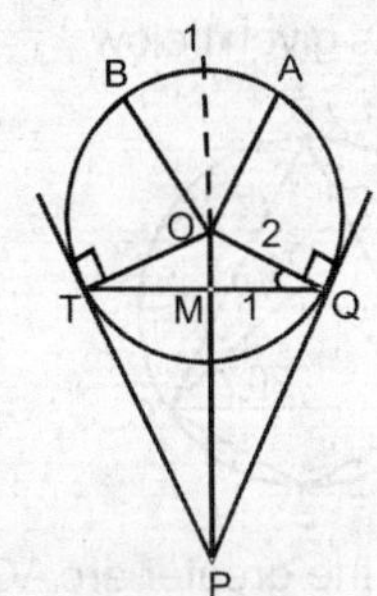

Since, OQ = TQ = 2 units, therefore ΔOTQ is an equilateral.

$\therefore \quad \angle TOQ = 60°$

Since, PQ is a tangent to the circle, therefore $\angle OQP = 90°$.

Since, PQ is a parallel to OA therefore $\angle AOQ = 90°$.

For the same reason $\angle BOT = 90°$.

$\therefore \quad \angle AOB = 360° - (\angle TOQ + \angle AOQ + \angle BOT)$

$= 120°$.

47. b

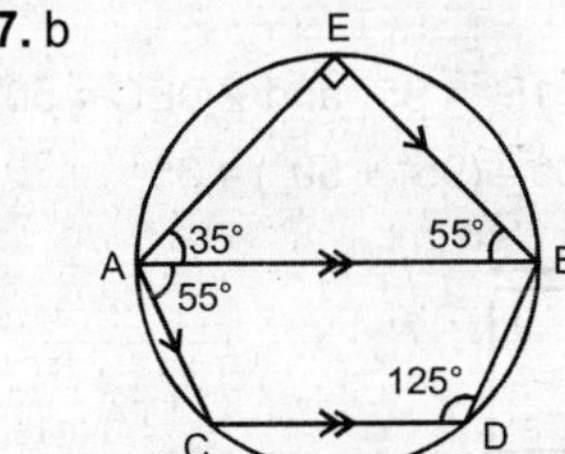

$\angle AEB = 90°$ (Angle in a semicircle)

$\therefore \quad \angle ABE = 180 - (90 + 35) = 55°$

$\therefore \quad \angle BAC = 55°$ (Alternate interior angles)

Now, $\angle CDB = 180 - 55 = 125°$ (Sum of opposite angles of a cyclic quadrilateral is 180°.)

$\therefore \quad \angle ABD = 180 - 125 = 55°$

(Sum of interior opposite angles is 180°.).

Hence $\angle CDB - \angle ABD = 125 - 55 = 70°$.

48. d There would be 2 cases.

Case I: When B lies in greater arc AC.

The figure would be as below.

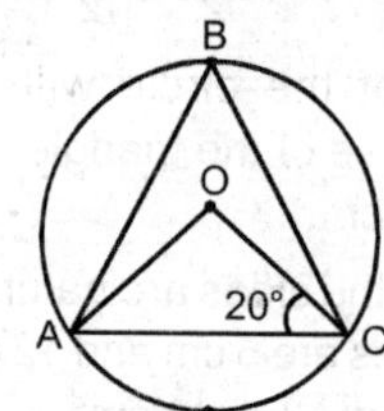

$\angle OAC = \angle OCA = 20°$

$\Rightarrow \quad \angle AOC = 140°$

$\therefore \quad \angle ABC = \frac{1}{2}\angle AOC = 70°$

Case II: When B lies in smaller arc AC.

The figure would be as given below.

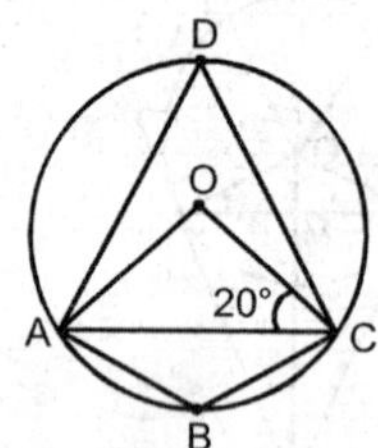

Let D be a point O is the greater arc AC.

$\angle OAC = \angle OCA = 20°$

$\Rightarrow \quad \angle OAC = 140°$

$\therefore \quad \angle ADC = \angle AOC = 70°$

ABCD is a cyclic quadrilateral

$\therefore \quad \angle ABC = 180° - 70° = 110°$.

49. c $\angle EOA = 85°, \angle BOD = 15°$

$\therefore \angle EOD = 180° - (85° + 15°) = 80°$

$\therefore$ In ΔOED, OE = OD (radius)

$\therefore \angle OED = \angle ODE = 50°$

In ΔEOC,

$\angle EOC = 80° + 15° = 95°$ and $\angle OEC = 50°$

$\therefore \angle ECA = 180° - (95° + 50°) = 35°$

50. c

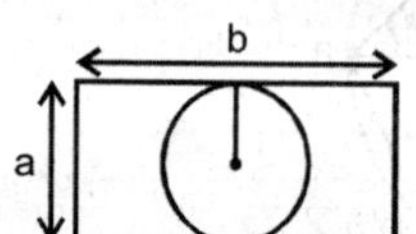

Let 'a' be the length of smaller side

$\therefore$ Radius $= \frac{a}{2}$

$\Rightarrow \pi\left(\frac{a}{2}\right)^2 = \frac{3}{2}\left[60 - \pi\left(\frac{a}{2}\right)^2\right]$

$\Rightarrow 5\pi\left(\frac{a}{2}\right)^2 = 180 \Rightarrow \frac{\pi a^2}{4} = 36$

$a = \sqrt{\frac{36 \times 4}{\pi}} = \frac{12}{\sqrt{\pi}}$ units .

51. b

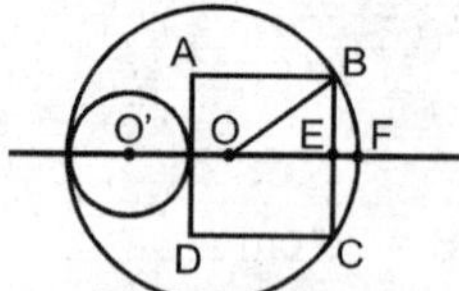

Let the radius of the bigger circle be R and that of the smaller circle be r and the side of the square is 2a.

$\therefore \quad OE = R - EF$

$= R - [2R - (2r + 2a)]$

$OE^2 + EB^2 = OB^2$

i.e $[2a + 2r - R]^2 + a^2 = R^2$

$a = 9$ ($\because$ 2a = 18); R = 15

$\therefore \quad (18 + 2r - 15)^2 + 9^2 = 15^2$

$\therefore \quad 2r + 3 = 12$

$\therefore \quad r = \frac{9}{2} = 4.5$ cm

52. c

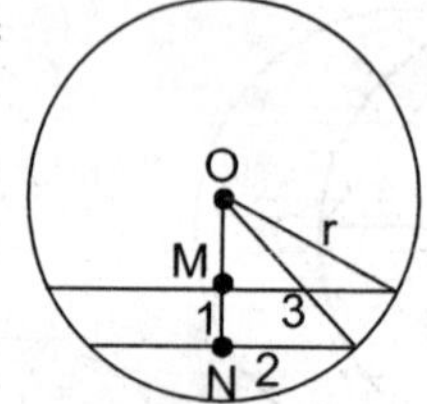

Using Pythagoras formula,

$r^2 - 9 = OM^2$.

$r^2 = 4 + (OM + 1)^2$.

$r^2 = 4 + OM^2 + 1 + 2\,OM$ ....(i)

Now put $OM = \sqrt{r^2 - 9}$ in eq. (i)

$r^2 = 4 + r^2 - 9 + 1 + 2\sqrt{r^2 - 9}$

$4 = 2\sqrt{r^2 - 9}$

$r^2 = 13$

$r = \sqrt{13}$ cm

53. b

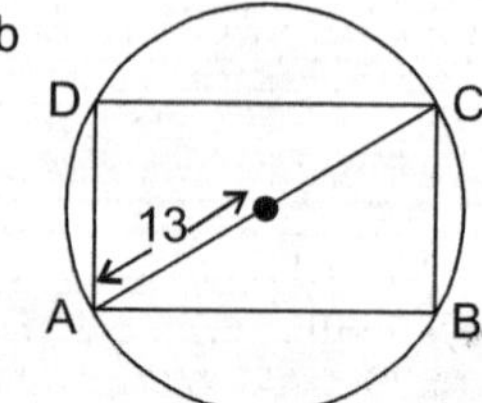

AC = 26 cm

So, $AB^2 + BC^2 = (26)^2 = 576$

Among the options, length = 24 and breadth = 10cm, will satisfy the above equation

$(24)^2 + (10)^2 = 576$

Hence, (24, 10) can be the possible pair.

54. c

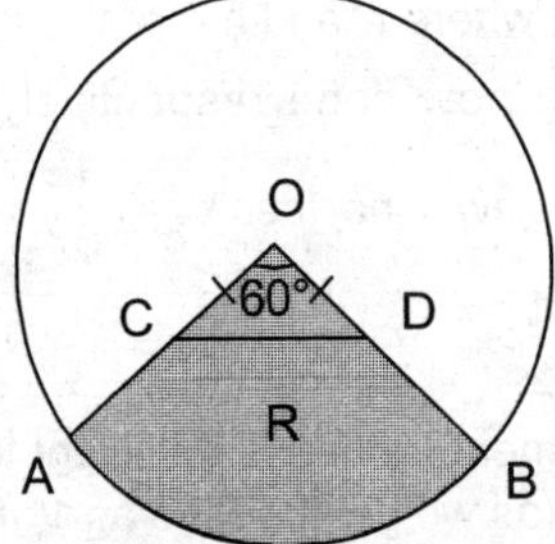

Area of $\Delta OCD = \frac{1}{2}$ Area of region R.

$$\frac{1}{2} \times \pi(1)^2 \times \frac{60}{360} = \frac{\pi}{12} \text{ sq. cm}$$

As OC = CD and $\angle COD = 60°$

$\therefore \angle OCD = \angle ODC = 60°$

Hence, ΔOCD is an equilateral Δ.

$$\therefore \frac{\sqrt{3}}{4} OC^2 = \frac{\pi}{12}$$

$$OC = \left(\frac{\pi}{3\sqrt{3}}\right)^{\frac{1}{2}} \text{ cm.}$$

55. 24 Triangles BPC and BQC will be right angled triangles as they are made inside semicircle.

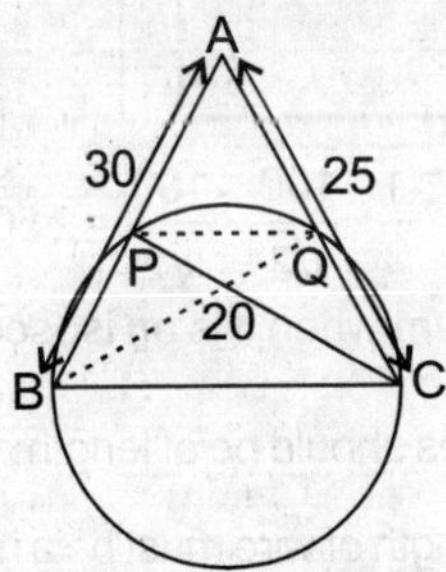

Since, area of triangle ABC

$$= \frac{1}{2} \times AB \times CP = \frac{1}{2} \times AC \times BQ$$

$\Rightarrow$ AB × CP = AC × BQ

$\Rightarrow$ 30 : 20 = 25 × BQ

Hence, BQ = 24 cm.

56. c The chord extends an angle of 60° at the center so an equilateral triangle will be formed with the other two sides being the radius of the circle.

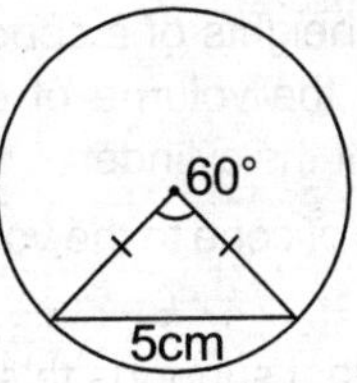

Thus, radius = 5 cm

Let the length of the chord that extends 120° be 'a' cm.

$\Rightarrow a^2 = 5^2 + 5^2 - 2 \times 5 \times 5\cos 120°$

....(using cosine rule)

Hence, $a = 5\sqrt{3}$ cm.

Mensuration

1. a If x = 1, then for the rectangular box : l = 8, b = 8 and h = 1, so volume = 64.

If x = 2, l = 6, b = 6 and h = 2 and volume = 72.

If x = 3, l = 4, b = 4 and h = 3 and volume = 48.

Therefore, we can see that for a value of x between 2 and 3, the volume of box decreases and will go on decreasing further as x increases.

Hence, the maximum volume that the box can have is 72 cubic inches.

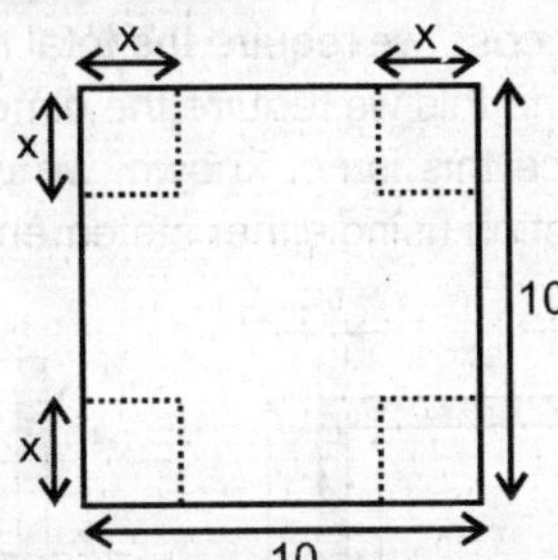

2. b Let l be the length of the rod, then

Volume of slab = Volume of rod

$$\Rightarrow \quad 8 \times 11 \times 2 = \pi\left(\frac{8}{2}\right)^2 \times l\pi$$

$\Rightarrow$ l = 3.5 inches.

3. c It can be seen that if a spherical ball is placed inside a hollow cone of same diameter, the ball won't go up to the diameter. In other words, because of the slanting edges of the cone, only less than 50% of the ball would enter the cone. i.e, more than 50% of the ball would be outside the cone.

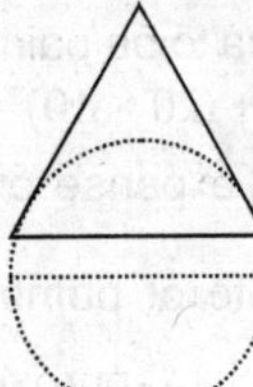

4. a If the diameters and the heights of a cone and a cylinder are same, then the volume of cone is always 1/3rd the volume of the cylinder.

So the ratio of the volume of cone to the volume of cylinder = 1 : 3.

The only answer choice that supports this is (a).

5. b Let the radius and height of original cone be 'r' and 'h' respectively.

$\therefore$ The volume of the original cone $(V) = \frac{\pi r^2 h}{3}$.

The height and radius of the smaller cone are $\frac{2h}{3}$ and $\frac{2r}{3}$ respectively.

So its volume $= \frac{\pi}{3} \times \left(\frac{2r}{3}\right)^2 \times \frac{2h}{3} = \frac{8V}{27}$.

$\therefore$ Volume of frustum = $\left(V - \frac{8V}{27}\right) = \frac{19V}{27}$.

$\therefore$ Ratio of the volumes = 8 : 19.

6. d From the statement I, we can find out the area that needs to be bordered. And from the statement II, we can find out the cost of each tile. But to find the total cost, we require the total number of tiles and to find this we require the dimension of each tile. Since this is not known, we cannot answer the question using either statements.

7. c

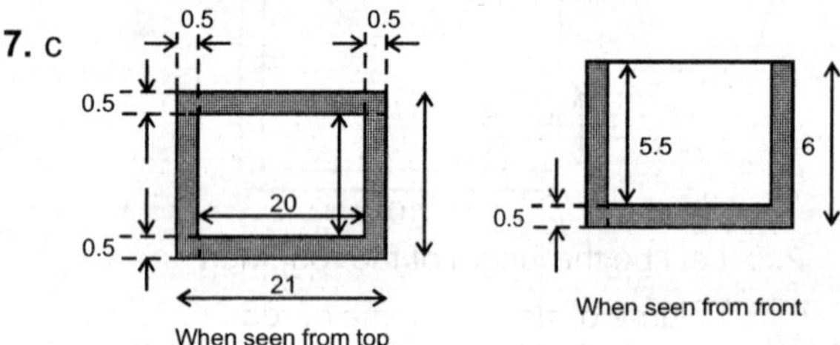

When seen from top

When seen from front

As it can be seen from the diagram, because of the thickness of the wall, the dimensions of the inside of the box is as follows: length = (21 – 0.5 – 0.5) = 20 cm, width = (11 – 0.5 – 0.5) = 10 cm and height = (6 – 0.5)= 5.5 cm.

Total number of faces to be painted = 4 walls + one base (as it is open from the top).

The dimensions of two of the walls = (10 × 5.5), that of the remaining two walls = (20 × 5.5) and that of the base = (20 × 10).

So the total area to be painted = 2 × (10 × 5.5) + 2 × (20 × 5.5) + (20 × 10) = 530 cm².

Since the total expense of painting this area is Rs. 70, the rate of painting = $\frac{70}{530}$ = 0.13 = Re. 0.1 per sq.cm. (approximately).

8. b Let V_1 be the original volume and r_1 and h_1 be the radius and height of the cone respectively.

$V_1 = \left(\frac{1}{3}\right) \times \pi \times (r_1)^2 \times h_1$. Consider statement I.

If the cone is cut parallel to base and dividing the height in the ratio 1 : 2, then $r_2 = (\frac{1}{2}) \times r_1$ and $h_2 = (\frac{1}{2}) \times h_1$, where r_2 and h_2 are the radius and height of the new cone respectively. If V_2 is the volume of new cone, then $V_2 = (\frac{1}{3}) \times \pi(r_2)^2 \times h_2$

$= (\frac{1}{3}) \times \pi \times (\frac{1}{2} \times r_1)^2 \times ((\frac{1}{2})h_1) = (\frac{1}{8}) \times V_1$

Hence, statement I alone is sufficient to answer the question (as we get the ratio as 1 : 8).

Similarly, based on statement II alone, we can find the ratio (which will be 1 : 27).

9. c Statement I gives the thickness of the wall which is of no use to find the volume of the tank since we do not know the radius of the sphere.

Statement II gives us the answer as the volume of water displaced is equal to the volume of the immersed tank (from Archimedes' principle).

So to find the exact storage volume of the tank both the statements are needed.

10. a

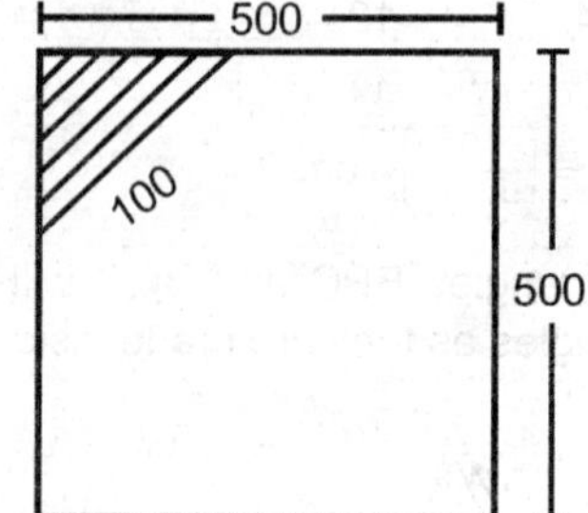

Area of shaded region $= \frac{1}{2} \times \frac{100}{\sqrt{2}} \times \frac{100}{\sqrt{2}} = 2{,}500$ sq m

Area of a Δ is maximum when it is an isosceles Δ.

So perpendicular sides should be of length $\frac{100}{\sqrt{2}}$ m.

11. d Work with options. Length of wire must be a multiple of 6 and 8. Number of poles should be one more than the multiple.

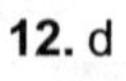

12. d

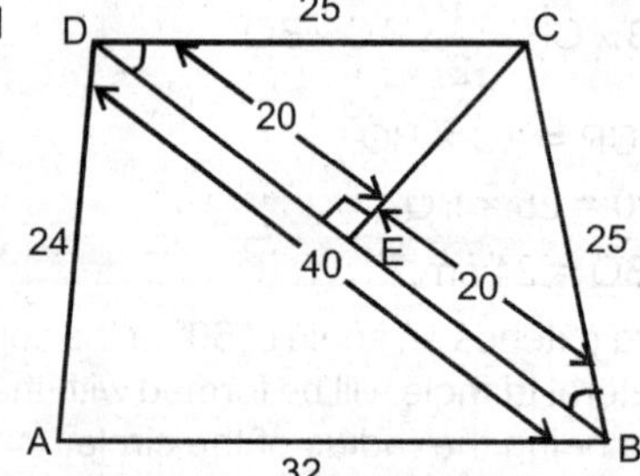

$CE = \sqrt{25^2 - 20^2} = 15$

(Since DBC is isosceles triangle.)

ABCD is a quadrilateral where AB = 32 m, AD = 24 m, DC = 25 m, CB = 25 m and $\angle DAB$ is right angle.

By Pythagoras Theorem: DB = 40 m

So area of Δ ADB $= \frac{1}{2} \times 32 \times 24 = 384$ sq. m

Now in isosceles ΔBCD, perpendicular CE from C to BD bisects BD.

$BE = DE = \frac{40}{2} = 20$ m.

Now by Pythagoras, Theorem:

$CE = \sqrt{25^2 - 20^2} = 15$ m.

So area of ΔBCD $= 2 \times \frac{1}{2} \times 15 \times 20 = 300$ sq. m

Hence, area of ABCD = 384 + 300 = 684 sq. m

13. c

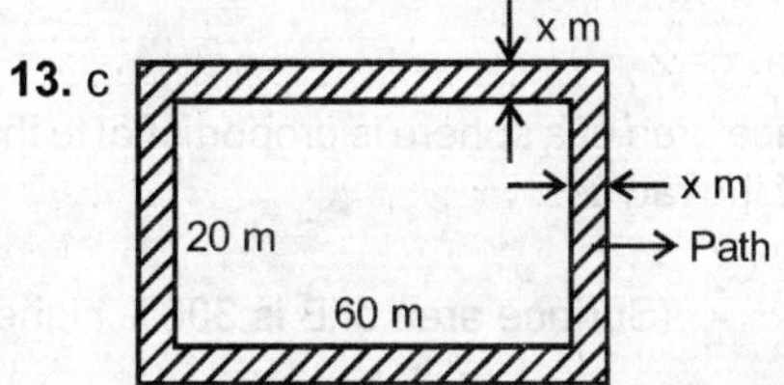

Let width of the path be x metres.

Then area of the path = 516 sq. m

$\Rightarrow$ (60 + 2x)(20 + 2x)– 60 × 20 = 516

$\Rightarrow$ 1200 + 120x + 40x + 4x² – 1200 = 516

$\Rightarrow$ 4x² + 160x – 516 = 0 $\Rightarrow$ x² + 40x – 129 = 0

Using the answer choices, we get x = 3 m.

14. b

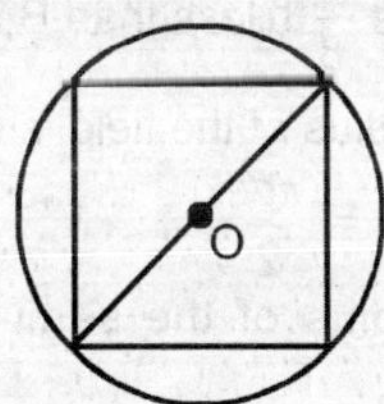

We know that the diameter of circle will be the diagonal of the square.

Thus, from any of the two statements, we can find out the areas of the circle and square.

15. a Total area = 14 × 14 = 196 m²

Grazed area $= \left(\frac{\pi \times r^2}{4}\right) \times 4 = \pi r^2 = 22 \times 7\ (r = 7\text{ m})$

= 154 m²

Ungrazed area is less than (196 – 154) = 42 m², for which there is only one option i.e. 22 m².

16. c Area = 40 × 20 = 800 m².

If 3 rounds are done, area = 34 × 14 = 476 m²

$\Rightarrow$ Area > 3 rounds

If 4 rounds $\Rightarrow$ Area left = 32 × 12 = 347 m²

Hence, area should be slightly less than 4 rounds.

For questions 17 to 19:

$A_1A_2 = 2r$, $B_1B_2 = 2r + r\sqrt{3}$, $C_1C_2 = 2r + 2r\sqrt{3}$

Hence, a = 3 × 2r;b = 3 × $(2r + r\sqrt{3})$; c = 3 × $\left(2r + 2r\sqrt{3}\right)$

17. a Difference between (a)and (b) is $3\sqrt{3}r$ and that between (b) and (c)is $3\sqrt{3}r$. Hence, (a) is the correct choice.

18. c Time taken by A $= \frac{2r}{20} + \frac{2r}{30} + \frac{2r}{15} = \left(\frac{2r \times 9}{60}\right) = \frac{3}{10}r$

Therefore, B and C will also travel for time $\frac{3}{10}r$.

Now speed of B $= \left(10\sqrt{3} + 20\right)$

Therefore, the distance covered

$= \left(10\sqrt{3} + 20\right) \times \frac{3}{10}r = \left(\sqrt{3} + 2\right) \times 10 \times \frac{3}{10}r$

$= \left(2r + \sqrt{3}r\right) \times 3 = B_1B_2 + B_2B_3 + B_3B_1$

$\therefore$ B will be at B_1.

Now time taken by for each distance are

$\frac{C_1C_2}{\frac{40}{3}\left(\sqrt{3}+1\right)}, \frac{C_2C_3}{\frac{40}{3}\left(\sqrt{3}+1\right)}, \frac{C_3C_1}{120}$

$\frac{3}{40} \times \frac{\left(2+2\sqrt{3}\right)r}{\left(\sqrt{3}+1\right)}, \frac{3}{40} \times \frac{\left(2+2\sqrt{3}\right)r}{\left(\sqrt{3}+1\right)}, \frac{\left(2+2\sqrt{3}\right)r}{120}$

i.e. $\frac{3}{40} \times 2r, \frac{3}{40} \times 2r, \frac{\left(1+\sqrt{3}\right)}{60}r$

i.e. $\frac{3}{20}r, \frac{3}{20}r, \frac{\left(1+\sqrt{3}\right)}{60}r$

We can observe that time taken for C_1C_2 and C_2C_3 combined is $\frac{3}{20}r + \frac{3}{20}r = \frac{3}{10}r$, which is same as time taken by A.Therefore, C will be at C_3.

19. b In similar triangles, ratio of Area = Ratio of squares of corresponding sides.

Hence, A and C reach A_3 and C_3 respectively.

20. a The whole height h will be divided into n equal parts. Therefore, spacing between two consecutive turns $= \frac{h}{n}$.

21. b The four faces through which string is passing can be shown as:

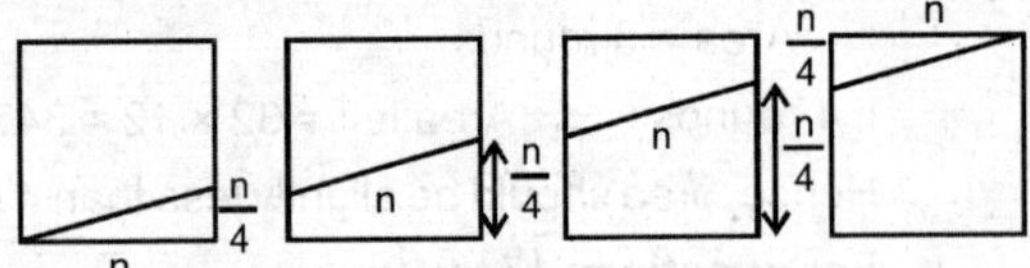

Therefore, length of string in each face

$$= \sqrt{n^2 + \left(\frac{n}{4}\right)^2} = \sqrt{n^2 + \frac{n^2}{16}} = \frac{\sqrt{17}n}{4}$$

Therefore, length of string through four faces

$$= \frac{\sqrt{17}n}{4} \times 4 = \sqrt{17}n$$

22. c Length of string is same.

Let us open 1 turn of string around cylinder.

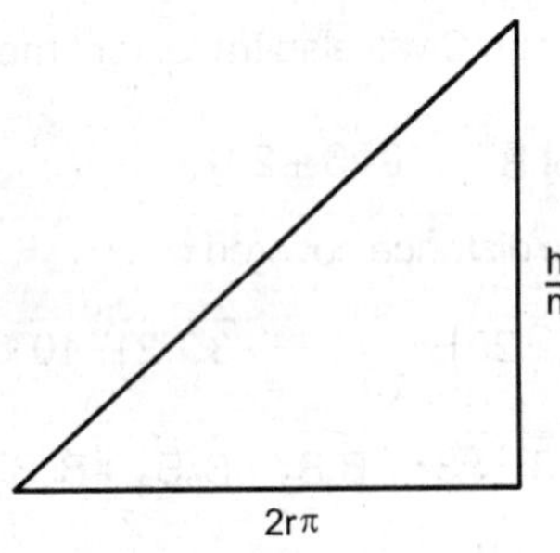

So length of string

$$= n \times \sqrt{(2\pi r)^2 + \frac{h^2}{n^2}} = n\sqrt{4^2 + \frac{h^2}{n^2}}$$

From previous question length of string $= \sqrt{17}n$.

$$\Rightarrow \sqrt{17}n = n\sqrt{16 + \frac{h^2}{n^2}} \Rightarrow h = n$$

23. a Consider a square of side x.

Therefore, its area = x^2

Therefore, area of the largest circle = $\pi\left(\frac{x}{2}\right)^2$,

which can be cut from square = $\frac{\pi x^2}{4}$.

Therefore, area scrapped = $x^2 - \frac{\pi}{4}x^2 = x^2\left(1 - \frac{\pi}{4}\right)$

$$\therefore \frac{\text{Area scrapped}}{\text{Area of square}} = \frac{x^2\left(1 - \frac{\pi}{4}\right)}{x^2} = 1 - \frac{\pi}{4} = \text{Contant}$$

As this ratio is constant whether we cut a circle from small square or larger square, scrapped area will be a fixed percentage of square. Therefore, in our problem as two squares are of the same size, the ratio will be 1 : 1.

24. c It's standard property among circle, square and triangle, for a given parameter, area of circle is the highest and area of the triangle is least whereas area of the square is in-between, i.e. c > s > t.

25. d The required answer is 34 × 0.65 × 0.65 = 14.365 Because we get two similar triangles and area is proportional to square of its side.

26. d

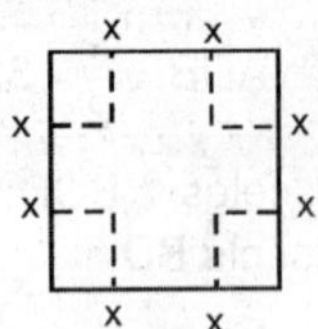

$$\text{Volume} = l \times b \times h$$
$$V = (12 - 2x)(12 - 2x) \times x$$
$$V' = (12 - 2x)\ (12 - 2x)\ 4x$$

Where V' = 4 V

Now sum = 12 – 2x + 12 – 2x + 4x = 24 [Constant]

As sum is constant for maximum product 12 – 2x = 12 – 2x = 4x

Therefore, x = 2

27. d The surface area of a sphere is proportional to the square of the radius.

Thus, $\frac{S_B}{S_A} = \frac{4}{1}$ (Surface area of B is 300% higher than A)

$\therefore \frac{r_B}{r_A} = \frac{2}{1}$

The volume of a sphere is proportional to the cube of the radius.

Thus, $\frac{V_B}{V_A} = \frac{8}{1}$

Or, V_A is $\frac{7}{8}$th less than B i.e. $\frac{7}{8} \times 100 = 87.5\%$.

28. b If the radius of the field is r, then the total area of the field $= \frac{\pi r^2}{2}$.

The radius of the semi-circles with centre's P and R $= \frac{r}{2}$.

Hence, their total area $= \frac{\pi r^2}{4}$

Let the radius if the circle with centre S be x.

Thus, OS = (r – x), OR = $\frac{r}{2}$ and RS $= \left(\frac{r}{2} + x\right)$.

Applying Pythagoras Theorem, we get

$$(r - x)^2 + \left(\frac{r}{2}\right)^2 = \left(\frac{r}{2} + x\right)^2$$

Solving this, we get $x = \frac{r}{3}$.

Thus the area of the circle with centre $S = \frac{\pi r^2}{9}$.

The total area that can be grazed

$$= \pi r^2\left(\frac{1}{4}+\frac{1}{9}\right) = \frac{13\pi r^2}{36}$$

Thus the fraction of the field that can be grazed

$$= \frac{26}{36}\left(\frac{\text{Area that can be grazed}}{\text{Area of the field}}\right)$$

The fraction that cannot be grazed $= \frac{10}{36} = 28\%$ (approx.)

29. c

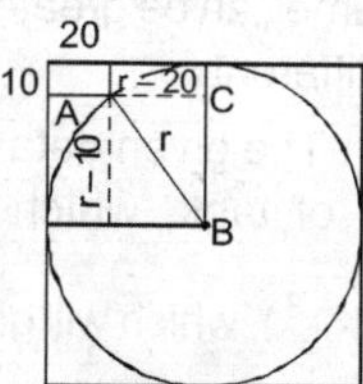

Let the radius be r. Thus by Pythagoras' theorem for ΔABC we have $(r-10)^2 + (r-20)^2 = r^2$

i.e. $r^2 - 60r + 500 = 0$. Thus r = 10 or 50.

It would be 10, if the corner of the rectangle had been lying on the inner circumference. But as per the given diagram, the radius of the circle should be 50 cm.

30. b

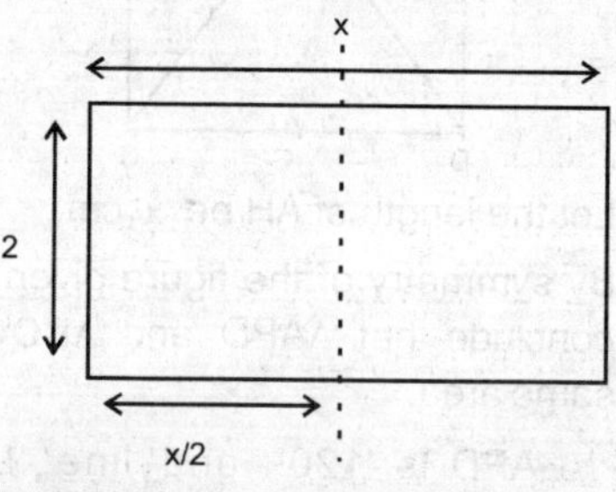

In original rectangle ratio $= \frac{x}{2}$

In smaller rectangle ratio $= \frac{2}{\left(\frac{x}{2}\right)}$

Given $\frac{x}{2} = \frac{2}{\frac{x}{2}} \Rightarrow x = 2\sqrt{2}$

Area of smaller rectangle

$$= \frac{x}{2}\times 2 = x = 2\sqrt{2} \text{ sq. units}.$$

31. d

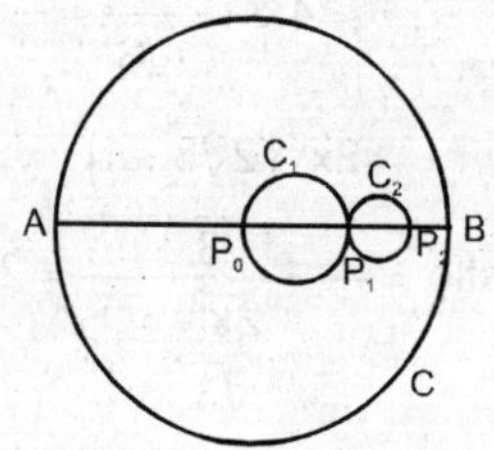

Circle	Radius
C	r
C_1	$\frac{r}{4}$
C_2	$\frac{r}{8}$
C_3	$\frac{r}{16}$
⋮	⋮

$$\Rightarrow \frac{\text{Area of unshaded portion of C}}{\text{Area of C}}$$

$$= 1 - \frac{\text{Area of shaded portion}}{\text{Area of C}}$$

$$= 1 - \frac{\pi\left(\left(\frac{r}{4}\right)^2 + \left(\frac{r}{8}\right)^2 + \ldots\right)}{\pi r^2}$$

$$= 1 - \left(\frac{1}{4^2} + \frac{1}{8^2} + \ldots\right) = 1 - \frac{\frac{1}{16}}{1-\frac{1}{4}} = \frac{11}{12}$$

32. a DF, AG and CE are body diagonals of cube.

Let the side of cube be a.

Therefore, body diagonal is $a\sqrt{3}$

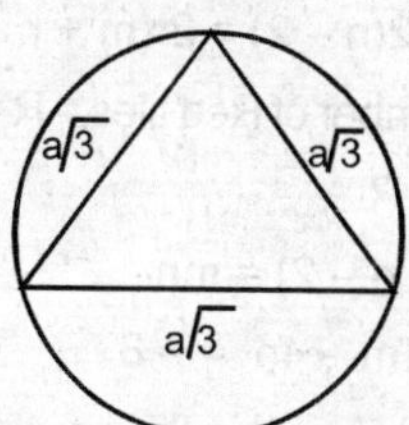

Circum radius for equilateral triangle $= \frac{\text{Side}}{\sqrt{3}}$

Therefore, $\frac{a\sqrt{3}}{\sqrt{3}} = a$

33. b

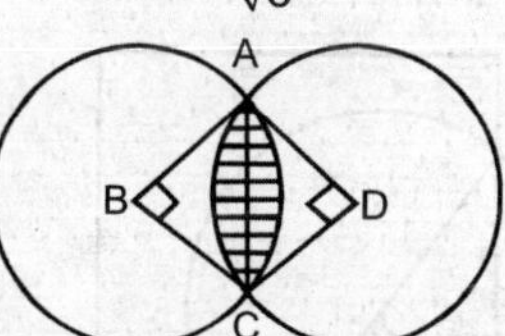

Shaded area = 2 × (area of sector ADC – area of ΔADC)

$$= 2\times\left(\frac{\pi}{4}\times 1^2 - \frac{1}{2}\times 1\times 1\right)$$

$$= \frac{\pi}{2} - 1$$

34. b

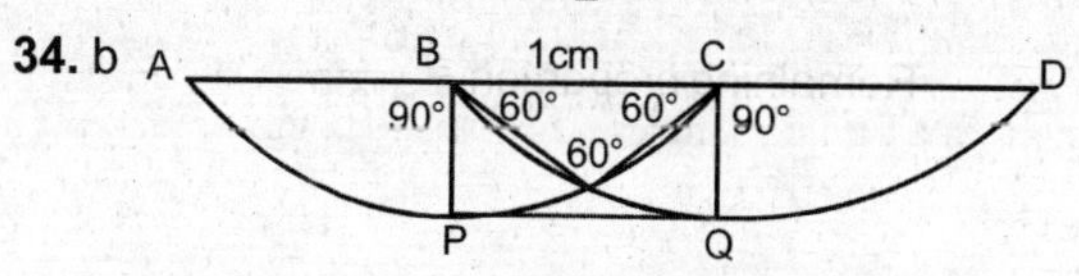

Drawn figure since it have not to be within distance of 1 m so it will go along APQD, which is the path of minimum distance.

$$AP = \frac{90}{360} \times 2\pi \times 1 = \frac{\pi}{2}$$

Also, $AP = QD = \frac{\pi}{2}$

So the minimum distance

$$= AP + PQ + QD$$

$$= \frac{\pi}{2} + 1 + \frac{\pi}{2} = 1 + \pi$$

35. c

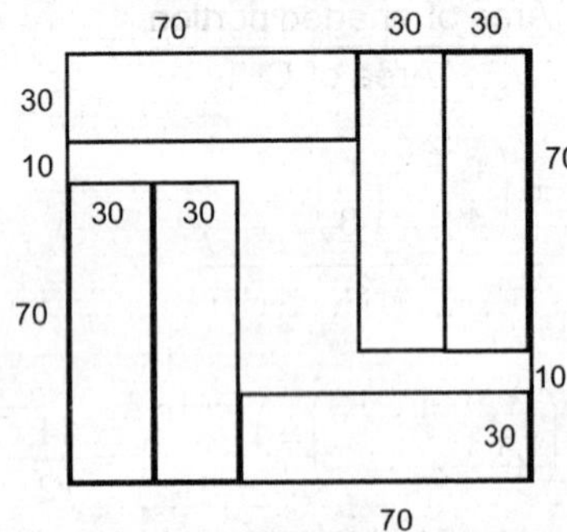

36. b Let the rectangle has m and n tiles along its length and breadth respectively.

The number of white tiles

$W = 2m + 2(n - 2) = 2(m + n - 2)$

And the number of Red tiles $= R = mn - 2(m + n - 2)$

Given $W = R$

$\Rightarrow 4(m + n - 2) = mn$

$\Rightarrow mn - 4m - 4n = -8$

$\Rightarrow (m - 4)(n - 4) = 8$

As m & n are integers so $(m - 4)$ & $(n - 4)$ are both integers. The possibilities are $(m - 4, n - 4) \equiv (1, 8)$ or $(2, 4)$ giving, (m, n) as $(5, 12)$ or $(6, 8)$ so the edges can have 5, 12, 6 or 8 tiles.

37. b

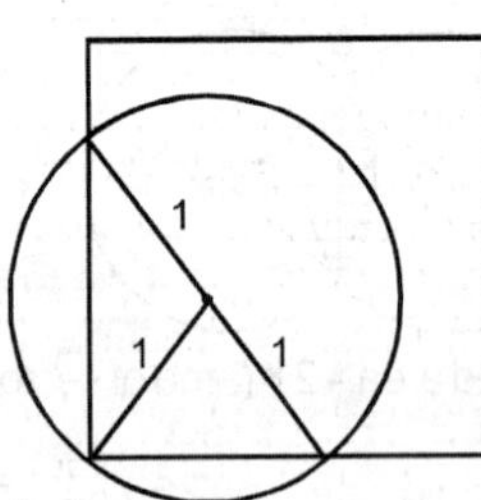

$$\text{Remaining area} = 4 - \left(\frac{\pi}{2} + \frac{1}{2} \times 1 \times 2\right) = \frac{6 - \pi}{2}$$

$$\text{Remaining proportion} = \frac{6 - \pi}{8}$$

38. d

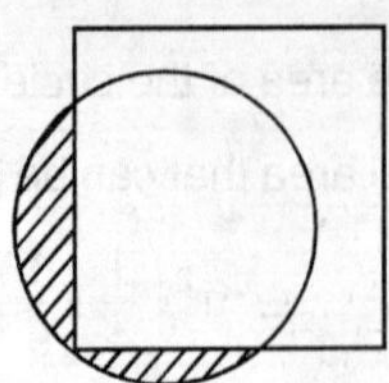

$$\text{Area} = \pi(1)^2 - \left(\frac{\pi}{2} + 1\right) = \pi - \frac{\pi}{2} - 1 = \frac{\pi - 2}{2}$$

39. b **Using A:** Inner radius of the tank is atleast 4 m.

So volume $= \frac{4}{3}\pi r^3$ where $4 < r < 10$

This volume can be greater as well as smaller than 400 for different r.

Using B: The given data gives the volume of the material of tank, which can be expressed as $\frac{4}{3}\pi(10^3 - r^3)$, which will give the value of r which is unique and sufficient to judge if the capacity is adequate.

Hence, option (b)is correct choice.

40. e

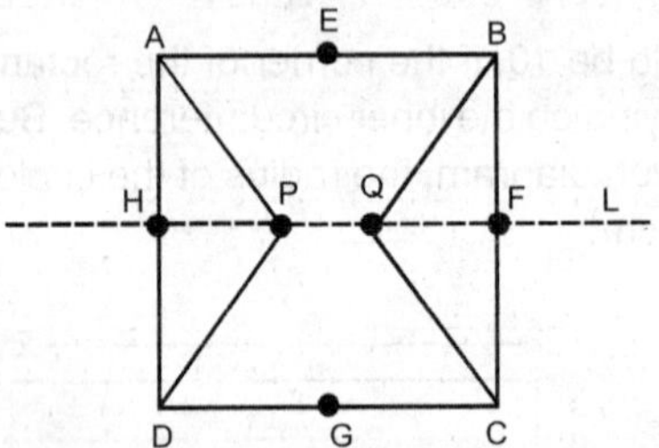

Let the length of AH be 'x' cm.

By symmetry of the figure given above, we can conclude that ΔAPD and ΔBQC will have the same area.

$\because \angle APD$ is $120°$ and line 'L' divides the square ABCD in 2 equal halves, therefore $\angle APH = \angle HPD = 60°$

In $\Delta AHP: \frac{AH}{HP} = \tan 60° = \sqrt{3} \Rightarrow HP = \frac{x}{\sqrt{3}}$ cm

Area of $\Delta APD = 2 \times \text{area}(\Delta AHP)$

$$= 2 \times \frac{1}{2} \times x \times \frac{x}{\sqrt{3}} = \frac{x^2}{\sqrt{3}} \text{ cm}$$

Area of ABQCDP = area (ABCD) – 2 area (ΔAPD)

$$= 4x^2 - \frac{2x^2}{\sqrt{3}} = \frac{2x^2\left(2\sqrt{3} - 1\right)}{\sqrt{3}}$$

$$\text{Required ratio} = \frac{\frac{2x^2\left(2\sqrt{3} - 1\right)}{\sqrt{3}}}{\frac{2x^2}{\sqrt{3}}} = 2\sqrt{3} - 1$$

Alternate method: Concepts used:

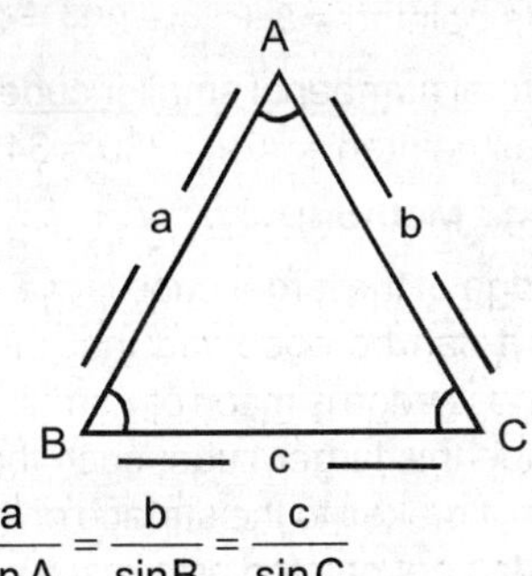

$\Rightarrow \frac{a}{\sin A} = \frac{b}{\sin B} = \frac{c}{\sin C}$

Also, area of $\Delta ABC = \frac{1}{2}$ ab sin C = $\frac{1}{2}$ bc sin A = $\frac{1}{2}$ ac sin B. In the given figure

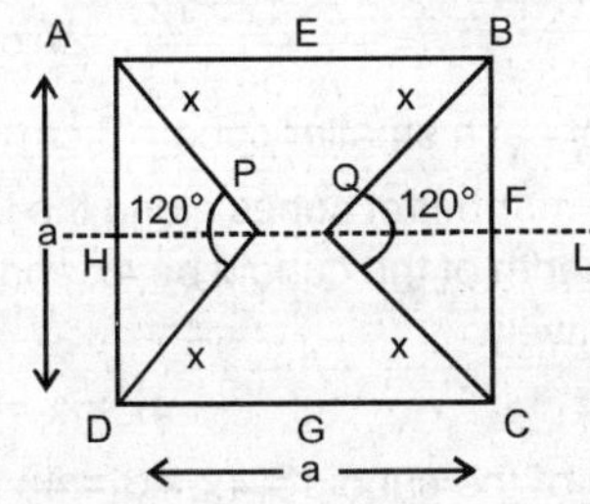

For ΔAPD, Let AP = PD = x cm

$\Rightarrow \frac{a}{\sin 120°} = \frac{x}{\sin 30°} = \frac{x}{\sin 30°}$

$\Rightarrow \sin 120° = \sin (90° + 30°)$

$= \cos 30° = \frac{\sqrt{3}}{2}$, $\sin 30° = \frac{1}{2}$

$\Rightarrow \frac{a}{\frac{\sqrt{3}}{2}} = \frac{x}{\frac{1}{2}}$

$\Rightarrow x = \frac{a}{\sqrt{3}}$ cm

Thus, area of ΔAPD is $\frac{1}{2} \times AP \times PD \times \sin 120°$

$= \frac{1}{2} \times \frac{a}{\sqrt{3}} \times \frac{a}{\sqrt{3}} \times \frac{\sqrt{3}}{2}$

$= \frac{a^2}{4\sqrt{3}}$ cm^2

by symmetry, Area of ΔAPD = Area of ΔBQC

Thus, ratio of $\frac{\text{Area of ABQCDP}}{\text{[Removing area inside square ABCD}}$

$= \frac{\text{Area of square ABCD} - 2 \times (\text{Area of } \Delta APD)}{2 \times (\text{Area of } \Delta APD)}$

$= 2\sqrt{3} - 1$

41. e

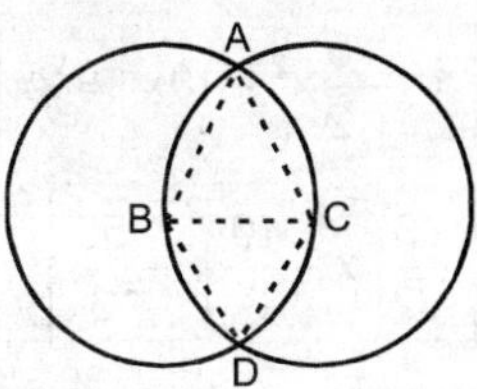

It is given that AB = BC = AC = BD = DC = 1 cm.

Therefore, ΔABC is an equilateral triangle.

Hence, $\angle ACB = 60°$

Now area of sector $\widehat{AB} = \frac{60}{360} \times \pi(1)^2 = \frac{\pi}{6}$

Area of equilateral triangle $\Delta ABC = \frac{\sqrt{3}}{4}(1)^2 = \frac{\sqrt{3}}{4}$

Area of remaining portion in the common region

$\widehat{ABC}$ excluding $\Delta ABC = 2 \times \left(\frac{\pi}{6} - \frac{\sqrt{3}}{4}\right)$

Hence, the total area of the intersecting region

$= 2 \times \frac{\sqrt{3}}{4} \times (1)^2 + 4 \times \left(\frac{\pi}{6} - \frac{\sqrt{3}}{4}\right)$

$= \frac{2\pi}{3} - \frac{\sqrt{3}}{2}$ sq. cm.

42. a

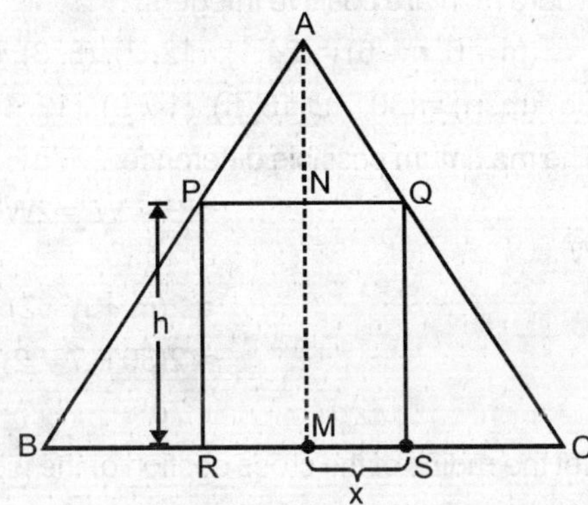

Let the height of the cylinder be 'h' cm and radius be 'x' cm.

ΔANQ is similar to ΔQSC

$\Rightarrow \frac{AN}{NQ} = \frac{QS}{SC} \Rightarrow \frac{10-h}{x} = \frac{h}{4-x}$

$\Rightarrow \frac{10}{h} - 1 = \frac{x}{4-x} \Rightarrow \frac{10}{h} = \frac{4}{4-x}$

$\therefore h = \frac{5}{2}(4-x)$

Surface area of the cylinder PQSR

$= 2\pi\left[x^2 + hx\right] = 2\pi\left[x^2 + \frac{5x}{2}(4-x)\right]$

$= 2\pi\left[x^2 - \frac{5}{2}x^2 + 10x\right] = 2\pi\left[10x - \frac{3}{2}x^2\right]$

$= 2\pi\left[-\frac{3}{2}\left(x - \frac{10}{3}\right)^2 + \frac{50}{3}\right]$

Maximum value of surface area of the cylinder will be at $x = \frac{10}{3}$.

43. a Let's assume that the rectangle has m and n tiles along its length and breadth respectively.

The number of white tiles

$W = 2m + 2(n - 2)$

$= 2(m + n - 2)$

The number of red tiles

$R = (m - 2)(n - 2)$

$= mn - 2m - 2n + 4$

Also, $2W = R$ (given)

$\Rightarrow$ $4m + 4n - 8 = mn - 2m - 2n + 4$

$\Rightarrow$ $mn - 6m - 6n + 12 = 0$

$\Rightarrow$ $(m - 6)(n - 6) - 36 + 12 = 0$

$\Rightarrow$ $(m - 6)(n - 6) = 24$

As m and n are integers, both (m – 6) and (n – 6) are integers as well. The possible sets of values where m, n are positive integers:

$(m - 6, n - 6) = (24,1), (12, 2), (8, 3), (6, 4)$

So $(m, n) = (30, 7), (18, 8), (14, 9), (12, 10)$

The maximum possible difference

$= R - W = 2W - W =$

W

$= 2(m + n - 2)$

$= 2(30 + 7 - 2)$

$= 70$

44. a Let the radius of the cross section of the pipe be r.

Speed (v) at which water flows

= 54 km/hr = 54000 m/hr

Rate of water flow

= (Cross-sectional area of the pipe) × v

$\therefore$ $\pi r^2 \times 54 \times 10^3 \times 14 = \frac{80}{100} \times 118800$

$\Rightarrow$ $r = \frac{2}{10} m = 20$ cm.

45. c There are 8 smaller cubes (on the corners) which have exactly three sides painted.

There are 7 × 12 i.e. 84 smaller cubes (on the edges) which have exactly two sides painted.

There are 7 × 7 × 6 i.e. 294 smaller cubes (on the faces) which have exactly one side painted.

The total number of smaller cubes with at least one side painted = 8 + 84 + 294 = 386

So the total number of smaller cubes with none of the sides painted = 729 – 386 = 343.

Alternate Method:

Each edge of the larger cube is made of 9 smaller cubes. It can be observed that there is another cube whose edge is made of 7 smaller cubes which lies inside this larger cube, such that none of the cubes in it makes to the surface of the larger cube (and didn't get painted as a result).

The total number of smaller cubes in this cube = $7^3 = 343$.

46. c Volume of each smaller cube

$= \frac{12 \times 12 \times 12}{64} = 27 \text{ cm}^3$

Edge of each smaller cube = 3 cm

Let the number of cubes along the length and the breadth of the cuboid be 4x and x respectively.

$4x \times x = 64$ or $x = 4$

Length of the cuboid = 4x × 3 = 48 cm

Breadth of the cuboid = x × 3 = 12 cm

Required surface area = 48 × 12 = 576 cm^2

47. a

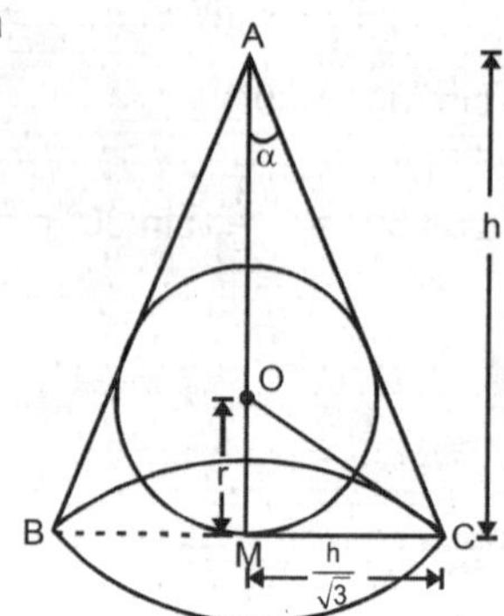

Let the semi vertical angle of the cone be α.

$\tan\alpha = \frac{h/\sqrt{3}}{h} \Rightarrow \tan\alpha = \frac{1}{\sqrt{3}} \Rightarrow \alpha = 30^\circ$

The vertical angle of the cone = 60°

Therefore, the triangle ABC is an equilateral triangle.

The given case i.e. placing of a sphere of the maximum volume inside a cone will be identical to the case of inscribing a circle inside a triangle. Therefore, the center (O) of the circle will coincide with the centroid of the triangle ABC.

In triangle ACM, OC is angle bisector of $\angle ACM$.

$\therefore$ $\angle OCM = 30^\circ$

In ΔOCM,

$\tan 30^\circ = \dfrac{r}{h/\sqrt{3}} \Rightarrow r = \dfrac{h}{3}$

Hence, the ratio of the volume of the sphere to that of the cone $= \dfrac{\frac{4}{3}\pi\left(\frac{h}{3}\right)^3}{\frac{1}{3}\pi\left(\frac{h}{\sqrt{3}}\right)^2 \times h} = 4:9.$

48. a

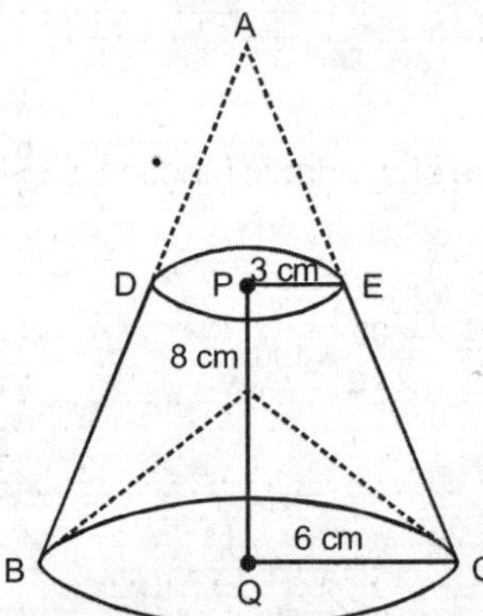

In the figure given above, ABC represents the actual cone from which the frustum was made. DEBC represents the frustum and BRC represents the conical cavity.

Now, the volume of the material in the solid can be calculated by subtracting the volume of the cone ADE and the conical cavity BRC from the cone ABC.

ΔAPE and ΔAQC are similar,

$\Rightarrow \quad \dfrac{AP}{AQ} = \dfrac{PE}{QC}$

$\Rightarrow \quad AP = 8$ cm.

Volume of cone ABC $= \dfrac{1}{3}\pi(6)^2 \times 16$

Volume of cone APE $= \dfrac{1}{3}\pi(3)^2 \times 8$

Volume of conical cavity BRC $= \dfrac{1}{3}\pi(6)^2 \times 3$

Required volume of solid

$= \dfrac{1}{3}\pi(6)^2 \times 16 - \dfrac{1}{3}\pi(3)^2 \times 8 - \dfrac{1}{3}\pi(6)^2 \times 3$

$= 132\pi$ cm^3.

49. b Since the HCF of 24 and 56 is 8, the side of the identical square plots must be one of the factors of 8.

The factors of 8 are 1, 2, 4 and 8

If side of the square plot is 1 m, the length of fencing material required is $(25 \times 56 + 57 \times 24) = 2768$ m

But 2768 m > 2700 m.

If side of the square plot is 2 m, the length of fencing material required is

$(29 \times 24 + 13 \times 56) = 1464$ m < 2600 m

$\therefore$ For minimum fencing material to be left the side of identical square plot = 2m.

50. Volume of a cylinder = $\pi r^2 h$, where

r = radius of the cylinder

h = height of the cylinder

Volume of the graphite cylinder

$= \pi\left(\dfrac{1}{10}\right)^2 \times 10 = \dfrac{\pi}{10}$ cm^3

Volume of the layer of wood

$= 10\pi\left[\left(\dfrac{7}{10}\right)^2 - \left(\dfrac{1}{10}\right)^2\right] = \dfrac{48\pi}{10}$ cm^3

Cost of the material in a pencil

$= \dfrac{\pi}{10} \times 2.10 + \dfrac{48\pi}{10} \times 0.70$ = Rs.11.22

51.

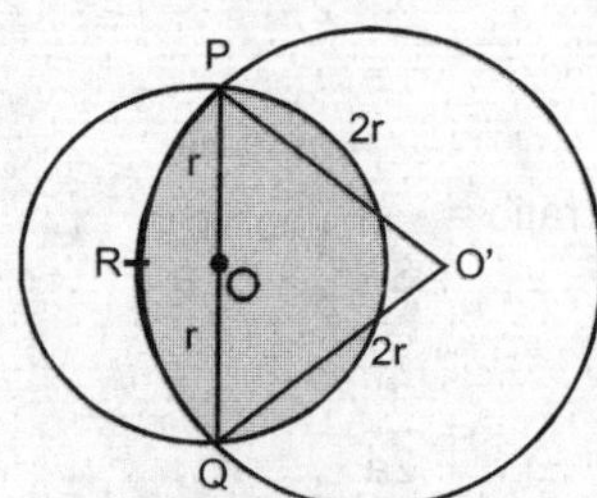

The common chord will be of the maximum length if it is the diameter of the smaller circle.

In ΔPO'Q, PQ = 2r and PO' = QO' = 2r, therefore, ΔPO'Q is an equilateral triangle.

Required area (in sq. units) of the shaded region

$= \dfrac{1}{2} \times$ Area of smaller circle + Area of segment PRQ

$= \dfrac{1}{2} \times$ Area of smaller circle + (Area of sector O'PQ − Area of triangle PO'Q)

$= \dfrac{\pi r^2}{2} + \left\{\dfrac{\pi(2r)^2}{6} - \dfrac{\sqrt{3}(2r)^2}{4}\right\} = \dfrac{7\pi r^2}{6} - \sqrt{3}r^2.$

52. Let the original volume of the raindrop be 'x' ml.

Therefore, initial volume of water in the raindrop will be 0.75x ml.

Remaining volume of water after evaporation

$= (0.75x - 2)$ ml

Remaining volume of water is 70% of $(x - 2)$ ml.

$\therefore \quad 0.75x - 2 = (x - 2) \times 0.7$

$\Rightarrow \quad x = 12.$

53. Let the length of the side of the octagon and the radius of the circle be 'a' units and 'r' units respectively. Therefore, the length of the side of the square will be $\left(\frac{2r}{\sqrt{2}}\right)$ units.

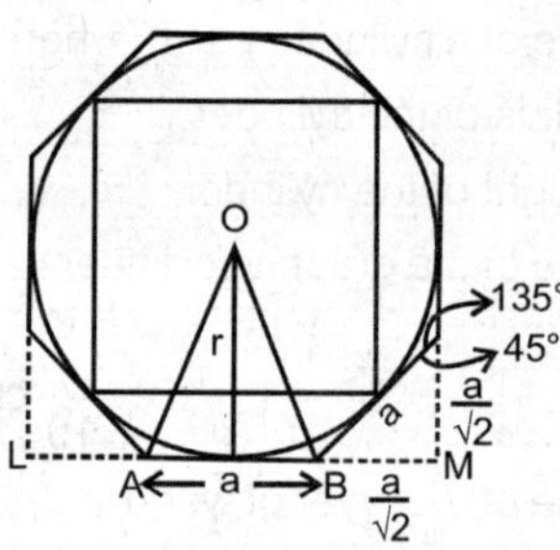

$$LM = LA + AB + BM$$

$$\Rightarrow \quad 2r = \frac{a}{\sqrt{2}} + a + \frac{a}{\sqrt{2}}$$

$$\Rightarrow \quad r = \frac{a(1+\sqrt{2})}{2}$$

Hence, the ratio $= \dfrac{\left(\frac{2r}{\sqrt{2}}\right)^2}{8 \times \frac{1}{2} \times r \times a}$

$$= \frac{r}{2a}$$

$$= \frac{a\left(\frac{1+\sqrt{2}}{2}\right)}{2a} = \left(1+\sqrt{2}\right) : 4.$$

54. Let the side of the squares be 'a' cm.

So the dimensions of the open box will be:

Length = (30 – 2a) cm

Breadth = (20 – 2a) cm

Height = a cm

$\therefore \quad (30 - 2a) \times (20 - 2a) \times a = 1056$

$\Rightarrow \quad (15 - a) \times (10 - a) \times a = 264 = 11 \times 6 \times 4$

Hence, a = 4.

55.

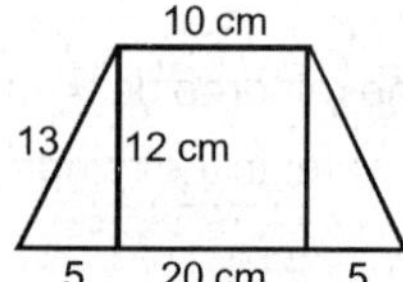

Area of a base $= \frac{1}{2}(10 + 20) \times 12 = 180$ cm

Total area of all six surfaces of the pillar is

$= 10 \times 20 + 20 \times 20 + 2 \times 180 + 2 \times (13 \times 20)$

$= 200 + 400 + 360 + 520 = 1480$ cm^2.

56. 00

So x + 2y = 400

x = 400 – 2y

Area = xy

= (400 – 2y)y

$= 400y - 2y^2$

Maximum value of quadratic function is $\frac{-b}{2a}$ (when a is –ve)

So, value of $y = \frac{-400}{-2 \times 2} = 100,$

So if y = 100

x = 200.

57. 6

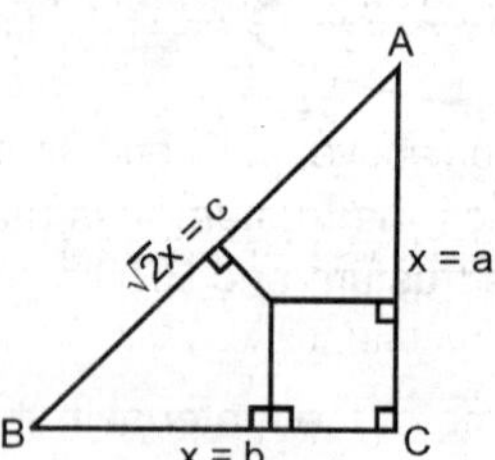

In-radius of a right $\angle\Delta$ is $r = \frac{a+b-c}{2}$

$\Rightarrow 4(\sqrt{2}-1) = \frac{x + x - \sqrt{2}x}{2}$

$\Rightarrow 4(\sqrt{2}-1) = \frac{2x - \sqrt{2}x}{2}$

$\Rightarrow 4(\sqrt{2}-1) = \frac{\sqrt{2}x(\sqrt{2}-1)}{2}$

$x = 4\sqrt{2}$ cm.

$\therefore$ Area $= \frac{1}{2} \times 4\sqrt{2} \times 4\sqrt{2}$

= 16 cm^2

58.

AB = 12 ft, MB = 9 ft

$\therefore$ AM = 3ft

As $\Delta AMN \sim \Delta ABC$

$\therefore \frac{12}{4} = \frac{3}{MN}$

$\Rightarrow MN = 1$ ft

$\therefore$ Volume of the remaining part of the cone

$$= \frac{1}{3}\pi(4)^2 \times 12 - \frac{1}{3} \times \pi(1)^2 \times 3.$$

$$= \frac{1}{3}\pi \times 3[64 - 1]$$

$$= \frac{22}{7} \times 63 = 198 \text{ cubic ft.}$$

Co-ordinate Geometry

1. c The distance between two points (x_1, y_1) and (x_2, y_2) is given as $\sqrt{(x_2 - x_1)^2 + (y_2 - y_1)^2}$

Hence, required distance

$= \sqrt{(-2-3)^2 + (-7-8)^2}$

$= 5\sqrt{10}$.

2. d The three lines can be expressed as

$$Y = \frac{5}{3} - \frac{2X}{3},\ Y = \frac{5X}{7} + \frac{2}{7} \text{ and } Y = \frac{9X}{5} - \frac{4}{5}.$$

Therefore, the slopes of the three lines are $\frac{-2}{3}, \frac{5}{7}$ and $\frac{9}{5}$ respectively and their Y intercepts are $\frac{5}{3}, \frac{2}{7}$ and $\frac{4}{5}$ respectively. For any two lines to be perpendicular to each other, the product of their slopes = –1. We find that the product of none of the slopes is –1. For any two be parallel, their slopes should be the same. This is again not the case. And finally for the two lines to be intersecting at the same point, there should be one set of values of (X, Y)that should satisfy the equations of 3 lines. Solving the first two equations, we get X = 1 and Y = 1. If we substitute this in the third equation, we find that it also satisfies that equation. So the solution set (1, 1)satisfies all three equations, suggesting that the three lines intersect at the same point, viz. (1, 1). Hence, they are coincident.

3. c If we solve the two given equations, we get the point of intersection as (3, 2). Let A = (3, 2). The lines of our interest (let it be L_1 and L_2)also pass through A. One of the lines passes through (0, 4). Let L_1 passes through (0, 4), but it also passes through (3, 2). Hence, we can find the slope of L_2 (which is equal to $-\frac{2}{3}$). Hence, slope of L_2 will be $\frac{3}{2}$ since L_1 and L_2 are perpendicular. Hence, equations of L_1 and L_2 can be obtained by using slope point form. (Students! we need not really find out the equations.) After getting both the equations, we can find the area bounded by L_1 and L_2 and coordinate axes.

4. c The final point is (6, 6). The previous point is (6, 2) and the one before is (4, 2).

5. a Two instructions are needed, one parallel to the X-axis and the other parallel to the Y-axis. i.e. WALKX(–x)and WALKY (–y)

6. a The gradient of the line AD is –1. Coordinates of B are (– 1, 0).

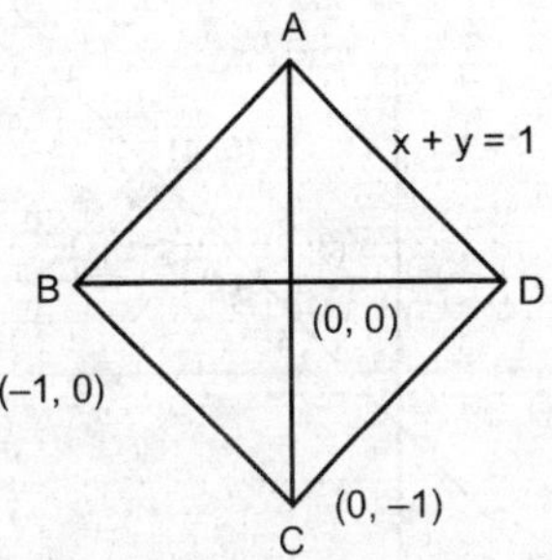

Equation of line BC is x + y = –1.

7. d Both the statements combined also do not tell us if they are intersecting or not. The two lines can be parallel also depending on the values of a, b, d, e.

8. b

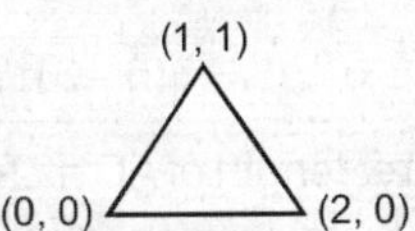

Let a = 0

Hence, area = $\frac{1}{2}(2)\ (1) - 1$

Note: Answer should be independent of a and area of the triangle does not have square root.

9. a

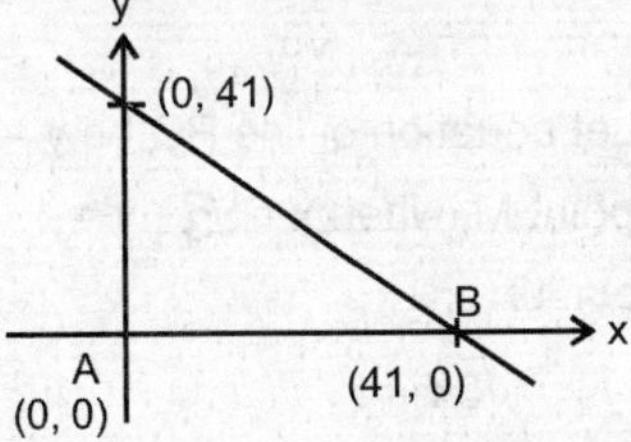

equation of line ≡ x + y = 41. If the (x, y) co-ordinates of the points are integer, their sum shall also be integers so that x + y = k (k, a variable) as we have to exclude points lying on the boundary of triangle; k can take all values from 1 to 40 only. k = 0 is also rejected as at k = 0 will give the point

A; which can't be taken.

Now, x + y = k, (k = 1, 2, 3, ...,40)

with k = 40; x + y = 40; taking integral solutions.

We get points (1, 39), (2, 38); (3, 37); ..., (39, 1)

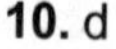
i.e. 39 points

x + y = 40 will be satisfied by 39 points.

Similarly, x + y = 39 is satisfied by 38 points.

x + y = 38 by 37 points.

x + y = 3 by 2 points.

x + y = 2 is satisfied by 1 point.

x + y = 1 is not satisfied by any point.

So, the total no. of all such points is:

$$39+38+37+36+...+3+2+1=\frac{39\times 40}{2}=780 \text{ points.}$$

10. d

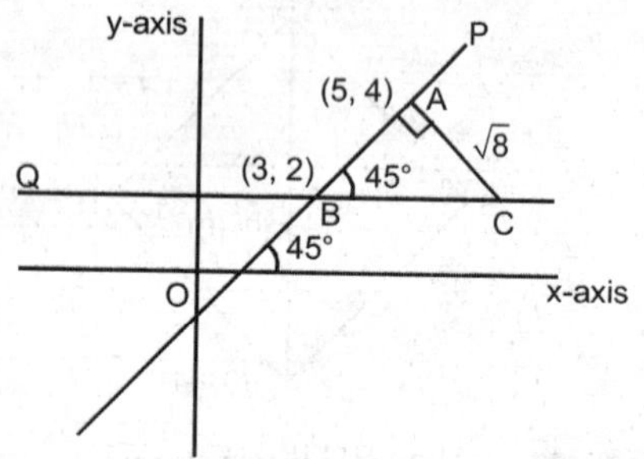

As slope of line P is 45°, $\angle ABC = 45°$.

(Corresponding angles)

In triangle ABC, length of AB

$$= \sqrt{(5-3)^2+(4-2)^2} = 2\sqrt{2} \text{ units}$$

Therefore, length of AC = $2\sqrt{2}$ units

Required area $= \frac{1}{2}\times 2\sqrt{2}\times 2\sqrt{2} = 4$ sq. units

11. d PQ is perpendicular to line $y=\frac{x}{\sqrt{3}}$

$\therefore$ Slop of PQ $= \frac{-1}{\frac{1}{\sqrt{3}}} = -\sqrt{3}$

$\therefore$ Let equation of line PQ be $y=-\sqrt{3}x + c$

At point M, when x = $\sqrt{3}$, y = 1.

$\therefore$ c = 4

$\Rightarrow y=-\sqrt{3}x+4$

$\therefore$ Co-ordinates of point Q = $\left(\frac{4}{\sqrt{3}}, 0\right)$ and Co-ordinates of point P = (0, 4).

Hence, PQ = $\sqrt{\left(\frac{4}{\sqrt{3}}\right)^2+4^2} = 4\sqrt{\frac{1}{3}+1} = \frac{8}{\sqrt{3}}$units

12. c

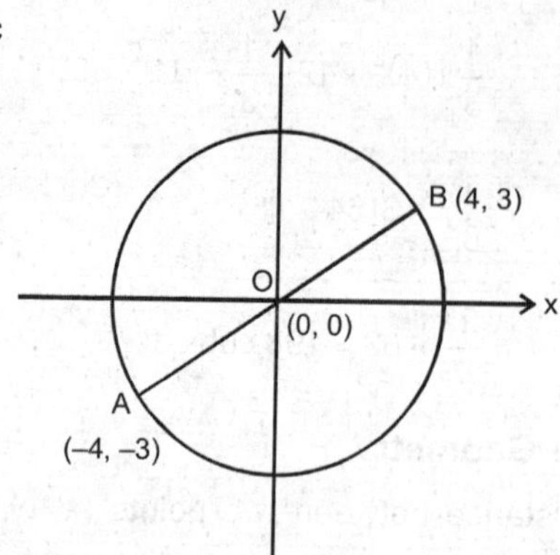

Other two vertices will make two right angled triangles with AB as the common hypotenuse. So they must lie on the circle with AB as the diameter and O as the centre. Radius of that circle will be 5 units.

There will be 5 such pairs in which both the coordinates are integers.

[(5, 0), (–5, 0)], [(–4, 3), (4, – 3)], [(–3, 4), (3, –4)] [(–3, –4), (3, 4)] and [(0, 5), (0, –5)]

13. d

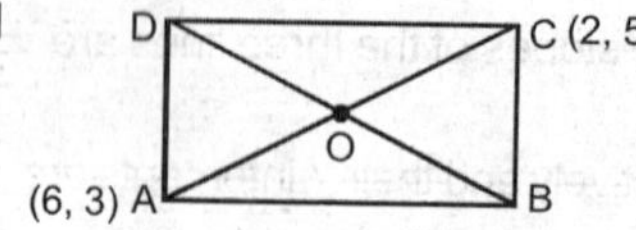

Since diagonals of a rectangle bisect each other so O is the mid point of AC.

Co-ordinates of O = $\left(\frac{6+2}{2}, \frac{5+3}{2}\right)$ = (4, 4)

Point O will satisfy the equation of the other diagonal too. So,

y = 3x + c

4 = 3 × 4 + c

c = – 8.

CHAPTER

Modern Maths

PERMUTATION AND COMBINATION

1990

1. There are six boxes numbered 1, 2, 3, 4, 5, 6. Each box is to be filled up either with a white ball or a black ball in such a manner that at least one box contains a black ball and all the boxes containing black balls are consecutively numbered. The total number of ways in which this can be done equals.

   (a) 15 (b) 21
   (c) 63 (d) 64

1991

2. How many 3-digit even numbers can you form such that if one of the digits is 5 then the following digit must be 7?

   (a) 5 (b) 405
   (c) 365 (d) 495

1993

3. Four cities are connected by a road network as shown in the figure. In how many ways can you start from any city and come back to it without travelling on the same road more than once?

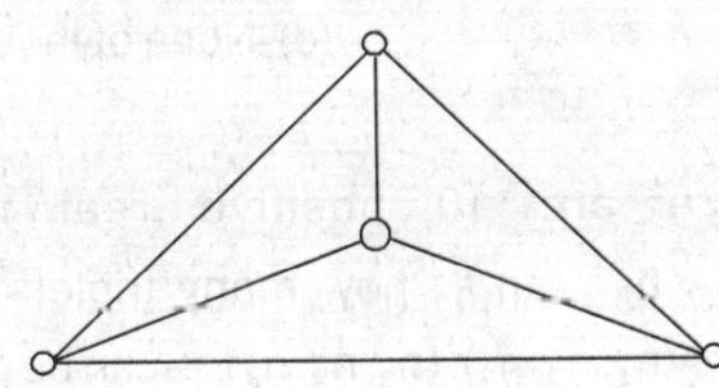

   (a) 8 (b) 12
   (c) 16 (d) 20

4. A five digit number is formed using digits 1, 3, 5, 7 and 9 without repeating any one of them. What is the sum of all such possible numbers?

   (a) 6666600 (b) 6666660
   (c) 6666666 (d) None of these

5. Consider the five points comprising of the vertices of a square and the intersection point of its diagonals. How many triangles can be formed using these points?

   (a) 4 (b) 6
   (c) 8 (d) 10

1995

6. Boxes numbered 1, 2, 3, 4 and 5 are kept in a row, and they are to be filled with either a red or a blue ball, such that no two adjacent boxes can be filled with blue balls. Then how many different arrangements are possible, given that all balls of a given colour are exactly identical in all respects?

   (a) 8 (b) 10
   (c) 15 (d) 22

7. A, B, C and D are four towns, any three of which are non-collinear. Then the number of ways to construct three roads each joining a pair of towns so that the roads do not form a triangle is

   (a) 7 (b) 8
   (c) 9 (d) 24

1996

8. A man has 9 friends: 4 boys and 5 girls. In how many ways can he invite them, if there have to be exactly 3 girls in the invitees?

   (a) 320 (b) 160
   (c) 80 (d) 200

Direction for Question 9: The question is followed by two statements, I and II. Mark the answer as

(a) if the question cannot be answered even with the help of both the statements taken together.

(b) if the question can be answered by any one of the two statements.

(c) if each statement alone is sufficient to answer the question, but not the other one (e.g. statement I alone is required to answer the question, but not statement II and vice versa).

(d) if both statements I and II together are needed to answer the question.

9. How many different triangles can be formed?

   I. There are 16 coplanar, straight lines.
   II. No two lines are parallel.

1997

10. In how many ways can eight directors, the vice chairman and chairman of a firm be seated at a round table, if the chairman has to sit between the vice chairman and a director?

   (a) $9! \times 2$ (b) $2 \times 8!$
   (c) $2 \times 7!$ (d) None of these

1998

11. How many numbers can be formed from 1, 2, 3, 4, 5, without repetition, when the digit at the unit's place must be greater than that in the ten's place?
(a) 54
(b) 60
(c) 17
(d) 2 × 4!

1999

12. Ten points are marked on a straight-line and 11 points are marked on another straight-line. How many triangles can be constructed with vertices from among the above points?
(a) 495
(b) 550
(c) 1045
(d) 2475

13. For a scholarship, at the most n candidates out of 2n + 1 can be selected. If the number of different ways of selection of at least one candidate is 63, the maximum number of candidates that can be selected for the scholarship is
(a) 3
(b) 4
(c) 6
(d) 5

2000

14. One red flag, three white flags and two blue flags are arranged in a line such that:
I. No two adjacent flags are of the same colour
II. The flags at the two ends of the line are of different colours
In how many different ways can the flags be arranged?
(a) 6
(b) 4
(c) 10
(d) 2

15. Sam has forgotten his friend's seven-digit telephone number. He remembers the following: the first three digits are either 635 or 674, the number is odd, and the number 9 appears once. If Sam were to use a trial and error process to reach his friend, what is the minimum number of trials he has to make before he can be certain to succeed?
(a) 10,000
(b) 2,430
(c) 3,402
(d) 3,006

16. ABCDEFGH is a regular octagon. A and E are opposite vertices of the octagon. A frog starts jumping from vertex to vertex, beginning from A. From any vertex of the octagon except E, it may jump to either of the two adjacent vertices. When it reaches E, the frog stops and stays there. Let a_n be the number of distinct paths of exactly n jumps ending in E. Then what is the value of a_{2n-1}?
(a) 0
(b) 4
(c) 2n – 1
(d) Cannot be determined

2001

17. Ashish is given Rs. 158 in one-rupee denominations. He has been asked to allocate them into a number of bags such that any amount required between Re 1 and Rs. 158 can be given by handing out a certain number of bags without opening them. What is the minimum number of bags required?
(a) 11
(b) 12
(c) 13
(d) None of these

18. The figure below shows the network connecting cities A, B, C, D, E and F. The arrows indicate permissible direction of travel. What is the number of distinct paths from A to F?

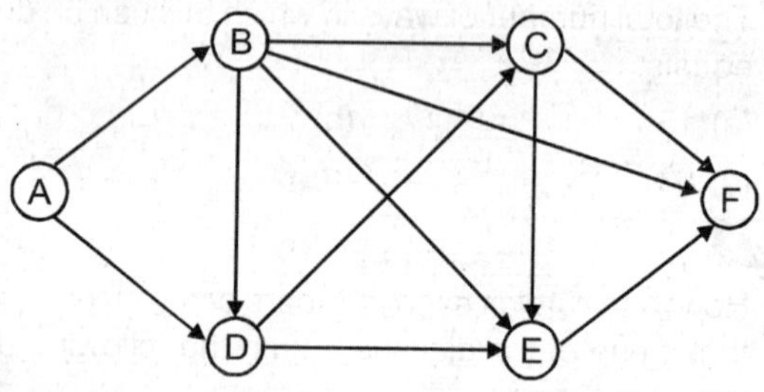

(a) 9
(b) 10
(c) 11
(d) None of these

19. Let n be the number of different five-digit numbers, divisible by 4 with the digits 1, 2, 3, 4, 5 and 6, no digit being repeated in the numbers. What is the value of n?
(a) 144
(b) 168
(c) 192
(d) None of these

2002

20. If there are 10 positive real numbers $n_1 < n_2 < n_3 ... < n_{10}$, how many triplets of these numbers $(n_1, n_2, n_3), (n_2, n_3, n_4)$, ... can be generated such that in each triplet the first number is always less than the second number, and the second number is always less than the third number?
(a) 45
(b) 90
(c) 120
(d) 180

21. Ten straight lines, no two of which are parallel and no three of which pass through any common point, are drawn on a plane. The total number of regions (including finite and infinite regions) into which the plane would be divided by the lines is
(a) 56
(b) 255
(c) 1024
(d) not unique

Directions for Questions 22 and 23: Answer the questions based on the following information.

Each of the 11 letters A, H, I, M, O, T, U, V, W, X and Z appears same when looked at in a mirror. They are called symmetric letters. Other letters in the alphabet are asymmetric letters.

22. How many four-letter computer passwords can be formed using only the symmetric letters (no repetition allowed)?

(a) 7,920 (b) 330

(c) 14,640 (d) 4,19,430

23. How many three-letter computer passwords can be formed (no repetition allowed)with at least one symmetric letter?

(a) 990 (b) 2,730

(c) 12,870 (d) 15,600

24. In how many ways is it possible to choose a white square and a black square on a chessboard so that the squares must not lie in the same row or column?

(a) 56 (b) 896

(c) 60 (d) 768

25. How many numbers greater than 0 and less than a million can be formed with the digits 0, 7 and 8?

(a) 486 (b) 1,084

(c) 728 (d) None of these

2003(R)

26. There are 12 towns grouped into four zones with three towns per zone. It is intended to connect the towns with a telephone lines such that every two towns are connected with three direct lines if they belong to the same zone, and with only one direct line otherwise. How many direct telephone lines are required?

(a) 72 (b) 90

(c) 96 (d) 144

27. An intelligence agency forms a code of two distinct digits selected from 0, 1, 2, …, 9 such that the first digit of the code is non-zero. The code, handwritten on a slip, can however potentially create confusion when read upside down— for example, the code 91 may appear as 16. How many codes are there for which no such confusion can arise?

(a) 80 (b) 78

(c) 71 (d) 69

Directions for Questions 28 and 29: Answer the questions on the basis of the information given below.

A string of three English letters is formed as per the following rules:

I. The first letter is any vowel.

II. The second letter is m, n or p.

III. If the second letter is m, then the third letter is any vowel which is different from the first letter.

IV. If the second letter is n, then the third letter is e or u.

V. If the second letter is p, then the third letter is the same as the first letter.

28. How many strings of letters can possibly be formed using the above rules?

(a) 40 (b) 45

(c) 30 (d) 35

29. How many strings of letters can possibly be formed using the above rules such that the third letter of the string is e?

(a) 8 (b) 9

(c) 10 (d) 11

2003(L)

30. How many three digit positive integers, with digits x, y and z in the hundred's, ten's and unit's place respectively, exist such that $x < y$, $z < y$ and $x \neq 0$?

(a) 245 (b) 285

(c) 240 (d) 320

31. There are 6 boxes numbered 1,2,… 6. Each box is to be filled up either with a red or a green ball in such a way that at least 1 box contains a green ball and the boxes containing green balls are consecutively numbered. The total number of ways in which this can be done is

(a) 5 (b) 21

(c) 33 (d) 60

32. A graph may be defined as a set of points connected by lines called edges. Every edge connects a pair of points. Thus, a triangle is a graph with 3 edges and 3 points. The degree of a point is the number of edges connected to it. For example, a triangle is a graph with three points of degree 2 each. Consider a graph with 12 points. It is possible to reach any point from any point through a sequence of edges. The number of edges, e, in the graph must satisfy the condition

(a) $11 \leq e \leq 66$ (b) $10 \leq e \leq 66$

(c) $11 \leq e \leq 65$ (d) $0 \leq e \leq 11$

2004

33. N persons stand on the circumference of a circle at distinct points. Each possible pair of persons, not standing next to each other, sings a two-minute song one pair after the other. If the total time taken for singing is 28 minutes, what is N?

(a) 5 (b) 7

(c) 9 (d) None of the above

34. In the adjoining figure, the lines represent one-way roads allowing travel only northwards or only westwards. Along how many distinct routes can a car reach point B from point A?

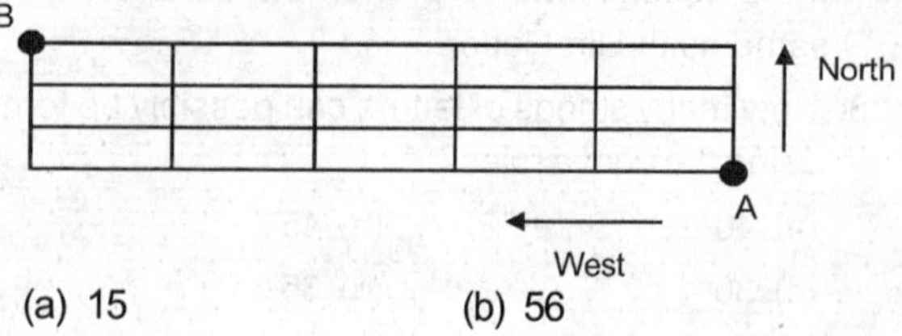

(a) 15 (b) 56
(c) 120 (d) 336

35. A new flag is to be designed with six vertical stripes using some or all of the colours yellow, green, blue and red. Then, the number of ways this can be done so that no two adjacent stripes have the same colour is

(a) 12 × 81 (b) 16 × 192
(c) 20 × 125 (d) 24 × 216

2005

36. In a chess competition involving some boys and girls of a school, every student had to play exactly one game with every other student. It was found that in 45 games both the players were girls, and in 190 games both were boys. The number of games in which one player was a boy and the other was a girl is

(a) 200 (b) 216
(c) 235 (d) 256

37. Let S be the set of five-digit numbers formed by digits 1, 2, 3, 4 and 5, using each digit exactly once such that exactly two odd position are occupied by odd digits. What is the sum of the digits in the rightmost position of the numbers in S?

(a) 228 (b) 216
(c) 294 (d) 192

38. Three Englishmen and three Frenchmen work for the same company. Each of them knows a secret not known to others. They need to exchange these secrets over person-to-person phone calls so that eventually each person knows all six secrets. None of the Frenchmen knows English, and only one Englishman knows French. What is the minimum number of phone calls needed for the above purpose?

(a) 5 (b) 10
(c) 9 (d) 15

2006

39. There are 6 tasks and 6 persons. Task 1 cannot be assigned either to person 1 or to person 2; task 2 must be assigned to either person 3 or person 4. Every person is to be assigned one task. In how many ways can the assignment be done?

(a) 144 (b) 180
(c) 192 (d) 360
(e) 716

2007

Directions for Questions 40 and 41: Answer the following questions based on the information given below.

Let S be the set of all pairs (i, j)where, $1 \le i < j \le n$ and $n \ge 4$. Any two distinct members of S are called "friends" if they have one constituent of the pairs in common and "enemies" otherwise. For example, if n = 4, then S = {(1, 2), (1, 3), (1, 4), (2, 3), (2, 4), (3, 4)}. Here, (1, 2) and (1, 3) are friends, (1, 2) and (2, 3) are also friends, but (1, 4) and (2, 3) are enemies.

40. For general 'n', how many enemies will each member of S have?

(a) $n-3$ (b) $\frac{1}{2}(n^2-3n-2)$
(c) $2n-7$ (d) $\frac{1}{2}(n^2-5n+6)$
(e) $\frac{1}{2}(n^2-7n+14)$

41. For general 'n', consider any two members of S that are friends. How many other members of S will be common friends of both these members?

(a) $\frac{1}{2}(n^2-5n+8)$ (b) $2n-6$
(c) $\frac{1}{2}n(n-3)$ (d) $n-2$
(e) $\frac{1}{2}(n^2-7n+16)$

42. In a tournament, there are n teams $T_1, T_2, \dots, T_n$, with n > 5. Each team consists of 'k' players, k > 3. The following pairs of teams have one player in common:

T_1 & T_2, T_2 & T_3, ..., T_{n-1} & T_n, and T_n & T_1

No other pair of teams has any player in common. How many players are participating in the tournament, considering all the 'n' teams together?

(a) n(k–1) (b) k(n–1)
(c) n(k–2) (d) k(n – 2)
(e) (n – 1)(k – 1)

2008

43. How many integers, greater than 999 but not greater than 4000, can be formed with the digits 0, 1, 2, 3 and 4, if repetition of digits is allowed?

(a) 499
(b) 500
(c) 375
(d) 376
(e) 501

2008

Directions for Questions 44 and 45:

The figure below shows the plan of a town. The streets are at right angles to each other. A rectangular park (P) is situated inside the town with a diagonal road running through it. There is also a prohibited region (D) in the town.

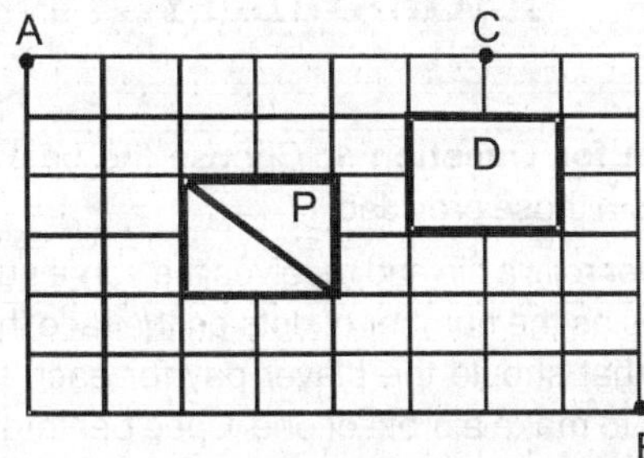

44. Neelam rides her bicycle from her house at A to her office at B, taking the shortest path. Then the number of possible shortest paths that she can choose is

(a) 60 (b) 75
(c) 45 (d) 90
(e) 72

45. Neelam rides her bicycle from her house at A to her club at C, via B taking the shortest path. Then the number of possible shortest paths that she can choose is

(a) 1170 (b) 630
(c) 792 (d) 1200
(e) 936

46. What is the number of distinct terms in the expansion of $(a + b + c)^{20}$?

(a) 231 (b) 253
(c) 242 (d) 210
(e) 228

MEMORY BASED QUESTIONS

2010

47. In how many ways can 18 identical balls be distributed among 3 identical boxes?

(a) 25 (b) 210
(c) 105 (d) 37

2011

48. There are four lines in a plane and exactly two of them are parallel. If P is the number of points of intersection of these lines, then how many different values of P are possible?

(a) 2 (b) 3
(c) 5 (d) 6

2012

49. All the two-digit natural numbers whose unit digit is greater than their ten's digit are selected. If all these numbers are written one after the other in a series, how many digits are there in the resulting number?

(a) 90 (b) 72
(c) 36 (d) 54

2013

50. How many triangles can be drawn by joining any three vertices of a pentagon?

(a) 8 (b) 9
(c) 11 (d) 10

51. In how many ways can 18 identical candies be distributed among 8 children such that the number of candies received by each child is a prime number?

(a) 4 (b) 8
(c) 28 (d) 12

2014

52. There are exactly sixty chairs around a circular table. There are some people sitting on these chairs in such a way that the next person to be seated around the table will have to sit next to someone. What is the least possible number of people sitting around the table currently?

(a) 10 (b) 20
(c) 30 (d) 40

53. Find the number of ways in which a batsman can score 100 runs by scoring runs in 2's, 4's and 6's, such that he hits at least one double, one boundary and one six.

(a) 184 (b) 185
(c) 192 (d) 208

54. Amar, Akbar and Antony are three students in a class of 9 students. A class photo is taken. The number of ways in which it can be taken such that no two of Amar, Akbar and Antony are sitting together is:

(a) 151200 (b) 120960
(c) 181440 (d) 241920

2015

55. x is the smallest positive integer such that when it is divided by 7, 8 and 9 leaves remainder as 4, 5 and 6 respectively. Find the remainder when $x^3 + 2x^2 - x - 3$ is divided by 132.

(a) 49 (b) 76
(c) 94 (d) 15

56. If we arrange the letters of the word 'KAKA' in all possible ways, what is the probability that vowels will not be together in an arrangement?

(a) $\frac{2}{3}$ (b) $\frac{1}{3}$

(c) $\frac{1}{2}$ (d) $\frac{5}{6}$

2016

57. A man, having $2 in his pocket, goes to play his favourite game at a casino. If he wins he gets $2 whereas if he loses he gets nothing. He plays the game multiple times and pays $1 for each game as the entry fee. He does not lose more than once and leaves the casino as soon as he has $4 in his pocket. How many different Win-Loss sequences are possible for him?

(a) 4 (b) 3

(c) 8 (d) 5

58. India fielded 'n' (> 3) bowlers in a test match, and they operated in pairs. If a particular bowler did not bowl in pair with at least two other bowlers in the team, then at most how many bowlers could have bowled in pair with every other bowler in the team?

(a) n – 3 (b) n – 1

(c) n – 2 (d) None of these

2017

59. In how many ways can 8 identical pens be distributed among Amal, Bimal, and Kamal so that Amal gets at least 1 pen, Bimal gets at least 2 pens, and Kamal gets at least 3 pens?

60. How many four digit numbers, which are divisible by 6, can be formed using the digits 0, 2, 3, 4, 6, such that no digit is used more than once and 0 does not occur in the left-most position?

2018 Slot 1

61. How many numbers with two or more digits can be formed with the digits 1,2,3,4,5,6,7,8,9, so that in every such number, each digit is used at most once and the digits appear in the ascending order?

2018 Slot 2

62. In a tournament, there are 43 junior level and 51 senior level participants. Each pair of juniors play one match. Each pair of seniors play one match. There is no junior versus senior match. The number of girl versus girl matches in junior level is 153, while the number of boy versus boy matches in senior level is 276. The number of matches a boy plays against a girl is

63. How many two-digit numbers, with a non-zero digit in the units place, are there which are more than thrice the number formed by interchanging the positions of its digits?

(a) 7 (b) 6

(c) 5 (d) 8

PROBABILITY

1991

Direction for Question 1: Choose the best answer choice from those provided

1. A player rolls a die and receives the same number of rupees as the number of dots on the face that turns up. What should the player pay for each roll if he wants to make a profit of one rupee per throw of the die in the long run?

(a) Rs. 2.50 (b) Rs. 2

(c) Rs.3.50 (d) Rs. 4

1993

2. A box contains 6 red balls, 7 green balls and 5 blue balls. Each ball is of a different size. The probability that the red ball selected is the smallest red ball, is

(a) 1/18 (b) 1/3

(c) 1/6 (d) 2/3

1994

Directions for Question 3: Data is provided followed by two statements – I and II – both resulting in a value, say I and II. As your answer,

Mark (a) if I > II.

Mark (b) if I < II.

Mark (c) if I = II.

Mark (d) if nothing can be said.

3. I. The probability of encountering 54 Sundays in a leap year.

II. The probability of encountering 53 Sundays in a non-leap year.

1995

4. If a 4 digit number is formed with digits 1, 2, 3 and 5. What is the probability that the number is divisible by 25, if repetition of digits is not allowed?

(a) $\frac{1}{12}$

(b) $\frac{1}{4}$

(c) $\frac{1}{6}$

(d) None of these

MEMORY BASED QUESTIONS

2009

5. How many arrangements of the letters of the word CATASTROPHE are there in which both the 'A's appear before both the 'T's?

(a) $\frac{11!}{4!}$ (b) $\frac{11!}{4!(2!)^2}$

(c) $\frac{11!}{6}$ (d) $\frac{11!(2!)^2}{4!}$

2010

6. There are two boxes – I and II. Each contains balls of two colours – White and Black. A ball is selected at random. It is known that $P(W \cap I) = 0.3$ and $P(B'|II) = 0.8$, where W, B, I and II represent the events White ball selected, Black ball selected, ball selected from Box I and ball selected from Box II respectively. Find $P(I|B)$.

(a) $\frac{2}{3}$ (b) $\frac{1}{3}$

(c) $\frac{1}{2}$ (d) $\frac{3}{4}$

2011

7. Two six-faced unbiased dice are thrown simultaneously. What is the probability that the sum of the numbers that appear on the two dice is a prime number?

(a) $\frac{7}{12}$ (b) $\frac{5}{12}$

(c) $\frac{1}{3}$ (d) $\frac{1}{2}$

2012

8. What is the probability that the product of two integers chosen at random has the same unit digit as the two integers?

(a) $\frac{3}{10}$ (b) $\frac{1}{25}$

(c) $\frac{4}{15}$ (d) $\frac{7}{15}$

2013

9. The coefficient of $a^{12}b^{8}$ in the expansion of $(a^2 + b)^{13}$ is

(a) $\frac{13!}{12!\,6!}$ (b) $-\frac{13!}{6!\,8!}$

(c) $\frac{13!}{6!\,8!}$ (d) None of these

2014

10. If p is the probability of head turning up in the toss of a coin (not necessarily fair) and q is the probability of a tail turning up. Find the minimum possible value of $X = pq + \left(\frac{1}{p}\right)\left(\frac{1}{q}\right)$.

(a) 4.25 (b) $2\sqrt{5}$

(c) 2 (d) None of these

2015

11. Three persons - A, B and C - are playing the game of death. 3 bullets are placed randomly in a revolver having 6 chambers. Each one has to shoot himself by pulling the trigger once after which the revolver passes to the next person. This process continues till two of them are dead and the survivor of the game becomes the winner. What is the probability that B is the winner if A starts the game and A, B and C take turns in that order.

(a) 0.33 (b) 0.3

(c) 0.25 (d) None of these

2016

12. A cube is painted with red colour and then cut into 64 small identical cubes. If two cubes are picked randomly from the heap of 64 cubes, what is the probability that both of them have exactly two faces painted red?

(a) $\frac{23}{168}$ (b) $\frac{47}{84}$

(c) $\frac{1}{4}$ (d) $\frac{3}{8}$

SET THEORY

1991

Direction for Question 1: The question is followed by two statements. As the answer,

Mark (a) If the question can be answered with the help of statement I alone,

Mark (b) If the question can be answered with the help of statement II alone,

Mark (c) If both the statement I and statement II are needed to answer the question, and

Mark (d) If the question cannot be answered even with the help of both the statements.

1. How many people (from the group surveyed) read both Indian Express and Times of India?

I. Out of total of 200 readers, 100 read Indian Express, 120 read Times of India and 50 read Hindu.

II. Out of a total of 200 readers, 100 read Indian Express, 120 read Times of India and 50 read neither.

2. Fifty college teachers are surveyed as to their possession of colour TV, VCR and tape recorder. Of them, 22 own colour TV, 15 own VCR and 14 own tape recorders. Nine of these college teachers own exactly two items out of colour TV, VCR and tape recorder; and, one college teacher owns all three. How many of the 50 teachers own none of the three, colour TV, VCR or tape recorder?

(a) 4 (b) 9
(c) 10 (d) 11

Directions for Questions 3 and 4: Answer the questions on the basis of the information given below.

There were a hundred schools in a town. Of these, the number of schools having a play – ground was 30, and these schools had neither a library nor a laboratory. The number of schools having a laboratory alone was twice the number of those having a library only. The number of schools having a laboratory as well as a library was one fourth the number of those having a laboratory alone. The number of schools having either a laboratory or a library or both was 35.

3. How many schools had none of the three viz., laboratory, library or play – ground?

(a) 20 (b) 5
(c) 30 (d) 35

4. What was the ratio of schools having laboratory to those having library?

(a) 1 : 2 (b) 5 : 3
(c) 2 : 1 (d) 2 : 3

5. There are 3 clubs A, B & C in a town with 40, 50 & 60 members respectively. While 10 people are members of all 3 clubs, 70 are members in only one club. How many belong to exactly two clubs?

(a) 20 (b) 25
(c) 50 (d) 70

1993

Directions for Questions 6 and 7 : Use the following information.

Eighty five children went to an amusement park where they could ride on the merry – go round, roller coaster, and Ferris wheel. It was known that 20 of them took all three rides, and 55 of them took at least two of the three rides. Each ride cost Re.1, and the total receipt of the amusement park was Rs.145.

6. How many children did not try any of the rides?

(a) 5 (b) 10
(c) 15 (d) 20

7. How many children took exactly one ride?

(a) 5 (b) 10
(c) 15 (d) 20

8. Out of 100 families in the neighbourhood, 45 own radios, 75 have TVs, 25 have VCRs. Only 10 families have all three and each VCR owner also has a TV. If 25 families have radio only, how many have only TV?

(a) 30 (b) 35
(c) 40 (d) 45

1994

Directions for Questions 9 to 11: Answer the questions based on the following information.

Ghoshbabu is staying at Ghosh Housing Society, Aghosh Colony, Dighospur , Calcutta. In Ghosh Housing Society 6 persons read daily Ganashakti and 4 read Anand Bazar Patrika; in his colony there is no person who reads both. Total number of persons who read these two newspapers in Aghosh Colony and Dighospur is 52 and 200 respectively. Number of persons who read Ganashakti in Aghosh Colony and Dighospur is 33 and 121 respectively; while the persons who read Anand Bazar Patrika in Aghosh Colony and Dighospur are 32 and 117 respectively.

9. Number of persons in Dighospur who read only Ganashakti is

(a) 121 (b) 83
(c) 79 (d) 127

10. Number of persons in Aghosh Colony who read both of these newspapers is

(a) 13 (b) 20
(c) 19 (d) 14

11. Number of persons in Aghosh Colony who read only one paper

(a) 29 (b) 19
(c) 39 (d) 20

1996

12. In a locality, two-thirds of the people have cable TV, one-fifth have VCR, and one-tenth have both. What is the fraction of people having either cable -TV or VCR?

(a) $\frac{19}{30}$ (b) $\frac{2}{3}$
(c) $\frac{17}{30}$ (d) $\frac{23}{30}$

1997

Directions for Questions 13 to 15: Answer the questions based on the following information.

A survey of 200 people in a community who watched at least one of the three channels — BBC, CNN and DD — showed that 80% of the people watched DD, 22% watched BBC and 15% watched CNN.

13. What is the maximum percentage of people who can watch all the three channels?

(a) 12.5% (b) 8.5%
(c) 15% (d) Data insufficient

14. If 5% of people watched DD and CNN, 10% watched DD and BBC, then what percentage of people watched BBC and CNN only?

(a) 2% (b) 5%
(c) 8.5% (d) Cannot be determined

15. Referring to the previous question, what percentage of people watched all the three channels?

(a) 3.5% (b) 0%
(c) 8.5% (d) Cannot be determined

1999

16. In a survey of political preferences, 78% of those asked were in favour of at least one of the proposals: I, II and III. 50% of those asked favoured proposal I, 30% favoured proposal II and 20% favoured proposal III. If 5% of those asked favoured all three of the proposals, what percentage of those asked favoured more than one of the three proposals?

(a) 10 (b) 12
(c) 17 (d) 22

Directions for Question 17 and 18: The questions is followed by two statements, I and II. Answer the question using the following instructions.

Mark the answer as

(a) if the question can be answered by one of the statements alone, but cannot be answered by using the other statement alone.
(b) if the question can be answered by using either statement alone.
(c) if the question can be answered by using both the statements together, but cannot be answered by using either statement alone.
(d) if the question cannot be answered even by using both statements together.

2000

17. How many people are watching TV programme P?

I. Number of people watching TV programme Q is 1,000 and number of people watching both the programmes P and Q, is 100.
II. Number of people watching either P or Q or both is 1,500.

2002

18. People in a club either speak French or Russian or both. Find the number of people in a club who speak only French.

A. There are 300 people in the club and the number of people who speak both French and Russian is 196.
B. The number of people who speak only Russian is 58.

2003(R)

19. Consider the sets $T_n = \{n, n+1, n+2, n+3, n+4\}$, where n = 1, 2, 3,..., 96. How many of these sets contain 6 or any integral multiple thereof (i.e. any one of the numbers 6, 12, 18, ...)?

(a) 80 (b) 81
(c) 82 (d) 83

20. A survey on a sample of 25 new cars being sold at a local auto dealer was conducted to see which of the three popular options — air conditioning, radio and power windows were already installed.

Following were the observation of the survey:

I. 15 had air conditioning
II. 2 had air conditioning and power windows but no radios
III. 12 had radio
IV. 6 had air conditioning and radio but no power windows
V. 11 had power windows
VI. 4 had radio and power windows
VII. 3 had all three options

What is the number of cars that had none of the options?

(a) 4 (b) 3
(c) 1 (d) 2

21. Seventy percent of the employees in a multinational corporation have VCD players, 75% have microwave ovens, 80% have ACS and 85% have washing machines. At least what percentage of employees has all four gadgets?

(a) 15 (b) 5
(c) 10 (d) Cannot be determined

2003(L)

Directions for Questions 22 and 23: Answer the questions on the basis of the information given below.

New Age Consultants have three consultants Gyani, Medha and Buddhi. The sum of the number of projects handled by Gyani and Buddhi individually is equal to the number of projects in which Medha is involved. All three consultants are involved together in 6 projects. Gyani works with Medha in 14 projects. Buddhi has 2 projects with Medha but without Gyani, and 3 projects with Gyani but without Medha. The total number of projects for New Age Consultants is one less than twice the number of projects in which more than one consultant is involved.

22. What is the number of projects in which Gyani alone is involved?

(a) Uniquely equal to zero.

(b) Uniquely equal to 1.

(c) Uniquely equal to 4.

(d) Cannot be determined uniquely.

23. What is the number of projects in which Medha alone is involved?

(a) Uniquely equal to zero.

(b) Uniquely equal to 1.

(c) Uniquely equal to 4.

(d) Cannot be determined uniquely.

2005

Directions for Questions 24 to 27: Answer the questions on the basis of the information given below:

Help Distress (HD)is an NGO involved in providing assistance to people suffering from natural disasters. Currently, it has 37 volunteers. They are involved in three projects: Tsunami Relief (TR)in Tamil Nadu, Flood Relief (FR in Maharashtra, and Earthquake Relief (ER) in Gujarat. Each volunteer working with Help Distress has to be involved in at least one relief work project.

- A maximum number of volunteers are involved in the FR project. Among them, the number of volunteers involved in FR project alone is equal to the volunteers having additional involvement in the ER project.
- The number of volunteers involved in the ER project alone is double the number of volunteers involved in all the three projects.
- 17 volunteers are involved in the TR project.
- The number of volunteers involved in the TR project alone is one less than the number of volunteers involved in ER project alone.
- Ten volunteers involved in the TR project are also involved in at least one more project.

24. Based on the information given above, the minimum number of volunteers involved in both FR and TR projects, but not in the ER project is

(a) 1 (b) 3

(c) 4 (d) 5

25. Which of the following additional information would enable to find the exact number of volunteers involved in various projects?

(a) Twenty volunteers are involved in FR.

(b) Four volunteers are involved in all the three projects.

(c) Twenty three volunteers are involved in exactly one project.

(d) No need for any additional information.

26. After some time, the volunteers who were involved in all the three projects were asked to withdraw from one project. As a result, one of the volunteers opted out of the TR project, and one opted out of the ER project, while the remaining ones involved in all the three projects opted out of the FR project. Which of the following statements, then, necessarily follows?

(a) The lowest number of volunteers is now in TR project.

(b) More volunteers are now in FR project as compared to ER project.

(c) More volunteers are now in TR project as compared to ER project.

(d) None of the above.

27. After the withdrawal of volunteers, as indicated in Question 25, some new volunteers joined the NGO. Each one of them was allotted only one project in a manner such that, the number of volunteers working in one project alone for each of the three projects became identical. At that point, it was also found that the number of volunteers involved in FR and ER projects was the same as the number of volunteers involved in TR and ER projects. Which of the projects now has the highest number of volunteers?

(a) ER (b) FR

(c) TR (d) Cannot be determined

2006

28. A survey was conducted of 100 people to find out whether they had read recent issues of Golmal, a monthly magazine. The summarized information regarding readership in 3 months is given below:

Only September: 18;

September but not August: 23;

September and July: 8;September: 28;

July: 48;

July and August: 10;

None of the three months: 24.

What is the number of surveyed people who have read exactly two consecutive issues (out of the three)?

(a) 7 (b) 9

(c) 12 (d) 14

(e) 17

MEMORY BASED QUESTIONS

2011

29. Two sets A and B are given below.

$A = \{2^0, 2^1, 2^2, 2^3, 2^4\}$

$B = \{3^0, 3^1, 3^2, 3^3, 3^4\}$

How many different proper fractions can be made by picking the numerator from one of the sets and the denominator from the other set?

(a) 24 (b) 20

(c) 12 (d) None of these

2013

30. Let S = {1, 2, 3, 4, 5, 6, 8, 9, 10, 11, 12}. The number of subsets of S comprising composite number(s) only and that of those comprising prime number(s) only are N_1 and N_2 respectively. What is the absolute difference between N_1 and N_2?

(a) 0 (b) 32
(c) 48 (d) 24

2015

31. All reputed B-schools place their students. One-sixth of those B-schools that place their students are reputed and one-fourth of all B-schools that are recognised, place their students. There are exactly 6 reputed B-schools that are recognised too and there are 39 B -schools that are recognised but do not place their students. If there is a total of 78 B-schools that place their students, then how many of these B-schools are neither recognised nor reputed but place their students?

32. A = {1, 4, 7, 10, ..., 20th term}
B = {9, 16, 23, 30, ..., 20th term}
If $S = A \cup B$, how many elements are there in S?

(a) 37 (b) 38
(c) 39 (d) 35

2018 Slot 1

33. Each of 74 students in a class studies at least one of the three subjects H, E and P. Ten students study all three subjects, while twenty study H and E, but not P. Every student who studies P also studies H or E or both. If the number of students studying H equals that studying E, then the number of students studying H is

34. If among 200 students, 105 like pizza and 134 like burger, then the number of students who like only burger can possibly be

(a) 26 (b) 96
(c) 23 (d) 93

2018 Slot 2

35. For two sets A and B, let $A\Delta B$ denote the set of elements which belong to A or B but not both. If P = {1, 2, 3, 4}, Q = {2, 3, 5, 6,}, R = {1, 3, 7, 8, 9}, S = {2, 4, 9, 10}, then the number of elements in $(P\Delta Q)\Delta(R\Delta S)$ is

(a) 7 (b) 8
(c) 9 (d) 6

ANSWERS

Permutation and Combination

1. (b)	2. (a)	3. (b)	4. (a)	5. (c)	6. (*)	7. (d)	8. (b)	9. (a)	10. (b)
11. (b)	12. (c)	13. (a)	14. (a)	15. (c)	16. (a)	17. (d)	18. (b)	19. (c)	20. (c)
21. (a)	22. (a)	23. (c)	24. (d)	25. (c)	26. (b)	27. (c)	28. (d)	29. (c)	30. (c)
31. (b)	32. (a)	33. (b)	34. (b)	35. (a)	36. (a)	37. (b)	38. (c)	39. (a)	40. (d)
41. (d)	42. (a)	43. (d)	44. (d)	45. (a)	46. (a)	47. (d)	48. (a)	49. (b)	50. (d)
51. (c)	52. (b)	53. (a)	54. (a)	55. (d)	56. (c)	57. (b)	58. (a)	59. 6	60. 50
61. 502	62. (1098)	63. (b)							

Probability

1. (a)	2. (c)	3. (b)	4. (a)	5. (a)	6. (a)	7. (b)	8. (b)	9. (d)	10. (a)
11. (b)	12. (a)								

Set Theory

1. (b)	2. (c)	3. (d)	4. (b)	5. (b)	6. (c)	7. (c)	8. (c)	9. (b)	10. (a)
11. (c)	12. (b)	13. (c)	14. (a)	15. (d)	16. (c)	17. (c)	18. (c)	19. (a)	20. (d)
21. (c)	22. (d)	23. (b)	24. (c)	25. (a)	26. (b)	27. (d)	28. (b)	29. (a)	30. (c)
31. 58	32. (a)	33. (52)	34. (d)	35. (a)					

EXPLANATIONS

Permutation and combination

1. b If there is only one box containing black ball, the boxes can be filled in 6 ways.

   If there are two boxes containing black ball, the boxes can be filled in 5 ways. (The two black balls can be in either of the boxes (1,2), (2,3), (3,4), (4,5) or (5,6)).

   If there are 3 boxes containing black ball the boxes can be filled in 4 ways viz.(123), (234), (345), (456).

   Similarly if there are 4 boxes, it can be done in 3 ways viz.(1234), (2345), (3456), if there are 5 boxes it can be done in 2 ways viz.(12345), (23456) and all 6 boxes can have a black ball only in 1 way.

   Hence, total number of ways = 6 + 5 + 4 + 3 + 2 + 1 = 21.

2. a Three digit number such that 7 follows 5 could be of the form 57_ or _57.

   Since, the number is an even number

   Therefore possible numbers are 570,572,574,576 or 578.

   Hence, 5 such numbers are possible.

3. b It can be seen that every city is connected to all the other 3 cities.

   If we start from city A, there are 3 ways in which we can proceed, viz. AB, AD or AC.

   Once we are at any of these cities, each one of them is connected to the other 3 cities. But since we cannot go back to city A, there are only 2 ways in which we can proceed from here.

   If we are at B, we can take either paths BD or BC. From this point, we have a choice of going directly to A (thus skipping 4th city) or go to 4th city and come back to A. Eg. If we are at D, we can either take DA or DCA. So there are 2 more ways to go from here. Hence, required number of ways = 3 x 2 x 2 = 12.

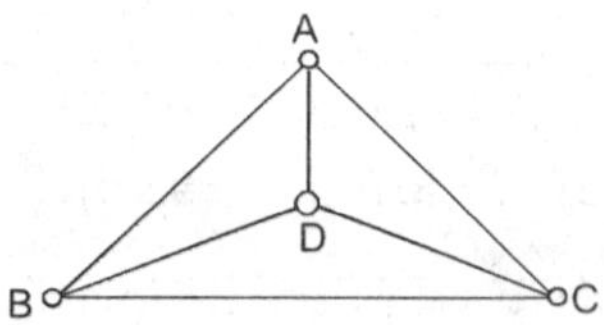

4. a If we assume that any digit is in a fixed position, then the remaining four digits can be arranged in 4! = 24 ways. So each of the 5 digits will appear in each of the five places 24 times. So the sum of the digits in each position is 24(1 + 3 + 5 + 7 + 9) = 600.

   Hence, the sum of all such numbers will be 600(1 + 10 + 100 + 1000 + 10000) = 6666600.

5. c We can form a triangle with any 3 points which are not collinear. 3 points out of 5 can be chosen in $^5C_3 = 10$ ways. But of these, the three points lying on the two diagonals will be collinear. So 10 – 2 = 8 triangles can be formed.

6. * There cannot be four or more blue balls.

   Case 1: If there are three blue balls, then they can be only in box 1, 3 and 5.

   Case 2: If there are two blue balls, then total number of cases = $^5C_2 = 10$

   But in 4 cases the blue ball will be in adjacent boxes. These cases are when blue balls in boxes 1 and 2 or 2 and 3 or 3 and 4 or 4 and 5.

   Therefore, total number of cases when there are two blue balls = 10 – 4 = 6

   Case 3: If there is one blue ball, then total number of cases = $^5C_1 = 5$

   Case 4: If there is no blue ball, then total number of cases = $^5C_5 = 1$

   Hence, total number of cases = 1 + 6 + 5 + 1 = 13.

   *** The correct answer is not available in the given options.**

7. d Let us choose a town, say A.

   If I were to consider this as the base town and construct two roads such that I connect any pair of towns, I get the following combinations:

   1. AB – BC, 2. AB – BD, 3. AC – CB, 4. AC – CD, 5. AD – DB and 6. AD – DC.

   From any of these combinations, if I were to construct a road such that it again comes back to A, then it would form a triangle.

   To avoid a triangle, the third road that I construct should not be connected to A but to the third town.

   Hence, the combination would be:

   1. AB – BC – CD, 2. AB – BD – DC, 3. AC – CB – BD, 4. AC – CD – DB, 5. AD – DB – BC and 6. AD – DC – CB.

   Thus, from each town, we can construct 6 such combinations.

   Hence, total number of combinations that we can have from four towns = (6 × 4) = 24.

8. b Out of the 5 girls, 3 girls can be invited in $^5C_3$ ways. Nothing is mentioned about the number of boys that he has to invite. He can invite one, two, three, four or even no boys. Each boy can be invited or not. He can invite them in 2^4 ways. Thus, the total number of ways is $^5C_3 \times (2)^4 = 10 \times 16 = 160$.

9. a The question cannot be answered until and unless number of concurrent lines are known.

10. b

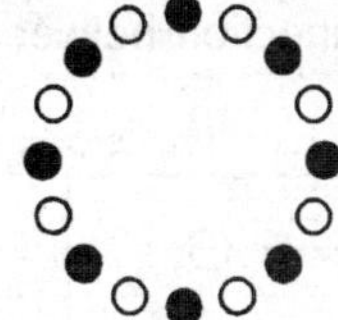

If we consider the Chairman and the vice chairman as one set, we can see that this set can fit 8 slots in between the 8 directors. Hence, this can be done in 8! ways. Between themselves, the chairman and the vice chairman can be arranged in 2 ways. Hence, the required answer = 2 x 8!.

11. b — — — $\underset{\text{Ten's place}}{t}$ $\underset{\text{Unit's place}}{u}$

$u > t$

Case (i): t = 1

u can be 2, 3, 4, 5 $\Rightarrow$ 4 possibilities

So total possible number that can be formed = 4 × 3 × 2 × 1

Case (ii): t = 2

u can be 3, 4, 5 $\Rightarrow$ 3 possibilities

So total possible number that can be formed = 3 × 3 × 2 × 1

Case (iii): t = 3

u can be 4, 5 $\Rightarrow$ 2 possibilities

So total possible number that can be formed = 2 × 3 × 2 × 1

Case (iv): t = 4

u can be 5 $\Rightarrow$ 1 possibility

So total possible number that can be formed = 1 × 3 × 2 × 1

Hence, total possible number = (4 + 3 + 2 + 1) $\underline{|3}$ = 60

12. c The answer is $^{10}C_2 \times 11 + {}^{11}C_2 \times 10 = 45 \times 11 + 55 \times 10 = 1045$.

13. a At least 1 and at most n are to be selected

$\Rightarrow {}^{2n+1}C_1 + {}^{2n+1}C_2 + \ldots + {}^{2n+1}C_n = 63$

$\Rightarrow \frac{1}{2}\left(2^{2n+1} - 2\right) = 63$

$\Rightarrow n = 3$

14. a The possibilities are W@W@W@ or @W@W@W, where 2 blue and 1 red flag occupy the space marked as @. Hence, the total permutation is $2 \times \frac{3!}{2!} = 6$.

15. c There are two possible cases. The number 9 comes at the end, or it comes at position 4, 5, or 6.

For the first case, the number would look like:

635 - - - 9 or 674 - - - 9

In both these cases, the blanks can be occupied by any of the available 9 digits (0, 1, 2, ..., 8).

Thus, total possible numbers would be

2 × (9 × 9 × 9) = 1458.

For the second case, the number 9 can occupy any of the given position 4, 5, or 6, and there shall be an odd number at position 7.

Thus, the total number of ways shall be 2[3(9 × 9 × 4)] = 1944.

Hence, answer is 3402.

16. a

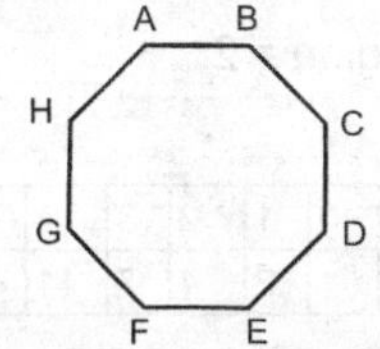

In order to reach E from A, it can walk clockwise as well as anticlockwise. In all cases, it will have to take odd number of jumps from one vertex to another. But the sum will be even. In simple case, if n = 4, then $a_n = 2$.

For $a_{2n-1} = 7$ (odd), we cannot reach the point E.

17. d Number of one-rupee coins = 158.

Possible arrangements of coins are listed as 1, 2, 4, 8, 16, 32, 64 and 31.

∴ Number of arrangements = 8.

So the least number of bags required = 8.

18. b

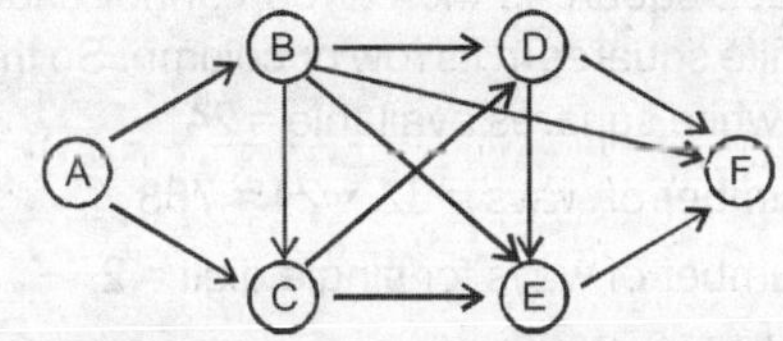

The number of distinct routes from A to F are listed below.

(1) ABDF	(2) ACEF	(3) ABF
(4) ABEF	(5) ACDF	(6) ABCDEF
(7) ACDEF	(8) ABDEF	(9) ABCDF
(10) ABCEF		

There are 10 way to reach F from A.

19. c The last two digits can be 12, 16, 24, 32, 36, 52, 56, and 64, i.e. 8 possibilities.

Remaining digits can be chosen in $^4P_3 = 24$ ways.

Hence, total number of such five-digit numbers = 24 × 8 = 192.

20. c Total possible arrangements = 10 × 9 × 8

Now 3 numbers can be arranged among themselves in 3! ways = 6 ways

Given condition is satisfied by only 1 out of 6 ways.

Hence, the required number of arrangements

$= \frac{10 \times 9 \times 8}{6} = 120$

Alternate solution:

$^{10}C_3 = 120$

Any three numbers selected out of 10 numbers will have only one possible arrangement.

21. a Number of regions $= \frac{n(n+1)}{2} + 1$, where n = Number of lines, i.e. for 0 line we have region = 1.

For 1 line we have region = 2.

It can be shown as:

Number of lines	0	1	2	3	4	5...	10
Number of regions	1	2	4	7	11	16...	56

Therefore, for n = 10, it is $\frac{10 \times 11}{2} + 1 = 56$

22. a Total number of passwords with atleast 1 symmetric letter = 11 × 10 × 9 × 8 = 7920

23. c Total number of passwords with atleast 1 symmetric letter

= Total number of passwords using all letters – Total number of passwords using no symmetric letters

= (26 × 25 × 24)– (15 × 14 × 13)

= 12870

24. d A black square can be chosen in 32 ways. Once a black square is there, you cannot choose the 8 white squares in its row or column. So the number of white squares available = 24

Number of ways = 32 × 24 = 768

25. c Number of ways for single digit = 2

2 digits = 2 × 3 = 6

3 digits = 2 × 3 × 3 = 18

4 digits = 2 × 3 × 3 × 3 = 54

5 digits = 2 × 3 × 3 × 3 × 3 = 162

6 digits = 2 × 3 × 3 × 3 × 3 × 3 = 486

Total number of ways = 728

26. b Consider first zone. The number of telephone lines can be shown a follows.

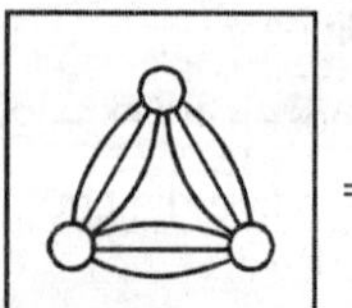

= 9 lines

Therefore, total number of lines required for internal connections in each zone = 9 × 4 = 36 lines.

Now consider the connection between any two zones.

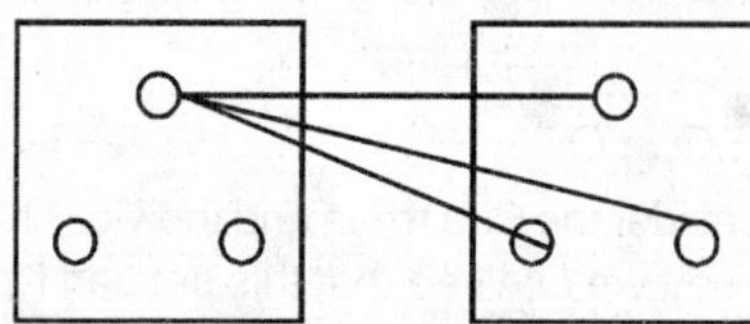

Each town in first zone can be connected to three towns in the second zone.

Therefore, the lines required = 3 × 3 = 9

Therefore, total number of lines required for connecting towns of different zones = $^4C_2$ × 9 = 6 × 9 = 54

Therefore, total number of lines in all = 54 + 36 = 90

27. c Total codes which can be formed = 9 × 9 = 81. (Distinct digit codes)

The digits which can confuse are 1, 6, 8, 9, from these digit we can form the codes = 4 × 3 = 12

Out of these 12 codes two numbers 69 and 96 will not create confusion.

Therefore, (12 – 2)= 10 codes will create a confusion.

Therefore, total codes without confusion= 81 – 10 = 71.

28. d **Case I:** ___ m ___

First place can be selected in five ways and hence the third in four ways.

$\therefore 5 \times 4 = 20$ ways

Case II: ___ n ___

First place can be selected in 5 ways and third in 2 ways.

$\therefore 5 \times 2 = 10$ ways

Case III: ___ p ___

First place can be selected in 5 ways and last letter will be same, i.e. one way.

$\therefore 5 \times 1 = 5$ way

$\therefore$ Total ways = 20 + 10 + 5 = 35 ways.

29. c As third letter is e, it can be selected in one way only.

Case I: 4 m e ⇒ 4 ways

Case II: 5 n e ⇒ 5 ways

Case III: e p e ⇒ 1 ways

⇒ 10 ways

30. c If y = 2 (it cannot be 0 or 1), then x can take 1 value and z can take 2 values.

Thus with y = 2, a total of 1 × 2 = 2 numbers can be formed. With y = 3, 2 × 3 = 6 numbers can be formed. Similarly checking for all values of y from 2 to 9 and adding up we get the answer as 240.

31. b GRRRRR, RGRRRR, RRGRRR, RRRGRR, RRRRGR, RRRRRG

GGRRRR, RGGRRR, RRGGRR, RRRGGR, RRRRGG

GGGRRR, RGGGRR, RRGGGR, RRRGGG

GGGGRR, RGGGGR, RRGGGG

GGGGGR, RGGGGG

GGGGGG

Hence 21 ways.

32. a The least number of edges will be when one point is connected to each of the other 11 points, giving a total of 11 lines. One can move from any point to any other point via the common point.

The maximum edges will be when a line exists between any two points. Two points can be selected from 12 points in $^{12}C_2$ i.e. 66 lines.

33. b Each person will form a pair with all other persons except the two beside him. Hence he will form (n – 3) pairs.

If we consider each person, total pairs = n (n – 3) but here each pair is counted twice.

Hence actual number of pairs $= \frac{n(n-3)}{2}$

They will sing for $\frac{n(n-3)}{2} \times 2 = n(n-3)$ min

Hence n(n -3)

$= 28 \Rightarrow n^2 - 3n - 28 = 0 \Rightarrow n = 7$ or – 4

Discarding the negative value: n = 7

34. b From A to B, there are 8 on-way roads out of which 3 roads are in Northwards and 5 roads are Westwards.

Therefore number of distinct routes is $= \frac{8!}{5!3!} = 56$

35. a The first strip can be of any of the four colours, The 2nd can be of any colour except that of the first (i.e. 3). Similarly, each subsequent strip can be of any colour except that of the preceding strip (=3)

Hence number of ways = 4 × 3^5 = 12 × 81

36. a Let there be m boys and n girls

$^nC_2 = 45 = \frac{n(n-1)}{2} \Rightarrow n(n-1) = 90 \Rightarrow n = 10$

$^mC_2 = 190 \Rightarrow \frac{m(m-1)}{2} = 190$

$\Rightarrow m(m-1) = 380 \Rightarrow m = 20$

Number of games between one boy and one girl

$= {}^{10}C_1 \times {}^{20}C_1 = 10 \times 20 = 200$

Hence, option (a)is the correct answer.

37. b

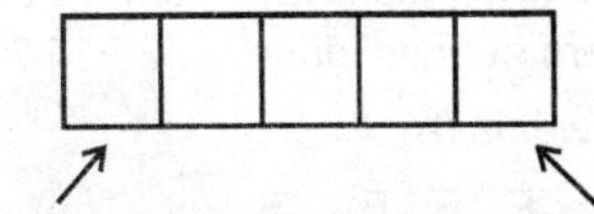

odd positions can be counted in 2 ways.

(i) Counting from the LMD-end:

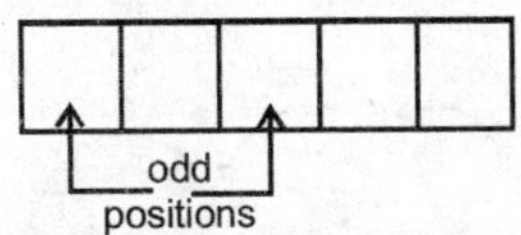

We have 1, 2, 3, 4 & 5 to be filled in these blocks. Odd nos. (1, 3, 5)to be filled in at odd positions. Other places are to be filled by even numbers (2 or 4) Let's count, how many such numbers are there with 2 at the unit's digit

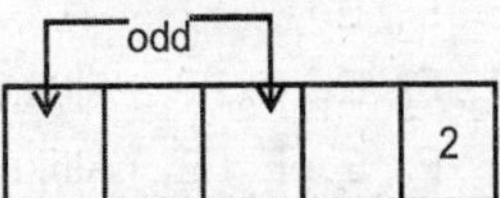

Odd numbers can be filled in $^3P_2$ = 6 way.

The remaining two places are to be filled by 2 numbers (one odd number left out of 1, 3, 5 & one even i.e. 4) in = 2 ways.

So, there are 6 × 2 = 12 number with 2 at the rightmost place. Similarly; there are 12 such numbers with 4 at the rightmost digits.

The sum of rightmost digits in all such number = 12(2 + 4) = 72

(ii) Now counting from the RMD-end.

Let's place 1 at the units place and check, how many numbers are possible with (1, 3) at the odd positions:

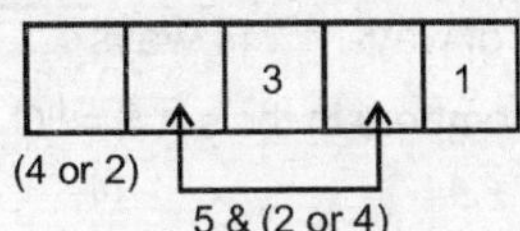

Number of such cases = 2 × 2 = 4 ways.

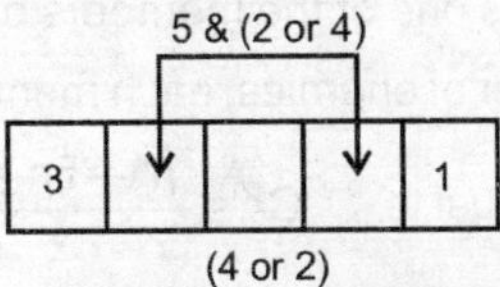

Here again number of ways = 2 × 2 = 4 ways.

So, there are 4 + 4 = 8 numbers, in which (1, 3) are at odd positions. Similarly there are 8 numbers in which (1, 5)are at odd positions. So, in all there are 16 numbers where 1 is at unit's place. Similarly there are 16 numbers with 3 at unit's place and 16 more with 5 at unit's place.

Summing up all the odd unit's digits = 16(1 + 3 + 5) = 144

From (i) and (ii)we can now, sum up all (even or odd)numbers at units place = 72 +144 = 216.

Hence answer is (b).

38. c Frenchmen : F_1, F_2, F_3

Englishmen: E_1, E_2, E_3

Let E_1 knows French

I round of calls:

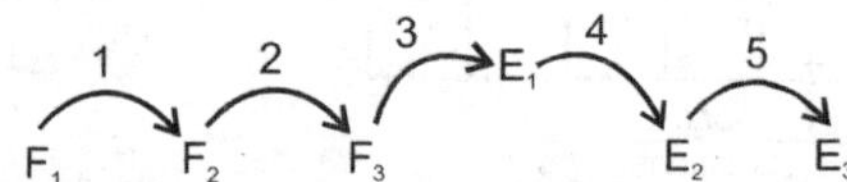

Persons	Secrets know after I-round
F_1	F_1, F_2
F_2	F_1, F_2, F_3
F_3	F_1, F_2, F_3, F_4
E_1	F_1, F_2, F_3, E_2
E_2	$F_1, F_2, F_3, E_1, E_2, E_3$) All known
E_3	$F_1, F_2, F_3, E_1, E_2, E_3$) All know

II round calls

F_1 F_2 F_3 E_1 E_2 or E_3

9 8 7 6

In the 6th call, E_1 knows all the secrets. Similarly, after 9th call, everybody know all the secrets.

39. a Task 2 can only be given to two persons i.e. (3 and 4)

∴ Number of ways = 2 ways

First task can be done in 3 ways by 3 persons.

Third task can be done by 4 persons.

∴ 4 ways similarly for fourth, five and six tasks, number of ways is 3, 2 and 1 respectively.

∴ Total number of ways = 144 ways

40. d The number of members in the set S = $^nC_2$, where n is greater than = 4

Each member of S has two distinct numbers.

Let us say (1, 2)is one of the members of S.

To find the number of enemies, each member of S will have to be equal to $^{n-2}C_2 = \dfrac{n^2 - 5n + 6}{2}$.

Alternative Method:

Number of enemies for this member is 6, i.e. (3, 4), (3, 5), (3, 6), (4, 5)(4, 6)and (5, 6).

Checking by options, this is only satisfied by $\dfrac{n^2 - 5n + 6}{2}$

Hence, $\dfrac{n^2 - 5n + 6}{2}$ is the correct choice.

41. d Considering any two members of S, that are friends there will be 1 number of the pairs that will be common.

The common element of these pairs will have n – 3 pairs, with the remaining n – 3 elements. There will be one more member made up of the remaining two constituent elements which are not same. In total there are n – 3 + 1 = n – 2 other members of S that are common friends of the chosen two pairs or numbers.

Alternative Method:

For n = 6 lets consider the members (1, 2) and (1, 3)

Friends of the member (1, 2)in the set S are (1, 4), (1, 5), (1, 6), (2, 3), (2, 4), (2, 5), (2, 6).

Friends of the member (1, 3) in the set S (1, 4), (1, 5), (1, 6), (2, 3), (3, 4), (3, 5), (3, 6).

The number of members of S that are common friends to the above member are 4, i.e. (1, 4), (1, 5), (1, 6), (2, 3).

So the answer is n – 2.

42. a In each team, T_j there are two players, one it shares with T_{j-1} and other with T_{j-1}. Other (k – 2)players team T_j shares with no other team. So, total players which play for only one team = (k – 2)n.

One player is common in T_1 and T_2, one in T_2 and T_3 and so on.

Number of such players = number of pairs = n

So, total players = (k – 2)n + n = n(k – 1)

43. d In other words we need to find the total number of 4-digit numbers not more than 4000 using the digits 0, 1, 2, 3 and 4.

The digit at the thousands place can be selected in 3 ways.

The digits at the hundreds place can be selected in 5 ways.

The digits at the tens place can be selected in 5 ways.

The digits at the units place can be selected in 5 ways.

Therefore, the total number of 4-digit numbers less than 4000 is equal to

3 × 5 × 5 × 5 = 375.

Therefore, the total number of 4-digit numbers not more than 4000 is equal to 375 + 1 = 376.

44. d

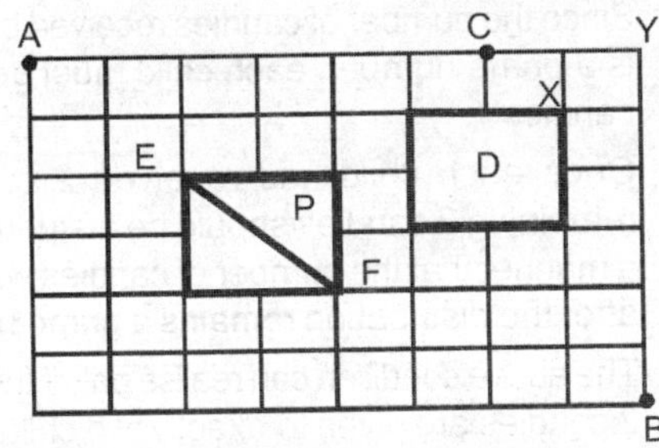

For the shortest route, Neelam follows the following path: A → E → F → B

Number of ways to reach from A to E: $\frac{(2+2)!}{2! \times 2!} = 6$

Number of ways to reach from E to F: 1

Number of ways to reach from F to B: $\frac{(4+2)!}{4! \times 2!} = 15$

⇒ Total number of possible shortest paths

= 6 × 1 × 15 = 90

45. a Neelam has to reach C via B.

From A to B, the number of paths are 90, as found in question 44.

From B to C, Neelam follows the route:

Case I: B → X → C

OR **Case II:** B → Y → C.

Case I: B → X → C

Number of ways to reach from B to X: $\frac{(5+1)!}{5! \times 1!} = 6$

Number of ways to reach from X to C : 2

So, total number of paths are 6 × 2 = 12 ways.

Case II: B → Y → C:

There is just one way.

Therefore, from B to C, there are 6 × 2 + 1 = 13 ways

∴ Total number of ways of reaching from A to C, via B = 90 × 13 = 1170.

46. a Number of terms in the given expansion is nothing but the non-negative integral solutions of the equation a + b + c = 20.

Total number of non-negative integral solutions $= {}^{20+3-1}C_{3-1} = {}^{22}C_2 = 231$

Alternative Method:

$(a+b+c)^{20} = \{(a+b)+c\}^{20}$

$= {}^{20}C_0(a+b)^{20}.C^0 + {}^{20}C_1(a+b)^{19}.C^1 + ... {}^{20}C_{20}(a+b)^0.C^{20}$

Number of terms = 21 + 20 + 19 + ... + 1 = 231

47. d (i) Let the box with the smallest number of balls does not contain any ball. Then 18 balls can go into 2 identical boxes in 10 ways (0, 18), (1, 17).... (9, 9).

(ii) Let the box with the smallest number of balls contains 1 ball. Then 17 balls can go into 2 identical boxes in 8 ways (1, 16), (2, 15).... (8, 9).

(iii) Let the box with the smallest number of balls contains 2 balls. Then 16 balls can go into 2 identical boxes in 7 ways (2, 14), (3, 13).... (8, 8).

(iv) Let the box with the smallest number of balls contains 3 balls. Then 15 balls can go into 2 identical boxes in 5 ways (3, 12), (4, 11).... (7, 8).

(v) Let the box with the smallest number of balls contains 4 balls. Then 14 balls can go into 2 identical boxes in 4 ways (4, 10), (5, 9).... (7, 7).

(vi) Let the box with the smallest number of balls contains 5 balls. Then 13 balls can go into 2 identical boxes in 2 ways (5, 8) and (6, 7).

(vii) Let the box with the smallest number of balls contains 6 balls. Then 12 balls can go into 2 identical boxes in just 1 way (6, 6).

The number of possible ways

= 10 + 8 + 7 + 5 + 4 + 2 + 1

= 37

Alternate Method:

Case I:

All the boxes contain an equal number of balls. There is only one possible case i.e. 6, 6 and 6.

Case II:

Exactly two boxes contain an equal number of balls. There are 9 possible cases i.e. (0, 0, 18), (1, 1, 16), (2, 2, 14), (3, 3, 12), (4, 4, 10), (5, 5, 8), (7, 7, 4), (8, 8, 2) and (9, 9, 0).

For each of these cases 3 combinations were possible had the boxes been non-identical.

Case III:

Each box contains a different number of balls.

Let the number of cases be x.

For each of these cases 6 combinations were possible had the boxes been non-identical.

∴ $1 + 9 \times 3 + 6x = {}^{18+3-1}C_{3-1}$

⇒ $28 + 6x = \frac{20 \times 19}{2} = 190$

⇒ $x = 27$

So the required number of ways

= 27 + 9 + 1 = 37

48. a Only two cases are possible:

Case I:

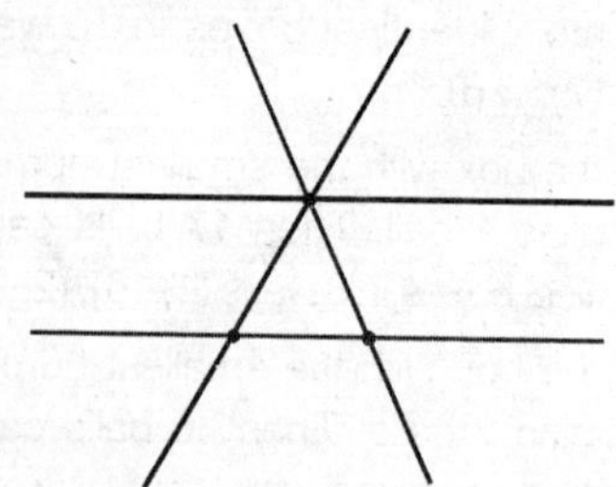

Points of intersection = 3

Case II:

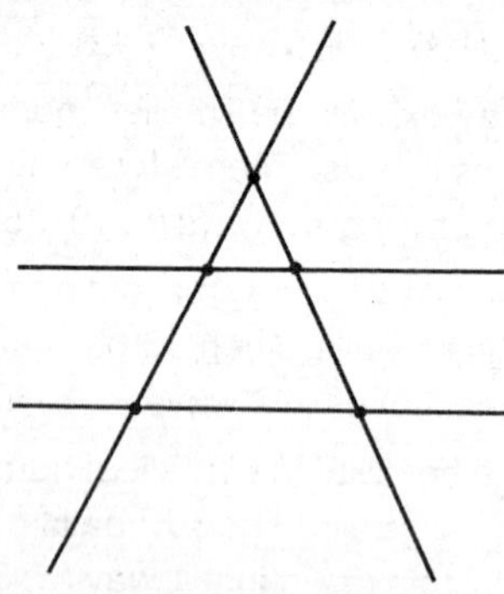

Points of intersection = 5

Hence, possible values of P are 3 and 5.

49. b It is equivalent to finding how many such 2-digit numbers are there.

In such numbers we cannot have 0 or 1 in unit's place.

When we have 2 in unit's place, we have 1 such number, 12.

When we have 3 in unit's place, we have 2 such numbers, 13 and 23.

.

.

.

When we have 9 in unit's place, we have 8 such numbers.

So number of such numbers is (1 + 2 + 3 + ... + 8)

= 36.

Hence the resulting number has 72 digits.

50. d ∴ No three points corresponding to the five vertices of a pentagon are collinear, by joining any of the three vertices of a pentagon, we get a triangle.

Hence, the number of triangles that can be drawn = $^5C_3$ = 10.

51. c Since the number of candies received by each child is a prime number, each child must get at least 2 candies.

Once each child has received 2 candies, the remaining 2 candies should be distributed in such a manner that the number of candies with any child after the distribution remains a prime number.

The above condition can realise only if the remaining 2 candies are given to exactly two children in such a way that both the children receive one candy each.

Hence, the number of ways of distribution = $^8C_2$ = 28.

52. b If there are 60 chairs around a circular table, consider a scenario wherein there are two chairs vacant between every two consecutive people. Thus, there will be exactly 20 people sitting and exactly 40 vacant seats between them and in such a scenario, next person coming to sit will have to sit next to someone.

53. a Let the batsman scored a 2's, b 4's and c 6's.

$\Rightarrow \quad 2a + 4b + 6c = 100$

$\Rightarrow \quad a + 2b + 3c = 50.$ ... (i)

When c = 1, (i) becomes a + 2b = 47

$\Rightarrow \quad a = 47 - 2b$ ... (ii)

Since $a \geq 1$ and $b \geq 1$, the number of solutions of (ii) is 23.

When c = 2, (i) becomes a + 2b = 44

$\Rightarrow \quad a = 44 - 2b$ ... (iii)

Since $a \geq 1$ and $b \geq 1$, the number of solutions of (iii) is 21.

When c = 3, (i) becomes a + 2b = 41

$\Rightarrow \quad a = 41 - 2b$ ... (iv)

Since $a \geq 1$ and $b \geq 1$, the number of solutions of (iv) is 20.

When c = 4, (i) becomes a + 2b = 38

$\Rightarrow \quad a = 38 - 2b$ ... (v)

Since $a \geq 1$ and $b \geq 1$, the number of solutions of (v) is 18.

Thus, we see a pattern emerging.

∴ The total number of ways

= 23 + 21 + 20 + 18 +...+ 3 + 2

= 184.

54. a First let the 6 other students be seated in 6 chairs.

The number of spaces between the 6 students = 7.

∴ Amar, Akbar and Anthony can be seated in the 7 places in $^7C_3$ ways.

Thus, the number of ways in the class photo can be taken such that no two of Amar, Akbar and Anthony are sitting together is

= 7C3 × 3! × 6!

= 151200.

55. d x = L.C.M. of (7, 8, 9) – 3 = 504 – 3 = 501

$x^3 + 2x^2 + x - 3 = (x - 1)(x + 1)(x + 2) - 1$

$= 500 \times 502 \times 503 - 1$

Remainder when $500 \times 502 \times 503 - 1$ is divided by:

11 = 4

3 = 0

4 = 3

Required remainder = least possible number which when divided by 11, 3 and 4 leavs remainder 4, 0 and 3 respectively

Such least no. is 15.

56. c Letters of the word 'KAKA' can be arranged in

$\left(\frac{4!}{2! \times 2!}\right) = 6$ ways

If we consider the cases where vowels are together, then considering two A's as single entity,

we have $\left(\frac{3!}{2!}\right) = 3$ arrangements.

So, there must be (6 – 3) = 3 arrangements, where vowels are not together.

Therefore, the required probability $= \frac{3}{6} = \frac{1}{2}$.

57. b Let the number of games won and those lost by the man be N_w and N_l respectively.

Since he gains $2, $N_w - N_l = 2$.

Also, he does not lose more than once.

The possible cases are (W → Win and L → Loss):

Case (i): $N_w = 2$ and $N_l = 0$.

The only possible sequence is WW.

Case (ii): $N_w = 3$ and $N_l = 1$.

Possible sequences: LWWW and WLWW.

Hence, the total number of possible Win-Loss sequences = 1 + 2 = 3.

58. a Let the bowlers be represented by $B_1, B_2, B_3, \ldots, B_n$.

If a particular bowler B_1 (say) did not bowl in pair with two other bowlers, B_2 and B_3 (say), then B_2 and B_3 also did not bowl in pair with every bowler in the team. Therefore, at least three bowlers must not have bowled in pair with every other bowler in the team.

Hence, the maximum number of bowlers who could have bowled in pair with every other bowler in the team is n – 3.

59. 6 Amal Bimal Kamal

≥ 1 ≥ 2 ≥ 3

	A	B	K
Pens	3	2	3
	1	4	3
	1	2	5
	2	3	3
	1	3	4
	2	2	4

Total cases = 6

60. 50 For divisibility by 6, last digit should be even and sum of digits is divisible by 3.

Case I :

2, 3, 4, 6

$3 \times 2 \times 1 \times 3$ = 18 ways

Case II:

(i) 2, 3, 4, 0(when last digit is zero)

$3 \times 2 \times 1 \times 1$ = 6 ways

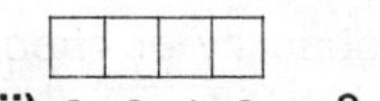

(ii) $2 \times 2 \times 1 \times 2$ = 8 ways

Total 8 + 6 = 14 ways

Case III:

0, 2, 4, 6

$3 \times 3 \times 2 \times 1$ = 18 ways

So, total possible ways = 50.

61. 502 Digits available = 1, 2, 3, 4, 5, 6, 7, 8, 9

The numbers will be ${}^9C_2 + {}^9C_3 + \ldots\ldots {}^9C_9$.

$= 2^9 - {}^9C_0 - {}^9C_1$.

= 512 – 1 – 9 = 502.

62. 1098 Let the number of girls in junior section be g, thus ${}^9C_2 = 153$

$\Rightarrow \frac{g(g-1)}{2} = 153$

$\Rightarrow g = 18$

Therefore, number of girls in junior section = 18 and that of boys = 25

Again, let the number of boys in senior section be b

$\Rightarrow \frac{b(b-1)}{2} = 276$

$\Rightarrow b = 24$

Therefore, number of boys in senior section = 24 and that of girls = 26

Hence, the number of matches played between boys and girls = 25 × 18 + 24 × 27 = 1098.

63. b Given that: $10a + b > 3(10b + a)$

$\Rightarrow 7a > 29b$

For b = 1 we get a = 5, 6, 7, 8 and 9

For b = 2 we get a = 9

Hence, required answer will be 6.

Probability

1. a Since in the long run the probability of each number appearing is the same, we can say in 'n' throws one can get 1, 2, 3, 4, 5 and 6, $\frac{n}{6}$ times each.

Hence he would earn

$$\frac{(1+2+3+4+5+6)n}{6} = Rs.\frac{7n}{2}.$$

In order to make a profit of 1 Re. per throw he has to totally earn a profit of Rs.n. Hence his cost for the n throws should be $\frac{7n}{2} - n$.

So his cost per throw should be

$$\left(\frac{7}{2} - 1\right) = \frac{5}{2} = Rs.2.50.$$

2. c Since there are 6 red balls and all six of them are of different sizes, probability of choosing the smallest among them is $\frac{1}{6}$.

3. b 53 Sundays can occur in a non-leap year, if 1st January is either a Saturday or a Sunday. But 54 Sundays can never occur.

Hence, I < II.

4. a Total number of four-digit numbers that can be formed = 4!.

If the number is divisible by 25, then the last two digits are 25.

So the first two digits can be arranged in 2! ways.

Hence, required probability $= \frac{2!}{4!} = \frac{1}{12}$.

5. a The total number of arrangements possible $= \frac{11!}{(2!)^2}$

The total arrangements of 2 'A's and 2 'T's $= \frac{4!}{(2!)^2} = 6$

Out of these 6 possible arrangements only 1 arrangement AATT is acceptable with the given condition.

So for every 6 arrangements of the letters of the word CATASTROPHE, only 1 would satisfy the given condition.

Hence, the required arrangements $= \frac{11!}{(2!)^2.6} = \frac{11!}{4!}$

6. a $P(I) = P(II) = \frac{1}{2}$

$\therefore P(B \cap I) = P(I) - P(W \cap I)$

$\Rightarrow P(B \cap I) = \frac{1}{2} - \frac{3}{10} = \frac{1}{5}$ ...(i)

Also, $P(B' | II) = \frac{P(B' \cap II)}{P(II)}$

$\Rightarrow P(B' \cap II) = \frac{8}{10} \times \frac{1}{2} = \frac{2}{5}$

$\because P(B' \cap II) = P(W \cap II)$

$\Rightarrow P(W \cap II) = \frac{2}{5}$

$\therefore P(B \cap II) = P(II) - P(W \cap II) = \frac{1}{2} - \frac{2}{5} = \frac{1}{10}$

Now, $P(I | B) = \frac{P(I \cap B)}{P(B)}$

As $P(B) = P(B \cap I) + P(B \cap II)$, therefore,

from (i) and (ii) $P(B) = \frac{1}{5} + \frac{1}{10} = \frac{3}{10}$

$\Rightarrow P(I | B) = \frac{1}{5} \div \frac{3}{10} = \frac{2}{3}$.

7. b The total number of possibe outcomes = 6 × 6 = 36.

The favourable values of the sum are 2, 3, 5, 7 and 11.

Favourable cases when the sum is:

I) 2 = (1, 1)

II) 3 = (1, 2) and (2, 1)

III) 5 = (1, 4), (4, 1), (2, 3) and (3, 2)

IV) 7 = (1, 6), (6, 1), (2, 5), (5, 2), (3, 4) and (4, 3)

V) 11 = (5, 6) and (6, 5)

The total number of favourable cases = 15.

Required probability $= \frac{15}{36} = \frac{5}{12}$.

8. b An integer can end with any of the ten digits (0, 1, 2 .... 9) out of which if it ends with one of the four (0, 1, 5, 6), the required condition will be satisfied. The probability of an integer ending with 0 or 1 or 5 or 6 is 4/10 = 2/5

Now the probability of 2nd integer also ending with the digit that has come in unit's place of the first integer is 1/10

$\therefore$ The required probability = (2/5) × (1/10) = 1/25

9. d The expression $a^{12}b^8$ can be rewritten as $(a^2)^6 b^8$.

We can observe that the sum of the powers of a^2 and b in $(a^2)^6 b^8$ is (6 + 8) i.e.14. But in the expansion of $(a^2 + b)^{13}$ the sum of the powers of a^2 and b must be 13 in each of the terms. Hence, the given term does not exist in the expansion i.e. the required coefficient is zero.

10. a p + q = 1, i.e. q = 1 – p (0 = p, q = 1)

Now when the sum of two variables is a constant then their multiplication is the maximum when they are equal. So, pq will be maximum and $\left(\frac{1}{p}\right)\left(\frac{1}{q}\right)$ the minimum when $p = q = \frac{1}{2}$.

Thus, the minimum value of X = 0.25 + 4 = 4.25.

11. b Total number of the cases = $^6C_3 = 20$.

The favourable cases for B surviving are:

(B : Bullet; N : No Bullet)

BNBBNN or BNBNBN or BNBNNB or BNNNBB or NNBBNB or NNBBBN.

Hence probability = $\frac{6}{20} = 0.3$

12. a The number of ways of picking two small cubes

$$= {}^{64}C_2 = 32 \times 63$$

The number of small cubes with exactly two faces painted red

= 2 × 12 = 24 (Since two such cubes will be obtained from each edge of the large cube.)

The number of ways of picking two such cubes

$$= {}^{24}C_2 = 23 \times 12$$

So the required probability $= \frac{23 \times 12}{63 \times 32} = \frac{23}{168}$.

Set Theory

1. b From the statement I, we have the following Venn diagram :

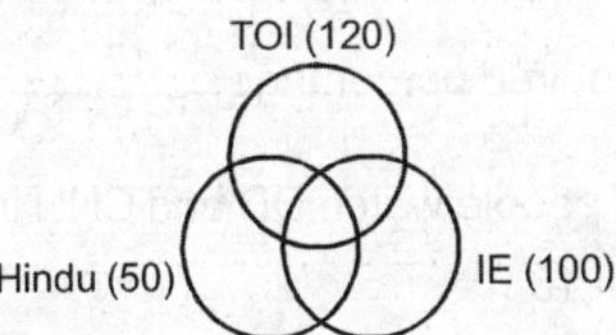

Using this we cannot find the answer.

From the statement II however we can find the answer, as we get the following Venn diagram.

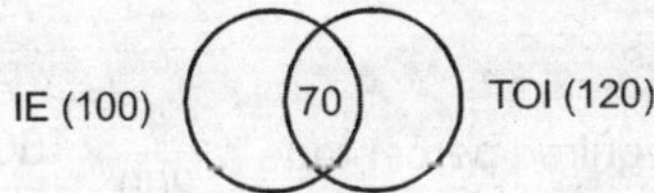

2. c We know that x + y + z = T and x + 2y + 3z = R_T, where

x = number of members belonging to exactly 1 set

y = number of members belonging to exactly 2 sets = 9

z = number of members belonging to exactly 3 sets = 1

T = Total number of members

R_T = Repeated total of all the members

= (22 + 15 + 14) = 51

R_T = T + y + 2z

Thus we have two equations and two unknowns. Solving this we get T = 40.

In other words, the number of teachers owing at least 1 out of the three items = 40. Hence the number of teachers owing none = 50 – 40 = 10.

For questions 3 and 4:

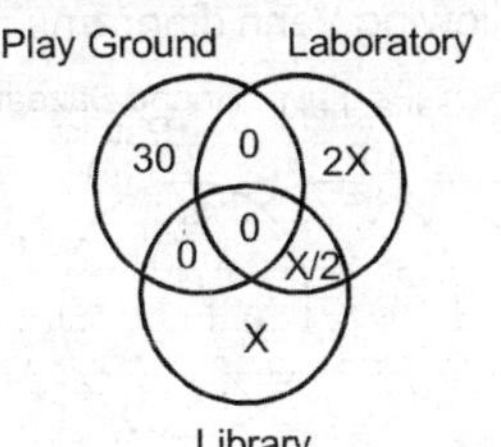

It is given that X + 2X + X/2 = 35

Therefore, X = 10.

3. d Total number of schools that had at least one of the three = 30 + 10 + 20 + 5 = 65. Hence the number of schools having none of them = 100 – 65 = 35.

4. b Number of schools having library = 15. And number of schools having laboratory = 25.

Hence the ratio = 25 : 15 = 5 : 3.

5. b

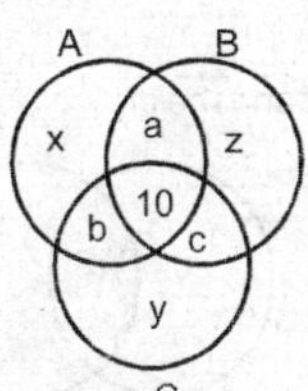

x + a + b = 40 – 10 = 30 ... (i)

y + b + c = 50 – 10 = 40 ... (ii)

z + a + c = 60 – 10 = 50 ... (iii)

From (i), (ii) and (iii)

a + b + c = 25.

For questions 6 and 7:

Let x, y and z be the number of children who took 1 rides, 2 rides and 3 rides respectively.

Since z = 20 and y + z = 55, y = 35.

Then, total number of rides = x + 2y + 3z = 145

$\Rightarrow$ x + 2 × 35 + 3 × 20 = 145 $\Rightarrow$ x = 15

6. c Number of children, who did not try any of the rides = 85 – (x + y + z)= 85 – (15 + 35 + 20) = 15

7. c Number of children, who took exactly one ride = x = 15

8. c

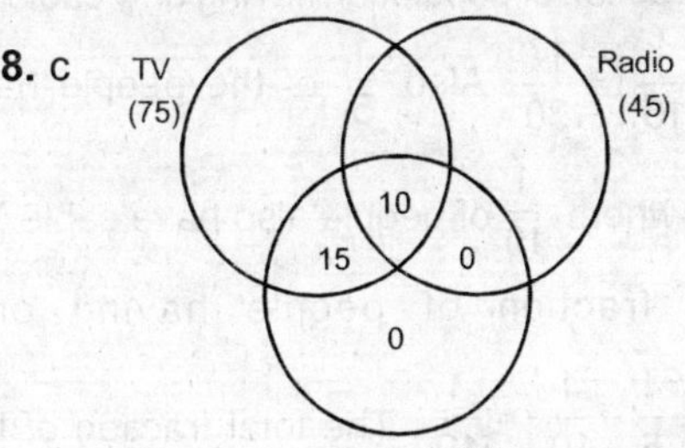

Since each VCR owner also has a TV, therefore, 15 families own both TV and VCR but not Radio.

Since 25 families have radio only, therefore, 10 families own both TV and Radio but not VCR.

Hence, number of families having only TV = 75 – 10 –10 – 15 = 40.

For questions 9 to 11: The data can be represented in the following Venn diagrams.

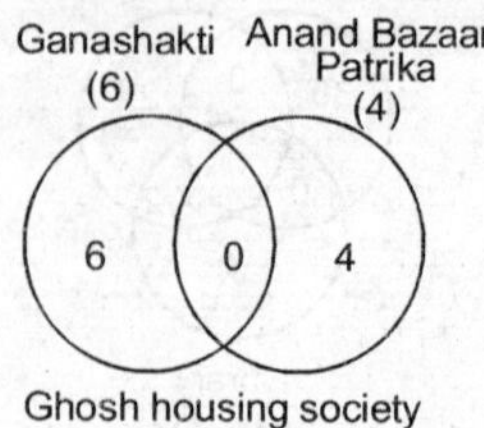

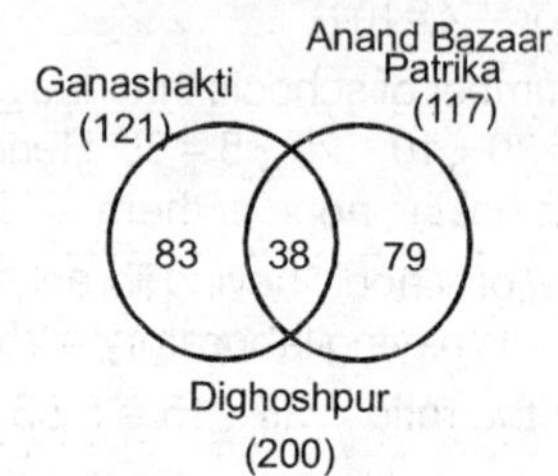

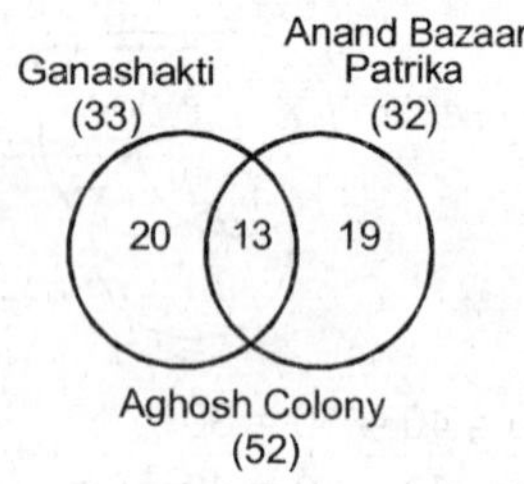

9. b Number of persons in Dighoshpur who read only Ganashakti = 83.

10. a Number of persons in Aghosh Colony who read both the newspapers = 13.

11. c Number of persons in Aghosh Colony who read only 1 newspaper = 20+19 = 39.

12. b We are supposed to find out what fraction of the population has exactly one among the two (since either cable TV or VCR indicates they do not have both). Now $\frac{2}{3}$ of the people have cable TV, of whom $\frac{1}{10}$ of people also have VCR.

Hence, fraction of population having only cable TV $= \left(\frac{2}{3} - \frac{1}{10}\right) = \frac{17}{30}$. Also $\frac{1}{5}$ of the people have VCR, of whom $\frac{1}{10}$ of people also have cable TV.

Hence, fraction of people having only VCR $= \left(\frac{1}{5} - \frac{1}{10}\right) = \frac{1}{10}$. The total fraction of the people who either have cable TV or VCR $= \left(\frac{17}{30} + \frac{1}{10}\right) = \frac{2}{3}$.

For questions 13 to 15:

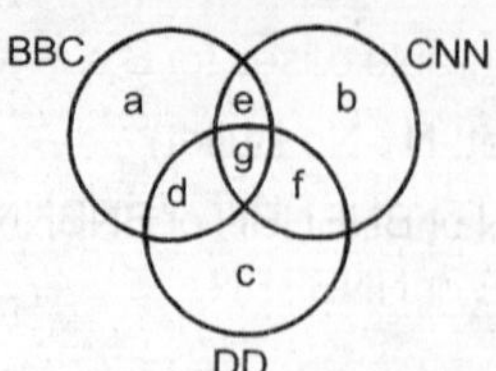

Here, $a + b + c + d + e + f + g = 200$ ...(i)

80% of the people watch DD implies

$c + d + f + g = 160$ ...(ii)

22% of the people watch BBC implies

$a + d + e + g = 44$ ...(iii)

15% of the people watch CNN implies

$b + e + f + g = 30$ ...(iv)

(ii) + (iii) + (iv) gives

$a + b + c + 2(d + e + f) + 3g = 234$

Subtracting (i) from this equation,

$d + e + f + 2g = 34$ ...(v)

13. c To maximize g, in equation (v), we put $d = e = f = 0$

$\therefore$ Maximum value of $g = \frac{34}{2} = 17$

$\therefore$ Required percentage $= \frac{17}{200} \times 100 = 8.5\%$

14. a 5% of people watch DD and CNN implies

$f + g = 10$ ...(vi)

10% of people watch DD and BBC implies

$d + g = 20$ ...(vii)

(v) – (vi) – (vii) gives

$e = 4$

$\therefore$ Required percentage $= \frac{4}{200} \times 100 = 2\%$

15. d From equation (v), we have

$(d + 4 + f) + 2g = 34$

$\Rightarrow (d + f) + 2g = 30$

Since we cannot find the values of d and f, the value of g cannot be ascertained.

16. c Let 'a' be the percentage of people who favoured exactly one proposal, 'b' be the percentage of people who favoured exactly by two proposals and 'c' be the percentage of people who favoured exactly three proposals.

$a + b + c = 78$ ... (i)

$a + 2b + 3c = 100$ ... (ii)

(ii) – (i) implies $b + 2c = 22$

Since $c = 5$, $b = 12$

Required percentage $= b + c = 12 + 5 = 17\%$.

17. c The Venn diagram arrived at from both I and II clearly indicates that 500 people are watching programme P.

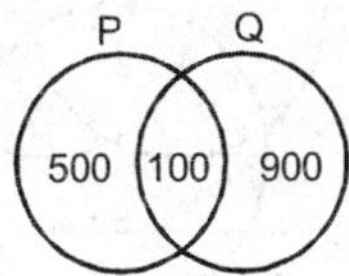

18. c From statement A, we cannot find anything.

From B alone we cannot find.

From A and B,

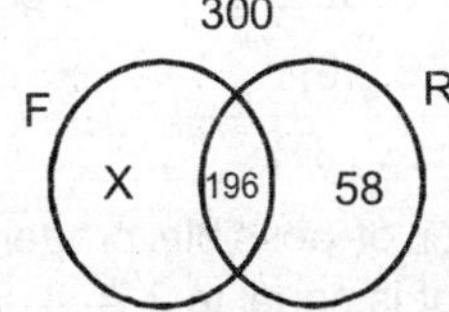

x + 196 + 58 = 300. Thus, x can be found.

19. a By observing, we see 6 will appear in 5 sets T_2, T_3, T_4, T_5 and T_6. Similarly, 12 will also appear in 5 sets and these sets will be distinct from the sets in which 6 appears, i.e. T_8, T_9, T_{10}, T_{11} and T_{12}. Thus, each multiple of 6 will appear in 5 distinct sets. Till T_{96}, there will be 16 multiples of 6. These 16 multiples of 6 will appear in 16 × 5 = 80 sets.

20. d

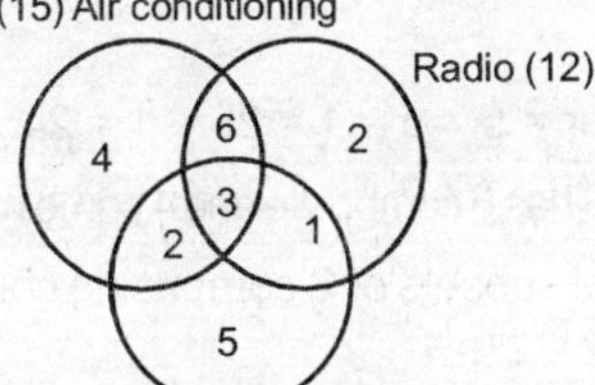

Total = 4 + 6 + 2 + 2 + 3 + 1 + 5 = 23

∴ Cars having none of the option = 25 – 23 = 2.

21. c VCD = 70%, Microwave = 75%, ACS = 80%, Washing M/c = 85%

Least percentage of employees having both VCD and Microwave = 70 + 75 – 100 = 45%

Least percentage having all three – VCD, Microwave, ACS = 45 + 80 – 100 = 25%

Least percentage having all four = 25% + 85% – 100% = 10%

For question 22 and 23: As per the given data, we get the following:

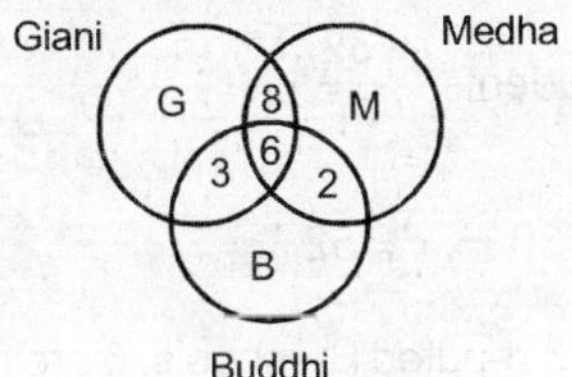

22. d Putting the value of M in either equation, we get G + B = 17.

Hence, neither of two can be uniquely determined.

23. b G + B = M + 16

Also, M + B + G + 19 = (2 × 19) – 1

i.e. (G + B) = 18 – M

Thus, M + 16 = 18 – M

i.e. M = 1

Questions 24 to 27:

- 17 in TR

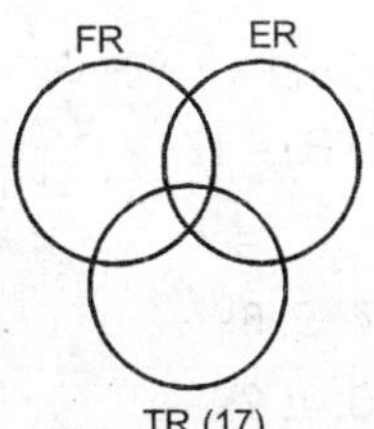

- 10 in TR also in at least one more ⇒ 7 in TR alone

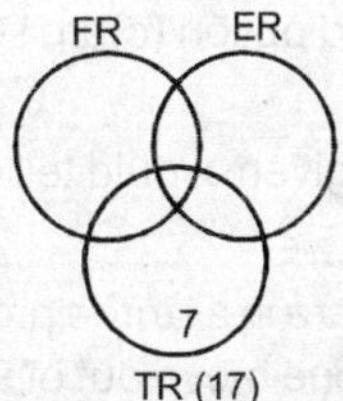

- TR alone = one less than ER alone ⇒ ER alone = 8
- ER alone = double of all 3 ⇒ In all three = $\frac{8}{2}$ = 4

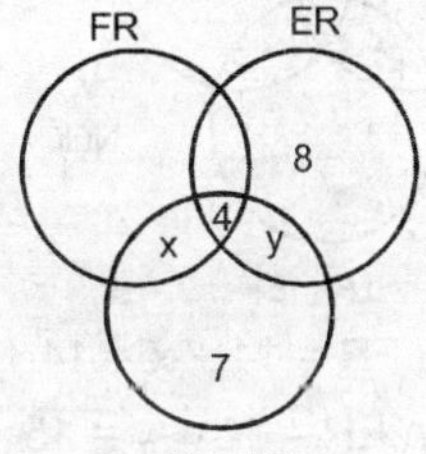

- FR alone = (FR and ER)

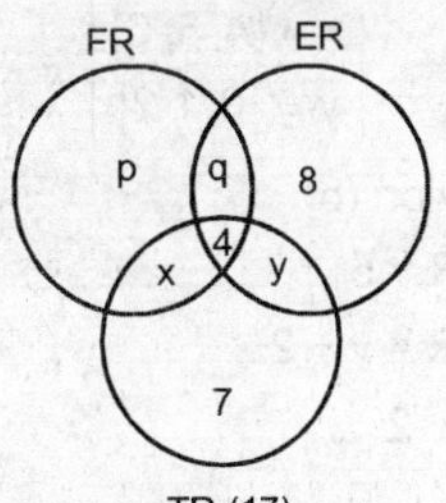

⇒ p = q + 4 ...(1)

Total = 37

[7 + 8 + p + (x + y + q) + 4] = 37 [p + q = 12]

⇒ p – a = 4

⇒ p = 8 and q = 4

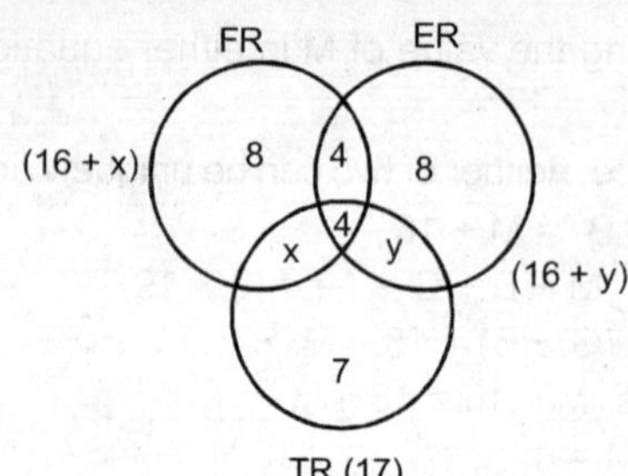

Now, total number of FR is maximum

$\Rightarrow$ $8 + 4 + 4 + x > 8 + 4 + 4 + y$

$\Rightarrow$ $x > y$ and $x + y = 6$

as $n(TR) = 17 = x + y + 4 + 7$

$\Rightarrow$ $x = \{4, 5, 6\}$

$y = \{0, 1, 2\}$

24. c Both FR and TR but not ER = x

Minimum x = 4

25. a Option (b) and option (c)are superfluous. They are not required.

Option (a), if given, would tell us the value of x = 4 and hence y = 2.

26. b Out of 4 who are in all three projects, 2 move out of FR and one-one move out of ER and TR.

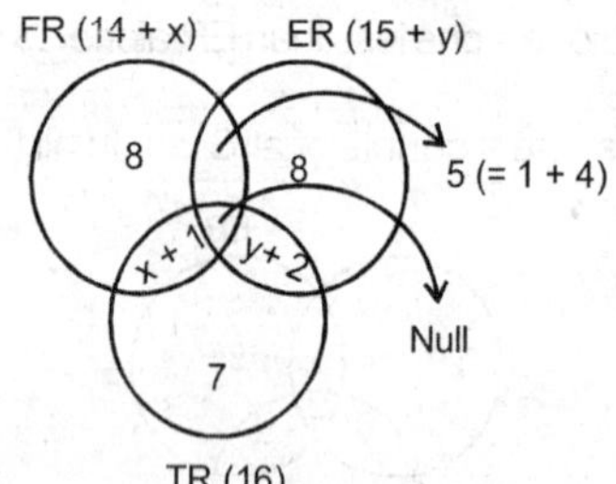

Minimum in FR = 14 + x = 14 + 4 = 18

Maximum in ER = 15 + y = 15 + 2 = 17

$$\left\{\begin{array}{c} \text{As} \\ x = \{4, 5, 6\} \\ y = \{0, 1, 2\} \end{array}\right\}$$

Hence, option (b).

27. d FR and ER = 5

ER and TR = y + 2

$\Rightarrow$ 5 = y + 2

$\Rightarrow$ y = 3;

which is not a possible value as y is 0, 1, or 2 only.

$\Rightarrow$ option (d)

Inconsistent data.

28. b

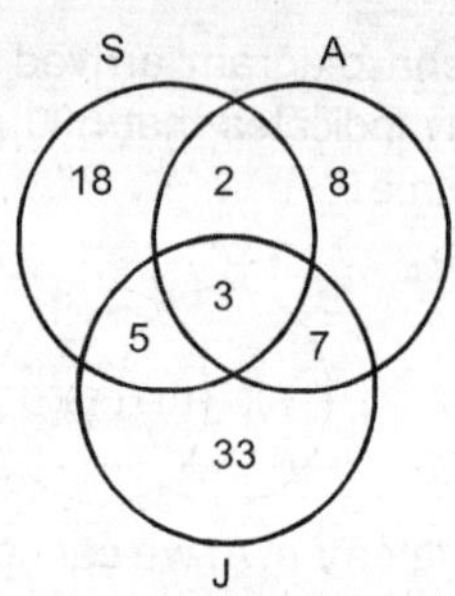

So, total people reading the newspaper in consecutive months i.e. July and August and August and Sept. is 2 + 7 = 9 people.

29. a A = {1, 2, 4, 8, 16}

B = {1, 3, 9, 27, 81}

The number of possible proper fractions when denominator is equal to 2, 4, 8 and 16 are 1, 2, 2 and 3 respectively.

The number of possible proper fractions when denominator is equal to 3, 9, 27 and 81 are 2, 4, 5 and 5 respectively.

Since no two of these fractions can be equal, the answer = 24.

Alternate method: All the combinations can result in a proper fraction except when 1 is chosen from both the sets.

So the answer = 5 × 5 – 1 = 25 – 1 = 24.

30. c The given set S has 6 composite and 4 prime numbers.

The number of subsets of S comprising composite numbers only = $2^6 - 1$

The number of subsets of S comprising prime numbers only = $2^4 - 1$

Hence, the required difference = $(2^6 - 1) - (2^4 - 1) = 48$.

31. 58 There are a total of 78 B-schools that place their students

$\therefore$ No. of B-schools which are reputed and place their students $= \frac{1}{6} \times 78 = 13$

Let No. of B-schools that are recognised = x

$\therefore$ No. of recognised B-schools that place their students $= \frac{1}{4}x$

$\therefore$ No. of recognised B-schools that do not place their students $= \frac{3x}{4}$

$\therefore \frac{3x}{4} = 39 \Rightarrow x = 52$

Out of 13 reputed B-schools, 6 are recognised too

∴ Number of B-schools that are either recognised and place their students or reputed and place their students = 13 + 13 – 6 = 20

∴ Number of B-school that are neither reputed nor recognised but place their students = 78 – 20 = 58.

32. a A = {1, 4, 7, 10, ..., 20 terms}

B = {9, 16, 23, 30, ..., 20 terms}

We first need to find $n(A \cap B)$.

The nth term of A = 1 + (n – 1)3 = 3n – 2.

The mth term of B = 9 + (m – 1)7 = 7m + 2.

$n(A \cap B)$ will be equal to the number of solutions of 3n – 2 = 7m + 2, where n and m are natural numbers not more than 20.

$$\Rightarrow \quad n = \frac{7m + 4}{3}$$

If m = 2, n = 6;

m = 5, n = 13;

m = 8, n = 20

$\Rightarrow$ $n(A \cap B) = 3$

Hence, $n(A \cup B) = n(A) + n(B) - n(A \cap B)$

$= 20 + 20 - 3 = 37.$

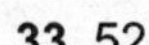

33. 52

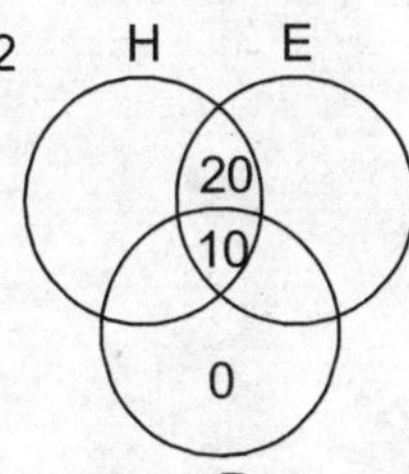

Number of students studying H equals that studying E = z + 30

As total number of students = 74

∴ z + z + 30 = 74

2z + 30 = 74

2z = 44

z = 22

So, the number of students studying H is z + 30 = 22 + 30 = 52.

34. d

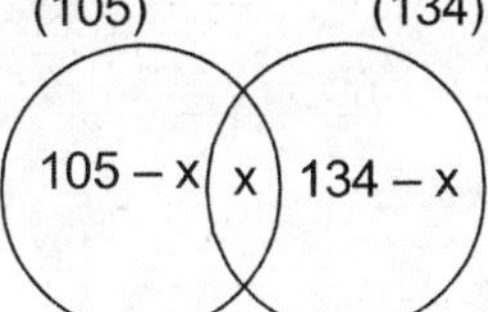

Total students = 200

So, the number of students who like only burger = 134 – x

first, check option 1,

134 – x = 26

x = 108 which is greater than the number of students who like Pizza. So, 26 cannot be the answer.

Similarly, 134 – x = 96

x = 38

So, the number of students who like only Pizza

= 105 – x = 105 – 38 = 67

So, the total number of students

= 67 + 38 + 96

= 201, which is wrong.

Hence, option 2 cannot be the answer.

Now, put option 3,

134 – x = 23

x = 111, which is again greater than the number of students who like Pizza, hence, option (3) cannot be the answer,

If 134 – x = 93

$\Rightarrow$ x = 41

∴ Number of students who like Pizza only

= 105 – 41 = 64

So, total number of these students who like one or more items = 93 + 41 + 64 = 198

Hence, 93 can be the possible answer.

35. a $(P \Delta Q) = (1, 4, 5, 6)$ and $(R \Delta S) = (1, 2, 3, 4, 7, 8, 10)$

$\Rightarrow (P \Delta Q) \Delta (R \Delta S) = (2, 3, 5, 6, 7, 8, 10)$

Hence, required number of elements = 7.

5 CHAPTER

Algebra

EQUATIONS, POLYNOMIALS AND INEQUATIONS

1990

1. The value of $\frac{1}{(1-x)}+\frac{1}{(1+x)}+\frac{2}{(1+x^2)}+\frac{4}{(1+x^4)}$ is

(a) $\frac{8}{(1-x^8)}$ (b) $\frac{4x}{(1+x^2)}$

(c) $\frac{4}{(1-x^6)}$ (d) $\frac{4}{(1+x^4)}$

2. Let a, b be any positive integers and x = 0 or 1, then

(a) $a^x b^{(1-x)} = xa + (1-x)b$

(b) $a^x b^{(1-x)} = (1-x)a + xb$

(c) $a^x b^{(1-x)} = a^{(1-x)}bx$

(d) None of the above is necessarily true.

3. The value of $\frac{(1-d^3)}{(1-d)}$ is

(a) > 1 if d > –1 (b) > 3 if d > 1

(c) > 2 if 0 < d < 0.5 (d) < 2 if d < –2

4. The roots of the equation $ax^2 + 3x + 6 = 0$ will be reciprocal to each other if the value of *a* is

(a) 3 (b) 4

(c) 5 (d) 6

5. If xy + yz + zx = 0, then $(x + y + z)^2$ equals

(a) $(x + y)^2 + xz$ (b) $(x + z)^2 + xy$

(c) $x^2 + y^2 + z^2$ (d) 2(xy + yz + xz)

Directions for Questions 6 and 7: Each of the following questions is followed by two statements. MARK,

(a) if the question can be answered with the help of statement I alone

(b) if the question can be answered with the help of statement II alone

(c) if both, statement I and statement II are needed to answer the question, and

(d) if the statement cannot be answered even with the help of both the statements.

6. A man distributed 43 chocolates to his children. How many of his children are more than five years old?

I. A child older than five years gets 5 chocolates.

II. A child 5 years or younger in age gets 6 chocolates.

7. Is $\left[\frac{(x^{-1}-y^{-1})}{(x^{-2}-y^{-2})}\right] > 1$?

I. x + y > 0.

II. x and y are positive integers and each is greater than 2.

1991

8. What is the value of k for which the following system of equations has no solution:

2x – 8y = 3 and kx + 4y = 10

(a) –2 (b) 1

(c) –1 (d) 2

9. Iqbal dealt some cards to Mushtaq and himself from a full pack of playing cards and laid the rest aside. Iqbal then said to Mushtaq. "If you give me a certain number of your cards, I will have four times as many cards as you will have. If I give you the same number of cards, I will have thrice as many cards as you will have". Of the given choices, which could represent the number of cards with Iqbal?

(a) 9 (b) 31

(c) 12 (d) 35

10. The number of integers n satisfying $-n + 2 \geq 0$ and $2n \geq 4$ is

(a) 0 (b) 1

(c) 2 (d) 3

11. In Sivakasi, each boy's quota of match sticks to fill into boxes is not more than 200 per session. If he reduces the number of sticks per box by 25, he can fill 3 more boxes with the total number of sticks assigned to him. Which of the following is the possible number of sticks assigned to each boy?

(a) 200 (b) 150

(c) 125 (d) 175

1993

Directions for Questions 12 and 13 : Each of these items has a question followed by two statements. As the answer,

Mark (a) If the question can be answered with the help of statement I alone

Mark (b) If the question can be answered with the help of statement II, alone

Mark (c) If both, statement I and statement II are needed to answer the question, and

Mark (d) If the question cannot be answered even with the help of both the statements.

12. Given that X and Y are non-negative. What is the value of X?

I. $2X + 2Y \leq 40$

II. $X - 2Y \geq 20$

13. What is the price of mangoes per kg?

I. Ten kg of mangoes and two dozens of oranges cost Rs.252.

II. Two kg of mangoes could be bought in exchange for one dozen oranges.

14. Two oranges, three bananas and four apples cost Rs.15. Three oranges, two bananas and one apple cost Rs 10. I bought 3 oranges, 3 bananas and 3 apples. How much did I pay?

(a) Rs.10 (b) Rs.8

(c) Rs.15 (d) cannot be determined

15. John bought five mangoes and ten oranges together for forty rupees. Subsequently, he returned one mango and got two oranges in exchange. The price of an orange would be

(a) Re. 1 (b) Rs. 2

(c) Rs. 3 (d) Rs. 4

1994

16. If *a + b + c = 0,* where $a \neq b \neq c$, then $\frac{a^2}{2a^2 + bc} + \frac{b^2}{2b^2 + ac} + \frac{c^2}{2c^2 + ab}$ is equal to

(a) zero (b) 1

(c) –1 (d) abc

17. If one root of $x^2 - 7 + 12 = 0$ is 4, while the equation $x^2 - 7x + q = 0$ has equal roots, then the value of *q* is

(a) $\frac{49}{4}$ (b) $\frac{4}{49}$

(c) 4 (d) $\frac{1}{4}$

Direction for Question 18: Data is provided followed by two statements – I and II – both resulting in a value, say I and II. As your answer,

Mark (a) if I > II.

Mark (b) if I < II.

Mark (c) if I = II.

Mark (d) if nothing can be said.

18. Nineteen year from now Jackson will be 3 times as old as Joseph is now. Johnson is three years younger than Jackson.

I. Johnson's age now.

II. Joseph's age now.

Direction for Question 19: The question is followed by two statements. As the answer,

Mark (a) If the question can be answered with the help of statement I alone

Mark (b) If the question can be answered with the help of statement II, alone

Mark (c) If both, statement I and statement II are needed to answer the question, and

Mark (d) If the question cannot be answered even with the help of both the statements.

19. If twenty sweets are distributed among some boys and girls such that each girl gets two sweets and each boy gets three sweets, what is the number of boys and girls?

I. The number of girls is not more than five.

II. If each girl gets 3 sweets and each boy gets 2 sweets, the number of sweets required for the children will still be the same.

1995

20. One root of $x^2 + kx - 8 = 0$ is square of the other. Then the value of k is

(a) 2 (b) 8

(c) –8 (d) –2

21. Two positive integers differ by 4 and sum of their reciprocals is $\frac{10}{21}$. Then one of the numbers is

(a) 3 (b) 1

(c) 5 (d) 21

22. What is the value of m which satisfies $3m^2 - 21m + 30 < 0$?

(a) m < 2 or m > 5

(b) m > 2

(c) 2 < m < 5

(d) Both (a) and (c)

Direction for Question 23: The question is followed by two statements, I and II. Mark the answer as

(a) if the question can be answered with the help of statement I alone.

(b) if the question can be answered with the help of statement II alone.

(c) if both statement I and statement II are needed to answer the question.

(d) if the question cannot be answered even with the help of both the statements.

23. What is the value of x, if x and y are consecutive positive even integers?
I. $(x-y)^2 = 4$
II. $(x+y)^2 < 100$

1996

24. Which of the following values of x do not satisfy the inequality $(x^2 - 3x + 2 > 0)$at all?
(a) $1 \le x \le 2$ (b) $-1 \ge x \ge -2$
(c) $0 \le x \le 2$ (d) $0 \ge x \ge -2$

25. Given the quadratic equation $x^2 - (A-3)x - (A-2) = 0$, for what value of A will the sum of the squares of the roots be zero?
(a) –2 (b) 3
(c) 6 (d) None of these

Direction for Question 26 : The question is followed by two statements, I and II. Mark the answer as:
(a) if the question cannot be answered even with the help of both the statements taken together.
(b) if the question can be answered by any one of the two statements.
(c) if each statement alone is sufficient to answer the question, but not the other one (e.g. statement I alone is required to answer the question, but not statement II and vice versa).
(d) if both statements I and II together are needed to answer the question.

26. If α and β are the roots of the equation $(ax^2 + bx + c = 0)$, then what is the value of $(\alpha^2 + \beta^2)$?
I. $\alpha + \beta = -\left(\frac{b}{a}\right)$
II. $2\alpha\beta = \left(\frac{c}{a}\right)$

27. Find the value of $\dfrac{1}{1+\dfrac{1}{3-\dfrac{4}{2+\dfrac{1}{3-\dfrac{1}{2}}}}} + \dfrac{3}{3-\dfrac{4}{3+\dfrac{1}{2-\dfrac{1}{2}}}}$
(a) $\frac{13}{7}$ (b) $\frac{15}{7}$
(c) $\frac{11}{21}$ (d) $\frac{17}{28}$

1997

28. A, B and C are defined as follows.
$$A = (2.000004) \div \left[(2.000004)^2 + (4.000008)\right]$$
$$B = (3.000003) \div \left[(3.000003)^2 + (9.000009)\right]$$
$$C = (4.000002) \div \left[(4.000002)^2 + (8.000004)\right]$$
Which of the following is true about the values of the above three expressions?
(a) All of them lie between 0.18 and 0.2
(b) A is twice of C
(c) C is the smallest
(d) B is the smallest

29. A student instead of finding the value of $\frac{7}{8}$ of a number, found the value of $\frac{7}{18}$ of the number. If his answer differed from the actual one by 770, find the number.
(a) 1584 (b) 2520
(c) 1728 (d) 1656

30. If the roots x_1 and x_2 of the quadratic equation $x^2 - 2x + c = 0$ also satisfy the equation $7x_2 - 4x_1 = 47$, then which of the following is true?
(a) $c = -15$
(b) $x_1 = -5, x_2 = 3$
(c) $x_1 = 4.5, x_2 = -2.5$
(d) None of these

Direction for Question 31: The question followed by two statements, I and II. Mark the answer
(a) if the question can be answered with the help of one statement alone.
(b) if the question can be answered with the help of any one statement independently.
(c) if the question can be answered with the help of both statements together.
(d) if the question cannot be answered even with the help of both statements together.

31. What is the value of x and y?
I. $3x + 2y = 45$
II. $10.5x + 7y = 157.5$

1998

Direction for Question 32: The question followed by two statements, I and II. Mark the answer
(a) if the question can be answered with the help of any one statement alone but not by the other statement.
(b) if the question can be answered with the help of either of the statements taken individually.
(c) if the question can be answered with the help of both statements together.
(d) if the question cannot be answered even with the help of both statements together.

32. In a group of 150 students, find the number of girls.

I. Each girl was given 50 paise, while each boy was given 25 paise to purchase goods totalling Rs. 49.

II. Girls and boys were given 30 paise each to buy goods totalling Rs. 45.

1999

33. The number of positive integer valued pairs (x, y) satisfying $4x - 17y = 1$ and $x \leq 1000$ is

(a) 59 (b) 57

(c) 55 (d) 58

Direction for Question 34: The question is followed by two statements I and II.

Mark:

(a) if the question can be answered by any one of the statements alone, but cannot be answered byusing the other statement alone.

(b) if the question can be answered by using either statement alone.

(c) if the question can be answered by using both the statements together, but cannot be answered by using either statement alone.

(d) if the question cannot be answered even by using both the statements together.

34. Find a pair of real numbers x and y that satisfy the following two equations simultaneously. It is known that the values of a, b, c, d, e and f are non-zero.

$ax + by = c$

$dx + ey = f$

I. $a = kd$ and $b = ke$, $c = kf$, $k \neq 0$

II. $a = b = 1$, $d = e = 2$, $f \neq 2c$

2000

35.

x	1	2	3	4	5	6
y	4	8	14	22	32	44

In the above table, for suitably chosen constants a, b and c, which one of the following best describes the relation between y and x?

(a) $y = a + bx$

(b) $y = a + bx + cx^2$

(c) $y = e^{a + bx}$

(d) None of these

36. If $x > 2$ and $y > -1$, then which of the following statements is necessarily true?

(a) $xy > -2$ (b) $-x < 2y$

(c) $xy < -2$ (d) $-x > 2y$

37. If the equation $x^3 - ax^2 + bx - a = 0$ has three real roots, then it must be the case that

(a) $b = 1$ (b) $b \neq 1$

(c) $a = 1$ (d) $a \neq 1$

38. There are three cities: A, B and C. Each of these cities is connected with the other two cities by at least one direct road. If a traveller wants to go from one city (origin)to another city (destination), she can do so either by traversing a road connecting the two cities directly, or by traversing two roads, the first connecting the origin to the third city and the second connecting the third city to the destination. In all there are 33 routes from A to B (including those via C). Similarly, there are 23 routes from B to C (including those via A). How many roads are there from A to C directly?

(a) 6 (b) 3

(c) 5 (d) 10

39. Two full tanks, one shaped like a cylinder and the other like a cone, contain jet fuel. The cylindrical tank holds 500 L more than the conical tank. After 200 L of fuel has been pumped out from each tank the cylindrical tank contains twice the amount of fuel in the conical tank. How many litres of fuel did the cylindrical tank have when it was full?

(a) 700 L (b) 1,000 L

(c) 1,100 L (d) 1,200 L

Direction for Question 40: The question is followed by two statements, I and II. Answer the question using the following instructions.

Mark the answer as:

(a) if the question can be answered by one of the statements alone, but cannot be answered by using the other statement alone.

(b) if the question can be answered by using either statement alone.

(c) if the question can be answered by using both the statements together, but cannot be answered by using either statement alone.

(d) if the question cannot be answered even by using both statements together.

40. Let X be a real number. Is the modulus of X necessarily less than 3?

I. $X(X + 3) < 0$

II. $X(X - 3) > 0$

2001

41. If $x > 5$ and $y < -1$, then which of the following statements is true?

(a) $(x + 4y) > 1$ (b) $x > -4y$

(c) $-4x < 5y$ (d) None of these

42. In a four-digit number, the sum of the first 2 digits is equal to that of the last 2 digits. The sum of the first and last digits is equal to the third digit. Finally, the sum of the second and fourth digits is twice the sum of the other 2 digits. What is the third digit of the number?

(a) 5 (b) 8
(c) 1 (d) 4

43. Three friends, returning from a movie, stopped to eat at a restaurant. After dinner, they paid their bill and noticed a bowl of mints at the front counter. Sita took one-third of the mints, but returned four because she had a momentary pang of guilt. Fatima then took one-fourth of what was left but returned three for similar reason. Eswari then took half of the remainder but threw two back into the bowl. The bowl had only 17 mints left when the raid was over. How many mints were originally in the bowl?

(a) 38 (b) 31
(c) 41 (d) None of these

44. Anita had to do a multiplication. In stead of taking 35 as one of the multipliers, she took 53. As a result, the product went up by 540. What is the new product?

(a) 1050 (b) 540
(c) 1440 (d) 1590

45. x and y are real numbers satisfying the conditions $2 < x < 3$ and $-8 < y < -7$. Which of the following expressions will have the least value?

(a) x^2y (b) xy^2
(c) $5xy$ (d) None of these

46. m is the smallest positive integer such that for any integer $n \geq m$, the quantity $n^3 - 7n^2 + 11n - 5$ is positive. What is the value of m?

(a) 4 (b) 5
(c) 8 (d) None of these

47. Every 10 years the Indian Government counts all the people living in the country. Suppose that the director of the census has reported the following data on two neighbouring villages Chota Hazri and Mota Hazri.

Chota Hazri has 4,522 fewer males than Mota Hazri.

Mota Hazri has 4,020 more females than males.

Chota Hazri has twice as many females as males.

Chota Hazri has 2,910 fewer females than Mota Hazri.

What is the total number of males in Chota Hazri?

(a) 11,264 (b) 14,174
(c) 5,632 (d) 10,154

48. At a certain fast food restaurant, Brian can buy 3 burgers, 7 shakes, and one order of fries for Rs. 120 exactly. At the same place it would cost Rs. 164.50 for 4 burgers, 10 shakes, and one order of fries. How much would it cost for an ordinary meal of one burger, one shake, and one order of fries?

(a) Rs. 31 (b) Rs. 41
(c) Rs. 21 (d) Cannot be determined

49. In some code, letters a, b, c, d and e represent numbers 2, 4, 5, 6 and 10. We just do not know which letter represents which number. Consider the following relationships:

I. $a + c = e$, II. $b - d = d$ and III. $e + a = b$

Which of the following statements is true?

(a) $b = 4, d = 2$ (b) $a = 4, e = 6$
(c) $b = 6, e = 2$ (d) $a = 4, c = 6$

50. Ujakar and Keshab attempted to solve a quadratic equation. Ujakar made a mistake in writing down the constant term. He ended up with the roots (4, 3). Keshab made a mistake in writing down the coefficient of x. He got the roots as (3, 2). What will be the exact roots of the original quadratic equation?

(a) (6, 1) (b) (–3, –4)
(c) (4, 3) (d) (–4, –3)

51. A change-making machine contains one-rupee, two-rupee and five-rupee coins. The total number of coins is 300. The amount is Rs. 960. If the numbers of one-rupee coins and two-rupee coins are interchanged, the value comes down by Rs. 40. The total number of five-rupee coins is

(a) 100 (b) 140
(c) 60 (d) 150

2002

52. If x, y and z are real numbers such that $x + y + z = 5$ and $xy + yz + zx = 3$, what is the largest value that x can have?

(a) $\frac{5}{3}$ (b) $\sqrt{19}$
(c) $\frac{13}{3}$ (d) None of these

53. A rich merchant had collected many gold coins. He did not want anybody to know about him. One day, his wife asked, " How many gold coins do we have?" After a brief pause, he replied, "Well! if I divide the coins into two unequal numbers, then 48 times the difference between the two numbers equals the difference between the squares of the two numbers." The wife looked puzzled. Can you help the merchant's wife by finding out how many gold coins the merchant has?

(a) 96 (b) 53
(c) 43 (d) None of these

54. Shyam visited Ram during his brief vacation. In the mornings they both would go for yoga. In the evenings they would play tennis. To have more fun, they indulge only in one activity per day, i.e. either they went for yoga or played tennis each day. There were days when they were lazy and stayed home all day long. There were 24 mornings when they did nothing, 14 evenings when they stayed at home, and a total of 22 days when they did yoga or played tennis. For how many days Shyam stayed with Ram?

(a) 32 (b) 24

(c) 30 (d) None of these

55. If $x^2 + 5y^2 + z^2 = 2y(2x + z)$, then which of the following statements is(are)necessarily true?

A. x = 2y B. x = 2z C. 2x = z

(a) Only A (b) B and C

(c) A and B (d) None of these

56. The number of real roots of the equation $\frac{A^2}{x} + \frac{B^2}{x-1} = 1$, where A and B are real numbers not equal to zero simultaneously, is

(a) None (b) 1

(c) 2 (d) 1 or 2

57. A piece of string is 40 cm long. It is cut into three pieces. The longest piece is three times as long as the middle-sized and the shortest piece is 23 cm shorter than the longest piece. Find the length of the shortest piece.

(a) 27 (b) 5

(c) 4 (d) 9

Directions for Questions 58 and 59: Each item is followed by two statements, A and B. Answer each question using the following instructions.

Choose (a) if the question can be answered by one of the statements alone but not by the other.

Choose (b) if the question can be answered by using either statement alone.

Choose (c) if the question can be answered by using both the statements together, but cannot be answered by using either statement alone.

Choose (d) if the question cannot be answered even by using both statements together.

58. Is x = y?

A. $(x + y)\left(\frac{1}{x} + \frac{1}{y}\right) = 4$

B. $(x - 50)^2 = (y - 50)^2$

59. Is $|x - 2| < 1$?

A. $|x| < 1$

B. $|x - 1| < 2$

2003(R)

60. If both a and b belong to the set {1, 2, 3, 4}, then the number of equations of the form $ax^2 + bx + 1 = 0$ having real roots is

(a) 10 (b) 7

(c) 6 (d) 12

61. If x and y are integers, then the equation 5x + 19y = 64 has

(a) no solution for x < 300 and y < 0

(b) no solution for x > 250 and y > –100

(c) a solution for 250 < x < 300

(d) a solution for –59 < y < –56

62. The number of roots common between the two equations $x^3 + 3x^2 + 4x + 5 = 0$ and $x^3 + 2x^2 + 7x + 3 = 0$ is

(a) 0 (b) 1

(c) 2 (d) 3

63. A real number x satisfying $1 - \frac{1}{n} < x \le 3 + \frac{1}{n}$, for every positive integer n, is best described by

(a) $1 < x < 4$ (b) $1 < x \le 3$

(c) $0 < x \le 4$ (d) $1 \le x \le 3$

64. If n is such that $36 \le n \le 72$, then

$$x = \frac{n^2 + 2\sqrt{n}(n+4) + 16}{n + 4\sqrt{n} + 4}$$ satisfies

(a) 20 < x < 54 (b) 23 < x < 58

(c) 25 < x < 64 (d) 28 < x < 60

65. If 13x + 1 < 2z and $z + 3 = 5y^2$, then

(a) x is necessarily less than y

(b) x is necessarily greater than y

(c) x is necessarily equal to y

(d) None of the above is necessarily true

Directions for Question 66: The question is followed by two statements, A and B. Answer the question using the following instructions:

Choose (a) if the question can be answered by using statement A alone but not by using B alone.

Choose (b) if the question can be answered by using statement B alone but not by using A alone.

Choose (c) if the question can be answered by using either statement alone and

Choose (d) if the question can be answered using both the statements together but not by either statement alone.

66. A family has only one kid. The father says, "After 'n' years, my age will be 4 times the age of my kid." The mother says, "After 'n' years, my age will be 3 times that of my kid." What will be the combined ages of the parents after 'n' years?

A. The age difference between the parents is 10 years.

B. After 'n' years the kid is going to be twice as old as she is now.

2003(L)

67. The number of non-negative real roots of $2^x - x - 1 = 0$ equals

(a) 0 (b) 1
(c) 2 (d) 3

68. Which one of the following conditions must p, q and r satisfy so that the following system of linear simultaneous equations has at least one solution, such that $p + q + r \neq 0$?

$$x + 2y - 3z = p$$
$$2x + 6y - 11z = q$$
$$x - 2y + 7z = r$$

(a) $5p - 2q - r = 0$ (b) $5p + 2q + r = 0$
(c) $5p + 2q - r = 0$ (d) $5p - 2q + r = 0$

69. A leather factory produces two kinds of bags, standard and deluxe. The profit margin is Rs. 20 on a standard bag and Rs. 30 on a deluxe bag. Every bag must be processed on machine A and on Machine B. The processing times per bag on the two machines are as follows:

	Time required (Hours/bag)	
	Machine A	Machine B
Standard Bag	4	6
Deluxe Bag	5	10

The total time available on machine A is 700 hours and on machine B is 1250 hours. Among the following production plans, which one meets the machine availability constraints and maximizes the profit?

(a) Standard 75 bags, Deluxe 80 bags
(b) Standard 100 bags, Deluxe 60 bags
(c) Standard 50 bags, Deluxe 100 bags
(d) Standard 60 bags, Deluxe 90 bags

70. A test has 50 questions. A student scores 1 mark for a correct answer, –1/3 for a wrong answer, and –1/6 for not attempting a question. If the net score of a student is 32, the number of questions answered wrongly by that student cannot be less than

(a) 6 (b) 12
(c) 3 (d) 9

71. Let p and q be the roots of the quadratic equation $x^2 - (\alpha - 2)x - \alpha - 1 = 0$. What is the minimum possible value of $p^2 + q^2$?

(a) 0 (b) 3
(c) 4 (d) 5

72. Let a, b, c, d be four integers such that $a + b + c + d = 4m + 1$ where m is a positive integer. Given m, which one of the following is necessarily true?

(a) The minimum possible value of $a^2 + b^2 + c^2 + d^2$ is $4m^2 - 2m + 1$
(b) The minimum possible value of $a^2 + b^2 + c^2 + d^2$ is $4m^2 + 2m + 1$
(c) The maximum possible value of $a^2 + b^2 + c^2 + d^2$ is $4m^2 - 2m + 1$
(d) The maximum possible value of $a^2 + b^2 + c^2 + d^2$ is $4m^2 + 2m + 1$

73. Given that $-1 \le v \le 1$, $-2 \le u \le -0.5$ and $-2 \le z \le -0.5$ and $w = vz/u$, then which of the following is necessarily true?

(a) $-0.5 \le w \le 2$ (b) $-4 \le w \le 4$
(c) $-4 \le w \le 2$ (d) $-2 \le w \le -0.5$

74. If x, y, z are distinct positive real numbers the $\dfrac{x^2(y+z)+y^2(x+z)+z^2(x+y)}{xyz}$ would be

(a) greater than 4. (b) greater than 5.
(c) greater than 6 (d) None of the above.

Direction for Question 75: In the question there are two statements: A and B.

Choose (a) if the question can be answered by one of the statements alone but not by the other.

Choose (b) if the question can be answered by using either statement alone.

Choose (c) if the question can be answered by using both the statements together but cannot be answered using either statement alone.

Choose (d) if the question cannot be answered even by using both the statements A and B.

75. Each packet of SOAP costs Rs. 10. Inside each packet is a gift coupon labelled with one of the letters S, O, A and P. If a customer submits four such coupons that make up the word SOAP, the customer gets a free SOAP packets. Ms. X kept buying packet after packet of SOAP till she could get one set of coupons that formed the word SOAP. How many coupons with label P did she get in the above process?

A. The last label obtained by her was S and the total amount spent was Rs. 210.

B. The total number of vowels obtained was 18.

Direction for Question 76: The question is followed by two statements, A and B. Answer the question using the following instructions.

Choose (a) if the question can be answered by one of the statements alone but not by the other.

Choose (b) if the question can be answered by using either statement alone.

Choose (c) if the question can be answered by using both the statements together, but cannot be answered by using either statement alone.

Choose (d) if the question cannot be answered even by using both the statements together.

76. What are the unique values of b and c in the equation $4x^2 + bx + c = 0$ if one of the roots of the equation is $(-1/2)$?

A. The second root is 1/2.

B. The ratio of c and b is 1.

2004

77. Let $y = \cfrac{1}{2+\cfrac{1}{3+\cfrac{1}{2+\cfrac{1}{3+\dots}}}}$

What is the value of y?

(a) $\frac{\sqrt{11}+3}{2}$ (b) $\frac{\sqrt{11}-3}{2}$

(c) $\frac{\sqrt{15}+3}{2}$ (d) $\frac{\sqrt{15}-3}{2}$

78. Each family in a locality has at most two adults, and no family has fewer than 3 children. Considering all the families together, there are more adults than boys, more boys than girls, and more girls than families, Then the minimum possible number of families in the locality is

(a) 4 (b) 5

(c) 2 (d) 3

79. The total number of integers pairs (x, y) satisfying the equation $x + y = xy$ is

(a) 0 (b) 1

(c) 2 (d) None of the above

Directions for Questions 80 and 81: Answer the questions on the basis of the information given below.

In an examination, there are 100 questions divided into three groups A, B and C such that each group contains at least one question. Each question in group a carries 1 mark, each question in group B carries 2 marks and each question in group C carries 3 marks. It is known that the questions in group A together carry at least 60% of the total marks.

80. If group B contains 23 questions, then how many questions are there in Group C?

(a) 1

(b) 2

(c) 3

(d) Cannot be determined

81. If group C contains 8 questions and group B carries at least 20% of the total marks, which of the following best describes the number of questions in group B?

(a) 11 or 12 (b) 12 or 13

(c) 13 or 14 (d) 14 or 15

Directions for Questions 82 and 83: Each question is followed by two statements, A and B. Answer each question using the following instructions.

Choose (a) if the question can be answered by using one of the statements alone but not by using the other statement alone.

Choose (b) if the question can be answered by using either of the statements alone.

Choose (c) if the question can be answered by using both statements together but not by either statement alone.

Choose (d) if the question cannot be answered on the basis of the two statements.

82. Ravi spent less than Rs. 75 to buy one kilogram each of potato, onion, and gourd. Which one of the three vegetables bought was the costliest?

A. 2 kgs potato and 1 kg gourd cost less than 1 kg potato and 2 kg gourd.

B. 1 kg potato and 2 kgs onion together cost the same as 1 kg onion and 2 kgs gourd.

83. Nandini paid for an article using currency notes of denominations Re. 1, Rs. 2, Rs. 5, and Rs. 10 using at least one note of each denomination. The total number of five and ten rupee notes used was one more than the total number of one and two rupee notes used. What was the price of the article?

A. Nandini used a total of 13 currency notes.

B. The price of the article was a multiple of Rs. 10.

2005

84. For which value of k does the following pair of equations yield a unique solution of x such that the solution is positive?

$$x^2 - y^2 = 0$$

$$(x-k)^2 + y^2 = 1$$

(a) 2 (b) 0

(c) $\sqrt{2}$ (d) $-\sqrt{2}$

85. Let $x = \sqrt{4+\sqrt{4-\sqrt{4+\sqrt{4-...\text{to infinity}}}}}$. Then x equals

(a) 3 (b) $\left(\frac{\sqrt{13}-1}{2}\right)$

(c) $\left(\frac{\sqrt{13}+1}{2}\right)$ (d) $\sqrt{13}$

86. A telecom service provider engages male and female operators for answering 1000 calls per day. A male operator can handle 40 calls per day whereas a female operator can handle 50 calls per day. The male and the female operators get a fixed wage of Rs. 250 and Rs. 300 per day respectively. In addition, a male operator gets Rs. 15 per call he answers and female operator gets Rs. 10 per call she answers. To minimize the total cost, how many male operators should the service provider employ assuming he has to employ more than 7 of the 12 female operators available for the job?

(a) 15 (b) 14

(c) 12 (d) 10

2006

Directions for Questions 87 and 88: Answer questions on the basis of the information given below:

An airline has a certain free luggage allowance and charges for excess luggage at a fixed rate per kg. Two passengers, Raja and Praja have 60 kg of luggage between them, and are charged Rs. 1,200 and Rs. 2,400 respectively for excess luggage. Had the entire luggage belonged to one of them, the excess luggage charge would have been Rs. 5,400.

87. What is the weight of Praja's luggage?

(a) 20kg (b) 25 kg

(c) 30 kg (d) 35 kg

(e) 40 kg

88. What is the free luggage allowance?

(a) 10 kg (b) 15 kg

(c) 20 kg (d) 25 kg

(e) 30 kg

89. What values of x satisfy $x^{\frac{2}{3}} + x^{\frac{1}{3}} - 2 \le 0$ ('x' is a real number)?

(a) $-8 \le x \le 1$ (b) $-1 \le x \le 8$

(c) $1 < x < 8$ (d) $1 \le x \le 8$

(e) $-8 \le x \le 8$

90. The number of solutions of the equation 2x + y = 40 where both x and y are positive integers and $x \le y$ is:

(a) 7 (b) 13

(c) 14 (d) 18

(e) 20

91. When you reverse the digits of the number 13, the number increases by 18. How many other two-digit numbers increase by 18 when their digits are reversed?

(a) 5 (b) 6

(c) 7 (d) 8

(e) 10

2007

92. Suppose you have a currency, named Miso, in three denominations: 1 Miso, 10 Misos and 50 Misos. In how many ways can you pay a bill of 107 Misos?

(a) 17 (b) 16

(c) 18 (d) 15

(e) 19

93. A confused bank teller transposed the rupees and paise when he cashed a cheque for Shailaja giving her rupees instead of paise and paise instead of rupees. After buying a toffee for 50 paise, Shailaja noticed that she was left with exactly three times as much as the amount on the cheque. Which of the following is a valid statement about the cheque amount?

(a) Over Rupees 13 but less than Rupees 14

(b) Over Rupees 7 but less than Rupees 8

(c) Over Rupees 22 but less than Rupees 23

(d) Over Rupees 18 but less than Rupees 19

(e) Over Rupees 4 but less than Rupees 5

94. How many pairs of positive integers m, n satisfy $\frac{1}{m}+\frac{4}{n}=\frac{1}{12}$, where, 'n' is an odd integer less than 60?

(a) 6 (b) 4

(c) 7 (d) 5

(e) 3

95. A quadratic function $f(x)$ attains a maximum of 3 at x = 1. The value of the function at x = 0 is 1. What is the value $f(x)$ at x = 10?

(a) –119 (b) –159

(c) –110 (d) –180

(e) –105

Direction for Question 96: The question is followed by two statements A and B. Indicate your response based on the following directives.

Mark (a) if the questions can be answered using A alone but not using B alone.

Mark (b) if the question can be answered using B alone but not using A alone.

Mark (c) if the question can be answered using A and B together, but not using either A or B alone.

Mark (d) if the question cannot be answered even using A and B together.

96. Consider integers x, y, z. What is the minimum possible value of $x^2 + y^2 + z^2$?

A: x + y + z = 89.

B: Among x, y, z two are equal.

2008

97. If the roots of the equation $x^3 - ax^2 + bx - c = 0$ are three consecutive integers, then what is the smallest possible value of b?

(a) $-\frac{1}{\sqrt{3}}$ (b) –1

(c) 0 (d) 1

(e) $\frac{1}{\sqrt{3}}$

98. Three consecutive positive integers are raised to the first, second and third powers respectively and then added. The sum so obtained is perfect square whose square root equals the total of the three original integers. Which of the following best describes the minimum, say m, of these three integers?

(a) $1 \le m \le 3$ (b) $4 \le m \le 6$

(c) $7 \le m \le 9$ (d) $10 \le m \le 12$

(e) $13 \le m \le 15$

99. A shop stores x kg of rice. The first customer buys half this amount plus half a kg of rice. The second customer buys half the remaining amount plus half a kg of rice. Then the third customer also buys half the remaining amount plus half a kg of rice. Thereafter, no rice is left in the shop. Which of the following best describes the value of x?

(a) $2 \le x \le 6$ (b) $5 \le x \le 8$

(c) $9 \le x \le 12$ (d) $11 \le x \le 14$

(e) $13 \le x \le 18$

MEMORY BASED QUESTIONS

2009

100. $x^2y^3 = 8$, where x, y > 0.

What is the minimum value of 4x + 3y?

(a) 8 (b) 11

(c) 9 (d) 10

101. If a, b are integers then how many ordered pairs (a, b) satisfy the equation $a^2 + ab + b^2 = 1$?

(a) 6 (b) 4

(c) 2 (d) 8

102. Champak takes a test called RAT which comprises 28 questions. In RAT three marks are awarded for each correct response, one mark is deducted for each incorrect response and there are no marks for unattempted questions. If he scores more than 22 marks in RAT, then what is the maximum possible number of incorrect responses that he could have marked?

(a) 14 (b) 15

(c) 16 (d) 17

103. If a, b, c are the roots of the equation

$$3x^3 + 42x + 93 = 0,$$

then what is the value of $a^3 + b^3 + c^3$?

(a) 81 (b) 92

(c) –85 (d) –93

2010

104. $P + \frac{1}{Q} = Q + \frac{1}{R} = 1$, where P, Q and R are real numbers. What is the value of $PQR + R + \frac{1}{P}$?

(a) –2 (b) –1

(c) 0 (d) Cannot be determined

105. Anant purchased x chocolates for Rs. y, where y is a natural number. The shopkeeper had offered to give him x+10 chocolates for Rs. 2. Anant declined the offer though it would have resulted in a saving of 80 paise per dozen chocolates for him. Which of the following can be the number of chocolates purchased by Anant?

(a) 1 (b) 3

(c) 5 (d) 15

106. If $n = \frac{a}{b+c} + \frac{b}{c+a} + \frac{c}{a+b}$, where a, b and c are the three sides of a triangle, then which of the following best describes the range in which n lies?

(a) $\left[\frac{3}{2}, 2\right)$ (b) $\left(\frac{2}{3}, \frac{3}{2}\right)$

(c) $\left(1, \frac{5}{2}\right]$ (d) $\left(\frac{4}{3}, \frac{5}{3}\right)$

107. What is the equation of the straight line which passes through the point of intersection of the straight lines 3x + 4y – 11 = 0 and x + y – 3 = 0 and is parallel to the line 2x + 5y = 0?

(a) 5x – 2y – 12 = 0 (b) 2x + 5y – 12 = 0

(c) 2x + 5y – 9 = 0 (d) 5x + 2y – 9 = 0

2011

108. The route taken by a bus from Delhi to Jaipur has 'n' stops, including the source and the destination. When 'm' new stops are added on the route of the bus (where m > 1) the number of different tickets that can be issued between two stops on the route increases by 11. What is the value of 'n'?

(a) 6 (b) 4

(c) 7 (d) 5

2012

109. If $\frac{bx-ay}{bc}=\frac{ay-cz}{ac}=\frac{cz-bx}{ab}$, then, given that $(bx \neq ay \neq cz)$

(a) ab + bc + ca = 0
(b) ab – bc + ca = 0
(c) ab + bc – ca = 0
(d) ab – bc – ca = 0

110. There are five consecutive integers a, b, c, d and e such that a < b < c < d < e and $a^2 + b^2 + c^2 = d^2 + e^2$. What is/are the possible value(s) of b?

(a) 0
(b) 11
(c) 0 and –11
(d) –1 and 11.

111. $ax^2 + bx + c = 0$ is a quadratic equation with rational coefficients such that a + b + c = 0, then which of the following is necessarily true?

(a) Both the roots of this equation are less than 1.
(b) One of the roots of the equation is c.
(c) One of the roots of the equation is $\frac{c}{a}$.
(d) Exactly one of the roots is 1.

112. If x + y = 1, then what is the value of $(x^3 + y^3 + 3xy)$?

(a) 1 (b) 3
(c) 9 (d) –1

2013

113. Let $f(x) = ax^2 + bx + c$, where a, b and c are real numbers and a ≠ 0. If f(x) attains its maximum value at x = 2, then what is the sum of the roots of f(x) = 0?

(a) 4 (b) –2
(c) 8 (d) –4

2014

114. A shopkeeper sells four qualities of rice A, B, C and D having cost price Rs. 40/kg, Rs. 55/kg, Rs. 50/kg and Rs. 65/kg respectively. Ankit purchased 'a' kg of A and 'b' kg of B to make 'a + b' kg of a new quality 'E' of rice worth Rs. 50/kg. Then he purchased 'c' kg of C and 'd' kg of D to make 'c + d' kg of a new quality 'F' of rice worth Rs. 60/kg.

Finally he took 'x' kg of rice and 'y' kg of rice from 'E' quality of rice and 'F' quality of rice respectively to make 'x + y' kg of rice worth Rs. 53/kg. Ensuring that a, b, c, d, x and y are all integers then what is the minimum value of a + b + c + d + x + y in kg?

(a) 28 (b) 22
(c) 16 (d) 26

115. What is the sum of the roots of all the quadratic equations that can be formed such that both the roots of the quadratic equation are common with the roots of equation (x – a)(x – b)(x – c) = 0?

(a) 3(a + b + c)
(b) 2(a + b + c)
(c) (a + b + c)
(d) 4(a + b + c)

116. If x(x – 3) = –1, then the value of $x^3(x^3 - 18)$ is

(a) 1 (b) 0
(c) –1 (d) 2

117. The sum of the coefficients of the polynomial $(x-1)^9 (x-2)^4 (x-4)$ is

(a) 0 (b) 16
(c) –20 (d) None of these

2015

118. Both the roots of the quadratic equation $x^2 + rx + s = 0$ are real and greater than 1. If $R = \left(\frac{r+s+1}{s-r}\right)$, then which of the following is definitely true?

(a) R = 0
(b) R < 0
(c) R > 0
(d) Cannot be determined

119. A certain sum of money is made up of Re. 1, 50 paise and 25 paise coins. The ratio of the number of these coins is 5 : 6 : 8. Then, 3/5th of the Re. 1 coins are changed to 50 paise and 25 paise coins, such that the ratio of the total number of these coins in the same order became 1: 2. Now, half of the 50 paise coins are changed to Re. 1 coins and all the 25 paise coins are changed to Re. 1 and 50 paise coins in the ratio 7: 4. What is the ratio of the Re. 1 and 50 paise coins at the end of the conversions? (Note:- If you change a Re.1 coin into 50 paise coins, then you will get two coins of 50 paise for a Re. 1 coin.)

(a) 11 : 23 (b) 16 : 13
(c) 54 : 71 (d) None of these

120. Let x, y, z and t be the positive numbers which satisfy the following conditions:

I. If x > y, then z > t and
II. If x > z, then y < t

Which of the following is necessarily true?

(a) If x < y, then z < t
(b) If x > z then x – y < z + t
(c) If x > y + z, then z > y
(d) None of these

2016

121. If 'a' and 'b' are the roots of the equation $x^2 + 7x + 4 = 0$, where $a > b$, then find the value of $\left(\frac{2}{7a}\right)+\left(\frac{1}{3.5b}\right)+ab.$

(a) $\frac{7}{2}$ (b) $\frac{14}{3}$

(c) $\frac{-7}{2}$ (d) $\frac{2}{7}$

122. If $a^2 + 6a - 1 = 0$, then what is the value of $\left(a+\frac{1}{a}\right)^2 - 5\left(a-\frac{1}{a}\right)$?

123. Find the minimum possible value of 'y' if $\frac{4}{7}<\frac{x}{y}<\frac{12}{13}$, where x and y are natural numbers.

(a) 4 (b) 5

(c) 3 (d) 2

124. If $f(x) = \max(x^2 - 4, x, -1)$, then what is the minimum value of f(x)?

(a) -4 (b) $\frac{1-\sqrt{17}}{2}$

(c) -1 (d) 0

125. $x+\frac{1}{y+\frac{1}{z}}=\frac{68}{21}$, where x, y and z are natural numbers. Find the value of $x + y + z$.

(a) 9 (b) 12

(c) 11 (d) 14

2017

126. The minimum possible value of the sum of the squares of the roots of the equation

$$x^2 + (a + 3)x - (a + 5) = 0$$ is

(a) 1 (b) 2

(c) 3 (d) 4

127. If $9^{x-\frac{1}{2}} - 2^{2x-2} = 4^x - 3^{2x-3}$, then X is

(a) $\frac{3}{2}$ (b) $\frac{2}{5}$

(c) $\frac{3}{4}$ (d) $\frac{4}{9}$

2018 Slot 1

128. If $u^2 + (u - 2v - 1)^2 = -4v(u + v)$, then what is the value of $u + 3v$?

(a) $-1/4$ (b) 1/4 (c) 1/2 (d) 0

2018 Slot 2

129. The smallest integer n such that $n^3 - 11n^2 + 32n - 28 > 0$ is

130. If N and x are positive integers such that $N^N = 2^{160}$ and $N^2 + 2^N$ is an integral multiple of 2^x, then the largest possible x is

131. If $A = \{6^{2n} - 35n - 1 : n = 1, 2, 3,...\}$ and $B = \{35(n - 1) : n = 1, 2, 3,...\}$ then which of the following is true?

(a) Every member of A is in B and at least one member of B is not in A

(b) At least one member of A is not in B

(c) Neither every member of A is in B nor every member of B is in A

(d) Every member of B is in A.

132. If a and b are integers such that $2x^2 - ax + 2 > 0$ and $x^2 - bx + 8 \geq 0$ for all real numbers x, then the largest possible value of $2a - 6b$ is

133. Let $t_1, t_2,...$ be real numbers such that $t_1 + t_2 + ... + t_n = 2n^2 + 9n + 13$, for every positive integer $n \geq 2$. If $t_k = 103$, then k equals

FUNCTIONS AND GRAPHS

1990

1. From any two numbers x and y, we define $x \times y = x + 0.5y - xy$. Suppose that both x and y are greater than 0.5. Then $x \times x < y \times y$ if

(a) $1 > x > y$ (b) $x > 1 > y$

(c) $1 > y > x$ (d) $y > 1 > x$

2. Consider a function f(k) defined for positive integers k = 1, 2, ... ; the function satisfies the condition

$f(1) + f(2) + ... = \frac{p}{(p-1)}$.

Where p is fraction i.e. $0 < p < 1$.

Then f(k) is given by

(a) $p(-p)^{k-1}$ (b) $p(1-p)^{k-1}$

(c) $\{p(1-p)\}^{k-1}$ (d) None of these

1991

3. A function can sometimes reflect on itself, i.e. if $y = f(x)$, then $x = f(y)$. Both of them retain the same structure and form. Which of the following functions has this property?

(a) $y=\frac{2x+3}{3x+4}$ (b) $y=\frac{2x+3}{3x-2}$

(c) $y=\frac{3x+4}{4x-5}$ (d) None of the above.

4. If $y = f(x)$ and $f(x) = (1-x)/(1 + x)$, which of the following is true?

(a) $f(2x) = f(x) - 1$ (b) $x = f(2y) - 1$

(c) $f(1/x) = f(x)$ (d) $x = f(y)$

5. Let Y = minimum of $\{(x + 2), (3 - x)\}$. What is the maximum value of Y for $0 \leq x \leq 1$?

(a) 1.0 (b) 1.5

(c) 3.1 (d) 2.5

1993

Directions for Questions 6 and 7: Answer the questions based on the following information.

A function f(x)is said to be even if f(–x)= f(x), and odd if f(–x) = –f(x). Thus, for example, the function given by $f(x) = x^2$ is even, while the function given by $f(x) = x^3$ is odd. Using this definition, answer the following questions.

6. The function given by $f(x) = |x|^3$ is

(a) even (b) odd

(c) neither (d) both

7. The sum of two odd functions

(a) is always an even function

(b) is always an odd function

(c) is sometimes odd and sometimes even

(d) may be neither odd nor even

8. The maximum possible value of $y = \min(1/2 - 3x^2/4, 5x^2/4)$ for the range $0 < x < 1$ is

(a) 1/3 (b) 1/2

(c) 5/27 (d) 5/16

1994

Directions for Questions 9 and 10: Answer the questions based on the following information.

If $md(x) = |x|$,

$mn(x, y) =$ minimum of *x* and *y* and

$Ma(a, b, c, ...) =$ maximum of *a, b, c, ...*

9. Value of

$Ma\left[md(a), mn(md(b), a), mn(ab, md(ac))\right]$

where *a* = –2, *b* = –3, *c* = 4 is

(a) 2 (b) 6

(c) 8 (d) –2

10. Given that a > b then the relation

Ma[md(a),mn(a, b)] = mn[a, md(Ma(a, b))] does not hold if

(a) a < 0, b < 0

(b) a > 0, b > 0

(c) a > 0, b < 0, $|a| < |b|$

(d) a > 0, b < 0, $|a| > |b|$

Directions for Questions 11 to 14: Answer the questions based on the following information.

If $f(x) = 2x + 3$ and $g(x) = \frac{x-3}{2}$, then

11. *fog*(x) is equal to

(a) 1 (b) gof(x)

(c) $\frac{15x+9}{16x-5}$ (d) $\frac{1}{x}$

12. For what value of x; $f(x) = g(x-3)$?

(a) –3 (b) $\frac{1}{4}$

(c) –4 (d) None of these

13. What is the value of (gofofogogof) (x) (fogofog)(x)?

(a) x (b) x^2

(c) $\frac{5x+3}{4x-1}$ (d) $\frac{(x+3)(5x+3)}{(4x-5)(4x-1)}$

14. What is the value of fo(fog)o(gof)(x)?

(a) x (b) x^2

(c) 2x + 3 (d) $\frac{x+3}{4x-5}$

1995

15. Largest value of $\min(2 + x^2, 6 - 3x)$, when x > 0, is

(a) 1 (b) 2

(c) 3 (d) 4

Directions for Questions 16 to 19: Answer the questions based on the following information.

le(x, y) = Least of (x, y)

mo(x) = |x|

me(x, y) = Maximum of (x, y)

16. Find the value of me(a + mo(le(a, b)), mo(a + me(mo(a), mo(b))), at a = –2 and b = –3.

(a) 1 (b) 0

(c) 5 (d) 3

17. Which of the following must always be correct for a, b > 0?

(a) mo(le(a, b)) ≥ (me(mo(a), mo(b))

(b) mo(le(a, b)) > (me(mo(a), mo(b))

(c) mo(le(a, b)) < (le(mo(a), mo(b))

(d) mo(le(a,b)) = le(mo(a), mo(b))

18. For what values of 'a' is $me(a^2 - 3a, a - 3) < 0$?

(a) a > 3 (b) 0 < a < 3

(c) a < 0 (d) a = 3

19. For what values of 'a' is $le(a^2 - 3a, a - 3) < 0$?

(a) a > 3 (b) 0 < a < 3

(c) a < 0 (d) Both b and c

1996

Directions for Questions 20 and 21: Answer the questions based on the following information.

A, S, M and D are functions of x and y, and they are defined as follows.

A(x, y) = x + y

S(x, y) = x – y

M(x, y) = xy

$D(x, y) = \frac{x}{y}, y \neq 0$

20. What is the value of M(M(A(M(x, y), S(y, x)), x), A(y, x)) for x = 2, y = 3?

(a) 60 (b) 140

(c) 25 (d) 70

21. What is the value of S[M(D(A(a, b), 2), D(A(a, b), 2)), M(D(S(a, b), 2), D(S(a, b), 2))]?

(a) $a^2 + b^2$ (b) ab

(c) $a^2 - b^2$ (d) $\frac{a}{b}$

1997

Directions for Questions 22 to 24: Answer the questions based on the following information.

For these questions the following functions have been defined. $la(x, y, z) = \min(x + y, y + z)$

$$le(x, y, z) = \max(x - y, y - z)$$

$$ma(x, y, z) = \frac{1}{2}[le(x, y, z) + la(x, y, z)]$$

22. Given that $x > y > z > 0$. Which of the following is necessarily true?

(a) $la(x, y, z) < le(x, y, z)$

(b) $ma(x, y, z) < la(x, y, z)$

(c) $ma(x, y, z) < le(x, y, z)$

(d) None of these

23. What is the value of ma(10,4, le(la(10, 5, 3), 5, 3))?

(a) 7 (b) 6.5

(c) 8 (d) 7.5

24. For $x = 15$, $y = 10$ and $z = 9$, find the value of $le(x, \min(y, x - z), le(9, 8, ma(x, y, z)))$.

(a) 5 (b) 12

(c) 9 (d) 4

1998

Directions for Questions 25 to 27: Answer the questions based on the following information.

The following operations are defined for real numbers.

a # b = a + b, if a and b both are positive else a # b = 1

a ∇ b = $(a \times b)^{a+b}$ if a × b is positive else a ∇ b = 1.

25. $\frac{(2\#1)}{(1\nabla 2)} =$

(a) $\frac{1}{8}$ (b) 1

(c) $\frac{3}{8}$ (d) 3

26. $\frac{\{((1\#1)\#2) - (10^{1.3}\nabla \log_{10} 0.1)\}}{(1\nabla 2)} =$

(a) $\frac{3}{8}$ (b) $\frac{4.\log_{10} 0.1}{8}$

(c) $\frac{(4+10^{13})}{8}$ (d) None of these

27. $\left(\frac{(X\#-Y)}{(-X\nabla Y)}\right) = \frac{3}{8}$, then which of the following must be true?

(a) X = 2, Y = 1 (b) X > 0, Y< 0

(c) X, Y both positive (d) X, Y both negative

1999

28. If $|r - 6| = 11$ and $|2q - 12| = 8$, what is the minimum possible value of $\frac{q}{r}$?

(a) $-\frac{2}{5}$ (b) $\frac{2}{17}$

(c) $\frac{10}{17}$ (d) None of these

Directions for Questions 29 to 31: Answer the questions based on the following information.

Let x and y be real numbers and

let $f(x,y) = |x + y|$, $F(f(x,y)) = -f(x,y)$

and $G(f(x, y)) = -F(f(x, y))$

29. Which of the following statements is true?

(a) F(f(x, y)) · G(f(x, y))= –F(f(x, y)) · G(f(x, y))

(b) F(f(x, y)) · G(f(x, y))> –F(f(x, y)) · G(f(x, y))

(c) F(f(x, y)) · G(f(x, y)) ≠ G(f(x, y)) · G(f(x, y))

(d) F(f(x, y)) + G(f(x, y))+ f(x, y) = f(–x, –y)

30. What is the value of f(G(f(1, 0)), f(F(f(1, 2)), G(f(1, 2))))?

(a) 3 (b) 2

(c) 1 (d) 0

31. Which of the following expressions yields x^2 as its result?

(a) $F(f(x, -x)) \cdot G(f(x, -x))$

(b) $F(f(x, x)) \cdot G(f(x, x)) \cdot 4$

(c) $-F(f(x, x)) \cdot G(f(x, x)) \div \log_2 16$

(d) $f(x, x) \cdot f(x, x)$

Directions for Questions 32 to 35: Answer the questions based on the following information.

In each of the following questions, a pair of graphs F(x) and F1(x) is given. These are composed of straight-line segments, shown as solid lines, in the domain $x \in (-2, 2)$.

Choose the answer as

(a) if F1(x) = –F(x)

(b) if F1(x) = F(–x)

(c) if F1(x) = –F(–x)

(d) if none of the above is true

32.

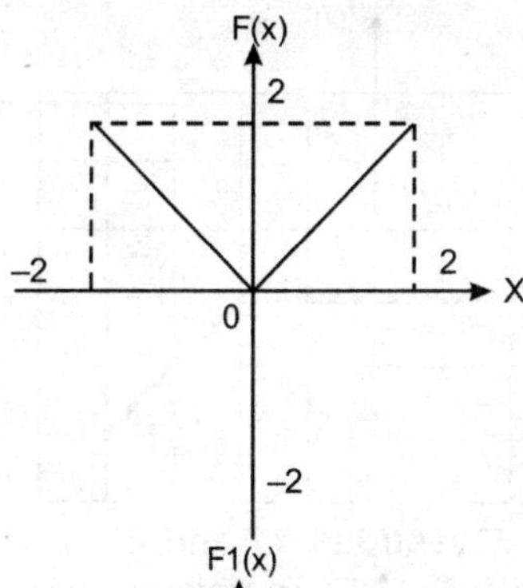

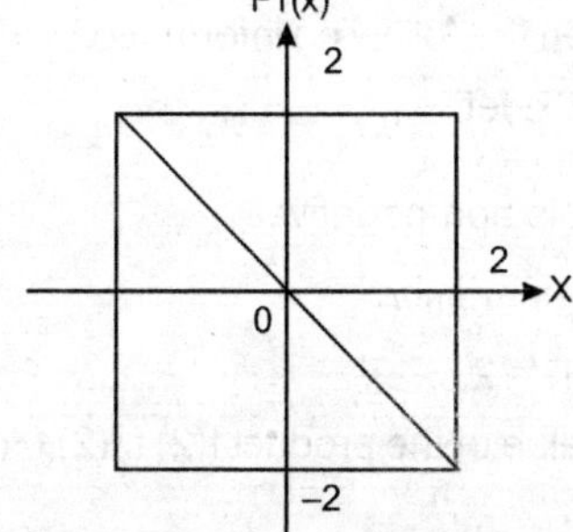

33.

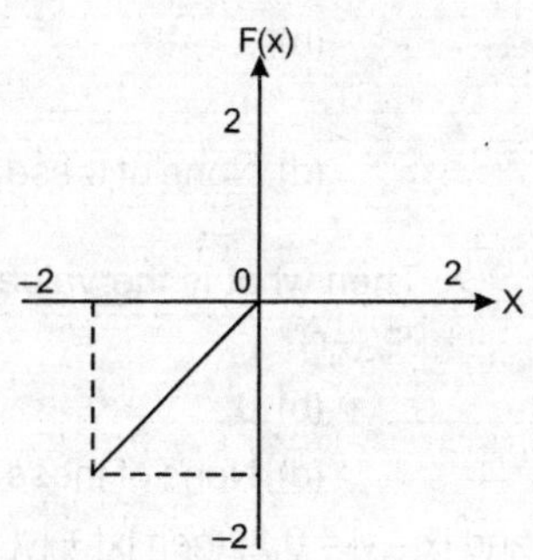

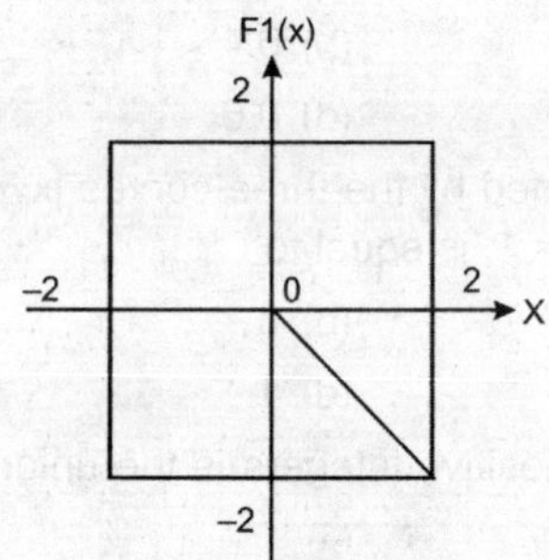

34.

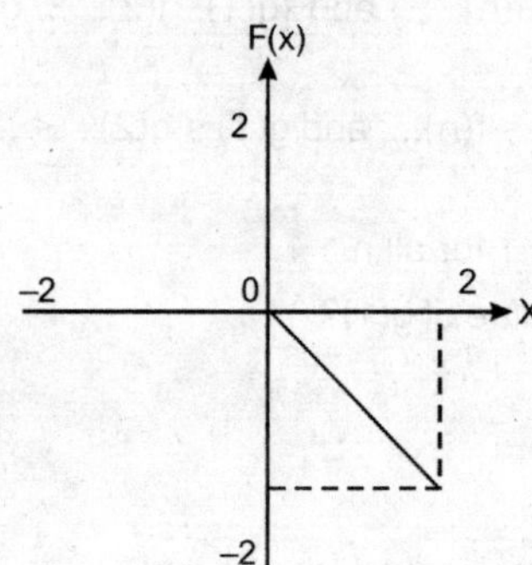

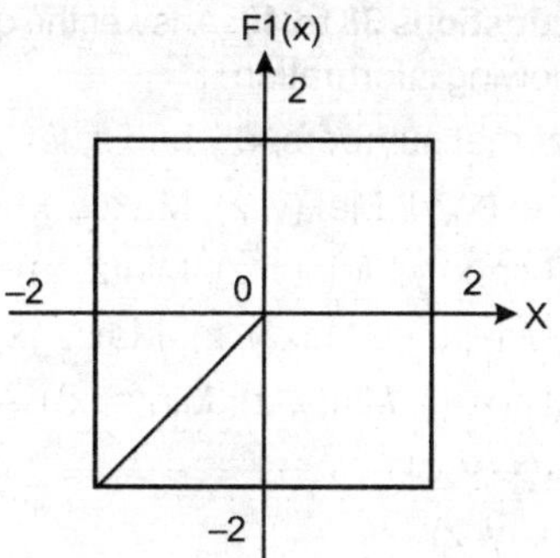

35.

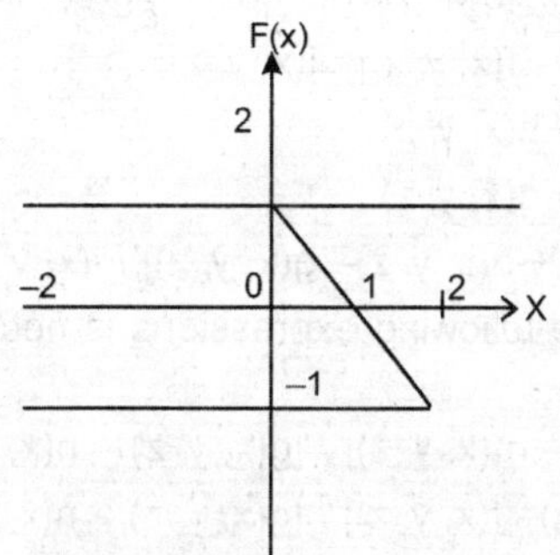

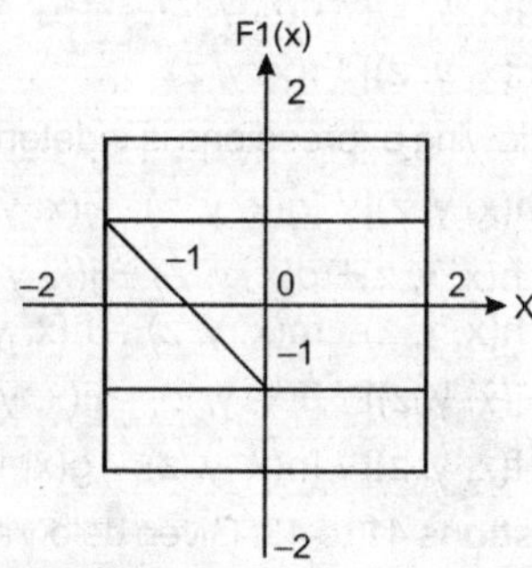

2000

Directions for Questions 36 and 37: Answer the questions based on the following information.

For real numbers x and y, let

$$f(x, y) = \begin{cases} \text{Positive square root of } (x + y), & \text{if } (x + y)^{0.5} \text{ is real} \\ (x + y)^2, & \text{otherwise} \end{cases}$$

$$g(x, y) = \begin{cases} (x + y)^2, & \text{if } (x + y)^{0.5} \text{ is real} \\ -(x + y), & \text{otherwise} \end{cases}$$

36. Which of the following expressions yields a positive value for every pair of non-zero real numbers (x, y)?

(a) $f(x, y) - g(x, y)$
(b) $f(x, y) - (g(x, y))^2$
(c) $g(x, y) - (f(x, y))^2$
(d) $f(x, y) + g(x, y)$

37. Under which of the following conditions is f(x, y) necessarily greater than g(x, y)?

(a) Both x and y are less than –1
(b) Both x and y are positive
(c) Both x and y are negative
(d) y > x

Directions for Questions 38 to 40: Answer the questions based on the following information.

For three distinct real numbers x, y and z, let

f(x, y, z)= Min(Max(x, y), Max(y, z), Max(z, x))

g(x, y, z)= Max(Min(x, y), Min(y, z), Min(z, x))

h(x, y, z)= Max(Max(x, y), Max(y, z), Max(z, x))

j(x, y, z)= Min(Min(x, y), Min(y, z), Min(z, x))

m(x, y, z) = Max(x, y, z)

n(x, y, z) = Min(x, y, z)

38. Which of the following is necessarily greater than 1?
(a) [h(x, y, z)– f(x, y, z)] / j(x, y, z)
(b) j(x, y, z) / h(x, y, z)
(c) f(x, y, z) / g(x, y, z)
(d) [f(x, y, z) + h(x, y, z)– g(x, y, z)] / j(x, y, z)

39. Which of the following expressions is necessarily equal to 1?
(a) [f(x, y, z)– m(x, y, z)] / [g(x, y, z) – h(x, y, z)]
(b) [m(x, y, z)– f(x, y, z)] / [g(x, y, z) – n(x, y, z)]
(c) [j(x, y, z)– g(x, y, z)] / h(x, y, z)
(d) [f(x, y, z)– h(x, y ,z)] / f(x, y, z)

40. Which of the following expressions is indeterminate?
(a) [f(x, y, z)– h(x, y, z)] / [g(x, y, z) – j(x, y, z)]
(b) [f(x, y, z) + h(x, y, z)+ g(x, y, z) + j(x, y, z)] / [j(x, y, z) + h(x, y, z)– m(x, y, z) – n(x, y, z)]
(c) [g(x, y, z)– j(x, y, z)] / [f(x, y, z) – h(x, y, z)]
(d) [h(x, y, z)– f(x, y, z)] / [n(x, y, z) – g(x, y, z)]

Directions for Questions 41 to 43: Given below are three graphs made up of straight line segments shown as thick lines. In each case choose the answer as

(a) if f(x) = 3 f(–x) (b) if f(x) = –f(–x)
(c) if f(x) = f(–x) (d) if 3f(x) = 6 f(–x), for $x \geq 0$

41.

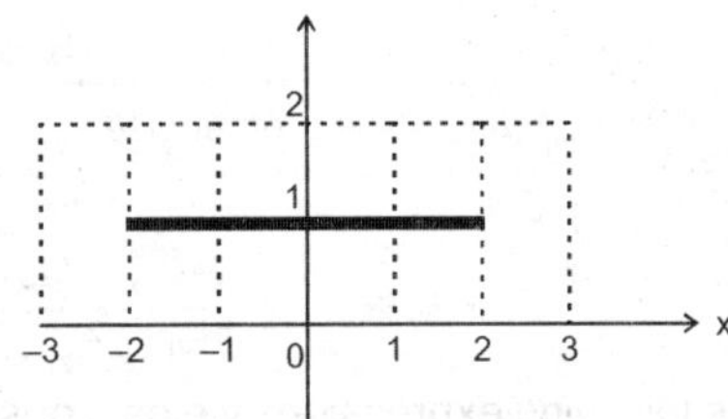

42.

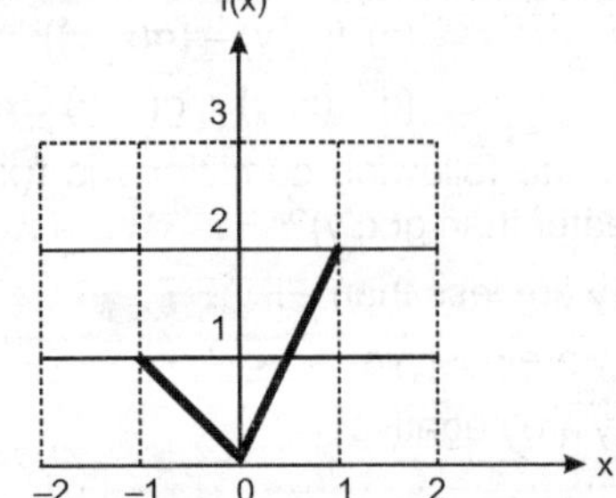

43.

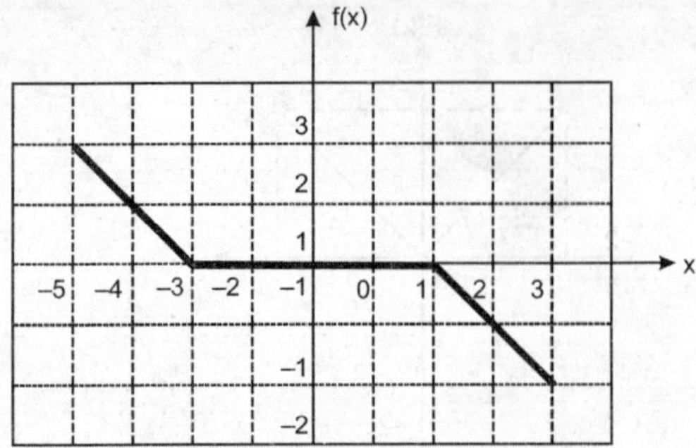

Directions for Questions 44 and 45: Answer the questions based on the following information.

For a real number x, let

$$f(x) = \frac{1}{1+x}, \text{ if x is non-negative}$$
$$= 1 + x \text{ if x is negative}$$

$f^n(x) = f(f^{n-1}(x))$, n = 2, 3, ...

44. What is the value of the product $f(2)\, f^2(2)\, f^3(2)\, f^4(2)\, f^5(2)$?
(a) $\frac{1}{3}$ (b) 3
(c) $\frac{1}{18}$ (d) None of these

45. r is an integer ≥ 2. Then what is the value of $f^{r-1}(-r) + f^r(-r) + f^{r+1}(-r)$?
(a) –1 (b) 0
(c) 1 (d) None of these

46. If $x^2 + y^2 = 0.1$ and $|x - y| = 0.2$, then $|x| + |y|$ is equal to
(a) 0.3 (b) 0.4
(c) 0.2 (d) 0.6

47. The area bounded by the three curves $|x + y| = 1$, $|x| = 1$, and $|y| = 1$, is equal to
(a) 4 (b) 3
(c) 2 (d) 1

48. The set of all positive integers is the union of two disjoint subsets:
{f(1), f(2), ..., f(n), ...} and {g(1), g(2), ..., g(n), ...}, where
f(1) < f(2) < ... < f(n)..., and g(1) < g(2) < ... < g(n) ..., and
g(n) = f(f(n)) + 1 for all $n \geq 1$.
What is the value of g(1)?
(a) 0
(b) 2
(c) 1
(d) Cannot be determined

49. For all non-negative integers x and y, f(x, y) is defined as below.

f(0, y) = y + 1

f(x + 1, 0) = f(x, 1)

f(x + 1, y + 1)= f(x, f(x + 1, y))

Then what is the value of f(1, 2)?

(a) 2 (b) 4

(c) 3 (d) Cannot be determined

Direction for Question 50: The question is followed by two statements, I and II. Answer the question using the following instructions.

Mark the answer as:

(a) if the question can be answered by one of the statements alone, but cannot be answered by using the other statement alone.

(b) if the question can be answered by using either statement alone.

(c) if the question can be answered by using both the statements together, but cannot be answered by using either statement alone.

(d) if the question cannot be answered even by using both statements together.

50. For any two real numbers:

$a \oplus b = 1$ if both a and b are positive or both a and b are negative.

$= -1$ if one of the two numbers a and b is positive and the other negative.

What is $(2 \oplus 0) \oplus (-5 \oplus -6)$?

I. $a \oplus b$ is zero if a is zero

II. $a \oplus b = b \oplus a$

2001

51. If a, b, c and d are four positive real numbers such that abcd = 1, what is the minimum value of (1 + a)(1 + b)(1 + c)(1 + d)?

(a) 4 (b) 1

(c) 16 (d) 18

52. Let x and y be two positive numbers such that x + y = 1.

Then the minimum value of $\left(x+\frac{1}{x}\right)^2+\left(y+\frac{1}{y}\right)^2$ is

(a) 12 (b) 20

(c) 12.5 (d) 13.3

Directions for Questions 53 and 54: Answer the questions based on the following information.

The batting average (BA)of a Test batsman is computed from runs scored and innings played — completed innings and incomplete innings (not out)in the following manner:

r_1 = Number of runs scored in completed innings

n_1 = Number of completed innings

r_2 = Number of runs scored in incomplete innings

n_2 = Number of incomplete innings $BA = \frac{r_1 + r_2}{n_1}$

To better assess a batsman's accomplishments, the ICC is considering two other measures MBA_1 and MBA_2 defined as follows:

$$MBA_1 = \frac{r_1}{n_1} + \frac{n_2}{n_1}\max\left[0, \left(\frac{r_2}{n_2} - \frac{r_1}{n_1}\right)\right]$$

$$MBA_2 = \frac{r_1 + r_2}{n_1 + n_2}$$

53. Based on the above information which of the following is true?

(a) $MBA_1 \le BA \le MBA_2$

(b) $BA \le MBA_2 \le MBA_1$

(c) $MBA_2 \le BA \le MBA_1$

(d) None of these

54. An experienced cricketer with no incomplete innings has BA of 50. The next time he bats, the innings is incomplete and he scores 45 runs. It can be inferred that

(a) BA and MBA_1 will both increase

(b) BA will increase and MBA_2 will decrease

(c) BA will increase and not enough data is available to assess change in MBA_1 and MBA_2

(d) None of these

2002

55. If $f(x) = \log\left\{\frac{(1+x)}{(1-x)}\right\}$, then f(x) + f(y) is

(a) f(x + y) (b) $f\left\{\frac{(x+y)}{(1+xy)}\right\}$

(c) $(x+y)f\left\{\frac{1}{(1+xy)}\right\}$ (d) $\frac{f(x)+f(y)}{(1+xy)}$

56. Suppose for any real number x, [x] denotes the greatest integer less than or equal to x. Let L(x, y) = [x] + [y] + [x + y] and R(x, y)= [2x] + [2y]. Then it is impossible to find any two positive real numbers x and y for which

(a) L(x, y) = R(x, y) (b) L(x, y) ≠ R(x, y)

(c) L(x, y) < R(x, y) (d) L(x, y) > R(x, y)

57. Davji Shop sells samosas in boxes of different sizes. The samosas are priced at Rs. 2 per samosa up to 200 samosas. For every additional 20 samosas, the price of the whole lot goes down by 10 paise per samosa. What should be the maximum size of the box that would maximise the revenue?

(a) 240 (b) 300

(c) 400 (d) None of these

2003(R)

58. If three positive real numbers x, y and z satisfy $y-x=z-y$ and $xyz=4$, then what is the minimum possible value of y?

(a) $2^{1/3}$ (b) $2^{2/3}$

(c) $2^{1/4}$ (d) $2^{3/4}$

59. If $|b| \geq 1$ and $x=-|a|b$, then which one of the following is necessarily true?

(a) $a-xb<0$ (b) $a-xb \geq 0$

(c) $a-xb>0$ (d) $a-xb \leq 0$

Directions for Questions 60 to 62: Answer the questions on the basis of the tables given below.

Two binary operations $\oplus$ and $*$ are defined over the set {a, e, f, g, h} as per the following tables:

⊕	a	e	f	g	h
a	a	e	f	g	h
e	e	f	g	h	a
f	f	g	h	a	e
g	g	h	a	e	f
h	h	a	e	f	g

*	a	e	f	g	h
a	a	a	a	a	a
e	a	e	f	g	h
f	a	f	h	e	g
g	a	g	e	h	f
h	a	h	g	f	e

Thus, according to the first table $f \oplus g = a$, while according to the second table $g * h = f$, and so on. Also, let $f^2 = f * f$, $g^3 = g * g * g$, and so on.

60. What is the smallest positive integer n such that $g^n = e$?

(a) 4 (b) 5

(c) 2 (d) 3

61. Upon simplification, $f \oplus [f * \{f \oplus (f * f)\}]$ equals

(a) e (b) f

(c) g (d) h

62. Upon simplification, $\{a^{10} * (f^{10} \oplus g^9)\} \oplus e^8$ equals

(a) e (b) f

(c) g (d) h

2003(L)

63. Let g(x)= max(5 – x, x + 2). The smallest possible value of g(x) is

(a) 4.0

(b) 4.5

(c) 1.5

(d) None of the above

64. The function $f(x) = |x-2| + |2.5-x| + |3.6-x|$, where x is a real number, attains a minimum at

(a) x = 2.3

(b) x = 2.5

(c) x = 2.7

(d) None of the above

65. Consider the following two curves in the x-y plane:

$$y = x^3 + x^2 + 5$$
$$y = x^2 + x + 5$$

Which of following statements is true for $-2 \leq x \leq 2$?

(a) The two curves intersect once.

(b) The two curves intersect twice.

(c) The two curves do not intersect

(d) The two curves intersect thrice.

2004

66. If $f(x) = x^3 - 4x + p$, and f(0) and f(1) are of opposite sings, then which of the following is necessarily true

(a) $-1 < p < 2$ (b) $0 < p < 3$

(c) $-2 < p < 1$ (d) $-3 < p < 0$

67. Let $f(x) = ax^2 - b|x|$, where a and b are constants. Then at x = 0, f(x) is

(a) maximized whenever a > 0, b > 0

(b) maximized whenever a > 0, b < 0

(c) minimized whenever a > 0, b > 0

(d) minimized whenever a > 0, b < 0

Directions for Questions 68 and 69: Answer the questions on the basis of the information given below.

$f_1(x) = x$ $\quad 0 \leq x \leq 1$

$= 1$ $\quad x \geq 1$

$= 0$ $\quad$ Otherwise

$f_2(x) = f_1(-x)$ $\quad$ for all x

$f_3(x) = -f_2(x)$ $\quad$ for all x

$f_4(x) = f_3(-x)$ $\quad$ for all x

68. How many of the following products are necessarily zero for every x?

$f_1(x)f_2(x),\ f_2(x)f_3(x),\ f_2(x)f_4(x)$

(a) 0 (b) 1

(c) 2 (d) 3

69. Which of the following is necessarily true?

(a) $f_4(x) = f_1(x)$ for all x

(b) $f_1(x) = -f_3(-x)$ for all x

(c) $f_2(-x) = f_4(x)$ for all x

(d) $f_1(x) = f_3(x) = 0$ for all x

2005

70. If $R = \dfrac{30^{65} - 29^{65}}{30^{64} + 29^{64}}$, then

(a) $0 < R \le 0.1$ (b) $0.1 < R \le 0.5$

(c) $0.5 < R \le 1.0$ (d) $R > 1.0$

71. In the X-Y plane, the area of the region bounded by the graph $|x+y| + |x-y| = 4$ is

(a) 8 (b) 12

(c) 16 (d) 20

72. Let g(x)be a function such that g(x + 1) + g(x – 1) = g(x)for every real x. Then for what value of p is the relation g(x + p) = g(x)necessarily true for every real x?

(a) 5 (b) 3

(c) 2 (d) 6

2006

73. If x = – 0.5, then which of the following has the smallest value?

(a) $2^{\frac{1}{x}}$ (b) $\dfrac{1}{x}$

(c) $\dfrac{1}{x^2}$ (d) 2^x

(e) $\dfrac{1}{\sqrt{-x}}$

74. The graph of y – x against y + x is as shown below. (All graphs in this question are drawn to scale and the same scale has been used on each axis.)

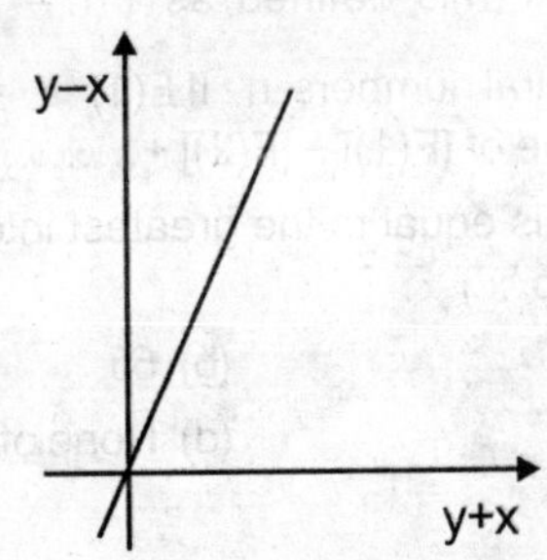

Which of the following shows the graph of y against x?

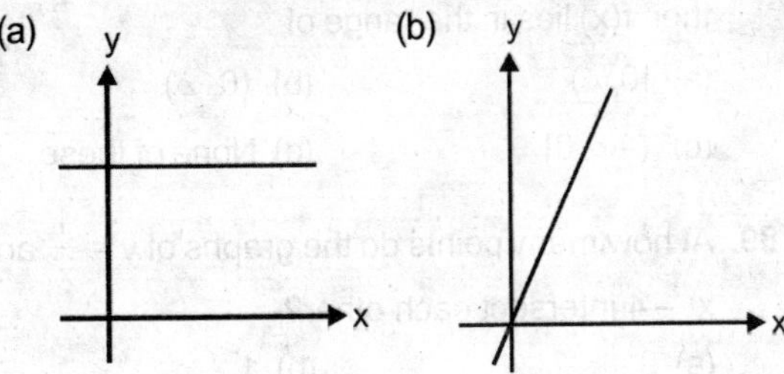

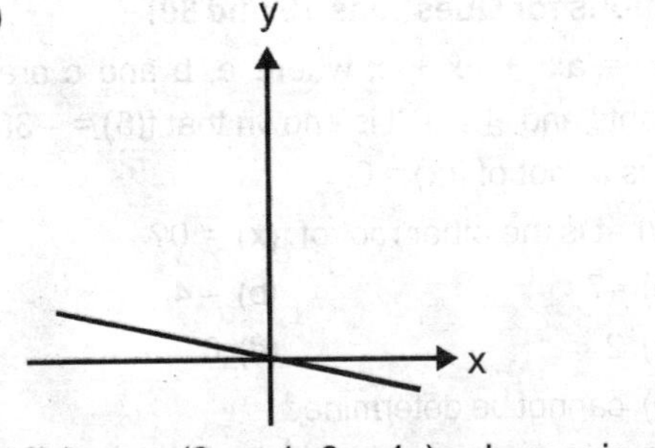

(e)

75. Let f(x)= max(2x + 1, 3 – 4x), where x is any real number. Then the minimum possible value of f(x)is:

(a) $\dfrac{1}{3}$ (b) $\dfrac{1}{2}$

(c) $\dfrac{2}{3}$ (d) $\dfrac{4}{3}$

(e) $\dfrac{5}{3}$

2007

76. A function $f(x)$ satisfies $f(1) = 3600$ and $f(1) + f(2) + \ldots + f(n) = n^2 f(n)$, for all positive integers n > 1. What is the value of $f(9)$?

(a) 80 (b) 240

(c) 200 (d) 100

(e) 120

Directions for Questions 77 and 78: Answer the following questions based on the information given below:

Mr. David manufactures and sells a single product at a fixed price in a niche market. The selling price of each unit is Rs. 30. On the other hand, the cost, in rupees, of producing 'x' units is $240 + bx + cx^2$, where 'b' and 'c' are some constants. Mr. David noticed that doubling the daily production from 20 to 40 units increases the daily production cost by $66\frac{2}{3}\%$. However, an increase in daily production from 40 to 60 units results in an increase of only 50% in the daily production cost. Assume that demand is unlimited and that Mr. David can sell as much as he can produce. His objective is to maximize the profit.

77. How many units should Mr. David produce daily?

(a) 130 (b) 100

(c) 70 (d) 150

(e) Cannot be determined

78. What is the maximum daily profit, in rupees, that Mr. David can realize from his business?

(a) 620 (b) 920
(c) 840 (d) 760
(e) Cannot be determined

2008

Directions for Questions 79 and 80:

Let $f(x) = ax^2 + bx + c$, where a, b and c are certain constants and $a \neq 0$ It is known that $f(5) = -3f(2)$ and that 3 is a root of $f(x) = 0$.

79. What is the other root of $f(x) = 0$?

(a) –7 (b) – 4
(c) 2 (d) 6
(e) cannot be determined

80. What is the value of a + b + c?

(a) 9 (b) 14
(c) 13 (d) 37
(e) cannot be determined

81. Let f(x)be a function satisfying $f(x)f(y) = f(xy)$ for all real x, y. If f(2)= 4, then what is the value of $f\left(\frac{1}{2}\right)$?

(a) 0 (b) $\frac{1}{4}$
(c) $\frac{1}{2}$ (d) 1
(e) cannot be determined

MEMORY BASED QUESTIONS

2009

82.

$$f(m, n) = \begin{cases} n + 1 \text{ if } m = 0 \\ f(m-1, 1) \text{ if } m > 0, n = 0 \\ f(0, f(m, n-1)) \text{ if } m > 0, n > 0 \end{cases}$$

What is the value of 20[f(1, 2) + f(1, 1) + 15]?

(a) 440 (b) 480
(c) 520 (d) 560

2010

83. A function f(x) is defined for all real values of x as $f(x) = \frac{x-1}{x+1}$. If $y_1 = f(x)$, $y_2 = f(f(x))$, $y_3 = f(f(f(x)))$ and so on, then what is the value of y_{501}?

(a) $\frac{-1}{x}$ (b) $\frac{x+1}{x-1}$
(c) $501x - 1$ (d) $\frac{x-1}{x+1}$

2011

84. A function f(x) is defined for all real values of x as $f(x) = ax^2 + bx + c$. If f(1) = f(–1), f(0) = 10 and f(2) = 14, then what is the value of f(10)?

(a) 100
(b) 110
(c) 64
(d) None of these

85. Two operations, for real numbers x and y, are defined as given below.

(i) $x \square y = (x + y)^2$

(ii) $x \Delta y = (x - y)^2$

If $x^2 \square y^2 = 169$ and $x^2 \Delta y^2 = 25$, then what is the value of x^2y^2?

(a) 81 (b) 36
(c) 64 (d) None of these

2012

86. A function f(x)is defined for real values of x as:

$$f(x) = \frac{1}{\log_{5-|x|}\sqrt{x^3 - 7x^2 + 14x - 8}}$$

What is the domain of f(x)?

(a) $x \in (0, \infty)$
(b) $x \in (-5, -4) \cup (-4, 4) \cup (4, 5)$
(c) $x \in (1, 2) \cup (4, 5)$
(d) $x \in (1, 2) \cup (4, \infty)$

87. A function F(n)is defined as $F(n-1) = \frac{1}{(2 - F(n))}$ for all natural numbers 'n'. If F(1) = 2, then what is the value of [F(1)] + [F(2)] +...........+ [F(50)]? (Here, [x] is equal to the greatest integer less than or equal to 'x')

(a) 51 (b) 55
(c) 54 (d) None of these

2013

88. If $f(x) = (\sec x + \operatorname{cosec} x)(\tan x - \cot x)$ and $\frac{\pi}{4} < x < \frac{\pi}{2}$, then f(x) lies in the range of

(a) $[0, \infty)$ (b) $(0, \infty)$
(c) $(-\infty, 0]$ (d) None of these

89. At how many points do the graphs of $y = \frac{1}{x}$ and $y = x^2 - 4$ intersect each other?

(a) 0 (b) 1
(c) 2 (d) 3

2014

90. If $f(n) = 1^4 + 2^4 + 3^4 + \ldots + n^4$, then how can $1^4 + 3^4 + 5^4 + \ldots + (2n-1)^4$ be expressed?

(a) $f(2n-1) - 16 \times f(n)$ (b) $f(2n-1) - 8 \times f(n)$
(c) $f(2n) - 16 \times f(n)$ (d) $f(2n) - 8 \times f(n)$

91. Find the range of 'x' if $\frac{1}{|x|-2} < 0.5$

(a) $x < -4$
(b) $(x > 4) \cup (x < -4)$
(c) $(x < -4) \cup (-2 < x < 2) \cup (x > 4)$
(d) $-2 < x < 2$

92. 'f' is a real function such that $f(x + y) = f(xy)$ for all real values of x and y. If $f(-7) = 7$, then the value of $f(-49) + f(49)$ is

(a) 7 (b) 14
(c) 0 (d) 49

93. Find the domain of the function

$$f(x) = \frac{3}{9-x^2} + \log_{10}(x^3 - x).$$

(a) (–1, 0) U (1, 3)
(b) (–1, 0) U (1, 3) U (3, ∞)
(c) (–3, 0) U (3, ∞)
(d) (–∞,–3) U (–3, 3) U (3, ∞)

94. A ray of light along the line $\sqrt{3}x + y = \sqrt{3}$ gets reflected on the x-axis to become a ray along the line

(a) $y = x + \sqrt{3}$ (b) $\sqrt{3}y = x - 1$
(c) $y = \sqrt{3}x - \sqrt{3}$ (d) $\sqrt{3}y = x - \sqrt{3}$

2015

95. Find the solution set for [x] + [2x] + [3x] = 8, where x is a real number and [x] is the greatest integer less than or equal to x.

(a) $1 \le x < \frac{4}{3}$ (b) $x < \frac{5}{3}$
(c) $\frac{3}{2} \le x < \frac{5}{3}$ (d) None of these

2016

96. A function f(x) is defined as $(x + 1) \times f(x + 1) + x \times f(x) + (x - 1) \times f(x - 1) = 0$ for $x \ge 2$. If f(a) = 40 and f(6) = 180, find the value of f(14).

(a) –80 (b) –160
(c) –1120 (d) Cannot be determined

2017

97. Let $f(x) = x^2$ and $g(x) = 2^x$, for all real x. Then the value of f(f(g(x)) + g(f(x))) at x = 1 is

(a) 16 (b) 18 (c) 36 (d) 40

98. If f(ab) = f(a)f(b) for all positive integers a and b, then the largest possible value of f(a) is

99. Let f(x) = 2x – 5 and g(x) = 7 – 2x. Then |f(x) + g(x)| = |f(x)| + |g(x)| if and only if

(a) $\frac{5}{2} < x < \frac{7}{2}$ (b) $x \le \frac{5}{2}$ or $x \ge \frac{7}{2}$
(c) $x < \frac{5}{2}$ or $\ge \frac{7}{2}$ (d) $\frac{5}{2} \le x \le \frac{7}{2}$

2018 Slot 1

100. If f(x + 2) = f(x) + f(x + 1) for all positive integers x, and f(11) = 91, f(15) = 617, then f(10) equals

101. Let $f(x) = \min\{2x^2, 52 - 5x\}$, where x is any positive real number. Then the maximum possible value of f(x) is

2018 Slot 2

102. Let $f(x) = \max\{5x, 52 - 2x^2\}$, where x is any positive real number. Then the minimum possible value of f(x) is

LOGARITHM AND EXPONENTS

1994

1. If $\log_7 \log_5 \left(\sqrt{x+5} + \sqrt{x}\right) = 0$, find the value of x.

(a) 1 (b) 0
(c) 2 (d) None of these

2. $\log_6 216\sqrt{6}$ is

(a) 3 (b) $\frac{3}{2}$
(c) $\frac{7}{2}$ (d) None of these

1997

3. If $\log_2\left[\log_7\left(x^2 - x + 37\right)\right] = 1$, then what could be the value of 'x'?

(a) 3 (b) 5
(c) 4 (d) None of these

1999

Direction for Question 4: The question followed by two statements, I and II. Mark the answer

(a) if the question can be answered by any one of the statements alone, but cannot be answered by using the other statement alone.
(b) if the question can be answered by using either statement alone.
(c) if the question can be answered by using both the statements together, but cannot be answered by using either statement alone.
(d) if the question cannot be answered even by using both the statements together.

4. What is the distance x between two cities A and B in integral number of kilometres?
   I. x satisfies the equation $\log_2 x = \sqrt{x}$
   II. $x \leq 10$ km

2003(R)

5. If $\log_{10}x - \log_{10}\sqrt{x} = 2\log_x 10$, then the possible value of x is given by
   (a) 10 (b) $\frac{1}{100}$
   (c) $\frac{1}{1000}$ (d) None of these

6. If $\frac{1}{3}\log_3 M + 3\log_3 N = 1 + \log_{0.008} 5$, then
   (a) $M^9 = \frac{9}{N}$ (b) $N^9 = \frac{9}{M}$
   (c) $M^3 = \frac{3}{N}$ (d) $N^9 = \frac{3}{M}$

7. What is the sum of 'n' terms in the series $\log m + \log\left(\frac{m^2}{n}\right) + \log\left(\frac{m^3}{n^2}\right) + \log\left(\frac{m^4}{n^3}+\right) + \ldots$?
   (a) $\log\left[\frac{n^{(n-1)}}{m^{(n+1)}}\right]^{\frac{n}{2}}$ (b) $\log\left[\frac{m^m}{n^n}\right]^{\frac{n}{2}}$
   (c) $\log\left[\frac{m^{(1-n)}}{n^{(1-m)}}\right]^{\frac{n}{2}}$ (d) $\log\left[\frac{m^{(n+1)}}{n^{(n-1)}}\right]^{\frac{n}{2}}$

2003(L)

8. When the curves $y = \log_{10}x$ and $y = x^{-1}$ are drawn in the x-y plane, how many times do they intersect for values $x \geq 1$?
   (a) Never
   (b) Once
   (c) Twice
   (d) More than twice

9. If $\log_3 2$, $\log_3(2^x - 5)$, $\log_3(2^x - 7/2)$ are in arithmetic progression, then the value of x is equal to
   (a) 5 (b) 4
   (c) 2 (d) 3

2004

10. Let $u = (\log_2 x)^2 - 6\log_2 x + 12$ where x is a real number. Then the equation $x^u = 256$, has
   (a) no solution for x
   (b) exactly one solution for x
   (c) exactly two distinct solutions for x
   (d) exactly three distinct solutions for x

2005

11. If $x \geq y$ and $y > 1$, then the value of the expression $\log_x\left(\frac{x}{y}\right) + \log_y\left(\frac{y}{x}\right)$ can never be
   (a) –1 (b) –0.5
   (c) 0 (d) 1

2006

12. If $\log_y x = (a \cdot \log_z y) = (b \cdot \log_x z) = ab$, then which of the following pairs of values for (a, b) is not possible?
   (a) $\left(-2, \frac{1}{2}\right)$ (b) (1, 1)
   (c) (0.4, 2.5) (d) $\left(\pi, \frac{1}{\pi}\right)$
   (e) (2, 2)

13. What are the values of x and y that satisfy both the equations?
   $$2^{0.7x} \cdot 3^{-1.25y} = \frac{8\sqrt{6}}{27}$$
   $$4^{0.3x} \cdot 9^{0.2y} = 8 \cdot (81)^{\frac{1}{5}}$$
   (a) x = 2, y = 5
   (b) x = 2.5, y = 6
   (c) x = 3, y = 5
   (d) x = 3, y = 4
   (e) x = 5, y = 2

MEMORY BASED QUESTIONS

2010

14. If a and b are integers such that $\log_2(a+b) + \log_2(a-b) = 3$, then how many different pairs (a, b) are possible?
   (a) 0 (b) 1
   (c) 2 (d) 3

2011

15. If $\log_{16}5 = m$ and $\log_5 3 = n$, then what is the value of $\log_3 6$ in terms of 'm' and 'n'?
   (a) $\frac{1+4mn}{4mn}$
   (b) $\frac{4mn}{1+4mn}$
   (c) $\frac{1}{1+4mn}$
   (d) Cannot be determined

2014

16. If $X=\sum_{i=1}^{i=n}\log_{10}(i)-\sum_{j=1}^{j=p}\log_{10}(j)-\sum_{k=1}^{k=(n-p)}\log_{10}(k)$, where $p \le n$, then the maximum value of X for n = 8 is:

(a) $1+\log_{10}24$

(b) $\log_{10}56$

(c) $1+\log_{10}7$

(d) $1+\log_{10}48$

17. If $\log_3 2$, $\log_3(2^x-5)$ and $\log_3\left(2^x-\frac{7}{2}\right)$ are in Arithmetic Progression, then x is equal to

(a) 2 (b) 3

(c) 2 or 4 (d) 2 or 3

2015

18. If $\log 2x = 2\log(x+1)$, find the number of real values of x?.

2016

19. If $\log_c a=\frac{1}{2}$, $\log_d b=\frac{1}{3}$, where a, b, c and d are distinct natural numbers and $a<b<c<d$, what is the minimum possible value of $a+b+c+d$?

(a) 10 (b) 22 (c) 34 (d) 36

2017

20. If x is a real number such that $\log_3 5=\log_5(2+x)$, then which of the following is true?

(a) $0<x<3$ (b) $23<x<30$

(c) $x>30$ (d) $3<x<23$

21. If $\log(2^a\times 3^b\times 5^c)$ is the arithmetic mean of $\log(2^2\times 3^3\times 5)$, $\log(2^6\times 3\times 5^7)$, and $\log(2\times 3^2\times 5^4)$, then a equals

2018 Slot 1

22. If $\log_2(5+\log_3 a)=3$ and $\log_5(4a+12+\log_2 b)=3$, then a + b is equal to

(a) 40 (b) 32 (c) 67 (d) 59

23. If $\log_{12}81=p$, the $3\left(\frac{4-p}{4+p}\right)$ is equal to

(a) $\log_4 16$ (b) $\log_2 8$

(c) $\log_6 8$ (d) $\log_6 16$

24. If x is a positive quantity such that $2^x=3^{\log_5 2}$, then x is equal to

(a) $\log_5 9$ (b) $\log_5 8$

(c) $1+\log_3\frac{5}{3}$ (d) $1+\log_5\frac{3}{5}$

25. The number of integers x such that $0.25\le 2^x\le 200$, and 2^x+2 is perfectly divisible by either 3 or 4, is

26. Given that $x^{2018}y^{2017}=1/2$ and $x^{2016}y^{2019}=8$, the value of x^2+y^3 is

(a) $\frac{33}{4}$ (b) $\frac{35}{4}$

(c) $\frac{37}{4}$ (d) $\frac{31}{4}$

2018 Slot 2

27. If $p^3=q^4=r^5=s^6$, then the value of $\log_s(pqr)$ is equal to

(a) $\frac{24}{5}$ (b) 1

(c) $\frac{16}{5}$ (d) $\frac{47}{10}$

28. $\frac{1}{\log_2 100}-\frac{1}{\log_4 100}+\frac{1}{\log_5 100}-\frac{1}{\log_{10} 100}+\frac{1}{\log_{20} 100}-\frac{1}{\log_{25} 100}+\frac{1}{\log_{50} 100}=?$

(a) 0 (b) 10

(c) –4 (d) $\frac{1}{2}$

PROGRESSIONS

1990

1. What is the sum of the series:

$$\frac{1}{(1\times 2)}+\frac{1}{(2\times 3)}+\frac{1}{(3\times 4)}+\ldots\ldots+\frac{1}{(100\times 101)}?$$

(a) $\frac{99}{100}$ (b) $\frac{1}{100}$

(c) $\frac{100}{101}$ (d) $\frac{101}{102}$

2. N the set of natural numbers is partitioned into subsets $S_1=(1)$, $S_2=(2, 3)$, $S_3=\{4, 5, 6\}$, $S_4=\{7, 8, 9, 10\}$ and so on. The sum of the elements of the subset S_{50} is

(a) 61250 (b) 65525

(c) 42455 (d) 62525

1993

3. Let $u_{n+1}=2u_n+1\ (n=0,1,2,\ldots)$ and $u_0=0$. Then u_{10} nearest to

(a) 1023 (b) 2047

(c) 4095 (d) 8195

1994

4. If the harmonic mean between two positive numbers is to their geometric mean as 12 : 13; then the numbers could be in the ratio

(a) 12 : 13 (b) 1/12 : 1/13

(c) 4 : 9 (d) 2 : 3

5. Fourth term of an arithmetic progression is 8. What is the sum of the first 7 terms of the arithmetic progression?

(a) 7

(b) 64

(c) 56

(d) Cannot be determined

6. Along a road lie an odd number of stones placed at intervals of 10m. These stones have to be assembled around the middle stone. A person can carry only one stone at a time. A man carried out the job starting with the stone in the middle, carrying stones in succession, thereby covering a distance of 4.8 km. Then the number of stones is

(a) 35

(b) 15

(c) 29

(d) 31

Direction for Question 7: The question is followed by two statements. As the answer:

Mark (a) if the question can be answered with the help of statement I alone

Mark (b) if the question can be answered with the help of statement II, alone

Mark (c) if both, statement I and statement II are needed to answer the question, and

Mark (d) if the question cannot be answered even with the help of both the statements.

7. Three boys had a few coffee Bite toffees with them. The number of toffees with the second were four more than those with the first and the number of toffees with the third were four more than those with the second. How many toffees were there in all?

I. The number of toffees with each of them is a multiple of 2.

II. The first boy ate up four toffees from what he had and the second boy ate up six toffees from what had and the third boy gave them two toffees each from what he had and the number of toffees remaining with each of them formed a geometric progression.

1995

Direction for Question 8: The question is followed by two statements, I and II. Mark the answer as:

(a) if the question can be answered with the help of statement I alone.

(b) if the question can be answered with the help of statement II alone.

(c) if both statement I and statement II are needed to answer the question.

(d) if the question cannot be answered even with the help of both the statements.

8. What is the first term of an arithmetic progression of positive integers?

I. Sum of the squares of the first and the second term is 116.

II. The fifth term is divisible by 7.

1996

Directions for Questions 9 to 13: Answer the questions based on the following information.

A series S_1 of five positive integers is such that the third term is half the first term and the fifth term is 20 more than the first term. In series S_2, the nth term defined as the difference between the (n+1)th term and the nth term of series S_1, is an arithmetic progression with a common difference of 30.

9. First term of S_1 is

(a) 80 (b) 90

(c) 100 (d) 120

10. Second term of S_2 is

(a) 50 (b) 60

(c) 70 (d) None of these

11. What is the difference between second and fourth terms of S_1?

(a) 10 (b) 20

(c) 30 (d) 60

12. What is the average value of the terms of series S_1?

(a) 60

(b) 70

(c) 80

(d) Average is not an integer

13. What is the sum of series S_2?

(a) 10 (b) 20

(c) 30 (d) 40

1998

14. One bacterium splits into eight bacteria of the next generation. But due to environmental condition only 50% survives and remaining 50% dies after producing next generation. If the seventh generation number is 4,096 million, what is the number in first generation?

(a) 1 million (b) 2 million

(c) 4 million (d) 8 million

Direction for Question 15: The question is followed by two statements, I and II. Answer the question based on the statements and mark the answer as:

(a) if the question can be answered with the help of any one statement alone but not by the other statement.

(b) if the question can be answered with the help of either of the statements taken individually.

(c) if the question can be answered with the help of both statements together.

(d) if the question cannot be answered even with the help of both statements together.

15. Find the value of X in terms of 'a'.

I. Arithmetic mean of X and Y is 'a' while the geometric mean is also 'a'.

II. $\frac{X}{Y} = R$; $X - Y = D$.

1999

Directions for Questions 16 to 18: Answer the questions based on the following information.

There are 50 integers $a_1, a_2, ..., a_{50}$, not all of them necessarily different. Let the greatest integer of these 50 integers be referred to as G, and the smallest integer be referred to as L. The integers a_1 through a_{24} form sequence S1, and the rest form sequence S2. Each member of S1 is less than or equal to each member of S2.

16. All values in S1 are changed in sign, while those in S2 remain unchanged. Which of the following statements is true?

(a) Every member of S1 is greater than or equal to every member of S2.

(b) G is in S1.

(c) If all numbers originally in S1 and S2 had the same sign, then after the change of sign, the largest number of S1 and S2 is in S1.

(d) None of the above

17. Elements of S1 are in ascending order, and those of S2 are in descending order. a_{24} and a_{25} are interchanged. Then which of the following statements is true?

(a) S1 continues to be in ascending order.

(b) S2 continues to be in descending order.

(c) S1 continues to be in ascending order and S2 in descending order.

(d) None of the above

18. Every element of S1 is made greater than or equal to every element of S2 by adding to each element of S1 an integer x. Then x cannot be less than

(a) 2^{10}

(b) the smallest value of S2

(c) the largest value of S2

(d) (G – L)

2000

19. If $a_1 = 1$ and $a_{n+1} = 2a_n + 5$, n = 1, 2, ... , then a_{100} is equal to

(a) $(5 \times 2^{99} - 6)$ (b) $(5 \times 2^{99} + 6)$

(c) $(6 \times 2^{99} + 5)$ (d) $(6 \times 2^{99} - 5)$

20. What is the value of the following expression?

$$\left(\frac{1}{(2^2-1)}\right)+\left(\frac{1}{(4^2-1)}\right)+\left(\frac{1}{(6^2-1)}\right)+\cdots+\left(\frac{1}{(20^2-1)}\right)$$

(a) $\frac{9}{19}$ (b) $\frac{10}{19}$

(c) $\frac{10}{21}$ (d) $\frac{11}{21}$

21. Each of the numbers $x_1, x_2, \cdots, x_n, n \geq 4$, is equal to 1 or –1. Suppose

$$x_1x_2x_3x_4 + x_2x_3x_4x_5 + x_3x_4x_5x_6 + \cdots + x_{n-3}x_{n-2}x_{n-1}x_n + x_{n-2}x_{n-1}x_nx_1 + x_{n-1}x_nx_1x_2 + x_nx_1x_2x_3 = 0,$$ then

(a) n is even

(b) n is odd

(c) n is an odd multiple of 3

(d) n is prime

2001

22. Two men X and Y started working for a certain company at similar jobs on January 1, 1950. X asked for an initial salary of Rs. 300 with an annual increment of Rs. 30. Y asked for an initial salary of Rs. 200 with a rise of Rs. 15 every 6 months. Assume that the arrangements remained unaltered till December 31, 1959. Salary is paid on the last day of the month. What is the total amount paid to them as salary during the period?

(a) Rs. 93,300 (b) Rs. 93,200

(c) Rs. 93,100 (d) None of these

23. All the page numbers from a book are added, beginning at page 1. However, one page number was added twice by mistake. The sum obtained was 1000. Which page number was added twice?

(a) 44 (b) 45
(c) 10 (d) 12

24. For a Fibonacci sequence, from the third term onwards, each term in the sequence is the sum of the previous two terms in that sequence. If the difference in squares of 7th and 6th terms of this sequence is 517, what is the 10th term of this sequence?

(a) 147
(b) 76
(c) 123
(d) Cannot be determined

2002

25. The nth element of a series is represented as

$X_n = (-1)^n X_{n-1}$

If $X_0 = x$ and $x > 0$, then which of the following is always true?

(a) X_n is positive if n is even
(b) X_n is positive if n is odd
(c) X_n is negative if n is even
(d) None of these

26. Let S denotes the infinite sum

$2 + 5x + 9x^2 + 14x^3 + 20x^4 + \ldots$, where $|x| < 1$ and the coefficient of x^{n-1} is $\frac{1}{2}n(n+3), (n = 1, 2, \ldots)$. Then S equals:

(a) $\frac{2-x}{(1-x)^3}$ (b) $\frac{2-x}{(1+x)^3}$
(c) $\frac{2+x}{(1-x)^3}$ (d) $\frac{2+x}{(1+x)^3}$

27. A child was asked to add first few natural numbers (i.e. $1 + 2 + 3 + \ldots$) so long his patience permitted. As he stopped, he gave the sum as 575. When the teacher declared the result wrong, the child discovered he had missed one number in the sequence during addition. The number he missed was

(a) less than 10
(b) 10
(c) 15
(d) more than 15

2003(R)

28. Let S_1 be a square of side a. Another square S_2 is formed by joining the mid-points of the sides of S_1. The same process is applied to S_2 to form yet another square S_3, and so on. If $A_1, A_2, A_3, \ldots$ be the areas and $P_1, P_2, P_3, \ldots$ be the perimeters of $S_1, S_2, S_3, \ldots$, respectively, then the ratio $\frac{P_1 + P_2 + P_3 + \cdots}{A_1 + A_2 + A_3 + \cdots}$ equals

(a) $\frac{2(1+\sqrt{2})}{a}$ (b) $\frac{2(2-\sqrt{2})}{a}$
(c) $\frac{2(2+\sqrt{2})}{a}$ (d) $\frac{2(1+2\sqrt{2})}{a}$

29. The infinite sum $1 + \frac{4}{7} + \frac{9}{7^2} + \frac{16}{7^3} + \frac{25}{7^4} + \cdots$ equals

(a) $\frac{27}{14}$ (b) $\frac{21}{13}$
(c) $\frac{49}{27}$ (d) $\frac{256}{147}$

2003(L)

30. The sum of 3rd and 15th elements of an arithmetic progression is equal to the sum of 6th, 11th and 13th elements of the same progression. Then which element of the series should necessarily be equal to zero?

(a) 1st (b) 9th
(c) 12th (d) None of the above

31. The 288th term of the series a,b,b,c,c,c,d,d,d,d,e,e,e,e,e,f,f,f,f,f,f,... is

(a) u (b) v
(c) w (d) x

32. There are 8436 steel balls, each with a radius of 1 centimeter, stacked in a pile, with 1 ball on top, 3 balls in the second layer, 6 in the third layer, 10 in the fourth, and so on. The number of horizontal layers in the pile is

(a) 34 (b) 38
(c) 36 (d) 32

33. If the product of n positive real numbers is unity, then their sum is necessarily

(a) a multiple of n (b) equal to $n + \frac{1}{n}$
(c) never less than n (d) a positive integer

34. Let T be the set of integers {3, 11, 19, 27, ..., 451, 459, 467} and S be a subset of T such that the sum of no two elements of S is 470. The maximum possible number of elements in S is

(a) 32 (b) 28
(c) 29 (d) 30

Directions for Question 35: The question is followed by two statements, A and B. Answer the question using the following instructions.

Choose (a) if the question can be answered by one of the statements alone but not by the other.

Choose (b) if the question can be answered by using either statement alone.

Choose (c) if the question can be answered by using both the statements together, but cannot be answered by using either statement alone.

Choose (d) if the question cannot be answered even by using both the statements together.

35. Is $\left(\frac{1}{a^2}+\frac{1}{a^4}+\frac{1}{a^6}+\cdots\right)>\left(\frac{1}{a}+\frac{1}{a^3}+\frac{1}{a^5}+\cdots\right)$?

A. $-3 \le a \le 3$

B. One of the roots of the equation $4x^2 - 4x + 1 = 0$ is a.

2004

36. If the sum of the first 11 terms of an arithmetic progression equals that of the first 19 terms, then what is the sum of the first 30 terms?

(a) 0 (b) –1

(c) 1 (d) Not unique

37. On January 1, 2004 two new societies s_1 and s_2 are formed, each n numbers. On the first day of each subsequent month, s_1 adds b members while s_2 multiples its current numbers by a constant factor r. Both the societies have the same number of members on July 2, 2004. If b = 10.5n, what is the value of r?

(a) 2.0 (b) 1.9

(c) 1.8 (d) 1.7

38. Consider the sequence of numbers a_1, a_2, a_3, ... to infinity where $a_1 = 81.33$ and $a_2 = -19$ and $a_j = a_{j-1} - a_{j-2}$ for $j \ge 3$. What is the sum of the first 6002 terms of this sequence?

(a) –100.33 (b) –30.00

(c) 62.33 (d) 119.33

2005

39. If $a_1 = 1$ and $a_{n+1} - 3a_n + 2 = 4n$ for every positive integer n, then a_{100} equals

(a) $3^{99} - 200$ (b) $3^{99} + 200$

(c) $3^{100} - 200$ (d) $3^{100} + 200$

2006

40. Consider a sequence where the nth term,

$$t_n = \frac{n}{(n+2)}, n = 1, 2, \ldots$$

The value of $t_3 \times t_4 \times t_5 \times \ldots \times t_{53}$ equals:

(a) $\frac{2}{495}$ (b) $\frac{2}{477}$

(c) $\frac{12}{55}$ (d) $\frac{1}{1485}$

(e) $\frac{1}{2970}$

41. A group of 630 children is arranged in rows for a group photograph session. Each row contains three fewer children than the row in front of it. What number of rows is not possible?

(a) 3 (b) 4

(c) 5 (d) 6

(e) 7

42. Consider the set S = {1, 2, 3, . . ., 1000}. How many arithmetic progressions can be formed from the elements of S that start with 1 and end with 1000 and have at least 3 elements?

(a) 3 (b) 4

(c) 6 (d) 7

(e) 8

2007

43. Consider the set S = {2, 3, 4, ……, 2n + 1}, where 'n' is a positive integer larger than 2007. Define X as the average of the odd integers in S and Y as the average of the even integers in S. What is the value of X – Y?

(a) 0 (b) 1

(c) $\frac{1}{2}n$ (d) $\frac{n+1}{2n}$

(e) 2008

44. The price of Darjeeling tea (in rupees per kilogram) is 100 + 0.10n, on the nth day of 2007 (n = 1, 2, ..., 100), and then remains constant. On the other hand, the price of Ooty tea (in rupees per kilogram) is 89 + 0.15n, on the nth day of 2007 (n = 1, 2, ..., 365). On which date in 2007 will the prices of these two varieties of tea be equal?

(a) May 21 (b) April 11

(c) May 20 (d) April 10

(e) June 30

Directions for Questions 45 and 46: Answer the following questions based on the information given below:

Let $a_1 = p$ and $b_1 = q$, where p and q are positive quantities. Define

$a_n = pb_{n-1}$, $b_n = qb_{n-1}$, for even n > 1,

and $a_n = pa_{n-1}$, $b_n = qa_{n-1}$, for odd n > 1.

45. Which of the following best describes $a_n + b_n$ for even 'n'?

(a) $q(pq)^{\frac{1}{2}n-1}(p+q)$ (b) $qp^{\frac{1}{2}n-1}(p+q)$

(c) $q^{\frac{1}{2}n}(p+q)$ (d) $q^{\frac{1}{2}n}(p+q)^{\frac{1}{2}n}$

(e) $q(pq)^{\frac{1}{2}n-1}(p+q)^{\frac{1}{2}n}$

46. If $p = \frac{1}{3}$ and $q = \frac{2}{3}$, then what is the smallest odd 'n' such that $a_n + b_n < 0.01$?

(a) 7 (b) 13

(c) 11 (d) 9

(e) 15

2008

47. The integers 1, 2, ..., 40 are written on a blackboard. The following operation is then repeated 39 times: In each repetition, any two numbers, say a and b, currently on the blackboard are erased and a new number a + b – 1 is written. What will be the number left on the board at the end?

(a) 820 (b) 821

(c) 781 (d) 819

(e) 780

48. The number of common terms in the two sequences 17, 21, 25,..., 417 and 16, 21, 26,..., 466 is

(a) 78 (b) 19

(c) 20 (d) 77

(e) 22

49. Find the sum

$$\sqrt{1+\frac{1}{1^2}+\frac{1}{2^2}}+\sqrt{1+\frac{1}{2^2}+\frac{1}{3^2}}+\ldots\ldots+\sqrt{1+\frac{1}{2007^2}+\frac{1}{2008^2}}$$

(a) $2008-\frac{1}{2008}$ (b) $2007-\frac{1}{2007}$

(c) $2007-\frac{1}{2008}$ (d) $2008-\frac{1}{2007}$

(e) $2008-\frac{1}{2009}$

MEMORY BASED QUESTIONS

2009

50. If the sum of the first 'n' terms of an Arithmetic Progression is 100 and the sum of the next 'n' terms of the Arithmetic Progression is 300, then what is the ratio of the first term and the common difference?

(a) 2 : 1

(b) 1 : 2

(c) 1 : 3

(d) Cannot be determined

2012

51. A sequence of terms is defined such that

$2a_n = a_{n+1} + a_{n-1}$; $a_0 = 1$; $a_1 = 3$.

What is the value of $a_0 + a_1 + a_2 + a_3 + \ldots\ldots + a_{50}$?

(a) 2551 (b) 2753

(c) 2601 (d) 2451

2013

52. If E = 3 + 8 + 15 + 24 + ... + 195, then what is the sum of the prime factors of E?

(a) 29 (b) 31

(c) 33 (d) 23

2014

53. An equation with all positive roots is written as $x^n + a_n x^{n-1} + a_{n-1} x^{n-2} + \ldots a_1 = 0$. Which of the following in necessarily true?

(a) $a_n^{\,n} \geq n^n \times a_1$ (b) $n^n \geq a_n^{\,n} \times a_1$

(c) $a_1^{\,n} \geq n^n \times a_n$ (d) None of these

54. The number of APs with 5 distinct terms that can be formed from the first 50 natural numbers is

(a) 325 (b) 300

(c) 375 (d) 288

55. $P = \frac{1}{1!+2!}+\frac{1}{2!+3!}+\frac{1}{3!+4!}+\ldots+\frac{1}{9!+10!}$. Find the value of P.

(a) $\frac{1}{2!}-\frac{1}{11!}$ (b) $\frac{1}{2!}-\frac{1}{10!}$

(c) $\frac{1}{1!}-\frac{1}{10!}$ (d) $\frac{1}{1!}-\frac{1}{11!}$

56. A set 'P' is formed from the set of first 'N' natural numbers by deleting all the perfect squares and all the perfect cubes. If the numbers are arranged in an ascending order then, what is the 476th number of the set 'P'?

(a) 500 (b) 501

(c) 502 (d) 503

57. P1, P2, P3, ..., P11 are 11 friends. The number of balls with P1 through P11 in that order is in an Arithmetic Progression. If the sum of the number of balls with P1, P3, P5, P7, P9 and P11 is 72, what is the number of balls with P1, P6 and P11 put together?

(a) 24 (b) 48

(c) 36 (d) Cannot be determined

2017

58. An infinite geometric progression $a_1, a_2, a_3, \ldots$ has the property that $a_n = 3(a_{n+1} + a_{n+2} + \ldots)$ for every $n \geq 1$. If the sum $a_1 + a_2 + a_3 + \ldots = 32$, then a_5 is

(a) $\frac{1}{32}$ (b) $\frac{2}{32}$

(c) $\frac{3}{32}$ (d) $\frac{4}{32}$

59. If $a_1 = \frac{1}{2\times5}, a_2 = \frac{1}{5\times8}, a_3 = \frac{1}{8\times11}, \ldots$, then $a_1 + a_2 + a_3 + \ldots + a_{100}$ is

(a) $\frac{25}{151}$ (b) $\frac{1}{2}$

(c) $\frac{1}{4}$ (d) $\frac{111}{55}$

2018 Slot 1

60. Let x, y, z be three positive real numbers in a geometric progression such that $x < y < z$. If 5x, 16y, and 12z are in an arithmetic progression then the common ratio of the geometric progression is

(a) $\frac{5}{2}$

(b) $\frac{3}{6}$

(c) $\frac{3}{2}$

(d) $\frac{1}{6}$

2018 Slot 2

61. Let $a_1, a_2, \ldots, a_{52}$ be positive integers such that $a_1 < a_2 < \ldots < a_{52}$. Suppose, their arithmetic mean is one less than the arithmetic mean of $a_2, a_3, \ldots, a_{52}$. If $a_{52} = 100$, then the largest possible value of a_1 is

(a) 20

(b) 23

(c) 45

(d) 48

ANSWERS

Equations, Polynomials and Inequations

1. (a)	**2.** (a)	**3.** (b)	**4.** (d)	**5.** (c)	**6.** (c)	**7.** (b)	**8.** (c)	**9.** (b)	**10.** (b)
11. (b)	**12.** (c)	**13.** (c)	**14.** (c)	**15.** (b)	**16.** (b)	**17.** (a)	**18.** (d)	**19.** (b)	**20.** (d)
21. (a)	**22.** (d)	**23.** (d)	**24.** (a)	**25.** (d)	**26.** (d)	**27.** (b)	**28.** (d)	**29.** (a)	**30.** (a)
31. (d)	**32.** (a)	**33.** (a)	**34.** (d)	**35.** (b)	**36.** (b)	**37.** (b)	**38.** (a)	**39.** (d)	**40.** (a)
41. (d)	**42.** (a)	**43.** (d)	**44.** (d)	**45.** (c)	**46.** (d)	**47.** (c)	**48.** (a)	**49.** (b)	**50.** (a)
51. (b)	**52.** (c)	**53.** (d)	**54.** (c)	**55.** (c)	**56.** (d)	**57.** (c)	**58.** (a)	**59.** (b)	**60.** (b)
61. (c)	**62.** (a)	**63.** (c)	**64.** (d)	**65.** (d)	**66.** (a)	**67.** (c)	**68.** (a)	**69.** (a)	**70.** (c)
71. (d)	**72.** (b)	**73.** (b)	**74.** (c)	**75.** (c)	**76.** (b)	**77.** (d)	**78.** (d)	**79.** (c)	**80.** (a)
81. (c)	**82.** (c)	**83.** (d)	**84.** (c)	**85.** (c)	**86.** (d)	**87.** (d)	**88.** (b)	**89.** (a)	**90.** (b)
91. (b)	**92.** (c)	**93.** (d)	**94.** (e)	**95.** (b)	**96.** (a)	**97.** (b)	**98.** (a)	**99.** (b)	**100.** (d)
101. (a)	**102.** (b)	**103.** (d)	**104.** (c)	**105.** (c)	**106.** (a)	**107.** (b)	**108.** (d)	**109.** (a)	**110.** (d)
111. (c)	**112.** (a)	**113.** (a)	**114.** (b)	**115.** (d)	**116.** (c)	**117.** (a)	**118.** (c)	**119.** (b)	**120.** (c)
121. (a)	**122.** (70)	**123.** (c)	**124.** (c)	**125.** (b)	**126.** (c)	**127.** (a)	**128.** (a)	**129.** (8)	**130.** (10)
131. (a)	**132.** (36)	**133.** (24)							

Functions and Graphs

1. (b)	**2.** (a)	**3.** (b)	**4.** (d)	**5.** (d)	**6.** (a)	**7.** (b)	**8.** (d)	**9.** (b)	**10.** (a)
11. (b)	**12.** (c)	**13.** (b)	**14.** (c)	**15.** (c)	**16.** (a)	**17.** (d)	**18.** (b)	**19.** (d)	**20.** (d)
21. (b)	**22.** (b)	**23.** (b)	**24.** (c)	**25.** (c)	**26.** (a)	**27.** (b)	**28.** (d)	**29.** (d)	**30.** (c)
31. (c)	**32.** (d)	**33.** (b)	**34.** (b)	**35.** (c)	**36.** (d)	**37.** (a)	**38.** (d)	**39.** (a)	**40.** (b)
41. (c)	**42.** (d)	**43.** (b)	**44.** (c)	**45.** (b)	**46.** (b)	**47.** (b)	**48.** (b)	**49.** (b)	**50.** (c)
51. (c)	**52.** (c)	**53.** (d)	**54.** (b)	**55.** (b)	**56.** (d)	**57.** (b)	**58.** (b)	**59.** (b)	**60.** (a)
61. (d)	**62.** (a)	**63.** (d)	**64.** (b)	**65.** (d)	**66.** (b)	**67.** (d)	**68.** (c)	**69.** (b)	**70.** (d)
71. (c)	**72.** (d)	**73.** (b)	**74.** (d)	**75.** (e)	**76.** (a)	**77.** (b)	**78.** (d)	**79.** (b)	**80.** (e)
81. (b)	**82.** (a)	**83.** (d)	**84.** (b)	**85.** (b)	**86.** (c)	**87.** (a)	**88.** (b)	**89.** (d)	**90.** (c)
91. (c)	**92.** (b)	**93.** (b)	**94.** (c)	**95.** (c)	**96.** (a)	**97.** (c)	**98.** (a)	**99.** (d)	**100.** (54)
101. (32)	**102.** (20)								

Logarithm and Exponents

1. (d)	**2.** (c)	**3.** (c)	**4.** (c)	**5.** (b)	**6.** (b)	**7.** (d)	**8.** (b)	**9.** (d)	**10.** (b)
11. (d)	**12.** (e)	**13.** (e)	**14.** (c)	**15.** (a)	**16.** (c)	**17.** (b)	**18.** 0	**19.** (d)	**20.** (d)
21. (c)	**22.** (d)	**23.** (c)	**24.** (d)	**25.** (5)	**26.** (a)	**27.** (d)	**28.** (d)		

Progressions

1. (c)	**2.** (d)	**3.** (a)	**4.** (c)	**5.** (c)	**6.** (d)	**7.** (b)	**8.** (a)	**9.** (c)	**10.** (d)
11. (a)	**12.** (c)	**13.** (b)	**14.** (a)	**15.** (a)	**16.** (d)	**17.** (a)	**18.** (d)	**19.** (d)	**20.** (c)
21. (a)	**22.** (a)	**23.** (c)	**24.** (c)	**25.** (d)	**26.** (a)	**27.** (d)	**28.** (c)	**29.** (c)	**30.** (c)
31. (d)	**32.** (c)	**33.** (c)	**34.** (d)	**35.** (a)	**36.** (a)	**37.** (a)	**38.** (c)	**39.** (c)	**40.** (a)
41. (d)	**42.** (d)	**43.** (b)	**44.** (c)	**45.** (a)	**46.** (d)	**47.** (c)	**48.** (c)	**49.** (a)	**50.** (b)
51. (c)	**52.** (b)	**53.** (d)	**54.** (d)	**55.** (a)	**56.** (d)	**57.** (c)	**58.** (c)	**59.** (a)	**60.** (a)
61. (b)									

EXPLANATIONS

Equations, Polynomials and Inequations

1. a $\frac{1}{(1-x)}+\frac{1}{(1+x)}+\frac{2}{(1+x^2)}+\frac{4}{(1+x^4)}$

$=\frac{2}{(1-x^2)}+\frac{2}{(1+x^2)}+\frac{4}{(1+x^4)}=\frac{4}{(1-x^4)}+\frac{4}{(1+x^4)}$

$=\frac{8}{(1-x^8)}$.

2. a When $x = 0$, $a^x b^{(1-x)} = b$

When $x = 1$, $a^x b^{(1-x)} = a$

Only option (a)always satisfies the given constraints.

3. b $\left(\frac{1-d^3}{1-d}\right)=\frac{(1-d)(1+d+d^2)}{(1-d)}=(1+d+d^2)$

If $d > 1$, then $d^2 > 1$ and $(1 + d + d^2) > 3$.

Hence, (b)is the correct option.

4. d If the roots are reciprocal of each other their product = 1.

Product of roots of the equation $=\frac{6}{a}$

Since $\frac{6}{a}=1 \Rightarrow a=6.$

5. c $(x + y + z)^2$

$= x^2 + y^2 + z^2 + 2(xy + yz + xz)$

$= x^2 + y^2 + z^2 + 2 \times 0$

$= x^2 + y^2 + z^2$.

6. c As 43 is neither a multiple of 5 nor 6, either statement alone is not sufficient to answer the question.

Using both statements together: Let the number of children older than 5 years be 'a' and that of 5 years or younger be 'b'.

As per the given information, $5a + 6b = 43$.

As a and b are non-negative integer, only possible value: $a = 5$ and $b = 3$.

7. b $\left[\frac{(x^{-1}-y^{-1})}{(x^{-2}-y^{-2})}\right]=\frac{\left(\frac{1}{x}-\frac{1}{y}\right)}{\left(\frac{1}{x^2}-\frac{1}{y^2}\right)}$

$=\frac{\left(\frac{1}{x}-\frac{1}{y}\right)}{\left[\left(\frac{1}{x}-\frac{1}{y}\right)\left(\frac{1}{x}+\frac{1}{y}\right)\right]}=\frac{1}{\left(\frac{1}{x}+\frac{1}{y}\right)}$

For above expression to be > 1, $\left(\frac{1}{x}+\frac{1}{y}\right)$ has to be less than 1.

For this both 'x' and 'y' have to be greater than 2. Statement I doesn't give any information about this, but statement II clearly specifies this. Hence, only statement II is required to answer the given question.

8. c For no solution, lines must be parallel and not over lapping

$\Rightarrow \frac{2}{k}=\frac{-8}{4}\neq\frac{3}{10}$

$\therefore k=-1$

9. b Let Mushtaq has M cards while Iqbal has got I cards with him.

Let number of cards exchanged be x.

Case 1: $I + x = 4(M - x)$ ... (i)

Case 2: $I - x = 3(M + x)$ ... (ii)

From (i) and (ii),

$I = 31x$.

Only possible value for I could be 31.

10. b The two equations can be simplified into $n \le 2$ and $n \ge 2$. The only value that satisfies both these conditions is $n = 2$.

11. b Let x be the total number of sticks assigned to each boy and y be the number of boxes in which he has to fill them. If he reduces number of sticks per box by 25, he would fill $\left(\frac{x}{y}-25\right)$ in each box and hence he would now fill $(y + 3)$ boxes.

$\therefore x=\left(\frac{x}{y}-25\right)(y+3)=x+\frac{3x}{y}-25y-75.$

$\Rightarrow 3x = (25y + 75)y$

$\Rightarrow x=\frac{(25y^2+75y)}{3}=\frac{25y(y+3)}{3}$

For x to have an integer value, $y(y + 3)$has to be a multiple of 3. This is possible only when y is a multiple of 3. Subsequently, $(y + 3)$ will be a multiple of 3. Therefore, $\frac{25y(y+3)}{3}=x$ will be a multiple of 3. Hence, the correct choice is (b).

12. c **From statement I:** $2X+2Y\le 40$ or $X+Y\le 20$

This statement alone cannot give the value of X.

From statement II: $X-2Y\ge 20$

This statement also alone cannot give the value of X.

On combining statements I and II:

Multiplying the second statement by –1 and adding both the statements, we get

$3Y \le 0$ i.e., $Y \le 0$, but it is given that Y is non negative.

$\therefore Y = 0$ and $X = 20$

Hence, using both statements together we can answer the question.

13. c **From statement I:** Let price per kg of mangoes be Rs.x and price per dozen of oranges be Rs.y.

$\therefore 10x + 2y = 252$

From this statement, we cannot find x.

From statement II: $2x = y$

From this statement also, we cannot find the price per kg of mangoes.

On combining statements I and II: $14x = 252$ i.e., $x = 18$

Hence, using both statements together we can answer the question.

14. c The two equations are : $2o + 3b + 4a = 15$ and $3o + 2b + a = 10$.

Adding the two equations, we get

$5o + 5b + 5a = 25$

$\Rightarrow o + b + a = 5$

$\therefore 3o + 3b + 3a = 15.$

15. b The price of 1 mango is equal to the price of 2 oranges. Hence, 5 mangoes will be equivalent to 10 oranges. So 20 oranges cost Rs.40, therefore one orange will cost Rs.2.

16. b Assume some values of a, b and c such that sum of a, b and c is 0 where $a \neq b \neq c$, and find the value of the given expression.

Let a = 1, b = –1 and c = 0.

$$\Rightarrow \frac{a^2}{2a^2+bc}+\frac{b^2}{2b^2+ac}+\frac{c^2}{2c^2+ab}$$

$$= \frac{1}{2}+\frac{1}{2}+0 = 1.$$

17. a If one root of $x^2 + px + 12 = 0$ is 4, then $4^2 + 4p + 12 = 0$, i.e. $p = -7$.

$x^2 - 7x + q = 0$ has equal roots.

If the roots are α each, $2\alpha = -\frac{(-7)}{1} = 7$, i.e.

$\alpha = \frac{7}{2}$, and $q = \alpha^2 \Rightarrow q = \frac{49}{4}$.

18. d Since the ages of none of them is mentioned and we have two equations and three unknowns.

Hence, we cannot say anything about the ages of any of them.

19. b $2g + 3b = 20$.

Since b & g should be integers the values that satisfy this equation are (g = 10 & b = 0), (g = 7 and b = 2), (g = 4 & b = 4), and (g = 1 and b = 6).

From the statement I, we can shortlist the last two possibilities i.e. g =4 or g = 1, but cannot get a unique answer.

The statement II suggests that the number of girls and boys have to be equal. Hence, we get a unique answer viz. g = 4 & b = 4. Only statement II is required to answer the question.

20. d If the roots are a and a^2, the product of roots = $a^3 = -8$.

$\therefore a = -2$.

Hence, sum of the roots = $k = -(a + a^2) = -(-2 + 4) = -2$.

21. a Let one of the numbers be x. So the other number would be (x + 4).

According to the question, we have

$\frac{1}{x}+\frac{1}{(x+4)} = 21$ or $x = 3$.

Hint: Please note that the sum of reciprocals is basically = $\frac{(\text{Sum of the integers})}{(\text{Product of the integers})}$. So we have to find two integers whose sum is 10 and whose product is 21.

So x + (x + 4)= 10 or x = 3.

22. d $3m^2 - 21m + 30 < 0$

$\therefore m^2 - 7m + 10 < 0 \Rightarrow (m - 5)(m - 2) < 0.$

So either $(m - 5) < 0$ and $(m - 2) > 0$ or $(m - 2) < 0$ and $(m - 5) > 0$.

Hence, either m < 5 and m > 2, i.e., 2 < m < 5 or m < 2 and m > 5.

23. d Statement I is useless as it only tells that if x and y are consecutive positive even integers, then $(x - y)^2$ has to be equal to 4.

Statement II suggests the possibility that the numbers could be 2 and 4. But it does not suggest which is x and which is y.

Hence, we cannot find the value of x using either statements.

24. a If we simplify the expression $x^2 - 3x + 2 > 0$, we get $(x - 1)(x - 2) > 0$. For this product to be greater than zero, either both the factors should be greater than zero or both of them should be less than zero. Therefore, $(x - 1) > 0$ and $(x - 2) > 0$ or $(x - 1) < 0$ and $(x - 2) < 0$. Hence, x > 1 and x > 2 or x < 1 and $x < 2$. If we were to club the ranges, we would get either $x > 2$ or $x < 1$. So for any value of x equal to or between 1 and 2, the above equation does not follow.

25. d If we write the given equation in the conventional form, i.e. $ax^2 + bx + c = 0$, $a = 1$, $b = -(A-3)$, i.e. $(3-A)$ and $c = -(A-2)$, i.e. $(2-A)$. Let the roots of this equation be α and β. So the sum of the squares of the roots $= \alpha^2 + \beta^2 = (\alpha+\beta)^2 - 2\alpha\beta$.

Now $(\alpha+\beta)$= Sum of the roots $= \frac{-b}{a} = \frac{(A-3)}{1}$ $= (A-3)$ and $\alpha\beta$ = Product of the roots $= \frac{c}{a}$ $= \frac{(2-A)}{1} = (2-A)$. Hence, $\alpha^2+\beta^2 = (A-3)^2 - 2(2-A)$ $= A^2 - 4A + 5 = 0$. None of the answer choices matches this.

26. d Using statement II, $2\alpha\beta = \frac{c}{a} = \alpha\beta$

$\Rightarrow \alpha = 0$ or $\beta = 0$ or α and $\beta = 0$

Hence, the question cannot be answered.

27. b $$\frac{1}{1+\frac{1}{3-\frac{4}{2+\frac{1}{3-\frac{1}{2}}}}} + \frac{3}{3-\frac{4}{3+\frac{1}{2-\frac{1}{2}}}}$$

$$= \frac{1}{1+\frac{1}{3-\frac{4}{2+\frac{2}{5}}}} + \frac{3}{3-\frac{4}{3+\frac{1}{\frac{3}{2}}}}$$

$$= \frac{1}{1+\frac{1}{3-\frac{4}{\frac{12}{5}}}} + \frac{3}{3-\frac{4}{3+\frac{1}{\frac{3}{2}}}}$$

$$= \frac{1}{1+\frac{1}{3-\frac{5}{3}}} + \frac{3}{3-\frac{4}{3+\frac{2}{3}}}$$

$$= \frac{1}{1+\frac{1}{\frac{4}{3}}} + \frac{3}{3-\frac{4}{\frac{11}{3}}} = \frac{1}{1+\frac{3}{4}} + \frac{3}{3-\frac{12}{11}}$$

$$= \frac{1}{1+\frac{3}{4}} + \frac{3}{3-\frac{12}{11}} = \frac{1}{\frac{7}{4}} + \frac{3}{\frac{21}{11}}$$

$$= \frac{4}{7} + \frac{11}{7} = \frac{15}{7}$$

28. d $$A = \frac{2.000004}{[(2.000004)^2 + 2(2.000004)]}$$

$$= \frac{2.000004}{2.000004[(2.000004)+2]}$$

$$= \frac{1}{[(2.000004)+2]}$$

$$= \frac{1}{4.000004}$$

$$= \frac{1}{4} = 0.25 \text{ (Approximately)}$$

$$B = \frac{3.000003}{[(3.000003)^2 + 3(3.000003)]}$$

$$= \frac{3.000003}{3.000003[(3.000003)+3]}$$

$$= \frac{1}{[(3.000003)+3]} = \frac{1}{6.000003}$$

$$C = \frac{4.000002}{[(4.000002)^2 + 2(4.000002)]}$$

$$= \frac{4.000002}{4.000002[(4.000002)+2]}$$

$$= \frac{1}{[(4.000002)+2]} = \frac{1}{6.000002}$$

Looking at the answer choices, we can see that the only (d)satisfies the relationship, viz. B is the smallest.

29. a This equation is very straightforward. If the number is 'x', then $\frac{7x}{8} - \frac{7x}{18} = 770$. On solving this equation, we get $x = 1584$.

Hint: Students please note that if the difference in $\frac{7}{8}$ and $\frac{7}{18}$ of a number is 770, then the difference in $\frac{1}{8}$ and $\frac{1}{18}$ of the number should be 110. If we express this as an equation, we get

$$\frac{x}{8} - \frac{x}{18} = 110$$

or $10x = 110 \times 18 \times 8$

or $x = 11 \times 18 \times 8$

You can further proceed from here in two ways: (i) the last digit of the required answer should be $(1 \times 8 \times 8) = 4$, (ii)number should be divisible by 11. In both cases, the answer that is obtained from the given choices is 1584.

30. a We know that the sum of the roots $= -\frac{b}{a}$.
Hence, $x_1 + x_2 = 2$. Now we have two equations, viz.

$x_1 + x_2 = 2$ ...(i)

and $7x_2 - 4x_1 = 47$ ...(ii)

Solving these two equations, we get $x_1 = -3$ and $x_2 = 5$. Since it does not satisfy options (b) and (c), we will verify it for option (a). The product of the roots $= (-3) \times 5 = -15$, $\frac{c}{a}$ in our case is c. Hence, $c = -15$.

Alternative method:

Put values of x_1, x_2 in equation (ii). Do not match. So put $c = -15$ in equation (i) to get the roots of equation. After finding the roots of equation (i), check whether they satisfy equation (ii) or not. The roots (5, –3)satisfy the equation (ii) so answer is (a).

31. d Students! be careful. Generally, as we see two unknowns (i.e. x and y in this case) and two equations, we tempt to mark the answer as (c), i.e. combining two statements, we can easily find the values of x and y.

But have a look at the equations $3x + 2y = 45$ and $10.5x + 7y = 157.5$. Multiplying 1st equation by 3.5, we get 2nd equation. Hence, these are not really two different equations. Hence, data is insufficient to answer the question. In general, remember the following rule. If we have two equations $Ax + By = k_1$ and $Cx + Dy = k_2$, and $A \times D = B \times C$, then the equations cannot be solved.

32. a

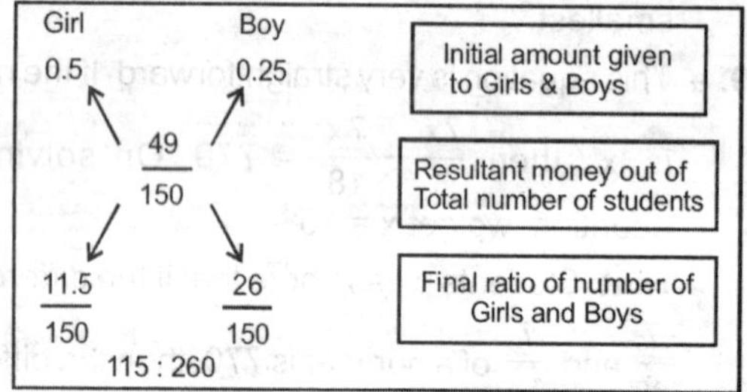

Using the first statement alone, we can alligate and find the ratio of boys to girls and hence the number of girls, i.e. as shown in the adjacent diagram, 150 students when divided in the ratio 115 : 260, give 46 girls and 104 boys. The second statement, however, does not throw any further light on the data given in the question as it simply suggests $0.3B + 0.3G = 45$ or $B + G = 150$, which is already known. Hence, only statement I is required to answer the question.

33. a The difference between two integers will be 1, only if one is even and the other one is odd. 4x will always be even, so 17y has to be odd and hence, y has to be odd.

Moreover, the number 17y should be such a number that is 1 less than a multiple of 4. In other words, we have to find all such multiples of 17, which are 1 less than a multiple of 4. The first such multiple is 51. Now you will find that as the multiples of 17 goes on increasing, the difference between it and its closest higher multiple of 4 is in the following pattern, 0, 3, 2, 1, E.g. $52 - 51 = 1$, $68 - 68 = 0$, $88 - 85 = 3$, $104 - 102 = 2$, $120 - 119 = 1$, $136 - 136 = 0$

So the multiples of 17 that we are interested in are 3, 7, 11, 15.

Now since $x \le 1000$, $4x \le 4000$. The multiple of 17 closest and less than 4000 is 3995 (17 × 235). And incidentally, 3996 is a multiple of 4, i.e. the difference is 4.

This means that in order to find the answer, we need to find the number of terms in the AP formed by 3, 7, 11, 15, ... 235, where a = 3, d = 4.

Since we know that $T_n = a + (n - 1)d$

$\Rightarrow 235 = 3 + (n - 1) \times 4$

Hence, n = 59.

Alternate Solution:

$4x - 17y = 1$ and $x \le 1000$

so $17y + 1 \le 4000$ i.e. $y \le 235$ and moreover every 4th value of y with give value of x.

So number of values $= \frac{235}{4} \approx 58$

Hence, total number of terms will be 58 + 1 = 59

34. d Statement I when used to solve the sum gives us the same equation as the second substituted in to the first equation.

$kdx + key = kf$

$\therefore\ k(dx + ey) = kf$

as $k \neq 0$, $dx + ey = f$ which is same as second equation.

So it is of no use as we get infinite solutions and not a unique one.

Statement II gives us the following equations.

$$x + y = c$$
$$2x + 2y = f.$$

These are two linear equations in x and y, such that $\frac{1}{2} = \frac{1}{2} \neq \frac{c}{f}$.

As $\frac{c}{f} \neq \frac{1}{2}$ (Given), the system will have no solution.

As the data given in both the statements is inconsistent, the question cannot be answered.

35. b The data is not linear. So check (b).

Let the equation be $y = a + bx + cx^2$.

Putting the values of x and y, we get the following result.

$\Rightarrow 4 = a + b + c, 8 = a + 2b + 4c$ and $14 = a + 3b + 9c$.

Solving these, we get a = 2, b = 1 and c = 1.

So the equation is $y = 2 + x + x^2$.

36. b Use choices. The answer is (b), because $-x < -2$ and $-2 < 2y \Rightarrow -x < 2y$.

37. b Use the choices. If b = 1, then the factors are (x – a) $(x^2 + 1)$. This cannot yield 3 real roots.

38. a Let the number of direct roads from A to B, B to C and C to A be x, y and z respectively. Then, x + yz = 33, y + xz = 23. Hence, by solving, we get z = 6.

39. d Work with options. If the cylinder has a capacity of 1,200 L, then the conical vessel shall have a capacity of 700 L. Once 200 L have been taken out from the same, the remaining volume in each of them shall be 1000 and 500.

Alternative method:

Let the volume of conical tank be x.

Then the volume of cylindrical tank = x + 500

$x + 300 = 2(x - 200)$

$\Rightarrow x = 700$

Volume of cylindrical tank = 700 + 500 = 1200L.

40. a The first statement implies that X must lie between 0 and – 3. Hence, it gives the answer. But from the second statement, we have either X > 3 or X < 0. This does not gives us any information about the modulus of X.

41. d $x > 5, y < -1$

Use answer choices.

Take x = 6, y = –6. We see none of the statements (a), (b) and (c) is true. Hence, the correct option is (d).

42. a Let the four-digit number be abcd.

$a + b = c + d$ ... (i)

$b + d = 2(a + c)$ ... (ii)

$a + d = c$ ... (iii)

From (i) and (iii), b = 2d

From (i) and (ii), 3b = 4c + d

$\Rightarrow 3(2d) = 4c + d$

$\Rightarrow 5d = 4c$

$\Rightarrow c = \frac{5}{4}d$

Now, d can be 4 or 8.

But if d = 8, then c = 10 not possible.

So d = 4 which gives c = 5.

43. d Let there be x mints originally in the bowl.

Sita took $\frac{1}{3}$, but returned 4. So now the bowl has

$\frac{2}{3}x + 4$ mints.

Fatima took $\frac{1}{4}$ of the remainder, but returned 3.

So the bowl now has $\frac{3}{4}\left(\frac{2}{3}x + 4\right) + 3$ mints.

Eshwari took half of remainder that is

$$\frac{1}{2}\left[\frac{3}{4}\left(\frac{2}{3}x + 4\right) + 3\right]$$

She returns 2, so the bowl now has

$$\frac{1}{2}\left[\frac{3}{4}\left(\frac{2}{3}x + 4\right) + 3\right] + 2 = 17 \Rightarrow x = 48$$

Short cut:

Since Sita was the first person to pick and she picks up $\frac{1}{3}$ of the mint, but if you see the options, none of the option is a multiple of 3.

44. d Let the number be x.

Increase in product = 53x – 35x = 18x

$\Rightarrow 18x = 540 \Rightarrow x = 30$

Hence, new product = 53 × 30 = 1590.

45. c The value of y would be negative and the value of x would be positive from the inequalities given in the question.

Therefore, from (a), y becomes positive. The value of xy^2 would be positive and will not be the minimum.

From (b)and (c), x^2y and 5xy would give negative values but we do not know which would be the minimum.

On comparing (a)and (c), we find that

$x^2 < 5x$ in $2 < x < 3$.

$\therefore x^2y > 5xy$ [Since y is negative.]

$\therefore$ 5xy would give the minimum value.

46. d Let $y = n^3 - 7n^2 + 11n - 5$

At n = 1, y = 0

$\therefore (n-1)(n^2 - 6n + 5) = (n-1)^2(n-5)$

Now $(n-1)^2$ is always positive.

For n < 5, the expression gives a negative quantity.

Therefore, the least value of n will be 6.

Hence, m = 6.

47. c Let 'x' be the number of males in Mota Hazri.

	Chota Hazri	Mota Hazri
Males	x – 4522	x
Females	2(x – 4522)	x + 4020

$x + 4020 - 2(x - 4522) = 2910 \Rightarrow x = 10154$

∴ Number of males in Chota Hazri = 10154 – 4522 = 5632

48. a Let the cost of 1 burger, 1 shake and 1 fries be x, y and z.

Then,

$3x + 7y + z = 120$ ... (i)

$\underline{4x + 10y + z = 164.50}$ ... (ii)

$x + 3y = 44.50$ ... (iii) (ii – i)

Multiplying (iii) by 4 and subtracting (ii) from it, we get

$2y - z = 13.50$ ...(iv)

Subtracting (iv) from (iii), we get x + y + z = 31.

49. b From II, b = 2d

Hence, b = 10, d = 5 or b = 4, d = 2

From III, e + a = 10 or e + a = 4

From I, a + c = e or e – a = c

From III and I, we get 2e = 10 + c or 2e = 4 + c

$\Rightarrow e = 5 + \frac{c}{2}$ ... (i)

or $e = 2 + \frac{c}{2}$ ... (ii)

From (i), we can take c = 2, 4, 6, 10.

For c = 2, e = 6

c = 4, e = 7 (Not possible)

c = 6, c = 8 (Not possible)

c = 10, e = 10 (Not possible since both c and e cannot be 10)

From (ii), we have c = 2, 4, 6, 10.

For c = 2, e = 3 (Not possible)

c = 4, e = 4 (Not possible)

c = 6, e = 5 (Possible)

c = 10, e = 7 (Not possible)

Considering the possibility from B that c = 6 and ⇒ e = 5 means e + a = 4

⇒ a = –1 (Not possible)

Hence, only possibility is b = 10, d = 5, c = 2, e = 6.

e + a = 10 ⇒ a = 4

50. a Quadratic equation having roots (4, 3) is

$(x - 4)(x - 3) = 0$

$\Rightarrow x^2 - 7x + 12 = 0$ ... (i)

Quadratic equation having roots (3, 2) is

$(x - 3)(x - 2) = 0$

$\Rightarrow x^2 - 5x + 6 = 0$ ... (ii)

Picking the coefficient of x from (i) and the constant term from (ii), we get the required equation

$x^2 - 7x + 6 = 0$

$\Rightarrow (x - 6)(x - 1) = 0$

∴ x = 1, 6

Hence, actual roots are (6,1).

Alternate method:

Since constant = [3 × 2] and coefficient of

⇒ x = [–4x – 3x] = –7

Since quadratic equation is

x^2 – (Sum of roots)x + Product of roots = 0

or $x^2 - 7x + 6 = 0$

Solving the equation,

(x – 6)(x – 1) = 0 or x = (6, 1).

51. b Let the number of five-rupee, two-rupee and one-rupee coins be x, y and z respectively.

$x + y + z = 300$

$5x + 2y + z = 960$

$\underline{5x + y + 2z = 920}$

$y - z = 40$

And $x + 2y = 340$

Using the answer choices, y = 140 satisfies all the given conditions.

52. c $xy + yz + zx = 3$

$\Rightarrow xy + (y + x)z = 3$

$\Rightarrow xy + (y + x)(5 - x - y) = 3$

$\Rightarrow x^2 + y^2 + xy - 5x - 5y + 3 = 0$

$\Rightarrow y^2 + (x - 5)y + x^2 - 5x + 3 = 0$

As it is given that y is a real number, the discriminant for above equation must be greater than or equal to zero.

Hence, $(x - 5)^2 - 4(x^2 - 5x + 3) \geq 0$

$\Rightarrow 3x^2 - 10x - 13 \leq 0$

$\Rightarrow 3x^2 - 13x + 3x - 13 \leq 0$

$\Rightarrow x \in \left[-1, \frac{13}{3}\right]$

Largest value that x can have is $\frac{13}{3}$.

53. d Let the number of gold coins = x + y

∴ $48(x - y) = x^2 - y^2$

$\Rightarrow 48(x - y) = (x - y)(x + y)$

$\Rightarrow x + y = 48$

Hence, the correct choice will be none of these.

54. c Let's assume that

p days : they played tennis

y days : they went for yoga

T days : total duration for which Ram and Shyam stayed together

$\Rightarrow$ p + y = 22

(T – y) = 24 and (T – p) = 14

Adding all of them,

2T = 22 + 24 + 14 $\Rightarrow$ T = 30 days.

55. c $x^2 + 5y^2 + z^2 = 4yx + 2yz$

$\Rightarrow \left(x^2 + 4y^2 - 4yx\right) + \left(z^2 + y^2 - 2yz\right) = 0$

$\Rightarrow (x - 2y)^2 + (z - y)^2 = 0$

It can be true only if x = 2y and z = y

56. d $\dfrac{A^2}{x} + \dfrac{B^2}{x-1} = 1 \Rightarrow A^2(x-1) + B^2x = x^2 - x$

When one of A or B is zero, it will be a linear equation which will have one real root. When both A and B are non-zero, it will be a quadratic equation which can have two real roots.

57. c Let the largest piece = 3x

Middle = x

Shortest = 3x – 23

$\therefore$ 3x + x + (3x – 23)= 40

$\Rightarrow$ x = 9

$\therefore$ the shortest piece = 3(9) – 23 = 4

58. a From (A), $(x + y\left(\dfrac{1}{x} + \dfrac{1}{y}\right)) = 4$ or $(x + y\left(\dfrac{y+x}{xy}\right)) = 4$

$\Rightarrow (x + y)^2 = 4xy$

$\Rightarrow (x - y)^2 = 0$

$\Rightarrow$ x = y ... (i)

From (B), $(x - 50)^2 = (y - 50)^2$

On solving,

x(x – 100) = y(y – 100) ... (ii)

This suggests that the values of x and y can either be 0 or 100.

59. b From statement A, we know that for all –1 < x < 1, we can determine |x – 2| < 1 is not true. Therefore, statement A alone is sufficient.

From statement B, –1 < x < 3, we cannot determinewhether |x – 2| < 1 or not. Therefore, statement B alone is sufficient.

60. b $ax^2 + bx + 1 = 0$

For real roots, $b^2 - 4ac \geq 0$

$\therefore b^2 - 4a(1) \geq 0$

$\Rightarrow b^2 \geq 4a$

For a = 1, 4a = 4 $\Rightarrow$ b = 2, 3, 4

a = 2, 4a = 8 $\Rightarrow$ b = 3, 4

a = 3, 4a = 12 $\Rightarrow$ b = 4

a = 4, 4a = 16 $\Rightarrow$ b = 4

$\therefore$ Number of equations possible = 7.

61. c 5x + 19y = 64

We see that if y =1, we get an integer solution for x = 9. Now, if y changes (increases or decreases) by 5x will change (decrease or increase) by 19. Looking at the options, if x = 294, we get y = –74. Using these values we see options (a), (b)and (d) are eliminated and also that there exists a solution for 250 < x ≤ 300.

62. a Let α be the common root.

$\therefore \alpha^3 + 3\alpha^2 + 4\alpha + 5 = 0$

$\Rightarrow \alpha^3 + 2\alpha^3 + 7\alpha + 3 = 0$

$\Rightarrow \alpha^2 - 3\alpha + 2 = 0$

$\alpha = 2,\ \alpha = 1$

But the above values of α do not satisfy any of the equations. Thus, no root is common.

63. c $1 - \dfrac{1}{n} < x \leq 3 + \dfrac{1}{n}$

Putting n = 1

$\therefore 0 < x \leq 4$

64. d $36 \leq n \leq 72$

$x = \dfrac{n^2 + 2\sqrt{n}(n+4) + 16}{n + 4\sqrt{n} + 4}$

Putting n = 36, we get

$x = \dfrac{(36)^2 + 2 \times 6 \times 40 + 16}{36 + 24 + 4} = 28$

which is least value of x.

65. d 13x + 1 < 2z and z + 3 = $5y^2$

$\Rightarrow 13x + 1 < 2(5y^2 - 3)$

$\Rightarrow 13x + 1 < 10y^2 - 6$

$\Rightarrow 13x + 7 < 10y^2$

Putting x = 1

$20 < 10y^2 \Rightarrow y^2 > 2$

$\Rightarrow (y^2-2)>0 \Rightarrow (y+\sqrt{2})(y-\sqrt{2})>0.$

$\therefore y \in (-\infty,-\sqrt{2}) \cup (\sqrt{2},\infty)$

x = 1

$-\sqrt{2}$ 0 $\sqrt{2}$ y

66. a $F + n = 4(k + n)$ ... (i)

$M + n = 3(k + n)$ ...(ii)

From the above equations

$F - M = (k + n)$

From statement A

$F - M = 10 \Rightarrow k + n = 10$

$F + n = 40$

$M + n = 30$

$\Rightarrow F + M + 2n = 70$

Hence, from statement A alone, we can get the answer.

67. c $2^x - x - 1 = 0$

$\Rightarrow 2^x - 1 = x$

If we put x = 0, then this is satisfied and if we put x = 1, then also this is satisfied.

Now, if we put x = 2, the equation this is not valid.

68. a It is given that $p+q+r \neq 0$. If we consider the option (a), and multiply the first equation by 5, second by –2 and third by –1, we see that the coefficients of x, y and z all add upto zero.

Thus, $5p - 2q - r = 0$

No other option satisfies this.

69. a Let 'x' be the number of standard bags and 'y' be the number of deluxe bags.

Thus, $4x + 5y \leq 700$ and $6x + 10y \leq 1250$

Among the choices, (c)and (d) do not satisfy the second equation.

Choice (b)is eliminated as, in order to maximize profits, the number of deluxe bags should be higher than the number of standard bags because the profit margin is higher in a deluxe bag.

70. c Let the number of correct answers be 'x', number of wrong answers be 'y' and number of questions not attempted be 'z'.

Thus, $x + y + z = 50$ ... (i)

And $x - \frac{y}{3} - \frac{z}{6} = 32$

The second equation can be written as,

$6x - 2y - z = 192$ ... (ii)

Adding the two equations we get,

$7x - y = 242$ or $x = \frac{242}{7} + y$

Since x and y are both integers, y cannot be 1 or 2. The minimum value that y can have is 3.

71. d $p + q = \alpha - 2$ and $pq = -\alpha - 1$

$(p + q)^2 = p^2 + q^2 + 2pq,$

Thus $(\alpha - 2)^2 = p^2 + q^2 + 2(-\alpha - 1)$

$p^2 + q^2 = \alpha^2 - 4\alpha + 4 + 2\alpha + 2$

$p^2 + q^2 = \alpha^2 - 2\alpha + 6$

$p^2 + q^2 = \alpha^2 - 2\alpha + 1 + 5$

$p^2 + q^2 = (\alpha - 1)^2 + 5$

Thus, minimum value of $p^2 + q^2$ is 5.

72. b $(a + b + c + d)^2 = (4m + 1)^2$

Thus, $a^2 + b^2 + c^2 + d^2 + 2(ab + ac + ad + bc + bd + cd) = 16m^2 + 8m + 1$

$a^2 + b^2 + c^2 + d^2$ will have the minimum value if $(ab + ac + ad + bc + bd + cd)$ is the maximum.

This is possible if $a = b = c = d = (m + 0.25)$ [since $a + b + c + d = 4m + 1$]

In that case, $2(ab + ac + ad + bc + bd + cd)$

$= 12(m + 0.25)^2 = 12m^2 + 6m + 0.75$

Thus, the minimum value of $a^2 + b^2 + c^2 + d^2$

$= (16m^2 + 8m + 1) - 2(ab + ac + ad + bc + bd + cd)$

$= (16m^2 + 8m + 1) - (12m^2 + 6m + 0.75)$

$= 4m^2 + 2m + 0.25$

Since it is an integer, the actual minimum value $= 4m^2 + 2m + 1$

73. b u is always negative. Hence, for us to have a minimum value of $\frac{vz}{u}$, vz should be positive. Also, for the least value, the numerator has to be the maximum positive value and the denominator has to be the smallest negative value. In other words, vz has to be 2 and u has to be –0.5.

Hence, the minimum value of $\frac{vz}{u} = \frac{2}{-0.5} = -4.$

To get the maximum value, vz has to be the smallest negative value and u has to be the highest negative value. Thus, vz has to be –2 and u has to be –0.5.

Hence, the maximum value of $\frac{vz}{u} = \frac{-2}{-0.5} = 4.$

74. c Here x, y, z are distinct positive real number

So $\dfrac{x^2(y+z)+y^2(x+2)+z^2(x+y)}{xyz}$

$=\dfrac{x}{y}+\dfrac{x}{z}+\dfrac{y}{x}+\dfrac{y}{z}+\dfrac{z}{x}+\dfrac{z}{y}$

$=\left(\dfrac{x}{y}+\dfrac{y}{x}\right)+\left(\dfrac{y}{z}+\dfrac{z}{y}\right)+\left(\dfrac{z}{x}+\dfrac{x}{z}\right)$

[We know that $\dfrac{a}{b}+\dfrac{b}{a}>2$ if a and b are distinct numbers]

> 2 + 2 + 2 i.e. > 6

75. c Since Ms. X bought 21 packets out of which there are 18 O's and A's in total. Since she got one S, there has to be 2 P's which she bought. Hence, both the statements are required to answer the question.

76. b Solution can be found using Statement A alone as we know both the roots for the equation (viz. $\frac{1}{2}$ and $-\frac{1}{2}$).

Also, statement B alone is sufficient.

Since ratio of c and b = 1, c = b.

Thus, the equation is $4x^2 + bx + b = 0$. Since $x = -\frac{1}{2}$ is one of the roots, substituting, we get $1 - \frac{b}{2} + b = 0$ or b = –2.

Thus, c = –2.

77. d $y=\dfrac{1}{2+\dfrac{1}{3+y}}$

$\Rightarrow y=\dfrac{3+y}{7+2y}$

$\Rightarrow 2y^2+6y-3=0$

$\Rightarrow y=\dfrac{-6\pm\sqrt{36+24}}{4}$

$=\dfrac{-6\pm\sqrt{60}}{4}=\dfrac{-3\pm\sqrt{15}}{2}$

Since 'y' is a +ve number, therefore:

$y=\dfrac{\sqrt{15}-3}{2}$.

78. d

Family	Adults	Children
I	0, 1, 2	3, 4, 5, ...
II	0, 1, 2	3, 4, 5, ...
III	0, 1, 2	3, 4, 5, ...

As per the question, we need to satisfy three conditions namely:

1. Adults (A) > Boys (B)
2. Boys (B) > Girls (G)
3. Girls (G) > Families (F)

Clearly, if the number of families is 2, maximum number of adults can only be 4. Now, for the second condition to be satisfied, every family should have atleast two boys and one girl each. This will result in non-compliance with the first condition because adults will be equal to boys. If we consider the same conditions for 3 families, then all three conditions will be satisfied.

79. c Given equation is x + y = xy

$\Rightarrow xy - x - y + 1 = 1$

$\Rightarrow (x-1)(y-1) = 1$

$\therefore x-1=1$ and $y-1=1$ or $x-1=-1$ and $y-1=-1$

Clearly, (0, 0) and (2, 2)are the only pairs that will satisfy the equation.

80. a Since Group (B)contains 23 questions, the marks associated with this group are 46.

Now check for option (a). If Group (C) has one question, then marks associated with this group will be 3. This means that the cumulative marks for these two groups taken together will be 49. Since total number of questions are 100, Group (A) will have 76 questions, the corresponding weightage being 76 marks. This satisfies all conditions and hence is the correct option. It can be easily observed that no other option will fit the bill.

81. c Since Group (C)contains 8 questions, the corresponding weightage will be 24 marks. This figure should be less than or equal to 20% of the total marks. Check from the options . Option (c) provides 13 or 14 questions in Group (B), with a corresponding weightage of 26 or 28 marks. This means that number of questions in Group (A) will either be 79 or 78 and will satisty the desired requirement.

82. c **Statement A:** 2 kg potato cost + 1 kg gourd cost < 1 kg potato cost + 1 kg gourd cost

⇒ 1 kg potato cost < 1 kg gourd cost.

Hence, statement A is not sufficient.

Statement B: 1 kg potato cost + 2 kg onion cost = 1 kg onion cost + 2 kg gourd cost

1 kg potato cost + 1 kg onion cost = 2 kg gourd cost.

Hence, statement B is also not sufficient.

Combining both statements, we get

1 kg potato cost < 1 kg gourd cost ...(i)

1 kg potato cost + 1 kg onion cost = 2 kg gourd cost ...(ii)

Hence, onion is the costliest.

83. d **Statement A:** 13 currency notes will give different values.

Statement B: Multiple of 10 and by many.

Even if you combine the statement, we can have various values. Hence, the correct option is (d).

84. c $y^2 = x^2$

$2x^2 - 2kx + k^2 - 1 = 0$

D = 0

$\Rightarrow 4k^2 = 8k^2 - 8$

$\Rightarrow 4k^2 = 8$

$\Rightarrow k^2 = 2$

$\Rightarrow k = \pm\sqrt{2}$.

$k = +\sqrt{2}$ gives the equation $2x^2 - 2\sqrt{2}x + 1 = 0$;

Its root is $\frac{-b}{2a} = +\frac{1}{\sqrt{2}}$, $k = -\sqrt{2}$ gives the equation $2x^2 + 2\sqrt{2}x + 1 = 0$. Its root is $-\frac{1}{\sqrt{2}}$ this root is –ve, will reject $k = -\sqrt{2}$.

Only answer is $k = +\sqrt{2}$.

Alternate:

Graph based.

$x^2 - y^2 = 0$ & $(x - k)^2 + y^2 = 1$ are plotted below.

We are solving for a unique positive x.

$x^2 - y^2 = 0$ is a pair of straight lines

y = x & y = –x

$(x - k)^2 + y^2 = 1$ is a circle with center (k, 0) & radius 1.

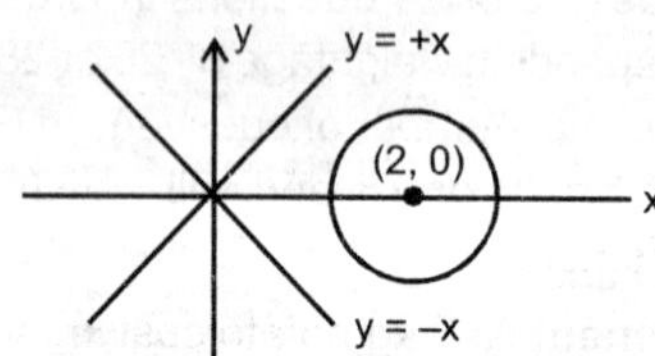

(a) k = 2; clearly, no solution

(b) k = 0

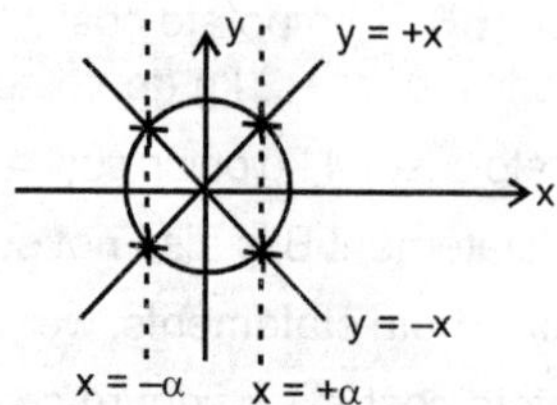

x = α, –α are its two solutions.

– rejected.

(c) $k = +\sqrt{2}$

unique value of x & a positive one as shown.

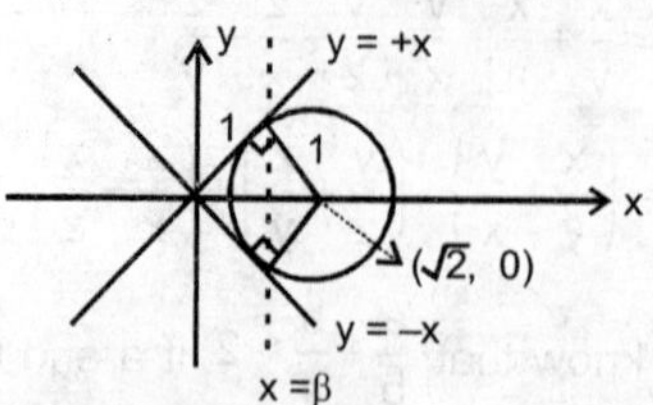

(d) $k = -\sqrt{2}$, also gives the unique value of x but it is negative one.

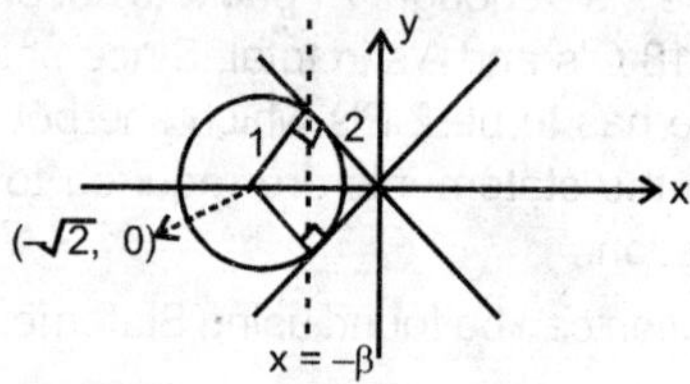

85. c $x = \sqrt{4 + \sqrt{4 - x}} \Rightarrow x^2 = 4 + \sqrt{4 - x}$

$\Rightarrow (x^2 - 4) = \sqrt{4 - x}$

Now putting the values from options, we find only option (c) satisfies the condition.

86. d There are two equations to be formed 40 m + 50 f = 1000

250 m + 300 f + 40 × 15 m + 50 × 10 × f = A

850 m + 8000 f = A

m and f are the number of males and females A is amount paid by the employer.

Then, the possible values of f = 8, 9, 10, 11, 12

If f = 8, m = 15.

If f = 9, 10, 11 then m will not be an integer while f = 12, then m will be 10.

By putting f = 8 and m = 15, A = 18800. When f = 12 and m = 10, then A = 18100

Therefore, the number of males will be 10.

For questions 87 and 88:

Let for Raja allowed luggage be A and excess luggage be E

∴ For Praja, his luggage must be A + 2E.

If all luggage belongs to one, (A + 3E) is the excess.

E corresponds to Rs. 1,200.

∴ A must correspond to (5400 – 3600) = Rs. 1,800

If E = 2x, A = 3x

So total weight = 2(A)+ 3E = 12x

$\Rightarrow$ x = 5

Hence, Praja's luggage weight = 7x = 35 kg

Alternate method:

Let Raja = x kg, Free allowance = F kg and Praja = (60 – x) kg

According to the question,

$(x - F)V = 1200$ ... (i)

{V = rate of levy on excess luggage}

$(60 - x - F)V = 2400$ ... (ii)

$(60 - F)V = 5400$ ... (iii)

Dividing equation (ii)by (i), we get $\frac{60 - x - F}{x - F} = 2$

$\Rightarrow 60 - x - F = 2x - 2F$

$\Rightarrow 3x - F = 60$ ...(iv)

Dividing (iii) by (i), we get

$\Rightarrow \frac{60 - F}{x - F} = 4.5$

$\Rightarrow 60 - F = 4.5x - 4.5F$

$\Rightarrow 4.5x - 3.5F = 60$ ...(v)

Multiplying equation (iv)by 1.5,

$4.5x - 1.5F = 90$

$4.5x - 3.5F = 60$

$2F = 30$

$\Rightarrow F = 15$

Putting value of F in (iv), we get

$3x = 75 \Rightarrow x = 25$

87. d Praja have 35 kg luggage

88. b 15 kg.

89. a $x^{2/3} + x^{1/3} - 2 \le 0$

$\Rightarrow x^{2/3} + 2x^{1/3} - x^{1/3} - 2 \le 0$

$\Rightarrow (x^{1/3} - 1)(x^{1/3} + 2) \le 0$

$\Rightarrow -2 \le x^{1/3} \le 1 \Rightarrow -8 \le x \le 1$

90. b $2x + y = 40$

$x \le y$

$\Rightarrow y = 40 - 2x$

Values of x and y that satisfy the equation

x	y
1	38
2	36
3	34
.	.
.	.
.	.
13	14

∴ 13 values of (x, y)satisfy the equation such that $x \le y$

91. b Let the number be 10x + y so when number is reversed the number because 10y + x. So, the number increases by 18

Hence, $(10y + x) - (10x + y) = 9(y - x) = 18$

$\Rightarrow y - x = 2$

So, the possible pairs of (x, y) are (3, 1) (4, 2)(5, 3) (6, 4), (7, 5) (8, 6) (9, 7)

But we want the number other than 13 so, there are 6 possible numbers, i.e. 24, 35, 46, 57, 68, 79.

So total possible numbers are 6.

92. c Let the number of currency 1 Miso, 10 Misos and 50 Misos be x, y and z respectively.

$\Rightarrow x + 10y + 50z = 107$

Now the possible values of z could be 0, 1 and 2.

For z = 0: $x + 10y = 107$

Number of integral pairs of values of x and y that satisfy the equation $x + 10y = 107$ will be 11. These values of x and y in that order are (7, 10); (17, 9); (27, 8); ... (107, 0).

For z = 1: $x + 10y = 57$

Number of integral pairs of values of x and y that satisfy the equation $x + 10y = 57$ will be 6. These values of x and y in that order are (7, 5); (17, 4); (27, 3); (37, 2); (47, 1) and (57, 0).

For z = 2: $x + 10y = 7$

There is only one integer value of x and y that satisfies the equation $x + 10y = 7$ in that order is (7, 0).

Therefore, total number of ways in which you can pay a bill of 107 Misos = 11 + 6 + 1 = 18

93. d Suppose the cheque for Shailaja is of Rs. X and Y paise

As per the question,

$3 \times (100X + Y) = (100Y + X) - 50$

$\Rightarrow 299X = 97Y - 50$

$\Rightarrow Y = \frac{299X + 50}{97}$

Now the value of Y should be a integer.

Checking by options only for X = 18, Y is a integer and the value of Y = 56

94. e $\frac{1}{m} + \frac{4}{n} = \frac{1}{12}, n < 60$

$\Rightarrow \frac{1}{m} = \frac{1}{12} - \frac{4}{n} = \frac{n - 48}{12n}$

$\Rightarrow m = \frac{12n}{n - 48}$

Positive integral values of m for odd integral values of n are for n = 49, 51 and 57.

Therefore, there are 3 integral pairs of values of m and n that satisfy the given equation.

95. b Let $f(x) = ax^2 + bx + c$

At x = 1, f(1)= a + b + c = 3

At x = 0, f(0) = c = 1

The maximum of the function f(x) is attained at

$$x = -\frac{b}{2a} = 1 = \frac{a-2}{2a}$$

$\Rightarrow$ a = –2 and b = 4

$\therefore \quad f(x) = -2x^2 + 4x + 1$

Therefore, f(10)= –159

96. a **Using statement A:** x = 30, y = 30 and z = 29 will give the minimum value.

Using statement B: Nothing specific can be said about the relation between x, y and z.

Hence, option (a)is the correct choice.

97. b $x^3 - ax^2 + bx - c = 0$

Let the roots of the above cubic equation be $(\alpha - 1), \alpha, (\alpha + 1)$

$\Rightarrow \alpha(\alpha - 1) + \alpha(\alpha + 1) + (\alpha + 1)(\alpha - 1) = b$

$\Rightarrow \alpha^2 - \alpha + \alpha^2 + \alpha + \alpha^2 - 1 = b \Rightarrow 3\alpha^2 - 1 = b$

Thus, the minimum possible value of 'b' will be equal to – 1 and this value is attained at $\alpha = 0$.

98. a Let the three consecutive positive integers be equal to 'n – 1', 'n' and 'n + 1'.

$\Rightarrow n - 1 + n^2 + (n+1)^3 = (3n)^2$

$\Rightarrow n^3 + 4n^2 + 4n = 9n^2$

$\Rightarrow n^2 - 5n + 4 = 0$

$\therefore n = 1$ or $n = 4$

Since the three integers are positive, the value of 'n' cannot be equal to 1, therefore the value of 'n' = 4 or m = n – 1 = 3.

Hence, the three consecutive positive integers are 3, 4 and 5.

99. b Amount of rice bought by the first customer

$$= \left(\frac{x}{2} + \frac{1}{2}\right) \text{kgs}$$

Amount of rice remaining

$$= x - \left(\frac{x}{2} + \frac{1}{2}\right) = \frac{x-1}{2} \text{kgs}$$

Amount of rice bought by the second customer

$$= \frac{1}{2} \times \left(\frac{x-1}{2}\right) + \frac{1}{2} = \frac{x+1}{4} \text{kgs}$$

Amount of rice remaining

$$= \left(\frac{x-1}{2}\right) - \left(\frac{x+1}{4}\right) = \frac{x-3}{4} \text{kgs}$$

Amount of rice bought by the third customer

$$= \frac{1}{2} \times \left(\frac{x-3}{4}\right) + \frac{1}{2} = \frac{x+1}{8} \text{kgs}$$

As per the information given in the question $\frac{x+1}{8} = \frac{x-3}{4}$ because there is no rice left after the third customer has bought the rice.

Therefore, the value of 'x' = 7 kgs.

100. d $\quad x^2.y^3 = 8$

$\Rightarrow$ (2x).(2x).y.y.y = 2.2.8 = 32

If the product of five variables is constant, then their sum would be minimum if the variables are equal.

For their sum, 4x + 3y, to be minimum all of them must be equal to 2.

$\Rightarrow \quad 2x = y = 2$

$\Rightarrow \quad x = 1, y = 2$

So the minimum value of 4x + 3y will be 10.

101. a $\quad a^2 + ab + b^2 = 1$

So $a(a + b) + b^2 = 1$

and $b(a + b) + a^2 = 1$.

Adding the two equations we get:

$(a + b)^2 + a^2 + b^2 = 2$

The integer pairs (a, b) satisfying the equation are: (1, –1), (–1, 1), (1, 0), (0, 1), (–1, 0), (0, –1)

So 6 ordered pairs (a, b) are possible in all.

102. b To maximise the number of incorrect responses, the number of correct responses should also be maximised.

Let the number of correct responses be x.

So the number of incorrect responses = 28 – x

Total marks scored = 3x – (28 – x) > 22

$\Rightarrow$ 4x – 28 > 22

$\Rightarrow \quad x > 12.5$

The least possible value of x = 13

So the answer = 28 – 13 = 15

103. d Since the coefficient of x^2 is 0, the sum of the three roots of the equation is 0.

If $\quad a + b + c = 0$, then

$$a^3 + b^3 + c^3 = 3abc = 3 \times \frac{-93}{3} = -93$$

104. c

$$P + \frac{1}{Q} = 1 \Rightarrow \frac{1}{P} = \frac{1}{1 - \frac{1}{Q}} = \frac{Q}{Q-1} \quad \text{...(i)}$$

$$Q + \frac{1}{R} = 1 \Rightarrow R = \frac{1}{1-Q} \quad \text{...(ii)}$$

From (i) and (ii), we get

$$R+\frac{1}{P}=\frac{1}{1-Q}-\frac{Q}{1-Q}=1 \quad ...(iii)$$

Also, $PQR=\left(\frac{Q-1}{Q}\right)Q\left(\frac{1}{1-Q}\right)=-1$ ...(iv)

From (iii) and (iv), we get $PQR+R+\frac{1}{P}=1-1=0.$

105. c Cost per dozen chocolates

$$=\frac{\frac{y}{x}}{12}=\text{Rs. }\frac{12y}{x}$$

Cost per dozen under the offer

$$=\frac{\frac{2}{x+10}}{12}=\text{Rs. }\frac{24}{x+10}$$

Saving per dozen $=\frac{12y}{x}-\frac{24}{x+10}=\frac{80}{100}$

$$\Rightarrow \frac{12y}{x}-\frac{24}{x+10}=\frac{4}{5}$$

$$\Rightarrow \frac{3y}{x}-\frac{6}{x+10}=\frac{1}{5}$$

$$\Rightarrow \frac{15y}{x}-\frac{30}{x+10}=1$$

The equation is satisfied for $x = 5$, $y = 1$.

106. a Assume that $a \le b \le c$.

So $\frac{a}{b+c}+\frac{b}{a+c}+\frac{c}{a+b}\ge\frac{a}{a+c}+\frac{b}{a+b}+\frac{c}{b+c},$

and

$$\frac{a}{b+c}+\frac{b}{a+c}+\frac{c}{a+b}\ge\frac{a}{a+b}+\frac{b}{b+c}+\frac{c}{c+a}.$$

Adding these two inequalities and dividing the resultant by 2, we get

$$\frac{a}{b+c}+\frac{b}{c+a}+\frac{c}{a+b}\ge\frac{3}{2}$$

$s=\frac{a+b+c}{2}$, where s is the semiperimeter of triangle.

$a + b > c$ and $a + b > s$.

$$\Rightarrow \frac{c}{a+b}<\frac{c}{s}, \frac{a}{b+c}<\frac{a}{s} \text{ and } \frac{b}{a+c}<\frac{b}{s}$$

But $\frac{a}{s}+\frac{b}{s}+\frac{c}{s}=\frac{a+b+c}{s}=2.$

Hence $\frac{a}{b+c}+\frac{b}{c+a}+\frac{c}{a+b}<2.$

107. b Solving the two linear equations $3x + 4y - 11 = 0$ and $x + y - 3 = 0$, we get $x = 1$ and $y = 2$.

Hence, the two lines intersect at the point (1, 2).

Any line which is parallel to $2x + 5y = 0$ should be of the form $2x + 5y - k = 0$ ...(i)

where k is a real number.

Putting $x = 1$ and $y = 2$ in (i), we get $k = 12$.

Hence, the equation of the straight line will be $2x + 5y - 12 = 0$.

108. d ${}^{n+m}C_2 = {}^{n}C_2 + 11$

$$\frac{(n+m)(n+m-1)}{2}=\frac{n(n-1)}{2}+11$$

$$n^2 + 2nm - n + m^2 - m = n^2 - n + 22$$

$$m^2 + (2n - 1)m = 22$$

$$m(m + 2n - 1) = 22$$

Hence, $m = 2$ and $n = 5$.

109. a Suppose $\frac{bx-ay}{bc}=\frac{ay-cz}{ac}=\frac{cz-bx}{ab}=k.$

So

$$bx - ay = kbc$$

$$ay - cz = kac$$

$$cz - bx = kab$$

On adding, $k(ab + bc + ca) = 0$

or, $ab + bc + ca = 0$.

110. d Solve the equation to find the answer.

$$(x - 1)^2 + x^2 + (x + 1)^2 = (x + 2)^2 + (x + 3)^2.$$

111. c Quadratic equation $ax^2 + bx + c = 0$ must have two roots which may or may not be identical.

Let $f(x) = ax^2 + bx + c.$

$$f(1) = a(1)^2 + b(1) + c$$

$$= a + b + c = 0$$

So, $x = 1$ is definitely a root of $ax^2 + bx + c = 0$.

Product of roots of $ax^2 + bx + c = 0$ is $\frac{c}{a}$.

So if one of the roots is 1 then the other root must be $\frac{c}{a}$.

112. a Given that

$$x + y = 1$$

$$\Rightarrow x + y - 1 = 0$$

$$\Rightarrow x^3 + y^3 - 1 = -3xy$$

$(a^3 + b^3 + c^3 = 3abc \text{ if } a + b + c = 0)$

$$\Rightarrow x^3 + y^3 + 3xy = 1$$

113. a The sum of the roots of $ax^2 + bx + c = 0$ is $\frac{-b}{a}$.

$ax^2 + bx + c$ attains its maximum value at $x = \frac{-b}{2a}$.

$\therefore \frac{-b}{2a} = 2 \Rightarrow \frac{-b}{a} = 4$

Hence, the sum of the roots = 4.

114. b Using allegation,

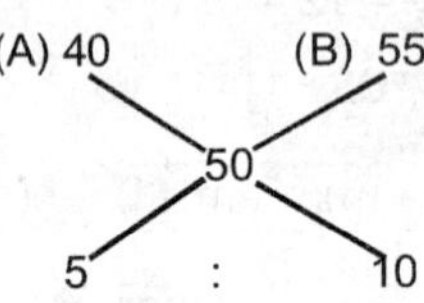

$\Rightarrow$ 1 : 2

Hence a : b = 1 : 2

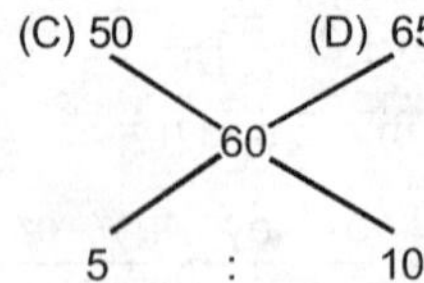

$\Rightarrow$ 1 : 2

Hence, c : d = 1 : 2

Also,

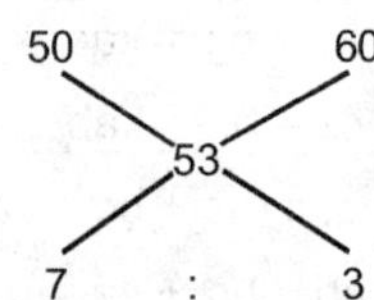

Hence, x : y = 7 : 3

To have minimum x (= 7 kg) and y (= 3 kg)

we need $(a + b) \geq 7$ and $(c + d) \geq 3$.

Hence, minimum a + b = 9 (as it has to be in the ratio of 1 : 2 it must be a multiple of 3)

Minimum c + d = 3.

Minimum a + b + c + d + x + y

= 9 + 3 + 7 + 3 = 22 kg.

115. d The equations formed by the roots of the equation $(x - a)(x - b)(x - c)$ can be as follows:

(i) $(x - a)(x - b) \Rightarrow$ Roots are a, b

(ii) $(x - b)(x - c) \Rightarrow$ Roots are b, c

(iii) $(x - c)(x - a) \Rightarrow$ Roots are c, a

(iv) $(x - a)^2 \Rightarrow$ Roots are a, a

(v) $(x - b)^2 \Rightarrow$ Roots are b, b

(vi) $(x - c)^2 \Rightarrow$ Roots are c, c

Adding all these roots, we get 4(a + b + c).

116. c By the question,

$x(x - 3) = -1$

$\Rightarrow x^3(x - 3)^3 = -1$

$\Rightarrow x^3(x^3 - 27 - 9x^2 + 27x) = -1$

$\Rightarrow x^3(x^3 - 18) + x^3(-9 - 9x^2 + 27x) = -1$

$\Rightarrow x^3(x^3 - 18) - 9x^3(x^2 - 3x + 1) = -1$

$\Rightarrow x^3(x^3 - 18) - 9x^3(-1 + 1) = -1$

$\Rightarrow x^3(x^3 - 18) = -1.$

117. a We obtain the sum of all the coefficients of a polynomial by equating all the variables to 1. Here by putting x = 1 in the polynomial, the required sum comes out to be zero.

118. c $x^2 + rx + s = 0$

r = – (sum of roots)   r = –ve

s = product of roots   s = +ve

s – r = +ve

r + s + 1

= – a – b + ab + 1 (where a & b are roots)

= (a – 1) (b – 1)

= +ve

$\Rightarrow \frac{+ve}{+ve} = +ve$

Alternative Method:

Take roots as 2, 2

$\Rightarrow r = -4$ & $s = 4 \Rightarrow \frac{r + s + 1}{s - r} = \frac{1}{8} = +ve$.

119. b Let the number of Re. 1, 50 paise and 25 paise coins be 360, 432 and 576 respectively (ratio 5 : 6 : 8).

Re. 1	50 paise	25 paise
360	432	576

I transaction: 3/5th of Re. 1 coins changed

216 coins of Re. 1 would be changed with 144 coins of 50 paise and 576 coins of 25 paise (so that total 50 paise coins = 576 and total 25 paise coins = 1152 in the ratio 1:2)

Re. 1	50 paise	25 paise
144	576	1152

II transaction: Half of 50 paise coins to Re. 1 and all 25 paise coins to Re. 1 and 50 paise in the ratio 7:4

Half of 50 paise coins $\Rightarrow$ 144 coins of Re. 1

1152 coins of 25 paise $\Rightarrow$ 224 coins of Re. 1 and 128 coins of 50 paise

Re. 1	50 paise	25 paise
512	416	0

Ratio = 512 : 416 = 16 : 13.

120. c By assuming the values of x, y, z and t, (a) and (b) can be very easily ruled out.

Checking option (c), if x > y + z, then x > y and x > z(since all numbers are positive).

So, using statements I and II, x > z > t > y.

So, option (c) is correct.

121. As 'a' and 'b' are the roots of the given equation,

$$a + b = -7$$

$$ab = 4$$

The given expression can be rewritten as

$$\frac{2}{7}\left(\frac{a+b}{ab}\right)+ab = \frac{2}{7}\left(\frac{-7}{4}\right)+4=\frac{7}{2}.$$

122. $a^2 - 1 = -6a$

$$\Rightarrow \quad a-\frac{1}{a} = -6$$

Now, $\left(a+\frac{1}{a}\right)^2 - 5\left(a-\frac{1}{a}\right) = \left(\left(a-\frac{1}{a}\right)^2+4\right)-5\left(a-\frac{1}{a}\right)$

$$= \left((-6)^2+4\right)-5\times-6$$

$$= 40 + 30 = 70.$$

123. $\frac{4}{7}<\frac{x}{y}<\frac{12}{13}, \Rightarrow \frac{13x}{12}<y<\frac{7x}{4}$

As 'x' increases, the interval in which 'y' lies also increases.

For x = 1, the intervals in which y lies is $\left(1\frac{1}{12}, 1\frac{3}{4}\right)$.

This interval does not contain any integer.

For x = 2, the interval in which y lies is $\left(2\frac{1}{6}, 3\frac{1}{2}\right)$ and 3 lies in the interval.

Hence, the minimum possible value of y is 3.

124. The graph of f(x) is shown below.

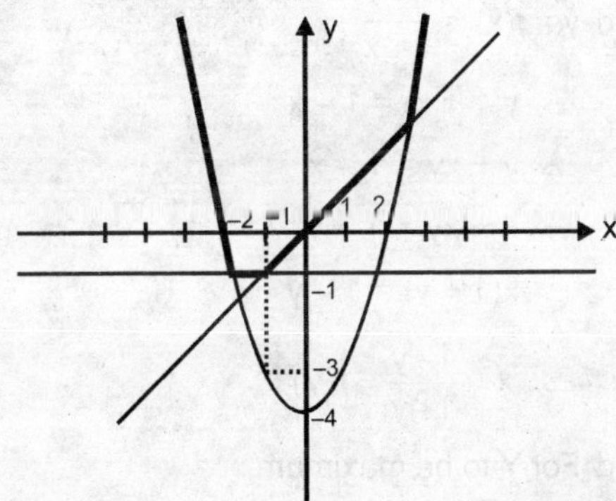

We can see from the graph that the minimum value of f(x) is –1.

125. Given, $x+\cfrac{1}{y+\cfrac{1}{z}}=\frac{68}{21}=3+\frac{5}{21}$.

As x is a natural number, the only possible value of x is 3.

$$\therefore \quad y+\frac{1}{z} = \frac{21}{5}=4+\frac{1}{5}$$

As y and z are natural numbers, the only possible values of y and z are 4 and 5 respectively.

$$\therefore \quad x + y + z = 3 + 4 + 5 = 12$$

126. $x^2 + (a + 3)x - (a + 5) = 0$

Let α and β are the roots of the above equation

So $\alpha + \beta = -\frac{(a+3)}{1}$

$\alpha\beta = -\frac{(a+5)}{1}$

Now, $\alpha^2 + \beta^2 = (\alpha + \beta)^2 - \alpha \times \beta$

$= (a + 3)^2 - 2(-(a + 5))$

$a = a^2 + 9 + 6a + 2a + 10$

$= a^2 + 8a + 19.$

$= (a + 4)^2 + 3$

At a = –4, minimum value = 3.

127. $9^{x-\frac{1}{2}} - 2^{2x-2} = 4^x - 3^{2x-3}$

$\Rightarrow 3^{2x-1} + 3^{2x-3} = 2^{2x} + 2^{2x-2}$

$\Rightarrow \frac{3^{2x}}{3}+\frac{3^{2x}}{27} = 2^{2x}+\frac{2^{2x}}{4}$

$\Rightarrow \frac{210\times 3}{27}=\frac{5\times 2}{4}$

$\Rightarrow \left(\frac{3}{2}\right)^{2x}=\frac{27}{8}=\left(\frac{3}{2}\right)^3 \Rightarrow 2x = 3 \Rightarrow x = 3/2.$

128. $u^2+(u-2v-1)^2=-4v(u+v)$

Put $u=\frac{1}{2}$ and $v=-\frac{1}{4}$ in the above equation,

$\text{L.H.S.} = \left(\frac{1}{2}\right)^2+\left(\frac{1}{2}+\frac{1}{2}-1\right)^2=\frac{1}{4}$

$\text{R.H.S} = -4\times-\frac{1}{4}\left(\frac{1}{2}-\frac{1}{4}\right)=\frac{1}{4}$

So, L.H.S = R.H.S.

$\therefore\ u+3v=\frac{1}{2}+3\times\left(-\frac{1}{4}\right)=-\frac{1}{4}$

129. Given equation is $n^3 - 11n^2 + 32n - 28$

$= (n - 4)^3 + n^2 - 16n + 36$

$= (n - 4)^3 + (n - 6)^2 - 4n$

We can straight away check the value for the given equation at n = 6, to quickly get – 16

Similarly, n = 7 gives the answer as zero thereby making the required answer as 8.

130. Given that: $N^N = 2^{160}$

$\Rightarrow N^N = 2^{5\times 2\times 16}$ or N = 32

Now, $N^2 + 2^N = 32^2 + 2^{32} = 2^{10} + 2^{32} = 2^{10}(1 + 2^{22})$

Hence, largest possible value of x = 10.

131. Given that, $A = \{6^{2n} - 35n - 1 : n = 1, 2, 3....\}$ and $B = \{35(n-1) : n = 1, 2, 3...\}$

Since, $B = 35(n-1)$ so $B = 35k$

and in $A = 6^{2n} - 35n - 1$, 35n will always be a multiple of 35

$\Rightarrow 6^{2n} - 1 = (6n+1)(6n-1)$

Therefore, putting n = 1, 6... we get multiples of 35 in A.

However, smaller multiples of 35 are not present in A such as 70, 105 etc.

Hence, every member of A is in B and at least one member of B is not in A.

132. Given equations are:

$2x^2 - ax + 2 > 0$

(Upward parabola that doesn't touch the x - axis)

and $x^2 - bx + 8 \geq 0$ (Upward parabola)

Therefore, $D_1 < 0$ for $(2x^2 - ax + 2 > 0)$ and $D_2 = 0$ for $(x^2 - bx + 8 \geq 0)$

$\Rightarrow a^2 - 16 < 0$ and $b^2 - 32 \leq 0$

Now, to find out the largest possible value of 2a – 6b we will take largest possible value of 'a' which is 3 and smallest possible value of 'b' which is – 5.

Hence, required answer = 2 × 3 – (6 × – 5) = 36.

133. For n = 2, we have $t_1 + t_2 = 39$

For n = 3, we have $t_1 + t_2 + t_3 = 58$ and thus $t_3 = 19$

For n = 4, we have $t_1 + t_2 + t_3 + t_4 = 81$ and thus $t_4 = 23$

For n = 5, we have $t_1 + t_2 + t_3 + t_4 + t_5 = 108$ and thus $t_5 = 27$

Thus we can see that from t_3 onwards an AP has been formed with first term as 19 and common difference as 4.

$\Rightarrow 19 + (n-1) \times 4 = 103$

$\Rightarrow 19 + 4n - 4 = 103$

Hence, n = 22 and k = 22 + 2 = 24.

Functions and Graphs

1. b $x \times x = 1.5x - x^2$ and $y \times y = 1.5y - y^2$.

For $x \times x < y \times y$ to be true, $1.5x - x^2 < 1.5y - y^2$

$\Rightarrow x(1.5 - x) < y(1.5 - y)$

Option I: $1 > x > y$

Thus, x × x and y × y must be greater than 0.5.

If x = 0.6 and y = 0.9

In this case x × x = y × y

Thus, this condition is not always true.

Option II: $x > 1 > y$

Here, y × y must be greater than 0.5 and x × x must be less than 0.5.

This condition is always true.

Option III: $1 > y > x$

Thus, x × x and y × y must be greater than 0.5.

If x = 0.6 and y = 0.9

In this case x × x = y × y

Thus, this condition is not always true.

Option IV: $y > 1 > x$

Here, x × x must be greater than 0.5 and y × y must be less than 0.5.

This condition can never be true.

2. a The summation of all terms $= \dfrac{p}{(p-1)} = \dfrac{-p}{(1-p)}$,

comparing this expression with sum of an infinite geometric progression with first term as 'a' and common ration = r, i.e. $\dfrac{a}{1-r}$ a = – p and r = p f(k) is the kth term of geometric progression.

Hence, $f(k) = -p \times p^{(k-1)}$.

3. b For each of the given expressions, you may have to simplify and express x in terms of y and hence verify for which one does the form and structure remain the same. In general, any function of the form $y = \dfrac{(ax+b)}{(bx-a)}$ reflects on to itself as we arrange it can be found that $x = \dfrac{(ay+b)}{(by-a)}$.

Hence, the answer is (b).

4. d $y = f(x) = \dfrac{1-x}{1+x}$

$\Rightarrow y(1+x) = 1 - x$

$\Rightarrow y + xy = 1 - x$

$\Rightarrow x + xy = 1 - y$

$\Rightarrow x(1+y) = 1 - y$

$\Rightarrow x = \dfrac{1-y}{1+y} = f(y)$

5. d For Y to be maximum,

$x + 2 = 3 - x \Rightarrow x = 0.5$

Maximum value of Y = x + 2 = 2.5

6. a $f(x) = |x|^3$

$\therefore f(-x) = |-x|^3 = |x|^3 = f(x)$.

Hence, the given function is even.

7. b Let f(x) = g(x) + h(x),

where g and h are odd functions.

$\therefore f(-x) = g(-x) + h(-x) = -g(x) - h(x) = -f(x)$.

Hence, f(x)is an odd function.

8. d

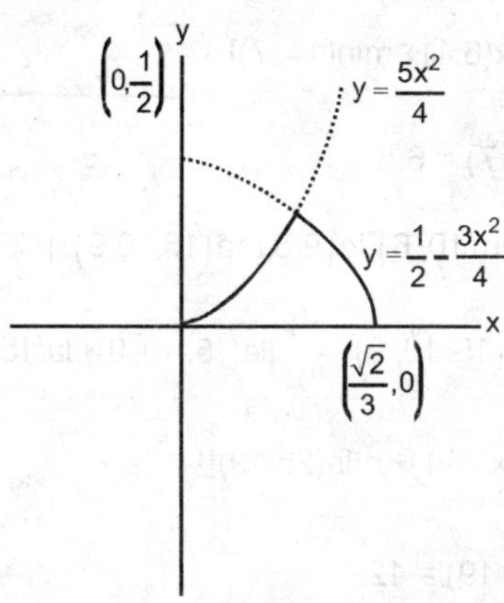

So maximum possible value will be at the point of intersection of the two graphs.

$\therefore \frac{1}{2} - \frac{3x^2}{4} = \frac{5x^2}{4}$

$\Rightarrow x^2 = \frac{1}{4}$

Hence, required maximum value

$= \frac{5x^2}{4} = \frac{5}{4} \times \frac{1}{4} = \frac{5}{16}$.

9. b $Ma\left[md(-2), mn(md(-3), -2), mn(6, md(-8))\right]$

$= Ma\left[2, mn(3, -2), mn(6, 8)\right] = Ma\left[2, -2, 6\right] = 6.$

10. a For a > b, the given equation reduces to $Ma\left[|a|, b\right] = mn\left[a, |a|\right]$.

If b < a < 0, then $|b| > |a| > 0 > a > b$.

$\therefore Ma\left[|a|, b\right] = |a|$ and $mn\left[a, |a|\right] = a$.

Hence, option (a)is correct.

11. b Let $g(x) = \frac{x-3}{2}$ be y. So, $fog(x) = f(y) = 2y + 3$.

Substituting $y = \frac{x-3}{2}$, we get

$fog(x) = (x-3) + 3 = x = \frac{[(2x+3)-3]}{2} = gof(x)$.

12. c If $2x + 3 = \frac{[(x-3)-3]}{2}$, then $x = -4$.

13. b From Question 11, $fog(x) = gof(x) = x$, you will realise that if you were to form a chain of these functions for even number of times, you would still end up getting x.

E.g. $fogofog(x) = fog(x) = x$. Since both the brackets have the functions repeated for even number of times, each of their value will be x and their product will be x^2.

14. c From question 11, gof(x)= fog(x) = x.

fo(fog)o(gof)(x) = fo(fog)(x) = f(x) = 2x + 3.

15. c If x = 1, we have min(3, 3)= 3.

If x = 2, we have min(6, 0)= 0.

If x = 3, we have min(11, –3) = –3.

If x = 0.5, we have min(2.25, 4.5) = 2.25.

If x = 0.3, we have min(2.09, 5.1) = 2.09.

Thus, we find that as x increases above 1 and when it decreases below 1, the value of the function decreases. It is maximum at x = 1 and the corresponding value = 3.

Hint: Please note that the highest value of the given fraction will be at a point where $(2 + x^2) = (6 - 3x)$, as even if one of the values increases beyond this, the other value will be the minimum value.

If we equate the two, we get $x^2 + 3x - 4 = 0$. Solving this, we get x = 1 or x = –4.

Since x > 0, it has to be 1 and hence the result.

16. a If a = –2 and b = –3, then our expression will be me(–2 + mo(le(–2, –3)), mo(–2 + me(mo(–2), mo(–3)))

= me(–2 + mo(–3), mo(–2 + me(2, 3)))

= me(–2 + 3, mo(–2 + 3))

= me(1, mo(1)) = me(1, 1) = 1.

17. d Please note that the fastest way to solve these sums is the method of simulation, i.e., select any arbitrary values in the range given and verify whether the option holds good. E.g. a = 2, b = 3.

In this case, option (a)LHS = mo(le(2, 3)) = mo(2) = 2.

RHS = (me(mo(2), mo(3))= (me(2, 3)) = 3. Hence, LHS < RHS.

(b) LHS = mo(lo(2, 3))= mo(2) = 2. RHS = (me(mo(2), mo(3)) = (me(2, 3))= 3. Hence, LHS < RHS.

(c) LHS = mo(le(2, 3))= mo(2) = 2. RHS = (le(mo(2), mo(3)) = le(2, 3)= 2. Hence, LHS = RHS.

(d) LHS = mo(le(2, 3))= mo(2) = 2. RHS = (le(mo(2), mo(3)) = le(2, 3)= 2. Hence, LHS = RHS.

18. b Let us verify by taking arbitrary values of a in the range specified.

(a) a > 3. Let a = 4.

So $me(a^2 - 3a, a - 3)$= me(4, 1) = 4 > 0.

(b) 0 < a < 3. Let a = 2.

So $me(a^2 - 3a, a - 3)$= me(–2, –1) = –1 < 0.

(c) a < 0. Let a = –1.

So $me(a^2 - 3a, a - 3)$= me(4, –4) = 4 > 0.

(d) a = 3, $me(a^2 - 3a, a - 3)$ = me(0, 0) = 0.

19. d We can work this on the above lines. E.g.

(a) $a > 3$. Let $a = 4$. So $le(a^2 - 3a, a - 3) = le(4, 1) = 1 > 0$.

(b) $0 < a < 3$. Let $a = 2$. So $le(a^2 - 3a, a - 3) = le(-2, -1) = -2 < 0$.

(c) $a < 0$. Let $a = -1$. So $le(a^2 - 3a, a - 3) = le(4, -4) = -4 < 0$.

20. d $M(M(A(M(x, y), S(y, x)), x), A(y, x)) = M(M(A(M(2, 3), S(3, 2)), 2), A(3, 2)) = M(M(A((2\times3), (3-2)), 2), A(3, 2))$

$= M(M(A(6, 1), 2), A(3, 2))$

$= M(M((6 + 1), 2), (3 + 2))$

$= M(M(7, 2), 5)$

$= M((7 \times 2), 5)$

$= M(14, 5)$

$= (14 \times 5)$

$= 70$.

21. b $S[M(D(A(a,b),2),D(A(a,b),2)),M(D(S(a,b),2), D(S(a, b),2))] = S[M(D((a + b),2),D((a + b),2)), M(D((a-b),2), D((a-b),2))]$

$$= S\left[M\left\{\frac{(a+b)}{2}, \frac{(a+b)}{2}\right\}, M\left\{\frac{(a-b)}{2}, \frac{(a-b)}{2}\right\}\right]$$

$$= S\left[\left\{\frac{(a+b)}{2}\right\}^2, \left\{\frac{(a-b)}{2}\right\}^2\right]$$

$$= \left\{\frac{(a+b)}{2}\right\}^2 - \left\{\frac{(a-b)}{2}\right\}^2$$

$$= \frac{4ab}{4} = ab$$

22. b This question can be done by assuming some values for x, y and z. E.g. let $x = 4$, $y = 3$ and $z = 1$. Thus,

$la(4, 3, 1) = \min(7, 4) = 4$; $le(x, y, z) = \max(1, 2) = 2$;

$ma(x, y, z) = \frac{1}{2}(4 + 2) = 3$. Hence, we can see that the only answer-choice that satisfies the relationship is $ma(x, y, z) < la(x, y, x)$.

23. b $ma(10,\ 4,\ le(la(10,\ 5,\ 3),\ 5,\ 3))$

$= ma(10, 4,\ le(\min(15,8), 5, 3))$

$= ma(10,\ 4,\ le(8,\ 5,\ 3))$

$= ma(10, 4, \max(3,2))$

$= ma(10,\ 4,\ 3)$

$= \frac{1}{2}[le(10, 4, 3) + la(10, 4, 3)]$

$= \frac{1}{2}[\max(6,1) + \min(14, 7)]$

$= \frac{1}{2}(6 + 7) = 6.5$

24. c $le(15, \min(10, 6), le(9, 8, ma(15, 10, 9)))$

Now $ma(15, 10, 9) = \frac{1}{2}[le(15, 10, 9) + la(15, 10, 9)]$

$= \frac{1}{2}[\max(5, 1) + \min(25, 19)]$

$= \frac{1}{2}(5 + 19) = 12$

Hence, our original expression would now be

$le(15, \min(10,6), le(9, 8, 12))$

$= le(15, 6, \max(1, -4))$

$= le(15, 6, 1) = \max(9, 5) = 9$

25. c Since both 2 and 1 are positive, $(2 \# 1) = 2 + 1 = 3$.

$(1\nabla2) = (1\times2)^{1+2} = 2^3 = 8$.

Thus, the given expression is equal to $\frac{3}{8}$.

26. a Let us first simplify the numerator. Since 1 is positive, $(1 \# 1)$ is $1 + 1 = 2$ which again is positive. Then

$(1 \# 1) \# 2 = 2 \# 2 = 2 + 2 = 4$

Now note that $\log_{10} 0.1 = \log_{10} 10^{-1} = -1$

Then $10^{1.3} \log_{10} 0.1 = 10^{1.3} \times (-1)$ is negative.

So $10^{1.3} \nabla \log_{10} 0.1 = 1$

Hence, the numerator is equal to $4 - 1 = 3$

Since $1 \times 2 = 2$ is positive, $(1\nabla2) = (1\times2)^{1+2} = 2^3 = 8$.

So the denominator = 8. Hence, the answer is $\frac{3}{8}$.

27. b The best possible way to solve this is to check each of the given answer choices. In options (a), (c) and (d), either both X and Y are positive or both X and Y are negative. Since we have (–Y) in the numerator of our expression and (–X) in the denominator, X and Y will never be both positive and neither will XY be positive. Hence, both the numerator and the denominator of our expression will be 1 and the value will always be 1. Hence, the only possible answer choice is (b).

28. d $|r - 6| = 11 \Rightarrow r - 6 = 11,\ r = 17$

or $-(r - 6) = 11$, $r = -5$

$|2q - 12| = 8 \Rightarrow 2q - 12 = 8$, $q = 10$

or $2q - 12 = -8$, $q = 2$

Hence, minimum value of $\frac{q}{r} = \frac{10}{-5} = -2$.

For questions 29 to 31:

$f(x,y)=|x+y|$ --- This is always positive

$F(f(x,y))=-f(x,y)=-|x+y|$ --- This is always negative $G(f(x,y))=-F(f(x,y))=-(-|x+y|)=|x+y|$ --- This is always positive

29. d $F(f(x,y))G(f(x,y))=-|x+y|^2$

and $G(f(x,y)).G(f(x,y))=|x+y|^2$

From the choices, we observe that:

Option (a): LHS of the expression is $-|x+y|^2$, which is always non positive. RHS of the expression is $|x+y|^2$, which is always non negative. The only situation when LHS is equal to RHS is when each is equal to zero. Hence, (a) is not necessarily true.

Option (b): The given expression can be written as

$-|x+y|^2>|x+y|^2$ or $0>2|x+y|^2$.

This implies that 0 > |x + y|, which is not true. Hence, (b) is not true.

Option (c): $F(f(x,y))G(f(x,y))=-|x+y|^2$

and $G(f(x,y)).G(f(x,y))=|x+y|^2$

These two expressions can be equal if |x + y| = 0. Hence, (c) is not necessarily true.

Option (d): $F(f(x,y))+G(f(x,y))+f(x,y)$

$$=-|x+y|+|x+y|+|x+y|=|x+y|$$

$$f(-x,-y)=|(-x)+(-y)|=|-x-y|=|-(x+y)|=|x+y|$$

Therefore, the two expressions are equal.

30. c $f(G(f(1,0)),f(F(f(1,2)),G(f(1,2))))$

$=f(G(f(1,0)),f(3,-3))$

$=f(G(f(1,0)),0)$

$=f(-1,0)=1.$

31. c The option (c) yields x^2.

$-F(f(x,x))\cdot G(f(x,x))\div\log_2 16$

$=-(-2x.2x)\div\log_2 16$

$=\dfrac{4x^2}{\log_2 2^4}=x^2$

32. d The graph F(x) represents the function F(x) = | x |, where x is any real number.

The graph of F1(x) represents the function F1(x) = – x, where x is any real number.

None of the given relationships are satisfied by these two functions.

Alternate solution:

F1(–2) = 2 = F(–2) and F1(2) = –2. But F(2) = 2. So the correct option is (d).

33. b $F(x)=\begin{cases}0 & \text{when } x\geq 0\\ x & \text{when } x<0\end{cases}$

and $F1(x)=\begin{cases}-x & \text{when } x>0\\ 0 & \text{when } x\leq 0\end{cases}$

Therefore, replacing x by (–x) in above functions, we get

$F(-x)=\begin{cases}0 & \text{when } x\leq 0\\ -x & \text{when } x>0\end{cases}$

and $F1(-x)=\begin{cases}x & \text{when } x<0\\ 0 & \text{when } x\geq 0\end{cases}$

Clearly, F1(x)= F(–x), hence, option (b) is the correct choice.

Alternate solution:

F1(–2) = 0 = F(2) and F1(2) = –2 = F(–2).

So the correct option is (b), i.e. F1(x) = F(–x).

34. b $F(x)=\begin{cases}0 & \text{when } x\leq 0\\ -x & \text{when } x>0\end{cases}$

and $F1(x)=\begin{cases}x & \text{when } x<0\\ 0 & \text{when } x\geq 0\end{cases}$

Therefore, replacing x by (–x) in above functions, we get

$F(-x)=\begin{cases}0 & \text{when } x\geq 0\\ x & \text{when } x<0\end{cases}$

and $F1(-x)=\begin{cases}-x & \text{when } x>0\\ 0 & \text{when } x\leq 0\end{cases}$

Clearly, F1(x)= F(–x), hence, option (b) is the correct choice.

Alternate solution:

F1(–2) = –2 = F(2) and F1(2) = 0 = F(–2).

So the correct option is (b), i.e. F1(x) = F(–x)

35. c $F(x)=\begin{cases}1-x & \text{when } 0\leq x<2\\ 1 & \text{when } -2<x<0\end{cases}$

and $F1(x)=\begin{cases}-1-x & \text{when} -2<x<0\\ -1 & \text{when } 0\leq x<2\end{cases}$

Therefore, replacing x by (–x) in above functions, we get

$F(-x)=\begin{cases}1+x & \text{when } -2<x<0\\ 1 & \text{when } 0\leq x<2\end{cases}$

and $F1(-x)=\begin{cases}-1+x & \text{when } 0\leq x<2\\ -1 & \text{when } -2<x<0\end{cases}$

$\therefore\ -F(-x)=-\begin{cases}1+x & \text{when } -2<x<0\\ 1 & \text{when } 0\leq x<2\end{cases}$

$=\begin{cases}-1-x & \text{when} -2<x<0\\ -1 & \text{when } 0\leq x<2\end{cases}=F1(x)$

Hence, option (c) is the correct option.

Alternate solution:

F1(2) = –1 = F(2) and F1(–2) = 1 = F(–2).

So the correct option is (c), i.e. F1(x) = – F(–x).

36. d Using choices, (a), (b) and (c) could be both negative as well as positive, depending on the values of x and y.

37. a For (a), x, y < – 1. Then value of f(x, y) = $(x + y)^2$ and value of g(x, y) = – (x + y).

Substituting any value of x, y < – 1, we get f(x, y) always greater than g(x, y).

38. d Use choices. For the given set of questions, function j(x, y, z), n(x, y, z) means minimum of x, y, z and h(x, y, z), m(x, y, z) means maximum of x, y, z.

f(x, y, z), g(x, y, z) means the middle value.

39. a Use choices.

40. b The answer is (b) because the denominator becomes zero.

41. c From the graph, x = 2 ⇒ f(2) = 1 and x = –2 ⇒ f(–2) = 1

Thus, f(2)= f(–2). Hence, f(x) = f(–x)

42. d From the graph, x = 1

⇒ f(1) = 2 and x = –1

⇒ f(–1) = 1

Thus, f(1) = 2f(–1)

Hence, 3f(x) = 6f(–x)

43. b From the graph, x = 4

⇒ f(4) = –2 and x = –4

⇒ f(–4) = 2

Thus, f(4) = –f(–4)

Hence, f(x) = –f(–x)

44. c $f(2)=\frac{1}{3},\ f^2(2)=\frac{3}{4},\ f^3(2)=\frac{4}{7},\ f^4(2)=\frac{7}{11},\ f^5(2)=\frac{11}{18}$

$\therefore\ f(2)f^2(2)f^3(2)f^4(2)f^5(2)=\frac{1}{18}.$

45. b $f^1(-2) = -1$

$f^2(-2) = 0$

$f^3(-2) = \frac{1}{1}$

$\therefore f^1(-2)+f^2(-2)+f^3(-2) = -1 + 0 + 1 = 0.$

46. b $x^2 + y^2 = 0.1$

$|x - y|^2 = x^2 + y^2 - 2xy$

$(0.2)^2 = 0.1 - 2xy$

⇒ 2xy = 0.06 ⇒ xy = 0.03

Now, $|x|+|y| = \sqrt{x^2+y^2+2xy} = \sqrt{0.1+0.06}$

∴ |x| + |y| = 0.40

Hence, x = 0.3, y = 0.1 or vice versa.

47. b Solving these equations, we get 6 distinct lines.

x + y = 1, x + y = –1, x = 1, x = –1, y = 1 and y = –1. Tracing these curves, we get the area common as 3 square units.

48. b g(1) = f[f(1)] + 1 = 2. Since f(1) has to be 1, else all the integers will not be covered. f(n) is the set of odd numbers and g(n)is the set of even numbers.

49. b f(1, 2) = f(0, f(1, 1));

Now f(1, 1)= f[0, f(1, 0)] = f[0, f(0, 1)] = f[0, 2] = 3

Hence, f(1, 2) = f(0, 3) = 4

50. c We cannot work the questions individually through I or II. But combining the two statements, we get (2 ⊕ 0) = (0 ⊕ 2)= 0 and 0 ⊕ (– 5 ⊕ – 6) = 0.

51. c Taking a = b = c = d = 1, we get the minimum value as (1 + 1) (1 + 1)(1 + 1) (1 + 1)

= 2 × 2 × 2 × 2 = 16.

52. c x + y = 1 and x > 0, y > 0

Taking $x = y = \frac{1}{2}$, value of $\left(x+\frac{1}{x}\right)^2+\left(y+\frac{1}{y}\right)^2$

$=\left(2+\frac{1}{2}\right)^2+\left(2+\frac{1}{2}\right)^2$

$=\frac{25}{4}+\frac{25}{4}=\frac{25}{2}$

It can be easily verified as it is the least value among options.

For questions 53 and 54:

$BA=\frac{r_1+r_2}{n_1},\ MBA_2=\frac{r_1+r_2}{n_1+n_2}$

and $MBA_1=\frac{r_1}{n_1}+\frac{n_2}{n_1}\max\left\{0,\frac{r_2}{n_2}-\frac{r_1}{n_1}\right\}$

From BA and MBA_2, we get $BA \geq MBA_2$ because $n_1+n_2 \geq n_1$.

From BA and MBA_1, we get $BA \geq MBA_1$ because

$\frac{r_1}{n_1}+\frac{r_2}{n_1}\geq\frac{r_1}{n_1}+\frac{r_2}{n_1}\times\frac{n_2}{r_2}\max\left\{0,\frac{r_2}{n_2}-\frac{r_1}{n_1}\right\}.$

Now from MBA_1 and MBA_2, we get

$\frac{r_1}{n_1}+\frac{r_2}{n_1}\times\frac{n_2}{r_2}\max\left\{0,\frac{r_2}{n_2}-\frac{r_1}{n_1}\right\}\geq\frac{r_1}{n_1+n_2}+\frac{r_2}{n_1+n_2}.$

53. d From the above information, $BA \geq MBA_1 \geq MBA_2$

None of these is the right answer.

54. b BA = 50 where there is no incomplete innings

means $r_2 = n_2 = 0 \Rightarrow \frac{r_1}{n_1} = 50$

$$MBA_1 = \frac{r_1}{n_1} + \frac{n_2}{n_1}\max\left[0, \left(\frac{r_2}{n_2} - \frac{r_1}{n_1}\right)\right]$$

$$= 50 + \frac{1}{n_1}\max\left[0, \left(\frac{45}{1} - 50\right)\right]$$

$= 50 + 0$

$= 50$

$$BA = \frac{r_1 + r_2}{n_1} = \frac{50n_1 + 45}{n_1} = 50 + \frac{45}{n_1} > 50$$

$$MBA_2 = \frac{r_1 + r_2}{n_1 + n_2} = \frac{50n_1 + 45}{n_1 + 1} = 50 - \frac{5}{n+1}$$

Hence, BA will increase, MBA_2 will decrease.

55. b $f(x) + f(y) = \log\left(\frac{1+x}{1-x}\right) + \log\left(\frac{1+y}{1-y}\right)$

$$= \log\left(\frac{(1+x)\ (1+y)}{(1-x)(1-y)}\right)$$

$$= \log\left(\frac{1+x+y+xy}{1+xy-x-y}\right)$$

$$= \log\left(\frac{1+xy+x+y}{1+xy-(x+y)}\right)$$

$$= \log\left(\frac{1+\left(\frac{x+y}{1+xy}\right)}{1-\left(\frac{x+y}{1+xy}\right)}\right)$$

$$= f\left(\frac{x+y}{1+xy}\right)$$

56. d $x - 1 \leq [x] \leq x$

$2x + 2y - 3 \leq L(x, y) \leq 2x + 2y \Rightarrow a - 3 \leq L \leq a$

$2x + 2y - 2 \leq R(x, y) \leq 2x + 2y \Rightarrow a - 2 \leq R \leq a$

Therefore, $L \leq R$

Note: Choice (b)is wrong, otherwise choice (a) and choice (c)are also not correct. Choose the numbers to check.

57. b Number of samosas = 200 + 20n, n is a natural number.

Price per samosa = Rs.(2 – 0.1n)

Revenue = (200 + 20n)(2 – 0.1n)

$= 400 + 20n - 2n^2$

$= 450 - 2(n-5)^2$

Revenue will be maximum if n – 5 = 0

$\Rightarrow n = 5$

∴ Maximum revenue will be at (200 + 20 × 5) = 300 samosas.

58. b xyz = 4

$y - x = z - y \Rightarrow 2y = x + z$

∴ y is the AM of x, y, z.

Also, $\sqrt[3]{xyz} = 4^{\frac{2}{3}} \Rightarrow \sqrt[3]{xyz} = 2^{\frac{1}{3}}$.

∵ AM ≥ GM

$\therefore y \geq 2^{\frac{2}{3}}$

Therefore, the minimum value of y is $2^{\frac{2}{3}}$.

59. b $x = -|a|\ b$

Now $a - xb = a - (-|a|\ b)b$

$= a + |a|\ b^2$

$$\therefore a - xb = \begin{cases} a + ab^2 & \text{if } a \geq 0 \\ a - ab^2 & \text{if } a < 0 \end{cases}$$

$$= \begin{cases} a(1+b^2) & \text{if } a \geq 0 \\ a(1-b^2) & \text{if } a < 0 \end{cases}$$

Consider first case:

As $a \geq 0$ and $|b| \geq 1$, therefore $(1 + b^2)$ is positive.

$\therefore a(1 + b^2) \geq 0 \Rightarrow a - xb \geq 0$

Consider second case.

As $a < 0$ and $|b| \geq 1$, therefore $(1 - b^2) \leq 0$

$\therefore a(1 - b^2) \geq 0$ (Since –ve × -ve = +ve and $1 - b^2$ can be zero also), i.e. $a - xb \geq 0$

Therefore, in both cases $a - xb \geq 0$.

60. a $g^2 = g * g = h$

$g^3 = g^2 * g = h * g = f$

$g^4 = g^3 * g = f * g = e$

$\therefore n = 4$

61. d $f \oplus [f * \{f \oplus (f * f)\}] = f \oplus [f * \{f \oplus h\}]$

$= f \oplus [f * e\}]$

$= f \oplus [f]]$

$= h$

62. a $e^8 = e^2 * e^2 * e^2$

$= e * e * e$

$= e$

If we observe a $*$ anything = a

$\therefore a^{10} = a$

$\therefore \{a^{10} * (f^{10} \oplus g^9)\} \oplus e^8$

$= a \oplus e$

$= e$

63. d We can see that x + 2 is an increasing function and 5 – x is a decreasing function. This system of equation will have smallest value at the point of intersection of the two. i.e. 5 – x = x + 2 or x = 1.5.

Thus, smallest value of g(x) = 3.5

64. b **Case 1:** If x < 2, then y = 2 – x + 2.5 – x + 3.6 – x = 8.1 – 3x.

This will be least if x is highest i.e. just less than 2. In this case, y will be just more than 2.1

Case 2: If $2 \le x < 2.5$, then y = x – 2 + 2.5 – x + 3.6 – x = 4.1 – x

Again, this will be least if x is the highest i.e. just less than 2.5. In this case, y will be just more than 1.6.

Case 3: If $2.5 \le x < 3.6$, then y = x – 2 + x – 2.5 + 3.6 – x = x – 0.9.

This will be least if x is least i.e. x = 2.5.

Case 4: If $x \ge 3.6$, then

y = x – 2 + x – 2.5 + x – 3.6 = 3x – 8.1

The minimum value of this will be at x = 3.6 and y = 2.7

Hence, the minimum value of y is attained at x = 2.5

Alternate method:

At x = 2, f(x) = 2.1

At x = 2.5, f(x) = 1.6

At x = 3.6, f(x) = 2.7

Hence, at x = 2.5, f(x)will be minimum.

65. d When we substitute two values of x in the above curves, at x = –2, we get

y = –8 + 4 + 5 = 1

y = 4 – 2 + 5 = 7

Hence, at x = –2 the curves do not intersect.

At x = 2, y_1 = 17 and y_2 = 11

At x = –1, y_1 = 5 and 2 and y_2 = 5

When x = 0, y_1 = 5 and y_2 = 5

And at x = 1, y_1 = 7 and y_2 = 7

Therefore, the two curves meet thrice when x = –1, 0 and 1.

66. b We have

$f(0) = 0^3 - 4(0) + p = p$

$f(1) = 1^3 - 4(1) + p = p - 3$

If p and p – 3 are of opposite signs, then p(p – 3) < 0

Hence, 0 < p < 3.

67. d When a > 0, b < 0,

ax^2 and $-b|x|$ are non negative for all x,

i.e. $ax^2 - b|x| \ge 0$

$\therefore ax^2 - b|x|$ is minimum at x = 0 when a > 0, b < 0.

68. c $f_1f_2 = f_1(x)f_1(-x)$

$$f_1(-x) = \begin{cases} -x & 0 \le -x \le 1 \\ 1 & -x \ge 1 \\ 0 & \text{other wise} \end{cases}$$

$$= \begin{cases} -x & -1 \le x \le 0 \\ 1 & x \le -1 \\ 0 & \text{other wise} \end{cases}$$

$f_1f_1(-x) = 0 \forall x$

Similarly, $f_2f_3 = -(f_1(-x))^2 \ne 0$ for some x

$f_2f_4 = f_1(-x).\, f_3(-x) = -f_1(-x)\, f_2(-x)$

$= -f_1(-x)\, f_1(x) = 0\ \forall x$

69. b Checking with options:

Option (b):

$f_3(-x) = -f_2(-x) = -f_1(x) \Rightarrow f_1(x) = -f_3(-x)\ \forall x$

70. d $R = \dfrac{30^{65} - (30-1)^{65}}{30^{64} + (30-1)^{64}} = \dfrac{30^{65} - 30^{65}\left(1 - \dfrac{1}{30}\right)^{65}}{30^{64} + 30^{64}\left(1 - \dfrac{1}{30}\right)^{64}}$

$$\Rightarrow R = \frac{36^{65}}{30^{64}}\left\{\frac{1 - \left(1 - \frac{1}{30}\right)^{65}}{1 + \left(1 - \frac{1}{30}\right)^{64}}\right\}$$

$$\Rightarrow R = 30\left\{\frac{1-(0.96)^{65}}{1+(0.96)^{64}}\right\}$$

In $\dfrac{1-(0.96)^{65}}{1+(0.96)^{64}}$, numerator is only slightly less than 1.

and denominator is only slightly more than 1.

Hence, R is certainly greater than 1.

71. c |x + y| + |x – y| = 4

Replacing "+x" by "– x" & "+y" by "–y" everywhere in the curve, we again get the same equation.

⇒ Curve is symmetric in the 4-quadrants of X–Y plane.

In I-quadrant (x, y > 0)

$|x + y| + |x - y| = 4$

$$= \begin{cases}(x+y)+(y-x)=4;\ y>x\\(x+y)-(y-x)=4;\ y<x\end{cases}$$

$$= \begin{cases}y=2;\ y>x\\x=2;\ y<x\end{cases}$$

The graph looks like below.

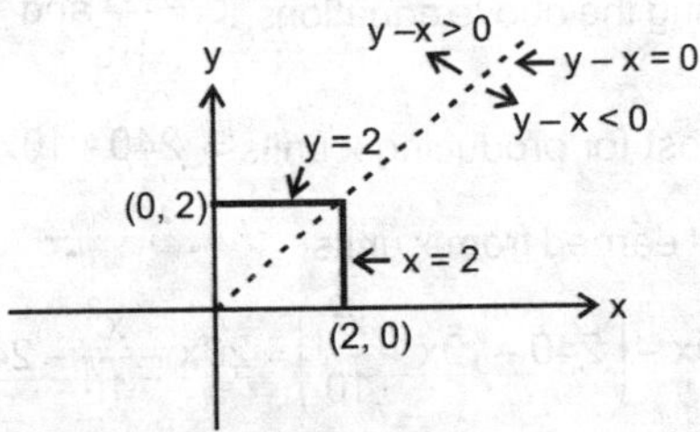

Area in I-quadrant = $(2)^2 = 4$

Total area of $|x + y| + |x - y| = 4$ is

4 × (area of I-quadrant)= 4 × 4 = 16.

72. d $g(x + 1) + g(x - 1) = g(x)$

$g(x+ 2) + g(x) = g(x + 1)$

Adding these two equations, we get

$g(x + 2) + g(x - 1) = 0$

$\Rightarrow g(x + 3) + g(x) = 0$

$\Rightarrow g(x + 4) + g(x + 1) = 0$

$\Rightarrow g(x + 5) + g(x + 2) = 0$

$\Rightarrow g(x + 6) + g(x + 3)= 0$

$\Rightarrow g(x + 6) - g(x) = 0$

73. b Going by options, we put $x = \dfrac{-1}{2}$

(a) $2^{-2} = \dfrac{1}{4}$

(b) $\dfrac{1}{x} \Rightarrow \dfrac{1}{-1/2} = -2$

(c) $\dfrac{1}{x^2} \Rightarrow \dfrac{1}{(-1/2)^2} = 4$

(d) $2^{-1/2} = \dfrac{1}{\sqrt{2}}$

(e) $\dfrac{1}{\sqrt{-x}} = \dfrac{1}{\frac{1}{\sqrt{2}}} = \sqrt{2}.$

Clearly, $\dfrac{1}{x}$ bears a negative value only and hence, is the smallest.

74. d From the graph of (y – x)vs. (y + x), it is obvious that inclination is more than 45°.

Slope of line $= \dfrac{y-x}{y+x} = \tan(45° + \theta)$

$\Rightarrow \dfrac{y-x}{y+x} = \dfrac{1+\tan\theta}{1-\tan\theta}$

By componendo-dividendo, $\dfrac{y}{x} = -\tan\theta$ which is nothing but the slope of the line that shows the graph of y vs. x.

And as $0° < \theta < 45°$, absolute value of tan θ is less than 1.

$\dfrac{-1}{\tan\theta}$ is negative and also, greater than 1.

⇒ The slope of the graph y vs. x must be negative and greater than 1. Accordingly, only option (d) satisfies.

We can also try by putting the values of (y + x) = 2(say) and (y – x)= 4(anything more than 2 for that matter). We can solve for values of y and x and cross check with the given options.

Alternate method:

In the normal X-Y coordinate plane the X-axis corresponds to y = 0

And Y-axis corresponds to x = 0

y + x = 0 and y – x = 0 are perpendicular lines on this plane.

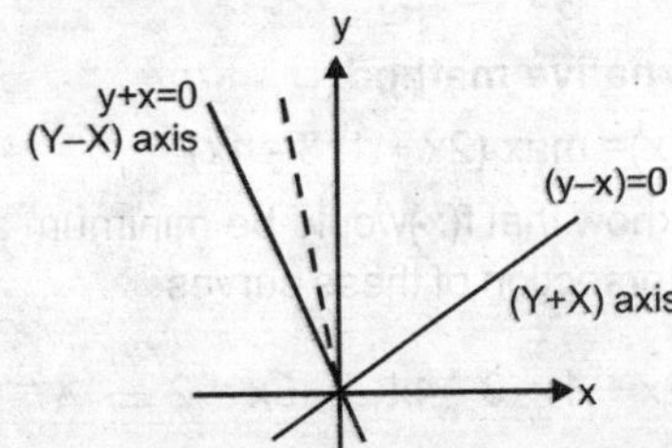

And y-x = 0 is the axis Y+X and y+x = 0 is the axis Y-X

So, the dotted line is the graph drawn in the question.

When you observe w.r.t to X-axis it looks like

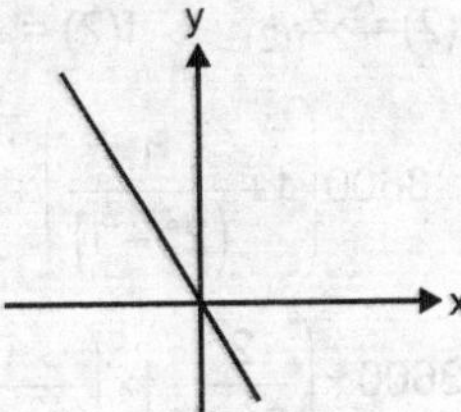

75. e f(x) = max (2x + 1, 3 - 4x)

So, the two equations are y = 2x + 1 and y = 3 - 4x

$y - 2x = 1$

$\Rightarrow \dfrac{y}{1} + \dfrac{x}{-1/2} = 1$

Similarly, y + 4x = 3

$\Rightarrow \frac{y}{3}+\frac{x}{3/4}=1$

Their point of intersection would be

2x + 1 = 3 - 4x $\Rightarrow$ 6x = 2 $\Rightarrow x=\frac{1}{3}$

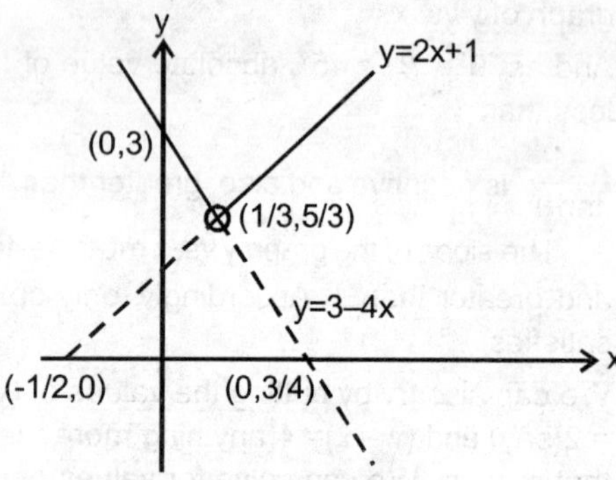

So when $x \le \frac{1}{3}$, then $f(x)_{max}=3-4x$

and when $x \ge \frac{1}{3}$, then $f(x)_{max}=2x+1$

Hence, the minimum of this will be at x = $\frac{1}{3}$

i.e. $y=\frac{5}{3}$

Alternative method:

As f(x)= max (2x + 1, 3 - 4x)

We know that f(x)would be minimum at the point of intersection of these curves

i.e. 2x + 1 = 3 - 4x $\Rightarrow$ 6x = 2 $\Rightarrow x=\frac{1}{3}$

Hence, min f(x) is $\frac{5}{3}$

76. a f(1) + f(2) + f(3)+ .... + f(n) = $n^2 f(n)$, f(1) = 3600.

For n = 2,

$\Rightarrow f(1)+f(2)=2^2 f(2) \Rightarrow f(2)=\frac{f(1)}{(2^2-1)}$

For n = 3, $3600\left(1+\frac{1}{(2^2-1)}\right)+f(3)=3^2 f(3)$

$\Rightarrow f(3)=3600\times\left(\frac{2^2}{2^2-1}\right)\times\left(\frac{1}{3^2-1}\right)$

Similarly,

$$f(9)=3600\times\frac{2^2\times3^2\times4^2...\times8^2}{(2^2-1)(3^2-1)(4^2-1)...(9^2-1)}$$

Therefore, f(9) = 80

77. b Using the given data –

$$\frac{(240+40b+40^2c)-(240+20b+20^2c)}{240+20b+20^2c}=\frac{2}{3}$$

and

$$\frac{(240+60b+60^2c)-(240+40b+40^2c)}{240+40b+40^2c}=\frac{1}{2}$$

Solving the above equations, $c=\frac{1}{10}$ and $b=10$

So cost for producing x units = $240+10x+\frac{x^2}{10}$

Profit earned from x units

$=30x-\left(240+10x+\frac{x^2}{10}\right)=20x-\frac{x^2}{10}-240$

$=760-\frac{1}{10}(x-100)^2$

For maximum profit, x – 100 = 0 $\Rightarrow$ x = 100.

78. d Maximum profit = Rs. 760

79. b Given that f(x) = ax^2 + bx + c

Also, f(5) = –3f(2) $\Rightarrow$ f(5) + 3f(2) = 0

$\Rightarrow$ (25a + 5b + c)+ 3(4a + 2b + c) = 0

$\Rightarrow$ 37a + 11b + 4c = 0...(i)

Also, as 3 is a root of f(x)= 0, thus, f(3) = 0.

Therefore, 9a + 3b + c = 0 ...(ii)

Using equation (i)and (ii), we get that a = b

Therefore, c = –12a

$\Rightarrow$ f(x) = a(x^2 + x –12)= a(x + 4) (x – 3)

Therefore, the other root of f(x) = 0 is –4.

80. e f(x) = a(x^2 + x –12)

Therefore, the value of a + b + c cannot be uniquely determined.

81. b f(x).f(y) = f(xy)

Given, f(2) = 4

We can also write,

f(2) = f(2 × 1) = f(2)× f(1)

OR f(1) × 4 = 4

$\Rightarrow$ f(1) = 1

Now we can also write,

$f(1)=f\left(2\times\frac{1}{2}\right)=f(2)\times f\left(\frac{1}{2}\right)$

$\Rightarrow f\left(\frac{1}{2}\right)=\frac{f(1)}{f(2)}=\frac{1}{4}$

82. a f(1, 2) = f(0, f(1, 2 – 1))

(as in f(1, 2): m > 0 and n > 0)

= f(0, f(1, 1))

$= f(0, f(0, f(1, 1-1)))$

(as in f(1, 1): m > 0 and n > 0)

$= f(0, f(0, f(1, 0)))$

$= f(0, f(0, f(1-1, 1)))$

(as in f(1, 0): m > 0 and n = 0)

$= f(0, f(0, f(0, 1)))$

$= f(0, f(0, 1+1))$

(as in f(0, 1): m = 0)

$= f(0, f(0, 2))$

$= f(0, 2+1)$

(as in f(0, 2): m = 0)

$= f(0, 3)$

$= 3 + 1 = 4.$

(as in f(0, 3): m = 0)

Also, from above:

$f(0, f(1, 1)) = f(0, 3)$ or $f(1, 1) = 3$.

Hence, $20[f(1, 2) + f(1, 1) + 15]$

$= 20\,[4 + 3 + 15] = 20 \times 22 = 440.$

83. d $y_1 = \dfrac{(x-1)}{(x+1)}$

$y_2 = f(y_1) = -\dfrac{1}{x}$

$y_3 = f(y_2) = -\dfrac{(x+1)}{(x-1)}$

$y_4 = f(y_3) = x$

$y_5 = f(y_4) = \dfrac{(x-1)}{(x+1)}$

It can be concluded that the given function has the cyclicity of 4 or $y_n = y_{n+4k}$, where k is a whole number.

Hence, $y_{501} = y_1 = \dfrac{(x-1)}{(x+1)}$.

84. b $f(0) = 10 = c$ ...(i)

$f(1) = a + b + c$ and $f(-1) = a - b + c$

$\therefore$ $b = -b = 0$ ...(ii)

$f(2) = 4a + 2b + c = 14$

$\therefore$ $a = 1$ ...(iii)

From equations (i), (ii) and (iii), we get

$f(10) = 100a + 10b + c = 110.$

85. b $(x^2 + y^2)^2 = 169$

$x^2 + y^2 = +13$ ...(i)

(since $x^2 + y^2 \geq 0$)

$(x^2 - y^2)^2 = 25$

$x^2 - y^2 = \pm 5$ ...(ii)

Case I:

$x^2 + y^2 = 13$

$x^2 - y^2 = 5$

Solving the equations, we get $x^2 = 9$ and $y^2 = 4$.

Case II:

$x^2 + y^2 = 13$

$x^2 - y^2 = -5$

Solving the equations, we get $x^2 = 4$ and $y^2 = 9$.

In both the cases, $x^2y^2 = 4 \times 9 = 36$.

86. c $f(x) = \dfrac{1}{\log_{5-|x|} \sqrt{x^3 - 7x^2 + 14x - 8}}$

$= \dfrac{1}{\log_{5-|x|} \sqrt{(x-1)(x-2)(x-4)}}$

Base of the logarithmic function $5 - |x| > 0$ and $5 - |x| \neq 1$

So, $x \in (-5, -4) \cup (-4, 4) \cup (4, 5)$ ...(i)

Also, $(x-1)(x-2)(x-4)$ must be greater than zero as well.

So, $x \in (1, 2) \cup (4, \infty)$ ...(ii)

Combining (i) and (ii): $x \in (1, 2) \cup (4, 5)$

87. a Given that $F(n-1) = \dfrac{1}{(2 - F(n))}$ and $F(1) = 2$.

For n = 2: $F(1) = \dfrac{1}{(2 - F(2))}$

$\Rightarrow F(2) = \dfrac{3}{2}$,

Similarly, one can find the values of F(3), F(4), F(5) as $\dfrac{4}{3}$, $\dfrac{5}{4}$ and $\dfrac{6}{5}$ respectively.

$\Rightarrow F(n) = \dfrac{n+1}{n}$

From this we can say that every term except [F(1)], of the series [F(1)] + [F (2)] +...........+ [F(50)] is equal to 1 as for 'n' > 0, F(n) lies between 1 and 2.

Therefore, [F(1)] + [F(2)] +......+ [F(50)] = 51.

Hence, option (a) is the correct choice.

88. b AT $x = \dfrac{\pi}{4}$, $f(x) = 0$

AT $x = \dfrac{\pi}{2}$, $f(x) = \infty$

Hence, f(x) lies in the range of $(0, \infty)$.

89. d The graphs of the two functions are shown below :

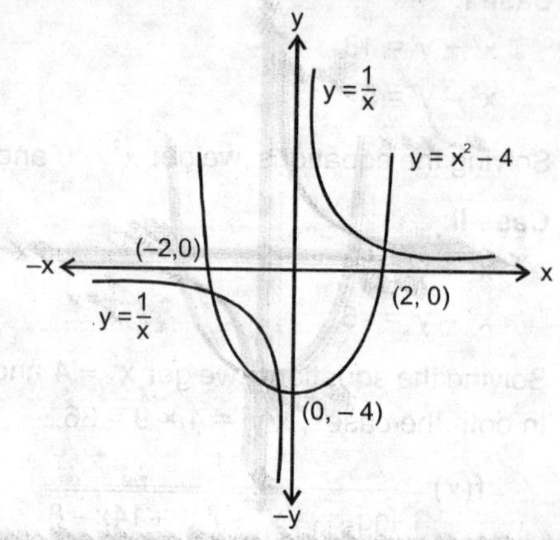

From the above figure, it is obvious that the graphs of the two functions intersect at three points.

90. c $f(2n) = 1^4 + 2^4 + 3^4 + 4^4 + 5^4 + \dots + (2n)^4$

$\Rightarrow f(2n) = (1^4 + 3^4 + 5^4 + \dots + (2n-1)^4) + (2^4 + 4^4 + 6^4 + \dots + (2n)^4)$

$\therefore 1^4 + 3^4 + 5^4 + \dots + (2n-1)^4$

$= f(2n) - (2^4 + 4^4 + 6^4 + \dots + (2n)^4)$

$= f(2n) - 2^4 \times (1^4 + 2^4 + 3^4 + \dots + n^4)$

$= f(2n) - 16 \times f(n)$.

91. c There would be two cases.

They are as follows:

Case I: $x \geq 0$ ... (i)

The inequality becomes,

$$\frac{1}{x-2} < 0.5$$

$\Rightarrow (x-2) < 0.5\,(x-2)^2$

$\Rightarrow (x-2)^2 - 2(x-2) > 0$

$\Rightarrow (x-2)(x-4) > 0$

$\Rightarrow x > 4$ or $x < 2$

Using (i), the range becomes

$x > 4$ or $0 \leq x < 2$ ...(ii)

Case II: $x < 0$ ...(iii)

The inequality becomes,

$$\frac{1}{-x-2} < 0.5$$

$\Rightarrow \frac{1}{x+2} > -0.5$

$\Rightarrow 2(x+2) + (x+2)^2 > 0$

$\Rightarrow (x+2)(x+4) > 0$

$\Rightarrow x > -2$ or $x < -4$

Using (iii), the range becomes

$-2 < x < 0$ or $x < -4$ ... (iv)

Combining (ii) and (iv),

The range is $(x < -4) \cup (-2 < x < 2) \cup (x > 4)$.

92. b Let us assume f(0) = K, where K' is a constant.

Then, $f(0 + y) = f(0.y) = f(0) = K$

and $f(x + 0) = f(x.0) = f(0) = K$.

This proves that the function is a constant function.

Thus, the value of

$f(-49) = f(49) = 7$

Hence, $f(-49) + f(49) = 14$.

93. b $f(x) = \frac{3}{9-x^2} + \log_{10}(x^3 - x)$

$9 - x^2 \neq 0$

$\Rightarrow x^2 \neq 9$

$\Rightarrow x \neq 3, -3$ ... (i)

$x^3 - x > 0$

$\Rightarrow (x-1)x(x+1) > 0$

$\Rightarrow x > 1$

or $-1 < x < 0$ ... (ii)

Combining (i) and (ii)

$x \in (-1, 0) \cup (1, 3) \cup (3, \infty)$.

94. c Replace y by – y.

The equation becomes

$\sqrt{3}x - y = \sqrt{3}$.

$\Rightarrow y = \sqrt{3}x - \sqrt{3}$.

95. c By observing we can find that $x > 1$ and $x < 2$. Else the RHS $\neq 8$.

So the combinations are [x] = 1, [2x] = 2 or 3, [3x] = 4 or 5

The combinations that give RHS = 8 are 1 + 2 + 5 or 1 + 3 + 4.

For any value of x, the case of "1 + 2 + 5" is not possible. Hence it has to be the case of "1 + 3 + 4". Which will occur

when $x \geq \frac{3}{2}$ and $x < \frac{5}{3}$.

Hence the solution is $\frac{3}{2} \leq x < \frac{5}{3}$.

96. (a) **97.** (c) **98**(a) **99.** (d) **100.** (54) **101.** (32) **102.** (20)

96. a $(x+1) \times f(x+1) + x\,f(x) + (x-1) \times f(x-1) = 0$ ...(i)

In the above equatin, replacing x by x – 1, we get

$x \times f(x) + (x-1) \times f(x-1) + (x-2) \times f(x-2) = 0$ ...(ii)

From equations (i) and (ii), we get

$(x+1) \times f(x+1) = (x-2) \times f(x-2)$ ...(iii)

Replacing x by x + 2in equation (iii), we get

$x \times f(x) = (x+3) \times f(x+3) = (x+6) \times f(x+6)$ and so on...

Hence, $f(1) = 4f(4) = 7f(7)\dots$, $2f(2) = 5f(5) = 8f(8)\dots$ and $3f(3) = 6f(6) = 9f(9)\dots$

Also, $3f(3) = 6f(6) \Rightarrow f(3) = 2f(6) \Rightarrow f(3) = 180 \times 2 = 360$

By putting the values of f(1) and f(3) in f(1) + 2f(2) + 3f(3) = 0, we get f(2) = –560

Also, 2f(2) = 14f(14) $\Rightarrow$ f(14) = $\frac{f(2)}{7}$ = –80

97. c $f(x) = x^2$, g(x) = 2

At x = 1, f(1) = 1, g(1) = 2

So, f(f(g(1)) + g(1)))

= f(f(2) + g(1))

$f(2) = 2^2 = 4$

So f(4 + 2) = f(6)

$f(6) = 6^2 = 36.$

98. a f(ab) = f(a) f(b)

$f(1) = f(1)^2$

$f(1)^2 - f(1) = 0$

f(1) [f(1) – 1] = 0

f(1) – 1 = 0

f(1) =

99. d To satisfy this, both function should be either less than or equal to zero or greater than equal to zero

Both cannot be less than zero

$f(x) \geq 0$ and $g(x) \geq 0$

$\Rightarrow 2x - 5 \geq 0$ and $7 - 2x \geq 0$

$\Rightarrow 2x \geq 5$ and $7 \geq 2x$

$\Rightarrow x \geq \frac{5}{2}$ and $x \leq \frac{7}{2}$

Hence, $\frac{5}{2} \leq x \leq \frac{7}{2}$

100. 54 f(x + 2) = f(x) + f(x + 1)

f(15) = f(13) + f(14)

f(15) = f(13) + f(12) + f(13)

[$\because$ f(14) = f(12) + f(13)]

617 = 2f(13) + f(12)

617 = 2 [f(11) + f(12)] + f(12)

[$\because$ f(13) = f(11) + f(12)]

617 = 2 [91] + 3f(12)

435 = 3 (f(10 + f(11))

435 = 3f(10) + 273

3f(10) = 162

f(10) = 54

101. 32 f(x) = min $\{2x^2, 52 - 5x\}$

The maximum possible value of f(x) is obtained when $52 - 5x = 2x^2$.

Solving further we get,

(x – 4) (2x + 13) = 0

x = 4 and $x = -\frac{13}{2}$

$x = -\frac{13}{2}$ will be rejected since x is a positive real number.

At x = 4, f(x) = 32.

102. 20 In order to find the point where the two graphs meet we need to equate the two equations:

$\Rightarrow 5x = 52 - 2x^2$

But we need only positive values of x, so the meeting point or x = 4

For x < 4, $52 - 2x^2$ will be maximum and for x > 4 the line 5x will be maximum.

Hence, f(x) will be minimum at x = 4 and the required value will be f(4) = 20.

Logarithm and Exponents

1. d $\log_7 \log_5 \left(\sqrt{x+5} + \sqrt{x}\right) = 0,$

We know

$\log_a b = x \Rightarrow a^x = b$

$\therefore \log_5\left(\sqrt{x+5} + \sqrt{x}\right) = 7^0$

$\Rightarrow \log_5\left(\sqrt{x+5} + \sqrt{x}\right) = 1$

$\Rightarrow \sqrt{x+5} + \sqrt{x} = 5^1$

$\Rightarrow \sqrt{x+5} = 5 - \sqrt{x}$

Squaring both sides, we get

$\Rightarrow x + 5 = 25 + x - 2 \times 5\sqrt{x}$

$\Rightarrow x + 5 = 25 + x + 10\sqrt{x}$

$\Rightarrow 10\sqrt{x} = 20$

$\Rightarrow \sqrt{x} = 2$

$\Rightarrow \left(\sqrt{x}\right)^2 = (2)^2$

$\Rightarrow x = 4$

2. c Let $\log_6 216\sqrt{6} = x$.

Then by rule, $\log_b a = x \Rightarrow b^x = a$ we have,

$6^x = 216\sqrt{6}$

$6^x = 6^3 \times 6^{\frac{1}{2}} \Rightarrow 6^x = 6^{\frac{7}{2}}$

$\therefore x = \frac{7}{2}$

3. c We know that if $\log_a x = y$, then $x = a^y$. So comparing this form with our equation, we can get $\log_7 (x^2 - x + 37) = 2^1 = 2$ and furthermore from this we can say that

$(x^2 - x + 37) = 7^2 = 49$

Thus, we have the equation

$x^2 - x - 12 = 0$

The solutions of this equation are,

$x = 4$ or $x = -3$.

The value that satisfies the given answer-choices is $x = 4$.

4. c **Statement I:** Given that x satisfies the equation, $\log_2 x = \sqrt{x}$

$\therefore x = 2^{\sqrt{x}}$

This equation is satisfied by the values $x = 4$ and 16.

Hence, statement I alone is not sufficient.

Statement II: Nothing concrete can be concluded from the fact that $x \le 10$ km.

Hence, statement II alone is not sufficient.

Combining statements I and II, we get a unique value of $x = 4$ km.

5. b $\log_{10} x - \log_{10}\sqrt{x} = 2\log_x 10$

$$\Rightarrow \log_{10}\left[\frac{x}{\sqrt{x}}\right] = \log_x 100$$

$$\Rightarrow \log_{10}\sqrt{x} = \frac{\log_{10} 100}{\log_{10} x}$$

$$\Rightarrow \frac{1}{2}\log_{10} x = \frac{2}{\log_{10} x}$$

$$\Rightarrow (\log_{10} x)^2 = 4$$

$$\Rightarrow \log_{10} x = \pm 2$$

$$\Rightarrow \log_{10} x = 2 \quad \text{or} \quad \log_{10} x = -2$$

$$\Rightarrow 10^2 = x \quad \text{or} \quad 10^{-2} = x$$

$$\therefore x = 100 \quad \text{or} \quad x = \frac{1}{100}$$

6. b $\frac{1}{3}\log_3 M + 3\log_3 N = 1 + \log_{0.008} 5$

$$\Rightarrow \log_3(M^{1/3}N^3) = 1 + \frac{(\log 10 - \log 2)}{\log 8 - \log 1000}$$

$$\Rightarrow \log_3(M^{1/3}N^3) = 1 - \frac{(1 - \log 2)}{3(1 - \log 2)}$$

$$\Rightarrow \log_3(M^{1/3}N^3) = 1 - \frac{1}{3} = \frac{2}{3}$$

$$\Rightarrow M^{1/3}N^3 = 3^{2/3}$$

$$\Rightarrow MN^9 = 3^2$$

$$\Rightarrow N^9 = \frac{9}{M}.$$

7. d Sum of $\log m + \log\left(\frac{m^2}{n}\right) + \log\left(\frac{m^3}{n^2}\right) + \cdots$ n terms such problem must be solved by taking the value of number of terms. Let's say 2 and check the given option. If we look at the sum of 2 terms of the given series it comes out to be

$$\log m + \log\frac{m^2}{n} \Rightarrow \log\frac{m \times m^2}{n} = \log\left(\frac{m^3}{n}\right)$$

Now look at the option and put number of terms as 2, only option (d)validates the above mentioned answer.

$$\log\left[\frac{m^{(n+1)}}{n^{(n-1)}}\right]^{\frac{n}{2}} = \log\left[\frac{m^3}{n}\right]^1 = \log\left(\frac{m^3}{n}\right)$$

8. b For the curves to intersect, $\log_{10} x = x^{-1}$

Thus, $\log_{10} x = \frac{1}{x}$ or $x^x = 10$

This is possible for only one value of x $(2 < x < 3)$.

9. d Using $\log a - \log b = \log\left(\frac{a}{b}\right)$, $\frac{2}{y-5} = \frac{y-5}{y-3.5}$, where $y = 2^x$

Solving we get y = 4 or 8

i.e. x = 2 or 3.

It cannot be 2 as log of negative number is not defined (see the second expression).

10. b $u = (\log_2 x)^2 - 6\log_2 x + 12$

$x^u = 256$

Let $\log_2 x = y \Rightarrow x = 2^y$

$$x^u = 2^8 \Rightarrow uy = 8 \Rightarrow u = \frac{8}{y}$$

$$\therefore \frac{8}{y} = y^2 - 6y + 12 \Rightarrow y^3 - 6y^2 + 12y - 8 = 0$$

$$\Rightarrow (y-2)^3 = 0 \Rightarrow y = 2$$

$$\therefore x = 4, \quad u = 4$$

11. d $P = \log_x\left(\frac{x}{y}\right) + \log_y\left(\frac{y}{x}\right)$

$$= \log_x x - \log_x y + \log_y y - \log_y x$$

$$= 2 - \log_x y - \log_y x$$

Let $t = \log_x y$

$$P = 2 - \frac{1}{t} - t = -\left[\sqrt{t} - \frac{1}{\sqrt{t}}\right]^2$$

which can never be positive. Out of given options, it can't assume a value of +1.

12. e $\log_y x = a.\log_z y = b.\log_x z = a \times b$

$$a = \frac{\log_y x}{\log_z y} \text{ and } b = \frac{\log_y x}{\log_z y}$$

$$\Rightarrow a \times b = \frac{\log_y x}{\log_z y} \times \left(\frac{\log_y x}{\log_z y}\right)$$

$$= \frac{\left(\frac{\log_k x}{\log_k y}\right)}{\left(\frac{\log_k y}{\log_k z}\right)} \times \frac{\left(\frac{\log_k x}{\log_k y}\right)}{\left(\frac{\log_k y}{\log_k z}\right)} \quad [\text{For some base } k]$$

$$= \left(\frac{\log_k x}{\log_k y}\right)^3 = \left(\log_y x\right)^3 = (ab)^3$$

So, $ab - a^3b^3 = 0$

$$\Rightarrow a \times b\left(1 - a^2b^2\right) = 0$$

$$\Rightarrow ab = \pm 1$$

Only option (e)does not satisfy.

13. e Equation (ii)can be written as

$$4^{0.3x} \times 9^{0.2y} = 8 \times (81)^{1/5}$$

$$\Rightarrow (2^2)^{0.3x}(3^2)^{0.2y} = 8 \cdot (81)^{1/5}$$

$$\Rightarrow 2^{0.6x}\, 3^{0.4y} = 2^3 \cdot (3^4)^{1/5} = 2^3 \cdot 3^{4/5}$$

$$\Rightarrow 0.6x = 3$$

$$\Rightarrow x = 5 \quad \text{and } 0.4y = \frac{4}{5}$$

$$\Rightarrow y = 2$$

If we put the values of x and y in first equation these values satisfy the first equation also.

So the answer is x = 5, y = 2

Hence, option (e)is the correct option

14. c $\log_2(a+b) + \log_2(a-b) = 3$

$$\Rightarrow \log_2(a+b)(a-b) = 3$$

$$\Rightarrow \log_2\left(a^2 - b^2\right) = \log_2 2^3$$

$$\Rightarrow a^2 - b^2 = 8$$

Solving the above equation for integer values of a and b, we get (a, b) ≡ (3, 1) or (3, –1).

Note: ‘a – b’ must be greater than zero.

15. a $\log_{16} 5 = \frac{1}{4} \times \frac{\log 5}{\log 2} = m$ ...(i)

$\log_5 3 = \frac{\log 3}{\log 5} = n$ ...(ii)

From equations (i) and (ii), we get

$$m \times n = \frac{\log 5}{\log 2} \times \frac{1}{4} \times \frac{\log 3}{\log 5} \text{ or } \frac{\log 2}{\log 3} = \frac{1}{4mn}$$

Let $\log_3 6$ be equal to k; therefore,

$$\log_3 6 = \frac{\log 6}{\log 3} = \frac{\log 3 + \log 2}{\log 3} = 1 + \frac{\log 2}{\log 3} = k$$

$$\therefore \quad k = \frac{1+4mn}{4mn}.$$

16. c $X = (\log_{10} 1 + \log_{10} 2 + \ldots + \log_{10} n)$
$- (\log_{10} 1 + \log_{10} 2 + \ldots + \log_{10} p)$
$- (\log_{10} 1 + \log_{10} 2 + \ldots + \log_{10}(n - p))$

$$\Rightarrow X = \log_{10} n! - \log_{10} p! - \log_{10}(n-p)!$$

$$\Rightarrow X = \log_{10} \frac{n!}{p!(n-p)!}.$$

X is maximum when $\frac{n!}{p!(n-p)!}$ is maximum.

$\Rightarrow \frac{8!}{p!(8-p)!}$ is maximum, i.e. ${}^8C_p$ is maximum

$$\Rightarrow p = 4$$

$$\Rightarrow X = \log_{10} \frac{8!}{4!(8-4)!} = \log_{10} 70 = 1 + \log_{10} 7.$$

17. b By the question,

$$\log_3(2^x - 5) - \log_3 2 = \log_3\left(2^x - \frac{7}{2}\right) - \log_3(2^x - 5)$$

$$\Rightarrow \log_3\left(\frac{2^x - 5}{2}\right) = \log_3\left(\frac{2^x - \frac{7}{2}}{2^x - 5}\right)$$

$$\Rightarrow \frac{2^x - 5}{2} = \frac{2^x - \frac{7}{2}}{2^x - 5}.$$

Let $2^x = a$

$$\Rightarrow \frac{a-5}{2} = \frac{a - \frac{7}{2}}{a-5}.$$

$$\Rightarrow a^2 - 10a + 25 = 2a - 7$$

$$\Rightarrow a^2 - 12a + 32 = 0$$

$$\Rightarrow (a-4)(a-8) = 0$$

$$\Rightarrow a = 4 \text{ or } 8$$

$$\therefore x = 2 \text{ or } 3.$$

Hence, $2^x - 5 = -1$,

when x = 2, which is not possible.

$$\therefore x = 3.$$

18. 0 Clearly, x > 0

The equation reduces to $2x = x^2 + 2x + 1$

$\Rightarrow 0 = x^2 + 1$

Which does not have real roots.

Hence, there are no solutions.

19. $\log_c a = \frac{1}{2}$ or $c = a^2$ ...(i)

$\log_d b = \frac{1}{3}$ or $d = b^3$ ...(ii)

Clearly, 'a' and 'b' cannot be equal to 1.

Therefore, $a_{min.} = 2$ and $b_{min.} = 3$

The minimum possible value of a + b + c + d

$= 2 + 3 + 4 + 27 = 36$

20. $\log_3 5 = \log_5 (2 + x)$

Only $3 < x < 23$ is true.

21. $\frac{\log(2^3 \times 3^3 \times 5) + \log(2^6 \times 3 \times 5^7) + \log(2 \times 3^2 \times 5^4)}{3}$

$= \log (2^a \times 3^b \times 5^c)$

$\Rightarrow \log(2^8 \times 3^4 \times 5^8) + \log(2 \times 3^2 \times 5^4)$

$= 3 \log(2^a \times 3^b \times 5^c)$

$\log (2^9 \times 3^6 \times 5^{12}) = 3 \log (2^a \times 3^b \times 5^c)$.

$\Rightarrow 2^9 \times 3^6 \times 5^{12} = (2^a \times 3^b \times 5^c)^3$

$\Rightarrow 3a = 9, a = 3.$

22. $\log_2 (5 + \log_3 a) = 3$

$2^3 = 5 + \log_3 a$

$\log_3 a = 3$

$3^3 = a$

$\Rightarrow a = 27$

$\log_5 (4a + 12 + \log_2 b) = 3$

$5^3 = 4a + 12 + \log_2 b.$

$\Rightarrow \log_2 b = 125 - 120$

$\log_2 b = 5$

$b = 2^5 = 32$

Hence, a + b = 27 + 32 = 59

23. $\log_{12} 81 = p$

$$3\left[\frac{4-p}{4+p}\right] = 3\left[\frac{4-\frac{\log 81}{\log 12}}{4+\frac{\log 81}{\log 12}}\right] = 3\left[\frac{4\log 12 - \log 81}{4\log 12 + \log 81}\right]$$

$$= 3\left[\frac{\log \frac{12^4}{81}}{\log(12)^4 \times 81}\right] = 3\frac{\log 4^4}{\log(12)^4 \times (3)^4}$$

$$= \frac{12\log 4}{4\log 36} = \frac{24\log 2}{8\log 6}$$

$$= \frac{3\log 2}{\log 6} = \frac{\log 8}{\log 6} = \log_6 8$$

24. $2^x = 3^{\log_5 2}$

Taking log both sides

$\log 2^x = \log 3^{\log_5 2}$

$x \log 2 = \log_5 2 \times \log 3$

$x \log 2 = \frac{\log 2}{\log 5} \times \log 3$

$x = \frac{\log 3}{\log 5} + 1 - 1$

$x = \frac{\log 3 - \log 5}{\log 5} + 1 = \frac{\log \frac{3}{5}}{\log 5} + 1 = 1 + \log_5 \frac{3}{5}$

25. $0.25 \le 2x \le 200$

So, the possible values of x

$= -2, -1, 0, 1, 2, 3, 4, 5, 6, 7.$

But $2^x + 2$ is perfectly divisible by either 3 or 4, so, on putting x = 0, 1, 2, 4, 6 in $2^x + 2$, the numbers obtained will be perfectly divisible by either 3 or 4. Hence, 5 values of x are possible.

26. Given that $x^{2018}\ y^{2017} = \frac{1}{2}$ and $x^{2016}\ y^{2019} = 8$

$x = \frac{1}{2}$ and $y = 2$ will satisfy the above equations.

As $\left(\frac{1}{2}\right)^{2018} \times (2)^{2017} = \frac{1}{2}$

$x^{2016}\ y^{2019} = \left(\frac{1}{2}\right)^2 \times (2)^{2019} = 8$

$\therefore x^2 + y^3 = \left(\frac{1}{2}\right)^2 + (2)^3$

$= \frac{1}{4} + 8 = \frac{33}{4}$

27. Let $p^3 = q^4 = r^5 = s^6 = k$

$\Rightarrow p = k^{1/3}, q = k^{1/4}, r = k^{1/5}$ and $s = k^{1/6}$

$\Rightarrow \log_s(pqr)$

$$= \frac{\log k^{\left(\frac{1}{3}+\frac{1}{4}+\frac{1}{5}\right)}}{\log k^{\frac{1}{6}}} = \frac{\frac{47}{60}\log k}{\frac{1}{6}\log k} = \frac{47}{60} \times 6 = \frac{47}{10}.$$

28. The given expression can be written as:

$\frac{1}{\log 100} \times (\log 2 - \log 4 + \log 5 - \log 10 + \log 20 - \log 25 + \log 50)$

$= \frac{1}{\log 100} \times (\log 2 \times 5 \times 20 \times 50 - \log 4 \times 10 \times 25)$

$= \frac{1}{2} \times \frac{1}{\log 10} \times \log \frac{10000}{1000} = \frac{1}{2}.$

Progressions

1. c $\frac{1}{(1\times 2)} + \frac{1}{(2\times 3)} + \frac{1}{(3\times 4)} + --- + \frac{1}{(100\times 101)}$

$= \left(1 - \frac{1}{2}\right) + \left(\frac{1}{2} - \frac{1}{3}\right) + \left(\frac{1}{3} - \frac{1}{4}\right)$

$+ --- + \left(\frac{1}{99} - \frac{1}{100}\right) + \left(\frac{1}{100} - \frac{1}{101}\right) = 1 - \frac{1}{101} = \frac{100}{101}.$

2. d First elements of each set = 1, 2, 4, 7, 11, 16, ... This series is neither an AP nor a GP, but the difference between the terms viz.1, 2, 3, 4, 5,..... is in AP with both first term and common difference as 1.

Hence, to find the 50th term of the original series we have to add the sum of 49 terms of the second series to the first term of the original series.

The sum of first 49 terms = $\frac{(49 \times 50)}{2}$ = 1225.

Therefore, the 50th term of the original series = (1225 + 1) = 1226.

This will be the first element of the set S_{50}, which will have 50 elements.

The last element of S_{50} will be = 1226 + 49 = 1275.

So the sum of the elements in this set

$= \frac{50 \times (1226 + 1275)}{2} = 62525.$

3. a $U_0 = 2^0 - 1 = 0$

$U_1 = 2^1 - 1 = 1$

$U_2 = 2^2 - 1 = 3$

$U_3 = 2^3 - 1 = 7$ and so on.

Hence, $U_{10} = 2^{10} - 1 = 1023$.

4. c The harmonic mean of two numbers *x* and *y* is $\frac{2xy}{(x+y)}$ and the geometric mean is $\sqrt{xy}$.

$\therefore \frac{\frac{2xy}{(x+y)}}{\sqrt{xy}} = \frac{12}{13} \Rightarrow \frac{4xy}{(x+y)^2} = \frac{144}{169}.$

Although this can be simplified to get the answer, the best way to proceed from here would be to look out for the answer choices and figure out which pair of x & y satisfies the above equation. You will find the answer is (c).

HINT : Students please note that this sum is a classic example of how you could have gone for intelligent guess work. Since we know that the denominator of the ratio is the geometric mean, which is $\sqrt{xy}$, the two numbers should be in such a ratio that their product should be a perfect square. The only pair from the answer choices that supports this is 4 & 9, as $\sqrt{4 \times 9} = \sqrt{36} = 6$.

5. c Middle term of an A.P. is average of all the terms in A.P.

Number of terms = 7

Middle term = Fourth term = 8

Therefore, sum of all the terms = 56.

6. d Let the number of stones be 'n'.

As the person covers 4.8 km, he covers 2.4 km on one side and 2.4 km on other side.

So total distance covered by him = 20 + 40 + 60 +......

$\therefore 2400 = \frac{n}{2}\left[2 \times 20 + (n-1)20\right] = 10n(n+1)$

(Here n is the number of stones)

After solving, we get n = 15

$\therefore$ Total number of stones = 15 + 15 + 1 = 31

7. b Let the number of toffees with the first, second and third boy be x, (x + 4) and (x + 8) respectively.

Hence, total number of toffees = (3x + 12).

The statement I merely suggests that (3x + 12) is a multiple of 2, which means that x is a multiple of 2. Nothing concrete can be concluded on the basis of this statement.

The statement II suggests that (x – 4 + 2), (x + 4 – 6 + 2) and (x + 8 – 4)are in GP or (x – 2), x and (x + 4) is in GP.

$\therefore x^2 = (x+4)(x-2)$

$\Rightarrow x = 4$

$\Rightarrow (3x + 12) = 24$

Question can be answered using statement II alone.

8. a Since 116 is less than 11^2, it can be figured out that both the first two terms of the AP should be less than 10.

There is only one pair of positive integers whose squares add up to 116 and they are 10 and 4.

Thus, these two should be the first two terms of the AP. Hence, the first term is 4, and can be obtained only from statement I.

Statement II merely suggests that the fifth term is of the form 7k. Nothing correct can be concluded from this.

For questions 9 to 13:

First series: $(S_1) = x,\ y,\ \frac{x}{2},\ z,\ x + 20$

Second series: $(S_2) = a_1, a_2, a_3, a_4$

Now $a_1 = y - x$, $a_2 = \frac{x}{2} - y$, $a_3 = z - \frac{x}{2}$

and $a_4 = x + 20 - z$

$a_2 - a_1 = 30$ gives $3x - 4y = 60$ ... (i)

$a_4 - a_3 = 30$ gives $3x - 4z = 20$ ... (ii)

and $a_4 - a_2 = 60$ gives $x - 2z + 2y = 80$ .. (iii)

Solving these equations we get the values of $x = 100, y = 60, z = 70$

$\therefore S_1 = 100, 60, 50, 70, 120$

$S_2 = -40, -10, 20, 50$

14. a Let there be x bacteria in the first generation i.e. $n_1 = x$.

$\therefore n_2 = 8x$, but only 50% survives

$\Rightarrow n_{2,survived} = \frac{8x}{2} = 4x$

$n_3 = 8(4x)$, but only 50% survives

$n_{3,survived} = 4^2x$

Similarly,

$n_{7survived} = 4^{7-1}x = 4096$ million

$\therefore x = 1$ million.

15. a Statement II is not required at all as no way can we express X in terms of 'a'.

Statement I implies that $X + Y = 2a$ and $XY = a^2$. Solving these two, we can say that $X = a$.

Hence, statement I alone is sufficient to answer the question.

16. d The ideal approach is to pick up the options one by one.

Option (a)– Let S1 and S2 be two sequences of positive numbers. After change of sign, S1 will consist of negative numbers while S2 remains unchanged. Clearly, the members of S1 would be less than that of S2. Hence, option (a) is not correct.

Option (b)- Let S1 and S2 be two sequences of positive numbers. After change of sign, S1 will consist of negative numbers while S2 remains unchanged. Clearly, G would remain in S2 itself. Hence, option (b)is not correct.

Option (c)– If S1 and S2 had same sign, say positive initially, then the largest number of S1 and S2 would be in S2. Then after the change of sign, every member of S1 will be negative and therefore, less than every member of S2. This implies that the largest number would remain in S2. Hence, option (c) is not correct.

17. a The elements of S1 are in the order : $a_1 < a_2 < a_3 < a_4 < \ldots < a_{24}$

The elements of S2 are in the order: $a_{25} > a_{26} > \ldots > a_{49} > a_{50}$

Even if a_{24} and a_{25} are interchanged, the elements of S1 continues to be in ascending order. However, nothing can be concluded about the elements of S2.

18. d Since every element of S1 is less than or equal to each member of S2, L will be in S1 and G in S2.

For some i $(1 \le i \le 24)$, $a_i = L$ and for some j $(25 \le j \le 50)$, $a_j = G$.

Every other element of S1 is greater than a_i and every other member of S2 is less than a_j.

Therefore, to make every element of S1 greater than or equal to that of S2, we need to add a minimum of $(a_j - a_i) = G - L$.

19. d $a_1 = 1, a_2 = 7, a_3 = 19, a_4 = 43$.

The difference between successive terms is in series 6, 12, 24, 48, ..., i.e. they are in GP. Hence,

$$a_{100} = a_1 + a\left(\frac{r^n - 1}{r - 1}\right) = 1 + 6\frac{(2^{99} - 1)}{(2 - 1)} = 6 \times 2^{99} - 5$$

20. c $\frac{1}{1.3} + \frac{1}{3.5} + \frac{1}{5.7} + \ldots + \frac{1}{19.21}$

$$= \frac{1}{2}\left(1 - \frac{1}{3}\right) + \frac{1}{2}\left(\frac{1}{3} - \frac{1}{5}\right) + \frac{1}{2}\left(\frac{1}{5} - \frac{1}{7}\right) + \ldots + \frac{1}{2}\left(\frac{1}{19} - \frac{1}{21}\right)$$

$$= \frac{1}{2} - \frac{1}{42} = \frac{(21 - 1)}{42} = \frac{20}{42} = \frac{10}{21}$$

21. a Each term has to be either 1 or –1.

Hence, if the sum of n such terms is 0, then n is even.

22. a Amount of money given to X

$= 12 \times 300 + 12 \times 330 + \ldots + 12 \times 570$

$= 12[300 + 330 + \ldots + 540 + 570]$

$= 12 \times \frac{10}{2}[600 + 9 \times 30] = 52200$

Amount of money given to Y is

$6 \times 200 + 6 \times 215 + 6 \times 230 + 6 \times 245 + \ldots$ to 20 terms

$= 6[200 + 215 + 280 + \ldots 485]$

$= 6 \times \frac{20}{2}[400 + 19 \times 15]$

$= 6 \times 10[400 + 285]$

$= 60 \times 685 = 41100$

$\therefore$ Total amount paid = 52200 + 41100 = Rs. 93,300.

23. c Let the total number of pages in the book be n.

Let page number x be repeated.

Then $\sum_{i=1}^{n} i + x = 1000$

$\frac{n(n+1)}{2} + x = 1000$

Thus, $\frac{n(n+1)}{2} \le 1000$ gives n = 44

Since $\frac{n(n+1)}{2} = 990$ (for n = 44), hence, x = 10.

24. c Let the 6th and the 7th terms be x and y.

Then 8th term = x + y

Also $y^2 - x^2 = 517$

$\Rightarrow (y + x)(y - x) = 517 = 47 \times 11$

So y + x = 47

y – x = 11

Taking y = 29 and x = 18, we have 8th term = 47,

9th term = 47 + 29 = 76 and 10th term = 76 + 47 = 123.

25. d $x_0 = x$

$x_1 = -x$

$x_2 = -x$

$x_3 = x$

$x_4 = x$

$x_5 = -x$

$x_6 = -x$

....

$\Rightarrow$ Choices (a), (b), (c) are incorrect.

26. a Coefficient of $x^n = \frac{1}{2}(n+1)(n+4)$

$S = 2 + 5x + 9x^2 + 14x^3 + ...$

$xS = 2x + 5x^2 + ...$

$S(1-x) = 2 + 3x + 4x^2 + 5x^3 + ...$

Let $S_1 = S(1-x) \Rightarrow S_1 = 2 + 3x + 4x^2 + ...$

$xS_1 = 2x + 3x^2 + ...$

$S_1(1-x) = 2 + x + x^2 + ...$

$S_1(1-x) = 2 + \frac{x}{1-x}$

$S(1-x^2) = 2 + \frac{x}{1-x} \Rightarrow S = \frac{2-x}{(1-x)^3}$

27. d $575 = \frac{n^2+n}{2} - x$

$1150 = n^2 + n - 2x$

$n(n+1) \ge 1150$

$n^2 + n \ge 1150$

The smallest value for it is n = 34.

For n = 34,

40 = 2x $\Rightarrow$ x = 20

28. c $\frac{P + \frac{P}{\sqrt{2}} + \cdots\infty}{A + \frac{A}{2} + \cdots\infty} = \frac{\frac{P}{1-\frac{1}{\sqrt{2}}}}{2A} = \frac{P\sqrt{2}}{(\sqrt{2}-1)} \times \frac{1}{2A}$

$= \frac{\sqrt{2}P(\sqrt{2}+1)}{2A} = \frac{\sqrt{2} \times 4a(\sqrt{2}+1)}{2 \times a^2}$

$= \frac{\sqrt{2} \times 2(\sqrt{2}+1)}{a} = \frac{2(2+\sqrt{2})}{a}$

29. c Let $S = 1 + \frac{4}{7} + \frac{9}{7^2} + \frac{16}{7^3} + \frac{25}{7^4}$ ... (i)

$\therefore \frac{1}{7}S = \frac{1}{7} + \frac{4}{7^2} + \frac{9}{7^3} + \frac{16}{7^4}$ ... (ii)

(i) – (ii) gives,

$S\left(1-\frac{1}{7}\right) = 1 + \frac{3}{7} + \frac{5}{7^2} + \frac{7}{7^3} + \frac{9}{7^4}$ ... (iii)

$\frac{1}{7} \times S\left(1-\frac{1}{7}\right) = \frac{1}{7} + \frac{3}{7^2} + \frac{5}{7^3} + \frac{7}{7^4}$ ... (iv)

(iii) – (iv) gives,

$S\left(1-\frac{1}{7}\right) - \frac{1}{7}S\left(1-\frac{1}{7}\right) = 1 + \frac{2}{7} + \frac{2}{7^2} + \frac{2}{7^3} + \frac{2}{7^4} \cdots$

$\Rightarrow S\left(1-\frac{1}{7}\right)\left(1-\frac{1}{7}\right) = 1 + \frac{2}{7}\left[1 + \frac{1}{7} + \frac{1}{7^2} + \cdots\infty\right]$

$\Rightarrow S\left(1-\frac{1}{7}\right)^2 = 1 + \frac{2}{7} \times \frac{1}{1-\frac{1}{7}}$

$\Rightarrow S\left(\frac{6}{7}\right)^2 = 1 + \frac{2}{7} \times \frac{7}{6} \Rightarrow S \times \frac{36}{49} = 1 + \frac{1}{3}$

$\Rightarrow S = \frac{49}{36} \times \frac{4}{3} \Rightarrow S = \frac{49}{27}$

30. c Let the 1st term be 'a' and common difference be 'd' then we have 3rd term = a + 2d

15th term = a + 14d

6th term = a + 5d

11th term = a + 10d

13th term = a + 12d

Since sum of 3rd and 15th term = sum of 6th, 11th and 13th term, therefore, we have

2a + 16d = 3a + 27d

$\Rightarrow$ a + 11d = 0

which is the 12th term.

31. d The number of terms of the series forms the sum of first n natural numbers i.e. $\frac{n(n+1)}{2}$.

Thus the first 23 letters will account for the first $\frac{23\times24}{2}$ = 276 terms of the series.

The 288th term will be the 24th letter which is x.

32. c Assume the number of horizontal layers in the pile be n.

So $\Sigma\frac{n(n+1)}{2} = 8436$

$\Rightarrow \frac{1}{2}\ [\Sigma n^2 + \Sigma n] = 8436$

$\Rightarrow \frac{n(n+1)\ (2n+1)}{12} + \frac{n(n+1)}{4} = 8436$

$\Rightarrow n(n+1)\left[\frac{2n+4}{12}\right] = 8436$

$\Rightarrow \frac{n(n+1)(n+2)}{6} = 8436$

$\Rightarrow n(n+1)(n+2) = 36\times37\times38$

So n = 36

33. c The best way to do this is to take some value and verify.

E.g. 2, $\frac{1}{2}$ and 1. Thus, n = 3 and the sum of the three numbers = 3.5.

Thus, options (a), (b)and (d) get eliminated.

Alternative method:

Let the n positive numbers be $a_1, a_2, a_3, \ldots a_n$

$a_1, a_2, a_3, \ldots a_n = 1$

We know that AM $\geq$ GM

Hence, $\frac{1}{n}(a_1 + a_2 + a_3 + \ldots + a_n) \geq (a_1a_2\ldots a_n)^{1/n}$

or $(a_1 + a_2 + a_3 + \ldots + a_n) \geq n$

34. d $T_n = a + (n-1)d$

$\Rightarrow 467 = 3 + (n-1)8$

$\Rightarrow n = 59$

Half of n = 29 terms

29th term is 227 and 30th term is 235 and when these two terms are added, the sum is less than 470.

Hence, the maximum possible values the set S can have is 30.

35. a Both the series are infinitely diminishing series.

For the first series: First term = $\frac{1}{a^2}$ and r = $\frac{1}{a^2}$

For the second series: First term = $\frac{1}{a}$ and r = $\frac{1}{a^2}$

The sum of the first series = $\frac{\frac{1}{a^2}}{1-\frac{1}{a^2}} = \frac{1}{a^2-1}$

The sum of the second series = $\frac{\frac{1}{a}}{1-\frac{1}{a^2}} = \frac{a}{a^2-1}$

Now, from the first statement, the relation can be anything (depending on whether a is positive or negative).

But the second statement tells us, $4a^2 - 4a + 1 = 0$ or a = $\frac{1}{2}$. For this value of a, the sum of second series will always be greater than that of the first.

36. a Given

$t_1 + t_2 + \ldots + t_{11} = t_1 + t_2 + \ldots + t_{19}$ (for an A.P.)

$\Rightarrow \frac{11}{2}[2a + (11-1)d] = \frac{19}{2}[2a + (19-1)d]$

$\Rightarrow 22a + 110d = 38a + 342d$

$\Rightarrow 16a + 232d = 0$

$\Rightarrow 2a + 29d = 0$

$\Rightarrow \frac{30}{2}[2a + (30-1)d] = 0$

$\Rightarrow S_{30\text{terms}} = 0$

37. a There will be an increase of 6 times.

Number of members s_1 will be in A.P.

On July 2nd , 2004, s_1 will have n + 6 b members = n + 6 × 10.5 n = 64n

Number of members in s_2 will be in G.P

On July 2nd, 2004, number of members in $s_2 = nr^6$

They are equal.

Hence, 64 n = nr^6

$\Rightarrow 64 = r^6 \Rightarrow r = 2$

38. c Given $a_1 = 81.33$; $a_2 = -19$

Also:

$a_j = a_{j-1} - a_{j-2}$, for $j \geq 3$

$\Rightarrow a_3 = a_2 - a_1 = -100.33$

$a_4 = a_3 - a_2 = -81.33$

$a_5 = a_4 - a_3 = 19$

$a_6 = a_5 - a_4 = +100.33$

$a_7 = a_6 - a_5 = +81.33$

$a_8 = a_7 - a_6 = -19$

Clearly, a_7 onwards there is a cycle of 6 and the sum of terms in every such cycle = 0. Therefore, when we add $a_1, a_2, a_3, \ldots$upto a_{6002}, we will eventually be left with $a_1 + a_2$ only i.e. 81.33 – 19 = 62.33.

39. c $a_1 = 1$, $a_{n+1} - 3a_n + 2 = 4n$

$a_{n+1} = 3a_n + 4n - 2$

when n = 2 then $a_2 = 3 + 4 - 2 = 5$

when n = 3 then $a_3 = 3 \times 5 + 4 \times 2 - 2 = 21$

from the options, we get an idea that a_n can be expressed in a combination of some power of 3 & some multiple of 100.

(a) $3^{99} - 200$; tells us that a_n could be: $3^{n-1} - 2 \times n$; but it does not fit a_1 or a_2 or a_3

(b) $3^{99} + 200$; tells us that a_n could be: $3^{n-1} + 2 \times n$; again, not valid for a_1, a_2 etc.

(c) $3^{100} - 200$; tells $3^n - 2n$: valid for all a_1, a_2, a_3.

(d) $3^{100} + 200$; tells $3^n + 2n$: again not valid.

Hence, (c)is the correct answer.

40. a $t_3 \times t_4 \times t_5 \times .... \times t_{53}$

$$= \frac{3}{5} \times \frac{4}{6} \times \frac{5}{7} \times .... \times \frac{51}{53} \times \frac{52}{54} \times \frac{53}{55} = \frac{3 \times 4}{54 \times 55} = \frac{2}{495}$$

Hence, option (a)is the correct answer.

41. d Let the no. of students in front row be x.

So, the no. of students in next rows be x – 3, x - 6, x – 9,.... so on

If n i.e. no. of rows be 3, then

$x + (x - 3) + (x - 6) = 630$

$\Rightarrow 3x = 639 \Rightarrow x = 213$

So possible.

Similarly, for n = 4,

$x + (x - 3) + (x - 6) + (x - 9) = 630$

$\Rightarrow 4x - 18 = 630$

$\Rightarrow x = \frac{648}{4} = 162$

$\therefore$ x = 4 to possible.

If n = 5,

$(4x - 18) + (x - 12) = 630$

$\Rightarrow 5x - 30 = 630$

$\Rightarrow x = 120$

Again n = 5 is possible.

If n = 6,

$(5x - 30) + (x - 15) = 630$

$\Rightarrow 6x - 45 = 630$

$\Rightarrow 6x = 675$

$\Rightarrow x \neq$ Integer

Hence, $n \neq 6$.

42. d Let number of elements in progression be n, then

$1000 = 1 + (n-1)d$

$\Rightarrow (n-1)d = 999 = 3^3 \times 37$

Possible values of d = 3, 37, 9, 111, 27, 333, 999

Hence, 7 progressions are possible.

43. b Sum of the odd integers in the set S

$= \frac{n}{2}(2 \times 3 + (n-1) \times 2)$

$= \frac{n}{2}(2n + 4) = n \times (n+2)$

Therefore, the average of the odd integers in set S = n + 2

Sum of the even integers in the set S

$= \frac{n}{2}(2 \times 2 + (n-1) \times 2)$

$= \frac{n}{2}(2n + 2) = n \times (n+1)$

Therefore, the average of the even integers in the set S = n + 1

Hence, X – Y = (n + 2)– (n + 1) = 1

44. c Price of Darjeeling tea (in rupees per kilo gram)is 100 + 0.10n

Price of Ooty tea (in rupees per kilo gram)is 89 + 0.15n

Price of the Darjeeling tea on the 100th day = 100 + 0.1 × 100 = 110 $\Rightarrow 89 + 0.15n = 110 \Rightarrow n = 140$

Number of days in the months of January, February, March and April in the year 2007 = 31 + 28 + 31 + 30 = 120.

Therefore, the price of both the tea will be equal on 20th May.

45. a $a_n + b_n (n \text{ is even}) = p^{\frac{n}{2}} q^{\frac{n}{2}} + p^{\frac{n}{2}-1} q^{\frac{n}{2}+1}$

$$= q(pq)^{\frac{n}{2}-1}(p+q)$$

46. d $a_n + b_n (n \text{ is odd}) = p^{\frac{n+1}{2}} q^{\frac{n-1}{2}} + p^{\frac{n-1}{2}} q^{\frac{n+1}{2}}$

$$= (p+q)(pq)^{\frac{n-1}{2}}$$

Substituting $p = \frac{1}{3}$ and $q = \frac{2}{3}$

$$a_n + b_n = \left(\frac{2}{9}\right)^{\frac{n-1}{2}}$$

Substituting n = 7, $a_n + b_n > 0.01$

Substituting n = 9, $a_n + b_n < 0.01$

Hence, smallest value of n is 9.

47. c Total sum of the numbers written on the blackboard $= \frac{40 \times 41}{2} = 820$

When two numbers 'a' and 'b' are erased and replaced by a new number a + b – 1, the total sum of the numbers written on the blackboard is reduced by 1.

Since this operation is repeated 39 times, therefore, the total sum of the numbers will be reduced by 1 × 39 = 39.

Therefore, after 39 operations there will be only 1 number that will be left on the blackboard and that will be 820 – 39 = 781.

48. c Total number of terms in the sequence 17, 21, 25, ... ,417 is equal to $\frac{417-17}{4}+1=101$.

Total number of terms in the sequence 16, 21, 26, ..., 466 is equal to $\frac{466-16}{5}+1=91$.

n^{th} term of the first sequence = 4n + 13.

m^{th} term of the second sequence = 5m + 11.

As per the information given in the question 4n + 13 = 5m + 11

$\Rightarrow$ 5m – 4n = 2.

Possible integral values of n that satisfy 5m = 2 + 4n are (2, 7, 12, ..., 97)

Therefore, the total number of terms common in both the sequences is 20.

49. a $S=\sqrt{1+\frac{1}{1^2}+\frac{1}{2^2}}+\sqrt{1+\frac{1}{2^2}+\frac{1}{3^2}}+\ldots+\sqrt{1+\frac{1}{2007^2}+\frac{1}{2008^2}}$

$$T_n=\sqrt{1+\frac{1}{n^2}+\frac{1}{(n+1)^2}}$$

$$=\sqrt{\frac{n^4+2n^3+3n^2+2n+1}{n^2(n+1)^2}}$$

$$=\frac{n^2+n+1}{n^2+n}=1+\frac{1}{n^2+n}$$

$$S=\sum_{n=1}^{2007}T_n=2007+\sum_{n=1}^{2007}\left\{\frac{1}{n}-\frac{1}{n+1}\right\}$$

$$=2008-\frac{1}{2008}$$

50. b Let the nth term of the A.P. be a_n and common difference be d.

$a_{n+1}=a_1+nd$

$a_{n+2}=a+(n+1)d=(a+d)+nd=a_2+nd$

$\ldots a_{2n}=a+(2n-1)d=(a+(n-1)d)+nd=a_n+nd$

Sum of first n terms = $a_1+a_2\ldots\ldots+a_n=100$

Sum of next n terms = $a_{n+1}+a_{n+2}\ldots\ldots+a_{2n}$

$=a_1+a_2\ldots\ldots+a_n+n(nd)$

$=100+n^2d=300$

Hence, $n^2d=200.$

Also, sum of the first n terms

$$=\left(\frac{n}{2}\right)(2a+(n-1)d)$$

$$=an+n^2\frac{d}{2}-n\frac{d}{2}$$

$$=an+\frac{200}{2}-n\frac{d}{2}=100$$

Hence, $an=n\frac{d}{2}$

$\Rightarrow$ a : d = 1 : 2

51. c Sum of $a_0+a_1+\ldots\ldots+a_{50}=1+3+\ldots\ldots+101$ = 2601

52. b E = 3 + 8 + 15 + 24 + ... + 195 = 1 × 3 + 2 × 4 + 3 × 5 + 4 × 6 + ...+ 13 × 15

$\therefore$ $T_n=n(n+2)$ and n = 13

$$\therefore\ E=\sum_{n=1}^{13}T_n=\sum_{n=1}^{13}n(n+2)$$

$$=\frac{n(n+1)(2n+1)}{6}+2\times\frac{n(n+1)}{2}$$

$$=\frac{13\times14\times27}{6}+2\times\frac{13\times14}{2}=1001$$

$$=7\times11\times13$$

Hence, the sum of the prime factors of E

= 7 + 11 + 13 = 31.

53. d Say you have an equation,

$(x-1)(x-2)(x-3)=0$

$\Rightarrow$ $(x^2-3x+2)(x-3)=0$

$\Rightarrow$ $x^3-6x^2+11x-6=0$

By the question, $x=3$, $a_n=-6$, $a_1=-6$.

Substitute the above values in the option.

Option (a): $(-6)^3\geq3^3\times-6$

$\Rightarrow$ $-216\geq-168$

This is incorrect, thus option (a) is incorrect.

Option (b): $3^3\geq(-6)^3\times-6$

$27\geq6^4$

This is incorrect, thus option (b) is incorrect.

Option (c): $(-6)^3\geq3^3\times-6$

$\Rightarrow$ $-216\geq-168$

This is incorrect, thus option (c) is incorrect.

Thus, none of the options is necessarily true.

54. d When common difference is 1, the first term can be anything from 1 to 46 i.e. 46 values.

When common difference is 2, the first term can be anything from 1 to 42 i.e. 42 values.

Similarly, when common difference is 12, the first term can be anything from 1 to 2 i.e. 2 values.

$\therefore$ Total possible AP's = 46 + 42 + ... + 2

$$=12\left(\frac{2+46}{2}\right)=288.$$

55. a nth term of the series can be written as

$$\frac{1}{n!+(n+1)!} = \frac{1}{n!(n+2)} = \frac{(n+1)}{(n+2)!}$$

$$= \frac{1}{(n+1)!} - \frac{1}{(n+2)!}.$$

Put n = 1, 2, ... 10 to get

$$\left(\frac{1}{2!}-\frac{1}{3!}\right)+\left(\frac{1}{3!}-\frac{1}{4!}\right)+\ldots+\left(\frac{1}{10!}-\frac{1}{11!}\right)$$

$$= \frac{1}{2!}-\frac{1}{11!}.$$

56. d If we take the 1st option, and delete all perfect squares and perfect cubes, a total of 22 perfect square will be deleted ($1^2, 2^2 \ldots\ldots 22^{22}$) and a total of 7 perfect cubes will be deleted ($1^3, 2^3, \ldots 7^3$).

Two numbers are common in between them viz. 1^6 and 2^6 which are perfect squares as well as perfect cubes.

Thus, 500 is the (500 – 22 – 7 + 2) = 473rd term.

Hence, the 476th term will be 500 + 3 = 503.

57. c Let the number of balls with

$$P_i = a_i \ (i = 1 \text{ to } 11)$$

$$a_1 + a_3 + a_5 \ldots + a_{11} = 6(a_6) = 72.$$

As a_6 would be the arithmetic mean of these 11 numbers and

$$2(a_6) = (a_1 + a_{11}) = (a_2 + a_{10})$$
$$= (a_3 + a_9) = (a_4 + a_8)$$
$$= (a_5 + a_7)$$

$$\therefore \quad a_1 + a_6 + a_{11} = 3(a_6) = 36.$$

58. c $a_1 = 3(a_2 + a_3 + \ldots\infty)$

let $a_2 + a_3 + \ldots\infty = x$

$a_1 = 3x$

So, $a_1 + a_2 + a_3 + \ldots. = 32$

$\Rightarrow 4x = 32$

$\Rightarrow x = 8$

$\Rightarrow a_1 = 24$ and $a_2 + a_3 + \ldots = 8$

Now $a_2 = 3(a_3 + a_4 + \ldots)$

Let $a_3 + a_4 + \ldots = y$

$\Rightarrow a_2 = 3y$

$\Rightarrow 24 + 3y + y = 32$

$\Rightarrow 4y = 8$

$\Rightarrow y = 2$

$\Rightarrow a_2 = 6$

As $a_1 = 24$ and $a_2 = 6$

$$\Rightarrow a_5 = 24 \times \frac{1}{4} \times \frac{1}{4} \times \frac{1}{4} \times \frac{1}{4} = 24\left(\frac{1}{4}\right)^4 = \frac{3}{32}.$$

59. a $a_1 + a_2 + a_3 + \ldots a_{100}$

$$= \frac{1}{2\times5}+\frac{1}{5\times8}+\frac{1}{8\times11}+\ldots\frac{1}{299\times302}$$

$$= \frac{1}{3}\left[\frac{3}{2\times5}+\frac{3}{5\times8}+\frac{3}{8\times11}+\ldots\frac{3}{299\times302}\right]$$

$$= \frac{1}{3}\left[\frac{1}{2}-\frac{1}{5}+\frac{1}{5}-\frac{1}{8}+\frac{1}{8}-\frac{1}{11}+\ldots\frac{1}{299}-\frac{1}{302}\right]$$

$$= \frac{1}{3}\left[\frac{1}{2}-\frac{1}{302}\right] = \frac{1}{3}\left[\frac{151-1}{302}\right] = \frac{150}{3\times302} = \frac{25}{151}.$$

60. a x, y and z are in G.P.

$\therefore \ y^2 = xz$

$$x = \frac{y^2}{z}.$$

5x, 16y and 12z are in A.P.

32y = 12z + 5x

$$32y = 12z + \frac{5y^2}{z} \quad \left[\because x = \frac{y^2}{z}\right]$$

$32yz = 12z^2 + 5y^2$.

$12z^2 - 32yz + 5y^2 = 0$

Divide by y^2

$$12\left(\frac{z}{y}\right)^2 \ 32\left(\frac{z}{y}\right) + 5 = 0$$

On solving this quadratic equation, we get

$$\frac{z}{y} = \frac{1}{6} \text{ or } \frac{5}{2}$$

But as z > y, therefore $\frac{z}{y} = \frac{5}{2}$ is the only possible value, which is the common ratio of G.P.

61. b Let the series starting with a_1 be A and that with a_2 be B

For a_1 to be maximum we need a_2 to be maximum as well which will be 50

Therefore, arithmetic mean of B $= \frac{50+100}{2} = 75$

and thus the arithmetic mean of A will be 75 – 1 = 74

Hence, maximum value of a_1 = 74 – 51 × 1 = 23.

CHAPTER

Miscellaneous Questions

MISCELLANEOUS QUESTIONS

1990

1. There were x pigeons and y mynahs in a cage. One fine morning p of them escaped to freedom. If the bird keeper, knowing only that p = 7, was able to figure out without looking into the cage that at least one pigeon had escaped, then which of the following does not represent a possible (x,y) pair?

(a) (10,8)

(b) (7,2)

(c) (25,6)

(d) (12,4)

2. Mr.X enters a positive integer Y in an electronic calculator and then goes on pressing the square – root key repeatedly. Then

(a) The display does not stabilize

(b) The display becomes closer to 0

(c) The display becomes closer to 1

(d) May not be true and the answer depends on the choice of Y

3. Consider the following steps :

1. Put x = 1, y = 2
2. Replace x by xy
3. Replace y by y +1
4. If y = 5 then go to step 6 otherwise go to step 5.
5. Go to step 2
6. Stop

Then the final value of x equals

(a) 1 (b) 24

(c) 120 (d) 720

Direction for Question 4: The question is followed by two statements. As the answer, MARK,

(a) if the question can be answered with the help of statement I alone,

(b) if the question can be answered with the help of statement II alone,

(c) if both, statement I and statement II are needed to answer the question, and

(d) if the statement cannot be answered even with the help of both the statements.

4. The unit price of product P1 is non-increasing and that of product P2 is decreasing. Which product will be costlier 5 years hence?

I. Current unit price of P1 is twice that of P2.

II. 5 years ago, unit price of P2 was twice that of P1.

5. 116 people participated in a singles tennis tournament of knock out format. The players are paired up in the first round, the winners of the first round are paired up in second round, and so on till the final is played between two players. If after any round, there is odd number of players, one player is given a bye, i.e. he skips that round and plays the next round with the winners. Find the total number of matches played in the tournament.

(a) 115 (b) 53

(c) 232 (d) 116

Directions for Questions 6 to 9: The pages of a book are numbered 0, 1, 2 ... upto M, M>0. There are four categories of instructions that direct a person in positioning the book at a page. The instruction types and their meanings are :

1. OPEN : Position the book at page No. 1
2. CLOSE : Position the book at page No. 0
3. FORWARD, n :From the current page move forward by n pages; if, in this process, page number M is reached, stop at M.
4. BACKWARD, n : From the current page, move backward by n pages; if in this process, page number 0 is reached, stop at page number 0.

In each of the following questions, you will find a sequence of instructions formed from the above categories. In each case, let n_1 be the page number before the instructions are executed and n_2 be the page number at which the book is positioned after the instructions are executed.

6. FORWARD, 25 ; BACKWARD, 10.

Which of the following statements is true about above set of instructions?

(a) $n_1 = n_2$ if M = 10 and $n_1 = 0$

(b) M = 20 provided $n_1 > 0$

(c) $n_1 > 30$ provided M = 900

(d) $n_1 = 37$ provided M = 25

7. BACKWARD, 5; FORWARD, 5.

Which of the following statements is true about the above set of instructions?

(a) $n_1 = n_2$ provided $n_1 \geq 5$
(b) $n_1 = n_2$ provided $n_1 > 0$
(c) $n_2 = 5$ provided $M > 0$
(d) $n_1 > n_2$ provided $M > 0$

8. FORWARD, 10; FORWARD, 10.

Which of the following statements about the above instructions is true?

(a) $n_2 - n_1 = 20$ only if $n_1 = 0$
(b) $n_2 - n_1 = 20$ if $M > 20$ and $n_1 = 1$
(c) $n_2 - n_1 = 10$ if $M = 21$ and $n_1 = 0$
(d) $n_2 > n_1$ if $M > 0$

9. FORWARD, 5; BACKWARD, 4.

Which of the following statements about the above instructions is true?

(a) $n_2 = n_1 + 4$ Provided $1 < n_1 < 7$
(b) $n_2 = n_1$ provided $M < 6$
(c) $n_2 = n_1 + 1$ provided $M - n_1 > 5$
(d) $n_2 - n_1 < 0$ provided $M > 0$

Directions for Questions 10 and 11: There are 5 cities, A, B, C, D and E connected by 7 roads as shown in the figure below:

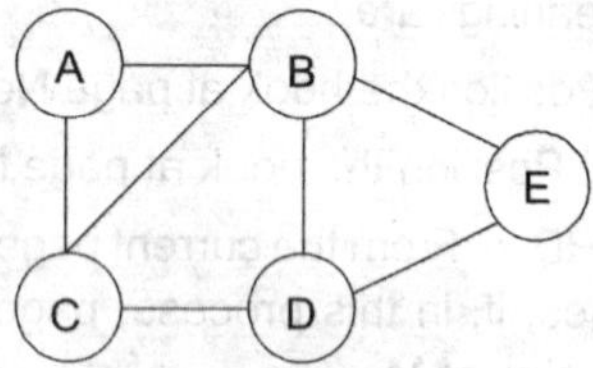

Design a route such that you start from any city of your choice and walk on each of the 7 roads once and only once, not necessarily returning to the city from which you started.

10. For a route that satisfies the above restrictions, which of the following statements is true?

(a) There is no route that satisfies the above restriction.
(b) A route can either start at C or end at C, but not both.
(c) D can be only an intermediate city in the route.
(d) The route has to necessarily end at E.

11. How many different starting cities are possible such that the above restriction is satisfied?

(a) One (b) Zero
(c) Three (d) Two

Directions for Questions 12 and 13: Answer the questions on the basis of the information given below.

In a game played by two people there were initially N match sticks kept on the table. A move in the game consists of a player removing either one or two matchsticks from the table. The one who takes the last matchstick loses. Players make moves alternately. The player who will make the first move is A. The other player is B.

12. The smallest value of N (greater than 5) that ensures a win for B is

(a) 7 (b) 6
(c) 10 (d) 8

13. The largest value of N (less than 50) that ensures a win for B is

(a). 46 (b) 47
(c) 48 (d) 49

1991

14. What is the total number of ways to reach A to B in the network given?

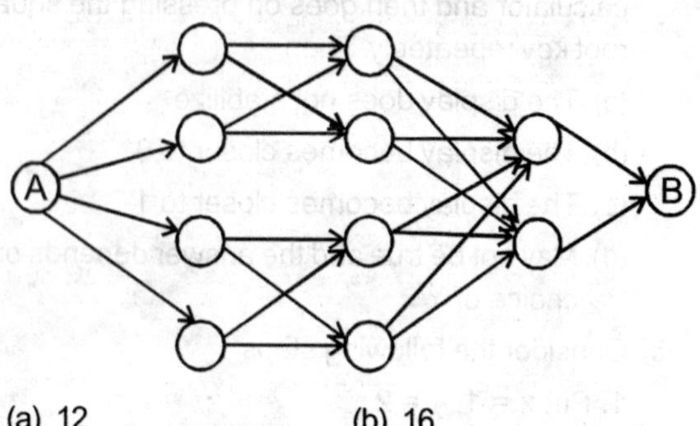

(a) 12 (b) 16
(c) 20 (d) 22

15. A calculator has two memory buttons, A and B. Value 1 is initially stored in both memory locations. The following sequence of steps is carried out five times:

add 1 to B

multiply A to B

store the result in A

What is the value stored in memory location A after this procedure?

(a) 120 (b) 450
(c) 720 (d) 250

16. In a six-node network, two nodes are connected to all the other nodes. Of the remaining four, each is connected to four nodes. What is the total number of links in the network?

(a) 13 (b) 15
(c) 7 (d) 26

1993

17. An intelligence agency decides on a code of 2 digits selected from 0, 1, 2, ... , 9. But the slip on which the code is hand–written allows confusion between top and bottom, because these are indistinguishable. Thus, for example, the code 91 could be confused with 16. How many codes are there such that there is no possibility of any confusion?

(a) 25
(b) 75
(c) 80
(d) None of these

18. 139 persons have signed up for an elimination tournament. All players are to be paired up for the first round, but because 139 is an odd number one player gets a bye, which promotes him to the second round, without actually playing in the first round. The pairing continues on the next round, with a bye to any player left over. If the schedule is planned so that a minimum number of matches is required to determine the champion, the number of matches which must be played is

(a) 136 (b) 137
(c) 138 (d) 139

19. There are ten 50 paise coins placed on a table. Six of these show tails, four show heads. A coin is chosen at random and flipped over (not tossed). This operation is performed seven times. One of the coins is then covered. Of the remaining nine coins, five show tails and four show heads. The covered coin shows

(a) a head
(b) a tail
(c) more likely a head
(d) more likely a tail

Directions for Questions 20 to 23: Use the following information:

Swetha, Swarna, Sneha and Soumya are four sisters who have an agreement that they share all snacks equally among themselves. One day, uncle Prem gave a box of cookies to Swetha. Since the other sisters were not around, Swetha divided the cookies into four parts, ate her share and put the rest into the box. As she was closing the box, Swarna came in, She took all the cookies from the box and divided them into four equal parts. Swetha and Swarna ate one part each and put the rest into the box. Just then Sneha walked in. She took all the cookies from the box, divided them into four equal parts. The three of them ate their respective shares and put the rest into the box. Later, when Soumya came, she divided all the cookies into four equal parts and all the four sisters ate their respective shares. In total, Soumya ate 3 cookies.

20. How many cookies, in total, did Sneha eat?

(a) 30 (b) 12
(c) 15 (d) 6

21. How many cookies did uncle Prem give to Swetha?

(a) 128 (b) 156
(c) 256 (d) 192

22. How many cookies, in total, did Swetha eat?

(a) 32 (b) 142
(c) 72 (d) 71

23. How many cookies, in total, did Swarna eat?

(a) 9 (b) 30
(c) 39 (d) 78

Directions for Questions 24 to 26 : The following functions have been defined for three numbers A, B and C:

@ (A, B) = average of A and B

*(A, B) = product of A and B

/(A, B) = A divided by B

Answer these questions with the above data.

24. If A = 2 and B = 4, the value of @(/(*(A, B), B), A) would be

(a) 2 (b) 4
(c) 6 (d) 16

25. The sum of A and B is given by

(a) *(@(A, B), 2)
(b) /(@(A, B), 2)
(c) @(*(A, B), 2)
(d) @(/(A, B), 2)

26. The sum of A, B, and C is given by

(a) *(@(*(@(B, A), 2), C), 3)
(b) /(@(*(@(B, A), 3), C), 2)
(c) /(*(@(*(B, A), 2), C), 3)
(d) None of these

1996

27. A cube of side 12 cm is painted red on all the faces and then cut into smaller cubes, each of side 3 cm. What is the total number of smaller cubes having none of their faces painted?

(a) 16 (b) 8
(c) 12 (d) 24

1998

Direction for Question 28: The question is followed by two statements, I and II. Answer the questions based on the statements and mark the answer as

(a) if the question can be answered with the help of any one statement alone but not by the other statement.

(b) if the question can be answered with the help of either of the statements taken individually.

(c) if the question can be answered with the help of both statements together.

(d) if the question cannot be answered even with the help of both statements together.

28. Find $2 \otimes 3$, where $2 \otimes 3$ need not be equal to $3 \otimes 2$.

I. $1 \otimes 2 = 3$

II. $a \otimes b = \frac{(a+b)}{a}$, where a and b are positive.

2001

29. If 09/12/2001(DD/MM/YYYY) happens to be Sunday, then 09/12/1971 would have been a

(a) Wednesday (b) Tuesday

(c) Saturday (d) Thursday

2002

30. The owner of a local jewellery store hired three watchmen to guard his diamonds, but a thief still got in and stole some diamonds. On the way out, the thief met each watchman, one at a time. To each he gave $\frac{1}{2}$ of the diamonds he had then, and 2 more besides. He escaped with one diamond. How many did he steal originally?

(a) 40 (b) 36

(c) 25 (d) None of these

Directions for Questions 31 and 32: Answer the questions based on the following information.

A boy is asked to put one mango in a basket when ordered '1', one orange when ordered '2', one apple when ordered '3', and is asked to take out from the basket one mango and an orange when ordered '4'. A sequence of orders is given as:

1 2 3 3 2 1 4 2 3 1 4 2 2 3 3 1 4 1 1 3 2 3 4

31. How many total oranges were in the basket at the end of the above sequence?

(a) 1 (b) 4

(c) 3 (d) 2

32. How many total fruits will be in the basket at the end of the above order sequence?

(a) 9 (b) 8

(c) 11 (d) 10

2003(R)

33. Using only 2, 5, 10, 25, and 50 paisa coins, what will be the minimum number of coins required to pay exactly 78 paise, 69 paise and Rs. 1.01 to three different persons?

(a) 19 (b) 20

(c) 17 (d) 18

2003(L)

34. Twenty-seven persons attend a party. Which one of the following statements can never be true?

(a) There is a person in the party who is acquainted with all the twenty-six others.

(b) Each person in the party has a different number of acquaintances.

(c) There is a person in the party who has an odd number of acquaintances.

(d) In the party, there is no set of three mutual acquaintances.

35. In a certain examination paper, there are n questions. For j = 1,2 …n, there are 2^{n-j} students who answered j or more questions wrongly. If the total number of wrong answers is 4095, then the value of n is

(a) 12 (b) 11

(c) 10 (d) 9

2004

Direction for Question 36: The question is followed by two statements, A and B. Answer the question using the following instructions.

Choose (a) if the question can be answered by using one of the statements alone but not by using the other statement alone.

Choose (b) if the question can be answered by using either of the statements alone.

Choose (c) if the question can be answered by using both statements together but not by either statement alone.

Choose (d) if the question cannot be answered on the basis of the two statements.

36. Tarak is standing 2 steps to the left of a red mark and 3 steps to the right of a blue mark. He tosses a coin. If it comes up heads, he moves one step to the right; otherwise he moves one step to the left. He keeps doing this until he reaches one of the two marks, and then he stops. At which mark does he stop?

A. He stops after 21 coin tosses.

B. He obtains three more tails than heads.

2008

Directions for Questions 37 and 38: The question is followed by two statements, A and B. Answer the question using the following instructions.

Mark (a) if Q can be answered from A alone but not from B alone.

Mark (b) if Q can be answered from B alone but not from A alone.

Mark (c) if Q can be answered from A alone as well as from B alone.

Mark (d) if Q can be answered from A and B together but not from any of them alone.

Mark (e) if Q cannot be answered even from A and B together.

In a single elimination tournament, any player is eliminated with a single loss. The tournament is played in multiple rounds subject to the following rules :

(a) If the number of players, say n, in any round is even, then the players are grouped into n/2 pairs. The players in each pair play a match against each other and the winner moves on to the next round.

(b) If the number of players, say n, in any round is odd, then one of them is given a bye, that is he automatically moves on to the next round. The remaining (n–1)players are grouped into (n–1)/2 pairs. The players in each pair play a match against each other and the winner moves on to the next round. No player gets more than one bye in the entire tournament.

Thus, if n is even, then n/2 players move on to the next round while if n is odd, then (n+1)/2 players move on to the next round. The process is continued till the final round, which obviously is played between two players. The winner in the final round is the champion of the tournament.

37. What is the number of Matches played by the champion?

A. The entry list for the tournament consists of 83 players.

B. The champion received one bye.

38. If the number of players, say n, in the first round was between 65 and 128, then what is the exact value of n?

A. Exactly one player received a bye in the entire tournament.

B. One player received a bye while moving on to the fourth round from the third round.

2016

39. A leap year X has exactly the same calendar as another leap year Y. What can be the absolute difference between the values of X and Y?

(a) 12 (b) 28

(c) 40 (d) All of these

ANSWERS

1. (a)	**2.** (c)	**3.** (b)	**4.** (d)	**5.** (a)	**6.** (a)	**7.** (a)	**8.** (b)	**9.** (c)	**10.** (b)
11. (d)	**12.** (a)	**13.** (d)	**14.** (b)	**15.** (c)	**16.** (a)	**17.** (c)	**18.** (c)	**19.** (a)	**20.** (c)
21. (a)	**22.** (d)	**23.** (c)	**24.** (a)	**25.** (a)	**26.** (a)	**27.** (b)	**28.** (a)	**29.** (d)	**30.** (b)
31. (d)	**32.** (c)	**33.** (a)	**34.** (b)	**35.** (a)	**36.** (b)	**37.** (d)	**38.** (d)	**39.** (d)	

EXPLANATIONS

1. a For the bird keeper to figure out that at least 1 pigeon had escaped, the number of mynahs has to be less than 7. In other words, $y < 7$. Hence, the pair (10,8)is not a valid one.

2. c Repeated square root of positive integer y

$$= \left(\left(\left(\left(y^{\frac{1}{2}}\right)^{\frac{1}{2}}\right)^{\frac{1}{2}}\right)^{\cdots\infty}\right) = (y)^{\frac{1}{2^{\infty}}} = y^0 = 1.$$

3. b The successive values of x and y are as follows:

Cycle	X	Y	XY	Y+1
1	1	2	2	3
2	2	3	6	4
3	6	4	24	5
4	24	5		

4. d Although using both the statements we can find out by how much has the price of P1 and P2 changed over the 5 years, we cannot answer the question that is being asked as it is no where mentioned that the rate of change is uniform.

5. a There are 116 players in all. If we have to choose 1 winner, there have to be 115 losers in all. And since 1 match gives 1 loser, there has to be 115 matches to be played in all in the tournament.

6. a FORWARD 25, BACKWARD 10 would effectively mean FORWARD 15 i.e. n_2-n_1 = 15, (if $M - n_1 > 25$) and $n_2 = M - 10$ (if $M - n_1 < 25$).

The only option satisfies is option (a).

So if M = 10 and n_1 = 0., then $M - n_1 < 25$ and so $n_2 = 10 - 10 = 0$. Hence, n_1=n_2.

7. a BACKWARD, 5; FORWARD, 5 would effectively mean $n_1 = n_2$ (in case $n_1 \geq 5$) or $n_2 = 5$ (in case n_1<5). The only option that satisfies this is (a).

8. b FORWARD, 10 ; FORWARD, 10 would effectively mean FORWARD 20 i.e. n_2-n_1 = 20, (if $M - n_1 \geq 20$).or $n_2 = M$ (if $M - n_1 < 20$).

The option that satisfies this condition is (b), as if M>20 and n_1=1, then $M - n_1 > 20$, and hence n_2-n_1 = 20.

9. c FORWARD, 5; BACKWARD, 4, would effectively mean FORWARD 1 i.e. n_2-n_1 = 1 (if $M - n_1 \geq 5$) or $n_2 = M - 4$ (if $M - n_1$< 5).

The option that satisfies this condition is (c).

10. b Option (a)cannot be true as there are many routes that satisfy the given condition. Option (c) is also not true as we can have a route starting from D (eg. DEBDCBAC). The route need not necessarily end at E, which is apparent from the given example.

Hence, the correct option is (b).

11. d City A is connected by 2 roads, B by 4 roads, C by 3 roads, D by 3 roads and E by 2 roads. For a city to be starting city for such a route, it has to be connected by odd number of roads. Hence, the required answer is 2 i.e. C and D are the stating cities.

For questions 12 and 13: Students please note that the best way to answer this question is by finding generally what would ensure a win for B. If B has to win, A has to pickup the last matchstick. This can be forced upon A if there are 2 or 3 matchsticks left on the table when it is B's turn. As then, B could pick-up 1 or 2 matchsticks and force upon A to pick-up the last one. For this to happen there should always be odd number of matchsticks initially. Eg. If there are 7 match sticks initially any of the following combinations will leave either 2 or 3 matchsticks on the table when it is B's turn.

A	B	B	A			
1	2	3	4	5	6	7

A	B	B	A	A		
1	2	3	4	5	6	7

A	A	B	A			
1	2	3	4	5	6	7

A	A	B	A	A		
1	2	3	4	5	6	7

Hence, the smallest value of N (greater than 5) to ensure a win for B is 7. Also the largest value of N (less than 50)to ensure a win for B is 49.

14. b Total number of ways to reach A to B = 4 × 2 × 2 × 1 = 16.

15. c

	A	B	Step I (B + 1)	Step II (A x B)	Step III A	Step III B
Beginning	1	1				
1st Time	1	1	B =2	(1 × 2) = 2	2	2
2nd Time	2	2	B = 3	(2 × 3) = 6	6	3
3rd Time	6	3	B = 4	(6 × 4) = 24	24	4
4th Time	24	4	B = 5	(24 × 5) = 120	120	5
5th Time	120	5	B = 6	(120 × 6) = 720	**720**	6

16. a We find that the total number of links in the network is 13. (Note : In the diagram given below, the top two nodes are connected to all the other nodes, while the remaining four are connected to only four other nodes).

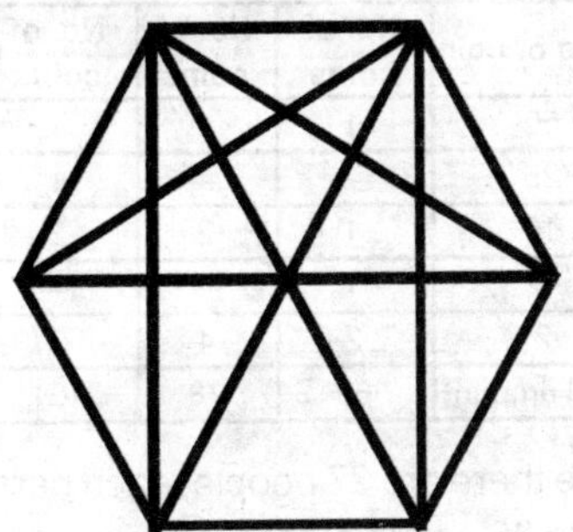

17. c Total number of two-digit codes that can be formed is 10 × 10 = 100

Out of them 0,1,6,8,9 can create confusion.

Using these five digits, total number of two-digit numbers that can be made is 5 × 5 = 25.

But out of these 25 numbers, 00, 11, 88, 69 and 96 will not make any confusion.

Hence, the required answer is 100 – 25 + 5 = 80.

18. c This can be logically done in the following manner. There are 139 players in all. We want to determine 1 champion among them. So all except the Champion should lose. A player can lose only once and since any match produces only one loser, to produce 138 losers, there should be 138 matches that should be played.

19. a The initial reading for 10 coins is : 6 Tails and 4 Heads

After repeating the process of flipping one coin at random for 7 times, the final reading for 9 coins is: 5 Tails and 4 Heads.

Therefore, possible final reading for 10 coins is:

6 Tails and 4 Heads or 5 Tails and 5 Heads.

If the final reading is 6T and 4H, it is same as the initial one. However, this is not possible as the process of flipping a coin has taken place an odd number of times, so there has to be atleast one change in the final reading.

Therefore, the final reading is 5T and 5H.

So the covered coin will certainly be a Head.

For questions 20 to 23: Since Soumya was the last one to eat the cookies and she ate 3 cookies, the total number of cookies left when she entered the room = (3 × 4) = 12. This should be Soumya's share that was left in the box uneaten. Hence, just before Soumya entered, Swetha, Sneha and Swarna would have eaten their share of 12 cookies each. Total number of cookies left when Sneha entered = (12 × 4) = 48. This in turn should have been the combined share of Sneha and Soumya (24 × 2) that was left in the box uneaten. So just before Sneha entered, Swetha and Swarna should have eaten 24 cookies each. In other, words number of cookies left, just before Swarna entered = (24 × 4) = 96. Now this should have been the combined share of Swarna, Sneha and Soumya (3 × 32) that was kept in the box by Swetha . So just before Swarna entered, Swetha must have eaten her share of 32 cookies. Hence, total number of cookies given by Prem uncle = (32 × 4) = 128.

The situation is also shown in the following table:-

		Number of cookies eaten					
		Swetha	**Swarna**	**Sneha**	**Soumya**	**Not Eaten**	**Total**
Girl entered	**Soumya**	3	3	3	3	-	12
	Sneha	12	12	12	-	12	48
	Swarna	24	24	-	-	(24×2) = 48	96
	Swetha	32	-	-	-	(32×3) = 96	128
	Total	71	39	15	3	-	-

20. c Sneha ate 15 cookies, in total.

21. a Prem uncle gave 128 cookies to Swetha.

22. d Swetha ate 71 cookies, in total.

23. c Swarna ate 39 cookies, in total.

24. a @(/(*(2, 4), 4), 2)= @(/(8, 4), 2) = @(2, 2) 2.

6.8 Miscellaneous Questions

25. a A + B = 2((A + B)/2)= 2(@(A, B)) = *(@(A, B), 2).

26. a Sum of A, B, C =[A + B + C] = 3{[2((A + B)/2) + C] / 3} =*(@(*(@(B, A), 2), C), 3).

(**HINT :** Students please note that for Q87 and Q88, if it doesn't strike you to simplify in this manner, the best way is to simplify the answer choices and work backwards.)

27. b Since each side of the smaller cube is 3 cm, it can be figured out that each face of the original cube is divided into 4 parts, or in other words, the original cube is divided into 64 smaller cubes. For a smaller cube to have none of its sides painted, it should not be a part of the face of the original cube (i.e. none of its faces should be exposed). We can find at the centre of the original cube there are (2 × 2 × 2)= 8 such cubes.

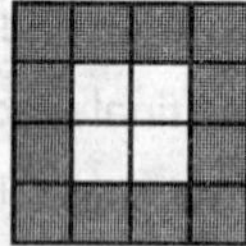

Hint: Students please note that the answer can only be a cube of some integer. The only cube among the answer choices is $(2)^3 = 8$.

28. a It is clear that statement II alone is enough to answer the question. This statement gives the value of the function $a \otimes b$, so we can find the value of $2 \otimes 3$.

So $2 \otimes 3 = \frac{(2+3)}{2} = 2.5$

29. d In 30 years from 1971 to 2001, number of odd days = 30 + (8 from leap years) = 38 and $38 \equiv 3 \bmod 7$

So December 9, 1971 is Sunday – 3 days = Thursday

30. b Since thief escaped with 1 diamond,

Before 3rd watchman he had (1 + 2) × 2 = 6 diamonds.

Before 2nd watchman he had (6 + 2) × 2 = 16 diamonds.

Before 1st watchman he had (16 + 2) × 2 = 36 diamonds.

31. d Number of oranges at the end of the sequence = Number of (2s)– Number of (4s) = 6 – 4 = 2

32. c Number of (1s + 2s + 3s)– 2(Number of 4s) = 19 – 8 = 11

33. a Let's make the given sum by using minimum number of coins as

Value of coin	No. of coins	No. of coins	No. of coins	Total no. of coins
50	1	1	1	3
25	—	—	1	1
10	1	2	2	5
5	1	—	—	1
2	2	4	3	9
Total amount	69	78	101	19

34. b Since there are 27 people, each person can have 0 upto 26 acquaintances.

If a person has zero acquaintances, then the maximum number of acquaintances any of the other persons can have is 25.

Similarly, if a person has one acquaintance, then the maximum number of acquaintances any of the other persons can have is 26.

Therefore, the number of acquaintances can be any number from 0 to 25 or from 1 to 26. This rules out options (a) and (c).

The congregation consists of 27 people whereas the number of acquaintances any person can have is 26 (either 0 to 25 or 1 to 26). This implies that there is one person who share the same number of acquaintances as atleast one of the other persons. This contradicts option (b).

Hence, (b)is the desired option.

Note: If we consider the situation other wise, to satisfy condition 2, the first person must have 26 acquaintances, the second 25, third 24 and so on. If we continue, the last one should have 0 acquaintance, which is not possible.

35. a Let us say there are only 3 questions. Then, there are $2^{3-1} = 4$ students who have done 1 or more questions wrongly, $2^{3-2} = 2$ students who have done 2 or more questions wrongly and $2^{3-3} = 1$ student who must have done all 3 wrongly. Thus, total number of wrong answers = 4 + 2 + 1 = 7 = $2^3 - 1 = 2^n - 1$.

In our question, the total number of wrong answers = 4095 = $2^{12} - 1$. Thus n = 12.

36. b [Blue] —— —— Tarak —— [Red]

Statement A: To reach the Red mark, Tarak needs to take even number of steps and to reach the Blue mark, he needs to take odd number of steps. Given that the number of steps taken by him is 21. Therefore, Tarak stops at the Blue mark.

Hence, statement A alone is sufficient.

Statement B: If the number of tails is 3 more than the heads, then the effective movement will be 3 steps to the left, i.e. Tarak will reach Blue mark.

Hence, statement B alone is sufficient.

37. d **Statement A:** If the number of players at the entry level is 83, we can get the following table.

Round	Number of players	Pair of players	Byes	Number of matches
1	83	41	1	41
2	41 + 1 = 42	21	0	21
3	21	10	1	10
4	10 + 1 = 11	5	1	5
5	5 + 1 = 6	3	0	3
6	3	1	1	1
7	1 + 1 = 2	1	0	1

Since we do not know the number of byes given to the champion, we cannot ascertain the number of matches played by him.

Hence, statement A alone is not sufficient.

Statement B: The champion received one bye, but no information is given regarding the number of entrants in the tournament.

Hence, statement B alone is not sufficient.

Combining statements A and B: We get that the total number of matches played by the champion = 7 - 1 = 6

Hence, statements A and B both are required to answer.

38. d **Using statement A:**

When n = 127, exactly one bye is given in round 1.

When = 96, exactly one bye is given in round 6.

As no unique value of n can be determined, hence, statement A alone is not sufficient.

Using statement B:

As we do not know exactly how many bye 5 are given in total, we cannot determine the value of n, uniquely.

Combining statement A and B:

There is a unique value of n = 124, for which exactly 1 bye is given from the third round to the fourth round.

39. d The calendars of two leap years with a gap of 28 years will be the same. E.g. the calendars of 1908 and 1936 are exactly the same.

The calendars of two leap years with a gap of 12 years will be the same if a century year, which is not a leap year, falls between the two years. E.g. since 1900 falls between 1896 and 1908, the calendars of 1896 and 1908 are exactly the same.

Also, we can see that the calendars of 1896 and 1936 (a gap of 40 (12 + 28) years) are exactly the same.

Logical Reasoning
&
Data Interpretation

1

CHAPTER

Logical Reasoning

ANALYTICAL REASONING

1990

Direction for Question 1: *The question is followed by two statements. MARK,*

(a) if the question can be answered with the help of statement I alone,

(b) if the question can be answered with the help of statement II alone,

(c) if both, statement I and statement II are needed to answer the question, and

(d) if the statement cannot be answered even with the help of both the statements.

1. X is older than Y, Z is younger than W and V is older than Y. Is Z younger than X?

I. W may not be older than V.

II. W is not older than V.

Directions for Questions 2 to 4 : *The following questions relate to a game to be played by you and your friend. The game consists of a 4 x 4 board (see below) where each cell contains a positive integer. You and your friend make moves alternately. A move by any of the players consists of splitting the current board configuration into two equal halves and retaining one of them. In your moves you are allowed to split the board only vertically and to decide to retain either the left or the right half. Your friend, in his/her moves, can split the board only horizontally and can retain either the lower or the upper half. After two moves by each player a single cell will remain which can no longer be split and the number in that cell will be treated as the gain (in rupees) of the person who has started the game. A sample game is shown below.*

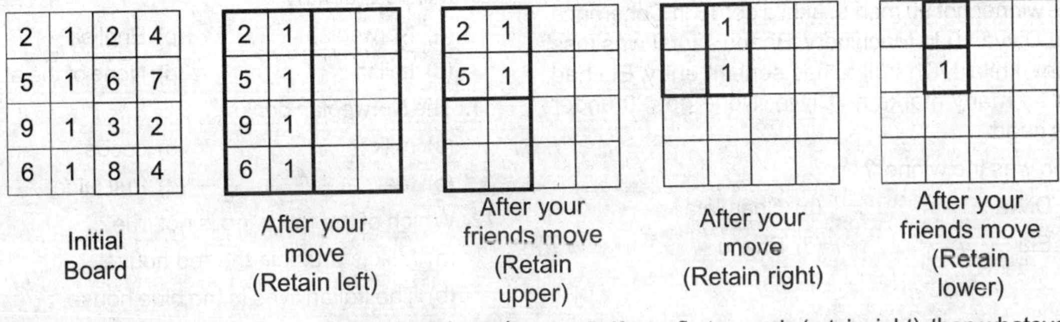

So your gain is Re.1. With the same initial board configuration as above and assuming that you have to make the first move, answer the following questions.

2. If you choose (retain right) (retain left) in your turns, the best move sequence for your friend to reduce your gain to a minimum will be

(a) (retain upper)(retain lower)

(b) (retain lower) (retain upper)

(c) (retain upper) (retain upper)

(d) (retain lower) (retain lower)

3. If both of you select your moves intelligently then at the end of the game your gain will be

(a) Rs.4 (b) Rs.3

(c) Rs.2 (d) None of these

4. If your first move is (retain right), then whatever moves your friend may select you can always force a gain of no less than

(a) Rs.3 (b) Rs.6

(c) Rs.4 (d) None of these

5. Saira, Mumtaz and Zeenat have a ball, a pen and a pencil, and each girl has just one object in hand. Among the following statements, only one is true and the other two are false.

I. Saira has a ball.

II. Mumtaz does not have the ball.

III. Zeenat does not have the pen.

Who has the ball?

(a) Saira

(b) Mumtaz

(c) Zeenat

(d) Cannot be determined

6. Albert, David, Jerome and Tommy were plucking mangoes in a grove to earn some pocket money during the summer holidays. Their earnings were directly related to the number of mangoes plucked and had the following relationship:

Jerome got less money than Tommy. Jerome and Tommy together got the same amount at Albert and David taken together. Albert and Tommy together got less than David and Jerome taken together.

Who earned the most pocket money? Who plucked the least number of mangoes?

(a) David, Jerome (b) David, Albert

(c) Jerome, Tommy (d) Jerome, Albert

7. I happened to be the judge in the all India Essay Competition on Nylon Dying, organized some time back by a dyestuff firm. Mill technicians were eligible to enter the competition. My work was simplified in assessing the essays, which had to be done under five heads-Language, Coherence, Subject Matter, Machinery and Recent Developments. Marks were to be given out of a maximum of 20 under each head. There were only five entries.

The winner got 90 marks. Akhila got 13 in Coherence and Divya 10 in Machinery. Bhanu's total was less than Akhila's. Charulata has sent an entry. Ela had got as many marks as Divya. None got 20 under any head.

Who was the winner?

(a) Divya (b) Charulata

(c) Ela (d) Bhanu

1991

Direction for Question 8 : *The question is followed by two statements. As the answer,*

Mark (a), If the question can be answered with the help of statement I alone,

Mark (b), If the question can be answered with the help of statement II alone,

Mark (c), If both the statement I and statement II are needed to answer the question, and

Mark (d), If the question cannot be answered even with the help of both the statements.

8. Mr. Murthy takes the morning train to his office from station A to station B, and his colleague Mr.Rahman joins him on the way. There are three stations C, D and E on the way not necessarily in that sequence.

What is the sequence of stations?

I. Mr. Rahman boards the train at D.

II. Mr. Thomas, who travels between C & D has two segments of journey in common with Mr. Murthy but none with Mr. Rahman.

1993

Directions for Questions 9 to 12: *Read the text and the numbered statements carefully and answer the questions given at the end.*

Four people of different nationalities live on the same side of a street in four houses each of different color. Each person has a different favorite drink. The following additional information is also known:

The Englishman lives in the red house.

The Italian drinks tea.

The Norwegian lives in the first house on the left.

In the second house from the right they drink milk.

The Norwegian lives adjacent to the blue house.

The Spaniard drinks fruit juice.

Tea is drunk in the blue house.

The white house is to the right of the red house.

9. The color of the Norwegian's house is

(a) yellow (b) white

(c) blue (d) red

10. Milk is drunk by

(a) Norwegian (b) English

(c) Italian (d) None of the above

11. The Norwegian drinks

(a) milk (b) cocoa

(c) tea (d) fruit juice.

12. Which of the following is not true?

(a) Milk is drunk in the red house.

(b) The Italian lives in the blue house.

(c) The Spaniard lives in a corner house.

(d) The Italian lives next to the Spaniard.

Directions for Questions 13 to 16: *Read the text and the numbered statements carefully and answer the questions given at the end.*

"Kya – Kya" is an island in the South Pacific. The inhabitants of "Kya – Kya" always answer any question with two sentences, one of which is always true and the other always false.

13. You find that your boat is stolen. You question three inhabitants of the island and they reply as follows:

John says, "I didn't do it. Mathew didn't do it."

Mathew says. "I didn't do it. Krishna didn't do it."

Krishna says. "I didn't do it. I don't know who did it."

Who stole your boat?

(a) John (b) Mathew

(c) Krishna (d) None of them

14. There is only one pilot on the island. You interview three men, Koik, Lony and Mirna. You also notice that Koik is wearing a cap.

Mirna says, "Lony's father is the pilot. Lony is not the priest's son."

Koik says, "I am the priest. On this island, only priests can wear caps."

Lony says, "I am the priest's son. Koik is not the priest."

Which of the following is true?

(a) Lony is not Koik's son.

(b) Koik is the pilot.

(c) Mirna is the pilot.

(d) Lony is the priest.

15. You are walking on the road and come to a fork. You ask the inhabitants Ram, Laxman and Lila. "Which road will take me to the village?"

Ram says, "I never speak to strangers. I am new to these parts."

Laxman says, "I am married to Lila. Take the left road."

Lila says, "I am married to Ram. He is not new to this place."

Which of the following is true?

(a) Left road takes you to the village.

(b) Right road takes you to the village.

(c) Lila is married to Laxman.

(d) None of these.

16. You want to speak to the chief of the village. You question three inhabitants. Amar, Bobby and Charles. Only Bobby is wearing a red shirt."

Amar says. "I am not Bobby's son. The chief wears a red shirt."

Bobby says, "I am Amar's father. Charles is the chief."

Charles says, "The chief is one among us. I am the chief."

Who is the chief?

(a) Amar (b) Bobby

(c) Charles (d) None of them

17. Amar, Akbar, and Anthony came from the same public school in the Himalayas. Every boy in that school either fishes for trout or plays frisbee. All fishermen like snow while no frisbee player likes rain. Amar dislikes whatever Akbar likes and likes whatever Akbar dislikes. Akbar likes rain and snow. Anthony likes whatever the other two like. Who is a fisherman but not a frisbee player?

(a) Amar (b) Akbar

(c) Anthony (d) None

1994

Directions for Questions 18 to 21: *Study the information below and answer questions based on it.*

A leading socialite decided to organize a dinner and invited a few of her friends. Only the host and the hostess were sitting at the opposite ends of a rectangular table, with three persons along each side. The pre-requisite for the seating arrangement was that each person must be seated such that atleast on one side it has a person of opposite sex. Maqbool is opposite Shobha, who is not the hostess. Ratan has a woman on his right and is sitting opposite a woman. Monisha is sitting to the hostess's right , next to Dhirubhai. One person is seated between Madhuri and Urmila who is not the hostess. The men were Maqbool, Ratan, Dhirubhai and Jackie, while the women were Madhuri, Urmila, Shobha and Monisha.

18. The eighth person present, Jackie, must be

I. the host

II. Seated to Shobha's right

III. Seated opposite Urmila

(a) I only (b) III only

(c) I and II only (d) II and III only

19. Which of the following persons is definitely not seated next to a person of the same sex?

(a) Maqbool (b) Madhuri

(c) Jackie (d) Shobha

20. If Ratan would have exchanged seats with a person four places to his left, which of the following would have been true after the exchange?

I. No one was seated between two persons of the opposite sex. (e.g. no man was seated between two women)

II. One side of the table consisted entirely of persons of the same sex.

III. Either the host or the hostess changed seats.

(a) I only (b) II only

(c) I and II only (d) II and III only

21. If each person is placed directly opposite her spouse, which of the following pairs must be married?

(a) Ratan and Monisha

(b) Madhuri and Dhirubhai

(c) Urmila and Jackie

(d) Ratan and Madhuri

Directions for Questions 22 to 24: *Study the information below and answer questions based on it.*

Five of India's leading models are posing for a photograph promoting "y'know, world peace and understanding". But then, Rakesh Shreshtha the photographer is having a tough time getting them to stand in a straight line, because Aishwarya refuses to stand next to Sushmita because Sushmita had said something about her in a leading gossip magazine. Rachel and Anu want to stand together because they are "such good friends, y'know". Manpreet on the other hand cannot get along well with Rachel, because there is some talk about Rachel scheming to get a contract already awarded to Manpreet. Anu believes her friendly astrologer who has asked her to stand at the extreme right for all group photographs. Finally, Rakesh managed to pacify the girls and got a beautiful picture of five beautiful girls smiling beautifully in a beautiful straight line, promoting world peace.

22. If Aishwarya is standing to the extreme left, which is the girl standing in the middle?

(a) Manpreet (b) Sushmita
(c) Rachel (d) Cannot say

23. If Aishwarya stands to the extreme left, which is the girl who stands second from left?

(a) Cannot say (b) Sushmita
(c) Rachel (d) Manpreet

24. If Anu's astrologer tells her to stand second from left and Aishwarya decides to stand second from right, then who is the girl standing on the extreme right?

(a) Rachel (b) Sushmita
(c) Cannot say (d) Manpreet

Directions for Questions 25 to 28: *Study the information below and answer the questions based on it.*

A, B, C, D, E, F and G are brothers. Two brothers had an argument and A said to B "You are as old as C was when I was twice as old as D, and will be as old as E was when he was as old as C is now". B said to A " You may be older than F but G is as old as I was when you were as old as G is, and D will be as old as F was when F will be as old as G is".

25. Who is the eldest brother?

(a) A (b) E
(c) C (d) Cannot be determined

26. Who is the youngest brother?

(a) B (b) D
(c) F (d) Cannot be determined

27. Which two are probably twins?

(a) D and G (b) E and C
(c) A and B (d) Cannot be determined

28. Which of the following is false?

(a) G has 4 elder brothers.
(b) A is older than G but younger than E.
(c) B has three elder brothers.
(d) There is a pair of twins among the brothers.

Directions for Questions 29 to 32: *Study the information below and answer the questions based on it.*

The primitive tribes – folk of the island of Lexicophobos have recently developed a language for themselves. Which has a very limited vocabulary. In fact, the words can be classified into only three types : the Bingoes, the Cingoes and the Dingoes.

The Bingoes type of words are : Grumbs, Harrumphs, Ihavitoo

The Cingoes type of words are : Ihavitoo, Jingongo, Koolodo

The Dingoes type of words are : Lovitoo, Metoo, Nana

They have also devised some rules of grammar:

Every sentence must have only five words.

Every sentence must have two Bingoes, one Cingo and two Dingoes.

If Grumbs is used in a sentence, Ihavitoo must also be used and vice versa.

Koolodo can be used in a sentence only if Lovitoo is used.

29. Which choice of words in a sentence is not possible, if no rules of grammar are to be violated?

(a) Grumbs and Harrumphs as the Bingoes and Ihavitoo as the Cingo.
(b) Harrumphs and Ihavitoo as the Bingoes.
(c) Grumbs and Ihavitoo as the Bingoes and Lovitoo and Nana as the Dingoes.
(d) Metoo and Nana as the Dingoes.

30. If Grumbs and Harrumphs are the Bingoes in a sentence, and no rule of grammar is violated, which of the following is / are true?

I. Ihavitoo is the Cingo.
II. Lovitoo is the Dingo.
III. Either Lovitoo or Metoo must be one of – or both – the Dingoes.

(a) I only (b) II only
(c) III only (d) I & III only

31. Which of the following is a possible sentence if no grammar rule is violated?
    (a) Grumbs harrumphs ihavitoo lovitoo metoo.
    (b) Grumbs harrumphs ihavitoo jingongo lovitoo.
    (c) Harrumphs ihavitoo jingongo lovitoo metoo.
    (d) Grumbs ihavitoo koolodo metoo nana.

32. If in a sentence Grumps is the Bingo and no rule of grammar is violated, which of the following cannot be true?
    (a) Harrumphs must be a Bingo.
    (b) Ihavitoo must be a Bingo.
    (c) Lovitoo may be used.
    (d) All three Bingoes are used.

1996

Directions for Questions 33 and 34: *Answer the questions based on the following information.*

In a locality, there are five small cities: A, B, C, D and E. The distances of these cities from each other are as follows.

AB = 2 km	AC = 2km	AD > 2 km
AE > 3 km	BC = 2 km	BD = 4 km
BE = 3 km	CD = 2 km	CE = 3 km
DE > 3 km		

33. If a ration shop is to be set up within 2 km of each city, how many ration shops will be required?
    (a) 2 (b) 3
    (c) 4 (d) 5

34. If a ration shop is to be set up within 3 km of each city, how many ration shops will be required?
    (a) 1 (b) 2
    (c) 3 (d) 4

1997

Direction for Question 35: *The question is followed by two statements, I and II. Mark the answer*

(a) if the question can be answered with the help of one statement alone.
(b) if the question can be answered with the help of any one statement independently.
(c) if the question can be answered with the help of both statements together.
(d) if the question cannot be answered even with the help of both statements together.

35. Three friends P, Q and R are wearing hats, either black or white. Each person can see the hats of the other two persons. What is the colour of P's hat?
    I. P says that he can see one black hat and one white hat.
    II. Q says that he can see one white hat and one black hat.

1998

36. P, Q, R and S are four statements. Relation between these statements is as follows.
    I. If P is true, then Q must be true.
    II. If Q is true, then R must be true.
    III. If S is true, then either Q is false or R is false.
    Which of the following must be true?
    (a) If P is true, then S is false
    (b) If S is false, then Q must be true
    (c) If Q is true, then P must be true
    (d) If R is true, then Q must be true

Directions for Questions 37 to 39: *Answer the questions based on the following information.*

A, B, C and D are to be seated in a row. But C and D cannot be together. Also B cannot be at the third place.

37. Which of the following must be false?
    (a) A is at the first place
    (b) A is at the second place
    (c) A is at the third place
    (d) A is at the fourth place

38. If A is not at the third place, then which of the following options does C have?
    (a) The first place only
    (b) The third place only
    (c) The first and third place only
    (d) Any of the places

39. If A and B are together, then which of the following must be necessarily true?
    (a) C is not at the first place
    (b) A is at the third place
    (c) D is at the first place
    (d) C is at the first place

Directions for Questions 40 and 41: *Answer the questions based on the following information.*

Amar, Akbar and Anthony are three friends. Only three colours are available for their shirts, viz. red, green and blue. Amar does not wear red shirt. Akbar does not wear green shirt. Anthony does not wear blue shirt.

40. If Akbar and Anthony wear the same colour of shirts, then which of the following is not true?
    (a) Amar wears blue and Akbar wears green
    (b) Amar wears green and Akbar wears red
    (c) Amar wears blue and Akbar does not wear blue
    (d) Anthony wears red

41. If two of them wear the same colour, then how many of the following must be false?

I. Amar wears blue and Akbar does not wear green
II. Amar does not wear blue and Akbar wears blue
III. Amar does not wear blue and Akbar does not wear blue
IV. Amar wears green, Akbar does not wear red, Anthony does not wear green

(a) None (b) One
(c) Two (d) Three

Directions for Questions 42 to 45: *Answer the questions based on the following information.*

Mr Bankatlal acted as a judge for the beauty contest. There were four participants, viz. Ms Andhra Pradesh, Ms Uttar Pradesh, Ms West Bengal and Ms Maharashtra. Mrs Bankatlal, who was very anxious about the result, asked him about it as soon as he was back home. Mr Bankatlal just told that the one who was wearing the yellow saree won the contest. When Mrs Bankatlal pressed for further details, he elaborated as follows:

All of them were sitting in a row.

All of them wore sarees of different colours, viz. green, yellow, white, red.

There was only one runner-up and she was sitting beside Ms. Maharashtra.

The runner-up was wearing the green saree.

Ms West Bengal was not sitting at the ends and was not the runner up.

The winner and the runner-up are not sitting adjacent to each other.

Ms Maharashtra was wearing white saree.

Ms Andhra Pradesh was not wearing the green saree.

Participants wearing yellow saree and white saree were at the ends.

42. W ho wore the red saree?

(a) Ms Andhra Pradesh (b) Ms West Bengal
(c) Ms Uttar Pradesh (d) Ms Maharashtra

43. Ms. West Bengal was sitting adjacent to

(a) Ms Andhra Pradesh and Ms Maharashtra
(b) Ms Uttar Pradesh and Ms Maharashtra
(c) Ms Andhra Pradesh and Ms Uttar Pradesh
(d) Ms Uttar Pradesh

44. Which saree was worn by Ms Andhra Pradesh?

(a) Yellow (b) Red
(c) Green (d) White

45. Who was the runner-up?

(a) Ms Andhra Pradesh (b) Ms West Bengal
(c) Ms Uttar Pradesh (d) Ms Maharashtra

46. A, B, C, D, ..., X, Y, Z are the players who participated in a tournament. Everyone played with every other player exactly once. A win scores 2 points, a draw scores 1 point and a loss scores 0 point. None of the matches ended in a draw. No two players scored the same score. At the end of the tournament, by ranking list is published which is in accordance with the alphabetical order. Then

(a) M wins over N
(b) N wins over M
(c) M does not play with N
(d) None of these

Directions for Questions 47 and 48: *Each question is followed by two statements, I and II. Answer the questions based on the statements and mark the answer as*

(a) if the question can be answered with the help of any one statement alone but not by the other statement.
(b) if the question can be answered with the help of either of the statements taken individually.
(c) if the question can be answered with the help of both statements together.
(d) if the question cannot be answered even with the help of both statements together.

47. There are four envelopes — E_1, E_2, E_3 and E_4 — in which one was supposed to put letters L_1, L_2, L_3 and L_4 meant for persons C_1, C_2, C_3 and C_4 respectively, but by mistake the letters got jumbled up and went in wrong envelopes. Now if C_2 is allowed to open an envelope at random, then how will he identify the envelope containing the letter for him?

I. L_2 has been put in E_1.
II. The letter belonging to C_3 has gone in the correct envelope.

48. There are four racks numbered 1, 2, 3, 4 and four books numbered 1, 2, 3, 4. If an even rack has to contain an odd-numbered book and an odd rack contains an even-numbered book, then what is the position of book 4?

I. Second book has been put in third rack.
II. Third book has been put in second rack.

1999

49. Three labelled boxes containing red and white cricket balls are all mislabelled. It is known that one of the boxes contains only white balls and another one contains only red balls. The third contains a mixture of red and white balls. You are required to correctly label the boxes with the labels red, white and red and white by picking a sample of one ball from only one box. What is the label on the box you should sample?

(a) white
(b) red
(c) red and white
(d) Not possible to determine from a sample of one ball

50. Abraham, Border, Charlie, Dennis and Elmer, and their respective wives recently dined together and were seated at a circular table. The seats were so arranged that men and women alternated and each woman was three places away from her husband. Mrs Charlie sat to the left of Mr Abraham. Mrs Elmer sat two places to the right of Mrs Border. Who sat to the right of Mr Abraham?
(a) Mrs Dennis
(b) Mrs Elmer
(c) Mrs Border
(d) Mrs Border or Mrs Dennis

Directions for Questions 51 and 52: *Answer the questions based on the following information.*

A, B, C, D, E and F are a group of friends from a club. There are two housewives, one lecturer, one architect, one accountant and one lawyer in the group. There are two married couples in the group. The lawyer is married to D who is a housewife. No lady in the group is either an architect or an accountant. C, the accountant, is married to F who is a lecturer. A is married to D and E is not a housewife.

51. What is the profession of E?
(a) Lawyer (b) Architect
(c) Lecturer (d) Accountant

52. How many members of the group are male?
(a) 2 (b) 3
(c) 4 (d) None of these

Directions for Questions 53 and 54: *Answer the questions based on the following information.*

Seven university cricket players are to be honoured at a special luncheon. The players will be seated on the dais along one side of a single rectangular table.

I. A and G have to leave the luncheon early and must be seated at the extreme right end of the table, which is closest to the exit.
II. B will receive the Man of the Match Award and must be in the centre chair.
III. C and D who are bitter rivals for the position of wicketkeeper, dislike one another and should be seated as far apart as possible.
IV. E and F are best friends and want to sit together.

53. Which of the following may not be seated at either end of the table?
(a) C (b) D
(c) G (d) F

54. Which of the following pairs may not be seated together?
(a) E and A (b) B and D
(c) C and F (d) G and D

Directions for Questions 55 to 57: *Each question is followed by two statements I and II.*

Mark:
(a) if the question can be answered by any one of the statements alone, but cannot be answered by using the other statement alone.
(b) if the question can be answered by using either statement alone.
(c) if the question can be answered by using both the statements together, but cannot be answered by using either statement alone.
(d) if the question cannot be answered even by using both the statements together.

55. Three professors A, B and C are separately given three sets of numbers to add. They were expected to find the answers to 1 + 1, 1 + 1 + 2, and 1 + 1 respectively. Their respective answers were 3, 3 and 2. How many of the professors are mathematicians?
I. A mathematician can never add two numbers correctly, but can always add three numbers correctly.
II. When a mathematician makes a mistake in a sum, the error is +1 or –1.

56. How many students among A, B, C and D have passed the examination?
I. The following is a true statement: A and B passed the examination.
II. The following is a false statement: At least one among C and D has passed the examination.

57. Mr Mendel grew 100 flowering plants from black seeds and white seeds, each seed giving rise to one plant. A plant gives flowers of only one colour. From a black seed comes a plant giving red or blue flowers. From a white seed comes a plant giving red or white flowers. How many black seeds were used by Mr Mendel?
I. The number of plants with white flowers was 10.
II. The number of plants with red flowers was 70.

2000

Directions for Questions 58 and 59: *Answer the questions based on the following information.*

There are three bottles of water — A, B, C, whose capacities are 5 L, 3 L, and 2 L respectively. For transferring water from one bottle to another and to drain out the bottles, there exists a piping system. The flow through these pipes is computer-controlled. The computer that controls the flow through these pipes can be fed with three types of instructions, as explained below.

Instruction type	Explanation of the instruction
Fill (X, Y)	Fill bottle labelled X from the water in bottle labelled Y, where the remaining capacity of X is less than or equal to the amount of water in Y.
Empty (X, Y)	Empty out the water in bottle labelled X into bottle labelled Y, where the amount of water in X is less than or equal to remaining capacity of Y.
Drain (X)	Drain out all the water contained in bottle labelled X

Initially, A is full with water, and B and C are empty.

58. After executing a sequence of three instructions, bottle A contains one litre of water. The first and the third of these instructions are shown below.

First instruction: FILL (C, A)

Third instruction: FILL (C, A)

Then which of the following statements about the instructions is true?

(a) The second instruction is FILL (B, A).

(b) The second instruction is EMPTY (C, B).

(c) The second instruction transfers water from B to C.

(d) The second instruction involves using the water in bottle A.

59. Consider the same sequence of three instructions and the same initial state mentioned above. Three more instructions are added at the end of the above sequence to have A contain 4 L of water. In this total sequence of six instructions, the fourth one is DRAIN (A). This is the only DRAIN instruction in the entire sequence. At the end of the execution of the above sequence, how much water is contained in C?

(a) 1 L (b) 2 L
(c) 0 (d) None of these

60. There is a vertical stack of books marked 1, 2 and 3 on Table A, with 1 at the bottom and 3 on the top. These are to be placed vertically on Table B with 1 at the bottom and 2 on the top, by making a series of moves from one table to the other. During a move, the topmost book, or the topmost two books, or all the three, can be moved from one of the tables to the other. If there are any books on the other table, the stack being transferred should be placed on top of the existing books, without changing the order of books in the stack that is being moved in that move. If there are no books on the other table, the stack is simply placed on the other table without disturbing the order of books in it. What is the minimum number of moves in which the above task can be accomplished?

(a) 1 (b) 2
(c) 3 (d) 4

Directions for Questions 61 to 65: *Answer the questions based on the following information.*

Sixteen teams have been invited to participate in the ABC Gold Cup cricket tournament. The tournament is conducted in two stages. In the first stage, the teams are divided into two groups. Each group consists of eight teams, with each team playing every other team in its group exactly once. At the end of the first stage, the top four teams from each group advance to the second stage while the rest are eliminated. The second stage comprises of several rounds. A round involves one match for each team. The winner of a match in a round advances to the next round, while the loser is eliminated. The team that remains undefeated in the second stage is declared the winner and claims the Gold Cup.

The tournament rules are such that each match results in a winner and a loser with no possibility of a tie. In the first stage, a team earns one point for each win and no points for a loss. At the end of the first stage, teams in each group are ranked on the basis of total points to determine the qualifiers advancing to the next stage. Ties are resolved by a series of complex tie-breaking rules so that exactly four teams from each group advance to the next stage.

61. What is the total number of matches played in the tournament?

(a) 28 (b) 55
(c) 63 (d) 35

62. The minimum number of wins needed for a team in the first stage to guarantee its advancement to the next stage is

(a) 5 (b) 6
(c) 7 (d) 4

63. What is the highest number of wins for a team in the first stage in spite of which it would be eliminated at the end of first stage?

(a) 1 (b) 2
(c) 3 (d) 4

64. What is the number of rounds in the second stage of the tournament?

(a) 1 (b) 2
(c) 3 (d) 4

65. Which of the following statements is true?

(a) The winner will have more wins than any other team in the tournament.
(b) At the end of the first stage, no team eliminated from the tournament will have more wins than any of the teams qualifying for the second stage.
(c) It is possible that the winner will have the same number of wins in the entire tournament as a team eliminated at the end of the first stage.
(d) The number of teams with exactly one win in the second stage of the tournament is 4.

Directions for Questions 66 to 70: *Read each of the five problems given below and choose the best answer from among the four given choices.*

66. Persons X, Y, Z and Q live in red, green, yellow or blue-coloured houses placed in a sequence on a street. Z lives in a yellow house. The green house is adjacent to the blue house. X does not live adjacent to Z. The yellow house is in between the green and red houses. The colour of the house, X lives in is

(a) blue
(b) green
(c) red
(d) Not possible to determine

67. My bag can carry not more than ten books. I must carry at least one book each of management, mathematics, physics and fiction. Also, for every management book I carry I must carry two or more fiction books, and for every mathematics book I carry I must carry two or more physics books. I earn 4, 3, 2 and 1 points for each management, mathematics, physics and fiction book, respectively. I carry in my bag. I want to maximise the points I can earn by carrying the most appropriate combination of books in my bag. The maximum points that I can earn is

(a) 20 (b) 21
(c) 22 (d) 23

68. Five persons with names P, M, U, T and X live separately in any one of the following: a palace, a hut, a fort, a house or a hotel. Each one likes two different colours from among the following: blue, black, red, yellow and green. U likes red and blue. T likes black. The person living in a palace does not like black or blue. P likes blue and red. M likes yellow. X lives in a hotel. M lives in a

(a) hut (b) palace
(c) fort (d) house

69. There are ten animals — two each of lions, panthers, bison, bears, and deer — in a zoo. The enclosures in the zoo are named X, Y, Z, P and Q and each enclosure is allotted to one of the following attendants: Jack, Mohan, Shalini, Suman and Rita. Two animals of different species are housed in each enclosure. A lion and a deer cannot be together. A panther cannot be with either a deer or a bison. Suman attends to animals from among bison, deer, bear and panther only. Mohan attends to a lion and a panther. Jack does not attend to deer, lion or bison. X, Y and Z are allotted to Mohan, Jack and Rita respectively. X and Q enclosures have one animal of the same species. Z and P have the same pair of animals. The animals attended by Shalini are

(a) bear and bison (b) bison and deer
(c) bear and lion (d) bear and panther

70. Eighty kilogram of store material is to be transported to a location 10 km away. Any number of couriers can be used to transport the material. The material can be packed in any number of units of 10, 20, or 40 kg. Courier charges are Rs. 10 per hour. Couriers travel at the speed of 10 km/hr if they are not carrying any load, at 5 km/hr if carrying 10 kg, at 2 km/hr if carrying 20 kg and at
1 km/hr if carrying 40 kg. A courier cannot carry more than 40 kg of load. The minimum cost at which 80 kg of store material can be transported to its destination will be

(a) Rs. 180 (b) Rs. 160
(c) Rs. 140 (d) Rs. 120

2001

Directions for Questions 71 to 73: *Answer the questions based on the pipeline diagram below.*

The following sketch shows the pipelines carrying material from one location to another. Each location has a demand for material. The demand at Vaishali is 400, at Jyotishmati is 400, at Panchal is 700, and at Vidisha is 200. Each arrow indicates the direction of material flow through the pipeline. The flow from Vaishali to Jyotishmati is 300. The quantity of material flow is such that the demands at all these locations are exactly met. The capacity of each pipeline is 1,000.

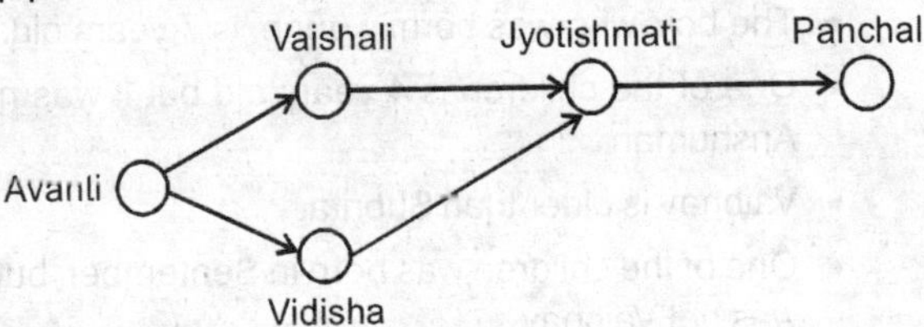

71. The quantity moved from Avanti to Vidisha is
(a) 200 (b) 800
(c) 700 (d) 1,000

72. The free capacity available at the Avanti-Vaishali pipeline is
(a) 0 (b) 100
(c) 200 (d) 300

73. What is the free capacity available in the Avanti-Vidisha pipeline?
(a) 300 (b) 200
(c) 100 (d) 0

74. At a village mela, the following six nautankis (plays) are scheduled as shown in the table below.

No.	Nautanki	Duration	Show Times
1	Sati Savitri	1 hr	9 a.m. and 2 p.m.
2	Joru ka Ghulam	1 hr	10.30 a.m. and 11: 30 a.m.
3	Sundar Kand	30 min	10 am and 11 a.m.
4	Veer Abhimanyu	1 hr	10 a.m. and 11a.m.
5	Reshma aur Shera	1 hr	9.30 a.m., 12 noon and 2 p.m.
6	Jhansi ki Rani	30 min	11 a.m. and 1: 30 p

You wish to see all the six nautankis. Further, you wish to ensure that you get a lunch break from 12.30 p.m. to 1.30 p.m. Which of the following ways can you do this?
(a) Sati Savitri is viewed first; Sundar Kand is viewed third, and Jhansi ki Rani is viewed last
(b) Sati Savitri is viewed last; Veer Abhimanyu is viewed third, and Reshma aur Shera is viewed first
(c) Sati Savitri is viewed first; Sundar Kand is viewed third, and Joru ka Ghulam is viewed fourth
(d) Veer Abhimanyu is viewed third; Reshma aur Shera is viewed fourth, and Jahansi ki Rani is viewed fifth

75. Mrs Ranga has three children and has difficulty remembering their ages and months of their birth. The clue below may help her remember.
- The boy, who was born in June, is 7 years old.
- One of the children is 4 years old but it was not Anshuman.
- Vaibhav is older than Suprita.
- One of the children was born in September, but it was not Vaibhav.
- Suprita's birthday is in April.
- The youngest child is only 2-year-old.

Based on the above clues, which one of the following statements is true?
(a) Vaibhav is the oldest, followed by Anshuman who was born in September, and the youngest is Suprita who was born in April
(b) Anshuman is the oldest being born in June, followed by Suprita who is 4-year-old, and the youngest is Vaibhav who is 2-year-old
(c) Vaibhav is the oldest being 7-year-old, followed by Suprita who was born in April, and the youngest is Anshuman who was born in September
(d) Suprita is the oldest who was born in April, followed by Vaibhav who was born in June, and Anshuman who was born in September

76. The Bannerjees, the Sharmas, and the Pattabhiramans each have a tradition of eating Sunday lunch as a family. Each family serves a special meal at a certain time of day. Each family has a particular set of chinaware used for this meal. Use the clues below to answer the following question.
- The Sharma family eats at noon.
- The family that serves fried brinjal uses blue chinaware.
- The Bannerjee family eats at 2 o'clock.
- The family that serves sambar does not use red chinaware.
- The family that eats at 1 o'clock serves fried brinjal.
- The Pattabhiraman family does not use white chinaware.
- The family that eats last likes makkai-ki-roti.

Which one of the following statements is true?
(a) The Bannerjees eat makkai-ki-roti at 2 o'clock, the Sharmas eat fried brinjal at 12 o'clock and the Pattabhiramans eat sambar from red chinaware
(b) The Sharmas eat sambar served in white chinaware, the Pattabhiramans eat fried brinjal at 1 o'clock, and the Bannerjees eat makkai-ki-roti served in blue chinaware
(c) The Sharmas eat sambar at noon, the Pattabhiramans eat fried brinjal served in blue chinaware, and the Bannerjees eat makkai-ki-roti served in red chinaware
(d) The Bannerjees eat makkai-ki-roti served in white chinaware, the Sharmas eat fried brinjal at 12 o'clock and the Pattabhiramans eat sambar from red chinaware

77. While Balbir had his back turned, a dog ran into his butcher shop, snatched a piece of meat off the counter and ran out. Balbir was mad when he realised what had happened. He asked three other shopkeepers, who had seen the dog, to describe it. The shopkeepers really did not want to help Balbir. So each of them made a statement which contained one truth and one lie.

- Shopkeeper number 1 said: "The dog had black hair and a long tail."
- Shopkeeper number 2 said: "The dog had a short tail and wore a collar."
- Shopkeeper number 3 said: "The dog had white hair and no collar."

Based on the above statements, which of the following could be a correct description?

(a) The dog had white hair, short tail and no collar
(b) The dog had white hair, long tail and a collar
(c) The dog had black hair, long tail and a collar
(d) The dog had black hair, long tail and no collar

Directions for Questions 78 and 79: *Answer the following questions based on the information given below.*

Elle is three times older than Yogesh. Zaheer is half the age of Wahida. Yogesh is older than Zaheer.

78. Which of the following can be inferred?

(a) Yogesh is older than Wahida
(b) Elle is older than Wahida
(c) Elle may be younger than Wahida
(d) None of these

79. Which of the following information will be sufficient to estimate Elle's age?

(a) Zaheer is 10-year-old
(b) Both Yogesh and Wahida are older than Zaheer by the same number of years
(c) Both (a) and (b)
(d) None of these

Directions for Questions 80 to 82: *Answer the questions based on the passage below.*

A group of three or four has to be selected from seven persons. Among the seven are two women: Fiza and Kavita, and five men: Ram, Shyam, David, Peter and Rahim. Ram would not like to be in the group If Shyam is also selected. Shyam and Rahim want to be selected together in the group. Kavita would like to be in the group only if David is also there. David, if selected, would not like Peter in the group. Ram would like to be in the group only if Peter is also there. David insists that Fiza be selected in case he is there in the group.

80. Which of the following is a feasible group of three?

(a) David, Ram and Rahim
(b) Peter, Shyam and Rahim
(c) Kavita, David and Shyam
(d) Fiza, David and Ram

81. Which of the following is a feasible group in four?

(a) Ram, Peter, Fiza and Rahim
(b) Shyam, Rahim, Kavita and David
(c) Shyam, Rahim, Fiza and David
(d) Fiza, David, Ram and Peter

82. Which of the following statements is true?

(a) Kavita and Ram can be part of a group of four
(b) A group of four can have two women
(c) A group of four can have all four men
(d) None of these

83. On her walk through the park, Hamsa collected 50 coloured leaves, all either maple or oak. She sorted them by category when she got home, and found the following:

The number of red oak leaves with spots is even and positive.

The number of red oak leaves without any spot equals the number of red maple leaves without spots.

All non-red oak leaves have spots, and there are five times as many of them as there are red spotted oak leaves.

There are no spotted maple leaves that are not red.

There are exactly 6 red spotted maple leaves.

There are exactly 22 maple leaves that are neither spotted nor red.

How many oak leaves did she collect?

(a) 22 (b) 17
(c) 25 (d) 18

84. Eight people carrying food baskets are going for a picnic on motorcycles. Their names are A, B, C, D, E, F, G, and H. They have 4 motorcycles M1, M2, M3 and M4 among them. They also have 4 food baskets O, P, Q and R of different sizes and shapes and each can be carried only on motorcycles M1, M2, M3 and M4 respectively. No more than 2 persons can travel on a motorcycle and no more than one basket can be carried on a motorcycle. There are 2 husband-wife pairs in this group of 8 people and each pair will ride on a motorcycle together. C cannot travel with A or B. E cannot travel with B or F. G cannot travel with F, or H, or D. The husband-wife pairs must carry baskets O and P. Q is with A and P is with D. F travels on M1 and E travels on M2 motorcycles. G is with Q, and B cannot go with R. Who is travelling with H?

(a) A (b) B
(c) C (d) D

85. In a family gathering there are 2 males who are grandfathers and 4 males who are fathers. In the same gathering there are 2 females who are grandmothers and 4 females who are mothers. There is at least one grandson or a granddaughter present in this gathering. There are 2 husband-wife pairs in this group. These can either be a grandfather and a grandmother, or a father and a mother. The single grandfather (whose wife is not present) has 2 grandsons and a son present. The single grandmother (whose husband is not present) has 2 grand daughters and a daughter present. A grandfather or a grandmother present with their spouses does not have any grandson or granddaughter present.

What is the minimum number of people present in this gathering?

(a) 10 (b) 12
(c) 14 (d) 16

86. I have a total of Rs. 1,000. Item A costs Rs. 110, item B costs Rs. 90, item C costs Rs. 70, item D costs Rs. 40 and item E costs Rs. 45. For every item D that I purchase, I must also buy two of item B. For every item A, I must buy one of item C. For every item E, I must also buy two of item D and one of item B. For every item purchased I earn 1,000 points and for every rupee not spent I earn a penalty of 1,500 points. My objective is to maximise the points I earn.

What is the number of items that I must purchase to maximise my points?

(a) 13 (b) 14
(c) 15 (d) 16

87. Four friends Ashok, Bashir, Chirag and Deepak are out for shopping. Ashok has less money than three times the amount that Bashir has. Chirag has more money than Bashir. Deepak has an amount equal to the difference of amounts with Bashir and Chirag. Ashok has three times the money with Deepak. They each have to buy at least one shirt, or one shawl, or one sweater, or one jacket that are priced Rs. 200, Rs. 400, Rs. 600, and Rs. 1,000 a piece respectively. Chirag borrows Rs. 300 from Ashok and buys a jacket. Bashir buys a sweater after borrowing Rs. 100 from Ashok and is left with no money. Ashok buys three shirts. What is the costliest item that Deepak could buy with his own money?

(a) A shirt (b) A shawl
(c) A sweater (d) A jacket

88. In a 'keep-fit' gymnasium class there are 15 females enrolled in a weight-loss programme. They all have been grouped in any one of the five weight-groups W1, W2, W3, W4, or W5. One instructor is assigned to one weight-group only. Sonali, Shalini, Shubhra and Shahira belong to the same weight-group. Sonali and Rupa are in one weight-group, Rupali and Renuka are also in one weight-group. Rupa, Radha, Renuka, Ruchika, and Ritu belong to different weight-groups. Somya cannot be with Ritu, and Tara cannot be with Radha. Komal cannot be with Radha, Somya, or Ritu. Shahira is in W1 and Somya is in W4 with Ruchika. Sweta and Jyotika cannot be with Rupali, but are in a weight-group with total membership of four. No weight-group can have more than five or less than one member. Amita, Babita, Chandrika, Deepika and Elina are instructors of weight-groups with membership sizes 5, 4, 3, 2 and 1 respectively. Who is the instructor of Radha?

(a) Babita (b) Elina
(c) Chandrika (d) Deepika

89. A king has unflinching loyalty from eight of his ministers M1 to M8, but he has to select only four to make a cabinet committee. He decides to choose these four such that each selected person shares a liking with at least one of the other three selected. The selected persons must also hate at least one of the likings of any of the other three persons selected.

M1 likes fishing and smoking, but hates gambling.

M2 likes smoking and drinking, but hates fishing.

M3 likes gambling, but hates smoking,

M4 likes mountaineering, but hates drinking,

M5 likes drinking, but hates smoking and mountaineering.

M6 likes fishing, but hates smoking and mountaineering.

M7 likes gambling and mountaineering, but hates fishing.

M8 likes smoking and gambling, but hates mountaineering.

Who are the four people selected by the king?

(a) M1, M2, M5 and M6
(b) M3, M4, M5 and M6
(c) M4, M5, M6 and M8
(d) M1, M2, M4 and M7

Directions for Questions 90 to 93: *Answer the questions based on the following information.*

A and B are two sets (e.g. A = Mothers, B = Women). The elements that could belong to both the sets (e.g. women who are mothers) is given by the set C = A . B. The elements which could belong to either A or B, or both, is indicated by the set D = A $\cup$ B . A set that does not contain any elements is known as a null set represented by φ (e.g. if none of the women in the set B is a mother, then C = A .B is a null set, or C = φ).

Let 'V' signify the set of all vertebrates, 'M' the set of all mammals, 'D' dogs, 'F' fish, 'A' alsatian and 'P', a dog named Pluto.

90. Given that X = M .D is such that X = D. Which of the following is true?

(a) All dogs are mammals
(b) Some dogs are mammals
(c) X = φ
(d) All mammals are dogs

91. If Y = F . (D . V) is not a null set, it implies that

(a) all fish are vertebrates
(b) all dogs are vertebrates
(c) some fish are dogs
(d) None of these

92. If Z = (P . D) ∪ M, then

(a) the elements of Z consist of Pluto, the dog, or any other mammal
(b) Z implies any dog or mammal
(c) Z implies Pluto or any dog that is a mammal
(d) Z is a null set

93. If P . A = φ and P ∪ A = D, then which of the following is true?

(a) Pluto and alsatians are dogs
(b) Pluto is an alsatian
(c) Pluto is not an alsatian
(d) D is a null set

2002

Directions for Questions 94 to 97: *Four students — Ashish, Dhanraj, Felix and Sameer sat for the Common Entrance Exam for Management (CEEM). One student got admission offers from three NIMs (National Institutes of Management), another from two NIMs, the third from one NIM, while the fourth got none. Below are some of the facts about who got admission offers from how many NIMs and what is their educational background.*

I. The one who is an engineer didn't get as many admissions as Ashish.
II. The one who got offer for admissions in two NIMs isn't Dhanraj nor is he a chartered accountant.
III. Sameer is an economist.
IV. Dhanraj isn't an engineer and received more admission offers than Ashish.
V. The doctor got the most number of admission offers.

94. Which one of the following statements is necessarily true?

(a) Ashish is a chartered accountant and got offer for admission in three NIMs.
(b) Dhanraj is a doctor and got admission offer in one NIM.
(c) Sameer is an economist who got admission offers in two NIMs.
(d) Felix who is not an engineer did not get any offer for admission.

95. Five boys went to a store to buy sweets. One boy had Rs. 40. Another boy had Rs. 30. Two other boys had Rs. 20 each. The remaining boy had Rs. 10. Below are some more facts about the initial and final cash positions.

I. Alam started with more than Jugraj.
II. Sandeep spent Rs. 1.50 more than Daljeet.
III. Ganesh started with more money than just only one other person.
IV. Daljeet started with $\frac{2}{3}$ of what Sandeep started with.
V. Alam spent the most, but did not end with the least.
VI. Jugraj spent the least and ended with more than Alam or Daljeet.
VII. Ganesh spent Rs.3.50.
VIII. Alam spent 10 times more than what Ganesh did.

In the choices given below, all statements except one are false. Which one of the following statements can be true?

(a) Alam started with Rs. 40 and ended with Rs. 9.50
(b) Sandeep started with Rs. 30 and ended with Re. 1
(c) Ganesh started with Rs. 20 and ended with Rs. 4.
(d) Jugraj started with Rs. 10 and ended with Rs. 7

96. In a hospital there were 200 diabetes, 150 hyperglycaemia and 150 gastro-enteritis patients. Of these, 80 patients were treated for both diabetices and hyperglycaemia. Sixty patients were treated for gastro-enteritis and hyperglycaemia, while 70 were treated for diabetes and gastro-enteritis. Some of these patients have all the three diseases. Dr. Dennis treats patients with only gastro-enteritis. Dr. Paul is a generalist. Therefore, he can treat patients with multiple diseases. Patients always prefer a specialist for their disease. If Dr. Dennis had 80 patients, then the other three doctors can be arranged in terms of the number of patients treated as:

(a) Paul > Gerard > Hormis
(b) Paul > Hormis > Gerard
(c) Gerard > Paul > Hormis
(d) None of these

97. Three children won the prizes in the Bournvita Quiz contest. They are from the schools: Loyola, Convent and Little Flowers, which are located at different cities. Below are some of the facts about the schools, the children and the city they are from.

I. One of the children is Bipin.

II. Loyola School's contestant did not come first.

III. Little Flower's contestant was named Riaz.

IV. Convent School is not in Hyderabad.

V. The contestant from Pune is not from Loyola School.

VI. The contestant from Bangalore did not come first.

VII. Convent School's contestant's name is not Balbir.

Which of the following statements is true?

(a) 1st prize: Riaz (Little Flowers), 2nd prize: Bipin (Convent), 3rd prize: Balbir (Loyola)

(b) 1st prize: Bipin (Convent), 2nd prize: Riaz (Little Flowers), 3rd prize: Balbir (Loyola)

(c) 1st prize: Riaz (Little Flowers), 2nd prize: Balbir (Loyola), 3rd prize: Bipin (Convent)

(d) 1st prize: Bipin (Convent), 2nd prize: Balbir (Loyola), 3rd prize: Riaz (Litttle Flowers)

98. Six persons are playing a card game. Suresh is facing Raghubir who is to the left of Ajay and to the right of Pramod. Ajay is to the left of Dhiraj. Yogendra is to the left of Pramod. If Dhiraj exchanges his seat with Yogendra and Pramod exchanges with Raghubir, who will be sitting to the left of Dhiraj?

(a) Yogendra (b) Raghubir

(c) Suresh (d) Ajay

2003

Directions for Questions 99 to 102: *Answer the questions on the basis of the following information.*

Four families decided to attend the marriage ceremony of one of their colleagues. One family has no kids, while the others have at least one kid each. Each family with kids has at least one kid attending the marriage. Given below is some information about the families, and who reached when to attend the marriage.

The family with two kids came just before the family with no kids.

Shanthi who does not have any kids reached just before Sridevi's family.

Sunil and his wife reached last with their only kid.

Anil is not the husband of Joya.

Anil and Raj are fathers.

Sridevi's and Anita's daughters go to the same school.

Joya came before Shanthi and met Anita when she reached the venue

Raman stays the farthest from the venue.

Raj said his son could not come because of his exams.

99. Who among the following arrived third?

(a) Shanthi (b) Sridevi

(c) Anita (d) Joya

100. Name the correct pair of husband and wife.

(a) Raj and Shanthi (b) Sunil and Sridevi

(c) Anil and Sridevi (d) Raj and Anita

101. Of the following pairs, whose daughters go to the same school?

(a) Anil and Raman (b) Sunil and Raman

(c) Sunil and Anil (d) Raj and Anil

102. Whose family is known to have more than one kid for certain?

(a) Raman's (b) Raj's

(c) Anil's (d) Sunil's

Directions for Questions 103 to 106: *Answer the questions on the basis of the following information.*

Seven faculty members at a management institute frequent a lounge for strong coffee and stimulating conversation. On being asked about their visit to the lounge last Friday we got the following responses.

JC: I came in first, and the next two persons to enter were SS and SM. When I left the lounge, JP and VR were present in the lounge. DG left with me.

JP: When I entered the lounge with VR, JC was sitting there. There was someone else, but I cannot remember who it was.

SM: I went to the lounge for a short while, and met JC, SS and DG in the lounge that day.

SS: I left immediately after SM left.

DG: I met JC, SS, SM, JP and VR during my first visit to the lounge, I went back to my office with JC. When I went to the lounge the second time, JP and VR were there.

PK: I had some urgent work, so I did not sit in the lounge that day, but just collected my coffee and left. JP and DG were the only people in the lounge while I was there.

VR: No comments.

103. Based on the responses, which of the two, JP or DG, entered the lounge first?

(a) JP

(b) DG

(c) Both entered together

(d) Cannot be determined

104. Who was sitting with JC when JP entered the lounge?

(a) SS (b) SM
(c) DG (d) PK

105. How many of the seven members did VR meet on Friday in the lounge?

(a) 2 (b) 3
(c) 4 (d) 5

106. Who were the last two faculty members to leave the lounge?

(a) JC and DG (b) PK and DG
(c) JP and PK (d) JP and DG

Directions for Questions 107 to 110: *Answer the questions on the basis of the following information.*

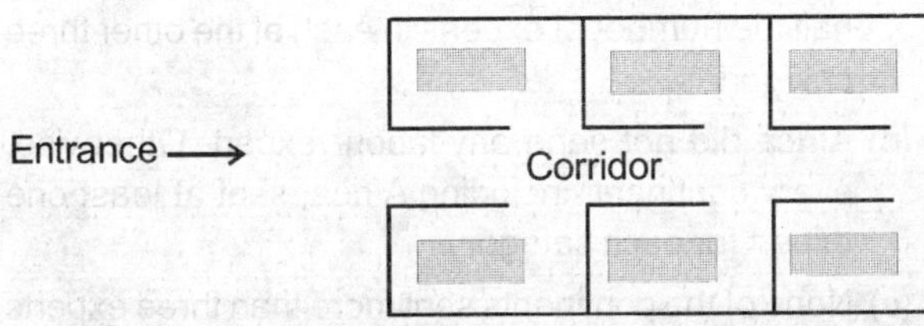

The plan above shows an office block for six officers — A, B, C, D, E and F. Both B and C occupy offices to the right of the corridor (as one enters the office block) and A occupies an office to the left of the corridor. E and F occupy offices on opposite sides of the corridor but their offices do not face each other. The offices of C and D face each other. E does not have a corner office. F's office is further down the corridor than A's, but on the same side.

107. If E sits in his office and faces the corridor, whose office is to his left?

(a) A (b) B
(c) C (d) D

108. Whose office faces A's office?

(a) B (b) C
(c) D (d) E

109. Who is/are F's neighbour(s)?

(a) A only (b) A and D
(c) C only (d) B and C

110. D was heard telling someone to go further down the corridor to the last office on the right. To whose room was he trying to direct that person?

(a) A (b) B
(c) C (d) F

Directions for Questions 111 to 113: *Answer the questions on the basis of the information given below.*

A, B, C, D, E, and F are a group of friends. There are two housewives, one professor, one engineer, one accountant and one lawyer in the group. There are only two married couples in the group. The lawyer is married to D, who is a housewife. No woman in the group is either an engineer or an accountant. C, the accountant, is married to F, who is a professor. A is married to a housewife. E is not a housewife.

111. Which of the following is one of the married couples?

(a) A & B (b) B & E
(c) D & E (d) A & D

112. What is E's profession?

(a) Engineer (b) Lawyer
(c) Professor (d) Accountant

113. How many members of the group are males?

(a) 2 (b) 3
(c) 4 (d) Cannot be determined

Directions for Questions 114 and 115: *Answer the questions on the basis of the information given below.*

The Head of a newly formed government desires to appoint five of the six elected members A, B, C, D, E and F to portfolios of Home, Power, Defence, Telecom and Finance. F does not want any portfolio if D gets one of the five. C wants either Home or Finance or no portfolio. B says that if D gets either Power or Telecom then she must get the other one. E insists on a portfolio if A gets one.

114. Which is a valid assignment?

(a) A-Home, B-Power, C-Defence, D-Telecom, E-Finance.
(b) C-Home, D-Power, A-Defence, B-Telecom, E-Finance.
(c) A-Home, B-Power, E-Defence, D-Telecom, F-Finance.
(d) B-Home, F-Power, E-Defence, C Telecom, A-Finance.

115. If A gets Home and C gets Finance, then which is NOT a valid assignment of Defense and Telecom?

(a) D-Defence, B-Telecom.
(b) F-Defence, B-Telecom.
(c) B-Defence, E-Telecom.
(d) B-Defence, D-Telecom.

Directions for Questions 116 to 118: *Answer the questions on the basis of the information given below.*

Rang Barsey Paint Company (RBPC) is in the business of manufacturing paints. RBPC buys RED, YELLOW, WHITE, ORANGE, and PINK paints. ORANGE paint can be also produced by mixing RED and YELLOW paints in equal proportions. Similarly, PINK paint can also be produced by mixing equal amounts of RED and WHITE paints. Among other paints, RBPC sells CREAM paint, (formed by mixing WHITE and YELLOW in the ratio 70:30) AVOCADO paint (formed by mixing equal amounts of ORANGE and PINK paint) and WASHEDORANGE paint (formed by mixing equal amounts of ORANGE and WHITE paint). The following table provides the price at which RBPC buys paints

Color	Rs./litre
RED	20
YELLOW	25
WHITE	15
ORANGE	22
PINK	18

116. The cheapest way to manufacture AVOCADO paint would cost
- (a) Rs. 19.50 per litre.
- (b) Rs. 19.75 per litre
- (c) Rs. 20.00 per litre.
- (d) Rs. 20.25 per litre.

117. WASHEDORANGE can be manufactured by mixing
- (a) CREAM and RED in the ratio 14:10.
- (b) CREAM and RED in the ratio 3:1.
- (c) YELLOW and PINK in the ratio 1:1.
- (d) RED, YELLOW, and WHITE in the ratio 1:1:2.

118. Assume that AVOCADO, CREAM and WASHEDORANGE each sells for the same price. Which of the three is the most profitable to manufacture?
- (a) AVOCADO
- (b) CREAM
- (c) WASHEDORANGE
- (d) Sufficient data is not available.

Directions for Questions 119 to 121: *Answer the questions on the basis of the information given below.*

Seven varsity basketball players (A, B, C, D, E, F, and G) are to be honoured at a special luncheon. The players will be seated on the dais in a row. A and G have to leave the luncheon early and so must be seated at the extreme right. B will receive the most valuable player's trophy and so must be in the centre to facilitate presentation. C and D are bitter rivals and therefore must be seated as far apart as possible.

119. Which of the following cannot be seated at either end?
- (a) C
- (b) D
- (c) F
- (d) G

120. Which of the following pairs cannot be seated together?
- (a) B & D
- (b) C & F
- (c) D & G
- (d) E & A

121. Which of the following pairs cannot occupy the seats on either side of B?
- (a) F & D
- (b) D & E
- (c) E & G
- (d) C & F

2004

Directions for Questions 122 to 125: *Answer the questions on the basis of the information given below.*

Twenty one participants from four continents (Africa, America, Australasia, and Europe) attended a United Nations conference. Each participant was an expert in one of four fields, labour, health, population studies, and refugee relocation. The following five facts about the participants are given.

(a) The number of labour experts in the camp was exactly half the number of experts in each of the other three categories.

(b) Africa did not send any labour expert. Otherwise, every continent, including Africa, sent at least one expert for each category.

(c) None of the continents sent more than three experts in any category.

(d) If there had been one less Australasian expert, then the Americas would have had twice as many experts as each of the other continents.

(e) Mike and Alfanso are leading experts of population studies who attended the conference. They are from Australasia.

122. Which of the following combinations is NOT possible?
- (a) 2 experts in population studies from the Americas and 2 health experts from Africa attended the conference.
- (b) 2 experts in population studies from the Americas and 1 health expert from Africa attended the conference.
- (c) 3 experts in refugee relocation from the Americas and 1 health expert from Africa attended the conference.
- (d) Africa and America each had 1 expert in population studies attending the conference.

123. If Ramos is the lone American expert in population studies, which of the following is NOT true about the numbers of experts in the conference from the four continents?
- (a) There is one expert in health from Africa.
- (b) There is one expert in refugee relocation from Africa.
- (c) There are two experts in health from the Americas.
- (d) There are three experts in refugee relocation from the Americas.

124. Alex, an American expert in refugee relocation, was the first keynote speaker in the conference. What can be inferred about the number of American experts in refugee relocation in the conference, excluding Alex?

i. At least one

ii. At most two

(a) Only i and not ii (b) Only ii and not i

(c) Both i and ii (d) Neither i nor ii

125. Which of the following numbers cannot be determined from the information given?

(a) Number of labour experts from the Americas.

(b) Number of health experts from Europe.

(c) Number of health experts from Australasia.

(d) Number of experts in refugee relocation from Africa.

Directions for Questions 126 to 129: *Answer the questions on the basis of the information given below.*

The year was 2006. All six teams in Pool A of World Cup hockey, play each other exactly once. Each win earns a team three points, a draw earns one point and a loss earns zero points. The two teams with the highest points qualify for the semifinals. In case of a tie, the team with the highest goal difference (Goal For - Goals Against) qualifies.

In the opening match, Spain lost to Germany. After the second round (after each team played two matches), the pool table looked as shown below.

Pool A

Teams	Games Played	Won	Drawn	Lost	Goals For	Goals Against	Points
Germany	2	2	0	0	3	1	6
Argentina	2	2	0	0	2	0	6
Spain	2	1	0	1	5	2	3
Pakistan	2	1	0	1	2	1	3
New Zealand	2	0	0	2	1	6	0
South Africa	2	0	0	2	1	4	0

In the third round, Spain played Pakistan, Argentina played Germany, and New Zealand played South Africa. All the third round matches were drawn. The following are some results from the fourth and fifth round matches

(a) Spain won both the fourth and fifth round matches.

(b) Both Argentina and Germany won their fifth round matches by 3 goals to 0.

(c) Pakistan won both the fourth and fifth round matches by 1 goal to 0.

126. Which one of the following statements is true about matches played in the first two rounds?

(a) Germany beat New Zealand by 1 goal to 0.

(b) Spain beat New Zealand by 4 goals to 0.

(c) Spain beat South Africa by 2 goals to 0.

(d) Germany beat South Africa by 2 goals to 1.

127. Which one of the following statements is true about matches played in the first two rounds?

(a) Pakistan beat South Africa by 2 goals to 1.

(b) Argentina beat Pakistan by 1 goal to 0.

(c) Germany beat Pakistan by 2 goals to 1.

(d) Germany beat Spain by 2 goals to 1.

128. If Pakistan qualified as one of the two teams from Pool A, which was the other team that qualified?

(a) Argentina (b) Germany

(c) Spain (d) Cannot be determined

129. Which team finished at the top of the pool after five rounds of matches?

(a) Argentina (b) Germany

(c) Spain (d) Cannot be determined

2006

Directions for Questions 130 to 134: *Answer the questions on the basis of the information given below:*

K, L, M, N, P, Q, R, S, U and W are the only ten members in a department. There is a proposal to form a team from within the members of the department, subject to the following conditions:

1. A team must include exactly one among P, R, and S.
2. A team must include either M or Q, but not both.
3. If a team includes K, then it must also include L, and vice versa.
4. If a team includes one among S, U, and W, then it must also include the other two.
5. L and N cannot be members of the same team.
6. L and U cannot be members of the same team.

The size of a team is defined as the number of members in the team.

130. Who cannot be a member of a team of size 3?

(a) L (b) M

(c) N (d) P

(e) Q

131. Who can be a member of a team of size 5?

(a) K (b) L

(c) M (d) P

(e) R

132. What would be the size of the largest possible team?
(a) 8 (b) 7
(c) 6 (d) 5
(e) Cannot be determined

133. What could be the size of a team that includes K?
(a) 2 or 3 (b) 2 or 4
(c) 3 or 4 (d) Only 2
(e) Only 4

134. In how many ways a team can be constituted so that the team includes N?
(a) 2 (b) 3
(c) 4 (d) 5
(e) 6

Directions for Questions 135 to 139: *Answer the questions on the basis of the information given below:*

Mathematicians are assigned a number called Erdös number (named after the famous mathematician, Paul Erdös). Only Paul Erdös himself has an Erdös number of zero. Any mathematician who has written a research paper with Erdös has an Erdös number of 1. For other mathematicians, the calculation of his/her Erdös number is illustrated below:

Suppose that a mathematician X has co-authored papers with several other mathematicians. From among them, mathematician Y has the smallest Erdös number. Let the Erdös number of Y be y. Then X has an Erdös number of y+1. Hence any mathematician with no co-authorship chain connected to Erdös has an Erdös number of infinity.

In a seven day long mini-conference organized in memory of Paul Erdös, a close group of eight mathematicians, call them A, B, C, D, E, F, G and H, discussed some research problems. At the beginning of the conference, A was the only participant who had an infinite Erdös number. Nobody had an Erdös number less than that of F.

1. On the third day of the conference F co-authored a paper jointly with A and C. This reduced the average Erdös number of the group of eight mathematicians to 3. The Erdös numbers of B, D, E, G and H remained unchanged with the writing of this paper. Further, no other co-authorship among any three members would have reduced the average Erdös number of the group of eight to as low as 3.
2. At the end of the third day, five members of this group had identical Erdös numbers while the other three had Erdös numbers distinct from each other.
3. On the fifth day, E co-authored a paper with F which reduced the group's average Erdös number by 0.5. The Erdös numbers of the remaining six were unchanged with the writing of this paper.
4. No other paper was written during the conference.

135. How many participants in the conference did not change their Erdös number during the conference?
(a) 2 (b) 3
(c) 4 (d) 5
(e) Cannot be determined

136. The person having the largest Erdös number at the end of the conference must have had Erdös number (at that time):
(a) 5 (b) 7
(c) 9 (d) 14
(e) 15

137. How many participants had the same Erdös number at the beginning of the conference?
(a) 2 (b) 3
(c) 4 (d) 5
(e) Cannot be determined

138. The Erdös number of C at the end of the conference was:
(a) 1 (b) 2
(c) 3 (d) 4
(e) 5

139. The Erdös number of E at the beginning of the conference was:
(a) 2 (b) 5
(c) 6 (d) 7
(e) 8

2008

Directions for Questions 140 to 142: *Answer the following questions based on the statements given below:*

(i) There are three houses on each side of the road.
(ii) These six houses are labeled as P, Q, R, S, T and U.
(iii) The houses are of different colours, namely, Red, Blue, Green, Orange, Yellow and White.
(iv) The houses are of different heights.
(v) T, the tallest house, is exactly opposite to the Red coloured house.
(vi) The shortest house is exactly opposite to the Green coloured house.
(vii) U, the Orange coloured house, is located between P and S.
(viii) R, the Yellow coloured house, is exactly opposite to P.
(ix) Q, the Green coloured house, is exactly opposite to U.
(x) P, the White coloured house, is taller than R, but shorter than S and Q.

140. What is the colour of the house diagonally opposite to the Yellow coloured house?
(a) White (b) Blue
(c) Green (d) Red
(e) none of these

141. Which is the second tallest house?

(a) P (b) S

(c) Q (d) R

(e) cannot be determined

142. What is the colour of the tallest house?

(a) Red (b) Blue

(c) Green (d) Yellow

(e) none of these

MEMORY BASED QUESTIONS

2009

143. Three people among A, B, C, D, E and F are to be selected to form a committee. Each selected person should share at least one 'liking' with at least one of the other two selected people. Each selected person should also hate at least one 'liking' of at least one of the other two people selected.

- A likes reading and travelling, and hates surfing and singing.
- B likes surfing and driving, and hates fishing.
- C likes dancing and travelling, and hates reading and fishing.
- D likes fishing and surfing, and hates driving.
- E likes singing and travelling, and hates dancing
- F likes reading and fishing, and hates surfing.

Which three can be selected together to form the committee?

(a) A, D and F (b) A, C and E

(c) B, D and F (d) Both (b) and (c)

144. Seven friends Salim, Govind, Sajid, Hasan, Sunil, Sanjay and Reeta are to be divided into two teams such that the difference between the number of people in the two teams is the least possible. Reeta and Sajid cannot be placed in the same team. Sunil can be placed in the same team with neither Salim nor Sanjay. Hasan and Govind must be placed in the same team.

How many of the following statements cannot be true?

(1) Hasan and Sunil are placed in the same team.

(2) Reeta and Hasan are placed in the same team.

(3) Hasan and Salim are placed in the same team.

(a) 0 (b) 1

(c) 2 (d) 3

145. Five dancers Angad, Bali, Gaurav, Monica and Shonali participate in a competition called DOD. Each participant gets some points from each of the five judges A, B, C, D and E for their performance in DOD. The final score of a participant is the sum of the points received by him/her from the five judges. The winner of the competition is the dancer whose final score is the maximum among the five dancers. The following details are also known:

- Bali gets 37 marks from judge B and Shonali gets 39 marks from judge C.
- The final score of Gaurav is less than the final score of Shonali.
- The winner of DOD gets a final score of 220.
- No contestant gets more than 45 marks from any of the five judges.
- The arithmetic mean of the final scores of Angad and Gaurav is greater than the arithmetic mean of the final scores of Monica and Shonali.

Who is the winner of DOD?

(a) Shonali (b) Monica

(c) Angad (d) Cannot be determined

2010

146. Each of the five children – Aman, Bhanu, Chaman, Deepak and Elhan – likes at least one activity among Rowing, Singing, Dancing, Sketching and Running. Each activity except Dancing is liked by at least three of the five children. There are two children who like exactly the same set of activities. Aman likes Rowing and Running. There is no activity which is liked by both Aman and Deepak. Both Bhanu and Deepak like Dancing but there is no other activity which is liked by both of them. Deepak likes Sketching. Who among the five children definitely like Running?

(a) Aman, Bhanu, Chaman and Elhan.

(b) Aman, Chaman, Deepak and Elhan.

(c) Aman, Chaman and Elhan.

(d) Aman, Bhanu and Chaman.

147. Six persons – Chetan, Kartik, Hari, Pankaj, Naresh and Vicky – are married to Radha, Kiran, Shama, Hema, Divya, and Charu, not necessarily in the same order. There is no person among the six whose name starts with the same letter as his wife's name. They are going on a picnic in three cars such that each car has two couples. It is known that:

(i) Charu is not in the same car as Hari.

(ii) Radha is in the same car as Pankaj.

(iii) Shama is in the same car as Hema.

(iv) Kiran is not in the same car as Naresh.

(v) Divya is not in the same car as Charu.

If Vicky is in a car in which nobody's name starts with the same letter as that of any of the other eleven persons, then which of the following statements cannot be true?

(a) Shama is married to Hari.
(b) Hema is married to Kartik.
(c) Radha is married to Vicky.
(d) Pankaj is married to Divya.

148. Eight persons – Anu, Bindu, Candy, Dolly, Emran, Fiza, Gauri and Hemant – are sitting at a square table, in the same order, in clockwise direction. Two persons are sitting on each side of the table. Two of them are Managers, two Executives, two Consultants and two Engineers.

The Executives are sitting opposite each other. One of the Executives is sitting on the same side of the table as an Engineer and on his/her left. The Consultants are sitting opposite each other and each of them is sitting next to an Engineer. The Managers are sitting next to each other. If Anu is a Consultant who is sitting next to a Manager, then which of the following statements is definitely false?

(a) Fiza is an Executive.
(b) Hemant is sitting next to a Manager.
(c) Emran is an Engineer.
(d) None of these

2013

Directions for questions 149 to 150: Answer the questions on the basis of the information given below.

A Cricket team of 11 players is to be formed from a group of 15 players—A, B, C, D, E, F, G, H, I, J, K, L, M, N and O. Among the players A, D, K, L, M, N and O are batsmen; B, C, E, F, G and H are bowlers; I and J are wicketkeepers. It is also known that:

I. The team must have at least 5 batsmen and exactly 1 wicketkeeper.
II. H can be selected only if B is selected.
III. F can be selected only if both G and N are selected.
IV. If I is selected, then F is also selected.
V. K and M cannot be selected together for the team. The same is true for B and G.

149. If G is one of the bowlers in the team, then who will be the wicketkeeper?

(a) J
(b) I
(c) Either (a) or (b)
(d) No such team is possible

150. If H is selected, then who among the following cannot be selected in the team?

(a) O (b) N
(c) G (d) J

2014

151. Read the following arguments and answer the questions that follow.

A study of the effect of language on memory was performed by Loftus and Loftus, in 1975. They showed subjects a film of a traffic accident to two groups, and then asked them questions about what they had seen. After a week, the subjects were asked about the film again. One group of subjects was asked, immediately after seeing the film, "How fast were the cars going when they hit each other?" The other group of subjects was asked, "How fast were the cars going when they smashed into each other?" When they were tested later, the subjects were asked if they had seen any broken glass in the film. (There hadn't been any.) Those subjects who had heard the word "smashed" remembered seeing broken glass scattered around after the accident.

The findings of the study have significant relevance for

(a) A move subscribing severe penalties for rash drivers who cause accidents amounting to culpable homicide.
(b) A memory-improvement course for students who score below the national average in IQ tests.
(c) People who are concerned about 'leading questions' in court, or in the police questioning of witnesses.
(d) None of the above

Directions for questions 152 to 154 : Answer the questions on the basis of the information given below.

Mr. Alfonso has six cars such that each car is of a different brand. The cars with Mr. Alfonso are of the six brands Chevrolet, Ferrari, Honda, Mercedes, BMW and Hyundai. In the months of January and February in the year 2008, Mr. Alfonso drove exactly one car each day. The following table gives details about the days in January and February 2008 on which he did not drive a car of each of the given six brands. Given that January 1, 2008 was a Tuesday.

Chevrolet	Sunday	Monday	Wednesday	Friday
Ferrari	Tuesday	Thursday	Saturday	Monday
Honda	Sunday	Wednesday	Thursday	Friday
Mercedes	Tuesday	Monday	Wednesday	Thursday
BMW	Friday	Monday	Saturday	Tuesday
Hyundai	Sunday	Tuesday	Wednesday	Saturday

The number of days in January and February 2008 on which he drove a car of brand Chevrolet, Ferrari, Honda, Mercedes, BMW and Hyundai is denoted by CH, FE, HO, ME, BM and HY respectively.

It is also known that HO > ME > CH > BM > HY > FE.

The following pie – chart gives details about the number of days in January and February 2008 on which he drove a car of brand Honda, BMW and Hyundai.

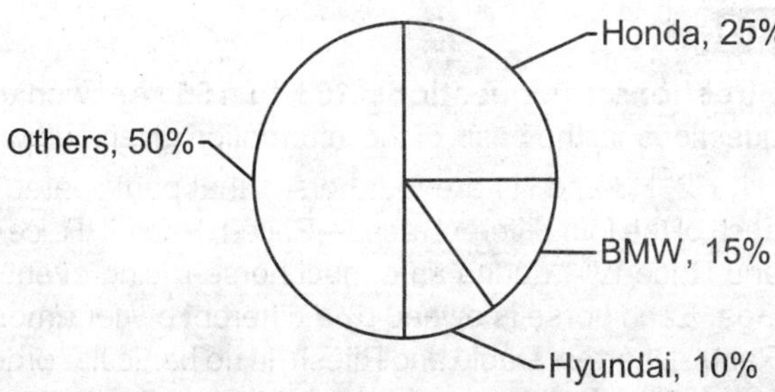

152. Given that the number of days in January 2008 on which Mr. Alfonso drove the car of brand Honda is the maximum. What is the number of days in February 2008 on which he drove the car of brand Honda?

(a) Zero (b) One
(c) Three (d) Two

153. If Mr. Alfonso drove the car of brand Chevrolet on all possible Saturdays in January 2008 and all possible Thursdays in January 2008 and February 2008, then what is the number of days on which he drove Ferrari in the given two months?

(a) Four (b) Two
(c) Three (d) Five

154. What is the difference between the maximum and minimum possible number of days on which Mr. Alfonso drove the car of brand Mercedes in the given two months?

(a) Four (b) Three
(c) Two (d) One

2015

Directions for questions 155 to 158: Answer the questions on the basis of the information given below.

In a given season of F1 racing, 9 races are to be held. There are 8 teams with two drivers in each team and the points are awarded to the drivers in each race as per to the following table.

Rank	1st	2nd	3rd	4th	5th	6th	7th	8th	9th to 16th
Points	10	8	6	5	4	3	2	1	0

Two championships viz. 'Driver's Championship' and 'Constructor's Championship' take place simultaneously. 'Driver's Championship' is given to the player who has the maximum number of points at the end of the season. 'Constructor's Championship' is given to the team for which the sum of the points of two its drivers is the maximum. A driver is said to get the podium finish only when he is among the top 3 rankers in a race.

After the first 6 races, the point standings of the 16 drivers is as follows:

Driver	Team	Points
Alonso	Renault	54
Schumacher	Ferrari	39
Kimi	Mclaren	29
Fisichella	Renault	27
Montoya	Mclaren	22
Massa	Ferrari	22
Button	Honda	21
Barichello	Honda	10
Villeneuve	Red Bull	4
Webber	Williams	3
Roseberg	Williams	2
Coulthard	BMW Soubers	1
Heidfeld	Red Bull	0
Klien	BMW Soubers	0
Liuzzi	Toro Rosso	0
Scott Speed	Toro Rosso	0

155. If Alonso got the podium finish in each of the first 6 races, then what was the maximum number of races in which he had 2nd rank?

(a) 4 (b) 3
(c) 2 (d) 1

156. Apart from the first six races, Alonso got the podium finish in the 7th race as well. However, he was not allowed to participate in the subsequent races due to mechanical failure. At the end of the season, if Schumacher won the 'Driver's Championship', then which of the following could have been his lowest rank in any of the last three races?

(a) 5th (b) 6th
(c) 7th (d) 4th

157. Which of the following statements CANNOT be true?

(a) Renault and Ferrari had a tie for the 'Constructor's Championship'.

(b) Alonso got the podium finish in each of the first 6 races out of which he did not have rank 1st in the 6th race.

(c) Fisichella got the podium finish in the 9th race and Honda won the 'Constructor's Championship'.

(d) Barichello got the podium finish in the 3rd race but he did not score any point in the 1st race.

158. If Schumacher ranked 9th in one of the first six races, then which of the following CANNOT be the points scored by him in any one of the first six races?

(a) 3 (b) 2
(c) 1 (d) 0

Directions for questions 159 to 162 : Answer the questions on the basis of the information given below.

From ISBT, buses ply on 6 different routes viz. 414, 413, 427, 966, 893 and 181 at an interval of 10 min, 10 min, 12 min, 15 min, 20 min and 30 min, not necessarily in that order, to four different destinations viz. Mehrauli, Badarpur, Uttam Nagar and Azadpur. There is at least one bus for each destination. Further information is also known:

i. Two buses to the same destination cannot start at the same time.
ii. If the timings of two buses plying different routes but heading towards the same destination clash, then the bus of the route number having the shorter time interval will skip this journey.
iii. Buses on two different routes ply between ISBT and Mehrauli.
iv. The difference between the time intervals of a route to Mehrauli and Uttam Nagar is equal to the difference between the time intervals of the two routes to Uttam Nagar.
v. Buses on a route to Mehrauli leaves after every 10 min.
vi. 414 leaves for Badarpur after every 30 min.
vii. Time intervals between two different routes heading towards the same destination cannot be equal.
viii. Buses on one of the routes to Uttam Nagar leave after every 15 min.
ix. Buses to any destination can leave from ISBT with an interval of at least one minute or an integral multiple of one minute.

159. If 427 leaves to Mehrauli after every 10 min, then in a given hour a minimum of how many buses can ply on route 427?

(a) 3 (b) 4
(c) 6 (d) 2

160. On a festival day, if frequency of all buses was increased by decreasing the time interval of all the routes by 5 min, then what can be the minimum time difference between any two buses plying to Mehrauli?

(a) 2 min (b) 5 min
(c) 1 min (d) None of these

161. Which of the following statements is necessarily TRUE?

(a) A maximum of 3 buses can depart at a given time.
(b) Maximum of 11 buses can depart for Mehrauli in 1 hour.
(c) Maximum difference between the intervals of the buses plying to Uttam Nagar and Badarpur is 10 min.
(d) The difference between the time intervals of buses plying to Uttam Nagar is an integral multiple of 5 min.

162. If condition (iii) is not there, then what can be the minimum difference between the time intervals between the buses plying to Uttam Nagar?

(a) 2 min (b) 3 min
(c) 4 min (d) 5 min.

2016

Directions for questions 163 to 166: Answer the questions on the basis of the information given below.

H1, H2, H3 and H4 are four horses that participated in each of the four different races – Race-I, Race-II, Race-III and Race-IV – during an annual horse-racing event in Goa. Each horse is owned by a different owner among Rahul, Dharma, Dablu and Ritesh, in no particular order. None of the four horses finished at the same position in more than two of the four races. In each race the four horses were given ranks 1, 2, 3 and 4 according to the positions at which they finished in the race. It is also known that:

(i) In Race-I, H2 finished third and Ritesh's horse finished first. Interestingly, in Race-II, H2 finished first and Ritesh's horse finished third.
(ii) In Race-IV, H2 finished third and H3 finished fourth.
(iii) Dablu's horse finished at the same position in Race-I and Race-II, and also in Race-III and Race-IV.
(iv) In Race-IV, H1 and H3 interchanged the positions at which they had finished in Race-II.
(v) In Race-III, H3 finished fourth and H4 finished second.
(vi) Rahul's horse did not finish first in any of the four races.

163. Who are the owners of H3 and H4 respectively?

(a) Ritesh and Rahul (b) Dablu and Ritesh
(c) Rahul and Dablu (d) Cannot be determined

164. Whose horse finished third in Race-III?

(a) Rahul (b) Ritesh
(c) Dharma (d) Either Rahul or Dablu

165. If the horse with the lowest sum of ranks in the four races won a Jackpot of Rs. 1 crore, which horse won the Jackpot?

(a) H1 (b) H2
(c) H3 (d) H4

166. Which of the following statements is definitely false?

(a) H2 is owned by Dharama
(b) H3 finished second in Race-II
(c) H4 finished fourth in Race-II
(d) None of these

Directions for questions 167 to 170: Answer the questions on the basis of the information given below.

Anu, Banu, Charu, Dhanu, Ellu, Fiza, Goru and Hina are eight friends, from eight different B-Schools. They perform in Nukkad Natak "LPG" held at Patna. During the performance they sit at a circular table such that four of them face inside i.e. towards the center and the rest four face outside i.e. away from the center of the table. Each of them uses one of the four props – Dholak, Danda, Dafli and Chunni. Anu and Hina sit diametrically opposite to each other and use the same prop. No other pair of friends sitting diametrically opposite uses the same prop. It is also known that:

(i) Hina from IMT uses Dafli. She sits immediately to the left of both Charu from IMI and Banu from FMS.

(ii) The person sitting diametrically opposite the person from IMI faces inside.

(iii) Goru from IIMS sits immediately to the left of Anu from CIMP.

(iv) Charu and both her immediate neighbours face inside.

(v) Dhanu from IIMA sits diametrically opposite Ellu.

(vi) The props used by Banu and Charu are Chunni and Dholak respectively.

(vii) Dhanu, who uses Chunni, sits third to the left of the person from IIMR.

(viii) The person from IIFT uses Danda and is the only person sitting between the two persons using Dholak.

167. Who is from IIMR and which prop does he/she use?

Fill 1 if "your answer is Fiza, Chunni"

Fill 2 if "your answer is Charu, Dholak"

Fill 3 if "your answer is Fiza, Dholak"

Fill 4 if "your answer is Cannot be determined"

168. How many of the following combinations of person-prop is/are correct?

(i) Goru - Dholak

(ii) Dhanu - Chunni

(iii) Ellu - Danda

(iv) Anu - Dafli

169. The number of friends sitting between Fiza and the friend from FMS is

170. The number of letters in the name of the person who is sitting opposite to Charu is

Directions for questions 171 to 174: Answer the questions on the basis of the information given below.

During a cycle racing event in 2012 Olympic Games, eight riders – Alex, Fausto, Hilton, Jason, Matt, Nathan, Rahsaan and Ryan – cycled in eight different lanes on a track. The lanes were numbered 1 to 8 from left to right in that order. In a strange coincidence, the finishing positions of all the riders were same as their lane numbers. E.g. the rider cycling in the lane numbered 1 finished first, the rider cycling in the lane numbered 2 finished second and so on. It is also known that:

(i) Exactly two riders finished between Hilton and Rahsaan.

(ii) Jason finished just ahead of Rahsaan.

(iii) Nathan finished just ahead of Alex.

(iv) Jason finished ahead of Hilton.

(v) Neither Matt nor Ryan finished last.

(vi) Exactly two riders finished ahead of Jason.

171. Who could not have finished fifth in the race?

(a) Alex (b) Matt

(c) Nathan (d) Ryan

172. Who finished seventh and eighth respectively in the race?

(a) Rahsaan and Fausto

(b) Hilton and Fausto

(c) Jason and Hilton

(d) Cannot be determined

173. The sum of all the possible positions to which Matt could finish the race was

(a) 14 (b) 11

(c) 12 (d) 13

174. If Ryan did not finish first, who finished first?

(a) Nathan (b) Matt

(c) Rahsaan (d) Cannot be determined

Directions for questions 175 to 178: Answer the questions on the basis of the information given below.

Amar went for a vacation to a different place every year from 2004 to 2008. His vacation lasted for a different number of day(s) among 1, 2, 3, 4 and 5 on each occasion, in no particular order. It is also known that:

(i) His vacation in 2007 lasted a day longer as compared to the year when he went to Singapore.

(ii) He went to Europe in the year next to the one in which he went to the USA.

(iii) He went to Bangkok in the year next to the one in which his vacation lasted for just 1 day.

(iv) He didn't go to Europe in 2008. His vacation in Europe lasted for less than 5 days.

(v) His vacation in 2006 lasted a day longer as compared to the year when he went to Nepal.

(vi) He went to Bangkok in 2005 and his vacation lasted for less than 5 days.

175. Which of the following combinations of the destination and the year of vacation is not correct?

(a) Nepal – 2008 (b) Europe – 2007

(c) Singapore – 2004 (d) None of these

176. How many days did Amar spend on his vacation in Europe?

(a) 1 (b) 2

(c) 3 (d) 4

177. Which of the following statement(s) is/are true?

I. He spent 1 day on his vacation in Nepal.

II. He spent 4 days on his vacation in the USA.

(a) Only I (b) Only II

(c) Both I and II (d) Neither I nor II

178. In which year did he visit Nepal?

(a) 2004 (b) 2006

(c) 2007 (d) 2008

2017

Question Numbers (179 to 182) : A tea taster was assigned to rate teas from six different locations - Munnar, Wayanad, Ooty, Darjeeling, Assam and Himachal. These teas were placed in six cups, numbered 1 to 6, not necessarily in the same order The tea taster was asked to rate these teas on the strength of their flavour on a scale of 1 to 10. He gave a unique integer rating to each tea. Some other information is given below:

1. Cup 6 contained tea from Himachal.
2. Tea from Ooty got the highest rating, but it was not in Cup 3.
3. The rating of tea in Cup 3 was double the rating of the tea in Cup 5.
4. Only two cups got ratings in even numbers.
5. Cup 2 got the minimum rating and this rating was an even number.
6. Tea in Cup 3 got a higher rating than that in Cup 1.
7. The rating of tea from Wayanad was more than the rating of tea from Munnar, but less than that from Assam.

179. What was the second highest rating given?

180. What was the number of the cup that contained tea from Ooty?

181. If the tea from Munnar did not get the minimum rating, what was the rating of the tea from Wayanad?

(a) 3 (b) 5

(c) 1 (d) 6

182. If cups containing teas from Wayanad and Ooty had consecutive numbers, which of the following statements may be true?

(a) Cup 5 contains tea from Assam

(b) Cup 1 contains tea from Darjeeling

(c) Tea from Wayanad has got a rating of 6

(d) Tea from Darjeeling got the minimum rating

Question Numbers : (183 to 186) : In an 8 × 8 chessboard a queen placed anywhere can attack another piece if the piece is present in the same row, or in the same column or in any diagonal position in any possible 4 directions, provided there is no other piece in between in the path from the queen to that piece.

The columns are labelled a to h (left to right) and the rows are numbered 1 to 8 (bottom to top). The position of a piece is given by the combination of column and row labels. For example, position c5 means that the piece is in c^{th} column and 5th row.

Sub questions

183. If the queen is at c5, and the other pieces at positions c2, g1, g3, g3 and a3, how many are under attack by the queen? There are no other pieces on the board.

(a) 2 (b) 3

(c) 4 (d) 5

184. If the other pieces are only at positions a1, a3, b4, d7, h7 and h8, then which of the following positions of the queen results in the maximum number of pieces being under attack?

(a) f8 (b) a7

(c) c1 (d) d3

185. If the other pieces are only at positions a1, a3, b4, d7, h7 and h8, then from how many positions the queen cannot attack any of the pieces?

(a) 0 (b) 3

(c) 4 (d) 6

186. Suppose the queen is the only piece on the board and it is at position d5.

In how many positions can another piece be placed on the board such that it is safe from attack from the queen?

(a) 32 (b) 33

(c) 36 (d) 37

Question Numbers : (187 to 190) : Eight friends: Ajit, Byomkesh, Gargi, Jayanta, Kikira, Manik, Prodosh and Tapesh are going to Delhi from Kolkata by a flight operated by Cheap Air. In the flight, sitting is arranged in 30 rows, numbered 1 to 30, each consisting of 6 seats, marked by letters A to F from left to right, respectively. Seats A to C are to the left of the aisle (the passage running from the front of the aircraft to the back), and seats D to F are to the right of the aisle. Seats A and F are by the windows and referred to as Window seats, C and D are by the aisle and are referred to as Aisle seats while B and E are referred to as Middle seats. Seats marked by consecutive letters are called consecutive seats (or seats next to each other). A seat number is a combination of the row number, followed by the letter indicating the position in the row; e.g., 1A is the left window seat in the first row, while 12E is the right middle seat in the 12th row.

Cheap Air charges Rs.1000 extra for any seats in Rows 1, 12 and 13 as those have extra legroom. For Rows 210, it charges Rs.500 extra for Window seats and Rs.300 extra for Aisle seats. For Rows 11 and 14 to 20, it charges Rs.200 extra for Window seats and Rs.400 extra for Aisle seats. All other seats are available at no extra charge.

The following are known:

1. The eight friends were seated in six different rows.
2. They occupied 3 Window seats, 4 Aisle seats and 1 Middle seat.
3. Seven of them had to pay extra amounts, totaling to Rs. 4600, for their choices of seat. One of them did not pay any additional amount for his/her choice of seat.
4. Jayanta, Ajit and Byomkesh were sitting in seats marked by the same letter, in consecutive rows in increasing order of row numbers; but all of them paid different amounts for their choices of seat. One of these amounts may be zero.
5. Gargi was sitting next to Kikira, and Manik was sitting next to Jayanta.
6. Prodosh and Tapesh were sitting in seats marked by the same letter, in consecutive rows in increasing order of row numbers; but they paid different amounts for their choices of seat. One of these amounts may be zero.

187. In which row was Manik sitting?

(a) 10 (b) 11

(c) 12 (d) 13

188. How much extra did Jayanta pay for his choice of seat?

(a) Rs. 300 (b) RS. 400

(c) Rs. 500 (d) RS. 1000

189. How much extra did Gargi pay for her choice of seat?

(a) 0 (b) Rs. 300

(c) Rs. 400 (d) Rs. 1000

190. Who among the following did not pay any extra amount for his/her choice of seat?

(a) Kikira (b) Manik

(c) Gargi (d) Tapesh

Question Numbers : (191 to 194) : A high security research lab requires the researchers to set a pass key sequence Passed on the scan of the five fingers of their left hands. When an employee first joins the lab, her fingers are scanned in an order of her choice, and then when she wants to re-enter the facility, she has to scan the five fingers in the same sequence.

The lab authorities are considering some relaxations of the scan order requirements, since it is observed that some employees often get locked-out because they forget the sequence.

191. The lab has decided to allow a variation in the sequence of scans of the five fingers so that at most two scans (out of five) are out of place. For example, if the original sequence is Thumb (T), index finger (I), middle finger (M), ring finger (R) and little finger (L) then TLMRI is also allowed, but TMRLI is not.

How many different sequences of scans are allowed for any given person's original scan?

192. The lab has decided to allow variations of the original sequence so that input of the scanned sequence of five fingers is allowed to vary from the original sequence by one place for any of the fingers. Thus, for example, if TIMRL is the original sequence, then ITRML is also allowed, but LIMRT is not.

How many different sequences are allowed for any given person's original scan?

(a) 7 (b) 5

(c) 8 (d) 13

193. The lab has now decided to require six scans in the pass key sequence, where exactly one finger is scanned twice, and the other fingers are scanned exactly once, which can be done in any order. For example, a possible sequence is TIMTRL.

Suppose the lab allows a variation of the original sequence (of six inputs) where at most two scans (out of six) are out of place, as long as the finger originally scanned twice is scanned twice and other fingers are scanned once.

How many different sequences of scans are allowed for any given person's original scan?

194. The lab has now decided to require six scans in the pass key sequence, where exactly one finger is scanned twice, and the other fingers are scanned exactly once, which can be done in any order. For example, a possible sequence is TIMTRL.

Suppose the lab allows a variation of the original sequence (of six inputs) so that input in the form of scanned sequence of six fingers is allowed to vary from the original sequence by one place for any of the fingers, as long as the finger originally scanned twice is scanned twice and other fingers are scanned once.

How many different sequences of scans are allowed if the original scan sequence is LRLTIM?

(a) 8 (b) 11

(c) 13 (d) 14

2018 Slot 1

195. Who are the students from the institute Z?

(a) Adriana and Bandita (b) Chitra and Daisy

(c) Adriana and Daisy (d) Bandita and Chitra

196. Which subject does Deb minor in?
(a) Cannot be determined uniquely from the given information
(b) Finance
(c) Operations
(d) Marketing

197. Which subject does Amit major in?
(a) Cannot be determined uniquely from the given information
(b) Finance
(c) Marketing
(d) Operations

198. If Chitra majors in Finance, which subject does Bandita major in?
(a) Marketing
(b) Cannot be determined uniquely from the given information
(c) Operations
(d) Finance

Question Numbers (199 to 202) :

An ATM dispenses exactly Rs. 5000 per withdrawal using 100, 200 and 500 rupee notes. The ATM requires every customer to give her preference for one of the three denominations of notes. It then dispenses notes such that the number of notes of the customer's preferred denomination exceeds the total number of notes of other denominations dispensed to her.

199. In how many different ways can the ATM serve a customer who gives 500 rupee notes as her preference?

200. If the ATM could serve only 10 customers with a stock of fifty 500 rupee notes and a sufficient number of notes of other denominations, what is the maximum number of customers among these 10 who could have given 500 rupee notes as their preferences?

201. What is the maximum number of customers that the ATM can serve with a stock of fifty 500 rupee notes and a sufficient number of notes of other denominations, if all the customers are to be served with at most 20 notes per withdrawal?
(a) 16 (b) 10
(c) 12 (d) 13

202. What is the number of 500 rupee notes required to serve 50 customers with 500 rupee notes as their preferences and another 50 customers with 100 rupee notes as their preferences, if the total number of notes to be dispensed is the smallest possible?
(a) 1400 (b) 800
(c) 750 (d) 900

Question Numbers (203 to 206) :

Fuel contamination levels at each of 20 petrol pumps P1, P2, ..., P20 were recorded as either high, medium, or low.

1. Contamination levels at three pumps among P1 - P5 were recorded as high.
2. P6 was the only pump among P1 - P10 where the contamination level was recorded as low.
3. P7 and P8 were the only two consecutively numbered pumps where the same levels of contamination were recorded.
4. High contamination levels were not recorded at any of the pumps P16 - P20.
5. The number of pumps where high contamination levels were recorded was twice the number of pumps where low contamination levels were recorded.

203. Which of the following MUST be true?
(a) The contamination level at P12 was recorded as high.
(b) The contamination level at P13 was recorded as low.
(c) The contamination level at P20 was recorded as medium.
(d) The contamination level at P10 was recorded as high.

204. What best can be said about the number of pumps at which the contamination levels were recorded as medium?
(a) At most 9 (b) At least 8
(c) More than 4 (d) Exactly 8

205. If the contamination level at P11 was recorded as low, then which of the following MUST be true?
(a) The contamination level at P12 was recorded as high.
(b) The contamination level at P18 was recorded as low.
(c) The contamination level at P15 was recorded as medium.
(d) The contamination level at P14 was recorded as medium.

206. If contamination level at P15 was recorded as medium, then which of the following MUST be FALSE?
(a) Contamination levels at P13 and P17 were recorded as the same.
(b) Contamination levels at P11 and P16 were recorded as the same.
(c) Contamination levels at P10 and P14 were recorded as the same.
(d) Contamination level at P14 was recorded to be higher than that at P15.

Question Numbers (207 to 210) :

You are given an n×n square matrix to be filled with numerals so that no two adjacent cells have the same numeral. Two cells are called adjacent if they touch each other horizontally, vertically or diagonally. So a cell in one of the four corners has three cells adjacent to it, and a cell in the first or last row or column which is not in the corner has five cells adjacent to it. Any other cell has eight cells adjacent to it.

207. What is the minimum number of different numerals needed to fill a 3 × 3 square matrix?

208. What is the minimum number of different numerals needed to fill a 5 × 5 square matrix?

209. Suppose you are allowed to make one mistake, that is, one pair of adjacent cells can have the same numeral. What is the minimum number of different numerals required to fill a 5 × 5 matrix?

(a) 16 (b) 4

(c) 9 (d) 25

210. Suppose that all the cells adjacent to any particular cell must have different numerals. What is the minimum number of different numerals needed to fill a 5 × 5 square matrix?

(a) 9 (b) 16

(c) 4 (d) 25

2018 Slot 2

Question Numbers: (212 to 214):

Fun Sports (FS) provides training in three sports – Gilli-danda (G), Kho-Kho (K), and Ludo (L). Currently it has an enrollment of 39 students each of whom is enrolled in at least one of the three sports. The following details are known:

1. The number of students enrolled only in L is double the number of students enrolled in all the three sports.
2. There are a total of 17 students enrolled in G.
3. The number of students enrolled only in G is one less than the number of students enrolled only in L.
4. The number of students enrolled only in K is equal to the number of students who are enrolled in both K and L.
5. The maximum student enrollment is in L.
6. Ten students enrolled in G are also enrolled in at least one more sport.

212. What is the minimum number of students enrolled in both G and L but not in K?

213. If the numbers of students enrolled in K and L are in the ratio 19:22, then what is the number of students enrolled in L?

(a) 17 (b) 18

(c) 19 (d) 22

214. Due to academic pressure, students who were enrolled in all three sports were asked to withdraw from one of the three sports. After the withdrawal, the number of students enrolled in G was six less than the number of students enrolled in L, while the number of students enrolled in K went down by one. After the withdrawal, how many students were enrolled in both G and K?

215. Due to academic pressure, students who were enrolled in all three sports were asked to withdraw from one of the three sports. After the withdrawal, the number of students enrolled in G was six less than the number of students enrolled in L, while the number of students enrolled in K went down by one. After the withdrawal, how many students were enrolled in both G and L?

(a) 8 (b) 5

(c) 6 (d) 7

Question Numbers: (216 to 219):

Seven candidates, Akil, Balaram, Chitra, Divya, Erina, Fatima, and Ganeshan, were invited to interview for a position. Candidates were required to reach the venue before 8 am. Immediately upon arrival, they were sent to one of three interview rooms: 101, 102, and 103. The following venue log shows the arrival times for these candidates. Some of the names have not been recorded in the log and have been marked as '?'.

Time	7:10 am	7:15 am	7:25 am	7:30 am	7:40 am	7:45 am
Person	Akil, ?	?	?	Chitra	Fatima	?

Additionally here are some statements from the candidates:

Balaram: I was the third person to enter Room 101.

Chitra: I was the last person to enter the room I was allotted to.

Erina: I was the only person in the room I was allotted to.

Fatima: Three people including Akil were already in the room that I was allotted to when I entered it.

Ganeshan: I was one among the two candidates allotted to Room 102.

216. What best can be said about the room to which Divya was allotted?

(a) Definitely Room 103

(b) Definitely Room 101

(c) Definitely Room 102

(d) Either Room 101 or Room 102

217. Who else was in Room 102 when Ganeshan entered?

(a) No one (b) Divya

(c) Akil (d) Chitra

218. When did Erina reach the venue?

(a) 7:15 am (b) 7:10 am

(c) 7:45 am (d) 7:25 am

219. If Ganeshan entered the venue before Divya, when did Balaram enter the venue?

(a) 7:25 am (b) 7:10 am
(c) 7:15 am (d) 7:45 am

Question Numbers: (220 to 223):

According to a coding scheme the sentence

Peacock is designated as the national bird of India is coded as

5688999 35 1135556678 56 458 13666689 1334 79 13366

This coding scheme has the following rules:

1. The scheme is case-insensitive (does not distinguish between upper case and lower case letters).
2. Each letter has a unique code which is a single digit from among 1,2,3, ..., 9.
3. The digit 9 codes two letters, and every other digit codes three letters.
4. The code for a word is constructed by arranging the digits corresponding to its letters in a non-decreasing sequence.

Answer these questions on the basis of this information.

220. What best can be concluded about the code for the letter L?

(a) 1 or 8 (b) 8
(c) 6 (d) 1

221. What best can be concluded about the code for the letter B?

(a) 3 or 4 (b) 3
(c) 1 or 3 or 4 (d) 1

222. For how many digits can the complete list of letters associated with that digit be identified?

(a) 0 (b) 2
(c) 3 (d) 1

223. Which set of letters CANNOT be coded with the same digit?

(a) S, E, Z
(b) S, U, V
(c) X, Y, Z
(d) I, B, M

Question Numbers: (224 to 227):

Each visitor to an amusement park needs to buy a ticket. Tickets can be Platinum, Gold, or Economy. Visitors are classified as Old, Middle-aged, or Young. The following facts are known about visitors and ticket sales on a particular day:

1. 140 tickets were sold.
2. The number of Middle-aged visitors was twice the number of Old visitors, while the number of Young visitors was twice the number of Middle-aged visitors.
3. Young visitors bought 38 of the 55 Economy tickets that were sold, and they bought half the total number of Platinum tickets that were sold.
4. The number of Gold tickets bought by Old visitors was equal to the number of Economy tickets bought by Old visitors.

224. If the number of Old visitors buying Platinum tickets was equal to the number of Middle-aged visitors buying Platinum tickets, then which among the following could be the total number of Platinum tickets sold?

(a) 34 (b) 32
(c) 38 (d) 36

225. If the number of Old visitors buying Platinum tickets was equal to the number of Middle-aged visitors buying Economy tickets, then the number of Old visitors buying Gold tickets was

226. If the number of Old visitors buying Gold tickets was strictly greater than the number of Young visitors buying Gold tickets, then the number of Middle-aged visitors buying Gold tickets was

227. Which of the following statements MUST be FALSE?

(a) The numbers of Gold and Platinum tickets bought by Young visitors were equal
(b) The numbers of Old and Middle-aged visitors buying Platinum tickets were equal
(c) The numbers of Old and Middle-aged visitors buying Economy tickets were equal
(d) The numbers of Middle-aged and Young visitors buying Gold tickets were equal

DATA SUFFICIENCY

2000

Direction for Question 1: *The question is followed by two statements, I and II. Answer the question using the following instructions.*

Mark the answer as

(a) if the question can be answered by one of the statements alone, but cannot be answered by using the other statement alone.
(b) if the question can be answered by using either statement alone.
(c) if the question can be answered by using both the statements together, but cannot be answered by using either statement alone.
(d) if the question cannot be answered even by using both statements together.

1. Consider three real numbers, X, Y and Z. Is Z the smallest of these numbers?

I. X is greater than at least one of Y and Z.
II. Y is greater than at least one of X and Z.

2003

Direction for Question 2: *In the question there are two statements: A and B.*

Choose (a) if the question can be answered by one of the statements alone but not by the other.

Choose (b) if the question can be answered by using either statement alone.

Choose (c) if the question can be answered by using both the statements together but cannot be answered using either statement alone.

Choose (d) if the question cannot be answered even by using both the statements A and B.

2. F and M are father and mother of S, respectively. S has four uncles and three aunts. F has two siblings. The siblings of F and M are unmarried. How many brothers does M have?

A. F has two brothers.

B. M has five siblings.

2004

Directions for Questions 3 and 4: *Each question is followed by two statements, A and B. Answer each question using the following instructions.*

Choose (a) if the question can be answered by using one of the statements alone but not by using the other statement alone.

Choose (b) if the question can be answered by using either of the statements alone.

Choose (c) if the question can be answered by using both statements together but not by either statement alone.

Choose (d) if the question cannot be answered on the basis of the two statements.

3. Four candidates for an award obtain distinct scores in a test. Each of the four casts a vote to choose the winner of the award. The candidate who gets the largest number of votes wins the award. In case of a tie in the voting process, the candidate with the highest score wins the award. Who wins the award?

A. The candidates with top three scores each vote for the top score amongst the other three.

B. The candidate with the lowest score votes for the player with the second highest score.

4. In a class of 30 students, Rashmi secured the third rank among the girls, while her brother Kumar studying in the same class secured the sixth rank in the whole class. Between the two, who had a better overall rank?

A. Kumar was among the top 25% of the boys merit list in the class in which 60% were boys.

B. There were three boys among the top five rank holders, and three girls among the top ten rank holders.

2007

Direction for Question 5: *The question is followed by two statements, A and B.*

Answer the question using the following instructions:

Mark (a) if the question can be answered by using the statement A alone but not by using the statement B alone.

Mark (b) if the question can be answered by using the statement B alone but not by using the statement A alone.

Mark (c) if the question can be answered by using either of the statements alone.

Mark (d) if the question can be answered by using both the statements together but not by either of the statements alone.

Mark (e) if the question cannot be answered on the basis of the two statements.

5. Five students Atul, Bala, Chetan, Dev and Ernesto were the only ones who participated in a quiz contest. They were ranked based on their scores in the contest. Dev got a higher rank as compared to Ernesto, while Bala got a higher rank as compared to Chetan. Chetan's rank was lower than the median. Who among the five got the highest rank?

A. Atul was the last rank holder.

B. Bala was not among the top two rank holders.

2003 (R)

Directions for Questions 6 and 7: *Each question is followed by two statements, A and B. Answer each question using the following instructions:*

Choose (a) if the question can be answered by using statement A alone but not by using B alone.

Choose (b) if the question can be answered by using statement B alone but not by using A alone.

Choose (c) if the question can be answered by using either statement alone and

Choose (d) if the question can be answered using both the statements together but not by either statement alone.

6. In a cricket match, the 'Man of the Match' award is given to the player scoring the highest number of runs. In case of a tie, the player (out of those locked in the tie) who has taken the higher number of catches is chosen. Even thereafter if there is a tie, the player (out of those locked in the tie) who has dropped fewer catches is selected. Aakash, Biplab, and Chirag who were contenders for the award dropped at least one catch each. Biplab dropped two catches more than Aakash did, scored 50, and took two catches. Chirag got two chances to catch and dropped both. Who was the 'Man of the Match'?

A. Chirag made 15 runs less than both Aakash and Bipla2.

B. The catches dropped less by Biplab are 1 more than the catches taken by Aakash.

7. Four friends — A, B, C and D got the top four ranks in a competitive examination, but A did not get the first, B did not get the second, C did not get the third, and D did not get the fourth rank. Who secured which rank?

A. Neither A nor D were among the first 2.

B. Neither B nor C was third or fourth.

MEMORY BASED QUESTIONS

2009

8. The question given below is followed by two statements, A and B. Mark the answer using the following instructions:

Mark (a) if the question can be answered by using Statement A alone, but cannot be answered by using Statement B alone.

Mark (b) if the question can be answered by using Statement B alone, but cannot be answered by using Statement A alone.

Mark (c) if the question cannot be answered even by using both the statements together.

Mark (d) if the question can be answered by using either statement alone.

Q. Uncle Gomes distributes 40 candies among five children in such a way that each child gets at least one candy and no two children get the same number of candies. What is the number of candies received by the child who gets the maximum number of candies among the five children?

A. Each child gets more than 4 candies.

B. The sum of the number of candies received by the child who gets the maximum and the child who gets the minimum number of candies among the five children is 29.

9. The question given below is followed by two statements, A and B. Mark the answer using the following instructions:

Mark (a) if the question can be answered by using one of the statements alone, but cannot be answered by using the other statement alone.

Mark (b) if the question can be answered by using either statement alone.

Mark (c) if the question can be answered by using both the statements together, but cannot be answered by using either statement alone.

Mark (d) if the question cannot be answered even by using both the statements together.

Q. Some students are standing in a row facing the West direction. Fourteen students are standing to the left of Mukesh and twenty two students are standing to the right of Rakesh. How many students are there in all?

A. Exactly 5 students are standing between Mukesh and Rakesh.

B. The total number of students is a prime number less than 37.

10. The question given below is followed by two statements, A and B. Mark the answer using the following instructions:

Mark (a) if the question can be answered by using either statement alone.

Mark (b) if the question can be answered by using one of the statements alone, but cannot be answered by using the other statement alone.

Mark (c) if the question cannot be answered even by using both the statements together.

Mark (d) if the question can be answered by using both the statements together, but cannot be answered by using either statement alone.

Q. ABCDEF is a hexagon in which all the interior angles are equal. If AB = 20 cm and DE = 10 cm, then what is the perimeter of the hexagon?

A. The shortest distance between AB and DE is 30 cm.

B. The line joining the midpoints of AB and DE is perpendicular to both AB and DE.

2010

11. The question given below is followed by two statements, A and B. Mark the answer using the following instructions:

Mark (a) if the question can be answered by using one of the statements alone, but cannot be answered by using the other statement alone.

Mark (b) if the question can be answered by using either statement alone.

Mark (c) if the question can be answered by using both the statements together, but cannot be answered by using either statement alone.

Mark (d) if the question cannot be answered even by using both the statements together.

Q. The houses of Pavan, Pranab, Mohit and Santosh are of different sizes and each house has some vehicle parking slots. Pavan stays in the second smallest house, which has the same number of parking slots as that in Pranab's house. The largest house is not the one with the highest number of parking slots. Santosh's house is not the smallest. The sum of the number of parking slots in Mohit's house and Pranab's house is an even number. Who among the four stays in the second largest house and how many parking slots does it have?

A. One house has two parking slots and the remaining three houses have one parking slot each.

B. The four houses have two, three, three and five parking slots, in no particular order.

Directions for questions 12 and 13: Answer the questions on the basis of the information given below.

Two stock traders – Hasan and Sajid – trade in the shares of Pineapple Group only. Each of them follows a different strategy for selling and buying the stocks. Sajid sells an equal number of shares at 9 a.m. and 10 a.m. and buys them back in equal numbers at 1 p.m. and 2 p.m. Hasan sells some shares at 11 a.m. and the rest at 12 noon such that the amount he gets on the two occasions is the same. He buys back the whole lot at 3 p.m. The chart given below displays the performance of Pineapple Group stock on two particular days – Day 1 and Day 2. The profit/loss made by a trader on a particular day is the difference between the amount that he obtains by selling the shares and the amount that he spends in buying the shares. "Margin" for a day is the profit/loss expressed as a percentage of the total amount obtained by selling the shares on that day.

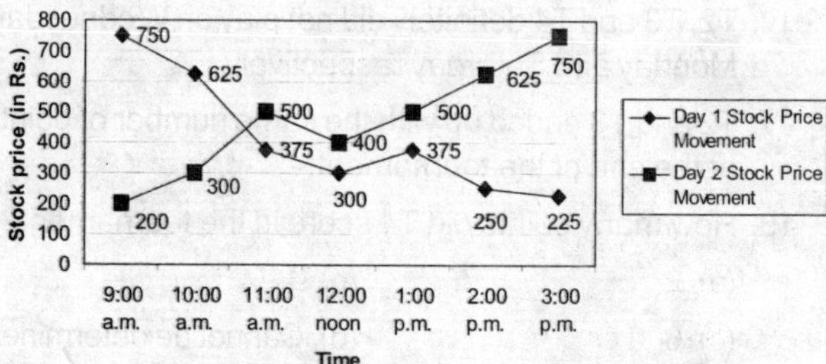

12. If Sajid and Hasan sold an equal number of shares on Day 1, then which of the following statements would definitely be true?

I. Hasan made more profit than Sajid on Day 1.

II. Hasan made less profit than Sajid on Day 1.

III. Hasan's Margin was more than Sajid's Margin on Day 1.

IV. Hasan's Margin was less than Sajid's Margin on Day 1.

(a) I only (b) I and IV
(c) II and IV (d) I and III

13. What was the ratio of Hasan's Margin to Sajid's Margin on Day 2?

(a) 13 : 20 (b) 11 : 20
(c) 20 : 13 (d) Cannot be determined

14. The question given below is followed by two statements, A and B. Mark the answer using the following instructions:

Mark (a) if the question can be answered by using one of the statements alone, but cannot be answered by using the other statement alone.

Mark (b) if the question can be answered by using either statement alone.

Mark (c) if the question can be answered by using both the statements together, but cannot be answered by using either statement alone.

Mark (d) if the question cannot be answered even by using both the statements together.

Q. ABCD is a cyclic quadrilateral in which AB = 8 cm and BC = 15 cm. What is the area of the quadrilateral?

A. AD = CD

B. The length of the diameter of the circumcircle of triangle BCD is 17 cm.

2011

15. The question given below is followed by two statements, A and B. Mark the answer using the following instructions:

Mark (a) if the question can be answered by using either statement alone.

Mark (b) if the question can be answered by using one of the statements alone, but cannot be answered by using the other statement alone.

Mark (c) if the question cannot be answered even by using both the statements together.

Mark (d) if the question can be answered by using both the statements together, but cannot be answered by using either statement alone.

Q. What is the sum of a, b and c?

A. The numbers a, b and c are in Arithmetic Progression.

B. $a^2 + b^2 + c^2 = 83$, where a, b and c are natural numbers.

16. The question given below is followed by two statements, A and B. Mark the answer using the following instructions:

Mark (a) if the question can be answered by using one of the statements alone, but cannot be answered by using the other statement alone.

Mark (b) if the question can be answered by using either statement alone.

Mark (c) if the question cannot be answered even by using both the statements together.

Mark (d) if the question can be answered by using both the statements together, but cannot be answered by using either statement alone.

Q. If p and q are natural numbers, then what is the remainder when (p + q) is divided by 7?

A. $6q - p = 5$

B. $8q + p = 45$

17. The question given below is followed by two statements, A and B. Mark the answer using the following instructions:

Mark (a) if the question can be answered by using Statement A alone, but cannot be answered by using Statement B alone.

Mark (b) if the question can be answered by using Statement B alone, but cannot be answered by using Statement A alone.

Mark (c) if the question can be answered by using either statement alone.

Mark (d) if the question cannot be answered by any of the two statements.

Q. Four friends – Ajay, Bikas, Chetan and Deepak – have different surnames among Rathore, Agarwal, Yadav and Sharma, not necessarily in the same order. They are standing in a queue one after the other. Either Rathore or Agarwal is standing immediately in front of Ajay and the other is standing immediately behind Ajay. Bikas and Chetan are standing at the two ends of the queue. What is the surname of Ajay?

A. The surname of Chetan is Agarwal.

B. The surname of Bikas is Yadav.

18. The question given below is followed by two statements, A and B. Mark the answer using the following instructions:

Mark (a) if the question can be answered by using Statement A alone, but cannot be answered by using Statement B alone.

Mark (b) if the question can be answered by using Statement B alone, but cannot be answered by using Statement A alone.

Mark (c) if the question can be answered by using either statement alone.

Mark (d) if the question cannot be answered by any of the two statements.

Q. Five people having different ages are standing in a row. They are Engineer, Professor, Manager, Doctor and Lawyer respectively by profession. The oldest among them is standing in the middle of the row and he is not a Lawyer. The youngest among them is an Engineer and he is not standing at any of the two ends of the row. The Professor is younger than exactly three people and he is standing at one of the ends of the row. The Doctor is standing beside the Engineer. The Lawyer is standing beside the Doctor. The Manager is standing beside the Lawyer. How many people are younger than the Manager?

A. The Lawyer is younger than the Doctor.

B. The Manager is younger than the Lawyer.

2013

Directions for questions 19 to 21: Answer the questions on the basis of the information given below.

Four teams—T1, T2, T3 and T4— participated in a tournament of 'Bat and trap', an English bat-and-ball pub game. In the tournament, each team played exactly one match with each of the other teams. The matches were played on six consecutive days of a week from Monday to Saturday. Two points were awarded to the winner of a match and no points to the loser. No match in the tournament resulted in a tie/draw. It is also known that:

I. T1 won only one match in the tournament and it was played on Monday.

II. The match played on Thursday was won by T4.

III. T3 won against T2 on Tuesday.

IV. T2, T3 and T4 definitely did not play on Wednesday, Monday and Saturday respectively.

V. T2 and T3 ended up with the same number of points at the end of the tournament.

19. How many points did T4 score in the tournament?

(a) 2 (b) 4
(c) 6 (d) Cannot be determined

20. T3 lost its match against

(a) T1 (b) T2
(c) T4 (d) Both T1 and T2

21. The match played on Friday was between

(a) T1 and T2 (b) T2 and T3
(c) T1 and T4 (d) T2 and T4

Directions for questions 22 to 24: Answer the questions on the basis of the information given below.

Eight persons are sitting at a rectangular table such that four persons are sitting along each of the longer sides of the table. Each person works in a different bank among PNB, SBI, HDFC, ICICI, CBI, BOB, BOI and Citi, and holds a different designation among IT Officer, Marketing Officer, Law Officer, Agricultural Officer, Rajbhasha Adhikari, Technical Officer, Finance Officer and HR Manager, not necessarily in the same order. It is also known that:

I. The Finance Officer, who works in BOI, is sitting to the immediate left of the HR Manager.

II. The Marketing Officer, who works in SBI, is sitting opposite the Technical Officer.

III. The Agricultural Officer, who works in ICICI, is sitting diagonally opposite the Rajbhasha Adhikari, who is sitting to the immediate left of the Technical Officer.

IV. The Law Officer, who works in HDFC, is sitting to the immediate left of the Marketing officer.

V. The persons who work in PNB and HDFC are sitting along the same side of the table.

VI. The Rajbhasha Adhikari, who works in CBI, is sitting at one of the extreme ends in his row.

22. Who is sitting to the immediate right of the Finance Officer?

(a) Agricultural Officer

(b) Technical Officer

(c) Marketing Officer

(d) None of these

23. For how many persons can we definitely determine the banks in which they work?

(a) 8 (b) 6

(c) 4 (d) None of these

24. The person who is sitting opposite the Law Officer works in

(a) BOI (b) ICICI

(c) BOB (d) Cannot be determined

2014

Directions for questions 25 to 28 : Answer the questions on the basis of information given below.

A farmer has 60 hens in his poultry farm. Each of these 60 hens lays one egg per day. On each day out of the eggs laid, some of the eggs are found to be rotten and some of the eggs get broken. Only the eggs that are neither rotten nor broken are taken to the market for sale but due to some unavoidable reasons some eggs are not sold. The eggs that are not sold are brought back to the poultry farm.

Additional Information Given:

I. Out of the eggs that are brought back on each day, 40% are rotten and 20% are broken the next morning (and they are always integers).

II. Out of the eggs that are brought back to the poultry farm on each day, the eggs that are neither broken nor rotten are taken along with the eggs that are laid by the hens on the next day to the market for sale.

III. On any particular day the number of eggs that are not sold is less than 20% of the number of eggs that are taken to be sold out of the eggs that are laid on each day.

IV. Out of the eggs that are laid on each day, the number of eggs that are rotten is greater than 1 but less than 5 and the number of eggs that got broken is greater than 3 and less than 7.

V. Every week has five days and each week starts from day 1 and ends on day 5. Assume there are no eggs with the farmer at the beginning of day 1 of the given week.

25. Find the minimum possible aggregate number of eggs sold on day 4 and day 5.

(a) 84 (b) 83

(c) 86 (d) 85

26. If the number of eggs that got rotten and broken is maximum possible in a particular week, then find the difference between the total number of eggs that got rotten and the total number of eggs that got broken across all the five days of the week.

(a) 4 (b) 2

(c) 6 (d) 8

27. What can be the maximum number of eggs (that are unbroken and not rotten) that were left unsold at the end of the fifth day?

(a) 10

(b) 50

(c) 25

(d) Cannot be determined

28. If the number of eggs sold on any day of the week is maximum possible then what is the aggregate sum of the total number of eggs sold in the entire week?

(a) 253 (b) 254

(c) 265 (d) 251

Directions for questions 29 to 32: Answer the questions on the basis of the information given below.

There are 6 friends — Gurvinder, Surinder, Mahinder, Bhupinder, Harinder and Joginder. Their wives are — Sita, Rama, Dolly, Monica, Trisna and Kaveri (not in the same order as their husbands). Each of these 6 friends belong to exactly one out of Ambala, Jaipur, Guntur, Kapurthala, Noida and Jammu (not necessarily in order). Each of them plays exactly one of the games — cricket, football, volleyball, snooker, TT and badminton (again not necessarily in that order). Each of the friends is married to one lady only.

— Husbands of Dolly, Trisna or Kaveri do not play football or volleyball.

— The one who is from Guntur plays cricket.

— Joginder plays football and is from Jammu.

— Mahinder and Harinder are married to Sita and Monica respectively but are not from Guntur.

— The men from Jaipur and Kapurthala are TT and volleyball players respectively.

— Bhupinder is from Noida.

— Rama is married to the man from Jammu.

— Mahinder plays snooker.

29. Who is married to the man from Kapurthala?

(a) Dolly (b) Monica
(c) Sita (d) Cannot be determined

30. The person who plays Snooker belongs to which place?

(a) Noida (b) Ambala
(c) Jammu (d) Cannot be determined

31. Which game is being played by Bhupinder?

(a) Badminton (b) Football
(c) Volleyball (d) Cannot be determined

32. Who is the wife of Surinder?

(a) Dolly (b) Trisna
(c) Kaveri (d) Cannot be determined

Directions for questions 33 to 36: Answer the questions on the basis of information given below.

Volleyball is a sport played by two teams on a playing court divided by a net.

The object of the game is to send the ball over the net in order to ground it on the opponent's court, and to prevent the same effort by the opponent.

The team has three hits for returning the ball.

The rally continues until the ball is grounded on the playing court, goes "out" or a team fails to return it properly. In Volleyball, the team winning a rally scores a point (Rally Point System).

There are six players on court in a volleyball team.

Matches are played in five sets. The first four sets are played to 25 points, with the final set being played to 15 points. A team must win a set by at least two points. There is no ceiling, so a set continues until one of the teams gains a two-point advantage.

A match was played between Brazil and Russia in which-

(i) Only three sets finished with the minimum threshold points.

(ii) The final score of Russia was same in two of the sets in which it won one of the sets.

(iii) In one of the sets, the final score of Brazil was less than half of Russia.

(iv) The score of Brazil in one of the sets is same as the score of Russia in one of the other set. Both of them lost their respective sets with a different margin.

(v) The total score of five sets of Brazil and Russia were 108 and 116 respectively. Also, Brazil won 3 sets.

(vi) The maximum score by any team in the five sets was 30 and the minimum was 12. Russia scored 23 points in one of the sets.

(vii) There were only three sets in which a team won by exactly two-point advantage.

33. What was the maximum difference by which a team won the set?

(a) 2 points (b) 12 points
(c) 13 points (d) 3 points

34. What was the score of Russia in the fifth set?

(a) 12 points (b) 13 points
(c) 15 points (d) Cannot be determined

35. In how many sets, the score of Brazil was an even number?

(a) 2 (b) 3
(c) 4 (d) 5

36. What was the score which was common with both the teams, and in which both won their respective sets?

(a) 28 (b) 12
(c) 25 (d) No such score

■■

ANSWERS

ANALYTICAL REASONING

1. (d)	**2.** (c)	**3.** (b)	**4.** (a)	**5.** (b)	**6.** (b)	**7.** (b)	**8.** (c)	**9.** (a)	**10.** (b)
11. (b)	**12.** (d)	**13.** (b)	**14.** (b)	**15.** (a)	**16.** (b)	**17.** (b)	**18.** (c)	**19.** (d)	**20.** (a)
21. (a)	**22.** (b)	**23.** (d)	**24.** (d)	**25.** (b)	**26.** (b)	**27.** (c)	**28.** (c)	**29.** (b)	**30.** (d)
31. (a)	**32.** (b)	**33.** (a)	**34.** (a)	**35.** (d)	**36.** (a)	**37.** (a)	**38.** (c)	**39.** (b)	**40.** (a)
41. (b)	**42.** (b)	**43.** (c)	**44.** (a)	**45.** (c)	**46.** (a)	**47.** (a)	**48.** (a)	**49.** (c)	**50.** (d)
51. (b)	**52.** (b)	**53.** (d)	**54.** (a)	**55.** (d)	**56.** (c)	**57.** (d)	**58.** (b)	**59.** (c)	**60.** (d)
61. (c)	**62.** (b)	**63.** *	**64.** (c)	**65.** (c)	**66.** (a)	**67.** (c)	**68.** (b)	**69.** (c)	**70.** (b)
71. (d)	**72.** (d)	**73.** (d)	**74.** (c)	**75.** (c)	**76.** (c)	**77.** (b)	**78.** (b)	**79.** (c)	**80.** (b)
81. (c)	**82.** (d)	**83.** (b)	**84.** (c)	**85.** (b)	**86.** (b)	**87.** (b)	**88.** (b)	**89.** (d)	**90.** (a)
91. (c)	**92.** (a)	**93.** (c)	**94.** (c)	**95.** (d)	**96.** (d)	**97.** (c)	**98.** (c)	**99.** (a)	**100.** (b)
101. (c)	**102.** (b)	**103.** (b)	**104.** (c)	**105.** (b)	**106.** (d)	**107.** (c)	**108.** (d)	**109.** (a)	**110.** (b)
111. (d)	**112.** (a)	**113.** (b)	**114.** (b)	**115.** (d)	**116.** (b)	**117.** (d)	**118.** (b)	**119.** (c)	**120.** (d)
121. (c)	**122.** (d)	**123.** (c)	**124.** (c)	**125.** (d)	**126.** (d)	**127.** (b)	**128.** (d)	**129.** (d)	**130.** (a)
131. (c)	**132.** (d)	**133.** (e)	**134.** (e)	**135.** (d)	**136.** (b)	**137.** (b)	**138.** (b)	**139.** (c)	**140.** (d)
141. (e)	**142.** (b)	**143.** (d)	**144.** (b)	**145.** (c)	**146.** (c)	**147.** (b)	**148.** (d)	**149.** (c)	**150.** (c)
151. (c)	**152.** (d)	**153.** (c)	**154.** (d)	**155.** (b)	**156.** (c)	**157.** (c)	**158.** (b)	**159.** (a)	**160.** (c)
161. (d)	**162.** (a)	**163.** (b)	**164.** (a)	**165.** (d)	**166.** (c)	**167.** 3	**168.** 3	**169.** 3	**170.** 4
171. (a)	**172.** (b)	**173.** (a)	**174.** (d)	**175.** (d)	**176.** (b)	**177.** (d)	**178.** (d)	**179.** 7	**180.** 4
181. (b)	**182.** (b)	**183.** (c)	**184.** (d)	**185.** (c)	**186.** (c)	**187.** (a)	**188.** (c)	**189.** (d)	**190.** (d)
191. 11	**192.** (c)	**193.** 15	**194.** (c)	**195.** (d)	**196.** (b)	**197.** (b)	**198.** (c)	**199.** 3	**200.** 6
201. (c)	**202.** (d)	**203.** (d)	**204.** (d)	**205.** (d)	**206.** (b)	**207.** 4	**208.** 4	**209.** (b)	**210.** (a)
211. 4	**212.** (d)	**213.** 2	**214.** (c)	**215.** (b)	**216.** (a)	**217.** (c)	**218.** (a)	**219.** (d)	**220.** (a)
221. (b)	**222.** (b)	**223.** (b)	**224.** 3	**225.** 0	**226.** (c)				

DATA SUFFICIENCY

1. (c)	**2.** (a)	**3.** (a)	**4.** (a)	**5.** (d)	**6.** (d)	**7.** (c)	**8.** (b)	**9.** (c)	**10.** (b)
11. (a)	**12.** (c)	**13.** (b)	**14.** (d)	**15.** (d)	**16.** (b)	**17.** (b)	**18.** (b)	**19.** (a)	**20.** (c)
21. (d)	**22.** (d)	**23.** (b)	**24.** (a)	**25.** (c)	**26.** (b)	**27.** (a)	**28.** (a)	**29.** (b)	**30.** (b)
31. (a)	**32.** (d)	**33.** (c)	**34.** (a)	**35.** (b)	**36.** (c)				

EXPLANATIONS

ANALYTICAL REASONING

1. d X > Y, Z < W and V > Y. If we were to look at all of them we can say that, X,V > Y & W > Z. The first statement gives a uncertain situation using "may", hence we cannot definitely say about the answer. The second statement says, V > W and hence V > Z. This again does not say anything because we do not know whether X>Z or X<Z. Hence, the answer is (d)

For question 2 to 4:

2. c

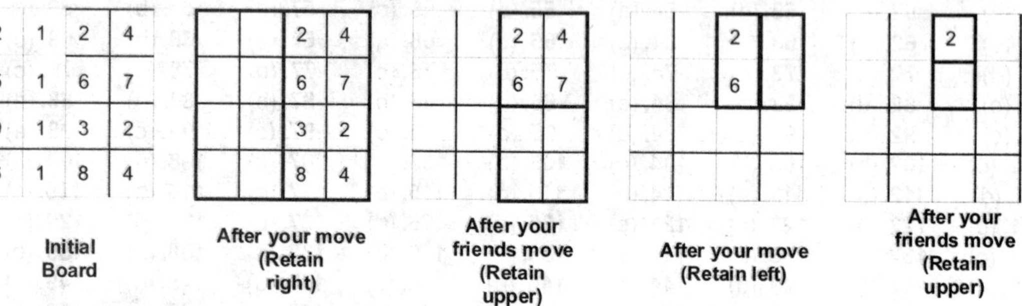

Since you choose to retain right and then left in your next move, the cells that would hence be retained contain 2,6,3,8. (look at the second grid) Hence, to reduce your gain to minimum, your friend has to retain 2 at the end. So his strategy has to be retain upper and retain upper.

3. b If both of you select the moves intelligently, you would both go for maximising your earnings.

In your first move you have to select either left or right and your friend has to then select either upper or lower. Hence the possibilities could be :

2	1	2	4
5	1	6	7
9	1	3	2
6	1	8	4

		2	4
		6	7

		3	2
		8	4

2	1		
5	1		

9	1		
6	1		

You Move	Your Friend Moves	Integers left for your 2nd move	Minimum gain ensured
(Retain Right)	(Retain Upper)	2, 4, 6, 7	4 (after you move retain right)
	(Retain Lower)	3, 2, 8, 4	3 (after you move retain left)
(Retain Left)	(Retain Upper)	2, 1, 5, 1	2 (after you move retain left)
	(Retain Lower)	9, 1, 6, 1	6 (after you move retain left)

So, if you move (retain right) you ensure a minimum gain of Rs.3 and if you move (retain left) you ensure a minimum gain of Rs.2. Hence if both of you play intelligently, you would first move retain right and ensure a minimum win of Rs.3, irrespective of what your friend moves.

4. a If your first move is (retain right) then the grid will look the same as in Q82. Your friend may hence choose either (retain upper), which will leave you to choose from 2,4,6,7 or he may choose (retain lower), which will leave you to choose from 3,2,8,4. In case he takes the former move, you can then move (retain right) and hence force a minimum gain of 4. But in case he chooses the latter move, you can then move (retain move) and force a minimum gain of 3. In either case you can force a minimum gain of Rs.3

5. b If statement (I) is true, the other 2 should be false. In other words it implies that both Saira and Mumtaz have the ball. This is not possible.

If statement (II) is true, then statements (I) and (III) are false, then Saira and Mumtaz does not have the ball and even Zeenat does not have the ball as she has the pen. This is contradictory.

Hence, the only possibility that is statement (III) is true and (I) and (II) are false. This implies that Mumtaz has the ball, Zeenat has the pencil and Saira has the pen.

6. b The equations can be expressed as :

$J < T$

$J + T = A + D$

$A + T < D + J$

Comparing (i) and (iii), we can see that D > A.

If we rearrange the statement (ii) we get : $(T - J) < (D - A)$. In other words the difference between J and T is less than that between D and A. Using this relationship and statement (ii), we can say that the right order is D > T > J > A. Hence, the answer is (b).

7. b As Bhanu's total was less than Akila's, Bhanu cannot be the winner. As Ela's and Divya's marks are the same, none of them could be winners. The winner could hence be either Bhanu or Charulata. Now, Akhila got 13 in Coherence. Even if she gets 19 in all of the remaining (as no one got 20 in any 1 head), her total would only be 89. But the winner's total is 90. So Charulata is the winner.

8. c From statement I alone no conclusion can be drawn.

From statement II following sequence of stations is possible

A	C/D	E	C/D	B

But, from I, Mr. Rahman boards the station at D which is possible at fourth position only because Mr. Thomas and Mr. Rahman have no common station.

For questions 9 to 12: If we were to number the houses 1-2-3-4 from left to right, the information given in the question can be depicted as:

Nationality	House Colour	Favourite Drink	House Number
English	Red	Milk	3
Italian	Blue	Tea	2
Norwegian	Yellow	Cocoa	1
Spaniard	White	Fruit Juice	4

Knowing this, we can answer all the questions.

9. a The colour of the Norwegian's house is yellow.

10. b Milk is drunk by the Englishman.

11. b The Norwegian drinks Cocoa.

12. d The only statement that is not true is (d), as the Italian lives in house no. 2 and the Spaniard lives in house no. 4, which are not next to each other.

For questions 13 to 16: The best way to solve these kinds of questions is to assume that one of the statements is either true or false and thus figure out whether there is consistency in what everyone is saying.

13. b Let us assume that John's first statement is true. So his second statement must be false. This implies that Mathew did it. This makes Mathew's first statement false. So the second statement has to be true. This implies that Krishna didn't do it. So Krishna's first statement is true and his second statement is false. Since all the statements are consistent with each other, the assumption made by us should be the correct one. So it is Mathew who stole the boat.

14. b The key here are the statements made by Koik. Since we know that he is wearing a cap, if his first statement is false, then his second statement cannot be true. So his first statement is true and his second statement is false. This implies that Koik is the priest. This makes Lony's second statement false and so his first statement is true. So Lony is Koik's son. This makes Mirna's second statement false and so his first statement is true. So Lony's father is a pilot. Thus, Koik is the pilot. (**Note:** Koik is also the priest).

15. a The first statement of Ram is obviously false, as he is saying that he never speaks to a stranger, when he actually is. So he must be new to those parts. This makes the second statement of Lila false. So she should be married to Ram. This makes the first statement of Ram false. So the left road should take you to the village.

16. b If you observe Charle's statement carefully, you will figure out that his first statement is true and second statement is false. For instance, if his first statement is false, then his second statement cannot be true. There would be inconsistency in what he is talking. So Charles is not the chief. This makes Bobby's second statement false and first statement true. So Bobby is Amar's father and hence, Amar's first statement is false. So his second statement must be true. This implies that the chief is wearing the red shirt. So Bobby is the chief.

17. b Since Akbar likes rain, he cannot be a frisbee player (as no frisbee player likes rain). And since every boy in the school does one of the two, Akbar has to be a fisherman.

For questions 18 to 21: The correct seating arrangement can be depicted as shown below:

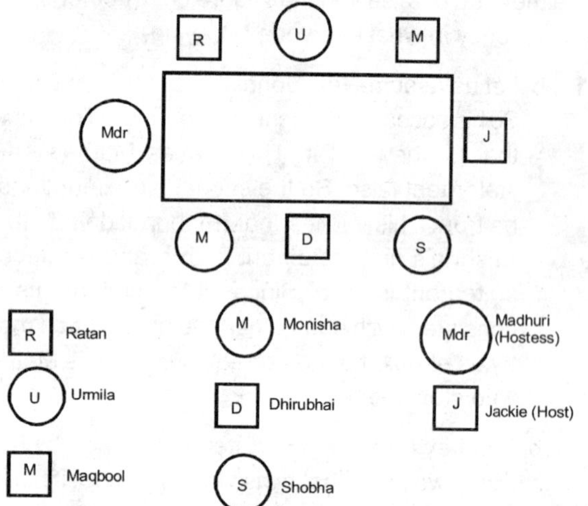

18. c Jackie is the host and also sitting on Shobha's right. Hence (c) is the correct answer.

19. d Shobha is sitting next to Jackie and Dhirubhai. So she is the only person who is not seated next to a person of the same sex.

20. a If Ratan would have exchanged seat with a person four places to his left, which is Shobha, the following arrangement would exist.

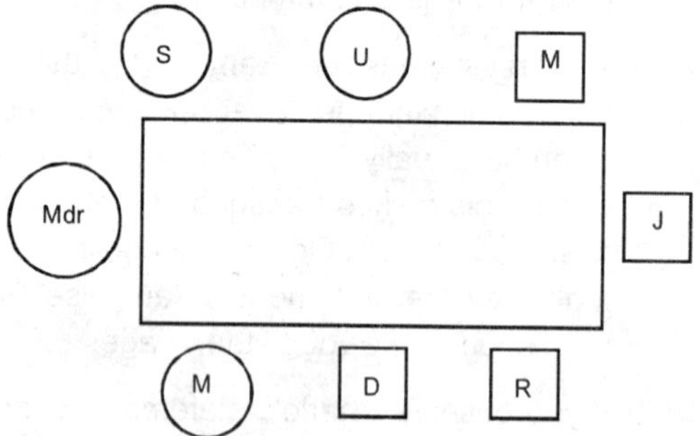

The first statement is hence true, since no man is sitting between two woman and no woman is sitting between two man. However statements II and III are not true. Hence the answer is (a).

21. a Among the given choices, only Ratan & Monisha are sitting opposite to each other and hence they must be married.

For questions 22 to 24:

From the given conditions the only arrangements that are possible is

Left / Right

Sushmita	Manpreet	Aishwarya	Rachel	Anu
1	2	3	4	5

Left / Right

Aishwarya	Manpreet	Sushmita	Rachel	Anu
1	2	3	4	5

22. b If Aishwarya is standing at the extreme left, the latter arrangement holds good. Hence it is Sushmita who is standing in the middle.

23. d Again the latter arrangement holds good. So the girl who is standing second from left is Manpreet.

24. d Under the given condition, following arrangement is possible:

Left / Right

Sushmita	Anu	Rachel	Aishwarya	Manpreet
1	2	3	4	5

Hence Rachel is standing on the extreme right.

For questions 25 to 28 :

The first statement suggests : B is now as old as C was in the past. Therefore, B < C. Also sometime in the past, A was twice as old as D. So A > D. C will be as old as E in future. Hence C < E.

The second statement suggests : A > F. A was as old as G in the past. Therefore, A > G. D will be as old as F in future. So F > D. F will be as old as G now in future. This implies G > F. G was as old as B, when A was as old as G. Hence, A = B.

Combining both the results, we get :

E > C > B = A > G > F > D (Note by A = B, it is meant that they are of similar age group, not necessarily the same).

25. b It could be figured out that E is the eldest brother.

26. b D is the youngest brother.

27. c Only A and B could probably be twins.

28. c It could be figured out that only statement (c) is false as B has only 2 elder brothers and not 3.

29. b All the sentences are possible except (b) as Grumbs have to be used with Ihavitoo and Grumbs cannot be used in any other type but Bingoes.

30. d Since Grumbs and Harrumphs are the Bingoes and Grumbs has to always go with Ihavitoo, so we will have to use Ihavitoo as the Cingo. Since statement I is true, the answer can only be (a) or (d). So we will only evaluate the option (d). Since we have not used Koolodo as Cingo, we can use either Lovitoo or Metoo or both as Dingos. Hence, statement III is also true, so the answer is (d).

31. a Option (b) uses two Cingo's instead of one, hence grammatically incorrect. Option (c) violates the same rule again and in addition it uses ihavitoo without using Grumbs. Option (d) again uses two Cingo's instead of one. Hence, the only option that is grammatically correct is (a).

32. b If Grumps is the Bingo, then Ihavitoo must also be used. And since Ihavitoo is common to Bingo and Cingo, Ihavitoo must be used as a Cingo . Also no other Cingo can be used. So obviously Harrumphs

must also be used as a Bingo. And since we are not using Koolodo as Cingo, we can use Lovitoo as Dingo. So (a), (c) and (d) can all be true. So (b) cannot be true.

For questions 33 and 34:

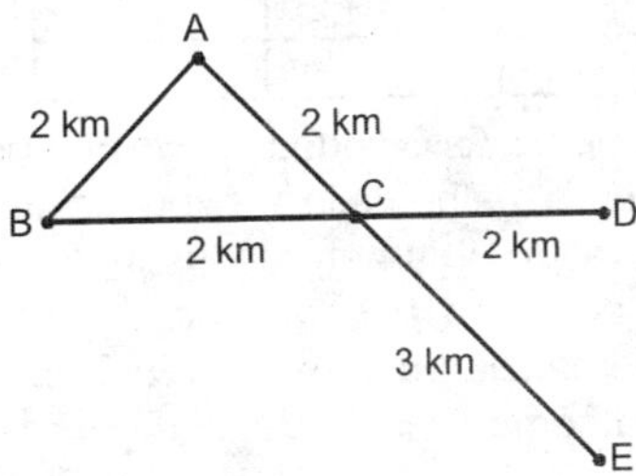

33. a If there is a shop at C, all A, B, C and D are within 2 km range. Another shop is needed for E. Hence, 2 shops are required.

34. a If there is a shop at C; all A, B, D and E are within 3 km range. Hence, 1 shop is required.

35. d P says he can see one black and one white hat. So either Q is wearing white and R is wearing black, or Q is wearing black and R is wearing white. Q also makes same statement. Still we cannot say the colour of the hat which P is wearing.

36. a If P is true, then both Q and R have to be true. For S to be true, either Q or R must be false. Hence, if P is true, S cannot be true.

37. a Since C and D cannot be together, they can occupy either of the following seats: (1st and 3rd), (1st and 4th) or (2nd and 4th). In the last two cases, since B cannot be in the 3rd place, A will have to be there. Thus, we can see that A can never be in the 1st place. Hence, statement (a) is false.

38. c Since neither A nor B can be at 3rd place, this place has to be occupied by either D or C. And if either of them occupies this place, the other one has to occupy the 1st place (since D and C cannot be together). Hence, C can only occupy either 1st or 3rd place.

39. b If A and B are together, but C and D are not, then the only places that A and B can occupy are 2nd and 3rd. And since B cannot be at 3rd place, A has to be at 3rd place.

40. a Amar does not wear red shirt.

Akbar does not wear green shirt.

Anthony does not wear blue shirt.

Since Akbar and Anthony wear same colour, it can neither be green nor blue.

Hence, option (a) is false.

41. b If two of them wear the same colour, the following six combinations will exist: since Amar does not wear red, he can either wear blue or green. In either case, the remaining two will have to wear red, Akbar does not wear green, and Anthony does not wear blue. This gives the combinations 1 and 2 below. Similarly, the other combinations can be worked out.

42. b Ms Maharashtra was wearing white. Since Ms West Bengal was not the runner-up, she was not wearing green and neither was Ms Andhra Pradesh. Hence, it was Ms Uttar Pradesh who was wearing green saree. So red could have either be worn by Ms West Bengal or by Ms Andhra Pradesh. Now participants wearing yellow saree and white saree were at the ends, but Ms West Bengal did not occupy any of these positions. Hence, it can be concluded that Ms Andhra Pradesh sat at one of the ends and wore yellow, while Ms West Bengal wore red.

43. c From the previous answer it can be concluded that Ms Maharashtra and Ms Andhra Pradesh occupied the seats at the end. So Ms West Bengal and Ms Uttar Pradesh, should occupy middle two seats. So the answers could be either (b) or (c). It can further be concluded that since Ms Andhra Pradesh wore yellow, she was the winner and since Ms Uttar Pradesh wore green, she was the runner-up. So these two cannot sit together. Option (b) would contradict this. Hence, (c) is the only option left.

44. a From answer to question 43, it can be seen that Ms Andhra Pradesh had worn the yellow saree.

45. c From answer to question 43, it can be seen that Ms Uttar Pradesh was the runner-up.

46. a It can be seen that each of the 26 players played 25 matches. Since none of the matches ended in a draw, the scores for each of the players has to be even (since a win gives 2 points). So the highest score possible for a player would be 50 and the lowest would be 0. Since all 26 of them had different scores varying between 0 and 50, the scores should indeed be all the even numbers between 0 and 50. And since the ranks obtained by players are in alphabetical order, it can be concluded that A scored 50, B scored 48, C scored 46 and so on and Z scored 0. Now the only way A can score 50 is, if he wins all his matches, i.e. he defeats all other players. Now B has scored 48. So he has lost only one of his matches, which incidentally is against A. He must have defeated all other players. Similarly, C has scored 46 matches. So he must have lost two matches, (i.e. to A and B) and defeated all other players. So we conclude that a player whose name appears alphabetically higher up in the order has defeated all the players whose name appear alphabetically lower down.

Hence, M should win over N.

47. a The issue at hand is to make C_2 identify in which envelope is the letter L_2. The first statement actually tells him this. Hence, it alone is sufficient to answer the question. The second statement only implies that his letter would be in either E_1, E_2 or E_4 and hence is not sufficient to answer the question.

48. a From the question itself, we can figure out that book 4 can either be in rack 1 or rack 3. The first statement says that book 2 has been kept in rack 3. Hence, book 4 has to be kept in rack 1. So this statement is sufficient to answer the question. The second statement, however, does not add any additional information to what we already know. As books 3 in rack 2 would still imply book 4 can be in rack 1 or 3.

49. c Test the boxes labelled — Red and White.

Now if the ball is Red, label the box — Red

Now the box which has the label White is either Red or Red and White.

However, it cannot be Red.

Hence, it is Red and White.

The last box is White.

50. d According to the given conditions, either Mrs Border or Mrs Dennis can sit to the right of Mr Abraham. It can't be Mrs. Elmer as she sat two places to the right of Mrs. Border.

For questions 51 and 52:

D, a lawyer is married to A, a housewife.

C, an accountant is married to F, a lecturer.

E is not a housewife.

Hence, E is an architect and B is a housewife.

Also, any lady is neither an architect nor an accountant

A	Lawyer	Male
B	Housewife	Female
C	Accountant	Male
D	Housewife	Female
E	Architect	Male
F	Lecturer	Female

For questions 53 and 54:

If the positions from left to right are 1 to 7

A and G take up positions 6 and 7

B takes up position 4

C and D are in places 1 and 5, so that they are as far as possible.

E and F are in positions 2 and 3.

1	2	3	4	5	6	7
C/D	E/F	F/E	B	D/C	A/G	G/A

55. d

A	B	C
1 + 1	1 + 1 + 2	1 + 1
3	3	2

Statement I: As C added up two numbers correctly, he is not a mathematician. However, from the given information, it is not necessary that any person who adds up two numbers incorrectly is a mathematician. Therefore, A or B may or may not be mathematicians.

Hence, statement I alone is not sufficient.

Statement II: If a mathematician makes a mistake in a sum, the error is +1 or -1. But it doesn't implies that if a person makes an error of +1 or -1, he is a mathematician.

Hence, statement II alone is not sufficient.

Even on combining the two statements, we cannot conclude anything concrete.

56. c From I, we know A and B passed the examination.

From II, we know the condition that among C and D at least one passed (or both passed) is false.

Therefore, it is obvious that both C and D have failed. Thus, both statements are necessary to find the answer.

57. d Statement I gives us the number of white flowers. But we know that a white seed gives both red or white flowers. Thus, proving statement II, gives the number of red flowers. But both black and white seeds give red flowers, again providing no solutions.

58. b The initial water in bottles A, B and C are 5 L, 0 L and 0 L respectively.

First instruction. FILL (C, A) means that 2 litres is transferred from A to C (leaving 3 litres A, and C is full)

Third instruction FILL (C, A) again means some water is transferred from A to C.

After the third instruction, 1 litre of water is left in bottle A.

Option (a) is not possible because if it were executed, there would not be any water left in A for executing the third instruction of FILL(C,A).

Option (b) is possible because C is emptied out and when third instruction is followed, of the 3 litres left in A (at the end of first instruction), two litres are transferred to C leaving only 1 litre in A.

Option (c) can be eliminated because, there was no water in B.

Option (d) is not possible because had it been executed, there would not be any water left in A for executing the third instruction.

59. c The first four instructions are:

1st : FILL (C, A)

2nd : EMPTY (C, B)

3rd : FILL (C, A)

4th : DRAIN (A)

Fourth instruction drains off 1 liter from A and the quantities with A, B and C at the end of 3rd instruction is 1 L, 2 L and 2 L respectively.

Amount of water in the system after 4th instruction = 5 – 1 = 4 L

If at the end of the 6th instruction, all the 4 L are in A, then B and C will definitely be empty.

60. d Shift 1, 2, 3 to the second table. Bring back 2, 3 to the first table. Take 3 only to the second table and finally shift 2 to the second table.

61. c There shall be 8 teams in each group. Each team in a group shall be playing with every other team. Hence, total number of matches shall be $\frac{(7 \times 8)}{2} = 28$ in one group. Hence, in both the groups, there shall be 56 matches. This is for the first stage. Thereafter, there are 8 teams in knockout rounds from which one winner emerges, or 7 losers are identified.

Hence, 7 more matches, i.e. in all 63 matches.

62. b In the first stage, there are 28 matches to be played by each group of 8 teams and eventually 4 from each group moved into second stage.

7 teams can win 4 matches each. Then, three of them will be eliminated on the basis of tiebreak rules. This doesn't assure any team a place in the second stage.

5 teams can win 5 matches each and there can be 3 more matches won by the remaining teams. Then, one of the teams winning 5 matches will be eliminated on the basis of tiebreak rules. This also doesn't assure any team a place in the second stage.

4 teams can win 6 matches and there can be 4 matches won by the remaining teams. This will guarantee a place for each team winning 6 matches a place in the second round.

63. * In order to maximize the number of wins of a team which would be eliminated at the end of first stage, we minimize the number of wins in the bottom 3 teams. The bottom 3 teams will play ${}^3C_2 = 3$ matches among themselves (i.e. there will be 3 wins). So the remaining wins (28 – 3) = 25 must be divided among top 5 teams, such that the 5th ranked team wins the maximum and yet fail to qualify for the second round. This is possible if each of the top 5 teams win an equal number of matches, i.e. $\frac{25}{5} = 5$. Hence, the 5th ranked team can win a maximum of 5 matches and would get eliminated at the end of first stage on the basis of tiebreak rules.

* **Note:** The answer given in the answer key of 'CAT 2001 Bulletin' is incorrect. Ideal answer should be 5 wins.

64. c There are 8 teams. Hence, there would be 7 matches in 3 rounds.

65. c Statement 1 is false. Consider a case where the points scored by the top three teams were 7, 6 and 5. Rest of the 10 points were distributed equally among the remaining five teams with 2 points to each. Any one of these five teams could have won the tournament with total of 5 wins.

Statement 2 is false, as only the top four teams were advanced to the stage II.

Statement 3 is true. Consider a case where five different teams of the same group got 5 points each. Also, a team with 2 points in the different group of stage I won could have won the tournament with total of 5 points.

Statement 4 is false as the number of teams with exactly one win in stage II is 2.

66. a Since yellow is between green and red, it should be house number 2 or 3. Also green is adjacent to blue house, it should have blue and yellow house on either side. Hence, the following table can be constructed.

House number	1	2	3	4
Colour	Blue	Green	Yellow	Red
Occupant	X		Z	

or

House number	1	2	3	4
Colour	Red	Yellow	Green	Blue
Occupant		Z		X

Since X does not live adjacent to Z, it has to live in blue house.

67. c The ratio of points for carrying books of various subjects is:

Management : Mathematics : Physics : Fiction = 4 : 3 : 2 : 1

Since the points are to be maximized, the number of books that Ramesh should carry in descending order is management, mathematics, physics and fiction.

The ratio which Ramesh has to maintain is:

Management : Fiction < 1 : 2,

Mathematics : Physics < 1 : 2.

This means that a combination of management and fiction books in the ratio of 1 : 2 will give 6 points while a combination of mathematics and physics books in the ratio of 1 : 2 will give 7 points, hence, Ramesh should carry the following combination of books to maximize the points; management 1, mathematics 2, physics 5 and fiction 2, a total of 22 points.

68. b The following table can be created using the data given.

Persons	P	M	U	T	X
Colour choice	Blue and Red	Yellow	Red and Blue	Black	
Stays in					Hotel
Does not stay in	Palace		Palace	Palace	

Since X stays in a hotel and P or U or T cannot stay in a palace, M stays in palace.

69. c The attendants of X, Y and Z are to be Mohan, Jack and Rita. The animals under Mohan's care is given in the data. Since Jack does not attend to deer, lion and bison, the following table can be created using the data given.

Attendants	Mohan	Jack	Rita
Animals	Lion and Panther	Bear and Panther	
Enclosure	X	Y	Z

Name	Mohan	Jack	Rita	Shalini	Suman
Animals	Lion and panther	Bear and panther	Deer and bison	Lion and bear	Deer and bison
Cage	X	Y	Z	Q	P

The data for Mohan and Jack can be filled directly. Similarly, X, Y, Z can be filled directly from data given. The key after filling in these animals is that Z and P have the same pair of animals, the only option is deer and bison.

70. b By trial and error, we can make different combinations and find the cost. Like 20 kg × 2 + 10 kg × 4, the cost would be Rs.180. The minimum cost comes in the case of 10 kg × 8, i.e. Rs.160.

71. d We can see that the flow from Vaishali to Jyotishmati is 300 whereas demand is 400, so the deficit 100 will be met by flow from Vidisha. Again, the demand of 700 in Panchal is to be met by flow from Jyotishmati which can get it from Vidisha.

Thus, the quantity moved from Avanti to Vidisha 200 + 100 + 700 = 1000

72. d Free capacity at Avanti-Vaishali pipeline is 300, since capacity of each pipeline is 1000 and demand at Vidisha is 400 and 300 flows to Jyotishmati.

Thus, free capacity = {1000 – (400 + 300)} = 300

73. d Free capacity in Avanti-Vidisha is zero. Explanation is similar as in previous answer.

74. c Sati-Savitri starts at the earliest.

So we view it first.

(1) Sati-Savitri — 9.00 a.m. to 10.00 a.m.

(2) Veer Abhimanu — 10.00 a.m. to 11.00 a.m.

(3) Jhansi Ki Rani/Sundar Kand — 11.00 a.m. to 11.30 a.m.

(4) Joru Ka Ghulam — 11.30 a.m. to 12.30 p.m.

Now lunch break from 12.30 p.m. to 1.30 p.m.

At 1.30 p.m. he can takes the show of only Jhansi Ki Rani so it cannot be viewed at 3rd.

(5) Jhansi Ki Rani — 1.30 p.m. to 2.00 p.m.

(6) Reshma aur Shera 2.00 p.m. to 3.00 p.m.

Hence, option (c) is best.

75. c Three children Vaibhav, Suprita and Anshuman.

Vaibhav > Suprita

↓

(Born in April)

One of children is born in September, but it is not Vaibhav, so it has to be Anshuman.

So Vaibhav is born in June and is 7-year-old. Vaibhav is 7-year-old and Anshuman is not 4-year-old.

So Suprita is 4-year-old.

Youngest child is 2-year-old and it has to be Anshuman.

Vaibhav > Suprita > Anshuman

(June, 7 years) (April, 4 years) (Sept., 2-year-old)

Hence, (c) is the answer.

76. c We can find out the time for lunch of respective families from the table below:

Family/Time	12:00	1:00	2:00
Sharma	✓		
Banerjee			✓
Pattabhiraman	✓		

Fried brinjal → Chinaware

Sambar → White Chinaware

Makkai-ki-roti → Red Chinaware

The family that eats at 1 o'clock serves fried brinjal, hence Pattabhiraman serves fried brinjal.

The family that eats last like makkai-ki-roti so Banaerjees like makkai-ki-roti. Sharmas are left with sambar.

Sharma - 12:00 - Sambar - White

Pattabhiraman - 1:00 - Fried brinjal - Blue

Bannerjees - 2:00 - Makkai-ki-roti - Red

Hence, (c) is the best option.

77. b We start making one true and other false.

Case I

	T	F
Shopkeeper 1:	Black hair	Long tail
Shopkeeper 2:	Short tail	Wore a collar
Shopkeeper 3:	White hair	No collar

Case II

	T	F
Shop keeper 1:	Black hair	Long tail
Shop keeper 2:	Short tail	Wore a collar
Shop keeper 3:	White hair	No collar

Both the cases are correct, and hence, we see only option (b) is correct.

78. b Elle is 3 times older than Yogesh and Zaheer is half the age of Wahida.

If Wahida is 2x-year-old, then Zaheer is x.

Now Yogesh > Zaheer

$\Rightarrow$ Yogesh > x

Elle is 3 times older than Yogesh.

This implies Elle is older than Wahida as 3x > 2x.

Alternative method:

$E = 3y$ ...(i)

$z = \frac{w}{2}$, or $2z = w$ ...(ii)

$y > z$, implies $2y > 2z$ implies $2y > w$ from (ii)

Now, if $2y > w$

$3y > w$, i.e. $E > w$ from (i)

Hence, Elle is older than Wahida.

79. c From (a) Zaheer is 10-year-old means Wahida is 20-year-old. From (b) Yogesh and Wahida are older than Zaheer by same number of years.

This means Yogesh is 20-year-old. Now Elle is 3 times older than Yogesh.

Elle is 20 × 3 = 60-year-old.

Hence, we see that both (a) and (b) statements are needed so the answer is (c).

80. b Checking from options,

(a) David, Rama and Rahim

Ram would like to be in the group only if Peter is there, so it is not feasible.

(b) Peter, Shyam and Rahim want to be selected together and none of them have problem or any conditions, hence feasible.

(c) Since Shyam is there, Rahim has to be but he is not also Fiza is not there which David insists so not feasible.

(d) Since Peter is not there Ram would not prefer that group, hence not feasible.

81. c Looking at options, we see (c) is best as Shyam and Rahim is selected and Fiza is there when David is selected.

In (a) we see Shyam is not there with Rahim.

In (b) Fiza is not there with David.

In (d) Peter and David cannot go together as David would not like Peter in the group.

82. d In Ist option — Kavita is in the group means David is there and David would not like Peter in the group, whereas Ram would like to be in the group if Peter is there so the statement cannot be true.

2nd option — If David is there, then only the group will have both women Kavita and Fiza, but in that case we see none of the rest could be the fourth person as Shyam and Rahim has to be together and Ram would be if Peter is there and David would not like Peter in the group, hence statement is false.

3rd option — It is not possible as Ram cannot go with Shyam and David with Peter.

So none of the above statements are true.

83. b Let S = spotted, NS = Non-spotted

There are 50 coloured leaves and is given as red and non-red.

We make the following table. Let 2n be number of red oak leaves where n is any natural number.

Oak				Maple			
Red		Non-red		Red		Non-red	
S	NS	S	NS	S	NS	S	NS
2n	x	10n	0	6	x	0	22

Now we have 2n + x + 10n + 6 + x + 22 = 50

$\Rightarrow$ 12n + 2x = 22

It is possible for only n = 1, x = 5

($\because$ n is not greater than 1)

Hence, number of oak leaves = 2 × 1 + 5 + 10 × 1 = 17

84. c O, P, Q and R carried on motorcycles M_1, M_2, M_3 and M_4 respectively. So

O P Q R

M_1 M_2 M_3 M_4

F E A + G C

B D H

Since B cannot be with R so it will go with O that is only left.

Hence, C and H will go together in M_4 with R.

85. b

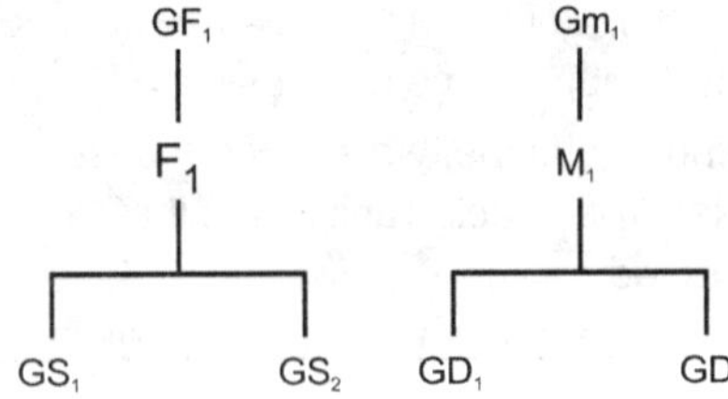

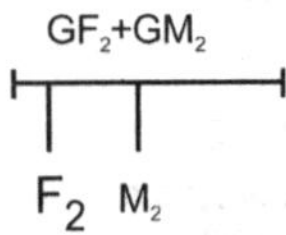

Thus, we have 2 grandfathers: GF_1, GF_2

4 fathers: GF_1, GF_2, F_1 and F_2

2 grandmothers: GM_1, GM_2

4 mothers: GM_1, GM_2, M_1 and M_2

Hence, minimum number will be 12.

86. b We have packages as follows:

3 item (D + 2B) = Rs.40 + Rs.180 = Rs.220 ... (i)

2 item (A + C) = Rs.180 ... (ii)

4 item (E + 2D + B) = 45 + 50 + 90 = Rs.215 ... (iii)

The combinations of purchase possible are:

Case 1: 220 × 4 = Rs.880

Points: 12 × 1000 – 120 × 1500 = – 1,68,000

Case 2: 180 × 5 = Rs.900

Points: 10 × 1000 – 100 × 1500 = – 1,40,000

Case 3: 215 × 4 = Rs.860

Points:16 × 1000 – 140 × 1500 = – 1,94,000

Case 4: 2(220 + 180) + 180 = Rs.980

Points: 12 × 1000 – 20 × 1500 = – 18,000

Case 5: 2(220 + 215) = Rs.890

Points : 14 × 1000 – 110 × 1500 = – 1,51,000

Case 6: 2(215 + 180) + 180 = Rs.970

Points :14 × 1000 – 30 × 1500 = – 31,000

By seeing the above figure, we see that we maximize the point in last case when purchase is 14 item for Rs.970.

87. b Bashir < Chirag.

Now Chirag borrows Rs. 300 and Bashir Rs. 100 from Ashok. Ashok buys 3 shirt so he must have at least Rs. 1,000.

Bashir is left with no money after buying a sweater and he had to borrow Rs.100 from Ashok which means he had Rs. 500 with him.

Ashok must have less than Rs. 1,500 and he has three times the money with Deepak.

So Deepak cannot have Rs. 300 because Ashok must have Rs.1,000. Again, Deepak cannot have Rs. 500 because Ashok should have less than Rs.1,500.

So Deepak has Rs. 400 for which he can purchase the shawl which is the costliest.

88. b

W1			**W4**	
Rupa	**Radha**	**Renuka**	**Ruchika**	**Ritu**
Sonali		**Rupali**	**Somya**	**Tara**
Shalini		**Komal**	**Sweta**	
Shubhra			**Jyotika**	
Shahira				**Deepika**
Amita	**Elina**	**Chandrika**	**Babita**	

Hence, Elina is the instructor of Radha.

89. d

	Fishing	Smoking	Drinking	Gambling	Mountaineering
Likes	M_1 M_6	M_1 M_2 M_8	M_2 M_5	M_3 M_7 M_8	M_4 M_7
Dislikes	M_2 M_7	M_3 M_5 M_6	M_4	M_1	M_5 M_6 M_8

Going by options, we have:

(a) M does not hate at least one of the liking of any of the other 3 persons selected.

(b) None of person shares the liking of at least one of the other selected.

(c) None of the person shares a liking with at least one of the other three selected.

(d) M_1 shares liking with M_2 and vice versa.

M_4 shares liking with M_7 and vice versa.

M_1, M_2 dislikes M_7 liking.

M_4, M_7 dislikes M_2 liking.

Hence, the answer is option (d).

90. a $X = M.D = M \cap D$

$X = D$

$M \cap D = D$

$\Rightarrow D \subset M$

Thus, all dogs are mammals.

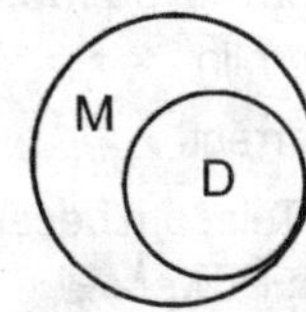

91. c $Y = F \cap (D \cap V)$ is not a null set means some F's are D's and sum D's are V's .

This implies some fish are dogs.

92. a $Z = (P \cap D) \cup M$

$P \cap D$ means Pluto, the dog.

$(P \cap D) \cup M$ means Pluto, the dog or any other mammal.

93. c $P.A = \phi$; $P \cup A = D$

$P \cap A = \phi$ means no alsatian is Pluto or Pluto is not an alsatian where dogs are composed of alsatian or Pluto or both.

94. c Statement I tells us that

(1) Ashish is not an engineer, (2) Ashish got more offers than the engineers.

Hence, Ashish did not have 0 offers.

After this the following table can be achieved.

Profession	Names	Offers				
		3	2	1	0	X Profession
CA	Ashish	×	×	✓	×	X Engineer
MD	Dhanraj	✓	×	×	×	X Engineer
Economist	Sameer	×	✓	×	×	
Engineer		×	×	×	✓	

From statement IV, Dhanraj is not at 0 and 1.

95. d Option (c) is ruled out by statement VII.

Option (a) is ruled out by statements VII and VIII.

From statement IV, Sandeep had Rs. 30 to start and Daljeet Rs. 20.

From statement II, option (b) is not possible as Sandeep was left with Re 1, he spent Rs. 29. But according to (b) he spent Rs. 1.50 more than Daljeet. But Daljeet had only Rs. 20. Hence, option (d) is correct.

96. d Data insufficient, please check the question.

97. c Statements V and VI rule out options (a) and (b). Since contestants from Bangalore and Pune did not come first, school from Hyderabad can come first. Convent is not in Hyderabad which rules out option (c).

98. c

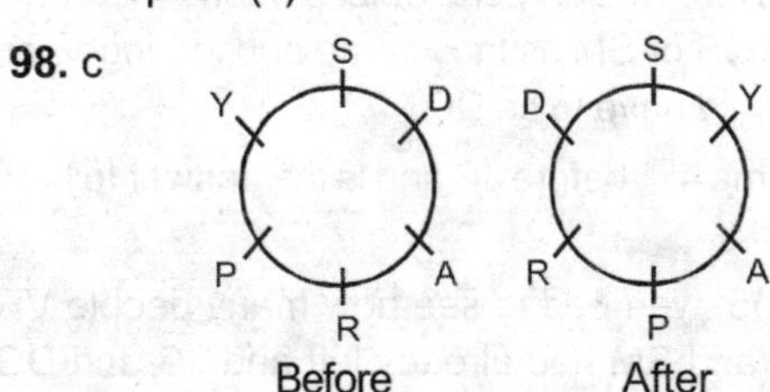

Suresh is sitting to the left of Dhiraj.

For questions 99 to 102:

The key to cracking this question is to follow the simple fundamentals in Analytical Reasoning of going 1 line at a time and making a simple table

Arrival Order	Husband	Wife	Kids
1		Joya	2
2		Shanthi	0
3		Sridevi	
4	Sunil		1

Sentence 1 – Family with 2 kids before no kids

Sentence 2 – Shanthi with no kids came before Sridevi

Sentence 3 – Sunil and wife came last with only kid

Sentence 4 – Anil and Joya not husband and wife

Sentence 5 – Anil and Raj are fathers – hence cannot be the family with no kids

Sentence 6 – Sridevi and Anita cannot be the persons with no kid

Sentence 7 – Anil and Joya not husband and wife

Sentence 8 – Joya before Shanti and Anita was already present.

Using the above informations, Anil and Raj cannot be married to Shanthi as Shanthi has no kids. Hence, Sunil has to be married to Sridevi (not with Joya already stated) and Raman with Shanthi.

Arrival Order	Husband	Wife	Kids
1	Anil	Anita	1
2	Raj	Joya	2
3	Raman	Shanthi	0
4	Sunil	Sridevi	1

For questions 103 to 106:

JC came in first and the next 2 people were SS and SM. When he left, DG left with him. JP and VR stayed behind.

Entry	Exit	Met
JC → SS → SM	JC and DG	JP and VR
JP and VR together		JC and one more person

SS left immediately after SM.

PK only met JP and DG.

The key to this question is that when JP and VR entered apart from JC there was only one other person. This could not have been SS or SM as they came and left together. Hence, this would have to be DG.

Hence, DG came 4th, before JP and is the answer to both 143 and 144.

Now for Qs 145, we need to see how many people VR met. Both SS and SM had already left and JC and DG were sitting. He entered with JP eliminating 2 and 5 from our answer choices. Since PK did not meet VR, the answer is 3 and not 4.

For questions 107 to 110:

	D	A	F
Entrance	Corridor		
	C	E	B

107. c If E faces the corridor, person to his left is C.
So the answer is (c).

108. d According to figure, E faces A's office.
So the answer is (d).

109. a According to figure, F's neighbour is A.
So the answer is (a).

110. b According to figure, B's room is last on the right.
So the answer is (b).

For questions 111 to 112:

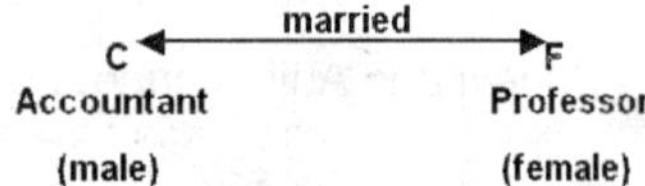

Since the Housewife D is married to the Lawyer and A is married to a Housewife, D and A is the other married couple.

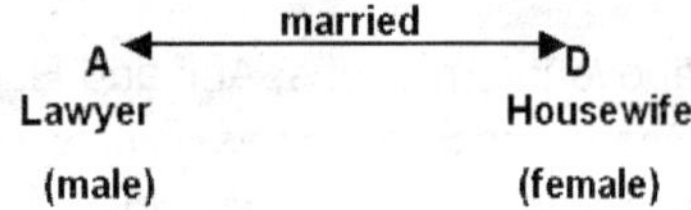

Since E is not the Housewife, it implies E is an Engineer and B is a Housewife. As no Engineer is female, E is a male. So the male members in the group are A, C and E and the female members are B, D and F.

111. d

112. a

113. b

For questions 114 and 115:

If D gets portfolio, F does not or vice-versa.

C wants only Home or Finance or none.

If D gets Power, B must get Telecom or if D gets Telecom, then B must get Power.

If A gets a portfolio, E should get the same.

114. b (a) gets eliminated because C can have either home or finance.

(c) gets eliminated because F and D cannot be in the same team.

(d) gets eliminated because C cannot have telecom portfolio.

Hence, (b) is correct.

115. d B-Defence, D - Telecom because if D gets Telcom then B must get Power.

116. b AVOCADO paint is mixture of ORANGE and PINK in equal quantities.

If ORANGE is made using RED and YELLOW, then the cost of ORANGE would be $\frac{20+25}{2} = 22.5$ which is greater than the cost of the ORANGE.

If we make PINK by RED and WHITE, the cost of PINK would be $\frac{20+15}{2} = 17.5$ which is less than the cost of the PINK paint.

Hence, the cost of the AVOCADO is $\frac{22+17.5}{2} = 19.75$

117. d Mixing equal amounts of ORANGE and WHITE can make WASHEDORANGE, ORANGE can be made by mixing equal amounts of RED and YELLOW. So the ratio of RED, YELLOW and WHITE is 1 : 1 : 2

118. b If cost of AVOCADO paint is Rs.19.75

The cost of the CREAM is $\frac{7 \times 15 + 3 \times 75}{10}$ = Rs. 18

And cost of WASHEDORANGE is Rs.18.50

So CREAM is the most profitable.

For questions 119 to 121:

1	2	3	4	5	6	7
C			B	D	A	G
D			B	C	A	G
C			B	D	G	A
D			B	C	G	A

119. c From given options, F is the only possibility.

120. d If we look at the options, D and G can sit together. C and F can sit together B and D can sit together. Hence, E and A is the only option which is not possible.

121. c E and G is the only possibility.

For questions 122 to 125: For solving these questions make a table like this:

	Africa	America	Australasia	Europe	
L	0	1	1	1	**3**
H			1	1	**6**
P			2	1	**6**
R			1	1	**6**
	4	**8**	**5**	**4**	**21**

(i) As the labour expert is half of each of the other, so the only possible combination is:

L – 3
H, P, R – 6 each

(ii) Statement (d): If the number of Australasia expert is 1 less, i.e. total export are 20 American be twice as each of other. The only combined possible is Americas = 8.

Australasia = 4 + 1 = 5

Europe = 4

Africa = 4

Now, we need to workout the various options possible in the blank cells.

	Africa	America	Australasia	Europe	
L	0	1	1	1	**3**
H	2	2	1	1	**6**
P	1	2	2	1	**6**
R	1	3	1	1	**6**
	4	**8**	**5**	**4**	**21**

	Africa	America	Australasia	Europe	
L	0	1	1	1	**3**
H	1	3	1	1	**6**
P	1	2	2	1	**6**
R	2	2	1	1	**6**
	4	**8**	**5**	**4**	**21**

	Africa	America	Australasia	Europe	
L	0	1	1	1	**3**
H	1	3	1	1	**6**
P	2	1	2	1	**6**
R	1	3	1	1	**6**
	4	**8**	**5**	**4**	**21**

For questions 126 to 129:

Germany has won both their matches, so possible winning combinations in first two rounds is

R1 : Won 1 - 0 and R2: Won 2 - 1

Or

R1 : Won 2 - 1 and R2: Won 1 - 0.

Argentina must have won R1 and R2 by 1 - 0.

If Germany won by 2 - 1 in R1 vs Spain, Spain won in R2 by 4 - 0, and if Germany won 1 - 0 in R1, then Spain won 5 - 1 in R2.

Since only New Zealand and South Africa conceded 4 or more than 4 goals, then Spain must have played either one in R2.

If Spain won 4 - 0 in R2 vs South Africa, then South Africa must win R1 by 1 - 0, which is a contradiction to the fact that South Africa has lost both R1 and R2. Also, Spain can never win 5 -1 vs South Africa in R2 (goals conceded by South Africa is 4).

Therefore, Spain won against New Zealand in R2.

Germany:

R1	vs	Spain	Won 2 -1	or	1 - 0
R2	vs	SA/Pak	Won 1 - 0	or	2 - 1
R3	vs	Arg	Draw		

Spain:

R1	vs	Germany	Lost 1 - 2	or	0 - 1
R2	vs	NZ	Won 4 - 0	or	5 - 1
R3	vs	Pak	Draw		

New Zealand:

R1	vs	Arg/Pak	Lost 1 - 2	or	0 - 1
R2	vs	Spain	Lost 0 - 4	or	1 - 5
R3	vs	SA	Draw		

Looking at the table, the only possible outcomes for Pakistan in the first two rounds are 2 -0 win and 0 - 1 loss.

In R1, New Zealand cannot lose 1 - 2 since Argentina conceded no goals and Pakistan's only loss was by a margin 0 - 1.

Therefore, NZ lost R1 0 - 1. This score is possible only if its opponent is Argentina. Consequently, NZ lost 1 - 5 in R2 vs Spain. Hence, Spain must have lost 0 - 1 to Germany.

The above information can be finally summarised as:

Germany:	R1	vs	Spain	Won 1 - 0
	R2	vs	SA	Won 2 - 1
	R3	vs	Arg	Draw
Spain:	R1	vs	Germany	Lost 0 - 1
	R2	vs	NZ	Won 5 - 1
	R3	vs	Pak	Draw
New Zealand:	R1	vs	Arg	Lost 0 - 1
	R2	vs	Spain	Lost 1 - 5
	R3	vs	SA	Draw
Pakistan:	R1	vs	SA	Won 2 -0
	R2	vs	Arg	Lost 0 - 1
	R3	vs	Spain	Draw
Argentina:	R1	vs	NZ	Won 1 - 0
	R2	vs	Pak	Won 1 - 0
	R3	vs	Germany	Draw
South Africa:	R1	vs	Pak	Lost 0 - 2
	R2	vs	Germany	Lost 1 - 2
	R3	vs	NZ	Draw

126. d

127. b

Additional information for Q.128-129:

* The given data set for rounds 4 and 5 appears to be inconsistent because from statements (a), (b) and (c) it is evident that four teams namely Spain, Argentina, Germany and Pakistan won their fifth round matches whereas the maximum possible wins in any round is only 3.

128. d

129. d

For questions 130 to 134:

From statement one, team would include exactly one among P, R, S

⇒ P (or) R (or) S.

From statement two, team would include either M, or Q

⇒ M but not Q

(or) Q but not M

From statement three, if a team includes K, it will include L or vice versa.

⇒ K, L always accompany each other.

From statement four, if one of S, U, W is included, then the other two also have to be included.

⇒ S, U, W are always together.

From statement five, L and N cannot be included together

⇒ L, N are never together.

From statement six, L and U cannot be included together.

⇒ L, U are never together.

130. a From statements one and two;

one of P, R, S and

one of M, Q are to be selected. We require one more member.

But from statement three; (K, L) are always together.

Hence 'L' cannot be included in a team of 3 members.

131. c Again, from statement one;

one of P, R, S has to be selected.

To make a team of '5'

'S' will be chosen (which leaves out P and R)

⇒ If 'S' is chosen 'U' and 'W' have to be chosen (statement four)

⇒ If 'U' is chosen 'L' cannot be chosen (statement five)

⇒ K cannot be chosen (statement three)

And from statement two; one of M (or) Q has to be chosen.

132. d From statements one and two

Two members are to be selected.

Of the remaining seven;

To maximize the size of the team.

We would chose S,

⇒ U and W are included in the team (statement four)

We cannot include K (or) L because we would then have to leave out N and U (from statements five and six)

133. e If 'K' is included, 'L' has to be included (statement (3))

If 'L' is chosen, neither N nor U can be chosen (statements (5) and (6))

⇒ S, W are also not included because S, U, W have to be always together. (Statement (4))

Hence one of P (or) R would be selected (statement (1)) and one of M (or) Q would be selected (statement (2))

(K, L) and two of the above five have to be included.

134. e If a team includes N, it cannot include 'L',

and therefore, not even 'K'. (from statement five and three)

According to statement (1), one of P or R or S has to be included.

According to statement (2), one of M or Q has to be selected.

So the following cases are possible

P Q N,

R Q N

P M N,

R M N

If 'S' is selected, then S U W M N and S U W Q N are the only possible cases.

Hence, in all 4 + 2 = 6 teams can be constituted.

For questions 135 to 139:

As only Paul Erdös was having an Erdös number of zero, so the minimum Erdös number among A, B, C, D, E, F, G, H should be 1 or greater than one. At the end of the third day, F co-authored a paper with A and C. F had the minimum Erdös number among the 8 people. So if F's Erdös number is y, then A and C's Erdös number should change to (y + 1) after third day. As A and C decreased the average by maximum possible extent, it means C had the second-height Erdös number among all eight, as A had an Erdös number of infinity. Suppose Erdös numbers of A, B, C, D, E, F, G, H are y + 1, b, y + 1, c, d, e, y, g, h respectively at the end of third day.

$\therefore$ (y + 1 + b + y + 1 + c + d + e + y + g + h) = 24 = (3 × 8)

$\Rightarrow$ 3y + 2 + b + d + e + g + h = 24

When E co-authored with F, the average Erdös number reduced again, it means, E's Erdös number was not the same with A & C initially. As at the end of third day, 5 people had same Erdös number, they should be A, C and any 3 out of B, D, G, H. Suppose those 3 people are B, D, G. Then

(3y + 2 + y + 1 + y + 1 + y + 1 + e + h) = 24

$\Rightarrow$ 6y + h + e = 19 ...(i)

On the fifth day, E co-authored a paper with F and hence, Erdös number of E changed to (y + 1). Also the average decreased by 0.5 which means the total decreased by 4.

Hence, e - (y + 1) = 4

$\Rightarrow$ e – y = 5

Putting the value of e in equation (i), we get

6y + h + (5 + y) = 19

$\Rightarrow$ 7y + h = 14

Only possible value of y = 1 as h cannot be zero.

So after 3rd round Erdös number of A, C, E, F were 2, 2, 6, 1 respectively.

135. d Only A, C, E changed their Erdös number, rest 5 did not change their Erdös number.

136. b At the end of conference 6 people including E were having an Erdös number of 2 and F was having 1 as Erdös number. So 8th person was having an Erdös number of [20 – (2 × 6 + 1)] = 7

137. b At the end of 3rd round, 5 people were having same Erdös number. A and C changed their Erdös number after coauthoring with F. So, the other 3 will have same Erdös number in the beginning.

138. b 2

139. c After co-authoring with F, E was having Erdös number of 2, which was 4 less than initial Erdös number of E. So answer is 2 + 4 = 6.

For questions 140 to 142:

The given information can be depicted as follows.

(i) 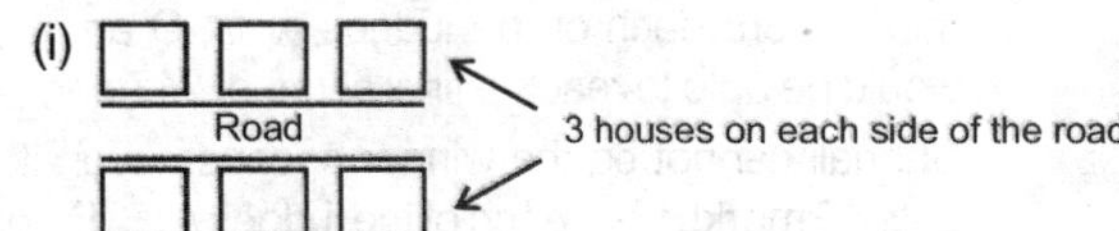

(ii) Six houses – P, Q, R, S, T, U

(iii) Colours – Red, Blue, Green, Orange, Yellow, White

(iv) Different heights

(v) T = tallest & opposite to Red

(vi) Shortest opposite to Green

(vii) U = orange & the position of U is: P/S U S/P

(viii) R = yellow & opposite to P

(ix) Q = Green & opposite to U

(x) P = White & (S, Q) > P > R (in height)

From (iv), (v), (vi), (ix) & (x), T > (S, Q) > P > R > U in terms of height

From (iv), (vii), (viii), (ix) & (x), we get the following two cases.

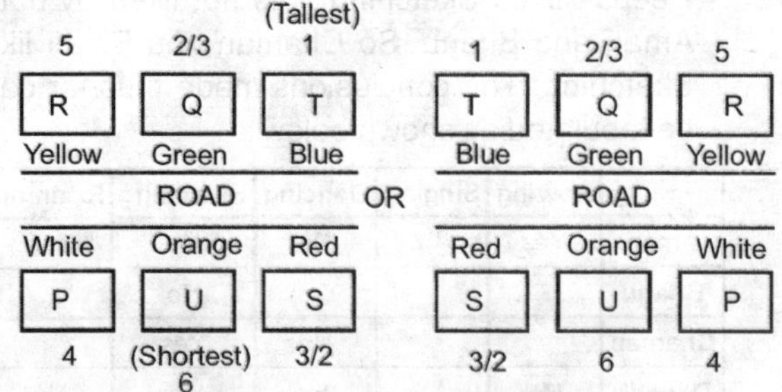

140. d Diagonally opposite to yellow is red.

141. e Second tallest house is either Q or S. So, we can not determine.

142. b Tallest house is T whose colour is Blue.

143. d A, D and F cannot be selected together as D doesn't hate any of the likings of A and F i.e. reading, travelling and fishing.

The rest two sets of people can be selected together.

144. b One team will have 3 members and the other will have 4 members. There are only two possible cases:

(i) 3-member team: Sajid, Salim, Sanjay
4-member team: Reeta, Sunil, Hasan, Govind

(ii) 3-member team: Reeta, Salim, Sanjay
4-member team: Sajid, Sunil, Hasan, Govind

Statement (1) is true in both the cases.

Statement (2) is true in case (i).

Statement (3) is false in both the cases.

145. c It's given that the winner gets a final score of 220 and no participants gets more than 45 marks from any of the judges.

Bali cannot be the winner because even if he gets 45 marks from each of the judges A, C, D and E, he would be able to reach a final score of 217 only.

Shonali cannot be the winner because even if she gets 45 marks from each of the judges A, B, D and E, she would be able to reach a final score of 219 only.

Gaurav cannot be the winner as his final score is less than that of Shonali.

Let the final scores of Angad, Gaurav, Monica and Shonali be 'a', 'g', 'm' and 's' respectively.

Therefore, as per the given condition

$\frac{a+g}{2} > \frac{m+s}{2}$.

Since 's' is greater than 'g', 'a' would be greater than 'm'. So Angad is the winner.

146. c It can be concluded that nobody except Bhanu and Deepak likes Dancing as the number of children who like Dancing cannot be more than two. Also, Deepak doesn't like Rowing and Running, both of which are liked by Aman. SInce Deepak likes Sketching, it is not liked by both Aman and Bhanu. So Chaman and Elhan like Sketching. The conclusions made thus far can be tabulated as shown below.

	Rowing	Singing	Dancing	Sketching	Running
Aman	Yes		No	No	Yes
Bhanu			Yes	No	
Chaman			No	Yes	
Deepak	No		Yes	Yes	No
Elhan			No	Yes	

The two children who like exactly the same set of activities must be Chaman and Elhan (this can be seen from the table). Since at least three children like Running, Chaman and Elhan must be two of them. It cannot be determined whether Bhanu likes Running or not.

147.b From (iii), as Shama and Hema are in the same car, Radha must be in a different car. From (v), either Divya or Charu must be in the same car as Radha and the other must be in the same car as Kiran. As Vicky cannot be in the same car as Hema, Kiran or Charu, he must be in the same car as Radha and Divya. From (i), Hari and Naresh are in the same car with Shama and Hema.

Further analysis leads to the following table:

Case I	Case II
Car I:	**Car I:**
Radha-Pankaj	Radha-Vicky
Divya-Vicky	Divya-Pankaj
Car II:	**Car II:**
Shama-Hari	Shama-Hari
Hema-Naresh	Hema-Naresh
Car III:	**Car III:**
Charu-Kartik	Charu-Kartik
Kiran-Chetan	Kiran-Chetan

148. d Let Anu, Bindu, Candy, Dolly, Emran, Fiza, Gauri and Hemant be represented by A, B, C, D, E, F, G and H respectively. The only possible arrangement is shown below.

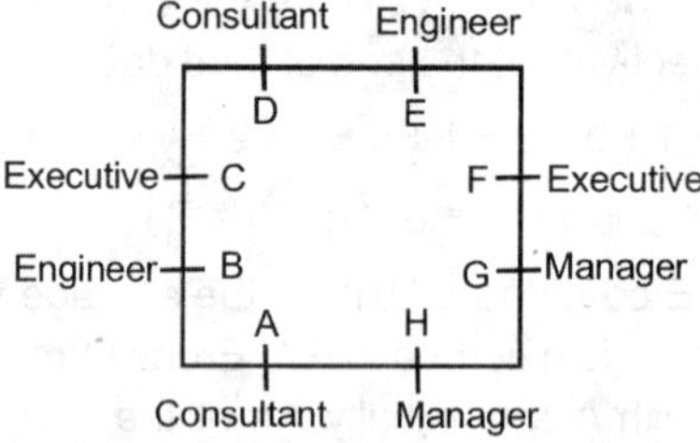

Hence, none of the statements is false.

For questions 149 to 151:

From statement (V), B and G cannot be together in the team. Therefore, there are three possible cases.

Case I: When B is selected.

F cannot be selected as F can only be selected when both G and N are selected. Thus, when B is selected, the team comprises exactly four bowlers. Also, J must be the wicketkeeper in the team, as selection of I ensures selection of F. Following table gives the possible compositions for the team.

Batsmen	Bowlers	Wicketkeeper
A, D, L, N, O, K/M	B, H, C, E	J

The number of ways in which the team can be formed

= 2 × 1 × 1 = 2

Case II: When G is selected.

H cannot be selected as H can only be selected when B is selected. Thus, when G is selected, then again the team comprises exactly four bowlers. Following table gives the possible compositions for the team.

Batsmen	Bowlers	Wicketkeeper
A, D, L, N, O, K/M	G, F, C, E	I/J

The number of ways in which the team can be formed

= 2 × 1 × 2 = 4.

Case III: When neither B nor G is selected.

When both B and G are not selected, then there is no possible composition for the team.

149. c If G is one of the bowlers in the team, then either of the two (i.e., I and J) can be selected as the wicketkeeper in the team.

150. c If H is selected, G cannot be selected.

151. c Options (a) and (b) are irrelevant. Loftus and Loftus found that the way in which questions were asked had a significant impact on what the subjects recalled. The implication of this is that when someone is asked to recall something, the phrasing/wording of the question may distort their recollections. Hence, option (c) is the correct answer.

For questions 152 to 154 :

The total number of different days of the week in January and February 2008 are as follows:

Mondays: 8 (4 each in January and February)

Tuesdays: 9 (5 in January and 4 in February)

Wednesdays: 9 (5 in January and 4 in February)

Thursdays: 9 (5 in January and 4 in February)

Fridays: 9 (4 in January and 5 in February)

Saturdays: 8 (4 each in January and February)

Sundays: 8 (4 each in January and February)

Total number of days in January and February 2008 = 60

Total number of days on which he drove the car of brand Honda

= 25 % of 60 = 15.

Total number of days on which he drove the car of brand BMW

= 15 % of 60 = 9.

Total number of days on which he drove the car of brand Hyundai

= 10 % of 60 = 6.

Given that HO > ME > CH > BM > HY > FE

So, we get that 15 > ME > CH > 9 > 6 > FE.

We also know that

ME + CH + FE = 60 – (15 + 9 + 6) = 30.

152. d Given that the number of days on which Mr. Alfonso drove the car of brand in January 2008 is the maximum.

Now, the car of brand Honda is only driven on either of the three days of any week, i.e. Monday, Tuesdays and Saturdays.

Total number of Mondays, Tuesdays and Saturdays in January 2008

= 4 + 5 + 4 = 13.

Total number of days in January and February 2008 on which he drove the car of brand Honda is equal to 15.

Required Answer = 15 – 13 = 2.

153. c Mr. Alfonso drove Chevrolet on all possible Saturdays in January 2008 i.e. 4 days and all possible Thursdays in January 2008 and February 2008 i.e. 9 days.

⇒ He drove Chevrolet on 13 days and Mercedes on 14 days as 15 > ME > CH

⇒ Number of days on which he drove Ferrari

= 30–(13 + 14) = 3 days.

154. d Maximum number of days on which Mr. Alfonso can drove the Mercedes in given two months = 14

To minimize the number of number of days when he drove Mercedes in the given two months, we will maximize the number of days on which he drove Ferrari and Chevrolet.

He could drove Ferrari for a maximum of 5 days as FE < 6.

⇒ ME + CH = 25 and ME > CH

⇒ The minimum value of ME = 13

Difference between maximum and minimum value of ME = 14 – 13 = 1.

155. b Alonso finished on podium in each of the first six races and scores 54 points.

He can score 54 points as

10, 10, 10, 8, 8, 8 [in any order]

10, 10, 10, 10, 8, 6

So, he can get 2nd rank in at most 3 races.

156. c Alonso finishes the next race on podium.

⇒ his total points are 60 or 62 or 64.

For finding lowest rank obtained by Schumacher, we take Alonso's score as 60 (lowest among 60, 62, 64)

To win the championship Schumacher needs 61 points.

⇒ in the last three races he has to score 61 – 39 = 22 points.

For lowest rank 22 can be scored as 10, 10, 2 (in any order).

Hence, the lowest rank obtained by Schumacher is 7th (corresponding to 2 points).

157. c If Fisichella finishes on podium in race 9 (or in any of the last 3 races), the points scored by Renault will be 87 (or more).

Hence, even if Honda drivers take top two ranks in all three races they will end up with 85 points.

i.e. 31 + 3 (8 + 10) = 31 + 54 = 85 points.

Hence, in this case Honda won't be able to win the 'Constructor's Championship'.

158. b After first six races Schumacher's total points are 39.

He didn't score any point in 1 race. Hence effectively, he scored 39 points in 5 races and 0 points in 1 race.

If in any of the 5 races he scores 7th rank or 2 points, then in other four races he has to score 37 points, which is not possible in any combination.

159. a A bus to Uttam Nagar departs after every 15 min.

One of the buses to Mehrauli leaves after every 10 min.

Other bus to Mehrauli can leave after every 12 min or 20 min

Let us assume bus on route no. 427 leaves after every 10 min between 9:00 a.m & 10:00 a.m i.e. at 9:00, 9:10, 9:20, 9:30, 9:40, 9:50 and 10:00 a.m.

<u>12 min</u>

If timings of buses plying after 12 & 10 min clash then the bus plying after every 12 min will go.

If timings of any of the buses plying after 12 min coincides with departure time of 427 then the next bus timings will clash only after 60 min(LCM of 12 & 10)

So maximum of 1 bus timings can clash with route no. 427 in a given hour.

Hence, a minimum 7 – 1= 6 buses on route 427 can depart in an hour.

<u>20 min</u>

If timings of buses plying after 20 & 10 min clash then the bus plying after every 20 min will go.

If timings of any of the bus plying after 20 min coincides with departure time of 427 then the next bus timings will clash again after 20 min(LCM of 20 & 10)

If the timings of two buses clash at 9:00 AM then timings will again clash at 9:20, 9:40 and 10:00

Hence, a minimum 7 – 4 = 3 buses on route 427 can depart in an hour.

160. c If frequency of all buses increases by 5 min then new time intervals become 5, 5, 7, 10, 15 and 25 min.

So now one of the bus to Mehrauli departs after every 5 min. The Other bus can depart after every 7 min or 15 min.

The minimum time difference between buses plying after 5 and 7 min can be 1 min (GCD of 5 and 7).

161. d The difference in time intervals between a particular bus to Mehrauli and Uttam Nagar is same as the difference in time intervals between two buses plying towards Uttam Nagar.

Hence, time intervals between Buses for Mehrauli and Uttam Nagar can only be:

Mehrauli – 10 and 12 / 20

Uttam Nagar – 15 and 10 / 20

So the time interval between two different routes to Uttam Nagar is always a multiple of 5.

162. a If condition (iii) is waved off then there can be possibility of 3 buses plying to Uttam Nagar. Then 3 buses to Uttam Nagar can ply between intervals 10,12 and 15 mins or between intervals of 10,15,20 mins.

So the minimum time interval can be in the first case i.e. when 3 buses ply after an interval of 10, 12, 15 mins.

Minimum difference between time interval

= 12 – 10 = 2 minute.

For questions 163 to 166:

After filling up the given data in a table, it can be concluded from statement (iv) that H3 could not have finished first, third or fourth in Race-II. Therefore, it must have finished second and so H4 and H1 must have finished third and fourth respectively in Race-II.

Now, H2 must have finished first in Race-III as it couldn't have finished at the same position in more than two races.

From statement (iii), Dablu's horse must be H3 and it must have finished second in Race-I.

Further analysis leads to the final tables as below.

Owner	Rahul	Dharma	Dablu	Ritesh
Horse	H1	H2	H3	H4

Rank / **Race**	**1**	**2**	**3**	**4**
Race-I	H4	H3	H2	H1
Race-II	H2	H3	H4	H1
Race-III	H2	H4	H1	H3
Race-IV	H4	H1	H2	H3

163. Dablu and Ritesh

164. Rahul

165. The sum of the ranks of H4 was the lowest and was equal to 7. Hence, H4 must have won the jackpot.

166. H4 finished third in Race-II. Hence, option (c) is the correct answer.

For questions 167 to 170:

From statement (iv), Charu and both her neighbours face inside. From statement (i), Hina sits to the immediate left of Charu as well as Banu; therefore, we can conclude that Banu must be facing outside. From statement (ii), the person sitting diametrically opposite Charu faces inside. Therefore, the rest of the persons must be facing outside.

Also, it is given that Anu sits diametrically opposite Hina and the two use the same prop i.e. Dafli. The conclusions made thus far can be shown with the help of a diagram.

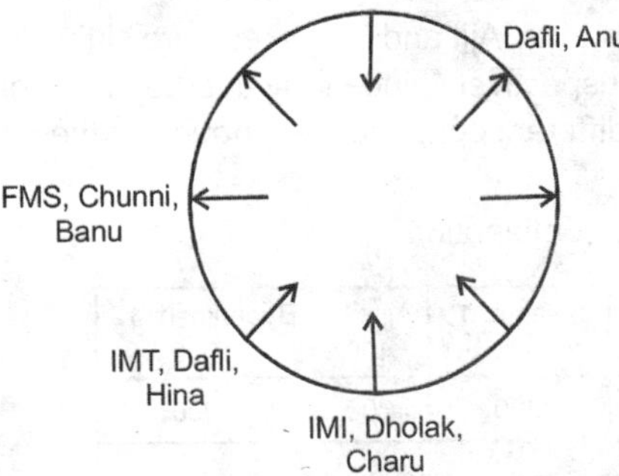

From statement (iii), Goru sits to the immediate left of Anu and must be facing inside. From statement (v), the only vacant positions, that are diametrically opposite, must have been occupied by Dhanu and Ellu. Now, Fiza from IIMR must be sitting immediately to the right of Anu. Further analysis leads to the final arrangement shown below.

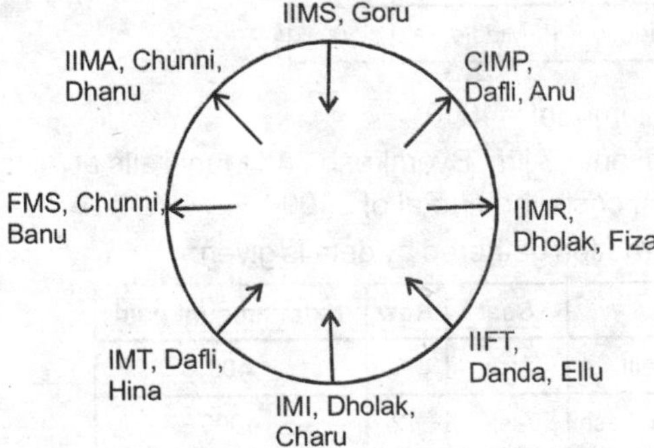

167. Fiza, Dholak

168. 3

169. Fiza is sitting opposite to the person who is from FMS.

Hence, the number of friends sitting between them is 3.

170. Goru is sitting opposite to Charu and thus the number of letters in the name of the friend sitting opposite to Charu is 4.

For questions 171 to 174:

From statements (ii) and (vi), Jason and Rahsaan were cycling in the lanes numbered 3 and 4 respectively. From statements (i) and (iv), Hilton was in the lane numbered 7. From statements (iii) and (v), either Alex or Fausto was in the lane numbered 8. But since Hilton was in the lane numbered 7, Alex could not have been in the lane numbered 8. Therefore, Fausto was in the lane numbered 8. Now two cases are possible:

Case I: Nathan and Alex were in the lanes numbered 1 and 2 respectively. Matt and Ryan were in the lanes numbered 5 and 6, in no particular order.

Lane No.	1	2	3	4	5	6	7	8
Rider	Nathan	Alex	Jason	Rahsaan	Matt/ Ryan	Ryan/ Matt	Hilton	Fausto

Case II: Nathan and Alex were in the lanes numbered 5 and 6 respectively. Matt and Ryan were in the lanes numbered 1 and 2, in no particular order.

Lane No.	1	2	3	4	5	6	7	8
Rider	Matt/ Ryan	Ryan/ Matt	Jason	Rahsaan	Nathan	Alex	Hilton	Fausto

171. Alex

172. Hilton and Fausto

173. The possible positions to which could have finished were 1, 2, 5 and 6.

Hence, the required sum = 1 + 2 + 5 + 6 = 14.

174. Either Nathan or Matt must have finished first in case Ryan did not finish first. Hence, the question cannot be answered.

For questions 175 to 178:

As he went to Bangkok in 2005, he must have gone to the USA and Europe respectively in either 2006 and 2007 or 2007 and 2008. But 2007 and 2008 is not possible as it violates statement (iv). From statement (iii), he spent 1 day on his vacation in 2004.

Let the number of days spent on vacation in Singapore and Nepal be x and y respectively. Therefore, he spent '$x + 1$' and '$y + 1$' days in Europe and the USA respectively. Let the number of days he spent in Bangkok be z.

Either x or y is equal to 1. Also, z as well as $(x + 1)$ cannot be equal to 5 (from statements (iv) and (vi)); the only possibility is $x = 1$ and $y = 4$. Further analysis leads to the final table shown below.

Year	Destination	No. of days
2004	Singapore	1
2005	Bangkok	3
2006	USA	5
2007	Europe	2
2008	Nepal	4

175. None of these

176. 2

177. Neither I nor II

178. He visited Nepal in 2008

For questions 179 to 182:

Only two cups got even ratings

even numbers from 1–10

$\Rightarrow$ 2, 4, 6, 8, 10

Other 4 places got odd ratings
1, 3, 5, 7, 7
Since, smallest rating is even
and rating of cup 3
= 2 × rating of cup 5
∴ Possible combinations are (3, 6) (5, 10)
Out of which the only acceptable scenario is
minimum rating is 2 which is of cup 2
cup 3 rating is 6 and cup 5 rating is 3
Since only 2 cups have even ratings. Therefore, cup 1, cup 4, cup 6 have ratings 5, 7 and 9 not necessarily in this order.

Also, since cup 3 got higher rating than cup 1, the only possibility is cup 1 got the rating of 5.

Tea from Himachal is cup 6 and Tea from Ooty got the highest rating.

Therefore Ooty is cup 4 and got rating of 9 and cup 6 that is Himachal got rating of 7.

The final information is tabulated below.

Places	Cup no	Rating	Rank
	1	5	4
	2	2	6
	3	6	3
Ooty	4	9	1
	5	3	5
Himachal	6	7	2

183.

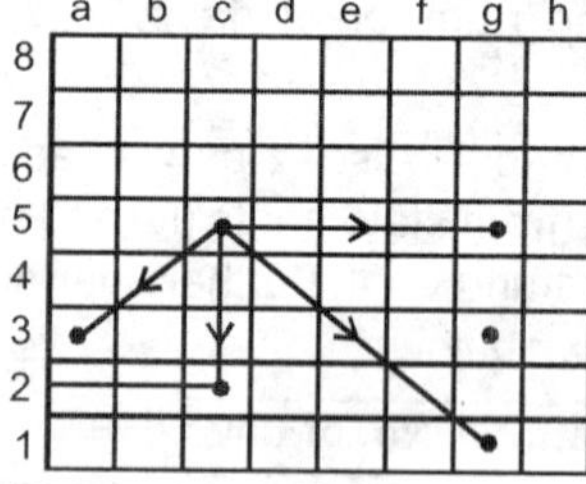

Figure 1

Directly from the diagram

184.

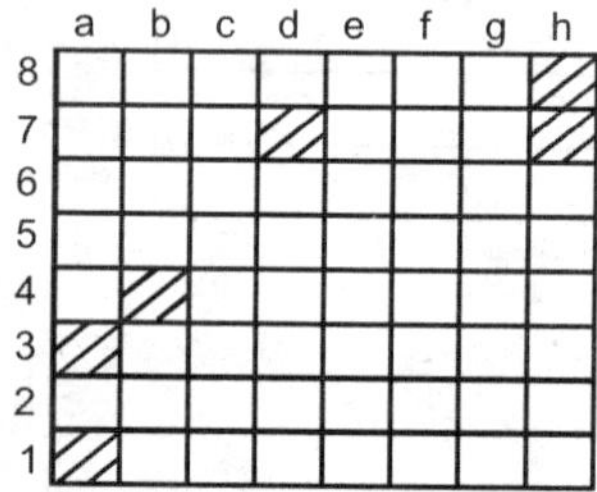

Figure 2

See the fgiure 2

If queen is at f8 then it can attack h8 and B4

Similarly, when queen is at a7 and c1 it can attack maximum of 2 piece

But when queen is at D3 then it can attack a3, d7 and h7.

185. Queen cannot attack 4 positions.

186. Another pieces can be at 36 positions.

For questions 187 to 190:

Since Jayanta, Ajit and Byomkesh are sitting in rows 10, 11, 12 respectively since only this combination of rows have 3 different consecutive amount for their choices of seat.

Possible combination

Aisle	Jayanta, 10 500	Ajit, 11 400	Byomkesh, 12 1000
Window	300	200	1000

Since, Manik is sitting next to Jayanta, so possible combinations for Manik is

Jayanta	Manik	Amount
Aisle, C	Auskem, D	500
Aisle, D	E, Middle	0
Window, A	Middle, B	0

Total amount = 4600

∴ Jayanta, Ajim, Byomkesh and Manik sits at Aisle seat, which costs them total of 24000.

Information gathered by details given:-

	Seat	Row	Extra amount paid
Ajit	Aisle	10	400
Byomkesh	Aisle	12	1000
Gargi	Middle	1/13	1000
Jayanta	Aisle	10	500
Kikira	Window	1/13	1000
Manik	Aisle	10	500
Prodosh	Window	20	200
Tapesh	Window	21	0
Total			4600

187. Since Jayanta is sitting in row 10, and Manik is next to Jayanta, therefore he is sitting in row 10.

188. Jayanta is sitting in row 10, seat C which is an Aisle seat, therefore she paid 500 extra.

189. Gargi was sitting at middle seat in either row 1 or 13, therefore she paid 1000 extra.

190. Tapesh sat in row 21, for which there extra amount.

191. 1 Let original sequence be abcde.

Therefore, possible combinations could be:

bacde			
cbade	acbde		
dbcae	adcbe	abdce	
ebcda	aecdb	abedc	abced

⇒ 11 sequences.

192. Let original sequence be abcde.

Therefore, possible combinations could be:

bacde			
badce	acbed		
baced	acbde	abdce	abced

$\Rightarrow$ 8 sequences.

193. 5 $5 + 4 + 3 + 2 + 1$

$\Rightarrow$ 15 sequences.

194. Let original sequence be LRLTIM.

Therefore, possible combinations could be:

RLLTIM				
RLTLIM				
RLTLMI	LLRTIM			
RLLITM	LLRITM	LRTLIM		
RLLTMI	LLRTMI	LRTLMI	LRLITM	LRLTMI

For questions 195 to 198:

By statement (2) and (6), Barun minor in Finance and by statement (3), Barun is the only male who major in Operations and three female students who did minor in Marketing are Adriano, Bandita & Chitra since Daisy did minors in operations.

By statement (1), (2) and (5) we get that Adriana and Deb are from same institute and does Daisy & Amit, therefore, the two girls that are form Z have to be Bandita and Chitra.

By statement (6) and (7) we get this initial table:

Gender	Students	Institute	Major	Minor
Female	Adriana	X/Y		Marketing
	Bandita	Z		Marketing
	Chitra	Z		Marketing
	Daisy	Y/X		Operations
Male	Amit	Y/X		
	Barun	Y	Operations	Finance
	Chetan	X	Finance	
	Deb	X/Y		

By statement (2), female student from Y that majors in Operations have to be Adriana, since, Daisy has her minor in Operations and cannot have the major in the same subject.

Therefore, by statement (5), we get, Adriana and Deb are from Y institute and Daisy and Amit are form X institute.

Gender	Students	Institute	Major	Minor
Female	Adriana	Y	Operations	Marketing
	Bandita	Z		Marketing
	Chitra	Z		Marketing
	Daisy	X		Operations
Male	Amit	X	Finance	
	Barun	Y	Operations	Finance
	Chetan	X	Finance	
	Deb	Y	Marketing	Finance

195. Students from the institute Z are Bandita and Chitra.

196. Deb minor in finance.

197. Amit major in finance.

198. If Chitra majors in Finance, then, Bandita major in Operations by statement (4).

199. To find: - Number of ways the ATM can serve a customer who gives 500 rupee notes as her preference.

Let number of 100, 200 and 500 rupee notes be a, b and c respectively, then

$a100 + b200 + c500 = 5000$ and,

$\Rightarrow a + 2b + 5c = 50.$

$c > a + b.$

If $c = 10$, $a + 2b = 0$

implies $a = 0 = b$

If $c = 9$, $a + 2b = 5$ then possible combinations of (a, b) are (5, 0), (1, 2), (3, 1)

if $c = 8$, $a + 2b = 10$, then possible combinations of (a, b) are (2, 4), (4, 3), (0, 5).

200. If a customer gives 500 rupee notes as their preference, then, the possible cases are given in the previous question answer from all those cases we will pick the case which has least number of 500 rupee notes i.e when $c = 8$ to maximise the number of customers.

$\therefore$ No of customers who could give 500 rupee as their preference are 6 customers ($\because 6 \times 8 = 48$)

201. If a customer gives 500 rupee notes as their preference then the minimum possible number of 500 rupee notes a customer gets is 8, but since we have to maximise the number of customers therefore we have to keep the number of 500 rupee notes minimum.

Let analyse the options.

Let no of customers be 16,

$\therefore$ therefore, number of fifty 500 rupee notes distributed among 16 customers will be

$$= \frac{50}{16} = 3.125 \approx 3$$

$a + 2b + 5c = 50$

$\Rightarrow a + 2b = 35.$

Also $a + b + c \leq 20$

$\Rightarrow a + b \leq 17$

Let $a + b = 17$

$a + 2b = 35$ and $a + b = 17$

then $b = 18$, $a = -1$, is not possible therefore no value of (a, b) will satisfy for $c = 3$

Let number of customers be 13

∴ Number of fifty 500 rupee notes distributed among 13 customers will be

$\frac{50}{13} = 3.84 \approx 3$ notes, which we know will not satisfy.

Let number of customers be 12.

∴ Number of fifty 500 rupee notes distributed among 12 customers will be $\frac{50}{12} = 4.167 \approx 4$

∴ a + 2b = 30

$a + b \leq 16$

Let in particular a + b = 16.

solving, a + 2b = 30 and a + b = 16, we get

b = 14 and a = 2

∴ a + b + c = 20 which satisfies the condition.

202. Number of 500 rupee notes required to serve 50 customers with 500 rupee notes as their preference, given, that the total number of notes to be dispensed is the smallest possible.

If a + 2b + 5c = 50, then c = 10, a = 0, b = 0 (combinations are given in explanation of first answer)

Total number = 50 × 10 = 500

Number of 500 notes dispensed to serve 50 customers with 100 rupee notes as their preference, given, that the total number of notes dispensed is the smallest possible.

If a + 2b + 5c = 50 and a > b + c, then a = 10, b = 0 and c = 8 is only such combination where a + b + c = 18 is the least.

Total number of 500 rupee notes = 50 × 8 = 400

∴ Total = 500 + 400 = 900

For questions 203 to 206:

Let the number of pumps where low, medium and high contamination levels were recorded by a, b and c respectively.

Then by statement (5),

c = 2a

Since by statement (1), atleast three pumps were recorded as high, which has to be P1, P3 and P5. and by statement (2) and (4), there are atleast three pumps that were recorded as low.

So, possible combinations of (a, b, c) are (3, 11, 6), (4, 8, 8), (5, 5, 10), (6, 2, 12);

Maximum number of petrol pumps with concentration level as high could be only 8. Therefore, the possible combinations now are (3, 11, 6) and (4, 8, 8)

Petrol pumps.

P1	High
P2	Medium
P3	High
P4	Medium
P5	High
P6	Low
P7	Medium
P8	Medium
P9	High
P10	Medium
P11	High
P12	Medium
P13	High
P14	Medium
P15	Medium
P16	Medium
P17	Low
P18	Medium
P19	Low
P20	Medium

This case is not possible

Case II: - when (a, b, c) = (4, 8, 8)

Petrol Pumps	Concentration Level			
	Case I	Case II	Case III	Case IV
P1	High	High	High	High
P2	Medium	Medium	Medium	Medium
P3	High	High	High	High
P4	Medium	Medium	Medium	Medium
P5	High	High	High	High
P6	Low	Low	Low	Low
P7	High	High	High	High
P8	High	High	High	High
P9	Medium	Medium	Medium	Medium
P10	High	High	High	High
P11	Medium	Medium	Medium	Low
P12	High	High	Low	Medium
P13	Medium	Medium	High	High
P14	High	High	Medium	Medium
P15	Low	Medium	High	High
P16	Medium	Low	Medium	Medium
P17	Low	Medium	Low	Low
P18	Medium	Low	Medium	Medium
P19	Low	Medium	Low	Low

203. Following all the subcases of case II: the contamination level at P10 was recorded as high is true.

204. Exactly 8 petrol pumps were recorded as medium.

205. If the contamination level at P11 was recorded as low, then, the contamination level at P14 was recorded as Medium (Case II : Subcase IV)

206. If contamination level at P15 was recorded as medium then, contamination levels at P11 and P16 were not recorded as the same

207. Consider a 3 × 3 square matrix:-

0	1	0
2	3	2
0	1	0

Therefore minimum 4 different numbers can fill a 3 × 3 square matrix.

208. Consider a 5 × 5 square matrix:-

0	1	0	1	0
2	3	2	3	2
0	1	0	1	0
2	3	2	3	2
0	1	0	1	0

Therefore minimum 4 different numerals can fill a 5 × 5 square matrix

209. In order to make one mistake the numeral at the corner or the boundary could be changed in the matrix given in the answer of the previous question, and still the minimum numerals required to fill a 5 × 5 matrix would be 4.

For example:-

0	1	0	1	0
2	3	2	3	2
0	1	0	1	0
2	3	2	3	2
1	1	0	1	0

210. Consider a 5 × 5 matrix:-

6	7	5	6	1
3	1	2	3	8
4	8	0	4	7
5	7	6	5	1
1	2	3	8	2

Therefore, a minimum of 9 different numerals can fill a 5 × 5 square matrix such that all the cells adjacent to any particular cell have different numerals.

Question Numbers: (211 to214):

Each of the 39 students is enrolled in at least one of the three sports.

A + B + C + D + E + F + G = 39 ... (1)

G = 2 × E ... (2)

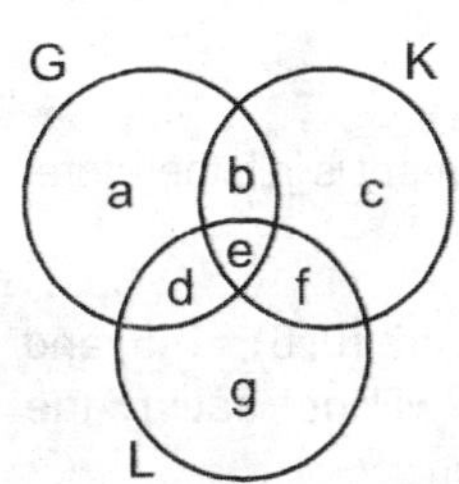

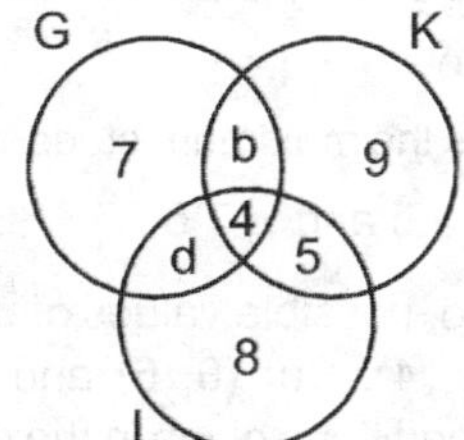

According to 1st statement

A + B + D + E = 17 ... (3)

According to 2nd statement

A = G – 1 ... (4)

According to 3rd statement

C = F + E ... (5)

According to 4th statement

B + D + E = 10 ... (6)

According to 6th statement

Now, solving 3, 6, 4, 2, we get

A = 7, G = 8, E = 4.

From 1 and 5, C = 9, F = 5.

So B + D = 6.

211. Maximum number of students are enrolled in L.

If B = 1, D = 5, then total number of students enrolled in L is 18 and that in K is 23, which is against the condition.

Using similar methods, if B = 4, D = 2, the total number of students enrolled in L is 21 and that in K is 20. So this satisfies the condition.

Therefore, minimum number of students enrolled in both G and L but not in K is 4.

212. Now B + D = 6. ... (1)

Number of students enrolled in K = 18 + B

Number of students enrolled in L = 17 + D.

$$\frac{(18+B)}{(17+D)} = \frac{19}{22} \quad \text{... (2)}$$

Solving 1 and 2, we get B = 1, D = 5.

Therefore, the total number of students enrolled in L = 22

213. 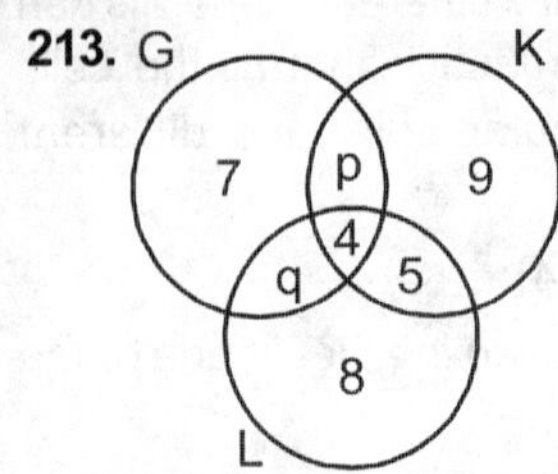

According to the given details, the venn diagram will be exactly like given above.

Now p + q = 6

As the maximum student enrollment is in L therefore,

q > p and q ≠ 0

So, possible values of p and q are (0, 6), (1, 5) and (2, 4). But (0, 6) and (2, 4) will not satisfy the conditions given in the question.

∴ Only p = 1 and q = 5 will satisfy the given conditions.

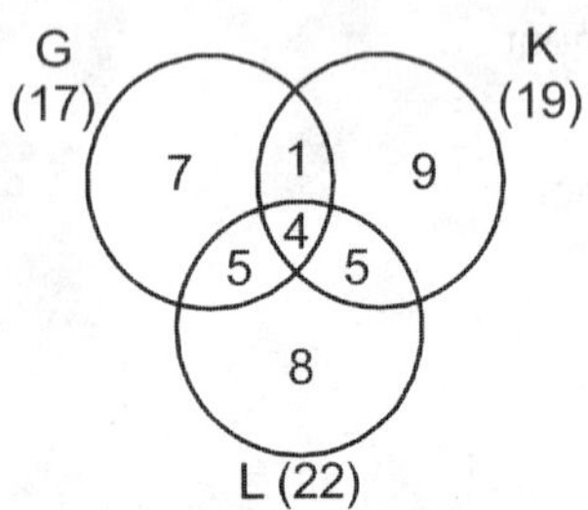

Now, it is given that the number of students who were enrolled in all three sports i.e. 4 students, were asked to withdraw from one of the three sports.

After withdrawal, the number of students enrolled in G was 6 less than the number of students enrolled in L, while the number of students enrolled in K went down by 1.

∴ Final diagram would be:

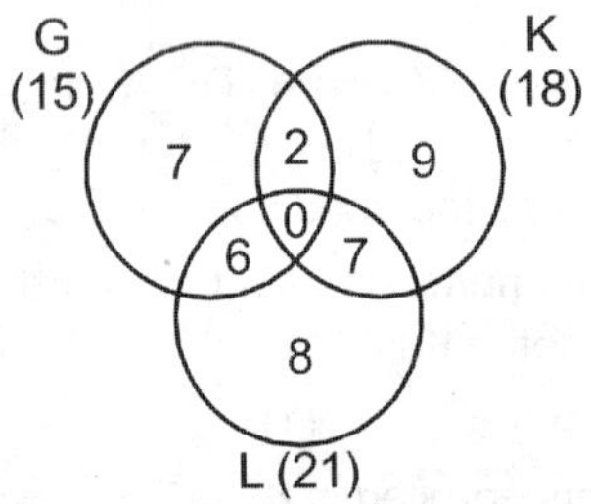

Clearly, 2 students were enrolled in both G and K.

214. 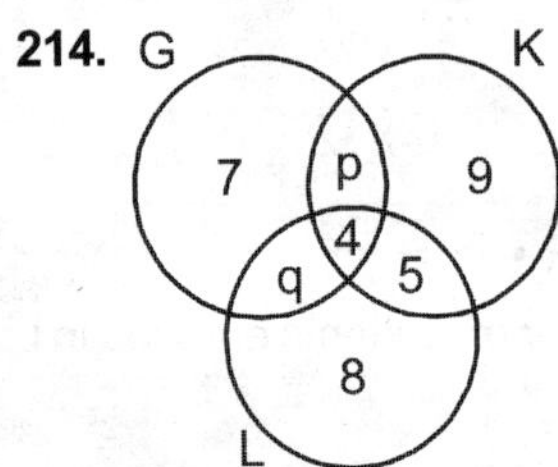

According to the directions, the venn diagram will be exactly like given above.

Now p + q = 6

As the maximum student enrollment is in L therefore,

q > p and q ≠ 0

So, possible values of p and q are (0, 6), (1, 5) and (2, 4). But (0, 6) and (2, 4) will not satisfy the conditions given in the question.

∴ Only p = 1 and q = 5 will satisfy the given conditions.

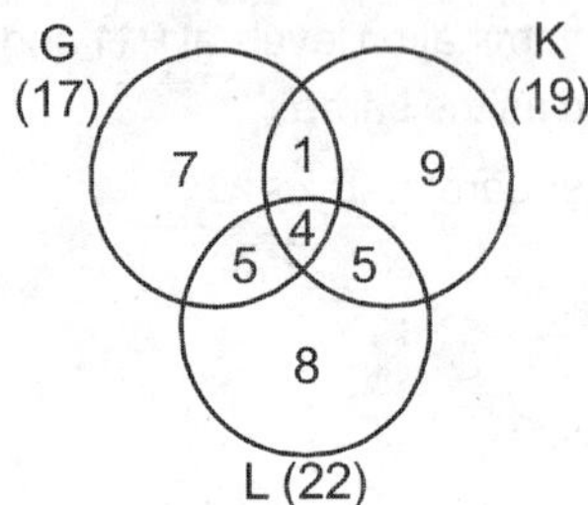

Now, it is given that the number of students who were enrolled in all three sports i.e. 4 students, were asked to withdraw from one of the three sports.

After withdrawal, the number of students enrolled in G was 6 less than the number of students enrolled in L, while the number of students enrolled in K went down by 1.

∴ Final diagram would be:

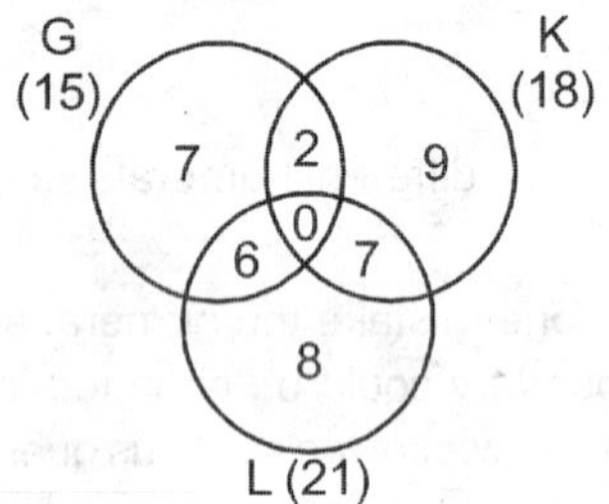

Clearly, 6 students were enrolled in both G and L.

Question Numbers: (215 to 218):

1. Through Balaram and Fatima's statements, it can be inferred that they were in a room having 4 candidates, and as Balaram was 3rd to enter room 101 so this room had 4 candidates.
2. Through Ganeshan's statement, it can be inferred that room 102 had 2 candidates.
3. Through Erina's statement, it can be inferred that Erina was in room 103 having only 1 candidate.
4. From Chitra's statement, it can be inferred that she was in room 102.
5. So, room 101 had Akil, Divya, Balaram and Fatima as 4 candidates.

From the given time table, following table can be filled as:

Timings / Room No	7:10 AM	7:15 AM	7:25 AM	7:30 AM	7:40 AM	7:45 AM
101	Akil				Fatima	
102				Chitra		
103						

215. From the above information provided, Divya was alloted room 101.

216. It is definite that Ganeshan and Chitra were the only two in room 102, and according to Chitra, she is the last one to enter the allotted room, so Ganeshan is the 1st one to enter room 102 and hence there was no one when Ganeshan entered.

217. In room 101, Fatima is the last one to enter and Balaram is the third one to enter. Therefore, David is either first or second person to enter room 101. In room 102, Ganeshan is the first one to enter.

David, Balaram, and Ganeshan must have entered before 7:30. So Erina must have entered at 7:45 am.

218. If Ganeshan reached before Divya, and Divya reaches before Balaram, then Ganeshan, Divya and Balaram must have reached at 7:10, 7:15 and 7:25 respectively.

Timings / Room No	7:10 AM	7:15 AM	7:25 AM	7:30 AM	7:40 AM	7:45 AM
101	Akil	Divya	Balaram		Fatima	
102	Ganeshan			Chitra		
103						Erina

Question Numbers: (219 to 222):

1. Looking at the code for words "is" and "as" it can be deduced that i = 3, s = 5, a = 6.
2. Now looking at the code for "Peacock", digit 9 has only two letters according to statement 3 and 9 comes 3 times in Peacocks code. Since 9 cannot be associated with 3 individual letters, a letter associated with 9 must occur twice. Only "c" occurs twice. So c = 9.
3. Similarly, looking at the code for "National", digit 6 occurs 4 times and code for i = 3. So 6 should be equal to two letters occurring twice respectively. Those digits are "a" and "n".
4. Between "Peacock" and "National", letter "o" and digits "8" and "9" are common. Since, a = 8. So o = 9.
5. Between "The" and "National", letter "t" and digit "8" are common. So t = 8, l = 1.
6. Similarly, between "The" and "Peacock", only letter "e" is common. So e = 5, h = 4.
7. In the code for "Of", o = 9, f = 7.
8. Looking at code for "Designated", i = 3, n = 6, a = 6, t = 8, e = 5 and between "Designated" and "Bird", letters "I" and "d" are common, digits "1" and "3" are common. Since i = 3, so d = 1.
9. In the code for "Designated", g=7.

Check the following table for final codes for every letter.

1	D, L
2	
3	I
4	H
5	S, E
6	A, N
7	F, G
8	T, P, K
9	C, O

219. Code for L = 1 from the above table.

220. In the code "Bird", i = 3, d = 1. So B can be either 3 or 4. Answer is 3 or 4.

221. For digits "8" and "9" can the complete list of letters be identified. So answer is 2.

222. For option 1, S and E have same code. So this can't be the answer

For option 3, X, Y, Z can have same code. So this can't be the answer.

For option 4, B can be 3 same as I. Again this is not the answer.

So only option is S, U, V. Since S and E are already associated with 5, and it can have a maximum of 3 letters. S, U, V cannot be associated to the same number.

Question Numbers: (223 to 226):

Let O, M, Y be the total number of Old, Middle-aged, and Young visitors respectively.

It is given that M = 2 × O, Y = 2 × M. So Y = 4 × O.

Total 140 tickets are sold. O + M + Y = 140.

Solving this we get O = 20, M = 40, Y = 80.

Total 55 Economy tickets were sold. Old visitors bought equal number of Gold and Economy tickets. Let this be x.

	Old (20)	Middle-aged (40)	Young (80)	Total
Platinum			P/2	P
Gold	x			G
Economy	x		38	55

223. Young visitors have half of the platinum tickets, thus old and middle aged will share equally the remaining half of Platinum tickets.

For values 34 and 38 the half is an odd number, and thus cannot be divided equally.

For value 36, Number of Old-aged buying Platinum will be 9, and the rest of the tickets bought by Old-aged visitors will be 11. But, Old-aged visitors buy Gold and Economy equally, which is not possible.

So only option remaining is 32.

224. Let number of Old visitors buying Platinum tickets be Y, then number of Middle aged visitors buying economy ticket is also Y.

According to the question,

Old-aged and Middle-aged visitors together buy 17 economy tickets.

So X + Y = 17 ...(1)

Also, 2 × X + Y = 20 ...(2)

Solving (1) and (2), we get

X = 3, Y = 14.

Therefore, number of Old visitors buying Gold tickets is 14.

225. Let the number of Gold, Platinum, and Economy tickets be equal to G, P, E respectively.

G + P + E = 140 ... (1)

E = 55, G + P = 85 ... (2)

Now, 38 Young visitors have bought Economy tickets. So let us assume that remaining 42 Young visitors have bought Platinum tickets.

As Number of Young visitors buying Platinum tickets is equal to the half of total Platinum tickets.

So P = 84. From (2), G = 1.

It is mentioned that number of Old visitors buying Gold tickets is strictly greater than the number of Young visitors. So number of middle aged visitors buying Gold tickets must be 0. Check from the following table.

	Old (20)	Middle-aged (40)	Young (80)	Total
Platinum	18	24	42	84
Gold	1	0	0	1
Economy	1	16	38	55

226. Number of Old and Middle-aged visitors buying Economy tickets together is equal to 17, which is an odd number.

So these two values cannot be equal to each other.

Therefore, statement saying The numbers of Old and Middle-aged visitors buying Economy tickets were equal" is false.

DATA SUFFICIENCY

1. c Statement I implies X > Y or X > Z or X > Y and Z Statement II implies Y > X or Y > Z or Y > X and Z.

Combining both statements, we can get Y > X > Z or

X > Y > Z. Hence, Z is the smallest.

2. a S has 4 uncles and from statement A. F has two brothers. Hence, the other 2 uncles of S must be the brothers of M. Statement B does not give any additional information.

3. a Assume A, B, C, D gets score 10, 8, 6, 4 respectively.

A B C D

10 8 6 4

Statement A:

With the conditions, A will give vote to B

With the conditions, B will give vote to A

With the conditions, C will give vote to A

Even if D gives to A/B/C - 2 situation arises.

Either A will win or there will a tie when D gives vote to B.

Even then A will win.

So we are getting the answer.

Statement B: Nothing concrete can be derived.

4. a Statement A: Nothing can be said.

Statement B: Since there are 3 boys in the top 5 rank holders, the other two are girls and Rashmi is not one of them. As Kumar is ranked sixth, Rashmi is either seventh or below. Hence, statement II alone is sufficient.

5. d Statements A and B alone are not sufficient but if both are combined, then we can form the following sequence:

1	2	3	4	5
D	E	B	C	A

So the answer is (d).

6. d From statement A, both Aakash and Biplab have the same scores. But we cannot find the man of the match.

From statement B only, we cannot find the man of the match.

Combining both statements we can find the man of the match i.e. Aakash.

7. c From statement A, their ranks will be A - 4, B -1, C - 2, D - 3.

From statement B, also their ranks will be A - 4, B -1, C - 2, D - 3.

8.b **From Statement A:**

There are multiple possibilities:

6, 7, 8, 9, 10

5, 7, 8, 9, 11 etc.

So the answer cannot be determined using A alone.

From Statement B:

There are only two possible cases:

(i) 1, 2, 4, 5, 28

(ii) 1, 2, 3, 6, 28

In both the cases the answer will be 28.

9. c **From Statement A:**

Two cases are possible (x means x students):

(i) 14 Mukesh 5 Rakesh 22

This gives a total of 14 + 1 + 5 + 1 + 22 = 43 students.

(ii) 8 Rakesh 5 Mukesh 16.

This gives a total of 8 + 1 + 5 + 1 + 16 = 31 students.

From Statement B:

Three cases are possible:

(i) Rakesh 13 Mukesh 8

This gives a total of 1 + 13 + 1 + 8 = 23 students.

(ii) 6 Rakesh 7 Mukesh 14

This gives a total of 6 + 1 + 7 + 1 + 14 = 29 students.

(iii) 8 Rakesh 5 Mukesh 16

This gives a total of 8 + 1 + 5 + 1 + 16 = 31 students.

Combining Statement A and Statement B:

The answer has to be 31.

10. b Since all the interior angles are equal (given), each interior angle must be 120^0. Though ABCDEF is not a regular hexagon (as AB is not equal to DE), the opposite sides would still be parallel.

From Statement A:

The shortest distance, d, between parallel lines is given as 30cm.

However it can be observed that exact position of the points D and E are still not known w.r.t. AB.

Let us draw one of the possible hexagons ABCDEF:

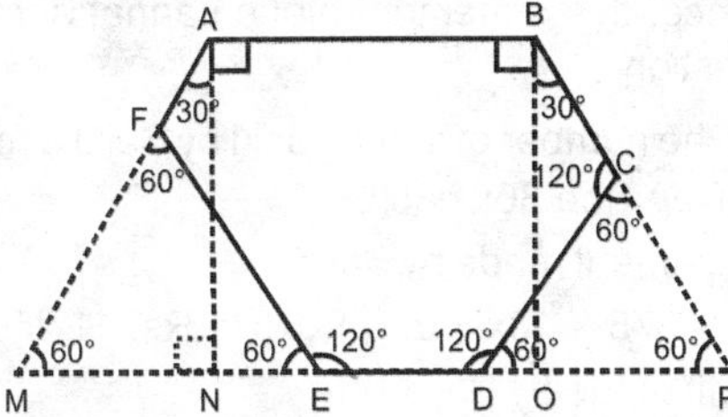

Here AF and BC may or may not be equal.

AF, BC and ED are extended to meet at points M and P (see the figure).

Also, AN and BO are perpendiculars drawn from A and B on ED extended.

It can be observed that both the triangles FME and DCP are equilateral.

Hence, AF + FE = AF + FM = AM

$$= \frac{AN}{\cos 30^\circ} = \frac{d}{\cos 30^\circ}$$

Similarly, BC + CD = BC + CP = BP

$$= \frac{BO}{\cos 30^\circ} = \frac{d}{\cos 30^\circ}$$

It can be observed that 'AF + FE' and 'BC + DC' both are same and also unique for all possible hexagons ABCDEF.

Hence, despite having many possible hexagons ABCDEF, the perimeter:

$$= 20 + 10 + \frac{2d}{\cos 30^\circ} = 99.28 \text{ cm}$$

(will be constant)

Hence, Statement A alone is sufficient to answer.

From Statement B:

Since Statement B gives no information about the distance between AB and DE, it is insufficient to calculate the perimeter of the hexagon.

11. a **From Statement A:**

As the sum of the number of parking slots in Mohit's house and Pranab's house is an even number, the number of parking slots in each of Pavan, Pranab and Mohit's house is one and the number of parking slots in Santosh's house is two. Also, Santosh must be staying in the second largest house. Hence, this statement alone can answer the question.

From Statement B:

The houses of Pavan, Pranab, Mohit and Santosh have three, three, five and two parking slots respectively. It is also known that the largest house cannot have five parking slots. But we cannot deduce anything about the second largest house. Hence, this statement alone cannot answer the question.

12. c Let the number of shares sold by Sajid and Hasan on Day 1 be 36x each.

Investment made by Sajid

$= 375 \times 18x + 250 \times 18x = \text{Rs. } 11{,}250x.$

Profit made by Sajid

$= 750 \times 18x + 625 \times 18x - 375 \times 18x - 250 \times 18x$

$= \text{Rs. } 13{,}500x.$

Sajid's Margin on Day 1 $\approx$ 54.5%.

Investment made by Hasan

$= 225 \times 36x = \text{Rs. } 8{,}100x.$

Profit made by Hasan

$= 375 \times 16x + 300 \times 20x - 225 \times 36x$

$= \text{Rs. } 3{,}900x.$

Hasan's Margin on Day 1 = 32.5%.

13. b **For Hasan:**

As the share price at 11:00 a.m. and 12:00 noon was Rs. 500 and Rs. 400 respectively, the number of shares sold by Hasan at 11:00 a.m. and 12:00 noon must be in the ratio 4 : 5 respectively. Let the number of shares sold by Hasan at 11:00 a.m. and 12:00 noon be 4x and 5x respectively.

Total sales amount $= 500 \times 4x + 400 \times 5x$

$= \text{Rs. } 4{,}000x$

Total investment in purchase

$= 750 \times 9x = \text{Rs. } 6{,}750x$

$$\text{Margin (loss)} = \frac{6750 - 4000}{4000} = 68.75\%$$

For Sajid:

Let the total number of shares sold by Sajid at 9 a.m. and 10 a.m. be 2y.

Total sales amount

$= 200 \times y + 300 \times y = \text{Rs. } 500y$

Total investment in purchase $= 500 \times y + 625y$

$= \text{Rs. } 1{,}125y$

$$\text{Margin (loss)} = \frac{1125 - 500}{500} = 125\%$$

Required ratio = 68.75 : 125 = 11 : 20

14. d **From Statement A:**

Since we do not know the angle between AB and BC, infinitely many cyclic quadrilaterals ABCD are possible, where AB = 8 cm, BC = 15 cm and AD = CD. Hence, this statement alone cannot answer the question.

From Statement B:

Circumcircle of BCD is also the circumcircle of ABCD. Since we do not know the lengths of AD and CD, infinitely many cyclic quadrilaterals ABCD are possible. Hence, this statement also cannot answer the question alone.

Combining Statements A and B:

In a circle of diameter 17 cm, construct a chord BC = 15 cm. This chord divides the circle into two unequal parts. On both these parts, chord AB of length 8 cm can be drawn. Even if AD = CD, we can arrive at two different quadrilaterals ABCD (see the figures given below). Hence, the question cannot be answered even by using both the statements together.

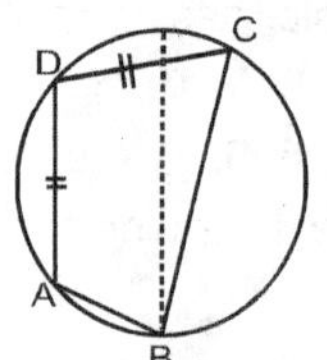

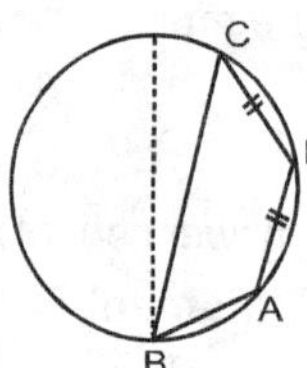

15. d **From Statement A:**

Statement A alone is clearly insufficient to answer the question.

From Statement B:

$$a^2 + b^2 + c^2 = 83$$

Case I:

$$(a, b, c) = (1, 1, 9)$$

Case II:

$$(a, b, c) = (3, 5, 7)$$

Statement B alone is also not sufficient to answer the question.

From Statements A and B:

The values of (a, b, c) are (3, 5, 7) and the sum of a, b and c is 15.

16. b **From Statement A:**

$$6q - p = 5$$
$$p = 6q - 5$$
$$p + q = 7q - 5$$

(7q – 5) when divided by 7 leaves remainder 2.

This statement alone is sufficient to answer the question.

From Statement B:

$$8q + p = 45$$
$$p = 45 - 8q$$
$$p + q = 45 - 7q$$

(45 – 7q) when divided by 7 leaves remainder 3.

This statement alone is sufficient to answer the question.

17. b The given information can be shown as:

Name	-	Ajay	-
Surname	Rathore/Agarwal	-	Agarwal/Rathore

Therefore, the surame of Ajay is either Yadav or Sharma.

From Statement A:

The surname of Chetan is Agarwal; but we still cannot conclude anything about the surname of Ajay. This statement alone is not sufficient to answer.

From Statement B:

The surname of Bikas is Yadav; therefore, the surname of Ajay is Sharma. This statement alone is sufficient to answer.

18. b Let the ages of the five people, from youngest to oldest, be represented by A1, A2, A3, A4 and A5 respectively. From the given information it can be concluded that the age of the Engineer is A1 and the age of the Professor is A2. As the age of the Lawyer is not A5 and he is standing between the Manager and the Doctor, the Manager must be standing at one of the ends of the row and the Professor must be standing at the other end of the row. The tables given below show the two possible cases.

Age	A2	A1	A5	-	-
Profession	Professor	Engineer	Doctor	Lawyer	Manager

or

Age	-	-	A5	A1	A2
Profession	Manager	Lawyer	Doctor	Engineer	Professor

From Statement A:

The given information is already present in the root of the question. This statement alone is not sufficient to answer.

From Statement B:

As the Manager is younger than the Lawyer, the age of the Manager must be A3. Hence, exactly two people are younger than him. This statement alone is sufficient to answer.

For questions 19 to 21 :

From statements (III) and (V), it can be concluded that both T2 and T3 ended up with either 2 or 4 points.

Case 1: When T2 and T3 scored 2 points each.

Since T3 won against T2, T3 must have lost its remaining matches and T4 must have won all its matches. Thus, T1 must have played on Monday against T3, but this was not the case as per the statement (IV). Hence, this case is invalid.

Case 2: When T2 and T3 scored 4 points each.

Since T2 lost against T3 on Tuesday, it must have won against T1 and T4. From statement (IV), T2 and T4 did not play on Wednesday and Saturday respectively. So T2 must have won its matches against T4 and T1 on Friday and Saturday respectively.

Further analysis leads to the following table.

Day	Match played between	Winner
Monday	T1 & T4	T1
Tuesday	T2 & T3	T3
Wednesday	T1 & T3	T3
Thursday	T3 & T4	T4
Friday	T2 & T4	T2
Saturday	T1 & T2	T2

19. a T4 scored 2 points.

20. c T3 lost against T4.

21. d The match played on Friday was between T2 and T4.

For questions 22 to 24 :

Consider the following table with marked positions.

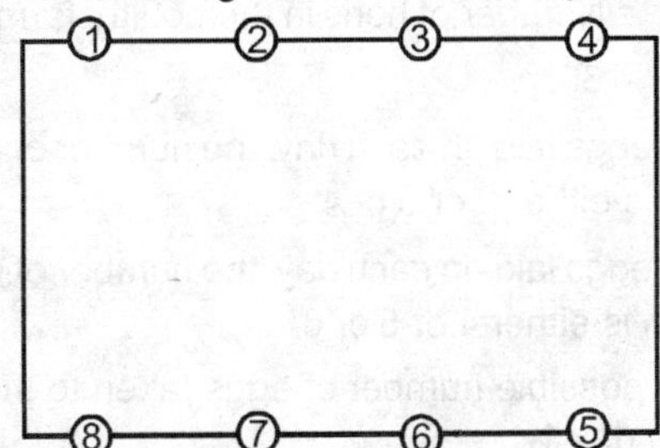

From statements (III) and (VI), Rajbhasa Adhikari is sitting on either chair 4 or chair 8. From statements (II), (IV) and (V), it can be deduced that the Law Officer, the Marketing Officer and the officer who works in PNB are sitting along the same side of the table. Now, from statements (I) and (III), it can be concluded that the Finance Officer, the HR Manager, the Technical Officer and the Rajbhasha Adhikari are sitting along the same side of the table. Therefore, IT Officer works in PNB.

Further analysis leads to the following arrangements.

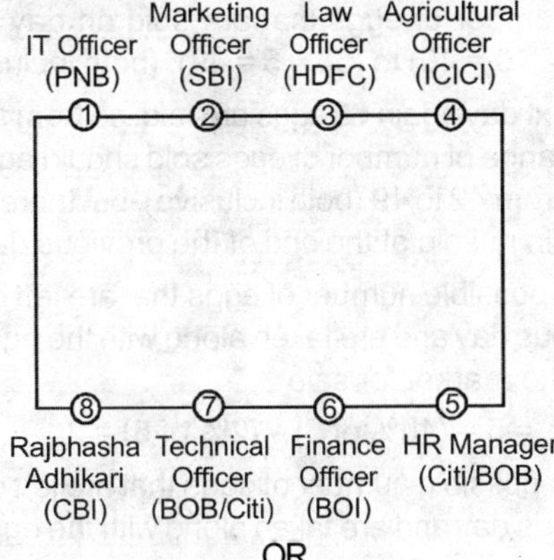

OR

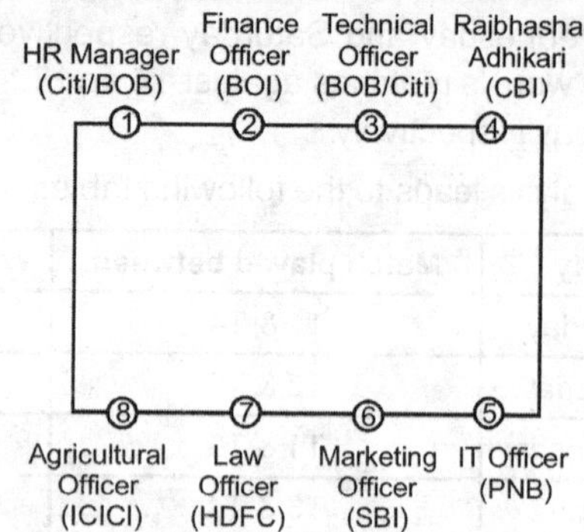

22. d HR Manager is sitting to the immediate right of Finance officer.

23. b For six persons, we can definitely determine the banks in which they work.

24. a The person who is sitting opposite the Law Officer works in BOI.

For questions 25 to 28 :

Number of eggs laid on each day

= Number of hens in the poultry farm

= 60.

Out of the eggs laid on each day, the number of eggs that got rotten is either 2 or 3 or 4.

Out of the eggs laid on each day, the number of eggs that got broken is either 4 or 5 or 6.

Maximum possible number of eggs taken to the market for sale on day 1

= 60 – (2 + 4)= 54.

Minimum possible number of eggs taken to the market for sale on day 1

= 60 – (4 + 6)= 50.

The minimum number of eggs that are left unsold each day must be 5, as the number of eggs that are rotten and broken among them needs to be an integer. It can be at max 10, since number of egg left unsold on any day is less than 20% of the number of eggs laid on each day, i.e. 20% of 60 = 12.

So, the number of eggs that are sold on day 1 ranges from (50 – 10 = 40) to (54 – 5 = 49), (both inclusive).

On the next day again 60 eggs are laid, so from the above logic the range of number of eggs sold should again come out to be from 42 to 49 (both inclusive), but there are eggs that remain unsold at the end of the previous day.

Minimum possible number of eggs that are left over from the previous day and are taken along with the eggs laid on a day to the market for sale

= 5 – (40% of 5) – (2% of 5) = 2.

Maximum possible number of eggs that are left over from the previous day and are taken along with the eggs laid on a day to the market for sale

= 10 – (40% of 10) – (20% of 10) = 4.

So, the range of number of eggs that are sold on day 2 varies from (40 + 2 = 42) to (49 + 4 = 53) (both inclusive) and this holds true for day 3, day 4 and day 5 also.

	Eggs Laid	Rotten	Broken	Sold	Unsold
Day 1	60	2 - 4	4 - 6	40 - 49	5 or 10
Day 2	60	2 - 4	4 - 6	42 - 53	5 or 10
Day 3	60	2 - 4	4 - 6	42 - 53	5 or 10
Day 4	60	2 - 4	4 - 6	42 - 53	5 or 10
Day 5	60	2 - 4	4 - 6	42 - 53	5 or 10

25. c The minimum possible number of eggs that were sold on day 4 can be 42.

42 eggs are sold in the scenorio when 10 eggs are left unsold.

So, the next day i.e. day 5, the minimum number of eggs that were sold can be calculated as

Out of the 60 eggs that were laid – maximum rotten and broken eggs can be removed which are 4 and 6 respectively. Thus, left with 50 eggs. Also, from the 10 eggs of the previous day maximum rotten and broken can be removed which are 4 and 2 respectively, thus left with 4 eggs only. So, out of the total 54 eggs, a maximum of only 10 eggs can be left unsold. Therefore, the minimum eggs that were sold on day 5 were 54 – 10 = 44.

Hence, aggregate sum of eggs is 42 + 44 = 86.

Note: Most of the students will make a mistake of considering 42 eggs for both the days but this is not possible on any two consecutive days simultaneously.

26. b Number of eggs that got rotten and broken is maximum possible.

So, assume that on each day 10 eggs remain unsold at the end of each day.

So, out of these 10 eggs that remain unsold at the end of each day, the number of eggs that get rotten and broken on the next day is 4 and 2 respectively.

The maximum number of eggs that got rotten and broken from among the eggs laid each day is 4 and 6 respectively.

So, the number of eggs that got broken across all the five days

= 6 × 5 + 2 × 4 = 38.

Number of eggs that got rotten across all the five days

= 4 × 5 + 4 × 4 = 36.

Required difference = 38 – 36 = 2.

27. a The maximum number of eggs that were left unsold at the end of the fifth day can be 10.

28. a The maximum number of eggs that were sold on day 1 can be 49, in a scenario when 5 eggs were left unsold. In this case, the maximum number of eggs that were sold on day 2 can be calculated as 60(laid on day 2) – 2 (minimum rotten out of 60) – 4 (minimum broken out of 60) + 5 (previous days unsold eggs) – 2(rotten out of 5) – 1(broken out of 5) – 5(minimum unsold) = 51

Since, on day 2 also, 5 eggs were left unsold the maximum number eggs sold on day 3 will again be 51. The same holds true for day 4 and day 5.

So, the maximum number of eggs that can be sold in the entire week can be 49 + 51 × 4 = 253.

Note: Most of the students will make a mistake of considering 53 eggs for any two consecutive days but this is not possible on any two consecutive days simultaneously.

For questions 29 to 32 :

Name	Wife	Place	Game
Gurvinder		Jaipur / Guntur	TT / Cricket
Surinder		Guntur / Jaipur	Cricket / TT
Mahinder	Sita	Ambala	Snooker
Bhupinder		Noida	Badminton
Harinder	Monica	Kapurthala	Volleyball
Joginder	Rama	Jammu	Football

29. b The man from Kapurthala is Harinder and is married to Monica.

30. b Mahinder plays Snooker and belongs to Ambala.

31. a Badminton is being played by Bhupinder.

32. d The wife of Surinder can be one of Dolly, Trisna or Kaveri, which cannot be determined.

For questions 33 to 36 :

According to the given conditions, the minimum score that a winning team can score in the first four sets is 25 and in the last set is 15.

From statements (iii) and (vi), it can be inferred that in one of the sets the score of Brazil and Russia were 12 and 25 respectively.

From statements (ii), (v) and (vi), there are two possibilities-

Case I: Russia scored the maximum score 30. In this case Russia cannot win any other set as it can win only two sets. In this scenario, Russia must lose a set with a score of either 25 or 30. With a score of 30 it cannot lose a set as 30 is the maximum score, thus it must have lost a set with a score of 25. In that case, Brazil must have scored 27.

Also, Russia scored 23 points in one of sets, which means Brazil must have scored 25 points (as Russia lost the set), Now, to make the total of Russia as 116, if must have scored 13 and to make the total of Brazil as 108, it must have scored 16 in the final set, which is not possible. Brazil can reach a score of 16 only when Russia scored 14 otherwise Brazil must have won at the score of 15. Thus, it can be said that Russia did not score 30 points.

	Brazil	Russia	
Set 1	12	25	
Set 2	28	30	
Set 3	27	25	
Set 4	25	23	
Set 5	16	13	(Not possible)
Total Score	108	116	

Case II: Brazil scored 30 points and Russia scored 28. Also, in one of the sets Russia scored 23 points. Now, there are again two possibilities - either Russia won the set as Brazil scored 21 points them it must be the fifth set or Russia lost the set as Brazil scored 25 points and it is one of the first four sets. If the first possibility is considered, in that case. Brazil must win the remaining two sets as Russia has already won two sets (12-25, 21-23) and to win two sets the minimum score of Brazil must be 25 in each set. But in this case, the total score of Brazil in all the five sets will become more than 108. Hence, Russia lost the set with the score of 23.

So the scores of three sets are tabulated below-

	Brazil	Russia
Set 1	12	25
Set 2	30	28
Set 3	25	23
Set 4		
Set 5		
Total Score	108	116

Now, the sum of the scores of Russia in the remaining two sets is 116 – (25 + 28 + 23) = 40.

Also, from statement (ii) one of the scores of the remaining two sets of Russia must be one of 23 or 25 or 28.

So, the possible scores of Russia in the remaining two sets are (23, 17), (25, 15) and (28, 12). Also, the sum of the scores of Brazil in the remaining two sets must be 108 – (12 + 30 + 25) = 41. The various possibilities are-

	Brazil	Russia
Set 4	23	25
Set 5 (NP)	18	15

	Brazil	Russia
Set 4	27	25
Set 5 (NP)	14	15

	Brazil	Russia
Set 4	21	23
Set 5 (NP)	20	17

	Brazil	Russia
Set 4	25	23
Set 5 (NP)	16	17

	Brazil	Russia
Set 4	30	28
Set 5 (NP)	11	12

	Brazil	Russia
Set 4	26	28
Set 5	15	12

* NP - Not Possible

33. c The maximum difference by which a team won a set is 13 points.

34. a The score of Russia in the fifth set is 12 points.

35. b In three of the sets the score of Brazil was an even number.

36. c The required common score was 25.

2 CHAPTER Data Interpretation

LOGIC BASED DI

1995

Directions for Questions 1 to 4: *Answer the questions based on the following information.*

Four sisters — Suvarna, Tara, Uma and Vibha are playing a game such that the loser doubles the money of each of the other players from her share. They played four games and each sister lost one game in alphabetical order. At the end of fourth game, each sister had Rs.32.

1. How many rupees did Suvarna start with?
   (a) Rs.60 (b) Rs.34
   (c) Rs.66 (d) Rs.28
2. Who started with the lowest amount?
   (a) Suvarna (b) Tara
   (c) Uma (d) Vibha
3. Who started with the highest amount?
   (a) Suvarna (b) Tara
   (c) Uma (d) Vibha
4. What was the amount with Uma at the end of the second round?
   (a) 36 (b) 72
   (c) 16 (d) None of these

2000

Directions for Questions 5 and 6: *Answer the questions based on the following information*

A, B and C are three numbers. Let

@ (A, B) = Average of A and B,

/ (A, B) = Product of A and B, and

× (A, B) = The result of dividing A by B.

5. The sum of A and B is given by
   (a) / (@ (A, B), 2)
   (b) × (@ (A, B), 2)
   (c) @ (/ A, B), 2)
   (d) @ (× (A, B), 2)
6. Average of A, B and C is given by
   (a) @ (/ (@ (/ (B, A), 2), C), 3)
   (b) × (@ (/ (@ (B, A), 3), C), 2)
   (c) / (×(× (@ (B, A), 2), C), 3)
   (d) / (× (@ (/ (@ (B, A) 2), C), 3), 2)

2002

7. Two boys are playing on a ground. Both the boys are less than 10 years old. Age of the younger boy is equal to the cube root of the product of the age of the two boys. If we place the digit representing the age of the younger boy to the left of the digit representing the age of the elder boy, we get the age of father of the younger boy. Similarly, if we place the digit representing the age of the elder boy to the left of the digit representing the age of the younger boy and divide the figure by 2, we get the age of mother of the younger boy. The mother of the younger boy is younger to his father by 3 years. Then, what is the age of the younger boy?
   (a) 3 (b) 4
   (c) 2 (d) None of these

Directions for Questions 8 to 11: *Answer the questions based on the information given below.*

A country has the following types of traffic signals.

3 red lights = stop

2 red lights = turn left

1 red light = turn right

3 green lights = go at 100 km/hr speed

2 green lights = go at 40 km/hr speed

1 green light = go at 20 km/hr speed

A motorist starts at a point on a road and follows all traffic signals. His car is heading towards the north. He encounters the following signals (the time mentioned in each case below is applicable after crossing the previous signal).

Starting point - 1 green light

After half an hour, 1st signal - 2 red and 2 green lights

After 15 min, 2nd signal - 1 red light

After half an hour, 3rd signal - 1 red and 3 green lights

After 24 min, 4th signal - 2 red and 2 green lights

After 15 min, 5th signal - 3 red lights

8. The total distance travelled by the motorist from the starting point till the last signal is
   (a) 90 km (b) 100 km
   (c) 120 km (d) None of these

9. What is the position (radial distance) of the motorist when he reaches the last signal?

(a) 45 km directly north of the starting point

(b) 30 km directly to the east of the starting point

(c) 50 km away to the north-east of the starting point

(d) 45 km away to the north-west of the starting point

10. After the starting point, if the 1st signal were 1 red and 2 green lights, what would be the final position of the motorist?

(a) 30 km to the west and 20 km to the south

(b) 30 km to the west and 40 km to the north

(c) 50 km to the east and 40 km to the north

(d) Directly 30 km to the east

11. If at the starting point, the car was heading towards south, what would be the final position of the motorist?

(a) 30 km to the east and 40 km to the south

(b) 50 km to the east and 40 km to the south

(c) 30 km to the west and 40 km to the south

(d) 50 km to the west and 20 km to the north

Directions for Questions 12 to 17: *Answer these questions based on the tables given below:*

There are 6 refineries, 7 depots and 9 districts. The refineries are BB, BC, BD, BE, BF and BG. The depots are AA, AB, AC, AD, AE, AF and AG. The districts are AAA, AAB, AAC, AAD, AAE, AAF, AAG, AAH, and AAI. Table A gives the cost of transporting one unit from refinery to depot. Table B gives the cost of transporting one unit from depot to a district.

Table A

	BB	BC	BD	BE	BF	BG
AA	928.2	537.2	567.8	589.9	589.9	800.1
AB	311.1	596.7	885.7	759.9	759.9	793.9
AC	451.1	0	320.1	780.1	720.7	1000.1
AD	371.1	150.1	350.1	750.1	650.4	980.1
AE	1137.3	314.5	0	1157.7	1157.7	1023.4
AF	617.1	516.8	756.5	1065.9	1065.9	406.3
AG	644.3	299.2	537.2	1093.1	1093.1	623.9

Table B

	AA	AB	AC	AD	AE	AF	AG
AAA	562.7	843.2	314.5	889.1	0	754.8	537.2
AAB	532.7	803.2	284.5	790.5	95.2	659.6	442
AAC	500.7	780.2	0	457.3	205.7	549.1	331.5
AAD	232.9	362.1	286.2	275.4	523.6	525.3	673.2
AAE	345.1	268.6	316.2	163.2	555.9	413.1	227.8
AAF	450.1	644.3	346.2	372.3	933.3	402.9	379.1
AAG	654.5	0	596.7	222.7	885.7	387.6	348.5
AAH	804.1	149.6	627.2	360.4	1035.3	537.2	498.1
AAI	646	255	433.5	137.7	698.7	112.2	161.5

12. What is the least cost of sending one unit from any refinery to any district?

(a) 95.2 (b) 0

(c) 205.7 (d) 284.5

13. What is the least cost of sending one unit from any refinery to the district AAB?

(a) 0 (b) 284.5

(c) 95.2 (d) None of these

14. What is the least cost of sending one unit from refinery BB to any district?

(a) 284.5 (b) 311.1

(c) 451.1 (d) None of these

15. What is the least cost of sending petrol from refinery BB to district AAA?

(a) 765.6 (b) 1137.3

(c) 1154.3 (d) None of these

16. How many possible ways are there for sending petrol from any refinery to any district?

(a) 63 (b) 42

(c) 54 (d) 378

17. The largest cost of sending petrol from any refinery to any district is

(a) 2172.6 (b) 2193.0

(c) 2091.0 (d) None of these

Directions for Questions 18 to 20: *Answer the questions based on the table given below.*

The table below gives information about four different crops, their different quality categories and the regions where they are cultivated. Based on the information given in the table answer the questions below.

Type of Crop	Quality	Region
Crop - 1	High	R1, R2, R3, R4, R5
	Medium	R6, R7, R8
	Low	R9, R10, R11
Crop - 2	High	R5, R8, R12
	Medium	R9, R13
	Low	R6, R7, R8
Crop - 3	High	R2, R6, R7, R13
	Medium	R3, R9, R11
	Low	R1, R4
Crop - 4	High	R3, R10, R11
	Medium	R1, R2, R4
	Low	R5, R9

18. How many regions produce medium qualities of Crop-1 or Crop-2 and also produce low quality of Crop-3 or Crop-4?
(a) Zero (b) One
(c) Two (d) Three

19. Which of the following statements is true?
(a) All medium quality Crop-2 producing regions are also high quality Crop-3 producing regions.
(b) All high quality Crop-1 producing regions are also medium and low Crop-4 producing regions.
(c) There are exactly four Crop-3 producing regions, which also produce Crop-4 but not Crop-2.
(d) Some Crop-3 producing regions produce Crop-1, but not high quality Crop-2.

20. How many low quality Crop-1 producing regions are either high quality Crop-4 producing regions or medium quality Crop-3 producing regions?
(a) One (b) Two
(c) Three (d) Zero

Direction for Question 21: *The question is followed by two statements, A and B. Answer the question using the following instructions.*

Choose (a) if the question can be answered by one of the statements alone but not by the other.
Choose (b) if the question can be answered by using either statement alone.
Choose (c) if the question can be answered by using both the statements together, but cannot be answered by using either statement alone.
Choose (d) if the question cannot be answered even by using both statements together.

21. In a hockey match, the Indian team was behind by 2 goals with 5 min remaining. Did they win the match?
A. Deepak Thakur, the Indian striker, scored 3 goals in the last 5 min of the match.
B. Korea scored a total of 3 goals in the match.

2003 (R)

Directions for Questions 22 and 23: *Answer the questions on the basis of the following information.*

Shown below is the layout of major streets in a city.

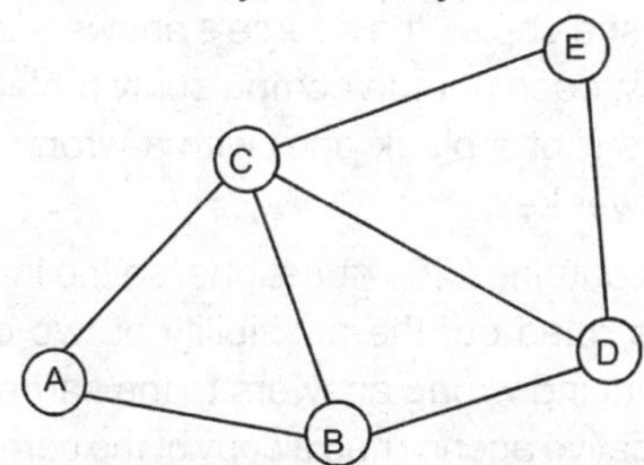

Two days (Thursday and Friday) are left for campaigning before a major election, and the city administration has received requests from five political parties for taking out their processions along the following routes.

Congress	: A-C-D-E	BJP	: A-B-D-E
SP	: A-B-C-E	BSP	: B-C-E
CPM	: A-C-D		

Street B-D cannot be used for a political procession on Thursday due to a religious procession. The district administration has a policy of not allowing more than one procession to pass along the same street on the same day. However, the administration must allow all parties to take out their procession during these two days.

22. Congress procession can be allowed
(a) only on Thursday
(b) only on Friday
(c) on either day
(d) only if the religious procession is cancelled

23. Which of the following is NOT true?
(a) Congress and SP can take out their processions on the same day.
(b) The CPM procession cannot be allowed on Thursday.
(c) The BJP procession can only take place on Friday.
(d) Congress and BSP can take out their processions on the same day.

Directions for Questions 24 to 28: *Answer the questions on the basis of the following information.*

Recently, the answers of a test held nationwide were leaked to a group of unscrupulous people. The investigative agency has arrested the mastermind and nine other people A, B, C, D, E, F, G, H and I in this matter. Interrogating them, the following facts have been obtained regarding their operation. Initially the mastermind obtains the correct answer-key. All the others create their answer-key in the following manner. They obtain the answer-key from one or two people who already possess the same. These people are called his/her 'sources'. If the person has two sources, then he/she compares the answer-keys obtained from both sources. If the key to a question from both sources is identical, it is copied, otherwise it is left blank. If the person has only one source, he/she copies the source's answers into his/her copy. Finally, each person compulsorily replaces one of the answers (not a blank one) with a wrong answer in his/her answer key.

The paper contained 200 questions; so the investigative agency has ruled out the possibility of two or more of them introducing wrong answers to the same question. The investigative agency has a copy of the correct answer key and has tabulated the following data. These data represent question numbers.

Name	Wrong Answer(s)	Blank Answer(s)
A	46	—
B	96	46, 90, 25
C	27, 56	17, 46, 90
D	17	—
E	46, 90	—
F	14, 46	92, 90
G	25	—
H	46, 92	—
I	27	17, 46, 90

24. Which one among the following must have two sources?

(a) A

(b) B

(c) C

(d) D

25. How many people (excluding the mastermind) needed to make answer-keys before C could make his answer-key?

(a) 2 (b) 3

(c) 4 (d) 5

26. Both G and H were sources to

(a) F (b) B

(c) I (d) None of the nine

27. Which of the following statements is true?

(a) C introduced the wrong answer to question 27.

(b) E introduced the wrong answer to question 46.

(c) F introduced the wrong answer to question 14.

(d) H introduced the wrong answer to question 46.

28. Which of the following two groups of people had identical sources?

I. A, D and G

II. E and H

(a) Only I

(b) Only II

(c) Neither I nor II

(d) Both I and II

2003 (L)

Directions for Questions 29 and 30: *Answer the questions on the basis of the information given below.*

Some children were taking free throws at the basketball court in school during lunch break. Below are some facts about how many baskets these children shot.

i. Ganesh shot 8 baskets less than Ashish.

ii. Dhanraj and Ramesh together shot 37 baskets.

iii. Jugraj shot 8 baskets more than Dhanraj.

iv. Ashish shot 5 baskets more than Dhanraj.

v. Ashish and Ganesh together shot 40 baskets.

29. Which of the following statements is true?

(a) Ramesh shot 18 baskets and Dhanraj shot 19 baskets.

(b) Ganesh shot 24 baskets and Ashish shot 16 baskets.

(c) Jugraj shot 19 baskets and Dhanraj shot 27 baskets.

(d) Dhanraj shot 11 baskets and Ashish shot 16 baskets.

30. Which of the following statements is true?

(a) Dhanraj and Jugraj together shot 46 baskets.

(b) Ganesh shot 18 baskets and Ramesh shot 21 baskets.

(c) Dhanraj shot 3 more baskets than Ramesh.

(d) Ramesh and Jugraj together shot 29 baskets.

Directions for Questions 31 to 33: *Answer the questions on the basis of the information given below.*

Five women decided to go shopping to M.G. Road, Bangalore. They arrived at the designated meeting place in the following order: 1. Archana, 2. Chellamma, 3. Dhenuka, 4. Helen, and 5. Shahnaz. Each woman spent at least Rs. 1000. Below are some additional facts about how much they spent during their shopping spree.

i. The woman who spent Rs.2234 arrived before the lady who spent Rs.1193.

ii. One woman spent Rs.1340 and she was not Dhenuka.

iii. One woman spent Rs.1378 more than Chellamma.

iv. One woman spent Rs.2517 and she was not Archana.

v. Helen spent more than Dhenuka.

vi. Shahnaz spent the largest amount and Chellamma the smallest.

31. What was the amount spent by Helen?

(a) Rs.1193 (b) Rs.1340

(c) Rs.2234 (d) Rs.2517

32. Which of the following amounts was spent by one of them?

(a) Rs. 1139 (b) Rs. 1378

(c) Rs. 2571 (d) Rs. 2718

33. The woman who spent Rs. 1193 is

(a) Archana (b) Chellamma

(c) Dhenuka (d) Helen

Directions for Questions 34 to 36: *Answer the questions on the basis of the information given below.*

Five friends meet every morning at Sree Sagar restaurant for an idli-vada breakfast. Each consumes a different number of idlis and vadas. The number of idlis consumed are 1, 4, 5, 6, and 8, while the number of vadas consumed are 0, 1, 2, 4, and 6. Below are some more facts about who eats what and how much.

i. The number of vadas eaten by Ignesh is three times the number of vadas consumed by the person who eats four idlis.

ii. Three persons, including the one who eats four vadas eat without chutney.

iii. Sandeep does not take any chutney.

iv. The one who eats one idli a day does not eat any vadas or chutney. Further, he is not Mukesh.

v. Daljit eats idli with chutney and also eats vada.

vi. Mukesh, who does not take chutney, eats half as many vadas as the person who eats twice as many idlis as he does.

vii. Bimal eats two more idlis than Ignesh, but Ignesh eats two more vadas than Bimal.

34. Which one of the following statements is true?

(a) Daljit eats 5 idlis (b) Ignesh eats 8 idlis

(c) Bimal eats 1 idli. (d) Bimal eats 6 idlis.

35. Which of the following statements is true?

(a) Sandeep eats 2 vadas.

(b) Mukesh eats 4 vadas.

(c) Ignesh eats 6 vadas.

(d) Bimal eats 2 vadas.

36. Which of the following statements is true?

(a) Mukesh eats 8 idlis and 4 vadas but no chutney.

(b) The person who eats 5 idlis and 1 vada does not take chutney.

(c) The person who eats equal number of vadas and idlis also takes chutney.

(d) The person who eats 4 idlis and 2 vadas also takes chutney.

Direction for question 37 : *The question has two statements: A and B.*

Choose (a) if the question can be answered by one of the statements alone but not by the other.

Choose (b) if the question can be answered by using either statement alone.

Choose (c) if the question can be answered by using both the statements together but cannot be answered using either statement alone.

Choose (d) if the question cannot be answered even by using both the statements A and B.

37. A game consists of tossing a coin successively. There is an entry fee of Rs. 10 and an additional fee of Re. 1 for each toss of coin. The game is considered to have ended normally when the coin turns heads on two consecutive throws. In this case the player is paid Rs. 100. Alternatively, the player can choose to terminate the game prematurely after any of the tosses. Ram has incurred a loss of Rs. 50 by playing this game. How many times did he toss the coin?

A. The game ended normally.

B. The total number of tails obtained in the game was 138.

2004

Directions for Questions 38 to 41: *Answer the questions on the basis of the information given below.*

The Dean's office recently scanned student results into the central computer system. When their character reading software cannot read something, it leaves the space blank. The scanner output reads as follows:

Name	Finance	Marketing	Statistics	Strategy	Operations	GPA
Aparna		B	F			1.4
Bikas	D	D	F	F		
Chandra		D	A	F	F	2.4
Deepak	A	B		D	D	3.2
Fazal	D	F	B		D	2.4
Gowri	C	C	A		B	3.8
Hari		B	A		D	2.8
Ismet			B		A	
Jagdeep	A	A	B		C	3.8
Kunal	F		A	F	F	1.8
Leena	B	A		B	F	3.2
Manab			A	B	B	
Nisha	A	D	B	A	F	3.6
Osman	C		B	B	A	4.6
Preeti	F	D		D		3.2
Rahul	A	C	A		F	4.2
Sameer		C	F	B		
Tara	B					2.4
Utkarsh			F	C	A	3
Vipul	A		C	C	F	2.4

In the grading system, A, B, C, D, and F grades fetch 6, 4, 3, 2, and 0 grade points respectively. The Grade Point Average (GPA) is the arithmetic mean of the grade points obtained in the five subjects. For example Nisha's GPA is (6 + 2 + 4 + 6 + 0) / 5 = 3.6. Some additional facts are also known about the students' grades. These are

(a) Vipul obtained the same grade in Marketing as Aparna obtained in Finance and Strategy.

(b) Fazal obtained the same grade in Strategy as Utkarsh did in Marketing.

(c) Tara received the same grade in exactly three courses.

38. What grade did Preeti obtain in Statistics?

(a) A (b) B
(c) C (d) D

39. In Operations, Tara could have received the same grade as

(a) Ismet (b) Hari
(c) Jagdeep (d) Manab

40. In Strategy, Gowri's grade point was higher than that obtained by

(a) Fazal (b) Hari
(c) Nisha (d) Rahul

41. What grade did Utkarsh obtain in Finance?

(a) B (b) C
(c) D (d) F

Directions for Questions 42 to 45: *Answer the questions on the basis of the information given below.*

Prof. Singh has been tracking the number of visitors to his homepage. His service provider has provided him with the following data on the country of origin of the visitors and the university they belong to:

Number of visitors

	DAY		
COUNTRY	1	2	3
Canada	2	0	0
Netherlands	1	1	0
India	1	2	0
UK	2	0	2
USA	1	0	1

	Number of visitors		
	DAY		
UNIVERSITY	1	2	3
University 1	1	0	0
University 2	2	0	0
University 3	0	1	0
University 4	0	0	2
University 5	1	0	0
University 6	1	0	1
University 7	2	0	0
University 8	0	2	0

42. To which country does University 5 belong?

(a) India or Netherlands but not USA

(b) India or USA but not Netherlands

(c) Netherlands or USA but not India

(d) India or USA but not UK

43. University 1 can belong to

(a) UK

(b) Canada

(c) Netherlands

(d) USA

44. Which among the listed countries can possibly host three of the eight listed universities?

(a) None

(b) Only UK

(c) Only India

(d) Both India and UK

45. Visitors from how many universities from UK visited Prof. Singh's homepage in the three days?

(a) 1 (b) 2

(c) 3 (d) 4

Directions for Questions 46 to 49: *Answer the questions on the basis of the information given below.*

A study was conduced to ascertain the relative importance that employees in five different countries assigned to five different traits in their Chief Executive Officers. The traits were compassion (C), decisiveness (D), negotiation skills (N), public visibility (P), and vision (V). The level of dissimilarity between two countries is the maximum difference in the ranks allotted by the two countries to any of the five traits. The following table indicates the rank order of the five traits for each country.

	Country				
Rank	India	China	Japan	Malaysia	Thailand
1	C	N	D	V	V
2	P	C	N	D	C
3	N	P	C	P	N
4	V	D	V	C	P
5	D	V	P	N	D

46. Which of the following pairs of countries are most dissimilar?

(a) China and Japan

(b) India and China

(c) Malaysia and Japan

(d) Thailand and Japan

47. Which of the following countries is least dissimilar to India?

(a) China

(b) Japan

(c) Malaysia

(d) Thailand

48. Which amongst the following countries is most dissimilar to India?

(a) China

(b) Japan

(c) Malaysia

(d) Thailand

49. Three of the following four pairs of countries have identical levels of dissimilarity. Which pair is the odd one out?

(a) Malaysia and China

(b) China and Thailand

(c) Thailand and Japan

(d) Japan and Malaysia

2005

Directions for Questions 50 to 52: *Answer the questions on the basis of the information given below:*

The table below reports the gender, designation and age-group of the employees in an organization. It also provides information on their commitment to projects coming up in the months of January (Jan), February (Feb), March (Mar) and April (Apr), as well as their interest in attending workshops on: Business Opportunities (BO), Communication Skills (CS), and E-Governance (EG).

Sl. No.	Name	Gender	Designation	Age group	Committed to projects during	Interested in workshop on
1	Anshul	M	Mgr	Y	Jan, Mar	CS, EG
2	Bushkant	M	Dir	I	Feb, Mar	BO, EG
3	Charu	F	Mgr	I	Jan, Feb	BO, CS
4	Dinesh	M	Exe	O	Jan, Apr	BO, CS, EG
5	Eashwaran	N	Dir	O	Feb, Apr	BO
6	Fatima	F	Mgr	Y	Jan, Mar	BO, CS
7	Gayatri	F	Exe	Y	Feb, Mar	EG
8	Hari	M	Mgr	I	Feb, Mar	BO, CS, EG
9	Indira	F	Dir	O	Feb, Apr	BO, EG
10	John	M	Dir	Y	Jan, Mar	BO
11	Kalindi	F	Exe	I	Jan, Apr	BO, CS, EG
12	Lavanya	F	Mgr	O	Feb, Apr	CS, EG
13	Mandeep	M	Mgr	O	Mar, Apr	BO, EG
14	Nandlal	M	Dir	I	Jan, Feb	BO, EG
15	Parul	F	Exe	Y	Feb, Apr	CS, EG
16	Rahul	M	Mgr	Y	Mar, Apr	CS, EG
17	Sunita	F	Dir	Y	Jan, Feb	BO, EG
18	Urvashi	F	Exe	I	Feb, Mar	EG
19	Yamini	F	Mgr	O	Mar, Apr	CS, EG
20	Zeena	F	Exe	Y	Jan, Mar	BO, CS, EG

M = Male, F = Female; Exe = Executive, Mgr = Manager, Dir = Director;

Y = Young, I = In between, O = Old

For each workshop, exactly four employees are to be sent, of which at least two should be Females and at least one should be Young. No employee can be sent to a workshop in which he she is not interested in. An employee cannot attend the workshop on

- Communication Skills, if he/she is committed to internal projects in the month of January.
- Business Opportunities, if he/she is committed to internal projects in the month of February.
- E-governance, if he/she is committed to internal projects in the month of March.

50. Assuming that Parul and Hari are attending the workshop on Communication Skills (CS), then which of the following employees can possibly attend the CS workshop?

(a) Rahul and Yamini (b) Dinesh and Lavanya

(c) Anshul and Yamini (d) Fatima and Zeena

51. How many Executives (Exe) cannot attend more than one workshop?

(a) 2 (b) 3

(c) 15 (d) 16

52. Which set of employees cannot attend any of the workshops?

(a) Anshul, Charu, Eashwaran and Lavanya

(b) Anshul, Bushkant, Gayatri, and Urvashi

(c) Charu, Urvashi, Bushkant and Mandeep

(d) Anshul, Gayatri, Eashwaran and Mandeep

Directions for Questions 53 to 56: *Answer the questions on the basis of the information given below:*

In the table below is the listing of players, seeded from highest (#1) to lowest (#32), who are due to play in an Association of Tennis Players (ATP) tournament for women. This tournament has four knockout rounds before the final, i.e., first round, second round, quarterfinals, and semi-finals. In the first round, the highest seeded player plays the lowest seeded player (seed #32) which is designated match No. 1 of first round; the 2nd seeded player plays the 31st seeded player which is designated match No. 2 of the first round, and so on. Thus, for instance, match No. 16 of first round is to be played between 16th seeded player and the 17th seeded player. In the second round, the winner of match No. 1 of first round plays the winner of match No. 16 of first round and is designated match No. 1 of second round. Similarly, the winner of match No. 2 of first round plays the winner of match No. 15 of first round, and is designated match No. 2 of second round. Thus, for instance, match No. 8 of the second round is to be played between the winner of match No. 8 of first round and the winner of match No. 9 of first round. The same pattern is followed for later rounds as well.

Seed#	Name of Player	Seed#	Name of Player	Seed#	Name of Player
1	Maria Sharapova	12	Mary Pierce	23	Silvia Farina Elia
2	Lindsay Davenport	13	Anastasia Myskina	24	Tatiana Golovin
3	Amelie Mauresmo	14	Alicia Molik	25	Shinobu Asagoe
4	Kim Clijsters	15	Nathalie Dechy	26	Francesca Schiavone
5	Svetlana Kuznetsova	16	Elena Bovina	27	Nicole Vaidisova
6	Elena Dementieva	17	Jelena Jankovic	28	Gisela Dulko
7	Justine Henin	18	Ana Ivanovic	29	Flavia Pennetta
8	Serena Williams	19	Vera Zvonareva	30	Anna Chakvetadze
9	Nadia Petrova	20	Elena Likhovtseva	31	Al Sugiyama
10	Venus Williams	21	Daniela Hantuchova	32	Anna-lena Groenefeld
11	Patty Schnyder	22	Dinara Safina		

53. If there are no upsets (a lower seeded player beating a higher seeded player) in the first round, and only match Nos. 6, 7, and 8 of the second round result in upsets, then who would meet Lindsay Davenport in quarter finals, in case Davenport reaches quarter finals?

(a) Justine Henin (b) Nadia Petrova

(c) Patty Schnyder (d) Venus Williams

54. If Elena Dementieva and Serena Williams lose in the second round, while Justine Henin and Nadia Petrova make it to the semi-finals, then who would play Maria Sharapova in the quarterfinals, in the event Sharapova reaches quarterfinals?

(a) Dinara Safina (b) Justine Henin

(c) Nadia Petrova (d) Patty Schnyder

55. If, in the first round, all even numbered matches (and none of the odd numbered ones) result in upsets, and there are no upsets in the second round, then who could be the lowest seeded player facing Maria Sharapova in semi-finals?

(a) Anastasia Myskina (b) Flavia Pennetta

(c) Nadia Petrova (d) Svetlana Kuznetsova

56. If the top eight seeds make it to the quarterfinals, then who, amongst the players listed below, would definitely not play against Maria Sharapova in the final, in case Sharapova reaches the final?

(a) Amelie Mauresmo

(b) Elena Dementieva

(c) Kim Clijsters

(d) Lindsay Davenport

Directions for Questions 57 to 60: *Answer the questions on the basis of the information given below:*

The table below presents the revenue (in million rupees) of four firms in three states. These firms, Honest Ltd., Aggressive Ltd., Truthful Ltd. and Profitable Ltd. are disguised in the table as A, B, C and D, in no particular order.

States	Firm A	Firm B	Firm C	Firm D
UP	49	82	80	55
Bihar	69	72	70	65
MP	72	63	72	65

Further, it is known that:

- In the state of MP, Truthful Ltd. has the highest market share.
- Aggressive Ltd.'s aggregate revenue differs from Honest Ltd.'s by Rs. 5 million.

57. What can be said regarding the following two statements?

Statement 1: Profitable Ltd. has the lowest share in MP market.

Statement 2: Honest Ltd.'s total revenue is more than Profitable Ltd.

(a) If Statement 1 is true then Statement 2 is necessarily true.

(b) If Statement 1 is true then Statement 2 is necessarily false.

(c) Both Statement 1 and Statement 2 are true.

(d) Neither Statement 1 nor Statement 2 is true.

58. What can be said regarding the following two statements?

Statement 1: Aggressive Ltd.'s lowest revenues are from MP.

Statement 2: Honest Ltd.'s lowest revenues are from Bihar.

(a) If Statement 2 is true then Statement 1 is necessarily false.
(b) If Statement 1 is false then Statement 2 is necessarily true.
(c) If Statement 1 is true then Statement 2 is necessarily true
(d) None of the above.

59. What can be said regarding the following two statements?

Statement 1: Honest Ltd. has the highest share in the UP market.

Statement 2: Aggressive Ltd. has the highest share in the Bihar market.

(a) Both statements could be true.
(b) At least one of the statements must be true.
(c) At most one of the statements is true.
(d) None of the above.

60. If Profitable Ltd.'s lowest revenue is from UP, then which of the following is true?

(a) Truthful Ltd.'s lowest revenues are from MP.
(b) Truthful Ltd.'s lowest revenues are from Bihar.
(c) Truthful Ltd.'s lowest revenues are from UP.
(d) No definite conclusion is possible.

2006

Directions for Questions 61 to 65: *Answer the questions on the basis of the information given below:*

A significant amount of traffic flows from point S to point T in the one-way street network shown below.

Points A, B, C, and D are junctions in the network, and the arrows mark the direction of traffic flow. The fuel cost in rupees for travelling along a street is indicated by the number adjacent to the arrow representing the street.

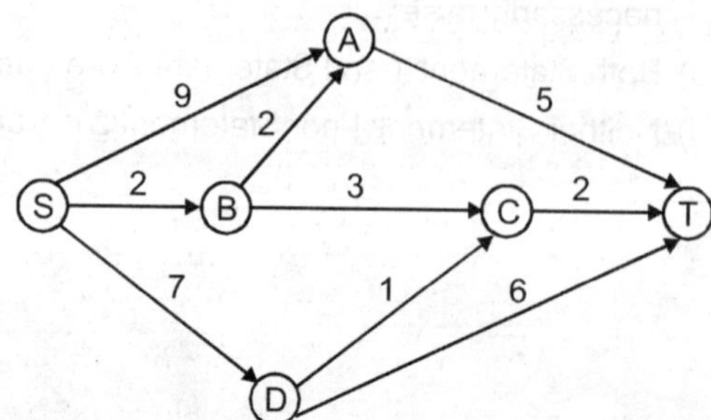

Motorists travelling from point S to point T would obviously take the route for which the total cost of travelling is the minimum. If two or more routes have the same least travel cost, then motorists are indifferent between them. Hence, the traffic gets evenly distributed among all the least cost routes.

The government can control the flow of traffic only by levying appropriate toll at each junction. For example, if a motorist takes the route S-A-T (using junction A alone), then the total cost of travel would be Rs 14 (i.e., Rs 9 + Rs 5) plus the toll charged at junction A.

61. If the government wants to ensure that no traffic flows on the street from D to T, while equal amount of traffic flows through junctions A and C, then a feasible set of toll charged (in rupees) at junctions A, B, C, and D respectively to achieve this goal is:

(a) 1,5,3,3
(b) 1,4,4,3
(c) 1,5,4,2
(d) 0,5,2,3
(e) 0,5,2,2

62. If the government wants to ensure that all motorists travelling from S to T pay the same amount (fuel costs and toll combined) regardless of the route they choose and the street from B to C is under repairs (and hence unusable), then a feasible set of toll charged (in rupees) at junctions A, B, C, and D respectively to achieve this goal is:

(a) 2,5,3,2
(b) 0,5,3, 1
(c) 1,5,3,2
(d) 2,3,5,1
(e) 1,3,5,1

63. If the government wants to ensure that the traffic at S gets evenly distributed along streets from S to A, from S to B, and from S to D, then a feasible set of toll charged (in rupees) at junctions A, B, C, and D respectively to achieve this goal is:

(a) 0,5,4,1
(b) 0,5,2,2
(c) 1,5,3,3
(d) 1,5,3,2
(e) 0,4,3,2

64. If the government wants to ensure that all routes from S to T get the same amount of traffic, then a feasible set of toll charged (in rupees) at junctions A, B, C, and D respectively to achieve this goal is:

(a) 0,5,2,2
(b) 0,5,4,1
(c) 1,5,3,3
(d) 1,5,3,2
(e) 1,5,4,2

65. The government wants to devise a toll policy such that the total cost to the commuters per trip is minimized. The policy should also ensure that not more than 70 per cent of the total traffic passes through junction B. The cost incurred by the commuter travelling from point S to point T under this policy will be:

(a) Rs. 7
(b) Rs. 9
(c) Rs. 10
(d) Rs. 13
(e) Rs. 14

2007

Directions for Questions 66 to 69: Answer the following questions based on the information given below:

A health-drink company's R&D department is trying to make various diet formulations, which can be used for certain specific purposes. It is considering a choice of 5 alternative ingredients (O, P, Q, R, and S), which can be used in different proportions in the formulations. The table below gives the composition of these ingredients. The cost per unit of each of these ingredients is O: 150, P: 50. Q: 200, R: 500, S: 100.

Ingredient	Composition			
	Carbohydrate%	Protein%	Fat%	Minerals%
O	50	30	10	10
P	80	20	0	0
Q	10	30	50	10
R	5	50	40	5
S	45	50	0	5

66. For a recuperating patient, the doctor recommended a diet containing 10% minerals and at least 30% protein. In how many different ways can we prepare this diet by mixing at least two ingredients?

(a) One
(b) Two
(c) Three
(d) Four
(e) None

67. Which among the following is the formulation having the lowest cost per unit for a diet having 10% fat and at least 30% protein? (The diet has to be formed by mixing two ingredients).

(a) P and Q
(b) P and S
(c) P and R
(d) Q and S
(e) R and S

68. In what proportion P, Q and S should be mixed to make a diet having at least 60% carbohydrate at the lowest cost per unit?

(a) 2 : 1 : 3
(b) 4 : 1 : 2
(c) 2 : 1 : 4
(d) 3 : 1 : 2
(e) 4 : 1 : 1

69. The company is planning to launch a balanced diet required for growth needs of adolescent children. This diet must contain at least 30% each of carbohydrate and protein, no more than 25% fat and at least 5% minerals. Which one of the following combinations of equally mixed ingredients is feasible?

(a) O and P
(b) R and S
(c) P and S
(d) Q and R
(e) O and S

Directions for Questions 70 to 74: *Answer the following questions based on the information given below:*

A low-cost airline company connects ten Indian cities, A to J. The table below gives the distance between a pair of airports and the corresponding price charged by the company. Travel is permitted only from a departure airport to an arrival airport. The customers do not travel by a route where they have to stop at more than two intermediate airports.

Sector No	Airport of Departure	Airport of Arrival	Distance between the Airports (km)	Price (Rs.)
1	A	B	560	670
2	A	C	790	1350
3	A	D	850	1250
4	A	E	1245	1600
5	A	F	1345	1700
6	A	G	1350	2450
7	A	H	1950	1850
8	B	C	1650	2000
9	B	H	1750	1900
10	B	I	2100	2450
11	B	J	2300	2275
12	C	D	460	450
13	C	F	410	430
14	C	G	910	1100
15	D	E	540	590
16	D	F	625	700
17	D	G	640	750
18	D	H	950	1250
19	D	J	1650	2450
20	E	F	1250	1700
21	E	G	970	1150
22	E	H	850	875
23	F	G	900	1050
24	F	I	875	950
25	F	J	970	1150
26	G	I	510	550
27	G	J	830	890
28	H	I	790	970
29	H	J	400	425
30	I	J	460	540

70. What is the lowest price, in rupees, a passenger has to pay for travelling by the shortest route from A to J?

(a) 2275

(b) 2850

(c) 2890

(d) 2930

(e) 3340

71. The company plans to introduce a direct flight between A and J. The market research results indicate that all its existing passengers travelling between A and J will use this direct flight if it is priced 5% below the minimum price that they pay at present. What should the company charge approximately, in rupees, for this direct flight?

(a) 1991 (b) 2161

(c) 2707 (d) 2745

(e) 2783

72. If the airports C, D and H are closed down owing to security reasons, then what would be the minimum price, in rupees, to be paid by a passenger travelling from A to J?

(a) 2275 (b) 2615
(c) 2850 (d) 2945
(e) 3190

73. If the prices include a margin of 10% over the total cost that the company incurs, then what is the minimum cost per kilometer that the company incurs in flying from A to J?

(a) 0.77 (b) 0.88
(c) 0.99 (d) 1.06
(e) 1.08

74. If the prices include a margin of 15% over the total cost that the company incurs, then which among the following is the distance to be covered in flying from A to J that minimizes the total cost per kilometer for the company?

(a) 2170 (b) 2180
(c) 2315 (d) 2350
(e) 2390

Direction for Questions 75: *The question is followed by two statements, A and B.*

Answer each question using the following instructions:

Mark (a) if the question can be answered by using the statement A alone but not by using the statement B alone.

Mark (b) if the question can be answered by using the statement B alone but not by using the statement A alone.

Mark (c) if the question can be answered by using either of the statements alone.

Mark (d) if the question can be answered by using both the statements together but not by either of the statements alone.

Mark (e) if the question cannot be answered on the basis of the two statements.

75. In a football match, at the half-time, Mahindra and Mahindra Club was trailing by three goals. Did it win the match?

A. In the second-half Mahindra and Mahindra Club scored four goals.

B. The opponent scored four goals in the match.

2008

Directions for Questions 76 and 77:

Five horses, Red, White, Grey, Black and Spotted participated in a race. As per the rules of the race, the persons betting on the winning horse get four times the bet amount and those betting on the horse that came in second get thrice the bet amount. Moreover, the bet amount is returned to those betting on the horse that came in third, and the rest lose the bet amount. Raju bets Rs. 3000, Rs. 2000 and Rs. 1000 on Red, White and Black horses respectively and ends up with no profit and no loss.

76. Which of the following cannot be true?

(a) At least two horses finished before Spotted
(b) Red finished last
(c) There were three horses between Black and Spotted
(d) There were three horses between White and Red
(e) Grey came in second

77. Suppose, in addition, it is known that Grey came in fourth. Then which of the following cannot be true?

(a) Spotted came in first
(b) Red finished last
(c) White came in second
(d) Black came in second
(e) There was one horse between Black and White

Directions for Questions 78 to 80: *Answer the following questions based on the information given below:*

For admission to various affiliated colleges, a university conducts a written test with four different sections, each with a maximum of 50 marks. The following table gives the aggregate as well as the sectional cut-off marks fixed by six different colleges affiliated to the university. A student will get admission only if he/she gets marks greater than or equal to the cut-off marks in each of the sections and his/her aggregate marks are at least equal to the aggregate cut-off marks as specified by the college.

	Sectional Cut – off Marks				Aggregate Cut-off Marks
	Section A	Section B	Section C	Section D	
College 1	42	42	42		176
College 2		45	45		175
College 3			46		171
College 4	43			45	178
College 5	45		43		180
College 6		41		44	176

78. Bhama got calls from all colleges. What could be the minimum aggregate marks obtained by her?

(a) 180 (b) 181
(c) 196 (d) 176
(e) 184

79. Charlie got calls from two colleges. What could be the minimum marks obtained by him in a section?

(a) 0 (b) 21
(c) 25 (d) 35
(e) 41

80. Aditya did not get a call from even a single college. What could be the maximum aggregate marks obtained by him?

(a) 181 (b) 176
(c) 184 (d) 196
(e) 190

Directions for Questions 81 to 84: *Answer the following questions based on the information given below:*

In a sports event, six teams (A, B, C, D, E and F) are competing against each other. Matches are scheduled in two stages. Each team plays three matches in stage – I and two matches in Stage – II. No team plays against the same team more than once in the event. No ties are permitted in any of the matches. The observations after the completion of Stage – I and Stage – II are as given below.

Stage-I:

- One team won all the three matches.
- Two teams lost all the matches.
- D lost to A but won against C and F.
- E lost to B but won against C and F.
- B lost at least one match.
- F did not play against the top team of Stage-I.

Stage-II:

- The leader of Stage-I lost the next two matches.
- Of the two teams at the bottom after Stage-I, one team won both matches, while the other lost both matches.
- One more team lost both matches in Stage-II.

81. The two teams that defeated the leader of Stage-I are:

(a) F & D (b) E & F
(c) B & D (d) E & D
(e) F & D

82. The only team(s) that won both matches in Stage-II is (are):

(a) B (b) E & F
(c) A, E & F (d) B, E & F
(e) B & F

83. The teams that won exactly two matches in the event are:

(a) A, D & F (b) D & E
(c) E & F (d) D, E & F
(e) D & F

84. The team(s) with the most wins in the event is (are):

(a) A (b) A & C
(c) F (d) E
(e) B & E

MEMORY BASED QUESTIONS

2009

Directions for questions 85 to 87: *Answer the following questions on the basis of the information given below.*

Priya, Qureshi, Rahul and Sonal are Lawyer, Engineer, Doctor and Cricketer by profession not necessarily in the same order. Each of them lives in a different house among the four adjacent houses that lie in a row. Each house has a distinct colour among red, green, blue and white in no particular order.

Additional Information:

(i) Priya is not a Cricketer and she lives in the house at the extreme left of the row.

(ii) The Engineer stays beside the Doctor and the Lawyer.

(iii) Qureshi is a Doctor and he stays in a green house beside the Cricketer's house.

(iv) Rahul stays in a white house and he is not an Engineer.

85. What is the profession of the person who stays in the blue house?

(a) Lawyer (b) Cricketer
(c) Engineer (d) Cannot be determined

86. Who is the Cricketer among the four people?

(a) Rahul (b) Sonal
(c) Qureshi (d) Cannot be determined

87. Which of the following cannot be a possible combination of name, profession and house-colour?

(a) Priya → Lawyer → red
(b) Sonal → Engineer → blue
(c) Qureshi → Doctor → green
(d) Rahul → Cricketer → red

2010

Directions for questions 88 to 90: *Answer the questions on the basis of the information given below.*

IILK organized a 2-day Indian Classical Music Event with three slots on each day. Four artists – Subbu, Kumar, Shankar and Kehsanloy – and three bands – Delhi Sea, GTH and Mitti – performed at the event. In each slot, an artist or a band or a combination of an artist and a band performed. No artist performed alone in the last slot of a day and no band performed alone in the first slot.

Whenever Delhi Sea and Mitti performed, they did it in two successive slots with Delhi Sea performing before Mitti. The number of performances given by Shankar was less than that given by GTH and the last performance of Shankar was held before the first performance of GTH. Subbu performed alone only once during the event and that was in the first slot on the second day. The sum of the number of performances given by Mitti, Kehsanloy and Kumar respectively wasn't a prime number. The total number of performances given by the artists was equal to the total number of performances given by the bands.

88. It is known that Kehsanloy performed in the last slot on both the days. If a combination of an artist and a band performed in two of the slots on the second day, then who performed in the second slot on the first day?

(a) Shankar-GTH

(b) Shankar-Mitti

(c) Mitti

(d) Kumar-Mitti

89. If Kumar performed on both the days, then he must have performed with which of the bands?

(a) Delhi Sea

(b) GTH

(c) Mitti

(d) Cannot be determined

90. Which of the following statements cannot be true?

(a) Kehsanloy and GTH performed in the third slot on the first day.

(b) Shankar and Mitti performed in the second slot on the first day.

(c) Kumar and GTH performed in the third slot on the second day.

(d) None of these

2011

Directions for questions 91 to 93: *Answer the questions on the basis of the information given below.*

The figure given below shows the plan of a housing complex, which has eight houses – P1, P2, P3, P4, P5, P6, P7 and P8. Each house is owned by a different person among Aadi, Bina, Cara, Diya, Ema, Fiza, Gauri and Hari, not necessarily in the same order. The houses are of two types – Bungalows and Quarters. All the Bungalows are identical; similarly, all the Quarters are also identical. P3, P6 and P8 are the Bungalows and each of them is owned by a different officer. Each Quarter is owned by a different servant. Two persons are called neighbours if their houses share a common wall. E.g. the one who lives in P1 is a neighbour of those who live in P2 and P6.

P1	P2	P3	P4	P5
P6		P7	P8	

It is also known that:

(i) The number of neighbours of Aadi is equal to the number of neighbours of Cara.

(ii) Diya is a neighbour of both Aadi and Fiza.

(iii) Ema is an officer and is a neighbour of Gauri who does not live in P7.

(iv) Bina and Hari are not neighbours.

(v) Fiza lives in P8 and Aadi is not her neighbour.

91. Who lives in P7?

(a) Cara (b) Hari

(c) Bina (d) Cannot be determined

92. How many neighbours does Aadi have?

(a) 2 (b) 3

(c) 4 (d) 5

93. Who among the following is definitely not a neighbour of Diya?

(a) Gauri (b) Bina

(c) Ema (d) Cara

Directions for questions 94 to 96: *Answer the questions on the basis of the information given below.*

Four people – Alfred, Buckley, Cherry and Dirk – went to a museum on a Sunday. No two of them reached the museum at the same time. They were wearing shirts of different colours among Purple, Red, White and Yellow, in no particular order. It is also known that:

(i) Cherry was not the first one to reach the museum and he was wearing the Red shirt.

(ii) The person wearing the Yellow shirt reached the museum earlier than Buckley.

(iii) The person wearing the White shirt was not the last one to reach the museum.

(iv) Alfred was not wearing the Yellow shirt.

(v) The person wearing the Purple shirt reached the museum earlier than the person wearing the White shirt.

(vi) Alfred reached the museum before Dirk.

94. Who among the four was wearing the White shirt?

(a) Alfred (b) Buckley
(c) Cherry (d) Dirk

95. Who among the four was the last to reach the museum?

(a) Alfred (b) Buckley
(c) Cherry (d) Dirk

96. Which of the following statement(s) is/are correct?

I. Dirk was wearing the Yellow shirt and he reached the museum before Cherry.

II. Alfred was wearing the White shirt and he reached the museum before Cherry.

(a) Only I (b) Only II
(c) Neither I nor II (d) Both I and II

2012

Directions for Questions 97 to 99 : Answer the questions on the basis of the information given below.

The following table provides partial details about the comparison of the increase in the number of applicants among four streams in education viz. Engineering, Medical Science, Commerce and Arts in the year 2008 as compared to the year 2007. The increase in the number of applicants in the Commerce stream in 2008 as compared to 2007 is 70000 and the average number of applicants in the four streams in 2008 is 400000. Assume that these are the only four streams in the education system. In the given table, the number 20000 under the title 'Commerce' means that the increase in the number of applicants in the Commerce stream in 2008 as compared to the year 2007 is 20000 less than the corresponding increase in the Engineering stream. All the other data in the table should be interpreted similarly.

	Engineering	Medical Sciences	Commerce
Engineering		69000	20000
Medical Sciences	A		B
Commerce	D	C	
Arts	E	59000	F

97. Which of the following is not true?

(a) E + F = 0
(b) C = 49000
(c) E + 10000 = 0
(d) None of these

98. The total number of applicants in the four given streams in 2007 was

(a) 1339000
(b) 1739000
(c) 1439000
(d) 1349000

99. The total increase in the number of applicants in the Arts stream in 2008 as compared to 2007 as a percentage (approximate)of the total number of applicants in the four given streams in 2007 is

(a) 9% (b) 6%
(c) 8% (d) 5%

Directions for Questions 100 to 102 : Answer the questions on the basis of the information given below.

Each of the six persons namely A, B, C, D, E and F took one ball from a box containing 300 balls of six different colours Blue, Black, Red, White, Green and Yellow. Also, the number of balls of each colour is the same. Following is the detail of three statements made by each of the persons. Exactly one of the statements made by each person is true and only one of the statements made about B is correct. Also, balls of two particular colours were not taken by any of the perons.

	Statement I	Statement II	Statement III
A	B took a green ball	C did not take a red ball	E took a blue ball
B	A took a green ball	D did not take a yellow ball	C took a black ball
C	F took a white ball	F did not take a white ball	A did not take a blue ball
D	E took a yellow ball	F took a yellow ball	One green ball was taken by me
E	F took a red ball	B took the same coloured ball as A	B took a blue ball
F	A took a white ball	C took a black ball	D did not take a red ball

100. What is the colour of the ball taken by A?

(a) Green (b) Yellow
(c) Blue (d) Red

101. What is the colour of the ball taken by C?

(a) Green (b) White
(c) Blue (d) Red

102. For how many of the mentioned persons, the exact colour of the balls taken by them can be determined?

(a) 6 (b) 4
(c) 3 (d) 5

Directions for Questions 103 to 105: Answer the questions on the basis of the information given below.

Five friends, viz. Ashok, Amit, Ajay, Akansh and Abhishek are living in five different cities named Kunnamangalam, Joka, Vastrapur, Banerghatta and Prabandhnagar, not necessarily in that order. Their salaries are 700000, 800000, 900000, 1100000, 1300000 (INR per annum), in no particular order. Further, the following information is given about them:

I. Akansh, who does not live in Banerghatta, earns a salary that is a prime number multiple of 100000.
II. Amit made a call to one of his four mentioned friends who lives in Prabandhnagar and earning a perfect square multiple of 100000 INR in salary.
III. Ajay's salary is 100000 INR more than the average salary of Akansh and Ashok
IV. Amit lives in the city, which has the shortest name amongst the above cities.

103. If Akansh lives in Vastrapur, then what is the average salary of the persons living in Banerghatta and Kunnamangalam?

(a) Rs.9 lakh (b) Rs.10 lakh
(c) Rs.12 lakh (d) Data Insufficient

104. Who stays in Prabandhnagar?

(a) Ashok (b) Amit
(c) Abhishek (d) Akansh

105. If Amit and Ajay live in cities with names starting with consecutive alphabets, then who lives in Vastrapur?

(a) Ashok (b) Amit
(c) Abhishek (d) Akansh

2013

Directions for questions 106 : Answer the questions on the basis of the information given below.

A Cricket team of 11 players is to be formed from a group of 15 players—A, B, C, D, E, F, G, H, I, J, K, L, M, N and O. Among the players A, D, K, L, M, N and O are batsmen; B, C, E, F, G and H are bowlers; I and J are wicketkeepers. It is also known that:

I. The team must have at least 5 batsmen and exactly 1 wicketkeeper.
II. H can be selected only if B is selected.
III. F can be selected only if both G and N are selected.
IV. If I is selected, then F is also selected.
V. K and M cannot be selected together for the team. The same is true for B and G.

106. In how many ways can the team be formed?

(a) 3 (b) 4
(c) 5 (d) 6

2014

Directions for questions 107 to 109 : Answer the questions on the basis of the information given below.

There are ten real numbers A, B, C, D, E, F, G, H, I. Differences between any two of them are given in the diagram below.

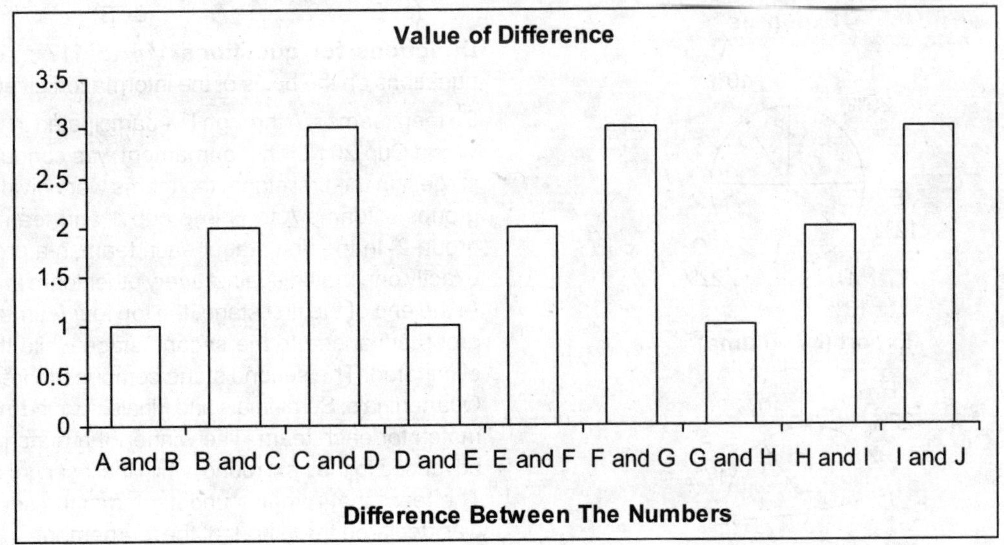

107. If the value of A is known then how many distinct values are possible for J?

(a) 512 (b) 256

(c) 128 (d) None of these

108. If all the 10 numbers from A to J are positive integers then at least how many of them are even?

(a) 3 (b) 4

(c) 5 (d) 6

109. If all the 10 numbers from A to J are positive integers and A is equal to 1 then at a time at most how many of them can be perfect squares?

(a) 7 (b) 9

(c) 8 (d) 6

2015

Directions for questions 110 to 113 : Answer the questions on the basis of the information given below.

The following pie chart gives details of the production, expenses and export of the six products manufactured by company KL Enterprises, which manufactures only the given six products, in the year 2014. In the given year, the company followed a very strict internal audit policy and any item that did not meet the specifications were rejected and disposed off. All the products exported were those manufactured in the same year itself.

Production

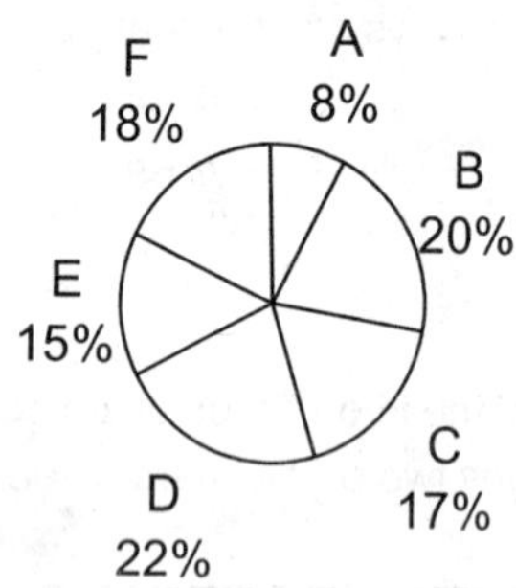

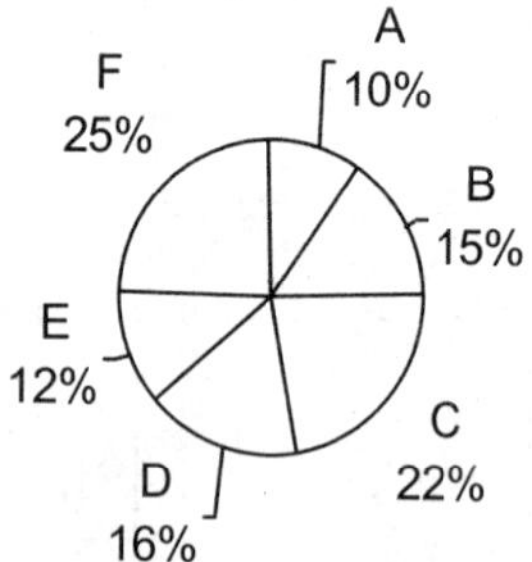

Export (by volume)

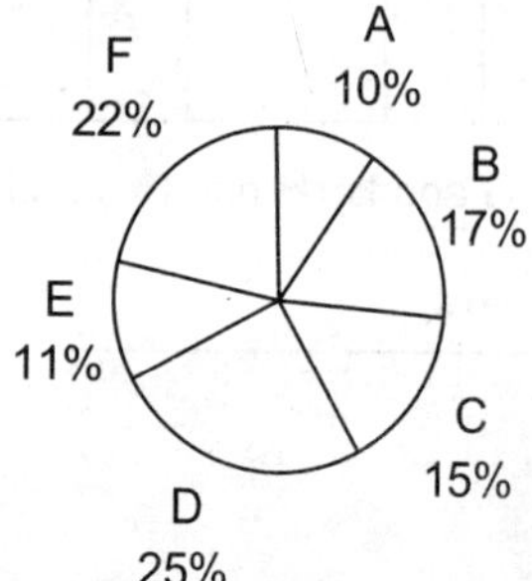

Export (by value)

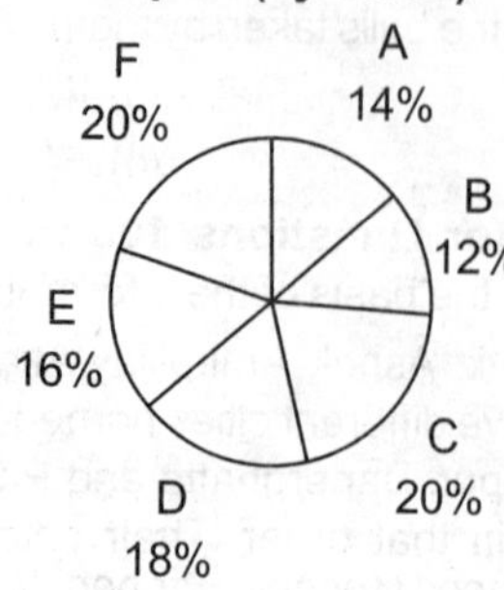

Profit = Sales – Expenses

$$\text{Profitability (\%)} = \frac{\text{Profit}}{\text{Expenses}} \times 100$$

Note: Export is the only source of sales.

110. In 2014, the products exported as a percentage of the products manufactured by the company could not be more than

(a) 73.3% (b) 81.81%

(c) 80% (d) 88%

111. In 2014, if product D was a profit making product for the company, what was the maximum number of products that were loss making products for the company?

(a) 2 (b) 3

(c) 4 (d) Zero

112. The export price per unit of which product was the highest?

(a) A (b) C

(c) D (d) E

113. For which product the rejection rate was maximum?

(a) C (b) F

(c) E (d) B

Directions for questions 114 to 117 : Answer the questions on the basis of the information given below.

Sixteen teams – A through P – participated in the Hockey World Cup, 2013. The tournament was conducted in two stages. In the first stage, the teams were divided into two groups – teams A to H in group 1 and teams I to P in group 2. In the first stage, each team in a group played exactly one match against every other team in that group. At the end of the first stage, the top four teams from each group advanced to the second stage while the rest got eliminated. The second stage comprised three rounds – Quarterfinals, Semi-finals and Finals. A round involves one match for each team. The winner of a match in a round advanced to the next round, while the loser got eliminated. The team that remains undefeated in the second stage was declared the winner of the tournament.

At the end of the first stage, top four teams in each group were determined on the basis of total number of matches won by individual teams; in case, two or more teams in a group were ended up with the same number of wins, ties were resolved by a series of complex tie-breaking rules to determine the top four positions. The teams qualifying for the second stage from group 1 were A, B, C and D and those from group 2 were I, J, K and L. No match in the tournament ended in a draw/tie.

114. In the tournament, if E and L won the same number of matches and L was the winner of the tournament, then what was the sum of the number of matches won by E and that by L?

115. The number of matches won in the first stage by a team that advanced to the second stage could not be less than

116. How many of the following statements is/are true?

(i) Maximum number of teams which could have one win in the first stage was 6.

(ii) Maximum number of teams which could have three wins in the first stage was 12.

(iii) Number of teams which had exactly 2 wins in the second stage was 2.

117. The value of the total of number of matches won, in the first stage, by teams A, B, C and D together could not be more than

Directions for questions 118 to 121 : Answer the questions on the basis of the information given below.

A group has to be selected from seven persons containing two women (Rehana and Kavya) and five men (Rohit, Rahul, Kamal, Nusarat and John). Rohit would not like to be in the group if Rahul is selected. Rahul and John want to be selected together in the group. Kavya would like to be in the group only if Kamal is also there. Kamal, if selected, would not like Nusarat in the group. Rohit would like to be in the group only if Nusarat is also there. Kamal insists that Rehana must be selected in case he is there in the group.

118. Which of the following is an acceptable combination of a group of three?

(a) Rohit, John, Kavya

(b) Rahul, Kamal, Nusarat

(c) Rohit, Nusarat, Rahul

(d) Rohit, Nusarat, Rehana

119. Which of the following is an acceptable combination of a group of four?

(a) Rohit, Nusarat, Rehana, John

(b) Rahul, John, Kavya, Kamal

(c) Rahul, John, Rehana, Kamal

(d) Rehana, Kamal, Rohit, Nusarat

120. Which of the following statements is true?

(a) Kavya and Rohit both can be selected in a group of four.

(b) A group of four can have both the women.

(c) A group of four can have four men.

(d) None of the above

121. If a group of five members has to be selected, then in how many ways is it possible such that Kamal is definitely a member of the group?

(a) 1 (b) 0

(c) 2 (d) 3

2016

Directions for questions 122 to 125: Answer the questions on the basis of the information given below.

Ina, Mina and Dika had some money with which they decided to buy the shares of two companies – Bindaas and Jhakkas. The amount with Mina was 1/3rd of the total money available with the three of them. Ina and Mina spent equal amounts of money in buying Bindaas shares. The amount spent by Mina on buying Jhakkas shares was twice that of Dika. The amount spent by Ina on buying Jhakkas shares was 50% more than the amount spent on Jhakkas shares by Mina and Dika together. The amount spent by Dika on Bindaas shares was 1/9th of the total initial money with the three of them. The amount spent on Jhakkas shares by the three of them together was 1/3rd of the total initial money with them. Mina and Dika had equal amounts of money left with them after making the purchases. The amount spent by Dika in buying Jhakkas shares was equal to the amount left with Mina after making the purchases. The money left with Ina after making the purchases was 1/15th of the total initial money with the three of them. The amount spent on Jhakkas shares by Mina and Dika together was Rs. 2,00,000 more than the money that was left with the two of them after making the purchases.

122. If the price of a Bindaas share was Rs. 5,000 then find the number of Bindaas shares bought by the three of them together.

(a) 420 (b) 440

(c) 460 (d) 480

123. What was the money available with Ina in the beginning?

(a) Rs. 21,00,000 (b) Rs. 30,00,000

(c) Rs. 24,00,000 (d) Rs. 18,00,000

124. Which of the following statement(s) is/are true?

I. The money spent on purchases as a percentage of the money available with an individual in the beginning was the highest for Dika among the three.

II. The three of them were left with a sum of Rs. 7,00,000 after making the purchases.

(a) Only I (b) Only II

(c) Both I and II (d) Neither I nor II

125. What was the total amount of money (in Rs.) with the three at the beginning?

(a) 45,00,000

(b) 40,00,000

(c) 42,50,000

(d) None of these

2017

Question Numbers: (126 to 129): Funky Pizzaria was required to supply pizzas to three different parties. The total number of pizzas it had to deliver was 800, 70% of which were to be delivered to Party 3 and the rest equally divided between Party 1 and Party 2.

Pizzas could be of Thin Crust (T) or Deep Dish (D) variety and come in either Normal Cheese (NC) or Extra Cheese (EC) versions. Hence, There are four types of pizzas: T-NC, T-EC, D-NC and D-EC. Partial information about proportions of T and NC pizzas ordered by the three parties is given below:

	Thin Crust (T)	Normal Cheese (NC)
Party 1	0.6	
Party 2	0.55	0.3
Party 3		0.65
Total	0.375	0.52

126. How many Thin Crust pizzas were to be delivered to Party 3?

(a) 398 (b) 162

(c) 196 (d) 364

127. How many Normal Cheese pizzas were required to be delivered to Party 1?

(a) 104 (b) 84

(c) 16 (d) 196

128. For Party 2, if 50% of the Normal Cheese pizzas were of Thin Crust variety, what was the difference between the numbers of T-EC and D-EC pizzas to be delivered to Party 2?

(a) 18 (b) 12

(c) 30 (d) 24

129. Suppose that a T-NC pizza cost as much as a D-NC pizza, but 3/5th of the price of a D-EC pizza. A D-EC pizza costs Rs.50 more than a T-EC pizza, and the latter costs Rs.500.

If 25% of the Normal Cheese pizzas delivered to Party 1 were of Deep Dish variety, what was the total bill for Party 1?

(a) Rs. 59480 (b) Rs. 59840

(c) RS. 42520 (d) Rs. 45240

Question Numbers : (130 to 133) : There were seven elective courses - E1 to E7 - running in a specific term in a college. Each of the 300 students enrolled had chosen just one elective from among these seven. However, before the start of the term, E7 was withdrawn as the instructor concerned had left the college. The students who had opted for E7 were allowed to join any of the remaining electives, Also, the students who had chosen other electives were given one chance to change their choice. The table below captures the movement of the students from one elective to another during this process. Movement from one elective to the same elective simply means no movement. Some numbers in the table got accidentally erased; however, it is known that these were either 0 or 1.

		To Elective					
		E1	E2	E3	E4	E5	E6
From Elective	E1	9	5	10	1	4	2
	E2		34	8		2	2
	E3	2	6	25			2
	E4		3	2	14		4
	E5		5			30	
	E6		7	3		2	9
	E7	4	16	30	5	5	41

Further, the following are known:

1. Before the change process there were 6 more students in E1 than in E4, but after the reshuffle, the number of students in E4 was 3 more than that in E1.
2. The number of students in E2 increased by 30 after the change process.
3. Before the change process, E4 had 2 more students than E6, while E2 had 10 more students than E3.

130. How many elective courses among E1 to E6 had a decrease in their enrollments after the change process?

(a) 4 (b) 1

(c) 2 (d) 3

131. After the change process, which of the following is the correct sequence of number of students in the six electives E1 to E6?

(a) 19, 76, 79, 21, 45, 60

(b) 19, 76, 78, 22, 45, 60

(c) 18, 76, 79, 23, 43, 61

(d) 18, 76, 79, 21, 45, 61

132. After the change process, which course among E1 to E6 had the largest change in its enrollment as a percentage of its original enrollment?

(a) E1 (b) E2

(c) E3 (d) E6

133. Later, the college imposed a condition that if after the change of electives, the enrollment in any elective (other than E7) dropped to less than 20 students, all the students who had left that course will be required to reenroll for that elective.

Which of the following is a correct sequence of electives in decreasing order of their final enrollments?

(a) E2, E3, E6, E5, E1, E4

(b) E3, E2, E6, E5, E4, E1

(c) E2, E5, E3, E1, E4, E6

(d) E2, E3, E5, E6, E1, E3

Question Numbers (134 to 137) : *An old woman had the following assets:*

(a) Rs.70 lakh in bank deposits

(b) 1 house worth Rs.50 lakh

(c) 3 flats, each worth Rs.30 lakh

(d) Certain number of gold coins, each worth Rs.1 lakh

She wanted to distribute her assets among her three children; Neeta, Seeta and Geeta.

The house, any of the flats or any of the coins were not to be split. That is, the house went entirely to one child; a flat went to one child and similarly, a gold coin went to one child.

134. Among the three, Neeta received the least amount in bank deposits, while Geeta received the highest. The value of the assets was distributed equally among the children, as were the gold coins.

How much did Seeta receive in bank deposits (in lakhs of rupees)?

(a) 30 (b) 40

(c) 20 (d) 10

135. Among the three, Neeta received the least amount in bank deposits, while Geeta received the highest. The value of the assets was distributed equally among the children, as were the gold coins.

How many flats did Neeta receive?

136. The value of the assets distributed among Neeta, Seeta and Geeta was in the ratio of 1 : 2 : 3, while the gold coins were distributed among them in the ratio of 2 : 3 : 4. One child got all three flats and she did not get the house. One child, other than Geeta, got Rs.30 lakh in bank deposits.

How many gold coins did the old woman have?

(a) 72 (b) 90

(c) 180 (d) 216

137. The value of the assets distributed among Neeta, Seeta and Geeta was in the ratio of 1 : 2 : 3, while the gold coins were distributed among them in the ratio of 2 : 3 : 4. One child got all three flats and she did not get the house. One child, other than Geeta, got Rs.30 lakh in bank deposits.

How much did Geeta get in bank deposits (in lakhs of rupees)?

2018 Slot 1

Question Numbers (138 to 141) :

Twenty four people are part of three committees which are to look at research, teaching, and administration respectively. No two committees have any member in common. No two committees are of the same size. Each committee has three types of people: bureaucrats, educationalists, and politicians, with at least one from each of the three types in each committee. The following facts are also known about the committees:

1. The numbers of bureaucrats in the research and teaching committees are equal, while the number of bureaucrats in the research committee is 75% of the number of bureaucrats in the administration committee.

2. The number of educationalists in the teaching committee is less than the number of educationalists in the research committee. The number of educationalists in the research committee is the average of the numbers of educationalists in the other two committees.

3. 60% of the politicians are in the administration committee, and 20% are in the teaching committee.

138. Based on the given information, which of the following statements MUST be FALSE?

(a) The size of the research committee is less than the size of the administration committee

(b) In the teaching committee the number of educationalists is equal to the number of politicians

(c) In the administration committee the number of bureaucrats is equal to the number of educationalists

(d) The size of the research committee is less than the size of the teaching committee

139. What is the number of bureaucrats in the administration committee?

140. What is the number of educationalists in the research committee?

141. Which of the following CANNOT be determined uniquely based on the given information?

(a) The total number of educationalists in the three committees

(b) The size of the research committee

(c) The total number of bureaucrats in the three committees

(d) The size of the teaching committee

142. What best can be said about the number of satellites serving C?

(a) Cannot be more than 800

(b) Must be at least 100

(c) Must be between 400 and 800

(d) Must be between 450 and 725

143. What is the minimum possible number of satellites serving B exclusively?

(a) 100 (b) 500

(c) 200 (d) 250

144. If at least 100 of the 1600 satellites were serving O, what can be said about the number of satellites serving S?

(a) At least 475

(b) At most 475

(c) No conclusion is possible based on the given information

(d) Exactly 475

145. If the number of satellites serving at least two among B, C, and S is 1200, which of the following MUST be FALSE?

(a) The number of satellites serving B is more than 1000

(b) All 1600 satellites serve B or C or S

(c) The number of satellites serving B exclusively is exactly 250

(d) The number of satellites serving C cannot be uniquely determined

2018 Slot 2

Question Numbers: (146 to 149):

An agency entrusted to accredit colleges looks at four parameters: faculty quality (F), reputation (R), placement quality (P), and infrastructure (I). The four parameters are used to arrive at an overall score, which the agency uses to give an accreditation to the colleges. In each parameter, there are five possible letter grades given, each carrying certain points: A (50 points), B (40 points), C (30 points), D (20 points), and F (0 points). The overall score for a college is the weighted sum of the points scored in the four parameters. The weights of the parameters are 0.1, 0.2, 0.3 and 0.4 in some order, but the order is not disclosed. Accreditation is awarded based on the following scheme:

Range	Accreditation
Overall score ≥ 45	AAA
$35 \leq$ Overall score < 45	BAA
$25 \leq$ Overall score < 35	BBA
$15 \leq$ Overall score < 25	BBB
Overall score < 15	Junk

Eight colleges apply for accreditation, and receive the following grades in the four parameters (F, R, P, and I):

	F	R	P	I
A-one	A	A	A	B
Best Ed	B	C	D	D
Cosmopolitan	B	D	D	C
Dominance	D	D	B	C
Education Aid	A	A	B	A
Fancy	A	A	B	B
Global	C	F	D	D
High Q	C	D	D	B

It is further known that in terms of overall scores:

1. High Q is better than Best Ed;
2. Best Ed is better than Cosmopolitan; and
3. Education Aid is better than A-one.

146. What is the weight of the faculty quality parameter?

(a) 0.2 (b) 0.1

(c) 0.4 (d) 0.3

147. How many colleges receive the accreditation of AAA?

148. What is the highest overall score among the eight colleges?

149. How many colleges have overall scores between 31 and 40, both inclusive?

(a) 3 (b) 0

(c) 1 (d) 2

Question Numbers: (150 to 153):

The base exchange rate of a currency X with respect to a currency Y is the number of units of currency Y which is equivalent in value to one unit of currency X. Currency exchange outlets buy currency at buying exchange rates that are lower than base exchange rates, and sell currency at selling exchange rates that are higher than base exchange rates.

A currency exchange outlet uses the local currency L to buy and sell three international currencies A, B, and C, but does not exchange one international currency directly with another. The base exchange rates of A, B and C with respect to L are in the ratio 100:120:1. The buying exchange rates of each of A, B, and C with respect to L are 5% below the corresponding base exchange rates, and their selling exchange rates are 10% above their corresponding base exchange rates.

The following facts are known about the outlet on a particular day:

1. The amount of L used by the outlet to buy C equals the amount of L it received by selling C.
2. The amounts of L used by the outlet to buy A and B are in the ratio 5:3.
3. The amounts of L the outlet received from the sales of A and B are in the ratio 5:9.
4. The outlet received 88000 units of L by selling A during the day.
5. The outlet started the day with some amount of L, 2500 units of A, 4800 units of B, and 48000 units of C.
6. The outlet ended the day with some amount of L, 3300 units of A, 4800 units of B, and 51000 units of C.

150. How many units of currency A did the outlet buy on that day?

151. How many units of currency C did the outlet sell on that day?

(a) 6000 (b) 22000

(c) 3000 (d) 19000

152. What was the base exchange rate of currency B with respect to currency L on that day?

153. What was the buying exchange rate of currency C with respect to currency L on that day?

(a) 1.90 (b) 0.95

(c) 1.10 (d) 2.20

CALCULATION BASED DI

1990

Directions for Questions 1 to 3 : *Answer the questions on the basis of the information given below.*

Ghosh Babu has a certain amount of property consisting of cash, gold coins and silver bars. The cost of a gold coin is Rs. 4000 and the cost of a silver bar is Rs. 1000. Ghosh Babu distributed his property among his daughters equally. He gave to his eldest daughter gold coins worth 20% of the total property and Rs. 25000 in cash. The second daughter was given silver bars worth 20% of the remaining property and Rs. 50000 cash. He then gave each of the third and fourth daughters equal number of gold coins and silver bars both together accounting each for 20% of the property remaining after the previous distribution and Rs. 25000 more than what the second daughter had received in cash.

1. The amount of property in gold and silver possessed by Ghosh Babu is

(a) 2,25,000 (b) 2,75,000

(c) Rs. 4,25,000 (d) None of these

2. Total property of Ghosh Babu (in Rs.lakh) is

(a) 5.0 (b) 7.5

(c) 10.0 (d) 12.5.

3. If Ghosh Babu had equal number of gold and silver bars, the number of silver bars he has is

(a) 90 (b) 60

(c) 75 (d) 55

Directions for Questions 4 to 7: *Answer the questions on the basis of the information given below.*

The following graph shows the value of liquor supplied by the 5 states in 1996 and the excise duty rates in each state.

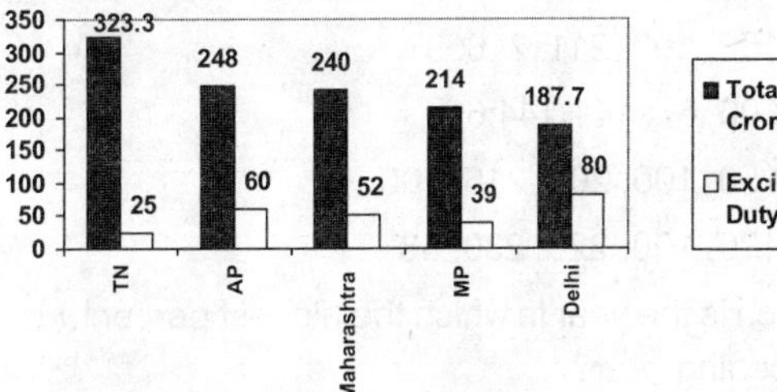

Amount of liquor supplied in Tamil Nadu Distilleries A, B, C, D, E (from bottom to top) in lakh litres.

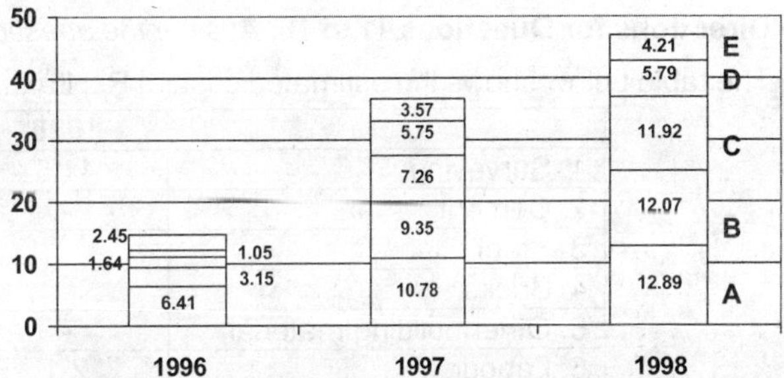

4. What is the lowest percentage difference in the excise duty rates for any two states?

(a) 12 (b) 15

(c) 20 (d) Cannot be determined.

5. Which of the five states manufactured liquor at the lowest cost?

(a) Tamil Nadu

(b) Delhi

(c) The states which has the lowest value for (wholesale price-Excise duty) per litre

(d) Cannot be determined.

6. If Excise duty is levied before the goods leave the factory (on the value of the liquor), then which of the following choices shows distilleries in ascending order of the excise duty paid by them for the year 1996? (Assume the total liquor in TN is supplied by only these 5 distilleries).

(a) ECABD (b) ADEBC

(c) DCEBA (d) Cannot be determined.

7. If the Tamil Nadu distillery, with the least average simple annual growth in amount of liquor supplied in the given period had shown the same rate of growth as the one which grew fastest, what would that company's supply have been in 1998, in lakh liters?

(a) 13 (b) 15.1 1

(c) 130 (d) Cannot be determined.

Directions for Questions 8 to 10: *Answer the questions on the basis of the information given below.*

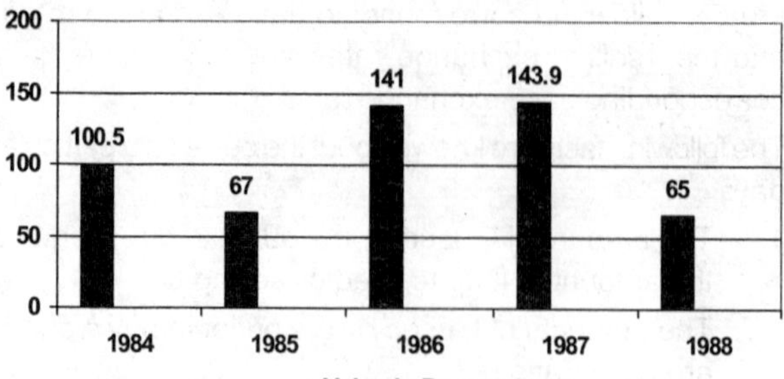

8. What is the average value of the contract secured during the years shown in the diagram?

(a) Rs. 103.48 crore (b) Rs. 105 crore

(c) Rs. 100 crore (d) Rs.125.2 crore

9. Compared to the performance in 1985 (i.e. taking it as the base), what can you say about the performances in the years '84, '85, '86, '87, '88 respectively, in percentage terms?

(a) 150, 100, 211, 216, 97

(b) 100, 67, 141,144,65

(c) 150, 100, 200, 215, 100

(d) 120, 100, 220, 230, 68

10. Which is the year in which the highest percentage decline is seen in the value of contract secured compared to the preceding year?

(a) 1985 (b) 1988

(c) 1984 (d) 1986

Directions for Questions 11 to 16: *Answer the questions on the basis of the information given below.*

The table below shows the estimated cost (in Rs. Lakh) of a project of laying a railway line between two places.

	1988	1989	1990	1991
1. Surveying	41.5	7.5	2.2	0.5
2. Cement	-	95.0	80.0	75.0
3. Steel	-	70.0	45.0	60.0
4. Bricks	-	15.0	12.0	16.0
5. Other building material	-	25.0	18.0	21.0
6. Labour	2.1'	25.0	20.0	18.0
7. Administration	7.5	15.0	15.0	14.0
8. Contingencies	1.0	15.0	4.2	5.0
Total	**52.1**	**267.5**	**196.4**	**209.5**

11. The total expenditure is required to be kept within Rs. 700 lakh by cutting the expenditure on administration equally in all the years. What will be the percentage cut for 1989?

(a) 22.6% (b) 32.6%

(c) 42.5% (d) 52.6%

12. If the length of line to be laid each year is in proportion to the estimated cost for material and labour, what fraction of the total length is proposed to be completed by the third year?

(a) 0.9 (b) 0.7

(c) 0.6 (d) 0.3

13. What is the approximate ratio of the total cost of materials for all the years to the total labour cost?

(a) 4 : 1 (b) 8 : 1

(c) 12:1 (d) 16 : 1

14. If the cost of materials rises by 5% each year from 1990 onwards, by how much will the estimated cost rise?

(a) Rs. 11.4 lakh

(b) Rs. 16.4 lakh

(c) Rs.21.4 lakh

(d) Rs.26.4 lakh

15. It is found at the end of 1990, that the entire amount estimated for the project has been spent. If for 1991, the actual amount spent was equal to that which was estimated, by what percent (approximately) has the actual expenditure exceeded the estimated expenditure?

(a) 39 (b) 29

(c) 19 (d) 9

16. After preparing the estimate, the provision for contingencies is felt inadequate and is therefore doubled. By what percent does the total estimate increase?

(a) 3.47 (b) 2.45

(c) 1.50 (d) 3.62

Directions for Questions 17 to 21: *Answer the questions on the basis of the information given below.*

The first table gives the number of saris (of all the eight colours) stocked in six regional showrooms. The second gives the number of saris (of all the eight colours) sold in these six regional showrooms. The third table gives the percentage of saris sold to saris stocked for each colour in each region. The fourth table gives the percentage of saris of a specific colour sold within that region. The fifth table gives the percentage of saris of a specific colour sold across all the regions. Study the tables and for each of the following questions, choose the best alternative.

Table 1

Region	Blue	Green	Magenta	Brown	Orange	Red	Violet	Yellow	Total
1	267	585	244	318	132	173	195	83	1994
2	341	480	99	199	234	119	200	109	1781
3	279	496	107	126	100	82	172	106	1468
4	198	307	62	221	65	96	124	91	1164
5	194	338	120	113	82	60	125	124	1156
6	158	261	133	104	71	158	128	82	1095
Total	**1437**	**2454**	**765**	**1081**	**684**	**688**	**944**	**595**	**8658**

Table 2

Region	Blue	Green	Magenta	Brown	Orange	Red	Violet	Yellow	Total
1	122	164	71	165	40	84	97	45	788
2	124	200	37	78	67	47	73	50	676
3	21	57	7	24	9	14	20	11	163
4	79	85	22	164	18	46	43	54	511
5	29	36	22	17	9	18	19	16	166
6	1	3	2	2	1	3	2	4	18
Total	**376**	**545**	**161**	**450**	**144**	**212**	**254**	**180**	**2322**

Table 3

Region	Blue	Green	Magenta	Brown	Orange	Red	Violet	Yellow	All
1	46	28	29	52	30	49	50	54	40
2	36	42	37	39	29	39	37	46	38
3	8	11	7	19	9	17	12	10	11
4	40	28	35	74	28	48	35	59	44
5	15	11	18	15	11	30	15	13	14
6	1	1	2	2	1	2	2	5	2
All	**26**	**22**	**21**	**42**	**21**	**31**	**27**	**30**	

Table 4

Region	Blue	Green	Magenta	Brown	Orange	Red	Violet	Yellow	Total
1	15	21	9	22	4	11	12	6	100
2	18	30	5	12	10	7	11	7	100
3	13	35	4	15	6	9	12	7	100
4	15	17	4	32	4	9	8	11	100
5	17	22	13	10	5	11	11	10	100
6	6	14	11	11	6	17	11	22	100

Table 5

Region	Blue	Green	Magenta	Brown	Orange	Red	Violet	Yellow
1	32	30	44	37	28	40	38	25
2	33	37	23	17	47	22	29	28
3	6	10	4	5	6	7	8	6
4	21	16	14	36	13	22	17	30
5	8	7	14	4	6	8	7	9
6	0	1	1	0	1	1	1	2
Total	**100**	**100**	**100**	**100**	**100**	**100**	**100**	**100**

17. Which region-colour combination accounts for the highest percentage of sales to stock?

(a) (1, Brown) (b) (2, Yellow)

(c) (4, Brown) (d) (5, Red)

18. Which colour is the most popular in region1?

(a) Blue (b) Brown

(c) Green (d) Violet

19. Which region sold the maximum percentage of magenta saris out of the total sales of magenta saris?

(a) 3 (b) 4

(c) 2 (d) 1

20. Out of its total sales, which region sold the minimum percentage of green saris?

(a) 1 (b) 6

(c) 4 (d) 2

21. In which region is the maximum percentage of blue saris sold?

(a) 2 (b) 3

(c) 1 (d) 4

Directions for Questions 22 to 25: *Answer the questions on the basis of the information given below.*

The table below gives the achievements of Agricultural Development Programmes from 1983 – 84 to 1988 – 89. Study the following table and for each of the following questions, choose the best alternative.

Programme	83 – 84	84 - 85	85 - 86	86 - 87	87 - 88	88 – 89
Irrigation (Cumulative in Million Hectares)						
Major & Medium	22.05	22.70	23.20	24.00	24.60	25.32
Minor	28.60	32.77	32.77	34.20	34.00	35.14
High yielding varieties (Million Hectares)						
1. Paddy	16.90	18.20	19.70	18.70	21.70	22.80
2. Wheat	15.90	16.10	16.80	17.80	19.40	19.10
3. Jowar	3.10	3.50	3.90	4.40	5.30	5.10
4. Bajra	2.90	3.60	4.60	4.70	5.40	5.20
5. Maize	1.40	1.60	1.60	1.70	1.90	2.00

Consumption of Chemical fertilizers (Million tons)

1. Nitrogen	3.42	3.68	4.07	4.22	5.20	5.49
2. Phosphate	1.11	1.21	1.32	1.44	1.73	1.89
3. Potash	0.59	0.62	0.67	0.73	0.78	0.84

Gross Cropped area (Million hectares)

	174.8	173.1	177.00	172.6	180.4	187.8

22. The consumption of chemical fertilizer per hectare of gross cropped area is lowest for the year

(a) 1984 – 85 (b) 1985 – 86
(c) 1986 – 87 (d) 1987 – 88

23. In which year does the area cropped under high yielding varieties show a decline for the maximum number of crops?

(a) 1988 – 89 (b) 1985 – 86
(c) 1986 – 87 (d) None of these

24. How much area, in million hectares, was brought under irrigation during the year 1986-87?

(a) 58.20 (b) 1.43
(c) 0.80 (d) 2.23

25. It is possible that a part of the minor irrigated area is brought under major and medium areas. In which year has this definitely happened?

(a) 1984 – 85 (b) 1985 – 86
(c) 1986 – 87 (d) 1987 – 88

1991

Directions for Questions 26 to 30: *Answer the questions on the basis of the information given below.*

The following table gives the national income and the population of a country for the years 1984 – 85 to 1989 –90. For each of the following questions choose the best alternative:

Year	National Income (in Rs. Crore)	Population (in crore)
1984-85	229,225	74.0
1985-86	261,174	75.0
1986-87	291,556	77.0
1987-88	329,934	78.5
1988-89	388,539	80.0
1989-90	433,500	81.5

26. The increase in the per capita income compared to the previous year is lowest for the year :

(a) 1985-86 (b) 1986-87
(c) 1987-88 (d) 1989-90

27. The per capita income is highest for the year :

(a) 1984-85 (b) 1985-86
(c) 1987-88 (d) 1989-90

28. The difference between the percentage increase in per capita income and the percentage increase in the population compared to the previous year is highest for the year:

(a) 1985-86 (b) 1986-87
(c) 1987-88 (d) 1988-89

29. The rate of increase in population was lowest in the year:

(a) 1985-86 (b) 1987-88
(c) 1989-90 (d) None of these

30. Increase in the per capita income compared to the previous year among the years given below was highest for the year:

(a) 1985-86 (b) 1986-87
(c) 1987-88 (d) 1989-90

Directions for Questions 31 to 35: *Answer the questions on the basis of the information given below.*

Ghosh Babu deposited a certain sum of money in a bank in 1986. The bank calculated interest on the principal at 10 percent simple interest, and credited it to the account once a year. After the 1st year, Ghosh Babu withdrew the entire interest and 20% of the initial amount. After the 2nd year, he withdrew the interest and 50% of the remaining amount. After the 3rd year, he withdrew the interest and 50% of the remaining amount. Finally after the 4th year, Ghosh Babu closed the account and collected the entire balance of Rs. 11,000.

31. The initial amount in rupees, deposited by Ghosh Babu was:

(a) 25,000 (b) 75,000
(c) 50,000 (d) None of these

32. The year, at the end of which, Ghosh Babu withdrew the smallest amount was:

(a) First (b) Second
(c) Third (d) Fourth

33. The year, at the end of which, Ghosh Babu collected the maximum interest was:

(a) First (b) Second
(c) Third (d) Fourth

34. The year, at the end of which, Ghosh Babu withdrew the maximum amount was:
(a) First (b) Second
(c) Third (d) Fourth

35. The total interest, in rupees, collected by Ghosh Babu was:
(a) 12,000 (b) 20,000
(c) 4,000 (d) 11,000

Directions for Questions 36 to 40 : *Answer the questions on the basis of the information given below.*

The graph below shows the end of the month market values of 4 shares for the period from January to June.

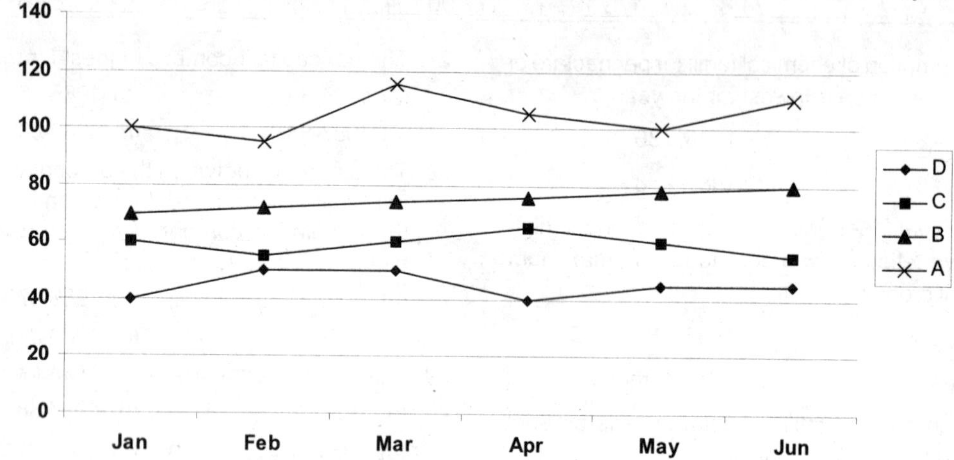

36. Which share showed the greatest percentage increase in market value in any month during the entire period?
(a) A (b) B
(c) C (d) D

37. In which month was the greatest absolute change in market value for any share recorded?
(a) March
(b) April
(c) May
(d) June

38. In which month was the greatest percentage increase in market value for any share recorded?
(a) February (b) March
(c) April (d) May

39. An individual wishes to sell 1 share of C and 1 share of D to buy 1 share of A at the end of a month. At which month-end would the individual's loss from this decision, due to share value changes, be the most?
(a) February (b) March
(c) April (d) June

40. An individual decides to sell 1 share of C and 1 share of D to buy 1 share of A at the end of the month. What can be the individual's greatest gain from this decision, due to share value changes?
(a) 5 (b) 10
(c) 15 (d) none

Directions for Questions 41 to 45: *Answer the questions on the basis of the information given below.*

Prakash has to decide whether or not to test a batch of 1000 widgets before sending them to the buyer. In case he decides to test, he has two options: (a) Use test I ; (b) Use test II. Test I cost Rs. 2 per widget. However, the test is not perfect. It sends 20% of the bad ones to the buyer as good. Test II costs Rs. 3 per widget. It brings out all the bad ones. A defective widget identified before sending can be corrected at a cost of Rs. 25 per widget. All defective widgets are identified at the buyer's end and penalty of Rs. 50 per defective widget has to be paid by Prakash.

41. Prakash should not test if the number of bad widgets in the lot is:
(a) less than 100 (b) more than 200
(c) between 120 & 190 (d) Cannot be found out.

42. If there are 120 defective widgets in the lot, Prakash:
(a) should either use Test I or not test.
(b) should either use Test II or not test.
(c) should use Test I or Test II.
(d) should use Test I only.

43. If the number of defective widgets in the lot is between 200 and 400, Prakash:
(a) may use Test I or Test II
(b) should use Test I only.
(c) should use Test II only
(d) cannot decide.

44. If Prakash is told that the lot has 160 defective widgets, he should:

(a) use Test I only

(b) use Test II only.

(c) do no testing.

(d) either use Test I or do not test.

45. If there are 200 defective widgets in the lot, Prakash:

(a) may use either Test I or Test II

(b) should use Test I or not use any test

(c) should use Test II or not use any test.

(d) cannot decide.

Directions for Questions 46 to 50: *Answer the questions on the basis of the information given below.*

In the following graph the x – axis denotes the years from 1983 to 1991.

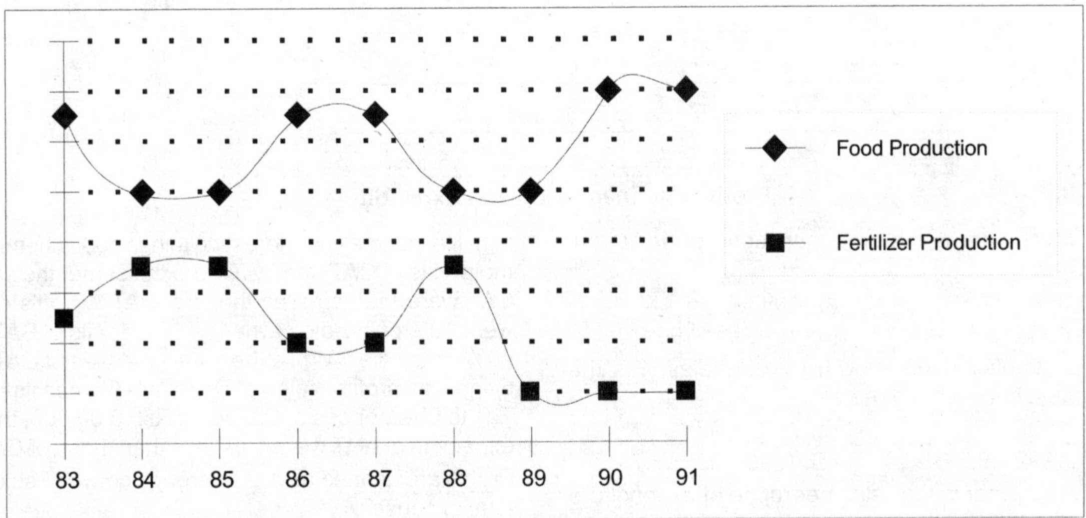

46. The sum of food and fertilizer production has shown a constant value for how many years?

(a) None of the years

(b) 2

(c) 4

(d) 5

47. If in 1988, the sum of the food and fertilizer production was 170 million tonnes, the value of food production must have been (approximately, in million tonnes) ...

(a) 90

(b) 70

(c) 100

(d) Insufficient data

48. From its apparent behaviour, the food production in year 1992 can be expected to ...

(a) go up

(b) go down

(c) remain the same as previous year.

(d) nothing can be said.

49. Going according to previous trends, one can say that the Fertilizer Production has shown an anomalous behaviour in which year?

(a) 1985

(b) 1984

(c) 1991

(d) 1989

50. A scholar observed that if the production of fertilizers in 1989 had been the same as that in 1988, then the total fertilizer production for all the given years would have been 450 million tonnes. Using this information, and knowing that the food production has been plotted on the same scale, one may say that the food production in 1983 was (approximately, in million tonnes) ...

(a) 80

(b) 130

(c) 105

(d) Cannot be determined

1993

Directions for Questions 51 to 54: *Answer the questions on the basis of the information given below.*

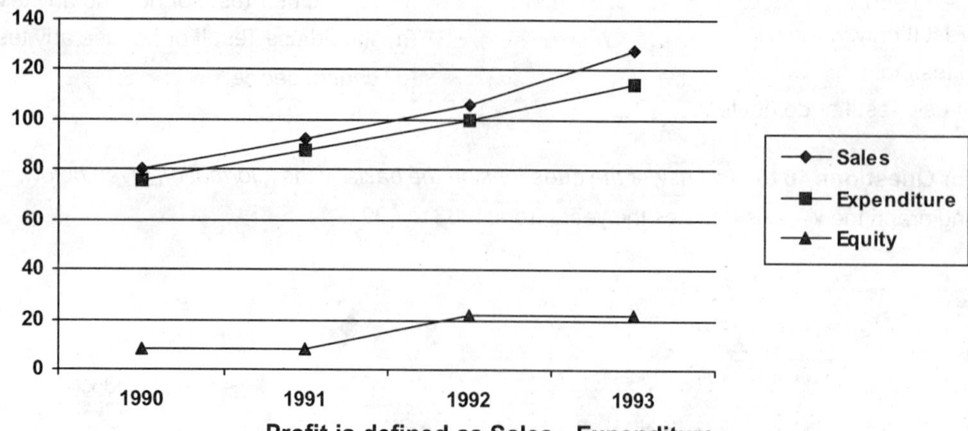

Profit is defined as Sales - Expenditure

51. In which year is the profit per rupee of equity the highest?

(a) 1991 (b) 1992
(c) 1993 (d) 1990 and 1991

52. The simple annual growth rate in sales was the highest between the years?

(a) 1990 – 91 (b) 1991 – 92
(c) 1992 – 93 (d) 1990 – 92

53. In which year is the sales per rupee of expenditure the lowest?

(a) 1990 (b) 1991
(c) 1992 (d) 1993

54. In which year is sales per rupee of equity the highest?

(a) 1990 (b) 1991
(c) 1992 (d) 1994

Directions for Questions 55 to 58: *Answer the questions on the basis of the information given below.*

Ghosh Babu has recently acquired four companies namely Arc – Net Technologies (ANT), Babu Anta Transport (BAT), Charles Anter Tailor (CAT) and Daud Akbar Transistors (DAT). When the results of the companies for the year 1992 – 93 were placed before him. He found a few interesting things about them. While the profits of CAT and DAT were the same, the sales of CAT were the same as those of BAT . Profits of ANT were 10% of its sales, where as the profits of BAT were 20% of its sales. While the total expenses of CAT were 5 times its profits, sales of DAT were 3 times its profits. The total expenses of CAT were Rs.10,00,000, the total expenses of ANT were 10% less than those of CAT.

Profits are defined as the difference between sales and total expenses.

55. Which company had the lowest sales?

(a) ANT (b) BAT
(c) CAT (d) DAT

56. Which company had the highest total expenses?

(a) ANT (b) BAT
(c) CAT (d) DAT

57. Which company had the lowest profits?

(a) ANT (b) BAT
(c) CAT (d) DAT

58. Which company had the highest profits.

(a) ANT (b) BAT
(c) CAT (d) DAT

Directions for Questions 59 to 62: *Answer the questions on the basis of the information given below.*

Study the graph below and answer the questions.

Total Assets are defined as Net Fixed Assets + Net Current Assets + Investments

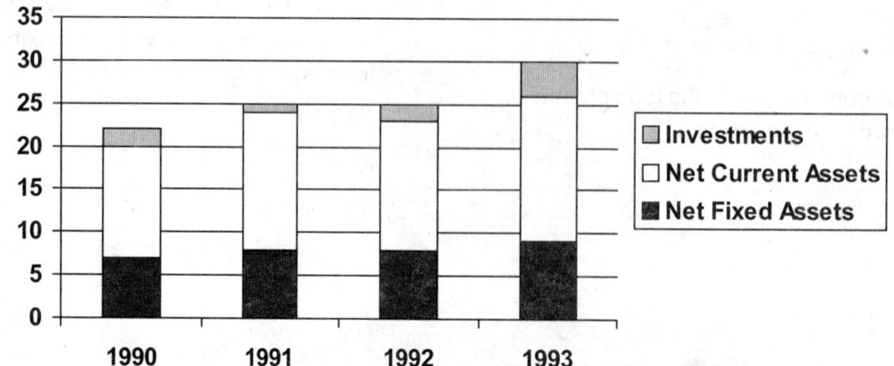

59. What is the approximate simple annual growth rate of Total Assets 1990 and 1993?

(a) 36% (b) 12%
(c) 9% (d) 27%

60. In any two consecutive years, the growth rate is lowest for

(a) Net Fixed Assets.
(b) Net Current Assets.
(c) Investments.
(d) Total Assets.

61. Between 1991 and 1992, the highest growth rate was seen for

(a) Net Fixed Assets
(b) Net Current Assets.
(c) Investments
(d) Total Assets.

62. The only item which has not shown a negative growth in every year between 1990 and 1993 is

(a) Net Fixed Assets. (b) Net Current Assets.
(c) Investments. (d) Total Assets.

Directions for Questions 63 to 67: *Answer the questions on the basis of the information given below.*

A professor keeps data on students tabulated by performance and sex of the student . The data is kept on a computer disk, but unfortunately some of it is lost because of a virus. Only the following could be recovered :

	Performance			Total
	Average	Good	Excellent	
Male			10	
Female				32
Total		30		

Panic buttons were pressed but to no avail. An expert committee was formed, which decided that the following facts were self evident:

Half the students were either excellent or good.

40% of the students were females.

One third of the male students were average.

63. How many students were both female and excellent?

(a) 0 (b) 8
(c) 16 (d) 32

64. How many students were both male and good?

(a) 10 (b) 16
(c) 22 (d) 48

65. Among average students, what was the ratio of male to female?

(a) 1 : 2 (b) 2 : 1
(c) 3 : 2 (d) 2 : 3

66. What proportion of female students were good?

(a) 0 (b) 0.25
(c) 0.5 (d) 1.0

67. What proportion of good students were male?

(a) 0 (b) 0.73
(c) 0.4 (d) 1.0

Directions for Questions 68 to 71: *Answer the questions on the basis of the information given below.*

Given below are the forecasts of the World and Asian energy demand for the years 1990, 2000 and 2010. The demand is given in million barrels per day, crude oil equivalent.

	1990		2000		2010	
	World	Asia	World	Asia	World	Asia
Petroleum	50.0	4.0	70.0	10.0	80.0	15.0
Natural Gas	30.0	0.5	40.0	2.5	50.0	5.0
Solid Fuels	50.0	4.0	60.0	5.0	75.0	10.0
Nuclear	10.0	0.5	20.0	1.0	25.0	1.3
Hydropower	10.0	1.0	10.0	1.5	20.0	2.0
Total	150.00	10.0	200.0	20.0	250.0	33.3

68. Over 1990 – 2010, which two fuels meet more than 60 percent of the total energy demand of both World and Asia?

(a) Petroleum & Natural Gas
(b) Petroleum & Solid Fuels
(c) Natural Gas & Solid Fuels
(d) None of the above

69. Which fuel's proportion in the total energy demand increases over the decade 1990–2000 and decreases over the decade 2000 – 2010 for both the World and Asia?

(a) Petroleum (b) Natural Gas
(c) Solid Fuels (d) Nuclear

70. Which is the fuel whose proportion in the total energy demand will decrease continuously over the period 1990 – 2010, in Asia?

(a) Natural Gas (b) Solid Fuels
(c) Nuclear (d) Hydropower

71. Which is the fuel whose proportion to the total energy demand of the world will remain constant over the period 1990 – 2010 but whose proportion will increase in the total energy demand in Asia?

(a) Solid Fuels (b) Nuclear
(c) Hydropower (d) Natural Gas

1994

Directions for Questions 72 to 74: *Answer the questions on the basis of the information given below.*

Alphonso, on his death bed, keeps half his property for his wife and divide the rest equally among his three sons Ben, Carl and Dave. Some years later Ben dies leaving half his property to his widow and half to his brothers Carl and Dave together, shared equally. When Carl makes his will he keeps half his property for his widow and the rest he bequeaths to his younger brother Dave. When Dave dies some years later, he keeps half his property for his widow and the remaining for his mother. The mother now has Rs. 1,575,000.

72. What was the worth of the total property?

(a) Rs. 30 lakh (b) Rs. 8 lakh
(c) Rs. 18 lakh (d) Rs.24 lakh

73. What was Carl's original share?

(a) Rs. 4 lakh (b) Rs. 12 lakh
(c) Rs. 6 lakh (d) Rs. 5 lakh

74. What was the ratio of the property owned by the widows of the three sons, in the end?

(a) 7 : 9 : 13 (b) 8 : 10 : 15
(c) 5 : 7 : 9 (d) 9 : 12 : 13

Directions for Questions 75 to 79: *Answer the questions on the basis of the information given below.*

Solubility-Temperature relationships for various salts.

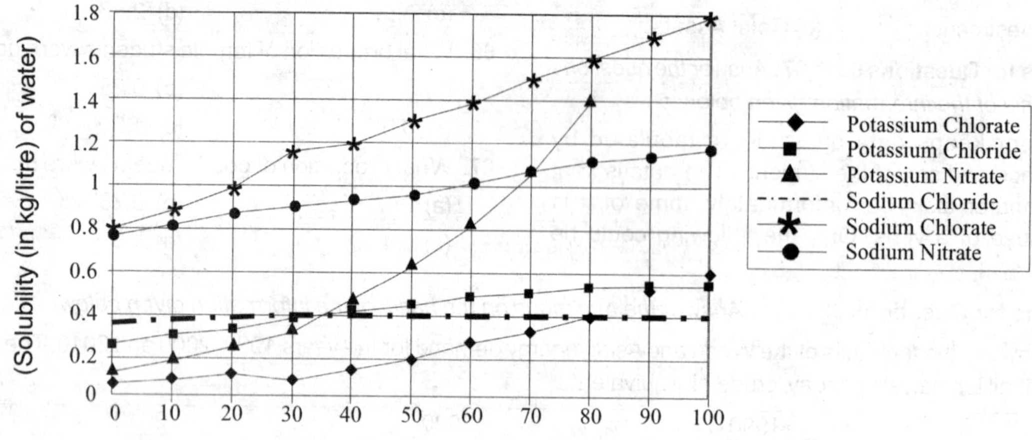

Temperature in Degree Celsius

75. Which of the following salts has greatest solubility?

(a) Potassium Chlorate at 80° C.
(b) Potassium Chloride at 35° C.
(c) Potassium Nitrate at 39° C.
(d) Sodium Chloride at 85° C.

76. Approximately, how many kg of Potassium Nitrate can be dissolved in 10 litres of water at 30°C?

(a) 0.04 (b) 0.4
(c) 4 (d) 0.35

77. By what percentage is the solubility of Potassium Chlorate in water increased as the water is heated from 30°C to 80°C?.

(a) 100 (b) 200
(c) 250 (d) 300

78. If 1 mole of Potassium Chloride weighs 0.07456 kg, approximately. How many moles of Potassium Chloride can be dissolved in 100 litres of water at 36°C?

(a) 700
(b) 650
(c) 480
(d) 540

79. Which of the salts has greater change in solubility in kg / litre of water between 15°C and 25°C?

(a) Potassium Chlorate
(b) Potassium Nitrate
(c) Sodium Chlorate
(d) Sodium Nitrate

Directions for Questions 80 to 83: *Answer the questions on the basis of the information given below.*

In 1984 – 85 value of exports of manufactured articles exceeds over the value of exports of raw materials by 100%.

In 1985 – 86 the ratio of percentage of exports of raw material to that of exports of manufactured articles is 3 : 4.

Exports of food in 1985 – 86 exceeds the 1984 – 85 figures by Rs. 1006 crore.

Item	1984-85	1985-86
Food		23%
Manufactured Articles		
Raw Material		
Total Value of Exports in Crore of Rs.	22400	25800

80. In 1984 – 85 what percentage of total values of exports accounts for items related to food

(a) 23% (b) 29.2%

(c) 32% (d) 22%

81. During 1984 – 85, how much more raw material than food was exported?

(a) Rs. 2580 crore

(b) Rs. 896 crore

(c) Rs. 1986 crore

(d) Rs. 1852 crore

82. Value of exports of raw materials during 1984 – 85 was how much percent less than that for 1985 – 86?

(a) 39

(b) 46.18

(c) 7

(d) 31.6

83. The change in value of exports of manufactured articles from 1984 – 85 to 1985 – 86 is

(a) 296 crore

(b) 629 crore

(c) 2064 crore

(d) 1792 crore

Directions for Questions 84 to 87: *Answer the questions on the basis of the information given below.*

Distribution of material in Ghosh Babu's body (as % of total body weight)

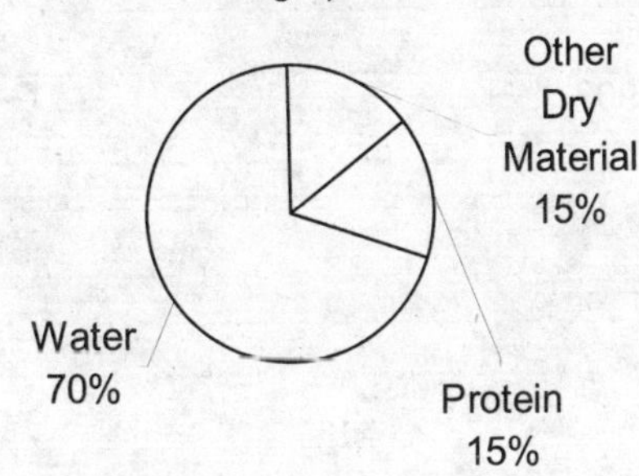

Occurance of Proteins in different organ's of Ghosh Babu's body

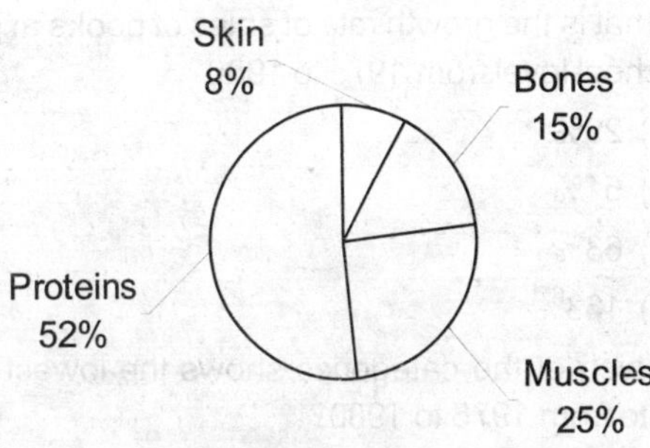

84. What fraction of Ghoshbabu's weight consists of muscular and skin protein?

(a) $\frac{1}{13}$ (b) $\frac{1}{30}$

(c) $\frac{1}{20}$ (d) Cannot be determined

85. Ratio of distribution of protein in muscle to the distribution of protein in skin is

(a) 3 : 1 (b) 3 : 10

(c) 1 : 3 (d) $3\frac{1}{2}:1$

86. What percent of Ghosh Babu's body weight is made up of skin

(a) 0.15 (b) 10

(c) 1.2 (d) Cannot be determined

87. In terms of total body weight, the portion of material other than water and protein is closest to

(a) $\frac{3}{20}$

(b) $\frac{1}{15}$

(c) $\frac{85}{100}$

(d) $\frac{1}{20}$

Directions for Questions 88 to 91: *Answer the questions on the basis of the information given below.*

The following table gives the sales details for text books and reference books at Primary/Secondary/Higher Secondary/Graduate Levels.

Year	Primary	Secondary	Higher Secondary	Graduate Level
1975	42137	8820	65303	25343
1976	53568	10285	71602	27930
1977	58770	16437	73667	28687
1978	56872	15475	71668	30057
1979	66213	17500	78697	33682
1980	68718	20177	82175	36697

88. What is the growth rate of sales of books at primary school level from 1975 to 1980?

(a) 29%

(b) 51%

(c) 63%

(d) 163%

89. Which of the categories shows the lowest growth rate from 1975 to 1980?

(a) Primary (b) Secondary

(c) Higher secondary (d) Graduate Level

90. Which category had the highest growth rate in the period?

(a) Primary (b) Secondary

(c) Higher secondary (d) Graduate Level

91. Which of the categories had either a consistent growth or a consistent decline in the period shown?

(a) Primary (b) Secondary

(c) Higher secondary (d) Graduate Level

Directions for Questions 92 to 95: *Answer the questions on the basis of the information given below.*

Number of Engineering Students (in hundreds) at institutions of different kinds

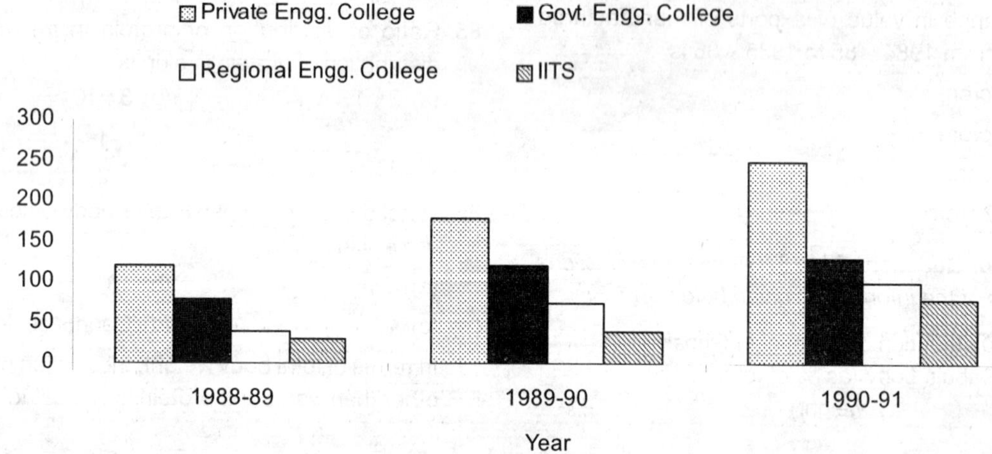

92. What was the total number of engineering students in 1989 – 90?

(a) 28500

(b) 4400

(c) 4200

(d) 42000

93. The growth rate in students of Govt. Engg. Colleges compared to that of Private Engg. Colleges between 1988 – 89 and 1989 – 90 is

(a) more (b) less

(c) equal (d) $\frac{3}{2}$

94. The total number of Engg. Students in 1991 – 92, assuming a 10% reduction in the number over the previous year, is

(a) 5700 (b) 57000

(c) 44800 (d) none of these

95. In 1990 – 91, what percent of Engg. Students were studying at IIT's?

(a) 16 (b) 15

(c) 14 (d) 12

Directions for Questions 96 to 99: *Answer the questions on the basis of the information given below.*

Bankatlal works x hours a day and rests y hours a day. This pattern continues for 1 week, with an exactly opposite pattern next week, and so on for four weeks. Every fifth week he has a different pattern. When he works longer than he rests, his wage per hour is twice what he earns per hour when he rests longer than he works.

The following are his daily working hours for the weeks numbered 1 to 13.

	1st week	5th week	9th week	13th week
Rest	2	3	4	-
Work	5	7	6	8

A week consists of six days and a month consists of 4 weeks.

96. If Bankatlal is paid Rs. 20 per working hour in the 1st week. What is his salary for the 1st month?

(a) Rs.1760 (b) Rs.1440

(c) Rs.1320 (d) Rs.1680

97. Referring to the data given in Q.187, Bankatlal's average monthly salary at the end of the first four months will be

(a) Rs.1780 (b) Rs.2040

(c) Rs.1830 (d) Rs.1680

98. The new manager Khushaldas stipulated that Rs.5 be deducted for every hour of rest and Rs. 25 be paid per hour starting 9th week, then what will be the change in Bankatlal's salary for the 3rd month? (Hourly deductions are constant for all weeks starting 9th week)

(a) Rs.540 (b) Rs.480

(c) Rs.240 (d) Rs.120

99. Using the data in the previous questions, what will be the total earning of Bankatlal at the end of sixteen weeks.

(a) Rs.7320 (b) Rs.7800

(c) Rs.8400 (d) Rs.9600

1995

Directions for Questions 100 to 104: *Answer the questions on the basis of the information given below.*

Ghosh Babu surveyed his companies and obtained the following data. Income tax is paid from profit before tax and the remaining amount is apportioned to dividend and retained earnings. The retained earnings were accumulated into reserves. The reserves at the beginning of 1991 were Rs.80 lakh.

Figure (in Rs. lakh)	1994	1993	1992	1991
Share capital	310	205	98	98
Sales	6435	4725	2620	3270
Profit before Tax	790	525	170	315
Dividends	110	60	30	30
Retained earnings	400	245	70	14

100. In which year was the tax per rupee of 'profit before tax' lowest?

(a) 1991 (b) 1992

(c) 1993 (d) 1994

101. In which year was the sales per rupee of share capital highest?

(a) 1991 (b) 1992

(c) 1993 (d) 1994

102. In which year was the profit before tax per rupee of sales highest?

(a) 1991 (b) 1992

(c) 1993 (d) 1994

103. In which year was the percentage addition to reserves over previous years reserves the highest?

(a) 1991 (b) 1992

(c) 1993 (d) 1994

104. Amount of the reserves at the end of 1994 is

(a) Rs.935 lakh

(b) Rs.915 lakh

(c) Rs.230 lakh

(d) None of these

Directions for Questions 105 to 109: *Answer the questions on the basis of the information given below.*

Market share in four metropolitan cities				
Period/ Product	**Mumbai 1993-94**	**Kolkata 1993-94**	**Delhi 1993-94**	**Chennai 1993-94**
HD	20-15	35-30	20-15	20-30
CO	20-25	30-15	15-10	20-15
BN	45-40	25-35	35-35	10-10
MT	15-20	10-20	10-10	50-45

105. The maximum percentage decrease in market share is

(a) 60% (b) 50%

(c) 53.3% (d) 20%

106. The city in which minimum number of products increased their market shares in 1993-94 is

(a) Mumbai

(b) Delhi

(c) Kolkata

(d) Chennai

107. The market shares of which products did not decrease between 1993-94 in any city?

(a) HD (b) CO

(c) BN (d) None of these

108. The number of products which had 100% market share in four metropolitan cities is

(a) 0 (b) 1

(c) 2 (d) 3

109. The number of products which doubled their market shares in one or more cities is

(a) 0 (b) 1

(c) 2 (d) 3

Directions for Questions 110 to 114: *Answer the questions on the basis of the information given below.*

110. The operating profit in 1991-92 increased over that in 1990-91 by

(a) 23% (b) 22%

(c) 25% (d) 24%

111. The interest burden in 1991-92 was higher than that in 1990-91 by

(a) 50% (b) Rs.25 lakh

(c) 90% (d) Rs.41 lakh

112. If on an average, 20% rate of interest was charged on borrowed funds, then the total borrowed funds used by this company in the given two years amounted to

(a) Rs.221 lakh (b) Rs.195 lakh

(c) Rs.368 lakh (d) Rs.515 lakh

113. The retained profit in 1991-92, as compared to that in 1990-91 was

(a) higher by 2.5% (b) higher by 1.5%

(c) lower by 2.5% (d) lower by 1.5%

114. The equity base of these companies remained unchanged. Then the total dividend earning by the share holders in 1991-92 is

(a) Rs.104 lakh (b) Rs.9 lakh

(c) Rs.12.8 lakh (d) Rs.15.6 lakh

Directions for Questions 115 to 119: *Answer the question on the basis of the information given below.*

Foreign trade (in billion dollars)

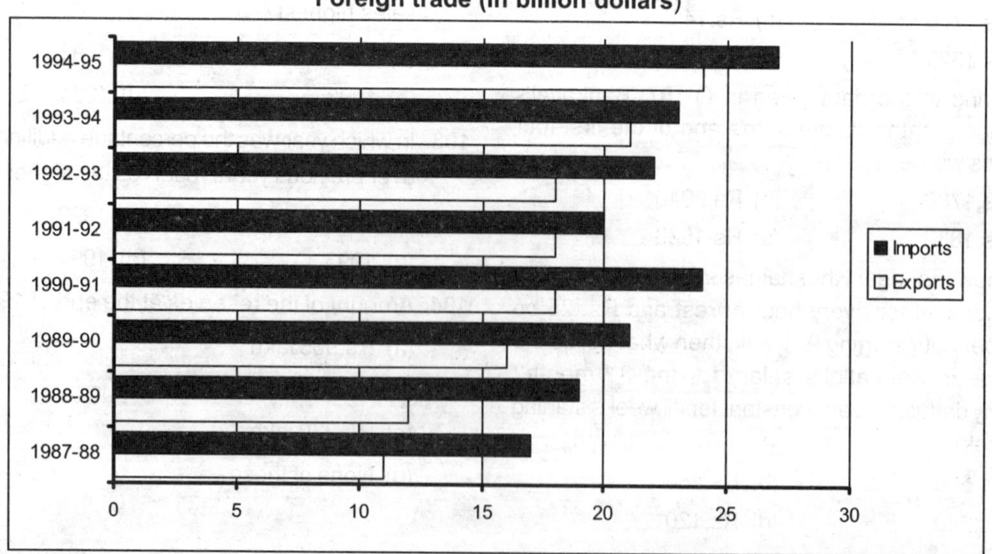

115. In which year was the trade deficit highest?
(a) 1987-88 (b) 1988-89
(c) 1989-90 (d) 1990-91

116. In how many years was the trade deficit less than the trade deficit in the succeeding year?
(a) 1 (b) 2
(c) 3 (d) 4

117. Export earning in 1990-91 is how many per cent of imports in 1991-92?
(a) 82% (b) 85%
(c) 90% (d) 15%

118. In the last three years, the total export earnings have accounted for how many per cent of the value of the imports?
(a) 80% (b) 83%
(c) 95% (d) 88%

119. Which of the following statements can be inferred from the graph?
I. In all the years shown in the graph, the trade deficit is less than the export earning.
II. Export earnings increased in every year between 1989-90 and 1991-92.
III. In all the years shown in the graph, the earning by exports is less than the expenditure on imports in the preceding year.
(a) I only
(b) II only
(c) III only
(d) I and III only

Directions for Questions 120 to 124: *Answer the questions on the basis of the information given below.*

Revenue obtained by a publishing house while selling books, magazines and journals (Rs.in lakh).

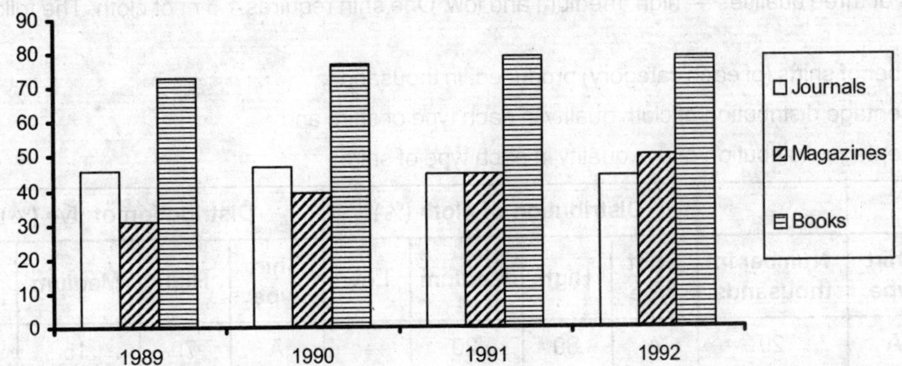

120. Which year shows the highest change in revenue obtained from journals?
(a) 1989 (b) 1990
(c) 1991 (d) 1992

121. In 1992, what per cent of the total revenue came from books?
(a) 45% (b) 55%
(c) 35% (d) 25%

122. The number of years in which there was an increase in revenue from at least two categories is
(a) 1 (b) 2
(c) 3 (d) 4

123. If 1993 were to show the same growth as 1992 over 1991, the revenue in 1993 must be
(a) Rs.194 lakh
(b) Rs.187 lakh
(c) Rs.172 lakh
(d) Rs.177 lakh

124. The growth in total revenue from 1989 to 1992 is
(a) 21% (b) 28%
(c) 15% (d) 11%

Directions for Questions 125 to 129: *Answer the questions on the basis of the information given below.*

Machine M1 as well as machine M2 can independently produce either product P or product Q. The time taken by machines M1 and M2 (in minutes) to produce one unit of product P and product Q are given in the table below: (Each machine works 8 hour per day).

Product	M1	M2
P	10	8
Q	6	6

125. What is the maximum number of units that can be manufactured in one day?
(a) 140 (b) 160
(c) 120 (d) 180

126. If M1 works at half its normal efficiency, what is the maximum number of units produced, if at least one unit of each must be produced?

(a) 96

(b) 89

(c) 100

(d) 119

127. What is the least number of machine hours required to produce 30 pieces of P and 25 pieces of Q respectively?

(a) 6 hr 30 min

(b) 7 hr 24 min

(c) 6 hr 48 min

(d) 4 hr 6 min

128. If the number of units of P is to be three times that of Q, what is the maximum idle time to maximize total units manufactured?

(a) 0 min

(b) 24 min

(c) 1 hr

(d) 2 hr

129. If equal quantities of both are to be produced, then out of the four choices given below, the least efficient way would be

(a) 48 of each with 3 min idle

(b) 64 of each with 12 min idle

(c) 53 of each with 10 min idle

(d) 71 of each with 9 min idle

Directions for Questions 130 to 134: *Answer the questions on the basis of the information given below.*

A company produces five types of shirts — A, B, C, D and E — using cloth of three qualities — high, medium and low —, using dyes of three qualities — high, medium and low. One shirt requires 1.5 m of cloth. The following table gives respectively:

1. The number of shirts (of each category) produced, in thousands,
2. The percentage distribution of cloth quality in each type of shirt, and
3. The percentage distribution of dye quality in each type of shirt.

		Distribution of cloth (%)				Distribution of dye (%)			
Shirt type	**Number in thousands**	**Shirt type**	**High**	**Medium**	**Low**	**Shirt type**	**High**	**Medium**	**Low**
A	20	A	80	20	–	A	70	15	15
B	30	B	30	40	30	B	20	50	30
C	30	C	–	70	30	C	–	60	40
D	10	D	–	60	40	D	–	40	60
E	10	E	–	10	90	E	–	20	80

130. What is the total requirement of cloth?

(a) 1,50,000 m (b) 2,00,000 m

(c) 2,25,000 m (d) 2,50,000 m

131. How many metres of low-quality cloth is consumed?

(a) 22,500 m (b) 46,500 m

(c) 60,000 m (d) 40,000 m

132. How many metres of high quality cloth is consumed by A-type shirts?

(a) 8,000 m

(b) 112,000 m

(c) 24,000 m

(d) 30,000 m

133. What is the ratio of the three qualities of dyes in high-quality cloth?

(a) 2 : 3 : 5

(b) 1 : 2 : 5

(c) 7 : 9 : 10

(d) Cannot be determined

134. What is the ratio of low-quality dye used for C-type shirts to that used for D- type shirts?

(a) 3 : 2

(b) 2 : 1

(c) 1 : 2

(d) 2 : 3

1996

Directions for Questions 135 to 139: *Answer the questions on the basis of the information given below.*

The data given in the table shows the investment details in country 'Fortune Land' of companies A, B, C, D, E and F. Figures in the table are in US dollars in billions.

	A	B	C	D	E	F
Year 1	2.5	4.6	5.8	3.11	10.6	7.8
Year 2	6.7	7.5	12.5	5.6	17.4	25.3
Year 3	11.5	18.7	21.2	7.7	29.8	60.1

135. What is the percentage increase in investment of B, C, D and E from year 1 to year 3?

(a) 121% (b) 321%
(c) 221% (d) 300%

136. What is the ratio of investments of E to F for the years 1 to 3?

(a) 31 : 19 (b) 19 : 31
(c) 20 : 29 (d) 41 : 53

137. What is D's contribution as a percentage of total investments in year 2?

(a) 8.2% (b) 4.5%
(c) 7.4% (d) 9.2%

138. For which company is investment not increased from year 1 to year 3?

(a) C (b) D
(c) F (d) None of these

139. What is the percentage difference in investments of companies A, B, C and companies D, E, F in year 2?

(a) 75% (b) 81%
(c) 67.5% (d) 42.3%

Directions for Questions 140 to 144: *Answer the questions on the basis of the information given below.*

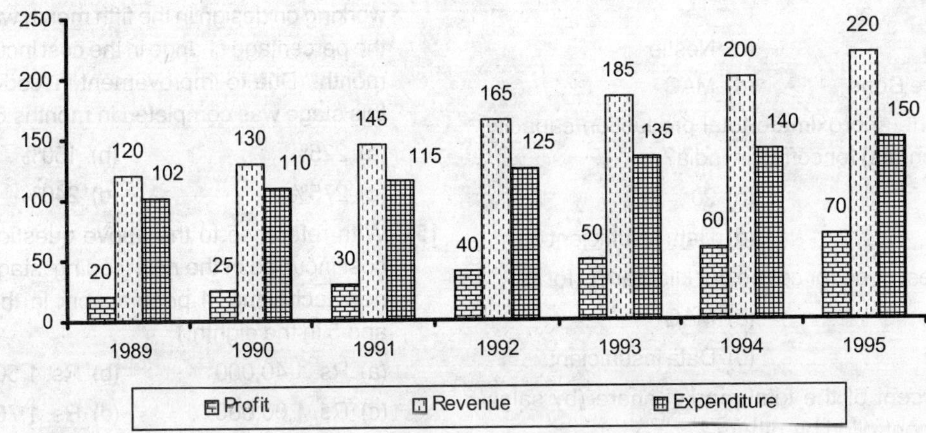

140. The average revenue collected in the given 7 years is approximately

(a) Rs. 164 lakh (b) Rs. 168 lakh
(c) Rs. 171 lakh (d) Rs. 175 lakh

141. The expenditure for the 7 years together form what per cent of the revenues during the same period?

(a) 75% (b) 67%
(c) 62% (d) 83%

142. Which year showed the greatest percentage increase in profit as compared to the previous year?

(a) 1993 (b) 1994
(c) 1990 (d) 1992

143. In which year was the growth in expenditure maximum as compared to the previous year?

(a) 1993
(b) 1995
(c) 1991
(d) 1992

144. If the profit in 1996 shows the annual rate of growth as it had shown in 1995 over the previous year, then what approximately will be the profit in 1996?

(a) Rs. 72 lakh
(b) Rs. 82 lakh
(c) Rs. 93 lakh
(d) Rs. 78 lakh

Directions for Questions 145 to 149: *Answer the questions on the basis of the information given below.*

The following table gives data about certain coffee producers in India.

	Production ('000 tonnes)	Capacity utilisation (%)	Sales ('000 tonnes)	Total sales value (Rs. in crores)
Brooke Bond	2.97	76.50	2.55	31.15
Nestle	2.48	71.20	2.03	26.75
Lipton	1.64	64.80	1.26	15.25
MAC	1.54	59.35	1.47	17.45
Total (including others)	11.60	61.30	10.67	132.80

145. What is the maximum production capacity (in '000 tonnes) of Lipton for coffee?

(a) 2.53 (b) 2.85
(c) 2.24 (d) 2.07

146. Which company out of the four companies mentioned above has the maximum unutilised capacity (in '000 tonnes)?

(a) Lipton (b) Nestle
(c) Brooke Bond (d) MAC

147. What is the approximate total production capacity (in '000 tonnes) for coffee in India?

(a) 18 (b) 20
(c) 18.7 (d) Data insufficient

148. The highest price for coffee per kilogram is for

(a) Nestle (b) MAC
(c) Lipton (d) Data insufficient

149. What percent of the total market share (by sales value) is controlled by 'others'?

(a) 60% (b) 32%
(c) 67% (d) insufficient data

Directions for Questions 150 to 154: *Answer the questions on the basis of the information given below.*

Mulayam Software Co., before selling a package to its clients, follows the given schedule.

Month	Stage	Cost (Rs. '000 per man / month)
1-2	Specification	40
3-4	Design	20
5-8	Coding	10
9-10	Testing	15
11-15	Maintenance	10

The number of people employed in each month is:

Month	1	2	3	4	5	6	7	8	9	10	11	12	13	14	15
Number of people employed	2	3	4	3	4	5	5	4	4	1	3	3	1	1	1

150. Due to overrun in 'design', the design stage took 3 months, i.e. months 3, 4 and 5. The number of people working on design in the fifth month was 5. Calculate the percentage change in the cost incurred in the fifth month. (Due to improvement in 'coding' technique, this stage was completed in months 6-8 only.)

(a) 225% (b) 150%
(c) 275% (d) 240%

151. With reference to the above question, what is the cost incurred in the new 'coding' stage? (Under the new technique, 4 people work in the sixth month and 5 in the eighth.)

(a) Rs. 1,40,000 (b) Rs. 1,50,000
(c) Rs. 1,60,000 (d) Rs. 1,70,000

152. What is the difference in cost between the old and the new techniques?

(a) Rs. 30,000 (b) Rs. 60,000
(c) Rs. 70,000 (d) Rs. 40,000

153. Under the new technique, which stage of software development is most expensive for Mulayam Software Co.?

(a) Testing (b) Specification
(c) Coding (d) Design

154. Which five consecutive months have the lowest average cost per man-month under the new technique?

(a) 1-5 (b) 9-13
(c) 11-15 (d) None of these

Directions for Questions 155 to 169: *Answer the questions on the basis of the information given below.*

The amount of money invested (rupees in crores) in the core infrastructure areas of two districts, Chittoor and Khammam of Andhra Pradesh, is as follows.

Chittor district			Khammam district		
Core area	**1995**	**1996**	**Core area**	**1995**	**1996**
Electricity	815.2	1054.2	**Electricity**	2065.8	2365.1
Chemical	389.5	476.7	**Chemical**	745.3	986.4
Thermal	632.4	565.9	**Thermal**	1232.7	1026.3
Solar	468.1	589.6	**Solar**	1363.5	1792.1
Nuclear	617.9	803.1	**Nuclear**	1674.3	2182.1
Total	2923.1	3489.5	**Total**	7081.6	8352.0

155. By what per cent was the total investment in the two districts more in 1996 as compared to 1995?

(a) 14% (b) 21%
(c) 24% (d) 18%

156. The investment in electricity and thermal energy in 1995 in these two districts formed what per cent of the total investment made in that year?

(a) 41% (b) 47%
(c) 52% (d) 55%

157. In Khammam district, the investment in which area in 1996 showed the highest percentage increase over the investment in that area in 1995?

(a) Electricity (b) Chemical
(c) Solar (d) Nuclear

158. Approximately how many times was the total investment in Chittoor to the total investment in Khammam?

(a) 2.8 (b) 2
(c) 2.4 (d) 1.7

159. If the total investment in Khammam shows the same rate of increase in 1997, as it had shown from 1995 to 1996, what approximately would be the total investment in Khammam in 1997?

(a) Rs. 9,850 crore
(b) Rs. 10,020 crore
(c) Rs. 9,170 crore
(d) Rs. 8,540 crore

Directions for Questions 160 to 164: *Answer the questions on the basis of the information given below.*

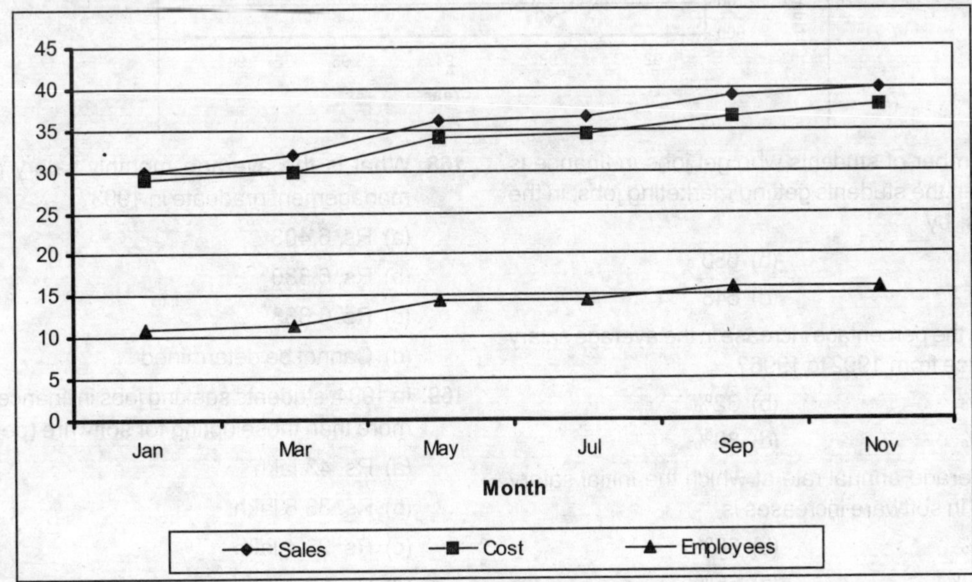

Employees in thousands Sales – Cost = Profit

160. Which month records the highest profit?
(a) September (b) July
(c) March (d) May

161. In which month is the total increase in the cost highest as compared to two months ago?
(a) March (b) September
(c) July (d) May

162. In which month is the percentage increase in sales two months before, the highest?
(a) March (b) September
(c) July (d) May

163. Which month has the highest profit per employee?
(a) September
(b) July
(c) January
(d) March

164. Assuming that no employees left the job, how many more people did the company take on in the given period?
(a) 4,600 (b) 5,000
(c) 5,800 (d) 6,400

Directions for Questions 165 to 169: *Answer the questions on the basis of the information given below.*

The first table gives the percentage of students in MBA class, who sought employment in the areas of finance, marketing and software. The second table gives the average starting salaries of the students per month, (rupees in thousands) in these areas. The third table gives the number of students who passed out in each year.

First table

	Finance	Marketing	Software	Others
1992	22	36	19	23
1993	17	48	23	12
1994	23	43	21	13
1995	19	37	16	28
1996	32	32	20	16

Second table

	Finance	Marketing	Software
1992	5450	5170	5290
1993	6380	6390	6440
1994	7550	7630	7050
1995	8920	8960	7760
1996	9810	10220	8640

Third table

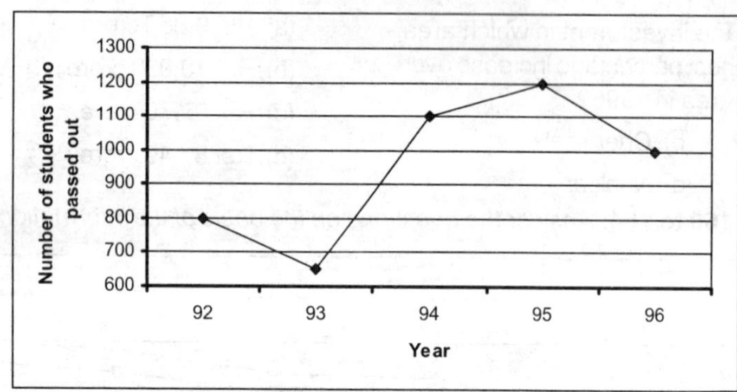

165. The number of students who get jobs in finance is less than the students getting marketing jobs, in the 5 years, by
(a) 826 (b) 650
(c) 750 (d) 548

166. What is the percentage increase in the average salary of finance from 1992 to 1996?
(a) 60% (b) 32%
(c) 96% (d) 80%

167. The average annual rate at which the initial salary offered in software increases is
(a) 21% (b) 33%
(c) 15.9% (d) 65%

168. What is the average monthly salary offered to a management graduate in 1993?
(a) Rs. 6,403
(b) Rs. 6,330
(c) Rs. 6,333
(d) Cannot be determined

169. In 1994, students seeking jobs in finance earned ___ more than those opting for software (per annum).
(a) Rs. 43 lakh
(b) Rs. 33.8 lakh
(c) Rs. 28.4 lakh
(d) Rs. 38.8 lakh

1997

Directions for Questions 170 to 174: Answer the questions on the basis of the information given below.

Hotels in Mumbai

Project	No. of rooms	Cost (Rs. in crores)	Year of completion	Company
Windsor Manor	600	275	1999	IHCL
Leela Hotels	310	235	1999	Leela Hotels
Mumbai Heights	250	250	1998	Bombay Hotels
Royal Holidays	536	225	1998	Lokhandwala Group
Majestic Holiday	500	250	1999	Raheja Group
Supremo Hotel	300	300	1999	ITC
Hyatt Regency	500	250	2000	Asian Hotels

Note: All projects start in 1997.

170. Which of the following had the least cost per room?
(a) Lokhandwala Group (b) Raheja Group
(c) IHCL (d) ITC

171. Which of the following has the maximum number of rooms per crore of rupees?
(a) IHCL (b) Raheja Group
(c) Lokhandwala Group (d) ITC

Additional directions for questions 172 to 174: *Assume that the cost of the project is incurred in the year of completion; interest is charged at the rate of 10% per annum.*

172. What is the cost incurred for projects completed in 1998?
(a) Rs. 475 crore (b) Rs. 500 crore
(c) Rs. 522.5 crore (d) Rs. 502.5 crore

173. What is the cost incurred for projects completed in 1999?
(a) Rs. 1,282.6 crore
(b) Rs. 1,270 crore
(c) Rs. 1,805.1 crore
(d) Rs. 1,535 crore

174. What is the approximate cost incurred for projects completed by 2000?
(a) Rs. 1,785 (b) Rs. 2,140
(c) Rs. 2,320 (d) None of these

Directions for questions 175 to 180: *Answer the questions on the basis of the information given below.*

The graph given below shows the quantity of milk and food grains consumed annually along with female and male population (in millions). Use the data to answer the questions that follow.

175. When was the per capita production of milk least?
(a) 1990 (b) 1992
(c) 1994 (d) 1996

176. When was the per capita production of foodgrains most?
(a) 1992 (b) 1993
(c) 1994 (d) 1995

177. In which year was the difference between the percentage increase in the production of foodgrains and milk maximum?
(a) 1993 (b) 1994
(c) 1995 (d) 1996

178. If milk contains 320 calories and foodgrains contain 160 calories, in which year was the per capita consumption of calories highest?
(a) 1993 (b) 1994
(c) 1995 (d) 1996

179. If one gallon milk contains 120 g of a particular nutrient and one tonne of foodgrains contains 80 g of the same nutrient, in which year was the availability of this nutrient maximum?
(a) 1993 (b) 1994
(c) 1995 (d) 1996

180. Referring to the above question, in which year was the per capita consumption of this nutrient highest?
(a) 1993 (b) 1994
(c) 1995 (d) 1996

Directions for Questions 181 to 186: *Answer the questions on the basis of the information given below.*

The graph given below gives the yearly details of money invested in producing a certain product over the years 1991 to 1995. It also gives the profit (in '000 rupees).

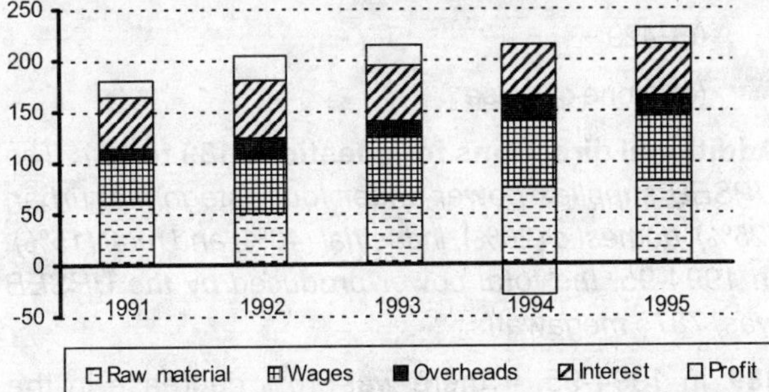

181. In which year was the increase in raw material maximum?
(a) 1992 (b) 1993
(c) 1994 (d) 1995

182. In which period was the change in profit maximum?

(a) 1991-92 (b) 1992-93

(c) 1993-94 (d) 1994-95

183. Which component of the cost production has remained more or less constant over the period?

(a) Interest (b) Overheads

(c) Wages (d) Raw material

184. In which year were the overheads, as a percentage of the raw material, maximum?

(a) 1995 (b) 1994

(c) 1992 (d) 1993

185. What percentage of the costs did the profits form over the period?

(a) 3% (b) 5%

(c) 8% (d) 11%

186. If the interest component is not included in the total cost calculation, which year would show the maximum profit per unit cost?

(a) 1991

(b) 1992

(c) 1993

(d) 1995

Directions for Questions 187 to 191: *Answer the questions on the basis of the information given below.*

The following table gives the tariff [in paise per kilo-watt-hour (kWh)] levied by the UPSEB in 1994-95, in four sectors and the regions within them. The table also gives the percentage change in the tariff as compared to 1991-92.

	Region 1		Region 2		Region 3		Region 4		Region 5	
	P/kWh	%	P/kWh	% incr.	P/kWh	% incr.	P/kWh	% incr.	P/kWh	% incr.
Sector 1	425	+15	472	+5	420	–4	415	+8	440	+10
Sector 2	430	+12	468	+8	448	+7	423	–3	427	+11
Sector 3	428	+8	478	–4	432	+6	441	+10	439	+8
Sector 4	434	–5	470	+15	456	+10	451	+12	446	–12

187. If the amount of power consumed by the various regions in sector 1 is the same, then as compared to 1991-92 the net tariff in 1994-95

(a) increased by 6.5%

(b) decreased by 3.5%

(c) increased by 10.2%

(d) decreased by 7.3%

188. What was the approximate average tariff in region 3 in 1991-92?

(a) 407

(b) 420

(c) 429

(d) None of these

Additional directions for questions 189 to 191: *The UPSEB supplies power under four categories: urban (25%), domestic (20%), industrial (40%) and rural (15%). In 1994-95, the total power produced by the UPSEB was, 7875 megawatts.*

189. In 1994-95, if there was 10% decrease in the domestic consumption of power as compared to that in 1991-92, what was the consumption of power in the rural sector in 1991-92?

(a) 1,312 megawatts

(b) 1,422 megawatts

(c) 1,750 megawatts

(d) None of these

190. In the given 2 years, what is the total tariff paid by the urban sector?

(a) Rs. 22.4 lakh

(b) Rs. 21.6 lakh

(c) Rs. 27.2 lakh

(d) Cannot be determined

191. Which of the following statements is true?

(a) The average tariff in region 4 is 437.5 p/kWh

(b) The average tariff in region 2 is greater than the average tariff in region 5

(c) In 1991-92, the industrial sector contributed to about 42% of the total revenue from power

(d) None of these

Directions for Questions 192 to 199: *Answer the questions on the basis of the information given below.*

The table given below gives the annual details of loans from rural banks and agricultural loans over the years 1970 to 1983. Using this data answer the questions that follow.

Year	Loan from Rural Banks			Agricultural Loans		
	Number of rural banks	Average number of loans	Average size (in Rs.)	No. ('000)	Value (Rs. in millions)	Consumer price index
1970	90	28	109	18.3	2.00	43
1971	115	39	133	20.4	3.58	49
1972	130	52	178	25.1	6.26	55
1974	260	98	243	41.2	34.54	70
1975	318	121	283	51.4	52.21	78
1980	605	288	567	135.7	498.4	131
1981	665	312	622	152.8	612.4	137
1983	840	380	711	211.6	915.7	149

192. In 1974, the amount of agricultural loans formed what percentage of the total loans?

(a) 85% (b) 71%
(c) 77% (d) Cannot be determined

193. From the given data, the number of rural loans up to 1980 formed approximately what percentage of those in 1983?

(a) 112% (b) 80%
(c) 97% (d) Cannot be determined

194. Which of the following pairs of years showed the maximum increase in the number of rural bank loans?

(a) 1971-72 (b) 1974-75
(c) 1970-71 (d) 1980-81

195. What is the value of the agricultural loans in 1983 at 1970 prices?

(a) Rs.326 (b) Rs.264
(c) Rs.305 (d) None of these

196. In which year was the number of rural bank loans per rural bank least?

(a) 1974 (b) 1971
(c) 1970 (d) 1975

197. What is the simple annual rate of increase in the number of agricultural loans from 1970 to 1983?

(a) 132% (b) 81%
(c) 75% (d) 1056%

Additional directions for questions 198 and 199: *If the consumer price index for 1970 is to be taken as 105 and the indices for the subsequent years are to be corrected accordingly, then answer 184 and 185.*

198. By roughly how many points do the indices for 1983 and 1975 differ?

(a) 174 (b) 180
(c) 188 (d) 195

199. What is the value of the loans in 1980 at 1983 prices?

(a) Rs.570 million
(b) Rs.680 million
(c) Rs.525 million
(d) Rs.440 million

1998

Directions for Questions 200 to 202: *Answer the questions on the basis of the information given below.*

A, B, C and D collected one-rupee coins following the given pattern.

Together they collected 100 coins.

Each one of them collected even number of coins.

Each one of them collected at least 10 coins.

No two of them collected the same number of coins.

200. The maximum number of coins collected by any one of them cannot exceed

(a) 64 (b) 36
(c) 54 (d) None of these

201. If A collected 54 coins, then the difference in the number of coins between the one who collected maximum number of coins and the one who collected the second highest number of coins must be at least

(a) 12 (b) 24
(c) 30 (d) None of these

202. If A collected 54 coins and B collected two more coins than twice the number of coins collected by C, then the number of coins collected by B could be

(a) 28 (b) 20
(c) 26 (d) 22

Directions for Questions 203 to 208: *Answer the questions on the basis of the information given below.*

The following table gives the quantity of apples (in tonnes) arriving at New Delhi market from various states in a particular year. The month in which demand was more than supply, the additional demand was met by the stock from cold storage.

Month	State			Cold storage	Total
	HP	UP	J & K		
April	7	0	7	59	73
May	12	1	0	0	13
June	9,741	257	8,017	0	18,015
July	71,497	0	18,750	0	90,247
August	77,675	0	20,286	0	97,961
September	53,912	0	56,602	0	1,10,514
October	12,604	0	79,591	24	92,219
November	3,499	0	41,872	42	45,413
December	1,741	0	14,822	15	16,578
January	315	0	10,922	201	11,438
February	25	0	11,183	77	11,285
March	0	0	683	86	769

203. What was the maximum percentage of apples supplied by any state in any of the months?

(a) 99%

(b) 95%

(c) 88%

(d) 100%

204. Which state supplied the maximum number of apples?

(a) UP

(b) HP

(c) J & K

(d) Cold storage

205. Which state supplied the highest percentage of apples from the total apples supplied?

(a) HP

(b) UP

(c) J & K

(d) Cannot be determined

206. In which of the following periods was the supply greater than the demand?

(a) August-March

(b) June-October

(c) May-September

(d) Cannot be determined

207. If the yield per tree was 40 kg, then from how many trees were the apples supplied to New Delhi (in millions) during the year?

(a) 11.5

(b) 12.5

(c) 13.5

(d) Cannot be determined

208. Using the data in question 207, if there were 250 trees per hectare, then how many hectares of land was used?

(a) 9,400 hectares

(b) 49,900 hectares

(c) 50,000 hectares

(d) 49,450 hectares

Directions for Questions 209 to 214: *Answer the questions on the basis of the information given below.*

The following bar chart gives the growth percentage in the number of households in middle, upper-middle and high income categories in the four regions for the period between 1987-88 and 1994-95.

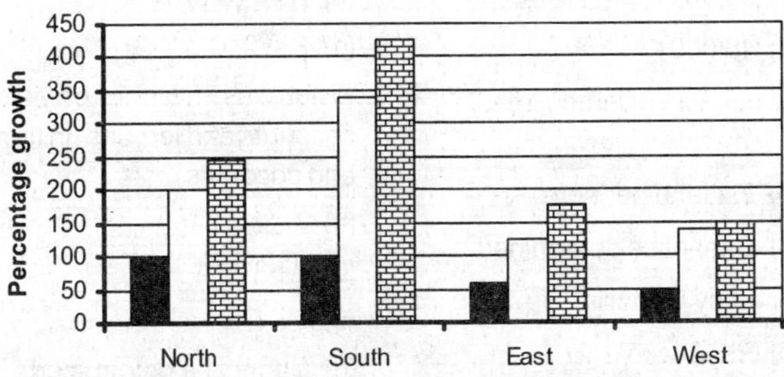

	Number of households in 1987–88 (in thousands)	Average household income in 1987–88	Growth in average household income (1994–95 over 1987–88)
Middle income	40	Rs. 30,000	50%
Upper- middle	10	Rs. 50,000	60%
High income	5	Rs. 75,000	90%

209. Which region showed the highest growth in number of households in all the income categories for the period?

(a) North (b) South
(c) West (d) None of these

210. What was the total household income in northern region for upper-middle class?

(a) Rs. 50 lakh (b) Rs. 500 million
(c) Rs. 300 million (d) Cannot be determined

211. What is the percentage increase in total number of households for the northern region (upper-middle) over the given period?

(a) 100%
(b) 200%
(c) 240%
(d) Cannot be determined

212. What was the average income of the high-income group in 1987-88?

(a) Rs. 75,000
(b) Rs. 25,000
(c) Rs. 2,25,000
(d) Cannot be determined

Additional directions for questions 213 and 214: *The numbers of households in each category were equally distributed in all the regions.*

213. The ratio of total income for the high-income category to the upper-middle class increased by how much percentage in the given period?

(a) 20% (b) 36%
(c) 25% (d) Cannot be determined

214. The average income for the northern region in 1987-88 was

(a) Rs. 37,727 (b) Rs. 37,277
(c) Rs. 35,000 (d) Cannot be determined

Directions for Questions 215 to 219: Answer the questions on the basis of the information given below.

Krishna distributed 10-acre land to Gopal and Ram who paid him the total amount in the ratio 2 : 3. Gopal invested a further Rs. 2 lakh in the land and planted coconut and lemon trees in the ratio 5 : 1 on equal areas of land. There were a total of 100 lemon trees. The cost of one coconut was Rs. 5. The crop took 7 years to mature and when the crop was reaped in 1997, the total revenue generated was 25% of the total amount put in by Gopal and Ram together. The revenue generated from the coconut and lemon trees was in the ratio 3 : 2 and it was shared equally by Gopal and Ram as the initial amount spent by them were equal.

215. What was the total output of coconuts?

(a) 24,000 (b) 36,000
(c) 18,000 (d) 48,000

216. What was the value of output per acre of lemon trees planted?

(a) 0.24 lakh per acre (b) 2.4 lakh per acre
(c) 24 lakh per acre (d) Cannot be determined

217. What was the amount received by Gopal in 1997?

(a) Rs. 1.5 lakh (b) Rs. 3 lakh
(c) Rs. 6 lakh (d) None of these

218. What was the value of output per tree for coconuts?

(a) Rs. 36
(b) Rs. 360
(c) Rs. 3,600
(d) Rs. 240

219. What was the ratio of yields per acre of land for coconuts and lemons (in terms of number of lemons and coconuts)?

(a) 3 : 2
(b) 2 : 3
(c) 1 : 1
(d) Cannot be determined

Directions for Questions 220 to 224: *Answer the questions on the basis of the information given below.*

Ghosh Babu has a manufacturing unit. The following graph gives the cost for various number of units. Given: Profit = Revenue – Variable cost – Fixed cost. The fixed cost remains constant up to 34 units after which additional investment is to be done in fixed assets. In any case, production cannot exceed 50 units.

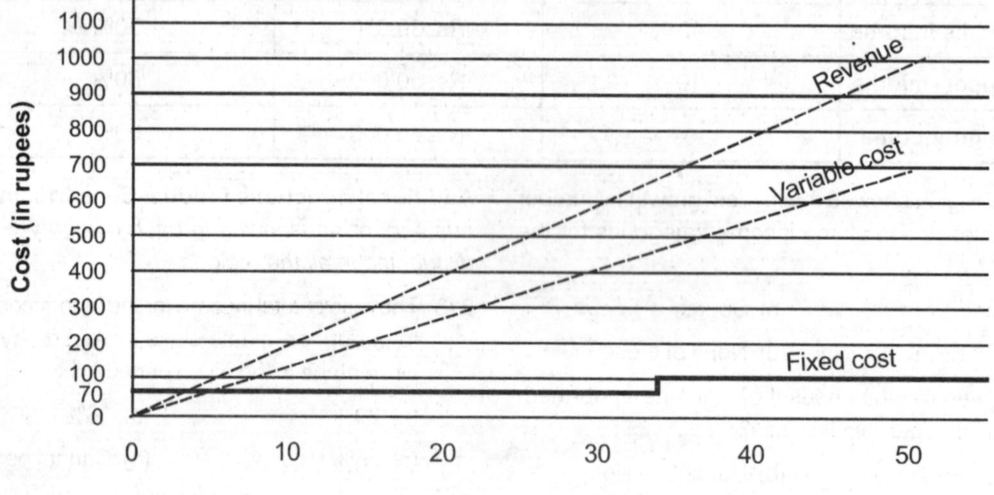

220. What is the minimum number of units that need to be produced to make sure that there was no loss?

(a) 5 (b) 10
(c) 20 (d) Indeterminable

221. How many units should be manufactured such that the profit was at least Rs. 50?

(a) 20 (b) 34
(c) 45 (d) 30

222. If at the most 40 units can be manufactured, then what is the number of units that can be manufactured to maximise profit per unit?

(a) 40 (b) 34
(c) 35 (d) 25

223. If the production cannot exceed 45 units, then what is the number of units that can maximise profit per unit?

(a) 40
(b) 34
(c) 45
(d) 35

224. If the fixed cost of production goes up by Rs. 40, then what is the minimum number of units that need to be manufactured to make sure that there is no loss?

(a) 10 (b) 19
(c) 15 (d) 20

Directions for Questions 225 to 230: *Answer the questions on the basis of the information given below.*

In the following chart, the price of logs shown is per cubic metre that of plywood and saw timber is per tonne.

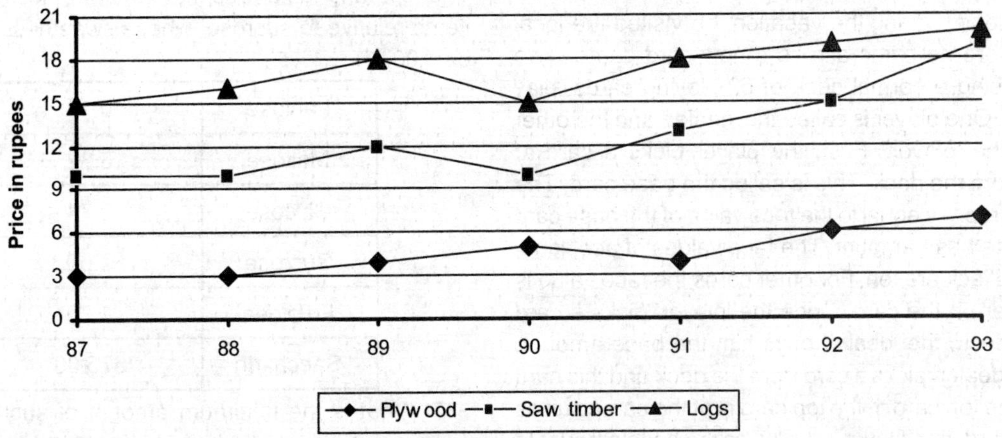

225. What is the maximum percentage increase in price per cubic metre or per tonne over the previous year?

(a) 33.33% (b) 85%

(c) 50% (d) Cannot be determined

226. Which product shows the maximum percentage increase in price over the period?

(a) Saw timber (b) Plywood

(c) Logs (d) Cannot be determined

227. If 1 m^3 = 750 kg for saw timber, find in which year was the difference in prices of saw timber and logs the least?

(a) 1989 (b) 1990

(c) 1991 (d) 1992

228. If one cubic metre = 700 kg for plywood and 800 kg for saw timber, find in which year was the difference in the prices of plywood and saw timber (per cubic metre) the maximum?

(a) 1989 (b) 1990

(c) 1991 (d) 1992

229. If the volume sales of plywood, saw timber and logs were 40%, 30% and 30% respectively, then what was the average realisation in 1993 per cubic metre of sales? (Weight of one cubic metre of saw dust and plywood both = 800 kg)

(a) 18 (b) 15

(c) 16 (d) 13

230. In the previous question, if in 1994, prices increased by 5%, 1% and 10% while the volume sales break-up was 40%, 30% and 30% for plywood, saw timber and logs respectively, then what was the average realisation?

(a) 18.95 (b) 16.45

(c) 13.15 (d) 10.25

1999

Directions for Questions 231 to 233: *Answer the questions on the basis of the information given below.*

A young girl Roopa leaves home with x flowers, goes to the bank of a nearby river. On the bank of the river, there are four places of worship, standing in a row. She dips all the x flowers into the river. The number of flowers doubles. Then she enters the first place of worship, offers y flowers to the deity. She dips the remaining flowers into the river, and again the number of flowers doubles. She goes to the second place of worship, offers y flowers to the deity. She dips the remaining flowers into the river, and again the number of flowers doubles. She goes to the third place of worship, offers y flowers to the deity. She dips the remaining flowers into the river, and again the number of flowers doubles. She goes to the fourth place of worship, offers y flowers to the deity. Now she is left with no flowers in hand.

231. If Roopa leaves home with 30 flowers, the number of flowers she offers to each deity is

(a) 30 (b) 31

(c) 32 (d) 33

232. The minimum number of flowers that could be offered to each deity is

(a) 0 (b) 15

(c) 16 (d) Cannot be determined

233. The minimum number of flowers with which Roopa leaves home is

(a) 16 (b) 15

(c) 0 (d) Cannot be determined

Directions for Questions 234 to 236: *Answer the questions on the basis of the information given below.*

Recently, Ghosh Babu spent his winter vacation on Kyakya Island. During the vacation, he visited the local casino where he came across a new card game. Two players, using a normal deck of 52 playing cards, play this game. One player is called the 'dealer' and the other is called the 'player'. First, the player picks a card at random from the deck. This is called the base card. The amount in rupees equal to the face value of the base card is called the base amount. The face values of ace, king, queen and jack are ten. For other cards the face value is the number on the card. Once the 'player' picks a card from the deck, the 'dealer' pays him the base amount. Then the 'dealer' picks a card from the deck and this card is called the top card. If the top card is of the same suit as the base card, the 'player' pays twice the base amount to the 'dealer'. If the top card is of the same colour as the base card (but not the same suit), then the 'player' pays the base amount to the 'dealer'. If the top card happens to be of a different colour than the base card, the 'dealer' pays the base amount to the 'player'.

Ghosh Babu played the game four times. First time he picked eight of clubs and the 'dealer' picked queen of clubs. Second time, he picked ten of hearts and the 'dealer' picked two of spades. Next time, Ghosh Babu picked six of diamonds and the 'dealer' picked ace of hearts. Lastly, he picked eight of spades and the 'dealer' picked jack of spades. Answer the following questions based on these four games.

234. If Ghosh Babu stopped playing the game when his gain would be maximized, the gain in Rs. would have been

(a) 12
(b) 20
(c) 16
(d) 4

235. The initial money Ghosh Babu had (before the beginning of the game sessions) was Rs. X. At no point did he have to borrow any money. What is the minimum possible value of X?

(a) 16
(b) 8
(c) 100
(d) 24

236. If the final amount of money that Ghosh Babu had with him was Rs. 100, what was the initial amount he had with him?

(a) 120 (b) 8
(c) 4 (d) 96

Directions for Questions 237 and 238: *Answer the questions on the basis of the information given below.*

The following table presents the sweetness of different items relative to sucrose, whose sweetness is taken to be 1.00.

Lactose	0.16
Maltose	0.32
Glucose	0.74
Sucrose	1.00
Fructose	1.70
Saccharin	675.00

237. What is the minimum amount of sucrose (to the nearest gram) that must be added to one gram of saccharin to make a mixture that will be at least 100 times as sweet as glucose?

(a) 7 (b) 8
(c) 9 (d) 100

238. Approximately how many times sweeter than sucrose is a mixture consisting of glucose, sucrose and fructose in the ratio of 1 : 2 : 3?

(a) 1.3 (b) 1.0
(c) 0.6 (d) 2.3

Directions for Questions 239 to 242: *Answer the questions on the basis of the information given below.*

The figure below represents sales and net profit in Rs. crore of IVP Ltd. for five years from 1994-95 to 1998-99. During this period the sales increased from Rs. 100 crore to Rs. 680 crore. Correspondingly, the net profit increased from Rs. 2.5 crore to Rs. 12 crore. Net profit is defined as the excess of sales over total costs.

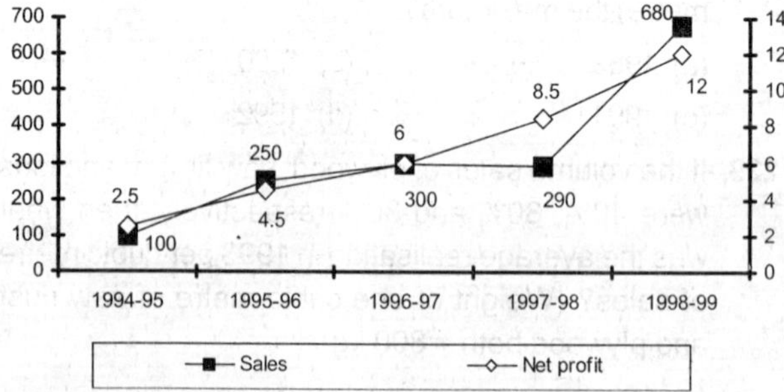

239. The highest percentage of growth in sales, relative to the previous year, occurred in

(a) 1995-96
(b) 1996-97
(c) 1997-98
(d) 1998-99

240. The highest percentage growth in net profit, relative to the previous year, was achieved in

(a) 1998-99 (b) 1997-98
(c) 1996-97 (d) 1995-96

241. Defining profitability as the ratio of net profit to sales, IVP Ltd., recorded the highest profitability in

(a) 1998-99 (b) 1997-98
(c) 1994-95 (d) 1996-97

242. With profitability as defined in question 241, it can be concluded that

(a) profitability is non-decreasing during the five years from 1994-95 to 1998-99.
(b) profitability is non-increasing during the five years from 1994-95 to 1998-99.
(c) profitability remained constant during the five years from 1994-95 to 1998-99.
(d) None of the above

Directions for Questions 243 to 248: *Answer the questions on the basis of the information given below.*

Consider the information provided in the figure below relating to India's foreign trade in 1997-98 and the first eight months of 1998-99. Total trade with a region is defined as the sum of exports and imports from that region. Trade deficit is defined as the excess of imports over exports. Trade deficit may be negative.

A. USA	G. Other East European countries
B. Germany	H. OPEC
C. Other EU	I. Asia
D. UK	J. Other LDCs
E. Japan	K. Others
F. Russia	

Source of imports

1997-98

Imports into India $40,779 million

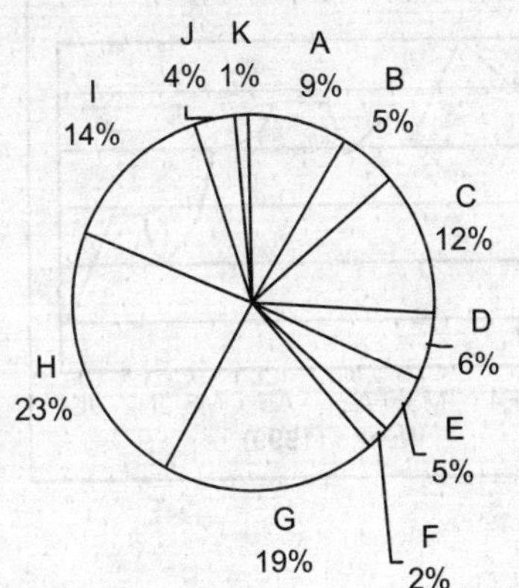

1998-99

Imports into India (April-November)

$28,126 million

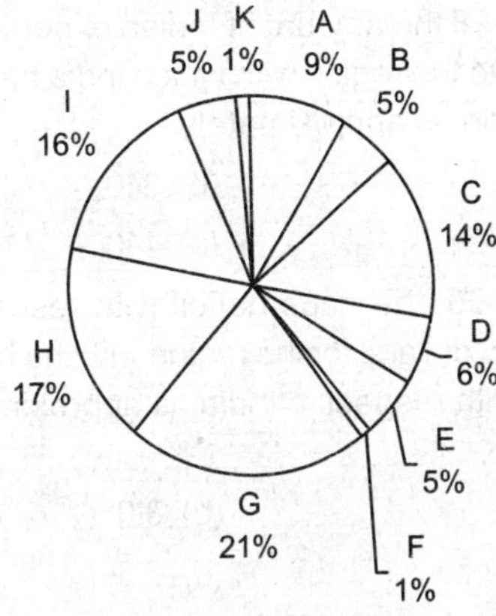

Destination of exports

1997-98

Exports from India: $33,979 million

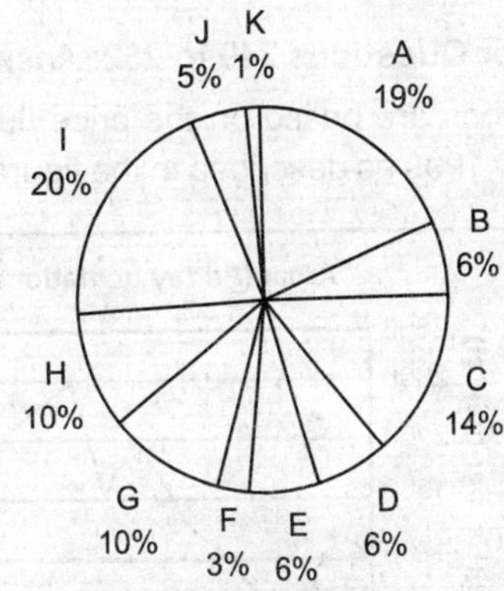

1998-99

Exports from India (April-November)

$21,436 million

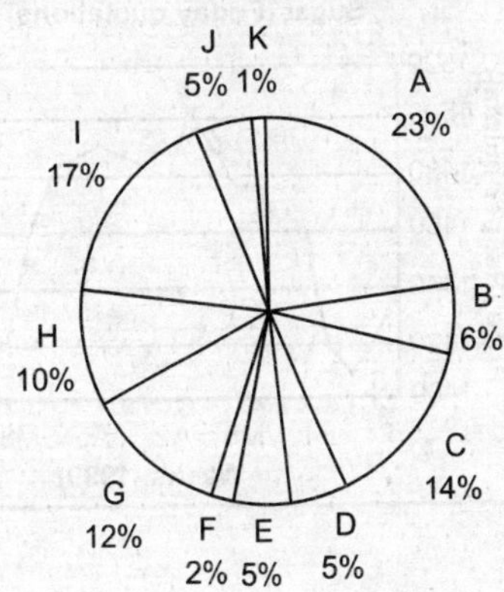

243. What is the region with which India had the highest total trade in 1997-98?

(a) USA (b) Other EU countries
(c) OPEC (d) Others

244. In 1997-98 the amount of Indian exports, million US dollars, to the region with which India had the lowest total trade, is approximately

(a) 750 (b) 340
(c) 220 (d) 440

245. In 1997-98, the trade deficit with respect to India, billion US dollars, for the region with the highest trade deficit with respect to India, is approximately equal to

(a) 6.0 (b) 3.0
(c) 4.5 (d) 7.5

246. What is the region with the lowest trade deficit with India in 1997-98?

(a) USA (b) Asia
(c) Others (d) Other EU countries

Additional directions for questions 247 and 248: *Answer the questions on the basis of the information given below.*

Assume that the average monthly exports from India and imports to India during the remaining four months of 1998-99 would be the same as that for the first eight months of the year.

247. What is the region to which India's exports registered the highest percentage growth between 1997-98 and 1998-99?

(a) Other East European countries
(b) USA
(c) Asia
(d) Exports have declined, no growth

248. What is the percentage growth rate in India's total trade deficit between 1997-98 and 1998-99?

(a) 43
(b) 47
(c) 50
(d) 40

Directions for Questions 249 to 252: *Answer the questions on the basis of the information given below.*

These questions are based on the price fluctuations of four commodities — arhar, pepper, sugar and gold during February-July 1999 as described in the figures below.

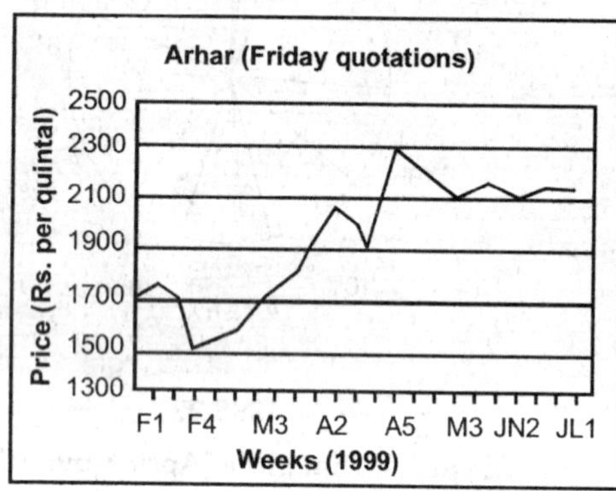

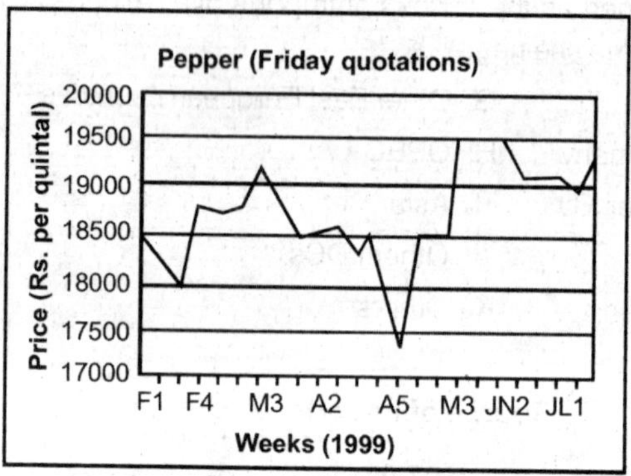

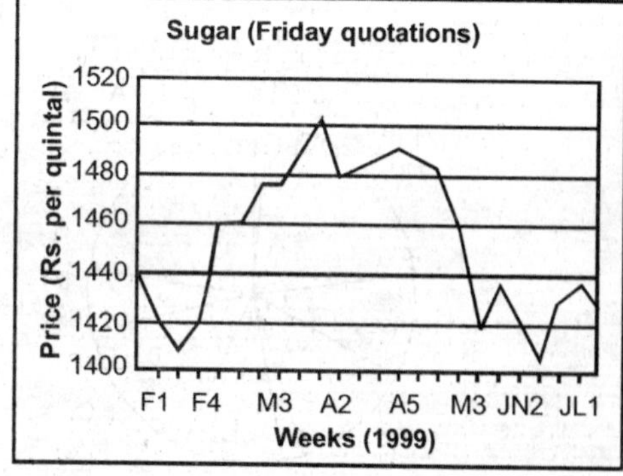

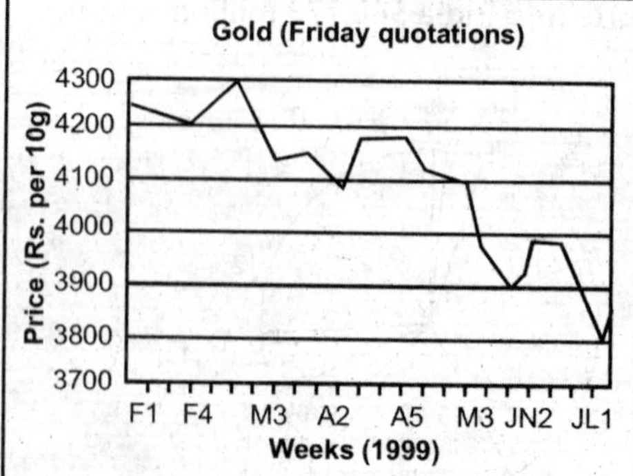

249. Price change of a commodity is defined as the absolute difference in ending and beginning prices expressed as a percentage of the beginning. What is the commodity with the highest price change?

(a) Arhar (b) Pepper
(c) Sugar (d) Gold

250. Price volatility (PV) of a commodity is defined as follows:

PV = (Highest price during the period – Lowest price during the period)/Average price during the period.
What is the commodity with the lowest price volatility?

(a) Arhar (b) Pepper
(c) Sugar (d) Gold

251. Mr X, a fund manager with an investment company invested 25% of his funds in each of the four commodities at the beginning of the period. He sold the commodities at the end of the period. His investments in the commodities resulted in

(a) 17% profit (b) 5.5% loss
(c) No profit, no loss (d) 5.4% profit

252. The price volatility(PV) of the commodity with the highest PV during the February-July period is approximately equal to

(a) 3% (b) 40%
(c) 20% (d) 12%

Directions for Questions 253 to 259: *Answer the questions on the basis of the information given below.*

The table below presents data on percentage population covered by drinking water and sanitation facilities in selected Asian countries.

Population covered by drinking water and sanitation facilities

Percentage coverage

	Drinking water			Sanitation facilities		
	Urban	Rural	Total	Urban	Rural	Total
India	85	79	81	70	14	29
Bangladesh	99	96	97	79	44	48
China	97	56	67	74	7	24
Pakistan	82	69	74	77	22	47
Philippines	92	80	86	88	66	77
Indonesia	79	54	62	73	40	51
Sri Lanka	88	52	57	68	62	63
Nepal	88	60	63	58	12	1

(*Source:* World Resources 1998-99, p. 251, UNDP, UNEP and World Bank.)

Country A is said to dominate B or A > B if A has higher percentage in total coverage for both drinking water and sanitation facilities, and, B is said to be dominated by A, or B < A.

A country is said to be on the coverage frontier if no other country dominates it. Similarly, a country is not on the coverage frontier if it is dominated by at least one other country.

253. Which countries are the countries on the coverage frontier?

(a) India and China
(b) Sri Lanka and Indonesia
(c) Philippines and Bangladesh
(d) Nepal and Pakistan

254. Which of the following statements are true?

A. India > Pakistan and India > Indonesia
B. India > China and India > Nepal
C. Sri Lanka > China
D. China > Nepal

(a) A and C (b) B and D
(c) A, B and C (d) B, C and D

255. Using only the data presented under 'sanitation facilities' columns, it can be concluded that rural population in India, as a percentage of its total population is approximately

(a) 76 (b) 70
(c) 73 (d) Cannot be determined

256. Again, using only the data presented under 'sanitation facilities' columns, sequence China, Indonesia and Philippines in ascending order of rural population as a percentage of their respective total population. The correct order is
(a) Philippines, Indonesia, China
(b) Indonesia, China, Philippines
(c) Indonesia, Philippines, China
(d) China, Indonesia, Philippines

257. India is not on the coverage frontier because
A. it is lower than Bangladesh in terms of coverage of drinking water facilities.
B. it is lower than Sri Lanka in terms of coverage of sanitation facilities.
C. it is lower than Pakistan in terms of coverage of sanitation facilities.
D. it is dominated by Indonesia.
(a) A and B (b) A and C
(c) D (d) None of these

Additional directions for questions 258 and 259: *These relate to the above table with the additional provision that the gap between the population coverages of 'sanitation facilities' and 'drinking water facilities' is a measure of disparity in coverage.*

258. The country with the most disparity in coverage of rural sector is
(a) India
(b) Bangladesh
(c) Nepal
(d) None of these

259. The country with the least disparity in coverage of urban sector is
(a) India
(b) Pakistan
(c) Philippines
(d) None of these

2000

Directions for Questions 260 to 264: *Answer these questions with reference to the table given below.*

Information Technology Industry in India
(Figures are in million US dollars)

		1994-95	1995-96	1996-97	1997-98	1998-99
Software						
	Domestic	350	490	670	950	1250
	Exports	485	734	1083	1750	2650
Hardware						
	Domestic	590	1037	1050	1205	1026
	Exports	177	35	286	201	4
Peripherals						
	Domestic	148	196	181	229	329
	Exports	6	6	14	19	18
Training		107	143	185	263	302
Maintenance		142	172	182	221	236
Networking and others		36	73	156	193	237
Total		2041	2886	3807	5031	6052

260. The total annual exports lies between 35 and 40% to the total annual business of the IT industry, in

(a) 1997-98 and 1994-95
(b) 1996-97 and 1997-98
(c) 1996-97 and 1998-99
(d) 1996-97 and 1994-95

261. The highest percentage growth in the total IT business, relative to the previous year was achieved in

(a) 1995-96
(b) 1996-97
(c) 1997-98
(d) 1998-99

262. Which one of the following statements is correct?

(a) The annual software exports steadily increased but annual hardware exports steadily declined during 1994-99.
(b) The annual peripheral exports steadily increased during 1994-99.
(c) The IT business in training during 1994-99 was higher than the total IT business in maintenance during the same period.
(d) None of the above

Additional directions for questions 263 and 264:

For any activity, A, year X dominates year Y if the IT business in activity A, in the year X is greater than the IT business in activity A in the year Y. For any two IT business activities, A and B, year X dominates year Y if

I. the IT business in activity A, in the year X, is greater than or equal to the IT business in activity A in the year Y,
II. the IT business in activity B, in the year X, is greater than or equal to the IT business in activity B in the year Y and
III. there should be strict inequality in the case of at least one activity.

263. For the IT hardware business activity, which one of the following is not true?

(a) 1997-98 dominates 1996-97
(b) 1997-98 dominates 1995-96
(c) 1995-96 dominates 1998-99
(d) 1998-99 dominates 1996-97

264. For the two IT business activities, hardware and peripherals, which one of the following is true?

(a) 1996-97 dominates 1995-96
(b) 1998-99 dominates 1995-96
(c) 1997-98 dominates 1998-99
(d) None of these

Directions for Questions 265 to 269: *Answer these questions based on the data provided in the table below.*

Factory Sector by Type of Ownership

All figures in the table are in percentage of the total for the corresponding column

Sector	Factories	Employment	Fixed capital	Gross output	Value added
Public:	7	27.7	43.2	25.8	30.8
Central Government	1	10.5	17.5	12.7	14.1
States or local government	5.2	16.2	24.3	11.6	14.9
Central and state or local government	0.8	1.0	1.4	1.5	1.8
Joint:	1.8	5.1	6.8	8.4	8.1
Wholly private	90.3	64.6	46.8	63.8	58.7
Others	0.9	2.6	3.2	2.0	2.4
Total	100	100	100	100	100

265. Suppose the average employment level is 60 per factory. The average employment in 'wholly private' factories is approximately

(a) 43 (b) 47
(c) 50 (d) 54

266. Among the firms in different sectors, value added per employee is highest in
(a) Central Government
(b) Central and States or Local Governments
(c) Joint sector
(d) Wholly private

267. Capital productivity is defined as the gross output value per rupee of fixed capital. The three sectors with the higher capital productivity, arranged in descending order are
(a) Joint, Wholly private, Central and States or Local Governments
(b) Wholly private, Joint, Central and States or Local Governments
(c) Wholly private, Central and States or Local Governments, Joint
(d) Joint, Wholly private, Central

268. A sector is considered 'pareto efficient' if its value added per employee and its value added per rupee of fixed capital is higher than those of all other sectors. Based on the table data, the pareto efficient sector is
(a) Wholly private
(b) Joint
(c) Central and State or Local
(d) others

269. The total value added in all sectors is estimated at Rs. 1,40,000 crore. Suppose the number of firms in the joint sector is 2,700. The average value added per factory, in the Central Government is
(a) Rs. 141 crore (b) Rs. 14.1 crore
(c) Rs. 131 crore (d) Rs. 13.1 crore

Directions for Questions 270 to 273: *Answer these questions based on the data presented in the figure below.*

FEI for a country in a year, is the ratio (expressed as a percentage) of its foreign equity inflows to its GDP. The following figure displays the FEIs for select Asian countries for 1997 and 1998.

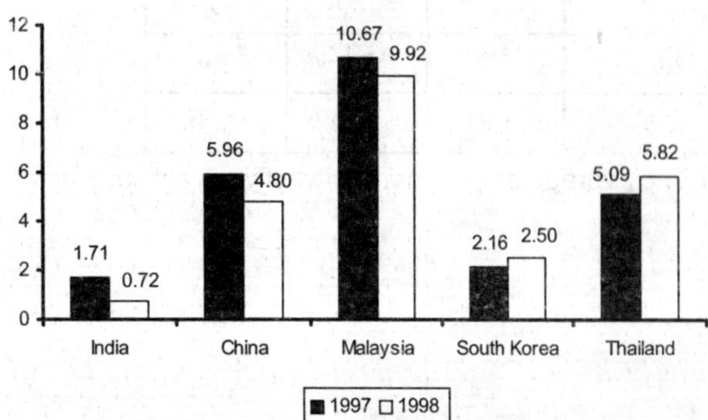

270. The country with the highest percentage change in FEI in 1998 relative to its FEI in 1997, is
(a) India (b) China
(c) Malaysia (d) Thailand

271. Based on the data provided, it can be concluded that
(a) absolute value of foreign equity inflows in 1998 was higher than that in 1997 for both Thailand and South Korea.
(b) absolute value of foreign equity inflows was higher in 1998 for Thailand and lower for China than the corresponding values in 1997.
(c) absolute value of foreign equity inflows was lower in 1998 for both India and China than the corresponding values in 1997.
(d) None of the above can be inferred

272. It is known that China's GDP in 1998 was 7% higher than its value in 1997, while India's GDP grew by 2% during the same period. The GDP of South Korea, on the other hand, fell by 5%. Which of the following statements is/are true?
I. Foreign equity inflows to China were higher in 1998 than in 1997.
II. Foreign equity inflows to China were lower in 1998 than in 1997.
III. Foreign equity inflows to India were higher in 1998 than in 1997.
IV. Foreign equity inflows to South Korea decreased in 1998 relative to 1997.
V. Foreign equity inflows to South Korea increased in 1998 relative to 1997.
(a) I, III and IV (b) II, III and IV
(c) I, III and V (d) II and v

273. China's foreign equity inflows in 1998 were 10 times that of India. It can be concluded that
(a) China's GDP in 1998 was 40% higher than that of India
(b) China's GDP in 1998 was 70% higher than that of India
(c) China's GDP in 1998 was 50% higher than that of India
(d) no inference can be drawn about relative magnitudes of China's and India's GDPs

Directions for Questions 274 to 275: *Answer the questions based on the table below.*

The table shows trends in external transactions of Indian corporate sector during the period 1993-94 to 1997-98. In addition, following definitions hold good:

$Sales_i$, $Imports_i$, and $Exports_i$ respectively denote the sales, imports and exports in year i.

Deficit for year i, $Deficit_i = Imports_i - Exports_i$

Deficit Intensity in year i, $DI_i = Deficit_i / Sales_i$

Growth rate of deficit intensity in year i,

$GDI_i = (DI_i - DI_{i-1}) / DI_{i-1}$

Further, note that all imports are classified as either raw material or capital goods.

Trends in External Transactions of Indian Corporate Sector

(All figures in per cent)

Year	1997-98	1996-97	1995-96	1994-95	1993-94
Export intensity*	9.2	8.2	7.9	7.5	7.3
Import intensity*	14.2	16.2	15.5	13.8	12.4
Imported raw material/Total cost of raw material	20.2	19.2	17.6	16.3	16
Imported capital goods/Gross fixed assets	17.6	9.8	11.8	16.3	19.5

* Ratio of Exports (or Imports) to sales.

274. The highest growth rate in deficit intensity was recorded in

(a) 1994-95 (b) 1995-96

(c) 1996-97 (d) 1997-98

275. The value of the highest growth rate in deficit intensity is approximately

(a) 8.45% (b) 2.15%

(c) 33.3% (d) 23.5%

276. In 1997-98 the total cost of raw material is estimated as 50% of sales of that year. The turnover of gross fixed assets, defined as the ratio of sales to gross fixed assets, in 1997-98 is, approximately

(a) 3.3

(b) 4.3

(c) 0.33

(d) Not possible to determine

277. Which of the following statements can be inferred to be true from the given data?

(a) During the 5-year period between 1993-94 and 1997-98 exports have increased every year.

(b) During the 5-year period 1993-94 and 1997-98, imports have decreased every year.

(c) Deficit in 1997-98 was lower than that in 1993-94.

(d) Deficit intensity has increased every year between 1993-94 and 1996-97.

Directions for Questions 278 to 283: *Answer the questions based on the data given below.*

The figures below present annual growth rate, expressed as the percentage change relative to the previous year, in four sectors of the economy of the Republic of Reposia during the 9-year period from 1990 to 1998. Assume that the index of production for each of the four sectors is set at 100 in 1989. Further, the four sectors: manufacturing, mining and quarrying, electricity, and chemicals, respectively, constituted 20%, 15%, 10% and 15% of total industrial production in 1989.

Manufacturing

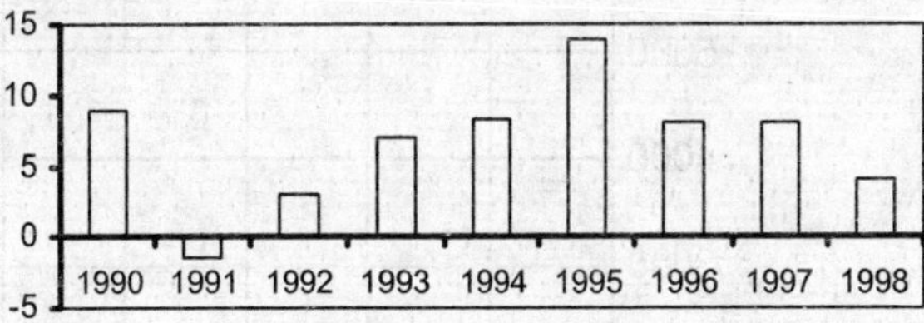

Mining and quarrying

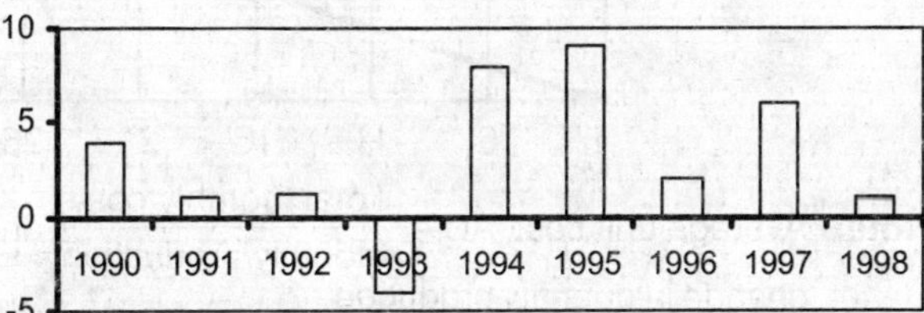

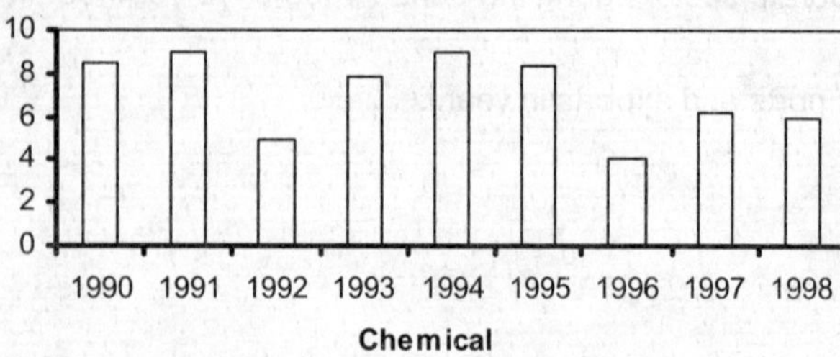

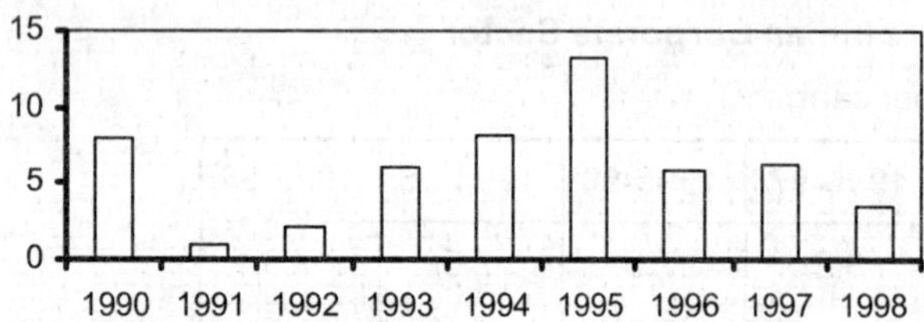

278. Which is the sector with the highest growth during the period 1989 to 1998?

(a) Manufacturing (b) Mining and quarrying
(c) Electricity (d) Chemical

279. The overall growth rate in 1991 of the four sectors together is approximately

(a) 10% (b) 1%
(c) 2.5% (d) 1.5%

280. When was the highest level of production in the manufacturing sector achieved during the 9-year period 1990-98?

(a) 1998 (b) 1995
(c) 1990 (d) Cannot be determined

281. When was the lowest level of production of the mining and quarrying sector achieved during the 9-year period 1990-98?

(a) 1996 (b) 1993
(c) 1990 (d) Cannot be determined

282. The percentage increase of production in the four sectors, namely, manufacturing, mining and quarrying, electricity and chemicals, taken together in 1994, relative to 1989 is approximately

(a) 25% (b) 20%
(c) 50% (d) 40%

283. It is known that the index of total industrial production in 1994 was 50% more than that in 1989. Then, the percentage increase in production between 1989 and 1994 in sectors other than the four listed above is

(a) 57.5% (b) 87.5%
(c) 127.5% (d) 47.5%

Directions for Questions 284 to 289: Answer the questions based on the following information.

ABC Ltd. produces widgets for which the demand is unlimited and they can sell all of their production. The graph below describes the monthly variable costs incurred by the company as a function of the quantity produced. In addition, operating the plant for the first shift results in a fixed monthly cost of Rs. 800. Fixed monthly costs for second shift operation is estimated at Rs. 1,200. Each shift operation provides capacity for producing 30 widgets per month.

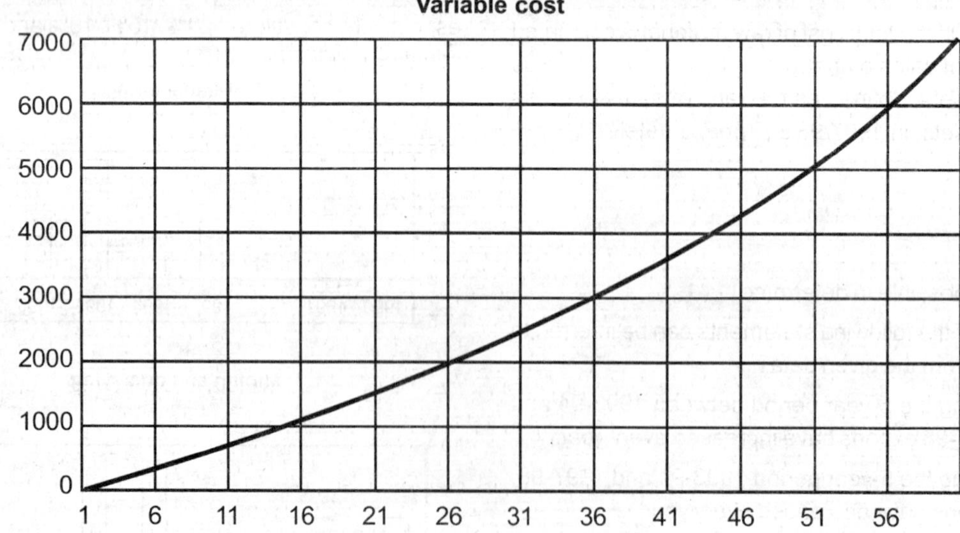

Note: Average unit cost, AC = $\frac{\text{Total monthly costs}}{\text{Monthly production}}$ and marginal cost, MC is the rate of change in total cost for unit change in quantity produced.

284. Total production in July is 40 units. What is the approximate average unit cost for July?

(a) 3,600 (b) 90

(c) 140 (d) 115

285. ABC Ltd. is considering increasing the production level. What is the approximate marginal cost of increasing production from its July level of 40 units?

(a) 110 (b) 130

(c) 150 (d) 160

286. From the data provided it can be inferred that, for production levels in the range of 0 to 60 units,

(a) MC is an increasing function of production quantity.

(b) MC is a decreasing function of production quantity.

(c) initially MC is a decreasing function of production quantity, attains a minimum and then it is an increasing function of production quantity.

(d) None of the above.

287. Suppose that each widget sells for Rs. 150. What is the profit earned by ABC Ltd. in July?

(Profit is defined as the excess of sales revenue over total cost.)

(a) 2,400 (b) 1,600

(c) 400 (d) 0

288. Assume that the unit price is Rs. 150 and profit is defined as the excess of sales revenue over total costs. What is the monthly production level of ABC Ltd. at which the profit is highest?

(a) 30 (b) 50

(c) 60 (d) 40

289. For monthly production level in the range of 0 to 30 units,

(a) AC is always higher than MC.

(b) AC is always lower than MC.

(c) AC is lower than MC up to a certain level and then is higher than MC.

(d) None of the above.

2001

Directions for Questions 290 to 293: *Answer the questions based on the table given below.*

The following table describes garments manufactured based upon the colour and size for each lay. There are four sizes: M – medium, L – large, XL – extra large and XXL – extra extra large. There are three colours: yellow, red and white.

Lay	Number of Garments											
	Yellow				Red				White			
Lay No.	M	L	XL	XXL	M	L	XL	XXL	M	L	XL	XXL
1	14	14	7	0	0	0	0	0	0	0	0	0
2	0	0	0	0	0	0	0	0	42	42	21	0
3	20	20	10	0	18	18	9	0	0	0	0	0
4	20	20	10	0	0	0	0	0	30	30	15	0
5	0	0	0	0	24	24	12	0	30	30	15	0
6	22	22	11	0	24	24	12	0	32	32	16	0
7	0	24	24	12	0	0	0	0	0	0	0	0
8	0	20	20	10	0	2	2	1	0	0	0	0
9	0	20	20	10	0	0	0	0	0	22	22	11
10	0	0	0	0	0	26	26	13	0	20	20	10
11	0	22	22	11	0	26	26	13	0	22	22	11
12	0	0	2	2	0	0	0	0	0	0	0	0
13	0	0	0	0	0	0	0	0	0	0	20	20
14	0	0	0	0	0	0	0	0	0	0	22	22
15	0	0	10	10	0	0	2	2	0	0	22	22
16	0	0	0	0	1	0	0	0	1	0	0	0
17	0	0	0	0	0	5	0	0	0	0	0	0
18	0	0	0	0	0	32	0	0	0	0	0	0
19	0	0	0	0	0	32	0	0	0	0	0	0
20	0	0	0	0	0	5	0	0	0	0	0	0
21	0	0	0	18	0	0	0	0	0	0	0	0
22	0	0	0	0	0	0	0	26	0	0	0	0
23	0	0	0	0	0	0	0	0	0	0	0	22
24	0	0	0	8	0	0	0	1	0	0	0	0
25	0	0	0	8	0	0	0	0	0	0	0	12
26	0	0	0	0	0	0	0	1	0	0	0	14
27	0	0	0	8	0	0	0	2	0	0	0	12
Production	76	162	136	97	67	194	89	59	135	198	195	156
Order	75	162	135	97	67	194	89	59	135	197	195	155
Surplus	1	0	1	0	0	0	0	0	0	1	0	1

290. How many lays are used to produce yellow fabrics?

(a) 10 (b) 11

(c) 12 (d) 14

291. How many lays are used to produce XXL fabrics?

(a) 15 (b) 16

(c) 17 (d) 18

292. How many lays are used to produce XXL yellow or XXL white fabrics?

(a) 8 (b) 9

(c) 10 (d) 15

293. How many varieties of fabrics, which exceed the order, have been produced?

(a) 3 (b) 4

(c) 5 (d) 6

Directions for Questions 294 to 297: *Answer the questions based on the table given below concerning the busiest 20 international airports in the world.*

No.	Name	International Airport Type	Code	Location	Passengers
1	Hartsfield	A	ATL	Atlanta, Georgia, USA	77939536
2	Chicago-O'Hare	A	ORD	Chicago, Illinois, USA	72568076
3	Los Angeles	A	LAX	Los Angeles, California, USA	63876561
4	Heathrow Airport	E	LHR	London, United Kingdom	62263710
5	DFW	A	DFW	Dallas/Ft. Worth, Texas, USA	60000125
6	Haneda Airport	F	HND	Tokyo, Japan	54338212
7	Frankfurt Airport	E	FRA	Frankfurt, Germany	45858315
8	Roissy-Charles de Gaulle	E	CDG	Paris, France	43596943
9	San Francisco	A	SFO	San Francisco, California, USA	40387422
10	Denver	A	DIA	Denver, Colorado, USA	38034231
11	Amsterdam Schiphol	E	AMS	Amsterdam, Netherlands	36781015
12	Minneapolis - St. Paul	A	MSP	Minneapolis-St. Paul, USA	34216331
13	Detroit Metropolitan	A	DTW	Detroit, Michigan, USA	34038381
14	Miami	A	MIA	Miami, Florida, USA	33899246
15	Newark	A	EWR	Newark, New Jersey, USA	33814000
16	McCarran	A	LAS	Las Vegas, Nevada, USA	33669185
17	Phoenix Sky Harbor	A	PHX	Phoenix, Arizona, USA	33533353
18	Kimpo	FE	SEL	Seoul, Korea	33371074
19	George Bush	A	IAH	Houston, Texas, USA	33089333
20	John F. Kennedy	A	JFK	New York, New York, USA	32003000

294. How many international airports of type 'A' account for more than 40 million passengers?

(a) 4

(b) 5

(c) 6

(d) 7

295. What percentage of top ten busiest airports is in the United States of America?

(a) 60%

(b) 80%

(c) 70%

(d) 90%

296. Of the five busiest airports, roughly, what percentage of passengers in handled by Heathrow Airport?

(a) 30

(b) 40

(c) 20

(d) 50

297. How many international airports not located in the USA handle more than 30 million passengers?

(a) 5

(b) 6

(c) 10

(d) 14

Directions for Questions 298 to 303: *Answer the questions based on the two graphs shown below.*

Figure I shows the amount of work distribution, in man-hours, for a software company between offshore and onsite activities. Figure 2 shows the estimated and actual work effort involved in the different offshore activities in the same company during the same period. [**Note:** Onsite refers to work performed at the customer's premise and offshore refers to work performed at the developer's premise.]

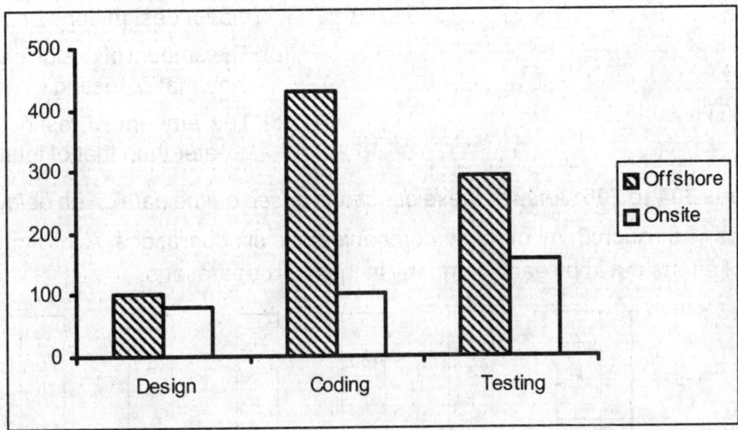

Figure 1

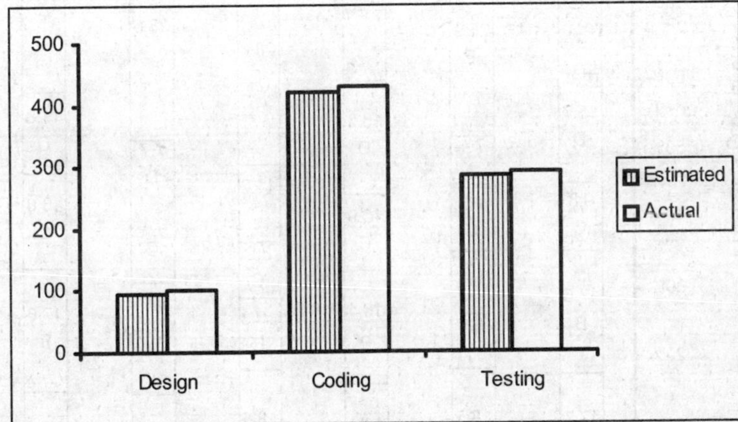

Figure 2

298. Which work requires as many man-hours as that spent in coding?

(a) Offshore, design and coding

(b) Offshore coding

(c) Testing

(d) Offshore, testing and coding

299. Roughly, what percentage of the total work is carried out onsite?

(a) 40%

(b) 20 %

(c) 30 %

(d) 10 %

300. The total effort in man-hours spent onsite is nearest to which of the following?

(a) The sum of the estimated and actual effort for offshore design.

(b) The estimated man-hours of offshore coding.

(c) The actual man-hours of offshore testing.

(d) Half of the man-hours of estimated offshore coding.

301. If the total working hours were 100, which of the following tasks will account for approximately 50 hr?

(a) Coding

(b) Design

(c) Offshore testing

(d) Offshore testing plus design

302. If 50% of the offshore work were to be carried out onsite, with the distribution of effort between the tasks remaining the same, the proportion of testing carried out offshore would be

(a) 40% (b) 30%

(c) 50% (d) 70%

303. If 50% of the offshore work were to be carried out onsite, with the distribution of effort between the tasks remaining the same, which of the following is true of all work carried out onsite?

(a) The amount of coding done is greater than that of testing.

(b) The amount of coding done onsite is less than that of design done onsite.

(c) The amount of design carried out onsite is greater than that of testing.

(d) The amount of testing carried out offshore is greater than that of total design.

Directions for Questions 304 to 306: *Answer these questions based on the data given below:*

There are six companies, 1 through 6. All of these companies use six operations, A through F. The following graph shows the distribution of efforts put in by each company in these six operations.

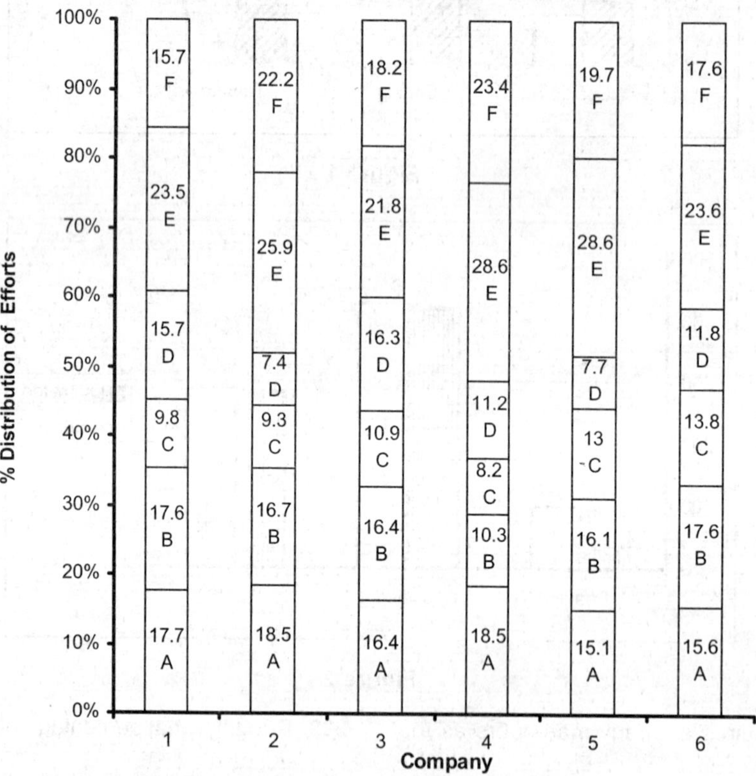

304. Suppose effort allocation is inter-changed between operations B and C, then C and D, and then D and E. If companies are then ranked in ascending order of effort in E, what will be the rank of company 3?

(a) 2 (b) 3

(c) 4 (d) 5

305. A new technology is introduced in company 4 such that the total effort for operations B through F get evenly distributed among these. What is the change in the percentage of effort in operation E?

(a) Reduction of 12.3 (b) Increase of 12.3

(c) Reduction of 5.6 (d) Increase of 5.6

306. Suppose the companies find that they can remove operations B, C and D and redistribute the effort released equally among the remaining operations. Then which operation will show the maximum across all companies and all operations?

(a) Operation E in company 1
(b) Operation E in company 4
(c) Operation F in company 5
(d) Operation E in company 5

Directions for Questions 307 to 309: *Answer the questions based on the pie charts given below.*

Chart 1 shows the distribution of 12 million tonnes of crude oil transported through different modes over a specific period of time. Chart 2 shows the distribution of the cost of transporting this crude oil. The total cost was Rs. 30 million

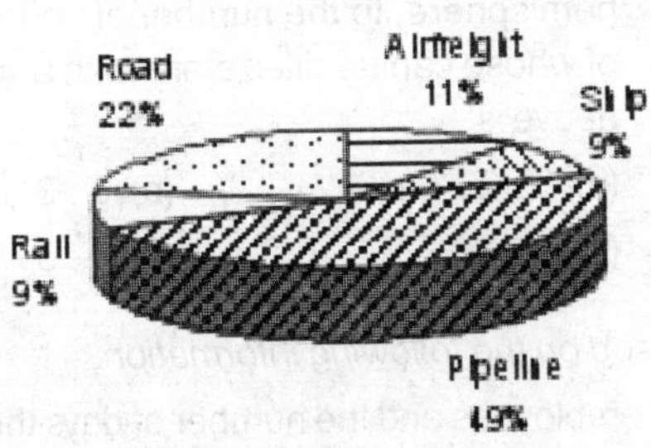

Chart 1: Volume transported

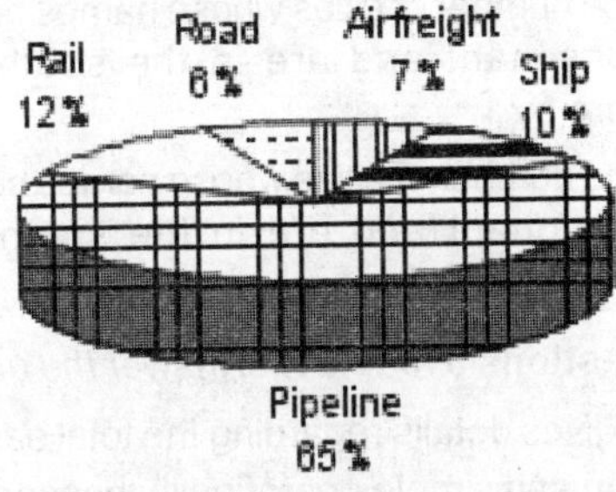

Chart 2: Cost of transportation

307. The cost in rupees per tonne of oil moved by rail and road happens to be roughly

(a) Rs. 3
(b) Rs. 1.5
(c) Rs. 4.5
(d) Rs. 8

308. From the charts given, it appears that the cheapest mode of transport is

(a) road
(b) rail
(c) pipeline
(d) ship

309. If the costs per tonne of transport by ship, air and road are represented by P, Q and R respectively, which of the following is true?

(a) R > Q > P
(b) P > R > Q
(c) P > Q > R
(d) R > P > Q

2002

Directions for Questions 310 to 312: *Answer these questions based on the table given below.*

The following table provides data on the different countries and location of their capitals. (the data may not match the actual Latitude, Longitudes) Answer the following questions on the basis of this table.

S.No.	Country	Capital	Latitude	Longitude
1	Argentina	Buenos Aires	34.30 S	58.20 E
2	Australia	Canberra	35.15 S	149.08 E
3	Austria	Vienna	48.12 N	16.22 E
4	Bulgaria	Sofia	42.45 N	23.20 E
5	Brazil	Brasilia	15.47 S	47.55 E
6	Canada	Ottawa	45.27 N	75.42 E
7	Cambodia	Phnom Penh	11.33 N	104.55 E
8	Equador	Quito	0.15 S	78.35 E
9	Ghana	Accra	5.35 N	0.60 E
10	Iran	Teheran	35.44 N	51.30 E
11	Ireland	Dublin	53.20 N	6.18 E
12	Libya	Tripoli	32.49 N	13.07 E
13	Malaysia	Kuala Lumpur	3.90 N	101.41 E
14	Peru	Lima	12.05 S	77.0 E
15	Poland	Warsaw	52.13 N	21.0 E
16	New Zealand	Wellington	41.17 S	174.47 E
17	Saudi Arabia	Riyadh	24.41 N	46.42 E
18	Spain	Madrid	40.25 N	3.45 W
19	Sri Lanka	Colombo	6.56 N	79.58 E
20	Zambia	Lusaka	15.28 S	28.16 E

310. What percentage of cities located within 10°E and 40°E (20° East and 40° East) lie in the Southern Hemisphere?

(a) 15% (b) 20%

(c) 25% (d) 30%

311. The number of cities whose names begin with a consonant and are in the Northern Hemisphere in the table

(a) exceeds the number of cities whose names begin with a consonant and are in the southern hemisphere by 1.

(b) exceeds the number of cities whose names begin with a consonant and are in the southern hemisphere by 2.

(c) is less than the number of cities whose names begin with a consonant and are in the east of the meridian by 1.

(d) is less than the number of countries whose name begins with a consonant and are in the east of the meridian by 3.

312. The ratio of the number of countries whose name starts with vowels and located in the southern hemisphere, to the number of countries, the name of whose capital cities starts with a vowel in the table above is

(a) 3 : 2 (b) 3 : 3

(c) 3 : 1 (d) 4 : 3

Directions for Questions 313 to 316: *Answer the questions based on the following information.*

The following table gives details regarding the total earnings of 15 employees and the number of days they have worked on complex, medium and simple operation in the month of June 2002. Even though the employees might have worked on an operation, they would be eligible for earnings only if they have minimum level of efficiency.

	Total Earnings				Total Days			
Emp. No	**Complex**	**Medium**	**Simple**	**Total**	**Complex**	**Medium**	**Simple**	**Total**
2001147	82.98		636.53	719.51	3.00	0.00	23.00	26.00
2001148	51.53		461.73	513.26	3.33	1.67	16.00	21.00
2001149	171.1		79.10	250.81	5.50	4.00	8.50	18.00
2001150	100.47		497.47	597.95	6.00	4.67	7.33	18.00
2001151	594.43	159.64		754.06	9.67	13.33	0.00	23.00
2001156	89.70			89.70	8.00	0.00	1.00	9.00
2001158	472.31	109.73		582.04	1.39	9.61	0.00	11.00
2001164	402.25	735.22	213.67	1351.14	5.27	12.07	0.67	18.00
2001170	576.57			576.57	21.00	0.00	0.00	21.00
2001171	286.48	6.10		292.57	8.38	4.25	0.38	13.00
2001172	512.10	117.46		629.56	10.00	8.50	3.50	22.00
2001173	1303.88			1303.88	25.50	0.00	0.50	26.00
2001174	1017.94			1017.90	26.00	0.00	0.00	26.00
2001179	46.56	776.19		822.75	2.00	19.00	0.00	21.00
2001180	116.40	1262.79		1379.19	5.00	19.00	0.00	24.00

313. The number of employees who have earned more than Rs. 50 per day in complex operations is

(a) 4

(b) 3

(c) 5

(d) 6

314. The number of employees who have earned more than Rs. 600 and having more than 80% attendance (there are 25 regular working days in June 2002; some might be coming on overtime too) is

(a) 4

(b) 5

(c) 6

(d) 7

315. The employee number of the person who has earned the maximum earnings per day in medium operation is

(a) 2001180

(b) 2001164

(c) 2001172

(d) 2001179

316. Among the employees who were engaged in complex and medium operations, the number of employees whose average earning per day in complex operations is more than average earning per day in medium operations is

(a) 2 (b) 3

(c) 5 (d) 7

Directions for Questions 317 to 324: *Answer the questions based on the table given below:*

The following table shows the revenue and expenses in millions of Euros (European currency) associated with REPSOL YPF company's oil and gas producing activities in operations in different parts of the world for 1998-2000.

REPSOL YPF'S Operations of Oil and Gas Producing Activities

S. No.	Item	Year	Total World	Spain	North Africa & Middle East	Argentina	Rest of Latin America	Far East	North Sea	Rest of the World
1	Revenue	1998	916	70	366	281	34	82	78	5
		1999	3374	55	666	2006	115	301	140	91
		2000	8328	394	1290	5539	482	603	0	20
2	Expenses	1998	668	39	255	187	57	63	52	15
		1999	1999	48	325	1168	131	204	65	58
		2000	3709	43	530	2540	252	311	0	33
3	Income before Taxes & Charges (Revenue-Expenses) =[(1)-(2)]	1998	248	31	111	94	–23	19	26	–10
		1999	1375	7	341	838	–16	97	75	33
		2000	4619	351	760	2999	230	292	0	–13
4	Taxes & Charges	1998	152	6	104	33	–3	9	6	–3
		1999	561	3	169	338	–6	39	21	–3
		2000	1845	126	404	1150	61	103	0	1
5	Net Income Taxes Charges [=(3)-(4)]	1998	96	25	7	61	–20	10	20	–7
		1999	814	4	172	500	–10	58	54	36
		2000	2774	225	356	1849	169	189	0	–14

317. How many operations (Spain, North Africa and Middle East,..) of the company accounted for less than 5% of the total revenue earned in 1999?

(a) 2 (b) 3

(c) 4 (d) None of these

318. How many operations (Spain, North Africa and Middle East...) of the company witnessed more than 200% revenue from 1999 to 2000?

(a) 1 (b) 2

(c) 3 (d) None of these

319. How many operations registered a sustained yearly increase in income before taxes and charges from 1998 to 2000?

(a) 3

(b) 4

(c) 5

(d) None of these

320. Ignoring the loss making operations of the company in 1998, for how many operations was the percentage increase in net income before taxes and charges higher than the average from 1998 to 1999?

(a) 0

(b) 1

(c) 2

(d) None of these

321. If profitability is defined as the ratio of net income after taxes and charges to expense, which of the following statements is true?

(a) The Far East operations witnessed its highest profitability in 1998.

(b) The North Sea operations increased its profitability from 1998 to 1999.

(c) The operations in Argentina witnessed a decrease in profitability from 1998 to 1999.

(d) Both 2 and 3 are true.

322. In 2000, which among the following countries had the best profitability?

(a) North Africa and Middle East

(b) Spain

(c) Rest of Latin America

(d) Far East

323. If efficiency is defined as the ratio of revenue to expenses, which operation was the least efficient in 2000?

(a) Spain (b) Argentina

(c) Far East (d) None of these

324. Of the following statements, which one is not true?

(a) The operations in Spain had the best efficiency in 2000.

(b) The Far East operations witnessed an efficiency improvement from 1999 to 2000.

(c) The North Sea operations witnessed an efficiency improvement from 1998 to 1999.

(d) In 1998, the operations in Rest of Latin America were the least efficient.

Directions for Questions 325 and 326: Answer the questions based on the pie charts given below.

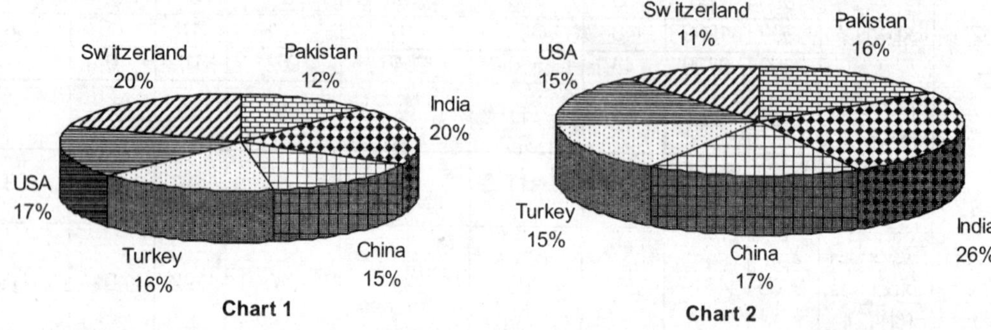

Chart 1 shows the distribution by value of top 6 suppliers of MFA Textiles in 1995. Chart 2 shows the distribution by quantity of top 6 suppliers of MFA Textiles in 1995. The total value is 5760 million Euro (European currency). The total quantity is 1.055 million tonnes.

325. The country which has the highest average price is

(a) USA (b) Switzerland

(c) Turkey (d) India

326. The average price in Euro per kilogram for Turkey is roughly

(a) 6.20 (b) 5.60

(c) 4.20 (d) 4.80

Directions for Questions 327 to 332: *Answer the questions based on the chart given below.*

The chart given below indicates the annual sales tax revenue collections (in rupees in crores) of seven states from 1997 to 2001. The values given at the top of each bar represents the total collections in that year.

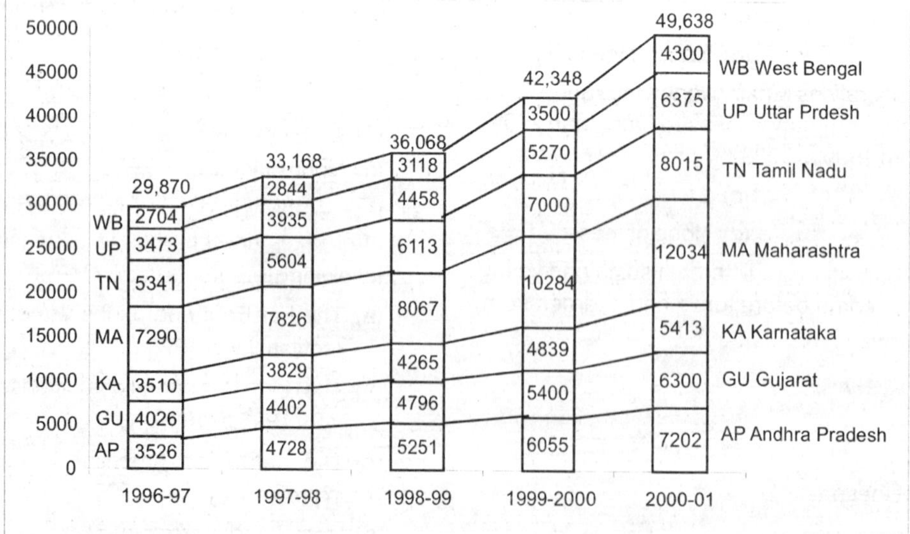

327. If for each year, the states are ranked in terms of the descending order of sales tax collections, how many states do not change the ranking more than once over the five years?

(a) 1 (b) 5
(c) 3 (d) 4

328. Which of the following states has changed its relative ranking most number of times when you rank the states in terms of the descending volume of sales tax collections each year?

(a) Andhra Pradesh (b) Uttar Pradesh
(c) Karnataka (d) Tamil Nadu

329. The percentage share of sales tax revenue of which state has increased from 1997 to 2001?

(a) Tamil Nadu (b) Karnataka
(c) Gujarat (d) Andhra Pradesh

330. Which pair of successive years shows the maximum growth rate of tax revenue in Maharashtra?

(a) 1997 to 1998 (b) 1998 to 1999
(c) 1999 to 2000 (d) 2000 to 2001

331. Identify the state whose tax revenue increased exactly by the same amount in two successive pair of years?

(a) Karnataka (b) West Bengal
(c) Uttar Pradesh (d) Tamil Nadu

332. Which state below has been maintaining a constant rank over the years in terms of its contribution to total tax collections?

(a) Andhra Pradesh
(b) Karnataka
(c) Tamil Nadu
(d) Uttar Pradesh

2003 (R)

Directions for Questions 333 to 335: *Answer the questions on the basis of the following information.*

In a Decathlon, the events are 100 m, 400 m, 100 m hurdles, 1,500 m, High jump, Pole vault, Long jump, Discus, Shot put and Javelin. The performance in the first four of these events is consolidated into Score-1, the next three into Score-2, and the last three into Score-3. Each such consolidation is obtained by giving appropriate positive weights to individual events. The final score is simply the total of these three scores. The athletes with the highest, second highest and the third highest final scores receive the gold, silver, and the bronze medals respectively. The table below gives the scores and performance of 19 top athletes in this event.

Name	Country	Final Score	Score-1	Score-2	Score-3	100m	High jump	Pole-vault
Eduard Hämäläinen	BLS	8802	491	5322	2989	10.74	2.08	4.8
Michael Smith	CAN	8855	174	5274	3407	11.23	1.97	4.9
Tomas Dvorak	CZE	8796	499	5169	3128	10.63	1.91	4.7
Uwe Freimuth	DDR	8799	441	5491	3124	11.06	1.97	4.8
Torsten Voss	DDR	8880	521	5234	2868	10.69	2.1	5.1
Erki Nool	EST	8768	408	5553	2808	10.71	1.99	5.4
Christian Plaziat	FRA	8775	563	5430	2781	10.72	2.1	5
Jürgen Hingsen	FRG	8792	451	5223	3033	10.95	2	4.9
Siegfried Wentz	FRG	8856	470	5250	3137	10.85	2.05	4.8
Guido Kratschmer	FRG	8861	575	5308	3064	10.58	2	4.6
Daley Thompson	GBR		582		3003	10.55	2.11	4.6
Frank Busemann	GER	8905	568	5392	2945	10.6	2.04	4.8
Alexandr Apaichev	SOV	8803	492	5370	3115	10.92	1.95	4.8
Grigory Degtyarov	SOV	8823	339	5196	3114	11.05	2.08	4.9
Robert Zmelik	TCH	8832	494	5455	2883	10.78	2.06	5.1
Dave Johnson	USA	8811	366	5370	3114	10.78	2.1	5
Steve Fritz	USA	8827	427	5163	3119	10.75	2.04	5
Bruce Jenner	USA	8846	483	5280	3200	10.94	2.03	4.8
Dan O'Brien	USA	8897	408	5331	3120	10.36	2.09	4.8

333. The athletes from FRG and USA decided to run a 4 × 100 m relay race for their respective countries with the country having three athletes borrowing the athlete from CZE. Assume that all the athletes ran their stretch of the relay race at the same speed as in Decathlon event. How much more time did the FRG relay team take as compared to the USA team?

(a) 0.18 (b) 0.28
(c) 0.78 (d) 0.00

334. What is the least that Daley Thompson must get in Score-2 that ensures him a bronze medal?

(a) 5309 (b) 5296
(c) 5271 (d) 5270

335. At least how many competitors (excluding Daley Thompson) must Michael Smith have out-jumped in the long jump event?

(a) One (b) Two
(c) Three (d) Four

Directions for Questions 336 to 338: *Answer the questions on the basis of the following charts.*

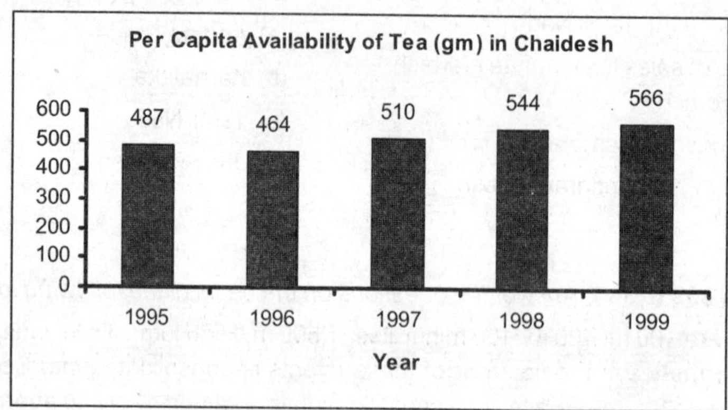

(**Note:** Availability is defined as production less export.)

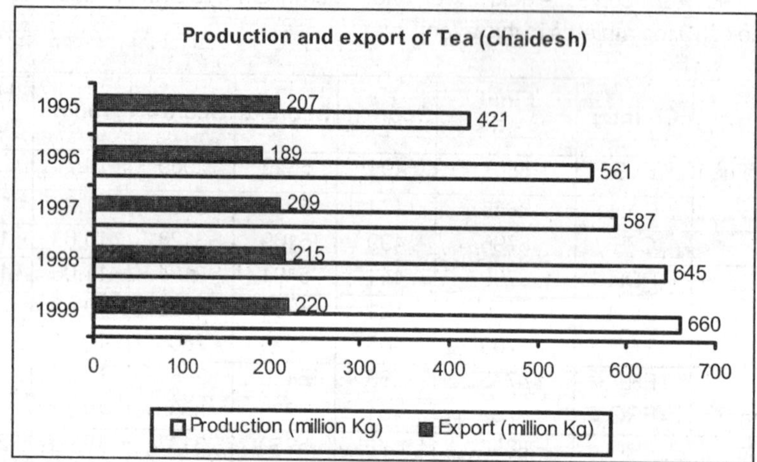

336. In which year during the period 1996-1999 was Chaidesh's export of tea, as a proportion of tea produced, the highest?

(a) 1996 (b) 1997
(c) 1998 (d) 1999

337. In which of the following years was the population of Chaidesh the lowest?

(a) 1995 (b) 1996
(c) 1997 (d) 1999

338. The area under tea cultivation continuously decreased in all four years from 1996 to 1999, by 10%, 7%, 4%, and 1%, respectively. In which year was tea productivity (production per unit of area) the highest?

(a) 1999
(b) 1998
(c) 1997
(d) 1996

Directions for Questions 339 to 342: *Answer the questions on the basis of the following information.*

The following is the wholesale price index (WPI) of a select list of items with the base year of 1993-94. In other words, all the item prices are made 100 in that year (1993-94). Prices in all other years for an item are measured with respect to its price in the base year. For instance, the price of cement went up by 1% in 1994-95 as compared to 1993-94. Similarly, the price of power went up by 3% in 1996-97 as compared to 1993-94.

	1993-94	1994-95	1995-96	1996-97	1997-98	1998-99	1999-2000	2000-01	2001-02	2002-03
All items	100	102.0	102.5	104.0	103.0	105.0	106.0	108.0	107.0	106.0
Cement	100	101.0	100.5	103.0	102.5	103.5	103.1	103.8	103.7	104.0
Limestone	100	102.0	102.5	102.75	102.25	103.0	104.0	105.0	104.5	105.0
Power	100	101.5	102.5	103.0	103.5	104.0	106.0	107.0	107.5	108.0
Steel	100	101.5	101.0	103.5	104.0	104.25	105.0	105.5	106.0	105.5
Timber	100	100.5	101.5	102.0	102.5	102.0	103.0	103.5	104.0	104.5
Wages	100	101.5	103.0	103.5	104.0	104.25	104.0	104.75	104.9	105.3

339. Let us suppose that one bag of cement (50 kg) consumes 100 kg of limestone and 10 units of power. The only other cost item in producing cement is in the form of wages. During 1993-94, limestone, power and wages contributed, respectively, 20%, 25% and 15% to the cement price per bag. The average operating profit (per cent of price per cement bag) earned by a cement manufacturer during 2002-03 is closest to

(a) 40%

(b) 39.5%

(c) 38.5%

(d) 37.5%

340. Steel manufacturing requires the use of iron ore, power and manpower. The cost of iron ore has followed the All Items index. During 1993-94 power accounted for 30% of the selling price of steel, iron ore for 25%, and wages for 10% of the selling price of steel. Assuming the cost and price data for cement as given in the previous question, the operating profit (per cent of selling price) of an average steel manufacturer in 2002-03

(a) is more than that of a cement manufacturer.

(b) is less than that of a cement manufacturer.

(c) is the same as that of a cement manufacturer.

(d) Cannot be determined.

341. Which item experienced continuous price rise during the ten-year period?

(a) Power

(b) Cement

(c) Wages

(d) Limestone

342. Which item(s) experienced only one decline in price during the ten-year period?

(a) Steel and limestone

(b) Steel and timber

(c) Timber

(d) Timber and wages

Directions for Questions 343 to 346: *Answer the questions on the basis of the following table.*

Below is a table that lists countries region-wise. Each region-wise list is sorted, first by birth rate and then alphabetically by name of country. We now wish to merge the region-wise list into one consolidated list and provide overall rankings to each country based first on birth rate and then on death rate. Thus, if some countries have the same birth rate, then the country with a lower death rate will be ranked higher. Further, countries having identical birth and death rates will get the same rank. For example, if two countries are tied for the third position, then both will be given rank 3, while the next country (in the ordered list) will be ranked 5.

Rank	Country	Birth Rate	Death Rate	Region
1	South Africa	36	12	Africa
2	Egypt	39	13	Africa
3	Cameroon	42	22	Africa
4	Mozambique	45	18	Africa
5	Zaire	45	18	Africa
6	Ghana	46	14	Africa
7	Angola	47	23	Africa
8	Madagascar	47	22	Africa
9	Morocco	47	16	Africa
10	Tanzania	47	17	Africa
11	Ethiopia	48	23	Africa
12	Ivory coast	48	23	Africa
13	Rhodesia	48	14	Africa
14	Uganda	48	17	Africa
15	Nigeria	49	22	Africa
16	Saudi Arabia	49	19	Africa
17	Sudan	49	17	Africa
18	Algeria	50	16	Africa
19	Kenya	50	14	Africa
20	Upper Volta	50	28	Africa

Rank	Country	Birth Rate	Death Rate	Region
1	Germany (FRG)	10	12	Europe
2	Austria	12	13	Europe
3	Belgium	12	12	Europe
4	Germany (DRG)	12	14	Europe
5	Sweden	12	11	Europe
6	Switzerland	12	9	Europe
7	U.K.	12	12	Europe
8	Netherlands	13	8	Europe
9	France	14	11	Europe
10	Italy	14	10	Europe
11	Greece	16	9	Europe
12	Bulgaria	17	10	Europe
13	Hungary	18	12	Europe
14	Spain	18	8	Europe
15	USSR	18	9	Europe
16	Yugoslavia	18	8	Europe
17	Czech. Rep.	19	11	Europe
18	Portugal	19	10	Europe
19	Romania	19	10	Europe
20	Poland	20	9	Europe

Rank	Country	Birth Rate	Death Rate	Region
1	Japan	16	6	Asia
2	Korea (ROK)	26	6	Asia
3	Sri Lanka	26	9	Asia
4	Taiwan	26	5	Asia
5	Malaysia	30	6	Asia
6	China	31	11	Asia
7	Thailand	34	10	Asia
8	Turkey	34	12	Asia
9	India	36	15	Asia
10	Burma	38	15	Asia
11	Iran	42	12	Asia
12	Vietnam	42	17	Asia
13	Korea (DPRK)	43	12	Asia
14	Pakistan	44	14	Asia
15	Nepal	46	20	Asia
16	Bangladesh	47	19	Asia
17	Syria	47	14	Asia
18	Iraq	48	14	Asia
19	Afghanistan	52	30	Asia

Rank	Country	Birth Rate	Death Rate	Region
1	U.S.A.	15	9	N. America
2	Canada	16	7	N. America
3	Cuba	20	6	N. America
4	Mexico	40	7	N. America
1	Australia	16	8	Pacific
2	Philippines	34	10	Pacific
3	Indonesia	38	16	Pacific
1	Argentina	22	10	S. America
2	Chile	22	7	S. America
3	Colombia	34	10	S. America
4	Brazil	36	10	S. America
5	Venezuela	36	6	S. America
6	Guatemala	40	14	S. America
7	Peru	40	13	S. America
8	Ecuador	42	11	S. America

343. In the consolidated list, what would be the overall rank of the Philippines?

(a) 32 (b) 33

(c) 34 (d) 35

344. In the consolidated list, how many countries would rank below Spain and above Taiwan?

(a) 9 (b) 8

(c) 7 (d) 6

345. In the consolidated list, which country ranks 37th?
(a) South Africa (b) Brazil
(c) Turkey (d) Venezuela

346. In the consolidated list, how many countries in Asia will rank lower than every country in South America, but higher than at least one country in Africa?
(a) 8 (b) 7
(c) 6 (d) 5

Directions for Questions 347 and 348: Answer the questions on the basis of the data presented in the figure below.

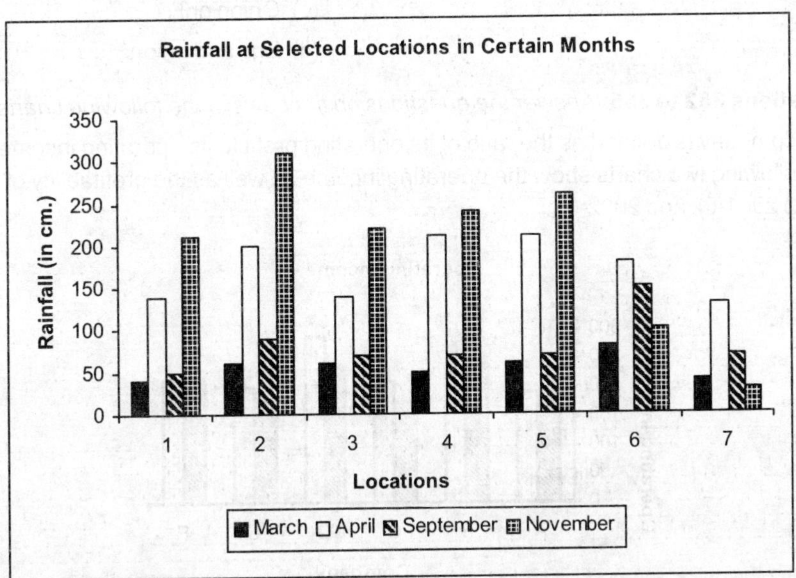

347. Which of the following statements is correct?
(a) November rainfall exceeds 100 cm in each location.
(b) September rainfall exceeds 50 cm in each location.
(c) March rainfall is lower than September rainfall in each location.
(d) None of these.

348. Locations 6 and 7 differ from all the rest because only in these two locations,
(a) April rainfall exceeds March rainfall.
(b) Peak rainfall occurs in April.
(c) November rainfall is lower than March rainfall.
(d) April rainfall is less than 200 cm.

Directions for Questions 349 to 351: *Answer the questions on the basis of the data presented in the figure below.*

Mid-year Prices of Essential Commodities

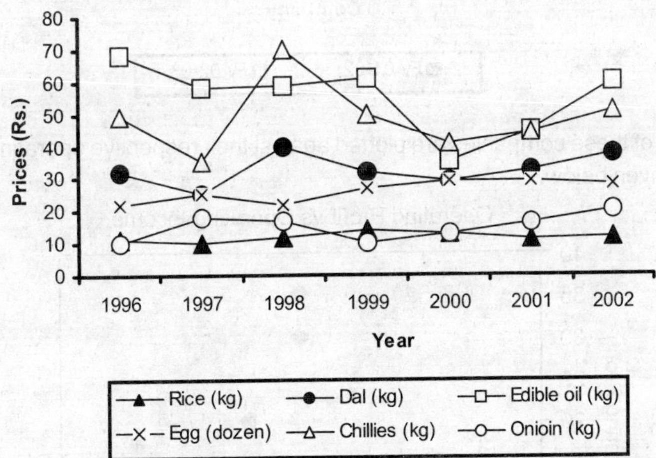

349. During 1996-2002, the number of commodities that exhibited a net overall increase and net overall decrease, respectively, were
(a) 3 and 3 (b) 2 and 4
(c) 4 and 2 (d) 5 and 1

350. The number of commodities that experienced a price decline for two or more consecutive years is

(a) 2 (b) 3

(c) 4 (d) 5

351. For which commodities did a price increase immediately follow a price decline only once in this period?

(a) Rice, edible oil and dal

(b) Egg and dal

(c) Onion only

(d) Egg and onion

Directions for Questions 352 to 355: *Answer the questions on the basis of the following charts.*

The profitability of a company is defined as the ratio of its operating profit to its operating income, typically expressed in percentage. The following two charts show the operating income as well as the profitability of six companies in the financial years (F.Ys.) 2001-02 and 2002-03.

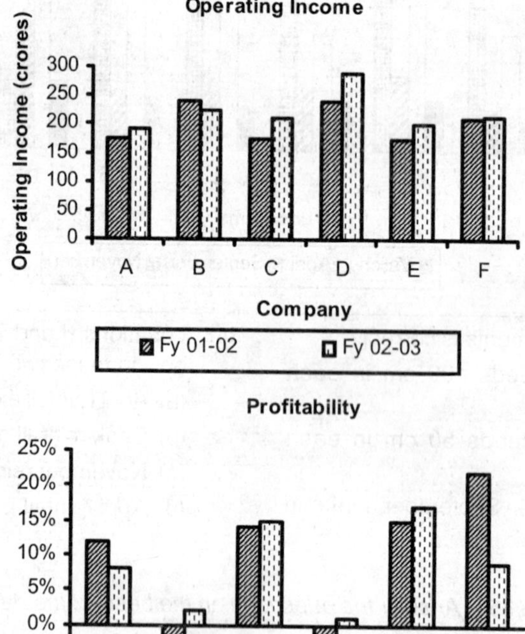

The operating profits of four of these companies are plotted against their respective operating income figures for the F.Y. 2002-03, in the third chart given below.

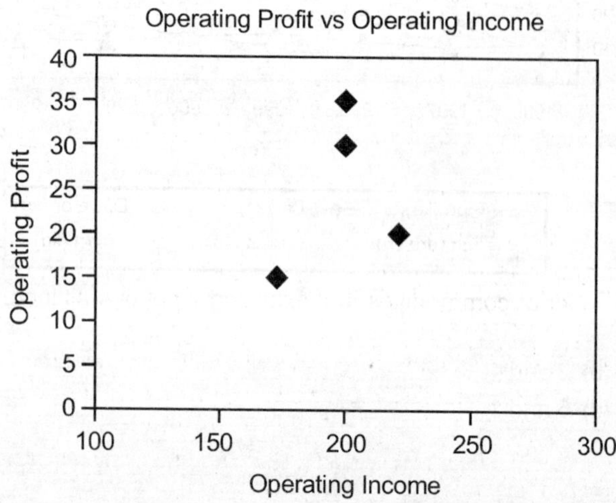

352. Which of the following statements is NOT true?

(a) The company with the third lowest profitability in F.Y. 2001-02 has the lowest operating income in F.Y. 2002-03.

(b) The company with the highest operating income in the two financial years combined has the lowest operating profit in F.Y. 2002-03.

(c) Companies with a higher operating income in F.Y. 2001-02 than in F.Y. 2002-03 have higher profitability in F.Y 2002-03 than in F.Y. 2001-02.

(d) Comanies with profitability between 10% and 20% in F.Y. 2001-02 also have operating incomes between 150 crore and 200 crore in F.Y. 2002-03.

353. Which company recorded the highest operating profit in F.Y. 2002-03?

(a) A (b) C

(c) E (d) F

354. What is the approximate average operating profit, in F.Y 2001-02, of the two companies excluded from the third chart?

(a) –7.5 crore (b) 3.5 crore

(c) 25 crore (d) Cannot be determined

355. The average operating profit in F.Y. 2002-03 of companies with profitability exceeding 10% in F.Y. 2002-03, is approximately

(a) 17.5 crore (b) 25 crore

(c) 27.5 crore (d) 32.5 crore

Directions for Questions 356 to 358: *Answer the questions on the basis of the table given below:*

Sex Ratio (Number of females per 1,000 males) of Selected States in India : 1901-2001

	1901	**1911**	**1921**	**1931**	**1941**	**1951**	**1961**	**1971**	**1981**	**1991**	**2001**
AP	985	992	993	987	980	986	981	977	975	972	978
Assam	919	915	896	874	875	868	869	896	910	923	932
Bihar	1061	1051	1020	995	1002	1000	1005	957	948	907	921
Goa	1091	1108	1120	1088	1084	1128	1066	981	975	967	960
Gujarat	954	946	944	945	941	952	940	934	942	934	921
Haryana	867	835	844	844	869	871	868	867	870	865	861
HP	884	889	890	897	890	912	938	958	973	976	970
J&K	882	876	870	865	869	873	878	878	892	896	900
Karnataka	983	981	969	965	960	966	959	957	963	960	964
Kerala	1004	1008	1011	1022	1027	1028	1022	1016	1032	1036	1058
MP	972	967	949	947	946	945	932	920	921	912	920
Maharashtra	978	966	950	947	949	941	936	930	937	934	922
Orissa	1037	1056	1086	1067	1053	1022	1001	988	981	971	972
Punjab	832	780	799	815	836	844	854	865	879	882	874
Rajasthan	905	908	896	907	906	921	908	911	919	910	922
TN	1044	1042	1029	1027	1012	1007	992	978	977	974	986
UP	938	916	908	903	907	998	907	876	882	876	898
WB	945	925	905	890	852	865	878	891	911	917	934
India	**972**	**964**	**955**	**950**	**945**	**946**	**941**	**930**	**934**	**927**	**933**

356. The two states which achieved the largest increases in sex ratio over the period 1901-2001 are

(a) Punjab and HP

(b) HP and Kerala

(c) Assam and J & K

(d) Kerala and J & K

357. Among the states which have a sex ratio exceeding 1000 in 1901, the sharpest decline over the period 1901-2001 was registered in the state of

(a) Goa (b) TN

(c) Bihar (d) Orissa

358. Each of the following statements pertains to the **number** of states with females outnumbering males in a given census year. Which of these statements is NOT correct?

(a) This number never exceeded 5 in any census year.

(b) This number registered its sharpest decline in 1971.

(c) The number of consecutive censuses in which this number remained unchanged never exceeded 3.

(d) Prior to the 1971 census, this number was never less than 4.

2003 (L)

Directions for Questions 359 to 361: *In each question, there are two statements: A and B, either of which can be true or false on the basis of the information given below.*

A research agency collected the following data regarding the admission process of a reputed management school in India.

Year	Gender	Number bought application forms	Number appeared for written test	Number called for interviews	Number selected for the course
2002	Male	61205	59981	684	171
	Female	19236	15389	138	48
2003	Male	63298	60133	637	115
	Female	45292	40763	399	84

Choose (a) if only A is true

Choose (b) if only B is true

Choose (c) if both A and B are true

Choose (d) if neither A nor B is true

359. Statement A: The success rate of moving from written test to interview stage for males was worse than for females in 2003.

Statement B: The success rate of moving from written test to interview stage for females was better in 2002 than in 2003.

360. Statement A: In 2002, the number of females selected for the course as a proportion of the number of females who bought application forms, was higher than the corresponding proportion for males.

Statement B: In 2002, among those called for interview, males had a greater success rate than females.

361. Statement A: The percentage of absentees in the written test among females decreased from 2002 to 2003.

Statement B: The percentage of absentees in the written test among males was larger than among females in 2003.

Directions for Questions 362 to 365: *Answer the questions on the basis of the information given below.*

The length of an infant is one of the measures of his/her development in the early stages of his/her life.

The figure below shows the growth chart of four infants in the first five months of life.

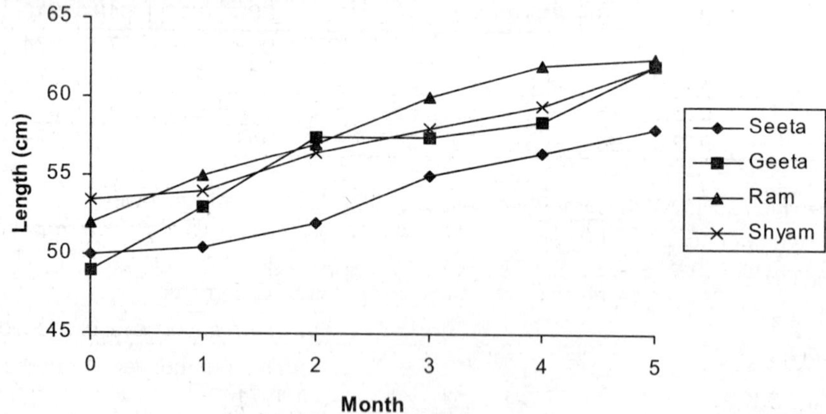

362. After which month did Seeta's rate of growth start to decline?

(a) Second month

(b) Third month

(c) Fourth month

(d) Never

363. Who grew at the fastest rate in the first two months of life?

(a) Geeta
(b) Seeta
(c) Ram
(d) Shyam

364. The rate of growth during the third month was the lowest for

(a) Geeta
(b) Seeta
(c) Ram
(d) Shyam

365. Among the four infants, who grew the least in the first five months of life?

(a) Geeta
(b) Seeta
(c) Ram
(d) Shyam

Directions for Questions 366 to 368: Answer the questions on the basis of the information given below.

The table below provides certain demographic details of 30 respondents who were part of a survey. The demographic characteristics are: gender, number of children, and age of respondents. The first number in each cell is the number of respondents in that group. The minimum and maximum age of respondents in each group is given in brackets. For example, there are five female respondents with no children and among these five, the youngest is 34 years old, while the oldest is 49.

No. of children	Male	Female	Total
0	1 (38, 38)	5 (34, 49)	6
1	1 (32, 32)	8 (35, 57)	9
2	8 (21, 65)	3 (37, 63)	11
3	2 (32, 33)	2 (27, 40)	4
Total	12	18	30

366. The percentage of respondents aged less than 40 years is at least

(a) 10%
(b) 16.67%
(c) 20.0%
(d) 30%

367. Given the information above, the percentage of respondents older than 35 can be at most

(a) 30%
(b) 73.33%
(c) 76.67%
(d) 90%

368. The percentage of respondents that fall into the 35 to 40 years age group (both inclusive) is at least

(a) 6.67%
(b) 10%
(c) 13.33%
(d) 26.67%

Directions for Questions 369 to 371: *Answer the questions on the basis of the information given below.*

Spam that enters our electronic mailboxes can be classified under several spam heads. The following table shows the distribution of such spam worldwide over time. The total number of spam emails received during December 2002 was larger than the number received in June 2003. The total number of spam emails received during September 2002 was larger than the number received in March 2003. The figures in the table represent the percentage of all spam emails received during that period, falling into those respective categories.

Category	Sep-02	Dec-02	Mar-03	Jun-03
Adult	38	33	19	17
Financial	25	30	37	45
Health	11	19	5	18
Internet	5	3	10	6
Products	3	7	10	11
Scams	5	6	11	2
Others	13	2	8	1

369. In which category was the percentage of spam emails increasing but at a decreasing rate?

(a) Financial
(b) Scams
(c) Products
(d) None of the above

370. In the health category, the number of spam emails received in December 2002 as compared to June 2003.

(a) was larger
(b) was smaller
(c) was equal
(d) cannot be determined

371. In the financial category, the number of spam emails received in September 2002 as compared to March 2003.

(a) was larger
(b) was smaller
(c) was equal
(d) cannot be determined

Directions for Questions 372 to 374: *Answer the questions on the basis of the information given below.*

One of the functions of the Reserve Bank of India is to mobilize funds for the Government of India by issuing securities. The following table shows details of funds mobilized during the period July 2002 - July 2003. Notice that on each date there were two rounds of issues, each with a different maturity.

Date of issue	Notified amount	Maturity	Competitive bids received	Non-competitive bids received	Competitive bids accepted		Non-competitive bids accepted		Total amount mobilized	Coupon rate %	Implicit yield %
	Rs. Crore	Years	No.	No.	No.	Value	No.	Value	Rs. Crore		
17-Jul-02	40	15	229	23	66	15.21	23	0.37	16	8.07	7.80
17-Jul-02	30	10	145	12	90	29.88	12	0.12	30	6.72	6.72
5-Aug-02	50	9	324	13	105	49.68	13	0.33	50	9.39	7.24
5-Aug-02	20	24	163	9	34	19.81	9	0.19	20	10.18	7.93
28-Aug-02	50	15	260	26	157	48.92	26	1.08	50	7.46	7.46
28-Aug-02	20	30	119	15	67	19.61	15	0.39	20	7.95	7.95
11-Sep-02	40	15	261	22	152	38.93	22	1.07	40	7.46	7.44
11-Sep-02	30	20	131	20	98	29.44	20	0.56	30	8.35	7.70
9-Oct-02	40	11	361	26	119	39.22	26	0.78	40	7.27	7.14
9-Oct-02	30	30	91	15	39	29.52	15	0.48	30	7.95	7.89
7-Nov-02	40	17	245	14	20	39.71	14	0.29	40	10.03	7.26
7-Nov-02	30	24	166	11	49	29.70	11	0.31	30	10.18	7.48
9-Apr-03	40	20	245	25	65	39.53	25	1.47	40	6.30	6.30
9-Apr-03	50	11	236	24	201	49.40	24	0.60	50	7.37	5.98
23-Apr-03	50	15	319	26	134	48.98	26	1.02	50	6.25	6.10
23-Apr-03	20	29	131	19	9	19.39	19	0.61	20	7.95	6.33
5-May-03	60	10	314	14	98	59.69	14	0.31	60	7.27	5.97
5-May-03	30	20	143	14	118	29.58	14	0.42	30	6.30	6.35
4-Jun-03	30	25	187	19	15	28.50	19	1.50	30	6.13	6.13
4-Jun-03	60	9	378	21	151	59.09	21	0.91	60	6.85	5.76
2-Jul-03	50	11	298	20	116	49.05	20	0.95	50	7.37	5.76
2-Jul-03	30	25	114	20	45	28.64	20	1.36	30	6.31	6.10
16-Jul-03	60	17	371	29	115	57.00	29	3.10	60	6.35	5.97
16-Jul-03	30	29	134	22	12	29.32	22	0.68	30	7.95	6.20
Total	930								906		

372. How many times was the issue of securities under-subscribed, i.e., how often did the total amount mobilized fall short of the amount notified?

(a) 0 (b) 1
(c) 2 (d) 3

373. Which of the following is true?

(a) The second round issues have a higher maturity than the first round for all dates.
(b) The second round issue of any date has a lower maturity only when the first round notified amount exceeds that of the second round.
(c) On at least one occasion, the second round issue having lower maturity received a higher number of competitive bids.
(d) None of the above three statements is true.

374. Which of the following statements is NOT true?

(a) Competitive bids received always exceed non-competitive bids received.
(b) The number of competitive bids accepted does not always exceed the number of non-competitive bids accepted.
(c) The value of competitive bids accepted on any particular date is never higher for higher maturity.
(d) The value of non-competitive bids accepted in the first round is always greater than that in the second round.

Directions for Questions 375 to 377: *Answer the questions on the basis of the information given below.*

Each point in the graph below shows the profit and turnover data for a company. Each company belongs to one of the three industries: textile, cement and steel.

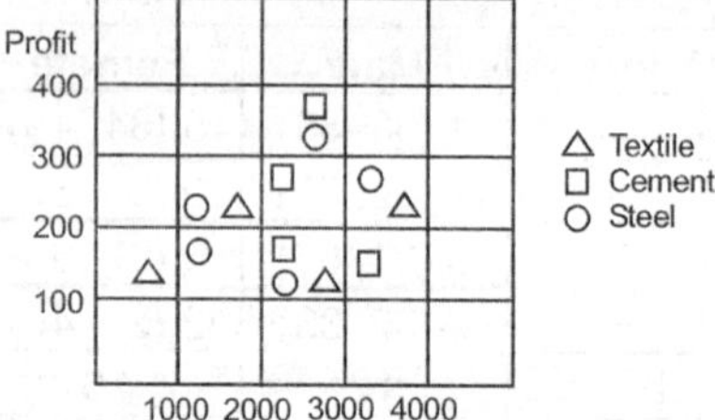

375. For how many companies does the profit exceed 10% of turnover?

(a) 8 (b) 7
(c) 6 (d) 5

376. For how many steel companies with a turnover of more than 2000 is the profit less than 300?

(a) 0 (b) 1
(c) 2 (d) 7

377. An investor wants to buy stock of only steel or cement companies with a turnover more than 1000 and profit exceeding 10% of turnover. How many choices are available to the investor?

(a) 4 (b) 5
(c) 6 (d) 7

Directions for Questions 378 to 380: Answer the questions on the basis of the information given below.

Details of the top 20 MBA schools in the US as ranked by US News and World Report, 1997 are given below.

School	Overall ranking	Ranking by Academics	Ranking by recruiters	Ranking by placement	Median starting salary	% employed	Annual tuition fee
Stanford University	1	1	3	1	$82,000	98.9	$23,100
Harvard University	2	1	2	4	$80,000	96.4	$23,840
University of Pennsylvania	3	1	4	2	$79,000	100.0	$24,956
Massachusetts Institute of Technology	4	1	4	3	$78,000	98.8	$23,900
University of Chicago	5	1	8	10	$65,000	98.4	$23,930
Northwestern University	6	1	1	11	$70,000	93.6	$23,025
Columbia University	7	9	10	5	$83,000	96.2	$23,830
Dartmouth College	8	12	11	6	$70,000	98.3	$23,700
Duke Univrsity	9	9	7	8	$67,500	98.5	$24,380
University of California—Berkeley	10	7	12	12	$70,000	93.7	$18,788
University of Virginia	11	12	9	9	$66,000	98.1	$19,627
University of Michigan—Ann Arbor	12	7	6	14	$65,000	99.1	$23,178
New York University	13	16	19	7	$70,583	97	$23,554
Carnegie Mellon University	14	12	18	13	$67,200	96.6	$22,200
Yale University	15	18	17	22	$65,000	91.5	$23,220
Univ. of North Carolina—Chapel Hill	16	16	16	16	$60,000	96.8	$14,333
University of California—Los Angeles	17	9	13	38	$65,000	82.2	$19,431
University of Texas—Austin	18	18	13	24	$60,000	97.3	$11,614
Indiana University—Bloomington	19	18	20	17	$61,500	95.2	$15,613
Cornell University	20	12	15	36	$64,000	85.1	$23,151

378. Madhu has received admission in all schools listed above. She wishes to select the highest overall ranked school whose a) annual tuition fee does not exceed $23,000 and b) median starting salary is at least $70,000. Which school will she select?

(a) University of Virginia.

(b) University of Pennsylvania

(c) Northwestern University

(d) University of California - Berkeley

379. In terms of staring salary and tuition fee, how many schools are uniformly better (higher median starting salary AND lower tuition fee) than Dartmouth College?

(a) 1 (b) 2

(c) 3 (d) 4

380. How many schools in the list above have single digit rankings on at least 3 of the 4 parameters (overall ranking, ranking by academics, ranking by recruiters and ranking by placement)?

(a) 10 (b) 5

(c) 7 (d) 8

Directions for Questions 381 to 383: Answer the questions on the basis of the information given below.

Table A below provides data about ages of children in a school. For the age given in the first column, the second column gives the number of children not exceeding the age. For example, first entry indicates that there are 9 children aged 4 years or less. Tables B and C provide data on the heights and weights respectively of the same group of children in a similar format. Assuming that an older child is always taller and weighs more than a younger child, answer the following questions.

Table A

Age (years)	Number
4	9
5	12
6	22
7	35
8	42
9	48
10	60
11	69
12	77
13	86
14	100

Table B

Height (cm.)	Number
115	6
120	11
125	24
130	36
135	45
140	53
145	62
150	75
155	81
160	93
165	100

Table C

Weight (kg.)	Number
30	8
32	13
34	17
36	28
38	33
40	46
42	54
44	67
46	79
48	91
50	100

381. What is the number of children of age 9 years of less whose height does not exceed 135 cm?

(a) 48
(b) 45
(c) 3
(d) Cannot be determined

382. How many children of age more than 10 years are taller than 150 cm and do not weigh more than 48 kg?

(a) 16
(b) 40
(c) 9
(d) Cannot be determined

383. Among the children older than 6 years but not exceeding 12 years, how many weigh more than 38 kg.?

(a) 34
(b) 52
(c) 44
(d) Cannot be determined

Directions for Questions 384 and 385: *Answer the questions on the basis of the information given below.*

An industry comprises four firms (A, B, C, and D). Financial details of these firms and of the industry as a whole for a particular year are given below. Profitability of a firm is defined as profit as a percentage of sales.

Figures in Rs.	A	B	C	D	Total
Sales	24568	25468	23752	15782	89570
Operating costs	17198	19101	16151	10258	62708
Interest costs	2457	2292	2850	1578	9177
Profit	4914	4075	4750	3946	17684

384. Which firm has the highest profitability?

(a) A
(b) B
(c) C
(d) D

385. If firm A acquires firm B, approximately what percentage of the total market (total sales) will they corner together?

(a) 55%
(b) 45%
(c) 35%
(d) 50%

2004

Directions for Questions 386 to 389: *Answer the questions on the basis of the information given below.*

The data points in the figure below represent monthly income and expenditure data of individual members of the Ahuja family (■), the Bose family (□), the Coomar family (○), and the Dubey family (●). For these questions, savings is defined as

Savings = Income – Expenditure

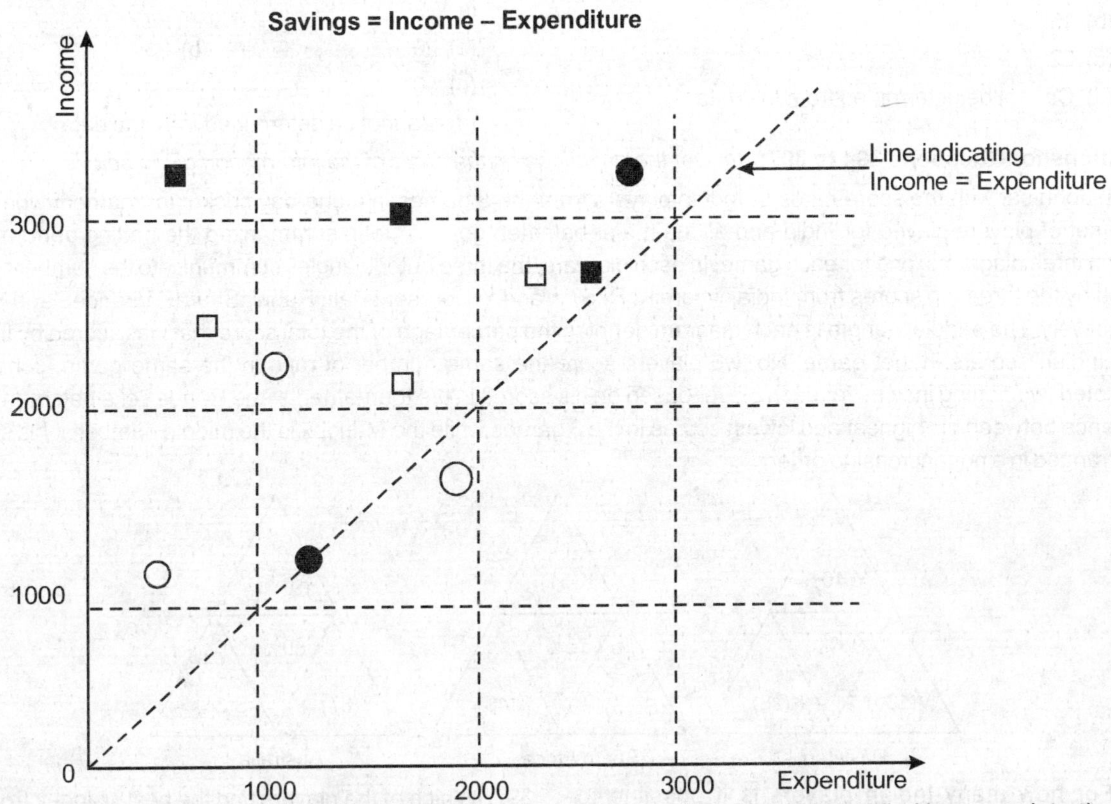

386. Which family has the lowest average income?

(a) Ahuja (b) Bose

(c) Coomar (d) Dubey

387. Which family has the highest average expenditure?

(a) Ahuja (b) Bose

(c) Coomar (d) Dubey

388. Which family has the lowest average savings?

(a) Ahuja (b) Bose

(c) Coomar (d) Dubey

389. The highest amount of savings accrues to a member of which family?

(a) Ahuja (b) Bose

(c) Coomar (d) Dubey

Directions for Questions 390 to 393: *Answer the questions on the basis of the information given below.*

Purana and Naya are two brands of kitchen mixer-grinders available in the local market. Purana is an old brand that was introduced in 1990, while Naya was introduced in 1997. For both these brands, 20% of the mixer-grinders bought in a particular year are disposed off as junk exactly two years later. It is known that 10 Purana mixer-grinders were disposed off in 1997. The following figures show the number of Purana and Naya mixer-grinders in operation from 1995 to 2000, as at the end of the year.

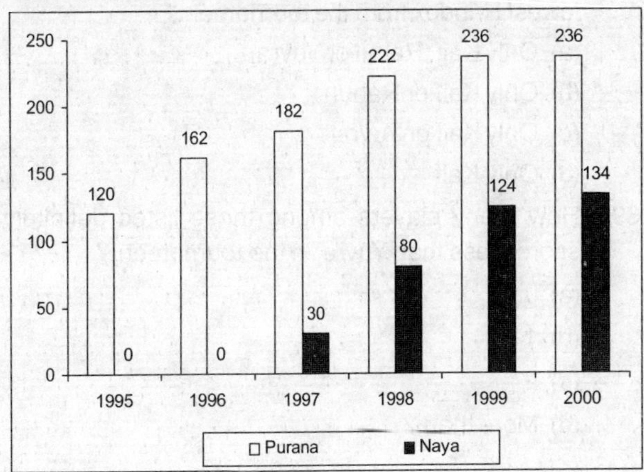

390. How many Naya mixer-grinders were purchased in 1999?
(a) 44 (b) 50
(c) 55 (d) 64

391. How many Naya mixer-grinders were disposed off by the end of 2000?
(a) 10
(b) 16
(c) 22
(d) Cannot be determined from the data

392. How many Purana mixer-grinders were disposed off in 2000?
(a) 0 (b) 5
(c) 6
(d) Cannot be determined from the data

393. How many Purana mixer-grinders were purchased in 1999?
(a) 20 (b) 23
(c) 50
(d) Cannot be determined from the data

Directions for Questions 394 to 397: *Answer the questions on the basis of the information given below.*

Coach John sat with the score cards of Indian players from the 3 games in a one-day cricket tournament where the same set of players played for India and all the major batsmen got out. John summarized the batting performance through three diagrams, one for each game. In each diagram, the three outer triangles communicate the number of runs scored by the three top scores from India, where K, R, S, V, and Y represent Kaif, Rahul, Saurav, Virender, and Yuvraj respectively. The middle triangle in each diagram denotes the percentage of the total score that was scored by the top three Indian scorers in that game. No two players score the same number of runs in the same game. John also calculated two batting indices for each player based on his scores in the tournaments; the R-index of a batsman is the difference between his highest and lowest scores in the 3 games while the M-index is the middle number, if his scores are arranged in a non-increasing order.

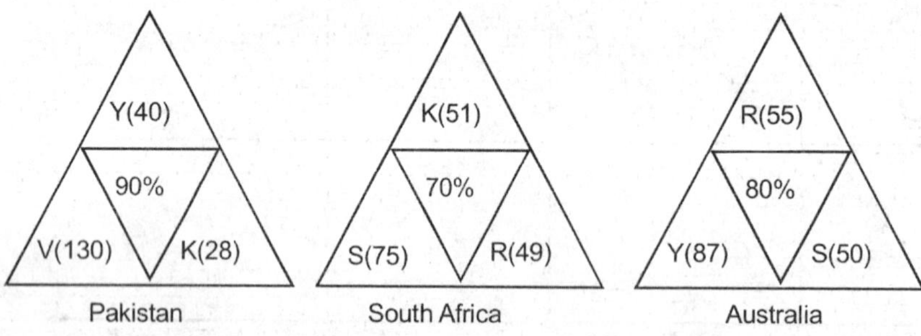

394. For how many Indian players is it possible to calculate the exact M-index?
(a) 0
(b) 1
(c) 2
(d) More than 2

395. Among the players mentioned, who can have the lowest R-index from the tournament?
(a) Only Kaif, Rahul or Yuvraj
(b) Only Kaif or Rahul
(c) Only Kaif or Yuvraj
(d) Only Kaif

396. How many players among those listed definitely scored less than Yuvraj in the tournament?
(a) 0
(b) 1
(c) 2
(d) More than 2

397. Which of the players had the best M-index from the tournament?
(a) Rahul
(b) Saurav
(c) Virender
(d) Yuvraj

2005

Directions for Questions 398 to 401: *Answer the questions on the basis of the information given below:*

A management institute was established on January 1, 2000 with 3, 4, 5, and 6 faculty members in the Marketing, Organisational Behaviour (OB), Finance, and Operations Management (OM) areas respectively, to start with. No faculty member retired or joined the institute in the first three months of the year 2000. In the next four years, the institute recruited one faculty member in each of the four areas. All these new faculty members, who joined the institute subsequently over the years, were 25 years old at the time of their joining the institute. All of them joined the institute on April 1. During these four years, one of the faculty members retired at the age of 60. The following diagram gives the area-wise average age (in terms of number of completed years) of faculty members as on April 1 of 2000, 2001, 2002, and 2003.

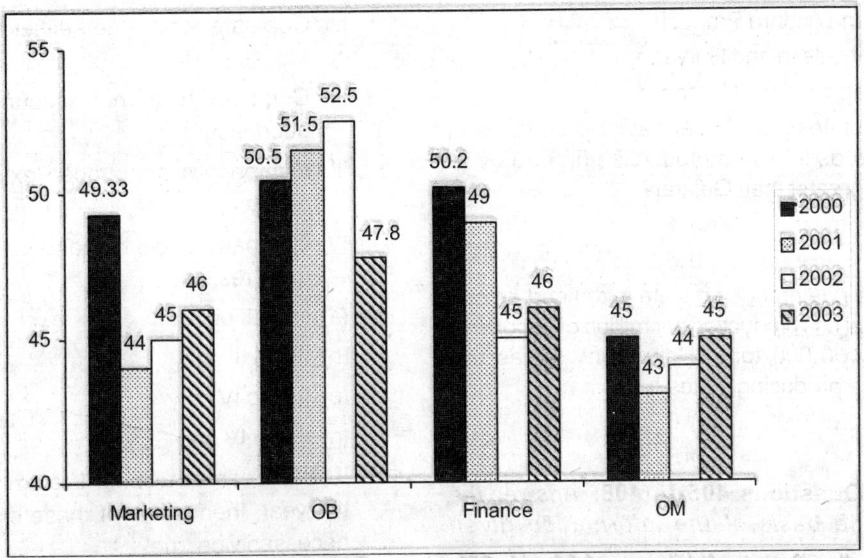

398. From which area did the faculty member retire?
(a) Finance (b) Marketing
(c) OB (d) OM

399. Professors Naresh and Devesh, two faculty members in the Marketing area, who have been with the Institute since its inception, share a birthday, which falls on 20th November. One was born in 1947 and the other one in 1950. On April 1 2005, what was the age of the third faculty member, who has been in the same area since inception?
(a) 47 (b) 50
(c) 51 (d) 52

400. In which year did the new faculty member join the Finance area?
(a) 2000
(b) 2001
(c) 2002
(d) 2003

401. What was the age of the new faculty member, who joined the OM area, as on April 1, 2003?
(a) 25 (b) 26
(c) 27 (d) 28

Directions for Questions 402 to 404: *Answer the questions on the basis of the information given below:*

The table below reports annual statistics related to rice production in select states of India for a particular year.

State	Total Area (in million hectares)	% of Area Under Rice Cultivation	Production (in million tons)	Population (in millions)
Himachal Pradesh	6	20	1.2	6
Kerala	4	60	4.8	32
Rajasthan	34	20	6.8	56
Bihar	10	60	12	83
Karnataka	19	50	19	53
Haryana	4	80	19.2	21
West Bengal	9	80	21.6	80
Gujarat	20	60	24	51
Punjab	5	80	24	24
Madhya Pradesh	31	40	24.8	60
Tamilnadu	13	70	27.3	62
Maharashtra	31	50	48	97
Uttar Pradesh	24	70	67.2	166
Andhra Pradesh	28	80	112	76

402. Which two states account for the highest productivity of rice (tons produced per hectare of rice cultivation)?

(a) Haryana and Punjab
(b) Punjab and Andhra Pradesh
(c) Andhra Pradesh and Haryana
(d) Uttar Pradesh and Haryana

403. How many states have a per capita production of rice (defined as total rice production divided by its population) greater than Gujarat?

(a) 3 (b) 4
(c) 5 (d) 6

404. An intensive rice producing state is defined as one whose annual rice production per million of population is at least 400,000 tons. How many states are intensive rice producing states?

(a) 5 (b) 6
(c) 7 (d) 8

Directions for Questions 405 to 408: *Answer the questions on the basis of the information given below:*

Venkat, a stockbroker, invested a part of his money in the stock of four companies — A, B, C and D. Each of these companies belonged to different industries, viz., Cement, Information Technology (IT), Auto, and Steel, in no particular order. At the time of investment, the price of each stock was Rs. 100. Venkat purchased only one stock of each of these companies. He was expecting returns of 20%, 10%, 30% and 40% from the stock of companies A, B, C and D, respectively. Returns are defined as the change in the value of the stock after one year, expressed as a percentage of the initial value. During the year, two of these companies announced extraordinarily good results. One of these two companies belonged to the Cement or the IT industry, while the other one belonged to either the Steel or the Auto industry. As a result, the returns on the stocks of these two companies were higher than the initially expected returns. For the company belonging to the Cement or the IT industry with extraordinarily good results, the returns were twice that of the initially expected returns. For the company belonging to the Steel or the Auto industry, the returns on announcement of extraordinarily good results were only one and a half times that of the initially expected returns. For the remaining two companies which did not announce extraordinarily good results, the returns realized during the year were the same as initially expected.

405. What is the minimum average return Venkat would have earned during the year?

(a) 30% (b) $31\frac{1}{4}\%$
(c) $32\frac{1}{2}\%$ (d) Cannot be determined

406. If Venkat earned a 35% return on average during the year, then which of these statements would necessarily be true?

I. Company A belonged either to Auto or to Steel Industry.
II. Company B did not announce extraordinarily good results.
III. Company A announced extraordinarily good results.
IV. Company D did not announce extraordinarily good results.

(a) I and II only
(b) II and III only
(c) III and IV only
(d) II and IV only

407. If Venkat earned a 38.75% return on average during the year, then which of these statement(s) would necessarily be true?

I. Company C belonged either to Auto or to Steel Industry.
II. Company D belonged either to Auto or to Steel Industry.
III. Company A announced extraordinarily good results.
IV. Company B did not announce extraordinarily good results.

(a) I and II only (b) II and III only
(c) I and IV only (d) II and IV only

408. If Company C belonged to the Cement or the IT industry and did announce extraordinarily good results, then which of these statement(s) would necessarily be true?

I. Venkat earned not more than 36.25% return on average.
II. Venkat earned not less than 33.75% return on average.
III. If Venkat earned 33.75% return on average, Company A announced extraordinarily good results.
IV. If Venkat earned 33.75% return on average, Company B belonged either to Auto or to Steel Industry.

(a) I and II only
(b) II and IV only
(c) II and III only
(d) III and IV only

Directions for Questions 409 to 412: *Answer the questions on the basis of the information given below:*

The year is 2089. Beijing, London, New York, and Paris are in contention to host the 2096 Olympics. The eventual winner is determined through several rounds of voting by members of the IOC with each member representing a different city. All the four cities in contention are also represented in IOC.

(a) In any round of voting, the city receiving the lowest number of votes in that round gets eliminated. The survivor after the last round of voting gets to host the event.

(b) A member is allowed to cast votes for at most two different cities in all rounds of voting combined. (Hence, a member becomes ineligible to cast a vote in a given round if both the cities (s)he voted for in earlier rounds are out of contention in that round of voting.)

(c) A member is also ineligible to cast a vote in a round if the city (s)he represents is in contention in that round of voting.

(d) As long as the member is eligible, (s)he must vote and vote for only one candidate city in any round of voting.

The following incomplete table shows the information on cities that received the maximum and minimum votes in different rounds, the number of votes cast in their favour, and the total votes that were cast in those rounds.

Round	Total votes cast	Maximum votes cast		Eliminated	
		City	No. of votes	City	No. of votes
1		London	30	New York	12
2	83	Paris	32	Beijing	21
3	75				

It is also known that:

- All those who voted for London and Paris in round, 1 continued to vote for the same cities in subsequent rounds as long as these cities were in contention. 75% of those who voted for Beijing in round 1, voted for Beijing in round 2 as well.
- Those who voted for New York in round 1, voted either for Beijing or Paris in round 2.
- The difference in votes cast for the two contending cities in the last round was 1.
- 50% of those who voted for Beijing in round 1, voted for Paris in round 3.

409. What percentage of members from among those who voted for New York in round 1, voted for Beijing in round 2?

(a) 33.33

(b) 50

(c) 66.67

(d) 75

410. What is the number of votes cast for Paris in round 1?

(a) 16

(b) 18

(c) 22

(d) 24

411. What percentage of members from among those who voted for Beijing in round 2 and were eligible to vote in round 3, voted for London?

(a) 33.33

(b) 38.10

(c) 50

(d) 66.67

412. Which of the following statements must be true?

I. IOC member from New York must have voted for Paris in round 2.

II. IOC member from Beijing voted for London in round 3.

(a) Only I

(b) Only II

(c) Both I and II

(d) Neither I nor II

2006

Directions for Questions 413 to 417: *Answer questions on the basis of the information given below:*

In a Class X Board examination, ten papers are distributed over five Groups - PCB, Mathematics, Social Science, Vernacular and English. Each of the ten papers is evaluated out of 100. The final score of a student is calculated in the following manner. First, the Group Scores are obtained by averaging marks in the papers within the Group. The final score is the simple average of the Group Scores. The data for the top ten students are presented below. (Dipan's score in English Paper II has been intentionally removed in the table.)

Name of the student	PCB Group			Mathematics Group	Social Science Group		Vernacular Group		English Group		Final Score
	Phy.	Chem.	Bio.		Hist.	Geo.	Paper I	Paper II	Paper I	Paper II	
Ayesha (G)	98	96	97	98	95	93	94	96	96	98	96.2
Ram (B)	97	99	95	97	95	96	94	94	96	98	96.1
Dipan (B)	98	98	98	95	96	95	96	94	96	??	96.0
Sagnik (B)	97	98	99	96	96	98	94	97	92	94	95.9
Sanjiv (B)	95	96	97	98	97	96	92	93	95	96	95.7
Shreya (G)	96	89	85	100	97	98	94	95	96	95	95.5
Joseph (B)	90	94	98	100	94	97	90	92	94	95	95
Agni (B)	96	99	96	99	95	96	82	93	92	93	94.3
Pritam (B)	98	98	95	98	83	95	90	93	94	94	93.9
Tirna (G)	96	98	97	99	85	94	92	91	87	96	93.7

Note: B or G against the name of a student respectively indicates whether the student is a boy or a girl.

413. How much did Dipan get in English Paper II?

(a) 94 (b) 96.5
(c) 97 (d) 98
(e) 99

414. Among the top ten students, how many boys scored at least 95 in at least one paper from each of the groups?

(a) 1 (b) 2
(c) 3 (d) 4
(e) 5

415. Had Joseph, Agni, Pritam and Tirna each obtained Group Score of 100 in the Social Science Group, then their standing in decreasing order of final score would be:

(a) Pritam, Joseph, Tirna, Agni
(b) Joseph, Tirna, Agni, Pritam
(c) Pritam, Agni, Tirna, Joseph
(d) Joseph, Tirna, Pritam, Agni
(e) Pritam, Tirna, Agni, Joseph

416. Students who obtained Group Scores of at least 95 in every group are eligible to apply for a prize. Among those who are eligible, the student obtaining the highest Group Score in Social Science Group is awarded this prize. The prize was awarded to:

(a) Shreya (b) Ram
(c) Ayesha (d) Dipan
(e) No one from the top ten

417. Each of the ten students was allowed to improve his/her score in exactly one paper of choice with the objective of maximizing his/her final score. Everyone scored 100 in the paper in which he or she chose to improve. After that, the topper among the ten students was:

(a) Ram (b) Agni
(c) Pritam (d) Ayesha
(e) Dipan

Directions for Questions 418 to 422: *Answer the questions on the basis of the information given below:*

Two traders, Chetan and Michael, were involved in the buying and selling of MCS shares over five trading days. At the beginning of the first day, the MCS share was priced at Rs 100, while at the end of the fifth day it was priced at Rs 110. At the end of each day, the MCS share price either went up by Rs 10, or else, it came down by Rs 10. Both Chetan and Michael took buying and selling decisions at the end of each trading day. The beginning price of MCS share on a given day was the same as the ending price of the previous day. Chetan and Michael started with the same number of shares and amount of cash, and had enough of both. Below are some additional facts about how Chetan and Michael traded over the five trading days.

1. Each day if the price went up, Chetan sold 10 shares of MCS at the closing price. On the other hand, each day if the price went down, he bought 10 shares at the closing price.
2. If on any day, the closing price was above Rs 110, then Michael sold 10 shares of MCS, while if it was below Rs 90, he bought 10 shares, all at the closing price.

418. If Chetan sold 10 shares of MCS on three consecutive days, while Michael sold 10 shares only once during the five days, what was the price of MCS at the end of day 3?

(a) Rs 90 (b) Rs 100
(c) Rs 110 (d) Rs 120
(e) Rs 130

419. If Chetan ended up with Rs 1300 more cash than Michael at the end of day 5, what was the price of MCS share at the end of day 4?

(a) Rs 90 (b) Rs 100
(c) Rs 110 (d) Rs 120
(e) Not uniquely determinable

420. If Michael ended up with 20 more shares than Chetan at the end of day 5, what was the price of the share at the end of day 3?

(a) Rs 90 (b) Rs 100
(c) Rs 110 (d) Rs 120
(e) Rs 130

421. If Michael ended up with Rs 100 less cash than Chetan at the end of day 5, what was the difference in the number of shares possessed by Michael and Chetan (at the end of day 5)?

(a) Michael had 10 less shares than Chetan.
(b) Michael had 10 more shares than Chetan.
(c) Chetan had 10 more shares than Michael.
(d) Chetan had 20 more shares than Michael.
(e) Both had the same number of shares.

422. What could have been the maximum possible increase in combined cash balance of Chetan and Michael at the end of the fifth day?

(a) Rs 3700
(b) Rs 4000
(c) Rs 4700
(d) Rs 5000
(e) Rs 6000

2007

Directions for Questions 423 to 426: *Answer the following questions based on the information given below:*

The following table shows the break-up of actual costs incurred by a company in last five years (year 2002 to year 2006) to produce a particular product:

	Year 2002	Year 2003	Year 2004	Year 2005	Year 2006
Volume of production and sale (units)	1000	900	1100	1200	1200
Costs (Rs.)					
Material	50,000	45,100	55,200	59,900	60,000
Labour	20,000	18,000	22,100	24,150	24,000
Consumables	2,000	2,200	1,800	1,600	1,400
Rent of building	1,000	1,000	1,100	1,100	1,200
Rates and taxes	400	400	400	400	400
Repair and maintenance expenses	800	820	780	790	800
Operating cost of machines	30,000	27,000	33,500	36,020	36,000
Selling and marketing expenses	5,750	5,800	5,800	5,750	5,800

The production capacity of the company is 2000 units. The selling price for the year 2006 was Rs. 125 per unit. Some costs change almost in direct proportion to the change in volume of production, while others do not follow any obvious pattern of change with respect to the volume of production and hence are considered fixed. Using the information provided for the year 2006 as the basis for projecting the figures for the year 2007, answer the following questions:

423. What is the approximate cost per unit in rupees, if the company produces and sells 1400 units in the year 2007?

(a) 104 (b) 107
(c) 110 (d) 115
(e) 116

424. What is the minimum number of units that the company needs to produce and sell to avoid any loss?

(a) 313 (b) 350
(c) 384 (d) 747
(e) 928

425. If the company reduces the price by 5%, it can produce and sell as many units as it desires. How many units the company should produce to maximize its profit?

(a) 1400 (b) 1600
(c) 1800 (d) 1900
(e) 2000

426. Given that the company cannot sell more than 1700 units, and it will have to reduce the price by Rs.5 for all units, if it wants to sell more than 1400 units, what is the maximum profit, in rupees, that the company can earn?

(a) 25,400 (b) 24,400
(c) 31,400 (d) 32,900
(e) 32,000

Directions for Questions 427 to 430: *Answer the following questions based on the information given below:*

The proportion of male students and the proportion of vegetarian students in a school are given below.

The school has a total of 800 students, 80% of whom are in the Secondary Section and rest are equally divided between Class 11 and 12.

	Male (M)	Vegetarian (V)
Class 12	0.6	
Class 11	0.55	0.5
Secondary Section		0.55
Total	0.475	0.53

427. What is the percentage of male students in the secondary section?

(a) 40 (b) 45
(c) 50 (d) 55
(e) 60

428. In Class 12, twenty five per cent of the vegetarians are male. What is the difference between the number of female vegetarians and male non-vegetarians?

(a) less than 8 (b) 10
(c) 12 (d) 14
(e) 16

429. What is the percentage of vegetarian students in Class 12?

(a) 40 (b) 45
(c) 50 (d) 55
(e) 60

430. In the Secondary Section, 50% of the students are vegetarian males. Which of the following statements is correct?

(a) Except vegetarian males, all other groups have same number of students.
(b) Except non-vegetarian males, all other groups have same number of students.
(c) Except vegetarian females, all other groups have same number of students.
(d) Except non-vegetarian females, all other groups have same number of students.
(e) All of the above groups have the same number of students.

Directions for Questions 431 to 434: *Answer the following questions based on the information given below:*

The Table below shows the comparative costs, in US Dollars, of major surgeries in USA and a select few Asian countries.

Procedure	Comparative Costs in USA and some Asian countries (in US Dollar)				
	USA	India	Thailand	Singapore	Malaysia
Heart Bypasss	130000	10000	11000	18500	9000
Heart Valve Replacement	160000	9000	10000	12500	9000
Angioplasty	57000	11000	13000	13000	11000
Hip Replacement	43000	9000	12000	12000	10000
Hysterectomy	20000	3000	4500	6000	3000
Knee Replacement	40000	8500	10000	13000	8000
Spinal Fusion	62000	5500	7000	9000	6000

The equivalent of one US Dollar in the local currencies is given below:

	1 US Dollar equivalent	
India	40.928	Rupees
Malaysia	3.51	Ringits
Thailand	32.89	Bahts
Singapore	1.53	S Dollars

A consulting firm found that the quality of the health services were not the same in all the countries above. A poor quality of a surgery may have significant repercussions in future, resulting in more cost in correcting mistakes. The cost of poor quality of surgery is given in the table below:

Procedure	Comparative cost of poor quality in USA and some Asian countries (in US Dollars '000)				
	USA	India	Thailand	Singapore	Malaysia
Heart Bypasss	0	3	3	2	4
Heart Valve Replacement	0	5	4	5	5
Angioplasty	0	5	5	4	6
Hip Replacement	0	7	5	5	8
Hysterectomy	0	5	6	5	4
Knee Replacement	0	9	6	4	4
Spinal Fusion	0	5	6	5	6

431. A US citizen is hurt in an accident and requires an angioplasty, hip replacement and a knee replacement. Cost of foreign travel and stay is not a consideration since the government will take care of it. Which country will result in the cheapest package, taking cost of poor quality into account?

(a) India

(b) Thailand

(c) Malaysia

(d) Singapore

(e) USA

432. Taking the cost of poor quality into account, which country/countries will be the most expensive for knee replacement?

(a) India

(b) Thailand

(c) Malaysia

(d) Singapore

(e) India and Singapore

433. Approximately, what difference in amount in Bahts will it make to a Thai citizen if she were to get a hysterectomy done in India instead of in her native country, taking into account the cost of poor quality? (It costs 7500 Bahts for one-way travel between Thailand and India).

(a) 23500

(b) 40500

(c) 57500

(d) 67500

(e) 75000

434. The rupee value increases to Rs.35 for a US Dollar, and all other things including quality, remain the same. What is the approximate difference in cost, in US Dollars, between Singapore and India for a Spinal Fusion, taking this change into account?

(a) 700

(b) 2500

(c) 4500

(d) 8000

(e) No difference

2008

Directions for Questions 435 to 437: *Answer the following questions based on the information given below:*

Telecom operators get revenue from transfer of data and voice. Average revenue received from transfer of each unit of data is known as ARDT. In the diagram below, the revenue received from data transfer as percentage of total revenue received and the ARDT in US Dollars (USD) are given for various countries.

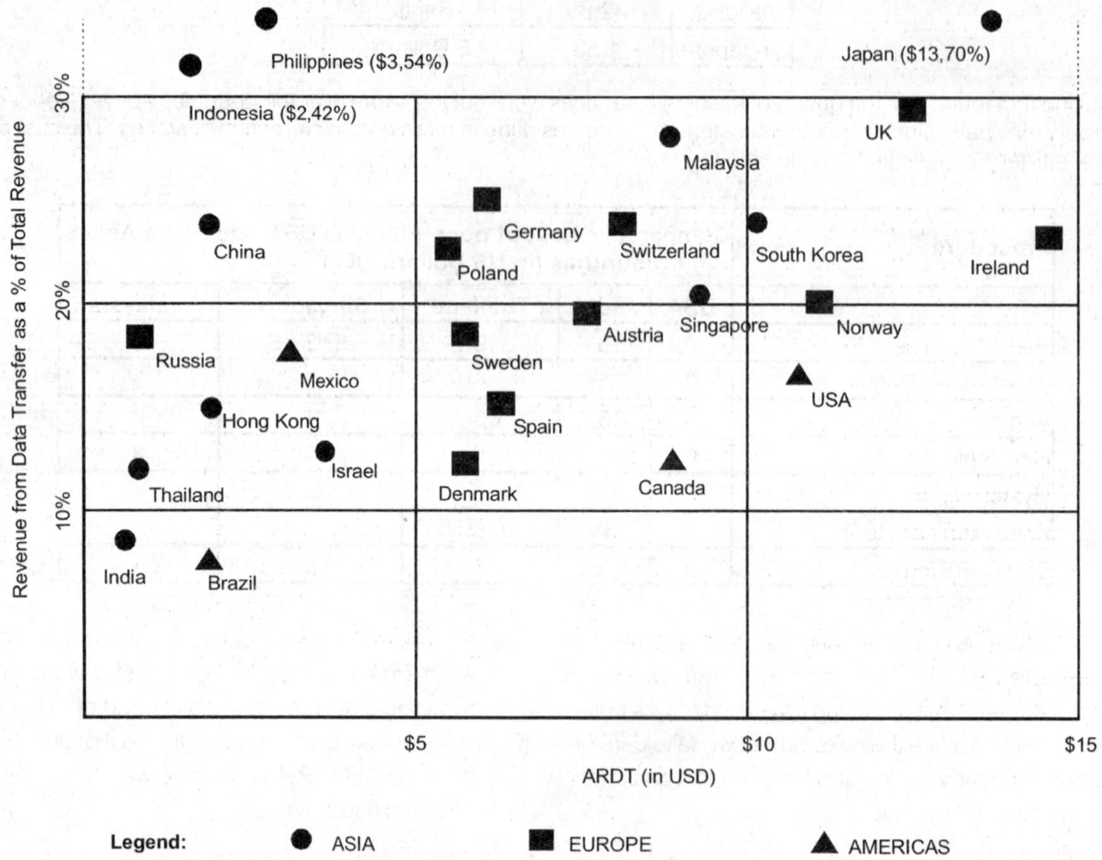

435. It was found that the volume of data transfer in India is the same as that of Singapore. Then which of the following statements is true?

(a) Total revenue is the same in both countries.

(b) Total revenue in India is about 2 times that of Singapore.

(c) Total revenue in India is about 4 times that of Singapore.

(d) Total revenue in Singapore is about 2 times that of India.

(e) Total revenue in Singapore is about 4 time that of India.

436. It is expected that by 2010, revenue from data transfer as a percentage of total revenue will triple for India and double for Sweden. Assume that in 2010, the total revenue in India is twice that of Sweden and that the volume of data transfer is the same in both the countries. What is the percentage increase of ARDT in India if there is no change in ARDT in Sweden?

(a) 400%

(b) 550%

(c) 800%

(d) 950%

(e) cannot be determined

437. If the total revenue received is the same for the pairs of countries listed in the choices below, choose the pair that has approximately the same volume of data transfer.

(a) Philippines and Austria

(b) Canada and Poland

(c) Germany and USA

(d) UK and Spain

(e) Denmark and Mexico

Directions for Questions 438 to 441: *Answer the following questions based on the information given below:*

The bar chart below shows the revenue received in million US Dollars (USD), from subscribers to a particular Internet service. The data covers the period 2003 to 2007 for the United States (US) and Europe. The bar chart also shows the estimated revenues from subscription to this service for the period 2008 to 2010.

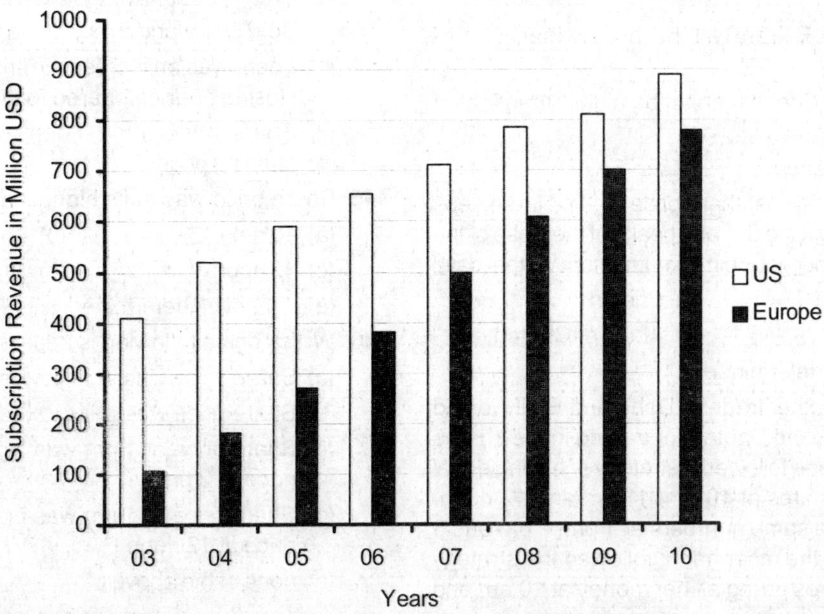

438. The difference between the estimated subscription in Europe in 2008 and what it would have been if it were computed using the percentage growth rate of 2007 (over 2006), is closest to:

(a) 50 (b) 80
(c) 20 (d) 10
(e) 0

439. In 2003, sixty percent of subscribers in Europe were men. Given that women subscribers increase at the rate of 10 percent per annum and men at the rate of 5 percent per annum, what is the approximate percentage growth of subscribers between 2003 and 2010 in Europe? The subscription prices are volatile and may change each year.

(a) 62 (b) 15
(c) 78 (d) 84
(e) 50

440. Consider the annual percent change in the gap between subscription revenues in the US and Europe. What is the year in which the absolute value of this change is the highest?

(a) 03 - 04 (b) 05 - 06
(c) 06 - 07 (d) 08 - 09
(e) 09 - 10

441. While the subscription in Europe has been growing steadily towards that of the US, the growth rate in Europe seems to be declining. Which of the following is closest to the percent change in growth rate of 2007 (over 2006) relative to the growth rate of 2005 (over 2004)?

(a) 17 (b) 20
(c) 35 (d) 60
(e) 100

Directions for Questions 442 to 446: *Answer the following questions based on the information given below:*

Abdul, Bikram and Chetan are three professional traders who trade in shares of a company XYZ Ltd. Abdul follows the strategy of buying at the opening of the day at 10 am and selling the whole lot at the close of the day at 3 pm. Bikram follows the strategy of buying at hourly intervals: 10 am, 11 am, 12 noon, 1 pm, and 2 pm, and selling the whole lot at the close of the day. Further, he buys an equal number of shares in each purchase. Chetan follows a similar pattern as Bikram but his strategy is somewhat different. Chetan's total investment amount is divided equally among his purchases. The profit or loss made by each investor is the difference between the sale value at the close of the day less the investment in purchase. The "return" for each investor is defined as the ratio of the profit or loss to the investment amount expressed as a percentage.

442. On a day of fluctuating market prices, the share price of XYZ Ltd. ends with a gain, i.e, it is higher at the close of the day compared to the opening value. Which trader got the maximum return on that day?

(a) Bikram (b) Chetan
(c) Abdul (d) Bikram or Chetan
(e) cannot be determined

443. Which one of the following statements is always true?
(a) Abdul will not be one with the minimum return
(b) Return for Chetan will be higher than that of Bikram
(c) Return for Bikram will be higher than that of Chetan
(d) Return for Chetan cannot be higher than that of Abdul
(e) none of the above

444. On a "boom" day the share price of XYZ Ltd. keeps rising throughout the day and peaks at the close of the day. Which trader got the minimum return on that day?
(a) Bikram (b) Chetan
(c) Abdul (d) Abdul or Chetan
(e) cannot be determined

One day, two other traders, Dane and Emily joined Abdul, Bikram and Chetan for trading in the shares of XYZ Ltd. Dane followed a strategy of buying equal numbers of shares at 10 am. 11 am and 12 noon, and selling the same numbers at 1 pm, 2 pm and 3 pm. Emily, on the other hand, followed the strategy of buying shares us ing all her money at 10 am and selling all of them at 12 noon and again buying the shares for all the money at 1 pm and again selling all of them at the close of the day at 3 pm. At the close of the day the following was observed.
i. Abdul lost money in the transactions.
ii. Both Dane and Emily made profits.
iii. There was an increase in share price during the closing hour compared to the price at 2 pm.
iv. Share price at 12 noon was lower than the opening price

445. Share price was at its highest at
(a) 10 am (b) 11 am
(c) 12 noon (d) 1 pm
(e) cannot be determined

446. Which of the following is necessarily false?
(a) Share price was at its lowest at 2 pm
(b) Share price was at its lowest at 11 am
(c) Share price at 1 pm was higher than the share price at 2 pm
(d) Share price at 1 pm was higher than the share price at 12 noon
(e) none of the above

Directions for Questions 447 to 449: *Answer the following questions based on the information given below:*

There are 100 employees in an organization across five departments. The following table gives the department-wise distribution of average age, average basic pay and allowances. The gross pay of an employee is the sum of his/her basic pay and allowances.

Department	Number of Employees	Average Age (Years)	Average Basic Pay (Rs.)	Allowances (% of Basic Pay)
HR	5	45	5000	70
Marketing	30	35	6000	80
Finance	20	30	6500	60
Business Development	35	42	7500	75
Maintenance	10	35	5500	50

There are limited numbers of employees considered for transfer/promotion across departments. Whenever a person is transferred/promoted from a department of lower average age to a department of higher average age, he/she will get an additional allowance of 10% of basic pay over and above his/her current allowance. There will not be any change in pay structure if a person is transferred/promoted from a department with higher average age to a department with lower average age.

Questions below are independent of each other.

447. What is the approximate percentage change in the average gross of the HR department due to transfer of a 40-year old person with basic pay of Rs. 8000 from the Marketing department?
(a) 9% (b) 11%
(c) 13% (d) 15%
(e) 17%

448. There was a mutual transfer of an employee between Marketing and Finance departments and transfer of one employee from Marketing to HR. As a result, the average age of Finance department increased by one year and that of Marketing department remained the same. What is the new average age of HR department?
(a) 30 (b) 35
(c) 40 (d) 45
(e) cannot be determined

449. If two employees (each with a basic pay of Rs. 6000) are transferred from Maintenance department to HR department and one person (with a basic pay of Rs. 8000) was transferred from Marketing department to HR department, what will be the percentage change in average basic pay of HR department?

(a) 10.5% (b) 12.5%
(c) 15% (d) 30%
(e) 40%

MEMORY BASED QUESTIONS

2009

Directions for Questions 450 to 452: *Answer the following questions on the basis of the information given below.* The table given below shows the production figures (in thousand tonnes) of the various types of crops produced in the country called Khetistan for three years. It also shows the percentage contribution of Charyana, one of the states of Khetistan, to the total production of Khetistan for each year.

	1991		1992		1993	
	Khetistan (in '000 tonnes)	Charyana (in %)	Khetistan (in '000 tonnes)	Charyana (in %)	Khetistan (in '000 tonnes)	Charyana (in %)
Wheat	1500	20	1800	25	2000	25
Rice	2000	15	2200	20	2400	20
Bajra	500	25	600	15	800	15
Maize	400	20	300	15	500	20
Others	1200	10	1400	10	1000	10
Total	5600		6300		6700	

450. In which year was the percentage contribution of Charyana to the total production of Khetistan (all the crops) maximum during the period 1991-1993?

(a) 1991 (b) 1992
(c) 1993 (d) Cannot be determined

451. Which crop showed a decline in production for two consecutive years in Charyana during the period 1991-1993?

(a) Bajra (b) Maize
(c) Rice (d) None of these

452. Which crop showed a decline in production for at least one year in Charyana despite showing an increase in production for two consecutive years in Khetistan during the period 1991-1993?

(a) Wheat (b) Rice
(c) Bajra (d) Maize

Directions for questions 453 to 456: *Answer the following questions on the basis of the information given below.*

The performance of six students of a class in five subjects is evaluated on a 9-point grading system. Each student is awarded a grade and grade points in each of the five subjects based on the marks obtained by him in that subject (See Table - 1). Table - 2 shows the marks obtained by each student in the five subjects. A student's GPA (Grade Point Average) is the average of the grade points awarded to him in the five subjects.

Marks Range	Grade	Grade Points
91-100	A1	10
81-90	A2	9
71-80	B1	8
61-70	B2	7
51-60	C1	6
41-50	C2	5
31-40	D	4
21-30	E	3
0-20	F	2

Table - 1

		Subject-wise Marks Scored				
		English	Hindi	Math	Science	S.Sc.
Student	Abhishek	56	67	92	97	51
	Saral	88	79	87	Z	88
	Himanshu	X	81	82	89	81
	Puneet	83	90	91	78	79
	Vijay	74	65	Y	67	77
	Sanjay	73	88	93	60	86

Table - 2

Additional Information:

- The sum of the GPAs of Saral and Puneet is equal to the sum of the GPAs of Himanshu and Sanjay.
- The GPAs of Abhishek and Vijay are equal.
- Saral, Himanshu, Puneet and Sanjay get distinct GPAs.

- Though the total marks (the sum of the marks obtained in the five subjects) of Himanshu are not the highest, his GPA is the highest among the six students.
- The sum of the marks obtained by the six students in Science is more than the sum of the marks obtained by the six students in exactly three of the other four subjects.

453. Which grade is awarded to Saral in Science?

(a) A1 (b) A2
(c) B1 (d) B2

454. Who gets the second highest GPA among the six students?

(a) Saral (b) Puneet
(c) Vijay (d) Sanjay

455. What is the sum of the marks obtained by Saral in the five subjects?

(a) 422 (b) 432
(c) 426 (d) Cannot be determined

456. How many values are possible for X?

(a) 1 (b) 10
(c) 8 (d) None of these

Directions for questions 457 to 460 : Answer the following questions on the basis of the information given below.

The figure given below shows a water distribution system consisting of tanks, pumps and the connecting pipelines. It supplies water to five cities C1, C2, C3, C4 and C5. The water can flow only in one direction in a pipeline. The water stored (in million gallons) initially in the tanks T1, T2, T3 and T4 was 200, 300, 100 and 500 respectively. The system starts when the water starts flowing out of each tank and is distributed equally among all the pipelines connected to a tank. The pumps do not consume any water and the volume of the water coming in and going out of a pump is the same. The consumption of water (in million gallons) in C1, C4 and C5 is 250, 200 and 150 respectively. The consumption of water in C2 and C3 is in the ratio 3 : 2. The water which is left after consumption in a city flows out of it through a pipeline.

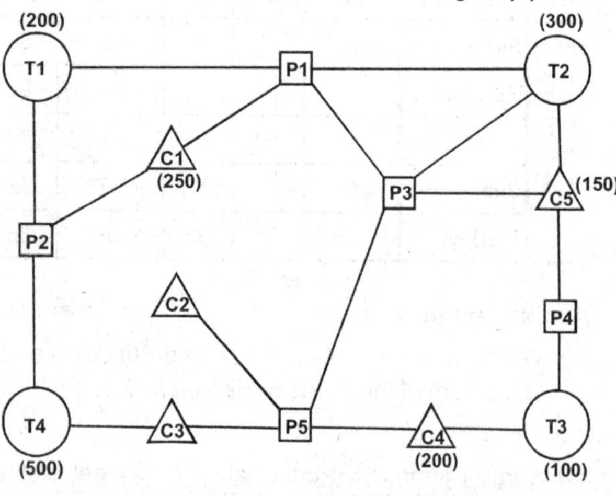

457. What is the ratio of the volume of the water coming in to the water going out of C1?

(a) 5 : 2 (b) 3 : 1
(c) 2 : 1 (d) 7 : 2

458. What is the consumption (in million gallons) of water in C2?

(a) 200 (b) 250
(c) 300 (d) 350

459. What is the volume of the water that flows through the pipeline joining C5 and P3?

(a) 50 (b) 100
(c) 150 (d) None of these

460. What is the ratio of the volume of the water that flows through P1 to the water that flows through P5?

(a) 1 : 3 (b) 2 : 3
(c) 3 : 4 (d) 5 : 9

2010

Directions for questions 461 and 462: *Answer the questions on the basis of the information given below.*

The performance appraisal of the employees of Hondai Motors Pvt Ltd. was done three times in the year 2010. The first appraisal was done in January, the second in July and the third in November. Only the employees who were appraised in January were eligible for appraisal in July and only those who were appraised in July were eligible for appraisal in November.

During an appraisal, an employee was appraised on exactly one of the three performance areas – Individual Performance, Team Performance and Moral Conduct. An employee already appraised on a particular performance area was not appraised on the same performance area in subsequent appraisal(s) during the year.

The table given below shows the number of employees appraised in each of the three appraisal months in 2010 for different performance areas.

Performance Area	Appraisal Month		
	January	July	November
Individual Performance	70	30	9
Team Performance	67	22	13
Moral Conduct	97	29	11

461. How many employees of Hondai Motors Pvt Ltd. were appraised on exactly one performance area in 2010?

(a) 235

(b) 121

(c) 154

(d) None of these

462. Among the employees of Hondai Motors Pvt Ltd. who were appraised in 2010, how many were not appraised on Individual Performance?

(a) 125 (b) 134
(c) 113 (d) 165

Directions for questions 463 to 465 : Answer the questions on the basis of the information given below.

Ten people – Chuck, Berry, David, Gilmour, Eric, Clapton, Jimmy, Page, Kirk and Hammett – live in a building that has six floors numbered 1 to 6 (lowest to highest). Each floor is occupied by at least one of the ten people. If N(x) represents the number of people living on floor x, then $N(1) = N(6) \neq N(3)$ and $N(2) = N(5)$. Also, $N(x) \neq N(x+1)$ for x = 1 to 5. It is also known that:

(i) Both Chuck and Berry live on the floor that is immediately above the floor on which Kirk lives.

(ii) David lives on a higher floor as compared to Clapton, Jimmy and Hammett but on a lower floor as compared to Chuck.

(iii) Gilmour and Page live on the same floor.

(iv) The number of people who live on the floor on which Jimmy lives is equal to that on which Eric lives.

463. What is the difference between the number of people who live on floor 3 and floor 5?

(a) 0 (b) 1
(c) 3 (d) 2

464. Who among the following lives on floor 6?

(a) Eric (b) David
(c) Chuck (d) Gilmour

465. How many people live on a floor higher than the one on which Jimmy lives?

(a) 7 (b) 5
(c) 9 (d) 6

Directions for questions 466 to 468: *Answer the questions on the basis of the information given below.*

The graph given below shows the statistics of five companies – Perfitti VM, UB Group, ITC, Unilever and Wipro – in India. Each point on the graph indicates the Total Revenue generated by a different department of one of these companies and the Average Revenue generated per Unit Energy Consumed by that particular department.

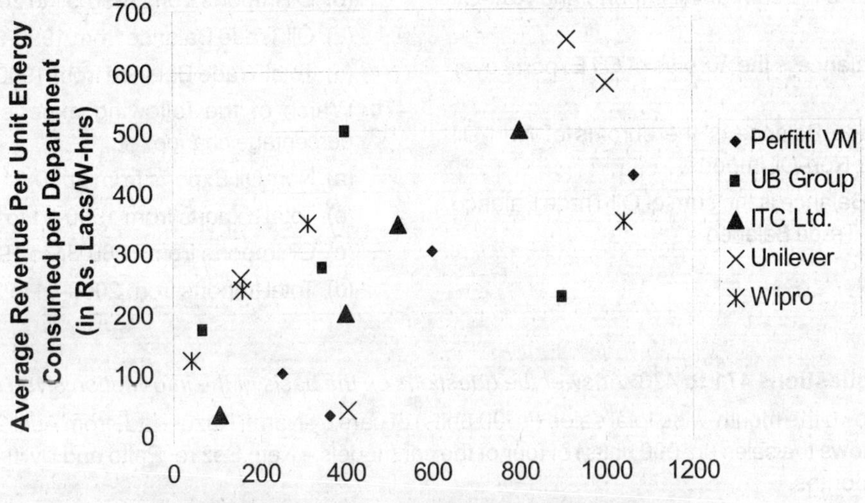

466. If the departments represented in the graph are the only departments in the five companies where energy is consumed, then for which company is the Energy Consumption the highest?

(a) Wipro (b) UB Group
(c) ITC Ltd. (d) None of these

467. How many of the represented departments across the five companies have consumed less than 100W-hrs of energy?

(a) Seven (b) Three
(c) Five (d) Six

468. Which of the five companies has the highest number of departments that generate more than Rs. 600 crores as the Total Revenue and consume less than 200W-hrs of energy?

(a) Perfitti VM (b) Unilever
(c) Wipro (d) ITC Ltd.

Directions for questions 469 and 470 : *Answer the questions on the basis of the information given below.*

The graph given below shows the total Exports and Imports of a country for four different years.

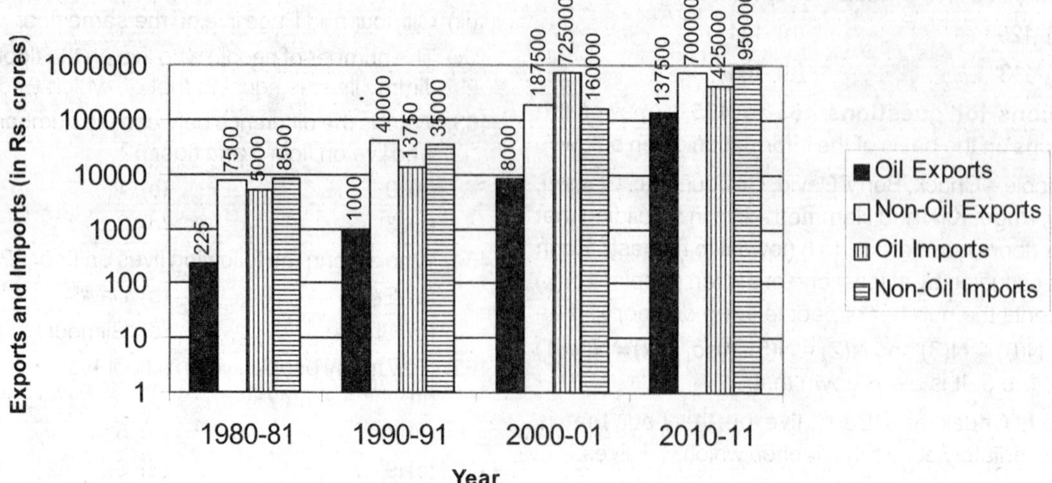

Please note:

(i) Total Exports is the sum of Oil Exports and Non-Oil Exports.

(ii) Total Imports is the sum of Oil Imports and Non-Oil Imports.

(iii) Oil Trade Balance is the surplus of Oil Exports over Oil Imports.

(iv) Non-Oil Trade Balance is the surplus of Non-Oil Exports over Non-Oil Imports.

(v) Total Trade Balance is the sum of Oil Trade Balance and Non-Oil Trade Balance.

469. Which of the following experiences the highest increase?

(a) Oil Exports from 2000-01 to 2010-11.

(b) Oil Imports from 1990-91 to 2000-01.

(c) Oil Trade Balance from 1990-91 to 2000-01.

(d) Total Trade Balance from 1990-91 to 2000-01

470. Which of the following experiences the lowest percentage change?

(a) Non-Oil Exports from 2000-01 to 2010-11.

(b) Total Exports from 1990-91 to 2000-01.

(c) Oil Imports from 1980-81 to 1990-91.

(d) Total Imports from 2000-01 to 2010-11.

2011

Directions for questions 471 to 473: *Answer the questions on the basis of the information given below.*

Bar Graph - I shows the month-wise total sales (in '00 units) of cars by Naruti Kuzuki Ltd. from April 2010 to July 2010. Bar Graph - II shows the sales (in '000 units) of four of the car models – Ken, Sezire, Palto and Dwift – of Naruti Kuzuki Ltd. in the four months.

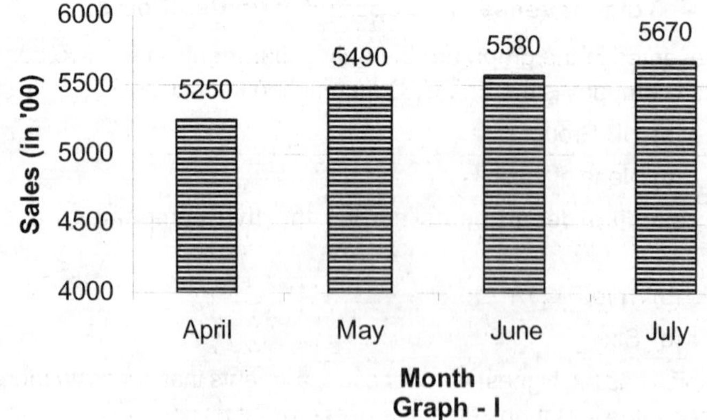

Graph - I

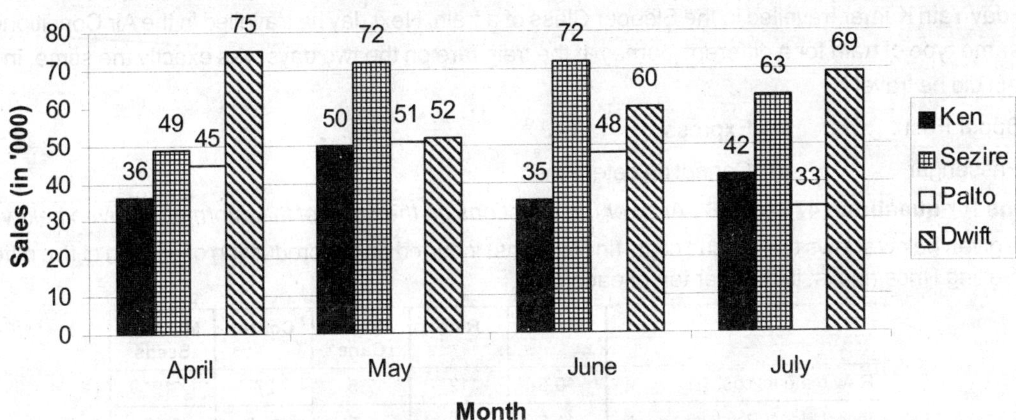

Graph - II

471. For which of the four car models is the absolute percentage change in the sales from April 2010 to July 2010 equal to the absolute percentage change in the total sales of cars by Naruti Kuzuki Ltd. during the same period?

(a) Dwift
(b) Ken
(c) Sezire
(d) Palto

472. What is the percentage increase in the sales of the rest of the car models (other than the given four) by Naruti Kuzuki Ltd. from May 2010 to July 2010?

(a) 7.5% (b) 8%
(c) 9.09% (d) None of these

473. For which month is the ratio of the sales of Sezire to the total sales of cars by Naruti Kuzuki Ltd. the highest?

(a) April (b) May
(c) June (d) July

Directions for questions 474 and 475 : *Answer the questions on the basis of the information given below.*

Travelabad is famous for its vast railway network. It has three types of trains – Super Fast, Express and Passenger – and each type of train has two classes of travel – Sleeper and Air Conditioned. The train fare in Travelabad has two components – fixed fare and variable fare. The fixed fare is based on the class of travel – Rs. 60 for Sleeper and Rs. 100 for Air Conditioned. The variable fare depends on the distance of the journey, the type of train and the class of travel. The table given below shows the variable fare (in Rs.) for different distance ranges from the source station to the destination station.

Distance Range	≤150 km		151 – 500 km		501 – 1000 km		1001 – 1800 km		≥1801 km	
Class	**SL**	**AC**	**SL**	**AC**	**SL**	**AC**	**SL**	**AC**	**SL**	**AC**
Super Fast	80	200	155	500	250	650	340	950	480	1250
Express	60	160	110	300	175	450	240	650	330	900
Passenger	45	120	80	225	125	325	160	425	225	550

AC = Air Conditioned Class

SL = Sleeper Class

474. Ghumakkad Das travels only in the Sleeper class of Super Fast trains. He travelled from Delhi to Bhopal and then took another train from Bhopal to Mumbai. Next day he returned to Delhi directly from Mumbai. The total train fare while going to Mumbai from Delhi via Bhopal exceeded the train fare while coming back to Delhi from Mumbai by Rs.125. If Bhopal lies on the only rail route connecting Delhi and Mumbai, in which range does Delhi-Mumbai rail distance fall?

(a) 151 – 500 km (b) 501 – 1000 km
(c) 1001 – 1800 km (d) ≥1801 km

475. One day Yatri Kumar travelled in the Sleeper Class of a train. Next day he travelled in the Air Conditioned Class of the same type of train for a different journey. If the train fare on the two days was exactly the same, in which type of train did he travel?

(a) Super Fast (b) Express

(c) Passenger (d) Cannot be determined

Directions for questions 476 to 478 : *Answer the questions on the basis of the information given below.*

The table given below shows the various costs (in Rs. lakhs) incurred on the production of one ton of five different crops and the Selling Price (in Rs. lakhs) per ton of each crop.

Crop	Maize	Rice	Sugar Cane	Cotton	Mustard Seeds
Raw material cost	10.5	12	7.5	27	19
Insecticides/ Pesticides cost	11.5	8	9.5	42.5	32.5
Fertilizers cost	13.5	10	17.5	20	21
Fuel Consumption Cost	20	15	12.5	10	22.5
Irrigation cost	8	11.5	22	33	16.5
Storage cost	14	8.5	21	20	11
Transportation cost	12.5	10	15	7.5	17.5
Selling Price	120	90	125	175	180

Note: Profit = Selling Price – Total Cost

476. For which crop is the profit percentage per ton the highest?

(a) Cotton (b) Maize

(c) Mustard Seeds (d) None of these

477. For how many of the given crops is the Irrigation cost more than 20% of the total cost?

(a) 0 (b) 1

(c) 2 (d) 3

478. If 1 kg of raw material of Cotton costs Rs. 54 and 200 grams of raw material is sown in 10 m^2 of land, then what is the area of land required for producing 1 ton of Cotton?

(a) 2500 m^2

(b) 500 m^2

(c) 2.5 km^2

(d) 5 km^2

2012

Directions for Questions 479 to 481 : Answer the questions on the basis of the information given below.

The bar charts given below shows the details of the "Budgeted I-Tax" collections and the "Actual I-Tax" collections of India in each of the years from 2004-05 to 2008-09. Bar Chart-I shows the details of the **Total I-Tax** collections and bar chart-II shows the details of the **Corporate I-Tax** collections. There are only two categories of taxpayers in India "Individual Taxpayers" and "Corporate Taxpayers". All the figures are in Rs. crores.

Total I-Tax collections

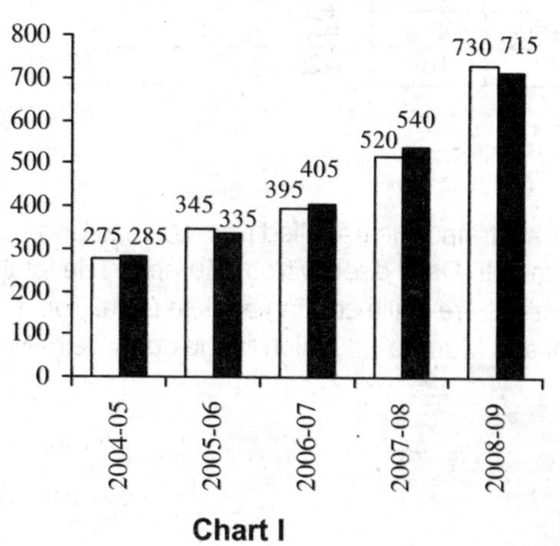

Chart I

Corporate I-Tax collections

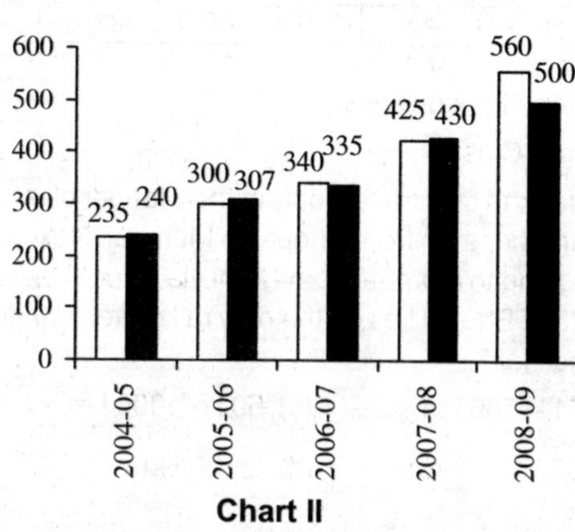

Chart II

□ Budgeted ■ Actual

$$\text{Efficacy Ratio} = \left(\frac{\text{Budgeted I-Tax Collections}}{\text{Actual I-Tax Collections}}\right)$$

479. For how many of the given years the Efficacy Ratio of at least two out of "Total I-Tax" collections, "Corporate I-Tax" collections and "Individual I-Tax" collections is greater than 1?

(a) 0 (b) 1

(c) 2 (d) Data Insufficient

480. In which of the following years, for either of the Corporate I-Tax collections or the Total I-Tax collections, the percentage growth of I-Tax over the previous year for both the Budgeted and the Actual is approximately the same?

(a) 2005-06 (b) 2006-07

(c) 2007-08 (d) Both (b) and (c)

481. Which of the following statements (is/are) true?

I. Percentage contribution of the corporate I-Tax (Actual) collections to the total I-Tax (Actual) collections has decreased in the year 2008-09 in comparison to the year 2005-06.

II. Simple Annual growth rate of Actual I-Tax paid by the individual taxpayers for the period 2004-05 to 2008-09 is more than 90 percent

III. Efficacy ratio for the "Corporate I-Tax" collections is the highest in the year 2008-09.

(a) I (b) II

(c) III (d) I, II and III

Directions for Questions 482 to 484 : Answer the following questions on the basis of the information given below.

The following table gives the sales turnover (in crore Rs.) of the five major detergent brands A, B, C, D, E and others in the 4 regions East, West, North and South of India. The data is for the years 2008 and 2009. The pie chart gives the breakup of the sales of the same brands in terms of the number of units sold. The total number of units sold for 2008 and 2009 was the same.

Region → / Brand ↓	East		West		North		South		Total	
	2008	2009	2008	2009	2008	2009	2008	2009	2008	2009
A	165	172	180	192	167	190	213	180	725	734
B	75	90	62	75	53	72	17	77	207	314
C	212	182	207	222	153	162	137	120	709	686
D	101	115	121	134	113	121	178	190	513	560
E	90	105	87	95	73	92	67	92	317	384
Others	250	310	152	175	143	162	57	83	602	730
Total	893	974	809	893	702	799	669	742		

Volumewise Breakup of Brands All India

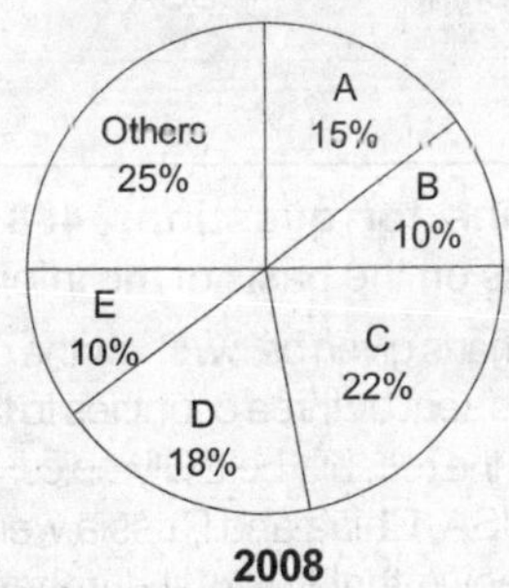

2008

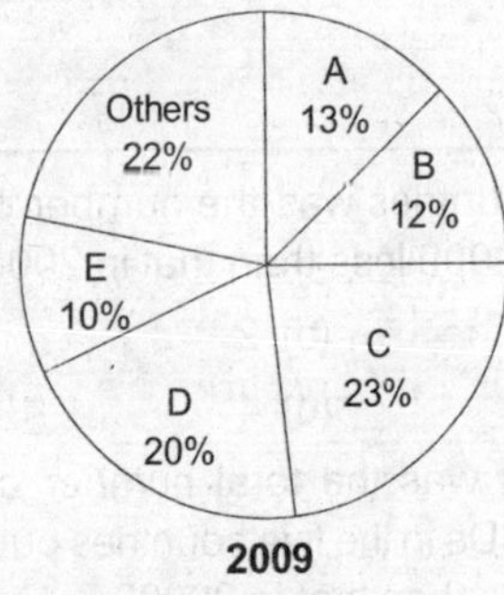

2009

482. What is the total sales turnover (in crore Rs.) of the detergent market in India in the year 2009?

(a) 3073 (b) 2842

(c) 2906 (d) 3408

483. Which brand registered the maximum percentage increase in the price per unit in 2009?

(a) A (b) B

(c) D (d) E

484. Which of the following statement(s) is/are true?

1. Exactly two brands could not register a growth in all the regions in 2009.
2. The number of units sold by B in 2009 has shown an increase of above 350% in South.
3. The number of units sold by C in 2009 was less than that sold by C in 2008.

(a) Only 1 (b) 1 and 2

(c) 1 and 3 (d) 2 and 3

2013

Directions for questions 485 to 487 : Answer the questions on the basis of the information given below.

The bar graphs given below show the gender-wise deaths (in '000) due to NCDs (Non Communicable Diseases) in five countries for the years 2008 and 2009.

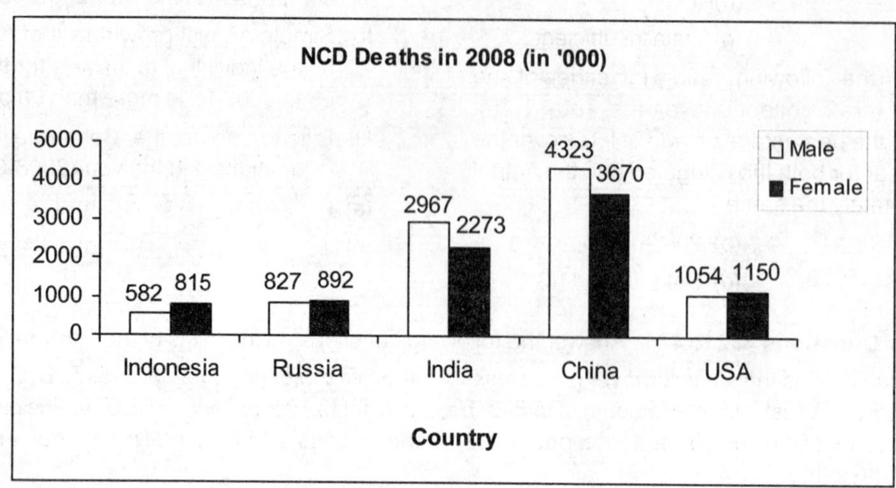

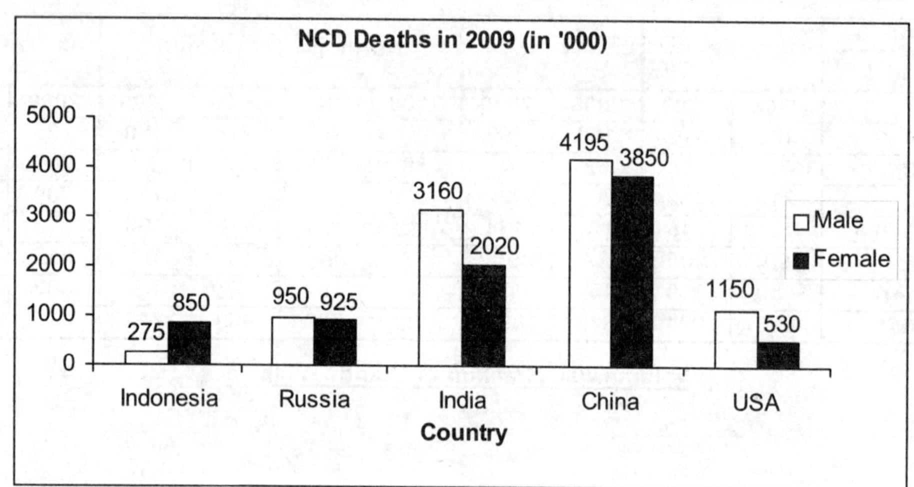

485. In how many countries was the number of deaths due to NCDs in 2009 less than that in 2008?

(a) 1 (b) 2
(c) 3 (d) 4

486. By what percent was the total number of female deaths due to NCDs in the five countries put together in 2009 more/less than that in 2008?

(a) 7.10 (b) 6.40
(c) 8.60 (d) 7.90

487. What was the absolute difference between the total number of male deaths due to NCDs in the five countries put together in 2008 and 2009?

(a) 22500 (b) 23000
(c) 24000 (d) None of these

Directions for questions 488 to 490: Answer the questions on the basis of the information given below.

The pie charts given below show the distribution of the number of athletes sent by three countries to take part in eight different games in the recently held Olympics. The numbers of athletes sent by USA, China and Russia were in the ratio 8 : 11 : 5. It is also known that the total number of athletes sent by the three countries put together was 2400.

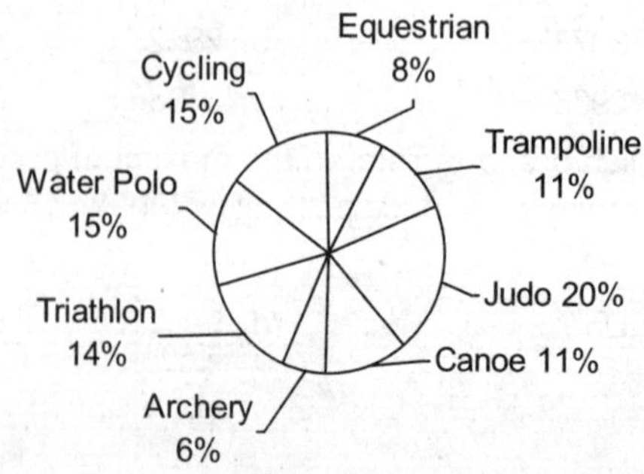

China

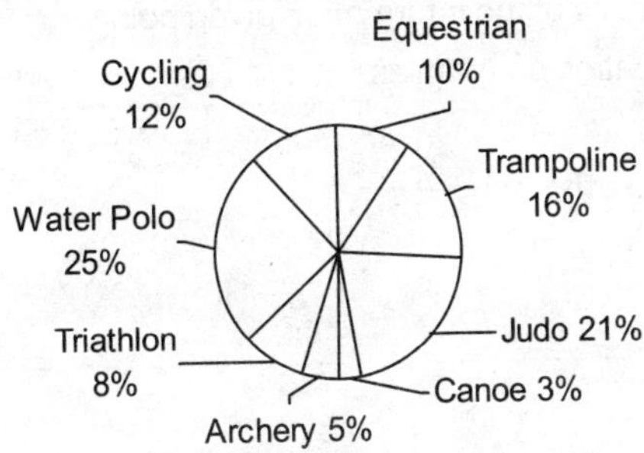

Russia

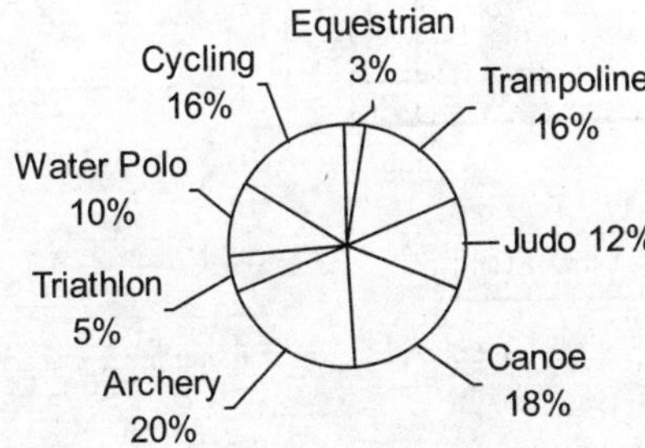

488. The female to male ratio for Cycling athletes from Russia and USA was 1 : 19 and 4 : 1 respectively. If the number of female Cycling athletes was equal to the number of male Cycling athletes for the three countries put together, then what was the number of female Cycling athletes from China?

(a) 4

(b) 96

(c) 66

(d) None of these

489. What was the absolute difference between the maximum number of athletes sent by China for a game and the minimum number of athletes sent by Russia for a game?

(a) 260

(b) 160

(c) 242

(d) 145

490. The number of Water Polo athletes constituted what percent of the total number of athletes sent by the three countries put together?

(a) 20.00 (b) 18.90

(c) 22.30 (d) 18.54

Directions for questions 491 to 493: Answer the questions on the basis of the information given below.

The table given below shows the data related to a few key financial indicators for fourteen European countries in the FY 2011-12.

Country	Inflation (%)	Long-term interest rate (% p.a.)	Debt to GDP ratio (in %)	Fiscal-deficit (as a % of GDP)
Austria	2.2	3.4	70.2	4.8
Belgium	3.4	3.9	100.8	4.8
Cyprus	2.2	4.6	61.1	5.7
Denmark	2.2	3	46.6	4.6
Estonia	2.4	5.7	7.7	1.7
Finland	1.1	3.1	45.4	3.4
France	1.5	3.3	83.5	8
Germany	1.9	2.9	74.8	4.5
Italy	1.4	4.6	118	5.1
Latvia	1.2	7.5	48	8.6
Malta	1.7	4.4	72	3.8
Netherlands	1.1	3.1	64.6	5.6
Poland	2.4	5.9	53.9	7.3
Portugal	1.1	6.5	83.2	7.3

491. If the Fiscal-deficit of France was x Euros, which was 50% more than that of Belgium, then what was the Debt (in Euros) of Belgium in FY 2011-12?

(a) 13x

(b) 7x

(c) 14x

(d) 6.5x

492. The countries with the Long-term interest rate less than 4% per annum, Debt to GDP ratio less than 60% and Fiscal-deficit not more than 4.6% were given a AAA rating. The number of countries rated AAA among the fourteen in FY 2011-12 was

(a) 0

(b) 1

(c) 2

(d) None of these

493. If the GDP (in Euros) of Finland was 50% more than that of Italy, then by what percent was the Fiscal-deficit (in Euros) of Italy more/less than that of Finland in FY 2011-12?

(a) 0

(b) 1.5

(c) 0.5

(d) Cannot be determined

2014

Direction for questions 494 to 497 : Answer the questions on the basis of the information given below.
The graphs given below show the revenues and profits of four IT education companies.
Profitability = (Profit/Revenue)

Total cost = Revenue – Profit

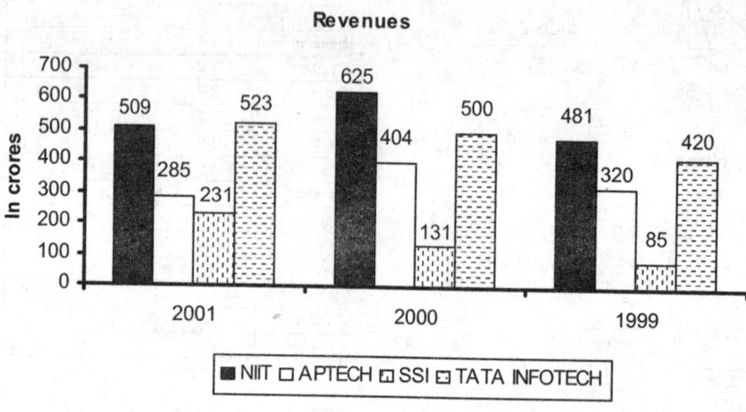

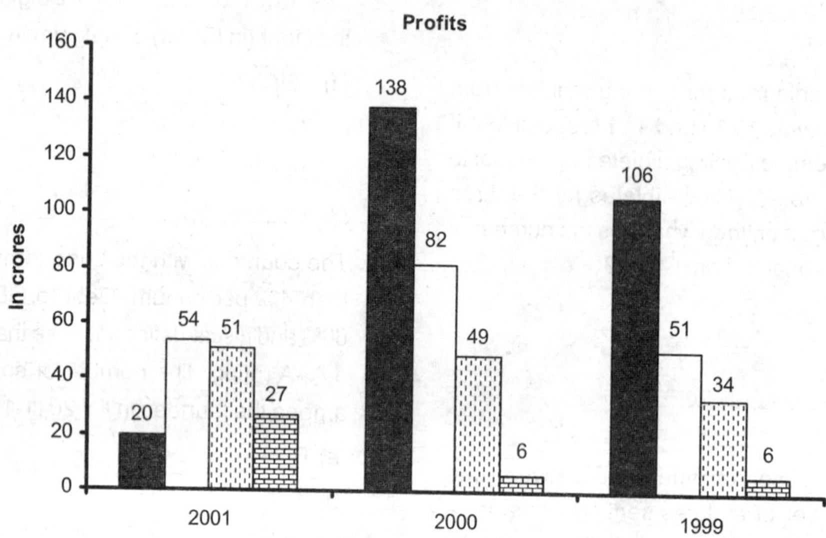

494. In 1999, how many companies have a profitability less than the average of the profitabilities of the four companies?

(a) 1 (b) 2
(c) 3 (d) 0

495. In 2002, if the cost in each company increased by 10% over 2001 and the revenue for each company decreased by 10% over 2001, what is the approximate profitability of all the companies taken together in 2002?

(a) 10.25% (b) –10.25%
(c) –9.25% (d) 8.75%

496. Arrange the companies in increasing order of their profitability in 2001.

(a) NIIT, Tata Infotech, Aptech, SSI
(b) NIIT, Tata Infotech, SSI, Aptech
(c) NIIT, Aptech, Tata Infotech, SSI
(d) SSI, Aptech, Tata Infotech, NIIT

497. Which company has the highest profitability in 2000?

(a) NIIT
(b) Aptech
(c) SSI
(d) Tata Infotech

Directions for questions 498 to 500 : Answer the questions on the basis of the information given below.

The average annual salary figures of five leading B-schools have been shown below.

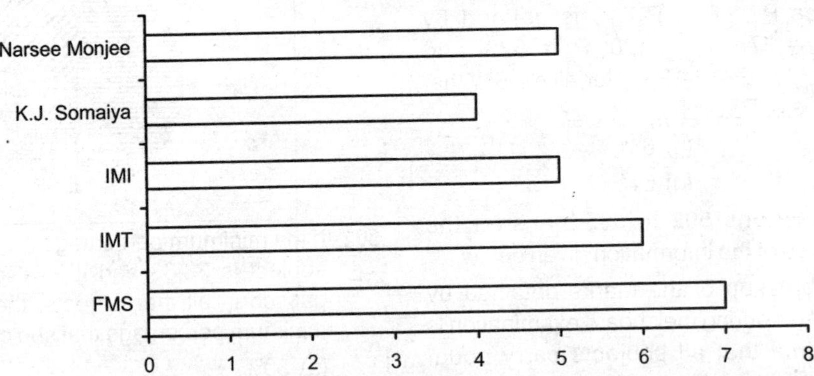

The percentage of students getting PPOs (Pre-Placement offers) and their average annual salary in lakhs is shown below.

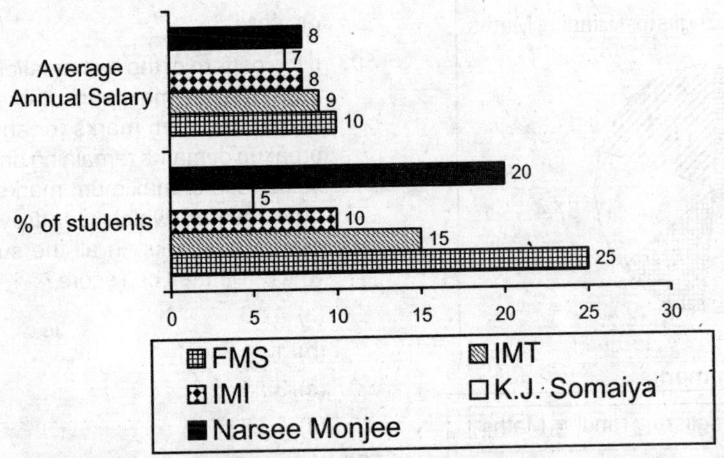

The number of students, the number of companies visiting the campus and total offers made (including PPO's) have been shown below for these five leading B-schools.

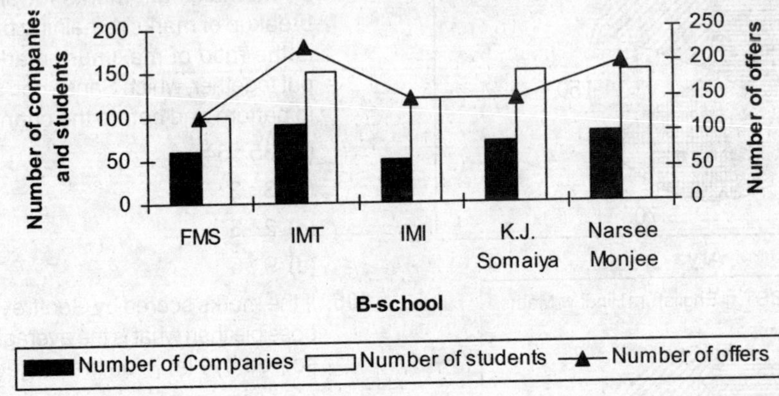

498. Which school has the highest total number of offers per student?

(a) IMT (b) Narsee Monjee

(c) IMI (d) FMS

499. The ratio of number of offers to the number of companies visiting the campus is highest for:

(a) IMT (b) K.J. Somaiya

(c) IMI (d) FMS

500. At FMS, what is the average salary of students, who did not get a PPO?

(a) Rs. 6.5 lakh (b) Rs. 4.5 lakh

(c) Rs. 8 lakh (d) Rs. 6 lakh

501. The sequence P_1, P_2, P_3, ... is defined by $P_1 = 211$, $P_2 = 375$, $P_3 = 420$, $P_4 = 523$, and $P_n = P_{n-1} - P_{n-2} + P_{n-3} - P_{n-4}$ for all $n \geq 5$. What will be the value of $P_{531} + P_{753} + P_{975}$?

(a) 898 (b) 631

(c) 364 (d) 544

Directions for questions 502 to 505 : Answer the questions on the basis of the information given below.

The subject wise breakup of the marks obtained by 4 students in 5 subjects during their board examination is given below. Assume that all subjects carry equal maximum marks unless specified.

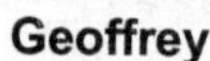

Geoffrey

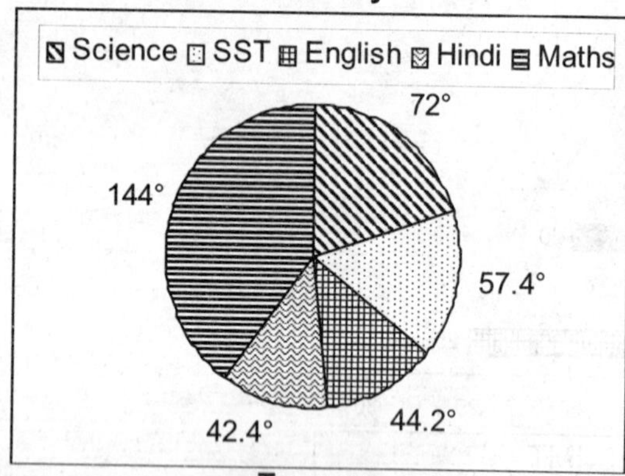

Tommen

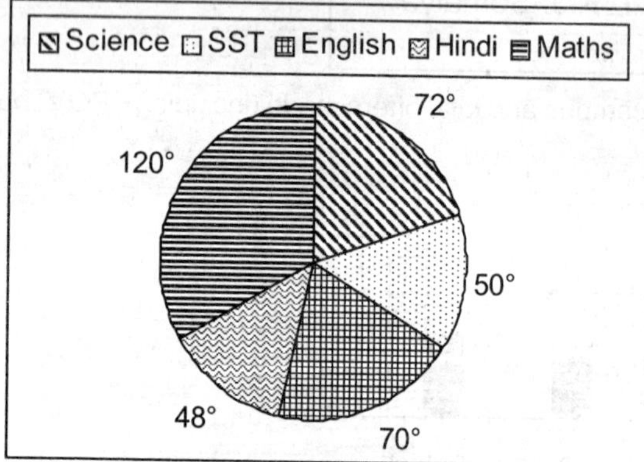

Arya

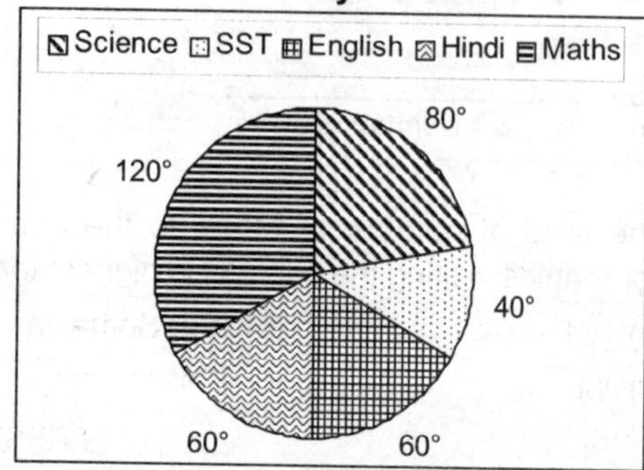

Sansa

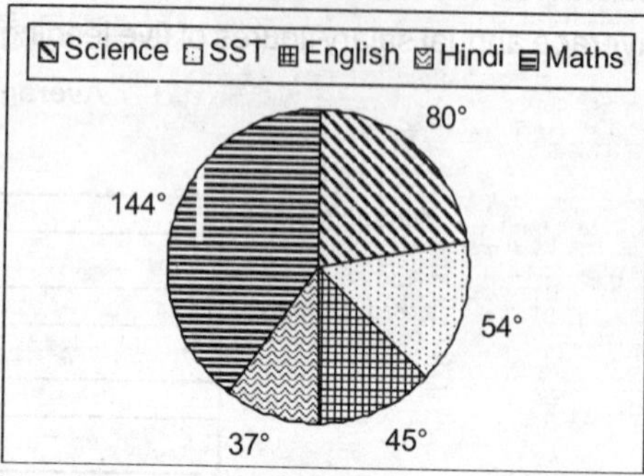

502. If the minimum percentage required to pass in any subject is 33.33 and it is also known that Arya passed in all the subjects, then what can be the minimum percentage that she can score in English?

(a) 30%

(b) 40%

(c) 50%

(d) 60%

503. If the pattern of the examination is changed in such a way that the maximum marks for Maths is double of the maximum marks for any other subject (the breakup of marks remaining unchanged), then what is the ratio of maximum marks, in all the subjects put together, which Geoffrey can score to the maximum marks, in all the subjects put together, which Tommen can score?

(a) 4 : 3

(b) 1 : 1

(c) 3 : 4

(d) 1 : 2

504. If the pattern of the examination is changed in such a way that the maximum marks for Maths is double of the maximum marks for any other subject (the breakup of marks remaining unchanged), then what is the ratio of maximum marks, in all the subjects put together, which Sansa can score after the change in pattern and before the change in pattern?

(a) 35 : 54

(b) 3 : 2

(c) 2 : 3

(d) 9 : 5

505. If the marks scored by Geoffrey in Maths is maximum possible then what is the average of percentage marks scored by him in all the subjects?

(a) 50%

(b) 25%

(c) 10%

(d) 12.5%

2015

Directions for questions 506 to 509 : Answer the questions on the basis of the information given below.

The following pie chart gives the distribution of the total loans disbursed by ADB in 2012 among eleven Asian countries. Total amount of loans disbursed = Rs. 7200 Cr

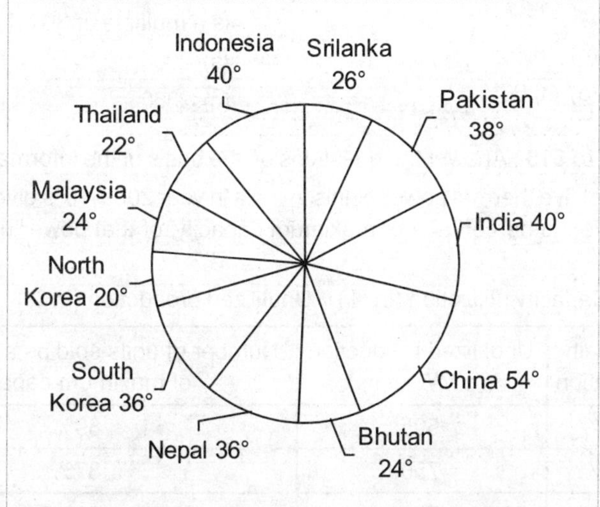

The following line graph gives the percentage contribution of loan from ADB in the total investment made in different sectors in the same year by India and China.

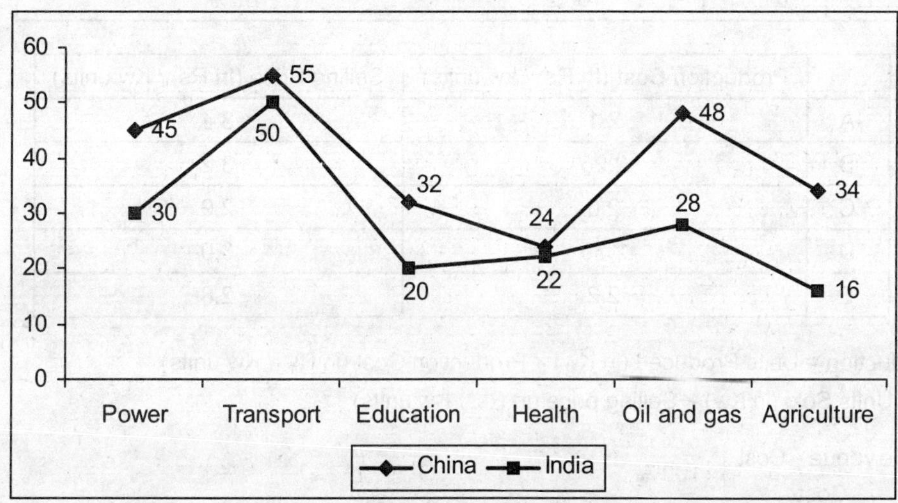

For both China and India, the loan received from ADB was utilized in the given sectors only.

506. If the total investment in Education sector in China was 60% higher than that in India, then what is the ratio of A and B, where

A : The percentage of loan from ADB invested in Education sector by China

B : The percentage of loan from ADB invested in Education sector by India

(a) 256 : 135

(b) 256 : 189

(c) 256 : 225

(d) Cannot be determined

507. The amount of loan invested in Transport sector by China was equal to 60% of the total loan given by ADB to Malaysia. The amount of loan invested in Transport sector by India was equal to 60% of the total loan given by ADB to North Korea. The total investment made in Transport sector by India was approximately what percent of that made by china?

(a) 75.76

(b) 91.67

(c) 80.80

(d) 81.81

508. If the total investments made in Education, Health and Agriculture sectors in India in 2012 was Rs. 150 cr., Rs. 120 cr and Rs. 400 cr. respectively, then the amount of ADB loan invested by India in these three sectors constitute what percentage of the total loan granted to India by ADB?

(a) 15.05% (b) 18.85%
(c) 12.33% (d) 16.66%

509. The total loan invested in Power, Transport and Education sectors by India was 500 cr. What was the maximum possible investment (in Rs. crore) in these three sectors made by India?

[The loan amount invested in all of these three sectors is a multiple of 30 cr]

(a) 2000 (b) 2100
(c) 2360 (d) 2400

Directions for questions 510 to 513 : Answer the questions on the basis of the information given below.

The total electricity production of five thermal power plants in India in year 2009-10 is given in the table below. Capacity utilization for any power plant is the percentage of maximum capacity, of that power plant, which is used for power production.

Maximum capacity (100%) = Capacity utilization (In %) + Unutilized production (In %)

Power Plant	Capacity Utilization	Unutilized production (In MW units)	Number of units sold as a percentage of maximum capacity
A	93%	595	89%
B	88%	750	87%
C	92.50%	750	90%
D	86%	1190	85%
E	81%	1805	80%

	Production Cost (In Rs. / kw units)	Selling Price (In Rs. / Kw units)
A	2.1	3.4
B	2.25	3.2
C	2.0	2.9
D	2.35	3.0
E	2.2	2.8

Total cost of production = Units Produced (in Kw) × Production Cost (in Rs. / Kw units)

Total Revenue = Units Sold (in Kw) × Selling price (in Rs. / Kw units)

$$\text{Profitability} = \left(\frac{\text{Revenue} - \text{Cost}}{\text{Cost}}\right) \times 100\%$$

510. In the given year, if capacity of power plant B had 12.5% of the total power capacity of India, and thermal power capacity of India is 95% of its total power capacity. The total capacity of these 5 thermal power plants was what percentage of the total thermal power capacity of India?

(a) 91.92% (b) 85.5%
(c) 77.73% (d) 90%

511. Which of the following represents the decreasing order of units sold by the given 5 power plants?

(a) E > C > D > A > B (b) C > E > A > D > B
(c) E > C > A > D > B (d) C > A > E > B > D

512. Which power plant had the third highest profitability?

(a) A (b) C
(c) D (d) B

513. Which of the following statements is true?

(a) The power plant with the lowest percentage capacity utilization sold minimum number of units.
(b) The power plant with the second highest per unit selling price sold minimum number of units.
(c) The power plant B had the second lowest capacity.
(d) The total capacity of E was more than 10,000 MW units.

Directions for questions 514 to 517: Answer the questions on the basis of the information given below.

The pie chart given below shows the break-up of production cost of six products – A through F – of Zen Private Ltd. in year 2011. The total production cost was Rs. 250 Cr.

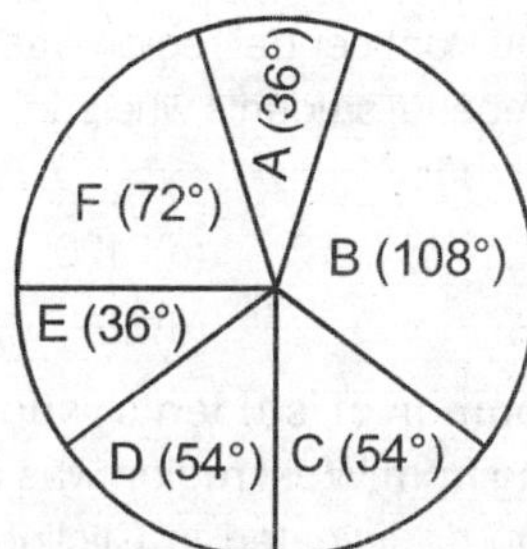

Each of the six products is produced in two varieties- Type P and Type Q. The ratio of the units produced for each product and the profit percentage on selling them is given in the table below.

Product	Ratio of production		Profit Percentage	
	Type P	Type Q	Type P	Type Q
A	3	2	15	30
B	4	3	25	20
C	5	6	15	20
D	1	1	15	10
E	5	3	25	20
F	5	4	20	15

Also for each product, the cost of production per item of Type P and Type Q varieties are in the ratio 4 : 5.

514. For how many of the six products, is the profit made on items of type Q not more than the profit made on items of type P?

515. For which product is the ratio of total profit to total production cost, the lowest?

(a) B (b) C
(c) D (d) F

516. For how many products, overall profit percentage is more than 20%?

517. The nearest integer to the total cost (In Rs. Cr.) incurred in producing type A of products A, D & F is

2016

Directions for questions 518 to 521: Answer the questions on the basis of the information given below.

The bar graph given below shows the data related to the number of people visiting a famous museum named 'Ancient Wax' in Putlabad from the year 2007 to the year 2011.

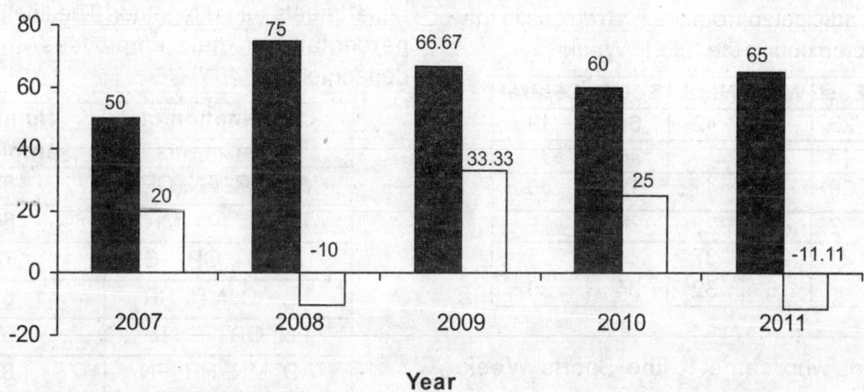

518. If the total number of visitors in the year 2006 was 46850, what was the number of female visitors in the year 2011?

519. How many of the following statement(s) is/are true?

(i) The only year in the given period when the number of female visitors decreased as compared to the previous year was 2008.

(ii) There was a growth of 40% in the number of male visitors from 2008 to 2009.

(iii) There was a growth of 50% in the number of female visitors from 2009 to 2010.

(iv) The year 2008 onwards, there was an increase each year in the number of male visitors as compared to the previous year.

520. The difference between the number of male visitors and the number of female visitors in a year is called "Gender Gap". For which of the following pairs of years is Gender Gap equal?

Fill 1 if "your answer is 2008 and 2011"

Fill 2 if "your answer is 2009 and 2010"

Fill 3 if "your answer is 2008 and 2010"

Fill 4 if "your answer is 2009 and 2011"

521. If the number of male visitors in 2010 was 14796, what was the total number of visitors in 2007?

Directions for questions 522 to 525: Answer the questions on the basis of the information given below.

The pie chart given below shows the percentage break-up of students who participated from five different regions in the Sports Week organized by Dharma Public Association in the year 2011.

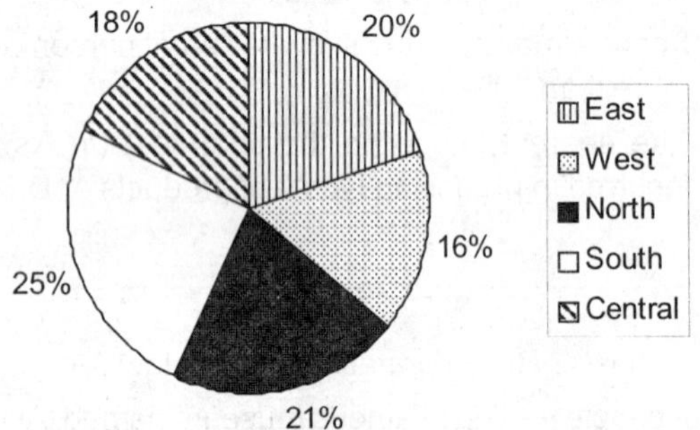

The partially filled-in table given below shows the number of students who participated from the five regions in the six events conducted during the Sports Week.

Activity	East	West	North	South	Central
Swimming	23		42	64	19
Lawn Tennis	45	27		46	31
Cycling	39		41	18	45
Badminton	52	49	23	38	
Hockey	21	24	37		25
Football		16	32	34	30

Note:

(i) Each student who came to the Sports Week participated in exactly one of the six events.

(ii) At least one student from each region participated in each of the six events.

(iii) Six cells in the table are left blank. The sum of the six missing values is 279.

522. Which of the following is not a possible ratio of the number of students who participated from the West region in Swimming and Cycling respectively?

(a) 7 : 8

(b) 3 : 5

(c) 5 : 7

(d) 1 : 9

523. Which of the six events witnessed the highest participation from the students of the five regions put together?

(a) Swimming (b) Cycling

(c) Badminton (d) Cannot be determined

524. The number of students who participated in Badminton from central region was what percentage of the number of students who participated in Football from East region?

(a) 80 (b) 120

(c) 125 (d) 75

525. If the number of students who participated in Swimming from West region was more than that of those who participated in Cycling from West and was also multiple of 5, what is the sum of all the possible values of the product of the number of students who participated in Swimming from West and that of those who participated in Hockey from South?

(a) 21375 (b) 18875

(c) 20325 (d) 16875

Directions for questions 526 to 529: Answer the questions on the basis of the information given below.

In an organization, there are seven departments – MR, HR, FN, OP, TC, TL and AD. The table given below shows the number of employees in a few combinations of four departments taken together. The line graph shows the percentage of male employees in the mentioned departments.

Combination of departments	Number of employees
MR, HR, FN, OP	870
TC, TL, AD, MR	600
HR, FN, OP, TC	780
TL, AD, MR, HR	670
FN, OP, TC, TL	630
AD, MR, HR, FN	850
OP, TC, TL, AD	640

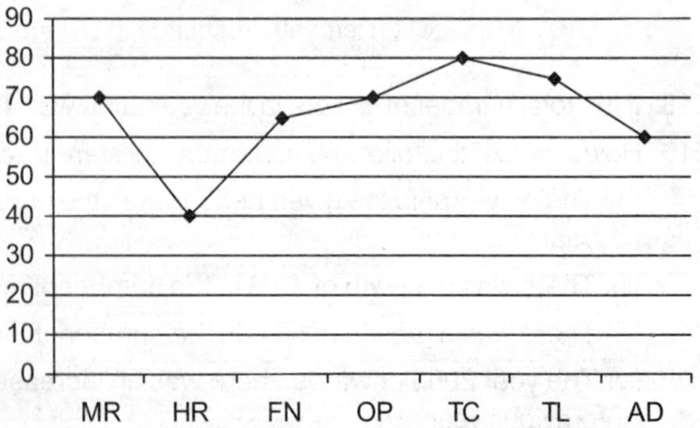

526. What is the ratio of the number of female employees in HR department to the number of male employees in TC department?

(a) 19 : 16 (b) 27 : 19
(c) 19 : 27 (d) 11 : 5

527. In which department is the difference between the number of male employees and the number of female employees the highest?

(a) FN (b) TC
(c) OP (d) MR

528. The number of male employees in MR, FN and AD departments taken together is approximately what percent more than the number of female employees in HR, OP and AD departments taken together?

(a) 43 (b) 57
(c) 52 (d) 63

529. What is the absolute difference between the total number of males and that of females across the seven departments?

(a) 347 (b) 350
(c) 351 (d) 343

2017

Question Numbers : (530 to 533) : At a management school, the oldest 10 dorms, numbered 1 to 10, need to be repaired urgently. The following diagram represents the estimated repair costs (in Rs. Crores) for the 10 dorms. For any dorm, the estimated repair cost (in Rs. Crores) is an integer. Repairs with estimated cost Rs. 1 or 2 Crores are considered light repairs, repairs with estimated cost Rs. 3 or 4 are considered moderate repairs and repairs with estimated cost Rs. 5 or 6 Crores are considered extensive repairs.

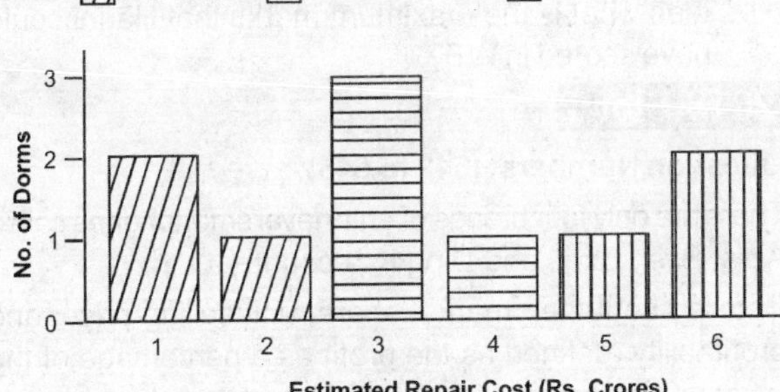

Further, the following are known:

1. Odd-numbered dorms do not need light repair; even-numbered dorms do not need moderate repair and dorms, whose numbers are divisible by 3, do not need extensive repair.
2. Dorms 4 to 9 all need different repair costs, with Dorm 7 needing the maximum and Dorm 8 needing the minimum.

530. Which of the following is NOT necessarily true?

(1) Dorm 1 needs a moderate repair
(2) Dorm 5 repair will cost no more than Rs. 4 Crores
(3) Dorm 7 needs an extensive repair
(4) Dorm 10 repair will cost no more than Rs. 4 Crores

531. What is the total cost of repairing the odd-numbered dorms (in Rs. Crores)?

532. Suppose further that:

(1) 4 of the 10 dorms needing repair are women's dorms and need a total of Rs.20 Crores for repair
(2) Only one of Dorms 1 to 5 is a women's dorm.

What is the cost for repairing Dorm 9 (in Rs. Crores)?

533. Suppose further that:

(1) 4 of the 10 dorms needing repair are women's dorms and need a total of Rs.20 Crores for repair.
(2) Only one of Dorms 1 to 5 is a women's dorm.

Which of the following is a women's dorm?

(a) Dorm 2 (b) Dorm 5
(c) Dorm 8 (d) Dorm 10

2018 Slot 1

Question Numbers (534 to 437) :

The multi-layered pie-chart below shows the sales of LED television sets for a big retail electronics outlet during 2016 and 2017. The outer layer shows the monthly sales during this period, with each label showing the month followed by sales figure of that month. For some months, the sales figures are not given in the chart. The middle-layer shows quarter-wise aggregate sales figures (in some cases, aggregate quarter-wise sales numbers are not given next to the quarter). The innermost layer shows annual sales. It is known that the sales figures during the three months of the second quarter (April, May, June) of 2016 form an arithmetic progression, as do the three monthly sales figures in the fourth quarter (October, November, December) of that year.

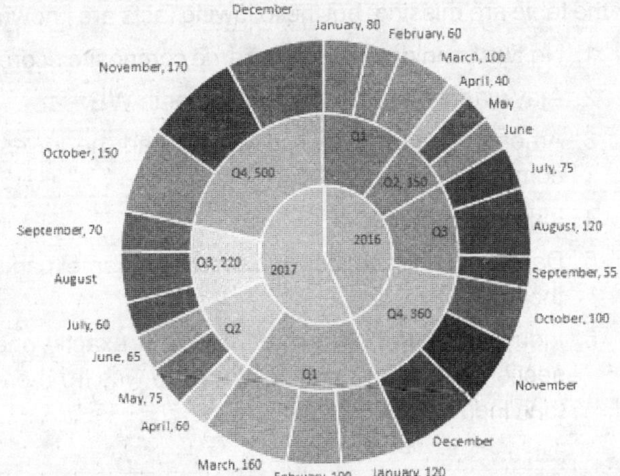

534. What is the percentage increase in sales in December 2017 as compared to the sales in December 2016?

(a) 38.46 (b) 28.57

(c) 50.00 (d) 22.22

535. In which quarter of 2017 was the percentage increase in sales from the same quarter of 2016 the highest?

(a) Q1 (b) Q2

(c) Q3 (d) Q4

536. During which quarter was the percentage decrease in sales from the previous quarter's sales the highest?

(a) Q1 of 2017

(b) Q4 of 2017

(c) Q2 of 2016

(d) Q2 of 2017

537. During which month was the percentage increase in sales from the previous month's sales the highest?

(a) March of 2016 (b) October of 2016

(c) October of 2017 (d) March of 2017

Question Numbers (538 to 541) :

A company administers a written test comprising of three sections of 20 marks each - Data Interpretation (DI), Written English (WE) and General Awareness (GA), for recruitment. A composite score for a candidate (out of 80) is calculated by doubling her marks in DI and adding it to the sum of her marks in the other two sections. Candidates who score less than 70% marks in two or more sections are disqualified. From among the rest, the four with the highest composite scores are recruited. If four or less candidates qualify, all who qualify are recruited.

Ten candidates appeared for the written test. Their marks in the test are given in the table below. Some marks in the table are missing, but the following facts are known:

1. No two candidates had the same composite score.
2. Ajay was the unique highest scorer in WE.
3. Among the four recruited, Geeta had the lowest composite score.
4. Indu was recruited.
5. Danish, Harini, and Indu had scored the same marks the in GA.
6. Indu and Jatin both scored 100% in exactly one section and Jatin's composite score was 10 more than Indu's.

Candidate	marks out of 20		
	DI	WE	GA
Ajay	8		16
Bala		9	11
Chetna	19	4	12
Danish	8	15	
Ester	12	18	16
Falak	15	7	10
Geeta	14		6
Harini	5		
Indu		8	
Jatin		16	14

538. Which of the following statements MUST be true?

1. Jatin's composite score was more than that of Danish.
2. Indu scored less than Chetna in DI.
3. Jatin scored more than Indu in GA.

(a) Only 2 (b) Only 1

(c) Both 1 and 2 (d) Both 2 and 3

539. Which of the following statements MUST be FALSE?

(a) Bala scored same as Jatin in DI

(b) Harini's composite score was less than that of Falak

(c) Bala's composite score was less than that of Ester

(d) Chetna scored more than Bala in DI

540. If all the candidates except Ajay and Danish had different marks in DI, and Bala's composite score was less than Chetna's composite score, then what is the maximum marks that Bala could have scored in DI?

541. If all the candidates scored different marks in WE then what is the maximum marks that Harini could have scored in WE?

2018 Slot 2

Question Numbers: (542 to 545):

There are only four brands of entry level smartphones called Azra, Bysi, Cxqi, and Dipq in a country.

Details about their market share, unit selling price, and profitability (defined as the profit as a percentage of the revenue) for the year 2016 are given in the table below:

Brand	Market share (%)	Unit Selling Price (Rs.)	Profitability
Azra	40	15,000	10
Bysi	25	20,000	30
Cxqi	15	30,000	40
Dipq	20	25,000	30

In 2017, sales volume of entry level smartphones grew by 40% as compared to that in 2016. Cxqi offered a 40% discount on its unit selling price in 2017, which resulted in a 15% increase in its market share. Each of the other three brands lost 5% market share. However, the profitability of Cxqi came down to half of its value in 2016. The unit selling prices of the other three brands and their profitability values remained the same in 2017 as they were in 2016.

542. The brand that had the highest revenue in 2016 is:

(a) Dipq (b) Cxqi
(c) Azra (d) Bysi

543. The brand that had the highest profit in 2016 is:

(a) Cxqi (b) Azra
(c) Dipq (d) Bysi

544. The brand that had the highest profit in 2017 is:

(a) Azra (b) Bysi
(c) Dipq (d) Cxqi

545. The complete list of brands whose profits went up in 2017 from 2016 is:

(a) Azra, Bysi, Cxqi (b) Azra, Bysi, Dipq
(c) Cxqi, Azra, Dipq (d) Bysi, Cxqi, Dipq

Question Numbers: (546 to 549):

Each of the 23 boxes in the picture below represents a product manufactured by one of the following three companies: Alfa, Bravo and Charlie. The area of a box is proportional to the revenue from the corresponding product, while its centre represents the Product popularity and Market potential scores of the product (out of 20). The shadings of some of the boxes have got erased.

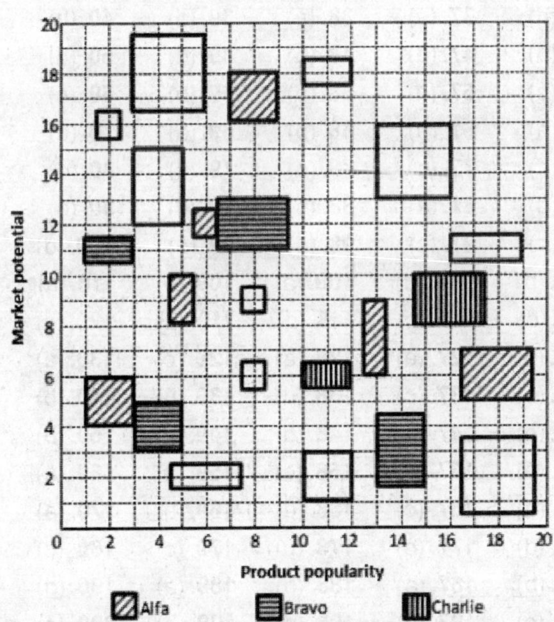

The companies classified their products into four categories based on a combination of scores (out of 20) on the two parameters – Product popularity and Market potential as given below:

	Promising	Blockbuster	Doubtful	No-hope
Product popularity score	>10	>10	≤10	≤10
Market potential score	>10	≤10	>10	≤10

The following facts are known:

1. Alfa and Bravo had the same number of products in the Blockbuster category.
2. Charlie had more products than Bravo but fewer products than Alfa in the No-hope category.
3. Each company had an equal number of products in the Promising category.
4. Charlie did not have any product in the Doubtful category, while Alfa had one product more than Bravo in this category.
5. Bravo had a higher revenue than Alfa from products in the Doubtful category.
6. Charlie had a higher revenue than Bravo from products in the Blockbuster category.
7. Bravo and Charlie had the same revenue from products in the No-hope category.
8. Alfa and Charlie had the same total revenue considering all products.

546. Considering all companies' products, which product category had the highest revenue?

(a) Promising (b) Blockbuster
(c) Doubtful (d) No-hope

547. Which of the following is the correct sequence of numbers of products Bravo had in No-hope, Doubtful, Promising and Blockbuster categories respectively?

(a) 1, 3, 1, 2 (b) 1, 3, 1, 3
(c) 3, 3, 1, 2 (d) 2, 3, 1, 2

548. Which of the following statements is NOT correct?

(a) Bravo and Charlie had the same revenues from No-hope products
(b) The total revenue from No-hope products was less than the total revenue from Doubtful products
(c) Alfa's revenue from Blockbuster products was the same as Charlie's revenue from Promising products
(d) Bravo's revenue from Blockbuster products was greater than Alfa's revenue from Doubtful products

549. If the smallest box on the grid is equivalent to revenue of Rs.1 crore, then what approximately was the total revenue of Bravo in Rs. crore?

(a) 34 (b) 40
(c) 30 (d) 24

ANSWERS

LOGIC BASED DI

1. (c) **2.** (d) **3.** (a) **4.** (b) **5.** (a) **6.** (d) **7.** (c) **8.** (a) **9.** (c) **10.** (c)
11. (c) **12.** (b) **13.** (c) **14.** (b) **15.** (a) **16.** (d) **17.** (b) **18.** (b) **19.** (d) **20.** (c)
21. (d) **22.** (a) **23.** (d) **24.** (b) **25.** (c) **26.** (d) **27.** (c) **28.** (d) **29.** (a) **30.** (a)
31. (b) **32.** (a) **33.** (c) **34.** (a) **35.** (c) **36.** (c) **37.** (b) **38.** (a) **39.** (d) **40.** (b)
41. (c) **42.** (a) **43.** (c) **44.** (a) **45.** (b) **46.** (d) **47.** (a) **48.** (b) **49.** (d) **50.** (a)
51. (b) **52.** (b) **53.** (d) **54.** (c) **55.** (a) **56.** (c) **57.** (b) **58.** (c) **59.** (c) **60.** (c)
61. (e) **62.** (b & c) **63.** (a) **64.** (d) **65.** (c) **66.** (a) **67.** (d) **68.** (e) **69.** (e) **70.** (d)
71. (b) **72.** (c) **73.** (b) **74.** (d) **75.** (e) **76.** (d) **77.** (c) **78.** (b) **79.** (c) **80.** (c)
81. (b) **82.** (d) **83.** (e) **84.** (e) **85.** (d) **86.** (a) **87.** (d) **88.** (c) **89.** (b) **90.** (d)
91. (*) **92.** (*) **93.** (*) **94.** (*) **95.** (*) **96.** (*) **97.** (d) **98.** (a) **99.** (b) **100.** (c)
101. (d) **102.** (b) **103.** (d) **104.** (c) **105.** (d) **106.** (d) **107.** (d) **108.** (b) **109.** (a) **110.** (c)
111. (b) **112.** (d) **113.** (c) **114.** 10 **115.** 2 **116.** 2 **117.** 22 **118.** (d) **119.** (c) **120.** (d)
121. (a) **122.** (c) **123.** (a) **124.** (b) **125.** (a) **126.** (b) **127.** (c) **128.** (b) **129.** (a) **130.** (c)
131. (d) **132.** (d) **133.** (a) **134.** (c) **135.** (2) **136.** (b) **137.** (20) **138.** (d) **139.** (4) **140.** (3)
141. (d) **142.** (d) **143.** (d) **144.** (b) **145.** (d) **146.** (b) **147.** (3) **148.** (48) **149.** (b) **150.** (1200)
151. (d) **152.** (240) **153.** (a)

CALCULATION BASED DI

1. (b) **2.** (a) **3.** (d) **4.** (d) **5.** (d) **6.** (c) **7.** (b) **8.** (a) **9.** (a) **10.** (b)
11. (c) **12.** (b) **13.** (b) **14.** (b) **15.** (b) **16.** (a) **17.** (c) **18.** (b) **19.** (d) **20.** (b)
21. (a) **22.** (a) **23.** (a) **24.** (d) **25.** (d) **26.** (b) **27.** (d) **28.** (d) **29.** (a) **30.** (a)
31. (c) **32.** (d) **33.** (a) **34.** (b) **35.** (a) **36.** (d) **37.** (a) **38.** (a) **39.** (d) **40.** (b)
41. (a) **42.** (d) **43.** (c) **44.** (a) **45.** (a) **46.** (d) **47.** (d) **48.** (b) **49.** (d) **50.** (d)
51. (c) **52.** (c) **53.** (b) **54.** (b) **55.** (d) **56.** (c) **57.** (a) **58.** (b) **59.** (b) **60.** (c)
61. (c) **62.** (d) **63.** (a) **64.** (c) **65.** (d) **66.** (b) **67.** (b) **68.** (b) **69.** (a) **70.** (d)
71. (d) **72.** (d) **73.** (a) **74.** (b) **75.** (c) **76.** (c) **77.** (d) **78.** (d) **79.** (c) **80.** (d)
81. (b) **82.** (d) **83.** (a) **84.** (c) **85.** (a) **86.** (d) **87.** (a) **88.** (c) **89.** (c) **90.** (b)
91. (d) **92.** (d) **93.** (c) **94.** (d) **95.** (c) **96.** (b) **97.** (c) **98.** (d) **99.** (d) **100.** (d)
101. (a) **102.** (d) **103.** (a) **104.** (a) **105.** (b) **106.** (b) **107.** (d) **108.** (a) **109.** (b) **110.** (a)
111. (b) **112.** (d) **113.** (d) **114.** (c) **115.** (b) **116.** (d) **117.** (c) **118.** (d) **119.** (a) **120.** (c)
121. (a) **122.** (b) **123.** (d) **124.** (c) **125.** (b) **126.** (d) **127.** (a) **128.** (a) **129.** (c) **130.** (a)
131. (b) **132.** (c) **133.** (d) **134.** (b) **135.** (c) **136.** (b) **137.** (c) **138.** (d) **139.** (b) **140.** (b)
141. (a) **142.** (d) **143.** (d) **144.** (b) **145.** (a) **146.** (d) **147.** (c) **148.** (d) **149.** (b) **150.** (b)
151. (a) **152.** (b) **153.** (d) **154.** (c) **155.** (d) **156.** (b) **157.** (b) **158.** (c) **159.** (a) **160.** (a)
161. (d) **162.** (d) **163.** (d) **164.** (b) **165.** (c) **166.** (d) **167.** (c) **168.** (d) **169.** (b) **170.** (a)
171. (c) **172.** (c) **173.** (a) **174.** (b) **175.** (a) **176.** (d) **177.** (c) **178.** (c) **179.** (c) **180.** (c)
181. (b) **182.** (c) **183.** (a) **184.** (c) **185.** (b) **186.** (b) **187.** (a) **188.** (b) **189.** (a) **190.** (d)
191. (b) **192.** (a) **193.** (b) **194.** (d) **195.** (b) **196.** (c) **197.** (b) **198.** (a) **199.** (b) **200.** (a)
201. (c) **202.** (d) **203.** (a) **204.** (c) **205.** (c) **206.** (c) **207.** (b) **208.** (d) **209.** (b) **210.** (d)
211. (b) **212.** (a) **213.** (b) **214.** (a) **215.** (b) **216.** (a) **217.** (a) **218.** (b) **219.** (d) **220.** (*)
221. (a) **222.** (b) **223.** (b) **224.** (b) **225.** (c) **226.** (b) **227.** (b) **228.** (d) **229.** (d) **230.** (c)

231. (c)	**232.** (c)	**233.** (b)	**234.** (a)	**235.** (b)	**236.** (d)	**237.** (c)	**238.** (a)	**239.** (a)	**240.** (d)
241. (b)	**242.** (d)	**243.** (c)	**244.** (b)	**245.** (a)	**246.** (a)	**247.** (b)	**248.** (b)	**249.** (a)	**250.** (c)
251. (d)	**252.** (b)	**253.** (c)	**254.** (b)	**255.** (c)	**256.** (a)	**257.** (d)	**258.** (a)	**259.** (c)	**260.** (b)
261. (a)	**262.** (c)	**263.** (d)	**264.** (d)	**265.** (a)	**266.** (b)	**267.** (b)	**268.** (c)	**269.** (d)	**270.** (a)
271. (d)	**272.** (d)	**273.** (c)	**274.** (a)	**275.** (d)	**276.** (b)	**277.** (d)	**278.** (c)	**279.** (d)	**280.** (a)
281. (b)	**282.** (a)	**283.** (b)	**284.** (c)	**285.** (b)	**286.** (a)	**287.** (c)	**288.** (a)	**289.** (a)	**290.** (d)
291. (b)	**292.** (d)	**293.** (b)	**294.** (b)	**295.** (a)	**296.** (c)	**297.** (b)	**298.** (a)	**299.** (c)	**300.** (c)
301. (a)	**302.** (b)	**303.** (a)	**304.** (b)	**305.** (a)	**306.** (d)	**307.** (b)	**308.** (a)	**309.** (c)	**310.** (b)
311. (d)	**312.** (a)	**313.** (c)	**314.** (d)	**315.** (a)	**316.** (c)	**317.** (c)	**318.** (b)	**319.** (b)	**320.** (b)
321. (b)	**322.** (b)	**323.** (d)	**324.** (d)	**325.** (b)	**326.** (b)	**327.** (b)	**328.** (b)	**329.** (d)	**330.** (c)
331. (a)	**332.** (c)	**333.** (a)	**334.** (b)	**335.** (d)	**336.** (b)	**337.** (a)	**338.** (a)	**339.** (c)	**340.** (b)
341. (a)	**342.** (d)	**343.** (b)	**344.** (a)	**345.** (d)	**346.** (a)	**347.** (c)	**348.** (b)	**349.** (c)	**350.** (d)
351. (d)	**352.** (d)	**353.** (c)	**354.** (a)	**355.** T	**356.** (b)	**357.** (c)	**358.** (c)	**359.** (d)	**360.** (d)
361. (a)	**362.** (b)	**363.** (a)	**364.** (a)	**365.** (d)	**366.** (d)	**367.** (c)	**368.** (c)	**369.** (c)	**370.** (a)
371. (d)	**372.** (b)	**373.** (c)	**374.** (d)	**375.** (b)	**376.** (c)	**377.** (b)	**378.** (d)	**379.** (b)	**380.** (d)
381. (b)	**382.** (a)	**383.** (c)	**384.** (d)	**385.** (a)	**386.** (c)	**387.** (d)	**388.** (d)	**389.** (a)	**390.** (b)
391. (b)	**392.** (d)	**393.** (a)	**394.** (c)	**395.** (a)	**396.** (b)	**397.** (b)	**398.** (c)	**399.** (d)	**400.** (c)
401. (c)	**402.** (a)	**403.** (b)	**404.** (d)	**405.** (a)	**406.** (b)	**407.** (c)	**408.** (b)	**409.** (d)	**410.** (d)
411. (d)	**412.** (a)	**413.** (c)	**414.** (a)	**415.** (a)	**416.** (d)	**417.** (e)	**418.** (c)	**419.** (b)	**420.** (a)
421. (e)	**422.** (d)	**423.** (b)	**424.** (c)	**425.** (e)	**426.** (a)	**427.** (b)	**428.** (e)	**429.** (a)	**430.** (*)
431. (c)	**432.** (a)	**433.** (d)	**434.** (b)	**435.** (e)	**436.** (c)	**437.** (d)	**438.** (a)	**439.** (a)	**440.** (d)
441. (c)	**442.** (e)	**443.** (e)	**444.** (a)	**445.** (a)	**446.** (a)	**447.** (c)	**448.** (c)	**449.** (b)	**450.** (c)
451. (d)	**452.** (c)	**453.** (c)	**454.** (b)	**455.** (a)	**456.** (c)	**457.** (d)	**458.** (c)	**459.** (d)	**460.** (b)
461. (c)	**462.** (a)	**463.** (b)	**464.** (a)	**465.** (c)	**466.** (d)	**467.** (d)	**468.** (b)	**469.** (b)	**470.** (d)
471. (a)	**472.** (d)	**473.** (b)	**474.** (c)	**475.** (c)	**476.** (b)	**477.** (c)	**478.** (c)	**479.** (c)	**480.** (a)
481. (d)	**482.** (c)	**483.** (b)	**484.** (a)	**485.** (c)	**486.** (a)	**487.** (b)	**488.** (c)	**489.** (a)	**490.** (d)
491. (c)	**492.** (c)	**493.** (a)	**494.** (b)	**495.** (b)	**496.** (a)	**497.** (c)	**498.** (a)	**499.** (c)	**500.** (d)
501. (a)	**502.** (c)	**503.** (b)	**504.** (d)	**505.** (a)	**506.** (a)	**507.** (b)	**508.** (a)	**509.** (c)	**510.** (d)
511. (b)	**512.** (d)	**513.** (b)	**514.** 4	**515.** (c)	**516.** 3	**517.** 55	**518.** 26236	**519.** 1	**520.** 4
521. 16440	**522.** (b)	**523.** (c)	**524.** (b)	**525.** (d)	**526.** (a)	**527.** (c)	**528.** (c)	**529.** (b)	**530.** (d)
531. (19)	**532.** (3)	**533.** (d)	**534.** (b)	**535.** (a)	**536.** (d)	**537.** (c)	**538.** (c)	**539.** (a)	**540.** (13)
541. (14)	**542.** (c)	**543.** (a)	**544.** (b)	**545.** (b)	**546.** (b)	**547.** (a)	**548.** (d)	**549.** (a)	

EXPLANATION

LOGIC BASED DI

For questions 1 to 4:

Please note that the best way to solve this question is by working backwards.

E.g. after the 4th round, each one of them had Rs.32. Since it is Vibha who lost in this round, all the remaining three must have doubled their share.

In other words, they would have had Rs.16 each after the 3rd round.

Since the increase is of Rs.16 in each one's share, i.e., Rs.48 overall which comes from Vibha's share, her share before the 4th round was (32 + 48) = Rs.80, after the 3rd round.

Working backwards in this manner, we can get the following table.

	Share of each			
	Suvarna	**Tara**	**Uma**	**Vibha**
4. Vibha	32	32	32	32
3. Uma	16	16	16	(32 + 48) = 80
2. Tara	8	8	(16 + 40 + 8 + 8) = 72	40
1. Suvarna	4	(8 + 4 + 36 + 20) = 68	36	20
Initial	(4 + 34 + 18 + 10) = 66	34	18	10

1. c Suvarna started with Rs.66.

2. d It was Vibha who started with the lowest amount, viz. Rs.10.

3. a It was Suvarna who started with the highest amount, viz. Rs.66.

4. b At the end of the second round, Uma had Rs.72.

5. a $A + B = \left(\frac{A+B}{2}\right) \times 2$ = @(A, B) × 2 = /(@(A, B), 2)

6. d To find the average of A, B, C we seek to find A + B + C and then divide by 3.

For A + B, we first find the average of A and B and multiply it by 2, i.e. /(@(A, B), 2).

This expression can be seen only in option (d).

So let us check option (d).

/(× (@ (/ (@(B, A,), 2), C), 3), 2)

$$= /\left(\times\left(@\left(/\left(\frac{B+A}{2}, 2\right), C\right), 3\right), 2\right)$$

$$= /\left(\times\left(@\left(\{B+A\}, C\right), 3\right), 2\right)$$

$$= /\left(\times\left(\frac{(B+A)+C}{2}, 3\right), 2\right)$$

$$= /\left(\frac{A+B+C}{2\times 3}, 2\right) = \frac{A+B+C}{3}$$

7. c The only two possible combinations are:

Younger	Older
2	4
3	9

Cubes of natural numbers are 1, 8, 27, 64, ... Here, 64 and above are not possible as the age will go above 10 years.

If younger boy is 2 years old, then older boy is 4 years old. Then, Father's age is 24 years and Mother's age is $\frac{42}{2} = 21$ years.

Also, 24 – 21 = 3

∴ Age of younger boy = 2 years

8. a

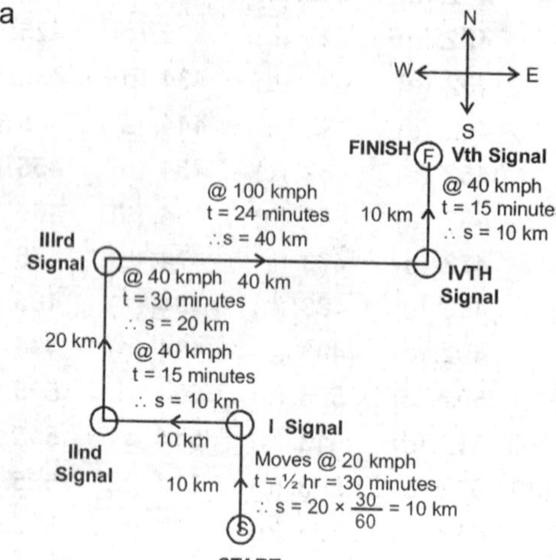

Note: s = Distance covered; v = Velocity (km/hr)

t = Time taken; s = v × t

The total distance travelled by the motorist from the starting point till last signal = 10 + 10 + 20 + 40 + 10 = 90 km.

9. c

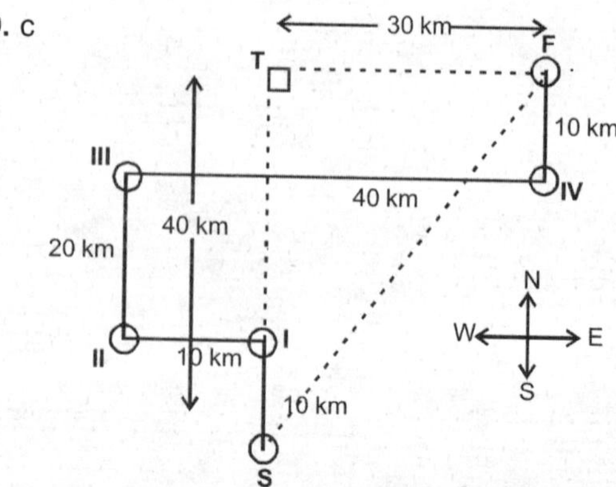

By Pythagoras' Theorem,

$SF = \sqrt{ST^2 + TF^2} = \sqrt{40^2 + 30^2} = \sqrt{2500} = 50$ km

10. c In the case when 1st signal were 1 red and 2 green lights, the surface diagram will be as given below.

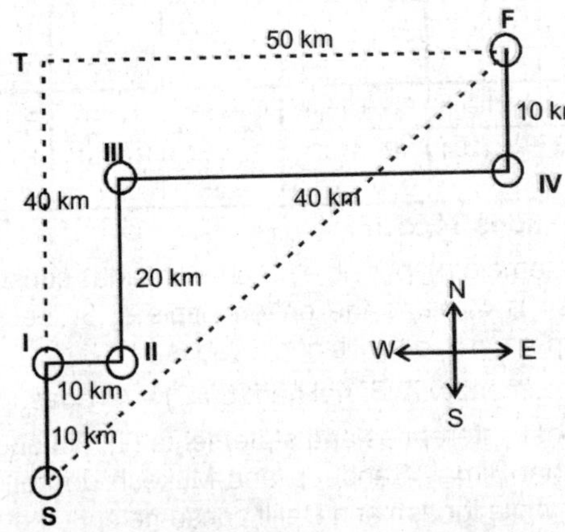

TF = 50 km; ST = 40 km

Considering the above figure, option (c) is correct, 50 km to the east and 40 km to the north.

11. c If the car was heading towards South from the start point, then the surface diagram will be as given below.

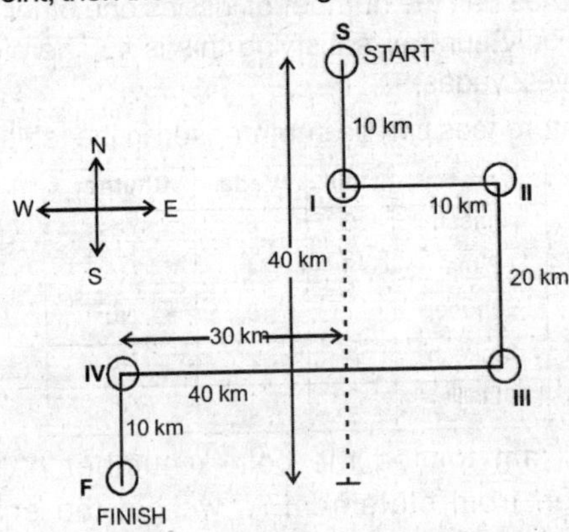

Hence, we can see that option (c) is correct.

12. b BC → AC → AAC = 0

13. c BD $\xrightarrow{0}$ AE $\xrightarrow{95.2}$ AAB

∴ Least cost of sending one unit from any refinery to AAB

= 0 + 95.2 = 95.2.

14. b BB → AB → AAG = 311.1

Same as above.

15. a First we will have to check the minimum cost for receiving at AAA. This is 0 for AE. But, BB to AE is very high. Next is AC [314.5]. BB to AC is 451.1. After AC, the others are high.

Hence, 314.5 + 451.1 = 765.6 is the least cost.

16. d Number of refineries = 6

Number of depots = 7

Number of districts = 9

Therefore, number of possible ways to send petrol from any refinery to any district = 6 × 7 × 9 = 378.

17. b The highest cost is for the route

BE → AE → AAH = 2193.0

18. b Only R9 is that region which produces medium quality of crop – 2 and low quality of crop – 4.

19. d Statement (a) is not satisfied by R9.

Statement (b) is not satisfied by R3.

Statement (c) is incorrect as there are six such regions R1, R2, R3, R4, R9 and R11.

Statement (d) is correct.

20. c Three regions namely R9, R10 and R11.

21. d From statement A, we know only the number of goals made by India is the last 5 minutes. But, as we don't know what the opponent team did in the last 5 minutes, we can't conclude anything. So statement A alone is not sufficient.

Similarly, statement B does not talk about the total number of goals scored by India. So statement B is not sufficient.

Using both the statements, we have two possibilities:

(I) If Korea had scored 3 goals 5 minutes before the end of the match India would have scored 1 goal. In the last 5 minutes as India made 3 goals and Korea on the whole made 3 goals, we can conclude that India had won the game.

(II) If Korea had scored 3 goals 5 minutes before the end of the match, India would have scored zero goals. In the last 5 minutes, as India made 3 goals and Korea on the whole made 3 goals, we can say the match was drawn.

Hence, we cannot answer the question even boy using both the statements together.

For questions 22 and 23:

Congress – Thursday

BJP – Friday

SP – Thursday

BSP – Friday

CPM – Friday

22. a Congress procession can only be allowed on Thursday.

23. d According to the data above, statement (d) is not true.

For questions 24 to 28:

If a person copies from one source, he must have the same blank answers as the source and exactly one wrong answer more than the source (as the copier has introduced one wrong answer on his own). If the person copies from two sources, the distinct wrong answers from the two sources would be left blank by the copier and the same wrong answers in the two sources would be copied as it is.

24. b A and D have only one source since they have only one wrong answer each.

C may have copied from only one source i.e. I and hence, only B has two sources.

25. c I did it before C since 27 is the wrong choice for I. Similarly, A, D and E made keys before C. Hence, 4 people made their keys before C.

26. d Both G and H can't be sources to any of F, B or I and hence, (d) is the correct option.

27. c F introduced wrong answer to question 14, because nobody else has done question 14 wrong.

28. d A, D and G have one distinct wrong answer and no blank answers. So they must have the same source. E and H also have a common wrong answer and no blanks.

Hence, both the groups had identical sources.

For questions 29 and 30:

G + 8 = A

D + R = 37

J = D + 8

A = D + 5

A + G = 40

Solving the above equations, we get

2G = 32, G = 16, A = 24

D = 19, J = 27, R = 18

29. a

30. a D + J = 46

For questions 31 to 33:

Four of the amounts spent by the five women are Rs.2234, Rs.1193, Rs.1340 ad Rs.2517.

Two cases arise:

(i) The lowest amount spent is Rs.1193(by Chellamma): Then, the fifth amount will be Rs(1193 + 1378) = Rs.2571, which will then be the highest amount and is spent by Shahnaz. As Archana arrived before Chellamma, so she must have spent Rs.2234. This implies Helen spent Rs.2517 and Dhenuka spent Rs.1340, which is a contradiction.

Hence, this case is not possible.

(ii) The highest amount spent is Rs.2517 (by Shahnaz): Then the fifth amount will be Rs.(2517 – 1378) = Rs.1139. Since it is the lowest amount, it will be spent by Chellamma. Further analysis leads to the following table:

Order of arrival	1	2	3	4	5
Name	Archana	Chellamma	Dhenuka	Helen	Shahnaz
Amount spent	Rs.2234	Rs.1139	Rs.1193	Rs.1340	Rs.2517

For questions 34 to 36:

From statement (i), possible number of vadas consumed by Ignesh is 6, being the only multiple of 3.Therefore, another person had 4 idlis and 2 vadas.

From statement (vii), Bimal had (6 – 2) = 4 vadas.

Using these inferences and statements (ii), (iii) and (vi), we get that Bimal, Sandeep and Mukesh do not have chutney, while Ignesh and Daljit consume cuhutney.

From (iii) and (iv), Sandeep has only one idli and no vada.

From (vii), Bimal has two more idlis than Ignesh. This implies that Bimal can have either 6 or 8 idlis. If Bimal had 6 idlis, then Ignesh had 4 idlis. This contradicts statement (i). Therefore, Bimal had 8 idlis and Ignesh had 6 idlis.

Mukesh has half the number of idlis as one other person and the only number satisfying this is 4. Therefore, he must have 2 vadas.

These inferences can be summarised in the table below:

	Idli	Vada	Chutney
Ignesh	6	6	Yes
Bimal	8	4	No
Sandeep	1	0	No
Mukesh	4	2	No
Daljit	5	1	Yes

37. b If Ram tossed the coin x number of times, then from statement A, we get the equation 10 + x – 100 = 50. Thus, x = 140.

From statement II individually, we have x > 138.

Thus, we are sure that he has paid up more than 148. If he incurs a loss of only Rs. 50, the game has to end normally. Thus, he must have played 150 shots and got first 138 as tails and 139 and 140 throws as heads. With no other scenario, a loss of just Rs.50 and 138 tails will show up.

38. a GPA of Preeti = 3.2

i.e., $\frac{F+D+x+D+y}{5} = 3.2$

$\Rightarrow$ 0 + 2 + x + 2 + y = 16

$\Rightarrow$ x + y = 12

The only possible combination is A, A.

Hence, Preeti obtained A grade in Statistics.

39. d Total points scored by Tara = 2.4 × 5 = 12

She scored same grade in three of the subjects, so her score is of the form 3x + y + z = 12

She cannot have scored 3 A's as her total points will exceed 12.

She can score 3 B's and 2 F's which will make her total points 3 × 4 + 2 × 0 = 12.

She cannot score 3 C's as the points in remaining two will be 12 – 3 × 3 = 3 and only possible breakup is (3, 0). This will contradict the fact that she had same grade in only three courses.

For a similar reason, she cannot score 3 D's.

She cannot score 3 F's, because for the remaining two courses she has to amass 12 points which is possible if she score A in both – a contradiction.

Hence, Tara could have scored a B or F grade in Operations.

40. b GPA of Gowri is 3.8

i.e. 3 + 3 + 6 + x + 4 = 3.8 × 5

16 + x = 19

x = 3

So in Strategy, Gowri's grade is C.

Rahul's grade in strategy = (4.2 × 5) – 15 = 6, i.e., A.

Fazal's grade in strategy = (2.4 × 5) – 8 = 4, i.e., B.

Hence, Gowri's grade will be higher than that of Hari.

41. c As Fazal's GPA = 2.4

So D + F + B + X + D = 2.4 × 5

⇒ 2 + 0 + 4 + X + 2 = 12

⇒ X = 4

So his grade in Strategy is B.

So grade of Utkarsh in Marketing is also B.

So for Utkarsh, Y + B + F + C + A = 3 × 5

⇒ Y + 4 + 0 + 3 + 6 = 15

⇒ Y = 2

So grade of Utkarsh in Finance = D.

For questions 42 to 45:

On day 3, there were 2 visitors from UK and 1 from USA. On the same day, the site was visited by 2 persons from University 4 and 1 from University 6. So University 4 is located in UK and University 6 is in USA.

Similar reasoning for day 2 gives us the conclusion that University 3 is located in Netherlands and University 8 is in India.

On day 1, the number of visitors from USA is 1 and that from University 6 is 1. University 6 is in USA (derived above), which implies no other university is in USA.

The number of visitors from India on day 1 is 1. Also, no visitor from University 8, which is in Idia has visited the site on day 1. This implies that one of University 1 and University 5 is in India and the other in Netherlands. A similar logic gives us that one of University 2 and University 6 is in UK and the other in Canada.

46. d Thailand and Japan (Maximum difference of 4 ranks (5 – 1) = 4.

47. a China (Maximum difference of 2 between 2 parameter's 2)

48. b Japan (Maximum difference of 4.)

49. d Japan and Malaysia (Inferring from question 46)

50. a Rahul and Yamini.

51. b Gayatri, Urvashi and Zeena cannot attend more than one workshop.

52. b Anshul, Bushkant, Gayatri and Urvashi cannot attend any of the workshops.

53. d

1	16
2	15
3	14
4	13
5	12
6	**11**
7	**10**
8	**9**

Winners after round two would be 1, 2, 3, 4, 5, 11, 10, 9 for 8 rounds respectively. As Lindsay is number two, she will play Venus Williams in quarter finals.

54. c Elena is at number 6 and Serena is at number 8.

If they lose, then table would be:

1	9
2	7
3	11
4	5

Maria is at number 1 and she will play the player at number 9. i.e., Nadia Petrova.

55. a

1	32
2	**31**
3	30
4	**29**
5	28
6	**27**
7	26
8	**25**
9	24
10	**23**
11	22
12	**21**
13	20
14	**19**
15	18
16	**17**

Matches in bold letters had upsets.

Then, from the table, winners would be:

1, 31, 3, 29, 5, 27, 7, 25, 9, 23, 11, 21, 13, 19, 15 and 17.

So for the next round, table would look like:

1	17
31	15
3	19
29	13
5	21
27	11
7	23
25	9

Since, there was no upset in the second round, so the table in the next round would look like:

1	9
15	7
3	11
13	5

We are given Maria is in the semi-finals. As we are not sure what is the result of other games, table for the next round can be drawn as follows:

1	5/13
7/15	3/11

Hence, Anastasia will play with Maria Sharapova.

56. c

1	8
2	7
3	6
4	5

In this case, Kim Clijster will either not reach semi-finals or she will play Maria in semi-finals.

Hence, she cannot play Maria in finals.

For questions 57 to 60: The given information can be tabulated as follows:

States	Firm A	Firm B	Firm C	Firm D
UP	49	82	80	55
Bihar	69	72	70	65
MP	72	63	72	65
Total	190	217	222	185

57. b As Truthful Ltd. has the highest market share, so Truthful Ltd. can be A or C.

From neutral statement, either B and C are Aggressive and Honest or A and D are Aggressive and Honest.

According to statement 1, B is Profitable. Then, A and D are Aggressive and Honest.

Then, Honest's total revenue cannot be more than that of Profitable. Hence, statement 2 is false.

58. c According to statement 1, Aggressive is B. Then, Honest has to be C (as given in the neutral statement).

Then, statement 2 is also true as Honest Ltd's. lowest revenue is from Bihar.

59. c B is Honest according to statement 1.

Atmost one statement can be true as both give Aggressive and Honest as firm B and firm B cannot have two names.

60. c Profitable can be either A or D. Then, Aggressive and Honest have to be B and C. Hence, Truthful is D or A. For both A and D, lowest revenue is from UP.

Hence, (c) is the correct option.

For questions 61 to 65:

In this set, the fuel cost for each of the path is given. In addition, there are four toll collection junctions.

61. e No traffic flows on the street from D to T.

Now, we have fuel cost on different paths as

SAT : 9 + 5 = Rs. 14 + toll at junction A

SBAT : 2 + 2 + 5 = Rs. 9 + toll at junction B and A

SBCT : 2 3 + 2 = Rs. 7 + toll at junction B and C

SDCT : 7 + 1 + 2 = Rs. 10 + toll at junction D and C

Now, checking the options we find that toll at junction A is 0 or 1.

When toll is 0, fuel cost on SAT = 14 + 0 = Rs. 14

When toll is 1, fuel cost on SAT = 14 + 1 = Rs. 15

The fuel cost on all the paths should be equal.

Options (a), (b), (c) can be ruled out as in all these options toll at C and D add up to more than Rs. 5. As fuel cost on SDCT is Rs. 10 without toll, so with toll it cannot exceed Rs. 15 (i.e. toll of path SAT).

Option (d) is ruled out as in this option SAT comes out to be Rs. 14 and SDCT sums up to Rs.15.

So correct answer is option (e).

62. b & c

Note: Both the options b and c are correct.

Available routes are:

SAT → Rs. 14

SBAT → Rs. 9

SDCT → Rs. 10

SDT → Rs. 13

Now, fuel cost of SAT - fuel of SDT = 14 – 13 = Rs. 1.

Hence toll at junction D should be 1 more than the toll at A. So option (a), (d) and (e) are ruled out.

Now, fuel cost of SAT - fuel cost of SBAT = 14 – 9 = Rs. 5. So toll at junction B should be Rs. 5. So answer could be either (b) or option (c).

63. a Available paths considering no toll are

SAT → Rs. 14

SBCT → Rs. 7

SBAT → Rs. 9

SDCT → Rs. 10

SDT → Rs. 13

It is very likely that option (d) is selected. But, if all the five routes have the same cost, then there will be an equal flow on all the five routes i.e., 20% on each route. But, then the percentage of traffic. on

S – A → 20%

S – B → 40% (As there are two routes involving S – B.)

S – D → 40% (As there are two routes involving S – D.)

But, it is given that traffic on S – A = traffic on S – B = traffic on S – D.

64. d Available routes are

SAT → Rs. 14

SBAT → Rs. 9

SBCT → Rs. 7

SDCT → Rs. 10

SDT → Rs. 13

Fuel cost on path SAT - fuel cost on path SDT

= 14 - 13 = Rs. 1.

So the toll at junction D should be 1 more than toll at junction A. So option a and c are ruled out.

Fuel cost on path SAT - fuel cost on path SBCT

= 14 - 7 = Rs. 7.

So sum of toll at junction B and C should be 7 more than the toll at A. Hence, only option (d) matches.

65. c We have to find a path on which minimum cost is incurred and such that total traffic through B does not exceed 70%.

So option (e) is ruled out because we can send all the traffic through SDCT or SDT and meet all conditions.

Option (a) is also ruled out as in that case all traffic will be passed through SBCT [not possible as traffic at B can't be more than 70%]

Option (b) is also ruled out as it is possible only when toll at junction C is 2. In that case also all traffic will pass through B.

Option (c) can be the answer, when toll at junction B is 4 and toll at junction C is 0. Then SDCT will have toll equal to Rs. 10.

As Rs. 10 is less than Rs. 13, so option (d) is also ruled out.

Hence, option (c) is the correct choice.

66. a The diet should contain 10% minerals and only two ingredient contain 10% minerals namely O and Q.

Hence, only by mixing O and Q, a diet with 10% minerals can be formed.

Hence, there is only one way.

67. d None of the choices among (a), (b) and (c) can be used to form the diet with 10% fat and atleast 30% protein. For Q and S to form the diet with 10% fat and at least 30% protein, let us suppose that they are mixed in x : y ration. Then,

$$\frac{x(50)+y(0)}{x+y}=10$$

$\Rightarrow$ x : y = 1 : 4

$$\text{Cost per unit} = \frac{1(200)+4(100)}{5} = \text{Rs.}120$$

Similarly, for R and S, cost per unit = Rs. 200

∴ Cost per unit is lowest for Q and S.

68. e To make a diet with P, Q and S having atleast 60% carbohydrates, the proportion of P should be the maximum and the other two should be minimum to get the lowest per unit cost. Options (b) and (e) satisfies this but the lowest cost per unit can be achieved when P, Q and S are mixed in the proportion 4 : 1 : 1.

69. e As the ingredients are mixed in equal amounts, so we can take the average of the constituent percentage of the elements used.

Only option (e) satisfies all the conditions.

70. d For the shortest route, we have to consider the path A-C-F-J.

The table given below shows the distance and the corresponding price.

Path	Distance	Price
A-C	790	1350
C-F	410	430
F-J	970	1150
Total	**2170**	**2930**

Hence, the price for travelling by the shortest route is Rs. 2930.

71. b For the lowest price we have to consider the path A-H-J.

The table given below shows the distance and the corresponding price.

Path	Distance	Price
A-H	1950	1850
H-J	400	425
Total	**2350**	**2275**

If the company charges 5% below the minimum price of Rs. 2275 then it should charge 0.95 × 2275 = Rs. 2161

72. c If the airports C, D and H are closed, then the passenger must follow the path A-F-J for minimum price.

The table given below shows the distance and the corresponding price.

Path	Distance	Price
A-F	1345	1700
F-J	970	1150
Total	2315	2850

So the corresponding minimum price paid by a passenger is Rs. 2850.

73. b For minimum cost per km, we have to consider the path A-H-J

From solution of question 71, we know that the distance of path A-H-J is 2350 km and the price is Rs. 2275.

The price includes a margin of 10%.

So the minimum cost per km

$$= 2275 \times \frac{10}{11} \times \frac{1}{2350} = 0.88$$

74. d For minimum cost per km, again we have to consider the path A-H-J as illustrated in the solution of question 73.

The distance of path A-H-J is 2350 km.

75. e Statement A alone is not sufficient because it is not giving any information about the opponent. Statement B alone is also not sufficient because it is not giving any information regarding the performance of Mahindra & Mahindra in the second half. Even if both the statements are used together, we will get two cases:

M & M	0	1
Opponent	3	4

So in one case, match is drawn and in the other case, it is won by Mahindra & Mahindra.

Hence, the answer is (e)

For questions 76 to 77:

Raju bets on the horses as follows:

Red – Rs.3000 , White – Rs.2000

and Black – Rs.1000 = Total of Rs.6000

He makes no profit no loss in the game. So the possible ways of recovering his money (Rs.6000) is as follows:

Case (i): 3000 + 3(1000)

Case (ii): 2000 + 4(1000)

Case (iii): 3(2000) + 0

Case (a): A breakup of 3000 + 3(1000) can be arrived at if the Black horse finished at 2nd and the Red horse at 3rd positions.

Then the White horse is either on the 4th or 5th position.

	1st	2nd	3rd	4th	5th
I	Grey/ Spotted	Black	Red	White	Spotted/ Grey
II	Grey/ Spotted	Black	Red	Spotted/ Grey	White

Case (b): A breakup of 2000 + 4(1000) can be arrived at if the Black horse finished at 1st and the White horse at 3rd positions.

Then the Red horse is either on the 4th or 5th position.

	1st	2nd	3rd	4th	5th
I	Black	Grey/ Spotted	White	Red	Spotted/ Grey
II	Black	Grey/ Spotted	White	Spotted/ Grey	Red

Case (c): A breakup of 3(2000) + 0 can be arrived at if the White horse finished at 2nd position.

Then the Red and Black horses must have finished at the 4th and 5th positions, not necessary in that order.

	1st	2nd	3rd	4th	5th
I	Spotted/ Grey	White	Grey/ Spotted	Red/ Black	Black/ Red

76. d None of the cases has three horses between White and Red horses.

77. c If Grey came fourth, we consider cases (a) and (b). All the options except (c) can hold true for these cases. White horse can either be 2nd or 5th in the race.

78. b Since Bhama got calls from all colleges, she has to score marks in each section equal to at least the maximum of the cut-offs across colleges which means 45, 45, 46 & 45 in section A, B, C & D respectively. This makes her total to be 181 with which she will clear the overall cut-offs of all the institutes.

79. c Since we have to minimise the marks in a particular section, we will have to maximise the marks in other 3 sections. Let us assume that marks obtained in each of the three sections in which we are going to maximize the score, is equal to 50. Now, the lowest overall cut-off is 171 & second lowest is 175. Hence, Charlie must have scored at least 175 – (50 + 50 + 50) = 25 marks in the remaining section.

Let us confirm whether he can clear sectional cut-offs also with such a distribution. On seeing the sectional cut-offs, we conclude that they can be cleared with 50 marks each in section A, B & C and 25 marks in section D, which may enable Charlie to clear the sectional cut-off of section D for college 1, 2, 3 or 5. Hence, 25 is the correct answer.

80. c Since we have to maximize Aditya's marks, let us take the base values of 50 marks in each section and try to reduce that by minimum values to ensure he doesn't get any call. We notice that by reducing the marks obtained in section C to 41, we ensure colleges 1, 2, 3 & 5 are ruled out. Now for colleges 4 & 6, reducing the marks obtained in section D to 43, ensures these colleges are also ruled out. Please note that we are reducing the score to 1 less than the minimum cut-off across all colleges for that particular section.

In the other two sections A and B, Aditya may score 50 each. So the maximum possible aggregate marks = 50 + 50 + 41 + 43 = 184.

For questions 81 to 84:

The given basic information can be collated as below:

(i) Six teams – A, B, C, D, E, F.

(ii) Matches scheduled in two stages – I & II.

(ii) No team plays against the same team more than once.

(iv) No ties permitted.

As per the instructions given for stage – I, we can reach the following conclusions:

(a) As B lost at least one match, A won all the 3 matches.

(b) The two teams who lost all the matches cannot be A (as explained above), cannot be B (E lost to B), cannot be D (D won against C & F). Hence, the two teams must be C and F.

(c) F did not play against the top team (i.e. A).

We get the following table for stage – I.

(To be read from rows)

	A	B	C	D	E	F
A	X	W	W	W		
B	L	X			W	W
C	L		X	L	L	
D	L		W	X		W
E		L	W		X	W
F		L		L	L	X

As per the instructions given for Stage-II, we can reach the following conclusions.

(d) A lost both its matches against E and F.

(e) F won against A, hence is the bottom team (out of C & F) which won both the matches

⇒ F won against C as well.

This also means that C lost both its matches against B and F.

(f) Apart from A and C, one more team lost both the matches in Stage-II.

That team can neither be E (A lost to E), nor B (as C lost to B), nor F (as F won both its matches).

Hence, the team must be D.

We get the following table for Stage-II.

(To be read from rows)

	A	B	C	D	E	F
A	X				L	L
B		X	W	W		
C		L	X			L
D		L		X	L	
E	W			W	X	
F	W		W			X

81. b E and F defeated A. **[Please note that in this question, options (a) and (e) were the same.]**

82. d B, E and F won both the matches in Stage-II.

83. e D and F won exactly two matches in the event.

84. e B and E have most wins, 4 each.

For questions 85 to 87:

Colour	Red/Blue	Blue/Red	Green	White
Name	Priya	Sonal	Qureshi	Rahul
Profession	Lawyer	Engineer	Doctor	Cricketer

For questions 88 to 90 :

As Subbu performed alone in the first slot on the second day, the bands could not have performed more than 5 times. So the number of performances given by the bands was either 4 or 5. If the number of performances given by the bands was 4, then each of the four artists would have given one performance. However, in that case the sum of the number of performances given by Mitti, Kehsanloy and Kumar respectively would be 3 (a prime number), which is not possible. So the number of performances given by the bands as well as by the artists must be 5. The number of performances given by Delhi Sea and Mitti must be the same and it should be 1 each only. The number of performances given by GTH was 3. Either Kehsanloy or Kumar gave 2 performances and the rest 3 artists gave 1 performance each.

As the last performance of Shankar was held before the first performance of GTH, Delhi Sea and Mitti must have performed successively in the first two slots on the first day. Shankar must have performed in either the first slot or the second slot on the first day.

The conclusions made thus far can be tabulated as given below.

Slot / Day	Slot-1	Slot-2	Slot-3
Day-1	-	-	-
	Delhi Sea	Mitti	GTH
Day-2	Subbu	-	-
	NA	GTH	GTH

88. c The given information can be tabulated as:

Slot / Day	Slot-1	Slot-2	Slot-3
Day-1	Shankar	NA	Kehsanloy
	Delhi Sea	Mitti	GTH
Day-2	Subbu	Kumar	Kehsanloy
	NA	GTH	GTH

89. b Kumar must definitely have performed with GTH as GTH performed in both the second and the third slot on the second day.

90. d All the given statements could be true.

For questions 91 to 93 :

Let Aadi, Bina, Cara, Diya, Ema, Fiza, Gauri and Hari be represented by A, B, C, D, E, F, G and H respectively. The number of neighbours of the person living in:

P1 and P5 = 2;

P2, P4 and P7 = 3;

P6 and P8 = 4;

P3 = 5.

From statement (v), it can be concluded that A lives in P1 or P2 or P6. From statement (i), A cannot live in P6 as then A and C will not have the same number of neighbours. From statement (ii), A and F have a common neighbour – D – and hence it can be concluded that A lives in P2 and D lives in P3. From statement (iii), E lives in P6 and hence G lives in P1. From statements (iv) and (i), it can be concluded that C lives in P4. Thus it can be concluded that one between B and H lives in P5 and the other lives in P7. The following figure illustrates these conclusions:

P1 (G)	P2 (A)	P3 (D)	P4 (C)	P5 (B/H)
P6 (E)		P7 (H/B)	P8 (F)	

91. Either Bina or Hari lives in P7.

92. Aadi has three neighbours.

93. Gauri is not a neighbour of Diya.

For questions 94 to 96:

From statements (i), (ii) and (vi), it can be concluded that Alfred was the first person to reach the museum. From statements (i), (ii) and (iv), it can be concluded that Dirk was wearing the Yellow shirt.

Hence, either Alfred or Buckley was wearing the Purple shirt and the other one was wearing the White shirt. From statement (v), it can be concluded that Alfred was wearing the Purple shirt while Buckley was wearing the White shirt. Further analysis leads to the following table:

	(Left to Right) First-to-last to arrive at museum			
Person	Alfred	Dirk	Buckley	Cherry
Shirt Colour	Purple	Yellow	White	Red

94. Buckley

95. Cherry

96. Only statement I is correct.

For questions 97 to 99 :

Given that the increase in the number of applicants in the Commerce stream in 2008 as compared to 2007 is 70000 and that the average number of applicants in the four given streams in 2008 is 400000.

Therefore, the increase in the number of applicants in the Engineering stream in 2008 will be 70000 + 20000 = 90000.

Thus, the corresponding increase in the number of applicants in the Medical Science stream in 2008 will be 90000 – 69000 = 21000 and subsequently the increase in the number of applicants in the Arts stream will be 21000 + 59000 = 80000.

97. d So, the values of C, E and F will be (70000 – 21000 = 49000), (80000 – 90000 = – 10000) and (80000 – 70000) respectively.

So, the options (a), (b) and (c) are true.

For questions 98 and 99:

Let the number of applicants in the Engineering, Medical Science, Commerce and Arts stream in 2007 be 'x', 'y', 'z' and 'w' respectively.

Therefore, the number of applicants in the Engineering, Medical Science, Commerce and Arts stream in 2008 will be (x + 90000), (y + 21000), (z + 70000) and (w + 80000) respectively.

So, $x + y + z + w + 261000 = 400000 \times 4 = 1600000$.

Or, $x + y + z + w = 1339000$.

99. b So, Required percentage

$$= \left(\frac{80000}{1339000}\right) \times 100 = 5.97\,\% \approx 6\%$$

For questions 100 to 102 :

100.c Considering the statements made by C, we can conclude that one of the two statements I and II must be true, which means that statement III is definitely false.

So, A took a blue ball.

101.d Considering the statements made by C, we can conclude that one of the two statements I and II must be true, which means that statement III is definitely false.

Considering the statements made by E and A: Both statements II and III by E state that B took a blue ball and hence both are false as only one statement made on B is true. So statement I of both A and E are correct.

So, F took a red ball and B took a green ball.

Hence statement II by A was false.

So, C took a red ball.

102.b Considering the statements made by C, we can conclude that one of the two statements I and II must be true, which means that statement III is definitely false.

Considering the statements made by B:

We know that statement I is definitely false as A took a blue ball. Also, statement III is false.

So, statement II made by B is true.

Considering the statements made by F: We already know that A took a blue ball and C took a green ball. Hence, both the statements I and II are false and therefore statement III made by F is true.

So, neither D took a yellow ball nor did he took a red ball.

Consider the statements made by D: We already know that statement II is false as F took a red ball. So, one of the statements I and III is true.

It is also given that balls of two different colours were not taken by any of the mentioned persons.

Case I: E took a yellow ball

D must have taken a blue ball and balls of white and black colour are not taken by any of the mentioned persons.

Case II: D took a green ball

E could have taken either a white or a black ball.

For four persons viz. A, F, C and B the exact color of the balls taken by them can be determined.

For questions 103 to 105 :

From the given information, we can summarize the data in the following table:

	Akansh	Ajay	Ashok	Abhishek	Amit
Salaries (In Rs. Lakh)	7 or 13	11	13 or 7	9	8
Cities:	K/V	B/K/V	B/K/V	Prabandhnagar	Joka

Where 'K', 'V' and 'B' stands for 'Kunnamangalam', 'Vastrapur' and 'Banerghatta' respectively.

103. d If Akansh, lives in Vastrapur, then Ajay and Ashok must be staying at Kunnamangalam and Banerghatta, not necessarily in that order. Their average salary in any case will be Rs.12 lakhs or 9 lakhs. So, the data is insufficient.

104. c Amit called a friend, who gets Rs. 9 lakh as his salary is a perfect square multiple of 100000 and stays in Prabandhnagar.

Abhishek stays in Prabandhnagar.

105. d Amit lives in Joka, so Ajay must be living at Kunnamangalam. Since Akansh is not staying at Banerghatta, he must be staying at Vastrapur.

For questions 106 :

From statement (V), B and G cannot be together in the team. Therefore, there are three possible cases.

Case I: When B is selected.

F cannot be selected as F can only be selected when both G and N are selected. Thus, when B is selected, the team comprises exactly four bowlers. Also, J must be the wicketkeeper in the team, as selection of I ensures selection of F. Following table gives the possible compositions for the team.

Batsmen	Bowlers	Wicketkeeper
A, D, L, N, O, K/M	B, H, C, E	J

The number of ways in which the team can be formed $= 2 \times 1 \times 1 = 2$

Case II: When G is selected.

H cannot be selected as H can only be selected when B is selected. Thus, when G is selected, then again the team comprises exactly four bowlers. Following table gives the possible compositions for the team.

Batsmen	Bowlers	Wicketkeeper
A, D, L, N, O, K/M	G, F, C, E	I/J

The number of ways in which the team can be formed $= 2 \times 1 \times 2 = 4$.

Case III: When neither B nor G is selected.

When both B and G are not selected, then there is no possible composition for the team.

106. d The total number of ways in which the team can be formed = 2 + 4 = 6.

For questions 107 to 109 :

The table below gives all the possible values of B, C, D, E, F, G, H, I and J if the value of A is assumed to be 'x'.

A	x
B	x ± 1
C	x ± 1; x ± 3
D	x; x ± 2; x ± 4; x ± 6
E	x ± 1; x ± 3; x ± 5; x ± 7
F	x ± 1; x ± 3; x ± 5; x ± 7; x ± 9
G	x; x ± 2; x ± 4; x ± 6; x ± 8; x ± 10; x ± 12
H	x ± 1; x ± 3; x ± 5; x ± 7; x ± 9; x ± 11; x ± 13
I	x ± 1; x ± 3; x ± 5; x ± 7; x ± 9; x ± 11; x ± 13; x ± 15
J	x; x ± 2; x ± 4; x ± 6; x ± 8; x ± 10; x ± 12; x ± 14; x ± 16; x ± 18

107. d Clearly only 19 distinct values are possible for J if the value of A is known.

Answer option (d) is the correct choice.

108.b If 'x' is even then A, D, G and J are even. If 'x' is odd then B, C, E, F, H and I are even.

Answer option (b) is the correct choice.

109. a If x = 1 then a possibility is that B = 2, C = 4, D = 1, E = 2, F = 4, G = 1, H = 2, I = 4 and J = 1 in which case 7 values are perfect squares. This is the maximum number of perfect squares which can occur at the same time i.e. in a single case.

110. c Let the production be 100x and export (volume) be 100y.

As the share in export for three products (I.e. A, D and F is more than that in production but A witness the maximum change in share.)

For maximizing the export (volume) assume all volume of A is exported

$\therefore$ 8x = 10y $\Rightarrow \frac{y}{x} = 0.8 = 80\%$.

111. b Let the expenses and export by value be 100 x and 100y respectively.

As D is making profit

$\therefore$ 16x > 18y $\Rightarrow x > \frac{9}{8}y$

Now, we can see that three products B, C and F can be in loss.

112. d Let export (by volume) and export by value be 100x and 100y respectively then price per unit for all products is shown below:

$A = \frac{14y}{10x}$, $B = \frac{12y}{17x}$,

$C = \frac{20y}{15x}$, $D = \frac{15y}{25x}$

$E = \frac{16y}{11x}$, $F = \frac{20y}{22x}$

Hence, E has the highest price per unit.

113. c Let the production and export is 100x and 100y respectively.

Rejection rate of all products is given below:

$A = 1 - \frac{10y}{8x}$, $B = 1 - \frac{17y}{20x}$, $C = 1 - \frac{15y}{20x}$

$D = 1 - \frac{25y}{22x}$, $E = 1 - \frac{11y}{15x}$, $F = 1 - \frac{22y}{18x}$

Hence, E has the maximum rejection rate.

114.10 Since, L is the winner of the tournament, it must have won at least five matches. E is not qualified for second stage, it means E definitely won less than six matches.

Only possible case is shown below:

Number of matches won by E = Number of matches won by L = 5

Hence, required number = 5 + 5 = 10.

115. 2 Any team who had won two matches, there is a possibilities that the team will qualify for second stage. A possible case for the number of wins = 2 2 2 2 2 6 6 6.

116. 2 Statement (i) is obviously true.

Three teams in group 1 and three teams in group 2 can win one match each in stage 1.

Statement (ii) is incorrect because maximum number of teams which could have three wins in the first stage would be 14.

Possible case: 3 3 3 3 3 3 3 7 i.e. seven teams in each group would have three wins in the first stage.

Statement (iii) is clearly correct.

Hence, statement (i) and (iii) are correct

117. 22 Four teams cannot have six wins each hence maximum number of matches won in the first stage by teams A, B, C and D together would be 22

Possible case for number of wins: 2 1 1 2 4 6 6 6.

Required number = 4 + 6 + 6 + 6 = 22.

118. d Option (a) Violates the condition that Rahul and John want to be selected together.

Option (b) Violates the condition that Kamal cannot be in the group with Nusarat.

Option (c) Violates the condition that Rahul and John are to be selected together.

Option (d) Rohit, Nusarat, Rehana – is acceptable

119. c Option (a) Violates the condition that John and Rahul are selected together.

Option (b) Violates the condition that Kamal has to be with Rehana.

Option (c) Rahul, John, Rehana, Kamal – is acceptable

Option (d) Violates the condition that Nusarat cannot be with Kamal.

120. d Option (a) is not correct as if Kavya and Rohit both the selected then Rahul and John cannot be selected and Kamal and Rehana must be selected. If Kamal is selected then Nusarat cannot be selected but as Rohit is selected Nusarat must be selected which is contradictory.

Option (b) is also incorrect.

Both women $\Rightarrow$ Rehana and Kavya

Kavya $\Rightarrow$ Kamal

Now, one more male is required. He cannot be Rahul or John because they should necessarily be together. Rohit cannot exist in the group without Nusarat and Nusarat cannot exist because Kamal is already selected. Hence, a group of 4 having both women is also not possible.

Option (c) is not correct as Kamal should not be with Nusarat and Rohit cannot be with Rahul.

121. a The only possible group:

Kamal, Kavya, Rehana, Rahul and John.

For questions 122 to 125: Let the total money with the three of them in the beginning be Rs. 45x, the amount left with Mina and Dika after making the purchases be Rs. y each and the money spent on Bindaas shares by Ina and Mina be Rs. z each. The initial table can be made as shown below.

Name	Ina	Mina	Dika	Total
Money spent (in Rs.) on Jhakkas shares	4.5y	2y	y	15x
Money spent (in Rs.) on Bindaas shares	z	z	5x	
Amount (in Rs.) left	3x	y	y	
Total (in Rs.)		15x		45x

Now,

$$(2y + y) - (y + y) = 2,00,000$$

$$\Rightarrow \quad y = 2,00,000 \quad \ldots(i)$$

$$4.5y + 2y + y = 15x$$

$$\Rightarrow \quad x = 1,00,000 \quad \ldots(ii)$$

$$2y + z + y = 15x$$

$$\Rightarrow \quad z = 9,00,000 \quad \ldots(iii)$$

The final table is given below.

Name	Ina	Mina	Dika	Total
Money spent (in Rs.) on Jhakkas Shares	9,00,000	4,00,000	2,00,000	15,00,000
Money spent (in Rs.) on Bindaas Shares	9,00,000	9,00,000	5,00,000	23,00,000
Amount (in Rs.) left	3,00,000	2,00,000	2,00,000	7,00,000
Total (in Rs.)	21,00,000	15,00,000	9,00,000	**45,00,000**

122. Total amount spent by the three of them on purchasing Bindaas shares

= Rs. 23,00,000

The number of Bindaas shares purchased

$$= \frac{2300000}{5000} = 460.$$

123. Total money available with Ina in the beginning = Rs. 21,00,000.

124. Mina, and not Dika, was the person. Hence, statement I is not correct.

They were left with Rs. 7,00,000 after making the purchases. Hence, statement II is correct.

125. The required amount = Rs. 45,00,000.

For questions 126 to 129:

Total number of pizza = 800

70% were delivered to party 3 = $\frac{70 \times 800}{100}$ = 560 pizza

800 – 560 = 240

∴ 120 pizza each were delivered to party 1 and party

	(T) THIN CRUST	Normal Cheese (NC)
Party 1	0.6 × 120 =– 112	416 – 364 – 36 = 16
Party 2	0.55 × 120 = 66	0.3 × 120 = 36
Party 3	300 – 72 – 66 = 162	0.66 × 560 = 364
Total	0.375 × 800 = 300	0.52 × 800 = 416

126. From table, 162 thin crust pizzas were to be delivered to party 3.

127. From table, 16 normal cheese pizzas were required to be delivered to party.

128. 50% of normal cheese of party 2 = $\frac{50 \times 36}{100}$ = 18 pizza were thin crust.

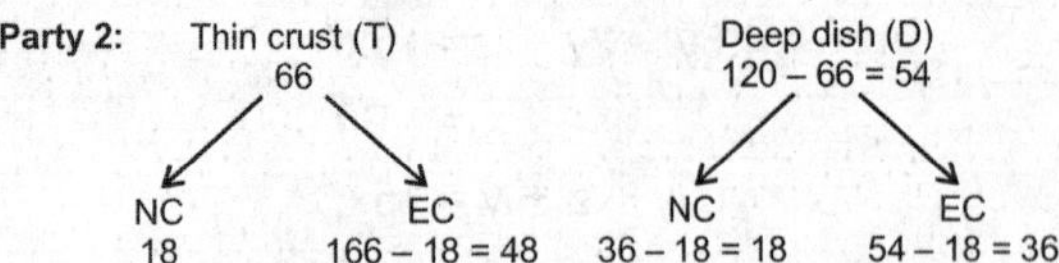

Difference between number of T – EC and D – EC

= 48 – 36 = 12

129. Party 1: Thin crust (T) 72 → NC: 16 – 4 = 12; EC: 72 – 12 = 60

Deep dish (D) 120 – 72 = 48 → NC: 25% of 16 = 4; EC: 48 – 4 = 44

Given: T-EC (Thin crust with extra cheese)

= Rs.500

D-EC = 500 + 50 = Rs.550

T-NC costs = $\frac{3}{5}$ of D-EC = $\frac{3}{5} \times 550 = 330$ Rs.

D-NC costs = Rs.330

Total biu for party 1

= (12 × 330) + (500 × 60) + 4 × (330) + (550 × 44)

= 3960 + 30,000 + 1320 + 24200 = 59480

For questions 130 to 133:

Total students = 300

After change process = 292

Missing information = 8 students

	E1	E2	E3	E4	E5	E6
E1	9	5	10	1	4	2
E2	D	34	8	0	2	2
E3	2	6	25	0	1	2
E4	1	3	2	14	1	4
E5	1	5	1	0	30	1
E6	1	7	3	1	2	9
E7	4	16	30	5	5	41

Before the change process

E1 = E4 + 6

E1 = 31 (With missing information)

E4 = 23 (With missing information)

After the change process E4 = E1 + 3

E1 = 16

E4 = 20

Number of E2 increased by 30

After reshuffling E2 = 76

Before = 76 – 36 = 46

With missing information E2 = 46, number change

Before reshuffling E4 = E6 + 2

Since with missing information E4 = 25, E6 = 21.

Before, reshuffling E2 = e3 + 10

E2 = 46, E3 = 35

Since after change, E4 = E1 + 3

E4 = 21, E1 = 17

Now, since total students are 300, fill out missing information

130.

	Before	After
E1	31	18
E2	46	76
E3	36	79
E4	25	21
E5	38	45
E6	23	61

131. 18, 76, 79, 21, 45, 61

132. $\frac{E3_{After} - E3_{Before}}{E3_{Before}} \times 100 = \frac{61-23}{61} \times 100 = 165.217.$

Which is largest.

133. After reshuffling E1 has 18 students which is less than 20. E1 + (5 + 10 + 1 + 4 + 2) = 18 + 22 = 40

From E1 to E2 = 5 students

E2 – 5 = (76 – 5) students = 71

From E1 to E3 = 10 students

E3 – 10 = (79 – 10) students = 69

From E1 to E4 = 1 students

E4 – 1 = 21 – 1 = 20 students

From E1 to E5 = 4 students

E5 – 4 = 45 – 4 = 41 students

From E1 to E6 = 2 students

E6 – 2 = (61 – 2) = 59 students

Decreasing order

E2 > E3 > E6 > E5 > E1 > E4.

134. Given value of the assets was distributed equally

∴ Neeta, Seeta & Geeta received 70 lakh each each.

Since, neeta received the least amount and Geeta received the highest amount in bank deposits

∴ The only possibility is

Neeta: 2 flats : 30 × 2 = 60 lakh and

70 – 60 = 10 lakh in bank deposit

Seeta: 1 house : 50 lakh and

70 – 50 = 20 lakh in bank deposit

Geeta: 70 – 10 – 20 = 40 lakh in bank deposit

Option (3).

135. Neeta received 2 flats.

136. Total assets is worth Rs = (210 + x) lakhs, where x is the number of Gold coins worth of 1 lakh each.

Given:

Ratio for assets is 1 : 2 : 3 and for gold coins is 2 : 3 : 4

∴ Seeta has $[210 + x] \times \frac{2}{6}$ lakhs of assets and $x \times \frac{3}{9}$ gold coins.

$\Rightarrow \left(70 + \frac{x}{3}\right)$ lakhs, where $\frac{x}{3}$ is the gold coins and 70 lakhs (bank deposits, home and flat)

Since, one child got all three flats which costs = 3 × 30 = 90 lakhs

∴ Seeta doesn't get flats

and other than Geeta, one child got 30 lakhs in deposits

⇒ Seeta gets home, i.e. she has (70 – 50) = 20 lakhs in bank deposit.

∴ Neeta gets 30 lakhs indeposits and Geeta gets (70 – 30 – 20) lakhs = 20 lakhs in bank deposits.

Also, Geeta gets 3 flats each of 30 lakhs.

Let the number of gold coins received by Neeta, Seeta and Geeta be 2a, 3a, 4a respectively.

$\Rightarrow \frac{30 + 2a}{70 + 3a} = \frac{1}{2}$

⇒ a = 10

Gold coins (x) = (2 × 10) + 3(10) + 4 × 10

= 90

137. 20 lakhs from above explanations.

For questions 138 to 141:

Note :- Each committee has at least one from each of the three types - bureaucrats, educationalists and politicians.

By statement 1:-

Let Bureaucrats in the administration committee = a

Then Bureaucrats in the research and teaching committee will be $\frac{a75}{100} = \frac{3a}{4}$ respectively.

∴ only possible value of 'a' can be 4

(since, if a takes values greater than 4 say 8, then $\frac{3a}{4} = 6$ and that gives the total 8 + 6 + 6 = 20 and according to the Note, this is not possible)

∴ Total numbers of people in Research Committee are 10.

By statement 2:-

Let the number of educationalists in the teaching committee and administration committee be b and d respectively then, number of educationalists in Research committee will be = $\frac{b+d}{2}$

Also $b < \frac{b+d}{2}$

⇒ 2b < b + d

⇒ b < d

Following the conditions stated above the possible combinations are:-

	Educationalists		
	Case I	**Case II**	**Case III**
Research	2	3	3
Teaching	1	1	2
Administration	3	5	4
Total	6	9	9

By statement 3:-

Let total number of politicians be 'P', then

	Politicians
Research	P/5
Taching	P/5
Adminsitration	3P/5

Therefore, P is a multiple of 5 and therefore (Case I) of statement 2 is eliminated. So, P = 5.

Final table looks like:-

		Research	Teaching	Administration
Bureaucrats		3	3	4
Educationalists	Case I	3	1	5
	Case II	3	2	4
Politicians		1	1	3
Total		7	5/6	12/11

138. The size of the research committee is less than the size of the teaching committee

139. Number of bureaucrats in the administration committee = 4

140. Number of educationalists in the research committee = 3.

141. The size of the teaching committee could be either 5 or 6, hence, cannot be determined uniquely.

For questions 142 to 145:

Given: The satellite serving either B, C or S do not serve O.

From statement (1), the number of satellites serving B, C and S are 2x, x, and x respectively.

Let number of satellites serving B exclusively are 'a', than the number of satellites serving C and S exclusively are $\frac{3a}{10}$ = 0.3a each.

Let number of satellites serving others (O) = b then b = satellites serving both C and S but not B.

Since the number of satellites serving C and S are equal, therefore number of satellites serving 'B and C but not S' is equal to the number of satellites serving 'S and B but not C', say d.

Further the following Venn diagram can be formed:-

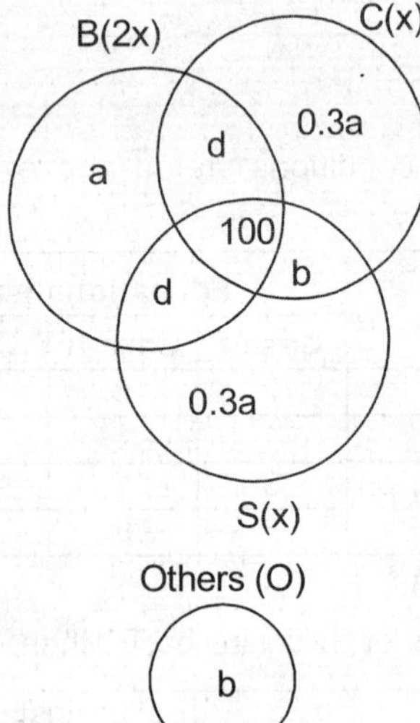

Others (O)

b

Now, $a + 2d + 2b + 100 + (0.3a)2 = 1600$

$1.6a + 2d + 2b = 1500$ ....(1)

By statement (1),

$a + 2d + 100 = 2(0.3a + d + b + 100)$

$a + 2d + 100 = 0.6a + 2d + 2b + 200$

$0.4\,a = 2b + 100$

$\boxed{a = 5b + 250}$ ....(2)

By (1) and (2), we get

$8b + 400 + 2d + 2b = 1500$

$10b + 2d = 1100.$

$5b + d = 550$

$\boxed{d = 550 - 5b}$

142. Number of satellites serving C

$= 0.3a + b + d + 100$

$= 0.3\,(5b + 250) + b + 550 - 5b + 100$

$= 1.5\,b + 75 + 650 - 4b$

$= 725 - 2.5b$

Maximum value when b = 0, is <u>725</u>.

Now $d \geq 0$

$\Rightarrow 550 - 5\,b \geq 0$

$\Rightarrow 110 \geq b.$

Maximum value of b = 10.

Minimum value when b = 110, is 450.

143. The minimum possible number of satellites serving B exclusively are:-

$a = 5b + 250.$

Minimum will be b = 0, i.e., a = 250.

144. The minimum value of O is 100, i.e., $b \geq 100$.

Now $S = C = 725 - 2.5b$.

This will be maximum when b is minimum

Minimum value of b = 100.

Maximum value of $S = 725 - 2.5(100) = 475$.

$\therefore$ At most 475.

145. Number of satellites serving at least two of B, C and S is 1200.

i.e, $d + d + b + 100 = 1200.$

$\Rightarrow 2[550 - 5b] + b + 100 = 1200$

$\Rightarrow 1100 - 10b + b + 100 = 1200$

$\Rightarrow -9b = 0$

$\Rightarrow$ This is only possible when b = 0

Then, d = 550 and a = 250.

Now satellites serving $C = d + b + 0.3a + 100$

$= 550 + 0 + 0.3\,(250) + 100 = 725$

The number of satellites serving C can be uniquely determined.

Hence Option (4).

For questions 146 to 149:

146. From the second condition, we know that R > I as Best Ed and Cosmopolitan have similar points in F i.e. B and in P i.e. D.

(a) From the third condition, we know that I > P, as Education Aid and A-one have similar points in F and R i.e. A. Therefore, R > I > P.

(b) Now, we have a few distinct possibilities for F.

Consider condition 1, if we take F = 0.4 then R = 0.3, I = 0.2, P = 0.1.

Then, Overall Score of High Q = 30 × 0.4 + 20 × 0.3 + 20 × 0.1 + 40 × 0.2 = 28

Overall Score of Best Ed = 40 × 0.4 + 30 × 0.3 + 20 × 0.1 + 20 × 0.2 = 31.

But High Q is better than Best Ed, so F is not equal to 0.4. Since, R > I > P therefore, F = 0.1.

Finally we get, R = 0.4, I = 0.3, P = 0.2, F = 0.1.

The weight of the faculty quality parameter is 0.1

147. Since, R = 0.4, I = 0.3, P = 0.2, F = 0.1.

We get the following table.

	F = 0.1	R = 0.4	P = 0.2	I = 0.3	Overall Score	Rating
A-one	50 × 0.1	50 × 0.4	50 × 0.2	40 × 0.3	47	AAA
Best Ed	40 × 0.1	30 × 0.4	20 × 0.2	20 × 0.3	26	BBA
Cosmopolitan	40 × 0.1	20 × 0.4	20 × 0.2	30 × 0.3	25	BBA
Dominance	20 × 0.1	20 × 0.4	40 × 0.2	30 × 0.3	27	BBA
Education Aid	50 × 0.1	50 × 0.4	40 × 0.2	50 × 0.3	48	AAA
Fancy	50 × 0.1	50 × 0.4	40 × 0.2	40 × 0.3	45	AAA
Global	30 × 0.1	0 × 0.4	20 × 0.2	20 × 0.3	13	Junk
High Q	30 × 0.1	20 × 0.4	20 × 0.2	40 × 0.3	27	BBA

∴ Only A-one, Education Aid, and Fancy have got AAA rating.

148. Check from the table given in the previous question. The highest score is 48 for Education Aid.

149. Check from the table given in the answer for the 10th question, no college has overall score between 31 and 40.

For questions 150 to 153:

(a) The outlet received 88000 units of L by selling A during the day.

Now as the amount received by the outlet by selling A and B is 5 : 9, the amount the outlet received by selling B = $\left(\frac{9}{5}\right)$ × 88000 = 158400 units of L.

(b) The outlet ended with the same amount of B it started the day with, that is, 4800 units. Thus, it must have bought the same amount of currency B that it sold.

Since the outlet received 158400 units of L by selling currency B,

∴ The base value of the amount will be = $\left(\frac{158400}{1.1}\right)$

= 144000

[Since the company charges 10% premium while selling exchange rates].

Since the base value is 144000, the amount in buying currency B = $\left(\frac{144000}{0.95}\right)$ = 136800.

(c) Now, we know that the amount the outlet received by selling A and B is in the ratio 5 : 3,

∴ The amount the outlet received is = 136800 × $\left(\frac{5}{3}\right)$ = 228000.

(d) The outlet started the day with 2500 units and ended the day with 3300 units of A. Therefore, it bought 800 units of A more than it sold.

Using similar methods, the base value of L that the company received by selling L = $\frac{88000}{1.1}$ = 80000.

The base amount the company bought A for is $\frac{228000}{0.95}$ = 240000.

Since the difference in the amounts of L denotes 800 extra units of A, (240000 – 80000) = 160000, units of L = 800 units of L. So, 200 units of L = 1 unit of A.

Following, 240 units of B = 1 unit of L, and 2 units of C = 1 unit of L.

(e) We know that the amounts of L used to buy and sell C is the same. Let that be X.

While buying, it's base value will be $\left(\frac{X}{0.95}\right)$, and while selling it will be $\frac{X}{1.1}$.

The outlet ends the day with 3000 units of C more than it started the day with, so, since the currency rate 2 : 1.

$$\frac{\left(\frac{X}{0.95}\right)}{2} = \left\{\frac{\left(\frac{X}{1.1}\right)}{2}\right\} + 3000$$

Solving, we get X = 41800

150. Base value of 228000 = $\frac{228000}{0.95}$ = 240000. (As company buys currency at 5% below the base exchange rate).

The number of units of currence C bought by the outlet on that day = $\frac{240000}{200}$ = 1200.

151. Base value of C in L while selling = 38000.

The number of units of currency C sold by the outlet on that day = $\frac{38000}{2}$ = 19000.

152. 240

153. 2 × 0.95 = 1.90

CALCULATION BASED DI

For question 1 to 3:

Since Ghosh babu distributed his property equally among his 4 daughters, each one of them should get 25% of the property. The eldest daughter got 20% of the total property and Rs.25000 in cash. So, Rs.25000 should constitute 5% of the total property. Hence the total property is worth Rs.5 lakhs.

Now, the total cash given by him = Rs.25000 (eldest daughter) + Rs.50000 (second daughter) + Rs.150000 (i.e. Rs.75000 each to his third and fourth daughters) = Rs.225000.

So, out of his total property of Rs.500000, Rs.225000 is cash, so the gold and silver should be worth Rs.275000.

3. d If Ghosh Babu has equal number of gold and silver bars, the value of 1 gold bar and 1 silver bar is Rs.5000 (i.e. Rs.4000 + Rs.1000) and the total worth of gold and silver bars is Rs.275000.

Hence, number of gold and silver bars would be equal i.e. $\frac{275000}{5000}$ = 55.

4. d The answer cannot be determined as the data for only five states is given and we don't know the excise duty rates for other states.

5. d We have been given the total value in the graph, but nothing is mentioned about the amount of liquor manufactured by states other than Tamil Nadu.

6. c Since Excise duty is levied on the total value of liquor produced by the 5 distilleries, this will be in the same order as the order of the amount of the liquor produced by them (as the excise duty rate remains constant). Hence the correct order is DCEBA.

7. b Average simple annual growth rate of five distilleries is as follows:

$$A = \frac{1}{2}\left(\frac{12.89 - 6.41}{6.41}\right) \times 100 = 50.54\%$$

$$B = \frac{1}{2}\left(\frac{12.07 - 3.15}{3.15}\right) \times 100 = 141.58\%$$

$$C = \frac{1}{2}\left(\frac{11.92 - 1.64}{1.64}\right) \times 100 = 313.41\%$$

$$D = \frac{1}{2}\left(\frac{5.79 - 1.05}{1.05}\right) \times 100 = 225.71\%$$

$$E = \frac{1}{2}\left(\frac{4.21 - 2.45}{2.45}\right) \times 100 = 35.91\%$$

So the distillery with highest growth rate is C and with lowest growth rate is E.

So had the amount of liquor manufactured by E grown by 313.41% in the 2 year period ie. Grown by 616.82% overall, its supply in 1998 would be $2.45 \times \frac{616.82}{100}$ = 15.11 liters.

8. a Required average

$$= \frac{(100.5 + 67 + 141 + 143.9 + 65)}{5} = 103.48$$

9. a The key here is figuring out that the only performance which is less than the 1985 performance is the 1988 performance. Hence the percentage corresponding to 1988 should be less than 100.

Thus we see that (c) cannot be the answer. Also (b) cannot be the answer as it shows two of the years having less than 100%.

Between options (a) and (d), the correct answer is (a), This is so because the difference between the 1985 and 1988 performance is only 2 units on 67 units. Hence percentage wise it has to be 97% and not 68%.

10. b The highest percentage decline over the previous year is seen for the year 1988, as in this year the performance almost halved.

11. c The estimated total expenditure

= 52.1+267.5+196.4+209.5

= 725.5 lakhs.

If it has to be kept within 700 lakhs, the expenditures have to be cut by 25.5 laks.

Cut in expenditure every year

$$= \left(\frac{25.5}{4}\right) = 6.375 \text{ lakhs.}$$

Hence, percentage cut for 1989

$$= \left(\frac{6.375}{15}\right) \times 100 = 42.5\%.$$

12. b The estimated costs of material and labour for different years are :

1988 = 2.1

1989 = 95+70+15+25+25 = 230

1990 = 80+45+12+18+20 = 175

1991 = 75+60+16+21+18 = 190

Required proportion

$$= \frac{2.1 + 230 + 175}{2.1 + 230 + 175 + 190} = 0.682$$

13. b Total material cost for all years

= (95+80+75+70+45+60+15+12+16+25+18+21)

= 532

Total labour cost for all years = (2.1+25+20+18)

= 65.1

Hence ratio = 532 : 65.1 $\approx$ 8 : 1

14. b In the given table we can see that the costs that can be taken under the head "Materials" are : Cement, Steel, Bricks and Other building materials.

The estimated cost of these heads in 1990

= 80 + 45 + 12 + 18 = 155

The estimated cost of these heads in 1991

= 75 + 60 + 16 + 21 = 172

Since the cost of material rises by 5%, or would rise by 0.05X (155 + 172) = Rs.16.35 lakhs.

15. b Till 1990, actual amount spent = Rs.725.5 lakhs

Expenditure for 1991 as estimated = 209.5 lakhs.

Required percentage increase $= \frac{209.5}{725.5} \times 100$

= 28.89%.

16. a Total estimate = Rs. 725.5 lakh;

Estimate of contingencies = (1 + 15 + 4.2 + 5)

= Rs.25.2 lakh.

Now as the estimate of contingencies is doubled, it increases by Rs.25.2 lakhs.

Hence, the percentage increase in the total estimate is $\left(\frac{25.2}{725.5}\right) \times 100 = 3.47\%$.

17. c From table 3 it can be seen that the highest percentage of sales to stock is 74% for the Region 4 and colour Brown.

18. b From Table 4 it can be seen that in region 1, the maximum percentage of saris were sold of Brown colour viz.22% and hence this is the most popular colour in this region.

19. d This can be answered from the fifth table. It can be seen that Region 1 has sold the maximum percentage of magenta saris out of its total magenta saris sold (viz.44%)

20. b This can be answered from the fourth table. It can be seen that Region 6 has sold the least percentage of green saris out of its total sale (viz.14%)

21. a This can be answered from the fifth table. It can be seen that the percentage of blue saris sold is maximum for Region 2 viz. (33%)

22. a

Year	Consumption of chemical fertilizers	Gross cropped area	Ratio
84-85	(3.68+1.21+0.62) = 5.51	173.1	0.032
85-86	(4.07+1.32+0.67) = 6.60	177	0.037
86-87	(4.22+1.44+0.73) = 6.39	172.6	0.037
87-88	(5.20+1.73+0.78) = 7.71	180.4	0.043

Hence the ratio is lowest for 84-85.

23. a It can be seen that in 88-89, area cropped shows a decline for 3 of the crops viz.wheat, jowar and bajra. This is the maximum number of crops for any year.

24. d The amount area brought under irrigation for Major and Medium in 86-87 = (24 – 23.2) = 0.8

The amount area brought under irrigation for Minor in 86-87 = (34.2 – 32.77) = 1.43

Hence total area brought under irrigation in 86-87

= 0.8+1.43 = 2.23 million hectares.

25. d It can be seen that only in the year 1987-88, the area under minor irrigated area has decreased (from 34.2 to 34). Hence it is obvious that this area should have been transferred to major and medium irrigated areas.

For questions 26 to 30:

$$\text{Per Capita Income} = \frac{\text{(National Income)}}{\text{(Population)}}$$

Year	Per Capita Income	increase over previous year
1984-85	3097.62	-
1985-86	3482.32	384.70
1986-87	3786.44	304.12
1987-88	4202.98	416.54
1988-89	4856.73	653.75
1989-90	5319.01	462.28

Year	Population (in crore)	Percentage increase over the previous year	Per Capita Income	Percentage increase over the previous year
1984-85	74	-	3097.63	-
1985-86	75	1.35%	3482.32	12.43%
1986-87	77	2.66%	3786.44	8.73%
1987-88	78.5	1.94%	4202.98	11.01%
1988-89	80	1.91%	4856.73	15.56%
1989-90	81.5	1.87%	5319.01	9.51%

26. b As it can be clearly seen, the increase is lowest for the year 1986 – 87 = Rs. 304 .12

27. d Per Capita Income is highest for the year 1989 – 90 $\approx$ 5319.

28. d Required difference is highest for the year 1988 - 98, 13.65.

29. a It is apparent that the rate of increase of population is lowest for the year 1985-86 viz.1.35%.

30. a Among the years given in the answer choices, the increase in per capita income compared to previous year is highest for the year 1985 - 86.

For questions 31 to 35:

Let us assume that Ghosh Babu had deposited Rs.100 initially.

Year	Opening Balance	Interest Earned	Withdrawn by Ghosh Babu	Closing Balance
1986	100	10	10 + 20 = 30	80
1987	80	8	8 + 40 = 48	40
1988	40	4	4 + 20 = 24	20
1989	20	2	22	0

31. c Had he deposited Rs.100 initially, he should have withdrawn Rs.22 at the end to close the account. Since he withdrew Rs.11000, at the end, he should have initially deposited Rs.50000.

32. d He withdrew the smallest amount after the 4th year.

33. a He collected the maximum interest after the 1st year.

34. b Ghosh Babu withdrew the maximum amount after the 2nd year.

35. a The total interest collected by Ghosh Babu is Rs.24 on Rs.100. Hence on Rs.50000, it would be Rs.12000.

For questions 36 to 40:

The values of the graph can be tabulated as given below:

	A	% Change	B	% Change	C	% Change	D	% Change
Jan	100	–	70	–	60	–	40	–
Feb	95	–5%	72	2.85%	55	-8.33%	50	25%
Mar	115	21%	74	2.77%	60	9.09%	50	–
Apr	105	–8.7%	76	2.70%	69	15%	41	–18%
May	100	–4.7%	78	2.63%	60	–13%	44	7.31%
Jun	110	10%	80	2.56%	55	–8.33%	45	2.27%

36. d As it is seen the highest % increase is for D in Feb. viz.25%.

37. a The greatest absolute change in the market value for any share recorded is 20 i.e. for share "A" for month of March = 115 – 95 = 20.

38. a The greatest percentage change in any share was recorded for share D for the month of February viz. 25%.

39. d

	C	D	Total Earning	A	Gain/ Loss
Jan	60	40	100	100	–
Feb	55	50	105	95	+10
Mar	60	50	110	115	–5
Apr	69	41	110	105	+5
May	60	44	104	100	+4
Jun	55	45	100	110	–10

Hence, the maximum loss due to share value changes is 10 for the month of Jun. Hence the answer is (d).

40. b Again referring to the above table it can be seen that the individual's highest gain is Rs.10.

For questions 41 to 45:

Let the number of defective tests be 'x'

Cost to Prakash if he does not use any test = 50x

Cost to Prakash if he uses test 1

$$= 2 \times 1000 + \frac{4x}{5} \times 25 + \frac{x}{5} \times 50 = 2000 + 30x$$

Cost to Prakash if he uses test 2 = 3000 + 25x

Prakash should not test when

$$50x \le 2000 + 30x \quad 20x \le 2000 \quad x \le 100$$

Prakash should use test 1 when

$$50x > 3000 + 25x \ge 2000 + 30x$$

$$3000 + 25x \ge 2000 + 30x$$

$$5x \le 1000 \quad x \le 200$$

For $x \ge 200$ he can use test 2.

41. a Below 100, no test would be cheaper.

42. d If there are 120 widgets, he should go for test I as it is cheaper.

43. c It is clear from the table that if the number of defectives is between 200 & 400, he should go for Test II as it is cheaper.

44. a In case of 160 defectives he should use test I as it is cheaper.

45. a If there are 200 defective widgets in the lot, Prakash may use either Test I or Test II as the cost of both the Tests is same= Rs.8000.

For questions 46 to 50:

Students please note that the values on the Y-axis are not given. For the sake of convenience let us assume that one step on y-axis is 'x' and starting value be k.

Years	Food production	Fertilizer production
83	6.5 + k	2.5x + k
84	5 + k	3.5x + k
85	5 + k	3.5x + k
86	6.5 + k	2x + k
87	6.5 + k	2x + k
88	5 + k	3.5x + k
89	5 + k	x +
90	7x + k	x + k
91	7x + k	x+ k

46. d If you see, for each year from 1984 to 1988 sum of food and fertilizers = 8.5x + 2k

Hence, it is constant for 5 years.

47. d Fertilizers production in 1988 = 3.5x + k

Food production in 1988 = 5x + k

As per the given information

8.5x + 2 k = 170

Value of x and k cannot be determined.

48. b The graph of food production shows an alternate increase and decrease in every 1 to 2 years. Hence looking at the trend of the graph in 1990 and 1991, it can be expected that the graph will go down in 1992.

49. d It is clear that the graph for fertilizer production remains constant for two consecutive years. But it breaks this trend in 1989 as it has a value lower than its value in 1988.

50. d If the fertilizer production in 1989 had been the same as that in 1988, its value for 1989 would have been 3.5x + k.

Hence total fertilizer production according to our values would have been (2.5x + k + 3.5x + k + 3.5x + k + 2x + k + 2x + k + 3.5x + k + 3.5x + k + x + k + x + k) = 22.5x + 9k. As per the given information 22.5x + k = 490

Value of x and k cannot be determined.

For questions 51 to 54:

The given graph can be represented in the following table:

Company	Sales (1)	Expend. (2)	Profit (3)=(1)–(2)	Equity (4)	Pro/Equ (3)/(4)	Sal/Equ (1)/(4)	Sal/Exp (1)/(2)	Growth Rate Sales
1990	80	76	4	8	0.5	10	1.05	-
1991	92	88	4	8	0.5	**11.5**	**1.04**	15%
1992	106	100	6	22	0.27	4.82	1.06	15.21%
1993	128	114	14	22	**0.64**	5.82	1.12	**20.75%**

51. c It is clear that the profit per rupee of equity is highest for 1993 viz. 0.64.

52. c The simple annual growth rate in sales is maximum for the year 1992-93 viz. 20.75%.

53. b Sales per rupee of the expenditure is lowest for the year 1991 viz. 1.04.

54. b Sales per rupee of equity is highest for 1991 viz. 11.5

For questions 55 to 58:

Let the profits of CAT and DAT be x, Sales of CAT and BAT be y and sales of ANT be z. So we have

COMPANY	SALES	EXPENDITURE	PROFIT
ANT	z	0.9z	0.1z
BAT	y	0.8y	0.2y
CAT	y	5x	x
DAT	3x	2x	x

Now, it is said that the total expenses of CAT were Rs.10 lakhs. Thus, 5x = Rs.10 lakhs or x = Rs.2 lakhs. Also, total expenses of ANT were 10% less than those of CAT = Rs.9 lakhs. Hence, 0.9z = 9 lakhs or z = 10 lakhs. Finally, in case of CAT, since Sales – Expenditure = Profit, Sales = Expenditure + Profit = 6x = 12 lakhs, y = 12 lakhs.

Our final table will become:

COMPANY	SALES	EXPENDITURE	PROFIT
ANT	10	9	1
BAT	12	9.6	2.4
CAT	12	10	2
DAT	6	4	2

(All values in lakh Rupees)

55. d Company with the lowest sales is DAT with a sales of Rs.6 lakhs.

56. c CAT had highest total expenses i.e. Rs.10 lakhs.

57. a ANT had lowest profits i.e. Rs.1 lakh.

58. b BAT had the highest profits i.e. Rs.2.4 lakhs.

For questions 59 to 62:

The given graph can be represented in the following manner:

Years	Net Fixed Assets (NFA)	Net Current Assets (NCA)	Investments	Total Assets (TA)
1990	7	13	2	22
1991	8	16	1	25
1992	7.5	15	2	25
1993	9	17	4	30

59. b The growth rate of total assets between 1990-93 = $\frac{(30-22)}{22}$ = 36%. But this is for a 3 year period.

Hence, simple average annual growth rate $= \frac{36}{3} = 12\%$.

60. c It can be seen that the growth rate is lowest for investments in 1990-91 viz. 50% decrease.

61. c Between 1991 and 1992, the highest growth rate was seen for investments viz. 100% increase.

62. d It can be seen that every individual item has shown a decrease in some year or the other. Only Total Assets has not followed this trend.

For questions 63 to 71:

Since 40% of the students were females, i.e., 32 students. Total number of students was 80 and total number of male students was 48. Since half of the students were either excellent or good, (number of average students) = (number of good students + number of excellent students) = 40, number of excellent students = 40 – 30 = 10.

As 1/3rd of male students were average, total number of male students that were average = $\left(\frac{1}{3} \times 48\right)$ = 16 and hence, total number of male students that were good = (48 – 16 – 10) = 22.

Based on the above revelations, the following table can be drawn:

	Performance			Total
	Average	Good	Excellent	
Male	16	22	10	48
Female	24	8	0	32
Total	40	30	10	80

63. a Number of students who were both female and excellent = 0.

64. c Number of students who were both male and good = 22.

65. d Ratio of male to female among average students = 16 : 24 = 2 : 3.

66. b Proportion of female students who were good $= \left(\frac{8}{32}\right) = 0.25$.

67. b Proportion of good students who are male $= \left(\frac{22}{30}\right) = 0.73$.

68. b Thus, we can see that Solid Fuels and Petroleum together constitute more than 60% of total energy in both World and Asia for the given period.

69. a As seen from the above table, Petroleum is the fuel whose proportion in the total energy demand increases during 1990-2000 and decreases during 2000-2010 for both World and Asia.

70. d In case of Asia, for the given answer choices, we can make the following table:

		1990	2000	2010
Total Energy		10	20	33
Natural Gas	Value	0.5	2.5	5
	Proportion	5%	12.50%	15.15%
Solid Fuels	Value	4	5	10
	Proportion	40%	25%	30.30%
Nuclear	Value	0.5	1	1.3
	Proportion	5%	5%	3.90%
Hydropower	Value	1	1.5	2
	Proportion	10%	7.50%	6.06%

Hence, we can see that the proportion of Hydropower goes on decreasing over the period.

71. d In case of the World, for the answer choices, we can make the following table.

		1990	2000	2010
Total Energy		150	200	250
Natural Gas	Value	30	40	50
	Proportion	20%	20%	20%
Solid Fuels	Value	50	60	75
	Proportion	33.30%	30%	30%
Nuclear	Value	10	20	25
	Proportion	6.66%	10%	10%
Hydropower	Value	10	10	20
	Proportion	6.66%	5%	8%

Hence, we can see that the proportion of Nuclear gas in total energy demand of the World remains constant over the given period and its proportion will increase in the total energy demand in Asia.

(Use information of the question number 70.)

For question 72 to 74 :

Let us assume that Alphonso's total property was of Rs.x.

Person on death bed	Property given to his relatives					Total Share
	Widow	Mother	Ben	Carl	Dave	
Aplhonso	x/2	-	x/6	x/6	x/6	x
Ben	x/12	-	-	x/24	x/24	x/6
Carl	5x/48	-	-	-	5x/48	5x/24
Dave	15x/96	15x/96	-	-	-	15x/48

72. d Since Alphonso's wife is also the mother of Dave, the total share of this lady would be $\left(\frac{x}{2} + \frac{15x}{96}\right) = \frac{63x}{96}$. And since, $\frac{63x}{96}$ = 1,575000

$\Rightarrow$ x = Rs.24 lakhs.

73. a Carl's original share was $\frac{x}{6} = \frac{24}{6}$ = Rs.4 lakhs.

74. b The ratio's of the property owned by the widows of the 3 sons = $\left(\frac{1}{12} : \frac{5}{48} : \frac{15}{96}\right)$ = 8 : 10 : 15.

75. c

Option	Description	Solubility
(a)	Potassium Chlorate at 80^0	0.4
(b)	Potassium Chloride at 35^0 C	0.4
(c)	Potassium Nitrate at 39^0 C	**0.48**
(d)	Sodium Chloride at 85^0 C	0.4

Hence (c) is the correct answer.

76. c At 30°C, solubility of potassium nitrate is 0.38 kg./lt. Hence in 10 litres 3.8 kg.($\approx$4 kg) of potassium nitrate can be dissolved.

77. d Percentage increase in solubility of potassium chlorate = $\frac{(0.4 - 0.1) \times 100}{0.1}$ = 300%.

78. d Solubility of potassium chloride at 36°C = 0.4 kg./lt. Hence the amount of Potassium chloride that can be dissolved in 100 lt. at 36°C = 40 kg.

Number of moles = $\frac{40}{0.07456} \approx \frac{40}{0.075} = 533$.

As we have approximated 0.07456 as 0.075 and 540 is closest to 533, it should be correct answer.

79. c From the graph it can be seen that between 15°C &25°C, solubility of sodium nitrate, potassium chloride, sodium chloride, is almost constant. It can clearly seen from graph that solubility of sodium chlorate is maximum.

For questions 80 to 83:

From the data that is given we can find the following data: (the explanation of how the following values were arrived, is given after the table).

Item	1984-85	1985-86
Food (Percentage)	22%	23%
Food (Value)	4928	5934
Manufactured Articles	11648	11352
Raw Material	5824	8514
Total Value of Exports in Crore of Rs.	22400	25800

80. d Food related exports in 1985-86 = 0.23 x 25800 = 5934.

So food related exports in 1984-95 = (5934 – 1006) = 4928.

Hence, percentage of food related exports in 1984 – 85 = $\frac{4928}{22400} \times 100$ = 22%.

81. b In 1984-85, Value of Manufactured articles & Raw materials exports = (22400 – 4928) = Rs.17472 crores.

Since Export of manufactured goods is twice that of raw materials, Rs.17472 has to be divided in the ratio 2:1.

Therefore, export of manufactured goods = Rs.11648 crores and Raw materials = Rs.5824 crores.

Hence, the difference between raw material and food = (5824 – 4928) = Rs.896 crores.

82. d In 1985-86, the combined percentage of Manufactured articles and Raw materials = 77% and this is in the ratio 4 : 3.

Hence, percentage of Manufactured articles export is 44% and that of Raw materials export is 33%.

Hence, value of manufactured = 0.44 × 25800 = Rs.11352 crores

and the value of Raw materials = Rs.8514 crores.

Hence, percentage difference between the value of Raw materials between 1984-85 and 1985-86

$= \left[\frac{(8514 - 5824)}{8514}\right] \times 100 = 31.6\%.$

83. a The change in the value of exports from 1984-85 to 1985-86 = (11648 – 11352) = Rs.296 crores.

84. c The skin & muscular protein totally constitutes 33% of the total proteins. The total proteins itself is 15% of the total body weight. Hence the percentage of skin & muscular protein as a fraction of the total body weight = 33% of 15% = 5 %. = $\frac{1}{20}$.

Required fraction

= (8 + 25)% of 15% = $\left(\frac{1}{3}\right) \times \left(\frac{3}{20}\right) = \frac{1}{20}$.

85. a Required Ratio = 25 : 8 $\approx$ 3 : 1.

86. d We can determine only the percentage of skin protein in Ghosh Babu's total body weight. But there is no data given about the percentage of skin in Ghosh Babu's body. Hence the answer is (d).

87. a Proportion of material other than water & protein in Ghosh Babu's body is $\frac{15}{100} = \frac{3}{20}$.

88. c Required percentage growth

$$= \frac{(68718 - 42137) \times 100}{42137}.$$

Students please note that to calculate the exact value of this expression, we need calculator. Since, options given are not very close to each other so we can approximate values. And using approximations we get the value of required ratio $= \frac{(68600 - 42000) \times 100}{42000} = \frac{2650}{42} = 63\%.$

89. c

Books	1975	1980	Percentage growth
Primary	42137	68718	63%
Secondary	8820	20177	125%
Higher Secondary	65303	82175	26%
Graduate Level	25343	36697	45%

Hence, percentage growth is least for higher secondary books viz.26%.

90. b Again referring to the above table we can see that the percentage growth rate is maximum for secondary level books viz.125%.

91. d It can be seen from the given table that though primary level books have shown a consistent growth, it has declined in the year 1978. On the other hand even Secondary and Higher secondary level books have shown a consistent increase except for the year 1977 when it had declined. But the graduate level books have shown a consistent growth over the period.

For questions 92 to 95:

The data given the graph can be tabulated as given below :

College	1988-89	1989-90	1990-91
Private Engg. College	120	180	250
Govt. Engg. College	80	130	130
Regional Engg. College	40	70	100
IIT	30	40	80

92. d Total number of students in 1989–90

$= (180 + 130 + 70 + 40) \times 100 = 42000.$

93. c Growth rate in number of students in Govt. Engg.

College $= \frac{(120 - 80)}{80} = 50\%$

Growth rate in number of students in Private Engg.

College $= \frac{(180 - 120)}{120} = 50\%$. Hence the growth rate is equal.

94. d Total number of students in 1990–91

$= (250 + 130 + 100 + 80)\ 100 = 56000$

Hence the total number of students in 1991-92 $= 0.9 \times 56000 = 50400.$

Hence (d) is the correct answer

95. c Percentage of IIT students in 1990 – 91

$$= \frac{80}{560} = \frac{1}{7} = 14.28\%$$

For questions 96 to 99:

The data given in the question can be computed as :

96. b From the first week data we can arrive at the following work pattern of Bankatlal for the 1st month.

First Month :

	1st week	2nd week	3rd week	4th week
Hours of rest	2	5	2	7
Working hrs.	5	2	5	3
Wage per hour	Rs.20	Rs.10	Rs.20	Rs.10
Total Wage per day	Rs.100	Rs.20	Rs.100	Rs.20
Total Wage per w eek	Rs.600	Rs.120	Rs.600	Rs.120

Thus his total wage = (600+120+600+120) = Rs.1440

97. c Let us compile the data for 2nd, 3rd and 4th month.

Second Month :

	5th week	6th week	7th week	8th week
Hours of rest	3	7	3	7
Working hrs.	7	3	7	3
Wage per hour	Rs.20	Rs.10	Rs.20	Rs.10
Total Wage per day	Rs.140	Rs.30	Rs.140	Rs.30
Total Wage per w eek	Rs.840	Rs.180	Rs.840	Rs.180

Third Month :

	9th week	10th week	11th week	12th week
Hours of rest	4	6	4	6
Working hrs.	6	4	6	4
Wage per hour	Rs.20	Rs.10	Rs.20	Rs.10
Total Wage per day	Rs.120	Rs.40	Rs.120	Rs.40
Total Wage per w eek	Rs.720	Rs.240	Rs.720	Rs.240

Fourth Month :

	13th week	14th week	15th week	16th week
Hours of rest	0	8	0	8
Working hrs.	8	0	8	0
Wage per hour	Rs.20	Rs.10	Rs.20	Rs.10
Total Wage per day	Rs.160	0	Rs.160	0
Total Wage per week	Rs.960	0	Rs.960	0

Total wage for 1st month = Rs.1440

Total wage for 2nd month = (840 +180 +840 +180) = Rs.2040

Total wage for 3rd month = (720 + 240 + 720 + 240) = Rs.1920

Total wage for 4th month = (960+960) = Rs.1920

Total wage for the 4 months = (1440+2040+1920+1920) = 7320

Hence the average salary = $\frac{7320}{4}$ = Rs.1830.

98. d Using the above data, we can revise the wage compilation for the third month as given below:

Third Month :

	9th week	10th week	11th week	12th week
Hours of rest	4	6	4	6
Working hrs.	6	4	6	4
Wage per hour or work	Rs.25	Rs.12.5	Rs.25	Rs.12.5
Fine per hour of rest	Rs.5	Rs.5	Rs.5	Rs.5
Total wage per day	Rs.150	Rs.50	Rs.150	Rs.50
Total fine per day	Rs.20	Rs.30	Rs.20	Rs.30
Effective wage per day	Rs.130	Rs.20	Rs.130	Rs.20
Total Wage per week	Rs.780	Rs.120	Rs.780	Rs.120

So now his third month age = (780+120+780+120) = Rs.1800.

Previously he used to earn Rs.1920 in the third month.

Hence change in Bankatlal's salary for the 3rd month = (1920 – 1800) = Rs.120.

99. d For the fourth month, the new wage compilation will be as given below :

Fourth Month :

	9th week	10th week	11th week	12th week
Hours of rest	0	8	0	8
Working hrs.	8	0	8	0
Wage per hour or work	Rs.25	Rs.12.5	Rs.25	Rs.12.5
Fine per hour of rest	Rs.5	Rs.5	Rs.5	Rs.5
Total wage per day	Rs.400	0	Rs.400	0
Total fine per day	0	Rs.40	0	Rs.40
Effective wage per day	Rs.400	-Rs.40	Rs.400	-Rs.40
Total Wage per week	Rs.2400	-Rs.240	Rs.2400	-Rs.240

So now his total wage for the 4th month = (2400 + 2400 – 240 – 240) = Rs.4320.

Since the calculations for the first two months are made as per the old scheme of things, this has already been computed.

Total wage for 1st month = Rs.1440

Total wage for 2nd month = Rs.2040

Calculation for the third and fourth month are as per new calculations and they are :

Total wage for 3rd month = Rs.1800

Total wage for 4th month = Rs.4320

Therefore, total salary for the four months = (1440 + 2040 + 1800 + 4320) = Rs.9600.

100. d We know, Dividends + Retained earnings = Profit before tax – Tax.

Tax = Profit before tax – (Dividends + Retained earnings).

Figure (In Rs. Lakh)	1991	1992	1993	1994
Profit before Tax	315	170	525	790
Dividends + Retained earnings	170	100	305	510
Tax	145	70	220	280
Tax per rupee of 'Profit before tax'	0.46	0.41	0.42	0.35

Hence, tax per rupee of 'Profit before Tax' was the lowest in 1994.

101. a

Figure (in Rs. Lakh)	1991	1992	1993	1994
Sales	3270	2620	4725	6435
Share Capital	98	98	205	310
Sales per rupee of share capital	33.36	26.73	23.04	20.75

Hence, sales per rupee of share capital was the highest in 1991.

102. d

Figure (in Rs. Lakh)	1991	1992	1993	1994
Profit before Tax	315	170	525	790
Sales	3270	2620	4725	6435
Profit before tax per rupee of sales	0.09	0.06	0.11	0.12

Hence, profit before tax per rupee of sales was the highest in 1994.

103. a

Figure (in Rs. Lakh)	1991	1992	1993	1994
Reserves	80	220	290	535
Retained earnings	140	70	245	400
Percentage addition to reserves	175%	31.81%	84.48%	74.76%

Hence, the highest percentage addition to reserves was in 1991.

104. a From the above table, it is clear that the amount of reserves at the end of 1994

= (535 + 400) = Rs.935 lakh.

105. b It can be seen that the market share of CO in Kolkata has halved in 1994. None of the other products show such a drastic decrease in any city. Hence, percentage decrease in market share = 50%.

106. b Mumbai and Kolkata have two products whose market shares were increased. Chennai has 1 while Delhi has none.

107. d We can see that among the given options, the market share of HD decreased in Mumbai, Kolkata and Delhi. The market share of CO decreased in Kolkata, Delhi and Chennai and the market share of BN decreased in Mumbai.

108. a None of the products had 100% market share.

109. b Only MT doubled its market share in Kolkata in 1993-94.

110. a Percentage increase = $(160-130)\frac{100}{130}$

$=\frac{300}{13} = 23\%$.

111. b Interest in 1990-91 = 30% of 130 = Rs.39 lakh

Interest in 1991-92 = 40% of 160 = Rs.64 lakh

Hence, required difference = (64 – 39)

= Rs.25 lakh

112. d Total interest = (30% of 130) + (40% of 160)

= (39 + 64) = Rs.103 lakh.

If this total interest is charged on borrowed funds, then (20% of borrowed funds) = 103. Hence, borrowed funds = (5 × 103) = Rs.515 lakh.

113. d Retained profit in 1990-91 = (25% of 130)

= Rs.32.5 lakh

Retained profit in 1991-92 = (20% of 160)

= Rs.32 lakh

Hence, percentage change in retained profit

$=\frac{(32.5-32)}{32.5} = 1.5\%$ lower.

114. c Total dividend earned by shareholders in 1991-92

= (8% of 160) = Rs.12.8 lakh.

For questions 115 to 119:

The graph given in the question can be expressed as a table given below.

Year	Import	Export	Trade Deficit
1987-88	17	11	6
1988-89	19	12	7
1989-90	21	16	5
1990-91	24	18	6
1991-92	20	18	2
1992-93	22	18	4
1993-94	23	21	2
1994-95	27	24	3
	173	138	

115. b Trade deficit = Imports – Exports, was the highest for the year 1988-89, viz. 7 billion dollars.

116. d Trade deficit is less than that in the succeeding year in 1987-88, 1989-90, 1991-92 and 1993-94.

117. c Required percentage = $\frac{18}{20}\times 100 = 90\%$

118. d In the last three years,

Imports = (22 + 23 + 27) = 72

and Exports = (18 + 21 + 24) = 63.

Hence, the required percentage = $\frac{63}{72}\times 100$ = 87.5% = 88% (approximately).

119. a The first statement is obviously true as the trade deficit in each year is less than the export earning. The export earning has remained constant for three years between 1990 and 1993. Hence, statement II is not true. Even statement III is not true as the exports in 1994-95 is more than the imports in 1993-94.

For questions 120 to 125:

The graph given in the question can be depicted in the following table:

	1989	1990	1991	1992
Journals	46	47	45	44
Magazines	31	39	45	50
Books	73	77	79	79
Total	150	163	169	173

120. c The highest change in the revenue obtained from journals is (47 – 45) = 2 in 1991.

121. a In 1992, percentage of total revenue that came from books = $\frac{79}{173} \times 100 = 45.6\% = 45\%$ (approximately).

122. b In 1990, there was an increase in revenue for all the 3 categories. In 1991, it increased for magazines and books.

And in 1992, it increased only for magazines. So the answer is b, viz. 2 years.

123. d Growth rate in 1992 over 1991 = $\frac{(173-169)}{169}$ = 2.36%. If this rate remained same in 1993 as well, then the revenue in 1993 would be $173 \times \left(1 + \frac{2.36}{100}\right)$ = Rs. 177 lakh.

124. c Percentage growth in the total revenue from 1989 to 1992

$= \frac{(173-150)}{150} = 15.33\% = 15\%$ (approximately).

125. b Since time taken to manufacture Q by both the machines is the least, we have to manufacture only Q in order to maximize the output for the day. In such a case, total number of units of Q produced by M1 = $\frac{(8 \times 60)}{6}$ = 80 units and that by M2 $= \frac{(8 \times 60)}{6}$ = 80 units. So the maximum number of units that can be produced in one day

= (80 + 80) = 160 units.

126. d If M1 works at half of its normal efficiency, time taken by M1 to manufacture 1 unit of P = 20 min and Q = 12 min. For producing maximum number of units, we have to produce Q on M2 first as it takes only 6 min per piece. Also since at least one unit of P has to be manufactured and it is more efficient to do so on M2, we would do that. So time taken to manufacture 1 unit of P on M2 = 8 min. Hence, time remaining on M2 = (480 – 8) = 472. In this remaining time number of units of Q that can be manufactured on M2 = $\frac{472}{6}$ = 78 (only completed units taken). Now since it takes less time to manufacture Q on M1 as well, we will maximize Q on M1. Since 1 unit of number of units that can be produced $= \frac{(8 \times 60)}{12}$ = 40. Hence, the total number of units manufactured = (1 + 78 + 40) = 119 units.

127. a In order to minimize time required, we will manufacture P on M2 and Q on M1. Number of machine hours required to manufacture 30 units of P on M2 = (30 × 8) = 240 min = 4 hr. Number of machine hours required to manufacture 25 units of Q on M1 = (25 × 6) = 150 min = 2.5 hr. So total time taken = (4 + 2.5) = 6.5 hr or 6 hr 30 min.

128. a Since P has to be produced in more number than Q and since time taken to produce P is least on M2, to maximize the output utilize the entire time available on M2 for producing P. Number of units of P produced in this time = $\frac{(8 \times 60)}{8}$ = 60 units. Now since the number of units of Q should be one -third that of P, we should manufacture 20 units of Q. To manufacture this on M1, it would take (20 × 6) = 120 min. So there are still (480 – 120) = 360 min of M1 to be utilized. Now for every 3 units of P that is manufactured, we have to manufacture 1 unit of Q. To run one such cycle on M1, it would take (3 × 10 + 1 × 6) = 36 min. Hence in 360 min, we have 10 such cycles and utilize all the idle time of M1. Hence, to maximize the output under the given condition it is possible to have no idle time on any of the machines.

129. c The least efficient way is the option that gives least production with highest idle time. So we can compare the options in the following two ways. Assume that production is constant (viz. LCM of 48, 64, 53 and 71) in all 4 options and compare the corresponding idle time. Or we can assume the idle time to be constant (viz. LCM of 3, 12, 10 and 9) in all 4 options and compare the corresponding production. The latter method is more preferable as finding LCM of idle time is easier. So LCM of 3, 12, 10, 9 = 180. If we assume that the idle time has to be 180 min, then as per option (a) we would get production $=\left(\frac{180}{3}\times 48\right)=2{,}880$ units, as per option (b), we would get production $=\left(\frac{180}{12}\times 64\right)$ = 960 units, as per option (c), production $=\left(\frac{180}{10}\times 53\right)$ = 954 units and as per option (d), production $=\left(\frac{180}{9}\times 71\right)$ = 1,420 units. Since option (c) gives the least production, it is the least efficient way.

130. a Total requirement of cloth
= Total number of shirts × Cloth required per shirt
= (20 + 30 + 30 + 10 + 10) × 1000 × 1.5 = 1,50,000 m.

131. b Total low quality cloth consumed
= 1.5 (30% of 30000 + 30% of 30000 + 40% of 10000 + 90% of 10000)
= 46,500 m.

132. c Total quantity of high quality cloth consumed by A-type shirts = (80% of 20000) × 1.5 = 24,000 m.

133. d We only know the relationship between the type of shirt and cloth used and type of shirt and dye used. We cannot find any relationship between type of cloth and dye used.

134. b Amount of low quality die used for C-type shirts
= (40% of 30000)
= 12,000 units.
Amount of low quality die used for D-type shirts
= (60% of 10000)
= 6,000 units.
Hence, required ratio $=\left(\frac{12000}{6000}\right)$ = 2 : 1.

135. c Amount invested on B, C, D and E in year 1
= 4.6 + 5.8 + 3.11 + 10.6 = 24.11
Amount invested on B, C, D and E in year 3
= 18.7 + 21.2 + 7.7 + 29.8 = 77.4
∴ Percentage increase
$$=\frac{77.4-24.11}{24.11}\times 100\approx 221\%$$

136. b Company E's investment for years 1 to 3
= 10.6 + 17.4 + 29.8 = 57.8
Company F's investment for years 1 to 3
= 7.8 + 25.3 + 60.1 = 93.2
∴ Ratio = 57 : 93 = 19 : 31

137. c Total investment in year 2
= 6.7 + 7.5 + 12.5 + 5.6 + 17.4 + 25.3 = 75
D's contribution in year 2 = 5.6
∴ Percentage contribution $=\frac{5.6}{75}=7.4\%$

138. d As we can see from the table, none of the investments increases from year 1 to 3.
Hence, none of these.

139. b In year 2,
A + B + C = 6.7 + 7.5 + 12.5 = 26.7
D + E + F = 5.6 + 17.4 + 25.3 = 48.3
Percentage difference
$$=\frac{48.3-26.7}{26.7}=80.8\%\approx 81\%$$

For questions 140 to 144:

To handle this type of questions, the best way is to express the data in tabular form.

Year	1989	1990	1991	1992	1993	1994	1995
Revenue	120	130	145	165	185	200	220
Expenditure	102	110	115	125	135	140	150
Profit	20	25	30	40	50	60	70

140. b The average revenue collected in the given 7 years
$$=\frac{(120+130+145+165+185+200+220)}{7}$$
= 166.42
which is approximately is Rs. 168 lakh.

141. a Expenses of 7 years add up to 877. Revenue of 7 years add up to 1165.
Hence, the required answer is $\frac{877}{1165}\approx\frac{880}{1170}$
≈ 75%.

142. d We need to find the profit in each year.

Year	Profit percentage
1990	(5/20) × 100 = 25%
1991	(5/25) × 100 = 20%
1992	(10/30) × 100 = 33.33%
1993	(10/40) × 100 = 25%
1994	(10/50) × 100 = 20%
1995	(10/60) × 100 = 16.66%

From the above table, clearly, the answer is 1992, as in 1992 the profit is maximum, i.e. 33.33%.

143. d The growth in expenditure over the previous year can be expressed as:

Year	Growth in expenditure
1990	(8/202) × 100 = 7.8%
1991	(5/110) × 100 = 4.5%
1992	(10/115) × 100 = 8.7%
1993	(10/125) × 100 = 8%
1994	(5/135) × 100 = 3.7%
1995	(10/140) × 100 = 7.14%

Hence, it is maximum for 1992.

144. b Profit in 1994 = 60. Profit in 1995 = 70. Growth percentage in profit in 1995 over 1994 = $\left(\frac{10}{60}\right) \times 100$ = 16.66%.

Profit in 1996 will be (16.66% of 70) + 70 = Rs. 82 lakh.

145. a Lipton production is 1.64 (in '000 tonnes) which corresponds to 64.8% capacity. Maximum capacity will be 100%. For 64.8% it is 1.64 .

∴ For 100% it will be

$$\left(\frac{100}{64.8}\right) \times 1.64 \approx \frac{100}{65} \times 1.64$$

$\approx$ 2.53 (in '000 tonnes).

146. d This can be represented in the following manner.

	Production ('000 tonnes)	Capacity utilisation (%)	Total capacity (100%)	Unutilised capacity
	A	sB	C = A/B ×100	C - A
Brooke Bond	2.97	76.50	3.88	0.912
Nestle	2.48	71.20	3.48	1.003
Lipton	1.64	64.80	2.53	0.89
MAC	1.54	59.35	2.59	1.05

Hence, we find that the maximum unutilised capacity is for MAC, viz. 1,050 tonnes.

147. c 61.3 % ≡ 11.6

$$\therefore 100\% \equiv \left(\frac{100}{61.3}\right) \times 11.6 \approx \left(\frac{100}{62}\right) \times 11.6 \approx 18.7$$

$\simeq$ 18.7 tonnes (in '000)

148. d From the data that is given, we cannot say anything about the price of coffee for the companies among others.

149. b Total sales of all brands

= (31.15 + 26.75 + 15.25 + 17.45) = Rs. 90.6 crore

Total sales value of others = 132.8 – 90.6 = Rs. 42.2 crore

$$\text{Required percentage} = \frac{42.2}{132.8} \times 100 \approx \frac{42}{132} \times 100$$

= 31.18 ≈ 32%.

150. b Originally for the fifth month, 4 people were scheduled to do coding. This would have cost them (10000 × 4) = Rs. 40,000. Now there are 5 people who are working on design in the fifth month.

The total cost for this would be (20000 × 5)

= Rs.1,00,000.

Hence, percentage change in the cost incurred in the fifth month = $\frac{(100000 - 40000)}{40000} \times 100 = 150\%$.

151. a As given in the previous question, it can be seen that the coding stage is now completed in 6th, 7th and 8th months. Number of people employed in the 6th month is 4 and in the 8th month is 5. In the 7th month also there are 5 people employed (from previous data). Hence, if we were to combine these months, we find that the total cost incurred in the coding stage = (5 + 5 + 4) × 10000 = Rs.1,40,000.

152. b The difference in the cost will arise only because of the following months: 5, 6 and 8. And we can compare the costs as given below

	Original scheme			New scheme		
Month	People	Cost per man/ month	Total cost for the month	People	Cost per man/ month	Total cost for the month
5	4	10000	40000	5	20000	1,00,000
6	5	10000	50000	4	10000	40,000
8	4	10000	40000	5	10000	50,000
		Total cost	Rs. 1,30,000		Total cost	Rs. 1,90,000

It can be clearly seen that the difference in the cost between the old and the new technique is Rs. 60,000.

153. d The cost incurred in various stages under the present scheme is as given below.

	Month	People	Cost per man/ month	Total cost for the month	Total cost for the stage
Specification	1	2	40000	80000	Rs. 2,00,000
	2	3	40000	120000	
Design	3	4	20000	80000	Rs. 2,40,000
	4	3	20000	60000	
	5	5	20000	100000	
Coding	6	4	10000	40000	Rs. 1,40,000
	7	5	10000	50000	
	8	5	10000	50000	
Testing	9	4	15000	60000	Rs. 75,000
	10	1	15000	15000	
Maintenance	11	3	10000	30000	Rs. 90,000
	12	3	10000	30000	
	13	1	10000	10000	
	14	1	10000	10000	
	15	1	10000	10000	

Hence, the most expensive stage is Design.

154. c If we look at the above table again, it is clear that the average cost for 5 consecutive month period is lowest for months 11 to 15.

155. d Total investment in the two districts in 1995

$$= 2932.1 + 7081.6 \approx 10,000.$$

Total investment in the two districts in 1996

$$= 3489.5 + 8352 \approx 11840.$$

$$\text{Required percentage} = \frac{(11840 - 10000)}{10000} \approx 18\ \%.$$

156. b Total investment in electricity and thermal energy in both the districts in 1995 = (815.2 + 632.4 + 2065.8 + 1232.7) = 4746.1. Total investment made in that year

$$= 2923.1 + 7081.6$$

$$= 10004.7 \approx 10000$$

$$\text{Hence, required percentage is } \frac{4746.1}{10,000} \approx 47\%.$$

157. b Percentage increase in investment in electricity $\approx \frac{300}{2070} = 14\%$. Percentage increase in investment in chemical $\approx \frac{(986.4 - 745.3)}{745.31} \times 100$

$$\approx \frac{240}{745} \approx 32\%.$$

Percentage increase in investment in solar

$$= \frac{428.6}{1792.1} \approx \frac{430}{1792} \approx 23\%$$

Percentage increase in investment in nuclear

$$= \frac{507.8}{1674.3} \approx \frac{500}{1670} \approx 29\%.$$

Clearly percentage increase in investment in chemical is the highest.

158. c Total investment in Chittoor = 2923.1 + 3489.5

$$= 6412.6 \approx 6410.$$

Total investment in Khammam = 7081.6 + 8352

$$\approx 15430.$$

$$\text{Required ratio} = \left(\frac{15430}{6410}\right) = 2.4.\ \text{times}.$$

159. a Percentage increase in the total investment in Khammam in 1996

$$= \left(\frac{(8352 - 7081.6)}{7081.6}\right) \times 100 \approx \frac{1270}{7080} \approx 18\%$$

Total investment in Khammam in 1997 will be $1.18 \times 8352 = 9855.36 \approx 9850$

160. a By observation gap between the Cost and the Sales is the highest in September. Thus, the highest profit is recorded in September.

161. d By observation difference between the Cost in March and May is the highest. Thus, in May total increase in Cost is the highest as compared to two months ago.

162. d By observation difference between the Cost in March and May is the highest. Also, the Sales in March is less as compared to the following months. Thus, in May percentage increase in sales two months before the highest.

163. d By observation increase in the number of employees from January to March is the less than the increase in profit from January to March. Thus, profit per employee is the highest in March.

164. b From January to November the number of employees that company takes = (16 – 11) × 1000 = 5000.

165. c

Year	Number of students employed	Number of students employed from finance	Number of students employed from marketing
1992	800	0.22 × 800 = 176	0.36 × 800 = 288
1993	640	0.17 × 650 = 110.5	0.48 × 650 = 312
1994	1100	0.23 × 1100 = 253	0.43 × 1100 =473
1995	1200	0.19 × 1200 = 228	0.37 × 1200 = 444
1996	1000	0.32 × 1000 = 320	0.32 × 1000 = 320
		1087.5	1837

∴ Difference in number of students employed from finance and marketing = 1837 – 1087.5 = 749.5 ≈ 750.

166. d Percentage increase in the average salary of finance

$$= \frac{9810 - 5450}{5450} \times 100 = 80\%$$

167. c Average annual rate at which the initial salary offered in software increases

$$= \frac{1}{4}\left[\frac{(8640 - 5290)}{5290} \times 100\right] = 15.83\% \approx 15.9\%$$

168. d As we don't have any information about the average monthly salary offered to 'Others', we cannot determine the answer.

169. b

Year	Number of candidates employed from finance	Number of candidates employed from software
1994	0.23 × 1100 = 253	0.21 × 110 = 231

Students seeking jobs in finance earned

= 253 × 7550 = Rs. 16,28,550

Difference in the amount earned

= 1910150 – 1628550

= Rs. 2.81 lakh per month

= Rs. 33.8 lakh per annum.

170. a

Company	Cost/Room
Lokhandwala	225/536 "225/535 = 0.42
Raheja	250/500 = 0.50
IHCL	275/600 = 0.45
ITC .	300/300 = 1

From the right hand side column, for Lokhandwala Group, cost per room is least.

171. c In previous question, we have found out for which group the cost per room is least. To answer the second question, we need to take the reciprocals of fractions in the first question. Naturally, the answer will be same, i.e. Lokhandwala Group.

172. c Two projects are completed in 1998, one is Mumbai Heights and the second is Royal Holidays.

The cost of project is 250 + 225 = 475 crore. *Cost incurred = 475 + 47.5 = 522.5. (Students please note the last step. Rather than doing 1.1 × 475, it is convenient to do 475 + 10% of 475, which is = 475 + 47.5)

173. a Four projects are completed in 1999. They are: (i) Majestic Holiday, (ii) Supremo Hotel, (iii) Windsor Manor and (iv) Leela Hotels. It is very much similar to previous situation.

The cost of project is 250 + 300 + 275 + 235 = 1060

Hence, the cost incurred = 1060 × $(1.1)^2$

= 1282.6 crore

174. b Students! read the question carefully. It says what is the cost of projects completed by 2000.

It will be addition of previous two answers + Cost incurred for the projects completed in 2000. Approximate cost of projects completed by 2000 is 1282.6 + 522.5 + (250 × $(1.1)^3$) ≈ 2140.

175. a

Year	Male population	Female population	Total	Per capita production
1990	34	36	70	5/70 = 0.071
1992	35	37	72	7/72 = 0.09
1994	39	37	76	7.6/76 = 0.1
1996	43	40	83	7/83 " 7/84 = 0.08

From the table, it is clear that in 1990, the per capita production of milk was least.

176. d We can prepare a similar kind of table that we prepared for previous question. This table prepared is for food grains.

Year	Total population	Per capita production
1992	72	20/72 = 0.27
1993	74	22/74 = 0.297
1994	76	25/76 " 25/75 = 0.33
1995	80	31/80 " 30/80 = 0.375

Hence, per capita production of foodgrains was maximum in 1995.

177. c Percentage increase in production of food

Year	Production of foodgrains	% increase = X	Production of milk	% increase = Y	X – Y
1992	20		7		
1993	22	2/20 = 10%	8	1/7 = 14.2%	-4.28%
1994	25	3/22 = 13.6%	7.5	–0.5/8 = –6.2%	19.8%
1995	31	6/25 = 24%	6.8	-0.7/7.5 = –9.3%	33.3%
1996	27	– 4/31 = – 12.9%	7	0.2/6.8 = 2.9%	15.8%

From the last table, it is clear that in 1995, the difference between percentage increase in production of foodgrains and percentage increase in production of milk was maximum.

178. c

Year	Per capita consumption of milk = A	Calories consumed = X(X = 320x A)	Per capita consumption of foodgrains = B	Calories consumed = Y(Y = 160 x B)	X + Y
1993	0.11	35.2	0.28	44.8	80
1994	0.1	32	0.33	52.8	84.8
1995	0.093	29.76	0.37	59.2	88.96
1996	0.08	25.6	0.33	52.8	78.4

From the last column of the table, it is clear that the per capita consumption of calories was highest in 1995.

179. c

Year	Production of milk = A	Availability of nutrient= 120A =X	Production of foodgrains = B	Availability of nutrient= 80B =Y	X +Y
1993	8	960	22	1760	2720
1994	7.5	900	25	2000	2900
1995	6.8	816	32	2560	3376
1996	7	840	27	2160	3060

Clearly, from the table, availability of nutrient is maximum in1995.

180. c

Year	Total population	Per capita consumption of nutrient
1993	74	2720/74 = 36.75
1994	76	2900/76 = 38.15
1995	80	3376/80 = 42.2
1996	83	3060/83 = 36.86

From the table, it is clear that the per capita consumption is maximum in 1995.

For questions 181 to 186:

The values in the graph can be represented in the table given below.

Here O.H. is overheads and Int. is interest, P/C is profit/cost.

Year	Raw Mat.	Wages	O.H.	Int.	Profit
1991	60	45	10	50	15
1992	50	55	20	55	25
1993	65	60	15	55	20
1994	75	65	25	50	-30
1995	80	65	20	50	15
Total	330	290	90	260	45

181. b We can see that the increase in raw material has been maximum in 1993, viz. 15 points increase.

182. c The change in the profit is maximum in 1993-94. In this year, there is a 50 points drop in the profits.

183. a It can be seen that the interest has remained more or less constant over the given period.

184. c

Year	Raw Mat.(RM)	O.H.	OH/RM x 100
1991	60	10	16.66%
1992	50	20	40%
1993	65	15	23.07%
1994	75	25	33.33%
1995	80	20	25%

Thus, it can be seen from the above table that the overheads as a percentage of raw material is maximum for 1992.

185. b The total profits over the period

$= (15 + 25 + 20 - 30 + 15) = 45$

Total costs = (330 + 290 + 90 + 260) = 970

Hence, profit/costs $= \frac{45}{970} = 4.6\% = 5\%$ (Approximately)

186. b If the interest component is not included in the cost, the data can be represented as follows.

Year	Cost	Profits	P/C x 100
1991	115	15	13.04%
1992	125	25	20%
1993	140	20	14.28%
1994	165	-30	-
1995	165	15	9.09%

Hence, we can see from the table that maximum profit per unit cost is in 1992.

187. a If the amount of tariff consumed by sector 1 is the same, then we can directly compare the tariffs to the two regions and get the answer.

	Tariff 1994-95	% change over 1991-92	Tariff 1991-92
Region 1	425	+15%	369.5
Region 2	472	+5%	449.5
Region 3	420	-4%	437.5
Region 4	415	+8%	384.25
Region 5	440	+10%	400
	2172		2040.75

Hence, we can see that as compared to 1991-92, the net tariff in 1994-95 increased by $\frac{(2172-2040)}{2040} = 6.5\%$

188. b

	Tariff 1994-95	% change over 1991-92	Tariff 1991-92
Sector 1	420	-4	437.5
Sector 2	448	+7	418.7
Sector 3	432	+6	407.5
Sector 4	456	+10	414.5
			1678.3

Hence, the average tariff for region 3 in 1991-92 is $\frac{1678.3}{4} = 419.5 = 420$ (Approximately)

189. a In 1994-95, the power consumed by various sectors out of 7875 megawatts can be given as follows.

Category	Percentage	Consumption in 94-95
Urban	25	1969
Domestic	20	1575
Industrial	40	3150
Rural	15	1181
		7875

Since there was a 10% decrease in domestic consumption of power in 1994-95, the domestic consumption in 1991-92 $= \left(\frac{1575}{0.9}\right) = 1750$ megawatts. But this constitutes 20% of total power consumed in 1991-92 and the rural consumption constitutes 15% of total power in 1991-92.

Hence, in 1991-92 the rural consumption

$= (1750 \times \frac{15}{20}) = 1312$ megawatts.

190. d We only know the tariff rates for the two years for various regions and sectors. But we do not know the category-wise break-up of tariffs, i.e. the rates for urban sector is not known. In the light of this, we cannot answer this question.

191. b Let us evaluate each of the above statements.

The average tariff in region 4

$= \frac{(415+423+441+451)}{4} = 432.5$ p/kwh

region 2 $= \frac{(472+468+478+470)}{4} = 472$ p/kwh

region 5 $= \frac{(440+427+439+446)}{4} = 438$ p/kwh

Hence, the average tariff in region 2 is higher than in region 5. This statement is true. Note that we cannot evaluate the third statement at all.

192. a In 1974, agricultural loans amounted to

= Rs. 34.54 million.

Loans from rural banks in 1974

$= (260 \times 98 \times 243)$

= Rs. 6.19 million.

Hence, total amount of loans

$= (34.54 + 6.19)$

= Rs. 40.73 million.

Hence, percentage of agricultural loans

$= \frac{34.54}{40.73} = 84.79\% = 85\%$ (Approximately)

193. b

Year	No. of rural banks	Average no. of loans	Total no. of loans
1970	90	28	2520
1971	115	39	4485
1972	130	52	6760
1974	260	98	25480
1975	318	121	38478
1980	605	288	174240
1981	665	312	207480
1983	840	380	319200

So the total number of loans up to 1980 $= (2520 + 4485 + 6760 + 25480 + 38478 + 174240) = 251963$

And the total number of rural loans in 1983 = 319200

Hence, $\frac{251963}{319200} = 78.93\%$

= 80% (Approximately).

194. d

Year	Total no. of loans	Increase
1970	2520	-
1971	4485	1965
1972	6760	2275
1974	25480	18720
1975	38478	12998
1980	174240	-
1981	207480	33240
1983	319200	-

Thus, we find that the maximum increase in the

number of loans for rural banks is in 1980-81.

Note: Students please note that we have not calculated the increase for 1970, 1980 and 1983 as their previous years' figure is not known.

195. b The value of agricultural loan in 1983 is Rs. 915.7 million. But this at consumer price index (CPI) = 149. So if we want this value at 1970 CPI, viz. 43, it would simply be

$$\frac{43 \times 915.7}{149} = 264.26.$$

196. c Students please note that what they are really asking is for which year the average number of loans is the least, and we can see in 1970.

197. b From 1970 to 1983, in 13 years the number of agricultural loans went up from 18,300 to 2,11,600, an increase of 1,93,300. So percentage increase in this $= \frac{193300}{18300} = 1057$. However, this growth is spread across 13 years. Hence, simple annual rate of increase $= \frac{1057}{13} = 81.3\% = 81$ (Approximately).

198. a The CPI in 1970 is 43. But it has to be taken as 105. Presently in 1983 and 1975, the CPI is 149 and 78 respectively. Hence, they should actually be taken as $\left(149 \times \frac{105}{43}\right) = 363.83$ and $\left(78 \times \frac{105}{43}\right) = 190.46$ respectively. Hence, their difference = (363.83 – 190.46) = 173.37 = 174 (Approximately).

199. b Total value of loans

= Rural bank loans + Agricultural loans.

Rural bank loan in 1980 = (605 × 288 × 567) = Rs. 98.79 million.

Total value of agricultural loan in 1980

= Rs.498.4 million.

Hence, total loans in 1980

= (98.79 + 498.4) = 597.19.

But this is at a CPI = 131

If it is to be calculated at 1983 CPI, viz. 149, then its value will be $597.19 \times \left(\frac{149}{131}\right)$ = Rs. 679.24 million

= Rs. 680 million (Approximately).

200. a For, if any one of them collects the maximum number of coins, the remaining three should collect the minimum number of coins. To have distinct, even, atleast 10 coins; they will have to collect 10, 12, 14 coins. So if the three of them collect (10 + 12 + 14) = 36 coins, the fourth one has to collect (100 – 36) = 64 coins which has to be the maximum by any one person.

201. c Since A has collected 54 coins out of 100, he should obviously be the person who collected the maximum number of coins. For the difference between him and the second highest person to be minimum, the second highest person should collect the maximum number of coins possible under the given conditions. And for this to happen, the remaining two should collect the minimum number of coins. So if the two of them collect 10 and 12 coins, i.e. 22 coins between themselves, the third person would have to collect (100 – 54 – 22) = 24 coins. Hence, the difference between him and the highest person should at least be (54 – 24) = 30.

202. d If A has collected 54 coins, the remaining three of them should collect (100 – 54) = 46 coins between themselves.

Let us assume that C has collected 10 coins. So B will collect (2 × 10) + 2 = 22. So A will collect (46 – 10 – 22) = 14 coins, which is a possible combination.

Let us now assume that C picks up 12 coins. So B should pick up (2 × 12) + 2 = 26. So A will have to collect (46 – 12 – 26) = 8 coins.

This combination is not possible. It can be concluded that C cannot pick up more than 10 coins and hence B has to pick up 22 coins to satisfy the given condition.

203. a If we were to take the highest quantity supplied from various states in different months, we will get the following table:

Month	Highest supply	Total	Total percentage
April	7	73	9.5%
May	12	13	92.3%
June	9741	18015	54.0%
July	71497	90247	79.2%
August	77675	97961	79.2%
September	56602	110514	51.2%
October	79591	92219	86.3%
November	41872	45413	92.2%
December	14822	16578	89.4%
January	10922	11438	95.4%
February	11183	11285	99.0%
March	683	769	88.8%

Hence, we find that the highest percentage of apples supplied by any state is 99% (J & K in February).

204. c If we were to add the quantity of apples supplied by various states, it can be found that HP supplied 2,31,028 tonnes, UP supplied 258 tonnes, and J & K supplied 2,62,735 tonnes. Thus, it was J & K that supplied the maximum number of apples.

205. c If J & K supplied the highest quantity of apples, it is obvious that it would supply the highest percentage of total apples supplied as well.

206. c It is given that in case demand is more than the supply, additional demand is met by taking the stock from the cold storage. So it can be figured out that in all those months when supply was greater than the demand, no stock would have been used from the cold storage. Looking at the table, we can find that during the period May to September, no stock was taken from the cold storage, and hence supply should have been greater than the demand.

207. b Total quantity of apples supplied to Delhi during the year was (231028 + 258 + 262735)

= 494021 tonnes = 494021000 kg

If one tree yields 40 kg of apple, then the number of trees required to yield 49,40,21,000 kg

$= \frac{494021000}{40}$ = 1,23,50,525 trees

= 12.5 million trees (approximately)

208. d If there are 250 trees per hectare, then area required to have 12350525 $= \frac{12350525}{250}$

= 49402 = 49450 (approximately)

209. b It can be seen from the graph that the southern region showed the highest growth in number of households in all the income categories for the period.

210. d We only know the total number of households for all four regions combined. Nowhere have they given the region-wise break-up of this value. In the light of this, the given question cannot be answered.

211. b It is very clear from the graph that the percentage increase in total number of households for the northern region for upper middle income category is 200%.

212. a As seen from the table, the average income of high-income group in 1987-88 is Rs. 75,000.

213. b The total income of high income category in 1987-88 is Rs. (5000 × 75000).

The total income of upper-middle class category in 1987-88 is Rs. (10000 × 50000).

Hence, the current ratio of their total incomes = 3 : 4 = 0.75

Since the number of households in each category were equally distributed in all regions, we can have the following table for high income category.

Region	Households in 1987-88	Percentage increase	Households in 1994-95
North	1250	240%	4250
South	1250	425%	6562.5
East	1250	175%	3437.5
West	1250	150%	3125
Total	5000		17375

The average household income for high-income category increased by 90%. Hence, average household income for this category in 1994-95

= (75000 × 1.9) = Rs. 1,42,500

Hence, the total income for high-income category in 1994-95 = (17375 × 142500) = Rs. 2,476 million

The same table can be drawn for upper-middle class category as follows:

Region	Households in 1987-88	Percentage increase	Households in 1994-95
North	2500	200%	7500
South	2500	340%	11000
East	2500	125%	5625
West	2500	140%	6000
Total	10000		30125

The average household income for upper-middle class category increased by 60%. Hence, the average household income for this category in 1994-95 = (50000 ×1.6) = Rs. 80,000

Hence, the total income for high-income category in 1994-95 = (30125 × 80000) = Rs. 2,410 million

Hence, the ratio of total income for these two categories in 1994-95 $= \frac{2476}{2410} = 1.02$.

Hence, percentage increase in ratio

$= \frac{(1.02 - 0.75)}{0.75} = 36\%$

214. a For northern region, we can draw the following table for 1987-88.

Category	Households in 1987-88	Average household income	Total income (Rs. in millions)
Middle income	10000	Rs. 30,000	300
Upper-middle	2500	Rs. 50,000	125
High income	1250	Rs. 75,000	93.75
Total	13750		518.75

Hence, the average income for northern region

$$= \frac{518.75}{13750} \times 10^6 = \text{Rs. } 37{,}727$$

215. b It is said that Gopal and Ram invested equal amounts initially. Let the amount paid by both of them to Krishna be 2x and 3x respectively. Gopal further invested Rs. 2 lakh. Hence, we can say (2x + 2) = 3x or x = 2 lakh. Hence, the initial amounts paid by Gopal and Ram to Krishna is 4 lakh and 6 lakh. So Gopal and Ram together put in (6 + 6) = 12 lakh initially (note that this includes Rs. 2 lakh put in by Gopal later). The total revenue generated is 25% of 12 lakh = 3 lakh.

The revenue from coconut and lemon trees are in the ratio 3 : 2. Hence, 3 lakh when divided in the ratio 3 : 2 gives Rs. 1,80,000 from coconut and Rs. 1,20,000 from lemons. And since each coconut costs Rs. 5, the total output of coconut would be $\left(\frac{180000}{5}\right) = 36000$

216. a Lemon and coconut trees were planted on equal areas of land, viz. 5 acres each. The value of lemon output per acre of land $= \left(\frac{120000}{5}\right) = 0.24$ lakh per acre.

217. a The total revenue of Rs. 3,00,000 was divided equally by Gopal and Ram.

Hence, the amount received by Gopal in 1997

$$= \frac{1}{2} \times 300000 = \text{Rs. } 1.5 \text{ lakh}$$

218. b The ratio of the number of trees of coconut and lemon was 5 : 1. Since the number of lemon trees is 100, the number of coconut trees is 500. So they totally obtained a revenue of Rs. 1,80,000 from 500 coconut trees.

Hence, the value per tree $= \left(\frac{180000}{500}\right) =$ Rs. 360.

219. d We have not been given the cost of one lemon. In the light of this fact, we cannot find the number of lemons produced and hence the required ratio cannot be determined.

220** .b* Profit = Revenue – Variable Cost – Fixed Cost = Revenue – (Variable Cost + Fixed Cost). If we consider (Fixed Cost + Variable cost) as total cost, then as long as the revenue is higher than the total cost, there is a profit. In case the revenue is less than the total cost there would be a loss. If we are to compile the data given in the question it would be as follows:

Production	Fixed cost (Rs.)	Variable cost (Rs.)	Total cost (Rs.)	Revenue (Rs.)	Profit /loss (Rs.)
9	70	126	196	180	–16
10	70	140	210	200	–10
12	70	168	238	240	+2
20	70	280	350	400	+50
30	70	420	490	600	+110
40	100	560	660	800	+140
50	100	700	800	1,000	+200

Thus, we can say that at a production of 12 units, there is a profit of Rs. 2. Above 12 units there is always a profit and below 12 units there is loss. Hence, to make sure there is no loss, one has to manufacture a minimum of 12 units.

* The answer is clearly not indeterminable, it should be 12 units, but among the options given the one closest to it is 10 units.

221. a It can be seen that at 20 units there is a profit of Rs. 50. Below this the profit will reduce.

Hence, to ensure that the profit is at least Rs. 50, then 20 units have to be manufactured.

222. b Let us verify for the given options.

Production	Fixed cost (Rs.)	Variable cost (Rs.)	Total cost (Rs.)	Revenue (Rs.)	Profit/loss (Rs.)	Profit/unit (Rs.)
25	70	350	420	500	+80	3.20
34	70	476	546	680	+134	3.94
35	100	490	590	700	+110	3.14
40	100	560	660	800	+140	3.50

Hence, we can see that to maximise profit per unit, we need to manufacture 34 units.

223. b Extending the above table for 45 units, we get

Production	Fixed cost (Rs.)	Variable cost (Rs.)	Total cost (Rs.)	Revenue (Rs.)	Profit/ loss (Rs.)	Profit/ unit (Rs.)
45	100	630	730	900	+170	3.77

Thus, it can be figured out that still he has to manufacture 34 units.

224. b Referring to the table in question 220, we can see that if the fixed cost increases by Rs. 40, the profit will reduce by Rs. 40.

Hence, we can see that at 10 units he will make a loss of Rs. 30 and at 20 units he will make a profit of Rs. 10.

Hence, the answer has to be between (b) and (c). Let us verify for them:

Production	Fixed cost (Rs.)	Variable cost (Rs.)	Total cost (Rs.)	Revenue (Rs.)	Profit/ loss (Rs.)
15	110	210	320	300	–20
19	110	266	376	380	+4

Thus, we see that to make sure there is no loss, he has to manufacture 19 units.

225. c The data can be represented in the following table.

	Plywood		Saw timber		Logs	
	Price	% increase	Price	% increase	Price	% increase
87	3	–	10	–	15	–
88	3	–	10	–	16	6.67%
89	4	33.33%	12	20%	18	12.5%
90	5	25%	10	–	15	–
91	4	–	13	30%	18	20%
92	6	50%	15	15.38%	19	5.55%
93	7	16.66%	19	27%	20	5.26%

Thus, we can see that the maximum increase is 50%.

226. b

	Price in 1987	Price in 1993	Percentage increase
Plywood	3	7	133.33%
Saw timber	10	19	90%
Logs	15	20	33.33%

Thus, we see that the maximum percentage increase over the period is shown by plywood.

227. b Since the price of saw timber is given in rupees per tonne and that of log is given in rupees per cubic metre, we cannot compare the two. Hence, using the given conversion, let us convert the price of saw timber in per cubic metre. The table will be as follows:

(**Note:** 1 tonne $= \frac{4}{3} = 1.33$ cubic m)

Year	Saw timber (Price in Rs./tonnes)	Saw timber (Price in Rs./cubic metres)	Logs price in (Rs./cubic metres)	Difference in price
1989	12	9	18	9
1990	10	7.50	15	7.50
1991	13	9.75	18	8.25
1992	15	11.25	19	7.75

Thus, we see that the difference is least in the year 1990.

228. d As in the previous table, we can draw a similar table for saw timber and logs.

(**Note**: One tonne of plywood $= \frac{10}{7}$ cubic m = 1.43 cubic m and one tonne of saw timber $= \frac{5}{4}$ cubic m = 1.25 cubic m.

Year	Saw timber (Price in Rs./ tonnes)	Saw timber (Price in Rs./cubic metres)	Plywood (Price in Rs./ tonnes)	Plywood (Price in Rs./cubic metres)	Difference in price
1989	12	9.60	4	2.80	6.80
1990	10	8.00	5	3.50	4.50
1991	13	10.40	4	2.80	7.60
1992	15	12.00	6	4.20	7.80

Hence, it can be seen that the difference is maximum for 1992.

229. d Note that one tonne $= \frac{4}{3}$ m^3 = 1.33 m^3, for both plywood and saw timber.

In 1993, price of logs = Rs. 20 per cubic metre.

Price of plywood $= \left(\frac{7}{1.33}\right)$ = Rs. 5.26 per cubic metre.

And price of saw timber $= \left(\frac{19}{1.33}\right)$ = 14.28 per cubic metre.

Now the sales volume of plywood, saw timber and logs are in the ratio 4 : 3 : 3. So the average realisation per cubic metre of sales is indeed the weighted average.

This is given as

$$\frac{[(4\times5.26)+(3\times14.28)+(3\times20)]}{(4+3+3)}$$

= Rs. 12.4

= Rs. 13 (Approximately)

230. c The only change would be the accounting for price increase. This is given as

$$\frac{(4\times5.26\times1.05)+(3\times14.28\times1.01)+(3\times20\times1.10)}{(4+3+3)}$$

= Rs. 13.15

For questions 231 to 233:

Place of worship	Number of flowers before offering	Number of flowers offered	Number of flowers left
1	(15/8)y	y	(7/8)y
2	(7/4) y	y	(3/4)y
3	(3/2) y	y	y/2
4	y	y	0

Starting from the fourth place of worship and moving backwards, we find that number of flowers before entering the first place of worship is $\frac{15}{8}$y.

231. c Hence, number of flowers before doubling = $\frac{15}{16}$y

(but this is equal to 30)

Hence, y = 32

232. c The minimum value of y so that $\frac{15}{16}$y is a whole number is 16.

Therefore, 16 is the minimum number of flowers that can be offered.

233. b For y = 16, the value of $\frac{15}{16}y = 15$.

Hence, the minimum number of flowers with which Roopa leaves home is 15.

For questions 234 to 236:

Game	Opening balance	Player's pick		Dealer's pick		Closing balance
		Debit (–)	Credit (+)	Debit (–)	Credit (+)	
1	0	0	8	16	0	-8
2	-8	0	10	0	10	12
3	12	0	6	6	0	12
4	12	0	8	16	0	4

234. a Hence, we see that the maximum gain is Rs. 12.

235. b Since the maximum negative that Ghosh Babu goes into is –8, he should begin with at least Rs. 8, so that he does not have to borrow any money at any point.

236. d From the above table it is evident that in four games, Ghosh Babu makes a profit of Rs. 4.

Hence, if the final amount left with Ghosh Babu is Rs. 100, the initial amount that he had would be Rs. 96.

237. c If the mixture is to be made 100 times as sweet as glucose, its sweetness should be 74. The ratio in which saccharin and sucrose be mixed to get the above level of sweetness is given by the following alligation table.

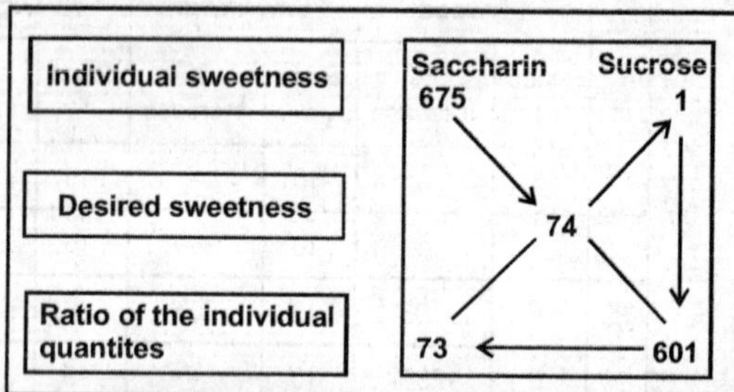

In other words, it means to achieve the given level of sweetness, you need to add 601 g of sucrose to 73 g of saccharin. Hence to 1 g of saccharin, the amount of sucrose to be added is $\frac{601}{73}$ = 8.23 g.

238. a $\frac{[(0.74)+(1.000)2+(1.7)3]}{6} = 1.31$.

239. a From the graph, we know the percentage growth in sales are:

	Previous sales	Current sales	Difference	Percentage
1995-96	100	250	150	150%
1996-97	250	300	50	20%
1997-98	300	290	-10	–3.33%
1998-99	290	680	390	134.5%

It is but obvious from the above table that the maximum percentage increase relative to previous year occurred in 1995-96.

240. d From the graph, we can again calculate the growth in profits.

	Previous profit	Current profit	Difference	Percentage
1995-96	2.5	4.5	2	80%
1996-97	4.5	6	1.5	33.33%
1997-98	6.0	8.5	2.5	41.66%
1998-99	8.5	12	3.5	41.2%

The highest percentage growth in net profit relative to the previous year was achieved in 1995-96.

241. b

	Net profit	Net sales	Ratio
1994-95	2.5	100	0.025
1995-96	4.5	250	0.02
1996-97	6	300	0.02
1997-98	8.5	290	0.03
1998-99	12	680	0.018

The profitability is maximum for 1997-98.

242. d It may be seen that profitability does not follow a fixed pattern as the first three statements try to generalize the profitability. They are not applicable.

243. c Total trade with a region is defined as: The sum of exports and imports from that region, from the pie charts for 1997-98, we have the following sectors occupying maximum area.

	Country	Exports	Imports	Trade
H	OPEC	3397.9	9379.2	12795.1
I	Asia	6796	5709	12505
G	East Europe	3397	7748	11145.9
C	EU	4757	4893.5	9650.5
A	USA	6456	3670	10126

H – OPEC has the maximum trade.

244. b From the pie chart, the region having lowest trade is K.

1% of imports + 1% of exports

∴ Indian exports are 1% of 3397.9 which is roughly 340 million USD.

245. a

	Imports to India	Exports from India	Trade deficit
A	3670.11	6456.01	–2785.9
B	2038.95	2038.74	0.21
C	4893.48	4757.06	136.42
D	2446.74	2038.74	408
E	2038.95	2038.74	0.21
F	815.58	1019.37	–203.79
G	7748.01	3397.9	4350.11
H	9379.17	3397.9	5981.27
I	5709.06	6795.8	–1086.74
J	1631.16	1698.95	–67.79

So, we see that region H has highest trade deficit of approximately \$6,000 million or \$6 billion.

246. a From the pie chart for 1997-98, we get that USA which is a region A has the lowest trade deficit.

(9% of imports – 19% of total exports)

$$\left(\frac{9}{100}\times 40779-\frac{19}{100}\times 33979\right)$$

= \$– 2785.9 million.

247. b From the pie chart, we know that the exports have increased from three regions A, G and H as follows.

	Country	1998-99	1997-98
A	USA	7395.4	6456
G	East European countries	3858.5	3397.9
H	OPEC	3215.4	3397.9

Also the exports for 8 months have been given. According to new directions, before question 247, we need to calculate exports for 12 months

$$\frac{21436\times 12}{8} = \$32{,}154 \text{ million.}$$

The maximum percentage increase is therefore from region A.

248. b India's total trade deficits are as follows.

	Imports	Exports	Deficit
1997-98	40779	33979	6800
1998-99	42189	32154	10035

Total imports for 1998-99

$$=\frac{28126\times 12}{8} = \$42{,}189 \text{ millions}$$

Similarly, exports for 1998-99 = $\frac{28126\times 12}{8}$

= \$32,154 millions

Percentage growth rate = $\frac{10035-6800}{6800}\times 100$

= 47.6%

249. a The price changes for each commodity are as follows.

	Ending	Beginning	Difference	Percentage
Arhar	2125	1700	425	25
Pepper	19275	18525	750	4
Sugar	1435	1440	5	–0.3
Gold	3820	4250	330	7.8

The highest price change from the graph and the above is definitely for Arhar.

250. c The price volatility for each individual.

	Highest price	Lowest price	Difference	Average price	PV
Arhar	2300	1500	800	1900	0.42
Pepper	19500	17350	2250	18425	0.12
Sugar	1500	1410	90	1455	0.062
Gold	4300	3800	480	4050	0.12

The price volatility for sugar is least, hence answer choice is (c).

Note: Average price can be calculated by highest price, lowest price, ending and beginning price.

251. d Let us assume Mr X invested Rs. 100 in each commodity.

	Price increase percentage	Income on Rs. 100
Arhar	25	25
Pepper	4	4.0
Sugar	–0.3	–0.3
Gold	–7.8	–7.8
		21.5

∴ His income is Rs. 21.5 on Rs. 400.

∴ $\frac{21.5}{400} \times 100 = 5.4\%$ profit

252. b As per the table in question 250, the maximum PV is around 40%.

253. c Bangladesh has highest drinking water facility and hence can not be dominated by any country.

Similarly Philippines has highest sanitation facilities and hence cannot be dominated.

254. b Statement A > Statement B only if statement A has higher percentage in total coverage for both drinking water and sanitation facilities taken independently and not as a total of the two facilities.

Thus, only statement B and statement D are

India > China

(81 > 67 and 29 > 24)

India > Nepal

(81 > 63 and 29 > 18)

Also China > Nepal (67 > 63 and 24 > 18)

255. c Let the urban population be x and rural population be y.

From the sanitation column, we have

$$0.7x + 0.14y = 0.29(x + y)$$

$$0.41x = 0.15y$$

$$\therefore \quad x = \frac{15}{41}y$$

∴ Percentage of rural population

$$= \frac{y}{x+y} \times 100 = \frac{y}{\frac{15}{41}y + y} \times 100$$

$$= \frac{41}{56} \times 100$$

$$= 73.2\%$$

256. a In the same way as the previous questions, we can find percentage of rural population for Philippines, Indonesia and China.

P	50%
I	66.66%
C	79.8%

Thus, P < I < C

257. d India is not on coverage frontier because

(i) it is below Bangladesh and Philippines for drinking water.

(ii) for sanitation facilities it is below Philippines, Sri Lanka, Indonesia and Pakistan.

For questions 258 and 259:

The disparity for the coverage of rural sector is as follows.

	Rural sector	**Urban sector**
I	65	15
B	52	20
C	49	23
P	47	5
P	20	4
I	22	6
S	–5	20
N	51	30

Note: Disparity = (Percentage denoting drinking facilities coverage – Percentage denoting sanitation coverage),

For example, rural sector of India = 79 – 14= 65%

Thus, as it can be seen from the table, in rural sector the country with most disparity is India (79 – 14) = 65%.

And the country with least disparity in urban sector is Philippines (92 – 88) = 4%

260. b Total exports = Software export + Hardware export + Peripherals export

Hence, total export as a percentage of IT business:

For 1994-95 $= \frac{668}{2041} \times 100 = 32.7\%$

For 1995-96 $= \frac{775}{2886} \times 100 = 26.8\%$

For 1996-97 $= \frac{1383}{3807} \times 100 = 36\%$

For 1997-98 $= \frac{1970}{5031} \times 100 = 39\%$

For 1998-99 $= \frac{2672}{6052} \times 100 = 44\%$

261. a Percentage growth for 1995-96 = 41%, 1996-97 = 32%, 1997-98 = 32%, 1998-99 = 20%.

262. c Annual hardware exports did not decline steadily during 1994-99.

Annual peripheral exports did not increase steadily during 1994-99.

IT business in training during 1994-99

= 107 + 143 + 185 + 263 + 302 = 1000

IT business in maintenance during 1994-99

= 142 + 172 + 182 + 221 + 236 = 953

Hence, option (c) is correct.

263. d Total IT business hardware activity

in 1995-96 = 1037 + 35 = 1072

in 1996-97 = 1050 + 286 = 1336

in 1997-98 = 1205 + 201 = 1406

in 1998-99 = 1026 + 4 = 1030

Clearly, 1998-99 does not dominate 1996-97.

264. d In this question, there are two activities — hardware and peripherals. Thus, for year X to dominate year Y, at least one activity in year X has to be greater than that in year Y and the other activity in year X has to be greater than or equal to that in year Y. In (a), (b) and (c), while hardware dominates in one year, the peripherals dominate in the other.

265. a If the total number of factories is 100, then the total number of employees = 60 × 100 = 6000 of which 64.6% = 3876 work in wholly private factories. Since the number of wholly private factories = 90.3,

the answer $= \frac{3876}{90.3} = 43.$

Short cut: $0.64 \times \frac{60}{0.903} < \left(\frac{2}{3}\right) \times 60 = 45.$

266. b Value added per employee $= \frac{\text{Value added}}{\text{Employment}}.$

267. b Compound productivity $= \frac{\text{Gross output}}{\text{Fixed capital}}.$

Hence, compound productivity for various sectors is: Public sector = 0.6, Central government = 0.725, States/Local = 0.47, Central and States or Local = 1.07, Joint sector = 1.23 and wholly private = 1.36.

Hence, the order should be: Wholly private, Joint, Central and State or Local Government, Central Government, Public sector and State or Local government.

268. c Calculate the ratios: Value added/employment and value added/fixed capital for the sectors mentioned in the choices. The respective values are:

Wholly private 0.9 and 1.25; Joint sector 1.59 and 1.19; Central/State/Local 1.8, 1.28; others 0.92 and 0.75.

269. d The number of factories in joint sector is 1.8% = 2700, thus, the number of factories in Central Government = 1% of (2700 x 100/1.8) = 1500.

Value added by Central Government = 14.1% of 1,40,000 crore = 19,740.

Hence, required average value added

$= \frac{19740}{1500}$ = Rs. 13.1 crore.

270. a Percentage change in FEI in 1998 relative to 1997 for various countries is:

For India $= \frac{(0.72-1.71)}{1.71} = -57.89\ \%$

For China $= \frac{(4.8-5.96)}{4.8} = -19.46\%$

For Malaysia $= \frac{(9.92-10.67)}{10.67} = -7.02\%$

For Thailand $= \frac{(5.282-5.09)}{5.2} = 14.34\%$

Hence, highest change (absolute) is for India.

271. d Since the absolute values are not given, it cannot be calculated.

272. d Assume GDP of India for 1997 to be x.

For 1998, India's FEI $= \frac{0.72 \times 102x}{100} = 0.7344x$

And foreign equity inflows for 1997 = 1.71x

For China, assume GDP as y. Then, FEI in 1998 $= \frac{107y}{100} \times 4.8 = 5.136y$. And FEI in 1997 = 5.96y.

For South Korea, let GDP be z.

FEI in 1998 $= \frac{95z}{100} \times 2.5 = 2.375z$ and FEI in 1997 = 2.16z.

FEI of India and China were lower in 1998 than in 1997, while that of South Korea was higher in 1998 than in 1997.

273. c Let x be the foreign equity inflow of India. Thus, China's foreign equity inflow is 10x.

Now in 1998, FEI in India was 0.72. Therefore,

$$0.72 = \frac{x}{\text{GDP of India}}$$

Similarly, FEI in China in 1998 was 4.8,

therefore, $4.8 = \frac{10x}{\text{GDP of China}}$

Hence, (GDP of China/GDP of India) = (10 × 0.72)/ 4.8 = 1.5.Thus, China's GDP is 50% higher than that of India.

274. a As from the table, the deficit intensity from 1993-94 to 1997-98 are 5.1, 6.3, 7.6, 8 and 5.

Therefore, the highest growth rate is $\frac{7.6-6.3}{6.3}$ = 23.5%, which is in 1994-95.

275. d The highest growth rate = $\frac{7.6-6.3}{6.3} \times 100 = 23.5\%$

276. b From the tables given,

Import of raw material = 10.1 × Sales (S) import of capital goods = 17.6 × Gross fixed assets (GFA)

Given imports = Raw materials + Capital goods

So import = 10.1 S + 17.6 GFA So imports = 14.2 S

Hence, 14.2 S = 10.1 S + 17.6 GFA

Hence, $\frac{S}{GFA} = \frac{17.6}{4.1} = 4.3$

277. d As the sales in different years are not given, the absolute value of exports and imports cannot be compared across years.

Deficit Intensity increases every year between 1993-94 and 1996-97.

278. c It is clear from the given graph.

279. d Let us first find out the growth in 1990 of the all four sectors. So manufacturing 9% of 20 = 1.8. Hence, 20 + 1.8

= 21.8. Similarly, for mining and quarrying it is 15.6.

For electrical, it is 10.85 and for chemical it is 16.1. Now in 1991 there is 1% negative growth in manufacturing. So 1% of 21.8 becomes 0.218. Thus, 21.8 – 0.218 = 21.582. Similarly, for mining and quarrying it is 15.44. For electrical it is 11.88 and for chemical it is 16.21.

Now we add the figures for 1991 of all the sectors which comes to 21.582 + 15.75 + 11.88 + 16.21 = 65.42. Now, 65.42 – 64.35 = 1.07, which comes to approximately 1.5% growth rate.

280. a It is clear from the graph that manufacturing is always growing in 1992 – 98. Hence, it will reach highest level in 1998.

281. b In 1990, there is 4% growth.

Hence, 4% of 15 = 0.6. So weightage in 1990 becomes 15.6.

Similarly, in 1991 it becomes 15.44, in 1992 it is 15.6, in 1993 it is 14.97, in 1994 it is 16.16.

Hence, it can be seen that the lowest level of production was in 1993.

282. a Find out the weightage for all the sectors for 1994. For manufacturing it is 25.54, for mining and quarrying it is 16, for electrical it comes out to be 14.5 and for chemical it is 19.5. The total comes to approximately 77. In 1989, it was 60. Hence, 77 – 60 = 17 which is approximately 25% increase.

283. b Since the index of total industrial production in 1994 is 50% more than in 1989, it becomes 150.

Now, total weightage for manufacturing, mining and quarrying, electrical and chemical in 1994 is approximately 77. So 150 – 77 = 73.

In 1989, it was 100 – 60 = 40.

So 73 – 40 = 33, which is approximately 87.5%.

284. c Cost in shift operation = 800 + 1200 = Rs. 2,000

Variable cost for 40 units = Rs. 3,600

Approximate average unit cost for July

$= \frac{3600+2000}{40} = \text{Rs. } 140$.

285. b The only change for change of production from 40 to 41 is the variable cost which is Rs. (3730 – 3600) = Rs. 130.

286. a As the graph is an increasing function graph, MC always increases with increase in the number of units produced.

287. c Total sales revenue = Rs. (150 × 40) = Rs. 6,000

Total production cost = Rs. (3600 + 2000) = Rs. 5600.

So profit = Rs. 400.

288. a Profit is the highest when there is no second shift.

289. a For production level in the range of 0 – 30 units, AC is always greater than Rs. 100 whereas MC is always less than or equal to Rs. 100.

290. d Count only those lays for which any size of yellow coloured fabric is produced.

They are lay number

1, 3, 4, 6, 7, 8, 9, 11, 12, 15, 21, 24, 25, 27

Hence, 14 is the answer.

291. b Count those lays for which extra-extra large fabric is produced of any colours, i.e. count the lay numbers for which at least one of XXL from 3 colours is non-zero.

They are lay number 7, 8, 9, 10, 11, 12, 13, 14, 15, 21, 22, 23, 24, 25, 26, 27 .

Hence, 16 is the answer.

292. d Again count lay number for which at least one of the XXL from yellow and white are non-zero.

Lay number 7, 8, 9, 10, 11, 12, 13, 14, 15, 21, 23, 24, 25, 26, 27.

Hence, 15 is the answer.

293. b The varieties for which there is surplus gives the answer. There are 4 such varieties.

294. b Put a decimal after the first two digit in the passengers column and it wil give the figure in millions.

In that case we have only 5 international airports of type A having more than 40 million passengers.

They are in serial number 1, 2, 3, 5, 9.

Rest all 'A' type airports are below 40 million.

295. a There are only six airports of USA among the top 10 busiest airports. They are in serial number 1, 2, 3, 5, 9, 10.

Hence, $\frac{6}{10} \times 100 = 60\%$.

296. c We have to calculate the percentage of passengers handled at Heathrow Airport.

Now total number of passengers in the 5 busiest airport is approximately

(77 + 72 + 63 + 62 + 60) million = 334 million

At Heathrow it is 62 million.

The approximate percentage is $\frac{60}{300} \times 100 \cong 20\%$

297. b All the international airports handle more than 30 million passengers. Among these only 6 airports are not located in USA. Hence, (b) is the correct option.

298. a Man-hours spent in coding is 420 + 100 = 520.

Now going by options, we see (a) is the only option.

299. c Total work is approximately

(100 + 80) + (420 + 100) + (280 + 140) = 1120

On-site work = 80 + 100 + 140 = 320

Percentage of total work carried out on-site is

$\frac{320}{1120} \times 100 = 30\%$ approximately.

300. c From figure the total effort In man-hours spent on-site is 320.

It is nearest to actual man-hours of offshore testing which is 280 (approximately.)

301. a Total man-hours

= (100 + 80) + (420 + 100) + (280 + 140) = 1120.

Total working hours = 100

Total man working $= \frac{1120}{100} = 11.2$ or 11.

For 50 hr the total man-hours is 50 × 11 = 550, which is near to coding (420 + 100)

Hence, (a) is the correct option.

302. b Initial offshore testing man-hours = 280.

Initial onshore testing man-hours = 140.

Final offshore testing man-hours

= 280 – 50% of 280 = 140

Final onshore testing man-hours = 140 + 140 = 280.

Hence, the proportion of testing offshore

$= \frac{140}{(140+280)} = 30\%$ approximately.

303. a

	Design	Coding	Testing
Initially	80	100	140
Finally	$80 + \frac{100}{2} = 130$	$100 + \frac{420}{2} = 310$	

$140 + \frac{294}{2} = 287$

304. b On interchanging the effort allocation between operations B and C, then C and D, and then D and E we find that B takes the E's position.

Looking at the effort in B and then ranking in ascending order we find that the company 3 ranks third.

305. a Total effort for operation B through F is 81.5%.

Even distribution will give effort allocation in each operation $= \frac{81.5}{5} = 16.3\%$

$\therefore$ Change in E = 28.6 – 16.3 = 12.3%

306. d Since we are given about company 1, 4, 5 in options so we will look for changes in these companies only.

Allocation of effort in B, C, D in companies 1 = 43.1

Remaining operations gets $\frac{43.1}{3} = 14.4\%$ each.

Allocation of effort in B, C, D operations of company 4 = 29.7

Remaining operation is allocated extra $\frac{29.7}{3} = 9.9\%$ each.

Allocation of effort in B, C, D operation of company 5 = 36.8

Remaining operation is allocated $\frac{36.8}{3} = 12.3\%$ each.

We see that operation E in company 5 will then show the maximum.

307. b Cost in rupees of oil moved by rail and road is 18% of 30 million = 5.4 million.

Volume of oil transported by rail and road

= 31% of 12 million tonnes

= 3.72 million tonnes.

Cost in rupees per tonnes $= \frac{5.4}{3.72} = 1.5$ approximately.

308. a From the chart, we can make out the least among road, rail, pipeline, ship by looking at the ratio of cost to volume.

Road = $\frac{6}{22}$

Rail = $\frac{12}{9}$

Pipeline = $\frac{65}{49}$

Ship = $\frac{10}{9}$

Since ratio of cost to volume for road is the lowest, it is the cheapest.

309. c Ship, air and road.

Like the previous answer again look at ratio of $\frac{10}{9}, \frac{7}{11}, \frac{6}{22}$

So $\frac{10}{9} > \frac{7}{11} > \frac{6}{22}$

Hence, P > Q > R.

310. b Total five lie between 10 E and 40 E.

Austria,	Bulgaria,	Libya,	Poland,	Zambia
N	N	N	N	S

$\frac{1}{5} = 20\%$

311. d Number of cities starting with consonant and in the northern hemisphere = 10.

Number of countries starting with consonant and in the east of the meridien = 13.

Hence, option (d) is the correct choice. The difference is 3.

312. a Three countries starting with vowels and in southern hemisphere — Argentina. Australia and Ecuador and two countries with capitals beginning with vowels — Canada and Ghana.

313. c Emp. numbers 51, 58, 64, 72, 73 earn more than 50 per day in complex operations.

Total = 5

314. d 80% attendance = 80% of 25 = 20 days

Emp. numbers 47, 51, 72, 73, 74, 79, 80.

Thus, total = 7

315. a

Emp. No.	Earnings E (medium)	No. of days D (medium)	E/D
2001151	159.64	13.33	11.97
2001158	109.72	9.61	11.41
2001164	735.22	12.07	60.91
2001171	6.10	4.25	-
2001172	117.46	8.50	13.81
2001179	776.19	19.00	40.85
2001180	1262.79	19.00	66.46

Hence, Emp. number 2001180 earns the maximum earnings per day.

316. c Emp. numbers 51, 58, 64, 71, 72 satisfy the condition.

[For emp. 64, you see 12 is not the double of 5. And 735 is not even double of 402.

Hence, $\frac{402}{5} > \frac{735}{12}$.

Note: Emp. numbers 48, 49, 50 are not eligible for earnings. Hence, they are not counted.

317. c Total revenue of 1999 = 3374

5% of 3374 = 3374 × $\frac{5}{100}$ = 168.7

For 1999, revenue for Spain is 55, Rest of Latin America is 115, North Sea is 140, Rest of the world is 91.

So total four operations of the company accounted for less than 5% of the total revenue earned in the year 1999.

318. b **The language in the question is ambiguous.**

Taking the question to be more than 200% growth in revenue, the revenue in 2000 will be more than 3 times that in 1999. Hence, (b) is the answer.

Taking the revenue in 2000 to be more than 200% of that in 1999, the revenue in 2000 should be more than twice of that in 1999. Then there will be 4 operations.

319. b Four operations, as given below:

(1) North Africa and Middle-East

(2) Argentina

(3) Rest of Latin America

(4) Far East

have registered yearly increase in income before taxes and charges from 1998 to 2000.

320. b Percentage increase in net income before tax and charges for total world (1998-99)

$$= \frac{1375 - 248}{248} \times 100 = 454.4\%$$

Spain is making loss.

Percentage increase for North Africa and Middle-East

$$\frac{341 - 111}{111} \times 100 = 207.2\%$$

Percentage increase for Argentina = $\frac{838 - 94}{94} \times 100$

= 791.5%

From the table one can directly say that there is no operation other than Argentina, whose percentage increase in net income before taxes and charges is higher than the average (world).

321. b Statement 1 is obviously wrong.

(b) $\frac{54}{65} > \frac{20}{52}$. Hence, (b) is correct.

(c) $\frac{500}{1168} > \frac{61}{187}$. Hence, (c) is wrong.

322. b Profitability of North Africa and Middle-East in 2000

$$= \frac{356}{530} = 0.67$$

Profitability of Spain in 2000 = $\frac{225}{43}$ = 5.23

Profitability of Rest of Latin America in 2000 = $\frac{169}{252}$, i.e. < 1.

Profitability of Far East in 2000 = $\frac{189}{311}$ = < 1

323. d Except Rest of Latin America and Rest of the World, all the operations are greater than 2.

324. d Options (a), (b) and (c), are ruled out. So the correct option is (d).

325. b It can be easily observed from the two charts that Switzerland's ratio of chart 1 to chart 2 is $\frac{20}{11}$ has the highest price per unit kilogram for its supply. Finding the ratio of the value and quantity is enough to reach the solution.

326. b Total value of distribution to Turkey is 16% of 5760 million Euro.

Total quantity of distribution to Turkey is 15% of 1.055 million tonnes.

So the average price in Euro per kilogram for Turkey is

$$\frac{\left(5760 \times \frac{16}{100}\right)}{\left(1055 \times \frac{15}{100}\right)} \simeq 5.6$$

For questions 327 to 332:

Position of States (Rank)	Year					
	96-97	97-98	98-99	99-00	00-01	
1	MA	MA	MA	MA	MA	
2	TN	TN	TN	TN	TN	
3	GU	AP	AP	AP	AP	
4	AP	GU	GU	GU	UP	changed twice
5	KA	UP	UP	UP	GU	
6	UP	KA	KA	KA	KA	
7	WB	WB	WB	WB	WB	

327. b From above table, we can conclude that option (b) is correct.

328. b On referring to the table, we can see that UP is the state which changed its relative ranking most number of times.

329. d We can say directly on observing the graph that the sales tax revenue collections for AP has more than doubled from 1997 to 2001.

330. c Growth rate of tax revenue can be calculated as:

(Sales tax revenue of correct year – Sales tax revenue of previous year)

For year 1997-98 $\frac{7826 - 7290}{7826} = 0.068$

For year 1998-99 $\frac{8067 - 7826}{7826} = 0.030$

For year 1999-2000 $\frac{10284 - 8067}{8067} = 0.274$

For year 2000-01 $\frac{12034 - 10284}{10284} = 0.170$

331. a For increase by the same amount for 2 successive years, eliminate the options by subtracting only the last digit.

For Karnataka, increase in 2000-01 is 5413 – 4839 = 574 and increase in 1999-2000 is 4839 – 4265 = 574.

Hence, (a) is the correct option.

332. c On referring to the table, we can see that Tamil Nadu has been maintaining a constant rank over the years in terms of its contribution to total tax collections.

333. a FRG + CZE = 43.01 and US Total = 42.83

Hence, difference in time = 43.01 – 42.83 = 0.18

334. b The first two rankers of final score are 8905 and 8897.

The third ranker is carrying a score of 8880. So he needs to score 8881 to get a bronze, whereas his sum is 582 + 3003 = 3585.

Least score required = 8881 – 3585 = 5296

335. d Let the positive weights given to a competitor in High Jump, Pole Vault and Long Jump be x, y and z respectively. Therefore, x + y + z = Score-2

In long jump event, Michael Smith must have out-jumped all those competitors (excluding Daley Thompson) who had scored more than or equal to Michael Smith in each of High Jump and Pole Vault but with consolidated Score-2 of less than the consolidated Score-2 of Michael Smith.

The four competitors whom Michael Smith must have out-jumped in the long jump event are Torsten Voss, Jurgen Hingsen, Grigory Degtyarov and Steve Fritz.

336. b Here you need to compare the ratio as which is the highest out of $\frac{189}{561}, \frac{209}{587}$ and rest of the options have equal value.

Now we can see that $\frac{209}{587}$ is greater than $\frac{189}{561}$, so 1997 has the highest ratio.

337. a Population in 1995

$= \frac{421-207}{487} \times 1000 \text{ million} \approx 440 \text{ million}$

Population in 1996

$= \frac{561-189}{464} \times 1000 \text{ million} \approx 802 \text{ million}$

Population in 1997

$= \frac{587-209}{510} \times 1000 \text{ million} \approx 740 \text{ million}$

Population in 1999

$= \frac{660-220}{566} \times 1000 \text{ million} \approx 777 \text{ million}$

Hence, Chaidesh had the lowest population in 1995.

338. a From 96 to 99, in each year the production has increased but the area has decreased. Therefore, the production in unit per area is highest in 1999.

339. c

	Cement	Limestone	Power	Wages
93 - 94	100	20	25	15
02 - 03	104	21	27	15.8

So percentage profit $= \frac{104-(21+27+15.8)}{104} \times 100$

$= \frac{40.2}{104} \times 100 = 38.65\%$

340. b

	Steel	Power	Wages	Iron Ore
93 – 94	100	30	10	25
02 – 03	105.5	32.4	10.53	26.5

So percentage profit

$= \frac{105.5-(32.4+10.53+26.5)}{105.5} \times 100 = 34.18\%$

341. a You only need to see the particular row in the table for the given options and for Power, it experienced continuous rise.

342. d Again for timber, wages experienced declined only once for the given period.

343. b There are 32 nations in all the four lists which have lower birth rates than Philippines. So they are ranked higher than it. Now, three nations namely Philippines, Thailand and Colombia have identical birth rates and death rates (34 and 10 respectively). Hence, they are ranked 33rd in the consolidated list.

344. a The rank of Spain is 17th overall, tied alongwith Yugoslavia. So the next country will be ranked 19th in the list. Taiwan is ranked 28th in the list. Hence, there will be (28 – 19) = 9 countries between Taiwan and Spain.

345. d In the consolidated list, there are 36 countries whose birth rate doesn't exceed 35. Now looking at the countries with birth rate of 36, we see that on the basis of lower death rates, Venezuela is placed at 37th position.

346. a There are 9 countries in Asia that are ranked lower than every country of South America, namely Iran, Vietnam, Korea(DPRK), Pakistan, Nepal, Bangladesh, Syria, Iraq and Afghanistan. Out of these nations, only Afghanistan is ranked below all the countries from Africa. Remaining 8 countries satisfy the given condition.

347. c March rainfall is lower than September rainfall in every location.

348. b Peak rainfall occurs in April only in locations 6 and 7.

For questions 349 to 351:

Based on observation only.

349. c By observation, 4 commodities namely Chillies, Onion, Egg and Dal showed a net overall increase and the remaining two , namely Edible Oil and Rice showed a net overall decrease.

350. d Except Edible Oil, all the other five commodities experienced a price decline for two or more consecutive years.

351. d Egg and Onion shows a price rise immediately after a price decline only once in this period.

For questions 352 to 355:

Operating profit = Profitability × Operating Income

Operating profits in 2002-03 for:

$A = \frac{8 \times 180}{100} = 14.4$ crore; $B = \frac{2 \times 220}{100} = 14.4$ crore;

$C = \frac{15 \times 200}{100} = 30$ crore; $D = \frac{1 \times 290}{100} = 2.9$ crore;

$E = \frac{17.5 \times 200}{100} = 35$ crore; $F = \frac{9 \times 210}{100} = 18.9$ crore

Looking at the values, two companies B and D are excluded in the third graph.

352. d Companies A, C and E have profitability between 10% and 20% in F.Y. 2001-02. But the operating income of C in F.Y. 2002-03 is greater than 200 crore. Hence, option (d) is the correct option.

353. c E has the highest operating profit of Rs.35 crore in F.Y. 2002-03.

354. a Operating profit of B in F.Y. 2001-02

$= \frac{(-4) \times 250}{100} = -10$ crore

and operating profit of D in F.Y. 2001-02

$$= \frac{(-2)\times 250}{100} = -5 \text{ crore}$$

Therefore, average operating profit for B and D in F.Y. 2001-02 $= \frac{(-5)+(-10)}{2}$ crore $= -7.5$ crore

355. Two companies C and E have profitability exceeding 10% in F.Y. 2002-03.

∴ Their average operating profit in F.Y. 2002-03

$$= \frac{30+35}{2} \text{ crore} = 32.5 \text{ crore.}$$

356. b Increase of HP is from 884 to 970, i.e. 86
Increase of Kerala is from 1004 to 1058, i.e. 54
Increase of Punjab is from 832 to 874, i.e. 42
Increase of Assam is 919 to 932, i.e. 13
Increase of J & K is 882 to 900, i.e. 18
Therefore, HP and Kerala are highest.

357. c Goa (1091 to 960) i.e. 131
Tamil Nadu (1044 to 986) i.e. 58
Bihar (1061 to 921) i.e. 140
Orissa (1037 to 972) i.e. 65
Therefore, Bihar should the sharpest decline over the period 1901 – 2001.

358. c Females outnumbering males means that the sex ratio is more than 1000.
Option (a), (b), and (d) are true.

359. d **Statement A:**

Success rate for males in 2003

$$= \frac{637}{60133}\times 100 \approx 1.06\%$$

Success rate for females in 2003

$$= \frac{399}{40763}\times 100 \approx 0.98\%$$

Hence, 'A' is false.

Statement B:

Success rate for females in 2002

$$= \frac{138}{15389}\times 100 \approx 0.89\%$$

Success rate for females in 2003

$$= \frac{399}{40763}\times 100 \approx 0.98\%.$$

Hence, 'B' is false.

360. d **Statement A:**

Females selected $= \frac{48}{19236}\times 100 \approx 0.25\%$

Males selected $= \frac{171}{61205}\times 100 \approx 0.28\%$

Hence, 'A' is false.

Statement B:

Success rate for Males $= \frac{17}{684}\times 100 = 25\%$

Success rate for Females $= \frac{48}{138}\times 100 \approx 34.8\%$

Hence, 'B' is false.

361. a **Statement A:**

Female absentees in 2002 (19236 – 15389) = 3847

$$= \frac{3847}{19236}\times 100 \approx 20\%$$

Female absentees in 2003 (45292 – 40763) = 4529

$$= \frac{4529}{45292}\times 100 \approx 10\%$$

Hence, 'A' is true.

Statement B:

Male absentees in 2003 (63298 – 60133) = 3165

$$= \frac{63298-60133}{63298}\times 100 \approx 5\%$$

Hence, 'B' is false.

362. b It is evident from the graph that Seeta's growth rate decreased from third month as this is the first time the slope has decreased.

363. a Geeta grew at the fastest rate in the first two months (the slope of the line in this period is steepest for Geeta).

364. a Geeta grew the lowest in the third month (during this period, the slope was least for Geeta).

365. d Seeta increased by 7 cm on 50 cm and Shyam by 7 cm on 53 cm. Hence, Shyam grew least.

366. d The possible combinations when the respondents are aged less than 40 years is minimum can be:

(i) No children – 1 male(aged 38) and atleast 1 female (aged 34)

(ii) 1 child – 1 male(aged 32) and atleast 1 female (aged 35)

(iii) 2 children – at least 1 male(aged 21) and at least 1 female (aged 37)

(iv) 3 children – 2 males(aged 32 and 33) and 1 female (aged 27)

i.e. there is at least 9 such respondents.

Required percentage $= \frac{9}{30}\times 100 = 30\%$.

367. c The possible combinations when the respondents are aged more than 35 years is maximum can be:

(i) No children – 1 male(aged 38) and atmost 4 females

(ii) 1 children – 0 male and at most 7 female

(iii) 2 children – at most 7 males and 3 females

(iv) 3 children – 0 male and 1 female(aged 40)

i.e. there can be at most 23 such respondents.

Required percentage = $\frac{23}{30} \times 100 = 76.67\%$

368. c The possible combinations when the respondents are aged between 35 and 40 years(both inclusive) is minimum can be:

(i) No children – 1 male(aged 38) and 0 female

(ii) 1 children – 0 male and at least 1 female (aged 35)

(iii) 2 children – 0 males and at least 1 female (aged 37)

(iv) 3 children – 0 male and 1 female (aged 40)

i.e. there can be at least 4 such respondents.

Required percentage = $\frac{4}{30} \times 100 = 13.33\%$.

369. c In case of Products, percentage of spam emails is increasing but at decreasing rate, from Sep 2002 to Dec 2002 products increased by $\frac{7-3}{3} \approx 133\%$ and in Mar 2003 about $\frac{7-4}{7} \approx 43\%$ and in Jun 2003 $\left(\frac{11-10}{10} \approx 10\%\right)$.

370. a Since percentage of spam is Dec 2002 is higher than June 2003, and the number of total e-mails received is higher, hence number received in Dec 2002 is higher.

371. d Cannot be determined as in Sept 2002 percentage is lower as compared to March 2003, however the total number of emails received in Sept 2003 is higher than that in March 2002. Thus, we cannot say anything.

372. b It happened only once i.e., on 17-Jul-02.

373. c From the table, we can see that for issue dated, 04 June-03, the 2nd round issue has a lower maturity and the competitive bids received are higher.

374. d On 07-Nov 02, the value of non-competitive bids in the 2nd round is greater than that of 1st round. So option (d) is not true.

375. b Here the scale of the profit axis is exactly 10% of the scale of turnover axis. Just draw a diagonal line from bottom left point to top right point. All companies lying above this line have profit in excess of 10% of turnover.

From the graph, there are 7 companies, has the profit 10% of turnover.

376. c From the graph, there are 2 steel companies with a turnover of more than 2000 and profit less than 300.

377. b From the graph, there are 5 companies.

378. d By looking up the table, in University of California - Berkeley median starting salary is $70,000 and annual tuition fee is $18,788.

379. b By looking up the table, the number of schools, uniformly better than Dartmouth College is 2, namely Stanford and New York University.

380. d 8 universities namely, Stanford, Harvard, Pennsylvania, Massachusetts, Chicago, Northwestern, Columbia and Duke university have single digit ranking on atleast 3 of the 4 parameters.

381. b Number of children with age $\leq$ 9 years = 45

Number of children with height $\leq$ 135 cm = 48

Therefore, the number of children of age 9 years or less whose height does not exceed 135 cm will be the common of the two (age $\leq$ 9 years and height $\leq$ 135 cm) = minimum(45, 48) = 45

382. a Number of children aged more than

10 years = 100 – 60 = 40

Number of children taller than

150 cm = 100 – 75 = 25

Number of children with weight more than

48 kg = 100 – 91 = 9

These 9 children are surely included in the 25 children taller than 150 cm and more than 10 years of age because of the assumption given. Thus, 25 – 9 = 16 children satisfy the given condition.

383. c Number of children older than 6 years but not exceeding 12 years = 77 – 22 = 55

Number of children with weights not exceeding 38 kg = 33

These 33 children includes the 22 children with age not exceeding 6 years. Therefore, the remaining (33 – 22) = 11 comes from the 55 children of ages older than 6 years but not exceeding 12 years.

Therefore, 55 – 11 = 44 children satisfy the given condition.

384. d Profitability is defined as percentage of sales. Approximately, Firm A has 20% profit, B has 16.66%, C has 20% and D has approximately 25% profit.

385. a $\frac{24568 + 25468}{89570} \times 100 \approx 55\%$

386. c Average incomes of Ahuja family

$=\frac{3200+3000+2800}{3}=\frac{9000}{3}=3000;$

Bose family $=\frac{2300+2100+2800}{3}$

$=\frac{7200}{3}=2400;$

Coomar family $=\frac{1200+2200+1600}{3}$

$=\frac{5000}{3}\approx 1667$

and Dubey family $=\frac{1200+3200}{2}=\frac{4400}{2}=2200.$

Hence, Coomar family has the lowest average income.

387. d The average expenditures (approximately) for the families:

Ahuja $=\frac{700+1700+2700}{3}\approx 1733;$

Bose $=\frac{800+1750+2300}{3}\approx 1617;$

Coomar $=\frac{500+1100+1900}{3}\approx 1167$ and

Dubey $=\frac{1200+2800}{2}=2000.$

Hence, Dubey family has the highest average expenditure.

388. d The average savings (approximately) for the families:

Ahuja $=\frac{2500+1300+100}{3}=1300;$

Bose $=\frac{1500+350+500}{3}\approx 783;$

Coomar $=\frac{700+1100+300}{3}=700$ and

Dubey $=\frac{0+400}{2}=200.$

Hence, Dubey family has the lowest average savings.

389. a The savings of a person is maximum if he/she has high income but less expenditure. From the graph, a member of Ahuja family has Rs.3200 as income and Rs.700 as expenditure. Hence, he/she will have the maximum savings among all.

390. b Number of Naya mixer-grinders disposed off in 1999 = 20% of 30 = 6

So the number of Naya mixer-grinders in 1999, i.e. 124 is inclusive of those mixer grinders produced in 1997 and 1998 and still in operation. The numbers are (30 – 6) = 24 and (80 – 30) = 50 respectively.

Therefore, number of new Naya mixer-grinders purchased in 1999 = 124 – (50 + 24) = 50.

391. b Number of Naya mixer-grinders disposed off in 1999 = 20% of 30 = 6

Number of Naya mixer-grinders disposed off in 2000 = 20% of (80 – 30) = 10

Therefore, total number of Naya mixer-grinders disposed by end of 2000 = 6 + 10 = 16.

392. d Sine information regarding the number of Purana mixer-grinders for the years prior to 1995 is not known, it cannot be ascertained as to how many of them were disposed off in 2000.

393. a It is given that 10 Purana mixer-grinders were disposed off as junk in 1997. So the number of mixer-grinders in operation in 1997 must have been 162 – 10 = 152. But it is given to be 182.

∴ Number of newly purchased Purana mixer-grinder in 1997 = 182 – 152 = 30

20% of this, i.e. 6 were disposed off in 1999. So the number of mixer-grinders in operation in 1999 must have been 222 – 6 = 216. But it is given to be 236.

∴ Number of newly purchased Purana mixer-grinder in 1999 = 236 – 216 = 20.

For questions 394 to 397:

Go through the following table.

	Pakistan	South Africa	Australia
K	28	51	< 48
R	< 22	49	55
S	< 22	75	50
V	130	< 49	< 48
Y	40	< 49	87
Top 3 batsmen	198	175	192
India Total	220	250	240

394. c **395.** a **396.** b **397.** b

For questions 398 to 401:

In any department in any given year, the average year ranges between 42-53 years.

(i) When a 25 year old will join, the average age will dip by a minimum of 5 years.

(ii) When a 60 year old will retire, the dip will be less compared to (i).

398. c In the bar graph, one dip corresponds to the new 25 year old joinee. However, two dips in the trend implies joining of a 25 year old and the retirement of a 60 year old employee. This trait is observed only in Finance department. Hence, the faculty member who retired belonged to Finance.

399. d From the graph of Marketing, it is clear that the new faculty joined in 2001.

On April 1, 2000, completed age of Professor Naresh and Devesh were 52 years and 49 years, in no particular order.

∴ Age of the third Professor on April 1, 2000

$= 49.33 \times 3 - (52 + 49) = 47$ years

Hence, his age on April 1, 2005 will be 52 years.

400. c As the dip will be less in case a faculty retired compared to that when a new faculty joined in, so the new faculty member joined the Finance area in 2002.

401. c For the OM area, the only dip comes in the year 2001. So the new 25 year old faculty joined in 2001. Hence, on April 1, 2003, his age will be 27 years old.

402. a **State Productivity (Tons per hectare)**

Haryana $\frac{19.2}{3.2} = 6$

Punjab $\frac{24}{4} = 6$

Andhra Pradesh $\frac{112}{22.4} = 5$

Uttar Pradesh $\frac{67.2}{16.8} = 4$

Hence, Haryana and Punjab have the highest productivity.

403. b Gujarat $\rightarrow \frac{24}{51} = 0.47$

Only per capita production of rice for Haryana, Punjab, Maharashtra and Andhra Pradesh are greater than 0.47.

404. d As seen from the table

Haryana, Gujarat, Punjab, MP, Tamil Nadu, Maharashtra, UP and AP are intensive rice producing states.

405. a The minimum return will be gained if the extraordinary performing stocks (double & 1.5 growth) are the ones whose expected returns are lowest (i.e. 10% & 20%). Taking the minimum value of the expected returns as 10. We have to see which of the two values of 10 and 20 multiplied by 2 and 1.5 and vice versa yields the minimum value.

Hence comparing the minimum value between $20 \times 2 + 10 \times 1.5$ and $20 \times 1.5 + 10 \times 2$, the 2nd one is minimum. Hence the minimum average return is

$$\frac{20 \times 1.5 + 10 \times 2 + 30 + 40}{4} = 30\%$$

406. b If the average return is 35%, then the total return is

$35 \times 4 =$ Rs.140.

The only possible arrangement of 140 is

$40 \times 1.5 + 30 + 20 \times 2 + 10.$

∴ $A = 20 \times 2$ (Cement or IT)

$B = 10$

$C = 30$

$D = 40\ (1.5)$ (Steel or Auto)

From the data given in the question, we see that A has to be Cement or IT.

D is Steel or Auto.

Hence, statements (II) and (III) are correct.

407. c Total return is $38.75 \times 4 =$ Rs.155

The possible arrangement is

$20 + 10 + 30 \times 1.5 + 40 \times 2$

Therefore, A = 20, B = 10, C = 30 (Steel or Auto), D = 40 (Cement or IT)

Hence, statements (I) and (IV) are correct.

Hence, (c) is the correct option.

408. b Given Company C is either Cement or IT industry

C's Return is $30 \times 2 = 60\%$

Among the other values we see that the possible arrangements can be

$10 \times 1.5 + 20 + 40$, $10 + 20 \times 1.5 + 40$, $40 + 20 + 40 \times 1.5$

The average returns will be in each case

$$\frac{10 \times 1.5 + 20 + 40 + 60}{4} = 33.75\%,$$

$$\frac{10 + 20 \times 1.5 + 40 + 60}{4} = 35\%,$$

$$\frac{40 + 20 + 40 \times 1.5 + 60}{4} = 45\%.$$

Considering 33.75% as the valid value, then B belongs to the Auto industry.

Hence, (II) and (IV) are correct.

Hence, (b) is the correct option.

For questions 409 to 412:

L = London, Paris = P, New York= NY, Beijing = B

In round III, one of the two cities, either London or Paris will get 38 votes and the other 37. Further:

(1) The persons representing London, Paris, Beijing and New York can not vote as long as their own cities are in contention. In round I, New York gets eliminated and hence the representative from NY becomes eligible for voting in the II round hence increasing the total votes by 1. This means the total votes in the first round must be 83 – 1 = 82.

(2) After round II, the representative from Beijing votes in the III round. This should have increased the number of total votes by 1 and the total votes must have become 83 + 1 = 84.

We are given that the total votes in round III are 75 only. We conclude that 84 – 75 = 9 people who voted in round I and II have become ineligible for voting in round III.

(3) 9 people who have voted in round I and II become ineligible for voting in round III. The reason of their ineligibility is that till round I and II, they have already voted for two different cities which are not available for contention in round III. All of these 9 voters are those who voted for NY in round I and then voted for Beijing in round II.

(4) Beijing's vote in round II is 21. This includes 9 votes from people who voted for NY in the first round. So 21 – 9 = 12 people voted for Beijing in both round I and II.

(5) We are given that 75% of the people who voted for Beijing in round I, voted again for Beijing in round II as well. So, 16 people must have voted for Beijing in round I.

(6) In round I we have:

$$82 = L + P + B + NY$$

Or

$$82 = 30 + P + 16 + 12$$

Giving P = 24

(7) In round II, we have:

$$83 = L + 32 + 21, \text{ giving } L = 30$$

(8) NY had 12 votes in round I. 9 of these votes went to B(see point 2 , again). The rest 3 went to P.

(9) 16 votes for B in round I. 12 of them still vote for B. The rest 4 voted for either L or P. L has the same number of votes in both the rounds I and II. This means in round II, these 4 votes must have gone to Paris only.

(10) The representative from NY did not vote in round I but has voted in round II. As L has the same people voting for it (30 votes in both the rounds I and II) and we know the exact break up of B in II. This NY-representative vote must go to Paris only. Further, in order to avoid ineligibility, this NY rep must vote for Paris only in round III also.

(11) Paris (in round II) break up is:

32 = 24 (from round I, who voted for Paris)

+ 4 (out of the 16, who voted for Beijing in round I)

+ 3(out of 12, who voted for NY in round I)

+ 1 (NY -Rep)

(12) Beijing gets eliminated in round II. So the rep of Beijing can vote in round III.

(13) 12 People (out of 21) who voted for Beijing in round II are still eligible for vote in round III.

(14) 50% of people who voted for Beijing in I (i.e. 8 People) voted for Paris in round III. These 8 People include 4 of those who voted for Paris in round II also. Therefore 4(out of 12 who voted for Beijing in round II and are still eligible for vote in round III) people have voted for Paris in round III.

(15) This implies that the rest 8(out of 12 who voted for Beijing in round II and are still eligible for vote in round III) can vote for London only. This makes London's vote = 30+ 8 or 38 in round III. Which implies that Paris got 37 votes.

(16) The Beijing Rep who is eligible to vote in round III must have voted for Paris only.

The following table sums up the Vote Pattern:

Round	Total Votes	London (L)	Paris(P)	Beijing (B)	New York (NY)
I	82	**30**	24	16	**12**
II	**83**	30	**32** = (24 + 4 + 3 + 1 of NY-rep)	**21** (12 + 9)	X
III	**75**	38 = (30 + 8)	37= (32 + 4 + 1 of B-rep)	X	X

(The data shown in **Bold** was already provided in the problem. The other data is deduced from the solution.)

409. d Required percentage

$$= \frac{9}{12} \times 100 = 75\%$$

410. d As seen from the table, Paris got 24 votes.

411. d Required percentage

$$= \frac{8}{12} \times 100 = 66.67\%$$

412. a Based on the table, IOC members from New York must have voted for Paris in Round II.

For questions 413 to 417:

413. c Let Dipan get x marks in paper II.

Dipan's average in PCB group = 98

Maths group = 95

S.S. group = 95.5

Vernacular group = 95

English group = $\left(\frac{96 + x}{2}\right)$

Sum of all = 96 × 5

So $95.5 + 96 \times 3 + 48 + \frac{x}{2} = 96 \times 5$

$$\Rightarrow \frac{x}{2} = 96 \times 2 - 95.5 - 48$$

$$x = 2(96.5 - 48) = 2 \times 48.5 = 97$$

So (c) is the correct option.

414. a The only boy getting 95 in atleast one of the subjects of the group among all the groups is Dipan.

So (a) is the correct option.

415. a A group score of 100 in Social Science would have increased the scores as follows:

	Score Increase	Group Score	Final Score Increase	Final group Score
Pritam	22	11	$\frac{11}{5}=2.2$	96.1
Joseph	9	4.5	$\frac{4.5}{5}=.9$	95.9
Tirna	21	10.5	$\frac{10.5}{5}=2.1$	95.8
Agni	9	4.5	$\frac{4.5}{5}=.9$	95.2

So the order is Pritam > Joseph > Trina > Agni.

So option (a) is the correct choice.

416. d The student having atleast 95 in every group is Dipan, so the answer is Dipan, option (d).

417. e Let us increase the score in one of the subjects of the following candidates

	Least Scores	Contribution in net Score	Final Score
Ram	94 in group of 2	3 in 5 groups	96.1 + .6 = 96.7
Agni	82 in group of 2	9 in 5 groups	94.3 + 1.8 = 96.1
Pritam	83 in group of 2	8.5 in 5 groups	93.9 + 1.7 = 95.6
Ayesha	93 in group of 2	3.5 in 5 groups	96.2 + .7 = 96.9
Dipan	95 in group of 1	5 in 5 groups	96 + 1 = 97.0

So, Dipan will end with a highest total.

So the answer is option (e).

For questions 418 to 422:

The MCS share price at the beginning of first day is Rs.100 and at the close of day 5 is Rs.110.

The following cases of the closing prices can be derived.

At the end of	Day 1	Day 2	Day 3	Day 4	Day 5
1	90	80	90	100	110
2	90	100	90	100	110
3	90	100	110	120	110
4	90	100	110	100	110
5	110	100	90	100	110
6	110	100	110	100	110
7	110	120	110	100	110
8	110	120	110	120	110
9	110	120	130	120	110
10	110	120	110	100	110

418. c As Chetan sold 10 shares on three consecutive days, therefore, of the five days, there must be an increase for three of the five days and a decrease for the remaining two days. It is given that Michael sold 10 shares only once.

Hence, the price is more than 110 for only one day and on all the remaining days, it cannot exceed 110. The only satisfying case is **(3)**.

Hence, the price at the end of Day 3 is Rs.110.

419. b The satisfying cases are **(1), (2), (4), (5), (6)**.

Hence, the price at the end of Day 4 is Rs.100.

420. a Let Chetan and Michael start with x number of shares initially.

From case **(1)**, we get that the number of shares with Michael = x + 10 and number of shares with Chetan = x + 10 + 10 – 10 – 10 – 10 = x – 10.

So Michael has 20 more shares than Chetan. This is the only satisfying case.

Hence, the share price at the end of Day 3 is Rs.90.

421. e Consider cases **(3) and (7)**. Only these two satisfies the condition that Michael had Rs.100 less than Chetan at the end of day 5.

For case **(3)**,

Number of shares with Chetan

= x + 10 – 10 – 10 – 10 + 10 = x – 10

And with Michael = x – 10

For case **(7)**,

Number of shares with Chetan

= x – 10 – 10 + 10 + 10 – 10 = x – 10

And with Michael = x – 10

In either case, number of shares with Michael and Chetan are the same.

422. d To maximise the amount gathered by both of them, we need to look into those cases wherein we have maximum number of 110 excess figures. It is only then that Michael and Chetan both will make money. So we check for case **(9)**.

For case **(9)**,

Extra cash with Chetan by the end of day 5

= 1100 + 1200 + 1300 – 1200 – 1100

= Rs.1300

And that with Michael

= 1200 + 1300 + 1200 = Rs.3700

Total extra cash with both of them

= 1300 + 3700 = Rs.5000

For questions 423 to 426:

Looking at the values in the table one can easily conclude that the costs which are directly proportional to the change in volume of proportion are 'Material', 'Labour' and 'Operating cost of machines'. Rest of the costs are all fixed costs. If 'x' is the number of units produced in 2007, then the total cost of production would be

C = 9600 (Fixed cost) + 100x (Variable cost),

Variable cost = 100x because as the number of units for 2006 is 1200 and variable cost for that is 120000 i.e. 100 times the number of units.

423. b Total cost = 9600 + 100 × 1400 = 149600

$$\text{Cost per unit} = \frac{149600}{1400} = 107 \text{ (approx.)}$$

424. c To avoid any loss the total selling price should be equal to the total cost price. If 'x' units are produced and selling price of each unit is 125 Rs.

Therefore, 125x = 9600 + 100x

25x = 9600

$\Rightarrow$ x = 384

Hence, 384 units should be produced.

425. e Here, fixed cost is Rs.9600 and the variable cost is Rs.100x, where x is number of units produced. Hence, profit is maximum if x is maximum. Therefore, 2000 units will give maximum profit.

426. a If the company sells a maximum of 1400 units, the selling price is fixed at Rs. 125 per unit. If more than 1400 units are sold, the selling price is reduced to Rs. 120 per unit. The company cannot sell more than 1700 units.

To earn maximum profit at a unit selling price of Rs. 125, the company must sell 1400 units. The maximum profit earned, denoted by P_0, is calculated as below:

Profit = (Selling Price) – (Cost Price)

P_0 = 125 × 1400 – (9600 + 100 × 1400)

= Rs. 25400

Now if the company sells an x number of units (x > 1400) then the profit earned will be:

P_x = 120 × x – (9600 + 100 × x)

= 20 × x – 9600

The minimum value of x for which P_x will be more than P_0 must satisfy the following inequality:

20 × x – 9600 > 25400

$\Rightarrow$ x > 1750

As only a maximum of 1700 units can be sold, P_x will never be more than P_0. Hence the maximum profit that can be earned is Rs. 25400 only.

Hence (a) is correct.

For questions 427 to 430:

From the given information the following table can be formed:

	M	F	V	NV	Total
Class 12	48	32	32	48	80
Class 11	44	36	40	40	80
Secondary Section	288	352	352	288	640
Total	380	420	424		800

427. b From the above table

Percentage of male students in the secondary section $= \frac{288}{640} \times 100 = 45\%$

428. e From the above table

Male vegetarians $= \frac{25}{100} \times 32 = 8$

Female vegetarians = 32 – 8 = 24

Male non-vegetarians = 48 – 8 = 40

So, their difference is 40 – 24 = 16.

429. a Percentage of vegetarian students in Class 12

$= \frac{32}{80} \times 100 = 40\%$

430.* From the main table

	M	F	V	Male Veg	Female Veg	Total
Class 12	48	32	32			80
Class 11	44	36	40			80
Secondary Section	288	352	352	320	320	640
Total	380	420	424			800

***This question is wrong** because the number of Male vegetarian cannot be greater than 288.

431. c The cost of angioplasty, hip replacement and a knee replacement (in US Dollars '000) in the given countries is as follows.

	India	Thailand	Malaysia	Singapore	USA
Angioplasty	11 + 5 = 16	13 + 5 = 18	11 + 6 = 17	13 + 4 = 17	57
Hip replacement	9 + 7 = 16	12 + 5 = 17	10 + 8 = 18	12 + 5 = 17	43
Knee replacement	8.5 + 9 = 17.5	10 + 6 = 16	8 + 4 = 12	13 + 4 = 17	40
Total cost	49.5	51	47	51	140

The cheapest is in Malaysia.

432. a

	India	Thailand	Malaysia	Singapore
Knee replacement	8.5 + 9 = 17.5	10 + 6 = 16	8 + 4 = 12	13 + 4 = 17

Clearly, India has the highest cost for knee replacement surgery.

433. d In India, total cost in US$ $= 3000 + 5000 + \frac{1500}{32.89}$ (transportation cost) = 8456.06

In Thailand, total cost in US$ = 4500 + 6000 = 10,500

Difference in amount is 10,500 – 8456.06 = US$ 2044 ≈ 67,500 Bahts

434. b In India, total cost for spirial fusion in US$

$= \frac{5500 \times 40.928}{35} = 6431.5$

In Singapore, total cost for spirial fusion in US$ = 9000

Difference (in US$) is 9000 – 6431.5 = 2568.5

≈ 2500

435. e Let volume of data transfer in India = Volume of data transfer in Singapore = x

For INDIA:

ARDT for India ≈ \$1 (approx)

∴ Revenue from data transfer = \$x (approx)

$$\frac{\text{Revenue from data transfer}}{\text{Total Revenue}} \times 100 = 9\% \text{ (approx)}$$

$$\Rightarrow \text{Total Revenue} = \frac{x}{9} \times 100 \text{ (approx)}$$

For SINGAPORE:

ARDT = \$9 (approx)

∴ Revenue from data transfer = \$9x (approx)

$$\frac{\text{Revenue from data transfer}}{\text{Total Revenue}} \times 100 = 20.5\% \text{ (approx)}$$

$$\Rightarrow \text{Total Revenue} = \frac{9x}{20.5} \times 100 \text{ (approx)}$$

$$\frac{\text{Total Revenue for Singapore}}{\text{Total Revenue for India}} = \frac{\frac{9x}{20.5} \times 100}{\frac{x}{9} \times 100}$$

$$\approx 4 \text{ (approx)}$$

436. c Let total revenue of Sweden in 2010 = x

Therefore total Revenue of India in 2010 = 2x

For Sweden in 2010:

ARDT = \$6

Revenue from data transfer = 2 × 18% of x

$$\therefore \text{ Volume of data transfer} = \frac{2 \times 18\% \text{ of } x}{6}$$

For India in 2010:

Let ARDT = y

Revenue from data transfer = $3 \times 9\%$ of 2x

$$\therefore \text{ Volume of data transfer} = \frac{3 \times 9\% \text{ of } 2x}{y}$$

$$\text{Therefore } \frac{2 \times 18\% \text{ of } x}{6} = \frac{3 \times 9\% \text{ of } 2x}{y} \Rightarrow y = \$9$$

Therefore % change in ARDT of India

$$= \frac{9-1}{1} \times 100 = 800\%$$

437. d **For UK**:

$$\frac{\text{Revenue from Data transfar}}{\text{Total Revenue}} \times 100 = 30\% \text{(approx)}$$

$$\text{Revenue from Data transfer} = \frac{30}{100} \times \text{Total Revenue}$$

ARDT = \$ 13 (approx)

$$\therefore \text{ Volume of Data transfer} = \frac{30}{100} \times \frac{\text{Total Revenue}}{13}$$

$$\approx \frac{3}{130} \times \text{Total Revenue}$$

For Spain:

$$\frac{\text{Revenue from Data transfar}}{\text{Total Revenue}} \times 100 = 15\% \text{(approx)}$$

ARDT = 6.5 (approx)

$$\therefore \text{ Volume of Data transfer} = \frac{15}{100} \times \frac{\text{Total Revenue}}{6.5}$$

$$\approx \frac{3}{130} \times \text{Total Revenue}$$

Similarly, we can check the other options and easily see that the volume of data transfer is NOT the same for given pair countries.

438. a Subscription in Europe in 2006 = 380 Mn USD

Subscription in Europe in 2007 = 500 Mn USD

$$\% \text{ change in 2007} = \frac{500-380}{380} \times 100 \approx 30\%$$

Therefore subscription (based upon the growth rate of 2007 over 2006) in 2008 should have been

= 500 × 1.3 = 650 Mn USD (approx)

Therefore difference from the estimated subscription

= 650 – 600 = 50 Mn USD (approx)

[Please note that the unit is mentioned neither in the question, nor in the options]

439. a Let the total number of subscribers = 100x

Number of men = 60x

Therefore number of men in 2010

$= 60x \times (1.05)^7 = 84.42x$ (approx)

Number of women = 40x

Therefore, number of women in 2010

$= 40x \times 1.1^7 = 77.94x$ (approx)

Therefore, total number of subscribers

= 84.42x + 77.94x = 162.36x

Percentage growth of subscribers

$$= \frac{162.36x - 100x}{100x} = 62.36 \text{ (approx)}$$

440. d Gap in 2008 = 780 – 600 = 180 Mn USD

Gap in 2009 = 810 – 700 = 110 Mn USD

$$\text{Annual \% change} = \frac{110-180}{180} \times 100 = -39\%$$

Absolute change = 39% which is the highest. Among the other options, option (c) '06-07' is closest, but it will lead to only 22% change in gap.

441. c $\text{Growth rate of 2007} = \frac{500-380}{380} \times 100 = 31.58\%$

$$\text{Growth rate of 2005} = \frac{280-190}{190} \times 100 = 47.37\%$$

Therefore % change in growth rate of 2007 relative to growth rate of 2005 is

$$\frac{47.37-31.58}{47.37}\times 100 \approx 35\%$$

442. e Since we do not know what the share prices are during different times of the day, we cannot come to any conclusion.

443. e Abdul buys all his shares at 10 am while the other two purchases once every hour. Since the share prices throughout the day is not specified, we cannot compare the returns of Abdul with the other two. Let us observe the strategies adopted by Bikram and Chetan.

Bikram buys equal number of shares every one hour, irrespective of their prices.

Chetan invests equal amount every one hour, irrespective of the share prices. This means that higher the share price, lesser the number of shares purchased by him. This in turn reduces his return. So whenever the prices are changing, Chetan's returns will be higher than Bikram's. In case, the share prices remain the same, the returns of Bikram and Chetan will be equal.

Hence, the correct option is (e) – none of the above.

444. a As the share prices are increasing throughout the day, the earlier a person invests, the more profitable it would be. Therefore, Abdul who invested in the beginning only, had reaped in the maximum return. Between Bikram and Chetan, Bikram bought a fixed number of shares every one hour, i.e. towards the end , he must have bought the same number of shares at an even higher rate. Meanwhile, Chetan invested same amount every one hour, i.e. he bought higher number of shares when the prices were low and vice versa. Hence, Chetan's return will be definitely higher than Bikram's.

Additional data for questions 445 to 446:

Let the share prices (in Rs.) at 10 am, 11 am, 12 noon, 1 pm, 2 pm and 3 pm be a, b, c, d, e and f respectively.

Abdul purchased all his shares at 10 am and sold off the same at 3 pm. It is given that he incurred a loss. If he bought n shares, then his investment = na must be more than his sale price = nf, i.e.

$$na > nf \Rightarrow a > f \quad \text{... (i)}$$

Similarly, Emily bought/sold same number of shares at 10 am/12 noon and 1 am/3 pm and finally made profit.

i.e. $c + f > a + d$ ... (ii)

Similar observation for Dane can be made

i.e. $d + e + f > a + b + c$ ... (iii)

It is given that share price at 12 noon is less than the opening price, i.e.

$a > c$ ... (iv)

Also, share price at 2 pm is lower than the closing price

i.e. $f > e$ ... (v)

From (i) and (ii), we get

$c > d$ ... (vi)

From (i), (iii) and (vi), we get e > b

Hence, we have a > f > e > b and a > c > d.

445. a The share price was the highest at 10 am.

446. a and d

Share price was lowest either at 11 am or 1 pm. Therefore, option (a) is false.

Share price at 1 pm was higher than that at 12 noon (equation (vi)).

447. c Average gross pay of HR department before transfer

= Rs. 5000 × 1.7

= Rs. 8500

Basic pay of the transferred person = Rs. 8000

New allowance of the transferred person = (80 + 10) = 90% of the basic pay

New Gross pay of the transferred person

= Rs. 8000 × 1.9

= Rs. 15,200

New average gross pay of HR dept.

$$= \text{Rs. } 8500 + \left(\frac{15200-8500}{6}\right) = \text{Rs. } (8500+1116)$$

$$\text{Percentage change} = \frac{1116}{8500}\times 100 \approx 13\%$$

448. c Since increase in average age of the Finance department. is one year, the age of the person moving from Marketing to Finance is more than that moving from Finance to Marketing, by 1 × 20 = 20 years.

Hence, due to this transfer, cumulative age of Marketing department has gone down by 20 yrs. But since the average age of Marketing department remaining unchanged, the person moving from Marketing to HR has age = (Avg. age of Marketing) – 20 = 15 years.

New average age of HR dept.

$$= \frac{(5\times 45)+(1\times 15)}{5+1} = 40 \text{ yrs.}$$

449. b Total basic pay of HR = 5 × 5000 (existing) + 2 × 6000 (from Maintenance) + 1 × 8000 (from Marketing) = Rs. 45,000

$$\text{New average} = \frac{45{,}000}{8} = \text{Rs. } 5{,}625$$

$$\text{Percentage change} = \frac{625}{5000}\times 100 = 12.5\%.$$

450. c The total production of Charyana in 1991 = 925

The percentage contribution

$$= \frac{925}{5600} \times 100 = 16.52$$

The total production of Charyana in 1992 = 1165

The percentage contribution

$$= \frac{1156}{6300} \times 100 = 18.49$$

The total production of Charyana in1993 = 1300

The percentage contribution

$$= \frac{1300}{6700} \times 100 = 19.40$$

451. d None of the three crops showed a decline in production for two consecutive years in Charyana.

452. c Bajra showed a decline in production in Charyana in 1992 despite showing an increase in production for two consecutive years in Khetistan.

For questions 44 to 47:

Let's assume that the grade points awarded to Himanshu in English, Vijay in Math and Saral in Science are x, y and z respectively.

The sum of the five grade points for:

Abhishek = 39
Saral = 35 + z
Himanshu = 36 + x
Puneet = 44
Vijay = 30 + y
Sanjay = 42

Since Abhishek and Vijay get equal GPAs,

39 = 30 + y

⇒ y = 9

⇒ Y lies in the range 81-90.

Since the sum of the GPAs of Saral and Puneet is equal to the sum of the GPAs of Himanshu and Sanjay,

(35 + z) + 44 = (36 + x) + 42

⇒ x = z + 1

Since the GPA obtained by Himanshu is the highest, x cannot be less than 9. (Otherwise Puneet's GPA would be either equal to or higher than Himanshu's GPA.)

If x = 10 then z = x – 1 = 9. In this case the GPAs of Saral and Puneet would become equal (which violates the condition given in the question).

So x = 9, z = 8.

⇒ X lies in the range 81-90, Z lies in the range 71 – 80.

Sum of the marks obtained by the six students in:

English = 374 + X
Hindi = 470
Math = 445 + Y
Science = 391 + Z
S.Sc. = 462

Since the total marks in Science are definitely less than the total marks in Math, the total marks in Science should be more than the total marks in Hindi.

So 391 + Z > 470

⇒ Z > 79

⇒ Z = 80

The total marks obtained by:

Abhishek = 363
Saral = 422
Himanshu = 333 + X
Puneet = 421
Vijay = 283 + Y
Sanjay = 400

Since the total marks obtained by Himanshu are not the highest, his total should be less than Saral's total.

So 333 + X < 422

⇒ X < 89

⇒ X lies in the range 81-88.

The final table looks like this:

	English	Hindi	Math	Science	S.Sc.
Abhishek	56	67	92	97	51
Saral	88	79	87	80	88
Himanshu	81-88	81	82	89	81
Puneet	83	90	91	78	79
Vijay	74	65	81-90	67	77
Sanjay	73	88	93	60	86

For questions 457 to 460 :

The figure can be completed on the basis of the given information. It would look like this:

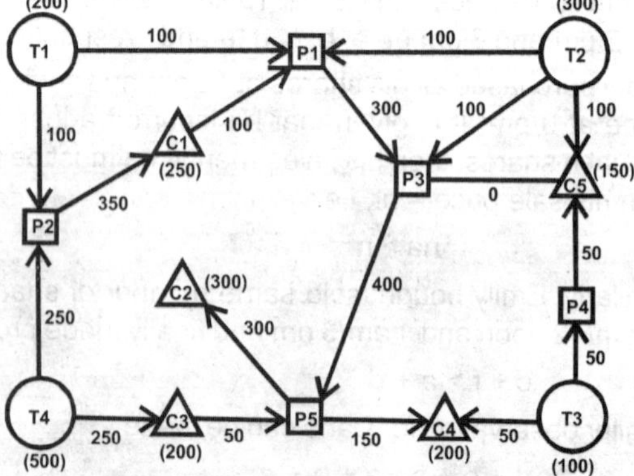

461. c The total number of employees who were appraised in January was 71 + 67 + 97 i.e. 235. These were the employees who were appraised on at least one performance area.

The total number of employees who were appraised in July was 30 + 22 + 29 i.e. 81. These were the employees who were appraised on at least two performance areas.

The number of employees who were appraised on exactly one performance area is 235 – 81 i.e. 154.

462. a The number of employees who were not appraised on Individual Performance in January was 67 + 97 i.e. 164. The employees who were appraised on Individual Performance in July and November were among these 164 employees only. So the number of employees who were not appraised on Individual Performance in 2010 was 164 – (30 + 9) = 125.

For questions 463 to 465 :

Let N(1) = N(6) = a, N(2) = N(5) = b, N(3) = c and N(4) = d. Here a, b and c are distinct (as given). Also, b and d cannot be the same.

Hence, 2a + 2b + c + d = 10 (the total number of people).

$\Rightarrow 2(a + b) + c + d = 10$

The least possible value of 'a + b' is 3 and it is evident from the above equation that none among a, b, c and d can be greater than or equal to 4. The only possible integer solution to the above equation is when a, b, c and d are equal 1, 2, 3 and 1 respectively.

The following table can thus be concluded:

	Number of occupants	Name of the occupants
Floor 6	1	?
Floor 5	2	?
Floor 4	1	?
Floor 3	3	?
Floor 2	2	?
Floor 1	1	?

From statement (ii) and the above table it is evident that Chuck's floor number is greater than 3 and hence from statement (i) and the above table it can be concluded that Chuck and Berry live on floor 5. Subsequently, Kirk and David live on floor 4 and floor 3 respectively. Clapton, Jimmy and Hammett must occupy floor 1 and floor 2 (in no particular order), as they live below David. From statement (iii) it can be concluded that Gilmour and Page live on floor 3 with David. Finally, it can be concluded from statement (iv) that Jimmy and Eric live on floor 1 and floor 6 respectively. The table can be completed as given below.

	Number of occupants	Name of the occupants
Floor 6	1	Eric
Floor 5	2	Chuck, Berry
Floor 4	1	Kirk
Floor 3	3	David, Gilmour, Page
Floor 2	2	Clapton, Hammett
Floor 1	1	Jimmy

463. b Difference = 3 – 2 = 1

464. a Eric lives on floor 6

465. c Jimmy lives alone on floor 1. The rest 9 people live on floors higher than his.

466. d The Energy Consumption of a department can be obtained by dividing the Total Revenue of that department by the Average Revenue per Unit Energy Consumed by that department. Among the five companies, the Energy Consumption is the highest for Perfitti VM at approximately 1900W-hrs.

467. d There are six departments in all whose Energy Consumption is less than 100W-hrs. They include two departments of UB Group, one of Unilever and three of Wipro.

468. b Unilever has two departments whose Total Revenue is more than Rs. 600 crores and Energy Consumption is less than 200W-hrs. The only other department that satisfies the given criteria is of ITC Ltd.

469. b Both Oil Trade Balance and Total Trade Balance decreased from 1990-91 to 2000-01. The increase in Oil Imports from 1990-91 to 2000-01 was more as compared to the increase in Oil Exports from 2000-01 to 2010-11.

470. d Non-Oil Exports increased by approximately 273% from 2000-01 to 2010-11.

Total Exports increased by approximately 377% from 1990-91 to 2000-01.

Oil Imports increased by 175% from 1980-81 to 1990-91.

Total Imports increased by approximately 55% from 2000-01 to 2010-11.

471. a Absolute percentage change in the total sales of Naruti Kuzuki Ltd. from April to July

$$= \frac{5670 - 5250}{5250} \times 100 = 8\%$$

Absolute percentage change in sales of Dwift from April to July $= \frac{75 - 69}{75} \times 100 = 8\%$

472. d Sales of the other car models of Naruti Kuzuki Ltd. in May 2010

$= 549000 - (50 + 72 + 51 + 52) \times 1000 = 324 \times 10^3$

Sales of the other car models of Naruti Kuzuki Ltd. in July 2010

$= 567000 - (42 + 63 + 33 + 69) \times 1000 = 360 \times 10^3$

Percentage increase

$$= \frac{360 - 324}{324} \times 100 = 11.11\%$$

473. b The ratio of the sales of Sezire to the total sales of cars by Naruti Kuzuki Ltd. in:

$$\text{April} = \frac{49\times1000}{5250\times100} = \frac{7}{75}$$

$$\text{May} = \frac{72\times1000}{5490\times100} = \frac{8}{61}$$

$$\text{June} = \frac{72\times1000}{5580\times100} = \frac{8}{62}$$

$$\text{July} = \frac{63\times1000}{5670\times100} = \frac{1}{9}$$

So the ratio is the highest for May.

474. c We can say that the total fare of:

Delhi-Bhopal + Bhopal-Mumbai

= Mumbai-Delhi + Rs.125.

Hence, the variable fare of:

Delhi-Bhopal + Bhopal-Mumbai

= Mumbai-Delhi + Rs.65.

This is possible only if Mumbai-Delhi falls in the distance range 1001 – 1800 km (Rs. 340). One of Delhi-Bhopal and Bhopal-Mumbai falls in the range 151 – 500 km (Rs. 155) and the other falls in the range 501 – 1000 km (Rs. 250).

475. c Yatri Kumar must have travelled in a Passenger train.

First day: Fare in the Sleeper Class for the distance range 1001 – 1800 km

= Rs. 160 + Rs. 60 = Rs. 220.

Second day: Fare in the Air Conditioned Class for the distance range $\leq$150 km

= Rs. 120 + Rs. 100 = Rs. 220.

For questions 476 to 478 : The table given below can be formed from the data given in the question.

Commodities	Maize	Rice	Sugar Cane	Cotton	Mustard Seeds
Total production cost (Rs. lakhs)	90	75	105	160	140
Profit per ton (Rs. lakhs)	30	15	20	15	40

476. b Profit percentage per ton for:

$$\text{Maize} = \frac{30}{90}\times100 = 33.33\%$$

$$\text{Rice} = \frac{15}{75}\times100 = 20\%$$

$$\text{Sugar Cane} = \frac{20}{105}\times100 = 19.05\%$$

$$\text{Cotton} = \frac{15}{160}\times100 = 9.375\%$$

$$\text{Mustard seeds} = \frac{40}{140}\times100 = 28.57\%$$

So the profit percentage per ton is the highest for Maize.

477. c Two - Sugar Cane and Cotton.

478. c Total quantity of raw material used in production of 1 ton of Cotton $= \frac{27\times10^5}{54} = 50{,}000$ kg

The total area of land required

$$= \frac{10}{200}\times50{,}000\times10^3$$

$$= 2500000\ \text{m}^2 = 2.5\text{km}^2$$

479. c For the year 2005-06 and 2008-09

	Efficacy Ratio		
	Total	Corporate	Individual
2004-05	0.96	0.98	0.89
2005-06	**1.03**	**0.98**	**1.5**
2006-07	0.98	1.01	0.79
2007-08	0.96	0.99	0.86
2008-09	**1.02**	**1.12**	**0.79**

Alternate method:

2004 - 05: By visual inspection for both "Total I-Tax" and "Corporate I-Tax" efficacy ratio is less than one, hence we need not check for "Individual I-Tax".

2005 - 06: Similarly, efficacy ratio of "Total I-Tax" collections is more than one but for "Corporate I-Tax" it is less than one, calculating for "Individual I-Tax" it comes out to be more than one.

2006 - 07: Similarly efficacy ratio of "Corporate I-Tax" is more than one but that of "Total I-Tax" collection is less than one. The same value for "Individual I-Tax" comes out to be less than one.

2007 - 08: By visual inspection for both "Total I-Tax" and "Corporate I-Tax" efficacy ratio is less than one, hence we need not check for "Individual I-Tax".

2008 - 09: Similarly by visual inspection for both "Total I-Tax" and "Corporate I-Tax", efficacy ratio is greater then one.

480. a For the year 2005-06 in the **Corporate I-Tax**

	Total (Budgeted)	% Growth	Total (Actual)	% Growth
2004-05	275	-	285	
2005-06	345	25.5	335	17.5
2006-07	395	14.5	405	20.9
2007-08	520	31.6	540	33.3
2008-09	730	40.4	715	32.4

	Corporate (Budgeted)	% Growth	Corporate (Actual)	% Growth
2004-05	235	-	240	-
2005-06	**300**	**27.7**	**307**	**27.9**
2006-07	340	13.3	335	9.1
2007-08	425	25	430	28.4
2008-09	560	31.8	500	16.3

481. d I. Percentage contribution of Corporate I-Tax to the Total I-Tax in the year 2005-06

$$= \left(\frac{307}{335}\right) \times 100 = 91.6\%$$

In the year 2008-09 = $\left(\frac{500}{715}\right) \times 100 = 70\%$

II. Simple Annual Growth Rate

$$= \frac{(215-45)}{45} \times 100 \times \left(\frac{1}{4}\right) = 94.4\%$$

III. This is also true as evident from the table provided.

482. c Sum of all the entries corresponding to the year 2009 = Rs. 3408 cr.

483. b Compare the values of

$$\frac{Sales_{09}}{Sales_{08}} \times \frac{(Market\ Share)_{08}}{(Market\ Share)_{09}}$$

for A = 1.168

B = 1.264

C = 0.925

D = 0.982

E = 1.211

484. a Let a total of 100N units be sold in both the years 2008 and 2009.

Statement 1:

A could not register growth in South and C could not register growth in both South and East.

Statement 1 is true.

Statement 2:

Number of units sold by B in 2009 in South

$$= \left(\frac{12}{100} \times 100N\right)\frac{77}{314} = 2.94N$$

Number of units sold by B in 2008 in South

$$= \left(\frac{10}{100} \times 100N\right)\frac{17}{214} = 0.79N$$

Percentage increase

$$= \left(\frac{2.94-0.79}{0.79}\right) \times 100 = 272\%$$

Statement 2 is false.

Statement 3:

Number of units sold by C in 2009 (23N) is greater than the number of units sold by C in 2008 (22N).

Statement 3 is false.

For questions 485 to 487 : The given data can be tabulated as shown below.

Counties	NCD deaths in 2008			NCD deaths in 2009		
	Male	Female	**Total**	Male	Female	**Total**
Indonesia	582	815	**1397**	275	850	**1125**
Russia	827	892	**1719**	950	925	**1875**
India	2967	2273	**5240**	3160	2020	**5180**
China	4323	3670	**7993**	4195	3850	**8045**
USA	1054	1150	**2204**	1150	530	**1680**
Total	**9753**	**8800**	**18553**	**9730**	**8175**	**17905**

485. c In three countries, viz. Indonesia, India and USA, the number of deaths due to NCDs in 2009 was less than that in 2008.

486. a Required percentage

$$= \frac{8800-8175}{8800} \times 100 = 7.10.$$

487. b Required difference = (9753 – 9730) × 1000 = 23000.

For questions 488 to 490 :

The total number of athletes sent by:

$$USA = 2400 \times \frac{8}{24} = 800$$

$$China = 2400 \times \frac{11}{24} = 1100$$

$$Russia = 2400 \times \frac{5}{24} = 500$$

488. c Total number of Cycling athletes sent by the three countries together

= 0.15 × 800 + 0.12 × 1100 + 0.16 × 500 = 332

Total number of female Cycling athletes sent by the three countries together = 166

Number of female Cycling athletes sent by Russia

$$= \frac{1}{20} \times (0.16 \times 500) = 4$$

Number of Cycling athletes sent by USA

$$= \frac{4}{5} \times (0.15 \times 800) = 96$$

Hence, the number of female Cycling athletes sent by China = 166 – (4 + 96) = 66.

489. a Maximum number of athletes sent by China for a game = 0.25 × 1100 = 275

Minimum number of athletes sent by Russia for a game = 0.03 × 500 = 15

Hence, the required difference = 275 – 15 = 260

490. d The total number of Water Polo athletes sent by the three countries put together

$= 0.15 \times 800 + 0.25 \times 1100 + 0.10 \times 500 = 445$

Hence, the required percentage

$$= \frac{445}{2400} \times 100 = 18.54.$$

491. c Let the GDP of Belgium be y Euros.

$$\therefore \quad y \times \frac{4.8}{100} \times 1.5 = x \Rightarrow y = \frac{100}{7.2}x$$

Hence, the debt (in Euros) of Belgium

$$= \frac{100.8}{100} \times \frac{100}{7.2}x = 14x.$$

492. c Two countries, viz. Denmark and Finland, were rated AAA.

493. a Let the GDP (in Euros) of Italy be x.

Therefore, the GDP (in Euros) of Finland = 1.5x.

The fiscal-deficit of:

Italy = 0.051x

Finland = 0.034 × 1.5x = 0.051x.

Hence, the required percentage = 0.

494. b Profitability of NIIT in 1999 is $\frac{106}{481} = 0.2204$

Profitability of Aptech in 1999 is $\frac{51}{320} = 0.1594$

Profitability of SSI in 1999 is $\frac{34}{85} = 0.4$

Profitability of Tata Infotech in 1999 is $\frac{6}{420} = 0.0143$

Average of the profitabilities of the four companies in 1999

$$= \frac{\frac{106}{481} + \frac{51}{320} + \frac{34}{85} + \frac{6}{420}}{4} = 0.1985.$$

∴ Only Tata Infotech and Aptech have a profitability less than the average of the profitabilities in 1999.

495. b Total revenues of four companies in 2001

= 509 + 285 + 231 + 523

= 1548 crore.

Total profit in 2001 = 20 + 54 + 51 + 27

= 152 crore

So total cost = (1548 – 152) = 1396 crore

In 2002, total revenue ≈ (1548 – 155) crore

= 1393 crore.

Total cost ≈ (1396 + 140) = 1536 crore

Hence, net profit = (1393 – 1536)

= –143 crore

$$\therefore \quad \text{Profitability} = \frac{-143}{1393} = -10.25\%.$$

496. a The profitability of NIIT, Aptech, SSI and Tata Infotech in 2001 is $\frac{20}{509}, \frac{54}{285}, \frac{51}{231}$ and $\frac{27}{523}$ respectively.

Thus, the correct order is:

NIIT, Tata Infotech, Aptech and SSI.

497. c The profitability SSI is highest in 2000 and it is $= \frac{49}{131}$.

For questions 498 to 499: The following table can be drawn.

B-school	No.of companies	No.of students	No. of offers	Offers per company	Offers per student
FMS	60	100	125	2.08	1.25
IMT	90	150	225	2.5	1.5
IMI	50	120	150	3	1.25
K.J.Somai	70	150	150	2.14	1
Narsee Monjee	80	150	200	2.5	1.33

498. a IMT has the highest number of offers per student.

499. c IMI has the highest ratio of offers per company.

500. d Total salary for FMS = 100 × 7

= ₹ 700 lakh.

Total salary of PPO holders = (25% of 100) × 10

= ₹ 250 lakh.

∴ Average annual salary of people not getting PPOs $= \frac{700 - 250}{75} = 6$ lakhs.

501. a Put n = 5, in the given relation to get $P_5 = 267$.

$P_6 = P_5 - P_4 + P_3 - P_2$

$\Rightarrow \quad P_6 = -P_1$

$P_7 = -P_2,$

Similarly, $P_8 = -P_3$

$P_9 = -P_4$

$P_{10} = -P_5.$

The sequence repeats its terms after every 10 terms.

Following this pattern, we observe that

$P_{531} = P_{(530+1)} = P_1 = 211$

$P_{753} = P_{(750+3)} = P_3 = 420$

$P_{975} = P_{(970+5)} = P_5 = 267$

So; $P_{531} + P_{753} + P_{975} = 211 + 420 + 267 = 898.$

502. c Minimum percentage to pass in a subject = 33.33%

Thus, 40° out of 360° represents 33.33%.

⇒ 60° represents 50%.

503. b Let maximum marks for each subject other than maths = 100

∴ Maximum marks in maths = 200.

For Geoffrey, 144° = 200 marks.

⇒ 360° = 500 marks.

For Tommen, if 120° = 200 marks then

72° > 100 marks,

which is not possible.

∴ For Tommen, 72° = 100 marks

⇒ 360° = 500 marks.

∴ Ratio of maximum marks, in all the subjects put together, which Geoffrey can score to the maximum marks, in all the subjects put together, which Tommen can score = 1 : 1.

504. d Before the change in pattern,

144° = 100 marks

⇒ 360° = 250 marks.

After the change in pattern,

80° = 100 marks

⇒ 360° = 450 marks.

∴ Desired ratio = 450 : 250 = 9 : 5.

505. a By the problem,

144° = 100 marks

⇒ 360° = 250 marks.

$\therefore$ Average percentage $= \frac{250}{500} \times 100$

= 50%.

506. a Let the total investment in education sector by India be Rs. 'P' crore the same in China will be Rs. 1.6 P crore.

For china, 32% of 1.6 P was from ADB loans which will constitute

$$A = \frac{0.32 \times 1.6P}{\left(\frac{54}{360} \times 7200\right)} \times 100\%$$

For India,

$$B = \frac{0.2 \times P}{\left(\frac{40}{360} \times 7200\right)} \times 100\%$$

A : B = 256 : 135.

507. b Amount of loan invested in transport sector by China

$= \frac{60}{100} \times \frac{24}{360} \times 7200$ cr

Total investment in transport by china

$= \frac{60}{100} \times \frac{24}{360} \times 7200 \times \frac{100}{55} = 523.63$ cr

Amount of loan invested in transport sector by India

$= \frac{60}{100} \times \frac{24}{100} \times 7200$ cr

Total investment in transport by India

$= \frac{60}{100} \times \frac{24}{360} \times 7200 \frac{100}{50} = 480$ cr

Required percentage $= \frac{480}{523.63} \times 100 = 91.67\%$.

508. a Loan amount invested in education

= 20% of 150 = Rs 30 cr

Loan amount invested in Health

= 22% of 120 = Rs 26.4 cr

Loan amount invested in Agriculture

= 16% of 400 = Rs 64 cr

The required percentage $= \frac{30 + 26.4 + 64}{\left(\frac{40}{360} \times 7200\right)} \times 100$

= 15.05.

509. c Total investment will be maximum when maximum loan amount is invested in education i.e. Rs. 440 cr. And Rs. 30 cr each is invested in other two sectors.

Total investment in the 3 sectors will be

$= 440 \times \frac{100}{20} + 30 \times \frac{100}{30} + 30 \times \frac{100}{50}$

= Rs. 2360 cr

For questions 510 to 513 :

	Total Capacity (n MW units)	Units Sold (In MW units)
A	8,500	7,565
B	6,250	5,437.50
C	10,000	9,000
D	8,500	7,225
E	9,500	7,600

510. d Total capacity of India $= 6{,}250 \times \frac{100}{12.5}$

= 50,000 MW units

Thermal capacity of India = 95% of total capacity

= 47,500 MW units

Total capacity of these five power plants

= 42,750 MW units

$$\text{Required percentage} = \frac{42,750}{47,500} \times 100 = 90\%.$$

511. b The correct order is C > E > A > D > B

512. d Profitability can be compared by comparing the ratio of total revenue to total cost.

$$\text{Profitability for A} = \frac{(89\% \text{ of TC}) \times 3.4}{(93\% \text{ of TC}) \times 2.1} = \frac{89 \times 3.4}{93 \times 2.1}$$

= 1.549.

where TC is the total capacity of that power plant.

Same values of others are

B → 1.406, C → 1.4108

D → 1.2617, E → 1.257

So, B has the third highest ratio and hence third highest profitability.

513. b Only statement 'b' is true.

Foq questions 514 to 517 :

Product	Total cost of production (In Rs. Crore)		Total profit (In Rs. Lakh)	
	Type P	Type Q	Type P	Type Q
A	13.64	11.36	204.6	340.8
B	38.71	36.29	967.8	725.8
C	15	22.5	225	450
D	16.67	20.83	250.1	208.3
E	14.3	10.7	357.5	214
F	25	25	500	375

514. 4 The profit made on items of Type Q is not more than the profit made on items of Type P for products B, D, E and F.

515. c For D, the desired ratio is lowest among all the products.

516. 3 For A, B and E, the overall profit percentage is more than 20%.

517. 55 Total Cost = 13.64 + 16.67 + 25

= Rs. 55.31 crore.

For questions 518 to 521:

The data given in the bar graph can be tabulated as shown below.

Let the total number of visitors in the year 2006 be 100x.

Year	Total number of visitors	Number of male visitors	Number of female visitors
2007	120x	60x	60x
2008	108x	81x	27x
2009	144x	96x	48x
2010	180x	108x	72x
2011	160x	104x	56x

518. The total number of female visitors in the year 2011

= 56x = 56 × 468.50 = 26236

519. Percentage growth in the number of female visitors from 2009 to 2010

$$= \frac{72x - 48x}{48x} \times 100$$

= 50%

520. Gender Gap in

the year 2009 = 96x – 48x = 48x

the year 2011 = 104x – 56x = 48x

Hence, it is equal in 2009 and 2011.

521. According to the question,

108x = 14796

⇒ x = 137

Hence, required number = 120 × 137

= 16440.

For questions 522 to 525:

Let the number of students who participated from East, West, North, South and Central regions be 20k, 16k, 21k, 25k and 18k respectively, where 'k' is a natural number.

The total number of students who participated from the five regions is equal to 100k.

⇒ (180 + 116 + 175 + 200 + 150) + 279 = 100k

⇒ 100k = 821 + 279

⇒ k = 11

Let the number of students who participated in Swimming and Cycling from the West region be x and y respectively, where x + y = 60.

The final table is given below.

	East	West	North	South	Central
Swimming	23	**x**	42	64	19
Lawn Tennis	45	27	**56**	46	31
Cycling	39	**y**	41	18	45
Badminton	52	49	23	38	**48**
Hockey	21	24	37	**75**	25
Football	**40**	16	32	34	30

522. The sum of the number of students who participated from the West region in Swimming and Cycling is 60. Since 60 when divided in the ratio 3 : 5 does not give integer values, 3 : 5 is the answer.

523. The number of students who participated in

Lawn Tennis = 205

Badminton = 210

Hockey = 182

Football = 152

In case of Swimming the number will be highest if x = 59, y = 1, and in case of Cycling the number will be highest if x = 1, y = 59. However, the number of students who participated in Badminton will still be the highest among the six events.

524. Required percentage = $\frac{48}{40} \times 100 = 120$.

525. We have x + y = 60.

According to the given condition, the possible values of x are 35, 40, 45, 50 and 55.

Hence, the required answer

= 75 (35 + 40 + 45 + 50 + 55)

= 16875.

For questions 526 to 529:

Since each department appears four times in the given combinations, the total number of employees in the organization

$$= \frac{870 + 600 + 780 + 670 + 630 + 850 + 640}{4}$$

= 1260.

The number of employees in MR department

= (MR, HR, FN, OP + TC, TL, AD, MR) – 1260

= (870 + 600) – 1260 = 210.

Similarly, the number of employees in HR, FN, OP, TC, TL and AD are 190, 220, 250, 120, 40 and 230 respectively.

Using the information given in the graph, the data can be tabulated as shown below.

Department	Total number of employees	Male employees	Female employees
MR	210	147	63
HR	190	76	114
FN	220	143	77
OP	250	175	75
TC	120	96	24
TL	40	30	10
AD	230	138	92

526. The ratio = $\frac{114}{96} = \frac{19}{16}$, i.e. 19:16.

527. The difference between the number of male employees and the number of female employees is the highest in OP department, i.e. 100.

528. The percentage

$$= \frac{(147 + 143 + 138) - (114 + 75 + 92)}{(114 + 75 + 92)} \times 100$$

$$= \frac{147}{281} \times 100 \approx 52.$$

529. The difference

= (147 + 76 + 143 + 175 + 96 + 30 + 138)

– (63 + 114 + 77 + 75 + 25 + 10 + 92)

= 350.

For questions 530 to 533:

Dorms 1, 3, 5, 7, 9 – either need moderate repair

Or

Extensive repair

Dorms 2, 4, 6, 8, 10 – either need light repair or extensive repair

Since 3/6, 3/9, dorm 6, light repair dorm 9 – moderate repair.

Since, dorm 8 needing the minimum repair = 1 crore.

We gather following information from the data given.

Dorms	Estimated repair cost (crore)
1	3–4
2	2
3	3–4
4	5
5	3–4
6	2
7	6
8	1
9	3–4
10	6

530. Dorm 10 estimated repair cost is 6 crore

531. 9 Odd number dorms are 1, 2, 5, 7, 9

Since there are 3 dorms whose repair cost is 3 crore and 1 dorm with repair cost of 4 crore

∴ total cost for odd-numbered dorms

= 3 × 3 + 4 + 6 = 19 crore.

532. Since total cost for repairing 4 women's dorm = 20 crores

The only possible combination is repair cost of dorm 4, 7, 9, 10.

$\therefore$ dorm 4 + dorm 7 + dorm 9 + dorm 10 = 20 crore

5 + 6 + dorm 9 + 6 = 20.

Dorm 9 = 3 crore.

533. Dorm 10 is a women's dorm

For questions 534 to 537:

Sales figures during second quarter of 2016:-

April, May and June form an A.P i.e. ,

40 + (40 + d) + (40 + 2d) = 150

d = 10

$\therefore$ Sales figures of April, May and June (2016) are 40, 50 and 60 respectively.

Similarly, sales figures of October, November, December (2016) are 100, 120 and 140 respectively, since, they also form an A.P.

Complete figure is:-

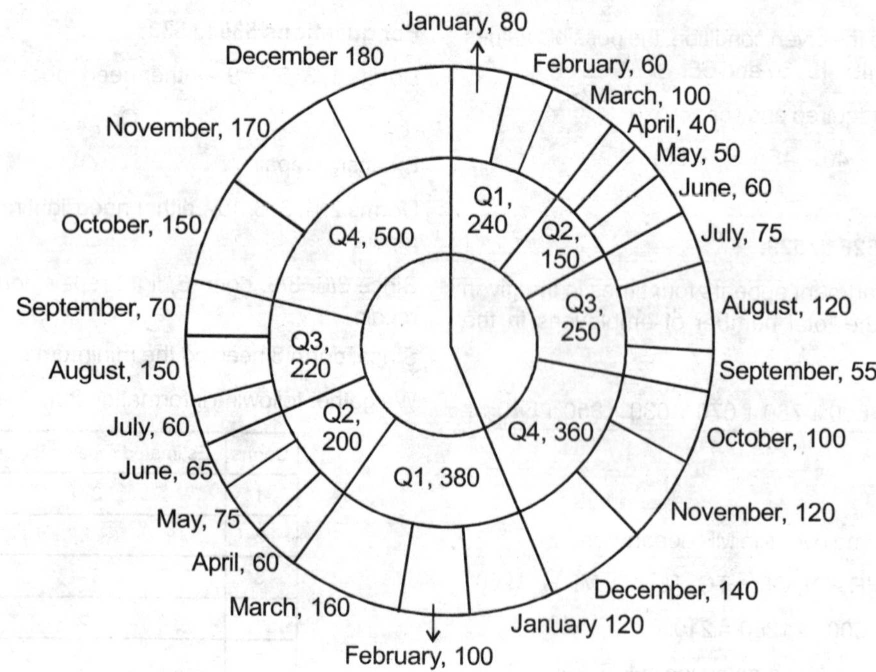

534. Percentage increase in sales in December 2017 as compared to the sales in December 2016 is:

$$\frac{180-140}{140} \times 100 = 28.57\%$$

535. Quarter 1 : $\frac{380-270}{270} \times 100 = 40.74\%$

Quarter 2 : $\frac{200-150}{150} \times 100 = 33.33\%$

Quarter 4 : $\frac{500-360}{360} \times 100 = 38.89\%$

Therefore, quarter 1.

536. In Q1 of 2007 and Q4 of 2017 increase in sales has been observed.

Q2 of 2016 : $\frac{240-150}{240}\times 100$

$=\frac{90}{240}\times 100 = 37.5\%$

Q2 of 2017 : $\frac{380-200}{380}\times 100$

$=\frac{180}{380}\times 100$

$= 47.37\%$

Therefore, Q2 of 2017.

537. March of 2016 : $\frac{100-60}{60}\times 100$

$=\frac{40}{60}\times 100$

$= 66.67\%$

October of 2016 : $\frac{100-55}{55}\times 100 = 81.82\%$

October of 2017 : 114.28%

March of 2017 : 60%

For questions 538 to 541:

By statement (6), Jatin scored 100% in exactly one section, therefore, that section has to be DI.

So composite score of Jatin will be:

2 × 20 + 16 + 14 = 70.

Indu's composite score is 60 (By statement 6)

Let Indu scored 100% in DI, then

2(20) + 8 + GA = 60

$\Rightarrow$ GA = 12

But since, Indu was recruited (by statement 4), therefore, she must have scored 70% or more in two or more sections.

Hence Indu scored 100% in, GA,

2(DI) + 8 + 20 = 60

DI =16

By statement (5), Danish, Harini and Indu had scored the same marks in GA, i.e., 20.

By statement (2), Ajay was the unique highest scorer in WE, i.e., he could score 19 or 20. But, if Ajay scores 19 in WE then his composite score will be 51, which is Danish's composite score.

Therefore, Ajay scored 20 in WE.

Since Indu was recruited (by statement 4), Jatin would be definitely recruited since his composite score is more than Indu.

Now, since Geeta is one of the recruited people with lowest composite score, therefore her score has to be definitely more than 52, hence, her score in WE will be either 19 or 20.

But her score in WE cannot be 20 as it will give the composite score of 54, which is already a composite score of Chetna and she is disqualified as she did not score 70% or more in two subjects.

Therefore, Geeta scored 19 in WE and have a composite score of 53.

So we get the table as:-

Candidate	Marks out of 20			Composite score	Status
	DI	WE	GA		
Ajay	8	20	16	52	qualified
Bala		9	11		disqualified
Chetna	19	4	12	54	disqualified
Danish	8	15	20	51	qualified
Ester	12	18	16	58	qualified
Falak	15	7	10	47	disqualified
Geeta	14	19	6	53	recruited
Harini	5		20		
Indu	16	8	20	60	recruited
Jatin	20	16	14	70	recruited

538. 1. Jatin scored 70 and Danish 51. True

2. Indu scored 16 in DI and Chetna scored 19 in DI. True.

3. Jatin and Indu scored 14 and 20 in GA. False.

Both (1) and (2)

539. If Bala scored same as Jatin in DI, i.e., 20 then composite score of Bala would be 2(20) + 9 + 11 = 60. Which is same as Indu's composite score, hence, not possible.

540. Chetna's composite score is 54.

Bala's composite score:-

2(DI) + 9 + 11 $\leq$ 50

DI $\leq$ 15, but 15 and 14 are already the scores in DI of Falak and Geeta respectively. Therefore, Bala could have scored maximum 13 marks in DI.

541. Harini could score maximum 14 marks in WE.

For questions 542 to 545:

542. Revenue = (Market Share) × (Unit Selling Price). Check the following table for the year 2016.

BRAND	Market Share (%)	Unit Selling Price	Profitability	Revenue = Market Share × Unit Selling Price
Azra	40	15000	10	6000
Bysi	25	20000	30	5000
Cxqi	15	30000	40	4500
Dipq	20	25000	30	5000

So Azra has the highest revenue in 2016.

543. Profit = (Market Share) × (Unit Selling Price) × (Profitability). Check the following table for the year 2016.

Brand	Profits
Azra	600
Bysi	1500
Cxqi	1800
Dipq	1500

Cxqi has the highest profit in 2016.

544. Profit = (Market Share) × (Unit Selling Price) × (Profitability).

Now for the year 2017, Cxqi offered 40% discount on its Unit Selling price.

New Unit Selling Price = 30000 – (0.4 × 30000) = 18000.

Due to this market share of Cxqi increased by 15%. So new market share for Cxqi = 30%.

There is a decrease of 5% in market share for Azra, Bysi, and Dipq respectively.

Also, profitability for Cxqi in 2017 = half of profitability in 2016.

Check the updated table for year 2017.

Brand	Market Share	Unit SP	Profitability	Profits
Azra	35	15000	10	525
Bysi	20	20000	30	1200
Cxqi	30	18000	20	1080
Dipq	15	25000	30	1125

Bysi has the highest profit in 2017.

545. Profit given in the previous table has increased by 40% in 2017. We get, the following table with comparing profits of brands in 2016 and 2017.

Brand	Profit (2016)	Profit (2017)
Azra	600	525 × 1.4 = 735
Bysi	1500	1200 × 1.4 = 1680
Cxqi	1800	1080 × 1.4 = 1512
Dipq	1500	1125 × 1.4 = 1575

As it can be observed from the table that for only Cxqi profit is decreasing. So, the answer is Azra, Bysi, Dipq.

For questions 546 to 549:

By looking at the table of conditions given for each product to fall under a category, we can easily make out that the four categories can be divided into four quadrants.

1. Promising is the top-right quadrant.
2. Blockbuster is the bottom-right quadrant.
3. No hope is the bottom left quadrant.
4. Doubtful is the top left quadrant.

546. Since product categories have been classified into 4 quadrants, just compare the sum of areas of the boxes in the quadrants to check which category has the maximum revenue as the area of a box is proportional to the revenue. Check the following table.

Promising	14
Blockbuster	36
No-hope	15
Doubtful	29

Blockbuster has the maximum area out of all the categories. So it has the maximum revenue.

547. From statement 1, it can be deduced that in the Blockbuster category, the number of products for A, B and C is 2, 2 and 3 respectively, as this category already has 2 Alfa products, 1 Bravo product, 2 Charlie products

From statement 2, it can be deduced that in the No-hope category, the number of products for A, B and C is 3, 1 and 2 respectively.

From statement 3, it can be deduced that in the Promising category, the number of products for A, B and C is 1 each. (Since there are 3 boxes in this category).

From statement 4, it can be deduced that in the doubtful category, the number of products for A, B and C is 4, 3 and 0 respectively.

Check the following table.

	A	B	C
Promising	1	1	1
Blockbuster	2	2	3
No-hope	3	1	2
Doubtful	4	3	0

So the number of products for B in No-hope, Doubtful, Promising, and Blockbuster is 1, 3, 1 and 2 respectively.

548. Using statement 5, 6, 7 and 8, it can be observed which box belongs to which company in the given different categories.

Check the following table to observe the revenues of different products in different categories.

	A	B	C
Promising	9	3	2
Blockbuster	9	10	17
No-hope	7	4	4
Doubtful	12	17	0
Total	37	34	23

So it can be seen from the table that Bravo's revenue from Blockbuster products is less than Alfa's revenue from Doubtful products. Hence, option (4) is incorrect.

549. Check the table given in the previous question, the total revenue of Bravo was Rs. 34 crore.

■■

CAT 2019 SOLVED PAPER (SLOT-1)

Section I: VRC

Question Numbers (1 to 5): The passage below is accompanied by a set of five questions. Choose the best answer to each question.

Contemporary internet shopping conjures a perfect storm of choice anxiety. Research has consistently held that people who are presented with a few options make better, easier decisions than those presented with many. . . . Helping consumers figure out what to buy amid an endless sea of choice online has become a cottage industry unto itself. Many brands and retailers now wield marketing buzzwords such as curation, differentiation, and discovery as they attempt to sell an assortment of stuff targeted to their ideal customer. Companies find such shoppers through the data gold mine of digital advertising, which can catalog people by gender, income level, personal interests, and more. Since Americans have lost the ability to sort through the sheer volume of the consumer choices available to them, a ghost now has to be in the retail machine, whether it's an algorithm, an influencer, or some snazzy ad tech to help a product follow you around the internet. Indeed, choice fatigue is one reason so many people gravitate toward lifestyle influencers on Instagram—the relentlessly chic young moms and perpetually vacationing 20-somethings—who present an aspirational worldview, and then recommend the products and services that help achieve it. . . .

For a relatively new class of consumer-products start-ups, there's another method entirely. Instead of making sense of a sea of existing stuff, these companies claim to disrupt stuff as Americans know it. Casper (mattresses), Glossier (makeup), Away (suitcases), and many others have sprouted up to offer consumers freedom from choice: The companies have a few aesthetically pleasing and supposedly highly functional options, usually at mid-range prices. They're selling nice things, but maybe more importantly, they're selling a confidence in those things, and an ability to opt out of the stuff rat race. . . .

One-thousand-dollar mattresses and $300 suitcases might solve choice anxiety for a certain tier of consumer, but the companies that sell them, along with those that attempt to massage the larger stuff economy into something navigable, are still just working within a consumer market that's broken in systemic ways. The presence of so much stuff in America might be more valuable if it were more evenly distributed, but stuff's creators tend to focus their energy on those who already have plenty. As options have expanded for people with disposable income, the opportunity to buy even basic things such as fresh food or quality diapers has contracted for much of America's lower classes.

For start-ups that promise accessible simplicity, their very structure still might eventually push them toward overwhelming variety. Most of these companies are based on hundreds of millions of dollars of venture capital, the investors of which tend to expect a steep growth rate that can't be achieved by selling one great mattress or one great sneaker. Casper has expanded into bedroom furniture and bed linens. Glossier, after years of marketing itself as no-makeup makeup that requires little skill to apply, recently launched a full line of glittering color cosmetics. There may be no way to opt out of stuff by buying into the right thing.

1. Which one of the following best sums up the overall purpose of the examples of Casper and Glossier in the passage?

1. They are exceptions to a dominant trend in consumer markets.
2. They are increasing the purchasing power of poor Americans.
3. They are facilitating a uniform distribution of commodities in the market.
4. They might transform into what they were exceptions to.

2. A new food brand plans to launch a series of products in the American market. Which of the following product plans is most likely to be supported by the author of the passage?

1. A range of 10 products priced between $5 and $10.
2. A range of 25 products priced between $10 and $25.
3. A range of 10 products priced between $10 and $25.
4. A range of 25 products priced between $5 and $10.

3. Which of the following hypothetical statements would add the least depth to the author's prediction of the fate of start-ups offering few product options?

1. Start-ups with few product options are no exception to the American consumer market that is deeply divided along class lines.
2. An exponential surge in their sales enables start-ups to meet their desired profit goals without expanding their product catalogue.
3. With Casper and Glossier venturing into new product ranges, their regular customers start losing trust in the companies and their products.
4. With the motive of promoting certain rival companies, the government decides to double the tax-rates for these start-ups.

4. Based on the passage, all of the following can be inferred about consumer behaviour EXCEPT that:

1. too many options have made it difficult for consumers to trust products.
2. consumers tend to prefer products by start-ups over those by established companies.
3. consumers are susceptible to marketing images that they see on social media.
4. having too many product options can be overwhelming for consumers.

5. All of the following, IF TRUE, would weaken the author's claims EXCEPT:

1. the annual sales growth of companies with fewer product options were higher than that of companies which curated their products for target consumers.
2. product options increased market competition, bringing down the prices of commodities, which, in turn, increased purchasing power of the poor.
3. the empowerment felt by purchasers in buying a commodity were directly proportional to the number of options they could choose from.
4. the annual sale of companies that hired lifestyle influencers on Instagram for marketing their products were 40% less than those that did not.

Question Numbers (6 to 10): The passage below is accompanied by a set of five questions. Choose the best answer to each question.

In the past, credit for telling the tale of Aladdin has often gone to Antoine Galland . . . the first European translator of . . . Arabian Nights [which] started as a series of translations of an incomplete manuscript of a medieval Arabic story collection. . . But, though those tales were of medieval origin, Aladdin may be a more recent invention. Scholars have not found a manuscript of the story that predates the version published in 1712 by Galland, who wrote in his diary that he first heard the tale from a Syrian storyteller from Aleppo named Hanna Diyab . . .

Despite the fantastical elements of the story, scholars now think the main character may actually be based on a real person's real experiences. . . . Though Galland never credited Diyab in his published translations of the Arabian Nights stories, Diyab wrote something of his own: a travelogue penned in the mid-18th century. In it, he recalls telling Galland the story of Aladdin [and] describes his own hard-knocks upbringing and the way he marveled at the extravagance of Versailles. The descriptions he uses were very similar to the descriptions of the lavish palace that ended up in Galland's version of the Aladdin story. [Therefore, author Paulo Lemos] Horta believes that "Aladdin might be the young Arab Maronite from Aleppo, marveling at the jewels and riches of Versailles." . . .

For 300 years, scholars thought that the rags-to-riches story of Aladdin might have been inspired by the plots of French fairy tales that came out around the same time, or that the story was invented in that 18th century period as a byproduct of French Orientalism, a fascination with stereotypical exotic Middle Eastern luxuries that was prevalent then. The idea that Diyab might have based it on his own life — the experiences of a Middle Eastern man encountering the French, not vice-versa — flips the script. [According to Horta,] "Diyab was ideally placed to embody the overlapping world of East and West, blending the storytelling traditions of his homeland with his youthful observations of the wonder of 18th-century France." . . .

To the scholars who study the tale, its narrative drama isn't the only reason storytellers keep finding reason to return to Aladdin. It reflects not only "a history of the French and the Middle East, but also [a story about] Middle Easterners coming to Paris and that speaks to our world today," as Horta puts it. "The day Diyab told the story of Aladdin to Galland, there were riots due to food shortages during the winter and spring of 1708 to 1709, and Diyab was sensitive to those people in a way that Galland is not. When you read this diary, you see this solidarity among the Arabs who were in Paris at the time. . . . There is little in the writings of Galland that would suggest that he was capable of developing a character like Aladdin with sympathy, but Diyab's memoir reveals a narrator adept at capturing the distinctive psychology of a young protagonist, as well as recognizing the kinds of injustices and opportunities that can transform the path of any youthful adventurer."

6. Which of the following is the primary reason for why storytellers are still fascinated by the story of Aladdin?

1. The traveller's experience that inspired the tale of Aladdin resonates even today.
2. The tale of Aladdin documents the history of Europe and Middle East.
3. The archetype of the rags-to-riches story of Aladdin makes it popular even today.
4. The story of Aladdin is evidence of the eighteenth century French Orientalist attitude.

7. Which of the following, if true, would invalidate the inversion that the phrase "flips the script" refers to?

1. The description of opulence in Hanna Diyab's and Antoine Galland's narratives bore no resemblance to each other.
2. Diyab's travelogue described the affluence of the French city of Bordeaux, instead of Versailles.
3. Galland acknowledged in the published translations of Arabian Nights that he heard the story of Aladdin from Diyab.
4. The French fairy tales of the eighteenth century did not have rags-to-riches plot lines like that of the tale of Aladdin.

8. The author of the passage is most likely to agree with which of the following explanations for the origins of the story of Aladdin?

1. The story of Aladdin has its origins in an undiscovered, incomplete manuscript of a medieval Arabic collection of stories.
2. Basing it on his own life experiences, Diyab transmitted the story of Aladdin to Galland who included it in Arabian Nights.
3. Galland received the story of Aladdin from Diyab who, in turn, found it in an incomplete medieval manuscript.
4. Galland derived the story of Aladdin from Diyab's travelogue in which he recounts his fascination with the wealth of Versailles.

9. All of the following serve as evidence for the character of Aladdin being based on Hanna Diyab EXCEPT:

1. Diyab's narration of the original story to Galland.
2. Diyab's humble origins and class struggles, as recounted in his travelogue.
3. Diyab's cosmopolitanism and cross-cultural experience.
4. Diyab's description of the wealth of Versailles in his travelogue.

10. Which of the following does not contribute to the passage's claim about the authorship of Aladdin?

1. Galland's acknowledgment of Diyab in his diary.
2. The depiction of the affluence of Versailles in Diyab's travelogue.
3. The story-line of many French fairy tales of the 18th century.
4. The narrative sensibility of Diyab's travelogue.

Question Numbers (11 to 15): The passage below is accompanied by a set of five questions. Choose the best answer to each question.

As defined by the geographer Yi-Fu Tuan, topophilia is the affective bond between people and place. His 1974 book set forth a wide-ranging exploration of how the emotive ties with the material environment vary greatly from person to person and in intensity, subtlety, and mode of expression. Factors influencing one's depth of response to the environment include cultural background, gender, race, and historical circumstance, and Tuan also argued that there is a biological and sensory element. Topophilia might not be the strongest of human emotions—indeed, many people feel utterly indifferent toward the environments that shape their lives—but when activated it has the power to elevate a place to become the carrier of emotionally charged events or to be perceived as a symbol.

Aesthetic appreciation is one way in which people respond to the environment. A brilliantly colored rainbow after gloomy afternoon showers, a busy city street alive with human interaction—one might experience the beauty of such landscapes that had seemed quite ordinary only moments before or that are being newly discovered. This is quite the opposite of a second topophilic bond, namely that of the acquired taste for certain landscapes and places that one knows well. When a place is home, or when a space has become the locus of memories or the means of gaining a livelihood, it frequently evokes a deeper set of attachments than those predicated purely on the visual. A third response to the environment also depends on the human senses but may be tactile and olfactory, namely a delight in the feel and smell of air, water, and the earth.

Topophilia—and its very close conceptual twin, sense of place—is an experience that, however elusive, has inspired recent architects and planners. Most notably, new urbanism seeks to counter the perceived placelessness of modern suburbs and the decline of central cities through neo-traditional design motifs. Although motivated by good intentions, such attempts to create places rich in meaning are perhaps bound to disappoint. As Tuan noted, purely aesthetic responses often are suddenly revealed, but their intensity rarely is long-lasting. Topophilia is difficult to design for and impossible to quantify, and its most articulate interpreters have been self-reflective philosophers such as Henry David Thoreau, evoking a marvelously intricate sense of place at Walden Pond, and Tuan, describing his deep affinity for the desert.

Topophilia connotes a positive relationship, but it often is useful to explore the darker affiliations between people and place. Patriotism, literally meaning the love of one's terra patria or homeland, has long been cultivated by governing elites for a range of nationalist projects, including war preparation and ethnic cleansing. Residents of upscale residential developments have disclosed how important it is to maintain their community's distinct identity, often by casting themselves in a superior social position and by reinforcing class and racial differences. And just as a beloved landscape is suddenly revealed, so too may landscapes of fear cast a dark shadow over a place that makes one feel a sense of dread or anxiety—or topophobia.

11. Which one of the following comes closest in meaning to the author's understanding of topophilia?

1. The tendency of many cultures to represent their land as "motherland" or "fatherland" may be seen as an expression of their topophilia
2. The French are not overly patriotic, but they will refuse to use English as far as possible, even when they know it well.
3. Scientists have found that most creatures, including humans, are either born with or cultivate a strong sense of topography.
4. Nomadic societies are known to have the least affinity for the lands through which they traverse because they tend to be topophobic.

12. Which one of the following best captures the meaning of the statement, "Topophilia is difficult to design for and impossible to quantify . . ."?

1. The deep anomie of modern urbanisation led to new urbanism's intricate sense of place.
2. People's responses to their environment are usually subjective and so cannot be rendered in design.
3. Philosopher-architects are uniquely suited to develop topophilic design.
4. Architects have to objectively quantify spaces and hence cannot be topophilic.

13. Which of the following statements, if true, could be seen as not contradicting the arguments in the passage?

1. The most important, even fundamental, response to our environment is our tactile and olfactory response.
2. Patriotism, usually seen as a positive feeling, is presented by the author as a darker form of topophilia.
3. Generally speaking, in a given culture, the ties of the people to their environment vary little in significance or intensity.
4. New Urbanism succeeded in those designs where architects collaborated with their clients.

14. In the last paragraph, the author uses the example of "Residents of upscale residential developments" to illustrate the:

1. social exclusivism practised by such residents in order to enforce a sense of racial or class superiority.
2. introduction of nationalist projects by such elites to produce a sense of dread or topophobia.
3. manner in which environments are designed to minimise the social exclusion of their clientele.
4. sensitive response to race and class problems in upscale residential developments.

15. The word "topophobia" in the passage is used:

1. to represent a feeling of dread towards particular spaces and places.
2. as a metaphor expressing the failure of the homeland to accommodate non-citizens.
3. to signify the fear of studying the complex discipline of topography.
4. to signify feelings of fear or anxiety towards topophilic people.

Question Numbers (16 to 19): The passage below is accompanied by a set of four questions. Choose the best answer to each question.

Scientists recently discovered that Emperor Penguins—one of Antarctica's most celebrated species—employ a particularly unusual technique for surviving the daily chill. As detailed in an article published today in the journal Biology Letters, the birds minimize heat loss by keeping the outer surface of their plumage below the temperature of the surrounding air. At the same time, the penguins' thick plumage insulates their body and keeps it toasty. . . .

The researchers analyzed thermographic images . . . taken over roughly a month during June 2008. During that period, the average air temperature was

0.32 degrees Fahrenheit. At the same time, the majority of the plumage covering the penguins' bodies was even colder: the surface of their warmest body part, their feet, was an average 1.76 degrees Fahrenheit, but the plumage on their heads, chests and backs were -1.84, -7.24 and -9.76 degrees Fahrenheit respectively. Overall, nearly the entire outer surface of the penguins' bodies was below freezing at all times, except for their eyes and beaks. The scientists also used a computer simulation to determine how much heat was lost or gained from each part of the body—and discovered that by keeping their outer surface below air temperature, the birds might paradoxically be able to draw very slight amounts of heat from the air around them. The key to their trick is the difference between two different types of heat transfer: radiation and convection.

The penguins do lose internal body heat to the surrounding air through thermal radiation, just as our bodies do on a cold day. Because their bodies (but not surface plumage) are warmer than the surrounding air, heat gradually radiates outward over time, moving from a warmer material to a colder one. To maintain body temperature while losing heat, penguins, like all warm-blooded animals, rely on the metabolism of food. The penguins, though, have an additional strategy. Since their outer plumage is even colder than the air, the simulation showed that they might gain back a little of this heat through thermal convection—the transfer of heat via the movement of a fluid (in this case, the air). As the cold Antarctic air cycles around their bodies, slightly warmer air comes into contact with the plumage and donates minute amounts of heat back to the penguins, then cycles away at a slightly colder temperature.

Most of this heat, the researchers note, probably doesn't make it all the way through the plumage and back to the penguins' bodies, but it could make a slight difference. At the very least, the method by which a penguin's plumage wicks heat from the bitterly cold air that surrounds it helps to cancel out some of the heat that's radiating from its interior. And given the Emperors' unusually demanding breeding cycle, every bit of warmth counts. . . . Since [penguins trek as far as 75 miles to the coast to breed and male penguins] don't eat anything during [the incubation period of 64 days], conserving calories by giving up as little heat as possible is absolutely crucial.

16. Which of the following best explains the purpose of the word "paradoxically" as used by the author?

1. Keeping their body colder helps penguins keep their plumage warmer.
2. Heat gain through radiation happens despite the heat loss through convection.
3. Keeping a part of their body colder helps penguins keep their bodies warmer.
4. Heat loss through radiation happens despite the heat gain through convection.

17. In the last sentence of paragraph 3, "slightly warmer air" and "at a slightly colder temperature" refer to ______AND ______respectively:

1. the cold Antarctic air whose temperature is higher than that of the plumage AND the fall in temperature of the Antarctic air after it has transmitted some heat to the plumage.
2. the air inside penguins' bodies kept warm because of metabolism of food AND the fall in temperature of the body air after it transfers some heat to the plumage.
3. the air trapped in the plumage which is warmer than the Antarctic air AND the fall in temperature of the trapped plumage air after it radiates out some heat.
4. the cold Antarctic air which becomes warmer because of the heat radiated out from penguins' bodies AND the fall in temperature of the surrounding air after thermal convection.

18. Which of the following can be responsible for Emperor Penguins losing body heat?

1. Food metabolism.
2. Thermal convection.
3. Reproduction process.
4. Plumage.

19. All of the following, if true, would negate the findings of the study reported in the passage EXCEPT:

1. the temperature of the plumage on the penguins' heads, chests and backs were found to be 1.84, 7.24 and 9.76 degrees Fahrenheit respectively.
2. the penguins' plumage were made of a material that did not allow any heat transfer through convection or radiation.
3. the average temperature of the feet of penguins in the month of June 2008 were found to be 2.76 degrees Fahrenheit.
4. the average air temperature recorded during the month of June 2008 in the area of study were –10 degrees Fahrenheit.

Question Numbers (20 to 24): The passage below is accompanied by a set of five questions. Choose the best answer to each question.

"Free of the taint of manufacture" – that phrase, in particular, is heavily loaded with the ideology of what the Victorian socialist WIlliam Morris called the "anti-scrape", or an anti-capitalist conservationism (not conservatism) that solaced itself with the vision of a pre-industrial golden age. In Britain, folk may often appear a cosy, fossilised form, but when you look more closely, the idea of folk – who has the right to sing it, dance it, invoke it, collect it, belong to it or appropriate it for political or cultural ends – has always been contested territory. . . .

In our own time, though, the word "folk" . . . has achieved the rare distinction of occupying fashionable and unfashionable status simultaneously. Just as the effusive floral prints of the radical William Morris now cover genteel sofas, so the revolutionary intentions of many folk historians and revivalists have led to music that is commonly regarded as parochial and conservative. And yet – as newspaper columns periodically rejoice – folk is hip again, influencing artists, clothing and furniture designers, celebrated at music festivals, awards ceremonies and on TV, reissued on countless record labels. Folk is a sonic "shabby chic", containing elements of the uncanny and eerie, as well as an antique veneer, a whiff of Britain's heathen dark ages. The very obscurity and anonymity of folk music's origins open up space for rampant imaginative fancies. . . .

[Cecil Sharp, who wrote about this subject, believed that] folk songs existed in constant transformation, a living example of an art form in a perpetual state of renewal. "One man sings a song, and then others sing it after him, changing what they do not like" is the most concise summary of his conclusions on its origins. He compared each rendition of a ballad to an acorn falling from an oak tree; every subsequent iteration sows the song anew. But there is tension in newness. In the late 1960s, purists were suspicious of folk songs recast in rock idioms. Electrification, however, comes in many forms. For the early-20th-century composers such as Vaughan Williams and Holst, there were thunderbolts of inspiration from oriental mysticism, angular modernism and the body blow of the first world war, as well as input from the rediscovered folk tradition itself.

For the second wave of folk revivalists, such as Ewan MacColl and AL Lloyd, starting in the 40s, the vital spark was communism's dream of a post-revolutionary New Jerusalem. For their younger successors in the 60s, who thronged the folk clubs set up by the old guard, the lyrical freedom of Dylan and the unchained melodies of psychedelia created the conditions for folk-rock's own golden age, a brief Indian summer that lasted from about 1969 to 1971. . . . Four decades on, even that progressive period has become just one more era ripe for fashionable emulation and pastiche. The idea of a folk tradition being exclusively confined to oral transmission has become a much looser, less severely guarded concept. Recorded music and television, for today's metropolitan generation, are where the equivalent of folk memories are seeded. . . .

20. The primary purpose of the reference to William Morris and his floral prints is to show:

1. that despite its archaic origins, folk continues to remain a popular tradition.
2. that what is once regarded as radical in folk, can later be seen as conformist.
3. the pervasive influence of folk on contemporary art, culture, and fashion.
4. that what was once derided as genteel is now considered revolutionary.

21. All of the following are causes for plurality and diversity within the British folk tradition EXCEPT:

1. that British folk forms can be traced to the remote past of the country.
2. paradoxically, folk forms are both popular and unpopular.
3. the fluidity of folk forms owing to their history of oral mode of transmission.
4. that British folk continues to have traces of pagan influence from the dark ages.

22. Which of the following statements about folk revivalism of the 1940s and 1960s cannot be inferred from the passage?

1. Freedom and rebellion were popular themes during the second wave of folk revivalism.
2. It reinforced Cecil Sharp's observation about folk's constant transformation.
3. Electrification of music would not have happened without the influence of rock music.
4. Even though it led to folk-rock's golden age, it wasn't entirely free from critique.

23. The author says that folk "may often appear a cosy, fossilised form" because:

1. folk is a sonic "shabby chic" with an antique veneer.
2. of its nostalgic association with a pre-industrial past.
3. it has been arrogated for various political and cultural purposes.
4. the notion of folk has led to several debates and disagreements.

24. At a conference on folk forms, the author of the passage is least likely to agree with which one of the following views?

1. The power of folk resides in its contradictory ability to influence and be influenced by the present while remaining rooted in the past.
2. Folk forms, despite their archaic origins, remain intellectually relevant in contemporary times.
3. The plurality and democratising impulse of folk forms emanate from the improvisation that its practitioners bring to it.
4. Folk forms, in their ability to constantly adapt to the changing world, exhibit an unusual poise and homogeneity with each change.

25. The four sentences (labelled 1, 2, 3, 4) given below, when properly sequenced would yield a coherent paragraph. Decide on the proper sequence of the order of the sentences and key in the sequence of the four numbers as your answer.

1. Metaphors may map to similar meanings across languages, but their subtle differences can have a profound effect on our understanding of the world.
2. Latin scholars point out carpe diem is a horticultural metaphor that, particularly seen in the context of its source, is more accurately translated as "plucking the day," evoking the plucking and gathering of ripening fruits or flowers, enjoying a moment that is rooted in the sensory experience of nature, unrelated to the force implied in seizing.
3. The phrase carpe diem, which is often translated as "seize the day and its accompanying philosophy, has gone on to inspire countless people in how they live their lives and motivates us to see the world a lillle differently from the norm
4. It's an example of one of the more telling ways that we mistranslate metaphors from one language to another, revealing in the process our hidden assumptions about what we really value.

26. Five sentences related to a topic are given below. Four of them can be put together to form a meaningful and coherent short paragraph. Identify the odd one out. Choose its number as your answer and key it in.

1. One argument is that actors that do not fit within a single, well-defined category may suffer an "illegitimacy discount".
2. Others believe that complex identities confuse audiences about an organization's role or purpose.
3. Some organizations have complex and multidimensional identities that span or combine categories, while other organizations possess narrow identities.
4. Identity is one of the most important features of organizations, but there exist opposing views among sociologists about how identity affects organizational performance.
5. Those who think that complex identities are beneficial point to the strategic advantages of ambiguity, and organizations' potential to differentiate themselves from competitors.

27. The passage given below is followed by four alternate summaries. Choose the option that best captures the essence of the passage.

Physics is a pure science that seeks to understand the behavior of matter without regard to whether it will afford any practical benefit. Engineering is the correlative applied science in which physical theories are put to some specific use, such as building a bridge or a nuclear reactor. Engineers obviously rely heavily on the discoveries of physicists, but an engineer's knowledge of the world is not the same as the physicist's knowledge. In fact, an engineer's know-how will often depend on physical theories that, from the point of view of pure physics, are false. There are some reasons for this. First, theories that are false in the purest and strictest sense are still sometimes very good approximations to the true ones, and often have the added virtue of being much easier to work with. Second, sometimes the true theories apply only under highly idealized conditions which can only be created under controlled experimental situations. The engineer finds that in the real world, theories rejected by physicists yield more accurate predictions than the ones that they accept.

1. Though engineering draws heavily from pure science, it contributes to knowledge, by incorporating the constraints and conditions in the real world.
2. Engineering and physics fundamentally differ on matters like building a bridge or a nuclear reactor.
3. The unique task of the engineer is to identify, understand, and interpret the design constraints to produce a successful result.
4. The relationship between pure and applied science is strictly linear, with the pure science directing applied science, and never the other way round.

28. The four sentences (labelled 1, 2, 3, 4) given below, when properly sequenced would yield a coherent paragraph. Decide on the proper sequence of the order of the sentences and key in the sequence of the four numbers as your answer.

1. If you've seen a little line of text on websites that says something like "customers who bought this also enjoyed that" you have experienced this collaborative filtering firsthand.
2. The problem with these algorithms is that they don't take into account a host of nuances and circumstances that might interfere with their accuracy.
3. If you just bought a gardening book for your cousin, you might get a flurry of links to books about gardening, recommended just for you! – the algorithm has no way of knowing you hate gardening and only bought the book as a gift.
4. Collaborative filtering is a mathematical algorithm by which correlations and co-occurrences of behaviors are tracked and then used to make recommendations.

29. Five sentences related to a topic are given below in a jumbled order. Four of them form a coherent and unified paragraph. Identify the odd sentence that does not go with the four. Key in the number of the option that you choose.

1. 'Stat' signaled something measurable, while 'matic' advertised free labour; but 'tron', above all, indicated control.
2. It was a totem of high modernism, the intellectual and cultural mode that decreed no process or phenomenon was too complex to be grasped, managed and optimized.
3. Like the heraldic shields of ancient knights, these morphemes were painted onto the names of scientific technologies to proclaim one's history and achievements to friends and enemies alike.
4. The historian Robert Proctor at Stanford University calls the suffix '-tron', along with '-matic' and '-stat', embodied symbols.
5. To gain the suffix was to acquire a proud and optimistic emblem of the electronic and atomic age.

30. The four sentences (labelled 1, 2, 3, 4) given below, when properly sequenced would yield a coherent paragraph. Decide on the proper sequence of the order of the sentences and key in the sequence of the four numbers as your answer.

1. We'll all live under mob rule until then, which doesn't help anyone.
2. Perhaps we need to learn to condense the feedback we receive online so that 100 replies carry the same weight as just one.
3. As we grow more comfortable with social media conversations being part of the way we interact every day, we are going to have to learn how to deal with legitimate criticism.
4. A new norm will arise where it is considered unacceptable to reply with the same point that dozens of others have already.

31. The passage given below is followed by four alternate summaries. Choose the option that best captures the essence of the passage.

Vance Packard's The Hidden Persuaders alerted the public to the psychoanalytical techniques used by the advertising industry. Its premise was that advertising agencies were using depth interviews to identify hidden consumer motivations, which were then used to entice consumers to buy goods. Critics and reporters often wrongly assumed that Packard was writing mainly about subliminal advertising. Packard never mentioned the word subliminal, however, and devoted very little space to discussions of "subthreshold" effects. Instead, his views largely aligned with the notion that individuals do not always have access to their conscious thoughts and can be persuaded by supraliminal messages without their knowledge.

1. Packard held that advertising as a 'hidden persuasion' builds on peoples' conscious thoughts and awareness, by understanding the hidden motivations of consumers and works at the subliminal level.
2. Packard argued that advertising as a 'hidden persuasion' works at the supraliminal level, wherein the people targeted are aware of being persuaded, after understanding the hidden motivations of consumers and works.
3. Packard held that advertising as a 'hidden persuasion' understands the hidden motivations of consumers and works at the supraliminal level, though the people targeted have no awareness of being persuaded.
4. Packard argued that advertising as a 'hidden persuasion' understands the hidden motivations of consumers and works at the subliminal level, on the subconscious level of the awareness of the people targeted.

32. The four sentences (labelled 1, 2, 3, 4) given below, when properly sequenced would yield a coherent paragraph. Decide on the proper sequence of the order of the sentences and key in the sequence of the four numbers as your answer.

1. People with dyslexia have difficulty with print-reading, and people with autism spectrum disorder have difficulty with mind-reading.
2. An example of a lost cognitive instinct is mind-reading: our capacity to think of ourselves and others as having beliefs, desires, thoughts and feelings.
3. Mind-reading looks increasingly like literacy, a skill we know for sure is not in our genes, since scripts have been around for only 5,000-6,000 years.
4. Print-reading, like mind-reading varies across cultures, depends heavily on certain parts of the brain, and is subject to developmental disorders.

33. Five sentences related to a topic are given below. Four of them can be put together to form a meaningful and coherent short paragraph. Identify the odd one out. Choose its number as your answer and key it in.

1. His idea to use sign language was not a completely new idea as Native Americans used hand gestures to communicate with other tribes.
2. Ancient Greek philosopher Aristotle, for example, observed that men who are deaf are incapable of speech.
3. People who were born deaf were denied the right to sign a will as they were "presumed to understand nothing; because it is not possible that they have been able to learn to read or write."
4. Pushback against this prejudice began in the 16th century when Pedro Ponce de León created a formal sign language for the hearing impaired.
5. For millennia, people with hearing impairments encountered marginalization becau se it was believed that language could only be learned by hearing the spoken word.

34. The passage given below is followed by four alternate summaries. Choose the option that best captures the essence of the passage.

A distinguishing feature of language is our ability to refer to absent things, known as displaced reference. A speaker can bring distant referents to mind in the absence of any obvious stimuli. Thoughts, not limited to the here and now, can pop into our heads for unfathomable reasons. This ability to think about distant things necessarily precedes the ability to talk about them. Thought precedes meaningful referential communication. A prerequisite for the emergence of human-like meaningful symbols is that the mental categories they relate to can be invoked even in the absence of immediate stimuli.

1. Thoughts are essential to communication and only humans have the ability to think about objects not present in their surroundings.
2. The ability to think about objects not present in our environment precedes the development of human communication.
3. Thoughts precede all speech acts and these thoughts pop up in our heads even in the absence of any stimulus.
4. Displaced reference is particular to humans and thoughts pop into our heads for no real reason.

Section II: DI & LR

Question Numbers (35 to 38): Answer the questions on the basis of the information given below.

The Ministry of Home Affairs is analysing crimes committed by foreigners in different states and union territories (UT) of India. All cases refer to the ones registered against foreigners in 2016.

The number of cases – classified into three categories: IPC crimes, SLL crimes and other crimes – for nine states/UTs are shown in the figure below. These nine belong to the top ten states/UTs in terms of the total number of cases registered. The remaining state (among top ten) is West Bengal, where all the 520 cases registered were SLL crimes.

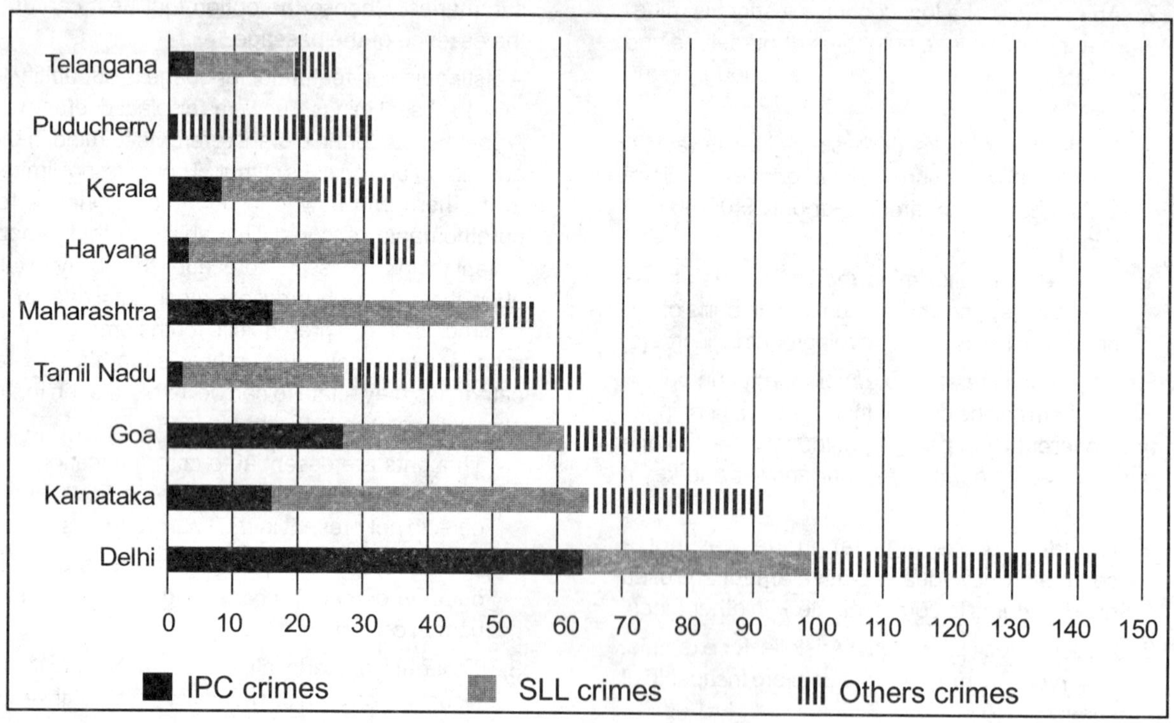

The table below shows the ranks of the ten states/UTs mentioned above among ALL states/UTs of India in terms of the number of cases registered in each of the three category of crimes. A state/UT is given rank r for a category of crimes if there are (r-1) states/UTs having a larger number of cases registered in that category of crimes. For example, if two states have the same number of cases in a category, and exactly three other states/UTs have larger numbers of cases registered in the same category, then both the states are given rank 4 in that category. Missing ranks in the table are denoted by *.

	IPC Crimes	SLL Crimes	Other Crimes
Delhi	*	*	*
Goa	*	4	*
Haryana	8	6	*
Karnataka	3	2	*
Kerala	*	9	*
Maharashtra	3	4	8
Puducherry	13	29	*
Tamil Nadu	11	7	*
Telangana	6	9	8
West Bengal	17	*	16

35. What is the rank of Kerala in the 'IPC crimes' category?

36. In the two states where the highest total number of cases are registered, the ratio of the total number of cases in IPC crimes to the total number in SLL crimes is closest to

(1) 19 : 20 (2) 1 : 9

(3) 3 : 2 (4) 11 : 10

37. Which of the following is DEFINITELY true about the ranks of states/UT in the 'other crimes' category?

i) Tamil Nadu: 2

ii) Puducherry: 3

(1) both i) and ii)

(2) only ii)

(3) neither i), nor ii)

(4) only i)

38. What is the sum of the ranks of Delhi in the three categories of crimes?

Question Numbers (39 to 42): Answer the questions on the basis of the information given below.

The following table represents addition of two six-digit numbers given in the first and the second rows, while the sum is given in the third row. In the representation, each of the digits 0, 1, 2, 3, 4, 5, 6, 7, 8, 9 has been coded with one letter among A, B, C, D, E, F, G, H, J, K, with distinct letters representing distinct digits.

		B	H	A	A	G	F
+		A	H	J	F	K	F
	A	A	F	G	C	A	F

39. Which digit does the letter A represent?

40. Which digit does the letter B represent?

41. Which among the digits 3, 4, 6 and 7 cannot be represented by the letter D?

42. Which among the digits 4, 6, 7 and 8 cannot be represented by the letter G?

Question Numbers (43 to 46): Answer the questions on the basis of the information given below.

A new game show on TV has 100 boxes numbered 1, 2, . . . , 100 in a row, each containing a mystery prize. The prizes are items of different types, a, b, c, . . . , in decreasing order of value. The most expensive item is of type a, a diamond ring, and there is exactly one of these. You are told that the number of items at least doubles as you move to the next type. For example, there would be at least twice as many items of type b as of type a, at least twice as many items of type c as of type b and so on. There is no particular order in which the prizes are placed in the boxes.

43. What is the minimum possible number of different types of prizes?

44. What is the maximum possible number of different types of prizes?

45. Which of the following is not possible?

(1) There are exactly 75 items of type e.

(2) There are exactly 45 items of type c.

(3) There are exactly 30 items of type b.

(4) There are exactly 60 items of type d.

46. You ask for the type of item in box 45. Instead of being given a direct answer, you are told that there are 31 items of the same type as box 45 in boxes 1 to 44 and 43 items of the same type as box 45 in boxes 46 to 100.

What is the maximum possible number of different types of items?

(1) 5 (2) 4

(3) 3 (4) 6

Question Numbers (47 to 50): Answer the questions on the basis of the information given below.

Princess, Queen, Rani and Samragni were the four finalists in a dance competition. Ashman, Badal, Gagan and Dyu were the four music composers who individually assigned items to the dancers. Each dancer had to individually perform in two dance items assigned by the different composers. The first items performed by the four dancers were all assigned by different music composers. No dancer performed her second item before the performance of the first item by any other dancers. The dancers performed their second items in the same sequence of their performance of their first items.

The following additional facts are known.

i) No composer who assigned item to Princess, assigned any item to Queen.

ii) No composer who assigned item to Rani, assigned any item to Samragni.

iii) The first performance was by Princess; this item was assigned by Badal.

iv) The last performance was by Rani; this item was assigned by Gagan.

v) The items assigned by Ashman were performed consecutively. The number of performances between items assigned by each of the remaining composers was the same.

47. Which of the following is true?

(1) The second performance was composed by Dyu.

(2) The second performance was composed by Gagan.

(3) The third performance was composed by Ashman.

(4) The third performance was composed by Dyu.

48. Which of the following is FALSE?

(1) Queen did not perform in any item composed by Gagan.

(2) Rani did not perform in any item composed by Badal.

(3) Samragni did not perform in any item composed by Ashman.

(4) Princess did not perform in any item composed by Dyu.

49. The sixth performance was composed by:

(1) Badal (2) Dyu

(3) Ashman (4) Gagan

50. Which pair of performances were composed by the same composer?

(1) The second and the sixth

(2) The first and the seventh

(3) The third and the seventh

(4) The first and the sixth

Question Numbers (51 to 54): Answer the questions on the basis of the information given below.

Six players – Tanzi, Umeza, Wangdu, Xyla, Yonita and Zeneca competed in an archery tournament. The tournament had three compulsory rounds, Rounds 1 to 3. In each round every player shot an arrow at a target. Hitting the centre of the target (called bull's eye) fetched the highest score of 5. The only other possible scores that a player could achieve were 4, 3, 2 and 1. Every bull's eye score in the first three rounds gave a player one additional chance to shoot in the bonus rounds, Rounds 4 to 6. The possible scores in Rounds 4 to 6 were identical to the first three.

A player's total score in the tournament was the sum of his/her scores in all rounds played by him/her. The table below presents partial information on points scored by the players after completion of the tournament. In the table, NP means that the player did not participate in that round, while a hyphen means that the player participated in that round and the score information is missing.

	Round-1	Round-2	Round-3	Round-4	Round-5	Round-6
Tanzi	-	4	-	5	NP	NP
Umeza	-	-	-	1	2	NP
Wangdu	-	4	-	NP	NP	NP
Xyla	-	-	-	1	5	-
Yonita	-	-	3	5	NP	NP
Zeneca	-	-	-	5	5	NP

The following facts are also known.

1. Tanzi, Umeza and Yonita had the same total score.
2. Total scores for all players, except one, were in multiples of three.
3. The highest total score was one more than double of the lowest total score.
4. The number of players hitting bull's eye in Round 2 was double of that in Round 3.
5. Tanzi and Zeneca had the same score in Round 1 but different scores in Round 3.

51. What was the highest total score?

(1) 23 (2) 25
(3) 21 (4) 24

52. What was Zeneca's total score?

(1) 23 (2) 22
(3) 24 (4) 21

53. Which of the following statements is true?

(1) Zeneca's score was 23.
(2) Xyla was the highest scorer.
(3) Xyla's score was 23.
(4) Zeneca was the highest scorer.

54. What was Tanzi's score in Round 3?

(1) 1 (2) 3
(3) 5 (4) 4

Question Numbers (55 to 58): Answer the questions on the basis of the information given below.

The figure below shows the street map for a certain region with the street intersections marked from a through l. A person standing at an intersection can see along straight lines to other intersections that are in her line of sight and all other people standing at these intersections. For example, a person standing at intersection g can see all people standing at intersections b, c, e, f, h, and k. In particular, the person standing at intersection g can see the person standing at intersection e irrespective of whether there is a person standing at intersection f.

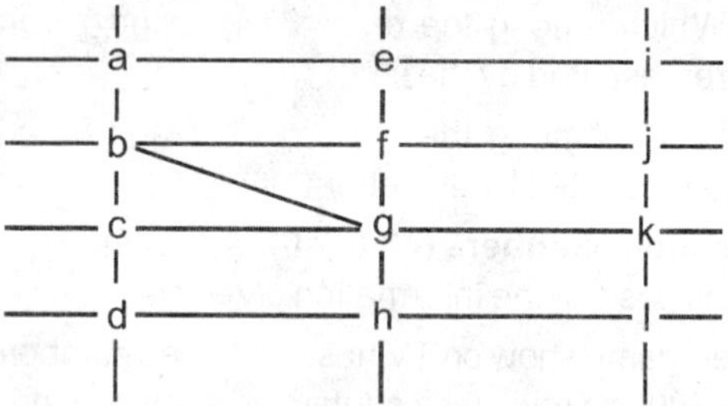

Six people U, V, W, X, Y, and Z, are standing at different intersections. No two people are standing at the same intersection.

The following additional facts are known.

1. X, U, and Z are standing at the three corners of a triangle formed by three street segments.
2. X can see only U and Z.
3. Y can see only U and W.
4. U sees V standing in the next intersection behind Z.
5. W cannot see V or Z.
6. No one among the six is standing at intersection d.

55. Who is standing at intersection a?

(1) W (2) V
(3) Y (4) No one

56. Who can V see?

(1) U and Z only (2) Z only
(3) U only (4) U, W and Z only

57. What is the minimum number of street segments that X must cross to reach Y?

(1) 1 (2) 4
(3) 3 (4) 2

58. Should a new person stand at intersection d, who among the six would she see?

(1) W and X only (2) V and X only
(3) U and W only (4) U and Z only

Question Numbers (59 to 62): Answer the questions on the basis of the information given below.

A supermarket has to place 12 items (coded A to L) in shelves numbered 1 to 16. Five of these items are types of biscuits, three are types of candies and the rest are types of savouries. Only one item can be kept in a shelf. Items are to be placed such that all items of same type are clustered together with no empty shelf between items of the same type and at least one empty shelf between two different types of items. At most two empty shelves can have consecutive numbers.

The following additional facts are known.

1. A and B are to be placed in consecutively numbered shelves in increasing order.
2. I and J are to be placed in consecutively numbered shelves both higher numbered than the shelves in which A and B are kept.
3. D, E and F are savouries and are to be placed in consecutively numbered shelves in increasing order after all the biscuits and candies.
4. K is to be placed in shelf number 16.
5. L and J are items of the same type, while H is an item of a different type.
6. C is a candy and is to be placed in a shelf preceded by two empty shelves.
7. L is to be placed in a shelf preceded by exactly one empty shelf.

59. In how many different ways can the items be arranged on the shelves?

(1) 8 (2) 4
(3) 2 (4) 1

60. Which of the following items is not a type of biscuit?

(1) A (2) L
(3) G (4) B

61. Which of the following can represent the numbers of the empty shelves in a possible arrangement?

(1) 1, 2, 8, 12 (2) 1, 2, 6, 12
(3) 1, 5, 6, 12 (4) 1, 7, 11, 12

62. Which of the following statements is necessarily true?

(1) All biscuits are kept before candies.
(2) All candies are kept before biscuits.
(3) There are at least four shelves between items B and C.
(4) There are two empty shelves between the biscuits and the candies.

Question Numbers (63 to 66): Answer the questions on the basis of the information given below.

Five vendors are being considered for a service. The evaluation committee evaluated each vendor on six aspects – Cost, Customer Service, Features, Quality, Reach, and Reliability. Each of these evaluations are on a scale of 0 (worst) to 100 (perfect). The evaluation scores on these aspects are shown in the radar chart. For example, Vendor 1 obtains a score of 52 on Reliability, Vendor 2 obtains a score of 45 on Features and Vendor 3 obtains a score of 90 on Cost.

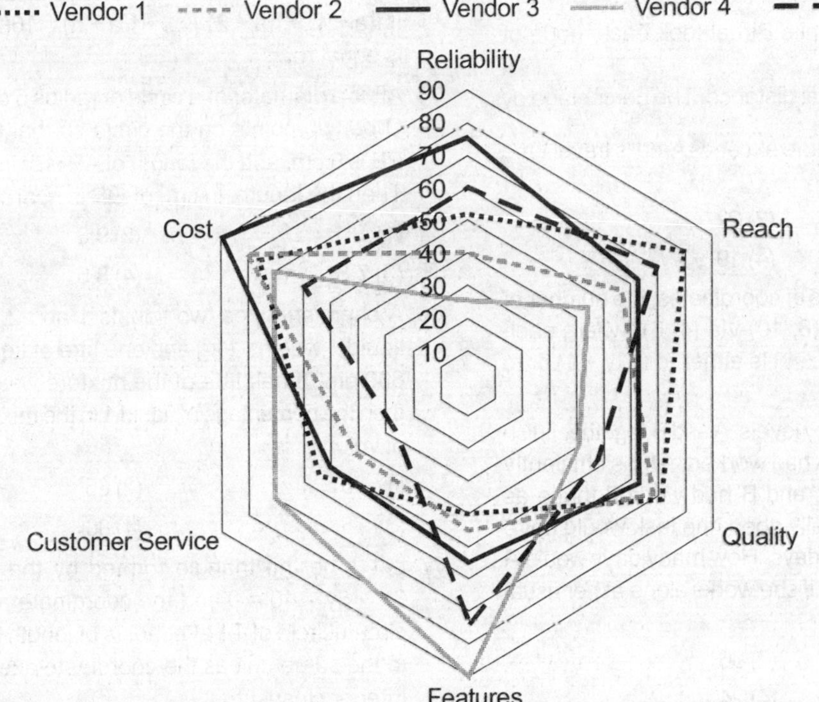

63. On which aspect is the median score of the five vendors the least?

(1) Quality (2) Cost

(3) Reliability (4) Customer Service

64. A vendor's final score is the average of their scores on all six aspects. Which vendor has the highest final score?

(1) Vendor 1 (2) Vendor 4

(3) Vendor 3 (4) Vendor 2

65. List of all the vendors who are among the top two scorers on the maximum number of aspects is:

(1) Vendor 1 and Vendor 5

(2) Vendor 1 and Vendor 2

(3) Vendor 2, Vendor 3 and Vendor 4

(4) Vendor 2 and Vendor 5

66. List of all the vendors who are among the top three vendors on all six aspects is:

(1) Vendor 3

(2) Vendor 1 and Vendor 3

(3) None of the Vendors

(4) Vendor 1

Section III: QA

67. Corners are cut off from an equilateral triangle T to produce a regular hexagon H. Then, the ratio of the area of H to the area of T is

(1) 2 : 3 (2) 4 : 5

(3) 3 : 4 (4) 5 : 6

68. Let x and y be positive real numbers such that $\log_5 (x + y) + \log_5 (x - y) = 3$, and $\log_2 y - \log_2 x = 1 - \log_2 3$. Then xy equals

(1) 25 (2) 100

(3) 150 (4) 250

69. One can use three different transports which move at 10, 20, and 30 kmph, respectively. To reach from A to B, Amal took each mode of transport $\frac{1}{3}$ of his total journey time, while Bimal took each mode of transport $\frac{1}{3}$ of the total distance. The percentage by which Bimal's travel time exceeds Amal's travel time is nearest to

(1) 21 (2) 22

(3) 20 (4) 19

70. With rectangular axes of coordinates, the number of paths from (1, 1) to (8, 10) via (4, 6), where each step from any point (x, y) is either to (x, y + 1) or to (x + 1, y), is

71. At their usual efficiency levels, A and B together finish a task in 12 days. If A had worked half as efficiently as she usually does, and B had worked thrice as efficiently as he usually does, the task would have been completed in 9 days. How many days would A take to finish the task if she works alone at her usual efficiency?

(1) 18 (2) 36

(3) 12 (4) 24

72. Meena scores 40% in an examination and after review, even though her score is increased by 50%, she fails by 35 marks. If her post-review score is increased by 20%, she will have 7 marks more than the passing score. The percentage score needed for passing the examination is

(1) 70 (2) 60

(3) 75 (4) 80

73. In a race of three horses, the first beat the second by 11 metres and the third by 90 metres. If the second beat the third by 80 metres, what was the length, in metres, of the racecourse?

74. Consider a function f satisfying $f(x + y) = f(x) f(y)$ where x, y are positive integers, and $f(1) = 2$. If $f(a + 1) + f(a + 2) + ... + f(a + n) = 16(2^n - 1)$ then a is equal to

75. AB is a diameter of a circle of radius 5 cm. Let P and Q be two points on the circle so that the length of PB is 6 cm, and the length of AP is twice that of AQ. Then the length, in cm, of QB is nearest to

(1) 9.1 (2) 9.3

(3) 7.8 (4) 8.5

76. A chemist mixes two liquids 1 and 2. One litre of liquid 1 weighs 1 kg and one litre of liquid 2 weighs 800 gm. If half litre of the mixture weighs 480 gm, then the percentage of liquid 1 in the mixture, in terms of volume, is

(1) 70 (2) 85

(3) 75 (4) 80

77. Let T be the triangle formed by the straight line $3x + 5y - 45 = 0$ and the coordinate axes. Let the circumcircle of T have radius of length L, measured in the same unit as the coordinate axes. Then, the integer closest to L is

78. On selling a pen at 5% loss and a book at 15% gain, Karim gains Rs. 7. If he sells the pen at 5% gain and the book at 10% gain, he gains Rs. 13. What is the cost price of the book in Rupees?

(1) 80 (2) 85

(3) 95 (4) 100

79. The income of Amala is 20% more than that of Bimala and 20% less than that of Kamala. If Kamala's income goes down by 4% and Bimala's goes up by 10%, then the percentage by which Kamala's income would exceed Bimala's is nearest to

(1) 29 (2) 31

(3) 28 (4) 32

80. The product of the distinct roots of $|x^2 - x - 6| = x + 2$ is

(1) –24 (2) –16

(3) –8 (4) –4

81. Two cars travel the same distance starting at 10:00 am and 11:00 am, respectively, on the same day. They reach their common destination at the same point of time. If the first car travelled for at least 6 hours, then the highest possible value of the percentage by which the speed of the second car could exceed that of the first car is

(1) 20 (2) 25

(3) 30 (4) 10

82. The number of solutions to the equation $|x|(6x^2 + 1) = 5x^2$ is

83. The wheels of bicycles A and B have radii 30 cm and 40 cm, respectively. While traveling a certain distance, each wheel of A required 5000 more revolutions than each wheel of B. If bicycle B traveled this distance in 45 minutes, then its speed, in km per hour, was

(1) 18π (2) 12π

(3) 16π (4) 14π

84. For any positive integer n, let f(n) = n(n + 1) if n is even, and f(n) = n + 3 if n is odd.

If m is a positive integer such that 8f(m + 1) – f(m) = 2, then m equals

85. The product of two positive numbers is 616. If the ratio of the difference of their cubes to the cube of their difference is 157:3, then the sum of the two numbers is

(1) 85 (2) 95

(3) 58 (4) 50

86. The number of the real roots of the equation $2\cos(x(x + 1)) = 2^x + 2^{-x}$ is

(1) 1 (2) 0

(3) infinite (4) 2

87. If $a_1 + a_2 + a_3 + ... + a_n = 3(2^{n+1} - 2)$, for every $n \geq 1$, then a_{11} equals

88. In a circle of radius 11 cm, CD is a diameter and AB is a chord of length 20.5 cm. If AB and CD intersect at a point E inside the circle and CE has length 7 cm, then the difference of the lengths of BE and AE, in cm, is

(1) 3.5 (2) 1.5

(3) 2.5 (4) 0.5

89. A person invested a total amount of Rs 15 lakh. A part of it was invested in a fixed deposit earning 6% annual interest, and the remaining amount was invested in two other deposits in the ratio 2 : 1, earning annual interest at the rates of 4% and 3%, respectively. If the total annual interest income is Rs 76000 then the amount (in Rs lakh) invested in the fixed deposit was

90. If m and n are integers such that $(\sqrt{2})^{19}\, 3^4\, 4^2\, 9^m\, 8^n = 3^n\, 16^m \left(\sqrt[4]{64}\right)$ then m is

(1) –24 (2) –16

(3) –12 (4) –20

91. Let S be the set of all points (x, y) in the x-y plane such that $|x| + |y| \leq 2$ and $|x| \geq 1$. Then, the area, in square units, of the region represented by S equals

92. A club has 256 members of whom 144 can play football, 123 can play tennis, and 132 can play cricket. Moreover, 58 members can play both football and tennis, 25 can play both cricket and tennis, while 63 can play both football and cricket. If every member can play at least one game, then the number of members who can play only tennis is

(1) 32 (2) 43

(3) 38 (4) 45

93. Three men and eight machines can finish a job in half the time taken by three machines and eight men to finish the same job. If two machines can finish the job in 13 days, then how many men can finish the job in 13 days?

94. Amala, Bina, and Gouri invest money in the ratio 3 : 4 : 5 in fixed deposits having respective annual interest rates in the ratio 6 : 5 : 4. What is their total interest income (in Rs) after a year, if Bina's interest income exceeds Amala's by Rs 250?

(1) 7000 (2) 6000

(3) 7250 (4) 6350

95. If $a_1, a_2, \ldots$ are in A.P., then

$$\frac{1}{\sqrt{a_1}+\sqrt{a_2}}+\frac{1}{\sqrt{a_2}+\sqrt{a_3}}+\ldots+\frac{1}{\sqrt{a_n}+\sqrt{a_{n+1}}}$$

is equal to

(1) $\frac{n-1}{\sqrt{a_1}+\sqrt{a_{n-1}}}$ (2) $\frac{n-1}{\sqrt{a_1}+\sqrt{a_n}}$

(3) $\frac{n}{\sqrt{a_1}+\sqrt{a_{n+1}}}$ (4) $\frac{n}{\sqrt{a_1}-\sqrt{a_{n+1}}}$

96. Ramesh and Gautam are among 22 students who write an examination. Ramesh scores 82.5. The average score of the 21 students other than Gautam is 62. The average score of all the 22 students is one more than the average score of the 21 students other than Ramesh. The score of Gautam is

(1) 51 (2) 53

(3) 48 (4) 49

97. If the rectangular faces of a brick have their diagonals in the ratio $3 : 2\sqrt{3} : \sqrt{15}$, then the ratio of the length of the shortest edge of the brick to that of its longest edge is

(1) $\sqrt{2} : \sqrt{3}$ (2) $2 : \sqrt{5}$

(3) $\sqrt{3} : 2$ (4) $1 : \sqrt{3}$

98. In a class, 60% of the students are girls and the rest are boys. There are 30 more girls than boys. If 68% of the students, including 30 boys, pass an examination, the percentage of the girls who do not pass is

99. If the population of a town is p in the beginning of any year then it becomes 3 + 2p in the beginning of the next year. If the population in the beginning of 2019 is 1000, then the population in the beginning of 2034 will be

(1) $(1003)2^{15} - 3$ (2) $(997)2^{14} + 3$

(3) $(997)^{15} - 3$ (4) $(1003)^{15} + 6$

100. If $(5.55)^x = (0.555)^y = 1000$, then the value of $\frac{1}{x} - \frac{1}{y}$ is

(1) 1 (2) $\frac{2}{3}$

(3) $\frac{1}{3}$ (4) 3

ANSWERS

1. (4)	**2.** (1)	**3.** (2)	**4.** (2)	**5.** (1)	**6.** (1)	**7.** (1)	**8.** (2)	**9.** (1)	**10.** (3)
11. (1)	**12.** (2)	**13.** (2)	**14.** (1)	**15.** (1)	**16.** (3)	**17.** (1)	**18.** (3)	**19.** (3)	**20.** (2)
21. (2)	**22.** (3)	**23.** (2)	**24.** (4)	**25.** (3241)	**26.** (1)	**27.** (1)	**28.** (4123)	**29.** (2)	**30.** (3241)
31. (3)	**32.** (2341)	**33.** (2)	**34.** (2)	**35.** (5)	**36.** (2)	**37.** (1)	**38.** (5)	**39.** (1)	**40.** (9)
41. (7)	**42.** (6)	**43.** (2)	**44.** (6)	**45.** (2)	**46.** (1)	**47.** (1)	**48.** (1)	**49.** (1)	**50.** (4)
51. (2)	**52.** (3)	**53.** (2)	**54.** (1)	**55.** (4)	**56.** (1)	**57.** (4)	**58.** (1)	**59.** (1)	**60.** (3)
61. (2)	**62.** (3)	**63.** (4)	**64.** (3)	**65.** (1)	**66.** (1)	**67.** (1)	**68.** (3)	**69.** (2)	**70.** (3920)
71. (1)	**72.** (1)	**73.** (880)	**74.** (3)	**75.** (1)	**76.** (4)	**77.** (9)	**78.** (1)	**79.** (2)	**80.** (2)
81. (1)	**82.** (5)	**83.** (3)	**84.** (10)	**85.** (4)	**86.** (1)	**87.** (6144)	**88.** (4)	**89.** (9)	**90.** (3)
91. (2)	**92.** (2)	**93.** (13)	**94.** (3)	**95.** (3)	**96.** (1)	**97.** (4)	**98.** (20)	**99.** (1)	**100.** (3)

EXPLANATIONS

1. In order to answer this question, we need to refer to the last paragraph of the passage. Consider the lines, 'For start-ups that promise accessible simplicity, their very structure still might eventually push them toward overwhelming variety......' Thus, the fourth option provides the right answer. While option 1 is only partially correct, options 2 and 3 are factually inconsistent with the information provided in the passage.

2. The central premise of the author's argument is two-fold:
   1. Fewer choices effectively result in better, easier decisions
   2. The creators of new products continue to focus on those who already have plenty while access to basic necessities has shrunk even further for the lower classes.

   Hence, the author is likely to support any scheme that offers a limited range of products at low prices. This makes the choice, *A range of 10 products priced between \$5 and \$10* the right answer.

3. In the last paragraph of the passage, the author states that starts-ups offering limited products also have revenue considerations and will have to eventually increase the range of products being offered, just like Casper and Glossier have done. The question asks you to identify the option that will add the least depth to the author's argument (in other words, a statement that weakens the argument).

   Option 1 which states that *start-ups with few product options are no exception to the American consumer market that is deeply divided along class lines* adds depth to the author's argument since it contends that there is nothing unique about start-ups. They are bound to fail or will have to change. Another option which states that *with the motive of promoting certain rival companies, the government decides to double the tax-rates for these start-ups* also predicts that start-ups are likely to fail, adding weight to author's argument about their fate mentioned in the last para.

   Option 2 adds least depth because it brings out a point that will not lead start-ups to offer more product varieties, after all they are experiencing a surge in revenue without expanding their product catalogue. This actually contradicts the author's prediction.

   The third statement strengthens the author's perspective and is thus negated.

4. In this question we need to identify the inference that can't be made based on the information provided in the passage. The statement *having too many product options can be overwhelming for consumers* can be easily inferred from the initial lines of the passage.

   Similarly, *consumers are susceptible to marketing images that they see on social media* can be inferred from the lines, 'Indeed, choice fatigue is one reason so many people gravitate toward lifestyle influencers on Instagram....'

   The statement *too many options have made it difficult for consumers to trust products* can be inferred from 'They're selling nice things, but maybe more importantly, they're selling a confidence in those things, and an ability to opt out of the stuff rat race. . . .'

   Thus, the only statement that can't be inferred is *'consumers tend to prefer products by start-ups over those by established companies.'*

5. Throughout the passage, the author is in favor of offering limited choices to customers. This particular option demonstrates that offering fewer products can bring positive results. Thus, it strengthens the author's content and is the right answer.

   The other options directly contradict the information provided in the passage and weaken the author's claims.

6. As can be inferred from the passage, the main reason for scholars' fascination with the story of Aladdin is that the experiences of the author are reflected in the story. The story of Aladdin, in a way, is a reflection of the author's life. This is what makes it so interesting. Therefore, the correct answer is option 1. Documentation of history and the concept of Orientalism is not necessarily something that would keep the interest alive. This negates options 2 and 4. Similarly, the concept of rags-to-riches is showcased in various stories. So, option 3 is also out of scope.

7. Scholars initially thought that the plot of Aladdin must have been inspired by 18th century French fairy tales, but to quote the author, "The idea that Diyab might have based it on his own life — the experiences of a Middle Eastern man encountering the French, not vice-versa — flips the script."

   In other words, the story of Aladdin was not inspired by the French fairy tales but that Diyab was the actual author. By invalidating the inversion, the question wants us to not give the credit to Diyab

Option 4 is negated because by pointing out the dissimilarity between Aladdin and the French fairy tales, it gives the credit to Diyab.

Option 2 is negated because even though Diyab described Bordeaux, he still saw the luxury and opulence of France.

Option 3 also gives the credit to Diyab, so it is not invalidating the inversion.

Option 1 is the right choice because, if the narratives bore no resemblance, then it disputes the evidence that Diyab ever narrated the story to Galland, as Galland claims in his diary. This would contradict, at least to some extent, the author's claim that Diyab was the inspiration for the character of Aladdin.

8. Options 1, 3 and 4 are out of scope and cannot be considered. The origin of the story of Aladdin was based on Diyab's life experiences. He transmitted this story to Galland who made it a part of Arabian Nights. Therefore, the correct answer is option 2.

9. Diyab's travelogue serves as evidence for the character of Aladdin being based on him. This negates options 2 and 4. Moreover, the second-last paragraph of the passage is suggestive of Diyab's cosmopolitanism and cross-cultural experience. So, option 3 is also negated. Refer to the following lines from the first paragraph of the passage, "Galland, who wrote in his diary that he first heard the tale from a Syrian storyteller from Aleppo named Hanna Diyab". There is no evidence of Diyab's narration of the story to Galland. This makes option 1 the correct answer.

10. Diyab and his life experiences have the authorship of the story of Aladdin. Since this is reflected in options 1, 2 and 4, they cannot be considered. This makes option 3 the correct answer as it proposes an entirely different theory to the authorship.

11. As per the passage, 'topophilia' has positive connotations and evokes feelings of love, affection and a strong emotional bond. Thus, all options that talk about lack of affinity or poor emotional connect can be negated. Thus, the statements '*Nomadic societies are known to have the least affinity for the lands through which they traverse because they tend to be topophobic*' and '*The French are not overly patriotic, but they will refuse to use English as far as possible, even when they know it well*' can be easily negated. There is no discussion regarding 'topography' in the passage. Hence, the correct answer is '*The tendency of many cultures to represent their land as "motherland" or "fatherland" may be seen as an expression of their topophilia.*'

12. Refer the lines *Topophilia is difficult to design for and impossible to quantify, and its most articulate interpreters have been self-reflective philosophers such as Henry David Thoreau, evoking a marvelously intricate sense of place at Walden Pond, and Tuan, describing his deep affinity for the desert.* Thus, there is an element of subjectiveness that underlies all topophilic expression. Hence, option 2 is the right answer.

13. This is a slightly difficult question. We have to read the options carefully and look for the one that is not against what the author has to say.

Option 1 is contradictory because the author says that olfactory response is the third most important factor, while the option says that it is the most important factor.

Option 3 can be ruled out because the author says in the first paragraph: the emotive ties with the material environment vary greatly from person to person and in intensity, subtlety, and mode of expression. The author says, 'vary greatly', while the option says, 'vary little'.

Refer the lines - *"As Tuan noted, purely aesthetic responses often are suddenly revealed, but their intensity rarely is long-lasting. Topophilia is difficult to design for and impossible to quantify..."* However, the option says that New Urbanism succeeded in those designs where architects collaborated with their clients. Thus, option 4 can also be negated.

Option 2 can be seen in the last paragraph and is parallel to what the author has to say. This is not contradicting the author's argument, and hence it is the right choice.

14. This example has been discussed in the last paragraph of the passage where the author is talking about the darker applications of topophilia while exploring the affiliations between people and places. This immediately negates statements 3 and 4 - *manner in which environments are designed to minimize the social exclusion of their clientele* and *sensitive response to race and class problems in upscale residential developments.* There is no discussion regarding nationalist projects of the elites. Hence, option 1 is the right answer.

15. The answer to this question can be found in the last lines of the passage - And just as a beloved landscape is suddenly revealed, so too may landscapes of fear cast a dark shadow over a place that makes one feel a sense of dread or anxiety—or topophobia.

16. This is a simple question. Just go through the relevant section of the passage - *"...by keeping their outer surface below air temperature, the birds might paradoxically be able to draw very slight amounts of heat from the air around them..."* Option 3 captures this precisely.

17. It is already given that the sentence can be found in the last part of the third paragraph. Let's see the context: *As the cold Antarctic air cycles around their bodies, slightly warmer air comes into contact with the plumage and donates minute amounts of heat back to the penguins, then cycles away at a slightly colder temperature.*

We know that the outer plumage of the penguins is even colder than the air, thus, the first blank refers to the cold air whose temperature is higher than that of the plumage and the second blank refers to the fall in temperature after some heat has been transmitted to the plumage.

18. We know that the plumage is responsible for maintaining body heat; it is the central idea of the passage. Food metabolism, too, helps generate heat, the passage says that clearly. We are left with two choices, thermal convection and reproduction process. The passage says that thermal convection helps them gain heat ("the simulation showed that they might gain back a little of this heat through thermal convection"). Thus, we see that thermal convection, food metabolism, and plumage all are responsible for heat gain, not heat loss. We are left with choice 3 as the right answer.

Choice 3 can be inferred from the following lines of the passage: "And given the Emperors' unusually demanding breeding cycle, every bit of warmth counts...". This suggests that the reproduction process results in heat loss.

19. The passage says that the outer air temperature is warmer than the plumage temperature, but if the outer air temperature becomes colder than the plumage temperature, as option 4 says, the author's argument would be invalidated, because the heat transfer from the outer colder air to the relatively warmer plumage will not happen.

Similarly, the plumage has to be colder than the outer Antarctic air, but in choice 1 the plumage is warmer than the outer Antarctic air, so this too would weaken the author's argument in the passage.

In option 2; thermal convection helps the penguins get some heat, if the plumage is not allowing thermal convection to take place, there would be no gain of warmth, thus this too weakens the argument.

Only option 3 does not weaken the argument. The passage says that the feet are the warmest part of the body of a penguin. If you make them a little warmer, they will still remain the warmest part of the body. Hence, it is the answer.

20. This is a simple question whose answer can be easily inferred from the following lines - *Just as the effusive floral prints of the radical William Morris now cover genteel sofas, so the revolutionary intentions of many folk historians and revivalists have led to music that is commonly regarded as parochial and conservative.* Option 4 distorts the idea by reversing its order.

21. This question can be answered by reading the options closely. A long history and varied influences will contribute to the diversity of an art form. Similarly, the presence of fluidity and oral traditions will also introduce diversity. However, the popularity and unpopularity of any art form has no correlation with the presence of diversity. Hence, this is the correct answer.

22. The question asks us to select an option that cannot be inferred from the passage. The statement that is made in the passage is: "In the late 1960s, purists were suspicious of folk songs recast in rock idioms. Electrification, however, comes in many forms." In other words, electrification need not always come through rock alone. It might come from any other form of music as well. Thus, this option surely cannot be inferred.

"...the lyrical freedom of Bob Dylan..." this phrase supports option 1.

Option 2 can be inferred because Cecil Sharp talks about folk music's ability to adapt. The music of 40s and 60s demonstrates that adaptation.

The passage says that in the late 1960s, Purists were suspicious of folk songs recast in rock idioms, this suggests that it had critics. Thus, option 4 can be inferred.

23. Fossilized refers to something belonging to/ associated with the past. Out of the options given, only the second option comes close in meaning. The other options don't correlate with the word fossilized.

24. The author appreciates how folk forms have been used by modern musicians and the fusion of folk with other forms of music throughout the passage.

Hence, he is likely to agree with all options except 4 because it says that folk music exhibits unusual homogeneity.
If there is homogeneity, then the idea of adapting and infusing with other kinds of music is not valid. Thus, the author will not agree with this.

25. Sentence 3 introduces the phrase 'carpe diem' so it comes in beginning. It is followed by statement 2 which further explains the meaning of the phrase. 4 and 1 form a mandatory pair as they talk about metaphors. Thus, the correct sequence is 3241.

26. Statement 4 is the introductory statement as it introduces the concept of complex identities. It will be followed by statement 3 as it further explains the phenomena of complex identities. Statements 2 and 5 form a pair because as they discuss two conflicting ideas of complex identities. Only statement 1 is the odd one out.

27. The passage discusses the difference between pure and applied science and the difference between the knowledge of an engineer and that of a physicist. This is not captured by option 2. Option 4 cannot be considered as it is untrue. Option 3 has no mention of pure science, so it cannot be considered. So, the correct answer is option 1 as it clearly captures the essence of the passage.

28. Sentence 4 is clearly the introductory line as it introduces the concept of collaborative filtering. Sentence 1 further discusses the experience of collaborative filtering, so it comes after 4. 2 and 3 form a mandatory pair as they throw light on the problems in collaborative filtering. So, the correct sequence is 4123.

29. 4 is the introductory sentence as it introduces 'suffix'. The author then talks about what these symbols mean in statement 1. This is followed by statement 5 which talks about gaining suffix. It is followed by statement 3 which throws light on how these symbols are painted on the names of scientific technologies. Statement 2 does not fit entirely with the context of the passage and is hence the odd one out.

30. Statement 3 acts as an introductory statement as it talks about dealing with legitimate criticism. It is followed by statement 2. Statement 4 and 1 form a mandatory pair, which is evident from the phrase "until then". So, the correct sequence is 3241.

31. Choices with respect to supraliminal and subliminal have a clear difference. Also, the passage mentions that Packard believed in supraliminal images, not subliminal. This makes options 1 and 4 incorrect. The passage mentions that people are not aware, which is also indicated in option 3. Thus, the correct answer is option 3.

32. Statement 2 is clearly the introductory line as it introduces the concept of mind-reading. It is followed by 3 which further elaborates on the concept. Statements 4 and 1 form a mandatory pair as they talk about the concept of print-reading, which is very similar to mind-reading. Thus, the correct sequence is 2341.

33. The five sentences discuss the issue of hearing impairments and marginalization because of this. Statements 5, 4, 1 and 3 revolve around the same concept. Sentence 2 seems a little out of context. Thus, the correct answer is option 2.

34. Option 1 cannot be considered because it mentions information that has not been described in the passage. Options 3 and 4 are untrue as they distort the information provided in the passage, so they cannot be considered. Option 2 does not have any distortions and clearly captures the essence of the passage. Thus, the correct answer is option 2.

35. Can simply observe from given graph that Kerala has rank 5 in IPC crimes, (Delhi, Karnataka, Goa, Maharashtra are ranked above it)

36. Two highest crime states are Delhi and West Bangal

	Delhi	W-B
IPC	64	0
SLL	34	520

$$\text{Ratio of IPC to SLL} = \frac{64+0}{34+520} = 1:9$$

37. Can observe from the graph that in "other crimes"
Delhi > Tamil Nadu > Puducherry > Karnataka
So option 1 is correct, where Tamil Nadu rank = 2, Puducherry = 3

38.

IPC	SLL	Other Crimes
1	3	1
(Observed from graph)	(WB = 1, Karnataka = 2, Delhi/Maharashtra = 3)	(Observed from graph)

∴ Sum of Ranks = 1 + 3 + 1 = 5

For questions 39 to 42:

We need to find the values of A, B, C, D, E, F, G, H, J and K which are distinct digits among 0 to 9 such that :-

		B	H	A	A	G	F
+		A	H	J	F	K	F
	A	A	F	G	C	A	F

The value of F must be 0 since F + F = F can hold only if F = 0

The value of H must be 5 since H + H = F and F = 0

Now, since, 1 will be carried forward by the sum of H(5) + H(5) = F(0), therefore, A has to be 1 and B must be 9, only then B + A = AA

Modified table will now look like,

		9	5	1	1	G	0
+		1	5	J	0	K	0
	1	1	0	G	C	I	0

Unknown variables :- J, G, C, K

Unused digits :- 2, 3, 4, 6, 7, 8

Clearly, the sum of G + K must be 11, So 1 will be carried forward and therefore, C = 2.

Possible combinations for (G, K) = (3, 8), (8, 3), (4, 7) and (7, 4)

Case I :- (G, K) = (3, 8)

		9	5	1	1	3	0
+		1	5	J	0	8	0
	1	1	0	3	2	I	0

This case is not possible, since J has to be 2 but C = 2

Case II :- (G, K) = (8, 3)

	9	5	1	1	8	0
+	1	5	J = 7	0	3	0
1	1	0	8	2	1	0

This case is possible.

A = 1, B = 9, C = 2, F = 0, G = 8, H = 5, J = 7, K = 3.

Case III :- (G, K) = (4, 7)

	9	5	1	1	4	0
+	1	5	J = 3	0	7	0
1	1	0	4	2	1	0

This case is possible

A = 1, B = 9, C = 2, F = 0, G = 4, H = 5, J = 3, K = 7

Case IV :- (G, K) = (7, 4)

	9	5	1	1	7	0
+	1	5	J = 6	0	4	0
1	1	0	7	2	1	0

This case is possible

A = 1, B = 9, C = 2, F = 0, G = 7, H = 5, J = 6, K = 4.

39. Letter A represent digit 1

40. Letter B represent digit 9

41. Digit 7 cannot be represented by D, as in all cases 7 is already represented by some other letter.

42. Letter G cannot be represented by digit 6.

43. It is given that the most expensive item is a diamond ring of type a and there is exactly one of these. Since the item b should be at least twice. The minimum number of items will be obtained when a = 1 and b = 99, which means there are only two different types of items.

44. It is given that the most expensive item is a diamond ring of type a and there is exactly one of these. Since the number of items of type b should be at least twice of that of a and the number of items of type c should be at least twice of that of b and so on. So the maximum number of different types of items of a, b and c will be obtained when a = 1, b = 2, c = 4, d = 8, e = 16, f = 69. Hence the maximum number of different types of items will be 6.

If the number of items is 7, then the minimum number of prizes should be 1 + 2 + 4 + 8 + 16 + 32 + 64 = 127 which is more than 100. Hence, 6 is the answer.

45. Option 1: There are exactly 75 items of type e. a = 1, b = 2, c = 4, d = 8, e = 85. Here the maximum value of e = 85. Hence it can take the value 75.

An example of such case is a = 1, b = 2, c = 4, d = 18, e = 75

Option 2: There are exactly 45 items of type c. Since the value of d should be at least 90, it means that d is not present because 45 + 90 will be more than 100(maximum number of items). Only a, b and c are present.

The maximum value of b = 22 and a = 1, but 45 + 22 + 1 = 68, which is less than 100. So this case is not possible.

Option 3: There are exactly 30 items of type b. a = 1, b = 30 and c = 69. Hence this case is also possible.

Option 4: There are exactly 60 items of type d. d = 60, c = 30, b = 9 and a = 1. a + b + c + d = 100. Hence, this case is possible.

2 is the answer.

46. The total number of items from 1 to 100, which are of same type as in box 45 = 31 + 1 + 43 = 75

Now to maximize the number of items, a = 1, b = 2, c = 4, d = 18 and e = 75(given)

There can be maximum 5 types of items.

If we consider number of items to be 6, then minimum number of items of 5th type will be 16,

1 + 2 + 4 + 8 + 16 + 75 = 106 which is more than 100.

Direction 47 to 50 :-

From statement (iii) and (iv) we get

	First item				Second item			
	I	II	III	IV	I	II	III	IV
Finalists	Princess							Rani
Composer	Badal		G			B		Gagan

By statement (V), since items assigned by Ashman were performed consecutively and first items performed by the four dancers were all assigned by different music composers therefore, fourth performance of first item and 1st performance of second items was assigned by Ashman.

Also, the number of performances between the items assigned by each of the remaining composers was the same, which is possible only if 4 performances happen between the items assigned.

	First item				Second item			
	I	II	III	IV	I	II	III	IV
Finalists	Princess							Rani
Composer	Badal	Dyu	Gagan	Ashman	Ashman	Badal	Dyu	Gagan

It is given that dancers performed their second items in the same sequence of their performance of their first items, i.e., princess performed first in both dance items and Rani performed the last.

Also by statement (i) and (ii), we get the final table as.

	First item				Second item			
	I	II	III	IV	I	II	III	IV
Finalists	Princess	Samragiri	Queen	Rani	Princess	Samragni	Queen	Rani
Composers	Badal	Dyu	Gagan	Ashman	Ashman	Badal	Dyu	Gagan

47. The second performance was composed by Dyu, is true.

48. Statement Queen didn't perform in any item composed by Gagan, is false

49. The sixth performance was composed by Badal.

50. The first and the sixth pair of performances were composed by the same composer.

For questios 51 to 54:

	Round-1	Round-2	Round-3	Round-4	Round-5	Round-6
Tanzi	-	4	-	5	NP	NP
Umeza	-	-	-	1	2	NP
Wangdu	-	4	-	NP	NP	NP
Xyla	-	-	-	1	5	-
Yonita	-	-	3	5	NP	NP
Zeneca	-	-	-	5	5	NP

It is given that every bull's eye score in the first three rounds gave a player one additional chance to shoot in the bonus rounds, Rounds 4 to 6, which means Tanzi scored Bull's eye only once in the first 3 rounds because she participated only once in round 4 to 6. Similarly, Umeza scored Bull's eye exactly 2 times in the first 3 rounds. Wangdu did not score Bull's eye in the first three rounds and so on.

Now from 1, Tanzi, Umeza and Yonita had the same total score.

So, Total score of Tanzi will be 4 + 5 + 5 + a = 14 + a, (She scored Bull's eye(a score of 5) in exactly one round and a is the unknown score)

Total score of Umeza = 1 + 2 + 5 + 5 + b = 13 + b (She scored Bull's eye(a score of 5) in exactly 2 rounds and b is the unknown score)

Total score of Yonita = 3 + 5 + 5 + c = 13 + c (She scored Bull's eye(a score of 5) in exactly one round and c is the unknown score)

Now 14 + a = 13 + b = 13 + c,

Also it is given that total scores for all players, except one, were in multiples of three, so these three will have to be a multiple of 3.

So, (a, b, c) can be either (1, 2, 2) or (4, 5, 5) in the same order. But the value (5, 5) for b and c is not possible. (Umeza scored Bull's eye in exactly 2 rounds and Yonita in exactly 1 round)

Hence, a = 1, b = 2 and c = 2. So, each of Tanzi, Umeza and Yonita had total score of 15.

Tabulating the data, we have

	Round-1	Round-2	Round-3	Round-4	Round-5	Round-6	Total
Tanzi	1/5	4	1/5	5	NP	NP	15
Umeza	5/5/2	5/5/2	5/5/2	1	2	NP	15
Wangdu	1/2/3/4	4	1/2/3/4	NP	NP	NP	6-12
Xyla	5	5	5	1	5	1/2/3/4/5	22-26
Yonita	2/5	2/5	3	5	NP	NP	15
Zeneca	-	-	-	5	5	NP	-

From 5, Tanzi and Zeneca had the same score in Round 1 but different scores in Round 3.

Zeneca score Bull's eye 2 times in round 1 to 3. If Tanzi scored 1 in round 1, then Zeneca also has to score 1 in round 1, which means both Tanzi and Zeneca scores in round 3 will be 5, which violates 5. Hence Tanzi scored 5 in round 1 and Zeneca also scored the same in round 1.

So the new table is:

	Round-1	Round-2	Round-3	Round-4	Round-5	Round-6	Total
Tanzi	5	4	1	5	NP	NP	15
Umeza	5/5/2	5/5/2	5/5/2	1	2	NP	15
Wangdu	1/2/3/4	4	1/2/3/4	NP	NP	NP	6-12
Xyla	5	5	5	1	5	1/2/3/4/5	22-26
Yonita	2/5	2/5	3	5	NP	NP	15
Zeneca	5	5/(2/34)	5/(2/3/4)	5	5	NP	-

From 4, the number of players hitting bull's eye in Round 2 was double of that in Round 3.

So, in round 3 either 1 or 2 Bull's eye can be scored and in round 2, 2 or 4 Bull's eye can be scored.

Case 1: If only 1 Bull's eye is scored in the round 3, then in round 3 Umeza will score 2 and Zeneca will score 2/3/4 in round 3, which means both will score 5 in round 2. So, minimum Bull's eye in round 2 will be 3. (Umeza, Zeneca, and Xyla). Hence, this case is rejected.

Case 2: 2 Bull's eye were scored in round 3 and 4 Bull's eye were scored in round 2. So in round 2 Umeza, Yonita and Zeneca scored 5. This can be tabulated as:

	Round-1	Round-2	Round-3	Round-4	Round-5	Round-6	Total
Tanzi	5	4	1	5	NP	NP	15
Umeza	5/2	5	5/2	1	2	NP	15
Wangdu	1/2/3/4	4	1/2/3/4	NP	NP	NP	6-12
Xyla	5	5	5	1	5	1/2/3/4/5	22-26
Yonita	2	5	3	5	NP	NP	15
Zeneca	5	5	(2/3/4)	5	5	NP	-

In round 3, 2 Bull's eye can only be scored by Xyla and Umeza.

	Round-1	Round-2	Round-3	Round-4	Round-5	Round-6	Total
Tanzi	5	4	1	5	NP	NP	15
Umeza	2	5	5	1	2	NP	15
Wangdu	1/2/3/4	4	1/2/3/4	NP	NP	NP	6-12
Xyla	5	5	5	1	5	1/2/3/4/5	22-26
Yonita	2	5	3	5	NP	NP	15
Zeneca	5	5	(2/3/4)	5	5	NP	22-24

The highest scorer can be either Xyla or Zeneca. The lowest scorer will be Wangdu.

Let Zeneca is the highest scorer.

From 3, the highest total score was one more than double of the lowest total score. So the only possible score for Zeneca is 23 and that for Wangdu is 11. ($11 \times 2 + 1 = 23$)

But this will violate condition 2, since both Zeneca and Wangdu do not have their scores as multiples of three in this case.

Hence, Xyla will be the highest scorer. The only possible total score for Xyla will be 25, and that for Wangdu is 12(4 + 4 + 4). ($12 \times 2 + 1 = 25$)

Since Xyla already has non-multiple of 3 as total score. Zeneca will have 24 as the total score. The complete table is:

	Round-1	Round-2	Round-3	Round-4	Round-5	Round-6	Total
Tanzi	5	4	1	5	NP	NP	15
Umeza	2	5	5	1	2	NP	15
Wangdu	4	4	4	NP	NP	NP	12
Xyla	5	5	5	1	5	4	25
Yonita	2	5	3	5	NP	NP	15
Zeneca	5	5	4	5	5	NP	24

51. The highest score is 25.

52. Zeneca total score is 24.

53. Xyla was the highest scorer.

54. Tanzi scored 1 in round 3.

For questios 55 to 58:

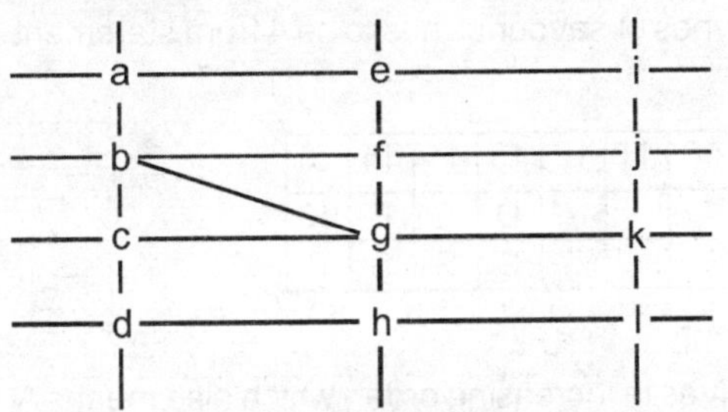

From 1, X, U, and Z are standing at the three corners of a triangle formed by three street segments.

From 2, X can see only U and Z.

From 4, U sees V standing in the next intersection behind Z. Also, no one among the six is standing at intersection d.

Only cases possible are:

1.

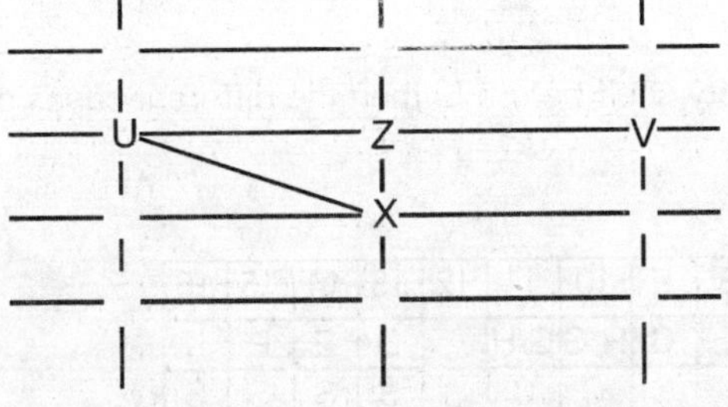

W cannot see V or Z. So, W can only be at the intersection a. Since Y can see only U and W, Y can only be at c where X can see him. Hence this case is rejected.

2.

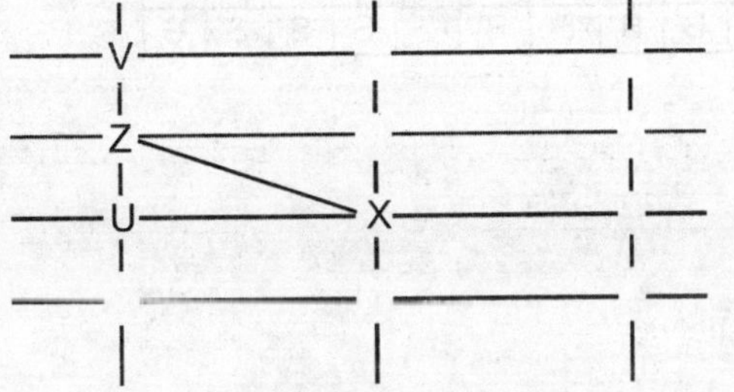

Y can only see U and W. Y cannot be placed anywhere. Hence this case is also rejected.

3.

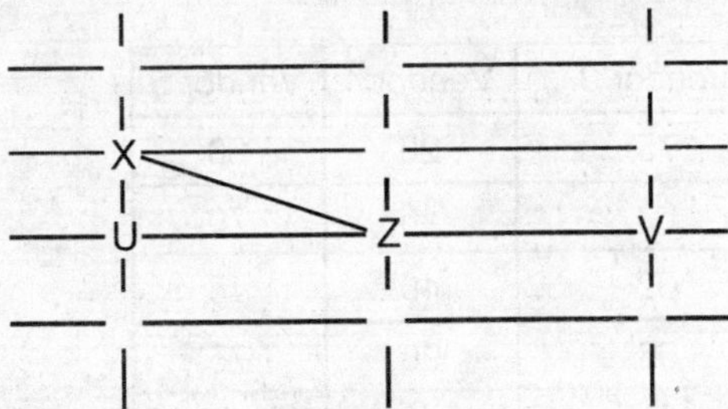

Y can only see U and W. Y cannot be placed anywhere. Hence this case is also rejected.

4.

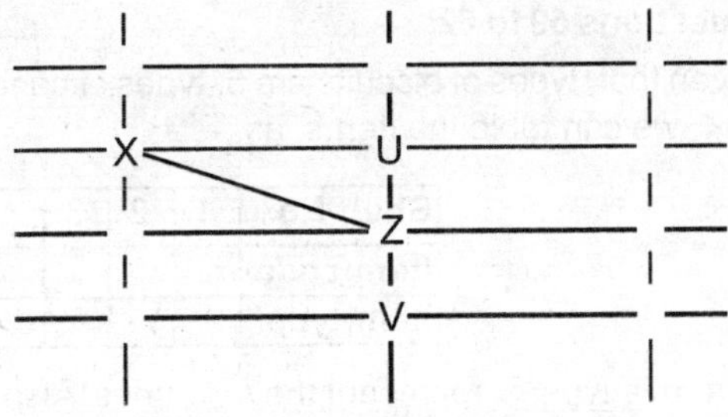

W cannot see V or Z. W can only be placed at i. Y can see only U and W. Y can only be placed at j or e, where he can see more people than U and W. Hence this case is also rejected.

5.

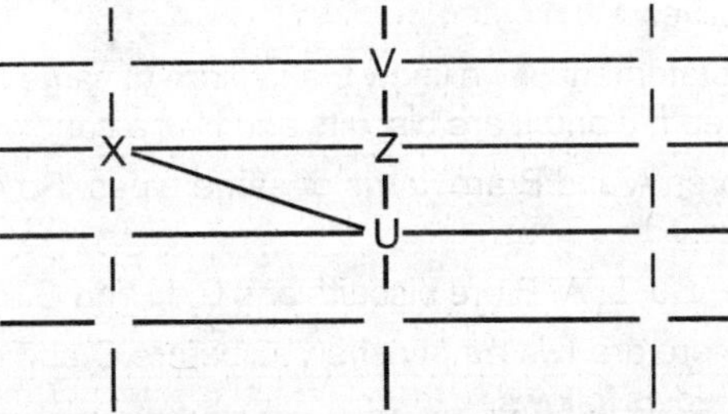

W cannot see V or Z. Y can only see U and W. Hence W and Y can only be placed as shown:

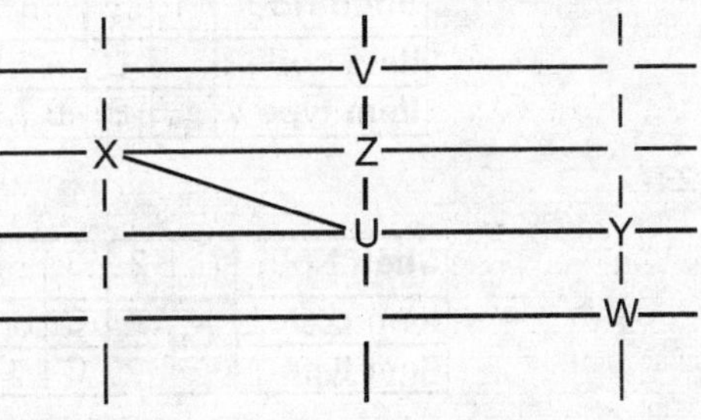

55. No one is standing at the intersection a. Hence (4) is the answer.

56. V can see U and Z only. Hence (1) is the answer.

57. To reach Y, X has to go from b to g and g to k, i.e. 2 streets.

58. If a new person stands at d(left down corner), they can see W and X only. Hence (1) is the answer.

For questions 59 to 62:

It is given that, types of biscuits are 5, types of candies are 3, therefore, types of savouries has to be 4 from statement 3 and 4, we can table the items as :-

Shelf No.	1	2	3	4	5	6	7	8	9	10	11	12	13	14	15	16
Item code													D	E	F	K
Item type													S	S	S	S

In the above type 'S' represent the savouries. Also, shelf 12 has to be empty

From statement 1, A and B are to placed in consecutively numbered shelves in increasing order, which also means A and B are of same kind, i.e, either biscuits or candies.

From statement 6 and 7 , C is a candy and is to be placed in a shelf preceded by two empty shelves and L is to be placed in a shelf preceded by exactly one empty shelf. Hence C and L are items of different types i.e., candy and biscuit respectively.

From statement 5, we know L and J are of same type and H is an items of a different type since I and J are clustered together, I, J and L are biscuits and H is a candy. So C, H are candies and I, J, L are biscuits.

It is given A and B are items of same types. So A, B should be biscuits because if they are candies there will be 4 candies.

Hence, I, J, L, A, B are biscuits and C, H and G are candies.

Now there are two empty shelves before C and exactly one empty shelf before L, then the different cases can be tabulated as follows :-

Case 1 :-

Shelf No :	1	2	3	4	5	6	7	8	9	10	11	12	13	14	15	16
Item code :		L	A	B	I/J	J/I			C	H/G	G/H		D	E	F	K
Item type :		B	B	B	B	B			C	C	C		S	S	S	S

Case 2 :-

Shelf No :	1	2	3	4	5	6	7	8	9	10	11	12	13	14	15	16
Item code :			C	H/G	G/H		L	A	B	I/J	J/I		D	E	F	K
Item type :			C	C	C		B	B	B	B	B		S	S	S	S

59. The number of arrangements for the first case = 2 × 2 = 4.

The number of arrangements for the second case = 2 × 2 = 4

The total number of arrangements = 4 + 4 = 8

60. G is not a type of biscuit.

61. 1, 2, 6, 12 can be the possible arrangement of the empty shelves.

62. There are at atleast four shelves between items B and C.

For questios 63 to 66:

The data can be tabulated as follows (approximately):

Parameters	Vendor 1	Vendor 2	Vendor 3	Vendor 4	Vendor 5
Reliability	52	40	75	26	60
Reach	80	58	63	46	70
Quality	72	69	62	40	48
Features	40	45	56	90	75
Customer Services	55	41	50	70	28
Cost	77	81	90	71	50

63. Customer Services: 28,41,50,55,70 (The median is 50)

Cost: 50,71,77,81,90 (The median is 77)

Reliability: 26, 40, 52, 60, 75 (The median is 52)

Quality: 40, 48, 62, 69, 72 (The median is 62)

Hence the customer services have the lowest median.

64. The average of the vendor will be highest which has highest total score. Hence vendor 3 has the highest average.

65. Top 3 on Reliability: Vendor 3, Vendor 5

Top 3 on Reach: Vendor 1, Vendor 5

Top 3 on Quality: Vendor 1, Vendor 2

Top 3 on Features: Vendor 4, Vendor 5

Top 3 on Customer Services: Vendor 4, Vendor 1

Top 3 on Cost: Vendor 3, Vendor 2

Vendor 1: 3 times, Vendor 2: Only once, Vendor 3: 2 times, Vendor 4: 2 times, Vendor 5: 3 times

Here, vendor 1 and 5 comes 3 times. Hence B is the answer.

66. Top 3 on Reliability: Vendor 3, Vendor 5, Vendor 1

Top 3 on Reach: Vendor 1, Vendor 5, Vendor 3

Top 3 on Quality: Vendor 1, Vendor 2, Vendor 3

Top 3 on Features: Vendor 4, Vendor 5, Vendor 3

Top 3 on Customer Services: Vendor 4, Vendor 1, Vendor 3

Top 3 on Cost: Vendor 3, Vendor 2, Vendor 1

Only Vendor 3 ranks among top 3 in all the six parameters.

67.

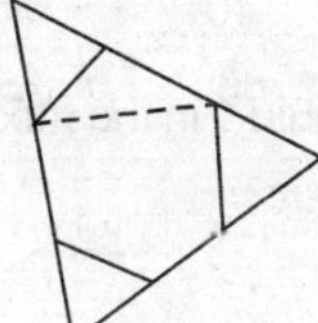

If the corners of the triangle are folded inside the hexagon, half of the area would be covered.

$$\therefore \frac{\Delta H}{\Delta T} = \frac{\Delta H}{\Delta H + \frac{\Delta H}{2}} = \frac{2}{3}$$

68. $\text{Log}_5 (x + y) + \log_5 (x - y) = 3$

$\Rightarrow \log_5 (x + y)(x - y) = 3.$

$\Rightarrow \log (x^2 - y^2) = 3 \log 5$

$\Rightarrow x^2 - y^2 = 5^3 \quad ...(1)$

$\log_2 y - \log_2 x = 1 - \log_2 3$

$\Rightarrow \log_2 \frac{y}{x} = \log_2 2 - \log_2 3$

$\Rightarrow \log_2 \frac{y}{x} = \log_2 \frac{2}{3}$

$\Rightarrow \frac{y}{x} = \frac{2}{3} \quad ...(2)$

Substitute the value of y from (2) in (1) and get,

$$\Rightarrow x^2 - \left(\frac{2x}{3}\right)^2 = 5^3$$

$$\Rightarrow x^2 \frac{5}{9} = 5^3$$

$\Rightarrow x = 15$ and $y = 10$

$\therefore xy = 150.$

69. Assume time taken by Amal = t

Then, the distance A and B = $d = \frac{t}{3}(10 + 20 + 30)$

$= 20\,t$

Total time taken by Bimal

$$= \frac{20t}{3}\left(\frac{1}{10} + \frac{1}{20} + \frac{1}{30}\right)$$

$$= \frac{20t}{3}\left(\frac{6+3+2}{60}\right) = \frac{11t}{9}$$

Hence, the time taken by Bimal will exceed Amal

by $= \dfrac{\frac{11t}{9} - t}{t} \times 100 = 22.22\%$

70. Paths from (1, 1) to (8, 10) via, (4, 6)

Means No. of paths from (1, 1) to (4, 6) multiplied by no. of paths from (4,6) to (8, 10)

Moving from (1, 1) to (4, 6) we have to take (4 – 1) + (6 – 1) steps = 8 steps, out of which '3' are horizontal and 5 are vertical. If we select '3' out of 8 steps, and assign them to horizontal, them all vertical steps are already assigned.

$\therefore$ No. of paths = ${}^8C_3 \times {}^8C_4 = 3920.$

71. Let A completes 'a' units of work in a day and B completes 'b' units of work in a day and the total work = 1 unit.

Hence, $12(a + b) = 1$ and, ...(1)

$9\left(\frac{a}{2} + 3b\right) = 1 \quad ...(2)$

Using both equations, we get

$$12(a + b) = 9\left(\frac{a}{2} + 3b\right)$$

$\Rightarrow 4a + 4b = \frac{3a}{2} + 9b. \Rightarrow a = 2b$

Substituting the value of b in equation (1),

$\Rightarrow 12\left(\frac{3a}{2}\right) = 1.$

$\therefore$ Number of days required = 18.

72. Let the maximum marks = 100a, then Meena got 40a.

After increasing her score by 50%, she will get

$\Rightarrow 40a\left(1 + \frac{50}{100}\right) = 60a.$

Given:- Passing score = 60a + 35.

Post review score after 20% increase

$= 60a \times 1.2 = 72a$

$\Rightarrow 60a + 35 + 7 = 72a$

$\Rightarrow 12a = 42$

$\Rightarrow a = 3.5$

$\therefore$ maximum marks = 350.

Passing marks = 210 + 35 = 245.

and, passing percentage $= \frac{245 \times 100}{350} = 70\%.$

73. Let the length of race course = x and the speed of three horses be a, b and c respectively.

Hence, $\frac{x}{a} = \frac{x-11}{b}$ ... (1)

and, $\frac{x}{a} = \frac{x-90}{c}$ ... (2)

Also, $\frac{x}{b} = \frac{x-80}{c}$ ... (3)

From (1) and (2) we get, $\frac{x-11}{b} = \frac{x-90}{c}$ ... (4)

Dividing (3) and (4) we get, $\frac{x-11}{x} = \frac{x-90}{x-80}$

$\Rightarrow (x - 11)(x - 80) = x(x - 90)$

$\Rightarrow 91x - 90x = 880$

$\Rightarrow x = 880$

74. Given f(x + y) = f(x) f(y) and f(1) = 2

$\Rightarrow f(a + 1) + f(a + 2) + ... + f(a + n) = 16(2^n - 1)$

Now f(2) = f(1 + 1) = f(1) f(1) = 4

f(3) = f(2 + 1) = f(2) f(1) = 8

f(4) = f(3 + 1) = f(3) f(1) = 16

$\therefore f(x) = 2^x$

Now, $f(a + 1) + f(a + 2) + ... + f(a + n) = 16(2^n - 1)$

on putting n = 1 in the equation, we get

f(a + 1) = 16

$\Rightarrow f(a) f(1) = 16$

$\Rightarrow 2^a . 2 = 16$

$\Rightarrow a = 3.$

75. 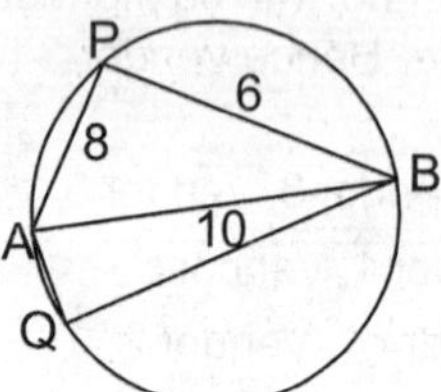

APB are vertices of a right angled triangle.

$\therefore AP = \sqrt{10^2 - 6^2} = 8$

$\therefore AQ = 4$

$\Rightarrow QB = \sqrt{10^2 - 4^2} = \sqrt{84} \simeq 9.1$

76. The weight/volume (g/L) for liquid 1 = 1000

The weight/volume (g/L) for liquid 2 = 800

The weight/volume (g/L) of the mixture $= \frac{480}{\left(\frac{1}{2}\right)} = 960$

using alligation the ratio of liquid 1 and liquid 2 in the mixture $= \frac{(960 - 800)}{(1000 - 960)} = \frac{160}{40} = 4$.

Hence, the percentage of liquid 1 in the mixture

$= \frac{4 \times 100}{4 + 1} = 80$

77. Equation of straight line = 3x + 5y – 45 = 0

It intersects 'X' axis when y = 0, $\Rightarrow$ at the point (15, 0)

It intersects Y axis, when x = 0, $\Rightarrow$ at the point (0, 9)

Diameter of circumcircle = length of hypotenuse

$= \sqrt{15^2 + 9^2}$

$\therefore$ Radius $= \frac{\sqrt{225 + 81}}{2} \simeq 9$

78. Let cost price of pen and book be x and y respectively. Then selling price of pen and book will be 0.95x and 1.15y respectively.

$(0.95x + 1.15y) - (x + y) = 7$ ... (1)

and

$(x1.05 + 1.10y) - (x + y) = 13$ ... (2)

Solving (1) and (2) we get,

$0.15y - 0.05x = 7$

$0.10y + 0.05x = 13$

$\Rightarrow \boxed{y = 80}$.

79. Let income of Bimala = 100

Then, Amala's income = 100 × 1.2 = 120.

Kamala's income = $\frac{120 \times 100}{80} = 150$.

Kamala income down by 4% = 144.

Bimala's income goes up by 10% = 110.

∴ Percentage by which Kamala's income would exceed Bimala's income

$= \frac{144 - 110}{110} \times 100 = 30.91\% \approx 31\%$

80. Given :- $|x^2 - x - 6| = x + 2$

$\Rightarrow |(x - 3)(x + 2)| = x + 2$

For $x < -2$, $(3 - x)(-x - 2) = x + 2$

$\Rightarrow x - 3 = 1 \Rightarrow x = 4$ (Not possible, as $x < -2$)

For $-2 \le x < 3$, $(3 - x)(x + 2) = (x + 2)$

$\Rightarrow x = 2, -2$

For $x \ge 3$, $(x - 3)(x + 2) = x + 2$

$\Rightarrow x = 4$

Hence the product = 4 × 2 × (–2) = –16

81. Let the speed of cars be a and b and the distance = d.

Minimum time taken by 1st car = 6 hours

For maximum difference in time taken by both of them, car 1 has to start at 10 : 00 AM and car 2 has to start at 11 : 00 AM

Hence, car 2 will take 5 hours.

Hence $a = \frac{d}{6}$ and $b = \frac{d}{5}$.

∴ The speed of car 2 will exceed the speed of car 1 by $\frac{\frac{d}{5} - \frac{d}{6}}{\frac{d}{6}} \times 100 = \frac{\frac{d}{30}}{\frac{d}{6}} \times 100 = 20\%$.

82. $|x|(6x^2 + 1) = 5x^2$

For $x < 0$, $(-x)(6x^2 + 1) = 5x^2$

$\Rightarrow 6x^3 + x + 5x^2 = 0$

$\Rightarrow x(6x^2 + 5x + 1) = 0$

$\Rightarrow x(6x^2 + 3x + 2x + 1) = 0$

$\Rightarrow x(3x + 1)(2x + 1) = 0$

$x = 0, \frac{-1}{3}, \frac{-1}{2}$

For $x > 0$, $(x)(6x^2 + 1) = 5x^2$

$\Rightarrow 6x^3 + x - 5x^2 = 0$

$\Rightarrow x(6x^2 + 1 - 5x) = 0$

$\Rightarrow x(6x^2 - 3x - 2x + 1) = 0$

$\Rightarrow x(2x - 1)(3x - 1) = 0$

$\therefore x = 0,\ x = \frac{1}{2}, \frac{1}{3}$

Hence, the total number of solutions = 5.

83. Distance covered by A in 1 revolution = $2\pi \times 30 = 60\pi$

Distance covered by B in 1 revolution = $2\pi \times 40 = 80\pi$

Now, $(5000 + n)(60\pi) = 80\pi n$

$\Rightarrow 15000 = 4n - 3n$

$\Rightarrow n = 15000$

Then distance travelled by B = $15000 \times 80\pi$ cm

$= 12\pi$ km

Hence the speed = $\frac{12\pi \times 60}{45} = 16\pi$

84. Let us assume that m is even, then, m + 1 will be odd and $\Rightarrow 8f(m + 1) - f(m) = 2$

$\Rightarrow 8(m + 1 + 3) - m(m + 1) = 2$

$\Rightarrow 8m + 32 - m^2 - m = 2$

$\Rightarrow m^2 - 7m - 30 = 0$

$\Rightarrow m = 10, -3.$

Rejecting the negative value, we get m = 10.

85. Let two positive numbers be x and y.

Given :- $xy = 616$ and $\frac{x^3 - y^3}{(x - y)^3} = \frac{157}{3}$.

To find :- $x + y = ?$

$\Rightarrow \frac{x^3 - y^3}{(x - y)^3} = \frac{(x - y)^3 + 3xy(x - y)}{(x - y)^3}$

$\Rightarrow \frac{x^3 - y^3}{(x - y)^3} = \frac{(x - y)^2 + 3xy}{(x - y)^2}$

$$\Rightarrow \frac{x^3 - y^3}{(x-y)^3} \cdot \frac{x^2 + y^2 - 2xy + 3xy}{x^2 + y^2 - 2xy}.$$

$$\Rightarrow \frac{x^2 + y^2 + xy}{x^2 + y^2 - 2xy} = \frac{157}{3}$$

$\Rightarrow 3[x^2 + y^2] + 3 \times xy = 157 [x^2 + y^2] - 2(xy) + 157$

$\Rightarrow 3(x^2 + y^2) + 1848 = 157 (x^2 + y^2) - 193424$

$\Rightarrow 195272 = 154 (x^2 + y^2)$

$\Rightarrow 1268 = x^2 + y^2$

Now, use $(x + y)^2 = x^2 + y^2 + 2xy$

$= 1268 + 2 \times 616 = (x + y)^2$

$\Rightarrow 2500 = (x + y)^2$

$\Rightarrow x + y = 50$ (Since, x and y are positive numbers)

86. $2 \cos (x (x + 1)) = 2^x + 2^{-x}$

The maximum value of L.H.S is 2 when cos (x (x + 1)) is 1 and the minimum value of R.H.S is 2.

Hence, L.H.S and R.H.S can only be equal when both sides are 2.

For L.H.S, $\cos (x (x + 1)) = 1$

$\Rightarrow x(x + 1) = 0$

$\Rightarrow x = 0, -1.$

For R.H.S minimum value, $x = 0$.

Hence, only one solution $x = 0$.

87. Given $a_1 + a_2 + a_3 + ... + a_n$

$= 3 (2^{n+1} - 2), n \geq 1$

11th term of series $= a_{11}$

= Sum of 11 terms – Sum of 10 terms

$= 3(2^{12} - 2) - 3(2^{11} - 2)$

$= 3[2^{12} - 2 - 2^{11} + 2]$

$= 3[2^{12} - 2^{11}]$

$= 3 \times 2^{11}$

$= 6144.$

88.

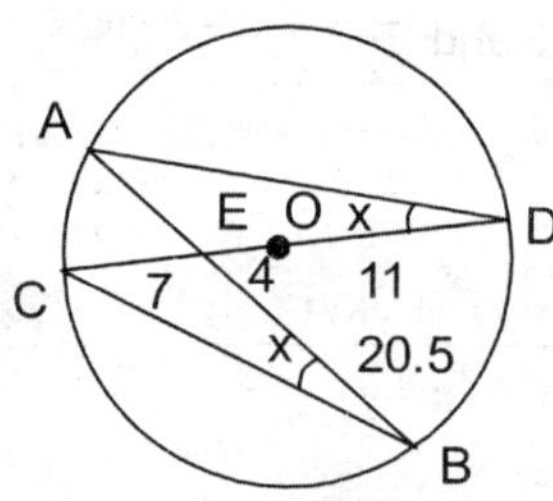

DE = 4, EC = 7, AB = 20.5

CD = 22

|BE – AE| = ?

In figure AE × BE = CE × DE (P tolemy Theorem)

$\Rightarrow 7 \times 15 = x(20.5 - x)$

(Let AE = x)

$\Rightarrow 210 = x(41 - 2x)$

$\Rightarrow 2x^2 - 41x + 210 = 0$

$\Rightarrow x = 10$ or 10.5

AE = 10 or AE = 10.5

Hence, BE = 20.5 – 10 = 10.5 or

BE = 20.5 – 10.5 = 10

Required difference = 10.5 – 10 = 0.5

89. Let the amount invested in the ratio 2 : 1 was 200 x and 100 x, then the fixed deposit investment = 1500000 – 300 x.

Hence, the interest $= 200x \times \frac{4}{100} = 8x$ and,

$100x \times \frac{3}{100} = 3x$

Interest from the fixed deposit

$= (1500000 - 300x) \frac{6}{100} = 90000 - 18x$

Hence the total interest $= 90000 - 18x + 8x + 3x$
$= 90000 - 7x$

$\Rightarrow 90000 - 7x = 76000$

$\Rightarrow 7x = 14000$

$\Rightarrow x = 2000$

Hence the fixed deposit investment

= 15000000 – 300 × 2000

= 9,00,000

= 9 lakhs.

90. $(\sqrt{2})^{19} 3^4 4^2 9^m 8^n = 3^n 16^m (\sqrt[4]{64})$

$$\Rightarrow 2^{\frac{19}{2}} 3^4 2^4 3^{2m} 2^{3n} = 3^n 2^{4m} (64)^{\frac{1}{4}}$$

$$\Rightarrow \left(2^{\frac{19}{2}+4+3n}\right)\left(3^{4+2m}\right) = 3^n 2^{4m} 2^{\frac{3}{2}}.$$

$$\Rightarrow 2^{\frac{27}{2}+3n} 3^{4+2m} = 3^n 2^{4m+\frac{3}{2}}$$

$$\therefore \frac{27}{2} + 3n = 4m + \frac{3}{2} \quad ...(1)$$

and $4 + 2m = n$ ...(2)

Solving (1) and (2), we get,

$m = -12$

91. $|x| + |y| \le 2$, $|x| \ge 1$

we have to find the shaded area

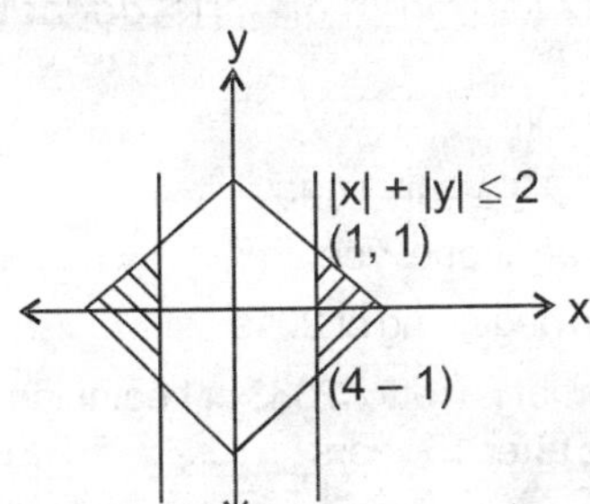

$$= 2 \times \frac{1}{2} \times 2 \times 1$$

$= \boxed{2}$ sq. units

92.

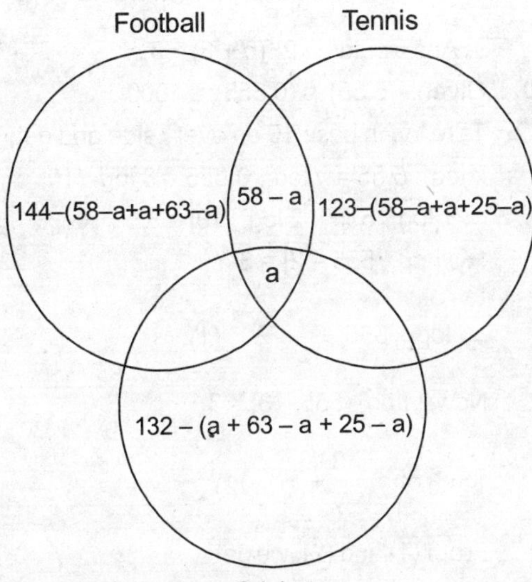

All players total = 256

$\Rightarrow 256 = 144 + 123 + 132 - (58 + 25 + 63) + a$

$\Rightarrow 256 = 399 - 146 - 2a$

$\Rightarrow 256 = 253 + a$

$\Rightarrow \boxed{a = 3}$

$\therefore$ only Tennis = 123 – 58 – 25 + 3

= 123 – 80 = 43

93. Let 'W' be work, M be efficiency of men, 'm' be efficiency of machines

3M + 8m = 2(8M + 3m) ... (1)

2m = 13 days

from eq^n (1) : 3M + 8m = 16M + 6m

$\Rightarrow \boxed{2m = 13M}$

If '2' machines complete work in 13 days

$\Rightarrow$ 13 Men will complete the work in 13 days.

94. Let the investment of Amala, Bina and Gouri be 300x, 400x and 500x, hence the interest incomes will be $(300x)\frac{6}{100} = 18x$, $(400x)\frac{5}{100} = 20x$ and $(500x)\frac{4}{100} = 20x$ respectively.

Given, Bina's interest income exceeds Amala by.
20x – 18x = 2x = 250 $\Rightarrow$ x = 125.

Now, total interest income = 18x + 20x + 20x
= 58x = 58 × 125 = 7250.

95. Given:- $a_1, a_2, \ldots\ldots$ are in A.P.

therefore, $a_1 = a_1$

$a_2 = a_1 + d$

$a_3 = a_2 + d$

and so on.

where d is the common difference.

Now consider

$$\frac{1}{\sqrt{a_1}+\sqrt{a_2}} + \frac{1}{\sqrt{a_2}+\sqrt{a_3}} + \ldots. + \frac{1}{\sqrt{a_n}+\sqrt{a_{n+1}}}$$

Rationalise each term and get,

$$\Rightarrow \frac{\sqrt{a_1}-\sqrt{a_2}}{a_1 - a_2} + \frac{\sqrt{a_2}-\sqrt{a_3}}{a_2 - a_3} + \ldots + \frac{\sqrt{a_n}-\sqrt{a_{n+1}}}{a_n - a_{n+1}}$$

$$\Rightarrow \frac{-1}{d}\left[\sqrt{a_1}-\sqrt{a_2}+\sqrt{a_2}-\sqrt{a_3}+\ldots+\sqrt{a_n}-\sqrt{a_{n+1}}\right]$$

$$\Rightarrow \frac{-1}{d}\left[\sqrt{a_1}-\sqrt{a_{n+1}}\right]$$

$$\Rightarrow \frac{-1}{d}\left[\frac{a_1 - a_{n+1}}{\sqrt{a_1}+\sqrt{a_{n+1}}}\right] \text{ [rationalise again]}$$

$$\Rightarrow \frac{n}{\sqrt{a_1}+\sqrt{a_{n+1}}}.$$

96. Let the score of Ramesh and Gautam be denoted by S_R and S_G respectively.

Given:- $S_R = 82.5$ and,

$$\frac{\text{sum of scores of 20 students} + S_R}{21} = 62$$

$\Rightarrow$ sum of scores of 20 students = 62 × 21 – 82.5
= 1219.5

Average score of 21 students other than Ramesh

$$= \frac{1219.5 + S_G}{21}$$

Average score of 22 students

$$= \frac{1219.5 + 82.5 + S_G}{22}$$

Given:- $\frac{1219.5 + 82.5 + S_G}{22} = 1 + \frac{1219.5 + S_G}{21}$

$\Rightarrow (1302 + S_G) \times 21 = (1240.5 + S_G)22$

$\Rightarrow 27342 - 27291 = S_G$

$\Rightarrow 51 = G$

97. Rectangular faces have diagonals

$3 : 2\sqrt{3} : \sqrt{15}$

Let's take sides in a ratio such that this case can be observed.

$\Rightarrow \sqrt{l^2 + b^2} : \sqrt{b^2 + h^2} : \sqrt{l^2 + h^2} = 3 : 2\sqrt{3} : 15$

or $l^2 + b^2 = 9$,

$b^2 + h^2 = 12$, $l^2 + h^2 = 15$

$\Rightarrow l^2 = 6$, $b^2 = 3$, $h^2 = 9$.

$\therefore$ shortest to longest edge $= \sqrt{\frac{3}{9}} = 1 : \sqrt{3}$

98. Let there be x students in the class

Girls = x × 0.6

Boys = x × 0.4

Given:- There are 30 more girls than boys i.e.,

$\Rightarrow x(0.6) = (x \times 0.4) + 30$

$\Rightarrow x(0.2) = 30$

$\Rightarrow x = 150$

68% pass the examination $\Rightarrow$102 students

since, 102 students, includes 30 boys, therefore, 72 will be Girls who passed.

Girls who do not pass = (150 × 0.6) – 72 = 18

$\therefore \frac{18 \times 100}{90} = 20\%$ of girls do not pass the examination.

99. popl^n = p at beginning,

3 + 2p after one year

1000 in beginning of 2019

Then what is it after 2033 or beginning of 2014 that means after 15 years

year 1	year 2	year 3	year3
p	3 + 2p	2(3 + 2p) + 3	2(4p + 9) + 3
		= 4p + 9	= 8p + 21
		= 4(p + 3) – 3	= 8(p + 3) – 3
		$= 2^2(p+3) - 3$	$= 2^3(p+3) - 3$

$\therefore$ Ans would be $2^{15}(p + 3) - 3$

100. Given;- $(5.55)^x = (0.555)^y = 1000$

Take log in base 10 on every side and get,

$x \log_{10} 5.55 = y \log_{10} 0.555 = 3 \log_{10} 10.$

$\Rightarrow x[\log_{10} 555 - 2 \log_{10} 10] = 3$

$\Rightarrow x[\log_{10} 555 - 2] = 3$

$\Rightarrow \log_{10} 555 = \frac{3}{x} + 2 \ldots (1)$

Now, $y[\log_{10} 555 - 3] = 3$

$\log_{10} 555 = \frac{3}{y} + 3 \ldots (2)$

From (1) and (2), we get

$\Rightarrow \frac{3}{x} + 2 = \frac{3}{y} + 3 \Rightarrow \frac{3}{x} - \frac{3}{y} = 1 \Rightarrow \frac{1}{x} - \frac{1}{y} = \frac{1}{3}.$

CAT 2019 SOLVED PAPER (SLOT-2)

Section I: VRC

Question Numbers (1 to 5): The passage below is accompanied by a set of five questions. Choose the best answer to each question.

War, natural disasters and climate change are destroying some of the world's most precious cultural sites. Google is trying to help preserve these archaeological wonders by allowing users access to 3D images of these treasures through its site.

But the project is raising questions about Google's motivations and about who should own the digital copyrights. Some critics call it a form of "digital colonialism."

When it comes to archaeological treasures, the losses have been mounting. ISIS blew up parts of the ancient city of Palmyra in Syria and an earthquake hit Bagan, an ancient city in Myanmar, damaging dozens of temples, in 2016. In the past, all archaeologists and historians had for restoration and research were photos, drawings, remnants and intuition.

But that's changing. Before the earthquake at Bagan, many of the temples on the site were scanned.... [These] scans ... are on Google's Arts & Culture site. The digital renditions allow viewers to virtually wander the halls of the temple, look up-close at paintings and turn the building over, to look up at its chambers. . . . [Google Arts & Culture] works with museums and other nonprofits . . . to put high-quality images online

The images of the temples in Bagan are part of a collaboration with CyArk, a nonprofit that creates the 3D scanning of historic sites.... Google ... says [it] doesn't make money off this website, but it fits in with Google's mission to make the world's information available and useful.

Critics say the collaboration could be an attempt by a large corporation to wrap itself in the sheen of culture. Ethan Watrall, an archaeologist, professor at Michigan State University and a member of the Society for American Archaeology, says he's not comfortable with the arrangement between CyArk and Google.... Watrall says this project is just a way for Google to promote Google. "They want to make this material accessible so people will browse it and be filled with wonder by it," he says. "But at its core, it's all about advertisements and driving traffic." Watrall says these images belong on the site of a museum or educational institution, where there is serious scholarship and a very different mission. ...

[There's] another issue for some archaeologists and art historians. CyArk owns the copyrights of the scans — not the countries where these sites are located. That means the countries need CyArk's permission to use these images for commercial purposes.

Erin Thompson, a professor of art crime at John Jay College of Criminal Justice in New York City, says it's the latest example of a Western nation appropriating a foreign culture, a centuries-long battle. . . . CyArk says it copyrights the scans so no one can use them in an inappropriate way. The company says it works closely with authorities during the process, even training local people to help. But critics like Thompson are not persuaded. . . . She would prefer the scans to be owned by the countries and people where these sites are located.

1. Of the following arguments, which one is LEAST likely to be used by the companies that digitally scan cultural sites?

(1) It enables people who cannot physically visit these sites to experience them.

(2) It helps preserve precious images in case the sites are damaged or destroyed.

(3) It provides images free of cost to all users.

(4) It allows a large corporation to project itself as a protector of culture.

2. Based on his views mentioned in the passage, one could best characterise Dr. Watrall as being:

(1) critical about the links between a non-profit and a commercial tech platform for distributing archaeological images.

(2) opposed to the use of digital technology in archaeological and cultural sites in developing countries.

(3) uneasy about the marketing of archaeological images for commercial use by firms such as Google and CyArk.

(4) dismissive of laypeople's access to specialist images of archaeological and cultural sites.

3. In Dr. Thompson's view, CyArk owning the copyright of its digital scans of archaeological sites is akin to:
   (1) digital platforms capturing users' data for market research.
   (2) the illegal downloading of content from the internet.
   (3) the seizing of ancient Egyptian artefacts by a Western museum.
   (4) tourists uploading photos of monuments onto social media.
4. Which of the following, if true, would most strongly invalidate Dr. Watrall's objections?
   (1) Google takes down advertisements on its website hosting CyArk's scanned images.
   (2) There is a ban on CyArk scanning archeological sites located in other countries.
   (3) CyArk uploads its scanned images of archaeological sites onto museum websites only.
   (4) CyArk does not own the copyright on scanned images of archaeological sites.
5. By "digital colonialism", critics of the CyArk–Google project are referring to the fact that:
   (1) countries where the scanned sites are located do not own the scan copyrights.
   (2) the scanning process can damage delicate frescos and statues at the sites.
   (3) CyArk and Google have not shared the details of digitisation with the host countries.
   (4) CyArk and Google have been scanning images without copyright permission from host countries.

Question Numbers (6 to 10): The passage below is accompanied by a set of five questions. Choose the best answer to each question.

Around the world, capital cities are disgorging bureaucrats. In the post-colonial fervour of the 20th century, coastal capitals picked by trade-focused empires were spurned for "regionally neutral" new ones .... But decamping wholesale is costly and unpopular; governments these days prefer piecemeal dispersal. The trend reflects how the world has changed. In past eras, when information travelled at a snail's pace, civil servants had to cluster together. But now desk-workers can ping emails and video-chat around the world. Travel for face-to-face meetings may be unavoidable, but transport links, too, have improved....

Proponents of moving civil servants around promise countless benefits. It disperses the risk that a terrorist attack or natural disaster will cripple an entire government. Wonks in the sticks will be inspired by new ideas that walled-off capitals cannot conjure up. Autonomous regulators perform best far from the pressure and lobbying of the big city. Some even hail a cure for ascendant cynicism and populism. The unloved bureaucrats of faraway capitals will become as popular as firefighters once they mix with regular folk.

Beyond these sunny visions, dispersing central-government functions usually has three specific aims: to improve the lives of both civil servants and those living in clogged capitals; to save money; and to redress regional imbalances. The trouble is that these goals are not always realised.

The first aim—improving living conditions—has a long pedigree. After the second world war Britain moved thousands of civil servants to "agreeable English country towns" as London was rebuilt. But swapping the capital for somewhere smaller is not always agreeable. Attrition rates can exceed 80%. . . . The second reason to pack bureaucrats off is to save money. Office space costs far more in capitals. . . . Agencies that are moved elsewhere can often recruit better workers on lower salaries than in capitals, where well-paying multinationals mop up talent.

The third reason to shift is to rebalance regional inequality. . . . Norway treats federal jobs as a resource every region deserves to enjoy, like profits from oil. Where government jobs go, private ones follow. . . . Sometimes the aim is to fulfil the potential of a country's second-tier cities. Unlike poor, remote places, bigger cities can make the most of relocated government agencies, linking them to local universities and businesses and supplying a better-educated workforce. The decision in 1946 to set up America's Centres for Disease Control in Atlanta rather than Washington, D.C., has transformed the city into a hub for health-sector research and business.

The dilemma is obvious. Pick small, poor towns, and areas of high unemployment get new jobs, but it is hard to attract the most qualified workers; opt for larger cities with infrastructure and better-qualified residents, and the country's most deprived areas see little benefit. . . .

Others contend that decentralisation begets corruption by making government agencies less accountable. . . . A study in America found that state-government corruption is worse when the state capital is isolated—journalists, who tend to live in the bigger cities, become less watchful of those in power.

6. The "long pedigree" of the aim to shift civil servants to improve their living standards implies that this move:
   (1) has become common practice in several countries worldwide.
   (2) is not a new idea and has been tried in the past.
   (3) takes a long time to achieve its intended outcomes.
   (4) is supported by politicians and the ruling elites.

7. People who support decentralising central government functions are LEAST likely to cite which of the following reasons for their view?

(1) It could weaken the nexus between bureaucrats and media in the capital.

(2) Policy makers may benefit from fresh thinking in a new environment.

(3) More independence could be enjoyed by regulatory bodies located away from political centres.

(4) It reduces expenses as infrastructure costs and salaries are lower in smaller cities.

8. According to the passage, colonial powers located their capitals:

(1) based on political expediency.

(2) to showcase their power and prestige.

(3) to promote their trading interests.

(4) where they had the densest populations.

9. The "dilemma" mentioned in the passage refers to:

(1) encouraging private enterprises to relocate to smaller towns or not incentivising them in order to keep government costs in those towns low.

(2) concentrating on decongesting large cities or focusing on boosting employment in relatively larger cities.

(3) keeping government agencies in the largest city with good infrastructure or moving them to a remote area with few amenities.

(4) relocating government agencies to boost growth in remote areas with poor amenities or to relatively larger cities with good amenities.

10. According to the author, relocating government agencies has not always been a success for all of the following reasons EXCEPT:

(1) the difficulty of attracting talented, well-skilled people in more remote areas.

(2) a rise in pollution levels and congestion in the new locations.

(3) increased avenues of corruption away from the capital city.

(4) high staff losses, as people may not be prepared to move to smaller towns.

Question Numbers (11 to 14): The passage below is accompanied by a set of four questions. Choose the best answer to each question.

For two years, I tracked down dozens of . . . Chinese in Upper Egypt [who were] selling lingerie. In a deeply conservative region, where Egyptian families rarely allow women to work or own businesses, the Chinese flourished because of their status as outsiders. They didn't gossip, and they kept their opinions to themselves. In a New Yorker article entitled "Learning to Speak Lingerie," I described the Chinese use of Arabic as another non-threatening characteristic. I wrote, "Unlike Mandarin, Arabic is inflected for gender, and Chinese dealers, who learn the language strictly by ear, often pick up speech patterns from female customers. I've come to think of it as the lingerie dialect, and there's something disarming about these Chinese men speaking in the feminine voice." . . .

When I wrote about the Chinese in the New Yorker, most readers seemed to appreciate the unusual perspective. But as I often find with topics that involve the Middle East, some people had trouble getting past the black-and-white quality of a byline. "This piece is so orientalist I don't know what to do," Aisha Gani, a reporter who worked at The Guardian, tweeted. Another colleague at the British paper, Iman Amrani, agreed: "I wouldn't have minded an article on the subject written by an Egyptian woman—probably would have had better insight." . . .

As an MOL (man of language), I also take issue with this kind of essentialism. Empathy and understanding are not inherited traits, and they are not strictly tied to gender and race. An individual who wrestles with a difficult language can learn to be more sympathetic to outsiders and open to different experiences of the world. This learning process—the embarrassments, the frustrations, the gradual sense of understanding and connection—is invariably transformative. In Upper Egypt, the Chinese experience of struggling to learn Arabic and local culture had made them much more thoughtful. In the same way, I was interested in their lives not because of some kind of voyeurism, but because I had also experienced Egypt and Arabic as an outsider. And both the Chinese and the Egyptians welcomed me because I spoke their languages. My identity as a white male was far less important than my ability to communicate.

And that easily lobbed word—"Orientalist"—hardly captures the complexity of our interactions. What exactly is the dynamic when a man from Missouri observes a Zhejiang native selling lingerie to an Upper Egyptian woman? . . . If all of us now stand beside the same river, speaking in ways we all understand, who's looking east and who's looking west? Which way is Oriental?

For all of our current interest in identity politics, there's no corresponding sense of identity linguistics. You are what you speak—the words that run throughout your mind are at least as fundamental to your selfhood as is your ethnicity or your gender. And sometimes it's healthy to consider human characteristics that are not inborn, rigid, and outwardly defined. After all, you can always learn another language and change who you are.

11. According to the passage, which of the following is not responsible for language's ability to change us?

(1) The ups and downs involved in the course of learning a language.

(2) The twists and turns in the evolution of language over time.

(3) Language's intrinsic connection to our notions of self and identity.

(4) Language's ability to mediate the impact of identity markers one is born with.

12. Which of the following can be inferred from the author's claim, "Which way is Oriental?"

(1) Globalisation has mitigated cultural hierarchies and barriers.

(2) Learning another language can mitigate cultural hierarchies and barriers.

(3) Orientalism is a discourse of the past, from colonial times, rarely visible today.

(4) Goodwill alone mitigates cultural hierarchies and barriers.

13. A French ethnographer decides to study the culture of a Nigerian tribe. Which of the following is most likely to be the view of the author of the passage?

(1) The author would encourage the ethnographer and recommend him/her to hire a good translator for the purpose of holding interviews.

(2) The author would encourage the ethnographer, but ask him/her to first learn the language of the Nigerian tribe s/he wishes to study.

(3) The author would discourage the ethnographer from conducting the study as Nigerian ethnographers can better understand the tribe.

(4) The author would encourage the ethnographer, but ask him/her to be mindful of his/her racial and gender identity in the process.

14. The author's critics would argue that:

(1) Language is insufficient to bridge cultural barriers.

(2) Linguistic politics can be erased.

(3) Orientalism cannot be practiced by Egyptians.

(4) Empathy can overcome identity politics.

Question Numbers (15 to 19): The passage below is accompanied by a set of five questions. Choose the best answer to each question.

British colonial policy . . . went through two policy phases, or at least there were two strategies between which its policies actually oscillated, sometimes to its great advantage. At first, the new colonial apparatus exercised caution, and occupied India by a mix of military power and subtle diplomacy, the high ground in the middle of the circle of circles. This, however, pushed them into contradictions. For, whatever their sense of the strangeness of the country and the thinness of colonial presence, the British colonial state represented the great conquering discourse of Enlightenment rationalism, entering India precisely at the moment of its greatest unchecked arrogance. As inheritors and representatives of this discourse, which carried everything before it, this colonial state could hardly adopt for long such a self-denying attitude. It had restructured everything in Europe—the productive system, the political regimes, the moral and cognitive orders—and would do the same in India, particularly as some empirically inclined theorists of that generation considered the colonies a massive laboratory of utilitarian or other theoretical experiments. Consequently, the colonial state could not settle simply for eminence at the cost of its marginality; it began to take initiatives to introduce the logic of modernity into Indian society. But this modernity did not enter a passive society. Sometimes, its initiatives were resisted by pre-existing structural forms. At times, there was a more direct form of collective resistance. Therefore the map of continuity and discontinuity that this state left behind at the time of independence was rather complex and has to be traced with care.

Most significantly, of course, initiatives for . . . modernity came to assume an external character. The acceptance of modernity came to be connected, ineradicably, with subjection. This again points to two different problems, one theoretical, the other political. Theoretically, because modernity was externally introduced, it is explanatorily unhelpful to apply the logical format of the 'transition process' to this pattern of change. Such a logical format would be wrong on two counts. First, however subtly, it would imply that what was proposed to be built was something like European capitalism. (And, in any case, historians have forcefully argued that what it was to replace was not like feudalism, with or without modificatory adjectives.) But, more fundamentally, the logical structure of endogenous change does not apply here. Here transformation agendas attack as an external force. This externality is not something that can be casually mentioned and forgotten. It is inscribed on every move, every object, every proposal, every legislative act, each line of causality. It comes to be marked on the epoch itself. This repetitive emphasis on externality should not be seen as a nationalist initiative that is so well rehearsed in Indian social science. . . .

Quite apart from the externality of the entire historical proposal of modernity, some of its contents were remarkable. . . . Economic reforms, or rather alterations . . . did not foreshadow the construction of a classical capitalist economy, with its necessary emphasis on extractive and transport sectors. What happened was the creation of a degenerate version of capitalism—what early dependency theorists called the 'development of underdevelopment'.

15. All of the following statements, if true, could be seen as supporting the arguments in the passage, EXCEPT:

(1) throughout the history of colonial conquest, natives have often been experimented on by the colonisers.

(2) the introduction of capitalism in India was not through the transformation of feudalism, as happened in Europe.

(3) the change in British colonial policy was induced by resistance to modernity in Indian society.

(4) modernity was imposed upon India by the British and, therefore, led to underdevelopment.

16. Which of the following observations is a valid conclusion to draw from the author's statement that "the logical structure of endogenous change does not apply here. Here transformation agendas attack as an external force"?

(1) The endogenous logic of colonialism can only bring change if it attacks and transforms external forces.

(2) Indian society is not endogamous; it is more accurately characterised as aggressively exogamous.

(3) The transformation of Indian society did not happen organically, but was forced by colonial agendas.

(4) Colonised societies cannot be changed through logic; they need to be transformed with external force.

17. "Consequently, the colonial state could not settle simply for eminence at the cost of its marginality; it began to take initiatives to introduce the logic of modernity into Indian society." Which of the following best captures the sense of this statement?

(1) The colonial enterprise was a costly one; so to justify the cost it began to take initiatives to introduce the logic of modernity into Indian society.

(2) The colonial state felt marginalised from Indian society because of its own modernity; therefore, it sought to address that marginalisation by bringing its modernity to change Indian society.

(3) The colonial state's eminence was unsettled by its marginal position; therefore, it developed Indian society by modernising it.

(4) The cost of the colonial state's eminence was not settled; therefore, it took the initiative of introducing modernity into Indian society.

18. Which one of the following 5-word sequences best captures the flow of the arguments in the passage?

(1) Military power—arrogance—laboratory—modernity—capitalism.

(2) Military power—colonialism—restructuring—feudalism—capitalism.

(3) Colonial policy—Enlightenment—external modernity—subjection—underdevelopment.

(4) Colonial policy—arrogant rationality—resistance—independence—development.

19. All of the following statements about British colonialism can be inferred from the first paragraph, EXCEPT that it:

(1) allowed the treatment of colonies as experimental sites.

(2) faced resistance from existing structural forms of Indian modernity.

(3) was at least partly an outcome of Enlightenment rationalism.

(4) was at least partly shaped by the project of European modernity.

Question Numbers (20 to 24): The passage below is accompanied by a set of five questions. Choose the best answer to each question.

The magic of squatter cities is that they are improved steadily and gradually by their residents. To a planner's eye, these cities look chaotic. I trained as a biologist and to my eye, they look organic. Squatter cities are also unexpectedly green. They have maximum density—1 million people per square mile in some areas of Mumbai—and have minimum energy and material use. People get around by foot, bicycle, rickshaw, or the universal shared taxi.

Not everything is efficient in the slums, though. In the Brazilian favelas where electricity is stolen and therefore free, people leave their lights on all day. But in most slums recycling is literally a way of life. The Dharavi slum in Mumbai has 400 recycling units and 30,000 ragpickers. Six thousand tons of rubbish are sorted every day. In 2007, the Economist reported that in Vietnam and Mozambique, "Waves of gleaners sift the sweepings of Hanoi's streets, just as Mozambiquan children pick over the rubbish of Maputo's main tip. Every city in Asia and Latin America has an industry based on gathering up old cardboard boxes." . . .

In his 1985 article, Calthorpe made a statement that still jars with most people: "The city is the most environmentally benign form of human settlement. Each city dweller consumes less land, less energy, less water, and produces less pollution than his counterpart in settlements of lower densities." "Green Manhattan" was the inflammatory title of a 2004 New Yorker article by David Owen. "By the most significant measures," he wrote, "New York is the greenest community in the United States, and one of the greenest cities in the world . . . The key to New York's relative environmental benignity is its extreme compactness. . . . Placing one and a half million people on a twenty-three-square-mile island sharply reduces their opportunities to be wasteful." He went on to note that this very compactness forces people to live in the world's most energy-efficient apartment buildings. . . .

Urban density allows half of humanity to live on 2.8 per cent of the land. . . . Consider just the infrastructure efficiencies. According to a 2004 UN report: "The concentration of population and enterprises in urban areas greatly reduces the unit cost of piped water, sewers, drains, roads, electricity, garbage collection, transport, health care, and schools." . . .

[T]he nationally subsidised city of Manaus in northern Brazil "answers the question" of how to stop deforestation: give people decent jobs. Then they can afford houses, and gain security. One hundred thousand people who would otherwise be deforesting the jungle around Manaus are now prospering in town making such things as mobile phones and televisions. . . .

Of course, fast-growing cities are far from an unmitigated good. They concentrate crime, pollution, disease and injustice as much as business, innovation, education and entertainment. . . . But if they are overall a net good for those who move there, it is because cities offer more than just jobs. They are transformative: in the slums, as well as the office towers and leafy suburbs, the progress is from hick to metropolitan to cosmopolitan . . .

20. According to the passage, squatter cities are environment-friendly for all of the following reasons EXCEPT:

(1) their transportation is energy efficient.

(2) their streets are kept clean.

(3) they recycle material.

(4) they sort out garbage.

21. Which one of the following statements would undermine the author's stand regarding the greenness of cities?

(1) The high density of cities leads to an increase in carbon dioxide and global warming.

(2) The compactness of big cities in the West increases the incidence of violent crime.

(3) Sorting through rubbish contributes to the rapid spread of diseases in the slums.

(4) Over the last decade the cost of utilities has been increasing for city dwellers.

22. In the context of the passage, the author refers to Manaus in order to:

(1) explain where cities source their labour for factories.

(2) promote cities as employment hubs for people.

(3) describe the infrastructure efficiencies of living in a city.

(4) explain how urban areas help the environment.

23. From the passage it can be inferred that cities are good places to live in for all of the following reasons EXCEPT that they:

(1) offer employment opportunities.

(2) have suburban areas as well as office areas.

(3) help prevent destruction of the environment.

(4) contribute to the cultural transformation of residents.

24. We can infer that Calthorpe's statement "still jars" with most people because most people:

(1) regard cities as places of disease and crime.

(2) do not regard cities as good places to live in.

(3) consider cities to be very crowded and polluted.

(4) do not consider cities to be eco-friendly places.

25. Five sentences related to a topic are given below in a jumbled order. Four of them form a coherent and unified paragraph. Identify the odd sentence that does not go with the four. Key in the number of the option that you choose.

(1) Socrates told us that 'the unexamined life is not worth living' and that to 'know thyself' is the path to true wisdom

(2) It suggests that you should adopt an ancient rhetorical method favored by the likes of Julius Caesar and known as 'illeism' – or speaking about yourself in the third person.

(3) Research has shown that people who are prone to rumination also often suffer from impaired decision making under pressure and are at a substantially increased risk of depression.

(4) Simple rumination – the process of churning your concerns around in your head – is not the way to achieve self-realization.

(5) The idea is that this small change in perspective can clear your emotional fog, allowing you to see past your biases.

26. The four sentences (labelled 1, 2, 3, 4) given below, when properly sequenced would yield a coherent paragraph. Decide on the proper sequence of the order of the sentences and key in the sequence of the four numbers as your answer.

(1) Such a belief in the harmony of nature requires a purpose presumably imposed by the goodness and wisdom of a deity.

(2) These parts, all fit together into an integrated, well-ordered system that was created by design.

(3) Historically, the notion of a balance of nature is part observational, part metaphysical, and not scientific in any way.

(4) It is an example of an ancient belief system called teleology, the notion that what we call nature has a predetermined destiny associated with its component parts.

27. Five sentences related to a topic are given below. Four of them can be put together to form a meaningful and coherent short paragraph. Identify the odd one out. Choose its number as your answer and key it in.

(1) A particularly interesting example of inference occurs in many single panel comics.

(2) It's the creator's participation and imagination that makes the single-panel comic so engaging and so rewarding.

(3) Often, the humor requires you to imagine what happened in the instant immediately before or immediately after the panel you're being shown.

(4) To get the joke, you actually have to figure out what some of these missing panels must be.

(5) It is as though the cartoonist devised a series of panels to tell the story and has chosen to show you only one – and typically not even the funniest.

28. The four sentences (labelled 1, 2, 3, 4) given below, when properly sequenced would yield a coherent paragraph. Decide on the proper sequence of the order of the sentences and key in the sequence of the four numbers as your answer.

(1) To the uninitiated listener, atonal music can sound like chaotic, random noise.

(2) Atonality is a condition of music in which the constructs of the music do not 'live' within the confines of a particular key signature, scale, or mode.

(3) After you realize the amount of knowledge, skill, and technical expertise required to compose or perform it, your tune may change, so to speak.

(4) However, atonality is one of the most important movements in 20th century music.

29. Five sentences related to a topic are given below. Four of them can be put together to form a meaningful and coherent short paragraph. Identify the odd one out. Choose its number as your answer and key it in.

(1) Ocean plastic is problematic for a number of reasons, but primarily because marine animals eat it.

(2) The largest numerical proportion of ocean plastic falls in small size fractions.

(3) Aside from clogging up the digestive tracts of marine life, plastic also tends to adsorb pollutants from the water column.

(4) Plastic in the oceans is arguably one of the most important and pervasive environmental problems today.

(5) Eating plastic has a number of negative consequences such as the retention of plastic particles in the gut for longer periods than normal food particles.

30. The four sentences (labelled 1, 2, 3, 4) given below, when properly sequenced would yield a coherent paragraph. Decide on the proper sequence of the order of the sentences and key in the sequence of the four numbers as your answer.

(1) Living things—animals and plants—typically exhibit correlational structure.

(2) Adaptive behaviour depends on cognitive economy, treating objects as equivalent.

(3) The information we receive from our senses, from the world, typically has structure and order, and is not arbitrary.

(4) To categorize an object means to consider it equivalent to other things in that category, and different—along some salient dimension—from things that are not.

31. The four sentences (labelled 1, 2, 3, 4) given below, when properly sequenced would yield a coherent paragraph. Decide on the proper sequence of the order of the sentences and key in the sequence of the four numbers as your answer.

(1) Conceptualisations of 'women's time' as contrary to clock-time and clock-time as synonymous with economic rationalism are two of the deleterious results of this representation.

(2) While dichotomies of 'men's time', 'women's time', clock-time, and caring time can be analytically useful, this article argues that everyday caring practices incorporate a multiplicity of times; and both men and women can engage in these multiple-times

(3) When the everyday practices of working sole fathers and working sole mothers are carefully examined to explore conceptualisations of gendered time, it is found that caring time is often more focused on the clock than generally theorised.

(4) Clock-time has been consistently represented in feminist literature as a masculine artefact representative of a 'time is money' perspective.

32. The passage given below is followed by four alternate summaries. Choose the option that best captures the essence of the passage.

Language is an autapomorphy found only in our lineage, and not shared with other branches of our group such as primates. We also have no definitive evidence that any species other than Homo sapiens ever had language. However, it must be noted straightaway that 'language' is not a monolithic entity, but rather a complex bundle of traits that must have evolved over a significant time frame.... Moreover, language crucially draws on aspects of cognition that are long established in the primate lineage, such as memory: the language faculty as a whole comprises more than just the uniquely linguistic features.

(1) Language is a distinctively human feature as there is no evidence of the existence of language in any other species.

(2) Language, a derived trait found only in humans, has evolved over time and involves memory.

(3) Language evolved with linguistic features building on features of cognition such as memory.

(4) Language is not a single, uniform entity but the end result of a long and complex process of linguistic evolution.

33. The passage given below is followed by four alternate summaries. Choose the option that best captures the essence of the passage.

Privacy-challenged office workers may find it hard to believe, but open-plan offices and cubicles were invented by architects and designers who thought that to break down the social walls that divide people, you had to break down the real walls, too. Modernist architects saw walls and rooms as downright fascist. The spaciousness and flexibility of an open plan would liberate homeowners and office dwellers from the confines of boxes. But companies took up their idea less out of a democratic ideology than a desire to pack in as many workers as they could. The typical open-plan office of the first half of the 20th century was a white-collar assembly line. Cubicles were interior designers' attempt to put some soul back in.

(1) Wall-free office spaces did not quite work out the way their utopian inventors intended, as they became tools for exploitation of labor.

(2) Wall-free office spaces did not quite work out as desired and therefore cubicles came into being.

(3) Wall-free office spaces did not quite work out as companies don't believe in democratic ideology.

(4) Wall-free office spaces could have worked out the way their utopian inventors intended had companies cared for workers' satisfaction.

34. The passage given below is followed by four alternate summaries. Choose the option that best captures the essence of the passage.

Social movement organizations often struggle to mobilize supporters from allied movements in their efforts to achieve critical mass. Organizations with hybrid identities—those whose organizational identities span the boundaries of two or more social movements, issues, or identities—are vital to mobilizing these constituencies. Studies of the post-9/11 U.S. antiwar movement show that individuals with past involvement in non-anti-war movements are more likely to join hybrid organizations than are individuals without involvement in non-anti-war movements. In addition, they show that organizations with hybrid identities occupy relatively more central positions in inter-organizational contact networks within the antiwar movement and thus recruit significantly more participants in demonstrations than do nonhybrid organizations.

(1) Hybrid organizations attract individuals that are deeply involved in anti-war movements.

(2) Movements that work towards social change often find it difficult to mobilize a critical mass of supporters.

(3) Organizations with hybrid identities are able to mobilize individuals with different points of view.

(4) Post 9/11 studies show that people who are involved in non anti-war movements are likely to join hybrid organizations.

Section II: DI & LR

Question Numbers (35 to 38): Answer the questions on the basis of the information given below.

The first year students in a business school are split into six sections. In 2019 the Business Statistics course was taught in these six sections by Annie, Beti, Chetan, Dave, Esha, and Fakir. All six sections had a common midterm (MT) and a common endterm (ET) worth 100 marks each. ET contained more questions than MT. Questions for MT and ET were prepared collectively by the six faculty members. Considering MT and ET together, each faculty member prepared the same number of questions.

Each of MT and ET had at least four questions that were worth 5 marks, at least three questions that were worth 10 marks, and at least two questions that were worth 15 marks. In both MT and ET, all the 5-mark questions preceded the 10-mark questions, and all the 15-mark questions followed the 10-mark questions.

The following additional facts are known.

i. Annie prepared the fifth question for both MT and ET. For MT, this question carried 5 marks.

ii. Annie prepared one question for MT. Every other faculty member prepared more than one questions for MT.

iii. All questions prepared by a faculty member appeared consecutively in MT as well as ET.

iv. Chetan prepared the third question in both MT and ET; and Esha prepared the eighth question in both.

v. Fakir prepared the first question of MT and the last one in ET. Dave prepared the last question of MT and the first one in ET.

35. The second question in ET was prepared by:

(1) Chetan (2) Dave
(3) Beti (4) Esha

36. How many 5-mark questions were there in MT and ET combined?

(1) 12 (2) 10
(3) 13 (4) Cannot be determined

37. Who prepared 15-mark questions for MT and ET?

(1) Only Dave, Esha and Fakir
(2) Only Dave and Fakir
(3) Only Esha and Fakir
(4) Only Beti, Dave, Esha and Fakir

38. Which of the following questions did Beti prepare in ET?

(1) Tenth question (2) Seventh question
(3) Fourth question (4) Ninth question

Question Numbers (39 to 42): Answer the questions on the basis of the information given below.

Ten players, as listed in the table below, participated in a rifle shooting competition comprising of 10 rounds. Each round had 6 participants. Players numbered 1 through 6 participated in Round 1, players 2 through 7 in Round 2,..., players 5 through 10 in Round 5, players 6 through 10 and 1 in Round 6, players 7 through 10, 1 and 2 in Round 7 and so on.

The top three performances in each round were awarded 7, 3 and 1 points respectively. There were no ties in any of the 10 rounds. The table below gives the total number of points obtained by the 10 players after Round 6 and Round 10.

Player No.	Player Name	Points after Round 6	Points after Round 10
1	Amita	8	18
2	Bala	2	5
3	Chen	3	6
4	David	6	6
5	Eric	3	10
6	Fatima	10	10
7	Gordon	17	17
8	Hansa	1	4
9	Ikea	2	17
10	Joshin	14	17

The following information is known about Rounds 1 through 6:

1. Gordon did not score consecutively in any two rounds.
2. Eric and Fatima both scored in a round.

The following information is known about Rounds 7 through 10:

1. Only two players scored in three consecutive rounds. One of them was Chen. No other player scored in any two consecutive rounds.
2. Joshin scored in Round 7, while Amita scored in Round 10.
3. No player scored in all the four rounds.

39. What were the scores of Chen, David, and Eric respectively after Round 3?

(1) 3, 3, 3 (2) 3, 3, 0
(3) 3, 6, 3 (4) 3, 0, 3

40. Which three players were in the last three positions after Round 4?

(1) Bala, Hansa, Ikea (2) Bala, Chen, Gordon
(3) Bala, Ikea, Joshin (4) Hansa, Ikea, Joshin

41. Which player scored points in maximum number of rounds?

(1) Chen (2) Joshin
(3) Amita (4) Ikea

42. Which players scored points in the last round?

(1) Amita, Bala, Chen (2) Amita, Eric, Joshin
(3) Amita, Chen, Eric (4) Amita, Chen, David

Question Numbers (43 to 46): Answer the questions on the basis of the information given below.
To compare the rainfall data, India Meteorological Department (IMD) calculated the Long Period Average (LPA) of rainfall during period June-August for each of the 16 states. The figure given below shows the actual rainfall (measured in mm) during June-August, 2019 and the percentage deviations from LPA of respective states in 2018. Each state along with its actual rainfall is presented in the figure.

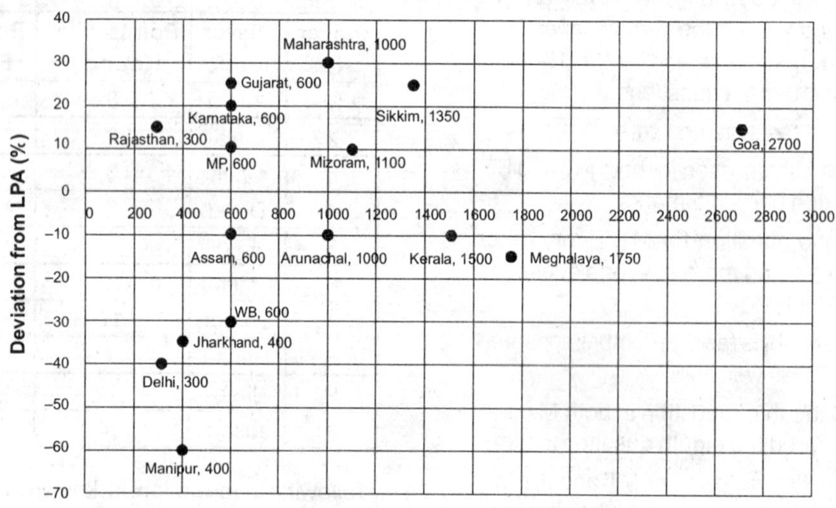

43. If a 'Heavy Monsoon State' is defined as a state with actual rainfall from June-August, 2019 of 900 mm or more, then approximately what percentage of 'Heavy Monsoon States' have a negative deviation from respective LPAs in 2019?

(1) 14.29 (2) 42.86
(3) 75.00 (4) 57.14

44. If a 'Low Monsoon State' is defined as a state with actual rainfall from June-August, 2019 of 750 mm or less, then what is the median 'deviation from LPA' (as defined in the Y-axis of the figure) of 'Low Monsoon States'?

(1) –30% (2) –20%
(3) 10% (4) –10%

45. What is the average rainfall of all states that have actual rainfall of 600 mm or less in 2019 and have a negative deviation from LPA?

(1) 460 mm (2) 367 mm
(3) 500 mm (4) 450 mm

46. The LPA of a state for a year is defined as the average rainfall in the preceding 10 years considering the period of June-August. For example, LPA in 2018 is the average rainfall during 2009-2018 and LPA in 2019 is the average rainfall during 2010-2019. It is also observed that the actual rainfall in Gujarat in 2019 is 20% more than the rainfall in 2009. The LPA of Gujarat in 2019 is closest to

(1) 525 mm (2) 505 mm
(3) 490 mm (4) 475 mm

Question Numbers (47 to 50): Answer the questions on the basis of the information given below.

A large store has only three departments, Clothing, Produce, and Electronics. The following figure shows the percentages of revenue and cost from the three departments for the years 2016, 2017 and 2018. The dotted lines depict percentage levels. So for example, in 2016, 50% of store's revenue came from its Electronics department while 40% of its costs were incurred in the Produce department.

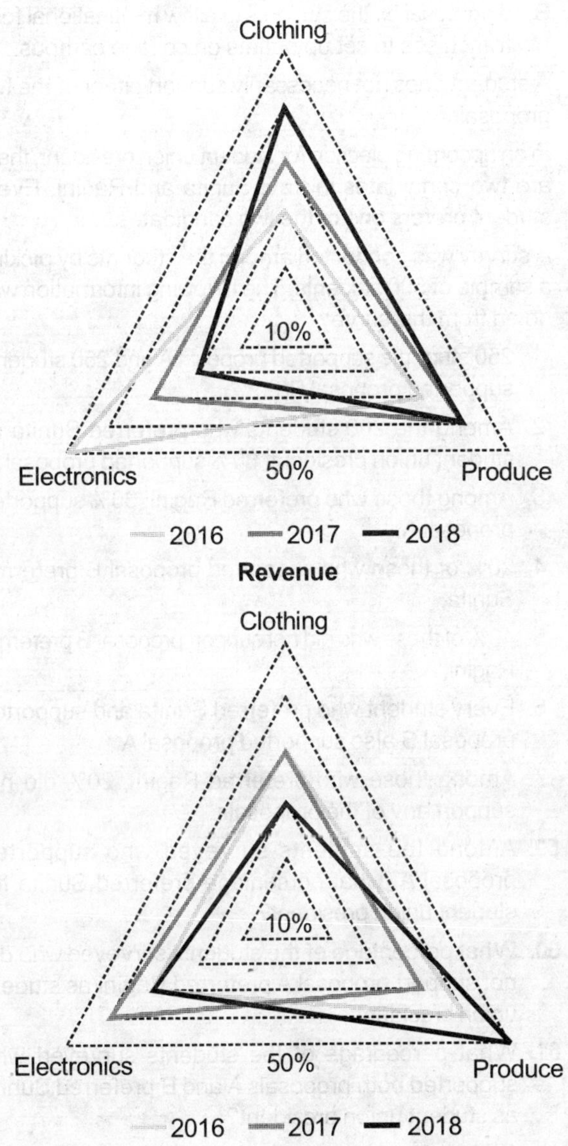

In this setup, Profit is computed as (Revenue – Cost) and Percentage Profit as Profit/Cost × 100%.

It is known that

1. The percentage profit for the store in 2016 was 100%.
2. The store's revenue doubled from 2016 to 2017, and its cost doubled from 2016 to 2018.
3. There was no profit from the Electronics department in 2017.
4. In 2018, the revenue from the Clothing department was the same as the cost incurred in the Produce department.

47. What was the percentage profit of the store in 2018?

48. What was the ratio of revenue generated from the Produce department in 2017 to that in 2018?

(1) 4 : 3 (2) 8 : 5

(3) 9 : 16 (4) 16 : 9

49. What percentage of the total profits for the store in 2016 was from the Electronics department?

50. What was the approximate difference in profit percentages of the store in 2017 and 2018?

(1) 25.0 (2) 8.3

(3) 33.3 (4) 15.5

Question Numbers (51 to 54): Answer the questions on the basis of the information given below.

column 1 column 2 column 3

row 1

row 2

row 3

	Column 1	Column 2	Column 3
Row 1	(2, 4)	(6, 8)	(1, 3)
Row 2	(3, 5)	(1, 1)	(6, 20)
Row 3	(1, 2)	(1, 2)	(2, 5)

Three pouches (each represented by a filled circle) are kept in each of the nine slots in a 3 × 3 grid, as shown in the figure. Every pouch has a certain number of one-rupee coins. The minimum and maximum amounts of money (in rupees) among the three pouches in each of the nine slots are given in the table. For example, we know that among the three pouches kept in the second column of the first row, the minimum amount in a pouch is Rs. 6 and the maximum amount is Rs. 8.

There are nine pouches in any of the three columns, as well as in any of the three rows. It is known that the average amount of money (in rupees) kept in the nine pouches in any column or in any row is an integer. It is also known that the total amount of money kept in the three pouches in the first column of the third row is Rs. 4.

51. What is the total amount of money (in rupees) in the three pouches kept in the first column of the second row?

52. How many pouches contain exactly one coin?

53. What is the number of slots for which the average amount (in rupees) of its three pouches is an integer?

54. The number of slots for which the total amount in its three pouches strictly exceeds Rs. 10 is

Question Numbers (55 to 58): Answer the questions on the basis of the information given below.

In the table below the check marks indicate all languages spoken by five people: Paula, Quentin, Robert, Sally and Terence. For example, Paula speaks only Chinese and English.

	Arabic	Basque	Chinese	Dutch	English	French
Paula			✓		✓	
Quentin				✓	✓	
Robert	✓					✓
Sally		✓			✓	
Terence			✓			✓

These five people form three teams, Team 1, Team 2 and Team 3. Each team has either 2 or 3 members. A team is said to speak a particular language if at least one of its members speak that language.

The following facts are known.

1. Each team speaks exactly four languages and has the same number of members.
2. English and Chinese are spoken by all three teams, Basque and French by exactly two teams and the other languages by exactly one team.
3. None of the teams include both Quentin and Robert.
4. Paula and Sally are together in exactly two teams.
5. Robert is in Team 1 and Quentin is in Team 3.

55. Who among the following four is not a member of Team 2?

(1) Paula (2) Terence

(3) Sally (4) Quentin

56. Who among the following four people is a part of exactly two teams?

(1) Sally (2) Paula

(3) Quentin (4) Robert

57. Who among the five people is a member of all teams?

(1) Paula (2) No one

(3) Terence (4) Sally

58. Apart from Chinese and English, which languages are spoken by Team 1?

(1) Arabic and French (2) Basque and French

(3) Arabic and Basque (4) Basque and Dutch

Question Numbers (59 to 62): Answer the questions on the basis of the information given below.

Students in a college are discussing two proposals --

A: a proposal by the authorities to introduce dress code on campus, and

B: a proposal by the students to allow multinational food franchises to set up outlets on college campus.

A student does not necessarily support either of the two proposals.

In an upcoming election for student union president, there are two candidates in fray: Sunita and Ragini. Every student prefers one of the two candidates.

A survey was conducted among the students by picking a sample of 500 students. The following information was noted from this survey.

1. 250 students supported proposal A and 250 students supported proposal B.
2. Among the 200 students who preferred Sunita as student union president, 80% supported proposal A.
3. Among those who preferred Ragini, 30% supported proposal A.
4. 20% of those who supported proposal B preferred Sunita.
5. 40% of those who did not support proposal B preferred Ragini.
6. Every student who preferred Sunita and supported proposal B also supported proposal A.
7. Among those who preferred Ragini, 20% did not support any of the proposals.

59. Among the students surveyed who supported proposal A, what percentage preferred Sunita for student union president?

60. What percentage of the students surveyed who did not support proposal A preferred Ragini as student union president?

61. What percentage of the students surveyed who supported both proposals A and B preferred Sunita as student union president?

(1) 50 (2) 20

(3) 40 (4) 25

62. How many of the students surveyed supported proposal B, did not support proposal A and preferred Ragini as student union president?

(1) 40 (2) 200

(3) 150 (4) 210

Question Numbers (63 to 66): Answer the questions on the basis of the information given below.

Three doctors, Dr. Ben, Dr. Kane and Dr. Wayne visit a particular clinic Monday to Saturday to see patients. Dr. Ben sees each patient for 10 minutes and charges Rs. 100/-. Dr. Kane sees each patient for 15 minutes and charges Rs. 200/-, while Dr. Wayne sees each patient for 25 minutes and charges Rs. 300/-.

The clinic has three rooms numbered 1, 2 and 3 which are assigned to the three doctors as per the following table.

Room No.	Monday & Tuesday	Wednesday & Thursday	Friday & Saturday
1	Ben	Wayne	Kane
2	Kane	Ben	Wayne
3	Wayne	Kane	Ben

The clinic is open from 9 a.m. to 11.30 a.m. every Monday to Saturday.

On arrival each patient is handed a numbered token indicating their position in the queue, starting with token number 1 every day. As soon as any doctor becomes free, the next patient in the queue enters that emptied room for consultation. If at any time, more than one room is free then the waiting patient enters the room with the smallest number. For example, if the next two patients in the queue have token numbers 7 and 8 and if rooms numbered 1 and 3 are free, then patient with token number 7 enters room number 1 and patient with token number 8 enters room number 3.

63. What is the maximum number of patients that the clinic can cater to on any single day?

(1) 15 (2) 31

(3) 30 (4) 12

64. The queue is never empty on one particular Saturday. Which of the three doctors would earn the maximum amount in consultation charges on that day?

(1) Dr. Wayne

(2) Both Dr. Wayne and Dr. Kane

(3) Dr. Ben

(4) Dr. Kane

65. Mr. Singh visited the clinic on Monday, Wednesday, and Friday of a particular week, arriving at 8:50 a.m. on each of the three days. His token number was 13 on all three days. On which day was he at the clinic for the maximum duration?

(1) Same duration on all three days

(2) Monday

(3) Friday

(4) Wednesday

66. On a slow Thursday, only two patients are waiting at 9 a.m. After that two patients keep arriving at exact 15 minute intervals starting at 9:15 a.m. -- i.e. at 9:15 a.m., 9:30 a.m., 9:45 a.m. etc. Then the total duration in minutes when all three doctors are simultaneously free is

(1) 15 (2) 0

(3) 10 (4) 30

Section III: QA

67. In an examination, Rama's score was one-twelfth of the sum of the scores of Mohan and Anjali. After a review, the score of each of them increased by 6. The revised scores of Anjali, Mohan, and Rama were in the ratio 11:10:3. Then Anjali's score exceeded Rama's score by

(1) 24 (2) 26

(3) 35 (4) 32

68. The base of a regular pyramid is a square and each of the other four sides is an equilateral triangle, length of each side being 20 cm. The vertical height of the pyramid, in cm, is

(1) $5\sqrt{5}$ (2) $8\sqrt{3}$

(3) 12 (4) $10\sqrt{2}$

69. Let ABC be a right-angled triangle with hypotenuse BC of length 20 cm. If AP is perpendicular on BC, then the maximum possible length of AP, in cm, is

(1) $6\sqrt{2}$ (2) 5

(3) $8\sqrt{2}$ (4) 10

70. The quadratic equation $x^2 + bx + c = 0$ has two roots 4a and 3a, where a is an integer. Which of the following is a possible value of $b^2 + c$?

(1) 361 (2) 549

(3) 427 (4) 3721

71. The strength of a salt solution is p% if 100 ml of the solution contains p grams of salt. Each of three vessels A, B, C contains 500 ml of salt solution of strengths 10%, 22%, and 32%, respectively. Now, 100 ml of the solution in vessel A is transferred to vessel B. Then, 100 ml of the solution in vessel B is transferred to vessel C. Finally, 100 ml of the solution in vessel C is transferred to vessel A. The strength, in percentage, of the resulting solution in vessel A is

(1) 13 (2) 15

(3) 14 (4) 12

72. In 2010, a library contained a total of 11500 books in two categories - fiction and non-fiction. In 2015, the library contained a total of 12760 books in these two categories. During this period, there was 10% increase in the fiction category while there was 12% increase in the non-fiction category. How many fiction books were in the library in 2015?

(1) 6000 (2) 6160

(3) 5500 (4) 6600

73. Two ants A and B start from a point P on a circle at the same time, with A moving clock-wise and B moving anti-clockwise. They meet for the first time at 10:00 am when A has covered 60% of the track. If A returns to P at 10:12 am, then B returns to P at

(1) 10:18 am (2) 10:27 am

(3) 10:25 am (4) 10:45 am

74. The number of common terms in the two sequences: 15, 19, 23, 27, ... , 415 and 14, 19, 24, 29, . . . , 464 is

(1) 21 (2) 20

(3) 18 (4) 19

75. Two circles, each of radius 4 cm, touch externally. Each of these two circles is touched externally by a third circle. If these three circles have a common tangent, then the radius of the third circle, in cm, is

(1) 1 (2) $\sqrt{2}$

(3) $\frac{1}{\sqrt{2}}$ (4) $\frac{\pi}{3}$

76. Let A be a real number. Then the roots of the equation $x^2 - 4x - \log_2 A = 0$ are real and distinct if and only if

(1) $A < \frac{1}{8}$ (2) $A < \frac{1}{16}$

(3) $A > \frac{1}{8}$ (4) $A > \frac{1}{16}$

77. In a triangle ABC, medians AD and BE are perpendicular to each other, and have lengths 12 cm and 9 cm, respectively. Then, the area of triangle ABC, in sq cm, is

(1) 78 (2) 80

(3) 68 (4) 72

78. What is the largest positive integer n such that $\frac{n^2+7n+12}{n^2-n-12}$ is also a positive integer?

(1) 16 (2) 12

(3) 6 (4) 8

79. John jogs on track A at 6 kmph and Mary jogs on track B at 7.5 kmph. The total length of tracks A and B is 325 metres. While John makes 9 rounds of track A, Mary makes 5 rounds of track B. In how many seconds will Mary make one round of track A?

80. If (2n + 1) + (2n + 3) + (2n + 5) ... + (2n + 47) = 5280, then what is the value of 1 + 2 + 3 + ... + n?

81. If x is a real number, then $\sqrt{\log_e \frac{4x - x^2}{3}}$ is a real number if and only if

(1) $1 \le x \le 3$ (2) $-1 \le x \le 3$

(3) $-3 \le x \le 3$ (4) $1 \le x \le 2$

82. Let A and B be two regular polygons having a and b sides, respectively. If b = 2a and each interior angle of B is $\frac{3}{2}$ times each interior angle of A, then each interior angle, in degrees, of a regular polygon with a + b sides is

83. How many pairs (m, n) of positive integers satisfy the equation $m^2 + 105 = n^2$?

84. The real root of the equation $2^{6x} + 2^{3x+2} - 21 = 0$ is

(1) $\log_2 9$ (2) $\log_2 27$

(3) $\frac{\log_2 3}{3}$ (4) $\frac{\log_2 7}{3}$

85. A man makes complete use of 405 cc of iron, 783 cc of aluminium, and 351 cc of copper to make a number of solid right circular cylinders of each type of metal. These cylinders have the same volume and each of these has radius 3 cm. If the total number of cylinders is to be kept at a minimum, then the total surface area of all these cylinders, in sq cm, is

(1) 928π (2) $1044(4 + \pi)$

(3) $1026(1 + \pi)$ (4) 8464π

86. If $5^x - 3^y = 13438$ and $5^{x-1} + 3^{y+1} = 9686$, then x + y equals

87. How many factors of $2^4 \times 3^5 \times 10^4$ are perfect squares which are greater than 1?

88. Let $a_1, a_2, ...$ be integers such that $a_1 - a_2 + a_3 - a_4 + ... + (-1)^{n-1} a_n = n$, for all $n \ge 1$. Then $a_{51} + a_{52} + ... + a_{1023}$ equals

(1) 0 (2) 1

(3) −1 (4) 10

89. Let a, b, x, y be real numbers such that $a^2 + b^2 = 25$, $x^2 + y^2 = 169$, and $ax + by = 65$. If $k = ay - bx$, then

(1) $0 < k \leq \frac{5}{13}$ (2) $k = \frac{5}{13}$

(3) $k = 0$ (4) $k > \frac{5}{13}$

90. Amal invests Rs 12000 at 8% interest, compounded annually, and Rs 10000 at 6% interest, compounded semi-annually, both investments being for one year. Bimal invests his money at 7.5% simple interest for one year. If Amal and Bimal get the same amount of interest, then the amount, in Rupees, invested by Bimal is

91. A cyclist leaves A at 10 am and reaches B at 11 am. Starting from 10:01 am, every minute a motor cycle leaves A and moves towards B. Forty-five such motor cycles reach B by 11 am. All motor cycles have the same speed. If the cyclist had doubled his speed, how many motor cycles would have reached B by the time the cyclist reached B?

(1) 23 (2) 20

(3) 15 (4) 22

92. In a six-digit number, the sixth, that is, the rightmost, digit is the sum of the first three digits, the fifth digit is the sum of first two digits, the third digit is equal to the first digit, the second digit is twice the first digit and the fourth digit is the sum of fifth and sixth digits. Then, the largest possible value of the fourth digit is

93. Anil alone can do a job in 20 days while Sunil alone can do it in 40 days. Anil starts the job, and after 3 days, Sunil joins him. Again, after a few more days, Bimal joins them and they together finish the job. If Bimal has done 10% of the job, then in how many days was the job done?

(1) 14 (2) 15

(3) 12 (4) 13

94. In an examination, the score of A was 10% less than that of B, the score of B was 25% more than that of C, and the score of C was 20% less than that of D. If A scored 72, then the score of D was

95. John gets Rs 57 per hour of regular work and Rs 114 per hour of overtime work. He works altogether 172 hours and his income from overtime hours is 15% of his income from regular hours. Then, for how many hours did he work overtime?

96. The average of 30 integers is 5. Among these 30 integers, there are exactly 20 which do not exceed 5. What is the highest possible value of the average of these 20 integers?

(1) 4.5 (2) 4

(3) 5 (4) 3.5

97. Mukesh purchased 10 bicycles in 2017, all at the same price. He sold six of these at a profit of 25% and the remaining four at a loss of 25%. If he made a total profit of Rs. 2000, then his purchase price of a bicycle, in Rupees, was

(1) 8000 (2) 2000

(3) 6000 (4) 4000

98. The salaries of Ramesh, Ganesh and Rajesh were in the ratio 6:5:7 in 2010, and in the ratio 3:4:3 in 2015. If Ramesh's salary increased by 25% during 2010-2015, then the percentage increase in Rajesh's salary during this period is closest to

(1) 10 (2) 8

(3) 7 (4) 9

99. Let f be a function such that f (mn) = f (m) f (n) for every positive integers m and n. If f (1), f (2) and f (3) are positive integers, f (1) < f (2), and f (24) = 54, then f (18) equals

100. A shopkeeper sells two tables, each procured at cost price p, to Amal and Asim at a profit of 20% and at a loss of 20%, respectively. Amal sells his table to Bimal at a profit of 30%, while Asim sells his table to Barun at a loss of 30%. If the amounts paid by Bimal and Barun are x and y, respectively, then $\frac{(x - y)}{P}$ equals

(1) 0.7 (2) 1

(3) 1.2 (4) 0.50

ANSWERS

1. (4)	**2.** (1)	**3.** (3)	**4.** (3)	**5.** (1)	**6.** (2)	**7.** (1)	**8.** (3)	**9.** (4)	**10.** (2)
11. (2)	**12.** (2)	**13.** (2)	**14.** (1)	**15.** (3)	**16.** (3)	**17.** (2)	**18.** (3)	**19.** (2)	**20.** (2)
21. (1)	**22.** (4)	**23.** (2)	**24.** (4)	**25.** (1)	**26.** (3421)	**27.** (2)	**28.** (2143)	**29.** (2)	**30.** (2431)
31. (4132)	**32.** (3)	**33.** (1)	**34.** (3)	**35.** (2)	**36.** (3)	**37.** (1)	**38.** (1)	**39.** (1)	**40.** (4)
41. (4)	**42.** (3)	**43.** (2)	**44.** (4)	**45.** (1)	**46.** (3)	**47.** (25)	**48.** (2)	**49.** (70)	**50.** (2)
51. (13)	**52.** (8)	**53.** (2)	**54.** (3)	**55.** (4)	**56.** (1)	**57.** (1)	**58.** (1)	**59.** (64)	**60.** (84)
61. (1)	**62.** (3)	**63.** (2)	**64.** (4)	**65.** (2)	**66.** (2)	**67.** (4)	**68.** (4)	**69.** (4)	**70.** (2)
71. (3)	**72.** (4)	**73.** (2)	**74.** (2)	**75.** (1)	**76.** (4)	**77.** (4)	**78.** (2)	**79.** (48)	**80.** (4851)
81. (1)	**82.** (150)	**83.** (4)	**84.** (3)	**85.** (3)	**86.** (13)	**87.** (44)	**88.** (2)	**89.** (3)	**90.** (20920)
91. (3)	**92.** (7)	**93.** (4)	**94.** (80)	**95.** (12)	**96.** (1)	**97.** (4)	**98.** (3)	**99.** (12)	**100.** (2)

EXPLANATIONS

1. Options 1 and 2 are categorically mentioned in the first three paragraphs. Hence, they cannot be the correct answers.

2. Ethan Watrall believes that Google's collaboration with CyArk is all about advertisements and driving traffic. Refer to the sentence, "But at its core, it's all about advertisements and driving traffic."

3. The answer can be found in the following sentences: Erin Thompson, a professor of art crime at John Jay College of Criminal Justice in New York City, says it's the latest example of a Western nation appropriating a foreign culture, a centuries-long battle ... CyArk says it copyrights the scans so no one can use them in an inappropriate way ... where these sites are located." The other options are out of scope.

4. Watrall believes that Google's initiative is all about advertisements and driving traffic. In other words, profit motive is evident. However, if CyArk uploads the images onto museum websites, Dr. Watrall's theory will be nullified. Uploading images onto museum websites will ensure that profit motive is absent. Hence, option 3 is the correct answer.

5. Refer to the sentences in the initial section of the passage: "But the project is raising questions about Google's motivations and about who should own the digital copyrights. Some critics call it a form of 'digital colonialism.'" The other options cannot be said to be interpretations of 'digital colonialism.'

6. The phrase "a long pedigree" is found in the first line of the 4th paragraph. The use of the phrase "long pedigree" in the given context indicates that the effort to move the civil servants from capitals to other places is not a new thing. So, option 2 is the answer.

7. Options 2, 3 and 4 are found in the given passage.

Option 2 – Refer to the 3rd sentence of the 2nd paragraph, "Wonks in the sticks will be inspired by new ideas that walled-off capitals cannot conjure up."

Option 3 – Refer to the 4th sentence the 2nd paragraph, "Autonomous regulators perform best far from the pressure and lobbying of the big city."

Option 4 – Refer to the 1st sentence of the 3rd paragraph and sentences 5 and 6 of the 4th paragraph respectively, "...to save money..." and "The second reason to pack bureaucrats off is to save money. Office space costs far more in capitals. . . . Agencies that are moved elsewhere can often recruit better workers on lower salaries than in capitals..."

Option 1 is not mentioned in the passage. Therefore, it is the answer.

8. Refer to the 2nd sentence of the 1st paragraph, "...capitals picked by trade-focused empires..." Here, the empires refer to the colonial powers and it is clearly seen from the quoted line that these colonial powers picked their capitals to promote their trades.

9. Option 4 – Refer to the 6th paragraph, "The dilemma is obvious. Pick small, poor towns, and areas of high unemployment get new jobs, but it is hard to attract the most qualified workers; opt for larger cities with infrastructure and better-qualified residents, and the country's most deprived areas see little benefit." This part of the passage talks about the dilemma. So, option 4 is the answer.

10. Options 1, 3 and 4 are found in the given passage.

Option 1 – Refer to the 2nd sentence of the 6th paragraph, "Pick small, poor towns, and areas of high unemployment get new jobs, but it is hard to attract the most qualified workers…"

Option 3 - Refer to the 1st sentence of the 7th paragraph "…decentralisation begets corruption by making government agencies less accountable."

Option 4 - Refer to the 3rd sentence of the 4th paragraph, "But swapping the capital for somewhere smaller is not always agreeable. Attrition rates can exceed 80%."

Option 2 is not mentioned in the given passage. Thus, it is the answer.

11. Option 1 is mentioned in the third paragraph. The author mentions the words 'wrestle' and 'frustrations' (third last paragraph) that indicate the ups and downs in the process of learning a language. Options 3 and 4 are mentioned in the last paragraph.

12. Refer to the third last paragraph for the answer. The author intends to say that familiarity with a language can actually blur the cultural differences. The other options are out of scope.

13. The author regards himself as a man of language. He speaks both Chinese and Arabic. Equipped with these languages, he studies Chinese cultural contact with the Egyptians. Therefore, option 2 is very likely to be his view.

14. The fact that the author speaks Arabic but still considers the Arabic as outsiders would clearly make the author's critics argue that language is insufficient to bridge the cultural barriers. So, option 1 is the answer.

15. Options 1, 2 and 4 support the argument as they are mentioned in the passage. Option 1 is mentioned in the first paragraph. Option 2 is mentioned in the second paragraph. Option 4 is mentioned towards the end concluding part of the passage where it says that modernity was an external thing that was imposed on the Indian society which eventually led to underdevelopment. Option 3 is the correct answer because it was not the modernity that caused the change in the colonial policy but the other way round.

16. 'Here' in the given context refers to India. This is supported by the parts of the passage which precede it. 'Endogenous change' means internal change and according to the quoted lines such change is not something which happens in India. Rather it is forced upon the Indians by the colonial policies. So, option 3 is the answer. Options 1 and 4 do not specifically talk about India.

17. Option 2 is the answer. Options 1, 3 and 4 do not make sense according to the given passage. The only reason why modernity was introduced to change the Indian society was to address the marginalization that the colonial state felt as it was already modern and the Indian society was not at that time.

18. The following sequence captures the flow of the arguments in the given passage: 1st line of the 1st paragraph, "British colonial policy…", 3rd sentence of the 1st paragraph, "…Enlightenment…", 6th sentence of the 1st paragraph, "…modernity…", 2nd sentence of the second paragraph, "…with subjection." and the last sentence of the last paragraph. In other words, the colonial policy included Enlightenment of the colonized people and modernity was forced upon them only to dominate them which eventually led to underdevelopment and dependency. So, option 3 is the answer.

19. Option 2 is directly mentioned in the given passage. Refer to the sentences, "But this modernity did not enter a passive society. Sometimes, its initiatives were resisted by pre-existing structural forms. At times, there was a more direct form of collective resistance."

20. Options 1, 3 and 4 are clearly mentioned in the passage; however, option 2 is not mentioned in the passage.

21. It is mentioned in the first paragraph that squatter cities are also unexpectedly green and they have minimum energy and material use as people get around by foot, bicycle, rickshaw, or the universal shared taxi. So, that makes the point that the author is defending these cities are green. Thus, option 1 would undermine his stand regarding the greenness of cities.

22. Refer to the 5th paragraph of the given passage. The reason why the city of Manus is mentioned in the passage is to emphasize the fact that subsidised city like Manaus could stop deforestation and this serves as an example that urban areas can help in protecting the environment. So, option 4 is the answer.

23. Options 1 and 4 are mentioned in the last paragraph and option 3 is mentioned in the fifth paragraph. Option 2 cannot be inferred from the given passage.

24. 'Jars' in the phrase "still jars" is used as a verb; it means 'to bear unpleasant effect on' or 'annoy'. Calthorpe's statements: "The city is the most environmentally benign form of human settlement. Each city dweller consumes less land, less energy, less water, and produces less pollution than his counterpart in settlements of lower densities." still bear an unpleasant effect on the people as his statements contradict what people think about cities.

25. Sentences 2 and 5 can be clubbed together. Sentence 2 talks about speaking from the third person's point of view while sentence 5 mentions a change in perspective. Sentences 3 and 4 can be clubbed together as well because both explain rumination. Therefore, sentence 1 is the odd sentence.

26. Sentence 4 explains sentence 3. Hence, 3 and 4 can be defined as a mandatory pair. 2 and 1 also form a mandatory pair because sentence 1 talks about harmony of nature which is an explanation of 'integrated, well-ordered system' mentioned in sentence 2.

27. Except sentence 2, the other sentences talk about single panel comics and the characteristic feature of being interesting, humorous, funny and possessing an element of joke. Thus, all the sentences, except sentence 2, can be clubbed together.

28. Sentence 2 mentions atonality and it is further explained in sentence 1. Sentence 4 follows and sentence 3 mentions how to compose or perform atonal music. Hence, sentence 3 closes the paragraph effectively.

29. Except sentence 2, the other sentences talk about the problem of plastic pollution and how marine animals eat plastic. Sentence 2 doesn't talk about the consumption of plastic. Hence, it is the odd sentence.

30. 2 and 4 form a mandatory pair. In sentence 2, there is the mention of 'treating objects as equivalent.' The same idea is explained further in sentence 4. Sentence 3 talks about structure and order and sentence 1 explains the word 'structure' further.'

31. Sentence 1 talks about a certain representation and this representation is given in sentence 4. Hence, 4 and 1 form a mandatory pair. Sentence 3 talks about caring practices and time that is further elaborated in sentence 2.

32. The other options are narrow in scope. The passage mentions memory and also, the gradual evolution of languages. There is also the mention of aspects or features of cognition that help a language to develop. Hence, option 3 is the correct answer.

33. Option 1 is the most appropriate summary because the mentions that open offices were originally conceived to break social walls. Later, open offices were preferred by employers because more number of people could be accommodated. The other options are narrow in scope.

34. Refer to the second sentence of the paragraph. The second sentence forms the crux of the passage. The other options are narrow in scope and don't encompass the entire passage.

For questions 35 to 38:

According to the given information, the table till now becomes–

MT			ET		
Question No.	**Prepared by**	**Marks**	**Question No.**	**Prepared by**	**Marks**
1	Fakir	5	1	Dave	5
2	Fakir	5	2		5
3	Chetan	5	3	Chetan	5
4	Chetan	5	4		5
5	Annie	5	5	Annie	
6			6		
7			7		
8	Esha		8	Esha	
⋮ Last Question	Dave	15	⋮ Last Question	Fakir	15

There would be definitely more than 18 questions in total considering MT and ET together as ET contained more questions than MT i.e., total 24. Also, each faculty member prepared the same number of questions so that means each faculty must have prepared 4 questions in MT and ET together.

There were atleast 4 questions worth 5 marks, atleast 3 questions worth 10 marks and atleast 2 questions worth 15 marks such that all 5 - mark questions preceded the 10 - mark questions and all the 15 - mark questions followed the 10 - mark questions.

From statement (ii) and (iii), we could say that the 2nd question and 4th question in MT were prepared by Fakir and Chetan respectively.

From statement (ii), Annie prepared one question for MT, that means, she prepared three questions for ET. From the above table, there are two possibilities now–

Case 1: Annie prepared 4th, 5th and 6th questions for ET.

Case 2: Annie prepared 5th, 6th and 7th questions for ET.

Case 1: If Annie prepared 4th, 5th and 6th questions for ET, then Chetan must have prepared 2nd and 3rd questions for ET, which further implies that Dave prepared only 1 question for ET and 3 questions for MT.

From statement 5th, we could also say that the last three questions were prepared by Dave for MT, and as total 24 questions were there in total so maximum 11 questions could be prepared for MT. This means 9th, 10th and 11th questions were prepared by Dave for MT. From statements 2nd and 4th, we could say 7th and 8th questions were prepared by Esha, so only 6th question remained left in MT which would be definitely prepared by Beti. But Beti must prepare more than 1 question for MT so this case is incorrect.

Case 2: If Annie prepared 5th, 6th and 7th questions for ET, then definitely the 4th question was prepared by Chetan and 2nd question was prepared by Dave for ET (from statement iii).

So, Dave prepared 1st and 2nd questions for ET, therefore he must have prepared the last two questions for MT.

Esha prepared 8th question, so she must have prepared 9th also for MT. Hence, Beti prepared 6th and 7th for MT.

ET had more number of questions than MT so, MT had 11 and ET had 13 questions in all.

Now, Esha prepared 2 questions for MT so, she must have prepared 2 questions for ET. Therefore, Esha prepared 8th and 9th for ET. Fakir prepared last two questions i.e., 12th and 13th, so Beti prepared 10th and 11th questions for ET.

So, the final table looks like.

MT			ET		
Question No.	Prepared by	Marks	Question No.	Prepared by	Marks
1	Fakir	5	1	Dave	5
2	Fakir	5	2	Dave	5
3	Chetan	5	3	Chetan	5
4	Chetan	5	4	Chetan	5
5	Annie	5	5	Annie	5
6	Boti	10	6	Annie	5
7	Beti	10	7	Annie	5
8	Esha	10	8	Esha	5
9	Esha	15	9	Esha	10
10	Dave	15	10	Beti	10
11	Dave	15	11	Beti	10
			12	Fakir	15
			13	Fakir	15

35. Clearly, from the table, we can see that the second question in ET was prepared by Dave.

36. In MT, 5 questions were there worth 5 marks and in ET, 8 questions were there. So, in total 13 questions were there in MT and ET combined.

37. Only Esha, Dave and Fakir prepared 15 - mark questions for MT and ET.

38. Beti prepared 10th question among the given options in ET.

For questions 39 to 42:

From the condition given in the statements, we can make the following table:

	1	2	3	4	5	6	T_1	7	8	9	10	T_2
A		X	X	X	X		8					18
B			X	X	X	X	2					5
C				X	X	X	3	X				6
D					X	X	6	X	X			6
E						X	3	X	X	X		10
F							10	X	X	X	X	10
G	X						17		X	X	X	17
H	X	X					1			X	X	4
I	X	X	X				2				X	17
J	X	X	X	X			14					17

Where T_1 = Total points after Round 6

T_2 = Total points after Round 10

The information known about Rounds 1 through 6:

1. Gordon (G) did not score consecutively in any two rounds.
2. Eric (E) and Fatima (F) both scored in a round.

   By observing the table:

   1. Jordan (J) scored 7 points in both the rounds 5th and 6th.
   2. Amita (A) scored 1, 7 points then she scored 7 in the first round.
   3. Bala (B) scored 1 point in both the rounds 1st and 2nd.
   4. Ikea (I) scored 1 point in the round 4th and 5th.
   5. Gordon (G- 7, 7, 3) did not score consecutively in any two rounds so it scored in 2nd, 4th and 6th rounds respectively.

   We can make the following table from the details given in the question.

	1	2	3	4	5	6	T_1	7	8	9	10	T_2
A	7	X	X	X	X	1	8					18
B	1	1	X	X	X	X	2					5
C	3	0	0	X	X	X	3	X				6
D	0	3	0	3	X	X	6	X	X			6
E	0	0	3	0	0	X	3	X	X	X		10
F	0	0	7	0	3	0	10	X	X	X	X	10
G	X	7	0	7	0	3	17		X	X	X	17
H	X	X	1	0	0	0	1			X	X	4
I	X	X	X	1	1	0	2				X	17
J	X	X	X	X	7	7	14					17

1. Only two players scored in three consecutive rounds. One of them was Chen. So He scored 1 point in the rounds 8th, 9th and 10th.
2. Ikea scored 15 points (1,7,7) in three rounds respectively.
3. Eric scored 7 in round 10.
4. Amita will score 3 in round 10, and 7 in round 7.

We can make the following table:

	1	2	3	4	5	6	T_1	7	8	9	10	T_2
A	7	X	X	X	X	1	8	7	0	0	3	18
B	1	1	X	X	X	X	2	0	0	3	0	5
C	3	0	0	X	X	X	3	X	1	1	1	6
D	0	3	0	3	X	X	6	X	X	0	0	6
E	0	0	3	0	0	X	3	X	X	X	7	10
F	0	0	7	0	3	0	10	X	X	X	X	10
G	X	7	0	7	0	3	17	0	X	X	X	17
H	X	X	1	0	0	0	1	0	3	X	X	4
I	X	X	X	1	1	0	2	1	7	7	X	17
J	X	X	X	X	7	7	14	3	0	0	0	17

39. The scores of Chen, David and Eric after round 3 were 3, 3, 3 respectively.

40. Hansa, Ikea and Joshin were in the last three positions after round 4.

41. Ikea scored points in maximum number of rounds.

42. Amita, Chen, and Eric scored points in the last round.

43. Heavy monsoon states = 1000 + 1350 + 1100 + 2700 + 1000 + 1500 + 1750 = 10400

Those having negative deviation from respective LPAs = 1000 + 1500 + 1750 = 4250.

$\therefore$ Required % $= \dfrac{4250}{10400} \times 100 \sim 42.86\%$.

44. There are 9 low monsoon states from the given figure and to find the median 'deviation from LPA', first we will arrange them in increasing order.

So, their deviations in terms of percentage are–

–60, –40, –35, –30, –10, 10, 15, 20, 25.

The middle number of this sequence is the median i.e., –10%.

45. There are 5 states that have actual rainfall of 600mm or less in 2019 and have a negative deviation from LPA.

$\therefore$ Average rainfall of these 5 states $= \dfrac{600+600+400+300+400}{5} = \dfrac{2300}{5} = 460$ mm.

46. The actual rainfall in Gujarat in 2019 = 600 mm

The actual rainfall in Gujarat in 2009 $= \dfrac{100}{120} \times 600 = 500$ mm

% deviation from LPP of Gujarat in 2018 = 25%

$\therefore 600 = \dfrac{125}{100} \times \text{LPA}$ in 2018 $\Rightarrow$ LPA ub 2018 = 480 mm

$\therefore$ Total sum of rainfall in Gujarat during 2009 – 18 = 480 × 10 = 4800 mm

Rainfall during 2010 – 18 = 4800 – 500 = 4300 mm

Total sum of rainfall during 2010 – 2019 = 4300 + 600 = 4900 mm

$\therefore$ Average rainfall $= \dfrac{4900}{10} = 490$ mm

So, the LPA of Gujarat in 2019 is closest to 490 mm.

For questions 47 to 50:

We can make the following table from the figure given in the question:

	Revenue			Cost		
	Clothing	Produce	Electronics	Clothing	Produce	Electronics
2016	20	30	50	30	40	30
2017	30	40	30	30	30	40
2018	40	40	20	20	50	30

If we consider the total cost in the year 2016 as 100, then according to statement 1, the total revenue in 2016 must be 200. The store's revenue doubled from 2016 to 2017, thus the total revenue in the year 2017 = 400. We can find the revenue for the individual department in the year 2017, from the table. There was no profit from the Electronics department in 2017, thus, we can find the total cost in 2017= 300. Considering the statement 4, we can find the total revenue in 2018 and tabulate the following table.

Cost							
	Clothing		Produce		Electronics		Total
2016	30%	30	40%	40	30%	30	100
2017	30%	90	30%	90	40%	120	300
2018	20%	40	50%	100	30%	60	200

Revenue							
	Clothing		Produce		Electronics		Total
2016	20%	40	30%	60	50%	100	200
2017	30%	120	40%	160	30%	120	400
2018	40%	100	40%	100	20%	50	250

47. The percentage profit of the store in 2018 = $\frac{250-200}{200}$ = 25%.

48. The ratio of revenue generated from the Produce department in 2017 to that in 2018 = 160 : 100 = 8 : 5.

49. Profit in 2016 = 200 – 100 = 100 Profit in the electronic department in 2016 = 100 – 30 = 70. So, the required profit is 70%.

50. Profit percentage in 2017 = $\frac{400-300}{300}$ = 33.33%.

Profit percentage in 2018 = $\frac{250-200}{200}$ = 25%.

The approximate difference in profit percentages of the store in 2017 and 2018 = (33.33 – 25)% = 8.33%.

For questions 51 to 54:

We can make the following table from "the total amount of money kept in the three pouches in the first column of the third row is Rs. 4."

If the minimum and maximum values are 1, then the sum of the three pouches in the middle will be Rs 3.

	Column 1	Column 2	Column 3
Row 1			
Row 2		3 (1,1,1)	
Row 3	4 (1,1,2)		

If we calculate the maximum and minimum value possible for each slot in column 1. For the slot, column 1 and row 1, the maximum value possible is 10{2,4,4} while the minimum value possible is 8{2,2,4}.

Similarly, for the slot, column 1 and row 2, the maximum value possible is 13{3,5,5} while the minimum value possible is 11{3,3,5}.

It is known that the average amount of money (in rupees) kept in the nine pouches in any column or in any row is an integer. Thus the sum of coins in a row or column must be a multiple of 9.

So, we can iterate that 10,13,4 ...{27} is the only sum possible for the slots of column 1.

We now know two elements of row 2, thus we can iterate from the maximum and the minimum value possible for the slot {column 3, row 2} that 38 is the only value possible for the slot.

We can make the following table:

	Column 1	Column 2	Column 3
Row 1	10 (2,4,4)		
Row 2	13 (3,5,5)	3 (1,1,1)	38 (6,12,20)
Row 3	4 (1,1,2)		

Similarly, we can find the amount for Column 2.

For the slot, column 2 and row 1, the maximum value possible is 22{6,8,8} while the minimum value possible is 20{6,6,8}.

For the slot, column 2 and row 3, the maximum value possible is 5{1,2,3} while the minimum value possible is 4{1,1,2}.

Thus {20,3,4} is the only solution possible.

	Column 1	Column 2	Column 3
Row 1	10 (2,4,4)	20 (6,6,8)	
Row 2	13 (3,5,5)	3 (1,1,1)	38 (6,12,20)
Row 3	4 (1,1,2)	4 (1,1,2)	

We can similarly make the following table for the last column.

	Column 1	Column 2	Column 3
Row 1	10 (2,4,4)	20 (6,6,8)	6 (1,2,3)
Row 2	13 (3,5,5)	3 (1,1,1)	38 (6,12,20)
Row 3	4 (1,1,2)	4 (1,1,2)	10 (2,3,5)

51. The total amount of money (in rupees) in the three pouches kept in the first column of the second row = 13.

52. 8 pouches contain exactly one coin

53. For 2 slots, the average amount in three pouches is an integer.

54. For 3 slots, the total amount in three pouches exceeds Rs. 10.

For questions 55 to 58:

From statement 1 and 2,Each team speaks exactly four languages. English and Chinese are spoken by all three teams, Basque and French by exactly two teams and the other languages by exactly one team, multiple options are possible.

In the following tables: A, B, C can be any team among Team 1, Team 2, Team 3.

A	B	C
English	English	English
Chinese	Chinese	Chinese
Basque	Basque	Arabic
French	French	Dutch

A	B	C
English	English	English
Chinese	Chinese	Chinese
Basque	Basque	Arabic
Dutch	French	French

A	B	C
English	English	English
Chinese	Chinese	Chinese
Basque	Basque	Dutch
Arabic	French	French

From the data given in the question, the person who speaks Arabic also speaks French. Thus the only option possible is 'Table 2'.

A	B	C
English	English	English
Chinese	Chinese	Chinese
Basque	Basque	Arabic
Dutch	French	French

According to statement 4, "Paula and Sally are together in exactly two teams." Sally knows Basque, thus, she will be in group A and B, with Paula. According to statement 5, Robert (Arabic) is in Team 1 and Quentin(Dutch) is in Team 3. Thus, Group C is Team 1 and Group A is Team 3.

Team 3		Team 2		Team 1	
English	Paula, Sally, Quentin	English	Paula, Sally	English	Paula
Chinese	Paula	Chinese	Paula, Terence	Chinese	Paula, Terence
Basque	Sally	Basque	Sally	Arabic	Terence, Robert
Dutch	Quentin	French	Terence	French	Robert

55. Quentin is not a member of team 2.

56. Sally is a part of exactly two teams.

57. Among the five people, Paula is the one who is a member of all teams.

58. Apart from Chinese and English, Arabic and French are spoken by Team 1.

For questions 59 to 62:

Total number of students surveyed = 500

Every student prefers one of the two candidates. Ragini(R) and Sunita(S).

Thus, R + S = 500.

According to statement 2, "Among the 200 students who preferred Sunita as student union president, 80% supported proposal A."

The number of students who support Sunita(S) = 200

The number of students who supported Ragini(R) = 300

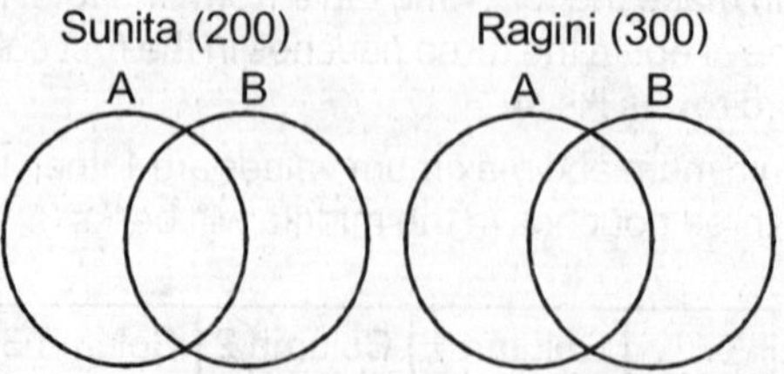

According to statements 2 and 3, 160 students who supported Sunita also supported the proposal A and 90 students who supported Ragini also supported proposal A.

According to statements 4 and 6, we can make the following Venn diagram for Sunita.

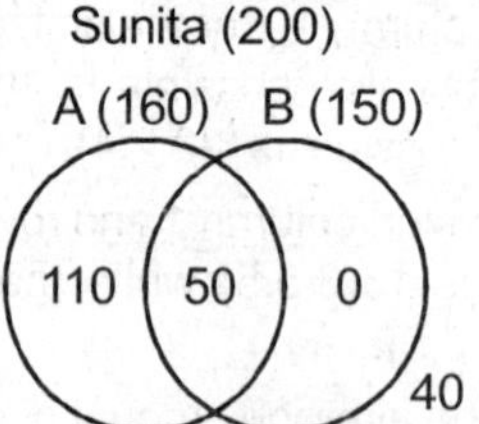

According to statement 5 and 7, we can make the following Venn diagram.

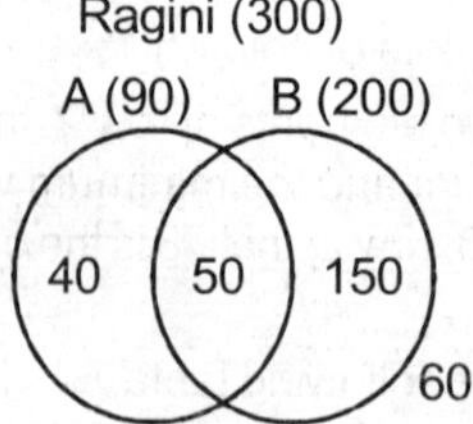

59. The number of students who preferred Sunita and the proposal A = 160 = $\frac{160}{250}$ = 64%

60. The percentage of the students surveyed who did not support proposal A preferred Ragini as student union president = $\frac{210}{250}$ = 84%.

61. According to the Venn diagram, the students surveyed who supported both proposals A and B preferred Sunita as student union president $= \frac{50}{(50+50)} = 50\%$.

62. From the venn diagram we can see that 150 students is the correct answer.

63. If all the doctors served the patients one after the other, then in 2.5 hrs, Ben will serve 15 patients, Kane will serve 10 patients and Wayne will serve 6 patients. A total of 31 patients can be served on a particular day.

64. If all the doctors served the patients one after the other, then in 2.5 hrs, Ben will serve 15 patients Kane will serve 10 patients and Wayne will serve 6 patients.

Ben will earn = 15 × 100 = Rs. 1500.

Kane will earn = 10 × 200 = Rs. 2000.

Wayne will earn = 6 × 300 = Rs. 1800.

So, Kane will earn the maximum amount in consultation charges on that day.

65. Mr. Singh is 13th in the sequence on all the three days.

The following table will show the sequence for Monday, Wednesday and Friday.

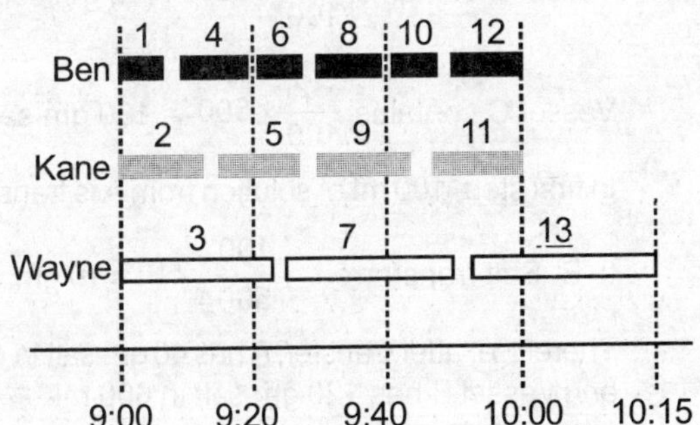

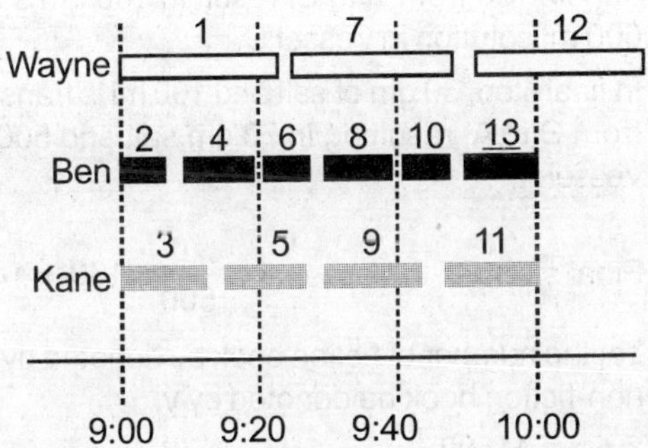

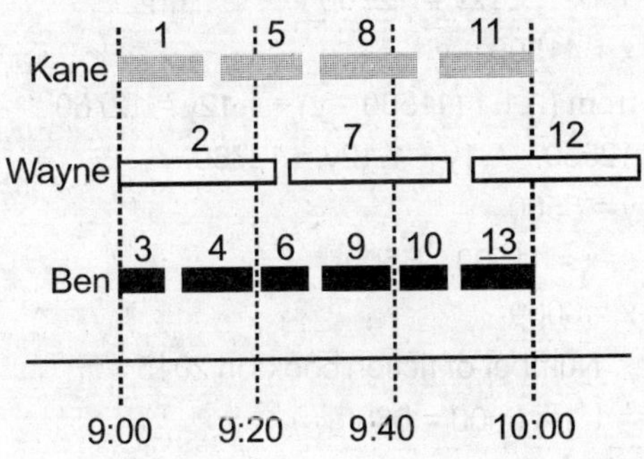

He will stay the longest when the 13th guy is served by Doctor Wayne. From the table, on Monday he had to wait at the clinic for the maximum duration: till 10 : 15.

66. On Thursday, the preference order for the patients is Wayne, Ben and Kane.

The first two customers will be served by Wayne and Ben. While Kane will be empty for the first 15 minutes. Then he and Ben will serve the next two customers and Wayne will be empty for 5 minutes as shown in the figure below.

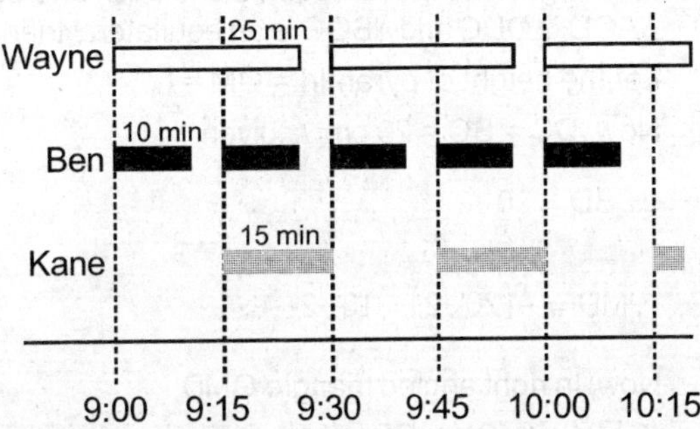

As we can see that the cycle will repeat after every 30 minutes. So, all three doctors are never simultaneously free.

67. Let the Rama's score be 'R', Mohan's score be 'M' and Anjali's score be 'A'

As per the question,

$$R = \frac{1}{2}(M + A) \quad \text{...(1)}$$

and (A + 6) : (m + 6) : (R + 6) = 11 : 10 : 3 ...(2)

$$\frac{A+6}{R+6} = \frac{11}{3}$$

$\therefore$ 3A = 11R + 48

and $\frac{M+6}{R+6} = \frac{10}{3}$

$\therefore$ 3M = 10R + 42

From (1) 12R = M + A

36R = 3M + 3A

36R = 11R + 48 + 10R + 42

15R = 90

$\boxed{R = 6}$

$$\therefore\ A = \frac{11(6)+48}{3} = 38$$

$$\text{and } M = \frac{10(6)+42}{3} = 36$$

$\therefore$ Anjali's score exceeded Rama's score by (38 – 6) = 32.

68.

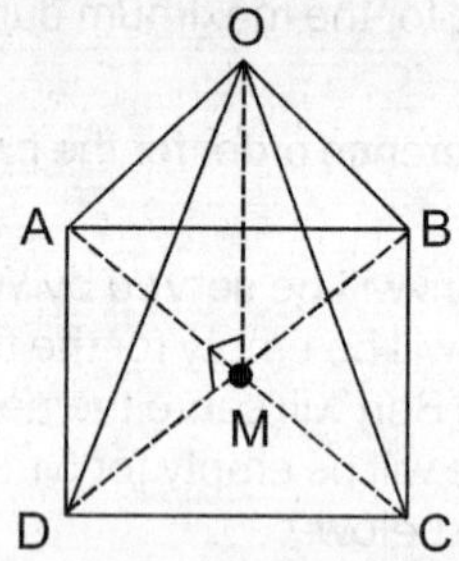

In the figure, ABCD is a square and each of Δ OAB, ΔAOD, ΔODC and ΔBOC is an equilateral triangle.

Let the height of pyramid = OM = h

Now, DC = BC = 20 cm ...given

$\therefore$ BD = $20\sqrt{2}$

$\therefore MD = \frac{1}{2}(20\sqrt{2}) = 10\sqrt{2}$

Now, In right angled triangle OMD,

$(OM)^2 + (MD)^2 = OD^2$

$h^2 = (20)^2 - (10\sqrt{2})^2$

$h = 10\sqrt{2}$

$\therefore$ The vertical height of the pyramid $= 10\sqrt{2}$ cm.

69.

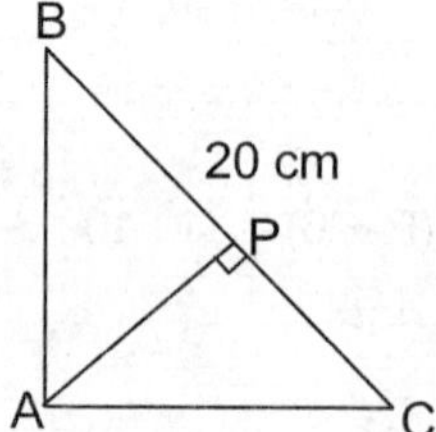

The length of AP will be maximum only when AB = AC

$\therefore$ In rt. ΔBAC,

$(AB)^2 + (AC)^2 = (20)^2$

$2(AC)^2 = 400$

$AC = 10\sqrt{2}$

Now, In ΔAPC

$(AP)^2 + (PC)^2 = AC^2$

(Right angled triangle)

$(AP)^2 = (10\sqrt{2})^2 - (10)^2 \qquad \left(\because PC = \frac{BC}{2}\right)$

$AP^2 = 100$

$\therefore$ AP = 10 cm.

70. The quadratic equation $x^2 + bx + c = 0$ has two roots '3a' and '4a'.

Sum of roots = 4a + 3a $= \frac{-b}{1}$

Product of roots = (4a) (3a) $= \frac{c}{1}$

$7a = -b$

$12a^2 = c$

Now, $b^2 + c = (-7a)^2 + (12a^2) = 49a^2 + 12a^2 = 61a^2$

Now, from options, the only possible value of $(b^2 + c)$ is 549 where a is an integer i.e., a = 3.

71. The three vessels A, B and C contain 500 ml of salt solution of strength 10%, 22% and 32% respectively

Vessel A contains $\frac{10}{100} \times 500 = 50$ gm salt

Vessel B contains $\frac{22}{100} \times 500 = 110$ gm salt

Vessel C contains $\frac{32}{100} \times 500 = 160$ gm salt

In first step, 100 ml of solution from A is transferred to B. Salt transferred $= \frac{100}{500} \times 50 = 10$ gm

Therefore, after transfer, A has 40 gm salt in 400 ml and vessel B has 120 gm salt in 600 ml.

In second step, similarly, 20 gm salt and 100 ml is transferred from B to C, result in 180 gm salt and 600 ml solution in vessel C.

In final step, 30 gm of salt and 100 ml is transferred from C to A, resulting in 70 gm salt and 500 ml in vessel A.

Final strength in vessel A $= \frac{70}{500} \times 100 = 14\%$.

72. Let the number of fiction book be denoted by x and non-fiction book be denoted by y.

$x + y = 11500$ ...(I)

$1.1x + 1.12y = 12760$ ...(II)

$x = 11500 - y$

from (I) $1.1(11500 - y) + 1.12y = 12760$

$12650 - 1.1y + 1.12y = 12760$

$y = 5500$

$\therefore x = 11500 - 5500$

$x = 6000$

$\therefore$ Number of fiction books in 2015

$= 1.1 \times 6000 = 6600$.

73. Two ants A and B meet for the first time at 10:00 am when A has covered 60% of the track.

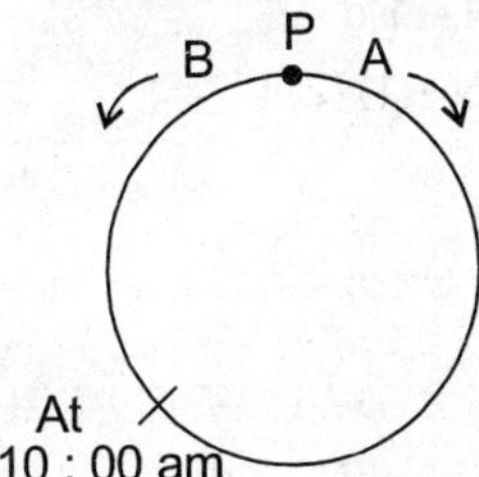

∴ At 10:00 am, B has covered 40% of the track.

Let the total length of track be T km.

Let the speed of ant A and B be S_A km/min and S_B km/min respectively.

Time taken by A to cover 60% of track = time taken by B to cover 40% of track.

$$\therefore \frac{0.6T}{S_A} = \frac{0.4T}{S_B}$$

$$\therefore \frac{S_A}{S_B} = \frac{3}{2}$$

A returns to P at 10:12 am

$$\therefore \frac{0.4T}{S_A} = 12$$

$$\Rightarrow S_A = \frac{0.4T}{12}$$

Now, Time in which B returns to P $= \frac{0.6T}{S_B}$

$$= \frac{0.6T}{\frac{2}{3}\left(\frac{0.4T}{12}\right)} = 27 \text{ min}$$

∴ B returns to P at 10:27 am.

74. 15, 19, 23, 27, ... 415 ...(1)

19, 24, 29, 34, ... 464 ...(2)

Common difference of 1st series $= d_1 = 4$

Common difference of 2nd series $= d_2 = 5$

The common terms in both series (1) and (2) will form an A.P with common difference = LCM (d_1, d_2) = LCM (4, 5) = 20

∴ Number of common terms (n) can be calculated by

$415 = 19 + (n - 1) 20$

$n = 20.8$

∴ 20 terms are common in both series.

75.

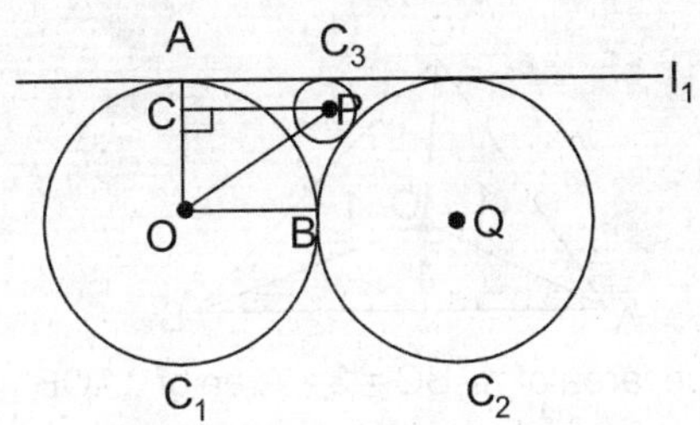

The circles C_1 and C_2 are each of radius 4 cm. Circle C_3 touches C_1 and C_2 such that line l_1 is a common tangent.

Now, Let the radius of C_3 be r.

OP = 4 + 4

OC = 4 – r

CP = OB = 4

In triangle OCP, which is right angled at C,

$OP^2 = OC^2 + CP^2$

$\Rightarrow (4 + r)^2 = (4 - r)^2 + 4^2$

$\Rightarrow (4 + r)^2 - (4 - r)^2 = 4^2$

$\Rightarrow 8 \times 2r = 16$

$\Rightarrow r = 1$ cm.

76. The roots of the equation $x^2 - 4x - \log_2 A = 0$ are real and distinct if $b^2 - 4ac > 0$

$\therefore (-4)^2 - 4(\log_2 A) > 0$

$16 > 4 \log_2 A$

$4 > \log_2 A$

$A < 2^4$

$A < 16$

i.e., $A > \frac{1}{16}$.

77.

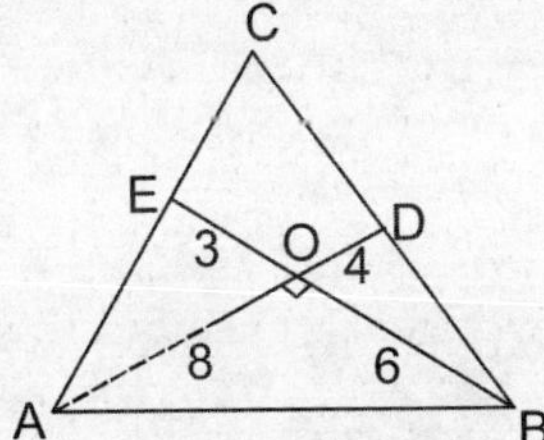

AD and BE are medians intersecting at point O which is the centroid.

A centroid divides the median in the ratio of 2 : 1

⇒ AO = 8 cm, OD = 4 cm and BO = 6 cm and OE = 3cm.

Hence, are of $\Delta AOB = \frac{1}{2} \times 8 \times 6 = 24 \text{ cm}^2$

In a triangle, all three medians meeting at centroid, divides the area of the triangle into three equal parts

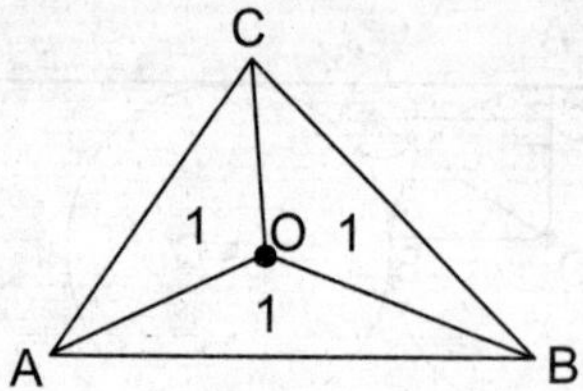

Hence, area of $\Delta ABC = 3 \times$ Area of ΔAOB
$= 3 \times 24 = 72\ cm^2$.

78. $\frac{n^2 7n+12}{n^2-n-12} = \frac{(n+4)(n+3)}{(n-4)(n+3)} = \frac{(n+4)}{(n-4)}$

From the options,

(i) Put n = 16, $\frac{(n+4)}{n-4} = \frac{16+4}{16-4} = \frac{5}{3}$

(ii) Put n = 12, $\frac{n+4}{n-4} = \frac{12+4}{12-4} = 2 \rightarrow$ is a positive integer.

$\therefore$ The largest positive integer, n = 12.

79. A + B = 325

John jogs on track A at 6 km/hr

$= 6 \times \frac{5}{18} = \frac{5}{3} m/sec.$

Mary jogs on track B at 7.5 km/hr

$= 7.5 \times \frac{5}{18} = \frac{25}{12} m/sec$

As per question, $\frac{9A}{\left(\frac{5}{3}\right)} = \frac{5(B)}{\frac{25}{12}}$

$\frac{27A}{5} = \frac{60B}{25}$

$\therefore A = \frac{4}{9}B$

$\because$ A + B = 325

$\left(\frac{4}{9}B\right) + B = 325$

$\therefore$ B = 225 m

$\therefore$ A = 325 – 225 = 100 m.

Required time $= \frac{100}{\left(\frac{25}{12}\right)} = 48\ sec.$

80. (2n + 1) + (2n + 3) + ... (2n + 47) = 5280

$\Rightarrow$ (N × 2n) + (1 + 3 + 5 + ... 47) = 5280

2Nn + (1 + 3 + 5 + ...47) = 5280 ...(1)

Here, N is the number of terms in the series (1 + 3 + 5 + ...47)

$t_N = a + (N-1)d$

47 = 1 + (N – 1) (2)

$\frac{46}{2} = N - 1$

N = 24

$\therefore S_N = \frac{N}{2}(2a + (N-1)d)$

$= \frac{24}{2}[2 + 23(2)] = 576$

$\therefore$ From (1)

48n = 5280 – 576

n = 98

$\therefore 1 + 2 + 3 + ...n = \frac{98}{2}(1+98) = 4851.$

81. $\sqrt{\log_e \frac{4x-x^2}{3}}$ is a real number.

$\therefore \log_e \frac{4x-x^2}{3} \geq 0$

$\frac{4x-x^2}{3} \geq e^{\circ}$

$\therefore 4x - x^2 \geq 3$

$x^2 - 4x \leq 3$

$x^2 - 4x - 3 \leq 0$

$(x-3)(x-1) \leq 0$

$x - 3 \geq 0$ and $x - 1 \leq 0$ or $(x-3) \leq 0$ & $(x-1) \geq 0$

$x \geq 3$ and $x \leq 1$ or $x \leq 3$ & $x \geq 1$

$\therefore 1 \leq x \leq 3.$

82. Interior angle of polygon A of a sides $= \frac{(a-2)180^{\circ}}{a}$

Given that,

$\left(\frac{b-2}{b}\right) \times 180 = \frac{3}{2}\left(\frac{a-2}{a}\right) \times 180$

$\Rightarrow 2ba - 4a = 3\ ab - 6b$

$\Rightarrow 2(2a)a - 4a = 3a(2a) - 6(2a)$

$\Rightarrow 4a^2 - 4a = 6a^2 - 12a$

$\Rightarrow 2a^2 = 8a$

$\Rightarrow a = 4$

Therefore, a = 4 and b = 8.

For polygon of a + b sides, a +b = 12.

Interior angle $= \left(\frac{12-2}{12}\right) \times 180 = 150^{\circ}.$

83. $m^2 + 105 = n^2$ $\quad$ m, n > 0

$m^2 - n^2 = 105$

$(m + n)(m - n) = 105 = 3 \times 5 \times 7$

Case I : $(m - n) = 3$ and $(m + n) = 35$

$\therefore m = 19, n = 16$

Case II : $(m - n) = 7$ and $(m + n) = 15$

$\therefore m = 11, n = 4$

Case III : $m - n = 5$ and $m + n = 21$

$\therefore m = 13, n = 8$

Case IV : $m - n = 1$ and $m + n = 105$

$\therefore m = 53, n = 52$

So, there are 4 pairs.

84. $2^{6x} + 2^{3x+2} - 21 = 0$

$(2^{3x})^2 + 2^{3x} . 2^2 - 21 = 0$

$(2^{3x})^2 + 2.2^{3x} . 2 + (2)^2 - 25 = 0$

$(2^{3x} + 2)^2 = 25$

$2^{3x} + 2 = 5$

$2^{3x} = 3$

Applying log to both side.

$3x \log 2 = \log 3$

$$x = \frac{1}{3}\log_2 3$$

85. To completely use the metal and to make whole cylinders from the metal, the volume of one metal must be the HCF of 405, 351 and 783.

HCF of 405, 351 and 783 = 27

$\therefore \pi r^2 h = 27$

$\Rightarrow (3)^2 h = 27$

$$\Rightarrow h = \frac{3}{\pi}$$

Surface area of one cylinder = $2\pi r(r + h)$

$$= 2\pi \times 3\left(3 + \frac{3}{\pi}\right)$$

$= 18(1 + \pi)$

$$\text{Number of cylinders} = \frac{405 + 351 + 783}{27} = 57$$

Total surface area = $57 \times 18(1 + \pi)$

$= 1026(1 + \pi)$

86. Let $5^x = a$ and $3^y = b$.

Then,

$a - b = 13438$ $\quad$ ...(i)

$$\frac{a}{5} + 3b = 9686 \quad ...(ii)$$

On multiplying (ii) by 5,

$a + 15b = 48,430$ $\quad$ ...(iii)

$\Rightarrow 13438 + b + 15b = 48,430$

$\Rightarrow b = 2187 = 3^7$

$a = 15625 = 5^6$

$\therefore x = 6\ y = 7$

$x + y = 13$

87. $2^4 \times 3^5 \times 10^4$

$2^4 \times 3^5 \times 2^4 \times 5^4$

$2^8 \times 3^5 \times 5^4$

For the factor to be a perfect square, the factor should be even power of the number.

In 2^8, the factors which are perfect squares are = 5

Similarly, in 3^5, the factors which are perfect squares are = 3

In 5^4, the factors which are perfect squares are = 3

Number of perfect squares greater than

$1 = 5 \times 3 \times 3 - 1 = 44$.

88. From the sequence given here,

$a_1 = 1$

$a_1 - a_2 = 2 \Rightarrow a_2 = -1$

$a_1 - a_2 + a_3 = 3 \Rightarrow a_3 = 1$

So, all odd numbered integers are +1 and even numbered integers are –1

Required sum = $a_{51} + a_{52} + ... + a_{1023}$

$= 1 - 1 + 1 - 1 + 1 - 1 ...... + 1$

$= 1$.

89. In the given set of equations, by hit and trial, the following results can be obtained:

Case 1: a = 5 ; b = 0 ; x = 13; y = 0

Case 2: a = 0 ; b = 5 ; x = 0; y = 13

In both the cases, $ay - bx = 0 - 0 = 0$

Therefore, k = 0

90. Interest earned by Amal

$$= 12000\left(1 + \frac{8}{100}\right)^1 - 12,000 + 10000\left(1 + \frac{3}{100}\right)^2 - 1000$$

$= 960 + 609 = 1569$.

$$\text{Interest earned by Bimal} = \frac{P \times 7.5 \times 1}{100} = \frac{7.5P}{100}$$

$$\text{Now, } \frac{7.5P}{100} = 1569 \Rightarrow P = 20,920.$$

91. Since 45 motor cycles reach point B and 11 pm, the last motorcycle must have left at 10 : 45 and reached by 11 pm. So the whole journey takes 15 minutes to cover by motor cycle.

If cyclist doubles his speed, he will reach point B in 30 minutes. Since motorcycle takes 15 minutes to cover the distance, the first motorcycle reaches at 10 : 16 and in total 15 motor cycles would reach by when B reached.

92. As per the instruction, let the first digit be a.

The second digit will be 2a

Third digit will be a

Fourth digit will be (2a + 2b + a) = 7a

Fifth digit will be 3a

Sixth digit will be 4a

$\therefore$ Largest value of fourth digit can only be 7.

93. Work done by Anil in one day $= \frac{1}{20}$

Work done by Sunil in one day $= \frac{1}{40}$

Let the days worked by Sunil be n.

Then, $\frac{3}{20} + n\left(\frac{1}{20} + \frac{1}{40}\right) + \frac{1}{10} = 1.$

$\Rightarrow \frac{6 + 3n + 4}{40} = 1$

$\Rightarrow 3n = 30 \Rightarrow n = 10$

Therefore total number of days taken

= 10 + 3 = 13 days.

94. Score of A = 72.

Score of B $= 72 \times \frac{100}{90} = 80$

Score of C $= 80 \times \frac{100}{125} = 64$

Score of D $= 64 \times \frac{100}{80} = 80$

So, the score of D was 80.

95. Let the numbers of hours worked in regular work be a and number of hours worked overtime be b.

$\frac{114b}{57a} = \frac{15}{100} \Rightarrow \frac{2b}{a} = \frac{3}{20}$

$\Rightarrow 40b = 3a$

a + b = 172

$\Rightarrow 3a + 3b = 516$

$\Rightarrow 43b = 516$

$\Rightarrow b = \frac{516}{43} = 12.$

$\therefore$ John did 12 hours of overtime.

96. Sum of the 30 integers = 30 × 5 = 150.

For the 10 integers greater than 5, they must be 6, so that the average of 20 integers can be the highest.

So, Sum of 10 integers = 6 × 10 = 60.

Sum of remaining 20 integers = 150 – 60 = 90

$\therefore$ Required average $= \frac{90}{20} = 4.5.$

97. Let the cost price of each bicycle be Rs x.

Total cost price = 10x

Selling price of 6 bicycles = 1.25x × 6 = 7.5x

Selling price of 4 bicycles = 0.75x × 4 = 3x

Total selling price = 7.5x + 3x = 10.5x

Profit = SP – CP = 10.5x – 10x = 0.5x

Now, 0.5x = 2000 $\Rightarrow$ x = Rs 4000.

98. Let the salaries be 6a, 5a, and 7a in 2010 for Ramesh, Ganesh and Rajesh respectively and 3b, 4b and 3b in 2015 respectively.

Given that

$1.25 \times 6a = 3b \Rightarrow 7.5a = 3b \Rightarrow 2.5a = b$

Then salary of Rajesh in 2015 is 3 × 2.5a = 7.5a

$\therefore$ Percentage increase $= \frac{0.5a}{7a} \times 100 = 7.14\%.$

99. Given, f(mn) = f(m)f(n)

when m = n = 1, f(1) = f(1) × f(1) $\Rightarrow$ f(1) = 1

when m = 1, n = 2, f(2) = f(1) × f(2) $\Rightarrow$ f(1) = 1

when m = n = 2, f(4) = f(2) × f(2) $\Rightarrow$ f(4) = $[f(2)]^2$

Similarly f(8) = f(4) × f(2) = $[f(2)]^3$

f(24) = 54

$[f(2)]^3 \times f(3) = 3^3 \times 2$

On comparing LHS and RHS, we get

f(2) = 3 and f(3) = 2

Now we have to find the value of f(18)

f(18) = f(2) × $[f(3)]^2$ = 3 × 4 = 12.

100. CP of the table at which the shopkeeper procured each table = p

It is given that shopkeeper sold the tables to Amal and Asim at a profit of 20% and at a loss of 20%, respectively.

The selling price of the tables = 1.2p and 0.8p to Amal and Asim respectively.

Amal sells his table to Bimal at a profit of 30%.

So, CP of the table by Bimal (x) = 1.2p × 1.3 = 1.56p.

Asim sells his table to Barun at a loss of 30%.

So, CP of the table by Barun (y) = 0.7 × 0.8p = 0.56p

$\frac{(x - y)}{p} = \frac{(1.56p - 0.56p)}{p} = \frac{p}{p} = 1.$

CAT 2020 SOLVED PAPER (SLOT-1)

Section I: VARC

Question Numbers (1 to 5): The passage below is accompanied by a set of questions. Choose the best answer to each question.

Vocabulary used in speech or writing organizes itself in seven parts of speech (eight, if you count interjections such as Oh! and Gosh! and Fuhgeddaboudit!). Communication composed of these parts of speech must be organized by rules of grammar upon which we agree. When these rules break down, confusion and misunderstanding result. Bad grammar produces bad sentences. My favorite example from Strunk and White is this one: "As a mother of five, with another one on the way, my ironing board is always up."

Nouns and verbs are the two indispensable parts of writing. Without one of each, no group of words can be a sentence, since a sentence is, by definition, a group of words containing a subject (noun) and a predicate (verb); these strings of words begin with a capital letter, end with a period, and combine to make a complete thought which starts in the writer's head and then leaps to the reader's.

Must you write complete sentences each time, every time? Perish the thought. If your work consists only of fragments and floating clauses, the Grammar Police aren't going to come and take you away. Even William Strunk, that Mussolini of rhetoric, recognized the delicious pliability of language. "It is an old observation," he writes, "that the best writers sometimes disregard the rules of rhetoric." Yet he goes on to add this thought, which I urge you to consider: "Unless he is certain of doing well, [the writer] will probably do best to follow the rules."

The telling clause here is Unless he is certain of doing well. If you don't have a rudimentary grasp of how the parts of speech translate into coherent sentences, how can you be certain that you are doing well? How will you know if you're doing ill, for that matter? The answer, of course, is that you can't, you won't. One who does grasp the rudiments of grammar finds a comforting simplicity at its heart, where there need be only nouns, the words that name, and verbs, the words that act.

Take any noun, put it with any verb, and you have a sentence. It never fails. Rocks explode. Jane transmits. Mountains float. These are all perfect sentences. Many such thoughts make little rational sense, but even the stranger ones (Plums deify!) have a kind of poetic weight that's nice. The simplicity of noun-verb construction is useful—at the very least it can provide a safety net for your writing. Strunk and White caution against too many simple sentences in a row, but simple sentences provide a path you can follow when you fear getting lost in the tangles of rhetoric—all those restrictive and nonrestrictive clauses, those modifying phrases, those appositives and compound-complex sentences. If you start to freak out at the sight of such unmapped territory (unmapped by you, at least), just remind yourself that rocks explode, Jane transmits, mountains float, and plums deify. Grammar is . . . the pole you grab to get your thoughts up on their feet and walking.

1. Inferring from the passage, the author could be most supportive of which one of the following practices?

(1) The critique of standardised rules of punctuation and capitalisation.

(2) A campaign demanding that a writer's creative license should allow the breaking of grammatical rules.

(3) The availability of language software that will standardise the rules of grammar as an aid to writers.

(4) A Creative Writing course that focuses on how to avoid the use of rhetoric.

2. Which one of the following quotes best captures the main concern of the passage?

(1) "The telling clause here is Unless he is certain of doing well."

(2) "Nouns and verbs are the two indispensable parts of writing. Without one of each, no group of words can be a sentence . . ."

(3) "Strunk and White caution against too many simple sentences in a row, but simple sentences provide a path you can follow when you fear getting lost in the tangles of rhetoric . . ."

(4) "Bad grammar produces bad sentences."

3. "Take any noun, put it with any verb, and you have a sentence. It never fails. Rocks explode. Jane transmits. Mountains float." None of the following statements can be seen as similar EXCEPT:
   (1) Take an apple tree, plant it in a field, and you have an orchard.
   (2) A collection of people with the same sports equipment is a sports team.
   (3) A group of nouns arranged in a row becomes a sentence.
   (4) Take any vegetable, put some spices in it, and you have a dish.
4. Which one of the following statements, if false, could be seen as supporting the arguments in the passage?
   (1) It has been observed that writers sometimes disregard the rules of rhetoric.
   (2) Perish the thought that complete sentences necessarily need nouns and verbs!
   (3) Regarding grammar, women writers tend to be more attentive to method and accuracy.
   (4) An understanding of grammar helps a writer decide if she/he is writing well or not.
5. All of the following statements can be inferred from the passage EXCEPT that:
   (1) sentences do not always have to be complete.
   (2) the primary purpose of grammar is to ensure that sentences remain simple.
   (3) the subject–predicate relation is the same as the noun–verb relation.
   (4) "Grammar Police" is a metaphor for critics who focus on linguistic rules.

Question Numbers (6 to 9): The passage below is accompanied by a set of questions. Choose the best answer to each question.

Few realise that the government of China, governing an empire of some 60 million people during the Tang dynasty (618–907), implemented a complex financial system that recognised grain, coins and textiles as money. . . . Coins did have certain advantages: they were durable, recognisable and provided a convenient medium of exchange, especially for smaller transactions. However, there were also disadvantages. A continuing shortage of copper meant that government mints could not produce enough coins for the entire empire, to the extent that for most of the dynasty's history, coins constituted only a tenth of the money supply. One of the main objections to calls for taxes to be paid in coin was that peasant producers who could weave cloth or grow grain – the other two major currencies of the Tang – would not be able to produce coins, and therefore would not be able to pay their taxes. . . .

As coins had advantages and disadvantages, so too did textiles. If in circulation for a long period of time, they could show signs of wear and tear. Stained, faded and torn bolts of textiles had less value than a brand new bolt. Furthermore, a full bolt had a particular value. If consumers cut textiles into smaller pieces to buy or sell something worth less than a full bolt, that, too, greatly lessened the value of the textiles. Unlike coins, textiles could not be used for small transactions; as [an official] noted, textiles could not "be exchanged by the foot and the inch" . . .

But textiles had some advantages over coins. For a start, textile production was widespread and there were fewer problems with the supply of textiles. For large transactions, textiles weighed less than their equivalent in coins since a string of coins . . . could weigh as much as 4 kg. Furthermore, the dimensions of a bolt of silk held remarkably steady from the third to the tenth century: 56 cm wide and 12 m long . . . The values of different textiles were also more stable than the fluctuating values of coins. . . .

The government also required the use of textiles for large transactions. Coins, on the other hand, were better suited for smaller transactions, and possibly, given the costs of transporting coins, for a more local usage. Grain, because it rotted easily, was not used nearly as much as coins and textiles, but taxpayers were required to pay grain to the government as a share of their annual tax obligations, and official salaries were expressed in weights of grain. . . .

In actuality, our own currency system today has some similarities even as it is changing in front of our eyes. . . . We have cash – coins for small transactions like paying for parking at a meter, and banknotes for other items; cheques and debit/credit cards for other, often larger, types of payments. At the same time, we are shifting to electronic banking and making payments online. Some young people never use cash [and] do not know how to write a cheque . . .

6. During the Tang period, which one of the following would not be an economically sound decision for a small purchase in the local market that is worth one-eighth of a bolt of cloth?
   (1) Making the payment with the appropriate weight of grain.
   (2) Paying with a faded bolt of cloth that has approximately the same value.

(3) Cutting one-eighth of the fabric from a new bolt to pay the amount.

(4) Using coins issued by the government to make the payment.

7. According to the passage, the modern currency system shares all the following features with that of the Tang, EXCEPT that:

(1) it uses different currencies for different situations.

(2) its currencies fluctuate in value over time.

(3) it is undergoing transformation.

(4) it uses different materials as currency.

8. In the context of the passage, which one of the following can be inferred with regard to the use of currency during the Tang era?

(1) Copper coins were more valuable and durable than textiles.

(2) Grains were the most used currency because of government requirements.

(3) Currency that deteriorated easily was not used for official work.

(4) Currency usage was similar to that of modern times.

9. When discussing textiles as currency in the Tang period, the author uses the words "steady" and "stable" to indicate all of the following EXCEPT:

(1) reliable transportation.

(2) reliable quality.

(3) reliable measurements.

(4) reliable supply.

Question Numbers (10 to 13): The passage below is accompanied by a set of questions. Choose the best answer to each question.

In the late 1960s, while studying the northern-elephant-seal population along the coasts of Mexico and California, Burney Le Boeuf and his colleagues couldn't help but notice that the threat calls of males at some sites sounded different from those of males at other sites. . . . That was the first time dialects were documented in a nonhuman mammal. . . .

All the northern elephant seals that exist today are descendants of the small herd that survived on Isla Guadalupe [after the near extinction of the species in the nineteenth century]. As that tiny population grew, northern elephant seals started to recolonize former breeding locations. It was precisely on the more recently colonized islands where Le Boeuf found that the tempos of the male vocal displays showed stronger differences to the ones from Isla Guadalupe, the founder colony.

In order to test the reliability of these dialects over time, Le Boeuf and other researchers visited Año Nuevo Island in California—the island where males showed the slowest pulse rates in their calls—every winter from 1968 to 1972. "What we found is that the pulse rate increased, but it still remained relatively slow compared to the other colonies we had measured in the past" Le Boeuf told me.

At the individual level, the pulse of the calls stayed the same: A male would maintain his vocal signature throughout his lifetime. But the average pulse rate was changing. Immigration could have been responsible for this increase, as in the early 1970s, 43 percent of the males on Año Nuevo had come from southern rookeries that had a faster pulse rate. This led Le Boeuf and his collaborator, Lewis Petrinovich, to deduce that the dialects were, perhaps, a result of isolation over time, after the breeding sites had been recolonized. For instance, the first settlers of Año Nuevo could have had, by chance, calls with low pulse rates. At other sites, where the scientists found faster pulse rates, the opposite would have happened—seals with faster rates would have happened to arrive first.

As the population continued to expand and the islands kept on receiving immigrants from the original population, the calls in all locations would have eventually regressed to the average pulse rate of the founder colony. In the decades that followed, scientists noticed that the geographical variations reported in 1969 were not obvious anymore. . . . In the early 2010s, while studying northern elephant seals on Año Nuevo Island, [researcher Caroline] Casey noticed, too, that what Le Boeuf had heard decades ago was not what she heard now. . . . By performing more sophisticated statistical analyses on both sets of data, [Casey and Le Boeuf] confirmed that dialects existed back then but had vanished. Yet there are other differences between the males from the late 1960s and their great-great-grandsons: Modern males exhibit more individual diversity, and their calls are more complex. While 50 years ago the drumming pattern was quite simple and the dialects denoted just a change in tempo, Casey explained, the calls recorded today have more complex structures, sometimes featuring doublets or triplets. . . .

10. From the passage it can be inferred that the call pulse rate of male northern elephant seals in the southern rookeries was faster because:

(1) a large number of male northern elephant seals migrated from the southern rookeries to Año Nuevo Island in the early 1970s.

(2) the calls of male northern elephant seals in the southern rookeries have more sophisticated structures, containing doublets and triplets.

(3) the male northern elephant seals of Isla Guadalupe with faster call pulse rates might have been the original settlers of the southern rookeries.

(4) a large number of male northern elephant seals from Año Nuevo Island might have migrated to the southern rookeries to recolonise them.

11. Which one of the following best sums up the overall history of transformation of male northern elephant seal calls?

(1) Owing to migrations in the aftermath of near species extinction, the average call pulse rates in the recolonised breeding locations exhibited a gradual increase until they matched the tempo at the founding colony.

(2) Owing to migrations in the aftermath of near species extinction, the calls have transformed from exhibiting complex composition, less individual variety, and great regional variety to simple composition, less individual variety, and great regional variety.

(3) The calls have transformed from exhibiting simple composition, less individual variety, and great regional variety to complex composition, great individual variety, and less regional variety.

(4) The calls have transformed from exhibiting simple composition, great individual variety, and less regional variety to complex composition, less individual variety, and great regional variety.

12. Which one of the following conditions, if true, could have ensured that male northern elephant seal dialects did not disappear?

(1) The call tempo of individual male seals in host colonies changed to match the average call tempo of immigrant male seals.

(2) The call tempo of individual immigrant male seals changed to match the average tempo of resident male seals in the host colony.

(3) Besides Isla Guadalupe, there was one more founder colony with the same average male call tempo from which male seals migrated to various other colonies.

(4) Besides Isla Guadalupe, there was one more surviving colony with the same average male call tempo from which no migration took place.

13. All of the following can be inferred from Le Boeuf's study as described in the passage EXCEPT that:

(1) changes in population and migration had no effect on the call pulse rate of individual male northern elephant seals.

(2) male northern elephant seals might not have exhibited dialects had they not become nearly extinct in the nineteenth century.

(3) the influx of new northern elephant seals into Año Nuevo Island would have soon made the call pulse rate of its male seals exceed that of those at Isla Guadalupe.

(4) the average call pulse rate of male northern elephant seals at Año Nuevo Island increased from the early 1970s till the disappearance of dialects.

Question Numbers (14 to 18): The passage below is accompanied by a set of questions. Choose the best answer to each question.

The word 'anarchy' comes from the Greek anarkhia, meaning contrary to authority or without a ruler, and was used in a derogatory sense until 1840, when it was adopted by Pierre-Joseph Proudhon to describe his political and social ideology. Proudhon argued that organization without government was both possible and desirable. In the evolution of political ideas, anarchism can be seen as an ultimate projection of both liberalism and socialism, and the differing strands of anarchist thought can be related to their emphasis on one or the other of these.

Historically, anarchism arose not only as an explanation of the gulf between the rich and the poor in any community, and of the reason why the poor have been obliged to fight for their share of a common inheritance, but as a radical answer to the question 'What went wrong?' that followed the ultimate outcome of the French Revolution. It had ended not only with a reign of terror and the emergence of a newly rich ruling caste, but with a new adored emperor, Napoleon Bonaparte, strutting through his conquered territories.

The anarchists and their precursors were unique on the political Left in affirming that workers and peasants, grasping the chance that arose to bring an end to centuries of exploitation and tyranny, were inevitably betrayed by the new class of politicians, whose first priority was to re-establish a centralized state power. After every revolutionary uprising, usually won at a heavy cost for ordinary populations, the new rulers had no hesitation in applying violence and terror, a secret police, and a professional army to maintain their control.

For anarchists the state itself is the enemy, and they have applied the same interpretation to the outcome of every revolution of the 19th and 20th centuries. This is not merely because every state keeps a watchful and sometimes punitive eye on its dissidents, but because every state protects the privileges of the powerful.

The mainstream of anarchist propaganda for more than a century has been anarchist-communism, which argues that property in land, natural resources, and the means of production should be held in mutual control by local communities, federating for innumerable joint purposes with other communes. It differs from state socialism in opposing the concept of any central authority. Some anarchists prefer to distinguish between anarchist-communism and collectivist anarchism in order to stress the obviously desirable freedom of an individual or family to possess the resources needed for living, while not implying the right to own the resources needed by others.

. . .

There are, unsurprisingly, several traditions of individualist anarchism, one of them deriving from the 'conscious egoism' of the German writer Max Stirner (1806–56), and another from a remarkable series of 19th-century American figures who argued that in protecting our own autonomy and associating with others for common advantages, we are promoting the good of all. These thinkers differed from free-market liberals in their absolute mistrust of American capitalism, and in their emphasis on mutualism.

14. According to the passage, what is the one idea that is common to all forms of anarchism?

(1) There is no idea common to all forms of anarchism; that is why it is anarchic.

(2) They all focus on the primacy of the power of the individual.

(3) They all derive from the work of Pierre-Joseph Proudhon.

(4) They are all opposed to the centralisation of power in the state.

15. Of the following sets of concepts, identify the set that is conceptually closest to the concerns of the passage.

(1) Anarchism, State, Individual, Freedom.

(2) Revolution, State, Strike, Egoism.

(3) Anarchism, Betrayal, Power, State.

(4) Revolution, State, Protection, Liberals.

16. The author makes all of the following arguments in the passage, EXCEPT:

(1) The failure of the French Revolution was because of its betrayal by the new class of politicians who emerged from it.

(2) Individualist anarchism is actually constituted of many streams, all of which focus on the autonomy of the individual.

(3) For anarchists, the state is the enemy because all states apply violence and terror to maintain their control.

(4) The popular perception of anarchism as espousing lawlessness and violence comes from a mainstream mistrust of collectivism.

17. The author believes that the new ruling class of politicians betrayed the principles of the French Revolution, but does not specify in what way. In the context of the passage, which statement below is the likeliest explanation of that betrayal?

(1) The new ruling class was constituted mainly of anarchists who were against the destructive impact of the Revolution on the market.

(2) The new ruling class struck a deal with the old ruling class to share power between them.

(3) The new ruling class rode to power on the strength of the workers' revolutionary anger, but then turned to oppress that very class.

(4) The anarchists did not want a new ruling class, but were not politically strong enough to stop them.

18. Which one of the following best expresses the similarity between American individualist anarchists and free-market liberals as well as the difference between the former and the latter?

(1) Both are sophisticated arguments for capitalism; but the former argue for a morally upright capitalism, while the latter argue that the market is the only morality.

(2) Both reject the regulatory power of the state; but the former favour a people's state, while the latter favour state intervention in markets.

(3) Both are founded on the moral principles of altruism; but the latter conceive of the market as a force too mystical for the former to comprehend.

(4) Both prioritise individual autonomy; but the former also emphasise mutual dependence, while the latter do not do so.

19. Five jumbled up sentences, related to a topic, are given below. Four of them can be put together to form a coherent paragraph. Identify the odd one out and key in the number of the sentence as your answer:

(1) Talk was the most common way for enslaved men and women to subvert the rules of their bondage,

to gain more agency than they were supposed to have.

(2) Even in conditions of extreme violence and unfreedom, their words remained ubiquitous, ephemeral, irrepressible, and potentially transgressive.

(3) Slaves came from societies in which oaths, orations, and invocations carried great potency, both between people and as a connection to the all-powerful spirit world.

(4) Freedom of speech and the power to silence may have been preeminent markers of white liberty in Colonies, but at the same time, slavery depended on dialogue: slaves could never be completely muted.

(5) Slave-owners obsessed over slave talk, though they could never control it, yet feared its power to bind and inspire—for, as everyone knew, oaths, whispers, and secret conversations bred conspiracy and revolt.

20. The passage given below is followed by four alternate summaries. Choose the option that best captures the essence of the passage.

For nearly a century most psychologists have embraced one view of intelligence. Individuals are born with more or less intelligence potential (I.Q.); this potential is heavily influenced by heredity and difficult to alter; experts in measurement can determine a person's intelligence early in life, currently from paper-and-pencil measures, perhaps eventually from examining the brain in action or even scrutinizing his/her genome. Recently, criticism of this conventional wisdom has mounted. Biologists ask if speaking of a single entity called "intelligence" is coherent and question the validity of measures used to estimate heritability of a trait in humans, who, unlike plants or animals, are not conceived and bred under controlled conditions.

(1) Biologists have criticised that conventional wisdom that individuals are born with more or less intelligence potential.

(2) Biologists have questioned the view that 'intelligence' is a single entity and the ways in which what is inherited.

(3) Biologists have questioned the long-standing view that 'intelligence' is a single entity and the attempts to estimate it's heritability.

(4) Biologists have started questioning psychologists' view of 'intelligence' as a measurable immutable characteristic of an individual.

21. Five jumbled up sentences, related to a topic, are given below. Four of them can be put together to form a coherent paragraph. Identify the odd one out and key in the number of the sentence as your answer:

(1) For feminists, the question of how we read is inextricably linked with the question of what we read.

(2) Elaine Showalter's critique of the literary curriculum is exemplary of this work.

(3) Androcentric literature structures the reading experience differently depending on the gender of the reader.

(4) The documentation of this realization was one of the earliest tasks undertaken by feminist critics.

(5) More specifically, the feminist inquiry into the activity of reading begins with the realization that the literary canon is androcentric, and that this has a profoundly damaging effect on women readers.

22. The passage given below is followed by four alternate summaries. Choose the option that best captures the essence of the passage.

As Soviet power declined, the world became to some extent multipolar, and Europe strove to define an independent identity. What a journey Europe has undertaken to reach this point. It had in every century changed its internal structure and invented new ways of thinking about the nature of international order. Now at the culmination of an era, Europe, in order to participate in it, felt obliged to set aside the political mechanisms through which it had conducted its affairs for three and a half centuries. Impelled also by the desire to cushion the emergent unification of Germany, the new European Union established a common currency in 2002 and a formal political structure in 2004. It proclaimed a Europe united, whole, and free, adjusting its differences by peaceful mechanisms.

(1) Europe has consistently changed in keeping with the changing world order and that has culminated in a united Europe.

(2) Europe has chosen to lower political and economic heterogeneity, in order to adapt itself to an emerging multi-polar world.

(3) Europe has consistently changed its internal structure to successfully adapt to the changing world order.

(4) The establishment of a formal political structure in Europe was hastened by the unification of Germany and the emergence of a multipolar world.

23. The passage given below is followed by four alternate summaries. Choose the option that best captures the essence of the passage.

For years, movies and television series like Crime Scene Investigation (CSI) paint an unrealistic picture of the "science of voices." In the 1994 movie Clear and Present Danger an expert listens to a brief recorded utterance and declares that the speaker is "Cuban, aged 35 to 45, educated in the [...] eastern United States." The recording is then fed to a supercomputer that matches the voice to that of a suspect, concluding that the probability of correct identification is 90%. This sequence sums up a good number of misimpressions about forensic phonetics, which have led to errors in real-life justice. Indeed, that movie scene exemplifies the so-called "CSI effect"—the phenomenon in which judges hold unrealistic expectations of the capabilities of forensic science.

(1) Although voice recognition is often presented as evidence in legal cases, its scientific basis can be shaky.

(2) Voice recognition as used in many movies to identify criminals has been used to identify criminals in real life also.

(3) Movies and televisions have led to the belief that the use of forensic phonetics in legal investigations is robust and fool proof.

(4) Voice recognition has started to feature prominently in crime-scene intelligence investigations because of movies and television series.

24. The four sentences (labelled 1, 2, 3, 4) below, when properly sequenced would yield a coherent paragraph. Decide on the proper sequencing of the order of the sentences and key in the sequence of the four numbers as your answer:

(1) Tensions and sometimes conflict remain an issue in and between the 11 states in South East Asia (Brunei Darussalam, Cambodia, Indonesia, Laos, Malaysia, Myanmar, the Philippines, Singapore, Thailand, Timor-Leste and Vietnam).

(2) China's rise as a regional military power and its claims in the South China Sea have become an increasingly pressing security concern for many South East Asian states.

(3) Since the 1990s, the security environment of South East Asia has seen both continuity and profound changes.

(4) These concerns cause states from outside the region to take an active interest in South East Asian security.

25. The four sentences (labelled 1, 2, 3, 4) below, when properly sequenced would yield a coherent paragraph. Decide on the proper sequencing of the order of the sentences and key in the sequence of the four numbers as your answer:

(1) Man has used poisons for assassination purposes ever since the dawn of civilization, against individual enemies but also occasionally against armies.

(2) These dangers were soon recognized, and resulted in two international declarations—in 1874 in Brussels and in 1899 in The Hague—that prohibited the use of poisoned weapons.

(3) The foundation of microbiology by Louis Pasteur and Robert Koch offered new prospects for those interested in biological weapons because it allowed agents to be chosen and designed on a rational basis.

(4) Though treaties were all made in good faith, they contained no means of control, and so failed to prevent interested parties from developing and using biological weapons.

26. The four sentences (labelled 1, 2, 3, 4) below, when properly sequenced would yield a coherent paragraph. Decide on the proper sequencing of the order of the sentences and key in the sequence of the four numbers as your answer:

(1) Relying on narrative structure alone, indigenous significances of nineteenth century San folktales are hard to determine.

(2) Using their supernatural potency, benign shamans transcend the levels of the San cosmos in order to deal with social conflict and to protect material resources and enjoy a measure of respect that sets them apart from ordinary people.

(3) Selected tales reveal that they deal with a form of spiritual conflict that has social implications and concern conflict between people and living or dead malevolent shamans.

(4) Meaning can be elicited, and the tales contextualized, by probing beneath the narrative of verbatim, original-language records and exploring the connotations of highly significant words and phrases.

Section II: DI & LR

Question Numbers (27 to 30): Answer the questions on the basis of the information given below.

1000 patients currently suffering from a disease were selected to study the effectiveness of treatment of four types of medicines — A, B, C and D. These patients were first randomly assigned into two groups of equal size, called treatment group and control group. The patients in the control group were not treated with any of these medicines; instead they were given a dummy medicine, called placebo, containing only sugar and starch. The following information is known about the patients in the treatment group.

a. A total of 250 patients were treated with type A medicine and a total of 210 patients were treated with type C medicine.

b. 25 patients were treated with type A medicine only. 20 patients were treated with type C medicine only. 10 patients were treated with type D medicine only.

c. 35 patients were treated with type A and type D medicines only. 20 patients were treated with type A and type B medicines only. 30 patients were treated with type A and type C medicines only. 20 patients were treated with type C and type D medicines only.

d. 100 patients were treated with exactly three types of medicines.

e. 40 patients were treated with medicines of types A, B and C, but not with medicines of type D. 20 patients were treated with medicines of types A, C and D, but not with medicines of type B.

f. 50 patients were given all the four types of medicines. 75 patients were treated with exactly one type of medicine.

27. How many patients were treated with medicine type B?

28. The number of patients who were treated with medicine types B, C and D, but not type A was:

29. How many patients were treated with medicine types B and D only?

30. The number of patients who were treated with medicine type D was:

Question Numbers (31 to 36): Answer the questions on the basis of the information given below.

In a certain board examination, students were to appear for examination in five subjects: English, Hindi, Mathematics, Science and Social Science. Due to a certain emergency situation, a few of the examinations could not be conducted for some students. Hence, some students missed one examination and some others missed two examinations. Nobody missed more than two examinations.

The board adopted the following policy for awarding marks to students. If a student appeared in all five examinations, then the marks awarded in each of the examinations were on the basis of the scores obtained by them in those examinations.

If a student missed only one examination, then the marks awarded in that examination was the average of the best three among the four scores in the examinations they appeared for.

If a student missed two examinations, then the marks awarded in each of these examinations was the average of the best two among the three scores in the examinations they appeared for.

The marks obtained by six students in the examination are given in the table below. Each of them missed either one or two examinations.

	English	Hindi	Mathematics	Science	Social Science
Alva	80	75	70	75	60
Bithi	90	80	55	85	85
Carl	75	80	90	100	90
Deep	70	90	100	90	80
Esha	80	85	95	60	55
Foni	83	72	78	88	83

The following facts are also known.

I. Four of these students appeared in each of the English, Hindi, Science, and Social Science examinations.

II. The student who missed the Mathematics examination did not miss any other examination.

III. One of the students who missed the Hindi examination did not miss any other examination. The other student who missed the Hindi examination also missed the Science examination.

31. Who among the following did not appear for the Mathematics examination?

(1) Alva

(2) Foni

(3) Esha

(4) Carl

32. Which students did not appear for the English examination?

(1) Cannot be determined

(2) Carl and Deep

(3) Esha and Foni

(4) Alva and Bithi

33. What BEST can be concluded about the students who did not appear for the Hindi examination?

(1) Alva and Deep

(2) Deep and Esha

(3) Alva and Esha

(4) Two among Alva, Deep and Esha

34. What BEST can be concluded about the students who missed the Science examination?

(1) Deep and Bithi

(2) Alva and Deep

(3) Alva and Bithi

(4) Bithi and one out of Alva and Deep

35. How many out of these six students missed exactly one examination?

36. For how many students can we be definite about which examinations they missed?

Question Numbers (37 to 42): Answer the questions on the basis of the information given below.

Four institutes, A, B, C, and D, had contracts with four vendors W, X, Y, and Z during the ten calendar years from 2010 to 2019. The contracts were either multi-year contracts running for several consecutive years or single-year contracts. No institute had more than one contract with the same vendor. However, in a calendar year, an institute may have had contracts with multiple vendors, and a vendor may have had contracts with multiple institutes. It is known that over the decade, the Institutes each got into two contracts with two of these vendors, and each vendor got into two contracts with two of these institutes.

The following facts are also known about these contracts.

I. Vendor Z had at least one contract in every year.

II. Vendor X had one or more contracts in every year up to 2015, but no contract in any year after that.

III. Vendor Y had contracts in 2010 and 2019. Vendor W had contracts only in 2012.

IV. There were five contracts in 2012.

V. There were exactly four multi-year contracts. Institute B had a 7-year contract, D had a 4-year contract, and A and C had one 3-year contract each. The other four contracts were single-year contracts.

VI. Institute C had one or more contracts in 2012 but did not have any contract in 2011.

VII. Institutes B and D each had exactly one contract in 2012. Institute D did not have any contract in 2010.

37. In which of the following years were there two or more contracts?

(1) 2015

(2) 2018

(3) 2017

(4) 2016

38. Which of the following is true?

(1) B had a contract with Y in 2019

(2) D had a contract with X in 2011

(3) B had a contract with Z in 2017

(4) D had a contract with Y in 2019

39. In how many years during this period was there only one contract?

(1) 3

(2) 5

(3) 2

(4) 4

40. What BEST can be concluded about the number of contracts in 2010?

(1) at least 3

(2) at least 4

(3) exactly 4

(4) exactly 3

41. Which institutes had multiple contracts during the same year?

(1) B and C only

(2) B only

(3) A only

(4) A and B only

42. Which institutes and vendors had more than one contracts in any year?

(1) A, D, W, and Z

(2) B, W, X, and Z

(3) A, B, W, and X

(4) B, D, W, and X

Question Numbers (43 to 46): Answer the questions on the basis of the information given below.

Ten musicians (A, B, C, D, E, F, G, H, I and J) are experts in at least one of the following three percussion instruments: tabla, mridangam, and ghatam. Among them, three are experts in tabla but not in mridangam or ghatam, another three are experts in mridangam but not in tabla or ghatam, and one is an expert in ghatam but not in tabla or mridangam. Further, two are experts in tabla and mridangam but not in ghatam, and one is an expert in tabla and ghatam but not in mridangam.

The following facts are known about these ten musicians.

1. Both A and B are experts in mridangam, but only one of them is also an expert in tabla.
2. D is an expert in both tabla and ghatam.
3. Both F and G are experts in tabla, but only one of them is also an expert in mridangam.
4. Neither I nor J is an expert in tabla.
5. Neither H nor I is an expert in mridangam, but only one of them is an expert in ghatam.

43. Who among the following is DEFINITELY an expert in tabla but not in either mridangam or ghatam?

(1) F
(2) A
(3) C
(4) H

44. Who among the following is DEFINITELY an expert in mridangam but not in either tabla or ghatam?

(1) B
(2) E
(3) J
(4) G

45. Which of the following pairs CANNOT have any musician who is an expert in both tabla and mridangam but not in ghatam?

(1) C and E
(2) F and G
(3) A and B
(4) C and F

46. If C is an expert in mridangam and F is not, then which are the three musicians who are experts in tabla but not in either mridangam or ghatam?

(1) E, G and H
(2) E, F and H
(3) C, E and G
(4) C, G and H

Question Numbers (47 to 50): Answer the questions on the basis of the information given below.

The local office of the APP-CAB company evaluates the performance of five cab drivers, Arun, Barun, Chandan, Damodaran, and Eman for their monthly payment based on ratings in five different parameters (P1 to P5) as given below:

P1: timely arrival
P2: behaviour
P3: comfortable ride
P4: driver's familiarity with the route
P5: value for money

Based on feedback from the customers, the office assigns a rating from 1 to 5 in each of these parameters. Each rating is an integer from a low value of 1 to a high value of 5. The final rating of a driver is the average of his ratings in these five parameters. The monthly payment of the drivers has two parts – a fixed payment and final rating-based bonus. If a driver gets a rating of 1 in any of the parameters, he is not eligible to get bonus. To be eligible for bonus a driver also needs to get a rating of five in at least one of the parameters.

The partial information related to the ratings of the drivers in different parameters and the monthly payment structure (in rupees) is given in the table below:

	P1	P2	P3	P4	P5	Fixed payment	Bonus
Arun				4		Rs. 1000	Rs.250 × Final Rating
Barun	3					Rs. 1200	Rs.200 × Final Rating
Chandan			2			Rs. 1400	Rs.100 × Final Rating
Damodaran		3				Rs. 1300	Rs.150 × Final Rating
Eman					2	Rs. 1100	Rs.200 × Final Rating

The following additional facts are known.

1. Arun and Barun have got a rating of 5 in exactly one of the parameters. Chandan has got a rating of 5 in exactly two parameters.
2. None of drivers has got the same rating in three parameters.

47. If Damodaran does not get a bonus, what is the maximum possible value of his final rating?

(1) 3.8
(2) 3.6
(3) 3.4
(4) 3.2

48. If Eman gets a bonus, what is the minimum possible value of his final rating?

(1) 2.8
(2) 3.4
(3) 3.0
(4) 3.2

49. If all five drivers get bonus, what is the minimum possible value of the monthly payment (in rupees) that a driver gets?

(1) 1740
(2) 1750
(3) 1600
(4) 1700

50. If all five drivers get bonus, what is the maximum possible value of the monthly payment (in rupees) that a driver gets?

(1) 1950
(2) 2050
(3) 1900
(4) 1960

Section III: QA

51. An alloy is prepared by mixing three metals A, B and C in the proportion 3 : 4 : 7 by volume. Weights of the same volume of the metals A, B and C are in the ratio 5 : 2 : 6. In 130 kg of the alloy, the weight, in kg, of the metal C is

(1) 84 (2) 70
(3) 48 (4) 96

52. A person spent Rs 50000 to purchase a desktop computer and a laptop computer. He sold the desktop at 20% profit and the laptop at 10% loss. If overall he made a 2% profit then the purchase price, in rupees, of the desktop is

53. If a, b and c are positive integers such that ab = 432, bc = 96 and c < 9, then the smallest possible value of a + b + c is

(1) 46 (2) 56
(3) 49 (4) 59

54. Among 100 students, x_1 have birthdays in January, x_2 have birthdays in February, and so on. If x_0 = max $(x_1, x_2, \ldots, x_{12})$, then the smallest possible value of x_0 is

(1) 12 (2) 10
(3) 8 (4) 9

55. If $\log_4 5 = (\log_4 y)(\log_6 \sqrt{5})$, then y equals

56. Two persons are walking beside a railway track at respective speeds of 2 and 4 km per hour in the same direction. A train came from behind them and crossed them in 90 and 100 seconds, respectively. The time, in seconds, taken by the train to cross an electric post is nearest to

(1) 78 (2) 87
(3) 75 (4) 82

57. A solution, of volume 40 litres, has dye and water in the proportion 2 : 3. Water is added to the solution to change this proportion to 2 : 5. If one-fourths of this diluted solution is taken out, how many litres of dye must be added to the remaining solution to bring the proportion back to 2 : 3?

58. If f(5 + x) = f(5 – x) for every real x, and f(x) = 0 has four distinct real roots, then the sum of these roots is

(1) 40 (2) 10
(3) 20 (4) 0

59. If y is a negative number such that $2^{y^2 \log_3 5} = 5^{\log_2 3}$, then y equals

(1) $\log_2 (1/3)$ (2) $-\log_2 (1/5)$
(3) $-\log_2 (1/3)$ (4) $\log_2 (1/5)$

60. How many distinct positive integer-valued solutions exist to the equation $(x^2 - 7x + 11)^{(x^2 - 13x + 42)} = 1$?

(1) 2 (2) 4
(3) 8 (4) 6

61. How many 3-digit numbers are there, for which the product of their digits is more than 2 but less than 7?

62. Veeru invested Rs 10000 at 5% simple annual interest, and exactly after two years, Joy invested Rs 8000 at 10% simple annual interest. How many years after Veeru's investment, will their balances, i.e., principal plus accumulated interest, be equal?

63. A gentleman decided to treat a few children in the following manner. He gives half of his total stock of toffees and one extra to the first child, and then the half of the remaining stock along with one extra to the second and continues giving away in this fashion. His total stock exhausts after he takes care of 5 children. How many toffees were there in his stock initially?

64. The number of distinct real roots of the equation $\left(x + \frac{1}{x}\right)^2 - 3\left(x + \frac{1}{x}\right) + 2 = 0$ equals

65. On a rectangular metal sheet of area 135 sq. in, a circle is painted such that the circle touches two opposite sides. If the area of the sheet left unpainted is two-thirds of the painted area then the perimeter of the rectangle in inches is

(1) $5\sqrt{\pi}\left(3 + \frac{9}{\pi}\right)$ (2) $3\sqrt{\pi}\left(5 + \frac{12}{\pi}\right)$

(3) $4\sqrt{\pi}\left(3 + \frac{9}{\pi}\right)$ (4) $3\sqrt{\pi}\left(\frac{5}{2} + \frac{6}{\pi}\right)$

66. A straight road connects points A and B. Car 1 travels from A to B and Car 2 travels from B to A, both leaving at the same time. After meeting each other, they take 45 minutes and 20 minutes, respectively, to complete their journeys. If Car 1 travels at the speed of 60 km/hr, then the speed of Car 2, in km/hr, is

(1) 90 (2) 70
(3) 100 (4) 80

67. The area of the region satisfying the inequalities $|x| - y \le 1$, $y \ge 0$ and $y \le 1$ is

68. A train travelled at one-thirds of its usual speed, and hence reached the destination 30 minutes after the scheduled time. On its return journey, the train initially travelled at its usual speed for 5 minutes but then stopped for 4 minutes for an emergency. The percentage by which the train must now increase its usual speed so as to reach the destination at the scheduled time, is nearest to

(1) 58 (2) 67
(3) 50 (4) 61

69. The number of real-valued solutions of the equation $2^x + 2^{-x} = 2 - (x-2)^2$ is

(1) infinite (2) 0
(3) 2 (4) 1

70. A circle is inscribed in a rhombus with diagonals 12 cm and 16 cm. The ratio of the area of circle to the area of rhombus is

(1) $\frac{3\pi}{25}$ (2) $\frac{2\pi}{15}$

(3) $\frac{6\pi}{25}$ (4) $\frac{5\pi}{18}$

71. A solid right circular cone of height 27 cm is cut into two pieces along a plane parallel to its base at a height of 18 cm from the base. If the difference in volume of the two pieces is 225 cc, the volume, in cc, of the original cone is

(1) 264 (2) 256
(3) 232 (4) 243

72. In a group of people, 28% of the members are young while the rest are old. If 65% of the members are literates, and 25% of the literates are young, then the percentage of old people among the illiterates is nearest to

(1) 59 (2) 55
(3) 62 (4) 66

73. If $x = (4096)^{7+4\sqrt{3}}$, then which of the following equals 64?

(1) $\frac{x^{\frac{7}{2}}}{x^{2\sqrt{3}}}$ (2) $\frac{x^7}{x^{2\sqrt{3}}}$

(3) $\frac{x^7}{x^{4\sqrt{3}}}$ (4) $\frac{x^{\frac{7}{2}}}{x^{\frac{4}{\sqrt{3}}}}$

74. The mean of all 4-digit even natural numbers of the form 'aabb', where $a > 0$, is

(1) 4864 (2) 5050
(3) 5544 (4) 4466

75. Leaving home at the same time, Amal reaches office at 10:15 am if he travels at 8 km/hr, and at 9:40 am if he travels at 15 km/hr. Leaving home at 9:10 am, at what speed, in km/hr, must he travel so as to reach office exactly at 10 am?

(1) 14 (2) 12
(3) 13 (4) 11

76. Let A, B and C be three positive integers such that the sum of A and the mean of B and C is 5. In addition, the sum of B and the mean of A and C is 7. Then the sum of A and B is

(1) 6 (2) 7
(3) 5 (4) 4

ANSWERS

1. (3)	**2.** (4)	**3.** (4)	**4.** (2)	**5.** (2)	**6.** (3)	**7.** (3)	**8.** (4)	**9.** (1)	**10.** (3)
11. (3)	**12.** (2)	**13.** (3)	**14.** (4)	**15.** (1)	**16.** (4)	**17.** (3)	**18.** (4)	**19.** (3)	**20.** (3)
21. (3)	**22.** (2)	**23.** (3)	**24.** (3124)	**25.** (1324)	**26.** (1432)	**27.** (340)	**28.** (10)	**29.** (150)	**30.** (325)
31. (4)	**32.** (3)	**33.** (1)	**34.** (4)	**35.** (3)	**36.** (4)	**37.** (1)	**38.** (4)	**39.** (1)	**40.** (4)
41. (4)	**42.** (3)	**43.** (4)	**44.** (3)	**45.** (1)	**46.** (2)	**47.** (2)	**48.** (3)	**49.** (4)	**50.** (4)
51. (1)	**52.** (20000)	**53.** (1)	**54.** (4)	**55.** (36)	**56.** (4)	**57.** (8)	**58.** (3)	**59.** (1)	**60.** (4)
61. (21)	**62.** (12)	**63.** (62)	**64.** (1)	**65.** (2)	**66.** (1)	**67.** (3)	**68.** (2)	**69.** (2)	**70.** (3)
71. (4)	**72.** (4)	**73.** (1)	**74.** (3)	**75.** (2)	**76.** (1)				

EXPLANATIONS

1. The author swears by the rules of grammar. Refer to paragraphs 1 and 5. Hence, option (3), if true, will most probably be supported by the author. Option (1) is wrong because the author is not critiquing the rules of grammar. He wants that the rules of grammar be followed. Option (2) is exactly the opposite of what the author says in the passage. Option (4) is incorrect because is out of scope.
2. The passage talks about the importance of grammar. Not knowing the fundamentals of grammar can impact framing a sentence. Refer to the last paragraph where the author sums up the main idea in the passage. The remaining options are narrow in scope.
3. Nouns and verbs are separate parts of speech. The quoted sentence implies juxtaposing 2 disparate things and the result is something that is coherent and meaningful. Hence, option (4) comes closest to the idea that is there in the quoted sentence.
4. Refer to the first sentence of the last paragraph. The author reiterates that a complete sentence needs a noun and verb. Hence, option (2), if false, will support the author's belief. Option (4), if true, will support the author's belief and hence, it is wrong. Option (3) is out of scope. Option (1) is a statement that is mentioned in the passage. It doesn't support the author's belief.
5. Option (1) can be inferred from the first paragraph. Option (3) can be inferred from the second paragraph. Option (4) can be inferred from the third last paragraph. Option (2) is not stated and so, is the answer.
6. Refer to the second paragraph where the author mentions that torn bolts of textiles had less value than a brand new bolt. Furthermore, the author mentions that textiles could not be exchanged by the foot and the inch. Hence, option (3), if true, would not have been a viable option. Option (2) is out of scope. Option (1) was an accepted mode of payment. Option (4) was again an accepted mode of payment that was considered to be viable.
7. Refer to the last paragraph where the author comments that the modern currency system is changing in front of our eyes. So, option (3) is true. Options (1) and (4) can be inferred from the second, third and fourth paragraphs. Option (2) can be inferred from the sentence, "Furthermore, the dimensions of a bolt of silk held remarkably steady from the third to the tenth century" (third paragraph) and "The values of different textiles were also more stable than the fluctuating values of coins.... (third paragraph).
8. Refer to the last paragraph where the author mentions the similarities between the modern times and the currency usage during the Tang period. The other 3 options are incorrect in the light of the passage. We don't know if grains were the most used currency.
9. Option (1) is not mentioned in the passage and so, it is the answer. Options (3) and (4) are mentioned in the third last paragraph. Option (2) can be inferred from the sentence, "The values of different textiles were also more stable than the fluctuating values of coins. . . ."
10. Option (3) can be inferred from the second and third paragraphs of the passage. Also, refer to the 4th paragraph where the author mentions the factor of immigration. Option (1) is not the reason behind the faster call pulse rate Option (2) is wrong because the elephant seals that have sophisticated structures containing doublets and triplets have migrated to the islands from the southern rookeries. Option (4) is out of scope.
11. This is a fact based question and the answer has been clearly given in the last paragraph. Refer to the last three sentences of the passage for the answer where the transition from simple to complex composition has been mentioned. Option (2) states exactly the opposite of what the passage says. Option (4) is factually incorrect. These days, modern males exhibit more individual diversity. Option (1) is out of scope.
12. In the light of the last sentence of the second paragraph, it can be said that option (2), if true, could have ensured that male northern elephant seal dialects didn't disappear. Option (1) is wrong in the light of the last sentence of the second paragraph. Options (3) and (4) are out of scope.
13. Option (1) can be inferred in the light of the first sentence of the last paragraph. Option (2) can be inferred in the last 4 sentences of the passage. Option (4) can be inferred in the light of the third sentence of the 4th paragraph.
14. Refer to the second sentence of the second last paragraph where the author mentions the common thread that binds forms of anarchism. The other options are out of scope.
15. The passage is on anarchism and its relation to the state. Hence, 'anarchism' and 'state' are two key areas mentioned in the passage. The passage also discusses the individual and his/her rights. Hence, 'individual' and 'freedom' are the other two key areas. Options (2) and (4) can be negated because they don't contain 'anarchism'. Option (3) can be negated because 'betrayal' is out of scope.

16. Option (1) has been discussed in the second paragraph. Option (2) has been discussed in the last paragraph. Option (3) has been discussed in the third last paragraph. Option (4) is not discussed in the passage and so, it is the answer.

17. Note the word 'strutting' in the second paragraph. Strutting refers to an arrogant behaviour. Furthermore, the French Revolution ended with a reign of terror. Hence, option (3) is the most plausible explanation. The other options cannot be inferred in the light of the passage.

18. This is again a fact based question. Refer to the last sentence of the last paragraph for the answer where the relationship between American individualist anarchists and free-market liberals has been mentioned. The remaining options are not stated in the passage.

19. Except sentence 3, the other sentences discuss the role of speech in conditions of slavery. So, 3 is the odd one out.

20. The passage questions the age old belief that intelligence is a single entity and also, the role of heredity in it. Hence, option (3) is the most appropriate summary of the given passage.

21. Except sentence 3, the other sentences talk about the feminists' way of looking at the literary works.

22. The passage provides the details of how Europe adopted a common currency in 2002 and a formal political structure in 2004. Hence, the political and economic heterogeneity have been reduced and this has happened because the world has become multi-polar. Therefore, option (2) is the most appropriate answer.

23. The passage talks about a television series Crime Scene Investigation (CSI) and how it portrayed a wrong impression of so called forensic phonetics being fool proof. Hence, option (3) is the most appropriate. Option (1) is narrow in scope in comparison with option (3). Options (2) and (4) are out of scope.

24. 3 and 1 form a mandatory pair. 3 opens the paragraph and 1 gives the details of the South East Asian countries that have witnessed tension and conflict. 4 sums up the paragraph because it talks about the concerns of the conflicts present in the South East Asian nations and China's rise as a regional military power.

25. 1 opens the paragraph because it gives the readers an idea of what the paragraph is all about. 3 and 2 form a mandatory pair. 3 talks about biological weapons while 2 talks about the dangers that the biological weapons presented. Sentence 4 sums up the paragraph because the sentence talks about the treaties mentioned in the preceding sentence 2. Therefore, 324 can be said to be a mandatory sequence.

26. Sentences 1 and 4 form a mandatory pair. Sentence 1 talks about how significances of San folktales are hard to determine. Sentence 4 says that their meanings can be elicited. Sentence 3 explains the significances of San folktales further. Sentence 2 sums up the paragraph by providing details of the significance of San folktales.

For questions 27 to 30:

Number of people in treatment group = 500

Let us make venn diagram for it

By using statement (a) and (b),

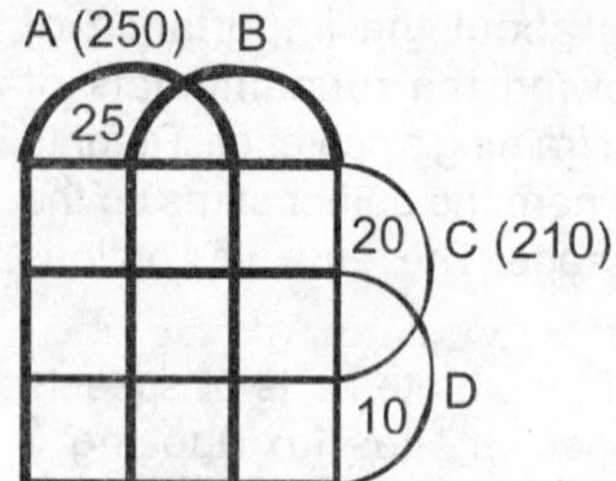

By using statement (c) and (f)

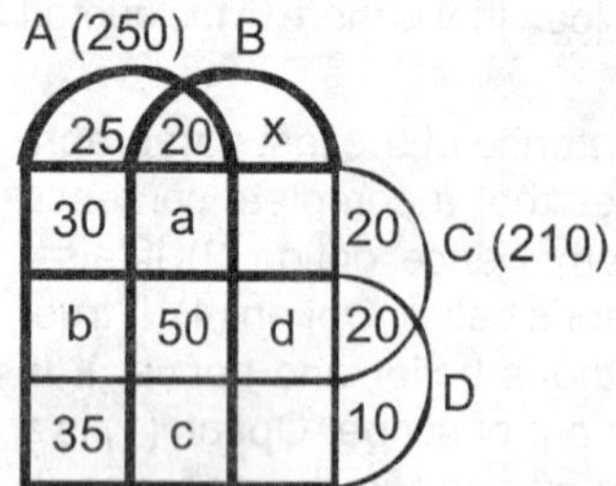

a + b + c + d = 100 [By using statement (d)]

a = 40, b = 20 [By using statement (e)]

So, c + d = 40

25 + x + 20 + 10 = 75 [By using statement (f)]

$\Rightarrow$ x = 20

Combining all statements:

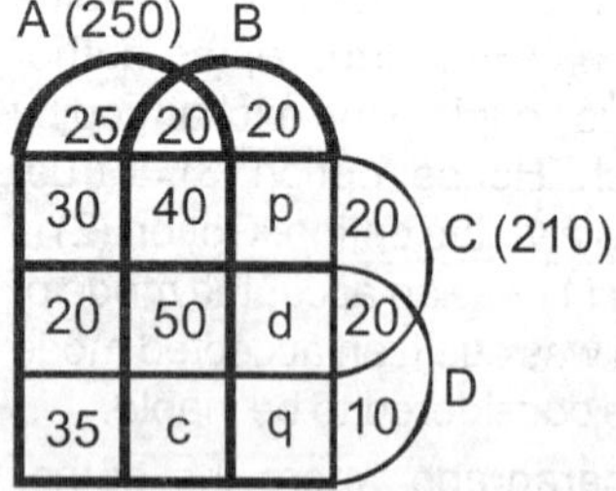

Total value of A = 250

So, c = 30 and d = 10

Total value of c = 210

$\Rightarrow$ p = 20

As total venn add upto = 500

$\Rightarrow$ q = 150.

27. 340 patients were treated with medicine type B.

28. The number of patients who were treated with medicine types B, C and D, but not type A was 10.

29. 150 patients were treated with medicine types B and D only.

30. The number of patients who were treated with medicine type D was 325.

For question 31 to 36:

From the known facts, the student who missed the Mathematics examination did not miss any other examination (statement II.), therefore, lets first find out who that can be by finding out the average of the best three among the four scores in the examinations they appeared for.

Alva: $\frac{75+75+80}{3} = 76.67 \neq 70$

Bithi: $\frac{85+85+90}{3} \neq 55$

Carl: $\frac{100+90+80}{3} = 90$

Deep: $\frac{90+90+80}{3} \neq 100$

Esha: $\frac{85+80+60}{3} \neq 95$

Foni: $\frac{88+83+83}{3} \neq 78$

Clearly, only Carl missed the mathematics examination.

By statement I and III together we know two students missed Hindi examination. By statement III, we know the student who missed the Hindi examination also missed the science examination, and therefore, there scores in two examinations will be same, which is clearly true for either Alva or Deep.

Let's find out who that can be by finding out the average of the best two among the three scores in the examinations they appeared for.

Alva: $\frac{80+70}{2} = 75$

Deep: $\frac{100+80}{2} = 90$

Also, one of the students who missed the Hindi examination did not miss any other examination, and this can also be either Alva or Deep only. The table we get so far looks like:

	English	Hindi	Mathematics	Science	Social Science
Alva	80	75	70	75	60
Bithi	90	80	55	85	85
Carl	75	80	90	100	90
Deep	70	90	100	90	80
Esha	80	85	95	60	55
Foni	83	72	78	88	83

Now, two out of Bithi, Esha and Foni missed English and Social Science examination and one out of Bithi, Esha and Foni missed Science examination.

Observing the scores of Bithi, it can be concluded that Bithi did not miss English examination or any combination of examination that includes English, since all her scores are less than 90 and noway the average will be equal to 90. Therefore, Esha and Foni must have missed the English examination. Similarly, Esha did not miss Social Science examination or any combination of examination that includes Social Science, since all her scores are greater than 55 and in no way the average will be equal to 55. Therefore, Foni and Bithi must have missed the Social Science examination.

So, the updated table will look like:

	English	Hindi	Mathematics	Science	Social Science
Alva	80	75	70	75	60
Bithi	90	80	55	85	85
Carl	75	80	90	100	90
Deep	70	90	100	90	80
Esha	80	85	95	60	55
Foni	83	72	78	88	83

31. Carl did not appear for the Mathematics examination.

32. Esha and Foni did not appear for the English examination.

33. Alva and Deep are the students who did not appear for the Hindi examination can be BEST concluded.

34. Bithi and one out of Alva and Deep

35. Three out of six students missed exactly one examination.

36. For 4 students we can be definite about which examinations they missed.

Questions 37 to 42:

From statement (V),

Institute	Contract
A	3-year, 1-year
B	7-year, 1-year
C	3-year, 1-year
D	4-year, 1-year

From statement (III), vendor Y had contracts in 2010 and 2019. So vendor Y had 1-year, 1-year contracts.

Also from statement (III), vendor W had contracts only in 2012. So vendor W had 1-year, 1-year contracts.

From statement (I), vendor Z had at least one contract in every year. So vendor Z had 7-year, 4-year or 7-year, 3-year contracts.

From statement (II), vendor X had one or more contracts in every year up to 2015, but no contract in any year after that. So vendor X had 3-year, 3-year or 3-year, 4-year contracts.

From the given information:

Case 1: Vendor Z had 7-year, 4-year contracts and vendor X had 3-year, 3-year contracts.

Year	Vendor				Institute				Total contracts
	W	X	Y	Z	A	B	C	D	
2010	×	A	A	B				×	3
2011	×	A	×	B			×		2
2012	D, C	A	×	B		1		1	5
2013	×	C	×	B					2
2014	×	C	×	B					2
2015	×	C	×	B					2
2016	×	×	×	B, D					2
2017	×	×	×	D					1
2018	×	×	×	D					1
2019	×	×	B	D					2
Contract (in year(s))	1, 1	3, 3	1, 1	7, 4	3, 1	7, 1	3, 1	4, 1	

From statement (IV), there were five contracts in 2012. So Case 1 is not possible.

Case 2: Vendor Z had 7-year, 3-year contracts and vendor X had 3-year, 4-year contracts.

Year	Vendor				Institute				Total contracts
	W	X	Y	Z	A	B	C	D	
2010	×	A	B	B				×	3
2011	×	A	×	B			×		2
2012	A, C	A, D	×	B		1		1	5
2013	×	D	×	B					2
2014	×	D	×	B					2
2015	×	D	×	B					2
2016	×	×	×	B					1
2017	×	×	×	C					1
2018	×	×	×	C					1
2019	×	×	D	C					2
Contract (in year(s))	1, 1	3, 4	1, 1	7, 3	3, 1	7, 1	3, 1	4, 1	

37. There were 2 contracts in 2015.

38. D had a contract with Y in 2019.

39. There were three years 2016, 2017 and 2018.

40. There were exactly three contracts in 2010.

41. A and B only

42. A, B, W, and X

Directions for 43 to 46:

From the given information it can be concluded that 6 musicians are experts in table, 5 in Mridangam and 2 in Ghatam. Since, only two are expert in Ghatam according to the statements given and they are D and I clearly, therefore, all others are not experts. Also, one out A and B and one out of C and E is expert in Tabla. Similarly, one out of F and G are expert in Mridangam and one out of C and E are experts in Mridangam.

From the five facts stated following table can be drawn.

	Table (6)	Mridangam (5)	Ghatam (2)
A		Expert	Not
B		Expert	Not
C			Not
D	Expert	Not	Expert
E			Not
F	Expert		Not
G	Expert		Not
H	Expert	Not	Not
I	Not	Not	Expert
J	Not	Expert	Not

43. Musician H is DEFINITELY an expert in table but not in either mridangam or ghatam.

44. Musician J is DEFINITELY an expert in mridangam but not in either tabla or ghatam.

45. Since, exactly two musicians are there who are experts in both table and mridangam but not ghatam, they have to be one out of A and B and one out of F and G. The possible combination left for C and E will have to be one out of (Tabla → Expert, Mridangam → Not expert, Ghatam → Not expert) and (Tabla → Not Expert, Mridangam → Expert, Ghatam → Not expert).

Therefore, pair C and E CANNOT have any musician who is an expert in both table and mridangam but not in Ghatam.

46. If C is an expert in mridangam and F is not, table will look like:

	Table (6)	Mridangam (5)	Ghatam (2)
A		Expert	Not
B		Expert	Not
C	Not	Expert	Not
D	Expert	Not	Expert
E	Expert	Not	Not
F	Expert	Not	Not
G	Expert	Expert	Not
H	Expert	Not	Not
I	Not	Not	Expert
J	Not	Expert	Not

The three musicians who are experts in tabla but not in either mridangam or ghatam will be: E, F and H.

47. If Damodaran does not get a bonus, it implies that Damodaran must have got a rating of 1 in one of the five parameters. Since, none of drivers has got the same rating in three parameters, means they can have same rating in at most two parameters. Therefore, in order to maximize the final rating of Damodaran, we can assume that the rating in five parameters could be 1, 3, 4, 5, and 5.

The average rating = (1 + 3 + 4 + 5 + 5)/5 = 3.6.

48. If Eman gets a bonus, it implies that Eman must have got a rating of 5 in atleast one of the five parameters. Since, none of drivers has got the same rating in three parameters, means they can have same rating in at most two parameters. Therefore, in order to minimize the final rating of Eman, we can assume that the rating in five parameters could be 2, 3, 3, 5, and **2**.

The average rating = (2 + 3 + 3 + 5 + 2)/5 = 3.

49. Since, everybody gets the bonus implies that each one of them must have got a rating of 5 in atleast one of the five parameters. Note that none of drivers has got the same rating in three parameters, means they can have same rating in at most two parameters. Therefore, in order to minimize the monthly payment (in rupees) that a driver gets we need to minimize the ratings in the parameters as per the conditions given.

	P1	P2	P3	P4	P5	Fixed payment	Bonus	Final
Arun	5	2	2	4	3	Rs. 1000	250 × 3.2 = 800	1800
Barun	3	5	2	2	3	Rs. 1200	200 × 3 = 600	1800
Chandan	2	3	2	5	5	Rs. 1400	100 × 3.4 = 340	1740
Damodaran	2	3	2	3	5	Rs. 1300	150 × 3 = 450	1750
Eman	2	3	3	5	2	Rs. 1100	200 × 3 = 600	1700

50. Since, everybody gets the bonus implies that each one of them must have got a rating of 5 in atleast one of the five parameters. Note that none of drivers has got the same rating in three parameters, means they can have same rating in at most two parameters. Therefore, in order to maximize the monthly payment (in rupees) that a driver gets we need to maximize the ratings in the parameters as per the conditions given.

	P1	P2	P3	P4	P5	Fixed payment	Bonus	Final
Arun	5	4	3	**4**	3	Rs. 1000	250 × 3.8 = 950	1950
Barun	**3**	5	3	4	4	Rs. 1200	200 × 3.8 = 760	1960
Chandan	4	4	**2**	5	5	Rs. 1400	100 × 3.6 = 360	1760
Damodaran	5	**3**	4	4	5	Rs. 1300	150 × 4.2 = 630	1930
Eman	4	4	5	5	**2**	Rs. 1100	200 × 4 = 800	1900

51. Ratio of three metals A, B and C in the alloy
= 3 : 4 : 7 by volume
Ratio of the weights of the same volume of the metals A, B and C = 5 : 2 : 6
Combined ratio = 3 × 5 : 4 × 2 : 7 × 6 = 15 : 8 : 42

Hence, the weight of metal C in 130 kg of the alloy = $130 \times \frac{42}{15+8+42} = 84$ kg.

52. Let the purchase price of the desktop be Rs. x.
Then, purchase price of laptop = Rs. (50000 – x)
According to problem,
$1.2x + 0.9 \times (50000 - x) = 50000 \times 1.02$
$\Rightarrow 1.2x + 45000 - 0.9x = 51000$
$x = 6000/0.3$ = Rs. 20,000.

53. Given ab = 432, bc = 96 and c < 9, where a, b and c are positive integers.
The value of c should be 8, 6, 4 or 2.
At c = 8, b = 12 and a = 36
At c = 6, b = 16 and a = 27
At c = 4, b = 24 and a = 18
At c = 2, b = 48 and a = 9
Hence, minimum value of a + b + c = 18 + 24 + 4 = 46.

54. $x_0 = \max(x_1, x_1, x_3, ..., x_{12})$
For smallest possible value of x_0: Among $x_1, x_1, x_3, ..., x_{12}$ eight will be equal to 8 and remaining four will be equal to 9.
So 8 × 8 + 9 × 4 = 100
Hence, smallest possible value of x_0 will be 9.

55. $\log_4 5 = (\log_4 y)(\log_6 \sqrt{5})$

$\Rightarrow \frac{\log_4 5}{\log_4 y} = \frac{1}{2}\log_6 5$

$\Rightarrow \log_y 5 = \log_{6^2} 5 = \log_{36} 5$

$\Rightarrow y = 36.$

56. Let 'x' and 's' be the length and speed of the train respectively.

Then, $\frac{x}{s-2\times\frac{5}{18}} = 90 \Rightarrow x = 90s - 50$ ... (i)

and $\frac{x}{s-4\times\frac{5}{18}} = 100 \Rightarrow x = 100s - \frac{1000}{9}$ ... (ii)

Solving (i) and (ii), we get s = 55/9 m/sec and x = 500 m

Hence, time taken by the train to cross the electric post

$= \frac{x}{s} = \frac{500}{55/9} \approx 81.81$ or 82 sec.

57. In 40 liter solution, dye = 40 × $\frac{2}{2+3}$ = 16 liters

and water = 40 – 16 = 24 liters

Let 'x' liters of water be added in the solution.

Then, $\frac{16}{24+x} = \frac{2}{5} \Rightarrow x = 16$

Let 'y' liters of dye be added in the 3/4 diluted solution.

Then, $\frac{16\times\frac{3}{4}+y}{40\times\frac{3}{4}} = \frac{2}{3} \Rightarrow$ y = 8 liters.

58. Since f(5 + x) = f(5 – x), the function is symmetric about x = 5.

Which means the graph should be the same on the left hand side and the right hand side of x = 5. And it would cut the X-axis on both sides an equal number of times, and at an equal distance from x = 5.

So, if one root is 5 + a, the corresponding root on the other side will be 5 – a.

Adding all such roots, we get sum of roots = 5 × 4 = 20.

Hence, the sum of roots is 20.

59. $2^{y^2 \log_3 5} = 5^{\log_2 3}$

$\Rightarrow y^2\log_3 5 \log 2 = \log_2 3 \log 5$

$\Rightarrow y^2 = \frac{\log_2 3\times\log 5}{\log 2\times\log_3 5}$

$\Rightarrow y^2 = \left(\frac{\log 3}{\log 2}\right)^2$

$\Rightarrow y = \pm\frac{\log 3}{\log 2}$

Since y < 0, therefore, $y = -\frac{\log 3}{\log 2} = \log_2\left(\frac{1}{3}\right)$

60. Given: $(x^2 - 7x + 11)^{(x^2 - 13x + 42)} = 1$

Case 1:

$x^2 - 7x + 11 = 1$

$\Rightarrow x^2 - 7x + 10 = 0$

$\Rightarrow x^2 - 5x - 2x + 10 = 0$

$\Rightarrow (x - 5)(x - 2) = 0$

$\therefore$ x = 5 and x = 2

Case 2:

$x^2 - 13x + 42 = 0$

$\Rightarrow x^2 - 7x - 6x + 42 = 0$

$\Rightarrow (x - 7)(x - 6) = 0$

$\therefore$ x = 7 and x = 6

Case 3:

$x^2 - 7x + 11 = -1$ and the power is even.

$\Rightarrow x^2 - 7x + 11 = -1$

$\Rightarrow x^2 - 7x + 12 = 0$

$\Rightarrow x^2 - 3x - 4x + 12 = 0$

$\Rightarrow (x - 3)(x - 4) = 0$

$\therefore$ x = 3 and x = 4

At x = 3 and x = 4, $x^2 - 13 + 42$ = even.

Hence, there are six possible values for 'x'.

61. Given that : 2 < Product of digits < 7

Digits	Number of ways
1, 1, 3	3
1, 1, 4	3
1, 1, 5	3
1, 1, 6	3
1, 2, 2	3
1, 2, 3	6

Hence, total number of 3-digit numbers = 3 + 3 + 3 + 3 + 3 + 6 = 21.

62. Let the required number of years be 'n'.

Then, 10000 + 10000 × 0.05 × n = 8000 + 8000 × 0.1 × (n – 2)

$\Rightarrow$ 10000 + 500n = 8000 + 800n – 1600

$\Rightarrow$ n = 12.

63. Let 'n' be the initial number of toffees.

Number of toffees received by 1st child = n/2 + 1

Remaining toffees = n/2 – 1

Number of toffees received by 2nd child = n/4 – 1/2 + 1

Remaining toffees = n/4 – 1/2 – 1

Number of toffees received by 3rd child = n/8 – 1/4 – 1/2 + 1

Remaining toffees = n/8 – 1/4 – 1/2 – 1

Number of toffees received by 4th child = n/16 – 1/8 – 1/4 – 1/2 + 1

Remaining toffees = n/16 – 1/8 – 1/4 – 1/2 – 1

Number of toffees received by 5th child = n/32 – 1/16 – 1/8 – 1/4 – 1/2 + 1

Remaining toffees = n/32 – 1/16 – 1/8 – 1/4 – 1/2 – 1

According to problem,

n/32 – 1/16 – 1/8 – 1/4 – 1/2 – 1 = 0

⇒ n/32 = 31/16

⇒ n = 62.

64. $$\left(x+\frac{1}{x}\right)^2 - 3\left(x+\frac{1}{x}\right)+2=0$$

Let $x+\frac{1}{x}=y$

Then, $y^2-3y+2=0$

$\Rightarrow (y-1)(y-2)=0$

$\Rightarrow y = 1$ or $y = 2$

$\therefore x+\frac{1}{x}=1$

$\Rightarrow x^2-x+1=0$

$\Rightarrow x=\frac{1\pm\sqrt{1-4}}{2}=\frac{1\pm\sqrt{3}i}{2}$ (Imaginary roots)

and $x+\frac{1}{x}=2 \Rightarrow x^2-2x+1=0$

$\Rightarrow (x-1)^2=0 \Rightarrow x = 1, 1$

Hence, number of distinct real roots is 1.

65. 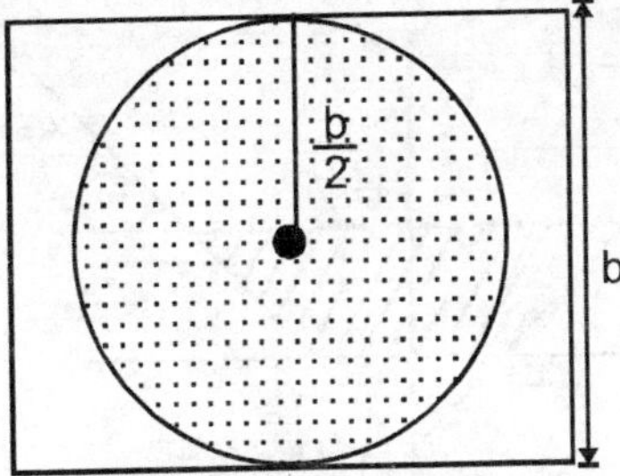

Area of the rectangle = 135 sq. in.

Let 'b' be the width of the rectangle.

Then, radius of the circle = b/2

Let A be area of the circle.

Then, according to problem,

$A+\frac{2}{3}A=135 \Rightarrow A = 81$ sq.in.

Therefore, $\pi(b/2)^2=81 \Rightarrow b=\frac{18}{\sqrt{\pi}}$ inches

Therefore, length of the rectangle

$=\frac{135}{18/\sqrt{\pi}}=\frac{15\sqrt{\pi}}{2}$ inches

Hence, the perimeter of the rectangle

$=2\left(\frac{15\sqrt{\pi}}{2}+\frac{18}{\sqrt{\pi}}\right)=3\sqrt{\pi}\left(5+\frac{12}{\pi}\right)$ inches.

66. 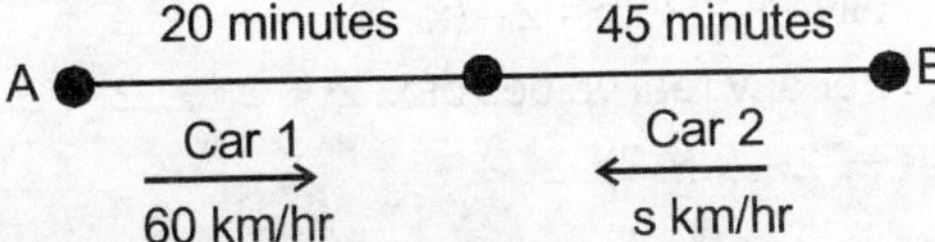

Let S be the speed of Car2.

Then, using the formula,

$\frac{S1}{S2}=\sqrt{\frac{t2}{t1}}$

$\Rightarrow \frac{60}{s}=\sqrt{\frac{20}{45}} \Rightarrow s = 90$ km/hr.

67. $|x| - y \le 1$, $y \ge 0$ and $y \le 1$

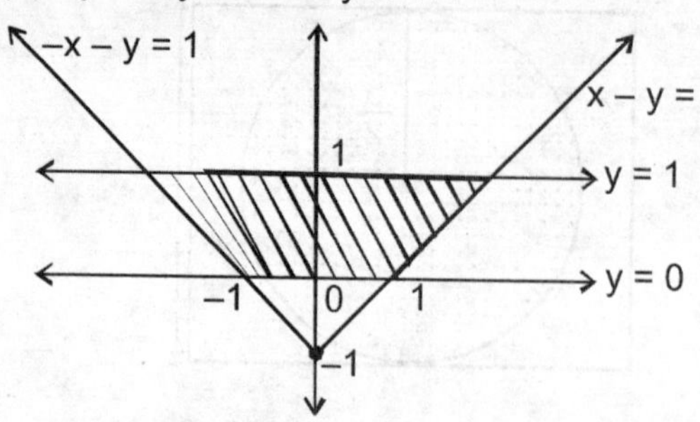

$$\text{Area} = \frac{1}{2} + \frac{1}{2} + 2 = 3$$

68. Let 's' km/hr be the usual speed of the train and 'd' km be the distance.

Then, $d/s = t$

and $\dfrac{d}{\frac{1}{3}s} = t + \dfrac{30}{60} \Rightarrow 3t = t + \dfrac{1}{2}$

$\Rightarrow t = 1/4$ hour = 15 minutes

Therefore, usual speed, $s = d/15$

Distance travelled in 5 minutes = $d/3$

Remaining distance = $2d/3$ and remaining time = 15 – 5 – 4 = 6 minutes

Therefore, new speed, $s' = 2d/18 = d/9$

Hence, required percentage increase

$$= \frac{d/9 - d/15}{d/15} \times 100 \approx 67\%.$$

69. Given: $2^x + 2^{-x} = 2 - (x-2)^2$

For any real values of x, $2^x + 2^{-x} \ge 2$

$\Rightarrow 2 - (x-2)^2 \ge 2$

$\Rightarrow 0 \ge (x-2)^2$

Which is not possible for any real value of x.

Hence, no solution is there for any value of x.

70.

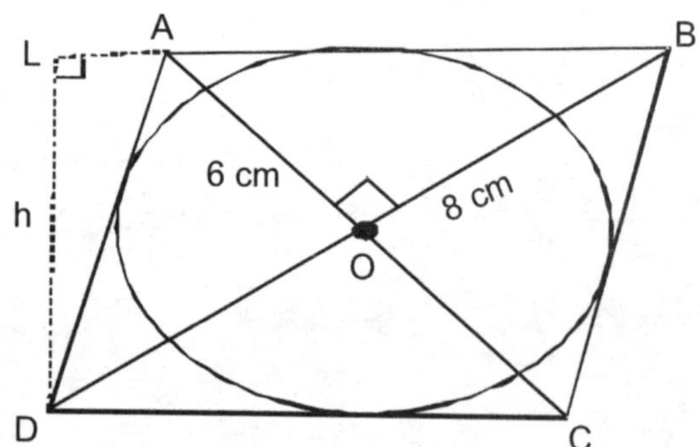

Side of rhombus = $\sqrt{8^2 + 6^2}$ = 10 cm

Let 'h' be the height of the rhombus.

Then, Area of rhombus = $\dfrac{1}{2} \times 12 \times 16$

Therefore, $h \times 10 = \dfrac{1}{2} \times 12 \times 16$

$\Rightarrow h = \dfrac{48}{5}$ cm

Radius of inscribed circle = h/2 = 24/5 cm

$$\text{Hence, required ratio of areas} = \frac{\pi\left(\frac{24}{5}\right)^2}{\frac{1}{2} \times 12 \times 16} = \frac{6\pi}{25}.$$

71.

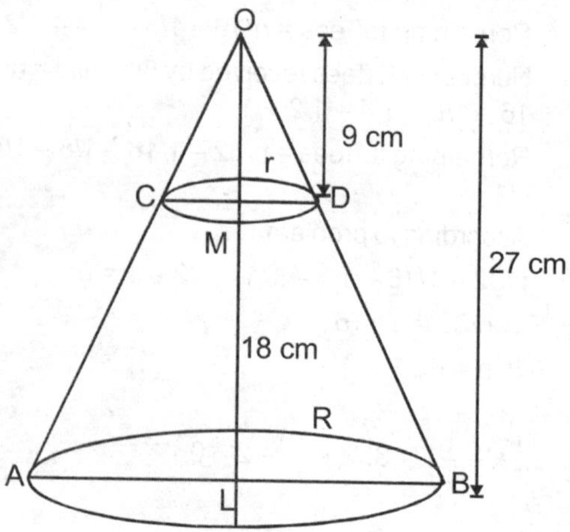

Triangles OMD and OLB are similar.

Therefore, $\dfrac{OM}{OL} = \dfrac{MD}{LB}$

$\Rightarrow \dfrac{9}{27} = \dfrac{r}{R} \Rightarrow R = 3r$

Difference in volume of the two pieces = 225

$$\Rightarrow \left(\frac{1}{3}\pi R^2 \times 27 - \frac{1}{3}\pi r^2 \times 9\right) - \frac{1}{3}\pi r^2 \times 9 = 225$$

$$\Rightarrow \frac{1}{3}\pi (3r)^2 \times 27 - 2 \times \frac{1}{3}\pi r^2 \times 9 = 225$$

$$\Rightarrow r^2 = \frac{3}{\pi}$$

Hence, volume of original cone

$$= \frac{1}{3}\pi R^2 \times 27$$

$$= \frac{1}{3}\pi (3r)^2 \times 27$$

$$= \frac{1}{3}\pi \times 9 \times \frac{3}{\pi} \times 27$$

= 243 cubic cm.

72. Let 100x be the total number of people in the group.

Then, young members = 28x and old members = 72x

Number of literates members = 65x

Number of literate young members = 0.25 × 65x = 16.25x

Number of literate old members = 0.75 × 65x = 48.75x

Hence, illiterate old members = 72x – 48.75x = 23.25x

Hence, percentage of illiterate old members in illiterate members = $\frac{23.25}{35} \times 100 \approx 66\%$.

73. $x = (4096)^{7+4\sqrt{3}} = (64^2)^{7+4\sqrt{3}} = (64)^{14+8\sqrt{3}}$

From option (1), $\frac{x^{\frac{7}{2}}}{x^{2\sqrt{3}}} = \frac{\left(64^{14+8\sqrt{3}}\right)^{\frac{7}{2}}}{\left(64^{14+8\sqrt{3}}\right)^{2\sqrt{3}}} = 64.$

74. aabb is an even natural number where $1 \le a \le 9$ and b = 0, 2, 4, 6, 8.

Total numbers possible are = 9 × 5 = 45

$$\frac{(1100 + 1122 + 1144 + 1166 + 1188) + (2200 + 2222 + ..+2288) + ... +(9900 + 9922 + 9944 +...+9988)}{45}$$

$$\Rightarrow \frac{1100(1+...+ 9) + 11[102 + 202 +...+ 902] +11[104 +...904]+...+11[108+...+908]}{45}$$

$$\Rightarrow \frac{\frac{1100 \times 9 \times 10}{2} + 11 \times (420 + 3620) \times \frac{9}{2}}{45}$$

= 1100 + 4444 = 5544.

75. Let 'd' be the distance between home and office.

Then, $\frac{d}{8} - \frac{d}{15} = \frac{35}{60}$

$\Rightarrow \frac{7d}{8 \times 15} = \frac{35}{60}$

$\Rightarrow$ d = 10 km

Let 's' be the required speed.

Then, 10/s = 50/60 $\Rightarrow$ s = 12 km/hr.

76. Given A, B and C are three positive integers.

A + (B + C)/2 = 5 $\Rightarrow$ 2A + B + C = 10 … (i)

B + (A + C)/2 = 7 $\Rightarrow$ A + 2B + C = 14 … (ii)

Subtracting (i) from (ii),

B – A = 4 $\Rightarrow$ B = 4 + A … (iii)

From (i), (ii) and (iii), A = 1.

If A > 1, then the conditions (i) and (ii) cannot hold.

Therefore, B = 4 + 1 = 5 and C = 3

Hence, A + B = 1 + 5 = 6.

CAT 2020 SOLVED PAPER (SLOT-2)

Section I: VARC

Question Numbers (1 to 5): The passage below is accompanied by a set of questions. Choose the best answer to each question.

In a low-carbon world, renewable energy technologies are hot business. For investors looking to redirect funds, wind turbines and solar panels, among other technologies, seem a straightforward choice. But renewables need to be further scrutinized before being championed as forging a path toward a low-carbon future. Both the direct and indirect impacts of renewable energy must be examined to ensure that a climate-smart future does not intensify social and environmental harm. As renewable energy production requires land, water, and labor, among other inputs, it imposes costs on people and the environment. Hydropower projects, for instance, have led to community dispossession and exclusion . . . Renewable energy supply chains are also intertwined with mining, and their technologies contribute to growing levels of electronic waste . . . Furthermore, although renewable energy can be produced and distributed through small-scale, local systems, such an approach might not generate the high returns on investment needed to attract capital.

Although an emerging sector, renewables are enmeshed in long-standing resource extraction through their dependence on minerals and metals . . . Scholars document the negative consequences of mining . . . even for mining operations that commit to socially responsible practices[:] "many of the world's largest reservoirs of minerals like cobalt, copper, lithium, [and] rare earth minerals"—the ones needed for renewable technologies—"are found in fragile states and under communities of marginalized peoples in Africa, Asia, and Latin America." Since the demand for metals and minerals will increase substantially in a renewable-powered future . . . this intensification could exacerbate the existing consequences of extractive activities.

Among the connections between climate change and waste, O'Neill . . . highlights that "devices developed to reduce our carbon footprint, such as lithium batteries for hybrid and electric cars or solar panels [,] become potentially dangerous electronic waste at the end of their productive life." The disposal of toxic waste has long perpetuated social injustice through the flows of waste to the Global South and to marginalized communities in the Global North . . .

While renewable energy is a more recent addition to financial portfolios, investments in the sector must be considered in light of our understanding of capital accumulation. As agricultural finance reveals, the concentration of control of corporate activity facilitates profit generation. For some climate activists, the promise of renewables rests on their ability not only to reduce emissions but also to provide distributed, democratized access to energy . . . But Burke and Stephens . . . caution that "renewable energy systems offer a possibility but not a certainty for more democratic energy futures." Small-scale, distributed forms of energy are only highly profitable to institutional investors if control is consolidated somewhere in the financial chain. Renewable energy can be produced at the household or neighborhood level. However, such small-scale, localized production is unlikely to generate high returns for investors. For financial growth to be sustained and expanded by the renewable sector, production and trade in renewable energy technologies will need to be highly concentrated, and large asset management firms will likely drive those developments.

1. Which one of the following statements best captures the main argument of the last paragraph of the passage?

(1) Renewable energy produced at the household or neighbourhood level is more efficient than mass-produced forms of energy.

(2) The development of the renewable energy sector is a double-edged sword.

(3) Renewable energy systems are not democratic unless they are corporate-controlled.

(4) Most forms of renewable energy are not profitable investments for institutional investors.

2. All of the following statements, if true, could be seen as supporting the arguments in the passage, EXCEPT:

(1) Marginalised people in Africa, Asia and Latin America have often been the main sufferers of corporate mineral extraction projects.

(2) The example of agricultural finance helps us to see how to concentrate corporate activity in the renewable energy sector.

(3) The possible negative impacts of renewable energy need to be studied before it can be offered as a financial investment opportunity.

(4) One reason for the perpetuation of social injustice lies in the problem of the disposal of toxic waste.

3. Which one of the following statements, if false, could be seen as best supporting the arguments in the passage?

(1) Renewable energy systems are as expensive as non-renewable energy systems.

(2) Renewable energy systems have little or no environmental impact.

(3) Renewable energy systems are not as profitable as non-renewable energy systems.

(4) The production and distribution of renewable energy through small-scale, local systems is not economically sustainable.

4. Based on the passage, we can infer that the author would be most supportive of which one of the following practices?

(1) Encouragement for the development of more environment-friendly carbon-based fuels.

(2) The study of the coexistence of marginalised people with their environments.

(3) The localised, small-scale development of renewable energy systems.

(4) More stringent global policies and regulations to ensure a more just system of toxic waste disposal.

5. Which one of the following statements, if true, could be an accurate inference from the first paragraph of the passage?

(1) The author has reservations about the consequences of non-renewable energy systems.

(2) The author's only reservation is about the profitability of renewable energy systems.

(3) The author has reservations about the consequences of renewable energy systems.

(4) The author does not think renewable energy systems can be as efficient as non-renewable energy systems.

Question Numbers (6 to 10): The passage below is accompanied by a set of questions. Choose the best answer to each question.

The claims advanced here may be condensed into two assertions: [first, that visual] culture is what images, acts of seeing, and attendant intellectual, emotional, and perceptual sensibilities do to build, maintain, or transform the worlds in which people live. [And second, that the] study of visual culture is the analysis and interpretation of images and the ways of seeing (or gazes) that configure the agents, practices, conceptualities, and institutions that put images to work. . . .

Accordingly, the study of visual culture should be characterized by several concerns. First, scholars of visual culture need to examine any and all imagery – high and low, art and nonart. . . . They must not restrict themselves to objects of a particular beauty or aesthetic value. Indeed, any kind of imagery may be found to offer up evidence of the visual construction of reality. . . .

Second, the study of visual culture must scrutinize visual practice as much as images themselves, asking what images do when they are put to use. If scholars engaged in this enterprise inquire what makes an image beautiful or why this image or that constitutes a masterpiece or a work of genius, they should do so with the purpose of investigating an artist's or a work's contribution to the experience of beauty, taste, value, or genius. No amount of social analysis can account fully for the existence of Michelangelo or Leonardo. They were unique creators of images that changed the way their contemporaries thought and felt and have continued to shape the history of art, artists, museums, feeling, and aesthetic value. But study of the critical, artistic, and popular reception of works by such artists as Michelangelo and Leonardo can shed important light on the meaning of these artists and their works for many different people. And the history of meaning-making has a great deal to do with how scholars as well as lay audiences today understand these artists and their achievements.

Third, scholars studying visual culture might properly focus their interpretative work on lifeworlds by examining images, practices, visual technologies, taste, and artistic style as constitutive of social relations. The task is to understand how artifacts contribute to the construction of a world. . . . Important methodological implications follow: ethnography and reception studies become productive forms of gathering information, since these move beyond the image as a closed and fixed meaning-event. . . .

Fourth, scholars may learn a great deal when they scrutinize the constituents of vision, that is, the structures of perception as a physiological process as well as the epistemological frameworks informing a system of visual representation. Vision is a socially and a biologically constructed operation, depending on the design of the human body and how it engages the interpretive devices developed by a culture in order to see intelligibly. . . . Seeing . . . operates on the foundation of covenants with images that establish the conditions for meaningful visual experience.

Finally, the scholar of visual culture seeks to regard images as evidence for explanation, not as epiphenomena.

6. Which set of keywords below most closely captures the arguments of the passage?

(1) Scholars, Social Analysis, Michelangelo and Leonardo, Interpretive Devices.

(2) Imagery, Visual Practices, Lifeworlds, Structures of Perception.

(3) Visual Construction of Reality, Work of Genius, Ethnography, Epiphenomena.

(4) Visual Culture, Aesthetic Value, Lay Audience, Visual Experience.

7. All of the following statements may be considered valid inferences from the passage, EXCEPT:

(1) artifacts are meaningful precisely because they help to construct the meanings of the world for us.

(2) visual culture is not just about how we see, but also about how our visual practices can impact and change the world.

(3) understanding the structures of perception is an important part of understanding how visual cultures work.

(4) studying visual culture requires institutional structures without which the structures of perception cannot be analysed.

8. Which one of the following best describes the word "epiphenomena" in the last sentence of the passage?

(1) Overarching collections of images.

(2) Phenomena amenable to analysis.

(3) Visual phenomena of epic proportions.

(4) Phenomena supplemental to the evidence.

9. "No amount of social analysis can account fully for the existence of Michelangelo or Leonardo." In light of the passage, which one of the following interpretations of this sentence is the most accurate?

(1) Michelangelo or Leonardo cannot be subjected to social analysis because of their genius.

(2) No analyses exist of Michelangelo's or Leonardo's social accounts.

(3) Social analytical accounts of people like Michelangelo or Leonardo cannot explain their genius.

(4) Socially existing beings cannot be analysed, unlike the art of Michelangelo or Leonardo which can.

10. "Seeing . . . operates on the foundation of covenants with images that establish the conditions for meaningful visual experience." In light of the passage, which one of the following statements best conveys the meaning of this sentence?

(1) Sight as a meaningful visual experience is possible when there is a foundational condition established in images of covenants.

(2) The way we experience sight is through images operated on by meaningful covenants.

(3) Images are meaningful visual experiences when they have a foundation of covenants seeing them.

(4) Sight becomes a meaningful visual experience because of covenants of meaningfulness that we establish with the images we see.

Question Numbers (11 to 14): The passage below is accompanied by a set of questions. Choose the best answer to each question.

Aggression is any behavior that is directed toward injuring, harming, or inflicting pain on another living being or group of beings. Generally, the victim(s) of aggression must wish to avoid such behavior in order for it to be considered true aggression. Aggression is also categorized according to its ultimate intent. Hostile aggression is an aggressive act that results from anger, and is intended to inflict pain or injury because of that anger. Instrumental aggression is an aggressive act that is regarded as a means to an end other than pain or injury. For example, an enemy combatant may be subjected to torture in order to extract useful intelligence, though those inflicting the torture may have no real feelings of anger or animosity toward their subject. The concept of aggression is very broad, and includes many categories of behavior (e.g., verbal aggression, street crime, child abuse, spouse abuse, group conflict, war, etc.). A number of theories and models of aggression have arisen to explain these diverse forms of behavior, and these theories/models tend to be categorized according to their specific focus. The most common system of categorization groups the various approaches to aggression into three separate areas, based upon the three key variables that are present whenever any aggressive act or set of acts is committed. The first variable is the aggressor him/herself. The second is the social situation or circumstance in which the aggressive act(s) occur. The third variable is the target or victim of aggression.

Regarding theories and research on the aggressor, the fundamental focus is on the factors that lead an individual (or group) to commit aggressive acts. At the most basic level, some argue that aggressive urges and actions are the result of inborn, biological factors. Sigmund Freud (1930) proposed that all individuals are born with a death instinct that predisposes us to a variety of aggressive behaviors, including suicide (self directed aggression) and mental illness (possibly due to an unhealthy or unnatural suppression of aggressive urges). Other influential perspectives supporting a biological basis for aggression conclude that humans evolved with an abnormally low neural inhibition of aggressive impulses (in comparison to other species), and that humans possess a powerful instinct for property accumulation and territorialism. It is proposed that this instinct accounts for hostile behaviors ranging from minor street crime to world wars. Hormonal factors also appear to play a significant role in fostering aggressive tendencies. For example, the hormone testosterone has been shown to increase aggressive behaviors when injected into animals. Men and women convicted of violent crimes also possess significantly higher levels of testosterone than men and women convicted of non violent crimes. Numerous studies comparing different age groups, racial/ethnic groups, and cultures also indicate that men, overall, are more likely to engage in a variety of aggressive behaviors (e.g., sexual assault, aggravated assault, etc.) than women. One explanation for higher levels of aggression in men is based on the assumption that, on average, men have higher levels of testosterone than women.

11. All of the following statements can be seen as logically implied by the arguments of the passage EXCEPT:

(1) if the alleged aggressive act is not sought to be avoided, it cannot really be considered aggression.

(2) the Freudian theory of suicide as self-inflicted aggression implies that an aggressive act need not be sought to be avoided in order for it to be considered aggression.

(3) a common theory of aggression is that it is the result of an abnormally low neural regulation of testosterone.

(4) Freud's theory of aggression proposes that aggression results from the suppression of aggressive urges.

12. The author identifies three essential factors according to which theories of aggression are most commonly categorised. Which of the following options is closest to the factors identified by the author?

(1) Extreme – Moderate – Mild.

(2) Psychologically – Sociologically – Medically.

(3) Hostile – Instrumental – Hormonal.

(4) Aggressor – Circumstances of aggression – Victim.

13. "[A]n enemy combatant may be subjected to torture in order to extract useful intelligence, though those inflicting the torture may have no real feelings of anger or animosity toward their subject." Which one of the following best explicates the larger point being made by the author here?

(1) Information revealed by subjecting an enemy combatant to torture is not always reliable because of the animosity involved.

(2) The use of torture to extract information is most effective when the torturer is not emotionally involved in the torture.

(3) In certain kinds of aggression, inflicting pain is not the objective, and is no more than a utilitarian means to achieve another end.

(4) When an enemy combatant refuses to reveal information, the use of torture can sometimes involve real feelings of hostility.

14. The author discusses all of the following arguments in the passage EXCEPT that:

(1) aggression in most societies is kept under control through moderating the death instinct identified by Freud.

(2) the nature of aggression can vary depending on several factors, including intent.

(3) men in general are believed to be more hormonally driven to exhibit violence than women.

(4) several studies indicate that aggression may have roots in the biological condition of humanity.

Question Numbers (15 to 18): The passage below is accompanied by a set of questions. Choose the best answer to each question.

174 incidents of piracy were reported to the International Maritime Bureau last year, with Somali pirates responsible for only three. The rest ranged from the discreet theft of coils of rope in the Yellow Sea to the notoriously ferocious Nigerian gunmen attacking and hijacking oil tankers in the Gulf of Guinea, as well as armed robbery off Singapore and the Venezuelan coast and kidnapping in the Sundarbans in the Bay of Bengal. For [Dr. Peter] Lehr, an expert on modern-day piracy, the phenomenon's history should be a source of instruction rather than entertainment, piracy past offering lessons for piracy present. . . .

But . . . where does piracy begin or end? According to St Augustine, a corsair captain once told Alexander the Great that in the forceful acquisition of power and wealth at sea, the difference between an emperor and a pirate was simply one of scale. By this logic, European empire-builders were the most successful pirates of all time. A more eclectic history might have included the conquistadors, Vasco da Gama and the East India Company. But Lehr sticks to the disorganised small fry, making comparisons with the renegades of today possible.

The main motive for piracy has always been a combination of need and greed. Why toil away as a starving peasant in the 16th century when a successful pirate made up to £4,000 on each raid? Anyone could turn to freebooting if the rewards were worth the risk . . . .

Increased globalisation has done more to encourage piracy than suppress it. European colonialism weakened delicate balances of power, leading to an influx of opportunists on the high seas. A rise in global shipping has meant rich pickings for freebooters. Lehr writes: "It quickly becomes clear that in those parts of the world that have not profited from globalisation and modernisation, and where abject poverty and the daily struggle for survival are still a reality, the root causes of piracy are still the same as they were a couple of hundred years ago." . . .

Modern pirate prevention has failed. After the French yacht Le Gonant was ransomed for $2 million in 2008, opportunists from all over Somalia flocked to the coast for a piece of the action. . . . A consistent rule, even today, is there are never enough warships to patrol pirate-infested waters. Such ships are costly and only solve the problem temporarily; Somali piracy is bound to return as soon as the warships are withdrawn. Robot shipping, eliminating hostages, has been proposed as a possible solution; but as Lehr points out, this will only make pirates switch their targets to smaller carriers unable to afford the technology.

His advice isn't new. Proposals to end illegal fishing are often advanced but they are difficult to enforce. Investment in local welfare put a halt to Malaysian piracy in the 1970s, but was dependent on money somehow filtering through a corrupt bureaucracy to the poor on the periphery. Diplomatic initiatives against piracy are plagued by mutual distrust: the Russians execute pirates, while the EU and US are reluctant to capture them for fear they'll claim asylum.

15. "Why toil away as a starving peasant in the 16th century when a successful pirate made up to £4,000 on each raid?" In this sentence, the author's tone can best be described as being:

(1) ironic, about the reasons why so many took to piracy in medieval times.

(2) analytical, to explain the contrasts between peasant and pirate life in medieval England.

(3) indignant, at the scale of wealth successful pirates could amass in medieval times.

(4) facetious, about the hardships of peasant life in medieval England.

16. We can deduce that the author believes that piracy can best be controlled in the long run:

(1) if we eliminate poverty and income disparities in affected regions.

(2) through lucrative welfare schemes to improve the lives of people in affected regions.

(3) through international cooperation in enforcing stringent deterrents.

(4) through the extensive deployment of technology to track ships and cargo.

17. "A more eclectic history might have included the conquistadors, Vasco da Gama and the East India Company. But Lehr sticks to the disorganised small fry . . ." From this statement we can infer that the author believes that:

(1) the disorganised piracy of today is no match for the organised piracy of the past.

(2) Vasco da Gama and the East India Company laid the ground for modern piracy.

(3) colonialism should be considered an organised form of piracy.

(4) Lehr does not assign adequate blame to empire builders for their past deeds.

18. The author ascribes the rise in piracy today to all of the following factors EXCEPT:

(1) the high rewards via ransoms for successful piracy attempts.

(2) the growth in international shipping with globalisation.

(3) decreased surveillance of the high seas.

(4) colonialism's disruption of historic ties among countries.

19. Five jumbled up sentences, related to a topic, are given below. Four of them can be put together to form a coherent paragraph. Identify the odd one out and key in the number of the sentence as your answer:

(1) You can observe the truth of this in every e-business model ever constructed: monopolise and protect data.

(2) Economists and technologists believe that a new kind of capitalism is being created - different from industrial capitalism as was merchant capitalism.

(3) In 1962, Kenneth Arrow, the guru of mainstream economics, said that in a free market economy the purpose of inventing things is to create intellectual property rights.

(4) There is, alongside the world of monopolised information and surveillance, a different dynamic growing up: information as a social good, incapable of being owned or exploited or priced.

(5) Yet information is abundant. Information goods are freely replicable. Once a thing is made, it can be copied and pasted infinitely.

20. The passage given below is followed by four alternate summaries. Choose the option that best captures the essence of the passage.

All humans make decisions based on one or a combination of two factors. This is either intuition or information. Decisions made through intuition are usually fast, people don't even think about the problem. It is quite philosophical, meaning that someone who made a decision based on intuition will have difficulty explaining the reasoning behind it. The decision-maker would often utilize her senses in drawing conclusions, which again is based on some experience in the field of study. On the other side of the spectrum, we have decisions made based on information. These decisions are rational — it is based on facts and figures, which unfortunately also means that it can be quite slow. The decision-maker would frequently use reports, analyses, and indicators to form her conclusion. This methodology results in accurate, quantifiable decisions, meaning that a person can clearly explain the rationale behind it.

(1) It is better to make decisions based on information because it is more accurate, and the rationale behind it can be explained.
(2) Decisions based on intuition and information result in differential speed and ability to provide a rationale.
(3) We make decisions based on intuition or information on the basis of the time available.
(4) While decisions based on intuition can be made fast, the reasons that led to these cannot be spelt out.

21. The four sentences (labelled 1, 2, 3, 4) below, when properly sequenced would yield a coherent paragraph. Decide on the proper sequencing of the order of the sentences and key in the sequence of the four numbers as your answer:

(1) While you might think that you see or are aware of all the changes that happen in your immediate environment, there is simply too much information for your brain to fully process everything.
(2) Psychologists use the term 'change blindness' to describe this tendency of people to be blind to changes though they are in the immediate environment.
(3) It cannot be aware of every single thing that happens in the world around you.
(4) Sometimes big shifts happen in front of your eyes and you are not at all aware of these changes.

22. The four sentences (labelled 1, 2, 3, 4) below, when properly sequenced would yield a coherent paragraph. Decide on the proper sequencing of the order of the sentences and key in the sequence of the four numbers as your answer:

(1) But the attention of the layman, not surprisingly, has been captured by the atom bomb, although there is at least a chance that it may never be used again.
(2) Of all the changes introduced by man into the household of nature, [controlled] large-scale nuclear fission is undoubtedly the most dangerous and most profound.
(3) The danger to humanity created by the so-called peaceful uses of atomic energy may, however, be much greater.
(4) The resultant ionizing radiation has become the most serious agent of pollution of the environment and the greatest threat to man's survival on earth.

23. Five jumbled up sentences, related to a topic, are given below. Four of them can be put together to form a coherent paragraph. Identify the odd one out and key in the number of the sentence as your answer:

(1) The victim's trauma after assault rarely gets the attention that we lavish on the moment of damage that divided the survivor from a less encumbered past.
(2) One thing we often do with narratives of sexual assault is sort their respective parties into different temporalities: it seems we are interested in perpetrators' futures and victims' pasts.
(3) One result is that we don't have much of a vocabulary for what happens in a victim's life after the painful past has been excavated, even when our shared language gestures toward the future, as the term "survivor" does.
(4) Even the most charitable questions asked about the victims seem to focus on the past, in pursuit of understanding or of corroboration of painful details.
(5) As more and more stories of sexual assault have been made public in the last two years, the genre of their telling has exploded --- crimes have a tendency to become not just stories but genres.

24. The passage given below is followed by four alternate summaries. Choose the option that best captures the essence of the passage.

The rural-urban continuum and the heterogeneity of urban settings pose an obvious challenge to identifying urban areas and measuring urbanization rates in a consistent way within and across countries. An objective methodology for distinguishing between urban and rural areas that is based on one or two metrics with fixed thresholds may not adequately capture the wide diversity of places. A richer combination of criteria would better describe the multifaceted nature of a city's function and its environment, but the joint interpretation of these criteria may require an element of human judgment.

(1) Current methodologies used to define urban and rural areas are no longer relevant to our being able to study trends in urbanisation.
(2) Distinguishing between urban and rural areas might call for some judgement on the objective methodology being used to define a city's functions.
(3) With the diversity of urban landscapes, measurable criteria for defining urban areas may need to be supplemented with human judgement.
(4) The difficulty of accurately identifying urban areas means that we need to create a rich combination of criteria that can be applied to all urban areas.

25. The passage given below is followed by four alternate summaries. Choose the option that best captures the essence of the passage.

With the Treaty of Westphalia, the papacy had been confined to ecclesiastical functions, and the doctrine of sovereign equality reigned. What political theory could then explain the origin and justify the functions of secular political order? In his Leviathan, published in 1651, three years after the Peace of Westphalia, Thomas Hobbes provided such a theory. He imagined a "state of nature" in the past when the absence of authority produced a "war of all against all." To escape such intolerable insecurity, he theorized, people delivered their rights to a sovereign power in return for the sovereign's provision of security for all within the state's border. The sovereign state's monopoly on power was established as the only way to overcome the perpetual fear of violent death and war.

(1) Thomas Hobbes theorized that sovereign states emerged out of people's voluntary desire to overcome the sense of insecurity and establish the doctrine of sovereign equality.

(2) Thomas Hobbes theorized the emergence of sovereign states based on a transactional relationship between people and sovereign state that was necessitated by a sense of insecurity of the people.

(3) Thomas Hobbes theorized the voluntary surrender of rights by people as essential for emergence of sovereign states.

(4) Thomas Hobbes theorized the emergence of sovereign states as a form of transactional governance to limit the power of the papacy.

26. The four sentences (labelled 1, 2, 3, 4) below, when properly sequenced would yield a coherent paragraph. Decide on the proper sequencing of the order of the sentences and key in the sequence of the four numbers as your answer:

(1) It also has four movable auxiliary telescopes 1.8 m in diameter.

(2) Completed in 2006, the Very Large Telescope (VLT) has four reflecting telescopes, 8.2 m in diameter that can observe objects 4 billion times weaker than can normally be seen with the naked eye.

(3) This configuration enables one to distinguish an astronaut on the Moon.

(4) When these are combined with the large telescopes, they produce what is called interferometry: a simulation of the power of a mirror 16 m in diameter and the resolution of a telescope of 200 m.

Section II: DI & LR

Question Numbers (27 to 30): Answer the questions on the basis of the information given below.

Twenty five coloured beads are to be arranged in a grid comprising of five rows and five columns. Each cell in the grid must contain exactly one bead. Each bead is coloured either Red, Blue or Green.

While arranging the beads along any of the five rows or along any of the five columns, the rules given below are to be followed:

1. Two adjacent beads along the same row or column are always of different colours.
2. There is at least one Green bead between any two Blue beads along the same row or column.
3. There is at least one Blue and at least one Green bead between any two Red beads along the same row or column.

Every unique, complete arrangement of twenty five beads is called a configuration.

27. The total number of possible configurations using beads of only two colours is:

28. What is the maximum possible number of Red beads that can appear in any configuration?

29. What is the minimum number of Blue beads in any configuration?

30. Two Red beads have been placed in 'second row, third column' and 'third row, second column'. How many more Red beads can be placed so as to maximise the number of Red beads used in the configuration?

Question Numbers (31 to 34): Answer the questions on the basis of the information given below.

A shopping mall has a large basement parking lot with parking slots painted in it along a single row. These slots are quite narrow; a compact car can fit in a single slot but an SUV requires two slots. When a car arrives, the parking attendant guides the car to the first available slot from the beginning of the row into which the car can fit.

For our purpose, cars are numbered according to the order in which they arrive at the lot. For example, the first car to arrive is given a number 1, the second a number 2, and so on. This numbering does not indicate whether a car is a compact or an SUV. The configuration of a parking lot is a sequence of the car numbers in each slot. Each single vacant slot is represented by letter V.

For instance, suppose cars numbered 1 through 5 arrive and park, where cars 1, 3 and 5 are compact cars and 2 and 4 are SUVs. At this point, the parking lot would be described by the sequence 1, 2, 3, 4, 5. If cars 2 and 5 now vacate their slots, the parking lot would now be described as 1, V, V, 3, 4. If a compact car (numbered 6) arrives subsequently followed by an SUV (numbered 7), the parking lot would be described by the sequence 1, 6, V, 3, 4, 7.

Answer the following questions INDEPENDENTLY of each other.

31. Initially cars numbered 1, 2, 3, and 4 arrive among which 1 and 4 are SUVs while 2 and 3 are compact cars. Car 1 then leaves, followed by the arrivals of car 5 (a compact car) and car 6 (an SUV). Car 4 then leaves. Then car 7 (an SUV) and car 8 (a compact car) arrive. At this moment, which among the following numbered car is parked next to car 3?

(1) 6 (2) 5

(3) 8 (4) 7

32. Suppose eight cars have arrived, of which two have left. Also suppose that car 4 is a compact and car 7 is an SUV. Which of the following is a POSSIBLE current configuration of the parking lot?

(1) V, 2, 3, 7, 5, 6, 8 (2) 8, 2, 3, V, 6, 5, 7

(3) 8, 2, 3, V, 5, 7, 6 (4) 8, 2, 3, V, 5, 6, 7

33. Suppose the sequence at some point of time is 4, 5, 6, V, 3. Which of the following is NOT necessarily true?

(1) Car 1 is an SUV.

(2) Car 5 is a compact.

(3) Car 4 is a compact.

(4) Car 3 is an SUV.

34. Suppose that car 4 is not the first car to leave and that the sequence at a time between the arrival of the car 7 and car 8 is V, 7, 3, 6, 5. Then which of the following statements MUST be false?

(1) Car 2 is a compact.

(2) Car 7 is a compact.

(3) Car 4 is an SUV.

(4) Car 6 is a compact.

Question Numbers (35 to 40): Answer the questions on the basis of the information given below.

The Humanities department of a college is planning to organize eight seminars, one for each of the eight doctoral students - A, B, C, D, E, F, G and H. Four of them are from Economics, three from Sociology and one from Anthropology department. Each student is guided by one among P, Q, R, S and T. Two students are guided by each of P, R and T, while one student is guided by each of Q and S. Each student is guided by a guide belonging to their department.

Each seminar is to be scheduled in one of four consecutive 30-minute slots starting at 9:00 am, 9:30 am, 10:00 am and 10:30 am on the same day. More than one seminars can be scheduled in a slot, provided the guide is free. Only three rooms are available and hence at the most three seminars can be scheduled in a slot. Students who are guided by the same guide must be scheduled in consecutive slots.

The following additional facts are also known.

1. Seminars by students from Economics are scheduled in each of the four slots.
2. A's is the only seminar that is scheduled at 10:00 am. A is guided by R.
3. F is an Anthropology student whose seminar is scheduled at 10:30 am.
4. The seminar of a Sociology student is scheduled at 9:00 am.
5. B and G are both Sociology students, whose seminars are scheduled in the same slot. The seminar of an Economics student, who is guided by T, is also scheduled in the same slot.
6. P, who is guiding both B and C, has students scheduled in the first two slots.
7. A and G are scheduled in two consecutive slots.

35. Which one of the following statements is true?

(1) Two seminars are scheduled in the first slot.

(2) Three seminars are scheduled in the last slot.

(3) Only one seminar is scheduled in the second slot.

(4) Three seminars are scheduled in the first slot.

36. Who all are NOT guiding any Economics students?

(1) P, Q and R (2) P, Q and S

(3) Q, R and S (4) P, R and S

37. Which of the following statements is necessarily true?

(1) S is guiding F.

(2) H is an Economics student.

(3) Q is guiding G.

(4) B is scheduled in the first slot.

38. If D is scheduled in a slot later than Q's, then which of the following two statement(s) is(are) true?

(i) E and H are guided by T.

(ii) G is guided by Q.

(1) Both (i) and (ii) (2) Neither (i) nor (ii)

(3) Only (i) (4) Only (ii)

39. If E and Q are both scheduled in the same slot, then which of the following statements BEST describes the relationship between D, H, and T?

(1) Both D and H are guided by T.

(2) Neither D nor H is guided by T.

(3) At least one of D and H is guided by T.

(4) Exactly one of D and H is guided by T.

40. If D is scheduled in the slot immediately before Q's, then which of the following is NOT necessarily true?

(1) E is guided by R. (2) F is guided by S.

(3) D is guided by T. (4) G is guided by Q.

Question Numbers (41 to 46): Answer the questions on the basis of the information given below.

In an election several candidates contested for a constituency. In any constituency, the winning candidate was the one who polled the highest number of votes, the first runner up was the one who polled the second highest number of votes, the second runner up was the one who polled the third highest number of votes, and so on. There were no ties (in terms of number of votes polled by the candidates) in any of the constituencies in this election.

In an electoral system, a security deposit is the sum of money that a candidate is required to pay to the election commission before he or she is permitted to contest. Only the defeated candidates (i.e., one who is not the winning candidate) who fail to secure more than one sixth of the valid votes polled in the constituency, lose their security deposits.

The following table provides some incomplete information about votes polled in four constituencies: A, B, C and D, in this election.

	Constituency			
	A	B	C	D
No. of candidates contesting	10	12	5	8
Total No. of valid votes polled	5,00,000	3,25,000	6,00,030	
No. of votes polled by the winning candidate	2,75,000	48,750		
No. of votes polled by the first runner up	95,000			37,500
No. of votes polled by the second runner up				30,000
% of valid votes polled by the third runner up				10%

The following additional facts are known:

1. The first runner up polled 10,000 more votes than the second runner up in constituency A.
2. None of the candidates who contested in constituency C lost their security deposit. The difference in votes polled by any pair of candidates in this constituency was at least 10,000.
3. The winning candidate in constituency D polled 5% of valid votes more than that of the first runner up. All the candidates who lost their security deposits while contesting for this constituency, put together, polled 35% of the valid votes.

41. What is the percentage of votes polled in total by all the candidates who lost their security deposits while contesting for constituency A?

42. How many candidates who contested in constituency B lost their security deposit?

43. What BEST can be concluded about the number of votes polled by the winning candidate in constituency C?

(1) between 1,40,005 and 1,40,010

(2) 1,40,006

(3) 1,40,010

(4) less than 2,00,010

44. What was the number of valid votes polled in constituency D?

(1) 1,75,000 (2) 62,500

(3) 1,25,000 (4) 1,50,000

45. The winning margin of a constituency is defined as the difference of votes polled by the winner and that of the first runner up. Which of the following CANNOT be the list of constituencies, in increasing order of winning margin?

(1) B, D, C, A (2) D, B, C, A

(3) D, C, B, A (4) B, C, D, A

46. For all the four constituencies taken together, what was the approximate number of votes polled by all the candidates who lost their security deposit expressed as a percentage of the total valid votes from these four constituencies?

(1) 32.00% (2) 23.91%

(3) 38.25% (4) 23.54%

Question Numbers (47 to 50): Answer the questions on the basis of the information given below.

A chain of departmental stores has outlets in Delhi, Mumbai, Bengaluru and Kolkata. The sales are categorized by its three departments – 'Apparel', 'Electronics', and 'HomeDecor'. An Accountant has been asked to prepare a summary of the 2018 and 2019 sales amounts for an internal report. He has collated partial information and prepared the following table.

	Sales Amounts (Crore Rupees)							
	Delhi		Mumbai		Bengaluru		Kolkata	
	2018	2019	2018	2019	2018	2019	2018	2019
Apparels	-	-	-	-	-	-	-	54
Electronics	78	98	82	102	90	70	80	100
HomeDecor	-	100	-	72	-	80	-	54

The following additional information is known.

1. The sales amounts in the Apparel departments were the same for Delhi and Kolkata in 2018.
2. The sales amounts in the Apparel departments were the same for Mumbai and Bengaluru in 2018. This sales amount matched the sales amount in the Apparel department for Delhi in 2019.
3. The sales amounts in the HomeDecor departments were the same for Mumbai and Kolkata in 2018.
4. The sum of the sales amounts of four Electronics departments increased by the same amount as the sum of the sales amounts of four Apparel departments from 2018 to 2019.
5. The total sales amounts of the four HomeDecor departments increased by Rs 70 Crores from 2018 to 2019.
6. The sales amounts in the HomeDecor departments of Delhi and Bengaluru each increased by Rs 20 Crores from 2018 to 2019.
7. The sales amounts in the Apparel departments of Delhi and Bengaluru each increased by the same amount in 2019 from 2018. The sales amounts in the Apparel departments of Mumbai and Kolkata also each increased by the same amount in 2019 from 2018.
8. The sales amounts in the Apparel departments of Delhi, Kolkata and Bengaluru in 2019 followed an Arithmetic Progression.

47. In HomeDecor departments of which cities were the sales amounts the highest in 2018 and 2019, respectively?

(1) Bengaluru and Delhi (2) Delhi and Delhi
(3) Mumbai and Delhi (4) Mumbai and Mumbai

48. What was the increase in sales amount, in Crore Rupees, in the Apparel department of Mumbai from 2018 to 2019?

(1) 8 (2) 12
(3) 10 (4) 5

49. Among all the 12 departments (i.e., the 3 departments in each of the 4 cities), what was the maximum percentage increase in sales amount from 2018 to 2019?

(1) 50 (2) 75
(3) 25 (4) 28

50. What was the total sales amount, in Crore Rupees, in 2019 for the chain of departmental stores?

(1) 750 (2) 900
(3) 600 (4) 150

Section III: QA

51. In a group of 10 students, the mean of the lowest 9 scores is 42 while the mean of the highest 9 scores is 47. For the entire group of 10 students, the maximum possible mean exceeds the minimum possible mean by

(1) 3 (2) 6
(3) 5 (4) 4

52. From an interior point of an equilateral triangle, perpendiculars are drawn on all three sides. The sum of the lengths of the three perpendiculars is s. Then the area of the triangle is

(1) $\frac{s^2}{2\sqrt{3}}$ (2) $\frac{2s^2}{\sqrt{3}}$

(3) $\frac{\sqrt{3}s^2}{2}$ (4) $\frac{s^2}{\sqrt{3}}$

53. If x and y are positive real numbers satisfying x + y = 102, then the minimum possible value of 2601 $\left(1+\frac{1}{x}\right)\left(1+\frac{1}{y}\right)$ is

54. The sum of the perimeters of an equilateral triangle and a rectangle is 90 cm. The area, T, of the triangle and the area, R, of the rectangle, both in sq cm, satisfy the relationship $R = T^2$. If the sides of the rectangle are in the ratio 1:3, then the length, in cm, of the longer side of the rectangle, is

(1) 18 (2) 27
(3) 21 (4) 24

55. In a car race, car A beats car B by 45 km, car B beats car C by 50 km, and car A beats car C by 90 km. The distance (in km) over which the race has been conducted is

(1) 475 (2) 550
(3) 450 (4) 500

56. A sum of money is split among Amal, Sunil and Mita so that the ratio of the shares of Amal and Sunil is 3:2, while the ratio of the shares of Sunil and Mita is 4:5. If the difference between the largest and the smallest of these three shares is Rs 400, then Sunil's share, in rupees, is

57. The distance from B to C is thrice that from A to B. Two trains travel from A to C via B. The speed of train 2 is double that of train 1 while traveling from A to B and their speeds are interchanged while traveling from B to C. The ratio of the time taken by train 1 to that taken by train 2 in travelling from A to C is

(1) 1:4 (2) 5:7
(3) 4:1 (4) 7:5

58. Two circular tracks T1 and T2 of radii 100 m and 20 m, respectively touch at a point A. Starting from A at the same time, Ram and Rahim are walking on track T1 and track T2 at speeds 15 km/hr and 5 km/hr respectively. The number of full rounds that Ram will make before he meets Rahim again for the first time is

(1) 4 (2) 2
(3) 5 (4) 3

59. How many 4-digit numbers, each greater than 1000 and each having all four digits distinct, are there with 7 coming before 3?

60. Anil buys 12 toys and labels each with the same selling price. He sells 8 toys initially at 20% discount on the labeled price. Then he sells the remaining 4 toys at an additional 25% discount on the discounted price. Thus, he gets a total of Rs 2112, and makes a 10% profit. With no discounts, his percentage of profit would have been

(1) 55 (2) 60
(3) 54 (4) 50

61. In how many ways can a pair of integers (x , a) be chosen such that $x^2 - 2|x| + |a - 2| = 0$?

(1) 7 (2) 6
(3) 5 (4) 4

62. In May, John bought the same amount of rice and the same amount of wheat as he had bought in April, but spent ₹ 150 more due to price increase of rice and wheat by 20% and 12%, respectively. If John had spent ₹ 450 on rice in April, then how much did he spend on wheat in May?

(1) ₹ 560 (2) ₹ 570
(3) ₹ 590 (4) ₹ 580

63. Let the m-th and n-th terms of a geometric progression be $\frac{3}{4}$ and 12, respectively, where m < n. If the common ratio of the progression is an integer r, then the smallest possible value of r + n – m is

(1) 6 (2) –4
(3) –2 (4) 2

64. The number of integers that satisfy the equality $(x^2 - 5x + 7)^{x+1} = 1$ is

(1) 2 (2) 3
(3) 4 (4) 5

65. Let C be a circle of radius 5 meters having center at O. Let PQ be a chord of C that passes through points A and B where A is located 4 meters north of O and B is located 3 meters east of O. Then, the length of PQ, in meters, is nearest to

(1) 7.2 (2) 6.6
(3) 8.8 (4) 7.8

66. For the same principal amount, the compound interest for two years at 5% per annum exceeds the simple interest for three years at 3% per annum by Rs 1125. Then the principal amount in rupees is

67. The number of pairs of integers (x, y) satisfying $x \geq y \geq -20$ and $2x + 5y = 99$ is

68. A and B are two points on a straight line. Ram runs from A to B while Rahim runs from B to A. After crossing each other, Ram and Rahim reach their destinations in one minute and four minutes, respectively. If they start at the same time, then the ratio of Ram's speed to Rahim's speed is

(1) $\frac{1}{2}$ (2) $\sqrt{2}$
(3) 2 (4) $2\sqrt{2}$

69. Let C1 and C2 be concentric circles such that the diameter of C1 is 2 cm longer than that of C2. If a chord of C1 has length 6 cm and is a tangent to C2, then the diameter, in cm, of C1 is

70. Aron bought some pencils and sharpeners. Spending the same amount of money as Aron, Aditya bought twice as many pencils and 10 less sharpeners. If the cost of one sharpener is ₹ 2 more than the cost of a pencil, then the minimum possible number of pencils bought by Aron and Aditya together is

(1) 30 (2) 27
(3) 33 (4) 36

71. Let $f(x) = x^2 + ax + b$ and $g(x) = f(x + 1) - f(x - 1)$. If $f(x) \geq 0$ for all real x, and g(20) = 72, then the smallest possible value of b is

(1) 1 (2) 4
(3) 0 (4) 16

72. If x and y are non-negative integers such that x + 9 = z, y + 1 = z and x + y < z + 5, then the maximum possible value of 2x + y equals

73. Students in a college have to choose at least two subjects from chemistry, mathematics and physics. The number of students choosing all three subjects is 18, choosing mathematics as one of their subjects is 23 and choosing physics as one of their subjects is 25. The smallest possible number of students who could choose chemistry as one of their subjects is

(1) 20 (2) 19
(3) 22 (4) 21

74. The value of $\log_a\left(\frac{a}{b}\right)+\log_b\left(\frac{b}{a}\right)$, for $1 < a \le b$ cannot be equal to

(1) 1 (2) –0.5
(3) –1 (4) 0

75. John takes twice as much time as Jack to finish a job. Jack and Jim together take one-thirds of the time to finish the job than John takes working alone. Moreover, in order to finish the job, John takes three days more than that taken by three of them working together. In how many days will Jim finish the job working alone?

76. For real x, the maximum possible value of $\frac{x}{\sqrt{1+x^4}}$ is

(1) $\frac{1}{\sqrt{3}}$ (2) $\frac{1}{\sqrt{2}}$
(3) $\frac{1}{2}$ (4) 1

ANSWERS

1. (2)	**2.** (3)	**3.** (2)	**4.** (4)	**5.** (3)	**6.** (2)	**7.** (4)	**8.** (4)	**9.** (3)	**10.** (4)
11. (3)	**12.** (4)	**13.** (3)	**14.** (1)	**15.** (1)	**16.** (1)	**17.** (3)	**18.** (3)	**19.** (2)	**20.** (2)
21. (1342)	**22.** (2413)	**23.** (4)	**24.** (3)	**25.** (2)	**26.** (2143)	**27.** (2)	**28.** (9)	**29.** (6)	**30.** (6)
31. (4)	**32.** (4)	**33.** (4)	**34.** (4)	**35.** (1)	**36.** (2)	**37.** (2)	**38.** (1)	**39.** (3)	**40.** (1)
41. (9)	**42.** (11)	**43.** (2)	**44.** (1)	**45.** (4)	**46.** (2)	**47.** (2)	**48.** (2)	**49.** (1)	**50.** (2)
51. (4)	**52.** (4)	**53.** (2704)	**54.** (2)	**55.** (3)	**56.** (800)	**57.** (2)	**58.** (4)	**59.** (315)	**60.** (4)
61. (1)	**62.** (1)	**63.** (3)	**64.** (2)	**65.** (3)	**66.** (90000)	**67.** (17)	**68.** (3)	**69.** (10)	**70.** (3)
71. (2)	**72.** (23)	**73.** (1)	**74.** (1)	**75.** (4)	**76.** (2)				

EXPLANATIONS

1. The passage says that renewable energy produced at the household or neighbourhood level is unlikely to generate high returns for investors but it does not say that renewable energy produced at this level is more efficient than mass-produced forms of energy. Therefore, option 1 is incorrect. Option 2 is correct because the passage dwells on both the advantages and disadvantages of renewable energy. Refer to "Both the direct and indirect impacts of renewable energy must be examined to ensure that a climate-smart future does not intensify social and environmental harm." Option 3 contradicts what is said in the passage about democratic distribution of renewable energy. Refer to "For some climate activists, the promise of renewables rests on their ability not only to reduce emissions but also to provide distributed, democratized access to energy . . . But Burke and Stephens . . . caution that "renewable energy systems offer a possibility but not a certainty for more democratic energy futures."" Option 4 is incorrect because the passage says the passage says that renewable technology is a hot business. It is also said that if renewable energy is produced and distributed at small scale it might not generate high returns on investment.

2. Option 1 is mentioned in the second paragraph of the given passage. Option 2 is found in the first and second sentences of the fourth paragraph, "While renewable energy is a more recent addition to financial portfolios, investments in the sector must be considered in light of our understanding of capital accumulation. As agricultural finance reveals, the concentration of control of corporate activity facilitates profit generation." The passage says that the renewable energy is already a hot or lucrative business and talks about looking at the social and environmental impact it would have, however, it does not say that the possible negative impacts of renewable energy need to be studied before it can be offered as a financial investment opportunity. Hence, option 3 is the answer. Option 4 is mentioned in the last sentence of the paragraph of the given passage, "The disposal of toxic waste has long perpetuated social injustice through the flows of waste to the Global South and to marginalized communities in the Global North..."

3. Refer to "As renewable energy production requires land, water, and labor, among other inputs, it imposes costs on people and the environment. Hydropower projects, for instance, have led to community dispossession and exclusion..." Hence, option 2 is correct as it is false according to the given passage. Option 1 is true because a lot of money needs to be invested in order to get high returns. Option 3 is true as non-renewable energy system is more profitable. Option 4 is also true. Refer to, "Renewable energy can be produced at the household or neighborhood level. However, such small-scale, localized production is unlikely to generate high returns for investors."

4. The passage talks about renewable energy. So, option 1 cannot be inferred from the given passage. The passage does not talk about the need for the study of the coexistence of marginalised people with their environments. It cannot be inferred from the given passage either. So, option is incorrect. The passage does not suggest the localised, small-scale development of renewable energy systems. Thus, option 2 is also incorrect. Option 4 can be inferred from "The disposal of toxic waste has long perpetuated social injustice through the flows of waste to the Global South and to marginalized communities in the Global North..."

5. The author does not suggest any thing about the non-renewable energy in the first paragraph of the given passage. So, option 1 cannot be inferred from it. Profitability of renewable energy was not the author's only reservation. In fact, the author's concern is whether renewable energy system would work without causing any harm to the environment. So, option 2 is incorrect. However, this very concern of the author makes option 3 the correct option. Option 4 cannot be inferred from the given passage.

6. Michelangelo and Leonardo are given as examples. So, they cannot be included as main arguments of the passage. Thus, option 1 can be eliminated. Similarly, option 3 can also be eliminated because 'epiphenomena' is not one of the main arguments of the given passage. Option 4 contains the phrase 'lay audience' which is also not one of the main points of the passage. Thus, option 2 is the correct choice. The keywords given in option 2 talk about the study of visual culture as mentioned in 2nd, 3rd, 4th and 5th paragraphs respectively.

7. Option 1 can be inferred from "The task is to understand how artifacts contribute to the construction of a world..." Option 2 can be inferred from "visual culture is what images, acts of seeing, and attendant intellectual, emotional, and perceptual sensibilities do to build, maintain, or transform the worlds in which people live." Option 3 can be inferred from the fourth paragraph of the given passage. However, option 4 cannot be inferred from the given passage.

8. 'Epiphenomena' means phenomena which is a supplementary to something else. Hence, option 4 is an obvious answer. The other options are incorrect.

9. The quoted sentence says that no amount of social analysis can explain the existence of Michelangelo and Leonardo. So, options 1, 2 and 4 are incorrect. Only option 3 is the most accurate interpretation of the given sentence.

10. Options 1, 2 and 3 fail to convey the meaning of the given statement. The given statement says that seeing becomes meaningful visual experience because of agreements of meaningfulness we establish with images that we perceive. Hence, option 4 is the answer.

11. Option 1 can be inferred from the first two sentences of the passage, "Aggression is any behavior that is directed toward injuring, harming, or inflicting pain on another living being or group of beings. Generally, the victim(s) of aggression must wish to avoid such behavior in order for it to be considered true aggression." Options 2 and 4 are implied in the sentence, "Sigmund Freud (1930) proposed that all individuals are born with a death instinct that predisposes us to a variety of aggressive behaviors, including suicide (self directed aggression) and mental illness (possibly due to an unhealthy or unnatural suppression of aggressive urges)." Option 3 is not logically implied by the passage as neural inhibition and testosterone are discussed separately. Hence, option 3 is the answer.

12. Options 1, 2 and 3 are incorrect. Option 4 is found in the sentences, "The first variable is the aggressor him/herself. The second is the social situation or circumstance in which the aggressive act(s) occur(s). The third variable is the target or victim of aggression."

13. Option 1 subverts the meaning of the quoted sentence. It is not mentioned that the use of torture to extract information is most effective when the torturer is not emotionally involved in the torture. So, option 2 can be eliminated. Option 3 best explains the quoted sentence in the question. It is said in the quoted sentence that no feelings are involved, so option 4 is incorrect.

14. Option 1 is the answer. Option 2 can be found in the sentences, "The concept of aggression is very broad, and includes many categories of behavior (e.g., verbal aggression, street crime, child abuse, spouse abuse, group conflict, war, etc.)...", "Aggression is any behavior that is directed toward injuring, harming, or inflicting pain on another living being or group of beings" and "Aggression is also categorized according to its ultimate intent." Option 3 is found in the sentence, "higher levels of aggression in men is based on the assumption that, on average, men have higher levels of testosterone than women." Option 4 is found in the sentence, "At the most basic level, some argue that aggressive urges and actions are the result of inborn, biological factors."

15. The author's tone in the given sentence is definitely ironic because he says why should one work very hard when one can earn handsomely by becoming a successful pirate who could make up to £4,000 on each raid. The sentence is not analytical, so option 2 is incorrect. The author is not annoyed by the wealth amassed by pirates. So, option 3 is also incorrect. The author does not deal with subject of piracy in the given sentence playfully, therefore, option 4 is also incorrect.

16. Option 1 can be deduced from what Lehr has written and the same has been quoted by the author, "It quickly becomes clear that in those parts of the world that have not profited from globalisation and modernisation, and where abject poverty and the daily struggle for survival are still a reality, the root causes of piracy are still the same as they were a couple of hundred years ago." So, option 1 is the answer. Option 2 cannot be the way to control piracy because it did not work in Malaysia because of corruption. Option 3 also cannot be the way to control piracy because diplomatic initiatives against piracy are plagued by mutual distrust. Option 2 is practically impossible.

17. Options 1, 2 and 4 cannot be inferred. Since conquistadors, Vasco da Gama and the East India Company were colonisers and if the scope of looting were to be widened colonialism should be regarded as an organised form of looting. Thus, from the given statement we can infer that the author believes that colonialism should be considered an organised form of piracy. Hence, option 3 is the answer.

18. Option 1 is found in the line, "...a successful pirate made up to £4,000 on each raid..." Option 2 can be found in the sentence, "Increased globalisation has done more to encourage piracy than suppress it." Although it is said in the passage that a consistent rule, even today, is there are never enough warships to patrol pirate infested waters, it not said that there is a decrease in the surveillances of the high seas. Hence, option 3 is the answer. Option 4 is found in the sentence, "European colonialism weakened delicate balances of power, leading to an influx of opportunists on the high seas."

19. Options 1 talks about monopoly and data protection. So, it can be connected with option 3 which talks about intellectual property rights. Options 4 and 5 also talk about monopoly of information. However, option 2 talks about different kinds of capitalism. Hence, option 2 is the odd one out.

20. Option 1 does not include intuition. Moreover, the author did not recommend a way to make a decision. Decision is not made according to the available time. So, option 3 is incorrect. Option 4 talks only about intuition. So, option 2 is the answer.

21. 'It' in sentence 3 refers to 'your brain' in sentence 1 making 13 a mandatory pair and also making 1 the opening sentence. The brain not being aware of every single thing that happens in the world around you, is furthered by "not at all aware of" in sentence 4. This is followed by 2. Hence, the correct sequence is 1342.

22. 'But' in sentence 1 and 'The resultant...' in sentence 4 clearly show that neither of these two sentences can be the opening sentence. Of the remaining two sentences, sentence 2 can be the opening sentence. 'The resultant ionizing radiation' in sentence 4 springs from 'large-scale nuclear fission...' in sentence 2, making 24 a mandatory pair. Sentence 1 talks about atom bomb unlike sentences 2 and 4 which talk about nuclear fission and the resultant radiation. 'Atomic energy' in sentence 3 refers to 'atom bomb' in sentence 1. Hence, the correct sequence is 2413.

23. Sentences 1, 2, 3 and 5 focus both on the past and the future of a victim of sexual assault. However, sentence 4 talks about questions focusing only on the victim's past. Hence, option 4 is the odd one out.

24. The heterogeneity of urban settings, measurement of urbanization and an element of human judgment are mentioned only in option 3, hence, it is the answer. Other options are incorrect.

25. Option 1 is incorrect because people delivered their rights to a sovereign power in return for the sovereign's provision of security. Option 3 is incorrect because sovereign states were already in existence. Option 4 is incorrect because papacy is not mentioned in Hobbes theory. Only option 2 best summarizes the given passage.

26. 'It' in sentence 1, 'This configuration' in sentence 3 and 'When these are...' in sentence 4 clearly indicate that none of these sentences can be the opening sentence. Thus, sentence 2 is the obvious opening sentence. 'It' in sentence 1 refers back to 'the Very Large Telescope (VLT)' in sentence 2 making 21 a mandatory pair. 'These' in sentence 4 refers back to the Very Large Telescope (VLT) with four reflecting telescopes mentioned in sentence 2 and 'four movable auxiliary telescopes 1.8 m in diameter' mentioned in sentence 1. This is followed by sentence 3. Hence, the correct sequence is 2143.

27. Making configuration using beads of only two colours will be possible only when we use Blue and Green coloured beads, otherwise it will contradict statement 3. Now, using the given data, there are two possibilities:

I.

G	B	G	B	G
B	G	B	G	B
G	B	G	B	G
B	G	B	G	B
G	B	G	B	G

II.

B	G	B	G	B
G	B	G	B	G
B	G	B	G	B
G	B	G	B	G
B	G	B	G	B

28. Using the information given in the statements, to maximise the number of Red beads, the configuration will be like:

R	G	B	R	G
G	R	G	B	R
B	G	R	G	B
R	B	G	R	G
G	R	B	G	R

Hence, the maximum number of Red beads is 9.

29. The minimum number of Blue beads in any configuration is 6, which is shown below.

R	G	B	R	G
G	R	G	B	R
B	G	R	G	B
R	B	G	R	G
G	R	B	G	R

30. Two Red beads have been placed in their respective positions. In order to maximise the number of Red beads, the configuration will be like:

R	G	B	R	G
G	B	R	G	B
B	R	G	B	R
R	G	B	R	G
G	B	R	G	B

Hence, 6 more Red beads can be placed.

31. According to the question, cars 1, 4, 6 and 7 are SUVs and cars 2, 3, 5 and 8 are compact cars. Now, their arrival and departure are described in the following steps.

I. 1, 2, 3, 4

II. V, V, 2, 3, 4

III. 5, V, 2, 3, 4

IV. 5, V, 2, 3, 4, 6

V. 5, V, 2, 3, V, V, 6

VI. 5, V, 2, 3, 7, 6

VII. 5, 8, 2, 3, 7, 6

Clearly, car 7 is parked next to car 3.

32. Check options:

Option 1 is not possible as car 7 cannot be parked between car 3 and car 5 because car 7 is an SUV.

Option 2 is not possible as car 6 cannot be parked just before car 5 because 4th slot is vacant and car 4 is a compact car. Option 3 is also not possible as car 7 which is an SUV cannot be parked between car 5 and car 6.

Option 4 is the possible current configuration of the parking lot (Car 1 and car 4 have left and in place of car 1, car 8 then arrived in that slot).

33. Seeing the sequence: 4, 5, 6, V, 3, we can conclude that car 1 and car 2 are definitely SUVs which occupied two slots each. After that car 4, car 5 and car 6 arrived and one slot is vacant which clearly means car 4 and car 5 are compact cars. We cannot say about the type of car 3 so option 4 is not necessarily true.

34. The sequence at a time between the arrival of the car 7 and car 8 is V, 7, 3, 6, 5. Also, that the car 4 is not the first car to leave so that means firstly, all the five car: cars: 1, 2, 3, 4 and 5 must have arrived and then car 2 is the one which left first. After that car 4 left the parking slot. Also, car 2 is a compact car and car 4 and car 6 are SUVs, otherwise car 6 would have occupied slot 2 where car 2 was parked initially which would contradict the given sequence.

∴ The sequence will be

1, V, 3, 6, 5

Then, car 7, which is a compact car will arrive and then the configuration will be

1, 7, 3, 6, 5

After that car 1 will left the parking slot, so the sequence will become like the given sequence in the question.

i.e, V, 7, 3, 6, 5

Hence, options 1, 2 and 3 are true where option 4 must be false.

For questions 35 to 40:

Using the information given in the first five statements (1 to 5), we can draw two cases:

Case 1:

9 am	9 : 30 am	10 am	10 : 30 am
Economics + B (Sociology) + G (Sociology)	Economics	A (Economics)	Economics + F (Anthropology)

Case 2:

9 am	9 : 30 am	10 am	10 : 30 am
Economics + Sociology	Economics + B(Sociology) + G (Sociology)	A (Economics)	Economics + F (Anthropology)

But using statement 7, case 1 is rejected so only case 2 is left. Again, using statement 6, the table becomes

Table 1:

9 am	9 : 30 am	10 am	10 : 30 am
Economics + C (Sociology)	Economics + B(Sociology) + G (Sociology)	A (Economics)	Economics + F (Anthropology)

Clearly, remaining students D, E and H are Economics students.

Also, it is given that two students are guided by each of P, R and T, while one student is guided by each of Q and S, therefore, based on that we can create another table.

Table 2:

Guide →	P	Q	R	S	T
	B (Sociology) + C (Sociology)	___ (Anthropology/ Sociology)	___ A (Economics) in 10 am slot + ___ (Economics) in 10 : 30 am slot	___ (Sociology/ Anthropology)	___ (Economics) in 9 am slot + ___ (Economics) in 9 : 30 am slot

35. Clearly from table 1, we can say that two seminars are scheduled in the first slot.

36. From table 2, we can see that R is guiding the Economics students so, options 1, 3 and 4 are rejected. Hence, option 2 will be the answer.

37. Options 1 and 3 are not necessarily true because we are not sure about it. S can guide either F or G. Similarly Q can guide either G or F. Option 4 is absolutely incorrect. Hence, option 2 is necessarily true.

38. If D is scheduled in a slot later than Q's, i.e., using both tables 1 and 2, we can say that Q is guiding Sociology student (G), and D is scheduled in 10 : 30 am slot i.e., R is guiding D, so table 2 becomes

Guide →	P	Q	R	S	T
	B (Sociology) + C (Sociology)	G (Sociology)	A (Economics) + D (Economics)	F (Anthropology)	E (Economics) + H (Economics)

Hence, both statement (i) and (ii) are true.

39. If E and Q are both scheduled in the same slot, then two cases arise:

Case 1: When Q guides the Sociology student i.e., G, then E is scheduled in 9 : 30 am slot, i.e., T is guiding E. Therefore, the remaining student who is guided by T is either D or H.

Case 2: When Q guides the Anthropology student i.e., F, then E is scheduled in 10 : 30 am slot, i.e. R is guiding E. Therefore, remaining two students of Economics D and H are guided by T.

Hence, from both the cases we can say that atleast one of D and H is guided by T.

40. If D is scheduled in the slot immediately before Q's then from tables 1 and 2, we can say that Q is scheduled in 9 : 30 am slot and D in 9 am slot. So, the table 2 becomes

Guide →	P	Q	R	S	T
	B (Sociology) + C (Sociology)	G (Sociology)	A (Economics) + E/H (Economics)	F (Anthropology)	D (Economics) + H/E (Economics)

Among the options, first option is NOT necessarily true as E is guided by either R or T, rest all other options are true.

For questions 41 to 46:

From additional information following can be concluded:

Statement 1: The second runner up polled 85,000 votes which is 10,000 less votes than the first runner up in constituency A.

Statement 2: Since none of the candidates who contested in constituency C lost their security deposit, therefore, all the candidates must have polled more than 1/6th of the valid votes, that is.,

$600030 \times \frac{1}{6} = 100005$. So, every candidate must have polled atleast 100006 votes. Also, the difference in votes polled by any pair of candidates in this constituency was at least 10,000, therefore, the only possible case is: 100006, 110006 (third runner up), 120006(second runner up), 130006 (first runner up), and 140006 (winning candidate). (The sum of the votes polled adds up to 600030).

Statement 3: Let the total number of valid votes polled in constituency D is y, then the winning candidate in constituency D must have got 37500 + 0.05y valid votes that is., 5% of valid votes more than that of the first runner up.

	Constituency			
	A	B	C	D
No. of candidates contesting	10	12	5	8
Total no. of valid votes polled	500000	325000	600030	y
No. of votes polled by the winning candidate	275000	48750	140006	37500 + 0.05y
No. of votes polled up by the first runner up	95000		130006	37500
No. of votes polled by the second runner up	85000		120006	30000
% of valid votes polled by the third runner up			110006	10%

Also, all the candidates who lost their security deposits while contesting for this constituency, put together, polled 35% of the valid votes, that is., 0.35y.

Let 7 out of 8 candidates lost their security deposit, then,

0.65y = 37500 + 0.05y

y = 62500 (Not possible)

Now, let 6 out of 8 candidates lost their security deposit, then,

0.65y = 37500 + 0.05y + 37500

y = 125000 (Not possible)

Now, let 5 out of 8 candidates lost their security deposit, then,

0.65y = 37500 + 0.05y + 37500 + 30000

y = 175000 (Possible)

Now, let 4 out of 8 candidates lost their security deposit, then,

0.65y = 37500 + 0.05y + 37500 + 30000 + 0.1y

0.5y = 105000

y = 2,10,000 (Not possible)

	Constituency			
	A	B	C	D
No. of candidates contesting	10	12	5	8
Total no. of valid votes polled	500000	325000	600030	175000
No. of votes polled by the winning candidate	275000	48750	140006	46250
No. of votes polled up by the first runner up	95000		130006	37500
No. of votes polled by the second runner up	85000		120006	30000
% of valid votes polled by the third runner up			110006	10%

41. The percentage of votes polled in total by all the candidates who lost their security deposits while contesting for constituency A is-

$$5,00,000 \times \frac{p}{100} = 5,00,000 - (2,75,000 - 95,000 - 85,000)$$

$$\Rightarrow 5,00,000 \times \frac{p}{100} = 45,000$$

$\Rightarrow p = 9\%$.

42. Number of candidates contested in constituency B who lost their security deposit are 11. Since $3,25,000 \times \frac{1}{6} = 54166.67$, and none of the candidates scored more than that, therefore, they all lost except the winning candidate.

43. The number of votes polled by the winning candidate in constituency C is 140006.

44. The number of valid votes polled in constituency D was 1,75,000.

45. In constituency A, the winning margin is = 275000 – 95000 = 180000

Constituency C, 140006 – 130006 = 10000

Constituency D, 46250 – 37500 = 8750.

Option 4: B, C, D, A is not possible since winning margin of D is definitely less than C.

46. The total valid votes from four constituencies = 1600030

In constituency A, 7 people lost their security deposit. The number of votes polled by all the candidates who lost their security deposit = 500000 – 455000 = 45000.

In constituency B, 11 people lost their security deposit. The number of votes polled by them = 325000 – 48750 = 276250.

In constituency D, 5 people lost their security deposit. The number of votes polled by them = 175000 – 113750 = 61250.

The approximate number of votes polled by all the candidates who lost their security deposit expressed as a percentage of the total valid votes from these four constituencies:

$$\Rightarrow p = \frac{382500}{1600030} \times 100 = 23.91\%$$

For questions 47 to 50:

From statements (1), (2), and (3), let x, y and z be the sales amount of Apparels deptt for Delhi and Kolkata in 2018, Apparels deptt for Mumbai and Kolkata in 2018 and Delhi in 2019, and Home décor deptt for Delhi and Kolkata in 2019 respectively. Let us assume the other values as a, b, c and d.

	Sales Amounts (Crore Rupees)							
	Delhi		Mumbai		Bengaluru		Kolkata	
	2018	2019	2018	2019	2018	2019	2018	2019
Apparels	x	y	y	a	Y	b	x	54
Electronics	78	98	82	102	90	70	80	100
HomeDecor	c	100	z	72	d	80	z	54

By statement 4, sum of the sales amounts of four Electronics departments increased by the same amount as the sum of the sales amounts of four Apparel departments from 2018 to 2019.

Sum of the sales amounts of four Electronics departments in 2018 = 78 + 82 + 90 + 80 = 330 and in 2019 = 98 + 102 + 70 + 100 = 370, therefore, the increase is of 40.

Sum of the sales amounts of four Apparels departments in 2018 = 2x + 2y, and in 2019 = 2x + 2y + 40 = y + a + b + 54.

⇒ 2x + y = a + b + 14.

Now, by statement 5, total sales amounts of the four HomeDecor departments in 2019 = 100 + 72 + 80 + 54 = 306, which is 70 more than the total sales amount of the four homedecor dept in 2018.

⇒ c + 2z + d + 70 = 306

⇒ c + 2z + d = 236

By statement 6, we can infer that, c = 80 and d = 60 and therefore, z = 48.

From statement 7, it can be concluded that y – x = b – y ⇒ 2y = b + x and a – y = 54 – x ⇒ a + x = 54 + y.

By statement 8, we know that, y, 54 and b are in arithmetic progression, therefore, for some p, y = 54 – p and b = 54 + p.

	Sales Amounts (Crore Rupees)							
	Delhi		Mumbai		Bengaluru		Kolkata	
	2018	2019	2018	2019	2018	2019	2018	2019
Apparels	x	54 – p	54 – p	a	54 – p	54 + p	X	54
Electronics	78	98	82	102	90	70	80	100
HomeDecor	80	100	48	72	60	80	48	54

Now substitute the values of y and b so as to calculate p.

⇒ 2(54 – p) = 54 + p + x

⇒ 108 – 2p = 54 + p + x

⇒ x = 54 – 3p

And,

⇒ a + 54 – 3p = 54 + 54 – p

⇒ a = 54 + 2p

Now,

⇒ 2(54 – 3p) + 54 – p = 54 + 2p + 54 + p + 14

⇒ 108 – 7p = 3p + 68

⇒ 10p = 40

⇒ p = 4

So, final updated table is:

	Sales Amounts (Crore Rupees)							
	Delhi		Mumbai		Bengaluru		Kolkata	
	2018	2019	2018	2019	2018	2019	2018	2019
Apparels	42	50	50	62	50	58	42	54
Electronics	78	98	82	102	90	70	80	100
HomeDecor	80	100	48	72	60	80	48	54

47. In HomeDecor departments the cities with highest sales amounts in 2018 and 2019 was Delhi.

48. The increase in sales amount, in Crore Rupees, in the Apparel department of Mumbai from 2018 to 2019 was 12.

49. Among all the 12 departments (i.e., the 3 departments in each of the 4 cities), the maximum percentage increase in sales amount from 2018 to 2019 is 50 % In Homedecor dept of Mumbai city.

50. The total sales amount, in Crore Rupees, in 2019 for the chain of departmental stores is 900.

51. Let us consider two scenarios:

I	II
2	42
47	42
47	42
47	42
47	42
47	42
47	42
47	42
47	42
47	87
Total = 425	Total = 465
Mean = 42.5	Mean = 46.5
Difference	= 4

In (I) and (II) both, all the conditions given in the question are satisfied.

$\therefore$ Difference between the maximum and minimum average scores = 4.

52.

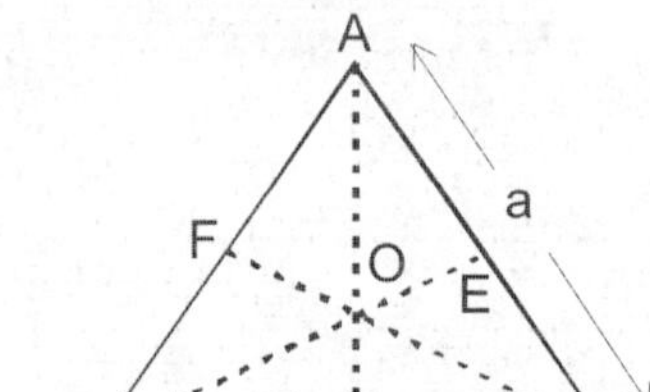

As ΔABC is an equilateral triangle.

$$\therefore AD = \frac{\sqrt{3}a}{2}$$

and $OD = \frac{1}{3} \times \frac{\sqrt{3}a}{2}$

Given that OD + OE + OF = s

Also, OD = OE = OF

$$\therefore 3\left(\frac{1}{3} \times \frac{\sqrt{3}a}{2}\right) = s$$

$$\therefore a = \frac{2s}{\sqrt{3}}$$

Hence, the area of $\Delta ABC = \frac{\sqrt{3}}{4} \times \left(\frac{2s}{\sqrt{3}}\right)^2 = \frac{s^2}{\sqrt{3}}$.

53. As x + y = 102 (given)

Now, 2601 = 51 × 51

So, $2601\left(1+\frac{1}{x}\right)\left(1+\frac{1}{y}\right)$ can be written as,

$$= 51 \times 51\left(1+\frac{1}{x}\right)\left(1+\frac{1}{y}\right)$$

$$= \left(51+\frac{51}{x}\right)\left(51+\frac{51}{y}\right)$$

We have to find the minimum possible value of the given expression, therefore put x = y = 51

$$\therefore \left(51+\frac{51}{51}\right)\left(51+\frac{51}{51}\right) = (52)(52) = 2704.$$

54. Let the side of the equilateral triangle be 'a' and the length and breadth of the rectangle be 'l' and 'b' respectively.

$\therefore$ According to the question,

$3a + 2(l + b) = 90$ ... (i)

Also, $\frac{b}{l} = \frac{1}{3}$

$$\Rightarrow b = \frac{l}{3}$$

$\therefore$ Equation (i) becomes,

$3a + \frac{8l}{3} = 90$ ... (ii)

Also, $R = T^2$

$$l \times \frac{l}{3} = \left(\frac{\sqrt{3}a^2}{4}\right)$$

$$\frac{l^2}{a^4} = \frac{9}{16}$$

$$\Rightarrow \frac{l}{a^2} = \frac{3}{4} \text{ or } l = \frac{3a^2}{4}$$

Put it in equation (ii), we get,

$$3a + \frac{8}{3} \times \frac{3}{4}a^2 = 90$$

$2a^2 + 3a - 90 = 0$

$\Rightarrow a = 6$

$$\Rightarrow l = \frac{3}{4} \times 6 \times 6 = 27\,cm.$$

55. Let the required distance be 'd'.

∴ When A covers 'd' km, B covers (d – 45) km

And when B covers 'd' km, C covers (d – 50) km

So, the distance covered by C when B covers

$(d-45)$ km $= \dfrac{(d-50)}{d} \times (d-45)$ km

⇒ When A covers 'd' km,

then C covers $\dfrac{(d-50)(d-45)}{d}$ km

$\therefore d - \left[\dfrac{(d-50)(d-45)}{d}\right] = 90$

Now, if we put options one by one, only option (3) satisfies the above equation.

Hence, the required distance = 450 km.

56. Let the amount of money with Amal and Sunil be 6x and 4x. Now the amount of money with Mita be 5x.

Difference between the largest and smallest amount is Rs. 400 i.e., 6x – 4x = 400 or 2x = 400 or x = 200. Amount of money with Sunil is 200 × 4 = 800.

57.

d 3d
A B C

Let the speeds of trains 1 and 2 be s and 2s respectively while travelling from A to B.

Similarly from B to C, their speeds are interchanged,

$\therefore$ Required ratio $= \dfrac{\frac{d}{s}+\frac{3d}{2s}}{\frac{d}{2s}+\frac{3d}{s}} = \dfrac{\frac{2d+3d}{2s}}{\frac{d+6d}{2s}} = 5:7.$

58.

Ram T_1 Rahim T_2 100m A 20m

Rahim moves on track T_2 with speed of 5 km/hr.

∴ Time taken by him to complete one round till

point A $= \dfrac{2\pi(20)}{5\times1000}$ hours $= \dfrac{\pi}{125}$ hours

Distance covered by Ram in one round = $2(\pi)(100)$ = 200π m

∴ Time taken by Ram to cover 200π

$= \dfrac{200\pi}{15\times1000}$ hours $= \dfrac{\pi}{75}$ hours

∴ Time after which both meet for the first time at point A = LCM$\left(\dfrac{\pi}{125}, \dfrac{\pi}{75}\right) = \dfrac{\pi}{25}.$

Hence, full rounds made by Ram $= \dfrac{\frac{\pi}{25}}{\frac{\pi}{75}} = 3$ rounds.

59. According to the question, the possibilities are:-

Case 1: 7 3 _ _

For its 3rd digit, 8 possibilities are there (0, 1, 2, 4, 5, 6, 8, 9) and for 4th digit, 7 possibilities.

Hence, total possibilities in this case = 8 × 7 = 56.

Case 2: 7 _ 3 _

Similarly, here, total possibilities = 8 × 7 = 56.

Case 3: 7 _ _ 3

Total possibilities = 8 × 7 = 56.

Case 4: _ 7 3 _

For 1st digit, 0 can't come, so 7 possibilities are there, and 7 for last digit. So, 7 × 7 = 49.

Case 5: _ 7 _ 3

Total possibilities = 7 × 7 = 49

Case 6: _ _ 7 3

Total possibilities = 7 × 7 = 49

Hence, total possible numbers = 3 × 56 + 3 × 49 = 315.

60. Let M.P. of 1 toy be 100x.

∴ M.P. of 12 toys will be 1200x.

At 20% discount,

S.P. of 8 toys = 8 × 80x = 640x

And, S.P. of remaining 4 toys $= 4\times80x\times\dfrac{3}{4}$ = 240x

Total S.P. = 640x + 240x = 880x

⇒ 880x = 2112

$\Rightarrow x = \dfrac{12}{5}$

$\therefore$ C.P. of 12 toys $= \dfrac{100}{110}\times2112 =$ Rs.1,920

With no discounts, M.P. of 12 toys = S.P. of 12 toys = 1200x $= 1200\times\dfrac{12}{5} =$ Rs.2880.

$\therefore$ Required profit% $= \dfrac{(2880-1920)}{1920}\times100 = 50\%.$

61. **Given:** $x^2 - 2|x| + |a - 2| = 0$

Case 1: $x \geq 0$ and $a \geq 2$

Then, $x^2 - 2x + a - 2 = 0$

Here, $x = 1 + \sqrt{3-a}$ and $x = 1 - \sqrt{3-a}$

Only two integer values are possible when a = 2 and a = 3.

At a = 2, x = 2 and x = 0

At a = 3, x = 1

Case 2: $x \geq 0$ and $a < 2$

Then, $x^2 - 2x - a + 2 = 0$

Here we get x = 1 and a = 1

Case 3: $x < 0$ and $a \geq 2$

we get a = 3, x = – 1 and a = 2, x = – 2

Case 4: $x < 0$ and $a < 2$

we get, a = 1 and x = – 1

Hence, total 7 pair of integers (x, a) are possible.

62. Let John buy x kg of rice and y kg of wheat.

In April, let price of rice be r, then price in May will be 1.2r.

Similarly, let price of wheat in April and May be w and 1.12w respectively.

Now he spent Rs 150 more in May, so -

$0.2(rx) + 0.12(yw) = 150.$

Also, rx = 450 (given)

So, $0.2(rx) = 0.2 \times 450 = 90$

$\therefore yw = \frac{150 - 90}{0.12} = 500$

$\therefore$ Amount spent on wheat in May will be

$= 1.12 \times 500 = 560.$

63. Let the first term of the GP be "a".

Given: $ar^{m-1} = \frac{3}{4}$ and, ... (1)

$ar^{n-1} = 12$ ... (2)

Divide both the equations and get,

$\Rightarrow r^{m-1-n+1} = \frac{1}{16}$

$\Rightarrow r^{m-n} = 16^{-1}$

$\Rightarrow r^{n-m} = 16$

In order to find the smallest possible value of r + n – m, give minimum possible value of 'r' i.e., '– 4' and n – m = 2.

$\therefore$ Minimum possible value of r + n – m = – 4 + 2 = –2.

64. **Given:** $(x^2 - 5x + 7)^{x+1} = 1$

There can be a solution when $x^2 - 5x + 7 = 1$ or $x^2 - 5x + 6 = 0$.

Solving further we get, x = 3 and x = 2.

Also, there can be a solution when x + 1 = 0 or x = –1.

Hence, three possible solutions exist.

65.

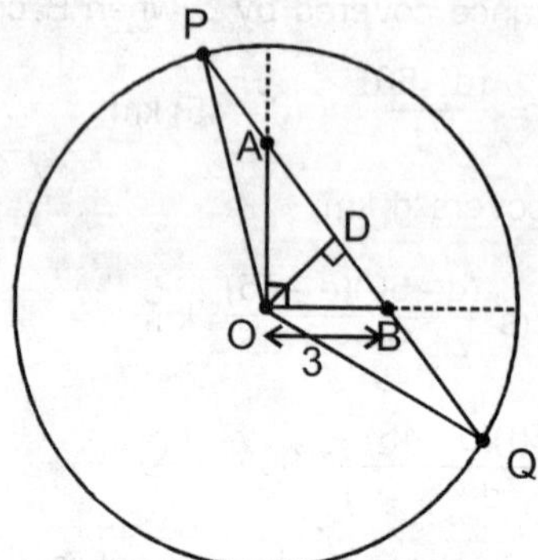

OA = 4m

OB = 3m

OP = OQ = radius = 5m

In ΔAOB,

AO = 4, OB = 3

$\Rightarrow AB = \sqrt{4^2 + 3^2} = 5m$ [ΔAOB is a right triangle]

$\Delta ODB \sim \Delta AOB$ (RHS similarity)

$\therefore \frac{OB}{AB} = \frac{OD}{AO}$

$\Rightarrow \frac{3}{5} = \frac{OD}{4} \Rightarrow OD = \frac{12}{5}m$

In ΔODQ,

$OQ = 5m,\ OD = \frac{12}{5}m$

$\therefore DQ = \sqrt{(5)^2 - \left(\frac{12}{5}\right)^2} = \sqrt{\frac{481}{25}} = 4.386$

Hence, $PQ = 2DQ = 2 \times 4.386 = 8.77 \approx 8.8m$.

66. Let the principal be 'P'.

$\therefore$ According to the question,

$$P\left[\left(1 + \frac{5}{100}\right)^2 - 1\right] - \frac{P \times 3 \times 3}{100} = 1125$$

$$\Rightarrow P\left(\frac{441}{400} - 1\right) - \frac{9P}{100} = 1125$$

$$\Rightarrow \frac{41P}{400} - \frac{9P}{100} = 1125$$

$$\Rightarrow \frac{5P}{400} = 1125$$

$\Rightarrow$ P = Rs. 90,000.

67. We have 2x + 5y = 99 or, $x = \frac{(99-54)}{2}$

Now $x \geq y \geq -20$

So, $\frac{99-5y}{2} \geq 2y$ or $99 \geq 9y$ or $11 \geq y$.

And since $y \geq -20$, therefore, $-20 \leq y \leq 11$

Now for this range of "y" we have to find all the integral values of "x". For which 99 – 5y must be even, which will happen only when y is odd'.

However, there are only 17 odd values of 'y' from – 20 to 11.

Hence, the number of possible values is 17.

68. $\frac{\text{Speed}_{\text{Ram}}}{\text{Speed}_{\text{Rahim}}} = \sqrt{\frac{\text{Time}_{\text{Rahim}}}{\text{Time}_{\text{Ram}}}} = \sqrt{\frac{4}{1}} = 2.$

69.

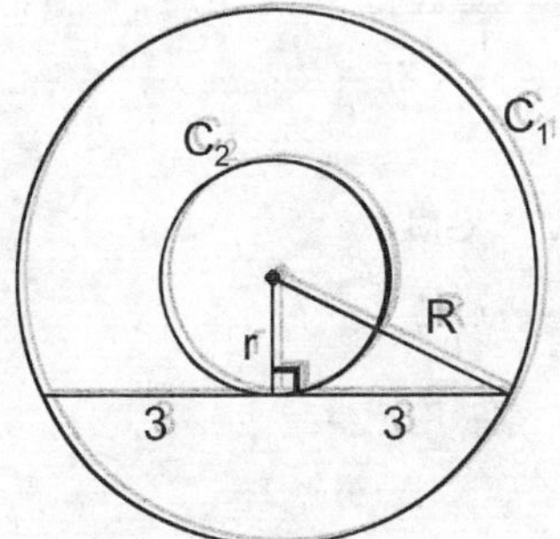

Let 'D' and 'd' be the diameters of circles C_1 and C_2 respectively.

$\therefore D = d + 2$

$2R = 2r + 2$ [Radius of both circles]

$\Rightarrow r = R - 1$

$\therefore r^2 + 9 = R^2$

$(R-1)^2 + 9 = R^2$

$\Rightarrow R = 5$ cm

$\Rightarrow D = 10$ cm.

70. Let the number of pencils and sharpeners bought by Aron are 'p' and 's' respectively.

∴	No. of pencils	No. of sharpeners
Aron	p	s
Aditya	2p	s – 10

Let the cost of one pencil be Rs. 'x'

∴ According to the question,

$px + (x+2)s = 2px + (s-10)(x+2)$

$\Rightarrow px = (x+2)s - (s-10)(x+2)$

$\Rightarrow px = sx + 2s - [sx + 2s - 10x - 20]$

$\Rightarrow px = sx + 2s - sx - 2s + 10x + 20$

$\Rightarrow x = \frac{20}{p-10}$.

Clearly, the value of 'p' should be more than 10.

The minimum possible number of pencils bought by Aron and Aditya together = $p + 2p = 3p_{min}$.

Now, check options:

1st option is $30 \Rightarrow p = 10$, so, not possible.

Similarly, 2nd option is also not possible.

Both 3rd and 4th options are possible but the minimum value of p, we get from option 3 i.e., $3p = 33 \Rightarrow p = 11$.

71. **Given:** $f(x) = x^2 + ax + b$

Then, $f(x+1) = (x+1)^2 + a(x+1) + b$

$= x^2 + 2x + 1 = ax + a + b$

$f(x-1) = (x-1)^2 + a(x-1) + b$

$= x^2 - 2x + 1 + ax - a + b$

$\therefore g(x) = f(x+1) - f(x-1)$

$= 4x + 2a$

Now, $g(20) = 72$

$\Rightarrow g(20) = 4 \times 20 + 2a$

$= 80 + 2a = 72$

$\Rightarrow a = -4$

$\therefore f(x) = x^2 - 4x + b$

For this expression to be greater than zero it has to be a perfect square which is possible for $b \geq 4$.

Hence, the smallest value of b is 4.

72. **Given:** x + 9 = z and y + 1 = z

$x + y < z + 5$ ... (3)

We can write $x = z - 9$ and $y = z - 1$ ... (4)

Now substitute these in inequality (3).

$\Rightarrow z - 9 + z - 1 < z + 5$

$\Rightarrow z < 15$

Hence, the maximum possible value of z is 14 maximum value of "x" is 5 and maximum value of y is 13.

$\therefore (2x + y)_{max} = 10 + 13 = 23$

73. Now 23 students choose maths as one of their subject.

This means (MPC) + (MC) + (PC) = 23 where MPC denotes students who choose all the three subjects maths, physics and chemistry and so on.

So, MC + PM = 5.

Similarly, we have PC + MP = 7.

We have to find the smallest number of students choosing chemistry. For that in the first equation let PM = 5 and MC = 0. In the second equation this PC = 2. Hence, minimum number of students choosing chemistry will be (18 + 2) = 20. Since 18 students chose all the three subjects.

74. $\log_a\left(\frac{a}{b}\right) + \log_b\left(\frac{b}{a}\right)$

$\Rightarrow \log_a a - \log_a b + \log_b b - \log_b a$

$\Rightarrow 1 - \log_a b + 1 - \log_b a$

$\Rightarrow 2 - \left(\frac{\log b}{\log a} + \frac{\log a}{\log b}\right)$

Now applying the property of AM $\geq$ GM, we get

$$\frac{\log_a b + \frac{1}{\log_a b}}{2} \geq 1 \text{ or,}$$

$$\log_a b + \frac{1}{\log_a b} \geq 2$$

Hence, from here we can conclude that the expression will always be equal to 0 or less than 0. Hence any positive value is not possible.

75. The ratio of time taken by John and Jack to finish a job = 2 : 1

∴ Their work efficiency ratio = 1 : 2

⇒ John : Jack = 1 : 2 ... (i)

Also, the ratio of the time taken by (Jack and Jim) together and by John = 1 : 3

So, their work efficiency = 3 : 1

⇒ (Jack + Jim) : John = 3 : 1 ... (ii)

So, from (i) and (ii), we can say in terms of their work efficiencies that the ratio given below will be John : (All three of them)

= 1 : 4

Then, their time taken ratio will become John : (All three of them)

Time ratio → 4 : 1

Diff. = 3

In the question, it is given that John takes 3 days more than that taken by three of them working together, so the above time ratio satisfies the condition.

Hence, John takes 4 days.

As the efficiency of both John and Jim is same, hence, Jim will finish the job in 4 days working alone.

76. To find maximum possible value of $\frac{x}{\sqrt{1+x^4}}$.

$$\Rightarrow \frac{1}{\sqrt{\frac{1+x^4}{x^2}}} = \frac{1}{\sqrt{\frac{1}{x^2}+x^2}}$$

Now apply AM $\geq$ GM

$$\Rightarrow \frac{\left(\frac{1}{x^2}+x^2\right)}{2} \geq 1$$

$$\Rightarrow \frac{1}{x^2}+x^2 \geq 2$$

Substituting we get the maximum value of the equation as $\frac{1}{\sqrt{2}}$.

CAT 2020 SOLVED PAPER (SLOT-3)

Section I: VARC

Question Numbers (1 to 5): The passage below is accompanied by a set of questions. Choose the best answer to each question.

Mode of transportation affects the travel experience and thus can produce new types of travel writing and perhaps even new "identities." Modes of transportation determine the types and duration of social encounters; affect the organization and passage of space and time; . . . and also affect perception and knowledge—how and what the traveler comes to know and write about. The completion of the first U.S. transcontinental highway during the 1920s . . . for example, inaugurated a new genre of travel literature about the United States—the automotive or road narrative. Such narratives highlight the experiences of mostly male protagonists "discovering themselves" on their journeys, emphasizing the independence of road travel and the value of rural folk traditions.

Travel writing's relationship to empire building— as a type of "colonialist discourse"—has drawn the most attention from academicians. Close connections have been observed between European (and American) political, economic, and administrative goals for the colonies and their manifestations in the cultural practice of writing travel books. Travel writers' descriptions of foreign places have been analyzed as attempts to validate, promote, or challenge the ideologies and practices of colonial or imperial domination and expansion. Mary Louise Pratt's study of the genres and conventions of 18th- and 19th-century exploration narratives about South America and Africa (e.g., the "monarch of all I survey" trope) offered ways of thinking about travel writing as embedded within relations of power between metropole and periphery, as did Edward Said's theories of representation and cultural imperialism. Particularly Said's book, *Orientalism*, helped scholars understand ways in which representations of people in travel texts were intimately bound up with notions of self, in this case, that the Occident defined itself through essentialist, ethnocentric, and racist representations of the Orient. Said's work became a model for demonstrating cultural forms of imperialism in travel texts, showing how the political, economic, or administrative fact of dominance relies on legitimating discourses such as those articulated through travel writing. . . .

Feminist geographers' studies of travel writing challenge the masculinist history of geography by questioning who and what are relevant subjects of geographic study and, indeed, what counts as geographic knowledge itself. Such questions are worked through ideological constructs that posit men as explorers and women as travelers—or, conversely, men as travelers and women as tied to the home. Studies of Victorian women who were professional travel writers, tourists, wives of colonial administrators, and other (mostly) elite women who wrote narratives about their experiences abroad during the 19th century have been particularly revealing. From a "liberal" feminist perspective, travel presented one means toward female liberation for middle- and upper-class Victorian women. Many studies from the 1970s onward demonstrated the ways in which women's gendered identities were negotiated differently "at home" than they were "away," thereby showing women's self-development through travel. The more recent poststructural turn in studies of Victorian travel writing has focused attention on women's diverse and fragmented identities as they narrated their travel experiences, emphasizing women's sense of themselves as women in new locations, but only as they worked through their ties to nation, class, whiteness, and colonial and imperial power structures.

1. American travel literature of the 1920s:

(1) developed the male protagonists' desire for independence.

(2) showed participation in local traditions.

(3) presented travellers' discovery of their identity as different from others.

(4) celebrated the freedom that travel gives.

2. From the passage, we can infer that feminist scholars' understanding of the experiences of Victorian women travellers is influenced by all of the following EXCEPT scholars':

(1) knowledge of class tensions in Victorian society.

(2) awareness of the ways in which identity is formed.

(3) perspective that they bring to their research.

(4) awareness of gender issues in Victorian society.

3. From the passage, we can infer that travel writing is most similar to:

(1) historical fiction.

(2) autobiographical writing.

(3) feminist writing.

(4) political journalism.

4. From the passage, it can be inferred that scholars argue that Victorian women experienced self-development through their travels because:

(1) they were from the progressive middle- and upper-classes of society.

(2) their identity was redefined when they were away from home.

(3) they were on a quest to discover their diverse identities.

(4) they developed a feminist perspective of the world.

5. According to the passage, Said's book, "Orientalism":

(1) explained the difference between the representation of people and the actual fact.

(2) demonstrated how cultural imperialism was used to justify colonial domination.

(3) argued that cultural imperialism was more significant than colonial domination.

(4) illustrated how narrow minded and racist westerners were.

Question Numbers (6 to 9): The passage below is accompanied by a set of questions. Choose the best answer to each question.

[There is] a curious new reality: Human contact is becoming a luxury good. As more screens appear in the lives of the poor, screens are disappearing from the lives of the rich. The richer you are, the more you spend to be off-screen. . . .

The joy — at least at first — of the internet revolution was its democratic nature. Facebook is the same Facebook whether you are rich or poor. Gmail is the same Gmail. And it's all free. There is something mass market and unappealing about that. And as studies show that time on these advertisement-support platforms is unhealthy, it all starts to seem déclassé, like drinking soda or smoking cigarettes, which wealthy people do less than poor people. The wealthy can afford to opt out of having their data and their attention sold as a product. The poor and middle class don't have the same kind of resources to make that happen.

Screen exposure starts young. And children who spent more than two hours a day looking at a screen got lower scores on thinking and language tests, according to early results of a landmark study on brain development of more than 11,000 children that the National Institutes of Health is supporting. Most disturbingly, the study is finding that the brains of children who spend a lot of time on screens are different. For some kids, there is premature thinning of their cerebral cortex. In adults, one study found an association between screen time and depression. . . .

Tech companies worked hard to get public schools to buy into programs that required schools to have one laptop per student, arguing that it would better prepare children for their screen-based future. But this idea isn't how the people who actually build the screen-based future raise their own children. In Silicon Valley, time on screens is increasingly seen as unhealthy. Here, the popular elementary school is the local Waldorf School, which promises a back-to-nature, nearly screen-free education. So as wealthy kids are growing up with less screen time, poor kids are growing up with more. How comfortable someone is with human engagement could become a new class marker.

Human contact is, of course, not exactly like organic food . . . . But with screen time, there has been a concerted effort on the part of Silicon Valley behemoths to confuse the public. The poor and the middle class are told that screens are good and important for them and their children. There are fleets of psychologists and neuroscientists on staff at big tech companies working to hook eyes and minds to the screen as fast as possible and for as long as possible. And so human contact is rare. . . .

There is a small movement to pass a "right to disconnect" bill, which would allow workers to turn their phones off, but for now a worker can be punished for going offline and not being available. There is also the reality that in our culture of increasing isolation, in which so many of the traditional gathering places and social structures have disappeared, screens are filling a crucial void.

6. Which of the following statements about the negative effects of screen time is the author least likely to endorse?

(1) It can cause depression in viewers.

(2) It is designed to be addictive.

(3) It is shown to have adverse effects on young children's learning.

(4) It increases human contact as it fills an isolation void.

7. The author claims that Silicon Valley tech companies have tried to "confuse the public" by:

(1) promoting screen time in public schools while opting for a screen-free education for their own children.

(2) pushing for greater privacy while working with advertisement-support platforms to mine data.

(3) developing new work-efficiency programmes while lobbying for the "right to disconnect" bill.

(4) concealing the findings of psychologists and neuroscientists on screen-time use from the public.

8. The author is least likely to agree with the view that the increase in screen-time is fuelled by the fact that:

(1) there is a growth in computer-based teaching in public schools.

(2) screens provide social contact in an increasingly isolating world.

(3) with falling costs, people are streaming more content on their devices.

(4) some workers face punitive action if they are not online.

9. The statement "The richer you are, the more you spend to be off-screen" is supported by which other line from the passage?

(1) ". . . studies show that time on these advertisement-support platforms is unhealthy . . ."

(2) "Gmail is the same Gmail. And it's all free."

(3) ". . . screens are filling a crucial void."

(4) "How comfortable someone is with human engagement could become a new class marker."

Question Numbers (10 to 13): The passage below is accompanied by a set of questions. Choose the best answer to each question.

Although one of the most contested concepts in political philosophy, human nature is something on which most people seem to agree. By and large, according to Rutger Bregman in his new book Humankind, we have a rather pessimistic view – not of ourselves exactly, but of everyone else. We see other people as selfish, untrustworthy and dangerous and therefore we behave towards them with defensiveness and suspicion. This was how the 17th-century philosopher Thomas Hobbes conceived our natural state to be, believing that all that stood between us and violent anarchy was a strong state and firm leadership.

But in following Hobbes, argues Bregman, we ensure that the negative view we have of human nature is reflected back at us. He instead puts his faith in Jean-Jacques Rousseau, the 18th-century French thinker, who famously declared that man was born free and it was civilisation – with its coercive powers, social classes and restrictive laws – that put him in chains.

Hobbes and Rousseau are seen as the two poles of the human nature argument and it's no surprise that Bregman strongly sides with the Frenchman. He takes Rousseau's intuition and paints a picture of a prelapsarian idyll in which, for the better part of 300,000 years, Homo sapiens lived a fulfilling life in harmony with nature . . . Then we discovered agriculture and for the next 10,000 years it was all property, war, greed and injustice. . . .

It was abandoning our nomadic lifestyle and then domesticating animals, says Bregman, that brought about infectious diseases such as measles, smallpox, tuberculosis, syphilis, malaria, cholera and plague. This may be true, but what Bregman never really seems to get to grips with is that pathogens were not the only things that grew with agriculture – so did the number of humans. It's one thing to maintain friendly relations and a property-less mode of living when you're 30 or 40 hunter-gatherers following the food. But life becomes a great deal more complex and knowledge far more extensive when there are settlements of many thousands.

"Civilisation has become synonymous with peace and progress and wilderness with war and decline," writes Bregman. "In reality, for most of human existence, it was the other way around." Whereas traditional history depicts the collapse of civilisations as "dark ages" in which everything gets worse, modern scholars, he claims, see them more as a reprieve, in which the enslaved gain their freedom and culture flourishes. Like much else in this book, the truth is probably somewhere between the two stated positions.

In any case, the fear of civilisational collapse, Bregman believes, is unfounded. It's the result of what the Dutch biologist Frans de Waal calls "veneer theory" – the idea that just below the surface, our bestial nature is waiting to break out. . . . There's a great deal of reassuring human decency to be taken from this bold and thought-provoking book and a wealth of evidence in support of the contention that the sense of who we are as a species has been deleteriously distorted. But it seems equally misleading to offer the false choice of Rousseau and Hobbes when, clearly, humanity encompasses both.

10. According to the passage, the "collapse of civilisations" is viewed by Bregman as:

(1) a sign of regression in society's trajectory.

(2) a temporary phase which can be rectified by social action.

(3) a time that enables changes in societies and cultures.

(4) resulting from a breakdown in the veneer of human nature.

11. The author has differing views from Bregman regarding:

(1) a property-less mode of living being socially harmonious.

(2) the role of agriculture in the advancement of knowledge.

(3) the role of pathogens in the spread of infectious diseases.

(4) a civilised society being coercive and unjust.

12. According to the author, the main reason why Bregman contrasts life in pre-agricultural societies with agricultural societies is to:

(1) bolster his argument that people are basically decent, but progress as we know it can make them selfish.

(2) advocate the promotion of less complex societies as a basis for greater security and prosperity.

(3) make the argument that an environmentally conscious lifestyle is a more harmonious way of living.

(4) highlight the enormous impact that settled farming had on population growth.

13. None of the following views is expressed in the passage EXCEPT that:

(1) Hobbes and Rousseau disagreed on the fundamental nature of humans, but both believed in the need for a strong state.

(2) most people agree with Hobbes' pessimistic view of human nature as being intrinsically untrustworthy and selfish.

(3) Bregman agrees with Hobbes that firm leadership is needed to ensure property rights and regulate strife.

(4) the author of the review believes in the veneer theory of human nature.

Question Numbers (14 to 18): The passage below is accompanied by a set of questions. Choose the best answer to each question.

I've been following the economic crisis for more than two years now. I began working on the subject as part of the background to a novel, and soon realized that I had stumbled across the most interesting story I've ever found. While I was beginning to work on it, the British bank Northern Rock blew up, and it became clear that, as I wrote at the time, "If our laws are not extended to control the new kinds of super-powerful, super-complex, and potentially super-risky investment vehicles, they will one day cause a financial disaster of global-systemic proportions." . . . I was both right and too late, because all the groundwork for the crisis had already been done—though the sluggishness of the world's governments, in not preparing for the great unraveling of autumn 2008, was then and still is stupefying. But this is the first reason why I wrote this book: because what's happened is extraordinarily interesting. It is an absolutely amazing story, full of human interest and drama, one whose byways of mathematics, economics, and psychology are both central to the story of the last decades and mysteriously unknown to the general public. We have heard a lot about "the two cultures" of science and the arts—we heard a particularly large amount about it in 2009, because it was the fiftieth anniversary of the speech during which C. P. Snow first used the phrase. But I'm not sure the idea of a huge gap between science and the arts is as true as it was half a century ago—it's certainly true, for instance, that a general reader who wants to pick up an education in the fundamentals of science will find it easier than ever before. It seems to me that there is a much bigger gap between the world of finance and that of the general public and that there is a need to narrow that gap, if the financial industry is not to be a kind of priesthood, administering to its own mysteries and feared and resented by the rest of us. Many bright, literate people have no idea about all sorts of economic basics, of a type that financial insiders take as elementary facts of how the world works. I am an outsider to finance and economics, and my hope is that I can talk across that gulf.

My need to understand is the same as yours, whoever you are. That's one of the strangest ironies of this story: after decades in which the ideology of the Western world was personally and economically individualistic, we've suddenly been hit by a crisis which shows in the starkest terms that whether we like it or not—and there are large parts of it that you would have to be crazy to like—we're all in this together. The aftermath of the crisis is going to dominate the economics and politics of our societies for at least a decade to come and perhaps longer.

14. All of the following, if true, could be seen as supporting the arguments in the passage, EXCEPT:

(1) The story of the economic crisis is also one about international relations, global financial security, and mass psychology.

(2) The difficulty with understanding financial matters is that they have become so arcane.

(3) The failure of economic systems does not necessarily mean the failure of their ideologies.

(4) Economic crises could be averted by changing prevailing ideologies and beliefs.

15. According to the passage, the author is likely to be supportive of which one of the following programmes?

(1) The complete nationalisation of all financial institutions.

(2) Economic policies that are more sensitively calibrated to the fluctuations of the market.

(3) An educational curriculum that promotes developing financial literacy in the masses.

(4) An educational curriculum that promotes economic research.

16. Which one of the following, if false, could be seen as supporting the author's claims?

(1) The economic crisis was not a failure of collective action to rectify economic problems.

(2) The huge gap between science and the arts has steadily narrowed over time.

(3) Most people are yet to gain any real understanding of the workings of the financial world.

(4) The global economic crisis lasted for more than two years.

17. Which one of the following best captures the main argument of the last paragraph of the passage?

(1) In the decades to come, other ideologies will emerge in the aftermath of the crisis.

(2) The ideology of individualism must be set aside in order to deal with the crisis.

(3) Whoever you are, you would be crazy to think that there is no crisis.

(4) The aftermath of the crisis will strengthen the central ideology of individualism in the Western world.

18. Which one of the following, if true, would be an accurate inference from the first sentence of the passage?

(1) The author has witnessed many economic crises by travelling a lot for two years.

(2) The economic crisis outlasted the author's preoccupation with it.

(3) The author is preoccupied with the economic crisis because he is being followed.

(4) The author's preoccupation with the economic crisis is not less than two years old.

19. The passage given below is followed by four alternate summaries. Choose the option that best captures the essence of the passage.

The dominant hypotheses in modern science believe that language evolved to allow humans to exchange factual information about the physical world. But an alternative view is that language evolved, in modern humans at least, to facilitate social bonding. It increased our ancestors' chances of survival by enabling them to hunt more successfully or to cooperate more extensively. Language meant that things could be explained and that plans and past experiences could be shared efficiently.

(1) Since its origin, language has been continuously evolving to higher forms, from being used to identify objects to ensuring human survival by enabling our ancestors to bond and cooperate.

(2) Most believe that language originated from a need to articulate facts, but others think it emerged from the need to promote social cohesion and cooperation, thus enabling human survival.

(3) Experts are challenging the narrow view of the origin of language, as being merely used to describe facts and label objects, to being necessary to promote more complex interactions among humans.

(4) From the belief that humans invented language to process factual information, scholars now think that language was the outcome of the need to ensure social cohesion and thus human survival.

20. Five jumbled up sentences, related to a topic, are given below. Four of them can be put together to form a coherent paragraph. Identify the odd one out and key in the number of the sentence as your answer:

(1) Machine learning models are prone to learning human-like biases from the training data that feeds these algorithms.

(2) Hate speech detection is part of the on-going effort against oppressive and abusive language on social media.

(3) The current automatic detection models miss out on something vital: context.

(4) It uses complex algorithms to flag racist or violent speech faster and better than human beings alone.

(5) For instance, algorithms struggle to determine if group identifiers like "gay" or "black" are used in offensive or prejudiced ways because they're trained on imbalanced datasets with unusually high rates of hate speech.

21. The four sentences (labelled 1, 2, 3, 4) below, when properly sequenced would yield a coherent paragraph. Decide on the proper sequencing of the order of the sentences and key in the sequence of the four numbers as your answer:

(1) Complex computational elements of the CNS are organized according to a "nested" hierarchic criterion; the organization is not permanent and can change dynamically from moment to moment as they carry out a computational task.

(2) Echolocation in bats exemplifies adaptation produced by natural selection; a function not produced by natural selection for its current use is exaptation -- feathers might have originally arisen in the context of selection for insulation.

(3) From a structural standpoint, consistent with exaptation, the living organism is organized as a complex of "Russian Matryoshka Dolls" -- smaller structures are contained within larger ones in multiple layers.

(4) The exaptation concept, and the Russian-doll organization concept of living beings deduced from studies on evolution of the various apparatuses in mammals, can be applied for the most complex human organ: the central nervous system (CNS).

22. Five jumbled up sentences, related to a topic, are given below. Four of them can be put together to form a coherent paragraph. Identify the odd one out and key in the number of the sentence as your answer:

(1) The logic of displaying one's inner qualities through outward appearance was based on a distinction between being a woman and being feminine.

(2) 'Appearance' became a signifier of conduct - to look was to be and conformity to the feminine ideal was measured by how well women could use the tools of the fashion and beauty industries.

(3) The makeover-centric media sets out subtly and not-so-subtly, 'good' and 'bad' ways to be a woman, layering these over inequalities of race and class.

(4) The denigration of working-class women and women of colour often centres on their perceived failure to embody feminine beauty.

(5) 'Woman' was considered a biological category, but femininity was a 'process' by which women became specific kinds of women.

23. The passage given below is followed by four alternate summaries. Choose the option that best captures the essence of the passage.

Brown et al. (2001) suggest that 'metabolic theory may provide a conceptual foundation for much of ecology just as genetic theory provides a foundation for much of evolutionary biology'. One of the successes of genetic theory is the diversity of theoretical approaches and models that have been developed and applied. A Web of Science (v. 5.9. Thomson Reuters) search on genetic* + theor* + evol* identifies more than 12000 publications between 2005 and 2012. Considering only the 10 most-cited papers within this 12000 publication set, genetic theory can be seen to focus on genome dynamics, phylogenetic inference, game theory and the regulation of gene expression. There is no one fundamental genetic equation, but rather a wide array of genetic models, ranging from simple to complex, with differing inputs and outputs, and divergent areas of application, loosely connected to each other through the shared conceptual foundation of heritable variation.

(1) Genetic theory has a wide range of theoretical approaches and application and is foundational to evolutionary biology and Metabolic theory has the potential to do the same for ecology.

(2) Genetic theory has a wide range of theoretical approaches and applications and Metabolic theory must have the same in the field of ecology.

(3) Genetic theory provides an example of how a range of theoretical approaches and applications can make a theory successful.

(4) Genetic theory has evolved to spawn a wide range of theoretical models and applications but Metabolic theory need not evolve in a similar manner in the field of ecology.

24. The passage given below is followed by four alternate summaries. Choose the option that best captures the essence of the passage.

Aesthetic political representation urges us to realize that 'the representative has autonomy with regard to the people represented' but autonomy then is not an excuse to abandon one's responsibility. Aesthetic autonomy requires cultivation of 'disinterestedness' on the part of actors which is not indifference. To have disinterestedness, that is, to have comportment towards the beautiful that is devoid of all ulterior references to use – requires a kind of aesthetic commitment; it is the liberation of ourselves for the release of what has proper worth only in itself.

(1) Disinterestedness, as distinct from indifference, is the basis of political representation.

(2) Disinterestedness is different from indifference as the former means a non-subjective evaluation of things which is what constitutes aesthetic political representation.

(3) Aesthetic political representation advocates autonomy for the representatives drawing from disinterestedness, which itself is different from indifference.

(4) Aesthetic political representation advocates autonomy for the representatives manifested through disinterestedness which itself is different from indifference.

25. The four sentences (labelled 1, 2, 3, 4) below, when properly sequenced would yield a coherent paragraph. Decide on the proper sequencing of the order of the sentences and key in the sequence of the four numbers as your answer:

(1) It advocated a conservative approach to antitrust enforcement that espouses faith in efficient markets and voiced suspicion regarding the merits of judicial intervention to correct anticompetitive practices.

(2) Many industries have consistently gained market share, the lion's share - without any official concern; the most successful technology companies have grown into veritable titans, on the premise that they advance 'public interest'.

(3) That the new anticompetitive risks posed by tech giants like Google, Facebook, and Amazon, necessitate new legal solutions could be attributed to the dearth of enforcement actions against monopolies and the few cases challenging mergers in the USA.

(4) The criterion of 'consumer welfare standard' and the principle that antitrust law should serve consumer interests and that it should protect competition rather than individual competitors was an antitrust law introduced by, and named after, the 'Chicago school'.

26. The four sentences (labelled 1, 2, 3, 4) below, when properly sequenced would yield a coherent paragraph. Decide on the proper sequencing of the order of the sentences and key in the sequence of the four numbers as your answer:

(1) Each one personified a different aspect of good fortune.

(2) The others were versions of popular Buddhist gods, Hindu gods and Daoist gods.

(3) Seven popular Japanese deities, the Shichi Fukujin, were considered to bring good luck and happiness.

(4) Although they were included in the Shinto pantheon, only two of them, Daikoku and Ebisu, were indigenous Japanese gods.

Section II: DI & LR

Question Numbers (27 to 32): Answer the questions on the basis of the information given below.

The Hi-Lo game is a four-player game played in six rounds. In every round, each player chooses to bid Hi or Lo. The bids are made simultaneously. If all four bid Hi, then all four lose 1 point each. If three players bid Hi and one bids Lo, then the players bidding Hi gain 1 point each and the player bidding Lo loses 3 points. If two players bid Hi and two bid Lo, then the players bidding Hi gain 2 points each and the players bidding Lo lose 2 points each. If one player bids Hi and three bid Lo, then the player bidding Hi gains 3 points and the players bidding Lo lose 1 point each. If all four bid Lo, then all four gain 1 point each.

Four players Arun, Bankim, Charu, and Dipak played the Hi-Lo game. The following facts are known about their game:

1. At the end of three rounds, Arun had scored 6 points, Dipak had scored 2 points, Bankim and Charu had scored -2 points each.
2. At the end of six rounds, Arun had scored 7 points, Bankim and Dipak had scored -1 point each, and Charu had scored -5 points.
3. Dipak's score in the third round was less than his score in the first round but was more than his score in the second round.
4. In exactly two out of the six rounds, Arun was the only player who bid Hi.

27. What were the bids by Arun, Bankim, Charu and Dipak, respectively in the first round?

(1) Hi, Lo, Lo, Hi

(2) Hi, Hi, Lo, Lo

(3) Lo, Lo, Lo, Hi

(4) Hi, Lo, Lo, Lo

28. In how many rounds did Arun bid Hi?

29. In how many rounds did Bankim bid Lo?

30. In how many rounds did all four players make identical bids?

31. In how many rounds did Dipak gain exactly 1 point?

32. In which of the following rounds, was Arun DEFINITELY the only player to bid Hi?

(1) Third

(2) Second

(3) First

(4) Fourth

Question Numbers (33 to 38): Answer the questions on the basis of the information given below.

A farmer had a rectangular land containing 205 trees. He distributed that land among his four daughters – Abha, Bina, Chitra and Dipti by dividing the land into twelve plots along three rows (X,Y,Z) and four Columns (1,2,3,4) as shown in the figure below:

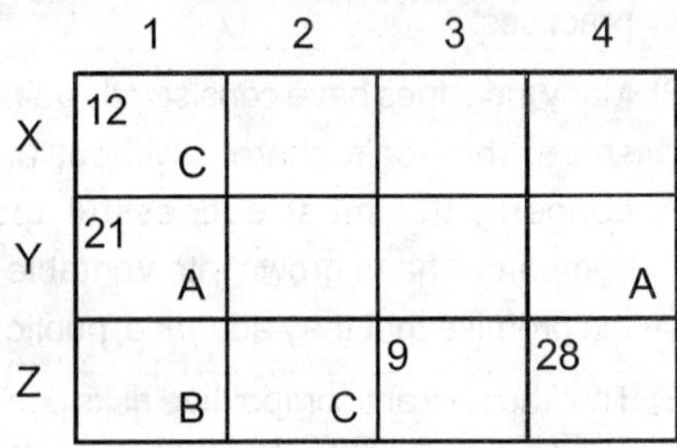

The plots in rows X, Y, Z contained mango, teak and pine trees respectively. Each plot had trees in non-zero multiples of 3 or 4 and none of the plots had the same number of trees. Each daughter got an even number of plots. In the figure, the number mentioned in top left corner of a plot is the number of trees in that plot, while the letter in the bottom right corner is the first letter of the name of the daughter who got that plot (For example, Abha got the plot in row Y and column 1 containing 21 trees). Some information in the figure got erased, but the following is known:

1. Abha got 20 trees more than Chitra but 6 trees less than Dipti.
2. The largest number of trees in a plot was 32, but it was not with Abha.
3. The number of teak trees in Column 3 was double of that in Column 2 but was half of that in Column 4.
4. Both Abha and Bina got a higher number of plots than Dipti.
5. Only Bina, Chitra and Dipti got corner plots.
6. Dipti got two adjoining plots in the same row.
7. Bina was the only one who got a plot in each row and each column.
8. Chitra and Dipti did not get plots which were adjacent to each other (either in row / column / diagonal).
9. The number of mango trees was double the number of teak trees.

33. How many mango trees were there in total?

(1) 49

(2) 126

(3) 84

(4) 98

34. Which of the following is the correct sequence of trees received by Abha, Bina, Chitra and Dipti in that order?

(1) 50, 69, 30, 56

(2) 60, 39, 40, 66

(3) 44, 87, 24, 50

(4) 54, 57, 34, 60

35. How many pine trees did Chitra receive?

(1) 15

(2) 21

(3) 30

(4) 18

36. Who got the plot with the smallest number of trees and how many trees did that plot have?

(1) Abha, 4 trees

(2) Dipti, 6 trees

(3) Bina, 3 trees

(4) Bina, 4 trees

37. Which of the following statements is NOT true?

(1) Chitra got 12 mango trees.

(2) Dipti got 56 mango trees.

(3) Abha got 41 teak trees.

(4) Bina got 32 pine trees.

38. Which column had the highest number of trees?

(1) Cannot be determined

(2) 3

(3) 2

(4) 4

Question Numbers (39 to 42): Answer the questions on the basis of the information given below.

XYZ organization got into the business of delivering groceries to home at the beginning of the last month. They have a two-day delivery promise. However, their deliveries are unreliable. An order booked on a particular day may be delivered the next day or the day after. If the order is not delivered at the end of two days, then the order is declared as lost at the end of the second day. XYZ then does not deliver the order, but informs the customer, marks the order as lost, returns the payment and pays a penalty for non-delivery.

The following table provides details about the operations of XYZ for a week of the last month. The first column gives the date, the second gives the cumulative number of orders that were booked up to and including that day. The third column represents the number of orders delivered on that day. The last column gives the cumulative number of orders that were lost up to and including that day.

It is known that the numbers of orders that were booked on the 11th, 12th, and 13th of the last month that took two days to deliver were 4, 6, and 8 respectively.

Day	Cumulative orders booked	Orders delivered on day	Cumulative orders lost
13th	219	11	91
14th	249	27	92
15th	277	23	94
16th	302	11	106
17th	327	21	118
18th	332	13	120
19th	337	14	129

39. Among the following days, the largest fraction of orders booked on which day was lost?

(1) 14th

(2) 13th

(3) 15th

(4) 16th

40. On which of the following days was the number of orders booked the highest?

(1) 14th

(2) 13th

(3) 12th

(4) 15th

41. The *delivery ratio* for a given day is defined as the ratio of the number of orders booked on that day which are delivered on the next day to the number of orders booked on that day which are delivered on the second day after booking. On which of the following days, was the *delivery ratio* the highest?

(1) 16th

(2) 15th

(3) 13th

(4) 14th

42. The average time taken to deliver orders booked on a particular day is computed as follows. Let the number of orders delivered the next day be x and the number of orders delivered the day after be y. Then the average time to deliver order is (x+2y)/(x+y). On which of the following days was the average time taken to deliver orders booked the least?

(1) 13th

(2) 14th

(3) 16th

(4) 15th

Question Numbers (43 to 46): Answer the questions on the basis of the information given below.

Sixteen patients in a hospital must undergo a blood test for a disease. It is known that exactly one of them has the disease. The hospital has only eight testing kits and has decided to pool blood samples of patients into eight vials for the tests. The patients are numbered 1 through 16, and the vials are labelled A, B, C, D, E, F, G, and H. The following table shows the vials into which each patient's blood sample is distributed.

Patient	Vials	Patient	Vials
1	B, D, F, H	9	A, D, F, H
2	B, D, F, G	10	A, D, F, G
3	B, D, E, H	11	A, D, E, H
4	B, D, E, G	12	A, D, E, G
5	B, C, F, H	13	A, C, F, H
6	B, C, F, G	14	A, C, F, G
7	B, C, E, H	15	A, C, E, H
8	B, C, E, G	16	A, C, E, G

If a patient has the disease, then each vial containing his/her blood sample will test positive. If a vial tests positive, one of the patients whose blood samples were mixed in the vial has the disease. If a vial tests negative, then none of the patients whose blood samples were mixed in the vial has the disease.

43. Suppose vial C tests positive and vials A, E and H test negative. Which patient has the disease?

(1) Patient 8

(2) Patient 2

(3) Patient 6

(4) Patient 14

44. Suppose vial A tests positive and vials D and G test negative. Which of the following vials should we test next to identify the patient with the disease?

(1) Vial E

(2) Vial H

(3) Vial C

(4) Vial B

45. Which of the following combinations of test results is NOT possible?

(1) Vials B and D positive, vials F and H negative

(2) Vials A and E positive, vials C and D negative

(3) Vials A and G positive, vials D and E negative

(4) Vial B positive, vials C, F and H negative

46. Suppose one of the lab assistants accidentally mixed two patients' blood samples before they were distributed to the vials. Which of the following correctly represents the set of all possible numbers of positive test results out of the eight vials?

(1) {5,6,7,8} (2) {4,5,6,7}

(3) {4,5} (4) {4,5,6,7,8}

Question Numbers (47 to 50): Answer the questions on the basis of the information given below.

A survey of 600 schools in India was conducted to gather information about their online teaching learning processes (OTLP). The following four facilities were studied.

F1: Own software for OTLP

F2: Trained teachers for OTLP

F3: Training materials for OTLP

F4: All students having Laptops

The following observations were summarized from the survey.

1. 80 schools did not have any of the four facilities – F1, F2, F3, F4.
2. 40 schools had all four facilities.
3. The number of schools with only F1, only F2, only F3, and only F4 was 25, 30, 26 and 20 respectively.
4. The number of schools with exactly three of the facilities was the same irrespective of which three were considered.
5. 313 schools had F2.
6. 26 schools had only F2 and F3 (but neither F1 nor F4).
7. Among the schools having F4, 24 had only F3, and 45 had only F2.
8. 162 schools had both F1 and F2.
9. The number of schools having F1 was the same as the number of schools having F4.

47. What was the total number of schools having exactly three of the four facilities?

(1) 80 (2) 64

(3) 200 (4) 50

48. What was the number of schools having facilities F2 and F4?

(1) 95 (2) 45

(3) 185 (4) 85

49. What was the number of schools having only facilities F1 and F3?

50. What was the number of schools having only facilities F1 and F4?

Section III: QA

51. Let k be a constant. The equations kx + y = 3 and 4x + ky = 4 have a unique solution if and only if

(1) $|k| \neq 2$ (2) k = 2
(3) $k \neq 2$ (4) $|k| = 2$

52. Vimla starts for office every day at 9 am and reaches exactly on time if she drives at her usual speed of 40 km/hr. She is late by 6 minutes if she drives at 35 km/hr. One day, she covers two-thirds of her distance to office in one-thirds of her usual time to reach office, and then stops for 8 minutes. The speed, in km/hr, at which she should drive the remaining distance to reach office exactly on time is

(1) 29 (2) 27
(3) 26 (4) 28

53. Let m and n be positive integers, If $x^2 + mx + 2n = 0$ and $x^2 + 2nx + m = 0$ have real roots, then the smallest possible value of m + n is

(1) 7 (2) 6
(3) 8 (4) 5

54. The area, in sq. units, enclosed by the lines $x = 2$, $y = |x - 2| + 4$, the X-axis and the Y-axis is equal to

(1) 6 (2) 8
(3) 12 (4) 10

55. How many pairs (a, b) of positive integers are there such that $a \leq b$ and $ab = 4^{2017}$?

(1) 2017 (2) 2018
(3) 2019 (4) 2020

56. If $x_1 = -1$ and $x_m = x_{m+1} + (m + 1)$ for every positive integer m, then x_{100} equals

(1) –5151 (2) –5150
(3) –5051 (4) –5050

57. A contractor agreed to construct a 6 km road in 200 days. He employed 140 persons for the work. After 60 days, he realized that only 1.5 km road has been completed. How many additional people would he need to employ in order to finish the work exactly on time?

58. The vertices of a triangle are (0, 0), (4, 0) and (3, 9). The area of the circle passing through these three points is

(1) $\frac{205\pi}{9}$ (2) $\frac{123\pi}{7}$
(3) $\frac{14\pi}{3}$ (4) $\frac{12\pi}{5}$

59. Dick is thrice as old as Tom and Harry is twice as old as Dick. If Dick's age is 1 year less than the average age of all three, then Harry's age, in years, is

60. $\frac{2 \times 4 \times 8 \times 16}{(\log_2 4)^2 (\log_4 8)^3 (\log_8 16)^4}$ equals

61. A and B are two railway stations 90 km apart. A train leaves A at 9:00 am, heading towards B at a speed of 40 km/hr. Another train leaves B at 10:30 am, heading towards A at a speed of 20 km/hr. The trains meet each other at

(1) 11 : 20 am (2) 11 : 45 am
(3) 11 : 00 am (4) 10 : 45 am

62. How many integers in the set {100, 101, 102, ..., 999} have at least one digit repeated?

63. If $f(x + y) = f(x)f(y)$ and $f(5) = 4$, then $f(10) - f(-10)$ is equal to

(1) 15.9375 (2) 0
(3) 3 (4) 14.0625

64. The points (2, 1) and (–3, –4) are opposite vertices of a parallelogram. If the other two vertices lie on the line $x + 9y + c = 0$, then c is

(1) 15 (2) 12
(3) 13 (4) 14

65. A person invested a certain amount of money at 10% annual interest, compounded half-yearly. After one and a half years, the interest and principal together became Rs 18522. The amount, in rupees, that the person had invested is

66. In the final examination, Bishnu scored 52% and Asha scored 64%. The marks obtained by Bishnu is 23 less, and that by Asha is 34 more than the marks obtained by Ramesh. The marks obtained by Geeta, who scored 84%, is

(1) 439 (2) 357
(3) 399 (4) 417

67. A man buys 35 kg of sugar and sets a marked price in order to make a 20% profit. He sells 5 kg at this price, and 15 kg at a 10% discount. Accidentally, 3 kg of sugar is wasted. He sells the remaining sugar by raising the marked price by p percent so as to make an overall profit of 15%. Then p is nearest to

(1) 31 (2) 25
(3) 22 (4) 35

68. If $\log_a 30 = A$, $\log_a\left(\frac{5}{3}\right) = -B$ and $\log_2 a = \frac{1}{3}$, then $\log_3 a$ is equal

(1) $\frac{A+B-3}{2}$ (2) $\frac{A+B}{2}-3$

(3) $\frac{2}{A+B}-3$ (4) $\frac{2}{A+B-3}$

69. Let m and n be natural numbers such that n is even and $0.2 < \frac{m}{20}, \frac{n}{m}, \frac{n}{11} < 0.5$. Then $m - 2n$ equals

(1) 4 (2) 3

(3) 1 (4) 2

70. If a, b, c are non-zero and $14^a = 36^b = 84^c$, then $6b\left(\frac{1}{c}-\frac{1}{a}\right)$ is equal to

71. Let N, x and y be positive integers such that N = x + y, 2 < x < 10 and 14 < y < 23. If N > 25, then how many distinct values are possible for N?

72. Anil, Sunil, and Ravi run along a circular path of length 3 km, starting from the same point at the same time, and going in the clockwise direction. If they run at speeds of 15 km/hr, 10 km/hr, and 8 km/hr, respectively, how much distance in km will Ravi have run when Anil and Sunil meet again for the first time at the starting point?

(1) 4.2 (2) 4.8

(3) 5.2 (4) 4.6

73. A batsman played n + 2 innings and got out on all occasions. His average score in these n + 2 innings was 29 runs and he scored 38 and 15 runs in the last two innings. The batsman scored less than 38 runs in each of the first n innings. In these n innings, his average score was 30 runs and lowest score was x runs. The smallest possible value of x is

(1) 1 (2) 2

(3) 4 (4) 3

74. How many of the integers 1, 2, … , 120, are divisible by none of 2, 5 and 7?

(1) 41 (2) 42

(3) 43 (4) 40

75. In a trapezium ABCD, AB is parallel to DC, BC is perpendicular to DC and $\angle BAD = 45°$. If DC = 5 cm, BC = 4 cm, the area of the trapezium in sq cm is

76. Two alcohol solutions, A and B, are mixed in the proportion 1:3 by volume. The volume of the mixture is then doubled by adding solution A such that the resulting mixture has 72% alcohol. If solution A has 60% alcohol, then the percentage of alcohol in solution B is

(1) 90% (2) 94%

(3) 89% (4) 92%

ANSWERS

1. (4)	**2.** (1)	**3.** (2)	**4.** (2)	**5.** (2)	**6.** (4)	**7.** (1)	**8.** (3)	**9.** (4)	**10.** (3)
11. (4)	**12.** (1)	**13.** (2)	**14.** (3)	**15.** (3)	**16.** (1)	**17.** (2)	**18.** (4)	**19.** (2)	**20.** (3)
21. (2431)	**22.** (3)	**23.** (1)	**24.** (3)	**25.** (4123)	**26.** (3142)	**27.** (1)	**28.** (4)	**29.** (4)	**30.** (2)
31. (1)	**32.** (2)	**33.** (4)	**34.** (1)	**35.** (4)	**36.** (3)	**37.** (4)	**38.** (4)	**39.** (3)	**40.** (2)
41. (4)	**42.** (2)	**43.** (3)	**44.** (1)	**45.** (2)	**46.** (4)	**47.** (3)	**48.** (3)	**49.** (42)	**50.** (20)
51. (1)	**52.** (4)	**53.** (2)	**54.** (4)	**55.** (2)	**56.** (4)	**57.** (40)	**58.** (1)	**59.** (18)	**60.** (24)
61. (3)	**62.** (252)	**63.** (1)	**64.** (4)	**65.** (16000)	**66.** (3)	**67.** (2)	**68.** (4)	**69.** (3)	**70.** (3)
71. (6)	**72.** (2)	**73.** (2)	**74.** (1)	**75.** (28)	**76.** (4)				

EXPLANATIONS

1. Refer the lines, *"The completion of the first U.S. transcontinental highway during the 1920s . . . for example, inaugurated a new genre of travel literature about the United States—the automotive or road narrative. ......"discovering themselves" on their journeys, emphasizing the independence of road travel and the value of rural folk traditions.* The other options distort the intended meaning of the statements.

2. In their analysis of Victorian women travelers, feminist scholars have drawn on their understanding of how identity is developed *(Such questions are worked through ideological constructs that posit men as explorers and women as travelers—or, conversely, men as travelers and women as tied to the home)*; their own perspective *(Feminist geographers' studies of travel writing challenge the masculinist history of geography by questioning who and what are relevant subjects of geographic study and, indeed, what counts as geographic knowledge itself)* and awareness of gender issues in Victorian societies *(From a "liberal" feminist perspective, travel presented one means toward female liberation for middle- and upper-class Victorian women. Many studies from the 1970s onward demonstrated the ways in which women's gendered identities were negotiated differently "at home" than they were "away," thereby showing women's self-development through travel)* There is no mention or reference to class tensions in Victorian societies.

3. Refer the lines, *"Mode of transportation affects the travel experience and thus can produce new types of travel writing and perhaps even new "identities."* The other options are not in consonance with the ideas discussed in the passage.

4. Refer the lines, *"Many studies from the 1970s onward demonstrated the ways in which women's gendered identities were negotiated differently "at home" than they were "away," thereby showing women's self-development through travel."* The other options are beyond the scope of the information given in the passage.

5. Refer the lines, *"Said's work became a model for demonstrating cultural forms of imperialism in travel texts, showing how the political, economic, or administrative fact of dominance relies on legitimating discourses such as those articulated through travel writing."* This makes 2 correct. The other options are factually inaccurate.

6. Throughout the passage, the author has highlighted the negative impacts of excessive screen time. Thus, statement 4, which can be interpreted as stating a positive impact of spending time on screens, is least likely to find endorsement by the author.

7. Refer the lines, *"Tech companies worked hard to get public schools to buy into programs that required schools to have one laptop per student, arguing that it would better prepare children for their screen-based future. But this idea isn't how the people who actually build the screen-based future raise their own children. In Silicon Valley, time on screens is increasingly seen as unhealthy."*

8. Statements 1, 2 and 4 are aligned with the various pieces of information shared by the author. 3 finds no evidence in the passage.

9. The idea behind the statement is that human contact is becoming a luxury good. The rich are opting for less screen time. The education of their children is also geared along these lines, whereas the poor and middle class does not have the resources to do so. This idea finds resonance in the statement- *"How comfortable someone is with human engagement could become a new class marker."*

10. Refer the lines, *"Whereas traditional history depicts the collapse of civilisations as "dark ages" in which everything gets worse, modern scholars, he claims, see them more as a reprieve, in which the enslaved gain their freedom and culture flourishes."* This makes 3 correct. The veneer theory was propounded by Dutch biologist Frans de Waal, not Bregman. There is no mention of rectification by social action in the passage.

11. Bregman believes that it was the rise of civilization that introduced war and decline in society. However, the author disagrees. Refer to the lines, *"Like much else in this book, the truth is probably somewhere between the two stated positions."*

12. Refer to the concluding lines of the passage- *"There's a great deal of reassuring human decency to be taken from this bold and thought-provoking book and a wealth of evidence in support of the contention that the sense of who we are as a species has been deleteriously distorted."* Thus, this is the reason that the author ascribes to the contrasts drawn by Bregman. The other options are limited in the explanations they offer.

13. None of the other options find support in the passage.

14. Option 1 - The story of the economic crisis is also one about international relations, global financial security, and mass psychology supports the following statement of the author - *It is an absolutely*

amazing story, full of human interest and drama, one whose byways of mathematics, economics, and psychology are both central to the story of the last decades and mysteriously unknown to the general public. Option 2 - The difficulty with understanding financial matters is that they have become so arcane supports the following information - *Many bright, literate people have no idea about all sorts of economic basics, of a type that financial insiders take as elementary facts of how the world works.* Option 4 - Economic crises could be averted by changing prevailing ideologies and beliefs echoes the following statement- *"If our laws are not extended to control the new kinds of super-powerful, super-complex, and potentially super-risky investment vehicles, they will one day cause a financial disaster of global-systemic proportions."* . . . Option 3 contradicts these statements and is hence, incorrect.

15. Refer the lines, *"It seems to me that there is a much bigger gap between the world of finance and that of the general public and that there is a need to narrow that gap, if the financial industry is not to be a kind of priesthood, administering to its own mysteries and feared and resented by the rest of us."* This makes option 3 correct. The other options are not supported by the information given in the passage.

16. The wording of the question is slightly tricky. The question is asking you to identify the option, which, if false, will support the author's argument. The first option states that-The economic crisis was not a failure of collective action to rectify economic problems. The author argues for the very opposite in the passage. He is surprised by the sluggishness of the world governments, by a collective lack of preparation by the various stakeholders involved. Thus, 1 is correct. The other options, if untrue, will weaken the author's claims.

17. The concluding paragraph of the passage highlights the larger impact and the need for a collective response to a crisis that is the result of an individualistic ideology. Thus, 2 is correct. The other options distort the information given in the paragraph.

18. The first line of the passage is-I've been following the economic crisis for more than two years now. Thus, the only inference that can be drawn is that the author's preoccupation with the economic crisis is not less than two years old.

19. The passage is making two points:

a. The prominent view is that language evolved to facilitate exchange of factual information about the world.

b. Another view holds that it evolved to facilitate social bonding which ensured the survival of the human race.

Only the second option captures these essential aspects of the argument. Option 1 is incorrect because there is no discussion on the evolution of language. There is no element of challenging of viewpoints. By the same logic even option 4 gets negated.

20. Sentences 1, 2, 4 and 5 are about detecting hate speech through machine learning and its process. Sentence 3, however, talks about the context in which certain words are used in social media which the machine is not able to understand or detect. Hence, the correct answer is sentence 3. The correct order of the sentences will be - Hate speech detection is part of the ongoing effort against oppressive and abusive language on social media. It uses complex algorithms to flag racist or violent speech faster and better than human beings alone. Machine learning models are prone to learning human-like biases from the training data that feeds these algorithms. For instance, algorithms struggle to determine if group identifiers like "gay" or "black" are used in offensive or prejudiced ways because they're trained on imbalanced datasets with unusually high rates of hate speech.

21. Exaptation is mentioned in 2 and elaborated upon in 4. Thus, 24 is a mandatory pair. Also, 2 is the opening sentence since it introduces the topic. Similarly, the reference to Russian dolls in 3 indicates that 3 follows next and the paragraph concludes with 1. Thus, the correct sequence is 2431.

22. The correct order will be 1524.

1. The logic of displaying one's inner qualities through outward appearance was based on a distinction between being a woman and being feminine.
2. 'Woman' was considered a biological category, but femininity was a 'process' by which women became specific kinds of women.
3. 'Appearance' became a signifier of conduct - to look was to be and conformity to the feminine ideal was measured by how well women could use the tools of the fashion and beauty industries.
4. The denigration of working-class women and women of colour often centres on their perceived failure to embody feminine beauty.

The reference to class and race in statement 3 makes it the odd one out.

23. The essence of the passage is captured in the opening line itself "metabolic theory may provide a conceptual foundation for much of ecology just as genetic theory provides a foundation for much of evolutionary biology'. It then goes on to talk about the various applications of genetic theory. Thus, the correct summarization is provided by option 1. The use of 'must' makes option 2 wrong. 3 is factually incorrect. There is no contrast presented between metabolic theory and genetic theory. Thus, 4 is also wrong.

24. The key aspects of the passage are – what constitutes aesthetic political representation and the meaning of disinterestedness in this respect. This is why 3 is correct. Option 1 distorts the flow of ideas while 'constitutes' makes 2 incorrect. The passage states that aesthetic autonomy requires the development of disinterestedness.

25. 'It' in 1 refers to the criterion of consumer welfare standard in 4. Thus, 41 becomes a pair. 'many industries' in 2 and the names of these industries in 3 makes 23 a pair. Since, 23 elaborates on the idea introduced in 4 and 1, 4123 becomes the correct sequence.

26. This is a relatively easy question. The mention of the seven deities in 3 and 'each' in 1 makes 31 a pair. The reference to two of them in 4 and the others in 2 makes 3142 the right order.

For questions 27 to 32:

Using statements 1 and 3, we can draw the following conclusion and lets tabulate it.

	Arun	Bankim	Charu	Dipak
Round 1	Hi(+2)	Lo(–2)	Lo(–2)	Hi(+2)
Round 2	Hi(+3)	Lo(–1)	Lo(–1)	Lo(–1)
Round 3	Lo(+1)	Lo(+1)	Lo(+1)	Lo(+1)
Points after round 3	6	–2	–2	+2

Now, using statements 2 and 4, we can further deduce that who bid 'Hi' or who bid 'Lo' in further 3 rounds..

	Arun	Bankim	Charu	Dipak
Round 1	Hi(+2)	Lo(–2)	Lo(–2)	Hi(+2)
Round 2	Hi(+3)	Lo(–1)	Lo(–1)	Lo(–1)
Round 3	Lo(+1)	Lo(+1)	Lo(+1)	Lo(+1)
Round 4/5/6	Hi(+3)	Lo(–1)	Lo(–1)	Lo(–1)
Round 5/6/4	Lo(–3)	Hi(+3)	Lo(–1)	Lo(–1)
Round 6/4/5	Hi(–1)	Hi(–1)	Hi(–1)	Hi(–1)
Points after round 6	7	–1	–5	–1

27. In the first round, the bids by Arun, Bankim, Charu and Dipak were Hi, Lo, Lo and Hi respectively.

28. In 4 rounds, Arun bid Hi.

29. Bankim bid Lo in 4 rounds.

30. All the four players make identical bids in 2 rounds.

31. Dipak gain exactly 1 point in only 1 round.

32. In second round, Arun was definitely the only player to bid Hi.

For questions 33 to 38:

Let the number of teak trees in column 3 be 2x.

Then using statement 3, the figure becomes

	1	2	3	4
Mango → X	12 C			
Teak → Y	21 A	x	2x	4x A
Pine → Z	B	C	9	28

Each plot had trees in non-zero multiples of 3 or 4 and none of the plots had the same number of trees.

∴ $x \neq 1, 2, 3, 5, 6,$ and 7 otherwise it will contradict the above condition and $x < 8$, otherwise it will exceed the total number of trees.

Hence, $x = 4$ is possible.

∴ Total number of trees in row Y = $21 + 7 \times 4 = 49$.

Using statement 9, number of trees in row X = $49 \times 2 = 98$

∴ Number of trees in row Z = 58

⇒ In row Z, number of trees in remaining two plots = $58 - (28 + 9) = 21$.

Using statement 2, someone has 32 trees in a plot, therefore it should be in row X. So, the sum of the trees in remaining two plots In row X will be $98 \quad (12 + 32) = 54$

As the number of trees in a plot is a multiple of 3 or 4, so the only possibility for the number of trees in these two plots in row X are 24 and 30 (sum is 54).

Similarly, for row Z, the number of trees in two blank plots are (3, 18) or (6, 15) as the sum is 21.

∴ The rectangular land looks like

	1	2	3	4
X	12 C	24/30/32	30/32/24	32/24/30
Y	21 A	4	8	16 A
Z	3/18 B	18/3	9	28

or

	1	2	3	4
X	12	24/30/32	30/32/24	32/24/30
Y	21	4	8	16 A
Z	6/15 B	15/6	9	28

Each daughter got an even number of plots and using statement 4, we can say that Abha and Bina got 4 plots each whereas Chitra and Dipti got 2 plots each.

Using statement 1, A = 20 + C and A = D – 6

Using statements 5 and 6, we can say that D got two adjoining plots in upper right corner i.e., one in row X and column 3 and other in row X and column 4.

Hence, 3 cases arise from here that the number of trees in two plots of D are (30, 32) or (24, 32) or (24, 30).

Case 1	Case 2	Case 3
D = 62 (=30 + 32)	D = 56 (=24 + 32)	D = 54 (= 24 + 30)
A = 62 – 6 = 56	A = 50	A = 48
C = 56 – 20 = 36	C = 30	C = 28
B = 102	B = 69	B = 75

Case 1 and case 3 are not possible.

Case 3 is rejected as it will not satisfy the condition given in statement 7 whereas case 1 is rejected because the total number of trees in B's plots cannot be 102.

∴ Case 2 is possible only.

∴ D = 24 + 32 = 56

A = 21 + 16 + 9 + 4 = 50

C = 12 + 18 = 30

B = 3 + 28 + 8 + 30 = 69

That means in row Z, the number of trees in two blank plots are 3 and 18.

(15 and 6 are rejected as they are not satisfying the above values of the sum)

Hence, the final figure is

	1	2	3	4	Sum
Mango → X	12 C	30 B	24/32 D	32/24 D	98
Teak → Y	21 A	4 A	8 B	16 A	49
Pine → Z	3 B	18 C	9 A	28 B	58

33. 98 mango trees were there in total.

34. The correct sequence is 50, 69, 30, 56.

35. Chitra received 18 pine trees.

36. Bina got the plot having number of trees equal to 3, which is the smallest.

37. Options 1, 2 and 3 are correct. Option 4 is not true as Bina got 31 pine trees.

38.

Columns	1	2	3	4
Total number of trees	36	52	41/49	76/68

Clearly, column 4 had the highest number of trees.

Directions for questions 39 to 42:

Based on the information given in the table we can deduce the number of orders booked on a particular day and the number of orders lost on a particular day. E.g., the cumulative orders booked upto 18th (including that day) is 332 and that upto 19th (including that day) is given as 337 which means that the number of orders booked on 19th day will be 337 – 332 = 5. Similarly for other days till 14th, we can calculate it.

Just like that, we can calculate the number of orders declared lost on 19th day = 129 – 120 = 9 and for other days too. Based on that, we can form a table.

Day	Orders booked on that day	Cumulative orders booked	Delivery of one day prior	Delivered on that day	Delivery of two days prior	Cumulative orders lost	Orders declared lost on that day
13th		219		11		91	
14th	30	249		27		92	1
15th	28	277		23		94	2
16th	25	302		11		106	12
17th	25	327		21		118	12
18th	5	332		13		120	2
19th	5	337		14		129	9

Now, according to the data given, the number of orders booked on 12th that took two days to deliver was 6. That means they were delivered on 14th. But, the total number of orders delivered on 14th was 27, therefore, $27 - 6 = 21$ was the number of orders that were booked one day prior to 14th i.e., on 13th.

Similarly, the number of orders that were booked on 13th but took two days to deliver i.e., delivered on 15th was 8. And we know, the total number of orders delivered on 15th = 23. This means, the number of orders that were booked one day prior to 15th i.e., on 14th = $23 - 8 = 15$. In this way, we can find out for other days.

Now, the number of orders booked but not delivered are declared lost at the end of the second day. Therefore, on 15th day, the number of orders declared lost is given as 2, which are actually the same orders that were booked on 13th.

Hence, the number of orders booked on 13th = $21 + 8 + 2 = 31$. The number of orders booked on 14th = 30 out of which the number of orders lost, declared on 16th = 12.

∴ The remaining number of orders that were delivered = $30 - 12 = 18$.

Out of these 18 orders, 15 orders were delivered the next day only (calculated above), that means $18 - 15 = 3$ orders were delivered the day after, i.e., on 16th. Total orders delivered on 16th = 11.

Therefore, the number of orders that were booked one day prior to 16th but delivered on 16th = $11 - 3 = 8$.

Now, accordingly, we will fill these data in the table.

Day	Orders booked on that day	Cumulative orders booked	Delivery of one day prior	Delivered on that day	Delivery of two days prior	Cumulative orders lost	Orders declared lost on that day
13th	31	219	7	11	4	91	
14th	30	249	21	27	6	92	1
15th	28	277	15	23	8	94	2
16th	25	302	8	11	3	106	12
17th	25	327	13	21	8	118	12
18th	5	332	3	13	10	120	2
19th	5	337	1	14	13	129	9

39. For 13th day,

Number of orders booked on 13th day = 31

Number of orders booked on 13th and was lost = 2

∴ Required fraction = $\frac{2}{31} = 0.064$

For 14th day, required fraction = $\frac{12}{30} = 0.4$

For 15th day required fraction = $\frac{12}{28} = 0.428$

For 16th day, required fraction = $\frac{2}{25} = 0.08$

Clearly, the largest value is 0.428, on 15th day.

40. The numbers of orders booked on 12th = $7 + 6 + 1 = 14$

The number of orders booked on 13th = 31

The number of orders booked on 14th = 30

The number of orders booked on 15th = 28

∴ It was highest on 13th day.

41. The delivery ratio for 13th day = $\frac{21}{8} = 2.625$

The delivery ratio for 14th day = $\frac{15}{3} = 5$

The delivery ratio for 15th day = $\frac{8}{8} = 1$

The delivery ratio for 16th day = $\frac{13}{10} = 1.3$

∴ Delivery ratio was highest on 14th day.

42. The average time taken on 13th day

$$= \frac{21 + 2 \times 8}{21 + 8} = \frac{21 + 16}{27} = \frac{37}{29} = 1.27$$

On 14th day = $\frac{15 + 2 \times 3}{15 + 3} = \frac{21}{18} = \frac{7}{6} = 1.16$

On 15th day = $\frac{8 + 2 \times 8}{8 + 8} = \frac{8 + 16}{16} = \frac{24}{16} = \frac{3}{2} = 1.5$

On 16th day = $\frac{13 + 2 \times 10}{13 + 10} = \frac{33}{23} = 1.43$

It was least on 14th day.

Directions for questions 43 to 46:

Vial A : Patient 9, 10, 11, 12, 13, 14, 15, 16

Vial B : Patient 1, 2, 3, 4, 5, 6, 7, 8

Vial C : Patient 5, 6, 7, 8, 13, 14, 15, 16

Vial D : Patient 1, 2, 3, 4, 9, 10, 11, 12

Vial E : Patient 3, 4, 7, 8, 11, 12, 15, 16

Vial F : Patient 1, 2, 5, 6, 9, 10, 13, 14

Vial G : Patient 2, 4, 6, 8, 10, 12, 14, 16

Vial H : Patient 1, 3, 5, 7, 9, 11, 13, 15

43. Since vial C tests positive it has to be one out of Patient 5, 6, 7, 8, 13, 14, 15, 16 who has the disease. But since vial A, E and H tests negative therefore, 13, 14, 15, 16, 7, 8, and 5 are not the ones with the disease. Hence, patient 6 has the disease.

44. Suppose vial A tests positive, then the patient with the disease is one out of 9, 10, 11, 12, 13, 14, 15, 16 but since vials D and G test negative, the patients 9, 10, 11, 12, 14, 16 are excluded. So only Patients left are 13 and 15.

Both patients present in vial H. Even if tested positive or negative we can't know who has got the disease. So (2) is not the answer.

Both patients present in vial C. Even if tested positive or negative we can't know who has got the disease. So (3) is not the answer.

Patient 13 or 15 are not present in vial B. So (4) is not the answer.

Only patient 15 is present in vial E, is tested positive then patient 15 has the disease else patient 13 has the disease.

Hence, option (1) is correct.

45. If vial C and D are negative then no patient could test negative. Hence, option (2) is the answer.

46. Suppose one of the lab assistants accidentally mixed two patients' blood samples before they were distributed to the vials. Then {4, 5, 6, 7, 8} correctly represents the set of all possible numbers of positive test results out of the eight vials.

For questions 47 to 50:

Let the number of schools with exactly three of the facilities was the same irrespective of which three were considered be 'a'.

Number of schools with only F1 and F2, only F1 and F3, and only F1 and F4 be 'b', 'c', and 'd' respectively.

Also, the number of schools with none of the facilities be 'n' from statement 1, i.e., n = 80.

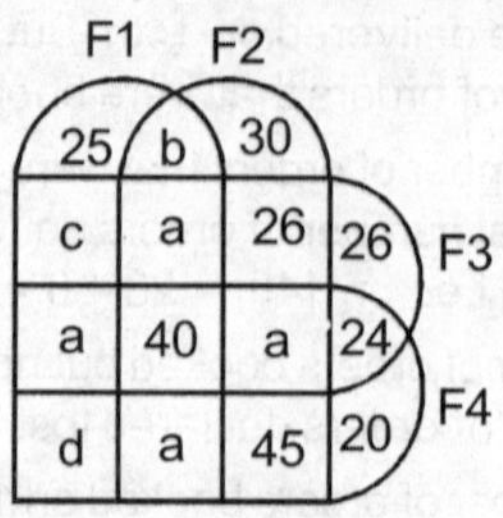

From statement 5, b + 141 + 3a = 313

$\Rightarrow$ b + 3a = 172 ... (i)

From statement 8, b + a + 40 + a = 162

$\Rightarrow$ b + 2a = 122 ... (ii)

(ii) – (i) gives a = 50 and b = 22.

From statement 9, 237 + 3a + c + d = 279 + 3a = d

$\Rightarrow$ c = 42

Total number of schools = 600, therefore,

313 + 25 + c + a + d + 26 + 24 + 20 + 80 = 600

$\Rightarrow$ d = 20.

The final venn diagram looks like:

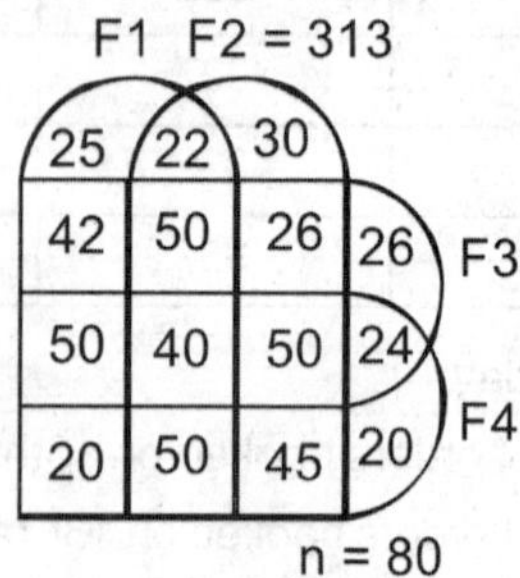

47. The total number of schools with exactly three of the four facilities = 4a = 200.

48. The total number of schools having facilities F4 and F2 = 45 + 50 + 50 + 40 = 185.

49. The total number of schools having only F1 and F3 = c = 42.

50. The total number of schools having only F1 and F4 = 20.

51. kx + y = 3 ... (i)

4x + ky = 4 ... (ii)

The equations (i) and (ii) have a unique solution if

$$\frac{a_1}{a_2} \neq \frac{b_1}{b_2} \Rightarrow \frac{k}{4} \neq \frac{1}{k}$$

$$\Rightarrow k^2 \neq 4 \Rightarrow |k| \neq 2.$$

52. Let the distance of his office be 'd' km.

Then, $\frac{d}{35}-\frac{d}{40}=\frac{6}{60}$

$\Rightarrow d = 28$ km

His usual time = $\frac{28}{40}=\frac{7}{10}$ hour

Let the required speed be 's' km/hr.

Then, $\left(1-\frac{2}{3}\right)\times\frac{28}{s}=\left(1-\frac{1}{3}\right)\times\frac{7}{10}-\frac{8}{60}$

$\Rightarrow s = 28$ km/hr.

53. For real roots of $x^2+mx+2n=0$,

$m^2-8n\ge 0$ ... (i)

If n = 1, then m = 3 or more

For real roots of $x^2+2nx+m=0$,

$(2n)^2-4m\ge 0$ or $n^2-m\ge 0$ ... (ii)

If m = 3, n = 2 or more

For n = 2,

From (i), $m^2-8n\ge 0\Rightarrow m^2-8\times 2\ge 0\Rightarrow m^2\ge 16$

Therefore, m = 4 or more

From (ii), $n^2-m\ge 0\Rightarrow 2^2-m\ge 0$

Therefore, m = 4 or less

Hence, smallest possible value of m + n

= 4 + 2 = 6.

54.

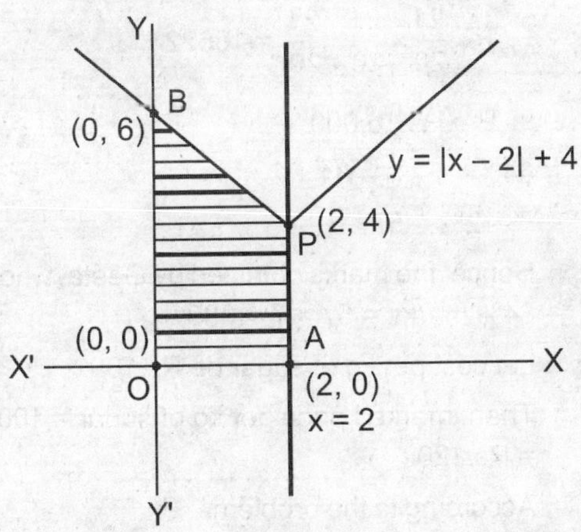

Required area = Area of trapezium formed by the points (0, 0), (2, 0), (2, 4) and (0, 6)

Hence, area of trapezium = 1/2 × Height × Sum of parallel sides

= 1/2 × 2 × (6 + 4) = 10 sq. units.

55. Given that: $a\le b$ and $ab=4^{2017}=2^{4034}$

$a=1=2^0,\ b=2^{4034}$

$a=2^1,\ b=2^{4033}$

$a=2^2,\ b=2^{4032}$

....

....

$a=2^{2017},\ b=2^{2017}$

Hence, total number of pairs (a, b) of positive integers = 2018.

56. $x_1=-1$ and $x_m=x_{m+1}+(m+1)$ (Given)

Therefore, $x_1=x_{1+1}+(1+1)\Rightarrow x_2=-1-2=-3$

$x_2=x_3+(2+1)\Rightarrow x_3=-1-2-3=-6$

$x_3=x_4+(3+1)\Rightarrow x_4=-1-2-3-4=-10$

Similarly, $x_{100}=-1-2-3-4-5-\ldots-100$

$=-\frac{100(100+1)}{2}=-5050.$

57. Let x be the number of additional people required to employ.

Then, $\frac{140\times 60}{1.5}=\frac{(140+x)\times 140}{4.5}$

$\Rightarrow x = 40.$

58.

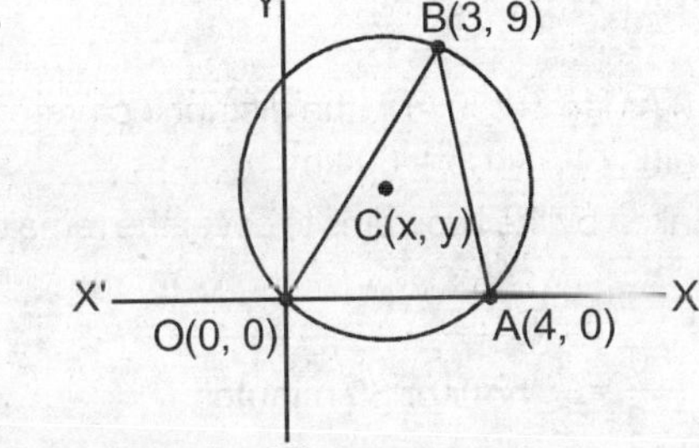

Let C(x, y) be the center of the circle.

OC = AC = BC = Radius

Then, $OC^2=(x-0)^2+(y-0)^2=x^2+y^2$ ... (i)

$AC^2=(x-4)^2+(y-0)^2=x^2+16-8x+y^2$ ... (ii)

$BC^2=(x-3)^2+(y-9)^2=x^2+9-6x+y^2+81-18x$ ... (iii)

From (i) and (ii), x = 2

From (i) and (iii), y = 39/9

Therefore, radius = OC = $\sqrt{4+\left(\frac{39}{9}\right)^2}$

Hence, area of the circle

$= \pi \times OC^2 = \pi\left[4+\left(\frac{39}{9}\right)^2\right] = \frac{205\pi}{9}$ sq. units.

59. Let x years be the age of Tom.

Then, Dick's age = 3x and Harry's age = 6x

According to question,

$$\frac{x+3x+6x}{3} = 3x + 1$$

$\Rightarrow x = 3$

Hence, Harry's age = 6x = 18 years.

60. $$\frac{2\times4\times8\times16}{(\log_2 4)^2(\log_4 8)^3(\log_8 16)^4}$$

$$= \frac{2\times4\times8\times16}{(2\log_2 2)^2\left(\frac{3}{2}\times\log_2 2\right)^3\left(\frac{4}{3}\times\log_2 2\right)^4}$$

$$= \frac{2\times4\times8\times16}{(2\times1)^2\left(\frac{3}{2}\times1\right)^3\left(\frac{4}{3}\times1\right)^4} = 24.$$

61. From 9 AM to 10:30 AM, the distance covered by first train = 40 × 1.5 = 60 km

Time taken by the two trains to cover the remaining distance

$= \frac{90-60}{40+20} = \frac{1}{2}$ hour or 30 minutes

Hence, the two trains meet each other at 11:00 AM.

62. There are 900 integers in the set {100, 101, 102, ... , 999}.

Let 'abc' be the three digit integer.

a	b	c
1 to 9	0 to 9 except a	0 to 9 except a and b
= 9	= 9	= 8

The number of integers which have no digits repeated = 9 × 9 × 8 = 648

Hence, the number of integers which have at least one digit repeated

= 900 – 648 = 252.

63. f(x) = f(x + 0) = f(x) × f(0)

$\Rightarrow$ f(x) = f(x) × f(0)

Let f(x) be non-zero. Then, f(0) = 1.

f(5) = 4 (Given)

f(10) = f(5 + 5) = f(5) × f(5) = 4 × 4 = 16

f(0) = f(10 – 10) = f(10 + (–10)) = f(10) × f(–10) = 16 × f(–10)

$\Rightarrow$ 1 = 16 × f(–10)

$\Rightarrow f(-10) = \frac{1}{16} = 0.0625$

Hence, f(10) – f(–10) = 16 – 0.0625 = 15.9375.

64. The midpoint of (2, 1) and (–3, –4)

$= \frac{2-3}{2}, \frac{1-4}{2} = -\frac{1}{2}, -\frac{3}{2}$

Since diagonals of a parallelogram bisect each other.

Therefore, $\left(-\frac{1}{2}, -\frac{3}{2}\right)$ lies on the line x + 9y + c = 0.

$-\frac{1}{2} + 9\times\left(-\frac{3}{2}\right) + c = 0$

$\Rightarrow$ c = 14.

65. Let P be the amount invested by the person.

Then, $P\left(1+\frac{5}{100}\right)^3 = 18522$

$\Rightarrow P\times\frac{21}{20}\times\frac{21}{20}\times\frac{21}{20} = 18522$

$\Rightarrow$ P = Rs.16,000.

66. 64% – 52% = 34 + 23

$\Rightarrow$ 12% = 57

Hence, the marks obtained by Geeta, who scored 84% marks = 57 × 7 = 399.

67. Let cost per kg of sugar be Rs.100x.

Then, marked price per kg of sugar = 100x × 1.2 = Rs.120x

According to the problem,

$5 \times 120x + 15 \times 120x \times 0.9 + 12 \times 120x\left(1+\frac{p}{100}\right)$

= 35 × 100x × 1.15

$\Rightarrow$ 600 + 1620 + 1440 + 14.4p = 4025

$\Rightarrow p \approx 25\%$.

68. $\log_a 30 = A$

$\Rightarrow \log_a 2\times3\times5 = A$

$\Rightarrow \log_a 2 + \log_a 3 + \log_a 5 = A$ ... (i)

$\log_a 5/3 = -B$

$\Rightarrow \log_a 5 - \log_a 3 = -B$

$\Rightarrow \log_a 5 = \log_a 3 - B$ ... (ii)

$\log_2 a = 1/3 \Rightarrow \log_a 2 = 3$ ... (iii)

From (i), (ii) and (iii),

$3 + \log_a 3 + \log_a 3 - B = A$

$\Rightarrow 2\log_a 3 = A + B - 3$

$\Rightarrow \log_a 3 = \dfrac{A+B-3}{2}$

Hence, $\log_3 a = \dfrac{2}{A+B-3}$.

69. We have $0.2 < \dfrac{m}{20}, \dfrac{n}{m}, \dfrac{n}{11} < 0.5$, where m and n are natural numbers and n is even.

$\Rightarrow 0.2 < \dfrac{m}{20} < 0.5$ or $4 < m < 10$

Therefore, m can take any of the values from the set (5, 6, 7, 8, 9).

and $0.2 < \dfrac{n}{11} < 0.5$ or $2.2 < n < 5.5$

Therefore, n can take any of the values from the set (3, 4, 5).

But n is an even natural number. Therefore, n = 4

Since $0.2 < \dfrac{n}{m} < 0.5$

Therefore, only m = 9 satisfies the above condition.

Hence, m – 2n = 9 – 2 × 4 = 1.

70. Let $14^a = 36^b = 84^c = k$

$14^a = k$

$\Rightarrow \log_{14} k = a \Rightarrow \log_k 14 = \dfrac{1}{a}$

$36^b = k$

$\Rightarrow \log_{36} k = b \Rightarrow \log_k 36 = \dfrac{1}{b}$

$\Rightarrow 2\log_k 6 = \dfrac{1}{b} \Rightarrow \log_k 6 = \dfrac{1}{2b}$

$84^c = k$

$\Rightarrow \log_{84} k = c \Rightarrow \log_k 84 = \dfrac{1}{c}$

Therefore, $\dfrac{1}{c} - \dfrac{1}{a} = \log_k 84 - \log_k 14 = \log_k 6$

$\Rightarrow \dfrac{1}{c} - \dfrac{1}{a} = \dfrac{1}{2b}$

Hence, $6b\left(\dfrac{1}{c} - \dfrac{1}{a}\right) = 6b \times \dfrac{1}{2b} = 3$.

71. $2 < x < 10 \Rightarrow$ x can take any of the values from the set (3, 4, 5, 6, 7, 8, 9)

$14 < y < 23 \Rightarrow$ y can take any of the values from the set (15, 16, 17, 18, 19, 20, 21, 22)

N = x + y, N > 25

The highest value of N (= x + y) can take = 9 + 22 = 31, at x = 9 and y = 22

30 can be obtained at x = 9, y = 21

29 can be obtained at x = 9, y = 20

28 can be obtained at x = 9, y = 19

27 can be obtained at x = 9, y = 18

26 can be obtained at x = 9, y = 17

Hence, N (= x + y) can take 6 distinct values.

72. Time taken by Anil to complete one round

$= \dfrac{3}{15} \times 60 = 12$ minutes

Time taken by Anil to complete one round

$= \dfrac{3}{10} \times 60 = 18$ minutes

Anil completing each round in 12 minutes, reaches the starting point at 12, 24, 36, 48, ... minutes

Sunil completing each round in 18 minutes, reaches the starting point at 18, 36, 54, 72, ... minutes

Clearly, both of them reach the starting point at (LCM of 12, 18 =) 36 minutes.

Hence, the distance covered by Ravi in 36 minutes

$= 8 \times \dfrac{36}{60} = 4.8$ km.

73. (n + 2) × 29 = n × 30 + (38 + 15)

$\Rightarrow$ n = 5

Since the average score of the first 5 innings is 30 and the batsman scored less than 38 runs in each of the first 5 innings.

Therefore, the maximum score that he can score is 37.

37 × 4 + x = 30 × 5

$\Rightarrow$ x = 2.

74. Number of multiples of (2 or 5 or 7) = Number of multiples of (2) + Number of multiples of (5) + Number of multiples of (7) - Number of multiples of (2 and 5) - Number of multiples of (2 and 7) - Number of multiples of (5 and 7) + Number of multiples of (2 and 5 and 7)

$= 60 + 24 + 17 - 12 - 8 - 3 + 1 = 79$

Hence, number of integers that are divisible by none of 2 or 5 or 7 = 120 – 81 = 41.

75. 

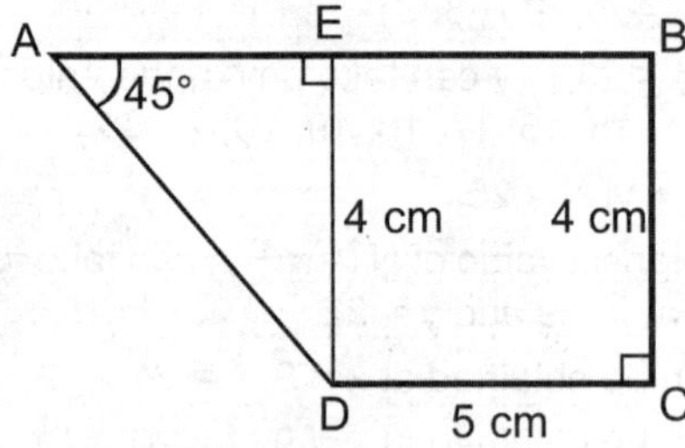

Draw DE perpendicular to AB.

In right angled triangle AED,

$\angle EAD = 45° = \angle ADE$

Therefore, AE = DE = 4 cm

and EB = DC = 5 cm

Therefore, AB = AE + EB = 4 + 5 = 9 cm

Hence, area of trapezium ABCD

$= 1/2 \times 4 \times (9 + 5) = 28$ sq. units.

76. A and B are mixed in the ratio 1: 3.

i.e., 1 unit of A is mixed with 3 units of B.

Total volume = 1 + 3 = 4 units

The volume is doubled by adding A, this implies that a quantity of 4 units of A is added to the existing 4 units of the mixture.

Now, total volume = 4 + 4 = 8 units

Thus, the ratio of A to B in the mixture = 5 : 3

Let b be the percentage of alcohol in solution B.

By Alligation Rule,

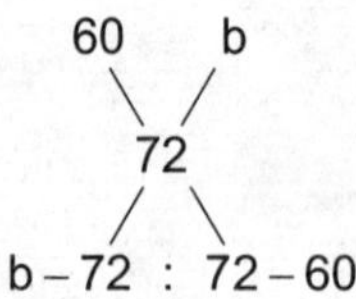

Hence, $\frac{b-72}{72-60} = \frac{5}{3} \Rightarrow b = 92\%$.

CAT 2021 SOLVED PAPER (SLOT-1)

Section I: VARC

Question Numbers (1 to 4): The passage below is accompanied by a set of questions. Choose the best answer to each question.

Cuttlefish are full of personality, as behavioral ecologist Alexandra Schnell found out while researching the cephalopod's potential to display self-control. . . . "Self-control is thought to be the cornerstone of intelligence, as it is an important prerequisite for complex decision-making and planning for the future," says Schnell . . .

[Schnell's] study used a modified version of the "marshmallow test" . . . During the original marshmallow test, psychologist Walter Mischel presented children between age four and six with one marshmallow. He told them that if they waited 15 minutes and didn't eat it, he would give them a second marshmallow. A long-term follow-up study showed that the children who waited for the second marshmallow had more success later in life. . . . The cuttlefish version of the experiment looked a lot different. The researchers worked with six cuttlefish under nine months old and presented them with seafood instead of sweets. (Preliminary experiments showed that cuttlefishes' favorite food is live grass shrimp, while raw prawns are so-so and Asian shore crab is nearly unacceptable.) Since the researchers couldn't explain to the cuttlefish that they would need to wait for their shrimp, they trained them to recognize certain shapes that indicated when a food item would become available. The symbols were pasted on transparent drawers so that the cuttlefish could see the food that was stored inside. One drawer, labeled with a circle to mean "immediate," held raw king prawn. Another drawer, labeled with a triangle to mean "delayed," held live grass shrimp. During a control experiment, square labels meant "never."

"If their self-control is flexible and I hadn't just trained them to wait in any context, you would expect the cuttlefish to take the immediate reward [in the control], even if it's their second preference," says Schnell . . . and that's what they did. That showed the researchers that cuttlefish wouldn't reject the prawns if it was the only food available. In the experimental trials, the cuttlefish didn't jump on the prawns if the live grass shrimp were labeled with a triangle—many waited for the shrimp drawer to open up. Each time the cuttlefish showed it could wait, the researchers tacked another ten seconds on to the next round of waiting before releasing the shrimp. The longest that a cuttlefish waited was 130 seconds.

Schnell [says] that the cuttlefish usually sat at the bottom of the tank and looked at the two food items while they waited, but sometimes, they would turn away from the king prawn "as if to distract themselves from the temptation of the immediate reward." In past studies, humans, chimpanzees, parrots and dogs also tried to distract themselves while waiting for a reward.

Not every species can use self-control, but most of the animals that can share another trait in common: long, social lives. Cuttlefish, on the other hand, are solitary creatures that don't form relationships even with mates or young. . . . "We don't know if living in a social group is important for complex cognition unless we also show those abilities are lacking in less social species," says . . . comparative psychologist Jennifer Vonk.

1. All of the following constitute a point of difference between the "original" and "modified" versions of the marshmallow test EXCEPT that:

(1) the former was performed over a longer time span than the latter.

(2) the former had human subjects, while the latter had cuttlefish.

(3) the former used verbal communication with its subjects, while the latter had to develop a symbolic means of communication.

(4) the former correlated self-control and future success, while the latter correlated self-control and survival advantages.

2. Which one of the following, if true, would best complement the passage's findings?

(1) Cuttlefish cannot distinguish between geometrical shapes.

(2) Cuttlefish are equally fond of live grass shrimp and raw prawn.

(3) Cuttlefish wait longer than 100 seconds for the shrimp drawer to open up.

(4) Cuttlefish live in big groups that exhibit sociability.

3. Which one of the following cannot be inferred from Alexandra Schnell's experiment?

(1) Cuttlefish exert self-control with the help of diversions.

(2) Intelligence in a species is impossible without sociability.

(3) Cuttlefish exercise choice when it comes to food.

(4) Like human children, cuttlefish are capable of self-control.

4. In which one of the following scenarios would the cuttlefish's behaviour demonstrate self-control?

(1) raw prawns are released while a live grass shrimp drawer labelled with a square is placed in front of the cuttlefish.

(2) Asian shore crabs and raw prawns are simultaneously released while a live grass shrimp drawer labelled with a triangle is placed in front of the cuttlefish, to be opened after one minute.

(3) raw prawns are released while an Asian shore crab drawer labelled with a triangle is placed in front of the cuttlefish, to be opened after one minute.

(4) live grass shrimp are released while two raw prawn drawers labelled with a circle and a triangle respectively are placed in front of the cuttlefish; the triangle-labelled drawer is opened after 50 seconds.

Question Numbers (5 to 8): The passage below is accompanied by a set of questions. Choose the best answer to each question.

We cannot travel outside our neighbourhood without passports. We must wear the same plain clothes. We must exchange our houses every ten years. We cannot avoid labour. We all go to bed at the same time . . . We have religious freedom, but we cannot deny that the soul dies with the body, since 'but for the fear of punishment, they would have nothing but contempt for the laws and customs of society'. . . . In More's time, for much of the population, given the plenty and security on offer, such restraints would not have seemed overly unreasonable. For modern readers, however, Utopia appears to rely upon relentless transparency, the repression of variety, and the curtailment of privacy. Utopia provides security: but at what price? In both its external and internal relations, indeed, it seems perilously dystopian.

Such a conclusion might be fortified by examining selectively the tradition which follows More on these points. This often portrays societies where . . . 'it would be almost impossible for man to be depraved, or wicked'. . . . This is achieved both through institutions and mores, which underpin the common life. . . . The passions are regulated and inequalities of wealth and distinction are minimized. Needs, vanity, and emulation are restrained, often by prizing equality and holding riches in contempt. The desire for public power is curbed. Marriage and sexual intercourse are often controlled: in Tommaso Campanella's *The City of the Sun (1623)*, the first great literary utopia after More's, relations are forbidden to men before the age of twenty-one and women before nineteen. Communal child-rearing is normal; for Campanella this commences at age two. Greater simplicity of life, 'living according to nature', is often a result: the desire for simplicity and purity are closely related. People become more alike in appearance, opinion, and outlook than they often have been. Unity, order, and homogeneity thus prevail at the cost of individuality and diversity. This model, as J. C. Davis demonstrates, dominated early modern utopianism. . . . And utopian homogeneity remains a familiar theme well into the twentieth century.

Given these considerations, it is not unreasonable to take as our starting point here the hypothesis that utopia and dystopia evidently share more in common than is often supposed. Indeed, they might be twins, the progeny of the same parents. Insofar as this proves to be the case, my linkage of both here will be uncomfortably close for some readers. Yet we should not mistake this argument for the assertion that all utopias are, or tend to produce, dystopias. Those who defend this proposition will find that their association here is not nearly close enough. For we have only to acknowledge the existence of thousands of successful intentional communities in which a cooperative ethos predominates and where harmony without coercion is the rule to set aside such an assertion. Here the individual's submersion in the group is consensual (though this concept is not unproblematic). It results not in enslavement but voluntary submission to group norms. Harmony is achieved without . . . harming others.

5. All of the following arguments are made in the passage EXCEPT that:

(1) there have been thousands of communities where homogeneity and stability have been achieved through choice, rather than by force.

(2) in early modern utopianism, the stability of utopian societies was seen to be achieved only with individuals surrendering their sense of self.

(3) in More's time, there was plenty and security, so people did not need restraints that could appear unreasonable.

(4) the tradition of utopian literature has often shown societies in which it would be nearly impossible for anyone to be sinful or criminal.

6. All of the following statements can be inferred from the passage EXCEPT that:

(1) many conceptions of utopian societies emphasise the importance of social uniformity and cultural homogeneity.

(2) it is possible to see utopias as dystopias, with a change in perspective, because one person's utopia could be seen as another's dystopia.

(3) utopian societies exist in a long tradition of literature dealing with imaginary people practicing imaginary customs, in imaginary worlds.

(4) utopian and dystopian societies are twins, the progeny of the same parents.

7. Following from the passage, which one of the following may be seen as a characteristic of a utopian society?

(1) A society where public power is earned through merit rather than through privilege.

(2) Institutional surveillance of every individual to ensure his/her security and welfare.

(3) The regulation of homogeneity through promoting competitive heterogeneity.

(4) A society without any laws to restrain one's individuality.

8. Which sequence of words below best captures the narrative of the passage?

(1) Utopia – Security – Homogeneity – Intentional community.

(2) Relentless transparency – Homogeneity – Utopia – Dystopia.

(3) Utopia – Security – Dystopia – Coercion.

(4) Curtailment of privacy – Dystopia – Utopia – Intentional community.

Question Numbers (9 to 12): The passage below is accompanied by a set of questions. Choose the best answer to each question.

The sleights of hand that conflate consumption with virtue are a central theme in A Thirst for Empire, a sweeping and richly detailed history of tea by the historian Erika Rappaport. How did tea evolve from an obscure "China drink" to a universal beverage imbued with civilising properties? The answer, in brief, revolves around this conflation, not only by profit-motivated marketers but by a wide variety of interest groups. While abundant historical records have allowed the study of how tea itself moved from east to west, Rappaport is focused on the movement of the idea of tea to suit particular purposes.

Beginning in the 1700s, the temperance movement advocated for tea as a pleasure that cheered but did not inebriate, and industrialists soon borrowed this moral argument in advancing their case for free trade in tea (and hence more open markets for their textiles). Factory owners joined in, compelled by the cause of a sober workforce, while Christian missionaries discovered that tea "would soothe any colonial encounter". During the Second World War, tea service was presented as a social and patriotic activity that uplifted soldiers and calmed refugees.

But it was tea's consumer-directed marketing by importers and retailers – and later by brands – that most closely portends current trade debates. An early version of the "farm to table" movement was sparked by anti-Chinese sentiment and concerns over trade deficits, as well as by the reality and threat of adulterated tea containing dirt and hedge clippings. Lipton was soon advertising "from the Garden to Tea Cup" supply chains originating in British India and supervised by "educated Englishmen". While tea marketing always presented direct consumer benefits (health, energy, relaxation), tea drinkers were also assured that they were participating in a larger noble project that advanced the causes of family, nation and civilization. . . .

Rappaport's treatment of her subject is refreshingly apolitical. Indeed, it is a virtue that readers will be unable to guess her political orientation: both the miracle of markets and capitalism's dark underbelly are evident in tea's complex story, as are the complicated effects of British colonialism. . . . Commodity histories are now themselves commodities: recent works investigate cotton, salt, cod, sugar, chocolate, paper and milk. And morality marketing is now a commodity as well, applied to food, "fair trade" apparel and eco-tourism. Yet tea is, Rappaport makes clear, a world apart – an astonishing success story in which tea marketers not only succeeded in conveying a sense of moral elevation to the consumer but also arguably did advance the cause of civilisation and community.

I have been offered tea at a British garden party, a Bedouin campfire, a Turkish carpet shop and a Japanese chashitsu, to name a few settings. In each case the offering was more an idea – friendship, community, respect – than a drink, and in each case the idea then created a reality. It is not a stretch to say that tea marketers have advanced the particularly noble cause of human dialogue and friendship.

9. The author of this book review is LEAST likely to support the view that:

(1) tea drinking was sometimes promoted as a patriotic duty.

(2) tea drinking has become a social ritual worldwide.

(3) the ritual of drinking tea promotes congeniality and camaraderie.

(4) tea became the leading drink in Britain in the nineteenth century.

10. This book review argues that, according to Rappaport, tea is unlike other "morality" products because it:
(1) appealed to a universal group and not just to a niche section of people.
(2) had an actual beneficial effect on social interaction and society in general.
(3) was marketed by a wide range of interest groups.
(4) was actively encouraged by interest groups in the government.

11. Today, "conflat[ing] consumption with virtue" can be seen in the marketing of:
(1) sustainably farmed foods.
(2) travel to pristine destinations.
(3) ergonomically designed products.
(4) natural health supplements.

12. According to this book review, A Thirst for Empire says that, in addition to "profit-motivated marketers", tea drinking was promoted in Britain by all of the following EXCEPT:
(1) factories to instill sobriety in their labour.
(2) the anti-alcohol lobby as a substitute for the consumption of liquor.
(3) tea drinkers lobbying for product diversity.
(4) manufacturers who were pressing for duty-free imports.

Question Numbers (13 to 16): The passage below is accompanied by a set of questions. Choose the best answer to each question.

For the Maya of the Classic period, who lived in Southern Mexico and Central America between 250 and 900 CE, the category of 'persons' was not coincident with human beings, as it is for us. That is, human beings were persons – but other, nonhuman entities could be persons, too. . . . In order to explore the slippage of categories between 'humans' and 'persons', I examined a very specific category of ancient Maya images, found painted in scenes on ceramic vessels. I sought out instances in which faces (some combination of eyes, nose, and mouth) are shown on inanimate objects. . . . Consider my iPhone, which needs to be fed with electricity every night, swaddled in a protective bumper, and enjoys communicating with other fellow-phone-beings. Does it have personhood (if at all) because it is connected to me, drawing this resource from me as an owner or source? For the Maya (who did have plenty of other communicating objects, if not smartphones), the answer was no. Nonhuman persons were not tethered to specific humans, and they did not derive their personhood from a connection with a human. . . . It's a profoundly democratising way of understanding the world. Humans are not more important persons – we are just one of many kinds of persons who inhabit this world. . . .

The Maya saw personhood as 'activated' by experiencing certain bodily needs and through participation in certain social activities. For example, among the faced objects that I examined, persons are marked by personal requirements (such as hunger, tiredness, physical closeness), and by community obligations (communication, interaction, ritual observance). In the images I examined, we see, for instance, faced objects being cradled in humans' arms; we also see them speaking to humans. These core elements of personhood are both turned inward, what the body or self of a person requires, and outward, what a community expects of the persons who are a part of it, underlining the reciprocal nature of community membership. . . .

Personhood was a nonbinary proposition for the Maya. Entities were able to be persons while also being something else. The faced objects I looked at indicate that they continue to be functional, doing what objects do (a stone implement continues to chop, an incense burner continues to do its smoky work). Furthermore, the Maya visually depicted many objects in ways that indicated the material category to which they belonged – drawings of the stone implement show that a person-tool is still made of stone. One additional complexity: the incense burner (which would have been made of clay, and decorated with spiky appliques representing the sacred ceiba tree found in this region) is categorised as a person – but also as a tree. With these Maya examples, we are challenged to discard the person/nonperson binary that constitutes our basic ontological outlook. . . . The porousness of boundaries that we have seen in the Maya world points towards the possibility of living with a certain uncategorisability of the world.

13. Which one of the following, if true, would not undermine the democratising potential of the Classic Maya worldview?
(1) They believed that animals like cats and dogs that live in proximity to humans have a more clearly articulated personhood.
(2) They understood the stone implement and the incense burner in a purely human form.
(3) They depicted their human healers with physical attributes of local medicinal plants.
(4) While they believed in the personhood of objects and plants, they did not believe in the personhood of rivers and animals.

14. Which one of the following best explains the "additional complexity" that the example of the incense burner illustrates regarding personhood for the Classic Maya?
(1) The example provides an exception to the nonbinary understanding of personhood that the passage had hitherto established.

(2) The example adds a new layer to the nonbinary understanding of personhood by bringing in a third category that shares a similar relation with the previous two.

(3) The example adds a new layer to the nonbinary understanding of personhood by bringing in a third category that shares a dissimilar relation with the previous two.

(4) The example complicates the nonbinary understanding of personhood by bringing in the sacred, establishing the porosity of the divine and the profane.

15. On the basis of the passage, which one of the following worldviews can be inferred to be closest to that of the Classic Maya?

(1) A tribe that perceives its utensils as person-utensils in light of their functionality and bodily needs.

(2) A tribe that perceives its hunting weapons as sacred person-artefacts because of their significance to its survival.

(3) A futuristic society that perceives robots to be persons as well as robots because of their similarity to humans.

(4) A tribe that perceives plants as person-plants because they form an ecosystem and are marked by needs of nutrition.

16. Which one of the following, if true about the Classic Maya, would invalidate the purpose of the iPhone example in the passage?

(1) The clay incense burner with spiky appliques was categorised only as a person and not as a tree by the Classic Maya.

(2) Classic Maya songs represent both humans and non-living objects as characters, talking and interacting with each other.

(3) Unlike modern societies equipped with mobile phones, the Classic Maya did not have any communicating objects.

(4) The personhood of the incense burner and the stone chopper was a function of their usefulness to humans

17. The four sentences (labelled 1, 2, 3, 4) below, when properly sequenced would yield a coherent paragraph. Decide on the proper sequencing of the order of the sentences and key in the sequence of the four numbers as your answer:

(1) In the central nervous systems of other animal species, such a comprehensive regeneration of neurons has not yet been proven beyond doubt.

(2) Biologists from the University of Bayreuth have discovered a uniquely rapid form of regeneration in injured neurons and their function in the central nervous system of zebrafish.

(3) They studied the Mauthner cells, which are solely responsible for the escape behaviour of the fish, and previously regarded as incapable of regeneration.

(4) However, their ability to regenerate crucially depends on the location of the injury.

18. Five jumbled up sentences, related to a topic, are given below. Four of them can be put together to form a coherent paragraph. Identify the odd one out and key in the number of the sentence as your answer:

(1) There is a dark side to academic research, especially in India, and at its centre is the phenomenon of predatory journals.

(2) But in truth, as long as you pay, you can get anything published.

(3) In look and feel thus, they are exactly like any reputed journal.

(4) They claim to be indexed in the most influential databases, say they possess editorial boards that comprise top scientists and researchers, and claim to have a rigorous peer-review structure.

(5) But a large section of researchers and scientists across the world are at the receiving end of nothing short of an academic publishing scam.

19. The four sentences (labelled 1, 2, 3, 4) below, when properly sequenced would yield a coherent paragraph. Decide on the proper sequencing of the order of the sentences and key in the sequence of the four numbers as your answer:

(1) The work is more than the text, for the text only takes on life, when it is realized and furthermore the realization is by no means independent of the individual disposition of the reader.

(2) The convergence of text and reader brings the literary work into existence and this convergence is not to be identified either with the reality of the text or with the individual disposition of the reader.

(3) From this polarity it follows that the literary work cannot be completely identical with the text, or with the realization of the text, but in fact must lie halfway between the two.

(4) The literary work has two poles, which we might call the artistic and the aesthetic; the artistic refers to the text created by the author, and the aesthetic to the realization accomplished by the reader.

20. Five jumbled up sentences, related to a topic, are given below. Four of them can be put together to form a coherent paragraph. Identify the odd one out and key in the number of the sentence as your answer:

(1) The legal status of resources mined in space remains ambiguous; and while the market for asteroid minerals is currently nonexistent, this is likely to change as technical hurdles diminish.

(2) Outer space is a commons, and all of it is open for exploration, however, space law developed in the 1950s and 60s is state-centric and arguably ill-suited to a commercial future.

(3) Laws adopted by the US and Luxembourg are first steps, but they only protect firms from competing claims by their compatriots; a Chinese company will not be bound by US law.

(4) Critics say the US is conferring rights that it has no authority to confer; Russia in particular has condemned this, citing the US' disrespect for international law.

(5) At issue now is commercial activity, as private firms—rather than nation states—look to space for profit.

21. The four sentences (labelled 1, 2, 3, 4) below, when properly sequenced would yield a coherent paragraph. Decide on the proper sequencing of the order of the sentences and key in the sequence of the four numbers as your answer:

(1) A popular response is the exhortation to plant more trees.

(2) It seems all but certain that global warming will go well above two degrees—quite how high no one knows yet.

(3) Burning them releases it, which is why the scale of forest fires in the Amazon basin last year garnered headlines.

(4) This is because trees sequester carbon by absorbing carbon dioxide.

22. The passage given below is followed by four alternate summaries. Choose the option that best captures the essence of the passage.

Foreign peacekeepers often exist in a bubble in the poor countries in which they are deployed; they live in posh compounds, drive fancy vehicles, and distance themselves from locals. This may be partially justified as they are outsiders, living in constant fear, performing a job that is emotionally draining. But they are often despised by the locals, and many would like them to leave. A better solution would be bottom-up peacebuilding, which would involve their spending more time working with communities, understanding their grievances and earning their trust, rather than only meeting government officials.

(1) Peacekeeping forces in foreign countries have tended to be aloof for valid reasons but would be more effective if they worked more closely with local communities.

(2) Extravagant lifestyles and an aloof attitude among the foreigners working as peacekeepers in poor countries have justifiably make them the target of local anger.

(3) Peacekeeping duties would be more effectively performed by local residents given their better understanding, knowledge and rapport with their own communities.

(4) The environment in poor countries has tended to make foreign peacekeeping forces live in enclaves, but it is time to change this scenario.

23. The passage given below is followed by four alternate summaries. Choose the option that best captures the essence of the passage.

McGurk and MacDonald (1976) reported a powerful multisensory illusion occurring with audio-visual speech. They recorded a voice articulating a consonant 'ba-ba-ba' and dubbed it with a face articulating another consonant 'ga-ga-ga'. Even though the acoustic speech signal was well recognized alone, it was heard as another consonant after dubbing with incongruent visual speech i.e., 'da-da-da'. The illusion, termed as the McGurk effect, has been replicated many times, and it has sparked an abundance of research. The reason for the great impact is that this is a striking demonstration of multisensory integration, where that auditory and visual information is merged into a unified, integrated percept.

(1) The McGurk effect which is a demonstration of multisensory integration has been replicated many times.

(2) Visual speech mismatched with auditory speech can result in the perception of an entirely different message: this illusion is known as the McGurk effect.

(3) When the auditory speech signal does not match the visual speech movements, the acoustic speech signal is confusing and integration of the two is imperfect.

(4) When the quality of auditory information is poor, the visual information wins over the auditory information.

24. The passage given below is followed by four alternate summaries. Choose the option that best captures the essence of the passage.

Developing countries are becoming hotbeds of business innovation in much the same way as Japan did from the 1950s onwards. They are reinventing systems of production and distribution, and experimenting with entirely new business models. Why are countries that were until recently associated with cheap hands now becoming leaders in innovation? Driven by a mixture of ambition and fear they are relentlessly climbing up the value chain. Emerging-market champions have not only proved highly competitive in their own backyards, they are also going global themselves.

(1) Production and distribution models are going through rapid innovations worldwide as developed countries are being challenged by their earlier suppliers from the developing world.

(2) Competition has driven emerging economies, once suppliers of cheap labour, to become innovators of business models that have enabled them to move up the value chain and go global.

(3) Innovations in production and distribution are helping emerging economies compete with countries to which they once supplied cheap labour.

(4) Developing countries are being forced to invent new business models which challenge the old business models, so they can remain competitive domestically.

Section II: DI & LR

Question Numbers (1 to 6): A journal plans to publish 18 research papers, written by eight authors (A, B, C, D, E, F, G, and H) in four issues of the journal scheduled in January, April, July and October. Each of the research papers was written by exactly one of the eight authors. Five papers were scheduled in each of the first two issues, while four were scheduled in each of the last two issues. Every author wrote at least one paper and at most three papers. The total number of papers written by A, D, G and H was double the total number of papers written by the other four authors. Four of the authors were from India and two each were from Japan and China. Each author belonged to exactly one of the three areas — Manufacturing, Automation and Logistics. Four of the authors were from the Logistics area and two were from the Automation area. As per the journal policy, none of the authors could have more than one paper in any issue of the journal.

The following facts are also known.

1. F, an Indian author from the Logistics area, wrote only one paper. It was scheduled in the October issue.
2. A was from the Automation area and did not have a paper scheduled in the October issue.
3. None of the Indian authors were from the Manufacturing area and none of the Japanese or Chinese authors were from the Automation area.
4. A and H were from different countries, but had their papers scheduled in exactly the same issues.
5. C and E, both Chinese authors from different areas, had the same number of papers scheduled. Further, E had papers scheduled in consecutive issues of the journal but C did not.
6. B, from the Logistics area, had a paper scheduled in the April issue of the journal.
7. B and G belonged to the same country. None of their papers were scheduled in the same issue of the journal.
8. D, a Japanese author from the Manufacturing area, did not have a paper scheduled in the July issue.
9. C and H belonged to different areas.

1. What is the correct sequence of number of papers written by B, C, E and G, respectively?

(1) 1, 2, 2, 3 (2) 3, 1, 1, 3
(3) 1, 2, 2, 1 (4) 1, 3, 3, 1

2. How many papers were written by Indian authors?

3. Which of the following statement(s) MUST be true?

Statement A: Every issue had at least one paper by author(s) from each country.

Statement B: Every issue had at most two papers by author(s) from each area.

(1) Neither of the statements
(2) Both the statements
(3) Only Statement A
(4) Only Statement B

4. Which of the following statements is FALSE?

(1) Every issue had at least one paper by author(s) from Automation area.
(2) Every issue had exactly one paper by a Chinese author.
(3) Every issue had exactly two papers by authors from Logistics area.
(4) Every issue had exactly two papers by Indian authors.

5. Which of the following statements is FALSE?

(1) There were exactly two papers by authors from Manufacturing area in the July issue.

(2) There were exactly two papers by authors from Manufacturing area in the January issue.

(3) There was exactly one paper by an author from Logistics area in the October issue.

(4) There was exactly one paper by an author from Manufacturing area in the April issue.

6. Which of the following is the correct sequence of number of papers by authors from Automation, Manufacturing and Logistics areas, respectively?

(1) 6, 6, 6

(2) 6, 5, 7

(3) 5, 6, 7

(4) 6, 7, 5

Question Numbers (7 to 10): Answer the questions on the basis of the information given below.

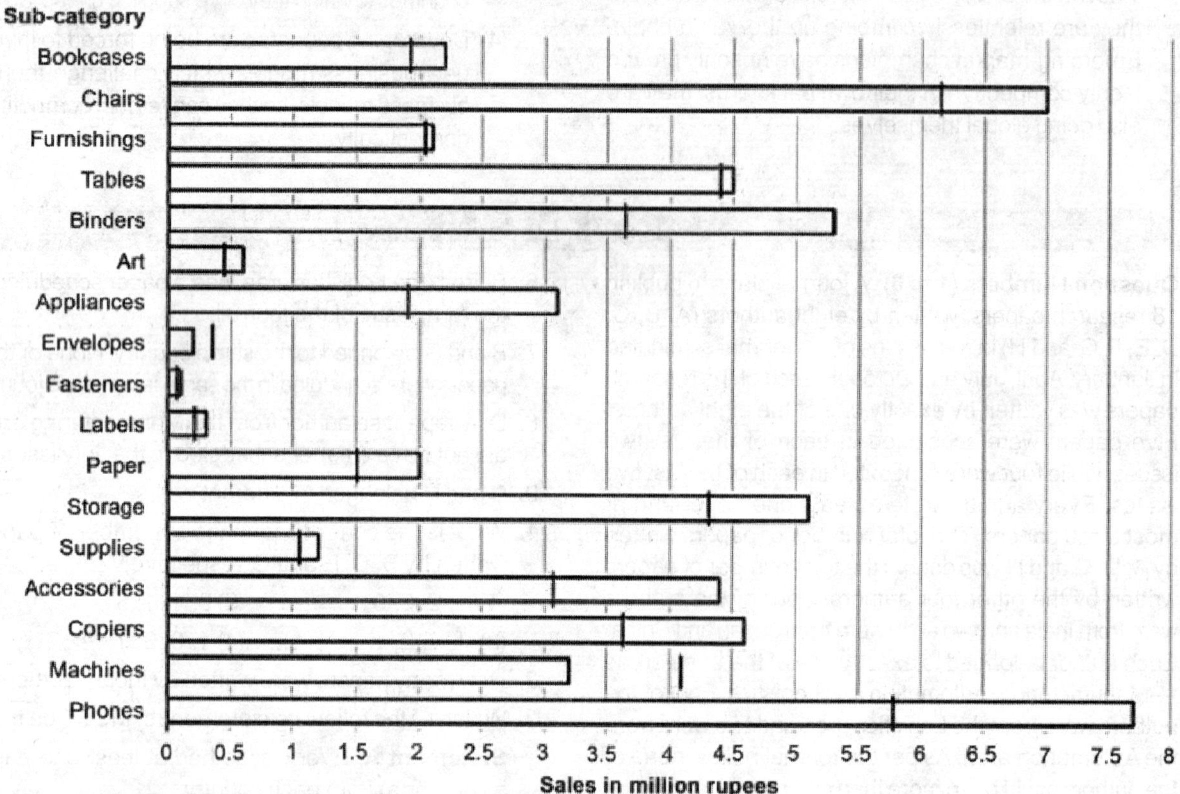

The horizontal bars in the above diagram represent 2020 aggregate sales (in Rs. million) of a company for the different subcategories of its products. The top four product subcategories (Bookcases, Chairs, Furnishings, Tables) belong to furniture product category; the bottom four product subcategories (Accessories, Copiers, Machines, Phones) belong to the technology product category while all other product subcategories belong to the office supply product category. For each of the product subcategories, there is a vertical line indicating the sales of the corresponding subcategory in 2019.

7. The total sales (in Rs. million) in 2019 from products in office supplies category is closest to

(1) 13.5 (2) 12.5

(3) 18.0 (4) 16.5

8. The percentage increase in sales in Furniture category from 2019 to 2020 is closest to

(1) 1% (2) 25%

(3) 20% (4) 8%

9. How many subcategories had sales of Rs. 4 million or more in 2019 and registered an increase in sales in excess of 25% in 2020?

10. The improvement index for a category is the maximum percentage increase in sales from 2019 to 2020 among any of its subcategories. The correct order of categories in increasing order of this improvement index is

(1) furniture, technology, office supply

(2) office supply, furniture, technology

(3) technology, furniture, office supply

(4) office supply, technology, furniture

Question Numbers (11 to 14): Answer the questions on the basis of the information given below.

Ganga, Kaveri, and Narmada are three women who buy four raw materials (Mango, Apple, Banana and Milk) and sell five finished products (Mango smoothie, Apple smoothie, Banana smoothie, Mixed fruit smoothie and Fruit salad). Table-1 gives information about the raw materials required to produce the five finished products. One unit of a finished product requires one unit of each of the raw materials mentioned in the second column of the table.

Table-1

Finished product	Raw materials required
Mango smoothie	Mango, Milk
Apple smoothie	Apple, Milk
Banana smoothie	Banana, Milk
Mixed fruit smoothie	Mango, Apple, Banana, Milk
Fruit salad	Mango, Apple, Banana

One unit of milk, mango, apple, and banana cost Rs. 5, Rs. 3, Rs. 2, and Rs. 1 respectively. Each unit of a finished product is sold for a profit equal to two times the number of raw materials used to make that product. For example, apple smoothie is made with two raw materials (apple and milk) and will be sold for a profit of Rs. 4 per unit. Leftover raw materials are sold during the last business hour of the day for a loss of Rs. 1 per unit.

The amount, in rupees, received from sales (revenue) for each woman in each of the four business hours of the day is given in Table-2.

Table-2

Business Hour	Ganga	Kaveri	Narmada
Hour 1	23	19	31
Hour 2	21	22	21
Hour 3	29	30	23
Hour 4 (last hour)	30	27	22

The following additional facts are known.

1. No one except possibly Ganga sold any Mango smoothie.
2. Each woman sold either zero or one unit of any single finished product in any hour.
3. Each woman had exactly one unit each of two different raw materials as leftovers.
4. No one had any banana leftover.

11. What BEST can be concluded about the number of units of fruit salad sold in the first hour?

(1) Exactly 1. (2) Either 0 or 1 or 2.

(3) Either 1 or 2. (4) Exactly 2.

12. Which of the following is NECESSARILY true?

(1) Ganga did not sell any leftover apples.

(2) Kaveri sold one unit of leftover mangoes.

(3) Narmada sold one unit of leftover milk.

(4) Ganga did not sell any leftover mangoes.

13. What BEST can be concluded about the total number of units of milk the three women had in the beginning?

(1) Either 18 or 19 units.

(2) Either 17 or 18 or 19 units.

(3) Either 18 or 19 or 20 units.

(4) Either 19 or 20 units.

14. If it is known that three leftover units of mangoes were sold during the last business hour of the day, how many apple smoothies were sold during the day?

Question Numbers (15 to 20): Answer the questions on the basis of the information given below.

Amudha, Bharatan, Chandran, Dhinesh, Ezhil, Fani and Gowtham are seven people in a town. Any pair of them could either be strangers, acquaintances, or friends. All relationships are mutual. For example, if Amudha is a friend of Bharatan, then Bharatan is also a friend of Amudha. Similarly, if Amudha is a stranger to Bharatan, then Bharatan is also a stranger to Amudha.

Partial information about the number of friends, acquaintances, and strangers of each of these people among them is given in the table below.

	No. of Friends	No. of Acquaintances	No. of Strangers
Amudha		1	4
Bharatan			
Chandran		1	
Dhinesh			2
Ezhil			1
Fani	1		
Gowtham		3	2

The following additional facts are also known.

1. Amudha, Bharatan, and Chandran are mutual strangers.
2. Amudha, Dhinesh, and Fani are Ezil's friends.
3. Chandran and Gowtham are friends.
4. Every friend of Amudha is an acquaintance of Bharatan, and every acquaintance of Bharatan is a friend of Amudha.
5. Every friend of Bharatan is an acquaintance of Amudha, and every acquaintance of Amudha is a friend of Bharatan.

15. Who are Gowtham's acquaintances?

(1) Dhinesh, Ezhil and Fani
(2) Amudha, Dhinesh and Fani
(3) Amudha, Bharatan and Fani
(4) Bharatan, Dhinesh and Ezhil

16. Which of these pairs share the same type of relationship?

(1) (Chandran, Ezhil) and (Dhinesh, Gowtham)
(2) (Bharatan, Chandran) and (Dhinesh, Ezhil)
(3) (Bharatan, Ezhil) and (Fani, Gowtham)
(4) (Amudha, Gowtham) and (Ezhil, Fani)

17. Who is an acquaintance of Amudha?

(1) Ezhil (2) Gowtham
(3) Dhinesh (4) Fani

18. Who is an acquaintance of Chandran?

(1) Bharatan (2) Dhinesh
(3) Ezhil (4) Fani

19. How many friends does Ezhil have?

20. How many people are either a friend or a friend-of-a-friend of Ezhil?

Section III: QA

1. If the area of a regular hexagon is equal to the area of an equilateral triangle of side 12 cm, then the length, in cm, of each side of the hexagon is

(1) $4\sqrt{6}$ (2) $2\sqrt{6}$
(3) $6\sqrt{6}$ (4) $\sqrt{6}$

2. $f(x) = \dfrac{x^2+2x-15}{x^2-7x-18}$ is negative if and only if

(1) $x < -5$ or $-2 < x < 3$ (2) $-5 < x < -2$ or $3 < x < 9$
(3) $-2 < x < 3$ or $x > 9$ (4) $x < -5$ or $3 < x < 9$

3. Amal purchases some pens at Rs. 8 each. To sell these, he hires an employee at a fixed wage. He sells 100 of these pens at Rs. 12 each. If the remaining pens are sold at Rs. 11 each, then he makes a net profit of Rs. 300, while he makes a net loss of Rs. 300 if the remaining pens are sold at Rs. 9 each. The wage of the employee, in INR, is

4. Two trains cross each other in 14 seconds when running in opposite directions along parallel tracks. The faster train is 160 m long and crosses a lamp post in 12 seconds. If the speed of the other train is 6 km/hr less than the faster one, its length, in m, is

(1) 184 (2) 192
(3) 190 (4) 180

5. If r is a constant such that $|x^2 - 4x - 13| = r$ has exactly three distinct real roots, then the value of r is

(1) 15 (2) 21
(3) 18 (4) 17

6. A basket of 2 apples, 4 oranges and 6 mangoes costs the same as a basket of 1 apple, 4 oranges and 8 mangoes, or a basket of 8 oranges and 7 mangoes. Then the number of mangoes in a basket of mangoes that has the same cost as the other baskets is

(1) 13 (2) 12
(3) 11 (4) 10

7. The amount Neeta and Geeta together earn in a day equals what Sita alone earns in 6 days. The amount Sita and Neeta together earn in a day equals what Geeta alone earns in 2 days. The ratio of the daily earnings of the one who earns the most to that of the one who earns the least is

(1) 11 : 3 (2) 3 : 2
(3) 7 : 3 (4) 11 : 7

8. Identical chocolate pieces are sold in boxes of two sizes, small and large. The large box is sold for twice the price of the small box. If the selling price per gram of chocolate in the large box is 12% less than that in the small box, then the percentage by which the weight of chocolate in the large box exceeds that in the small box is nearest to

(1) 135 (2) 124
(3) 127 (4) 144

9. The strength of an indigo solution in percentage is equal to the amount of indigo in grams per 100 cc of water. Two 800 cc bottles are filled with indigo solutions of strengths 33% and 17%, respectively. A part of the solution from the first bottle is thrown away and replaced by an equal volume of the solution from the second bottle. If the strength of the indigo solution in the first bottle has now changed to 21% then the volume, in cc, of the solution left in the second bottle is

10. A circle of diameter 8 inches is inscribed in a triangle ABC where $\angle ABC = 90°$. If BC = 10 inches then the area of the triangle in square inches is

11. How many three-digit numbers are greater than 100 and increase by 198 when the three digits are arranged in the reverse order?

12. The number of groups of three or more distinct numbers that can be chosen from 1, 2, 3, 4, 5, 6, 7 and 8 so that the groups always include 3 and 5, while 7 and 8 are never included together is

13. Onion is sold for 5 consecutive months at the rate of Rs. 10, 20, 25, 25, and 50 per kg, respectively. A family spends a fixed amount of money on onion for each of the first three months, and then spends half that amount on onion for each of the next two months. The average expense for onion, in rupees per kg, for the family over these 5 months is closest to

(1) 16 (2) 26
(3) 20 (4) 18

14. If $x_0 = 1$, $x_1 = 2$, and $x_{n+2} = \frac{1+x_{n+1}}{x_n}$, n = 0, 1, 2, 3, ..., then x_{2021} is equal to

(1) 1 (2) 2
(3) 3 (4) 4

15. Suppose hospital A admitted 21 less Covid infected patients than hospital B, and all eventually recovered. The sum of recovery days for patients in hospitals A and B were 200 and 152, respectively. If the average recovery days for patients admitted in hospital A was 3 more than the average in hospital B then the number admitted in hospital A was

16. Suppose the length of each side of a regular hexagon ABCDEF is 2 cm. It T is the mid point of CD, then the length of AT, in cm, is

(1) $\sqrt{15}$ (2) $\sqrt{12}$
(3) $\sqrt{14}$ (4) $\sqrt{13}$

17. Anu, Vinu and Manu can complete a work alone in 15 days, 12 days and 20 days, respectively. Vinu works everyday. Anu works only on alternate days starting from the first day while Manu works only on alternate days starting from the second day. Then, the number of days needed to complete the work is

(1) 8 (2) 5
(3) 7 (4) 6

18. If $5 - \log_{10}\sqrt{1+x} + 4\log_{10}\sqrt{1-x} = \log_{10}\frac{1}{\sqrt{1-x^2}}$, then 100x equals

19. Amar, Akbar and Anthony are working on a project. Working together Amar and Akbar can complete the project in 1 year, Akbar and Anthony can complete in 16 months, Anthony and Amar can complete in 2 years. If the person who is neither the fastest nor the slowest works alone, the time in months he will take to complete the project is

20. The number of integers n that satisfy the inequalities $|n - 60| < |n - 100| < |n - 20|$ is

(1) 19 (2) 18
(3) 20 (4) 21

21. Anil invests some money at a fixed rate of interest, compounded annually. If the interests accrued during the second and third year are Rs. 806.25 and Rs. 866.72, respectively, the interest accrued, in INR, during the fourth year is nearest to

(1) 931.72 (2) 926.84
(3) 929.48 (4) 934.65

22. The natural numbers are divided into groups as (1), (2, 3, 4), (5, 6, 7, 8, 9), ... and so on. Then, the sum of the numbers in the 15th group is equal to

(1) 4941 (2) 6090
(3) 6119 (4) 7471

ANSWERS

VARC

1. (4)	**2.** (4)	**3.** (2)	**4.** (2)	**5.** (3)	**6.** (4)	**7.** (2)	**8.** (1)	**9.** (4)	**10.** (2)
11. (1)	**12.** (3)	**13.** (3)	**14.** (2)	**15.** (4)	**16.** (4)	**17.** (2341)	**18.** (5)	**19.** (4312)	**20.** (4)
21. (2143)	**22.** (1)	**23.** (2)	**24.** (2)						

DI & LR

1. (1)	**2.** (8)	**3.** (3)	**4.** (3)	**5.** (1)	**6.** (2)	**7.** (1)	**8.** (4)	**9.** (1)	**10.** (1)
11. (3)	**12.** (1)	**13.** (3)	**14.** (6)	**15.** (1)	**16.** (3)	**17.** (3)	**18.** (4)	**19.** (3)	**20.** (4)

QA

1. (2)	**2.** (2)	**3.** (1000)	**4.** (3)	**5.** (4)	**6.** (1)	**7.** (1)	**8.** (3)	**9.** (200)	**10.** (120)
11. (70)	**12.** (47)	**13.** (4)	**14.** (2)	**15.** (35)	**16.** (4)	**17.** (3)	**18.** (99)	**19.** (32)	**20.** (1)
21. (1)	**22.** (3)								

EXPLANATIONS

VARC

1. As the passage states, there were several points of divergence between the marshmallow test done on children and its cuttlefish version. The time span over which these tests were performed, the type of subjects and the mode of communication used were different in these two versions. However, while the test on humans did find a correlation between self-control and future success, there is no mention of 'survival advantages' with respect to the experiment on cuttlefish.

2. The passage states that "Not every species can use self-control, but most of the animals that can share another trait in common: long, social lives." However, even though the cuttlefish are solitary creatures that don't form relationships even with mates or young, they did prove capable of exhibiting self-control when trained under the right circumstances. Thus, if it was established that cuttlefish also live in big groups and are sociable, the passages' findings will be reinforced. The other options, if true, are likely to contradict the information given and not complement it.

3. 1 – Can be inferred from "....... but sometimes, they would turn away from the king prawn "as if to distract themselves from the temptation of the immediate reward."

   3 – Can be inferred from "(Preliminary experiments showed that cuttlefishes' favorite food is live grass shrimp, while raw prawns are so-so and Asian shore crab is nearly unacceptable.)"

   4 – This was the finding of the research experiments.

   2 cannot be inferred from the passage. In fact, the success with the cuttlefish seems to suggest otherwise.

4. 1 – If the drawer with the live grass shrimp is labelled with a square, it means that it will 'never' be opened. In this scenario, the cuttlefish will automatically reach for raw prawns as their preferred food – the live grass shrimp – is not going to be available. Thus, there is no need for them to demonstrate any self-control.

   2 – This is the correct answer. In this case, the cuttlefish will have to choose between immediate gratification with a secondary preference – raw prawns and Asian shore crabs – and delayed gratification with their first choice– live grass shrimps. Notice that the drawer is labelled with a 'triangle' which means that the drawer will be opened after a delay (one minute in this case).

   3 – The cuttlefish prefer the raw prawns to Asian shore crabs. So, there is no need for them to exhibit any self-control since their preferred food is being released first.

   4 – Similar to the previous option, the cuttlefish prefer the live grass shrimp the most. Hence, they don't need to exhibit any self-control in this situation also.

5. 1 – Refer the lines: "For we have only to acknowledge the existence of thousands of successful intentional communities in which a cooperative ethos predominates and where harmony without coercion is the rule to set aside such an assertion."

   2 – Refer the lines: "People become more alike in appearance, opinion, and outlook than they often have been. Unity, order, and homogeneity thus prevail at the cost of individuality and diversity."

   4 – Refer the lines: "This often portrays societies where . . . 'it would be almost impossible for man to be depraved, or wicked'."

   3 is contradicted by the following lines: "In More's time, for much of the population, given the plenty and security on offer, such restraints would not have seemed overly unreasonable."

6. 1 – Refer the lines: "People become more alike in appearance, opinion, and outlook than they often have been. Unity, order, and homogeneity thus prevail at the cost of individuality and diversity."

   2 – Refer the lines: "....it is not unreasonable to take as our starting point here the hypothesis that utopia and dystopia evidently share more in common than is often supposed. Indeed, they might be twins, the progeny of the same parents."

   3 – Refer the lines: "And utopian homogeneity remains a familiar theme well into the twentieth century."

   4 is in direct contrast to the information given in the concluding paragraph of the passage.

7. 2 can be inferred from the following lines of the passage: "This is achieved both through institutions and mores, which underpin the common life. . .. The passions are regulated and inequalities of wealth and distinction are minimized. Needs, vanity, and emulation are restrained, often by prizing equality and holding riches in contempt. The desire for public power is curbed." The other options contradict the aspects of utopian societies as described in the passage.

8. The passage opens by describing utopia. It then ponders the question that even though utopia provides security: but at what price? The discussion then moves towards the emphasis placed on homogeneity and the passage closes by mentioning intentional communities where the individual's submersion in the group is consensual and not coerced. 1 captures this flow of ideas comprehensively and in the correct order.

9. All the other statements have been mentioned in the passage.

10. The answer is clearly inferable from the following lines: "Yet tea is, Rappaport makes clear, a world apart – an astonishing success story in which tea marketers not only succeeded in conveying a sense of moral elevation to the consumer but also arguably did advance the cause of civilisation and community."

11. Refer the lines: "An early version of the "farm to table" movement was sparked by anti-Chinese sentiment and concerns over trade deficits, as well as by the reality and threat of adulterated tea containing dirt and hedge clippings". Thus, this conflation of consumption with virtue is now seen in the marketing and promotion of sustainably farmed food.

12. All the other statements have been mentioned in the passage.

13. 1 – This is negated by the lines: "Nonhuman persons were not tethered to specific humans, and they did not derive their personhood from a connection with a human. . . ."

2 – This is negated by: "One additional complexity: the incense burner (which would have been made of clay, and decorated with spiky appliques representing the sacred ceiba tree found in this region) is categorised as a person – but also as a tree."

4 – This is challenged by information given throughout the passage.

14. The answer can be inferred from the lines: "With these Maya examples, we are challenged to discard the person/ nonperson binary that constitutes our basic ontological outlook."

15. For the Mayans, man was by all account not the only significant thing. Everything was similarly significant and similarly human. Choice 4 is aligned with this perspective. The other options are not consistent with the ideas expressed in the passage.

16. The author says that a thing (iPhone) has a personality for us because it's connected or useful to us, but that was not the case with the Maya people. To them the non-human were not tied to specific human beings. To invalidate this example, we must choose an alternative that is against it. Option 4 does exactly that. It makes the personality of incense sticks and stone choppers a function of their usefulness to humans, something the author seeks to negate through the example of the thing (iPhone). All the other three options do not invalidate the iPhone instance in any way. So, the correct answer is option 4.

17. 2 opens the discussion by introducing the theme of the paragraph. 'They' in 3 refers to the 'biologists' in 2. 'However' in 4 points to a caveat in this ability and 1 closes the discussion by drawing a parallel.

18. The correct sequence is: There is a dark side to academic research, especially in India, and at its centre is the phenomenon of predatory journals. They claim to be indexed in the most influential databases, say they possess editorial boards that comprise top scientists and researchers, and claim to have a rigorous peer-review structure. In look and feel, they are exactly like any reputed journal. But in truth, as long as you pay, you can get anything published.

The passage talks about elements of predatory journals. 5, by talking about an academic scam, goes against the ideas expressed in it.

19. 4 is the opening sentence as it talks about the two aspects of a literary work. 'This polarity' in 3 makes it the next sentence in the sequence. 1 talks about the interdependence between the reader and the text and 2 closes the discussion by talking about the impact of this convergence.

20. Option 4 is the odd sentence. The other options are talking about the legalities in relation to the resources mined in outer space while 4 is vaguely referring to rights conferred by USA.

21. The correct order is: It seems all but certain that global warming will go well above two degrees—quite how high no one knows yet. A popular response is the exhortation to plant more trees. This is because trees sequester carbon by absorbing carbon dioxide. Burning them releases it, which is why the scale of forest fires in the Amazon basin last year garnered headlines.

22. The key summary of the paragraph is: Foreign peacekeepers often exist in a bubble and though this may be partially justified, a better solution would be conducting bottom-up peacebuilding. Option 1 captures this argument concisely and is the correct answer.

23. The passage essentially defines the McGurk effect and its relevance. That is why option 2 is the correct answer.

24. The core message of the passage is captured in the following lines: "Why are countries that were until recently associated with cheap hands now becoming leaders in innovation? Driven by a mixture of ambition and fear they are relentlessly climbing up the value chain"

DI & LR

For questions 1 to 6:

Step 1:

Since the total number of papers written by A, D, G and H was double the total number of papers written by the other authors.

A + D + G + H = 12 papers and B + C + E + F = 6 papers

So A = D = G = H = 3 papers

From conditions (1) and (5), B, C, E and F had 1, 2, 2, 1 papers respectively.

Step 2:

From condition (3), A was Indian author.

From condition (7), B and G were Indian authors.

From condition (4), A and H were Indian and Japanese authors respectively. So F was Indian author and G was from Automation area.

From condition (9), C and H were from Manufacturing and Logistics areas respectively. So E was from Logistics.

The given information can be shown as:

Author	Papers	Month	Country	Area
A	3	xOctober	India	Automation
B	1	April	India	Logistics
C	2		China	Manufacturing
D	3	xJuly	Japan	Manufacturing
E	2		China	Logistics
F	1	October	India	Logistics
G	3		India	Automation
H	3		Japan	Logistics

Step 3:

From condition (4), A and H had their issues in January, April and July months.

From condition (5), E had issues in April, July and C had in January, October months.

From condition (7), G had issues in January, July and October months.

From condition (8), D had issues in January, April and October months.

The final table can be shown as:

Author	Papers	Month	Country	Area
A	3	January, April, July	India	Automation
B	1	April	India	Logistics
C	2	January, October	China	Manufacturing
D	3	January, April, October	Japan	Manufacturing
E	2	April, July	China	Logistics
F	1	October	India	Logistics
G	3	January, July, October	India	Automation
H	3	January, April, July	Japan	Logistics

1. The correct sequence of number of papers written by B, C, E and G is 1, 2, 2, 3 respectively.
2. The number of papers written by Indian authors is 8.
3. Only statement A must be correct.
4. The statement given in option (3) is false.
5. The statement given in option (1) is false.
6. The correct sequence is 6, 5, 7.

For questions 7 to 10:

From the given information, the table can be shown as:

Product Category	Product Subcategory	Sales (in Rs. Million) 2020	Sales (in Rs. Million) 2019	Increase/ Decrease
Furniture	Bookcases	2.2	1.9	0.3
	Chairs	7	6.15	0.85
	Furnishings	2.05	2	0.05
	Tables	4.5	4.35	0.15
		15.75	14.4	
Office Supply	Binders	5.3	3.65	1.65
	Art	0.6	0.45	0.15
	Appliances	3.1	1.9	1.2
	Envelopes	0.2	0.4	–0.2
	Fasteners	0.1	0.05	0.05
	Labels	0.3	0.2	0.1
	Paper	2	1.5	0.05
	Storage	5.1	4.3	0.8
	Supplies	1.2	1.05	0.15
		17.9	13.5	
Technology	Accessories	4.4	3.05	1.35
	Copiers	4.6	3.65	0.95
	Machines	3.2	4.1	–0.9
	Phones	7.7	5.8	1.9
		19.9	16.65	

7. The total sales (in Rs. Million) in 2019 from products in office supplies category is closest to 13.5.
8. Percentage increase in sales from 2019 to 2020 for Furniture category

$$= \frac{15.75 - 14.4}{14.4} \times 100 \approx 9.375\%$$

Hence, from the given options, the correct answer is 8%.

9. Only 5 subcategories had sales of Rs. 4 million or more in 2019 and registered an increase in sales only for Phones in excess of 25% in 2020.

The percentage increase = 1.9/5.8 × 100 ≈ 32.75%

Hence, increase in sales only for one product in excess of 25% in 2020.

10. Percentage increase in sales from 2019 to 2020 for Furniture category

$$= \frac{15.75 - 14.4}{14.4} \times 100 \approx 9.375\%$$

Percentage increase in sales from 2019 to 2020 for Office Supply category

$$= \frac{17.9 - 13.5}{13.5} \times 100 \approx 32.59\%$$

Percentage increase in sales from 2019 to 2020 for Technology category

$$= \frac{19.9 - 16.65}{16.65} \times 100 \approx 19.52\%$$

Hence, required increasing order is Furniture, Technology, Office Supply.

For questions 11 to 14:

Step 1:

From the 1st table and the given information:

Finished Product	Cost Price (in Rs./Unit)	Selling Price (in Rs./Unit)
Mango Smoothie	3 + 5 = 8	8 + 2 × 2 = 12
Apple Smoothie	2 + 5 = 7	7 + 2 × 2 = 11
Banana Smoothie	1 + 5 = 6	6 + 2 × 2 = 10
Mixed Fruit Smoothie	3 + 2 + 1 + 5 = 11	11 + 4 × 2 = 19
Fruit Salad	3 + 2 + 1 = 6	6 + 3 × 2 = 12

Step 2:

From the 2nd table and the conditions (i) to (v):

The leftover should have been either Milk + Apple or Mango + Apple or Milk + Mango. So leftover realization should have been Rs. 5 or Rs. 3 or Rs. 6.

The given information can be shown as:

Business Hour	Ganga	Kaveri	Narmada
Hour 1	1 Mango S + 1 Apple S **or** 1 Apple S + 1 Fruit Salad	1 Mixed Fruit S	1 Mixed Fruit S + 1 Fruit Salad
Hour 2	1 Apple S + 1 Banana S	1 Banana S + 1 Fruit Salad	1 Apple S + 1 Banana S
Hour 3	1 Banana S + 1 Mixed Fruit S	1 Apple S + 1 Mixed Fruit S	1 Apple S + 1 Fruit Salad
Hour 4 (Last hour)	1 Milk + 1 Apple = Rs. 5	1 Mango + 1 Apple = Rs. 3	1 Milk + 1 Mango = Rs. 6
Ganga	x25	x27	24
Kaveri	22	x24	21
Narmada	x17	19	x16

11. Either 1 or 2 units of fruit salad sold in first hour.

12. The statement given in option (1) is necessarily true.

13. Either 18 or 19 or 20 units of milk the three women had in the beginning.

14. If 3 leftover units of mangoes were sold during the last business hour of the day, then 6 apple smoothies were sold during the day.

For questions 15 to 20:

Let A, B, C, D, E, F, and G represent the people Amudha, Bharatan, Chandran, Dhinesh, Ezhil, Fani, and Gowtham respectively.

From conditions (1) to (5):

	No. of Friends	No. of Acquaintances	No. of Strangers
Amudha	1 E	1 D	4 B, C, F, G
Bharatan	1 D	1 E	4 A, C, F, G
Chandran	1 G	1 F	4 A, B, D, E
Dhinesh	2 B, E	2 A, G	2 C, F
Ezhil	3 A, D, F	2 B, G	1 C
Fani	1 E	2 C, G	3 A, B, D
Gowtham	1 C	3 D, E, F	2, A, B

15. Gowtham's acquaintances are Dhinesh, Ezhil and Fani.

16. (Bharatan, Ezhil) and (Fani, Gowtham) pairs share the same type of relationship.

17. Dhinesh is an acquaintance of Amudha.

18. Fani is an acquaintance of Chandran.

19. Ezhil have 3 friends.

20. The four people are either a friend or a friend-of-a-friend of Ezhil.

QA

1. Let 'a' be the side of the regular hexagon.

Then, area of regular hexagon = Area of equilateral triangle of side 12 cm

$$\Rightarrow 6 \times \frac{\sqrt{3}}{4} \times a^2 = \frac{\sqrt{3}}{4} \times 12^2$$

$$\Rightarrow a = 2\sqrt{6} \text{ cm.}$$

2. $$f(x) = \frac{x^2 + 2x - 15}{x^2 - 7x - 18} = \frac{(x+5)(x-3)}{(x-9)(x+2)} < 0$$

Or, $$\frac{(x+5)(x-3)(x-9)(x+2)}{(x-9)^2(x+2)^2} < 0$$

Or, $(x+5)(x-3)(x-9)(x+2) < 0$

–5 –2 +3 +9

X X X

Substituting x = 0, we get

$5 \times (-3) \times (-2) \times 9 > 0$

Hence, not satisfying $-5 < x < -2$ or $3 < x < 9$.

3. Let the number of pencils be x and the fixed wages be 'w'.

Profit = $4 \times 100 + 3(x - 100) - w = 300$

$\Rightarrow 3x - w = 200$ ... (i)

Loss = $4 \times 100 + 1(x - 100) - w = -300$

$\Rightarrow x - w = -600$ ... (ii)

From (i) and (ii), x = 400 and w = Rs. 1,000.

4. Speed of the faster train = 160/12 = 40/3 m/s or $40/3 \times 18/5 = 48$ km/h

Speed of the other train = 48 – 6 = 42 km/s

Relative speed = 48 + 42 = 90 km/h or 25 m/s

Distance travelled by both trains in 14 seconds = $25 \times 14 = 350$ m

Hence, the length of the other trains = 350 – 160 = 190 m.

5. $|x^2 - 4x - 13| = r$ should have 3 roots.

⇒ One quadratic equation should be a perfect square.

Going from choices if r = 17,

$|x^2 - 4x - 13| = 17x^2 - 4x - 13 = -17$ (One case)

$x^2 - 4x + 4 = 0$

$\Rightarrow (x-2)^2 = 0$

$\Rightarrow x = 2$

Hence, r = 17.

6. Let A, O and M represents the Apples, Oranges and Mangoes respectively.

2A + 4O + 6M = A + 4O + 8M = 8O + 7M

Therefore, A = 2M and 2A = 4O + M

⇒ 4M = 4O + M

⇒ 3M = 4O

So A + 4O + 8M = 2M + 3M + 8M = 13M

Hence, the number of mangoes in the basket is 13.

7. Let N, G and S be the amount that Neeta, Geeta and Sita earn in a day respectively.

Then, N + G = 6S and S + N = 2G

⇒ N + G = 6(2G – N) and S = 2G – N

⇒ N + G = 12G – 6N and S = 2G – N

⇒ 7N = 11G and S = 2G – N

Therefore, S = 2G – 11G/ 7

⇒ S = 3G/7 and N = 11G/7

⇒ If G = 7, S = 3, N = 11

Hence, one who earns the most : one who earns the least = 11 : 3.

8. Let 2x and x be the selling price of large and small box respectively.

Then, required percentage

$$= \frac{\frac{2x}{88} - \frac{x}{100}}{\frac{x}{100}} \times 100 \approx 127\%.$$

9. Even after throwing away some solution from 1st bottle, % Indigo would be 33%.

Applying allegation rule:

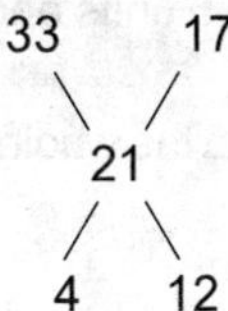

So ratio = 4 : 12 or 1 : 3.

So 600 from 2nd bottle were put into bottle 1.

Hence, 200 ml is left in bottle 2.

10.

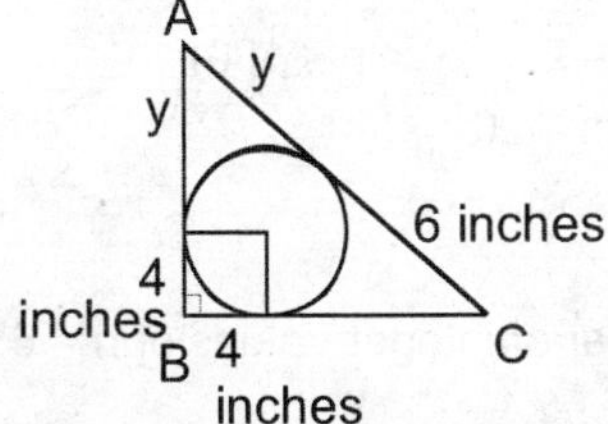

$(6 + y)^2 = (4 + y)^2 + 10^2$

$\Rightarrow 36 + y^2 + 12y = 16 + y^2 + 8y + 100$

$\Rightarrow 4y = 80 \Rightarrow y = 20$

Hence, area of triangle = 1/2 × 10 × 24 = 120 square inches.

11. Let xyz be the number by reversing it become xyz value difference

= 100x + 10y + z – (100z + 10y + x)

= 99x – 99z = 198

$\Rightarrow$ x – z = 2

3 – 1 = 10 numbers

4 – 2 = 10 numbers

....

9 – 7 = 10 numbers

Hence, total numbers are 7 × 10 = 70.

12. Given numbers are 1, 2, 3, 4, 5, 6, 7, 8.

A group of 3 digits with 3 and 5 included would be 3, 5, __

Number of 3 digits groups = 6

A group of 4 digits with 3 and 5 included 3, 5, __ __

Number of 4 digits groups = $^6C_2 - 1 = 14$ (1 case would be wherein both 7 and 8 are included.)

Similarly, 3, 5, _ _ _

Number of 5 digits groups = $^6C_3 - {}^4C_1 = 16$ (both 7, 8 included)

3, 5, _ _ _ _

Number of 6 digits groups = $^6C_4 - {}^4C_2 = 9$

3, 5, _ _ _ _ _

Number of 7 digits groups = $^6C_5 - {}^4C_3 = 2$

Hence, total number of groups = 6 + 14 + 16 + 9 + 2 = 47.

13. Let the family spend Rs. 100/month for the first 3 months.

Then, number of kg of onions = 100/10 = 10 kg; 100/20 = 5 kg; 100/25 = 4 kg

Rs. 50 for the next two months.

Number of kg of onions = 50/25 = 2 kg; 50/50 = 1 kg

Total onion in kg = 10 + 5 + 4 + 2 + 1 = 22 kg

Hence, the average price of onions = 400/22 ≈ Rs.18.

14. $x_0 = 1;\ x_1 = 2;\ x_{n+2} = \dfrac{1 + x_{n+1}}{x_n}$

$$x_2 = \frac{1+x_1}{x_0} = \frac{1+2}{1} = 3$$

$$x_3 = \frac{1+x_2}{x_1} = \frac{1+3}{2} = 2$$

$$x_4 = \frac{1+x_3}{x_2} = \frac{1+2}{3} = 1$$

$$x_5 = \frac{1+x_4}{x_3} = \frac{1+1}{2} = 1$$

$$x_6 = \frac{1+x_5}{x_4} = \frac{1+1}{1} = 2$$

$$x_7 = \frac{1+x_6}{x_5} = \frac{1+2}{1} = 3$$

The terms are 1, 2, 3, 2, 1, 1, 2, 3, 2, 1, ...

Hence, $x_{2019} = 1;\ x_{2020} = 1;\ x_{2021} = 2$.

15. Let the number of patients admitted in hospital B be x.

Then, the number of patients admitted in hospital A will be x – 21.

According to the question,

$$\frac{200}{x-21} - \frac{158}{x} = 3$$

$\Rightarrow$ x = 56

Hence, x – 21 = 35.

16.

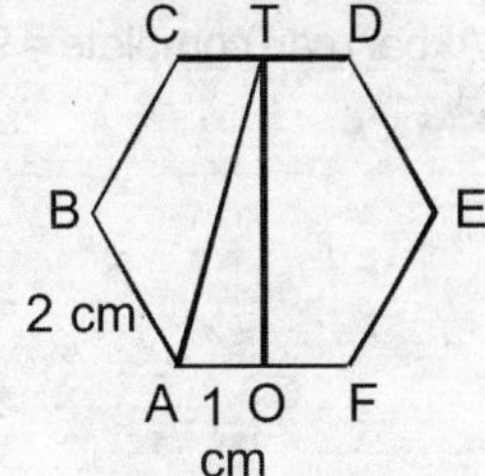

AO = 2/2 = 1 cm

$$OT = 2 \times \frac{\sqrt{3}}{2} \times 2 = 2\sqrt{3} \text{ cm}$$

$$\text{Hence, } AT = \sqrt{(2\sqrt{3})^2 + 1} = \sqrt{13} \text{ cm.}$$

17. Total work = LCM (15, 12, 20) = 60 units
Work done by Anu, Vinu and Manu in one day = 4, 5, 3 units respectively
Work done on Day 1 = 5 + 4 = 9 units
Work done on Day 2 = 5 + 3 = 8 units
Therefore, 9 + 8 + 9 + 8 + 9 + 8 + 9 = 60 units
Hence, number of days needed to complete the work = 7 days.

18. $5\log_{10}10 - \log_{10}\sqrt{1+x} + 4\log_{10}\sqrt{1-x}$

$= \log_{10}\sqrt{1-x^2}$

$\Rightarrow \frac{10^5}{\sqrt{1-x}} \times \sqrt{1-x^2} = \frac{1}{\sqrt{1-x} \times \sqrt{1+x}}$

$\Rightarrow 10^5 = \frac{1}{(1-x)^{\frac{5}{2}}}$

$\Rightarrow 10^5 = (1-x)^{-\frac{5}{2}}$

$\therefore 5 = -\frac{5}{2}\log_{10}(1-x)$

$\Rightarrow -2 = \log_{10}(1-x)$

$\Rightarrow 1-x = 10^{-2} = \frac{1}{100}$

$\Rightarrow x = \frac{99}{100}$

Hence, 100x = 99.

19. Total work = LCM (12, 16, 24) = 48 units
Work done by Amar and Akbar in 1 month = 4 units
Work done by Akbar and Anthony in 1 month = 3 units
Work done by Anthony and Amar in 1 month = 2 units
2(Amar + Anthony + Akbar) can complete = 9 units/month
Amar + Akbar + Anthony can complete = 4.5 units/month
Therefore, Anthony can complete = 0.5 units/month, Amar can complete = 1.5 units and Akbar can complete = 2.5 units
Hence, Amar can alone complete the whole project = 48/1.5 = 32 months.

20. $|n - 60| < |n - 100| < |n - 20|$
$|n - 60| < |n - 100|$ $(60 < n < 100)$
Or, $n - 60 < 100 - n$
Or, $2n < 160$
Or, $n < 80$
$|n - 100| < |n - 20|$ $(20 < n < 100)$
Or, $100 - n < n - 20$
Or, $2n > 120$
Or, $n > 60$
Hence, number of integer values of n = 61 to 79 = 19.

21. Compound interest in 2nd year = Rs.806.25
Compound interest in 3rd year = Rs.866.72
Percentage increase in interest

$= \frac{866.72 - 806.25}{806.25} \times 100 \approx 7.5\%$

Compound interest in 4th year = 866.72 + 866.72

$\times \frac{7.5}{100} \approx$ Rs.931.72.

22. 1st group = (1); 2nd group = (2, 3, 4); 3rd group = (5, 6, 7, 8, 9); …
In every bracket the last term is $(\text{bracket})^2$.
So in the 15th bracket the last term is $15^2 = 225$ and the number of terms in each bracket is consecutive odd number so the 15th bracket will have 29 terms.
15th bracket = {197, 198, 199, … , 225}

Hence, sum = $\frac{29}{2}(197 + 225) = 6119$.

CAT 2021 SOLVED PAPER (SLOT-2)

Section I: VARC

Question Numbers (1 to 4): The passage below is accompanied by a set of questions. Choose the best answer to each question.

Many people believe that truth conveys power. . . . Hence sticking with the truth is the best strategy for gaining power. Unfortunately, this is just a comforting myth. In fact, truth and power have a far more complicated relationship, because in human society, power means two very different things.

On the one hand, power means having the ability to manipulate objective realities: to hunt animals, to construct bridges, to cure diseases, to build atom bombs. This kind of power is closely tied to truth. If you believe a false physical theory, you won't be able to build an atom bomb. On the other hand, power also means having the ability to manipulate human beliefs, thereby getting lots of people to cooperate effectively. Building atom bombs requires not just a good understanding of physics, but also the coordinated labor of millions of humans. Planet Earth was conquered by Homo sapiens rather than by chimpanzees or elephants, because we are the only mammals that can cooperate in very large numbers. And large-scale cooperation depends on believing common stories. But these stories need not be true. You can unite millions of people by making them believe in completely fictional stories about God, about race or about economics. The dual nature of power and truth results in the curious fact that we humans know many more truths than any other animal, but we also believe in much more nonsense. . . .

When it comes to uniting people around a common story, fiction actually enjoys three inherent advantages over the truth. First, whereas the truth is universal, fictions tend to be local. Consequently if we want to distinguish our tribe from foreigners, a fictional story will serve as a far better identity marker than a true story. . . . The second huge advantage of fiction over truth has to do with the handicap principle, which says that reliable signals must be costly to the signaler. Otherwise, they can easily be faked by cheaters. . . If political loyalty is signaled by believing a true story, anyone can fake it. But believing ridiculous and outlandish stories exacts greater cost, and is therefore a better signal of loyalty. . . . Third, and most important, the truth is often painful and disturbing. Hence if you stick to unalloyed reality, few people will follow you. An American presidential candidate who tells the American public the truth, the whole truth and nothing but the truth about American history has a 100 percent guarantee of losing the elections. . . . An uncompromising adherence to the truth is an admirable spiritual practice, but it is not a winning political strategy. . . .

Even if we need to pay some price for deactivating our rational faculties, the advantages of increased social cohesion are often so big that fictional stories routinely triumph over the truth in human history. Scholars have known this for thousands of years, which is why scholars often had to decide whether they served the truth or social harmony. Should they aim to unite people by making sure everyone believes in the same fiction, or should they let people know the truth even at the price of disunity?

1. The central theme of the passage is about the choice between:

(1) stories that unite people and those that distinguish groups from each other.

(2) attaining social cohesion and propagating objective truth.

(3) truth and power.

(4) leaders who unknowingly spread fictions and those who intentionally do so.

2. The author implies that, like scholars, successful leaders:

(1) use myths to attain the first type of power.

(2) know how to balance truth and social unity.

(3) need to leverage both types of power to remain in office.

(4) today know how to create social cohesion better than in the past.

3. Regarding which one of the following quotes could we argue that the author overemphasises the importance of fiction?

(1) ". . . scholars often had to decide whether they served the truth or social harmony. Should they aim to unite people by making sure everyone believes in the same fiction, or should they let people know the truth . . .?"

(2) "In fact, truth and power have a far more complicated relationship, because in human society, power means two very different things."

(3) "On the one hand, power means having the ability to manipulate objective realities: to hunt animals, to construct bridges, to cure diseases, to build atom bombs."

(4) "Hence sticking with the truth is the best strategy for gaining power. Unfortunately, this is just a comforting myth."

4. The author would support none of the following statements about political power EXCEPT that:

(1) manipulating people's beliefs is politically advantageous, but a leader who propagates only myths is likely to lose power.

(2) there are definite advantages to promoting fiction, but there needs to be some limit to a pervasive belief in myths.

(3) while unalloyed truth is not recommended, leaders should stay as close as possible to it.

(4) people cannot handle the unvarnished truth, so leaders retain power by deviating from it.

Question Numbers (5 to 8): The passage below is accompanied by a set of questions. Choose the best answer to each question.

I have elaborated . . . . a framework for analyzing the contradictory pulls on [Indian] nationalist ideology in its struggle against the dominance of colonialism and the resolution it offered to those contradictions. Briefly, this resolution was built around a separation of the domain of culture into two spheres—the material and the spiritual. It was in the material sphere that the claims of Western civilization were the most powerful. Science, technology, rational forms of economic organization, modern methods of statecraft—these had given the European countries the strength to subjugate the non-European people . . . To overcome this domination, the colonized people had to learn those superior techniques of organizing material life and incorporate them within their own cultures. . . . But this could not mean the imitation of the West in every aspect of life, for then the very distinction between the West and the East would vanish—the self-identity of national culture would itself be threatened. . . .

The discourse of nationalism shows that the material/spiritual distinction was condensed into an analogous, but ideologically far more powerful, dichotomy: that between the outer and the inner. . . . Applying the inner/outer distinction to the matter of concrete day-to-day living separates the social space into ghar and bāhir, the home and the world. The world is the external, the domain of the material; the home represents one's inner spiritual self, one's true identity. The world is a treacherous terrain of the pursuit of material interests, where practical considerations reign supreme. It is also typically the domain of the male. The home in its essence must remain unaffected by the profane activities of the material world—and woman is its representation. And so one gets an identification of social roles by gender to correspond with the separation of the social space into ghar and bāhir . . . .

The colonial situation, and the ideological response of nationalism to the critique of Indian tradition, introduced an entirely new substance to [these dichotomies] and effected their transformation. The material/spiritual dichotomy, to which the terms world and home corresponded, had acquired ... a very special significance in the nationalist mind. The world was where the European power had challenged the non-European peoples and, by virtue of its superior material culture, had subjugated them. But, the nationalists asserted, it had failed to colonize the inner, essential, identity of the East which lay in its distinctive, and superior, spiritual culture.... [I]n the entire phase of the national struggle, the crucial need was to protect, preserve and strengthen the inner core of the national culture, its spiritual essence. ... Once we match this new meaning of the home/world dichotomy with the identification of social roles by gender, we get the ideological framework within which nationalism answered the women's question. It would be a grave error to see in this, as liberals are apt to in their despair at the many marks of social conservatism in nationalist practice, a total rejection of the West. Quite the contrary: the nationalist paradigm in fact supplied an ideological principle of selection.

5. On the basis of the information in the passage, all of the following are true about the spiritual/material dichotomy of Indian nationalism EXCEPT that it:

(1) helped in safeguarding the identity of Indian nationalism.

(2) represented a continuation of age-old oppositions in Indian culture.

(3) constituted the premise of the ghar / bāhir dichotomy.

(4) was not as ideologically powerful as the inner/outer dichotomy.

6. Which one of the following explains the "contradictory pulls" on Indian nationalism?

(1) Despite its fight against colonial domination, Indian nationalism had to borrow from the coloniser in the spiritual sphere.

(2) Despite its scientific and technological inferiority, Indian nationalism had to fight against colonial domination.

(3) Despite its fight against colonial domination, Indian nationalism had to borrow from the coloniser in the material sphere.

(4) Despite its spiritual superiority, Indian nationalism had to fight against colonial domination.

7. Which one of the following, if true, would weaken the author's claims in the passage?

(1) The colonial period saw the hybridisation of Indian culture in all realms as it came in contact with British/European culture.

(2) Forces of colonial modernity played an important role in shaping anti-colonial Indian nationalism.

(3) Indian nationalists rejected the cause of English education for women during the colonial period.

(4) The Industrial Revolution played a crucial role in shaping the economic prowess of Britain in the eighteenth century.

8. Which one of the following best describes the liberal perception of Indian nationalism?

(1) Indian nationalist discourses reaffirmed traditional gender roles for Indian women.

(2) Indian nationalism embraced the changes brought about by colonialism in Indian women's traditional gender roles.

(3) Indian nationalist discourses provided an ideological principle of selection.

(4) Indian nationalism's sophistication resided in its distinction of the material from the spiritual spheres.

Question Numbers (9 to 12): The passage below is accompanied by a set of questions. Choose the best answer to each question.

It's easy to forget that most of the world's languages are still transmitted orally with no widely established written form. While speech communities are increasingly involved in projects to protect their languages – in print, on air and online – orality is fragile and contributes to linguistic vulnerability. But indigenous languages are about much more than unusual words and intriguing grammar: They function as vehicles for the transmission of cultural traditions, environmental understandings and knowledge about medicinal plants, all at risk when elders die and livelihoods are disrupted.

Both push and pull factors lead to the decline of languages. Through war, famine and natural disasters, whole communities can be destroyed, taking their language with them to the grave, such as the indigenous populations of Tasmania who were wiped out by colonists. More commonly, speakers live on but abandon their language in favor of another vernacular, a widespread process that linguists refer to as "language shift" from which few languages are immune. Such trading up and out of a speech form occurs for complex political, cultural and economic reasons – sometimes voluntary for economic and educational reasons, although often amplified by state coercion or neglect. Welsh, long stigmatized and disparaged by the British state, has rebounded with vigor.

Many speakers of endangered, poorly documented languages have embraced new digital media with excitement. Speakers of previously exclusively oral tongues are turning to the web as a virtual space for languages to live on. Internet technology offers powerful ways for oral traditions and cultural practices to survive, even thrive, among increasingly mobile communities. I have watched as videos of traditional wedding ceremonies and songs are recorded on smartphones in London by Nepali migrants, then uploaded to YouTube and watched an hour later by relatives in remote Himalayan villages . . .

Globalization is regularly, and often uncritically, pilloried as a major threat to linguistic diversity. But in fact, globalization is as much process as it is ideology, certainly when it comes to language. The real forces behind cultural homogenization are unbending beliefs, exchanged through a globalized delivery system, reinforced by the historical monolingualism prevalent in much of the West.

Monolingualism – the condition of being able to speak only one language – is regularly accompanied by a deep-seated conviction in the value of that language over all others. Across the largest economies that make up the G8, being monolingual is still often the norm, with multilingualism appearing unusual and even somewhat exotic. The monolingual mindset stands in sharp contrast to the lived reality of most the world, which throughout its history has been more multilingual than unilingual. Monolingualism, then, not globalization, should be our primary concern.

Multilingualism can help us live in a more connected and more interdependent world. By widening access to technology, globalization can support indigenous and scholarly communities engaged in documenting and protecting our shared linguistic heritage. For the last 5,000 years, the rise and fall of languages was intimately tied to the plow, sword and book. In our digital age, the keyboard, screen and web will play a decisive role in shaping the future linguistic diversity of our species.

9. The author lists all of the following as reasons for the decline or disappearance of a language EXCEPT:

(1) governments promoting certain languages over others.

(2) a catastrophic event that entirely eliminates a people and their culture.

(3) people shifting away from their own language to study or work in another language.

(4) the focus on only a few languages as a result of widespread internet use.

10. From the passage, we can infer that the author is in favour of:

(1) cultural homogenisation.

(2) "language shifts" across languages.

(3) an expanded state role in the preservation of languages.

(4) greater multilingualism.

11. We can infer all of the following about indigenous languages from the passage EXCEPT that:

(1) they are repositories of traditional knowledge about the environment and culture.

(2) people are increasingly working on documenting these languages.

(3) they are in danger of being wiped out as most can only be transmitted orally.

(4) their vocabulary and grammatical constructs have been challenging to document.

12. The author mentions the Welsh language to show that:

(1) efforts to integrate Welsh speakers in the English-speaking fold have been fruitless.

(2) languages can revive even after their speakers have gone through a "language shift".

(3) vulnerable languages can rebound with state effort.

(4) while often pilloried, globalisation can, in fact, support linguistic revival.

Question Numbers (13 to 16): The passage below is accompanied by a set of questions. Choose the best answer to each question.

It has been said that knowledge, or the problem of knowledge, is the scandal of philosophy. The scandal is philosophy's apparent inability to show how, when and why we can be sure that we know something or, indeed, that we know anything. Philosopher Michael Williams writes: 'Is it possible to obtain knowledge at all? This problem is pressing because there are powerful arguments, some very ancient, for the conclusion that it is not . . . Scepticism is the skeleton in Western rationalism's closet'. While it is not clear that the scandal matters to anyone but philosophers, philosophers point out that it should matter to everyone, at least given a certain conception of knowledge. For, they explain, unless we can ground our claims to knowledge as such, which is to say, distinguish it from mere opinion, superstition, fantasy, wishful thinking, ideology, illusion or delusion, then the actions we take on the basis of presumed knowledge – boarding an airplane, swallowing a pill, finding someone guilty of a crime – will be irrational and unjustifiable.

That is all quite serious-sounding but so also are the rattlings of the skeleton: that is, the sceptic's contention that we cannot be sure that we know anything – at least not if we think of knowledge as something like having a correct mental representation of reality, and not if we think of reality as something like things-as-they-are-in-themselves, independent of our perceptions, ideas or descriptions. For, the sceptic will note, since reality, under that conception of it, is outside our ken (we cannot catch a glimpse of things-in-themselves around the corner of our own eyes; we cannot form an idea of reality that floats above the processes of our conceiving it), we have no way to compare our mental representations with things-as-they-are-in-themselves and therefore no way to determine whether they are correct or incorrect. Thus the sceptic may repeat (rattling loudly), you cannot be sure you 'know' something or anything at all – at least not, he may add (rattling softly before disappearing), if that is the way you conceive 'knowledge'.

There are a number of ways to handle this situation. The most common is to ignore it. Most people outside the academy – and, indeed, most of us inside it – are unaware of or unperturbed by the philosophical scandal of knowledge and go about our lives without too many epistemic anxieties. We hold our beliefs and presumptive knowledges more or less confidently, usually depending on how we acquired them (I saw it with my own eyes; I heard it on Fox News; a guy at the office told me) and how broadly and strenuously they seem to be shared or endorsed by various relevant people: experts and authorities, friends and family members, colleagues and associates. And we examine our convictions more or less closely, explain them more or less extensively, and defend them more or less vigorously, usually depending on what seems to be at stake for ourselves and/or other people and what resources are available for reassuring ourselves or making our beliefs credible to others (look, it's right here on the page; add up the figures yourself; I happen to be a heart specialist).

13. The author of the passage is most likely to support which one of the following statements?

(1) For the sceptic, if we think of reality as independent of our perceptions, ideas or descriptions, we should aim to know that reality independently too.

(2) The actions taken on the basis of presumed knowledge are rational and justifiable if we are confident that that knowledge is widely held.

(3) The confidence with which we maintain something to be true is usually independent of the source of the alleged truth.

(4) The scandal of philosophy is that we might not know anything at all about reality if we think of reality as independent of our perceptions, ideas or descriptions.

14. According to the last paragraph of the passage, "We hold our beliefs and presumptive knowledges more or less confidently, usually depending on" something. Which one of the following most broadly captures what we depend on?

(1) All of the options listed here.

(2) How we come to hold them; how widely they are held in our social circles.

(3) Remaining outside the academy; ignoring epistemic anxieties.

(4) How much of a stake we have in them; what resources there are to support them.

15. ". . . we cannot catch a glimpse of things-in-themselves around the corner of our own eyes; we cannot form an idea of reality that floats above the processes of our conceiving it . . ." Which one of the following statements best reflects the argument being made in this sentence?

(1) Our knowledge of reality floats above our subjective perception of it.

(2) Our knowledge of reality cannot be merged with our process of conceiving it.

(3) If the reality of things is independent of our eyesight, logically we cannot perceive our perception.

(4) If the reality of things is independent of our perception, logically we cannot perceive that reality.

16. The author discusses all of the following arguments in the passage, EXCEPT:

(1) philosophers maintain that the scandal of philosophy should be of concern to everyone.

(2) sceptics believe that we can never fully know anything, if by "knowing" we mean knowledge of a reality that is independent of the knower.

(3) if we cannot distinguish knowledge from opinion or delusion, we will not be able to justify our actions.

(4) the best way to deal with scepticism about the veracity of knowledge is to ignore it.

17. The passage given below is followed by four alternate summaries. Choose the option that best captures the essence of the passage.

Biologists who publish their research directly to the Web have been labelled as "rogue", but physicists have been routinely publishing research digitally ("preprints"), prior to submitting in a peer-reviewed journal. Advocates of preprints argue that quick and open dissemination of research speeds up scientific progress and allows for wider access to knowledge. But some journals still don't accept research previously published as a preprint. Even if the idea of preprints is gaining ground, one of the biggest barriers for biologists is how they would be viewed by members of their conservative research community.

(1) One of the advantages of digital preprints of research is they hasten the dissemination process, but these are not accepted by most scientific communities.

(2) While digital publication of research is gaining popularity in many scientific disciplines, almost all peer-reviewed journals are reluctant to accept papers that have been published before.

(3) Compared to biologists, physicists are less conservative in their acceptance of digital pre-publication of research papers, which allows for faster dissemination of knowledge.

(4) Preprints of research are frowned on by some scientific fields as they do not undergo a rigourous reviewing process but are accepted among biologists as a quick way to disseminate information.

18. Five jumbled up sentences, related to a topic, are given below. Four of them can be put together to form a coherent paragraph. Identify the odd one out and key in the number of the sentence as your answer:

(1) It has taken on a warm, fuzzy glow in the advertising world, where its potential is being widely discussed, and it is being claimed as the undeniable wave of the future.

(2) There is little enthusiasm for this in the scientific arena; for them marketing is not a science, and only a handful of studies have been published in scientific journals.

(3) The new, growing field of neuromarketing attempts to reveal the inner workings of consumer behaviour and is an extension of the study of how choices and decisions are made.

(4) Some see neuromarketing as an attempt to make the "art" of advertising into a science, being used by marketing experts to back up their proposals with some form of real data.

(5) The marketing gurus have already started drawing on psychology in developing tests and theories, and advertising people have borrowed the idea of the focus group from social scientists.

19. Five jumbled up sentences, related to a topic, are given below. Four of them can be put together to form a coherent paragraph. Identify the odd one out and key in the number of the sentence as your answer:

(1) The care with which philosophers examine arguments for and against forms of biotechnology makes this an excellent primer on formulating and assessing moral arguments.

(2) Although most people find at least some forms of genetic engineering disquieting, it is not easy to articulate why: what is wrong with re-engineering our nature?

(3) Breakthroughs in genetics present us with the promise that we will soon be able to prevent a host of debilitating diseases, and the predicament that our newfound genetic knowledge may enable us to enhance our genetic traits.

(4) To grapple with the ethics of enhancement, we need to confront questions that verge on theology, which is why modern philosophers and political theorists tend to shrink from them.

(5) One argument is that the drive for human perfection through genetics is objectionable as it represents a bid for mastery that fails to appreciate the gifts of human powers and achievements.

20. The passage given below is followed by four alternate summaries. Choose the option that best captures the essence of the passage.

Creativity is now viewed as the engine of economic progress. Various organizations are devoted to its study and promotion; there are encyclopedias and handbooks surveying creativity research. But this proliferating success has tended to erode creativity's stable identity: it has become so invested with value that it has become impossible to police its meaning and the practices that supposedly identify and encourage it. Many people and organizations committed to producing original thoughts now feel that undue obsession with the idea of creativity gets in the way of real creativity.

(1) The obsession with original thought, how it can be promoted and researched, has made it impossible for people and organizations to define the concept anymore.

(2) Creativity has proliferated to the extent that is no longer a stable process, and its mutating identity has stifled the creative process.

(3) The value assigned to creativity today has assumed such proportions that the concept itself has lost its real meaning and this is hampering the engendering of real creativity.

(4) The industry that has built up around researching what comprises and encourages creativity has destroyed the creative process itself.

21. The four sentences (labelled 1, 2, 3 and 4) below, when properly sequenced would yield a coherent paragraph. Decide on the proper sequencing of the order of the sentences and key in the sequence of the four numbers as your answer:

(1) The US has long maintained that the Northwest Passage is an international strait through which its commercial and military vessels have the right to pass without seeking Canada's permission.

(2) Canada, which officially acquired the group of islands forming the Northwest Passage in 1880, claims sovereignty over all the shipping routes through the Passage.

(3) The dispute could be transitory, however, as scientists speculate that the entire Arctic Ocean will soon be ice-free in summer, so ship owners will not have to ask for permission to sail through any of the Northwest Passage routes.

(4) The US and Canada have never legally settled the question of access through the Passage, but have an agreement whereby the US needs to seek Canada's consent for any transit.

22. The four sentences (labelled 1, 2, 3, 4) below, when properly sequenced would yield a coherent paragraph. Decide on the proper sequencing of the order of the sentences and key in the sequence of the four numbers as your answer:

(1) But today there is an epochal challenge to rethink and reconstitute the vision and practice of development as a shared responsibility – a sharing which binds both the agent and the audience, the developed world and the developing, in a bond of shared destiny.

(2) We are at a crossroads now in our vision and practice of development.

(3) This calls for the cultivation of an appropriate ethical mode of being in our lives which enables us to realize this global and planetary situation of shared living and responsibility.

(4) Half a century ago, development began as a hope for a better human possibility, but in the last fifty years, this hope has lost itself in the dreary desert of various kinds of hegemonic applications.

23. The passage given below is followed by four alternate summaries. Choose the option that best captures the essence of the passage.

The unlikely alliance of the incumbent industrialist and the distressed unemployed worker is especially powerful amid the debris of corporate bankruptcies and layoffs. In an economic downturn, the capitalist is more likely to focus on costs of the competition emanating from free markets than on the opportunities they create. And the unemployed worker will find many others in a similar condition and with anxieties similar to his, which will make it easier for them to organize together. Using the cover and the political organization provided by the distressed, the capitalist captures the political agenda.

(1) An unlikely alliance of the industrialist and the unemployed happens during an economic downturn in which they come together to unite politically and capture the political agenda.

(2) An economic downturn creates competition because of which the capitalists capture the political agenda created by the political organisation provided by the unemployed.

(3) In an economic downturn, the capitalists use the anxieties of the unemployed and their political organisation to set the political agenda to suit their economic interests.

(4) The purpose of an unlikely alliance between the industrialist and the unemployed during an economic downturn is to stifle competition in free markets.

24. The four sentences (labelled 1, 2, 3 and 4) below, when properly sequenced would yield a coherent paragraph. Decide on the proper sequencing of the order of the sentences and key in the sequence of the four numbers as your answer:

(1) Look forward a few decades to an invention which can end the energy crisis, change the global economy and curb climate change at a stroke: commercial fusion power.

(2) To gain meaningful insights, logic has to be accompanied by asking probing questions of nature through controlled tests, precise observations and clever analysis.

(3) The greatest of all inventions is the über-invention that has provided the insights on which others depend: the modern scientific method.

(4) This invention is inconceivable without the scientific method; it will rest on the application of a diverse range of scientific insights, such as the process transforming hydrogen into helium to release huge amounts of energy.

Section II: DI & LR

Question Numbers (1 to 6): Ten objects o1, o2, ..., o10 were distributed among Amar, Barat, Charles, Disha, and Elise. Each item went to exactly one person. Each person got exactly two of the items, and this pair of objects is called her/his bundle.

The following table shows how each person values each object.

	o1	o2	o3	o4	o5	o6	o7	o8	o9	o10
Amar	4	9	9	3	7	3	8	7	9	5
Barat	5	9	7	5	5	3	6	8	10	8
Charles	8	8	8	3	6	4	5	8	9	6
Disha	8	8	8	5	5	3	6	4	9	8
Elise	6	8	9	5	6	5	6	3	7	10

The value of any bundle by a person is the sum of that person's values of the objects in that bundle. A person X envies another person Y if X values Y's bundle more than X's own bundle.

For example, hypothetically suppose Amar's bundle consists of o1 and o2, and Barat's bundle consists of o3 and o4. Then Amar values his own bundle at 4 + 9 = 13 and Barat's bundle at 9 + 3 = 12. Hence Amar does not envy Barat. On the other hand, Barat values his own bundle at 7 + 5 = 12 and Amar's bundle at 5 + 9 = 14. Hence Barat envies Amar.

The following facts are known about the actual distribution of the objects among the five people.

1. If someone's value for an object is 10, then she/he received that object.
2. Objects o1, o2, and o3 were given to three different people.
3. Objects o1 and o8 were given to different people.
4. Three people value their own bundles at 16. No one values her/his own bundle at a number higher than 16.
5. Disha values her own bundle at an odd number. All others value their own bundles at an even number.
6. Some people who value their own bundles less than 16 envy some other people who value their own bundle at 16. No one else envies others.

1. What BEST can be said about object o8?

(1) o8 was given to Amar, Charles, or Disha

(2) o8 was given to Charles or Disha

(3) o8 was given to Charles

(4) o8 was given to Disha

2. Who among the following envies someone else?

(1) Amar (2) Charles

(3) Elise (4) Barat

3. What is Amar's value for his own bundle?

4. Object o4 was given to
(1) Barat (2) Charles
(3) Elise (4) Disha

5. Object o5 was given to
(1) Disha (2) Elise
(3) Charles (4) Amar

6. What BEST can be said about the distribution of object o1?
(1) o1 was given to Charles or Disha
(2) o1 was given to Charles, Disha, or Elise
(3) o1 was given to Charles
(4) o1 was given to Disha

Question Numbers (7 to 10): Answer the questions on the basis of the information given below.

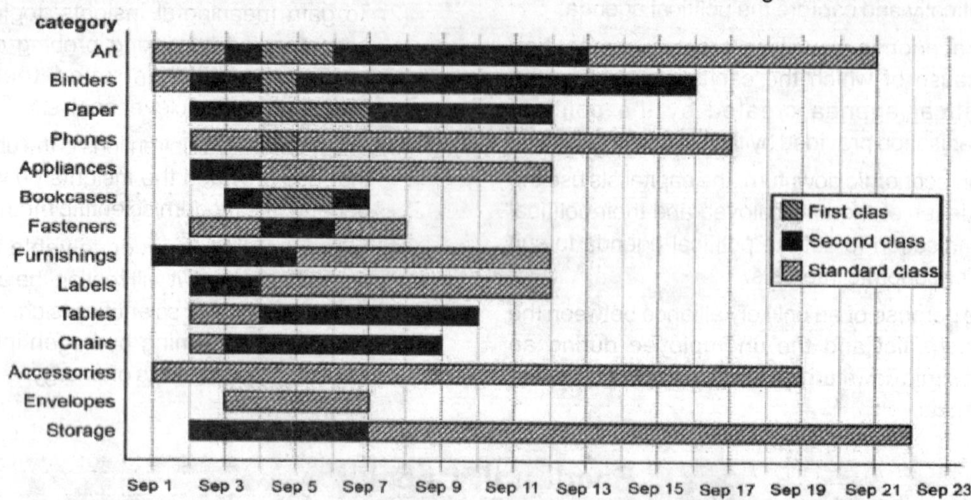

The different bars in the diagram above provide information about different orders in various categories (Art, Binders, ...) that were booked in the first two weeks of September of a store for one client. The colour and pattern of a bar denotes the ship mode (First Class / Second Class / Standard Class). The left end point of a bar indicates the booking day of the order, while the right end point indicates the dispatch day of the order. The difference between the dispatch day and the booking day (measured in terms of the number of days) is called the processing time of the order. For the same category, an order is considered for booking only after the previous order of the same category is dispatched. No two consecutive orders of the same category had identical ship mode during this period.

For example, there were only two orders in the furnishing category during this period. The first one was shipped in the Second Class. It was booked on Sep 1 and dispatched on Sep 5. The second order was shipped in the Standard class. It was booked on Sep 5 (although the order might have been placed before that) and dispatched on Sep 12. So the processing times were 4 and 7 days respectively for these orders.

7. How many days between Sep 1 and Sep 14 (both inclusive) had no booking from this client considering all the above categories?

8. What was the average processing time of all orders in the categories which had only one type of ship mode?

9. The sequence of categories -- Art, Binders, Paper and Phones -- in decreasing order of average processing time of their orders in this period is:
(1) Phones, Binders, Art, Paper
(2) Phones, Art, Binders, Paper
(3) Art, Binders, Paper, Phones
(4) Paper, Binders, Art, Phones

10. Approximately what percentage of orders had a processing time of one day during the period Sep 1 to Sep 22 (both dates inclusive)?
(1) 20% (2) 22%
(3) 16% (4) 25%

Question Numbers (11 to 16): Answer the questions on the basis of the information given below.

Ravi works in an online food-delivery company. After each delivery, customers rate Ravi on each of four parameters – Behaviour, Packaging, Hygiene, and Timeliness, on a scale from 1 to 9. If the total of the four rating points is 25 or more, then Ravi gets a bonus of Rs. 20 for that delivery. Additionally, a customer may or may not give Ravi a tip. If the customer gives a tip, it is either Rs. 30 or Rs. 50.

One day, Ravi made four deliveries - one to each of Atal, Bihari, Chirag and Deepak, and received a total of Rs. 120 in bonus and tips. He did not get both a bonus and a tip from the same customer.

The following additional facts are also known.

1. In Timeliness, Ravi received a total of 21 points, and three of the customers gave him the same rating points in this parameter. Atal gave higher rating points than Bihari and Chirag in this parameter.
2. Ravi received distinct rating points in Packaging from the four customers adding up to 29 points. Similarly, Ravi received distinct rating points in Hygiene from the four customers adding up to 26 points.
3. Chirag gave the same rating points for Packaging and Hygiene.
4. Among the four customers, Bihari gave the highest rating points in Packaging, and Chirag gave the highest rating points in Hygiene.
5. Everyone rated Ravi between 5 and 7 in Behaviour. Unique maximum and minimum ratings in this parameter were given by Atal and Deepak respectively.
6. If the customers are ranked based on ratings given by them in individual parameters, then Atal's rank based on Packaging is the same as that based on Hygiene. This is also true for Deepak.

11. What was the minimum rating that Ravi received from any customer in any parameter?

12. The COMPLETE list of customers who gave the maximum total rating points to Ravi is

(1) Bihari and Chirag (2) Atal and Bihari

(3) Bihari (4) Atal

13. What rating did Atal give on Timeliness?

14. What BEST can be concluded about the tip amount given by Deepak?

(1) Either Rs. 30 or Rs. 50

(2) Rs. 30

(3) Either Rs. 0 or Rs. 30 or Rs. 50

(4) Rs. 50

15. In which parameter did Atal give the maximum rating points to Ravi?

(1) Packaging (2) Hygiene

(3) Timeliness (4) Behaviour

16. What rating did Deepak give on Packaging?

(1) 8 (2) 5

(3) 6 (4) 7

Question Numbers (17 to 20): Answer the questions on the basis of the information given below.

The game of Chango is a game where two people play against each other; one of them wins and the other loses, i.e., there are no drawn Chango games. 12 players participated in a Chango championship. They were divided into four groups: Group A consisted of Aruna, Azul, and Arif; Group B consisted of Brinda, Brij, and Biju; Group C consisted of Chitra, Chetan, and Chhavi; and Group D consisted of Dipen, Donna, and Deb.

Players within each group had a distinct rank going into the championship. The players have NOT been listed necessarily according to their ranks. In the group stage of the game, the second and third ranked players play against each other, and the winner of that game plays against the first ranked player of the group. The winner of this second game is considered as the winner of the group and enters a semi-final.

The winners from Groups A and B play against each other in one semi-final, while the winners from Groups C and D play against each other in the other semi-final. The winners of the two semi-finals play against each other in the final to decide the winner of the championship.

It is known that:

1. Chitra did not win the championship.
2. Aruna did not play against Arif. Brij did not play against Brinda.
3. Aruna, Biju, Chitra, and Dipen played three games each, Azul and Chetan played two games each, and the remaining players played one game each.

17. Who among the following was DEFINITELY NOT ranked first in his/her group?

(1) Dipen (2) Aruna

(3) Chitra (4) Brij

18. Which of the following pairs must have played against each other in the championship?

(1) Deb, Donna (2) Azul, Biju

(3) Donna, Chetan (4) Chitra, Dipen

19. Who won the championship?

(1) Chitra (2) Brij

(3) Aruna (4) Cannot be determined

20. Who among the following did NOT play against Chitra in the championship?

(1) Dipen

(2) Biju

(3) Chetan

(4) Aruna

Section III: QA

1. Consider the pair of equations: $x^2 - xy - x = 22$ and $y^2 - xy + y = 34$. If $x > y$, then $x - y$ equals
(1) 7 (2) 4
(3) 6 (4) 8

2. In a football tournament, a player has played a certain number of matches and 10 more matches are to be played. If he scores a total of one goal over the next 10 matches, his overall average will be 0.15 goals per match. On the other hand, if he scores a total of two goals over the next 10 matches, his overall average will be 0.2 goals per match. The number of matches he has played is

3. For all possible integers n satisfying $2.25 \le 2 + 2^{n+2} \le 202$, the number of integer values of $3 + 3^{n+1}$ is

4. Let D and E be points on sides AB and AC, respectively, of a triangle ABC, such that AD : BD = 2 : 1 and AE : CE = 2 : 3. If the area of the triangle ADE is 8 sq cm, then the area of the triangle ABC, in sq cm, is

5. A person buys tea of three different qualities at Rs. 800, Rs. 500, and Rs. 300 per kg, respectively, and the amounts bought are in the proportion 2 : 3 : 5. She mixes all the tea and sells one-sixth of the mixture at Rs. 700 per kg. The price, in INR per kg, at which she should sell the remaining tea, to make an overall profit of 50%, is
(1) 688 (2) 692
(3) 653 (4) 675

6. For all real values of x, the range of the function f(x) $= \dfrac{x^2+2x+4}{2x^2+4x+9}$ is
(1) $\left[\frac{3}{7}, \frac{8}{9}\right)$ (2) $\left(\frac{3}{7}, \frac{1}{2}\right)$
(3) $\left[\frac{3}{7}, \frac{1}{2}\right)$ (4) $\left[\frac{4}{9}, \frac{8}{9}\right]$

7. The number of ways of distributing 15 identical balloons, 6 identical pencils and 3 identical erasers among 3 children, such that each child gets at least four balloons and one pencil, is

8. Three positive integers x, y and z are in arithmetic progression. If $y - x > 2$ and $xyz = 5(x + y + z)$, then $z - x$ equals
(1) 8 (2) 12
(3) 10 (4) 14

9. If $\log_2 [3 + \log_3 \{4 + \log_4 (x - 1)\}] - 2 = 0$ then 4x equals

10. From a container filled with milk, 9 litres of milk are drawn and replaced with water. Next, from the same container, 9 litres are drawn and again replaced with water. If the volumes of milk and water in the container are now in the ratio of 16 : 9, then the capacity of the container, in litres, is

11. Raj invested Rs. 10000 in a fund. At the end of first year, he incurred a loss but his balance was more than Rs. 5000. This balance, when invested for another year, grew and the percentage of growth in the second year was five times the percentage of loss in the first year. If the gain of Raj from the initial investment over the two year period is 35%, then the percentage of loss in the first year is
(1) 10 (2) 5
(3) 70 (4) 15

12. For a real number x the condition $|3x - 20| + |3x - 40| = 20$ necessarily holds if
(1) $9 < x < 14$ (2) $6 < x < 11$
(3) $10 < x < 15$ (4) $7 < x < 12$

13. Two pipes A and B are attached to an empty water tank. Pipe A fills the tank while pipe B drains it. If pipe A is opened at 2 pm and pipe B is opened at 3 pm, then the tank becomes full at 10 pm. Instead, if pipe A is opened at 2 pm and pipe B is opened at 4 pm, then the tank becomes full at 6 pm. If pipe B is not opened at all, then the time, in minutes, taken to fill the tank is
(1) 264 (2) 140
(3) 120 (4) 144

14. The sides AB and CD of a trapezium ABCD are parallel, with AB being the smaller side. P is the midpoint of CD and ABPD is a parallelogram. If the difference between the areas of the parallelogram ABPD and the triangle BPC is 10 sq cm, then the area, in sq cm, of the trapezium ABCD is
(1) 40 (2) 30
(3) 25 (4) 20

15. Two trains A and B were moving in opposite directions, their speeds being in the ratio 5 : 3. The front end of A crossed the rear end of B 46 seconds after the front ends of the trains had crossed each other. It took another 69 seconds for the rear ends of the trains to cross each other. The ratio of length of train A to that of train B is
(1) 2 : 3 (2) 5 : 3
(3) 2 : 1 (4) 3 : 2

16. A box has 450 balls, each either white or black, there being as many metallic white balls as metallic black balls. If 40% of the white balls and 50% of the black balls are metallic, then the number of non-metallic balls in the box is

17. If a rhombus has area 12 sq cm and side length 5 cm, then the length, in cm, of its longer diagonal is

(1) $\frac{\sqrt{37}+\sqrt{13}}{2}$ (2) $\sqrt{37}+\sqrt{13}$

(3) $\frac{\sqrt{13}+\sqrt{12}}{2}$ (4) $\sqrt{13}+\sqrt{12}$

18. For a 4-digit number, the sum of its digits in the thousands, hundreds and tens places is 14, the sum of its digits in the hundreds, tens and units places is 15, and the tens place digit is 4 more than the units place digit. Then the highest possible 4-digit number satisfying the above conditions is

19. For a sequence of real numbers $x_1, x_2 ..., x_n$, if $x_1 - x_2 + x_3 - ... + (-1)^{n+1} x_n = n^2 + 2n$ for all natural numbers n, then the sum $x_{49} + x_{50}$ equals

(1) –2 (2) 2

(3) –200 (4) 200

20. Anil can paint a house in 60 days while Bimal can paint it in 84 days. Anil starts painting and after 10 days, Bimal and Charu join him. Together, they complete the painting in 14 more days. If they are paid a total of Rs. 21000 for the job, then the share of Charu, in INR, proportionate to the work done by him, is

(1) 9100 (2) 9150

(3) 9000 (4) 9200

21. Anil, Bobby and Chintu jointly invest in a business and agree to share the overall profit in proportion to their investments. Anil's share of investment is 70%. His share of profit decreases by Rs. 420 if the overall profit goes down from 18% to 15%. Chintu's share of profit increases by Rs. 80 if the overall profit goes up from 15% to 17%. The amount, in INR, invested by Bobby is

(1) 2200 (2) 2400

(3) 1800 (4) 2000

22. Suppose one of the roots of the equation $ax^2 - bx + c = 0$ is $2 + \sqrt{3}$, where a, b and c are rational number and $a \neq 0$. If $b = c^3$ then |a| equals

(1) 3 (2) 1

(3) 4 (4) 2

ANSWERS

VARC

1. (2)	**2.** (2)	**3.** (1)	**4.** (4)	**5.** (2)	**6.** (3)	**7.** (1)	**8.** (1)	**9.** (4)	**10.** (4)
11. (4)	**12.** (2)	**13.** (4)	**14.** (2)	**15.** (4)	**16.** (4)	**17.** (3)	**18.** (5)	**19.** (1)	**20.** (3)
21. (2143)	**22.** (2413)	**23.** (3)	**24.** (3214)						

DI & LR

1. (3)	**2.** (1)	**3.** (12)	**4.** (4)	**5.** (2)	**6.** (4)	**7.** (6)	**8.** (11)	**9.** (2)	**10.** (1)
11. (5)	**12.** (1)	**13.** (6)	**14.** (1)	**15.** (4)	**16.** (4)	**17.** (1)	**18.** (4)	**19.** (3)	**20.** (2)

QA

1. (4)	**2.** (10)	**3.** (7)	**4.** (30)	**5.** (1)	**6.** (3)	**7.** (1000)	**8.** (4)	**9.** (5)	**10.** (45)
11. (1)	**12.** (4)	**13.** (4)	**14.** (2)	**15.** (4)	**16.** (250)	**17.** (2)	**18.** (4195)	**19.** (1)	**20.** (9100)
21. (4)	**22.** (4)								

EXPLANATIONS

VARC

1. The entire passage is about uniting people and a discourse on objective truth. Therefore, option (2) comprehensively covers the entire passage. The other options are narrow in scope and so, cannot be the answer. Option (3) is too generic. (3) is incorrect because the author is not talking about the choice between truth and power.
2. The dilemma is between fiction and telling the public the truth. So, option (2) is the answer.
3. The only option that talks about fiction is (1). The other options are mentioned in the context of fiction. So, option (1) is the answer. Refer to the key words 'same fiction' in option (1).
4. The author had used the term 'unalloyed reality' in the second last paragraph. Truth is often painful and disturbing and people cannot accept it. So, leaders deviate from it in order to retain power. So, (4) is the answer.
5. Options (1), (3) and (4) are mentioned in the passage. Refer to the repeated use of binaries in the passage. Option (2) is not what the author says and so, is the answer.
6. The 'contradictory pull' refer to the superior western civilisation compared to India. Refer to the 1st paragraph. Option (1) is factually correct in the light of the 1st paragraph. We were fighting against the colonisers and also, we learnt the material aspect from the colonisers. Therefore, (3) is the answer.
7. The author mentions how the West was superior in the material aspects of culture. Refer to the 1st paragraph. Also, refer to the last sentence of the 1st paragraph. The author observes that the West should not be imitated in all aspects of life. Option (1) if true, would weaken the author's observation. So, (1) is the answer. The other options are irrelevant.
8. Refer to the 2>nd paragraph where gender roles are mentioned. So, option (1) is the answer.
9. Refer to the first 2 paragraphs of the passage where options (1), (2) and (3) are mentioned. Option (4) is not mentioned and therefore, is the answer.
10. Refer to the last paragraph. The author is definitely in favour of multilingualism. Therefore, option (4) is the right answer.
11. The author doesn't say that vocabulary and grammatical constructs have been challenging. Therefore, option (4) is the answer. The other 3 options have been mentioned. Refer to the first 2 paragraphs of the passage.
12. Refer to the last sentence of the second paragraph where the author mentions the revival of the Welsh language. So, option (2) is the answer. The other options are not mentioned.
13. Refer to the second paragraph where the author mentions the relation between reality and perception. So, option (4) is the answer.
14. Refer to the last paragraph, especially the sentence, "We hold out beliefs ...." The author also refers to how we acquired those beliefs. Therefore, option (2) is the answer.
15. The reality of something is defined by our perception. If it is not, we cannot perceive that reality. Option (2) is narrow in scope. The author has only given the example of eyesight. So, option (4) is the answer.
16. The author hasn't mentioned that it is the best way to deal with scepticism about the veracity of knowledge is to ignore it. So, (4) is the answer.
17. The passage talks about how physicists can publish digitally. Also, note the last sentence of the passage where the author talks about 'biggest barriers'. So, option (3) is the most appropriate summary. Option (1) doesn't compare biologists with physicists.
18. Sentences 3 and 4 are talking about neuro marketing. Sentences 1 and 2 are also thematically linked. Sentence 5 is the odd sentence out so, it is the answer.
19. Other than sentence 1, the other sentences are talking about genetic engineering. So, (1) is the odd sentence out.
20. The passage talks about the futility of too much obsession about creativity so much so that real creativity is being diluted. So, option (3) is the most appropriate summary. Note the use of real creativity in the passage as well as in the 3rd option.
21. Sentences 2 and 1 present divergent views of the US and Canada on the same issue. So, sentences 2 and 1 form a mandatory pair. Sentence 4 talks about the dispute mentioned in sentences 2 and 1 and so, sentences 214 form a mandatory sequence. Sentence 3 comes last and concludes the paragraph.
22. Sentence 4 is telling us why we are at a crossroads (mentioned in sentence 2). Therefore, sentences 2 and 4 form a mandatory pair. Sentence 1 logically follows next. Note the relation between what happened half a century back and today. Therefore, 241 can form a mandatory sequence. 3 closes the paragraph.

23. Refer to the last sentence of the paragraph. Option (3) is basically a rephrasing of the last sentence. Option (3) is the correct answer.

24. Sentence 3 opens the paragraph. Sentence 2 talks about the insights mentioned in sentence 3. So, Sentences 3 and 2 form a mandatory pair. Sentences 1 and 4 form a mandatory pair because both talk about an invention.

DI & LR

For questions 1 to 6:

From statement 1, If someone's value for an object is 10, then she/he received that object. So, Barat and Elise received object o9 and o10 respectively. Also, value of own bundles of three people is 16 and Disha values her own bundle at odd number. Now note that Amar's value for Barat's bundle o7 and o9 is 8 + 9 = 17, therefore, Amar envies Barat and therefore, he must have value his own bundle at less than 16, which implies, Charles must be the third person to value his bundle at 16. From this information, we get following two cases:

Case 1:

	o1	o2	o3	o4	o5	o6	o7	o8	o9	o10	Total
Amar	4	9	9	3	7	3	8	7	9	5	even
Barat	5	9	7	5	5	3	6	8	10	8	16
Charles	8	8	8	3	6	4	5	8	9	6	16
Disha	8	8	8	5	5	3	6	4	9	8	Odd
Elise	6	8	9	5	6	5	6	3	7	10	16

Now here Amar, Charles, and Disha must have received itemso1, o2, o3, o4, o6 or o8. Also, items o1, o2, and o3 were received by different people and items o1, and o8 were also received by different people.

Case 2:

	o1	o2	o3	o4	o5	o6	o7	o8	o9	o10	Total
Amar	4	9	9	3	7	3	8	7	9	5	even
Barat	5	9	7	5	5	3	6	8	10	8	16
Charles	8	8	8	3	6	4	5	8	9	6	16
Disha	8	8	8	5	5	3	6	4	9	8	Odd
Elise	6	8	9	5	6	5	6	3	7	10	16

Here, since Amar envies Barat, Amar could not receive items (o2/o3, o5/o8), because this will lead to the value of his own bundle at 16. So, possible items are o4, o5 and o6. Any bundle will lead to the value of either 6 or 10 and therefore, Amar will be envy Disha too, which is contradictory to the statement 6, "Some people who value their own bundles less than 16 envy some other people who valuetheir own bundle at 16. No one else envies others." Hence, this case is discarded.

Final table looks like:

	o1	o2	o3	o4	o5	o6	o7	o8	o9	o10	Total
Amar	4	9	9	3	7	3	8	7	9	5	12
Barat	5	9	7	5	5	3	6	8	10	8	16
Charles	8	8	8	3	6	4	5	8	9	6	16
Disha	8	8	8	5	5	3	6	4	9	8	13
Elise	6	8	9	5	6	5	6	3	7	10	16

1. BEST can be said about object o8: o8 was given to Charles.
2. Amar envies someone else.
3. Amar's value for his own bundle is 12.
4. Object o4 was given to Disha.
5. Object o5 was given to Elise.
6. BEST can be said about the distribution of object o1: o1 was given to Disha.

For questions 7 to 10:

7. Sept 1 – 4 bookings
Sept 2 – 9 bookings
Sept 3 – 4 bookings
Sept 4 – 9 bookings
Sept 5 – 3 bookings
Sept 6 – 3 bookings
Sept 7 – 2 bookings
Sept 8 – 0
Sept 9 – 0
Sept 10 – 0
Sept 11 – 0
Sept 12 – 0
Sept 13 – 1
Sept 14 – 0
On 6 days, no bookings from this client were there considering all the categories.

8. The categories which had only one type of ship mode are Accessories and envelopes. In accessories exactly one order is placed whose processing time is 18 days (1 sept to 19 sept) and in Envelopes category also one order is placed whose processing time is 4 days (3 sept to 7 sept).
Average processing time = (18 + 4)/2 = 11

9. Average processing time in art category
= (2 + 1 + 2 + 7 + 8)/5 = 4
Average processing time in Binder's category
= (1+2+1 + 11)/4 = 3.75
Average processing time in Paper category
= (2 + 3 + 5)/3 = 3.33
Average processing time in phones category
= (2 + 1 + 12)/3 = 5
Correct decreasing order is → Phones, Art, Binders, Paper

10. Total number of orders placed from Sep 1 to Sep 22 are 35. Number of orders which had a processing time of one day during the period Sep 1 to Sep 22 (both dates inclusive) are 7.

Required percentage = (7/35)*100 = 20%

For questions 11 to 16:

Ravi received a total of Rs. 120 in bonus and tips, therefore, two out of four customers must have given a total rating of 25 or more thus giving a bonus of Rs. 20 for that delivery and other two customers must have given a total rating of less than 25, thus giving a tip of Rs. 30 and Rs. 50 respectively.

From statement 1, in Timeliness, Ravi received a total of 21 points, and three of the customers gave him the same rating points in this parameter. So, let the same ratings be 'a' and one different rating be 'b'. Given: b > a and 3a + b = 21. Possible combinations are: (4, 9) and (5, 6).

From statement 5, since everyone rated Ravi between 5 and 7 in Behaviour such that unique maximum and minimum ratings in this parameter were given by Atal and Deepak respectively which implies that Atal must have rated 7 and Deepak must have rated 5 and other two must have rated 6.

From statement 2, "Ravi received distinct rating points in Packaging from the four customers adding up to29 points.", so the only possible combination is (5,7,8,9) in any order. Also, "Ravi received distinct rating points in Hygiene from the four customers adding up to 26 points.", so the only possible combinations are (2, 7, 8, 9), (3, 6, 8, 9), (4, 5, 8, 9), (4, 6, 7, 9), and (5, 6, 7, 8). But from statement 4, among the four customers, Bihari gave the highest rating points in Packaging, so that must be 9, and Chirag gave the highest rating points in Hygiene, so that must be 8.

Table thus obtained from the information concluded is:

	Atal	Bihari	Chirag	Deepak	Total
Behaviour	7	6	6	5	25
Packaging	5	9	8	7	29
Hygiene	5	7	8	6	26
Timeliness	6	5	5	5	21
Total	23 (Tip of 30 or 50)	27 (Bonus)	27 (Bonus)	23 (Tip 30 or 50)	

11. The minimum rating that Ravi received from any customer in any parameter was 5.

12. The COMPLETE list of customers who gave the maximum total rating points to Ravi is Bihari and Chirag.

13. Rating that Atal give on Timeliness is 6.

14. BEST can be concluded about the tip amount given by Deepak – either Rs 30 or 50.

15. Atal give the maximum rating points to Ravi in Behaviour.

16. Rating that Deepak give on Packaging is 7.

For questions 17 to 20:

From statement 2, "Aruna did not play against Arif. Brij did not play against Brinda.", therefore, either Aruna must have played with Azul or Azul must have played with Arif, where in Arif must be the rank 1 in the group or Aruna must be the rank 1 in the group respectively. But since Aruna and Azul played more than 1 game, so, former case is not possible. Hence Azul must have played with Arif and Aruna must be ranked 1 in their group.

Similarly, either Brij must have played with Biju or Brinda must have played with Biju, wherein Brinda must be the rank 1 in the group or Brij must be the rank 1 in the group respectively.

<table>
<tr><td>Group Match</td><td>First Match –
Azul – Arif (Lost)
Aruna (Rank 1)
Second Match –
Azul (Lost) – Aruna</td><td>First Match –
Brij – Biju
Brinda (Group Rank 1)
Second Match –
Biju–Brinda
Or,
First Match –
Brinda – Biju
Brij (Group Rank 1)
Second Match –
Biju–Brij</td><td>First Match –
Chetan – Chhavi (Lost)
Chitra (Rank 1)
Second Match –
Chetan (Lost) – Chitra</td><td>First Match –
Donna – Dipen
Deb (Group Rank 1)
Second Match –
Dipen–Deb
Or,
First Match –
Deb – Dipen
Donna (Group Rank 1)
Second Match –
Dipen–Donna</td></tr>
<tr><td>Semi-final</td><td colspan="2">Aruna – Biju(Lost)</td><td colspan="2">Chitra–Dipen (Lost)</td></tr>
<tr><td>Final</td><td colspan="4">Aruna(Won) – Chitra (Lost)</td></tr>
</table>

17. Dipen was DEFINITELY NOT ranked first in his/her group.

18. Chitra, Dipen must have played against each other in the championship.

19. Aruna won the championship.

20. Biju did NOT play against Chitra in the championship.

QA

1. Given equations: $x^2 - xy - x = 22$ and $y^2 - xy + y = 34$

Add these two equations.

$(x - y)^2 - x + y = 56$ or $(y - x)^2 - x + y = 56$

Since $x > y$, we should take $(x - y)^2 - x + y = 56$ and solve for $x - y$.

$(x - y)^2 - (x - y) = 56$

$(x - y)(x - y - 1) = 56$

Let $x - y = n$, then $n(n - 1) = 56$ which gives $n = -7$ or $n = 8$. Since $x > y$, therefore $x - y > 0$ and hence, $x - y = 8$.

2. Let the number of matches already played be x, then over the next ten matches if one more goal is scored, the average goals become 0.15. Further, if the player scores two goals the average becomes 0.2.

It can be observed that one extra goal is increasing the average by 0.05 (0.2 – 0.15). Hence it can be said that the total number of matches played till the end is 20.

Therefore, $x + 10 = 20 \Rightarrow x = 10$

3. Given: $2.25 \le 2 + 2^{n+2} \le 202$

Since, $2 + 2^{n+2} \le 202$, the highest value of 'n' that satisfies the condition is 5.

Because $2^7 = 128$, but $2^8 = 256$.

Therefore, $n + 2 = 7 \Rightarrow n = 5$.

Further, subtracting 2 from the first two parts of the inequality,

$0.25 \le 2^{n+2}$

Or, $2^{-2} \le 2^{n+2}$

Hence, $n \ge -4$

So, from the inequality we can say that the integral value of n can be [–4, 5].

For $3 + 3^{n+1}$ to have integral values, n must be greater than or equal to –1 and go up till 5.

4. The triangle as per the information given looks like:

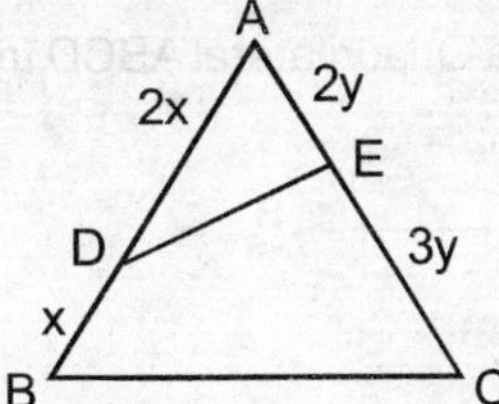

Given: Area of the triangle ADE = 8 sq cm.

$\Rightarrow 1/2 \times (AD)(AE) \times \sin(A) = 8$

$\Rightarrow 1/2 \times (2x)(2y) \times \sin(A) = 8$

$\Rightarrow xy \times \sin(A) = 4$ ... (1)

The area of the triangle ABC = $1/2 \times (AB)(AC) \times \sin(A)$

$= 1/2 \times (3x)(5y) \times \sin(A)$

$= 15/2 \times (xy) \times \sin(A)$

$= 15/2\,(4)$ (From (1))

$= 30$ sq cm

5. Given: Tea of three different qualities is bought in amounts which are in the proportion 2 : 3 : 5 costing Rs. 800, Rs. 500, and Rs. 300 per kg, respectively.

Since later 1/6th of the quantity has to be calculated thus let the amounts in which the Tea is bought be 6 : 9 : 15.

So, Total C.P = 800 × 6 + 500 × 9 + 300 × 15 = Rs. 13,800

Profit = 50% of C.P = 50% of Rs. 13,800 = Rs. 6,900

Therefore, S.P = C.P + Profit = 13,800 + 6,900 = Rs. 20,700

Since 1/6(6 + 9 + 15) = 1/6 × (30) = 5 kgs is sold at Rs. 700 per kg.

The S.P of these 5 kgs is 5 × 700 = Rs. 3,500

The remaining 20,700 – 3,500 = 17,200 must be generated from selling the remaining 30 – 5 = 25 kgs.

So, the S.P of the remaining tea per kg must be 17,200/25 = 172 × 4 = Rs. 688 per kg.

6. Given: $f(x) = \dfrac{x^2 + 2x + 4}{2x^2 + 4x + 9}$.

Now complete the squares in the numerator and denominator as follows:

$$f(x) = \frac{x^2 + 2x + 1 + 3}{2x^2 + 4x + 2 + 7}$$

$$= \frac{(x+1)^2 + 3}{2(x+1)^2 + 7}$$

Let $(x + 1)^2 + 3 = k$, then $f(x) = k/(2k+1)$.

The minimum value of k = 3, as the square part is always positive and it will be zero only at x = –1.

$f(x) = 3/(2(3) + 1) = 3/7$

And, the maximum value when k approaches its maximum value. We can observe that the fraction has a 2k + 1 in the denominator and so it will always be one more than twice the numerator. As the value of k increases the value of the addition of one gets less and less of a value to the overall denominator. The fraction approaches 1/2, but never 1/2 itself.

Hence the range becomes [3/7,1/2).

7. Given: 15 identical balloons, 6 identical pencils, and 3 identical erasers has to be distributed among 3 children, such that each child gets at least four balloons and one pencil.

So, after every person gets four balloons and one pencil - 3 balloons, 3 pencils, and 3 erasers will remain. So, let's first arrange the balloons in all possible combinations: (3, 0, 0), (2, 1, 0), (1, 1, 1).
We can arrange (3, 0, 0) in three ways.
We can arrange (2, 1, 0) in six ways.
We can arrange (1, 1, 1) in only one way.
So, we can arrange balloons among three children in 10 ways.

Likewise, we can also arrange 3 pencils in 10 ways and 3 erasers in 10 ways.

Therefore, the total number of ways is 10 x 10 x 10 = 1000 ways

8. Given: x, y, and z are in arithmetic progression and xyz = 5(x + y + z).

xyz = 5(3y). Since x, y, z are in arithmetic progression.

xz = 15.

The possible combinations for x and z are (3, 5) (1, 15).
z – x > 4 (Since y – x > 2).
Therefore,
x = 1, y = 8, z = 15
Therefore, z – x = 14.

9. Given: $\log_2[3 + \log_3\{4 + \log_4(x-1)\}] - 2 = 0$
$\Rightarrow \log_2[3 + \log_3\{4 + \log_4(x-1)\}] = 2$
$\Rightarrow 3 + \log_3\{4 + \log_4(x-1)\} = 4$
$(\because \log_a N = \Rightarrow N = a^x)$
$\Rightarrow \log_3\{4 + \log_4(x-1)\} = 1$
$\Rightarrow 4 + \log_4(x-1) = 3$
$\Rightarrow \log_4(x-1) = -1$
$\Rightarrow x - 1 = 1/4$
$\Rightarrow 4x = 5$

10. Ratio of milk and complete solution = 16 : (16 + 9) = 16 : 25 = $(4 : 5)^2$

So, $4/5^{th}$ is remaining it means $1/5^{th}$ of mixture is drawn. Hence $1/5^{th}$ of original mixture = 9 L
So, original mixture = 45L

11. Let the total investment be P, then at the end of the first year, after a loss of x percentage the value of the investment becomes P(1 – x).

Then in the next year the value of the investment increases by 5x.

So, the overall value of the investment becomes P(1 – x)(1 + 5x).

This is an increase of 35% from the initial investment amount.

Hence, 1.35 P = P (1 – x)(1 + 5x)

From the options given x = 10 satisfies the equation.

12. Equation 1:
3x – 20 + 3x – 40 = 20
6x – 60 = 20
6x = 80
x = 80/6 = 13.33
Equation 2:
– (3x – 20) – (3x – 40) = 20
– 6x + 60 = 20
– 6x = –40
x = 40/6 = 6.67
As per the options, for 7 < x < 12, the condition necessarily holds.

13. Let the filling rate of pipe A be 'a' and the rate of emptying the tank of pipe B be 'b'.

Then from the given information we can say that, when pipe A is kept open from 2PM to 10PM, i.e., for 8 hours and pipe B drains from 3PM till 10PM (7 hours), the tank gets filled up.

So, 8a – 7b = 1 ... eq(1)

Also, from the second statement,

A is kept open from 2 PM to 6 PM (4 hours), and B is kept open for 2 hours (4 PM to 6PM), the tank gets filled up.

4a – 2b = 1 ... eq(2)

Multiplying eq(2) with 2 and subtracting eq(1) from it we get,

⇒ 8a – 4b – (8a – 7b) = 2 – 1
⇒ b = 1/3 and a = 5/12

Hence the rate of filling is 5/12.

If only pipe 'a' is kept open, the tank will get filled in, say 'n' hours.
⇒ n a = 1
⇒ n (5/12) = 1
So, n = 12/5 = 2.4 hours = 144 minutes

14. We can construct a Quadrilateral ABCD from the given information:

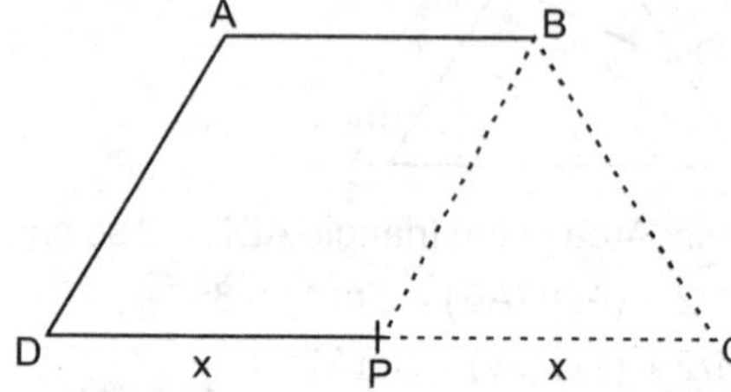

Point P divides the line CD into two equal halves,

Further we know that the area of the parallelogram ABPD is twice the area of the triangle BCP, and hence the heights of both will also be the same.

Now, from here we can say that the area of the parallelogram will be twice the area of the triangle.

Let the area of the triangle be 'A'. Then the area of the parallelogram BCP will be 2A.

So, this difference will be 2A – A = 10

Hence, A = 10

Then the area of the parallelogram would be 2A + A = 30 sq cm

15. Given: Speed of two trains A and B moving in opposite directions is 5 : 3.

Let speed of train A and B be 5x and 3x respectively.

Let lengths of train A and train B be L_a and L_b

The front end of A crossed the rear end of B, 46 seconds after the front ends of the trains had crossed each other.

So, the distance travelled is L_b. For this, the time taken is 46 sec.

Trains took another 69 seconds for the rear ends of the trains to cross each other.

So, the distance travelled is L_a. For this, the time taken is 69 sec.

$(L_a/5x + 3x)/(L_b/5x + 3x) = 69/46$

The relative speed is (5x + 3x), since they are moving opposite to each other.

$L_a/L_b = 3/2$

16. The box contains 450 balls. Let the number of white and black balls be 'x' and 'y' respectively.

The number of white metallic balls is the same as black metallic balls.

40% of the white balls and 50% of the black balls are metallic.

So, 0.4x = 0.5y

x : y = 5 : 4.

The number of White balls is 250 (100 - metallic and 150 - Non-metallic) and the number of Black balls is 200 (100 - metallic and 100 - Non-metallic). Therefore, the total number of non-metallic balls is 250.

17. Let the length of longer and shorter diagonal of the rhombus be '2a' and '2b' respectively.

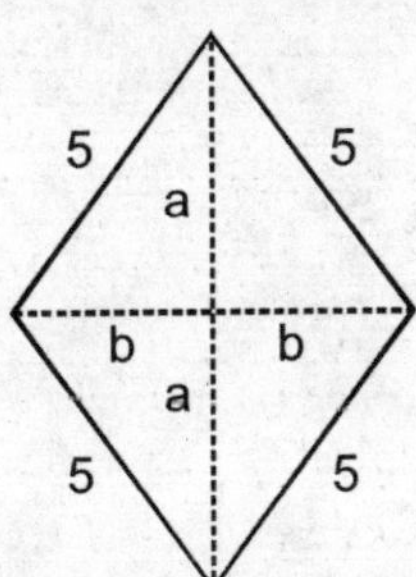

The area of the rhombus = 12 sq cm

12 × 2a × 2b = 12 sq cm ⇒ ab = 6.

The side of the rhombus = 5 cm.

So, $a^2 + b^2 = 25$.

$(a + b)^2 = a^2 + b^2 + 2ab$

$(a + b)^2 = 25 + 2(6) = 37$

$a + b = \sqrt{(37)}$ ...(1)

$(a - b)^2 = a^2 + b^2 - 2ab$

$(a - b)^2 = 25 - 2(6) = 13$

$a - b = \sqrt{(13)}$ ...(2)

By solving eq(1) & (2) we get

Long diagonal = $2a = \sqrt{(37)} + \sqrt{(13)}$

18. Given: the sum of the thousands, hundreds and the tens place digit is 14, and the sum of the hundreds, tens and the units place digit is 15.

So, we can conclude that the unit's digit is one unit greater than the thousandth place.

<u>n</u> __ <u>n + 5</u> <u>n + 1</u>

To maximize the 4-digit number the value of 'n' should be as large as possible. And the value of the tens digit can be 9 at most. So, the maximum value of 'n' is 4.

<u>4</u> __ <u>4 + 5</u> <u>4 + 1</u>

To satisfy the sum of the thousands, hundreds and the tens place digit, the value of the hundreds place should be equal to 1.

<u>4</u> <u>1</u> <u>9</u> <u>5</u>

Hence the largest possible number is 4195.

19. Given: $S_n = x_1 - x_2 + x_3 - x_4 + ... + (-1)^{n+1} x_n = n^2 + 2n = n(n + 2)$

$S_{50} = 50 (50 + 2) = 50 (52) = 50 (2) (26) = 2600$

$S_{49} = 49 (49 + 2) = 49 (51) = 2499$

$S_{48} = 48 (48 + 2) = 48 (50) = (24) (2) (50) = 2400$

$S_{50} = S_{49} - x_{50}$

$x_{50} = S_{49} - S_{50} = 2499 - 2600 = -101$

$S_{49} = S_{48} + x_{49}$

$x_{49} = S_{49} - S_{48} = 2499 - 2400 = 99$

$x_{49} + x_{50} = 99 - 101 = -2$

20. Anil can paint a house in 60 days.

So, he can do 1/60 of work per day.

Bimal can paint it in 84 days.

So, he can do 1/84 of work per day.

Let's assume Charu can paint it in 'c' days.

So, she can do 1/c of work per day.

Anil alone does the work for 10 days.

So, 1/6 of the work is completed.

The remaining work is 5/6.

After that, for 14 days they worked together.

14/60 + 14/84 + 14/c = 5/6

1/c = 13/(30 × 14)

Charu does his work for 14 days. So, the total work done by Charu is 13/30.

The amount earned by Charu = 13/30 × 21000 = Rs. 9100

21. Anil's share of investment is 70%. His share of profit decreases by Rs. 420 if the overall profit goes down from 18% to 15%.

Let the total amount invested be 'x'.

So, 70% of (18% of x – 15% of x) = 420.

70% of 3% of x = 420

x = 20,000.

Chintu's share of profit increases by Rs. 80 if the overall profit goes up from 15% to 17%.

Let Chintu's percentage share to be 'c'.

So, c% of 2% of 20,000 = 80.

So, c = 20%.

Therefore, the percentage of the amount invested by Bobby is 10%.

Hence, 10% of 20,000 is 2000.

22. For a quadratic equation, $ax^2 + bx + c = 0$ the roots are given by $x = (-b \pm \sqrt{b^2 - 4ac})/2a$

Since the roots, a, b, c are all rational and one of the roots, $2 + \sqrt{3}$ is irrational, the other root of the equation will also be irrational and a conjugate of $2 + \sqrt{3}$.

That is, the other root is, $2 - \sqrt{3}$.

Sum of roots is given by $-b/a = (2 + \sqrt{3}) + (2 - \sqrt{3}) = 4$.

And Product of roots is given by $c/a = (2 + \sqrt{3})(2 - \sqrt{3}) = 2^2 - (\sqrt{3})^2 = 4 - 3 = 1$

But here the quadratic equation is $ax^2 - b x + c = 0$.

Therefore,

$b/a = 4$ and $c/a = 1$

$b = 4a$; $c = a$.

We are also given that $b = c^3$

$4a = a^3$

$4 = a^2$

$|a| = 2$

CAT 2021 SOLVED PAPER (SLOT-3)

Section I: VARC

Question Numbers (1 to 4): The passage below is accompanied by a set of questions. Choose the best answer to each question.

Today we can hardly conceive of ourselves without an unconscious. Yet between 1700 and 1900, this notion developed as a genuinely original thought. The "unconscious" burst the shell of conventional language, coined as it had been to embody the fleeting ideas and the shifting conceptions of several generations until, finally, it became fixed and defined in specialized terms within the realm of medical psychology and Freudian psychoanalysis.

The vocabulary concerning the soul and the mind increased enormously in the course of the nineteenth century. The enrichments of literary and intellectual language led to an altered understanding of the meanings that underlie time-honored expressions and traditional catchwords. At the same time, once coined, powerful new ideas attracted to themselves a whole host of seemingly unrelated issues, practices, and experiences, creating a peculiar network of preoccupations that as a group had not existed before. The drawn-out attempt to approach and define the unconscious brought together the spiritualist and the psychical researcher of borderline phenomena (such as apparitions, spectral illusions, haunted houses, mediums, trance, automatic writing); the psychiatrist or alienist probing the nature of mental disease, of abnormal ideation, hallucination, delirium, melancholia, mania; the surgeon performing operations with the aid of hypnotism; the magnetizer claiming to correct the disequilibrium in the universal flow of magnetic fluids but who soon came to be regarded as a clever manipulator of the imagination; the physiologist and the physician who puzzled over sleep, dreams, sleepwalking, anesthesia, the influence of the mind on the body in health and disease; the neurologist concerned with the functions of the brain and the physiological basis of mental life; the philosopher interested in the will, the emotions, consciousness, knowledge, imagination and the creative genius; and, last but not least, the psychologist.

Significantly, most if not all of these practices (for example, hypnotism in surgery or psychological magnetism) originated in the waning years of the eighteenth century and during the early decades of the nineteenth century, as did some of the disciplines (such as psychology and psychical research). The majority of topics too were either new or assumed hitherto unknown colors. Thus, before 1790, few if any spoke, in medical terms, of the affinity between creative genius and the hallucinations of the insane . . .

Striving vaguely and independently to give expression to a latent conception, various lines of thought can be brought together by some novel term. The new concept then serves as a kind of resting place or stocktaking in the development of ideas, giving satisfaction and a stimulus for further discussion or speculation. Thus, the massive introduction of the term unconscious by Hartmann in 1869 appeared to focalize many stray thoughts, affording a temporary feeling that a crucial step had been taken forward, a comprehensive knowledge gained, a knowledge that required only further elaboration, explication, and unfolding in order to bring in a bounty of higher understanding. Ultimately, Hartmann's attempt at defining the unconscious proved fruitless because he extended its reach into every realm of organic and inorganic, spiritual, intellectual, and instinctive existence, severely diluting the precision and compromising the impact of the concept.

1. "The enrichments of literary and intellectual language led to an altered understanding of the meanings that underlie time-honored expressions and traditional catchwords." Which one of the following interpretations of this sentence would be closest in meaning to the original?

(1) Literary and intellectual language was altered by time-honored expressions and traditional catchwords.

(2) All of the options listed here.

(3) The meanings of time-honored expressions were changed by innovations in literary and intellectual language.

(4) Time-honored expressions and traditional catchwords were enriched by literary and intellectual language.

2. Which one of the following statements best describes what the passage is about?

(1) The identification of the unconscious as an object of psychical research.

(2) The growing vocabulary of the soul and the mind, as diverse processes.

(3) The discovery of the unconscious as a part of the human mind.

(4) The collating of diverse ideas under the single term: unconscious.

3. Which one of the following sets of words is closest to mapping the main arguments of the passage?

(1) Unconscious; Latent conception; Dreams.

(2) Literary language; Unconscious; Insanity.

(3) Language; Unconscious; Psychoanalysis.

(4) Imagination; Magnetism; Psychiatry.

4. All of the following statements may be considered valid inferences from the passage, EXCEPT:

(1) Unrelated practices began to be treated as related to each other, as knowledge of the mind grew in the nineteenth century.

(2) Eighteenth century thinkers were the first to perceive a connection between creative genius and insanity.

(3) Without the linguistic developments of the nineteenth century, the growth of understanding of the soul and the mind may not have happened.

(4) New conceptions in the nineteenth century could provide new knowledge because of the establishment of fields such as anaesthesiology.

Question Numbers (5 to 8): The passage below is accompanied by a set of questions. Choose the best answer to each question.

Back in the early 2000s, an awesome thing happened in the New *X-Men* comics. Our mutant heroes had been battling giant robots called Sentinels for years, but suddenly these mechanical overlords spawned a new threat: Nano-Sentinels! Not content to rule Earth with their metal fists, these tiny robots invaded our bodies at the microscopic level. Infected humans were slowly converted into machines, cell by cell.

Now, a new wave of extremely odd robots is making at least part of the Nano-Sentinels story come true. Using exotic fabrication materials like squishy hydrogels and elastic polymers, researchers are making autonomous devices that are often tiny and that could turn out to be more powerful than an army of Terminators. Some are 1-centimetre blobs that can skate over water. Others are flat sheets that can roll themselves into tubes, or matchstick-sized plastic coils that act as powerful muscles. No, they won't be invading our bodies and turning us into Sentinels – which I personally find a little disappointing – but some of them could one day swim through our bloodstream to heal us. They could also clean up pollutants in water or fold themselves into different kinds of vehicles for us to drive. . . .

Unlike a traditional robot, which is made of mechanical parts, these new kinds of robots are made from molecular parts. The principle is the same: both are devices that can move around and do things independently. But a robot made from smart materials might be nothing more than a pink drop of hydrogel. Instead of gears and wires, it's assembled from two kinds of molecules – some that love water and some that avoid it – which interact to allow the bot to skate on top of a pond.

Sometimes these materials are used to enhance more conventional robots. One team of researchers, for example, has developed a different kind of hydrogel that becomes sticky when exposed to a low-voltage zap of electricity and then stops being sticky when the electricity is switched off. This putty-like gel can be pasted right onto the feet or wheels of a robot. When the robot wants to climb a sheer wall or scoot across the ceiling, it can activate its sticky feet with a few volts. Once it is back on a flat surface again, the robot turns off the adhesive like a light switch.

Robots that are wholly or partly made of gloop aren't the future that I was promised in science fiction. But it's definitely the future I want. I'm especially keen on the nanometre-scale "soft robots" that could one day swim through our bodies. Metin Sitti, a director at the Max Planck Institute for Intelligent Systems in Germany, worked with colleagues to prototype these tiny, synthetic beasts using various stretchy materials, such as simple rubber, and seeding them with magnetic microparticles. They are assembled into a finished shape by applying magnetic fields. The results look like flowers or geometric shapes made from Tinkertoy ball and stick modelling kits. They're guided through tubes of fluid using magnets, and can even stop and cling to the sides of a tube.

5. Which one of the following statements, if true, would be the most direct extension of the arguments in the passage?

(1) X-Men may be created by injecting people with mutant nano-gels that will respond to the brain's magnetic field.

(2) In the future, robots will be used to search and destroy diseases even in the deepest recesses of the human body.

(3) Sentinel robots will be used in warfare to cause large-scale destructive mutations amongst civilians.

(4) 1-centimetre blobs of gel that have nano-robots in them will be used to send messages.

6. Which one of the following statements best summarises the central point of the passage?

(1) Once the stuff of science fiction, nano-robots now feature in cutting-edge scientific research.

(2) Robots will use nano-robots on their feet and wheels to climb walls or move on ceilings.

(3) The field of robotics is likely to be feature more and more in comics like the New *X-Men*.

(4) Nano-robots made from molecules that react to water have become increasingly useful.

7. Which one of the following statements best captures the sense of the first paragraph?
   (1) Tiny sentinels called X-Men infected people, turning them into mutant robot overlords.
   (2) None of the options listed here.
   (3) The X-Men were mutant heroes who now had to battle tiny robots called Nano-Sentinels.
   (4) People who were infected by Nano-Sentinel robots became mutants who were called X-Men.

8. Which one of the following scenarios, if false, could be seen as supporting the passage?
   (1) There are two kinds of molecules used to make some nano-robots: one that reacts positively to water and the other negatively.
   (2) Some hydrogels turn sticky when an electric current is passed through them; this potentially has very useful applications.
   (3) Nano-Sentinel-like robots are likely to be used to inject people to convert them into robots, cell by cell.
   (4) Robots made from smart materials are likely to become part of our everyday lives in the future.

Question Numbers (9 to 12): The passage below is accompanied by a set of questions. Choose the best answer to each question.

Starting in 1957, [Noam Chomsky] proclaimed a new doctrine: Language, that most human of all attributes, was innate. The grammatical faculty was built into the infant brain, and your average 3-year-old was not a mere apprentice in the great enterprise of absorbing English from his or her parents, but a "linguistic genius." Since this message was couched in terms of Chomskyan theoretical linguistics, in discourse so opaque that it was nearly incomprehensible even to some scholars, many people did not hear it. Now, in a brilliant, witty and altogether satisfying book, Mr. Chomsky's colleague Steven Pinker . . . has brought Mr. Chomsky's findings to everyman. In "The Language Instinct" he has gathered persuasive data from such diverse fields as cognitive neuroscience, developmental psychology and speech therapy to make his points, and when he disagrees with Mr. Chomsky he tells you so. . . .

For Mr. Chomsky and Mr. Pinker, somewhere in the human brain there is a complex set of neural circuits that have been programmed with "super-rules" (making up what Mr. Chomsky calls "universal grammar"), and that these rules are unconscious and instinctive. A half-century ago, this would have been pooh-poohed as a "black box" theory, since one could not actually pinpoint this grammatical faculty in a specific part of the brain, or describe its functioning. But now things are different. Neurosurgeons [have now found that this] "black box" is situated in and around Broca's area, on the left side of the forebrain. . . .

Unlike Mr. Chomsky, Mr. Pinker firmly places the wiring of the brain for language within the framework of Darwinian natural selection and evolution. He effectively disposes of all claims that intelligent nonhuman primates like chimps have any abilities to learn and use language. It is not that chimps lack the vocal apparatus to speak; it is just that their brains are unable to produce or use grammar. On the other hand, the "language instinct," when it first appeared among our most distant hominid ancestors, must have given them a selective reproductive advantage over their competitors (including the ancestral chimps)....

So according to Mr. Pinker, the roots of language must be in the genes, but there cannot be a "grammar gene" any more than there can be a gene for the heart or any other complex body structure. This proposition will undoubtedly raise the hackles of some behavioral psychologists and anthropologists, for it apparently contradicts the liberal idea that human behavior may be changed for the better by improvements in culture and environment, and it might seem to invite the twin bugaboos of biological determinism and racism. Yet Mr. Pinker stresses one point that should allay such fears. Even though there are 4,000 to 6,000 languages today, they are all sufficiently alike to be considered one language by an extraterrestrial observer. In other words, most of the diversity of the world's cultures, so beloved to anthropologists, is superficial and minor compared to the similarities. Racial differences are literally only "skin deep." The fundamental unity of humanity is the theme of Mr. Chomsky's universal grammar, and of this exciting book.

9. Which one of the following statements best summarises the author's position about Pinker's book?
   (1) Anatomical developments like the voice box play a key role in determining language acquisition skills.
   (2) Culture and environment play a key role in shaping our acquisition of language.
   (3) The evolutionary and deterministic framework of Pinker's book makes it racist.
   (4) The universality of the "language instinct" counters claims that Pinker's book is racist.

10. According to the passage, all of the following are true about the language instinct EXCEPT that:
   (1) all intelligent primates are gifted with it.
   (2) it confers an evolutionary reproductive advantage.
   (3) developments in neuroscience have increased its acceptance.
   (4) not all intelligent primates are gifted with it.

11. On the basis of the information in the passage, Pinker and Chomsky may disagree with each other on which one of the following points?
   (1) The inborn language acquisition skills of humans.
   (2) The Darwinian explanatory paradigm for language.
   (3) The language instinct.
   (4) The possibility of a universal grammar.

12. From the passage, it can be inferred that all of the following are true about Pinker's book, "The Language Instinct", EXCEPT that Pinker:

(1) draws extensively from Chomsky's propositions.

(2) disagrees with Chomsky on certain grounds.

(3) writes in a different style from Chomsky.

(4) draws from behavioural psychology theories.

Question Numbers (13 to 16): The passage below is accompanied by a set of questions. Choose the best answer to each question.

Keeping time accurately comes with a price. The maximum accuracy of a clock is directly related to how much disorder, or entropy, it creates every time it ticks. Natalia Ares at the University of Oxford and her colleagues made this discovery using a tiny clock with an accuracy that can be controlled. The clock consists of a 50-nanometre-thick membrane of silicon nitride, vibrated by an electric current. Each time the membrane moved up and down once and then returned to its original position, the researchers counted a tick, and the regularity of the spacing between the ticks represented the accuracy of the clock. The researchers found that as they increased the clock's accuracy, the heat produced in the system grew, increasing the entropy of its surroundings by jostling nearby particles . . . "If a clock is more accurate, you are paying for it somehow," says Ares. In this case, you pay for it by pouring more ordered energy into the clock, which is then converted into entropy. "By measuring time, we are increasing the entropy of the universe," says Ares. The more entropy there is in the universe, the closer it may be to its eventual demise. "Maybe we should stop measuring time," says Ares. The scale of the additional entropy is so small, though, that there is no need to worry about its effects, she says.

The increase in entropy in timekeeping may be related to the "arrow of time", says Marcus Huber at the Austrian Academy of Sciences in Vienna, who was part of the research team. It has been suggested that the reason that time only flows forward, not in reverse, is that the total amount of entropy in the universe is constantly increasing, creating disorder that cannot be put in order again.

The relationship that the researchers found is a limit on the accuracy of a clock, so it doesn't mean that a clock that creates the most possible entropy would be maximally accurate – hence a large, inefficient grandfather clock isn't more precise than an atomic clock. "It's a bit like fuel use in a car. Just because I'm using more fuel doesn't mean that I'm going faster or further," says Huber.

When the researchers compared their results with theoretical models developed for clocks that rely on quantum effects, they were surprised to find that the relationship between accuracy and entropy seemed to be the same for both. . . . We can't be sure yet that these results are actually universal, though, because there are many types of clocks for which the relationship between accuracy and entropy haven't been tested. "It's still unclear how this principle plays out in real devices such as atomic clocks, which push the ultimate quantum limits of accuracy," says Mark Mitchison at Trinity College Dublin in Ireland. Understanding this relationship could be helpful for designing clocks in the future, particularly those used in quantum computers and other devices where both accuracy and temperature are crucial, says Ares. This finding could also help us understand more generally how the quantum world and the classical world are similar and different in terms of thermodynamics and the passage of time.

13. The author makes all of the following arguments in the passage, EXCEPT that:

(1) The relationship between accuracy and entropy may not apply to all clocks.

(2) Researchers found that the heat produced in a system is the price paid for increased accuracy of measurement.

(3) There is no difference in accuracy between an inefficient grandfather clock and an atomic clock.

(4) In designing clocks for quantum computers, both precision and heat have to be taken into account.

14. Which one of the following sets of words and phrases serves best as keywords of the passage?

(1) Electric current; Heat; Quantum effects.

(2) Silicon Nitride; Energy; Grandfather Clock.

(3) Measuring Time; Accuracy; Entropy.

(4) Membrane; Arrow of time; Entropy.

15. None of the following statements can be inferred from the passage EXCEPT that:

(1) the arrow of time has not yet been tested for atomic clocks.

(2) quantum computers are likely to produce more heat and, hence, more entropy, because of the emphasis on their clocks' accuracy.

(3) grandfather clocks are likely to produce less heat and, hence, less entropy, because they are not as accurate.

(4) a clock with a 50-nanometre-thick membrane of silicon nitride has been made to vibrate, producing electric currents.

16. "It's a bit like fuel use in a car. Just because I'm using more fuel doesn't mean that I'm going faster or further . . ." What is the purpose of this example?

(1) If you go faster in a car, you will tend to consume more fuel, but the converse is not necessarily true. In the same way, increased entropy does not necessarily mean greater accuracy of a clock.

(2) The further you go in a car, the more fuel you use. In the same way, the faster you go in a car, the less time you use.

(3) If you measure the speed of a car with a grandfather clock, the result will be different than if you measured it with an atomic clock.

(4) The further and faster you go in a car, the greater the amount of fuel you will use, the greater the amount of heat produced and, hence, the greater the entropy.

17. The passage given below is followed by four alternate summaries. Choose the option that best captures the essence of the passage.

People view idleness as a sin and industriousness as a virtue, and in the process have developed an unsatisfactory relationship with their jobs. Work has become a way for them to keep busy, even though many find their work meaningless. In their need for activity people undertake what was once considered work (fishing, gardening) as hobbies. The opposing view is that hard work has made us prosperous and improved our levels of health and education. It has also brought innovation and labour and time-saving devices, which have lessened life's drudgery.

(1) Hard work has overtaken all aspects of our lives and has enabled economic prosperity, but it is important that people reserve their leisure time for some idleness.

(2) Some believe that hard work has been glorified to the extent that it has become meaningless, and led to greater idleness, but it has also had enormous positive impacts on everyday life.

(3) While the idealisation of hard work has propelled people into meaningless jobs and endless activity, it has also led to tremendous social benefits from prosperity and innovation.

(4) Despite some detractors, hard work is essential in today's world to enable economic progress, for education and health and to propel innovations that make life easier.

18. The passage given below is followed by four alternate summaries. Choose the option that best captures the essence of the passage.

Brazil's growth rate has been low, yet most Brazilians say their financial situation has improved, and they expect it to get even better. This is because most incomes are rising fast, with higher minimum wages and very low unemployment. The result is falling inequality and a growing middle class — the result of economic stabilization, improved social security and universal primary education. But despite recent improvements the Brazilian economy is still painfully unequal, with poor Brazilians paying the biggest share of their income in taxes and getting the least back in government services.

(1) With rising incomes and falling unemployment, most Brazilians are being misled into thinking that their economy is doing well.

(2) Most Brazilians feel they have benefitted from recent economic events, but the poor continue to be dealt unfairly by the state.

(3) Economic reforms have benefitted many Brazilians, but they are unaware of the impending problems from rising inequalities in their society.

(4) Good economic indicators have masked the unfair taxation of the poor that is likely to destabilise the Brazilian economy in the next few years.

19. The four sentences (labelled 1, 2, 3, 4) below, when properly sequenced would yield a coherent paragraph. Decide on the proper sequencing of the order of the sentences and key in the sequence of the four numbers as your answer:

(1) It is regimes of truth that make certain relationships speakable – relationships, like subjectivities, are constituted through discursive formations, which sustain regimes of truth.

(2) Relationships are nothing without the communication that brings them into being; interpersonal communication is connected to knowledge shared by interlocutors, and scholars should attend to relational histories in their analyses.

(3) A Foucauldian approach to relationships goes beyond these conceptions of discourse and history to macrolevel regimes of truth as constituting relationships.

(4) Reconsidering micropractices within relationships that are constituted within and simultaneously contributors to regimes of truth acknowledges the central position of power/knowledge in the constitution of what has come to be considered true and real.

20. Five jumbled up sentences, related to a topic, are given below. Four of them can be put together to form a coherent paragraph. Identify the odd one out and key in the number of the sentence as your answer:

(1) They often include a foundation course on navigating capitalism with Chinese characteristics and have replaced typical cases from US corporates with a focus on how Western theories apply to China's buzzing local firms.

(2) The best Chinese business schools look like their Western rivals but are now growing distinct in terms of what they teach and the career boost they offer.

(3) Western schools have enhanced their offerings with double degrees, popular with domestic and overseas students alike—and boosted the prestige of their Chinese partners.

(4) For students, a big draw is the chance to rub shoulders with captains of China's private sector.

(5) Their business courses now largely cater to the growing demand from China Inc which has become more global, richer and ready to recruit from this sinocentric student body.

21. The four sentences (labelled 1, 2, 3 and 4) below, when properly sequenced would yield a coherent paragraph. Decide on the proper sequencing of the order of the sentences and key in the sequence of the four numbers as your answer:

(1) Restitution of artefacts to original cultures could faces legal obstacles, as many Western museums are legally prohibited from disposing off their collections.

(2) This is in response to countries like Nigeria, which are pressurising European museums to return their precious artefacts looted by colonisers in the past.

(3) Museums in Europe today are struggling to come to terms with their colonial legacy, some taking steps to return artefacts but not wanting to lose their prized collections.

(4) Legal hurdles notwithstanding, politicians and institutions in France and Germany would now like to defuse the colonial time bombs, and are now backing the return of part of their holdings.

22. Five jumbled up sentences, related to a topic, are given below. Four of them can be put together to form a coherent paragraph. Identify the odd one out and key in the number of the sentence as your answer:

(1) A typical example is Wikipedia, where the overwhelming majority of contributors are male and so the available content is skewed to reflect their interests.

(2) Without diversity of thought and representation, society is left with a distorted picture of future options, which are likely to result in augmenting existing inequalities.

(3) Gross gender inequality in the technology sector is problematic, not only for the industry-wide marginalisation of women, but because technology designs embody the values of their makers.

(4) While redressing unequal representation in the workplace is a step in the right direction, broader social change is needed to address the structural inequalities embedded within the current organisation of work and employment.

(5) If technology merely reflects the perspectives of the male stereotype, then new technologies are unlikely to accommodate the diverse social contexts within which they operate.

23. The passage given below is followed by four alternate summaries. Choose the option that best captures the essence of the passage.

The human mind is wired to see patterns. Not only does the brain process information as it comes in, it also stores insights from all our past experiences. Every interaction, happy or sad, is catalogued in our memory. Intuition draws from that deep memory well to inform our decisions going forward. In other words, intuitive decisions are based on data, and not contrary to data as many would like to assume. When we subconsciously spot patterns, the body starts firing neurochemicals in both the brain and gut. These "somatic markers" are what give us that instant sense that something is right ... or that it's off. Not only are these automatic processes faster than rational thought, but our intuition draws from decades of diverse qualitative experience (sights, sounds, interactions, etc.) – a wholly human feature that big data alone could never accomplish.

(1) Intuitions are neuro-chemical firings based on pattern recognition and draw upon a rich and vast database of experiences.

(2) Intuition is infinitely richer than big data which is based on rational thought and accomplishes more than what big data can.

(3) Intuitions are automatic processes and are therefore faster than rational thought, and so decisions based on them are better.

(4) Intuition draws from deep memory, and may not be related to data, but to decades of diverse qualitative experience.

24. The four sentences (labelled 1, 2, 3 and 4) below, when properly sequenced would yield a coherent paragraph. Decide on the proper sequencing of the order of the sentences and key in the sequence of the four numbers as your answer:

(1) Businesses find automation, such as robotic employees, a big asset in terms of productivity and efficiency.

(2) But in recent years, robotics has had increasing impacts on unemployment, not just of manual labour, as computers are rapidly handling some white-collar and service-sector work.

(3) For years politicians have promised workers that they would bring back their jobs by clamping down on trade, offshoring and immigration.

(4) Economists, based on their research, say that the bigger threat to jobs now is not globalisation but automation.

Section II: DI & LR

Question Numbers (1 to 6): Answer the questions on the basis of the information given below.

10 players – P1, P2, ..., P10 - competed in an international javelin throw event. The number (after P) of a player reflects his rank at the beginning of the event, with rank 1 going to the topmost player. There were two phases in the event with the first phase consisting of rounds 1, 2, and 3, and the second phase consisting of rounds 4, 5, and 6. A throw is measured in terms of the distance it covers (in meters, up to one decimal point accuracy), only if the throw is a 'valid' one. For an invalid throw, the distance is taken as zero. A player's score at the end of a round is the maximum distance of all his throws up to that round. Players are re-ranked after every round based on their current scores. In case of a tie in scores, the player with a prevailing higher rank retains the higher rank. This ranking determines the order in which the players go for their throws in the next round.

In each of the rounds in the first phase, the players throw in increasing order of their latest rank, i.e. the player ranked 1 at that point throws first, followed by the player ranked 2 at that point and so on. The top six players at the end of the first phase qualify for the second phase. In each of the rounds in the second phase, the players throw in decreasing order of their latest rank i.e. the player ranked 6 at that point throws first, followed by the player ranked 5 at that point and so on. The players ranked 1, 2, and 3 at the end of the sixth round receive gold, silver, and bronze medals respectively.

All the valid throws of the event were of distinct distances (as per stated measurement accuracy). The tables below show distances (in meters) covered by all valid throws in the first and the third round in the event.

Distances covered by all the valid throws in the first round

Player	Distance (in m)
P1	82.9
P3	81.5
P5	86.4
P6	82.5
P7	87.2
P9	84.1

Distances covered by all the valid throws in the third round

Player	Distance (in m)
P1	88.6
P3	79
P9	81.4

The following facts are also known.

i. Among the throws in the second round, only the last two were valid. Both the throws enabled these players to qualify for the second phase, with one of them qualifying with the least score. None of these players won any medal.

ii. If a player throws first in a round AND he was also the last (among the players in the current round) to throw in the previous round, then the player is said to get a double. Two players got a double.

iii. In each round of the second phase, exactly one player improved his score. Each of these improvements was by the same amount.

iv. The gold and bronze medalists improved their scores in the fifth and the sixth rounds respectively. One medal winner improved his score in the fourth round.

v. The difference between the final scores of the gold medalist and the silver medalist, as well as the difference between the final scores of the silver medalist and the bronze medalist was 1.0 m.

1. Which two players got the double?
(1) P8, P10 (2) P2, P4
(3) P1, P10 (4) P1, P8

2. Who won the silver medal?
(1) P7 (2) P9
(3) P1 (4) P5

3. Who threw the last javelin in the event?
(1) P10 (2) P9
(3) P1 (4) P7

4. What was the final score (in m) of the silver-medalist?
(1) 87.2 (2) 88.6
(3) 89.6 (4) 88.4

5. Which of the following can be the final score (in m) of P8?
(1) 0 (2) 81.9
(3) 85.1 (4) 82.7

6. By how much did the gold medalist improve his score (in m) in the second phase?
(1) 2.4 (2) 2.0
(3) 1.0 (4) 1.2

Question Numbers (7 to 10): Answer the questions on the basis of the information given below.

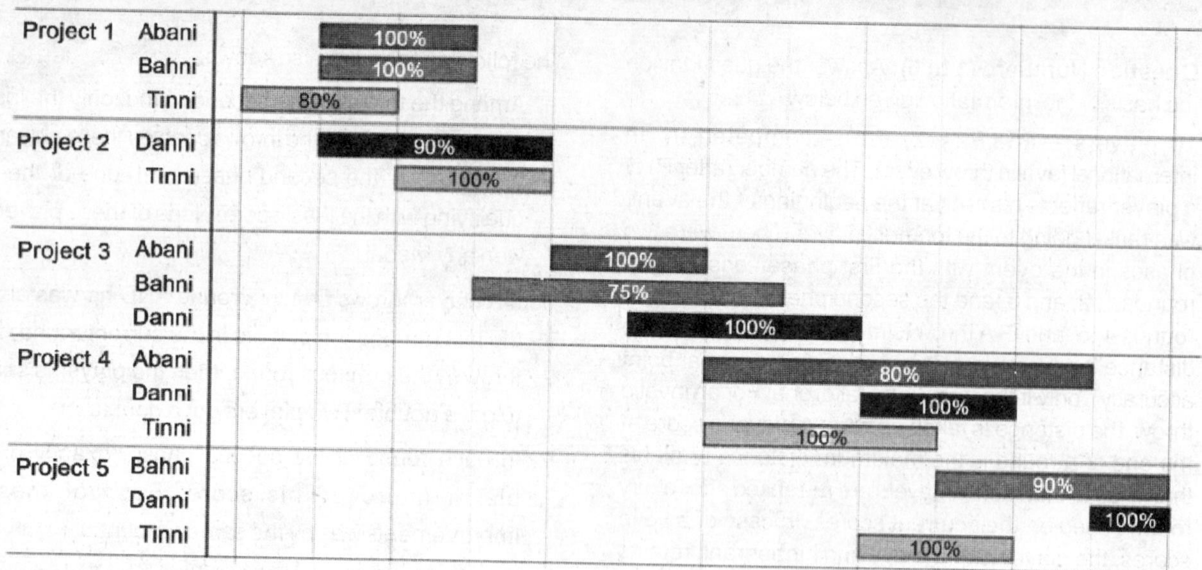

The figure above shows the schedule of four employees – Abani, Bahni, Danni and Tinni – whom Dhoni supervised in 2020. Altogether there were five projects which started and concluded in 2020 in which they were involved. For each of these projects and for each employee, the starting day was at the beginning of a month and the concluding day was the end of a month, and these are indicated by the left and right end points of the corresponding horizontal bars. The number within each bar indicates the percentage of assigned work completed by the employee for that project, as assessed by Dhoni.

For each employee, his/her total project-month (in 2020) is the sum of the number of months (s)he worked across the five project, while his/her annual completion index is the weightage average of the completion percentage assigned from the different projects, with the weights being the corresponding number of months (s)he worked in these projects. For each project, the total employee-month is the sum of the number of months four employees worked in this project, while its completion index is the weightage average of the completion percentage assigned for the employees who worked in this project, with the weights being the corresponding number of months they worked in this project.

7. Which of the following statements is/are true?

I: The total project-month was the same for the four employees.

II: The total employee-month was the same for the five projects.

(1) Only II

(2) Neither I nor II

(3) Both I and II

(4) Only I

8. Which employees did not work in multiple projects for any of the months in 2020?

(1) All four of them

(2) Only Tinni

(3) Only Abani and Bahni

(4) Only Abani, Bahni and Danni

9. The project duration, measured in terms of the number of months, is the time during which at least one employee worked in the project. Which of the following pairs of the projects had the same duration?

(1) Project 3, Project 5

(2) Project 1, Project 5

(3) Project 4, Project 5

(4) Project 3, Project 4

10. The list of employees in decreasing order of *annual completion index* is:

(1) Danni, Tinni, Abani, Bahni

(2) Tinni, Danni, Abani, Bahni

(3) Bahni, Abani, Tinni, Danni

(4) Danni, Tinni, Bahni, Abani

Question Numbers (11 to 16): Answer the questions on the basis of the information given below.

Three reviewers Amal, Bimal, and Komal are tasked with selecting questions from a pool of 13 questions (Q01 to Q13). Questions can be created by external "subject matter experts" (SMEs) or by one of the three reviewers. Each of the reviewers either approves or disapproves a question that is shown to them. Their decisions lead to eventual acceptance or rejection of the question in the manner described below.

If a question is created by an SME, it is reviewed first by Amal, and then by Bimal. If both of them approve the question, then the question is accepted and is not reviewed by Komal. If both disapprove the question, it is rejected and is not reviewed by Komal. If one of them approves the question and the other disapproves it, then the question is reviewed by Komal. Then the question is accepted only if she approves it.

A question created by one of the reviewers is decided upon by the other two. If a question is created by Amal, then it is first reviewed by Bimal. If Bimal approves the question, then it is accepted. Otherwise, it is reviewed by Komal. The question is then accepted only if Komal approves it. A similar process is followed for questions created by Bimal, whose questions are first reviewed by Komal, and then by Amal only if Komal disapproves it. Questions created by Komal are first reviewed by Amal, and then, if required, by Bimal.

The following facts are known about the review process after its completion.

1. Q02, Q06, Q09, Q11, and Q12 were rejected and the other questions were accepted.
2. Amal reviewed only Q02, Q03, Q04, Q06, Q08, Q10, Q11, and Q13.
3. Bimal reviewed only Q02, Q04, Q06 through Q09, Q12, and Q13.
4. Komal reviewed only Q01 through Q05, Q07, Q08, Q09, Q11, and Q12.

11. How many questions were DEFINITELY created by Amal?

12. How many questions were DEFINITELY created by Komal?

13. How many questions were DEFINITELY created by the SMEs?

14. How many questions were DEFINITELY disapproved by Bimal?

(1) 3 (2) 4
(3) 5 (4) 7

15. The approval ratio of a reviewer is the ratio of the number of questions (s)he approved to the number of questions (s)he reviewed. Which option best describes Amal's approval ratio?

(1) lies between 0.25 and 0.50
(2) either 0.25 or 0.75
(3) 0.25
(4) lies between 0.25 and 0.75

16. How many questions created by Amal or Bimal were disapproved by at least one of the other reviewers?

(1) 2 (2) 5
(3) 7 (4) 4

Question Numbers (17 to 20): Answer the questions on the basis of the information given below.

Each of the bottles mentioned in this question contains 50 ml of liquid. The liquid in any bottle can be 100% pure content (P) or can have certain amount of impurity (I). Visually it is not possible to distinguish between P and I. There is a testing device which detects impurity, as long as the percentage of impurity in the content tested is 10% or more.

For example, suppose bottle 1 contains only P, and bottle 2 contains 80% P and 20% I. If content from bottle 1 is tested, it will be found out that it contains only P. If content of bottle 2 is tested, the test will reveal that it contains some amount of I. If 10 ml of content from bottle 1 is mixed with 20 ml content from bottle 2, the test will show that the mixture has impurity, and hence we can conclude that at least one of the two bottles has I. However, if 10 ml of content from bottle 1 is mixed with 5 ml of content from bottle 2. the test will not detect any impurity in the resultant mixture.

17. 5 ml of content from bottle A is mixed with 5 ml of content from bottle B. The resultant mixture, when tested, detects the presence of I. If it is known that bottle A contains only P, what BEST can be concluded about the volume of I in bottle B?

(1) Less than 1 ml (2) 10 ml
(3) 10 ml or more (4) 1 ml

18. There are four bottles. Each bottle is known to contain only P or only I. They will be considered to be "collectively ready for despatch" if all of them contain only P. In minimum how many tests, is it possible to ascertain whether these four bottles are "collectively ready for despatch"?

19. There are four bottles. It is known that three of these bottles contain only P, while the remaining one contains 80% P and 20% I. What is the minimum number of tests required to definitely identify the bottle containing some amount of I?

20. There are four bottles. It is known that either one or two of these bottles contain(s) only P, while the remaining ones contain 85% P and 15% I. What is the minimum number of tests required to ascertain the exact number of bottles containing only P?

(1) 2 (2) 4
(3) 3 (4) 1

Section III: QA

1. A four-digit number is formed by using only the digits 1, 2 and 3 such that both 2 and 3 appear at least once. The number of all such four-digit numbers is

2. Let ABCD be a parallelogram. The lengths of the side AD and the diagonal AC are 10 cm and 20 cm, respectively. If the angle $\angle ADC$ is equal to 30° then the area of the parallelogram, in sq. cm, is

(1) $25(\sqrt{3}+\sqrt{15})$ (2) $\frac{25(\sqrt{5}+\sqrt{15})}{2}$

(3) $\frac{25(\sqrt{3}+\sqrt{15})}{2}$ (4) $25(\sqrt{5}+\sqrt{15})$

3. Bank A offers 6% interest rate per annum compounded half yearly. Bank B and Bank C offer simple interest but the annual interest rate offered by Bank C is twice that of Bank B. Raju invests a certain amount in Bank B for a certain period and Rupa invests Rs. 10,000 in Bank C for twice that period. The interest that would accrue to Raju during that period is equal to the interest that would have accrued had he invested the same amount in Bank A for one year. The interest accrued, in INR, to Rupa is

(1) 1436 (2) 2346

(3) 2436 (4) 3436

4. The cost of fencing a rectangular plot is Rs. 200 per ft along one side, and Rs. 100 per ft along the three other sides. If the area of the rectangular plot is 60000 sq. ft, then the lowest possible cost of fencing all four sides, in INR, is

(1) 120000 (2) 100000

(3) 160000 (4) 90000

5. For a real number a, if $\frac{\log_{15} a + \log_{32} a}{(\log_{15} a)(\log_{32} a)} = 4$ then a must lie in the range

(1) $a > 5$ (2) $3 < a < 4$

(3) $2 < a < 3$ (4) $4 < a < 5$

6. If n is a positive integer such that $(\sqrt[7]{10})(\sqrt[7]{10})^2 \ldots (\sqrt[7]{10})^n > 999$, then the smallest value of n is

7. In a triangle ABC, $\angle BCA = 50°$. D and E are points on AB and AC, respectively, such that AD = DE. If F is a point on BC such that BD = DF, then $\angle FDE$, in degrees, is equal to

(1) 96 (2) 100

(3) 80 (4) 72

8. Anil can paint a house in 12 days while Barun can paint it in 16 days. Anil, Barun, and Chandu undertake to paint the house for Rs. 24000 and the three of them together complete the painting in 6 days. If Chandu is paid in proportion to the work done by him, then the amount in INR received by him is

9. The arithmetic mean of scores of 25 students in an examination is 50. Five of these students top the examination with the same score. If the scores of the other students are distinct integers with the lowest being 30, then the maximum possible score of the toppers is

10. If $f(x) = x^2 - 7x$ and $g(x) = x + 3$, then the minimum value of $f(g(x)) - 3x$ is

(1) −15 (2) −20

(3) −16 (4) −12

11. Mira and Amal walk along a circular track, starting from the same point at the same time. If they walk in the same direction, then in 45 minutes, Amal completes exactly 3 more rounds than Mira. If they walk in opposite directions, then they meet for the first time exactly after 3 minutes. The number of rounds Mira walks in one hour is

12. A park is shaped like a rhombus and has area 96 sq m. If 40 m of fencing is needed to enclose the park, the cost, in INR, of laying electric wires along its two diagonals, at the rate of Rs. 125 per m, is

13. In a tournament, a team has played 40 matches so far and won 30% of them. If they win 60% of the remaining matches, their overall win percentage will be 50%. Suppose they win 90% of the remaining matches, then the total number of matches won by the team in the tournament will be

(1) 86 (2) 84

(3) 80 (4) 78

14. The total of male and female populations in a city increased by 25% from 1970 to 1980. During the same period, the male population increased by 40% while the female population increased by 20%. From 1980 to 1990, the female population increased by 25%. In 1990, if the female population is twice the male population, then the percentage increase in the total of male and female populations in the city from 1970 to 1990 is

(1) 68.75 (2) 68.25

(3) 69.25 (4) 68.50

15. Consider a sequence of real numbers $x_1, x_2, x_3, \ldots$ such that $x_{n+1} = x_n + n - 1$ for all $n \geq 1$. If $x_1 = -1$ then x_{100} is equal to

(1) 4949 (2) 4850

(3) 4849 (4) 4950

16. If a certain weight of an alloy of silver and copper is mixed with 3 kg of pure silver, the resulting alloy will have 90% silver by weight. If the same weight of the initial alloy is mixed with 2 kg of another alloy which has 90% silver by weight, the resulting alloy will have 84% silver by weight. Then, the weight of the initial alloy, in kg, is

(1) 3 (2) 2.5

(3) 3.5 (4) 4

17. A shop owner bought a total of 64 shirts from a wholesale market that came in two sizes, small and large. The price of a small shirt was INR 50 less than that of a large shirt. She paid a total of INR 5000 for the large shirts, and a total of INR 1800 for the small shirts. Then, the price of a large shirt and a small shirt together, in INR, is

(1) 150 (2) 225

(3) 175 (4) 200

18. One day, Rahul started a work at 9 AM and Gautam joined him two hours later. They then worked together and completed the work at 5 PM the same day. If both had started at 9 AM and worked together, the work would have been completed 30 minutes earlier. Working alone, the time Rahul would have taken, in hours, to complete the work is

(1) 10 (2) 12

(3) 11.5 (4) 12.5

19. One part of a hostel's monthly expenses is fixed, and the other part is proportional to the number of its boarders. The hostel collects Rs. 1600 per month from each boarder. When the number of boarders is 50, the profit of the hostel is Rs. 200 per boarder, and when the number of boarders is 75, the profit of the hostel is Rs. 250 per boarder. When the number of boarders is 80, the total profit of the hostel, in INR, will be

(1) 20200 (2) 20500

(3) 20000 (4) 20800

20. If $3x + 2|y| + y = 7$ and $x + |x| + 3y = 1$, then $x + 2y$ is

(1) $-\frac{4}{3}$ (2) 1

(3) 0 (4) $\frac{8}{3}$

21. A tea shop offers tea in cups of three different sizes. The product of the prices, in INR, of three different sizes is equal to 800. The prices of the smallest size and the medium size are in the ratio 2 : 5. If the shop owner decides to increase the prices of the smallest and the medium ones by INR 6 keeping the price of the largest size unchanged, the product then changes to 3200. The sum of the original prices of three different sizes, in INR, is

22. The number of distinct pairs of integers (m, n) satisfying $|1 + mn| < |m + n| < 5$ is

ANSWERS

VARC

1. (3)	**2.** (4)	**3.** (3)	**4.** (4)	**5.** (2)	**6.** (1)	**7.** (3)	**8.** (3)	**9.** (4)	**10.** (1)
11. (2)	**12.** (4)	**13.** (2)	**14.** (3)	**15.** (2)	**16.** (1)	**17.** (3)	**18.** (2)	**19.** (2314)	**20.** (3)
21. (3214)	**22.** (4)	**23.** (1)	**24.** (3412)						

DI & LR

1. (1)	**2.** (3)	**3.** (4)	**4.** (2)	**5.** (4)	**6.** (1)	**7.** (4)	**8.** (4)	**9.** (4)	**10.** (1)
11. (3)	**12.** (1)	**13.** (3)	**14.** (2)	**15.** (4)	**16.** (2)	**17.** (3)	**18.** (1)	**19.** (2)	**20.** (4)

QA

1. (50)	**2.** (1)	**3.** (3)	**4.** (1)	**5.** (4)	**6.** (6)	**7.** (3)	**8.** (3000)	**9.** (92)	**10.** (3)
11. (8)	**12.** (3500)	**13.** (2)	**14.** (1)	**15.** (2)	**16.** (1)	**17.** (4)	**18.** (1)	**19.** (2)	**20.** (3)
21. (34)	**22.** (12)								

EXPLANATIONS

VARC

1. 3 is the correct option. The phrase clearly states that the new literary and intellectual language because of the rise of unconscious as a literary tool has provided a change to the then systematic understanding of time-honoured expressions and traditional catchwords.

Incorrect options:

1. The phrase "altered by…" makes it incorrect. It talks about change in time honoured expressions and not by it.
2. All options are not correct.
4. The word enriched has a sense of judgement in it, which cannot be inferred from the passage. Whether enriching or uninspiring is open to debate.

2. The passage deals with the word "unconscious" and how over time since it was introduced in the late 19th century has changed the way we have perceived not only the psychological aspect but language in whole and how it has changed everyday understanding of everyday traditions and ideas. Be it the psychical research or the study of the human mind. The passage encompasses all of these changes. This makes 4, the correct choice.

Incorrect options:

All the other options, 1, 2 and 3 denote parts of the given passage. They are not factually incorrect but can be rendered incomplete.

3. Refer to "*Today we can hardly conceive of ourselves without an unconscious. Yet between 1700 and 1900, this notion developed as a genuinely original thought. The "unconscious" burst the shell of conventional language, coined as it had been to embody the fleeting ideas and the shifting conceptions of several generations until, finally, it became fixed and defined in specialized terms within the realm of medical psychology and Freudian psychoanalysis.*" The opening sentence of the passage clearly maps the sequence the rest of the passage is going to follow. First, it talks about the existence of language before "unconscious". Then comes "unconscious" itself and how it has changed the understanding of linguistics. And, finally the study of the "unconscious" through medical psychology and psychoanalysis.

All other options therefore can be rendered incorrect.

4. The term or the explanation of the term "anaesthesiology" cannot be found in the given passage. To understand the unconscious, many lateral ways of treating the mind has opened like hypnotic treatment, psychoanalysis, psychological magnetism etc. But anaesthesiology means the branch of medicine concerned with anaesthesia and anaesthetics. It is a completely different branch of study. Hence, it cannot be inferred.

Incorrect options:

1. Refer to, "At the same time, once coined, powerful new ideas attracted to themselves a whole host of seemingly unrelated issues, practices, and experiences, creating a peculiar network of preoccupations that as a group had not existed before." Hence can be inferred.
2. Refer to," Thus, before 1790, few if any spoke, in medical terms, of the affinity between creative genius and the hallucinations of the insane . . ." Can be inferred.
3. Refer to, "The vocabulary concerning the soul and the mind increased enormously in the course of the nineteenth century."

5. Refer to,"– but some of them could one day swim through our bloodstream to heal us. They could also clean up pollutants in water or fold themselves into different kinds of vehicles for us to drive. . ." The author is clearly vouching for thse nano robots if they can be used for better good. We can again refer from the last paragraph, "But it's definitely the future I want. I'm especially keen on the nanometre-scale "soft robots" that could one day swim through our bodies."

Incorrect options:

1 is a farfetched assumption that does not correspond to the argument given in the passage.

3 is incorrect as it is false according to the stated argument of the author.

4 4 is also an assumption that is farfetched.

6. The passage begins with an example from X-Men, how nano robots are used in the comics. Following that introduction, the entire passage deals how this nano robotic technology is playing an important role in robotic industry and research. Hence 1 is the correct option.

Incorrect Option:

2 is not factually incorrect. Passage does mention that but it does not capture the entire idea of the passage.

3 is incorrect because author does not state anything about field of robotics to feature more in X-Men.

4 is incorrect because again it captures a part of the passage, does not summarise the passage in whole.

7. The entire 1st paragraph showcase the rise of nano-sentinels in X-Men comics, which along with the sentinels but unlike them, invade our bodies at the microscopic level. So, the X-Men has to now fight both categories of villains. 3 captures the correct essence of the paragraph.

    Incorrect options:

    1 is incorrect because sentinels are not X-Men.

    2 is incorrect because 3 is the correct answer.

    4 is factually incorrect.

8. Refer to, "No, they won't be invading our bodies and turning us into Sentinels – which I personally find a little disappointing – but some of them could one day swim through our bloodstream to heal us." This makes option 3 the correct answer.

    Incorrect Options:

    Other options can be rendered incorrect. Although they are false but they are not supporting the passage.

9. The entire passage deals with the fact that "language, that most human of all attributes, was innate". So, it is instinctive in nature as far Pinker and Chomsky are concerned. So, exactly at this point though the claims of Pinker may seem racist to some, transcends all sort of differences and become universal. "The fundamental unity of humanity is the theme of Mr. Chomsky's universal grammar, and of this exciting book."

    1 is incorrect. It is an incorrect assumption.

    2 is incorrect. The passage counters that argument.

    3 is also factually incorrect.

10. Refer to, "He effectively disposes of all claims that intelligent nonhuman primates like chimps have any abilities to learn and use language. It is not that chimps lack the vocal apparatus to speak; it is just that their brains are unable to produce or use grammar." This clearly makes option 1 false and hence the correct answer.

    Since in the question it is written, "all of the following are true about the language instinct

    EXCEPT", we can conclude that other options are true.

11. Refer to, "Unlike Mr. Chomsky, Mr. Pinker firmly places the wiring of the brain for language within the framework of Darwinian natural selection and evolution." This proves that Chomsky did not agree with Darwinian explanatory paradigm for language. Hence 2 is the correct option.

    Chomsky and Pinker agree with all the other mentioned options.

12. "This proposition will undoubtedly raise the hackles of some behavioral psychologists and anthropologists, for it apparently contradicts the liberal idea that human behavior may be changed for the better by improvements in culture and environment, and it might seem to invite the twin bugaboos of biological determinism and racism." So, it becomes clear that Pinker's theory was criticised from the behavioural psychology standpoint.

13. Option 2 may seem close but the fact is that it is vague. It talks about an arbitrary system. The passage clearly talks about the increased accuracy in clocks. Compared to other options which are present in the passage quite distinctively, option 2 seems incomplete.

14. The entire passage deals with the measurement of time, how entropy is created while producing accurate time. Hence 3 is the correct option.

    1 is incorrect as the passage hardly talks about electric current.

    2 is also incorrect as it doesn't cover the entire passage.

    4 is also incorrect based on the same reason.

15. Refer to, "When the researchers compared their results with theoretical models developed for clocks that rely on quantum effects, they were surprised to find that the relationship between accuracy and entropy seemed to be the same for both. . . ." Hence option 2 can be inferred.

16. If we provide more fuel, it doesn't mean that the car will go faster. It will depend on the speed of the car at which it is travelling. In the same way if we increase entropy, doesn't mean the accuracy will increase, to gain more accuracy more entropy is produced. Hence, 1 is the correct option.

    Refer to, ""It's a bit like fuel use in a car. Just because I'm using more fuel doesn't mean that I'm going faster or further," says Huber."

17. 1 is incorrect because it depicts the passage exactly in a reverse manner. The use of the phrase, "Hard work has overtaken all aspects of our lives…" makes it more incorrect.

    2 is incorrect because of the phrase "greater idleness". The passage does not indicate that.

    4 is incorrect because it is incomplete and does not capture the entire essence of the passage.

    3 therefore is the correct option as it portrays the purpose of the passage, that although people have considered hard work as alternative to idleness, the world is benefitting from all the hard work.

18. 1 is incorrect because of the phrase ", most Brazilians are being misled into". There is no such mention of being misled to believe that the economy is doing well.

    3 is factually incorrect. Refer to," The result is falling inequality and a growing middle class…"

    4 is a far-fetched assumption that cannot be inferred from the given passage.

    2 is the correct option as it captures the essence of the passage. The passage talks about the improving financial condition of Brazil. It also states that the treatment of poor is "still painfully inequal".

19. 2 introduces the argument that relationships are nothing without communication and "is connected to knowledge shared by interlocutors, and scholars..." It is followed by 3 where the topic is expanded on the basis of regimes of truth. 1 therefore logically follows 3 extending the argument.

20. Option 3 talks about the western schools in particular whereas the other 4statements talk about the Chinese business schools in particular and the curses they offer and how the students are benefitting from that. Hence 3 is the odd one out.

21. 3 opens the paragraph stating that the Museums in Europe want to return the artifacts to their then colonised countries but do not want to lose their prized possessions. It is logically followed by 2 which provides the reason behind this. 1 and 4 form a logical pair depicting the obstacles faced while returning the artifacts.

22. Other than 4, all other sentences if arranged logically form a paragraph depicting gender inequality in workplace and how it has a severe effect on social contexts. 4 on the other hand addresses "the structural inequalities embedded within the current organisation of work and employment." Hence it is the odd one out.

23. The intuitions are created by neurochemicals which form somatic markers that our brain and gut identifies because of past experiences. Only option 1 depicts this. Hence it is the correct summary.

 2 is partially correct.

 3 is incorrect as it states that decisions based on intuitions are better. This is missing from the passage.

 4 is again an incomplete summary.

24. 3 opens the paragraph. 4 and 1 form a mandatory pair discussing how automation is a greater threat than globalisation. The sue of 'But' in 2 makes it follow 1.

DI & LR

For questions 1 to 6:

From the given information we can make the following conclusions:

The last 2 throws of R2 were valid and the participants qualified (among top 6) for next round.

In R4 and R5 only one improvement happened, (which means the last participant cannot become first until he beats all the others).

Hence, R2 to R3 and R3 to R4 we have a double, which means P10 has to be 1st in R3 (double). His throw in R2 is > 87.2.

Also P8 gets 6th rank in R3 and is the first to throw in R4. Since P8 has qualified, he beats P6 and P3 but not P1. So his throw in R3 is > 82.5 but < 82.9

In R4 P8 is the first one to throw. In R3 either P1 or P10 will be the best but P10 has not won a medal and there are only 3 improvements possible in the second phase.

So P10 cannot throw more than 88.6. Hence, P1 is the best in R3.

So the results of the first three rounds can be tabulated as follows:

Round 1		Round 2		Round 3	
P1	82.9	P7	87.2	P10	$87.2 < w < 87.6$
P2	-	P5	86.4	P7	87.2
P3	81.5	P9	84.1	P5	86.4
P4	-	P1	82.9	P9	84.1
P5	86.4	P6	82.5	P1	88.6
P6	82.5	P3	81.5	P8	$82.5 < y < 82.9$
P7	87.2	P2	-	P6	82.5
P8	-	P4	-	P3	81.5
P9	84.1	P8	qualified in top 6	P2	-
P10	-	P10	qualified in top 6	P4	-

Given that the gold and bronze medalists improved their scores in the 5th and the 6th rounds respectively. One medalist improved in the 4th round. Hence, we can say that the three medal winners are out of P1, P5, P7 and P9. Only 3 improvements and every improvement is by the same difference (say x). We see that P9 (84.1) is way behind the other three, so he cannot improve and become a medal winner, which means the three medal winners are P1, P5 and P7.

Let us see their throws at the beginning of R4.

P1 (88.6), P5 (86.4) and P7(87.2)

We have to make 3 improvements and keep each improvement the same.

It is obvious that we cannot improve the largest number that corresponds to P1.

Let the lowest (P7) improve in the 4th round (87.2 + x)

Now if we look at the throw of P5, it is obvious that he cannot be the gold medalist.

Also the difference between the throws of each of the medalists in the final tally is 1 m.

Let us assume P5 is the bronze medalist (one improvement in R6) and P1 is the silver medalist (no improvement in R5 or R6). Hence, P7 is the gold medalist. So his score improves in R5.

We have (87.2 + 2x), 88.6 and (86.4 + x). For the difference to be 1 m, the value of x has to be 1.2.

So the final lengths thrown by the gold, silver and bronze medalists are 89.6, 88.6 and 87.6.

(Let us go back to R3 now, the length of throw of P10 has to be less than 87.6).

Let us represent all the data for the remaining 3 rounds also in the form of a table:

Round 1		Round 2		Round 3		Round 4		Round 5		Round 6	
P1	82.9	P7	87.2	P10	87.2<w<87.6	P8	82.5<y<82.9	P8	82.5<y<82.9	P8	82.5<y<82.9
P2	-	P5	86.4	P7	87.2	P9	84.1	P9	84.1	P9	84.1
P3	81.5	P9	84.1	P5	86.4	P5	86.4	P5	86.4	P10	87.2<w<87.6
P4	-	P1	82.9	P9	84.1	P7	88.4	P10	87.2<w<87.6	P5	87.6
P5	86.4	P6	82.5	P1	88.6	P10	87.2<w<87.6	P7	89.6	P1	88.6
P6	82.5	P3	81.5	P8	82.5<y<82.9	P1	88.6	P10	88.6	P7	89.6
P7	87.2	P2	-	P6	82.5	-	-	-	-	-	-
P8	-	P4	-	P3	81.5	-	-	-	-	-	-
P9	84.1	P8	qualified in top 6	P2	-	-	-	-	-	-	-
P10	-	P10	qualified in top 6	P4	-	-	-	-	-	-	-

5. Between 82.5 and 82.9

6. Improved by 2.4.

For questions 7 to 10:

Total project month for each person:

A = 2 + 2 + 5 = 9 months

B = 2 + 4 + 3 = 9 months

D = 3 + 3 + 2 + 1 = 9 months

T = 2 + 2 + 3 + 2 = 9 months

Total employee month for each project:

P1 = 2 + 2 + 2 = 6 months

P2 = 3 + 2 = 5 = 5 months

P3 = 2 + 4 + 3 = 9 months

P4 = 5 + 2 + 3 = 10 months

P5 = 3 + 1 + 2 = 6 months

7. Statement 1 is true.
Statement 2 is false.
So option 4 is correct.

8. There is no overlap for A, B and D whereas there is an overlap for T in the month of September.

9. We can observe from the graph that the duration in months of each project is:

P1 = 3 months

P2 = 3 months

P3 = 5 months

P4 = 5 months

P5 = 4 months

So P1 and P2 have the same duration whereas P3 and P4 have the same duration.

10. Annual completion index for each person:

A = 800/9

B = 770/9

D = 870/9

T = 860/9

Hence, decreasing order is D > T > A > B.

For questions 11 to 16:

Based on the information given we can say that if SME creates a question then six cases are possible:

A	B	K	Accept / Reject
√	√	–	√
√	×	√	√
√	×	×	×
×	√	√	√
×	√	×	×
×	×	–	×

If A creates, B reviews first and then K.

If B creates, K reviews first and then A.

If K creates, A reviews first and then B.

Note that there is a cyclic pattern in reviewing.

Based on the information given regarding the questions we can create the following table:

Question	√ or ×	A	B	K	Created by
Q.1	√	–	–	√	B
Q.2	×	√ or ×	√ or ×	×	SME
Q.3	√	√	–	×	B
Q.4	√	√ or ×	√ or ×	√	SME
Q.5	√	–	–	√	B
Q.6	×	×	×	–	SME / K
Q.7	√	–	×	√	A
Q.8	√	√ or ×	√ or ×	√	SME
Q.9	×	–	×	×	A
Q.10	√	√	–	–	K
Q.11	×	×	–	×	B
Q.12	×	–	×	×	A
Q.13	√	×	√	–	SME / K

11. Three questions (q.7, 9 and 12) were definitely created by Amal, namely.

12. One question (q.10) was definitely created by Komal.

13. Three questions (q.2, 4, 8) were definitely created by SME.

14. Four questions (q.6, 7, 9, 12) were definitely disapproved by Bimal.

15. Amal's minimum approval ratio = 2/8 = 0.25; maximum approval ratio = 6/8 = 0.75.

16. Five questions (q.3, 7, 9, 11, 12) which were created by Amal or Bimal were definitely disapproved by one of the other reviewers.

17. Given that 5 ml each from A and B are mixed and presence of I is detected in the mixture, which means that the impurity in the mixture is 10% or more. Since A is 100% pure, it means that purity of B is 80% or less.

Given that bottle B contains 50 ml of liquid, so impurity present is 20% or more.

Hence, the impurity in B is 20 ml or more.

18. Given 4 bottles that contain only P or only I. To find the minimum number of tests to check if they are collectively ready for dispatch.

Mix one part each from all 4 bottles. If there are 3P and one I, then purity of the mixture is 75%, which will be detected.

If more than one bottle contains impurity, then the presence of purity of the mixture will be less than 75%, so it will be detected.

Hence, only one test is required to ascertain whether the 4 bottles are ready for dispatch.

19. Given 4 bottles such that 3 bottles contain 100% pure liquid and one contains 80% pure liquid. To find the minimum number of tests to identify the impure bottle.

Case 1	Test 1 (A + B) √	Test 2 (A + C) √	D is impure
		Test 2 (A + C) ×	C is impure
Case 2	Test 1 (A + B) ×	Test 2 (A + C) ×	A is impure
		Test 2 (A + C) √	B is impure

Hence, only 2 tests are required to detect the impure bottle.

20. Given that out of 4 bottles either 1 or 2 contain 100% pure liquid, which means either 3 or 2 contain 85% pure liquid. Equal quantities of liquid from all 4 bottles are mixed and tested.

Case 1: If one bottle with 100% liquid and three bottles have 85% liquid are there, then weighted average = (100 + 3 x 85)/4 = 355/4 < 90 (impurity will be detected).

Case 2: If two bottles with 100% liquid and two bottles have 85% liquid are there, then weighted average = (200 + 2 x 85)/4 = 370/4 > 90 (impurity will not be detected).

QA

1. If no conditions are there, then total number of ways in which 4 digits can be chosen from 1, 2 and 3 = 3^4

According to the question both 2 and 3 have to be present, so all numbers formed using (1, 2) and (1, 3) are rejected. The total number of such cases = $2^4 + 2^4$, out of which 1111 occurs in both sets.

Hence, total number of ways of forming a 4 digit number using 1, 2 and 3 such that 2 and 3 are always present = $3^4 - 2^4 - 2^4 + 1 = 50$.

2. 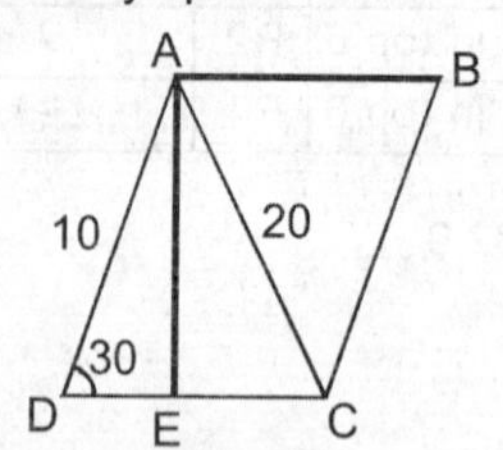

In the figure,

sin 30 = AE/10 = 1/2 ⇒ AE = 5 cm.

cos 30 = DE/10 = √3/2 ⇒ DE = 5√3.

In triangle AEC, EC = √(202 – 52) = √375 = 5√15

CD = 5√3 + 5√15

Area = 5 × (5√3 + 5√15) = 25(√3 + √15) sq. cm.

3. Given that the interest accrued by Raju"s investment in Bank B is equal to the interest accrued in Bank A for one year.

Bank A rate = 6% ; take time as 1 year.

⇒ A = P[1.03]2 = P * 1.0609

⇒ Rate in Bank B = 6.09%

⇒ Rate in Bank C = 2 x 6.09%

⇒ Required interest = (10000 × 2 × 6.09 × 2)/100 = Rs.2,436.

4. Let the length and breadth of the rectangle be a and b.

Given a × b = 60000

Cost = 200 × a + 100 (2b + a) = 100 [3a + 2b]

We need to minimize the cost.

Given a × b = 60000

Also AM ≥ GM ⇒ (a + b)/2 ≥ √(ab)

Here (3a + 2b)/2 ≥ √(60000 × 6)

Min will be when 3a = 2b = 600.

Lowest cost = 100[600 + 600] = Rs.1,20,000.

5. $$\left[\frac{\log_{15} a + \log_{32} a}{\log_{15} a \log_{32} a}\right] = 4$$

$$\Rightarrow \frac{1}{\log_{32} a} + \frac{1}{\log_{15} a} = 4$$

$\Rightarrow \log_a (32 \times 15) = 4 \Rightarrow a^4 = 32 \times 15 = 480$

Now, 480 his between 4^4 and 5^4.

Hence, $4 < a < 5$.

6. $(\sqrt[7]{10})(\sqrt[7]{10})^2...(\sqrt[7]{10})^n > 999$

$10^{\frac{1}{7}+\frac{2}{7}+\frac{3}{7}+...+\frac{n}{7}} > 999$

$10^{\left[\frac{n(n+1)}{2\times7}\right]} > 999$

Take $999 \approx 10^3$

$10^{\left[\frac{n(n+1)}{2\times7}\right]} > 10^3$

$\Rightarrow \frac{n(n+1)}{14} > 3$

$\Rightarrow n(n + 1) > 42$

Hence, smallest value of n = 6.

7.

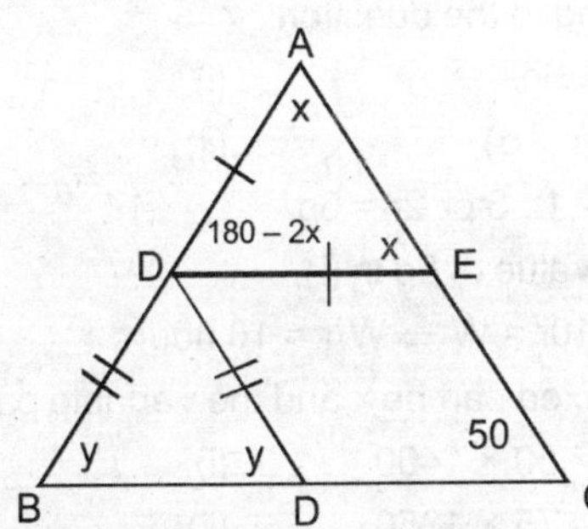

In the figure x + y + 50 = 180.

So x + y = 130

180 – 2y + ∠FDE + 180 – 2x = 180

⇒ ∠FDE = 2(x + y) – 180 = 80.

8. Give that Anil and Barun alone can do the work in 12 days and 16 days respectively.

Along with Chandu they complete the work in 6 days.

Let the total work be 48 units (LCM of 12 and 16).

Together they do 48/6 = 8 units in one day.

Out of these 8 units Anil does 48/12 = 4 units and Barun does 48/16 = 3 units.

So work done in a day by Chandu = 8 – 7 = 1 unit, which means Chandu takes 48 days to complete the work alone.

Ratio of wages of Anil : Barun : Chandu is in proportion to the work done = 4 : 3 :

Hence, Chandu's share = 1/8 × 24000 = Rs.3,000.

9. Given that 5 of them got the same scores. Let the score be x.

⇒ 5x + [30 + 31 + ….. + 49] = 25 × 50

⇒ x = 92.

10. Given $f(x) = x^2 - 7x$ and $g(x) = x + 3$

$f(g(x)) - 3x = (x + 3)^2 - 7(x + 3) - 3x = x^2 - 4x - 12$

So the minimum value will be at x = –b/2a = –(–4)/2 = 2

This function will have a graph like this:

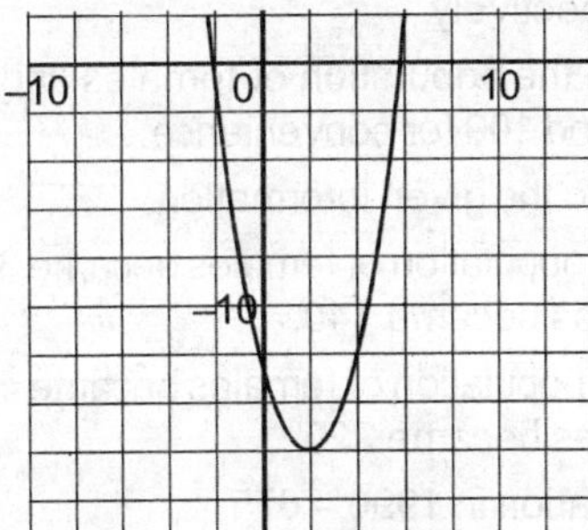

At x = 2 the value of the above function will be = 4 –4 × 2 – 12 = –16.

11. Let the speeds of Mira and Amal be Sm and Sa respectively.

Let the length of the track be x m.

According to the question:

3/4 × (Sm – Sa) = 3x ⇒ Sm – Sa = 4x …(i)

1/20 x (Sm + Sa) = x ⇒ Sm + Sa = 20x …(ii)

Solving (i) and (ii) we get Sm = 8x ⇒ 8 rounds of the track.

In one hour Mira walks 8 rounds of the track.

12. Perimeter is 40 m, so the length of one side is 10 m.

Given Area = $1/2 \times d_1 \times d_2 = 96 \Rightarrow d_1 \times d_1 = 192$.

Using Pythagoras theorem we get $(d_1^2 + d_2^2)/4 = a^2$.

$\Rightarrow (d_1^2 + d_2^2) = 400$

$\Rightarrow (d_1 + d_2)^2 = 400 + 384 = 784 \Rightarrow d_1 + d_2 = 28$

Hence, required cost = 125 × 28 = Rs.3,500.

13. Let the remaining number of matches be x

Using alligation:

Over Upcoming

30% 60%

50%

10 20

Given 40 : x = 10 : 20 ⇒ x = 80.

Out of 80 they win 90% ⇒ 0.9 × 80 = 72

Out of 40 they won 30% ⇒ 0.3 × 40 = 12

Hence, total number of matches won = 84.

14. Given that 40% increase in males and 20% increase in females from 1970 to 1980 results in a 25% increase in the total population. So using alligation we can find the ratio of the initial population of females and males.

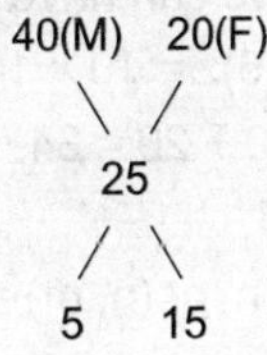

Hence, the initial population of females and males is 3 : 1 respectively.

Let us take the population of females and males to be 300 and 100 for convenience.

According to the given information,

In 1980 the population of females became 360 and that of males became 140.

In 1990 the population of females became 450 and that of males became 225.

Total population in 1990 = 675.

Required percentage increase in population from 1970 = (675 – 400)/400 × 100 = 68.75%.

15. Given $x_1 = -1$ and $x_{n+1} = x_n + (n-1)$

$\Rightarrow x_2 - x_1 = 0 \Rightarrow x_3 - x_2 = 1$

.....

$\Rightarrow x_{100} - x_{99} = 98$

On adding all the above we get, $x_{100} - x_1$

$= 0 + 1 + 2 + \ldots + 98$

$\Rightarrow x_{100} = (98 \times 99)/2 - 1 = 4850.$

16. Let the weight of the alloy used be x kg and percentage of silver in it be k%.

According to the question:

(kx + 300)/(x + 3) = 90 ...(i)

(kx + 180)/(x + 2) = 84 ...(ii)

Solving (i) and (ii) we get, k = 80 and x = 3.

17. Let the number of large shirts be n and small shirts be (64 – n). Let the price of large and small shirts be Rs.x and Rs.(x - 50) respectively.

Given that nx = 5000 and (64 – n)(x – 50) = 1800

The sum of prices of a large and a small shirt = 2x + 50

Going by the options:

If (2x + 50) = 100, x = 75 and n is not an integer. So this is not possible.

If (2x + 50) is equal to 225 or 175, we do not get integer values for n.

If (2x + 50) = 200, we get x = 125 and n = 40 which satisfies both equations.

18. Rahul worked for 8 hours and Gautam worked for 6 hours.

Let units of work done by Rahul and Gautam be r and g respectively.

According to the question:

W = 8r + 6g ...(i)

W = 7.5(r + g) ...(ii)

⇒ r : g = 1 : 3 or 2r = 6g

Put this value of 6g in (i).

We get 10r = W ⇒ W/r = 10 hours.

19. Let the fixed part be x and the variable part be y.

x + 50y = 50 × 1400 ...(i)

x + 75y = 75 × 1350 ...(ii)

In case of 80 persons, x + 80y = k × 80

Solving (i) and (ii) we get x = 7500 and y = 1250.

Profit = 80 × 1600 – [7500 + 80 × 1250] = 128000 – 107500 = 20500.

20. Given 3x + 2|y| + y = 7 and x + |x| + 3y = 1

If x > 0, y > 0	3x + 2y + y = 7 x + x + 3y = 1	We get x = 6 and y = –ve This is a contradiction as y < 0.
If x > 0, y < 0	3x – 2y + y = 7 x + x + 3y = 1	We get x = 2 and y = –1. This is a possible solution
If x < 0, y > 0	3x + 2y + y = 7 x – x + 3y = 1	We get x = 2 and y = 1/3 This is a contradiction as x > 0.
If x < 0, y < 0	–3x – 2y + y = 7 x – x + 3y = 1	We get y = 1/3 and x = –ve This is a contradiction as y > 0.

So x + 2y = 2 - 2 = 0 for (x, y) = (2, -1).

21. According to the question: There are three sizes x, y and z.

Let the prices of the three sizes be 2k, 5k and z, initially and $10k^2z = 800$.

After the change; (2k + 6)(5k + 6)z = 3200.

Let z = 20

If xyz = 800, putting z = 20, we can have x = 4 and y = 10, which satisfy 2k and 5k.

After increase, (2k + 6)(5k + 6)z = 10 × 16 × 20 = 3200 is also true.

Hence, required sum = 4 + 10 + 20 = 34.

22. Given : |1 + mn| < |m + n| < 5

This inequality is true for (m, n) or (n, m) = (±2, 0), (±3, 0), (±4, 0)

Hence, there are 12 possible pairs of integers.

CAT 2022 SOLVED PAPER (SLOT-1)

Section I: VARC

Question Numbers (1 to 4): The passage below is accompanied by a set of questions. Choose the best answer to each question.

Stoicism was founded in 300 BC by the Greek philosopher Zeno and survived into the Roman era until about AD 300. According to the Stoics, emotions consist of two movements. The first movement is the immediate feeling and other reactions (e.g., physiological response) that occur when a stimulus or event occurs. For instance, consider what could have happened if an army general accused Marcus Aurelius of treason in front of other officers. The first movement for Marcus may have been (internal) surprise and anger in response to this insult, accompanied perhaps by some involuntary physiological and expressive responses such as face flushing and a movement of the eyebrows. The second movement is what one does next about the emotion. Second movement behaviors occur after thinking and are under one's control. Examples of second movements for Marcus might have included a plot to seek revenge, actions signifying deference and appeasement, or perhaps proceeding as he would have proceeded whether or not this event occurred: continuing to lead the Romans in a way that Marcus Aurelius believed best benefited them. In the Stoic view, choosing a reasoned, unemotional response as the second movement is the only appropriate response.

The Stoics believed that to live the good life and be a good person, we need to free ourselves of nearly all desires such as too much desire for money, power, or sexual gratification. Prior to second movements, we can consider what is important in life. Money, power, and excessive sexual gratification are not important. Character, rationality, and kindness are important. The Epicureans, first associated with the Greek philosopher Epicurus . . . held a similar view, believing that people should enjoy simple pleasures, such as good conversation, friendship, food, and wine, but not be indulgent in these pursuits and not follow passion for those things that hold no real value like power and money. As Oatley (2004) states, "the Epicureans articulated a view–enjoyment of relationship with friends, of things that are real rather than illusory, simple rather than artificially inflated, possible rather than vanishingly unlikely–that is certainly relevant today" . . . In sum, these ancient Greek and Roman philosophers saw emotions, especially strong ones, as potentially dangerous. They viewed emotions as experiences that needed to be [reined] in and controlled.

As Oatley (2004) points out, the Stoic idea bears some similarity to Buddhism. Buddha, living in India in the 6th century BC, argued for cultivating a certain attitude that decreases the probability of (in Stoic terms) destructive second movements. Through meditation and the right attitude, one allows emotions to happen to oneself (it is impossible to prevent this), but one is advised to observe the emotions without necessarily acting on them; one achieves some distance and decides what has value and what does not have value. Additionally, the Stoic idea of developing virtue in oneself, of becoming a good person, which the Stoics believed we could do because we have a touch of the divine, laid the foundation for the three monotheistic religions: Judaism, Christianity, and Islam . . . As with Stoicism, tenets of these religions include controlling our emotions lest we engage in sinful behavior.

1. On the basis of the passage, which one of the following statements can be regarded as true?

(1) There were no Stoics in India at the time of the Roman civilisation.

(2) The Epicureans believed in controlling all emotions.

(3) The Stoic influences can be seen in multiple religions.

(4) The Stoics valorised the pursuit of money, power, and sexual gratification.

2. Which one of the following statements would be an accurate inference from the example of Marcus Aurelius?

(1) Marcus Aurelius was humiliated by the accusation of treason in front of the other officers.

(2) Marcus Aurelius was a Stoic whose philosophy survived into the Roman era.

(3) Marcus Aurelius was one of the leaders of the Roman army.

(4) Marcus Aurelius plotted revenge in his quest for justice.

3. "Through meditation and the right attitude, one allows emotions to happen to oneself (it is impossible to prevent this), but one is advised to observe the emotions without necessarily acting on them; one achieves some distance and decides what has value and what does not have value." In the context of the passage, which one of the following is not a possible implication of the quoted statement?
   (1) Emotional responses can make it difficult to distinguish valuable experiences from valueless experiences.
   (2) Meditation allows certain out-of-body experiences that permit us to gain the distance necessary to control our emotions.
   (3) The observation of emotions in a distant manner corresponds to the second movement referred to earlier in the passage.
   (4) "Meditation and the right attitude", in this instance, implies an initially passive reception of all experiences.
4. Which one of the following statements, if false, could be seen as contradicting the facts/arguments in the passage?
   (1) In the Stoic view, choosing a reasoned, unemotional response as the first movement is an appropriate response to emotional situations.
   (2) The Greek philosopher Zeno survived into the Roman era until about AD 300.
   (3) Despite practising meditation and cultivating the right attitude, emotions cannot ever be controlled.
   (4) In the Epicurean view, indulging in simple pleasures is not desirable.

Question Numbers (5 to 8): The passage below is accompanied by a set of questions. Choose the best answer to each question.

Critical theory of technology is a political theory of modernity with a normative dimension. It belongs to a tradition extending from Marx to Foucault and Habermas according to which advances in the formal claims of human rights take center stage while in the background centralization of ever more powerful public institutions and private organizations imposes an authoritarian social order.

Marx attributed this trajectory to the capitalist rationalization of production. Today it marks many institutions besides the factory and every modern political system, including so-called socialist systems. This trajectory arose from the problems of command over a disempowered and deskilled labor force; but everywhere [that] masses are organized - whether it be Foucault's prisons or Habermas's public sphere - the same pattern prevails. Technological design and development is shaped by this pattern as the material base of a distinctive social order. Marcuse would later point to a "project" as the basis of what he called rather confusingly "technological rationality." Releasing technology from this project is a democratic political task.

In accordance with this general line of thought, critical theory of technology regards technologies as an environment rather than as a collection of tools. We live today with and even within technologies that determine our way of life. Along with the constant pressures to build centers of power, many other social values and meanings are inscribed in technological design. A hermeneutics of technology must make explicit the meanings implicit in the devices we use and the rituals they script. Social histories of technologies such as the bicycle, artificial lighting or firearms have made important contributions to this type of analysis. Critical theory of technology attempts to build a methodological approach on the lessons of these histories.

As an environment, technologies shape their inhabitants. In this respect, they are comparable to laws and customs. Each of these institutions can be said to represent those who live under their sway through privileging certain dimensions of their human nature. Laws of property represent the interest in ownership and control. Customs such as parental authority represent the interest of childhood in safety and growth. Similarly, the automobile represents its users in so far as they are interested in mobility. Interests such as these constitute the version of human nature sanctioned by society.

This notion of representation does not imply an eternal human nature. The concept of nature as non-identity in the Frankfurt School suggests an alternative. On these terms, nature is what lies at the limit of history, at the point at which society loses the capacity to imprint its meanings on things and control them effectively. The reference here is, of course, not to the nature of natural science, but to the lived nature in which we find ourselves and which we are. This nature reveals itself as that which cannot be totally encompassed by the machinery of society. For the Frankfurt School, human nature, in all its transcending force, emerges out of a historical context as that context is [depicted] in illicit joys, struggles and pathologies. We can perhaps admit a less romantic . . . conception in which those dimensions of human nature recognized by society are also granted theoretical legitimacy.

5. Which one of the following statements best reflects the main argument of the fourth paragraph of the passage?
   (1) Automobiles represent the interest in mobility present in human nature.

(2) Technological environments privilege certain dimensions of human nature as effectively as laws and customs.

(3) Technology, laws, and customs are comparable, but dissimilar phenomena.

(4) Technology, laws, and customs are not unlike each other if considered as institutions.

6. Which one of the following statements contradicts the arguments of the passage?

(1) Marx's understanding of the capitalist rationalisation of production and Marcuse's understanding of a "project" of "technological rationality" share theoretical inclinations.

(2) Paradoxically, the capitalist rationalisation of production is a mark of so-called socialist systems as well.

(3) Masses are organised in patterns set by Foucault's prisons and Habermas' public sphere.

(4) The problems of command over a disempowered and deskilled labour force gave rise to similar patterns of the capitalist rationalisation of production wherever masses were organised.

7. Which one of the following statements could be inferred as supporting the arguments of the passage?

(1) It is not human nature, but human culture that is represented by institutions such as law and custom.

(2) The romantic conception of nature referred to by the passage is the one that requires theoretical legitimacy.

(3) Technologies form the environmental context and shape the contours of human society.

(4) Nature decides the point at which society loses its capacity to control history.

8. All of the following claims can be inferred from the passage, EXCEPT:

(1) analyses of technologies must engage with their social histories to be able to reveal their implicit and explicit meanings for us.

(2) the critical theory of technology argues that, as issues of human rights become more prominent, we lose sight of the ways in which the social order becomes more authoritarian.

(3) the significance of parental authority to children's safety does not therefore imply that parental authority is a permanent aspect of human nature.

(4) technologies seek to privilege certain dimensions of human nature at a high cost to lived nature.

Question Numbers (9 to 12): The passage below is accompanied by a set of questions. Choose the best answer to each question.

Stories concerning the Undead have always been with us. From out of the primal darkness of Mankind's earliest years, come whispers of eerie creatures, not quite alive (or alive in a way which we can understand), yet not quite dead either. These may have been ancient and primitive deities who dwelt deep in the surrounding forests and in remote places, or simply those deceased who refused to remain in their tombs and who wandered about the countryside, physically tormenting and frightening those who were still alive. Mostly they were ill-defined–strange sounds in the night beyond the comforting glow of the fire, or a shape, half-glimpsed in the twilight along the edge of an encampment. They were vague and indistinct, but they were always there with the power to terrify and disturb. They had the power to touch the minds of our early ancestors and to fill them with dread. Such fear formed the basis of the earliest tales although the source and exact nature of such terrors still remained very vague.

And as Mankind became more sophisticated, leaving the gloom of their caves and forming themselves into recognizable communities–towns, cities, whole cultures–so the Undead travelled with them, inhabiting their folklore just as they had in former times. Now they began to take on more definite shapes. They became walking cadavers; the physical embodiment of former deities and things which had existed alongside Man since the Creation. Some still remained vague and ill-defined but, as Mankind strove to explain the horror which it felt towards them, such creatures emerged more readily into the light.

In order to confirm their abnormal status, many of the Undead were often accorded attributes, which defied the natural order of things–the power to transform themselves into other shapes, the ability to sustain themselves by drinking human blood, and the ability to influence human minds across a distance. Such powers–described as supernatural–only [lent] an added dimension to the terror that humans felt regarding them.

And it was only natural, too, that the Undead should become connected with the practice of magic. From very early times, Shamans and witchdoctors had claimed at least some power and control over the spirits of departed ancestors, and this has continued down into more "civilized" times. Formerly, the invisible spirits and forces that thronged around men's earliest encampments, had spoken "through" the tribal Shamans but now, as entities in their own right, they were subject to magical control and could be physically summoned by a competent sorcerer. However, the relationship between the magician and an Undead creature was often a very tenuous and uncertain one. Some sorcerers might have even become Undead entities once they died, but they might also have been susceptible to the powers of other magicians when they did.

From the Middle Ages and into the Age of Enlightenment, theories of the Undead continued to grow and develop. Their names became more familiar–werewolf, vampire, ghoul–each one certain to strike fear into the hearts of ordinary humans.

9. Which one of the following statements best describes what the passage is about?

(1) The passage describes the failure of human beings to fully comprehend their environment.

(2) The writer describes the ways in which the Undead come to be associated with Shamans and the practice of magic.

(3) The writer discusses the transition from primitive thinking to the Age of Enlightenment.

(4) The passage discusses the evolution of theories of the Undead from primitive thinking to the Age of Enlightenment.

10. "In order to confirm their abnormal status, many of the Undead were often accorded attributes, which defied the natural order of things . . ." Which one of the following best expresses the claim made in this statement?

(1) According the Undead an abnormal status is to reject the natural order of things.

(2) Human beings conceptualise the Undead as possessing abnormal features.

(3) The natural attributes of the Undead are rendered abnormal by changing their status.

(4) The Undead are deified in nature's order by giving them divine attributes.

11. All of the following statements, if false, could be seen as being in accordance with the passage, EXCEPT:

(1) the relationship between Shamans and the Undead was believed to be a strong and stable one.

(2) the transition from the Middle Ages to the Age of Enlightenment saw new theories of the Undead.

(3) the Undead remained vague and ill-defined, even as Mankind strove to understand the horror they inspired.

(4) the growing sophistication of Mankind meant that humans stopped believing in the Undead.

12. Which one of the following observations is a valid conclusion to draw from the statement, "From out of the primal darkness of Mankind's earliest years, come whispers of eerie creatures, not quite alive (or alive in a way which we can understand), yet not quite dead either."?

(1) Mankind's primal years were marked by creatures alive with eerie whispers, but seen only in the darkness.

(2) Long ago, eerie creatures used to whisper in the primal darkness that they were not quite dead.

(3) Mankind's early years were marked by a belief in the existence of eerie creatures that were neither quite alive nor dead.

(4) We can understand the lives of the eerie creatures in Mankind's early years through their whispers in the darkness.

Question Numbers (13 to 16): The passage below is accompanied by a set of questions. Choose the best answer to each question.

The Chinese have two different concepts of a copy. Fangzhipin . . . are imitations where the difference from the original is obvious. These are small models or copies that can be purchased in a museum shop, for example. The second concept for a copy is fuzhipin . . . They are exact reproductions of the original, which, for the Chinese, are of equal value to the original. It has absolutely no negative connotations. The discrepancy with regard to the understanding of what a copy is has often led to misunderstandings and arguments between China and Western museums. The Chinese often send copies abroad instead of originals, in the firm belief that they are not essentially different from the originals. The rejection that then comes from the Western museums is perceived by the Chinese as an insult. . . .

The Far Eastern notion of identity is also very confusing to the Western observer. The Ise Grand Shrine [in Japan] is 1,300 years old for the millions of Japanese people who go there on pilgrimage every year. But in reality this temple complex is completely rebuilt from scratch every 20 years. . . .

The cathedral of Freiburg Minster in southwest Germany is covered in scaffolding almost all year round. The sandstone from which it is built is a very soft, porous material that does not withstand natural erosion by rain and wind. After a while, it crumbles. As a result, the cathedral is continually being examined for damage, and eroded stones are replaced. And in the cathedral's dedicated workshop, copies of the damaged sandstone figures are constantly being produced. Of course, attempts are made to preserve the stones from the Middle Ages for as long as possible. But at some point they, too, are removed and replaced with new stones.

Fundamentally, this is the same operation as with the Japanese shrine, except in this case the production of a replica takes place very slowly and over long periods of time. . . . In the field of art as well, the idea of an unassailable original developed historically in the Western world. Back in the 17th century [in the West], excavated artworks from antiquity were treated quite differently from today. They were not restored in a way that was faithful to the original. Instead, there was massive intervention in these works, changing their appearance. . . .

It is probably this intellectual position that explains why Asians have far fewer scruples about cloning than Europeans. The South Korean cloning researcher Hwang Woo-suk, who attracted worldwide attention with his cloning experiments in 2004, is a Buddhist. He found a great deal of support and followers among Buddhists, while Christians called for a ban on human cloning. . . . Hwang legitimised his cloning experiments with his religious affiliation: 'I am Buddhist, and I have no philosophical problem with cloning. And as you know, the basis of Buddhism is that life is recycled through reincarnation. In some ways, I think, therapeutic cloning restarts the circle of life.'

13. Which one of the following statements does not correctly express the similarity between the Ise Grand Shrine and the cathedral of Freiburg Minster?

(1) Both were built as places of worship.

(2) Both can be regarded as very old structures.

(3) Both are continually undergoing restoration.

(4) Both will one day be completely rebuilt.

14. The value that the modern West assigns to "an unassailable original" has resulted in all of the following EXCEPT:

(1) it allows regular employment for certain craftsmen.

(2) it discourages them from making interventions in ancient art.

(3) it discourages them from carrying out human cloning.

(4) it discourages them from simultaneous displays of multiple copies of a painting.

15. Which one of the following scenarios is unlikely to follow from the arguments in the passage?

(1) A 20th century Japanese Buddhist monk would value a reconstructed shrine as the original.

(2) A 17th century British painter would have no problem adding personal touches when restoring an ancient Roman painting.

(3) A 17th century French artist who adhered to a Christian worldview would need to be completely true to the original intent of a painting when restoring it.

(4) A 21st century Christian scientist is likely to oppose cloning because of his philosophical orientation.

16. Based on the passage, which one of the following copies would a Chinese museum be unlikely to consider as having less value than the original?

(1) Pablo Picasso's painting of Vincent van Gogh's original painting, identical in every respect.

(2) Pablo Picasso's painting of Vincent van Gogh's original painting, bearing Picasso's signature.

(3) Pablo Picasso's miniaturised, but otherwise faithful and accurate painting of Vincent van Gogh's original painting.

(4) Pablo Picasso's photograph of Vincent van Gogh's original painting, printed to exactly the same scale.

17. The four sentences (labelled 1, 2, 3 and 4) below, when properly sequenced, would yield a coherent paragraph. Decide on the proper sequencing of the order of the sentences and key in the sequence of the four numbers as your answer:

(1) Fish skin collagen has excellent thermo-stability and tensile strength making it ideal for use as bandage that adheres to the skin and adjusts to body movements.

(2) Collagen, one of the main structural proteins in connective tissues in the human body, is well known for promoting skin regeneration.

(3) Fish skin swims in here as diseases and bacteria that affect fish are different from most human pathogens.

(4) The risk of introducing disease agents into other species through the use of pig and cow collagen proteins for wound healing has inhibited its broader applications in the medical field.

18. The passage given below is followed by four alternate summaries. Choose the option that best captures the essence of the passage.

Petitioning is an expeditious democratic tradition, used frequently in prior centuries, by which citizens can bring issues directly to governments. As expressions of collective voice, they support procedural democracy by shaping agendas. They can also recruit citizens to causes, give voice to the voteless, and apply the discipline of rhetorical argument that clarifies a point of view. By contrast, elections are limited in several respects: they involve only a few candidates, and thus fall far short of a representative democracy. Further, voters' choices are not specific to particular policies or laws, and elections are episodic, whereas the voice of the people needs to be heard and integrated constantly into democratic government.

(1) Citizens become less inclined to petitioning as it enables vocal citizens to shape political agendas, but this needs to change to strengthen democracies today.

(2) Petitioning has been important to democratic functioning, as it supplements the electoral process by enabling ongoing engagement with the government.

(3) By giving citizens greater control over shaping political and democratic agendas, political petitions are invaluable as they represent an ideal form of a representative democracy.

(4) Petitioning is definitely more representative of the collective voice, and the functioning of democratic government could improve if we relied more on petitioning rather than holding periodic elections.

19. There is a sentence that is missing in the paragraph below. Look at the paragraph and decide in which blank (option 1, 2, 3, or 4) the following sentence would best fit.

Sentence: Easing the anxiety and pressure of having a "big day" is part of the appeal for many couples who marry in secret.

Paragraph: Wedding season is upon us and - after two years of Covid chaos that saw nuptials scaled back- you may think the temptation would be to go all out. ___**(1)**___. But instead of expanding the guest list, many couples are opting to have entirely secret ceremonies. With Covid case numbers remaining high and the cost of living crisis meaning that many couples are feeling the pinch, it's no wonder that some are less than eager to send out invites. ___**(2)**___. Plus, it can't hurt that in celebrity circles getting married in secret is all the rage. ___**(3)**___. "I would definitely say that secret weddings are becoming more common," says Landis Bejar, the founder of a therapy practice, which specialises in helping brides and grooms manage wedding stress. "People are looking for ways to get out of the spotlight and avoid the pomp and circumstance of weddings. ___**(4)**___. They just want to get to the part where they are married."

(1) Option 1 (2) Option 2
(3) Option 3 (4) Option 4

20. The four sentences (labelled 1, 2, 3 and 4) below, when properly sequenced, would yield a coherent paragraph. Decide on the proper sequencing of the order of the sentences and key in the sequence of the four numbers as your answer:

(1) The creative element in product design has become of paramount importance as it is one of the few ways a firm or industry can sustain a competitive advantage over its rivals.

(2) In fact, the creative element in the value of world industry would be larger still, if we added the contribution of the creative element in other industries, such as the design of tech accessories.

(3) The creative industry is receiving a lot of attention today as its growth rate is faster than that of the world economy as a whole.

(4) It is for this reason that today's trade issues are increasingly involving intellectual property, as Western countries have an interest in protecting their revenues along with freeing trade in non-tangibles.

21. The passage given below is followed by four alternate summaries. Choose the option that best captures the essence of the passage.

It's not that modern historians of medieval Africa have been ignorant about contacts between Ethiopia and Europe; they just had the power dynamic reversed. The traditional narrative stressed Ethiopia as weak and in trouble in the face of aggression from external forces, so Ethiopia sought military assistance from their fellow Christians to the north. But the real story, buried in plain sight in medieval diplomatic texts, simply had not yet been put together by modern scholars. Recent research pushes scholars of medieval Europe to imagine a much more richly connected medieval world: at the beginning of the so-called Age of Exploration, there is evidence that the kings of Ethiopia were sponsoring their own missions of diplomacy, faith and commerce.

(1) Medieval texts have documented how strong connections between the Christian communities of Ethiopia and Europe were invaluable in establishing military and trade links between the two civilisations.

(2) Historians were under the illusion that Ethiopia needed military protection from their neighbours, but in fact the country had close commercial and religious connections with them.

(3) Medieval texts have been 'cherry-picked' to promote a view of Ethiopia as weak and in need of Europe's military help with aggressive neighbours, but recent studies reveal it was a well-connected and outward-looking culture.

(4) Medieval historical sources selectively promoted the narrative that powerful European forces were called on to protect weak African civilisations such as Ethiopia, but this is far from reality.

22. The passage given below is followed by four alternate summaries. Choose the option that best captures the essence of the passage.

All that we think we know about how life hangs together is really some kind of illusion that we have perpetrated on ourselves because of our limited vision. What appear to be inanimate objects such as stones turn out not only to be alive in the same way that we are, but also in many infinitesimal ways to be affected by stimuli just as humans are. The distinction between animate and inanimate simply cannot be made when you enter the world of quantum mechanics and try to determine how those apparent subatomic particles, of which you and everything else in our universe is composed, are all tied together.

The point is that physics and metaphysics show there is a pattern to the universe that goes beyond our capacity to grasp it with our brains.

(1) Quantum physics indicates that an astigmatic view of reality results in erroneous assumptions about the universe.

(2) The inanimate world is both sentient and cognizant like its animate counterpart.

(3) The effect of stimuli is similar in inanimate objects when compared to animate objects or living beings.

(4) Arbitrary distinctions between inanimate and animate objects disappear at the scale at which quantum mechanics works.

23. There is a sentence that is missing in the paragraph below. Look at the paragraph and decide in which blank (option 1, 2, 3, or 4) the following sentence would best fit.

Sentence: Having made citizens more and less knowledgeable than their predecessors, the Internet has proved to be both a blessing and a curse.

Paragraph: Never before has a population, nearly all of whom has enjoyed at a least a secondary school education, been exposed to so much information, whether in newspapers and magazines or through YouTube, Google, and Facebook. ___(1)___. Yet it is not clear that people today are more knowledgeable than their barely literate predecessors. Contemporary advances in technology offered more serious and inquisitive students access to realms of knowledge previously unimaginable and unavailable. ___(2)___. But such readily available knowledge leads many more students away from serious study, the reading of actual texts, and toward an inability to write effectively and grammatically. ___(3)___. It has let people choose sources that reinforce their opinions rather than encouraging them to question inherited beliefs. ___(4)___.

(1) Option 1 (2) Option 2

(3) Option 3 (4) Option 4

24. The four sentences (labelled 1, 2, 3 and 4) below, when properly sequenced, would yield a coherent paragraph. Decide on the proper sequencing of the order of the sentences and key in the sequence of the four numbers as your answer:

(1) Some company leaders are basing their decisions on locating offices to foster innovation and growth, as their best-performing inventors suffered the greatest productivity losses when their commutes grew longer.

(2) Shorter commutes support innovation by giving employees more time in the office and greater opportunities for in-person collaboration, while removing the physical strain of a long commute.

(3) This is not always the case: remote work does not automatically lead to greater creativity and productivity as office water-cooler conversations are also very important for innovation.

(4) Some see the link between long commutes and productivity as support for work-from-home scenarios, as many workers have grown accustomed to their commute-free arrangements during the pandemic.

Section II: DI & LR

Question Numbers (1 to 5): The management of a university hockey team was evaluating performance of four women players - Amla, Bimla, Harita and Sarita for their possible selection in the university team for next year. For this purpose, the management was looking at the number of goals scored by them in the past 8 matches, numbered 1 through 8. The four players together had scored a total of 12 goals in these matches. In the 8 matches, each of them had scored at least one goal. No two players had scored the same total number of goals.

The following facts are known about the goals scored by these four players only. All the questions refer only to the goals scored by these four players.

1. Only one goal was scored in every even numbered match.
2. Harita scored more goals than Bimla.
3. The highest goal scorer scored goals in exactly 3 matches including Match 4 and Match 8.
4. Bimla scored a goal in Match 1 and one each in three other consecutive matches.
5. An equal number of goals were scored in Match 3 and Match 7, which was different from the number of goals scored in either Match 1 or Match 5.
6. The match in which the highest number of goals was scored was unique and it was not Match 5.

1. How many goals were scored in Match 7?

(1) 1

(2) Cannot be determined

(3) 2

(4) 3

2. Which of the following is the correct sequence of goals scored in matches 1, 3, 5 and 7?
(1) 3, 1, 2, 1
(2) 5, 1, 0, 1
(3) 3, 2, 1, 2
(4) 4, 1, 2, 1

3. Which of the following statement(s) is/are true?
Statement-1: Amla and Sarita never scored goals in the same match.
Statement-2: Harita and Sarita never scored goals in the same match.
(1) Statement-2 only
(2) Both the statements
(3) Statement-1 only
(4) None of the statements

4. Which of the following statement(s) is/are false?
Statement-1: In every match at least one player scored a goal.
Statement-2: No two players scored goals in the same number of matches.
(1) Both the statements
(2) None of the statements
(3) Statement-1 only
(4) Statement-2 only

5. If Harita scored goals in one more match as compared to Sarita, which of the following statement(s) is/are necessarily true?
Statement-1: Amla scored goals in consecutive matches.
Statement-2: Sarita scored goals in consecutive matches.
(1) Both the statements
(2) Statement-2 only
(3) None of the statements
(4) Statement-1 only

Question Numbers (6 to 10): There are 15 girls and some boys among the graduating students in a class. They are planning a get-together, which can be either a 1-day event, or a 2-day event, or a 3-day event. There are 6 singers in the class, 4 of them are boys. There are 10 dancers in the class, 4 of them are girls. No dancer in the class is a singer.

Some students are not interested in attending the get-together. Those students who are interested in attending a 3-day event are also interested in attending a 2-day event; those who are interested in attending a 2-day event are also interested in attending a 1-day event.

The following facts are also known:

1. All the girls and 80% of the boys are interested in attending a 1-day event. 60% of the boys are interested in attending a 2-day event.
2. Some of the girls are interested in attending a 1-day event, but not a 2-day event; some of the other girls are interested in attending both.
3. 70% of the boys who are interested in attending a 2-day event are neither singers nor dancers. 60% of the girls who are interested in attending a 2-day event are neither singers nor dancers.
4. No girl is interested in attending a 3-day event. All male singers and 2 of the dancers are interested in attending a 3-day event.
5. The number of singers interested in attending a 2-day event is one more than the number of dancers interested in attending a 2-day event.

6. How many boys are there in the class?

7. Which of the following can be determined from the given information?
I. The number of boys who are interested in attending a 1-day event and are neither dancers nor singers.
II. The number of female dancers who are interested in attending a 1-day event.
(1) Only II
(2) Both I and II
(3) Only I
(4) Neither I nor II

8. What fraction of the class are interested in attending a 2-day event?
(1) $\frac{7}{10}$ (2) $\frac{7}{13}$
(3) $\frac{2}{3}$ (4) $\frac{9}{13}$

9. What BEST can be concluded about the number of male dancers who are interested in attending a 1-day event?
(1) 6 (2) 5
(3) 4 or 6 (4) 5 or 6

10. How many female dancers are interested in attending a 2-day event?
(1) Cannot be determined
(2) 1
(3) 0
(4) 2

Question Numbers (11 to 15): Adhara, Bithi, Chhaya, Dhanavi, Esther, and Fathima are the interviewers in a process that awards funding for new initiatives. Every interviewer individually interviews each of the candidates individually and awards a token only if she recommends funding. A token has a face value of 2, 3, 5, 7, 11, or 13. Each interviewer awards tokens of a single face value only.

Once all six interviews are over for a candidate, the candidate receives a funding that is Rs.1000 times the product of the face values of all the tokens. For example, if a candidate has tokens with face values 2, 5, and 7, then they get a funding of Rs.1000 × (2 × 5 × 7) = Rs.70,000.

Pragnyaa, Qahira, Rasheeda, Smera, and Tantra were five candidates who received funding. The funds they received, in descending order, were Rs.390,000, Rs.210,000, Rs.165,000, Rs.77,000, and Rs.66,000.

The following additional facts are known:

1. Fathima awarded tokens to everyone except Qahira, while Adhara awarded tokens to no one except Pragnyaa.
2. Rashida received the highest number of tokens that anyone received, but she did not receive one from Esther.
3. Bithi awarded a token to Smera but not to Qahira, while Dhanavi awarded a token to Qahira but not to Smera.

11. How many tokens did Qahira receive?

12. Who among the following definitely received a token from Bithi but not from Dhanavi?

(1) Rasheeda

(2) Qahira

(3) Tantra

(4) Pragnyaa

13. How many tokens did Chhaya award?

14. How many tokens did Smera receive?

15. Which of the following could be the amount of funding that Tantra received?

(a) Rs. 66,000

(b) Rs. 165,000

(1) Only (b)

(2) Both (a) and (b)

(3) Neither (a) nor (b)

(4) Only (a)

Question Numbers (16 to 20):

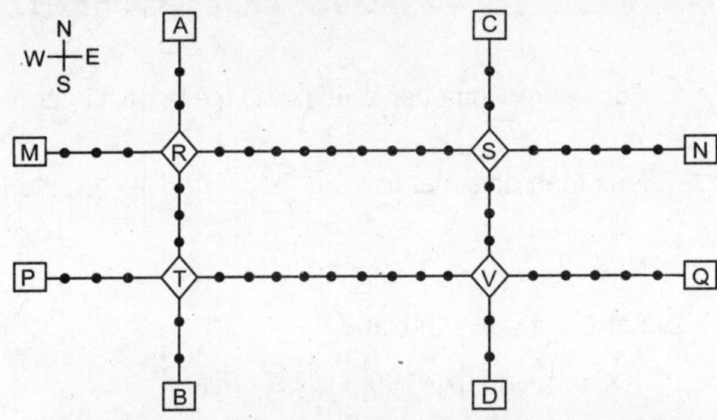

Given above is the schematic map of the metro lines in a city with rectangles denoting terminal stations (e.g. A), diamonds denoting junction stations (e.g. R) and small filled-up circles denoting other stations. Each train runs either in east-west or north-south direction, but not both. All trains stop for 2 minutes at each of the junction stations on the way and for 1 minute at each of the other stations. It takes 2 minutes to reach the next station for trains going in east-west direction and 3 minutes to reach the next station for trains going in north-south direction. From each terminal station, the first train starts at 6 am; the last trains leave the terminal stations at midnight. Otherwise, during the service hours, there are metro service every 15 minutes in the north-south lines and every 10 minutes in the east-west lines. A train must rest for at least 15 minutes after completing a trip at the terminal station, before it can undertake the next trip in the reverse direction. (All questions are related to this metro service only. Assume that if someone reaches a station exactly at the time a train is supposed to leave, (s)he can catch that train.)

16. If Hari is ready to board a train at 8:05 am from station M, then when is the earliest that he can reach station N?

(1) 9:13 am (2) 9:01 am

(3) 9:11 am (4) 9:06 am

17. If Priya is ready to board a train at 10:25 am from station T, then when is the earliest that she can reach station S?

(1) 11:28 am (2) 11:12 am

(3) 11:22 am (4) 11:07 am

18. Haripriya is expected to reach station S late. What is the latest time by which she must be ready to board at station S if she must reach station B before 1 am via station R?

(1) 11:49 am (2) 11:43 pm

(3) 11:35 pm (4) 11:39 pm

19. What is the minimum number of trains that are required to provide the service on the AB line (considering both north and south directions)?

20. What is the minimum number of trains that are required to provide the service in this city?

Section III: QA

1. For any real number x, let [x] be the largest integer less than or equal to x. If $\sum_{n=1}^{N}\left[\frac{1}{5}+\frac{n}{25}\right]=25$ then N is

2. Let $0 \le a \le x \le 100$ and $f(x)=|x-a|+|x-100|+|x-a-50|$.

   Then the maximum value of f(x) becomes 100 when a is equal to

   (1) 0 (2) 50
   (3) 100 (4) 25

3. Ankita buys 4 kg cashews, 14 kg peanuts and 6 kg almonds when the cost of 7 kg cashews is the same as that of 30 kg peanuts or 9 kg almonds. She mixes all the three nuts and marks a price for the mixture in order to make a profit of Rs. 1752. She sells 4 kg of the mixture at this marked price and the remaining at a 20% discount on the marked price, thus making a total profit of Rs. 744. Then the amount, in rupees, that she had spent in buying almonds is

   (1) 2520 (2) 1440
   (3) 1176 (4) 1680

4. Amal buys 110 kg of syrup and 120 kg of juice, syrup being 20% less costly than juice, per kg. He sells 10 kg of syrup at 10% profit and 20 kg of juice at 20% profit. Mixing the remaining juice and syrup, Amal sells the mixture at Rs. 308.32 per kg and makes an overall profit of 64%. Then, Amal's cost price for syrup, in rupees per kg, is

5. A mixture contains lemon juice and sugar syrup in equal proportion. If a new mixture is created by adding this mixture and sugar syrup in the ratio 1 : 3, then the ratio of lemon juice and sugar syrup in the new mixture is

   (1) 1 : 6
   (2) 1 : 4
   (3) 1 : 7
   (4) 1 : 5

6. In a class of 100 students, 73 like coffee, 80 like tea and 52 like lemonade. It may be possible that some students do not like any of these three drinks. Then the difference between the maximum and minimum possible number of students who like all the three drinks is

   (1) 48 (2) 47
   (3) 52 (4) 53

7. In a village, the ratio of number of males to females is 5 : 4. The ratio of number of literate males to literate females is 2 : 3. The ratio of the number of illiterate males to illiterate females is 4 : 3. If 3600 males in the village are literate, then the total number of females in the village is

8. For natural numbers x, y, and z, if xy + yz = 19 and yz + xz = 51, then the minimum possible value of xyz is

9. The average of three integers is 13. When a natural number n is included, the average of these four integers remains and odd integer. The minimum possible value of n is

   (1) 3 (2) 1
   (3) 5 (4) 4

10. Trains A and B start traveling at the same time towards each other with constant speeds from stations X and Y, respectively. Train A reaches station Y in 10 minutes while train B takes 9 minutes to reach station X after meeting train A. Then the total time taken, in minutes, by train B to travel from station Y to station X is

    (1) 12 (2) 10
    (3) 15 (4) 6

11. The largest real value of a for which the equation $|x+a|+|x-1|=2$ has an infinite number of solutions for x is

    (1) 0 (2) 2
    (3) –1 (4) 1

12. Let ABCD be a parallelogram such that the coordinates of its three vertices A, B, C are (1, 1), (3, 4) and (–2, 8), respectively. Then, the coordinates of the vertex D are

    (1) (–4, 5) (2) (4, 5)
    (3) (0, 11) (4) (–3, 4)

13. All the vertices of a rectangle lie on a circle of radius R. If the perimeter of the rectangle is P, then the area of the rectangle is

    (1) $\frac{P^2}{16}-R^2$ (2) $\frac{P^2}{2}-2PR$
    (3) $\frac{P^2}{8}-\frac{R^2}{2}$ (4) $\frac{P^2}{8}-2R^2$

14. Let a and b be natural numbers. If $a^2 + ab + a = 14$ and $b^2 + ab + b = 28$, then (2a + b) equals

    (1) 10 (2) 8
    (3) 9 (4) 7

15. Let A be the largest positive integer that divides all the numbers of the form $3^k + 4^k + 5^k$, and B be the largest positive integer that divides all the numbers of the form $4^k + 3(4^k) + 4^{k+2}$, where k is any positive integer. Then (A + B) equals

16. The average weight of students in a class increases by 600 gm when some new students join the class. If the average weight of the new students is 3 kg more than the average weight of the original students, then the ratio of the number of original students to the number of new students is

(1) 1 : 2 (2) 1 : 4
(3) 3 : 1 (4) 4 : 1

17. Let a, b, c be non-zero real numbers such that $b^2 < 4ac$, and $f(x) = ax^2 + bx + c$. If the set S consists of all integers m such that f(m) < 0, then the set S must necessarily be

(1) the empty set
(2) the set of all integers
(3) either the empty set or the set of all integers
(4) the set of all positive integers

18. Alex invested his savings in two parts. The simple interest earned on the first part at 15% per annum for 4 years is the same as the simple interest earned on the second part at 12% per annum for 3 years. Then, the percentage of his savings invested in the first part is

(1) 62.5% (2) 40%
(3) 60% (4) 37.5%

19. Pinky is standing in a queue at a ticket counter. Suppose the ratio of the number of persons standing ahead of Pinky to the number of persons standing behind her in the queue is 3 : 5. If the total number of persons in the queue is less than 300, then the maximum possible number of persons standing ahead of Pinky is

20. The number of ways of distributing 20 identical balloons among 4 children such that each child gets some balloons but no child gets an odd number of balloons, is

21. A trapezium ABCD has side AD parallel to BC, $\angle BAD = 90°$, BC = 3 cm and AD = 8 cm. If the perimeter of this trapezium is 36 cm, then its area, in sq. cm, is

22. For any natural number n, suppose the sum of the first n terms of an arithmetic progression is $(n + 2n^2)$. If the nth term of the progression is divisible by 9, then the smallest possible value of n is

(1) 8 (2) 7
(3) 9 (4) 4

ANSWERS

VARC

1. (3)	**2.** (3)	**3.** (2)	**4.** (4)	**5.** (4)	**6.** (3)	**7.** (3)	**8.** (4)	**9.** (4)	**10.** (2)
11. (2)	**12.** (3)	**13.** (3)	**14.** (3)	**15.** (3)	**16.** (1)	**17.** (2431)	**18.** (2)	**19.** (2)	**20.** (3214)
21. (3)	**22.** (4)	**23.** (4)	**24.** (2143)						

DI & LR

1. (1)	**2.** (4)	**3.** (2)	**4.** (2)	**5.** (3)	**6.** (50)	**7.** (1)	**8.** (2)	**9.** (4)	**10.** (3)
11. (2)	**12.** (4)	**13.** (3)	**14.** (3)	**15.** (2)	**16.** (3)	**17.** (2)	**18.** (4)	**19.** (8)	**20.** (48)

QA

1. (44)	**2.** (2)	**3.** (4)	**4.** (160)	**5.** (3)	**6.** (2)	**7.** (43200)	**8.** (34)	**9.** (3)	**10.** (3)
11. (4)	**12.** (1)	**13.** (4)	**14.** (2)	**15.** (82)	**16.** (4)	**17.** (3)	**18.** (4)	**19.** (111)	**20.** (84)
21. (66)	**22.** (2)								

EXPLANATIONS

VARC

1. 3 Refer the concluding lines of the passage: "Additionally, the Stoic idea of developing virtue in oneself, of becoming a good person, which the Stoics believed we could do because we have a touch of the divine, laid the foundation for the three monotheistic religions: Judaism, Christianity, and Islam . . .This makes option 3 the correct answer. The other options are either not mentioned or are extreme.

2. 3 This is a largely factual question. The reference to Marcus Aurelius comes in the first paragraph and his role can be deduced from the from lines: "an army general accused Marcus Aurelius of treason in front of other officers...or perhaps proceeding as he would have proceeded whether or not this event occurred: continuing to lead the Romans in a way that Marcus Aurelius believed best benefited them."

3. 2 The implied meaning of this line is that rather than reacting on emotions, one should aim to observe them and then decide on what is important. There is no reference to any out-of-body experience.

4. 4 Consider the following lines: "The Epicureans, first associated with the Greek philosopher Epicurus . . . held a similar view, believing that people should enjoy simple pleasures, such as good conversation, friendship, food, and wine, but not be indulgent in these pursuits and not follow passion for those things that hold no real value like power and money." Now, if the fourth option is false, it would contradict the views quoted above.

5. 4 The main idea of the fourth paragraph is encapsulated in its opening line: "As an environment, technologies shape their inhabitants. In this respect, they are comparable to laws and customs." The rest of the paragraph is elaborating upon this point.

6. 3 The reference to Foucault's prisons or Habermas's public sphere is an example of ways in which masses are organized. These are not the only ways in which this is done.

7. 3 Consider the following lines: "critical theory of technology regards technologies as an environment rather than as a collection of tools. We live today with and even within technologies that determine our way of life. Along with the constant pressures to build centers of power, many other social values and meanings are inscribed in technological design." Also, "As an environment, technologies shape their inhabitants." This makes option 3 correct.

8. 4 1 can be inferred from: ". A hermeneutics of technology must make explicit the meanings implicit in the devices we use and the rituals they script." 2 can be inferred from: "Critical theory of technology is a political theory of modernity with a normative dimension. .....according to which advances in the formal claims of human rights take center stage while in the background centralization of ever more powerful public institutions and private organizations imposes an authoritarian social order." 3 can be inferred from: "Customs such as parental authority represent the interest of childhood in safety and growth.....This notion of representation does not imply an eternal human nature." 4 is an extreme statement that finds no support in the passage.

9. 4 The passage is primarily concerned with the manner in which our fears and beliefs about certain unexplained phenomenon – the Undead – have evolved over a period of time and how the changing theories regarding the Undead reflect this.

10. 2 These lines simply mean that for humans, the Undead were an abnormality and in accordance with this idea, they were believed to possess certain unnatural attributes.

11. 2 The transition from the Middle Ages to the Age of Enlightenment did see new theories of the Undead. Thus, if this statement is false, it would not be aligned with the information given in the passage.

12. 3 The simple meaning of the statement is - Mankind's early years were marked by a belief in the existence of eerie creatures that were neither quite alive nor dead. The other options are distortions.

13. 3 Both are not continually undergoing restoration. While the Japanese shrine is rebuilt completely every 20 years, it is the German cathedral than is constantly being renovated.

14. 3 All the other options are correct inferences. The reference to cloning is not in the context of the unassailable original'.

15. 3 As the passage states: "Back in the 17th century [in the West], excavated artworks from antiquity were treated quite differently from today. They were not restored in a way that was faithful to the original. Instead, there was massive intervention in these works, changing their appearance. . ." The reference to religion comes in the context of cloning.

16. 1 Refer the following lines from the first paragraph: "The second concept for a copy is fuzhipin ... They are exact reproductions of the original, which, for the Chinese, are of equal value to the original. It has absolutely no negative connotations." The other options are examples of Fangzhipin and these are likely to have less value than the original.

17. 2431

2 is the obvious opener. It is the topic sentence and introduces the theme of the discussion – collagen. 'The risk – fish skin swims in here' makes 43 a pair (problem-likely solution). 1 closes the paragraph by elaborating on the benefits of fish skin collagen.

Original Paragraph:

(Edits have been made to the passage)

Collagen is one of the main structural proteins in connective tissues in the human body. Pig and cow collagen proteins have been used to promote wound healing successfully in the past, but the risk of introducing disease agents from these mammalian species inhibits broader applications in the medical field. And that's where fish skin swims in. Diseases and bacteria that affect fish are different from most human pathogens, and fish skin is also a cheap, readily available material for bandage production.

In considering the versatility of fish skin collagen, the researchers noted that the protein had excellent thermo-stability and tensile strength. This allows the bandage to adhere to the skin and adjust to body movements.

(**Source:**https://www.nature.com/scitable/blog/student-voices/fish_skin_bandaids_a_natural/)

18. 2 The passage is not promoting petitioning over elections. It is simply saying that it is an important democratic process. As expressions of collective voice, petitions support procedural democracy by shaping agendas. This makes 2 the correct summary. There is no mention of citizens' inclinations. 3 is extreme and 4 is a distortion.

19. 2 Blank 2 presents a context where couples will be reluctant to send out invitations. Therefore, option (2) is the appropriate answer because it fits the blank space thematically.

20. 3214

Sentences 3 and 2 talk about the creative industry and so, they form a mandatory pair. Note the transition words 'in fact'. So, sentence 2 logically follows sentence 3. Sentences 1 and 4 form another mandatory pair as well because sentence 4 provides additional information on product design mentioned in sentence 1.

21. 3 Option 3 is the most appropriate summary because the passage mentions how history was tweaked. Option 3 mentions how Ethiopiawas perceived to be weak but in reality, the picture was somewhat different.

Incorrect answers: Option 1 is narrow in scope.Option 2 is close but option 3 is a better answer because it provides a convincing summary of the given passage. Again, option (3) is better than option (4) because option (4) is a little sketchy. Option (3) is the most comprehensive summary.

22. 4 Quantum Mechanics blur the distinction between the animate and inanimate objects. Option (4) therefore, is the most convincing summary of the given passage. Option (1) is verbose and therefore, can be counted as irrelevant. Option (2) is narrow in scope. Option (3) is wrong because it is again narrow in scope.

23. 4 The sentence preceding blank 4 discusses the role of the internet. Thematically, the given sentence best fits blank space 4 because it provides both the pros and cons of internet.

24. 2143

Sentences 2 and 1 form a mandatory pair because it provides information about shorter commutes. Sentences 4 and 3 form a mandatory pair as well because both sentences present the pros and cons of working from home and working at office.

DI & LR

For questions 1 to 5:

Step 1:

From condition (1), In matches 2, 4, 6 and 8, only one goal was scored in each.

From condition (4), Bimla scored a goal in Match 1 and she scored a total of 4 goals.

From condition (2), Harita scored more goals than Bimla. Since no two players had scored the same total number of goals. So Harita scored a total of 5 goals. So remaining 3 goals were scored by Amla and Sarita.

From condition (3), The highest goal scorer was Harita. She scored goals in exactly 3 matches including Match 4 and Match 8.

From condition (4), Bimla scored one goal each in three consecutive matches 5, 6 and 7.

Player	Match								Total No. of goals
	1	2	3	4	5	6	7	8	
Amla				X		X		X	1/2
Bimla	1	X	X	X	1	1	1	X	4
Harita				1		X		1	5
Sarita				X		X		X	2/1
Total No. of goals		1		1		1		1	12

Step 2:

From conditions (5), An equal number of goals were scored in Match 3 and Match 7, which was different from the number of goals scored in Match 1 or Match 5.

From condition (6), The match in which the highest number of goals was scored was unique and it was not Match 5.

Also, in the 8 matches, each of them had scored at least one goal.

Hence, Harita scored 3 goals in Match 1.

Also, in matches 3 and 7, one goal was scored in each. So in Match 5, 2 goals were scored.

Hence, the final table can be shown as:

Player	Match								Total No. of goals
	1	2	3	4	5	6	7	8	
Amla	X			X		X	X	X	1/2
Bimla	1	X	X	X	1	1	1	X	4
Harita	3	X	X	1	X	X	X	1	5
Sarita	X			X		X	X	X	2/1
Total No. of goals	4	1	1	1	2	1	1	1	12

1. 1 In Match 7, one goal was scored.

2. 4 The correct sequence of goals scored in matches 1, 3, 5 and 7 is 4, 1, 2, 1.

3. 2 Both the statements are true.

4. 2 None of the statements is false.

5. 3 None of the statements is true.

For questions 6 to 10:

Let the number of boys be 'b'.

As per facts 1 and 2,

	Boys	Girls
1-day event	0.8b	15 = x + y
2-day event	0.6b	x
3-day event		

And,

	Boys	Girls	Total
Singers	4	2	6
Dancers	6	4	10
Total	10	6	

As per fact 3, b × 0.6 × 0.7, are neither singers nor dancers and b 0.6 × 0.3 are either singers or dancers which is equivalent to $\frac{21}{50}$b and $\frac{9}{50}$b.

Since 6 boys who are singers or dancers were interested in attending 3-day event therefore, $\frac{9}{50}$b must be 6, 7, 8, 9 or 10.

Hence, b must be 50.

	Boys	Girls	
		Case 1	Case 2
1-day event	0.8b = 40	15 = (5 + 10) or	(10 + 5)
2-day event	0.6b = 30	5 = (3 + 2) or	(6 + 4)
3-day event	(4 + 2 + P)	×	

Here in this table.

In case 2:- 9 + 4 = 13 singers or dancers will be interested to attend 2-day event.

And as per fact 5, number of singers = 7 and number of dancers = 6, which is not possible.

Since there are exactly 6 singers.

Final table can be shown as:

	Boys	Girls
1-day event	40	15 = 5 + 10
2-day event	30 = 21 + 9*	5 = 3 + 2*
3-day event		×

(*) means 2 girls are singers who are interested in 2-day event.

and 9 boys out of which 4 are singers and other 5 are dancers are interested in 2-day event.

6. 50 50 boys are there in the class.

7. 1 Statement I cannot be determined.

8. 2 The fraction of the class interested in attending a 2-day event is 7/13.

9. 4 The numbers of male dancers who are interested in attending a 1-day event can be either 5 or 6.

10. 3 Number of female dancers interested in attending a 2-day event is equal to 'O'.

For questions 11 to 15:

Note that the face values of the tokens are prime numbers and the funds received are numbers that are products of these prime numbers. We shall start by factorizing the numbers that represent the funds received (after dividing by 1000)

390 = 13 × 5 × 3 × 2

210 = 7 × 5 × 3 × 2

165 = 11 × 5 × 3

77 = 11 × 7

66 = 11 × 3 × 2

Fathima awarded tokens to everyone except Qahira, which means that Fatima had tokens with face value 3 and Qahira received funds worth 77000.

Adhara awarded tokens to no one except Pragnyaa, which means that Adhara had tokens with face value 13 and Pragnyaa received funds worth 390000.

Rashida received the highest number of tokens that anyone received, which is 4 and funds received by her is 210000.

(**Note:** Pragnyaa also received 4 tokens)

Bithi awarded a token to Smera but not to Qahira,
Dhanavi awarded a token to Qahira but not to Smera, which means that Dhanavi had tokens of face value 7.
The total funds received by Smera and Tantra are not clear as well as the face values of tokens with Bithi and Chaya.
The data can be tabulated as follows:

Interviewer (face value of token)	Pragnyaa	Qahira	Rashida	Smera	Tantra	Total tokens
Adhara (13)	✔					1
Bithi (2 / 5)	✔		✔	✔	?	3
Chaya (5 / 2)	✔		✔	?	?	3
Dhanavi (7)		✔	✔			2
Esther (11)		✔		✔	✔	3
Fatima (3)	✔		✔	✔	✔	4
Total tokens	4	2	4	3	3	
Total funds (Rs.)	390000	77000	210000	66000 / 165000	165000 / 66000	

11. 2 Qahira received 2 tokens.

12. 4 Pragnyaa definitely received a token from Bithi but not from Dhanavi.

13. 3 Chhaya awarded 3 tokens – Pragnyaa, Rashida and either Smera or Tantra.

14. 3 Total funds received by Smera was either 66000 or 165000, so tokens received were either (3, 2, 11) or (3, 5, 11). In either case the total number of tokens was 3.

15. 2 The funds received by Tantra could be either Rs.66,000 or Rs.1,65,000. Hence, option (2) is correct.

For questions 16 to 20:

Let us indicate the travel time and stoppages between the junctions in the schematic map.

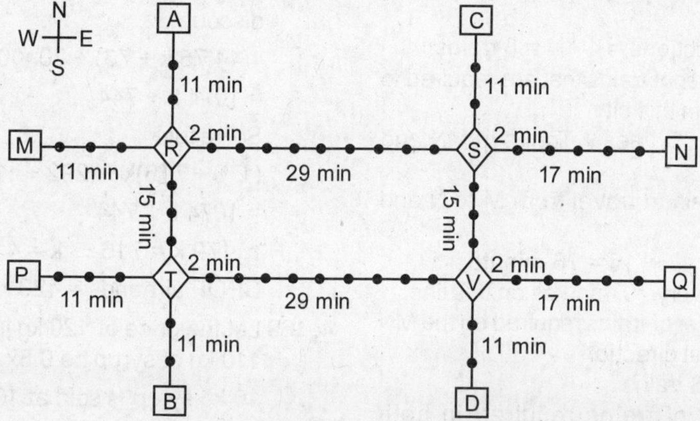

16. 3 Given that Hari is ready to board a train at 8:05 am from station M.
Trains leave after every 10 minutes. So Hari can catch the 8:10 train from M.
There are 17 stations, 2 junctions and 20 intervals, so time taken to travel = 20 × 2 + 17 × 1 + 2 × 2 = 61 minutes
Hence, time at which Hari reaches station N = 8:10 + 1:01 = 9:11 am.

17. 2 There can be two routes that Priya can take.
Case 1: First travel by East-West line and then North-South line.
Trains leave after every 10 minutes on the East-West line.
The 10:20 am train from P reaches and then leaves T at = 10:20 + 00:11 + 00:02 = 10:33 am
In the first case Priya will have to wait for 8 minutes at the station before boarding the train.
So let us see if the waiting time is reduced in case 2.
Case 2: First travel by North-South line and then East-West line.
Trains leave after every 15 minutes on the North-South line. The 10:15 am train from B will reach T at = 10:15 + 00:11 = 10:26 am and leave T at 10:28 am. In this case Priya's train leaves within 3 minutes of her reaching the station. This train reaches R at = 10:28 + 00:15 = 10:43 am.
From R Priya has to catch the East-West train for station S.
The 10:30 am train from M reaches R at = 10:30 + 00:11 = 10:41 am and leaves at 10:43 am.
Priya can catch this train and reach station S at = 10:43 + 00:29 = 11:12 am.

18. 4 The last (midnight) train from A reaches R at 12:11 am and leaves at 12:13 am. It will reach B at = 12:13 + 00:17 + 00:11 = 12:41 am.
From S to R the travel time is 29 minutes. To catch the 12:13 am train Haripriya will have to start from S at = 12:13 – 00:29 = 11:44 pm or before that.
Trains start from N after every 10 minutes and the time taken to reach S is 17 minutes.
There is a stoppage of 2 minutes at S.
The 11:30 pm train from N reaches S at 11:47 pm, which does not serve the purpose.
The 11:20 pm train from N reaches S at 11:37 pm and leaves at 11:39 pm.
This train will reach R by 11:39 + 00:29 = 12:08 am.
Then she can catch the last train from A going to B at 12:13 am.
Haripriya can catch the train at S if she reaches the station latest by 11:39 pm.

19. 8 Total time for a train to travel from A to B and to start back = 11 + 2 + 15 + 2 + 11 + 15 = 56 minutes.
Trains leave after every 15 minutes.
The minimum number of trains that are required to provide the service on the AB line
(in the North-South direction) = [56/15] = [3.733] = 4 trains
Hence, for both directions = 4 + 4 = 8 trains.

20. 48 The minimum number of trains that are required to provide the service in this city
= Trains in AB and CD lines + Trains in MN and PQ lines.
Time taken for a train to travel from M to N and start back
= 11 + 2 + 29 + 2 + 17 + 15 = 76 minutes.
Trains leave after every 10 minutes on this line.
The minimum number of trains required on the MN line in the East-West direction
= [76/10] = [7.6] = 8 trains
Minimum number of trains required in both directions on the MN line = 16 trains
Hence, total number of trains required = (AB + CD) + (MN + PQ) = (8 + 8) + (16 + 16) = 48.

QA

1. 44 Given that [x] = greatest integer less than x

$$\Rightarrow \left[\frac{1}{5}+\frac{n}{25}\right]=\left[\frac{5+n}{25}\right]$$

For n = 1, 2, ...,19 the above expression is zero.
For n = 20, 21, ..., 44 the expression has values 1.
From 20 to 44 these are 25 terms, hence, the sum from 1 to 44 will be 25.

2. 2 Given $0 \le a \le x \le 100$
$f(x) = |x - a| + |x - 100| + |x - a - 50|$
Since $x \ge a \Rightarrow |x - a| = x - a$
and $x \le 100 \Rightarrow |x - 100| = 100 - x$
$\Rightarrow f(x) = x - a + 100 - x + |x - a - 50|$
$f(x) = 100 - a + |x - a - 50|$
Let us go by options.
(1) Put a = 0; f(x) = 150 if x = 100
150 if x = 0
(2) Put a = 25; f(x) = 125 if x = 25
(3) Put a = 50; f(x) = 100 if x = 50
(4) Put a = 100; f(x) = 50 if x = 100
we can see that max f(x) = 100
f(x) = 100 for a = 50.

3. 4

	Cashew	Peanut	Almond	Total
Weight	4	14	6	24 kg
Cost	90 k	21k	70 k	

Given 7c = 30p = 9a
LCM of (7, 30, 9) = 630
$\Rightarrow$ c = 90 k; p = 21 k; a = 70 k
Price of mixture = 1074 k
Given that MP = 1074 k + 1752
4 kg is sold at MP and 20 kg is sold at 20% discount.
4(44.75 k + 73) + 20 × 0.8 (44.75 k + 73)
= 1074 k + 744
Solve for k
(179 + 716)k + (292 + 1168)
= 1074 k + 744
$\therefore$ 179 k = 716 $\Rightarrow$ k = 4
CPOF almonds = 420 k = 4 × 420 = Rs. 1,680.

4. 160 Let the price of 120 kg juice be Rs. x and price of 110 kg of syrup be 0.8x.
10 kg syrup is sold at 10% profit
20 kg juice is sold at 20% profit
The SP of remaining 100 kg juice and 100 kg syrup is Rs. 308.32

$$\frac{(1\times 1.1\times 0.8x)+(2\times 1.2x)+20\times 308.32}{11\times 0.8x+12\times x}=1.44$$

$\Rightarrow$ x = 200
$\therefore$ Cost of syrup = 0.8 × 200
= Rs. 160.

5. 3 Let leman juice be L.
Let syrup be S.
Given that ratio of these mixture and syrup = 1 : 3
L : S = 1 : 1 $\Rightarrow$ Total quantity is (1 + 1) = 2
$\Rightarrow$ 2 Portions of the mixture are mixed with 6 portions of syrup.

$\therefore$ In the new mixture,

Quantity of juice = 1 part quantity of syrup = 1 + 6 = 7 parts

$\therefore$ Required ratio = 1 : 7.

6. 2 Total = 100; coffee = 73

Tea = 80; Lemonade = 52

Max (all three) = 52

Min (all three) = 205 – 2 × 100 = 5

Required difference = 52 – 5 = 47.

7. 43200

	Literate	Illiterate	Total
Male	2x	4y	5k
Female	3x	3y	4k

$\Rightarrow \frac{2x+4y}{3x+3y} = \frac{5}{4}$

$\Rightarrow 7x = y$

$\Rightarrow \frac{x}{y} = \frac{1}{7}$

Given 2x = 3600

$\Rightarrow (3x + 3y) = (3 + 21) \times \frac{3600}{2} = 43200.$

8. 34 xy + yz = 19

$\Rightarrow y(x + z) = 19$ ... (i)

19 is prime $\Rightarrow$ Either y = 19

and (x + z) = 1

or (x + z) = 19 and y = 1

yz + xz = 51 ... (ii)

z(y + x) = 3 × 17

Either y = 3 and (y + x) = 17

or z = 17 and (y + x) = 3

Case 1: z = 17 (x, y) = (1, 2)

$\Rightarrow$ xyz = 34

Case 2: z = 3 (x, y) = (16, 1)

$\Rightarrow$ xyz = 48

z = 3 (x, y) = (15, 2)

$\Rightarrow$ xyz = 90

On checking for other possible values of x, y and z we can observe that the minimum possible value of xyz = 34.

9. 3 Average = 13 $\Rightarrow$ Sum = 39

Let the new number be x.

Given $\frac{(n-39)}{4}$ = odd integer

Let us check with the options.

1. $\frac{39+3}{4}$ = not an odd integer
2. $\frac{39+1}{4}$ = 10 (not odd)
3. $\frac{39+5}{4}$ = 11 = odd integer
4. $\frac{39+4}{4}$ = not an odd integer

10. 3

X ———————————— Y

A→ t / 9 ⋮ 10 – t / t ←B

t = GM of (9, 10 – t)

$\Rightarrow t^2 = 90 - 9t$

$\Rightarrow t^2 + 9t - 90 = 0$

$\Rightarrow t = 6$

Total time taken by B = 6 + 9 = 15 minutes.

11. 4 The given equation will have infinite number of solutions if x in |x + a| and x in |x – 1| cancel out.

Case 1: $x + a < 0$ and $x - 1 \geq 0$

$\Rightarrow -a - x + x - 1 = 2 \Rightarrow a = -3$

Case 2: $x + a = 0$ and $x - 1 < 0$

$\Rightarrow x + a - x + 1 = 2 \Rightarrow a = 1$

Hence, the largest value of a that will give an infinite number of solutions for the given equation is 1.

12. 1

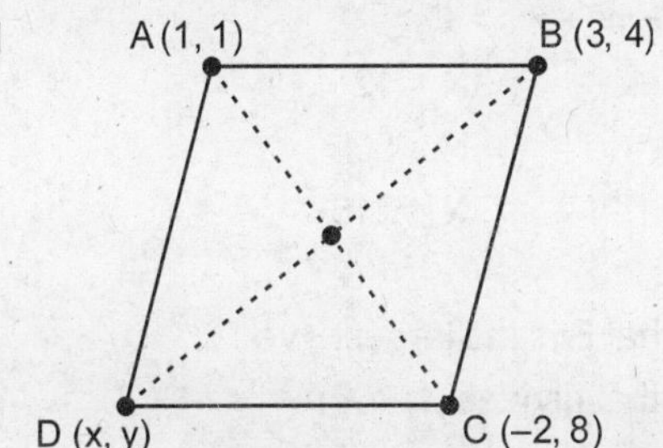

The mid points of AC and BD coincide

$\Rightarrow \frac{1+(-2)}{2} = \frac{x+3}{2} \Rightarrow x = -4$

$\frac{(1+8)}{2} = \frac{y+4}{2} \Rightarrow y = 5$

Hence, co-ordinates of D are (–4, 5).

13. 4

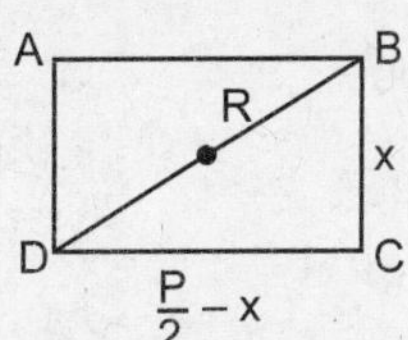

Given perimeter = P

Area of $\Delta BCD = \frac{1}{2} \times \left(\frac{P}{2} - x\right) \times n$

By Pythagoras theorem,

$4R^2 = x^2 + \frac{P^2}{4} - Px + x^2$

$\Rightarrow 4R^2 - \frac{P^2}{4} = 2x\left(x - \frac{P}{2}\right)$

$\Rightarrow x\left(\frac{P}{2} - x\right) = \frac{P^2}{8} - 2R^2$

Hence, area of rectangle ABCD $= \frac{P^2}{8} - 2R^2$

14. 2 $a^2 + ab + a = 14$ ... (i)

$b^2 + ab + b = 28$ ... (ii)

Add (i) and (ii),

$a^2 + b^2 + 2ab + a + b = 42$

$(a + b)(a + b + 1) = 42$

$\Rightarrow a + b = 6$ and $(a + b + 1) = 7$

From (i) $a(a + b + 1) = 14$

$\Rightarrow a = 2$

$\therefore 2a + b = a + a + b = 2 + 6 = 8.$

15. 82 Given A is the largest +ve integer that divides

$N = (3^k + 4^k + 5^k)$

For $k = 1$; $N = 12$

$k = 2$ $N = 50$

$k = 3$ $N = 216$

$\therefore A = 2$

Given that B is the largest +ve integer that divides

$M = 4^k(1 + 3 + 16)$

For $k = 1$ $M = 20 \times 4$

$k = 2$ $M = 20 \times 4^2$

$k = 3$ $M = 20 \times 4^3$

$\therefore B = 80$

Hence, $(A + B) = 2 + 80 = 82.$

16. 4 Using Aligation

Original New

w w + 3000

w + 600

2400 600

Required ratio = 4 : 1.

17. 3 $f(x) = ax^2 + bx + c$

The above equation represents a parabola and f(x) < 0 means it is below the x – axis.

$b^2 < 4ac \Rightarrow$ roots are imaginary and the graph does not touch x axis.

$\Rightarrow$ S = empty set or the set of all integers.

18. 4 Let the two parts be x and y.

Given: $x \times \frac{15}{100} \times 4 = y \times \frac{12}{100} \times 3$

$\Rightarrow 5x = 3y$

Let $x = 3k$ and $y = 5k$

$\therefore$ Required percentage $= \frac{3}{(3+5)} \times 100 = 37.5\%.$

19. 111

Let the number of people ahead of Pinky be 3k and the number of people behind Pinky be 5k.

Given $(3k + 1 + 5k) < 300$

Or, $8k < 299$

Or, $k < 37.37$

Or, Max (k) = 37

Required number = $3 \times 37 = 111.$

20. 84 Let the number of balloons that each child receives be 2a, 2b, 2c and 2d.

We know that $2a + 2b + 2c + 2d = 20$

and $a + b + c + d = 10$

Each of them should get some balloons.

Therefore, total number of ways = ${}^{(10-1)}C_{(4-1)}$

$= {}^9C_3 = 84.$

21. 66

ΔCED is right angled at E. We know of a Pythagorean triplet (5, 12, 13) that can satisfy the above condition

$\therefore$ Area of trapezium

$= \frac{1}{2}(3 + 8) \times 12 = 66 \text{ cm}^2.$

22. 2 Sum of n terms = $n + 2n^2$

For $n = 1$ $S = 3$

$n = 2$ $S = 10$

$n = 3$ $S = 21$

$\therefore$ The series is : 3, 7, 11, 15, 19, 23, 27

We know that 27 is divisible by 9.

Hence, the smallest possible value of n is 7.

CAT 2022 SOLVED PAPER (SLOT-2)

Section I : VARC

Question Numbers (1 to 4): The passage below is accompanied by a set of questions. Choose the best answer to each question.

[Octopuses are] misfits in their own extended families . . . They belong to the Mollusca class Cephalopoda. But they don't look like their cousins at all. Other molluscs include sea snails, sea slugs, bivalves – most are shelled invertebrates with a dorsal foot. Cephalopods are all arms, and can be as tiny as 1 centimetre and as large at 30 feet. Some of them have brains the size of a walnut, which is large for an invertebrate....

It makes sense for these molluscs to have added protection in the form of a higher cognition; they don't have a shell covering them, and pretty much everything feeds on cephalopods, including humans. But how did cephalopods manage to secure their own invisibility cloak? Cephalopods fire from multiple cylinders to achieve this in varying degrees from species to species. There are four main catalysts – chromatophores, iridophores, papillae and leucophores....

[Chromatophores] are organs on their bodies that contain pigment sacs, which have red, yellow and brown pigment granules. These sacs have a network of radial muscles, meaning muscles arranged in a circle radiating outwards. These are connected to the brain by a nerve. When the cephalopod wants to change colour, the brain carries an electrical impulse through the nerve to the muscles that expand outwards, pulling open the sacs to display the colours on the skin. Why these three colours? Because these are the colours the light reflects at the depths they live in (the rest is absorbed before it reaches those depths)....

Well, what about other colours? Cue the iridophores. Think of a second level of skin that has thin stacks of cells. These can reflect light back at different wavelengths. . . . It's using the same properties that we've seen in hologram stickers, or rainbows on puddles of oil. You move your head and you see a different colour. The sticker isn't doing anything but reflecting light – it's your movement that's changing the appearance of the colour. This property of holograms, oil and other such surfaces is called "iridescence"....

Papillae are sections of the skin that can be deformed to make a texture bumpy. Even humans possess them (goosebumps) but cannot use them in the manner that cephalopods can. For instance, the use of these cells is how an octopus can wrap itself over a rock and appear jagged or how a squid or cuttlefish can imitate the look of a coral reef by growing miniature towers on its skin. It actually matches the texture of the substrate it chooses.

Finally, the leucophores: According to a paper, published in Nature, cuttlefish and octopuses possess an additional type of reflector cell called a leucophore. They are cells that scatter full spectrum light so that they appear white in a similar way that a polar bear's fur appears white. Leucophores will also reflect any filtered light shown on them . . . If the water appears blue at a certain depth, the octopuses and cuttlefish can appear blue; if the water appears green, they appear green, and so on and so forth.

1. Which one of the following statements is not true about the camouflaging ability of Cephalopods?

(1) Cephalopods can blend into the colour of their surroundings.

(2) Cephalopods can take on the colour of their predator.

(3) Cephalopods can change their colour.

(4) Cephalopods can change their texture.

2. Based on the passage, we can infer that all of the following statements, if true, would weaken the camouflaging adeptness of Cephalopods EXCEPT:

(1) the hydrostatic pressure at the depths at which Cephalopods reside renders radial muscle movements difficult.

(2) the temperature of water at the depths at which Cephalopods reside renders the transmission of neural signals difficult.

(3) the number of chromatophores in Cephalopods is half the number of iridophores and leucophores.

(4) light reflects the colours red, green, and yellow at the depths at which Cephalopods reside.

3. Based on the passage, it can be inferred that camouflaging techniques in an octopus are most dissimilar to those in:

(1) squids (2) polar bears

(3) cuttlefish (4) sea snails

4. All of the following are reasons for octopuses being "misfits" EXCEPT that they:

(1) are consumed by humans and other animals.

(2) do not possess an outer protective shell.

(3) have several arms.

(4) exhibit higher intelligence than other molluscs.

Question Numbers (5 to 8): The passage below is accompanied by a set of questions. Choose the best answer to each question.

When we teach engineering problems now, we ask students to come to a single "best" solution defined by technical ideals like low cost, speed to build, and ability to scale. This way of teaching primes students to believe that their decision-making is purely objective, as it is grounded in math and science. This is known as technical-social dualism, the idea that the technical and social dimensions of engineering problems are readily separable and remain distinct throughout the problem-definition and solution process.

Nontechnical parameters such as access to a technology, cultural relevancy or potential harms are deemed political and invalid in this way of learning. But those technical ideals are at their core social and political choices determined by a dominant culture focused on economic growth for the most privileged segments of society. By choosing to downplay public welfare as a critical parameter for engineering design, we risk creating a culture of disengagement from societal concerns amongst engineers that is antithetical to the ethical code of engineering.

In my field of medical devices, ignoring social dimensions has real consequences.... Most FDA-approved drugs are incorrectly dosed for people assigned female at birth, leading to unexpected adverse reactions. This is because they have been inadequately represented in clinical trials.

Beyond physical failings, subjective beliefs treated as facts by those in decision-making roles can encode social inequities. For example, spirometers, routinely used devices that measure lung capacity, still have correction factors that automatically assume smaller lung capacity in Black and Asian individuals. These racially based adjustments are derived from research done by eugenicists who thought these racial differences were biologically determined and who considered nonwhite people as inferior. These machines ignore the influence of social and environmental factors on lung capacity.

Many technologies for systemically marginalized people have not been built because they were not deemed important such as better early diagnostics and treatment for diseases like endometriosis, a disease that afflicts 10 percent of people with uteruses. And we hardly question whether devices are built sustainably, which has led to a crisis of medical waste and health care accounting for 10 percent of U.S. greenhouse gas emissions.

Social justice must be made core to the way engineers are trained. Some universities are working on this.... Engineers taught this way will be prepared to think critically about what problems we choose to solve, how we do so responsibly and how we build teams that challenge our ways of thinking.

Individual engineering professors are also working to embed societal needs in their pedagogy. Darshan Karwat at the University of Arizona developed activist engineering to challenge engineers to acknowledge their full moral and social responsibility through practical self-reflection. Khalid Kadir at the University of California, Berkeley, created the popular course Engineering, Environment, and Society that teaches engineers how to engage in place-based knowledge, an understanding of the people, context and history, to design better technical approaches in collaboration with communities. When we design and build with equity and justice in mind, we craft better solutions that respond to the complexities of entrenched systemic problems.

5. All of the following are examples of the negative outcomes of focusing on technical ideals in the medical sphere EXCEPT the:

(1) neglect of research and development of medical technologies for the diagnosis and treatment of diseases that typically afflict marginalised communities.

(2) continuing calibration of medical devices based on past racial biases that have remained unadjusted for changes.

(3) exclusion of non-privileged groups in clinical trials which leads to incorrect drug dosages.

(4) incorrect assignment of people as female at birth which has resulted in faulty drug interventions.

6. We can infer that the author would approve of a more evolved engineering pedagogy that includes all of the following EXCEPT:

(1) making considerations of environmental sustainability intrinsic to the development of technological solutions.

(2) a more responsible approach to technical design and problem-solving than a focus on speed in developing and bringing to scale.

(3) design that is based on the needs of communities using local knowledge and responding to local priorities.

(4) moving towards technical-social dualism where social community needs are incorporated in problem-definition and solutions.

7. In this passage, the author is making the claim that:
   (1) engineering students today are taught to focus on objective technical outcomes, independent of the social dimensions of their work.
   (2) the objective of best solutions in engineering has shifted the focus of pedagogy from humanism and social obligations to technological perfection.
   (3) technical-social dualism has emerged as a technique for engineering students to incorporate social considerations into their technical problem-solving processes.
   (4) engineering students today are trained to be non-subjective in their reasoning as this best enables them to develop much-needed universal solutions.
8. The author gives all of the following reasons for why marginalised people are systematically discriminated against in technology-related interventions EXCEPT:
   (1) "Beyond physical failings, subjective beliefs treated as facts by those in decision-making roles can encode social inequities."
   (2) "These racially based adjustments are derived from research done by eugenicists who thought these racial differences were biologically determined and who considered nonwhite people as inferior."
   (3) "And we hardly question whether devices are built sustainably, which has led to a crisis of medical waste and health care accounting for 10 percent of U.S. greenhouse gas emissions."
   (4) "But those technical ideals are at their core social and political choices determined by a dominant culture focused on economic growth for the most privileged segments of society."

Question Numbers (9 to 12): The passage below is accompanied by a set of questions. Choose the best answer to each question.

Humans today make music. Think beyond all the qualifications that might trail after this bald statement: that only certain humans make music, that extensive training is involved, that many societies distinguish musical specialists from nonmusicians, that in today's societies most listen to music rather than making it, and so forth. These qualifications, whatever their local merit, are moot in the face of the overarching truth that making music, considered from a cognitive and psychological vantage, is the province of all those who perceive and experience what is made. We are, almost all of us, musicians — everyone who can entrain (not necessarily dance) to a beat, who can recognize a repeated tune (not necessarily sing it), who can distinguish one instrument or one singing voice from another. I will often use an antique word, recently revived, to name this broader musical experience. Humans are musicking creatures....

The set of capacities that enables musicking is a principal marker of modern humanity. There is nothing polemical in this assertion except a certain insistence, which will figure often in what follows, that musicking be included in our thinking about fundamental human commonalities. Capacities involved in musicking are many and take shape in complicated ways, arising from innate dispositions . . . Most of these capacities overlap with nonmusical ones, though a few may be distinct and dedicated to musical perception and production. In the area of overlap, linguistic capacities seem to be particularly important, and humans are (in principle) language-makers in addition to music-makers — speaking creatures as well as musicking ones.

Humans are symbol-makers too, a feature tightly bound up with language, not so tightly with music. The species Cassirer dubbed Homo symbolicus cannot help but tangle musicking in webs of symbolic thought and expression, habitually making it a component of behavioral complexes that form such expression. But in fundamental features musicking is neither language-like nor symbol-like, and from these differences come many clues to its ancient emergence.

If musicking is a primary, shared trait of modern humans, then to describe its emergence must be to detail the coalescing of that modernity. This took place, archaeologists are clear, over a very long durée: at least 50,000 years or so, more likely something closer to 200,000, depending in part on what that coalescence is taken to comprise. If we look back 20,000 years, a small portion of this long period, we reach the lives of humans whose musical capacities were probably little different from our own. As we look farther back we reach horizons where this similarity can no longer hold — perhaps 40,000 years ago, perhaps 70,000, perhaps 100,000. But we never cross a line before which all the cognitive capacities recruited in modern musicking abruptly disappear. Unless we embrace the incredible notion that music sprang forth in full-blown glory, its emergence will have to be tracked in gradualist terms across a long period.

This is one general feature of a history of music's emergence . . . The history was at once sociocultural and biological . . . The capacities recruited in musicking are many, so describing its emergence involves following several or many separate strands.

9. Which one of the following statements, if true, would weaken the author's claim that humans are musicking creatures?

(1) Nonmusical capacities are of far greater consequence to human survival than the capacity for music.

(2) Musical capacities are primarily socio-cultural, which explains the wide diversity of musical forms.

(3) From a cognitive and psychological vantage, musicking arises from unconscious dispositions, not conscious ones.

(4) As musicking is neither language-like nor symbol-like, it is a much older form of expression.

10. Which one of the following sets of terms best serves as keywords to the passage?

(1) Humans; Musicking; Linguistic capacities; Symbol-making; Modern humanity.

(2) Humans; Capacities; Language; Symbols; Modernity.

(3) Humans; Psychological vantage; Musicking; Cassirer; Emergence of music.

(4) Musicking; Cognitive psychology; Antique; Symbol-makers; Modernity.

11. "Think beyond all the qualifications that might trail after this bald statement . . ." In the context of the passage, what is the author trying to communicate in this quoted extract?

(1) Thinking beyond qualifications allows us to give free reign to musical expressions.

(2) Although there may be many caveats and other considerations, the statement is essentially true.

(3) A bald statement is one that is trailed by a series of qualifying clarifications and caveats.

(4) A bald statement is one that requires no qualifications to infer its meaning.

12. Based on the passage, which one of the following statements is a valid argument about the emergence of music/musicking?

(1) 20,000 years ago, human musical capacities were not very different from what they are today.

(2) Although musicking is not language-like, it shares the quality of being a form of expression.

(3) Anyone who can perceive and experience music must be considered capable of musicking.

(4) All musical work is located in the overlap between linguistic capacity and music production.

Question Numbers (13 to 16): The passage below is accompanied by a set of questions. Choose the best answer to each question.

We begin with the emergence of the philosophy of the social sciences as an arena of thought and as a set of social institutions. The two characterisations overlap but are not congruent. Academic disciplines are social institutions. . . . My view is that institutions are all those social entities that organise action: they link acting individuals into social structures. There are various kinds of institutions. Hegelians and Marxists emphasise universal institutions such as the family, rituals, governance, economy and the military. These are mostly institutions that just grew. Perhaps in some imaginary beginning of time they spontaneously appeared. In their present incarnations, however, they are very much the product of conscious attempts to mould and plan them. We have family law, established and disestablished churches, constitutions and laws, including those governing the economy and the military. Institutions deriving from statute, like joint-stock companies are formal by contrast with informal ones such as friendships. There are some institutions that come in both informal and formal variants, as well as in mixed ones. Consider the fact that the stock exchange and the black market are both market institutions, one formal one not. Consider further that there are many features of the work of the stock exchange that rely on informal, noncodifiable agreements, not least the language used for communication. To be precise, mixtures are the norm . . . From constitutions at the top to by-laws near the bottom we are always adding to, or tinkering with, earlier institutions, the grown and the designed are intertwined.

It is usual in social thought to treat culture and tradition as different from, although alongside, institutions. The view taken here is different. Culture and tradition are sub-sets of institutions analytically isolated for explanatory or expository purposes. Some social scientists have taken all institutions, even purely local ones, to be entities that satisfy basic human needs – under local conditions . . . Others differed and declared any structure of reciprocal roles and norms an institution. Most of these differences are differences of emphasis rather than disagreements. Let us straddle all these versions and present institutions very generally . . . as structures that serve to coordinate the actions of individuals. . . . Institutions themselves then have no aims or purpose other than those given to them by actors or used by actors to explain them . . .

Language is the formative institution for social life and for science . . . Both formal and informal language is involved, naturally grown or designed. (Language is all of these to varying degrees.) Languages are paradigms of institutions or, from another perspective, nested sets of institutions. Syntax, semantics, lexicon and alphabet/character-set are all institutions within the larger institutional framework of a written language. Natural languages are typical examples of what Ferguson called 'the result of human action, but not the execution of any human design'[;] reformed natural languages and artificial languages introduce design into their modifications or refinements of natural language. Above all, languages are paradigms of institutional tools that function to coordinate.

13. Consider the fact that the stock exchange and the black market are both market institutions, one formal one not." Which one of the following statements best explains this quote, in the context of the passage?

(1) Market instruments can be formally traded in the stock exchange and informally traded in the black market.

(2) The stock exchange and the black market are both organised to function by rules.

(3) The stock exchange and the black market are examples of how, even within the same domain, different kinds of institutions can co-exist.

(4) The stock exchange and the black market are both dependent on the market to survive.

14. Which of the following statements best represents the essence of the passage?

(1) The stock exchange and the black market are both market institutions.

(2) It is usual in social thought to treat culture and tradition as different from institutions.

(3) Institutions are structures that serve to coordinate the actions of individuals.

(4) Language is the fundamental formal institution for social life and for science.

15. All of the following inferences from the passage are false, EXCEPT:

(1) as concepts, "culture" and "tradition" have no analytical, explanatory or expository power, especially when they are treated in isolation.

(2) "natural language" refers to that stage of language development where no conscious human intent is evident in the formation of language.

(3) the institution of friendship cannot be found in the institution of joint-stock companies because the first is an informal institution, while the second is a formal one.

(4) institutions like the family, rituals, governance, economy, and the military are natural and cannot be consciously modified.

16. In the first paragraph of the passage, what are the two "characterisations" that are seen as overlapping but not congruent?

(1) "the philosophy of the social sciences" and "a set of social institutions".

(2) "individuals" and "social structures".

(3) "an arena of thought" and "academic disciplines".

(4) "academic disciplines" and "institutions".

17. The four sentences (labelled 1, 2, 3 and 4) below, when properly sequenced, would yield a coherent paragraph.

Decide on the proper sequencing of the order of the sentences and key in the sequence of the four numbers as your answer:

(1) From chemical pollutants in the environment to the damming of rivers to invasive species transported through global trade and travel, every environmental issue is different and there is no single tech solution that can solve this crisis.

(2) Discourse on the threat of environmental collapse revolves around cutting down emissions, but biodiversity loss and ecosystem collapse are caused by myriad and diverse reasons.

(3) This would require legislation that recognises the rights of future generations and other species that allows the judiciary to uphold a much higher standard of environmental protection than currently possible.

(4) Clearly, our environmental crisis requires large political solutions, not minor technological ones, so, instead of focusing on infinite growth, we could consider a path of stable-state economies, while preserving markets and healthy competition.

18. There is a sentence that is missing in the paragraph below. Look at the paragraph and decide in which blank (option 1, 2, 3, or 4) the following sentence would best fit.

Sentence: Most were first-time users of a tablet and a digital app.

Paragraph: Aage Badhein's USP lies in the ethnographic research that constituted the foundation of its development process. Customizations based on learning directly from potential users were critical to making this self-paced app suitable for both a literate and non-literate audience. ___(1)___ The user interface caters to a Hindi-speaking audience who have minimal to no experience with digital services and devices. ___(2)___ The content and functionality of the app are suitable for a wide audience. This includes youth preparing for an independent role in life or a student ready to create a strong foundation of financial management early in her life. ___(3)___ Household members desirous of improving their family's financial strength to reach their aspirations can also benefit. We piloted Aage Badhein in early 2021 with over 400 women from rural areas. ___(4)___ The digital solution generated a large amount of interest in the communities.

(1) Option 1 (2) Option 2

(3) Option 3 (4) Option 4

19. The passage given below is followed by four alternate summaries. Choose the option that best captures the essence of the passage.

Several of the world's earliest cities were organised along egalitarian lines. In some regions, urban populations governed themselves for centuries without any indication of the temples and palaces that would later emerge; in others, temples and palaces never emerged at all, and there is simply no evidence of a class of administrators or any other sort of ruling stratum. It would seem that the mere fact of urban life does not, necessarily, imply any particular form of political organization, and never did. Far from resigning us to inequality, the picture that is now emerging of humanity's past may open our eyes to egalitarian possibilities we otherwise would have never considered.

(1) We now have the evidence in support of the existence of an egalitarian urban life in some ancient cities, where political and civic organisation was far less hierarchical.

(2) Contrary to our assumption that urban settlements have always involved hierarchical political and administrative structures, ancient cities were not organised in this way.

(3) The lack of hierarchical administration in ancient cities can be deduced by the absence of religious and regal structures such as temples and palaces.

(4) The emergence of a class of administrators and ruling stratum transformed the egalitarian urban life of ancient cities to the hierarchical civic organisations of today.

20. The passage given below is followed by four alternate summaries. Choose the option that best captures the essence of the passage.

There's a common idea that museum artworks are somehow timeless objects available to admire for generations to come. But many are objects of decay. Even the most venerable Old Master paintings don't escape: pigments discolour, varnishes crack, canvases warp. This challenging fact of art-world life is down to something that sounds more like a thread from a morality tale: inherent vice. Damien Hirst's iconic shark floating in a tank – entitled The Physical Impossibility of Death in the Mind of Someone Living – is a work that put a spotlight on inherent vice. When he made it in 1991, Hirst got himself in a pickle by not using the right kind of pickle to preserve the giant fish. The result was that the shark began to decompose quite quickly – its preserving liquid clouding, the skin wrinkling, and an unpleasant smell wafting from the tank.

(1) Artworks may not last forever; they may deteriorate with time, and the challenge is to slow down their degeneration.

(2) The role of museums has evolved to ensure that the artworks are preserved forever in addition to guarding and displaying them.

(3) Museums have to guard timeless art treasures from intrinsic defects such as the deterioration of paint, polish and canvas.

(4) Museums are left with the moral responsibility of restoring and preserving the artworks since artists cannot preserve their works beyond their life.

21. The four sentences (labelled 1, 2, 3 and 4) below, when properly sequenced, would yield a coherent paragraph.

Decide on the proper sequencing of the order of the sentences and key in the sequence of the four numbers as your answer:

(1) Women may prioritize cooking because they feel they alone are responsible for mediating a toxic and unhealthy food system.

(2) Food is commonly framed through the lens of individual choice: you can choose to eat healthily.

(3) This is particularly so in a neoliberal context where the state has transferred the responsibility for food onto individual consumers.

(4) The individualized framing of choice appeals to a popular desire to experience agency, but draws away from the structural obstacles that stratify individual food choices.

22. The passage given below is followed by four alternate summaries. Choose the option that best captures the essence of the passage.

Today, many of the debates about behavioural control in the age of big data echo Cold War-era anxieties about brainwashing, insidious manipulation and repression in the 'technological society'. In his book Psychopolitics, Han warns of the sophisticated use of targeted online content, enabling 'influence to take place on a pre-reflexive level'. On our current trajectory, "freedom will prove to have been merely an interlude." The fear is that the digital age has not liberated us but exposed us, by offering up our private lives to machine-learning algorithms that can process masses of personal and behavioural data. In a world of influencers and digital entrepreneurs, it's not easy to imagine the resurgence of a culture engendered through disconnect and disaffiliation, but concerns over the threat of online targeting, polarisation and big data have inspired recent polemics about the need to rediscover solitude and disconnect.

(1) The notion of freedom and privacy is at stake in a world where artificial intelligence is capable of influencing behaviour through data gathered online.

(2) The role of technology in influencing public behaviour is reminiscent of the manner in which behaviour was manipulated during the Cold War.

(3) Rather than freeing us, digital technology is enslaving us by collecting personal information and influencing our online behaviour.

(4) With big data making personal information freely available, the debate on the nature of freedom and the need for privacy has resurfaced.

23. The four sentences (labelled 1, 2, 3 and 4) below, when properly sequenced, would yield a coherent paragraph.

Decide on the proper sequencing of the order of the sentences and key in the sequence of the four numbers as your answer:

(1) The trajectory of cheerfulness through the self is linked to the history of the word 'cheer' which comes from an Old French meaning 'face'.

(2) Translations of the Bible into vernacular languages, expanded the noun 'cheer' into the more abstract 'cheerful-ness', something that circulates as an emotional and social quality defining the self and a moral community.

(3) When you take on a cheerful expression, no matter what the state of your soul, your cheerfulness moves into the self: the interior of the self is changed by the power of cheer.

(4) People in the medieval 'Canterbury Tales' have a 'piteous' or a 'sober' cheer; 'cheer' is an expression and a body part, lying at the intersection of emotions and physiognomy.

24. There is a sentence that is missing in the paragraph below. Look at the paragraph and decide in which blank (option 1, 2, 3, or 4) the following sentence would best fit.

Sentence: This was years in the making but fast-tracked during the pandemic, when "people started being more mindful about their food", he explained.

Paragraph: For millennia, ghee has been a venerated staple of the subcontinental diet, but it fell out of favour a few decades ago when saturated fats were largely considered to be unhealthy. ___(1)___ But more recently, as the thinking around saturated fats is shifting globally, Indians are finding their own way back to this ingredient that is so integral to their cuisine. ___(2)___ For Karmakar, a renewed interest in ghee is emblematic of a return-to-basics movement in India. ___(3)___ This movement is also part of an overall trend towards "slow food". In keeping with the movement's philosophy, ghee can be produced locally (even at home) and has inextricable cultural ties. ___(4)___ At a basic level, ghee is a type of clarified butter believed to have originated in India as a way to preserve butter from going rancid in the hot climate.

(1) Option 1 (2) Option 2
(3) Option 3 (4) Option 4

Section II : DI & LR

Question Numbers (1 to 5): Every day a widget supplier supplies widgets from the warehouse (W) to four locations – Ahmednagar (A), Bikrampore (B), Chitrachak (C), and Deccan Park (D). The daily demand for widgets in each location is uncertain and independent of each other. Demands and corresponding probability values (in parenthesis) are given against each location (A, B, C, and D) in the figure below. For example, there is a 40% chance that the demand in Ahmednagar will be 50 units and a 60% chance that the demand will be 70 units. The lines in the figure connecting the locations and warehouse represent two-way roads connecting those places with the distances (in km) shown beside the line. The distances in both the directions along a road are equal. For example, the road from Ahmednagar to Bikrampore and the road from Bikrampore to Ahmednagar are both 6 km long.

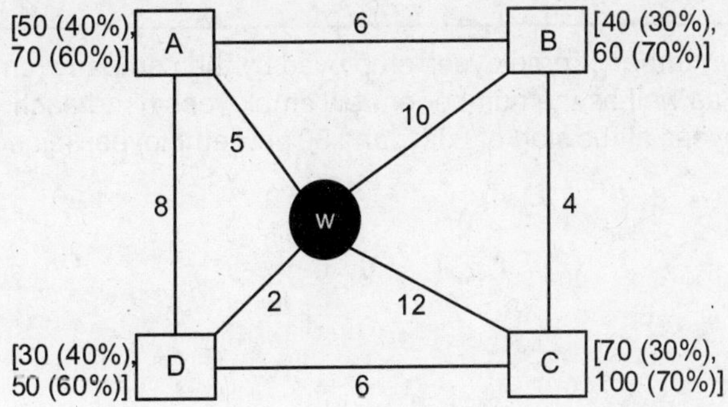

Every day the supplier gets the information about the demand values of the four locations and creates the travel route that starts from the warehouse and ends at a location after visiting all the locations exactly once. While making the route plan, the supplier goes to the locations in decreasing order of demand. If there is a tie for the choice of the next location, the supplier will go to the location closest to the current location. Also, while creating the route, the supplier can either follow the direct path (if available) from one location to another or can take the path via the warehouse. If both paths are available (direct and via warehouse), the supplier will choose the path with minimum distance.

1. If the last location visited is Ahmednagar, then what is the total distance covered in the route (in km)?
2. If the total number of widgets delivered in a day is 250 units, then what is the total distance covered in the route (in km)?
3. What is the chance that the total number of widgets delivered in a day is 260 units and the route ends at Bikrampore?
   (1) 7.56% (2) 33.33%
   (3) 10.80% (4) 17.64%
4. If the first location visited from the warehouse is Ahmednagar, then what is the chance that the total distance covered in the route is 40 km?
   (1) 30% (2) 3.24%
   (3) 18% (4) 5.4%
5. If Ahmednagar is not the first location to be visited in a route and the total route distance is 29 km, then which of the following is a possible number of widgets delivered on that day?
   (1) 220 (2) 250
   (3) 200 (4) 210

Question Numbers (6 to 10): The two plots below show data for four companies code-named A, B, C, and D over three years - 2019, 2020, and 2021.

The first plot shows the revenues and costs incurred by the companies during these years. For example, in 2021, company C earned Rs.100 crores in revenue and spent Rs.30 crores. The profit of a company is defined as its revenue minus its costs.

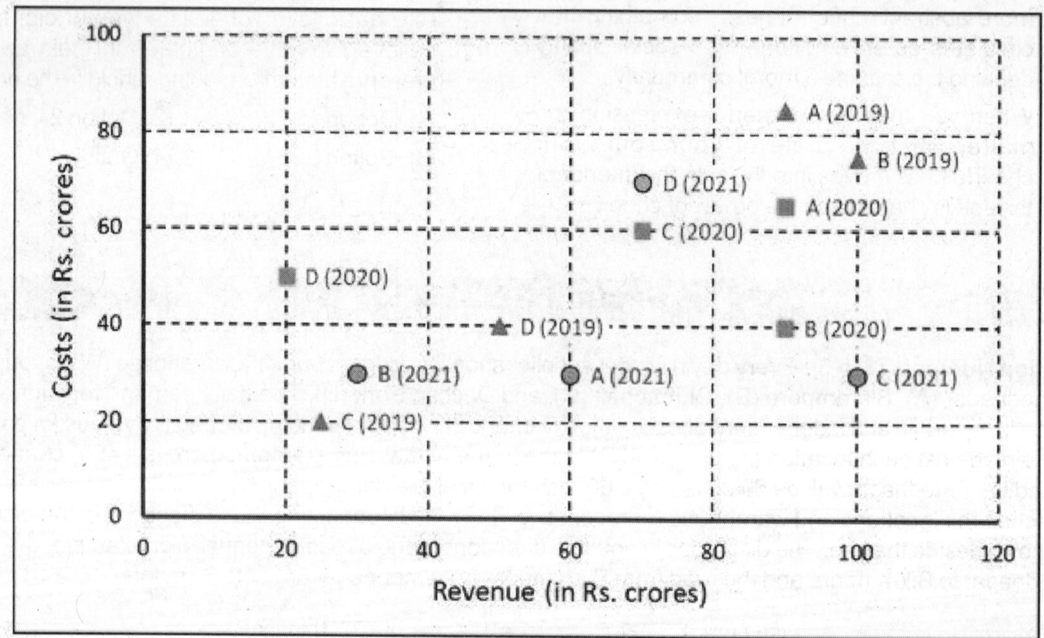

The second plot shows the number of employees employed by the company (employee strength) at the start of each of these three years, as well as the number of new employees hired each year (new hires). For example, Company B had 250 employees at the start of 2021, and 30 new employees joined the company during the year.

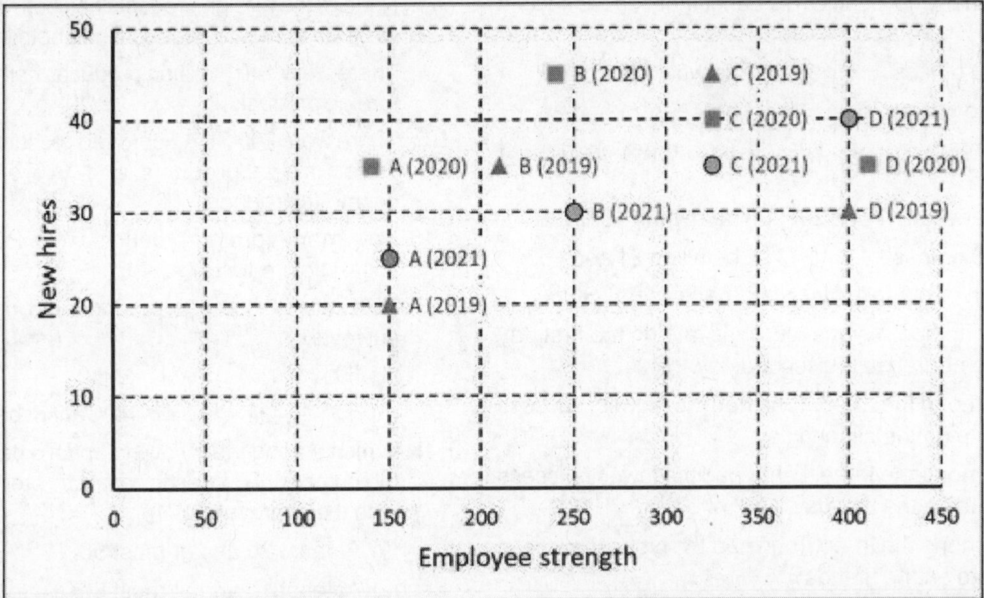

6. Considering all three years, which company had the highest annual profit?
(1) Company A (2) Company B
(3) Company C (4) Company D

7. Which of the four companies experienced the highest annual loss in any of the years?
(1) Company A (2) Company C
(3) Company B (4) Company D

8. The ratio of a company's annual profit to its annual costs is a measure of its performance. Which of the four companies had the lowest value of this ratio in 2019?
(1) Company D (2) Company C
(3) Company B (4) Company A

9. The total number of employees lost in 2019 and 2020 was the least for:
(1) Company D (2) Company A
(3) Company C (4) Company B

10. Profit per employee is the ratio of a company's profit to its employee strength. For this purpose, the employee strength in a year is the average of the employee strength at the beginning of that year and the beginning of the next year. In 2020, which of the four companies had the highest profit per employee?
(1) Company D (2) Company B
(3) Company A (4) Company C

Question Numbers (11 to 15): A few salesmen are employed to sell a product called TRICCEK among households in various housing complexes. On each day, a salesman is assigned to visit one housing complex. Once a salesman enters a housing complex, he can meet any number of households in the time available. However, if a household makes a complaint against the salesman, then he must leave the housing complex immediately and cannot meet any other household on that day. A household may buy any number of TRICCEK items or may not buy any item. The salesman needs to record the total number of TRICCEK items sold as well as the number of households met in each day. The success rate of a salesman for a day is defined as the ratio of the number of items sold to the number of households met on that day. Some details about the performances of three salesmen - Tohri, Hokli and Lahur, on two particular days are given below.

1. Over the two days, all three of them met the same total number of households, and each of them sold a total of 100 items.
2. On both days, Lahur met the same number of households and sold the same number of items.
3. Hokli could not sell any item on the second day because the first household he met on that day complained against him.
4. Tohri met 30 more households on the second day than on the first day.
5. Tohri's success rate was twice that of Lahur's on the first day, and it was 75% of Lahur's on the second day.

11. What was the total number of households met by Tohri, Hokli and Lahur on the first day?

12. How many TRICCEK items were sold by Tohri on the first day?

13. How many households did Lahur meet on the second day?

(1) 20 or less (2) between 30 and 35

(3) more than 35 (4) between 21 and 29

14. How many households did Tohri meet on the first day?

(1) between 11 and 20 (2) more than 40

(3) 10 or less (4) between 21 and 40

15. Which of the following statements is FALSE?

(1) Tohri had a higher success rate on the first day compared to the second day.

(2) Among the three, Tohri had the highest success rate on the second day.

(3) Among the three, Lahur had the lowest success rate on the first day.

(4) Among the three, Tohri had the highest success rate on the first day.

Question Numbers (16 to 20): A speciality supermarket sells 320 products. Each of these products was either a cosmetic product or a nutrition product. Each of these products was also either a foreign product or a domestic product. Each of these products had at least one of the two approvals – FDA or EU.

The following facts are also known:

1. There were equal numbers of domestic and foreign products.
2. Half of the domestic products were FDA approved cosmetic products.
3. None of the foreign products had both the approvals, while 60 domestic products had both the approvals.
4. There were 140 nutrition products, half of them were foreign products.
5. There were 200 FDA approved products. 70 of them were foreign products and 120 of them were cosmetic products.

16. How many foreign products were FDA approved cosmetic products?

17. How many cosmetic products did not have FDA approval?

(1) 60 (2) 10

(3) 50 (4) Cannot be determined

18. Which among the following options best represents the number of domestic cosmetic products that had both the approvals?

(1) At least 20 and at most 50

(2) At least 10 and at most 80

(3) At least 20 and at most 70

(4) At least 10 and at most 60

19. If 70 cosmetic products did not have EU approval, then how many nutrition products had both the approvals?

(1) 20 (2) 30

(3) 50 (4) 10

20. If 50 nutrition products did not have EU approval, then how many domestic cosmetic products did not have EU approval?

Section III : QA

1. There are two containers of the same volume, first container half-filled with sugar syrup and the second container half-filled with milk. Half the content of the first container is transferred to the second container, and then the half of this mixture is transferred back to the first container. Next, half the content of the first container is transferred back to the second container. Then the ratio of sugar syrup and milk in the second container is

(1) 4 : 5 (2) 5 : 6

(3) 6 : 5 (4) 5 : 4

2. In an examination, there were 75 questions. 3 marks were awarded for each correct answer, 1 mark was deducted for each wrong answer and 1 mark was awarded for each unattempted question. Rayan scored a total of 97 marks in the examination. If the number of unattempted questions was higher than the number of attempted questions, then the maximum number of correct answers that Rayan could have given in the examination is

3. The length of each side of an equilateral triangle ABC is 3 cm. Let D be a point on BC such that the area of triangle ADC is half the area of triangle ABD. Then the length of AD, in cm, is

(1) $\sqrt{7}$ (2) $\sqrt{8}$

(3) $\sqrt{6}$ (4) $\sqrt{5}$

4. Two ships meet mid-ocean, and then, one ship goes south and the other ship goes west, both travelling at constant speeds. Two hours later, they are 60 km apart. If the speed of one of the ships is 6 km per hour more than the other one, then the speed, in km per hour, of the slower ship is

(1) 20 (2) 18

(3) 24 (4) 12

5. The number of integers greater than 2000 that can be formed with the digits 0, 1, 2, 3, 4, 5, using each digit at most once, is

(1) 1440 (2) 1480

(3) 1420 (4) 1200

6. The number of integer solutions of the equation $(x^2 - 10)^{(x^2 - 3x - 10)} = 1$ is

7. Five students, including Amit, appear for an examination in which possible marks are integers between 0 and 50, both inclusive. The average marks for all the students is 38 and exactly three students got more than 32. If no two students got the same marks and Amit got the least marks among the five students, then the difference between the highest and lowest possible marks of Amit is

(1) 20 (2) 21
(3) 22 (4) 24

8. If a and b are non-negative real numbers such that a + 2b = 6, then the average of the maximum and minimum possible values of (a + b) is

(1) 3 (2) 4.5
(3) 4 (4) 3.5

9. Regular polygons A and B have number of sides in the ratio 1 : 2 and interior angles in the ratio 3 : 4. Then the number of sides of B equals

10. Mr. Pinto invests one-fifth of his capital at 6%, one-third at 10% and the remaining at 1%, each rate being simple interest per annum. Then, the minimum number of years required for the cumulative interest income from these investments to equal or exceed his initial capital is

11. In an election, there were four candidates and 80% of the registered voters casted their votes. One of the candidates received 30% of the casted votes while the other three candidates received the remaining casted votes in the proportion 1 : 2 : 3. If the winner of the election received 2512 votes more than the candidate with the second highest votes, then the number of registered voters was

(1) 60288 (2) 62800
(3) 50240 (4) 40192

12. Let r and c be real numbers. If r and –r are roots of $5x^3 + cx^2 - 10x + 9 = 0$, then c equals

(1) 4 (2) –9/2
(3) –4 (4) 9/2

13. Suppose for all integers x, there are two functions f and g such that $f(x) + f(x-1) - 1 = 0$ and $g(x) = x^2$. If $f(x^2 - x) = 5$, then the value of the sum $f(g(5)) + g(f(5))$ is

14. Let f(x) be a quadratic polynomial in x such that $f(x) \geq 0$ for all real numbers x. If f(2) = 0 and f(4) = 6, then f(–2) is equal to

(1) 12 (2) 6
(3) 36 (4) 24

15. Consider the arithmetic progression 3, 7, 11, ... and let A_n denote the sum of the first n terms of this progression. Then the value of $\frac{1}{25}\sum_{n=1}^{25} A_n$ is

(1) 442 (2) 415
(3) 455 (4) 404

16. Working alone, the times taken by Anu, Tanu and Manu to complete any job are in the ratio 5 : 8 : 10. They accept a job which they can finish in 4 days if they all work together for 8 hours per day. However, Anu and Tanu work together for the first 6 days, working 6 hours 40 minutes per day. Then, the number of hours that Manu will take to complete the remaining job working alone is

17. For some natural number n, assume that (15,000)! is divisible by (n!)!. The largest possible value of n is

(1) 4 (2) 6
(3) 7 (4) 5

18. In triangle ABC, altitudes AD and BE are drawn to the corresponding bases. If ∠BAC = 45° and ∠ABC = θ, then AD/BE equals

(1) 1 (2) $\frac{(\sin\theta + \cos\theta)}{\sqrt{2}}$
(3) $\sqrt{2}\cos\theta$ (4) $\sqrt{2}\sin\theta$

19. The average of a non-decreasing sequence of N numbers $a_1, a_2, \ldots, a_N$ is 300. If a_1 is replaced by $6a_1$, the new average becomes 400. Then the number of possible values of a_1 is

20. On day one, there are 100 particles in a laboratory experiment. On day n, where $n \geq 2$, one out of every n particles produces another particle. If the total number of particles in the laboratory experiment increases to 1000 on day m, then m equals.

(1) 18 (2) 19
(3) 16 (4) 17

21. Manu earns Rs. 4000 per month and wants to save an average of Rs. 550 per month in a year. In the first nine months, his monthly expense was Rs. 3500, and he foresees that, tenth month onward, his monthly expense will increase to Rs. 3700. In order to meet his yearly savings target, his monthly earnings, in rupees, from the tenth month onward should be

(1) 4300 (2) 4200
(3) 4350 (4) 4400

22. The number of distinct integer values of n satisfying $\frac{4 - \log_2 n}{3 - \log_4 n} < 0$, is

ANSWERS

VARC

1. (2) **2.** (3) **3.** (4) **4.** (1) **5.** (4) **6.** (4) **7.** (1) **8.** (3) **9.** (2) **10.** (1)
11. (2) **12.** (1) **13.** (3) **14.** (3) **15.** (2) **16.** (4) **17.** (2143) **18.** (4) **19.** (1) **20.** (1)
21. (2431) **22.** (4) **23.** (3142) **24.** (3)

DI & LR

1. (35) **2.** (38) **3.** (1) **4.** (3) **5.** (4) **6.** (3) **7.** (4) **8.** (4) **9.** (4) **10.** (2)
11. (84) **12.** (40) **13.** (4) **14.** (3) **15.** (2) **16.** (40) **17.** (1) **18.** (4) **19.** (4) **20.** (50)

QA

1. (2) **2.** (24) **3.** (1) **4.** (2) **5.** (1) **6.** (4) **7.** (1) **8.** (2) **9.** (10) **10.** (20)
11. (2) **12.** (2) **13.** (12) **14.** (4) **15.** (3) **16.** (6) **17.** (3) **18.** (4) **19.** (14) **20.** (2)
21. (4) **22.** (47)

EXPLANATIONS

VARC

1. 2 Option 2 is nowhere stated or implied in the passage. Rest of the options can be inferred from the third, fourth and fifth paragraphs.

2. 3 The argument that the number of chromatophores in Cephalopods is half the number of iridophores and leucophores.does not imply that the Cephalopods are not capable of practicing camouflage. Therefore, option 3 is the correct answer.

3. 4 Cuttlefish, squid and polar bear have been mentioned in the last twp paragraphs of the passage. Snails have been termed dissimilar in the first paragraph of the passage.

4. 1 Options 2 and 3 can be inferred from the first paragraph of the passage. Option 4 can be inferred from the second paragraph.

5. 4 Option 4 distorts the implication of these lines of the passage: 'Most FDA-approved drugs are incorrectly dosed for people assigned female at birth, leading to unexpected adverse reactions.' Therefore, option 4 is the correct answer.

6. 4 Refer to these lines of the passage: 'Nontechnical parameters such as access to a technology, cultural relevancy or potential harms are deemed political and invalid in this way of learning. But those technical ideals are at their core social and political choices determined by a dominant culture focused on economic growth for the most privileged segments of society. By choosing to downplay public welfare as a critical parameter for engineering design, we risk creating a culture of disengagement from societal concerns amongst engineers that is antithetical to the ethical code of engineering.' Options 1, 2 and 3 can be inferred from these lines. Option 4 contradicts the main idea of the first paragraph.

7. 1 Option 1 can be inferred from the first paragraph of the passage: **'When we teach engineering ... and solution process.'** Option 2 does not present the author's main point as the passage does not mentions any shift in the engineering pedagogy.

Option 3 contradicts the arguments of the passage. So does option 4.

8. 3 All options except 3 relate to why marginalized people are systematically discriminated against in technology-related interventions: racially-based adjustments are derived from research done by eugenicists; subjective beliefs treated as facts encodes social inequities and the supposed technical 'ideals' are determined by a culture focused on the privileged.

9. 2 Option 1 does not question the claim that humans are mucking by nature. Option 3 strengthens the claim that humans are musicking creatures. Option 4 states about how old musicking is. It, by no means, weakens the claim humans are musicking creatures. Option 2 questions the argument stated through these lines:' capacities involved in musicking are many and take shape in complicated ways, arising from *innate* dispositions...' Therefore, option 2 is the correct answer.

10. 1 Option 2 misses out musicking. Therefore, it loses the main essence of the passage. Option 3 omits linguistic capacities and narrows down to Cassirer, which is not representative of any key arguments of the passage. Option 4 omits 'capacities'. Therefore, option 1 serves as the keywords to the passage.

11. 2 "Think beyond all the qualifications that might trail after this bald statement . . ." Through these lines the author wants to state that despite multiple qualifications that one might think about while thinking about musicians, humans are necessarily musicking. Therefore, option 2 is correct.

12. 1 Refer to these lines of the passage: '**If we look back 20,000 years, a small portion of this long period, we reach the lives of humans whose musical capacities were probably little different from our own.**' Option 1 can be inferred from these lines. Therefore, option 1 is the correct answer.

13. 3 Refer to these lines of the passage: '**here are some institutions that come in both informal and formal variants, as well as in mixed ones. Consider the fact that the stock exchange and the black market are both market institutions, one formal one not.**' Clearly, through these lines, the author wants to imply exactly what option 3 states.

14. 3 Option 1 is too narrow in its scope.

Option 2 incorporates culture in the main idea which is unfounded in the passage.

Option 4 captures solely the language aspect of institutions. Thus, it is narrow in its scope.

Option 3 correctly states the main idea of the passage.

15. 2 Natural languages are typical examples of what Ferguson called 'the result of human action, but not the execution of any human design". In other words, there is no conscious human intent in this stage of language development. So, option 2 can be inferred to be true based on the passage. Therefore, option 2 is the correct answer.

16. 4 Refer to these lines: "We begin with the emergence of the philosophy of the social sciences as an arena of thought and as a set of social institutions. The two characterisations overlap but are not congruent." The two characterisations seen here as overlapping but not congruent are social sciences as an arena of thought and social sciences as a set of social institutions. Therefore, option 4 is the correct answer.

17. 2143

2 is the opening statement as it argues ecosystem collapse is caused by myriad of factors. 1 further strengthens the claim of 2. Thus, 21 is a meaningful pair. 43 is a mandatory pair as 3 describes how the solutions stated in 4 would be enforced. 4 states the solution of the problem highlighted in 21. Therefore, the correct sequence is 2143.

18. 4 Refer to these statement of the given paragraph: Household members desirous of improving their family's financial strength to reach their aspirations can also benefit. We piloted Aage Badhein in early 2021 with over 400 women from rural areas.

'Them' in the sentence to be placed refers to the 400 women mentioned in the above mentioned statements. Therefore, blank 4 would be replaced with the given sentence.

19. 1 Option 3 contradicts the arguments of the passage.

Option 4 finds no reference in the passage.

Option 2:It takes on an extreme stance as the given passage does not imply that all the ancient cities were organized along egalitarian lines. Thus, it is incorrect.

Option 1 correctly implies the essence of the passage.

20. 1 Options 2, 3 and 4 are incorrect for simple reason that they ascribe some responsibilities to museums that, by no means, has been implied in the given passage.

21. 2431

2 is the opening sentence as it is a general statement introducing the argument that is centered around food. 2 states that food is framed through the lens of individual choice; 4 begins with 'the individualized framing of choice' and explains what this leads to. Therefore, 24 is a mandatory pair. 3 further supports 4 by stating the case in which the argument of 4 stands true. 3 and 1 make a logical pair. Therefore, 2431 is the correct sequence.

22. 4 Option 1: It misses out the argument implied by the last two statements of the passage

Option 2: It is too narrow as it focys only on the message implied by the first statement of the passage.

Option 3: It does the same mistake as option 2.

Option 4: It captures all the key arguments of the passage.

23. 3142

'Cheerfulness travelling through the self' in 1 refers to the idea implied in 3. Therefore, 31 is a mandatory pair. 4 provides further explains 1 through illustrations. 2, then, describes how 'cheer' gave rise to 'cheerful'. Thus, 3142 is the correct sequence.

24. 3 Refer to these lines of the passage: For Karmakar, a renewed interest in ghee is emblematic of a return-to-basics movement in India.

'This' in the given sentence refers back to the 'return-to-basics movement' mentioned in the above mentioned line. Therefore, blank 3 will be replaced by the sentence.

DI & LR

For questions 1 to 5:

Let us represent Ahmednagar by A, Bikrampore by B, Chitrachak by C and Deccan Park by D.

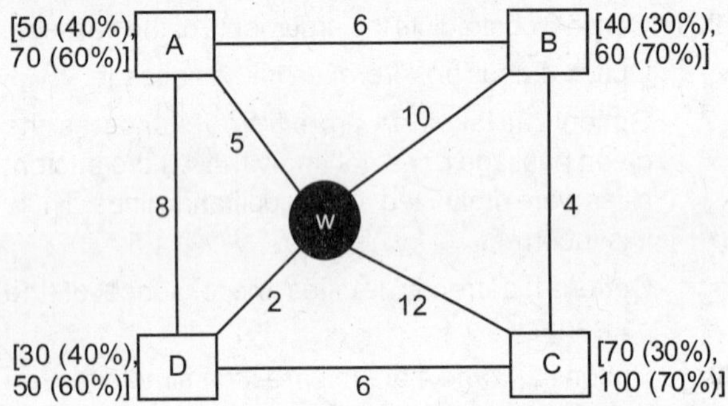

1. 35 Given that the last location is Ahmednagar, which means that the demand at A was the least among the four locations.

So the demand at A is 50. Then demand at B will be 60 and demand at D will be 50 (because these values cannot be less than the demand at A). Demand at C can be either 70 or 100, whichever be the case he will go from the warehouse to C first, thereby c traveling 12 km. From C he will go the the location with the next highest demand, which is B, thereby covering 4 km. Then he will go to D and cover (10 + 2 =) 12 km. Finally he will go to A, taking the path with the least distance, thereby covering (2 + 5 =) 7 km.

Total distance covered = 12 + 4 + 12 + 7 = 35 km.

2. 38 Given that the total number of widgets delivered is 250. The maximum possible number of widgets delivered can be 280 and the minimum possible number is 190. Note that 250 is 30 less than 280. Also the minimum and maximum demand in three out of four locations differ by 20 whereas in C it differs by 30. So the only possible way in which 250 widgets are delivered is:

A(70), B(6), C(70) and D(50). The first location visited is A, then C, Third is B and last location is D.

Distance covered = 5 + 5 + 12 + 4 + 10 + 2 = 38 km.

3. 1 Number of ways in which 260 widgets can be delivered can be shown in the following table:

	A	B	C	D
Case 1	50	60	100	50
Case 2	70	60	100	30
Case 3	70	40	100	50

We know that the route ends at B, which means that the demand at B was the least. Hence, only Case 3 is possible.

From the figure we take the given probabilities for the required remand.

Hence, required probability = 0.6 × 0.3 × 0.7 × 0.6 = 7.56%.

4. 3 Given that the first location is A, which means that the demand at A is highest, that is 70. Now demand at C will also be 70, as it cannot be more than that at A. So distance covered from W to A and from A to C will be = 5 + 5 + 12 = 22 km.

The following table shows the demands at B and C and the respective distances covered:

B	D	Total distance covered
40	30	22 + 4 + 16 = 38 km
40	50	22 + 6 + 12 = 40 km
60	30	2 + 4 + 16 = 38 km
60	50	2 + 4 + 16 = 38 km

The only possible case when the distance covered is 40 km is when the demand at B is 40 and that at D is 50.

Required probability = 0.6 × 0.3 = 0.18 or 18%.

5. 4 Given that A is not the first location to be visited, this means that C is definitely visited first. The only route that will have a total distance of 29 km is C-B-A-D. The demand at C may be 100 or 70, at B it is 60, at A it is 50 and at D it may be 30 or 50.

The total distance covered is 12 + 4 + 6 + 5 + 2 = 29 km. So the total number of widgets delivered can be 210, 230, 240 or 260.

Hence, 210 is a possible number of widgets that was delivered on that day.

For questions 6 to 10:

Let us represent the data given in the two scatter charts in the form of a table.

	2019				2020				2021			
	Cost	**Rev**	**Emp**	**New**	**Cost**	**Rev**	**Emp**	**New**	**Cost**	**Rev**	**Emp**	**New**
A	85	90	150	20	65	90	140	35	30	60	150	25
B	75	100	210	35	40	90	240	45	30	30	250	30
C	20	25	325	45	60	70	325	40	30	100	325	35
D	40	50	400	30	50	20	410	35	70	70	400	40

6. 3 Let us calculate the profit for all the three years for the four companies:

A = 90 + 90 + 60 – 85 – 65 – 60 = 30

B = 100 + 90 + 30 – 75 – 40 – 30 = 75

C = 25 + 70 + 100 – 20 – 60 – 30 = 85

D = 50 + 20 + 70 – 40 – 50 – 70 = –20

So the highest profit was for Company C.

7. 4 A company will be at a loss only if Cost is higher than revenue.

We can see from the table that this happens only in the case of Company D in 2020.

8. 4 The ratio of each company's annual profit to its annual costs in 2019:

A = 5/85 = 1/17; B = 25/75 = 1/3; C = 5/20 = 1/4; D = 10/40 = 1/4

Hence, the lowest value of this ratio is for Company A.

9. 4 Let us calculate the number of employees lost in 2019 and 2020.

Company	Employees lost in 2019	Employees lost in 2020	Total employees lost
A	150 + 20 – 140 = 30	140 + 35 – 150 = 25	55
B	210 + 35 – 240 = 5	240 + 45 – 250 = 35	40
C	325 + 45 – 325 = 45	325 + 40 – 325 = 40	85
D	400 + 30 – 410 = 20	410 + 35 – 400 = 45	65

The least number of employees lost was in Company B.

10. 2 Given that profit per employee is the ratio of a company's profit to its employee strength. Let us find the ratio for the four companies in 2020. Since Company D does not have a profit in 2020, we can rule it out.

Company	Profit	Employee strength	Ratio
A	90 – 65 = 25	(140 + 150)/2 = 145	25/145
B	90 – 40 = 50	(240 + 250)/2 = 245	50/245
C	70 – 60 = 10	(325 + 325)/2 = 325	10/325

We can see that the largest ratio is for Company B.

For questions 11 to 15:

Given that On both days, Lahur met the same number of households (say x) and sold the same number of items. Since the total number of items sold is 100, which means 50 were sold on each day.

Since Hokli could not sell any item on the second day, he must have sold all 100 on day 1. Also, he must have visited only one household on day 2.

Tohri met 30 more households on day 2 than on day 1. Total number of households is 2x, so he must have visited (x – 15) households on day 1 and (x + 15) households on day 2.

Tohri's success rate was twice that of Lahur's on day 1, and it was 75% of Lahur's on day 2.

Lahur's success rate on day 1 = 50/x ⇒ Tohri's success rate on day 1 = 100/x

Lahur's success rate on day 2 = 50/x ⇒ Tohri's success rate on day 2 = 75/2x

Success rate = items/households ⇒ items = households x success rate.

Salesman	Day 1		Day 2	
	Households visited	Items sold	Households visited	Items sold
Tohri	x – 15	[100/x](x – 15)	x + 15	[75/2x](x + 15)
Hokli	2x – 1	100	1	0
Lahur	x	50	x	50

Equating the total number of items sold by Tohri with 100 we can find the value of x.

⇒ [100/x](x – 15) + [75/2x](x + 15) = 100 ⇒ x = 25.

Hence, the table can be rewritten as follows:

Salesman	Day 1			Day 2		
	Households visited	Items sold	Success rate	Households visited	Items sold	Success rate
Tohri	10	40	4	40	60	3/2
Hokli	49	100	100/49	1	0	0
Lahur	25	50	2	25	50	2

11. 84 Total number of households met by Tohri, Hokli and Lahur on day 1 = 10 + 49 + 25 = 84.

12. 40 Total items sold by Tohri on day 1 = 40.

13. 4 Number of households visited by Lahur on day 2 = 25, which lies between 21 and 29.

14. 3 Tohri visited 10 households on day 1.

15. 2 Let us go by options (observe the success rates in the above table):

(1) Tohri had a higher success rate on the first day compared to the second day. This is true.

(2) Among the three, Tohri had the highest success rate on the second day. This is false.

(3) Among the three, Lahur had the lowest success rate on the first day. This is true.

(4) Among the three, Tohri had the highest success rate on the first day. This is true.

For questions 16 to 20:

	Cosmetic (180)		Nutrition (140)	
	Foreign (90)	Domestic (90)	Foreign (70)	Domestic (70)
FDA	p	a	s	b
EU	q	r	t	u
FDA & EU	0	x	0	y

As per statement (4), there were 140 nutrition product so, 180 must be cosmetic product.

Also, half of the nutrition products were foreign products i.e., $\frac{140}{2} = 70$, other 70 must be domestic products. Since there are equal number of domestic and foreign products, therefore, there must be 90 foreign and domestic cosmetic products.

As per statement (3), x + y = 60

p + q = 90

a + r + x = 90

s + t = 70

b + u + y = 70

As per statement (5),

$p + q + x + s + b + y = 200$

$p + s = 70$

$a + x + b + y = 130$

$p + a + x = 120$

$s + b + y = 80$

Also, as per statement (2), $a + x = 80$ (half of the domestic products were FDA approved).

Since $a + x = 80$, $a + r + x = 90 \Rightarrow r = 10$

Similarly, we get,

$p = 40$, $q = 50$, $r = 10$, $s = 30$, $t = 40$, $u = 20$

And,

$a + x = 80$

$x + y = 60$

$b + y = 50$

and $a + b = 70$

So unknown variables are a, b, x and y.

	Cosmetic (180)		Nutrition (140)	
	Foreign (90)	Domestic (90)	Foreign (70)	Domestic (70)
FDA	40	a	30	b
EU	50	10	40	20
FDA & EU	0	x	0	y

16. 40 40 foreign products were FDA approved cosmetic products.

17. 1 60 cosmetic products did not have FDA approval.

18. 4 Since $a + x = 80$ and $x + y = 60$

Therefore, x can be maximum 60.

and because $b + y = 50$, y can be 50 max, which implies b can be 0, x can be 10, a can be minimum 70.

So x can be at least 10 and at most 60.

19. 4 If 70 cosmetic products did not have EU approval, then $40 + a = 70 \Rightarrow a = 30$

And $a + b = 70 \Rightarrow b = 40$

And, $b + y = 50 \Rightarrow y = 10$

20. 50 If 50 nutrition products did not have EU approval, then

$30 + b = 50 \Rightarrow b = 20$

And, $a + b = 70 \Rightarrow a = 50$

50 domestic cosmetic products did not have EO approval.

QA

1. 2 Let initial volume of two containers be 200 unit and container A is filled with 100 unit of sugar syrup (SS) and container B is filled with 100 unit of milk.

	A	B
	100 unit SS	100 unit Milk
Step 1	50-SS	100-Milk, 50-SS
Step 2	75-SS, 50-Milk	50-Milk, 25-SS
Step 3	37.5-SS, 25-Milk	75-Milk, 62.5-SS

Required Ratio = 62.5 : 75 = 5 : 6.

2. 24 Let the number of questions correctly answered, wrongly answered and questions unattempted were a, b and c then,

$a + b + c = 75$ ...(i) and

$3a - b + c = 97$ ...(ii)

and $c > a + b$

We need to find maximum value of 'a'.

Since $c > a + b$

$\Rightarrow c > 75 - c \Rightarrow c > 37.5$

So, c can be 38.

From equation (i) and (ii) we get,

$2a + c = 86$

at $c = 38$, $a = 24$, which is the maximum number of correct answers.

3. 1 **Given:** D is the point on BC such that area of ΔADC is half the area of ΔABD.

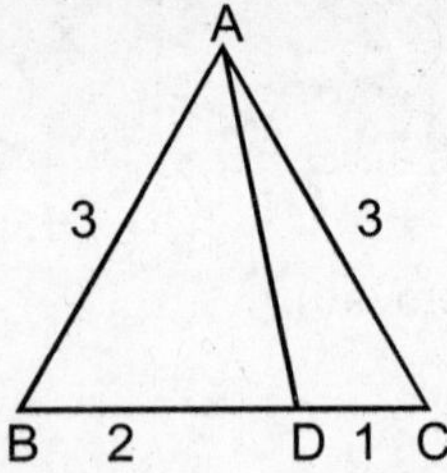

Let $\angle ADB = \theta$

$$\frac{1}{2}(AD)(BD)\sin\theta = 2\left(\frac{1}{2}(AD)(CD)\sin(180^\circ - \theta)\right)$$

BD = 2CD

Therefore, BD = 2 and CD = 1 in the figure above.

We know $\angle ABC = \angle ACB = 60°$

Apply cosine rule in ΔADC and get,

$$\cos\angle ACD = \frac{AC^2 + CD^2 - AD^2}{2(AC)(CD)}$$

$$\frac{1}{2} = \frac{9 + 1 - AD^2}{6} \Rightarrow AD^2 = 7 \Rightarrow AD = \sqrt{7}.$$

4. 2 Let the speed of two ships be 's' and 's + 6' km/hr and distance covered in 2 hours will be 2d and 2d + 12.

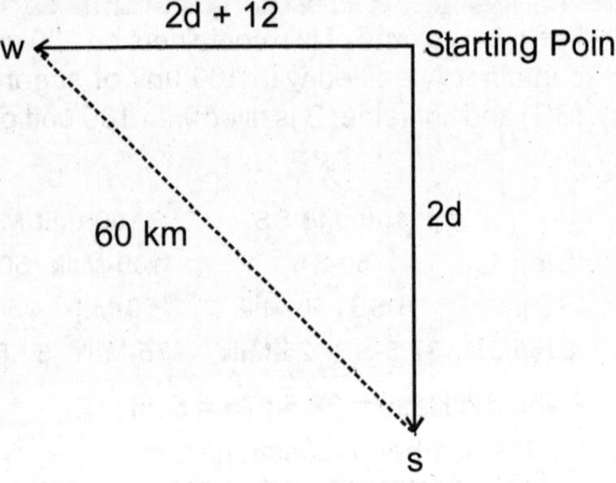

Now,

$(2d)^2 + (2d + 12)^2 = 60^2$

$\Rightarrow d^2 + (d + 6)^2 = 30^2$

$\Rightarrow 2d^2 + 12d + 36 = 900$

$\Rightarrow d^2 + 6d + 18 = 450$

d = –24, and d = 18 (Valid value)

Hence, the speed of slower ship is 18 km/hr.

5. 1 **Case 1:** If the number is 4-digit.

Since number is greater than 2000, therefore first digit can be 2, 3, 4 and 5.

Possible numbers are: $4 \times (5 \times 4 \times 3) = 240$

Case 2: If the number is 5-digit.

First digit can be 1, 2, 3, 4 and 5.

Possible numbers are = $5 \times 5 \times 4 \times 3 \times 2 = 600$

Case 3: If the number is 6-digit.

Possible numbers are $5 \times 5 \times 4 \times 3 \times 2 \times 1 = 600$

Total number of possibilities = 600 + 600 + 240 = 1440.

6. 4 **Given:** $(x^2 - 10)^{(x^2 - 3x - 10)} = 1$

Case 1: $x^2 - 3x - 10 = 0$ and $x^2 - 10 \neq 0$

$\Rightarrow (x - 5)(x + 2) = 0$

$\Rightarrow x = 5, x = -2$

Case 2: $x^2 - 10 = 1$

$\Rightarrow x^2 - 11 = 0$

This equation has no integral solution.

Case 3: $x^2 - 10 = -1$ and $x^2 - 3x - 10$ = even

$\Rightarrow x^2 - 9 = 0$

$\Rightarrow (x - 3)(x + 3) = 0$

$\Rightarrow x = 3, -3$

For x = –3, and x = 3, $x^2 - 3x - 10$ is even

Hence, total 4 integral values of x are possible.

7. 1 The sum of marks of all the students = 5×38 = 190

We need to find the minimum marks scored by Amit for that maximise the score of remaining students.

Sum of maximum scores of remaining students = 50 + 49 + 48 + 32 = 179

Minimum possible score of Amit = 190 – 179 = 11

Also, it is given that Amit scored least, which implies maximum possible scores of Amit can be 31.

$\therefore$ Required difference = 31 – 11 = 20.

8. 2 Given a + 2b = 6

Possible non-negative values of a, b are:-

a	b	a + b
0	3	3
2	2	4
4	1	5
6	0	6

$\therefore$ Maximum possible value of a + b = 6

and, minimum possible value of a + b = 3

Required average $= \frac{6+3}{2} = 4.5.$

9. 10 Let the number of sides of polygons A and B be 'n' and '2n', respectively.

Then,

$$\Rightarrow \frac{\frac{(n-2)180}{n}}{\frac{(2n-2)180}{2n}} = \frac{3}{4}$$

$$\Rightarrow \frac{n-2}{n-1} = \frac{3}{4} \Rightarrow n = 5$$

The number of sides of polygon B = 2 × 5 = 10.

10. 20 Let Mr. Pinto invested 15x for 't' years.

Then,

$$\Rightarrow \frac{3x \times 6 \times t}{100} \times \frac{5x \times 10 \times t}{100} + \frac{7x \times 1 \times t}{100} \geq 15x$$

$$\Rightarrow \frac{75xt}{100} \geq 15x \Rightarrow t \geq 20$$

So, minimum value of t is 20 years.

11. 2 Let the number of registered votes be 100x, then number of votes casted = 80x.

Votes received by one of the candidates

$$= \frac{30}{100} \times 80x = 24x$$

Remaining votes = 80x – 24x = 56x

Votes received by other three candidates

$$= \frac{56x}{6}, \frac{2 \times 56x}{6}, \frac{3 \times 56x}{6}$$

We know, 28x – 24x = 2512

$\Rightarrow 4x = 2512 \Rightarrow x = 628$

$\therefore$ The number of registered votes = 100x = 62800.

12. 2 Since $5x^3 + cx^2 - 10x + 9 = 0$ is a cubic equation so let 'p' be the third root.

Now,

$$r - r + p = \frac{-c}{5}$$

$$\Rightarrow p = \frac{-c}{5} \qquad \text{...(i)}$$

$$-r^2 - rp + rp = -2$$

$$\Rightarrow r^2 = 2 \qquad \text{...(ii)}$$

$$-r^2 p = \frac{-9}{5}$$

$$\Rightarrow p = \frac{9}{10} \qquad \text{...(iii)}$$

Substitute p in equation (i) and get

$$\frac{9}{10} = \frac{-c}{5}$$

$$\Rightarrow \frac{-9}{2} = c$$

13. 12 Given: $f(x) + f(x-1) = 1$ and $f(x^2 - x) = 5$

For x = 1

f(1) + f(0) = 1 and f(0) = 5

$\Rightarrow f(1) = -4$

Again

f(2) + f(1) = 1 and f(2) = 5

$\therefore$ f(n) = 5 if n is even and f(n) = –4 if n is odd

So, f(g(5)) + g(f(5)) = f(25) + g(–4)

= –4 + 16

= 12

14. 4 Given: $f(x) \geq 0$ for all real numbers x which implies discriminant $D \leq 0$.

Since f(2) = 0, therefore, x = 2 is a root of f(x).

Note that the discriminant $D \leq 0$ and 2 is a root of f(x).

So, D = 0

Therefore, $f(x) = a(x-2)^2$

$\Rightarrow f(4) = 6$

$\Rightarrow 6 = a(4-2)^2$

$$\Rightarrow a = \frac{3}{2}$$

$$\therefore f(-2) = \frac{3}{2}(-4)^2 = 24.$$

15. 3 Sum of n terms of AP is given by

$A_n = \frac{n}{2}(2a + (n-1)d)$ where 'a' is the first term and 'd' is the common difference.

$$A_n = \frac{n}{2}(6 + (n-1)4) = n(2n+1)$$

$$\Rightarrow \Sigma A_n = \Sigma n(2n+1)$$

$$= \Sigma 2n^2 + \Sigma n$$

$$= \frac{2n(n+1)(2n+1)}{6} + \frac{n(n+1)}{2}$$

Substitute n = 25 and get,

$$\frac{1}{25} \cdot \sum_{n=1}^{25} A_n = \frac{1}{25}\left(\frac{2(25)(25+1)(50+1)}{6} + \frac{25(26)}{2}\right)$$

= 455.

16. 6 Let the time taken by Anu, Tanu and Manu be 5x, 8x and 10x hours respectively.

Total work = LCM(5, 8, 10) = 40x

Anu, Tanu, and Manu can complete 8 units, 5 units, 4 units in one hour respectively.

It is given that three of these together can complete in 32 hours.

32(8 + 5 + 4) = 40x

$\Rightarrow x = \frac{68}{5}$

Now we know, Anu and Tanu work together for the first 6 days, working 6 hours 40 minutes per day i.e., 36 + 4 = 40 hours.

$\Rightarrow 40(8 + 5) + 4y = 40x$

$\Rightarrow y = 6$

$\therefore$ Manu alone can complete the remaining work in 6 hours.

17. 3 We need to find largest possible value of 'n' such that (n!)! divides 15000! for that n! < 15000

Note: 7! = 5040 and 8! = 40320 > 15000 which implies 15000! is not divisible by 40320!

Therefore, maximum value n can take is 7.

18. 4 Consider the triangle.

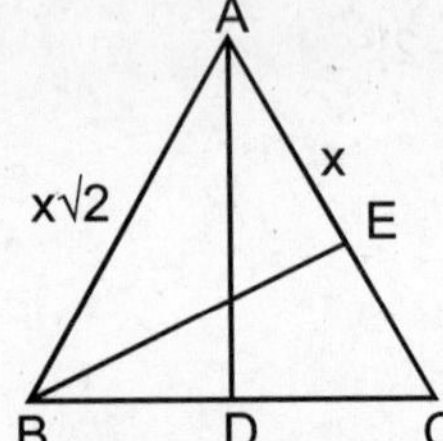

Here $\angle BAE = 45°$

Which implies AE = BE

Let AE = BE = x

In ΔABD, which is right angled triangle, let $\angle ABC = \theta$.

$\Rightarrow \sin\theta = \frac{AD}{AB}$

$\Rightarrow \sin\theta = \frac{AD}{x\sqrt{2}}$

$\Rightarrow \sqrt{2}\sin\theta = \frac{AD}{BE}$.

19. 14 Given: $a_1 + a_2 + ... + a_N = 300N$

and $6a_1 + a_2 + ... + a_N = 400N$

$\Rightarrow 5a_1 = 100N$

$\Rightarrow a_1 = 20N$

Since the sequence of numbers is non-decreasing N can takes values from 2 to 15.

[**Note:** $N \neq 1$, if N = 1 then average of N numbers as 300 would not satisfy.]

Therefore, N can take 14 values.

20. 2 The number of particles on day 1 = 100

On day 2, one out of every 2 article produces another articles.

On day 2, the number of particles $= \frac{100}{2}$

= 50 particles

On day 3, one out of every 3 articles produces another particle.

On day 3, the number of particles $= \frac{100 + 50}{3} = 50$

So, series thus formed is 100, 50, 50, 50, ...

It is given that,

100 + (m – 1) 50 = 1000

m = 19

21. 4 Total earnings of Manu = 4000 × 12 = 48000

He wants to save the total amount of Rs. 6600.

Manu's total expenses = 3500 × 9 + 3700 × 3 = Rs. 42600

So, 48000 – 42600 = 5400

and 6600 – 5400 = 1200

So, $\frac{1200}{3}$ = Rs.400

His monthly earnings should be Rs. 4400 from tenth month onwards.

22. 47 Given: $\frac{4 - \log_2 n}{3 - \log_4 n} < 0$

Let $\log_2 n = x$, then

$\Rightarrow \frac{4 - x}{3 - \frac{x}{2}} < 0$

$\Rightarrow (4 - x)\left(3 - \frac{x}{2}\right) < 0$

$\Rightarrow (4 - x)(6 - x) < 0$

$\Rightarrow (x - 4)(x - 6) < 0$

$\Rightarrow 4 < x < 6$

$\Rightarrow 4 < \log_2 n < 6$

$\Rightarrow 2^4 < n < 2^6$

$\Rightarrow 16 < n < 64$

So, n take total 47 values (17 to 63).

CAT 2022 SOLVED PAPER (SLOT-3)

Section I: VARC

Question Numbers (1 to 4): The passage below is accompanied by a set of questions. Choose the best answer to each question.

Sociologists working in the Chicago School tradition have focused on how rapid or dramatic social change causes increases in crime. Just as Durkheim, Marx, Toennies, and other European sociologists thought that the rapid changes produced by industrialization and urbanization produced crime and disorder, so too did the Chicago School theorists. The location of the University of Chicago provided an excellent opportunity for Park, Burgess, and McKenzie to study the social ecology of the city. Shaw and McKay found . . . that areas of the city characterized by high levels of social disorganization had higher rates of crime and delinquency.

In the 1920s and 1930s Chicago, like many American cities, experienced considerable immigration. Rapid population growth is a disorganizing influence, but growth resulting from in-migration of very different people is particularly disruptive. Chicago's in-migrants were both native-born whites and blacks from rural areas and small towns, and foreign immigrants. The heavy industry of cities like Chicago, Detroit, and Pittsburgh drew those seeking opportunities and new lives. Farmers and villagers from America's hinterland, like their European cousins of whom Durkheim wrote, moved in largo numbers into cities. At the start of the twentieth century, Americans were predominately a rural population, but by the century's mid-point most lived in urban areas. The social lives of these migrants, as well as those already living in the cities they moved to, were disrupted by the differences between urban and rural life. According to social disorganization theory, until the social ecology of the "new place" can adapt, this rapid change is a criminogenic influence. But most rural migrants, and even many of the foreign immigrants to the city, looked like and eventually spoke the same language as the natives of the cities into which they moved. These similarities allowed for more rapid social integration for these migrants than was the case for African Americans and most foreign immigrants.

In these same decades America experienced what has been called "the great migration": the massive movement of African Americans out of the rural South and into northern (and some southern) cities. The scale of this migration is one of the most dramatic in human history. These migrants, unlike their white counterparts, were not integrated into the cities they now called home. In fact, most American cities at the end of the twentieth century were characterized by high levels of racial residential segregation . . . Failure to integrate these migrants, coupled with other forces of social disorganization such as crowding, poverty, and illness, caused crime rates to climb in the cities, particularly in the segregated wards and neighborhoods where the migrants were forced to live.

Foreign immigrants during this period did not look as dramatically different from the rest of the population as blacks did, but the migrants from eastern and southern Europe who came to American cities did not speak English, and were frequently Catholic, while the native born were mostly Protestant. The combination of rapid population growth with the diversity of those moving into the cities created what the Chicago School sociologists called social disorganization.

1. Which one of the following is not a valid inference from the passage?

(1) According to social disorganisation theory, fast-paced social change provides fertile ground for the rapid growth of crime.

(2) According to social disorganisation theory, the social integration of African American migrants into Chicago was slower because they were less organised.

(3) The differences between urban and rural lifestyles were crucial factors in the disruption experienced by migrants to American cities.

(4) The failure to integrate in-migrants, along with social problems like poverty, was a significant reason for the rise in crime in American cities.

2. The author notes that, "At the start of the twentieth century, Americans were predominately a rural population, but by the century's mid-point most lived in urban areas." Which one of the following statements, if true, does not contradict this statement?

(1) A population census conducted in 1952 showed that more Americans lived in rural areas than in urban ones.

(2) Demographic transition in America in the twentieth century is strongly marked by an out-migration from rural areas.

(3) The estimation of per capita income in America in the mid-twentieth century primarily required data from rural areas.

(4) Economists have found that throughout the twentieth century, the size of the labour force in America has always been largest in rural areas.

3. A fundamental conclusion by the author is that:

(1) rapid population growth and demographic diversity give rise to social disorganisation that can feed the growth of crime.

(2) to prevent crime, it is important to maintain social order through maintaining social segregation.

(3) according to European sociologists, crime in America is mainly in Chicago.

(4) the best circumstances for crime to flourish are when there are severe racial disparities.

4. Which one of the following sets of words/phrases best encapsulates the issues discussed in the passage?

(1) Rapid population growth; Heavy industry; Segregation; Crime

(2) Chicago School; Social organisation; Migration; Crime

(3) Durkheim; Marx; Toennies; Shaw

(4) Chicago School; Native-born Whites; European immigrants; Poverty

Question Numbers (5 to 8): The passage below is accompanied by a set of questions. Choose the best answer to each question.

Nature has all along yielded her flesh to humans. First, we took nature's materials as food, fibers, and shelter. Then we learned to extract raw materials from her biosphere to create our own new synthetic materials. Now Bios is yielding us her mind—we are taking her logic.

Clockwork logic—the logic of the machines—will only build simple contraptions. Truly complex systems such as a cell, a meadow, an economy, or a brain (natural or artificial) require a rigorous nontechnological logic. We now see that no logic except bio-logic can assemble a thinking device, or even a workable system of any magnitude.

It is an astounding discovery that one can extract the logic of Bios out of biology and have something useful. Although many philosophers in the past have suspected one could abstract the laws of life and apply them elsewhere, it wasn't until the complexity of computers and human-made systems became as complicated as living things, that it was possible to prove this. It's eerie how much of life can be transferred. So far, some of the traits of the living that have successfully been transported to mechanical systems are: self-replication, self-governance, limited self-repair, mild evolution, and partial learning.

We have reason to believe yet more can be synthesized and made into something new. Yet at the same time that the logic of Bios is being imported into machines, the logic of Technos is being imported into life. The root of bioengineering is the desire to control the organic long enough to improve it. Domesticated plants and animals are examples of technos-logic applied to life. The wild aromatic root of the Queen Anne's lace weed has been fine-tuned over generations by selective herb gatherers until it has evolved into a sweet carrot of the garden; the udders of wild bovines have been selectively enlarged in a "unnatural" way to satisfy humans rather than calves. Milk cows and carrots, therefore, are human inventions as much as steam engines and gunpowder are. But milk cows and carrots are more indicative of the kind of inventions humans will make in the future: products that are grown rather than manufactured.

Genetic engineering is precisely what cattle breeders do when they select better strains of Holsteins, only bioengineers employ more precise and powerful control. While carrot and milk cow breeders had to rely on diffuse organic evolution, modern genetic engineers can use directed artificial evolution—purposeful design—which greatly accelerates improvements.

The overlap of the mechanical and the lifelike increases year by year. Part of this bionic convergence is a matter of words. The meanings of "mechanical" and "life" are both stretching until all complicated things can be perceived as machines, and all self-sustaining machines can be perceived as alive. Yet beyond semantics, two concrete trends are happening: (1) Human-made things are behaving more lifelike, and (2) Life is becoming more engineered. The apparent veil between the organic and the manufactured has crumpled to reveal that the two really are, and have always been, of one being.

5. None of the following statements is implied by the arguments of the passage, EXCEPT:

(1) the biological realm is as complex as the mechanical one; which is why the logic of Bios is being imported into machines.

(2) historically, philosophers have known that the laws of life can be abstracted and applied elsewhere.

(3) genetic engineers and bioengineers are the same insofar as they both seek to force evolution in an artificial way.

(4) purposeful design represents the pinnacle of scientific expertise in the service of human betterment and civilisational progress.

6. The author claims that, "The apparent veil between the organic and the manufactured has crumpled to reveal that the two really are, and have always been, of one being." Which one of the following statements best expresses the point being made by the author here?

(1) Organic reality has crumpled under the veil of manufacturing, rendering the apparent and the real as the same being.

(2) Scientific advances are making it increasingly difficult to distinguish between organic reality and manufactured reality.

(3) Apparent reality and organic reality are distinguished by the fact that the former is manufactured.

(4) The crumpling of the organic veil between apparent and manufactured reality reveals them to have the same being.

7. Which one of the following sets of words/phrases best serves as keywords to the passage?

(1) Nature; Computers; Carrots; Milk cows; Genetic engineering

(2) Nature; Bios; Technos; Self-repair; Holsteins

(3) Complex systems; Bio-logic; Bioengineering; Technos-logic; Convergence

(4) Complex systems; Carrots; Milk cows; Convergence; Technos-logic

8. The author claims that, "Part of this bionic convergence is a matter of words". Which one of the following statements best expresses the point being made by the author?

(1) "Mechanical" and "life" are words from different logical systems and are, therefore, fundamentally incompatible in meaning.

(2) "Mechanical" and "life" were earlier seen as opposite in meaning, but the difference between the two is increasingly blurred.

(3) A bionic convergence indicates the meeting ground of genetic engineering and artificial intelligence.

(4) "Bios" and "Technos" are both convergent forms of logic, but they generate meanings about the world that are mutually exclusive.

Question Numbers (9 to 12): The passage below is accompanied by a set of questions. Choose the best answer to each question.

Interpretations of the Indian past . . . were inevitably influenced by colonial concerns and interests, and also by prevalent European ideas about history, civilization and the Orient. Orientalist scholars studied the languages and the texts with selected Indian scholars, but made little attempt to understand the world-view of those who were teaching them. The readings therefore are something of a disjuncture from the traditional ways of looking at the Indian past. . . .

Orientalism [which we can understand broadly as Western perceptions of the Orient] fuelled the fantasy and the freedom sought by European Romanticism, particularly in its opposition to the more disciplined Neo-Classicism. The cultures of Asia were seen as bringing a new Romantic paradigm. Another Renaissance was anticipated through an acquaintance with the Orient, and this, it was thought, would be different from the earlier Greek Renaissance. It was believed that this Oriental Renaissance would liberate European thought and literature from the increasing focus on discipline and rationality that had followed from the earlier Enlightenment. . . . [The Romantic English poets, Wordsworth and Coleridge,] were apprehensive of the changes introduced by industrialization and turned to nature and to fantasies of the Orient.

However, this enthusiasm gradually changed, to conform with the emphasis later in the nineteenth century on the innate superiority of European civilization. Oriental civilizations were now seen as having once been great but currently in decline. The various phases of Orientalism tended to mould European understanding of the Indian past into a particular pattern. . . . There was an attempt to formulate Indian culture as uniform, such formulations being derived from texts that were given priority. The so-called 'discovery' of India was largely through selected literature in Sanskrit. This interpretation tended to emphasize non-historical aspects of Indian culture, for example the idea of an unchanging continuity of society and religion over 3,000 years; and it was believed that the Indian pattern of life was so concerned with metaphysics and the subtleties of religious belief that little attention was given to the more tangible aspects.

German Romanticism endorsed this image of India, and it became the mystic land for many Europeans, where even the most ordinary actions were imbued with a complex symbolism. This was the genesis of the idea of the spiritual east, and also, incidentally, the refuge of European intellectuals seeking to distance themselves from the changing patterns of their own societies. A dichotomy in values was maintained, Indian values being described as 'spiritual' and European values as 'materialistic', with little attempt to juxtapose these values with the reality of Indian society. This theme has been even more firmly endorsed by a section of Indian opinion during the last hundred years.

It was a consolation to the Indian intelligentsia for its perceived inability to counter the technical superiority of the west, a superiority viewed as having enabled Europe to colonize Asia and other parts of the world. At the height of anti-colonial nationalism it acted as a salve for having been made a colony of Britain.

9. In the context of the passage, all of the following statements are true EXCEPT:

(1) Indian texts influenced Orientalist scholars.

(2) India's spiritualism served as a salve for European colonisers.

(3) Orientalist scholarship influenced Indians.

(4) Orientalists' understanding of Indian history was linked to colonial concerns.

10. It can be inferred from the passage that the author is not likely to support the view that:

(1) India became a colony although it matched the technical knowledge of the West.

(2) Indian culture acknowledges the material aspects of life.

(3) the Orientalist view of Asia fired the imagination of some Western poets.

(4) India's culture has evolved over the centuries.

11. Which one of the following styles of research is most similar to the Orientalist scholars' method of understanding Indian history and culture?

(1) Reading 18th century accounts by travellers to India to see how they viewed Indian life and culture of the time.

(2) Analysing Hollywood action movies that depict violence and sex to understand contemporary America.

(3) Reading about the life of early American settlers and later waves of migration to understand the evolution of American culture.

(4) Studying artefacts excavated at a palace to understand the lifestyle of those who lived there.

12. It can be inferred from the passage that to gain a more accurate view of a nation's history and culture, scholars should do all of the following EXCEPT:

(1) examine the complex reality of that nation's society.

(2) examine their own beliefs and biases.

(3) read widely in the country's literature.

(4) develop an oppositional framework to grasp cultural differences.

Question Numbers (13 to 16): The passage below is accompanied by a set of questions. Choose the best answer to each question.

As software improves, the people using it become less likely to sharpen their own know-how. Applications that offer lots of prompts and tips are often to blame; simpler, less solicitous programs push people harder to think, act and learn.

Ten years ago, information scientists at Utrecht University in the Netherlands had a group of people carry out complicated analytical and planning tasks using either rudimentary software that provided no assistance or sophisticated software that offered a great deal of aid. The researchers found that the people using the simple software developed better strategies, made fewer mistakes and developed a deeper aptitude for the work. The people using the more advanced software, meanwhile, would often "aimlessly click around" when confronted with a tricky problem. The supposedly helpful software actually short-circuited their thinking and learning.

[According to] philosopher Hubert Dreyfus . . . . our skills get sharper only through practice, when we use them regularly to overcome different sorts of difficult challenges. The goal of modern software, by contrast, is to ease our way through such challenges. Arduous, painstaking work is exactly what programmers are most eager to automate—after all, that is where the immediate efficiency gains tend to lie. In other words, a fundamental tension ripples between the interests of the people doing the automation and the interests of the people doing the work.

Nevertheless, automation's scope continues to widen. With the rise of electronic health records, physicians increasingly rely on software templates to guide them through patient exams. The programs incorporate valuable checklists and alerts, but they also make medicine more routinized and formulaic—and distance doctors from their patients. . . . Harvard Medical School professor Beth Lown, in a 2012 journal article . . . warned that when doctors become "screen-driven," following a computer's prompts rather than "the patient's narrative thread," their thinking can become constricted. In the worst cases, they may miss important diagnostic signals. . . .

In a recent paper published in the journal Diagnosis, three medical researchers . . . examined the misdiagnosis of Thomas Eric Duncan, the first person to die of Ebola in the U.S., at Texas Health Presbyterian Hospital Dallas. They argue that the digital templates used by the hospital's clinicians to record patient information probably helped to induce a kind of tunnel vision. "These highly constrained tools," the researchers write, "are optimized for data capture but at the expense of sacrificing their utility for appropriate triage and diagnosis, leading users to miss the forest for the trees." Medical software, they write, is no "replacement for basic history-taking, examination skills, and critical thinking." . . .

There is an alternative. In "human-centered automation," the talents of people take precedence. . . . In this model, software plays an essential but secondary role. It takes over routine functions that a human operator has already mastered, issues alerts when unexpected situations arise, provides fresh information that expands the operator's perspective and counters the biases that often distort human thinking. The technology becomes the expert's partner, not the expert's replacement.

13. From the passage, we can infer that the author is apprehensive about the use of sophisticated automation for all of the following reasons EXCEPT that:

(1) it stops users from exercising their minds.

(2) it could mislead people.

(3) it stunts the development of its users.

(4) computers could replace humans.

14. In the Ebola misdiagnosis case, we can infer that doctors probably missed the forest for the trees because:

(1) the digital templates forced them to acquire tunnel vision.

(2) they used the wrong type of digital templates for the case.

(3) the data collected were not sufficient for appropriate triage.

(4) they were led by the data processed by digital templates.

15. It can be inferred that in the Utrecht University experiment, one group of people was "aimlessly clicking around" because:

(1) they did not have the skill-set to address complicated tasks.

(2) the other group was carrying out the tasks more efficiently.

(3) they wanted to avoid making mistakes.

(4) they were hoping that the software would help carry out the tasks.

16. In the context of the passage, all of the following can be considered examples of human-centered automation EXCEPT:

(1) software that offers interpretations when requested by the human operator.

(2) a smart-home system that changes the temperature as instructed by the resident.

(3) medical software that provides optional feedback on the doctor's analysis of the medical situation.

(4) software that auto-completes text when the user writes an email.

17. The passage given below is followed by four alternate summaries. Choose the option that best captures the essence of the passage.

"It does seem to me that the job of comedy is to offend, or have the potential to offend, and it cannot be drained of that potential," Rowan Atkinson said of cancel culture. "Every joke has a victim. That's the definition of a joke. Someone or something or an idea is made to look ridiculous." The Netflix star continued, "I think you've got to be very, very careful about saying what you're allowed to make jokes about. You've always got to kick up? Really?" He added, "There are lots of extremely smug and self-satisfied people in what would be deemed lower down in society, who also deserve to be pulled up. In a proper free society, you should be allowed to make jokes about absolutely anything."

(1) All jokes target someone and one should be able to joke about anyone in the society, which is inconsistent with cancel culture.

(2) Every joke needs a victim and one needs to include people from lower down the society and not just the upper class.

(3) Victims of jokes must not only be politicians and royalty, but also arrogant people from lower classes should be mentioned by comedians.

(4) Cancel culture does not understand the role and duty of comedians, which is to deride and mock everyone.

18. The passage given below is followed by four alternate summaries. Choose the option that best captures the essence of the passage.

Tamsin Blanchard, curator of Fashion Open Studio, an initiative by a campaign group showcasing the work of ethical designers says, "We're all drawn to an exquisite piece of embroidery, a colourful textile or even a style of dressing that might have originated from another heritage. [But] this magpie mentality, where all of culture and history is up for grabs as 'inspiration', has accelerated since the proliferation of social media... Where once a fashion student might research the history and traditions of a particular item of clothing with care and respect, we now have a world where images are lifted from image libraries without a care for their cultural significance. It's easier than ever to steal a motif or a craft technique and transfer it on to a piece of clothing that is either mass produced or appears on a runway without credit or compensation to their original communities."

(1) Copying an embroidery design or pattern of textile from native communities who own them is tantamount to stealing and they need to be compensated.

(2) Cultural collaboration is the need of the hour. Beautiful design ideas of indigenous people need to be showcased and shared worldwide.

(3) Taking fashion ideas from any cultural group without their consent is a form of appropriation without giving due credit, compensation, and respect.

(4) Media has encouraged mass production; images are copied effortlessly without care or concern for the interests of ethnic communities.

19. There is a sentence that is missing in the paragraph below. Look at the paragraph and decide in which blank (option 1, 2, 3, or 4) the following sentence would best fit.

Sentence: When people socially learn from each other, they often learn without understanding why what they're copying—the beliefs and behaviours and technologies and know-how—works.

Paragraph: ___(1)___. The dual-inheritance theory ....says....that inheritance is itself an evolutionary system. It has variation. What makes us a new kind of animal, and so different and successful as a species, is we rely heavily on social learning, to the point where socially acquired information is effectively a second line of inheritance, the first being our genes.... ___(2)___. People tend to home in on who seems to be the smartest or most successful person around, as well as what everybody seems to be doing—the majority of people have something worth learning. ___(3)___. When you repeat this process over time, you can get, around the world, cultural packages—beliefs or behaviours or technology or other solutions—that are adapted to the local conditions. People have different psychologies, effectively. ___(4)___.

(1) Option 1 (2) Option 2
(3) Option 3 (4) Option 4

20. The four sentences (labelled 1, 2, 3 and 4) below, when properly sequenced, would yield a coherent paragraph. Decide on the proper sequencing of the order of the sentences and key in the sequence of the four numbers as your answer:

(1) Various industrial sectors including retail, transit systems, enterprises, educational institutions, event organizing, finance, travel etc. have now started leveraging these beacons solutions to track and communicate with their customers.

(2) A beacon fixed on to a shop wall enables the retailer to assess the proximity of the customer, and come up with a much targeted or personalized communication like offers, discounts and combos on products in each shelf.

(3) Smart phones or other mobile devices can capture the beacon signals, and distance can be estimated by measuring received signal strength.

(4) Beacons are tiny and inexpensive, micro-location-based technology devices that can send radio frequency signals and notify nearby Bluetooth devices of their presence and transmit information.

21. The passage given below is followed by four alternate summaries. Choose the option that best captures the essence of the passage.

To defend the sequence of alphabetisation may seem bizarre, so obvious is its application that it is hard to imagine a reference, catalogue or listing without it. But alphabetical order was not an immediate consequence of the alphabet itself. In the Middle Ages, deference for ecclesiastical tradition left scholars reluctant to categorise things according to the alphabet — to do so would be a rejection of the divine order. The rediscovery of the ancient Greek and Roman classics necessitated more efficient ways of ordering, searching and referencing texts. Government bureaucracy in the 16th and 17th centuries quickened the advance of alphabetical order, bringing with it pigeonholes, notebooks and card indexes.

(1) Unlike the alphabet, once the efficacy of the alphabetic sequence became apparent to scholars and administrators, its use became widespread.

(2) The ban on the use by scholars of any form of categorisation – but the divinely ordained one – delayed the adoption of the alphabetic sequence by several centuries.

(3) The alphabetic order took several centuries to gain common currency because of religious beliefs and a lack of appreciation of its efficacy in the ordering of things.

(4) While adoption of the written alphabet was easily accomplished, it took scholars several centuries to accept the alphabetic sequence as a useful tool in their work.

22. The four sentences (labelled 1, 2, 3 and 4) below, when properly sequenced, would yield a coherent paragraph. Decide on the proper sequencing of the order of the sentences and key in the sequence of the four numbers as your answer:

(1) The more we are able to accept that our achievements are largely out of our control, the easier it becomes to understand that our failures, and those of others, are too.

(2) But the raft of recent books about the limits of merit is an important correction to the arrogance of contemporary entitlement and an opportunity to reassert the importance of luck, or grace, in our thinking.

(3) Meritocracy as an organising principle is an inevitable function of a free society, as we are designed to see our achievements as worthy of reward.

(4) And that in turn should increase our humility and the respect with which we treat our fellow citizens, helping ultimately to build a more compassionate society.

23. There is a sentence that is missing in the paragraph below. Look at the paragraph and decide in which blank (option 1, 2, 3, or 4) the following sentence would best fit.

Sentence: This has meant a lot of uncertainty around what a wide-scale return to office might look like in practice.

Paragraph: Bringing workers back to their desks has been a rocky road for employers and employees alike. The evolution of the pandemic has meant that best laid plans have often not materialised. ___**(1)**___ The flow of workers back into offices has been more of a trickle than a steady stream. ___**(2)**___ Yet while plenty of companies are still working through their new policies, some employees across the globe are now back at their desks, whether on a full-time or hybrid basis. ___**(3)**___ That means we're beginning to get some clarity on what return-to-office means — what's working, as well as what has yet to be settled. ___**(4)**___

(1) Option 1 (2) Option 2

(3) Option 3 (4) Option 4

24. The four sentences (labelled 1, 2, 3 and 4) below, when properly sequenced, would yield a coherent paragraph. Decide on the proper sequencing of the order of the sentences and key in the sequence of the four numbers as your answer:

(1) If I wanted to sit indoors and read, or play Sonic the Hedgehog on a red-hot Sega Mega Drive, I would often be made to feel guilty about not going outside to "enjoy it while it lasts".

(2) My mum, quite reasonably, wanted me and my sister out of the house, in the sun.

(3) Tales of my mum's idyllic-sounding childhood in the Sussex countryside, where trees were climbed by 8 am and streams navigated by lunchtime, were passed down to us like folklore.

(4) To an introverted kid, that felt like a threat - and the feeling has stayed with me.

Section II: DI & LR

Question Numbers (1 to 5): All the first-year students in the computer science (CS) department in a university take both the courses (i) AI and (ii) ML. Students from other departments (non-CS students) can also take one of these two courses, but not both. Students who fail in a course get an F grade; others pass and are awarded A or B or C grades depending on their performance. The following are some additional facts about the number of students who took these two courses this year and the grades they obtained.

1. The numbers of non-CS students who took AI and ML were in the ratio 2 : 5.
2. The number of non-CS students who took either AI or ML was equal to the number of CS students.
3. The numbers of non-CS students who failed in the two courses were the same and their total is equal to the number of CS students who got a C grade in ML.
4. In both the courses, 50% of the students who passed got a B grade. But, while the numbers of students who got A and C grades were the same for AI, they were in the ratio 3 : 2 for ML.
5. No CS student failed in AI, while no non-CS student got an A grade in AI.

6. The numbers of CS students who got A, B and C grades respectively in AI were in the ratio 3 : 5 : 2, while in ML the ratio was 4 : 5 : 2.
7. The ratio of the total number of non-CS students failing in one of the two courses to the number of CS students failing in one of the two courses was 3 : 1.
8. 30 students failed in ML.

1. How many students took AI?

(1) 270 (2) 90
(3) 210 (4) 60

2. How many CS students failed in ML?

3. How many non-CS students got A grade in ML?

4. How many students got A grade in AI?

(1) 63 (2) 42
(3) 99 (4) 84

5. How many non-CS students got B grade in ML?

(1) 165 (2) 90
(3) 25 (4) 75

Question Numbers (6 to 10): Pulak, Qasim, Ritesh, and Suresh participated in a tournament comprising of eight rounds. In each round, they formed two pairs, with each of them being in exactly one pair. The only restriction in the pairing was that the pairs would change in successive rounds. For example, if Pulak formed a pair with Qasim in the first round, then he would have to form a pair with Ritesh or Suresh in the second round. He would be free to pair with Qasim again in the third round. In each round, each pair decided whether to play the game in that round or not. If they decided not to play, then no money was exchanged between them. If they decided to play, they had to bet either Rs. 1 or Rs. 2 in that round. For example, if they chose to bet Rs. 2, then the player winning the game got Rs. 2 from the one losing the game.

At the beginning of the tournament, the players had Rs. 10 each. The following table shows partial information about the amounts that the players had at the end of each of the eight rounds. It shows every time a player had Rs. 10 at the end of a round, as well as every time, at the end of a round, a player had either the minimum or the maximum amount that he would have had across the eight rounds. For example, Suresh had Rs.10 at the end of Rounds 1, 3, and 8 and not after any of the other rounds. The maximum amount that he had at the end of any round was Rs. 13 (at the end of Round 5), and the minimum amount he had at the end of any round was Rs. 8 (at the end of Round 2). At the end of all other rounds, he must have had either Rs. 9, Rs. 11, or Rs. 12.

It was also known that Pulak and Qasim had the same amount of money with them at the end of Round 4.

	Pulak	Qasim	Ritesh	Suresh
Round 1		Rs. 8	Rs. 10	Rs. 10
Round 2	Rs. 13	Rs. 10		Rs. 8
Round 3				Rs. 10
Round 4				
Round 5	Rs. 10	Rs. 10		Rs. 13
Round 6				
Round 7		Rs. 12	Rs. 4	
Round 8	Rs. 13			Rs. 10

6. What BEST can be said about the amount of money that Ritesh had with him at the end of Round 8?

(1) Rs. 4 or Rs. 5 (2) Rs. 5 or Rs. 6
(3) Exactly Rs. 6 (4) Exactly Rs. 5

7. What BEST can be said about the amount of money that Pulak had with him at the end of Round 6?

(1) Rs. 11 or Rs. 12 (2) Rs. 12 or Rs. 13
(3) Exactly Rs. 11 (4) Exactly Rs. 12

8. How much money (in Rs.) did Ritesh have at the end of Round 4?

9. How many games were played with a bet of Rs. 2?

10. Which of the following pairings was made in Round 5?

(1) Pulak and Ritesh (2) Qasim and Suresh
(3) Pulak and Suresh (4) Pulak and Qasim

Question Numbers (11 to 15): There are only four neighbourhoods in a city – Levmisto, Tyhrmisto, Pesmisto and Kitmisto. During the onset of a pandemic, the number of new cases of a disease in each of these neighbourhoods was recorded over a period of five days. On each day, the number of new cases recorded in any of the neighbourhoods was either 0, 1, 2 or 3.

The following facts are also known:

1. There was at least one new case in every neighbourhood on Day 1.
2. On each of the five days, there were more new cases in Kitmisto than in Pesmisto.
3. The number of new cases in the city in a day kept increasing during the five-day period.

   The number of new cases on Day 3 was exactly one more than that on Day 2.
4. The maximum number of new cases in a day in Pesmisto was 2, and this happened only once during the five-day period.
5. Kitmisto is the only place to have 3 new cases on Day 2.
6. The total numbers of new cases in Levmisto, Tyhrmisto, Pesmisto and Kitmisto over the five-day period were 12, 12, 5 and 14 respectively.

11. What BEST can be concluded about the total number of new cases in the city on Day 2?

(1) Exactly 8 (2) Exactly 7

(3) Either 6 or 7 (4) Either 7 or 8

12. What BEST can be concluded about the number of new cases in Levmisto on Day 3?

(1) Exactly 2 (2) Either 2 or 3

(3) Either 0 or 1 (4) Exactly 3

13. On which day(s) did Pesmisto not have any new case?

(1) Only Day 2

(2) Only Day 3

(3) Both Day 2 and Day 3.

(4) Both Day 2 and Day 4

14. Which of the two statements below is/are necessarily false?

Statement A: There were 2 new cases in Tyhrmisto on Day 3.

Statement B: There were no new cases in Pesmisto on Day 2.

(1) Statement A only

(2) Statement B only

(3) Neither Statement A nor Statement B

(4) Both Statement A and Statement B

15. On how many days did Levmisto and Tyhrmisto have the same number of new cases?

(1) 2 (2) 3

(3) 4 (4) 5

Question Numbers (16 to 20): In the following, a year corresponds to 1st of January of that year.

A study to determine the mortality rate for a disease began in 1980. The study chose 1000 males and 1000 females and followed them for forty years or until they died, whichever came first. The 1000 males chosen in 1980 consisted of 250 each of ages 10 to less than 20, 20 to less than 30, 30 to less than 40, and 40 to less than 50. The 1000 females chosen in 1980 also consisted of 250 each of ages 10 to less than 20, 20 to less than 30, 30 to less than 40, and 40 to less than 50. The four figures below depict the age profile of those among the 2000 individuals who were still alive in 1990, 2000, 2010, and 2020. The blue bars in each figure represent the number of males in each age group at that point in time, while the pink bars represent the number of females in each age group at that point in time. The numbers next to the bars give the exact numbers being represented by the bars. For example, we know that 230 males among those tracked and who were alive in 1990 were aged between 20 and 30.

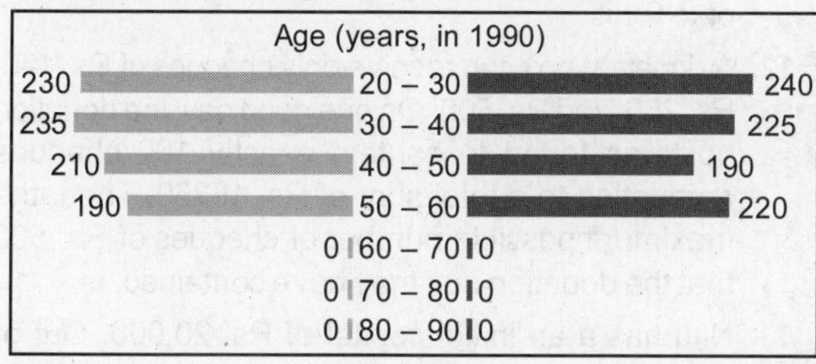

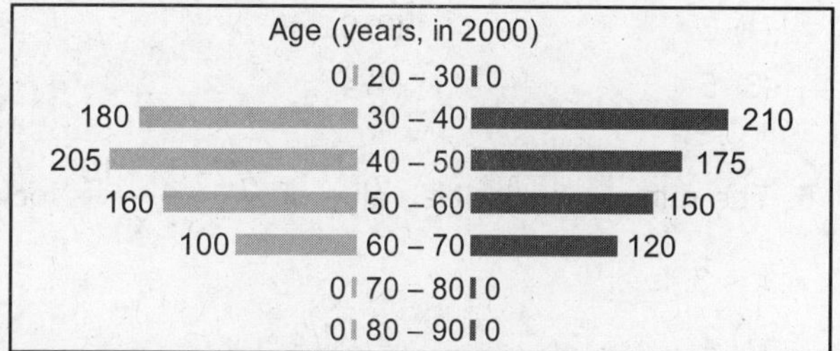

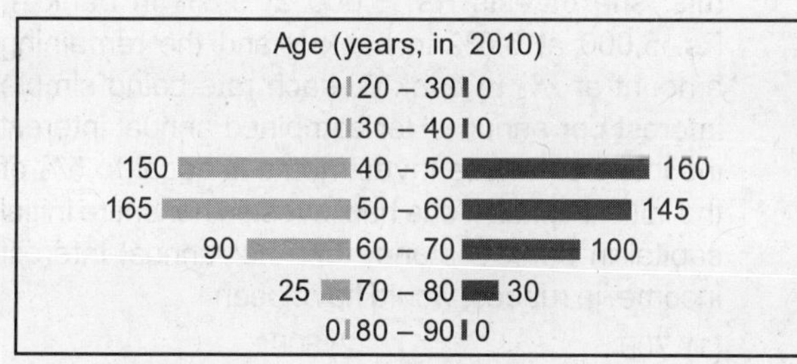

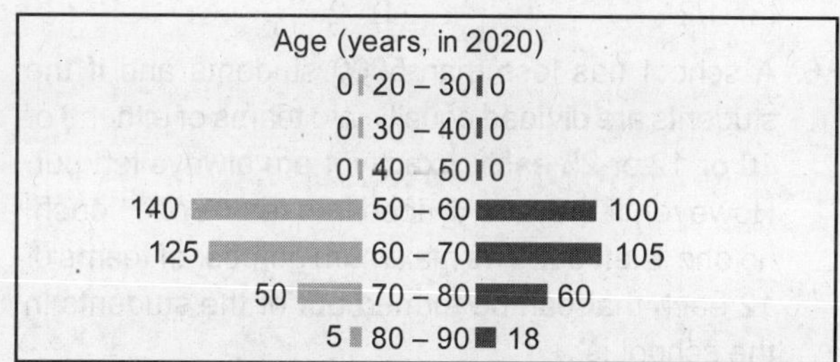

16. In 2000, what was the ratio of the number of dead males to dead females among those being tracked?

(1) 41 : 43 (2) 129 : 131

(3) 71 : 69 (4) 109 : 107

17. How many people who were being tracked and who were between 30 and 40 years of age in 1980 survived until 2010?

(1) 110 (2) 90

(3) 310 (4) 190

18. How many individuals who were being tracked and who were less than 30 years of age in 1980 survived until 2020?

(1) 580 (2) 240

(3) 230 (4) 470

19. How many of the males who were being tracked and who were between 20 and 30 years of age in 1980 died in the period 2000 to 2010?

20. How many of the females who were being tracked and who were between 20 and 30 years of age in 1980 died between the ages of 50 and 60?

Section III: QA

1. The arithmetic mean of all the distinct numbers that can be obtained by rearranging the digits in 1421, including itself, is

(1) 2222 (2) 2442
(3) 3333 (4) 2592

2. The average of all 3-digit terms in the arithmetic progression 38, 55, 72, ..., is

3. Two ships are approaching a port along straight routes at constant speeds. Initially, the two ships and the port formed an equilateral triangle with sides of length 24 km. When the slower ship travelled 8 km, the triangle formed by the new positions of the two ships and the port became right-angled. When the faster ship reaches the port, the distance, in km, between the other ship and the port will be

(1) 6 (2) 4
(3) 8 (4) 12

4. The lengths of all four sides of a quadrilateral are integer valued. If three of its sides are of length 1 cm, 2 cm and 4 cm, then the total number of possible lengths of the fourth side is

(1) 3 (2) 6
(3) 5 (4) 4

5. The minimum possible value of $\frac{x^2-6x+10}{3-x}$, for $x < 3$, is

(1) 2 (2) –1/2
(3) 1/2 (4) –2

6. A school has less than 5000 students and if the students are divided equally into teams of either 9 or 10 or 12 or 25 each, exactly 4 are always left out. However, if they are divided into teams of 11 each, no one is left out. The maximum number of teams of 12 each that can be formed out of the students in the school is

7. A glass contains 500 cc of milk and a cup contains 500 cc of water. From the glass, 150 cc of milk is transferred to the cup and mixed thoroughly. Next, 150 cc of this mixture is transferred from the cup to the glass. Now, the amount of water in the glass and the amount of milk in the cup are in the ratio

(1) 1 : 1 (2) 3 : 10
(3) 10 : 13 (4) 10 : 3

8. If $(3 + 2\sqrt{2})$ is a root of the equation $ax^2 + bx + c = 0$, and $(4 + 2\sqrt{3})$ is a root of the equation $ay^2 + my + n = 0$, where a, b, c, m and n are integers, then the value of $\left(\frac{b}{m}+\frac{c-2b}{n}\right)$ is

(1) 0 (2) 4
(3) 1 (4) 3

9. If $c = \frac{16x}{y}+\frac{49y}{x}$ for some non-zero real numbers x and y, then c cannot take the value

(1) – 70 (2) – 60
(3) – 50 (4) 60

10. Suppose the medians BD and CE of a triangle ABC intersect at a point O. If area of triangle ABC is 108 sq. cm., then, the area of the triangle EOD, in sq. cm., is

11. If $\left(\sqrt{\frac{7}{5}}\right)^{3x-y} = \frac{875}{2401}$ and $\left(\frac{4a}{b}\right)^{6x-y} = \left(\frac{2a}{b}\right)^{y-6x}$, for all non-zero real values of a and b, then the value of x + y is

12. A donation box can receive only cheques of Rs. 100, Rs. 250, and Rs. 500. On one good day, the donation box was found to contain exactly 100 cheques amounting to a total sum of Rs. 15250. Then, the maximum possible number of cheques of Rs. 500 that the donation box may have contained, is

13. Nitu has a an initial capital of Rs. 20,000. Out of this, she invests Rs. 8,000 at 5.5% in bank A, Rs. 5,000 at 5.6% in bank B and the remaining amount at x% in bank C, each rate being simple interest per annum. Her combined annual interest income from these investments is equal to 5% of the initial capital. If she had invested her entire initial capital in bank C alone, then her annual interest income, in rupees, would have been

(1) 700 (2) 800
(3) 1000 (4) 900

14. In a triangle ABC, AB = AC = 8 cm. A circle drawn with BC as diameter passes through A. Another circle drawn with center at A passes through B and C. Then the area, in sq. cm, of the overlapping region between the two circles is

(1) $32(\pi-1)$ (2) $16(\pi-1)$
(3) 32π (4) 16π

15. In an examination, the average marks of students in sections A and B are 32 and 60, respectively. The number of students in section A is 10 less than that in section B. If the average marks of all the students across both the sections combined is an integer, then the difference between the maximum and minimum possible number of students in section A is

16. Let r be a real number and $f(x) = \begin{cases} 2x - r & \text{if } x \geq r \\ r & \text{if } x < r \end{cases}$.

Then, the equation $f(x) = f(f(x))$ holds for all real values of x where

(1) $x \leq r$ (2) $x > r$

(3) $x \geq r$ (4) $x \neq r$

17. Two cars travel from different locations at constant speeds. To meet each other after starting at the same time, they take 1.5 hours if they travel towards each other, but 10.5 hours if they travel in the same direction. If the speed of the slower car is 60 km/hr, then the distance traveled, in km, by the slower car when it meets the other car while traveling towards each other, is

(1) 90 (2) 150

(3) 100 (4) 120

18. Bob can finish a job in 40 days, if he works alone. Alex is twice as fast as Bob and thrice as fast as Cole in the same job. Suppose Alex and Bob work together on the first day, Bob and Cole work together on the second day, Cole and Alex work together on the third day, and then, they continue the work by repeating this three-day roster, with Alex and Bob working together on the fourth day, and so on. Then, the total number of days Alex would have worked when the job gets finished, is

19. A group of N people worked on a project. They finished 35% of the project by working 7 hours a day for 10 days. Thereafter, 10 people left the group and the remaining people finished the rest of the project in 14 days by working 10 hours a day. Then the value of N is

(1) 36 (2) 140

(3) 23 (4) 150

20. Suppose k is any integer such that the equation $2x^2 + kx + 5 = 0$ has no real roots and the equation $x^2 + (k - 5)x + 1 = 0$ has two distinct real roots for x. Then, the number of possible values of k is

(1) 13 (2) 9

(3) 8 (4) 7

21. Moody takes 30 seconds to finish riding an escalator if he walks on it at his normal speed in the same direction. He takes 20 seconds to finish riding the escalator if he walks at twice his normal speed in the same direction. If Moody decides to stand still on the escalator, then the time, in seconds, needed to finish riding the escalator is

22. Consider six distinct natural numbers such that the average of the two smallest numbers is 14, and the average of the two largest numbers is 28. Then, the maximum possible value of the average of these six numbers is

(1) 24 (2) 23.5

(3) 22.5 (4) 23

ANSWERS

VARC

1. (2)	**2.** (2)	**3.** (1)	**4.** (2)	**5.** (3)	**6.** (2)	**7.** (3)	**8.** (2)	**9.** (2)	**10.** (1)
11. (2)	**12.** (4)	**13.** (4)	**14.** (4)	**15.** (4)	**16.** (4)	**17.** (1)	**18.** (3)	**19.** (2)	**20.** (4312)
21. (3)	**22.** (3214)	**23.** (2)	**24** (2314)						

DI & LR

1. (1)	**2.** (12)	**3.** (27)	**4.** (1)	**5.** (4)	**6.** (3)	**7.** (4)	**8.** (6)	**9.** (6)	**10.** (3)
11. (1)	**12.** (4)	**13.** (2)	**14.** (4)	**15.** (4)	**16.** (3)	**17.** (4)	**18.** (4)	**19.** (40)	**20.** (30)

QA

1. (1)	**2.** (548)	**3.** (4)	**4.** (3)	**5.** (1)	**6.** (150)	**7.** (1)	**8.** (2)	**9.** (3)	**10.** (9)
11. (14)	**12.** (12)	**13.** (2)	**14.** (1)	**15.** (63)	**16.** (1)	**17.** (1)	**18.** (11)	**19.** (2)	**20.** (2)
21. (60)	**22.** (3)								

Then, the number of non-CS students who got C grade in ML course be 150 – 75 – a – 18 = 57 – a.

Also, from condition (4), (72 + a)/(36 + 57 – a) = 3/2

$\Rightarrow$ 144 + 2a = 279 – 3a

$\Rightarrow$ 5a = 135 $\Rightarrow$ a = 27.

Hence, the final table can be shown below.

	CS	A	B	C	F
210	AI	63	105	42	0
210	ML	72	90	36	12
	Non-CS	**A**	**B**	**C**	**F**
60	AI	0	21	21	18
150	ML	27	75	30	18

1. 1 Number of students took AI = 210 + 60 = 270.

2. 12 Number of CS students failed in ML is 12.

3. 27 Number of non-CS students got A grade in ML is 27.

4. 1 Number of students got A grade in AI is 63 + 0 = 63.

5. 4 Number of non-CS students got B grade in ML is 75.

For questions 6 to 10:

Step 1:

We know that only an exchange of Rs.2, Re.1 or 0 can happen. There cannot be an exchange between the same two persons consecutively. The total amount after each exchange remains Rs.40, so for Rounds 1, 2 and 5 the vacant places can be filled using this information.

The maximum and minimum amounts are mentioned in the table, so we can make the following conclusions regarding all of the remaining exchanges: Pulak can have Rs.12 or Rs.11. Qasim can have Rs.9 or Rs.11 Ritesh can have Rs.5, Rs.6, Rs.7, Rs.8 or Rs,9 Suresh can have Rs.9, Rs.11 or Rs.12

In Round 8 Qasim and Ritesh together have Rs.17. Now, Qasim can have only Rs.11 or Rs.9. If he has Rs.9, then Ritesh will have Rs.8, which is not possible as in Round 7 Ritesh has Rs.4 and an increase of 2, 1 or 0 is only possible. So after Round 8 Qasim and Ritesh have Rs.11 and Rs.6 respectively. In Round 8 we can see that Ritesh witnessed an increase of 2 and Qasim a decrease of 1. Consequently, Pulak must have had an increase of 1 (If not, then for a decrease of 2 he should have had Rs.15 after Round 7, which is not possible) and Suresh must have had a decrease of 2. So after Round 7 the respective amounts with Pulak, Qasim, Ritesh and Suresh will be Rs.12, Rs.12, Rs.4 and Rs.12.

Step 2:

In Round 3 Suresh had Rs.10, which was an increase of 2 from Round 2. Now Suresh cannot have a match against Qasim, also Ritesh cannot have an increase of 2, which will make his amount Rs.11, which is not possible. So Pulak will have a decrease of 2, which will make his amount equal to Rs.11 and Ritesh will have Rs.8 after Round 3.

In Round 4 Pulak and Qasim had equal amounts, which can only be Rs.11 each. The remaining amount is Rs.18 between Ritesh and Suresh. This can happen only if Ritesh and Suresh have Rs.6 and Rs.12. (Note that Suresh cannot have Rs.11 as there will be a contradiction in the next round).

In Round 5 Pulak and Qasim's amounts have both increased by 1, so obviously Ritesh and Suresh's amounts will both decrease by 1. Hence, their respective amounts are Rs.6 and Rs.12.

Step 3:

After Round 6 Qasim's amount has to be Rs.11 (it cannot be 9 because in Round 7 Qasim's amount is Rs.12, an increase of 3 from Rs.9 will be a contradiction). Now, Ritesh's amount will be Rs.5 only (Note that for Rs.6, there will be a contradiction for the amounts in Round 7). Now, Ritesh's Rs.5 is a decrease of 2, so an increase of Rs.2 can happen only with Pulak making his amount equal to Rs.12. Hence, Suresh will have Rs.12 at the end of Round 6.

Based on the given information we can complete the table as follows:

Round	Pulak (Rs.10)	Qasim (Rs.10)	Ritesh (Rs.10)	Suresh (Rs.10)	Cash Exchange Between
Round 1	Rs.12	Rs.8	Rs.10	Rs.10	P-Q, R-S
Round 2	Rs.13	Rs.10	Rs.9	Rs.8	P-R, Q-S
Round 3	Rs.11	Rs.11	Rs.8	Rs.10	P-S, Q-R
Round 4	Rs.11	Rs.11	Rs.6	Rs.12	P-Q, R-S
Round 5	Rs.10	Rs.10	Rs.7	Rs.13	P-S, Q-R
Round 6	Rs.12	Rs.11	Rs.5	Rs.12	P-R, Q-S
Round 7	Rs.12	Rs.12	Rs.4	Rs.12	P-S, Q-R
Round 8	Rs.13	Rs.11	Rs.6	Rs.10	P-Q, R-S

6. 3 Ritesh had exactly Rs.6 at the end of Round 8.

7. 4 Pulak had exactly Rs.12 at the end of Round 6.

8. 6 Ritesh had exactly Rs.6 at the end of Round 4.

9. 6 From the table we can see that the amounts increased or decreased by 2 at 12 instances, so there are exactly 6 matches that were paid with a bet of Rs.2.

10. 3 In Round 5 Pulak and Ritesh played against each other.

For questions 11 to 15:

Step 1:

On each day, the number of new cases recorded in any of the neighbourhoods was either 0, 1, 2 or 3.

From condition (1), There was at least one new case in every neighbourhood on Day 1.

From condition (2), On each of the five days, there were more new cases in Kitmisto than in Pesmisto.

From condition (3), The number of new cases in the city in a day kept increasing during the five-day period. The number of new cases on Day 3 was exactly one more than that on Day 2.

Let the number of new cases on Day 2 be n. Then, the number of new cases on Day 3 will be n + 1.

From condition (5), Kitmisto is the only place to have 3 new cases on Day 2.

From condition (6), The total numbers of new cases in Levmisto, Tyhrmisto, Pesmisto and Kitmisto over the five-day period were 12, 12, 5 and 14 respectively.

From condition (4), The number of new cases in the five-day period in Pesmisto was 2, 1, 1, 1, 0 in any order.

The information can be shown in the table below.

	Neighbourhood	Day 1	Day 2	Day 3	Day 4	Day 5	Total	
	Levmisto						12	
	Tyhrmisto						12	
Kitmisto > Pesmisto	Pesmisto						5	2, 1, 1, 1, 0
	Kitmisto		3				14	
		× 0	< n	< n + 1	<	<		

Step 2:

Sum 14 is possible only in 3, 3, 3, 3, 2.

The maximum sum for Day 5 will be 3 + 3 + 2 + 3 = 11.

Sum of 12 + 12 + 5 + 14 = 43

Sum for Day 4 = 10, Sum for Day 3 = 9, Sum for Day 2 = 8 and sum for Day 1 = 5

This is possible.

If we take for Day 5 = 11, Day 3 = 8, Day 2 = 7

Then, for Day 4 = 9 or 10 and for Day 1 = 8 or 7, which is not possible.

Hence, the final table can be shown in the table given below.

	Neighbourhood	Day 1	Day 2	Day 3	Day 4	Day 5	Total
	Levmisto	1	2	3	3	3	12
	Tyhrmisto	1	2	3	3	3	12
Kitmisto > Pesmisto	Pesmisto	1	1	0	1	2	5
	Kitmisto	2	3	3	3	3	14
		5	8	9	10	11	43

11. 1 The total number of new cases in the city on Day 2 was 8.

12. 4 The number of new cases in Levmisto on Day 3 was 3.

13. 2 Only on Day 3 Pesmisto did not have any new case.

14. 4 Both Statement A and Statement B are necessarily false.

15. 4 All 5 days Levmisto and Tyhrmisto have the same number of new cases.

For questions 16 to 20:

The table given below shows the age profile of those among the 2000 individuals who were still alive in 1990, 2000, 2010, and 2020.

Males					Females				
Age Group	10-20	20-30	30-40	40-50	Age Group	10-20	20-30	30-40	40-50
1980	250	250	250	250	1980	250	250	250	250
1990	230	235	210	190	1990	240	225	190	220
2000	180	205	160	100	2000	210	175	150	120
2010	150	165	90	25	2010	160	145	100	30
2020	140	125	50	5	2020	100	105	60	18

16. 3 In 2020, number of dead males
= 1000 – (180 + 205 + 160 + 100) = 355
In 2020, number of dead females
= 1000 – (210 + 175 + 150 + 120) = 345
Hence, required ratio = 355 : 345 = 71 : 69.

17. 4 The number of people who were being tracked and who were between 30 and 40 years of age in 1980 survived until 2010 = 90 + 100 = 190.

18. 4 The number of individuals who were being tracked and who were less than 30 years of age in 1980 survived until 2020 = 140 + 125 + 100 + 105 = 470.

19. 40 Number of the males who were being tracked and who were between 20 and 30 years of age in 1980 died in the period 2000 to 2010 = 205 – 165 = 40.

20. 30 Number of the females who were being tracked and who were between 20 and 30 years of age in 1980 died between the ages of 50 and 60 = 175 – 145 = 30.

QA

1. 1 The number of possible rearrangements of the number 1421 = 4!/2! = 12

Now, consider only the units place.

1 occurs 6 times in the unit's place.

2 occurs 3 times in the unit's place.

4 occurs 3 times in the unit's place.

The total sum of digits of the units place in all the 12 arrangements combined

= 1 × 6 + 2 × 3 + 4 × 3 = 24

Similarly, the sum of digits in ten's, hundred's or thousand's place will also be 24.

So the sum of all the 12 rearrangements = 24 × 1111

Hence, the average of all these rearrangements = 24 × 1111/12 = 2222.

2. 548

The common difference of the AP 38, 55, 72, ... is 17.

The smallest 3-digit number in the AP is 106 and the largest 3-digit number in it is 990.

So 106 + 123 + ... + 973 + 990

= 106 + (106 + 17) + (106 + 2 × 17) + ... + (106 + 52 × 17)

= 53 × 106 + 17(1 + 2 + 3 + ... + 52)

= 53 × 106 + 17 × 52 × 53/2

= 53 × 106 + 17 × 26 × 53

Hence, average of all 3-digit numbers

= (53 × 106 + 17 × 26 × 53)/53 = 106 + 442 = 548.

3. 4 Let the port be denoted by P, the slower ship by S and the faster ship by F.

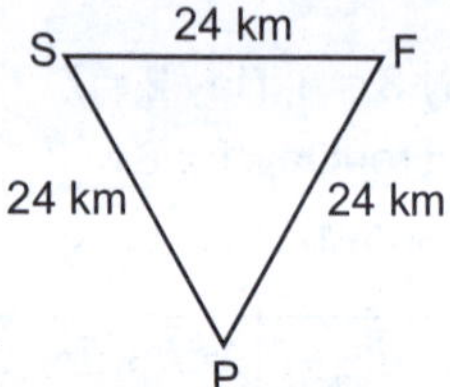

Let their new positions be A and B.

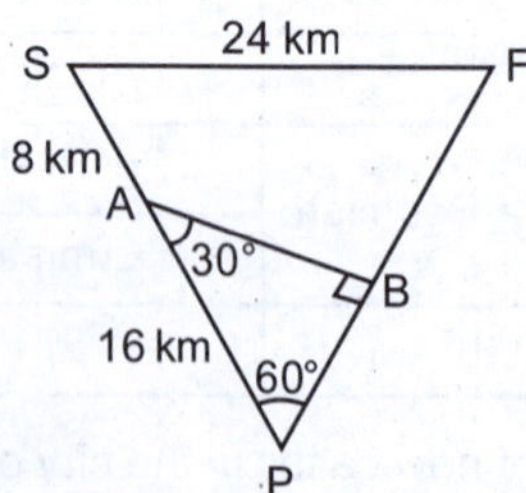

BP/AP = sin 30° = 1/2

⇒ BP = 16 × 1/2 = 8 km

BF = PF – BP = 24 – 8 = 16 km

This means, the faster ship is twice as fast as the slower one.

Hence, when the faster ship reaches the port covering 24 km, the slower ship covers only 12 km and has remaining 12 km left to cover.

4. 3 In any polygon, the largest side length should be less than the sum of the lengths of the other sides.

Let the fourth side be x.

Case 1: x is the largest side.

$x < 1 + 2 + 4$ or, $x < 7$

So x can take the values 4, 5, 6.

Case 2: 4 is the largest side and x is less than 4.

$4 < x + 1 + 2$ or, $x > 1$

So x can take the values of 2 or 3.

Hence, x can take 5 values i.e., 2, 3, 4, 5, 6.

5. 1 $\frac{x^2-6x+10}{3-x} = \frac{x^2-6x+9+1}{3-x}$

$= \frac{(x-3)^2}{3-x} + \frac{1}{3-x} = \frac{(x-3)^2}{3-x} + \frac{1}{3-x}$

$= \frac{(3-x)^2}{3-x} + \frac{1}{3-x} = 3-x+\frac{1}{3-x}$

Since $x < 3$, $3 - x$ is positive.

Let $3 - x = k$

Since k is positive, the minimum value of $k + 1/k$ is 2.

6. 150

Let the number of students in the school be N.

$N < 5000$

N leaves a remainder of 4 when divided by 9, 10, 12, or 25.

N leaves a remainder of 4 when divided by LCM (9, 10, 12, 25) = 900.

N leaves a remainder of 4 when divided by 900.

$N = 900x + 4$

Since $N < 5000$, x can take range from 0 to 5.

But $900x + 4$ is a multiple of 11 only when $x = 2$.

So $N = 900 \times 2 + 4 = 1804$

Since $1804 = 12 \times 150 + 4$

Hence, when we divide these 1804 students into groups of 12, we get 150 groups.

7. 1 Glass contains 500 cc of milk and cup contains 500 cc water.

After first transfer, glass contains 500 – 150 = 350 cc milk and the cup contains 150 cc milk and 500 cc water.

Now, the ratio of milk and water in the cup = 150 : 500 = 3 : 10

After second transfer, water in the glass = 150 × 3/13 cc and milk in the cup will be same i.e., 150 × 3/13 cc.

Hence, required ratio = 1 : 1.

8. 2 $3 + 2\sqrt{2}$ is a root of the equation $ax^2 + bx + c = 0$.

So the other root of the equation will be $3 - 2\sqrt{2}$.

Sum of roots

$= -b/a = 3 + 2\sqrt{2} + 3 - 2\sqrt{2} = 6$ ... (i)

Product of roots

$= c/a = (3 + 2\sqrt{2})(3 - 2\sqrt{2}) = 1$ ... (ii)

$4 + 2\sqrt{3}$ is a root of the equation $ax^2 + mx + n = 0$.

So the other root of the equation will be $4 - 2\sqrt{3}$.

Sum of roots

$= -m/a = 4 + 2\sqrt{3} + 4 - 2\sqrt{3} = 8$ ... (iii)

Product of roots

$= n/a = (4 + 2\sqrt{3})(4 - 2\sqrt{3}) = 4$ ... (iv)

From (i) and (iii), $b/m = 3/4$ ... (v)

From (ii) and (iv), $c/n = 1/4$ ... (vi)

From (i) and (iv),

$-b/n = 3/2$ or $-2b/n = 3$ ... (vii)

Hence, $b/m + (c - 2b)/n = 3/4 + 1/4 + 3 = 16/4 = 4$.

9. 3 $c = \frac{16x}{y} + \frac{49y}{x}$

Let $k = x/y$, since x and y are real, k is also real.

So $c = 16k + \frac{49}{k}$

$\Rightarrow 16k^2 - ck + 49 = 0$

For k to be real, it has to be rational first.

This means, $c^2 > (2 \times 4 \times 7)^2$

or, $c^2 > 56^2$

or, $|c| > 56$

Hence, c cannot take the value –50.

10. 9

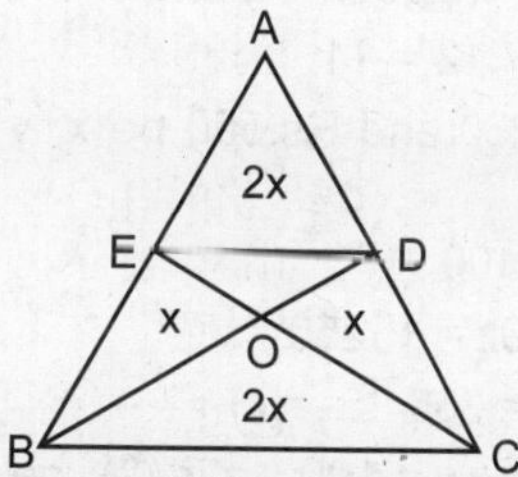

O is the centroid of the triangle ABC.

BO : OD = 2 : 1

CO : OE = 2 : 1

Area of triangle BOC : Area of triangle ODC = 2 : 1

Area of triangle COB : Area of triangle OEB = 2 : 1

Since BD is median, Area of triangle BDA = Area of triangle BDC

Area of quadrilateral AEOD = 2x

So $2x + x + x + 2x = 108$

$\Rightarrow 2x = 36$ sq. cm

Area of triangle AED = 1/4 × 108 = 27 sq. cm

Hence, area of triangle EOD = Area of quadrilateral AEOD – Area of triangle AED

= 36 – 27 = 9 sq. cm.

11. 14 $\left(\sqrt{\frac{7}{5}}\right)^{3x-y} = \frac{875}{2401}$

$\Rightarrow \left(\frac{7}{5}\right)^{\frac{3x-y}{2}} = \frac{125}{343}$

$\Rightarrow \left(\frac{7}{5}\right)^{\frac{3x-y}{2}} = \left(\frac{7}{5}\right)^{-3}$

So 3x – y = – 6 ... (i)

$\left(\frac{4a}{b}\right)^{6x-y} = \left(\frac{2a}{b}\right)^{y-6x}$

$(2)^{6x-y} = \left(\frac{2a}{b}\right)^{2y-12x}$

Let 2a/b = k, since a and b are real numbers, k is also real.

$k = \frac{1}{\sqrt{2}}$, but $\frac{1}{\sqrt{2}}$ is not real.

So the given equation can be satisfied only when the powers are zero.

Therefore, 6x – y = 0

⇒ y = 6x ... (ii)

Solving (i) and (ii), we get x = 2 and y = 12

Hence, x + y = 2 + 12 = 14.

12. 12 Let Rs.100, Rs. 250 and Rs.500 be x, y and z respectively.

Then, x + y + z = 100 ... (i)

100x + 250y + 500z = 15250

⇒ 2x + 5y + 10z = 305 ... (ii)

From (i), putting x + y = 100 – z in (ii), we get

2(100 – z) + 3y + 10z = 305

⇒ 3y + 8z = 105

From the above equation, the maximum possible value of z is 12, then y = 3 and x = 85.

Hence, the maximum possible number of cheques of Rs.500 is 12.

13. 2 According to the question,

8000 × 0.055 × 1 + 5000 × 0.056 × 1 + 7000 × x/100 × 1 = 20000 × 0.05 × 1

⇒ 0.44 + 0.28 + 7x/100 = 1

⇒ 7x/100 = 0.28

⇒ x = 4%

Hence, the required annual interest

= 20000 × 0.04 × 1 = Rs.800.

14. 1

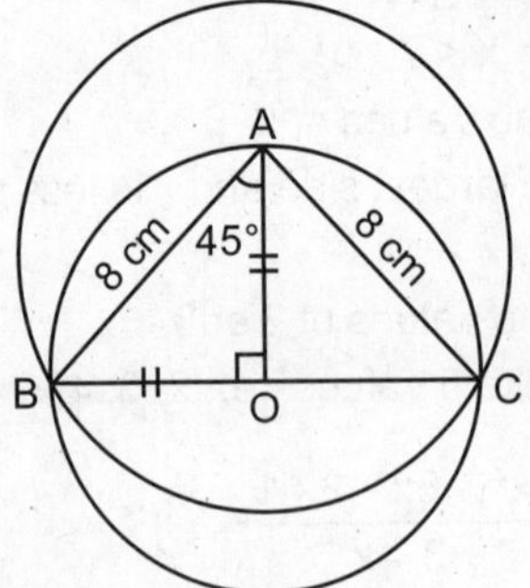

In triangle AOB, $AO^2 + OB^2 = AB^2$

⇒ $AO^2 + AO^2 = 8^2$ (AO = OB = Radii)

⇒ AO = 4√2 cm

The radius of the circle of diameter AB is 4√2 cm.

The radius of the circle with center at A is 8 cm.

Hence, the overlapping region between the two circles

$= \frac{1}{2} \times \pi \times (4\sqrt{2})^2 + \frac{1}{4} \times \pi \times (8)^2 - \frac{1}{2} \times 4\sqrt{2} \times 4\sqrt{2}$

= 16(π – 1)sq. cm.

15. 63 Let the possible average marks of all the students combined be n.

Then, 32 < n < 60

The ratio of the number of students in section A to the number of students in section B is

(60 – n) : (n – 32).

Also, when there are equal numbers of students in section A and section B, the value of n is (60 + 32)/2 = 46

Since there are 10 students in section B is more than that of section A, then 46 < n < 60

The extreme values of the number of students depend upon the extreme values of n.

When n = 47, the ratio of the number of students in section A to section B is

(60 – 47) : (47 – 32) = 13 : 15

So 15x – 13x = 10 ⇒ x = 5

So the number of students in section A = 13 × 5 = 65

When n = 56, the ratio of the number of students in section A to section B is

(60 – 56) : (56 – 32) = 1 : 6

So 6x – x = 10 ⇒ x = 2

So the number of students in section A = 1 × 2 = 2

Hence, the difference between the maximum and minimum possible number of students in section A is 65 – 2 = 63.

16. 1 For $x = r$,

$f(r) = 2r - r = r$

So $f(f(r)) = f(r) = r$

For $x < r$,

$f(x) = r$

$f(f(x)) = f(r) = r$

For $x > r$,

Let $x = kr$, where k is some number greater than 1.

$f(x) = f(kr) = 2kr - r = (2k - 1)r$

Since $k > 0$, $2k - 1 > k$

So for any $x > r$, $f(f(x)) \neq f(f(r))$

Hence, for $f(f(x)) = f(x)$ to be satisfied, the necessary condition is, $x \leq r$.

17. 1 Speed of slower car = 60 km/h and they take 1.5 hours if they travel towards each other, to meet each other after starting at the same time.

In this case the distance covered by the slower car = 60 × 1.5 = 90 km.

18. 11 Since Bob can finish a job in 40 days.

Then, Alex and Cole can finish this job in 20 and 60 days respectively.

Total work = LCM (20, 40, 60) = 120 units

Alex, Bob and Cole can finish 6, 3 and 2 units of the job per day.

In 3 days, they can finish 2(6 + 3 + 2) = 22 units

In 15 days, they can finish 5 × 22 = 110 units

Out of remaining 10, 9 units of work can finish by Alex and Bob and 1 unit by Bob and Cole.

Hence, the total number of days Alex would have worked when the job gets finished, is

2 × 5 + 1 = 11 days.

19. 2 According to the question,

$N \times 7 \times 10/35 = (N - 10) \times 10 \times 14/65$

$\Rightarrow N \times 7 \times 10 \times 65 = (N - 10) \times 10 \times 14 \times 35$

$\Rightarrow 13N = 14N - 140$

$\Rightarrow N = 140.$

20. 2 $2x^2 + kx + 5 = 0$

Since this quadratic equation has no real roots,

$k^2 < 4 \times 2 \times 5$ or $k^2 < 40$

Since k is an integer, the possible values of k are (–6, –5, ... , 5, 6).

$x^2 + (k - 5)x + 1 = 0$

Since this quadratic equation has real and distinct roots,

$(k - 5)^2 > 4 \times 1 \times 1$ or $(k - 5)^2 > 4$

Since k is an integer, the possible values of k are (..., 1, 2, 8, 9, ...).

So the possible values of k are (–6, –5, –4, –3, –2, –1, 0, 1, 2).

Hence, k can take 9 values.

21. 60 When Moody walks for 30 s, let the steps rolled out by the escalator be 3a and the steps walked by Moody be 3b.

Therefore, when the escalator runs for only 20 s, the steps rolled out by the escalator equals 2a. Since Moddy is also spending only 20 s instead of 30 s on the escalator, but walking at double the speed, he walks 4b steps.

The total steps of the escalator remain the same in both scenarios.

$3a + 3b = 2a + 4b$

$\Rightarrow a = b$

Total length of the escalator = 3a + 3b = 6a

When Moody doesn't walk on the Escalator, the Escalator has to roll out all the 6a steps for him.

Since the Escalator takes 30 s to roll out 3a steps, it would take 60 s to roll out all the 6a steps.

22. 3 The sum of the two smallest numbers = 14 × 2 = 28

The sum of the two largest numbers = 28 × 2 = 56

To maximize the average of all the 6 numbers, we must try to maximize the two numbers in between. This is possible when the two largest numbers are 27 and 29.

The maximum average case is

a, b, 25, 26, 27, 29; where a + b = 28

Hence, the average of these 6 numbers

= (a + b + 25 + 26 + 27 + 29)/6

= (28 + 25 + 26 + 27 + 29)/6 = 22.5.